Disordered Minds

Disordered Minds

Minette Walters

THORNDIKE
WINDSOR
PARAGON

This Large Print edition is published by Thorndike Press®, Waterville, Maine USA and by BBC Audiobooks, Ltd, Bath, England.

Published in 2005 in the U.S. by arrangement with The Berkley Publishing Group, a division of Penguin Group (USA) Inc.

Published in 2005 in the U.K. by arrangement with Pan Macmillan Ltd.

U.S. Hardcover 0-7862-7347-X (Core)
U.K. Hardcover 0-7540-7956-2 (Windsor Large Print)
U.K. Softcover 0-7540-9701-3 (Paragon Large Print)

This is a work of fiction. Names, characters, places, and incidents either are the product of the author's imagination or are used fictitiously. Any resemblance to actual persons, living or dead, business establishments, events, or locales is entirely coincidental.

The text of this Large Print edition is unabridged. Other aspects of the book may vary from the original edition.

Set in 16 pt. Plantin by Elena Picard.

Printed in the United States on permanent paper.

British Library Cataloguing-in-Publication Data available

Library of Congress Cataloging-in-Publication Data

Walters, Minette.
Disordered minds / by Minette Walters.
p. cm. — (Thorndike Press large print core)
ISBN 0-7862-7347-X (lg. print : hc : alk. paper)
1. Older women — Crimes against — Fiction. 2. People with mental disabilities — Fiction. 3. Anthropologists — Fiction. 4. Suicide victims — Fiction. 5. Judicial error — Fiction. 6. Large type books. I. Title. II. Thorndike Press large print core series.

PR6073.A444D57 2005
823′.914—dc22 2004027408

For Benson & Hedges

No man is so good as to be free from all evil,
nor so bad as to be worth nothing.

Michael Crichton

Chapter One

Colliton Park, Highdown, Bournemouth
Monday, May 4, 1970, 1:30 p.m.

It wasn't much of a park, barely half an acre of wilted grass off Colliton Way where local people walked their dogs in the mornings and evenings. During the day it was hardly frequented at all, except by truants who hung around the trees that lined the fences. The police rarely visited it and, anyway, there was a hundred yards of open space between the only entrance and the offenders. In the time it took two overweight coppers to lumber across, the teens were long gone, vaulting the low fences into the gardens that formed the rear perimeter. As complaints came in thick and fast from homeowners whenever this happened, the police, preferring an easy life, tended to leave the youngsters alone.

The logic ran that while they were in the

park they weren't thieving, and it was better to turn a blind eye and concentrate official efforts in the city center. To the cynical police mind, truanting came low on their list of criminal behavior.

Situated at the poorer end of Highdown, Colliton Way had little going for it. Unemployment was high, school attendance poor, and the proposed new buildings on the acres of waste ground behind it, which had promised jobs and houses, had faltered to a halt. The only site under construction was the Brackham & Wright tool factory, which was a planned replacement for the present, antiquated building on Glazeborough Road. This was no consolation to its workers, many of whom lived in Colliton Way, because up-to-date technology and automation always brought redundancies.

The most persistent truants were three boys. They were charismatic and generous as long as their leadership wasn't challenged, dangerously violent when it was. It made them a magnet for unhappy children who misinterpreted generosity for affection and cruelty for regard, and none of the children understood how damaged the boys were. How could they, when the boys didn't know it themselves? Barely able to read or write, only interested in immediate gratification and with no rein over their aggressive impulses, they thought they were in control of their lives.

That May Monday followed the aimless pattern of the many before. So entrenched was the boys' truancy that their mothers no longer bothered to get them out of bed. Better to let sleeping dogs lie, was the women's thinking, than face a beating because their overgrown sons were angry at being woken. The boys were incapable of getting up. None of them came home before the early hours — if they came home at all — and they were always so drunk their sleep was stupor. All three mothers had asked for them to be taken into care at one time or another, but their resolve had never lasted very long. Fear of reprisal, and misguided love for their absent firstborns, had always effected a change of mind. It might have been different if there had been men around, but there weren't, so the women did what their sons told them.

The boys had picked up a couple of thirteen-year-old girls in the center of town and brought them to the park. The skinny one, who had her ten-year-old brother in tow, held no interest for them; the other, a well-developed girl with flirtatious eyes, did. The girls sat opposite each other on a bench seat with their knees drawn up to their chins and toes touching while the four boys sprawled on the grass at their feet, staring at their knickers. Wearing knee-high boots, miniskirts and crocheted see-through tops with black bras underneath, the girls understood exactly where their power lay and it amused them. They spoke to each other about sex, and pointedly ignored the boys.

The response was lackluster. The boys passed round a bottle of stolen vodka but showed no interest in the crude flirting and, without an endgame, all sport grows tedious, even cock-teasing. The skinny girl, annoyed by the boys' lack of interest in her, teased them for being virgins, but the taller girl, Cill, swung her legs to the ground and shuffled her skirt down her bum. "This is silly," she said. "C'mon, Lou. We're going back down town."

Her friend, a small undernourished clone with smudged black eyes and pale pink lips, performed her own skirt-wriggling act and stood up. They both aped the fashion sense of Cathy McGowan from their favorite pop show, *Ready, Steady, Go!*, with belts worn at hip level and hair ironed straight to fall in heavy fringes over their forehead. It suited Cill, whose face was strong enough to take it, but Lou, who was tiny, like Twiggy, wanted to cut her hair in an urchin style. Cill wouldn't allow it. It was part of their friendship pact that they looked alike, or as near alike as was possible for a well-developed teenager and one who had to stuff Kleenex down her bra.

"You coming, or what?" Cill demanded of Lou's ten-year-old brother, nudging him with her toe. "Your dad'll string you up if the cops catch you, Billy. You see if he don't."

"Leave me alone," the child mumbled tipsily.

"Jee-sus!" The drink had made her quarrelsome and she cast a scornful eye over the prone bodies. "Blokes are so fucking pathetic. Me and Lou's had the same as you, but we ain't passed out."

"Don't push your luck," said one of the boys. He wasn't the tallest, but he was dark-haired and dark-eyed, and to her immature mind he looked like Paul McCartney.

Another, a freckle-faced redhead, reached a hand up Lou's thigh. "Slut," he jeered, squeezing hard.

She squeaked and pulled away, smacking

at him. “Virgin, virgin, virgin!” she chanted. “You ain’t never gonna get it, you’re too fucking ugly.” He made a grab for her foot and she wailed at Cill to get him off. “He’s gonna pull me over.”

The taller girl put a boot on his chest. “Let her go!”

He relaxed his hold with a grin. “What d’you expect? You’re a coupla tarts, ain’t you?”

She maneuvered a stiletto heel over his nipple. “You wanna say that again?”

He was visibly pubescent, with hair above his lip and acne crowding his neck, and he was too drunk to be intimidated. “You’re a fat tart,” he slurred lazily, “ ’n’ you’ve been laid so often I could park a car up yer cunt. Want me to try?”

His two friends rolled onto their fronts and watched the tableau with a gleam in their eye. To a girl with more experience, it would have been a warning sign, but Cill was a novice. She brought her full weight down on her heel as she stepped over him, dancing away before he could catch her. “ ’N’ don’t never call me fat again or I’ll put my heel on your cock next time.”

The redhead clutched at his chest. “That bloody hurt!”

“It was supposed to, dickhead.” She

jerked her chin at the other girl as she started to walk away.

But there was no such easy escape for Lou. She was trapped against the bench and lost her balance when the dark-haired boy made a lunge for her. He grabbed her arms as she fell and spread-eagled her on the grass, and her wails of fear brought Cill running back. Their mothers should have warned them about the dangers of whipping up testosterone, but the only advice either had been given was: if you dress like a tart, you'll get yourself raped, and it'll be your own fault when it happens.

Believing she was streetwise, it was Cill who was the more naive. With animal instinct, Lou became catatonic immediately and held no attraction for the aroused adolescents. Cill fought back determinedly and took the full brunt of the assault. She kept calling on Billy to run for help but, at ten and drunk, all he could do was bury his head in his arms.

It was when they pulled her by her hair into the lee of the trees that Cill gave up. The pain was indescribable and sent tears coursing down her made-up cheeks. It masked all the other pains she experienced. All three wanted her — she was the dominatrix — and they took it in turns to have her. The dark one raped her twice. She was too young to understand psychological trauma, but the ripping of her clothes — so loved and so longed for — the sweat, heat and filth of a prolonged gang bang and their leering, triumphant faces as they repeatedly violated her destroyed her in a way that their overexcited, briefly sustained penetrations could not.

"That's the last time anyone calls me a virgin," said the redhead, standing over her and zipping himself with a flourish.

The dark boy kicked her. "Bitch! If you run to the cops, you'll get more of the same. Understood?"

With a belated sense of self-preservation, Cill closed her eyes and shut him out. She could name each one, although she never would. Her dad would kill her if he knew she'd been raped, and the police wouldn't believe her anyway. *It was broad daylight in a park in Bournemouth, and no one had done a thing to help her.* Part of her brain wondered if the road was too far away for passersby to see what was happening, the other part reproached her for dressing sexy. Her mum was right — she *had* brought it on herself — but all Cill had ever wanted was for people to say she was pretty.

Lou crawled across the grass to lie beside her. "They've gone," she whispered, stealing her small hand into Cill's. "You OK?"

No-oo-oo! It was a scream that would reverberate in her head for days. "Yeah. What about you?"

The child curled into a fetal ball with her head on Cill's chest. "Your dad'll tan your hide when he finds out."

"I ain't telling him."

"What if you get pregnant?"

"I'll kill it."

"Billy'll tell our mum."

"Then I'll fucking kill him, too." She pushed Lou off and sat up. "Where is he?"

"Over there." She jerked her head toward the bench. "You shouldn't've stood on him, Cill. Ma says it's always the girl's fault when a man gets angry."

Cill tugged her torn top over her exposed breasts and stared at the hymenal blood on her thighs. She didn't need a lecture on blame, she needed to get home without being seen. With a vicious grab she caught Lou's hair and twisted it round her fist. "I wouldn't've 'ad to if you hadn't called him a virgin. Now, are you gonna help me, or you gonna drop me in it again?"

Tears sprouted in the other child's eyes. "You're hurting me," she pleaded.

"Yeah," said Cill unemotionally.

"It weren't my fault it happened."

"Bloody was. It was you called them virgins. You're a fucking stupid bitch, Lou, and you didn't do nothing to stop it."

"I was scared."

"So was I . . . but I came back."

Lou gave an uneasy wiggle of her shoulders. "There weren't no sense us both getting done."

"No," said Cill, taking another twist of hair and digging her knuckles into the smaller girl's scalp. "But you fucking well will be if you or Billy ever tell on me." She stared into Lou's eyes, her own full of tears. "You got that? Because if my dad has a go at me again, I'm off . . . and I ain't never coming back."

The cooling between the two girls was noticed by their families and their teachers. Once or twice Louise Burton's father tried to find out what had caused it, but Lou, who kept pestering to have her hair cut in the urchin style she so craved, shrugged and said Cill had found another friend. Billy slipped out of the room each time, but it didn't occur to either of his parents that he knew anything. Nor were they interested enough to pursue it. Free of Cill's influence, Louise reverted to dressing appropriately for a thirteen-year-old, and the brief flurry of truanting that had brought her to the unwelcome attention of her headmistress ceased abruptly.

For Priscilla Trevelyan's parents, the break was equally welcome. Their daughter had become wayward in puberty, but Louise Burton's unquestioning subservience had exacerbated it. Mr. Trevelyan, disappointed by Cill's unwillingness to apply herself and troubled by her early maturity, had exercised a tough, physical discipline to control her, and the sudden loss of affection between the two girls was acknowledged with relief but never mentioned. He was worried that talking about it would rekindle the dependence and he forbade his wife to show sympathy. He put Cill's bad temper down to the broken friendship, but overlooked it because of her new-found commitment to attending school.

The girls' teachers were less sanguine after a fight broke out between them during a PE lesson on Friday, May 29. There had been three weeks of hostile silence before Louise said something that prompted Priscilla to react. It was a cat-fight of teeth and claws with the smaller child taking the brunt of it before the pair were finally pulled apart by a furious games teacher and marched in front of the headmistress. Priscilla stood in stony-faced silence, refusing to speak, while Louise sobbed about having her hair pulled and Cill trying to persuade her to truant again. The headmistress, who didn't believe her, nevertheless made the decision, in the absence of apology or explanation, that Priscilla should be punished with a week's suspension while Louise was let off with a caution.

Predictably, Cill's father took out his disapproval in a thrashing and, as she had threatened, she ran away some time during the early hours of Saturday, May 30. Mr. Trevelyan described the punishment as "a couple of smacks" when the police asked if there was a reason for his daughter absconding, but otherwise he could not account for the out-of-character behavior. She had never done it before, she had a good home and was doing well academically. Yes, there had been a few truancy problems in the past, but that was the fault of the secondary-modern system. Priscilla was easily bored by lessons that were geared to the less intelligent.

Louise, under questioning by a sympathetic policewoman, began by saying that Cill would kill her if she told the truth, then confessed the rape. She couldn't name the boys, but her description led to them being rounded up and their homes searched for any sign of the missing girl. They denied any knowledge of rape, Priscilla Trevelyan or Louise Burton, and nothing was found to connect them with an assault or the girls. It didn't help that Louise hadn't known their names, could only give vague descriptions, couldn't remember how they were dressed, and that Cill's crocheted top, miniskirt and knickers had been thrown away. Nor, when Louise tearfully insisted that Cill had brought it on herself by getting drunk and talking sexy, did the police believe an assault had taken place. Heavy petting, perhaps, but not full-on gang rape.

However, as the major stumbling block was the alleged victim's absence, the boys were released after token questioning at 1323 on Monday, June 1. Rape was taken less seriously in 1970.

The following is a single-chapter excerpt from Dr. Jonathan Hughes's *Disordered Minds*

DISORDERED MINDS

Dr. Jonathan Hughes

"An important study into judicial blunder."
— JEREMY CROSSLEY

Jonathan Hughes, 34, was born in London where he now lives. He graduated with a first-class honors degree from Oxford University in 1992 and has made a particular study of the Middle East. He lectures widely on comparative religion and internecine conflicts. His first two books, *Racial Stereotyping*, 1995, and *Banishment*, 1997, explore the problems of ghettoization and social exile. In *Disordered Minds* he reexamines some infamous twentieth-century miscarriages of justice, where the rights of vulnerable defendants were exploited by the system. He is critical of Western democracies that take their morality and virtue for granted.

Dr. Hughes is a research fellow in European anthropology at London University.

12.

Howard Stamp — Victim or Murderer?

Many would argue that the brutal murder of fifty-seven-year-old Grace Jefferies in June 1970 in Bournemouth, Dorset, was another case where public pressure influenced police handling of an investigation. Press outrage over the slashing and stabbing of shy, disabled Grace whipped the public into a frenzy, and pressure was on the police to find a culprit. The headlines of Saturday, June 6, 1970, drew parallels with the Manson family's killing of Sharon Tate less than a year earlier.[1]

"Police fear copycat murder as Manson

[1]The trial of Charles Manson, Susan Atkins, Leslie Van Houten and Patricia Krenwinkel began six weeks later on July 24, 1970.

trial approaches"; "Grandmother tortured in California-style bloodletting"; "Orgy of bloodlust"; "Walls daubed with blood." We must assume that these ideas came from the police, because there's too much unanimity to lay the blame on journalists. If so, it was criminally misleading. Grace was alone when she was murdered, unlike Sharon Tate whose five guests were slaughtered with her, and "daubed" was a fanciful description for the arterial splatters of blood on Grace's wall. It gave the impression that Bournemouth police had found something similar to the "Pig" scrawled in blood on Sharon Tate's front door.

Not unreasonably, the public was terrified. The "Tate murders" in Los Angeles on August 9, 1969, followed twenty-four hours later by the "La Bianca murders," had shocked the world. Newspapers obsessed on "drug-induced cult horror" after details of the massacres emerged. The Beatles were in the dock for their song "Helter Skelter," along with the Vietnam War, Californian "flower power," Woodstock, long hair, pot-smoking and free love. The idea that these American diseases had crossed the Atlantic to erupt in savage murder in respectable Bournemouth was so shocking that there was a collective sigh of relief on

Sunday, June 7, when Howard Stamp confessed.

There was no gang involvement. It was a "domestic." Stamp, a retarded twenty-year-old with a noticeable harelip, was Grace's grandson. He had a history of truancy, bizarre behavior, refusal to work and an unhealthy obsession with the rock group Cream, particularly the drummer, Ginger Baker. He was held for questioning for thirty-six hours and finally admitted the murder at four o'clock on the Sunday morning. There was no solicitor present, and because he was illiterate his statement was written for him. It was an open-and-shut case and the accused was duly sent to trial and convicted in August 1971.

Disturbing Parallels

Open-and-shut cases had similarly led to the convictions of Timothy Evans and Derek Bentley in the 1950s, and the later convictions of Stephen Downing for the murder of Wendy Sewell in 1973 and Stefan Kiszko for the murder of Lesley Molseed in 1975. Like Stamp, all four were illiterate or semiliterate with physical or mental disabilities, and all were highly vulnerable to police suggestion.

Timothy Evans, twenty-six at the time of his conviction, was retarded and illiterate; Derek Bentley, nineteen, was mentally handicapped; Downing, a physically immature seventeen-year-old, had a reading age of eleven; and Kiszko, twenty-four, who suffered from XYY syndrome, hypogonadism, had undeveloped testes and was described as "a child in a man's body." Three of these men were denied the services of a solicitor and made confessions that they later retracted, claiming the police had used coercion to obtain the statements or had written the statements themselves; the fourth, Derek Bentley, who was under arrest when his sixteen-year-old codefendant, Christopher Craig, shot PC Sidney Miles, accused the police of lying when they claimed he shouted an order at Craig to commit the murder and was therefore guilty of "joint enterprise."

Police and prosecution confidence in each man's guilt resulted in botched investigations and the suppression of evidence. Although it was recognized at the time that all four men were emotionally immature with learning difficulties, these factors were not taken into account during their interrogations or at their trials. Indeed, many would argue the opposite: their vulnerability was exploited to secure a quick indictment. It has taken years to exonerate them — in Bentley's case nearly half a century — but they are now known to have been victims of four of the twentieth century's most notorious miscarriages of justice.

Reforms of the System

Two pieces of legislation, PACE (the Police and Criminal Evidence Act), 1984, and CPIA (the Criminal Procedure and Investigations Act), 1996, belatedly addressed many of the issues raised by both the Downing and Kiszko interrogations, although neither man's case had been reviewed at the time of the 1984 Act. The mainspring for that reform was almost certainly "Operation Countryman," an internal police investigation during the 1970s, which revealed terrifying levels of corruption in the Metropolitan Police. In its wake, Chief Superintendent Ken Drury of the Flying Squad was jailed, along with twelve other Scotland Yard detectives, for accepting bribes to falsify evidence.

Public confidence in the police was irreparably damaged and discontent with the whole criminal-justice system grew as doubts were raised about the safety of individual convictions. Prominent campaigns, claiming miscarriages of justice, centered around the Guildford Four — released in 1989; the Birmingham Six — released in 1991; and the Bridgwater Four — released in 1997. Other notable releases were the Cardiff Three and the M25 Three. In 1999 thirty convictions were quashed when it was revealed that the West Midlands Serious Crime Squad had fabricated evidence, tortured suspects and concocted false confessions. At the time of writing, dozens of appeals are still in the pipeline.

Stephen Downing

Stephen Downing served twenty-eight years before the Court of Appeal freed him in 2002. A small, shy seventeen-year-old with learning difficulties, he was interrogated by detectives for nine hours before, near to exhaustion, he agreed to sign a statement in which he admitted battering a young woman with a pickax handle in the cemetery in Bakewell, Derbyshire, where he worked. No solicitor was present to advise the teenager, nor was his father allowed to see him. At the time he signed the statement the victim, Wendy Sewell, was unconscious but still alive, and detectives assured the youngster that if he wasn't guilty Wendy would exonerate him when she came round. She died two days later and Downing was charged with her murder.

He retracted his statement immediately but his confession became the mainstay of the prosecution's case at Nottingham Crown Court the following year. He was found guilty and sentenced to life, with a recommendation that he serve seventeen years. This would have made him eligible for release in 1989, but, because he consistently denied his guilt, his applications were refused. It is a cornerstone of the U.K. penal system that remorse is a precondition for parole, so an IDOM (in denial of murder) prisoner will not be considered. To innocent men and women who are prepared to put their good name above a lifetime in prison, this rule is a catch-22.

Nearly three decades after Wendy Sewell's murder, the presiding appeal judge, Lord Justice Pill, acknowledged that errors had been made in Downing's interrogation. The court could not be sure, he said, that Mr. Downing's initial confessions to the police were reliable and it followed that his conviction was "unsafe." Downing's freedom and good name were returned to him but warning shots were fired across the Court of Appeal's bows. Don Hale, a crusading journalist who had worked for seven years to bring Downing's plight to public attention, said, "What worries me is how many similar cases lie buried in the prison system."

Stefan Kiszko

One such was Stefan Kiszko who was interrogated by police in 1975 for the murder of eleven-year-old Lesley Molseed in Rochdale. Convinced of Kiszko's guilt, police ignored the immaturity and social backwardness that had led to a lifetime's bullying, failed to tell him of his right to have a solicitor present, refused to allow him to see his mother (his only friend) and did not caution him until long after they had decided he was the prime suspect. When he finally confessed, he did so because police told him he would be allowed home as soon as he said what they wanted to hear.

Like Downing, he retracted his confession immediately but, again, the confession became the main plank of the prosecution case. Part of Kiszko's statement was a false admission that he had exposed himself some weeks earlier to two teenage girls who had named and identified him. Sixteen years later, when Kiszko was released by the Court of Appeal, these two girls, now grown women, admitted they had invented the story after seeing a taxi driver urinating behind a bush. More criminally, police withheld semen evidence at the trial which they knew would exculpate Kiszko.

As a sufferer of XYY syndrome, Kiszko was sterile. This was known to the police in 1975 because a sample of Kiszko's semen taken during the investigation contained no sperm. Yet the pathologist who examined Lesley Molseed's clothing had found sperm in the semen stains on her underwear. The police kept this evidence from the defense and the court, and it was only discovered when an inquiry into the case was ordered in 1990. Two years later, when an application on behalf of Kiszko was heard by the Court of Appeal, Lord Chief Justice Lane said, "It has been shown that this man cannot produce sperm. This man cannot have been responsible for . . . [the semen found on] . . . the girl's knickers and skirt, and consequently cannot have been her murderer."

Kiszko was released immediately. However, his brutal treatment at the hands of other prisoners, who had frequently beaten him, had driven him into a world of delusion where conspiracies abounded. Convinced that his mother — a lonely and steadfast voice on the outside claiming his innocence — had been part of the conspiracy to condemn him, he needed nine months' rehabilitation before he could return home to her care. He died after eighteen months, his physical and mental health destroyed, followed six months later by Mrs. Kiszko herself.

Public outrage at Kiszko's treatment was immense, although few recognized that by baying for blood in the wake of a child's murder they had added to the pressure on the police to find a culprit.

Howard Stamp

Bullied mercilessly at school for his harelip and defective speech, Stamp had a miserable attendance record. Described as "work-shy" at his trial, he had withdrawn into self-imposed isolation, too frightened to go out. "He was teased every time he left the house," said his mother in his defense. "He looked funny and he couldn't read or write."

Today he would have been dubbed a self-abuser. Not only is it clear that he suffered from an eating disorder — he was painfully thin with an immature physique — he made a habit of cutting his arms with razors. His mother, unable to understand or cope with behavioral difficulties that were barely recognized in the 1960s, begged her GP to certify him before he "used the razor on somebody else."

It was this request that convinced police he was guilty of the brutal murder of his fifty-seven-year-old grandmother, Grace Jefferies, on Wednesday, June 3, 1970. Found in a "bloodbath" at her home in Mullin Street, Highdown, on the border between Bournemouth and Poole, Grace had been stabbed and slashed thirty-three times. The press dubbed it "murder by a thousand cuts" because most of the nonfatal injuries were to her arms and legs, suggesting she had been tortured for some time before her throat was slit. The inescapable conclusion, according to the pathologist, was that she had staggered upstairs to her bedroom while her tormentor slashed at her arms and legs with a carving knife.

Suspicion focused on Stamp when witnesses came forward to say they'd seen him running from Grace's house on Wednesday, June 3, two days before her body was discovered on Friday, June 5. Bloodstains on his clothes seemed to confirm his guilt, and after thirty-six hours of interrogation he confessed to the murder. As with Downing and Kiszko, he had no solicitor present and retracted his confession shortly afterward. He admitted running from Grace's house, but claimed that his grandmother was already dead when he entered with his duplicate key. Horrified by what he had found, he fled home and locked himself in his bedroom, too shocked to tell anyone what he'd seen. It was another forty-eight hours before a postman reported that Grace's curtains had been drawn for several days.

It seemed a straightforward case, yet there were many inconsistencies in the evidence. The pathologist's first estimate suggested Grace had been dead four days before her body was found. This was later amended to forty-eight hours to tie in with the witness statements. At the trial, the pathologist explained the mistake as a "slip of the pen" and the defense failed to press him. In a similar volte-face, the postman who alerted police to Grace's drawn curtains told the court that when he'd said "several days" he had meant "two at the most." Again, the defense did not press the issue.

The flakes of dried blood on Stamp's trouser knees and shirt cuffs are consistent with his second statement: that he knelt beside his grandmother's body (two days after the murder if the pathologist's initial estimate was correct) to see if she was dead. They are less consistent with police and prosecution claims that he took a bath to wash off Grace's blood, then, dressed in fresh clothes, brushed against a blood-spattered wall on his departure. If this were true, some of the blood would still have been viscous enough to be absorbed by the fibers, and Stamp's back, behind, shoulders or thighs would have been the contact points, not his knees and cuffs.

The defense made some attempt to challenge the forensic evidence, most of which centered on hair and dried scum taken from the sides and plughole of the bathtub. The prosecution alleged that Stamp had immersed himself in water after the murder in order to clean himself. Both sides agreed that whoever killed Grace would have been covered in blood. The prosecution case was that Stamp had either committed the murder naked or removed bloodstained clothes from the property. This latter suggestion gained credibility after a witness said Stamp was carrying a black polythene bag when he ran from the house. (This bag was never recovered despite an intensive police search.)

The scum showed traces of Grace's blood group, and the hairs were identified as Stamp's. In addition, Stamp's fingerprints were found on the bathroom door and lavatory seat. Adam Fanshaw, Queen Counsel, counsel for the defense, succeeded in striking out the fingerprint evidence by arguing that Stamp was a regular visitor to the house. However, he was hampered over the hair evidence by Stamp's own insistence that he had never taken a bath in Grace's house.

The pathologist for the defense, Dr. John Foyle, put up a strong argument against the hairs being Stamp's by quoting Professor Keith Simpson, the noted Home Office pathologist, in a comment made during the 1943 Leckey trial.[2]

> The word "identical" does not mean the hairs necessarily came from the same person, only that they *could* have. That is the most one can ever say about hairs. Identical hairs are not compelling evidence like fingerprints, for they carry so much less detail.

Unfortunately, Dr. Foyle crumpled under cross-examination when Fanshaw failed to protect him against prosecution jibes of inexperience and publicity seeking. In a damaging about-face which implied the hairs were Stamp's, he said it was just as probable that "the hairs had been deposited in the bath on a previous occasion."

Stamp's mother, Wynne, made a poor witness for her son and should never have

[2]Gunner Dennis Leckey was tried for the murder of Caroline Traylor in 1943. Although found guilty and sentenced to death, Leckey was acquitted by the Court of Criminal Appeal on a technicality and allowed to walk free. Although Professor Simpson's comments referred to a 1943 case, they were still true thirty-five years later when he repeated them in *Professor Keith Simpson: An Autobiography*, published by Harrap Limited in 1978.

been called. Timid and of low intelligence, she stammered through her evidence, misunderstanding many of the questions that were put to her. She used her day in court to highlight her own problems — "I've had a terrible time because of Howard's physical and mental troubles . . . no one knows what I've had to put up with . . . there ought to be help for people like me . . ." She could give no explanation for why Howard had been at Grace's house on the Wednesday when he'd been due to start a job at Jannerway & Co. (a local dairy) that afternoon, except to say that he was "lazy." Nevertheless, she held firmly to her belief that Howard would never have hurt his grandmother. "He always went to her when he was depressed. She understood him because she had a cleft palate too. It runs in the family."

Grace's disability (an untreated cleft palate had left her with a severe speech impediment) had made her as reclusive as her grandson. Sent into service in 1928 at the age of fifteen, she gave birth to Wynne a year later. Nothing was known about the father, although the fact that she continued to be employed by the same family, and was allowed to keep her child, suggests that she may have been raped by a member of the household. Ten years later, aged twenty-six, she married Arthur Jefferies, forty-three, a merchant seaman who adopted Wynne and provided the home in Highdown, Bournemouth, where Grace lived for the rest of her life.

Tragically for Grace, Arthur was killed in 1942 during an attack on a North Sea convoy, and she became a widow before she was thirty. Three years later, aged just sixteen, Wynne met, and subsequently married, Fred Stamp, a farm worker from Bere Regis in Dorset. The marriage was of short duration — Wynne blamed their baby's "ugliness" for the break-up — and mother and son returned to Bournemouth to live in council accommodation in Colliton Way, half a mile from Grace's home in Mullin Street. While there is no evidence that Grace and Wynne did not get on, it seems there was little communication between the two women.

Grace was variously described by neighbors as "odd," "eccentric," "a bit of a recluse," "shy," "not very friendly." She was probably all of these things because, like her grandson, she would have found social interaction difficult. Certainly she had few callers, although a more likely reason for Wynne's failure to visit was that she didn't have a car and worked full-time as a packer at Brackham & Wright's tool factory in Glazeborough Road.

There is some evidence that Stamp went to his grandmother's house whenever he bunked off school. Neighbors mentioned seeing a child in the garden during the summers of the 1950s. If so, Grace never reported it to his mother or the truancy officer, and this would have persuaded Stamp that his grandmother was a safe refuge from bullies. Certainly, as he grew older he became a more frequent visitor, which is why he was identified so easily by the witnesses who saw him running away. "It was that skinny grandson," said one. "He used to hide with Grace instead of signing-on [for work]."

The prosecution argued at trial that Stamp's instability and self-abuse had increased to such a point that Grace had become afraid of him. As proof they quoted a letter to Wynne in which she said, "Howard's started shouting again even though he knows it frightens me. I've told him I'll put the police on to him if it goes on." Further on in the letter, and not quoted by the prosecution, she added, "I said if only he could meet a nice girl he'd start to feel better about things but he told me to shut up. You should have had words with the police when they laughed at him about the bullying. That's what did for him. He says it's a waste of time, but I got Arthur, didn't I?"

The defense failed to pick up on this, yet there are two reasons why they should have done so. First, Grace's meaning was surely this: Howard's been shouting again and it frightens me because I don't know how to help him. I've persuaded him to stop by threatening him with the police. We both know he's scared of them. They made fun of him when he told them he was being bullied, and he hasn't trusted them since. Second, if Stamp found the police intimidating, then nothing he said during his interrogation was reliable. Indeed his confession suggests that shocking them by admitting to a brutal murder was preferable to being jeered at for locking himself in his bedroom out of terror.

Stamp's case was never reopened because he hanged himself in 1973. However, even the most cursory comparison between Wynne Stamp's evidence and the prosecution case reveals alarming disparities. Wynne described her son as "not interested in cash because he hated going to the shops." The prosecution said, "Every drawer in Grace's house had been pulled out, either in a search for money and valuables or suggesting that Grace had disturbed a burglar." Wynne claimed she wasn't "a good housekeeper" and her son was always "tidying up" after her. The prosecution described Grace's house as "thoroughly vandalized." Wynne said her son was ashamed of his cut arms and wore long-sleeved jumpers and shirts to hide them from her. The prosecution said that "a man who reveled in using a razor on himself would take pleasure in slashing at a woman who was afraid of him."

There's no question that Stamp was badly let down by his defense team, and the inescapable conclusion is that they were as convinced of his guilt as the police and prosecution were. It's hard to understand why. However inadequate his social skills, however unattractive his appearance, he was clearly a vulnerable young man of low self-esteem and serious emotional difficulties. One theory that would fit the prosecution case is that Stamp was an undiagnosed paranoid schizophrenic who erupted one day in a fit of delusional violence against a woman who loved him.

There is no evidence to support this. He was examined by two psychiatrists to establish if he was fit to plead, and neither diagnosed schizophrenia. The verdict of the prosecution psychiatrist was that Stamp was "self-absorbed and introverted, but otherwise normal." The defense psychiatrist found him "depressed and suicidal."

> Howard is illiterate with a low IQ which means he has difficulty understanding simple instructions . . . He is deeply reserved, particularly when speaking about himself, refuses to look his interlocutor in the eye and covers the lower half of his face with his hands. This self-consciousness, amounting to obsession, is attributable to a poorly reconstructed harelip . . . Howard shows symptoms of agoraphobia and regularly betrays a sense of worthlessness . . . These emotional difficulties are not helped by being on remand, as he is fearful of interacting with officers and other inmates . . . these feelings of inadequacy are making him depressed and suicidal.
>
> I am concerned by his lack of confidence both in himself and in his relations with others. He has no amour propre and seems to feel he

deserves punishment. It is for this reason that he made a habit of cutting his arms during and postadolescence and is now refusing to eat in prison. I am confident that he is, and has been for some time, suffering from anorexia nervosa, an eating disorder, which is rare in young men but not unknown. This disorder is triggered when an individual persuades himself he is unattractive . . . In Howard's case, the deformity of his lip is clearly the major contributory cause.

. . . I consider him unfit to stand trial because he is incapable of taking a necessarily objective view if the charges are to be countered. In addition, he will be so distressed by his public display in court that he will be unable to function successfully.[3]

The defense psychiatrist's recommendations were ignored and Stamp was ruled competent to plead.

With the knowledge that we now have about eating disorders, it is more likely

[3]Taken from *Clinical Studies* by Dr. Andrew Lawson (Random House, U.S., 1975).

that the young man was suffering from body dysmorphic disorder. BDD is associated with obsessive-compulsive disorder and is not a variant of anorexia nervosa or bulimia nervosa, although self-harm and a refusal to eat are typical symptoms as the condition worsens. In most cases, an individual's obsession relates to facial features — defects can be real, imagined or exaggerated — and the sufferer comes to fear ridicule in social situations. The disorder usually begins in adolescence, becomes chronic and, if untreated, can lead to loneliness, isolation, severe depression and even suicide.

If this is indeed what Stamp was suffering from, then it becomes less probable that he killed his grandmother. She was the one person he could feel comfortable with, because she shared his disability. She may not have had a harelip, but her speech impediment was more severe than his, her friends as few and her dislike of going out as great. They were two of a kind, both preferring isolation to ridicule, and it stretches belief that Stamp's personality could alter so radically that he would move outside his self-harming, self-obsessive, self-hating introversion to slash and stab the one person who protected him.

Even if Grace had attempted to jolt him

out of depression by suggesting he "find a nice girl" because things had improved for her after she "got Arthur," and Stamp had become angry, it seems that shouting was the worst he did. Perhaps Wynne had tried making the same suggestion with the same result. She said at the trial, "He liked ladies better than men, but they didn't like him. It made him angry."

This was interpreted by the prosecution as "anger against women — one woman, his grandmother, Grace Jefferies, who had become frightened of him," but a more credible explanation is that Stamp voiced frustration when his mother and grandmother urged him to trawl for a date because he knew how painful and futile the exercise would be. Certainly, his suicide three years later is testimony that he found making friends of either sex difficult. A prison officer said at the inquest, "He was very timid. The other inmates picked on him because of it. He wouldn't come out of his cell unless he was ordered."

One can only imagine how lonely and desperate Stamp must have felt when even his mother believed in his guilt. "I stopped visiting when they moved him to Dartmoor," Wynne said at the inquest. "We had nothing to say to each other and it was a long way to go." The coroner, presumably wanting to rule out any suggestion of murder by other prisoners, asked Wynne if she thought Howard was the type to kill himself. She answered, "He had a lot on his conscience."

But Did He?

Police pay lip service to reopening cases, but the constraints of limited budgets and the time pressures of rising crime rates mean there is no realistic chance of anyone else facing charges. There is too little data on file, and precious little physical evidence, to indict a second individual a quarter of a century after the event. It's axiomatic — hence the reforms in PACE and CPIA — that if police believe a man to be guilty, they do not waste time looking for evidence that will exonerate him. In addition, and this is pertinent to a trial, the memories of witnesses who failed to come forward at the time or were never followed up will be deemed "unreliable" twenty or thirty years later.

Nevertheless, since DNA fingerprinting was first introduced in evidence in England in 1987,[4] the balance has swung against murderers who've "got away with it." While, to date, no prominent miscarriage of justice has been satisfactorily rectified by this technique, belated convictions have been achieved in a number of unsolved murders.

In 1970, DNA fingerprinting was a distant dream, yet inferences from press coverage of the trial in April 1971 suggest police did collect physical evidence from Grace's house that could even now exonerate Stamp.

> "The prosecution alleges that a T-shirt found in the house belonged to Stamp. This was denied by the defense although Wynne Stamp later admitted that her son had owned one 'like it'" (*The Times*, Tuesday, April 13, 1971). "Discarded gloves linked to orgy of bloodletting" (Headline — *Sun*, Wednesday, April 14, 1971). "A pair of bloodstained gloves thought to belong to the victim was found in a litter bin near the home of Grace Jefferies. Police believe they were worn by her murderer and then

[4]Robert Melias in the U.K. was the first man in history to be convicted on DNA evidence.

discarded" (*Daily Telegraph*, Wednesday, April 14, 1971). "The ace in the prosecution case is that hair found in Grace Jefferies's bath has been identified as the defendant's. Dr. James Studeley (Home Office pathologist) said the hairs were identical with Stamp's" (*The Times*, Wednesday, April 14, 1971).

"Adam Fanshaw, counsel for the defense, denied that hair recovered from Grace's bath could have belonged to Stamp. 'The defendant has never taken a bath in his grandmother's house,' he said, 'therefore any similarities shown by Dr. Studeley (Home Office pathologist) between the defendant's hair and hair retrieved from the bath must be coincidence'" (*Daily Telegraph*, Thursday, April 15, 1971). "In his summing up, Adam Fanshaw, QC said, 'Dr. Foyle (pathologist for the defense) has shown that the defendant's hair is comparable in character, color and form to his mother's hair, yet no one is suggesting Wynne Stamp committed this murder. The prosecution has failed to prove that the hairs found in the bath are the defendant's, merely that they are similar. Any ginger-haired person could have committed this crime . . . However, it is equally probable that hair from the defendant may have dropped into the bathtub during a previous visit'" (*The Times*, Friday, April 16, 1971).

This indecisiveness was damaging to Stamp's cause. Fanshaw, later to become a High Court judge, ran an inconsistent defense. On the horns of a dilemma because his client insisted he had never taken a bath in his grandmother's house, he offered alternative explanations to the jury. The hairs weren't Stamp's but, if the jury decided they were, then they must have dropped into the bath by accident. However, Wynne Stamp gave evidence that her son had not visited his grandmother's house between Thursday, May 28, and Wednesday, June 3. As she also insisted that her mother was too house-proud to leave her bath dirty, that left Wednesday as the only day for Howard's hairs to drop in "accidentally." Not unreasonably, the jury preferred prosecution claims that there was too much hair for this to have happened. The quantity was only consistent with someone immersing his head in water and rubbing it with shampoo.

If the pathologist's second estimate is to be believed, the crime took place between 1200 and 1400 on Wednesday, June 3, 1970. From the pattern of blood on the stairs, walls and floors, it was estimated that Grace had taken between one and two hours to die, and this fitted conveniently with sightings of Stamp. He was known to have left his mother's house at 1145 when he was seen by a neighbor. She described him as "looking normal" although she was unable to say what he was wearing. All the witnesses who saw him leaving his grandmother's house put the time at between 1400 and 1430 and their descriptions of his clothing were similar: "white shirt, not tucked in, and blue jeans," "shirt and trousers," "white T-shirt and Levi's." They all agreed his behavior was "peculiar." One said he was "running like a bat out of hell." Another: "He wasn't looking where he was going and bumped into the back of a parked car." A third: "He tried to hide his face but I saw it before he turned away. His eyes were mad and staring."

None said his hair was wet, nor that it looked different from normal. But they should have done if the prosecution was correct in its assumptions. In appearance,

Stamp aped his hero, Ginger Baker, the legendary drummer with the 1960s rock group Cream. A photograph of Stamp taken by his mother three months before the murder shows him with a pale, pinched face, straggly mustache and beard, and a tangled mat of wiry hair hanging over his face and down to his shoulders. Wynne said he rarely washed it because it "frizzed up when it dried and stuck out round his head." She also claimed he "put Vaseline on it to make it heavier." In his summing-up Adam Fanshaw drew attention to these discrepancies — "if the defendant shampooed his hair, it must have been wet or sticking out when he left the house . . . there were no residues of Vaseline on the hairs in the bath." But the jury wasn't impressed.

Perhaps they thought frizzy hair and matted hair looked much the same. Perhaps they found Stamp's clean-cut appearance at trial — he had been persuaded to shave and accept a short-back-and-sides to present a boyish appearance — inconsistent with his mother's descriptions of him as "always plastering his hair over his face to hide his lip." They certainly accepted the prosecution's claim that shampoo, a detergent, dissolves Vaseline, a petroleum-based product, despite the defense's attempts to prove that Vaseline residues would have remained on the sides of the bath.

In one last twist, Stamp's mugshot, taken four days after he was said to have had a bath, presents an identical appearance to the photograph taken three months earlier. Pale, pinched face, straggly mustache and beard, and a tangled mat of *Vaselined* hair to his shoulders.

Irreconcilable Evidence

The earliest Stamp could have reached Grace's house was 1200, and the latest he could have left it was 1430. This would have given him two and a half hours in which to work up a rage, slash and stab his grandmother before cutting her throat, take a bath, wipe his fingerprints from the bath taps (they were clean), vandalize her house to cast the blame elsewhere, pull the curtains and secure the windows.

Even assuming all this were possible in so comparatively short a time, he also had to remember to dispose of a pair of gloves in a litter bin after he left. Yet witnesses described him as behaving peculiarly, running like a bat out of hell, bumping into things and having mad, staring eyes. In other words, he was a man in a panic.

It's difficult to see how this mad flight in the middle of a summer afternoon can be reconciled with the thoughtful way he appears to have acted in the wake of the murder. Why draw attention to himself after leaving the scene if he'd made an attempt — however poor — to cover his tracks? Indeed why was it necessary to leave the house in such a hurry? Wynne said he rarely returned from visits to his grandmother until the early hours — "they watched telly together" — so why didn't he do the same that day? Not only would it have given him longer to lay a false trail, it would also have allowed him to slip out under cover of darkness.

The more obvious explanation for his flight is that his second statement was true. He let himself into his grandmother's house and was so shocked by what he discovered that he ran home in terror to lock himself in his bedroom.

When Was Grace Jefferies Killed?

The pathologist's first estimate, later dismissed as a "slip of the pen," suggested Grace died on Monday, June 1, 1970. The postman's statement, amended at trial, referred to her curtains having been drawn for several days before he decided to report his concerns to police on Friday, June 5. The blood deposits on Stamp's clothes were described as "flakes," which implies dried blood. In his second statement Stamp said, "I knew Nan was dead the minute I pushed her hand. It was cold and her fingers fell open. When I touched her shoulder it felt stiff."

This gives us the beginnings of a time frame. Rigor mortis starts after three to four hours in the small muscles of the face, hands and feet, before affecting the larger muscles. As it wears off, it follows the same pattern. Stamp's description implies rigor was still present in the major muscle of the shoulder, but had started to disappear in the smaller ones of the hand.

Because it's a chemical process, rigor can be affected by a number of variables: environmental temperature, body temperature, illness, activity before death, the physical conditions in which the corpse is left. Typically, a body that is described as cold and stiff has been dead between twelve and thirty-six hours, and one that is described as cold but *not* stiff may have been dead up to seventy-two hours. Cool environments and obesity delay onset, thereby extending the overall time frame. Warm environments and high metabolic activity before death advance it, thereby shortening the time frame.

Because of these variables, rigor is a poor indication of time of death. In Grace's case, there are conflicting factors. She was a large lady, but her metabolic rate must have been high in the hour before her death as she tried to avoid her tormentor. It was summer and the ambient temperature outside was warm; however, her curtains had been pulled to shut out the sunlight and police described the house as "chilly" when they entered. Loss of blood would have lowered blood pressure, while fear would have heightened metabolic activity.

The only records we now have of Dr. Studeley's findings come from newspapers:

> "The pathologist detailed the post-mortem results and said they were consistent with Mrs. Jefferies having been dead some forty-eight hours before he examined the body . . . In cross-examination, counsel for the defense challenged some of his conclusions. 'Isn't it true,' he asked,

'that the staining of the abdomen suggests decomposition was of longer duration than two days?' Dr. Studeley denied this. 'The process is faster when a body is exposed to air.' Fanshaw then asked why he'd found no evidence of rigor mortis. 'Grace Jefferies was a heavy woman. Wouldn't you have expected lingering stiffness in the larger muscles?' 'By no means,' said Dr. Studeley. 'The weather was warm and Mrs. Jefferies suffered horribly before she died. In such circumstances the onset and completion of rigor would be comparatively quick'" (*Daily Telegraph*, Tuesday, April 13, 1971). "After taking into account various factors, Dr. James Studeley said the postmortem results accorded with Mrs. Jefferies meeting her death during the morning or afternoon of June 3. He rejected defense claims that some of his conclusions were questionable" (*The Times*, Tuesday, April 13, 1971).

Dr. Foyle's testimony for the defense put the death twenty-four to thirty-six hours earlier. However, he faltered under cross-examination.

"The pathologist for the defense argued that putrefaction was too advanced for the forty-eight-hour estimate. 'Green staining appears on the right side of the abdomen in the first couple of days. Thereafter the discoloration spreads and the abdomen begins to swell with gas.' He pointed out that Dr. Studeley's notes from the postmortem mentioned 'pervasive staining and some bloating.' 'This is more consistent with three to four days,' he concluded. When asked by prosecuting counsel if he'd examined the body himself, Dr. Foyle admitted he hadn't" (*Daily Telegraph*, Wednesday, April 14, 1971). "Dr. Foyle said he believed the defendant's statement 'had the ring of truth.' 'Mr. Stamp's description suggests the process of rigor mortis wasn't complete at the time he found the body. This would agree with my estimate that Mrs. Jefferies died during the night of June 1 or by the evening of June 2 at the latest.' Asked under cross-examination if he'd seen the body, he said he hadn't. 'It's a matter of interpretation,' he said. 'Assuming Dr. Studeley recorded his findings accurately, then I cannot support his conclusions. In cases like this, time of death is always difficult to establish, but there's no doubt in my mind that Mrs. Jefferies was killed much earlier than is being suggested.' However, when pressed by prosecution counsel, Dr. Foyle agreed that Dr. Studeley's conclusions were 'not beyond the bounds of possibility'" (*The Times*, Wednesday, April 14, 1971).

Interestingly, it was the prosecuting counsel, Robert Tring, QC, who referred to Dr. Studeley's "slip of the pen."

"Robert Tring asked the witness why he had written four days in his postmortem notes if he was now claiming that Mrs. Jefferies had been dead only two days. Dr. Studeley said it was 'a slip of the pen' which he corrected on the official report" (*The Times*, Wednesday, April 14, 1971).

It's hard to understand why Adam Fanshaw didn't challenge this error when his own pathologist was arguing that three to four days was a more likely estimate. One explanation is that he planned to recall Studeley after his own pathologist had successfully established the night of June 1/day of June 2 as a possibility, and/or use the mistake as the main focus of his summing-up. Another explanation is that he didn't want to alienate the jury by badgering an elderly pathologist for a lapse of concentration, and intended to infer that Studeley had changed his mind under pressure from the police. In either event, the ground was cut from under his feet when Dr. Foyle agreed that Studeley's findings were "not beyond the bounds of possibility."

There was no reason why Foyle should have examined the body. Cause of death wasn't the issue; it was *time* of death that was in dispute. Stamp had alibis for June 1 and 2 — Wynne had taken a two-day "sickie" in order to "make him look for a job" — and June 3 was his first opportunity to visit Grace. Nevertheless, even had the defense insisted on their own postmortem, which was their right, it wouldn't have been helpful.

The significant factors in establishing time of death — ambient temperature, rigor mortis, algor mortis (body temperature), livor mortis (settling of the blood), autolysis and putrefaction (indicators of decomposition) — are useful only when the body is first examined, not after a week's refrigeration. Nor was there any reason to assume Studeley's data was wrong. An important fact brought out at the trial was the reference to "pervasive staining and bloating" of the abdomen. If, as Foyle claimed, this was more consistent with three to four days of decomposition, then the algor-mortis readings were important[5] and may explain why he was confident Grace had died "much earlier." In simple terms, if hourly readings showed an increase, then Grace's body had already cooled to the ambient temperature and was on the rise again.

Without more information, we can only guess what the debate was about, but the fact that it took place at all does seem to indicate the data was open to interpretation.

[5]After death, body temperature cools until it reaches the level of its surroundings. This process takes between eight and twelve hours on the skin, and twenty-four to thirty-six hours in the center of the body. Once putrefaction begins (about two days after death) the temperature rises again due to the metabolic activity of bacteria.

Despite prosecution claims that Stamp rifled his grandmother's drawers for money, or set out to pretend someone else had, there's no evidence that Grace had anything worth stealing. Wynne thought she "kept some cash in a shoe box," but couldn't suggest anything else that might have been stolen. The obvious person to ask was Stamp himself, since he knew Grace's house better than anyone, but as he was the main suspect, asking him was never in the cards.

The house was described as "vandalized" and a brief description was given by the policeman who broke in through the front door.

> "'I knew something was wrong when I saw the downstairs rooms. The place was a mess. Everything was broken: chairs, mirrors, even the plants had been torn out of their pots. It looked as if a kid had had a tantrum. I became alarmed when I saw blood on the stairs'" (*The Times*, Monday, April 12, 1971).

The prosecution alleged that Stamp lost

his temper and started breaking things, and when his grandmother remonstrated with him he pursued her upstairs with a carving knife from the kitchen. But if Stamp was innocent, then what does the destruction in the house tell us? Was it done for fun? Out of frustration? Anger? What kind of person vandalizes other people's property?

Research suggests he will be a young male with a history of truancy who associates with other delinquent youngsters. He will be living in a family with multiple problems, where there is little or no discipline and negligible supervision. Among his character traits will be aggressiveness, impulsiveness, self-centeredness, an inability to see another's point of view and a lack of forward thinking, all of which will make it difficult for him to understand the consequences of his actions and lead him to act on emotion and whim.

This is reflected in the policeman's remark: "It looked as if a kid had had a tantrum." Stamp certainly conformed to one of the above rules. He was a persistent truant, but he displayed the opposite character traits to a delinquent. He was too frightened to go out, too conscious of other people's opinions to forget his deformity, too aware of the consequences of his actions to attempt dating. Indeed, his vandalism was directed against himself. The more likely scenario if he'd killed his grandmother was that the police would have found two bodies when they broke in: Grace with a slit throat; Howard with multiple cuts on his arms before a last remorseful slice to his wrist brought peace.

Both prosecution and defense agreed that someone with frizzy or kinked ginger hair took a bath after the murder. The defense drew similarities between Wynne's hair and her son's hair not to suggest that Wynne murdered Grace but to demonstrate that hair was an unreliable method of identification in 1970.[6]

If either Grace or Wynne had had siblings, it would be tempting to look in their direction, but Wynne was an only child and there is no record that Grace had brothers or sisters. The kinked gene may have come from Wynne's unknown father, but any links with him seem to have been severed very quickly and it's unlikely that he or his subsequent children would have sought out Grace to murder her.

[6]Since DNA fingerprinting was introduced in 1987 it has become one of the *most* reliable methods.

More likely, Stamp was the victim of malign coincidence. Ginger hair is a characteristic shared by a significant number of British people and is frequently kinked — it appears to be one of its properties. Some past and present celebrities who've had it are Henry VIII, Queen Elizabeth I, Vincent Van Gogh, Ginger Baker, Art Garfunkel, Bette Midler, Mick Hucknall. To recognize how such a coincidence might happen, it's important to recall the words of Professor Simpson: "Identical hairs are not compelling evidence like fingerprints, for they carry so much less detail."

In the end, the most convincing evidence for Stamp's innocence of this crime are the pristine bath taps and the bloodstained gloves in the litter bin. These point unfailingly to someone else being in Grace's house. The gloves were used to search her drawers, vandalize her house and take up a knife to stab her, and the taps had to be cleaned because her murderer removed the gloves when he got into the bath.

The prosecution painted Howard Stamp as an angry young man of low intelligence who erupted one day in a fit of violence against the loving grandmother who protected him. In order to get away with it he donned a pair of gloves, took a bath, wiped his fingerprints from the taps but failed to remove them from any other surface. Why? His prints were found elsewhere in the bathroom, even on the lavatory seat, but if, in the wake of the crime, he recognized that to leave them on the bath taps would be harmful, why go on to insist that he'd never used the bath?

His detractors would argue that he wasn't bright enough to do anything else. Having confessed to everything at the beginning, he then rushed to denial. Indeed, the prosecution inferred that his denial was a tacit admission of guilt.

"In his summing-up, Robert Tring . . . drew the jury's attention to the evidence from the bathtub. 'The defendant claims he never used it,' he said, 'yet we have shown that he did. You must ask yourselves why he lied when only a guilty man would have been afraid to admit he'd taken a bath in Grace Jefferies' house'" (*Daily Telegraph*, Friday, April 16, 1971).

Unfortunately for Stamp the jury accepted this at face value instead of questioning why, if he was willing to say his confession had been coerced, he wasn't equally willing to "remember" a recent bath. While it would have been wrong for his barrister to suggest such a thing, there is no doubt Fanshaw would have discussed the evidential conflicts his client faced in such a way that the implications were clear. "My job would be a great deal easier if you'd used your grandma's tub, Howard. Are you *sure* you never did?" Wouldn't a guilty man have jumped at a way out?

In light of the Evans, Bentley, Kiszko and Downing miscarriages of justice, it's impossible to examine Stamp's case without having similar misgivings. He was an immature man with learning difficulties who was convicted on a retracted confession and disputed evidence. It's arguable if he even understood the case against him, let alone had the clarity of thought to present a viable defense.

Less than three years after his trial Howard Stamp was dead, driven to suicide by loneliness and despair. In his comparatively short life he had been teased and bullied for his harelip, mocked for his stupidity, accused and convicted of murdering the one person who protected him, then abandoned to fend for himself in the harsh environment of prison. Most would say it was a fitting punishment if he had murdered his grandmother. All would raise their hands in horror if DNA evidence proved tomorrow that he did not.[7]

[7]Anyone who has information relating to the murder of Grace Jefferies and/or the conviction of Howard Stamp can contact Dr. Jonathan Hughes, c/o Spicer & Hardy, Authors' Agents, 25 Blundell St., London W4 9TP.

Appendix

When I consulted Michael Williams, professor of behavioral science at Durham University, he suggested a profile of Grace Jefferies' murderer. "I have drawn some general conclusions, based on limited facts. Normally, I would visit the scene and study all available evidence. This is clearly impossible when the event happened thirty years ago, therefore much of this offender profile is informed guesswork. Victim-profiling has gained in importance in the last decade since it was recognized that a victim's pattern of behavior can also give clues to his/her murderer. Without more information about Grace Jefferies' character and lifestyle, my deductions are again guesswork."

This murder was an isolated event and not part of a series. As there was no evidence of a break-in, and Grace was described as "reclusive," it's reasonable to assume she knew her killer. This persuaded her to open her door. Because she was protective of her grandson, we can also assume she was protective of herself, which means her visitor was a regular caller or someone she recognized from the neighborhood. The murderer may not have intended to kill when he entered the house but, once inside, he lost his temper. He wreaked destruction out of frustration, possibly when he realized there was nothing worth stealing. Grace's speech impediment may have been the trigger for torture. He slashed at her to make her "talk" (either because it amused him or because he wanted her to tell him where her money was hidden). Oblivious both to the passage of time and the consequences of being caught on the premises, he took a bath to wash off her blood.

If we absolve Howard Stamp,[1] then

[1]Professor Williams added a caveat: "It was not unreasonable for the police to fix on Stamp as the prime suspect. He was Grace's only regular visitor, she thought of him as safe, he was frustrated with

the crime took place earlier than midday on June 3, 1970. This would expand the time frame during which the killer was able to operate. A significant factor was the closing of the curtains, which suggests he was in the house during the hours of darkness and feared being seen. It also explains why he was able to come and go without being noticed. Nevertheless, Grace was unlikely to open her door after dark unless she thought her visitor was "safe," and this implies an accomplice, almost certainly a girl, who was known to Grace and had a good excuse for being there. If this girl stayed to witness the crime, it is certain she experienced the same terror that Grace experienced; if she left after her boyfriend gained entry, then she was easily persuaded of his innocence and/or terrified into silence. In either case, she would not have spoken to the police.

---

himself and his life and he was known to lose his temper. There remains a question mark over his guilt, although I agree with Jonathan Hughes that (1) the time frame appears to have been distorted and (2) Stamp would have reacted differently if he'd committed the murder.

Significant features of the crime are: an expectation that there was something worth stealing; limited knowledge of forensic techniques (he left evidence of himself behind); sudden uncontrollable anger (he started destroying furniture); cruelty (he tortured his victim); a lack of forward thinking (he killed her regardless of the consequences); inexperience (he didn't expect to be covered in blood); no concern about being caught in the act (he took a bath afterward).

The killer was an immature person with a disorganized mind and anger/emotional problems. He may have been high on drugs, drink or glue. He believed Grace would be an easy "score" and was unnaturally confident about getting away with it. He was used to making threats — "land me in trouble and you're dead" — and he expected to be obeyed. This suggests a disdain for people in general, a disdain for the police in particular and a history of criminal behavior. There was no prior planning — he'd heard rumors that Grace kept cash in the house but he didn't bother to find out whether they were true. He was used to having his own way and became violent when he was thwarted.

Today he will be in his late forties and he may have a drinking or drug problem. He has, or had, ginger hair and will have spent time in prison. While in his teens he lived in or around Mullin Street in Highdown, Bournemouth. He was part of a deadbeat family who were disliked by their neighbors. He rarely attended school and regularly ran into trouble with the police. He was charismatic enough to attract a girlfriend (probably because he ran with a charismatic gang). He was the dominant partner in the relationship, although she was probably brighter. Because he is illiterate or semiliterate, he is unemployed or works as an unskilled laborer. He is easily roused to anger. If he lives with a partner and children they will be terrified of him; if he doesn't, then there are women and children in hiding who know him.

A selection of the 100-plus letters received by Jonathan Hughes

Tithe Cottage
West Staington
Dorset DT2 UVY

Sunday, August 12, 2001

Dear Dr. Hughes

I have just finished your book *Disordered Minds.* I was particularly interested by the chapter on the Grace Jefferies murder as my wife and I were living in Bournemouth at the time. As you know, it was a cause célèbre which filled many column inches in the national press. Indeed nothing so dreadful had happened in the town since Neville Heath's atrocious murder of Doreen Marshall in 1946.

With respect, I cannot accept your proposition that Howard Stamp was innocent. My wife and I were personally acquainted with one of his schoolteachers at St. David's Primary School, and she said he was a "wrong-un" from the age of six. While I accept that this is hardly evidence of guilt, I do believe that teachers have a feel for these things.

I fear you have fallen into the fashionable trap of looking to excuse sin, either by laying the blame at someone else's door or by portraying the sinner as a victim of circumstance.

Yours sincerely

Brendan McConnell

Replied, asking for name of teacher. Followed up on 10/3/01 and 11/14/01.

No response.

The man you're looking for is Barry Morton. He's got red hair and lives at 3 Springhill Close, Christchurch, nr Bournemouth. He regularly beats his wife and kids.

Received on 9/15/01. No address or signature. Checked out Barry Morton — too young (2 yrs. old in 1970).

Bournemouth

Dear Dr. Hughes,

I was at school with Howard Stamp. He was bullied all the time. Not that he turned up very often. Sometimes his mother dragged him in by his ear when the school inspectors got on to her. She wasn't a nice woman, she was always hitting him. I felt badly about the way he was treated. He was called terrible names. Even the teachers were nasty to him. I never believed he killed his nan but I don't know who did.

Yours sincerely,

Jan

Unable to reply without a full name and address.

Councillor G. Gardener
25 Mullin Street, Highdown,
Bournemouth, Dorset BH15 6VX

Dr. Jonathan Hughes
c/o Spicer & Hardy Authors' Agents
25 Blundell Street
London W4 9TP

December 17, 2002

Dear Jonathan Hughes:

After hearing an interview with you on Radio 4 some weeks ago, I was prompted to buy your book *Disordered Minds*. You will have noted that I live in the street where Grace Jefferies was murdered although, as I'm sure you're aware, her house and the two on either side were pulled down in 1972 to make way for a block of flats. I moved here from London in 1985 and by then her story was forgotten. I became aware of it after a spate of burglaries in the area when a neighbor mentioned that she hadn't seen so many police since

Grace's body was found. Naturally, I was curious and she gave me the details.

For over a century, Bournemouth has been depicted as a tranquil place of substantial villas, beautiful beaches and conservative (with both small and big Cs) inclinations, where the wealthy middle classes choose to retire. In some ways that is still what it represents, but an influx of service industries — finance, insurance, tourism — plus the inauguration of the university in 1992 and the success of the international airport, has brought a multitude of job opportunities to the town. It is now regarded as one of the "buzz" cities on the south coast.

With that in mind, it's difficult to imagine the "ghetto" that Highdown was in the 1960s. Trapped between the borders of Poole and Bournemouth, it was a dumping ground for difficult families where two, and sometimes three, generations were dependent on the dole. Most lived in council accommodation, while the 35% who owned their homes were widows or retired couples surviving on small pensions. The crime rate was disproportionately high compared with more affluent wards, although it tended to be opportunist thieving from property and gratuitous vandalism rather than the mugging and stealing of cars which is prevalent in other cities today.

This may go some way to explaining the shock that local people experienced when Grace was murdered. There was always concern among homeowners about the "deadbeat" families on their doorsteps, but they had learned to lock their doors and protect their possessions. A "California-style" killing was a different matter altogether, particularly when the victim was a shy widow with few friends. You make some reference to that in the book, but by no means enough. The local panic engendered by press headlines on the Saturday after the body was found was enormous.

The police in all parts of Bournemouth

were besieged by terrified women convinced they were going to be next. There was a mass exodus from Highdown as widowed ladies went to live with their sons or daughters rather than face a madman. Most remembered the murder of Doreen Marshall by Neville Heath, who was an early "serial killer." The convictions of Ian Brady and Myra Hindley for the Moors murders in April 1966 were still fresh in the mind. Charles Manson and his family were about to go on trial in America. It seemed as if the world was turning to multiple murder.

You mention the "collective sigh of relief" when Howard Stamp was arrested and charged, but it wasn't until the evidence was heard at trial that local people felt able to relax. My neighbor said they all thought the police had arrested the wrong person. She described Stamp as "someone who wouldn't say boo to a goose let alone murder anyone." In fact it was widely believed that the police had frightened him into making his confession, especially as none of the witnesses who saw him running away remembered seeing any blood on his clothes. There was a continuing fear that the real murderer was still at large.

As you make clear in your book, it was the forensic evidence that not only swung the jury against Stamp but also persuaded local people that he must be guilty. One detail you omitted was that Dr. James Studeley for the prosecution had trained under Sir Bernard Spilsbury — the "father" of forensic medicine — in the 1930s. Much was made of this by the prosecution during their cross-examination of Dr. Foyle, whose qualifications were "pedestrian by comparison," since he had trained in Australia under an "unknown." At one point, Robert Tring, Queen's Counsel, asked him to name a pathologist with whom he'd worked that a member of the jury might have heard of. He was unable to do so, and could only claim to have read their work. As this came after a similar question to Studeley, who cited not just Spilsbury but also

Sir Sydney Smith, Professor Keith Simpson, Dr. Francis Camps and Dr. Donald Teare, who between them had founded the "Association of Forensic Medicine" in the late 1940s, Foyle appeared to be a lightweight.

In particular, his quoting of Keith Simpson's comments on "identical hairs" lost credibility when Studeley was able to counter with remarks made by Simpson at another trial. "The supporting evidence of identical hair is useful when everything else is pointing in the same direction." In Stamp's case, of course, the "everything else" was his confession.

I applaud your efforts to bring Stamp's case to public attention, although I gather from your Radio 4 interview that you've had little success to date. From my own research I support your view that he was convicted on a coerced confession and unreliable evidence. However, in the absence of another suspect, it will be hard to prove. Sadly, my only neighbor who was here in 1970 died five years ago and, while I believe Wynne Stamp is still alive, I have never been able to find out where she went. Rumor had it she changed her name to escape publicity, but I have no firm evidence of that.

If I can be of any further assistance, please feel free to write.

Yours sincerely

George Gardener

George Gardener

Replied 1/5/03. During subsequent correspondence arranged a meeting for 2/13/03 at the Crown and Feathers pub in Highdown.

Chapter Two

Heathrow Airport, London
Wednesday, February 12, 2003, 11:00 p.m.

The news that evening was bleak. The government had ordered a ring of steel around Heathrow Airport. Scimitar lightweight reconnaissance tanks were parked menacingly along the perimeter walls, soldiers and armed policemen patrolled the terminals. London felt ominous. Even leaderless. The threat of looming war with Iraq — an unstoppable war if the BBC and the broadsheets were to be believed — depressed and worried its inhabitants. For many, the argument for a preemptive strike against a crippled country and a broken-backed dictator hadn't been made, and few understood why it was necessary to rattle sabers at Saddam Hussein when for fifteen months the enemy had been Al Qaeda.

There were rumors of splits in the Cabinet, and the Prime Minister's popularity had reached an all-time low. The Government had looked weak since a negotiating shambles had persuaded the firefighters to go on national strike, sucking soldiers away from the front line in order to man the pumps at home. People talked gloomily of a return to the "British disease" of the 1970s, when strikes had been commonplace. Patriotism was quoted as a reason why firefighters should remain at their stations. The air was thick with recrimination as the country took sides . . .

It was felt by every returning traveler to Heathrow that evening. They were warned to expect tanks and troops, but the reality of hard-faced soldiers and armed policemen in and around the terminals was shocking. It smacked of the military dictatorships they were being urged to mobilize against, and the more skeptical among them questioned the political convenience of unspecified terrorist threats so close to war. It was clever propaganda if it meant a reluctant population was frightened into accepting the necessity of preemptive strikes.

This was certainly Dr. Jonathan Hughes's position as he emerged, tired and angry, from Terminal 4 at eleven o'clock that night and lit a much-needed cigarette outside the exit doors. He was a tall, good-looking man with close-cropped dark hair and gold-rimmed spectacles, but that night he looked ill and drawn. He'd had trouble at both ends of the journey: four hours of checking in at JFK airport and a tailback of queues at Heathrow's passport control. Depression swamped him as he looked at the tanks and thought how easy it was for demagogues to whip up religious and racist hatred.

New York had been bad, but this was worse. He watched a woman wearing hijab cross the pavement toward him with lowered head, her tight shoulders betraying her fear. Airports were uneasy places since 9/11, and it wasn't just police and immigration officers who looked with suspicion at anyone with Arab features or Islamic dress.

Perhaps the Muslim woman felt Jonathan's gaze because she glanced up as she approached. The hijab, a pale green scarf wrapped like a nun's wimple round her forehead, cheeks and neck, performed its intended job of stripping her of her allure, and not for the first time Jonathan wondered why so many women were prepared to cover themselves rather than put the onus on men to behave with decency. At times like these the hijab bore such obvious witness to a woman's faith that it was dangerous. He felt his usual contempt for Muslim men. Not only did they want their wives to take responsibility for their own chastity — *"a woman should be concealed, for when she goes out the devil looks at her"* — they were too cowardly to advertise their own belief. Where was the male equivalent of the veil?

The woman scurried by, dropping her eyes the minute she met his angry ones. If she expected sympathy, she was out of luck. Jonathan studied comparative religions, but only for academic reasons. He didn't admire or approve of any of them. For him, the world was a godless desert where belief systems clashed because man's aggression was untameable. God was just an excuse for conflict, like capitalism or communism, and he found it laughable when leaders quoted morality as justification for their actions. There was no morality in killing people — a peasant's genes were as valuable to the species as a president's — merely expediency.

He dropped his cigarette and crushed it underfoot, the expression on his face showing his irritation as he stared after the woman. He deeply resented the implication behind the hijab, that every man was a potential rapist. Jet-lagged and cynical from a week in New York where reasoned discussion on a Palestinian state and the problems of Islamic fundamentalism had been impossible, Jonathan found his homecoming deeply dispiriting. It might have been Hiram Johnson who said the first casualty of war was truth, but to Jonathan's jaundiced eyes the first casualty was tolerance. As far as he was concerned, the world had gone mad since the attacks on the World Trade Center and the Pentagon.

Chapter Three

Highdown, Bournemouth
Thursday, February 13, 2003

He was in no better frame of mind by the morning. If anything, another sleepless night had made his depression worse. He should be using the day to recover instead of flogging himself to death to meet George Gardener. His interest in Howard Stamp was intellectual — a careless judicial system was indicative of a tired democracy — but he had no real desire to launch a crusade to clear one individual's name. He was a man of letters, not a man of action. He stared impassively out of the train window and wondered why he'd left it too late to cancel.

Sleet driving in on an icy east wind rattled the panes every time the train slowed. The other passengers, wary of meeting Jonathan's eyes, pointedly read their newspapers. He was an unsmiling man whose spectacles made him look older than his thirty-four years. The spectacles were cosmetic, his eyesight was perfect, but he wore them because he disliked not being taken seriously as an academic. He was dismissive of poor teaching and lazy thinking and had a reputation for departmental infighting. It won him few friends but it meant his intellectual authority was recognized. Certainly his fellow travelers found the brooding, introspective stare intimidating.

"For God's sake, Jon, everyone takes you seriously . . . they wouldn't dare do anything else . . ."

In the gardens and parks on the outskirts of town, thick layers of ice had formed on lakes and fish ponds, but when Jonathan finally disembarked at Branksome Station, after a cold wait at Bournemouth Central for a local train, the sleet was turning to water on the pavements. Shopkeepers, already suffering the knock-on effects of war jitters and plunging stockmarkets, stared despondently out of their windows as the wind-chill factor persuaded customers to stay at home. The weather would make the headlines on the local news that evening when Age Concern made a plea for help with pensioners' heating bills. Zero temperatures were a rarity in Dorset, which was why so many elderly chose to live there.

"Blair orders in tanks" read a stand outside a newsagent halfway up Highdown Road. It was a solitary shop, a tiny trading post in a run of shabby terraced housing. Jonathan glanced at the front pages of the newspapers on the racks inside the door. It was old news about the tanks at Heathrow. The war was still phoney. He crossed a side road and sheltered in the lee of a house to consult his map, cursing himself for coming. A jet-lagged body was unequal to the task of providing warmth, and his lightweight raincoat was about as waterproof as a piece of gauze. Worse, he had stomach cramps because he hadn't eaten since eight o'clock last night.

He screwed his eyes against the wind and sleet to read the street sign and wished he'd had the sense to look at a weather forecast. Irritation bubbled briefly against George Gardener. The councillor's last letter had said the Crown and Feathers was within easy walking distance of Branksome Station, but the man probably belonged to the Ramblers' Association and hiked twenty miles for pleasure every weekend. Easy walking distance to Jonathan was a couple of blocks, not a trek through a snowstorm. His fingers were numb, his shoes were leaking and he didn't believe this wild goose chase would lead to anything. His depression rode him like a black dog.

He took out a cigarette and cupped his hand round the flame of his lighter. The wind blew it out immediately. It was symptomatic of the day. Walking in Howard Stamp's footsteps thirty years after his death in order to talk to someone who'd never met him was pointless. He flicked the lighter again with the same result and blamed himself for ever allowing Andrew Spicer to include a contact address in the book. "If you believe what you write, then do something about it," Andrew had said. "If you don't then stop lecturing the rest of us on injustice." Jonathan tossed the cigarette into the gutter and clamped down on his simmering anger.

What did Andrew know about injustice? Jonathan should have taken him to New York and introduced him to some of his black and Islamic friends who were too frightened to go out. Hate crimes were increasing as troops were dispatched to the Gulf. If the whites weren't worried about war, they were worried about their investments. It was not a good time to be an American Arab or American Muslim. Even Jews were being targeted because of Israel's perceived intransigence toward a Palestinian state. At the bottom of the heap were north Africans on educational scholarships. As Jonathan knew well. He'd flown out to attend the funeral of Jean-Baptiste Kamil, a twenty-three-year-old student of his, who'd asked directions of the wrong man.

Divorced old Etonian Andrew Spicer, whose mouth had been stuffed with shiny white silver on the day he was born, was never going to suffer that kind of discrimination. Instead, he needled Jonathan. "It's time you left your ivory tower and got your hands dirty," he told him after reading Gardener's letter. "It'll make a good follow-up if you can prove your theory, and I won't have trouble getting an advance either."

Jonathan was reluctant. "It'll be time-consuming."

"You need the money."

It was true . . . "Not that badly." Certainly not badly enough to have another book "spiced up" by Andrew's editing. It had turned a thoughtful study on injustice into an unashamedly commercial book.

"You ruined the last one."

"It wouldn't have sold if you'd done it your way. As it is, you made a nice little profit. You'll stand to make a bigger one if you mount a campaign for Howard. Look at Ludovic Kennedy's *10 Rillington Place*. It was made into a film." Andrew folded his fat little hands on his desk. "You need the money, Jon. You can't buy Paul Smith suits and go to the opera every night on an academic's salary."

Money. With it, a man could lock his resentments in a box and be the person he wanted to be. Without it, he was nobody. Jonathan checked his map, saw with relief that Friar Road was the next on the left and battled on, head down. He didn't notice the BMW that drew quietly into the curb behind him.

The Crown and Feathers was on the corner, a dark Victorian building with pebble-dashed walls and signs in the windows advertising live music on Saturdays and discounted meals for senior citizens on Mondays, Wednesdays and Fridays. Jonathan's misery deepened. He loathed cheap and cheerful. No doubt the pub was a pit stop for coachloads of old-age pensioners on day trips to the coast. Or, worse, a drop-in center for the ones who lived there. There would be piped Vera Lynn singing "The White Cliffs of Dover" and "We'll Meet Again," the food would be inedible and the wine, if it was offered at all, would be vinegar. He should have stuck to his guns and insisted on a restaurant in town, but he might have had to foot the bill. With a sigh he shouldered open the door to the lounge bar and was surprised to find it almost deserted.

An elderly man sat on a bar stool, sipping beer and staring into space. A middle-aged couple were tucked away in a corner, heads together, sharing secrets. All three looked in Jonathan's direction when he entered, but the lack of response told him neither of the men was George Gardener. There was no one serving. He peered through a doorway marked "saloon," but it was empty except for a snooker table. The only food on offer appeared to be a list of sandwiches tacked to a wooden post; the only wine a couple of bottles beside the till with their corks pushed in. It was a place of cheap ale and no frills, and he wondered what sort of man would choose it for a meeting. Old Labor, Jonathan decided gloomily, and still fighting the class war.

Cold and wet, he shrugged off his raincoat and parked himself beside the bar. As an afterthought he took off his spectacles and tucked them into his breast pocket. Looking like an academic was the least of his problems. It was sporting the designer suit and shirt that was the mistake. He looked like a peacock in a chicken run, as out of place in the Crown and Feathers as the ancient beer drinker beside him would have been at Covent Garden. He felt the old man slide off his stool to move closer and studiously avoided his gaze. He was never in the mood for small talk — it was a talent he didn't possess — and especially not with a stranger who looked as if beer was his staple diet. The marbled hands were shaking so much that the decrepit Methuselah needed both of them to lift his glass.

"Don't get many of your sort in here."

Jonathan ignored him. It didn't take any deep intellect to guess what he meant by "your sort" and he wondered why it was always the elderly who came out with such statements.

A bony finger poked his arm. "I'm talking to you."

Jonathan lowered his leather briefcase to the floor and retrieved his cigarette pack from his raincoat pocket. "What sort is that?" he asked, ducking his head to the lighter. "Men who wear suits?" He shifted his glance to stare pointedly at the jabbing finger. "Or men on *very* short fuses?" He made a fist of his right hand and rested it on the bar.

The old man, perhaps mistaking the signet ring for a knuckle-duster, put some space between them. "Landlord's out back," he said. "Keep telling him he's losing customers, but he don't pay no heed. There's been a couple come and gone before you walked in."

"Mm."

"You should help yourself. Roy won't mind . . . long as you pay, of course."

"Mm."

"Maybe you don't go for ale? Not used to it, eh?"

"Mm."

"Don't say much, do you? Cat got your tongue?"

Jonathan made an effort. It wasn't the old man's fault he was overdressed for the occasion. He should have built in time to go home and change before a night with Verdi at the Royal Opera. "I'm in no hurry. I'm meeting a man called George Gardener. Do you know him? He's a local councillor."

The rheumy eyes gave a flicker of amusement, presumably anticipating that an Old Labor dinosaur and a peacock would make uneasy bedfellows. "Maybe."

"Is he a regular?"

"Comes in a couple of times a week. Sits over there to listen to the moaners." He nodded toward a window table. "Calls it a surgery or some such nonsense. Bloody waste of time *I* call it. How's a councillor going to increase benefits, eh? That's the government's job."

Jonathan gave a noncommittal nod.

"They should get off their arses and look for work," the old man grumbled. "No sense bellyaching to someone who can't do nothing."

"No."

"What you want with George, then? Looking for somewhere to live?"

"No."

"Good thing, too. Them as can afford it buy off the council . . . them like me what ain't got two farthings to rub together get down on bended knee and pray we don't get turned out." He stared into his beer. "It isn't right."

"No."

Belligerence sparked abruptly as if the repeated monosyllables annoyed him. Or perhaps it was the chill in the air — there didn't appear to be any heating in the room. "What would you know about it?" he snapped. "Where you from?"

"London."

The old man gave a derisive snort. "Timbuktu, more like."

"It's only two hours by train," said Jonathan mildly. "I did the trip this morning. It wasn't that difficult."

He was rewarded with a suspicious glare. "You making fun of me?"

"No."

"You'd better not be. I fought in the war so the likes of you could make something of yourselves. I got medals for it."

Jonathan took a thoughtful puff of his cigarette. The sensible thing would be to move to one of the tables, but he was damned if he'd give the old brute the satisfaction. He loathed senility with a passion. It was rude, it was self-absorbed and it contributed nothing to man's advancement. Rather the opposite, in fact. It was a destructive force, both in families and in society, because of the insatiable demands it made on the next generation.

The finger started jabbing again. "You listening to me?"

Jonathan took a deep breath through his nose before whipping up his hand and grasping the frail wrist. "You don't want to do this," he said, lowering his hand to the counter. "I'm cold, I'm wet, I'm tired and I am not in the best of moods." He relaxed his grip. "I sympathize with your housing problems but they are not my responsibility. I suggest you take them up with your MP, although he'll probably tell you to be grateful to taxpayers like me if you've been living on benefit all your life."

"Don't you lecture *me*," the old man snapped. "I got rights. More'n you'll ever have. I'm a Christian, I am, and it's a Christian country . . . or would be if we didn't keep opening our doors to heathens."

"This man bothering you?" asked a burly, dark-haired man, appearing through the saloon door.

Jonathan shook his head.

"I wasn't talking to you, mate. I was talking to my regular. I don't tolerate assaults on old guys. Certainly not by jumped-up wogs in fancy dress."

It was like a punch to the midriff. Jonathan hadn't been called a wog for years.

"That's a bit strong," said the old man. "He'll have you in court if you're not careful, Roy."

"What did he have hold of your hand

for? Was he hurting you?"

"No," Jim admitted fairly. "Didn't like me poking him."

"Then I apologize. No insult intended," Roy said, raising a trap in the counter and moving behind the bar. "Should have called you a black." He stood with his arms crossed, eyes narrowed aggressively, as if pulling a pint for this customer was the last thing he wanted to do. "What can I get you?"

"Nothing." Jonathan squashed his cigarette into the ashtray with a shaking hand and reached for his raincoat. "I'd rather take my chances in town." He took a card from his pocket and flicked it onto the bar. "If George Gardener comes in, tell him he can reach me on that mobile number. I'll give him the time it takes me to eat lunch, then I'll leave."

The landlord's expression changed. "Christ! Are you Jonathan Hughes? Listen, mate, I'm sorry. You should have said."

"What?"

"Who you were, for Christ's sake. I've been expecting a white bloke. Does *George* know you're a darkie?"

Jonathan took another calming breath. "Don't worry about it," he said, shrugging into the sodden coat and lifting his briefcase. “I’ll chalk it down to experience.” He retrieved his card and tucked it into his pocket. “On reflection, you can tell your friend I’ve changed my mind about meeting him. I don’t like the company he keeps.” He headed for the exit.

The landlord called after him, “Hang on, mate . . .” But his words were lost in the wind as Jonathan flung open the door.

After two hundred yards his furious pace slackened as a sense of proportion returned. He told himself to follow his own advice and chalk it down to experience. It wasn’t the first time it had happened and it wouldn’t be the last. His passport was scrutinized by zealous immigration officers every time he entered the country. He’d learned to bite his tongue, particularly since the events of 9/11, but it still maddened him. As a child his brain had churned with hatred every time he was slighted — *ignorant racists . . . low-grade trash . . . foul-mouthed illiterates* — but he had never said the words out loud.

If Andrew was to be believed, he should have done it. Holding back anger during adolescence had led to repression.

“You never stood up to your bullies, pal. You’ll argue a point to death in an article or a letter, but you won't do it face to face. Christ knows why. You're aggressive enough . . . on paper, anyway."

"I confront my colleagues and students every day."

"Where it's safe. It's not as if your students are ever going to hit you. You're two different people, Jon. A Rottweiler inside your department, an obedient whippet outside."

"They're dogs."

"Don't split hairs. You'll write damning critiques of your colleagues — it's made you a hero with your students — but you shy away from confrontation on the street. You spend a fortune on flashy suits to get yourself noticed, then hunch your shoulders and wear old men's glasses in case you are. You go to the opera, but you always go alone because you think an invitation might commit you to a relationship. It's a pity you didn't deck a skinhead when you were fifteen. You've been suppressing your feelings for so long you don't have any anymore."

"What makes you think it was whites who were the only problem? The Jamaicans and the Chinese were just as bad, and they ran in bigger gangs." Jonathan's face hardened at some distant memory. "They were illiterate and stupid, and none of them could speak English well enough to be understood." He gave a cynical shrug. "You try being half Iranian, half Libyan in that kind of environment . . . with a dark skin, Caucasian features and an English name that no one believes you're entitled to. Trust me, you keep your head down and work like crazy to get yourself out of it. The last thing you do is take a swing at anyone."

"For an anthropologist, you have a great dislike of people, Jon."

"It has nothing to do with anthropology. Abstract science doesn't generate hate."

"Then what does?"

War, thought Jonathan. His anger and aggression had increased by leaps and bounds since his passport had started being questioned. At the back of his mind was a constant fear that if he lost it, he would lose everything. As always, he patted his breast pocket to reassure himself it was there. The gesture was so automatic it had become a nervous tic.

A car drew up to the pavement beside him. It was an ancient Mini Cooper with its backseat piled high with books and files. "Excuse me . . . excuse me!" a woman called in a shrill voice as she wound down her window. "Are you Jonathan Hughes?" The voice rose to hideous vowel-strangled stridency. "*Excuse* me . . . *excuse* me!"

Jonathan ignored her.

He heard the gears crunch as she set off in pursuit on the wrong side of the road. "*Please* stop!" she shouted, pulling round a parked car to draw ahead of him. "Oh, *help!*" Her wail reached him as a van appeared out of the sleet in front of her and she slammed on her brakes.

Jonathan screwed up his eyes in pained disbelief and waited for the inevitable to happen. She was lucky. The reactions of the van driver were as quick as hers and he stopped his vehicle a yard from her bumper. His views on women drivers, mouthed through his windshield with his finger pointing skywards, were inaudible but intelligible, and none of it was complimentary. In particular, he didn't like *fat* women drivers. With a shake of his fist, he reversed up and pulled away.

Jonathan bent down to look through the window. "You'd better pull over before anyone else comes," he said. "I'll wait."

She was red-faced and shaking, but she had the presence of mind to do as he said. "God, that was stupid," she said, opening her door and climbing out. "I am so, so sorry. What must you be thinking?" She was zipped into a padded red coat with Wellingtons on her feet and a lime green woolen hat clamped to her head like a Roman helmet, none of which did anything for her figure or her complexion. She looked like a squat garden gnome and Jonathan wondered if she ever bothered to consult a mirror. He put her age at about sixty.

"What do you want?" he asked.

"I'm George Gardener." She offered an apologetic hand which he shook reluctantly. "I can't tell you how embarrassed I am about this. I could murder Roy and Jim for being so crass. I'm not going to make excuses for Jim — he's rude to everybody — but I'm afraid Roy thought you were a crack-cocaine dealer." She pulled a wry face. "The police keep warning us about London-based gangs moving in and he thought you were one of them."

"Is that supposed to make me feel better?"

The color deepened in her roughened cheeks. "I'm just trying to explain why he said what he did."

"I thought crack-cocaine dealers were Jamaican Yardies. Do I look like a Jamaican?"

"No, but . . . well, you have a very English name and you don't look like an Englishman either," she said in a rush.

Jonathan was unimpressed. "And you have a very male name, Mrs. Gardener, but I didn't insult women because I was expecting to meet a man." His mouth twisted cynically. "Does your friend assume all *white* men who enter his pub are drug dealers?"

She hesitated, considering the wisdom of answering. "As long as you don't mind my quoting him, then yes, he would . . . if they were flash bastards in smart suits . . . and the police had told him the gangs were white. People like that don't go into his pub." She wrung her hands. "*Please* don't be offended. Roy wasn't being racist, he was just trying to explain why he hadn't recognized you. He works very hard to keep drugs out of that pub, which is why most of his customers are elderly and he doesn't make any money. It's not a trendy place. The young wouldn't be seen dead in it."

Jonathan could well believe that. He wouldn't frequent the Crown and Feathers if he were paid. But he wondered at her naivety and was tempted to repeat the conversation from his point of view. There was no question in his mind that Roy was as racist as they came, but there was little point arguing about it. "All right," he said with a curt nod. "I am not offended."

"Then you'll come back?" she asked eagerly.

"No. I'm freezing to death and I'm not a beer and sandwiches man, Mrs. Gardener. I'll find somewhere with a more substantial menu."

She sighed. "It's Miss actually, but I can't stand being called Ms. I'd rather you called me George."

Why wasn't he surprised? No man in his right mind would want this earnest little bumpkin with her terrible fashion sense and bulky body.

"Roy made a hotpot specially," she told him. "He's a good chef — *truly* — and he's given us one of the private rooms. There's a *fire* going. The only reason I chose the Crown and Feathers was because Roy knew Howard Stamp." She placed a small, pleading hand on his arm. "It all went wrong because my car wouldn't start. It's the cold. I should have put newspaper under the hood last night, but I wasn't expecting a freeze. *You* wait: statistics say that at least two of my constituents will have broken a hip by this evening and fifty percent of the rest will be shivering in blankets to avoid upping their heating bills. Those are the pensioners like Jim."

Jonathan might have said that Bournemouth was holding fewer and fewer attractions for him, but he hesitated when she mentioned Howard Stamp, and she saw the interest in his face.

"Oh, *brilliant!*" she said, clapping her hands like a born-again Christian. "Hop in and I'll drive."

He almost abandoned it there and then. "I'd rather walk, thank you."

"Oh, come *on,*" she said, shepherding him round the hood. "I need Roy to charge the battery for me, so there's no point leaving the car here. You don't want to pay any attention to what that van driver said. My eyesight's fine and I've had a license for years. Also, I don't usually drive on the wrong side of the road."

She didn't seem to understand "no" and, with resignation, he folded his tall frame into the cramped passenger seat. She was sorry she couldn't adjust the seat, but the Mini doubled as a filing cabinet and there wasn't enough room. Jonathan's knees were almost touching his chin and he smiled rather sourly. The only thing he was grateful for was that none of his students could see him. Slumming it wasn't Dr. Hughes's style at all. George chattered like a little bird back to the pub, parked in a courtyard at the back, then solicitously helped him unfurl in order to march him upstairs to the private room where he was forced to accept the landlord's apologies.

It didn't go as well as she'd hoped. Roy Trent wasn't the type to eat humble pie, and Jonathan, who struggled with his own racism in a way that whites would never understand, was immediately reoffended to be called black. Despite his dark skin, he never thought of himself as black, only as an Arab. His irritation increased as George urged him forward, butting against his back with a large plastic carrier bag that she'd retrieved from the back of her car. *She* looked like a tramp, the landlord — the *chef* — looked as if he hadn't washed his hands in weeks, and Jonathan's fastidious nature recoiled at the whole idea of breaking bread with them.

"I could probably take the racism . . . I don't agree with it, but I suppose I understand the history. It's the snobbery I hate. You have such an inflated opinion of your intelligence, Jon. You think it puts you above everybody else . . . but clever people do not *set out to patronize everyone they meet . . ."*

Chapter Four

Inside, the two men eyed each other like a couple of silverback gorillas preparing to fight over a ripe female. Roy Trent, at a disadvantage because he was on his knees trying to bring the fire to life, or because he genuinely cared for the fat little gnome behind Jonathan, capitulated first. "Listen, mate, I'm sorry," he said, shoveling coal into the grate. "I saw this big black geezer gripping old Jim's hand and giving him the evil eye, and I thought, shit, he's dressed up like a dog's dinner and he's talking like Laurence bloody Olivier. I mean, it's not normal, is it? We all know Jim's a miserable old sod, but we tend to switch off and let him get on with it. It's George's fault really. All she told me was that an author was coming — some fellow who'd written about poor old Howard — so I was expecting a puny little critter in an anorak. I mean, Howard's hardly front-page news, is he?" He flicked

Jonathan an assessing gaze. "The real trouble is, you don't have a foreign name. I mean, Jonathan Hughes — what could be more English than that? Now, if you'd been called Mohammed or Ali, there wouldn't have been a problem." He stood up, wiping his coal-blackened hands on his trousers. "Apology accepted?" he asked, proffering his right.

Jonathan, well aware that he'd been purposely maligned, grasped the hand firmly in his and bore down heavily on the man's metacarpal bones. "As long as you accept mine."

There was a flicker of irritation in Roy's eyes but he answered pleasantly enough. "OK. What do you want to apologize for?"

"Making wrong-headed judgments about whites," said Jonathan. "It's a bad habit of mine. You all look the same to me."

"Go on, I can take it. What's the punchline?"

"Germans are well educated, the French are well dressed, the Irish have talent and Americans are polite." He shrugged. "As the British are none of these things, I invariably make mistakes in my dealings with them." He removed his raincoat and hung it on a hook beside the door before smoothing his jacket and hoping the shiny patches on the elbows wouldn't be noticed. "I apologize for the suit. I wore it as a courtesy to the person I was meeting —" he felt George stir uncomfortably behind him — "but I should have realized how inappropriate it would be. Of course, if your pub had been called the Pig and Wallow, there wouldn't have been a problem — I'd have had an idea what to expect — but the Crown and Feathers suggested a classier establishment."

There was a long pause while Roy thoughtfully massaged his fist. "Just for the record, so you don't get it wrong another time, you can't tell a pub by its name, mate. The Pig and Wallow could be the best inn you'll ever come across."

Jonathan smiled slightly. "Thank you for enlightening me," he murmured. "Being black and foreign does make the vagaries of English naming traditions very difficult to understand."

Roy jutted his chin aggressively. "You left out our good qualities. We don't take life as seriously as the Germans . . . we don't bellyache like the French . . . we don't emigrate at the drop of a hat like the Irish . . . and we don't worship money like the Americans." He tugged his old jumper over his beer gut. "I'll concede the bad dressing, though. So what nationality are you?"

"As British as you, Mr. Trent."

"Except I'm English."

The room was a small one with a table laid for two and a couple of leather armchairs on either side of the fire. Jonathan motioned to one of the chairs, inviting George to sit down. "May I take your coat?"

She clamped her arms over her chest. "No, I'm fine."

He wondered what she was wearing underneath. *Pajamas?* It wouldn't surprise him. Nothing would surprise him today. "Do you mind if I sit down?"

"Please."

He crossed one elegant leg over the other and put on his spectacles. "If you're asking what my racial roots are, Mr. Trent, then my father's family is Iranian and my mother's family is north African. I have an English name courtesy of my paternal great-grandfather, who was called Robert Hughes, and the reason I'm British is because I was born here and hold a U.K. passport. I attended a London comprehensive school, won a place at Oxford and am now a research fellow in European anthropology at the University of London. I speak English, French and Farsi fluently and can get by in German and Spanish." He steepled his hands under his chin. "So what are your racial roots? I'd say there's a lot of Welsh in you."

"None at all," said the burly man suspiciously. "My parents are both Dorset folk."

"Interesting. Yet your Celtic genes are so strong."

"How do you make that out?"

"Body shape, stature, eye color, facial type. A true Englishman would have Anglo-Saxon characteristics. He'd be taller and fairer, with blue or gray eyes and a finer bone structure. You have strong Celtic features — wiry dark hair and brown eyes — and your body shape is endomorphic. It's why the Norsemen called the Welsh trolls, because they were short, dark, hairy men with big bellies." He glanced at George as she made small tut-tutting noises. "I'd say you're at least seventy-five percent Welsh, Mr. Trent."

"That's rubbish," said the other man crossly. "You can't tell an Englishman just by looking at him. I'm fat because I eat too much. It doesn't make me bloody Welsh."

Jonathan touched his hands to his forehead in obeisance. "I do apologize. I hadn't realized being Welsh was such a problem for you. It's another area of the English psyche that I've never understood. I thought it was the Scots and Irish you didn't like."

"I am *not* Welsh."

George gave a nervous little wave. "He's teasing you, Roy. The Angles and Saxons were Germanic peoples who invaded England in the fourth century . . . at the same time as the Jutes and Vikings. The Jutes were Danes, the Vikings were Norwegian. Prior to that we were conquered by the Romans — who were *Italians* — and seven centuries later we were taken over by the Normans who were *French*." She squeezed her eyes at Jonathan in painful pleading. "Dr. Hughes was joking about endomorphs — *I'm* one, *you're* one — an *Iranian* could be one. It's got nothing do with nationality, anymore than color has. For most of us nationality's a *choice,* Roy . . . not a birthright."

"Not for me it isn't," he said stubbornly. "I was born here. It's the asylum seekers who look around for something better that choose."

George gave a disheartened shrug as if his xenophobia was not new to her. "At least recognize that it was the whites who invented economic migration, Roy. Everyone who went to America was looking for a better life."

Jonathan watched the man's mouth set into even more obstinate lines. He was tempted to tell him they both belonged to the same racial group, Caucasian — the non-Negroid peoples of Europe, the Middle East, north Africa and western Asia — including the Welsh — but it would only offend him. Instead he took pity on George's red face and extended a hand. "Shall we start again? I'm afraid I've been very ill-tempered since last night when I flew in from New York and was put through the wringer by an immigration officer. He asked me my views on Osama bin Laden. When I refused to answer, he kept me hanging around for an hour while he checked to see if my passport was genuine."

Roy accepted the olive branch. "Why did you refuse?"

"Because there was only one answer. Even bin Laden's most fanatical supporters are hardly likely to admit it to an immigration officer."

Roy appreciated the point. "Did he ask the whites the same question?"

"What do you think?"

"No."

Jonathan nodded. "You learn to live with it, Mr. Trent. At times like this, when people are frightened, there's always a presumption of guilt if your face doesn't fit. It's depressing. It happened to the Irish living in England every time an IRA bomb went off. It happened to Howard Stamp when people thought a Manson-style killer was roaming Highdown."

But mention of Howard Stamp brought an immediate cooling. Roy glanced at his watch. "I'd better see what's going on downstairs. Can I get you something to drink? Are you allowed alcohol? George suggested a Gevrey-Chambertin to go with the hotpot but perhaps you'd prefer something else? Wouldn't want to offend your religion or anything."

"I'm an atheist," said Jonathan, watching him, "and the Gevrey-Chambertin sounds excellent. Thank you."

"I'll be back shortly." He patted George's arm as he passed. "If you don't take that coat off soon, girl," he murmured, loud enough to carry, "you'll spontaneously combust . . . and the hat's not doing you any favors either, trust me. If you're going to be judged on your looks, you might as well get it over and done with as quickly as possible."

* * *

Trent closed the door behind him, but listened for a minute or two before he walked away. His first remark to Hughes had been accurate. "A jumped-up wog in fancy dress." The man was certainly doing himself no favors with George. Apart from anything else, he was insisting on calling her Miss Gardener. With an amused smile he walked down the stairs and pushed open the kitchen door, only for his amusement to turn to anger when he saw his ex-wife watching the CCTV monitor in the corner.

"What the hell are you doing here?" he asked angrily. "I told you to stay away."

She glanced at him. "I fancied a look at the famous author."

"Why?"

"So I'd recognize him again. I don't trust you, Roy, never have. When were you planning to tell me he was black?"

"I didn't know myself." He stared at her for a moment before taking a couple of wine glasses from a cupboard and transferring them to a tray. Age had been kind to her, whereas George looked every one of her years. The difference was character. George was ugly, unassuming and kind; his ex was a good-looking bitch.

She flicked the fringes of her cashmere

scarf. "A sad little anorak, you said, who doesn't know shit except what he's got from old newspapers. Instead Denzel Washington turns up."

"He says he's an Iranian."

"Who cares? He's black enough to be a nigger." The woman's pale eyes narrowed aggressively. "Your girlfriend's going to bust a gut to help him whatever he is. She's a do-gooder, for Christ's sake, and it's PC to be nice to wogs."

"Yeah, well this one's an arrogant bastard. I don't think George likes him much." He grinned suddenly. "You can thank me for that. I put his back up before she even arrived, and now she's having to grovel."

The woman looked interested. "Did you do it on purpose?"

He nodded toward the monitor. "Seemed worth a shot. I watched that old fool Jim Longhurst needle him for ten minutes, then went out and added to his grief. He's easily offended . . . but it doesn't stop him looking down his nose at proles. He's treating poor old George like something the cat brought in."

"I watched her go after him. She'd have licked his black arse if he'd given her half a chance."

Roy gave a contemptuous snort. "You might . . . she wouldn't."

"He's not bad looking."

"Looks like a woofter to me," said Roy, wiping his hand on his trousers as if it had been contaminated. "It won't cut any ice with George. She's only interested in what he can do for Howard."

"You sure she doesn't know anything?"

Roy shrugged as he reached for the Gevrey-Chambertin. "What's to know? If it wasn't Howard who killed Grace, then it was some other kid with ginger hair. The best either of them can do is clear the little sod's name." He placed the bottle on the tray with a corkscrew. "But there isn't a chance in hell they'll put anyone else in the frame —" he flicked her a speculative glance — "unless you know something I don't, Cill."

"Don't call me that," she snarled. "What about DNA? He mentions it in the book."

He could feel the heat of her impatience. "There's nothing to test it against," he said calmly. "All the evidence was destroyed after Howard died. George pestered the police for years until they told her it was incinerated." He hefted the tray and pushed past her. "Now get lost before someone sees you."

* * *

"I suppose you heard that," said George with a sigh as the door closed behind Roy.

Jonathan nodded.

"Oh, well." She tugged off her hat and sent her stubbly gray hair shooting skyward with static electricity. "I had an argument with the hairdresser," she explained apologetically, before discarding her coat to reveal an old yellow jumper with car oil down the front and a pair of equally grubby gray leggings tucked into her boots. "And I'm on nights at the moment so I didn't wake up till eleven. I thought I'd check the car before I put on my glad rags and, when it wouldn't start . . ." She gave a self-deprecating shrug. "I agree with you about it being courteous to dress up, Dr. Hughes, but I ran out of time to change. I rather hoped you'd be an elderly, short-sighted professor . . . and wouldn't notice."

Her hair looked more like the aftereffects of chemotherapy, and he wondered if the glad rags included a wig. He rose to his feet and pulled the other chair forward. "The only reason I'm wearing a suit, Miss Gardener, is because I'm going to Verdi's *Falstaff* tonight." He smiled as he sat down again, but it was a mechanical civility rather than an expression of friendship. "Let's just agree that first impressions aren't always right . . . and take it from there."

Her enthusiasm returned immediately. "Oh, thank goodness," she said with feeling, dropping into the other chair. "I was beginning to wonder how we'd get through this meal if I had to watch my p's and q's for hours. Putting on airs isn't my strong point — as you've probably noticed." Her voice had no accent until her pitch rose and the vowels betrayed London roots. "My poor mother despaired of me. She wanted a dainty, well-behaved daughter and she got a bull in a china shop."

"Is she still alive?"

"No. Died of breast cancer when I was fourteen." She pulled another face as if screwing her eyes and lips into gargoyle twists was a nervous mannerism, and Jonathan thought how astonishingly ugly she was. "She was ill for a long time before that so I was effectively brought up by my father. He had no airs and graces either, which is why I never learned them."

"What did he do?"

She smiled affectionately, bobbing forward to sit on the edge of her seat. "He was a postman."

Jonathan stretched his feet toward the fire and leaned back to put distance between them. "Is he still alive?"

She shook her head. "Heart attack fifteen years ago. That's when I upped stumps and came to Bournemouth. I'm afraid the genes aren't healthy on either side. If I make old bones it'll be a miracle, though it won't upset me hugely if I don't," she said matter-of-factly. "There's a lot of misery in old age."

"Jim being the perfect example," Jonathan said dryly.

Her eyes twinkled mischievously. "You can't blame old age for that. According to Roy, he's always been miserable. Did he tell you about his medals?"

Jonathan nodded.

"You have to feel sorry for him. He has flat feet so he spent the war emptying dustbins. He's told the medal story so often that I think he believes it now, but it's sad when someone has to invent a history because their lives have been such a disappointment." The eyes, a bright blue, examined him closely. "My father always said the hardest cross to bear was a chip on the shoulder. The more you resent it, the heavier it gets."

He wondered if she was having a dig at him. "How come the night shifts? What do you do?"

"Nothing very grand. I work in a nursing home."

"As a nurse?"

"Just a care assistant. I used to be a tax inspector when I lived in London." She smiled at his expression. "We don't all have horns, you know. Some of us are quite nice."

"Why give up? Couldn't you have transferred to a tax office down here?"

"It seemed like the right time to reassess priorities. In any case, I enjoy working with dementia. All my patients have amazing imaginations, none of which bears any relation to logic or reality. I have one old lady who's convinced her husband was murdered. She tells everyone he was bludgeoned to death by angry neighbors."

Jonathan looked doubtful. "Doesn't it upset her?"

"Only when she's told it's not true. It's her fifteen minutes of fame to produce a conversation stopper while a naive young nurse is trying to feed her. She sulks if people point out that her memory's at fault. It's like telling Michael Jackson he's black." She squeezed her eyes shut. "Oh lord! Foot in mouth. Didn't mean to use the b-word. Sorry!"

"Just don't use the w-word," Jonathan

said, hiding his irritation.

"What's that?"

"Welsh."

She gave a squeak of laughter. "Oh dear! That was quite funny, wasn't it? What's wrong with the *Welsh,* for goodness sake?"

"King Offa built a dyke in the eighth century to keep them in Wales," he said ironically. "I expect it has something to do with that."

Another giggle. "How did you know Roy would react the way he did?"

"Because he wants to be thought of as English. If I'd accused him of being Scottish or Irish, he'd have been just as angry. He probably doesn't like Lancastrians or Yorkshiremen either, so his Englishness is very much West Country based." He raised an eyebrow. "If you scratched him hard enough, his preferred passport would say Dorset. That's the only tribe he wants to belong to."

She examined his face for a moment. "And you, Dr. Hughes? What tribe do you want to belong to?"

It was a question he couldn't answer. Indeed, it was easier to list the tribes he didn't want to join — blacks, whites, yellows, browns, mulattos — than to name the one he did. His father wanted him to acknowledge his paternal roots, his mother hers, and all he could do was make the best of being British. And that wasn't easy. *Easy* would have been for his warring parents to have remained in their own countries, rather than emigrate to England, produce a single child and wait eighteen years to declare their hatred for each other. Had Jonathan been born in the homeland of either of his parents, he might have felt he belonged. Instead they'd left him rudderless, with only a flimsy passport to prove who, and what, he was.

He reached for his briefcase. "Shall we talk about Howard Stamp? I thought you might be interested in some of the letters I've received."

"If you like," George agreed.

"He's the reason we're here," Jonathan reminded her.

"Oh, I doubt it," she said. "I can't think of a single occasion when I've had just one reason for doing anything. Can you?"

He snapped the catches on his briefcase. He had no intention of discussing philosophy with her. "There's a woman who was at school with him — Jan — but she didn't give me an address or surname. Roy might be able to identify her. Another correspondent mentioned a schoolteacher. It would be useful to find her if she's still alive." He extracted the letters and handed them over.

George didn't read them immediately. "Have you ever thought that Howard's only purpose in life was to be a scapegoat? That's rather sad, don't you think?"

Jonathan flicked through the remaining letters. She'd be telling him God moved in mysterious ways next. "I'm more interested in the shortcomings of the police and judicial systems," he said patronizingly, "particularly when they have to deal with inadequate personalities or accused from different cultures who don't have a facility with language."

"I see," was all she said, before bending her head to the first piece of paper.

Chapter Five

The Gevrey-Chambertin made George's face even redder, a fact remarked on by Roy when he reappeared with their lunch. "You want to watch it," he warned her. "You'll be done for drink-driving if you're not careful."

He was solicitous of her in a ham-fisted way, and Jonathan wondered about the exact nature of their relationship. She certainly took Trent's comments in better spirit than he would have done, but then friendship for him meant mutual respect. Anything less wasn't friendship. "You'll die a lonely old man," Andrew had warned once. "Loyalty is worth more than respect."

"Same difference."

"Hardly. Your sycophantic friends wouldn't dream of pointing out your flaws."

"What makes you think they're sycophants?"

"Because you choose them carefully. You

need to be admired, Jon. It's a gaping flaw in your character."

"So what does that make you?"

"A loyal friend from Oxford days — your *only* friend from Oxford. You should think about that. It may be my easygoing personality, though I suspect it has more to do with the fact that I'm eight inches shorter than you, took over the family business and cheated on my wife."

"Meaning what?"

"That you can look down on me, literally and figuratively, so I've never threatened your self-esteem. My business success, such as it is, is transparently inherited, and my failed marriage means I'm no better at keeping women than you are. It's an interesting paradox in your character. You demand respect for yourself, but you can't give it. The minute you decide you're being eclipsed, you move on. I assume it's fear of perceived failure and not jealousy of another's good fortune that makes you do it, but it's a damned odd way to conduct your life."

Jonathan watched George use a letter to fan her face and tamped down a sudden rush of contempt. He looked away to hide it, questioning quite seriously whether there was something wrong with him. He felt divorced from the room, from the people in it, even from himself — this level of detachment wasn't a normal symptom of jet lag. He wondered if the wine was to blame. Strange tremors, like electric shocks, shot up his arm every time he lifted the glass to his lips, although only he seemed aware of them.

"You can't go on like this . . . you should see a doctor . . ."

The room was too warm. He took out a handkerchief and wiped a bead of sweat from his upper lip. "I gather you knew Howard Stamp," he said to Roy as the man laid the table.

"Depends what you mean by 'know,' mate. He used to pop into my dad's shop once in a while to pick up stuff for his gran but, as he never said much, we weren't exactly close."

"Where was the shop?"

"You'll have passed it on your way here. It's the newsagent in Highdown Road."

Jonathan remembered. "Was he older than you? He'd be in his midfifties if he was still alive."

"Yup," Roy agreed unhelpfully, retrieving salt and pepper pots from a cupboard. "You wouldn't have thought it at the time, though. He managed to grow a bit of a mustache and a scrappy little beard, but he never looked his age. He was a right little wimp . . . even his voice failed to develop. My dad called him 'sparrow chest' and told him to get a Bullworker . . . but he never did." He paused, thinking back. "He should've done. He'd have had more confidence with a muscle or two."

"You called him 'poor old Howard' earlier. I assumed you had some sympathy for him."

"In retrospect I do — he was bullied rotten — but at the time . . ." He broke off with a shake of his head. "A bloke couldn't afford to feel sympathy then. The kids today think they invented street cred but it's been around for decades. Only a loser would have admitted friendship with Howard."

"Classic torture tactics," murmured Jonathan mildly. "The Scylla of isolation and the Charybdis of fear."

Roy paused in what he was doing. "Scylla" — *Cill?* — at least, had struck a chord. "If you spoke English," he said carefully, "I'd know what you were talking about."

"Scylla and Charybdis were six-headed monsters who inhabited rocks in the Mediterranean," said George. "Ulysses had to steer his ship between them without being snared by either in Homer's *Odyssey*."

Roy relaxed noticeably. "I expect you're right," he drawled, "but it still isn't English."

"Howard was between a rock and a hard place," Jonathan explained, "bullied because he was friendless, and friendless because he was bullied. He had nowhere to go except inside himself. The outward sign of his distress was cutting his arms."

Roy shrugged. "Not my fault, mate. You can't hold the rest of us responsible because Howard didn't have the bottle to stand up for himself. We all got teased, but most of us learned to deal with it." He removed the casserole dish from a hotplate on the sideboard and placed it on a mat in the middle of the table. "Good eating," he said, before vanishing again.

"Was he one of the bullies?" Jonathan asked, clenching his fist involuntarily on the arm of his chair.

George noticed it and heard the edge to his voice. "Probably," she answered honestly, "but then all the children were. I don't think it would be right to single Roy out as an aggressor. He was five or six years younger than Howard, so he wasn't at school with him, and the school bullies were the worst." She heaved her bottom out of the chair and moved to the table. "Perhaps scapegoat was the wrong description. Whipping boy might have been better. The first had the sins of the Jews laid on his back before he was chased into the wilderness, the second was flogged for the failings of others. In either case, the guilty escaped punishment. It's a very twisted concept."

"But an old one." Jonathan pulled out the other chair. "Jesus died on the cross to take the sins of the world on himself. Or have I got that wrong?"

She smiled slightly. "You know you haven't," she said, unfolding her napkin, "but there's a difference between the son of God absolving the world and some poor goat being expected to do it." She took his plate and spooned lamb hotpot onto it. "Here's another animal sacrifice," she joked, handing it to him. "Help yourself to vegetables. As far as I know, they've never had to atone for anyone's sins. Or am I wrong, Dr. Hughes?"

There was more of the same during the meal. Serious remarks interspersed with teasing darts. She seemed intent on proving her general knowledge to him, and he let her do most of the talking while he struggled to eat the lamb hotpot. His appetite, as usual, was negligible and after five minutes he pushed his half-finished plate away and lit a cigarette without asking permission in case she refused. He wanted to remove his jacket, but he was worried she'd notice his fraying shirt cuffs.

Every so often he tried to break her garrulous flow. His questions were factual. Was Howard's primary school still in existence? Would they have records? Which secondary school did he attend? Was *that* still in existence? Would *they* have records? She answered readily enough, only to go off on a tangent immediately, and his frustration grew. He wanted to remind her that this was a fact-sharing meeting, instigated at her invitation, but he didn't know how to do it because he wasn't used to voluble middle-aged women who pulled faces and giggled under the influence of drink.

After half an hour she pushed her plate aside and propped her chubby elbows on the table. "Do you mind if *I* asked some questions now?"

"What about?"

"You." She shook her head as his expression closed immediately. "Not personal questions, Dr. Hughes, questions about why you became interested in Howard's case. For example, how did you come across it and where did you research it? Downing and Kiszko's cases were fairly well known even before their convictions were quashed, but interest in Howard died with him. He's not mentioned in books or on the Internet and, as I said in my first letter, the story was dead long before I moved to Mullin Street. So what brought you to him?"

"A *book*," said Jonathan with unnecessary emphasis, "although, admittedly, it's only available in academic libraries — *Clinical Studies* by Dr. Andrew Lawson. It was published in 1975 and has been out of print for years. It's a collection of psychiatric assessments, one of which was Stamp's. I quote it in *Disordered Minds* . . . the attribution is in a footnote." He smiled the mechanical smile again. "I always assume readers share my interest in bibliographic references, but obviously I'm wrong."

George's cheeks turned a brighter crimson. "I hadn't realized that's what sparked your interest. May I ask why it did?"

He shrugged. "I thought I made it clear in what I wrote. There were parallels between Stamp's case and the other cases I detailed. It seemed obvious to me that, had he lived, his conviction would have been quashed."

She nodded. "Most of your information comes from newspaper coverage. Is that the only research you did?"

He saw a criticism immediately. "It's a common enough resource tool, Miss Gardener . . . but, no, I also had some correspondence with Adam Fanshaw, who in turn put me in touch with Stamp's solicitor. They're both retired now, but they were able to fill in some of the gaps, particularly about Grace's history. The solicitor sent me a copy of a letter that was quoted at the trial, but it contained some rather more interesting information that I referred to in my book. I also consulted a psychological profiler."

She toyed with the edge of her plate. "Do you ever consider the advantages your dark skin gives you?" she asked abruptly.

He frowned. "I'm sorry?"

"Most decent people would hate to be thought of as racist. Surely that works in your favor some of the time?"

It was another tangent, but he didn't understand where it was leading. "I don't follow."

She held his gaze for a moment. "Presumably most educated whites, meeting you for the first time, make a point of expressing interest in what you say . . . even if it bores them. Isn't that an advantage of being dark-skinned? They wouldn't show the same courtesy to an overweight, middle-aged white woman." She smiled slightly. "But then being fat is a lifestyle choice — and being colored isn't."

"I wouldn't know, Miss Gardener. You're the first person who's accused me of being boring. I don't see how it relates to Howard."

"I was wondering how far he contributed to his own bullying," she mused. "How far does *anyone* contribute to their own bullying?"

"They don't. Howard became a target because of his harelip. He couldn't help it, anymore than blacks and Asians can help having dark skin. Bullying's a form of terror — and terrorists always choose the easiest targets."

She reverted to the subject of research. "Were documents your only tool? Did you never think of coming down to Bournemouth to find people who knew Howard?"

It was another criticism. "Not until today, no. But neither did I go to Rochdale to research the Kiszko case, nor Bakewell to research the Downing case."

"Didn't you think it was important?"

"My expertise lies in examining and analyzing available records, not in hammering on doors looking for long-lost witnesses. The Stamp case was one chapter in a long book that took over a year to write. I felt there was enough documentary evidence to posit the possibility of a mistrial, and you clearly agreed, otherwise you wouldn't have written to me. The idea now is to take the case further."

"I'm not trying to offend you," she said. "I'm just interested in how an academic approaches a subject like this. I'd love to have gone to an established university myself, but it wasn't easy for a postman's daughter at the tail end of the sixties."

Oh, please! Did she think it was any easier for a half-breed from a sink estate to win a place at Oxford at the tail end of the eighties? "It's precisely because I thought it was important to find people who knew Howard that I included a contact address in the book," he said patiently. "It's also why I'm here today —" he took out another cigarette — "although I don't seem to be making much progress."

"Only because you think your agenda's

more important than mine."

He flicked his lighter to the tip. "What makes you say that?"

"Body language."

"For Christ's sake, stop being so bloody stuffy. You look as if someone's rammed a broomstick up your backside."

He forced a smile to his face. "Do you mind if I take off my jacket?"

She noticed he was sweating. "Be my guest." She watched him stand up and meticulously empty his pockets before carefully draping the fine wool over the back of the chair. He tucked his wallet, passport and a couple of pens into his briefcase, then unbuttoned his shirtsleeves and folded them back. It was an interesting routine, she thought — very Pavlovian. "The reason I'm asking these questions," she went on as he took his seat at the table again, "is because, unlike you, I *have* done the legwork . . . on and off since I first heard Howard's story." She took a folder from the carrier bag she'd brought with her. "These are my notes."

The file was a good two inches thick. "May I see them?"

"Not yet," she said with surprising firmness. "First I'd like you to tell me what you plan to do with them."

"Assuming they add to the knowledge I already have — and with your permission of course — I'll include them in a new book."

"About what? Howard . . . or the iniquities of the judicial system?"

"Both, but Howard principally."

"May I ask why?"

Jonathan saw no reason not to be honest. "My agent's impressed by the number of letters I've received — not all of them sympathetic — but there does seem to be considerable interest in Howard."

"And your agent thinks the book will sell?"

He nodded.

"That's good." She propped her chin in her hands. "Now let me tell you why I'm interested in the case. As I said in my first letter, my introduction to it was through one of my neighbors who knew Grace by sight. They had a nodding acquaintance, but they weren't friends and they didn't socialize. Whenever my neighbor talked about the murder she always concentrated on the horror of it and the impact it had on the street. She said it was months before she dared go out and years before she opened her door without worrying about being murdered . . . in other words, long after Howard was convicted." She fell into a brief silence while she marshaled her thoughts.

"I asked her if she believed they'd caught the right man," she went on after a moment, "and she said no. Others were persuaded by his confession and the evidence, but she wasn't." She placed a hand on the folder. "She was one of the witnesses who came forward to say she'd seen Howard on the day of the murder, but she wasn't called at trial. At the time she was relieved, because she'd never been in court before and she'd found the police questioning intimidating. *Afterward* she questioned why her evidence had been excluded. She even wrote to her MP about it, although she never received an answer." She pulled a face. "It's not atypical, but considering what she had to say it should have been taken up." She fell silent again.

"What was it?"

"That she'd seen Howard's *arrival* and not his departure. She was cleaning her sitting-room window when she watched him let himself into his grandmother's house with his key. She had the radio on and she was listening to the lunchtime news on the Home Service. The presenter signed off just after Howard closed the door." George smiled impatiently at his lack of understanding. "In 1970 Radio 4 was called the Home Service, and the lunchtime news finished at two o'clock. It was followed by *The Archers*, and my father tuned in every day." She rapped her knuckles on the edge of the table. "There really is *no way* that Howard could have done everything he was accused of in half an hour."

Jonathan felt a stirring of excitement. "Did this woman make a statement?"

"Yes. I used my contacts on the police committee to try to get hold of the original, but we didn't have any success. If the file's still in existence, no one knows where it is — the best guess is that it was destroyed after Howard died. However, I do have a copy that my neighbor dictated to me from memory in 1997. It won't be exactly the same, of course, but she signed it and we had it officially notarized." She heaved a sigh. "Poor woman. She died shortly afterward, riddled with guilt that she hadn't made more of an effort to keep him out of prison."

He dropped ash onto his plate. "Why didn't she?"

"Because she was a humble little person who had absolute faith in the police. Before the trial she assumed her evidence wasn't important enough to call her as a witness; afterward she started to worry about it. She said she spoke to the local bobby, and he told her it was done and dusted. She made an attempt to contact Wynne, but Wynne had already been rehoused because of the furor . . . then Howard hanged himself."

"And she gave up?"

"Yes."

"When did she write to the MP?"

"Three days before Howard died. She assumed that's why she never had a reply. Then I came along and stirred her up again." She paused. "I still don't know if it was the right thing to do. She'd managed to persuade herself he wouldn't have confessed if he hadn't done it, and her conscience would have been easier if she could have gone on believing that."

"You can't blame yourself."

She gave a small laugh. "You'd be surprised what I can blame myself for, Dr. Hughes. At the moment I'm beating myself up because the car wouldn't start. They say a good beginning makes a good ending, so the reverse must be equally true . . . start badly and it goes downhill from then on."

Jonathan ignored the comment. From

his perspective, things had improved considerably since she'd started taking the meeting seriously, and he wondered how long she intended to make excuses. It was a peculiarly English characteristic to keep worrying at the vomit. He took a notepad and pen from his briefcase. "What was your neighbor's name?"

Her blue eyes searched his black ones for a moment before, with obvious regret, she screwed her face into pained apology. "Oh dear, this is where we hit the buffers at the bottom of the slope. I'm afraid I'm not going to tell you, Dr. Hughes, nor will I allow you to read my notes. I've made free with one piece of information that points to Howard's innocence because I'm embarrassed to have brought you all the way down here only to send you away empty-handed. However, if you want to write this book, then you'll have to put in the hours yourself — as I have done."

He stared at her with contempt, saying nothing, and she wiggled her shoulders uncomfortably. "I'm sure you'll believe it's a racist thing, but it isn't. I've spent fifteen years researching Howard's case, the last ten trying to bring it to public attention. I was so optimistic when I heard your interview on Radio 4 and read your book, but now . . ." She broke off with a shake of her head.

He gave a cynical laugh. "But now that you know *Disordered Minds* has raised the interest to a commercial level," he finished for her, "you'll try to write the book yourself. Have you ever written anything before, Miss Gardener? It's not easy, you know."

She tucked the folder back into its carrier bag and stood up, reaching for her coat. "You misunderstood me. The reason I won't share my information with you, Dr. Hughes, is because I don't like you." She shrugged. "You exploit your color to intimidate people, and in my book that's a form of abuse. You might not have treated me like dirt if I'd been better dressed or hadn't arrived late, but I doubt it. As my father was fond of saying, what can you expect from a pig but a grunt?"

Chapter Six

There was no sign of George when Jonathan followed her downstairs five minutes later, but her Mini was still parked where she'd left it in the yard, with a wire trailing from a battery charger under the hood to a plug inside the kitchen. The sleet had turned to rain and he stood irresolutely by the back door, wondering what to do. Leave? Seek her out to apologize? If so, what for? He didn't understand the accusation of abuse at all. He'd taken Roy's slights, even accepted his apology with the best grace he could muster. What more could he have done? He certainly hadn't inflicted his color on George over lunch.

Nevertheless, he'd clearly said something to make her angry, although he had no idea what it was. It certainly wasn't his reference to her writing the book, because she'd made up her mind by then. Nor had he challenged any of her theories — which was the reason his colleagues usually took umbrage. Perhaps she'd been offended that the flaring pain in his gut had prevented him eating Trent's lard-filled hotpot? His natural inclination was to pin her down and argue the logic of her position. If she wanted publicity for Howard, then whether she liked Jonathan or not was immaterial as long as he was able to generate it. But hers had been an emotional response and he didn't think she'd appreciate a lesson in logic.

The sound of rising voices came from the kitchen. ". . . sake, woman. Keep the volume down," said Roy firmly. "You'll have Jim quoting you all over the shop if you're not careful."

"What does it matter if he does?"

"You'll be done for slander."

"I couldn't give a damn. He's not even very *bright*, Roy, just a miserable little hick who's taught himself to speak properly. I don't believe a word he says. I'll eat my bloody hat if he ever went to Oxford — a polytechnic more like. God *knows* how he got a doctorate."

"Jesus! Will you calm *down*, girl!"

"Why should I? He never once asked if I had any qualifications, just wrote me off as a postman's daughter. You should have seen his reaction when I told him what Dad did, he couldn't put enough distance between us."

"What makes you think he's a hick? He sounds like a right ponce to me."

"Only because you've never lived in London. You can take the man out of the city, Roy, but you can never take the city out of the man. I should *know,* I was born and brought up in the blasted place. His accent's all over the shop. He's a fake, a bloody little con man who'd rather exploit other people than do the work himself. He's not interested in justice, he just wants to make money. I'm so *angry,* Roy."

"Disappointed, more like." There was the sound of chair legs scraping across the floor. "Buck up, girl. There'll be others. Like you say, it took fifty years before Derek Bentley got his pardon."

"But I haven't *got* fifty years, Roy."

"Then you'll have to prove the doctors wrong, darlin'. Stay put. I'll get rid of him, then I'll take a look at your battery. It's had over an hour so it ought to be charged."

There was a click as a door swung open, and Jonathan turned toward it, his face unusually apprehensive. The pain in his abdomen was like an acid burn eating through his stomach wall, and he wished to

God he'd brought some indigestion tablets with him. He swallowed bile, blaming the hotpot for his problems, and Roy grinned, seeing only discomfort at George's trashing of his character.

"You're all right, mate," he said, closing the kitchen door behind him. "I'm not going to bite you. It's pissing with rain, so I came to find out if you want a taxi to the station. If I ring now, it'll take ten minutes or thereabouts. You can wait in the bar or hop back upstairs." His grin broadened. "You're safe as long as I keep George in the kitchen."

Jonathan made a feeble attempt to regain the moral high ground. "I don't know what I did to upset her."

"Then you'll have something to puzzle over on the train ride home. So . . . shall I call a taxi or would you rather walk?"

"Why did she write to me if she wasn't willing to pool information?"

"Because she's been trying for years to get someone interested. She was pleased as punch when she heard you on the radio. Thought you were the guy to get things moving."

"I am."

"George doesn't think so. As far as she's concerned, you're just after the credit.

Howard can go hang himself — excuse the pun — if you can make money out of it. That's not George's way. Never has been."

"I'm happy to acknowledge her input. I'll pay her a percentage of the royalties if her information leads to something."

Roy shook his head. "You really don't get it, do you? She spent half an hour apologizing for my big mouth, then she realized you're more of a bigot than I am. For the record, she has two Open University degrees — one in psychology and one in criminology — also an external Ph.D. from Sussex in behavioral science." The amusement returned to his voice. "You shouldn't make assumptions, mate. George is far too modest to call herself a doctor — unlike you — but she's *just* as entitled. The difference is, she earned her qualifications the hard way: in the evenings while she held down a full-time job. You got yours the easy way: *free* — paid for by the likes of George. That's where being the token black pays dividends."

"You're wrong," said Jonathan flatly.

"Not according to George. You shouldn't look down your nose at people, mate, not if you want their cooperation. She's a good old girl, she'll bust a gut for anyone, but she doesn't like bullies, she doesn't like people who take advantage and she doesn't like snobs." He pointed a thumb at the floor. "And you're all three. *Now* . . . do you wanna taxi or do you wanna walk?"

It was the accusation of bullying that gave Jonathan most pause for thought as he retraced his steps along Highdown Road. Anger had always simmered behind his insecurity, erupting sometimes in uncontrollable tantrums against his mother and his demented grandfather, but he had never thought of himself as a bully. That was a title he reserved for his father, whose frustration could explode into violence with terrifying speed. There had been no joy in Clarence Hughes's life, merely a daily grind of menial toil for the local council that had stultified his intellect and driven him to rage against the only people who were safe — his family.

From early childhood Jonathan had understood what fueled his father's resentment even though he hated him for it. Clarence had wanted to amount to something in life, but immigration to Britain — far from offering him the opportunity to shine — had been a soul-destroying move. He wasn't a stupid man, but his heavily accented English, and his lack of recognized qualifications, had closed the door to jobs that would have given him status. Instead, he labored at menial tasks and hid his contempt for the people he worked with. The victims of so much repressed emotion were his family, in particular his only child, on whom all hopes of a better future were placed.

Such weighty expectations had taught Jonathan to compartmentalize his life early, hiding his secrets as fearfully as a thief. To his mother, he was a popular boy whose late returns from school were due to visits to friends. To his father, he was an intelligent, hard-working student who stayed on after hours to work in the school library. To his teachers, he was the son of an Indian lawyer and Ugandan doctor who'd been expelled by Idi Amin in the 1970s and had their wealth confiscated. To his bullies, he was invisible.

The truth — that he'd hidden in the school lavatories because he was too frightened to walk home, and had invented a background for his parents because he was ashamed of them — became obscured even in his own mind. It was easier to embroider fantasies of popularity and forced exile than to question his own timidity and his yearning to be respected. He'd even grown comfortable in the role of victim, gaining strength from it by logging each new slight on his tally stick of revenge.

At what point he decided to convert fantasy to fact, he didn't know. When he gained the place at Oxford? When he started aping the long vowels and clear diction of the upper middle class? When he realized that an appearance of wealth was almost as valuable as wealth itself? Or that the myth of good breeding was easily established by the simple expedient of cutting his family out of his life? Perhaps there was no defining moment, perhaps his descent into pathological deceit had been so gradual that no lie had ever seemed shocking enough to call a halt.

"Why do you push people away? Are you afraid they're going to see your flaws? What's the big deal, anyway? No one's perfect . . ."

He read the new placard outside the newsagent as he passed: "U.S. accused of bully-boy diplomacy." The pedant in him questioned the juxtaposition of "bully-boy" and "diplomacy." The two were irreconcilable . . . or should be. The one suggested brute ignorance, the other deft intelligence, though in a phoney war the rattling saber was a powerful propaganda tool for friend and foe alike.

Jonathan couldn't count the number of times his father had wept for the man he had become, but it hadn't changed his behavior. Fear of his heavy hand — a more potent weapon than the hand itself — had been the dominant discipline in both his marriage and his only child's upbringing. The injustice had been Jonathan's demented grandfather's regularly mistaking his growing grandson for his hated son-in-law. With a courage he'd never possessed, even in his prime, the old man had belabored the adolescent for the sins of the father while his mother held her finger to her lips and begged him with her eyes to let her Abba vent his spleen. "It's good medicine," she would say. "Now he'll sleep."

As he trudged on, contempt for his mother wound like a snake about Jonathan's heart. She was an ill-educated peasant who had fawned over her idiot father and paid lip service to her responsibilities to her son. What can I do? I'm just a woman. Clarence won't allow it . . . Clarence will lose his temper . . . Clarence has problems . . . Clarence will hit me . . . Clarence . . . Clarence . . . Clarence . . .

"Women make you so angry, Jon . . . one day you'll cross the line and you won't know you've done it until it's too late . . ."

★ ★ ★

Trains came and went at Branksome Station, but Jonathan felt too ill to take any notice. He stood under cover, leaning against a wall, loose-limbed and swaying slightly, clutching his briefcase to his midriff and staring into the middle distance. As they left, several passengers reported an Arab-looking man, sweating profusely and behaving strangely. The acting station master assessed him carefully through a window and wondered what to do. He couldn't imagine that a suicide bomber would choose Branksome Station as a target, but he reminded himself that Palestinian bombers blew themselves up on buses; trains were just a different mode of transport. He was about to call the transport police when another passenger, a woman, approached the man and shook him by the hand.

"Are you all right?" the dark-haired woman asked Jonathan kindly as she reached for his right hand and clasped it warmly. She wore an expensive overcoat with the collar turned up and a cashmere scarf looped around her neck, obscuring the lower part of her face. "You look as if you're about to fall over. Do you want some help?"

He glanced at her briefly, then reverted to staring across the track. Nausea threatened every time he moved his eyes. He'd persuaded himself it was weeks of sleepless nights followed by jet lag. It would pass, he'd been telling himself for nearly an hour. Everything passed eventually. But the gnawing pain in his stomach said it was something worse.

The woman moved in front of him. "You need to talk to me," she encouraged him. "There are two policemen watching you." She was pretty in a manufactured way — most of it was paint — but she looked genuinely concerned. Jonathan, who had seen the way everyone else had been giving him a wide berth, wondered why she was bothering with him.

Policemen . . . ? He wedged his back more firmly against the wall. "I'm all right," he managed.

She laughed and touched a gloved hand to his arm as if she were greeting an old friend. "You need to smile and play up a bit," she said. "They're very suspicious of you." She tilted her head toward the platform entrance. "They're behind the wall over there and they're afraid there's a bomb in your briefcase."

A bomb . . . ? The absurdity of the concept struck Jonathan forcibly even as he felt something give way inside his head — the first of the retaining walls that held his emotions in check. There was nothing in his briefcase except his wallet, letters about Howard Stamp, his ticket to the Royal Opera House and his passport. *If a single lie unraveled* . . . "Why would they think that?"

"You're black," she said bluntly, "you're sweating like a pig and you look shit-scared. It doesn't take much these days to get the cops excited."

Another wall collapsed. *Why did everyone keep calling him black? Why did everyone keep likening him to a pig?* Hysteria rocketed round his gut, searching for an exit, before converting into painful tears behind his eyes. He was scared and sweating because he didn't know what was happening to him. He tried to bolster the myth of jet lag. No one this tired could take the funeral of a murdered boy, anti-Arab bigotry, hostile immigration officers, tanks, soldiers, critical spinsters, dirty landlords . . . *war* . . . without suffering an emotional backlash. But he knew it wasn't true. The truth was that his fabricated personality was disintegrating in front of a total stranger because someone at last was showing him a little kindness.

The woman moved closer and he caught a waft of her scent. "I guess you've had too much to drink, but if you don't want the cops poking their noses in, then talk to me, pretend we know each other . . . even better, give me your briefcase." She held out a hand. "That's what's got them twitched. They'll go away if you let me open it."

He handed it to her, suddenly dizzy. "I'm not drunk."

"You're giving a damn good impression." She rested the case on her knee and flicked the latches, pulling the leather flap open so any watcher could see. Her scurrying fingers rummaged through the letters before she took them all out and handed them to him. "Look at me," she told him. "Make out we've met on purpose. Select something and give it to me."

He steeled himself to look down, quelling the sickness that rose in his throat. "Who are you?"

"It doesn't matter. Just give me a piece of paper. Good." She took the page and scanned it. "Talk to me. Say rhubarb if you want, but at least give the impression that we're having a conversation."

How did she know the police thought he

had a bomb in his briefcase? "Rhubarb?"

"Again."

"Rhubarb . . . rhubarb . . . rhubarb."

She pointed to something in the letter and flicked him a smile. "Now laugh. People who laugh don't blow up trains."

"I don't want to blow up a train. I'm a British academic. My passport's in the case. All I have to do is show it to them."

"They'll still question you. Everyone's been reporting a mad-looking Arab on the platform. I slipped round the back; otherwise they wouldn't have let me through."

"Why aren't you afraid?"

"I know who you are. I saw you at the Crown and Feathers."

Jonathan groped through his memory. There had been a couple in the bar, he recalled, but he didn't think the woman had been this one. "I don't remember you."

She stuffed the letters into the briefcase and tucked it under one arm. "It's a big place," she said cryptically, glancing toward the platform entrance. "You're all right now, I think. They seem to have gone. Come on, there's a seat down here." She put her other hand under his elbow and urged him along the platform. "You'll feel better if you sit down. You're so wet already, a little more water on your bum won't matter." She lowered him to the metal bench and sat beside him. "Did Roy say something to upset you? He can be a right jerk at times."

Jonathan leaned back to stare at the sky and felt the nausea begin to subside. The rain had eased off and a weak sun had broken through the clouds although it was still very cold. Her scent, an attractive one, filled his nostrils, and, for the first time in months, he found the closeness of a woman comforting. He couldn't account for it, nor did he bother to try, he was just grateful for the human contact. "Is he a friend of yours?"

"Not really. I know his ex-wife, so I get to hear about his faults. He's famous for opening mouth before engaging brain. Did he say something insulting?"

"That's where being the token black pays dividends . . ." Was the truth ever an insult? Perversely, Jonathan found himself defending the man. "If he did, it probably wasn't intentional."

"I wouldn't bet on it," she said with an easy laugh. "He may not be the brightest thing on two legs but he knows how to get under people's skin. You don't want to dwell on it. It gives him a buzz if he thinks one of his jibes has hit the spot."

Despite her expensive clothes, he didn't think she'd been born to wealth. Her voice had a rough Dorset burr, much like Roy Trent's. "Does he do it to you?"

"He does it to everyone. That's why he has so few customers."

It was a different explanation from George's, but it appealed to Jonathan rather more. "Do you know Councillor Gardener?"

"Roy's girlfriend? Only by sight." She turned to look at him. "Don't tell me *she* upset you? She got religion after the cancer — wants the world to accept Jesus and all that cr—" She broke off. "I'm being a bitch. Forget I said that. She's very well-meaning . . . crusades for the poor. I can't believe she'd say anything unkind."

Fleetingly, Jonathan wondered why she was so intent on blaming someone else for his problems. "It's just exhaustion," he said. "I flew in from the States last night and didn't sleep. I'd have done better to stay at home."

"Was the trip worth the effort?"

"To the States?"

"No . . . today's . . . down here."

He shook his head.

"Will you come back?"

He glanced at her. The question wasn't

overly intrusive, but somewhere in the recesses of his mind her persistence struck a suspicious chord. "Did Roy send you after me?"

"Hardly," she said with a small laugh. "He'll have forgotten all about you by now." She nestled her chin into her scarf. "To be honest, I was surprised to find you here. You left the pub a long time before I did. So . . . are you feeling better?"

"I am, yes." He was surprised. The nausea had gone, and even the tremors in his arms had ceased. "You've been very kind."

"I'm in a charitable mood." She looked along the track. "Your train's coming. I'll see you onto it, then all you have to do is make the connection at Bournemouth Central. Can you manage that?"

He pushed himself to the edge of the seat. "What about you?"

"I'm going the other way," she said, standing up and offering him his briefcase as the train drew in. She'd relocked it at some point, and he took it gratefully.

"Then why are you on this platform?"

"I could see you were in trouble."

He shook his head. "I don't even know who you are."

"A good Samaritan," was all she said, as

she opened a carriage door and urged him inside.

His last view of her was muffled in her scarf with a gloved hand raised in farewell but, as he waved back, it occurred to him that he wouldn't recognize her again. All he had seen was a pair of painted eyes beneath a dark fringe. It wasn't important until he opened his briefcase at Bournemouth Central and discovered that she'd stolen everything that mattered to him. She'd taken his wallet, his train ticket, his opera ticket, and worst of all she'd left him with nothing to prove who he was. His passport was gone.

After that he lost it. He ran about the station, barging into people and shouting at them. Some thought he was a pathetic lunatic. Some thought he was dangerous. When two transport policemen tackled him to the ground, he called them fascist scum and struck at them with the briefcase until one of them wrenched it from his grasp and kneed him in the gut.

Chapter Seven

Central police station, Bournemouth
Thursday, February 13, 2003, 8:30 p.m.

Andrew Spicer was not amused to be summoned from his office in London at five o'clock that evening to drive to Bournemouth to vouch for his friend. The most basic checks on Jonathan's identity had revealed that a man with his name had had his passport queried the night before when he flew in from America, and police, unimpressed by his behavior after he was arrested for running amok at Bournemouth's main station, insisted on proof of who he was before they would consider releasing him.

It was the opinion of the doctor summoned to test Jonathan Hughes for drugs and excessive alcohol — both of which proved negative — that further tests were required. The man was clearly ill. Jonathan was advised of his right to go to hospital, but as he retreated into silence, refusing both medical assistance and a solicitor, there was little to be done except approach Andrew Spicer, literary agent, whose name and address were on several letters in Jonathan's briefcase. An attempt was made to contact Councillor George Gardener, whose correspondence suggested a lunch appointment at the Crown and Feathers, but every call was intercepted by an answerphone. There was a similarly negative response from the pub itself, which wasn't due to open again until five-thirty.

How seriously ill was he? At death's door? Mental, rather than physical, said the doctor, so hardly an emergency. Once Andrew was persuaded to drive from London, the police lost interest. They had other fish to fry, and a safely contained, tearful Arab posed less of a threat than impatient drivers on freezing roads.

When Andrew finally arrived at eight-thirty, tired and hungry after sitting in gridlock on the M3, he was shown Jonathan through a two-way mirror. "Do you know this man?" he was asked by a uniformed sergeant who introduced himself as Fred Lovatt.

"Yes."

"Who is he?"

"Jonathan Hughes."
"What's your relationship with him?"
"I'm his literary agent."
"How long have you known him?"
Andrew unbuttoned his jacket and pointed to a chair. "Am I allowed to sit down? I haven't eaten since breakfast and I'm dead on my feet." He slumped onto it when the sergeant nodded. "What's he done?"
"Just answer the question, please, Mr. Spicer."
"Twelve years . . . thirteen years. We were at Oxford together, but I didn't get to know him well until he brought his first manuscript to me in 'ninety-two. We've been friends ever since."
"What's his profession?"
"Academic. He's a lecturer and research fellow in European anthropology at London University. Rather a good one, as a matter of fact . . . and much appreciated by his students because he takes the trouble to make the subject interesting."
The sergeant pulled out another chair. "Is there a reason why he wouldn't tell us that? Why would he have a problem if his university was approached for verification?"
Andrew studied his friend's face through

the window. "What are you charging him with?"

"Nothing at the moment."

"Then why are you holding him?"

"Because he's committed an offense and he's refusing to answer questions on it. He won't be released until we're satisfied it's safe to do so."

"What offense?"

Sergeant Lovatt consulted a piece of paper. "Running amok at Bournemouth Central. He collided with passengers and screamed about being —" he arched an eyebrow — "assuming this is right . . . *fall* staff? Possibly *full* staff? He's refusing to explain what it means. Do you have any ideas, sir?"

Andrew frowned. "It's a Verdi opera. It's on at Covent Garden tonight. *Falstaff* . . . Sir John Falstaff. He's a comic character from Shakespeare's *Merry Wives of Windsor*, also *Henry IV Parts 1 and 2* and *Henry V.* He's a big fat man with large appetites."

The sergeant looked doubtfully toward Jonathan, whose shirt was hanging off his thin shoulders. "Why would Mr. Hughes claim to be this man?"

"He wouldn't have said *being* Falstaff, but he might have said *going*. He's opera-mad. He told me he had a ticket for it . . . that's why he flew home last night. Otherwise he'd have canceled today's appointment and waited for a cheaper flight."

Lovatt read the paper again. "According to the witnesses, he said, 'I am Falstaff.' One of them claims he also said, 'The devil's a woman.' Is he married? Does he have problems at home?"

Andrew shook his head. "He had a steady girlfriend for a while, but they split up after Christmas. I don't think it affected him much; he never gave the impression it was serious."

"Is he a Muslim?"

"No." The fat little man smiled slightly. "Nor is that question sequential on 'the devil's a woman,' Sergeant. As far as I'm aware, it is not Islamic doctrine that Satan wears a dress. They believe the opposite: it's the devil in men — the trouser snake — that's the problem. That's why their women cover themselves."

The sergeant was unmoved. "Does this Falstaff character have problems with women?"

Andrew looked interested suddenly. "He certainly does in the opera. Verdi took the story from Shakespeare's *Merry Wives*, where Falstaff is portrayed as a figure of fun. He loses all his money and comes up with a plan to improve his finances by seducing the rich wives of Windsor. When the women find out about it, they devise humiliating punishments for him."

"What kind of punishments?"

"Slapstick stuff. I haven't seen it for a while but, as far as I recall, they dump him in a river, then make him parade around in fancy dress. It's the trouser-snake theme. The women lead him on by pretending to like him — get him excited, in other words — then slap him down when he thinks he's about to score. It's a tale of male mockery by feisty ladies. The lesson is that women are intellectually and ethically superior to men."

The sergeant gave a grunt of disapproval, as if the lesson didn't appeal to him. "Pretty topical then. That's all anything's about these days."

Andrew didn't disagree. "It always has been. It's the battle of the sexes . . . men are from Mars and women from Venus. Human nature never changes. We can analyze our DNA, email each other across the world, transplant hearts . . . but the fundamentals remain the same. Men hunt, and women control the family. Simple as that. Shakespeare's perceptions are as true now as they were when he recorded them four hundred years ago. He was a behavioral scientist before behavioral science was invented —" he ticked the air — "a genius of a psychologist, with a very real understanding of the dynamics of relationships — particularly male-female relationships."

"Mm."

"Sorry," said Andrew. "I'm a fan . . . tend to get carried away."

"I've only ever seen *Hamlet.* Someone told me the whole play could be reduced down to the speech about suicide. 'To be or not to be.' Is that right?"

"He's certainly a man who explores his own tormented identity. In that respect, it's a precursor of modern theater."

Sergeant Lovatt studied Jonathan through the window. "Does Mr. Hughes have a tormented identity?"

Andrew followed his gaze. "Don't we all?"

"Some more than others, I suspect," the other said blandly. "Has he ever displayed any mental problems that you're aware of?"

Too many to count, Andrew thought. *Envy . . . resentment . . . insecurity . . . self-loathing . . . just like his agent and every other poor sod on the planet who didn't measure up to expectation.* "No," he said. "What makes you ask?"

"Your friend resisted arrest and refuses to explain himself. We're interested why."

"Presumably because he doesn't believe he's done anything wrong. He writes books about the pitfalls of social stereotyping and the failings of the criminal justice system when it treats the stereotype and ignores the individual. I imagine he's working on the principle that if you haven't charged him, then he shouldn't have been arrested in the first place."

The sergeant shook his head. "There was nothing wrong with the arrest, sir. Mr. Hughes was detained under stop-and-search powers after going berserk in a public place. When he was taken into custody, he tried to hit an officer with his briefcase."

"Did he make contact?"

"Barely. If he wasn't such a big girl's blouse, he'd be facing a charge of assault, and that's a serious offense." A muscle twitched at the side of his mouth. "He's not much of a fighter, your friend. The transport policeman who detained him said it was like wrestling with a stick insect."

"What about the people he bumped into?"

"They were willing to let it go."

"So what's left, other than refusing to answer questions? I thought that was a right, not a crime."

"Unless you make a habit of it. He flew in from America last night and was detained for an hour for the same reason."

"Oh, for Christ's sake!" said Andrew impatiently. "It happens every time. If it's not his views on bin Laden, it's which bloody cricket team he supports. I'm never asked questions like that, and if I were I'd say Osama was a splendid fellow just to see what reaction I got." He leaned forward. "If no one else wants to pursue it, you've no reason to hold him."

"We still want an explanation, Mr. Spicer. Heathrow's on heightened alert because of terrorist threats, and the same applies in the major conurbations. Unusual behavior is taken seriously."

"More so when the suspect looks like an Arab, I suppose."

The man didn't say anything.

"If you have his passport, then you know he's British. It *used* to mean something."

"He isn't carrying anything that can

identify him, sir. That's why we asked you to drive down here."

Andrew looked surprised. "He must have his passport. He's irrational about the damn thing . . . so terrified of losing it he pats his breastpocket all the time."

The sergeant shook his head. "No passport."

"What about his wallet?"

"No wallet. No money. No credit cards. No train ticket. Certainly no opera ticket to Verdi's *Falstaff*. He's a bit of a mystery, your friend. All he has in his briefcase are a pay-as-you-go mobile telephone — with a rundown battery — and some letters addressed to him care of Spicer & Hardy —" he eyed Andrew thoughtfully — "which makes his refusal to cooperate rather surprising. You'd think he'd be falling over himself to prove who he is."

"Or explains it," Andrew countered. "When was the last time you had your identity questioned twice in twenty-four hours? You haven't questioned mine. How come I'm squeaky clean without a passport, but Jonathan isn't? Is he right? Are you a nonperson if you're paperless and dark-skinned in this country?"

"You came voluntarily, sir, and Mr. Hughes did not. He was detained legitimately and asked to account for himself. When he refused, he was arrested and brought here. Had he been willing to answer a few straightforward questions, he would have been released as soon as we had confirmation that his answers were true."

"What sort of questions?"

"Address, job, next-of-kin details, what took him to America. Nothing out of the ordinary . . . and nothing we wouldn't ask a white man in the same circumstances."

"I've told you his job, so to be strictly accurate it's *Dr.* Hughes, not Mr. Hughes. He lives in a flat in West Kensington — off the top of my head it's 2b Columbia Street or Road — and his next of kin are his parents, though he hasn't seen them for years. They divorced shortly before he went up to Oxford, and I believe his mother repatriated. He doesn't know — or care — what happened to his father. As for the trip to America, he was attending the funeral of one of his students who was killed in a racist attack on the streets of New York." He glanced at the window again. "Jon's the one who pulled strings to win him an educational scholarship, so I shouldn't think he's feeling too happy that the lad was murdered."

"How does he afford it on an academic's salary?"

"What?"

"Trips to America, Paul Smith suits, Versace shirts, tickets to the opera, Armani glasses. What kind of books does he write? Bestsellers?"

Andrew hesitated before he answered. "Not exactly. He's a single man with no dependents."

"It's an expensive lifestyle, Mr. Spicer. Does he own his flat?"

"I've no idea."

"Does he have any other income that you know of?"

"No." He studied the sergeant's deadpan face for several moments. "What are you suggesting?"

"These are uncertain times, Mr. Spicer."

Andrew laughed. "If you're thinking he's some sort of terrorist, you're way off beam. He hates violence."

The sergeant allowed himself a small smile. "Does he live alone, sir?"

"I believe so, yes."

"Rent and mortgages in Kensington don't come cheap, Mr. Spicer."

This was a policeman with a great capacity for taking in knowledge, Andrew thought, as he watched Jonathan take off his designer specs and polish them on the end of his tie, revealing how red his eyes were. In repose and under the bright lights, his face looked gaunt, while his shoulders had the skinny rigidity of a clothes hanger. Andrew's feelings for Jon had always been ambivalent. Their friendship was based on mutual liking and a shared interest in literature and good wine; however, Andrew despised Jonathan's adopted accent, he despised the snobbery, and, very particularly, he despised the lies. Until today he had never had reason to believe they were anything but a cloak for insecurity, but now he wondered. It was certainly true that the cloak had become increasingly transparent in the last few months.

He turned back to the policeman. "That suit's come out so often you could check your face in the elbows, and the specs are purely for show. I'm not his bank manager so I don't know how he conducts his finances, but it wouldn't surprise me if he's up to his eyes in debt. Money talks loudly, and to someone like Jon a place in Kensington and tickets to the opera are probably worth the interest on a loan."

"Meaning what?"

"Some people need to promote a false image of themselves. You can flaunt a trip to Verdi's *Falstaff*, but you can't flaunt an empty fridge." He saw the skepticism in the other man's eyes, although whether it was for Jonathan's stupidity in wasting money on the opera or disbelief of Andrew's analysis, it was impossible to say. "I know very little about how terrorists work, but I assume the first rule is, don't draw attention to yourself. Is running amok normal behavior?"

The sergeant shrugged. "We had a doctor check him for drugs and alcohol. His view is that Mr. Hughes is close to a breakdown. I'm no expert in terrorists either, Mr. Spicer, but I imagine it wreaks havoc with the mind . . . particularly if your own death is part of the process."

Andrew couldn't disagree with that. "It's more likely his house of cards is collapsing. Maybe the split with his girlfriend caused it . . . maybe he was more serious about her than I thought." He paused, recalling a remark Jon had made in the wake of Emma's departure. *"I couldn't love her the way she wanted . . ."* "He's not an easy man to read. Most of what he thinks and feels stays locked inside his head."

"Go on."

"I'm guessing it started at Oxford. I didn't know him so well then, he moved in a smarter circle than I did. It's a precious place . . . or can be," he corrected himself. "The mythology of dreaming spires and gilded youth. To a cynic like me, it's pretentious nonsense — even corrupting — but to someone who comes from the wrong side of the tracks, it's seductive."

"He doesn't sound like someone from the wrong side of the tracks."

"That's part of the fiction. He bought into the idea that image was everything — if you can pass yourself off as one of the elite, then you're made. The problem is, you have to support the lifestyle — and if you can't afford it, you lose your friends." Andrew shrugged. "I think he's afraid he's about to be exposed as a fraud. Which probably answers your question about why he didn't ask one of his colleagues at the university to vouch for him."

The sergeant looked thoughtful. "It's an offense to misrepresent yourself in a job application."

Andrew shook his head. "There's nothing wrong with his qualifications," he said with a wry smile. "It's his breeding he's worried about. The man's an anthropologist. It won't be easy admitting he's the unlikely product of a Jamaican road sweeper and a Hong Kong maid when he's made a habit of passing himself off as a dark-skinned Caucasian."

Andrew, given half an hour to persuade his friend to answer questions, eschewed sympathy in favor of brutal honesty. He listed the options. Assuming Jonathan had nothing criminal to hide, he had a choice of explaining himself and hitching a ride home with Andrew that evening, or keeping up the silence and spending a night in the cells while police made inquiries of his friends and colleagues in London. If he chose the latter, his detention would become public knowledge and he would have to make his own way home if and when he was released. As the police had found no credit cards, cash or return ticket in his pockets or in his briefcase, that could prove difficult.

If Jonathan could not afford his own lawyer, there was a duty paralegal kicking her heels in the waiting room. However, unless he wanted to prolong his agony by explaining his actions to a stranger — bearing in mind the potential charges were minimal — he'd be mad to waste time on a bored young woman who hadn't taken her exams yet. The police doctor who'd tested his urine had hinted at depression, and if

Jon persisted in silence there was a strong possibility his next stop would be the psychiatric department at the local hospital. The knock-on effects of this, when an explanation for his absence reached the university, would be rather more serious than a quiet consultation with a GP in London.

Finally, his agent, who knew more about his author than his author realized, had already blown the gaffe on Jonathan's financial situation, self-esteem problems and inability to sustain relationships . . . so it was pointless continuing to save face.

"You could lend me some money to get home," Jonathan muttered, staring at the floor.

"I could, but I'm not going to. What happened to yours?"

"It was stolen."

"Why didn't you tell the police?"

"Because they're fascists, and they only arrested me because I'm black."

There was some truth in that, thought Andrew, but now wasn't the time to say it. "Grow up, Jon!" he said curtly. "Football hooligans are regularly arrested for running amok, and ninety-nine point nine percent of them are white. Your color didn't come into it. In any case, you are where you are. You can either keep licking your wounds, or you can show some sense. Rightly or wrongly, you're banged up in a provincial nick with question marks over your behavior. God knows what's been going on, but you can either tell me about it . . . or you can tell the sergeant. Either way, you need to tell someone."

Jonathan dropped his head into his hands but didn't answer.

"What happened with Councillor Gardener? How did that go?"

"She called me a pig."

"She? I thought it was a man."

"Short, fat and bossy. A bit like you, except she's a hideously ugly middle-aged spinster who spends most of her time making faces."

Andrew lined up a chair beside him and sat down. "Why did she call you a pig?"

Jonathan ground his knuckles into his eyes. "She didn't like me. Accused me of bullying her and said, 'What you can expect from a pig but a grunt?' "

"What did you do?"

"I left."

"I meant, how did you bully her?"

"I didn't ask her what her flaming qualifications were."

It wasn't much of an explanation but Andrew made a reasonable guess at what had happened. "By which I presume you patronized her . . . and she didn't like it."

Jonathan gave an indifferent shrug which Andrew took for assent.

"Who stole your wallet?"

More knuckle-grinding. "I think it was the woman at the station, but it could have been any of them."

"What woman?"

"The one who helped me."

"What was her name?"

"I don't know, she wouldn't tell me."

"Was this before or after you ran amok?"

"Before."

"Why did you need help?"

"The police thought I had a bomb in my briefcase so she opened it to prove I was harmless." Jonathan gave a stifled laugh. "She said she was being charitable . . . and I believed her. That's how stupid I was. Since when did a woman do anything for free?"

Wondering if that was an oblique reference to Emma, Andrew filed the statement away. The minutes were ticking away and he couldn't afford to be sidetracked. "The sergeant didn't mention a bomb. He said you bumped into other passengers and shouted about being Falstaff."

"It was a different station. They were

watching me from the entrance because I was sweating."

"Which station?"

"Branksome."

"It's been freezing all day. Why were you sweating?"

"I felt ill. You can't be ill in this country if you're black. It frightens the natives."

"Don't talk crap, Jon! We have our ups and downs but, by and large, we're pretty peaceful."

"Then why are we going to war?"

Andrew turned to look at him. "Is that what this is about? Were you given a hard time in the States?"

His friend gave a hollow laugh. "It's an Arab thing. We're all potential terrorists."

Andrew shook his head. "Except you're not an Arab. You're half Jamaican, half Chinese and by some freak of genetics you ended up looking like a Bedouin."

Jonathan's jaw set in a hard line. "How do you know what my parentage is?"

"You got rat-arsed the week after Emma left. I couldn't follow most of it but I had the Caribbean-Asian conflict rammed down my throat." A confused loathing of his parents mixed with racist hatred of anyone of Afro-Caribbean or Chinese descent because of the vicious gangs who had terrorized him as a child.

"Why haven't you mentioned it before? Why let me go on pretending?"

"It wasn't my business. If you want to be an Arab or an Iranian, then so be it. I don't see it matters very much unless it causes problems for you. Does it?"

Nationality's a choice, not a birthright . . . "No."

"Then why are you here? Why were you feeling ill at the station?"

"It was jet lag. I just needed a bit of time, so I leaned against a wall."

"How long for?"

"I can't remember."

"Then this woman appeared and went through your briefcase?"

"Yes."

"Didn't you think that was a bit peculiar?"

Jonathan glanced at him, showing eyes bloodshot with exhaustion. "I do now," he muttered. "At the time I believed her. I even thanked her for her kindness. You can't get much stupider than that . . . allowing a woman to make a fool of you, then thanking her for doing it."

It explained the Falstaff reference, Andrew thought. "Oh, come on, pal, you were conned. It sounds like a professional scam . . . look for people in trouble, then rip them off while you're pretending to help them. You should have told the police. She's probably well known to them."

Jonathan didn't say anything.

"All right, *I'll* tell them. What did she look like? What sort of age?"

"I don't know."

"You must have some idea."

He went back to staring at the floor. "I felt sick every time I moved my eyes, so I never really looked at her."

Andrew shook his head. The whole story was becoming more and more bizarre, and he found himself sympathizing with the sergeant's view that Jon was suffering mental problems. "This isn't a figment of your imagination, is it?" he asked bluntly. "Does this woman actually exist?"

"Why would I invent her?"

"Because you're up shit creek without a paddle, mate. You've lost your passport, your money and your return ticket. You've alienated the only useful contact for a book on Howard Stamp and had yourself arrested for behaving like a maniac. What the *hell's* been going on?"

No answer.

Andrew stood up. "This is crazy. I'll ask them to phone George Gardener. At least she can tell us what happened at the pub."

"She said she knew Roy Trent and saw me at the Crown and Feathers."

"George Gardener?"

"The woman. She had a dark fringe and spoke with a Dorset accent."

"Who's Roy Trent?"

"The landlord." There was a long pause. "He's the bully, Andrew. He pretends to be helping her, but he does it in a cruel way. He called me a wog and a darkie and said I only got the place at Oxford because I was the token black."

"Ri-i-ight." Andrew watched him for a moment before turning the door handle. "When did you last have a decent night's sleep, Jon?"

His friend gave another muted laugh. "I think too much," he answered cryptically.

Chapter Eight

The sergeant agreed to telephone the Crown and Feathers but, rather than throwing any light on Jonathan's story, Roy Trent said the pub had been virtually empty at lunchtime and he didn't remember a dark-haired woman. He knew a number of brunettes and auburns but, without a name, he couldn't be anymore helpful. In any case, he'd found Jonathan's wallet and passport on the floor of the upstairs room when he'd come to clean it. He'd assumed Jonathan would phone as soon as he realized they were missing but, as he hadn't, he was planning to ask George Gardener to return them because she knew his address. "What's with the dark-haired woman?" he finished curiously.

"A female of that description gave Dr. Hughes assistance at Branksome Station. She claimed to know you."

"So?"

"Dr. Hughes says she went through his briefcase."

"And he thought she'd stolen his wallet?"

"Yes."

"How come it's taken you so long to call? It's hours since he left."

"He didn't tell us anything was missing until a few minutes ago, sir."

Roy gave a surprised laugh. "He's got real problems, that fellow. Why didn't he phone? The first place you'd check is where you took your jacket off. I'd've put his mind at rest quick as winking."

The sergeant caught Andrew's eye and looked away. "What sort of problems?"

"The whole-world's-out-to-get-me sort. He's just the type to jump to the conclusion his stuff's been stolen instead of thinking it might have been his fault. Mind, he'd've found out he'd dropped it a damn sight sooner if he'd let me call a taxi. But he wouldn't have one. Insisted on walking, even though it was bucketing down. Why did he need assistance?"

"We're not sure. Was he drunk when he left your pub?"

"Couldn't have been, not on what he had here . . . couple of glasses of wine, maximum. He might have been drinking before he arrived, of course, but he didn't look like it. He was sweating when he left, but that was because he'd blotted his copybook with George and she was rabbiting on at full blast about what a jerk he was. He couldn't get out fast enough, which probably explains why he didn't check his pockets properly."

"Do you have George Gardener's number?"

"Sure. She's on nights this week so you'll have to call her at work. Hang on, I'll find it for you." He came back with a nursing-home number a few seconds later. "It's the Birches," he said when the sergeant asked which one it was.

"The Birches," repeated the sergeant, writing the number on his notepad. "Is that the big place on Hathaway Avenue?"

"Yup."

"How easy will it be to get hold of Ms. Gardener?"

"Not difficult. She carries a pager."

"Right. Thank you, Mr. Trent."

"Hang on! What about this bloody wallet and passport? Does Hughes want to pick them up or should I post them?"

"I'll send a car."

A wary note crept into Roy's voice. "This isn't some sort of insurance scam, is it? There's not much in the wallet, you know . . . just a couple of twenties and some tickets. I assumed, as he didn't come back for it, he keeps his credit cards somewhere else. I'll be bloody angry if he tries to accuse me of stealing from him."

"He's not accusing anyone of anything at the moment, sir."

"Then what's the story? It all seems mighty peculiar to me."

You and me both, thought the sergeant, as he avoided the question by thanking the landlord again and cutting the line. He tapped his pen on his desk for a moment, then asked Andrew to find out from Jonathan what was in the wallet. "It's important, Mr. Spicer. If you think you're being lied to, please tell me."

While Andrew was out of the room, he consulted with the Transport Police, then checked for any call outs of the regular force to Branksome Station that afternoon. Both came up negative. There was no response at Branksome, which had closed for the night, but an operative at Bournemouth Central said the only information logged on the line about an Arab acting suspiciously was the "running amok" episode for which Jonathan had been arrested.

Andrew listened to the tail end of the conversation when he returned. "Do you think he imagined this woman?"

The sergeant shrugged. "Not necessarily, but he may have embroidered the encounter when he found his wallet was missing. He seems to like painting himself as a victim of injustice."

"Is that what the landlord said?"

The other man ignored the question. "I'm not unsympathetic, Mr. Spicer. It can't be easy for any dark-skinned person with all the anti-Muslim feeling that's in the world at the moment. What does he say was in the wallet?"

"Nothing worth stealing . . . except to him: a return ticket which he needed to get back in time for the opera, the *Falstaff* seat and forty-odd quid. He wasn't asked to show his ticket at Branksome, which is why he didn't discover it was missing till he reached Bournemouth Central. He says he should have just got on the train and blagged his way back to London, but he was too tired to think of it."

"What about credit cards?"

Andrew shrugged. "He wouldn't say where they were, but he's not claiming they were in the wallet."

George Gardener was as surprised as

Roy to be answering police questions about Dr. Hughes six hours after she thought she'd seen the back of him. She knew nothing about the missing wallet and passport, but she'd left the pub shortly after Jonathan. Like Roy, she had no recollection of a dark-haired woman. "There was hardly anyone there," she told the sergeant. "I only remember seeing Jim Longhurst. I suppose people may have come in while Dr. Hughes and I were upstairs, but he left by the back door, and that's not visible from the bar."

"Mr. Trent said you had a row with Dr. Hughes. May I ask what it was about?"

"We didn't row," she said. "Roy's probably talking about me voicing my opinions in the kitchen. I believe Dr. Hughes heard me, which is why he refused to wait for a taxi."

"Did he come by taxi?"

She hesitated. "I don't know . . . no, I don't think so. His raincoat was very wet when he got into my car, too wet for the few minutes before I caught up with him."

"Was this before or after you voiced your opinions?"

"Before. I was late for our meeting and there was a misunderstanding between him and Roy. I went after him in my car."

"What sort of misunderstanding?"

She sighed. "Roy made a remark that Dr. Hughes interpreted as racist. We were both expecting a white man — it's not a foreign name, you see, which is how the misunderstanding occurred." She paused. "Has he lodged a complaint against Roy?"

"Not that I'm aware of."

"Then what's this about?"

"That's what I'm trying to find out, Ms. Gardener. It would help if you gave me a summary — *brief,* if possible — of this meeting. What was the reason for it? What happened to make you voice opinions about Dr. Hughes?"

"Oh dear! It all seems very petty now."

"Please."

Sergeant Lovatt was expecting a rambling account but, in the event, it was surprisingly concise. George explained their common interest in Howard Stamp and referred to the differences between herself and Jonathan as a "personality clash." Their dislike had been mutual, and she'd recognized very early that she'd be walking on eggshells if she tried to work with him. Their attitudes to life were diametrically opposed — possibly because she was a generation older and Dr. Hughes aspired to more sophisticated standards than she cared about or was capable of achieving — so she had found it impossible to take the meeting further.

"I'm sorry if he's offended," she finished, "but I did explain that it wasn't a racist issue. Sometimes chemistry works and sometimes it doesn't. Sadly, in this case it didn't . . . and I wasn't prepared to hand my notes to someone whose motives I distrusted."

"Mm."

"Does that help, Sergeant?"

Not really . . . "Did he say he was feeling ill while he was with you, Ms. Gardener?"

"No."

"Did he *look* ill?"

Another hesitation. "If you'll forgive what appears to be another racist remark . . . his skin was too dark to tell. I know when white people are ill — even strangers — but I'm not well enough acquainted with black faces to recognize symptoms. He mopped his brow fairly regularly and didn't eat much — but there was a fire in the room and I assumed he didn't like Roy's food." Her concern sounded in her voice. "Now I feel awful. *Is* he ill? Is that why you've called?"

"He appears to have left his wallet and passport at the Crown and Feathers, Ms.

Gardener. It upset him. Without a return ticket, he had no means of getting back to London in time for the opera."

"I see," she said, although the lack of conviction in her voice suggested the opposite. "Why didn't he phone Roy?"

The sergeant stared across his desk at Andrew. "Perhaps he was embarrassed. There seem to have been some very unfortunate remarks made at this meeting. Thank you for your help."

He replaced the receiver. "I need verifiable contact details before he leaves, Mr. Spicer. However, I see no reason to detain him any longer tonight. I believe your assessment of your friend is right — that he has money difficulties and that the loss of his wallet pushed him off balance. It can be retrieved from the Crown and Feathers where he left it. I'll give you directions there, although I suggest you leave Dr. Hughes in the car and collect it from Mr. Trent yourself. If your friend gets himself into anymore trouble tonight, he will not go back to London. Understood?"

Andrew nodded. "Is this the end of it?"

Lovatt's expression was unreadable. "I've no idea, Mr. Spicer. I shall submit a report but I can't say whether any further action will be taken." He stood up. "If your reading of your friend is accurate, then you should encourage him to seek professional help. I repeat, unusual behavior is taken seriously these days . . . whatever the reasons for it."

Andrew checked his watch as he shut the passenger door on Jonathan. It was after ten o'clock and he was desperately hungry. He toyed with the idea of finding something to eat before driving to Highdown, but he didn't think he could do it and reach the Crown and Feathers before closing time. It made him irritable, and he slammed his own door with unnecessary force as he climbed in behind the wheel.

"I'm sorry," said Jonathan quietly. "I'd have chucked those letters in a bin if I'd known they were going to call you."

Andrew fired the engine and reversed out of the police car park. "Not your fault," he said with commendable control. "Better someone who knows you than someone who doesn't."

Jonathan clamped his hands between his knees. "Better no one at all. I should have taken the first train."

Andrew never held grudges. "You were a breakdown waiting to happen, pal. All you'd have done is postpone it." In an uncharacteristic gesture of affection he punched Jonathan lightly on the shoulder. "Be grateful it didn't happen at the opera. You'd have gone to pieces watching poor old Falstaff being pilloried — and that would have been horribly public."

"You can't get more public than Bournemouth Central."

"Certainly not if you're Jamaican. The brothers don't seem to have found Dorset yet."

Jonathan turned away to stare out of the window.

"You're black, Jon, and it's tearing you apart. However much you don't want to admit it, you have to address it at some point."

"What do you want me to say? I'm black and I'm proud?"

"Why not? It's my mantra. I say it all the time. I'm a short, fat, ugly white bloke so I tell myself, 'I'm black and I'm proud' and I go out and strut my stuff. It doesn't mean anyone sees anything except a short, fat, ugly white bloke, but it gives me a hell of a buzz. I'd swap with you any day."

"No, you wouldn't. It's hell being black."

"Would *you* swap with me?"

"Yes."

Andrew laughed. "Like hell you would!

It's no fun being five foot five. I can't even reach the pedals on this blasted car without jamming the seat against the steering wheel. You need a big personality to be a midget."

"At least you've *got* a car."

Andrew refused to rise and a silence fell. He wanted more explanation than Jonathan had given but he was wary of provoking further self-indulgent misery. Whether Jon was genuinely depressive, or simply depressed by a combination of circumstances, he was in no mood to view his situation objectively. And that was a pity because his best opportunity to learn how to do it was now. Objectivity was a talent Andrew had in spades, and not for the first time he wondered what Jonathan would say if he knew the truth about his agent.

Jonathan watched Andrew follow two signs to Highdown before he spoke. "Where are we going?"

"You dropped your wallet and passport at the Crown and Feathers. We're stopping off for them on the way."

"Who says?"

"The sergeant phoned the landlord. He found them after you left."

Jonathan leaned his head back and closed his eyes. "He can't have done," he murmured. "I took everything out of my breast pocket and put it in my briefcase when I removed my jacket. George Gardener watched me do it. I put the passport in the wallet and the wallet in the flapped pocket."

"Then it fell out," said Andrew reasonably.

"No. I checked when I put the correspondence back in the case. It's habit. The last wallet I had was stolen at a party when I left my jacket lying around. Now I always remove it and put it somewhere safe. And I never go anywhere without my passport."

"OK."

The corner's of Jonathan's mouth lifted in a faint smile. "Don't you believe me?"

"I'm too tired to care," Andrew said bluntly, drawing up behind a black BMW. "It doesn't make any difference anyway. The sergeant told me to pick the damn stuff up from the Crown and Feathers, and that's what I'm going to do . . . the emphasis being on *I*, Jon. You can wait in the car while I go inside."

There were a few more customers in the bar than when Jonathan had been there but Andrew's impressions were no more favorable than his friend's. He approached a young woman behind the bar. "Is Roy Trent around?" he asked.

"He's at the back. Can I help?"

"A friend of mine left his wallet here at lunchtime. I believe Roy's expecting someone to call for it."

"Oh, yes." She looked doubtful. "He told me it'd be a policeman."

"The man he spoke to was Sergeant Lovatt. He said he would send a car . . . but he didn't specify who would be in it. I was volunteered." He took out a card. "My name's Andrew Spicer and I'm a literary agent. The wallet belongs to one of my authors, Jonathan Hughes. Would you mind asking Roy to bring it out?"

"I guess it's OK." She raised the hatch in the counter. "If you go through that door over there, it takes you past the saloon and into the kitchen. It's a white door. He's in there."

Andrew questioned the business's viability as he negotiated the walkway behind the counter of the darkened, empty saloon. Overheads alone must have been crippling, and to keep a room that size unoccupied was financial suicide. Nor did it make any sense. All the manager had to do was recruit a decent chef and build a reputation for good eating. He crossed the hall where

Jonathan had stood listening to George's outburst, tapped on the white door opposite and pushed it open.

A man was sitting at the table watching a couple of television monitors in the corner. He switched one off as Andrew came in, then rose aggressively to his feet. "You're in the wrong room, mate. This is private."

"The barmaid told me to come through. Are you Roy Trent?"

"Yes."

Andrew proffered his card. "My name's Andrew Spicer. I'm Jonathan Hughes's agent. Sergeant Lovatt asked me to pick up his wallet and passport from you."

Trent glanced at the card, then used his bulk to shepherd Andrew out of the room. "She's a complete dipstick, that girl," he said with irritation. "I left them behind the till in the bar and told her to hand them over when the car arrived. If you retrace your steps and tell her I said you could have them, you'll be fine." He looked up the stairs as footsteps sounded on the landing.

Andrew followed his gaze. "It wasn't her fault. She was expecting a policeman."

A woman appeared on the landing and started down the steps, only to pause when she saw Roy had company. The light was dim but Andrew had a glimpse of a pale face beneath a dark fringe before the landlord thrust against him and forced him to step backward. "I'll come with you," he said affably. "Knowing Tracey, she probably won't be able to find them. You know the saying the lights are on but there's no one at home — it was written for her. She's pretty enough — decorates the bar nicely — but that's about all."

Andrew, annoyed by the shoving, recognized that Trent was talking for the sake of talking and decided to dig his heels in. "Is that the woman who helped Jonathan at the station?" he asked, coming to an abrupt halt and turning round. "If so, I'd like to thank her."

Trent shook his head. "No."

"No what? No, it wasn't her . . . or no, I can't thank her?"

"It wasn't her."

Andrew showed surprise. "How do you know without asking? She matches the description Jon gave, and the woman said she knew you."

Trent's smile didn't reach his eyes. "A lot of people know me, mate, but that's not the lady that helped your friend. This one's just arrived." He gestured impatiently to Andrew to proceed. "Now . . . do you want this wallet or not?"

Andrew led the way back into the lounge bar and watched Trent retrieve a slim black leather holder from behind the till with a passport tucked between its folds. "Check it by all means," he said, "but, like I told the copper who phoned, there's very little in it. If anything's missing, it went missing before Dr. Hughes got here."

Andrew opened it and flicked through the contents. "Nothing's missing," he agreed. "The only thing unaccounted for is how it came to drop out of his briefcase. It's the old-fashioned upright sort and it doesn't fall over very easily. Even if it did, it wouldn't lose its contents."

There was a lull in the conversation on the other side of the bar as curiosity drew the customers to listen. Suddenly, Trent had time on his hands. "Listen, mate, I'm just the guy who found it," he said good-humoredly. "If it wasn't in his briefcase, then it was in his jacket pocket. I don't see it matters one way or the other — long as he gets it back. You just tell him I'm glad it worked out for the best."

Andrew smiled. "Ms. Gardener watched him transfer it from his jacket to the case . . . and Dr. Hughes checked that it was still there before he left the pub."

Trent shrugged. "Then he made a mistake. What's the big deal, anyway? You said yourself there's nothing missing." He caught the eye of one of his customers and pulled a comical face. "What's the world coming to, eh, Tom? You keep a guy's wallet safe, and the next thing you know you're being hauled over the coals for it. Me, I was expecting thanks . . . but I might as well have been pissing in the wind. Forget gratitude —" he shifted his attention back to Andrew — "it's all about compensation these days."

Andrew chuckled as he tucked the wallet into his own breast pocket. "At least be honest — er — *mate*. The police have already told you there's no question of compensation." His eyes snapped in challenge. "I'm sure you know as well as anyone that truth is in the detail . . . and I'm one of those boring people who finds detail interesting." He extended an open palm. "Thank you. Jon will be very grateful to have everything back intact." He gripped Trent's hand, very much as Jonathan had done earlier, crunching the metacarpals in a surprisingly strong grasp for a small man. "It's been interesting seeing the way you do business."

Chapter Nine

Andrew folded himself into the car and leaned across Jonathan to retrieve his mobile from the dashboard pocket. He punched in the numbers for directory inquiries. "Yes, please, Bournemouth. The Birches, Hathaway Avenue . . . it's a nursing home." The sergeant wasn't the only one with a retentive memory, he thought, as he clicked onto the nursing home number. "Yes, hello, I'm sorry to bother you at such a late hour but I was wondering if I could have a quick word with George Gardener . . . no, it's not personal . . . it's a follow-up on the call she had earlier from Sergeant Lovatt." He absorbed the irritation from the other end. "I do apologize. You have my guarantee I'll only keep her for a minute or two. Yes, I'll wait . . . thank you."

He plugged the mobile into the car microphone, then took out Jonathan's wallet and handed it to him. "Trent's a bastard," he said cheerfully, "and I think I've just seen your dark-haired thief."

Jonathan looked at him in surprise. "You don't know what she looks like."

"No," Andrew agreed, "but she had a dark fringe and Trent didn't want me anywhere near her. He frog-marched me away."

A breathy voice came through the car speakers. "Hello. This is George Gardener."

"Andrew Spicer, Ms. Gardener. Jonathan's agent. You contacted him through my office, if you remember."

"They said it was the sergeant again."

"It's the same matter. I was with Sergeant Lovatt when you spoke to him earlier. I wonder if you'd be kind enough to confirm one small detail for me. Jon tells me you watched him take off his jacket and put his wallet and passport in his briefcase. Is that right?"

"Yes," she said without hesitation. "He was very meticulous about it."

"Did he take it out again at any point?"

"No . . . well, not when I was in the room with him at least. He may have done so after I left." There was a beat of silence. "I don't understand what's going on. Why all these questions? What's happened to Dr. Hughes?"

Andrew stared through the windshield. *What the hell . . . ?* There'd almost certainly be a piece about it in the local newspaper tomorrow. "He became distressed after his wallet was stolen," he said curtly, "and, unfortunately — the way things are at the moment — a dark-skinned Arab who shows visible agitation is viewed as a threat. He's been under arrest for six hours and was only released after I drove down from London to vouch for him."

She sounded baffled. "I thought Roy found the wallet at the pub."

"Let's just say it was in his possession, Ms. Gardener. I picked it up from there ten minutes ago. Whether Dr. Hughes dropped it is another matter altogether."

"I still don't understand."

"No," agreed Andrew, "neither do we, so I suggest you ask Mr. Trent for an explanation. It's not as though the wallet was even worth stealing."

"Was anything missing?"

"No."

"Is Dr. Hughes saying Roy stole it?"

"No," said Andrew again. "He believes it was a dark-haired woman on Branksome Station who helped him when he wasn't feeling well."

She took time to assimilate this information. "Well, I'm sorry he was ill, but I still don't understand what it has to do with Roy."

"The woman claimed to be a friend of Mr. Trent's . . . and she clearly must be, Ms. Gardener, otherwise he wouldn't have been able to return the wallet to me."

"She said she was a friend of his ex-wife's," corrected Jonathan in an undertone.

"Did you hear that, Ms. Gardener?"

"Was that Dr. Hughes speaking?"

"Yes."

"Oh dear, I'm so sorry. I can't help feeling partly to blame. None of this would have happened if I hadn't been late."

Jonathan shook his head but didn't say anything.

"He said the woman claimed to be a friend of Mr. Trent's ex-wife," Andrew prompted her. "She has a dark fringe and speaks with a Dorset accent. Does that ring any bells?"

"I'm afraid not. I've never met his wife, and certainly none of her friends. Perhaps she was lying?"

"Then how did Mr. Trent get the wallet back?"

Another silence while she considered the conundrum. "Perhaps Dr. Hughes is mistaken," she said unhappily. "Perhaps he took it out again after I left. We were both rather rattled." She waited for Andrew to respond, and when he didn't: "It all seems very strange," she finished lamely.

"I agree. If Mr. Trent provides you with an explanation, I'll be interested to hear it."

She didn't answer immediately. "If nothing's missing, he'll say it's a storm in a teacup."

"Of course he will," Andrew acknowledged. "He's obviously more used to lying than telling the truth."

She tut-tutted indignantly. "That's a terrible accusation to make against a man you don't know."

"Surely not," said Andrew ironically. "As the saying goes: what can you expect from a pig but a grunt?"

Cill lit a cigarette and blew the smoke into Roy's face. He'd backed her into a corner of the kitchen and his thrashing finger had been lambasting her for what seemed like hours. It reminded her of their tempestuous marriage before she left him for Nick. "Give it a rest," she said sulkily. "There's no harm done. I got the sodding thing back to you quick enough, didn't I?

How was I to know he'd go running to the cops instead of making a phone call?"

"He's a wog, you stupid bitch. They always go to the police. Why the fuck did you do it?"

"Because it seemed like a good idea at the time." She whooshed out another cloud of smoke to force him into retreat. "I wanted his address, and the letters only had his agent's address."

"Why?"

"In case you've been lying to me."

His eyes narrowed. "About what?"

"How much you've told the fat spinster. You're too damn friendly with her. I thought maybe she's been pricking your conscience. Nick thinks you've gone soft, Roy — there was a time when the only thing a bleeding heart liberal was worth was a damn good kicking."

He gave a snort of angry laughter. "*Nick* thinks!" He turned to the CCTV monitor. "You're married to a gorilla, Cill. All he thinks about is sex and food. You made a bad bargain there, darlin'."

She ignored him. "All right, *I* think you've gone soft. What difference does it make? Nick always agrees with me if I give him what he wants."

"Jesus, you're so thick! What were you

planning to do if you did get his address? Kill him? Thanks to me, he was away and done with. George didn't want anything more to do with him." He jabbed the finger in her face again. "He's a faggot — no fucking guts; I knew the minute I clapped eyes on him he'd be a pushover. *I* riled *him,* so *he* riled George . . . happens every time. Then you have to stick your nose in and land me with his sodding agent."

She smacked his finger away. "What's he going to do?" she demanded crossly. "The wog's got his wallet back intact. If you stick to your story, there won't be a problem."

"I know blokes like Spicer. Once they get the bit between their teeth, they never stop. He knows damn well Hughes didn't drop his wallet here."

"He's a midget," she said dismissively. "Since when were you frightened of midgets?"

"Since I was taught some sense. It's a pity you never learned any, darlin'. Small guys use their brains . . . big guys like your brain-dead husband put all their energy into getting atop the nearest available tart."

"What's he gonna do?" she repeated sulkily.

"Talk to George," Roy said grimly. "I'll put money on it."

"So?"

"She'll be at me with the questions again." He brought his fist up and rested it under her chin. "If you'd let it alone, Cill, she'd've gone on with her research and got precisely nowhere because I was the only source she had." He moved his knuckles up her soft skin, caressing it gently, before pressing them against her cheekbone. "Now she'll come looking for you, and if you drop me in it one more time —" he spread his lips in an evil smile — "I'll use this in such a way that even the gorilla you married won't recognize you."

Cill ignored him again. Roy's threats were never more than bluster. "Nick's getting worse, you know. He's been dropping things, but he won't go near the doctors. I think the paralysis is spreading."

Roy lowered his fist and turned away. "Well, you won't be shedding any tears over it. He's worth more to you dead than alive."

"Maybe I have feelings for him."

"Don't talk crap," said Roy dismissively. "The only feelings you have are for his money. You're getting quite a taste for the high life one way and another."

"Someone had to look after him."

He gave an angry laugh. "You're so full of it, darlin'. You thought you'd get a pussycat . . . instead you get a drooling lunatic whose anger control mechanism's shot to pieces."

Her pale eyes glittered malevolently. "He adores me," she said, "always has. I make him feel better about himself."

"Only because he doesn't know who you are."

It was true, but she was damned if she'd admit it. Half of Nick's brain had been scrambled seven years ago in London when two Metropolitan coppers ran him head first into a lamppost before taking their boots to him. They claimed they mistook him for a drug baron who was known to carry a gun. The fact that a gun was never found, the only drugs he had on him were class-C tranquilizers and he was held in a cell for three hours before he was given medical attention meant compensation of two hundred thousand for brain damage, wrongful arrest and imprisonment. It had taken his solicitors five years to win it through the courts, but Cill had thought dumping Roy to play Florence Nightingale to a cripple was a gamble worth taking.

"You won't be shedding tears neither, darlin'," she said, running a soft hand up between Roy's shoulder blades. "I always said I'd share it, and I will." She dug her fingernails into the nape of his neck. "In any case, it was you told me to do it."

He pressed his fingers into his eye sockets. "I'll swing for you one of these days, Cill."

She touched her lips to his cheek. "Don't be silly, darlin'. I'm the only girl you've ever loved."

It wasn't until Andrew turned onto the A31 and put his foot down that Jonathan roused himself to speak. "Thanks."

"Pleasure. We'll stop at the first service station and get something to eat. There's one on the M27."

"I'm OK. Don't worry about me."

"I'm not. I'm worrying about myself. I haven't eaten since breakfast." He glanced at Jonathan's tired face. "You'll be eating, too, pal, whether you like it or not. You can't go on starving yourself . . . not if you want to remain sane."

"I'm not starving myself."

"Then why are your clothes hanging off you?" He flicked the indicator and pulled out into the fast lane of the dual carriageway. "You can stay with me tonight, then tomorrow I'm taking you to my doctor."

"I can't. I have a tutorial at eleven."

"I'll phone your department and say you won't be in till Monday."

"I really —"

"Cut the crap," Andrew said sharply. "I've hauled my arse halfway across the country to bail you out. The least you can do is humor me. If nothing else, the doc will give you some knockout pills to help you sleep."

Jonathan hunched his shoulders. "They don't work. I've tried . . . nothing works when your brain won't switch off."

"Is it Emma?"

His friend gave a mirthless laugh. "No."

"Then what's the problem?"

It was a moment before Jonathan answered. "The usual," he said with sudden resignation, as if recognizing that Andrew needed something for his trouble. "Rueing the day I was born into this bloody awful country . . . wishing I was white and rich. It's an apartheid thing. Either you belong or you don't."

He spoke with such bitterness that Andrew didn't doubt he believed what he was saying. Perhaps it was true. "Who said you don't belong?"

Another humorless laugh. "You mean apart from immigration officials, policemen, Dorset landlords and anyone else who fancies a swipe?"

"Apart from them," Andrew agreed calmly.

"Everyone's prejudiced — it's been worse since the attack on the Trade Center."

"That was eighteen months ago, and you've only been twitched since Emma left."

Anger sparked briefly in Jonathan's eyes. "Drop it, OK. If it makes you feel comfortable, then go ahead, blame my problems on a failed relationship — it's how you excuse yours."

"I don't recall ever discussing my problems with you, Jon. We usually pore over yours for hours on end."

"Yes, well, stop blaming Emma. The truth is what happened today. Strangers don't see *me*, they see someone who isn't a member of their cozy club. You try dealing with that day after day and then tell me you sleep soundly at night."

"We're all in the same boat. When strangers look at me, they see a bald short-arse with zero status. It's just as painful . . . particularly when women do it. I watch their eyes skate over my head while they look around for a big, handsome fellow with a full head of hair —" he gave an amused chuckle — "and I wouldn't mind if I didn't have a preference for tall women. That's life. You have to recognize it's going to happen and be willing to make a few compromises."

"Like what?"

"Don't wear your heart on your sleeve. People react badly if you show you care. They either take advantage or leg it as fast as they can." He slowed as they approached a roundabout. "Calling the police fascists wasn't the best idea you've ever had."

Jonathan stared grimly through the windshield. "Do you know how many times I've been stopped and searched in the last six months? Four, including last night. How many times has it happened to you?"

"In the last six months? Not at all. In my life? Once, when a fight broke out as I left a pub."

"Point made then. As a kid, I was stopped every other week."

"Only because you were expecting to be. If you flag a prophecy, it'll fulfill itself immediately. I'm not saying it's fair, but suspicion breeds suspicion."

"And which came first?" Jonathan growled. "Police suspicion of me or mine of them? Try applying your simplistic rules to that little conundrum. I was hoping for some sympathy, not another damn lecture on the dangers of alienation. I'd tolerate it if I thought you'd ever experienced it, but you haven't. A broken marriage hardly counts, not when your wife still invites you to dinner and your girls stay weekends."

"You'll be telling me next how lucky I am," said Andrew mildly. "All the joys of family life without the irritation of living with any of them. Despite their age, the parents are fit and independent — courtesy of a share in a thriving little agency — the wife and kids are safely parked with a man who appreciates them — courtesy of a generous divorce settlement — and I can dedicate myself to what I really enjoy doing: working to support them all."

"Considering the divorce was your fault, you're damn lucky Jenny didn't break off all contact."

"Mm . . . except she was having an affair too. It's easier to maintain relationships when both parties feel guilty."

Jonathan looked at him. This was something he hadn't known. "I thought it was only you."

"I know you did."

"You should have told me."

"Why?"

"I always thought what an idiot you were to chuck Jenny over for a woman who only lasted a few months. I can't even remember her name now. Claire? Carol?"

"Claire," said Andrew, "a blonde, blue-eyed bombshell, just like Jenny. They say men are always attracted to the same type of woman, but it doesn't seem to work the other way. Greg — Jenny's lover — is ten feet tall and looks like Brad Pitt. I can see exactly why she was attracted to him. The girls, too. They adore him as much as she does."

Something in his tone caused Jonathan to frown. "If Jenny was equally to blame, how come she did so well out of the divorce?"

Andrew glanced at him. "I made it easy for her."

"Then you're a fool. She got the house, the bloke and the kids —" he made a dismissive gesture — "and you got a miserable two-up, two-down in Peckham. What kind of trade was that, for Christ's sake? No wonder Claire buggered off."

Andrew gave a small laugh. "I'll take that as a compliment. Obviously, I mistook my profession."

"What does that mean?"

"I'm a better actor than Greg."

There was a short silence.

"I don't understand."

"Claire never existed. The only blonde, blue-eyed bombshells I've ever had relationships with are Jenny and the girls. You don't have a monopoly on pride, Jon. What did you expect me to do? Get down on my knees and beg? I was happy as a sandboy — beautiful wife, beautiful children, house, secure job, good social life — then, *wham,* the wife hits me between the eyes with the muscled actor from next door who's been shafting her for months. The irony was, I really liked him . . . still do, as a matter of fact."

"You're mad," said Jonathan in disbelief. "Why would you lie about a thing like that? It's cost you a fortune in guilt money."

"It depends what you value. As long as the business isn't threatened, I'd rather be thought of as a bit of a dog than an embarrassing burden on my wife's conscience. Do you think Jenny would be on the phone all the time, or Greg would invite me to dinner, if they thought I was a sad, lonely git who still hankered after his ex-wife? Would the girls be happy to stay overnight if I'd slagged off their mother for two-timing me?" He spoke matter-of-factly without any attempt at sympathy. "More importantly, the parents see their grandchildren whenever they want. They castigate me regularly for causing the breakup but go on treating Jenny as their daughter-in-law. All in all, I'd say it was cheap at the price."

Jonathan's incredulity deepened. What did a man have to gain by turning himself into a whipping boy for an errant wife and critical parents? *"They were flogged for the failings of others . . . it's a very twisted concept . . ."* "Why let Jenny off scot-free? She bad-mouthed you enough at the time. I remember her telling me what a shit you were."

"I hope you agreed with her. I was never too sure she totally believed in Claire."

"I did as a matter of fact. I said you'd married too young, and the marriage was bound to fail." He thought back. "She wasn't very happy about it."

"Her pride was dented. She thought she was the only woman in my life."

"What about your pride?"

"Shot to pieces till I invented Claire. She was a great restorative."

"I'd have wanted revenge."

Andrew shrugged. "I couldn't see the point of going to war over something I couldn't control. You can't force people to love you . . . you can't force them to be loyal. All you can do is keep affection alive and hope for the best."

He was living in cloud cuckoo land, thought Jonathan. "Are you expecting Jenny to come back?"

"No."

"Then I don't get it. What's the quid pro quo for acting honorably if no one knows you're doing it?"

"I don't have to walk around with a neon sign on my forehead, saying 'loser.' "

Jonathan felt the familiar anger knot inside his jaw. "Meaning that I do, I suppose?"

" 'Fraid so. You're a sitting duck for the Roy Trents of this world."

Councillor G. Gardener
25 Mullin Street, Highdown,
Bournemouth, Dorset BH15 6VX

Andrew Spicer
Spicer & Hardy Authors' Agents
25 Blundell Street
London W4 9TP

April 2, 2003

Dear Mr. Spicer:

I hesitate to write to Dr. Hughes as he may not wish to correspond with me, but I would be grateful if you could pass on my apologies to him and my best wishes for his recovery. I have had a long conversation with Sergeant Lovatt and, though he refused to go into details, he did say that Dr. Hughes had been unwell.

The circumstances of our meeting were unfortunate, and I take much of the blame. I have some experience of illness, and I should have realized that

Dr. Hughes's reticence was physiologically based. He was clearly exhausted, but I made no allowances for poor health, jet lag or even the severity of the weather that day. My only excuse is blind dedication to exculpating Howard Stamp, and a long history of disappointment in the attempts I've made to do so. I am now so programmed for failure that I see it before I need to.

Re: our short phone call on the evening of February 13: Roy Trent stands by his story that Dr. Hughes left his wallet at the pub. However, after Sergeant Lovatt gave me the details of Dr. Hughes's arrest, I made inquiries at Branksome Station. The clerk in the ticket office remembers Dr. Hughes well because some passengers expressed concern about his behavior. The gist of the clerk's story is as follows:

He thought Dr. Hughes was drunk as he was swaying and trying to focus on the other platform to keep his balance. His face was wet — the clerk thought it was rain until he realized Dr. Hughes was sweating — and he was clutching his briefcase to his chest. Several trains went through but he didn't take them. At least two people thought he was a suicide bomber trying to pluck up the courage to go through with it. The clerk was worried enough to consider phoning the police. However, a woman approached Dr. Hughes for what appeared to be a prearranged meeting. They smiled and talked and Dr. Hughes gave her his briefcase from which she removed some papers. The clerk remembered seeing the woman earlier in the ticket hall, and assumed Dr. Hughes had misunderstood where the meeting was to take place. He admitted he wouldn't have been worried if Dr. Hughes hadn't been an Arab — he would have dismissed him as a drunk. He was relieved when the woman helped him onto a train and took the problem out of his hands. She had dark hair and held a scarf to her mouth, but he couldn't remember anything else about her except that she left in a black BMW that had been parked for forty-five minutes in the "drop-off only" zone.

Because this seemed to validate Dr. Hughes's version of events, I made some discreet inquiries about Roy Trent's ex-wife. Her name is Priscilla Fletcher, formerly known as Cill Trent. I was unable to discover her maiden name, but she has been described to me as midforties, medium height, slim, dark hair cut in a straight fringe, light-colored eyes (possibly blue) and attractive. Her current husband, Nicholas Fletcher, is in "business" — there's some mystery over exactly what he does — and they live in Sandbanks, an expensive part of Poole. She had a child by Roy — a son, now in his thirties (!) — but none by Fletcher. Because of the son, she and Roy remain on good terms. While there is no evidence that this is the woman who approached Dr. Hughes, the description seems to fit.

Nevertheless, I remained puzzled as to why Priscilla Fletcher, an apparently wealthy woman (or indeed one of her friends) would have taken the wallet. For this reason I related the clerk's story to Roy Trent, embroidering the description of the woman to more closely resemble Priscilla Fletcher, and asked him what he made of it in view of Dr. Hughes's certainty that she was the thief. Roy's reaction was interesting. He treated it as a joke and said if Dr. Hughes was right, the woman must have returned to the pub after it closed for the afternoon in order to leave the wallet on the floor of the room where Dr. Hughes and I had lunch. And that hadn't happened. I agreed the story was absurd, pointing out that she must also have known where the lunch took place, which would suggest someone very familiar with the running of the pub. Therefore, unless Roy recognized the woman's description, Dr. Hughes must be mistaken. Roy agreed that he did *not* recognize the woman's description.

I should say at this point that I've never had reason to disbelieve anything Roy has told me in the past. Our relationship is an informal one, based on two years of friendship after he gave me permission to use his pub as a "surgery." I don't claim to know him well — he is not a forthcoming man — but I've always found him pleasant and supportive, particularly with the help he's given me in unearthing information about Howard Stamp. Of course I was intrigued by the lie, particularly as I could see no reason for it. He might easily have said, "I know several women who match that description, my ex-wife being one, but none of them came to the pub that day." I was, after all, agreeing with him that Dr. Hughes was mistaken.

I was interested enough to do some further research and began by making a number of assumptions, any one of which might have been false, but which seemed worth testing. These are the assumptions I made:

1. Roy's ex-wife stole the wallet.
2. She did so because she: (a) is an opportunist thief; or (b) was told to; or (c) was interested in Dr. Hughes; or (d) a combination of the three.
3. If it was an opportunistic theft, how did she know: (a) to return the wallet to Roy; (b) that he would protect her?

4. Because she returned it, she must have known: (a) that Dr. Hughes had been at the pub earlier; (b) what he looked like.
5. She knew these facts because: (a) she had been at the pub herself; or (b) they had been given to her by someone else.
6. Apart from myself, Roy Trent is the only other person who knew when, where and why I was meeting with Dr. Hughes.
7. The only way Priscilla Fletcher could have known these details is if Roy told her.
8. If theft of money wasn't her motivation, then she wanted to know more about Dr. Hughes.
9. She did not ask Roy for details because: (a) she didn't think he would tell her; or (b) he didn't know the answers; or (c) it was he who told her to commit the theft.
10. If (b) or (c), Roy did not want to display undue interest in Dr. Hughes by quizzing me about him.
11. Dr. Hughes's only reason for coming to Bournemouth was his interest in Howard Stamp.

I already knew that Roy Trent was acquainted with Howard Stamp, if only "by sight" (Roy's words), but it seemed reasonable to infer that Priscilla Fletcher was also connected with him in some way. Out of curiosity, I went back to the newspaper coverage at the time of Grace Jefferies' murder to see if there was anything I'd overlooked. I came across an unrelated story about a thirteen-year-old called Priscilla "Cill" Trevelyan who went missing from her home in Highdown a week before Grace's body was found. As yet, I have been unable to establish whether Cill Trevelyan and Priscilla Fletcher are one and the same. However, there are similarities between the photograph of the missing girl and the one I've managed to track down of Priscilla Fletcher/Trent, taken five years ago at a Crown and Feathers barbecue, courtesy of Jim Longhurst. I hope Dr. Hughes will appreciate the irony! (Copies enclosed.)

While I am reluctant to jump to conclusions at this stage, it seems that Cill was subjected to a gang rape before she ran away and this would accord with Priscilla Fletcher (midforties) having a son in his thirties. I attach photocopies of the newspaper clippings which might be of interest to Dr. Hughes when he's well enough to read them. He will, of course, note immediately that Cill Trevelyan had shoulder-length dark hair. He will also note the descriptions of her assailants — none of whom was named and none of whom was charged through lack of evidence. Interestingly, the story of this missing thirteen-year-old never made it into the national press, presumably because she was posted immediately as a "runaway."

There is nothing to link Cill's story with Howard's except the coincidences of time and place and some thought-provoking descriptions. However, the synchronicity of events, coupled with the unnecessary theft of a wallet thirty years later, does raise questions. At the moment I have no idea what the linkage might be, but I am left with the suspicion that Priscilla Fletcher feels she has something to lose if Howard's case is resurrected. I am willing to forward further information that comes my way, if you think Dr. Hughes would be interested. I will, of course, understand if he prefers to wash his hands of it.

In conclusion, Roy Trent is not party to this information and, for the foreseeable future, I intend to remain on good terms with him. I would be grateful if you and Dr. Hughes would avoid doing anything to prejudice that position. Thanking you in advance,

Yours sincerely

George Gardener

Encs

Bournemouth Evening News —
Saturday, May 30, 1970

Concern For Missing Girl

Bournemouth Police today asked for help in the search for Priscilla Trevelyan, 13, who went missing from her home in Highdown during the early hours of this morning. She is 5' 5" tall, weighing approximately 8 stone, with shoulder-length dark hair, possibly dressed in blue jeans and a long-sleeved white T-shirt. Known as Cill, the youngster is believed to have run away after an argument with her father.

Mrs. Jean Trevelyan, 35, blamed her daughter's school. "Her father was upset because she was given a week's suspension for fighting. But it takes two to make a fight and the other girl wasn't punished at all. Cill's bright and she knew that wasn't fair." She broke down as she made a plea for her daughter to come home. "We love her and we want her back. No one's going to be angry."

Police are following various lines of

inquiry. "She's mature for her age," said a spokesman, "and she was in the company of some older boys three weeks ago. There's a possibility she may be with one of them now. Two were described as dark-haired and of medium build, the third as tall and thin with ginger hair. We are asking these boys to come forward. They have nothing to fear if they know where Cill is. The imperative is her safe return."

Police have not ruled out abduction. "Runaways of this age are vulnerable. They may accept offers of help from people who seek only to exploit them." The Metropolitan Police has been alerted. "London is a magnet for unhappy children," said the spokesman.

Bournemouth Evening News —
Monday, June 1, 1970

Hunt for 13-Year-Old Continues

Three teenage boys were released without charge today after being questioned by police over the disappearance of Priscilla Trevelyan. They matched descriptions given by one of her school friends, but all three denied knowing Priscilla or having any knowledge of her disappearance. A police spokesman says there is no evidence to link them with the missing girl.

Priscilla's father, David Trevelyan, 37 was also questioned after neighbors mentioned constant rows between the two. "They didn't get on," said one. "He was worried about her truanting." Police denied that Trevelyan was a suspect. "Parents are always questioned in these circumstances," said a spokesman, "but we are satisfied Mr. and Mrs. Trevelyan know nothing of their daughter's disappearance."

He admitted that the authorities are baffled. "Several sightings of a girl matching Cill's description have come to nothing, and we are no further forward. After leaving her house she appears to have vanished." They have made a fresh appeal to the public by issuing a series of photographs of the girl in the hope of jogging memories.

Bournemouth Evening News —
Saturday, July 25, 1970

Mother's Anguish Over Missing Teen

It's just two months since 13-year-old Priscilla Trevelyan left home after an argument with her father, yet her file has been shelved and the team looking into her disappearance disbanded. In simple terms, a runaway does not command the same level of police attention as a child who's been abducted, and Priscilla has joined the frightening statistic of 75,000 children under 16 who run away from homes or institutions in this country every year.

While most of these children return after one night away, some 1,000 will still be missing months later. They are in danger of physical and sexual assault, and many of them resort to crime and prostitution to stay alive. "Cases like these are always difficult," said PC Gary Prentice, who holds a watching brief over Priscilla's file. "If a runaway doesn't want to be found, there's little the police can do. We've circulated her photograph to other forces and we hope someone will recognize her. Many children return home at Christmas when memories of family are strong. I hope this happens in Cill's case."

Priscilla's mother, Jean Trevelyan, is heartbroken. She acknowledges that trouble at home was a contributory factor but she insists it's out of character for her daughter not to have telephoned. "The police say there's no evidence of abduction, but little girls don't vanish into thin air. I wish I'd never mentioned the row with her father. He was trying to support the school's punishment, but it gave the police an excuse to stop looking for her."

PC Prentice denies this. "We pursued every lead we were given. Sadly, Cill was a disturbed adolescent with complications at home and at school. She'd been truanting for some time before she decided to run away. There's always concern when a 13-year-old goes missing, but we're optimistic that Cill is bright enough to survive. Her friends described her as 'street-smart,' which is an American expression she taught them after reading it in a magazine. She used it to describe herself."

Jean Trevelyan remembers it differently. "Cill was always in trouble. People expected her to behave responsibly because she was well-developed for her age, but at heart she was like any other 13-year-old. One of her friends told the police she was gang raped before she ran away, but they were less interested in that than they were in the argument she had with her father."

PC Prentice admits the rape allegation but says there was no evidence to support it. "If it happened, then it's tragic that Cill was too ashamed to tell anyone about it." He agreed that the stigma of rape is a disincentive to reporting it. "Police forces are working on ways to encourage women and girls to come forward," he said, "but there's still a long way to go."

This is no consolation for Jean Trevelyan who sits by her window, praying for Priscilla to come home. "We've lost more than our daughter," she weeps, "we've lost our good name. People say we were unkind, but she was our only child and we wanted the best for her. The police claim to be sympathetic, but they've never once portrayed us as loving parents."

The photographs of Priscilla that line the room endorse Jean's love for her daughter, but she admits they've only been on display since Priscilla vanished. Like so many mothers, she found the balance between disciplining an errant adolescent and continuing to show love a difficult one. "We were strict because we worried about her, but we didn't know what worry was until she left. David is devastated by it all. It's a terrible way to learn that the time to show your child affection is when you're most angry. We disciplined her because we loved her, yet she must have believed it was done out of hate or she wouldn't have run away."

Her greatest anguish is that Priscilla felt unable to tell anyone she'd been raped. "Her friend said she thought people would say it was her fault because she was wearing a miniskirt, but we live in a terrible society if a 13-year-old thinks she'll be blamed for what happens to her. The police have cast doubt on the rape, but I know it happened because Cill threw her skirt away. She saved up for it and it was her favorite. She wouldn't have done that if she had nothing to feel ashamed about."

One is left with a sense of enormous tragedy. A grieving mother, indefinitely confined to her house for fear her daughter comes back to find no one at home. A father crippled by guilt because he upheld a school punishment. A house empty of laughter. A child missing because there was no one she could ask for help.

Bronwen Sherrard

SPICER & HARDY
Author's Agents
25 Blundell Street London W4 9TP

Cllr. George Gardener
25 Mullin Street
Highdown
Bournemouth
DORSET BH15 6VX

Monday, April 7, 2003

Dear George Gardener,

Thank you for your letter of April 2, and your kind wishes for Jonathan's recovery. Prior to your meeting he had been suffering for some time from severe stomach cramps and nausea which he foolishly put down to stress and overwork when the problem was a bleeding ulcer. His trip to the U.S. only exacerbated the problem and he developed complications on the day he visited you. Fortunately, it was caught in time and he's now well on the road to recovery. No thanks to him! I am telling you this because he won't tell you himself as he feels there are no excuses for his behavior. My own view, as I understand from Sergeant Lovatt that you are not well yourself, is that it was a clash of illnesses and is best forgotten. May I return the compliment you paid Jon, and send you my good wishes for *your* speedy recovery.

I enclose a letter from Jonathan re: Priscilla Fletcher/Cill Trevelyan. However, I wish to stress: (a) his willingness to be involved in your project; and (b) the expertise he can bring to it. Jon has many strong points but self-promotion isn't one of them. When he tries, he sounds patronizing. When he doesn't, he looks smug. Both traits are deeply infuriating, but they're easier to ignore if you view them as a disability.

Yours sincerely,

Andrew Spicer

Andrew Spicer
Enc.

DR. JONATHAN HUGHES
Flat 2b Columbia Road
West Kensington
London W14 2DD
Email: jon.hughes@london.ac.uk

Saturday, April 5

Dear George,

I'm embarrassed to think how badly I behaved the day we met, so please don't feel you have anything to apologize for. My trip to Bournemouth was a salutory lesson in my own stupidity. They say every cloud has a silver lining, and mine certainly has. I won't bore you with the Damascene conversion — you probably hate the cliché as much as I do — suffice it to say that I have taken Andrew's advice to live at peace with myself.

I was fascinated by your letter and the enclosures. You may by now have validated or refuted your assumptions. However, I draw your attention to the following:

- Having studied the photograph of Priscilla Fletcher, I believe she may have been the woman who approached me on Branksome Station.
- While there is a similarity between the photographs of Priscilla Fletcher and Cill Trevelyan, it appears superficial. It may be a result of the child having lost baby fat, or the fact that her picture is in black and white, but to my eyes the bone structure of the faces is very different. Cill has a heavier jaw and more pronounced cheekbone than Priscilla's rather delicate equivalents. Cill's eyes look darker, although this may be due to the monochrome.
- Priscilla is extremely fair-skinned, giving her a "Snow White" look — dark hair, pale face. While it's a common enough combination, fair skin is more usually associated with red or blonde hair, except in the Irish and Welsh(!!). Interestingly, my impression of the woman at Branksome Station was that her look was a manufactured one. The photograph gives the same impression. (Painted eyes, reshaped eyebrows, dyed [?] hair.)

- If these are the same person, then there are some interesting discrepancies.
- If they are two different people, then the similarity is striking, particularly as they are both called Priscilla, and Cill Trevelyan would now be in her midforties.

I imagine you have already scoured the newspaper archives for any information on Cill Trevelyan's return. You may even have located her parents, assuming they remained in the Bournemouth area. But if, as I suspect, you've found no evidence that she ever came back — (I'm guessing you did this research before you wrote to Andrew) — then the obvious question is: if Priscilla is *not* Cill, then why would she want to adopt the name and looks of a girl who vanished thirty-plus years ago?

Here are some other details that struck me as I read the newspaper clippings:

- Compare: "Three teenage boys . . . matched descriptions given by one of her [Cill's] school friends . . ." with Jean Trevelyan's claim: "One of her friends told the police she was gang raped . . ." There are various inferences to be drawn from these two statements: the friend either witnessed the incident or was told about it afterward; the friend only revealed what had happened after Cill went missing.

- Compare: "the youngster is believed to have run away after an argument with her father . . ."; "neighbors mentioned constant rows between the two . . ."; "[her father] was worried about her truanting . . ."; "Cill was always in trouble . . ."; "[Jean Trevelyan's] greatest anguish is that Priscilla felt unable to tell anyone she'd been raped . . . [Cill] thought people would say it was her fault . . ." The strong presumption in all these statements is that David Trevelyan would *not* have been sympathetic if Cill had admitted to being raped.
- "It takes two to make a fight and the other girl wasn't punished at all." Again, there are various inferences to

be drawn from this. The most common reason for children to fall out is when one says, "I'll tell on you." If "the friend" was also "the other girl," then the rape was the secret they shared and a threat to reveal it may have been the cause of the fight. If it was a different girl, then either Cill lost her temper over anything and everything *or* the secret was out. The fact that Cill was punished and the other girl wasn't suggests Cill started it and/or was the more violent and/or refused to give a reason.

- From all of the above references, it is reasonable to accept PC Prentice's analysis: "Cill was a disturbed adolescent with complications at home and at school." (There was an unusual amount of aggression in her life — hitting out at school suggests she was no stranger to being hit at home.) While a child like that may well abscond — research suggests that most runaways have suffered physical or sexual abuse — she was unlikely to keep her name. Indeed, if she hadn't been found in two months, and was still alive, she must have been calling herself something else. I believe that's the name she would continue to go by — *even if she returned home* — because it would have been a demonstration to her father that the rules had changed and a new "she" was setting the agenda.

I don't pretend to know any better than you which assumptions are correct. However, I do believe it might be worth trying to put a name to Cill Trevelyan's school friend. Presumably she was the same age as Cill, and a 13-year-old would have been deeply traumatized by the rape (more so if she witnessed it and did nothing to help), closely followed by the guilt of not speaking out, a spiteful threat to "tell" and Cill's disappearance.

I am no psychologist so I'll rely on your expertise to throw the idea out if it's too far-fetched. *The schoolfriend seems a more likely contender for Priscilla Fletcher than Cill Trevelyan.* (Transference reaction?

Mitigation of guilt by "resurrecting" the wronged person? Envy/hero worship — Cill got away and she didn't?) Are any of these credible? Can trauma in childhood define behavior through to middle age?

I have failed dismally to make a connection between Cill's story and Howard's, although I have noted the skinny, ginger-haired "rapist." (Also the medium-build dark-haired duo, one of whom may have been Roy? Is that your thinking?) All I can say re: the boys is that it would require considerable chutzpah to leave a police station following questioning about a rape, only to break in on a vulnerable woman a few hours later and torture her to death. Again, I rely on you for an analysis of juvenile behavior.

Finally — unless you come back with evidence that Cill resurfaced — my strongest suspicion from reading the newspaper reports is that she never ran away at all, but was killed by her father. According to one of the articles, David

Trevelyan was exonerated after being questioned by police, but I would need some very strong evidence to believe that. Statistics don't lie. Children who vanish into "thin air" are usually dead, and children who "vanish" are usually victims of their parents. David Trevelyan was a violent man, and I fear Cill may have made the mistake of trying to excuse "the fight" by telling him about her rape.

I look forward to hearing from you again.

Yours sincerely

Jonathan Hughes

From: George Gardener [geo.gar@mullinst.co.uk]
Sent: Tues. 4/8/03 19:20
To: jon.hughes@london.ac.uk
Subject: Cill Trevelyan

Dear Jonathan, You are absolutely right. I can find no record that Cill Trevelyan ever resurfaced. David & Jean Trevelyan left Highdown in the 80s but I have no forwarding address as yet. My new friend (!) Sergeant Lovatt is looking into it for me. He is also trying to locate the file on Howard. Apparently records from all the divisions were collected together in a central archive 20+ years ago. However, as redundant files are usually destroyed, he isn't holding out much hope. I'm keeping my fingers crossed.

Re: the schoolfriend and transference. Transference is commonly an emotional response — often experienced during therapy — where people transfer personality characteristics of parents/

partners/friends to someone else. It's an immature reaction, where neurotic patterns of behavior, often formed in childhood, color subsequent relationships — e.g. in very simple terms, a child who grows up afraid of a stern father will fear all men in authority. Clearly, it's more complicated than that but, generally, transference relates to an imbalance, or perceived imbalance, of power within a relationship, which is taken forward to other relationships and will *certainly persist into middle age.* [NB: It's not necessarily a negative response. If a child grows up admiring his father, he will look up to men in authority.]

If you're right that Priscilla Fletcher is the school friend, then it's highly likely that trauma at 13 has lingered into adult life. However, the most obvious contender for that is Cill herself as she's the one who experienced the abusive relationships! In some ways, I'd say idolatry or hero worship is closer to what you're looking for.

Interestingly, Howard was a case study

in hero worship. You made the point yourself when you said he aped his hero, Ginger Baker. He wanted to look like Baker, wanted to have the courage to rebel in the same way, wanted to be admired in the way Baker was. It was a displacement of his unloved self to a more acceptable substitute. I shall have to do more research, but it's not inconceivable that Cill became a "totem" to a traumatized child, particularly if her disappearance meant the loss of a best friend. I question how long those feelings would have lasted, however.

I shall certainly follow your advice to track down the friend. If nothing else, she will be able to tell us something about Highdown in 1970. Fred Lovatt suggested that one of the reasons Cill's disappearance dropped out of the headlines so quickly was because attention shifted within days to Grace's murder and Howard's arrest. The coincidences of time and place continue to fascinate me, however. It seems so unlikely that two unrelated events should happen within such a short period in the same area, although I take your point about the boys and chutzpah. It's not unknown, of course. Jack the Ripper killed two women within half an hour of each other, even though he'd been disturbed performing the first murder and the hue and cry was up. Adrenaline does strange things to the mind as well as the body.

Best wishes, George

Chapter Ten

9 Galway Road, Boscombe, Bournemouth
Friday, April 11, 2003, 6:30 p.m.

George drew up in front of a smart semi-detached house and left the motor running while she listened to the end of a dispatch from Baghdad. The news was still dominated by the fall of the Iraqi capital, although reports of rampant looting now took precedence over correspondents' and politicians' surprise at the lack of opposition to the U.S. army. For George, a longtime peace campaigner, the three weeks of over-the-top war coverage had been depressing. State-sponsored killing had become a showpiece for technology — smart bombs, laser-guided missiles, embedded journalists with videophones — when the reality on the ground was chaos and death.

She sighed as she switched off the engine. Ideas and words were being twisted to distance sensitive Western consciences from what was being done on their behalf. The killing of Iraqi civilians was "collateral damage"; the deaths of British servicemen at the hands of their own side were "friendly fire" or "blue on blue"; questions about the failure to find weapons of mass destruction — the excuse for war — the *only* excuse — were brushed aside with "we know they exist." How? In the same way the police had "known" that Howard Stamp was a murderer?

Justice demanded honesty, and there was no honesty in validating war through euphemism and vague suspicion. She particularly disliked assertions that the aim of invasion was to bring democracy to the Iraqi people. You have no vote, was the overbearing message. Do as we say because we know what's good for you. It was the same sanctimonious self-righteousness that had caused every miscarriage of justice in every democracy in the world.

I accuse you because I dislike you . . . I accuse you because I can . . .

J'accuse . . .

It had been easier to obtain the name of Priscilla Trevelyan's school friend than

George had feared. A request to the *Bournemouth Evening News* to find out whether Bronwen Sherrard, the byline on the piece "Mother's anguish over missing teen," was still on the staff had come up with a negative. However, the name was uncommon enough to prompt a not very hopeful look in the local telephone directory. Even when she found an entry and dialed the number, she wasn't optimistic it would be the same woman. Or if it was, that she'd remember details from an article she'd written in 1970.

However, it was indeed the same woman, now retired, and though she couldn't recall the information off the top of her head, she had kept meticulous files of all her work. George explained her interest by saying she was researching Highdown of the 1960s and 1970s, and Bronwen phoned back the next day with the name Louise Burton and the additional bonus that the family had been rehoused in Galway Road, Boscombe. "I never spoke to her or her parents," she finished. "When I went to the house, her mother called the police."

"Why?"

"I imagine they'd had enough of doorstepping journalists," said the woman with a laugh, "so let's hope you have better luck than I did."

"Do you know where they lived when they were in Highdown?"

There was rustle of paper. "Number 18, Mullin Street," said Bronwen helpfully, completely unaware of the extraordinary face that George Gardener was pulling at the other end of the line.

A check of the electoral register had shown that a Mr. William Burton and a Mrs. Rachel Burton were still living at 9 Galway Road, and George rang the bell in the full expectation that she was about to meet Louise's parents. But it was a man of around forty who answered the door. "Mr. Burton?"

"Yes." He was tall and broad-shouldered, with rolled-up shirtsleeves and tattoos on his muscular arms. Behind him, somewhere down the corridor, a television blared at full blast, overlayed by the sound of girls arguing. He wiped his hands on a towel and smiled inquiringly. "Sorry about the row. What can I do for you?"

George pulled one of her faces. "If they're killing each other, I can always come back later."

He listened for a moment. "Nn-nn. It's

fairly mild tonight. They only get really het up when they find the other one's nicked their clothes."

"Your daughters?"

He nodded. "Identical twins with fiery hair and fiery tempers." He grinned amiably. "You can have them if you like. We'll pay good money to be rid . . . the wife's close to strangling them."

George laughed. "How old?"

"Sixteen. I keep telling them they're old enough to marry but they won't take the hint." He flicked the towel over his shoulder and started to unroll his sleeves. "To be honest, I'm not sure there'd be any takers. The lads can hear 'em coming a mile off and they do a runner immediately." He chuckled. "How can I help?"

He was too nice to be related to Priscilla Fletcher, George thought, raising a clipboard with a photocopied page from the electoral register. "Are you William Burton?"

"That's me."

She offered a hand. "My name's George Gardener. I'm a councillor. I'm canvasing for the local elections on May 1." It had seemed a reasonable cover story to detain him long enough to ask a few questions — the elections were certainly happening —

but she realized it was a mistake when his face closed immediately.

He released her hand and started to close the door. "Sorry, not interested. We won't be voting."

"May I ask why not?"

"I'm a fireman," he said, nodding to a cap and uniform jacket hanging on a hook in his hallway, "and I'm sick to death of politicians telling me I'm unpatriotic because they chose to declare war while I was trying to strike for a decent salary. How does that make me unpatriotic?"

"Oh dear," said George, pulling a face. The withdrawal of labor had been very divisive. "The only answer I can give you is that I'm against both the war and the strikes. I've always believed that negotiation is the only way to solve problems."

"Yes, well, war was declared in our names without anyone asking our permission to do it." He obviously felt strongly enough to elevate George to the position of Prime Minister because he glared at her as if she were responsible for sending the troops in. "Over a million people said no, and that was just the tip of the iceberg. For every *one* who slogged up to the peace march in London, there were another *ten* who couldn't make it."

"Were you on it, Mr. Burton?"

"Mm. Fat lot of good it did."

"Me, too." She put a hand on the door to prevent him closing it. "Were your daughters with you?"

"Yes."

"Then that's the good it did, Mr. Burton," she said earnestly. "Youth's been quiet for too long, but it found a voice over this. I've been campaigning for nuclear disarmament for thirty years but I've never seen anything like that march." She lowered her clipboard but kept her other hand on the door. "You can't vote for me because this isn't my ward — and I'm an independent, so I have no clout at Westminster. My view is that abstention is a perfectly honorable tradition, so I won't waste your time trying to persuade you out of it."

He exerted mild pressure against her hand and came up against resistance. "But?"

"The person I really want to speak to is Louise Burton. I assumed the Mr. and Mrs. Burton in this house were her parents, but obviously not. You must be her brother, unless it's pure coincidence that Burtons have been registered here since the seventies."

The question was clearly one he'd answered before, because he didn't seem put out by it. "It's getting on for thirty years since Lou left. The folks bought the house off the council at the end of the 1980s and I took it over seven years ago when they retired to Cornwall. I don't think Lou's been back once in all that time."

"Do you know where she is now?"

He shook his head. "We lost track of her after she got married."

"Do you know what she's calling herself?"

Billy didn't answer immediately. "Are you a private detective?"

"No," she said in surprise. "I'm what I said I was — a councillor . . . for Highdown ward. Also a care worker at the Birches in Hathaway Avenue. I live in Mullin Street, where you and your family used to live before you were transferred here." She paused. "Do you have many private detectives looking for your sister?"

"I presume it's Cill Trevelyan you're interested in — it was Lou's only fifteen minutes of fame." She nodded. "OK, well, the Trevelyan parents pay up every so often to see if a private agency can track her down. The last one came about three years ago. They always get to Lou eventually — at least to the fact that she used to live here — but it doesn't help them. Apart from the fact we don't know where she is, she had no more idea than the rest of us what happened to Cill." He shrugged apologetically. "Sorry."

"What about your parents? Have they kept in touch with her?"

"No." He seemed to feel his parents needed defending. "It wasn't their fault. They did their best, but she always thought the grass was greener somewhere else. She left school at sixteen, became a hairdresser and got married almost immediately . . . then we lost track. There was a rumor she went to Australia, but I don't know if that's true."

George looked crestfallen. "Oh dear! I was so hopeful of being able to speak to her when I found that Burtons were still registered here."

"Sorry," he said again, stepping back to end the conversation.

She kept her hand on the door. "What was the name of her husband?"

He smiled rather cynically. "No idea. We weren't invited to the wedding. As far as I remember, she referred to him as Mike when I managed to track her down for the folks, but he was in jail so I didn't meet him." He shook his head at her expression.

"It happens," he said. "I was luckier. I married a gem."

George nodded. "I know it's a terribly personal question, but did she have a baby when she was fourteen or fifteen?"

He hesitated. "Not that I'm aware of."

It was a strangely evasive answer. "Surely you'd have noticed," said George with a smile.

"I was a lot younger than she was, so I probably wouldn't have understood what was going on. Put it this way: I don't recall a baby suddenly arriving in the family."

"Was she ever married to a man called Roy Trent who runs the Crown and Feathers pub in Highdown?"

His eyes held hers for a moment and she thought she saw a flicker of indecision. "Not that I'm aware of," he repeated, "but, like I say, we lost track of her."

Perhaps it was his hesitations, or the fact that he didn't give a firm negative, that prompted George to pose her next question. "Was Louise raped at the same time as Cill?" she asked bluntly. "Is that why the family was rehoused?"

"No." He was back on firm ground. "She saw it happen but she wasn't involved. Look, there's no mystery about it. We were moved because she was frightened out of her wits — first the rape, then Cill running away, then the police questions. My parents put her in a different school so she wouldn't keep being reminded about it."

"Would she have told your parents if she'd been raped? Cill didn't tell hers."

"It was a different time. Mini-teens today wear crop tops, but if they did it then they were accused of being tarts. Cill's dad went ape-shit every time she put on a miniskirt."

"And *your* parents?"

"The same." Another shrug. "Me, too, if it comes to that. I'm shotgun Dad. I hate it when my kids prance around half naked . . . it's an open invitation to the first predator to have a go."

"Then Louise may have been raped as well, but never admitted to it," George said reasonably.

"She wasn't raped," he said bluntly, "and she didn't get pregnant as a result . . . which I assume is the point you're trying to make." His eyes hardened suddenly. "Look, there was enough damn gossip at the time. None of us needs it resurrected."

George dropped her hand. "I'm sorry. I didn't mean to upset you. It's just that —" She broke off on a sigh. "Does the name

Priscilla Fletcher mean anything to you?"

"No."

She thought he was going to slam the door in her face, but he didn't. He waited, as if he expected her to go on. "Priscilla lives in Sandbanks," she said. "She's in her midforties and looks like an older version of Cill Trevelyan. She used to be married to Roy Trent and had a son by him when she was in her early teens. At that time, she was calling herself Cill. Do you know if your sister named Roy Trent to the police as one of the rapists?"

Billy avoided the question. "Half a minute ago you were making out this woman was Lou, now you're saying she's Cill Trevelyan. Who is she?"

"I don't know, Mr. Burton. That's what I'm trying to find out." She flipped over the top page on the clipboard and turned the pad toward him. "This photograph was taken five years ago. Do you recognize her?"

His expression was unreadable. "No."

"Does it remind you of Cill Trevelyan?"

He shook his head. "I barely remember her. I was ten years old when she left."

George flipped to the next page. "This is the picture of her that was in the newspapers."

Billy stared at it for several seconds and

his expression was genuinely appalled. "Christ! She's so *young!*"

"She was only thirteen, Mr. Burton, just a child still."

"Yes, but . . . I've always had it in my head she was quite grown-up. Christ!" he said again, taking the board and staring at the image. "She still has her baby fat. My two looked older than this at thirteen." With an abrupt movement he flipped back to the photograph of Priscilla Fletcher. "Maybe you should tell the Trevelyans . . . give 'em a chance to talk to this woman. Far as I know, they've never come close to finding a match."

"Do you have an address or a phone number for them?"

He shook his head. "No, but I think I kept the card of the last agency that came looking. They'd know." He glanced at his watch. "I can't look for it now — I'm on shift in an hour — but if you give me a contact number I'll see what I can do tomorrow."

George took back the clipboard and wrote her name and number on the back of the electoral register duplicate. "Why do you remember Cill as quite grown-up?" she asked curiously as she handed the page to him.

"She was a bit of a tart . . . liked talking sexy. It's what got her raped."

"How do you know?"

Billy's expression blanked immediately. "Guesswork," he said, before nodding a curt farewell and closing the door.

George would have put money on him trying to avoid any future contact so she was surprised to receive a call the following morning. He was briskly matter of fact, quoting the name and details of a Bristol-based detective agency. "You need to be careful how you go about it," he warned. "I talked it over with my wife last night and she said it would be cruel to raise the Trevelyans' hopes if it isn't Cill."

Privately, George agreed with him. She was back on night shifts and she'd mulled the problem over during her quiet periods. Without any expectation of William Burton coming through with the name of the detective agency, she had considered hiring one herself to find out who Priscilla Fletcher was. A quick browse on the Internet on her return home gave promises of "confidentiality," "discretion" and "caution," with hourly prices and flat fees not entirely beyond her bank balance.

Even so, there were too many ethical dilemmas for someone of George's sensibilities. Whoever Priscilla Fletcher was, she had the same right to privacy as anyone else — unless she'd committed a crime — and George could hardly argue that the theft of a wallet was justifiable grounds for breaking her cover. If she was Cill Trevelyan or Louise Burton, then it was a moral minefield. Both women had chosen to distance themselves from their families, and George had no entitlement to expose them. Yet that would be the inevitable outcome if a detective agency made a link with Cill, for George had no confidence that the Trevelyans' long search for their daughter wouldn't prompt a sympathetic — but *discreet* — approach in return for a fee.

Nor, from a selfish point of view, could George see what use the information would be to her. If the woman turned out to be Cill or Louise, George would still have to persuade her to tell her story; and what leverage could she use except threats of exposure? *"Tell me what I want to know or I'll give this information to your parents."* Apart from the absurdly childish nature of the menace, George wouldn't be able to carry it through. It rubbed against the grain of all her principles — namely the inalienable right of every individual to life, liberty and the pursuit of happiness.

In the early hours she'd recognized how much easier it would be if she could approach the Trevelyans' detective agency as a concerned citizen who'd spotted a similarity between Cill and a woman living in Sandbanks. Whatever the outcome, they'd feel obliged to tell her something, if only to stop her pursuing the search herself. Nevertheless, she appreciated as soon as William Burton gave her the agency's details that one avenue had been closed. George didn't believe he'd have given them to her if he thought Priscilla Fletcher was his sister. *Or would he?* Was it a double bluff? "Perhaps I should just abandon it," she said with a disingenuous sigh. "If it is Cill Trevelyan, then she obviously doesn't want to be found."

He didn't answer immediately. "That's what I thought until my wife asked me how I'd feel if one of the twins went missing. You'd never get over it, particularly if you found out she'd been raped and hadn't told you. I've been thinking about it all night and I reckon the parents have rights, too, even if just to know she's still alive." He paused again. "If it's any help, I made the point about Cill not wanting to be found to this Bristol agency, and they said she couldn't be forced to see her parents if she didn't want to."

"What's changed your mind, Mr. Burton?" George asked curiously.

"About what?"

"You've lived with this for thirty years but you're suddenly taking it personally. Why?"

"No one bothered to show me a photograph before," he said flatly. "They were looking for Lou, so it wasn't necessary . . . but it made me realize how young Cill was. My dad always said she was a flighty piece who was too forward for her own good and, once you get an idea into your head, it's difficult to shift. There wasn't much sympathy for her in our house, not after Lou started refusing to go out. The folks blamed Cill for everything. 'If only Louise had never met that bloody girl . . .' — that was all they could say for months." He fell silent.

"Cill seemed to have suffered a lot of abuse," George said unemotionally. "Reading between the lines of the newspaper articles, I got the impression her father didn't think twice about hitting her."

"He was always taking his belt to her. It didn't stop her acting up, though, just made her run away rather than face another larruping."

"Because of the fight with Louise?"

"Yes."

George made a pencil tick on a notepad in front of her. "It seems odd the school only punished Cill for it," she said mildly. "You'd think they'd both be suspended."

"Lou said Cill wouldn't explain, so the head gave her her marching orders. That's how it worked in those days."

"What was Lou's explanation?"

"Probably what she told our folks — that Cill had tried to persuade her to truant again."

"It doesn't sound like the truth, though, does it? It's more likely she was teasing Cill about the rape . . . maybe even threatening her. Something along the lines of: do what I want in this relationship or I'll tell on you." She waited through a brief silence. "It takes a lot of imagination to understand how devastating rape can be to the victim, particularly gang rape. It's as much a violation of the mind as it is of the body. The poor child was probably scrubbing herself raw every day in order to wash off their filth. Would Louise have understood how badly her friend had been damaged?"

"No."

"Which is why she did nothing to help her?"

"She was too scared. They dragged Cill by her hair, then kicked the shit out of her. There was blood all over her legs . . . that's why Lou went back for some trousers." His voice took on a sudden urgency. "You don't think about psychological stuff when you're a kid . . . you *can't* . . . most of the time you're struggling to understand why your parents never stop arguing. It might have been different if Cill hadn't launched in on us. She kept saying she'd kill us if we blabbed —" He broke off abruptly.

George let the admission ride. "She must have been very frightened of her father. Have you never asked yourself *why* she talked sexy? How did she know so much about it? Physical and sexual abuse often go hand in hand."

There was a long silence. "Why does he keep sending people to look for her?"

"Any number of reasons. Guilt . . . love . . . obsession. A friend of mine's convinced he went too far and killed her, so perhaps he's trying to pretend she's still alive."

"That's what my folks thought at the time — lots of people did — but I remember Dad saying he'd been questioned and let go because there was nothing in the house to show Cill had died. Plus, they never found a body."

"And when they did find one, Cill was promptly forgotten," said George with deliberate flippancy.

"I don't get you."

"Grace Jefferies. She was murdered in Mullin Street a few days after Cill went missing. I've been wondering if the two events were connected."

He sounded surprised. "It was Howard Stamp did that. I remember Dad telling me what a miserable little wanker he was."

George took a breath to calm her irritation. "If they'd had DNA testing in 1970, Mr. Burton, Howard wouldn't even have been charged, let alone sent for trial. It was someone else who killed Grace, but in those days no one gave a damn if a miserable little *wanker* got sent down for something he didn't do. It was par for the course."

"What makes you think Cill's disappearance was linked to the murder?"

"Statistics," said George bluntly. "Lightning never strikes in the same place twice . . . or if it does, there's a reason. Louise said one of the rapists was ginger-haired. Do you know what his name was?"

"What's ginger hair got to do with it?"

"Grace's murderer had ginger hair."

This time the silence was interminable, as if the man at the other end was putting together pieces of a jigsaw. "I knew them by sight," he said at last, "but the only name I remember was Roy. He's the one kept kicking Cill."

Chapter Eleven

West London
Sunday, April 13, 2003, midday

The Spicer & Hardy offices were on the third floor of a converted townhouse in a smart Victorian terrace in west London. Courtesy of Andrew's ex-wife, who made a living as an interior designer, it had been revamped six years previously to reflect a more modern taste than Mr. Spicer and Mr. Hardy's (deceased without issue) penchant for a donnish library look of dark walls, heavy leather furniture and mahogany bookcases. Andrew, who had loved the old style and still recalled the happiness of childhood days curled in an armchair in his father's office reading whatever was available, had never come to terms with the acres of space that Jenny had created using glass, color and artificial lighting. However, no one shared his feelings. To everybody else, the frequently photographed decor was a triumph.

George Gardener was no exception. “Goodness!” she said admiringly as Andrew escorted her up a flight of unremarkable stairs into the reception area, where a trompe l’œil reflection converted a quadrant of glass and chrome into a sweeping semicircular desk. “It’s huge.”

“Smoke and mirrors,” said Andrew, opening another door. “Be careful you don’t walk into a pane of glass by mistake.”

She caught a glimpse of her reflection and hastily buttoned her jacket. “You must have a very confident receptionist. I’m not sure I’d want to be looking at myself all day long.”

Andrew chuckled. “We’re not big enough to afford one, so the phones are all inside. It was my wife’s least good idea. She was either planning for a future that was never going to happen, or she got it into her head that agents’ offices are like doctors’ waiting rooms, and people drop in off the street clutching manuscripts to their chests.” He invited her to go in front of him. “It makes a good quiet room for reading or one-on-one meetings, so it isn’t entirely wasted.”

The next room was open plan with three desks, isolated from each other by glass screens, foliage plants and pools of artificial light. There were no drawers below the L-shaped ebony tabletops, and only computers and telephones stood on them. "Goodness!" said George again, astonished by so much neatness. "Isn't this room used either?"

"It certainly is. This is the hub of the whole operation. All the paperwork's done in here . . . correspondence, contracts, payments, manuscript returns." He nodded to the first desk. "That's where my rights manager sits. She works on a stack of files every day."

"Where are they?"

He stooped to release a catch under the table top, and a mirrored panel swung back to reveal shelves of papers. "The doors are set at a slight angle to reflect the carpet but the illusion vanishes the minute you open them. Personally I think it's awful, but then I'm boring and old-fashioned. The staff love it. It's about creating space, even imaginary space. I'm told it's good for stress levels."

"It makes sense," said George, thinking of the tiresome clutter in her Mini, "but it wouldn't do to put me in here. I'm far too untidy. I'd never be bothered to clear away at the end of the day and that would spoil the impression for everyone else."

"Me neither," said Andrew, leading her down a short corridor to a room at the end, "so you'll feel at home in here. This is where I drew the line."

The room wasn't exactly as his father had left it, but it was close enough for comfort. The leather armchair, double-sided partners' desk and mahogany bookcases remained, but it was lighter and cleaner than when Mr. Spicer Sr. had dropped cigarette ash on the floor, coated the books and ceiling with nicotine and allowed a single walkway through the piles of manuscripts that littered the floor. Secretly, Andrew still hankered after the old man's eccentricity, but Jenny had convinced him that image was everything. Visitors viewed a man's surroundings as a reflection of his professionalism.

He hadn't seen the truth of that until she left him for the actor. There was a tragic irony that he'd allowed her virtually free rein with his business premises while failing to appreciate that "image is everything" was a coded message for him. Occasionally he indulged in depressive navel-gazing, when he wondered whether she'd have stuck by him if he'd lost weight, worn lifts in his shoes and bought a toupee. There was no argument that the business had perked up since the refurbishments, which was a good indication that superficiality worked.

As if to prove the point, George gazed about the room with approval. "If you drew the line, does that mean your wife didn't have a say in what was done?"

"No, but we agreed I could keep the antiques and make it a mirror-free zone." He gestured for her to sit down and placed himself in his ergonomic swivel seat. "To be strictly accurate, she's my ex-wife, but don't let it worry you. We parted on amicable terms." He watched her settle herself in the worn armchair and wondered why she and Jon had come to blows. She was smartly dressed in a navy blue suit, makeup had toned down the ruddiness of her cheeks and soft gray hair lay in fluffy curls on her forehead. She reminded Andrew of one of his aunts — a favorite of his — and he was predisposed to like her. "I'd have invited you to my house, but it's in south London and difficult to find, so I thought this would be easier for both of you."

"Is Jonathan coming?"

Andrew nodded. "I told him twelve-thirty so that you and I could have a quick chat before he arrived." He put his elbows on the desk and leaned forward. "He's placed himself under a self-denying ordinance, George — keeps telling me this is your story, not his. He's happy to assist, but he wants you to write it and take the credit." He lifted an eyebrow. "How do you feel about that? If you have a facility with words you can make some money as well as highlighting the injustice against Howard. Jon's keen for me to act for you, and I'm willing to do so if you want to give it a shot."

She watched him closely. "Shouldn't you argue against that if you're his agent?"

"Not if he instructs me otherwise. In any case, he's not an easy man to argue with."

"It sounds as if there's a 'but' coming."

Andrew smiled. "The book will be much easier to sell if Jon's the author. He's the one who put Howard on the map, and his publisher will be interested in a follow-up if there's good evidence that Howard was innocent."

George shrugged. "I didn't expect anything else. I only know how to write dissertations." She flipped open the small case that she'd brought with her and removed a pile of notes. "I'm quite happy for Jonathan to take what he can from these . . . although I'm starting to question how valuable they are. I have a feeling I've been steered away from anything important, which is why I asked for this meeting. I hoped if we put our heads together we might come up with some fruitful leads."

"Mm." Andrew folded his hands under his chin. "The trouble is, Jon wants to play the martyr at the moment. It's a very tedious side to his character. He beats himself up every time he falls short of whatever unachievable standard he's set himself. If he wasn't an atheist I'd sign him into a monastery and give myself a break." He watched her face screw into a sympathetic twist. "What I'd like to suggest is a joint enterprise, with Jon's name at the top because he'll be writing the book and your name underneath because you'll be providing the bulk of the research. You can negotiate percentages between yourselves, or I can give you the name of an arbiter. Either way, you should end up with a fair return for your work. Does that appeal to you?"

"Not at all," she protested. "I wasn't expecting to be paid when I first approached Jonathan, and I certainly wouldn't have proposed a second meeting if I thought it was going to be a discussion about property rights and money. I was hoping to do what we should have done the first time — pool information and see where it takes us."

"Gre-eat!" said Andrew with mild irony. "Now I have two martyrs on my hands. We have the potential for a book that can exonerate a man's name . . . and no one to write it. What do you suggest I do? Postpone this meeting until I can find a ghostwriter to sit in on it and take notes? Offer the idea to another agent?"

George was a sensible woman whose only affectations were comical expressions and an inclination to giggle. "I misunderstood," she said. "Do I gather the joint enterprise was less a suggestion than an order? Am I to insist on my name on the cover in order to make your friend feel comfortable?"

Andrew tipped a finger at her. "The more insistent you are the better, as far as I'm concerned. Self-denying ordinances don't suit him. He's easier to live with when he's battling for his rights, a pain in the neck when he turns himself into a doormat."

She looked amused. "How's his blood pressure? Perhaps being a doormat is better for his health."

"No chance. Sitting around twiddling

his thumbs is sending it way up."

"I'm no actress," George warned. "If you're expecting me to be angry, I won't be able to do it. I'm a negotiator, not a table-thumper."

"Is that a yes?"

She shrugged. "I suppose so . . . as long as you ask him in front of me if he's still refusing to run with the project himself. I'd like to hear him say no for myself."

"Agreed. If he does, are you willing for me to act as agent in the joint enterprise?"

"Do I have a choice?"

"Most certainly. I'm sure any agent would be willing to represent you — I can even recommend the better ones. The difficulty will be if Jon prefers to stay with me."

"Then it'll have to be you."

"Excellent!" He stood up and reached across the desk to shake her warmly by the hand. "I'll have a contract drawn up tomorrow, but in the meantime you've given me authority to fight for your best interests . . . which means I'd rather you said nothing until I ask for your agreement on a deal. Can you do that?"

"As long as you don't misrepresent anything I've said."

"Other than emphasizing your insistence

on a joint enterprise, there's nothing to misrepresent," said Andrew. "As part of the Spicer & Hardy stable, you're as valuable to me now as Jon is."

When she looked back on it, George could only admire Andrew's skillful manipulation of his friend. As predicted, Jonathan arrived in metaphorical (*and* literal) sackcloth and ashes, having taken the trouble to dress down for the meeting while George had put on her glad rags, but he wasn't so crass as to draw attention to either. He merely complimented George on the work she'd done on the Cill Trevelyan story, then refused outright to take on the project when Andrew asked the question. His arguments were persuasive.

He had come across Howard by accident after reading *Clinical Studies* and most of his theories about the case were guesswork. To prepare a compelling rebuttal would require more definitive research, including interviews and legwork, and he couldn't commit the necessary time or energy. Andrew had worked with first-time authors before and was perfectly capable of editing an amateur up to publishable standard, or paying a mentor to help George achieve it herself. While Jonathan had a known interest in miscarriages of justice, his real commitment was to the mistakes made in the areas of asylum-seeking and economic migration. By contrast, George's known commitment was to Howard Stamp, and Howard's interests were best served by someone who had absolute faith in his innocence — which Jonathan didn't have.

Andrew showed his impatience. "I explained all this to George before you arrived," he said, "and it doesn't pass the so-what test, pal. I'm starting to question whether this book's worth anyone's time . . . *mine* included." He leveled an accusing finger at Jonathan. "*You* are having second thoughts about Howard's innocence and *George* —" he swiveled the finger toward her — "suspects her research is compromised. I'm willing to act for either of you if you offer me something solid, but I'm not interested in half measures. Any editor worth his salt will throw it straight back at me if the case for miscarriage isn't proven."

Jonathan turned a surprised face toward George. "How is your research compromised?"

She looked at Andrew.

"If you're not interested in the project then it's none of your business," Andrew answered for her. "George was hoping to negotiate a fifty-fifty split, but as you're not keen I suggested we approach Jeremy Crossley."

Jonathan's eyes narrowed immediately. "Why him?"

"He's an historian, and it's the sort of project he enjoys." He raised a calming hand. "I know, I know . . . he slated *Disordered Minds*, but that should work in George's favor, especially when I tell him you've changed your mind about Howard's innocence." He grinned. "He'll bust a gut to prove you wrong."

"You're doing this on purpose," said Jonathan curtly.

"What?"

"Riling me. You know bloody well what I think of Jeremy Crossley. I wouldn't wish him on my worst enemy, let alone someone like George. He'll take every piece of research she can give him, then cut her out of the equation. That's how he works."

"Don't be an idiot," said Andrew dismissively. "I'm acting for George, so no one will have access to her information until we've agreed a contract. She won't get a fifty-fifty split with Crossley, of course, but she'll get something, as long as her research has demonstrable value." He tapped the desk with the tip of his forefinger. "But that's the issue, I'm afraid. The message I'm getting from both of you is that there are major flaws in your analyses . . . so the scheme looks dead in the water before we even start."

"I see you've learned Crossley's review by heart," said Jonathan sarcastically.

"I can't even remember it," said Andrew indifferently.

"Like hell you can't. Every other sentence referred to 'flawed analysis' of data. It was a hatchet job by a second-rate academic who thinks he can write." He turned abruptly to George. "Don't let Andrew railroad you into this. It's a bad idea. Write it yourself . . . you're perfectly capable."

"You know that's not true," said Andrew firmly. He nodded to a pile of manuscripts beside his desk. "That's my slush pile," he told George. "If there's one halfway reasonable script in there, I'll be surprised. Writing's a craft — no one can expect to master it the first time they put pen to paper — and Jon knows that as well as I do."

"There are other authors," said Jonathan. "It doesn't have to be Crossley."

"Agreed. What about that fellow you work with . . . published by Hodder?

Henry Carr. He might be interested. I was talking to his editor the other day and she said he's green with envy . . . wants to find any idea that will outclass *Disordered Minds*."

Jonathan bared his teeth. "Even you wouldn't stoop that low."

"You'd better believe it," Andrew warned. "I'm after the best deal for George, and Evans will agree to a sixty-forty split if it means he can get one over on you."

"You're being ridiculous. There are plenty of good young authors on your list who'd jump at this chance. Why aren't you offering it to one of them?"

"Because the advance will be higher with an established name, and that's to George's advantage, particularly if she can earn the money before a word's been written."

Jonathan considered for a moment, then shifted his attention back to George. "Are you sure this is the route you want to go, because I'd be happy to advise you if you think you can do it yourself."

She opened her mouth to say something.

"Jon's not the best person to do that," Andrew warned her. "You want someone who believes in Howard's innocence."

"Stop putting words in my mouth," said Jonathan irritably. "The expression I used was 'absolute faith.' It's important to keep an open mind when looking at issues like this. You can't ignore contrary evidence just because it doesn't suit your theory. You have to examine it even more rigorously."

"Which is the opposite of what you said earlier. Now you're advocating healthy skepticism in George's coauthor. I wish you'd make up your mind." He looked at his watch. "To be honest, I can't see the point of this . . . we're just going round in circles. If you're not interested, then you might as well leave so that George can convince me she's got something worth selling. It's a waste of time arguing over coauthors if there isn't enough proof even to get them excited."

"Is there a link with the Cill Trevelyan story?" Jonathan asked.

George spoke before Andrew could. "I'm not sure," she said. "That's why I wanted to talk to you. You were right about the school friend — her name was Louise Burton. I've managed to locate her brother and he —"

Andrew broke in. "You're doing this against my advice, George. Jon should only be party to this information if you've agreed a contract with him."

She gave a guilty sigh. "I'm sorry, but it's obvious he doesn't want one . . . and we *are* going round in circles. I told you half an hour ago that I'd like to work with Dr. Hughes, but he's not obliged to return the favor if he doesn't want to. I'm no writer —" she smiled apologetically at Jonathan — "and I'm not much of an academic either . . . so I quite understand your reluctance. The trouble is, if what William Burton told me is true, then Roy Trent was one of Cill's rapists. I rather hoped . . ." She petered into an unhappy silence.

Jonathan hunched his shoulders. "I'll go with fifty-fifty."

Clever girl, thought Andrew, staring at his hands.

"I know it's tempting to see linkage in synchronicity," said Jonathan, "but it's very dangerous. Coincidences happen. It's why PACE and CPIA were introduced, and why DNA has become the major plank in police investigations. Everyone's looking to eliminate malign chance."

"But if Howard was innocent then malign chance is precisely what convicted him," George protested. "It was the hair in the bath that persuaded the jury, but the prosecution proved it could only have come from the murderer. Yet Howard wasn't the murderer."

"All the more reason not to fixate on another ginger-haired suspect. A goodly percentage of the population carries the gene." He smiled to take the sting from the words. "Which isn't to say we'll ignore your rapist — he certainly fits the profile — just be wary. The real pity is that the only name William Burton remembers is Roy . . . it was a popular name in the fifties and sixties so there were probably quite a few of them."

"Not *that* popular," said George. "Surely it's Roy Trent?"

"Roy Rogers . . . Roy Orbison . . . Roy of the Rovers . . . Roy Castle . . ."

"At least one of those was a comic-book character," said Andrew.

"So? Bill Clinton and David Beckham named their children after places. All I'm saying is we can't assume Roy Trent from Roy."

"It's a reasonable guess, though," said Andrew. "The man's an ape."

"That doesn't make him a rapist. Or let me put it another way — which of you is willing to go in and suggest it to him with no evidence to back it up . . . and what do you think his answer is going to be?" He glanced from one to the other. "Right! We need to find Louise or, even better, the Burton parents. They might be able to give us a surname."

"Assuming they'll talk to us," said George doubtfully. "I got the impression from William that they're extremely reluctant to be involved."

Jonathan flicked to the end of the transcript. "Did you tape these conversations or make notes?"

"I made notes in the car after the first one and used shorthand for the telephone call. I typed them up immediately afterward so I'm confident they're accurate."

He read the description of William Burton that she'd added at the end. "Forties, six foot approx, well-built, tattoos on his arms, thinning sandy hair, gray eyes, pleasant smiling face, fireman. Married with twin daughters." "You liked him," he said more in statement than question.

"Yes. He was very upfront and friendly at the beginning. We talked about his daughters who were arguing inside the house, and he was very amusing. He only tightened up when I mentioned his sister.

He kept saying he hadn't heard from her for years, but I didn't entirely believe him."

"You say here that he 'looked troubled' after you asked him if Louise had had a baby when she was fourteen," remarked Andrew, tapping a page of the transcript copy that she'd given him. "He answered: 'Not that I'm aware of.' You've put 'evasive' with a question mark. Is that how it struck you at the time?"

George nodded. "He went on to say he was a lot younger than she was and wouldn't have understood what was going on — it's a couple of lines down. I thought that was a very strange response . . . as if something *had* happened and he didn't want to lie about it. I've also put a question mark beside the 'a lot younger.' Louise would be forty-five or forty-six now, and William looked a good forty plus."

Jonathan drew her attention to some notes that came after William Burton's description. "(1) He wouldn't have phoned if he'd recognized Priscilla Fletcher as Louise. [Double bluff?] (2) Did he recognize her as Cill Trevelyan? (3) Why does he feel so 'connected' suddenly? [Because of Cill's photo? Because of his daughters? Because Priscilla F. is Cill and he knows it?]"

"What's the significance of his daughters?" he asked.

"It's at the beginning of the telephone transcript. He said his wife had asked him how he'd have felt if one of them had gone missing at thirteen. Also, he was very struck by how young Cill looked. He remembers her as quite adult and was shocked to see she still had her baby fat." She paused. "It's as if he saw her as a person for the first time . . . and I'm wondering if that was because he recognized her in Priscilla Fletcher."

"I should think it's more likely your first statement was correct. Thirty years after the event, he saw Cill for what she really was — a vulnerable child — and it shocked him."

"He said his parents blamed her for everything that went wrong. They called her 'that bloody girl' and made out she was a tart."

"What sort of things?"

She shrugged. "The rape . . . Louise becoming agoraphobic . . . the police questioning. Those are the ones he mentioned, but he said it went on for months."

"The agoraphobia?"

"Presumably."

"Interesting," Jonathan said slowly.

"What was she frightened of? The boys? Being raped herself?"

"He didn't say. There was a passing reference to her parents moving her to a different school so she wouldn't be reminded of Cill's disappearance, but that's all."

Andrew clicked his fingers suddenly. "Go back to the first paragraph where George has given a synopsis of the conversation about the girls," he told Jonathan. "Second line: 'Mr. Burton joked about his daughters' fiery hair and fiery tempers . . . said he'd pay to be rid of them.' "

"And?"

"Red hair runs in families, but I'm damn sure the gene has to be on both sides to produce fiery red."

Jonathan ran a thoughtful finger down his jawline. "Go on."

"You're hooked on the ginger-haired rapist, but what color hair did Louise have?"

From: George Gardener [geo.gar@mullinst.co.uk]
Sent: Thurs. 4/17/03 15:07
To: jon.hughes@london.ac.uk
Cc: Andrew Spicer
Subject: Louise Burton

Dear Jonathan and Andrew,

The Bristol agency was very unhelpful, refusing to share any details of their investigation or divulge the Trevelyans' address. They cited issues of confidentiality, but they refused to phone the Trevelyans for permission. I'm afraid they thought I was a journalist. In the circumstances I decided against making them a free gift of Priscilla Fletcher, and re: Louise they simply referred me back to William Burton.

Our friend Fred Lovatt has had no success with the archives, nor has he found any colleagues who were involved in Howard's case or Cill's disappearance. PC Prentice, who was mentioned in the newspaper clippings, retired in 1982 and is believed to have died of a stroke some time in the 1990s.

As I am reluctant to "scare" William Burton away, I have decided to approach this from a different angle. The school the girls attended prior to Cill's disappearance was almost certainly Highdown Secondary Modern, situated in Wellingborough Road. It was reinvented during the 1970s as Highdown Community School and subsequently moved to new, larger premises in Glazeborough Road (*coincidentally* utilizing the site of the demolished Brackham & Wright factory where Wynne Stamp worked!) They only keep records of past staff and pupils who sign up for the OH (Old Highdowners) Register. However, I have the name and address of the headmistress who was in charge from 1968 to '73. It is: Miss Hilda Brett, 12 Hardy Mansions, Poundbury, Dorchester, Dorset.

I have made some inquiries and I understand that Hardy Mansions is sheltered accommodation for "active" elderly — i.e., people who still have their marbles. This is very good news as Miss Brett *must* be the one who suspended Cill and should remember both girls. I am willing to talk to her on my own, though I would prefer Jonathan to come with me, not only because his status of research fellow and author will lend the questions academic authority — and may persuade her to be more forthcoming — but also because I am unsure how to structure the interview.

Do we say we're looking for Cill Trevelyan? For Louise? Do we mention Howard? None of them . . . just say we're researching Highdown of 1970 and were given her name by her old school? Help, please!

Best, George

P.S. If Jonathan can come I shall need some dates when he's free. On balance, I think we should just turn up, rather than attempt to book a meeting with her, as if she says "no" we will lose this opportunity.

Chapter Twelve

Dorchester, Dorset
Wednesday, April 23, 2003, morning

This time Jonathan had opted for smartness, and he was relieved to see George had done the same when she met him at Dorchester South Station. "What happened to the mobile filing cabinet?" he asked as he climbed into the car. "I hope you didn't move it on my account."

"I had a spring-cleaning," she told him, starting the engine. "Everything's in its proper place at home." She flashed him a smile. "I decided Andrew's ex-wife is right: 'Fine feathers make fine birds.' "

Jonathan grinned. "Except Andrew doesn't agree. He prefers, 'Don't judge a book by its cover.' "

"Me, too," she said cheerfully, pulling away from the curb, "but we're in a minority, so I'm going for the two-second sound bite — smart car . . . smart home . . . smart clothes . . . *smart* mind."

Jonathan laughed. "How long will it last?"

"It depends how determined I am." She turned right onto Weymouth Avenue before filtering left to head toward the western outskirts of Dorchester. She drove hunched over her steering wheel as if she couldn't see where she was going, and Jonathan closed his eyes to avoid flinching at every near miss.

"To do what?"

"Strike the right impression from the off. I realize I've only myself to blame that I'm never taken seriously."

Jonathan had known it was a conversation that would come eventually. Unresolved issues never vanished of their own accord. "If it's any consolation," he said lamely, "I said far worse things to Sergeant Lovatt. According to Andrew I called him a fascist . . . although I honestly don't remember it."

"Oh, for goodness sake! I'm not doing this for you."

"Who then?"

"Roy. He's been running rings around me because he thinks I'm a woolly headed spinster." There was a hiatus while she maneuvered between oncoming traffic and parked cars on her left. "I've tucked a map of Poundbury behind your sunblind," she told him, negotiating a five-way junction. "We're looking for Bridport Road and then Western Crescent. I'm fairly sure of the way but it's two years since I was here and, what with all the new building, the layout of the roads has probably changed."

He pulled out the map and spread it on his knee. "What sort of rings?"

She sighed and took her eyes off the road to look at him. "I didn't bring enough rigor to the information he's been giving me. Instead, I've wasted two years talking to people who were even more ignorant than I was about Howard."

"Names supplied by Roy?"

"Mm. Mrs. So-and-so who worked at Brackham & Wright in the 1960s and might have known what happened to Wynne. Mr. So-and-so who used to buy newspapers from Roy's dad and might have known Grace. Ms. So-and-so who was at St. David's Primary around the time Howard was there. I must have spoken to about twenty people who had vague connections with the story . . . but none of them actually *knew* anything."

Jonathan pressed his feet into the floor

as they drew up six inches behind a juggernaut. "Irritating!"

"I'd call it devious," George said, mounting the pavement to bypass the lorry and pull left onto Bridport Road as Jonathan stared stoically ahead. She nodded toward a cream-colored building ahead of them with a Germanic red-tiled spire. "That's where Poundbury begins. Have you visited it before? Do you know what it is?"

"No."

"Then you're in for a treat. It's Prince Charles's whack at modern architects and developers who build cheap estates full of identical redbrick boxes and expect people to be grateful. I mean, who wants to live in something *boring?*"

Roy Trent was promptly forgotten in her enthusiasm for the Prince of Wales's vision of how to build a new community. She insisted on making a detour into phase one of Poundbury which was less than ten years old but which, through its architecture and design — irregular roads, variety of building styles, use of local materials and housing arranged in mews, lanes, squares and courtyards — suggested history and permanence.

Jonathan was more impressed than he

thought he'd be, although he doubted a similar estate would work in London. "It would be difficult to translate to a city," he said as she pulled out onto the main road again.

"I don't see why," said George. "The principle of local tradition and local materials would work just as well in Harlesden as they do in Dorset. It's the uniformity of cheap brick and reinforced concrete that people hate. A house should be an expression of its owner's individuality, not a clone of the one next door."

"What about Victorian terraces?" he murmured ironically. "They were built to off-the-shelf blueprints and you can't get more uniform than that. In a hundred years people may be as fond of redbrick boxes as we are of the nineteenth-century equivalent."

George chuckled. "Assuming the boxes are still standing in a hundred years. Victorian terraces were built to last . . . these days everything's obsolete within a year." She slowed to read a street sign. "Poundbury Close," she announced.

Jonathan traced the map with his finger. "Which makes Western Crescent the second on the right," he told her, "over there." She flicked her indicator and pulled into the center of the road. "Tell me about Roy's deviousness," he invited.

"What's to tell?" she said dispassionately. "He's been sending me on wild goose chases because he doesn't want me finding out he was involved."

"You can't be sure of that," Jonathan warned. "He may be quite innocent but keeps his ear to the ground because he knows it's important to you. The fact that he's never come up with anything valuable might be evidence that he's as ignorant as you and I."

George gave a derisive snort. "You don't believe that anymore than I do. He's been playing me for a patsy. He wasn't remotely friendly until I mentioned an interest in Howard Stamp, then he became my newest pal. I should have smelled a rat then." She was driving slowly up the road looking for house names. She came to a halt beside a large building built in Purbeck stone. "Here we are . . . Hardy Mansions."

They were both surprised by the ease with which they gained entry to the old woman. They expected to pass their request through a warden, but it took just the press of a buzzer with "Hilda Brett" beside it, and George's mention of

Highdown Secondary Modern into the intercom, for the door to swing open and a barked instruction to come to Flat 12. "She's far too trusting," said George disapprovingly as they followed arrows marked 5–12 down a corridor. "We could be anyone."

"Perhaps she likes living dangerously," said Jonathan.

"I'm surprised it's allowed."

"Then she's rebelling against living in a prison," he murmured.

George pulled a face. "It's supposed to be the exact opposite — liberation from care and worry."

"Mm, but are undesirables being kept out or the inhabitants kept in? You can pay too high a price for freedom from care — fear of crime is more isolating than crime itself."

George's protest against this slur on sheltered accommodation remained unsaid, because the door to Number 12 opened and a gaunt woman gestured them inside. "Hello, hello!" she said happily. "Come on in." She leaned on a walking stick and drew back to let them pass. "Into the sitting room on your right . . . my chair's the upright one with the cushions." She closed the door and followed, examining her visitors brightly as she lowered herself into her seat. "Sit down . . . sit down. Make yourselves comfortable."

Jonathan folded his tall frame onto the sofa while George chose an armchair. "This is very good of you, Miss Brett," she said. "We were given your address by the school, but as they didn't have your phone number we decided to take a chance on finding you at home."

The woman was frail and looked well into her eighties, but her faded eyes were full of intelligence. "You'll have to help me," she said. "I'm afraid I don't recognize you at all. Obviously this young man was well after my time, but when were you there, my dear?"

George screwed her face into immediate apology. "Oh, goodness, I didn't mean to suggest we were ever pupils of yours." She watched disappointment cloud the old woman's expression. "May we introduce ourselves? My name's Georgina Gardener and I'm a councillor for Highdown ward where your school still is, and this is Dr. Jonathan Hughes —" she gestured toward the sofa — "who's an author and research fellow in European Anthropology at London University."

Jonathan stood up and bent to shake her

hand. "This is a great privilege, Miss Brett. I've long wanted to meet a headteacher who had responsibility for steering a school into the comprehensive era. It must have been a difficult and stressful time . . . but exciting too, perhaps?"

She frowned slightly, as if doubting this was the purpose of their visit. "All of those," she agreed, "but, of course, there was a strong crusading zeal at the time which carried us through. My staff and I had seen too many children relegated to what was effectively a second-class education because of their failure at the eleven-plus examination."

"With little or no chance of going to university," said Jonathan, sitting down again.

"Certainly. The direct route to higher education was through the grammar schools and private schools, which made it so pernicious that a child's future was decided at eleven." She paused, glancing doubtfully from one to the other. "Is this really what you came to talk to me about? I can't believe the opinions of a doddery headmistress — *long* past her sell-by date — add anything useful to the current debate on education."

George looked guilty. "Well . . ."

"In a way it is," said Jonathan, hunching

forward to address her more directly. "We're doing a case study of troubled children in the decades after the Second World War. There are two from Highdown that interest us. Howard Stamp, who was convicted of murdering his grandmother, and Priscilla Trevelyan, who disappeared in 1970. Howard was certainly before your time, but I believe Priscilla was one of your pupils?" He raised an inquiring eyebrow which she answered with a nod. "Would you be willing to tell us what you remember of her?"

She sighed wearily as her disappointments were compounded. "If you're detectives, then you're wasting your time. As I told your predecessors, I have no idea what happened to the poor child."

Jonathan took a card and security pass from his inside pocket and passed them to her. "That's my photograph, name and title . . . and at the bottom of the card is my departmental telephone number. I am more than happy for you to call and verify that I am who and what I say I am. Councillor Gardener can be similarly verified through her office or by telephoning one of her colleagues at the Birches Nursing Home in Highwood."

George promptly took one of her own

cards from her case and offered it across. "We aren't detectives," she assured the woman, "although I had the same response from Louise Burton's brother. I understand the Trevelyans have been trying to find their daughter for years."

Miss Brett barely glanced at the cards before shifting herself forward, preparatory to standing up. "I'm sorry but I can't help you. It was a devastating event . . . if I'd known anything useful I would have told the police."

It was a clear dismissal but Jonathan ignored it. "Georgina and I are approaching this from a very different angle," he told her. "We're more interested in why Priscilla became a statistic rather than where she is now. If her parents are to be believed from the press coverage, most of her problems stemmed from the fact that she was brighter than her peers . . . and that's not an unreasonable assumption. The links between truancy and delinquent behavior are well documented, and boredom is a trigger for both. Do you agree — indeed *did* you agree at the time — with Mr. and Mrs. Trevelyan's assessment of their daughter? Would Priscilla have been a less disturbed juvenile if she'd won a place at grammar school?"

It was a question that was pitched at the educationalist in her, and it worked. She remained sitting. "Truancy is commonly a symptom of *under*achievement, Dr. —" she consulted Jonathan's card again — "Hughes, while disruptive behavior in class can be a symptom of an above-average IQ that is not being thoroughly tested. Priscilla certainly fell into the latter category . . . so in that respect I did agree with Mr. and Mrs. Trevelyan. But although her brightness made her a difficult and unruly child, I don't believe it was the cause of her truancy . . . or, more importantly, her disappearance."

"What was?"

Miss Brett tapped her forefingers together. "You must put that question to her father."

Jonathan glanced at George, who stepped seamlessly into the conversation. "William Burton told me she was knowledgeable about sex," she said matter-of-factly. "I know it was less understood in those days but — looking back — do you think she was sexually abused?"

"Yes."

"By her father?"

"Yes."

George reached for a notepad and pen. "Is that something you told the police?"

There was a short silence. "No," said the old woman, then, "it's a conclusion I've come to in the last ten years. For a long time I blamed myself — it's a devastating event in a teacher's career to feel responsible for a child's disappearance. I liked to think I was approachable — I *should* have been approachable . . ." She broke off abruptly.

George's inclination was to stretch out a sympathetic hand, but Jonathan spoke before she could do it. "A student of mine was murdered in New York recently after I sponsored him to a scholarship out there," he said evenly, "and I'm left with 'if onlys': if only he hadn't been black . . . if only America and the U.K. hadn't whipped up hysteria against world terrorism . . . if only the man in the street could recognize that Muslim and terrorist are not synonymous." He smiled. "I'm guessing your 'if only' was to do with the rape? If only Priscilla had told you about it, you wouldn't have punished her for fighting with Louise, her father wouldn't have had an excuse to hit her . . . or *worse* . . . and she wouldn't have run away."

Miss Brett nodded. "That and more. She had a precocious, sexual vocabulary and didn't think twice about using it, particularly around the male teachers, but it never occurred to any of us that that might be a symptom of abuse." She gave another sigh. "I'm afraid it just made her unpopular in the staff room and her punishments were always more severe because of it. I regret that deeply. One wonders where the poor child found kindness if she wasn't getting it at home."

"There was so much ignorance then," said George. "It seems incredible now, but it wasn't until the Maria Colwell inquiry in '74 that the issue of child abuse really surfaced." She caught Jonathan's eye. "It wasn't until poor little Maria was dumped at hospital by her stepfather that the authorities recognized they should have protected her. He was her *murderer,* for goodness sake . . . he'd beaten a starving seven-year-old to death and he didn't think anyone would *object*."

"Things haven't improved much," said Jonathan, thinking of his own upbringing. "The trouble is, there's a thin dividing line between child protection and eugenic experimentation. We object to children being forcibly removed from inadequate parents, but complain when the same children die of neglect and brutality. It's a catch-22 for the authorities."

Miss Brett looked interested. "First define inadequacy," she said dryly. "There were many other parents I came into contact with who would have fitted the description better than the Trevelyans. Who's to say which father is harming his child?"

"Or how?" said George thoughtfully. "There's evidence that David Trevelyan hit Priscilla — even the mother seemed to admit it by talking about his strictness — but I'm less sure about the sexual abuse. William Burton's account of the rape suggests Cill was still a virgin. He said there was so much blood on her legs that Louise had to go home to find a pair of trousers to hide it. It may have been a period, of course, but I'm more inclined to think her hymen was broken . . . and that would make the rape the first time she was penetrated."

"It doesn't mean she hadn't been introduced to sexual activity," said Jonathan.

"I agree. And if her father was responsible it would explain why she didn't want him to know about the assault. He'd certainly believe she provoked it. It's how molesters and rapists excuse their behavior — it's not their fault, it's the fault of the victim for arousing them." She tapped her pen on her notepad. "The same arguments would apply to her mother. I came across a case study that showed that as many as twenty-five percent of sex-abuse offenses are committed by women. Any number of dynamics might have been operating within the family."

"Or *outside* it," said Jonathan. "A neighbor or relative might have been grooming her — perhaps her father was as troubled by her sexual precocity as her teachers, and didn't know how to deal with it. He may have been guilty only of heavy-handed discipline." He looked inquiringly at the headmistress. "What sort of man was he? Did you know him well?"

"Not really. I spoke to him once about Priscilla's truanting and once after she disappeared. On both occasions he was very angry. There was no meeting of minds. On the first occasion he told me it was the school's responsibility to ensure his daughter's attendance, and on the second he took me to task for suspending Priscilla and not Louise. He said that had he realized that Louise Burton was the other girl in the fight, he wouldn't have upheld my punishment."

"Why would he say that?"

She considered for a moment. "Each set of parents thought the other child was to blame for the truanting, but I believed then — and *still* believe — that Mr. Trevelyan was trying to shift the blame onto me. If he could place on record that all he'd done was reinforce a school punishment, then he could excuse whatever it was that caused Priscilla to run away."

"You didn't like him?" said George.

"Indeed I did not," said the old woman firmly. "He was an overweight bully who shook his fist under my nose and expected me to agree with him. I made it clear both times that I had no responsibility for Priscilla when she was off the premises — other than to report the fact to her parents and the relevant authorities — so he promptly blamed the school for her difficulties." She shook her head. "We'd held her back . . . she was bored . . . we weren't challenging her enough . . . she was too bright to be at Highdown. It was very depressing."

"And all reported in the press?"

"Indeed." Another sigh. "And there was nothing we could say in rebuttal. It would have been shabby to contradict their assessment of Priscilla, shabbier still to suggest the Trevelyans were —" she canted her head toward Jonathan — "*inadequate*. It was very much a case of: *de mortuis nil nisi bonum*."

Jonathan eyed her curiously. "Is that a figure of speech or did you believe she was dead?"

"Both. A missing child inspires intense emotion . . . we all grieved for her. Everyone expected a shallow grave to be found somewhere, and when it wasn't . . ." She broke off with an unhappy shrug. "Her parents continued to hope, but no one else believed she could survive on her own."

He nodded. "So why did the police abandon the investigation?"

"I don't think they did. They kept the case open for years, but they were really just waiting for a skeleton to turn up. As one of the inspectors said, she vanished into thin air after she left her parents' house, almost certainly abducted by one of these monsters who prey on children. She could be buried anywhere."

"Her father was questioned and ruled out," said George. "Do you know why? He seems the most obvious suspect."

"He was working a night shift that week and her mother said Priscilla was still at home after he left for work. He reported her missing when he came home at six o'clock in the morning and found her bed hadn't been slept in, but his work colleagues said he hadn't left the factory all night."

"What was his job?" asked Jonathan.

"He was a foreman at Brackham & Wright's tool factory. It closed a few years later and they used the site for the new comprehensive school."

There was a long and thoughtful silence.

"What was that you said about linkage and synchronicity?" asked George, leveling her pen at Jonathan. " 'Don't be tempted by it . . . coincidences happen.' Well, I *am* tempted." She switched her attention back to Miss Brett. "Do you remember Grace Jefferies's murder? Her body was discovered a week after Priscilla went missing."

The old woman nodded. "It was very shocking. You mentioned her killer earlier."

"Howard Stamp," said George. "His mother, Wynne — Grace's daughter — also worked at Brackham & Wright. It stretches the imagination to think a single workforce should be hit by an abduction and a murder within seven days of each other. Surely the two events must have been connected in some way? Did the police ever suggest that to you?"

"Not to me, although I do remember being surprised during the trial to learn that Mrs. Stamp worked there . . . but that was a year after Priscilla vanished, of course." Miss Brett fell into a brief reverie, staring toward her window as she sifted through memories. "It seems an obvious connection to make with hindsight," she said, "but it wasn't obvious at the time. Brackham & Wright was a major employer in Highdown in the 1960s — at a rough estimate there were two thousand on the payroll — and a large number of my parents worked there. I believe Louise Burton's father was also a foreman, and many of our pupils went into their training schemes."

"What sort of people were the Burtons?" Jonathan asked before George could speak.

"I don't believe I ever met the husband — there wasn't a great deal of contact with parents in those days — but I spoke to Mrs. Burton about Louise's truanting. She was rather more amenable than Mr. Trevelyan, accepting some responsibility for her daughter's behavior, but she blamed Priscilla for it. She wanted me to separate the girls but, as I pointed out, it would achieve nothing while they continued living so close to each other."

"How close were they? We know the

Burtons lived in Mullin Street but we haven't been able to find an address for the Trevelyans."

"If memory serves me right, they were in Lacey Street."

"Two on," said George, making a note. "Do you know which number in Lacey Street?" she asked Miss Brett.

She shook her head regretfully. "It was a long time ago."

"Was Mrs. Burton right?" Jonathan prompted. "Was Priscilla the leader in the friendship?"

"Oh, yes. She was by far the stronger character. Also, it was she who started the truanting — afternoons at first, then whole days."

"Every day? How long did it go on?"

Miss Brett considered for a moment. "I can't be precise . . . perhaps once or twice a week during the spring term. Both sets of parents were given warnings when we broke up for Easter, but I do remember the girls were absent for much of the first two weeks of the summer term. It ceased abruptly after the rape, although we only learned afterward that that was the cause. I'm afraid I assumed the sudden improvement was because of a letter I wrote to their fathers, threatening immediate expulsion if the behavior persisted."

"When were the letters sent?"

"As far as I could judge from what the police told me, it was the same day as the rape. They failed to register again that morning, which is why I decided to take action."

"And Louise just went along for the ride? She wasn't an instigator?"

Another pause for reflection. "She was a strange child . . . rather deceitful. I felt she maligned Priscilla to the police. It was a damning picture she painted. A violent, promiscuous, out-of-control teen who hated her parents, truanted to have sex with boys and used threats to make other children do what she wanted. There may have been elements of truth in it — Priscilla was big for her age and she could retaliate strongly when she was teased — but she wasn't a bully, not by my understanding of the word, anyway. She was a magnet to smaller, shyer children, but I don't recall her being unkind to them . . . rather the reverse, in fact; she tended to protect them."

"William Burton said the police questioning frightened Louise. Perhaps she was trying to win sympathy?"

"Indeed," said Miss Brett with an

acerbic edge to her voice. "It was certainly her character. She was prone to tears and fainting and wouldn't look you in the eye when she spoke to you — quite the opposite of Priscilla, who squared up and tried to battle her way out of it. It didn't mean Louise had no hand in the mischief, merely that her friend took the punishment for both of them."

"As in the rape?"

"I would think so."

"And the fight that caused Priscilla's suspension?"

"Yes. That was very typical of Louise. I was told by their teacher that she'd been whispering in Priscilla's ear all morning, but Louise insisted it was the other way round — that Priscilla had been trying to persuade her to truant again and attacked her when she refused."

"What did Priscilla say?"

"Nothing," said the woman regretfully. "I warned her she'd be suspended if she didn't give me an explanation, I even suggested it was Louise who'd provoked her —" she sighed again — "but she wasn't prepared to lie."

"Unlike Louise."

"Mm."

"Do you think with hindsight she was

teasing Priscilla about the rape?" George put in.

"Oh, yes."

"It would suggest a cruel streak, if she were . . . either that or a complete lack of imagination."

Miss Brett thought for a moment. "As to being cruel . . . well, possibly. She was certainly very pleased about Priscilla's suspension. But I've never met a deceitful child who lacked imagination," she finished with a small smile. "Telling stories against one's peers rather demands it, don't you think?"

Chapter Thirteen

Sandbanks Peninsula, Bournemouth
Wednesday, April 23, 2003, morning

Billy Burton had been sitting in his elderly Renault station wagon for over an hour watching the Fletchers' house for signs of life. It was getting on for two weeks since he'd passed the Bristol detective agency's address to Georgina Gardener, and he'd given up hope that she'd done anything about it. He wore a baseball cap over his thinning hair and a pair of cheap, black-rimmed reading glasses from Boots to break up his face. On the steering wheel in front of him was an open file of documents which he was pretending to study, but as time went by he became increasingly nervous that someone would mistake him for a thief and call the police.

The house was in a side street behind Panorama Road, where property prices were exorbitant because of the uninterrupted views of Poole Harbor and Brownsea Island but, even without a view, Billy would have been surprised if the Spanish-style, balconied villa he was watching was worth less than a million pounds. He'd read somewhere that the Sandbanks Peninsula commanded the fourth highest price per square foot of land in the world, with only Tokyo, Hong Kong and London's Belgravia coming in more expensive. But why this should be so was a complete mystery to him. Given the choice, he'd prefer a property on Malibu Beach in California, where the weather was temperate all the year round.

He hunkered down in his seat as a car cruised past, his heart beating fiercely. This was crazy. Celebrities bought weekend retreats here — half the houses were empty for months on end. He'd probably been under surveillance from a CCTV camera. Who the hell was this Fletcher guy and how could he afford to live cheek by jowl with pop stars and footballers? It didn't make sense. Every inquiry Billy had made had come up blank. "Never heard of him . . ." "Sorry . . ." "If he's on Sandbanks, he's out of my league, mate . . ." "What does he do?"

Billy had been tempted to visit the Crown and Feathers and put some questions to Roy Trent, but had thought better of it. There were a number of adages governing ill-conceived action against animals like Trent, but "beware of stirring up a hornets' nest" seemed appropriate. Trent had been a forgotten secret in Billy's brain for over thirty years and he cursed Georgina Gardener for resurrecting him.

Now he was trying to function on two hours' sleep in twenty-four, and driving his daughters mad by monitoring their every movement. He'd relived every minute of Cill's rape, but from the perspective of a grown man, not that of a naive, tipsy ten-year-old who hadn't a clue what was going on. He even knew what he was suffering from — post-traumatic stress disorder — because he'd been a firefighter long enough to recognize the symptoms. It was a disease of the job — the lingering trauma of dealing with car deaths and burn victims was devastating — although he could not account for the thirty-year delay in the onset — nor the intensity — of his guilt.

Why now? He'd dealt with detectives looking for Cill without blinking an eyelid, but a dumpy little stranger turns up, shows him a photograph and he promptly goes to pieces. The woman had told him too much, that was the trouble. *"It's more likely she was teasing Cill about the rape . . . It takes a lot of imagination to understand how devastating gang rape can be to the victim . . . the poor child was probably scrubbing herself raw every day in order to wash off their filth . . ."*

Thirty years on, he could work out what the blood on Cill's legs had signified, and it made him sick even to think about it. In the way of dreams, it was his twins who wandered in and out of his nightmares, hymenal blood pouring down their thighs and baby fat swelling their tiny breasts. Had Louise understood? She must have. He recalled her smirk when she came back with some trousers and dropped them on the ground. "Blokes can tell," she'd said. "You'll never get married now." And he remembered Cill's tearful answer: "At least I'm not a coward."

He'd never spoken to Cill again. The friendship with Louise had ceased abruptly and Cill was gone within a month. There had been some weeks of unease until the family moved to Boscombe, and then the child had been excised from their minds. Billy had never asked his sister why she hadn't told the police he was a witness to the rape. At ten years old, he'd thought she was trying to keep him out of trouble and loved her for it. In his forties, he wasn't so sure.

"Grace's murderer had ginger hair . . ."

He remembered the day the police came to Mullin Street. He'd thought it was to do with Cill, until a uniformed officer rang their bell and said Mrs. Jefferies was dead. His mother had been watching anxiously from behind a curtain as teams of coppers worked their way from house to house, then she'd ordered Billy upstairs to Louise's bedroom before she opened the door. Billy remembered her hands were shaking, and he remembered wondering why she was scared.

He'd stood just inside his sister's bedroom, listening to the conversation downstairs, while Louise's eyes grew huge in her white face. His mother's voice had been higher than usual as she said she'd never spoken to Mrs. Jefferies and didn't know which house she lived in. The policeman pointed it out to her — Number 11 — and asked her if she'd seen anyone enter or leave during the week. No, said his mother, but then she hadn't been out much. She'd been looking after her daughter, who was Cill Trevelyan's best friend. The man was sympathetic. He had daughters of his own.

They'd never been troubled again. Howard Stamp was arrested and charged within two days of Grace's body being found, and the "Mullin Street murder" was as little visited in the Burton household as Cill's disappearance. "Don't upset your sister," had been the watchword for months. Billy's knowledge of both events had been gleaned from friends whose parents were willing to share information with their children. The accepted story on Cill was that she ran away to London. The accepted story on Grace was that Howard went berserk after she ticked him off for slacking.

It was a conclusion that had puzzled Billy when he was ten, because Howard hadn't seemed capable of hacking anyone to pieces. He was even afraid of Billy and Louise, sliding into shadow whenever he saw them because Louise giggled every time he passed and called him a spastic. She even tried to trip him up once and Billy remembered how frightened he looked. On one occasion, Mrs. Jefferies came to their house and asked their mother to put a stop to it. She was a plump, gray-haired woman who wrung her hands nervously and had difficulty getting her words out. Billy remembered her saying please, all the time, as if she were the one at fault.

Their mother hadn't been particularly angry with them — *"Everyone knows there's something wrong with that boy"* — but she had warned them to leave Howard alone. *"According to his grandmother he's suicidal, and I don't want anyone saying you two were to blame when he does something silly."* Afterward, Billy assumed the "something silly" was murder and that his mother had lied to the police about talking to Mrs. Jefferies because she didn't want the family involved again. Their father was already furious that Louise had been questioned about Cill's disappearance. He kept talking about a terrible atmosphere at work where rumors were rife that if his daughter knew about Cill's rape, so must her parents.

It was a bewildering few months until they moved. Louise's fainting fits meant she stayed at home, while Billy was expected to go to school. He was suspicious and jealous of his mother's relationship with his sister and fearful of his morose father, who bit his head off every time he asked what was wrong. The Trevelyans featured strongly in his parents' invective. When it wasn't that "little tart Cill" who'd ruined Louise's life, it was "that bastard David" who was forcing his father out of Brackham & Wright. Grace Jefferies was never mentioned at all, except in passing. *"The whole damn street wants to move since that bloody woman's murder . . ."*

When they transferred to Boscombe life settled down again. Their father took a new job, Louise changed her name to Daisy and wore her hair differently and Billy found new friends. Only their mother seemed to carry the baggage of Highdown with her, spying from behind the curtains every time the bell rang. Once in a while Billy thought he recognized a face in a crowd, but after a couple of years even that ceased to trouble him. In the great scheme of things, the events of three short weeks in the life of a ten-year-old — events he hadn't understood and couldn't control — became irrelevant. It wasn't his fault that Cill had disappeared or that Mrs. Jefferies had been murdered.

"If they'd had DNA testing in 1970, Mr. Burton, Howard wouldn't even have been charged, let alone sent for trial. It was someone else who killed Grace . . ."

". . . someone with ginger hair . . ."

George retrieved the photographs of

Priscilla Fletcher and Cill Trevelyan from her case and handed Priscilla Fletcher's to Miss Brett. "Could this be Cill Trevelyan? Do you remember her well enough to say?"

The old woman studied the picture for a long time before shaking her head. She admitted to a vague sense of recognition, but it was over thirty years since she'd last seen the child and all she remembered was long brown hair and an overgrown body. George offered her the duplicate of Cill's photograph from the newspaper clipping and Miss Brett's response was the same as William Burton's. "Oh dear, dear, dear! I'd forgotten how young she was. What a *terrible* tragedy."

"Do you think they're the same person?"

She compared the pictures. "I really couldn't say. Some of my ex-pupils have barely changed at all in adulthood, others are unrecognizable. There are strong similarities, of course . . ." She broke off with another shake of her head.

"We did wonder if it was Louise Burton," said George.

The woman gave a surprised laugh. "Goodness me, no. Louise was a ferrety little thing with a pinched face and sharp nose. It was why she latched on to

Priscilla's coattails — I think she hoped some of the other child's appeal would wash off." She stared at Cill's smiling face. "It was rather pathetic, to be honest. She went through a phase of trying to ape Priscilla's looks and mannerisms and merely succeeded in turning herself into a mimic. It was an unbalanced friendship, of course. There was a lot of jealousy on Louise's side."

"What color hair did she have?" asked Jonathan mildly.

"She was a carrottop," said Miss Brett, returning to the photograph of Priscilla Fletcher. "This certainly isn't her."

A black BMW slowed as it came up behind Billy's Renault and he had a glimpse of a dark-haired woman in his rearview mirror before the car turned left into the driveway in front of the Fletchers' house. He dropped the spectacles into his lap and lifted a pair of mini-binoculars to his eyes, using his hand to shield them.

He watched the car door open and the woman climb out. She was slim and smartly dressed in navy blue trousers and a pink polo-neck cashmere jumper with dark hair brushing her shoulders. He couldn't see her face because she had her back to him and, when she let herself into her house, he thought he'd put himself through the wringer for nothing. But she reappeared almost immediately, looking directly at him as she went to the rear of the car and released her boot. It was a trip she repeated several times in order to carry her shopping bags inside and, even if Billy hadn't recognized her the first time, he couldn't have failed to identify the way she walked. Quick, small steps that spoke of an impatient nature.

"The Burtons moved after Priscilla disappeared so that Louise could go to a different school," George said. "Do you know what became of her after that?"

"No. She went to Highdown's equivalent in Boscombe, but where she went from there . . ." Miss Brett shook her head. "I did follow up with her new headmaster but I'm afraid he wasn't very flattering. I believe 'unteachable' was the expression he used. Her parents changed her name and encouraged her to put the past behind her, but the headmaster said it was a mistake."

"Why?"

"Oh, I imagine because it sent the wrong message. Changing one's name is such an easy way to wriggle out of one's difficulties, don't you think?" She was looking at Jonathan as she spoke, as if she suspected him of doing the same thing, and he felt his face heat up.

"What name did she take?" he asked.

"I believe it was Daisy."

"Did she keep her surname?"

Miss Brett nodded. "It was common enough not to worry about." She paused. "To be honest, I thought the Burtons overreacted. It's true Louise was picked on when she returned to school the following week, but it would have passed. The other girls thought she was responsible for Priscilla being punished — and indirectly for the child running away — so she had a difficult two days. I urged her mother to take a tougher line, but I'm afraid she wasn't up to it. In the end it seemed sensible to compromise on a move."

"You don't think it was Louise who was overreacting?"

"Without question," said the old woman dryly, "but, as I wasn't privy to what had gone on between the two girls, it was difficult to know how genuine she was being. I understood from her mother that her greatest fear was bumping into the Trevelyans, so clearly guilt played a part." She gave a regretful shrug. "It was desperately sad. None of us was immune. We all felt responsible."

There was a wistful note in her voice as if her own guilt still lingered and George wondered if that was one of the reasons why she needed to paint David Trevelyan as an abuser. "I'm sure you're right about it being trouble at home that caused Cill to leave," she said gently. "It's impossible to read her story without seeing her as a victim. Do you know if she had ever run away before? It tends to be a pattern of behavior that's repeated until the child decides to leave for good."

Miss Brett eyed her for a moment before leaning back to stare thoughtfully toward the window again. "Do you know I've never considered that? How very interesting. I always put her absences down to truanting." She fell silent for a moment or two. "I think it's unlikely. On the one occasion when she was absent for three days in a row, Louise was also absent, and neither set of parents reported their daughters missing, which suggests they were going home at night."

"Did the mothers work?" asked George. "Perhaps the girls stayed in all day."

"Oh, no, that wouldn't have been tolerated by either woman. I believe Mrs.

Burton had an office-cleaning job, but she was home at lunchtime. Mr. Trevelyan worked nights, of course, so he'd have been sleeping during the day." Miss Brett's mouth thinned with irritation. "We had several persistent truants, particularly among the boys. It was an impossible problem, made worse when the leaving age was raised to sixteen. Short of tying them to their desks, there was little we could do if their parents wouldn't cooperate."

"And ninety-nine percent of teachers would rather turn a blind eye and be shot of the disruptive element, anyway," said Jonathan lightly. "The job's hard enough without having to cope with an illiterate Neanderthal dragging his knuckles along the ground."

The old woman gave a grunt of amusement. "Are you referring to the students or their parents, Dr. Hughes? The more disruptive the child, the more ignorant and ill-disciplined the parents, I usually found. So many of the underachievers were lost causes before they ever reached Highdown. All one could ever do was pass the buck to the police and juvenile detention."

"Was Roy Trent one of those lost causes?"

She studied him for a moment, a small

frown creasing her forehead. "I remember the name but I don't know why."

"Dark-haired, medium height . . . his father ran a newsagent in Highdown Road. We believe Louise may have described him as one of Priscilla's rapists."

Her eyes widened as memory surged back. "Good heavens, you are well informed. Roy Trent, Micky Hopkinson and Colley Hurst." She watched George make a note. "In fact, Louise was insistent she didn't know who they were and could only give a vague description. It was the police who settled on those three because of their past history. They denied it, of course."

"Were they on the school roll?"

"Not at that time. They had a history of expulsion and transfer to different schools but I don't know where they were registered in 1970 . . . if at all, frankly. I believe social services tried various supervision orders but it was an intractable problem. They should have been sent to approved schools to break the links with home — but there were too few specialist units left after the Government cut the funding." She fell silent while she marshaled her thoughts. "I don't remember Micky's or Colley's circumstances, but Roy's father remarried and wouldn't have anything to do with him. It was a cruel way to treat a child . . . did the poor boy no good at all."

"We've been told that one of them had ginger hair," said George.

"Colley Hurst," she agreed.

"Where did he live?"

Miss Brett closed her eyes briefly as if looking back down a passage of time. "I believe all three boys were in Colliton Way. It was a dumping ground for difficult families. Most of our underachievers came from there."

George glanced at Jonathan. "I hope that rings some bells."

He gave a doubtful shake of his head. "Should it?"

"It's in your book," she said mischievously, "and it's another example of synchronicity. Wynne and Howard lived at 48 Colliton Way."

Miss Brett was as intrigued by the coincidences as George was. "One wonders why the police settled so quickly on Howard Stamp," she said. "As I remember it, he was taken in for questioning almost immediately."

"Several witnesses saw him running from Grace's house," said George. "He was a regular visitor, so everyone knew who he was, and when he confessed the police didn't need to look for anyone else."

"But you don't accept the confession?"

"No. Dr. Hughes and I believe it was coerced and that the story he gave in his defense fits the facts rather better. Do you remember it?"

"Only that he said his grandmother was already dead when he found her."

George took a copy of *Disordered Minds* from her case. "This is Dr. Hughes's book, which includes Howard's case in Chapter Twelve. You might like to read it. It's a very well-argued rebuttal of the prosecution evidence." She handed it across. "He questions the pathologist's timing of the murder, the psychological profile of the murderer or murderers and whether that profile fitted Howard, as well as the forensic hair evidence which, along with the confession, persuaded the jury of Howard's guilt."

"May I keep it?"

"Please. You have our cards and phone numbers. We'd be interested in any ideas you might have."

Miss Brett reached for some spectacles. "I remember Howard was a redhead," she said, examining the cover, "and if hair evidence was involved, that presumably explains your interest in Louise and Colley

Hurst? You think one of them was the murderer?"

"It's a possibility. Colley fits the psychological profile, and Louise was living in the same road as Grace."

"Mm." She lowered the book to her lap and folded her hands over it.

"You're not even tempted by the idea?" asked Jonathan with a smile.

The old woman studied him over the rims of her tortoiseshell half-moons. "I won't know until I've read it," she said, "but I fear you're clutching at straws . . . certainly where Louise is concerned. She would never have done something like that on her own — she was far too frightened — and if she had any knowledge of it she'd have spilled the beans immediately; that was her nature. She was a tale-teller."

"Perhaps she wasn't asked?"

Miss Brett shook her head. "She'd have found a way. Her favorite trick was to do what she did with Priscilla: needle away at whoever had annoyed her until they lost their temper, then plead innocence. I assume the aim was to get her own back on Priscilla for publicly breaking their friendship . . . but I never doubted that she was genuinely shocked by the poor child's disappearance." She shrugged. "You need to understand Louise's personality. She was a beastly little girl whose sole aim in life was to be the center of attention — and telling tales on others was the only way she knew how."

Priscilla Fletcher gave a frightened start as she slammed her boot and turned round to find a tall, well-built man in a baseball cap behind her. "My God!" she snapped angrily. "What the hell do you think you're doing?"

Billy removed the cap and smoothed his balding scalp. "Hello, sis," he said. "I was about to ask you the same thing."

Chapter Fourteen

Close up, Billy could see the tail end of bruising under Louise's left eye, a yellow crescent, masked with makeup. He put a hand under her chin and lifted her face. "Who's been hitting you?" he asked.

She pushed his arm away and pulled down a pair of dark glasses that had been holding back her hair. "No one," she snapped.

"I thought you'd done with all that, Lou. Never again, you said, the last time I saw you."

She spun on her heel and marched purposefully toward the front door. "You've got the wrong woman," she called over her shoulder. "My name's Priscilla Fletcher and I don't have a brother. I want you to leave."

Billy followed her. "And if I don't?"

"I'll call the police."

He blocked her attempt to close the

door. “Don’t be an idiot, sis. What would you tell them? That you’ve never seen me before in your life? All I’d have to do is phone the folks and get them to come up. Mum’ll know you immediately. You’ve probably still got that mole on your thigh and the scald mark where you spilled boiling tea on your stomach.” He watched her shoulders slump in resignation. “They’ve been worrying about you for twenty bloody years. We were told you’d gone to Australia.”

She stood irresolutely in the doorway, her head to one side as if she were listening for something in the farther reaches of the house. “Look, you can’t come in,” she said, touching a small hand to his arm. “Nick’s in his office and I don’t need anymore aggro. I’ll meet you somewhere. When are you free?”

“Now. I’ll take you for a drive.”

“I can’t. He knows I’m home.” They both heard the sound of a door opening. “Oh Jesus!” she hissed. “I’ll meet you outside Dingles at four this afternoon. Now, piss off quick, or I’ll get my face smashed in again.”

He put his hand out instinctively to stop her closing the door. “This is crazy. Tell him I’m your brother.”

But she was too fast for him. "He won't believe me," she whispered as the latch locked against him.

"I hate meeting women like that," said George of Miss Brett as she unlocked her car door.

"Really?" said Jonathan in surprise. "I thought she was incredible. Brain like a laser . . . memory like a computer. If I'm like that when I'm in my eighties I won't have any complaints."

"Exactly," said George, slinging her case onto the backseat. "Life is so *bloody* unfair."

He waited while she reached in to release the lock on the passenger side then stooped to face her across the seat. "Loads of people beat cancer, George. There's no reason why you shouldn't make eighty if you do what your doctors tell you. You mustn't get hung up on genetic history — it's the curse of modern living. Just because your mother died of it doesn't mean you're going to."

She settled herself on the seat. "That's not why I don't like meeting women like Miss Brett. She's a *wonder,* Jonathan. She should have had *babies*. Imagine what they would have been like — intelligent, healthy, *wise*. It makes my heart bleed, it really does. What's *wrong* with men that they can't recognize a peach when it's under their nose?"

He wondered if she was talking about herself. "Genes aren't everything. Nurture's just as important. Miss Brett's role in life has been to mold other people's children, and that's a far harder prospect than thirty seconds' drunken copulation that produces a random selection of dodgy chromosomes. In any case," he finished with a grin as he attached his seat belt, "how do you *know* she hasn't had a child?"

"If she did, she wouldn't have been allowed to keep it . . . or talk about it. They'd never have put an unmarried mother in charge of a secondary school in the sixties." She fed her key into the ignition and locked her own belt. "It's a crazy world that helps the least able in society to go on reproducing but discourages intelligent career women."

It was a surprisingly illiberal view for a woman who portrayed herself as the opposite. "It's better than it was," he murmured. "At least women aren't stigmatized for having children out of wedlock these days."

"Maybe not," she said roundly, "but

you're certainly penalized for it financially. You try holding down a full-time job and paying for forty-plus hours of childcare on what remains of a single salary after taxes have been deducted. *That's* the disincentive. It's a ridiculous waste of good genetic material. If I were in government, I'd make it a requirement of law that every workplace had a crèche."

"Too expensive and impossible to manage," said Jonathan. "Imagine the cost to a small company if only one female employee had a baby at any given time."

"Then they form a cooperative crèche with other businesses in the area," said George, starting the engine. "What's the alternative? I read a report recently that said over thirty percent of professional women are choosing to remain childless. That's a *disaster.* What happens if the rate reaches sixty percent? What happens if we end up with a society produced entirely by *under*achievers?"

"That's a very bleak view."

"I wish it were," she answered, pulling away from the curb and performing a three-point turn.

"It's just as hard for men," said Jonathan.

"Except your clocks take longer to run

down," George said with a smile, "and you can father a baby a week if you find enough accommodating women."

"It's not that easy," he said morosely.

She glanced at him as she drew to a halt at the junction with the main road. "Then start making compromises," she said bluntly. "You're an attractive and talented man, Jonathan, and you should be a father."

He gave a low chuckle. "Thank you, George. Sadly, the more usual response to my clumsy efforts is: 'I wouldn't have a baby with you if you were the last man on earth.' "

"Then do something about it."

"Like what?"

"Make compromises," she repeated, waiting for a car to pass.

"Did you?"

"No. There was always something better round the corner . . . and by the time I realized what a flawed philosophy that was, I'd become redundant." She flashed him a bright smile to quell any attempt at sympathy. "Don't make the same mistake, Jon. There's nothing worse than living with regrets."

In an uncharacteristic gesture, Jonathan put his hand on hers and gave it a quick squeeze. "If it's any consolation," he said, "you're just as redundant if you *do* pass on your genes. Once a child is born — and barring the few years of nurturing that allows him to achieve independence — there's nothing you can add to him that isn't already there. It may be good, it may be bad, but by the third generation your genes will have become so diluted that your great-grandchild will carry only a tiny percentage of you. People's value is in their achievements, George, not in their ever diminishing gene pool."

It was on the tip of her tongue to say achievements were empty when there was no one to share them with, but instead she gave a relaxed laugh. "Then let's find somewhere to eat while we work out who really killed Grace," she said, pulling left onto Bridport Road. "That would be one *hell* of an achievement."

She drove to the Smugglers Inn at Osmington Mill, to the east of Dorchester, which had been built in the thirteenth century, beside a stream, in a cleft between two swooping downlands that rose to meet the spectacular Jurassic cliffs of the Dorset coast. The car park overlooked the sea — a turbulent gray that April lunchtime, whipped by an easterly wind — with the thatched inn accessible via a steep ramp and a flight of steps. "My treat," said George firmly, leading the way. "I had a paycheck this morning so I'm feeling flush."

Jonathan made a halfhearted protest. "Why don't we go Dutch?"

"Because you're broke and I'm old enough to be your mother," said George, pushing open the door. "Also I'm starving, and I refuse to feel embarrassed about eating three courses while you pick away at some miserable little starter because it's all you can afford. Reason enough?"

He followed her inside. "I suppose Andrew's been dishing the dirt on me again?"

"It depends how you define dirt. Most of what he said was highly laudatory." She turned to look at him. "What do you think?"

"That you're feeling sorry for me."

"The *pub*, Jonathan. What do you think of the *pub*?"

"It'll do," he said, taking in the impressive oak beams that crisscrossed the low ceiling, the open fireplaces with glowing embers and blackboards advertising local lobster and a healthy wine list. "At least it's an improvement on the Crown and Feathers."

"You're very difficult to please," she said with a sigh. "*Anything*'s better than the Crown and Feathers. I hoped you'd appreciate some atmosphere."

He laughed and steered her toward the bar. "I was teasing, George. If you want to pass yourself off as my mother, you'll have to learn to take it."

This sharing of a meal was so different from the first that Jonathan wondered whether George's remark about a bad beginning making a bad ending was true. If so, he blamed Roy Trent for it. However ill Jonathan had been feeling that day, it was the other man's use of "black" and "wog" that had really raised his hackles. "Tell me something," he invited when a natural lull came in the conversation. "Did you phone Roy to tell him you were going to be late for the lunch in February?"

George paused with her fork, laden with steak-and-kidney pudding, halfway to her mouth. "Of course I did. I said I'd be lucky to be there before twelve-forty-five and asked him to take you up to the room. Why do you ask?"

"Just interested in why he was so aggressive. He left me standing at the bar for a good ten minutes before he put in an appearance, then the first thing he did was call me a wog, but he must have had some suspicion of who I was. The only other people there were a middle-aged couple and Jim Longhurst, so it's not as though there were droves of potential Jonathan Hugheses to choose from."

George looked appalled. "Did he *really* call you a wog?"

Jonathan nodded. "Wog . . . black . . . darkie — the only thing he didn't call me was a nigger."

George's face went through several gargoyle gyrations. "Good *lord!* That's *outrageous!* No wonder you were so cross."

Jonathan grinned as he cut into his fillet of salmon. "I think he was trying to get rid of me before you arrived."

"He'd have succeeded, too, if my neighbor hadn't come home when he did. I'd reckoned another half hour on the charger before there was enough juice in the battery to give me a spark, then Barry turned up with jump leads and had me ticking over in a couple of minutes." Her forehead creased in a frown. "I phoned just after midday, and Roy said you were already there."

"Then he was watching me through a spyhole," said Jonathan bluntly, "because he didn't emerge till twelve-fifteen. I thought at the time it was a damn strange way to run a pub."

"He has a CCTV camera above the till and a couple of monitors in the kitchen." She chewed a piece of steak. "I'm completely shocked. He told me the only racist remark he made was that he was expecting a white man and you took off like a rocket. Do you still think he isn't involved?"

Jonathan shook his head. "I'd probably agree a ninety percent certainty that he was one of Cill's rapists, but I can't see the connection with Grace unless the police missed a hell of a lot of evidence. Even if Colley Hurst was the murderer and bath taker, there was nothing to indicate the other two boys were there." He shrugged. "I suppose Colley might have told them about it afterward, but it doesn't explain why Roy would want to protect him now."

"Perhaps we should ask him," said George lightly.

"He'd laugh."

"Not if we concentrate on Cill's rape," she said. "We know he was taken in for questioning about it and we know the names of his friends. It'll be interesting to see his reaction." Impatiently, she pushed her plate aside and propped her elbows on the table. "He's so smug, Jonathan. At least let's put him on the back foot."

The idea was tempting. "What good will it do if we can't link him to Grace?"

"It'll scare the bejabbers out of him," she said, "particularly if we ask him who Priscilla Fletcher is and why she would want to steal your wallet. As far as he's aware, his ex-wife is completely unknown to us. In any case, I can't *believe* he called you a wog — it's so *rude*."

The closer they came to Bournemouth the more Jonathan regretted agreeing to accompany her. Sticks and stones might break his bones but rudeness had never killed him. In one form or another, he'd lived with it all his life. It had turned him into a deeply repressed individual, but it was the sticks and stones that frightened him.

"You're such a coward, Jon . . . it's embarrassing. When are you going to stand up for yourself?"

"I'm not sure I can do this," he said suddenly.

George, who had been prattling through his increasingly long silences, was unsurprised. A couple of glasses of wine had released his inhibitions long enough for him to accept the challenge, but the Dutch courage hadn't lasted the fifty-minute drive. "He'll avoid any difficult confrontations for as long as he can," Andrew had warned her. "His expertise, as he'll tell you again and again, is researching documents. He'll want the longest paper trail you've ever seen before he'll tackle Roy Trent. It's a defense mechanism."

"Against what?"

"Being in a situation he can't control . . . being found wanting . . . being afraid. I had the devil's own job persuading him down to Bournemouth to talk to you."

"Why?"

Andrew shrugged. "He didn't know who you were, or what to expect. He's a fish out of water with strangers."

"Is it shyness?"

"Not entirely. He was badly bullied at school and it's left him paranoid about everything — rejection, in particular."

"Like Howard."

Andrew nodded. "Except Jon's scars don't show, and I think that makes it harder for him. He doesn't have an obvious excuse to feel like an outsider — except his color — which is why he portrays himself as a victim of racism. It's easier than admitting that what he's really afraid of is derision."

George made no response to Jonathan's remark until she was able to pull off the main road and draw up behind a parked car in the first side street she could find. "What don't you think you can do?" she asked, killing the engine.

"Talk to Roy," he said, rubbing his face furiously with his hands.

"Why not?"

"We don't have enough information. What are we going to say to him?"

She watched him for a moment, not doubting that he was in a genuine funk. "I'm planning to describe Cill Trevelyan's gang rape as told to me by William Burton," she said unemotionally, "then make it clear that I believe Roy was involved along with his friends, Colley Hurst and Micky Hopkinson."

"He won't like it."

"Should I *give* a damn?" asked George with an amused laugh.

"He'll deny it. You don't have any proof."

"I'm not planning to arrest him, Jonathan, just let him know what I know and see where it takes us."

He lowered his fists to his lap and banged them against each other. "I can't see the point of putting him on his guard before we need to. Supposing he gets angry?"

"You should be more worried about me getting angry," she said mildly. "I hate rape with a passion, Jonathan, particularly gang rape of a child. If Cill had been *my* daughter — if *I'd* been Jean Trevelyan — I'd have camped on Roy's doorstep thirty-three years ago till he confessed, then I'd have ripped his head off. He should count himself lucky I wasn't."

Jonathan stared at her in wide-eyed desperation. "I really can't do it."

She put a hand on his arm. "What are you afraid of? That he'll hit me? I quite hope he does, as a matter of fact — I'll have him charged with assault — but he won't do it for that reason."

Jonathan shook his head. "You can't be sure."

"No," George agreed, "but I'm damned if I'll let that stop me. In any case, I have a pepper spray in my bag. It's highly illegal — I bought it in America — but I'd rather be in prison for zapping a mugger than dead because he had a knife." She paused to let him take the information in. "I'm not easily intimidated, Jonathan. I may not be the fittest thing on two legs but my dad taught me to stand up for myself, and it was a good lesson. I'll tackle Roy alone, if necessary, but it won't help you if I do."

He raised a mirthless smile. "It'll do me more good than having my jaw broken."

"Has that happened before?"

"Once."

"By bullies?"

"*A* bully," he said flatly.

"Did you report him?"

"No. I pretended I'd fallen off my bike."

"Why?"

"Because he said he'd break it again if I didn't." His smile became twisted. "I didn't have a father like yours, George. The last thing you did with mine was stand up for yourself . . . unless you wanted more of the same, of course."

There was no point telling him it was a variation on a theme repeated in every case study of physical abuse George had ever read. For Jonathan, and every abused child, their individual story was unique. A low-income family, struggling to survive. Secrecy, coupled with threats of retaliation if the abuse was exposed. A child who hid in the school lavatories because he was too frightened to go home. An angry father whose violent tendencies were aggravated by alcohol. A despised mother who allowed her son to be beaten in preference to herself. A dysfunctional parental relationship made worse by an elderly grandfather whose demands for attention increased the stress within the family. A skinny, fast-growing adolescent with ill-fitting clothes who was targeted by bullies because he wore his timidity too openly. A reinvention of history because lies were less painful than the truth. Repressed emotions, limited social skills, inability to commit to relationships, fear of criticism, fear of failure . . .

"Andrew told me you had a steady girlfriend until Christmas," George said. "What happened to her?"

"You're such a coward, Jon . . . it's embarrassing."

This was not a story Jonathan wanted to narrate, and he wouldn't have done so if George hadn't retreated into a deadening silence which became more insistent the longer it went on. He understood that hers was a far more determined character than his, and he began to wonder if she and Andrew had cooked up this plot to persuade him to talk about Emma.

"Were you lying about wanting this

meeting with Roy?" he asked angrily, as if George were party to his thought processes.

And perhaps she was, because she addressed his unspoken question. "Is it really so hard to tell me about her?"

"There's nothing to tell," he said harshly. "It didn't work out so we split up. It happens every day."

Again the silence drifted, nagging at Jonathan's nerves like a toothache. An interminable number of cars drove past while George sat calmly on, more prepared than he to wait it out. He wanted to despise her for her inquisitiveness, but he couldn't. An inquisitive woman would have pestered for an answer. He wanted to feel angry at her attempts to manipulate him, but he couldn't, for when he finally told the story it was because he wanted to.

Chapter Fifteen

Dingles Department Store, Bournemouth
Wednesday, April 23, 2003, 4:30 p.m.

Billy Burton took another look at his watch, then dropped his cigarette butt to the pavement and crushed it underfoot. He'd arrived early and had been standing close to the store entrance for forty-five minutes and, though crowds of shoppers had passed, Louise had not been among them. He was disappointed but not surprised. She'd failed to make several such rendezvous before the family lost touch with her, and the circumstances had been tediously similar.

At first, spurred on by his father, Billy had tracked her down each time she moved — always when her useless husband was given another stretch in prison — made an appointment to meet, only to hang around on a street corner waiting for her to show. In the end he became impatient, and he told his father to let her stew for a while. She'll call you when she's ready, he'd said confidently. But he was wrong. All contact with her had been lost, and they'd been out of touch for more than two decades.

There were no recriminations. Indeed, sometimes he thought they were secretly relieved to be shot of her. His father said he'd always expected it, his mother said Billy had tried his best, and, like a cracked record — never mind a whole river had passed under Lou's bridge — the parents returned to blaming Cill Trevelyan. Louise had never been the same since the "little tart" had run away. If they'd understood how much influence the beastly girl had wielded over their own naive Lou, they'd have strangled the friendship at birth.

Nevertheless, Billy had always felt guilty. Once in a while — usually under pressure from his wife — he would ask himself why his parents had never gone knocking on doors themselves in search of their errant daughter, but it wasn't an excuse that sat easily with him. Louise's prostitution and heroin addiction had been so inexplicable that on the rare occasions when she paid a visit home the Burtons' initial pleasure at seeing her had invariably degenerated into a blazing row, leaving Billy — no less puzzled by his sister's rapid descent from wife to hooker — as the only conduit of communication. The one thing he'd never told his folks was that among her various aliases was the name Cill.

Their mother was convinced she'd died in Australia, either from drugs or AIDS, and there was endless speculation about children. Had she had any? Where were they? Who was looking after them? Councillor Gardener believed she'd had a baby by Roy Trent in her teens, and, while Billy knew that to be untrue, he was less sure about a marriage. Her name changes had been as hard to keep track of as her changes of address.

He took another look at his watch, toying with the idea of driving back to Sandbanks. Lou hadn't denied it when he suggested she was still on the game, but her remark about having her face smashed in *again* implied it was Fletcher who'd given her the black eye. God knows she'd had plenty in her time, from either her husband or customers, but what kind of pimp lived on millionaire's row and sent his wife out prostituting?

He lit another cigarette and promised himself he'd leave when it was finished. He couldn't make anymore sense of Lou's situation today than he had twenty years before, but he'd give her another five minutes . . .

"It was *Guess Who's Coming to Dinner*, but without the happy ending," said Jonathan. "We lived together for a year before Emma allowed me to meet her parents — she insisted we wait until we were sure we wanted to get married." He smiled painfully. "So we invited them to the flat on Christmas Eve to give them the good news . . . and it was worse than anything I'd imagined. She warned me her father wouldn't like it, but she didn't tell me he'd call me a 'dirty nigger' and then start lamming into her. I left the room when he slapped her . . . and she moved out on Christmas Day. She hasn't spoken to me since."

"Where did you go?"

"I hid in the lavatory."

"What did Emma say?"

"That I was a coward and I'd embarrassed her — nothing I didn't deserve. She was looking for a man who would stand up to her father, and I couldn't . . . so we split up."

"Is she with anyone else?"

"I don't know."

"Have you called her?"

"No."

"Why not?"

He closed his eyes. "Why do you think?"

"I don't know, Jon, but I can *guess*. Because suffering in silence makes you feel better about yourself? Because you've persuaded yourself Emma would rather have a relationship with a brutish father who abuses her than with a coward who hides in the lavatory?" George's tone was abrasive. "Perhaps you're afraid he'll come round and hit you, and you've decided Emma isn't worth the thirty seconds of pain? Perhaps you *agree* with her . . . you *are* a coward and an embarrassment and she'll be better off without you? Or you're like Howard . . . and you hope that if you self-mutilate long enough someone like me will come along and rehabilitate you."

He took to rubbing his face again. "She'll refuse to speak to me," he said harshly. "*That's* why I haven't phoned."

"Oh, I see," said George in mock surprise, "you're afraid of rejection. Well, well, well! What a man of double standards you are, Jonathan. It doesn't matter whose feelings *you've* hurt . . . just so long as *yours* don't suffer. Are those the rules you operate by?"

"You know they aren't."

"I don't, I'm afraid. You shared a bed with the girl and made love to her. At the very *least* you have an obligation to find out if she's all right." She gave him an ironic smile. "Or am I being very old-fashioned?"

"You look like shit," said Billy, examining the new bruises under his sister's makeup. "Are you all right?"

"Yeah," she said, pulling her scarf over her mouth. "Nick's got a fucking awful temper, but he doesn't mean to hurt me . . . not really. He's powerfully jealous, which I guess means he loves me."

Billy took her arm and steered her toward a cafe in the alleyway opposite Dingles. "You're such a tit, Lou," he said, using a term he'd often called her in childhood. "When are you going to learn that guys who love their wives don't beat them up?"

"Don't start," she said crossly. "I had enough of the lectures before. I wouldn't be here except I was afraid you'd come banging on the door again."

He pushed open the cafe door and led the way to an empty table. "What do you want? Tea? Coffee? Something to eat?"

"Black coffee," she said ungraciously,

"but I can't pay for it because he took all my money."

So what's new? Billy thought, as he went to the counter. The only difference between now and twenty years ago was that she was better dressed and lived in an expensive house. The beatings still happened . . . she was still having to touch her family for spending money . . . she still didn't want her brother knocking on her door. It was damn weird whichever way he looked at it.

He returned with two coffees and put one in front of her. "So who's Nick Fletcher?" he asked, sitting down. "What does he do?"

"He's a businessman," she said.

"What kind of business?"

"He's a bookie."

"Never heard of him."

"No reason why you should." She changed the subject abruptly. "So what have you been doing with yourself, Billy? Are you married? Got kids?"

He nodded. "Do you remember Rachel Jennings? Sister of Mark Jennings who was in your year? We got hooked up in 'eighty-five and had twin daughters two years later — Paula and Jules — they're sixteen now."

"God!" said Louise. "You mean I'm an aunt?"

Billy grinned. "Of two redheads. What about you? Did you have any? Am I an uncle?"

She stared into her coffee cup. "I had a miscarriage once but that's the closest I came. It's a bit of a bugger really. I'd have liked kids."

There was too much regret in her voice for him not to believe her, and he wondered who'd told Councillor Gardener otherwise. "I'm sorry."

"Yeah. So how are the folks? Are they still in the old house?"

"No, Rachel and I bought it off them so they could move to Cornwall." He gave her a potted history of the family's fortunes since 1980. "Dad's supposed to have retired but he works as a jobbing gardener to avoid going stir-crazy at home, and Mum got born-again religion two years ago. She's a parish visitor or something: calls on old people who can't leave their houses . . . then spends every Sunday in church. Dad can't understand it at all, keeps telling her she must have a lot on her conscience."

It was seeing the smile vanish suddenly from Louise's face that made him think about what he'd said. He'd heard Robert

Burton use the expression several times, but he'd always assumed it was a mild joke to account for Eileen's sudden obsession with Jesus. Billy knew it annoyed his father, even made him jealous to have his pliant wife find an interest in life that excluded him, but he'd never taken the teasing seriously.

He watched his sister's gaze drop to the coffee cup again. "*Is* there something on her conscience?" he asked curiously.

"How would I know?" she snapped. "I haven't spoken to her in years."

"Then why are you looking so guilty?"

She didn't answer.

He stirred sugar into his own coffee. "Do you want to know how I found you?"

"Not particularly, but you'll tell me anyway. It used to give you a hell of a buzz to prove how clever you were tracking me down. You were a real pain, Billy. The folks'd click their fingers and you'd come messing up my life again . . . and you never even asked yourself if I wanted to be found."

"The first time I did, we lost touch with you," he said prosaically. "Was that what you wanted? I can't believe it. You couldn't take their money off me quick enough every time I turned up. You had upward of a thousand quid in a couple of years . . . but you were damned if you'd come by and say thank you. That's all they wanted, to see you once in a while and know you were still alive." He sipped his coffee. "It was you got the buzz out of me traipsing around after you, made you think you were important. It's the same reason you let men hit you — you want the attention."

"Cut the crap," she said with a bitter edge to her voice, "I'm not in the mood. I had a habit up to three years ago and it turned me into a zombie." She raised her eyes again. "Go on, tell me how you found me. I know you're dying to."

"I had a visit from a woman councillor about ten days ago. Her name was George Gardener . . ."

Jonathan took out a handkerchief and blew his nose. He was still painfully thin, with wrists and hands protruding from his cuffs like paddles, and George wondered if he had ever developed beyond the bullied adolescent who grew too fast for his clothes. She recalled Roy's derisive comments about Howard Stamp's "scrappy little beard" and "sparrow chest," and wondered if Roy had spotted the same similarities between Howard and Jonathan as she had. It would certainly explain his attempt to see Jonathan "off." George doubted Howard had ever left his house without running a gauntlet of abuse, which raised the question, how did he find the courage to leave it at all?

"What would I say to her?" Jonathan asked. "I'm sorry? It'll never happen again? It *will,* George. If her father slapped her twenty times, I'd still run away. I'm like my mother. I'd rather anyone had their jaw broken than me . . . *including* Emma. I'm everything she called me . . . I'm everything my mother was." He drew a shuddering breath. "And I *hated* my mother."

"Therefore Emma hates you," said George flatly.

"I don't blame her."

"Except it's a grand example of transference, Jon — a cockeyed view of the world where past relationships poison present ones." She gave a small laugh. "Let me put it another way — if you chose to play your mother, then what role did you give Emma? What did you want her to be?"

"Girlfriend . . . partner . . . lover. We didn't have any problems till her father showed up."

"Are you sure?"

Jonathan had been watching an elderly

man approach along the pavement. He had a tiny Yorkshire terrier on a lead and every time the dog showed an interest in a lamppost, he yanked it away like a hairy yo-yo. It was obvious he resented the animal, either because it belonged to his wife or because he thought the red ribbon in its fringe reflected badly on him, but the harshly snapping lead was an easy cruelty.

". . . you can be so unkind, Jon. I'm not your keeper . . . nor am I responsible when things go wrong for you . . ."

He shifted his attention back to George. "I don't know," he said honestly. "I was never that close to anyone before. I was a disappointment sometimes, but I didn't mean to be. I usually received a lecture when it happened."

George looked intrigued. "So you turned her into a nanny? How interesting. I'm not surprised she packed her bags. Women today don't even want to be nannies to their children, let alone their husbands."

"I did not," said Jonathan irritably. "She may have acted like one sometimes, but that wasn't my choice. I wanted an equal."

"Then your signals are confusing. We all get treated according to the reactions we provoke, Jon. I've known you half a second but it's obvious everyone nannies you . . . Emma, Andrew, me . . . even Priscilla Fletcher while she was stealing your wallet. I expect you have secretaries at work who do it." She raised her eyebrows in inquiry. "It's wonderful for your ego — means there's always nanny to blame when things go wrong — but quite incompatible with a mature relationship between equals."

He turned away angrily to watch the old man. "I didn't ask you to do this," he said in a strained voice. "I made a simple statement. I said I didn't want to talk to Roy. If you'd respected that, we wouldn't be having this conversation." He paused briefly, as if wondering about the wisdom of saying anything else, before letting rip: "You're like Emma . . . you go *on* and *on* . . . pick, pick, pick . . . and for what? So that I'll stand up to some *fucking* bastard I hardly know, just because you don't like the way he treats you."

"We all have transference reactions of some degree or other," George countered mildly. "My father blighted my life."

Jonathan glared at her suspiciously. "That's not the impression you give. You always talk as if you were fond of him."

"I was. No other man came close. Why do you think I've never married?"

* * *

Louise looked very shaken by the time Billy had finished the account of his meeting and telephone call with George Gardener. Her hands were trembling so much that she couldn't lift her cup without spilling the coffee. "If you knew it was me, why the hell did you tell her to go to the Trevelyans?" she hissed.

"Because she was going to go anyway . . . maybe not immediately, but she'd have got round to it eventually." He lit a cigarette and offered it to her. "I thought it was quite clever of me," he said with as much artistry as she used in her lies, "so a thank-you wouldn't come amiss."

Tears glittered on her lashes as she fumbled the cigarette into her mouth. "What's clever about it? I'll have a sodding detective on my doorstep next."

"So? You can prove you aren't Cill Trevelyan. I'm sure the folks still have your birth certificate." He lit a cigarette for himself and leaned forward. "The reason it was clever is that, by being helpful, I persuaded this Gardener woman that Priscilla Fletcher isn't Louise Burton. That's not to say she won't find out, but at least it gives you time to come up with an explanation."

She stared at him with suspicion. "For what?"

"For a kickoff, why you've turned yourself into Cill's clone. Why *have* you, as a matter of interest?"

"None of your business."

"Is it guilt? Did something happen to her?"

"She was raped."

"Other than that."

She wouldn't look at him. "Why did it take you so long to find me? You said your meeting with George was ten days ago."

"I've been on days for a while, so I haven't had time. And you're ex-directory. I had to persuade a mate at the post office to give me your address." He took note of the way she said "George." "Do you know this woman, Lou?"

"No."

"All right, do you know *of* her? She seems pretty clued up about you . . . or rather Priscilla Fletcher. She told me you live in Sandbanks, that you were married to Roy Trent and that you had a son by him when you were in your teens." Billy's heart sank as he watched fear widen his sister's eyes. "Oh Christ, Lou!" he muttered, lowering his voice. "What the hell did you get into? Was she right about Roy?

Were you lying when you said you hadn't had kids?"

He could read her expressions as easily as when she'd been a child, and he watched her face as her mind manufactured alternative versions of history, only to discard them. None was convincing enough to persuade him that she wasn't in trouble. "I wasn't lying about kids," she said finally, "but Roy had one. A boy. He's grown up now and lives in London — courtesy of Wandsworth prison — but he stayed with us for a while when we first married. That'll be where the nosy cow got the son bit from, I should think, though I'd bloody well like to know who told her. The kid was a nightmare . . . always on the take, always in trouble with the cops . . . he's the one caused me and Roy to split up."

"Who was his mother?"

"One of Roy's tarts. I told him he didn't need to take the boy on, but he had a thing about his own dad dumping him, so he wouldn't listen. The kid ended up in prison —" her mouth twisted — "*surprise, surprise* — he was sixteen when we took him on and nineteen when they banged him up — and in three years he managed to ruin everything Roy and I had going."

"When was this?"

She wiped the glowing end of her cigarette around the sides of the ashtray, then took another drag before squashing it. "We got married in 'ninety-two, split up after nine years of me being told his bloody son's problems were my fault and divorced last year. It was a fucker, Billy. Roy and me would have done OK — he still fancies me something chronic — it was the bloody kid caused all the trouble."

There was too much information and Billy wasn't practiced enough to sort the wheat from the chaff. Why had Louise married Roy at all? Had she been one of his tarts? What had she done to make his son's problems her fault? What happened after the divorce? When did she marry Nick Fletcher? How did she know Roy still fancied her? Was he the reason for her black eye and swollen lip?

In the end he asked the question that troubled him the most. "Did you ever go inside Grace Jefferies's house?" he demanded, gripping her wrist between his strong fingers. "I want the truth, Lou."

The change of expression was too obvious. This was an explanation she'd rehearsed. "Don't be an idiot!" she said scornfully, wriggling her hand free. "You know damn well I didn't. I was barely thirteen years old and I'd had my head done in because my best friend went missing. Ask Mum if you don't believe me. She stood guard over my door in case I did something stupid."

"I said *ever,* Lou. I didn't say, 'Were you in there the day she was murdered?' "

Louise reached for his pack and lighter and took another cigarette. Her hands were trembling again. "I never went in Mrs. Jefferies's house. *Satisfied?*"

"No." Billy shook his head. "I think you and Cill hid out with her when you truanted. I remember you telling me once that she had a bigger telly than ours."

Her mouth started working fiercely and she lifted her scarf to hide it. "You haven't changed much, have you, Billy?" The tears glimmered on her lids again. "You always were a fucking nuisance."

Chapter Sixteen

25 Mullin Street, Highdown, Bournemouth
Wednesday, April 23, 2003, 5:00 p.m.

George's house was a 1930s semi, with white pebble-dashed walls and anachronistic mock-tudor features in contrasting black. There was an embossed petal motif beneath the eaves, diamond leaded panes in the windows and two skimpy wooden beams set at right angles to each other to suggest a structural wooden frame. "It's typical of its period," she said with irony, when Jonathan made no comment.

He smiled back. "Rather like Poundbury, then — relatively new but pretending to be old."

"Just good old prewar sham," she said, leading the way up a short path to the front door, "but at least it was built to last. I'm not a big fan of the outside either but the inside's all right." She turned her key in the lock. "According to the neighbor who saw Howard's arrival, it's an exact replica of Grace's house." She nodded toward a block of flats fifty yards down the road. "That's where it was before it was pulled down."

"Where did the Burtons live?"

George swung the door open and held it ajar with her knee. "Number 18," she said, pointing to a terrace of brick houses opposite the flats. "They used to be council-owned but they were sold to the tenants in the eighties."

She took him into her sitting room and dropped her case onto a chair. It was a big, open room with a French window to the garden and an archway through to a dining area and kitchen. George clearly liked clutter, because every available surface was covered with knickknacks and curios. Her taste in color was interesting, thought Jonathan, while wondering if he liked the combination of mustard yellow walls and chocolate brown carpet. Very baked earth, and not always complimentary to the paintings on the walls, but the whole feel of the room was a good reflection of George's personality. Warm, full of ideas, but not entirely comfortable to be around.

"The phone's in the kitchen," she told

him, shrugging off her suit jacket and folding it over her arm. "I'm going upstairs to change, and it'll take me about half an hour. The coffee's by the kettle and there's an open bottle of wine in the fridge. Help yourself to whatever you want."

"What if I don't do it?"

George shrugged. "You'll never know what the next chapter might have been." She pulled a wry face. "But don't do it to please me. Dad always said I was far too curious for my own good. Do it because you want to, Jon."

He waited until he heard her footsteps on the stairs, then walked through the archway to look for the telephone. It was on the wall at the end of an L-shaped worktop that split the kitchen area from the dining table. He put his briefcase on the table and took off his jacket, automatically removing his wallet and tucking it into the case. Even as he did it, he recalled performing the same routine in the Crown and Feathers, right down to the brush of the briefcase lining against the backs of his fingers. He raised his eyes to stare through the lead-paned windows at George's unkempt garden. He was certainly curious about that chapter. Why had Priscilla Fletcher taken his wallet if she hadn't wanted to draw attention to herself?

With a sigh, he moved to the worktop and took the receiver from the hook. In the pit of his stomach he knew the call would end in tears, but he also knew that George was right. He couldn't live in an emotional vacuum forever. Not without going mad.

Louise flung Billy's hand off her arm as she stormed out of the cafe. "If you don't leave me alone, I'll start screaming," she hissed under her breath, "and I'll tell anyone who asks that you gave me the bruises." Her pale, obstinate eyes raked him. "You know I'll do it."

He did. She'd always been ready to lie about his involvement if it meant getting off scot-free herself — except on the one occasion of Cill's rape. "Go ahead," he said, with mirrored obstinacy in his own eyes. "Scream your head off . . . and when the police arrive, I'll tell them I was a witness to Cill Trevelyan's rape, that I can name all three of the bastards involved and that Howard Stamp wasn't the only person with ginger hair who spent time in Grace Jefferies's house."

Louise gave a shuddering laugh. "You wouldn't do it," she said. "You're too like Mum. You'll worry about what the neighbors'll say and keep your mouth shut."

"Don't rely on it, Lou."

There was a tiny hiatus before, with an unexpected show of affection, she touched a hand to his cheek. "It's forgotten history," she told him, "and you can't reopen it without hurting your wife and kids. Do you think they'll thank you for dragging their name through the mud? It's never the guilty who suffer, Billy."

She turned away and this time Billy let her go, fear rising like a sickness in his throat. *"Your mother has a lot on her conscience . . ."*

Jonathan was in the garden when George returned downstairs. He was picking his way rather aimlessly about her overgrown patch of lawn, head determinedly down, hands crumpling a handkerchief. She knew he'd made the call because she'd heard his voice through her bedroom floorboards.

"Oh, *bugger!*" she muttered to herself as she took the wine from the fridge. "Bugger! Bugger! Bugger!" She poured a couple of glasses and took them outside. "Chin up," she said with false cheer, handing one to Jonathan and clinking it with hers. "Try thinking of it as a beginning . . . when a door closes behind you it means you can move on. And that's healthy. It's how it's supposed to be."

"Your grass needs cutting," he said, scuffing his foot across the lawn. "Do you have a mower? Do you want me to do it for you?"

"Wouldn't you rather go home? I can give you a lift to the station." She lowered her wine glass. "I can finish this when I get back."

Jonathan put a slender finger under the stem and pushed it up. "Drink away. Andrew lent me thirty quid, so I'll take a taxi when the time comes."

She waited for him to continue, and when he didn't: "Do you want to talk about it? What did Emma say?"

"Nothing, I didn't speak to her." He smiled wryly at her expression. "Her father answered her phone. He said he'd '*rip* my black nuts off' if I ever called again. I presume she's living with them, or he's confiscated her mobile."

"What did *you* say?"

He played his foot across the grass again. "That I'd be round tomorrow morning to rip his white ones off if he didn't put Emma on immediately."

George gave a surprised laugh. "Oh, well done! And?"

"He doesn't think I've got the nerve. He hung up."

She let a beat of silence pass while she watched his fidgeting toe. "*Do* you have the nerve?"

"Maybe . . . if I do a trial run first."

"Who with?"

"Roy Trent," he said with a smile, "because the way I'm feeling at the moment, I'll rip *his* nuts off if he makes a remark I don't like."

From: wandr.burton@compuline.
com
Sent: Wed. 4/23/03 17:31
To: robandeileen.burton@uknet.
co.uk
Subject: Louise

I know its rachel or the twins usually does this but I can't ring because I'm angry and I don't know how to say this without getting in another row about the strikes Ive found louise and she's living with another abuser plus there's stuff going on here that's doing my head in lou looks like cill trevelyan and she was married to one of cills rapists for a while she says there's things mum kept to herself to save the family embarrassment and I want to know what they are

There's a woman councillor saying Howard stamp didn't kill grace jefferies and I remember mum lying about knowing her when the cops came round I always knew something bad happened round that time because you were both mad with worry this woman says it was someone with ginger hair killed grace but it wasn't Howard I know you both know lou was in grace's house every time she skipped school so is that the only thing mum kept quite about why do you keep saying mums got things on her conscience

I need some answers dad otherwise Im thinking of going to the cops.

Billy

From: Rob Burton [robandeileen.burton@uknet.co.uk]
Sent: Wed. 4/23/03 18:40
To: wandr.burton@compuline.com
Subject: Louise

Dear Son,

I've had great difficulty trying to make out what on earth you're talking about. I wish you'd learned to use punctuation when you were younger. Spellchecks can only do so much. As to rows, you know my feelings. The strikes are unpatriotic, son, and browbeating will not make me change my mind.

As to this ridiculous nonsense you've written, I can only presume Louise has been filling your head with lies again. Obviously, it's the drugs talking and I'm afraid you're even more foolish than I thought if you pay any mind to her.

I don't know who this woman is you're

referring to or why you say your mother lied about knowing her. Nor do I understand what you mean by "Lou looks like Cill Trevelyan." Of course Howard Stamp killed his grandmother, he confessed immediately and was convicted, and if your mother and I were "mad with worry" at that time, it was because David Trevelyan was making life difficult for me at work. He accused the family of spreading lies about Cill, saying there was only Louise's word the rape had happened. According to him, if both girls were together then they would both have suffered the same fate, and he was angry with Louise for suggesting his daughter was "easy" and "asked for it" while Louise was left alone. Unfortunately, his thinking was muddled. Another accusation he made was that if the rape had happened, Louise must have told your mother and me because she was so quick to tell the police. The implication was that we failed to pass the information to him, and instead allowed Cill to be punished for the fight with Louise while knowing that Cill was in a vulnerable state. By some rather twisted logic, that made us responsible for his wretched child running away.

I should say, we were never convinced about the rape, although we certainly believed Cill had had sex with some boys in front of Louise, and your sister had misinterpreted what was happening. From your mother's and my point of view, it was a friendship made in hell, with your sister being introduced to things she shouldn't have known at 13. I'm afraid we had our doubts about David Trevelyan from the beginning. He was unnaturally keen to thrash the girl, particularly after she started to develop, and neither of us was comfortable with it. If your mother has anything to regret it is certainly that. She has said many times that she should have found the courage to speak out and accuse him of abuse. I should add that we have often wondered if some of Louise's problems stem from the fact that he may also have abused her. She spent a lot of time in their house, and there's no doubt she became very frightened of him after Cill went missing. We tried to keep an open mind but that became increasingly hard when David started drumming up sympathy at work by making my life difficult. He was under a lot of pressure from the police because, despite an alibi, he would certainly have been charged had Cill's body ever been found. Yet he was able to deflect attention from that among our colleagues by accusing your sister of lying. On two or three occasions Jean had a screaming match in public with Mum on the same subject, and your mother found it embarrassing and stressful. It was this as much as anything that turned Louise into a frightened little mouse and persuaded us to move.

Re: your mother's "conscience': I have no idea what secrets she keeps in her heart but I am quite certain she had no knowledge of Louise playing truant in Grace Jefferies's house because it wasn't true.

Who put that idea into your head? And

as to Louise marrying one of Cill's rapists, where did that piece of nonsense come from? Louise herself didn't know the names of the boys and the police never revealed which ones they questioned. As a matter of fact, I believe several were taken in because Cill was rather too easy with her "favors," but there was nothing to connect any of them with the alleged rape or the disappearance. If Louise is your source, then I ask you to remember how drugs affect her brain. She was never able to be truthful about anything once she was caught in the cycle of addiction and prostitution, and I doubt much has changed if she's with another "abuser." It's a terrible waste of a life, but I'm out of sympathy with her now. Your mother and I couldn't have done more to get her away from it, but she made it clear she preferred the squalor of selling herself for heroin-induced stupors to behaving like a mature adult.

I have no problem with you giving her our address and phone number, though I doubt she'll bother to call. I expect, as usual, she left you in the lurch with threats of doing something silly if you interfere again. It's all so predictable, and not something I will ever understand. Mum is out at the moment but should be back by 7:00 p.m. If you want to talk to either of us, feel free to call, though I'd prefer it if we didn't have a row. Louise has caused so many in the past, and I don't have the energy for them these days. Your mother is well, as I hope are Rachel and the girls.

Dad

From: wandr.burton@compuline.com
Sent: Wed. 4/23/03 18:55
To: robandeileen.burton@uknet.co.uk
Subject: Louise

Dear dad it wasn't just lou saw the rape it was me too roy trent was part of the gang he's the one lou married there were three in the gang and one had red hair he was called colley hunt or something like that roy was the worst and now I find lou married him and has turned herself into a cill trevelyan clone looks just like her plus lou did go into grace jefferies house cill too I watched them sneak out the back a couple of times ask mum she knows its true grace came round one time to complain about the way me and lou teased Howard and she said shed tried being nice to lou to get it to stop by letting her in to watch tv I need you and mum to talk this over and see what you remember at the moment I don't know what to do for the best I'll call later but I don't want you telling me to keep my mouth shut I feel really bad about not saying anything before but seeing cills photo the other day makes me realize she could never have looked after herself I reckon her dad killed her and got away with it and I think lou knows he did that's why she went so peculiar plus I always thought it was weird that Howard killed his gran because he was so frightened of everything he cried once when lou called him a spastic

Billy

Roy flicked Louise a brief stare of dislike when she sidled into his kitchen and told him George Gardener had been asking her brother about Cill Trevelyan's disappearance. "I told you she'd find out about it, but you wouldn't listen to me."

He was sitting at the table, eating his supper and watching the CCTV monitors. He concentrated on his food and didn't bother to answer.

Louise's eyes flashed angrily. "Don't ignore me, Roy. You think you can control everyone . . . but you can't. George knows my name, she knows I was married to you and she's showing my picture around and one of Cill just before she went missing. Billy let her think I'm Cill by giving her the number of the last detective agency that came snooping, but the minute the Trevelyans see my photo, they'll tell her Priscilla Fletcher's Louise Burton. Then what are we going to do?"

He pushed his plate away and lit a cigarette before tilting his chair back and propping his feet on the table. "More to the point, what are *you* going to do, my darlin'? *I'm* not the one pretending to be someone else. Maybe I'll just wash my hands of you the way I should have done the day you took my son to bed." He blew a smoke ring into the air and watch it drift and expand toward the ceiling. "What say I throw you to the wolves, eh?"

She moved behind him to rest her cheek against his hair and link her wrists over his chest. "You'd never do it. Nick'd kill you first."

He stroked the soft down of her forearm. "Has he been hitting you again," he asked, squinting up at her bruised lip, "or was that for Billy's benefit?"

She smiled as she dropped a kiss on the top of his head. "Billy's putty in my hands when he's feeling sorry for me. I always got more money if he told Dad I was being done over."

Roy dropped his feet to the floor. "What are you up to?"

"Nothing."

He shook her off abruptly and stood up. "I should never have helped you get off the white stuff. You were halfway controllable when you were stoned, a sodding nuisance since you started thinking for yourself. I wouldn't mind so much if you didn't have sawdust for brains. You act before you think, Cill, that's always been your trouble." He moved away to put some distance between them.

"Don't call me that," she said irritably.

"You know I hate it."

Roy shrugged. "It's what you've been called for most of your life." He watched her expression sour. "You're carrying too many ghosts, darlin'. They come back to haunt you every time you feel sorry for yourself. You should have kept your clothes on and left the lad alone, then maybe I wouldn't have been so keen to let Nick take his turn in the queue."

She lifted her scarf to hide her mouth. It was an automatic gesture, learned from long experience of avoiding inquisitive eyes, but it was a waste of energy with someone who knew her as well as Roy. "Billy told me Mum's got religion," she said with a sudden little giggle, "and when he asked Dad why, Dad said she had things on her conscience. That's pretty funny, isn't it?"

Roy eyed her thoughtfully. "What else did Billy say?"

"That George knows about the rape and thinks you and me had a baby when we were in our teens." She flicked him a sly glance. "She's confused because she thinks I'm Cill — which makes the kid the product of rape, and you its daddy."

Roy's jaw tightened. "And?"

"I told Billy he was your son by one of

your tarts and I mothered him as best I could in the circumstances."

"What circumstances?"

"That he took after his dad," she said lightly. "A highly sexed, out-of-control teen with a habit, who couldn't keep his hands to himself and ended up in prison."

"My *God!*" he said with loathing. "You really *are* a bitch, aren't you?"

She raised an indifferent shoulder. "It's as near the truth as damn it."

Roy had a momentary understanding that he had never controlled her — *even when she was on her knees, begging for a hit* — but the idea was too radical to hold for long. "You're one sick bitch, Lou."

She let the comment go. "So what am I going to say to Billy? He'll come back, he always does."

Roy squeezed out the glowing tip of his cigarette and let it drop to the floor. "Not my problem," he said harshly. "You've brought this one on yourself. You should have left George to me, like I told you."

Louise wrapped her thin arms around herself. "Maybe I didn't want to," she said, with a catch in her voice. "Maybe I hoped she'd find out about Cill . . . maybe I can't live with ghosts as easily as you can, Roy."

He gave an angry laugh. "Don't do this,"

he warned. "It might work on your brother but it never worked on me. There's the phone." He jerked his chin toward a receiver on one of the worktops. "*Use* it. Call her. See how well the damaged-little-girl act works on a woman. Better still, call the cops. If you're lucky, they won't believe you —" He broke off as she leaned forward to stare at the monitor. "What's up?"

"You've got visitors," she said in a remarkably steady voice, all pretense at sympathy-seeking forgotten.

He followed her gaze and saw George and Jonathan talking to the barmaid. "Bloody hell!" he growled, as the girl lifted the trapdoor and gestured toward the kitchen. He manhandled Louise out of the door. "Upstairs and stay put till I tell you," he ordered, crushing her arm in an iron fist, "because I'm warning you . . . if Hughes catches even a glimpse of you, I'll drop you in it so fast your feet won't touch the ground."

Louise glanced at him scornfully as she placed her foot on the first step.

Chapter Seventeen

The Crown and Feathers,
Friar Road, Highdown
Wednesday, April 23, 2003, 7:35 p.m.

George had predicted that Roy would be affable, at least at the start, so his hostile demeanor when they entered the kitchen worried her. She wasn't much of a psychologist, she realized, as she glanced at the CCTV monitor showing the bar. Forewarned was forearmed, and a man like Roy would always favor attack as the best form of defense. As usual, the second monitor was dead, and, not for the first time, she wondered why he needed two. Jonathan reacted to the animosity immediately, jutting his jaw and clenching his fists at his sides, instinctively bracing himself for assault. It was reminiscent of their first meeting but this time there was no coerced apology from Roy to oil the water.

The man was facing the door, bottom propped on the table, a beer mug in his right hand which he was carelessly wiping with a tea towel. But he held it by its handle, as if polishing were not the aim of the exercise. He appeared very relaxed and, owing to where he'd stationed himself, George and Jonathan were unable to move out of the doorway into the room. They were too close together and it put them at a disadvantage, not least because it made them look comical.

Roy grinned. "Well, well, well . . . if it isn't the Odd Couple. What can I do for you?"

"We wanted a chat," said George lightly.

He stared at her for a moment, his expression unreadable. "It's not a good time. If you come back tomorrow morning, I'll see what I can do." He shifted his attention to Jonathan. "Not you, mate, you're barred." His eyes narrowed threateningly. "I don't like people who accuse me of lying, and I sure as hell don't want them in my pub."

"Jon never —" George began.

"Let him speak for himself," Roy cut in. "He's got a tongue, hasn't he? Or is he too scared to use it?"

Jonathan didn't say anything.

"That figures. I sussed you as a wimp the first time I saw you." He pushed himself upright and took a step forward. "End of conversation. Now sling your hook before I phone the cops and have you arrested for causing a nuisance."

George was the first to retreat. "Come on," she said, plucking at Jonathan's jacket. "He's within his rights, unfortunately. A licensee can exclude anyone he wants from his premises and he doesn't have to give a reason for doing it."

But for the first time in his life, Jonathan stood his ground. "Then I'll have to change his mind."

Roy dropped his right hand and took another step forward, holding the glass at his side. "And how are you planning to do that?"

"Not by fighting you," said Jonathan mildly, relaxing his clenched fists. "In the first place I'm not armed and in the second place it would give you an even better excuse to exclude me." He indicated the courtyard. "There's a black BMW parked in the road, registration number R848 OXR. It was there when I met George — I saw it when I left — and again in the evening when Andrew Spicer drove me back here to collect my wallet. Is it yours, Mr. Trent?"

"None of your business."

"Do you know what car he drives, George?"

She frowned, remembering a reference to a BMW but unable to recall why. "As far as I know, it's a van. He keeps it in a garage at the back."

"The ticket clerk at Branksome Station said the woman who went through my briefcase drove away in a black BMW. I think it's your ex-wife's car, Mr. Trent. She said she'd seen me here and knew who I was, and she was certainly here when my agent came for my wallet." He glanced toward the stairs. "Is she upstairs now? If so, we'd like to talk to her."

Roy raised his left palm and shoved it against Jonathan's chest. "Out!" he ordered. "Now! Go on! Piss off, the pair of you!"

Jonathan backed away immediately. "There's no need for violence, Mr. Trent." He raised his voice. "Tell Priscilla Fletcher we'll wait by her car till she comes out. We'd like to ask her about Cill Trevelyan's gang rape by Roy Trent, Colley Hurst and Micky Hopkinson."

"Keep your voice down," Roy snarled. "There's customers can hear you."

Jonathan ignored him. "We also want to

ask her about Grace Jefferies's murder," he called. "We know Roy Trent lived in the same road as Howard Stamp, and Louise Burton lived opposite Grace. We think Priscilla can tell us the connections. We're prepared to wait as long as it takes. She can't leave her car out there forever."

It was George who thwarted any attempt Roy might have made to shut Jonathan up. She used her briefcase to block his upswinging arm. "How *dare* you do that?" she squeaked, her face turning brilliant red. "You can't intimidate us the way you intimidated those defenseless children. What happened to Cill? What happened to Louise? How many other little girls did you rape?"

Roy might have reacted if his barmaid and one of his regulars hadn't appeared in the corridor behind Jonathan. They stood openmouthed, listening to what George was saying. "In the kitchen," he told George and Jonathan tersely. "And *you* —" he pointed to the girl — "back behind the bar. It's a private argument . . . none of your business."

But Tracey wasn't inclined to go that easily. "It didn't sound very private. Everyone could hear it. Should I phone the police?"

"No."

Tracey turned to George, her expression alight with curiosity. Perhaps she felt a sisterhood with the other woman after the remarks about "rape," or perhaps she didn't like her boss much. "What about you, love? Are you OK? Has someone been hurting you?"

George shook her head. "I'm all right for the moment, Tracey, but if there's anymore shouting, I believe you should call the police. We haven't come for a fight, but things get out of hand very quickly when people lose their tempers."

"That's for sure," said the girl with feeling. She took a last look at Roy and there was a hint of derision in her eyes, as if things had been said that struck chords with her. "I'll see you later then."

Roy gave an abrupt nod and shut the door on her, but it was a while before he said anything. He stood with head bowed, staring at the floor, and it was obvious to both George and Jonathan that he was working out what to do. Jonathan, buoyed up by success, wanted to seize the advantage, but George put a finger to her lips and persuaded him to stay quiet. Every so often, the boards creaked on the floor above, although whether from the natural contraction and expansion of wood or under the weight of an eavesdropper's stealthy footsteps it was impossible to tell.

When Roy finally spoke, it was without heat. "By rights, I should put a lawyer on to you," he said, looking up. "What you've done is slander me in front of my customers and staff. It's true that I was taken in for questioning about Cill Trevelyan's rape, along with Colley and Mick, but we denied it and there was no evidence to connect us with it. The girl who gave the information, Louise Burton, didn't know the names of the boys and didn't identify us —" he shrugged — "so the cops ended up questioning if a rape had even happened."

He moved away from the door and reached for his cigarette pack on the table. "I'm not going to say we weren't wild, because we were. Everyone despaired of us, including ourselves. We were never in school . . . couldn't read . . . always on the make." He bent his head to the lighter. "About the only thing that made life bearable was alcohol and, when we couldn't get it, we'd be thinking of more extreme ways to top ourselves. In that respect, we were no different from Howard." He fixed his attention on Jonathan. "You talked the other day about him having nowhere to go except inside himself. Well, we were no different. We did similar stuff . . . not to ourselves so much, though it happened —" he flexed his fingers — "Mick was the worst, always carving spirals on the back of his hands — but mostly we targeted other people." His mouth twisted cynically. "This isn't easy to say, and you probably don't want to hear it, but we felt good when someone else was hurting. It meant we weren't the only people living shit lives."

He fell into a brief silence while he took a drag on his cigarette. "We were awful to Howard," he said abruptly. "It went on for years . . . started when we were nippers and he was in his teens. He lived down the road from us and we were at him all the time. Mick used to prod him in the back with his knife . . . drew blood quite often till Howard got himself a leather jacket. It was too damn easy. He was such a miserable little wimp." Again he focused his attention on Jonathan. "I guess we hoped he'd fight back — show a bit of spirit — but he never did. Too much common sense, perhaps." His eyes hardened as if he were making the point for Jonathan. "Like George said earlier, things get out of hand when people lose their tempers, and

Howard was really scared of Mick's knife."

Jonathan leaned his hands on the back of a chair. "There were three of you and one of him," he said matter-of-factly. "What kind of odds were those?"

"Not good," Roy admitted, "which is why he showed sense by ducking and weaving. The trouble is, it made us worse. Most days he hid — either in his house or at his gran's — but we were always on the lookout for him. You both keep saying he didn't kill his gran. Well, he *did*. And the reason I know is because we wound him up for it. Mick was always on his back, jeering at him because he didn't have a weapon, and one day Howard pulls a sodding great carving knife and starts slashing at Colley. They said at the trial he went berserk and slashed his gran . . . well that's what he did with Colley. He was completely out of it . . . mad as a bloody hatter and so wild Mick and me couldn't get close. He cut Colley on the arm a couple of times before we legged it, and our next stop was the hospital. Far as I remember, Colley had twenty stitches, and he was still carrying the scars five years later."

He turned to George. "I'm not proud of it, which is why I didn't want you finding out. We were scared Howard was going to blame us for turning him into a raving lunatic, but the cops never came near us even though most of the street knew we'd been bullying him. The strange one was Wynne. She used to hiss at us every time she saw us, but she didn't say anything, not even at the trial. He flicked ash to the floor. "I've never understood why not. If they'd gone with diminished responsibility, he'd have been sent to Broadmoor and given some psychiatric help. Instead they banged him up in Dartmoor, where he was never going to make it."

George pulled out a chair and sat down, clearing a space for her case. "He pleaded not guilty," she said, flicking the catches, "therefore your treatment of him was irrelevant to his defense. You know that as well as I do, Roy. Rather more interesting is why the prosecution didn't quote this episode with the carving knife to strengthen their case." She took out her notepad. "Did Colley report it? What explanation did he give the hospital?"

"He said he'd been in a fight but didn't give any names."

"Why not?"

Roy shrugged. "We spent all our time avoiding the cops. No point getting involved if we didn't have to."

"When did it happen?"

"A month or two before Grace was murdered. I don't remember exactly."

Jonathan stirred. "How well did you know her?" he asked.

"Not at all."

"Then why call her Grace?"

There was a small hesitation. "Everyone did. It's how she was labeled in the newspapers."

"You said you couldn't read."

Irritation flickered briefly in the dark eyes. "So? It was the main topic of conversation in my dad's shop. He read every damn newspaper . . . told anyone who wanted to hear what the latest update was."

Jonathan reached over to flick back a page of George's notepad. "According to our information, you were estranged from your father. Your parents' marriage failed and you went to live in Colliton Way with your mother. Your father remarried and refused to have anything more to do with you." He looked up. "Presumably your stepmother had children of her own and didn't want an illiterate thug for a role model?"

Roy's jaw tightened. "What's the big deal? George always refers to her as Grace, and so do you in your book, Dr. Hughes." He smiled grimly. "And before you jump on me for that, I learned to read in a young offenders' institution when I was sixteen. I did twelve months for burglary . . . and it taught me a few things — mostly that prison was a mug's game."

Jonathan straightened and took out his own cigarettes. "The big deal is that I don't believe you, Mr. Trent," he said, flicking his lighter. "Howard going berserk with a knife a month before Grace was murdered is a little too convenient, don't you think? It's quite impressive if you managed to concoct it in the last few minutes, but it sounds more like a story you and your friends invented at the time."

"Why would we do that?"

"In case you were questioned."

Roy shook his head dismissively. "We wouldn't have been. We were never in the frame. Call me a liar as much as you like — it's water off a duck's back — but you're trying to prove a negative. Our patch was Colliton Way and the rundown buildings on the industrial estate at the back of it. We didn't know Grace from Adam, never went near her house and wouldn't have wanted to. It was when we strayed outside our boundaries that we got into trouble . . . sticking close to home meant we were left in peace. And that's how we liked it."

Jonathan stared him down. "The only reason you weren't in the frame was because Howard confessed. If he hadn't, you'd have been high on the list of suspects. The police had questioned the three of you only five days before about the rape of a missing girl who lived just two streets away from Grace. You matched the description given by that girl's best friend, Louise Burton, who lived *opposite* Grace. You were well acquainted with Howard Stamp, knew that he had a grandmother, knew that he took refuge in her house and knew that he bought goods for her at your father's shop. One of your gang, Micky Hopkinson, regularly carried a knife. Another, Colley Hurst, had red hair, as did Louise Burton, who was truanting regularly and was certainly associated with you."

"Then why couldn't she identify us?" Roy snapped.

"*Didn't,* is the word you're looking for, Mr. Trent. Why *didn't* she identify you?"

"Because it wasn't us."

George looked up from her note-taking. "It's easily proved, Roy. Her brother, William, witnessed the rape and, if you're agreeable, I'll show him a photograph of you and see what he says. Do you have any from when you were a teenager? Better still, do you have a group picture of yourself with Colley and Micky?"

This time the hesitation was a long one. "No," said Roy at last. "It's a period of my life that I'd rather forget." He crushed the butt of his cigarette into the ashtray and moved to look at the monitor. "Have you any idea how difficult it is to try to make something of yourself after the kind of childhood I had? You have to cut yourself off from everyone you know and start again. I've no idea where Colley and Mick are now . . . what happened to them . . . if they're still alive." He gave a grunt of amusement. "I don't think there *were* any pictures — you'd have to know someone with a camera to have your photo taken — and *we* didn't. Only the rich sods went in for that kind of crap."

It was an excuse that might have appealed to Jonathan — there was hardly any record of his childhood either — but George just laughed. "Oh, *please!* Spare us the violins. I bought a little Brownie in 1960 for about three and fourpence . . . which is under twenty pence in today's money. It was hardly a rich man's pastime. There must be some snaps of you. Anything from your late teens or early twenties would do. You wouldn't have changed much. What about a wedding photo?"

"The wife took them."

"Priscilla Fletcher?"

"First wife . . . mother of my kid."

George eyed him for a moment. "How many wives have you had?"

"Two," he said harshly. "Not that it's any of your business."

"What was the name of the first one?"

He didn't answer.

"Not my business?" she asked with a smile. "Well, you're probably right." She removed a digital camera from her case, then eased back her chair preparatory to standing up. "If you've no objections, I'll take a photograph of you now. There's a function on my computer that allows me to airbrush out the signs of aging, so I should be able to produce something that approximates to what you looked like in 1970."

Roy turned his back immediately. "Don't even think about it," he warned, "not if you want your camera intact when you leave."

"It's to your advantage," she pointed out mildly. "If you had nothing to do with the rape then William Burton will exonerate you." She placed the camera on the table in front of her and shuffled through her case. "Let me show you a photograph of Cill Trevelyan just before she went missing . . . see if that jogs your memory at all. She bears a striking resemblance to your second wife." George slid the copy across the table toward his rigid back and paused to see if he'd bite. "I also have one of Priscilla, taken by Jim Longhurst at a barbecue here." She lined the second picture up beside the first. "The ticket clerk confirmed that she was the dark-haired woman who went through Jonathan's briefcase at Branksome Station."

Roy lit another cigarette but wouldn't look at the photographs. "What's the point you're trying to make? That I married Cill Trevelyan?"

"Did you?"

He gave an angry laugh. "Of course I bloody didn't. The kid vanished. If the cops had done their job properly, they'd have put her father in the dock."

"He had an alibi," said Jonathan. "He was at work all night."

Roy half turned. "There was only his wife's word he didn't do it before he left. The cops didn't believe Mrs. Trevelyan anymore than anyone else did. She was protecting her husband."

Jonathan watched George scribble notes across a page. "Why would she want to?" he asked.

"Because she was just as guilty. She should have taken better care of the girl."

"In what way?"

"Kept her out of harm's way. That's what mothers are for."

It was a remark that begged a number of questions, thought Jonathan, recalling his own situation. How far was any mother responsible for her child's victimization — unless she was the abuser? What if she were being abused herself? Where did responsibility to others end and the drive for self-preservation take over? What was anyone's duty in life when terror was an all-consuming emotion? How far was Roy projecting his mother's neglect of him onto Mrs. Trevelyan? How far was he simply trying to divert attention from his own involvement?

"What harm are you talking about?" Jonathan asked bluntly. "The rape?"

"The beltings her father used to give her . . . that'll be how he killed her."

"Was it Cill who told you about them?"

Roy flicked him a withering glance.

"Couldn't have been, could it, as I never met her. It was in the newspapers, mate. It was given to me secondhand, like everything else, till a halfway decent screw decided I needed an education."

George intervened. "If David Trevelyan killed her, then when and how did he get rid of the body?" she asked matter-of-factly. "According to Miss Brett, he reported her missing as soon as he reached home on the Saturday morning, which means he had to kill her and bury her between the time she was sent home on the Friday afternoon and before he started his night shift. That's a tall order. The body would have to be deep enough — and far enough away from his house — to prevent it ever being found . . . or, if it *was*, to make it feasible that she'd been killed by an abductor."

Neither man said anything.

"The only Trevelyan who had all night was *Jean*," George went on slowly, "and a woman would have to be Myra Hindley to dispose of her daughter and appear normal afterward."

"It happens," said Roy.

"Except the psychology's wrong," George protested. "I should have thought this through before. Look —" she tapped her pencil on the newspaper clippings — "first Mrs. Trevelyan told the police that there were difficulties at home and that her husband had had a row with Cill, *then* she gave an interview to the press about her regret and anguish that they'd both been so strict with her." She turned a perplexed face to Jonathan. "But she'd have said the opposite if she knew the child was dead. She'd have stressed what a *good* relationship she and her husband had had with their daughter."

"Perhaps she was being clever."

"The kid was always in trouble with her dad, and everyone knew it," said Roy. "If her mum had pretended different, there'd've been even more eyebrows raised."

"A person would have to be psychopathic to work that out after a night's digging and no sleep," said George sarcastically. "Not to mention cleaning the house of every shred of evidence that a murder had been committed."

"All I know is what people said at the time," Roy countered stubbornly. "*He* killed the kid and *she* was protecting him. It forced them out in the end."

Chapter Eighteen

9 Galway Road, Boscombe, Bournemouth
Wednesday, April 23, 2003, 8:00 p.m.

Robert Burton picked up the receiver after a single ring and Billy pictured him in the cramped hallway of his bungalow, standing, waiting for the call to come, then pouncing on the telephone before it disturbed his wife. Billy had always had an easy, if distant, relationship with his father, but suspicion corroded trust and he didn't bother with pleasantries. "I want to talk to Mum," he said.

"She's not here."

"You said she'd be back by seven."

"She's on one of her parish visits. It's obviously taking longer than she expected." There was a ten-second hiatus as his hand muffled the receiver, but not before Billy had heard his mother's voice in the background. "Sorry, son, the cat was after the wire. Why don't I ask Mum to call you when she comes in?"

"No thanks," Billy responded curtly. "I'd rather you put her on now. I know she's there. I heard her."

"She doesn't want to talk to you."

"Then tell her I'll drive down tomorrow."

Another brief pause. "Why aren't you at work?" his father asked. "You know what I think about these twenty-four-hour strikes. You're letting the country down, expecting the army to cover for you while they're trying to fight a war in Iraq. It's unpatriotic, son."

Billy stared irritably at the wall. It was the sort of diversionary tactic his father always used. "Give it a rest, Dad, I'm not in the mood. I'm between shifts . . . back on days from Friday. Now, put Mum on, please. I really do need to talk to her."

"I'll try, but I don't think she'll come."

The receiver was placed beside the telephone and Billy heard his father walk into the sitting room. He couldn't make out what was being said because his parents spoke in whispers, but his mother's lighter tread returned. "Hello, dear," she said in her usual inexpressive tone. "Dad says you've found Louise again. How is she?"

"Hasn't Dad told you? I sent him an email."

"He said she was back to her old tricks." His mother sighed with what sounded like a genuine regret. "There's nothing to be done about it, Billy. I pray every day that she'll be given back to us but Jesus can only work miracles with people who have faith."

Billy wasn't interested in metaphysical solutions. "There's a woman asking questions about Grace Jefferies's murder," he said baldly. "According to her, Howard Stamp didn't do it, and I remember you lying to the police about knowing Mrs. Jefferies. You said you didn't know where she lived and had never talked to her . . . but you did and you had. So why did you lie, Mum?"

He expected her to deny it, or say she didn't remember, but she surprised him with honesty. "Because I was worried for the family," she said. "We were already connected with one scandal and I didn't want us dragged into another. You were so young you've forgotten how awful it was — everyone was terrified — we thought it was going to happen again until Howard Stamp was arrested."

Billy refused to be diverted from the lie. "You were worried even before the police came to the house," he said. "I was watching you. Your hands were shaking."

Eileen hesitated, as if debating the merits of truth. "I thought it was to do with Cill," she said after a moment. "I was afraid they'd found her body and the whole thing was going to become even more of a nightmare." She made a small noise that sounded like a laugh. "It was such a relief when they said Mrs. Jefferies was dead. I thought, oh, thank goodness, no one can say *we* had anything to do with that. It was a small lie, Billy, and I wasn't the only one," she went on. "No one admitted to knowing her. It was bad enough what happened, without being singled out for questioning. We all just wanted it to go away, and it did, of course, as soon as the wretched grandson confessed."

Billy stared at the wall again. "Why would you think Cill's body was in Mullin Street?"

More hesitation. "I didn't mean it to sound like that. I just meant I was afraid they'd found her body . . . not *where* it might be, just that it was somewhere. I'd been thinking about nothing else for days . . . when were they going to find the poor child's body? And with all those policemen around . . ." She petered into silence.

Billy wanted to believe her. Even at ten years old, it had been his first thought — that the police had come to Mullin Street because of Cill Trevelyan. "Cill and Lou used to go into Mrs. Jefferies's house to watch her telly. I know you knew that because I heard Mrs. Jefferies tell you."

Eileen didn't answer.

"Did you never think Cill might have gone there when she ran away? You should have told the police, Mum. So should Lou."

A tiny edge of malice entered his mother's voice. "And what do you think the Trevelyans' reaction would have been if I'd suggested Cill was involved in a murder? Jean was already screaming at me like a fishwife every time she saw me." She took a breath. "It's all very well criticizing, Billy, but I had two seconds to make up my mind and I'm still sure I did the right thing."

Perplexed, Billy rubbed his head. "I'm not saying she had anything to with the murder," he protested, "I'm just saying she might have gone there when she ran away."

"Well, if she did, it was nothing to do with us."

"Except everyone was trying to find her. Why didn't you or Lou say something when Lou was questioned about the rape?"

There was a catch in his mother's voice. "She wasn't asked, neither was I . . . and I don't understand why you're being so beastly to me —"

The receiver was taken by his father. "You're upsetting your mother, son. What's the point you're trying to make? Because if you're suggesting *she* had something to do with that bloody woman's death, you'll have me to deal with. Understood?"

Billy thought of his mother's long, red hair, which he used to fumble into loose plaits whenever she let him. It had been an intimacy they shared until she dyed it a deep auburn when they moved. After that he was never allowed so close again, and the intimacy was reserved for Louise, who, at the same time, became a brown-haired urchin called Daisy. Until now he'd forgotten how jealous he'd been. "Did she have anything to do with it, Dad?" he asked harshly. "Councillor Gardener said it was someone with ginger hair killed Mrs. Jefferies . . . and Ma sure as hell had ginger hair before you made us cut and run from Mullin Street. So did Louise. You called them 'the terrible twins.' Remember?"

The line went dead immediately.

The Crown and Feathers,
Highdown, Bournemouth
Wednesday, April 23, 2003, 8:15 p.m.

George was intensely skeptical. "That would mean three people were all suspected of murder in the same place, at the same time —" she ticked them off on her fingers — "Howard Stamp, David Trevelyan and Jean Trevelyan — and with *two* different victims. Don't you think that's a trifle unlikely, Roy? It's not as though murder's a common crime in this country. Manslaughter, maybe, but not *murder.* There wouldn't have been more than three to four hundred during 1970, and to have two of them happen a couple of streets apart and within days of each other is a statistical improbability."

"Unless they were connected," said Jonathan.

"We don't even know if Cill's dead," George pointed out, leveling the tip of her pencil at the photograph of Priscilla Fletcher. "*That* might be her."

Jonathan watched Roy's gaze stray toward the picture. "Is it, Mr. Trent?"

"No."

"Do you mind telling us who she is?"

The other man shrugged. He was

growing more relaxed as each minute passed, and Jonathan wondered why. *Because they'd strayed from Howard Stamp?* "She was calling herself Priscilla Curtis when I wed her."

"Then how can you be so certain she wasn't Cill Trevelyan? She looks just like her." He watched for a reaction, but Roy's expression remained deadpan. "You can't have it both ways, Mr. Trent," he went on. "If you never met Cill, then you have no way of knowing if she *was* the woman you married."

Roy stared at George's busily writing hand. "You're on the wrong track, mate," he said, allowing irritation into his voice. "I don't deny I was caught up in a bad crowd when I was a lad, but I wasn't involved in murder and I don't know what happened to Cill Trevelyan —" he jabbed a finger at the tabletop to reinforce his next sentence — "and *neither* does my ex. Now you can take my word for that or you can go to the cops and run this crap past them, because I've had enough. I may not have told George precisely how I knew Howard — I wasn't proud of teasing the poor little bugger — but everything else I've said is true." He stood up and moved toward the door in clear dismissal. "Take it or leave it, because this conversation ends now."

Jonathan exchanged a glance with George. "Then you won't object if we ask Priscilla to corroborate this," she said to Roy.

He eyed her with some amusement. "Go ahead, but you'll have to find her first." He nodded at the monitor. "I watched her sneak out about ten minutes ago."

George frowned at the screen. "Why does that please you?" she asked. "I'd be mad as a hatter if the only person who could prove I was telling the truth left me in the lurch."

"She'll back me up when you find her."

"Depending on how well you prime her," said George sarcastically. She shook her head. "You haven't done much of a job so far, Roy. She seems to drop you in it more often than she helps you out. I presume it wasn't your idea to steal Jonathan's wallet . . . you didn't need to, you'd already seen him off. So why did she do it?"

"You're plucking at straws," he said dismissively. "There was no crime committed. Your friend got everything back intact."

George made an abrupt decision. "I think we'll go with your second option and take what we've got to Sergeant Lovatt," she said, gathering her bits and pieces together and cramming them into her case. "Neither Jon nor I believes that Cill Trevelyan's disappearance and Grace Jefferies's murder weren't connected, and if the sergeant suspects that Priscilla's Cill, then he'll certainly want to talk to her . . . and to you."

Roy opened the kitchen door and stood back. "Feel free," he told her, "but you'll be making idiots of yourselves. You've got nothing at all if Priscilla can prove she wasn't Cill — which she can — and the cops won't resurrect Howard just so you can make money out of a book. They had him bang to rights at the time, and everyone knows it —" his lip curled — "except you two."

Jonathan took the case and gestured to George to precede him. "I'm sure they said the same about James Watson and Francis Crick," he murmured, "and look how right they proved to be. The discovery of the double helix was a conceptual step, but Watson and Crick were the only two who believed it at the beginning."

The other man's jaw jutted aggressively. "You should learn to speak English, mate. I don't know what you're talking about."

Jonathan halted in front of him. "Of course you don't, but that's not my problem — *mate* — it's yours. You're an ignorant sociopath."

Roy made a grab at his arm but Jonathan was ready for it. He wrapped his fist around Roy's in a surprisingly gentle gesture and pushed it away. "I'm talking about the three-dimensional structure of the DNA molecule, Mr. Trent. If the police haven't destroyed all the evidence from Grace's murder, then it may be Watson and Crick's discovery that sends you to prison."

George tut-tutted severely as she wedged herself behind the steering wheel. "You're lucky he didn't hit you."

Jonathan grinned. "He was afraid you were going to scratch his eyes out."

She smiled automatically, but her mood had turned to despondency. "So what do we do now? He's right about the police, you know. It wouldn't be fair to waste Fred Lovatt's time with this. We haven't anything concrete — it's all just speculation. We don't even know who Priscilla Fletcher is, let alone if she was in Highdown in 1970. She might have grown up in Sydney for all we know."

"She speaks with a Dorset accent."

"That's not proof of anything."

Jonathan was on top of the world, buoyed up by adrenaline, so her sudden depression took him by surprise. "What's up?"

"We're no further forward than we were an hour ago."

"Did you expect to be?"

"Yes," she said wearily, leaning her elbows on the wheel, perversely worn out by the excitement. "What was the point of doing it otherwise?"

To triumph over a phobia, thought Jonathan, wondering if that was his single, most powerful reason for doing anything. He felt better than he had for months and he couldn't understand why George was being so negative.

"I can't see how we move on," she continued. "I suppose we can corner Priscilla Fletcher but even if she agrees to speak to us, it won't get us anywhere. All she has to do is tell us her name was Mary Smith and we won't be able to prove any different. We haven't the authority to insist on a birth certificate."

"What about her husband? He must know as much of her history as Roy does."

George gave an impatient sigh. "And how do we approach him? If we go knocking on the door, it'll certainly be

Priscilla who answers, and she'll slam it in our faces. I don't know anything about him, except that he's some sort of bookie, and even that's a bit doubtful." She nodded toward the pub door. "My source was Tracey and she had it second-hand off Jim Longhurst. I don't even know the man's Christian name."

"Well, we can't do anything tonight," said Jonathan firmly, consulting his watch, "so let's just sleep on it. I need to be at the station by nine, otherwise I won't be home till after one-thirty. If you can drop me at Branksome, I'll take a taxi into town."

George wouldn't hear of it. "Don't be ridiculous," she said, starting the engine and pulling away from the kerb. "Andrew would be furious if you spent borrowed money on a cab. I'm sure he meant you to buy food with it."

"Probably."

"Then buy a sandwich on the train and start taking care of yourself."

He wasn't listening. "What about William Burton?" he suggested. "I'd say he's worth another shot, particularly if we can persuade him to come to the police station with us and name the boys who raped Cill. Lovatt can hardly ignore that, not if we show him your two photos. He's bound to interview Priscilla Fletcher in those circumstances . . . Roy, too, if he's one of the three that Burton accuses."

George cheered up immediately. "Do you think he'll do it?"

"I don't know," said Jonathan, "but it has got to be worth a try." His mind worked through the possibilities. "We also need to find the Trevelyans. If they didn't have anything to do with Cill's disappearance, then they'll be ahead of us in the queue, piling on the pressure. I need to listen to the tape because I'm guessing Roy told us a lot more than you think he did — it's just a question of isolating what's important."

"Did you get it all?"

"I hope so." He took a recorder from his pocket and pressed "rewind," letting it run for five seconds before touching "play." Roy's jeering tones broke into the silence inside the car. ". . . *You'll be making idiots of yourselves. You've got nothing at all if Priscilla can prove she wasn't Cill* . . ." Jonathan cut the voice short. "That's the first thing that needs sleeping on," he murmured.

"You think he's lying?"

"No," said Jonathan regretfully.

George was promptly downcast again. "That's what I thought when he said it."

"So?"

"There's no point looking for Cill's parents."

"Wrong," said Jonathan affectionately. "It makes it even more important. How would you feel if someone was masquerading as your daughter? You'd want to know *why*, wouldn't you?"

George glanced at him in surprise. "Is that what she's doing?"

"It's as plausible as my transference theory. One's conscious, the other's unconscious . . . I guess it depends whether you think the lights are on and no one's at home or if there's method in her madness."

George was doubtful. "What's the point?"

"Of a masquerade? Perhaps she's doing an Anna Anderson — reemerging as the Grand Duchess Anastasia in order to lay claim to the Romanov fortune. Cill was an only child, don't forget, so there might be some money to be made out of it."

"Priscilla lives on Sandbanks," protested George. "Her husband must be rolling in it."

Jonathan shrugged. "Perhaps Fletcher doesn't own the house . . . perhaps he insisted on a prenuptial agreement."

"Yes, but . . . it's *absurd,*" she said forcefully. "Even if the Trevelyans managed to buy a house in the West Country, it'll be worth a pittance. They were living in council accommodation when they were in Lacey Street, so the best they could have done was make an exchange, then buy whatever property they ended up in . . . and council property's never that valuable."

"It'll still be worth something."

"Then why isn't she calling herself Cill Trevelyan? Why hasn't she made herself known to the parents? It's the most far-fetched theory I've ever heard," she finished indignantly.

"OK, OK," said Jonathan with a small laugh. "It was just an idea. The only other theory I've come up with is coincidence — that a woman called Priscilla looks just like a Priscilla who went missing and happened to marry her rapist, Roy Trent — but that seems equally far-fetched. And you know how much I hate coincidences."

George concentrated on her driving for several minutes. "Anna Anderson led a comfortable life," she said, breaking her silence. "I saw a documentary on her a while back and there were a number of people who believed she was Anastasia. She lived on their charity for years, then ended up marrying a rich American who treated her like royalty."

"She was a fraud," said Jonathan. "They used DNA samples to prove she was a Polish factory worker."

"That wouldn't worry her . . . not once she was dead. It's living like a princess while you're *alive* that's important." There was a gleam in her eye. "Put it this way, if she was Anastasia, then she was robbed of her inheritance, but if she was a Polish factory worker, then she did extremely well out of the deception. But it wasn't the Romanov *family* who kept her in clover — they refused to recognize her — it was the people she *conned* . . ."

From: Dr. Jonathan Hughes [jon.hughes@london.ac.uk]
Sent: Thurs. 5/1/03 11:16
To: geo.gar@mullinst.co.uk
Cc: Andrew Spicer
Subject: Roy Trent

Dear George,

Herewith some thoughts re: the tape. As agreed, I have conferred with a psychologist colleague and we have divided Trent's statements into four categories.

Category 1 (statements that we both believe to be true)

1. The gang bullied Howard with a knife.
2. Howard subsequently acquired a knife and went berserk.
3. The gang experienced similar suicidal thoughts to Howard's.
4. Their stamping ground was Colliton Way.

5. They got into trouble when they left it.
6. Trent detested prison and did not want a repeat.
7. He regrets his behavior.
8. Priscilla Fletcher is not Cill Trevelyan.

Category 2 (statements that we are undecided about)

1. Trent and his gang did not know Grace.
2. David Trevelyan killed his daughter.
3. Jean Trevelyan told lies to protect him.

Category 3 (statements that may not be true but that Trent himself believes)

1. Howard killed Grace Jefferies.
2. He did so as a direct result of being bullied by Trent, Hurst and Hopkinson.
3. Wynne Stamp could have helped her son's defense by citing the gang.

Category 4 (statements that we both believe to be false)

1. Trent did not know Cill Trevelyan — *he did.*
2. Louise Burton did not know the names of the rapists — *she did.*
3. She did not identify them because they weren't involved — *they were.*
4. Trent has not seen Hurst or Hopkinson since they were youngsters — *he has.*
5. His ex-wife knows nothing about Cill's disappearance or Grace's murder — *she does.*

I should stress that *our conclusions may be wrong* — deciphering content and tone of voice is not an exact science by any stretch of the imagination (!) — nevertheless, Trent's responses were interesting. My colleague was impressed by the way he dealt with questions about himself, his gang and Howard Stamp, less impressed by his answers about Cill Trevelyan. As you will see from Category 4 above, most of the "lies" are associated with Cill and the rape.

Despite this, my colleague made the point that Trent was prepared for questions about Cill, viz. his calm response after you and I accused him of it. “It’s true that I was taken in for questioning . . .” etc. This suggests he knew we’d found out about it. Yet only two people were aware of that — William Burton and Miss Brett. It is highly unlikely that Miss Brett reported the fact to Roy Trent or anyone who knew him, but quite probable that William Burton passed it on, either directly to Trent or to Priscilla Fletcher.

Had our accusation come out of the blue, my colleague believes Trent would have postured and protested rather more strongly while he tried to collect his thoughts. In addition, he employed some fairly aggressive diversionary tactics at the beginning in order to prevent us asking anything at all. Since he seemed fairly comfortable talking about Howard, it was questions about Cill Trevelyan and/or Priscilla Fletcher that he wanted to avoid.

Of particular notice is that he shifts the conversation very quickly to Howard — where he feels on stronger ground — and only becomes comfortable talking about Cill when he knows Priscilla Fletcher has left the building. In light of what's on the tape and also Trent's attempts to keep you away from the Cill Trevelyan story, it seems reasonable to make the following assumptions:

1. William Burton repeated details of your conversation with him.
2. Priscilla Fletcher knew Cill Trevelyan well enough to copy her look.
3. Trent does not want us to talk to Priscilla.

I am left with the conviction that Trent was not involved in any way with Grace's murder — and genuinely believes that Howard was guilty. However, I have an equal conviction that he (a) raped Cill; and (b) knows what happened to her. If those conclusions are right, then Priscilla Fletcher was party to the crime(s), and my best guess at the moment — whatever Miss Brett may have said to the contrary — is that Priscilla Fletcher is Louise Burton, that William Burton knows it and that he almost certainly alerted his sister to your interest in the story.

Where that leaves us on Howard, I don't know. I won't abandon his "miscarriage of justice" lightly, but I am concerned about the "slashing and stabbing" incident described by Trent. When I wrote Howard's chapter in *Disordered Minds*, there was nothing to suggest a history of "manic" behavior against others. But if the episode happened — and we find proof of it through hospital records/Hurst/Hopkinson and/or their families/neighbors — then we will have to *rethink*. It indicates that Howard had a breaking point, was ready to ignore injury to himself and had a knife. You can't blame him — he had a miserable existence — but it makes our job harder.

For the moment I suggest we concentrate on bearding William Burton in his den and attempt through him to gain access to Priscilla Fletcher. I'm afraid it may turn out that the two stories are unconnected, as the police decided at the time, but we need to establish this for our own satisfaction.

Best wishes, Jon

P.S. Am sending a copy of the tape by snail mail.

From: George Gardener [geo.gar@mullinst.co.uk]
Sent: Sun. 5/4/03 14:29
To: jon.hughes@london.ac.uk
Cc: Andrew Spicer
Subject: Conclusions

Oh dear! Snail mail delivered, and I do rather agree with you. It's so disappointing. I set such high hopes on Louise Burton or Colley Hurst and it's wretched to have them dashed. If you remember, I was depressed on the way to the station because, even while Roy was speaking, I thought what he said about Howard and his gang sounded like the truth. I was especially struck by Roy's references to "suicidal tendencies" and "shit lives," both of which are well documented in literature about alienated youth.

I shall email some possible dates tomorrow, but at the moment I'm questioning the sense of wasting anymore time on Cill or Louise. I fear it's what you said at the beginning — coincidences are seductive — and if the police didn't make a link in 1970, then it's doubtful there was one.

Best, George

P.S. What happened with Emma's father?

From: Andrew Spicer [Andrew@spicerandhardy.co.uk]
Sent: Mon. 5/5/03 10:46
To: jon.hughes@london.ac.uk; geo.gar@mullinst.co.uk
Subject: Earning advances

Dear both,

I am in the middle of negotiating a delicate — but healthy — deal which is based on a presumption of Howard Stamp's innocence. While I have listened to a copy of the tape and also been mildly entertained by your hand-wringing emails on the subject of whether or not Roy Trent was telling the truth about his revoltingly unpleasant behavior as an adolescent, may I remind you that the object of the exercise is to make him tell you *everything* he remembers about the Stamp family.

Personally, I couldn't give a monkey's toss how suicidal he felt in his teens. If it's of any interest to you, I experienced feelings at fourteen when I contemplated my preordained fate of gaining huge amounts of weight like my mother, failing to score with attractive women like my father, then taking on the family firm in order to deal with authors who *keep* changing their minds.

Despite these miserably unappealing prospects, I did *not* go out and rape a 13-yr-old because I enjoyed watching people hurt; *nor* did I provoke a sad young man with a harelip and learning difficulties into producing a knife because my psychopathic friend had sliced his back whenever he felt like it. Should I now be worrying about you, Jon, because you stood up to Trent and called him a sociopath? Was that a "manic" incident? And what about your "berserk" episode on Bournemouth Station? Does this mean none of us is safe anymore?

You know Howard had a knife because he was a self-mutilator, and there was no point going against Trent and his gang without it. Give the poor chap credit for finding some courage at last, instead of assuming that one desperate attempt at gaining self-esteem led to an automatic downward spiral of murderous behavior. In your shoes, I'd be looking for evidence that his confidence improved in the wake of the incident. Find Wynne. Talk to her. Ask her why Howard agreed to go job-hunting on the Monday and Tuesday before Grace was found. Whose idea was that? Hers or his?

Meanwhile, go back to George's neighbor's testimony which states that Howard could not have committed the murder on the Wednesday because he did not arrive at Grace's house until 2:00 p.m. Then reread Jon's chapter on Howard where the defense pathologist argued that the murder happened on the Monday while the above job search was happening. If the knife-wielding episode worries you so much, then concentrate on *opportunity*. How and when could Howard have done it?

I hate to be a Victorian parent, but get *real,* for God's sake! Anthropologists who invite pretentious colleagues to listen to a tape over a cup of tea and councillors with politically correct leanings are persuadable enough to make me weep. Of course Roy Trent was convincing. He's had years of practice . . . he even persuaded one of his victims to marry him, if Jon's theory about P. Fletcher being Louise Burton is correct. *Plus* he's managed to keep George at arm's length from this story ever since he met her, by allowing her free access to his pub for "surgeries" in order to woo voters.

Next time you see him ask him how the Crown and Feathers survives without customers. Who owns it? Where's the money coming from? These are the interesting questions, and if either of you had ever run a business, you'd know it. You were a tax inspector, George. Trent's finances should be grist to your mill. The man's a crook, so of course he doesn't want to go back to prison. Name me one who does!

Best,

Andrew Spicer

P.S. OK, pal, give us the dirt. What *did* happen with Emma's father?

From: Dr. Jonathan Hughes [jon.hughes@london.ac.uk]
Sent: Thurs. 5/8/03 14:33
To: geo.gar@mullinst.co.uk; Andrew@spicerandhardy.co.uk
Subject: Emma's father

The bastard called me an asylum seeker, punched me in the gut and manhandled me out the door. And yes — *pal* — much as I hate to admit it, you're right! One swallow doesn't make a summer, so unless Howard had better luck than I did the next time he stood up to someone, he probably went back to carving his initials on his arm. *However,* the odds are high that the "next time" was Grace, and the poor little sod lost it when she didn't run away. My pretentious colleague says there's no going back after the first cut, unless you're clearheaded enough to realize what you're doing . . . and that's well-nigh impossible when there's a red mist in front of your eyes. 99% of murders are committd in anger, and the reason the cases are tried as murder, not manslaughter, is because the culprits try to cover their tracks afterward. Be warned! If Jenny or Greg test your patience too far, and you bop one or other of them on the head with a crowbar, phone the police immediately and plead provocation. You may get five years if the judge recognizes what a saint you've been toward a couple of shysters . . . but you won't get life.

Nevertheless, I have taken on board your Victorian strictures. You always were a bully, Andrew. I think it comes from being small and fat . . . although galloping baldness clearly isn't helping. The real mystery is why you have so much self-esteem. Considering what you look like, and the fact that beautiful women ignore you, it *ought* to be zero. J.

P.S. To avoid further emails on the subject of my love life, Emma wasn't there and I haven't heard from her. According to her mother, who followed me out, she is getting married on August 9 to a white Anglo-Saxon Protestant with a double-barreled name. I have written to congratulate her.

Chapter Nineteen

9 Galway Road, Boscombe, Bournemouth
Saturday, May 10, 2003, 9:00 p.m.

Rachel Burton moved the cursor to "send," then hovered her finger over the mouse. "Are you sure about this, sweetheart?" she asked her husband, looking up from the monitor. "Once it's gone there's no bringing it back."

Billy rested a hand on her shoulder and leaned forward to stare at the message on the screen. "It's not my choice. It's what you think that matters." He sighed despondently. "I just wish to God that stupid Gardener woman had done something, instead of making us do the dirty work."

"OK, then we send it." Rachel pressed the mouse button and watched the email vanish. "I'd rather have a husband with a clear conscience than a galloping insomniac, and if you change your mind, you don't have to give them her address." She reached up to squeeze his hand. "Look, it may not be as bad as you think. Louise could be squeaky clean . . . your mother's conscience might only be troubled by a few white lies. Blame your parents for refusing to talk to you . . . blame me and the twins for forcing you into it."

He dropped a kiss on the top of her head. It hadn't taken much forcing once he came clean about what was worrying him, because her attitude was the same as his. Neither of them was confident that George Gardener would let the issue of Priscilla Fletcher drop, and if there were skeletons in the Burton closet, then it was better to open the door themselves than wait for a stranger to do it. They wouldn't have a leg to stand on if the press arrived on their doorstep demanding to know why Billy had failed to recognize his sister, was Rachel's argument, so the best solution was to make Louise tell her story herself.

"And how do we do that?" Billy had asked gloomily. "She's never 'fessed up to a damn thing in her life."

"Tell the detective agency where she is," suggested Rachel. "You've got their card. Persuade *them* to ask the questions. That way, the police won't be involved . . . or not immediately."

"She'll lie."

"At least they might find out why she's pretending to be Cill."

"How's it going to help us if they don't report back?" Billy said. "We'll be just as much in the dark as we are now."

Rachel had a more positive character than her husband. "Then we need to find a way of making them." She stroked his face. "You can't go on like this, love. Right's right and wrong's wrong, and you'll have a breakdown if you don't do something pretty damn quick. You were ten years old. Whatever happened wasn't your fault."

"Perhaps it wasn't Louise's either. Perhaps that's why she went the way she did."

"Then the truth won't hurt her," said Rachel, with a minimum of sympathy. Her own knowledge of Louise was confined to a brief period at school when the older girl had singled her out for spiteful attention. Chubby, freckle-faced, copper-haired, and very unsure of herself, Rachel Jennings had been teased mercilessly by dark-haired Daisy Burton who reveled in calling her a "fat gingerbread freak." Her hatred for Daisy had made her avoid Billy for years, and it wasn't until he admitted that his sister's name was Louise, that she was a redhead herself, and, better still, had probably died of a drug overdose, that Rachel had discovered the eternal truth — siblings are rarely alike.

Nevertheless, it was no surprise when Billy explained his preoccupation of the last few weeks on Louise's resurfacing. Rachel had always feared it would happen one day. She'd asked him why he hadn't told her that he'd recognized the photograph Councillor Gardener had shown him, and he'd answered, "Because I hoped I was wrong. Nothing good ever came from Louise. She's been easier to live with since I thought she was dead. At least that way, I could feel sadness for her."

From: wandr.burton@compuline.com
Sent: Sat. 5/10/03 21:10
To: info@WCHinvestigations.com
Subject: Cill Trevelyan

Dear Sir,

I am Louise Burton's brother. One of your detectives came looking for her three years ago and gave me your card. It was in connection with Mr. and Mrs. Trevelyan's search for their daughter, Cill. I can supply you with Louise's name and address. However, I have only recently found her again and am concerned about her welfare. If you decide to talk to her, then I would appreciate a follow-up meeting with you afterward in return for me telling you where she is. I am finding it difficult to speak to her and hope you will have more success, but I would need some guarantees before I release the information. It might be of interest to you to know that she is calling herself Priscilla and styling herself to look like

Cill Trevelyan. I understand that all dealings are confidential.

I wait to hear from you.

Yours sincerely

William Burton

Peckham, London
Saturday, May 10, 2003, 9:30 p.m.

When his doorbell rang, Andrew looked up from the manuscript he was reading with a frown of irritation. Off the top of his head, he couldn't think of a single acquaintance who would be so crass as to visit unannounced at nine thirty on a Saturday evening. As his daughters were asleep upstairs, he didn't immediately leap to the idea that it was the police, but waited to see if the bell rang again. When it did, he rose reluctantly from his seat.

One of the downsides of living in a poky mews cottage, where every window faced forward and table lamps threw his shadow against the curtains, was that whoever was at his door certainly knew he was there, and he was too courteous a man to pretend otherwise. But he wasn't pleased about it. He was wearing scruffy corduroy trousers and an old denim shirt with soup stains down the front, and he had a sinking feeling that he was going to find Jenny and Greg outside, dressed to the nines for a party and hiding their smiles at his sad old man's appearance.

He slipped the Yale latch and opened the door, and if he hadn't recognized his visitor immediately as the woman he'd seen at the Crown and Feathers, he would certainly have known her from George's photograph. Priscilla Fletcher. He was quick-witted enough to see that he had two choices — to acknowledge her or pretend ignorance — and he rapidly assessed the advantages of each while hiding his astonishment behind a polite smile. "Can I help you?"

"Do you know who I am?" she asked bluntly.

Andrew prevaricated. "I believe so. You're Jonathan Hughes's mystery woman. I saw you at Roy Trent's pub in February."

Close to, she looked nothing like the black-and-white snapshot of plump, unlined Cill Trevelyan. Her face was thin and drawn, with signs of aging around her eyes, and Andrew was surprised at how dyed her hair looked. She reminded him more of an anorexic Wallis Simpson playing at being queen to a vacillating Edward VIII than she did of a vibrant thirteen-year-old on the threshold of life.

"Do you know my name?"

Andrew chose to play it straight. "It depends which one you're answering to," he said dryly. "Priscilla Fletcher . . . Cill Trent . . . possibly Daisy Burton or Louise

Burton? Which do you prefer?"

"Louise," she said. "I never really got used to the others." She jerked her chin toward the room behind him. "Are you going to let me in?"

He examined her face for a moment, then pulled the door wide. "As long as you're not planning to steal my wallet. I'm even poorer than Jonathan, so it won't do you any good."

"I didn't steal it," she said, walking past him. "I borrowed it for an hour to see what I could find out about him." She looked critically about the small, open-plan room that had a kitchen at one end, stairs rising out of the middle and a couple of armchairs and a coffee table at the other. "It's not much of a place, is it? I guess being an agent doesn't pay."

Andrew closed the door. "Who told you where I lived?"

She drew some business cards from her pocket and handed them to him. "These were in your friend's wallet. Yours has your home address written on the back of it."

Andrew flicked through the cards, most of which carried New York zip codes, until he came to his, dog-eared, at the bottom. He could even remember the fit of loneliness, shortly after he moved, that had prompted him to jot the number and street in Peckham on the back of it. He'd spun the card across a restaurant table at Jonathan and asked him to drop by one evening when he had nothing better to do. He never had. "Did you take anything else?"

"No. It was Hughes's address I wanted, but he didn't have any cards of his own." She glanced toward the stairs as if wondering if there was anyone else in the house. "He's a bit of a weird bastard, isn't he? His eyes were rolling the whole time I was talking to him . . . I thought he was a junkie."

"He was ill."

She wasn't interested enough to pursue it. "Do you mind if I sit down?"

"Be my guest."

She took off her jacket and dropped into one of the armchairs. "How about offering me a drink?"

He opened a kitchen cupboard and took out some wineglasses. "Red or white? I've a halfway decent Margaux or an excellent Pouilly-Fumé."

"What about vodka?"

"Wine's my limit, I'm afraid."

"Jesus!" she grumbled. "It's not much of a life, is it? I thought people made a fortune out of books." She eyed the two bottles that he held up for her. “OK, give me some of the red.” She watched him cut the foil from the neck and insert the corkscrew. “Aren’t you going to ask me why I’m here?”

“Do I need to?” he murmured, sniffing the cork to make sure it wasn’t tainted. “Aren’t you going to tell me anyway?”

She scowled at what she clearly thought was a piece of effete snobbery. “Not if you’re gonna act like a ponce.”

He poured some wine into one of the glasses and held it briefly to his nose before filling them both. “This isn’t a particularly expensive Margaux,” he said mildly, “but it still costs around twenty pounds a bottle.” He took the glasses in one hand and the bottle in the other and brought them to the coffee table. “How much is vodka these days?”

“Twelve . . . fifteen quid, but you’d have to be an alky to drink that much every night.”

“Mm. Well, corked wine’s about as disgusting as drinking sour milk,” said Andrew, handing her a glass and lowering himself into the other chair. He raised his glass to her. “Cheers.”

She took a tentative sip. “I guess it’ll do,” she said churlishly. “I prefer vodka and lime, though. Are you going to let me smoke?"

"Do I have a choice?"

She gave an abrupt laugh. "Not if you want to hear what I came to say."

Andrew rose to his feet again and fetched an ashtray from one of the cupboards. "Feel free," he said, handing it to her. "I'll open the window." He pulled the curtains back and unlatched one of the panes, glad of the excuse to make his affairs public. He didn't think she was going to pull a knife on him, but at the back of his mind was what happened to Grace.

"You're a strange bloke," she said, lighting up. "Don't you ever say no?"

He resumed his seat. It wasn't a question he'd ever been asked before and he was surprised by its perspicuity. "Not often," he admitted. "I turn down manuscripts fairly regularly, but those are business decisions."

"So what are you? A soft touch . . . a bit lonely?" Her gaze traveled about the room again and came to rest on the soup stains on his shirt. "You're not married, that's for sure. Are you gay?"

Andrew shook his head. "Heterosexual and divorced. My two daughters are in bed upstairs."

She glanced toward the ceiling. "How old?"

"Old enough to phone the police if I raise my voice," he said good-humoredly. "Young enough to stay asleep if this encounter remains peaceful and legal."

She gave a small laugh. "What do you think I am?"

He tilted his glass to the light and gently turned it, watching the Margaux run legs down the curved inside. "I don't know, Louise. I'm waiting for you to tell me. Your old headmistress, Miss Brett, says you're a liar . . . Jonathan Hughes says you're a thief . . . and both he and George Gardener think you witnessed Grace Jefferies's murder." He watched her for a moment before savoring a mouthful of wine. "Does anyone have anything good to say about you?"

He expected her to take offense, but she didn't. "I doubt it. I've been a fuckup most of my life. What did Billy say?"

Billy. "Is that your brother?"

Louise nodded.

"Nothing much," said Andrew, recalling George's transcript. "I believe he said you were married and your family thought you were in Australia. But he didn't recognize your photograph . . . or claimed he didn't."

She drained her glass at one swallow and put it on the coffee table, leaning forward to stare at the floor. "He's OK, is Billy, except he only sees what he wants to see . . . wouldn't notice a fucking elephant if it sat on his bed unless it flattened him in the process." She dedicated herself to smoking her cigarette.

Strange expression, thought Andrew, reaching for the bottle and topping her up again. She didn't seem to notice.

"I hated that bitch," she said suddenly. "She was always hauling Cill in for a lecture, but it never amounted to much — everyone knew she liked her. It was me she dumped on. People think an upfront punishment's a bad thing, but it's the drip-drip stuff that's worse. She'd tell Cill she was too bright to hang around with the likes of me . . . then tell me I was thick as pig shit and only good for bringing other kids down. It wasn't true. Cill was a maniac — stubbed a cigarette out on my arm once when I told her to get stuffed."

Andrew guessed the "bitch" was Miss Brett. "What did Miss Brett say to you after the fight?"

"The usual," she said cynically. " 'You're a nasty piece of work, Louise Burton, and one day you'll get your comeuppance. You provoked that fight deliberately to get Cill into trouble.' Bloody old cow! I'm sure she was a dyke."

"Was she right? Did you provoke it?"

Louise looked up, a gleam of amusement lighting her eyes. "What do you think?"

"Yes."

She gave an indifferent shrug. "It served Cill right. I took so much shit off her about the rape — why hadn't I jumped them? . . . why hadn't I screamed? . . . why didn't Billy do something? . . . why did I keep telling her to forget it?" Her small, glittering eyes held Andrew's for a moment before sliding away. "It wasn't even that bad . . . three puny fourteen-year-olds who couldn't keep it up for five seconds. OK, she had a bit of a kicking, but that was all." Louise jammed her cigarette into the ashtray and immediately lit another one. "She was shit-scared she was pregnant but even that was a no-no. She had a period ten days later and rammed it down my throat because she knew she was in the clear." She lapsed into silence, revisiting memories.

"What happened to her?"

There was barely a pause for reflection. "Her dad thrashed her for the fight, so she hid out with Grace." She smiled sourly at his expression. "That's what you wanted to hear, isn't it? It's where we went when we couldn't think of anything better to do. Grace let us watch telly all day as long as we could show her some bruises."

Andrew waited for her to explain. "Try running that past me again," he encouraged, after another silence. "You lost me between the telly and the bruises. At the moment I don't see a connection."

She rolled up the sleeve of her shirt. "Like this," she said, showing him a naked forearm with blue weals striping the flesh. "Enough of them and you could lounge around on her settee till the cows came home . . . if you had a mind to it, of course." She licked her finger and rubbed a white line through the stripes. "Eyeshadow," she said laconically. "Pretty effective, eh? I put it on in the car before I came in. Grace fell for it every time."

Andrew took another slow mouthful of Margaux. "Why?"

"She was a moron . . . just like her stupid grandson. Me and Cill could run rings around the pair of them." She paused, waiting for him to react. "It was Cill started it," she went on when he didn't. "She knew Howard hung out there all the time, doing eff all, so she rang the bell one day and told Grace her dad had been beating up on her. It worked a treat." She lifted a shoulder in a disdainful shrug. "We couldn't understand a word she said — she was worse than Howard like that — but she let us watch telly and gave us something to eat."

Andrew showed his skepticism. "Why?" he asked again. "What did she have to gain by it?"

"I don't know. She just did."

"Bullshit," he said without emphasis. "Grace may have had speech problems, but that wouldn't have affected her IQ. Your parents lived across the road. Why would she make enemies of them by letting you truant at her place?"

"She let Howard."

"He was her grandson. She felt sorry for him."

"Then maybe she felt sorry for us. Cill's dad had beaten her black and blue that first time. It was only afterward we used the eyeshadow." Louise took a curl of smoke into her mouth and stared at him with dislike. "You reckon you know it all, don't you? So when did your dad take a stick to you?"

"Never."

She pointed toward the ceiling. "How

many times have you beaten *them* within an inch of their lives?"

"Never."

"Then don't tell me what Grace would or wouldn't do. She knew about people's lives being fucked. Why do you think Howard was the way he was?"

"He had a disability."

Louise shook her head. "His mother used to thrash the living daylights out of him. She was a right bitch. He was so scared of her, he kept running away to Grace."

Andrew remembered a couple of lines from a letter Jonathan had received. *"Sometimes his mother dragged him in by his ear . . . she wasn't a nice woman . . . she was always hitting him."* "Did you know Howard well?"

"Well enough," she said dismissively. "He had a thing for Cill."

"Was he in the house when you were there?"

"Sometimes. Cill used to let him feel her tits whenever his gran was out of the room. It got him really excited."

Andrew looked toward the window, quelling a prudish distaste. "It's hardly unusual," he said. "Adolescents explore each other all the time."

"Yeah, but he wasn't an adolescent, was he? He was twenty years old." The pale eyes fixed on Andrew again. "Actually, it was pretty funny watching him. He'd get a hard-on just looking at her, and when he touched her he'd start juddering as if he was having an orgasm." Another scornful shrug. "He probably was, too — he was a sad little git . . . shot his load early every time, I reckon, assuming anyone let him get that close."

It wasn't just the remarks but the brutal way she said them that set Andrew's teeth on edge. Perhaps she thought shock tactics would make her more believable. "Who instigated it? Cill or Howard?"

"Cill, of course. She was a right little tart."

"What about you? Was Howard interested in you?"

"Like hell he was," said Louise bluntly, taking up her glass again. "I was the gooseberry so his gran wouldn't ask questions. He'd have gone the whole way with Cill if he could've got rid of Grace. He was always pressuring the silly old cow to go to the shops, but she never did because she hated leaving the house."

Andrew watched her drain the glass. It wasn't hard to see where she was going with this. "So because he was sexually obsessed with Cill, he killed his grandmother?"

"Had to've done," she agreed. "He was a dirty little pervert."

"*Had* to have done?" he queried. "You don't know?"

"Oh, I know all right," she said confidently. "I just can't prove it."

Andrew let a silence develop. "What was the point of coming here?" he asked at last. "I may be a soft touch in some areas of my life, Louise, but I'm not entirely stupid. Were you expecting me to believe this rigmarole?"

"What's not to believe?"

"That Grace would have allowed Cill to stay in her house once the police became involved. They were appealing for sightings on the Saturday morning. Grace wouldn't have hidden her in those circumstances."

Louise shrugged. "Maybe she was already dead."

"She can't have been," he said with conviction. "There was a debate over time of death at the trial, but the disparity between the two sides was twenty-four to forty-eight hours. If Cill disappeared on the Friday evening, then Grace would have had to have died on the Saturday in order to be ignorant of police involvement . . . which would have meant her body lying for nearly a week before it was found." He shook his head. "And that isn't possible. Decomposition would have been well into the second and third stages."

"Not my problem," she said indifferently. "I'm telling you how it was. It's up to you to work out how it fits."

He gave an abrupt laugh. "Then it's a pity you didn't make your story match the facts before you brought it to me. Let's start with Cill. If you knew where she was, why didn't you tell the police?"

"She'd have killed me." She reached forward to stub out her second cigarette. "Like I said, she was a psycho. If they'd hauled her kicking and screaming back to her dad for another larruping, she'd have got me in a corner, first opportunity, and scratched my eyes out."

"So why tell them about the rape?"

"Because they wanted to know what the fight was about. Plus, I reckoned that if the police knew she'd been raped and got social services involved, her dad wouldn't be able to take her apart for it." Her expression became almost rueful. "I was trying to do her a favor, though you wouldn't think it the way things turned out. It's no good looking at it with twenty-twenty vision, you have to picture what it was like then. Far as I knew, Cill'd sneak home when she got bored and that'd be the end of it. I didn't know she was going to vanish and Grace was going to die. No one did."

It was a fair point, he thought. "How did you know she was in Grace's house?"

"Soon as her mum phoned to see if she was round our place, I went and checked. We used to go through the gate in the fence at the back and in the kitchen door. I watched her through the window, stuffing her face with ice cream."

"Did you talk to her?"

"No chance. She'd have gone for me. It was my fault that cow Brett suspended her."

"What about Grace?"

"Didn't see her."

"Howard?"

She shook her head.

"What time was it?"

Louise shrugged. "Nine o'clock or thereabouts."

"Morning? Evening?"

"Morning. I was down at the nick two hours later, being quizzed by the cops."

It sounded convincing, but Andrew wasn't much of a judge in these matters.

Women had always run rings around him. He couldn't forget that, at the period Louise was describing, she was only thirteen years old — and, if her ex-headmistress was to be believed, not very bright. "Had you had dealings with the police before?" he asked. "I can't imagine withholding information at thirteen."

Her eyes glittered scornfully, but whether in contempt for Andrew's boyhood fear or impatience with his questioning, he couldn't tell. "It was my mother did most of the talking, and she was mad as hell that anyone'd think we knew where Cill was and wouldn't tell."

"But *you* knew."

"Right." She lit another cigarette. "That's why I talked about the rape." She forestalled his next attempt at a question. "Oh, come on, lighten up, for Christ's sake! What was the big deal? I wasn't going to rat on Cill, even if I did think she was a little bitch. All she'd done was take herself off for the night . . . hundreds of kids do it every day. In any case, I didn't want the cops finding out we'd been truanting round there because I didn't know what they'd do to Grace. Or *me* for that matter," she added reflectively. "My plan was to go round as soon as I got home and give Cill a bollocking, but Mum got fired up about the rape and wouldn't let me out of her sight. After that it all went pear-shaped."

"How?"

"How do you think?" she said morosely. "When I next went round, it looked as if a bloody war had broken out."

Chapter Twenty

It was like watching a battery-operated toy run down. Whatever had stimulated Louise to come to Andrew's house and tell her story was rapidly being neutralized by the wine and exhaustion. She rested her head against the back of the chair and stared at the ceiling.

"Did you go inside the house?"

"I was too damn scared."

"Why?"

"Everything was on the floor."

"Where?"

"In the kitchen . . . in the sitting room . . ."

"What sort of things?"

"*Everything*. Drawers, broken bottles, plants. It looked like a bomb had hit it."

Andrew flicked her a sideways glance. "How could you see into the sitting room? I thought the curtains were pulled."

"Not at the back they weren't. There

were some French windows onto the garden. I looked through them." She flicked ash onto his carpet before taking another drag on her cigarette. "It did my head in as a matter of fact. I knew something bad had happened. There was blood on the pane . . . right in front of my eyes. I thought it was Cill's."

"Why?"

She turned her head toward him. "Because Grace was a loony," she said flatly, "and I always knew she'd turn nasty one day. Cill used to tease her something chronic about the way she spoke and I reckoned she'd gone too far and made Grace flip."

"So what did you do?"

"Ran home, kept my mouth shut and refused to go out for weeks." She gave a faint smile at his expression. "I thought the cops'd come down on me like a ton of bricks for not telling them where she was on the Saturday. I should have done . . . *would* have done if my stupid mother hadn't stuck her oar in first."

"Which day was this?"

She thought for a moment. "It had to be the Tuesday. I ducked in on my way back from school because I was hacked off with everyone asking questions about Cill.

Come the Wednesday I had a fit, and the folks kept me back till we moved to Boscombe."

Andrew filed that piece of information away. "Why didn't you tell your mother what you'd seen?"

Louise didn't answer immediately but returned to staring at the ceiling as if wisdom could be found in its matte white paint. "What makes you think I didn't?" she asked then.

"There's no record of her going to the police."

"That doesn't mean I didn't tell her." She bent forward abruptly to kill the cigarette. "She went off like a rocket, so did my dad. How could I let the family down? What were the neighbors going to say? Didn't I understand what a dreadful position I'd put them in? First a rape . . . then keeping quiet about where Cill was . . . now telling stories about blood on Grace's windows . . ." She gave a hollow laugh. "They never liked me much so I'm sure they thought I was involved in some way."

Andrew placed his glass on the floor to avoid looking at her. "*Were* you?"

"Course not," she said without heat. "I hadn't a clue what was going on. Even when they arrested Howard, it didn't make any better sense. I kept asking Mum what had happened to Cill, till she boxed my ears and told me never to mention her again. It was a weird time . . . I couldn't make head or tail of anything. In the end I worked out that Howard'd killed Cill, too, as being the only thing that made sense . . . but it was way too late to say anything. The cops would've crucified the folks for keeping quiet."

She was very believable, thought Andrew. Everything dovetailed neatly until he thought about the questions she hadn't answered. "He couldn't have done," he said evenly. "He didn't have a car and there was only one body in the house. So how did he get rid of her?"

"Who knows?" she said glibly. "Promised to take her home? Took her for a walk? He was a right little pedophile . . . if he'd got away with Grace's murder, he'd've been picking kiddies off the street. It suits you to think he was innocent, but it doesn't mean he was. I was *there*, I *knew* him." She flashed him another contemptuous look. "He was a slimeball."

Andrew propped his elbows on the arms of his chair and steepled his hands under his chin. "Except there was no evidence anyone else had been in Grace's house," he told her. "Why weren't Cill's fingerprints all over the place? Why weren't *yours?* Even if the police couldn't identify them, they'd have questioned why two unknown sets were in there. Grace was a known recluse. The first thing everyone said about her was that she didn't have visitors."

"Not my problem," she said again. "*You* explain it. I can only tell you what I know. She was always cleaning up after us."

It was a clever tack — a challenge of belief — and he wondered fleetingly why her headmistress had thought her stupid. "Howard couldn't have killed anyone on the Monday or Tuesday, Louise. His movements were accounted for all day . . . which is why the prosecution pathologist argued strongly that the murder took place on the Wednesday." He lifted a cynical eyebrow. "But that's not your problem either, I suppose?"

She flashed him a mischievous smile. "Right."

"So why pick on Howard? Nothing you've said so far proves he was even there."

"Who else could it have been?" she said with a shrug. "There was no one else went near Grace, except us and him."

"How about Roy Trent, Colley Hurst

and Micky Hopkinson?"

She was ready for that, he thought. Her answer was too quick. "Dream on," she said scornfully. "They never left Colliton Way. What the hell would they be doing at Grace's?"

"Looking for Cill," Andrew suggested. "They'd raped her once, maybe they fancied another go." He watched her mouth turn down. "Perhaps they were looking for you?"

"What for?"

"To teach you a lesson for giving their description to the police." For the first time lines of indecision appeared around her eyes. "I should think they were mad as hell to have a two-bit kid rat on them."

"I didn't name them."

"You didn't need to. They must have been so well known to the police that saying there were three of them was probably enough." He watched her for a moment. "If you added in the bonus of Colley Hurst's red hair, then you might just as well have named them."

"It wasn't them," she said dismissively, "and I should bloody well know. I married one of the bastards."

Andrew smiled. "That's hardly proof of innocence."

"You think I'd marry a murderer?"

"No reason not to. They don't have 'M' tattooed on their foreheads."

She considered for a moment. "Meaning he might have done it, but I didn't know."

"That's one interpretation."

"What's the other?"

"That you could marry him safely because no one else knew he was a murderer." He watched a look of amusement crinkle her eyes. "So why *did* you marry him?"

"Why does anyone marry anyone? He was like Everest . . . he was *there*."

"Didn't it worry you what he did to Cill?"

"Not particularly. He was a damn sight better prospect than the bastard I had before. At least Roy had a place to live with some money coming in." She shrugged. "Name me a man who hasn't gone in for a bit of rough sex at some point in his life. It's natural, isn't it? You're all just Stone-Age types under the suits."

Andrew gave an abrupt laugh. "So that's where I've been going wrong. I had no idea sex was supposed to be painful. I thought it was about pleasuring women."

"Oh, *sure*," she murmured sarcastically. "And you can tell when a woman's having an orgasm, I suppose?"

He'd always thought he could, until Greg moved into his bed. "No," he confessed. "I wouldn't be divorced otherwise."

"Jesus!" Louise wasn't used to honesty in men. "You shouldn't admit to things like that."

"I'm not very good at lying." He grinned as she pulled a face. "And I don't have the kind of personality that measures itself by the length of its penis." He tapped the side of his head. "I'm more interested in this. What makes people tick? Why are some of us a success and others a failure?" He let a moment pass. "How does Roy make money when his pub doesn't have any customers?"

Louise reached for her jacket. "Not my problem. It was fine when I was there."

"Who owns it?"

"Maybe Roy does."

Andrew shook his head. "No chance. It's prime development property. He'd be under siege from potential buyers . . . and one of them would have persuaded him to sell by now."

She threaded her arms into the sleeves of her jacket. "How come you know so much? I thought it was your mate who was writing the book."

Andrew looked amused. "He consults with me . . . so does George Gardener. Is that a disappointment? Did you choose me because you thought I was too ignorant to ask questions?"

"Apart from George's, yours was the only address I had," she told him matter-of-factly, "and I wasn't going to talk to George. She'd have spilled the beans to Roy, and I don't need that at the moment."

"Why not? You said he wasn't involved."

"Different stuff," she said rather bleakly, "nothing to do with Cill or Grace." She pushed herself forward in the chair. "Are you going to tell George and your friend what I've said?"

"It's why you came, isn't it?" He took her silence for assent. "They'll want to talk to you themselves, though. If what you've told me is true, then you're only guessing that Howard took his obsession with Cill too far . . . but you know for a fact that Roy and his friends did. You were *there*," he said in a conscious echo of what she'd said earlier, "and gang rape is a better indication of sociopathic behavior than a bit of clumsy groping on a sofa."

"She'd been geeing them up to it for weeks," she said with an edge of malice in her voice. "They were drunk as skunks and she talked dirty for half an hour to get them excited. I told her she was asking for trouble, but she wouldn't listen to me." Her mouth thinned as she remembered. "She was an arrogant little cow. She thought she knew everything. It drove me mad sometimes."

Andrew watched her eyes smolder with irritation. "Then why try to look like her?"

This was another question she was prepared for. "If she was beside me, you wouldn't think there was any similarity, except for the hair. And you can blame my mother for that. She was the one who dyed it to avoid difficult questions after we moved. Now no one knows me as anything other than a brunette —" she gave a small laugh — "and I'm too vain to let the gray show through."

"You've been calling yourself Priscilla," he reminded her.

She stood up and buttoned her jacket. "Yeah. Shouldn't have done, should I?" she said ingenuously. "George wouldn't've kept digging if I'd stuck with Daisy." She tucked her cigarettes into her pocket. "I changed to Priscilla when I was married to my first loser."

Andrew pushed himself out of his chair. "Why?"

"It sounded glamorous," she said with a strange wistfulness, "and that's crazy when you think what happened to Cill." She moved toward the door. "I guess Miss Brett was right, eh?"

He moved ahead of her to turn the latch. "In what way?"

" 'Louise Burton acts before she thinks,' " she said with a twisted smile. "Story of my life." In a surprisingly warm gesture, she offered him her hand. "I'm hoping you're one of the good guys. Otherwise I'll end up regretting this, too."

He took the hand in his. "Are you safe to drive?"

"Better be."

She didn't give him time to respond, but turned away and headed up the mews. As she rounded the corner at the end she glanced back at him, her pale face lit by a streetlamp. It was impossible to read her expression from that distance, but there was no mistaking the small wave she gave him. He had no idea whether anything she'd told him was true but, as he returned the farewell courtesy, he was surprised at how much he wanted to believe her.

Jonathan was working through some student essays in bed when the telephone rang at eleven-thirty. He had a surge of hope that it was Emma, until he picked it up and heard Andrew babbling excitedly about "something important." It was so out of character that he assumed his friend was drunk and told him to call back in the morning, but Andrew insisted on giving him bullet points of the conversation while they were still fresh in his mind. "She was pretty convincing."

"Who was?"

"Priscilla Fletcher. Larger than life in my house and calling herself Louise Burton." He heard Jonathan's intake of breath. "Right! So get your pencil out, you lazy sod, and take some notes."

"Why can't you write them yourself?"

"Because I'm only getting a tenth of your earnings and I'm bored with doing all the work."

"You don't sound bored," said Jonathan dryly, pulling a notepad forward. "What did she do to you?"

"Charmed me," said Andrew succinctly.

Jonathan remembered the Good Samaritan act on Branksome Station. "And what's she stolen?"

"Belief."

"If Cill was in Grace's house, then she's

the obvious suspect for the murder," said Jonathan thoughtfully, running his pencil down his notes. "She was big for her age, she was there, she was a disturbed adolescent . . . recently raped with a possible history of sexual abuse. Put that with a volatile cocktail of hormones, and God knows what might have happened." He tapped the pencil against his teeth. "I can imagine a scenario where Grace tried to make her leave because she was worried about police involvement and Cill lost her temper and lashed out. The timing would work. She hid with Grace over the weekend, killed her on the Monday, then took herself off that night. It would explain why there were no sightings of her at the beginning . . . although it's odd she wasn't spotted afterward."

Andrew yawned at the other end. "Who took the bath and left ginger hair behind?"

"Pass."

"What about Howard fancying Cill? That sounded fairly convincing. She was an attractive girl."

"She was thirteen."

"Oh, come on! What's age got to do with anything? He was a retarded adolescent himself, so a grown woman's expectations would have terrified him. Maybe that's why he lost his rag when his grandmother told him to put himself about a bit. If he was besotted with Cill, he wouldn't have been interested in anyone else. More to the point, it would explain why he haunted Grace's house. Men'll do anything if there's half a chance of a shag at the end of it."

"Speak for yourself," Jonathan said tartly.

"I am," said Andrew with a laugh. "I abase myself regularly before beautiful women, and they all think I'm a comedian." He paused to take what sounded like a drink. "You should run this past your psychologist friend, but I'll put money on Louise being honest when she described Howard as a pervert. I'm not saying he *was,*" he went on when Jonathan attempted to break in, "I'm saying that was her perception of him. She called him a 'slimeball,' and it sounded too strong to be a latter-day invention. I think it's what she genuinely felt at the time."

Jonathan leaned his head against the pillows and rubbed the grit of tiredness from his eyes. "I need to sleep on this," he told Andrew. "I still don't understand why she came to you instead of me or George."

Andrew explained about his business card and the handwritten address. "I wouldn't think that was her reason, though. I'm guessing she expected me to swallow it whole without asking questions . . . either that, or it was a practice run."

"For what? She can't change the details now, not without eyebrows being raised." He looked at his notes again. "What was the punchline, anyway? Which bit were you supposed to believe?"

"Presumably that Howard was guilty and Roy and his gang weren't involved."

"Then she was sent by Roy," said Jonathan matter-of-factly. "He told us she'd back him up."

"Not very successfully. If Grace was already dead on the Tuesday, that exonerates Howard."

"There's only Wynne's evidence that he didn't go out on the Monday night," Jonathan warned. "It's not something we can prove. She was never cross-examined in court because the prosecution plumped for the Wednesday."

"Whose side are you on?" Andrew demanded. "Howard wouldn't have gone back if he knew Grace was dead . . . or if he did, he wouldn't have run away like a bat out of hell and refused to tell anyone. This is a gift, for God's sake! It's precisely the piece of evidence you and George have been looking for."

"That's what's making me suspicious," said Jonathan gloomily. "Why would Roy Trent tell Louise to say Tuesday? It doesn't make sense if he's read *Disordered Minds*."

Chapter Twenty-one

9 Galway Road, Boscombe, Bournemouth
Thursday, May 15, 2003, 11:30 a.m.

The well-endowed young woman from WCH Investigations was nothing like Rachel or Billy's idea of a private detective. She was young and rather nervous and they both thought she resembled an Eskimo, with her sallow skin, heavy black hair, flat cheekbones and narrow eyes. She gave her name as Sasha Spencer and began by explaining that her firm's contract with David and Jean Trevelyan had long since expired, but that she had been interested enough by William's email to look up the file, as it was the second approach on Cill Trevelyan that the firm had had in four weeks.

"Who was the first?" asked Rachel.

"I can't answer that, Mrs. Burton. We take confidentiality seriously."

"Georgina Gardener," said Billy. "She's

the one who put me on to Louise, although she doesn't know who she is . . . just spotted a similarity to Cill that wasn't real. Why didn't you respond to her approach? Why wait for ours?"

Sasha glanced uncertainly at her notes as if to confirm the name. It was a reverse-psychology technique that usually worked for her. Signs of indecisiveness and nerves persuaded interviewees that they knew more than she did, and it encouraged them to set her straight by telling her more than they intended. "I didn't speak to the person in question, but I understand they were trying to discover the Trevelyans' address." She looked up again. "It's not the sort of information we can reveal, so the meeting ended fairly rapidly."

"Meaning you didn't tell her anything?"

The young woman nodded. "We couldn't take it any further at that stage, because we were given no details about why the person was interested in Cill or her parents. However, when we received your email I called Mr. Trevelyan and explained that we'd had two approaches from two different sources in under a month and asked him if he wanted me to pursue either of them. He told me he did."

Rachel leaned forward with a frown.

"Are you saying that because your contract's with him, you won't be able to report back to us?"

"Not necessarily. I explained there was a quid pro quo — in return for divulging a name and address, one of the sources was asking for information for themselves. When I pointed out that it might be the only way to progress the search, Mr. Trevelyan instructed me to proceed as I thought best." She looked from one to the other. "I could, of course, approach the other party — whose contact details I have — and that person might give me the name and address for free, but I doubt they can give me the sort of background information that you can."

"Not if it's Georgina Gardener," Billy agreed. "I think she only came across Cill by accident when she was looking into Howard Stamp's story."

Sasha Spencer eyed him for a moment, then took a mini-cassette player out of her case and placed it on the coffee table between them. "Do you have any objections to my recording this? I'll be taking notes at the same time but it's useful to have a backup."

Billy looked unhappy. "Who are you going to play it to?"

"No one. It's just a memory aid."

But Rachel shook her head firmly as she reached for the recorder and tucked it under a cushion. "Sorry, love," she said, "but it's more than Billy's life's worth. His folks'll kill him if it ever gets out that he talked on tape about family secrets. Plus, there's no guarantee he's right, so he'll spend another few months tossing and turning because there's a cassette somewhere with his voice on it." She nodded to the notepad. "Let's stick to the old-fashioned way."

"No problem," said Sasha cheerfully, recognizing that the wife was tougher and cannier than the husband. "I tend to concentrate better on what people are saying if the tape's running, but it's no big deal." She sent Rachel a laughing smile that went all the way up to her eyes, deliberately courting her, while working out ways to persuade her to leave the room.

Listening in Robert and Eileen's old sitting room to Billy's account of his sister's upbringing gave substance to Louise in a way that hearing the same story in an office might not have done. There was an album of childhood photographs in a sideboard, items of furniture which had moved with them from Highdown and passed on to Billy when his parents left for Cornwall, even a china doll that Rachel said had once belonged to his sister.

Nevertheless, there were glaring holes in Billy's picture of the girl he grew up with. He claimed his mother was very protective of her after Cill's disappearance, but couldn't explain why — "I used to think she was worried Lou would abscond as well, but I'm not so sure now . . ." He said his father allowed her to behave like a prima donna — "He hardly ever told her off" — but again couldn't explain why — "I assumed he shared Mum's fear of frightening her away . . ." Nor was he able to give a clear sense of Louise's character, vacillating between describing her as a lying bitch — "She was always telling stories about people . . ." — and as being scared of her own shadow — "She'd go catatonic at the drop of a hat." When he went on to describe her descent into prostitution and drugs, his clear implication was that her life had been wrecked by her parents' sudden relaxation of her moral boundaries when she was thirteen.

Sasha looked up from her notes. "I'm not sure I understand," she said carefully. "Are you saying they backed off after Cill vanished because they knew Louise was involved in some way?"

Billy exchanged a glance with his wife.

"It just seems odd," said Rachel. "When you look at what became of her, you have to ask yourself why. It didn't happen with Billy. He turned out OK, but only because his folks never let up on him." She put a supporting arm through Billy's, hugging him close. "So why didn't they do the same with Louise instead of making excuses for her all the time?"

"It doesn't necessarily follow," said Sasha. "Siblings' characters vary hugely because of the different dynamics that operate inside families." She paused to consolidate her thoughts. "It's interesting, though, particularly as you're both suggesting it was Louise who was in control. It may have been straightforward emotional blackmail — 'Lay off me or I'll run away' — or you were right at the time," she told Billy, "they were afraid she'd imitate Cill."

He flicked another sideways look at his wife, as if seeking permission to be more forthright. "Maybe she had something on *them*," he muttered uncomfortably.

"What sort of thing?"

"I don't know."

Sasha frowned. "You must have *some* idea."

Billy stared at her rather helplessly for a moment, then hunched forward and concentrated on the floor. "It all happened together. The rape . . . Cill vanishing . . . Lou being questioned . . . Grace's murder . . ." He lapsed into silence.

"We don't think it's coincidence," Rachel put in. "I mean, if Eileen lied about Louise going to Grace's house, then she probably lied about other stuff." She moved her hand to her husband's back and rubbed it gently. "It's what we want you to find out. Billy's worried there's things he was never told, and it's driving him bananas."

Sasha watched them both for a long moment then sculpted an ironic "T" with her hands. "Time out?" she suggested. "I'm quite good at what I do, but I'm not a policeman. My forte is tracking down missing people — mostly children — and I succeed more often than I fail. Murder is something else entirely."

"It was a long time ago," said Billy.

"It makes no difference. If you think you have information about a murder, you should take it to the police." She closed her notebook. "Apart from anything else, you're putting me in a difficult position. Withholding evidence is a serious crime and I can't be a party to it."

Billy would have abandoned it there and then but Rachel gave a disparaging laugh. "No wonder none of you has ever found Cill. How can you go looking for a girl and not know there was a murder on her doorstep a few days later? OK, I don't know how old you are, or if you were even born then, but David Trevelyan bloody well ought to have mentioned it. If it hadn't been for Grace's death, the police would have spent more time looking for Cill. Didn't he tell you that?"

"Are you saying the two events were linked?"

Rachel shrugged. "All we know is that Lou was questioned about Cill going missing, then Eileen lied about knowing Grace." She gave Billy's back another comforting stroke. "And we don't know why, since Lou and Cill spent time in Grace's house . . . and Eileen knew it."

Sasha pondered for a moment, then reached into her case for a file. "I think you should read the Trevelyans' statements." She took out a file and extracted some papers. "These are copies of the ones they made to the police." She passed them across. "Jean's is a factual account of sending Cill to bed on the Friday night and waking up in the morning to find her bed empty. David's is more interesting, because it was made in response to some tough police questioning."

She watched Rachel split the copies and pass one to Billy. "Last night I listened to tapes of the interviews my predecessor had with both of them. They mention the names of numerous children and adults that Cill was friendly with — I have a list in here —" she tapped the file on her lap — "but there's no one called Grace and there's no mention of murder." She jerked her chin at the papers. "As far as I'm aware, those statements represent the limit of their knowledge."

INCIDENT REPORT

Date: 5.30.70
Time: 0930
Officers attending:
PC Lawrence Reed and
PC Paul Prentice
Incident: Missing child — mother,
Jean Trevelyan,
interviewed at home

Mrs. Jean Trevelyan reported her daughter missing at 0917. Officers Reed and Prentice responded immediately. After taking and transmitting details of Priscilla (Cill) Trevelyan's description, the officers questioned Jean Trevelyan (mother). She was extremely upset and not very coherent. However, she dictated the following statement and agreed it was an accurate and chronological record of events:

Cill was sent home from Highdown School yesterday afternoon [Friday, 5.29.70] at about two o'clock. She told me she'd been suspended for a week because she'd had a fight with another girl. The girl's name is Louise Burton and she was Cill's best friend until they fell out at the beginning of this month. They haven't talked to each other since, and my husband and I were pleased about it because Louise was a bad influence on our daughter.

Cill refused to tell me what the fight was about and I warned her that her father would be angry about the suspension. She lost her temper and stormed off to her bedroom, saying it wasn't her fault. I understood from something she said that Louise Burton had not been punished in the same way. As this seemed unreasonable, I telephoned Miss Brett at Highdown School and asked for an explanation. She told me Louise had said the fight started when Cill tried to persuade her to truant again, and Cill had not denied it. In the circumstances, she felt it proper to punish Cill.

The last three months have been a big worry to us. For no obvious reason Cill started truanting, and the school warned us a few weeks ago that she would be asked to leave if her poor attendance continued. She was encouraged to truant by Louise Burton, who struggles with schoolwork and finds lessons difficult. Both my husband and I have spoken to Miss Brett about moving Cill into a more challenging class. We have also asked Mr. and Mrs. Burton on two occasions to address Louise's behavior. Nothing has come of either approach.

My husband, David, works the night shift at Brackham & Wright's tool factory. At the time Cill arrived home he was asleep, and I decided to keep her in her room until he left for work at 8 p.m. I knew he'd be angry and felt it would be better to tell him about the suspension this morning [Saturday]. However, Cill was making so much noise that she woke him up. When he demanded an explanation, she swore at him and said she didn't have to say anything if she didn't want to.

Cill is our only child and David worries about her a great deal. She's well developed for her age and brighter than average, but she's easily led. We never had any problems with her until she went to Highdown School. Cill has accused David many times of being too strict, citing other children's parents as examples. She is angry that she isn't allowed to go out in the evenings or wear provocative clothing, and this has led to arguments with her father.

When she refused to say why she'd had a fight with Louise, he gave her three lashes of his belt. David has always taken the view that school punishments should be upheld and he ordered Cill to stay in her room until she was ready to explain and apologize. She went upstairs immediately and slammed her door again.

I knocked on her door shortly after David went to work and asked her if she wanted something to eat. She didn't answer but I could hear her crying. Her radio was playing pop music in the background. I decided against going into her room but spoke to her for several minutes through the door. I can't remember exactly what I said, because I was angry myself, but I did urge her to show some sense in the morning and to apologize to her father at the first opportunity.

When I went to bed at ten-thirty there was

no light under her door and the radio had been turned off. She certainly did not leave the house while I was downstairs, because I would have seen her. I am a light sleeper and I remember waking during the night. I believe the time was about twelve-fifteen.

I assume now that it may have been the front door closing, although I can't be sure.

When David returned from work this morning [Saturday] at seven-thirty I got up to make breakfast. We discussed Cill for about an hour in the kitchen before he asked me to call her down. We both agreed that confining her to the house and insisting she did chores was the best way forward. However, she was not in her room and her bed hadn't been slept in. A small rucksack is missing from her wardrobe along with her nightdress, two skirts and some T-shirts.

I immediately telephoned the parents of Louise Burton and three of her other friends [Rosie Maine, Ginny Lawson, Katey Cropper] but none of them knows where she is. I decided to call the police after David set off in his car to see if he could find her. She has never run away before and we cannot think of anywhere she could go at twelve-fifteen in the morning. If she was with a friend, the parents would have alerted us. We are desperately worried that she's put herself in danger by hitching a lift with a stranger.

It has been made clear to me by Officers Prentice and Reed that runaways are treated differently from abductions. I understand that in most circumstances children who leave home after a row with their parents return within twenty-four hours.

Jean Trevelyan

WITNESS STATEMENT

Date: 6.02.70
Time: 1130
Officers interviewing:
DC Williams and PC Prentice
Witness: David Trevelyan
Incident: Disappearance of Priscilla (Cill) Trevelyan on 5.30.70

Mr. David Trevelyan was invited for interview at Highdown Police Station. He presented himself voluntarily but was hostile to many of the questions that were put to him. The following statement was dictated and signed by Mr. Trevelyan.

I know nothing about my daughter's disappearance. You can call ours a love-hate relationship if you like, but it wouldn't be true. I have never hated Cill from the moment she was born. If I thought it would have done her any good, I'd have spoiled her rotten and given her everything she asked for. Instead, I put pressure on her to work because I know she is bright enough to do better than her parents. We had few problems with her until she reached puberty, but her difficult adolescence is putting a strain on the family.

I was upset when she didn't make it to grammar school. She has a good brain, but she was let down by her primary school. There's so much rubbish talked about the eleven-plus. It's supposed to be a test of IQ, but the more you practice the skills the better you are at them. Anyone can bump their level up by ten points when they know what's expected. Cill sat it blind and missed by a point, and you're not going to tell me that's fair. There's people I work with whose sons got through on lower scores. The system's rigged in favor of the middle classes.

I am strict because I want the best for her. The world's changing and women should have as good an education as men. I don't want her to be a packer at Brackham & Wright's or a lowly-paid hairdresser. I want her to find a decent job in London where she'll meet a good man who earns enough to buy his own house. My greatest fear has always been that some boy will take advantage and get her pregnant before she's sixteen.

It has caused a great number of arguments between us. My daughter developed early and thought she could look after herself. I have told her many times that she doesn't understand how vulnerable young girls are, and when the truanting began last term I felt I had no option but to take a sterner line. My wife and I have tried everything from delivering and collecting her from school ourselves to enforcing a curfew after six o'clock at night, but the only discipline that seems to work is physical punishment.

I object strongly to any suggestion that I take enjoyment from this. My relationship with my daughter has never strayed beyond a parental one with all my efforts geared to ensuring her future success. I recognize that my ambitions for her may exceed her own, but my hope has always been that she would never suffer my frustrations. If this has led me to be too severe on a child I love, then I am deeply sorry, but my intentions are good.

I was horrified to learn that Louise Burton made a statement on Saturday saying my daughter was gang raped at the beginning of May, and "brought it on herself." I understand that Louise blames my strictness for the fact that Cill was unable to tell my wife and me that it happened. We are deeply upset about this as we have long had concerns about Louise's truthfulness and fail to understand why this story of rape is believed when she could neither name the perpetrators nor identify the three suspects who were brought in for questioning. Nor do I understand why Louise failed to tell her own parents at the time. The Burtons take a relaxed view of their daughter's behavior and I cannot believe they were unaware of the rape if it happened. In summary, there is no evidence to support Louise's allegation and I am angry that it has been given credence when it reflects so badly on our daughter.

In reference to the argument I had with Cill on the afternoon of Friday, May 29, it was no different from the ones that had gone before. She and I are forceful people and there was a lot of shouting. My recollection is that she swore profusely and called me a "Victorian parent," "Hitler," "Methuselah," and accused me of "playing God." She then turned on her mother and called her a "telltale creep" and a "sniveling bitch." She also accused us of trying to live her life, and of caring more about what the other parents at school would say than we did about her.

I insisted on an explanation for the fight with Louise Burton. When she refused, I asked her if Louise's version was true — namely that she'd tried to persuade Louise to truant again. Cill began throwing things about the room and I felt I had no option but to give her three lashes of the belt. I then sent her to her room and instructed her mother to make sure she remained there. It was an unhappy experience for all of us, but I was confident that the outcome would be the same as usual: Cill would apologize in the morning and her behavior would improve in the short term. Our difficulty, as ever, was how to deal with her behavior in the long term, specifically the truanting.

I left for work at eight o'clock [Friday] and at that time Cill was in her bedroom. As a foreman in the engineering department at Brackham & Wright's, I oversee a night workforce of approximately fifty. Louise Burton's father, Robert, has similar responsibilities in the packing department. A female work colleague of mine, Deborah Handley, noticed that I was upset on arrival and asked me if something was wrong. Deborah has two daughters in their late teens and I've regularly asked her advice about Cill's behavior. During the shift I explained what had happened and told Deborah that Jean and I were at our wits' end. She suggested I talk to Robert Burton and find out what the fight was really about. I believe her words were, "If Cill was too worked up to invent a reason, then I bet there's more to it than meets the eye."

I approached Robert in the canteen at approximately one o'clock in the morning. He was unwilling to talk to me, claiming the school's punishment showed that Cill was at fault, not Louise. I pointed out that Louise's version of events was very convenient, since she knew how worried we and Miss Brett had been about Cill's truanting. He asked me if I was accusing his daughter of lying, and when I said it was a possibility, he became abusive and a fight broke out. I did not do this to draw attention to myself and create an alibi or to disguise any bruises from a previous encounter with Cill. It happened as a result of my deep concern and anxiety for my daughter's welfare, which boiled over when Robert Burton referred to her as "a cheap little tart who deserved what she got."

I have no idea why he made this remark unless Louise had already told him about the alleged rape. If so, he had a responsibility to pass that information to myself and my wife.

In conclusion, I have accounted for my movements during the night of Friday, May 29, and Saturday, May 30, 1970. Also, my fifty-minute drive on the morning of Saturday, May 30, when I went to Branksome Station and Bournemouth Central in the hope of finding my daughter. I confirm that I know nothing about Cill's disappearance and that I am ignorant of her current whereabouts.

David Trevelyan

By the time Billy had finished reading and laid the pages on the coffee table, his hands were shaking. "God!" he said with feeling. "Do you think Mr. Trevelyan's right? Do you think my folks *did* know about the rape?"

Assuming he was addressing her, Sasha Spencer demurred. "David's never been convinced the rape happened," she said. "He thinks your sister was lying to shift attention away from her part in Cill's suspension. Jean believes it, though, and she beats herself up regularly for being a lousy mother. It's a very sad situation. Rightly or wrongly — and for different reasons — they each hold themselves responsible."

Billy lowered his face into his hands. "It certainly happened," he muttered. "I was there, I saw it. They took it in turns . . . kept kicking her . . . she had blood all down her legs. It makes me sick just thinking about it."

Rachel saw the distaste on Sasha's face. "He was ten years old and they'd filled him with vodka," she said, leaping to Billy's defense, "so he didn't understand what was going on. He thought it was a fight. If the police had included him in the questioning, it would have been different, but no one knew he'd been with Cill and Louise that day."

"Cill was that scared of her dad, she said she'd kill us if we ever breathed a word," Billy went on unhappily, "so I never did. And it wasn't until a bloke at school told me his mum had read it in the newspapers that I found out Louise had told the police . . . I didn't even know what rape meant — he had to explain it to me . . . and that was a good two months after Cill vanished. It wasn't mentioned in our house. *Nothing* was." He dropped a hand to David Trevelyan's statement. "I didn't know Mr. Trevelyan cared about his kid that much . . . I didn't know my dad and him had a fight . . . I sure as hell didn't know Dad was calling Cill a tart *before* anyone knew she was missing."

There was a long silence.

Sasha opened her notebook again. "Why is that important?" she asked.

"He said Cill 'deserved what she got.' I think it means he knew about the rape."

Sasha eyed him with a frown. "I still don't understand why it's important. It may not reflect well on your parents, but it doesn't mean they had anything to do with Cill running away."

Billy took a printout of his father's email

from his shirt pocket. “Read this,” he said harshly, “then ask yourself what else he’s been lying about. You don’t tell a man his kid deserves what she gets if you think he’s abusing her . . . and you damn well talk to the police if you think that man’s been after your own daughter as well.”

Chapter Twenty-two

25 Mullin Street, Highdown, Bournemouth
Thursday, May 15, 2003, midday

Jonathan suggested they sit in the garden so that he could inspect the rear of George's house, but she told him there was only one chair and no table. She seemed depressed, and he thought it sad that she had no one to share her garden with. He said the day was too glorious to miss and insisted on moving furniture out from the kitchen. Puffs of high cloud drifted across a turquoise sky and the scent of wisteria on her neighbor's wall was heavy on the air. He collected a cushion from the sitting room and tucked it behind George's back, worried about the signs of pain and weariness that were showing round her eyes. "What's wrong?"

"Nothing," she said. "I'm just aching a bit."

He took the chair next to her. "You look tired."

"It goes with the job. I'm on nights again."

"I hope you're not playing the martyr," he warned her. "I'm investing a lot of time and energy into this book."

She gave a faint smile. "You're *such* a bully."

"I've been taking lessons from Andrew. Have you been to the doctor?"

"I'm going tomorrow."

He didn't press it. Instead he produced a printout of Andrew's bullet points which he'd emailed George at the beginning of the week. He began with what could be proved. If, as George's previous neighbor had told her, her house was an exact replica of Grace's, then Louise could certainly have seen into the sitting room through the French windows. Jonathan was less convinced about the girls entering through a gate in the fence at the back in order to truant. He nodded at George's rear boundary. "Their only access would have been through other people's gardens," he pointed out, "so why were they never seen by Grace's neighbors?"

George sorted through a folder that she'd asked him to fetch from her sitting room. "I think I've solved that." She drew out a photocopy of a street map and spread it on the table. "I found this in the library. It's from an early *A–Z* of Bournemouth, printed in 1969." She took up a pencil and placed the tip on Mullin Street. "This is where the houses were demolished to make the apartment block and, as near as I can get it, *this* —" she drew a small circle — "was Grace's house. If I'm right, then there was a narrow cul-de-sac at the back which was reached from Bladen Street." She ran her pencil up a road at right angles. "The alleyway doesn't exist anymore, because these two houses adjacent to Bladen Street appear to have extended their gardens, and the flats have garages along the boundary . . . but it was obviously there in 1970."

Jonathan gave a nod of approval. "Good stuff."

George pulled a face. "It doesn't prove anything. What about fingerprints? The police would have found some if Cill had been there for any length of time. Children's fingers are smaller than adults' so, if juvenile prints had been there, the police *couldn't* have missed them. Particularly Louise's. Miss Brett said she was a skinny little thing. Even if she didn't go inside, she'll have touched the windows when she looked in. It's the natural thing to do."

"Did Lovatt have any ideas?"

"He said eyebrows would have been raised by children's prints. He also thinks there would have been a comparison set on file as Cill's would have been lifted from her bedroom in case a body was found."

"So Louise is lying?"

"That's his view."

Jonathan linked his hands and stretched them toward the sky, cracking the joints at the back of his neck. "Louise told Andrew he'd have to explain it himself," he murmured, "which was very clever of her, because he's a competitive little man and he loves winning."

George tut-tutted. "You shouldn't keep drawing attention to his height. You'll give him a complex."

"Fat chance!"

"He thinks that's why his wife left him."

Jonathan relaxed again, dropping his arms to the tabletop and favoring George with a grin. "I did what you told me to do and went to see her a couple of days ago. She's bored with the parasitic stud, stressed to the eyeballs with work and kept asking me if Andrew had a girlfriend."

"What did you say?"

"That she didn't deserve a second chance because she was a two-timing bitch."

"You *didn't!*"

"Bloody did."

"No, you didn't."

He laughed. "OK! I may not have used those exact words, but I did say Andrew was a prince among men and if she had a blind bit of sense she'd recognize the fact. I also said he'd never had a bad word for her and was eating his heart out because she and the children were the best thing that ever happened to him."

George's eyes sparkled with delight. "What did she say?"

"That both girls had told her he'd had a woman in the house on Saturday, and the place stank of smoke on Sunday morning." He smiled at her deflated expression. "What's wrong with that? It means he's desirable."

"I hope you explained."

He shook his head. "I said the ladies were queuing up for him so she'd better get a move on."

"Do you think it'll work?" she asked, her soft heart visible in the pleasure that showed in her face.

"Should do, assuming he hasn't been seduced by Louise."

"Don't be silly!"

Jonathan tapped the bullet points. "He's very keen to believe her. His theory is that the house was cleaned either after Cill left it or after Grace was murdered."

"Who by?"

"Anyone you like. If it was after Cill left, then it might have been Grace herself. If it was after Grace died, then it was her murderer."

George pondered for a moment. "Why weren't Howard's prints wiped away at the same time?"

"They would have been, but he left enough on the Wednesday to satisfy the police. There's a clear suggestion in the prosecution case that part of his attempt to cast the blame elsewhere was to clean his prints from anything that looked suspicious — such as the bathroom taps — but that he was too stupid to do a thorough job."

She looked doubtful again. "It would have meant him using the lavatory after he found Grace's body. Do you think that's likely?"

"Very likely," said Jonathan dryly. "He probably vomited into it."

"What about Grace's prints?"

Jonathan eyed her with approval. "What about them?"

"If her murderer had cleaned up, there wouldn't have been any."

"Go on."

"Wouldn't the police have noticed?" she asked with a frown. "I mean, if they were arguing that Howard wasn't thorough enough to remove all of his, then Grace's should have been all over the place. Do you see the point I'm making? It would have been very peculiar if the only prints found were Howard's. The defense team would have picked up on it straight away because it would have supported his story."

Jonathan pulled a letter from his briefcase. "That's more or less what I thought, so I wrote to Howard's solicitor first thing Monday morning and this is his reply. I'll read the relevant paragraph . . . it's quite brief: 'By recollection, the main sets were Grace Jefferies's and Howard's. In addition, policemen touched objects in the hallway and kitchen before the house was sealed. These prints were accounted for. Two or three unidentifiable sets were found on objects in the sitting room, which was considered unusual (most houses contain many more) until it became clear that

Grace was a recluse. These sets were not considered suspicious. There were a number of partial prints about the house, which were thought to be Grace's, but they were too degraded for comparison.' " He looked up. "The rest is a diatribe about my suggestion that the defense team was negligent."

"Oh dear!"

He consulted the letter again. " 'We made every effort to substantiate our client's story, but I remain in no doubt that the verdict was a correct one.' " He pushed the letter across the table. "So unless they were even more negligent than I painted them," he said lightly, "which will be hotly disputed by my friend here, then Louise is lying and Cill was never there *or* — and this is Andrew's view — Grace cleaned the house of Cill's presence herself."

"Why?"

"Because someone told her she'd be arrested if the police discovered she'd been harboring a runaway."

"Who?"

Jonathan shrugged. "Anyone you like," he said again, "but Andrew's guessing Mr. or Mrs. Burton."

It was only when Rachel asked Billy to make a pot of tea that Sasha Spencer found out what he really believed, and she made a mental note never again to make assumptions about protective wives. Rachel waited until the door closed, then leaned forward and spoke urgently into the silence. “He’s not going to tell you this because he’s trying to convince himself he’s imagining it. He’s been surfing the Net researching recovered-memory syndrome. Half the sites talk about it being a recognized psychological phenomenon, the other half say the memories are invented . . . and he doesn’t know which is the case. I keep telling him the false stuff comes out of dodgy therapy sessions, but he doesn’t want to believe me. He’s off his head because he can’t sleep, and he’s worried he’s developed a thing about his dad because Robert keeps lecturing him about the firemen being on strike . . .”

George closed her eyes and lifted her face to the sun while Jonathan explained Andrew’s theory. “It’s in bullet points again,” he said, extracting another sheet of paper. “Cill took refuge at Grace’s on the Friday night . . . Louise saw her there on the Saturday morning . . . she told her parents about it — probably on the Saturday afternoon —”

"I thought she told them on the Wednesday," George broke in.

Jonathan put a finger on the line and looked up. "Andrew says she never specified a day, only *implied* the Wednesday. Now, he thinks it's more likely she owned up after the police questioning because her mother had been so insistent the Burtons didn't know where Cill was."

"OK. Next point."

He returned to the page. "One of the Burton parents went round to Grace's . . . read Cill the riot act and told her to go home . . . put the fear of God into Grace about harboring truants and runaways . . . became anxious when Cill remained missing . . . started to lose it when Louise reported the state of Grace's house on the Tuesday or Wednesday . . . and lost it completely when Grace's body was found. Result: withdrawal of Louise from school in case she said anything, total clampdown on the story in the Burton household and enormous effort to distance themselves from Mullin Street and the Trevelyans."

"So what does he think happened to Cill?"

"Pass."

"Who killed Grace?"

"Pass."

George shielded her eyes from the sun and squinted at him. "They'd have known by the Monday morning that Cill hadn't returned home," she pointed out, "so why weren't they worried about Louise spilling the beans at school that day?"

"They told her not to."

She eyed him with amusement. "Did she always do what she was told? They couldn't stop her truanting, don't forget."

"They threatened her with the police. Billy said she was frightened of them."

George shook her head. "I've never heard such a half-baked theory. There's only one explanation for why she wasn't confined to the house until the Wednesday: she didn't tell her parents she'd seen Cill in Grace's house until after she saw the blood on the window."

Jonathan gave his head a thoughtful scratch. "Maybe," he mused.

"What other explanation is there?"

"The parents were worried someone would come asking questions if Louise didn't turn up on the Monday . . . she was threatened with a thrashing if she didn't keep her mouth shut . . . they told her she was to blame for not telling the police where Cill was . . . she was a fluent liar and was used to keeping secrets, so they were confident she'd keep that one."

"What sort of secrets?"

Jonathan shrugged. "The rape? The reason for the fight?"

"Why didn't they make her go in on the Wednesday? All the same reasons apply."

"The circumstances had changed. The blood on the window was a secret too far and she threw a fit."

"Assuming she's telling the truth," said George cynically. "I'm not as easily seduced as Andrew."

"She's an incredible flirt."

"Oh dear!" George sighed. "*Please* don't tell me Andrew fell for her."

"Probably," said Jonathan. "He's a randy little beast — short arses always are — but I meant, she flirted with information. She told him it was Howard who did it, but what she was really doing was hooking him into her father and Roy Trent."

Rachel pulled nervously at her hair. "This isn't easy," she said. "I've known Robert for ages and I'd never have thought . . . Billy's saying now that he doesn't want the girls anywhere near him. He's even wondering if his dad had a go when they were younger. I keep telling him he can't have done because they never stayed overnight with the folks, and his mum was always around in the daytime. But it's funny, looking back. It was Billy who insisted they had to come home before bedtime . . . and I never really thought about it till now. I asked him the other day if it was because of all this —" she made a vague gesture toward Robert's email — "and he said, no, he'd forgotten. He just needed to know his kids were safe with me while he was on nights shifts. He thought it was because he was afraid of fire breaking out . . . now he thinks it was these unrecovered memories working like instinct. That's weird, isn't it?"

She didn't expect a reply because she wasn't even looking at Sasha. Instead, she twined a strand of hair about her fingers and concentrated determinedly on the carpet. "The trouble is, there's nothing specific. Billy never *saw* anything — it's just stuff he heard and things that Louise said . . . like she hated her mother's cleaning job because it meant their dad had to get them ready for school. Eileen did offices from six to ten in the morning and the kids'd be left to sleep till Robert came off his night shift around seven. Billy was never woken till eight, but Louise was always up and her dad'd be giving her breakfast and laughing with her. He didn't do it with Billy . . . just whacked some food at him and told him to get a move on." She paused. "You could say it was a daughter-dad thing — opposites attract and all that — but a few times Billy woke early and heard his dad talking to Louise in her bedroom. As a kid, it made him jealous because Robert never bothered to talk to him, but now . . ." She lapsed into a troubled silence.

Sasha watched her for a moment. "It doesn't prove he was an abuser, Rachel. The daughter-dad thing is just as likely."

The woman sighed. "I know, that's the trouble." She clasped her fingers in her lap. "It's why Billy keeps surfing the Net. There are other things that are just as vague — but nothing that proves abuse. They just look suspicious when you put it all together."

"Try me."

Billy returned with a tray of cups while Rachel was talking and resumed his seat without interrupting her. He appeared relieved that she'd taken a lead and after a while began to interject memories himself. To Sasha, watching him, it was clear that some of these memories were coming back to him even as he was speaking. Did that make them true? She had no idea, but the picture he painted of his childhood was a disturbing one.

"You try to make sense of things when you're a kid," he said at one point, "so I thought Dad only liked ladies. He called Mum and Louise his 'beautiful girls,' but it was always Lou got the attention . . . never Mum. She used to make me plait her hair in front of him, then push me away the minute he left the room." He smiled rather crookedly. "She said if I got a taste for it, I'd turn into a pansy. I thought she was talking about flowers."

On another occasion: "It was Lou started the Cathy McGowan thing. Dad slipped her some money and she came back with a miniskirt and loads of makeup. She was prancing around the sitting room in front of him, and Mum went completely crazy. Lou had this black eyeliner all round her eyes and pale pink lipstick, and Mum called her a tart and started hitting her. Dad just laughed . . .

". . . He gave Cill money as well, so she could buy the same stuff as Lou. He called them his princesses. That's when Lou started getting uppity and saying she didn't want to be friends with Cill anymore. She was really jealous. I mean, she was skinny as a rake. You'd have to be blind not to see that Cill looked better than she did . . .

". . . I don't know if my father abused Cill. You don't think about things like that when you're a kid. All I know is he liked her. He'd sit her on his lap when Mum wasn't around and play with her hair."

"Why did your mother go out if she was worried about him?" asked Sasha.

Billy buried his head in his hands for the hundredth time that morning. "I don't know if she was. I don't even know if I'm imagining all of this."

Rachel squeezed his hand. "Eileen worked in the evenings as well — four to eight. She was only at home when the kids were at school and her husband was asleep."

"She hated being a mother," said Billy. "It was Dad looked after us."

"Perhaps they needed the money," said Sasha.

"Then why didn't she work in a supermarket? That's what Rach does."

"Perhaps it was the only job available," the woman said. "Did Louise have any other friends who came to the house?"

"A few."

"Did your father sit them on his lap?"

"Sometimes, but Cill was the only one who'd let him play with her hair. I think she did it to make Lou jealous." He shook his head. "He can't have done anything really bad to her because I'm sure she was a virgin when those bastards raped her. There was too much blood on her legs."

"He may have been grooming her. That's usually how child molesters work."

Billy stared at her with a sick expression in his eyes. "It was never talked about in those days. There were kids like Cill who were given a larruping by their dads every time they stepped out of line, but this other stuff . . ." He shook his head. "There was Ian Brady and Myra Hindley, but they were psychopaths and went for other people's children. It's as if sex in families only started in the last ten–fifteen years."

"It's been going on for centuries," said Sasha, who'd researched the subject in depth. "It's society's attitude that's changed. We know now that if a child's forced into a relationship where the balance of power is unequal, the damage is irreparable. They tend to replicate that imbalance in future relationships, which is what Louise seems to have been doing."

Jonathan shielded his own eyes against

the sun. “Louise persuaded Andrew not to look at it with the benefit of hindsight, but to keep in mind that no one knew Grace was going to die. In those circumstances the only thing the Burtons were guilty of was failing to ensure that Cill returned home. They’d have been as shocked as anyone when the police continued to report her missing.”

“Why didn’t they say something then?”

Jonathan shrugged. “They were worried about what the neighbors would say.”

George pulled a disapproving face. “I can’t believe any parent would behave so irresponsibly.”

“You’re looking at it with hindsight again. As far as they were concerned, it was perfectly straightforward. Cill was alive, she was streetwise, her house was round the corner, she promised to go straight back to it. They probably thought she’d be spotted before she even reached the end of the road.”

“Why wasn’t she?”

“Pass.”

“Dear, dear, dear! You’re expecting me to swallow more coincidences than I ever offered you. It’s complete nonsense, Jon. You must see that.”

He held up his hands in mock surrender.

"I'm simply playing devil's advocate on behalf of the fat controller. I said I'd run it past you and I have."

"Do *you* believe it?"

Jonathan considered for a moment. "Andrew's looking for anyone other than Howard to be guilty . . . and he prefers Mr. Burton or Mr. Trevelyan because he likes the symmetry of child abuse running through the story."

George pulled a face. "You're supposed to be bringing a critical eye to bear on the evidence."

He grinned. "Then I'll tell you what I do believe. When Louise told Andrew she looked through Grace's window on the Tuesday, it was done deliberately to implicate Roy and his friends."

George squinted at him again. "Why?"

"I don't know . . . unless it's the truth . . ."

"She always picks blokes who're violent," Rachel said. "The one she's got at the moment gave her a black eye a few weeks ago. That's why Billy's worried about her. You could argue it's bad luck, except that, for a while, she was married to one of the boys who raped Cill. We don't understand that at all, because she must have known what she was getting into. She'll tell you she didn't know their names and couldn't identify them, but she'll be lying."

"It wasn't an accident that we all hooked up on the day of the rape," said Billy. "Cill and Lou knew where to find them, so they must have been with them before. There's no way she wouldn't have recognized Roy when she saw him."

"Who's Roy?"

"Roy Trent . . . manages a pub in Highdown. He's the one Lou married." Billy shook his head. "He's a right bastard . . . raped Cill twice then kicked her. So why would Lou want to marry a man like that? I can't get my head round it at all."

Sasha smiled slightly. "Better the devil you know?" she suggested. "She'd have had more power in a relationship where she held a bargaining chip. Secrets are powerful weapons. You made that point yourselves in reference to the way your parents treated her."

"Then why leave him for someone she *can't* control?" asked Rachel. "It doesn't make sense."

"Only because you're assuming a rationale behind her behavior which probably doesn't exist. If Roy was an inadequate lover, she'd move on to a man who was better."

"She can't go on doing it forever," said Rachel with a moue of disapproval. "She's no spring chicken anymore."

"I shouldn't think age has anything to do with it but, in any case, you said she's trying to look like Cill at thirteen, so perhaps she wants to act thirteen as well."

"That's pathetic."

"Yes," Sasha agreed soberly, "but, if your husband's right about his father, then she's a very damaged woman. Louise would have learned at ten or eleven that orgasm equals relationship . . . so how can a relationship exist without it? It would explain why she cut Billy out of her life, and why she isn't interested in you or your children. She lacks the skill to handle nonsexual relationships."

"She hasn't spoken to Dad in years," said Billy, "just took money off him."

"I expect she felt she'd earned it."

There was a brief silence while Billy and Rachel digested this.

"God!" said Rachel abruptly. "I hope we're not wrong about this. It's a hell of an accusation against a seventy-year-old."

Billy looked at Sasha. "What do *you* think?"

She hesitated, wondering how blunt she could be. "I'm no expert," she warned, "but you've described a common background for abuse. Absent mother, touchy-feely father, secretive behavior, taboo subjects — he certainly had the opportunity."

"Is that a yes?"

"I'd certainly like to talk to him about Cill. As far as I know, he wasn't interviewed at the time of her disappearance." She watched Billy's expression turn to anxiety. "It's what you suspect, isn't it? That he knows what happened to her? Your mother, too?"

He looked devastated, as if he'd wanted her to say the opposite. "Yes," he admitted. "And Louise."

"It certainly sounds as if he was using your sister as a procurer, although I wouldn't think she understood what role she was playing until she brought Cill into the house. You said she was jealous and uppity, so I'm guessing she realized that your father was getting bored with her." She paused. "As a matter of interest, how did she react when the boys paid more attention to Cill on the day of the rape?"

"She teased them about being virgins. It's what got them steamed up."

"So she contributed to what happened?"

Billy covered his eyes again. "She made Cill come back to help her, and that's when they jumped her."

"What did Louise do?"

"Curled into a ball," he said harshly. "Me, too, if it comes to that. Neither of us did a damn thing . . . just let it happen."

Sasha exchanged a glance with Rachel. "What happened after the boys had gone?" she asked. "How did Cill clean herself up?"

"She didn't, not then. Lou sneaked off and got her some clothes so she could cover up, then the girls left." He paused. "I've never been so scared in my life. I tried to go after them, but Lou said she'd drop me in it if I did."

"Did they say where they were going?"

"No."

"What time was it?"

"Afternoon . . . two-ish."

"What did you do?"

He raised his head. "Hid in the park till school ended, then went home. I felt ill from the vodka, but no one noticed. Dad was in the garden, so I went to my room and stayed there till Lou came back. I was shaking like a leaf . . . kept thinking Cill had died or something and the police were going to come. Then Lou waltzes in as if nothing had happened — it was weird."

"Did you ask her where she and Cill had gone?"

"I didn't need to," said Billy flatly. "I guessed where she got the clothes from, because she couldn't go to Cill's house or ours in case she was caught. Grace Jefferies," he explained. "Had to be. She came back with some trousers that were way too big for Cill. She had to bunch them at her waist to stop them falling down."

The sun was so strong that George decided they needed hats. Her face had turned the color of beetroot and she reappeared from upstairs with a pink straw confection on her head. "Friend's daughter's wedding," she said succinctly. "Total waste of money. They were divorced two years later. Here!" She plonked a cap on his head. "This was my father's postman's hat. At least it'll keep the sun off your face."

Jonathan turned it round so that the peak was shading his neck. "It's the boiling brain that's the problem. The face was bred for this sort of weather."

She giggled as she sat down. "You look as if you've got a saucepan on your head."

He eyed her with amusement. "And you look *great,* George! I've always thought red and pink were the perfect combination."

She giggled again. "Wasn't it a terrible choice? Some wretched shop assistant told me it suited me, and I *believed* her!" She tapped the table. "Here's a question. I was thinking about it upstairs: why did Grace allow the girls to truant in her house? I don't believe that nonsense Louise told Andrew about bruises. Grace was a mature woman. If she was concerned about the girls, she would have phoned the NSPCC, or social services, or the school, even the police . . . and she could have done it anonymously. So why didn't she?"

"For the same reason she didn't rat on Howard."

"And what reason was that?"

"She felt sorry for him."

George pondered for a moment. "Any normal grandmother would have bust a gut to find him some help, particularly when he was younger."

"Perhaps there wasn't any to be had."

George ignored him. "The only person who did anything for him was Wynne. She may not have been very effective, but at least she had a go. She dragged him to school by his ear, beat him up to make him stay there, went out to work to support him, took a two-day sickie to help him find a job, tried to get help from the GP." She raised her eyebrows. "Don't you think it's interesting that as soon as the two-day job search was over, he went straight back to Grace's house?"

"Not really. It's where he always went."

George wagged a finger at him. "Exactly."

"So?"

"Grace kept undermining Wynne's efforts. Every time Wynne got him up to the mark, Grace seduced him back again."

"She wouldn't have needed to seduce him. He preferred it there."

"Then she should have made it uncomfortable for him. It explains why Wynne never went to see her. They probably rowed all the time about Grace ruining Howard's chances. *I'd* have blooming well rowed with my mother if she'd kept my son from school." She smiled at Jonathan's continued skepticism. "Oh, come on! At least try to be objective. She did the same with Louise and Cill . . . reinforced their truanting against their parents' wishes. But none of us volunteers for anything unless it works to our advantage. Grace was a recluse. She hardly ever went out, didn't have a job, rarely saw her daughter, couldn't socialize with her neighbors because she had a speech impediment. What does that tell you?"

He shrugged. "She was difficult? Unlikeable? Divorced from reality?"

"Probably all of those things . . . but why did children like being with her?"

"She let them watch her television."

More finger pointing. "Right. And why did she do that?"

Jonathan shook his head. "Pass."

"She was *lonely,* Jon. I'll bet Louise could have had a party in there, and Grace would have baked the biscuits."

He stared thoughtfully down the garden, more taken by one of her earlier points. "Howard was supposed to be starting a job at the local dairy that Wednesday afternoon," he murmured. "Perhaps he was intending to do it until he found Grace's body."

"Why go to her house at all?"

"To see if Cill was there?"

Chapter Twenty-three

Sandbanks Peninsula, Bournemouth
Thursday, May 15, 2003, 2:45 p.m.

Sasha Spencer drew up outside the Fletchers' house in full view of a CCTV camera on a lamppost and reached into the backseat for her briefcase. Whether she was being monitored or not, she could see no point in pretending to be anything other than she was. She stepped out of the car, smoothed her skirt and took stock of the adobe facade before opening the gate. She had taken the trouble to consult an estate agent before she drove onto the peninsula and had discovered not only that Palencia was a rented property but also that the present tenant had announced his intention not to renew the lease. Was Ms. Spencer interested in taking it on?

There were no cars in the driveway and no answer to her persistent ringing of the doorbell. A garage to the left of the house was also empty. She looked for cameras but, if they existed, they were well hidden. Ostentatiously consulting her watch, she followed a path down the right-hand side, looking in windows as she went, before knocking loudly on the kitchen door. There was no response. Indeed, the only sign that the house was inhabited was a sun lounger on the lawn with a towel over it.

According to Billy Burton, Louise had said her husband was in his study the day Billy called, but Sasha had seen only a sitting room and a small dining room. With another quick scan for cameras, she moved past the kitchen and peered through the next set of windows, shading her eyes to cut out the glare of the sun. This room, too, was unoccupied but she could see the back of a computer console on the desk and a large flat-screen television on the wall behind it. Light flickered across its surface and she wondered if it was active until she realized it was a reflection from the computer monitor. She narrowed her eyes to see if she could make out the image but, even as she watched, the reflection vanished.

It was a moment or two before she questioned why. Then she straightened abruptly and stepped back. The monitor had shut down automatically because the computer hadn't been used for a preset number of minutes, usually fifteen. Someone was in the house, and a reactive prickling between her shoulders told Sasha she was being watched. With a look of annoyance, she consulted her watch again, then retraced her steps to the front. She took a business card from her pocket, scribbled, "FAO Louise Burton. Please call me. Need to speak to you urgently re: Cill Trevelyan" on the back and pushed it through the door. As she left, she had a strong suspicion that, even though she hadn't seen any cameras, all her movements had been recorded.

25 Mullin Street, Highdown, Bournemouth
Thursday, May 15, 2003, 3:30 p.m.

George opened the door and smiled inquiringly at the visitor on her doorstep. "How can I help?" she asked, assuming the young woman was a constituent.

Sasha took in the bizarre hat and red face without flinching. "Are you Councillor Georgina Gardener?"

"Yes."

Sasha produced her operating license. "I'm Sasha Spencer. I work for WCH Investigations. You visited our offices a month ago asking for information on Mr. and Mrs. Trevelyan. My colleague took your details but was unable to assist you for confidentiality reasons. I was wondering if you'd be willing to give me a few minutes of your time now."

George was too surprised to say anything for several seconds. "Well, well, well!" she then declared. "And Jonathan doesn't believe in coincidences!" She chuckled at Sasha's expression. "You'd better come in. We're in the garden."

Sasha felt at a distinct disadvantage as she was shepherded outside, introduced to Dr. Hughes, whose head attire was even more peculiar, and given a kitchen chair to sit on. She had no idea who he was, didn't take greatly to his amused smile and wasn't given a chance to run through her spiel before Councillor Gardener piled in with her own comments. She was better informed than Billy Burton realized and canny enough to recognize that Sasha wouldn't be there unless the Trevelyans had authorized it. She asked the young woman bluntly what had made them decide to do it. "It can't have been my approach to your colleague, because I didn't explain why I was there. And you wouldn't have driven all this way just to find out why I asked for their address."

"I'm afraid the issues of confidentiality remain the same, Councillor Gardener. I'm not at liberty to say."

"Has someone else contacted you?" She took the woman's silence for assent and looked at Jonathan. "It must have been William Burton. Interesting, eh? Why does he want his sister investigated?" She turned back to Sasha. "Have you spoken to her?"

"Who?"

"Priscilla Fletcher."

There was a pronounced pause before Jonathan took pity on Sasha. In a funny sort of way, she reminded him of George. A little on the chubby side, inappropriately dressed for a warm day in Bournemouth and certainly no beauty. Her mouth kept reaching nervously for a smile, as if she'd been trained to defuse difficult situations by offering a symbol of good will, but it wasn't something that came naturally to her. As usual, he failed to take into account the effect his intense gaze had on people and decided she hadn't been long in her job.

"Why don't you let Ms. Spencer tell us why she's here?" he suggested to George. "At the moment she's looking a trifle shell-shocked . . . which was rather my experience the first time I met you."

George promptly pulled an apologetic face. "I'm so sorry, dear. I thought it would be simpler if we just got on with it . . . but Jonathan's right. Please —" she made an inviting gesture — "go ahead."

Sasha wondered what to say. She had been taught to go through certain formalities, but she was more used to the nervous responses she'd had from the Burtons than to this amused impatience. She played for time by opening her briefcase and taking out her notebook. "If I may, I'll begin by explaining my company's policy with regard to your rights and the rights of my clients. You are under no obligation to answer my questions, however —" She broke off as Jonathan cleared his throat. "Who *are* you?" she demanded abruptly. "Why are you so interested in Cill Trevelyan?"

Jonathan gave a nod of approval. "How prepared are you to share information?" he asked. "We're fairly well informed on her story, but there are gaps in our knowledge that you might be able to fill."

"I can't breach client confidentiality."

He exchanged a glance with George. "Then there's no incentive for us to help you," he said. "We've put time and effort into researching Cill's story, and you wouldn't know Priscilla Fletcher was worth investigating if Councillor Gardener hadn't paid a visit to William Burton."

Sasha tried another smile. "Do you know where Cill Trevelyan is?"

"No."

"Do you know if she's still alive?"

"No."

"Then what *do* you know that's worth my breaking company rules?"

"Enough to give you a helping hand," said George. "Have you spoken to Priscilla Fletcher?"

Sasha shook her head. "I've just come from her house. I'm pretty sure someone was inside but they refused to answer the door. I've no idea if it was her or her husband." She hesitated. "Her brother says you have a photograph of her as she is now. May I see it?"

"As long as you show us one of Cill as a child," said George. "The Trevelyans must have given you one, but all we have is a black-and-white newspaper cutting. Trade for trade? We'll tell you something . . . you tell us something."

Sasha wasn't as naive as Jonathan thought, so she played with her pencil and pretended to think about it. They'd be freer with their own information if they thought hers had to be enticed out of her.

As if to prove her point, Jonathan leaned forward. "Live dangerously," he encouraged her, "otherwise George'll psychoanalyze you . . . and that's a nightmare."

Louise spotted the card the minute she entered her front door. It lay on the carpet a meter from the doormat as if a current of air had wafted it from the letter box. She picked it up and read it, then thrust it hurriedly into her pocket. If she gave any thought at all to the cameras and tapes that ran in twenty-four-hour loops in Nick's office, it was only in relation to her own arrival. She retreated through the door, her busy mind already working out excuses for her rapid turnaround, and left as quietly as she'd arrived.

Jonathan passed David Trevelyan's statement to George and bent his head to read Jean's. The noise of an occasional car filtered through from the road outside, but otherwise the only sounds were a distant motor-mower and the hum of crickets in the grass. Sasha sat patiently waiting, wishing there was an umbrella. Her skin was reddening in the sun and sweat was running down her back.

"Why don't you take off your jacket?" said Jonathan suddenly. "You'll fry if you're not careful."

Sasha gave her automatic smile. "I'm fine, thank you."

"Have a hat," said George, whipping off the pink straw creation and offering it across.

"No . . . I'm all right . . . thank you."

Jonathan came to the end of the page and pushed it away. "Very interesting." He turned his attention to Sasha again. "Have you met either of them? What are they like?"

"No, it was a predecessor who interviewed them. He noted down his impressions afterward." She sorted through her briefcase, looking for them. "I've listened to the tapes and spoken to Mr. Trevelyan on the phone, but that's all. Here we are." She read from the page: " 'David Trevelyan: Big, impressive man with easy manner. Did most of the talking. Clearly blames himself for what happened. No sense that he was keeping anything back. Jean Trevelyan: Slender, good-looking woman. More subdued than her husband. Spent most of the interview in tears. Also blames herself. No sense that she was keeping anything back. Some disagreement between them over the rape. Jean believes it happened. David can only focus on the way it allowed Cill to be portrayed as a tart. This still makes him angry.' " She looked up. "That's it."

"Does he talk on the tapes about the argument with Robert Burton?"

"All the time. He's convinced the Burtons set out to blacken Cill's name deliberately."

"Why?"

"He's not very sure. He keeps talking about the end result — that the police decided she was promiscuous, probably had a boyfriend she'd never told anyone about, and therefore wrote her off as a runaway." She paused to collect her thoughts. "He accuses Louise of lying about everything, including the rape. He says she was diverting attention from something she'd done and accuses the Burtons of backing her up to avoid the police taking too close an interest in their own daughter."

"That last bit is probably true," said George thoughtfully, mulling over what Sasha had told them. "They wouldn't want *anyone* taking an interest in Louise if William's right about the abuse." She folded her hands over David Trevelyan's statement. "I wonder how much the mother knew."

"She enabled it to happen," said Sasha.

"Mm." George pursed her lips in thought. "Except she couldn't know about the abuse *and* the rape. One or other, perhaps . . . but not both."

"Why do you say that?" asked Jonathan.

"Because she'd have told Louise to keep her mouth shut at the police station. There was no guarantee they'd accept Louise's story. If they'd had her examined to see if she'd been raped as well, then her father's abuse might have shown up."

There was a short silence.

"So what do you think happened?" asked Sasha.

"God knows," said George despondently. "There's too much to take in . . . I can't see the wood for the trees."

"It's not that bad," said Jonathan reassuringly, reaching for a clean sheet of paper. "Let's start with what we know to be true." He jotted them down as he spoke. "The rape. The names of the rapists. Cill and Louise's connection with Grace. Mrs. Burton's knowledge of it. Her readiness to lie to the police." He glanced from one to the other. "Anything else?"

"Abuse," said Sasha.

"We'll come to that in a minute. I'm after anything that's supported by an independent witness."

"The fight between the girls," said George, "presumably also the fight between Robert Burton and David Trevelyan . . . and Robert Burton's remark about Cill deserving what she got. The fact that Cill didn't disappear until after her father left for work." She gestured toward Sasha. "The Trevelyans' known commitment to trying to trace their daughter. The Burtons' willingness to let theirs go. Louise's troubled history — marriage to one of the rapists . . . *remarriage* to a man of the same type —"

"Do we know that for a fact?" Jonathan broke in.

"She had a black eye when William saw her," said Sasha.

"We don't know it was given to her by her husband —" he tapped Andrew's bullet points — "and it may not have been real, anyway. She turned up with fake bruises when she went to see our agent."

"What do you know about her husband?" Sasha asked. "William tells me his name's Nicholas Fletcher and he's a bookie, but he hasn't been able to find out anything else."

George shrugged. "We haven't done much better. He had a fight with Roy Trent over Priscilla on one occasion —" she pulled a wry face — "assuming you believe my not very reliable source at the Crown and Feathers who got the information secondhand off a customer. The barmaid," she explained. "She told me the other day after Jonathan and I had a set-to with him."

Sasha looked interested. "Did Mr. Trent report it? I might be able to find out Fletcher's details if he did."

"I shouldn't think so. He gives the police a fairly wide berth."

"When was this?"

"Two years ago. It was before Tracey started working there, which is why it's hearsay."

Sasha consulted her own notes. "Didn't you say Priscilla was at the pub in February when she stole Dr. Hughes's wallet?"

George nodded.

"Does her husband know she's still seeing him?"

"No idea . . . and it may not be relevant, anyway, if she's still working as a prostitute and her husband's her pimp." Her mouth turned down disapprovingly. "It's all very murky, whichever way you look at it. My father would be spinning in his grave if he knew the antics people get up to these days. What's wrong with being loyal to one partner? It always used to work."

Sasha caught Jonathan's gaze and a flicker of amusement shivered between them.

George pretended not to notice. "If she isn't in her house now, then she may well be at the Crown and Feathers. She's like a bee to a honeypot where Roy's concerned. I never noticed her car before, but now, almost every time I pass the pub, it's there in the road. You'd think she'd be worried about Nicholas seeing it. I mean, if *I've* noticed it, why hasn't he?"

"What sort of car is it?"

"Black BMW," said Jonathan. "We can even give you the registration number."

Sasha eyed him thoughtfully. "What about Nicholas? What does he drive?"

"Pass."

"Then perhaps the BMW's his. It's worth a try." She took out her mobile telephone. "There were no cars at the house when I was there," she explained, "but I'm sure there was someone in the house." She punched in a number. "Can you write out the registration?" she asked Jonathan. "This is a check I can run quite quickly through the office."

Louise slid through the kitchen doorway and watched Roy peeling potatoes. He was working at a chopping board near the monitor, and he had his back to her. It was funny how he reminded her of her father. They had similar builds and similar ways of speaking, but she didn't think either of those triggered memories of Robert. It had more to do with the fact that Roy was always preparing meals. "I don't know why you bother," she said into the silence. "Who's going to eat them?"

He'd known she was there. Just like her father, he always heard her come in. "Private room's booked out till midnight," he told her. "Card game." He wiped his hands on a towel and turned round. "What's up?"

She walked round the table to give him Sasha Spencer's card. "That bitch George must have told them. What should I do?"

Roy squinted at the writing on the back. "How did you get it?"

"It was posted through the letter box."

"Did you tell Nick?"

"Don't be an idiot!"

Roy jerked his head toward the monitor. "I've been watching him. He was waiting by the letter box when this Spencer woman poked it through." He tucked the card back into her pocket. "You'd better start working out how to tell him who Louise Burton is. He'll probably kill you for it . . . but I'm past caring."

She raised her mouth to his and teased him with her tongue. "Nick I can handle. What do I do about Sasha Spencer?"

He stared into her eyes before pulling her into a rough embrace. "What you always do," he said with a grim smile. "Tell her it was someone else. Cill'll not stay buried this time. There's too many people asking questions."

When George went inside to make a pot of tea, Jonathan suggested moving the table to a spot further down the garden where a neighbor's tree offered some shade. Sasha accepted gratefully. He tucked her chair well under the tree, then retrieved the other two, placing his in the sunshine, at an angle to the table, and stretching his long legs in front of him. "Do you mind if I ask you a personal question?"

"Strange things genes," said Jonathan nonchalantly. "My father was a Jamaican road sweeper and my mother was a Chinese maid."

Sasha glanced at his card. "You've done well," she said. "They must be proud of you."

Perhaps they were, he thought. "So what got you into tracing children?" he asked.

"An ad in the local newspaper," she admitted honestly. "I thought it sounded more interesting than my previous job."

"Which was?"

"Office work."

"What sort?"

"I worked for the Inland Revenue." She laughed at his expression. "Now you know why I wanted to leave."

"It's not that," he said. "George used to be a tax inspector in London." He laughed. "You'll be telling me you have degrees in psychology and behavioral science next."

"I wish I had. They'd be more useful in this game than medieval history." She paused. "She's an interesting person. Have you known her long?"

"Not really." He rearranged the postman's hat so that the peak settled more comfortably on his neck. "It just seems as if I have." He smiled at Sasha's expression.

"That was a compliment. She has a disproportionate effect on the people she meets . . . her influence on them is stronger than theirs on her."

"Some people are like that. Louise Burton, for example."

"Do you think so?" Jonathan asked curiously. "To me, she has all the attributes of a loose cannon."

Sasha shrugged. "Then why does everyone protect her? Her brother . . . Roy Trent . . . possibly even Nicholas Fletcher. Why does your agent want to believe she's telling the truth? There must be something about her that attracts people. You said yourself you felt comfortable with her until you discovered your wallet was missing."

"It's a man thing," he answered cynically. "Miss Brett wouldn't agree with you. She didn't like her at all."

"But she didn't punish her the way she punished Cill," Sasha pointed out.

George picked up the tail end of the conversation as she brought out a tray of cups and a teapot. "Cill went back to rescue her before the rape," she reminded Jonathan as she resumed her seat, "which suggests she perceived Louise as more vulnerable than she was. Weakness can be a strength in certain situations, particularly if it's used to manipulate emotions."

"It didn't work for Howard or Grace," he said.

"No," she agreed, "but they weren't manipulators."

"And Louise is?"

"She was very successful at persuading you to let her look through your briefcase . . . and Andrew into feeling sorry for her." She wagged a finger at him. "She had a good teacher, Jon. There's no more manipulative personality than an abusive father . . . and no one with less moral sense. It's an appalling role model for an impressionable child. You should know that better than anyone."

"Are you saying I'm manipulative?"

George chuckled. "You could write a book on it, my dear."

Louise lit a cigarette. "Don't tell me what to do, Roy. You're not my bloody keeper. Never have been. You all think you own me because of what happened, but you *don't . . . I* own *you!*" She moved away from him. "You're so like my dad, darlin', you wouldn't believe. Love you, love you, love you, baby . . . now gimme what I want or I'll thrash the living daylights out of you." Her eyes flared disparagingly. "I used to think he was God till he started feeling up Cill . . . then I realized what a dirty little creep he was . . . and I hated him. It was OK when he told me he loved me better than Mum. It wasn't OK when he said Cill was his favorite."

Roy had heard it all before. Every time she was stoned or drunk the shabby family secrets poured out, contaminating her, contaminating him. He wondered sometimes if he would ever have been drawn into this suicidally symbiotic relationship if she'd told him the truth at thirteen, but he was honest enough to recognize that he would. The sort of madness that had possessed them all that fatal May in 1970 was generated by drink and self-loathing, and the problems of a skinny child who held no attraction for them wouldn't have been heeded, much less understood.

She was right about ownership. She had held their fate in her hands for thirty-plus years, and the only thing that had kept her alive was heroin. Stumbling from one fix to another, she had been a threat to no one. Clean, she was a walking time bomb. "Take care, Lou," he warned. "I can't protect you forever."

She blew a lungful of smoke in his direction. "You're so arrogant," she said scornfully. "Did you never think I might be protecting you? You're the one Nick's worried about, darlin'. You know what he's like — gets a bee in his bonnet and there's no shifting it. I told you months ago he didn't like you buddying up to George, but you wouldn't listen."

"That's crap."

She gave an indifferent shrug. "Why do you think he lets me come here? He doesn't trust you . . . wouldn't trust Micky either if he was still alive. It's him told me to go through the wog's briefcase. He's round the bloody twist . . . sees ghouls and goblins everywhere."

It was partially true. The bits of Nick's memory that remained intact had fused into a looped tape of events that bore little resemblance to reality. Somewhere in the regions of his mad mind, it was only Grace's death he remembered.

Sasha closed her palm over her mobile's mouthpiece. "The car's registered in the name of Priscilla Fletcher Hurst." She frowned at George. "Where does the Hurst come from? I thought you said her previous husband was Roy Trent."

"Colley Hurst," said George slowly. "How very stupid of me. It's an old-fashioned abbreviation of Nicholas." She sorted through her folder for the transcript she'd made of her conversations with Billy Burton. "Her brother said her first husband was called Mike," she said, looking at Jonathan. "Could that have been Micky Hopkinson?"

"Wouldn't he have recognized him?"

"He said he was in prison so he never saw him."

Jonathan hunched forward in his chair. "What kind of a databank are you accessing?" he asked Sasha. "Is it worth telling your colleague to feed in Nicholas Hurst — maybe Michael Hopkinson, too — and see if he comes up with anything?"

"We'll give it a try but I wouldn't think so, not unless they've been convicted in the last ten years." She spoke into the phone again, giving both names, then hung up. "He'll call back in a couple of minutes with a yea or a nay." She pondered for a moment. "We have a sister company of inquiry agents who can find out anything you want to know — bank account details, family details, employment and car history, even medical and social service records — but, as most of that information's privileged, the costs are higher, to cover the company's risk. I know for a fact that Mr. Trevelyan can't afford it, but if either of you can, it might be worth a try."

"How much?" asked George.

"Upward of five hundred pounds."

George pulled a face. "Is it ethical?"

Jonathan exchanged another amused glance with Sasha. "Absolutely not," he said. "I should think it breaches every privacy law that's ever been written . . . but *bloody* interesting, George. We could use some of this famous advance Andrew keeps promising us."

"What about your debts?"

He bared his teeth at her. "Don't keep reminding me."

"*Someone* has to. You'll be grateful —"

She broke off as the mobile rang and Sasha put it to her ear. "Yup," she said, "go ahead." She wrote fast in shorthand across her pad. "Got that. What about Michael Hopkinson? OK . . . thanks." She laid the phone on the table. "Nothing on Hopkinson, but three years ago the Metropolitan Police was ordered to pay Nicholas Hurst two hundred thousand in compensation for brain damage, wrongful arrest, wrongful imprisonment and loss of earnings. At the time of his injuries he was managing a William Hill betting shop in the East End. He was in and out of hospital for three years and returned to Bournemouth in 2001 when the compensation came through. Last known address —" she raised her head — "the Crown and Feathers, Friar Road, Highdown."

"Good lord!" exclaimed George. "How very incestuous it all is. Do you realize that if Mike was Micky Hopkinson, then she's been married to all three of them at one time or another? Why aren't the men jealous of each other?"

"Because they have no more feelings for Louise than they do for each other," said Jonathan.

"There used to be a law that said wives couldn't testify against their husbands," put in Sasha. "I don't know when it was repealed, but perhaps they think it still applies."

Jonathan shook his head. "They're a tribe," he said. "Marriage is just a device to keep Louise within the fold." He paused. "The interesting question is why she goes along with it . . . unless she has more to gain than they have."

"Like what?"

"Security?" he suggested. "It's a primary tribal instinct."

From: Sasha Spencer [S.Spencer@WCHinvestigations.com]
Sent: Wed. 5/21/03 1002
To: jon.hughes@london.ac.uk; geo.gar@mullinst.co.uk
Subject: Report on Roy Trent, Crown and Feathers, Friar Road, Highdown

---

Dear George and Jonathan

Re: the report from Bentham Inquiry Agents

Bentham's agent has given me a verbal account of his investigation into Roy Trent. Copies of the full report will be posted on to you as soon as they're ready, but in the meantime the following is a summary of his findings:

1. Roy Trent has ownership of the pub until his death. His first wife, Robyn Hapgood, was the daughter of the previous owner. She OD'd on heroin in 1988, leaving the property

to Trent for his lifetime, and after that to their son, Peter (12 years old at the time of her death). The property's heavily mortgaged — possibly to pay inheritance tax at the time of Robyn's father's death (1984) — but Trent keeps up the repayments. The debts will be cleared in 2009.

2. Peter Hapgood, now aged 28, has a criminal record and a history of drug abuse. He was first sentenced in 1994 and is currently in the second year of a 5-year term for aggravated burglary.
3. Trent has received numerous offers on the pub and has rejected them all. It is not clear why as he has *insufficient* funds to develop it himself. There may be a clause in the will preventing him from selling it — but this is unlikely as such clauses can be challenged. Bentham's view is that he is holding on until the property's free of debt.
4. He married Louise Burton a.k.a. Daisy Burton a.k.a. Priscilla Hopkinson in 1992.

5. Michael Hopkinson OD'd in 1986 after several terms in prison. He and Louise married in 1974 (she was 17). She became chronically drug-addicted (heroin/crack cocaine) and maintained her own and her husband's addictions through prostitution.
6. Following their marriage, Trent made some attempts to wean her off drugs (e.g. obtained a placement in a rehab center where she lasted 6 weeks before relapsing). One source, not corroborated, says she had an affair with Peter while he was under his father's roof. The same source suggests it was Louise who got the boy (a) addicted and (b) into crime to supply them both.
7. Trent offered Nicholas "Colley" Fletcher Hurst free accommodation in 2000 and applied for a "quickie" divorce which came through in June 2001.
8. Louise began an affair with Nicholas while he was at the Crown and Feathers and they moved into

rented accommodation on Sandbanks in August 2001. Hurst's compensation came through in October 2001 and he and Louise married in November 2001. Louise has been "clean" since she hooked up with Hurst.

9. Louise continues to be a regular visitor to the pub.
10. Trent is well regarded by the local community (cf. George's initial impressions). The consensus view is that he has not jumped on the "leisure bandwagon" but continues to provide a service for the poor of Highdown who can't afford expensive prices. He has a reputation for being anti-drugs.
11. Full details of Trent's bank balance and mortgage history are in the report. Also, Peter Hapgood's criminal record. Trent himself spent 6 months in a juvenile institution for 5 counts of theft.

The Bentham agent suggests you look very closely at the drug connections. Despite Trent's publicly expressed views on the subject, there's been a high level of abuse among the people he's associated with. The main source (ex-prostitute who claims Trent was her pimp in the late '70s) claims she was buying class-A drugs off him until 1985 when she quit. No evidence that he's still dealing, but there are question marks over the profitability of the pub and Trent's apparent ability to make repayments on the loans.

There's a garage at the back which the agent was unable to investigate without blowing his cover, but it's heavily alarmed, has a CCTV coaxial cable supply and a hatch that faces onto an alleyway. (He obtained some digitally enhanced photographs from his car which are supplied with the report.) It would be possible to mount a surveillance operation from one of the neighboring houses to establish if it's being used for dealing, but the operation would be extremely expensive in manpower and fees, with no guarantee of success, and would be better done by the police. The agent's words to me were, “There may just be a Ferrari in there.”

Re: Robert and Eileen Burton

After discussing the Burtons with my senior colleague, I have decided to put them on hold until I/we’ve had a chance to talk to Louise. It would, of course, be a great advantage to interview her from an informed position but, as Robert Burton’s email to his son and the conversation William had with his mother both suggest that they will deny everything, no advantage would be gained. A premature meeting would only alert them to a possible police investigation, which in turn might prejudice future cooperation, particularly from Eileen Burton.

Re: Louise Burton/Priscilla Fletcher

I can confirm that her initial contact last Friday, May 16, was followed up yesterday with a proposal to meet at her house on Monday, May 26, at 1100. In this first instance, I suggest I meet with her alone and allow her to set the agenda. Assuming you're both free, I will report to you at George's house afterward.

Hoping this meets with your approval,

My best wishes

Sasha Spencer

From: Dr. Jonathan Hughes [jon.hughes@london.ac.uk]
Sent: Wed. 5/21/03 1706
To: S.Spencer@WCH investigations.com
Cc: geo.gar@mullinst.co.uk
Subject: Playing safe

Dear Sasha

Thank you for this, but I question the wisdom of holding the meeting in the lions' den. I urge you to go back to Louise and suggest neutral territory. N.B. Colley Hurst is a brain-damaged rapist who may have been party to Grace Jefferies' murder.

These are not sane people you're planning to confront, Sasha. George and I may have agreed to fund a rather dodgy investigation into Roy Trent. We did not authorize ill-considered interviews with possible murderers.

Please do something, George! You're the psychologist. Is this sensible?

Best, Jon

From: George Gardener
[geo.gar@mullinst.co.uk]
Sent: Thurs. 5/22/03 0841
To: S.Spencer@WCH
investigations.com
Cc: jon.hughes@london.ac.uk
Subject: Playing safe

Dear Sasha

Written in haste. Jonathan is right. At least question why Louise would let you into her house when her brother's experience was the exact opposite — no entry under any circumstances. Please reconsider. Everything we know about Colley Hurst suggests he's a violent man. Best,

George

From: Sasha Spencer [S.Spencer@WCHinvestigations.com]
Sent: Thurs. 5/22/03 1207
To: jon.hughes@london.ac.uk; geo.gar@mullinst.co.uk
Subject: Trust me

Dear Jon & George

I'm over 21. I don't need nannies!

Sasha

Chapter Twenty-four

Palencia, Frean Street,
Sandbanks, Bournemouth
Monday, May 26, 2003, 11:00 a.m.

As Andrew Spicer had found, the close-up reality of Louise was nothing like Cill Trevelyan. She was finer boned, smaller featured and her eyes were the wrong color. She was also prettier and younger looking than Sasha had expected, with only a vague resemblance to the scowling, sulky child in William Burton's album. She answered the door in a crisp, well-fitting jade green dress that accentuated her slim figure. Sasha, bulky in an overtight brown suit and wearing unattractive spectacles, felt fat and gauche by comparison, and showed it by tugging her jacket down to cover her hips. With an amused smile, Louise led her across the hall to the sitting room.

Sasha would have known it was a rented

house even if she hadn't been told by the estate agent. It was painted throughout in standard cream with unexceptional furniture and framed prints of Impressionist paintings and Dorset scenes on the walls. There was very little of a personal nature and the only point of interest in the sitting room was a large television screen similar to the one in the study. It was showing a horse race but the sound was muted. Louise noticed Sasha looking at it.

"My husband's an Internet gambler," she said, gesturing to an armchair before lowering herself to the sofa. "We have wall-to-wall racing off the digital channels."

Sasha went into her smiling routine as she took the chair. "I didn't know there were meetings in the morning."

Louise glanced at the screen. "It'll be a recording. There's a video link to his study that means I have to watch whatever he's watching. Is it bothering you? Do you want me to turn it off?"

Sasha listened to the silence. "No, it's fine. I wouldn't want to upset him."

"He won't know unless he joins us," said the older woman, reaching for the remote and killing the picture. "Turning one off doesn't affect the others." She crossed a neat leg over the other and looked encouragingly at the younger woman. "How can I help?"

Sasha went nervously into her preamble about confidentiality, while recognizing that she might easily have been persuaded that William's story was fantasy if Louise had opened the door twelve days ago. The woman was composed, charming and elegant, and there was nothing to indicate a violent husband or a history of drugs and sexual abuse. Her voice was more educated than William's rough Dorset burr, although Sasha wondered how natural it was.

Louise allowed Sasha to finish her presentation without interruption. "You mentioned Cill Trevelyan on your card," she said then. "Does that mean David and Jean are your clients?"

Sasha nodded. "Do you remember them, Mrs. Fletcher?"

"Of course," she said easily. "Cill was my best friend . . . as you know, or you wouldn't have written 'FAO Louise Burton' on your card."

Sasha ran her tongue across her lips. "I did, yes."

Louise was watching too closely not to notice the signs of nerves. "So how are the Trevelyans?" she asked. "I often think of them — it must be desperate to lose a child like that."

It was a very different start from the one Sasha had been expecting — more like the opening courtesies at a social function — but she went along with it, explaining that Jean hadn't been well recently. Louise produced several amusing memories of visiting the Trevelyan home in Highdown, then spoke of her shock when she learned that Cill had run away. "We were incredibly close," she murmured, before lapsing into an abrupt silence and waiting for Sasha to continue.

There was a sliver of sound from somewhere in the house and this time Sasha's nervousness was genuine. "I expect you're wondering how I found you."

"Not really," said Louise. "I'm hardly in hiding. You can't get more high profile than Sandbanks."

Sasha fixed her automatic smile to her face. "In fact it was your brother who passed your details to us, Mrs. Fletcher, because he knew we were acting for Mr. and Mrs. Trevelyan. I gather he reestablished contact with you a month or so ago?" She was watching equally closely and saw the sudden narrowing of Louise's eyes. "As you'll appreciate, David and Jean have never given up hope of finding Cill and we periodically reactivate the investigation when new information comes our way."

She retrieved her file and notebook from her case and placed them on her lap. "You may not be aware that various agencies have tried to locate you over the years without success," she went on. "Presumably because of your various name changes." She bent her head to her notes, holding her glasses in place with a finger. "First Louise Burton, then Daisy Burton, then Daisy Hopkinson, then Cill Trent, now Priscilla Fletcher Hurst." She looked up again, inviting Louise to respond. "I'm a little puzzled why you chose to take Cill's Christian name and marry her rapists, Mrs. Fletcher."

Louise answered readily enough. "Not that it's any of your business," she said mildly, "but I've known all three of them since I was a youngster. I'd have stayed with Michael if he hadn't died . . . and with Roy if Colley hadn't come back. There's nothing sinister about it. Sensible people always marry their friends. That way, you know what you're getting."

Sasha held her gaze for a moment. "Except that, in this case, you knew you were getting three violent young men who gang raped your best friend. It traumatized your brother — he's still having flashbacks thirty years after the event. Were you not similarly affected . . . especially as Cill vanished into thin air three weeks later?"

"Billy reinvents history to make his life more exciting," Louise said dismissively. "I expect you would, too, if you'd married the most boring person you'd ever met, always done what your father told you and only ever lived in one house. He was ten years old and he was drunk. Whatever he remembers is bound to be distorted."

Sasha made a note. "You make him sound too unimaginative to reinvent history," she remarked. "He certainly believes his flashbacks are real."

The classy accent began to slip a little. "It was hardly a rape. Cill was desperate for sex with Roy, couldn't lift her skirt quick enough . . . and it was only when Micky and Colley piled in on top that she started complaining. They were fourteen-year-old virgins, drunk as skunks on vodka, and at least two of them ejaculated before they even got in." She shrugged. "I'm not saying it's fun to have three teenage drunks wank over you, but Cill was as big as they were and gave as good as she got." She paused. "It's not what made her run away either. That was her dad taking the strap to her. She'd been saying for weeks she'd bugger off if he tried it on again."

Sasha refused to be sidetracked. "Your brother remembers it differently, Mrs. Fletcher. He describes a sickening level of brutality that was inexcusable whatever the age of the participants."

"Then you'll have to choose which of us you want to believe . . . though I can't say I'm happy about having my brother slander my husbands. The only time he spoke to any of them was that day, and he was so paralytic he could hardly string two words together."

Sasha removed copies of the newspaper clippings that George had found and extracted Jean Trevelyan's interview. "You told the police at the time that it was a gang rape," she said, handing her the page. "Jean Trevelyan refers to it as such in this article."

Louise glanced at the headline, then laid it on the coffee table without reading it. "How could I use a phrase I didn't know?" she countered. "All I did was describe what happened. Gang rape was what the police called it . . . and it's probably why Billy's embroidering his memories now." She took a breath and went on in a more conciliatory tone. "Look, is this really necessary? It's not going to help the Trevelyans to have Billy's version accepted. The boys were questioned at the time, but they weren't charged because it wasn't considered serious enough."

"No charges were brought because Cill was missing and you refused to identify the culprits."

"It wasn't a refusal. I *couldn't* . . . not then. It was only later we became friendly, when Micky and I started going together. I never remembered he was one of them until I saw all three together and twigged who they were, and by that time Micky'd persuaded me they were OK." She smoothed a hand down the crisp cotton of her dress. "Maybe you should ask Nick?" she suggested. "He'll tell you it's true." She tilted her head to one side. "Do you want me to fetch him?"

Sasha quelled a nervous tremor in her stomach. "That would be helpful," she said. "Thank you."

Louise gave an abrupt laugh and reached for her cigarette packet on the mantelpiece. "I wouldn't advise it. He suffered brain damage a while back and doesn't take too kindly to being quizzed about his past . . . mostly because he can't remember it and hates being made to look a fool." She lit a cigarette. "It's weird the way the brain works. He's forgotten whole chunks of his life, but he can remember the form of all the horses back to 1980 and still work out odds in half a second flat. On a good day he can make ten grand just by sitting at his computer."

"Does he remember the rape?"

"I don't know," said Louise, with a malicious glint in her eye. "I've never been stupid enough to ask. Feel free, though. His study's past the kitchen."

"Does he remember you?"

"What's that supposed to mean?"

"Are you part of a chunk that he remembers?"

Louise didn't answer immediately, as if fearing a trap. "I've known him for years," she said. "He'd have to've forgotten his whole fucking life to cut me out completely."

"Interesting," remarked Sasha idly, thinking that Louise's language and accent were falling apart by the second. "So what does he call you, Mrs. Fletcher? Louise? Daisy? Cill? Priscilla? It would be a very good indication of which . . . er . . . *chunks* . . . he remembers."

"Priscilla," she said, watching the younger woman through the smoke from her cigarette. "The same name I've had for twenty years." She smiled cynically. "And, before you ask why, I was stoned when I chose it, so any thoughts of Cill were in subconscious. I used to think it was classier than Louise or Daisy . . . probably because the Trevelyans were such snobs."

Sasha let a pulse of silence pass. "Why didn't you tell the police that Billy was a witness to the rape? He knew the names of the boys."

"I was protecting him. The folks didn't know he'd been truanting."

"Why didn't the school notice his absence?"

"I phoned in for him, pretending to be Mum. Said he was sick."

"Why?"

"To get him off the hook, of course." She took a pull at her cigarette. "It was his one and only time . . . he was so scared he never did it again. He should be grateful for small mercies instead of turning it into a drama."

Sasha smiled again. "I'm not sure he'd agree with you, Mrs. Fletcher." She paused to push her spectacles up her nose. "I meant, why did you want him with you that day? He told me the meeting with the boys was preplanned, and that you and Cill talked sex nonstop to get them excited. I can't see the point of having a ten-year-old tagging along in those circumstances."

"That's rubbish," retorted Louise angrily. "There's no way it was preplanned

. . . couldn't have been. We'd never seen them before. We went down the arcade and bumped into them by accident, and Cill promptly got the hots for Roy. The only reason we were stuck with Billy was because he couldn't go into school without being quizzed and he couldn't go home because the folks were there."

Sasha flicked back a few pages of her notepad. "I understood it was Cill who persuaded him to go with you, and you were furious about it."

There was a pronounced hesitation. "I don't remember, but it's probably right," she said. "It made Cill feel better about herself if she could get the rest of us to bunk off with her."

"Billy's interpretation is different. He says Cill wanted him along because she wasn't as keen to meet the boys as you were. He says you contributed to the rape . . . and may even have ordered it because you were jealous that Roy fancied Cill more than he fancied you."

"Dream on," said Louise scornfully. "If I'd ever wanted Roy that much, I'd still be married to him."

Sasha located the page she wanted from a follow-up interview with Billy. "Your brother doesn't buy into the idea that you were protecting him, Mrs. Fletcher, so he's looking for reasons why you didn't tell the police he was there. His childhood experience of you is that you got him into trouble at the drop of a hat to save your own skin." She ran her finger down the lines of the notepad. "These are some of the explanations he's offered. The boys were friends of yours and, as you didn't want them arrested, you couldn't afford to have Billy name them." She briefly raised her eyes. "No? Then perhaps you wanted a free hand to malign Cill because you knew how much your father liked her, and you didn't want Billy standing up for her?"

Louise squashed her cigarette into an ashtray. "Dad couldn't have given a shit. It was Mr. Trevelyan got excited about it. How *dare* Louise Burton suggest his daughter was a slut? It was quite funny, really. Everyone knew it was true except her tight-arsed parents."

Sasha let that go. "How about this one? You knew where Cill was but you didn't want to be asked questions about it, so you diverted attention onto something that had happened three weeks earlier. If Billy was involved, he might have mentioned Grace Jefferies's name, and you didn't want that." She deliberately echoed some of Louise's own words to Andrew Spicer. "It was no big deal. Cill was alive . . . she was safe while she was with Grace . . . and as far as you were concerned she'd go home as soon as she was bored." She looked up again and met the pale gaze.

"Billy never told you that."

"No," Sasha agreed, "but he's not the only person I've spoken to, Mrs. Fletcher. Let's go back to the rape for a moment. Billy says you went to Grace for replacement clothes because Cill's were torn and bloody. What happened then? Did you take her to Grace's house so that she could have a bath and clean up?"

Louise's expression hardened, but she didn't say anything.

"Should I take that as a yes?" She looked for a reaction which she didn't get. "Clearly, you couldn't tell the police about going to Grace's house," she went on evenly, "otherwise they'd have put two and two together and gone straight round to interview her about Cill's disappearance. And for some reason you didn't want that. Why not?"

"Because she'd have killed me for ratting on her. We'd had one fight already — I didn't want another one." Louise's lips twisted into a bitter smile. "Everyone pictures her as this poor little girl who ran away because she was unhappy, but she wasn't like that . . . she was a bully. You didn't cross her unless you wanted your head caved in."

"What did you and she fight about?"

"What girls always fight about. Who's more attractive, me or you?" She shook her head at Sasha's expression of incomprehension. "Oh for *Christ's* sake! What planet are you from, sweetheart? Lose some weight . . . get your hair done . . . talk dirty once in a while. You'll be a spinster all your life, if you don't. *Sex* — darlin' — *men!* She kept boasting that she was more fanciable than me, so I said I'd tell her folks about the rape if she didn't shut up. It was getting on my wick something chronic."

Sasha concentrated on her notes. "So you did know it was a rape?"

"Figure of speech," Louise said scornfully. "Who the hell cared what it was? As far as Cill was concerned, it was a walk in the park . . . proof that she was attractive enough to be fucked." She watched a look of distaste cloud Sasha's face. "Don't fret yourself. It'll never happen to you. You're not the type to get jumped. You have to show a bit of flesh if you want guys to be interested."

Sasha's fingers fled automatically to her spectacles, but she stuck gamely to her interview plan. "If Billy had been questioned, he'd have mentioned Grace. Is that the real reason you didn't want him involved?"

Louise lit another cigarette, then leaned her head against the back of the sofa and stared at the ceiling. "If you got all this off Andrew Spicer or his tame author, then I might as well save my breath. None of it would have mattered if the stupid girl had gone home. I was trying to do her a favor — give her an excuse for a bit of sympathy. Instead, she landed me in it by vanishing. She'd've been mad as hell if I'd let Billy name the boys, because she still fancied Roy. She'd have milked her mum's heart and thrown a wobbly if the police had tried to take it any further. That's the way she worked."

"You, too?" Sasha asked curiously. "Your mother became very protective of you afterward."

Scorn sparked in her eyes. "Protective of herself, you mean. She wet herself every time she thought of what the neighbors'd say when they found out I'd seen Cill at Grace's on the Saturday. The whole bloody family would've been hung out to dry."

"When did you tell her?"

"About Cill being at Grace's?" She lifted an indifferent shoulder. "Can't remember."

"It's important, Mrs. Fletcher."

Louise lowered her gaze. "Why? What difference does it make? Mum'll tell you I'm lying. She's like Billy — been rewriting history for years."

"So you told her on the Saturday?"

A brief nod.

"Before or after you went to the police station?"

"Before."

It was like pulling teeth, thought Sasha, as a silence developed. She wondered how contrived the strategy was, and who had instigated it. "How exactly?"

"It was a Saturday. She didn't work on Saturdays."

"And?"

"We were in the kitchen when the phone rings. It was Jean Trevelyan wanting to know if Cill was at our house. Mum says no, and hangs up, then gives me the third degree. What had I done? Why would Cill run away? What did I know? So I go looking round Grace's place. By the time I got back Dad was home, and he was in a right schiz because David Trevelyan had thumped him at work. Mum said it'd serve them right if Cill stayed away for good, so I told them she was holed up with Grace."

"Your mother told the police she had no idea where Cill was."

"Only because Dad was pissed off with David Trevelyan. He said it'd do him good to worry a bit. Then the cops turned up saying I had to go down the nick for interview because I was Cill's best friend. That *really* fired Dad up. He wanted them to talk to me at home, but they quoted the rules about questioning kids and Dad jumped to the idea that David had grassed him up about their fight. Dad's the one wanted me to tell the cops about Cill having sex, so the Trevelyans would know what a slut their daughter was."

"Your parents knew about that?"

A curl of smoke drifted out of Louise's mouth. "Dad did," she said curtly. "I don't know about Mum."

"Who told him?"

"Who do you think?"

"You?"

"Like hell!" she said dismissively. "There was nothing in it for me. Why would I want to give him a reason to get worked up over her? You seem to have worked out that he liked her." She regarded the other woman cynically. "It was Cill. That's how she operated. As long as men were fighting over her, she had what she wanted. It drove Dad crazy to think she'd let Roy have a bit of the action. It drove *David* crazy the amount of time she spent round our place." She gave a mirthless laugh at Sasha's shocked expression. "Oh, come on! You weren't born yesterday. Why the hell do you think the bastard kept thrashing her? It wasn't because he needed the exercise. It was because his wife was frigid and he creamed every time he lammed into Cill's arse."

Shock tactics were effective, thought Sasha, as she stared at the photocopy of Jean Trevelyan's interview on the table — "Mother's Anguish over Missing Teen" — and remembered David's forceful voice on the taped interviews. "Did Mr. and Mrs. Trevelyan know that you and Cill truanted at Grace's house?" she asked.

Louise shook her head. "Not unless Cill told them."

"But your parents knew?"

"Only after we'd stopped it. Howard kept pestering me about Cill, so I told him to fuck off and he went whining to his gran. Next thing I knew, Grace was on our doorstep wanting to know what was going on, and Mum sussed the whole thing in half a second flat. She gave Grace a right drubbing, told her she was lucky she wasn't going to report her for harboring truants just so her useless grandson could drool over a couple of teenagers."

It was like the pieces of a jigsaw slotting together. Every snippet of information that Sasha had been given, directly or indirectly, was finding its place. She pondered for a moment. "What was your father doing while you and your mother were at the police station?" she asked.

"No idea. Sleeping probably. He'd been at work all night."

"Was he in the house when you got back?"

"I presume so. We had to keep our voices down on Saturday mornings, and I don't recall that day being different." She paused. "He was there in the afternoon. I remember watching *Grandstand* with him, because he kept talking over it to ask me what the police had said."

"Where was your mother?"

Louise took a drag of her cigarette. "No idea," she said, with an amused smile. "Probably round at Grace's giving her another bollocking."

"Do you know that for a fact?"

"Of course not!" she said disparagingly. "The only facts I know are that Cill was there on the Saturday morning and was gone by the time the police found Grace's body."

"What about the Tuesday evening?"

"I didn't see her, but it doesn't mean she wasn't there." Another teasing smile. "Maybe she was upstairs, slashing at poor old Grace."

"Unlikely," said Sasha. "Her fingerprints weren't found anywhere in the house."

"Jesus!" Louise said with an abrupt return to scorn. "It wasn't a serious suggestion. How the hell would I know where she was? I kept my mouth shut because the folks got twitched when the silly bitch was still missing on the Monday. Maybe one of them went round to see what was going on, but if they did, they didn't tell me . . . and come the Friday, none of us fancied owning up to anything."

"You must have thought about it, though. What do you think happened?"

"What does it matter what I *think?* What I *know* is, it was a fucking nightmare."

"I'd be interested."

Louise looked toward the door into the hall. "All right," she said abruptly. "Howard went to Grace's on the Saturday afternoon, found Cill there, persuaded Grace she was mad to be hiding her and told her he'd take her home. Whatever happened after that wouldn't have been good, because Howard was a pervert. I'm guessing Cill wound him up by telling him about having sex with Roy, and he probably said he wanted it too. They got into a fight and she ended up dead."

Sasha felt the same prickling sensation between her shoulders as she'd felt the first time she came to this house, but she forced herself not to look at the door. "Why weren't they seen?"

"Because it was dark. If they'd left in daylight, everyone would've known Grace was involved."

"Where did he put the body?"

"How would I know? Somewhere close to where he killed her, I guess. It depends where he took her. He lived down Colliton Way and there was a lot of waste ground at the back of it."

"Her body would have been found."

Louise shrugged. "It's an industrial estate now, so maybe she ended up in someone's foundations. They were building the new Brackham & Wright's factory around that time, and Howard was always going on about it because they were putting in state-of-the-art automation and his mum was scared there'd be redundancies."

So neat. *Too neat?* "What happened then?"

Louise frowned. "He went home."

"No, I meant, what happened with Grace?"

"Howard took a carving knife to her. Had to've done. I expect she kept asking him why Cill hadn't gone home. She was on his back all the time to get himself a girl, but she wouldn't have wanted him having a go at a thirteen-year-old. She married a guy who was much older than her, so that's what she wanted for Howard . . . someone motherly who'd give him confidence but wouldn't expect sex. It wasn't what *he* wanted. Sex was the only thing he ever thought about." She smiled at Sasha's expression. "Just because a person's disabled doesn't make them pleasant, you know. They were both bloody strange, and they both thought it was everyone else's fault they were lonely. They rowed about it all the time."

Sasha pointedly returned to her notes. "It's difficult to see when he could have done it, Mrs. Fletcher. His mother gave him an alibi for the Monday and Tuesday, but you say you saw blood on Grace's window on the Tuesday afternoon. That suggests someone else killed Grace."

"Don't see why. What was to stop Howard doing it Monday night?"

"His mother alibied him. She said she was awake all night worrying about his job prospects."

"You talking about Wynne?"

"Yes."

"She was lying through her teeth."

"The prosecution didn't think so. That's why they argued that Grace died on the Wednesday."

"Not my problem," Louise said frankly, reaching forward to stub out her cigarette. "You asked me what I thought and I told you. Wynne was a lush — put away half a bottle of gin a night because she couldn't stand Howard and she couldn't stand her job — and I've never heard of a chronic alky lying awake worrying. Everyone at Brackham & Wright's knew. Her shift followed Dad's, and she was so hungover sometimes, she'd collapse over her bench with her head in her hands. Why do you think she was so worried about getting the chop?" Her pale eyes flashed with sudden humor. "Ask David Trevelyan. He'll tell you it's true. Everyone knows the whole Howard thing did her a favor. She ended up with the money from the sale of Grace's house and got shot of her useless son."

Sasha rested her pencil against the arm of her spectacles and stared at her notepad.

"Is that it? Are you done?"

"Just a couple more questions, Mrs. Fletcher. You said it was Cill who told your father about the rape . . . yet, according to your brother, you and she fell out so badly that she stopped coming to your house." She looked up with a smile. "When did she have an opportunity to talk to him?"

Louise didn't answer immediately. "Probably on the phone when Mum was at work. It's the kind of thing she did."

"Not easy if she was at school all day. There were no mobiles in 1970." No answer. "And if it wasn't Cill, there were only two other people who could have told him: you or Grace."

"Why not Billy?"

"He wouldn't have said that Cill deserved it, Mrs. Fletcher, but Grace might have done if you fed her your version first when you collected the clothes." She paused in face of Louise's incomprehension. "I'm trying to understand why your father encouraged you to tell the police about the rape on the Saturday morning, when David Trevelyan had punched him only a few hours earlier for saying Cill was a cheap little tart who deserved what she got. Most men — particularly men with unhealthy passions for little girls — don't do that. They damp down police interest as fast as they possibly can."

Out came another cigarette. "He always called her a tart."

"Only after the rape. Before the rape he wanted her on his lap all the time. That must have made you jealous."

"Why should it?"

"He was an abuser, Mrs. Fletcher, and you were his little princess. Did he show his disappointment too obviously when Cill stopped coming to the house? What did you tell him? That she preferred rough sex with Roy Trent to letting a dirty old man grope her?"

It was a second or two before Louise could bring the flame into contact with her cigarette. "What if I did? It doesn't change anything."

"It changes everything, Mrs. Fletcher. It says you're a liar and that you were jealous of your friend. And that lends credence to your brother's version of events." She paused. "It must have made you very angry that everyone you ever met — male or female — preferred Cill."

Chapter Twenty-five

There was so much hatred in the pale eyes that Sasha moved warily to the edge of her seat. On paper, there was no contest. She was taller, heavier and younger, but she didn't know how crazy Louise was and she certainly didn't fancy her chances if the woman seized on the heavy glass ashtray as a weapon. "I'm sorry if I offended you," she said, reaching down to put her notepad in her case. "It was a flippant remark and I apologize."

Louise watched her suspiciously. "What are you doing?" she demanded.

"I've taken up enough of your time."

"You haven't finished yet," she snapped. "Aren't you going to ask me how my father reacted when he heard I'd told the police Cill had been raped?"

This time there was no pretense when Sasha ran her tongue across her lips. There was too much emotion in the room and she lacked the experience to deal with it. "Certainly. If you want to tell me."

"The usual. Said he'd have me the minute Mum was out of the house."

"And did he?"

The cigarette trembled violently in Louise's fingers. "He sent Mum and Billy shopping, then buggered the life out of me in front of *Grandstand*. I even remember what was on — a horse race. I hate the fucking animals and they're on every television screen in this house." She gave a harsh laugh. "You're all obsessed with Cill's rape. What about *mine?*"

"Leave," said Sasha's boss in her ear. *"Trevor's watching her . . . says she's about to blow."*

It was true. Anger flared in the woman's eyes again like a forest fire fanned by wind. "Why don't you say something? What sort of damage do you think a grown man does to a skinny little kid? Why do you think I've never had babies?"

Sasha fluttered a hand to her mouth. "I'm trying to find some . . . *words.* I'm not qualified for this, Mrs. Fletcher. You should consult a lawyer or someone who works in the field of abuse."

Louise's derision was colossal. "How often have you been buggered, darlin'? Have you even had sex? Maybe you consult a lawyer every time a man looks at you, just so your fat little arse remains intact. *Cill* never got buggered — rogered by a trio of clowns, maybe, but never buggered. She should have been. It would've taken some of the heat off me."

"Humor her . . ."

"I'm sorry," said Sasha inadequately. "Have you ever thought about having your father prosecuted? There's no time limit on this sort of case . . . and I'm sure your brother would support you. He's the one who first suggested to us that your father abused you."

The woman stared at her. "Dad paid me and Micky a small fortune in blood money to keep quiet."

"About what?"

"Micky had a knife . . . said he'd chop my dad's dick off if he didn't pay for what he'd done." She fell silent, looking back down some dark corridor of time. "He was *so* scared . . . couldn't look at me without shaking. I reminded him of Cill. It gives you a buzz when you get that kind of reaction."

Sasha ignored her boss's voice in her audio specs telling her to leave. "Did he kill Cill, Mrs. Fletcher? Your brother says you know what happened to her."

The woman stirred. "It was Howard," she said automatically.

"Is that what Roy Trent told you to say?"

Louise's mouth twisted into a cynical smile and, for a moment, she looked as if she were about to agree.

"Don't be an idiot, Lou," said a man's voice from the doorway. "There's no harm done except your pride's been dented. Let's cool it, eh?"

Sasha's heart leaped in her chest. *Colley Hurst?* She flicked a rapid sideways glance at the newcomer, but he had dark hair flecked with gray. *"Leave now,"* said her boss's voice in her ear. She reached for her briefcase again.

The woman looked murderously toward the visitor. "This is my house, Roy. I'm the one who says what happens in it."

"Except you're making a fool of yourself," he said harshly, before jerking his head at Sasha. "Get your stuff together, girl, and I'll see you out."

There was a pulse of time in which Louise seemed ready to accept his authority. A look of resignation crossed her face and she leaned forward to abandon her cigarette in the ashtray before pushing herself to her feet. But something happened. Perhaps Roy was too insistent. Perhaps Sasha drew attention to herself by moving. Perhaps Louise heard the tinny voice in the spectacle arm. The end result was the same — a manic fury that was beyond anything Sasha had ever imagined or witnessed.

It happened so fast she could only watch in horrified paralysis as Louise swamped Roy with a burst of energy, battering at his head and eyes with the ashtray, kneeing, kicking, forcing him to the floor. "It's always about *you* . . . protect *you* . . . keep *your* fucking secrets."

At the back of Sasha's mind was a bizarre hope that it was a performance put on for her benefit, and she was only halfway to her feet when Louise brought the heavy glass weight crashing down on Roy's temple. She lurched forward in a panic, sending the coffee table crashing onto its back. "Mrs. Fletcher! MRS. FLETCHER! For God's sake, STOP! You're killing him."

Either the woman didn't hear her or Sasha was too insignificant to worry about, but there was no time to debate the rights and wrongs of any particular action. Sasha's instinctive response was to stop the terrible battering and she lunged forward to grab at Louise's wrists. It was like being caught up by a tornado, a whirling frenzy of movement as Louise turned on her, knocking her to the floor. Sasha felt her shoulder glance off a coffee-table leg before the underside rim slammed into her spine and knocked the wind from her lungs.

If a sensible thought about tactics entered her head, she had no recollection of it. She just gritted her teeth and clung grimly to the other woman's hands, thwarting every attempt to bring the ashtray in contact with her face. Flat on her back, and unable to gain an advantage because she was trapped between the legs of the table, she fought a desperate, sweaty struggle to hold the other woman at bay.

She remembered thinking her boss would be furious because the audio specs were somewhere beneath her, broken. She remembered thinking she needed to lose weight, as she felt the back of her jacket rip. She remembered thinking her mother had taught her that nice girls never got into fights. Most of all, she remembered thinking that if she got through this she would hand in her notice immediately. Fear grew as Louise's knee jammed into her midriff and made the struggle for breath even harder. Why hadn't she heeded George's and Jonathan's advice?

After how long she decided to bullshit the woman, she didn't know. Hours? Seconds? "You don't . . . need to do this," she grated out of half-starved lungs. "We *know* . . . what happened."

Louise released her left hand from the ashtray. "No one does except me and Roy," she snarled, thrusting her hands apart and slamming Sasha's arms against the sharp edges of the table legs to break her hold. "Micky's dead and Nick can't remember."

"Then *you* . . . tell us," Sasha managed despairingly.

Louise dragged her hands together again, preparing to repeat the exercise. "Nick'll kill me."

Sasha exerted all her strength to hold her wrists together. "Not if we . . . can *prove* it," she grunted.

There was the briefest relaxation of pressure, and this time it was Sasha who whipped her arms out, gasping from the pain as the sharp edge of the wood cut into the flesh of her arm in the same place as before. As a tactic, it worked spectacularly. The shock of the impact catapulted the ashtray to the far side of the room and, by luck rather than judgment, toppled the smaller woman off balance, pulling Sasha into an ungainly roll. As the table legs gave way beneath her weight, she took a lungful of air and then flailed a leg across the writhing woman, pinning her to the ground.

"ENOUGH!" she roared. "I am NOT Cill Trevelyan."

POOLE POLICE STATION

CIVIC CENTER POOLE DORSET BH15 2SE

INCIDENT REPORT

Date: 5.26.03
Time: 1223
Officers attending:
PC Alan Clarke,
WPC Mary Chambers
Incident: Disturbance at Palencia,
Frean Street, Sandbanks.

The disturbance was reported at 1223 by Duncan Bartholomew of WCH Investigations. An ambulance was requested at the same time. Officers Clark and Chambers arrived at Palencia within ten minutes. Five persons were in the house: Mrs. Priscilla Fletcher (tenant/occupier), Mr. Roy Trent (visitor), Mr. Duncan Bartholomew (partner with WCH Investigations), Ms. Sasha Spencer (WCH Investigations employee), Mr. Trevor Paul (Bentham Inquiry Agents employee). Bartholomew, Spencer and Paul are licensed operators.

Ms. Spencer reported a fight between Mr. Trent and Mrs. Fletcher, and subsequently between herself and Mrs. Fletcher when she tried to intervene. Mr. Trent had been hit on the head several times by a heavy ashtray but was sitting up by the time the officers reached the scene.

Paramedics arrived within five minutes. Although Mr. Trent initially refused medical assistance, he was persuaded to go in the ambulance and receive treatment at Poole General Hospital. He had difficulty focusing and standing, and severe concussion was diagnosed. He was asked to remain at the hospital until Officers Clarke and Chambers could take his statement. His address — Crown and Feathers, Highdown — was supplied by Mrs. Fletcher.

Mrs. Fletcher agreed that Ms. Spencer had come to her house by invitation and that Mr. Bartholomew and Mr. Paul had come to Ms. Spencer's assistance when the fighting got out of hand. They deny trespass. Mrs. Fletcher admitted that she left her front door open when Ms. Spencer arrived, which is how Mr. Bartholomew and Mr. Paul gained entry. She thanked them for their assistance.

Mrs. Fletcher said that she had taken her husband Mr. Nicholas Fletcher for a checkup at Poole General this morning. She expressed considerable fear of both him and Mr. Trent and said she couldn't remain in the house in case either of them returned. She refused to give a statement at this time, asking instead to be taken to Poole police station to make a written statement there.

After escorting everyone off the premises, Officers Clarke and Chambers secured the house and drove Mrs. Fletcher to Poole police station. A statement was subsequently taken from Mr. Trent at the General Hospital. On his advice, Officers Clarke and Chambers allowed him to inform Mr. Fletcher of the incident. Mr. Fletcher reacted angrily but accepted Mr. Trent's offer to stay at the Crown and Feathers in Highdown until the matter is resolved.

POOLE POLICE STATION

CIVIC CENTER POOLE DORSET BH15 2SE

WITNESS STATEMENT

Date: 5.26.03
Time: 1630
Witness: Priscilla Fletcher aka Priscilla Fletcher Hurst aka Louise Burton aka Daisy Hopkinson aka Cill Trent
Officers present:
DS John Wyatt, DC Peter Hughes
Also present:
Ms. Sasha Spencer (at the request of the witness)
Incident: The murder of Priscilla "Cill" Trevelyan on the night of May 30/31, 1970.

This statement was written from notes made during an interview with Priscilla Fletcher. She agrees that it is a true and complete record of what she said, and she has signed it accordingly.

My father started abusing me when I was

eleven years old. I believe my mother knew what was happening, although the subject has never been discussed between us. When Cill and I became friendly, I tried to keep her away from our house because I knew my father liked her. She was unhappy at home and preferred spending time in other people's houses. When we bunked off school we usually went to Grace Jefferies's, where we spent time with Howard Stamp.

I became jealous of Cill because she was popular and I wasn't. I had few girlfriends at school because none of them liked the way my father behaved toward them. Howard didn't like me because I'd teased him in the past. Our teachers blamed me for leading Cill astray, and Cill's parents reported me to my parents, saying that Cill's problems were my fault. The fight we had at school on Friday, May 29, was sparked by my jealousy.

After Mrs. Trevelyan phoned on the Saturday morning May 30 to say that Cill had not slept in her bed the previous night, I went round to Grace Jefferies's house. Cill was eating ice cream in the kitchen. I thought it was funny because my mother had said how upset Jean Trevelyan had sounded. That is what made me decide not to say anything to my parents or the police. This decision was reinforced when my mother became angry after the police suggested we might know where Cill was. I couldn't contradict her without being punished.

I told the police about the rape to get Cill into even more trouble with her father. He always said he'd wash his hands of her if he found out she'd had sex with a boy. I was still angry about our fight the day before when she had punched me and pulled my hair. It seemed a good revenge to make her life even more difficult.

I hadn't told my father that Cill had been raped because I didn't want him feeling sorry for her. Instead, I told him she'd had consensual sex with three boys. He became upset and started referring to her as "a tart." When he told Mr. Trevelyan that "she deserved what she got," he was referring to a possible pregnancy, as I'd told him that Cill had missed a period. This wasn't true, but my father was pleased about it because he thought the Trevelyans were snobs. After Cill went missing, he told me to repeat the story to the police so that David Trevelyan would know the sort of daughter he had.

Soon after my mother and I returned from the police station on Saturday, May 30, my mother ordered me to go to my bedroom so that she could tell my father what I'd said to the police. I disobeyed. Instead, I went to the public telephone in Bladen Street to call Roy Trent. I had made friends with Roy Trent, Micky Hopkinson and Colley Hurst after Howard kept complaining to Cill and Grace about the way they bullied him. Even at the time I understood that I had more in common with alienated teens than I did with losers like Howard Stamp and Grace Jefferies. Now I realize that I was looking for anyone who shared my sense of unhappiness and lack of worth.

It is true that I sought out Trent, Hopkinson and Hurst and asked them to give Cill

Trevelyan a fright. It is also true that I engineered the meeting and was angry when Cill insisted on bringing my brother along. At no point did I suggest rape. I asked them to pretend to like her, then treat her unkindly afterward. My feelings about the rape were mixed. I was glad that Cill was violated but I became obsessed with the idea that Trent, Hopkinson and Hurst only did it because they fancied her.

This made me angry. Although I didn't name the boys, I described them well enough to be identified. They were well known to the police at that time as persistent truants, petty thieves and vandals, and they were regularly taken home in a drunk and disorderly state from Colliton Park and the waste ground behind Colliton Way (now Colliton Industrial Estate). I hoped Trent, Hopkinson and Hurst would be scared and embarrassed by being taken in for questioning. I hoped the same would happen to Cill when she went home.

I spoke to Roy Trent at his mother's house at approximately 12:30 p.m. on Saturday, May 30, 1970, and told him what I'd said to the police. I did this because I wanted him to know how angry the rape had made me. He told me I was a fool because Micky Hopkinson carried a knife and would cut me at the first opportunity. I said they should deny they were the boys involved because I hadn't named them and wouldn't identify them. I had also kept secret from the police that my brother, William, had been a witness. Roy said none of that mattered because Cill would identify them.

He asked me where Cill Trevelyan was, and I said she was at Grace Jefferies's house. He told me to go back to Grace's and persuade Cill to go to Howard Stamp's house in Colliton Way. I said she would never agree because she knew Trent, Hurst and Hopkinson also lived in Colliton Way. Roy accepted that. Instead, he told me to persuade her to go home by leaving the house via the alleyway at the back. He asked me to wait until it got dark at around 8:30 p.m.

I refused, saying I didn't care if Cill never went home again and, in any case, I wanted Mr. and Mrs. Trevelyan to suffer. The money ran out before the conversation ended. I did not understand what Roy Trent intended to do. I believed he wanted to threaten Cill to make her keep her mouth shut. If neither of us identified Trent, Hurst and Hopkinson as the boys who committed the rape, then the police would let the matter drop.

I had no intention at that time of doing what Roy Trent asked, but my mother had told my father that I'd described the incident to the police as a gang rape. He was angry with me because of what he'd said to David Trevelyan the night before. By way of punishment, he sent my mother and my brother shopping and anally raped me in front of the television. All I could think about was that it was worse than anything Cill had suffered. My bottom bled for days but I couldn't tell anyone. On Wednesday I started having fainting fits. My mother made my father call the doctor, and though I didn't tell the doctor what was really wrong, my father was frightened.

I became very upset in the wake of this

incident on Saturday afternoon. I realize now that I was deeply confused and frightened, but I believed that I would be blamed for everything: the rape, the fight, Cill running away, my failure to tell the police that I'd seen her at Grace's. I was also afraid that Trent, Hurst and Hopkinson would take revenge on me if Cill identified them. I see now that I directed all my hate at Cill when I should have been directing it at my father, but I was too disturbed to understand this at the time.

At 8:15 p.m. on Saturday, May 30, I told my parents I was going to bed. They were watching television with my brother and weren't interested in me. I shut the sitting-room door and let myself out onto the street. I was absent for approximately half an hour, but I do not know if either of my parents was aware of this. They have never mentioned it.

I ran down Mullin Street to Bladen Street and turned into the alleyway at the back of Grace's house. Trent, Hurst and Hopkinson were waiting there, even though I'd told Trent I wasn't going to do what he'd asked. They said they planned to give Cill a fright so that she wouldn't name them to the police, and I believed them. They threatened me similarly if I changed my mind about identifying them. I said I wouldn't.

I had no trouble entering Grace's house because the kitchen door was open. She and Cill were watching television in the sitting room with the curtains closed. Cill wasn't pleased to see me, but Grace was. She was worried about news coverage of Cill's disappearance and had already told her that she must go home. I told Grace that I'd been questioned that morning, and that the police were saying that anyone found harboring Cill would be arrested. Grace was so concerned that she became angry with Cill and ordered her to leave. Cill burst into tears and refused, so I helped Grace drag her through the kitchen into the garden. Grace locked the door behind us.

I knew Cill would lash out at me so I ran straight to the fence. I saw Trent, Hurst and Hopkinson in the shadow of Grace's garden shed. I did not speak to them, nor did I hear them speak to Cill. I let myself out through the gate and ran home. I expected to hear the following morning that Cill had returned home.

I remember very little of the next few days because I was so frightened, by both my anal bleeding and Cill's continued disappearance. I attended school on the Monday and Tuesday but spent most of the time hiding or crying. I was shown no sympathy by the teachers or students because they held me responsible for Cill's suspension. On Tuesday afternoon I began to wonder if Cill was still in Grace Jefferies's house, so I sneaked into her garden on my way home from school.

I looked through the French windows into the sitting room. There was blood on one of the panes and the room had been vandalized. I was too scared to try the kitchen door and went straight home. From this point on, my fainting fits and convulsions became so serious that I was taken out of school and my family was eventually rehoused.

I had no contact with Trent, Hurst and

Hopkinson until after Howard Stamp had confessed to Grace's murder. I was aware that they had been questioned and released about Cill's rape, but I wasn't confident enough to phone Roy Trent until it became clear that Stamp had killed his grandmother. Roy set my mind at rest immediately. He said they'd threatened Cill with a beating if she named them, then sent her home. He and his friends had no idea what had happened afterward, but they believed she'd gone looking for Howard Stamp and he'd lost his temper with her in the same way he'd lost it with Grace. He described Howard as behaving like a lunatic in the days between Cill's disappearance and his arrest. However, none of us could report it because of our own involvement.

This is the extent of my firsthand knowledge and involvement in the murder of Cill Trevelyan. Anything else I know was told to me by my first husband, Michael "Micky" Hopkinson, many years afterward.

Micky was always more troubled by his conscience than either Roy Trent or Colley

Hurst. He stifled it with drugs and alcohol. He was chronically addicted to heroin by the time he was seventeen and he remained addicted until his death from overdose in 1986. We were married for twelve years and he was thirty when he died. During that time he persuaded me into drugs, forced me into prostitution to fund our habits and had several prison sentences for possession and theft. He also blackmailed my father to buy my silence about the abuse.

I realize now that my relationship with Micky was just another form of abuse. It's a pattern I repeated in my subsequent marriages to Roy Trent and Nicholas "Colley" Fletcher Hurst.

We were bound together by our knowledge of what happened on May 30, 1970, but I had no idea how dangerous my knowledge was to them until Micky confessed to Cill's murder shortly before he died.

The story he told me was as follows:

Trent, Hurst and Hopkinson had caught

Cill as she was leaving Grace's garden and Colley Hurst put his hand over her mouth to stop her screaming. Because she struggled, Micky showed her his knife and said he'd use it if she didn't do as she was told. She allowed Roy to put a handkerchief in her mouth and tie her hands behind her back, then they walked her to Colliton Way waste ground. Roy and Colley draped their arms over her shoulders, and Micky walked behind with his knife in her back. He said she cried the whole way there but, even though some pedestrians and cars passed them, no one noticed that anything was wrong.

They hadn't intended to kill her, but everything got out of hand when Roy and Colley decided to rape her again. Both boys had been drinking heavily since my phone call to Roy at lunchtime, and Micky thinks she died of suffocation because they didn't untie her or remove the handkerchief in case she started screaming. He said it was similar to the first rape and they only realized she was dead when she hadn't moved for several minutes. He never said whether he raped her, but I think he must have done.

He told me they put her body in one of the test pits that had been dug during the construction of the new Brackham & Wright factory. They shoveled rubble in on top of her, then went home to get some clean clothes. Roy had sobered up enough to realize that if the police took them in for the first rape, they'd find Cill's blood and hair on what they were wearing that night. Micky said he made them change and then slog across town to dispose of the clothes in someone's dustbin.

They never expected to get away with it, but all the test pits were filled in a few weeks later without being examined. Micky told me that Cill's body is under the grassed area where the factory workers eat their lunch in the summer.

I have no knowledge of the murder of Grace Jefferies. Micky never spoke about it, and Roy has always denied any involvement in it. I can only assume that Howard learned from Grace that Cill had been in her house and became angry because she hadn't told him. His interest in Cill was perverted, which may explain why he never mentioned the connection at his trial.

My life has been regulated and controlled by Roy Trent since May 30, 1970. My dependence on him was fueled for many years by my addiction to heroin. While I was married to Micky, he was our main supplier. After Micky's death in 1986, Roy took over as my pimp in order to retain control. He had a stable of prostitutes, one of whom was his wife, Robyn Hapgood. Roy married me in 1992 when I was at a low ebb in my life and close to suicide. At the time I was grateful to him.

When Colley Hurst suffered brain damage because of his treatment at the hands of the Metropolitan Police in 1998, Roy recognized that the damages would be high. He invited Colley to stay with us at the Crown and Feathers in order to access the money when it came through. Colley's life expectancy was low and he had no surviving relatives. Roy's idea was to take power of attorney during Colley's lifetime and to construct a will that made him sole beneficiary.

I had been calling myself Priscilla for

some time, although Roy always shortened it to Cill because it amused him. Colley is a very sick man with extensive amnesia, but he has a lasting memory of Cill Trevelyan. He has no recollection of killing her but he does remember that she was important to him. He believes I am Cill Trevelyan because Roy was calling me Cill when he first arrived at the Crown and Feathers, and he recognized me as someone he knew.

Since the assault, Colley finds contact with people frightening and it brings on his violence. During his stay with us, he and Roy came to blows regularly over Colley's fear of the customers. In the same disturbed way that he remembers Cill as someone he loved, he remembers Roy as someone to fear and distrust. Roy was the leader when they were a gang, and I'm sure part of Colley remembers that he led them into trouble. During these outbursts I was the only person who could control him, and Roy conceived the idea that I should marry Colley and move to a secluded house where contact with people would be minimal. In return, he promised to watch over me via webcams which would be connected twenty-four hours a day to a monitor in the Crown and Feathers kitchen.

I freely admit that I went along with this plan. As Colley's wife I would inherit everything automatically, and it is an indication of Roy's arrogance and controlling nature that he never questioned my willingness to return to him once Colley was dead. Colley and I moved into Palencia on Sandbanks in August 2001 (initially paid for by Roy) and we married in November 2001, subsequently calling ourselves Mr. and Mrs. Nicholas Fletcher.

This was the first time in thirty years that I was truly free of Roy Trent's influence and I used the opportunity to kick my drug habit by going cold turkey. It was made easier because Colley's paranoias meant I had to keep him tied to me all the time. He may be a violent and dangerous man, but he understood the pain I was going through and helped me in a way that no one else has ever done.

I also freely admit that I have planned for

the last two years to "out" Roy Trent, Colley Hurst and Micky Hopkinson as Cill Trevelyan's murderers. I also admit that by doing this I will secure Nicholas "Colley" Fletcher Hurst's money for myself. It has been suggested to me that it is convenient that one witness to Cill's murder is dead (Micky), and the other is an amnesiac (Nick/Colley). I can only answer that I was afraid of being killed in the same way Cill was if I'd told my story earlier.

I believe Roy has been suspicious of me ever since I came off drugs. One of his reasons for placing webcams about Palencia was to monitor anyone who came to the house. He knew, for example, that my brother had visited me before I told him. He also knew that Ms. Sasha Spencer had left her card. I told him about both incidents in order to allay his suspicions, but I did not tell him that I'd agreed to an interview with Ms. Spencer.

I hoped that by turning off the computer at my end he would think it was a glitch, but it merely made him suspicious. He has had keys to the house since August 2001 when we first moved in and he entered via the back door because he was suspicious of WCH Investigations' van in the road. I heard him come in, which is why I gave Ms. Spencer the version of events involving Howard Stamp that Roy instructed me to tell after Councillor Gardener and Dr. Hughes discovered Cill's story. However, when he attempted to remove Ms. Spencer, I realized I would be severely punished for stepping out of line.

Had I known that Ms. Spencer's colleagues were monitoring our conversation, I might have found the courage to tell the true version. They believed my husband was in the house and were ready to intervene because of his violent nature. While I understand that I have certain rights in law relating to privacy and security of information, I do not wish anyone to be prosecuted as a result of this morning's intervention by Mr. Duncan Bartholomew and Mr. Trevor Paul. I am grateful for their assistance in calling the police and the ambulance service.

I am relieved to have finally cleared my conscience.

I confirm that everything I have said in this statement is true.

Priscilla Fletcher

POOLE POLICE STATION
CIVIC CENTER POOLE DORSET BH15 2SE

WITNESS STATEMENT

Date: 5/27/03
Time: 1700
Witness: Roy Trent
In the presence of:
DS John Wyatt, DC Peter Hughes
Also present:
n/a (Witness refused a lawyer)
Incident: The alleged murder of Priscilla "Cill" Trevelyan on the night of May 30/31, 1970.

Mr. Roy Trent presented himself voluntarily at Poole police station in order to answer allegations made against him by Priscilla Fletcher on May 26, 2003. This statement was written by him and he agrees that it is a true and complete record of what he said. He has signed it accordingly.

Priscilla Fletcher's story is a complete fabrication. I deny absolutely that I, Micky

Hopkinson or Colley Hurst had any involvement in or knowledge of the alleged murder of Priscilla "Cill" Trevelyan on the night of May 30/31, 1970.

It is almost thirty-three years, to the day, that Cill Trevelyan went missing and it is impossible to prove or refute these allegations when so many witnesses are dead or, as in Nicholas "Colley" Hurst's case, severely brain damaged.

I do not deny that we raped Cill in early May 1970, nor that we bullied Howard Stamp mercilessly until he pulled out a knife and attacked us. I cannot recall precisely when this incident happened but I believe it was some time in late March or early April 1970.

Priscilla Fletcher is a deeply damaged woman who suffered appalling abuse at the hands of her father when she was a child. She has been a prostitute and a drug addict, although I deny that I ever pimped for her or supplied her with class-A narcotics.

I cite my reputation in Highdown for being

anti-drugs and the attempts I made when Priscilla and I first married to put her into rehab. I would also ask for my son, Peter, to be interviewed, who will testify on my behalf re: Priscilla's corrupting influence. By the time he was seventeen years old she had ensnared him into the drug culture, with all that that entails.

We became inextricably linked with Louise Burton a.k.a. Priscilla Fletcher long before Cill Trevelyan's disappearance and Grace Jefferies's murder. Louise gravitated toward us because of her own unhappiness at home, and because she knew we had a similar ill feeling toward Howard Stamp as she had. In her case it was fueled by jealousy of Cill.

In the wake of the above two events, she became a natural ally because of her refusal to name us to the police. None of the secrets we shared were so bad that we couldn't have revealed them at the time, but we weren't bright enough to understand that.

I have no explanation for why she is now

accusing us of murdering Cill on the night of May 30/31, 1970 unless it is to rid herself of the nuisance of looking after Nicholas "Colley" Fletcher Hurst. She genuinely loved Micky Hopkinson and was married to him for twelve years. I allowed her to move in with me after my first wife died because I felt some responsibility for her as Micky's widow. I became fond of her and we married in 1992 on the understanding that she would kick her habit. She didn't.

We had been living apart for six months when I offered to take on the care of Nicholas "Colley" Hurst in 2000. Louise immediately saw an advantage in marrying him. I made no objection because he was difficult to manage at the pub. In exchange for a percentage of the inheritance, I agreed to monitor them via webcams in case he became violent. He carries a mobile telephone which I have trained him to answer. In this way I can defuse difficult situations before they happen. His "violent" episodes are rare.

Contrary to what Louise has told you,

Colley readily responds to me, but is easily roused to anger when she becomes impatient with him. I cite yesterday's example at the hospital when he agreed to come home with me, as witnessed by two police officers.

I went to Palencia yesterday because the webcam link had failed and I wanted to check it. I deny that I ordered Ms. Sasha Spencer from the house to prevent Louise talking to her. I did it because I could see that Ms. Spencer's unwise remark about Cill Trevelyan's popularity had fired Louise into a temper. Cill Trevelyan is an obsession with her. I believe it comes from guilt. She needs to be told all the time that it wasn't her fault Cill vanished.

I agree that Nicholas "Colley" Hurst believes that Louise is Cill Trevelyan. I also agree that neither she nor I has attempted to correct this assumption. I have no explanation for why he retains a memory of Cill unless the rape remains on his conscience.

I have never raised a hand to Louise, although I threaten it from time to time when she attacks me as she did yesterday. She has an aggressive nature and is willing to provoke fights. I cite the fact that I could easily have defended myself, but chose not to because I would have done more damage to her than she did to me.

I believe now, as I have always done, that Howard Stamp was responsible for the murder of Grace Jefferies and the probable murder of Cill Trevelyan. I have no knowledge of either crime, but I have always wondered why Stamp never mentioned Cill's connection with Grace to the police or his defense team. If he was innocent of Grace's murder then he would have given the names of anyone remotely connected with her in order to shift police attention away from him. For example, he would have named myself, Hurst and Hopkinson, since he would have known about the rape. If Cill didn't tell him herself because they were friends, then Grace would certainly have done after Cill used her bathroom to clean up.

I admit that we lived in fear of this happening. I admit, too, that we made a pact to deny everything as the safest course of action. There have been many times in the past thirty-three years when I have wanted to come clean about the events of May 1970, but it wasn't my story to tell. Whatever Louise may say now about clearing her conscience, she has always been the main instigator in keeping the truth suppressed.

In conclusion, I repeat the point made above. If Howard Stamp had been innocent of Grace's murder, then he would have told the whole story. If he was guilty of two murders, then he would have selected the pieces that best suited his defense.

I confirm that everything in this statement is true.

Roy Trent

Chapter Twenty-six

25 Mullin Street, Highdown, Bournemouth
Friday, May 30, 2003, 2:30 p.m.

Duncan Bartholomew, a lean, gray-haired man in his fifties, reached forward to switch off the tape recorder as Sasha's voice called out, *"Mrs. Fletcher! For God's sake, stop! You're killing him."* "We lost sound a few seconds later, but you get an idea of Louise's mood in the lead-up to the attack. Not quite the reasonable individual that she presented at Poole police station when she made her statement."

"I *do* find that odd," said George. "Why did she want Sasha listening in?"

"So that we'd know the allegations against Trent," said Bartholomew. "I imagine she wanted us to do exactly what we have done. Report them to Mr. and Mrs. Trevelyan and, with their permission, repeat them to you and William Burton.

The police are unlikely to mount an investigation unless there's considerable pressure put on them. At the moment it's just Louise's word against Trent's."

"Have the police heard the tape?" asked Jonathan.

Sasha, who was sitting beside her boss on the sofa, shook her head. "They're wary of compromising a prosecution — illicit gathering of information," she explained. "But I made it clear in my statement that I thought Louise was stringing me along until Roy arrived. I'm sure she'd have given me twenty anecdotes of her visits to the Trevelyan house if she hadn't heard the back door open. *I* certainly heard it."

"So what was it all in aid of?" asked George. "Why didn't she tell you straight out what she told the police?"

It was Duncan Bartholomew who answered. "If you believe Mrs. Fletcher, then it was because Roy Trent was listening and she was too afraid to stray from the version he'd taught her. If you take Sasha's view that she was playing a game, then she wanted to engineer a confrontation that would involve the police being called. She said afterward that she'd expected Sasha to dial 999 immediately instead of weighing into the fight." He folded his hands in his lap. "Her statement *is* very convincing."

"I know," said George with sigh, "and you can understand how reluctant she might have been to make it without some strong guarantees that it was taken seriously. Talking to a private detective agency, or a couple of amateurs like me and Jon, wouldn't have got her anywhere. Even talking to the police without support from people like you would have been a gamble."

Bartholomew nodded. "Trent denies it, of course."

"He sent George a copy of his statement," said Jonathan. "Did he send you one?"

"Yes."

"It's a spinning war. You pays your money and you takes your choice. Roy makes a good point at the end when he questions why Howard never mentioned Cill in his defense. I checked it with Howard's solicitor. He was astonished to discover that two schoolgirls were regularly truanting in Grace's house. He said that if they'd known there was a disturbed adolescent in the house on the Saturday, they'd have concentrated their efforts on her. According to him, Cill was the reasonable doubt that might have swung the jury in Howard's favor."

"Assuming he didn't kill her," said Bartholomew dryly.

"Oh dear!" sighed George. "It's *so* depressing. Fred Lovatt says it's stalemate. He pointed to the fact that Louise's hearsay evidence came from a dead heroin addict with a history of criminal behavior who probably fantasized his life to make himself more interesting. He says the CPS will drop it for lack of evidence and Howard will go down in the annals of crime as a serial killer." She pulled a comical face. "Which is the exact opposite of what Jon and I set out to do when we first embarked on this wretched story."

Jonathan stood up and walked to the kitchen area to plug in the kettle. "Is there anything going for Howard?" he asked.

Sasha took out her notepad. "There's one small discrepancy," she said. "Louise authorized Nicholas Hurst's consultant to give me whatever information I requested. He vouched for his patient's brain damage, catastrophic amnesia and unpredictable aggression. He also paid tribute to Mrs. Fletcher for her care of a man who's greatly disabled." She looked up. "That's why she wanted me to talk to him. He couldn't praise her enough . . . said that if she hadn't stayed with him, Nicholas would have died a year ago. As far as the consultant's concerned, whatever she inherits is cheap at the price."

Bartholomew's thin face broke into a smile. "He was very insistent about it, apparently . . . says he's known grizzly bears with more charm. He's never understood how Louise put up with it."

"She didn't have to," said George cynically, propping her chin on her clasped hands. "She watched him on the monitor at the Crown and Feathers."

Sasha moved to the next point on her pad. "The consultant also confirmed some old knife-wound scars on Hurst's right arm. The scars healed well, so he clearly received treatment for them, which I believe is what Roy Trent told you."

George nodded. "They took him to hospital."

"I also checked with David Trevelyan about Wynne Stamp's drinking. That's true, I'm afraid — apparently she was quite notorious — so the alibi she gave Howard for the Monday night isn't reliable."

"Does he know what happened to her?" asked Jonathan, spooning tea leaves into the teapot.

"He said her drinking spiraled out of

control in the lead-up to Howard's trial, so Brackham & Wright's paid her off and she was rehoused somewhere along the south coast — possibly Weymouth. We've made inquiries there, but we haven't found a Wynne Stamp or a Wynne Jefferies."

"It's the name that's the problem," Bartholomew put in. "If she changed it, we've virtually no hope of locating her. We've tried the Public Record Office at Kew to see if she registered a new one, but they have no record of anyone called Stamp changing his or her name between 1963 and 1983. It doesn't mean she didn't do it, of course — it's not compulsory to place it on public record. Her most likely course was to do it free by adopting a new one through usage . . . but that makes tracing her impossible."

"Is that legal?"

"Perfectly legal. You can't alter your birth certificate, but you're entitled to call yourself anything you like. You can change your name every other day if you want to. Louise Burton's been doing it for years. That's why she remained hidden for so long."

Sasha moved down her pad. "I've tried the Dorset crematoria in case Wynne died," she said, "but I've had no success there either. No Wynne Stamps or Jefferies have been cremated in the time frame we're looking at. I wondered if the housing department might have kept her details."

George shook her head. "They were the first people I went to when my neighbor told me Grace's story, but they'd shredded their files from the 1970s long before I arrived."

"If you really want to find her, then the best course is to advertise in the local newspapers," said Bartholomew, "but I wouldn't pin your hopes on her coming forward."

Jonathan nodded. "What about Robert Burton?" he asked. "Did he agree to see you?"

The man nodded. "He did . . . heavily chaperoned by his wife. Very strange characters, both of them. We don't have a tape because they refused to be recorded, but they were in bullish denial for half an hour." He gave an abrupt laugh. "How dare we believe anything their drug-addicted daughter said about her wholesome, upright father? How dare we suggest that a good Christian woman like Eileen would lie to the police?" He jerked his head at the tape recorder. "When we got bored, we played them that interview with Louise."

"And?"

"Robert went to pieces," said Sasha, "but Eileen continued to deny everything. It was interesting. She's a tough woman — there's no way she's going to take responsibility for anything her husband did. She described Louise as a compulsive liar and was adamant they never knew Cill was with Grace." She turned to George. "She latched onto your point immediately: why would they have sent Louise to school on the Monday if they'd known where Cill was? She says Louise could never have kept the secret because all the children were firing questions at her about the fight on the Friday."

"So why did they take her out from the Wednesday?" Jonathan asked.

"For the reasons that Louise and William gave. She kept throwing fits. Her father called a doctor, who diagnosed delayed shock and put her on sedatives. The idea was to wean her back to school gently but, what with Grace's murder and Cill's continued disappearance, the doctor's advice was to start again somewhere else. He even helped them by putting a recommendation for a move to the housing department." Sasha shrugged. "I asked Mrs. Burton about the hair dyeing and the name change and she said they were done to give Louise courage. She dyed her own hair to make the child comfortable. She was completely immovable on the subject of abuse. As far as she's concerned, it never happened . . . Louise invented it to excuse her prostitution and drug addiction."

"What did Mr. Burton say to that?"

"Very little," said Bartholomew. "I don't know if he realized she was hanging him out to dry if Louise makes the abuse allegations public . . . but he managed to pull himself together enough to bluster a bit. It wasn't very convincing. He went white as a sheet when Sasha repeated what William had said about his visits to Louise's bedroom. He obviously thought he'd kept it secret from his son."

"The chances are he'd react the same if he were innocent," George said fairly. "It's a terrible accusation . . . and very frightening if both your children are making it."

"The abuse isn't in question," said Bartholomew. "He had no answers for anything . . . couldn't explain why he visited her bedroom and not Billy's . . . why he wanted her in provocative clothes and makeup . . . why he encouraged her to bring her friends home so that he could sit them on his lap. If we'd had him on his own he'd have given us chapter and verse, but Sasha's right — Eileen's a different kettle of fish entirely."

"Was she telling the truth?" asked George.

"About what?"

"Anything."

"I'd say she was being truthful about what she knew at the time," said Duncan. "Whether she's worked out since that things were happening behind her back — and has chosen to close her mind to it — I don't know."

"Then Louise lied about telling her Cill was at Grace's?"

"We think so."

"What about Robert?"

"He denied it very strongly. It's the only time we believed him."

"Then there's only Louise's word that Cill was ever there?"

"I'm afraid so."

"And that's not enough to convict Roy Trent?"

"No. He can draw on the evidence from the time that the only fingerprints found were Grace Jefferies's and Howard Stamp's."

There was a short silence.

"So what's this small discrepancy?" asked Jonathan.

"The scars on Nicholas Hurst's arm," said Sasha. "He's right-handed and they're on his right forearm — on the ventral surface — and there's some muscle wastage and loss of mobility in his hand. He can't touch his fifth finger with his thumb. This is characteristic of median nerve damage and it takes a long time to repair, apparently. Sometimes, as in Hurst's case, minor losses of function can become permanent."

Jonathan was ahead of her. "And it can't be attributed to the brain damage?"

"Unlikely. The arm's not paralyzed or semi-paralyzed. It's just the hand that's affected. One thing the consultant was very clear about was that anyone with the sort of scars Hurst presents would have been in considerable pain at the beginning and his hand would have been seriously — and *visibly* — disabled for months." She smiled. "William Burton didn't notice anything wrong on the day of the rape, he even says Hurst had charge of the vodka bottle. Yet, according to what Roy Trent told you about the fight with Howard, his hand should have been a useless claw."

Jonathan gave a small whistle. "I'm surprised Roy forgot that."

"How does it help us?" asked George.

"He'll just say he made a mistake on the dates."

"Except the details are in Hurst's medical records," said Sasha with a grin, "and when I asked the consultant when the damage occurred, he told me the treatment was dated 1972 — the year after Howard was convicted."

Extracts from a report compiled by Sasha Spencer, on the instructions of Mr. and Mrs. Trevelyan, requesting that Priscilla Trevelyan's disappearance on Saturday, May 30, 1970 be reopened as a murder inquiry

WCH INVESTIGATIONS

REPORT

Subject: Priscilla "Cill" Trevelyan, aged 13

Incident: Went missing from her parents' home in Lacey Street, Highdown, Bournemouth on the night of May 29/30, 1970

Present whereabouts:
Believed buried under the Colliton Way industrial estate

Circumstances:
Murdered by Roy Trent, Nicholas Hurst and Michael Hopkinson (deceased) on the night of Saturday/Sunday May 30/31, 1970

The full details of WCH Investigations'

examination of Cill Trevelyan's disappearance are available on request. Much of the evidence is circumstantial. However, WCH Investigations is confident that if the case is reopened as a murder inquiry, further proof will be found. It is outside of the scope of WCH Investigations to carry out searches, trace witnesses who have left the area, fully substantiate medical evidence or locate police files from 1970. Nevertheless, the case for murder is a compelling one.

(Attachments include transcripts of interviews and statements made by: Louise Burton, William Burton, Robert Burton, Eileen Burton and Roy Trent, and additional material supplied by Councillor George Gardener and Dr. Jonathan Hughes.)

IN CONCLUSION

It is clear that Roy Trent and Louise Burton have conspired for many years:

1. to suppress any connection between Cill Trevelyan's disappearance and the murder of Grace Jefferies;

2. to protect Trent, Hurst and Hopkinson from accusations of rape;
3. to maintain the fiction that Cill Trevelyan ran away and vanished;
4. to throw blame for that onto David and Jean Trevelyan;
5. *when that failed,* to involve Howard Stamp by painting him as a "pervert."

The remit of this investigation was to "find the present whereabouts of Priscilla 'Cill' Trevelyan." As demonstrated, we believe her body is buried in or around the Colliton Way industrial estate. However, questions have been raised about the murder of Grace Jefferies and the conviction of her grandson, Howard Stamp. While we have no evidence to dispute the jury's verdict, we believe the following facts should be considered:

1. At Stamp's trial the prosecution convinced the court that Grace Jefferies's murder happened on Wednesday, June 3. The time of death was disputed by the defense.
2. Louise Burton claims to have visited Grace's house on Tuesday, June 2, 1970, and seen blood on the windows.

3. Robert Burton, Eileen Burton, William Burton and Louise herself all testify that she had a fit on the morning of Wednesday, June 3, and refused to go to school. William Burton has testified that his sister threw fits, curled into the fetal position or became catatonic whenever she was frightened. Her GP was called and she was prescribed sedatives. This record, giving the date, may have survived.
4. Grace Jefferies was fond of Cill Trevelyan, and regularly harbored her and Louise Burton. If either of them came to her door late at night, she would have admitted them. Roy Trent, Nicholas Hurst and Michael Hopkinson knew this, and might have used one or both girls as a means of entry to Grace's house.
5. Councillor George Gardener has a signed and notarized statement from Grace Jefferies's neighbor (now deceased) that Howard Stamp did not arrive at Grace's house on Wednesday, June 3, 1970, until 2:00 p.m. — allowing only half an hour for him to commit a vicious murder *and* take the bath that condemned him.

It is the contention of WCH Investigations that Stamp's conviction was unsafe and should be reexamined.

At Stamp's trial he failed to give a convincing explanation for why he chose to visit his grandmother on Wednesday, June 3, 1970, instead of following up on a job at the local dairy (Jannerway & Co.). There was a suggestion that he became angry when she took him to task for shirking work. We believe a more likely explanation is that he made a detour via Grace Jefferies's house on his way to Jannerway's in order to ask her if she knew what had happened to Cill Trevelyan. *This suggests he was ignorant of her fate.* Finding Grace dead, he was too shocked to do anything other than run home.

The transcript of Roy Trent's interview makes much of the fact that Stamp did not cite his friendship with Cill Trevelyan in his defense. Yet, despite their questioning by the police, Trent, Hurst, Hopkinson and Burton never mentioned it either. Stamp's excuse is that he was never asked about the missing girl.

There is no such excuse for Trent, Hurst, Hopkinson and Burton, whose questioning related *only* to Cill Trevelyan.

Bournemouth Evening News,
Friday, June 27, 2003

New Evidence in 33-Year-Old Mysteries

Police announced today that they have reopened the investigation into the disappearance of Priscilla Trevelyan who vanished from her parents' home in Highdown in 1970. "New evidence has come to light," said Deputy Sergeant Wyatt, the officer in charge of the case, "and we now believe Priscilla was murdered."

No one has been arrested for the crime but three Bournemouth residents who were teenagers in 1970 are thought to be implicated. "We've been given a possible site where Priscilla's body was buried," said DS Wyatt, "and we hope to excavate it within the next few weeks." He refused to say where the site was, although he agreed it was somewhere in the Highdown area.

Mr. David Trevelyan, father of the missing girl, said, "My wife and I have lived with this tragedy for over 30 years.

It will be a relief to have closure at last." He thanked Councillor George Gardener of Highdown for her efforts in bringing the case to public attention. "Without her persistence, Priscilla would have remained a statistic."

Councillor Gardener came across the story while she was researching a book on Howard Stamp. Stamp was charged with the murder of his grandmother nine days after Priscilla Trevelyan went missing, and the police now believe the two cases may have been linked.

Councillor Gardener described Stamp's conviction as a terrible miscarriage of justice which couldn't happen with today's DNA testing. "I am optimistic of clearing his name," she said, "even though he isn't alive to see it happen." Tragically, Howard Stamp committed suicide in prison in 1973.

The police are asking for witnesses from the time to come forward. "We are keen to talk to anyone who was living in Colliton Way during the first half of 1970," said Deputy Sergeant Wyatt. "They may have information that will lead to an arrest."

From: Dr. Jonathan Hughes [jon.hughes@london.ac.uk]
Sent: Tues. 7/15/03 19:23
To: Andrew@spicerandhardy.co.uk
Subject: George

Dear A, This is a P.S. to the previous email which I'm not copying to George. The bad news is she's developed secondary cancer of the bone — in the ribs. The good news is it doesn't seem to have spread anywhere else. She's on some hefty hormone therapy and starts a course of radiation next week to deal with the pain. I've invited myself to stay with her for the duration of the summer vacation in order to act as chauffeur and get the book written. She seems happy about it. There shouldn't be a problem with the meeting next week as her radiation appointments are in the mornings, but she'll certainly be tired. She's a remarkable lady, refuses to give in to anything, although I've finally managed to persuade her to take some sick leave from the nursing home. I shall tell her I've told you, but I suggest you don't dwell on the sympathy too much. She's willing to talk about it, but won't tolerate pity!

Best, Jon

Chapter Twenty-seven

Spicer & Hardy's offices, West London
Wednesday, July 23, 2003, 2:30 p.m.

Jonathan waited for George to take a seat, then dropped into the spare visitor's chair and surveyed his friend with amusement. "You look like the cat that's got the cream," he said. "Let me guess. You've managed to double the advance?"

"Bugger off," said Andrew.

"Don't tease," said George as she settled herself in the other chair.

Jonathan's eyes gleamed wickedly. "Then it must be the clash of the Titans. Tall, glamorous actor-stud with full head of hair loses out to short, fat, bald bloke with embarrassing parents."

George wagged a finger at him. "Embarrassing *friends* more like. I don't recall you rushing to talk about your love life."

"Mine's nonexistent."

"That's not what I've heard," said Andrew. "Who's this Mongolian bareback rider that George keeps talking about?"

"Oh, for goodness *sake!*" said George crossly. "You're like a couple of children."

Andrew dropped her a wink. "How's the radiotherapy going?"

"Fine," she said, "apart from Jon's chauffeuring skills. I'm not at all convinced his license is genuine. We spend most of our time reversing."

"It's worse than driving Miss Daisy," groaned Jonathan. "Yack, yack, yack from the backseat — and me expected to tug my forelock so the nurses'll treat her like royalty. I wouldn't mind if we weren't using that miserable old rust bucket of hers." He leveled his forefinger at Andrew. "I'm not just the official chauffeur, you know, I'm also the resident gigolo. The neighbors are having a field day."

George's eyes sparkled. "That's *such* a lie. He's told everyone he's my son."

"Except they don't believe it. They're much happier thinking their upright local councillor has moved a black toyboy into her mock-Tudor semi. It's doing her reputation no end of good." He pulled a face, as if living with George had taught him to ape her mannerisms. "It's like sharing a house with a Mexican bean. She gets zapped with X-rays in the morning and bounces around all afternoon. When she's not on the phone, tracking down witnesses, she forces me onto the streets to get a sense of location. It's wearing me out."

Andrew watched spots of pleased color brighten George's cheeks. "I can't let you do everything," she protested. "I have to earn my fifty percent."

"Less Andrew's ten," Jonathan reminded her, "which he seems to think he earned by entertaining a mad woman for half an hour . . . and swallowing everything she told him hook, line and sinker, not to mention being charmed out of his socks."

Andrew grinned. "Some of it was true."

"Such as?"

"There was blood on Grace's windows by the Tuesday evening."

"There's only her word for that. Roy Trent denies it."

"The police believe her. Otherwise he wouldn't have been charged."

Jonathan bared his teeth. "I'd rather believe Roy. At the moment Louise looks like washing her hands of both murders."

Andrew looked inquiringly at George.

"She's squeaky clean," she agreed with a sigh. "All she's admitted to is persuading

Grace to unlock her door on Monday, then running away once the boys gained entry. Roy's been under the microscope since they found poor Cill's skeleton with the remains of the balled gag still in her mouth. They're being very cagey about the chances of recovering any DNA off it — probably vanished now — but it supports the version that Louise gave."

"Then perhaps she's innocent," said Andrew. "It makes sense that she went back to Grace's house on the Tuesday to check that everything was all right . . . and only started throwing fits and fainting when she realized it wasn't."

"It's not credible," said Jonathan irritably. "Why would Roy and his friends want to murder Grace? Even Louise says they were hiding behind the shed — so there's no evidence Grace ever saw them. *Louise* is the one with the problem, because she took Cill out of the house."

"I'm playing devil's advocate," said Andrew mildly. "However much you dislike Louise, you must at least weigh her innocence in the balance. You're the one who'll be complaining when Jeremy Crossley accuses you of 'flawed analysis.' " He tapped his forefingers together. "How does Louise explain it?"

"By playing the abused-child card. She was a damaged thirteen-year-old with rectal bleeding . . . confused about why Cill hadn't returned home . . . turned to her only friends, the boys, who told her the police would give them another grilling if they didn't persuade Grace to keep her mouth shut as well. Of *course* she worried that they'd killed her when she saw the blood on the window . . . but then Howard was arrested and she realized they *couldn't* have done." He arched a sardonic eyebrow. "The DS in charge finds her very convincing."

"What's Fred Lovatt's view?" Andrew asked George.

"Deeply skeptical — but he's prejudiced in our favor. Poole police are milking her for all she's worth because it's her testimony that will convict Roy. She's very cunning," George finished with reluctant admiration. "Each new statement gives the police a little more of what they want while Roy's are so full of holes you can drive a coach and horses through them."

"Mm." Andrew looked from one to the other. "So what's the problem? Why are you here?"

"We want to name her in the book as the main instigator in the murder of Cill

Trevelyan and the only murderer of Grace Jefferies," said Jonathan.

"Can you prove she murdered Grace?"

"No. The police have lost or destroyed the physical evidence from Grace's house."

"Then she'll sue," said Andrew.

"That's the idea," murmured George. "As things stand at the moment she'll get Colley Hurst's damages, compensation from the state for the abuse she suffered in childhood and a small fortune off the newspapers for selling her story. It's *so* unjust."

Andrew shook his head. "And another small fortune off your publisher when she wins. They'll never go for it."

"Then find us a publisher who will." George urged him. "She might just as well have persuaded Roy to murder Howard as well. The end result was the same." She leaned forward. "Do you know what I find most appalling? The way she uses her father's abuse to excuse all her actions. He was a *disgusting* man — and I would *never* condone what he did to her — I even have sympathy for her when I consider her objectively —" she sighed — "but hundreds of children a year are abused by their parents, and they don't become murderers. Look at Roy. He was as damaged as she was, but he's not claiming his father was responsible for what he did to Cill."

"Are you feeling sorry for him, George?"

She pulled one of her gargoyle faces. "Yes," she admitted. "Whatever Louise says, I don't think Roy and his friends murdered Grace. Only *one* person took a bath in Grace's tub that day and only *one* pair of gloves was recovered. There'll be as gross a miscarriage of justice the second time round as there was with Howard. At least Roy tried to *learn* from his mistakes. He didn't abandon his son. He honored Robyn's wishes to keep the pub and pass it on to the boy. His garage is a storeroom for Peter's possessions. He gave Louise a home . . . gave Colley a home. He's watched over everyone in one way or another. Me, too, when I first got cancer. What he hasn't done is continue to *destroy* people."

"And Louise has?"

"Yes."

Andrew exchanged a glance with Jonathan, who knew as well as he did that no publisher would countenance a potential libel suit. "What do you think?" he asked his friend.

"She's guilty as sin," said Jonathan. "Her nature is pathologically jealous and deceitful. She loses her temper at the drop of a hat and provokes fights when it suits her. She's the only one who had anything to lose if Grace spoke to the police about Cill's continued disappearance. She wielded the knife herself and enjoyed watching Grace die. She took a bath afterward and got a buzz from doing it because the last time she was in that room was when Cill was washing hymenal blood off her legs." He shrugged. only thing we might be able to prove is a negative: if all she did was gain entry for Roy and his friends, then why did the police find no evidence of them?"

"What are you waiting for?"

"Advice," said Jonathan. "Neither of us has yet worked out how to prove a negative."

Chapter Twenty-eight

Winchester Prison
Tuesday, July 29, 2003, 3:00 p.m.

George waited with DS Wyatt in a side room off the entry corridor of Winchester Prison for ten minutes before Roy was brought from the remand wing. The sergeant had been more open to persuasion on this project than George had expected, and she wondered if Fred Lovatt had dropped a word in his ear. Or perhaps Louise's charm was beginning to wear thin. Unable to repress her curiosity indefinitely, she asked him why he'd agreed to do it, and he told her he was beginning to find both her and Dr. Hughes's arguments persuasive. But he warned her that they undermined the case for Howard Stamp's innocence.

"You'll never persuade a jury that a skinny thirteen-year-old was capable of slashing an adult to death on her own," he said.

"She had no trouble pinning Roy and Sasha to the floor," George reminded him, "and she isn't much bigger now."

When Roy finally arrived, he showed immediate antagonism toward George. "What's she doing here?" he demanded, taking a seat on the other side of the table and looking at Wyatt. "I was told it was another police interview."

The sergeant offered him a cigarette. "I've agreed to let Ms. Gardener ask the questions."

"What if I refuse to answer them?"

"I'll put the questions for her. It'll take a lot longer, Roy, but you aren't going anywhere."

Grudgingly, he accepted a light. "Where's the wog?" he said with a sneer for George. "Why isn't he part of this jolly little party?"

"Dr. Hughes is waiting outside," she told him. She wasn't surprised Roy was angry, but she did wonder whether he felt the same kinship for her as she did for him. Their friendship had had its lighter moments and there was a sort of recognition in his eyes as if he remembered them. No man was so evil, she thought, that he had no redeeming qualities, and Roy had been kind to her. "He didn't think you'd talk in front of him."

Roy watched her for a moment. "Too damn right," he said bluntly, "but I'm not going to talk in front of you either, girl, so you've wasted your time coming. I should have given you your marching orders the first time I saw you."

"Why didn't you?"

"Because that stupid old fool Jim Longhurst told you I knew Howard, and I thought you'd be suspicious if I didn't show some interest." He propped his elbows on the table and stared belligerently from one to the other.

"Ms. Gardener's on your side, Roy," said DS Wyatt mildly. "She doesn't believe you killed Grace."

"More fool her. If it wasn't me and Colley, then it was Howard, and she's been scraping the barrel for years trying to prove *that* little wanker innocent."

Wyatt gave a faint smile. "I've explained that to her, but I'm still interested to hear how you respond to her questions. This isn't a formal interview so you aren't obliged to talk to her . . . but I suggest you do. You've nothing to lose by it."

"I've got everything to lose if she twists my words so she and her tame author can claim Howard was innocent."

"That's why I'm here, to ensure fair

play." The sergeant tapped his forefinger on the table. "You're on remand because the magistrates agreed you pose a threat to a witness — Mrs. Fletcher. But that threat only relates to Grace Jefferies's murder."

"She's lying through her teeth," said Roy angrily. "We never went near Grace's house after the Saturday evening."

"Then persuade us of that and there's a possibility the remand order will be revoked. We wouldn't have opposed bail on Cill Trevelyan's manslaughter. You've already said you won't contest the charges, and your clean record since 1974 and the fact that you were a juvenile when the crime was committed work in your favor." He paused for emphasis. "But I need something more convincing than denials, and 'she's lying through her teeth,' if you expect a review on the Jefferies' murder."

Roy stared him down. "If I had anything more convincing, don't you think I'd have told you? How am I supposed to prove the bitch is lying when Micky's dead and Colley can't remember a damn thing? She can say what the hell she likes . . . and you'll believe her."

George leaned forward. "Negatives are such difficult things to prove, Roy. In your favor is the fact that the police found no evidence that there was more than one person in Grace's house when she died. Against you are Louise's testimony that she engineered your access to Grace . . . that you had a motive . . . and that you'd already committed one murder."

He refused to look at her, not out of anger or resentment, she decided, but out of shame. "It was an accident," he said. "Mr. Wyatt's accepted we didn't mean to kill her."

"The end result was the same," said George.

"I'm not denying that," he said curtly, "which is why I'm holding my hands up to manslaughter."

"Do you regret it?" she asked.

Anger sparked in his face again. "Of course I bloody regret it," he snarled. "The poor kid would have lived if she'd listened to her father and steered clear of the likes of us."

"You were quite happy to smear David Trevelyan when Jonathan and I spoke to you," she reminded him. "Why should any of us believe that you aren't doing the same to Louise? Her story holds water. Yours doesn't." She watched his fingers clench involuntarily round his cigarette. "Perhaps whoever killed Grace didn't mean to do it either, but she was still dead by the time they left . . . and at the moment you and your friends are the only people apart from Louise and Howard who had any close connection with her."

He took a breath. "We — never — had — *any* — connection — with — Grace," he said with painstaking emphasis. "We knew her name from Howard, and we knew where she lived, but the *only* time we came anywhere close to her was when she shut the door behind Cill on the Saturday night."

"Then help me prove it," she urged. "If it wasn't you who killed her, who was it?"

"Howard," he said.

"What about Colley Hurst or Micky Hopkinson?"

Roy shook his head. "We were always together. One of us couldn't have done it without the others knowing."

"Then why is Louise saying you did?"

He raised impatient eyes to hers. "To get me banged up in here and Colley confined to a loony bin. It's like Mr. Wyatt says, we'd rip her miserable heart out if we had the chance. She only came up with this stuff when I looked like making bail on Cill."

George pulled a wry expression. "So

your only regret is being caught? As long as no one ever found out about Cill, you could pretend to yourself her death was just an unfortunate accident."

He pressed his thumb and forefinger into the corners of his eyes. "Don't lecture me," he warned her, with a dangerous edge to his voice. "You haven't lived my life. You don't know what I regret and what I don't."

"Was Grace another unfortunate accident? Did it start as a joke and end up as a murder because Micky pricked her with his knife and she started squealing the way Howard did?" She moistened her mouth in face of his naked anger. "You said it yourself," she went on. "If Howard didn't commit the murder, then it had to be the three of you. You were the only other people with a motive."

Roy glared at Wyatt. "I *told* you. She's stitching me up."

"It's a reasonable inference," the sergeant said. "If Grace knew you were in her garden when Cill left, then you certainly had a motive."

Roy arched forward, stabbing his cigarette at the other man. "I've told you a thousand times, she *couldn't* have done so. There was no way she could have seen us.

Even Lou's saying we were hiding behind the shed."

"Perhaps Louise told her you were waiting," said George.

"Oh sure!" he said scathingly. "And you think Cill would have come out if she knew her rapists were planning to jump her." He took a pensive drag on his cigarette. "We'd have been mad to go near Grace after the grilling we had on the Monday morning. All we could think about was putting distance between ourselves and anyone who'd known Cill. If we'd seen Howard, we'd have run a mile in case he guessed what we'd done." He paused, remembering. "We were scared out of our wits the cops had only let us go to follow us back to the body. We were a mess for months . . . shat bricks every time we saw bulldozers on the waste ground."

"Then why lie about Howard attacking Colley with a knife?" she asked reasonably. "It was so easily disproved, and it makes everything else you say suspect."

"Because I was sick to the back teeth of you and that damned author bleating on about Howard's innocence. I knew he was guilty . . . *everyone* knew he was guilty. About the only thing Lou's said that's true is that he was a pervert. He was always creeping around the kids in Colliton Way."

"That's tantamount to saying all perverts are murderers, Roy. On that basis, Louise's father could have murdered Grace."

He shrugged. "She'd go for it if there was a shred of evidence to support it. He didn't think twice about destroying *her*. She hates him with a passion."

George nodded. "She certainly flew that kite when she talked to Andrew Spicer."

Roy showed a reluctant interest. "When did she talk to him?"

"Nearly three months ago."

That surprised him. "She never told me."

"It was also the first time she mentioned seeing blood on Grace's window on the Tuesday," George said. "It suited us, of course, because it pointed toward Howard's innocence . . . but it didn't suit you or your friends. Jonathan believes she started trying to set you up from the minute he arrived on the scene."

Roy frowned. "She told Sasha Spencer it was Howard. I heard her. She even gave chapter and verse on how he did it . . . by sneaking out when his mother was drunk. *That* was the truth. It's this garbage about getting us into the house that's the lie."

"She only named Howard to give the impression that she was frightened of you." George watched a frown draw his heavy eyebrows together. "She wanted the police involved. It's probably why she stole Jonathan's wallet and passport. She's a sexy woman and she's *bored* with playing nurse to a mental cripple." She pulled a face. "To be honest, I don't think she cares who gets dragged into the net, just so long as she can walk away and start again. She doesn't have your loyalties . . . or your conscience."

"What's that supposed to mean?"

"Has she ever expressed remorse for delivering Cill into your hands?"

He squeezed the glowing end out of his cigarette and dropped it into the ashtray. "We don't talk about it."

"What did you say at the time? How did you explain the fact that Cill was still missing?"

He thought back. "I said she'd run away from us when we left the alleyway."

"And Louise believed you?"

"I didn't ask."

DS Wyatt leaned forward. "When did you speak to her?"

"On the Monday afternoon. She called from a pay phone on her way home from school wanting to know if the police had questioned us about the rape. I said they had and they'd let us go."

"What else?"

"I told her to keep her mouth shut about Saturday night, otherwise the police'd know we'd been lying about the rape."

"Did you threaten her?"

Roy nodded.

"What with?"

"I said we'd tell the cops it was her idea."

"The rape, or abducting Cill from Grace's house?"

"Both. It was Lou delivered the poor kid to us each time." He stared bleakly at the wall behind Wyatt's head. "I don't know why we went along with it now, except we knew Howard liked her. It was him we were really after." He shook himself suddenly as if to rid himself of phantoms. "It was Lou's big mouth that was the problem. I told her we'd have her if she made it any worse for us."

"Are we talking about the lunchtime conversation on the Saturday or the Monday afternoon one?"

"Saturday. She'd already dropped us in it by describing us."

"Is that when she said Cill was at Grace's?"

He nodded.

"And?" asked Wyatt.

"She came up with the idea of giving Cill a scare. Problem solved if she didn't name us."

"What about Grace?" put in George. "She must have known about the rape, and almost certainly knew, or could guess, that you were responsible. Why didn't you think it was necessary to give her a scare as well?"

Roy's eyes narrowed suspiciously. "We weren't that bloody thick. If Cill denied it was us, then it didn't matter what Grace said."

"Did you consider the idea at all?" Wyatt asked mildly.

Roy hesitated. "I'm not answering that," he said then, jerking his chin at George. "I'll have my words twisted if I do."

"Fair enough. Let me put it another way. Did Louise suggest for the Saturday night what she's now claiming happened on the Monday — that she engineered entry for you, Micky and Colley in order to scare Grace into keeping quiet?"

A tic started working violently at the side of Roy's mouth. "I'm not answering that either."

"Grace couldn't have died on the Saturday," George told him, "otherwise Cill's fingerprints would have been found." She saw incomprehension in his eyes. "No one's saying you killed Grace on the Saturday," she explained. "All we're asking is if Louise suggested you go into the house with her."

He didn't answer.

"Should we take that as a yes?" Wyatt asked. "Presumably you'd be denying it if she hadn't?"

Roy gave a terse nod. "We didn't go in, though."

"Because you didn't want Grace to see you?"

Another nod.

"But you didn't have a problem if she saw Louise?"

He shrugged. "It was her idea. She'd have talked her way out of it. We didn't have much of a say except to be waiting in the alley at the back by eight-thirty."

"But all this was before Cill died," Wyatt pointed out. "How did Louise react on the Monday when you said you'd take her down with you if she ever talked about the events of Saturday night."

"She got uppity and we had a row. I told her not to ring again. I was scared witless the police were going to find out we knew each other."

"What was the relationship between you?" George asked. "Was she keen on you?"

"Must have been," he said. "She was always on the phone, wanting to talk to me. I didn't feel the same way about her — not then — she was nothing to look at in those days. More of a joke, really."

"So you dumped her?" said Wyatt.

Roy shrugged. "It was for her sake as well as ours. She'd been acting pretty damn crazy since the rape — kept accusing us of fancying Cill. It was driving Micky round the bend, and he was never too stable at the best of times." He paused. "I'm not saying it's fair, but we all blamed her for what happened. If she hadn't told us where Cill was, we'd never have done it."

"Weren't you worried she'd take revenge?" Wyatt asked. "She was disturbed enough."

Roy shook his head. "She couldn't — not without getting herself into trouble."

"Until Grace was murdered," said George. "She was the only other person who knew Louise was involved."

There was a short silence.

"Whoever killed Mrs. Jefferies had red hair," said DS Wyatt. "It was someone she was willing to open her door to . . . and someone who was deeply disturbed."

Roy flicked a wary glance between the two of them.

"Louise was in a dangerously unstable mood after that weekend," George said. "Far more unstable than Howard, for example, who was looking for a job and was given one by Jannerway's Dairy. She was being blamed at school for provoking the fight that led indirectly to Cill running away . . . being accused by the Trevelyans of telling lies. She hated her father for what he was doing to her, hated you for abandoning her, and most certainly hated Cill. By the Wednesday, a doctor was prescribing tranquilizers to control her panic attacks."

"How could she have done it? She was a skinny little kid."

"Who was wielding a carving knife against a woman who tried to escape upstairs. She was slashing at her legs as she went after her."

Roy ground his fists into his eyes. "What was the point? Lou didn't know Cill was dead. The kid could have returned the next day, and the heat would have been off."

George shook her head. "She wouldn't

have been thinking as rationally as that, but are you sure she didn't know Cill was dead . . . or at least guess? If she was watching while you walked away up Bladen Street, she'd have known Cill didn't run away when you left the alley. Perhaps you said something on the Monday that allowed her to put two and two together?"

He stared at her. "Are you saying she did it after she spoke to me?"

"We think Tuesday's more likely. If she was ostracized for a second day at school — which she was — then it's probable her resentments spilled over in the evening. Everyone was blaming her. Her mother was furious because Jean Trevelyan had screamed at her in the street, and her father was angry because David Trevelyan was souring the atmosphere at work. She may even have gone to Grace's for sympathy and lost her temper when she didn't get it."

Wyatt offered him another cigarette. "You described her as 'uppity,' " he prompted. "What did she say?"

Roy dredged his memory. "I know she kept on about me fancying Cill, because that's what got me riled," he said. "The kid was already dead but she wouldn't let it drop. Lou was obsessed with her even then. Did I think Cill was prettier? Did I think Cill was sexier? I told her I'd kill her if she didn't shut up." He fell into a morose, brooding silence.

"She gives a great deal of detail in her statement," said Wyatt. "She claims it all came from Micky Hopkinson shortly before he died but it's very accurate for a story that was told her fifteen years after the event. She knew about the handkerchief . . . Cill's hands being tied . . . Micky holding a knife to her back . . . Cill crying the whole way to the waste ground . . . burial in one of the test pits . . . you getting rid of your clothes in a dustbin on the other side of town."

Roy lowered his head into his hands. "She'd have to've followed us to know all that for herself . . . and she didn't. I'm not *thick,* Mr. Wyatt. Do you think I wouldn't've caught her out by now? Do you think I'd've let her call the shots all these years if there was a chance she'd murdered Grace?"

"Did she have Micky or Colley's number?"

He hesitated. "She might have had Colley's. Micky's family didn't have a phone."

"Would she have called Colley?"

"Maybe . . . but it's not something you

can prove. He's forgotten the whole thing now."

"When did you next see her?" asked George.

"After she and Micky hooked up. I recognized her immediately. She'd changed everything else, but she couldn't change her eyes."

"Was she calling herself Priscilla?"

"Not then. She was Daisy at that point. She changed to Priscilla about three years after she married Micky."

"Did she explain why she chose it?"

He stirred the dirt in the ashtray with the end of his cigarette. "She liked it better than Daisy or Louise." He pondered for a moment. "Actually, I think she said *Micky* liked Priscilla better than Daisy or Louise, and she probably meant it that way, too. She never believed any of us liked her for who she was . . . you could say Colley's proved it by forgetting Louise completely."

"Did she ever mention Grace's murder or Howard's conviction?" Wyatt asked.

"Only since George came on the scene and started asking questions."

"What did she say?"

"That if George ferreted around too much she'd find out about Cill."

"Anything else?"

"She was worried about DNA evidence."

"In what connection?" asked George. "Cill's murder or Grace's?"

Roy eyed her for a moment. "Grace's," he said slowly. "She read Dr. Hughes's book where he mentioned that if some of the physical evidence had been kept, it would clear Howard. She was frightened that if that happened, the police would reopen the case and almost certainly look at Cill's disappearance again —" he paused — "and that would put her, Colley and me in the firing line because we were all questioned at the time."

"What was your answer to that?"

He didn't speak for a moment, and George could almost hear his brain working. "That you'd already told me the physical evidence had been destroyed and there wasn't much chance of anyone else being put in the frame."

George frowned at him. "I never said that, Roy. Even the police don't know if the evidence still exists. Fred Lovatt's looked through the archives and he hasn't found anything . . . but I live in hope. The Black Museum in London still has bits of evidence from the Ripper murders."

Roy's mouth twisted into a cynical smile. "She was acting paranoid. I wanted her out of the pub before she drew attention to herself. Bloody joke, eh? I wouldn't be here if I'd kept my stupid mouth shut."

Wyatt exchanged a questioning glance with George.

"Two hours later she stole Jonathan's wallet and passport," George said. "That's the only reason we became interested in Cill Trevelyan." She pulled a wry expression at Roy's dawning disillusionment. "I did say she didn't have your loyalties, Roy, and perhaps, after all, we should blame her father for it. If he hadn't made her the whipping boy for his frustrations, and forced her to lie about it, she wouldn't have learned how easy — or *pleasurable* — it was to see someone else punished for *hers.*"

From: wandr.burton@compuline.com
Sent: Tues. 7/29/03 15:23
To: robandeileen.burton@uknet.co.uk
Subject: Louise

Dear Robert and Eileen,

I'm writing to you without Billy's knowledge because he's forbidden me and the girls to talk to you, but someone has to say something before this awful situation gets any worse. You can't be so stupid that you'd go on lying for Louise when she's lining up Eileen as Grace's murderer if Roy Trent can wriggle out of it. Maybe you think you owe her something because of Robert's abuse. Maybe you think that by giving her an alibi, you're helping her. You're not. You're just accusing YOURSELVES. I'm guessing you're sticking to a story you invented years ago, but all you're doing is digging a bigger and bigger hole for yourselves because the police haven't told you what Louise has been saying.

Billy KNOWS that Eileen went to work on the Monday and Tuesday afternoons as usual, which means she COULDN'T have got home until after Robert clocked on at Brackham & Wright's. It wasn't until the Wednesday, when Louise started her fainting fits, that she gave up work. Robert, you know this too, so why are you lying about it? The police keep asking Billy the same questions over and over again. What time did his mother come home on the Tuesday? Was Louise there? Did his mother go out again later?

Eileen's already under suspicion because she said she collected Louise from school on the Monday afternoon and kept her at home for the rest of the day. That's contradicting Louise's OWN story about phoning Trent from a call box after school, then helping him and his friends gain access to Grace that evening. Because of that, they're now questioning whether Eileen collected Louise on the Tuesday. If you've been lying to protect the family, then you're MAD. At the moment, Eileen's next in the firing line. If you're guilty of Grace's murder, Eileen, then I have no sympathy for you, but if you're NOT, then you must tell the truth.

The worst I think you might have done is cover for Louise afterward. I'd know if either of my girls had done something bad. I bet she came home in a state on the Tuesday, long after you'd got back from work, probably in something of Grace's because she'd left hers on the bathroom floor. I expect she lied and said Grace was already dead when she got there. So what did you do? Go back for the clothes? Was it you who wiped the taps? It's the sort of thing you'd think of. I wonder why you didn't clean the bath as well, but maybe the blood and hair didn't show when it was wet. You must have been very frightened, of course, so perhaps you felt too sick to do the job properly. Was it you who vandalized the house to make it look like a burglary?

I'm not surprised you were shaking

when the police came door to door. I bet you couldn't believe your luck when the police didn't find any fingerprints. I wonder if it was you who picked up the bloodstained gloves and carried them away to a bin. You probably hoped Louise wouldn't have been clever enough to wear them, so you left them where they could be found in case they proved someone else was responsible.

I don't know what I would have done in your shoes, Eileen, but I hope I'd have had the courage — and sense — to do the right thing. You didn't solve anything for her, or for yourselves, by closing your mind to her guilt. I'm sure the whole idea of it was unbearable, particularly because you KNEW that only a very disturbed person could have murdered Grace in that way. Perhaps you even understood why Louise was disturbed — or at least guessed — so you share some of her guilt. Robert carries the most blame, though, because he treated her like a plaything that could be discarded when he got bored.

Then Howard confessed and you were able to persuade yourself that Louise had been telling the truth. Poor little bloke. He didn't have a mother who was prepared to cover and lie for him. Wynne just made his situation worse by saying he cut himself because he thought he was ugly. Billy's been having dreams about Cill. Well, I've been having them about Howard Stamp. I can't get out of my mind that, in his whole life, no one except his gran and Cill was ever kind to him. But, when he needed them — when he was at his most lonely — they weren't there.

Louise has no conscience, Eileen, because you and Robert taught her that it's OK to lie. Half of me thinks it would be natural justice for you to take the blame for her this time — you SHOULD have spoken out in 1970 — the other half revolts at it. She's already sent one innocent person to prison for this. Can't you see how WRONG it would be to let her do it again? Louise is not your only child. You are BILLY'S mother, too.

Rachel

Chapter Twenty-nine

Winchester Prison Car Park
Tuesday, July 29, 2003, 4:00 p.m.

Jonathan was standing by the car listening to the radio through the open window when George and DS Wyatt emerged through the judas gate in the huge oak doors that formed the entrance to Winchester Prison. He watched them walk the two hundred yards to the car park while a commentator talked about a forthcoming inquiry into the events surrounding the mysterious death of the Iraqi arms expert Dr. David Kelly.

"Campbell and Blair to give evidence to Hutton Inquiry . . . Government stands accused . . ."

To Jonathan, still as skeptical as he'd been in February, the idea that an inquiry could get at the truth when the major player was dead was laughable. There were no absolute truths. Only half-truths and interpretations that begged to be spun by anyone strong enough — or *determined* enough — to force his opinions on everyone else. It was single-minded zealots who ruled the world — politicians, religious leaders, terrorists, media and business moguls — and most of them were too arrogant or stupid to see that their beliefs were flawed.

He cocked an eyebrow as George and DS Wyatt drew close. "Any luck?"

"Nothing we can use as yet," said George, "but at least he's started thinking for himself." She gave a small giggle. "I shouldn't laugh — not after what he did to poor Cill — but he was huffing and puffing by the end. He can't *believe* what a fool he's been . . . he swallowed everything Louise ever told him and never thought for one *minute* that she had anything to hide."

Jonathan reached into the car and switched off the radio. "His memories won't help us," he warned her. "He'll come up with a stream of them if it gets him off the hook. We need something we can prove if we're going to name her."

"Oh, don't be so miserable," she said cheerfully, tapping his wrist. "Mr. Wyatt's very optimistic. He tells me persistence is everything. If he keeps asking questions,

Louise will trip herself up. She's not bright enough to do anything else — *none* of us is." Her wise eyes smiled into his. "She's already handed us a wealth of ammunition because of the numerous different versions she's produced. It's the tangled-web syndrome, Jon. Roy fell into it the minute he tried to sex up Howard's guilt. Lies always unravel under pressure. *You* know that."

He gave her a fond smile. "But I wasn't fully committed to mine, George."

She clucked like a mother hen. "Of course you weren't, my dear. You're far too honorable . . . and Emma wasn't worth the heartache it caused you. Sasha's a much better prospect. There are no sides to her . . . probably because her Mongolian blood is so obvious. It's not the sort of thing you can hide, is it?"

Jonathan opened his mouth to protect what little mystery he had left, but Wyatt forestalled him with an outrageous wink. "Never argue with a lady, Dr. Hughes . . . particularly when she's right. Ms. Spencer's a fine young woman, and I *am* optimistic. Mrs. Fletcher's never been questioned about Grace's murder and she's already contradicted her original statement where she claimed ignorance. It's just a matter of time before she ties herself in knots."

Jonathan looked into George's face. "You'd better not start feeling sorry for her," he warned.

"She was only thirteen."

He held up a finger. "I'm a man, George, and I can't cope with any more emotion."

"But —"

With a fond smile, he pulled her into his arms. "She's my mother," he told Wyatt over her head. "She had a one-night stand with a Jamaican road sweeper thirty-five years ago and she's been regretting it ever since. I wouldn't mind so much but she keeps trying to pass me off as her toyboy."

The policeman gave a doubtful smile.

WEBSTER'S REFERENCE LIBRARY

CONCISE EDITION DICTIONARY AND THESAURUS

WEBSTER'S REFERENCE LIBRARY

CONCISE EDITION

DICTIONARY AND THESAURUS

GEDDES & GROSSET

Published 2009 by Geddes & Grosset

David Dale House, New Lanark ML11 9DJ, Scotland

First published in this edition 2002.
Reprinted 2002 (twice), 2003 (twice), 2004, 2005,
2006 (twice), 2007 (twice), 2008, 2009

ISBN 978 1 84205 190 0

Printed and bound in the UK

Contents

Abbreviations used in this Book

abbr	abbreviation
adj	adjective
adv	adverb
anat	anatomy
approx	approximately
arch	archaic
archit	architecture
astrol	astrology
astron	astronomy
Austral	Australia, Australasia
aux	auxiliary
biol	biology
bot	botany
Brit	Britain, British
c	*circa*, about
cap	capital
cent	century
chem	chemical, chemistry
compar	comparative
comput	computing
conj	conjunction
demons	demonstrative
derog	derogatory, derogatorily
econ	economics
eg	*exempli gratia*, for example
elect	electricity
esp	especially
fig	figuratively
geog	geography
geol	geology
geom	geometry
gram	grammar
her	heraldry
hist	history
ie	*id est*, that is
imper	imperative
incl	including
inf	informal
interj	interjection
math	mathematics
mech	mechanics
med	medicine
mil	military
myth	mythology
n	noun
naut	nautical
neut	neuter
news	news media
nf	noun feminine
npl	noun plural
n sing	noun singular
orig	original, originally, origin
p	participle
pers	person, personal
philos	philosophy
photog	photography
pl	plural
poet	poetical
poss	possessive
pp	past participle
prep	preposition
pres t	present tense
print	printing
pron	pronoun
pr p	present participle
psychol	psychology
pt	past tense
RC	Roman Catholic
reflex	reflexive
Scot	Scotland
sing	singular
sl	slang
superl	superlative
theat	theatre
TV	television
UK	United Kingdom
US	United States
USA	United States of America
usu	usually
vb	verb
vb aux	auxiliary verb
vi	intransitive verb
vt	transitive verb
vti	transitive or instransitive verb
vulg	vulgar, vulgarly
zool	zoology

A

A *abbr* = ampere(s).
a *adj* the indefinite article; one; any; per.
AA *abbr* = Alcoholics Anonymous; anti-aircraft; Automobile Association.
aback *adv* **taken aback** startled.
abandon *vt* to leave behind; to desert; to yield completely to an emotion or urge. * *n* freedom from inhibitions.—**abandonment** *n*.
abate *vti* to make or become less; (*law*) to end.—**abatement** *n*.
abattoir *n* a slaughterhouse.
abbey *n* a building occupied by monks or nuns; a church attached to an abbey; the community of monks or nuns.
abbot *n* the head of an abbey of monks.
abbreviate *vt* to make shorter, esp to shorten (words) by omitting letters.
abbreviation *n* the process of abbreviating; a shortened form of a word.
abdicate *vti* to renounce an official position or responsibility, etc.—**abdication** *n*.
abdomen *n* the region of the body below the chest containing the digestive organs; the belly; (*insects, etc*) the section of the body behind the thorax.—**abdominal** *adj*.
abduct *vt* to carry off (a person) by force.—**abduction** *n*.—**abductor** *n*.
abet *vt* (*pt* **abetted**) to encourage or assist.—**abetter**.
abhor *vt* (*pt* **abhorred**) to detest, despise.
abide *vt* (*pt* **abode** *or* **abided**) to endure; to put up with.
ability *n* being able; power to do; talent; skill.
ablaze *adj* burning, on fire.
able *adj* having the competence or means (to do); talented; skilled.—**ably** *adv*.
abnormal *adj* unusual, not average or typical; irregular.—**abnormality** *n*.
aboard *adv* on or in an aircraft, ship, train, etc.—*also prep*.
abolish *vt* to bring to an end, do away with.
abolition *n* the act of abolishing; (*with cap*) in UK, the ending of the slave trade (1807) or slavery (1833), in US, the emancipation of the slaves (1863).—**abolitionist** *n*.
abominable *adj* despicable, detestable; (*inf*) very unpleasant.—**abominably** *adv*.
aborigine *n* any of the first known inhabitants of a region; (*with cap*) one of the original inhabitants of Australia.
abort *vti* to undergo or cause an abortion; to terminate or cause to terminate prematurely. * *n* the premature termination of a rocket flight, etc.
abortion *n* the premature expulsion of a foetus, esp if induced.
abortive *adj* failing in intended purpose; fruitless; causing abortion.
abound *vi* to be in abundance; to have in great quantities.
about *prep* on all sides of; near to; with; on the point of; concerning. * *adv* all around; near; to face the opposite direction.
above *prep* over, on top of; better or more than; beyond the reach of; too complex to understand. * *adv* in or to a higher place; in addition; (*text*) mentioned earlier.
abrasive *adj* causing abrasion; harsh, irritating. * *n* a substance or tool used for grinding or polishing, etc.
abreast *adv* side by side and facing the same way; informed (of); aware.
abridge *vt* to shorten by using fewer words but keeping the substance.—**abridgement, abridgment** *n*.
abroad *adv* in or to a foreign country; over a wide area; out in the open; in circulation, current.
abrupt *adj* sudden; unexpected; curt.—**abruptly** *adv*.
abscess *n* an inflamed area of the body containing pus.
abscond *vi* to hide, run away, esp to avoid punishment.
absence *n* the state of not being present; the time of this; a lack; inattention.
absent[1] *adj* not present; not existing; inattentive.
absent[2] *vt* to keep (oneself) away.
absentee *n* a person who is absent, as from work or school.
absenteeism *n* persistent absence from work, school, etc.
absent-minded *adj* inattentive; forgetful.
absolute *adj* unrestricted, unconditional; complete; positive; perfect, pure; not relative; (*inf*) utter, out-and-out.
absolutely *adv* completely; unconditionally; (*inf*) I completely agree, certainly.
absolve *vt* to clear from guilt or blame; to give

religious absolution to; to free from a duty, obligation, etc.

absorb *vt* to take in; to soak up; to incorporate; to pay for (costs, etc); to take in (a shock) without recoil; to occupy one's interest completely.—**absorber** *n*.—**absorption** *n*.

absorbent *adj* capable of absorbing moisture, etc.—**absorbency** *n*.

abstain *vi* to keep oneself from some indulgence, esp alcohol; to refrain from using one's vote.—**abstainer** *n*.—**abstention** *n*.

abstemious *adj* sparing in consuming food or alcohol.

abstinence *n* an abstaining or refraining, esp from food or alcohol.—**abstinent** *adj*.

abstract *adj* having no material existence; theoretical; (*art*) non-representational. * *n* (*writing, speech*) a summary or condensed version. * *vt* to remove or extract; to separate; to summarize.

absurd *adj* against reason or common sense; ridiculous.—**absurdity** *n*.

abundance *n* a plentiful supply; a considerable amount.

abundant *adj* plentiful; rich (in).—**abundantly** *adv*.

abuse *vt* to make wrong use of; to mistreat; to insult, attack verbally. * *n* misuse; mistreatment; insulting language.

abusive *adj* insulting.

abysmal *adj* extremely bad, deplorable.

abyss *n* a bottomless depth; anything too deep to measure.

academic *adj* pertaining to a school, college or university; scholarly; purely theoretical in nature. * *n* a member of a college or university; a scholarly person.

academy *n* a school for specialized training; (*Scot*) a secondary school; (*with cap*) a society of scholars, etc.

accede *vi* to take office; to agree or assent to (a suggestion).

accelerate *vti* to move faster; to happen or cause to happen more quickly; to increase the speed of (a vehicle).

acceleration *n* the act of accelerating or condition of being accelerated; the rate of increase in speed or change in velocity; the power of accelerating.

accelerator *n* a device for increasing speed; a throttle; (*physics*) an apparatus that imparts high velocities to elementary particles.

accent *n* emphasis on a syllable or word; a mark used to indicate this; any way of speaking characteristic of a region, class, or an individual; the emphasis placed on something; rhythmic stress in music or verse.

accept *vt* to receive, esp willingly; to approve; to agree to; to believe in; to agree to pay.—**acceptance** *n*.

acceptable *adj* satisfactory; welcome; tolerable.

access *n* approach, or means of approach; the right to enter, use, etc. * *vt* (*comput*) to retrieve (information) from a storage device; to gain access to.

accessory *adj* additional; extra. * *n* a supplementary part or item, esp of clothing; a person who aids another in a crime.

accident *n* an unexpected event; a mishap or misfortune, esp one resulting in death or injury; chance.

accidental *adj* occurring or done by accident; non-essential; (*mus*) a sign prefixed to a note indicating a departure from the key signature.—**accidentally** *adv*.

acclaim *vt* to praise publicly; to welcome enthusiastically. * *vi* to shout approval. * *n* a shout of welcome or approval.—**acclamation** *n*.

acclimatize *vt* to adapt to a new climate or environment * *vi* to become acclimatized.—**acclimatization** *n*.

accommodate *vt* to provide lodging for; to oblige, supply; to adapt, harmonize.

accommodating *adj* obliging, willing to help.

accommodation *n* lodgings; the process of adapting; willingness to help.

accompaniment *n* an instrumental part supporting a solo instrument, a voice, or a choir; something that accompanies.—**accompanist** *n*.

accompany *vt* (*person*) to go with; (*something*) to supplement.

accomplice *n* a partner, esp in committing a crime.

accomplish *vt* to succeed in carrying out; to fulfil.

accomplished *adj* done; completed; skilled, expert; polished.

accomplishment *n* a skill or talent; the act of accomplishing; something accomplished.

accord *vi* to agree; to harmonize (with). * *vt* to grant. * *n* consent; harmony.

accordance *n* agreement; conformity.

accordingly *adv* consequently; therefore.

accordion *n* a portable keyboard instrument with manually operated folding bellows that force air through metal reeds.—**accordionist** *n*.

accost *vt* to approach and speak to.

account *n* a description; explanatory statement; business record or statement; a credit arrangement with a bank, department store, etc; importance, consequence. * *vt* to think of as; to consider. * *vi* to give a financial reckoning (to); (*with* **for**) to give reasons (for); (*with* **for**) to kill, dispose of.

accountable *adj* liable; responsible.—**accountability** *n.*

accountancy *n* the profession or practice of an accountant.

accountant *n* one whose profession is auditing business accounts.

accumulate *vti* to collect together in increasing quantities, to amass.—**accumulation** *n.*—**accumulative** *adj.*

accurate *adj* conforming with the truth or an accepted standard; done with care, exact.—**accuracy** *n.*—**accurately** *adv.*

accusation *n* the act of accusing or being accused; an allegation.

accuse *vt* to charge with a crime, fault, etc; to blame.—**accuser** *n.*—**accusingly** *adv.*

accustom *vt* to make used (to) by habit, use, or custom.

accustomed *adj* usual, customary.

ace *n* the one spot in dice, cards, etc; a point won by a single stroke; an expert. * *adj* (*inf*) excellent.

ache *n* a dull, continuous pain. * *vi* to suffer a dull, continuous mental or physical pain; (*inf*) to yearn.

achieve *vt* to perform successfully, accomplish; to gain, win. —**achievable** *adj.*—**achiever** *n.*

acid *adj* sharp, tart, sour; bitter. * *n* a sour substance; (*chem*) a corrosive substance that turns litmus red; (*sl*) LSD.

acknowledge *vt* to admit that something is true and valid; to show that one has noticed or recognized.—**acknowledgement** *n.*

acne *n* inflammation of the skin glands producing pimples.

acorn *n* the nut of the oak tree.

acoustic *adj* of the sense of hearing or sound; of acoustics.

acoustics *npl* (*room, concert hall, etc*) properties governing how clearly sounds can be heard in it; (*in sing*) the physics of sound.—**acoustical** *adj.*—**acoustically** *adv.*

acquaint *vt* to make (oneself) familiar (with); to inform.

acquaintance *n* a person whom one knows only slightly.

acquire *vt* to gain by one's own efforts; to obtain.

acquisition *n* gaining, acquiring; something that is acquired.

acquisitive *adj* eager or greedy for possessions.—**acquisitively** *adv.*—**acquisitiveness** *n.*

acquit *vt* (*pt* **acquitted**) to free from an obligation; to behave or conduct (oneself); to declare innocent.—**acquittal** *n.*

acre *n* land measuring 4840 sq yards.

acrimony *n* bitterness of manner or language.—**acrimonious** *adj.*—**acrimoniously** *adv.*

acrobat *n* a skilful performer of spectacular gymnastic feats.—**acrobatic** *adj.*—**acrobatically** *adv.*

acrobatics *npl* acrobatic feats.

across *prep* from one side to the other of; on or at an angle; on the other side of. * *adv* crosswise; from one side to the other.

act *vi* to perform or behave in a certain manner; to perform a specific function; to have an effect; to perform on the stage. * *vt* to portray by actions, esp on the stage; to pretend, simulate; to take the part of, as a character in a play. * *n* something done, a deed; an exploit; a law; a main division of a play or opera; the short repertoire of a comic, etc; something done merely for effect or show.

acting *n* the art of an actor. * *adj* holding an office or position temporarily.

action *n* process of doing something; an operation; a movement of the body, gesture; a land or sea battle; a lawsuit; the unfolding of events in a play, etc.

activate *vt* to make active; to set in motion.—**activation** *n.*—**activator** *n.*

active *adj* lively, physically mobile; engaged in practical activities; energetic, busy; (*volcano*) liable to erupt; capable of producing an effect; radioactive; (*armed forces*) in full-time service. * *n* (*gram*) the verb form having as its subject the doer of the action.—**actively** *adv.*

activity *n* being active; energetic, lively action; specific occupations (*indoor activities*).

actor *n* a person who acts in a play, film, etc.—**actress** *nf.*

actual *adj* real; existing in fact or reality.—**actually** *adv.*

acumen *n* sharpness of mind, perception.

acupuncture *n* the insertion of the tips of fine needles into the skin at certain points to treat various common ailments.—**acupuncturist** *n.*

acute *adj* (*hearing*) sensitive; (*pain*) severe; very serious; (*angles*) less than 90 degrees; (*disease*) severe but not long lasting.—**acutely** *adv*.—**acuteness** *n*.

AD *abbr* = *anno Domini* (in the year of Our Lord) in dates of the Christian era, indicating the number of years since the birth of Christ.

Adam's apple *n* the hard projection of cartilage in the front of the neck.

adapt *vti* to make or become fit; to adjust to new circumstances.—**adaptability** *n* —**adaptable** *adj*.

adaptation *n* the process or condition of being adapted; something produced by modification; a version of a literary composition rewritten for a different medium.

adapter, adaptor *n* a device that allows an item of equipment to be put to new use; a device for connecting parts of differing size and shape.

add *vt* to combine (two or more things together); to combine numbers or amounts in a total; to remark or write further. * *vi* to perform or come together by addition.

adder *n* the venomous viper.

addict *n* a person who is dependent upon a drug.—**addiction** *n*.

addition *n* the act or result of adding; something to be added; an extra part.—**additional** *adj*.

additive *adj* produced by addition. * *n* a substance added (to food, etc) to improve texture, flavour, etc.

address *vt* to write directions for delivery on (a letter, etc); to speak or write directly to; to direct one's skills or attention (to); (*golf*) to adjust one's stance and aim before hitting the ball; * *n* a place where a person or business resides, the details of this on a letter for delivery; a speech, esp a formal one; (*comput*) a specific memory location where information is stored.

adenoids *npl* enlarged masses of tissue in the throat behind the nose.

adept *adj* highly proficient. * *n* a highly skilled person.

adequate *adj* sufficient for requirements; barely acceptable. —**adequacy** *n* —**adequately** *adv*.

adhere *vi* to stick, as by gluing or suction; to give allegiance or support (to); to follow.—**adherence** *n*.—**adherent** *n*.

adhesion *n* the action or condition of adhering; the attachment of normally separate tissues in the body.

adhesive *adj* sticky; causing adherence. * *n* a substance used to stick, such as glue, paste, etc.—**adhesiveness** *n*.

adjacent *adj* nearby; adjoining.

adjective *n* a word used to add a characteristic to a noun or pronoun.—**adjectival** *adj*.

adjoining *adj* beside, in contact with.

adjourn *vt* to suspend (a meeting) temporarily. * *vi* (*inf*) to retire (to another room, etc).—**adjournment** *n*.

adjust *vt* to arrange in a more proper or satisfactory manner; to regulate or modify by minor changes; to decide the amount to be paid in settling (an insurance claim). * *vi* to adapt oneself.—**adjustable** *adj*.—**adjuster** *n*.—**adjustment** *n*.

adjutant *n* a military staff officer who assists the commanding officer.—**adjutancy** *n*.

ad-lib *vti* (*pt* **ad-libbed**) (*speech, etc*) to improvise. * *n* an ad-libbed remark. * *adv* spontaneous, freely.

administer *vt* to manage, direct; to give out as a punishment; to dispense (medicine, punishment, etc); to tender (an oath, etc).

administration *n* management; the people who administer an organization; the government; (*with cap*) the executive officials of a government, their policies, and term of office.—**administrative** *adj*.

administrator *n* a person who manages or supervises; (*law*) one appointed to settle an estate.

admiral *n* the commanding officer of a fleet; a naval officer of the highest rank.

admiration *n* a feeling of pleasurable and often surprised respect; an admired person or thing.

admire *vt* to regard with honour and approval; to express admiration for.—**admirer** *n*.—**admiring** *adj*. —**admiringly** *adv*.

admission *n* an entrance fee; a conceding, confessing, etc; a thing conceded, confessed, etc.

admit *vb* (*pt* **admitted**)*vt* to allow to enter or join; to concede or acknowledge as true. * *vi* to give access; (*with* **of**) to allow or permit.

admittance *n* the act of admitting; the right to enter.

admittedly *adv* acknowledged as fact, willingly conceded.

admonish *vt* to remind or advise earnestly; to reprove gently.—**admonition** *n*.—**admonitory** *adj*.

ado *n* fuss, excitement, esp over trivia.

adolescent *adj* between childhood and maturity; (*inf*) immature. * *n* an adolescent person.—**adolescence** *n.*

adopt *vt* to take legally into one's family and raise as one's child; to take as one's own.—**adoption** *n.*

adore *vt* to worship; to love deeply.—**adoringly** *adv.*

adorn *vt* to decorate; to make more pleasant or attractive.—**adornment** *n.*

adrenaline *n* a hormone that stimulates the heart rate, blood pressure, etc in response to stress and that is secreted by the adrenal glands or manufactured synthetically.

adrift *adj, adv* afloat without mooring, drifting; loose.

adroit *adj* skilful and clever.—**adroitly** *adv.*—**adroitness** *n.*

adult *adj* fully grown; mature; suitable only for adults, as in pornography, etc. * *n* a mature person, etc.

adulterate *vt* to make impure or inferior, etc by adding an improper substance.—**adulteration** *n.*

adultery *n* sexual intercourse between a married person and someone other than their legal partner.—**adulterous** *adj.*

advance *vt* to bring or move forward; to promote; to raise the rate of; (*money*) to lend. * *vi* to go forward; to make progress; to rise in rank, price, etc. * *n* progress; improvement; a rise in value; payment beforehand; (*pl*) friendly approaches. * *adj* in front; beforehand.

advanced *adj* in front; old; superior in development.

advancement *n* promotion to higher rank; progress in development.

advantage *n* superiority of position or condition; a gain or benefit; (*tennis*) the first point won after deuce. * *vt* to produce a benefit or favour to.

advantageous *adj* producing advantage, beneficial.—**advantageously** *adv.*

advent *n* an arrival or coming.

adventure *n* a strange or exciting undertaking; an unusual, stirring, often romantic, experience.—**adventurous** *adj.*—**adventurously** *adv.*

adventurer *n* a person who seeks adventure; someone who seeks money or power by unscrupulous means.—**adventuress** *nf.*

adverb *n* a word that modifies a verb, adjective, another adverb, phrase, clause or sentence and indicates how, why, where, etc.—**adverbial** *adj.*

adversary *n* an enemy or opponent.

adverse *adj* hostile; contrary or opposite; unfavourable.—**adversely** *adv.*

adversity *n* trouble, misery, misfortune.

advert *n* (*inf*) an advertisement.

advertise *vt* to call public attention to by buying space or time in the media, etc. * *vi* to call public attention to things for sale; to ask (for) by public notice.—**advertiser** *n.*

advertisement *n* advertising; a public notice, usu paid for by the provider of a good or service.

advertising *n* the promotion of goods or services by public notices; advertisements; the business of producing adverts.

advice *n* recommendation with regard to a course of action; formal notice or communication.

advisable *adj* prudent, expedient.—**advisability** *n.*

advise *vt* to give advice to; to caution; to recommend; to inform. * *vi* to give advice.—**adviser, advisor** *n.*

advisory *adj* having or exercising the power to advise; containing or giving advice.

advocate *n* a person who argues or defends the cause of another, esp in a court of law; a supporter. * *vt* to plead in favour of.

aegis *n* protection, sponsorship.

aerial *adj* belonging to or existing in the air; of aircraft or flying. * *n* a metal device for transmitting and receiving radio waves, an antenna.

aerie, aery *n* variant spellings of **eyrie**.

aeroplane, airplane (*US*) *n* a power-driven aircraft.

aerosol *n* a suspension of fine solid or liquid particles in gas, esp as held in a container under pressure, with a device for releasing it in a fine spray.

aesthetics, esthetics (*US*) *n* the philosophy of art and beauty.—**aesthetic** *adj.*—**aesthetically** *adv.*

affable *adj* friendly; approachable.—**affability** *n* —**affably** *adv.*

affair *n* a thing done or to be done; (*pl*) public or private business; (*inf*) an event; a temporary romantic or sexual relationship.

affect[1] *vt* to have an effect on; to produce a change in; to act in a way that alters or affects the feelings of.

affect[2] *vt* to pretend or feign (an emotion); to incline to or show a preference for.

affect[3] *n* an emotion, feeling or desire associated with a certain stimulus.

affectation *n* a striving after or an attempt to

assume what is not natural or real; pretence.
affected *adj* (*manner, etc*) assumed artificially.
affection *n* tender feeling; liking.
affectionate *adj* showing affection, loving.—**affectionately** *adv*.
affiliate *vt* to connect as a subordinate member or branch; to associate (oneself with). * *vi* to join. * *n* an affiliated person, club, etc.—**affiliation** *n*.
affinity *n* attraction, liking; a close relationship, esp by marriage; similarity, likeness; (*chem*) a tendency in certain substances to combine.
affirmation *n* affirming; an assertion; a solemn declaration made by those declining to swear an oath, eg on religious grounds.
affix *vt* to fasten; to add, esp in writing; to attach.
afflict *vt* to cause persistent pain or suffering to; to trouble greatly.
affliction *n* persistent pain, suffering; a cause of this.
affluent *adj* rich, well provided for.—**affluence** *n* —**affluently** *adv*.
afford *vt* to be in a position to do or bear without much inconvenience; to have enough time, money, or resources for; to supply, produce.
affront *vi* to insult or offend openly or deliberately. * *n* a deliberate insult.
afield *adv* far away from home; to or at a distance; astray.
afloat *adj* floating; at sea, on board a ship; debt-free; flooded.—*also adv*.
afraid *adj* full of fear or apprehension; regretful.
afresh *adv* anew, starting again.
aft *adv* at, near, or toward the stern of a ship or rear of an aircraft.
after *prep* behind in place or order; following in time, later than; in pursuit of; in imitation of; in view of, in spite of; according to; about, concerning; subsequently. * *adv* later; behind. * *conj* at a time later than. * *adj* later, subsequent; nearer the stern of a ship or aircraft.
aftereffect *n* an effect that occurs some time after its cause.
afterlife *n* life after death.
aftermath *n* the result, esp an unpleasant one.
afternoon *n* the time between noon and sunset or evening.—*also adj*.
aftershave *n* lotion for use after shaving.
afterthought *n* a thought or reflection occurring later.
afterwards *adv* at a later time.
again *adv* once more; besides; on the other hand.
against *prep* in opposition to; unfavourable to; in contrast to; in preparation for; in contact with; as a charge on.
age *n* the period of time during which someone or something has lived or existed; a stage of life; later years of life; a historical period; a division of geological time; (*inf: often pl*) a long time. * *vti* (*pr p* **ageing** *or* **aging,** *pt* **aged**) to grow or make old, ripe, mature, etc.
aged *adj* very old; of a specified age.
agency *n* action; power; means; a firm, etc, empowered to act for another; an administrative government division.
agenda *n* a list of items or matters of business that need attention.
agent *n* a person or thing that acts or has an influence; a substance or organism that is active; one empowered to act for another; a government representative; a spy.
aggravate *vt* to make worse; (*inf*) to annoy, irritate.—**aggravation** *n*.
aggregate *adj* formed of parts combined into a mass or whole; taking all units as a whole. * *n* a collection or sum of parts; sand, stones, etc, mixed with cement to form concrete. * *vt* to collect or form into a mass or whole; to amount to (a total).
aggression *n* an unprovoked attack; a hostile action or behaviour.
aggressive *adj* boldly hostile; quarrelsome; self-assertive, enterprising.—**aggressively** *adv*.—**aggressiveness** *n*.
aghast *adj* utterly horrified.
agile *adj* quick and nimble in movement; mentally acute.—**agility** *n*.
agitate *vt* to shake, move; to disturb or excite the emotions of. * *vi* to stir up public interest for a cause, etc.—**agitation** *n*.—**agitator** *n*.
ago *adv* in the past. * *adj* gone by; past.
agony *n* extreme mental or physical suffering.
agree *vb* (*pt* **agreed**) *vi* to be of similar opinion; to consent or assent (to); to come to an understanding about; to be consistent; to suit a person's digestion; (*gram*) to be consistent in gender, number, case, or person. * *vt* to concede, grant; to bring into harmony; to reach terms on.
agreeable *adj* likeable, pleasing; willing to agree.—**agreeably** *adv*.
agreement *n* harmony in thought or opinion, correspondence; an agreed settlement between two people, etc.

agriculture *n* the science or practice of producing crops and raising livestock; farming.—**agricultural** *adj*.—**agriculturally** *adv*.
aground *adj* on or onto the shore.—*also adv*.
ahead *adj* in or to the front; forward; onward; in advance; winning or profiting.—*also adv*.
aid *vti* to help, give assistance to. * *n* anything that helps; a specific means of assistance, eg money; a helper.
aide *n* an aide-de-camp; assistant.
AIDS, Aids *n* (*acronym for* acquired immune deficiency syndrome) a condition caused by a virus, in which the body loses immunity to infection.
ailment *n* a slight illness.
aim *vti* to point or direct towards a target so as to hit; to direct (one's efforts); to intend. * *n* the act of aiming; purpose, intention.
air *n* the mixture of invisible gases surrounding the earth; the earth's atmosphere; empty, open space; a light breeze; aircraft, aviation; outward appearance, demeanour; a pervading influence; (*mus*) a melody; (*pl*) an affected manner. * *vt* to expose to the air for drying; to expose to public notice; (*clothes*) to place in a warm place to finish drying.
airborne *adj* carried by or through the air; aloft or flying.
air conditioning *n* regulation of air humidity and temperature in buildings, etc.
air-cooled *adj* cooled by having air passed over, into, or through.
aircraft *n* (*pl* **aircraft**) any machine for travelling through air.
aircraft carrier *n* a warship with a large flat deck, for carrying aircraft.
airgun *n* a gun that fires pellets by compressed air.
air hostess *n* a stewardess on a passenger aircraft.
air letter *n* a sheet of light writing paper that is folded and sealed for sending by airmail.
airline *n* a system or company for transportation by aircraft.
airlock *n* a blockage in a pipe caused by an air bubble; an airtight compartment giving access to a pressurized chamber.
airmail *n* mail transported by aircraft.
airplane *n* the US spelling of **aeroplane**.
airport *n* a place where aircraft can land and take off, with facilities for repair, etc.
air raid *n* an attack by military aircraft on a surface target.
airship *n* a self-propelled steerable aircraft that is lighter than air.
airstrip *n* an area of land cleared for aircraft to land on; a runway.
airtight *adj* too tight for air or gas to enter or escape; (*alibi, etc*) invulnerable.
airy *adj* (**airier, airiest**) open to the air; breezy; light as air; graceful; light-hearted; flippant.—**airily** *adv*.
aisle *n* a passageway, as between rows of seats; a side part of a church.
ajar *adv* partly open, as a door.
alarm *n* a signal warning of danger; an automatic device to arouse from sleep or to attract attention; fear arising from apprehension of danger. * *vt* to give warning of danger; to fill with apprehension or fear.
album *n* a book with blank pages for the insertion of photographs, autographs, etc; a long-playing record, cassette, or CD.
alchemy *n* chemistry as practised during medieval times, with the aim of transmuting base metals into gold.—**alchemist** *n*.
alcohol *n* a liquid, generated by distillation and fermentation, that forms the intoxicating agent in wine, beer and spirits; a liquid containing alcohol; a chemical compound of this nature.
alcoholic *adj* of or containing alcohol; caused by alcohol. * *n* a person suffering from alcoholism.
alcoholism *n* a disease caused by excessive consumption of alcohol.
alcove *n* a recess off a larger room.
ale *n* beer.
alert *adj* watchful; active, brisk. * *n* a danger signal. * *vt* to warn of impending danger, put in a state of readiness.—**alertly** *adv*.—**alertness** *n*.
algebra *n* the branch of mathematics dealing with the properties and relations of numbers; the generalization and extension of arithmetic.—**algebraic** *adj*.
alias *adv* otherwise called. * *n* (*pl* **aliases**) an assumed name.
alibi *n* (*pl* **alibis**) (*law*) the plea that a person charged with a crime was elsewhere when it was committed; (*inf*) any excuse.
alien *adj* foreign; strange. * *n* a person from another country, place, etc; a person of foreign birth who has not been naturalized; a being from outer space.
alienate *vt* to render hostile or unfriendly; to make less affectionate or interested.—**alienation** *n*.
alight[1] *vi* to come down, as from a bus; to descend after a flight.
alight[2] *adj* on fire; lively.

align *vt* to place in a straight line, to bring into agreement, etc. * *vi* to line up.—**alignment** *n*.

alike *adj* like one another. * *adv* equally; similarly.

alimony *n* an allowance for support made by one spouse to the other; maintenance.

alive *adj* having life; active, alert; in existence, operation, etc.

alkali *n* (*pl* **alkalis**) (*chem*) any salt or mixture that neutralizes acids.—**alkaline** *adj*.

all *adj* the whole amount or number of; every one of. * *adv* wholly; supremely, completely; entirely. * *n* the whole number, quantity; everyone; everything.

allay *vt* to lighten, alleviate; to pacify or make calm.

allege *vt* to assert or declare, esp without proof; to offer as an excuse.—**allegation** *n*.

allegedly *adv* asserted without proof.

allegiance *n* the obligation of being loyal to one's country, etc; devotion, as to a cause.

allegory *n* a fable, story, poem, etc, in which events depicted are used to convey a deeper, usu moral or spiritual, meaning.—**allegorical** *adj*.

allergy *n* an abnormal reaction of the body to substances (certain foods, pollen, etc) normally harmless; antipathy.—**allergic** *adj*.

alleviate *vt* to lessen or relieve (pain, worry, etc).—**alleviation** *n*.

alley *n* a narrow street between or behind buildings; a bowling lane.

alliance *n* a union by marriage or treaty for a common purpose; an agreement for this; the countries, groups, etc in such an association.

alligator *n* a large reptile similar to the crocodile but having a short, blunt snout.

all-in *adj* (*inf*) exhausted.

allocate *vt* to distribute or apportion in shares; to set apart for a specific purpose.—**allocation** *n*.

allot *vt* (*pt* **allotted**) to distribute, allocate.

allotment *n* allotting; a share allotted; a small area of land rented for cultivation.

all-out *adj* using maximum effort.

allow *vt* to permit; to acknowledge, admit as true; (*money*) to give, grant as an allowance at regular intervals; to estimate as an addition or deduction. * *vi* to admit the possibility (of).

allowance *n* an amount or sum allowed; a discount; a portion of income not subject to income tax; permission; admission, concession.

alloy *n* a solid substance comprising a mixture of two or more metals; something that degrades the substance to which it is added. * *vt* to make into an alloy; to degrade or spoil by mixing with an inferior substance.

all-round *adj* efficient in all respects, esp sport.

all-time *adj* unsurpassed until now.

allude *vi* to refer indirectly to.

allure *vt* to entice, charm. * *n* fascination; charm.

alluring *adj* attractive.

allusion *n* alluding; an implied or indirect reference.—**allusive** *adj*.

ally *vti* to join or unite for a specific purpose; to relate by similarity of structure, etc. * *n* a country or person joined with another for a common purpose.

almighty *adj* all-powerful. * *n* (*with cap*) God, the all-powerful.

almond *n* the edible kernel of the fruit of a tree of the rose family; the tree bearing this fruit. * *adj* (*eyes, etc*) oval and pointed.

almost *adv* all but, very nearly but not quite all.

alms *npl* money, food, etc, given to the poor.

alone *adj* isolated; without anyone or anything else; unassisted; unique. * *adv* exclusively.

along *adv* onward, forward; over the length of; in company and together with; in addition. * *prep* in the direction of the length of; in accordance with.

alongside *prep* close beside. * *adv* at the side.

aloof *adv* at a distance; apart. * *adj* cool and reserved.—**aloofness** *n*.

aloud *adv* with a normal voice; loudly.

alphabet *n* the characters used in a language arranged in conventional order.—**alphabetical** *adj*.—**alphabetically** *adv*.

alpine *adj* of the Alps; of high mountains. * *n* a mountain plant, esp a small herb.

already *adv* by or before the time specified; before the time expected.

also *adv* in addition, besides.

altar *n* a table, etc for sacred purposes in a place of worship.

alter *vti* to make or become different in a small way; to change.—**alteration** *n*.

alternate[1] *vt* to do or use by turns. * *vi* to act, happen, etc, by turns; to take turns regularly.

alternate[2] *adj* occurring or following in turns.—**alternately** *adv*.

alternating current *n* an electric current that reverses its direction at regular intervals.

alternative *adj* presenting a choice between two things. * *n* either of two possibilities.—**alternatively** *adv*.

alternator *n* an electric generator that pro-

duces alternating current.
although *conj* though; in spite of that.
altitude *n* height, esp above sea level.
alto *n* (*pl* **altos**) the range of the highest male voice; a singer with this range.
altogether *adv* in all; on the whole; completely.
aluminium, aluminum (*US*) *n* a silvery-white malleable metallic element notable for its lightness.
always *adv* at all times; in all cases; repeatedly; forever.
am *see* **be**.
a.m. *abbr = ante meridiem,* before noon.
amalgamate *vt* to combine, unite.—**amalgamation** *n*.
amass *vt* to bring together in a large quantity; to accumulate.
amateur *n* one who engages in a particular activity as a hobby, and not as a profession. * *adj* of or done by amateurs.
amateurish *adj* lacking expertise.—**amateurishly** *adv*.
amaze *vt* to fill with wonder, astonish.—**amazement** *n*.—**amazing** *adj*.
ambassador *n* the highest-ranking diplomatic representative from one country to another; an authorized messenger.—**ambassadorial** *adj*.
amber *n* a hard yellowish fossil resin, used for jewellery and ornaments, etc; the colour of amber; a yellow traffic light used to signal "caution."
ambiguous *adj* capable of two or more interpretations; indistinct, vague.—**ambiguity** *n*.—**ambiguously** *adv*.
ambition *n* desire for power, wealth and success; an object of ambition.
ambitious *adj* having or governed by ambition; resulting from or showing ambition; requiring considerable effort or ability.—**ambitiously** *adv*.
amble *vi* to walk in a leisurely way.
ambulance *n* a special vehicle for transporting the sick or injured.
ambush *n* the concealment of soldiers, etc to make a surprise attack; the bushes or other cover in which they are hidden. * *vti* to lie in wait; to attack from an ambush.
amenable *adj* easily influenced or led, tractable; answerable to legal authority.—**amenably** *adv*.
amend *vt* to remove errors, esp in a text; to modify, improve; to alter in minor details.—**amendment**.
amends *npl* (*used as sing*) compensation or recompense for some loss, harm, etc.
amenity *n* pleasantness, as regards situation or convenience.
amethyst *n* a gemstone consisting of bluish-violet quartz.
amiable *adj* friendly in manner, congenial.—**amiably** *adv*.
amicable *adj* friendly; peaceable.—**amicably** *adv*.
amid, amidst *prep* in or to the middle of; during.
amiss *adj* wrong, improper. * *adv* in an incorrect manner.
ammunition *n* bullets, shells, rockets, etc; any means of attack or defence; facts and reasoning used to prove a point in an argument.
amnesia *n* a partial or total loss of memory.—**amnesiac** *n*.
amnesty *n* a general pardon, esp of political prisoners.
among, amongst *prep* in the number of, surrounded by; in the group or class of; within a group, between; by the joint efforts of.
amoral *adj* neither moral nor immoral; without moral sense.
amorous *adj* displaying or feeling love or desire.—**amorously** *adv*.—**amorousness** *n*.
amorphous *adj* lacking a specific shape, shapeless; unrecognizable, indefinable.
amount *vi* to be equivalent (to) in total, quantity or significance. * *n* the total sum; the whole value or effect; a quantity.
ampere *n* the standard SI unit by which electric current is measured.
amphibious *adj* living on both land and water; (*mil*) involving both sea and land forces.
amphitheatre *n* an oval or circular building with rising rows of seats around an open arena.
ample *adj* large in size, scope, etc; plentiful.—**amply** *adv*.
amplifier *n* a device that increases electric voltage, current, or power, or the loudness of sound.
amplify *vt* to expand more fully, add details to; (*electrical signals, etc*) to strengthen.—**amplification** *n*.
amputate *vt* to cut off, esp by surgery.—**amputation** *n*.
amuse *vt* to entertain or divert in a pleasant manner; to cause to laugh or smile.—**amusement** *n*.
an *adj* the indefinite article ("a"), used before words beginning with the sound of a vowel

except "u" as pronounced "y."

anaemia, anemia (*US*) *n* a condition in which the blood is low in red cells or in haemoglobin, resulting in paleness, weakness, etc.

anaemic, anemic (*US*) *adj* suffering from anaemia; weak; pale; listless.

anaesthetic, anesthetic (*US*) *n* a drug, gas, etc used to produce anaesthesia, as before surgery. * *adj* of or producing anaesthesia.

anaesthetist, anesthetist (*US*) *n* a person trained to give anaesthetics.

analogy *n* a similarity or correspondence in certain respects between two things.

analyse, analyze (*US*) *vt* to separate (something) into its constituent parts to investigate its structure and function, etc; to examine in detail; to psychoanalyse.

analysis *n* (*pl* **analyses**) the process of analysing; a statement of the results of this; psychoanalysis.

analyst *n* a person who analyses; a psychoanalyst.

analytic, analytical *adj* pertaining to analysis.—**analytically** *adv*.

anarchist *n* a person who believes that all government is unnecessary and should be abolished.—**anarchism** *n*.

anarchy *n* the absence of government; political confusion; disorder, lawlessness.—**anarchic** *adj*.

anathema *n* anything greatly detested; an ecclesiastical denunciation with excommunication.

anatomy *n* the science of the physical structure of plants and animals; the structure of an organism.—**anatomical** *adj*.—**anatomically** *adv*.

ancestor *n* one from whom a person is descended, a forefather; an early animal or plant from which existing types are descended; something regarded as a forerunner.—**ancestral** *adj*.—**ancestress** *nf*.

ancestry *n* ancestors collectively; lineage.

anchor *n* a heavy metal implement that lodges at the bottom of the sea or a river to hold a ship in position; something that gives support or stability. * *vt* to fix by an anchor; to secure firmly.

anchorage *n* a safe anchoring place for ships; the charge for anchoring.

anchovy *n* a small Mediterranean fish resembling a herring with a very salty taste.

ancient *adj* very old; dating from the distant past; of the period and civilizations predating the fall of the Roman Empire; old-fashioned. * *n* a person who lived in the ancient period; (*pl*) the members of the classical civilizations of antiquity.

and *conj* in addition to; together with; plus; increasingly; as a consequence, afterwards; expressing contrast.

anecdote *n* a short entertaining account about an amusing or interesting event or person.

anew *adv* afresh; again, once more; in a new way or form.

angel *n* a messenger of God; an image of a human figure with wings and a halo; a very beautiful or kind person.—**angelic** *adj*.

anger *n* strong displeasure, often because of opposition, a hurt, etc. * *vti* to make or become angry.

angina *n* sharp stabbing pains in the chest, usu caused by angina pectoris.

angle[1] *n* a corner; the point from which two lines or planes extend or diverge; a specific viewpoint; an individual method or approach (eg to a problem). * *vt* to bend at an angle; to move or place at an angle; to present, news, etc from a particular point of view.

angle[2] *vi* to fish with a hook and line; to use hints or artifice to get something.—**angler** *n*.

Anglican *adj* belonging to or of the Church of England or churches in communion with it. * *n* a member of the Anglican Church.—**Anglicanism** *n*.

angry *adj* (**angrier, angriest**) full of anger; inflamed.—**angrily** *adv*.

anguish *n* agonizing physical or mental distress.

angular *adj* having one or more angles; forming an angle; measured by an angle; stiff and clumsy in manner, thin and bony.—**angularity** *n*.

animal *n* any living organism except a plant or bacterium, typically able to move about; a lower animal as distinguished from man, esp mammals; a brutish person. * *adj* of or like an animal; bestial; sensual.

animate *vt* to give life to; to liven up; to inspire, encourage. * *adj* alive; lively.

animosity *n* strong dislike; hostility.

aniseed *n* the seed of the anise plant, used as a flavouring.

ankle *n* the joint between the foot and leg, the part of the leg between the foot and calf.

annex *vt* to attach, esp to something larger; to incorporate into a state the territory of (another state).—**annexation** *n*.

annihilate *vt* to destroy completely; (*inf*) to defeat convincingly, as in an argument.—**annihilation** *n*.

anniversary *n* the yearly return of the date of some event; a celebration of this.—*also adj.*
annotate *vti* to provide with explanatory notes.—**annotation** *n.*
announce *vt* to bring to public attention; to give news of the arrival of; to be an announcer for. * *vi* to serve as an announcer.—**announcement** *n.*
annoy *vt* to vex, tease, irritate, as by a repeated action.—**annoyance** *n.*
annual *adj* of or measured by a year; yearly; coming every year; living only one year or season. * *n* a plant that lives only one year; a periodical published once a year.—**annually** *adv.*
annuity *n* an investment yielding fixed payments, esp yearly; such a payment.
annul *vt* (*pt* **annulled**) to do away with; to deprive of legal force, nullify.—**annulment** *n.*
anoint *vt* to rub with oil; to apply oil in a sacred ritual as a sign of consecration.—**anointment** *n.*
anomaly *n* abnormality; anything inconsistent or odd.—**anomalous** *adj.*
anonymous *adj* having or providing no name; written or provided by an unnamed person; lacking individuality.—**anonymity** *n.*—**anonymously** *adv.*
anorak *n* a waterproof jacket with a hood.
another *adj* a different or distinct (thing or person); an additional one of the same kind; some other.—*also pron.*
answer *n* a spoken or written reply or response; the solution to a problem; a reaction, response. * *vt* to speak or write in reply; to satisfy or correspond to (eg a specific need); to justify, offer a refutation of. * *vi* to reply; to act in response (to); to be responsible (for); to conform (to).
answerable *adj* capable of being refuted; (*with* **for** *or* **to**) responsible, accountable.
ant *n* any of a family of small, generally wingless insects of many species, all of which form and live in highly organized groups.
antagonism *n* antipathy, hostility; an opposing force, principle, etc.
antagonist *n* an adversary; an opponent.—**antagonistic** *adj.*—**antagonistically** *adv.*
antagonize *vt* to arouse opposition.
Antarctic *adj* of the South Pole or its surroundings. * *n* the Antarctic regions; the Antarctic Ocean.
antelope *n* any of the family of fast-running and graceful deer-like animals of Africa and Asia.
antenatal *adj* occurring or present before birth.
antenna *n* (*pl* **antennae**) either of a pair of feelers on the head of an insect, etc; (*pl* **antennas**) an aerial.
anthem *n* a religious choral song; a song of praise or devotion, as to a nation.
anthill *n* a mound thrown up by ants or termites in digging their nests.
anthology *n* a collection of poetry or prose.—**anthologist** *n.*
anthropology *n* the scientific study of human beings, their origins, distribution, physical attributes and culture.—**anthropological** *adj.*—**anthropologist** *n.*
anti- *prefix* opposed to; against.
antibiotic *n* any of various chemical, fungal or synthetic substances used against bacterial or fungal infections.
anticipate *vt* to give prior thought and attention to; to use, spend, act on in advance; to foresee and take action to thwart another; to expect. * *vi* to speak, act, before the appropriate time.—**anticipation** *n.*
anticlimax *n* a sudden drop from the important to the trivial; an ending to a story or series of events that disappoints one's expectations.
anticlockwise *adj* moving in a direction contrary to the hands of a clock as viewed from the front.—*also adv.*
anticyclone *n* a body of air rotating about an area of high atmospheric pressure.
antidote *n* a remedy that counteracts a poison; something that counteracts harmful effects.
antifreeze *n* a substance used, as in car radiator, to prevent freezing up.
antipathy *n* a fixed dislike; aversion; an object of this.
antiquated *adj* old-fashioned; obsolete.
antique *adj* from the distant past; old-fashioned. * *n* a relic of the distant past; a piece of furniture, pottery, etc dating from an earlier historical period and sought after by collectors.
antiquity *n* the far distant past, esp before the Middle Ages; (*pl*) relics dating from the far distant past.
antiseptic *n* a substance that destroys or prevents the growth of disease-producing microorganisms. * *adj* destroying harmful organisms; very clean.
antisocial *adj* avoiding the company of other people, unsocial; contrary to the interests of society in general.
antler *n* the branched horn of a deer or related animal.—**antlered** *adj.*

anus *n* the excretory orifice of the alimentary canal.
anvil *n* the heavy iron block on which metal objects are shaped with a hammer.
anxiety *n* the condition of being anxious; eagerness, concern; a cause of worry.
anxious *adj* worried; uneasy; eagerly wishing; causing anxiety.—**anxiously** *adv*.
any *adj* one out of many, some; every.
anybody *pron* any person; an important person.
anyhow *adv* in any way whatever; in any case.
anymore *adv* now; nowadays.
anyone *pron* any person; anybody.
anything *pron* any object, event, fact, etc. * *n* a thing, no matter what kind.
anyway *adv* in any manner; at any rate; haphazardly.
anywhere *adv* in, at, or to any place.
apart *adv* at a distance, separately, aside; into two or more pieces.
apartheid *n* a policy of racial segregation implemented in South Africa.
apartment *n* a room or rooms in a building; a flat.
apathy *n* lack of feeling; lack of concern, indifference.—**apathetic** *adj*.—**apathetically** *adv*.
ape *n* a chimpanzee, gorilla, orang-utan, or gibbon; any monkey; a mimic. * *vt* to imitate.
apéritif *n* an alcoholic drink taken before a meal.
aperture *n* an opening; a hole.
apex *n* the highest point, the tip; the culminating point; the vertex of a triangle.
aphrodisiac *adj* arousing sexually. * *n* a food, drug, etc that excites sexual desire.
apiece *adv* to, by, or for each one.
aplomb *n* poise; self-possession.
apologetic *adj* expressing an apology; contrite; presented in defence.—**apologetically** *adv*.
apologize *vi* to make an apology.
apology *n* an expression of regret for wrongdoing; a defence or justification of one's beliefs, etc; (*with* **for**) a poor substitute.
apoplexy *n* a sudden loss of consciousness and subsequent partial paralysis, usu caused by a broken or blocked artery in the brain.
apostle *n* the first or principal supporter of a new belief or cause.
apostrophe *n* a mark (') showing the omission of letters or figures, also a sign of the possessive case or the plural of letters and figures.
appal, appall (*US*) *vt* (*pt* **appalled**) to fill with terror or dismay.
appalling *adj* shocking, horrifying.—**appallingly** *adv*.
apparatus *n* the equipment used for a specific task; any complex machine, device, or system.
apparent *adj* easily seen, evident; seeming, but not real.—**apparently** *adv*.
apparition *n* an appearance or manifestation, esp something unexpected or unusual; a ghost.
appeal *vi* to take a case to a higher court; to make an earnest request; to refer to a witness or superior authority for vindication, confirmation, etc; to arouse pleasure or sympathy. * *n* the referral of a lawsuit to a higher court for rehearing; an earnest call for help; attraction, the power of arousing sympathy; a request for public donations to a charitable cause.
appear *vi* to become or be visible; to arrive, come in person; to be published; to present oneself formally (before a court, etc); to seem, give an impression of being.
appearance *n* the act or occasion of appearing; that which appears; external aspect of a thing or person; outward show, semblance.
appease *vt* to pacify; to allay; to conciliate by making concessions.—**appeasement** *n*.
appendage *n* something appended; an external organ or part, as a tail.
appendicitis *n* inflammation of the appendix of the intestine.
appendix *n* (*pl* **appendixes, appendices**) a section of supplementary information at the back of a book, etc; a small tube of tissue that forms an outgrowth of the intestine.
appetite *n* sensation of bodily desire, esp for food; (*with* **for**) a strong desire or liking, a craving.
appetizing *adj* stimulating the appetite.—**appetizingly** *adv*.
applaud *vt* to show approval, esp by clapping the hands.
applause *n* approval expressed by clapping; acclamation.
apple *n* a round, firm, fleshy, edible fruit.
appliance *n* a device or machine, esp for household use.
applicable *adj* that may be applied; appropriate, relevant (to).—**applicability** *n*.
applicant *n* a person who applies, esp for a job.
application *n* the act of applying; the use to which something is put; a petition, request; concentration, diligent effort; relevance or practical value.
apply *vt* to bring to bear; to put to practical use;

to spread, lay on; to devote (oneself) with close attention. * *vi* to make a formal, esp written, request; to be relevant.

appoint *vt* to fix or decide officially; to select for a job; to prescribe.

appraise *vt* to estimate the value or quality of.—**appraisal** *n*.

appreciable *adj* capable of being perceived or measured; fairly large.—**appreciably** *adv*.

appreciate *vt* to value highly; to recognize gratefully; to understand, be aware of; to increase the value of. * *vi* to rise in value.

appreciation *n* gratitude, approval; sensitivity to aesthetic values; an assessment or critical evaluation; a favourable review; an increase in value.—**appreciative** *adj*.

apprehend *vt* to arrest, capture; to understand, to perceive.

apprehension *n* anxiety; the act of arresting; understanding; an idea.

apprehensive *adj* uneasy; anxious.—**apprehensively** *adv*.

apprentice *n* one being taught a trade or craft; a novice.—**apprenticeship** *n*.

approach *vi* to draw nearer. * *vt* to make a proposal to; to set about dealing with; to come near to. * *n* the act of approaching; a means of entering or leaving; a move to establish relations; the final descent of an aircraft.—**approachable** *adj*.

appropriate *adj* fitting, suitable. * *vt* to take for one's own use, esp illegally; (*money, etc*) to set aside for a specific purpose.—**appropriately** *adv*.—**appropriateness** *n*.

approval *n* approving; favourable opinion; official permission.

approve *vt* to express a good opinion of; to authorize. * *vi* (*with* **of**) to consider to be favourable or satisfactory.

approximate *adj* almost exact or correct. * *vt* to come near to; to be almost the same as. * *vi* to come close.—**approximately** *adv*.

approximation *n* a close estimate; a near likeness.

apricot *n* a small, oval orange-pink fruit resembling the plum and peach.

apron *n* a garment worn to protect clothing; anything resembling the shape of an apron used for protection; the paved surface on an airfield where aircraft are parked, etc.

apt *adj* ready or likely (to); suitable, relevant; able to learn easily.—**aptness** *n*.

aptitude *n* suitability; natural talent, esp for learning.

aqualung *n* portable diving gear comprising air cylinders connected to a face mask.

aquarium *n* (*pl* **aquariums**) a tank, pond, etc for keeping aquatic animals or plants; a building where collections of aquatic animals are exhibited.

Aquarius *n* (*astrol*) the eleventh sign of the zodiac, the Water-carrier, operative 20 January-18 February.

aquatic *adj* of or taking place in water; living or growing in water.

aqueduct *n* a large pipe or conduit for carrying water; an elevated structure supporting this.

arbiter *n* an arbitrator.

arable *adj* (*land*) suitable for ploughing or planting crops.—*also n*.

arbitrary *adj* not bound by rules; despotic, absolute; capricious, unreasonable.—**arbitrarily** *adv*.—**arbitrariness** *n*.

arbitrate *vi* to act as an arbitrator. * *vt* to submit to or act as an arbitrator.

arbitration *n* the settlement of disputes by arbitrating.

arbitrator *n* a person chosen to settle a dispute between contending parties.

arc *n* a portion of the circumference of a circle or other curve; a luminous discharge of electricity across a gap between two electrodes or terminals. * *vi* (*pt* **arced** *or* **arcked**) to form an electric arc.

arcade *n* an arched passageway; a covered walk or area lined with shops.

arch[1] *n* a curved structure spanning an opening; the curved underside of the foot. * *vti* to span or cover with an arch; to curve, bend into an arch.

arch[2] *adj* (*criminal, etc*) principal, expert; clever, sly; mischievous.

archaeology, archeology *n* the study of past human societies through their extant remains.—**archaeological, archeological** *adj*.—**archaeologist, archeologist** *n*.

archaic *adj* belonging to ancient times; (*language*) no longer in use.

archbishop *n* a bishop of the highest rank.

archer *n* a person who shoots with a bow and arrow.

archery *n* the art or sport of shooting arrows from a bow.

archetype *n* the original pattern or model; a prototype.—**archetypal** *adj*.

archipelago *n* (*pl* **archipelagos**) a sea filled with small islands; a group of small islands.

architect *n* a person who designs buildings and supervises their erection; someone who plans something.

architecture *n* the art, profession, or science of designing and constructing buildings; the style of a building or buildings.—**architectural** *adj*.—**architecturally** *adv*.

archives *npl* the location in which public records are kept; the public records themselves.

archway *n* an arched or vaulted passage, esp leading into a castle.

arctic *adj* (*often with cap*) of, near, or relating to the North Pole or its surroundings; (*inf*) very cold, icy.

ardent *adj* passionate; zealous.—**ardently** *adv*.

arduous *adj* difficult, laborious; steep, difficult to climb.—**arduously** *adv*.

are *see* **be**.

area *n* an expanse of land; a total outside surface, measured in square units; a part of a house, district, etc; scope or extent.

arena *n* an area within a sports stadium, etc where events take place; a place or sphere of contest or activity.

aren't = are not.

arguable *adj* able to be asserted; plausible.—**arguably** *adv*.

argue *vt* to try to prove by reasoning; to debate, dispute; to persuade (into, out of). * *vi* to offer reasons for or against something; to disagree, exchange angry words.

argument *n* a disagreement; a debate, discussion; a reason offered in debate; an abstract, summary.

arid *adj* very dry, parched; uninteresting; dull.—**aridity** *n*.—**aridly** *adv*.—**aridness** *n*.

Aries *n* (*astrol*) the first sign of the zodiac, the Ram, operative 21 March-21 April.

aright *adv* correctly.

arise *vi* (*pt* **arose**, *pp* **arisen**) to get up, as from bed; to rise, ascend; to come into being, to result (from).

aristocracy *n* (a country with) a government dominated by a privileged minority class; the privileged class in a society, the nobility; those people considered the best in their sphere.

aristocrat *n* a member of the aristocracy; a supporter of aristocratic government; a person with the manners or taste of a privileged class.

aristocratic *adj* relating to or characteristic of the aristocracy; elegant, stylish in dress and manners.—**aristocratically** *adv*.

arithmetic *n* (*math*) computation (addition, subtraction, etc) using real numbers; calculation.—**arithmetic, arithmetical** *adj*.—**arithmetically** *adv*.

ark *n* (*Bible*) the boat in which Noah and his family and two of every kind of creature survived the flood; an enclosure in a synagogue for the scrolls of the Torah.

arm[1] *n* the upper limb from the shoulder to the wrist; something shaped like an arm, as a support on a chair; a sleeve; power, authority; an administrative division of a large organization.

arm[2] *n* (*usu pl*) a weapon; a branch of the military service; (*pl*) heraldic bearings. * *vt* to provide with weapons, etc; to provide with something that protects or strengthens, etc; to set a fuse ready to explode. * *vi* to prepare for war or any struggle.

armchair *n* a chair with side rests for the arms. * *adj* lacking practical experience.

armful *n* as much as the arms can hold.

armistice *n* a truce, preliminary to a peace treaty.

armour, armor (*US*) *n* any defensive or protective covering.

armpit *n* the hollow underneath the arm at the shoulder

arms *see* **arm**[2].

army *n* a large body of soldiers for waging war, esp on land; any large number of persons, animals, etc.

aroma *n* a pleasant smell; a fragrance.—**aromatic** *adj*.

arose *see* **arise**.

around *prep* on all sides of; on the border of; in various places in or on; approximately, about. * *adv* in a circle; in every direction; in circumference; to the opposite direction.

arouse *vt* to wake from sleep; to stir, as to action; to evoke.

arrange *vt* to put in a sequence or row; to settle, make preparations for; (*mus*) to prepare a composition for different instruments other than those intended.* *vi* to come to an agreement; to make plans.—**arrangement** *n*.—**arranger** *n*.

array *n* an orderly grouping, esp of troops; an impressive display; fine clothes; (*comput*) an ordered data structure that allows information to be easily indexed. * *vt* to set in order, to arrange; to dress, decorate.

arrears *npl* overdue debts; work, etc still to be completed.

arrest *vt* to stop; to capture, apprehend esp by legal authority; to catch and hold the attention of. * *n* a stoppage; seizure by legal authority.

arrival *n* arriving; a person or thing that has arrived.

arrive *vi* to reach any destination; to come; to achieve success, celebrity.

arrogance *n* an exaggerated assumption of importance.

arrogant *adj* overbearing; aggressively self-important.—**arrogantly** *adv*.

arrow *n* a straight, pointed weapon, made to be shot from a bow; a sign used to indicate direction.

arsenal *n* a workshop or store for weapons and ammunition.

arsenic *n* a soft grey metallic element, highly poisonous.

arson *n* the crime of using fire to destroy property deliberately.—**arsonist** *n*.

art *n* human creativity; skill acquired by study and experience; any craft and its principles; the making of things that have form and beauty; any branch of this, as painting, sculpture, etc; drawings, paintings, statues, etc; (*pl*) the creative and nonscientific branches of knowledge, esp as studied academically.

artefact, artifact *n* a product of human craftsmanship, esp a simple tool or ornament.

artery *n* a tubular vessel that conveys blood from the heart; any main channel of transport or communication.—**arterial** *adj*.

artful *adj* skilful at attaining one's ends; clever, crafty.—**artfully** *adv*.—**artfulness** *n*.

arthritis *n* painful inflammation of a joint.—**arthritic** *adj*.

artichoke *n* a thistle-like plant with a scaly flower head, parts of which are eaten as a vegetable.

article *n* a separate item or clause in a written document; an individual item on a particular subject in a newspaper, magazine, etc; a particular or separate item; (*gram*) a word placed before a noun to identify it as definite or indefinite.

articulate *adj* capable of distinct, intelligible speech, or expressing one's thoughts clearly; jointed. * *vti* to speak or express clearly; to unite or become united (as) by a joint.

artificial *adj* lacking natural qualities; man-made.—**artificiality** *n*.—**artificially** *adv*.

artillery *n* large, heavy guns; the branch of the army that uses these.

artisan *n* a skilled workman.

artist *n* one who practises fine art, esp painting; one who does anything very well.—**artistic** *adj*.

artistry *n* artistic quality, ability, work, etc.

artless *adj* simple, natural; without art or skill.—**artlessly** *adv*.—**artlessness** *n*.

as *adv* equally; for instance; when related in a certain way. * *conj* in the same way that; while; because. * *prep* in the role or function of.

asbestos *n* a fine fibrous mineral used for making incombustible and chemical-resistant materials.

ascend *vti* to go up; to succeed to (a throne).

ascendancy, **ascendency** *n* dominating influence.

ascent *n* ascending; an upward slope, means of ascending.

ascertain *vt* to acquire definite knowledge of.—**ascertainable** *adj*.

ascetic *adj* self-denying, austere. * *n* a person who practises rigorous self-denial as a religious discipline; any severely abstemious person.—**ascetically** *adv*.—**asceticism** *n*.

ascribe *vt* to attribute.—**ascribable** *adj*.

ash[1] *n* a tree with silver-grey bark; the wood of this tree.

ash[2] *n* powdery residue of anything burnt; fine, volcanic lava.

ashamed *adj* feeling shame or guilt.

ashen *adj* like ashes, esp in colour; pale.

ashore *adv* to or on the shore; to or on land.—*also adj*.

ashtray *n* a small receptacle for tobacco ash and cigarette stubs.

aside *adv* on or to the side; in reserve; notwithstanding. * *n* words uttered and intended as inaudible, esp as spoken by an actor to the audience and supposedly unheard by the others on the stage.

ask *vt* to put a question to, inquire of; to make a request of or for; to invite; to demand, expect. * *vi* to inquire about.

askance, askant *adv* with a sideways glance; with distrust.

askew *adv, adj* to one side; awry.

asleep *adj* sleeping; inactive; numb. * *adv* into a sleeping condition.

asparagus *n* a plant cultivated for its edible young shoots.

aspect *n* the look of a person or thing to the eye; a particular feature of a problem, situation, etc; the direction something faces; (*astrol*) the position of the planets with respect to one another, regarded as having an influence on human affairs.

aspersions *npl* slander; an attack on a person's reputation.

asphalt *n* a hard, black bituminous substance,

used for paving roads, etc. * *vt* to surface with asphalt.

asphyxiate *vt* to suffocate.—**asphyxiation** *n*.

aspiration *n* strong desire; ambition; aspirating; the act of breathing; the withdawal of air or fluid from a body cavity.

aspire *vi* to desire eagerly; to aim at high things.

aspirin *n* a pain-relieving drug.

ass *n* a donkey; a silly, stupid person; (*sl*) the arse, the buttocks.

assail *vt* to attack violently either physically or verbally.

assailant *n* an attacker.

assassin *n* a murderer, esp one hired to kill a leading political figure, etc.

assassinate *vt* to kill a political figure, etc; to harm (a person's reputation, etc).—**assassination** *n*.

assault *n* a violent attack; (*law*) an unlawful threat or attempt to harm another physically. * *vti* to make an assault (on).

assemble *vti* to bring together; to collect; to fit together the parts of; (*comput*) to translate.

assembly *n* assembling or being assembled; a gathering of persons, esp for a purpose; the fitting together of parts to make a whole machine, etc.

assembly line *n* a series of machines, equipment and workers through which a product passes in successive stages to be assembled.

assent *vi* to express agreement to something. * *n* consent or agreement.

assert *vt* to declare, affirm as true; to maintain or enforce (eg rights).

assertion *n* asserting; a statement that something is a fact, usu without evidence.

assertive *adj* self-assured, positive, confident.—**assertively** *adv*.—**assertiveness** *n*.

assess *vt* to establish the amount of, as a tax; to impose a tax or fine; to value, for the purpose of taxation; to estimate the worth, importance, etc of.—**assessment** *n*.

asset *n* anything owned that has value; a desirable thing; (*pl*) all the property, accounts receivable, etc of a person or business; (*pl*: *law*) property usable to pay debts.

assign *vt* to allot; to appoint to a post or duty; to ascribe; (*law*) to transfer (a right, property, etc).—**assignable** *adj*.

assignment *n* the act of assigning; something assigned to a person, such as a share, task, etc.

assimilate *vt* to absorb; to digest; to be ascribed; to be like.—**assimilation** *n*.

assist *vti* to support or aid.—**assistance** *n*.—**assistant** *n*.

associate *vt* to join as a friend, business partner or supporter; to bring together; to unite; to connect in the mind. * *vi* to combine or unite with others; to come together as friends, business partners or supporters. * *adj* allied or connected; having secondary status or privileges. * *n* a companion, business partner, supporter, etc; something closely connected with another; a person admitted to an association as a subordinate member.

association *n* an organization of people with a common aim; the act of associating or being associated; a connection in the mind, etc.

assorted *adj* distributed according to sorts; miscellaneous.

assortment *n* a collection of people or things of different sorts.

assume *vt* to take on, to undertake; to usurp; to take as certain or true; to pretend to possess.

assumption *n* something taken for granted.

assurance *n* a promise, guarantee; a form of life insurance; a feeling of certainty, self-confidence.

assure *vt* to make safe or certain; to give confidence to; to state positively; to guarantee, ensure.

asterisk *n* a sign (*) used in writing or printing to mark omission of words, etc. * *vt* to mark with an asterisk.

astern *adv* behind a ship or aircraft; at or toward the rear of a ship, etc; backward.

asthma *n* a chronic respiratory condition causing difficulty with breathing.—**asthmatic** *adj*.—**asthmatically** *adv*.

astir *adv* moving or bustling about; out of bed.

astonish *vt* to fill with sudden or great surprise.—**astonishing** *adj*.—**astonishment** *n*.

astound *vt* to astonish greatly.—**astounding** *adj*.

astray *adv* off the right path; into error.

astride *adv* with a leg on either side. * *prep* extending across.

astrology *n* the study of planetary positions and motions to determine their supposed influence on human affairs.—**astrologer** *n*.—**astrological** *adj*.—**astrologically** *adv*.

astronaut *n* one trained to make flights in outer space.

astronomy *n* the scientific investigation of the stars and other planets. —**astronomer** *n*.

astute *adj* crafty, shrewd.—**astutely** *adv*.—**astuteness** *n*.

asylum *n* a place of safety, a refuge; (*formerly*)

an institution for the blind, the mentally ill, etc.

at *prep* on; in; near; by; used to indicate location or position.

ate *see* **eat**.

atheism *n* belief in the nonexistence of God.—**atheist** *n*.

athlete *n* a person trained in games or exercises requiring skill, speed, strength, stamina, etc.

athletic *adj* of athletes or athletics; active, vigorous.—**athletically** *adv*. —**athleticism** *n*.

athletics *n* (*used as sing or pl*) running, jumping, throwing sports, games, etc.

atlas *n* a book containing maps, charts and tables.

atmosphere *n* the gaseous mixture that surrounds the earth or the other stars and planets; a unit of pressure equal to the pressure of the atmosphere at sea level; any dominant or surrounding influence.—**atmospheric** *adj*.

atom *n* the smallest particle of a chemical element; a tiny particle, bit.

atomic bomb *n* a bomb whose explosive power derives from the atomic energy released during nuclear fission or fusion.

atomizer *n* a device for atomizing liquids, usu perfumes or cleaning agents.

atone *vi* to give satisfaction or make amends (for).

atrocious *adj* extremely brutal or wicked; (*inf*) very bad, of poor quality.—**atrociously** *adv*.

atrocity *n* a cruel act; something wicked or repellent.

attach *vt* to fix or fasten to something; to appoint to a specific group; to ascribe, attribute. * *vi* to become attached; to adhere.—**attachable** *adj*.

attack *vt* to set upon violently; to assault in speech or writing; to invade, as of a disease. * *vi* to make an assault. * *n* an assault; a fit of illness; severe criticism; a beginning of a performance, undertaking, etc.

attain *vt* to succeed in getting or arriving at; to achieve. * *vi* to come to or arrive at by growth or effort.—**attainable** *adj*.

attainment *n* something attained; an accomplishment.

attempt *vt* to try to accomplish, get, etc. * *n* an endeavour or effort to accomplish; an attack, assault.

attend *vt* to take care of; to go with, accompany; to be present at. * *vi* to apply oneself (to); to deal with, give attention to.

attendance *n* attending; the number of people present; the number of times a person attends.

attendant *n* a person who serves or accompanies another; someone employed to assist or guide. * *adj* accompanying, following as a result; being in attendance.

attention *n* the application of the mind to a particular purpose, aim, etc; awareness, notice; care, consideration; (*usu pl*) an act of civility or courtesy; (*mil*) a soldier's formal erect posture.

attentive *adj* observant, diligent; courteous.—**attentively** *adv*.—**attentiveness** *n*.

attest *vt* to state as true; to certify, as by oath; to give proof of. * *vi* to testify, bear witness (to).—**attestation** *n*.

attic *n* the room or space just under the roof; a garret.

attire *vt* to clothe; to dress up. * *n* dress, clothing.

attitude *n* posture, position of the body; a manner of thought or feeling; the position of an aircraft or spacecraft in relation to certain reference points.

attorney *n* (*pl* **attorneys**) one legally authorized to act for another; a lawyer.

attract *vt* to pull towards oneself; to get the admiration, attention, etc of. * *vi* to be attractive.

attraction *n* the act of attraction; the power of attracting, esp charm; (*physics*) the mutual action by which bodies tend to be drawn together.

attractive *adj* pleasing in appearance, etc; arousing interest; able to draw or pull.—**attractively** *adv*.—**attractiveness** *n*.

attribute *vt* to regard as belonging to; to ascribe, impute (to). * *n* a quality, a characteristic of.—**attributable** *adj*.—**attribution** *n*.

attrition *n* a grinding down by or as by friction; a relentless wearing down and weakening.

aubergine, eggplant (*US*) *n* the dark purple fruit of the egg plant used as a vegetable; its colour.

auburn *adj* reddish brown.

auction *n* a public sale of items to the highest bidder. * *vt* to sell by or at an auction.

auctioneer *n* one who conducts an auction.

audacious *adj* daring, adventurous; bold; rash; insolent.—**audaciously** *adv*.—**audacity** *n*.

audible *adj* heard or able to be heard. —**audibly** *adv*.—**audibility** *n*.

audience *n* a gathering of listeners or spectators; the people addressed by a book, play, film, etc; a formal interview or meeting.

audiovisual *adj* using both sound and vision, as in teaching aids.

audit *n* the inspection and verification of business accounts by a qualified accountant. * *vt* to make such an inspection.

audition *n* a trial to test a performer. * *vti* to test or be tested by audition.

auditor *n* a person qualified to audit business accounts.

auditorium *n* the part of a building allotted to the audience; a building or hall for speeches, concerts, etc.

augment *vti* to increase.—**augmentation** *n.*

augur *vti* to prophesy; to be an omen (of).

August *n* the eighth month of the year, having 31 days.

august *adj* imposing; majestic.

aunt *n* a father's or mother's sister; an uncle's wife.

au pair *n* a person, esp a young woman, from abroad who performs domestic chores, child-minding, etc, in return for board and lodging.

aura *n* a particular quality or atmosphere surrounding a person or thing.

auspice *n* an omen; (*pl*) sponsorship; patronage.

auspicious *adj* showing promise, favourable.—**auspiciously** *adv.*

austere *adj* stern, forbidding in attitude or appearance; abstemious; severely simple, plain.—**austerely** *adv.*—**austerity** *n.*

authentic *adj* genuine, conforming to truth or reality; trustworthy, reliable.—**authentically** *adv.*—**authenticity** *n.*

author *n* a person who brings something into existence; the writer of a book, article, etc. * *vt* to be the author of.—**authoress** *nf.*

authoritarian *adj* favouring strict obedience; dictatorial. * *n* a person advocating or practising authoritarian principles.

authoritative *adj* commanding or possessing authority; accepted as true; official.—**authoritatively** *adv.*

authority *n* the power or right to command; (*pl*) officials with this power; influence resulting from knowledge, prestige, etc; a person, writing, etc cited to support an opinion; an expert.

authorize *vt* to give authority to, to empower; to give official approval to, sanction.—**authorization** *n.*

auto *n* (*pl* **autos**) (*US inf*) a motor car.

autobiography *n* the biography of a person written by himself or herself.—**autobiographer** *n.*—**autobiographical** *adj.*

autocrat *n* an absolute ruler; any domineering person.—**autocratic** *adj.*—**autocratically** *adv.*

autograph *n* a person's signature. * *vt* to write one's signature in or on.

automate *vt* to control by automation; to convert to automatic operation.

automatic *adj* involuntary or reflexive; self-regulating; acting by itself. * *n* an automatic pistol or rifle.—**automatically** *adv.*

automation *n* the use of automatic methods, machinery, etc, in industry.

automaton *n* (*pl* **automatons, automata**) any automatic device, esp a robot; a human being who acts like a robot.

automobile *n* a motor car.

autonomy *n* freedom of self-determination; independence, self-government.—**autonomous** *adj.*

autopsy *n* a post-mortem examination to determine the cause of death.

autumn *n* the season between summer and winter; in US, fall.—**autumnal** *adj.*

auxiliary *adj* providing help, subsidiary; supplementary. * *n* a helper; (*gram*) a verb that helps form tenses, moods, voices, etc of other verbs, as *have*, *be*, *may*, *shall*, etc.

avail *vti* to be of use or advantage to. * *n* benefit, use or help.

available *adj* ready for use; obtainable, accessible.—**availability** *n.*

avalanche *n* a mass of snow, ice, and rock tumbling down a mountainside; a sudden overwhelming accumulation or influx.

avant-garde *n* (*arts*) those ideas and practices regarded as in advance of those generally accepted. * *adj* pertaining to these and their creators.

avarice *n* greed for wealth.—**avaricious** *adj.*—**avariciously** *adv.*

Ave, ave *abbr* = avenue.

avenge *vt* to get revenge for.—**avenger** *n.*

avenue *n* a street, drive, etc, esp when broad; means of access.

average *n* the result of dividing the sum of two or more quantities by the number of quantities; the usual kind, amount, etc. * *vt* to calculate the average of; to achieve an average number of.

averse *adj* unwilling; opposed (to).

aversion *n* antipathy; hatred; something arousing hatred or repugnance.

avert *vt* to turn away or aside from; to prevent, avoid.

aviation *n* the art or science of flying aircraft.

avid *adj* eager, greedy.—**avidly** *adv*.
avocado (pear) *n* a thick-skinned, pear-shaped fruit with yellow buttery flesh.
avoid *vt* to keep clear of, shun; to refrain from.
avoidable *adj* able to be avoided.
await *vti* to wait for; to be in store for.
awake *vb* (*pt* **awoke** *or* **awaked,** *pp* **awoken** *or* **awaked**) *vi* to wake; to become aware. * *vt* to rouse from sleep; to rouse from inaction. * *adj* roused from sleep, not asleep; active; aware.
award *vt* to give, as by a legal decision; to give (a prize, etc); to grant. * *n* a decision, as by a judge; a prize.
aware *adj* realizing, having knowledge; conscious.—**awareness** *n*.
awash *adj* filled or overflowing with water.
away *adv* from a place; in another place or direction; off, aside; far. * *adj* absent; at a distance.
awe *n* a mixed feeling of fear, wonder and dread. * *vt* to fill with awe.
awesome *adj* inspiring awe.
awful *adj* very bad; unpleasant. * *adv* (*inf*) very.—**awfulness** *n*.
awhile *adv* for a short time.
awkward *adj* lacking dexterity, clumsy; graceless; embarrassing; embarrassed; inconvenient; deliberately obstructive or difficult to deal with.—**awkwardly** *adv*.—**awkwardness** *n*.
awning *n* a structure, as of canvas, extended above or in front of a window, door, etc to provide shelter against the sun or rain.
awoke, awoken *see* **awake**.
awry *adv* twisted to one side. * *adj* contrary to expectations, wrong.
axe, ax (*US*) *n* a tool with a long handle and bladed head for chopping wood, etc. * *vt* to trim, split, etc with an axe.
axiom *n* a widely held or accepted truth or principle.—**axiomatic** *adj*.
axis *n* (*pl* **axes**) a real or imaginary straight line about which a body rotates; the centre line of a symmetrical figure; a reference line of a coordinate system; a partnership, alliance.—**axial** *adj*.
axle *n* a rod on or with which a wheel turns; a bar connecting two opposite wheels, as of a car.

B

babble *vi* to make sounds like a baby; to talk incoherently; to murmur, as a brook. * *n* incoherent talk; chatter; a murmuring sound.—**babbler** *n*.
baby *n* a newborn child or infant; a very young animal; (*sl*) a girl or young woman; a personal project. * *vt* to pamper.—*also adj*.—**babyish** *adj*.
baby-sit *vti* to look after a baby or child while the parents are out.—**baby-sitter** *n*.
bachelor *n* an unmarried man; a person who holds a degree from a college or university.—**bachelorhood** *n*.
back *n* the rear surface of the human body from neck to hip; the corresponding part in animals; a part that supports or fits the back; the part farthest from the front; (*sport*) a player or position behind the front line. * *adj* at the rear; (*streets, etc*) remote or inferior; (*pay, etc*) of or for the past; backward. * *adv* at or toward the rear; to or toward a former condition, time, etc; in return or requital; in reserve or concealment. * *vti* to move or go backward; to support; to bet on; to provide or be back for; (*with* **down**) to withdraw from a position or claim; (*with* **off**) to move back (or away, etc); (*with* **out**) to withdraw from an enterprise; to evade keeping a promise, etc; (*with* **up**) to support; to move backward; to accumulate because of restricted movement; (*comput*) to make a copy (of a data file, etc) for safekeeping.
backache *n* an ache or pain in the back.
backbencher *n* a Member of Parliament who does not hold an important office.
backbiting *n* spiteful talk behind a person's back.—**backbite** *vt*.
backbone *n* the spinal column; main support; strength, courage.
backdate *vt* to declare valid from some previous date.
backfire *vi* (*automobiles*) to ignite prematurely causing a loud bang from the exhaust; to have the opposite effect from that intended, usu with unfortunate consequences.—*also n*.
backgammon *n* a board game played by two people with pieces moved according to throws of the dice.
background *n* the distant part of a scene or picture; an inconspicuous position; social

class, education, experience; circumstances leading up to an event.

backhand *n* (*tennis, etc*) a stroke played with the hand turned outwards.

backhanded *adj* backhand; (*compliment*) indirect, ambiguous.—*also adv*.

backhander *n* a backhanded stroke; (*inf*) a backhanded remark; (*sl*) a bribe.

backing *n* support; supporters; a lining to support or strengthen the back of something; musical accompaniment to a (esp pop) singer.

backlash *n* a violent and adverse reaction; a recoil in machinery.

backlog *n* an accumulation of work, etc still to be done.

backside *n* (*inf*) buttocks.

backstroke *n* (*swimming*) a stroke using backward circular sweeps of the arms whilst lying face upward.

backward *adj* turned toward the rear or opposite way; shy; slow or retarded. * *adv* backwards.—**backwardness** *n*.

backwards *adv* towards the back; with the back foremost; in a way opposite the usual; into a less good or favourable state or condition; into the past.

backwater *n* a pool of still water fed by a river; a remote, backward place.

backyard *n* a yard at the back of a house.

bacon *n* salted and smoked meat from the back or sides of a pig.

bacteria *npl* (*sing* **bacterium**) microscopic unicellular organisms.—**bacterial** *adj*.

bad *adj* (**worse, worst**) not good; not as it should be; inadequate or unfit; rotten or spoiled; incorrect or faulty; wicked; immoral; mischievous; harmful; ill; sorry, distressed.—**badness** *n*.

bade *see* **bid**.

badge *n* an emblem, symbol or distinguishing mark.

badger *n* a hibernating, burrowing black and white mammal related to the weasel. * *vt* to pester or annoy persistently.

badly *adv* poorly; inadequately; unsuccessfully; severely; (*inf*) very much.

badminton *n* a court game for two or four players played with light rackets and a shuttlecock volleyed over a net.

baffle *vt* to bewilder or perplex; to frustrate; to make ineffectual. * *n* a plate or device used to restrict the flow of sound, light or fluid.—**bafflement** *n*.—**baffling** *adj*.

bag *n* a usu flexible container of paper, plastic, etc that can be closed at the top; a satchel, suitcase, etc; a handbag; game taken in hunting; a bag-like shape or part; (*derog*) an old woman; (*inf: in pl*) plenty (of). * *vti* (*pt* **bagged**) to place in a bag; to kill in hunting; (*inf*) to get; to make a claim on; to hang loosely.

baggage *n* suitcases; luggage.

baggy *adj* (**baggier, baggiest**) hanging loosely in folds.—**baggily** *adv*.—**bagginess** *n*.

bagpipe *n* (*often pl*) a musical instrument consisting of an air-filled bag fitted with pipes.

bail[1] *n* money lodged as security that a prisoner, if released, will return to court to stand trial; such a release; the person pledging such money. * *vt* to free a person by providing bail; (*with* **out**) to help out of financial or other difficulty.

bail[2] *vti* (*usu with* **out**) to scoop out (water) from (a boat).

bail[3] *n* (*cricket*) either of two wooden crosspieces that rest on the three stumps; a bar separating horses in an open stable; a metal bar that holds the paper against the roller of a typewriter.

bailiff *n* in UK, the agent of a landlord or landowner; a sheriff's officer who serves writs and summonses; a minor official in some US courts.

bait *n* food attached to a hook to entice fish or make them bite; any lure or enticement. * *vt* to put food on a hook to lure; to set dogs upon (a badger, etc); to persecute, worry or tease, esp by verbal attacks; to lure, to tempt; to entice.

bake *vt* (*pottery*) to dry and harden by heating in the sun or by fire; (*food*) to cook by dry heat in an oven. * *vi* to do a baker's work; to dry and harden in heat; (*inf*) to be very hot.

baker *n* a person who bakes and sells bread, cakes, etc.

bakery *n* a room or building for baking; a shop that sells bread, cakes, etc; baked goods.

baking powder *n* a leavening agent containing sodium bicarbonate and an acid-forming substance.

balance *n* a device for weighing, consisting of two dishes or pans hanging from a pivoted horizontal beam; equilibrium; mental stability; the power to influence or control; a remainder. * *vt* to weigh; to compare; to equalize the debit and credit sides of an account. * *vi* to be equal in power or weight, etc; to have the debits and credits equal.

balance sheet *n* a statement of assets and liabilities.

balcony *n* a projecting platform from an upper storey enclosed by a railing; an upper floor of seats in a theatre, etc.—**balconied** *adj.*

bald *adj* lacking a natural or usual covering, as of hair, vegetation, nap; (*tyre*) having little or no tread; (*truth*) plain or blunt; bare, unadorned.—**baldly** *adv.*—**baldness** *n.*

bale[1] *n* a large bundle of goods, as raw cotton, compressed and bound. * *vt* (*hay etc*) to make into bales. * *vi* (*with* **out**) to parachute from an aircraft.

bale[2] *n* great evil; woe.—**baleful** *adj.*

balk *vt* to obstruct or foil. * *vi* to stop and refuse to move and act.—*also* **baulk**.

ball[1] *n* a spherical or nearly spherical body or mass; a round object for use in tennis, football, etc; a throw or pitch of a ball; a missile for a cannon, rifle, etc; (*pl*) testicles; any rounded part or protuberance of the body. * *vti* to form into a ball.

ball[2] *n* a formal social dance; (*inf*) a good time.—**ballroom** *n.*

ballad *n* a narrative song or poem; a slow, sentimental, esp pop, song.

ballast *n* heavy material carried in a ship or vehicle to stabilize it when it is not carrying cargo; crushed rock or gravel, etc used in railway tracks.

ballerina *n* a female ballet dancer.

ballet *n* a theatrical representation of a story, set to music and performed by dancers; the troupe of dancers.

ballistics *n* (*used as sing*) the scientific study of projectiles and firearms.

balloon *n* a large airtight envelope that rises up when filled with hot air or light gases, usu with a basket for passengers; a small inflatable rubber pouch used as a toy; a balloon-shaped line enclosing speech or thoughts in a strip cartoon. * *vti* to inflate; to swell, expand; to travel in a balloon.—**balloonist** *n.*

ballot *n* a paper used in voting; the process of voting; the number of votes cast. * *vi* (*pt* **balloted**) to vote.

ballot box *n* a secure container for ballot papers.

ballpoint pen *n* a pen with a tiny ball, which rotates against an inking cartridge, as its writing tip.

balsam *n* a fragrant, resinous substance or the tree yielding it.

bamboo *n* any of various, often tropical, woody grasses, used for furniture.

bamboozle *vt* (*inf*) to deceive; to mystify.

ban *n* a condemnation, an official prohibition. * *vt* (*pt* **banned**) to prohibit, esp officially; to forbid.

banal *adj* trite, commonplace.—**banality** *n.*

banana *n* a herbaceous plant bearing its fruit in compact, hanging bunches.

band[1] *n* a strip of material used for binding; a stripe; (*radio*) a range of wavelengths.

band[2] *n* a group of people with a common purpose; a group of musicians. * *vti* to associate together for a particular purpose.

bandage *n* a strip of cloth for binding wounds and fractures. * *vt* to bind a wound.

bandit *n* a robber.

bandwagon *n* a wagon for carrying a band in a parade; a movement, idea, etc that is (thought to be) heading for success.

bandy[1] *vt* to pass to and fro; (*often with* **about**) (*rumours, etc*) to spread freely; to exchange words, esp angrily.

bandy[2] *adj* (**bandier, bandiest**) having legs curved outward at the knee.—*also* **bandy-legged**.

bang *n* a hard blow; a sudden loud sound. * *vt* to hit or knock with a loud noise; (*door*) to slam. * *vi* to make a loud noise; to hit noisily or sharply. * *adv* with a bang, abruptly; (*inf*) precisely.

bangle *n* a bracelet worn on the arm or ankle.

banish *vt* to exile from a place; to drive away; to get rid of.—**banishment** *n.*

banister *n* the railing or supporting posts in a staircase.—*also* **bannister**.

banjo *n* (*pl* **banjos**) a stringed musical instrument with a drum-like body and a long fretted neck.

bank[1] *n* a mound or pile; the sloping side of a river; elevated ground in a lake or the sea; a row or series of objects, as of dials, switches. * *vti* to form into a mound; to cover (a fire) with fuel so that it burns more slowly; (*aircraft*) to curve or tilt sideways.

bank[2] *n* an institution that offers various financial services, such as the safekeeping, lending and exchanging of money; the money held by the banker or dealer in a card game; any supply or store. * *vti* (*cheques, cash, etc*) to deposit in a bank.

banker *n* a person who runs a bank; the keeper of the bank at a gaming table.

banking *n* the activity or occupation of running a bank. * *adj* of or concerning a bank.

banknote *n* a note issued by a bank, which serves as money.

bankrupt *n* a person, etc legally declared unable to pay his debts; one who becomes insolvent. * *adj* judged to be insolvent; financially ruined. * *vt* to make bankrupt.—**bankruptcy** *n*.

banner *n* a flag or ensign; a headline running across a newspaper page; a strip of cloth bearing a slogan or emblem carried between poles in a parade.

bannister *see* **banister**.

banns *npl* public declaration of intention, esp in church, to marry.

banquet *n* a feast; an elaborate and sometimes formal dinner in honour of a person or occasion. * *vt* to hold a banquet.

banter *vt* to tease good-humouredly.

baptise, baptize *vt* to immerse in or sprinkle with water, esp as a religious rite; to christen, name.

baptism *n* the sprinkling of water on the forehead, or complete immersion in water, as a rite of admitting a person to a Christian church; an initiating experience.—**baptismal** *adj*.—**baptismally** *adv*.

bar[1] *n* a straight length of wood or metal; a counter where drinks etc are served; a place with such a counter; an oblong piece, as of soap; anything that obstructs or hinders; a band or strip; barristers or lawyers collectively; the legal profession; (*mus*) a vertical line dividing a staff into measures; (*mus*) a measure. * *vt* (*pt* **barred**) to secure or fasten as with a bar; to exclude or prevent; to oppose. * *prep* except for.

bar[2] *n* a unit of atmospheric pressure.

barbecue *n* a metal frame for grilling food over an open fire; an open-air party where barbecued food is served. * *vt* to cook on a barbecue.

barber *n* a person who cuts hair and shaves beards.

barbiturate *n* a sedative drug.

bare *adj* without covering; unclothed, naked; simple, unadorned; mere; without furnishings. * *vt* to uncover; to reveal.—**bareness** *n*.

bareback *adj* on a horse with no saddle.—*also adv*.

barefaced *adj* with the face shaven or uncovered; shameless.

barefoot, barefooted *adj* with the feet bare.—*also adv*.

barely *adv* openly; merely, scarcely.

bargain *n* an agreement laying down the conditions of a transaction; something sold at a price favourable to the buyer. * *vt* to make a bargain, haggle.

barge *n* a flat-bottomed vessel, used to transport freight along rivers and canals; a large boat for excursions or pleasure trips. * *vi* to lurch clumsily; (*with* **in**) to interrupt (a conversation) rudely; (*with* **into**) to enter abruptly.

baritone *n* the adult male voice ranging between bass and tenor; a singer with such a voice.

bark[1] *n* the harsh or abrupt cry of a dog, wolf, etc; a similar sound, such as one made by a person. * *vi* to make a loud cry like a dog; to speak sharply.

bark[2] *n* the outside covering of a tree trunk. * *vt* to remove the bark from; (*inf*) to scrape; to skin (the knees, etc).

barley *n* a grain used in making beer and whisky, and for food.

barmaid *n* a woman serving alcohol in a bar.

barman *n* a man serving alcohol in a bar.

barmy *adj* (**barmier, barmiest**) (*sl*) crazy.

barn *n* a farm building used for storing grain, hay, etc.

barnacle *n* a hard-shelled marine animal that attaches itself to rocks and ship-bottoms.

barometer *n* an instrument for measuring atmospheric pressure and imminent changes in the weather; anything that marks change.—**barometric** *adj*.

baron *n* a member of a rank of nobility, the lowest in the British peerage; a powerful businessman.—**baroness** *nf*.

barracks *n* (*used as sing*) a building for housing soldiers.

barrage *n* a man-made dam across a river; heavy artillery fire; (*of protests*) continuous and heavy delivery.

barrel *n* a cylindrical container, usu wooden, with bulging sides held together with hoops; the amount held by a barrel; a tubular structure, as in a gun. * *vt* (*pt* **barrelled**) to put into barrels.

barrel organ *n* a mechanical piano or organ played by a revolving cylinder with pins that operate the keys or valves to produce sound.

barren *adj* infertile; incapable of producing offspring; unable to bear crops; unprofitable.

barricade *n* a barrier or blockade used in defence to block a street; an obstruction. * *vt* to block with a barricade.

barrier *n* anything that bars passage, prevents access, controls crowds, etc.

barrister *n* a qualified lawyer who has been called to the bar in England.

barrow *n* a wheelbarrow or hand-cart used for carrying loads.

barter *vt* to trade commodities or services

without exchanging money. * *vi* to haggle or bargain. * *n* trade by the exchanging of commodities.

base[1] *n* the bottom part of anything; the support or foundation; the fundamental principle; the centre of operations (eg military); (*baseball*) one of the four corners of the diamond. * *vt* to use as a basis; to found (on).—**basal** *adj*.

base[2] *adj* low in morality or honour; worthless; menial.—**basely** *adv*.—**baseness** *n*.

baseball *n* the US national game, involving two teams that score runs by hitting a ball and running round four bases arranged in a diamond shape on the playing area.

basement *n* the part of a building that is partly or wholly below ground level.

bash *vt* (*inf*) to hit hard.

bashful *adj* easily embarrassed, shy.—**bashfully** *adv*.

basic *adj* fundamental. * *n* (*often pl*) a basic principle, factor, etc.—**basically** *adv*.

basil *n* a plant with aromatic leaves used for seasoning food.

basin *n* a wide shallow container for liquid; its contents; any large hollow, often with water in it; a tract of land drained by a river.

basis *n* (*pl* **bases**) a base or foundation; a principal constituent; a fundamental principle or theory.

bask *vi* to lie in sunshine or warmth; to enjoy someone's approval.

basket *n* a container made of interwoven cane, wood strips, etc; the hoop through which basketball players throw the ball to score.

basketball *n* a game in which two teams compete to score by throwing the ball through an elevated net basket or hoop; this ball.

bass[1] *n* (*mus*) the range of the lowest male voice; a singer or instrument with this range. * *adj* of, for or in the range of a bass.

bass[2] *n* any of numerous freshwater food and game fishes.

bassoon *n* an orchestral, deep-toned woodwind instrument.—**bassoonist** *n*.

bastard *n* a person born of unmarried parents; (*offensive*) an unpleasant person; (*inf*) a person (*lucky bastard*). * *adj* illegitimate (by birth); false; not genuine.—**bastardy** *n*.

baste[1] *vt* to drip fat over (roasting meat, etc).

baste[2] *vt* to sew with long loose stitches as a temporary seam.

bat[1] *n* a wooden club used in cricket, baseball, etc; one who bats; a paddle used in table tennis. * *vb* (*pt* **batted**) *vt* to hit as with a bat. * *vi* to take one's turn at bat.

bat[2] *n* a mouse-like flying mammal with forelimbs modified to form wings.

bat[3] *vt* (*pt* **batted**) (*one's eyelids*) to wink or flutter.

batch *n* the quantity of bread, etc produced at one time; one set, group, etc; an amount of work for processing by a computer in a single run.

bath *n* water for washing the body; a bathing; a tub for bathing; (*pl*) a building with baths for public use; a municipal swimming pool. * *vti* to give a bath to; to bathe.

bathe *vt* to dampen with any liquid. * *vi* to have a bath; to go swimming; to become immersed.—**bather** *n*.

bathroom *n* a room with a bath or shower and usually a toilet and washbasin.

baton *n* a staff serving as a symbol of office; a thin stick used by the conductor of an orchestra to beat time; a hollow cylinder carried by each member of a relay team in succession; a policeman's truncheon.

battalion *n* an army unit consisting of three or more companies; a large group.

batter *vt* to beat with repeated blows; to wear out with heavy use. * *vi* to strike heavily and repeatedly. * *n* a mixture of flour, egg, and milk or water used in cooking.

battery *n* a set of heavy guns; a small unit of artillery; an electric cell that supplies current; unlawful beating.

battle *n* a combat or fight between two opposing individuals or armies; a contest. * *vti* to fight; to struggle.

battlefield *n* the land on which a battle is fought.

battlement *n* a parapet or wall with indentations, from which to shoot.

battleship *n* a large, heavily armoured warship.

baulk *see* **balk**.

bawdy *adj* (**bawdier, bawdiest**) humorously indecent; obscene, lewd.—**bawdily** *adv*.—**bawdiness** *n*.

bawl *vti* to shout; to weep loudly. * *n* a loud shout; a noisy weeping.—**bawler** *n*.—**bawling** *n*.

bay[1] *n* a type of laurel tree.

bay[2] *n* a wide inlet of a sea or lake; an inward bend of a shore.

bay[3] an alcove or recess in a wall; a compartment used for a special purpose.

bay[4] *vti* to bark (at). * *n* the cry of a hound or a pursuing pack; the position of one forced to turn and fight.

bay[5] *adj* reddish brown. * *n* a horse of this colour.

bayonet *n* a blade for stabbing attached to the muzzle of a rifle. * *vt* (*pt* **bayoneted** *or* **bayonetted**) to kill or stab with a bayonet.

bay window *n* a window projecting from the outside wall of a house.

bazaar *n* a market-place; a street full of small shops; a benefit sale for a church, etc.

BBC *abbr* = British Broadcasting Corporation.

BC *abbr* = Before Christ.

be *vi* (*pres t* **am, are, is**, *pt* **was, were**, *pp* **been**) to exist; to live; to take place.

beach *n* a flat, sandy shore of the sea. * *vi* to bring (a boat) up on the beach from the sea.

beacon *n* a light for warning or guiding.

bead *n* a small ball pierced for stringing; (*pl*) a string of beads; (*pl*) a rosary; a bubble or droplet of liquid; the sight of a rifle.—**beaded** *adj*.

beading *n* moulding or edging in the form of a series of beads; a wooden strip, rounded on one side, used for trimming.—*also* **beadwork**.

beak *n* a bird's bill; any projecting part; the nose.—**beaked** *adj*.

beaker *n* a large drinking cup, or the amount it holds; a cylindrical vessel with a pouring lip used by chemists and pharmacists.

beam *n* a long straight piece of timber or metal; the crossbar of a balance; a ship's breadth at its widest point; a slender shaft of light, etc; a radiant look, smile, etc; a steady radio or radar signal for guiding aircraft or ships. * *vt* (*light, etc*) to send out; to smile with pleasure.

bean *n* a plant bearing kidney-shaped seeds; a seed or pod of such a plant; any bean-like seed.

bear[1] *vb* (*pt* **bore**, *pp* **borne**) *vt* to carry; to endure; to support, to sustain; to conduct (oneself); to produce or bring forth; (*with* **out**) to confirm. * *vi* to be productive; (*with* **down**) to press or weigh down; to overwhelm; (*with* **on** *or* **upon**) to have reference to; (*with* **up**) to endure with courage.

bear[2] *n* a large mammal with coarse fur, short legs, strong claws and feeding mainly on fruit and insects; a gruff or ill-mannered person; a teddy bear; a speculator who sells stock in anticipation of a fall in price.

bearable *adj* endurable.—**bearably** *adv*.

beard *n* hair covering a man's chin; similar bristles on an animal or plant. * *vt* to defy, oppose openly.—**bearded** *adj*.

bearer *n* a person who bears or presents; a person who carries something (a coffin, etc).

bearing *n* demeanour; conduct; a compass direction; (*followed by* **to** *or* **upon**) relevance; a machine part on which another part slides, revolves, etc.

beast *n* a large, wild, four-footed animal; a brutal, vicious person; (*inf*) something difficult, an annoyance.

beastly *adj* (**beastlier, beastliest**) (*inf*) disagreeable. * *adv* (*inf*) very (*beastly cold*).

beat *vb* (*pt* **beat**, *pp* **beaten**) *vt* to strike, dash or pound repeatedly; to flog; to overcome or counteract; to find too difficult for; (*mus*) to mark (time) with a baton, etc; (*eggs, etc*) to mix by stirring vigorously; (*esp wings*) to move up and down; (*a path, way, etc*) to form by repeated trampling; (*sl*) to baffle. * *vi* to hit, pound, etc repeatedly; to throb; (*naut*) to sail against the wind. * *n* a recurrent stroke, pulsation, as in a heartbeat or clock ticking; rhythm in music or poetry; the area patrolled by a police officer.

beater *n* an implement for beating, such as an attachment for an electric food mixer.

beating *n* the act of striking or thrashing; throbbing, pulsation; a defeat.

beautician *n* one who offers cosmetic treatments.

beautiful *adj* having beauty; very enjoyable.—**beautifully** *adv*.

beauty *n* the combination of qualities in a person or object that cause delight or pleasure; an attractive woman or girl; good looks.

beaver *n* a large semi-aquatic dam-building rodent; its fur; a hat made from beaver fur. * *vi* (*often with* **away**) to work hard (at).

became *see* **become**.

because *conj* since; for the reason that.

beckon *vti* to summon by a gesture.

become *vb* (*pt* **became**, *pp* **become**) *vi* to come or grow to be. * *vt* to be suitable for.

becoming *adj* appropriate; seemly; suitable to the wearer.—**becomingly** *adv*.

bed *n* a piece of furniture for sleeping on; a plot of soil where plants are raised; the bottom of a river, lake, etc; any flat surface used as a foundation; a stratum. * *vt* (*pt* **bedded**) to put to bed; to embed; to plant in a bed of earth; to arrange in layers.

bedraggle *vt* to make untidy or dirty by dragging in the wet or dirt.—**bedraggled** *adj*.

bedridden *adj* confined to bed through illness.

bedroom *n* a room for sleeping in. * *adj* suggestive of sexual relations; inhabited by commuters.

bedside *n* the space beside a bed. * *adj* situated or conducted at the bedside; suitable for someone bedridden.

bedsit, bedsitter, bedsitting room *n* a single room with sleeping and cooking facilities.

bee *n* a social, stinging four-winged insect that is often kept in hives to make honey; any of numerous insects that also feed on pollen and nectar and are related to wasps.

beech *n* a tree with smooth silvery-grey bark; its wood.

beef *n* the meat of a full-grown cow, steer, etc; (*inf*) muscular strength; (*inf*) a complaint, grudge; (*pl* **beeves**) cows, ox, steers, etc bred for their meat. * *vt* (*with* **up**) to add weight, strength or power to.

beeline *n* a direct line or course.

been *see* **be**.

beer *n* an alcoholic drink made from malt, sugar, hops and water fermented with yeast.

beetle *n* any of an order of insects having hard wing covers.

beetroot *n* the fleshy root of beet used as a vegetable, in salads, etc.

befall *vti* (*pt* **befell,** *pp* **befallen**) to happen or occur to.

before *prep* ahead of; in front of; in the presence of; preceding in space or time; in preference to; rather than. * *adv* beforehand; previously; until now. * *conj* earlier than the time that; rather than.

befriend *vt* to be a friend to, to favour.

beg *vti* (*pt* **begged**) to ask for money or food; to ask earnestly; to implore.

began *see* **begin**.

beggar *n* a person who begs or who lives by begging; a pauper; (*inf*) a person. * *vt* to reduce to poverty; (*description*) to render inadequate.

begin *vti* (*pr p* **beginning**, *pt* **began**, *pp* **begun**) to start doing, acting, etc; to originate.

beginner *n* one who has just started to learn or do something; a novice.

beginning *n* source or origin; commencement.

begrudge *vt* to grudge; to envy.

begun *see* **begin**.

behalf *n*: **in** *or* **on behalf of** in the interest of; for.

behave *vti* to act in a specified way; to conduct (oneself) properly.

behaviour, behavior (*US*) *n* way of behaving; conduct or action.—**behavioural** *adj*.

beheld *see* **behold**.

behind *prep* at the rear of; concealed by; later than; supporting. * *adv* in the rear; slow; late.

behold *vb* (*pt* **beheld**) *vt* to look at; to observe. * *vi* to see.—**beholder** *n*.

beige *n* a very light brown.

being *n* life; existence; a person or thing that exists; nature, substance.

belated *adj* coming late.—**belatedly** *adv*.

belch *vti* to expel gas from the stomach by the mouth; to eject violently from inside.—*also n*.

belfry *n* the upper part of a tower in which bells are hung.

belie *vt* to show to be a lie; to misrepresent; to fail to live up to (a hope, promise).

belief *n* a principle or idea considered to be true; religious faith.

believe *vt* to accept as true; to think; to be convinced of. * *vi* to have religious faith.—**believer** *n*.

belittle *vt* (*a person*) to make feel small; to disparage.

bell *n* a hollow metal object which rings when struck; anything bell-shaped; the sound made by a bell.

belligerent *adj* at war; of war; warlike; ready to fight or quarrel.—**belligerence** *n*.

bellow *vi* to roar; to make an outcry. * *vt* to utter loudly. * *n* the roar of a bull; any deep roar.

bellows *n* (*used as pl or sing*) a device for creating and directing a stream of air by compression of its collapsible sides.

belly *n* the lower part of the body between the chest and the thighs; the abdomen; the stomach; the underside of an animal's body; the deep interior, as of a ship. * *vti* to swell out; to bulge.

belong *vi* to have a proper place; to be related (to); (*with* **to**) to be a member; to be owned.

belongings *npl* personal effects, possessions.

beloved *adj* dearly loved. * *n* one who is dearly loved.

below *prep* lower than; unworthy of. * *adv* in or to a lower place; beneath; later (in a book, etc).

belt *n* a band of leather, etc worn around the waist; any similar encircling thing; a continuous moving strap passing over pulleys and so driving machinery; a distinctive region or strip; (*sl*) a hard blow. * *vt* to surround, attach with a belt; to thrash with a belt; (*sl*) to deliver a hard blow; (*sl*) to hurry; (*with* **out**) (*sl*) to sing or play loudly; (*with* **up**) to fasten with a belt. * *vi* (*with* **up**) (*inf*) to wear a seat-belt; (*sl*: *often imper*) to be quiet.

bench *n* a long hard seat for two or more persons; a long table for working at; the place where judges sit in a court of law; the status of a judge; judges collectively; (*sport*) the place where reserves, etc, sit during play.

bend *vb* (*pt*, *pp* **bent**) *vt* to form a curve; to make crooked; to turn, esp from a straight line; to adapt to one's purpose, distort. * *vi* to turn, esp from a straight line; to yield from pressure to form a curve; (*with* **over** *or* **down**) to curve the body; to give in. * *n* a curve, turn; a bent part; (*pl*) decompression sickness.

beneath *prep* underneath; below; unworthy. * *adv* in a lower place; underneath.—*also adj*.

benefactor *n* a patron.

beneficial *adj* advantageous.—**beneficially** *adv*.

benefit *n* advantage; anything contributing to improvement; (*often pl*) allowances paid by a government, employer, etc; a public performance etc, whose proceeds are to help some person or cause. * *vb* (*pt* **benefited**) *vt* to help. * *vi* to receive advantage.

benevolence *n* inclination to do good; kindness; generosity.—**benevolent** *adj*.—**benevolently** *adv*.

bent[1] *see* **bend**.

bent[2] *n* aptitude; inclination of the mind. * *adj* curved or crooked; (*with* **on**) strongly determined; (*sl*) dishonest.

bequeath *vt* (*property, etc*) to leave by will; to pass on to posterity.

bequest *n* act of bequeathing; something that is bequeathed, a legacy.

bereave *vt* to deprive (of) a loved one through death.—**bereaved** *adj*.—**bereavement** *n*.

beret *n* a flat, round, soft cap.

berry *n* any small, juicy, stoneless fruit (eg blackberry, holly berry).

berserk *adj* frenzied; destructively violent.—*also adv*.

berth *n* a place in a dock for a ship at mooring; a built-in bed. * *vt* to put into or furnish with a berth; to moor a ship. * *vi* to occupy a berth.

beseech *vt* (*pt* **besought**) to implore, to entreat; to beg earnestly for.

beset *vt* (*pr p* **besetting,** *pt* **beset**) to surround or hem in; to attack from all sides; to harass.

beside *prep* at, by the side of, next to; in comparison with; in addition to; aside from.

besides *prep* other than; in addition; over and above. * *adv* in addition; except for that mentioned; moreover.

besiege *vt* to hem in with armed forces; to close in on; to overwhelm, harass.

besought *see* **beseech**.

best *adj* (*superl of* **good**) most excellent; most suitable, desirable, etc; largest; above all others. * *n* one's utmost effort; the highest state of excellence. * *adv* (*superl of* **well**) in or to the highest degree. * *vt* to defeat, outdo.

best man *n* the principal attendant of the bridegroom at a wedding.

bestow *vt* to present as a gift.—**bestowal** *n*.

best seller *n* a book or other commodity that sells in vast numbers; the author of such a book.—**best-selling** *adj*.

bet *n* a wager or stake; the thing or sum staked; a person or thing likely to bring about a desired result. * *vti* (*pt* **bet** *or* **betted**) to declare as in a bet; to stake (money, etc) in a bet (with someone).

betray *vt* to aid an enemy; to expose treacherously; to be a traitor to; to reveal unknowingly.—**betrayal** *n*.—**betrayer** *n*.

better[1] *adj* (*compar of* **good**) more excellent; more suitable; improved in health; larger. * *adv* (*compar of* **well**) in a more excellent manner; in a higher degree; more. * *n* a person superior in position, etc; a more excellent thing, condition, etc. * *vt* to outdo; to surpass.

better[2] *n* someone who bets.

between *prep* the space, time, etc separating (two things); (*bond, etc*) connecting from one or the other.

beverage *n* a drink, esp one other than water.

beware *vti* to be wary or careful (of).

bewilder *vt* to perplex; to confuse hopelessly.—**bewilderment** *n*.

bewitching *adj* fascinating, enchanting.

beyond *prep* further on than; past; later than; outside the reach of (*beyond help*). * *adv* further away.

bias *n* a slanting or diagonal line, cut or sewn across the grain in cloth; partiality; prejudice. * *vt* (*pt* **biased** *or* **biassed**) to prejudice.

bib *n* a cloth or plastic cover tied around a baby or child to prevent food spillage on clothes; the upper part of dungarees or an apron.

Bible *n* the sacred book of the Christian Church; the Old and New Testaments.

bicker *vi* to squabble, quarrel.—*also n*.

bicycle *n* a vehicle consisting of a metal frame on two wheels, driven by pedals and having handlebars and a seat. * *vti* to ride or travel on a bicycle.—**bicyclist** *n*.

bid[1] *n* an offer of an amount one will pay or accept; (*cards*) a statement of the number of tricks that a player intends to win. * *vi* (*pr p* **bidding,** *pt* **bid**) to make a bid.—**bidder** *n*.

bid[2] *vt* (*pr p* **bidding,** *pt* **bade** *or* **bid**, *pp* **bidden** *or* **bid**) to command or ask; (*farewell, etc*) to express.

bide *vi* to wait; to dwell.

bier *n* a portable framework on which a coffin is put.

big *adj* (**bigger, biggest**) large; of great size; important; grown-up; boastful.—**bigness** *n*.

bigamy *n* the act of marrying a second time when one is already legally married.—**bigamous** *adj*.—**bigamously** *adv*.

bigot *n* an intolerant person who blindly supports a particular political view or religion.—**bigoted** *adj*.—**bigotry** *n*.

bike *n* (*inf*) a bicycle; a motorcycle.

bikini *n* (*pl* **bikinis**) a scanty two-piece swimsuit for women.

bile *n* a thick bitter fluid secreted by the liver; bad temper.—**bilious** *adj*.—**biliousness** *n*.

bilingual *adj* written in two languages; able to speak two languages.

bill[1] *n* a bird's beak.

bill[2] *n* a statement for goods supplied or services rendered; a list, as a menu or theatre programme; a poster or handbill; a draft of a proposed law, to be discussed by a legislature; a bill of exchange; a piece of paper money; (*law*) a written declaration of charges and complaints filed. * *vt* to make out a bill of (items); to present a statement of charges to; to advertise by bills; (*performer*) to book.

billet *n* a written order to provide lodging for military personnel; the lodging; a position or job. * *vt* (*pt* **billeted**) to assign to lodging by billet.

billiards *n* a game in which hard balls are driven by a cue on a felt-covered table with raised, cushioned edges.

billion *n* a thousand millions, the numeral 1 followed by 9 zeros; (UK) a million million.—**billionaire** *n*.

bin *n* a box or enclosed space for storing grain, coal, etc; a dustbin.

bind *vb* (*pt* **bound**) *vt* to tie together, as with rope; to hold or restrain; to encircle with a belt, etc; (*often with* **up**) to bandage; to fasten together the pages of (a book) and protect with a cover; to obligate by duty, love, etc; to compel, as by oath or legal restraint. * *vi* to become tight or stiff; to stick together; to be obligatory. * *n* anything that binds; (*inf*) a difficult situation.

binding *n* the covering of a book holding the pages together.

bingo *n* a game of chance in which players cover numbers on their cards according to the number called aloud.

binoculars *npl* a viewing device for use with both eyes, consisting of two small telescope lenses joined together.

biochemistry *n* the chemistry of living organisms.—**biochemical** *adj*.—**biochemist** *n*.

biography *n* an account of a person's life written by another; biographical writings in general.—**biographer** *n*.—**biographical** *adj*.

biology *n* the study of living organisms.—**biological** *adj*.—**biologically** *adv*.—**biologist** *n*.

birch *n* a tree with a smooth white bark and hard wood; a bundle of birch twigs used for thrashing. * *vt* to flog.

bird *n* any class of warm-blooded, egg-laying vertebrates with a feathered body, scaly legs, and forelimbs modified to form wings; (*sl*) a woman.

birth *n* the act of being born; childbirth; the origin of something; ancestry.

birth control *n* the use of contraceptive drugs or devices to limit reproduction.

birthday *n* the day of birth; the anniversary of the day of birth.

birth rate *n* the number of births per thousand of population per year.

biscuit *n* a small, flat, dry, sweet or plain cake baked from dough. * *adj* pale brown in colour.

bishop *n* a high-ranking clergyman governing a diocese or church district; a chessman that can move in a diagonal direction.

bit[1] *n* a small amount or piece; a small part in a play, film, etc.

bit[2] *n* a metal mouthpiece in a bridle used for controlling a horse; a cutting or boring attachment for use in a brace, drill, etc.

bit[3] *n* (*comput*) a unit of information equivalent to either of two digits, 0 or 1.

bitch *n* a female dog or wolf; (*sl*) a spiteful woman; (*inf*) an unpleasant or difficult situation. * *vi* (*inf*) to grumble.

bite *vti* (*pt* **bit**, *pp* **bitten**) to grip or tear with the teeth; to sting or puncture, as an insect; to cause to smart; to take the bait. * *vi* to press or snap the teeth (into, at, etc). * *n* the act of biting with the teeth; a sting or puncture by an insect.

biting *adj* severe; critical, sarcastic.

bitter *adj* having an acrid or sharp taste; sorrowful; harsh; resentful; cynical.—**bitterly**

adj.—**bitterness** *n*.

bivouac *n* a temporary camp, esp one without tents. * *vi* (*pt* **bivouacked**) to spend the night in a bivouac.

bizarre *adj* odd, unusual.

blab *vti* (*pt* **blabbed**) to reveal (a secret); to gossip. * *n* a gossip.—**blabber** *n*.

black *adj* of the darkest colour, like coal or soot; having dark-coloured skin and hair, esp Negro; without light; dirty; evil, wicked; sad, dismal; sullen. * *n* black colour; (*often with cap*) a Negro, Australian Aborigine; black clothes, esp as mourning; (*chess, draughts*) black pieces. * *vt* to make black; to blacken; (*shoes*) to polish; to boycott; (*with* **out**) (*lights*) to extinguish, obliterate; (*broadcast*) to prevent transmission. * *vi* (*with* **out**) to lose consciousness or vision.—**blackness** *n*.

blackberry *n* a woody bush with thorny stems and berry-like fruit; its black or purple edible fruit. * *vt* to gather blackberries.

blackboard *n* a black or dark green board written on with chalk.

blacken *vt* to make black; to defame.

black eye *n* (*inf*) bruising around the eye caused by a blow.

blackjack *see* **pontoon**[2].

blacklist *n* a list of those censored, refused employment, etc.—*also vt*.

blackmail *vt* to extort money by threatening to disclose discreditable facts. * *n* the crime of blackmailing.—**blackmailer** *n*.

black market *n* the illegal buying and selling of goods.—**black marketeer** *n*.

blackout *n* the darkness when all lights are switched off; temporary loss of consciousness or electricity.

black sheep *n* a person regarded as disreputable or a disgrace by their family.

blacksmith *n* a metal worker, esp one who shoes horses.

bladder *n* a sac that fills with fluid, esp one that holds urine flowing from the kidneys; any inflatable bag.

blade *n* the cutting edge of a tool or knife; the broad, flat surface of a leaf; a straight, narrow leaf of grass; the flat part of an oar or paddle; the runner of an ice skate.—**bladed** *adj*.

blame *vt* to hold responsible for; to accuse. * *n* responsibility for an error; reproof.—**blamable, blameable** *adj*.

blameless *adj* innocent; free from blame.—**blamelessly** *adv*.—**blamelessness** *n*.

bland *adj* mild; gentle; insipid.—**blandly** *adv*.—**blandness** *n*.

blank *adj* (*paper*) bearing no writing or marks; vacant; (*mind*) empty of thought; (*denial, refusal*) utter, complete; (*cheque*) signed but with no amount written in. * *n* an empty space, esp one to be filled out on a printed form; an empty place or time; a powder-filled cartridge without a bullet.—**blankly** *adv*.—**blankness** *n*.

blanket *n* a large, soft piece of cloth used for warmth, esp as a bed cover; (*of snow, smoke*) a cover or layer. * *adj* applying to a wide variety of cases. * *vt* (*pt* **blanketed**) to cover.

blare *vti* to sound harshly or loudly. * *n* a loud, harsh sound.

blasphemy *n* speaking irreverently of God, a divine being or sacred things.

blast *n* a sharp gust of air; the sound of a horn; an explosion; an outburst of criticism. * *vt* to wither; to blow up, explode; to criticize sharply. * *vi* to make a loud, harsh sound; to set off explosives; (*with* **off**) to be launched.

blastoff *n* the launch of a space vehicle or rocket.

blatant *adj* noisy; glaringly conspicuous.—**blatantly** *adv*.

blaze *n* an intensive fire; a bright light; splendour; an outburst (of emotion). * *vi* to burn brightly; to shine with a brilliant light; to be excited, as with anger.

blazer *n* a lightweight jacket, often in a bright colour representing membership of a sports club, school, etc.

bleach *vti* to make or become white or colourless. * *n* a substance for bleaching.

bleak *adj* cold; exposed; bare; harsh; gloomy; not hopeful.—**bleakly** *adv*.—**bleakness** *n*.

bleat *vi* to cry as a sheep, goat or calf. * *n* a bleating cry or sound.

bleed *vb* (*pt* **bled**) *vi* to lose blood; to ooze sap, colour or dye. * *vt* to remove blood or sap from; (*inf*) to extort money or goods from.

bleep *vi* to emit a high-pitched sound or signal (eg a car alarm). * *n* a small portable electronic radio receiver that emits a bleep to convey a message (—*also* **bleeper**).

blemish *n* a flaw or defect, as a spot. * *vt* to mar; to spoil.

blend *vt* (*varieties of tea, etc*) to mix or mingle; to mix so that the components cannot be distinguished. * *vi* to mix, merge; to shade gradually into each other, as colours; to harmonize. * *n* a mixture.

bless *vt* (*pt* **blessed** *or* **blest**) to consecrate; to praise; to call upon God's protection; to grant happiness; to make the sign of the cross over.

blessed *adj* holy, sacred; fortunate; blissful.—**blessedly** *adv*.—**blessedness** *n*.
blessing *n* a prayer or wish for success or happiness; a cause of happiness; good wishes or approval; a grace said before or after eating.
blew *see* **blow**².
blight *n* any insect, disease, etc that destroys plants; anything that prevents growth or destroys. * *vt* to destroy; to frustrate.
blind *adj* sightless; unable to discern or understand; not directed by reason; (*exit*) hidden, concealed; closed at one end. * *n* something that deceives; a shade for a window. * *vti* to make sightless, to deprive of insight; to dazzle (with facts, a bright light, etc); to deceive.—**blindly** *adv*.—**blindness** *n*.
blindfold *adj* having the eyes covered, so as not to see. * *n* a cloth or bandage used to cover the eyes.—*also vt*.
blind spot *n* a point on the retina of the eye that is insensitive to light; a place where vision is obscured; a subject on which one is ignorant.
blink *vi* to open and close the eyes rapidly; (*light*) to flash on and off; (*with* **at**) to ignore. * *vt* (*with* **at**) to be amazed or surprised. * *n* a glance, a glimpse; a momentary flash.
bliss *n* supreme happiness; spiritual joy.—**blissful** *adj*.—**blissfully** *adv*.
blister *n* a raised patch on the skin, containing water, as caused by burning or rubbing; a raised bubble on any other surface. * *vti* to cause or form blisters; to lash with words.
blithe *adj* happy, cheerful, gay.—**blithely** *adv*.
blitz *n* any sudden destructive attack. * *vt* to subject to a blitz.
blizzard *n* a severe storm of wind and snow.
bloat *vti* to swell as with water or air; to puff up, as with pride.—**bloated** *adj*.
blob *n* a drop of liquid; a round spot (of colour, etc).
block *n* a solid piece of stone or wood, etc; a piece of wood used as a base (for chopping, etc); a group or row of buildings; a number of things as a unit; the main body of a petrol engine; a building divided into offices; an obstruction. * *vt* to impede or obstruct; to shape; (*often with* **out**) to sketch roughly. * *vi* to obstruct an opponent in sports.
blockade *n* (*mil*) the obstruction of an enemy seaport by warships; any strategic barrier.—*also vt*.
blockage *n* an obstruction.
block letter *n* a handwritten capital letter similar to a printed letter.
bloke *n* (*inf*) a man.
blond, blonde *adj* having light-coloured hair and skin; light-coloured. * *n* a blonde person.
blood *n* the red fluid that circulates in the arteries and veins of animals; the sap of a plant; the essence of life; kinship; descent; hatred; bloodshed.
blood donor *n* a person who donates blood for transfusion.
blood group *n* any of the classes of human blood.
bloodshed *n* killing.
bloodshot *adj* (*eye*) suffused with blood, red and inflamed.
bloodstream *n* the flow of blood through the blood vessels in the human body.
bloodthirsty *adj* eager for blood, warlike.—**bloodthirstiness** *n*.
bloody *adj* (**bloodier, bloodiest**) stained with or covered in blood; bloodthirsty; cruel, murderous; (*sl*) as an intensifier (*a bloody good hiding*). * *vt* to cover with blood.
bloody-minded *adj* (*inf*) deliberately obstructive.—**bloody-mindedness** *n*.
bloom *n* a flower or blossom; the period of being in flower; a period of most health, vigour, etc; a youthful, healthy glow; the powdery coating on some fruit and leaves. * *vi* to blossom; to be in one's prime; to glow with health etc.
blossom *n* a flower, esp one that produces edible fruit; a state or time of flowering. * *vi* to flower; to begin to develop.
blot *n* a spot or stain, esp of ink; a blemish in reputation. * *vt* (*pt* **blotted**) to spot or stain; to obscure; to disgrace; to absorb with blotting paper.
blotch *n* a spot or discoloration on the skin; any large blot or stain. * *vt* to cover with blotches.—**blotched** *adj*.—**blotchy** *adj*.
blotting paper *n* absorbent paper used to dry freshly written ink.
blouse *n* a shirt-like garment worn by women.
blow¹ *n* a hard hit, as with the fist; a sudden attack; a sudden misfortune; a setback.
blow² *vb* (*pt* **blew**, *pp* **blown**) *vi* to cause a current of air; to be moved or carried (by air, the wind, etc); (*mus*) to make a sound by forcing in air with the mouth; (*often with* **out**) to burst suddenly; to breathe hard; (*with* **out**) to become extinguished by a gust of air; (*gas or oil well*) to erupt out of control. * *vt* to move along with a current of air; to make a sound by blowing; to inflate with air; (*a fuse, etc*) to melt; (*inf*) to spend (money) freely;

(*sl*) to bungle; (*with* **out**) to extinguish by a gust; (*storm*) to dissipate (itself) by blowing; (*with* **over**) to pass over or pass by; (*with* **up**) to burst by an explosion; to enlarge a photograph; (*inf*) to lose one's temper.

blowlamp, blowtorch *n* a gas-powered torch that produces a hot flame for welding, etc.

blowout *n* (*inf*) a festive social event; a bursting of (a tyre) by pressure on a weak spot; an uncontrolled eruption of a gas or oil well.

blubber[1] *n* whale fat; excessive fat on the body.

blubber[2] *vi* to weep loudly.

bludgeon *n* a short, heavy stick used for striking. * *vti* to strike with a bludgeon; to bully or coerce.

blue *adj* (**bluer, bluest**) of the colour of the clear sky; depressed; (*film*) indecent, obscene. * *n* the colour of the spectrum lying between green and violet; (*with* **the**) the sky, the sea; (*pl: with* **the**) (*inf*) a depressed feeling; a style of vocal and instrumental jazz.

bluebottle *n* a large fly.

blueprint *n* a blue photographic print of plans; a detailed scheme, template of work to be done.

bluff[1] *adj* rough in manner; abrupt, outspoken; ascending steeply with a flat front. * *n* a broad, steep bank or cliff.—**bluffness** *n*.

bluff[2] *vti* to mislead or frighten by a false, bold front.* *n* deliberate deception.—**bluffer** *n*.

blunder *vi* to make a foolish mistake; to move about clumsily. * *n* a foolish mistake.—**blunderer** *n*.

blunt *adj* not having a sharp edge or point; rude, outspoken. * *vti* to make or become dull.—**bluntly** *adv*.—**bluntness** *n*.

blur *n* a stain, smear; an ill-defined impression. * *vti* (*pt* **blurred**) to smear; to make or become indistinct in shape, etc; to dim.

blurt *vt* (*with* **out**) to utter impulsively.

blush *n* a red flush of the face caused by embarrassment; any rosy colour. * *vi* (*with* **for**, **at**) to show embarrassment, modesty, joy, etc, involuntarily by blushing; to become rosy.

bluster *vi* to make a noise like the wind; to bully. * *n* a blast, as of the wind; bullying or boastful talk.—**blusterer** *n*.—**blustery** *adj*.—**blusteringly, blusterously** *adv*.

boar *n* a male pig, a wild hog.

board *n* meals, esp when provided regularly for pay; a long, flat piece of sawed wood, etc; a flat piece of wood, etc for some special purpose; a council; a group of people who supervise a company; the side of a ship. * *vt* to provide with meals and lodging at fixed terms; to come onto the deck of (a ship); to get on (a train, bus, etc). * *vi* to provide room and/or meals, regularly for pay; (*with* **up**) to cover with boards.

boarding house *n* a house where board is provided.

boardroom *n* a room where meetings of a company's board are held.

boast *vi* to brag. * *vt* to speak proudly of; to possess with pride. * *n* boastful talk.—**boaster** *n*.—**boastful** *adj*.—**boastfully** *adv*.

boat *n* a small, open, waterborne craft; a ship. * *vi* to travel in a boat, esp for pleasure.

boater *n* a stiff flat straw hat.

boating *n* rowing, sailing, etc.

bob *vb* (*pt* **bobbed**) *vi* to move abruptly up and down; to curtsey. * *vt* (*hair*) to cut short. * *n* a jerking motion up and down; the weight on a pendulum, plumb line, etc; a woman's or girl's short haircut.

bobbin *n* a reel or spool on which yarn or thread is wound.

bobby clip *n* a grip for holding hair in position.

bobsleigh, bobsled (*US*) *n* a long racing sledge. * *vi* to ride or race on a bobsleigh.

bodice *n* the upper part of a dress.

bodily *adj* physical; relating to the body. * *adv* in the flesh; as a whole; altogether.

body *n* the whole physical substance of a person, animal, or plant; the trunk of a person or animal; a corpse; the principal part of anything; a distinct mass; substance or consistency, as of liquid; a richness of flavour; a person; a distinct group. * *vt* to give shape to.

bodyguard *n* a person or persons assigned to guard someone.

bog *n* wet, spongy ground; quagmire.—**boggy** *adj*.

boggle *vi* to be surprised; to hesitate (at). * *vt* to confuse (the imagination, mind, etc).

bogus *adj* counterfeit, spurious.

boil[1] *vi* to change rapidly from a liquid to a vapour by heating; to bubble when boiling; to cook in boiling liquid; to be aroused with anger; (*with* **down**) to reduce by boiling; to condense; (*with* **over**) to overflow when boiling; to burst out in anger. * *vt* to heat to boiling point; to cook in boiling water.

boil[2] *n* an inflamed, pus-filled, painful swelling on the skin.

boiler *n* a container in which to boil things; a tank in which water is heated and steam generated; a device for providing central heating and hot water.

boisterous *adj* wild, noisy; stormy; loud and exuberant.—**boisterously** *adv*.

bold *adj* daring or courageous; fearless; impudent; striking to the eye.—**boldly** *adv*.—**boldness** *n*.

bollard *n* a strong post on a wharf around which mooring lines are secured; one of a line of posts closing off a street to traffic; an illuminated marker on a traffic island.

bolster *n* a long narrow pillow; any bolster-like object or support. * *vt* (*often with* **up**) to support or strengthen.

bolt *n* a bar used to lock a door, etc; a type of arrow; a flash of lightning; a threaded metal rod used with a nut to hold parts together; a roll (of cloth, paper, etc); a sudden dash. * *vt* to lock with a bolt; to eat hastily; to say suddenly; to blurt (out); to abandon (a party, group, etc). * *vi* (*horse*) to rush away suddenly * *adv* erectly upright.

bomb *n* a projectile containing explosives, incendiary material, or chemicals used for destruction; (*sl*) a lot of money. * *vt* to attack with bombs.

bombard *vt* to attack with bombs or artillery; to attack verbally.—**bombardment** *n*.

bombast *n* pretentious or boastful language.—**bombastic** *adj*.

bomber *n* a person who bombs; an aeroplane that carries bombs.

bombshell *n* a shocking surprise.

bona fide *adj* in good faith; genuine or real.

bond *n* anything that binds, fastens, or unites; (*pl*) shackles; an obligation imposed by a contract, promise, etc; the status of goods in a warehouse until taxes are paid; an interest-bearing certificate issued by the government or business, redeemable on a specified date; surety against theft, absconding, etc. * *vt* to join, bind, or otherwise unite; to provide a bond for; to place or hold (goods) in bond. * *vi* to hold together by means of a bond.

bone *n* the hard material making up the skeleton; any constituent part of the skeleton. * *vti* to remove the bones from, as meat; (*with* **up**) (*inf*) to study hard.—**boneless** *adj*.

bonnet *n* a hat with a chin ribbon, a cap.

bonus *n* an amount paid over the sum due as interest, dividend, or wages.

bony *adj* (**bonier, boniest**) of or resembling bones; having large or prominent bones; full of bones.

booby trap *n* a trap for playing a practical joke on someone; a camouflaged explosive device triggered by an unsuspecting victim.

book *n* a bound set of printed or blank pages; a literary composition of fact or fiction; (*pl*) written records of accounts. * *vt* to make a reservation in advance; to note a person's name and address for an alleged offence. * *vi* to make a reservation.

bookcase *n* a piece of furniture with shelves for books.

book-keeping *n* the systematic recording of business accounts.—**book-keeper** *n*.

booklet *n* a small book, usu with a paper cover; a pamphlet.

bookmaker *n* a person who takes bets on horse races, etc, and pays out winnings.

boom[1] *n* a spar on which a sail is stretched; a barrier across a harbour; a long pole carrying a microphone.

boom[2] *vi* to make a deep, hollow sound. * *n* a resonant sound, as of the sea.

boom[3] *vi* to flourish or prosper suddenly. * *n* a period of vigorous growth (eg in business, sales, prices).

boomerang *n* a curved stick that, when thrown, returns to the thrower; an action that unexpectedly rebounds and harms the agent.—*also vi*.

boon *n* something useful or helpful.

boost *vt* (*sales etc*) to increase; to encourage, to improve; to push. * *n* a push.

boot *n* a strong covering for the foot and lower part of the leg; (*sl*: *with* **the**) dismissal from employment; the rear compartment of a car used for holding luggage, etc. * *vt* to kick; (*comput*) to bring a program from a disc into the memory.

booth *n* a stall for selling goods; a small enclosure for voting; a public telephone enclosure.

booty *n* spoils obtained as plunder.

booze *vi* (*inf*) to drink alcohol excessively. * *n* alcohol.—**boozy** *adj*.

border *n* the edge, rim, or margin; a dividing line between two countries; a narrow strip along an edge. * *vi* (*with* **on, upon**) to be adjacent. * *vt* to form a border.

borderline *n* a boundary. * *adj* on a boundary; doubtful, indefinite.

bore[1] to drill so as to form a hole; to weary, by being dull or uninteresting. * *n* a hole made by drilling; the diameter of a gun barrel; a dull or uninteresting person.

bore[2] *see* **bear**[1].

boring *adj* dull, tedious; making holes.

born *adj* by birth, natural.

borne *see* **bear**[1].

borough *n* a self-governing, incorporated town;

an administrative area of a city, as in London or New York.

borrow *vt* to obtain (an item) with the intention of returning it; (*an idea*) to adopt as one's own; (*loan, money*) to obtain from a financial institution at definite rates of interest.—**borrower** *n*.

bosom *n* the breast of a human being, esp a woman; the part of a dress that covers it; the seat of the emotions. * *adj* (*friend*) very dear, intimate.

boss *n* (*inf*) the manager or foreman; a powerful local politician. * *vt* to domineer.

botany *n* the scientific study of plants.—**botanical** *adj*.—**botanist** *n*.

botch *n* a poorly done piece of work. * *vt* to mend or patch clumsily; to put together without sufficient care.

both *adj, pron* the two together; the one and the other. * *conj* together equally.—*also adv*.

bother *vt* to perplex or annoy; to take time or trouble. * *n* worry; trouble; someone who causes problems, etc.

bottle *n* a glass or plastic container for holding liquids; its contents; (*sl*) courage, nerve. * *vt* to put in bottles; to confine as if in a bottle.

bottleneck *n* a narrow stretch of a road where traffic is held up; a congestion in any stage of a process.

bottom *n* the lowest or deepest part of anything; the base or foundation; the lowest position (eg in a class); the buttocks; (*naut*) the part of a ship's hull below water; the seabed. * *vt* to be based or founded on; to bring to the bottom, to get to the bottom of. * *vi* to become based; to reach the bottom; (*with* **out**) to flatten off after dropping sharply.

bottomless *adj* very deep.

bough *n* a branch of a tree.

bought *see* **buy**.

boulder *n* a large stone or mass of rock rounded by the action of erosion.

bounce *vi* to rebound; to jump up suddenly; (*sl: cheque*) to be returned. * *vt* to cause a ball to bounce; (*sl*) to put (a person) out by force; (*sl*) to fire from a job. * *n* a leap or springiness; capacity for bouncing.

bouncer *n* (*sl*) a man hired to remove people from nightclubs, etc.

bound[1] *see* **bind**.

bound[2] *n* (*usu pl*) the limit or boundary. * *vt* to limit, confine or surround; to name the boundaries of.

bound[3] *n* a jump or leap. * *vi* to jump or leap.

bound[4] *adj* intending to go to, on the way to.

boundary *n* the border of an area; the limit.

boundless *adj* unlimited, vast.

bout *n* a spell, a turn, a period spent in some activity; a contest or struggle.

bovine *adj* relating to cattle; dull, sluggish. * *n* an ox, cow, etc.

bow[1] *vi* to lean the head (and chest) forward as a form of greeting or respect; to submit. * *vt* to bend downwards; to weigh down; to usher in or out with a bow. * *n* a lowering of the head (and chest) in greeting.

bow[2] *n* a weapon for shooting arrows; an implement for playing the strings of a violin; a decorative knot of ribbon, etc. * *vti* to bend, curve.

bow[3] *n* the forward part of a ship.

bowel *n* the intestine; (*pl*) the deep and remote part of anything.

bowl[1] *n* a wooden ball having a bias used in bowling; (*pl*) a game played on a smooth lawn with bowls. * *vti* to play the game of bowls; to send a ball to a batsman; (*cricket*) to dismiss by hitting the wicket with a bowled ball; (*with* **over**) to knock over; (*inf*) to astonish.

bowl[2] *n* a deep, rounded dish; the rounded end of a pipe; a sports stadium.

bowler[1] *n* a person who plays bowls or cricket.

bowler[2] *n* a stiff felt hat.

bowling *n* a game in which a heavy wooden ball is bowled along a bowling alley at ten wooden skittles; the game of bowls.

bowling alley *n* a long narrow wooden lane, usu one of several in a building designed for them.

bowling green *n* a smooth lawn for bowls.

bow tie *n* a tie tied in the shape of a bow.

box[1] *n* a container or receptacle for holding anything; (*theatre*) a compartment with seats; (*inf*) a television set. * *vt* to put into a box; to enclose.

box[2] *vt* to hit using the hands or fists. * *vi* to fight with the fists. * *n* a blow on the head or ear with the fist.

boxer *n* a person who engages in boxing; a breed of dog with smooth hair and a stumpy tail.

boxing *n* the skill or sport of fighting with the fists.

box office *n* a theatre ticket office; the popularity of a play, film, etc.—*also adj*.

boy *n* a male child; a son; a lad; a youth. * *interj* an exclamation of surprise or joy.—**boyish** *adj*.

boycott *vt* to refuse to deal with or trade with

in order to punish or coerce.—*also n.*

boyfriend *n* a male friend with whom a person is romantically or sexually involved.

bra *n* a woman's undergarment for protecting and supporting the breasts, a brassiere.

brace *n* a prop; a support to stiffen a framework; a hand tool for drilling; (*pl* **brace**) a pair, esp of game; (*pl*) straps for holding up trousers; a dental appliance for straightening the teeth. * *vt* to steady.

bracelet *n* an ornamental chain or band for the wrist.

bracing *adj* refreshing, invigorating.

bracken *n* a large, coarse fern.

bracket *n* a projecting metal support for a shelf; a group or category of people classified according to income; (*pl*) a pair of characters ( ), [ ], { }, used in printing or writing as parentheses. * *vt* (*pt* **bracketed**) to support with brackets; to enclose by brackets; (*people*) to group together.

brag *vti* (*pt* **bragged**) to boast. * *n* a boast or boastful talk.

braid *vt* to weave three or more strands (of hair, straw, etc) together; to make in this way. * *n* a narrow band made for decorating clothing; a plait.

brain *n* nervous tissue contained in the skull of vertebrates that controls the nervous system; intellectual ability; (*inf*) a person of great intelligence; (often *pl*) the chief planner of an organization or enterprise. * *vt* to shatter the skull of; (*sl*) to hit on the head.

brainwash *vt* to change a person's ideas or beliefs by physical or mental conditioning, usu over a long period.—**brainwashing** *n.*

brain wave *n* an electrical impulse in the brain; (*inf*) a bright idea.

braise *vt* (*meat, vegetables, etc*) to fry lightly and cook slowly in liquid in a covered pan.

brake *n* a device for slowing or stopping the motion of a wheel by friction. * *vt* to retard or stop by a brake. * *vi* to apply the brake on a vehicle; to become checked by a brake.

bramble *n* a prickly shrub or vine, esp of raspberries and blackberries.

bran *n* the husks of cereal grain separated from the flour by sieving.

branch *n* an offshoot extending from the trunk or bough of a tree or from the parent stem of a shrub; a separately located subsidiary or office of an enterprise or business; a part of something larger. * *vi* to possess branches; to divide into branches; to come out (from a main part) as a branch; (*with* **out**) to extend one's interests, activities, etc.

brand *n* an identifying mark on cattle, imprinted with hot iron; a burning piece of wood; a mark of disgrace; a trademark; a particular make (of goods). * *vt* to burn a mark with a hot iron; to denounce.

brandish (*a weapon, etc*) *vt* to wave or flourish in a threatening manner.

brand-new *adj* entirely new and unused.

brandy *n* an alcoholic liquor made from distilled wine or fermented fruit juice.

brash *adj* bold; reckless.—**brashly** *adv.*—**brashness** *n.*

brass *n* an alloy of copper and zinc; (*inf*) showy; impudent; nerve; cheek; (often *pl*) the brass instruments of an orchestra or band; (*sl*) officers or officials of high rank.

brass band *n* a band that uses brass and percussion instruments.

brasserie *n* a bar and restaurant.

brassiere *n* a bra.

brat *n* an ill-mannered, annoying child.

bravado *n* pretended confidence; swaggering.

brave *adj* showing courage; not timid or cowardly; fearless. * *vt* to confront boldly; to defy. * *n* a North American Indian warrior.—**bravely** *adv.*—**bravery** *n.*

brawl *vi* to quarrel loudly.—*also n.*

brawn *n* strong, well-developed muscles; physical strength.

brawny *adj* (**brawnier, brawniest**) muscular.

bray *n* the sound of a donkey; any harsh sound. * *vi* to make similar sounds.

brazen *adj* made of brass; shameless. * *vt* to face a situation boldly and shamelessly.

brazier *n* a metal container for hot coals.

breach *n* a break or rupture; violation of a contract, promise etc; a break in friendship. * *vt* to make an opening in.

bread *n* a dough, made from flour, yeast and milk, that is baked; nourishment; (*sl*) money.

breadth *n* measurement from side to side, width; liberality (eg of interests).

breadwinner *n* the principal wage-earner of a family.

break *vb* (*pt* **broke**, *pp* **broken**) *vt* to smash or shatter; to tame; (*rules*) to violate; to discontinue; to cause to give up a habit; to ruin financially; (*news*) to impart; to decipher or solve; (*with* **down**) to crush or destroy; to analyse; (*with* **in**) to intervene; to train. * *vi* to fall apart; (*voice*) to assume a lower tone at puberty; to cut off relations with; to suffer a collapse, as of spirit; (*news*) to become public in a sudden and sensational way; (*with*

down) to fail completely; to succumb emotionally; (*with* **even**) to suffer neither profit nor loss (after taking certain action); (*with* **in**) to force a way in; (*with* **out**) to appear, begin; to erupt; to throw off restraint, escape; (*with* **up**) to disperse; to separate; to collapse. * *n* a breaking; an interruption; a gap; a sudden change, as in weather; an escape; (*snooker, billiards*) a continuous run of points; (*sl*) a fortunate opportunity.

breakable *adj* able to be broken. * *n* a fragile object.

breakage *n* the action of breaking; something broken.

breakdown *n* a mechanical failure; failure of health; nervous collapse; an analysis.

breakfast *n* the first meal of the morning; the food consumed. * *vi* to have breakfast.

break-out *n* an escape, esp from prison.

breakthrough *n* the action of breaking through an obstruction; an important advance or discovery.

breakwater *n* a barrier that protects a harbour or area of coast against the force of the waves.

breast *n* the chest; one of the two mammary glands; the seat of the emotions. * *vt* to oppose, confront.

breaststroke *n* a swimming stroke in which both arms are brought out sideways from the chest.

breath *n* the inhalation and exhalation of air in breathing; the air taken into the lungs; life; a slight breeze.

Breathalyser, Breathalyzer *n* (*trademark*) a device for measuring the amount of alcohol in a person's breath.—**breathalyze, breathalyse** *vt*.

breathe *vi* to inhale and exhale, to respire air; to take a rest or pause; to exist or live; to speak or sing softly; to whisper. * *vt* to emit or exhale; to whisper or speak softly.

breather *n* a pause during exercise to recover one's breath.

breathless *adj* out of breath; panting; gasping; unable to breathe easily because of emotion.—**breathlessness** *n*.

breathtaking *adj* very exciting.

breed *vb* (*pt* **bred**) *vt* to engender; to bring forth; (*dogs*) to raise; to give rise to. * *vi* to produce young; to be generated. * *n* offspring; origin or race; species (of animal).—**breeder** *n*.

breeze *n* a light gentle wind. * *vi* (*inf*) to move quickly or casually.

breezy *adj* (**breezier, breeziest**) windy; nonchalant; light-hearted.

brevity *n* briefness; conciseness.

brew *vt* to make (beer, ale, etc) from malt and hops by boiling and fermenting; to infuse (tea, etc); to plot, scheme. * *vi* to be in the process of being brewed. * *n* a brewed drink.

brewer *n* a person who brews, usu beer.

brewery *n* a place where beer, etc is brewed.

bribe *n* money or gifts offered illegally to gain favour or influence; the gift to do this. * *vt* to offer or give a bribe to.

bribery *n* the process of giving or taking bribes.

brick *n* a baked clay block for building; a similar shaped block of other ma-terial. * *vt* to lay or wall up with brick.

bricklayer *n* a person who lays bricks.

bridal *adj* relating to a bride or a wedding.

bride *n* a woman about to be married or recently married.

bridegroom *n* a man about to be married or recently married.

bridesmaid *n* a young girl or woman attending the bride during a wedding.

bridge[1] *n* a structure built to convey people or traffic over a river, road, railway line, etc; the platform on a ship where the captain gives directions; the hard ridge of bone in the nose; an arch to raise the strings of a guitar, etc; a mounting for false teeth.—*also vt*.

bridge[2] *n* a card game based on whist.

bridle *n* the headgear of a horse; a restraint or check. * *vt* to put a bridle on (a horse); to restrain or check. * *vi* to draw one's head back as an expression of anger, scorn, etc.

bridle path *n* a trail suitable for horse riding.

brief *n* a summary of a client's case for the instruction of a barrister in a trial at law; an outline of an argument, esp that setting out the main contentions; (*pl*) snug, legless underpants. * *vt* to provide with a precise summary of the facts. * *adj* short, concise.—**briefly** *adv*.—**briefness** *n*.

briefcase *n* a flat case for carrying documents, etc.

brigade *n* an army unit, smaller than a division; a group of people organized to perform a particular function.

bright *adj* clear, shining; brilliant in colour or sound; favourable or hopeful; intelligent, illustrious. * *adv* brightly.—**brightly** *adv*.—**brightness** *n*.

brighten *vti* to make or become brighter.

brilliant *adj* sparkling, bright; splendid; very intelligent.—**brilliantly** *adv*.—**brilliance** *n*.

brim *n* the rim of a hollow vessel; the outer

edge of a hat. * *vti* (*pt* **brimmed**) to fill or be filled to the brim; (*with* **over**) to overflow.

brine *n* salt water.

bring *vt* (*pt* **brought**) to fetch, carry or convey "here" or to the place where the speaker will be; (*rain, relief, etc*) to cause to happen, to result in; to lead to an action or belief; to sell for; (*with* **about**) to induce, to effect; (*with* **down**) to cause to fall by or as if by shooting; (*with* **round, around**) to restore to consciousness; (*with* **up**) to educate, rear; to raise (a matter) for discussion; to vomit.—**bringer** *n*.

brink *n* the verge of a steep place; the point of onset; the threshold of danger.

brisk *adj* alert; vigorous; sharp in tone.—**briskly** *adv*.—**briskness** *n*.

bristle *n* a short, coarse hair. * *vi* to stand up, as bristles; to have the bristles standing up; to show anger or in-dignation; to be thickly covered (with).

brittle *adj* easily cracked or broken; fragile.—**brittleness** *n*.

broach *vt* (*a topic*) to introduce for discussion; to pierce (a container) and draw out liquid.

broad *adj* of large extent from side to side; wide; spacious; strongly marked in dialect or pronunciation. * *n* (*sl*) a woman.—**broadly** *adv*.

broadcast *n* a programme on radio or television. * *vti* (*pt* **broadcast**) to transmit on radio or television; to make known widely.—**broadcaster** *n*.

broaden *vti* to grow or make broad.

brochure *n* a booklet.

broil *vti* to cook by exposure to direct heat; to grill.

broke *pt* of **break**. * *adj* (*inf*) hard up, having no money.

broken *pp* of **break**. * *adj* splintered, fractured; violated; ruined; tamed; disconnected, interrupted; (*speech*) imperfect.—**brokenly** *adv*.

broken-down *adj* extremely infirm; worn out.

broker *n* an agent who negotiates contracts of purchase and sale; a power broker.

bronchitis *n* inflammation of the lining of the windpipe.—**bronchitic** *adj*.

bronze *n* a copper and tin alloy, sometimes other elements; any object cast in bronze; a reddish-brown colour. * *adj* made of, or like, bronze.

brooch *n* an ornament held by a pin or a clasp and usu worn near the neck.

brood *vi* to incubate or hatch (eggs); to ponder over or worry about. * *n* a group having a common nature or origin, esp the children in a family; the number produced in one hatch.

brook[1] *n* a freshwater stream.

brook[2] *vt* to tolerate.

broom *n* a bundle of fibres or twigs attached to a long handle for sweeping.

broomstick *n* the handle of a broom.

broth *n* a thin soup made by boiling meat, etc in water.

brothel *n* a house where prostitutes work.

brother *n* a male sibling; a friend who is like a brother; a fellow member of a group, profession or association; a lay member of a men's religious order; (*pl* **brethren**) used chiefly in formal address or in referring to the members of a society or sect.

brother-in-law *n* the brother of a husband or wife; the husband of a sister.

brotherly *adj* like a brother; kind; affectionate.—**brotherliness** *n*.

brought *see* **bring**.

brow *n* the forehead; the eyebrows; the top of a cliff; the jutting top of a hill.

browbeat *vt* (*pt* **browbeat**, *pp* **browbeaten**) to intimidate with threats, to bully.

brown *adj* having the colour of chocolate, a mixture of red, black and yellow; tanned. * *n* a brown colour. * *vti* to make or become brown.—**brownish** *adj*.

brownie *n* a square of flat, rich chocolate cake; a friendly helpful elf; (*with cap*) a junior Guide.

browse *vti* to nibble, graze; to examine casually.

bruise *vt* to injure and discolour (body tissue) without breaking the skin; to break down (as leaves and berries) by pounding; to inflict psychological pain on. * *vi* to inflict a bruise; to undergo bruising. * *n* contusion of the skin; a similar injury to plant tissue; an injury, esp to the feelings.

brunette *n* a girl or woman with black or dark-brown hair, often with dark eyes and complexion.—*also adj*.

brunt *n* the main force or shock of a blow; the hardest part.

brush *n* a device made of bristles set in a handle, used for grooming the hair, painting or sweeping; a fox's, etc bushy tail; a light stroke or graze, made in passing. * *vt* to groom or sweep with a brush; to remove with a brush. * *vi* to touch lightly or graze.

brush-off *n* a curt dismissal.

Brussels sprout *n* a plant with a small edible green head.

brutal *adj* inhuman; savage, violent; severe.—**brutality** *n.*—**brutally** *adv.*

brute *n* any animal except man; a brutal person; (*inf*) an unpleasant or difficult person or thing. * *adj* (*force*) sheer.

bubble *n* a film of liquid forming a ball around air or gas; a tiny ball of gas or air in a liquid or solid; a transparent dome; a scheme that collapses. * *vi* to boil; to rise in bubbles; to make a gurgling sound.

buck *n* the male of animals such as the deer, hare, rabbit, antelope; (*inf*) a dashing young man; (*sl*) a dollar. * *vti* (*horse*) to rear upward quickly; (*inf*) to resist; (*with* **up**) (*inf*) to make or become cheerful; to hurry up.

bucket *n* a container with a handle for carrying liquids, etc.

buckle *n* a fastening or clasp for a strap or band; a bend or bulge. * *vti* to fasten with a buckle; to bend under pressure, etc; (*with* **down**) (*inf*) to apply oneself.

bud *n* an embryo shoot, flower, or flower cluster of a plant; an early stage of development. * *vi* (*pt* **budded**) to produce buds; to begin to develop.

Buddha *n* the state of perfect enlightenment; an image of Siddharta Gautama, founder of Buddhism.—**Buddhist** *adj, n.*

budding *n* being in an early stage of development; promising.

buddy *n* (*inf*) a friend; a term of informal address.

budge *vti* to shift or move.

budgerigar *n* a small Australian parrot.—*also* (*coll*) **budgie**.

budget *n* an estimate of income and expenditure within specified limits; the total amount of money for a given purpose; a stock or supply. * *vb* (*pt* **budgeted**) *vi* to make a budget. * *vt* to put on a budget; to plan.

buff *n* a heavy, soft, brownish-yellow leather; a dull brownish yellow; (*inf*) a devotee, fan; (*inf*) a person's bare skin. * *adj* made of buff; of a buff colour. * *vt* to clean or shine, orig with leather or a leather-covered wheel.

buffer *n* anything that lessens shock, as of collision; something that serves as a protective barrier; a temporary storage area in a computer.

buffet[1] *n* a blow with the hand or fist. * *vb* (*pt* **buffeted**) *vt* to hit with the hand or fist; to batter (as of the wind). * *vi* to make one's way esp under difficult conditions.

buffet[2] *n* a counter where refreshments are served; a meal at which guests serve themselves food.

buffoon *n* a clown, a jester.

bug[1] *n* a continuing source of irritation.

bug[2] *n* an insect with sucking mouth parts; any insect; (*inf*) a germ or virus; (*sl*) a defect, as in a machine; (*sl*) a hidden microphone. * *vt* (*sl*) to plant a hidden microphone; (*sl*) to annoy, anger, etc.

bugbear *n* an object that causes great fear and anxiety.

bugle *n* a valveless brass instrument like a small trumpet, used esp for military calls. * *vti* to signal by blowing a bugle.—**bugler** *n.*

build *vb* (*pt* **built**) *vt* to make or construct, to establish, base; (*with up*) to create or develop gradually. * *vi* to put up buildings; (*with* **up**) to grow or intensify; (*health, reputation*) to develop. * *n* the way a thing is built or shaped; the shape of a person.—**builder** *n.*

building *adj* the skill or occupation of constructing houses, boats, etc; something built with walls and a roof.

building society *n* a company that pays interest on deposits and issues loans to enable people to buy their own houses.

built-in *adj* incorporated as an integral part of a main structure; inherent.

built-up *adj* made higher, stronger, etc with added parts; having many buildings on it.

bulb *n* the underground bud of plants such as the onion and daffodil; a glass bulb in an electric light.—**bulbous** *adj.*

bulge *n* a swelling; a rounded projected part. * *vti* to swell or bend outward.—**bulgy** *adj.*

bulk *n* magnitude; great mass; volume; the main part. * *adj* total, aggregate; not packaged.

bulkhead *n* a wall-like partition in the interior of a ship, aircraft or vehicle.

bulky *adj* (**bulkier, bulkiest**) large and unwieldy.—**bulkiness** *adj.*

bull[1] *n* an adult male bovine animal; a male whale or elephant; a speculator who buys in anticipation of reselling at a profit; the bull's-eye; (*sl*) nonsense. * *adj* male; rising in price.

bull[2] *n* an official edict issued by the pope, with the papal seal on it.

bulldozer *n* an excavator with caterpillar tracks for moving earth.

bullet *n* a small metal missile fired from a gun or rifle.

bulletin *n* an announcement; a short statement of news or of a patient's progress.

bullfighting *n* the sport of goading and then killing bulls, popular in Spain, etc.—**bullfighter** *n.*

bullion *n* gold or silver in mass before coinage.
bullock *n* a gelded bull; steer.
bull's-eye *n* (*darts, archery*) the centre of a target; something resembling this; a direct hit.
bully *n* a person, esp a child, who hurts or intimidates others weaker than himself. * *vt* to intimidate, oppress or hurt.
bum *n* (*inf*) a tramp; (*inf*) a devotee, as of skiing, etc; (*sl*) buttocks or anus.
bumblebee *n* a large, furry bee.
bump *vi* to knock with a jolt. * *vt* to hurt by striking or knocking; (*with* **off**) (*sl*) to murder. * *n* a jolt; a knock; a swelling or lump.
bumper *n* a shock-absorbing bar fixed to the front and rear of a motor vehicle. * *adj* exceptionally large.
bumptious *adj* offensively conceited or self-assertive.—**bumptiously** *adv*.—**bumptiousness** *n*.
bun *n* a roll made of bread dough and currants, spices and sugar; a bun-shaped coil of hair at the neck.
bunch *n* a cluster; a number of things growing or fastened together; (*inf*) a group of people. * *vi* to group together. * *vt* to make into a bunch.
bundle *n* a number of things fastened together; a fastened package; (*sl*) a large sum of money. * *vt* to put together in bundles; to push hurriedly into.
bung *n* a cork or rubber stopper. * *vt* to close up with a bung; (*sl*) to throw, toss.
bungalow *n* a one-storey house.
bungle *n* a mistake or blunder; something carried out clumsily. * *vt* to spoil something through incompetence or clumsiness.—**bungler** *n*.
bunion *n* a lump on the side of the first joint of the big toe.
bunk[1] *n* a narrow, shelf-like bed.
bunk[2] *n* (*sl*) a hurried departure.
bunker *n* a large storage container, esp for coal; a sand pit forming an obstacle on a golf course; an underground shelter.
bunting *n* a cotton fabric used for making flags; a line of pennants and decorative flags.
buoy *n* a bright, anchored, marine float used for mooring. * *vt* to keep afloat; (*usu with* **up**) to hearten or raise the spirits of; to mark with buoys.
buoyancy *n* ability to float or rise; cheerfulness; resilience.—**buoyant** *adj*.
burden *n* a load; something worrisome that is difficult to bear; responsibility. * *vt* to weigh down, to oppress.—**burdensome** *adj*.
bureau *n* (*pl* **bureaus, bureaux**) a writing desk; a chest of drawers; a branch of a newspaper, magazine or wire service in an important news centre; a government department.
bureaucracy *n* a system of government where the administration is organized in a hierarchy; the government collectively; excessive paperwork and red tape.
bureaucrat *n* an official in a bureaucracy.—**bureaucratic** *adj*.
burglar *n* a person who trespasses in a building with the intention of thieving.—**burglary** *n*.
burgle, burglarize *vt* to commit burglary.
burial *n* the act of burying.
burly *adj* (**burlier, burliest**) heavily built; sturdy.—**burliness** *n*.
burn *vb* (*pt* **burned** *or* **burnt**) *vt* to destroy by fire; to injure by heat. * *vi* to be on fire; to feel hot; to feel passion; (*inf*) to suffer from sunburn. * *n* a mark or injury caused by burning.
burnish *vt* to make shiny by rubbing; to polish. * *n* lustre; polish.
burnt *see* **burn**.
burp *vi* to belch. * *vt* to pat a baby on the back to cause it to belch.—*also n*.
burrow *n* an underground hide or tunnel dug by a rabbit, badger or fox, etc for shelter. * *vi* to dig a burrow; to live in a burrow; to hide (oneself).
bursar *n* a treasurer; a student holding a bursary.
bursary *n* a scholarship awarded to a student.
burst *vb* (*pt* **burst**) *vt* to break open; to cause to explode. * *vi* to emerge suddenly; to explode; to break into pieces; to give vent to. * *n* an explosion; a burst; a volley of shots.
bury *vt* (*bone, corpse*) to place in the ground; to conceal, to cover; to blot out of the mind.
bus *n* a motor coach for public transport. * *vti* (*pt* **bused** *or* **bussed**) to transport or travel by bus.
bush *n* a low shrub with many branches; a cluster of shrubs forming a hedge; woodland; uncultivated land.
bushy *adj* (**bushier, bushiest**) covered with bushes; (*hair*) thick.—**bushiness** *n*.
business *n* trade or commerce; occupation or profession; a firm; one's concern or responsibility; a matter.
businesslike *adj* efficient, methodical, practical.
businessman *n* a person who works for an industrial or commercial company.—**businesswoman** *nf*.

busker *n* a street entertainer.

bust[1] *n* the chest or breast of a human being, esp a woman; a sculpture of the head and chest.

bust[2] *vti* (*pt* **busted** *or* **bust**) (*inf*) to burst or break; to make or become bankrupt or demoted; to hit; to arrest. * *n* (*inf*) a failure; financial collapse; a punch; a spree; an arrest.

bustle[1] *vi* to move or act noisily or fussily. * *n* noisy activity, stir.

bustle[2] *n* a pad placed beneath a skirt to cause it to puff up at the back.

busy *adj* (**busier, busiest**) occupied; active; industrious; (*painting*) having too much detail; (*room, telephone*) in use. * *vt* to occupy; to make or keep busy (esp oneself).—**busily** *adv*.

busybody *n* a meddlesome person.

but *prep* save; except. * *conj* in contrast; on the contrary, other than. * *adv* only; merely; just.

butane *n* a flammable gas used as fuel.

butcher *n* a person who slaughters meat; a retailer of meat; a ruthless murderer. * *vt* to slaughter; to murder ruthlessly; to make a mess of or spoil.

butler *n* a male servant, esp the head servant of a household with several servants.

butt[1] *vti* to strike or toss with the head or horns, as a bull, etc.—*also n.*

butt[2] *n* a large cask for wine or beer.

butt[3] *n* a mound of earth behind targets; a person who is the target of ridicule or jokes; (*pl*) the target range.

butt[4] *n* the thick or blunt end; the stump; (*sl*) a cigarette; (*sl*) the buttocks. * *vti* to join end to end.

butter *n* a solidified fat made from cream by churning. * *vt* to spread butter on; (*with* **up**) (*inf*) to flatter.

butterfly *n* an insect with a slender body and four usu brightly coloured wings; a swimming stroke.

buttock *n* one half of the human rump.

button *n* a disc or knob of metal, plastic, etc used as a fastening; a badge. * *vti* to fasten with a button or buttons.

buttonhole *n* the slit through which a button is passed; a flower in the buttonhole. * *vt* to keep in conversation.

buttress *n* a projecting structure for strengthening a wall. * *vt* to support.

buxom *adj* plump and healthy; (*woman*) big-bosomed.

buy *vt* (*pt* **bought**) to purchase (for money); to bribe, corrupt; to acquire in exchange; (*inf*) to believe.—**buyer** *n*.

buzz *vi* to hum like an insect; to gossip; to hover (about). * *vt* to spread gossip secretly; (*inf*) to telephone. * *n* the humming of bees or flies; a rumour; (*sl*) a telephone call; (*sl*) a thrill.

buzzard *n* a large bird of prey.

buzzer *n* a device producing a buzzing sound.

by *prep* beside; next to; via; through the means of; not later than. * *adv* near to; past; in reserve.

bye-bye *interj* (*inf*) goodbye.

by-election, bye-election *n* an election other than a general election.

bylaw, bye-law *n* a rule or law made by a local authority or a company.

bypass *n* a main road avoiding a town; a channel redirecting the flow of something; (*med*) an operation to redirect the flow of blood into the heart. * *vt* to go around; to avoid.

by-product *n* a secondary product in the process of making something else.

bystander *n* a chance onlooker.

byte *n* (*comput*) a set of eight bits treated as a unit.

byword *n* a familiar saying; a perfect example; an object of derision.

C

C *abbr* = Celsius, centigrade; (*chem symbol*) = carbon.

© (*symbol*) = copyright.

cab *n* a taxicab; the place where the driver sits in a truck, crane, etc.

cabaret *n* entertainment given in a restaurant or nightclub.

cabbage *n* a garden plant with thick leaves formed usu into a compact head, used as a vegetable.

cabin *n* a small house, a hut; a room in a ship; the area where passengers sit in an aircraft.

cabin cruiser *n* a powerful motorboat with living accommodation.

cabinet *n* a case with drawers or shelves; a case containing a TV, radio, etc; a body of official advisers to a government.

cabinetmaker *n* a person who makes fine furniture.

cable *n* a strong thick rope often of wire strands; an anchor chain; an insulated cord that carries electric current; a cablegram; a bundle of insulated wires for carrying cablegrams, TV

signals, etc. * *vti* to send a message by cablegram.
cable car *n* a car drawn by a moving cable, as up a steep incline.
cablegram *n* a message transmitted by telephone line, submarine cable, etc, a cable.
cache *n* a secret hiding place; a store of food left for use by travellers, etc. * *vt* to place in a cache.
cackle *n* the clucking sound of a hen; shrill or silly talk or laughter. * *vti* to utter with a cackle.
cactus *n* (*pl* **cacti**, **cactuses**) a plant with a fleshy stem that stores water and is often studded with prickles.
caddie, caddy[1] *n* a person who carries a golfer's clubs. * *vi* to perform as a caddie.
caddy[2] *n* a small box or tin for storing tea.
cadet *n* a student at an armed forces academy.
cadge *vti* to beg or get by begging.—**cadger** *n*.
Caesarean section *n* the removal of a child from the womb by a surgical operation.
café *n* a small restaurant, a coffee bar, a nightclub, etc.
cafeteria *n* a self-service restaurant.
caffeine *n* a stimulant present in coffee and tea.
cage *n* a box or enclosure with bars for confining an animal, bird, prisoner, etc; a car for raising or lowering miners. * *vt* to shut in a cage, to confine.
cagey, **cagy** *adj* (**cagier, cagiest**) (*inf*) wary, secretive, not frank.—**cagily** *adv*.—**caginess** *n*.
cajole *vti* to persuade or soothe by flattery or deceit.
cake *n* a mixture of flour, eggs, sugar, etc baked in small, flat shapes or a loaf; a small block of compacted or congealed matter. * *vti* to encrust; to form into a cake or hard mass.
calamity *n* a disastrous event, a great misfortune; adversity.—**calamitous** *adj*.
calcium *n* the chemical element prevalent in bones and teeth.
calculate *vti* to reckon or compute by mathematics; to suppose or believe; to plan.—**calculable** *adj*.
calculating *adj* shrewd, scheming.
calculation *n* the act of calculating; the result obtained; an estimate.
calculator *n* a device, esp a small, electronic, hand-held one, for doing mathematical calculations rapidly; one who calculates.
calculus *n* (*pl* **calculi, calculuses**) an abnormal, stony mass in the body; (*math*) a mode of calculation using symbols.
calendar *n* a system of determining the length and divisions of a year; a chart or table of months, days and seasons; a list of scheduled events.
calf[1] *n* (*pl* **calves**) the young of a cow, seal, elephant, whale, etc; the leather skin of a calf.
calf[2] *n* (*pl* **calves**) the fleshy back part of the leg below the knee.
calibre, caliber (*US*) *n* the internal diameter of a gun barrel or tube; capacity, standing, moral weight.
call *vi* to shout or cry out; to pay a short visit; to telephone; (*with* **in**) to pay a brief or informal visit; (*with* **on**) to pay a visit; to ask, to appeal to. * *vt* to summon; to name; to describe as specified; to awaken; to give orders for; (*with* **down**) to invoke; (*with* **in**) to summon for advice or help; to bring out of circulation; to demand payment of (a loan); (*with* **off**) to cancel; (*an animal*) to call away in order to stop; (*with* **out**) to cry aloud; (*workers*) to order to strike; (*troops*) to summon to action; (*with* **up**) to telephone; to summon to military action, as in time of war; to recall. * *n* a summons; the note of a bird; a vocation, esp religious; occasion; a need; a demand; a short visit; the use of a telephone; a cry, shout.
call box *n* a telephone box.
caller *n* one who calls, esp by telephone.
call girl *n* a prostitute who is called by telephone to assignations.
callous *adj* (*skin*) hardened; (*person*) unfeeling.—**calloused** *adj*.—**callously** *adv*.—**callousness** *n*.
calm *adj* windless; still, unruffled; quiet, peaceful. * *n* the state of being calm; stillness; tranquillity. * *vti* to become or make calm.—**calmly** *adv*.—**calmness** *n*.
calorie, calory *n* a unit of heat; a measure of food energy.
calve *vti* to give birth to a calf.
camber *n* a slight upward curve in the surface of a road, etc. * *vti* to curve upwards slightly.—**cambered** *adj*.
came *see* **come**.
camel *n* a large four-footed, long-necked animal with a humped back; a fawny-beige colour.—*also adj*.
cameo *n* an onyx or other gem carved in relief; an outstanding bit role, esp in a motion picture; a short piece of fine writing.
camera *n* the apparatus used for taking still photographs or television or motion pictures; a judge's private chamber.

cameraman *n* a film or television camera operator.
camouflage *n* a method (esp using colouring) of disguise or concealment used to deceive an enemy; a means of putting people off the scent. * *vt* to conceal by camouflage.
camp[1] *n* the ground on which tents or temporary accommodation is erected; the occupants of this, such as holiday-makers or troops; the supporters of a particular cause. * *vi* to lodge in a camp; to pitch tents.—**camper** *n*.
camp[2] *adj* (*sl*) theatrical, exaggerated; effeminate.
campaign *n* a series of military operations; a series of operations with a particular objective, such as election of a candidate or promotion of a product; organized course of action. * *vi* to take part in or conduct a campaign.—**campaigner** *n*.
camp site *n* a camping ground, often with facilities for holiday-makers.
campus *n* (*pl* **campuses**) the grounds, and sometimes buildings, of a college or university.
can[1] *vt* (**could**) to be able to; to have to have the right to; to be allowed to.
can[2] *n* a container, usu metal, with a separate cover in which petrol, film, etc is stored; a tin in which meat, fruit, drinks, etc, are hermetically sealed; the contents of a can; (*sl*) jail; (*sl*) a toilet. * *vti* (*pt* **canned**) to preserve (foods) in a can.—**canner** *n*.
canal *n* an artificial waterway cut across land; a duct in the body.
canary *n* a small finch, usu greenish to yellow in colour, kept as a songbird.
cancel *vt* (*pt* **cancelled**) to cross out; to obliterate; to annul, suppress; (*reservation, etc*) to call off; to countermand.
cancellation *n* the act of cancelling; annulment; something cancelled; the mark made by cancelling.
Cancer *n* (*astron*) the Crab, a northern constellation; (*astrol*) the 4th sign of the zodiac, operative 21 June-21 July.
cancer *n* the abnormal and uncontrollable growth of the cells of living organisms, esp a malignant tumour; an undesirable or dangerous expansion of something.—**cancerous** *adj*.
candela *n* a unit of luminous intensity.
candid *adj* frank, outspoken; unprejudiced; (*photograph*) informal.—**candidly** *adv*.—**candidness** *n*.
candidate *n* a person who has nomination for an office or qualification for membership or award; a student taking an examination.—**candidacy** *n*.—**candidature** *n*.
candle *n* a stick of wax with a wick that burns to give light.
candlelight *n* the light produced by a candle or candles.
candour, candor (*US*) *n* sincerity, openness, frankness.
candy *n* a solid confection of sugar or syrup with flavouring, fruit, nuts, etc, a sweet.
candyfloss *n* a confection of spun sugar.
cane *n* the slender, jointed stem of certain plants, as bamboo; a plant with such a stem, as sugar cane; a stick of this used for corporeal punishment (*usu with* **the**) or supporting plants; strips of this used in furniture making etc; a walking stick. * *vt* to thrash with a cane; to weave cane into.
canine *adj* of or like a dog; of the family of animals that includes wolves, dogs and foxes; pertaining to a canine tooth. * *n* a dog or other member of the same family of animals; in humans, a pointed tooth next to the incisors.
canister *n* a small box or container for storing tea, flour, etc; a tube containing tear gas which explodes and releases its contents on impact.
cannabis *n* a narcotic drug obtained from the hemp plant; the hemp plant.—also **hashish, marijuana**.
canned *adj* stored in sealed tins; recorded for reproduction; (*sl*) drunk.
cannibal *n* a person who eats human flesh; an animal that feeds on its own species. * *adj* relating to or indulging in this practice.—**cannibalism** *n*.—**cannibalistic** *adj*.
cannon *n* (*pl* **cannon**) a large mounted piece of artillery; (*pl* **cannons**) an automatic gun on an aircraft; (*billiards*) a shot in which the cue ball hits two others successively. * *vi* to collide with great force (*with* **into**); to rebound; (*billiards*) to make a cannon.
cannonball *n* the heavy, round shot fired from a cannon. * *vi* to move along at great speed.
cannot = can not.
canoe *n* a narrow, light boat propelled by paddles.—*also vi*.—**canoeist** *n*.
canon *n* a decree of the Church; a general rule or standard, criterion; a list of the books of the Bible accepted as genuine; the works of any author recognized as genuine; a member of a cathedral chapter; a part of the mass containing words of consecration; (*mus*) a round.—**canonical** *adj*.—**canonically** *adv*.
canonize *vt* (*RC Church*) to officially declare

(a person) a saint. —**canonization** *n*.

canopy *n* a tent-like covering over a bed, throne, etc; any roof-like projection.

cant[1] *n* insincere or hypocritical speech; language specific to a group (eg thieves, lawyers); cliched talk, jargon. * *vi* to talk in or use cant.

cant[2] *n* an inclination or tilt; a slanting surface, bevel. * *vti* to slant, to tilt.

can't = can not.

cantaloupe, cantaloup *n* a variety of melon with orange flesh.

cantankerous *adj* ill-natured, bad-tempered, quarrelsome.—**cantankerously** *adv*.—**cantankerousness** *n*.

canteen *n* a restaurant attached to factory, school, etc, catering for large numbers of people; a flask for carrying water; (a box containing) a set of cutlery.

canter *n* a horse's 3-beat gait resembling a slow, smooth gallop.—*also vti*.

cantilever *n* a projecting beam that supports a balcony, etc.

canvas *n* a strong coarse cloth of hemp or flax, used for tents, sails, etc, and for painting on; sails; a tent or tents; an oil painting on canvas.

canvass *vti* to go through (places) or among (people) asking for votes, opinions, orders, etc.—also *n*.—**canvasser** *n*.

canyon *n* a long, narrow valley between high cliffs.

cap *n* any close-fitting head gear, visored or brimless; a cap-like thing, as an artificial covering for a tooth; a top, a cover; a percussion cap in a toy gun; a type of contraceptive device; (*sport*) the head gear presented to a player chosen for a team. * *vt* (*pt* **capped**) to put a cap on; to cover (the end of); to seal (an oil or gas well); to equal, outdo or top; (*sport*) to choose a player for a team.

capability *n* the quality of being capable; an undeveloped faculty.

capable *adj* able or skilled to do; competent, efficient; susceptible (of); adapted to.—**capably** *adv*.

capacity *n* the power of holding or grasping; cubic content; mental ability or power; character; legal competence; the greatest possible output or content.

cape[1] *n* a headland or promontory running into the sea.

cape[2] *n* a sleeveless garment fastened at the neck and hanging over the shoulders and back.

capital[1] *adj* of or pertaining to the head; (*offence*) punishable by death; serious; chief, principal; leading, first-class; of, or being the seat of government; of capital or wealth; relating to a large letter, upper case; (*inf*) excellent. * *n* a city that is the seat of government of a country; a large letter; accumulated wealth used to produce more; stock or money for carrying on a business; a city, town, etc pre-eminent in some special activity.

capital[2] *n* the head or top part of a column or pillar.

capital gain *n* the profit made on the sale of an asset.

capitalism *n* the system of individual ownership of wealth; the dominance of such a system.

capitalist *n* a person who has money invested in business for profit; a supporter of capitalism. * *adj* of or favouring capitalism.—**capitalistic** *adj*.

capital punishment *n* the death penalty for a crime.

capitulate *vi* to surrender on terms; to give in.—**capitulation** *n*.

capricious *adj* unstable, inconstant; unreliable.—**capriciously** *adv*.—**capriciousness** *n*.

Capricorn *n* (*astron*) the Goat, a southern constellation; (*astrol*) the tenth sign of the zodiac, operative 21 December-19 January.

capsize *vti* to upset or overturn.

capstan *n* an upright drum around which cables are wound to haul them in; the spindle in a tape recorder that winds the tape past the head.

capsule *n* a small gelatin case enclosing a drug to be swallowed; a metal or plastic container; (*bot*) a seed case; the orbiting and recoverable part of a spacecraft.

captain *n* a chief, leader; the master of a ship; the pilot of an aircraft; a rank of army, naval and marine officer; the leader of a team, as in sports. * *vt* to be captain of.—**captaincy** *n*.

caption *n* a heading in a newspaper, to a chapter, etc ; a legend or title describing an illustration; a subtitle. * *vti* to provide with a caption.

captivate *vt* to fascinate; to charm.—**captivating** *adj*.—**captivation** *n*.

captivity *n* the state of being a captive; a period of imprisonment.

capture *vt* to take prisoner; (*fortress, etc*) to seize; to catch; to gain or obtain by skill, attraction, etc, to win. * *n* the act of taking a prisoner or seizing by force; anything or anyone so taken.

car *n* a self-propelled motor vehicle, an automobile, a motorcar; the passenger compartment of a train, airship, lift, cable railway, etc; a railway carriage.

carafe *n* an open-topped bottle for serving water or wine at table.

caramel *n* burnt sugar, used in cooking to colour or flavour; a type of sweet tasting of this.

carat *n* a measure of weight for precious stones; a measure of the purity of gold.—*also* **karat**.

caravan *n* a large enclosed vehicle equipped to be lived in (—*also* **trailer**); a band of merchants travelling together for safety. * *vi* (*pt* **caravanned**) to travel with a caravan, esp on holiday.

caraway *n* a biennial plant with pungent aromatic seeds used as a flavouring.

carbohydrate *n* a compound of carbon, hydrogen and oxygen, esp in sugars and starches as components of food. * *npl* starchy foods.

carbon *n* a nonmetallic element, a constituent of all organic matter; a duplicate made with carbon paper.

carbon copy *n* a copy of typed or written material made by using carbon paper; an exact copy.

carburettor *n* a device in an internal-combustion engine for making an explosive mixture of air and fuel vapour.

carcass, carcase *n* the dead body of an animal; a framework, skeleton or shell.

card[1] *n* a small piece of cardboard; a piece of this with a figure or picture for playing games or fortune-telling; a piece of this with a person or firm's name, address or with an invitation, greeting, message, etc; (*inf*) an entertaining or eccentric person; a small piece of plastic identifying a person for banking purposes (eg a cheque card, credit card); (*pl*) card games; (*pl*) card playing; (*pl*) employees' documents held by the employer.

card[2] *n* a toothed instrument for combing cotton, wool or flax fibres off. * *vt* (*wool, etc*) to comb.

cardboard *n* thick stiff paper, often with a clay coating. * *adj* made of this; lacking substance.

cardiac *adj* relating to the heart.

cardigan *n* a knitted sweater fastening up the front.

cardinal *adj* of chief importance, fundamental; of a bright red. * *n* an official appointed by the Pope to his councils; bright red.

cardinal numbers *npl* numbers that express how many (1, 2, 3, etc).

care *n* anxiety; concern; serious attention, heed; consideration; charge, protection; the cause or object of concern or anxiety. * *vt* to feel concern; to agree or be willing (to do something). * *vi* (*usu with* **for, about**) to feel affection or regard; to have a desire (for); to provide for, have in one's charge.

career *n* progress through life; a profession, occupation, esp with prospects for promotion. * *vi* to rush rapidly or wildly.

carefree *adj* without cares, lively, light-hearted.

careful *adj* painstaking; cautious; thoughtful.—**carefully** *adv*.—**carefulness** *n*.

careless *adj* not careful; unconcerned, insensitive; carefree.—**carelessly** *adv*.—**carelessness** *n*.

caress *vt* to touch or stroke lovingly.—*also n*.

caretaker *n* a person put in charge of a place or thing; (*government*) one temporarily in control.

cargo *n* (*pl* **cargoes**) the load carried by a ship, truck, aircraft, etc; freight.

Caribbean *adj* of or pertaining to the Caribbean Sea and its islands. * *n* the Caribbean Sea.

caricature *n* a likeness made ludicrous by exaggeration or distortion of characteristic features. * *vt* to make a caricature of, to parody.—**caricaturist** *n*.

carnal *adj* of the flesh; sexual; sensual; worldly.—**carnally** *adv*.

carnation *n* a garden flower.

carnival *n* public festivities and revelry; a travelling fair with sideshows, etc.

carnivore *n* a flesh-eating mammal.

carnivorous *adj* (*animals*) feeding on flesh; (*plants*) able to trap and digest insects.

carol *n* a joyful song of joy; a Christmas hymn. * *vi* (*pt* **carolled**) to sing carols.

carp[1] *vi* to find fault, esp continually.

carp[2] *n* a brown and yellow freshwater fish.

car park, parking lot (*US*) *n* land or premises intended for parking cars.

carpenter *n* a person skilled in woodwork, esp house building.—**carpentry** *n*.

carpet *n* a woven fabric for covering floors; any thick covering. * *vt* (*pt* **carpeted**) to cover with carpet.

carriage *n* the act of carrying, transport; the cost of this; deportment, bearing; behaviour; a railway coach or compartment; the moving part of a typewriter.

carriageway *n* a road bearing single-line traffic.

carrier *n* one who carries or transports goods, esp for hire; a device for carrying; a person or animal transmitting an infectious disease without being affected by it; an aircraft carrier; a carrier bag.

carrier bag *n* a plastic bag with handles for holding shopping, etc.

carrot *n* a plant grown for its edible, fleshy orange root; an inducement, often illusory.

carry *vt* to convey or transport; to support or bear; to involve, have as a result; to hold (oneself); to extend or prolong; to gain by force; to win over; to stock; (*with* **off**) to cause to die; to remove by force; (*situation*) to handle successfully; (*with* **out**) to perform (a task, etc); to accomplish. * *vi* (*with* **on**) to persevere; to conduct a business, etc; (*inf*) to have an affair; (*inf*) to cause a fuss.

carrycot *n* a baby's portable cot.

carry-on *n* (*inf*) a fuss.

carry-out *n* food or drink sold by a restaurant but consumed elsewhere.—*also adj.*

cart *n* a two-wheeled vehicle drawn by horses; any small vehicle for carrying loads. * *vt* to carry in a cart; (*inf*) to transport with effort.

cartilage *n* tough, elastic tissue attached to the bones of animals; gristle.

carton *n* a cardboard box or container.

cartoon *n* a humorous picture dealing with current events; a comic-strip; an animated cartoon; a full-size preparatory sketch for reproduction on a fresco, etc.—**cartoonist** *n.*

cartridge *n* the case that contains the explosive charge and bullet in a gun or rifle; a sealed case of film for a camera; the device containing the stylus on the end of the pick-up arm of a record player.

carve *vt* to shape by cutting; to adorn with designs; to cut up (meat, etc).

carving *n* a figure or design carved from wood, stone, etc; the act of carving.

cascade *n* a small, steep waterfall; a shower, as of sparks, etc. * *vti* to fall in a cascade.

case[1] *n* a covering; a suitcase; its contents.

case[2] *n* an instance; a state of affairs; a condition, circumstance; a lawsuit; an argument for one side; (*sl*) character; (*med*) a patient under treatment; (*gram*) the relationship between nouns, pronouns and adjectives in a sentence.

cash *n* money in coins or notes; immediate payment, as opposed to that by cheque or on credit. * *vt* to give or get cash for.

cashew *n* the small, edible nut of a tropical tree.

cashier *n* a person in charge of the paying and receiving of money in a bank, shop, etc.

cashmere *n* a fine wool from Kashmir goats; a material made from this.

cash register *n* an automatic or electronic till that shows and records the amount placed in it.

casing *n* a protective or outer covering; the material for this.

casino *n* (*pl* **casinos**) a room or building where gambling takes place.

cask *n* a barrel of any size, esp one for liquids; its contents.

casket *n* a small box or chest for jewels, etc; a coffin.

casserole *n* a covered dish for cooking and serving; the food so cooked and served. * *vt* to cook in a casserole.

cassette *n* a usu plastic box that holds an audio or video tape.

cast *vb* (*pt* **cast**) *vt* to throw or fling; to throw off or shed; to record; to direct; to shape in a mould; to calculate; to select actors, etc for a play. * *vi* to throw, hurl; (*with* **off**) to untie a ship from its moorings; (*knitting*) to loop off stitches from a needle without letting them unravel; (*with* **on**) to loop the first row of stitches onto a needle. * *n* act of casting; a throw; a plaster form for immobilizing an injured limb; a mould for casting; type or quantity; a tinge of colour; the actors assigned roles in a play; the set of actors; a slight squint in the eye.

castanets *npl* hollow shell-shaped pieces of wood held between the fingers and rattled together, esp to accompany Spanish dancing.

castaway *n* a shipwrecked person.

caste *n* any of the Hindu hereditary social classes; an exclusive social group.

casting vote *n* the deciding vote used by the chairman of a meeting when the the votes on each side are equal.

cast iron *n* iron melted and run into moulds.—*also adj.*

castle *n* a fortified building; a chess piece (—*also* **rook**).

castor *n* a small container with a perforated top for sprinkling salt, sugar, etc; a small swivelled wheel on a table leg, etc.

castor oil *n* a vegetable oil used as a purgative and lubricant.

castor sugar *n* finely ground sugar.

castrate *vt* to remove the testicles of, to geld.—**castration** *n.*

casual *adj* accidental, chance; unplanned; occasional; careless, unmethodical; informal.—**casually** *adv.*

casualty *n* a person injured or killed in a war or in an accident; something damaged or destroyed.

cat *n* a small, domesticated feline mammal kept as a pet; a wild animal related to this; lions, tigers, etc (*inf*) a spiteful person.

catalogue, catalog (*US*) *n* a list of books, names, etc in systematic order. * *vti* to list, to make a catalogue of.—**cataloguer** *n.*

catalyst *n* a substance which accelerates or retards a chemical reaction without itself undergoing any permanent chemical change; a person or thing which produces change.

catapult *n* a contraption with elastic for shooting small stones (—*also* **slingshot**); a device for launching aircraft from the deck of an aircraft carrier. * *vt* to shoot forward as from a catapult.

cataract *n* a waterfall, esp a large sheet one; a disease of the eye causing dimming of the lens and loss of vision.

catarrh *n* inflammation of a mucous membrane, esp in the nose.—**catarrhal** *adj.*

catastrophe *n* a great disaster.—**catastrophic** *adj.*—**catastrophically** *adv.*

catch *vb* (*pt* **caught**) *vt* to take hold of, to grasp; to capture; to ensnare or trap; to be on time for; to detect; to apprehend; to become infected with (a disease); (*inf*) to see, hear, etc; to grasp (a meaning); (*with* **out**) (*inf*) to detect (a person) in a mistake; (*cricket*) to catch a ball hit by a batsman before it touches the ground, making him "out." * *vi* to become entangled; to begin to burn; (*with* **on**) (*inf*) to become popular; to understand; (*with* **up**) to reach or come level with (eg a person ahead); to make up for lost time, deal with a backlog. * *n* the act of catching; a device for fastening; someone worth catching; a hidden difficulty.

catching *adj* infectious; attractive.

catchment area *n* a geographic area served by an institution.

catch phrase *n* a well-known phrase or slogan, esp one associated with a particular group or person.

catchup *see* **ketchup**.

catchy *adj* (**catchier, catchiest**) easily remembered, as a tune.

catechism *n* a simple summary of the principles of religion in question and answer form, used for instruction.

categorical *adj* unconditional, absolute; positive, explicit.—**categorically** *adv.*

categorize *vt* to place in a category.

category *n* a class or division of things.

cater *vi* (*with* **for, to**) to provide with what is needed or desired, esp food and service, as for parties.—**caterer** *n.*

caterpillar *n* the worm-like larvae of a butterfly or moth; the ribbed band in place of wheels on a heavy vehicle; a vehicle (eg tank, tractor) equipped with such tracks.

cathedral *n* the chief church of a diocese. * *adj* of a cathedral.

Catholic *n* a member of the Roman Catholic Church. * *adj* relating to the Roman Catholic Church; embracing the whole body of Christians.—**Catholicism** *n.*

catholic *adj* universal, all-embracing; broad-minded, liberal; general, not exclusive.

catsup *see* **ketchup**.

cattle *npl* domesticated bovine mammals such as bulls and cows.

caught *see* **catch**.

cauliflower *n* a kind of cabbage with an edible white flower-head used as a vegetable.

cause *n* that which produces an effect; reason, motive, justification; a principle for which people strive; a lawsuit. * *vt* to bring about, to effect; to make (to do something).

causeway *n* a raised road across wet ground or water.

caustic *adj* burning tissue, etc by chemical action; corrosive; sarcastic, cutting. * *n* a caustic substance.—**caustically** *adv.*—**causticity** *n.*

caution *n* care for safety, prudence; warning. * *vt* to warn (against); to admonish.

cautious *adj* careful, circumspect.—**cautiously** *adv.*—**cautiousness** *n.*

cavalry *n* combat troops originally mounted on horseback.

cave *n* a hollow place inside the earth open to the surface. * *vti* (*with* **in**) to collapse or make collapse.

caveman *n* a prehistoric cave dweller; (*inf*) a person who acts in a primitive or crude manner.

cavern *n* a cave, esp a large cave.—**cavernous** *adj.*

caviar, caviare *n* pickled roe of the sturgeon.

cavity *n* a hole; a hollow place, esp in a tooth.

cavort *vi* to frolic, prance.

CBI *abbr* = Confederation of British Industry; Central Bureau of Investigation

cc *abbr* = carbon copy; cubic centimetre(s).

cease *vti* to stop, to come to an end; to discontinue.

ceasefire *n* a period of truce in a war, uprising, etc.
ceaseless *adj* without ceasing; incessant.—**ceaselessly** *adv*.
cedar *n* a large coniferous evergreen tree; its wood.—**cedarwood** *n*.
cede *vt* to yield to another, give up, esp by treaty; to assign or transfer the title of.
ceiling *n* the inner roof of a room; the lining of this; an upper limit; the highest altitude a particular aircraft can fly.
celebrate *vt* to make famous; to praise, extol; to perform with proper rites; to mark with ceremony; to keep (festival).—**celebrant** *n*.
celebrated *adj* famous.
celebration *n* the act of celebrating; an observance or ceremony to celebrate anything.
celebrity *n* fame; a famous or well-known person.
celery *n* a vegetable with long juicy edible stalks.
celestial *adj* in or of the sky; heavenly; divine.
celibacy *n* the unmarried state; complete sexual abstinence.
cell *n* a small room for one in a prison or monastery; a small cavity as in a honeycomb; a device that converts chemical energy into electricity; a microscopic unit of living matter; a small group of people bound by common aims within an organization or political party.—**cellular** *adj*.
cellar *n* a basement; a stock of wines.
cello *n* (*pl* **cellos**) a large bass instrument of the violin family.—**cellist** *n*.
cellophane *n* a thin transparent paper made from cellulose.
cellulose *n* a starch-like carbohydrate forming the cell walls of plants, used in making paper, textiles, film, etc.
Celtic *adj* of or relating to the Celts; the language of the Celts, including Scots or Irish Gaelic, Manx, Welsh, Cornish and Breton.
cement *n* a powdered substance of lime and clay, mixed with water, etc to make mortar or concrete, which hardens upon drying; any hard-drying substance. * *vt* to bind or glue together with or as if with cement; to cover with cement.
cemetery *n* a place for the burial of the dead.
cenotaph *n* a monument to a person who is buried elsewhere.
censor *n* an official with the power to examine literature, mail, etc and remove or prohibit anything considered obscene, objectionable, etc. * *vt* to act as a censor.—**censorship** *n*.
censure *n* an expression of disapproval or blame. * *vt* to condemn as wrong; to reprimand.—**censurable** *adj*.
cent *n* a hundredth of a dollar; (*inf*) a negligible amount of money.
centenary *n* a hundredth anniversary or its celebration. * *adj* of a hundred years.
centi- *prefix* one hundredth.
centigrade *adj* of a scale of a hundred degrees, of the Celsius scale. * *n* a hundredth part of a grade.
centimetre, centimeter (*US*) *n* one hundredth of a metre.
centipede *n* a a crawling creature with a long body divided into numerous segments each with a pair of legs.
central *adj* in, at, from or forming the centre; main, principal; important.—**centrally** *adv*.—**centrality** *n*.
central heating *n* a system of heating by pipes carrying hot water from a central boiler.
centralize *vt* to draw to the centre; to place under the control of a central authority, esp government.—**centralization** *n*.
centre, center (*US*) *n* the approximate middle point or part of anything, a pivot; interior; point of concentration, source; political moderation; (*sport*) a player at the centre of the field, etc, a centre-forward. * *adj* of or at the centre. * *vt* (*pr p* **centring**, *pt* **centred**) to place in the centre; to concentrate; to be fixed; (*football, hockey*) to kick or hit the ball into the centre of the pitch.
centre forward *n* (*football, hockey*) the central player in the forward attack.
centrifugal *adj* moving away from the centre of rotation.
century *n* a period of a hundred years; a set of a hundred; (*cricket*) 100 runs made by a batsman in a single innings; a company of a Roman legion.
ceramic *adj* of earthenware, porcelain, or brick. * *n* something made of ceramic; (*pl*) the art of pottery.
cereal *n* a grass grown for its edible grain, e.g. wheat, rice; the grain of such grasses; a breakfast food made from such grains. * *adj* of corn or edible grain.
ceremony *n* a sacred rite; formal observance or procedure; behaviour that follows rigid etiquette.
certain *adj* sure, positive; unerring, reliable; sure to happen, inevitable; definite, fixed; some; one.
certainly *adv* without doubt; yes.

certainty *n* something undoubted, inevitable; the condition of being certain.

certificate *n* a document formally attesting a fact; a testimonial of qualifications or character.—**certificated** *adj*.

certify *vt* to declare in writing or attest formally; to endorse with authority.

cervix *n* the neck of the womb.

cessation *n* a stoppage; a pause.

cesspit, cesspool *n* a covered cistern for collecting liquid waste or sewage.

cf. *abbr* = compare (Latin *confer*).

chafe *vti* to restore warmth by rubbing; to make or become sore by rubbing; to irritate; to feel irritation, to fret.

chaffinch *n* a European songbird.

chain *n* a series of connected links or rings; a continuous series; a series of related events; a bond; a group of shops, hotels, etc owned by the same company; a unit of length equal to 66 feet. * *vt* to fasten with a chain or chains.

chain reaction *n* a process in which a chemical, atomic or other reaction stimulates further reactions, eg combustion or nuclear fission; a series of events, each of which stimulates the next.

chain-smoke *vti* to smoke (cigarettes) one after the other.—**chain-smoker** *n*.

chain store *n* one of a series of shops owned by one company.

chair *n* a separate seat for one; a seat of authority; a chairman; a professorship; the electric chair. * *vt* to preside as chairman of.

chair lift *n* a series of seats suspended from a cable for carrying sightseers or skiers uphill.

chairman *n* a person who presides at a meeting; the president of a board or committee.—**chairwoman** *nf*.—*also* **chairperson**.

chalet *n* a Swiss hut; any similar building used in a holiday camp, as a ski lodge, etc.

chalice *n* a large cup with a base; a communion cup.

chalk *n* calcium carbonate, a soft white limestone; such a stone or a substitute used for drawing or writing. * *vt* to write, mark or draw with chalk; (*with* **up**) (*inf*) to score, get, achieve; to charge or credit.—**chalky** *adj*.

challenge *vt* to summon to a fight or contest; to call in question; to object to; to hail and interrogate. * *n* the act of challenging; a summons to a contest; a calling in question; a problem that stimulates effort.—**challenger** *n*.—**challenging** *adj*.

chamber *n* a room, esp a bedroom; a deliberative body or a division of a legislature; a room where such a body meets; a compartment; a cavity in the body of an organism; (*pl*) a judge's office.

chambermaid *n* a woman employed to clean bedrooms in a hotel, etc.

chamber music *n* music for performance by a small group, as a string quartet.

chamois *n* a small antelope found in Europe and Asia; a piece of chamois leather.

chamois leather *n* soft, pliable leather formerly made from chamois skin, and now obtained from sheep, goats and deer.

champagne *n* a sparkling white wine; a pale straw colour.

champion *n* a person who fights for another; one who upholds a cause; a competitor successful against all others. * *adj* first-class; (*inf*) excellent. * *vt* to defend; to uphold the cause of.

championship *n* the act of championing; the process of determining a champion; a contest held to find a champion.

chance *n* a course of events; fortune; an accident, an unexpected event; opportunity; possibility; probability; risk. * *vti* to risk; to happen. * *adj* accidental, not planned.

chancel *n* the part of a church around the altar, for the clergy and the choir.

chancellor *n* a high government official, as, in certain countries, a prime minister; in some universities, the president or other executive officer.—**chancellorship** *n*.

chandelier *n* an ornamental hanging frame with branches for holding lights.

change *vt* to make different, to alter; to transform; to exchange; to put fresh clothes on. * *vi* to become different, to undergo alteration; to put on fresh clothes; to continue one's journey by leaving one station, etc, or mode of transport and going to and using another. * *n* alteration, modification; substitution; variety; a fresh set, esp clothes; money in small units; the balance of money returned when given in a larger denomination as payment.

changeable *adj* able to be changed; altering rapidly between different conditions; inconstant.

channel *n* the bed or the deeper part of a river, harbour, etc; a body of water joining two larger ones; a navigable passage; a means of passing or conveying; a band of radio frequencies reserved for a particular purpose, eg television station; a path for an electrical signal; a groove or line along which liquids, etc may flow. * *vt* (*pt* **channelled**) to form a channel in; to groove; to direct.

chant *vti* to sing; to recite in a singing manner; to sing or shout (a slogan) rhythmically. * *n* sacred music to which prose is sung; singsong intonation; a monotonous song; a rhythmic slogan, esp as sung or shouted by sports fans, etc.

chaos *n* utter confusion, muddle.

chaotic *adj* completely without order or arrangement.—**chaotically** *adv*.

chap[1] *vti* (*pt* **chapped**) (*skin*) to make or become split or rough in cold weather. * *n* a chapped place in the skin.

chap[2] *n* (*inf*) a man.

chapel *n* a building for Christian worship, not as large as a church; an association of printers in a printing office.

chaperon, chaperone *n* a woman who accompanies a girl at social occasions for propriety. * *vt* to attend as a chaperon.

chaplain *n* a clergyman serving in a religious capacity with the armed forces, or in a prison, hospital, etc.—**chaplaincy** *n*.

chapter *n* a main division of a book; the body or meeting of canons of a cathedral or members of a monastic order; a sequence of events; an organized branch of a society or association.

char[1] *n* a charwoman. * *vt* (*pt* **charred**) to work as a charwoman.

char[2] *vb* (*pt* **charred**) *vt* to burn to charcoal or carbon. * *vti* to scorch.

char[3] *n* (*sl*) tea.

character *n* the combination of qualities that distinguishes an individual person, group or thing; moral strength; reputation; disposition; a person of marked individuality; a person in a play or novel; a guise, role; a letter or mark in writing, printing, etc.

characteristic *adj* marking or constituting the particular nature (of a person or thing). * *n* a characteristic feature.

characterize *vt* to describe in terms of particular qualities; to designate; to be characteristic of, mark.—**characterization** *n*.

charade *n* a game of guessing a word from the acted representation of its syllables and the whole; a travesty; an absurd pretence.

charcoal *n* the black carbon matter obtained by partially burning wood and used as fuel, as a filter or for drawing.

charge *vt* to ask as the price; to record as a debt; to load, to fill, saturate; to lay a task or trust on; to burden; to accuse; to attack at a run; to build up an electric charge (in). * *n* a price charged for a good or service; a build-up of electricity; the amount which a receptacle can hold at one time; the explosive required to fire a weapon; trust, custody; a thing or person entrusted; a task, duty; accusation; an attack.

chariot *n* a two-wheeled vehicle driven by two or more horses in ancient warfare, races, etc.—**charioteer** *n*.

charitable *adj* of or for charity; generous to the needy, benevolent; lenient in judging others, kindly.—**charitably** *adv*.

charity *n* leniency or tolerance towards others; generosity in giving to the needy; a benevolent fund or institution.

charm *n* an alluring quality, fascination; a magic verse or formula; something thought to possess occult power; an object bringing luck; a trinket on a bracelet. * *vt* to delight, captivate; to influence as by magic.—**charmer** *n*.

chart *n* a map, esp for use in navigation; an information sheet with tables, graphs, etc; a table, graph, etc; (*pl with* **the**) a list of the most popular music recordings. * *vt* to make a chart of; to plan (a course of action).

charter *n* a document granting rights, privileges, ownership of land, etc; the hire of transportation. * *vt* to grant by charter; to hire.

chartered accountant *n* an accountant who has qualified by passing the examinations of the Institute of Chartered Accountants.

charwoman *n* a woman employed to clean a house.

chase *vt* to pursue; to run after; to drive (away); to hunt; (*inf: usu with* **up**) to pursue in a determined manner. * *n* pursuit; a hunt; a quarry hunted; a steeplechase.

chasm *n* a deep cleft, an abyss, a gaping hole; a wide difference in opinions, etc.

chassis *n* (*pl* **chassis**) the frame of a car, aeroplane or other vehicle.

chastity *n* sexual abstinence; virginity.

chat *vi* (*pt* **chatted**) to talk in an easy or familiar way. * *n* informal conversation.

chatter *vi* to talk aimlessly and rapidly; (*animal, etc*) to utter rapid cries; (*teeth*) to rattle together. * *n* idle rapid talk; the sound of chattering.— **chatterer** *n*.

chatterbox *n* an incessant talker.

chatty *adj* (**chattier, chattiest**) talkative, full of gossip.—**chattily** *adv*.—**chattiness** *n*.

chauffeur *n* a person who drives a car for

someone else. * *vt* to drive as a chauffeur.—**chauffeuse** *nf*.

cheap *adj* low-priced, inexpensive; good value; of little worth, inferior.—**cheaply** *adv*.—**cheapness** *n*.

cheapen *vti* to make or become cheap.

cheat *vti* to defraud, to swindle; to deceive; to play unfairly. * *n* a fraud, deception; a person who cheats.—**cheater** *n*.

check *vti* to bring or come to a stand; to restrain or impede; to admonish, reprove; to test the accuracy of, verify; (*with* **out**) to settle the bill and leave a hotel; to investigate. * *n* repulse; stoppage; a pattern of squares; a control to test accuracy; a tick against listed items; a bill in a restaurant; a cheque; (*chess*) a threatening of the king.

checker[1] *n* a cashier in a supermarket (esp in US); a cloakroom attendant.

checker[2] *see* **draughtsman**[2].

checkers *n* the game of draughts.

checkmate *n* (*chess*) the winning position when the king is threatened and unable to move; defeat. * *vt* (*chess*) to place in checkmate; to defeat, foil.

checkroom *n* a left luggage office.

cheek *n* the side of the face below the eye; (*sl*) buttock; impudence.

cheeky *adj* (**cheekier, cheekiest**) disrespectful, impudent.—**cheekily** *adv*.—**cheekiness** *n*.

cheer *n* a shout of applause or welcome; a frame of mind, spirits; happiness. * *vt* to gladden; to encourage; to applaud.

cheerful *n* in good spirits; happy.—**cheerfully** *adv*.—**cheerfulness** *n*.

cheese *n* the curds of milk pressed into a firm or hard mass.

chef *n* a professional cook.

chemical *n* a substance used in, or arising from, a chemical process. * *adj* of, used in, or produced by chemistry.—**chemically** *adv*.

chemist *n* a pharmacy; a manufacturer of medicinal drugs; a person skilled in chemistry.

chemistry *n* the science of the properties of substances and their combinations and reactions; chemical structure.

cheque, check (*US*) *n* a money order to a bank.

chequebook, checkbook (*US*) *n* a book containing blank cheques to be drawn on a bank.

chequered, checkered (*US*) *adj* marked with a variegated pattern; having a career of fluctuating fortunes.

cherish *vt* to tend lovingly, foster; to keep in mind.

cherry *n* a small red, pitted fruit; the tree bearing it; a bright red colour.

chess *n* a game played by two people with 32 pieces on a chessboard.

chessboard *n* a board chequered with 64 squares used for playing chess or draughts.

chessman *n* any of the 16 pieces used by each player in chess.

chest *n* a large strong box; the part of the body enclosed by the ribs, the thorax.

chestnut *n* a tree or shrub of the beech family; the edible nut of a chestnut; the wood of the chestnut; a horse with chestnut colouring. * *adj* of the colour of a chestnut, a deep reddish brown.

chest of drawers *n* a piece of furniture containing several drawers.

chew *vt* to grind between the teeth, to masticate; to ponder, think over. * *n* the act of chewing; something to chew, as a sweet.

chewing gum *n* a flavoured gum made from chicle, for chewing.

chic *n* elegance, style. * *adj* stylish.

chick *n* a young bird; (*sl*) a youthful person.

chicken *n* a young, domestic fowl; its flesh. * *adj* cowardly, timorous.

chicken feed *n* poultry food; (*inf*) a trifling amount.

chickenpox *n* a contagious viral disease that causes a rash of red spots on the skin.

chicory *n* a salad plant; its dried, ground, roasted root used to flavour coffee.

chief *adj* principal, most important. * *n* a leader; the head of a tribe or clan.

chiefly *adv* especially; mainly; for the most part.

chiffon *n* a thin gauzy material.

chilblain *n* an inflamed swelling on the hands, etc, due to cold.

child *n* (*pl* **children**) a young human being; a son or daughter; offspring.

childbirth *n* the process of giving birth to children.

childhood *n* the period between birth and puberty in humans.

childish *adj* of, like or suited to a child; foolish.—**childishly**.—**childishness** *n*.

childlike *adj* like a child; innocent, simple, candid.

child minder *n* a person employed to look after children.

chill *n* a sensation of coldness; an illness caused by exposure to cold and marked by shivering; anything that dampens or depresses. * *adj* shivering with cold; feeling cold; unemotional, formal. * *vti* to make or become cold; to harden by cooling; to depress.

chilly *adj* (**chillier, chilliest**) cold; unfriendly.—**chilliness** *n.*

chime *n* the harmonious sound of a bell; accord; harmony; (*pl*) a set of bells or metal tubes, etc tuned in a scale; their ringing. * *vi* to ring (a bell); (*with* **with**) to agree. * *vt* to indicate the hour by chiming, as a clock.

chimney *n* (*pl* **chimneys**) a passage for smoke, hot air or fumes, a funnel.

chimpanzee *n* an African anthropoid ape.

chin *n* the part of the face below the mouth.

china *n* fine porcelain; articles made from this.

chink[1] *n* a narrow opening; a crack or slit.

chink[2] *n* the sound of coins clinking together.

chip *vt* (*pt* **chipped**) to knock small pieces off; to shape or make by chipping. * *n* a small piece cut or broken off; a thin strip of fried potato; a potato crisp; a counter used in games; a tiny piece of semi-conducting material, such as silicon, printed with a microcircuit and used as part of an integrated circuit.

chirp *n* the sharp, shrill note of some birds or a grasshopper. * *vi* to make this sound.

chisel *n* a tool with a square cutting end. * *vt* (*pt* **chiselled**) to cut or carve with a chisel; (*sl*) to defraud.

chit[1] *n* a voucher or a sum owed for drink, food, etc; a note; a requisition.

chit[2] *n* a child; (*derog*) an impudent girl.

chivalry *n* the medieval system of knighthood; knightly qualities, bravery, courtesy, respect for women.—**chivalrous** *adj.*—**chivalrously**.

chive, chives *n* a plant whose onion-flavoured leaves are used in cooking and salads.

chloride *n* any compound containing chlorine.

chlorine *n* a non-metallic element, a yellowish-green poisonous gas used in bleaches, disinfectants, and in industry.

chock *n* a block of wood or other material used as a wedge. * *vt* to secure with a chock.

chock-a-block, chock-full *adj* completely full.

chocolate *n* a powder or edible solid made of the roasted, pounded cacao bean; a drink made by dissolving this powder in boiling water or milk; a sweet with a centre and chocolate coating. * *adj* flavoured or coated with chocolate; dark reddish brown.

choice *n* act of choosing; the power to choose; selection; alternative; a thing chosen; preference; the best part. * *adj* of picked quality, specially good; fastidious.

choir *n* an organized group of singers, esp of a church; the part of a church used by them.

choke *vti* to stop the breath of, stifle; to throttle; to suffocate; to block (up). * *n* a fit of choking; a choking sound; a valve that controls the flow of air in a carburettor.

cholera *n* a severe, infectious intestinal disease.

choose *vt* (*pt* **chose**, *pp* **chosen**) to select (one thing) rather than another. * *vi* to decide, to think fit.—**chooser** *n.*

chop *vt* (*pt* **chopped**) to cut by striking; to cut into pieces. * *n* a cut of meat and bone from the rib, loin, or shoulder; a downward blow or motion.

choppy *adj* (**choppier, choppiest**) (*sea*) running in rough, irregular waves; jerky.—**choppiness** *n.*

chopsticks *n* a pair of wooden or plastic sticks used in Asian countries to eat with.

choral *adj* relating to, sung by, or written for, a choir or chorus.

chord[1] *n* (*mus*) three or more notes played simultaneously.

chord[2] *n* a straight line joining the ends of an arc.

chore *n* a piece of housework; a regular or tedious task.

choreography *n* the art of devising ballets or dances.—**choreographer** *n.* —**choreographic** *adj.*

chorister *n* a member of a choir.

chortle *vi* to chuckle exultantly.—*also n.*

chorus *n* a group of singers and dancers in the background to a play, musical, etc; a group of singers, a choir; music sung by a chorus; a refrain; an utterance by many at once. * *vt* to sing, speak or shout in chorus.

chose, chosen *see* **choose**.

Christ *n* Jesus of Nazareth, regarded by Christians as the Messiah. * *interj* (*taboo*) an oath expressing annoyance.

christen *vt* to enter the Christian Church by baptism; to give a name to; (*inf*) to use for the first time.—**christening** *n.*

Christian *n* a person who believes in Christianity. * *adj* relating to, believing in, or based on the doctrines of Christianity; kind, gentle, humane.

Christianity *n* the religion based on the teachings of Christ.

Christian name *n* a name given when one is christened; (*loosely*) any forename.

Christmas *n* an annual festival (25 December) in memory of the birth of Christ.

Christmas tree *n* an evergreen tree decorated at Christmas; an imitation tree.

chrome *n* chromium; a chromium pigment; something plated with an alloy of chromium.
chromium *n* a hard metallic element used in making steel alloys and electroplating to give a tough surface.
chromosome *n* any of the microscopic rod-shaped bodies bearing genes.
chronic *adj* (*disease*) long-lasting; (*sl*) bad, extremely unpleasant.—**chronically** *adv*.
chronicle *n* a record of events in chronological order; an account; a history. * *vt* to record in a chronicle.—**chronicler** *n*.
chronological *adj* arranged in order of occurrence.—**chronologically** *adv*.
chrysanthemum *n* a plant with a brightly coloured flower head.
chubby *adj* (**chubbier, chubbiest**) plump.—**chubbiness** *n*.
chuck[1] *vt* to throw, to toss; (*inf*) to stop, to give up.
chuck[2] *n* a device on a lathe, etc, that holds the work or drill; a cut of beef from the neck to the ribs.
chuckle *vt* to laugh softly; to gloat. * *n* a quiet laugh.
chum *n* (*inf*) a close friend, esp of the same sex.
chunk *n* a short, thick piece or lump, as wood, bread, etc.—**chunky** *adj*.
church *n* a building for public worship, esp Christian worship; the clerical profession; a religious service; (*with cap*) all Christians; (*with* **the**) a particular Christian denomination.
churchyard *n* the yard around a church often used as a burial ground.
churn *n* a large metal container for milk; a device that can be vigorously turned to make milk or cream into butter. * *vt* to agitate in a churn; to make (butter) this way; to stir violently.
chute *n* an inclined trough or a passage for sending down water, logs, rubbish, etc; a fall of water, a rapid.
CID *abbr* = Criminal Investigation Department.
cider *n* fermented apple juice as a drink.
cigar *n* a compact roll of tobacco leaf for smoking.
cigarette *n* shredded tobacco rolled in fine paper for smoking.
cinch *n* (*sl*) a firm hold, an easy job.
cinder *n* a tiny piece of partly burned wood, etc; (*pl*) ashes from wood or coal.
cine- *prefix* motion picture or cinema, as *cinecamera*, *cinefilm*.
cinema *n* a place where motion pictures are shown; film as an industry or art form.
cinnamon *n* a tree of the laurel family; its aromatic edible bark; a spice made from this; a yellowish brown colour.—*also adj*.
cipher *n* the numeral 0, zero; any single Arabic numeral; a thing or person of no importance, a nonentity; a method of secret writing. * *vt* to convert (a message) into cipher.—*also* **cypher**.
circle *n* a perfectly round plane figure; the line enclosing it; the curved seating area above the stalls in a theatre; a group, set or class (of people); extent, scope, as of influence. * *vti* to encompass; to move in a circle; to revolve (round).
circuit *n* a distance round; a route or course; an area so enclosed; the path of an electric current; a visit to an area by a judge to hold courts; the area itself; a chain or association.
circuitous *adj* roundabout, indirect.
circular *adj* shaped like a circle, round; (*argument*) using as evidence the conclusion which it is seeking to prove; moving round a circle. * *n* an advertisement, etc addressed to a number of people.
circulate *vti* to pass from hand to hand or place to place; to spread or be spread about; to move round, finishing at the starting point.—**circulatory** *adj*.
circulation *n* the act of circulating; a movement to and fro; the number of copies sold of a newspaper, etc; currency.
circumcise *vt* to cut off the foreskin of (a male) or the clitoris of (a female), esp as a religious rite.—**circumcision** *n*.
circumference *n* the line bounding a circle, a ball, etc; the length of this line.
circumstance *n* an occurrence, an incident; a detail; ceremony; (*pl*) a state of affairs; condition in life.
circus *n* a large arena for the exhibition of games, feats of horsemanship etc; a travelling show of acrobats, clowns, etc; a company of people travelling round giving displays.
cistern *n* a tank or reservoir for storing water, esp in a toilet.
cite *vt* to summon officially to appear in court; to quote; to give as an example or authority.
citizen *n* a member of a city, state or nation.—**citizenship** *n*.
citrus *n* a genus of trees including the lemon, orange, etc; the fruit of these.
city *n* an important or cathedral town; a town

created a city by charter; the people of a city; business circles, esp financial services.

civic *adj* of a city, citizen or citizenship. * *npl* the principles of good citizenship; the study of citizenship.

civil *adj* of citizens or the state; not military or ecclesiastical; polite, obliging; (*law*) relating to crimes other than criminal ones or to private rights.

civil engineer *n* an engineer who designs and constructs roads, bridges, etc.

civilian *n* a person who is not a member of the armed forces.

civilization, civilisation *n* the state of being civilized; the process of civilizing; an advanced stage of social culture; moral and cultural refinement.

civil service *n* those employed in the service of a state apart from the military.

civil war *n* a war between citizens of the same state or country.

claim *vt* to demand as a right; to call for; to require; to profess (to have); to assert. * *n* the act of claiming; a title, right to something; a thing claimed, esp a piece of land for mining.

claimant *n* one who makes a claim.

clam *n* an edible marine bivalve mollusc.

clamber *vi* to climb with difficulty, using the hands as well as the feet. * *n* a climb performed in this way.—**clamberer** *n*.

clammy *adj* (**clammier, clammiest**) damp and sticky.—**clamminess** *n*.

clamp *n* a device for gripping objects tightly together. * *vt* to grip with a clamp; to attach firmly.

clan *n* a group of people with a common ancestor, under a single chief; people with the same surname; a party or clique.

clang *n* a loud metallic sound. * *vti* to make or cause to make a clang.

clap[1] *vti* (*pt* **clapped**) to strike (the hands) together sharply; to applaud in this way; to slap; to put or place suddenly or vigorously. * *n* the sound of hands clapping; a sudden sharp noise; a sudden sharp slap.

clap[2] *n* (*vulg*) venereal disease, gonorrhoea.

claret *n* a dry red wine of Bordeaux in France.

clarify *vti* to make or become clear or intelligible; to free or become free from impurities.—**clarification** *n*.

clarinet *n* an orchestral woodwind instrument.—**clarinettist** *n*.

clarity *n* clearness.

clash *n* a loud noise of striking weapons, cymbals, etc; a contradiction, disagreement; a collision. * *vti* to make or cause to make a clash by striking together; to conflict; to collide; to be at variance (with).

clasp *n* a hold, an embrace; a catch or buckle. * *vt* to grasp firmly, to embrace; to fasten with a clasp.

class *n* a division, a group; a kind; a set of students who are taught together; a grade of merit or quality; standing in society, rank. * *vt* to put into a class.

classic *adj* of the highest class or rank, esp in literature; of the best Greek and Roman writers; of music conforming to certain standards of form, complexity, etc; traditional; authoritative. * *n* a work of literature, art, cinema, etc, of the highest excellence; a definitive work of art.

classical *adj* influenced by, of or relating to ancient Roman and Greek art, literature and culture; traditional; serious; refined.—**classically** *adv*.

classification *n* the organization of knowledge into categories; a category or a division of a category into which knowledge or information has been put.

classify *vt* to arrange in classes, to categorize; to restrict for security reasons.

classmate *n* a member of the same class in a school, college, etc.

classroom *n* a room where pupils or students are taught.

clatter *n* a rattling noise; noisy talk. * *vti* to make or cause a clatter.

clause *n* a single article or stipulation in a treaty, law, contract, etc; (*gram*) a short sentence; a part of a sentence.

claustrophobia *n* a morbid fear of confined spaces.—**claustrophobic** *adj*.

claw *n* the sharp hooked nail of an animal or bird; the pointed end or pincer of a crab, etc; a claw-like thing. * *vti* to seize or tear with claws or nails; to clutch (at).

clay *n* a sticky ductile earthy material.

clean *adj* free from dirt or impurities; unsoiled; morally or ceremonially pure; complete, decisive. * *adv* entirely; outright; neatly. * *vti* to remove dirt from.—**cleanness** *n*.

cleaner *n* a substance or device used for cleaning; a person employed to clean; (*pl*) a dry cleaner.

cleanse *vt* to make clean or pure.

cleanser *n* something that cleanses, esp a detergent, face cream, etc.

clear *adj* bright, not dim; transparent; without blemish; easily seen or heard; unimpeded,

open; free from clouds; quit (of); plain, distinct, obvious; keen, discerning; positive, sure. * *adv* plainly; apart from. * *vti* to make or become clear; to rid (of), remove; to to free from suspicion, vindicate; to disentangle; to pass by or over without touching; to make as a profit.—**clearness** *n*.
clearance *n* the act of clearing; permission, authority to proceed; the space between two objects in motion.
clearing *n* a tract of land cleared of trees, etc for cultivation.
clearly *adv* in a clear manner; evidently.
clearway *n* a main road where it is illegal for vehicles to stop.
clef *n* a sign on a music stave that indicates the pitch of the notes.
clench *vt* (*teeth, fist*) to close tightly; to grasp. * *n* a firm grip.
clergy *n* ministers of the Christian church collectively.
clergyman *n* a member of the clergy.
clerical *adj* of or relating to the clergy or a clergyman; of or relating to a clerk or a clerk's work.
clerk *n* an office worker who types, keeps files, etc; a layman with minor duties in a church; a public official who keeps the records of a court, town, etc.
clever *adj* able; intelligent; ingenious; skilful, adroit.—**cleverly** *adv*.—**cleverness** *n*.
cliché *n* a hackneyed phrase; something that has become commonplace.—**cliché'd, clichéd** *adj*.
click *n* a slight, sharp sound. * *vi* to make such a sound.
client *n* a person who employs another professionally; a customer.
clientele *n* clients, customers.
cliff *n* a high steep rock face.
climate *n* the weather characteristics of an area; the prevailing attitude, feeling, atmosphere.—**climatic** *adj*.
climax *n* the highest point; a culmination; sexual orgasm. * *vti* to reach, or bring to a climax.—**climactic** *adj*.
climb *vti* to mount with an effort; to ascend; (*plants*) to grow upwards by clinging onto walls, fences or other plants. * *n* an ascent.
climber *n* a mountaineer or rock climber; a climbing plant.
clinch *vt* (*argument, etc*) to confirm or drive home. * *vi* (*boxing*) to grip the opponent with the arms to hinder his punching. * *n* the act of clinching; (*inf*) an embrace.
cling *vi* (*pt* **clung**) to adhere, to be attached (to); to keep hold by embracing or entwining.
clinic *n* a place where outpatients are given medical care or advice; a place where medical specialists practice as a group; a private or specialized hospital; the teaching of medicine by treating patients in the presence of students.
clinical *adj* of or relating to a clinic; based on medical observation; plain, simple; detached, cool, objective.—**clinically** *adv*.
clink[1] *n* a slight metallic ringing sound. * *vti* to make or cause to make such a sound.
clink[2] *n* (*sl*) prison.
clip[1] *vt* (*pt* **clipped**) to cut or trim with scissors or shears; to punch a small hole in, esp a ticket; (*words*) to shorten or slur; (*inf*) to hit sharply. * *n* the piece clipped off; a yield of wool from sheep; an extract from a film; (*inf*) a smart blow; speed.
clip[2] *vt* (*pt* **clipped**) to hold firmly; to secure with a clip. * *n* any device that grips, clasps or hooks; a magazine for a gun; a piece of jewellery held in place by a clip.
clique *n* a small exclusive group, a set.—**cliquey** *adj*.—**cliquish** *adj*.
cloak *n* a loose sleeveless outer garment; a covering; something that conceals, a pretext. * *vt* to cover as with a cloak; to conceal.
cloakroom *n* a room where overcoats, etc, may be left.
clock *n* a device for measuring time; any timing device with a dial and displayed figures. * *vt* to time (a race, etc) using a stopwatch or other device; (*inf*) to register a certain speed; (*sl*) to hit.
clockwise *adv* moving in the direction of a clock's hands.—*also adj*.
clockwork *n* the mechanism of a clock or any similar mechanism with springs and gears. * *adj* mechanically regular.
clog *n* a wooden-soled shoe. * *vt* (*pt* **clogged**) to cause a blockage in; to impede, obstruct.
cloister *n* a roofed pillared walk, usu with one side open, in a convent, college, etc; a religious retreat. * *vt* to confine or keep apart as if in a convent.
close[1] *adj* near; reticent, secret; nearly alike; nearly even or equal; dense, compact; sultry, airless; narrow; restricted. * *adv* closely; near by. * *n* a courtyard; the entrance to a courtyard; the precincts of a cathedral.—**closely** *adv*.—**closeness** *n*.
close[2] *vt* to make closed; to stop up (an opening); to draw together; to conclude; to shut.

* *vi* to come together; to complete; to finish. * *n* a completion, end.

closed *adj* shut up; with no opening; restricted; not open to question or debate; not open to the public, exclusive.

closet *n* a small room or a cupboard for clothes, supplies, etc; a small private room. * *vt* (*pt* **closeted**) to enclose in a private room for a confidential talk.

close-up *n* a film or television shot taken from very close range; a close examination.

closure *n* closing; the condition of being closed; something that closes; (*parliament, etc*) a decision to end further debate and move to an immediate vote.

clot *n* a thickened mass, esp of blood; (*sl*) an idiot. * *vti* (*pt* **clotted**) to form into clots, to curdle, coagulate.

cloth *n* woven, knitted or pressed fabric from which garments, etc are made; a piece of this; a tablecloth; clerical dress.

clothe *vt* (*pt* **clothed** *or* **clad**) to cover with a garments; to dress; to surround, endow (with).

clothes *npl* garments, apparel.

clothesline *n* a rope on which washing is hung to dry.

clothespeg, clothespin *n* a plastic, wooden or metal clip for attaching washing to a line.

clothing *n* clothes.

cloud *n* a visible mass of water vapour floating in the sky; a mass of smoke, etc; a threatening thing, a gloomy look; a multitude. * *vt* to darken or obscure as with clouds.—**cloudless** *adj*.

cloudburst *n* a sudden rainstorm.

cloudy *adj* (**cloudier, cloudiest**) of or full of clouds; not clear; gloomy.—**cloudiness** *n*.

clout *n* a blow; (*sl*) power, influence.

clove[1] *n* a segment of a bulb, as garlic.

clove[2] *n* the dried flower bud of a tropical tree, used as a spice.

clover *n* a low-growing plant with three leaves used as fodder; a trefoil; (*inf*) luxury.

clown *n* a person who entertains with jokes, antics, etc, esp in a circus; a clumsy or boorish person. * *vi* to act the clown, behave comically or clumsily.—**clownish** *adj*.

club *n* a heavy stick used as a weapon; a stick with a head for playing golf, etc; an association of people for athletic, social, or common purposes; its premises; a suit of playing cards with black clover-like markings. * *vt* to beat with or use as a club. * *vi* to form into a club for a common purpose.

clubhouse *n* premises used by a club.

cluck *n* the call of a hen. * *vi* to make such a noise.

clue *n* a guide to the solution of a mystery or problem. * *vt* (*pt* **clued**) to provide with helpful information.

clump *n* a cluster of trees; a lump; (*of hair*) a handful; the sound of heavy footsteps.

clumsy *adj* (**clumsier, clumsiest**) unwieldy; awkward; lacking tact, skill or grace.—**clumsily** *adv*.—**clumsiness** *n*.

clung *see* **cling**.

cluster *n* a bunch; a swarm; a group. * *vti* to form or arrange in a cluster.

clutch[1] *vt* to seize, to grasp tightly; to snatch at. * *n* a tight grip; a device for throwing parts of a machine into or out of action; the pedal operating this device.

clutch[2] *n* a nest of eggs; a brood of chicks.

clutter *n* a disordered mess; confusion. * *vti* to litter; to put into disorder.

Co. *abbr* = Company; County.

c/o *abbr* = care of.

coach *n* a long-distance bus; a railway carriage; a large, covered four-wheeled horse-drawn carriage; a sports instructor; a tutor in a specialized subject. * *vti* to teach or train.

coagulate *vti* to change from a liquid to partially sold state, to clot, curdle.—**coagulation** *n*.

coal *n* a black mineral used for fuel; a piece of this; an ember.

coalfield *n* a region yielding coal.

coalition *n* a temporary union of parties or states.

coarse *adj* rough; large in texture; rude, crude; inferior.—**coarsely** *adv*. —**coarseness** *n*.

coast *n* an area of land bordering the sea; the seashore. * *vi* to sail along a coast; to travel down a slope without power; to proceed with ease.—**coastal** *adj*.

coastguard *n* an organization which monitors the coastline and provides help for ships in difficulties, prevents smuggling, etc.

coat *n* a sleeved outer garment; the natural covering of an animal; a layer. * *vt* to cover with a layer or coating.

coating *n* a surface coat; material for coats.

coat of arms *n* the heraldic bearings of a family, city, institution, etc.

coax *vt* to persuade gently; to obtain by coaxing.—**coaxingly** *adv*.

cobble[1] *n* a cobblestone, a rounded stone used for paving. * *vt* to pave with cobblestones.

cobble[2] *vt* to repair, to make (shoes); to put together roughly or hastily.

cobra *n* a venomous hooded snake of Africa and India.

cobweb *n* a spider's web; a flimsy thing; an entanglement.

cocaine *n* an intoxicating addictive drug obtained from coca leaves, used in anaesthesia.

cock *n* the adult male of the domestic fowl; the male of other birds; a tap or valve; the hammer of a gun; a cocked position; (*vulg*) the penis. * *vt* to set erect, to stick up; to set at an angle; to bring the hammer (of gun) to firing position.

cockerel *n* a young cock.

cockeyed *adj* (*inf*) having a squint; slanting; daft, absurd.

cockle *n* an edible shellfish with a rounded shell.

cockney *n* a person born in the East End of London; the dialect of this area.

cockpit *n* the compartment of a small aircraft for the pilot and crew, the flight deck; an arena for cock fighting; the driver's seat in a racing car.

cockroach *n* a nocturnal beetle-like insect.

cocktail *n* an alcoholic drink containing a mixture of spirits or other liqueurs; an appetizer, usu containing shellfish, served as the first course of a meal.

cocoa *n* a powder of ground cacao seeds; a drink made from this.

coconut *n* the fruit of the coconut palm.

cocoon *n* a silky case spun by some insect larvae for protection in the chrysalis stage; a cosy covering. * *vt* to wrap in a cocoon.

cod *n* a large edible fish of the North Atlantic.

code *n* a system of letters, numbers or symbols used to transmit secret messages, or to simplify communication; a systematic body of laws; a set of rules or conventions; (*comput*) a set of program instructions. * *vt* to put into code.

codify *vt* to collect or arrange (laws, rules, regulations, etc) into a system.—**codifier** *n*.—**codification** *n*.

coeducation *n* the teaching of students of both sexes in the same institution.—**coeducational** *adj*.

coerce *vt* to compel; to force by threats.—**coercion** *n*.

coexist *vi* to exist together at the same time; to live in peace together.—**coexistence** *n*.—**coexistent** *adj*.

coffee *n* a drink made from the seeds of the coffee tree; the seeds, or the shrub; a light-brown colour.

coffee table *n* a low table for holding drinks, books, etc. * *adj* (*book*) large and for looking at, not reading.

coffin *n* a chest for a dead body to be buried in.

cog *n* a tooth-like projection on the rim of a wheel.

cogent *adj* persuasive, convincing.—**cogently** *adv*.—**cogency** *n*.

cogwheel *n* a wheel with a toothed rim for gearing.

coherent *adj* cohering; capable of intelligible speech; consistent.— **coherently** *adv*.—**coherence** *n*.

coil *vti* to wind in rings or folds; to twist into a circular or spiral shape. * *n* a coiled length of rope; a single ring of this; (*elect*) a spiral wire for the passage of current; an intra-uterine contraceptive device.

coin *n* a piece of legally stamped metal used as money. * *vt* to invent (a word, phrase); to make into money, to mint.

coinage *n* the act of coining; the issue of coins, currency; a coined word.

coincide *vi* to occupy the same portion of space; to happen at the same time; to agree exactly, to correspond.

coincidence *n* the act of coinciding; the occurrence of an event at the same time as another without apparent connection.

coke[1] *n* coal from which gas has been expelled. * *vt* to convert (coal) into coke.

coke[2] *n* (*sl*) cocaine.

colander *n* a bowl with holes in the bottom for straining cooked vegetables, pasta, etc.

cold *adj* lacking heat or warmth; lacking emotion, passion or courage; unfriendly; (*scent*) faint; (*sl*) unconscious. * *n* absence of heat; the sensation caused by this; cold weather; a virus infection of the respiratory tract.—**coldly** *adv*.—**coldness** *n*.

cold feet *n* (*inf*) fear.

coleslaw *n* raw shredded cabbage in a dressing, used in salads.

collaborate *vi* to work jointly or together, esp in literature; to side with the invaders of one's country.—**collaboration** *n*.—**collaborator** *n*.

collage *n* art made up from scraps of paper, material and other odds and ends pasted onto a hard surface.

collapse *vi* to fall down; to come to ruin, to fail; to break down physically or mentally. * *n* the act of collapsing; a breakdown, prostration.

collapsible *adj* designed to fold compactly.

collar *n* the band of a garment round the neck; a decoration round the neck, a choker; a band of leather or chain put round an animal's neck. * *vt* to put a collar on; (*inf*) to seize.

collarbone *n* one of the two bones that connect the shoulder blades with the breast bone, the clavicle.

colleague *n* an associate in the same profession or office; a fellow worker.

collect *vti* to bring together, gather or assemble; to regain command of (oneself); to concentrate (thoughts, etc). * *n* a short prayer for a particular occasion.

collected *adj* self-possessed, cool.—**collectedly** *adv*.

collection *n* act of collecting; an accumulation; money collected at a meeting, etc; a group of things collected for beauty, interest, rarity or value; the periodic showing of a designer's fashions.

collector *n* a person who collects things, eg stamps, butterflies, as a hobby or so as to inspect them, as tickets.

college *n* an institution of higher learning; a school offering specialized knowledge; the buildings housing a college; an organized body of professionals.

collide *vi* to come into violent contact (with); to dash together; to conflict.

colliery *n* a coal mine and its associated buildings.

collision *n* state of colliding together; a violent impact of moving bodies, a crash; a clash of interests, etc.

colloquial *adj* used in familiar but not formal talk, not literary.—**colloquially** *adv*.

colon[1] *n* the part of the large intestine from the caecum to the rectum.—**colonic** *adj*.

colon[2] *n* a punctuation mark (:) between the semicolon and the full stop.

colonel *n* a commissioned officer junior to a brigadier but senior to a lieutenant colonel.

colonial *adj* of or pertaining to a colony or colonies; (*with cap*) pertaining to the thirteen British colonies that became the US. * *n* a person who takes part in founding a colony, a settler.

colonize *vt* to establish a colony in; to settle in a colony.

colony *n* an area of land acquired and settled by a distant state and subject to its control; a community of settlers; a group of people of the same nationality or interests living in a particular area; a collection of organisms in close association.

colossal *adj* gigantic, immense; (*inf*) amazing, wonderful.

colour, color (*US*) *n* the eye's perception of wavelengths of light with different colours corresponding to different wavelengths; the attribute of objects to appear different according to their differing ability to absorb, emit, or reflect light of different wavelengths; colour of the face or skin; pigment; dye; paint; (*literature*) use of imagery, vividness; (*mus*) depth of sound; (*pl*) a flag. * *vt* to give colour to, paint; to misrepresent; to influence. * *vi* to emit colour; to blush.—**coloration** *n*.

colour bar *n* discrimination based on race, esp by white races against other races.

colour-blind *adj* unable to distinguish colours, esp red and green.

coloured, colored (*US*) *adj* possessing colour; biased, not objective; of a darker skinned race. * *n* a person of a darker skinned race.

colourful, colorful (*US*) *adj* full of colour; vivid.—**colourfully** *adv*.

colt *n* a young male horse.

column *n* a round pillar for supporting or decorating a building; something of this shape; a vertical division of a page; a narrow-fronted deep formation of troops; a feature article appearing regularly in a newspaper, etc.

columnist *n* a journalist who contributes a regular column.

coma *n* deep prolonged unconsciousness.

comb *n* a toothed instrument for separating hair, wool, etc; a part of a machine like this; the crest of a cock; a honeycomb. * *vt* to arrange (hair) or dress (wool) with a comb; to seek for thoroughly.

combat *vti* (*pt* **combated**) to strive against, oppose; to do battle. * *n* a contest; a fight; struggle.

combination *n* the act of combining; a union of separate parts; persons allied for a purpose; a sequence of numbers which opens a combination lock.

combine *vti* to join together; to unite intimately; to possess together; to cooperate; (*chem*) to form a compound with. * *n* an association formed for commercial or political purposes; a machine for harvesting and threshing grain.

combustible *adj* capable of burning; easily set alight; excitable. * *n* a combustible thing.—**combustibility** *n*.

combustion *n* the process of burning; the process in which substances react with oxygen in air to produce heat.

come *vi* (*pt* **came,** *pp* **come**) to approach; to arrive; to reach; to happen (to); to originate; to turn out (to be); to occur in a certain order; to be derived or descended; to be caused; to result; to be available; (*sl*) to experience a sexual orgasm.

comeback *n* (*inf*) a return to a career or to popularity; (*inf*) a witty answer.

comedian *n* an actor of comic parts; an entertainer who tells jokes; a person who behaves in a humorous manner.

comedy *n* an amusing play or film; drama consisting of amusing plays; an amusing occurrence; humour.

comet *n* a celestial body that travels round the sun, with a visible nucleus and a luminous tail.

comfort *vti* to bring consolation to; to soothe; to cheer. * *n* consolation; relief; bodily ease; (*pl*) things between necessities and luxuries.

comfortable *adj* promoting comfort; at ease; adequate; (*inf*) financially well off.—**comfortably** *adv*.

comic *adj* of comedy; causing amusement. * *n* a comedian; an entertaining person; a paper or book with strip cartoons.

comical *adj* funny, laughable; droll, ludicrous.—**comically** *adv*.

comic strip *n* a series of drawings that depict a story in stages.

coming *adj* approaching next; of future importance.

comma *n* a punctuation mark (,) indicating a pause or break in a sentence, or separating items in a list.

command *vti* to order; to bid; to control; to have at disposal; to evoke, compel; to look down over; to be in authority (over), to govern. * *n* an order; control; disposal; position of authority; something or someone commanded; an instruction to a computer.

commandeer *vt* to seize for military purposes; to appropriate for one's own use.

commander *n* a person who commands, a leader; a naval officer ranking next below a captain.

commando *n* (*pl* **commandos**) a member of an elite military force trained to raid enemy territory.

commemorate *vt* to keep in the memory by ceremony or writing; to be a memorial of.—**commemoration** *n*.—**commemorative** *adj*.

commence *vti* to begin.

commend *vt* to speak favourably of, to praise; to recommend; to entrust.—**commendable** *adj*.

commendation *n* the act of com-mending, praise; an award.

commensurate *adj* having the same extent or measure; proportionate.

comment *n* a remark, observation, criticism; an explanatory note; talk, gossip. * *vi* to make a comment (upon); to annotate.

commentary *n* a series of explanatory notes or remarks.

commentator *n* one who reports and analyses events, trends, etc, as on TV.

commerce *n* trade in goods and services on a large scale between nations or individuals.

commercial *adj* of or engaged in commerce; sponsored by an advertiser; intended to make a profit. * *n* a broadcast advertisement.

commercialize *vt* to put on a business basis; to exploit for profit.—**commercialization** *n*.

commiserate *vti* to sympathize (with); to feel pity for.—**commiseration** *n*.

commission *n* authority to act; a document bestowing this; appointment as a military officer of the rank of lieutenant or above; a body of people appointed for specified duties; business committed to someone; a percentage on sales paid to a salesman or agent; brokerage. * *vt* to empower or appoint by commission; to employ the service of; to authorize.

commissionaire *n* a uniformed attendant at the entrance to an office building, shop, etc.

commissioner *n* a person empowered by a commission; various types of civil servant; a member of a commission.

commit *vti* (*pt* **committed**) to entrust; to consign (to prison); to do, to perpetrate; to pledge, to involve.

commitment *n* the act of committing; an engagement that restricts freedom; an obligation; an order for imprisonment or confinement in a mental institution.—**committal** *n*.

committee *n* a body of people appointed from a larger body to consider or manage some matter.

commodity *n* an article of trade; a useful thing; (*pl*) goods.

common *adj* belonging equally to more than one; public; usual, ordinary; widespread; familiar; frequent; easily obtained, not rare; low, vulgar; (*noun*) applying to any of a class. * *n* a tract of open public land; (*pl*) the common people; the House of Commons.—**commonly** *adv*.—**commonness** *n*.

commoner *n* an ordinary person, not a member of the nobility.

common law *n* the body of law based on custom and judicial precedent, as distinct from statute law. * *adj* denoting a marriage recognized in law not by an official ceremony, but after a couple have cohabited for a number of years.

Common Market *n* (*with* **the**) an unofficial name for the European Community, a grouping of nations formed to facilitate trade by removing tariff barriers.

commonplace *adj* ordinary, unremarkable. * *n* a platitude; an ordinary thing.

common sense *n* ordinary, practical good sense.—**common-sense** *adj*.

commonwealth *n* a political community; a sovereign state, republic; a federation of states; (*with cap*) an association of sovereign states and dependencies ruled or formerly ruled by Britain.

commotion *n* a violent disturbance; agitation; upheaval.

communal *adj* of a commune or community; shared in common.—**communally** *adv*.

commune[1] *n* a group of people living together and sharing possessions; the smallest administrative division in several European countries.

commune[2] *vi* to converse intimately; to communicate spiritually.

communicate *vti* to impart, to share; to succeed in conveying information; to be connected.

communication *n* the act of communicating; information; a connecting passage or channel; (*pl*) connections of transport; (*pl*) means of imparting information, as in newspapers, TV.

communication cord *n* a cord, by pulling which a passenger can stop a train in an emergency.

communion *n* common possession, sharing; fellowship; union in a religious body; (*with cap*) Holy Communion, the Christian sacrament of the Eucharist when bread and wine are consecrated and consumed.

communiqué *n* an official communication, esp to the press or public.

communism *n* a social system under which private property is abolished and the means of production are owned by the people; (*with cap*) a political movement seeking the overthrow of capitalism based on the writings of Karl Marx; the system as instituted in the former USSR and elsewhere.—**communist** *n*, *adj*.

community *n* an organized political or social body; a body of people in the same locality; the general public, society; any group having work, interests, etc in common; joint ownership; common character.

community centre *n* a place providing social and recreational facilities for a local community.

commute *vti* to travel daily from a suburban home to a city office; to exchange (for); to change (to); to reduce (a punishment) to one less severe.—**commutation** *n*.

commuter *n* a person who commutes to and from work.

compact[1] *n* an agreement; a contract, a treaty.

compact[2] *adj* closely packed; condensed; terse. * *vt* to press or pack closely; to compose (of). * *n* a small cosmetic case, usu containing powder and a mirror.—**compactly** *adv*.—**compactness** *n*.

companion *n* an associate in an activity; a partner; a friend; one of a pair of matched things.—**companionship** *n*.

company *n* any assembly of people; an association of people for carrying on a business, etc; a society; a military unit; the crew of a ship; companionship, fellowship.

comparable *adj* able or suitable to be compared (*with* **with**); similar.—**comparably** *adv*.—**comparability** *n*.

comparative *adj* estimated by comparison; relative, not absolute; (*gram*) expressing more.—**comparatively** *adv*.

compare *vt* to make one thing the measure of another; to observe similarity between, to liken; to bear comparison; (*gram*) to give comparative and superlative forms of (an adjective). * *vi* to make comparisons; to be equal or alike.

comparison *n* the act of comparing; an illustration; (*gram*) the use of *more* or *er* with an adjective.

compartment *n* a space partitioned off; a division of a railway carriage; a separate section or category.—**compartmental** *adj*.

compass *n* a circuit, circumference; an extent, area; the range of a voice; an instrument with a magnetic needle indicating north, south, east, west; (*often pl*) a two-legged instrument for drawing circles, etc.

compassion *n* sorrow for another's sufferings; pity.

compassionate *adj* showing compassion; merciful.—**compassionately** *adv*.

compatible *adj* agreeing or fitting in (with);

consistent.—**compatibly** *adv*.—**compatibility** *n*.
compel *vt* (*pt* **compelled**) to force, constrain; to oblige; to obtain by force.
compendium *n* (*pl* **compendiums, compendia**) an abridgement; a summary; a collection.
compensate *vti* to counterbalance; to make up for; to recompense.—**compensatory** *adj*.
compensation *n* the act of compensating; a sum given to compensate.
compere, compère *n* a person who introduces cabaret performers, television acts, etc. * *vt* to act as a compere (for).
compete *vi* to strive; to contend; to take part in a competition.
competence *n* the quality of being capable; sufficiency; capacity; an adequate income to live on.
competent *adj* fit, capable; adequate; legally qualified.—**competently** *adv*.
competition *n* act of competing; rivalry; a contest in skill or knowledge; a match.
competitive *adj* of, or involving, competition; of sufficient value in terms of price or quality to ensure success against rivals.—**competitively** *adv*.—**competitiveness** *n*.
competitor *n* a person who competes; an opponent; a rival.
compile *vt* to collect or make up from various sources; to amass; (*comput*) to translate high-level programme instructions into machine code using a compiler.—**compilation** *n*.
complacent *adj* self-satisfied.—**complacently** *adv*.—**complacency** *n*.
complain *vi* to find fault, to grumble; to be ill; (*poet*) to express grief, to make a mourning sound.
complaint *n* a statement of some grievance; a cause of distress or dissatisfaction; an illness.
complement *n* something making up a whole; a full allowance (of equipment or number). * *vt* to make complete.
complementary *adj* completing; together forming a balanced whole.
complete *adj* entire; free from deficiency; finished; thorough. * *vt* to make complete; to finish.—**completeness** *n*.
completely *adv* entirely, utterly.
completion *n* the act of completing; accomplishment; fulfilment.
complex *adj* having more than one part; intricate, not simple; difficult. * *n* a complex whole; a collection of interconnected parts, buildings or units; a group of mostly unconscious impulses, etc strongly influencing behaviour.—**complexity** *n*.
complexion *n* a colour, texture and look of the skin; aspect, character.
compliance *n* the act of complying with another's wishes; acquiescence.
compliant *adj* yielding, submissive.—**compliantly** *adv*.
complicate *vt* to make intricate or involved; to mix up.
complicated *adj* intricately involved; difficult to understand.
complication *n* a complex or intricate situation; a circumstance that makes (a situation) more complex; (*med*) a condition or disease following an original illness.
compliment *n* a polite expression of praise, a flattering tribute; (*pl*) a formal greeting or expression of regard. * *vt* to pay a compliment to, to flatter; to congratulate (on).
complimentary *adj* conveying or expressing a compliment; given free of charge.
comply *vi* to act in accordance (with); to yield, to agree.
component *adj* going to the making of a whole, constituent. * *n* a component part.
compose *vt* to make up, to form; to construct in one's mind, to write; to arrange, to put in order; to settle, to adjust; to tranquillize; (*print*) to set up. * *vi* to create musical works, etc.
composed *adj* calm, self-controlled.—**composedly** *adv*.
composer *n* a person who composes, esp music.
composition *n* the act or process of composing; a work of literature or music, a painting; a short written essay; the general make-up of something; a chemical compound.
compost *n* a mixture of decomposed organic matter for fertilizing soil.
composure *n* the state of being composed, calmness.
compound[1] *n* a substance or thing made up of a number of parts or ingredients, a mixture; a compound word. * *vt* to combine (parts, ingredients) into a whole, to mix; to intensify by adding new elements; to settle (debt) by partial payment. * *vi* to become joined in a compound; to come to terms of agreement. * *adj* compounded or made up of several parts; not simple.
compound[2] *n* an enclosure in which a building stands.
compound fracture *n* a fracture in which the bone pierces the skin.

compound interest *n* interest paid on the principal sum of capital and the interest that it has accrued.

comprehend *vt* to grasp with the mind, to understand; to include, to embrace.—**comprehension** *n*.

comprehensive *adj* wide in scope or content, including a great deal. * *n* a comprehensive school.—**comprehensively** *adv*.—**comprehensiveness** *n*.

comprehensive school *n* in Britain, a secondary school for local pupils of all abilities.

compress *vt* to press or squeeze together; to bring into a smaller bulk; to condense. * *n* a soft pad for compressing an artery, etc; a wet bandage to for relieving inflammation.

compression *n* the act of compressing; the increase in pressure in an engine to compress the gases so that they explode.

comprise *vt* to consist of, to include.

compromise *n* a settlement of a dispute by mutual concession; a middle course or view between two opposed ones. * *vti* to adjust by compromise; to lay open to suspicion, disrepute, etc.

compulsion *n* the act of compelling; something that compels; an irresistible urge.

compulsive *adj* compelling; acting as if compelled.—**compulsively** *adv*.

compulsory *adj* enforced, obligatory, required by law, etc; involving compulsion; essential.—**compulsorily** *adv*.

computer *n* an electronic device that processes data in accordance with programmed instructions.

computerize *vt* to equip with computers; to control or perform (a process) using computers; to store or process data using a computer.—**computerization** *n*.

comrade *n* a companion; a fellow member of a Communist party.—**comradely** *adv*.—**comradeship** *n*.

con[1] *vt* (*pt* **conned**) (*inf*) to swindle, trick. * *n* (*inf*) a confidence trick.

con[2] *n* against, as in **pro and con**.

con[3] *prep* with.

concave *adj* curving inwards, hollow. * *n* a concave line or surface.—**concavity** *n*.

conceal *vt* to hide, to keep from sight; to keep secret.—**concealment** *n*.

concede *vt* to grant; to admit to be true, to allow.

conceit *n* an over-high opinion of oneself; vanity; a far-fetched comparison, a quaint fancy.

conceited *adj* full of conceit, vain.—**conceitedly** *adv*.

conceivable *adj* capable of being imagined or believed.—**conceivably** *adv*.

conceive *vti* to become pregnant (with); to form in the mind; to think out, to imagine; to understand; to express.

concentrate *vt* to bring or converge together to one point; to direct to a single object or purpose; to collect one's thoughts or efforts; (*chem*) to increase the strength of by diminishing bulk, to condense. * *n* a concentrated product, esp a food reduced in bulk by eliminating fluid; a foodstuff relatively high in nutrients.

concentration *n* the act or process of concentrating; the direction of attention to a single object.

concern *vt* to relate or apply to; to fill with anxiety; to interest (oneself) in; to take part, to be mixed up (in). * *n* a thing that concerns one; anxiety, misgiving; interest in or regard for a person or thing; a business or firm.

concerned *adj* troubled, worried; interested.—**concernedly** *adv*.

concerning *prep* about; regarding.

concert *n* a musical entertainment; harmony; agreement or union.

concerted *adj* planned or arranged by mutual agreement; combined; (*mus*) arranged in separate parts for musicians or singers.

concertina *n* a hexagonal musical instrument, which produces sound by squeezing bellows that pass air over metal reeds. * *vi* to collapse or fold like the bellows of a concertina.

concerto *n* (*pl* **concertos**) a musical composition for a solo instrument and orchestra.

concession *n* the act of conceding; something conceded; a grant of rights, land, etc by a government, corporation, or individual; a reduction in price (of admission, travel, etc) for certain people.—**concessionary** *adj*.

conciliate *vt* to win over from hostility; to make friendly; to appease; to reconcile.—**conciliation** *n*.—**conciliator** *n*.—**conciliatory** *adj*.

concise *adj* brief, condensed, terse.—**concisely** *adv*.—**conciseness** *n*.

conclave *n* a private or secret meeting; a meeting of cardinals in seclusion to choose a pope; the meeting place.

conclude *vti* to bring or come to an end, to finish; to effect, to settle; to infer; to resolve.

conclusion *n* concluding; the end or close; an inference; a final opinion; (*logic*) a proposition deduced from premises.

conclusive *adj* decisive; convincing.—**conclusively** *adv*.

concoct *vt* to make by combining ingredients; to devise, to plan; to invent (a story).

concourse *n* an open space or hall where crowds gather, eg a railway or airport terminal.

concrete *adj* having a material existence; (*gram*) denoting a thing, not a quality, not abstract; made of concrete. * *n* anything concrete; a mixture of sand, cement, etc, used in building. * *vti* to form into a mass, to solidify; to cover with concrete.

concur *vi* (*pt* **concurred**) to happen together, to coincide; to cooperate; to be of the same opinion, to agree.—**concurrence** *n*.

concurrent *adj* existing, acting or occurring at the same time; coinciding.—**concurrently** *adv*.

concussion *n* the violent shock of an impact or explosion; loss of consciousness caused by a violent blow to the head.

condemn *vt* to express strong disapproval of; to find guilty; to blame or censure; to declare unfit for use.—**condemnation** *n*.—**condemnatory** *adj*.

condense *vt* to reduce to a smaller compass, to compress; to change from a gas into a liquid; to concentrate; to express in fewer words. * *vi* to become condensed.—**condenser** *n*.—**condensation** *n*.

condensed milk *n* milk that has been reduced by evaporation and sweetened.

condescend *vi* to waive one's superiority; to deign, to stoop; to act patronizingly.—**condescension** *n*.

condiment *n* a seasoning or relish.

condition *n* anything required for the performance, completion or existence of something else; physical state of health; an abnormality, illness; a prerequisite; (*pl*) attendant circumstances. * *vt* to be essential to the happening or existence of; to stipulate; to agree upon; to make fit; to make accustomed (to).—**conditioner** *n* a person or thing that conditions; a creamy substance for bringing the hair into a glossy condition.

conditional *adj* depending on conditions; not absolute; (*gram*) expressing condition. * *n* a conditional clause or conjunction.—**conditionally** *adv*.

condolence *n* sympathy.

condone *vt* to overlook, to treat as non-existent.

conducive *adj* leading or helping to cause or produce.

conduct *vti* to lead; to convey; to direct (an orchestra); to carry on or manage (a business); to transmit (electricity, heat); to behave (oneself). * *n* management, direction; behaviour.

conductor *n* a person who conducts an orchestra; one in charge of passengers on a train, or who collects fares on a bus; a substance that conducts heat or electricity.—**conductress** *nf*.

conduit *n* a channel or pipe that carries water, etc.

cone *n* a solid pointed figure with a circular or elliptical base; any cone-shaped object; the scaly fruit of the pine, fir, etc.

confectionery *n* sweets.

confederation *n* the act or state of confederating; an alliance of individuals, organizations or states.

confer *vt* (*pt* **conferred**) to grant or bestow; to compare views or take counsel; to consult.

conference *n* a meeting for discussion or consultation.

confess *vt* to acknowledge or admit; to disclose (sins) to a confessor; (*priest*) to hear confession of. * *vi* to make or hear a confession.

confession *n* admission or acknowledgement of a fault or sin, esp to a confessor; a thing confessed; a statement of one's religious beliefs, creed.

confessional *n* an enclosure in a church where a priest hears confessions.

confessor *n* a priest who hears confessions and grants absolution; one who confesses.

confetti *npl* bits of coloured paper thrown at weddings.

confide *vti* to put confidence (in); to entrust; to impart.

confidence *n* firm trust, faith; belief in one's own abilities; boldness; something revealed confidentially.

confidence trick *n* the persuading of a victim to hand over valuables as proof of confidence.

confident *adj* full of confidence; positive, assured.—**confidently** *adv*.

confidential *adj* spoken or written in confidence, secret; entrusted with secrets.—**confidentially** *adv*.—**confidentiality** *n*.

confine *vt* to restrict, to keep within limits; to keep shut up, as in prison, a sickbed, etc; to imprison. * *n* (*pl*) borderland, edge, limit.

confined *adj* narrow, enclosed.

confinement *n* a being confined; the period of childbirth.

confirm *vt* to make stronger; to establish firmly; to make valid, to ratify; to corroborate; to administer rite of confirmation to.

confirmation *n* the act of confirming; convincing proof; the rite by which people are admitted to full communion in Christian churches.

confirmed *adj* habitual; have undergone the rite of confirmation.

confiscate *vt* to appropriate to the state as a penalty; to seize by authority. —**confiscation** *n.*

conflict *n* a fight; a contest; strife, quar-rel; emotional disturbance. * *vi* to be at variance; to clash (with); to struggle.

conform *vi* to comply, to be obedient (to); to act in accordance with. * *vt* to adapt; to make like.

conformist *n* one who conforms to established rules, standards, etc; compliance with the rites and doctrines of an established church.—**conformism** *n.*

confound *vt* to mix up, to obscure; to perplex, to astound; to overthrow; to mistake one thing for another.

confounded *adj* astonished; confused; annoying; (*inf*) damned.—**confoundedly** *adv.*

confront *vt* to stand in front of, face; to bring face to face (with); to encounter; to oppose.—**confrontation** *n.*

confuse *vt* to throw into disorder; to mix up; to mistake one thing for another; to perplex, to disconcert; to embarrass; to make unclear.—**confusedly** *adv.*

confusion *n* the act or state of being confused; disorder; embarrassment, discomfiture; lack of clarity.

congeal *vti* to change from a liquid to a solid by cooling, to jell.—**congealment** *n.*

congenial *adj* of a similar disposition or with similar tastes, kindred; suited, agreeable (to).—**congenially** *adv.*—**congeniality** *n.*

congenital *adj* existing or dating since birth, as in certain defects.—**congenitally** *adv.*

conger eel *n* a large marine eel.

congestion *n* an overcrowding; (*med*) an excessive accumulation of blood in any organ; an accumulation of traffic causing obstruction.

congratulate *vt* to express sympathetic pleasure at success or good fortune of, to compliment.—**congratulation** *n.*—**congratulatory** *adj.*

congratulations *npl* an expression of joy or pleasure.

congregate *vti* to flock together, to assemble; to gather into a crowd or mass.

congregation *n* a gathering, an assembly; a body of people assembled for worship.

congress *n* an association or society; an assembly or conference, esp for discussion and action on some question; (*with cap*) the legislature of the US, comprising the Senate and the House of Representatives.

Congressman *n* a member of Congress.—**Congresswoman** *nf.*

conic, conical *adj* of a cone; cone-shaped.

conifer *n* any evergreen trees and shrubs with true cones (as pines) and other (as yews).—**coniferous** *adj.*

conjecture *n* a guess, guesswork. * *vt* to make a conjecture, to guess, surmise.—**conjectural** *adj.*

conjugal *adj* of or relating to marriage.—**conjugally** *adv.*

conjunction *n* (*gram*) a word connecting words, clauses or sentences; a union; a simultaneous occurrence of events; the apparent proximity of two or more planets.

conjunctivitis *n* inflammation of the membrane (conjunctiva) that covers the eyeball and inner eyelid.

conjure *vti* to practise magical tricks; to call up (spirits) by invocation.—**conjurer, conjuror** *n.*

conk *n* (*sl*) the nose or head. * *n* a blow to the nose or head.

con man *n* (*inf*) a swindler, one who defrauds by means of a confidence trick.

connect *vti* to fasten together, to join; to relate together, to link up; (*trains, buses, etc*) timed to arrive as another leaves so that passengers can continue their journey; to establish a link by telephone.—**connector, connecter** *n.*

connection, connexion *n* the act of connecting; the state of being connected; a thing that connects; a relationship, bond; a train, bus, etc timed to connect with another; an opportunity to transfer between trains, buses, etc; context; a link between components in an electric circuit; a relative; (*pl*) clients, customers.

connive *vi* to permit tacitly; to wink (at); to plot.—**connivance** *n.*

connoisseur *n* a trained discriminating judge, esp of the fine arts.

connotation *n* a consequential meaning, an implication—**connotative** *adj.*

conquer *vt* to gain victory (over), to defeat; to acquire by conquest; to overcome, to master.

* *vi* to be victor.—**conqueror** *n*.
conquest *n* conquering; the winning of a person's affection; a person or thing conquered.
conscience *n* the knowledge of right and wrong that affects action and behaviour; the sense of guilt or virtue induced by actions, behaviour, etc; an inmost thought; conscientiousness.
conscientious *adj* following the dictates of the conscience; scrupulous; careful, thorough.—**conscientiously** *adv*.—**conscientiousness** *n*.
conscientious objector *n* a person who refuses to serve in the military forces on moral or religious grounds.
conscious *adj* aware (of); awake to one's surroundings; (*action*) realized by the person who does it.—**consciously** *adv*.
consciousness *n* the state of being conscious; perception; the whole body of a person's thoughts and feelings.
conscript *adj* enrolled into service by compulsion; drafted. * *n* a conscripted person (as a military recruit). * *vt* to enlist compulsorily.—**conscription** *n*.
consecrate *vt* to set apart as sacred, to sanctify; to devote (to).—**consecration** *n*.
consecutive *adj* following in regular order without a break; successive; (*gram*) expressing consequence.—**consecutively** *adv*.
consensus *n* an opinion held by all or most; general agreement, esp in opinion.
consent *vi* to agree (to); to comply; to acquiesce * *n* agreement, permission; concurrence.
consequence *n* a result, an outcome; importance; (*pl*) a game in which each player writes part of a story without knowing what has gone before.
consequent *adj* occurring as a result.—**consequently** *adv*.
conservation *n* conserving; preservation of the environment and natural resources.—**conservationist** *n*.
conservative *adj* traditional; cautious; moderate. * *n* a conservative person; (*with cap*) a member of the Conservative Party in Britain and other countries.—**conservatively** *adv*.
conservatory *n* a greenhouse attached to a house; a conservatoire.
conserve *vt* to keep from loss or injury; to preserve (food) with sugar. * *n* a type of jam using whole fruit.
consider *vti* to reflect (upon), to contemplate; to examine, to weigh the merits of; to take into account; to regard as; to be of the opinion.
considerable *adj* a fairly large amount; worthy of respect.—**considerably** *adv*.
considerate *adj* careful of the feelings of others.—**considerately** *adv*.
consideration *n* the act of considering; deliberation; a point of importance; an inducement; thoughtfulness; deference.
considering *prep* in view of. * *adv* all in all. * *conj* seeing that.
consign *vt* to hand over, to commit; to send goods addressed (to).
consignment *n* consigning; goods, etc consigned.
consist *vi* to be made up (of); to be comprised (in).
consistency *n* degree of density, esp of thick liquids; the state of being consistent.
consistent *adj* compatible, not contradictory; uniform in thought or action.—**consistently** *adv*.
consolation *n* someone or something that offers comfort in distress.
console[1] *vt* to bring consolation to, to cheer in distress.—**consolable** *adj*.
console[2] *n* a desk containing the controls of an electronic system; the part of an organ containing the pedals, stops, etc; an ornamental bracket supporting a shelf or table.
consolidate *vti* to solidify; to establish firmly, to strengthen; to combine into a single whole.—**consolidation** *n*.
consonant *n* a letter of the alphabet that is not a vowel; the sound representing such a letter. * *adj* consistent, in keeping (with).
consortium *n* (*pl* **consortia**) an international banking or financial combination.
conspicuous *adj* easily seen, prominent; outstanding, eminent.—**conspicuousness** *n*.—**conspicuously** *adv*.
conspiracy *n* a secret plan for an illegal act; the act of conspiring.
conspire *vti* to combine secretly for an evil purpose; to plot, to devise.
constable *n* a policeman or policewoman of the lowest rank.
constant *adj* fixed; unchangeable; faithful; continual.—**constancy** *n*.
constellation *n* a group of fixed stars.
consternation *n* surprise and alarm; shock; dismay.
constipation *n* infrequent and difficult movement of the bowels.
constituency *n* a body of electors; the voters in a particular district.
constituent *adj* forming part of a whole, component; having the power to revise the consti-

tution. * *n* a component part; a member of an elective body; a voter in a district.

constitute *vt* to set up by authority, to establish; to frame, to form; to appoint; to compose, to make up.

constitution *n* fundamental physical condition; disposition; temperament; structure, composition; the system of basic laws and principles of a government, society, etc; a document stating these specifically.

constitutional *adj* of or pertaining to a constitution; authorized or limited by a constitution, legal; inherent, natural. * *n* a walk for the sake of one's health.—**constitutionally** *adv*.—**constitutionality** *n*.

constrain *vt* to compel, to force; to hinder by force; to confine, to imprison.

constrained *adj* enforced; embarrassed, inhibited; showing constraint.

constraint *n* compulsion; forcible confinement; repression of feeling; embarrassment.

constrict *vt* to draw together, to squeeze, to compress.

construct *vt* to make, to build, to fit together; to compose. * *n* a structure; an interpretation; an arrangement, esp of words in a sentence.—**constructible** *adj*.—**constructor, constructer** *n*.

construction *n* constructing; anything constructed; a structure, building; interpretation, meaning; (*gram*) two or more words grouped together to form a phrase, clause or sentence.—**constructional** *adj*.

constructive *adj* helping to improve, promoting development.—**constructively** *adv*.

construe *vti* to translate word for word; to analyse grammatically; to take in a particular sense, to interpret.

consul *n* a person appointed to live in a foreign city to attend to the interests of his country's citizens and business there.—**consular** *adj*.

consulate *n* the official residence of a consul; the office of a Roman consul.

consult *vti* to seek advice from, esp a doctor or lawyer; to deliberate, to confer.

consultant *n* a specialist who gives professional or technical advice; a senior physician or surgeon in a hospital; a person who consults another.—**consultancy** *n*.

consultation *n* the act of consulting; a conference, esp with a doctor or lawyer.—**consultative** *adj*.

consume *vti* to destroy; to use up; to eat or drink up; to waste away; to utilize economic goods.—**consumable** *adj*.

consumer *n* a person who uses goods and services, the end user.

consummate[1] *vt* to bring to perfection, to be the crown of; (*marriage*) to complete by sexual intercourse.—**consummation** *n*.

consummate[2] *adj* complete, perfect.

consumption *n* the act of consuming; the state of being consumed or used up; (*econ*) expenditure on goods and services by consumers; tuberculosis.

contact *n* touch, touching; connection; an acquaintance, esp in business; a connection allowing the passage of electricity; (*med*) a person who has been in contact with a contagious disease.* *vti* to establish contact with.

contact lens *n* a thin correctional lens placed over the cornea of the eye.

contagious *adj* (*disease*) spread by contact; capable of spreading disease by contact; (*influence*) catching, infectious.

contain *vt* to hold, to enclose; to comprise, to include; to hold back or restrain within fixed limits.

container *n* a receptacle, etc designed to contain goods or substances; a standardized receptacle used to transport commodities.

contaminate *vt* to render impure, to pollute.—**contaminant** *n*.—**contamination** *n*.—**contaminator** *n*.

contemplate *vti* to look at steadily; to reflect upon, to meditate; to have in view, to intend.—**contemplation** *n*.

contemporary *adj* living or happening at the same time; of about the same age; present day. * *n* a person living at the same time; a person of the same age.

contempt *n* the feeling one has toward someone or something considered low, worthless etc; the condition of being despised.

contemptible *adj* deserving contempt.—**contemptibly** *adv*.—**contemptibility** *n*.

contemptuous *adj* showing or feeling contempt; disdainful.—**contemptuously** *adv*.—**contemptuousness** *n*.

contend *vti* to take part in a contest, to strive (for); to quarrel; to maintain (that), to assert.—**contender** *n*.

content[1] *n* (*usu pl*) what is in a container; (*usu pl*) what is in a book; substance or meaning.

content[2] *adj* satisfied (with), not desiring more; willing (to); happy; pleased. * *n* satisfaction. * *vt* to make content; to satisfy.—**contentment** *n*.

contention *n* contending, struggling, arguing;

a point in dispute; an assertion in an argument.

contest *vti* to call in question, to dispute; to fight to gain, to compete for; to strive. * *n* a struggle, an encounter; a competition; a debate; a dispute.

contestant *n* a competitor in a contest; a person who contests.

context *n* the parts of a written work or speech that precede and follow a word or passage, contributing to its full meaning; associated surroundings, setting.—**contextual** *adj*.

continent[1] *n* one of the six or seven main divisions of the earth's land; (*with cap*) the mainland of Europe, excluding the British Isles; a large extent of land.

continent[2] *adj* able to control urination and defecation; practising self-restraint; chaste.—**continence** *n*.

continental *adj* of a continent; (*with cap*) of or relating to Europe, excluding the British Isles; of or relating to the former 13 British colonies later forming the USA. * *n* an inhabitant of the Continent.

contingency *n* a possibility of a future event or condition; something dependent on a future event.

contingent *adj* possible, that may happen; chance; dependent (on); incidental (to). * *n* a possibility; a quota of troops.—**contingently** *adv*.

continual *adj* frequently repeated, going on all the time.—**continually** *adv*.

continuation *n* a continuing; prolongation; resumption; a thing that continues something else, a sequel, a further instalment.

continue *vt* to go on (with); to prolong; to extend; to resume, to carry further. * *vi* to remain, to stay; to last; to preserve.

continuity *n* continuousness; uninterrupted succession; a script or scenario in a film or broadcast.

continuous *adj* continuing; occurring without interruption.—**continuously** *adv*.—**continuousness** *n*.

contort *vti* to twist out of a normal shape, to pull awry.—**contortion** *n*.

contortionist *n* a person who can twist his or her body into unusual postures.

contour *n* the outline of a figure, land, etc; the line representing this outline; a contour line.

contour line *n* a line on a map that passes through all points at the same altitude.

contra- *prefix* against.

contraband *n* smuggled goods; smuggling. * *adj* illegal to import or export.

contraception *n* the deliberate prevention of conception, birth control.

contraceptive *n* a contraceptive drug or device.—*also adj*.

contract *vt* to draw closer together; to confine; to undertake by contract; (*debt*) to incur; (*disease*) to become infected by; (*word*) to shorten by omitting letters. * *vi* to shrink; to become smaller or narrower; to make a contract. * *n* a bargain; an agreement to supply goods or perform work at a stated price; a written agreement enforceable by law.

contraction *n* the act of contracting; the state of being contracted; a contracted word; a labour pain in childbirth.

contractor *n* a person who makes a business contract, esp a builder.

contractual *adj* of a contract.—**contractually** *adv*.

contradict *vti* to assert the contrary or opposite of; to deny; to be at variance (with).

contradiction *n* the act of contradicting; a denial.—**contradictory** *adj*.

contralto *n* (*pl* **contraltos**) a singing voice having a range between tenor and mezzo-soprano; a person having this voice.

contraption *n* (*inf*) a device, a gadget.

contrary *adj* opposed; opposite in nature; wayward, perverse. * *n* the opposite. * *adv* in opposition to; in conflict with.—**contrarily** *adv*.—**contrariness** *n*.

contrast *vi* to show marked differences. * *vt* to compare so as to point out the differences. * *n* the exhibition of differences; difference of qualities shown by comparison; the degree of difference between colours or tones.

contravene *vt* to infringe (a law), to transgress; to conflict with, to contradict.—**contravention** *n*.

contribute *vti* to give to a common stock or fund; to write (an article) for a magazine, etc; to furnish ideas, etc.—**contributory** *adj*.

contribution *n* the act of contributing; something contributed; a literary article; a payment into a collection.

contributor *n* a person who contributes, esp the writer of a newspaper article, etc; a contributing factor.

contrite *adj* deeply repentant, feeling guilt.—**contritely** *adv*.—**contrition** *n*.

contrivance *n* something contrived, esp a mechanical device, invention; inventive ability; an artificial construct; a stratagem.

contrive *vt* to plan ingeniously; to devise, to

design, to manage; to achieve, esp by some ploy; to scheme.—**contriver** *n*.

control *n* restraint; command, authority; a check; a means of controlling; a standard of comparison for checking an experiment. * *vt* (*pt* **controlled**) to check; to restrain; to regulate; to govern; (*experiment*) to verify by comparison.

controversial *adj* causing controversy, open to argument.

controversy *n* a discussion of contrary opinions; dispute, argument.

convalesce *vi* to recover health and strength after an illness; to get better. —**convalescence** *n*.

convalescent *adj* recovering health; aiding the recovery of full health. * *n* a patient recovering after an illness.

convector *n* a heater that circulates warm air.

convene *vti* to call together for a meeting.—**convener** *n*.

convenience *n* what suits one; a useful appliance; a public lavatory.

convenient *adj* handy; suitable; causing little or no trouble.—**conveniently** *adv*.

convent *n* a house of a religious order, esp an establishment of nuns.

convention *n* a political or ecclesiastical meeting; an agreement between nations, a treaty; established usage, social custom.

conventional *adj* of or based on convention or social custom; not spontaneous; following accepted rules; (*weapons*) non-nuclear.—**conventionality** *n* —**conventionally** *adj*.

converge *vti* to come or bring together.—**convergence** *n*.—**convergent** *adj*.

conversant *adj* well acquainted; proficient; familiar (with).

conversation *n* informal talk or exchange of ideas, opinions, etc between people.—**conversational** *adj*.—**conversationally** *adv*.

converse[1] *vi* to engage in conversation (with). * *n* familiar talk, conversation.

converse[2] *adj* opposite, contrary. * *n* something that is opposite or contrary.—**conversely** *adv*.

conversion *n* change from one state, or from on religion, to another; something converted from one use to another; an alteration to a building undergoing a change in function; (*rugby*) a score after a try by kicking the ball over the crossbar.

convert *vt* to change from one thing, condition or religion to another; to alter; to apply to a different use; (*rugby*) to make a conversion after a try. * *n* a converted person, esp one who has changed religion.—**convertibility** *n*.

convertible *adj* able to be converted. * *n* a car with a folding or detachable roof.

convex *adj* curving outward like the surface of a sphere.—**convexly** *adv*.—**convexity** *n*.

convey *vt* to transport; to conduct, to transmit; to make known, to communicate; (*law*) to make over (property). —**conveyable** *adj*.—**conveyor** *n*.

conveyor belt *n* a continuous moving belt or linked plates for moving objects in a factory.

convict *vt* to prove or pronounce guilty. * *n* a convicted person serving a prison sentence.

conviction *n* act of convicting; a settled opinion; a firm belief.

convince *vt* to persuade by argument or evidence; to satisfy by proof.

convincing *adj* compelling belief.—**convincingly** *adv*.

convivial *adj* sociable, jovial.—**conviviality** *n*.—**convivially** *adv*.

convulse *vt* to agitate violently; to shake with irregular spasms. * *vi* (*inf*) to cause to shake with uncontrollable laughter.—**convulsive** *adj*.—**convulsively** *adv*.

convulsion *n* a violent involuntary contraction of a muscle or muscles; an agitation, tumult; (*pl*) a violent fit of laughter.

cook *vt* to prepare (food) by heat; (*inf*) to fake (accounts, etc); to subject to great heat. * *vi* to be a cook; to under go cooking. * *n* a person who cooks; one whose job is to cook.

cookbook, cookery book *n* a book of recipes and other information for preparing food.

cooker *n* an electric or gas appliance for cooking.

cookery *n* the art or practice of cooking.

cookie *n* a biscuit.

cool *adj* moderately cold; calm; indifferent. * *vti* to make or become cool. * *n* coolness; composure.—**cooler** *n*.—**coolly** *adv*.—**coolness** *n*.

coop[1] *n* a small pen for poultry. * *vt* to confine as in a coop.

coop[2], **co-op** *n* a cooperative society or shop run by a cooperative society.

cooperate, co-operate *vi* to work together, to act jointly.—**cooperation, co-operation** *n*.—**cooperator, co-operator** *n*.

cooperative, co-operative *adj* willing to co-operate; helpful. * *n* an organization or enterprise owned by, and operated for the benefit of, those using its services.—**cooperatively, co-operatively** *adv*.

coordinate, co-ordinate *vt* to integrate (different elements, etc) into an efficient relationship; to adjust to; to function harmoniously. * *n* an equal person or thing; any of a series of numbers that, in a given frame of reference, locate a point in space; (*pl*) separate items of clothing intended to be worn together. * *adj* equal in degree or status.—**coordinately**, **co-ordinately** *adv*.

coordination, **co-ordination** *n* the act of coordinating; the state of being coordinated; balanced and harmonious movement of the body.

coot *n* a European water-bird with dark plumage, similar to a duck.

cop *vb* (*pt* **copped**) *vt* (*sl*) to arrest, catch. * *vi* (*with* **out**) (*sl*) to fail to perform, to renege. * *n* (*sl*) capture; a policeman.

cope *vi* to deal successfully with; to contend on even terms (with).

copilot *n* a second pilot in an aircraft.

copious *adj* plentiful, abundant.—**copiously** *adv*.

copper[1] *n* a reddish ductile metallic element; a bronze coin. * *adj* made of, or of the colour of, copper.

copper[2] *n* (*sl*) a police officer.

copulate *vi* to have sexual intercourse.—**copulation** *n*.—**copulative** *adj*.

copy *n* a reproduction; a transcript; a single specimen of a book; a model to be copied; a manuscript for printing; text for an advertisement; subject matter for a writer. * *vt* to make a copy of, to reproduce; to take as a model, to imitate.

copyright *n* the exclusive legal right to the publication and sale of a literary, dramatic, musical, or artistic work in any form. * *adj* protected by copyright.

copywriter *n* a writer of advertising or publicity copy.—**copywriting** *n*.

coral *n* the hard skeleton secreted by certain marine polyps. * *adj* made of or like coral.

cord *n* a thick string or thin rope; something that binds; a slender electric cable; a ribbed fabric, esp corduroy; (*pl*) corduroy trousers.

cordial *adj* hearty, warm; friendly; affectionate. * *n* a fruit-flavoured drink.—**cordiality** *n*.—**cordially** *adv*.

cordon *n* a chain of police or soldiers preventing access to an area; a piece of ornamental cord or ribbon given as an award. * *vt* (*with* **off**) (*area*) to prevent access to.

corduroy *n* a strong cotton fabric with a velvety ribbed surface; (*pl*) trousers of this.

core *n* the innermost part, the heart; the inner part of an apple, etc containing seeds; the region of a nuclear reactor containing the fissile material; (*comput*) a form of magnetic memory used to store one bit of information. * *vt* to remove the core from.

cork *n* the outer bark of the cork oak used esp for stoppers and insulation; a stopper for a bottle, esp made of cork. * *adj* made of cork. * *vt* to stop up with a cork; to give a taste of cork to (wine).

corkage *n* a charge made by a restaurant for serving wine, esp when brought in by the customer from outside.

corkscrew *n* a tool for drawing corks from wine bottles. * *adj* resembling a corkscrew.

cormorant *n* a large voracious sea bird with dark plumage and webbed feet.

corn[1] *n* a grain or seed of a cereal plant; plants that yield grain; maize; (*sl*) something corny.

corn[2] *n* a small hard painful growth on the foot.

corn cob *n* the central part of an ear of maize to which the corn kernels are attached.

cornea *n* the transparent membrane in front of the eyeball.—**corneal** *adj*.

corner *n* the point where sides or streets meet; an angle; a secret or confined place; a difficult or dangerous situation; (*football, hockey*) a free kick from the corner of the pitch; a monopoly over the supply of a good or service giving control over the market price; one of the opposite angles in a boxing ring. * *vt* to force into a corner; to monopolize supplies of (a commodity). * *vi* to turn round a corner; to meet at a corner or angle.

cornerstone *n* the principal stone, esp one at the corner of a foundation; an indispensable part.

cornet *n* a tapering valved brass musical instrument; a cone-shaped wafer for ice cream.

cornflour *n* a type of maize flour used for thickening sauces.

cornice *n* a plaster moulding round a ceiling or on the outside of a building.

corny *adj* (**cornier, corniest**) (*inf*) hackneyed; banal; trite; overly sentimental.—**cornily** *adv*.—**corniness** *n*.

corollary *n* an additional inference from a proposition already proved; a result.

coronary *adj* pertaining to the arteries supplying blood to the heart. * *n* a coronary artery.

coronation *n* the act or ceremony of crowning a sovereign.

coroner *n* a public official who inquires into the causes of sudden or accidental deaths.

coronet *n* a small crown; an ornamental headdress.

corporal[1] *n* a non-commissioned officer below the rank of sergeant.
corporal[2] *adj* of or relating to the body; physical, not spiritual.—**corporally** *adv*.
corporal punishment *n* physical punishment, such as beating.
corporate *adj* legally united into a body; of or having a corporation; united.—**corporately** *adv*.
corporation *n* a group of people authorized by law to act as one individual; a city council.
corps *n* (*pl* **corps**) an organized subdivision of the military establishment; a group or organization with a special function (*medical corps*).
corpse *n* a dead body.
corpuscle *n* a red or white blood cell.—*also* **corpuscule**.—**corpuscular** *adj*.
corral *n* a pen for livestock; an enclosure with wagons; a strong stockade. * *vt* (*pt* **corralled**) to form a corral; to put or keep in a corral.
correct *vt* to set right, to remove errors from; to reprove, to punish; to counteract, to neutralize. * *adj* free from error; right, true, accurate; conforming to a fixed standard; proper.—**correctly** *adv*.—**correctness** *n*.
correction *n* the act of correcting; punishment.—**correctional** *adj*.
correlate *vti* to have or to bring into mutual relation; to correspond to one another.—**correlation** *n*.—**correlative** *adj*.
correspond *vi* to answer, to agree; to be similar (to); to communicate by letter.
correspondence *n* communication by writing letters; the letters themselves; agreement.
correspondent *n* a person who writes letters; a journalist who gathers news for newspapers, radio or television from a foreign country. * *adj* similar, analogous.
corridor *n* a long passage into which compartments or rooms open.
corroborate *vt* to confirm; to make more certain; to verify.—**corroboration** *n*.—**corroborative** *adj*.—**corroborator** *n*.
corrode *vti* to eat into or wear away gradually, to rust; to disintegrate.—**corrosion** *n*.
corrugated iron *n* sheet iron pressed in alternate parallel ridges and grooves and galvanized.
corrupt *adj* dishonest; taking bribes; depraved; rotten, putrid. * *vti* to make or become corrupt; to infect; to taint.—**corruptly** *adv*.—**corruptness** *n*.
corset *n* a close-fitting undergarment, worn to support the torso.
cortege, cortège *n* a train of attendants; a retinue; a funeral procession.
cosmetic *n* a preparation for improving the beauty, esp of the face. * *adj* beautifying or correcting faults in the appearance.—**cosmetically** *adv*.
cosmonaut *n* a Russian astronaut.
cosmopolitan *adj* of all parts of the world; free from national prejudice; at home in any part of the world.—**cosmopolitanism** *n*.
cosmos *n* the universe as an ordered whole; any orderly system.
cosset *vt* (*pl* **cosseted**) to make a pet of; to pamper.
cost *vt* (*pt* **cost**) to involve the payment, loss, or sacrifice of; to have as a price; (*pt* **costed**) to fix the price of. * *n* a price; expenditure of time, labour, etc; (*pl*) the expenses of a lawsuit.
costly *adj* (**costlier, costliest**) expensive; involving great sacrifice.—**costliness** *n*.
costume *n* a style of dress, esp belonging to a particular period, fashion, etc; clothes of an unusual or historical nature, as worn by actors in a play, etc.
costume jewellery *n* imitation gems or cheap jewellery worn for decorative effect.
cosy, cozy (*US*) *adj* (**cosier, cosiest**) warm and comfortable; snug.
cot *n* a child's box-like bed; a narrow collapsible bed.
cottage *n* a small house, esp in the country.
cottage cheese *n* a soft cheese made from loose milk curds.
cotton *n* soft white fibre of the cotton plant; fabric or thread made of this; thread. * *adj* made of cotton.
cotton wool *n* raw cotton that has been bleached and sterilized for use as a dressing, etc; a state of being protected.
couch *n* a piece of furniture, with a back and armrests, for seating several persons; a bed, esp as used by psychiatrists for patients. * *vt* to express in words in a particular way.
cough *vi* to expel air from the lungs with a sudden effort and noise. * *n* the act of coughing; a disease causing a cough.
could *see* **can**[1].
council *n* an elected or appointed legislative or advisory body; a central body uniting a group of organizations; an executive body whose members are equal in power and authority.
councillor, **councilor** (*US*) *n* a member of a council.
counsel *n* advice; consultation, deliberate purpose or design; a person who gives counsel,

a lawyer or a group of lawyers; a consultant. * *vb* (*pt* **counselled**) *vt* to advise; to recommend. * *vi* to give or take advice.

counsellor, counselor (*US*) *n* an adviser; a lawyer.

count[1] *n* a European noble.

count[2] *vt* to number, add up; to reckon; to consider to be; to call aloud (beats or time units); to include or exclude by counting. * *vi* to name numbers or add up items in order; to mark time; to be of importance; to rely (upon). * *n* act of numbering or reckoning; the total counted; a separate and distinct charge in an indictment; rhythm.

countdown *n* the descending count backwards to zero, eg to the moment a rocket lifts off.

countenance *n* the whole form of the face; appearance; support. * *vt* to favour, give approval to.

counter[1] *n* one who or that which counts; a disc used for scoring, a token; a table in a bank or shop across which money or goods are passed.

counter[2] *adv* contrary; adverse; in an opposite direction; in the wrong way. * *adj* opposed; opposite. * *n* a return blow or parry; an answering move. * *vti* to oppose; to retort; to give a return blow; to retaliate.

counteract *vt* to act in opposition to so as to defeat or hinder; to neutralize.—**counteraction** *n*.—**counteractive** *adj*.

counterattack *n* an attack in response to an attack. * *vt* to make a counterattack.

counterbalance *n* a weight balancing another. * *vt* to act as a counterbalance; to act against with equal power.

counterespionage *n* spying on or exposing enemy spies.

counterfeit *vt* to imitate; to forge; to feign, simulate. * *adj* made in imitation, forged; feigned, sham. * *n* an imitation, a forgery.

counterfoil *n* a detachable section of a cheque or ticket, kept as a receipt or record.

counterpart *n* a thing exactly like another, a duplicate; a corresponding or complementary part or thing.

countess *n* a woman with the rank of count or earl; the wife or widow of an earl or count.

countless *adj* innumerable.

country *n* a region or district; the territory of a nation; a state; the land of one's birth or residence; rural parts; country-and-western. * *adj* rural.

countryman *n* a person who lives in the country; a person from the same country as another.—**countrywoman** *nf*.

countryside *n* a rural district.

county *n* an administrative subdivision for local government.—*also adj*.

coup *n* a sudden telling blow; a masterstroke; a coup d'état.

coup d'état *n* a sudden and unexpected bold stroke of policy; the sudden overthrow of a government.

coupé *n* a closed, four-seater, two-door car with a sloping back.

couple *n* two of the same kind connected together; a pair; a husband and wife; a pair of equal and parallel forces. * *vt* to link or join together. * *vi* to copulate.

couplet *n* two consecutive lines of verse that rhyme with each other.

coupling *n* a device for joining parts of a machine or two railway carriages.

coupon *n* a detachable certificate on a bond, presented for payment of interest; a certificate entitling one to a discount, gift, etc; an entry form, as for a competition.

courage *n* bravery; fortitude; spirit.—**courageous** *adj*.—**courageously** *adv*.—**courageousness** *n*.

courier *n* a messenger; a tourist guide; a carrier of illegal goods between countries.

course *n* a race; a path or track; a career; a direction or line of motion; a regular sequence; the portion of a meal served at one time; conduct; behaviour; the direction a ship is steered; a continuous level range of brick or masonry of the same height; the chase of a hare by greyhounds; a series of studies; any of the studies. * *vt* to hunt. * *vi* to move swiftly along an indicated path; to chase with greyhounds.

court *n* an uncovered space surrounded by buildings or walls; a short street; a playing space, as for tennis, etc; a royal palace; the retinue of a sovereign; (*law*) a hall of justice; the judges, etc engaged there; address; civility; flattery. * *vt* to seek the friendship of; to woo; to flatter; to solicit. * *vi* to carry on a courtship.

courteous *adj* polite; obliging.—**courteously** *adv*.—**courteousness** *n*.

courtesan, courtezan *n* (*formerly*) a prostitute, or mistress of a courtier.

courtesy *n* politeness and kindness; civility; a courteous manner or action.

courthouse *n* a public building that houses law courts or local authority offices.

courtier *n* one in attendance at a royal court.

court martial *n* (*pl* **courts martial**) a court of

justice composed of naval or military officers for the trial of disciplinary offences.

court-martial *vt* (*pt* **court-martialled**) to try by court martial.

cousin *n* the son or daughter of an uncle or aunt.

cove *n* a small sheltered bay or inlet in a body of water; a curved moulding at the juncture of a wall and ceiling (—*also* **coving**).

covenant *n* a written agreement; a solemn agreement of fellowship and faith between members of a church. * *vt* to promise by a covenant. * *vi* to enter into a formal agreement.—**covenanted** *adj*.

cover *vt* to overspread the top of anything with something else; to hide; to save from punishment; to shelter; to clothe; to understudy; to insure against damage, loss, etc; to report for a newspaper; (*male animal*) to copulate. * *vi* to spread over, as a liquid does; to provide an excuse (for). * *n* that which is laid on something else; a shelter; a covert; an understudy; something used to hide one's real actions, etc; insurance against loss or damage; a place laid at a table for a meal.

coverage *n* the amount, extent, etc covered by something; the amount of reporting of an event for newspaper, television, etc.

cover charge *n* a charge made by a restaurant over and above the cost of the food and service.

covet *vt* (*pt* **coveted**) to desire earnestly; to lust after; to long to possess (what belongs to another).—**covetous** *adj*.—**covetousness** *n*.

coving *see* **cove**.

cow[1] *n* the mature female of domestic cattle; the mature female of various other animals, as the whale, elephant, etc; (*sl*) a disagreeable woman.

cow[2] *vt* to take the spirit out of, to intimidate.

coward *n* a person lacking courage; one who is afraid.

cowardice *n* lack of courage.

cowardly *adj* of, or like, a coward.—**cowardliness** *n*.

cowboy *n* a person who tends cattle or horses.—*also* **cowhand**.

cower *vi* to crouch or sink down through fear, etc; to tremble.

coxswain *n* a person who steers a boat, esp in a race.

coy *adj* playfully demure; bashful.—**coyly** *adv*.—**coyness** *n*.

cozy *see* **cosy**.

crab *n* any of numerous chiefly marine broadly built crustaceans. * *vi* (*pt* **crabbed**) to fish for crabs; to complain.

crack *vt* to burst, break or sever; to utter a sharp, abrupt cry; to injure; to damage mentally; to open a bottle; (*sl*) to make (a joke); (*inf*) to break open (a safe); to decipher (a code). * *vi* to make a sharp explosive sound; (*inf*) to lose control under pressure; to shift erratically in vocal tone. * *n* a chink or fissure; a narrow fracture; a sharp sound; a sharp resonant blow; an altered tone of voice; a chat, gossip; a wisecrack.

cracker *n* a firework that explodes with a crack; a paper tube that when pulled explodes harmlessly and releases a paper hat, etc; a thin, crisp biscuit.

crackle *vi* to make a slight, sharp explosive noise. * *vt* to cover with a delicate network of minute cracks. * *n* a noise of frequent and slight cracks and reports; a surface glaze on glass or porcelain.—**crackly** *adj*.

crackling *n* the browned crisp rind of roast pork.

cradle *n* a baby's crib or a small bed, often on rockers; infancy; birthplace or origin; a case for a broken limb; a framework of timbers, esp for supporting a boat. * *vt* to rock or place in a cradle; to nurse or train in infancy.

craft *n* manual skill; a skilled trade; the members of a skilled trade; cunning; (*pl* **craft**) a boat, ship, or aircraft.

craftsman *n* a person skilled in a particular craft.—**craftsmanship** *n*.

crag *n* a rough steep rock or cliff.—**craggy** *adj* (**craggier, craggiest**).—**cragginess** *n*.

cram *vt* (*pt* **crammed**) to pack tightly, to stuff; to fill to overflowing; (*inf*) to prepare quickly for an examination. * *vi* to eat greedily.

cramp *n* a spasmodic muscular contraction of the limbs; (*pl*) abdominal spasms and pain; a clamp. * *vt* to affect with muscular spasms; to confine narrowly; to hamper; to secure with a cramp. * *vi* to suffer from cramps.

cramped *adj* restricted, narrow; (*handwriting*) small and irregular.

crampon, crampoon *n* a metal frame with spikes attached to boots for walking or climbing on ice.

cranberry *n* a small red sour berry; the shrub it grows on.

crane *n* a large wading bird with very long legs and neck, and a long straight bill; a machine for raising, shifting, and lowering heavy weights. * *vti* to stretch out (the neck).

cranium *n* (*pl* **craniums, crania**) the skull, esp

the part enclosing the brain.—**cranial** *adj*.

crank *n* a right-angled arm attached to a shaft for turning it; (*inf*) an eccentric person. * *vt* to provide with a crank; to turn or wind.

cranny *n* a fissure, crack, crevice.

crash *n* a loud, sudden confused noise; a violent fall or impact; a sudden failure, as of a business or a computer; a collapse, as of the financial market. * *adj* done with great speed, suddenness or effort. * *vti* to clash together with violence; to make a loud clattering noise; (*aircraft*) to land with a crash; to collapse, to ruin; (*inf*) to intrude into (a party).

crash helmet *n* a cushioned helmet worn by airmen, motorcyclists, etc for protection.

crash-land *vti* (*aircraft*) to make an emergency landing without lowering the undercarriage, or to be landed in this way.—**crash-landing** *n*.

crate *n* an open box of wooden slats, for shipping; (*sl*) an old car or aircraft. * *vt* to pack in a crate.

crater *n* the mouth of a volcano; a cavity caused by the explosion of a bomb, shell, etc; an ancient Greek goblet.

cravat *n* a neckcloth.

crave *vt* to have a strong desire (for); to ask humbly, to beg.—**craving** *n*.

crawl *vi* to move along the ground on hands and knees; to move slowly and with difficulty; to creep; (*inf*) to seek favour by servile behaviour; to swarm (with). * *n* the act of crawling; a slow motion; a racing stroke in swimming.—**crawler** *n*.

crayfish *n* any of numerous freshwater crustaceans; the spiny lobster.

crayon *n* a stick or pencil of coloured chalk; a drawing done with crayons. * *vt* to draw with a crayon.

craze *n* a passing infatuation; excessive enthusiasm; a crack in pottery glaze. * *vt* to produce cracks; to render insane.

crazy *adj* (**crazier, craziest**) (*inf*) mad, insane; foolish; ridiculous; unsound; (*paving*) composed of irregular pieces.—**crazily** *adv*.—**craziness** *n*.

creak *vi* to make a shrill grating sound. * *n* such a sound.—**creaky** *adj*.

cream *n* the rich, fatty part of milk; the choicest part of anything; a yellowish white colour; a type of face or skin preparation. * *vt* to add or apply cream to; to beat into a soft, smooth consistency; to skim cream from; to remove the best part of. * *vi* to form cream or scum; to break into a creamy froth. —**creamy** *adj*.—**creaminess** *n*.

cream cheese *n* soft cheese made from soured milk or cream.

crease *n* a line made by folding; (*cricket*) a line made by a batsman or bowler marking the limits of their position. * *vti* to make or form creases; to become creased.

create *vt* to cause to come into existence; to form out of nothing. * *vi* to make something new, to originate; (*sl*) to make a fuss.

creation *n* the act of creating; the thing created; the whole world or universe; a production of the human mind.

creative *adj* of creation; having the power to create; imaginative, original, constructive.—**creatively** *adv*.—**creativeness** *n*.—**creativity** *n*.

creator *n* one who creates, esp God.

creature *n* a living being; a created thing; one dependent on the influence of another.

crèche *n* a day nursery for very young children.

credence *n* belief or trust, esp in the reports or testimony of another.

credentials *npl* documents proving the identity, honesty or authority of a person.

credible *adj* believable; trustworthy.—**credibility** *n*.—**credibly** *adv*.

credit *n* belief; trust; honour; good reputation; trust in a person's ability to pay; time allowed for payment; a sum at a person's disposal in a bank; the entry in an account of a sum received; the side of the account on which this is entered; (*educ*) a distinction awarded for good marks in an examination; (*pl*) a list of those responsible for a film, television programme, etc. * *vt* to believe; to trust; to have confidence in; to attribute to; to enter on the credit side of an account.

creditable *adj* worthy of praise.—**creditably** *adv*.

credit card *n* a card issued by a bank, department store, etc authorizing the purchase of goods and services on credit.

creditor *n* a person to whom money is owed.

creed *n* a system of religious belief or faith; a summary of Christian doctrine; any set of principles or beliefs.

creek *n* a natural stream of water smaller than a river.

creep *vi* (*pt* **crept**) to move slowly along the ground, as a worm or reptile; (*plant*) to grow along the ground or up a wall; to move stealthily or slowly; to fawn; to cringe; (*flesh*) to feel as if things were creeping over it. * *n* (*inf*) a

dislikable or servile person; (*pl: inf*) shrinking horror.
creeper *n* a creeping or climbing plant.
creepy *adj* (**creepier, creepiest**) making one's flesh crawl; causing fear or disgust.—**creepily** *adv*.—**creepiness** *n*.
cremate *vt* to burn (a corpse) to ashes.—**cremation** *n*.
crematorium *n* (*pl* **crematoriums, crematoria**) a place where bodies are cremated.
creosote *n* an oily substance derived from tar used as a wood preservative. * *vt* to treat with creosote.
crepe, crêpe *n* a thin, crinkled cloth of silk, rayon, wool, etc; thin paper like crepe; a thin pancake.
crept *see* **creep**.
crescendo *adv* (*mus*) gradually increasing in loudness or intensity; moving to a climax. * *n* (*pl* **crescendos**) a crescendo passage or effect.
crescent *n* the figure of the moon in its first or last quarter; a narrow, tapering curve; a curving street. * *adj* crescent-shaped, increasing.
cress *n* any of various plants with pungent leaves, used in salads.
crest *n* a plume of feathers on the head of a bird; the ridge of a wave; the summit of a hill; a distinctive device above the shield on a coat of arms. * *vti* to mount to the top of; to take the form of a crest; to provide or adorn with a crest, to crown.
crestfallen *adj* dejected.
crevasse *n* a deep cleft in a glacier; a deep crack.
crevice *n* a crack, a fissure.
crew *n* the people operating a ship or aircraft; a group of people working together. * *vi* to act as a member of the crew of a ship, etc.
crib *n* a rack for fodder, a manger; a child's cot with high sides; a model of the manger scene representing the birth of Jesus; (*inf*) something copied from someone else; (*inf*) a literal translation of foreign texts used (usu illicitly) by students in examinations, etc. * *vti* (*pt* **cribbed**) (*inf*) to copy illegally, plagiarize.
crick *n* a painful stiffness of the muscles of the neck. * *vt* to produce a crick in.
cricket[1] *n* a leaping grasshopper-like insect.
cricket[2] *n* a game played with wickets, bats, and a ball, by eleven players on each side.—**cricketer** *n*.
crime *n* a violation of the law; an offence against morality or the public welfare; wrongdoing; (*inf*) a shame, disappointment.
criminal *adj* of the nature of, or guilty of, a crime. * *n* a person who has committed a crime.
crimson *n* a deep-red colour inclining to purple. * *adj* crimson-coloured. * *vti* to dye with crimson; to blush.
cringe *vi* to shrink in fear or embarrassment; to cower; to behave with servility; to fawn.
crinkle *vt* to wrinkle; to corrugate; to crimp. * *vi* to curl; to be corrugated or crimped. * *n* a wrinkle.—**crinkly** *adj*.
cripple *vt* to deprive of the use of a limb; to disable. * *n* a lame or otherwise disabled person. * *adj* lame.
crisis *n* (*pl* **crises**) a turning point; a critical point in a disease; an emergency; a time of serious difficulties or danger.
crisp *adj* dry and brittle; bracing; brisk; sharp and incisive; decided. * *n* a potato snack; in US, a potato chip. * *vt* to make crisp.
criterion *n* (*pl* **criteria**) a standard, law or rule by which a correct judgment can be made.
critic *n* a person skilled in judging the merits of literary or artistic works; one who passes judgment; a fault-finder.
critical *adj* skilled in criticism; censorious; relating to the turning point of a disease; crucial.—**critically** *adv*.
criticism *n* a being critical; a critical comment; a review or analysis of a book, play, work of art, etc, by a critic.
criticize *vt* to pass judgment on; to find fault with; to examine critically.
croak *n* a deep hoarse discordant cry. * *vti* to utter a croak; (*inf*) to die, to kill.
crochet *n* a kind of knitting done with a hooked needle. * *vti* to do this; to make crochet articles.
crockery *n* china dishes, earthenware vessels, etc.
crocodile *n* large amphibious reptile, similar to an alligator; its skin, used to make handbags, shoes, etc; a line of schoolchildren walking in pairs.
crocus *n* a bulbous plant with yellow, purple, or white flowers.
croft *n* a small plot of land with a rented farmhouse, esp in Scotland.—**crofter** *n*.
crook *n* a shepherd's hooked staff; a bend, a curve; a swindler, a dishonest person. * *vti* to bend or to be bent into the shape of a hook.
crooked *adj* bent, twisted; dishonest.—**crookedly** *adv*.—**crookedness** *n*.
crop *n* a year's or a season's produce of any cultivated plant; harvest; a pouch in a bird's

gullet; a hunting whip; hair cut close or short. * *vti* (*pt* **cropped**) to clip short; to bite off or eat down (grass); (*land*) to yield; to sow, to plant; (*geol*) to come to the surface; to appear unexpectedly; to sprout.

croquet *n* a game played with mallets, balls and hopes.

croquette *n* a ball of minced meat, fish or potato seasoned and fried brown.

cross *n* a figure formed by two intersecting lines; a wooden structure, consisting of two beams placed across each other, used in ancient times for crucifixion; the emblem of the Christian faith; a burden, or affliction; a device resembling a cross; a cross-shaped medal; a hybrid. * *vti* to pass across; to intersect; to meet and pass; to place crosswise; to make the sign of the cross over; to thwart, to oppose; to modify (a breed) by intermixture (with). * *adj* transverse; reaching from side to side; intersecting; out of temper, peevish.—**crossly** *adv*.—**crossness** *n*.

crossbar *n* a horizontal bar, as that across goal posts or as bicycle frame.

crossbreed *vt* (*pt* **crossbred**) to breed animals by mating different varieties. * *n* an animal produced in this way.

cross-country *adj* across fields; denoting cross-country racing or skiing.

cross-examine *vt* to question closely; (*law*) to question (a witness) who has already been questioned by counsel on the other side.—**cross-examination** *n*.

cross-eyed *adj* squinting.

crossing *n* an intersection of roads or railway lines; a place for crossing a street.

crossroad *n* a road crossing another; (*pl*) where two roads cross; (*fig*) the time when a decisive action has to be made.

cross section *n* a cutting at right angles to length; the surface then shown; a random selection of the public.

crossword *n* a puzzle in which interlocking words to be inserted vertically and horizontally in a squared diagram are indicated by clues.

crotch *n* the region of the body where the legs fork, the genital area; any forked region.

crotchet *n* (*mus*) a note equal to a half-minim.

crotchety *adj* peevish, whimsical.

crouch *vi* to squat or lie close to the ground; to cringe.

crouton *n* a small piece of fried or toasted bread, sprinkled onto soups.

crow *n* any of various usu large, glossy, black birds; a cawing cry, the shrill sound of a cock. * *vi* (*pt* **crowed** *or* **crew**) to make a sound like a cock; to boast in triumph; to utter a cry of pleasure.

crowbar *n* an iron bar used to lever.

crowd *n* a number of people or things collected closely together; a dense multitude, a throng; (*inf*) a set; a clique. * *vti* to press closely together; to fill to excess; to push, to thrust; to importune.—**crowded** *adj*.

crown *n* a wreath worn on the head; the head covering of a monarch; regal power; the sovereign; the top of the head; a summit; a reward; the part of a tooth above the gum. * *vt* to invest with a crown; to adorn or dignify; to complete; to reward.

crucial *adj* decisive; severe; critical. —**crucially** *adv*.

crucifix *n* a cross with the sculptured figure of Christ.

crucifixion *n* a form of execution by being nailed or bound to a cross by the hands and feet; (*with cap*) the death of Christ in this manner.

crucify *vt* to put to death on a cross; to cause extreme pain to; to utterly defeat in an argument.

crude *adj* in a natural state; unripe; raw; immature; harsh in colour; unfinished, rough; lacking polish; blunt; vulgar. * *n* crude oil.—**crudely** *adv*.—**crudity** *n*.

cruel *adj* (**crueller, cruellest**) disposed to give pain to others; merciless; hard-hearted; fierce; painful; unrelenting. —**cruelly** *adv*.—**cruelty** *n*.

cruet *n* a small glass bottle for vinegar and oil, used at the table.

cruise *vi* to sail to and fro; to wander about; to move at the most efficient speed for sustained travel. * *vt* to cruise over or about. * *n* a voyage from place to place for military purposes or for pleasure.

crumb *n* a fragment of bread; the soft part of bread; a little piece of anything.

crumble *vt* to break into crumbs; to cause to fall into pieces. * *vi* to disappear gradually, to disintegrate.—**crumbly** *adj*.

crumpet *n* a soft cake, usu eaten toasted; (*sl*) a sexually attractive woman.

crumple *vti* to twist or crush into wrinkles; to crease; to collapse. * *n* a wrinkle or crease made by crumpling.

crunch *vti* to crush with the teeth; to tread underfoot with force and noise; to make a sound like this; to chew audibly. * *n* the sound or act of crunching.

crusade *n* a medieval Christian military expedition to recover the Holy Land; a vigorous concerted action defending a cause or advancing an idea. * *vi* to engage in a crusade.—**crusader** *n*.

crush *vt* to press between two opposite bodies; to squeeze; to break by pressure; to bruise; to ruin; to quell. * *vi* to be pressed out of shape or into a smaller compass. * *n* a violent compression or collision; a dense crowd; (*inf*) a large party; a drink made from crushed fruit; (*sl*) an infatuation.

crust *n* a hard external coating or rind; the exterior solid part of the earth's surface; a shell or hard covering. * *vti* to cover or become covered with a crust.—**crusty** *adj*.—**crustily** *adv*.—**crustiness** *n*.

crutch *n* a staff with a crosswise head to support the weight of a lame person; a prop; the crotch.

crux *n* (*pl* **cruxes, cruces**) a difficult problem; the essential or deciding point.

cry *vi* to call aloud; to proclaim; to exclaim vehemently; to implore; to shed tears. * *vt* to utter loudly and publicly. * *n* an inarticulate sound; an exclamation of wonder or triumph; an outcry; clamour; an urgent appeal; a spell of weeping; a battle cry; a catchword.

crypt *n* an underground chamber or vault, esp under a church, used as a chapel or for burial.

cryptic *adj* hidden, secret; mysterious.

crystal *n* very clear, brilliant glass; articles of such glass, as goblets. * *adj* made of crystal.—**crystalline** *adj*.

crystallize *vti* to form crystals; to give definite form.—**crystallization** *n*.

cu. *abbr* = cubic.

cub *n* a young carnivorous mammal; a young, inexperienced person; (*with cap*) a Cub Scout.

cube *n* a solid body with six equal square sides or faces; a cube-shaped block; the product of a number multiplied by itself twice. * *vt* to raise (number) to the third power, or cube; to cut into cube-shaped pieces.

cubic *adj* having the form or properties of a cube; three-dimensional.

cubicle *n* a small separate sleeping compartment in a dormitory, etc.

cuckoo *n* a bird with a dark plumage, a curved bill and a characteristic call that lays its eggs in the nests of other birds.

cuckoo clock *n* a clock that strikes the hours with a cuckoo call.

cucumber *n* a long juicy fruit used in salads and as a pickle; the creeping plant that bears it.

cud *n* the food that a ruminating animal brings back into the mouth to chew again.

cuddle *vt* to embrace or hug closely. * *vt* to nestle together. * *n* a close embrace.

cudgel *n* a short thick stick for beating.

cue[1] *n* the last word of a speech in a play, serving as a signal for the next actor to enter or begin to speak; any signal to do something; a hint. * *vt* (*pr p* **cuing** *or* **cueing**) to give a cue to.

cue[2] *n* a tapering rod used in snooker, billiards, and pool to strike the cue ball.

cuff[1] *n* a blow with the fist or the open hand. * *vt* to strike such a blow.

cuff[2] *n* the end of a sleeve; a covering round the wrist; the turn-up on a trouser leg.

cufflink *n* a decorative clip for fastening the edges of a shirt cuff.

cuisine *n* a style of cooking or preparing food; the food prepared.

cul-de-sac *n* a street blocked off at one end; a blind alley.

culinary *adj* of or relating to cooking.

culminate *vti* to reach the highest point of altitude, rank, power, etc; (*astron*) to reach the meridian; to bring to a head or the highest point.—**culmination** *n*.

culpable *adj* deserving censure; criminal; blameworthy.—**culpably** *adv*.—**culpability** *n*.

culprit *n* a person accused, or found guilty, of an offence.

cult *n* a system of worship; devoted attachment to a person, principle, etc; a religion regarded as unorthodox or spurious; its body of adherents.

cultivate *vt* to till; to improve by care, labour, or study; to seek the society of; to civilize or refine.

cultivation *n* the act of cultivating; the state of being cultivated; tillage; culture.

cultural *adj* pertaining to culture.—**culturally** *adv*.

culture *n* appreciation and understanding of the arts; the skills, arts, etc of a given people in a given period; the customary beliefs, social forms, and material traits of a religious, social, or racial group; improvement of the mind, manner, etc; a growth of bacteria, etc in a prepared substance. * *vt* to cultivate bacteria for study or use.

cultured *adj* educated to appreciate the arts; having good taste; artificially grown, as cultured pearls.

cumbersome *adj* inconveniently heavy or large, unwieldy.
cunning *adj* ingenious; sly; designing; subtle. * *n* slyness, craftiness.
cup *n* a small, bowl-shaped container for liquids, usu with a handle; the amount held in a cup; an ornamental cup used as a trophy. * *vt* (*pt* **cupped**) to take or put as in a cup; to curve (the hands) into the shape of a cup.
cupboard *n* a closet or cabinet with shelves for cups, plates, utensils, food etc.
cupola *n* a dome.
curate *n* an assistant of a vicar or rector.
curator *n* a superintendent of a a museum, art gallery, etc.
curb *vt* to to restrain; to check; to keep in subjection. * *n* that which checks, restrains, or subdues; a kerb.
curd *n* the coagulated part of soured milk, used to make cheese.
curdle *vti* to turn into curds; to coagulate.
cure *n* the act or art of healing; a remedy; restoration to health. * *vt* to heal; to rid of; to preserve, as by drying, salting, etc.—**curable** *adj*.
curfew *n* a signal, as a bell, at a fixed evening hour as a sign that everyone must be indoors; the signal or hour.
curio *n* (*pl* **curios**) an item valued as rare or unusual.
curiosity *n* the quality of being curious; inquisitiveness; a rare, strange or interesting object.
curious *adj* anxious to know; prying, inquisitive; strange, remarkable, odd.—**curiously** *adv*.—**curiousness** *n*.
curl *vti* to form into a curved shape, to coil; to twist into ringlets; to proceed in a curve, to bend; to play at curling. * *n* a ringlet of hair; a spiral form, a twist; a bend or undulation.
curler *n* a small pin or roller used for curling the hair; a person who plays curling.
curling *n* a game in which two teams slide large smooth stones on ice into a target circle.
curly *adj* (**curlier, curliest**) full of curls.—**curliness** *n*.
currant *n* a small variety of dried grape; a shrub that yields a red or black fruit.
currency *n* the time during which a thing is current; the state of being in use; the money current in a country.
current *adj* generally accepted; happening now; presently in circulation. * *n* a body of water or air in motion, a flow; the transmission of electricity through a conductor; a general tendency.
currently *adv* at the present time.
curriculum *n* (*pl* **curricula, curriculums**) a prescribed course of study.
curriculum vitae *n* a brief survey of one's career.
curry *n* a spicy dish with a hot sauce; curry seasoning. * *vt* to flavour with curry.
curse *n* a calling down of destruction or evil; a profane oath; a swear word; a violent exclamation of anger; a scourge. * *vti* to invoke a curse on; to swear, to blaspheme; to afflict, to torment.
cursor *n* a flashing indicator on a computer screen indicating position; the transparent slide on a slide-rule.
cursory *adj* hasty, passing; superficial, careless.—**cursorily** *adv*.
curt *adj* short; abrupt; concise; rudely brief.—**curtly** *adv*.—**curtness** *n*.
curtail *vt* to cut short; to reduce; to deprive of part (of).—**curtailment** *n*.
curtain *n* a cloth hung as a screen at a window, etc; the movable screen separating the stage from the auditorium; (*pl*) (*sl*) the end. * *vt* to enclose in, or as with, curtains.
curtsy, curtsey *n* a formal gesture of greeting, involving bending the knees, made by women and children. * *vi* to make a curtsy.
curve *n* a bending without angles; a bent form or thing; (*geom*) a line of which no part is straight. * *vti* to form into a curve, to bend.—**curvy** *adj*.
cushion *n* a case stuffed with soft material for resting on; the elastic border around a snooker table; the air mass supporting a hovercraft. * *vt* to furnish with cushions; to protect by padding.
custard *n* a sauce mixture of milk, eggs and sugar.
custody *n* guardianship; imprisonment; security.—**custodial** *adj*.—**custodian** *n*.
custom *n* a regular practice; usage; frequent repetition of the same act; business patronage; (*pl*) duties on imports.
customary *adj* habitual; conventional; common.—**customarily** *adv*.
customer *n* a person who buys from a shop or business, esp regularly.
cut *vb* (*pr p* **cutting,** *pt* **cut**) *vb* to cleave or separate with a sharp instrument; to make an incision in; to divide; to trim; to intersect; to abridge; to diminish; to pass deliberately without recognition; to wound deeply; to reduce or curtail; to grow a new tooth through

the gum; to divide (a pack of cards) at random; (*inf*) to stay away from class, school, etc. * *vi* to make an incision; to perform the work of an edged instrument; to grow through the gums; (*cinema*) to change to another scene, to stop photographing. * *n* an incision or wound made by a sharp instrument; a gash; a sharp stroke; a sarcastic remark; a passage or channel cut out; a slice; a block on which an engraving is cut; the fashion or shape of a garment; the deliberate ignoring of an acquaintance; the division of a pack of cards; a diminution in price below another merchant; (*sl*) a share, as of profits. * *adj* divided or separated; gashed; having the surface ornamented or fashioned; not wrought or hand-made.

cutback *n* a reduction, esp in expenditure.

cute *adj* (*inf*) acute, shrewd; pretty or attractive, esp in a dainty way.—**cutely** *adv*.—**cuteness** *n*.

cuticle *n* the skin at the base of the fingernail or toe nail; epidermis.

cutlery *n* knives, forks, etc for eating and serving food.

cutlet *n* a neck chop of lamb, etc; a small slice cut off from the ribs or leg; minced meat in the form of a cutlet.

cutthroat *n* a murderer. * *adj* merciless; (*razor*) having a long blade in a handle.

cutting *n* a piece cut off or from; an incision; a newspaper clipping; a slip from a plant for propagation; a passage or channel cut out; the process of editing a film or recording; a recording. * *adj* (*remarks*) hurtful.

cuttlefish *n* a marine creature with a flattened body that squirts ink when threatened.

CV *abbr* = curriculum vitae.

cwt. *abbr* = hundredweight.

cyanide *n* a poison.

cyclamen *n* a plant of the primrose family, with pink, purple or white flowers.

cycle *n* a recurring series of events or phenomena; the period of this; a body of epics or romances with a common theme; a bicycle, motorcycle, or tricycle. * *vi* to go in cycles; to ride a bicycle or tricycle.

cyclic, cyclical *adj* moving or recurring in cycles.—**cyclically** *adj*.

cyclist *n* a person who rides a bicycle.

cyclone *n* a violent circular storm; an atmospheric movement in which the wind blows spirally round towards a centre of low barometric pressure.—**cyclonic** *adj*.

cygnet *n* a young swan.

cylinder *n* a hollow figure or object with parallel sides and circular ends; an object shaped like a cylinder; any machine part of this shape; the piston chamber in an engine.—**cylindrical** *adj*.

cymbal *n* (*mus*) one of a pair of two brass plates struck together to produce a ringing or clashing sound.—**cymbalist** *n*.

cynic *n* a morose, surly, or sarcastic person; one of a sect of ancient Greek philosophers.—**cynicism** *n*.

cynical *adj* sceptical of or sneering at goodness; shameless in admitting unworthy motives.—**cynically** *adv*.

cypher *see* **cipher**.

cypress *n* an evergreen tree with hard wood.

cyst *n* a closed sac developing abnormally in the structure of plants or animals.—**cystic** *adj*.

czar *see* **tsar**.

D

dab[1] *vt* (*pt* **dabbed**) to touch lightly with something moist or soft. * *n* a quick light tap; a small lump of anything moist or soft.

dab[2] *n* a species of European flounder.

dabble *vi* to move hands, feet etc gently in water or another liquid; (*usu with* **at, in, with**) to do anything in a superficial or dilettante way. * *vt* to splash.—**dabbler** *n*.

dad, daddy *n* (*inf*) father.

daddy-longlegs *n* (*inf*) a crane fly; (*inf*) in US, any of various spiders or insects with long, slender legs.

daffodil *n* a yellow spring flower, a narcissus; its pale yellow colour.

daft *adj* (*inf*) silly, weak-minded; giddy; mad.—**daftness** *n*.

dagger *n* a short weapon for stabbing; a reference mark used in printing (†).—*also* **obelisk**.

daily *adj*, *adv* (happening) every day; constantly, progressively. * *n* a newspaper published every weekday; (*inf*) a charwoman.

dainty *adj* (**daintier, daintiest**) delicate; choice; nice, fastidious. * *n* a titbit, a delicacy.—**daintily** *adv*.—**daintiness** *n*.

dairy *n* a building or room where milk is stored and dairy products made; a shop selling these; a company supplying them.

daisy *n* any of various plants with a yellow centre and white petals, esp the English daisy.

dale *n* a valley.

dally *vi* to lose time by idleness or trifling; to play or trifle (with); to flirt.

dam[1] *n* an artificial embankment to retain water; water so contained. * *vt* (*pt* **dammed**) to retain (water) with such a barrier; to stem, obstruct, restrict.

dam[2] *n* the mother of a four-footed animal.

damage *n* injury, harm; loss; (*inf*) price, cost; (*pl*) (*law*) payment in compensation for loss or injury. * *vt* to do harm to, to injure.—**damaging** *adj*.

damn *vt* to condemn, censure; to ruin; to curse; to consign to eternal punishment. * *vti* to prove guilty. * *interj* (*sl*) expressing irritation or annoyance. * *n* (*sl*) something having no value. * *adj, adv* damned.—**damnatory** *adj*.

damp *n* humidity, moisture; in mines, poisonous or foul gas. * *adj* slightly wet, moist. * *vt* to moisten; (*with* **down**) to stifle, reduce.—**dampness** *n*.

dampen *vti* to make or become damp. * *vt* to stifle.—**dampener** *n*.

damson *n* a small, dark-purple variety of plum; the colour of this; the tree on which this fruit grows.

dance *vti* to move rhythmically, esp to music; to skip or leap lightly; to execute (steps); to cause to dance or to move up and down. * *n* a piece of dancing; a dance performance of an artistic nature; a party with music for dancing; music for accompanying dancing.—**dancer** *n*.

dandelion *n* a common wild plant with ragged leaves, a yellow flower and a fluffy seed head.

dandruff *n* scales of skin on the scalp, under the hair, scurf.

danger *n* exposure to injury or risk; a source of harm or risk.

dangerous *adj* involving danger; unsafe; perilous.—**dangerously** *adv*.

dangle *vi* to hang and swing loosely. * *vt* to carry something so that it hangs loosely; to display temptingly.

dapper *adj* nimble; neat in appearance, spruce.

dare *vti* to be bold enough; to venture, to risk; to defy, to challenge. * *n* a challenge.

daredevil *n* a rash, reckless person. * *adj* daring, bold; courageous.

daring *adj* fearless; courageous; unconventional. * *n* adventurous courage.

dark *adj* having little or no light; of a shade of colour closer to black than white; (*person*) having brown or black skin or hair; gloomy; (*inf*) secret, unknown; mysterious. * *n* a dark state or colour; ignorance; secrecy.—**darkly** *adv*.—**darkness** *n*.

darken *vti* to make or become dark or darker.

darkroom *n* a room for processing photographs in darkness or safe light.

darling *n* a dearly loved person; a favourite. * *adj* lovable; much admired.

darn[1] *vt* to mend a hole in fabric or a garment with stitches. * *n* an area that has been darned.

darn[2] *interj* a form of **damn** as a mild oath.—*also adj*.

dart *n* a small pointed missile; a sudden movement; a fold sewn into a garment for shaping it; (*pl*) an indoor game in which darts are thrown at a target. * *vti* to move rapidly; to send out rapidly.

dartboard *n* a circular cork or wooden target used in the game of darts.

dash *vti* to fling violently; to rush quickly; (*hopes*) to shatter; (*one's spirits, etc*) to depress, confound; to write quickly. * *n* a short race; a rush; a small amount of something added to food; a tinge; a punctuation mark (—); a dashboard; vigour, verve; display.

dashboard *n* an instrument panel in a car.

dashing *adj* spirited, stylish, dapper.

data *npl* (*sing* **datum**) (*often used as sing*) facts, statistics, or information either historical or derived by calculation or experimentation.

data processing *n* the analysis of information stored in a computer for various uses, eg stock control, statistical research, mathematical modelling, etc.

date[1] *n* a day or time of occurrence; a statement of this in a letter, etc; a period to which something belongs; a duration; an appointment, esp with a member of the opposite sex. * *vt* to affix a date to; to note the date of; to reckon the time of; (*inf*) to make a date with; (*inf*) to see frequently a member of the opposite sex. * *vi* to reckon from a point in time; to show signs of belonging to a particular period.

date[2] *n* the sweet fruit of the date palm, a palm tree of tropical regions.

date line *n* the line running north to south along the 180-degree meridian, east of which is one day earlier than west of it; a line on a newspaper story giving the date and place of writing.

daub *vt* to smear or overlay (with clay, etc); to paint incompetently. * *n* a smear; a poor painting.

daughter *n* a female child or descendant.
daughter-in-law *n* the wife of one's son.
dauntless *adj* intrepid.—**dauntlessly** *adv*.
dawdle *vi* to move slowly and waste time, to loiter.—**dawdler** *n*.
dawn *vi* (*day*) to begin to grow light; to begin to appear. * *n* daybreak; a first sign.
day *n* the time when the sun is above the horizon; the twenty-four hours from midnight to midnight; daylight; a particular period of success or influence; (*usu pl*) a period, an epoch.
daybreak *n* the first appearance of daylight, dawn.
daydream *n* a reverie. * *vi* to have one's mind on other things; to fantasize.—**daydreamer** *n*.
daylight *n* the light of the sun; dawn; publicity; a visible gap; the dawning of sudden realization or understanding.
daytime *n* the time of daylight.
daze *vt* to stun, to bewilder. * *n* confusion, bewilderment.
dazzle *vt* to confuse the sight of or be partially blinded by strong light; to overwhelm with brilliance. * *n* an overpoweringly strong light; bewilderment. —**dazzler** *n*.—**dazzling** *adj*.—**dazzlingly** *adv*.
dead *adj* without life; inanimate, inert; no longer used; lacking vegetation; emotionally or spiritually insensitive; without motion; (*fire, etc*) extinguished; (*limb, etc*) numb; (*colour, sound etc*) dull; (*a ball*) out of play; complete, exact; unerring. * *adv* in a dead manner; completely; utterly. * *n* a dead person; the quietest time.
deaden *vt* to render numb or insensible; to deprive of vitality; to muffle.
dead-end *n* a cul-de-sac; a hopeless situation.
dead heat *n* a race in which two or more finish equal, a tie.
deadline *n* the time by which something must be done.
deadlock *n* a clash of interests making progress impossible; a standstill.—*also vt*.
deadly *adj* (**deadlier, deadliest**) fatal; implacable; (*inf*) tedious. * *adv* death-like; intensely.
deadpan *adj* (*inf*) deliberately expressionless or emotionless.—*also adv*.
deaf *adj* unable to hear; hearing badly; not wishing to hear.—**deafness** *n*.
deafen *vt* to deprive of hearing.—**deafeningly** *adv*.
deal[1] *vb* (*pt* **dealt**) *vt* (*a blow*) to deliver, inflict; (*cards, etc*) to distribute; (*with* **with**) to do business with; (*problem, task*) to solve. * *vi* to do business (with); to trade (in). * *n* a portion, quantity; (*inf*) a large amount; a dealing of cards; a business transaction.
deal[2] *n* fir or pine wood.—*also adj*.
dealer *n* a trader; a person who deals cards; (*sl*) a seller of illegal drugs.
dealings *npl* personal or business transactions.
dean *n* the head of a cathedral chapter; a college fellow in charge of discipline; the head of a university or college faculty.
dear *adj* loved, precious; charming; expensive; a form of address in letters. * *n* a person who is loved. * *adv* at a high price.—**dearly** *adv*.—**dearness** *n*.
dearth *n* scarcity, lack.
death *n* the end of life, dying; the state of being dead; the destruction of something.
deathbed *n* the bed in which a person dies or is about to die.
death certificate *n* an official document with details of the date, place and cause of a person's death.
death duties *npl* taxes paid on an inheritance after a death.
deathly *adj* like death, pale still; deadly.—*also adv*.
debar *vt* (*pt* **debarred**) to exclude, bar. —**debarment** *n*.
debase *vt* to lower in character or value; (*coinage*) to degrade.—**debasement** *n*.
debatable, debateable *adj* open to question, disputed.
debate *n* a formal argument; a discussion, esp in parliament. * *vt* to consider, contest. * *vi* to discuss thoroughly; to join in debate.—**debater** *n*.
debauchery *n* depraved over-indulgence; corruption; profligacy.
debit *n* the entry of a sum owed, opposite to the credit; the left side of a ledger used for this. * *vt* to charge to the debit side of a ledger.
debris, débris *n* broken and scattered remains, wreckage.
debt *n* a sum owed; a state of owing; an obligation.
debtor *n* a person, company, etc who owes money to another.
debut *n* a first appearance as a public performer or in society.
decade *n* a period of ten years; a group of ten.
decadence, decadency *n* a state of deterioration in standards, esp of morality.
decadent *adj* deteriorating; self-indulgent.
decay *vti* to rot, decompose; to deteriorate,

wither. * *n* the act or state of decaying; a decline, collapse.
decease *n* death. * *vi* to die.
deceased *adj* dead. * *n* the dead person.
deceit *n* the act of deceiving; cunning; treachery; fraud.
deceitful *adj* treacherous; insincere; misleading.—**deceitfully** *adv*.—**deceitfulness** *n*.
deceive *vt* to cheat; to mislead; to delude; to impose upon.—**deceiver** *n*.
December *n* the twelfth and last month of the year with 31 days.
decency *n* being decent; conforming to accepted standards of behaviour.
decent *adj* respectable, proper; moderate; not obscene; (*inf*) quite good; (*inf*) kind, generous.—**decently** *adv*.
decentralize *vt* (*government, organization*) to divide among local centres. —**decentralization** *n*.
deception *n* the act of deceiving or the state of being deceived; illusion; fraud.
deceptive *adj* apt to mislead; ambiguous; unreliable.—**deceptively** *adv*.—**deceptiveness** *n*.
decibel *n* a unit for measuring sound level.
decide *vti* to determine, to settle; to give a judgment on; to resolve.
decided *adj* unhesitating; clearly marked.
decidedly *adv* definitely, certainly.
deciduous *adj* (*trees, shrubs*) shedding all leaves annually, at the end of the growing season.
decimal *adj* of tenths, of numbers written to the base 10.
decimal point *n* a dot written before the numerator in a decimal fraction (eg $0.5 = ^1/_2$).
decimate *vt* to kill every tenth person; to reduce by one tenth; to kill a great number.—**decimation** *n*.
decipher *vt* to decode; to make out (indistinct writing, meaning, etc).—**decipherable** *adj*.—**decipherment** *n*.
decision *n* a settlement; a ruling; a judgment; determination, firmness.
decisive *adj* determining the issue, positive; conclusive, final.—**decisively** *adv*.
deck *n* the floor on a ship, aircraft, bus or bridge; a pack of playing cards; the turntable of a record-player; the playing mechanism of a tape recorder; (*sl*) the ground, the floor. * *vt* to cover; to adorn.
deck chair *n* a folding chair made of canvas suspended in a frame.
declare *vt* to affirm, proclaim; to admit possession of (dutiable goods). * *vi* (*law*) to make a statement; (*with* **against, for**) to announce one's support; (*cricket*) to choose to close an innings before ten wickets have fallen.—**declaration** *n*.—**declarative** *adj*.—**declaratory** *adj*.
decline *vi* to refuse; to move down; to deteriorate, fall away; to fail; to diminish; to draw to an end; to deviate. * *vt* to reject, to refuse; (*gram*) to give the cases of a declension. * *n* a diminution; a downward slope; a gradual loss of physical and mental faculties.
decode *vt* to translate a code into plain language.—**decoder** *n*.
decompose *vti* to separate or break up into constituent parts, esp as part of a chemical process; to resolve into its elements. * *vi* to decay.—**decomposition** *n*.
decontaminate *vt* to free from (radioactive, etc) contamination.—**decontamination** *n*.
décor, decor *n* general decorative effect, eg of a room; scenery and stage design.
decorate *vt* to ornament; to paint or wallpaper; to honour with a badge or medal.
decoration *n* decorating; an ornament; a badge or an honour.
decorative *adj* ornamental, pretty to look at.—**decoratively** *adv*.
decorator *n* a person who decorates, esp houses.
decoy *vt* to lure into a trap. * *n* anything intended to lure into a snare.
decrease *vti* to make or become less. * *n* a decreasing; the amount of diminution.
decree *n* an order, edict or law; a judicial decision. * *vt* (*pt* **decreed**) to decide by sentence in law; to appoint.
decrepit *adj* worn out by the infirmities of old age; in the last stage of decay.—**decrepitude** *n*.
dedicate *vt* to consecrate (to some sacred purpose); to devote wholly or chiefly; to inscribe (to someone) —**dedication** *n*.—**dedicator** *n*.—**dedicatory** *adj*.
deduce *vt* to derive (knowledge, a conclusion) from reasoning; infer.—**deducible** *adj*.
deduct *vt* to take (from); to subtract.
deduction *n* deducting; the amount deducted; deducing; a conclusion that something is true because it necessarily follows from a set of general premises known to be valid.—**deductive** *adj*.
deed *n* an act; an exploit; a legal document recording a transaction.
deep *adj* extending or placed far down or far from the outside; fully involved; engrossed;

profound, intense; heartfelt; penetrating; difficult to understand; secret; cunning; sunk low; low in pitch; (*colour*) of high saturation and low brilliance. * *adv* in a deep manner; far in, into. * *n* that which is deep; the sea.—**deeply** *adv*.—**deepness** *n*.

deepen *vt* to make deeper in any sense; to increase. * *vi* to become deeper.

deepfreeze *n* a refrigerator in which food is frozen and stored.

deep-freeze *vt* to freeze (food) so that it keeps for a long period of time. * *n* a freezer.

deer *n* (*pl* **deer, deers**) a four-footed animal with antlers, esp on the males, including stag, reindeer, etc.

deface *vt* to disfigure; to obliterate. —**defacement** *n*.

default *n* neglect to do what duty or law requires; failure to fulfil a financial obligation; (*comput*) a basic setting or instruction to which a program reverts. * *vi* to fail in one's duty (as honouring a financial obligation, appearing in court).—**defaulter** *n*.

defeat *vt* to frustrate; to win a victory over; to baffle. * *n* a frustration of plans; overthrow, as of an army in battle; loss of a game, race, etc.

defeatism *n* disposition to accept defeat.—**defeatist** *n*.

defect *n* a deficiency; a blemish, fault. * *vi* to desert one's country or a cause.

defective *adj* having a defect; faulty; incomplete. * *n* a person defective in physical or mental powers.—**defectively** *adv*.—**defectiveness** *n*.

defence, defense (*US*) *n* resistance or protection against attack; a means of resisting an attack; protection; vindication; (*law*) a defendant's plea; the defending party in legal proceedings; (*sport*) defending (the goal, etc) against the attacks of the opposing side; the defending players in a team.—**defenceless** *adj*.

defend *vt* to guard or protect; to maintain against attack; (*law*) to resist, as a claim; to contest (a suit).

defendant *n* a person accused or sued in a lawsuit.

defensive *adj* serving to defend; in a state or posture of defence.—**defensively** *adv*.

defer[1] *vt* (*pt* **deferred**) to put off to another time; to delay.—**deferment, deferral** *n*.—**deferrable, deferable** *adj*.

defer[2] *vi* (*pt* **deferred**) to yield to another person's wishes, judgment or authority.

deference *n* a deferring or yielding in judgment or opinion; polite respect.

defiance *n* the act of defying; wilful disobedience; a challenge.—**defiant** *adj*.

deficiency *n* being deficient; lack, shortage; deficit.

deficient *adj* insufficient, lacking.

deficit *n* the amount by which an amount falls short of what is required; excess of expenditure over income, or liabilities over assets.

defile[1] *vt* to pollute or corrupt.

defile[2] *n* a long, narrow pass or way, through which troops can pass only in single file. * *vt* to march in single file.

define *vt* to fix the bounds or limits of; to mark the limits or outline of clearly; to describe accurately; to fix the meaning of.—**definable** *adj*.

definite *adj* defined; having distinct limits; fixed; exact; clear.—**definitely** *adv*.

definition *n* a description of a thing by its properties; an explanation of the exact meaning of a word, term, or phrase; sharpness of outline.

definitive *adj* defining or limiting; decisive, final.—**definitively** *adv*.

deflate *vt* to release gas or air from; to reduce in size or importance; to reduce the money supply, restrict credit, etc to reduce inflation in the economy. —**deflation** *n*.—**deflationary** *adj*.

deflect *vti* to turn or cause to turn aside from a line or proper course.—**deflection** *n*.—**deflector** *n*.

deform *vt* to spoil the natural form of; to put out of shape.—**deformation** *n*.

deformity *n* the condition of being deformed; a deformed part of the body; a defect.

defraud *vt* to remove (money, rights, etc) from a person by cheating or deceiving.—**defrauder** *n*.

defray *vt* to provide money (to pay expenses, etc).—**defrayal, defrayment** *n*.

defrost *vt* to unfreeze; to free from frost or ice.—*also vi*.

deft *adj* skilful, adept; nimble.—**deftly** *adv*.—**deftness** *n*.

defunct *adj* no longer being in existence or function or in use.

defuse *vt* to disarm an explosive (bomb or mine) by removing its fuse; to decrease tension in a (crisis) situation.

defy *vt* to resist openly and without fear; to challenge (a person) to attempt something considered dangerous or impossible; to resist attempts at, to elude.

degenerate *adj* having declined in physical or moral qualities; sexually deviant. * *vi* become or grow worse. * *n* a degenerate person.—**degeneracy** *n*.—**degeneration** *n*.

degrading *adj* humiliating.

degree *n* a step in a series; a stage in intensity; the relative quantity in intensity; a unit of measurement in a scale; an academic title awarded as of right or as an honour.

dehydrate *vt* to remove water from. * *vi* to lose water, esp from the bodily tissues.—**dehydration** *n*.

de-ice *vt* to prevent the formation of or to remove ice from a surface.—**de-icer** *n*.

deign *vi* to condescend; to think it worthy to do (something).

deity *n* a god or goddess; the rank or essence of a god; (*with cap and* **the**) God.

dejected *adj* morose, depressed.—**dejectedly** *adv*.

dejection *n* depression; lowness of spirits.

delay *vt* to postpone; to detain, obstruct. * *vi* to linger. * *n* a delaying or being delayed; the time period during which something is delayed.

delectable *adj* delightful, delicious.—**delectably** *adv*.

delegate *vt* to appoint as a representative; to give powers or responsibilities to (an agent or assembly). * *n* a deputy or an elected representative.

delegation *n* the act of delegating; a group of people empowered to represent others.

delete *vt* to strike out (something written or printed); to erase.—**deletion** *n*.

deliberate *vt* to consider carefully. * *vi* to discuss or debate thoroughly; to consider. * *adj* well thought out; intentional; cautious.—**deliberately** *adv*.

delicacy *n* delicateness; sensibility; a luxurious food.

delicate *adj* fine in texture; fragile, not robust; requiring tactful handling; of exquisite workmanship; requiring skill in techniques.—**delicately** *adv*. —**delicateness** *n*.

delicatessen *n* a store selling prepared foods, esp imported delicacies.

delicious *adj* having a pleasurable effect on the senses, esp taste; delightful.—**deliciously** *adv*.—**deliciousness** *n*.

delight *vt* to please greatly. * *vi* to have or take great pleasure (in). * *n* great pleasure; something that causes this.

delightful *adj* giving great pleasure.—**delightfully** *adv*.

delinquent *adj* negligent; guilty of an offence. * *n* a person guilty of a misdeed, esp a young person who breaks the law.—**delinquency** *n*.

delirium *n* a state of mental disorder, esp caused by a feverish illness; wild enthusiasm.—**delirious** *adj*.

deliver *vt* (*goods, letters, etc*) to transport to a destination; to distribute regularly; to liberate, to rescue; to give birth; to assist at a birth; (*blow*) to launch; (*baseball*) to pitch; (*speech*) to utter.—**deliverer** *n*.

delivery *n* act of delivering; anything delivered or communicated; the manner of delivering (a speech, etc); the manner of bowling in cricket, etc; the act of giving birth.

delta *n* the fourth letter of the Greek alphabet; an alluvial deposit at the mouth of a river.

delude *vt* to mislead, to deceive.

deluge *n* a flood; anything happening in a heavy rush. * *vt* to inundate.

delusion *n* a false belief; a persistent false belief that is a symptom of mental illness.—**delusive** *adj*.—**delusory** *adj*.

delve *vti* to search deeply; to dig.

demagogue, demagog *n* a political orator who derives power from appealing to popular prejudices.—**demagogic** *adj*.—**demagogy** *n*.

demand *vt* to ask for in an authoritative manner. * *n* a request or claim made with authority for what is due; an urgent claim; desire for goods and services shown by consumers.

demanding *adj* constantly making demands; requiring great skill, concentration or effort.

demarcation, demarkation *n* the act of marking off a boundary or setting a limit to; a limit; the strict separation of the type of work done by members of different trade unions.

demean *vt* to lower in dignity.—**demeaning** *adj*.

demeanour, demeanor (*US*) *n* behaviour; bearing.

demented *adj* crazy, insane.—**dementedly** *adv*.

demise *n* (*formal*) death; termination, end.

demobilize *vt* to discharge from the armed forces.—**demobilization** *n*.

democracy *n* a form of government by the people through elected representatives; a country governed by its people; political, social or legal equality.

democrat *n* a person who believes in or promotes democracy; (*with cap*) a member of the Democratic Party in the US.

democratic *adj* of, relating to, or supporting the principles of democracy; favouring or upholding equal rights.—**democratically** *adv*.

demolish *vt* (*a building*) to pull down or knock down; (*an argument*) to defeat; (*inf*) to eat up.—**demolition** *n*.

demonstrate *vt* to indicate or represent clearly; to provide certain evidence of, to prove; to show how something (a machine, etc) works. * *vi* to show one's support for a cause, etc by public parades and protests; to act as a demonstrator of machinery, etc.—**demonstrator** *n*.

demonstration *n* proof by evidence; a display or exhibition; a display of feeling; a public manifestation of opinion, as by a mass meeting, march, etc; a display of armed force.

demonstrative *adj* displaying one's feelings openly and unreservedly; indicative; conclusive; (*gram*) describing an adjective or pronoun indicating the person or thing referred to.—**demonstratively** *adv*.—**demonstrativeness** *n*.

demoralize *vt* to lower the morale of, discourage.—**demoralization** *n*.

demote *vt* to reduce in rank or position.—**demotion** *n*.

demur *vi* (*pt* **demurred**) to raise objections.

den *n* a cave or lair of a wild beast; a place where people gather for illegal activities; a room in a house for relaxation or study.

denial *n* the act of denying; a refusal of a request, etc; a refusal or reluctance to admit the truth of something.

denigrate *vt* to disparage the character of; to belittle.—**denigration** *n*.

denim *n* a hard-wearing cotton cloth, esp used for jeans; (*pl*) denim trousers or jeans.

denomination *n* a name or title; a religious group comprising many local churches, larger than a sect; one of a series of related units, esp monetary.—**denominational** *adj*.

denominator *n* the part of a fractional expression written below the fraction line.

denote *vt* to indicate, be the sign of; to mean.—**denotation** *n*.

denounce *vt* to condemn or censure publicly; to inform against; to declare formally the ending of (treaties, etc). —**denouncement** *n*.

dense *adj* difficult to see through; massed closely together; dull-witted, stupid.—**densely** *adv*.—**denseness** *n*.

density *n* the degree of denseness or concentration; stupidity; the ratio of mass to volume.

dent *n* a depression made by pressure or a blow. * *vti* to make a dent or become dented.

dental *adj* of or for the teeth.

dentifrice *n* toothpowder or toothpaste.

dentist *n* a person qualified to treat tooth decay, gum disease, etc.—**dentistry** *n*.

denture *n* (*usu pl*) a set of artificial teeth.

deny *vt* to declare to be untrue; to repudiate; to refuse to acknowledge; to refuse to assent to a request, etc.

deodorant *n* a substance that removes or masks unpleasant odours.

depart *vi* to go away, leave; to deviate (from).

department *n* a unit of specialized functions into which an organization or business is divided; a province; a realm of activity.—**departmental** *adj*.

department store *n* a large shop divided into various departments selling different types of goods.

departure *n* departing; deviating from normal practice; a new venture, course of action, etc.

depend *vi* to be determined by or connected with anything; to rely (on), put trust (in); to be reliant on for support, esp financially.

dependable *adj* able to be relied on.—**dependably** *adv*.—**dependability** *n*.

dependant *n* a person who is dependent on another, esp financially.

dependence, dependance *n* the state of being dependent; reliance, trust; a physical or mental reliance on a drug, person, etc.

dependent *adj* relying on another person, thing etc for support, money, etc; contingent; subordinate.

depict *vt* to represent pictorially; to describe.—**depiction** *n*.

deplete *vt* to use up a large quantity of. —**depletion** *n*.

deplorable *adj* shocking; extremely bad.—**deplorably** *adv*.

deplore *vt* to regret deeply; to complain of; to deprecate.

deploy *vt* (*military forces*) to distribute and position strategically. * *vi* to adopt strategic positions within an area.—**deployment** *n*.

depopulate *vt* to reduce the population of.—**depopulation** *n*.

deport *vt* to expel (an undesirable person) from a country; to behave (in a certain manner).—**deportation** *n*.

deportment *n* manners; behaviour.

depose *vt* to remove from power; to testify, esp in court.

deposit *vt* to place or lay down; to pay money into a bank or other institution for safekeeping, to earn interest, etc; to pay as a first instalment; to let fall, leave. * *n* something

deposited for safekeeping; money put in a bank; money given in part payment or security; material left in a layer, eg sediment.
depositor *n* a person who deposits money in a bank, etc.
depot *n* a warehouse, storehouse; a place for storing military supplies; a military training centre; a bus or railway station.
deprave *vt* to pervert; to corrupt morally.—**depravation** *n*.—**depraved** *adj*.
depravity *n* moral corruption; extreme wickedness.
depreciate *vti* to make or become lower in value.
depreciation *n* a fall in value, esp of an asset through wear and tear; an allowance for this deducted from gross profit; disparagement.
depress *vt* to push down; to sadden, dispirit; to lessen the activity of.—**depressing** *adj*.—**depressingly** *adv*.
depression *n* excessive gloom and despondency; an abnormal state of physiological inactivity; a phase of the business cycle characterized by stagnation, widespread unemployment, etc; a falling in or sinking; a lowering of atmospheric pressure, often signalling rain.
deprive *vt* to take a thing away from; to prevent from using or enjoying.—**deprivation** *n*.
deprived *adj* lacking the essentials of life, such as adequate food, shelter, education, etc.
depth *n* deepness; the distance downwards or inwards; the intensity of emotion or feeling; the profundity of thought; intensity of colour; the mid point of the night or winter; the lowness of sound or pitch; the quality of being deep.
depth-charge *n* a bomb designed to explode under water, used against submarines.
deputation *n* a person or group appointed to represent others.
deputize *vi* to act as deputy.
deputy *n* a delegate, representative, or substitute.
derail *vti* (*train*) to cause to leave the rails.—**derailment** *n*.
derange *vt* to throw into confusion; to disturb; to make insane.—**derangement** *n*.
derelict *adj* abandoned, deserted and left to decay; negligent. * *n* a person abandoned by society; a wrecked ship or vehicle.
deride *vt* to scorn, mock.
derision *n* ridicule.
derisive *adj* full of derision; mocking, scornful.
derisory *adj* showing or deserving of derision.
derivation *n* the tracing of a word to its root; origin; descent.
derivative *adj* derived from something else; not original. * *n* something that is derived; a word formed by derivation; (*math*) the rate of change of one quantity with respect to another.
derive *vt* to take or receive from a source; to infer, deduce (from). * *vi* to issue as a derivative (from).
derogatory *adj* disparaging; deliberately offensive.
derrick *n* any crane-like apparatus; a tower over an oil well, etc, holding the drilling machinery.
descend *vi* to come or climb down; to pass from a higher to a lower place or condition; (*with* **on, upon**) to make a sudden attack upon, or visit unexpectedly; to sink in morals or dignity; to be derived. * *vt* to go, pass, or extend down.
descendant *n* a person who is descended from an ancestor; something derived from an earlier form.
descent *n* a descending; a downward motion or step; a way down; a slope; a raid or invasion; lineage, ancestry.
describe *vt* to give a verbal account of; to trace out.
description *n* a verbal or pictorial account; sort, kind.
descriptive *adj* tending to or serving to describe.
desecrate *vt* to violate a sacred place by destructive or blasphemous behaviour.—**desecration** *n*.
desert[1] *n* (*often pl*) a deserved reward or punishment.
desert[2] *vt* to leave, abandon, with no intention of returning; to abscond from the armed forces without permission.—**deserter** *n*.—**desertion** *n*.
desert[3] *n* a dry, barren region, able to support little or no life; a place lacking in some essential quality.
deserve *vt* to merit or be suitable for (some reward, punishment, etc).—**deservedly** *adv*.
deserving *adj* worthy of support, esp financially.
design *vt* to plan; to create; to devise; to make working drawings for; to intend. * *n* a working drawing; a mental plan or scheme; the particular form or disposition of something; a decorative pattern; purpose; (*pl*) dishonest intent.

designate *vt* to indicate, specify; to name; to appoint to or nominate for a position, office. * *adj* (*after noun*) appointed to office but not yet installed.

designation *n* the act of designating; nomination; a distinguishing name or title.

designer *n* a person who designs things; a person who is renowned for creating high-class fashion clothes. * *adj* (*inf*) trendy, of the latest, esp expensive, fashion.

desirable *adj* arousing (sexual) desire; advisable or beneficial; worth doing.—**desirably** *adv*.—**desirability** *n*.

desire *vt* to long or wish for; to request, to ask for. * *n* a longing for something regarded as pleasurable or satisfying; a request; something desired; sexual craving.—**desirous** *adj*.

desk *n* a piece of furniture with a writing surface and usu drawers; a counter behind which a cashier, etc sits; the section of a newspaper responsible for a particular topic.

desolate *adj* solitary, lonely; devoid of inhabitants; laid waste.

desolation *n* destruction, ruin; a barren state; loneliness; wretchedness.

despair *vi* to have no hope. * *n* utter loss of hope; something that causes despair.

despatch *see* **dispatch**.

desperate *adj* (almost) hopeless; reckless through lack of hope; urgently requiring (money, etc); (*remedy*) extreme, dangerous.—**desperately** *adv*.

desperation *n* loss of hope; recklessness from despair.

despicable *adj* contemptible, worthless.—**despicably** *adv*.

despise *vt* to regard with contempt or scorn; to consider as worthless, inferior.

despite *prep* in spite of.

despondent *adj* dejected; lacking hope.—**despondence, despondency** *n*.—**despondently** *adv*.

dessert *n* the sweet course at the end of a meal.

dessertspoon *n* a spoon in between a teaspoon and a tablespoon in size, used for eating desserts.

destination *n* the place to which a person or thing is going.

destine *vt* to set aside for some specific purpose; to predetermine; intend.

destiny *n* the power supposedly determining the course of events; the future to which any person or thing is destined; a predetermined course of events.

destitute *adj* (*with* **of**) lacking some quality; lacking the basic necessities of life, very poor.

destroy *vt* to demolish, ruin, to put an end to; to kill.

destroyer *n* a fast small warship.

destructible *adj* able to be destroyed.

destruction *n* the act or process of destroying or being destroyed; ruin.

destructive *adj* causing destruction; (*with* **of** *or* **to**) ruinous; (*criticism*) intended to discredit, negative.—**destructively** *adv*.—**destructiveness** *n*.

detach *vt* to release; to separate from a larger group; (*mil*) to send off on special assignment.

detachable *adj* able to be detached.

detached *adj* separate; (*house*) not joined to another; aloof; free from bias or emotion.

detachment *n* indifference; freedom from emotional involvement or bias; the act of detaching; a thing detached; a body of troops detached from the main body and sent on special service.

detail *vt* to describe fully; (*mil*) to set apart for a particular duty. * *n* an item; a particular or minute account; (*art*) treatment of smaller parts; a reproduction of a smaller part of a picture, statue, etc; a small detachment for special service.

detailed *adj* giving full details; thorough.

detain *vt* to place in custody or confinement; to delay.

detect *vt* to discover the existence or presence of; to notice.

detection *n* a discovery or being discovered; the job or process of detecting.

detective *n* a person or a police officer employed to find evidence of crimes.

detector *n* a device for detecting the presence of something.

detention *n* the act of detaining or withholding; a being detained; confinement; being kept in (school after hours) as a punishment.

deter *vt* (*pt* **deterred**) to discourage or prevent (from acting).—**determent** *n*.

detergent *n* a cleaning agent—*also adj*.

deteriorate *vt* to make or become worse.—**deterioration** *n*.

determination *n* the act or process of making a decision; a decision resolving a dispute; firm intention; resoluteness.

determine *vt* to fix or settle officially; to find out; to regulate; to impel. * *vi* to come to a decision.

determined *adj* full of determination, resolute.—**determinedly** *adv*.

deterrent *n* something that deters; a nuclear weapon that deters attack through fear of retaliation. * *adj* deterring.—**deterrence** *n*.

detest *vt* to dislike intensely.—**detestation** *n*.

detestable *adj* intensely disliked, abhorrent.—**detestably** *adv*.

detonate *vti* to explode or cause to explode rapidly and violently.—**detonation** *n*.

detonator *n* a device that sets off an explosion.

detour *n* a deviation from an intended course, esp one serving as an alternative to a more direct route. * *vti* to make or send by a detour.

detract *vt* to take away. * *vi* to take away (from).—**detraction** *n*.—**detractor** *n*.

detriment *n* (a cause of) damage or injury.—**detrimental** *adj*.

devalue, devaluate *vt* to reduce the exchange value of (a currency).—**devaluation** *n*.

devastate *vt* to lay waste; to destroy; to overwhelm.—**devastation** *n*.

develop *vt* to evolve; to bring to maturity; to show the symptoms of (eg a habit, a disease); to treat a photographic film or plate to reveal an image; to improve the value of. * *vi* to grow (into); to become apparent.

developer *n* a person who develops; a person or organization that develops property; a reagent for developing photographs.

developing country *n* a poor country that is attempting to improve its social conditions and encourage industrial growth.

development *n* the process of growing or developing; a new situation that emerges; a piece of land or property that has been developed.

deviate *vi* to diverge from a course, topic, principle, etc.—**deviation** *n*.

device *n* a machine, implement, etc for a particular purpose; an invention; a scheme, a plot.

devil *n* (*with cap*) in Christian and Jewish theology, the supreme spirit of evil, Satan; any evil spirit; an extremely wicked person; (*inf*) a reckless, high-spirited person; (*inf*) someone or something difficult to deal with; (*inf*) a person. * *vb* (*pt* **devilled**) *vt* to cook food with a hot seasoning. * *vi* to act as a drudge to someone; to do research for an author or barrister.

devilish *adj* fiendish; mischievous. * *adv* (*inf*) very.

devious *adj* indirect; not straightforward; underhand, deceitful.—**deviously** *adv*.—**deviousness** *n*.

devise *vt* to invent, contrive; to plan.—**deviser, devisor** *n*.

devoid *adj* lacking (*with* **of**); free from.

devote *vt* to give or use for a particular activity or purpose.

devoted *adj* zealous; loyal; loving. —**devotedly** *adv*.

devotion *n* given to religious worship; piety; strong affection or attachment (to); ardour; (*pl*) prayers. —**devotional** *adj*.

devour *vt* to eat up greedily; to consume; to absorb eagerly by the senses or mind.

devout *adj* very religious, pious; sincere, dedicated.—**devoutly** *adv*.—**devoutness** *n*.

dew *n* air moisture, deposited on a cool surface, esp at night.

dexterity *n* manual skill, adroitness.

diabetes *n* a medical disorder marked by the persistent and excessive discharge of urine.

diabetic *adj* suffering from diabetes.—*also n*.

diagnose *vt* to ascertain by diagnosis.

diagnosis *n* (*pl* **diagnoses**) the identification of a disease from its symptoms; the analysis of the nature or cause of a problem.—**diagnostic** *adj*.—**diagnostician** *n*.

diagonal *adj* slanting from one corner to an opposite corner of a polygon. * *n* a straight line connecting opposite corners.—**diagonally** *adv*.

diagram *n* a figure or plan drawn in outline to illustrate the form or workings of something.—**diagrammatic** *adj*.

dial *n* the face of a watch or clock; a graduated disc with a pointer used in various instruments; the control on a radio or television set indicating wavelength or station; the numbered disc on a telephone used to enter digits to connect calls; an instrument for telling the time by the sun's shadow. * *vt* (*pt* **dialled**) to measure or indicate by a dial; to make a telephone connection by using a dial or numbered keypad.

dialect *n* the form of language spoken in a particular region or social class.

dialogue, dialog (*US*) *n* a conversation, esp in a play or novel; an exchange of opinions, negotiation.

diameter *n* a straight line bisecting a circle; the length of this line.

diamond *n* a valuable gem, a crystallized form of pure carbon; (*baseball*) the playing field, esp the infield; a suit of playing cards denoted by a red lozenge. * *adj* composed of, or set with diamonds; shaped like a diamond.

diaper *n* a nappy.

diaphragm *n* the midriff, a muscular structure separating the chest from the abdomen; any thin dividing membrane; a device for regulating aperture of a camera lens; a contraceptive cap covering the cervix; a thin vibrating disc used in a telephone receiver, microphone, etc.

diarrhoea, diarrhea (*US*) *n* excessive looseness of the bowels.

diary *n* a daily record of personal thoughts, events, or business appointments; a book for keeping a daily record.

dice *n* (*the pl of* **die**[2] *but used as sing*) a small cube with numbered sides used in games of chance. * *vt* to gamble using dice; to cut (food) into small cubes.

dictate *vt* to say or read for another person to write or for a machine to record; to pronounce, order with authority. * *vi* to give dictation; to give orders (to). * *n* an order, rule, or command; (*usu pl*) an impulse, ruling principle.—**dictation** *n*.

dictator *n* a ruler with absolute authority, usu acquired by force.

dictatorship *n* the office or government of a dictator; a country governed by a dictator; absolute power.

diction *n* a way of speaking, enunciation; a person's choice of words.

dictionary *n* a reference book containing the words of a language or branch of knowledge alphabetically arranged, with their meanings, pronunciation, origin, etc.

did *see* **do**.

die[1] *vi* (*pr p* **dying**, *pt* **died**) to cease existence; to become extinct; to stop functioning; to feel a deep longing.

die[2] *n* a dice.

die[3] *n* an engraved stamp for pressing coins; a casting mould.

diesel *n* a vehicle driven by diesel engine.

diesel engine *n* an internal combustion engine in which ignition is produced by the heat of highly compressed air alone.

diet[1] *n* food selected to adjust weight, to control illness, etc; the food and drink usually consumed by a person or animal. * *vt* to put on a diet. * *vi* to eat according to a special diet.—**dieter** *n*.

diet[2] *n* a legislative assembly in some countries.

differ *vi* to be unlike, distinct (from); to disagree.

difference *n* the act or state of being unlike; disparity; a distinguishing feature; the amount or manner of being different; the result of the subtraction of one quantity from another; a disagreement or argument.

different *adj* distinct, separate; unlike, not the same; unusual.—**differently** *adv*.

differential *adj* of or showing a difference; (*math*) relating to increments in given functions. * *n* something that marks the difference between comparable things; the difference in wage rates for different types of labour, esp within an industry.

differentiate *vt* to make different; to become specialized; to note differences; (*math*) to calculate the derivative of.—**differentiation** *n*.

difficult *adj* hard to understand; hard to make, do, or carry out; not easy to please.

difficulty *n* being difficult; a problem, etc that is hard to deal with; an obstacle; a troublesome situation; a disagreement.

diffident *adj* shy, lacking self-confidence, not assertive.—**diffidence** *n*.—**diffidently** *adv*.

diffuse[1] *vt* to spread widely in all directions. * *vti* (*gases, fluids, particles*) to intermingle.—**diffuser, diffusor** *n*.

diffuse[2] *adj* spread widely, not concentrated; wordy, not concise.—**diffusely** *adv*.

dig *vt* (*pr p* **digging**, *pt* **dug**) to use a tool or hands, claws, etc in making a hole in the ground; to unearth by digging; to excavate; to investigate; to thrust (into); to nudge; (*sl*) to understand, approve. * *n* (*sl*) a thrust; an archaeological excavation; a cutting remark.

digest[1] *vt* to convert (food) into assimilable form; to reduce (facts, laws, etc) to convenient form by classifying or summarizing; to form a clear view of (a situation) by reflection. * *vi* to become digested.

digest[2] *n* an abridgment of any written matter; a periodical synopsis of published or broadcast material.

digestible *adj* capable of being digested.—**digestibility** *n*.

digestion *n* the act or process of digesting.

digit *n* any of the basic counting units of a number system, including zero; a human finger or toe.

digital *adj* of or using digits.—**digitally** *adv*.

dignified *adj* possessing dignity; noble; serious.

dignitary *n* a person in a high position or rank.

dignity *n* noble, serious, formal in manner and appearance; sense of self-respect, worthiness; a high rank, eg in the government.

digress *vi* to stray from the main subject in

speaking or writing.—**digression** *n*.
digs *npl* (*inf*) lodgings.
dilapidated *adj* in a state of disrepair; shabby.
dilate *vti* to enlarge or become enlarged.—**dilation** *n*.—**dilator, dilater** *n*.
dilatory *adj* tardy; causing or meant to cause delay.—**dilatorily** *adv*.—**dilatoriness** *n*.
dilemma *n* a situation where each of two alternative courses is undesirable; any difficult problem or choice.
diligent *adj* industrious; done with proper care and effort.—**diligently** *adv*.—**diligence** *n*.
dilute *vt* to thin down, esp by mixing with water; to weaken the strength of. * *adj* diluted.—**dilution** *n*.
dim *adj* (**dimmer, dimmest**) faintly lit; not seen, heard, understood, etc clearly; gloomy; unfavourable; (*inf*) stupid. * *vti* to make or cause to become dark.—**dimly** *adv*.—**dimness** *n*.
dime *n* a US or Canadian coin worth ten cents.
dimension *n* any linear measurement of width, length, or thickness; extent; size.—**dimensional** *adj*.
diminish *vti* to make or become smaller in size, amount, or importance.
diminutive *adj* very small. * *n* a word formed by a suffix to mean small (eg *duckling*) or to convey affection (eg *Freddie*).
dimple *n* a small hollow, usu on the cheek or chin. * *vti* to make or become dimpled; to reveal dimples.
din *n* a loud persistent noise. * *vt* (*pt* **dinned**) to make a din; (*with* **into**) to instil by continual repetition.
dine *vi* to eat dinner. * *vt* to entertain to dinner.
dinghy *n* a small open boat propelled by oars or sails; a small inflatable boat.
dingy *adj* (**dingier, dingiest**) dirty-looking, shabby.—**dinginess** *n*.
dinner *n* the principal meal of the day; a formal meal in honour of a person or occasion.
dinner jacket *n* a man's usu black jacket for semiformal evening wear.
diocese *n* the district over which a bishop has authority.—**diocesan** *adj*.
dip *vt* (*pt* **dipped**) to put (something) under the surface (of a liquid) and lift quickly out again; to immerse (sheep) in an antiseptic solution. * *vi* to go into water and come out quickly; to drop down or sink out of sight; to read superficially; to slope downward. * *n* a dipping of any kind; a sudden drop; a mixture in which to dip something.
diphtheria *n* an acute infectious disease causing inflammation of the throat and breathing difficulties.
diphthong *n* the union of two vowel sounds pronounced in one syllable; a ligature.
diploma *n* a certificate given by a college or university to its graduating students.
diplomacy *n* the management of relations between nations; skill in handling affairs without arousing hostility.
diplomat *n* a person employed or skilled in diplomacy.
diplomatic, diplomatical *adj* of diplomacy; employing tact and conciliation; tactful.—**diplomatically** *adv*.
dipstick *n* a rod with graduated markings to measure fluid level.
dire *adj* dreadful; ominous; desperately urgent.
direct *adj* straight; in an unbroken line, with nothing in between; frank; truthful. * *vt* to manage, to control; to tell or show the way; to point to, to aim at; (*a letter or parcel*) to address; to carry out the organizing and supervision of; to train and lead performances; to command. * *vi* to determine a course; to act as a director.—**directness** *n*.
direct current *n* an electric current that flows in one direction only.
direction *n* management, control; order, command; a knowing or telling what to do, where to go, etc; any way in which one may face or point; (*pl*) instructions.
directly *adv* in a direct manner; immediately; in a short while.
director *n* person who directs, esp the production of a show for stage or screen; one of the persons directing the affairs of a company or an institution. —**directorial** *adj*.—**directorship** *n*.
directory *n* an alphabetical or classified list, as of telephone numbers, members of an organization, charities, etc.
dirt *n* filth; loose earth; obscenity; scandal.
dirt-cheap *adj* (*inf*) very cheap.
dirty *adj* (**dirtier, dirtiest**) filthy; unclean; dishonest; mean; (*weather*) stormy; obscene. * *vti* to make or become dirty.—**dirtily** *adv*.—**dirtiness** *n*.
disability *n* a lack of physical, mental or social fitness; something that disables, a handicap.
disabled *adj* having a physical handicap.
disadvantage *n* an unfavourable condition or situation; loss, damage. * *vt* to put at a disadvantage.
disadvantageous *adj* causing disadvantage.

disagree *vi* to differ in opinion; to quarrel; (*with* **with**) to have a bad effect on.—**disagreement** *n*.
disagreeable *adj* nasty, bad tempered. —**disagreeably** *adv*.
disallow *vt* to refuse to allow or to accept the truth or value of.
disappear *vi* to pass from sight completely; to fade into nothing.—**disappearance** *n*.
disappoint *vt* to fail to fulfil the hopes of (a person).—**disappointed** *adj*.—**disappointing** *adj*.—**disappointingly** *adv*.
disappointment *n* the frustration of one's hopes; annoyance due to failure; a person or thing that disappoints.
disapprove *vti* to express or have an unfavourable opinion (of).—**disapproval** *n*.
disarm *vt* to deprive of weapons or means of defence; to defuse (a bomb); to conciliate. * *vi* to abolish or reduce national armaments.
disarmament *n* the reduction or abolition of a country's armed forces and weaponry.
disaster *n* a devastating and sudden misfortune; utter failure.—**disastrous** *adj*.—**disastrously** *adv*.
disband *vt* to disperse; to break up and separate.—**disbandment** *n*.
disc *n* any flat, thin circular body; something resembling this, as the sun; a cylindrical pad of cartilage between the vertebrae; a gramophone record; (*comput*) a variant spelling of **disk**.
discard *vti* to cast off, get rid of; (*cards*) to throw away a card from one's hand. * *n* something discarded; (*cards*) a discarded card.
disc brake *n* one in which two flat discs press against a central plate on the wheel hub.
discern *vt* to perceive; to see clearly. —**discernible** *adj*.—**discernibly** *adv*.
discerning *adj* discriminating; perceptive.—**discernment** *n*.
discharge *vt* to unload; to send out, emit; to release, acquit; to dismiss from employment; to shoot a gun; to fulfil, as duties. * *vi* to unload; (*gun*) to be fired; (*fluid*) to pour out. * *n* the act or process of discharging; something that is discharged; an authorization for release, acquittal, dismissal, etc.
disciple *n* a person who believes in and helps to spread another's teachings, a follower; one of the twelve apostles of Christ.
disciplinary *adj* of or for discipline.
discipline *n* a field of learning; training and conditioning to produce obedience and self-control; punishment; the maintenance of order and obedience as a result of punishment; a system of rules of behaviour. * *vt* to punish to enforce discipline; to train by instruction; to bring under control.
disc jockey *n* (*inf*) a person who announces records on a programme of broadcast music, or in discotheques.
disclaim *vi* to deny connection with; to renounce all legal claim to.
disclose *vt* to bring into the open, to reveal.—**disclosure** *n*.
disco *n* (*inf*) a discotheque.
discolour, discolor (*US*) *vti* to ruin the colour of; to fade, stain.—**discoloration** *n*.
discomfort *n* uneasiness; something causing this. * *vt* to make uncomfortable; to make uneasy.
disconcert *vt* to confuse; to upset.
disconnect *vt* to separate or break the connection of.
disconnected *adj* disjointed; incoherent.
disconsolate *adj* miserable; dejected. —**disconsolately** *adv*.
discontent *n* lack of contentment, dissatisfaction.—**discontentment** *n*.
discontented *adj* feeling discontent; unhappy, unsatisfied.
discontinue *vti* to stop or come to a stop; to give up.—**discontinuance** *n*.
discord *n* lack of agreement, strife; (*mus*) a lack of harmony; harsh clashing sounds.—**discordance** *n*.—**discordant** *adj*.—**discordantly** *adv*.
discotheque *n* an occasion when people gather to dance to recorded pop music; a club or party, etc where this takes place; equipment for playing such music.
discount *n* a reduction in the amount or cost; the percentage charged for doing this. * *vt* to deduct from the amount, cost; to allow for exaggeration; to disregard; to make less effective by anticipation. * *vi* to make and give discounts.
discourage *vt* to deprive of the will or courage (to do something); to try to prevent; to hinder.—**discouraging** *adj*.—**discouraged** *adj*.—**discouragement** *n*.
discourteous *adj* lacking in courtesy, rude.—**discourteously** *adv*.—**discourtesy** *n*.
discover *vt* to see, find or learn of for the first time.—**discoverable** *adj*.—**discoverer** *n*.
discovery *n* the act of discovering or being discovered; something discovered.
discredit *n* damage to a reputation; doubt; disgrace; lack of credibility. * *vt* to damage

the reputation of; to cast doubt on the authority or credibility of.

discreet *adj* wisely cautious, prudent; unobtrusive.—**discreetly** *adv*.—**discreetness** *n*.

discrepancy *n* difference; a disagreement, as between figures in a total.

discretion *n* the freedom to judge or choose; prudence; wise judgment; skill.

discriminate *vi* to be discerning in matters of taste; to make a distinction; to treat differently, esp unfavourably due to prejudice.—**discrimination** *n*.—**discriminatory** *adj*.

discriminating *adj* judicious; discerning; discriminatory.

discus *n* a heavy disc with a thickened middle, thrown by athletes.

discuss *vt* to talk over; to investigate by reasoning or argument.—**discussion** *n*.

disdain *vt* to scorn, treat with contempt. * *n* scorn; a feeling of contemptuous superiority.—**disdainful** *adj*.—**disdainfully** *adv*.

disease *n* an unhealthy condition in an organism caused by infection, poisoning, etc; sickness; a harmful condition or situation.—**diseased** *adj*.

disembark *vti* to land from a ship, debark.—**disembarkation** *n*.

disembodied *adj* (*soul, spirit, etc*) free of the body.

disembowel *vt* (*pt* **disembowelled**) to remove the entrails of; to remove the substance of.

disenchant *vt* to disillusion.—**disenchantment** *n*.

disengage *vt* to separate or free from engagement or obligation; to detach, to release.—**disengaged** *adj*.—**disengagement** *n*.

disentangle *vt* to untangle; to free from complications.—**disentanglement** *n*.

disfavour, disfavor (*US*) *n* dislike; disapproval. * *vt* to treat with disfavour.

disfigure *vt* to spoil the beauty or appearance of.—**disfigurement** *n*.

disgrace *n* a loss of trust, favour, or honour; something that disgraces. * *vt* to bring disgrace or shame upon.

disgraceful *adj* causing disgrace, shameful.—**disgracefully** *adv*.

disgruntled *adj* dissatisfied, resentful.

disguise *vt* to hide what one is by appearing as something else; to hide what (a thing) really is. * *n* the use of a changed appearance to conceal identity; a false appearance.

disgust *n* sickening dislike. * *vt* to cause disgust in.—**disgustedly** *adv*.

dish *n* any of various shallow concave vessels to serve food in; the amount of food served in a dish; the food served; a shallow concave object, as a dish aerial; (*inf*) an attractive person.

dishcloth *n* a cloth for washing dishes.

dishearten *vt* to discourage.

dishevelled, disheveled (*US*) *adj* rumpled, untidy.—**dishevelment** *n*.

dishonest *adj* not honest.—**dishonestly** *adv*.—**dishonesty** *n*.

dishonour, dishonor (*US*) *n* loss of honour; disgrace, shame. * *vt* to bring shame on, to disgrace; to refuse to pay, as a cheque.

dishonourable, dishonorable (*US*) *adj* lacking honour, disgraceful.—**dishonourably** *adv*.

dishwasher *n* an appliance for washing dishes; a person employed to wash dishes.

disillusion *vt* to free from (mistaken) ideals or illusions. * *n* the state of being disillusioned.—**disillusionment** *n*.

disinfect *vt* to destroy germs.—**disinfection** *n*.

disinfectant *n* any chemical agent that inhibits the growth of or destroys germs.

disintegrate *vti* to break or cause to break into separate pieces.—**disintegration** *n*.

disinterested *adj* impartial; objective. —**disinterestedly** *adv*.

disjointed *adj* incoherent, muddled, esp of speech or writing.

disk *n* an alternative spelling of **disc**; (*comput*) a storage device in a computer, either floppy or hard.

dislike *vt* to consider unpleasant. * *n* aversion, distaste.—**dislikable, dislikeable** *adj*.

dislocate *vt* to put (a joint) out of place, to displace; to upset the working of.—**dislocation** *n*.

dislodge *vt* to force or move out of a hiding place, established position, etc. —**dislodgement, dislodgment** *n*.

dismal *adj* gloomy, miserable, sad; (*inf*) feeble, worthless. —**dismally** *adv*.

dismantle *vt* to pull down; to take apart.

dismay *n* apprehension, discouragement. * *vt* to fill with dismay.

disobedient *adj* failing or refusing to obey.—**disobediently** *adv*.—**disobedience** *n*.

disobey *vt* to refuse to follow orders.

disorder *n* lack of order; untidiness; a riot; an illness or interruption of the normal functioning of the body or mind. * *vt* to throw into confusion; to upset.—**disorderly** *adj*.

disorganize *vt* to confuse or disrupt an orderly arrangement.—**disorganization** *n*.

disown *vt* to refuse to acknowledge as one's own.

disparage *vt* to belittle.—**disparagingly** *adv*.—**disparagement** *n*.

disparity *n* essential difference; inequality.

dispassionate *adj* unemotional; impartial.—**dispassionately** *adv*.

dispatch *vt* to send off somewhere; to perform speedily; to kill. * *n* a sending off (of a letter, a messenger etc); promptness; haste; a written message, esp of news.—*also* **despatch**.

dispel *vt* (*pt* **dispelled**) to drive away and scatter.

dispensary *n* a place in a hospital, a chemist shop, etc where medicines are made up and dispensed.

dispense *vt* to deal out, distribute; to prepare and distribute medicines; to administer.

disperse *vt* to scatter in different directions. * *vi* to separate, become dispersed.—**dispersal** *n*.

dispirited *adj* depressed, discouraged.

displace *vt* to take the place of, to oust; to remove from a position of authority.—**displacement** *n*.

display *vt* to show, expose to view; to exhibit ostentatiously. * *n* a displaying; an eye-catching arrangement, exhibition; a computer monitor for presenting visual information.

displease *vt* to cause offence or annoyance to.

displeasure *n* a feeling of being displeased; dissatisfaction.

disposable *adj* designed to be discarded after use; available for use. * *n* something disposable, eg a baby's nappy.

disposal *n* a disposing of something; order, arrangement.

dispose *vt* to place in order, arrange; to influence. * *vi* to deal with or settle; to give, sell or transfer to another; to throw away.

disposed *adj* inclined (towards something).

disposition *n* a natural way of behaving towards others; tendency; arrangement.

disproportionate *adj* out of proportion.—**disproportionately** *adv*.

disprove *vt* to prove (a claim, etc) to be incorrect.

dispute *vt* to make the subject of an argument or debate; to query the validity of. * *vi* to argue. * *n* an argument; a quarrel.

disqualify *vt* to make ineligible because of a violation of rules; to make unfit or unsuitable, to disable.—**disqualification** *n*.

disquiet *n* anxiety, worry.—*also vt*.—**disquieting** *adj*.—**disquietude** *n*.

disregard *vt* to pay no attention to; to consider as of little or no importance. * *n* lack of attention, neglect.

disrepair *n* a worn-out condition through neglect of repair.

disreputable *adj* of bad reputation.

disrespect *n* lack of respect, rudeness. —**disrespectful** *adj*.—**disrespectfully** *adv*.

disrupt *vti* to break up; to create disorder or confusion; to interrupt.—**disruption** *n*.

dissect *vt* to cut apart (a plant, animal, etc) for scientific examination; to analyse and interpret in fine detail.—**dissection** *n*.—**dissector** *n*.

disseminate *vt* to spread or scatter (ideas, information, etc) widely.—**dissemination** *n*.

dissent *vi* to hold a different opinion; to withhold assent. * *n* a difference of opinion.—**dissenter** *n*.

dissident *adj* disagreeing. * *n* a person who disagrees strongly with government policies, esp one who suffers harassment or imprisonment as a result.—**dissidence** *n*.

dissipate *vt* to scatter, dispel; to waste, squander (money, etc). * *vi* to separate and vanish.

dissipated *adj* dissolute, indulging in excessive pleasure; scattered, wasted.

dissociate *vti* to separate or cause to separate the association of (people, things, etc) in consciousness; to repudiate a connection with.—**dissociation** *n*.

dissolute *adj* lacking moral discipline.

dissolve *vt* to cause to pass into solution; to disperse (a legislative assembly); to melt; (*partnership, marriage*) to break up legally, annul. * *vi* to become liquid; to fade away; to be overcome by emotion.

dissuade *vt* to prevent or discourage by persuasion.—**dissuasion** *n*.—**dissuasive** *adj*.

distance *n* the amount of space between two points or things; a distant place or point; remoteness, coldness of manner. * *vt* to place at a distance, physically or emotionally; to outdistance in a race, etc.

distant *adj* separated by a specific distance; far-off in space, time, place, relation, etc; not friendly, aloof.—**distantly** *adv*.

distaste *n* aversion; dislike.

distasteful *adj* unpleasant, offensive. —**distastefully** *adv*.

distemper *n* an infectious and often fatal disease of dogs and other animals; a type of paint made by mixing colour with egg or glue instead of oil; a painting made with this.

distend *vti* to swell or cause to swell, esp from internal pressure.

distil, **distill** (*US*) *vti* (*pt* **distilled**) to treat by, or cause to undergo, distillation; to purify; to extract the essence of; to let or cause to fall in drops.

distillery *n* a place where distilling, esp of alcoholic spirits, is carried on.

distinct *adj* different, separate (from); easy to perceive by the mind or senses.—**distinctly** *adv*.—**distinctness** *n*.

distinction *n* discrimination, separation; a difference seen or made; a distinguishing mark or characteristic; excellence, superiority; a mark of honour.

distinctive *adj* clearly marking a person or thing as different from another; characteristic.

distinguish *vt* to see or recognize as different; to mark as different, characterize; to see or hear clearly; to confer distinction on; to make eminent or known. * *vi* to perceive a difference. —**distinguishable** *adj*.

distinguished *adj* eminent, famous; dignified in appearance or manners.

distort *vt* to pull or twist out of shape; to alter the true meaning of, misrepresent.—**distortion** *n*.

distract *vt* to draw (eg the mind or attention) to something else; to confuse.

distracted *adj* bewildered, confused.

distraction *n* something that distracts the attention; an amusement; perplexity; extreme agitation.

distraught *adj* extremely distressed.

distress *n* physical or emotional suffering, as from pain, illness, lack of money, etc; a state of danger, desperation. * *vt* to cause distress to.

distribute *vt* to divide and share out; to spread, disperse throughout an area.—**distribution** *n*.

distributor *n* an agent who sells goods, esp wholesale; a device for distributing current to the spark plugs in an engine.

district *n* a territorial division defined for administrative purposes; a region or area with a distinguishing character.

distrust *n* suspicion, lack of trust.—*also vt*.—**distrustful** *adj*.

disturb *vt* to interrupt; to cause to move from the normal position or arrangement; to destroy the quiet or composure of.

disturbance *n* a disturbing or being disturbed; an interruption; an outbreak of disorder and confusion.

ditch *n* any long narrow trench dug in the ground. * *vt* to make a ditch in; (*sl*) to drive (a car) into a ditch; (*sl*) to make a forced landing of (an aircraft); (*sl*) to get rid of.

dither *vi* to hesitate, vacillate.—**ditherer** *n*.

ditto *n* the same again, as above—used in written lists and tables to avoid repetition. * *vt* to repeat.

divan *n* a long couch without back or sides; a bed of similar design.

dive *vi* (*pt* **dived** *or* **dove**) to plunge headfirst into water; (*aircraft*) to descend or fall steeply; (*diver, submarine*) to submerge; to plunge (eg the hand) suddenly into anything; to dash headlong, lunge. * *n* a headlong plunge; a submerging of a submarine, etc; a sharp descent; a steep decline; (*sl*) a disreputable public place.

diver *n* a person who dives; a person who works or explores underwater from a diving bell or in a diving suit; any of various aquatic birds.

diverge *vi* to branch off in different directions from a common point; to differ in character, form, etc; to deviate from a path or course.—**divergent** *adj*.—**divergence** *n*.

diverse *adj* different; assorted, various.

diversify *vt* to vary; to invest in a broad range of securities to lessen risk of loss. * *vi* to engage in a variety of commercial operations to reduce risk.—**diversification** *n*.

diversion *n* turning aside from a course; a recreation, amusement; a drawing of attention away from the principal activity; a detour when a road is temporarily closed to traffic.—**diversionary** *adj*.

diversity *n* variety.

divert *vt* to turn aside from one course onto another; to entertain, amuse.

divide *vt* to break up into parts; to distribute, share out; to sort into categories; to cause to separate from something else; to separate into opposing sides; (*Parliament*) to vote or cause to vote by division; (*math*) to ascertain how many times one quantity contains another. * *vi* to become separated; to diverge; to vote by separating into two sides. * *n* a watershed; a split.

dividend *n* a number which is to be divided; the money earned by a company and divided among the shareholders; a bonus derived from some action.

divine *adj* of, from, or like God or a god; (*inf*) excellent. * *n* a clergyman; a theologian. * *vt* to foretell the future by supernatural means; to discover intuitively; to dowse. * *vi* to practise divination.—**divinely** *adv*.—**diviner** *n*.

diving board *n* a platform or springboard for diving from.
divinity *n* any god; theology; the quality of being God or a god.
division *n* a dividing or being divided; a partition, a barrier; a portion or section; a military unit; separation; (*Parliament*) a separation into two opposing sides to vote; a disagreement; (*math*) the process of dividing one number by another.—**divisional** *adj.*
divorce *n* the legal dissolution of marriage; separation. * *vt* to terminate a marriage by divorce; to separate.
divorcé, divorcee *n* a divorced person.—**divorcée** *nf.*
divulge *vt* to tell or reveal.—**divulgence** *n.*
DIY *abbr* = do-it-yourself.
dizzy *adj* (**dizzier, dizziest**) confused; causing giddiness or confusion; (*sl*) silly; foolish. * *vt* to make dizzy; to confuse.—**dizzily** *adv.*
DJ *abbr* = disc jockey; dinner jacket.
do *vt* (*pres t* **does,** *pt* **did**, *pp* **done**) to perform; to work; to end, to complete; to make; to provide; to arrange, to tidy; to perform; to cover a distance; to visit; (*sl*) to serve time in prison; (*sl*) to cheat, to rob; (*sl*) to assault. * *vi* to act or behave; to be satisfactory; to manage. * *n* (*pl* **dos, do's**) (*inf*) a party; (*inf*) a hoax. *Do* has special uses where it has no definite meaning, as in asking questions (*Do you like milk?*), emphasizing a verb (*I do want to go*), and standing for a verb already used (*My dog goes where I do*).
docile *adj* easily led; submissive.—**docilely** *adv.*—**docility** *n.*
dock[1] *vt* (*an animal's tail*) to cut short; (*wages, etc*) to deduct a portion of.
dock[2] *n* a wharf; an artificial enclosed area of water for ships to be loaded, repaired, etc; (*pl*) a dockyard. * *vt* to come or bring into dock; to join (spacecraft) together in space.
dock[3] *n* an enclosed area in a court of law reserved for the accused.
docker *n* a labourer who works at the docks.
dockyard *n* an area with docks and facilities for repairing and refitting ships.
doctor *n* a person qualified to treat diseases or physical disorders; the highest academic degree; the holder of such a degree. * *vt* to treat medically; (*machinery, etc*) to patch up; to tamper with, falsify; (*inf*) to castrate or spay. —**doctoral** *adj.*
doctrine *n* a principle of belief.—**doctrinal** *adj.*
document *n* a paper containing information or proof of anything. * *vt* to provide or prove with documents. —**documentation** *n.*
documentary *adj* consisting of documents; presenting a factual account of an event or activity. * *n* a non-fiction film.
dodge *vi* to move quickly in an irregular course. * *vt* to evade (a duty) by cunning; to avoid by a sudden movement or shift of position; to trick. * *n* a sudden movement; (*inf*) a clever trick.—**dodger** *n.*
dog *n* a canine mammal of numerous breeds, commonly kept as a domestic pet; the male of the wolf or fox; a despicable person; a device for gripping things. * *vt* (*pt* **dogged**) to pursue relentlessly.—**dog-like** *adj.*
dog-collar *n* (*inf*) a clerical collar.
dog-eared *adj* (*book*) having the corners of the pages turned down; worn, shabby.
dogma *n* a belief taught or held as true, esp by a church; a doctrine.
dogmatic, dogmatical *adj* pertaining to a dogma; forcibly asserted as if true; overbearing.—**dogmatically** *adv.*
doings *npl* things done; actions.
doldrums *npl* inactivity; depression; boredom; the regions of the ocean about the equator where there is little wind.
dole *n* (*inf*) money received from the state while unemployed; a small portion. * *vt* to give (out) in small portions.
doleful *adj* sad, gloomy.—**dolefully** *adv.*
doll *n* a toy in the form of a human figure; a ventriloquist's dummy; (*sl*) a woman
dollar *n* the unit of money in the US, Canada, Australia and many other countries.
dolphin *n* a marine mammal with a beak-like snout, larger than a porpoise but smaller than a whale.
domain *n* an area under the control of a ruler or government; a field of thought, activity, etc.
dome *n* a large, rounded roof; something high and rounded.—*also vt.*
domesday *see* **doomsday**.
domestic *adj* belonging to the home or family; not foreign; (*animals*) tame. * *n* a servant in the home.—**domestically** *adv.*
domesticate *vt* to tame; to make home-loving and fond of household duties.—**domestication** *n.*
domicile *n* a house; a person's place of residence.—**domiciliary** *adj.*
dominant *adj* commanding, prevailing over others; overlooking from a superior height. * *n* (*mus*) the fifth note of a diatonic scale.—**dominance** *n.*

dominate *vt* to control or rule by strength; to hold a commanding position over; to overlook from a superior height.—**domination** *n*.
dominion *n* a territory with one ruler or government; the power to rule, authority.
domino *n* (*pl* **dominoes, dominos**) a flat oblong tile marked with up to six dots; (*pl*) a popular game usu using a set of 28 dominoes; a loose cloak, usu worn with an eye mask, at masquerades.
don[1] *vt* (*pt* **donned**) to put on.
don[2] *n* a head, fellow or tutor at Oxford or Cambridge universities; (*loosely*) any university teacher.
donate *vt* to give as a gift or donation, esp to a charity.—**donator** *n*.
donation *n* donating; a contribution.
done *see* **do**.
donkey *n* a small animal resembling a horse.
donor *n* a person who donates something, a donator; a person who gives blood, organs, etc, for medical use.
don't = do not.
donut *n* (*inf*) a doughnut.
doom *n* a grim destiny; ruin. * *vt* to condemn to failure, destruction, etc.
doomsday *n* the day of God's Last Judgment of mankind.—*also* **domesday**.
door *n* a movable barrier to close an opening in a wall; a doorway; a means of entry or approach.
doorman *n* a uniformed attendant stationed at the entrance to large hotels, offices, etc.
doormat *n* a mat placed at the entrance to a doorway for wiping one's feet; (*inf*) a submissive or easily bullied person.
dope *n* a thick pasty substance used for lubrication; (*inf*) any illegal drug, such as cannabis or narcotics; (*sl*) a stupid person; (*sl*) information. * *vt* to treat with dope. * *vi* to take addictive drugs.
dopey, dopy *adj* (**dopier, dopiest**) (*sl*) stupid; (*inf*) half asleep.—**dopiness** *n*.
dormant *adj* sleeping; quiet, as if asleep; inactive.—**dormancy** *n*.
dormitory *n* a large room with many beds, as in a boarding school.
dormouse *n* (*pl* **dormice**) a small mouse-like creature that hibernates in winter.
dose *n* the amount of medicine, radiation, etc administered at one time; a part of an experience; (*sl*) a venereal disease. * *vt* to administer a dose (of medicine) to.—**dosage** *n*.
dosshouse *n* (*sl*) a cheap lodging house.
dot *n* a small round speck, a point; the short signal in Morse code. * *vt* (*pt* **dotted**) to mark with a dot; to scatter (about).
dote *vi* (*with* **on** *or* **upon**) to show excessive affection.
double *adj* twice as large, as strong, etc; designed or intended for two; made of two similar parts; having two meanings, characters, etc; (*flowers*) having more than one circle of petals. * *adv* twice; in twos. * *n* a number or amount that is twice as much; a person or thing identical to another; (*film*) a person closely resembling an actor and who takes their place to perform stunts, etc; (*pl*) a game between two pairs of players. * *vti* to make or become twice as much or as many; to fold, to bend; to bend sharply backwards; to sail around; to have an additional purpose.—**doubly** *adv*.
double bass *n* the largest instrument of the violin family.
double-breasted *adj* (*suit*) having one half of the front overlap the other.
double-cross *vt* to betray an associate, to cheat.—*also n*.
double-park *vt* to park alongside a car which is already parked beside the kerb.
doubt *vi* to be uncertain or undecided. * *vt* to hold in doubt; to distrust; to be suspicious of. * *n* uncertainty; (*often pl*) lack of confidence in something, distrust.—**doubter** *n*.
doubtful *adj* feeling doubt; uncertain; suspicious.—**doubtfully** *adv*.
doubtless *adv* no doubt.
dough *n* a mixture of flour and water, milk, etc used to make bread, pastry, or cake; (*inf*) money.—**doughy** *adj*.
doughnut *n* small, fried, usu ring-shaped, cake.
dove[1] *see* **dive**.
dove[2] *n* a small bird of the pigeon family; (*politics, diplomacy*) an advocate of peace or a peaceful policy.
dovetail *n* a wedge-shaped joint used in woodwork. * *vt* to fit or combine together.
dowdy *adj* (**dowdier, dowdiest**) poorly dressed, not stylish.—**dowdily** *adv*.—**dowdiness** *n*.
down[1] *n* soft fluffy feathers or fine hairs.
down[2] *adv* toward or in a lower physical position; to a lying or sitting position; toward or to the ground, floor, or bottom; to a source or hiding place; to or in a lower status or in a worse condition; from an earlier time; in cash; to or in a state of less activity. * *adj* occupying a low position, esp lying on the ground; depressed, dejected. * *prep* in a descending direction in, on, along, or through.

* *n* a low period (as in activity, emotional life, or fortunes); (*inf*) a dislike, prejudice. * *vti* to go or cause to go or come down; to defeat; to swallow.

downcast *adj* dejected; (*eyes*) directed downwards.

downfall *n* a sudden fall (from power, etc); a sudden or heavy fall of rain, etc.

down payment *n* a deposit.

downpour *n* a heavy fall of rain.

downright *adj* frank; absolute. * *adv* thoroughly.

downtown *n* the main business district of a town or city.—*also adj*.

downward[1] *adj* moving from a higher to a lower level, position or condition. * *adv* downwards.

downwards, downward[2] *adv* towards a lower place, position, etc; from an earlier time to a later.

dowry *n* the money or possessions that a woman brings to her husband at marriage.

doze *vi* to sleep lightly. * *n* a light sleep, a nap.—**dozer** *n*.

dozen *n* a group of twelve.—**dozenth** *adj*.

Dr *abbr* = Doctor; debtor.

drab *adj* (**drabber, drabbest**) dull, un-interesting.—**drably** *adv*.—**drabness** *n*.

draft *n* a rough plan, preliminary sketch; an order for the payment of money by a bank; a smaller group selected from a larger for a specific task; in US, conscription; a draught. * *vt* to draw a rough sketch or outline of; to select for a special purpose; in US, to conscript.

drain *vt* to draw off liquid gradually; to make dry by removing liquid gradually; to exhaust physically or mentally; to drink the entire contents of a glass * *vi* to flow away gradually; to become dry as liquid trickles away. * *n* a sewer, pipe, etc by which water is drained away; something that causes exhaustion or depletion.

drainage *n* a draining; a system of drains; something drained off.

draining-board *n* a sloping, usu grooved, surface beside a sink for draining washed dishes.

drainpipe *n* a pipe that carries waste liquid, sewage, etc out of a building.

drama *n* a play for the stage, radio or television; dramatic literature as a genre; a dramatic situation or a set of events.

dramatic *adj* of or resembling drama; exciting, vivid.—**dramatically** *adv*.

dramatist *n* a person who writes plays.

drank *see* **drink**.

drape *vt* to cover or hang with cloth; to arrange in loose folds; to place loosely or untidily. * *n* a hanging cloth or curtain; (*pl*) curtains.

draper *n* a seller of cloth.

drastic *adj* acting with force and violence.—**drastically** *adv*.

draught, draft (*US*) *n* a current of air, esp in an enclosed space; the pulling of a load using an animal, etc; something drawn; a dose of medicine or liquid; an act of swallowing; the depth of water required to float a ship; beer, wine, etc stored in bulk in casks; a flat counter used in the game of draughts.

draughts *n* a board game for two players using 24 round pieces.—*also* **checkers**.

draughtsman[1], **draftsman** (*US*) *n* a person who makes detailed drawings or plans.—**draughtsmanship** *n*.

draughtsman[2] *n* a flat counter used in the game of draughts.—*also* **checker**.

draw *vti* (*pt* **drew**, *pp* **drawn**) to haul, to drag; to cause to go in a certain direction; to pull out; to attract; to delineate, to sketch; to receive (as a salary); to bend (a bow) by pulling back the string; to leave (a contest) undecided; to write up, to draft (a will); to produce or allow a current of air; to draw lots; to get information from; (*ship*) to require a certain depth to float. * *n* the act of drawing; (*inf*) an event that attracts customers, people; the drawing of lots; a drawn game.

drawback *n* a hindrance, handicap.

drawbridge *n* a bridge (eg over a moat) designed to be drawn up.

drawer *n* a person who draws; a person who draws a cheque; a sliding box-like compartment (in a table, chest, or desk); (*pl*) knickers, underpants.

drawing *n* a figure, plan, or sketch drawn by using lines.

drawing pin *n* a flat-headed pin used for fastening paper, drawings, etc, to a board.

drawing room *n* a room where visitors are entertained, a living room.

drawl *vt* to speak slowly and with elongated vowel sounds.—*also n*.

drawn *pp of* **draw**. * *adj* looking strained because of tiredness or worry.

dread *n* great fear or apprehension. * *vt* to fear greatly.—**dreadful** *adj*.—**dreadfully** *adv*.

dream *n* a stream of thoughts and images in sleep; a day-dreaming state, a reverie; an ambition; an ideal. * *vb* (*pt* **dreamt** *or* **dreamed**) *vi* to have a dream in sleep; to fantasize. * *vt* to dream of; to imagine as a reality.—**dreamer** *n*.

dreamy *adj* (**dreamier, dreamiest**) given to dreaming, unpractical; (*inf*) attractive, wonderful.

dreary *adj* (**drearier, dreariest**) dull; cheerless.—**drearily** *adv*.—**dreariness** *n*.

dredge[1] *n* a device for scooping up material from the bottom of a river, harbour, etc.—*also vt*.

dredge[2] *vt* to coat (food) by sprinkling.

dredger[1] *n* a vessel fitted with dredging equipment.

dredger[2] *n* a container with a perforated lid for sprinkling.

dregs *npl* solid impurities that settle on the bottom of a liquid; residue; (*inf*) a worthless person or thing.

drench *vt* to soak, saturate.

dress *n* clothing; a one-piece garment worn by women and girls comprising a top and skirt; a style or manner of clothing. * *vt* to put on or provide with clothing; to decorate; (*wound*) to wash and bandage; (*animal*) to groom; to arrange the hair; to prepare food (eg poultry, fish) for eating by cleaning, gutting, etc. * *vi* to put on clothes; to put on formal wear for an occasion.

dress circle *n* the first tier of seats in a theatre above the stalls.

dresser *n* a person who assists an actor to dress; a type of kitchen sideboard.

dressing *n* a sauce or stuffing for food; manure spread over the soil; dress or clothes; the bandage, ointment, etc applied to a wound.

dressing-down *n* a severe scolding.

dressing-gown *n* a loose garment worn when one is partially clothed.

dress rehearsal *n* rehearsal in full costume.

drew *see* **draw**.

dribble *vi* to flow in a thin stream or small drips; to let saliva to trickle from the mouth. * *vt* (*soccer, basketball, hockey*) to move (the ball) along little by little with the foot, hand, stick, etc. * *n* the act of dribbling; a thin stream of liquid.—**dribbler** *n*.

drier *see* **dryer**.

drift *n* a heap of snow, sand, etc deposited by the wind; natural course, tendency; the general meaning or intention (of what is said); the extent of deviation (of an aircraft, etc) from a course; an aimless course; the action or motion of drifting. * *vt* to cause to drift. * *vi* to be driven or carried along by water or air currents; to move along aimlessly; to be piled into heaps by the wind.

drill[1] *n* an implement with a pointed end that bores holes; the training of soldiers, etc; repetitious exercises or training as a teaching method; (*inf*) correct procedure or routine. * *vt* to make a hole with a drill; to instruct or be instructed by drilling.

drill[2] *n* a machine for planting seeds in rows; a furrow in which seeds are planted; a row of seeds planted in this way.—*also vt*.

drink *vb* (*pt* **drank**, *pp* **drunk**) *vt* to swallow (a liquid); to take in, absorb; to join in a toast. * *vi* to consume alcoholic liquor, esp to excess. * *n* liquid to be drunk; alcoholic liquor; (*sl*) the sea.—**drinker** *n*.

drip *vti* (*pt* **dripped**) to fall or let fall in drops. * *n* a liquid that falls in drops; the sound of falling drops; (*med*) a device for injecting a fluid slowly and continuously into a vein; (*inf*) a weak or ineffectual person.

drip-dry *adj* (*clothing*) drying easily and needing little ironing.—*also vti*.

dripping *n* fat that drips from meat during roasting.

drive *vb* (*pt* **drove**, *pp* **driven**) *vt* to urge, push or force onward; to direct the movement or course of; to convey in a vehicle; to carry through strongly; to impress forcefully; to propel (a ball) with a hard blow. * *vi* to be forced along; to be conveyed in a vehicle; to work, to strive (at). * *n* a trip in a vehicle; a stroke to drive a ball (in golf, etc); a driveway; a military attack; an intensive campaign; dynamic ability; the transmission of power to machinery.

driver *n* one who or that which drives; a chauffeur; (*golf*) a wooden club used from the tee.

driveway *n* a road for vehicles, often on private property.

drizzle *n* fine light rain.—*also vi*.—**drizzly** *adj*.

droll *adj* oddly amusing; whimsical. —**drolly** *adv*.

dromedary *n* a one-humped camel.

drone *n* a male honey-bee; a lazy person; a deep humming sound; a monotonous speaker or speech; an aircraft piloted by remote control. * *vi* to make a monotonous humming sound; to speak in a monotonous manner.

drool *vi* to slaver, dribble; to show excessive enthusiasm for.

droop *vi* to bend or hang down; to become weak or faint. * *n* the act or an instance of drooping.—**droopy** *adj*.

drop *n* a small amount of liquid in a roundish shape; something shaped like this; a tiny quantity; a sudden fall; the distance down. * *vb* (*pt* **dropped**) *vi* to fall in drops; to fall suddenly; to go lower, to sink; to come (in); (*with* **in**) to visit (with) informally; (*with* **out**) to abandon or reject (a course, society, etc). * *vt* to let fall, to cause to fall; to lower or cause to descend; to set down from a vehicle; to mention casually; to cause (the voice) to be less loud; to give up (as an idea).—**dropper** *n*.

dropout *n* a student who abandons a course of study; a person who rejects normal society.—*also vi*.

droppings *npl* animal dung.

dross *n* a surface scum on molten metal; rubbish, waste matter.

drought *n* a long period of dry weather.

drove[1] *see* **drive**.

drove[2] *n* a group of animals driven in a herd or flock, etc; a large moving crowd of people.

drown *vti* to die or kill by suffocation in water, etc. * *vt* to flood; to drench; to become immersed in some activity; to blot out (a sound) with a louder noise; to remove (sorrow, etc) with drink.

drowse *vi* to be nearly asleep.

drowsy *adj* (**drowsier, drowsiest**) sleepy.—**drowsily** *adv*.—**drowsiness** *n*.

drudge *vi* to do boring or very menial work.—*also n*.—**drudgery** *n*.

drug *n* any substance used in medicine; a narcotic. * *vt* (*pt* **drugged**) to administer drugs to; to stupefy

druggist *n* a pharmacist.

drugstore *n* a retail store in the US selling medicines and other miscellaneous articles such as cosmetics, film, etc.

drum *n* a round percussion instrument, played by striking a membrane stretched across a hollow cylindrical frame; the sound of a drum; anything shaped like a drum, as a container for liquids. * *vb* (*pt* **drummed**) *vi* to play a drum; to beat or tap rhythmically. * *vt* (*with* **in**) to instil (knowledge) into a person by constant repetition; (*with* **up**) to summon as by drum.

drummer *n* a person who plays a drum.

drunk[1] *see* **drink**.

drunk[2] *adj* intoxicated with alcohol. * *n* a drunk person.

drunkard *n* an habitual drunk.

drunken *adj* intoxicated; caused by excessive drinking.—**drunkenly** *adv*.—**drunkenness** *n*.

dry *adj* (**drier, driest**) free from water or liquid; thirsty; marked by a matter-of-fact, ironic or terse manner of expression; uninteresting, wearisome; (*bread*) without butter, etc; (*wine*) not sweet; not selling alcohol. * *vti* to make or become dry.—**drily, dryly** *adv*. —**dryness** *n*.

dry-clean *vt* to clean with solvents as opposed to water.—**dry-cleaner** *n*.—**dry-cleaning** *n*.

dryer *n* a device for drying, as a tumble-drier; a clothes horse.—*also* **drier**.

dry rot *n* decay of timber caused by a fungus; any form of moral decay or corruption.

dual *adj* double; consisting of two.—**duality** *n*.

dubious *adj* doubtful (about, of); uncertain as to the result; untrustworthy. —**dubiously** *adv*.

duchess *n* the wife or widow of a duke; a woman having the same rank as a duke in her own right.

duck[1] *vt* to dip briefly in water; to lower the head suddenly, esp to avoid some object; to avoid, dodge. * *vi* to dip or dive; to move the head or body suddenly; to evade a duty, etc. * *n* a ducking movement.

duck[2] *n* a water bird related to geese and swans; the female of this bird; its flesh used as food.

duct *n* a channel or pipe for fluids, electric cable, etc; a tube in the body for fluids to pass through.

dud *n* (*sl*) anything worthless.—*also adj*.

due *adj* owed as a debt; immediately payable; fitting, appropriate; appointed or expected to do or arrive. * *adv* directly, exactly. * *n* something due or owed; (*pl*) fees.

duel *n* combat with weapons between two persons over a matter of honour, etc; conflict of any kind between two people, sides, ideas, etc. * *vi* (*pt* **duelled**) to fight in a duel.—**duellist** *n*.

duet *n* a musical composition for two performers.

dug *see* **dig**.

duke *n* the highest order of British nobility; the title of a ruler of a European duchy.—**dukedom** *n*.

dull *adj* not sharp or pointed; not bright or clear; stupid; boring; not active. * *vti* to make or become dull. —**dully** *adv*.—**dullness** *n*.

duly *adv* properly; suitably.

dumb *adj* not able to speak; silent; (*inf*) stupid.—**dumbly** *adv*.—**dumbness** *n*.

dumbfound, dumfound *vti* to astonish, surprise.

dummy *n* a figure of a person used to display clothes; (*sl*) a soother or pacifier for a baby; a stupid person; an imitation; (*bridge*) the exposed cards of the dealer's partner.

dump *vt* to drop or put down carelessly in a heap; to deposit as rubbish; to abandon or get rid of; to sell goods abroad at a price lower than the market price abroad. * *n* a place for refuse; a temporary store; (*inf*) a dirty, dilapidated place.

dumpling *n* a rounded piece of dough cooked by boiling or steaming; a short, fat person.

dunce *n* a person who is stupid or slow to learn.

dune *n* a hill of sand piled up by the wind.

dung *n* excrement; manure.

dungarees *npl* overalls or trousers made from a coarse cotton cloth.

dungeon *n* an underground cell for prisoners.

dupe *n* a person who is cheated. * *vt* to deceive; to trick.

duplicate *adj* in pairs, double; identical; copied exactly from an original. * *n* one of a pair of identical things; a copy. * *vt* to make double; to make an exact copy of; to repeat.—**duplication** *n*.

durable *adj* enduring, resisting wear, etc.—**durability** *n*.—**durably** *adv*.

duration *n* the time in which an event continues.

duress *n* compulsion by use of force or threat; unlawful constraint; imprisonment.

during *prep* throughout the duration of; at a point in the course of.

dusk *n* (the darker part of) twilight.

dusky *adj* (**duskier, duskiest**) having a dark colour.—**duskiness** *n*.

dust *n* fine particles of solid matter. * *vt* to free from dust; to sprinkle with flour, sugar, etc.

dustbin *n* a container for household refuse.

dust jacket *n* a paper cover for a book.

dustman *n* a person employed to empty dustbins.

Dutch *adj* pertaining to Holland, its people, or language. * *n* the Dutch language.

duty *n* an obligation that must be performed for moral or legal reasons; respect for one's elders or superiors; actions and responsibilities arising from one's business, occupation, etc; a tax on goods or imports, etc.

duty-free *adj* free from tax or duty.

dwarf *n* (*pl* **dwarfs**) a person, animal, plant of abnormally small size. * *vt* to stunt; to cause to appear small.

dwell *vi* (*pt* **dwelt** *or* **dwelled**) to live (in a place); (*with* **on**) to focus the attention on; to think, talk, or write at length about.—**dweller** *n*.

dwelling *n* the house, etc where one lives, habitation.

dwindle *vi* to shrink, diminish; to become feeble.

dye *vt* (*pr p* **dyeing**, *pt* **dyed**) to give a new colour to. * *n* a colouring substance, esp in solution; a colour or tint produced by dyeing.

dynamic *adj* relating to force that produces motion; (*person*) forceful, energetic.—**dynamically** *adv*.

dynamics *n* (*used as sing*) the branch of science that deals with forces and their effect on the motion of bodies.

dynamite *n* a powerful explosive; a potentially dangerous situation; (*inf*) an energetic person or thing. * *vt* to blow up with dynamite.

dynamo *n* (*pl* **dynamos**) a device that generates electric current.

dynasty *n* a line of hereditary rulers or leaders of any powerful family or similar group.—**dynastic** *adj*.

dysentery *n* painful inflammation of the large intestine with associated diarrhoea.

E

E. *abbr* = east; eastern.

each *adj* every one of two or more.

eager *adj* enthusiastically desirous (of); keen (for); marked by impatient desire or interest.—**eagerly** *adv*.—**eagerness** *n*.

eagle *n* a bird of prey with keen eyes and powerful wings; (*golf*) a score of two strokes under par.

ear[1] *n* (the external part of) the organ of hearing; the sense or act of hearing; attention; something shaped like an ear.

ear[2] *n* the part of a cereal plant (eg corn, maize) that contains the seeds.

earache *n* a pain in the ear.

eardrum *n* the membrane within the ear that vibrates in response to sound waves.

earl *n* a member of the British nobility ranking between a marquis and a viscount.—**countess** *nf*.

early *adj* (**earlier, earliest**) before the expected or normal time; of or occurring in the first part of a period or series; of or occurring in the distant past or near future.—*also adv*.—**earliness** *n*.

earmark *vt* to set aside for a specific use; to put

an identification mark on. * *n* a distinguishing mark.

earn *vt* to gain (money, etc) by work or service; to acquire; to deserve; to earn interest (on money invested, etc).

earnest *adj* sincere in attitude or intention.—**earnestly** *adv*.—**earnestness** *n*.

earnings *npl* wages or profits; something earned.

earring *n* an ornament worn on the ear lobe.

earth *n* the world that we inhabit; solid ground, as opposed to sea; soil; the burrow of a badger, fox, etc; a connection between an electric device or circuit with the earth; (*inf*) a large amount of money. * *vt* to cover with or bury in the earth; to connect an electrical circuit or device to earth.

earthenware *n* pottery, etc made from baked clay.

earthquake *n* a violent tremor of the earth's crust.

earthy *adj* (**earthier, earthiest**) of or resembling earth; crude.—**earthiness** *n*.

earwig *n* a small insect with a pincer-like appendage at the end of its body.

ease *n* freedom from pain, discomfort or disturbance; rest from effort or work; effortlessness; lack of inhibition or restraint, naturalness. * *vt* to relieve from pain, trouble, or anxiety; to relax, make less tight, release; to move carefully and gradually. * *vi* (*often with* **off**) to become less active, intense, or severe.

easel *n* a supporting frame, esp one used by artists to support their canvases while painting.

easily *adv* with ease; by far; probably.

east *n* the direction of the sunrise; the compass point opposite west; (*with cap and* **the**) the area of the world east of Europe. * *adj, adv* in, towards, or from the east.

Easter *n* the Christian festival observed on a Sunday in March or April in commemoration of the resurrection of Christ.

easterly *adj* situated towards or belonging to the east, coming from the east. * *n* a wind from the east.

eastern *adj* of or in the east.

eastward *adj* towards the east.—**eastwards** *adv*.

easy *adj* (**easier, easiest**) free from pain, trouble, anxiety; not difficult or requiring much effort; (*manner*) relaxed; lenient; compliant; unhurried; (*inf*) open to all alternatives. * *adv* with ease.—**easiness** *n*.

easy chair *n* a comfortable chair.

easygoing *adj* placid, tolerant, relaxed.

eat *vt* (*pt* **ate,** *pp* **eaten**) to take into the mouth, chew and swallow as food; to have a meal; to consume, to destroy bit by bit; (*also with* **into**) to corrode; (*inf*) to bother, cause anxiety to; (*pl: inf*) food.—**eater** *n*.

eatable *adj* suitable for eating; fit to be eaten. * *n* (*pl*) food.

eaves *npl* the overhanging edge of a roof.

eavesdrop *vi* (*pt* **eavesdropped**) to listen secretly to a private conversation.—**eavesdropper** *n*.

ebb *n* the flow of the tide out to sea; a decline. * *vi* (*tide water*) to flow back; to become lower, to decline.

ebony *n* a hard heavy wood. * *adj* black as ebony.

ebullient *adj* exuberant, enthusiastic; boiling.—**ebullience, ebulliency** *n*.—**ebulliently** *adv*.

EC *abbr* = European Community; East Central.

eccentric *adj* deviating from a usual pattern; unconventional in manner or appearance, odd; (*circles*) not concentric; off centre. * *n* an eccentric person.—**eccentrically** *adv*.—**eccentricity** *n*.

ecclesiastic[1] *n* a member of the clergy.

ecclesiastic[2], **ecclesiastical** *adj* of or relating to the Christian Church or clergy.

echo *n* (*pl* **echoes**) a repetition of sound caused by the reflection of sound waves; imitation; the reflection of a radar signal by an object. * *vb* (*pr p* **echoing**, *pt* **echoed**) *vi* to resound; to produce an echo. * *vt* to repeat; to imitate; to send back (a sound) by an echo.

eclipse *n* the obscuring of the light of the sun or moon by the intervention of the other; a decline into obscurity, as from overshadowing by others. * *vt* to cause an eclipse of; to overshadow, darken; to surpass.

ecology *n* (the study of) the relationships between living things and their environments.—**ecological** *adj*.—**ecologist** *n*.

economic *adj* pertaining to economics or the economy; (*business, etc*) capable of producing a profit.

economical *adj* thrifty.—**economically** *adv*.

economics *n* (*used as sing*) the social science concerned with the production, consumption and distribution of goods and services; (*as pl*) financial aspects.—**economist** *n*.

economize *vti* to spend money carefully; to save; to use prudently.—**economization** *n*.

economy *n* careful use of money and resources

to minimize waste; an instance of this; the management of the finances and resources, etc of a business, industry or organization; the economic system of a country.

ecstasy *n* intense joy; (*sl*) a synthetic amphetamine-based drug that reduces social and sexual inhibitions. —**ecstatic** *adj*.—**ecstatically** *adv*.

ecumenical *adj* of the whole Christian Church; seeking Christian unity worldwide.—**ecumenicalism** *n*.

eczema *n* inflammation of the skin causing itching and the formation of scaly red patches.—**eczematous** *adj*.

eddy *n* a swiftly revolving current of air, water, fog, etc. * *vi* to move round and round.

edge *n* the border, brink, verge, margin; the sharp cutting side of a blade; sharpness, keenness; force, effectiveness. * *vt* to supply an edge or border to; to move gradually.

edgeways, edgewise *adv* with the edge forwards; sideways.

edgy *adj* (**edgier, edgiest**) irritable.—**edginess** *n*.

edible *adj* fit or safe to eat.

edict *n* a decree.

edifice *n* a substantial building; any large or complex organization or institution.

edit *vt* to prepare (text) for publication; to be in charge of a publication; (*cinema*) to prepare a final version of a film by selection and arrangement of sequences.

edition *n* a whole number of copies of a book, etc printed at a time; the form of a particular publication.

editor *n* a person in charge of a newspaper or other publication; a person who edits written material for publication; one who prepares the final version of a film; a person in overall charge of the form and content of a radio or television programme.

editorial *adj* of or produced by an editor. * *n* an article expressing the opinions of the editor or publishers of a newspaper or magazine.—**editorially** *adv*.

educate *vt* to train the mind, to teach; to provide schooling for.—**educator** *n*.

education *n* the process of learning and training; instruction as imparted in schools, colleges and universities; a course or type of instruction; the theory and practice of teaching.—**educational** *adj*.—**educationally** *adv*.

EEC *abbr* = (*formerly*) European Economic Community.

eel *n* a snake-like fish.

eerie *adj* (**eerier, eeriest**) causing fear; weird.—**eerily** *adv*.—**eeriness** *n*.

effect *n* the result of a cause or action by some agent; the power to produce some result; the fundamental meaning; an impression on the senses; an operative condition; (*pl*) personal belongings; (*pl: theatre, cinema*) sounds, lighting, etc to accompany a production. * *vt* to bring about, to accomplish.—**effectible** *adj*.

effective *adj* producing a specified effect; forceful, striking in impression; actual, real; operative.—**effectively** *adv*.—**effectiveness** *n*.

effeminate *adj* (*man*) displaying what are regarded as feminine qualities.—**effeminately** *adv*.—**effeminacy** *n*.

efficacious *adj* achieving the desired result.—**efficacy** *n*.

efficient *adj* achieving results without waste of time or effort; competent.—**efficiently** *adv*.—**efficiency** *n*.

effigy *n* a sculpture or portrait; a crude figure of a person, esp for exposure to public contempt and ridicule.

effort *n* exertion; an attempt, try; a product of great exertion.

effortless *adj* done with little effort, or seemingly so.—**effortlessly** *adv*.—**effortlessness** *n*.

effrontery *n* impudent boldness, insolence.

e.g., eg, eg. *abbr* = for example (Latin *exempli gratia*).

egalitarian *adj* upholding the principle of equal rights for all.—*also n*.—**egalitarianism** *n*.

egg[1] *n* the oval hard-shelled reproductive cell laid by birds, reptiles and fish; the egg of the domestic poultry used as food; ovum.—**eggy** *adj*.

egg[2] *vt* (*with* **on**) to incite (someone to do something).

eggplant *n* a plant producing a smooth, dark-purple fruit; this fruit used as a vegetable, aubergine.

eggshell *n* the hard outer covering of an egg. * *adj* fragile; (*paint*) having a slight sheen.

ego *n* the self; self-image, conceit.

eiderdown *n* the down of the eider duck used for stuffing quilts, etc; a thick quilt with a soft filling.

eight *n, adj* one more than seven; the symbol for this (8, VIII, viii); (the crew of) an eight-oared rowing boat.

eighteen *n, adj* one more than seventeen; the symbol for this (18, XVIII, xviii).—**eighteenth** *adj*.

eighth *adj, n* one after seventh; one of eight equal parts.
eighty *n* eight times ten; the symbol for this (80, LXXX, lxxx); (*pl*) the numbers from 80 to 89.—**eightieth** *adj, n*.
either *adj, n* the one or the other of two; each of two. * *conj* correlative to *or*.
eject *vt* to turn out, to expel by force. * *vi* to escape from an aircraft or spacecraft using an ejector seat.—**ejection** *n*.—**ejector** *n*.
ejector seat *n* an escape seat, esp in combat aircraft, that can be ejected with its occupant in an emergency by means of explosive bolts.
eke *vt* (*with* **out**) to supplement; to use (a supply) frugally; to make (a living) with difficulty.
elaborate *adj* highly detailed; planned with care and exactness. * *vt* to work out, explain in detail.—**elaborately** *adv*.—**elaboration** *n*.
elapse *vi* (*time*) to pass by.
elastic *adj* returning to the original size and shape if stretched or squeezed; springy; adaptable. * *n* fabric, tape, etc incorporating elastic thread.—**elastically** *adv*.—**elasticity** *n*.
elbow *n* the joint between the forearm and upper arm; the part of a piece of clothing covering this; any sharp turn or bend, as in a pipe. * *vt* to shove away rudely with the elbow; to jostle.
elder[1] *n* a tree or shrub with flat clusters of white or pink flowers.
elder[2] *n* an older person; an office bearer in some churches.
elderly *adj* quite old.
eldest *n* oldest, first born.
elect *vti* to choose by voting; to make a selection (of); to make a decision on. * *adj* chosen for an office but not installed.
election *n* the public choice of a person for office, esp a politician.
elector *n* a person who has a vote at an election.
electoral *adj* of elections or electors.
electorate *n* the whole body of qualified electors.
electric *adj* of, producing or worked by electricity; exciting, thrilling. * *npl* electric fittings.
electrical *adj* of or relating to electricity.—**electrically** *adv*.
electric blanket *n* a blanket heated by an internal electric element.
electrician *n* a person who installs and repairs electrical devices.
electricity *n* a form of energy comprising certain charged particles; an electric current.
electrify *vt* to charge with electricity; to modify or equip for the use of electric power; to astonish or excite.—**electrification** *n*.
electrode *n* a conductor through which an electric current enters or leaves a gas discharge tube, etc.
electromagnetic *adj* having electric and magnetic properties.—**electromagnetism** *n*.
electron *n* a negatively charged elementary particle that forms the part of the atom outside the nucleus.
electronic *adj* of or worked by streams of electrons flowing through devices, vacuum or gas; of or concerned with electrons or electronics. —**electronically** *adv*.
electronics *n* (*used as sing*) the study, development and application of electronic devices; (*as pl*) electronic circuits.
elegant *adj* graceful; refined; dignified, tasteful in manner and appearance.—**elegantly** *adv*.—**elegance** *n*.
element *n* a constituent part; any of the 105 known substances composed of atoms with the same number of protons in their nuclei; a favourable environment for a plant or animal; a wire that produces heat in an electric cooker, kettle, etc; any of the four substances (earth, air, fire, water) that in ancient and medieval thought were believed to constitute the universe; (*pl*) atmospheric conditions (wind, rain, etc); (*pl*) the basic principles, rudiments.
elementary *adj* concerned with the basic principles of a subject.
elephant *n* a large heavy mammal with a long trunk, thick skin, and ivory tusks.
elevate *vt* to lift up; to raise in rank; to improve in intellectual or moral stature.
elevation *n* a raised place; the height above the earth's surface or above sea level; the angle to which a gun is aimed above the horizon; a drawing that shows the front, rear, or side view of something.
elevator *n* a cage or platform for moving something from one level to another; a moveable surface on the tailplane of an aircraft to produce motion up and down; a lift; a building for storing grain.
eleven *adj, n* one more than ten; the symbol for this (11, XI, xi); (*cricket, football, etc*) a team of eleven players. —**eleventh** *adj, n*.
elevenses *npl* (*inf*) a light snack taken around mid-morning.
elf *n* (*pl* **elves**) a mischievous fairy. —**elfin** *adj*.—**elfish** *adj*.

elicit *vt* to draw out (information, etc).
eligible *adj* suitable to be chosen, legally qualified; desirable, esp as a marriage partner.—**eligibility** *n*.
eliminate *vt* to expel, get rid of; to eradicate completely; (*sl*) to kill; to exclude (eg a competitor) from a competition, usu by defeat.—**elimination** *n*.—**eliminator** *n*.
elite, élite *n* a superior group; (*typewriting*) a letter size having twelve characters to the inch.
ellipse *n* (*geom*) a closed plane figure formed by the plane section of a right-angled cone; a flattened circle.
elm *n* a tall deciduous shade tree with spreading branches and broad top; its hard heavy wood.
elocution *n* skill in public speaking.—**elocutionary** *adj*.—**elocutionist** *n*.
elongate *vti* to make or become longer.—**elongation** *n*.
elope *vi* to run away secretly with a lover, esp to get married.
eloquence *n* skill in the use of words; speaking with fluency, power or persuasiveness.
eloquent *adj* (*speaking, writing, etc*) fluent and powerful.
else *adv* besides; otherwise.
elucidate *vt* to make clear, to explain. —**elucidation** *n*.—**elucidatory** *adv*.
elude *vt* to avoid stealthily; to escape the understanding or memory of a person.
elusive *adj* escaping; baffling; solitary, difficult to contact.
emanate *vi* to issue from a source.—**emanation** *n*.
emancipate *vt* to liberate, esp from bondage or slavery.—**emancipation** *n*.—**emancipator** *n*.
embalm *vt* to preserve (a dead body) with drugs, chemicals, etc.—**embalmment** *n*.
embankment *n* an earth or stone mound made to hold back water or to carry a roadway.
embargo *n* (*pl* **embargoes**) an order of a government forbidding ships to enter or leave its ports; any ban or restriction on commerce by law; a prohibition, ban. * *vt* to lay an embargo on; to requisition.
embark *vti* to put or go on board a ship or aircraft to begin a journey; to make a start in any activity or enterprise.—**embarkation** *n*.
embarrass *vt* to make (a person) feel confused, uncomfortable or disconcerted.—**embarrassment** *n*.
embassy *n* a person or group sent abroad as ambassadors; the official residence of an ambassador.
embed *vt* (*pt* **embedded**) to fix firmly in surrounding matter.
embellish *vt* to decorate, to adorn.—**embellishment** *n*.
ember *n* a piece of glowing coal or wood in fire; (*pl*) the smouldering remains of a fire.
embezzle *vt* to steal (money, securities, etc entrusted to one's care).—**embezzlement** *n*.—**embezzler** *n*.
embitter *vt* to cause to feel bitter.—**embitterment** *n*.
emblem *n* a symbol; a figure adopted and used as an identifying mark.
embody *vt* to express in definite form; to incorporate in a single book, law, system, etc.—**embodiment** *n*.
emboss *vt* to ornament with a raised design.—**embossment** *n*.
embrace *vt* to take and hold tightly in the arms as a sign of affection; to accept eagerly (eg an opportunity); to adopt (eg a religious faith); to include.—*also n*.
embroider *vt* to ornament with decorative stitches; to embellish (eg a story).
embroidery *n* decorative needlework; elaboration or exaggeration.
embryo *n* (*pl* **embryos**) an animal during the period of its growth from a fertilized egg up to the third month; a human product of conception up to about the second month of growth; a thing in a rudimentary state.
emerald *n* a rich green gemstone; its colour.
emerge *vi* to appear up out of, to come into view; to be revealed as the result of investigation.—**emergence** *n*.—**emergent** *adj*.
emergency *n* an unforeseen situation demanding immediate action; a serious medical condition requiring instant treatment.
emery *n* a hard granular mineral used for grinding and polishing; a hard abrasive powder.
emery board *n* a nailfile made from cardboard covered with crushed emery.
emery paper *n* a stiff paper covered with powdered emery.
emetic *n* a medicine that induces vomiting.—*also adj*.
emigrant *n* a person who emigrates.
emigrate *vi* to leave one's country for residence in another.—**emigration** *n*.
eminence, eminency *n* high rank or position; a person of high rank or attainments; (*with cap: RC Church*) the title for a cardinal; a raised piece of ground, a high place.
eminent *adj* famous; conspicuous; distin-

guished.—**eminently** *adv*.

emit *vt* (*pt* **emitted**) to send out (light, heat, etc); to put into circulation; to express, to utter.—**emission** *n*.—**emissive** *adj*.—**emitter** *n*.

emotion *n* a strong feeling of any kind.

emotional *adj* of emotion; inclined to express excessive emotion.—**emotionally** *adv*.—**emotionalism** *n*.

emotive *adj* characterized by or arousing emotion.

emperor *n* the sovereign ruler over an empire.—**empress** *nf*.

emphasis *n* (*pl* **emphases**) particular stress or prominence given to something; force or vigour of expression; clarity of form or outline.

emphasize *vt* to place stress on.

emphatic *adj* spoken, done or marked with emphasis; forceful, decisive.—**emphatically** *adv*.

empire *n* a large state or group of states under a single sovereign, usu an emperor; nations governed by a single sovereign state; a large and complex business organization.

empirical *adj* based on observation, experiment or experience only, not theoretical.—**empirically** *adv*.

employ *vt* to give work and pay to; to make use of.

employee *n* a person who is hired by another person for wages.

employer *n* a person, business, etc that employs people.

employment *n* an employing; a being employed; occupation or profession.

empower *vt* to give official authority to.

empress *n* the female ruler of an empire; the wife or widow of an emperor.

empty *adj* (**emptier, emptiest**) containing nothing; not occupied; lacking reality, substance, or value; hungry. * *vt* to make empty; to transfer or discharge (the contents of something) by emptying. * *vi* to become empty; to discharge contents. * *n* empty containers or bottles.—**emptily** *adv*.—**emptiness** *n*.

emulate *vt* to try to equal or do better than; to imitate; to rival or compete.—**emulation** *n*.—**emulative** *adj*.—**emulator** *n*.

emulsion *n* a mixture of mutually insoluble liquids in which one is dispersed in droplets throughout the other; a light-sensitive substance on photographic paper or film.

enable *vt* to give the authority or means to do something; to make easy or possible.

enamel *n* a glasslike substance used to coat the surface of metal or pottery; the hard outer layer of a tooth; a usu glossy paint that forms a hard coat. * *vt* (*pt* **enamelled**) to cover or decorate with enamel.

enamour, enamor (*US*) *vt* to inspire with love.—**enamoured** *adj*.

enchant *vt* to bewitch, to delight.—**enchanter** *n*.—**enchantment** *n*.—**enchantress** *nf*.

encircle *vt* to surround; to move or pass completely round.—**encirclement** *n*.

enclose *vt* to shut up or in; to put in a wrapper or parcel, usu together with a letter.

enclosure *n* an enclosing; an enclosed area; something enclosed with a letter in a parcel, etc.

encore *interj* once more! * *n* a call for the repetition of a performance.—*also vt*.

encounter *vt* to meet, esp unexpectedly; to fight, engage in battle with; to be faced with (problems, etc). * *n* a meeting; a conflict, battle.

encourage *vt* to inspire with confidence or hope; to urge, incite; to promote the development of.—**encouragement** *n*.

encroach *vi* to infringe another's territory, rights, etc; to advance beyond an established limit.—**encroachment** *n*.

encyclopaedia, encyclopedia *n* a book or books containing information on all branches of knowledge, or treating comprehensively a particular branch.

end *n* the last part; the place where a thing stops; purpose; result, outcome. * *vt* to bring to an end; to destroy. * *vi* to come to an end; to result (in). * *adj* final; ultimate.

endanger *vt* to put in danger.

endear *vt* to make loved or more loved.—**endearing** *adj*.

endeavour, endeavor (*US*) *vi* to try or attempt (to). * *n* an attempt.

ending *n* reaching or coming to an end; the final part.

endless *adj* unending; uninterrupted; extremely numerous.

endorse *vt* to write one's name, comment, etc, on the back of to approve; to record an offence on a driving licence; to support.—**endorsement** *n*.

endow *vt* to give money or property to provide an income for; to provide with a special power or attribute.

endurance *n* the ability to withstand pain, hardship, strain, etc.

endure *vt* to undergo, tolerate (hardship, etc) esp with patience. * *vi* to continue in existence, to last out.—**endurable** *adj*.—**endurably** *adv*.

enemy *n* a person who hates or dislikes and wishes to harm another; a military opponent; something harmful or deadly.

energetic *adj* lively, active; done with energy.—**energetically** *adv*.

energy *n* capacity of acting or being active; vigour, power; (*physics*) capacity to do work.

enforce *vt* to compel obedience by threat; to execute with vigour.—**enforceable** *adj*.—**enforcement** *n*.

engage *vt* to pledge as security; to promise to marry; to keep busy; to hire; to attract and hold, esp attention or sympathy; to cause to participate; to bring or enter into conflict; to begin or take part in a venture; to connect or interlock, to mesh.

engaged *adj* entered into a promise to marry; reserved, occupied or busy.

engagement *n* the act or state of being engaged; a pledge; an appointment agreed with another person; employment; a battle.

engaging *adj* pleasing, attractive.

engender *vt* to bring into existence.

engine *n* a machine by which physical power is applied to produce a physical effect; a locomotive; (*formerly*) a mechanical device, such as a large catapult, used in war.

engineer *n* a person trained in engineering; a person who operates an engine, etc; a member of a military group devoted to engineering work; a designer or builder of engines. * *vt* to contrive, plan, esp deviously.

engineering *n* the art or practice of constructing and using machinery; the art and science by which natural forces and materials are utilized in structures or machines.

English *adj* of, relating to, or characteristic of, England, the English people, or the English language. * *n* the language of the British people, the US and other areas; English language and literature as a subject of study.

engrained *see* **ingrained**.

engrave *vt* to produce by cutting or carving a surface; to cut to produce a representation that may be printed from; to lodge deeply (in the mind, etc).—**engraver** *n*.

engraving *n* a print made from an engraved surface.

engulf *vt* to flow over and enclose; to overwhelm.

enhance *vt* to increase in value, importance, attractiveness, etc; to heighten.—**enhancement** *n*.

enigma *n* someone or something that is puzzling or mysterious.—**enigmatic** *adj*.—**enigmatically** *adv*.

enjoy *vt* to get pleasure from, take joy in; to use or have the advantage of; to experience.—**enjoyment** *n*.

enjoyable *adj* giving enjoyment.—**enjoyably** *adv*.

enlarge *vti* to make or grow larger; to reproduce (a photograph) in a larger form; to speak or write at length (on).

enlargement *n* an act, instance, or state of enlarging; a photograph, etc that has been enlarged.

enlighten *vt* to instruct; to inform.—**enlightenment** *n*.

enlightened *adj* well-informed, tolerant, unprejudiced.

enlist *vt* to engage for service in the armed forces; to secure the aid or support of. * *vi* to register oneself for the armed services.—**enlistment** *n*.

enmity *n* hostility, esp mutual hatred.

enormity *n* great wickedness; a serious crime; huge size, magnitude.

enormous *adj* extremely large.—**enormously** *adv*.

enough *adj* adequate, sufficient. * *adv* so as to be sufficient; very; quite. * *n* a sufficiency. * *interj* stop!

enquire *see* **inquire**.

enrich *vt* to make rich or richer; to ornament; to improve in quality by adding to.—**enrichment** *n*.

enrol, **enroll** (*US*) *vti* (*pt* **enrolled**) to enter or register on a roll or list; to become a member of a society, club, etc; to admit as a member.—**enrolment** *n*.

ensign *n* a flag; the lowest commissioned officer in the US Navy.

enslave *vt* to make into a slave; to subjugate.—**enslavement** *n*.

ensue *vi* to occur as a consequence or in time.

ensure *vt* to make certain, sure or safe.

entail *vt* to involve as a result; to restrict the inheritance of property. * *n* the act of entailing or the estate entailed.

enter *vi* to go or come in or into; to come on stage; to begin, start; (*with* **for**) to register as an entrant. * *vt* to come or go into; to pierce, penetrate; (*organization*) to join; to insert; (*proposal, etc*) to submit; to record (an item) in a diary, etc.

enterprise *n* a difficult or challenging undertaking; a business project; readiness to engage in new ventures.

entertain *vt* to show hospitality to; to amuse, please (a person or audience); to have in mind; to consider.

entertainer *n* a person who entertains in public, esp professionally.

entertainment *n* entertaining; amusement; an act or show intended to amuse and interest.

enthusiasm *n* intense interest or liking; something that arouses keen interest.

enthusiast *n* a person filled with enthusiasm for something.

enthusiastic *adj* filled with enthusiasm.—**enthusiastically** *adv*.

entice *vt* to attract by offering some pleasure or reward.—**enticement** *n*.

entire *adj* whole; complete.—**entirely** *adv*.

entirety *n* completeness; the total.

entitle *vt* to give a title to; to give a right (to).—**entitlement** *n*.

entrance[1] *n* the act of entering; the power or authority to enter; a means of entering; an admission fee.

entrance[2] *vt* to put into a trance; to fill with great delight.—**entrancement** *n*.—**entrancing** *adj*.

entrant *n* a person who enters (eg a competition, profession).

entreat *vt* to request earnestly; to implore, beg.—**entreaty** *n*.

entrench *vt* to dig a trench as a defensive perimeter; to establish (oneself) in a strong defensive position.—**entrenchment** *n*.

entrust *vt* (*with* **with**) to confer as a responsibility, duty, etc; (*with* **to**) to place something in another's care.

entry *n* the act of entering; a place of entrance; an item recorded in a diary, journal, etc; a person or thing taking part in a contest.

entwine *vt* to twine together or around.

enumerate *vt* to count; to list.—**enumeration** *n*.—**enumerator** *n*.

enunciate *vt* to state definitely; to pronounce clearly.—**enunciation** *n*.

envelop *vt* (*pt* **enveloped**) to enclose completely (as if) with a covering.—**envelopment** *n*.

envelope *n* something used to wrap or cover, esp a gummed paper container for a letter.

envious *adj* filled with envy.—**enviously** *adv*.

environment *n* external conditions and surroundings, esp those that affect the quality of life of plants, animals and human beings.—**environmental** *adj*.

envisage *vt* to have a mental picture of.

envoy *n* a diplomatic agent; a representative.

envy *n* resentment or discontent at another's achievements, possessions, etc; an object of envy. * *vt* to feel envy of.

enzyme *n* a complex protein, produced by living cells, that induces or speeds chemical reactions in plants and animals.

ephemeral *adj* existing only for a very short time.

epic *n* a long poem narrating the deeds of a hero; any literary work, film, etc in the same style. * *adj* relating to or resembling an epic.

epidemic *adj, n* (a disease) attacking many people at the same time in a community or region.

epilepsy *n* a disorder of the nervous system marked typically by convulsive attacks and loss of consciousness.—**epileptic** *adj*, *n*.

epilogue *n* the concluding section of a book or other literary work; a short speech addressed by an actor to the audience at the end of a play.

epiphany *n* a moment of sudden revelation or insight; (*with cap*) a festival of the Christian Church in commemoration of the coming of the Magi to Christ.

episode *n* a piece of action in a dramatic or literary work; an incident in a sequence of events.

epistle *n* (*formal*) a letter; (*with cap*) a letter written by one of Christ's Apostles.

epitaph *n* an inscription in memory of a dead person, usu on a tombstone.

epitome *n* a typical example; a paradigm; personification; a condensed account of a written work.

epitomize *vt* to be or make an epitome of.

epoch *n* a date in time used as a point of reference; an age in history associated with certain characteristics; a unit of geological time.—**epochal** *adj*.

equable *adj* level, uniform; (*climate*) free from extremes of hot and cold; even-tempered.—**equably** *adv*.

equal *adj* the same in amount, size, number, or value; impartial, regarding or affecting all objects in the same way; capable of meeting a task or situation. * *n* a person that is equal. * *vt* (*pt* **equalled**) to be equal to, esp to be identical in value; to make or do something equal to.—**equality** *n*.—**equally** *adv*.

equalize *vti* to make or become equal; (*games*) to even the score.—**equalization** *n*.

equanimity *n* evenness of temper; composure.

equate *vt* to make, treat, or regard as comparable. * *vi* to correspond as equal.

equation *n* an act of equalling; the state of being equal; (*logic, math*) a usu formal statement of equivalence with the relations denoted by the sign =; (*chem*) an expression representing a reaction in symbols.

equator *n* an imaginary circle passing round the globe, equidistant from the poles.—**equatorial** *n.*

equilibrium *n* (*pl* **equilibriums, equilibria**) a state of balance of weight, power, force, etc.

equinox *n* the two times of the year when night and day are equal in length (around 21 March and 23 September).—**equinoctial** *adj.*

equip *vt* (*pt* **equipped**) to provide with all the necessary tools or supplies.

equipment *n* the tools, supplies and other items needed for a particular task, expedition, etc.

equitable *adj* just and fair; (*law*) pertaining to equity as opposed to common or statute law.—**equitably** *adv.*

equity *n* fairness; (*law*) a legal system based on natural justice developed into a body of rules supplementing the common law; (*pl*) ordinary shares in a company.

equivalent *adj* equal in amount, force, meaning, etc; virtually identical, esp in effect or function. * *n* an equivalent thing.

equivocal *adj* ambiguous; uncertain; questionable; arousing suspicion.—**equivocally** *adv.*

era *n* an historical period typified by some special feature; a chronological order or system of notation reckoned from a given date as a basis.

eradicate *vt* to obliterate.—**eradication** *n.*—**eradicator** *n.*

erase *vt* to rub out, obliterate; to remove a recording from magnetic tape; to remove data from a computer memory or storage medium.

erect *adj* upright; not leaning or lying down; (*sexual organs*) rigid and swollen with blood from sexual stimulation. * *vt* to construct, set up.—**erecter, erector** *n.*—**erectness** *n.*

erection *n* construction; something erected, as a building; swelling, esp of the penis, due to sexual excitement.

ermine *n* (*pl* **ermines**, **ermine**) the weasel in its winter coat; the white fur of the winter coat; a rank or office whose official robe is edged with ermine.

erode *vt* to eat or wear away gradually.—**erosion** *n.*—**erosive** *adj.*

erotic *adj* of sexual love; sexually stimulating.—**erotically** *adv.*

eroticism *n* erotic nature; sexually arousing themes in literature and art; sexual desire.

err *vi* to be or do wrong.

errand *n* a short journey to perform some task, usu on behalf of another; the purpose of this journey.

erratic *adj* capricious; irregular; eccentric, odd.—**erratically** *adv.*

erroneous *adj* incorrect; mistaken.—**erroneously** *adv.*

error *n* a mistake, an inaccuracy; a mistaken belief or action.

erudite *adj* scholarly, having great knowledge.—**erudition** *n.*

erupt *vi* to burst forth; to break out into a rash; (*volcano*) to explode, ejecting ash and lava into the air.—**eruption** *n.*—**eruptive** *adj.*

escalate *vi* to increase rapidly in magnitude or intensity.—**escalation** *n.*

escalator *n* a motorized set of stairs arranged to ascend or descend continuously.

escapade *n* a wild or mischievous adventure.

escape *vt* to free oneself from confinement, etc; to avoid, remain unnoticed; to be forgotten. * *vi* to achieve freedom; (*gas, liquid*) to leak. * *n* an act or instance of escaping; a means of escape; a leakage of liquid or gas; a temporary respite from reality.—**escaper** *n.*

escort *n* a person, group, ship, aircraft, etc accompanying a person or thing to give protection, etc. * *vt* to attend as escort.

espionage *n* spying or the use of spies to obtain information.

esquire *n* a general courtesy title used instead of Mr in addressing letters.

essay *n* a short prose work usu dealing with a subject from a limited or personal point of view; an attempt. * *vt* to try, to attempt.

essence *n* that which makes a thing what it is; a substance extracted from another substance and having the special qualities of the original; a perfume.

essential *adj* of or containing the essence of something; indispensable, of the greatest importance. * *n* (*often pl*) indispensable elements or qualities.—**essentially** *adv.*

establish *vt* to set up (eg a business) permanently; to settle (a person) in a place or position; to get generally accepted; to place beyond dispute, prove as a fact.

establishment *n* the act of establishing; a commercial organization or other large institution; the staff and resources of an organization; a household; (*with cap*) those in power who work to preserve the status quo.

estate *n* landed property; a large area of residential or industrial development; a person's total possessions, esp at their death; a social or political class.
estate agent *n* a person whose business is selling and leasing property.
estate car *n* a car with extra carrying space reached through a rear door.
esteem *vt* to value or regard highly; to consider or think. * *n* high regard, a favourable opinion.
estimate *vt* to judge the value, amount, significance of; to calculate approximately. * *n* an approximate calculation; a judgment or opinion; a preliminary calculation of the cost of a particular job.
estimation *n* estimating; an opinion, judgment; esteem.
estuary *n* an arm of the sea at the mouth of a river.
etching *n* the art or process of producing designs on and printing from etched plates; an impression made from an etched plate.
eternal *adj* continuing forever without beginning or end, everlasting; unchangeable; (*inf*) seemingly endless. —**eternally** *adv*.
eternity *n* infinite time; the timelessness thought to constitute life after death; (*inf*) a very long time.
ether *n* (*chem*) a light flammable liquid used as an anaesthetic or solvent; the upper regions of space.
ethic *n* a moral principle or set of principles. * *adj* ethical.
ethical *adj* of or pertaining to ethics; conforming to the principles of proper conduct, as established by society, a profession, etc; (*med*) legally available only on prescription.—**ethically** *adv*.
ethics *n* (*used as sing*) the philosophical analysis of human morality and conduct; system of conduct or behaviour, moral principles.
ethnic *adj* of races or large groups of people classed according to common traits and customs.—**ethnically** *adv*.
etiquette *n* the form of conduct or behaviour prescribed by custom or authority to be observed in social, official or professional life.
eulogy *n* a speech or piece of writing in praise or celebration of someone or something.
euphemism *n* a mild or inoffensive word substituted for a more unpleasant or offensive term; the use of such words.—**euphemistic** *adj*.—**euphemistically** *adv*.
euthanasia *n* the act or practice of killing painlessly, esp to relieve incurable suffering.
evacuate *vti* to move (people, etc) from an area of danger to one of safety; to leave or make empty; to discharge wastes from the body.—**evacuation** *n*.
evade *vt* to manage to avoid, esp by dexterity or slyness.—**evadable, evadible** *adj*.—**evader** *n*.
evaluate *vt* to determine the value of; to assess.—**evaluation** *n*.—**evaluator** *n*.
evangelist *n* a person who preaches the gospel; one of the writers of the four Gospels.—**evangelistic** *adj*.
evaporate *vti* to change into a vapour; to remove water from; to give off moisture; to vanish; to disappear.—**evaporation** *n*.
evasion *n* the act of evading; a means of evading, esp an equivocal reply or excuse.—**evasive** *adj*.—**evasively** *adv*.—**evasiveness** *n*.
eve *n* the evening or the whole day, before a festival; the period immediately before an event; (*formerly*) evening.
even *adj* level, flat; smooth; regular, equal; balanced; exact; divisible by two. * *vti* to make or become even; (*with* **up**) to balance (debts, etc). * *adv* exactly; precisely; fully; quite; at the very time; used as an intensive to emphasize the identity of something (*he looked content, even happy*), to indicate something unexpected (*she refused even to look at him*), or to stress the comparative degree (*she did even better*).—**evenly** *adv*.—**evenness** *n*.
even-handed *adj* impartial, fair.
evening *n* the latter part of the day and early part of the night.
event *n* something that happens; a social occasion; contingency; a contest in a sports programme.
eventful *adj* full of incidents; momentous
eventual *adj* happening at some future unspecified time; ultimate.—**eventually** *adv*.
eventuality *n* a possible occurrence.
ever *adv* always, at all times; at any time; in any case.
evergreen *adj* (*plants, trees*) having foliage that remains green all year.—*also n*.
everlasting *adj* enduring forever; (*plants*) having flowers that may be dried without loss of form or colour.—**everlastingly** *adv*.
every *adj* being one of the total.
everybody, everyone *pron* every person.
everyday *adj* happening daily; commonplace; worn or used on ordinary days.
everything *pron* all things, all; of the utmost importance.

everywhere *adv* in every place.
evict *vt* to expel from land or from a building by legal process; to expel.—**eviction** *n.*
evidence *n* an outward sign; proof, testimony, esp matter submitted in court to determine the truth of alleged facts. * *vt* to demonstrate clearly; to give proof or evidence for.
evident *adj* easy to see or understand.—**evidently** *adv.*
evil *adj* wicked; causing or threatening distress or harm. * *n* a sin; a source of harm or distress.—**evilly** *adv.*
evoke *vt* to call forth or up.—**evocation** *n.*—**evocative** *adj.*
evolution *n* a process of change in a particular direction; the process by which something attains its distinctive characteristics; a theory that existing types of plants and animals have developed from earlier forms.—**evolutionary** *adj.*
evolve *vi* to develop by or as if by evolution.—**evolvement** *n.*
ewe *n* a female sheep.
ex[1] *n* (*inf*) a former husband, wife, etc.
ex[2] *prep* out of, from.
ex- *prefix* out, forth; quite, entirely; formerly.
exact *adj* without error, absolutely accurate; detailed. * *vt* to compel by force, to extort; to require.—**exactness** *n.*
exacting *adj* greatly demanding; requiring close attention and precision.
exactitude *n* (the state of) being exact.
exactly *adv* in an exact manner; precisely. * *interj* quite so!
exaggerate *vt* to enlarge (a statement, etc) beyond what is really so or believable.—**exaggeration** *n.*
exalt *vt* to raise up, esp in rank, power, or dignity.—**exaltation** *n.*
exam *n* (*inf*) an examination.
examination *n* an examining, close scrutiny; a set of written or oral questions designed as a test of knowledge; the formal questioning of a witness on oath.
examine *vt* to look at closely and carefully, to investigate; to test, esp by questioning.—**examiner** *n.*
example *n* a representative sample; a model to be followed or avoided; a problem to be solved in order to show the application of some rule; a warning to others.
exasperate *vt* to annoy intensely.—**exasperation** *n.*
excavate *vt* to form a hole or tunnel by digging; to unearth; to expose to view (remains, etc) by digging away a covering.—**excavation** *n.*—**excavator** *n.*
exceed *vt* to be greater than or superior to; to go beyond the limit of.
exceedingly *adv* very, extremely.
excellence *n* that in which one excels; superior merit or quality; (*with cap*) a title of honour given to certain high officials (—*also* **Excellency**).
excellent *adj* very good, outstanding.—**excellently** *adv.*
except *vt* to exclude, to take or leave out. * *prep* not including; other than.
exception *n* the act of excepting; something excepted; an objection.
exceptional *adj* unusual, forming an exception; superior.
excerpt *n* an extract from a book, film, etc.
excess *n* the exceeding of proper established limits; the amount by which one thing or quantity exceeds another; (*pl*) overindulgence in eating or drinking; unacceptable conduct.
excessive *adj* greater than what is acceptable, too much.—**excessively** *adv.*
exchange *vt* to give and take (one thing in return for another); to give to and receive from another person. * *n* the exchanging of one thing for another; the thing exchanged; the conversion of money from one currency to another; the system of settling commercial debts between foreign governments; a place where things and services are exchanged, esp a marketplace for securities; a centre or device in which telephone lines are interconnected.—**exchangeable** *adj.*
exchequer *n* (*with cap*) the British governmental department in charge of finances; (*inf*) personal finances.
excise[1] *n* a tax on the manufacture, sale, or use of certain articles within a country.
excise[2] *vt* to remove by cutting out.—**excision** *n.*
excitable *adj* easily excited.—**excitability** *n.*
excite *vt* to arouse the feelings of, esp to generate feelings of pleasurable anticipation; to cause to experience strong emotion; to stir up, agitate; to rouse to activity; to stimulate a response, eg in a bodily organ.
excited *adj* experiencing or expressing excitement.—**excitedly** *adv.*
excitement *n* a feeling of strong, esp pleasurable, emotion; something that excites.
exciting *adj* causing excitement; stimulating.
exclaim *vti* to shout out or utter suddenly and with strong emotion.

exclamation *n* a sudden crying out; a word or utterance exclaimed.

exclamation mark, exclamation point *n* the punctuation mark (!) placed after an exclamation.

exclude *vt* to shut out, to keep out; to reject or omit; to eject.—**exclusion** *n*.

exclusive *adj* excluding all else; reserved for particular persons; snobbishly aloof; fashionable, high-class, expensive; unobtainable or unpublished elsewhere; sole, undivided. —**exclusively** *adv*.—**exclusiveness** *n*.—**exclusivity** *n*.

excommunicate *vt* to bar from association with a church; to exclude from fellowship.—**excommunication** *n*.

excrement *n* waste matter discharged from the bowels.—**excremental** *adj*.

excruciating *adj* intensely painful or distressful; (*inf*) very bad.

excursion *n* a pleasure trip; a short journey.

excuse *vt* to pardon; to forgive; to give a reason or apology for; to be a reason or explanation of; to let off.—*also n*.

execute *vt* to carry out, put into effect; to perform; to produce (eg a work of art); to make legally valid; to put to death by law.

execution *n* the act or process of executing; the carrying out or suffering of a death sentence; the style or technique of performing, eg music.

executioner *n* a person who executes a death sentence upon a condemned prisoner.

executive *n* a person or group concerned with administration or management of a business or organization; the branch of government with the power to put laws, etc into effect. * *adj* having the power to execute decisions, laws, decrees, etc.

exemplary *adj* deserving imitation; serving as a warning.

exemplify *vt* to illustrate by example; to be an instance or example of.—**exemplification** *n*.

exempt *adj* not liable, free from the obligations required of others.—*also vt*.—**exemption** *n*.

exercise *n* the use or application of a power or right; regular physical or mental exertion; something performed to develop or test a specific ability or skill; (*often pl*) manoeuvres for military training. * *vt* to use, exert, employ; to engage in regular physical activity; to train (troops) by drills and manoeuvres; to engage the attention of; to perplex.

exert *vt* to bring (eg strength, influence) into use.

exhaust *vt* to use up completely; to make empty; to use up, tire out; (*subject*) to deal with or develop completely. * *n* the escape of waste gas or steam from an engine; the device through which these escape. —**exhausted** *adj*.—**exhaustible** *adj*. —**exhausting** *adj*.

exhaustion *n* the act of exhausting or being exhausted; extreme weariness.

exhaustive *adj* comprehensive, thorough.—**exhaustively** *adv*.

exhibit *vt* to display, esp in public; to present to a court in legal form. * *n* an act or instance of exhibiting, something exhibited; something produced and identified in court for use as evidence.—**exhibitor** *n*.

exhibition *n* a showing, a display; a public show.

exhilarate *vt* to make very happy; to invigorate.—**exhilaration** *n*.

exhort *vt* to urge or advise strongly. —**exhortation** *n*.—**exhortative** *adj*. —**exhortatory** *adj*.

exile *n* prolonged absence from one's own country, either through choice or as a punishment; an exiled person.—*also vt*.

exist *vi* to have being; to just manage a living; to occur in a specific place under specific conditions.

existence *n* the state or fact of existing; continuance of life; everything that exists.

exit *n* a way out of an enclosed space; death; a departure from a stage. * *vi* to leave, withdraw; to go offstage.

exonerate *vt* to absolve from blame; to relieve from a responsibility, obligation.—**exoneration** *n*.

exorcise *vt* to expel an evil spirit (from a person or place) by ritual and prayer.—**exorcism** *n*.—**exorcist** *n*.

exotic *adj* foreign; strange; excitingly different or unusual.—**exotically** *adv*.

expand *vt* to increase in size, bulk, extent, importance; to describe in fuller detail. * *vi* to become larger; to become more genial and responsive.

expanse *n* a wide area of land, etc; the extent of a spread-out area.

expansion *n* the act of expanding or being expanded; something expanded; the amount by which something expands; the fuller development of a theme, etc.

expatriate *adj* living in another country; self-exiled or banished. * *n* an expatriate person. * *vti* to exile (oneself) or banish (another person).—**expatriation** *n*.

expect *vt* to anticipate; to regard as likely to arrive or happen; to consider necessary, reasonable or due; to think, suppose.

expectant *adj* expecting, hopeful; filled with anticipation; pregnant.—**expectantly** *adv*.—**expectancy** *n*.

expectation *n* the act or state of expecting; something that is expected to happen; (*pl*) prospects for the future, esp of inheritance.

expediency, expedience *n* fitness, suitability; an inclination towards expedient methods.

expedient *adj* suitable or desirable under the circumstances. * *n* a means to an end; a means devised or used for want of something better.—**expediently** *adv*.

expedite *vt* to carry out promptly; to facilitate.—**expediter, expeditor** *n*.

expedition *n* a journey to achieve some purpose, as exploration, etc; the party making this journey; speedy efficiency, promptness.

expel *vt* (*pt* **expelled**) to drive out, to eject; to banish.

expend *vt* to spend (money, time, energy, etc); to use up, consume.

expenditure *n* the act or process of expending money, etc; the amount expended.

expense *n* a payment of money for something, expenditure; a cause of expenditure; (*pl*) money spent on some business activity; reimbursement for this.

expense account *n* an account of expenses to be repaid to an employee.

expensive *adj* causing or involving great expense; costly.—**expensively** *adv*.—**expensiveness** *n*.

experience *n* observation or practice resulting in or tending towards knowledge; knowledge gained by seeing and doing; a state of being affected from without (as by events); an affecting event. * *vt* to have experience of.

experienced *adj* wise or skilled through experience.

experiment *n* any test or trial to find out something; a controlled procedure carried out to discover, test, or demonstrate something. * *vi* to carry out experiments.—**experimentation** *n*.

experimental *adj* of, derived from, or proceeding by experiment; empirical; provisional.—**experimentalism** *n*.

expert *adj* thoroughly skilled; knowledgeable through training and experience. * *n* a person with special skills or training in any art or science.—**expertly** *adv*.

expertise *n* expert knowledge or skill.

expire *vti* to come to an end; to lapse or become void; to breathe out; to die.—**expiration** *n*.

explain *vt* to make plain or clear; to give a reason for, account for.

explanation *n* an act or process of explaining; something that explains, esp a statement.

explanatory *adj* serving as an explanation.

explicit *adj* clearly stated, not merely implied; outspoken, frank; graphically detailed.—**explicitly** *adv*.—**explicitness** *n*.

explode *vti* to burst or cause to blow up with a loud noise, as in the detonation of a bomb; (*emotions*) to burst out; (*population*) to increase rapidly; to expose (a theory, etc) as false.

exploit *n* a bold achievement. * *vt* to utilize, develop (raw materials, etc); to take unfair advantage of, esp for financial gain.—**exploitation** *n*.

exploratory, explorative *adj* for the purpose of exploring or investigating.

explore *vti* to examine or inquire into; to travel through (a country) for the purpose of discovery; to examine minutely.—**exploration** *n*.—**explorer** *n*.

explosion *n* an act or instance of exploding; a sudden loud noise caused by this; an outburst of emotion; a rapid increase or expansion.

explosive *adj* liable to or able to explode; liable or threatening to burst out with violence and noise. * *n* an explosive substance.—**explosively** *adv*.

exponent *n* a person who explains or interprets something; a person who champions, advocates, or exemplifies; (*math*) an index of the power to which an expression is raised.

export *vt* to send out (goods) of one country for sale in another. * *n* the act of exporting; the article exported.—**exportable** *adj*.—**exportation** *n*.—**exporter** *n*.

expose *vt* to deprive of protection or shelter; to subject to an influence (as light, weather); to display, reveal; to uncover or disclose.

exposure *n* an exposing or state of being exposed; time during which light reaches and acts on a photographic film, paper or plate; publicity.

expound *vt* to explain or set forth in detail.

express *vt* to represent in words; to make known one's thoughts, feelings, etc; to represent by signs, symbols, etc; to squeeze out. * *adj* firmly stated, explicit; (*train, bus, etc*) travelling at high speed with few or no stops. * *adv* at high speed, by express service. * *n* an express train, coach, etc; a system or company for sending freight, etc at rates higher than standard.

expression *n* an act of expressing, esp by words; a word or phrase; a look; intonation; a manner of showing feeling in communicating or performing (eg music); (*math*) a collection of symbols serving to express something. —**expressionless** *adj*.

expressive *adj* serving to express; full of expression.

expressly *adv* explicitly; for a specific purpose.

expulsion *n* the act of expelling or being expelled.—**expulsive** *adj*.

exquisite *adj* very beautiful, refined; sensitive, showing discrimination; acutely felt, as pain or pleasure.—**exquisitely** *adv*.

extend *vt* to stretch or spread out; to stretch fully; to prolong in time; to cause to reach in distance, etc; to enlarge, increase the scope of; to hold out (eg the hand); to accord, grant; to give, offer, (eg sympathy). * *vi* to prolong in distance or time; to reach in scope.

extension *n* act of extending or state of being extended; extent, scope; an added part, eg to a building; an extra period; a programme of extramural teaching provided by a college, etc; an additional telephone connected to the principal line.

extensive *adj* large; having a wide scope or extent.—**extensively** *adv*. —**extensiveness** *n*.

extent *n* the distance over which a thing is extended; the range or scope of something; the limit to which something extends.

exterior *adj* of, on, or coming from the outside; external; (*paint, etc*) suitable for use on the outside. * *n* the external part or surface; outward manner or appearance.

exterminate *vt* to destroy completely.—**extermination** *n*.—**exterminator** *n*.

external *adj* outwardly perceivable; of, relating to, or located on the outside or outer part. * *n* an external feature. —**externally** *adv*.

extinct *adj* (*animals*) not alive, no longer existing; (*fire*) not burning, out; (*volcano*) no longer active.—**extinction** *n*.

extinguish *vt* to put out (a fire, light, etc); to bring to an end.

extinguisher *n* a device for putting out a fire.

extort *vt* to obtain (money, promises, etc) by force or improper pressure.—**extortion** *n*.—**extortioner** *n*.

extortionate *adj* excessively high in price.

extra *adj* additional. * *adv* unusually; in addition. * *n* something extra or additional, esp a charge; a special edition of a newspaper; a person who plays a non-speaking role in a film.

extra- *prefix* outside, beyond.

extract *vt* to take or pull out by force; to withdraw by chemical or physical means; to abstract. * *n* the essence of a substance obtained by extraction; a passage taken from a book, play, film, etc.

extraction *n* the act of extracting; lineage; something extracted.

extradite *vt* to surrender (an alleged criminal) to the country where the offence was committed.—**extradition** *n*.

extramarital *adj* occurring outside marriage, esp sexual relationships.

extraneous *adj* coming from outside; not essential.—**extraneously** *adv*.

extraordinary *adj* not usual or regular; remarkable, exceptional.—**extraordinarily** *adv*.

extravagant *adj* lavish in spending; (*prices*) excessively high; wasteful; (*behaviour, praise, etc*) lacking in restraint, flamboyant, profuse.—**extravagantly** *adv*.—**extravagance** *n*.

extravert *see* **extrovert**.

extreme *adj* of the highest degree or intensity; excessive, immoderate, unwarranted; very severe, stringent; outermost. * *n* the highest or furthest limit or degree; (*often pl*) either of the two points marking the ends of a scale or range.—**extremely** *adv*.

extremist *n* a person of extreme views, esp political.—**extremism** *n*.

extremity *n* the utmost point or degree; the most remote part; the utmost violence, vigour, or necessity; the end; (*pl*) the hands or feet.

extricate *vt* to release from difficulties; to disentangle.—**extrication** *n*.

extrovert *n* a person more interested in the external world than his own feelings. —*also* **extravert**.

exuberant *adj* lively, high-spirited; profuse.—**exuberantly** *adv*.—**exuberance** *n*.

exude *vt* to cause or allow to ooze through pores or incisions, as sweat, pus; to display (confidence, emotion) freely.—**exudation** *n*.

exult *vi* to rejoice greatly.—**exultation** *n*.

eye *n* the organ of sight; the iris; the faculty of seeing; the external part of the eye; something resembling an eye. * *vt* (*pr p* **eyeing** *or* **eying**, *pt* **eyed**) to look at; to observe closely.

eyeball *n* the ball of the eye. * *vt* (*sl*) to stare at.

eyebrow *n* the hairy ridge above the eye.
eye-catching *adj* attractive or striking in appearance.
eyelash *n* the fringe of fine hairs along the edge of each eyelid.
eyelid *n* the lid of skin and muscle that moves to cover the eye.
eye-opener *n* something that comes as a shock or surprise.
eye-shadow *n* a coloured powder applied to accentuate or decorate the eyelids.
eyesight *n* the faculty of seeing.
eyesore *n* anything offensive to the sight.
eye-witness *n* a person who sees an event.
eyrie *n* the nest of an eagle or other bird of prey; any high inaccessible place or position.

F

F *abbr* = Fahrenheit; (*chem symbol*) fluorine.
fable *n* a story, often with animal characters, conveying a moral; a lie, fabrication; a story involving mythical, legendary or supernatural characters or events.
fabric *n* cloth made by knitting, weaving, etc; framework, structure.
fabulous *adj* told in fables; incredible, astonishing; (*inf*) very good.—**fabulously** *adv*.
façade, facade *n* the main front or face of a building; an outward appearance, esp concealing something.
face *n* the front part of the head containing the eyes, nose, etc; facial expression; the front or outer surface of anything; external show or appearance; dignity, self-respect; impudence, effrontery; a coal face. * *vt* to be confronted by (a problem, etc); to deal with (an opponent, etc) resolutely; to be opposite to; to turn (a card) face upwards; to cover with a new surface. * *vi* to turn the face in a certain direction; to be situated in or have a specific direction.
face-lift *n* plastic surgery to smooth and firm the face; an improvement or renovation, esp to the outside of a building.
facet *n* a small plane surface (as on a cut gem); an aspect of character, a problem, issue, etc.
facetious *adj* joking, esp in an inappropriate manner.—**facetiously** *adv*.—**facetiousness** *n*.
facia *see* **fascia**.
facial *adj* of or pertaining to the face. * *n* a beauty treatment for the face.—**facially** *adv*.
facile *adj* easy to do; superficial.
facilitate *vt* to make easier.
facility *n* the quality of being easily done; aptitude, dexterity; something, eg a service or equipment, that makes it easy to do something.
facsimile *n* an exact copy of a book, document, etc; a method of transmitting printed matter through the telephone system.—*also* **fax**.
fact *n* a thing known to have happened or to exist; reality; a piece of verifiable information; (*law*) an event, occurrence, etc as distinguished from its legal consequences.
faction[1] *n* a small group of people in an organization working together in a common cause against the main body; dissension within a group or organization.—**factional** *adj*.—**factionally** *adv*.—**factious** *adj*.
faction[2] *n* a book, film, etc based on facts but presented as a blend of fact and fiction.
factor *n* any circumstance that contributes towards a result; (*math*) any of two or more numbers that, when multiplied together, form a product; a person who acts for another.
factory *n* a building or buildings where things are manufactured.
factual *adj* based on, or containing, facts; actual.—**factually** *adv*.
faculty *n* any natural power of a living organism; special aptitude; a teaching department of a college or university, or the staff of such a department.
fad *n* a personal habit or idiosyncrasy; a craze.—**faddish, faddy** *adj*.
fade *vi* to lose vigour or brightness of colour gradually; to vanish gradually. * *vt* to cause (an image or a sound) to increase or decrease in brightness or intensity gradually.—*also n*.
fag *vti* (*pt* **fagged**) to become or cause to be tired by hard work. * *n* (*formerly*) a British public schoolboy who performs chores for senior pupils; (*inf*) drudgery; (*sl*) a homosexual; (*sl*) a cigarette.
fag-end *n* the useless remains of anything; (*sl*) a cigarette-end.
fail *vi* to weaken, to fade or die away; to stop operating; to fall short; to be insufficient; to be negligent in duty, expectation, etc; (*exam, etc*) to be unsuccessful; to become bankrupt. * *vt* to disappoint the expectations or hopes of; to be unsuccessful in an exam, etc; to leave, to abandon; to grade (a candidate) as not passing a test, etc. * *n* failure in an examination.
failing *n* a fault, weakness. * *prep* in default or absence of.

failure *n* failing, non-performance, lack of success; the ceasing of normal operation of something; a deficiency; bankruptcy; an unsuccessful person or thing.

faint *adj* dim, indistinct; weak, feeble; timid; on the verge of losing consciousness. * *vi* to lose consciousness temporarily from a decrease in the supply of blood to the brain, as from shock. * *n* an act or condition of fainting.—**faintly** *adv*.—**faintness** *n*.

faint-hearted *adj* lacking courage and resolution.

fair[1] *adj* pleasing to the eye; clean, unblemished; (*hair*) light-coloured; (*weather*) clear and sunny; (*handwriting*) easy to read; just and honest; according to the rules; moderately large; average. * *adv* in a fair manner; squarely.—**fairness** *n*.

fair[2] *n* a gathering for the sale of goods, esp for charity; a competitive exhibition of farm, household, or manufactured goods; a funfair.

fairly *adv* in a fair manner; justly; moderately.

fairy *n* an imaginary supernatural being, usu in human form; (*sl*) a male homosexual.

fairy story, fairy tale *n* a story about fairies; an incredible story; a fabrication.

faith *n* trust or confidence in a person or thing; a strong conviction, esp a belief in a religion; any system of religious belief; fidelity to one's promises, sincerity.

faithful *adj* loyal; true; true to the original, accurate.—**faithfully** *adv*.

fake *vt* to make (an object) appear more real or valuable in order to deceive; to pretend, simulate. * *n* a faked article, a forgery; an impostor. * *adj* counterfeit, not genuine.—**faker** *n*.

falcon *n* a type of hawk trained for use in falconry.

fall *vi* (*pt* **fell**, *pp* **fallen**) to descend by force of gravity; to come as if by falling; to collapse; to drop to the ground; to become lower, weaker, less; to lose power, status, etc; to lose office; to slope downwards; to be wounded or killed in battle; to pass into a certain state; to become pregnant; to take place, happen; to be directed by chance; to come by inheritance; (*with* **back**) to retreat; (*with* **out**) to quarrel; to leave one's place in a military formation. * *n* act or instance of falling; something which falls; the amount by which something falls; a decline in status, position; overthrow; a downward slope; a decrease in size, quantity, value; in US, autumn; (*wrestling*) a scoring move by pinning both shoulders of an opponent to the floor at once.

fallacy *n* a false idea; a mistake in reasoning.

fallible *adj* liable to make mistakes.—**fallibly** *adv*.— **fallibility** *n*.

fall-out *n* a deposit of radioactive dust from a nuclear explosion; a by-product.

fallow[1] *adj* (*lan d*) ploughed and left unplanted for a season or more.

fallow[2] *adj* yellowish-brown.

false *adj* wrong, incorrect; deceitful; artificial; disloyal, treacherous; misleading, fallacious.—**falsely** *adv*.—**falseness** *n*.

falsehood *n* a being untrue; the act of deceiving; a lie.

falter *vi* to move or walk unsteadily, to stumble; to hesitate or stammer in speech; to be weak or unsure, to waver.

fame *n* the state of being well known; good reputation.—**famed** *adj*.

familiar *adj* well-acquainted; friendly; common; well-known; too informal, presumptuous. * *n* a spirit or demon supposed to aid a witch, etc; an intimate. —**familiarly** *adv*.—**familiarity** *n*.

familiarize *vt* to make well known or acquainted; to make (something) well known.—**familiarization** *n*.

family *n* parents and their children; a person's children; a set of relatives; the descendants of a common ancestor; any group of persons or things related in some way; a group of related plants or animals; a unit of a crime syndicate (as the Mafia).

famine *n* an acute scarcity of food in a particular area; an extreme scarcity of anything.

famous *adj* renowned; (*inf*) excellent.—**famously** *adv*.

fan[1] *n* a handheld or mechanical device used to set up a current of air. * *vt* (*pt* **fanned**) to cool, as with a fan; to ventilate; to stir up, to excite; to spread out like a fan.

fan[2] *n* an enthusiastic follower of some sport, hobby, person, etc.

fanatic *n* a person who is excessively enthusiastic about something.—**fanatical** *adj*.—**fanatically** *adv*.

fan belt *n* the belt that drives the cooling fan in a car engine.

fanciful *adj* not factual, imaginary; indulging in fancy; elaborate or intricate in design.—**fancifully** *adv*.

fancy *n* imagination; a mental image; a whim; fondness. * *adj* (**fancier, fanciest**) not based on fact, imaginary; elegant or ornamental. * *vt* to imagine; to have a fancy or liking for;

(*inf*) to be sexually attracted to.

fancy dress *n* a costume worn at masquerades or parties, usu representing an animal, historical character, etc.

fang *n* a long sharp tooth, as in a canine; the long hollow tooth through which venomous snakes inject poison.

fanlight *n* a semicircular window with radiating bars like the ribs of a fan.

fantastic *adj* unrealistic, fanciful; unbelievable; imaginative; (*inf*) wonderful.—**fantastically** *adv*.

fantasy *n* imagination; a product of the imagination, esp an extravagant or bizarre notion or creation; an imaginative poem, play or novel.

far *adj* (**farther, farthest** *or* **further, furthest**) remote in space or time; long; (*political views, etc*) extreme * *adv* very distant in space, time, or degree; to or from a distance in time or position, very much.

faraway *adj* distant, remote; dreamy.

farce *n* a style of light comedy; a drama using such comedy; a ludicrous situation.—**farcical** *adj*.

fare *n* money paid for transportation; a passenger in public transport; food. * *vi* to be in a specified condition.

farewell *interj* goodbye.—*also n*.

far-fetched *adj* unlikely.

farm *n* an area of land (with buildings) on which crops and animals are raised. * *vt* to grow crops or breed livestock; to cultivate, as land; to breed fish commercially; (*with* **out**) to put out (work, etc) to be done by others, to subcontract.

farmer *n* a person who manages or operates a farm.

farmhouse *n* a house on a farm.

farmyard *n* a yard close to or surrounded by farm buildings.

far-reaching *adj* having serious or widespread consequences.

far-seeing *adj* having foresight.

fart *vi* (*vulg*) to expel wind from the anus.—*also n*.

farther *adj* at or to a greater distance. * *adv* to a greater degree.

farthest *adj* at or to the greatest distance. * *adv* to the greatest degree.

fascia *n* (*pl* **fasciae**) the instrument panel of a motor vehicle, the dashboard; the flat surface above a shop front, with the name, etc.—*also* **facia**.

fascinate *vt* to hold the attention of, to attract irresistibly.—**fascination** *n*.

fashion *n* the current style of dress, conduct, speech, etc; the manner or form of appearance or action. * *vt* to make in a particular form; to suit or adapt.

fashionable *adj* conforming to the current fashion; attracting or frequented by people of fashion.—**fashionably** *adv*.

fast[1] *adj* swift, quick; (*clock*) ahead of time; firmly attached, fixed; (*colour, dye*) non-fading; wild, promiscuous. * *adv* firmly, thoroughly, rapidly, quickly.

fast[2] *vi* to go without all or certain foods. * *n* a period of fasting.

fasten *vti* to secure firmly; to attach; to fix (the eyes, attention) steadily.

fastener, fastening *n* a clip, catch, etc for fastening.

fastidious *adj* hard to please; daintily refined; over-sensitive.—**fastidiously** *adv*.—**fastidiousness** *n*.

fat *adj* (**fatter, fattest**) plump; thick; fertile; profitable. * *n* an oily or greasy material found in animal tissue and plant seeds; the richest or best part of anything; a superfluous part.—**fatness** *n*.

fatal *adj* causing death; disastrous (to); fateful.—**fatally** *adv*.

fatalism *n* belief that all events are predetermined by fate and therefore inevitable; acceptance of this doctrine. —**fatalist** *n*.—**fatalistic** *adj*.

fatality *n* a death caused by a disaster or accident; a person killed in such a way; a fatal power or influence.

fate *n* the ultimate power that predetermines events, destiny; the ultimate end, outcome; misfortune, doom, death.

fateful *adj* having important, usu unpleasant, consequences.—**fatefully** *adv*.

father *n* a male parent; an ancestor; a founder or originator; (*with cap*) God; a title of respect applied to monks, priests, etc. * *vt* to be the father of; to found, originate.—**fatherhood** *n*.

father-in-law *n* the father of one's husband or wife.

fathom *n* a nautical measure of 6 feet (1.83 m). * *vt* to measure the depth of; to understand.

fatigue *n* tiredness from physical or mental effort; the tendency of a material to break under repeated stress; any of the menial or manual tasks performed by military personnel; (*pl*) the clothing worn on fatigue or in the field. * *vti* to make or become tired.

fatten *vt* to make fat or fleshy; to make abundant.—**fattening** *adj*.
fatty *adj* (**fattier, fattiest**) resembling or containing fat. * *n* (*inf*) a fat person.
fatuous *adj* foolish, idiotic.—**fatuously** *adv*.—**fatuousness** *n*.—**fatuity** *n*.
faucet *n* a fixture for draining off liquid (as from a pipe or cask); a tap.
fault *n* a failing, defect; a minor offence; (*tennis, etc*) an incorrect serve or other error; a fracture in the earth's crust causing displacement of strata. * *vt* to find fault with, blame. * *vi* to commit a fault.
faultless *adj* without fault.—**faultlessly** *adv*.—**faultlessness** *n*.
faulty *adj* (**faultier, faultiest**) imperfect.—**faultily** *adv*.—**faultiness** *n*.
fauna *n* (*pl* **faunas, faunae**) the animals of a region, period, or specific environment.
favour, favor (*US*) *n* goodwill; approval; a kind or helpful act; partiality; a gift given out at a party; (*usu pl*) a privilege conceded, esp sexual. * *vt* to regard or treat with favour; to show support for; to oblige (with); to afford advantage to, facilitate.
favourable, favorable (*US*) *adj* expressing approval; pleasing; propitious; conducive (to).—**favourably** *adv*.
favourite, favorite (*US*) *n* a favoured person or thing; a competitor expected to win. * *adj* most preferred.
favouritism, favoritism (*US*) *n* the showing of unfair favour.
fawn[1] *n* a young deer; a yellowish-brown colour. * *adj* fawn-coloured.
fawn[2] *vi* (*dogs, etc*) to crouch to show affection; to flatter obsequiously.—**fawner** *n*.—**fawning** *n*.
fax *see* **facsimile**.
fear *n* an unpleasant emotion excited by danger, pain, etc; a cause of fear; anxiety; deep reverence. * *vt* to feel fear, be afraid of; to be apprehensive, anxious; to be sorry. * *vi* to be afraid or apprehensive.—**fearless** *adj*.—**fearlessly** *adv*.—**fearlessness** *n*.
fearful *adj* causing intense fear; timorous; apprehensive (of); (*inf*) very great, very bad.—**fearfully** *adv*.
feasible *adj* able to be done or implemented, possible.—**feasibly** *adv*.—**feasibility** *n*.
feast *n* an elaborate meal prepared for a special occasion; something that gives abundant pleasure; a periodic religious celebration. * *vi* to have or take part in a feast. * *vt* to entertain with a feast.
feat *n* an action of remarkable strength, skill, or courage.
feather *n* any of the light outgrowths forming the covering of a bird, a hollow central shaft with a vane of fine barbs on each side; a plume; something resembling a feather; the water thrown up by the turn of the blade of an oar. * *vt* to ornament with feathers; to turn (a blade) so that the edge is foremost.—**feathering** *n*.—**feathery** *adj*.
feature *n* any of the parts of the face; a characteristic trait of something; a special attraction or distinctive quality of something; a prominent newspaper article, etc; the main film in a cinema programme. * *vti* to make or be a feature of (something).
featureless *adj* lacking prominent or distinctive features.
February *n* the second month of the year, having 28 days (or 29 days in leap years).
federal *adj* designating, or of a union of states, etc, in which each member surrenders some of its power to a central authority; of a central government of this type.—**federalism** *n*.—**federalist** *n*.—**federally** *adv*.
federation *n* a union of states, groups, etc, in which each subordinates its power to a central authority; a federated organization.
fee *n* the price paid for the advice or service of a professional; a charge for some privilege, as membership of a club; (*law*) an inheritance in land.
feeble *adj* weak, ineffective.—**feebly** *adv*.—**feebleness** *n*.
feeble-minded *adj* mentally defective; of low intelligence.
feed *vb* (*pt* **fed**) *vt* to give food to; to give as food to; to supply with necessary material; to gratify. * *vi* to consume food. * *n* food for animals; material fed into a machine; the part of a machine supplying this material.
feedback *n* a return to the input of part of the output of a system; information about a product, service, etc returned to the supplier for evaluation.
feel *vb* (*pt* **felt**) *vt* to perceive or explore by the touch; to find one's way by cautious trial; to be conscious of, experience; to have a vague or instinctual impression of; to believe, consider. * *vi* to be able to experience the sensation of touch; to be affected by; to convey a certain sensation when touched. * *n* the sense of touch; feeling; a quality as revealed by touch.
feeler *n* a tactile organ (as a tentacle or an-

tenna) of an animal; a tentative approach or suggestion to test another person's reactions.
feeling *n* the sense of touch; mental or physical awareness; a physical or mental impression; a state of mind; sympathy; emotional sensitivity; a belief or opinion arising from emotion; (*pl*) emotions, sensibilities.
feet *see* **foot**.
feign *vt* to invent; to pretend.
fell[1] *see* **fall**.
fell[2] *vt* to cut, beat, or knock down; to kill, to sew (a seam) by folding one raw edge under the other.
fell[3] *n* a skin, hide, pelt.
fell[4] *adj* (*poet*) cruel, fierce, bloody, deadly.
fellow *n* an associate; a comrade; an equal in power, rank, or position; the other of a pair, a mate; a member of the governing body in some colleges and universities; a member of a learned society; (*inf*) a man or boy. * *adj* belonging to the same group or class.
fellowship *n* companionship; a mutual sharing; a group of people with the same interests; the position held by a college fellow.
felony *n* (*formerly*) a grave crime.
felt[1] *see* **feel**.
felt[2] *n* a fabric made from woollen fibres, often mixed with fur or hair, pressed together. * *vti* to make into or become like felt.
female *adj* of the sex that produces young; of a woman or women; (*pipe, plug, etc*) designed with a hollow part for receiving an inserted piece. * *n* a female animal or plant.
feminine *adj* of, resembling, or appropriate to women; (*gram*) of that gender to which words denoting females belong.—**femininity** *n*.
feminism *n* the movement to win political, economic and social equality for women.—**feminist** *adj, n*.
fence *n* a barrier put round land to mark a boundary, or prevent animals, etc from escaping; a receiver of stolen goods. * *vt* to surround with a fence; to keep (out) as by a fence. * *vi* to practise fencing; to make evasive answers; to act as a fence for stolen goods.—**fencer** *n*.
fencing *n* fences; material for making fences; the art of fighting with foils or other types of sword.
fend *vi* (*with* **for**) to provide a livelihood for.
fender *n* anything that protects or fends off something else, as old tyres along the side of a vessel, or the part of a car body over the wheel.
ferment *n* an agent causing fermentation, as yeast; excitement, agitation. * *vti* to (cause to) undergo fermentation; to (cause to) be excited, agitated.
fermentation *n* the breakdown of complex molecules in organic components caused by the influence of yeast or other substances.
fern *n* any of a large class of non-flowering plants having roots, stems, and fronds, and reproducing by spores.—**ferny** *adj*.
ferocious *adj* savage, fierce.—**ferociously** *adv*.—**ferocity** *n*.
ferry *vt* to convey (passengers, etc) over a stretch of water; to transport from one place to another, esp along a regular route. * *n* a boat used for ferrying; a ferrying service; the location of a ferry.—**ferryman** *n*.
fertile *adj* able to bear offspring; (*land*) easily supporting plants and vegetation; (*animals*) capable of breeding; (*eggs*) able to grow and develop; prolific; (*mind, brain*) inventive.—**fertility** *n*.
fertilize *vt* to make (soil) fertile by adding nutrients; to impregnate; to pollinate.—**fertilization** *n*.
fertilizer *n* natural organic or artificial substances used to enrich the soil.
fervent, fervid *adj* passionate; zealous.—**fervently, fervidly** *adv*.—**fervency** *n*.
fester *vti* to become or cause to become infected; to suppurate; to rankle.
festival *n* a time of celebration; performances of music, plays, etc given periodically.
festive *adj* merry, joyous.
fetch *vt* to go for and bring back; to cause to come; (*goods*) to sell for (a certain price); (*inf*) to deal (a blow, slap, etc).
fetching *adj* attractive.
fête, fete *n* a festival; a usu outdoor sale, bazaar or entertainment in aid of charity. * *vt* to honour or entertain (as if) with a fête.
fetish *n* an object believed by primitive peoples to have magical properties; any object or activity regarded with excessive devotion.
fetus, *n* (*pl* **fetuses**) the unborn young of an animal, esp in its later stages; in humans, the offspring in the womb from the fourth month until birth.—*also* **foetus** (*pl* **foetuses**).—**fetal, foetal** *adj*.
feud *n* a state of hostilities, esp between individuals, families, or clans; a dispute.—*also* *vi*.
feudal *adj* pertaining to feudalism; (*inf*) old-fashioned, redundant.
feudalism *n* the economic and social system in medieval Europe, in which land, worked by

serfs, was held by vassals in exchange for military and other services to overlords.

fever *n* an abnormally increased body temperature; any disease marked by a high fever; a state of restless excitement.—**fevered** *adj*.

feverish *adj* having a fever; indicating a fever; restlessly excited.—**feverishly** *adv*.—**feverishness** *n*.

few *adj, n* a small number, not many.—**fewness** *n*.

fiancé *n* a person engaged to be married.—**fiancée** *nf*.

fiasco *n* (*pl* **fiascos, fiascoes**) a complete and humiliating failure.

fib *n* a lie about something unimportant.—*also vi*.—**fibber** *n*.

fibre, fiber (*US*) *n* a natural or synthetic thread, eg from cotton, nylon, which is spun into yarn; a material composed of such yarn; texture; strength of character; a fibrous substance, roughage.—**fibrous** *adj*.

fibreglass, fiberglass (*US*) *n* glass in fibrous form, often bonded with plastic, used in making various products.

fickle *adj* inconstant; capricious.—**fickleness** *n*.

fiction *n* an invented story; any literary work with imaginary characters and events, as a novel, play, etc; such works collectively.—**fictional** *adj*.—**fictionally** *adv*.

fictitious *adj* imaginary, not real; feigned.—**fictitiously** *adv*.

fiddle *n* (*inf*) a violin; (*sl*) a swindle. * *vt* (*inf*) to play on a violin; (*sl*) to swindle; to falsify. * *vi* to handle restlessly, to fidget.—**fiddler** *n*.

fidelity *n* faithfulness, loyalty; truthfulness; accuracy in reproducing sound.

fidget *vi* to (cause to) move restlessly.—*also n*.—**fidgety** *adj*.

field *n* an area of land cleared of trees and buildings, used for pasture or crops; an area rich in a natural product (eg gold, coal); a battlefield; a sports ground; an area affected by electrical, magnetic or gravitational influence, etc; the area visible through an optical lens; a division of activity, knowledge, etc; all competitors in a contest; (*comput*) a section of a record in a database. * *vt* (*cricket, baseball, etc*) to catch or stop and return the ball as a fielder; to put (eg. a team) into the field to play; (*inf*) to handle (eg questions) successfully.

field glasses *npl* small, portable binoculars for use outdoors.

fieldwork *n* research done outside the laboratory or place of work by scientists, archaeologists, social workers, etc. —**fieldworker** *n*.

fiend *n* an evil spirit; an inhumanly wicked person; (*inf*) an avid fan.—**fiendish** *adj*.—**fiendishly** *adv*.

fierce *adj* ferociously hostile; angry, violent; intense; strong, extreme.—**fiercely** *adv*.—**fierceness** *n*.

fiery *adj* (**fierier, fieriest**) like or consisting of fire; the colour of fire; intensely hot; spicy; passionate, ardent; impetuous; irascible.—**fierily** *adv*.—**fieriness** *n*.

fifteen *adj, n* one more than fourteen; the symbol for this (15, XV, xv); the first point scored by a side in a game of tennis.—**fifteenth** *adj, n*.

fifth *adj, n* last of five; being one of five equal parts.

fifty *adj, n* five times ten; the symbol for this (50, L, l).—**fiftieth** *adj*.

fig *n* a tree yielding a soft, pear-shaped fruit; a thing of little or no importance.

fight *vb* (*pt* **fought**) *vi* to engage in battle in war or in single combat; to strive, struggle (for). * *vt* to engage in or carry on a conflict with; to achieve (one's way) by fighting; to strive to overcome. * *n* fighting; a struggle or conflict of any kind; a boxing match.

fighter *n* a person who fights; a person who does not yield easily; an aircraft designed to destroy enemy aircraft.

figment *n* something imagined or invented.

figurative *adj* metaphorical; using figures of speech.—**figuratively** *adv*.

figure *n* a character representing a number; a number; value or price; bodily shape or form; a graphic representation of a thing, person or animal; a design; a geometrical form; a statue; appearance; a personage; (*dancing, skating*) a set of steps or movements; (*pl*) arithmetic. * *vt* to represent in a diagram or outline; to imagine; (*inf*) to consider; (*inf*) to believe. * *vi* to take a part (in), be conspicuous (in); to calculate.

figurehead *n* a carved figure on the bow of a ship; a nominal head or leader.

filament *n* a slender thread or strand; a fibre; the fine wire in a light bulb.

file[1] a container for keeping papers, etc, in order; an orderly arrangement of papers; a line of persons or things; (*comput*) a collection of related data under a specific name. * *vt* to dispatch or register; to put on public record. * *vi* to move in a line; to apply.

file[2] *n* a tool, usu steel, with a rough surface for smoothing or grinding. * *vt* to cut or smooth with, or as with, a file; to polish, improve.

filing *n* a particle rubbed off with a file.

fill *vt* to put as much as possible into; to occupy wholly; to put a person into (a position or job, etc); to supply the things called for (in an order, etc); to close or plug (holes, etc). * *vi* to become full. * *n* enough to make full or to satisfy; anything that fills.

fillet *n* a thin boneless strip of meat or fish; a ribbon, etc worn as a headband; (*archit*) a narrow band used between mouldings. * *vt* to bone and slice (fish or meat).

filling *n* a substance used to fill a tooth cavity; the contents of a sandwich, pie, etc. * *adj* (*meal, etc*) substantial.

filling station *n* a place where petrol is sold to motorists, a service station.

fillip *n* a blow with the nail of the finger; a stimulus.

film *n* a fine, thin skin, coating, etc; a flexible cellulose material covered with a light-sensitive substance used in photography; a haze or blur; a motion picture. * *vti* to cover or be covered as with a film; to photograph or make a film (of).

filter *n* a device or substance straining out solid particles, impurities, etc, from a liquid or gas; a device for removing or minimizing electrical oscillations, or sound or light waves, of certain frequencies; a traffic signal that allows cars to turn left or right while the main lights are red. * *vti* to pass through or as through a filter; to remove with a filter.

filth *n* dirt; obscenity.

filthy *adj* (**filthier, filthiest**) dirty, disgusting; obscene; (*inf*) extremely unpleasant.—**filthily** *adv*.—**filthiness** *n*.

fin *n* an organ by which a fish, etc steers itself and swims; a rubber flipper used for underwater swimming; any fin-shaped object used as a stabilizer, as on an aircraft or rocket.

final *adj* of or coming at the end; conclusive. * *n* (*often pl*) the last of a series of contests; a final examination. —**finally** *adv*.

finale *n* the concluding part of any public performance; the last section in a musical composition.

finalist *n* a contestant in a final.

finalize *vt* to make complete, to bring to an end.—**finalization** *n*.

finance *n* the management of money; (*pl*) money resources. * *vt* to supply or raise money for.—**financial** *adj*.—**financially** *adv*.

financier *n* a person skilled in finance.

find *vb* (*pt* **found**) *vt* to discover by chance; to come upon by searching; to perceive; to recover (something lost); to reach, attain; to decide and declare to be. * *vi* to reach a decision (as by a jury). * *n* a discovery, something found.

finding *n* a discovery; the conclusion reached by a judicial enquiry.

fine[1] *adj* very good; with no impurities, refined; (*weather*) clear and bright; not heavy or coarse; very thin or small; sharp; subtle; elegant. * *adv* in a fine manner; (*inf*) very well.—**finely** *adv*.—**fineness** *n*.

fine[2] *n* a sum of money imposed as a punishment. * *vt* to punish by a fine.

fine arts *npl* painting, sculpture, music, etc valued for their aesthetic qualities.

finery *n* elaborate clothes, jewellery, etc.

finesse *n* delicacy or subtlety of performance; skilfulness, diplomacy in handling a situation; (*bridge*) an attempt to take a trick with a card lower than a higher card held by an opponent. * *vt* to achieve by finesse; to play (a card) as a finesse.

finger *n* one of the digits of the hand, usu excluding the thumb; anything shaped like a finger; (*inf*) the breadth of a finger. * *vt* to touch with fingers; (*mus*) to use the fingers in a certain way when playing.

fingernail *n* the nail on a finger.

fingerprint *n* the impression of the ridges on a fingertip, esp as used for purposes of identification.—*also vt*.

finicky, finicking *adj* too particular, fussy.

finish *vt* to bring to an end, to come to the end of; to consume entirely; to perfect; to give a desired surface effect to. * *vi* to come to an end. * *n* the last part, the end; anything used to finish a surface; the finished effect; means or manner of completing or perfecting; polished manners, speech, etc.—**finisher** *n*.

finite *adj* having definable limits; (*verb form*) having a distinct grammatical person and number.

fiord *see* **fjord**.

fir *n* a kind of evergreen, cone-bearing tree; its timber.

fire *n* the flame, heat and light of combustion; something burning; burning fuel in a grate to heat a room; an electric or gas fire; a destructive burning; a strong feeling; a discharge of firearms. * *vti* to ignite; to supply with fuel; to bake (bricks, etc) in a kiln; to excite or become excited; to shoot (a gun, etc); to hurl or direct with force; to dismiss from a position.

fire alarm *n* a device that uses a bell, hooter, etc to warn of a fire.

firearm *n* a handgun.

fire brigade *n* an organization of men trained and equipped to fight fires.

fire escape *n* a means of exit from a building, esp a stairway, for use in case of fire.

fireman *n* a member of a fire brigade; a person employed to tend furnaces.

fireplace *n* a place for a fire, esp a recess in a wall; the surrounding area.

fireside *n* the area in a room nearest the fireplace; home.

firework *n* a device packed with explosive and combustible material used to produce noisy and colourful displays; (*pl*) such a display; (*pl*) a fit of temper, an outburst of emotions.

firing squad *n* a detachment with the task of firing a salute at a military funeral or carrying out an execution.

firm[1] *adj* securely fixed; solid, compact; steady; resolute; definite. * *vti* to make or become firm.—**firmly** *adv*.—**firmness** *n*.

firm[2] *n* a business partnership; a commercial company.

first *adj* before all others in a series; 1st; earliest; foremost, as in rank, quality, etc. * *adv* before anyone or anything else; for the first time; sooner. * *n* any person or thing that is first; the beginning; the winning place, as in a race; low gear; the highest award in a university degree.

first aid *n* emergency treatment for an injury, etc, before regular medical aid is available.

first-class *adj* of the highest quality, as in accommodation, travel.—*also n*.

firsthand *adj* obtained directly.

First Lady *n* the wife of the US president.

firstly *adv* in the first place.

first-rate *adj, adv* of the best quality; (*inf*) excellent.

fiscal *adj* of or relating to public revenue; financial. * *n* a prosecuting official in some countries.

fish *n* (*pl* **fish, fishes**) any of a large group of cold-blooded animals living in water, having backbones, gills and fins; the flesh of fish used as food. * *vi* to catch or try to catch fish; (*with* **for**) to try to obtain by roundabout methods. * *vt* (*often with* **out**) to grope for, find, and bring to view.

fisherman *n* a person who fishes for sport or for a living; a ship used in fishing.

fishery *n* the fishing industry; an area where fish are caught.

fish finger *n* a small oblong piece of fish covered in breadcrumbs.

fishmonger *n* a shop that sells fish.

fishy *adj* (**fishier, fishiest**) like a fish in odour, taste, etc; (*inf*) creating doubt or suspicion.—**fishily** *adv*.—**fishiness** *n*.

fission *n* a split or cleavage; the reproductive division of biological cells; the splitting of the atomic nucleus resulting in the release of energy, nuclear fission.—**fissionable** *adj*.

fissure *n* a narrow opening or cleft.—*also vti*.

fist *n* the hand when tightly closed or clenched.

fit[1] *adj* (**fitter, fittest**) suited to some purpose, function, etc; proper, right; healthy; (*sl*) inclined, ready. * *n* the manner of fitting. * *vb* (*pt* **fitted**) *vt* to be suitable to; to be the proper size or shape for; to adjust so as to fit; to equip, to outfit. * *vi* to be suitable or proper; to have the proper size or shape. —**fitly** *adv*.—**fitness** *n*.

fit[2] *n* any sudden, uncontrollable attack, as of coughing; an outburst, as of anger; a short period of impulsive activity; a seizure involving convulsions or loss of consciousness.

fitful *adj* marked by intermittent activity; spasmodic.—**fitfully** *adv*.—**fitfulness** *n*.

fitment *n* a piece of equipment, esp fixed furniture.

fitter *n* a person who specializes in fitting clothes; a person skilled in the assembly and operation of a particular piece of machinery.

fitting *adj* appropriate. * *n* an act of one that fits, esp a trying on of altered clothes; a small often standardized electrical part.—**fittingly** *adv*.

five *adj, n* one more than four; the symbol for this (5, V, v).

fiver *n* (*inf*) a £5 note.

fix *vt* to fasten firmly; to set firmly in the mind; to direct (one's eyes) steadily at something; to make rigid; to make permanent; to establish (a date, etc) definitely; to set in order; to repair; to prepare (food or meals); (*inf*) to influence the result or action of (a race, jury, etc) by bribery; (*inf*) to punish. * *vi* to become fixed; (*inf*) to prepare or intend. * *n* the position of a ship, etc, determined from the bearings of two known positions; (*inf*) a predicament; (*inf*) a situation that has been fixed; (*inf*) something whose supply becomes continually necessary or greatly desired, as a drug, activity, etc.

fixture *n* what is fixed to anything, as to land or to a house; a fixed article of furniture; a firmly established person or thing; a fixed or appointed time or event.

fizz *vi* to make a hissing or sputtering sound. * *n* this sound; any effervescent drink.—**fizzy** *adj*.—**fizziness** *n*.

fizzle *vi* to make a weak fizzing sound; (*with* **out**) (*inf*) to end feebly, die out, esp after a promising start.

fjord *n* a long, narrow inlet of the sea between high cliffs, esp in Norway. —*also* **fiord**.

flabbergast *vt* (*inf*) to astonish, startle.

flabby *adj* (**flabbier, flabbiest**) fat and soft; weak and ineffective.—**flabbiness** *n*.

flag[1] *vi* (*pt* **flagged**) to grow limp; to become weak, listless.

flag[2] *n* a piece of cloth, usu with a design, used to show nationality, party, a particular branch of the armed forces, etc, or as a signal. * *vt* (*pt* **flagged**) to decorate with flags; to signal to (as if) with a flag; (*usu with* **down**) to signal to stop.

flag[3] *n* a hard, flat stone used for paving, a flagstone. * *vt* (*pt* **flagged**) to pave.

flagon *n* a pottery or metal container for liquids with a handle and spout and often a lid.

flagrant *adj* conspicuous, notorious.—**flagrantly** *adv*.—**flagrancy** *n*.

flair *n* natural ability, aptitude; discernment; (*inf*) stylishness, sophistication.

flake *n* a small piece of snow; a small thin layer chipped from a larger mass of something. * *vt* to form into flakes.—**flaky** *adj*.

flamboyant *adj* brilliantly coloured; ornate; strikingly elaborate; dashing, exuberant.—**flamboyantly** *adv*.—**flamboyance** *n*.

flame *n* the burning gas of a fire, appearing as a tongue of light; the state of burning with a blaze; a thing like a flame; an intense emotion; (*inf*) a sweetheart. * *vi* to burst into flame; to become bright red with emotion.

flamingo *n* any of several wading birds with rosy-white plumage and long legs and neck.

flammable *adj* easily set on fire.—**flammability** *n*.

flan *n* an open case of pastry or sponge cake with a sweet or savoury filling.

flange *n* a projecting or raised edge.

flank *n* the fleshy part of the side from the ribs to the hip; the side of anything; the right or left side of a formation of troops. * *vt* to attack the flank of; to skirt the side of; to be situated at the side of.

flannel *n* a soft light cotton or woollen cloth; a small cloth for washing the face and hands; (*sl*) nonsense, equivocation; (*pl*) trousers of such cloth. * *vt* (*pt* **flannelled**) to wash with a flannel; (*inf*) to flatter.

flannelette *n* a soft cotton fabric.

flap *vi* (*pt* **flapped**) to move up and down, as wings; to sway loosely and noisily; to move or hang like a flap; (*inf*) to get into a fluster. * *n* the motion or noise of a flap; anything broad and flexible, either hinged or hanging loose; a light blow with a flat object; (*inf*) agitation, panic.

flare *vi* to burn with a sudden, bright, unsteady flame; to burst into emotion, esp anger; to widen out gradually. * *n* an unsteady flame; a sudden flash; a bright light used as a signal or illumination; a widened part or shape.

flare-up *n* a sudden burst of fire; (*inf*) a sudden burst of emotion.

flash *n* a sudden, brief light; a brief moment; a sudden brief display; (*TV, radio*) a sudden brief news item on an important event; (*photog*) a device producing a brief intense light; a sudden onrush of water. * *vi* to emit a sudden, brief light; to sparkle; to come or pass suddenly; (*sl*) to expose the genitals indecently. * *vt* to cause to flash; to send (news, etc) swiftly; (*inf*) to show off. * *adj* (*inf*) flashy.—**flasher** *n*.

flashback *n* an interruption in the continuity of a story, etc, by telling or showing an earlier episode.

flashbulb *n* a small bulb giving an intense light used in photography.

flashlight *n* a torch.

flashy *adj* (**flashier, flashiest**) pretentious; showy, gaudy.

flask *n* a slim-necked bottle; a vacuum flask.

flat *adj* (**flatter, flattest**) having a smooth level surface; lying spread out; broad, even, and thin; not fluctuating; (*tyre*) deflated; dull, tedious; (*drink*) not fizzy; (*battery*) drained of electric current. * *adv* in a flat manner or position; exactly; (*mus*) below true pitch. * *n* anything flat, esp a surface, part, or expanse; a flat tyre; a set of rooms on one floor of a building.—**flatly** *adv*.—**flatness** *n*.

flatten *vti* to make or become flat.

flatter *vt* to praise excessively or insincerely, esp to win favour; to display to advantage; to represent as more attractive, etc than reality; to gratify the vanity of; to encourage falsely.—**flatterer** *n*.—**flattery** *n*.

flaunt *vi* to move or behave ostentatiously; (*flag*) to wave in the wind. * *vt* to display.

flavour, flavor (*US*) *n* the taste of something in the mouth; a characteristic quality. * *vt* to give flavour to.

flavouring, flavoring (*US*) *n* any substance used to give flavour to food.

flaw *n* a defect; a crack. * *vti* to make or become flawed.—**flawless** *adj*.

flax *n* a blue-flowered plant cultivated for its fibre and seed; its fibre.

flaxen *adj* made of flax; pale yellow.

flea *n* a small wingless jumping bloodsucking insect.

fledge *vt* (*birds*) to rear until ready to fly; to cover or provide with feathers.

fledgling *n* a young bird just fledged; an inexperienced person, a trainee.

flee *vti* (*pt* **fled**) to run away from danger, etc; to pass away quickly, to disappear.

fleece *n* the woollen coat of sheep or similar animal. * *vt* to remove wool from; to defraud.—**fleecy** *adj*.

fleet[1] *n* a number of warships under one command; (*often with cap*) a country's navy; any group of cars, ships, buses, etc, under one control.

fleet[2] *adj* swift moving; nimble.—**fleetly** *adv*.—**fleetness** *n*.

fleeting *adj* brief, transient.

flesh *n* the soft substance of the body, esp the muscular tissue; the pulpy part of fruits and vegetables; meat; the body as distinct from the soul; all mankind; a yellowish-pink colour. * *vt* to give substance to (*usu with* **out**).—**fleshy** *adj*.

flexible, flexile *adj* easily bent; adaptable, versatile; docile.—**flexibly** *adv*. —**flexibility** *n*.

flick *n* a light stroke or blow; (*inf*) a cinema film. * *vt* to strike or propel with a flick; a flicking movement.

flicker *vi* to burn unsteadily, as a flame; to move quickly to and fro. * *n* a flickering moment of light or flame; a flickering movement.

flier *see* **flyer**.

flight[1] *n* the act, manner, or power of flying; distance flown; a group of creatures or things flying together; an aircraft scheduled to fly a certain trip; a trip by aircraft; a set of stairs, as between landings; a mental act of soaring beyond the ordinary; a set of feathers on a dart or arrow.

flight[2] *n* an act or instance of fleeing.

flimsy *adj* (**flimsier, flimsiest**) weak, insubstantial; light and thin; (*excuse etc*) unconvincing.—**flimsily** *adv*.—**flimsiness** *n*.

flinch *vi* to draw back, as from pain or fear; to wince.

fling *vb* (*pt* **flung**) *vt* to cast, throw aside, esp with force; to put or send suddenly or without warning. * *vi* to kick out violently; to move or rush quickly or impetuously. * *n* the act of flinging; a lively dance; a period of pleasurable indulgence.

flint *n* a very hard rock that produces sparks when struck with steel; an alloy used for producing a spark in lighters.

flip[1] *n* a drink made from any alcoholic beverage sweetened and mixed with beaten egg.

flip[2] *vb* (*pt* **flipped**) *vt* to toss with a jerk, to flick; to snap (a coin) in the air with the thumb; to turn or turn over. * *vi* to move jerkily; (*inf*) to burst into anger.

flippant *adj* impertinent; frivolous.—**flippancy** *n*.—**flippantly** *adv*.

flirt *vi* to make insincere amorous approaches; to trifle or toy (eg with an idea). * *n* a person who toys amorously with the opposite sex.—**flirtation** *n*.

flit *vi* (*pt* **flitted**) to move lightly and rapidly; to vacate (a premises) stealthily.—*also n*.

float *vi* to rest on the surface of or be suspended in a liquid; to move lightly; to wander aimlessly. * *vt* to cause to float; to put into circulation; to start up a business, esp by offering shares for sale. * *n* anything that floats; a cork or other device used on a fishing line to signal that the bait has been taken; a low flat vehicle decorated for exhibit in a parade; a small sum of money available for cash expenditures.

flock[1] *n* a group of certain animals as birds, sheep, etc, living and feeding together; a group of people or things. * *vi* to assemble or travel in a flock or crowd.

flock[2] *n* a tuft of wool or cotton fibre; woollen or cotton waste used for stuffing furniture.

flog *vt* (*pt* **flogged**) to beat harshly with a rod, stick or whip; (*sl*) to sell.—**flogging** *n*.

flood *n* an overflowing of water on an area normally dry; the rising of the tide; a great outpouring, as of words. * *vt* to cover or fill, as with a flood; to put too much water, fuel, etc on or in. * *vi* to gush out in a flood; to become flooded.

floodlight *n* a strong beam of light used to illuminate a stage, sports field, stadium, etc. * *vt* (*pt* **floodlit**) to illuminate with floodlights.

floor *n* the inside bottom surface of a room; the bottom surface of anything, as the ocean; a storey in a building; the area in a legislative assembly where the members debate; the lower limit, the base. * *vt* to provide with a floor; to knock down (a person) in a fight; (*inf*) to defeat; (*inf*) to shock, to confuse.

floorboard *n* one of the boards making up a floor.

flop *vi* (*pt* **flopped**) to sway or bounce loosely; to move in a heavy, clumsy or relaxed manner; (*inf*) to fail. * *n* a flopping movement; a collapse; (*inf*) a complete failure.

floppy *adj* (**floppier, floppiest**) limp, hanging loosely.—**floppiness** *n*.

flora *n* (*pl* **floras, florae**) the plants of a region or a period.

floral *adj* pertaining to flowers.

florid *adj* flowery; elaborate; (*complexion*) ruddy.

florist *n* a person who sells or grows flowers and ornamental plants.

flotation *n* the act or process of floating; a launching of a business venture.

flounce[1] *vi* to move in an emphatic or impatient manner.—*also n*.

flounce[2] *n* a frill of material sewn to the skirt of a dress. * *vt* to add flounces to.

flounder[1] *vi* to move awkwardly and with difficulty; to be clumsy in thinking or speaking.

flounder[2] *n* a small flatfish used as food.

flour *n* the finely ground powder of wheat or other grain. * *vt* to sprinkle with flour.—**floury** *adj*.

flourish *vi* (*plants*) to grow luxuriantly; to thrive, prosper; to live and work at a specified time. * *vt* to brandish dramatically. * *n* embellishment; a curve made by a bold stroke of a pen; a sweeping gesture; a musical fanfare.

flout *vt* to treat with contempt, to disobey openly.—**flouter** *n*.—**floutingly** *adv*.

flow *vi* (*liquids*) to move (as if) in a stream; (*tide*) to rise; to glide smoothly; (*conversation, etc*) to continue effortlessly; to be characterized by smooth and easy movement; to hang free or loosely; to be plentiful. * *n* a flowing; the rate of flow; anything that flows; the rising of the tide.

flow chart *n* a diagram representing the sequence of and relationships between different steps or procedures in a complex process, eg manufacturing.

flower *n* the seed-producing structure of a flowering plant, blossom; a plant cultivated for its blossoms; the best or finest part. * *vt* to cause to bear flowers. * *vi* to produce blossoms; to reach the best stage.

flowery *adj* full of or decorated with flowers; (*language*) full of elaborate expressions.

flown *see* **fly**.

flu *n* (*inf*) influenza.

fluctuate *vi* (*prices, etc*) to be continually varying in an irregular way.—**fluctuation** *n*.

fluent *adj* able to write and speak a foreign language with ease; articulate, speaking and writing easily and smoothly; graceful.—**fluency** *n*.—**fluently** *adv*.

fluff *n* soft, light down; a loose, soft mass, as of hair; (*inf*) a mistake, bungle. * *vt* to pat or shake until fluffy; (*inf*) to bungle.

fluffy *adj* (**fluffier, fluffiest**) like fluff; feathery.—**fluffiness** *n*.

fluid *n* a substance able to flow freely, as a liquid or gas does. * *adj* able to flow freely; able to change rapidly or easily.—**fluidity** *n*.

fluke[1] *n* a flatfish; a flattened parasitic worm.

fluke[2] *n* the part of an anchor that fastens in the sea bed, river bottom, etc; the barbed end of a harpoon; one of the lobes of a whale's tail.

fluke[3] *n* a stroke of luck.—**fluky** *adj*.

flung *see* **fling**.

fluoride *n* any of various compounds of fluorine.

flurry *n* a sudden gust of wind, rain, or snow; a sudden commotion. * *vti* to (cause to) become flustered.

flush[1] *n* a rapid flow, as of water; sudden, vigorous growth; a sudden excitement; a blush; a sudden feeling of heat, as in a fever. * *vi* to flow rapidly; to blush or glow; to be washed out by a sudden flow of water. * *vt* to wash out with a sudden flow of water; to cause to blush; to excite. * *adj* level or in one plane with another surface; (*inf*) abundant, well-supplied, esp with money.

flush[2] *vt* to make game birds fly away suddenly.

flush[3] *n* (*poker, etc*) a hand of cards all of the same suit.

fluster *vti* to make or become confused. * *n* agitation or confusion.

flute *n* an orchestral woodwind instrument in the form of a straight pipe (with finger holes and keys) held horizontally and played through a hole located near one end; a decorative groove. * *vi* to play or make sounds like a flute; to cut grooves in.

flutter *vi* (*birds*) to flap the wings; to wave about rapidly; (*heart*) to beat irregularly or spasmodically. * *vt* to cause to flutter. * *n* rapid, irregular motion; nervous excitement;

commotion, confusion; (*inf*) a small bet.—**fluttery** *adj*.

flux *n* a continual flowing or changing; a substance used to help metals fuse together, as in soldering.

fly[1] *n* a two-winged insect; a natural or imitation fly attached to a fish-hook as bait.

fly[2] *vb* (*pt* **flew**, *pp* **flown**) *vi* to move through the air, esp on wings; to travel in an aircraft; to control an aircraft; to take flight, flee; to pass quickly; (*inf*) to depart quickly. * *vt* to cause to fly, as a kite; to escape, flee from; to transport by aircraft. * *n* a flap that hides buttons, a zip, etc on trousers; material forming the outer roof of a tent; a device for regulating machinery, a flywheel.

fly[3] *adj* (*inf*) sly, astute.

flyer *n* something that flies or moves very fast; a pilot.—*also* **flier**.

flying *adj* capable of flight; fleeing; fast-moving. * *n* the act of flying an aircraft, etc.

flying saucer *n* an unidentified flying disc-shaped object, purportedly from outer space.

flying start *n* a start in a race when the competitor is already moving at the starting line; a promising start.

flyover *n* a bridge that carries a road or railway over another; a fly-past.

fly-past *n* a processional flight of aircraft.

flywheel *n* a heavy wheel which stores energy by inertia, used to regulate machinery.

foal *n* the young of a horse or related animal. * *vti* to give birth to a foal.

foam *n* froth or fine bubbles on the surface of liquid; something like foam, as frothy saliva; a rigid or springy cellular mass made from liquid rubber, plastic, etc. * *vi* to cause or emit foam.—**foamy** *adj*.

fob[1] *n* the chain or ribbon for attaching a watch to a waistcoat; any object attached to a watch chain; a small pocket in a waistcoat for a watch.

fob[2] *vt* (*pt* **fobbed**) (*with* **off**) to cheat; to put off; to palm off (upon).

focal *adj* of or pertaining to a focus.

focus *n* (*pl* **focuses, foci**) a point where rays of light, heat, etc meet after being bent by a lens, curved mirror, etc; correct adjustment of the eye or lens to form a clear image; a centre of activity or interest. * *vt* (*pt* **focused** *or* **focussed**) to adjust the focus of; to bring into focus; to concentrate.

fodder *n* dried food for horses, etc.

foe *n* an enemy, an adversary.

foetus *see* **fetus**.

fog *n* (a state of poor visibility caused by) a large mass of water vapour condensed to fine particles just above the earth's surface; a state of mental confusion; (*photog*) cloudiness on a developed photograph. * *vti* (*pt* **fogged**) to make or become foggy.

foggy *adj* (**foggier, foggiest**) thick with fog; mentally confused; indistinct, opaque.—**fogginess** *n*.

foible *n* a slight weakness or failing; an idiosyncrasy.

foil[1] *vt* to defeat; to frustrate.

foil[2] *n* a very thin sheet of metal; anything that sets off or enhances another by contrast.

foil[3] *n* a long, thin blunted sword used for fencing.

fold[1] *vt* to cover by bending or doubling over so that one part covers another; to wrap up, envelop; to interlace (one's arms); to clasp (one's hands); to embrace; to incorporate (an ingredient) into a food mixture by gentle overturnings. * *vi* to become folded; to fail completely; to collapse, esp to go out of business. * *n* something folded, as a piece of cloth; a crease or hollow made by folding.

fold[2] *n* a pen for sheep; a group of people or institutions having a common belief, etc. * *vt* to pen in a fold.

folder *n* a folded cover or large envelope for holding loose papers.

foliage *n* leaves, as of a plant or tree.

folk *n* a people of a country or tribe; people in general, esp those of a particular area; relatives; folk music. * *adj* of or originating among the ordinary people.

folklore *n* the traditional beliefs, legends, etc of a people.

folk song *n* a traditional song.

follow *vt* to go or come after; to pursue; to go along (a path, road, etc); to copy; to obey; to adopt, as an opinion; to watch fixedly; to focus the mind on; to understand the meaning of; to monitor the progress of; to come or occur after in time; to result from; (*with* **through**) to pursue (an aim) to a conclusion; (*with* **up**) to pursue a question, inquiry, etc, that has been started. * *vi* to go or come after another; to result; (*with* **on**) (*cricket*) to take a second innings immediately after a first; (*with* **through**) (*sport*) to continue a stroke or motion of a bat, club, etc after the ball has been struck.

follower *n* a disciple or adherent; a person who imitates another.

following *n* a body of adherents or believers.

* *adj* next after; now to be stated.
folly *n* a lack of sense; a foolish act or idea; an extravagant and fanciful building which serves no practical purpose.
fond *adj* loving, affectionate; doting, indulgent; (*with* **of**) having a liking for. —**fondly** *adv*.— **fondness** *n*.
fondle *vt* to caress.
font[1] *n* a receptacle for baptismal water; a receptacle for holy water.
font[2] *see* **fount**[1].
food *n* any substance, esp a solid, taken in by a plant or animal to enable it to live and grow; anything that nourishes.
foodstuff *n* a substance used as food.
fool *n* a person lacking wisdom or common sense; (*Middle Ages*) a jester; a dupe; a cold dessert of whipped cream and fruit purée. * *vt* to deceive, make a fool of. * *vi* to act jokingly; to spend time idly; to tease or meddle with.—**foolery** *n*.
foolhardy *adj* foolishly bold; rash.—**foolhardiness** *n*.
foolish *adj* unwise; ridiculous; ill-judged.—**foolishly** *adv*.—**foolishness** *n*.
foolproof *adj* proof against failure; easy to understand; easy to use.
foot *n* (*pl* **feet**) the end part of the leg, on which one stands; anything resembling foot, as the lower part of a chair, table, etc; the lower part or edge of something, bottom; a measure of length equal to 12 inches (30.48 cm); the part of a garment that covers the foot; an attachment on a sewing machine that grips the fabric; a group of syllables serving as a unit of metre in verse. * *vi* to dance. * *vt* to walk, dance over or on; to pay the entire cost of (a bill).
foot-and-mouth disease *n* a contagious diasease of cattle.
football *n* a field game played with an inflated leather ball by two teams; the ball used.—**footballer** *n*.
footbridge *n* a narrow bridge for pedestrians.
foothill *n* a hill at the foot of higher hills.
foothold *n* a ledge, etc, for placing the foot when climbing, etc; a place from which further progress may be made.
footing *n* the basis upon which something rests; status, relationship; a foothold.
footlights *npl* a row of lights in front of a stage floor.
footman *n* a liveried servant.
footnote *n* a note or comment at the foot of a page.
footpath *n* a narrow path for pedestrians.
footsore *adj* having painful feet from excessive walking.
footwear *n* shoes and socks, etc.
for *prep* because of, as a result of; as the price of, or recompense of; in order to be, to serve as; appropriate to, or adapted to; in quest of; in the direction of; on behalf of; in place of; in favour of; with respect to; notwithstanding, in spite of; to the extent of; throughout the space of; during. * *conj* because.
forage *n* food for domestic animals, esp when taken by browsing or grazing; a search for provisions. * *vi* to search for food.—**forager** *n*.
foray *n* a sudden raid. * *vti* to plunder.
forbade *see* **forbid**.
forbear *vb* (*pt* **forbore**, *pp* **forborne**) *vi* to endure, to avoid. * *vt* to hold oneself back from.—**forbearance** *n*.
forbid *vt* (*pt* **forbad** *or* **forbade**, *pp* **forbidden**) to command (a person) not to do something; to render impossible, prevent.
forbidding *adj* unfriendly, solemn, strict.—**forbiddingly** *adv*.
force *n* strength, power, effort; (*physics*) (the intensity of) an influence that causes movement of a body or other effects; a body of soldiers, police, etc prepared for action; effectiveness; violence, compulsion; legal or logical validity. * *vt* to compel or oblige by physical effort, superior strength, etc; to achieve by force; to press or drive against resistance; to produce with effort; to break open, penetrate; to impose, inflict; to cause (plants, animals) to grow faster than normal.
forceful *adj* powerful, effective.—**forcefully** *adv*.—**forcefulness** *n*.
forceps *n* an instrument for grasping and holding firmly, or exerting traction upon objects, esp by jewellers and surgeons.
ford *n* a shallow crossing place in a river, etc.—*also vt*.—**fordable** *adj*.
fore *adj* in front. * *n* the front. * *adv* in, at or towards the front. * *interj* (*golf*) a warning cry to anybody who may be hit by the ball.
forearm[1] *n* the arm between the elbow and the wrist.
forearm[2] *vt* to arm in advance.
forecast *vt* (*pt* **forecast** *or* **forecasted**) to predict (events, weather, etc) through rational analysis; to serve as a forecast of.—*also n*.
forecourt *n* an enclosed space in front of a building, as in a filling station.
forefathers *npl* ancestors.

forefinger *n* the finger next the thumb.
forego[1] *see* **forgo**.
forego[2] *vt* (*pt* **forewent**, *pp* **foregone**) to precede.
foregone conclusion *n* an inevitable result, easily predictable.
foreground *n* the part of a picture or view nearest the spectator's vision.
forehead *n* the part of the face above the eyes.
foreign *adj* of, in, or belonging to another country; involving other countries; alien in character; introduced from outside.
foreigner *n* a person from another country.
foreman *n* a person who supervises workers in a factory, etc; the spokesperson of a jury.—**forewoman** *nf*.
foremost *adj* first in importance; most advanced in rank or position.
forensic *adj* belonging to or used in courts of law.—**forensically** *adv*.
forensic medicine *n* the application of medical expertise to legal and criminal investigations.
forerunner *n* a person or thing that comes in advance of another; a portent.
foresee *vt* (*pt* **foresaw**, *pp* **foreseen**) to be aware of beforehand.
foresight *n* foreseeing; the power to foresee; provision for the future.
forest *n* a thick growth of trees, etc covering a large tract of land; something resembling a forest.
forestall *vt* to prevent by taking action beforehand; to anticipate.
forestry *n* the science of planting and cultivating forests.
foretell *vt* (*pt* **foretold**) to forecast, to predict.
for ever, forever *adv* for all future time; continually.
foreword *n* a preface to a book.
forfeit *n* something confiscated or given up as a penalty for a fault. * *vt* to lose or be penalized by forfeiture.—**forfeiture** *n*.
forgave *see* **forgive**.
forge[1] *n* (a workshop with) a furnace in which metals are heated and shaped. * *vt* to shape (metal) by heating and hammering; to counterfeit (eg a signature). * *vi* to commit forgery.
forge[2] *vt* to move steadily forward with effort.
forgery *n* fraudulently copying; a forged copy.
forget *vti* (*pt* **forgot**, *pp* **forgotten**) to be unable to remember; to overlook or neglect.
forgetful *adj* apt to forget, inattentive. —**forgetfully** *adv*.—**forgetfulness** *n*.
forgive *vt* (*pt* **forgave**, *pp* **forgiven**) to cease to feel resentment against (a person); to pardon. * *vi* to be merciful or forgiving.—**forgiveness** *n*.
forgo *vt* (*pt* **forwent**, *pp* **forgone**) to give up, abstain from.—*also* **forego**.
fork *n* a small, usu metal, instrument with two or more thin prongs set in a handle, used in eating and cooking; a pronged agricultural or gardening tool for digging, etc; anything that divides into prongs or branches; one of the branches into which a road or river divides; the point of separation. * *vi* to divide into branches; to follow a branch of a fork in a road, etc. * *vt* to form as a fork; to dig, lift, etc with a fork.
fork-lift truck *n* a vehicle with power-operated prongs for raising and lowering loads.
form *n* general structure; the figure of a person or animal; a mould; a particular mode, kind, type, etc; arrangement; a way of doing something requiring skill; a conventional procedure; a printed document with blanks to be filled in; a class in school; condition of mind or body; a chart giving information about racehorses; changed appearance of a word to show inflection; (*sl*) a criminal record. * *vt* to shape; to train; to develop (habits); to constitute. * *vi* to be formed.
formal *adj* in conformity with established rules or habits; regular; relating to outward appearance only; ceremonial; punctilious; stiff.—**formally** *adv*.
format *n* the size, form, shape in which books, etc are issued; the general style or presentation of something, eg a television programme; (*comput*) the arrangement of data on magnetic disk, etc for access and storage. * *vt* (*pt* **formatted**) to arrange in a particular form, esp for a computer.
formation *n* form of making or producing; that which is formed; structure; regular array or prearranged order.
formative *adj* pertaining to formation and development; shaping.
former *adj* of or occurring in a previous time; the first mentioned (of two). —**formerly** *adv*.
formidable *adj* causing fear or awe; difficult to defeat or overcome; difficult to handle.—**formidably** *adv*.
formula *n* (*pl* **formulas, formulae**) a set of symbols expressing the composition of a substance; a general expression in algebraic form for solving a problem; a prescribed form; a formal statement of doctrines; a list of ingredients, as for a prescription or recipe;

a fixed method according to which something is to be done; a prescribed recipe for baby food.

formulate *vt* to express in a formula; to devise.—**formulation** *n*.

forsake *vt* (*pt* **forsook**, *pp* **forsaken**) to desert; to give up, renounce.

fort *n* a fortified place for military defence.

forte[1] *n* something at which a person excels.

forte[2] *adv* (*mus*) loudly.

forth *adv* forwards; onwards; out.

forthcoming *adj* about to appear; readily available; responsive.

forthright *adv* frank, direct, outspoken.—**forthrightness** *n*.

fortification *n* act or process or fortifying; a wall, barricade, etc built to defend a position.

fortify *vt* to strengthen physically, emotionally, etc; to strengthen against attack, as with forts; to support; (*wine, etc*) to add alcohol to; (*milk*) to add vitamins to.

fortitude *n* courage in adversity.

fortnight *n* a period of two weeks or fourteen consecutive days.

fortnightly *adj, adv* once a fortnight.

fortress *n* a strong fort or fortified town.

fortuitous *adj* happening by chance. —**fortuitously** *adv*.—**fortuitousness** *n*.—**fortuity** *n*.

fortunate *adj* having or occurring by good luck.—**fortunately** *adv*.

fortune *n* the supposed arbitrary power that determines events; luck; destiny; prosperity, success; vast wealth.

fortune-teller *n* a person who claims to foretell a person's future.

forty *n* four times ten, the symbol for this (40, XL, xl).—*also adj*.—**fortieth** *adj*.

forum *n* an assembly or meeting to discuss topics of public concern; a medium for public debate, as a magazine; the marketplace and centre of public affairs in ancient Rome.

forward *adj* at, toward, or of the front; advanced; onward; prompt; bold; presumptuous; of or for the future. * *vt* to promote; to send on. * *n* (*sport*) an attacking player in various games. * *adv* toward the front; ahead.—**forwardness** *n*.

forwent *see* **forgo**.

fossil *n* the petrified remains of an animal or vegetable preserved in rock; (*inf*) a thing or person regarded as outmoded or redundant. * *adj* of or like a fossil; dug from the earth.

foster *vt* to encourage; to bring up (a child that is not one's own).

fought *see* **fight**.

foul *adj* stinking, loathsome; extremely dirty; indecent; wicked; (*language*) obscene; (*weather*) stormy; (*sports*) against the rules. * *vt* to make filthy; to dishonour; to obstruct; to entangle (a rope, etc); to make a foul against, as in a game. * *vi* to be or become fouled. * *n* (*sports*) a hit, blow, move, etc that is foul.—**foully** *adv*.

found[1] *see* **find**.

found[2] *vt* to bring into being; to establish (as an institution) often with provision for future maintenance.

found[3] *vt* to melt and pour (metal) into a mould to produce castings.

foundation *n* an endowment for an institution; such an institution; the base of a house, wall, etc; a first layer of cosmetic applied to the skin; an underlying principle, etc; a supporting undergarment, as a corset.

founder[1] *n* one who founds an institution, a benefactor.

founder[2] *n* a person who casts metal.

founder[3] *vi* (*ship*) to fill with water and sink; to collapse; to fail.

foundry *n* a workshop or factory where metal castings are produced.

fount[1] *n* a set of printing type or characters of one style and size.—*also* **font**.

fount[2] *n* a source.

fountain *n* a natural spring of water; a source; an artificial jet or flow of water; the basin where this flows; a reservoir, as for ink. * *vti* to (cause to) flow or spurt like a fountain.

four *n* one more than three; the symbol for this (4, IV, iv); the fourth in a series or set; something having four units as members (as a four-cylinder engine).—*also adj*.

fourteen *n, adj* four and ten; the symbol for this (14, XIV, xiv).—**fourteenth** *adj*.

fourth *adj* next after third. * *n* one of four equal parts of something.—**fourthly** *adv*.

fowl *n* any of the domestic birds used as food, as the chicken, etc; the flesh of these birds. * *vi* to hunt or snare wildfowl.—**fowling** *n*.—**fowler** *n*.

fox *n* any of various small, alert wild mammals of the dog family; the fur of the fox; a sly, crafty person. * *vt* to deceive by cunning. * *vi* (*inf*) to bemuse, puzzle.

foyer *n* an anteroom; an entrance hallway, as in a hotel or theatre.

fraction *n* a small part, amount, etc; (*math*) a quantity less than a whole, expressed as a decimal or with a numerator and denominator.—**fractional** *adj*.—**fractionally** *adv*.

fracture *n* the breaking of any hard material, esp a bone. * *vti* to break; to cause or suffer a fracture.

fragile *adj* easily broken; frail; delicate.—**fragilely** *adv*.—**fragility** *n*.

fragment *n* a piece broken off or detached; an incomplete portion. * *vti* to break or cause to break into fragments.

fragmentary *adj* consisting of fragments; incomplete.

fragrance, fragrancy *n* a pleasant scent, a perfume.

fragrant *adj* sweet-scented.—**fragrantly** *adv*.

frail *adj* physically or morally weak; fragile.

frame *vt* to form according to a pattern; to construct; to put into words; to enclose (a picture) in a border; (*sl*) to falsify evidence against (an innocent person). * *n* something composed of parts fitted together and united; the physical make-up of an animal, esp a human body; the framework of a house; the case enclosing a window, door, etc; an ornamental border, as round a picture; (*snooker*) a triangular mould for setting up balls before play; (*snooker*) a single game.—**framer** *n*.

framework *n* a structural frame; a basic structure; frame of reference.

franchise *n* the right to vote in public elections; authorization to sell the goods of a manufacturer in a particular area. * *vt* to grant a franchise.

frank *adj* free and direct in expressing oneself; honest, open. * *vt* to mark letters, etc with a mark denoting free postage. * *n* a mark indicating free postage.—**frankness** *n*.

frantic *adj* violently agitated; furious, wild.—**frantically** *adv*.

fraternal *adj* of or belonging to a brother or fraternity; friendly, brotherly.—**fraternally** *adv*.

fraternity *n* brotherly feeling; a society of people with common interests.

fraternize *vt* to associate in a friendly manner.—**fraternization** *n*.

fraud *n* deliberate deceit; an act of deception; (*inf*) a deceitful person; an impostor.

fraudulent *adj* deceiving or intending to deceive; obtained by deceit.—**fraudulence** *n*.—**fraudulently** *adv*.

fraught *adj* filled or loaded (with).

fray[1] *n* a fight, a brawl.

fray[2] *vti* (*fabric, etc*) to (cause to) wear away into threads, esp at the edge of; (*nerves, temper*) to make or become irritated or strained.

freak *n* an unusual happening; any abnormal animal, person, or plant; (*inf*) a person who dresses or acts in a notably unconventional manner; an ardent enthusiast.—**freakish** *adj*.

freckle *n* a small, brownish spot on the skin. * *vti* to make or become spotted with freckles.—**freckled, freckly** *adj*.

free *adj* (**freer, freest**) not under the control or power of another; having social and political liberty; independent; able to move in any direction; not burdened by obligations; not confined to the usual rules; not exact; generous; frank; with no cost or charge; exempt from taxes, duties, etc; clear of obstruction; not fastened. * *adv* without cost; in a free manner. * *vt* (*pt* **freed**) to set free; to clear of obstruction, etc.—**freely** *adv*.

freedom *n* being free; exemption from obligation; unrestricted use; a right or privilege.

freelance *n* a person who pursues a profession without long-term commitment to any employer (—*also* **freelancer**). * *vt* to work as a freelance.

Freemason *n* a member of the secretive fraternity (Free and Accepted Masons) dedicated to mutual aid.

free trade *n* trade based on the unrestricted international exchange of goods with tariffs used only as a source of revenue.—**freetrader** *n*.

freeway *n* in North America, a fast road, a motorway.

freewheel *n* a device for temporarily disconnecting and setting free the back wheel of a bicycle from the driving gear. * *vi* to ride a bicycle with the gear disconnected; to drive a car with the gear in neutral.—**freewheeler** *n*.

free will *n* voluntary choice or decision; freedom of human beings to make choices that are not determined by prior causes or by divine intervention.

freeze *vb* (*pt* **froze**, *pp* **frozen**) *vi* to be formed into, or become covered by ice; to become very cold; to be damaged or killed by cold; to become motionless; to be made speechless by strong emotion; to become formal and unfriendly. * *vt* to harden into ice; to convert from a liquid to a solid with cold; to make extremely cold; to act towards in a stiff and formal way; to act on usu destructively by frost; to anaesthetize by cold; to fix (prices, etc) at a given level by authority; to make (funds, etc) unavailable to the owners by authority.

freezer *n* a container that freezes and preserves food for long periods.

freezing point *n* the temperature at which a liquid solidifies.

freight *n* the transport of goods by water, land, or air; the cost for this; the goods transported. * *vt* to load with freight; to send by freight.

freighter *n* a ship or aircraft carrying freight.

French *adj* of France, its people, culture, etc. * *n* the language of France.

French fries, french fries *npl* thin strips of potato fried in oil, etc, chips.

French windows, French doors *npl* a pair of floor-length casement windows in an outside wall, opening on to a patio, garden, etc.

frenzy *n* wild excitement; violent mental derangement.—**frenzied** *adj*.—**frenziedly** *adv*.

frequency *n* repeated occurrence; the number of occurrences, cycles, etc in a given period.

frequent *adj* coming or happening often. * *vi* to visit often; to resort to.—**frequently** *adv*.

fresco *n* (*pl* **frescos, frescoes**) a picture painted on walls covered with damp freshly laid plaster.

fresh *adj* recently made, grown, etc; not salted, pickled, etc; not spoiled; lively, not tired; not worn, soiled, faded, etc; new, recent; inexperienced; cool and refreshing; (*wind*) brisk; (*water*) not salt; (*inf*) presumptuous, impertinent.—**freshly** *adv*.—**freshness** *n*.

freshen *vi* to make or become fresh.—**freshener** *n*.

freshwater *adj* of a river; not sea-going.

fret[1] *vti* (*pt* **fretted**) to make or become worried or anxious; to wear away or roughen by rubbing.

fret[2] *n* a running design of interlacing small bars. * *vt* (*pt* **fretted**) to furnish with frets.

fret[3] *n* any of a series of metal ridges along the finger-board of a guitar, banjo, etc used as a guide for depressing the strings.

friar *n* a member of certain Roman Catholic religious orders.

friction *n* a rubbing of one object against another; conflict between differing opinions, ideas, etc; the resistance to motion of things that touch.—**frictional** *adj*.

Friday *n* the sixth day of the week.

fridge *n* (*inf*) a refrigerator.

fried *see* **fry**[1].

friend *n* a person whom one knows well and is fond of; an ally, supporter—**friendless** *adj*.—**friendship** *n*.

friendly *adj* (**friendlier, friendliest**) like a friend; kindly; favourable. * *n* a sporting game played for fun, not in competition.—**friendliness** *n*.

frieze *n* a decorative band along the top of the wall of a room.

frigate *n* a warship smaller than a destroyer used for escort, anti-submarine, and patrol duties.

fright *n* sudden fear; a shock; (*inf*) something unsightly or ridiculous in appearance.

frighten *vt* to terrify, to scare; to force by frightening.

frightful *adj* terrible, shocking; (*inf*) extreme, very bad.—**frightfully** *adv*.

frigid *adj* extremely cold; not warm or friendly; unresponsive sexually.—**frigidly** *adv*.—**frigidity** *n*.

frill *n* a piece of pleated or gathered fabric used for edging; something superfluous, an affectation. * *vt* to decorate with a frill or frills.—**frilled** *adj*.—**frilly** *adj*.

fringe *n* a decorative border of hanging threads; hair hanging over the forehead; an outer edge; a marginal or minor part. * *vt* to be or make a fringe for. * *adj* at the outer edge; additional; minor; unconventional.

frisk *vi* to leap playfully. * *vt* (*inf*) to search (a person) by feeling for concealed weapons, etc.

frisky *adj* (**friskier, friskiest**) lively, playful.—**friskiness** *n*.

fritter[1] *n* a slice of fruit or meat fried in batter.

fritter[2] *vt* (*with* **away**) to waste; to break into tiny pieces.

frivolity *n* a trifling act, thought, or action.

frivolous *adj* irresponsible; trifling; silly.—**frivolously** *adv*.

fro *adv* away from; backward.

frock *n* a dress.

frog *n* a small tailless web-footed jumping amphibian; a decorative loop used to fasten clothing; (*offensive*) a French person.

frogman *n* a person who wears rubber suit, flippers, oxygen supply, etc and is trained in working underwater.

frolic *n* a lively party or game; merriment, fun. * *vi* (*pt* **frolicked**) to play happily.

from *prep* beginning at, starting with; out of; originating with; out of the possibility or use of.

front *n* outward behaviour; (*inf*) an appearance of social standing; etc; the part facing forward; the first part; a forward or leading position; the promenade of a seaside resort; the advanced battle area in warfare; a person or group used to hide another's activity; an advancing mass of cold or warm air. * *adj* at, to, in, on, or of the front. * *vti* to face; to serve as a front (for).

frontal *adj* of or belonging to the front; of or pertaining to the forehead. * *n* a decorative covering for the front of an altar.

frontier *n* the border between two countries; the limit of existing knowledge of a subject.

frost *n* temperature at or below freezing point; a coating of powdery ice particles; coldness of manner. * *vt* to cover (as if) with frost or frosting; to give a frost-like opaque surface to (glass).

frostbite *n* injury to a part of the body by exposure to cold.

frosting *n* icing.

frosty *adj* (**frostier, frostiest**) cold with frost; cold or reserved in manner.—**frostily** *adv*.—**frostiness** *n*.

froth *n* foam; foaming saliva; frivolity. —*also vi*.—**frothily** *adv*.—**frothy** *adj*.

frown *vi* to contract the brow as in anger or thought; (*with* **upon**) to regard with displeasure or disapproval.—*also n*.

froze, frozen *see* **freeze**.

frugal *adj* economical, thrifty; inexpensive, meagre.—**frugally** *adv*.—**frugality** *n*.

fruit *n* the seed-bearing part of any plant; the fleshy part of this used as food; the result or product of any action. * *vti* to bear or cause to bear fruit.

fruitful *adj* producing lots of fruit; productive.—**fruitfulness** *n*.

fruition *n* a coming to fulfilment, realization.

fruit machine *n* a coin-operated gambling machine, using symbols of fruit to indicate a winning combination.

frustrate *vt* to prevent from achieving a goal or gratifying a desire; to discourage, to irritate, to tire.—**frustration** *n*.

fry[1] *vti* (*pt* **fried**) to cook over direct heat in hot fat. * *n* a dish of things fried.

fry[2] *n* recently hatched fishes.

f-stop *see* **stop**.

ft. *abbr* = foot or feet.

fuchsia *n* any of a genus of decorative shrubs.

fudge *n* a soft sweet made of butter, milk, sugar, flavouring, etc. * *vi* to refuse to commit oneself; to cheat. * *vt* to fake; to fail to come to grips with.

fuel *n* material burned to supply heat and power, or as a source of nuclear energy; anything that serves to intensify strong feelings. * *vti* (*pt* **fuelled**) to supply with fuel.

fugitive *n* a person who flees. * *adj* fleeing, as from danger or justice; fleeting, transient.

fugue *n* a polyphonic musical composition with its theme taken up successively by different voices.—**fugal** *adj*.

fulfil, fulfill (*US*) *vt* (*pt* **fulfilled**) to carry out (a promise, etc); to achieve the completion of; to satisfy; to bring to an end, complete.—**fulfilment** *n*.

full *adj* having or holding all that can be contained; having eaten all one wants; having a great number (of); complete; having reached to greatest size, extent, etc. * *n* the greatest amount, extent etc. * *adv* completely, directly, exactly.

fullback *n* (*football, rugby, hockey, etc*) one of the defensive players at the back; the position held by this player.

full-stop *n* the punctuation mark (.) at the end of a sentence.—*also* **period**.

full time *n* the finish of a match.

full-time *adj* working or lasting the whole time.—**full-timer** *n*.

fully *adv* thoroughly; at least.

fumble *vi* to grope about. * *vt* to handle clumsily; to say or act awkwardly; to fail to catch (a ball) cleanly.—*also n*.

fume *n* (*usu pl*) smoke, gas or vapour, esp if offensive or suffocating. * *vi* to give off fumes; to express anger.

fumigate *vt* to disinfect or exterminate (pests, etc) using fumes.—**fumigation** *n*.

fun *n* (what provides) amusement and enjoyment.

function *n* the activity characteristic of a person or thing; the specific purpose of a certain person or thing; an official ceremony or social entertainment. * *vi* to perform a function; to act, operate.

functional *adj* of a function or functions; practical, not ornamental.

fund *n* a supply that can be drawn upon; a sum of money set aside for a purpose; (*pl*) ready money. * *vt* to provide funds for.

fundamental *adj* basic; essential. * *n* that which serves as a groundwork; an essential.—**fundamentally** *adv*.

funeral *n* the ceremony associated with the burial or cremation of the dead; a procession accompanying a coffin to a burial.

fungus *n* (*pl* **fungi, funguses**) any of a major group of lower plants, as mildews, mushrooms, yeasts, etc, that lack chlorophyll and reproduce by spores.—**fungal** *adj*.

funnel *n* an implement, usually a cone with a wide top and tapering to a narrow tube, for pouring fluids, powders, into bottles, etc; a metal chimney for the escape of smoke, steam, etc. * *vti* (*pt* **funnelled**) to (cause) to pour through a funnel.

funny *adj* (**funnier, funniest**) causing laughter; puzzling, odd; (*inf*) unwell, queasy.—**funnily** *adv*.—**funniness** *n*.

fur *n* the short, soft, fine hair on the bodies of certain animals; their skins with the fur attached; a garment made of fur; a fabric made in imitation of fur; a fur-like coating, as on the tongue. * *vti* (*pt* **furred**) to cover or become covered with fur.

furious *adj* full of anger; intense, violent.—**furiously** *adv*.

furlong *n* 220 yards, one-eighth of a mile.

furlough *n* leave of absence from duty, esp for military personnel. * *vt* to grant a furlough to.

furnace *n* an enclosed chamber in which heat is produced to burn refuse, smelt ore, etc.

furnish *vt* to provide (a room, etc) with furniture; to equip with what is necessary; to supply.

furnishings *npl* furniture, carpets, etc.

furniture *n* the things in a room, etc that equip it for living, as chairs, etc.

furrow *n* the groove in the earth made by a plough; a groove or track resembling this; a wrinkle. * *vti* to make furrows in; to wrinkle.

furry *adj* (**furrier, furriest**) like, made of, or covered with, fur.

further *adv* at or to a greater distance or degree; in addition. * *adj* more distant, remote; additional. * *vt* to help forward, promote.

furthermore *adv* moreover, besides.

furthest *adj* at or to the greatest distance.

furtive *adj* stealthy; sly.—**furtively** *adv*. —**furtiveness** *n*.

fury *n* intense rage; a frenzy; a violently angry person.

fuse *vti* to join or become joined by melting; to (cause to) melt by the application of heat; to equip a plug, circuit, etc with a fuse; to (cause to) fail by blowing a fuse. * *n* a tube or wick filled with combustible material for setting off an explosive charge; a piece of thin wire that melts and breaks when an electric current exceeds a certain level.

fuselage *n* the body of an aircraft.

fusible *adj* able to be fused.—**fusibly** *adv*.

fusion *n* the act of melting, blending or fusing; a product of fusion; union, partnership; nuclear fusion.

fuss *n* excited activity, bustle; a nervous state; (*inf*) a quarrel; (*inf*) a showy display of approval. * *vi* to worry over trifles; to whine, as a baby.—**fusser** *n*.

fussy *adj* (**fussier, fussiest**) worrying over details; hard to please; fastidious; over-elaborate.—**fussily** *adv*.—**fussiness** *n*.

futile *adj* useless; ineffective.—**futility** *n*.

future *adj* that is to be; of or referring to time yet to come. * *n* the time to come; future events; likelihood of eventual success.

futuristic *adj* forward-looking in design, appearance, intention, etc.

fuzzy *adj* (**fuzzier, fuzziest**) like fuzz; fluffy; blurred.—**fuzzily** *adv*.—**fuzziness** *n*.

G

g *abbr* = gallons(s); gram(s); gravity; acceleration due to gravity.

gabble *vti* to talk or utter rapidly or incoherently; to utter inarticulate or animal sounds.—**gabbler** *n*.

gable *n* the triangular upper part of a wall enclosed by the sloping ends of a pitched roof.—**gabled** *adj*.

gadget *n* a small, often ingenious, mechanical or electronic tool or device.

gag *n* something put over or into the mouth to prevent talking; any restraint of free speech; a joke. * *vb* (*pt* **gagged**) *vt* to cause to retch; to keep from speaking, as by stopping the mouth of. * *vi* to retch; to tell jokes.

gaiety *n* happiness, liveliness; colourful appearance.

gaily *adv* in a cheerful manner; with bright colours.

gain *vt* to obtain, earn, esp by effort; to win in a contest; to attract; to get as an addition (esp profit or advantage); to make an increase in; to reach. * *vi* to make progress; to increase in weight. * *n* an increase esp in profit or advantage; an acquisition.

gainful *adj* profitable.—**gainfully** *adv*.

gainsay *vt* (*pt* **gainsaid**) (*formal*) to dispute; to deny.

gait *n* a manner of walking or running; the sequence of footsteps made by a moving horse.

gala *n* a celebration, festival.

galaxy *n* any of the systems of stars in the universe; any splendid assemblage; (*with cap*) the galaxy containing the Earth's solar system; the Milky Way.

gale *n* a strong wind, specifically one between 39 to 46 mph; an outburst.

gallant *adj* dignified, stately; brave; noble; (*man*) polite and chivalrous to women.—**gallantly** *adv*.—**gallantry** *n*.

gall bladder *n* a membranous sac attached to the liver in which bile is stored.

gallery *n* a covered passage for walking; a long narrow outside balcony; a balcony running along the inside wall of a building; (the occupants of) an upper area of seating in a theatre; a long narrow room used for a special purpose, eg shooting practice; a room or building designed for the exhibition of works of art; the spectators at a golf tournament, tennis match, etc.

galley *n* a long, usu low, ship of ancient or medieval times, propelled by oars; the kitchen of a ship, aircraft; (*print*) a shallow tray for holding type; proofs printed from such type (—*also* **galley proof**).

gallon *n* a unit of liquid measure comprising 277.42 cubic inches (in US, 231 cubic inches); (*pl*) (*inf*) a large amount.

gallop *n* the fastest gait of a horse, etc; a succession of leaping strides; a fast pace. * *vti* to go or cause to go at a gallop; to move swiftly.

gallows *n* (*pl* **gallowses, gallows**) a wooden frame used for hanging criminals.

gallstone *n* a small solid mass in the gall bladder.

gambit *n* (*chess*) an opening in which a piece is sacrificed to gain an advantage; any action to gain an advantage.

gamble *vi* to play games of chance for money; to take a risk for some advantage. * *vt* to risk in gambling, to bet. * *n* a risky venture; a bet.—**gambler** *n*.

game[1] *n* any form of play, amusement; activity or sport involving competition; a scheme, a plan; wild birds or animals hunted for sport or food, the flesh of such animals. * *vi* to play for a stake. * *adj* (*inf*) brave, resolute; (*inf*) willing.—**gamely** *adv*.—**gameness** *n*.

game[2] *adj* (*limbs*) injured, crippled.

gamekeeper *n* a person who breeds and takes care of game birds and animals, as on an estate.

gammon *n* cured or smoked ham; meat from the hindquarters of a side of bacon.

gander *n* an adult male goose; (*inf*) a quick look.

gang *n* a group of persons, esp labourers, working together; a group of persons acting or associating together, esp for illegal purposes. * *vti* to form into or act as a gang.

gangrene *n* death of body tissue when the blood supply is obstructed.—**gangrenous** *adj*.

gangster *n* a member of a criminal gang.

gangway *n* a passageway, esp an opening in a ship's side for loading, etc; a gangplank.

gaol, gaoler *see* **jail, jailer**.

gap *n* a break or opening in something, as a wall or fence; an interruption in continuity, an interval; a mountain pass; a divergence, disparity. * *vt* (*pt* **gapped**) to make a gap in.—**gappy** *adj*.

gape *vi* to open the mouth wide; to stare in astonishment, esp with the mouth open; to open widely. * *n* the act of gaping; a wide opening.

garage *n* an enclosed shelter for motor vehicles; a place where motor vehicles are repaired and serviced, and fuel sold. * *vt* to put or keep in a garage.

garbage *n* food waste; unwanted or useless material; rubbish.

garden *n* an area of ground for growing herbs, fruits, flowers, or vegetables, usu attached to a house; a fertile, well-cultivated region; a public park or recreation area, usu laid-out with plants and trees. * *vi* to make, or work in, a garden.—**gardener** *n*.—**gardening** *n*.

gargle *vti* to rinse the throat by breathing air from the lungs through liquid held in the mouth. * *n* a liquid for this purpose; the sound made by gargling.

gargoyle *n* a grotesquely carved face or figure, usu acting as a spout to drain water from a gutter; a person with an ugly face.

garish *adj* crudely bright, gaudy.—**garishly** *adv*.

garland *n* a wreath of flowers or leaves worn or hung as decoration. * *vt* to decorate with a garland.

garlic *n* a bulbous herb cultivated for its compound bulbs used in cookery; its bulb.—**garlicky** *adj*.

garment *n* an item of clothing.

garnish *vt* to decorate; to decorate (food) with something that adds colour or flavour. * *n* something used to garnish food.—**garniture** *n*.

garret *n* an attic.

garrison *n* troops stationed at a fort; a fortified place with troops. * *vt* to station (troops) in (a fortified place) for its defence.

garrulous *adj* excessively talkative. —**garrulity** *n*. —**garrulous** *adv*.—**garrulousness** *n*.

garter *n* an elasticated band used to support a stocking or sock.

gas *n* (*pl* **gases**) an air-like substance with the capacity to expand indefinitely and not liquefy or solidify at ordinary temperatures; any mixture of flammable gases used for lighting or heating; any gas used as an anaesthetic; any poisonous substance dispersed in the air, as in war; (*inf*) empty talk; gasoline. * *vt* (*pt* **gassed**) to poison or disable with gas; (*inf*) to talk idly.

gash *n* a long, deep, open cut.—*also vt*.

gasket *n* a piece or ring of rubber, metal, etc sandwiched between metal surfaces to act as a seal.

gas mask *n* a protective breathing device worn over the face, which filters out poisonous gases.

gasoline, gasolene *n* petrol.

gasp *vi* to draw in the breath suddenly and audibly, as from shock; to struggle to catch the breath. * *vt* to utter breathlessly. * *n* the act of gasping.

gastric *adj* of, in, or near the stomach.

gastronomy *n* the art and science of good eating.—**gastronomic** *adj*.

gate *n* a movable structure controlling passage through an opening in a fence or wall; a gateway; a movable barrier; a structure controlling the flow of water, as in a canal; a device (as in a computer) that outputs a signal when specified input conditions are met; the total amount or number of paid admissions to a football match, etc. * *vt* to supply with a gate; to keep within the gates (of a university) as a punishment.

gate-crasher *n* a person who attends a party, etc without being invited.—**gatecrash** *vi*.

gateway *n* an opening for a gate; a means of entrance or exit.

gather *vt* to bring together in one place or group; to get gradually; to collect (as taxes); to harvest; to draw (parts) together; to pucker fabric by pulling a thread or stitching; to understand, infer. * *vi* to come together in a body; to cluster around a focus of attention; (*sore*) to swell and fill with pus.

gathering *n* the act of gathering or assembling together; an assembly; folds made in a garment by gathering.

gauche *adj* socially inept; graceless, tactless.—**gauchely** *adv*.

gaudy *adj* (**gaudier, gaudiest**) excessively ornamented; tastelessly bright. —**gaudily** *adv*.—**gaudiness** *n*.

gauge, gage (*US*) *n* measurement according to some standard or system; any device for measuring; the distance between rails of a railway; the size of the bore of a shotgun; the thickness of sheet metal, wire, etc. * *vt* to measure the size, amount, etc, of.—**gaugeable** *adj*.—**gauger** *n*.

gaunt *adj* excessively thin as from hunger or age; looking grim or forbidding.—**gauntness** *n*.

gauntlet[1] *n* a knight's armoured glove; a long glove, often with a flaring cuff.

gauntlet[2] *n* (*formerly*) a type of military punishment in which a victim was forced to run between two lines of men who struck him as he passed.

gauze *n* any very thin, loosely woven fabric, as of cotton or silk; a firm woven material of metal or plastic filaments; a surgical dressing.—**gauzy** *adj*.—**gauzily** *adv*.

gave *see* **give**.

gawp *vi* (*inf*) to stare stupidly.

gay *adj* joyous and lively; colourful; homosexual.—**gayness** *n*.

gaze *vi* to look steadily. * *n* a steady look.

gazelle *n* any of numerous small swift Asian or African antelopes.

gazump *vti* to force up a price (esp of a house) after a price has been agreed. —**gazumper** *n*.

GB *abbr* = Great Britain.

GCE *abbr* = General Certificate of Education.

gear *n* clothing; equipment, esp for some task or activity; a toothed wheel for meshing with another; (*often pl*) a system of such gears meshed to transmit motion; a specific adjustment of such a system; a part of a mechanism with a specific function. * *vt* to connect by or furnish with gears; to adapt (one thing) to conform with another.

gearbox *n* a metal case enclosing a system of gears.

gear lever *n* a lever used to engage or change gear, esp in a motor vehicle.

geese *see* **goose**.

gelatin, gelatine *n* a tasteless, odourless substance extracted by boiling bones, hoofs, etc and used in food, photographic film, medicines, etc.

gelignite *n* an explosive consisting of nitroglycerin absorbed in a base of wood pulp mixed with sodium or potassium nitrate.

gem *n* a precious stone, esp when cut and polished for use as a jewel; a person or thing regarded as extremely valuable or beloved.

Gemini *n* the third sign of the zodiac, represented by the twins Castor and Pollux, operative 21 May-20 June.

gender *n* the classification by which words are grouped as feminine, masculine, or neuter; (*inf*) the sex of a person.

general *adj* not local, special, or specialized; of or for a whole genus, relating to or covering all instances or individuals of a class or group; widespread, common to many; not specific or precise; holding superior rank, chief. * *n* something that involves or is applicable to the whole; a commissioned officer above a lieutenant general; a leader, commander; the title of the head of some religious orders.

general election *n* a national election to choose parliamentary representatives in every constituency.

generalize *vti* to form general conclusions from specific instances; to talk (about something) in general terms.—**generalization** *n*.

generally *adv* widely; popularly; usually; not specifically.

general practitioner *n* a non-specialist doctor who treats all types of illnesses in the community.

generate *vt* to bring into existence; to produce.

generation *n* the act or process of generating; a single succession in natural descent; people of the same period; production, as of electric current.

generator *n* one who or that which generates; a machine that changes mechanical energy to electrical energy.

generosity *n* the quality of being generous; liberality; munificence.

generous *adj* magnanimous; of a noble nature; willing to give or share; large, ample.—**generously** *adv*.

genetic *adj* of or relating to the origin, development or causes of something; of or relating to genes or genetics.—**genetically** *adv*.

genial *adj* kindly, sympathetic and cheerful in manner; mild, pleasantly warm.—**genially** *adv*.—**geniality** *n*.

genitals, genitalia *npl* the (external) sexual organs.

genitive *adj* (*gram*) of or belonging to the case of nouns, pronouns and adjectives expressing ownership or relation. * *n* the genitive case.

genius *n* (*pl* **geniuses**) a person possessing extraordinary intellectual power; (*with* **for**) natural ability.

gent *n* (*inf*) a gentleman.

genteel *adj* polite or well-bred; affectedly refined.—**genteelly** *adv*.

gentle *adj* belonging to a family of high social station; refined, courteous; generous; kind; kindly; patient; not harsh or rough.—**gently** *adv*.

gentleman *n* a man of good family and social standing; a courteous, gracious and honourable man; a polite term of address.—**gentlemanly** *adj*.

gentry *n* people of high social standing; (*formerly*) landed proprietors not belonging to the nobility.

genuine *adj* not fake or artificial, real; sincere.—**genuinely** *adv*.—**genuineness** *n*.

geography *n* the science of the physical nature of the earth, such as land and sea masses, climate, vegetation, etc, and their interaction with the human population; the physical features of a region.—**geographer** *n*.—**geographic, geographical** *adj*.—**geographically** *adv*.

geology *n* the science relating to the history and structure of the earth's crust, its rocks and fossils.—**geologist** *n*.—**geological** *adj*.—**geologically** *adv*.

geometry *n* the branch of mathematics dealing with the properties, measurement, and relationships of points, lines, planes, and solids.—**geometric, geometrical** *adj*.—**geometrically** *adv*.

geranium *n* a garden plant with red, pink or white flowers.

germ *n* a simple form of living matter capable of growth and development into an organism; any microscopic, disease-causing organism; an origin or foundation capable of growing and developing.

German *adj* of or relating to Germany, its people or their language. * *n* a native of Germany.

German measles *n* (*used as sing*) a mild contagious disease similar to measles.—*also* **rubella**.

germinate *vti* to start developing; to sprout, as from a seed.—**germination** *n*.—**germinator** *n*.

gestate *vt* to carry (young) in the womb during pregnancy; to develop (a plan, etc) gradually in the mind. —**gestation** *n*.

gesticulate *vi* to make expressive gestures, esp when speaking.—**gesticulation** *n*.

gesture *n* movement of part of the body to express or emphasize ideas, emotions, etc. * *vi* to make a gesture. —**gestural** *adj*.

get *vb* (*pr p* **getting,** *pt* **got**, *pp* **got** *or* **gotten**) *vt* to obtain, gain, win; to receive; to acquire; to go and bring; to catch; to persuade; to cause to be; to prepare; (*inf*) (*with* **have** *or* **has**) to be obliged to; to possess; (*inf*) to strike, kill, baffle; defeat, etc; (*inf*) to understand; (*with* **out of**) to avoid doing; (*with* **over**) to communicate effectively. * *vi* to come; to go; to arrive; to come to be; to manage or contrive; (*with* **at**) to reach; (*inf*) to imply; (*inf*) to criticize; (*inf*) to corrupt, bribe; (*with* **away**) to escape; (*with* **by**) (*inf*) to manage, to survive; (*with* **off**) to come off, down, or out of; to be acquitted; to depart; (*with* **on**) to go on or into; to put on; to proceed; to grow older; to manage; to succeed; (*with* **on with**) to establish a friendly relationship; (*with* **out**) to go out or away; to take out; to disclose, publish; (*with* **over**) to recover from; to forget; (*with* **through**) to finish; to manage to survive; to succeed; (*with* **up**) to rise to one's feet; to get out of bed; (*inf*) to organize; (*inf*) to dress in a certain style; (*inf*) to be involved in (mischief, etc).

getaway *n* the act of escaping; a start in a race, etc.

get-together *n* (*inf*) an informal social gathering or meeting.

get-up *n* (*inf*) dress, costume.

geyser *n* a natural spring from which columns of boiling water and steam gush into the air at intervals; a water heater.

ghastly *adj* (**ghastlier, ghastliest**) terrifying, horrible; (*inf*) intensely disagreeable; pale, unwell looking.—**ghastliness** *n*.

gherkin *n* a small cucumber used for pickling.

ghetto *n* (*pl* **ghettos**) a section of a city in which members of a minority group live, esp because of social, legal or economic pressure.

ghost *n* the supposed disembodied spirit of a dead person, appearing as a shadowy apparition; a faint trace or suggestion; a false image in a photographic negative.—**ghostly** *adj*.—**ghostliness** *n*.

giant *n* a huge legendary being of great strength; a person or thing of great size, strength, intellect, etc. * *adj* incredibly large.—**giantess** *nf*.

gibberish *n* unintelligible talk, nonsense.

gibe *n* a taunt, sneer. * *vti* to jeer, scoff (at).—*also* **jibe**.

giblets *npl* the edible internal organs of a bird.

giddy *adj* (**giddier, giddiest**) frivolous, flighty; having a feeling of whirling around as if about to lose balance and fall; causing giddiness.—**giddily** *adv*.—**giddiness** *n*.

gift *n* something given; the act of giving; a natural ability. * *vt* to present with or as a gift.

gifted *adj* having great natural ability.

gigantic *adj* exceedingly large.—**gigantically** *adv*.

giggle *vi* to laugh in a nervous or silly manner. * *n* a laugh in this manner; (*inf*) a prank, a joke.—**giggler** *n*.

gild *vt* (*pt* **gilded** *or* **gilt**) to coat with gold leaf; to give a deceptively attractive appearance to.—**gilder** *n*—**gilding** *n*.

gill[1] *n* an organ, esp in fish, for breathing in water.

gill[2] *n* a liquid measure equal to a quarter of a pint.

gills *npl* the fold of skin below the beak of certain birds; one of the radiating plates under the cap of a mushroom; a person's cheeks or jowls.

gilt[1] *see* **gild**.

gilt[2] *n* gilding; a substance used for this.

gimlet *n* a small tool with a screw point for boring holes.

gimmick *n* a trick or device for attracting notice, advertising or promoting a person, product or service. —**gimmickry** *n*.—**gimmicky** *adj*.

gin[1] *n* an alcoholic spirit distilled from grain and flavoured with juniper berries.

gin[2] *n* a trap for catching small animals; a type of crane; a machine for separating seeds from raw cotton.

ginger *n* a tropical plant with fleshy roots used as a flavouring; spice prepared by drying and grinding; (*inf*) vigour; a reddish-brown.—**gingery** *adj*.

ginger ale, ginger beer *n* a carbonated soft drink flavoured with ginger.

gingerbread *n* a cake flavoured with ginger.

gingerly *adv* with care or caution. * *adj* cautious.

gingham *n* a cotton fabric with stripes or checks.

gipsy *see* **gypsy**.

giraffe *n* a large cud-chewing mammal of Africa, with very long legs and neck.

girder *n* a large steel beam for supporting joists, the framework of a building, etc.

girdle *n* a belt for the waist.

girl *n* a female child; a young woman; (*inf*) a woman of any age.—**girlhood** *n*.—**girlish** *adj*.

girlfriend *n* a female friend, esp with whom one is romantically involved.

girth *n* the thickness round something; a band put around the belly of a horse, etc to hold a saddle or pack.

gist *n* the principal point or essence of anything.

give *vb* (*pt* **gave**, *pp* **given**) *vt* to hand over as a present; to deliver; to hand over in or for payment; to pass (regards etc) along; to act as host or sponsor of; to supply; to yield; (*advice*) to offer; (*punishment, etc*) to inflict; to sacrifice; to perform; (*with* **away**) to make a gift of; to give (the bride) to the bridegroom; to sell cheaply; to reveal, betray; (*with* **in**) to deliver (a document, etc); (*with* **off**) to emit (fumes, etc); (*with* **out**) to discharge; to make public; to distribute; (*with* **over**) to devote time to a specific activity; to cease (an activity); (*with* **up**) to hand over; to renounce; to cease; to stop trying; to despair of; to devote wholly. * *vi* to bend, move, etc from force or pressure; (*inf*) to be happening. * *n* capacity or tendency to yield to force or strain; the quality or state of being springy; (*with* **in**) to submit; (*with* **out**) to become worn out; (*with* **up**) to surrender.

give-away *n* (*inf*) an unintentional revelation.

glacier *n* a large mass of snow and ice moving slowly down a mountain.

glad *adj* (**gladder, gladdest**) happy; causing joy; very willing; bright.—**gladly** *adv*.—**gladness** *n*.

gladden *vti* to make or become glad.

gladiator *n* (*ancient Rome*) a person trained to fight with men or beasts in a public arena.—**gladiatorial** *adj*.

glamour, glamor (*US*) *n* charm, allure; attractiveness, beauty.—**glamorous** *adj*.—**glamorously** *adv*.

glance *vi* to strike obliquely and go off at an angle; to flash; to look quickly. * *n* a glancing off; a flash; a quick look. —**glancingly** *adv*.

gland *n* an organ that separates substances from the blood and synthesizes them for further use in, or for elimination from, the body.—**glandular** *adj*.

glare *n* a harsh uncomfortably bright light, esp painfully bright sunlight; an angry or fierce stare. * *vi* to shine with a steady, dazzling light; to stare fiercely.

glass *n* a hard brittle substance, usu transparent; glassware; a glass article, as a drinking vessel; (*pl*) spectacles or binoculars; the amount held by a drinking glass. * *adj* of or made of glass. * *vt* to equip, enclose, or cover with glass.

glasshouse *n* a large greenhouse for the commercial cultivation of plants; (*inf*) a military prison.

glassware *n* objects made of glass, esp drinking vessels.

glassy *adj* (**glassier, glassiest**) resembling glass; smooth; expressionless, lifeless.—**glassily** *adv*.—**glassiness** *n*.

glaze *vt* to provide (windows etc) with glass; to give a hard glossy finish to (pottery, etc); to cover (foods, etc) with a glossy surface. * *vi* to become glassy or glossy. * *n* a glassy finish or coating.—**glazer** *n*.

glazier *n* a person who fits glass in windows.—**glaziery** *n*.

gleam *n* a subdued or moderate beam of light; a brief show of some quality or emotion, esp hope. * *vi* to emit or reflect a beam of light.

glee *n* joy and gaiety; delight; (*mus*) a song in parts for three or more male voices.—**gleeful** *adj*.—**gleefully** *adv*.

glen *n* a narrow valley.

glib *adj* (**glibber, glibbest**) speaking or spoken smoothly, to the point of insincerity; lacking depth and substance.—**glibly** *adv*.—**glibness** *n*.

glide *vti* to move smoothly and effortlessly; to descend in an aircraft or glider with little or no engine power. * *n* a gliding movement.

glider *n* an engineless aircraft carried along by air currents.

gliding *n* the sport of flying gliders.

glimmer *vi* to give a faint, flickering light; to appear faintly.—*also n*.

glimpse *n* a brief, momentary view. * *vt* to catch a glimpse of.

glint *n* a brief flash of light; a brief indication. * *vti* to (cause to) gleam brightly.

glisten *vi* to shine, as light reflected from a wet surface.

glitter *vi* to sparkle; (*usu with* **with**) to be brilliantly attractive. * *n* a sparkle; showiness, glamour; tiny pieces of sparkling material used for decoration.—**glittery** *adj*.

gloaming *n* twilight.

gloat *vi* to gaze or contemplate with wicked or malicious satisfaction.

global *adj* worldwide; comprehensive.—**globally** *adv*.

globe *n* anything spherical or almost spherical; the earth, or a model of it.

gloom *n* near darkness; deep sadness. * *vti* to

look sullen or dejected; to make or become cloudy or murky.

gloomy *adj* (**gloomier, gloomiest**) almost dark, obscure; depressed, dejected.—**gloomily** *adv*.—**gloominess** *n*.

glorify *vt* to worship; to praise, to honour; to cause to appear more worthy, important, or splendid than in reality.—**glorification** *n*.

glorious *adj* having or deserving glory; conferring glory or renown; beautiful; delightful.—**gloriously** *adv*.

glory *n* great honour or fame, or its source; adoration; great splendour or beauty; heavenly bliss. * *vi* (*with* **in**) to exult, rejoice proudly.

gloss[1] *n* the lustre of a polished surface; a superficially attractive appearance. * *vt* to give a shiny surface to; (*with* **over**) to hide (an error, etc) or make seem right or inconsequential.

gloss[2] *n* an explanation of an unusual word (in the margin or between the lines of a text); a misleading explanation; a glossary. * *vt* to provide with glosses; to give a misleading sense of.

glossary *n* a list of specialized or technical words and their definitions.

glossy *adj* (**glossier, glossiest**) having a shiny or highly polished surface; superficial; (*magazines*) lavishly produced.—**glossily** *adv*.—**glossiness** *n*.

glove *n* a covering for the hand; a baseball player's mitt; a boxing glove. * *vt* to cover (as if) with a glove.

glow *vi* to shine (as if) with an intense heat; to emit a steady light without flames; to be full of life and enthusiasm; to flush or redden with emotion. * *n* a light emitted due to intense heat; a steady, even light without flames; a reddening of the complexion; warmth of emotion or feeling.

glower *vi* to scowl; to stare sullenly or angrily.—*also n*.—**gloweringly** *adv*.

glucose *n* a crystalline sugar occurring naturally in fruits, honey, etc.

glue *n* a sticky, viscous substance used as an adhesive. * *vt* (*pr p* **gluing,** *pt* **glued**) to join with glue.—**gluey** *adj*.

glum *adj* (**glummer, glummest**) sullen; gloomy.—**glumly** *adv*.—**glumness** *n*.

glut *vt* (*pt* **glutted**) to over-supply (the market). * *n* a surfeit, an excess of supply.

glutton *n* a person who eats and drinks to excess; a person who has a tremendous capacity for something (eg for work).—**gluttonous** *adj*.—**gluttony** *n*.

gm *abbr* = gram(s).

gnarled *adj* (*tree trunks*) full of knots; (*hands*) rough, knobbly; crabby in disposition.

gnat *n* any of various small, two-winged insects that bite or sting.

gnaw *vti* (*pp* **gnawed** *or* **gnawn**) to bite away bit by bit; to torment, as by constant pain.

gnome *n* (*folklore*) a dwarf who dwells in the earth and guards its treasure; a small statue of a gnome used as a garden decoration; a small and ugly person; (*sl*) an international banker or financier.

go[1] *vb* (*pt* **went**, *pp* **gone**) *vi* to move on a course; to proceed; to work properly; to act, sound, as specified; to result; to become; to be accepted or valid; to leave, to depart; to die; to be allotted or sold; to be able to pass (through); to fit (into); to be capable of being divided (into); to belong; (*with* **about**) to handle (a task, etc) efficiently; to undertake (duties, etc); (*sailing*) to change tack; (*with* **off**) to explode; to become stale; to fall asleep; to take place as planned; to cease to like; (*with* **slow**) to work at a slow rate as part of an industrial dispute. * *vt* to travel along; (*inf*) to put up with. * *n* (*pl* **goes**) a success; (*inf*) a try; (*inf*) energy.

go[2] *n* a Japanese board game.

goad *n* a sharp-pointed stick for driving cattle, etc; any stimulus to action. * *vt* to drive (as if) with a goad; to irritate, nag persistently.

go-ahead *n* (*inf*) permission to proceed. * *adj* (*inf*) enterprising, ambitious.

goal *n* the place at which a race, trip, etc is ended; an objective; the place over or into which (the ball) must go to score in some games; the score made.

goalkeeper *n* a player who defends the goal.

goat *n* a mammal related to the sheep that has backward curving horns, a short tail, and usu straight hair; a lecherous man.

gobble *vt* to eat greedily; (*often with* **up**) to take, accept or read eagerly. * *vi* to make a gurgling noise, as a turkey.

go-between *n* a messenger, an intermediary.

goblet *n* a large drinking vessel with a base and stem but without a handle.

goblin *n* an evil or mischievous elf.

god *n* any of various beings conceived of as supernatural and immortal, esp a male deity; an idol; a person or thing deified; (*with cap*) in monotheistic religions, the creator and ruler of the universe.

godchild *n* (*pl* **godchildren**) the child a god-

parent sponsors.
goddess *n* a female god; a lovely woman.
godfather *n* a male godparent; the head of a Mafia crime family or other criminal organization.
god-forsaken *adj* desolate, wretched.
godmother *n* a female godparent.
godparent *n* a person who sponsors a child, as at baptism, taking responsibility for its faith.
godsend *n* anything that comes unexpectedly when needed or desired.
godson *n* a male godchild.
goggle *vi* to stare with bulging eyes. * *npl* large spectacles fitting snugly against the face, to protect the eyes.
going *n* an act or instance of going, a departure; the state of the ground, eg for walking, etc; rate of progress. * *adj* that goes; commonly accepted; thriving; existing.
gold *n* a malleable yellow metallic element used esp for coins and jewellery; a precious metal; money, wealth; a yellow colour. * *adj* of, or like, gold.
golden *adj* made of or relating to gold; bright yellow; priceless; flourishing.
golden rule *n* a guiding principle.
goldfish *n* (*pl* **goldfish**) a small gold-coloured fish of the carp family, kept in ponds and aquariums.
golf *n* an outdoor game in which the player attempts to hit a small ball with clubs around a turfed course into a succession of holes in the smallest number of strokes.—**golfer** *n*.
golf club *n* a club with a wooden or metal head used in golf; a golf association or its premises.
golf course, golf links *n* a tract of land laid out for playing golf.
gondola *n* a long, narrow, black boat used on the canals of Venice; a cabin suspended under an airship or balloon; an enclosed car suspended from a cable used to transport passengers, esp skiers up a mountain; a display structure in a supermarket, etc.
gone[1] *see* **go**[1].
gone[2] *adj* departed; dead; lost; (*inf*) in an excited state; (*inf*) pregnant for a specified period.
gong *n* a disk-shaped percussion instrument struck with a usu padded hammer; (*sl*) a medal. * *vi* to sound a gong.
good *adj* (**better, best**) having the right or proper qualities; beneficial; valid; healthy or sound; virtuous, honourable; enjoyable, pleasant, etc; skilled; considerable. * *n* something good; benefit; something that has economic utility; (*with* **the**) good persons; (*pl*) personal property; commodities; (*pl*) the desired or required articles. * *adv* (*inf*) well; fully.
goodbye *interj* a concluding remark at parting; farewell.—*also n*.
Good Friday *n* the Friday before Easter, commemorating the Crucifixion of Christ.
good-looking *adj* handsome.
goodness *n* the state of being good; the good element in something; kindness; virtue. * *interj* an exclamation of surprise.
goodwill *n* benevolence; willingness; the established custom and reputation of a business.
goose *n* (*pl* **geese**) a large, long-necked, webfooted bird related to swans and ducks; its flesh as food; a female goose as distinguished from a gander; (*inf*) a foolish person.
gooseberry *n* the berry of a shrub related to the currant, used in jams, etc.
goose bumps, goose pimples, goose flesh *n* a roughening of the skin caused usu by cold or fear.
gore[1] *n* (clotted) blood from a wound.
gore[2] *n* a tapering section of material used to shape a garment, sail, etc.
gore[3] *vt* to pierce or wound as with a tusk or horns.
gorge *n* a ravine. * *vt* to swallow greedily; to glut. * *vi* to feed gluttonously.
gorgeous *adj* strikingly attractive; brilliantly coloured; (*inf*) magnificent.—**gorgeously** *adv*.—**gorgeousness** *n*.
gorilla *n* an anthropoid ape of western equatorial Africa related to the chimpanzee but much larger.
gorse *n* a spiny yellow-flowered European shrub.
gory *adj* (**gorier, goriest**) bloodthirsty; causing bloodshed; covered in blood. —**gorily** *adv*.—**goriness** *n*.
go-slow *n* a deliberate slowing of the work rate by employees as a form of industrial action.
gospel *n* the life and teachings of Christ contained in the first four books of the New Testament; (*with cap*) one of these books; anything proclaimed or accepted as the absolute truth.
gossamer *n* very fine cobwebs; any very light and flimsy material. * *adj* light as gossamer.
gossip *n* one who chatters idly about others; such talk. * *vi* to take part in or spread gossip.—**gossipy** *adj*.
got, gotten *see* **get**.
gout *n* a disease causing painful inflammation

of the joints; esp of the great toe.—**gouty** *adj*.

govern *vti* to exercise authority over; to rule, to control; to influence the action of; to determine.

governess *n* a woman employed in a private home to teach children.

government *n* the exercise of authority over a state, organization, etc; a system of ruling, political administration, etc; those who direct the affairs of a state, etc.—**governmental** *adj*.

governor *n* a person appointed to govern a province, etc; the elected head of any state of the US; the director or head of a governing body of an organization or institution; (*sl*) an employer; a mechanical device for automatically controlling the speed of an engine.

gown *n* a loose outer garment, specifically a woman's formal dress, a nightgown, a long, flowing robe worn by clergymen, judges, university teachers, etc; a type of overall worn in the operating room.

GP *abbr* = general practitioner.

grab *vt* (*pt* **grabbed**) to take or grasp suddenly; to obtain unscrupulously; (*inf*) to catch the interest or attention of. * *n* a sudden clutch or attempt to grasp; a mechanical device for grasping and lifting objects.

grace *n* beauty or charm of form, movement, or expression; good will; favour; a delay granted for payment of an obligation; a short prayer of thanks for a meal. * *vt* to decorate; to dignify.

graceful *adj* having beauty of form, movement, or expression.—**gracefully** *adv*.—**gracefulness** *n*.

gracious *adj* having or showing kindness, courtesy, etc; compassionate; polite to supposed inferiors; marked by luxury, ease, etc. * *interj* an expression of surprise.—**graciously** *adv*.—**graciousness** *n*.

gradation *n* a series of systematic steps in rank, degree, etc; arranging in such stages; a single stage in a gradual progression; progressive change.

grade *n* a stage or step in a progression; a degree in a scale of quality, rank, etc; a group of people of the same rank, merit, etc; the degree of slope; a sloping part; a mark or rating in an examination, etc. * *vt* to arrange in grades; to give a grade to; to make level or evenly sloping.

gradient *n* a sloping road or railway; the degree of slope in a road, etc.

gradual *adj* taking place by degrees. —**gradually** *adv*.

graduate *n* a person who has completed a course of study at a school, college, etc; a receptacle marked with figures for measuring contents. * *adj* holding an academic degree or diploma; of or relating to studies beyond the first or bachelor's degree.

graduation *n* graduating or being graduated; the ceremony at which degrees are conferred by a college or university; an arranging or marking in grades or stages.

graft *n* a shoot or bud of one plant inserted into another, where it grows permanently; the transplanting of skin, bone, etc; the getting of money or advantage dishonestly.

grain *n* the seed of any cereal plant, as wheat, corn, etc; cereal plants; a tiny, solid particle, as of salt or sand; a unit of weight, 0.0648 gram; the arrangement of fibres, layers, etc of wood, leather, etc; the markings or texture due to this; natural disposition. * *vt* to form into grains; to paint in imitation of the grain of wood, etc. * *vi* to become granular.

gram, gramme *n* the basic unit of weight in the metric system, equal to one thousandth of a kilogram (one 28th of an ounce).

grammar *n* the study of the forms of words and their arrangement in sentences; a system of rules for speaking and writing a language; a grammar textbook; the use of language in speech or writing judged with regard to correctness of spelling, syntax, etc.

grammatical *adj* conforming to the rules of grammar.—**grammatically** *adv*.

gramophone *n* a record player, esp an old mechanical model with an acoustic horn.

granary *n* a building for storing grain.

grand *adj* higher in rank than others; most important; imposing in size, beauty, extent, etc; distinguished; illustrious; comprehensive; (*inf*) very good; delightful. * *n* a grand piano; (*inf*) a thousand pounds or dollars. —**grandly** *adv*.—**grandness** *n*.

grandchild *n* the child of a person's son or daughter.

granddad *n* (*inf*) grandfather; an old man.

granddaughter *n* the daughter of a person's son or daughter.

grandfather *n* the father of a person's father or mother.

grandiose *adj* having grandeur; imposing; pompous and showy.—**grandiosity** *n*.

grandmother *n* the mother of a person's father or mother.

grand piano *n* a large piano with a horizontal harp-shaped case.

grandson *n* the son of a person's son or daughter.
grandstand *n* the main structure for seating spectators at a sporting event.
granite *n* a hard, igneous rock consisting chiefly of feldspar and quartz; unyielding firmness of endurance.
granny, grannie *n* (*inf*) a grandmother; (*inf*) an old woman.
grant *vt* to consent to; to give or transfer by legal procedure; to admit as true. * *n* the act of granting; a thing granted, esp a gift for a particular purpose; a transfer of property by deed; the instrument by which such a transfer is made.
granule *n* a small grain or particle.
grape *n* a small round, juicy berry, growing in clusters on a vine; a dark purplish red.
grapefruit *n* a large, round, sour citrus fruit with a yellow rind.
graph *n* a diagram representing successive changes in the value of a variable quantity or quantities.—*also vt*.
graphic, graphical *adj* described in realistic detail; pertaining to a graph, lettering, drawing, painting, etc.
grapple *vt* to seize or grip firmly. * *vi* to struggle hand-to-hand with; to deal or contend with. * *n* a grapnel; an act of grappling, a wrestle; a grip.
grasp *vt* to grip, as with the hand; to seize; to understand. * *vi* to try to clutch, seize; (*with* **at**) to take eagerly. * *n* a firm grip; power of seizing and holding; comprehension.
grasping *adj* greedy, avaricious.
grass *n* any of a large family of plants with jointed stems and long narrow leaves including cereals, bamboo, etc; such plants grown as lawn; pasture; (*sl*) marijuana; (*sl*) an informer. * *vi* to cover with grass; (*sl*) to inform, betray.
grasshopper *n* any of a group of plant-eating, winged insects with powerful hind legs for jumping.
grassy *adj* (**grassier, grassiest**) abounding in, covered with, or like, grass.—**grassiness** *n*.
grate[1] *n* a frame of metal bars for holding fuel in a fireplace; a fireplace; a grating.
grate[2] *vt* to grind into particles by scraping; to rub against (an object) or grind (the teeth) together with a harsh sound; to irritate. * *vi* to rub or rasp noisily; to cause irritation.
grateful *adj* appreciative; welcome. —**gratefully** *adv*.—**gratefulness** *n*.
grater *n* a metal implement with a jagged surface for grating food.
gratify *vt* to please; to indulge.—**gratification** *n*.
grating[1] *n* a open framework or lattice of bars placed across an opening.
grating[2] *adj* harsh; irritating.—**gratingly** *adv*.
gratitude *n* a being thankful for favours received.
gratuity *n* money given for a service, a tip.
grave[1] *n* a hole dug in the ground for burying the dead; any place of burial, a tomb.
grave[2] *adj* serious, important; harmful; solemn, sombre; (*sound*) low in pitch. * *n* an accent (ˋ) over a vowel. —**gravely** *adv*.
gravel *n* coarse sand with small rounded stones. * *vt* (*pt* **gravelled**) to cover, spread with gravel.
gravestone *n* a stone marking a grave, usu inscribed with the name and details of the deceased.
graveyard *n* a burial ground, cemetery.
gravitate *vi* to move or tend to move under the force of gravitation.
gravity *n* importance, esp seriousness; weight; the attraction of bodies toward the centre of the earth, the moon, or a planet.
gravy *n* the juice given off by meat in cooking; the sauce made from this juice; (*sl*) money easily obtained.
graze[1] *vi* to feed on growing grass or pasture. * *vt* to put (animals) to feed on growing grass or pasture.
graze[2] *vt* to touch lightly in passing; to scrape, scratch. * *n* an abrasion, esp on the skin, caused by scraping.
grease *n* melted animal fat; any thick, oily substance or lubricant. * *vt* to smear or lubricate with grease.
greasy *adj* (**greasier, greasiest**) covered with grease; full of grease; slippery; oily in manner.—**greasily** *adv*. —**greasiness** *n*.
great *adj* of much more than ordinary size, extent, etc; much above the average; intense; eminent; most important; more distant in a family relationship by one generation; (*often with* **at**) (*inf*) skilful; (*inf*) excellent; fine. * *n* (*inf*) a distinguished person.—**greatly** *adv*.—**greatness** *n*.
greed *n* excessive desire, esp for food or wealth.
greedy *adj* (**greedier, greediest**) wanting more than one needs or deserves; having too strong a desire for food and drink.—**greedily** *adv*.—**greediness** *n*.
Greek *adj* of Greece, its people, or its language. * *n* a native of Greece; the language used by Greeks; (*inf*) something unintelligible.

green *adj* of the colour green; covered with plants or foliage; environmentally conscious; having a sickly appearance; unripe; inexperienced, naive; not fully processed or treated; (*inf*) jealous. * *n* a colour between blue and yellow in the spectrum; the colour of growing grass; something of a green colour; (*pl*) green leafy vegetables, as spinach, etc; a grassy plot, esp the end of a golf fairway.—**greenish** *adj*.—**greeny** *adj*.—**greenly** *adv*.—**greenness** *n*.
greengrocer *n* a dealer in vegetables and fruit.—**greengrocery** *n*.
greenhouse *n* a heated building, mainly of glass, for growing plants.
greet *vt* to address with friendliness; to meet (a person, event, etc) in a specified way; to present itself to.
greeting *n* the act of welcoming with words or gestures; an expression of good wishes; (*pl*) a message of regards.
gregarious *adj* (*animals*) living in flocks and herds; (*people*) sociable, fond of company.—**gregariously** *adv*.
grenade *n* a small bomb thrown manually or projected (as by a rifle or special launcher).
grew *see* **grow**.
grey, gray (*US*) *n* any of a series of neutral colours ranging between black and white; something (as an animal, etc) of a grey colour. * *adj* grey in colour; having grey hair; darkish; dreary; vague, indeterminate.—**greyish** *adj*.—**greyness** *n*.
greyhound *n* any of a breed of tall and slender dogs noted for its great speed and keen sight.
grid *n* a gridiron, a grating; an electrode for controlling the flow of electrons in an electron tube; a network of squares on a map used for easy reference; a national network of transmission lines, pipes, etc for electricity, water, gas, etc.
grief *n* extreme sorrow caused as by a loss; deep distress.
grievance *n* a circumstance thought to be unjust and cause for complaint.
grieve *vti* to feel or cause to feel grief.
grill *vt* to cook by direct heat using a grill or gridiron; (*inf*) to question relentlessly. * *n* a device on a cooker that radiates heat downward for grilling; a gridiron; grilled food; a grille; a grillroom.
grille, grill *n* an open grating forming a screen.
grillroom *n* a restaurant that specializes in grilled food.
grim *adj* (**grimmer, grimmest**) hard and unyielding, stern; appearing harsh, forbidding; repellent, ghastly in character.—**grimly** *adv*.—**grimness** *n*.
grimace *n* a contortion of the face expressing pain, anguish, humour, etc.—*also vi*.
grime *n* soot or dirt, rubbed into a sur-face, as the skin. * *vt* to dirty, soil with grime.—**grimy** *adj*.—**griminess** *n*.
grin *vi* (*pt* **grinned**) to smile broadly as in amusement; to show the teeth in pain, scorn, etc. * *n* a broad smile.
grind *vb* (*pt* **ground**) *vt* to reduce to powder or fragments by crushing; to wear down, sharpen, or smooth by friction; to rub (teeth) harshly together; to oppress, tyrannize; to operate by a crank. * *vi* to be crushed, smoothed, or sharpened by grinding; to jar or grate; to work monotonously; to rotate the hips eroticically. * *n* the act or sound of grinding; hard monotonous work.
grip *n* a secure grasp; the manner of holding a bat, club, racket, etc; the power of grasping firmly; mental grasp; mastery; a handle; a small travelling bag. * *vt* (*pt* **gripped**) to take firmly and hold fast.
gripe *vt* to cause sharp pain in the bowels of; (*sl*) to annoy. * *vi* (*sl*) to complain.
grisly *adj* (**grislier, grisliest**) terrifying; ghastly; arousing horror.
gristle *n* cartilage, esp in meat.—**gristly** *adv*.
grit *n* rough particles, as of sand; firmness of spirit; stubborn courage. * *vt* (*pt* **gritted**) to clench or grind together (eg the teeth); to spread grit on (eg an icy road).
groan *vi* to utter a deep moan; to make a harsh sound (as of creaking) under sudden or prolonged strain.—*also n*.
grocer *n* a dealer in food and household supplies.
groggy *adj* (**groggier, groggiest**) (*inf*) weak and unsteady, usu through illness, exhaustion or alcohol.—**groggily** *adv*.—**grogginess** *n*.
groin *n* the fold marking the junction of the lower abdomen and the thighs; the location of the genitals.
groom *n* one employed to care for horses; a bridegroom. * *vt* to clean and care for (animals); to make neat and tidy; to train (a person) for a purpose.
groove *n* a long, narrow channel; a spiral track in a gramophone record for the stylus; a settled routine. * *vt* to make a groove in.
grope *vi* to search about blindly as in the dark; to search uncertainly for a solution to a problem. * *vt* to find by feeling; (*sl*) to fondle

sexually. * *n* the act of groping.—**gropingly** *adv*.

gross *adj* fat and coarse-looking; flagrant, dense, thick; lacking in refinement; earthy; obscene; total, with no deductions. * *n* (*pl* **grosses**) an overall total; (*pl* **gross**) twelve dozen. * *vt* to earn as total revenue.

grotesque *adj* distorted or fantastic in appearance, shape, etc; ridiculous; absurdly incongruous. * *n* a grotesque person or thing; a decorative device combining distorted plant, animal and human forms.—**grotesquely** *adv*.—**grotesqueness** *n*.

grotto *n* (*pl* **grottoes, grottos**) a cave, esp one with attractive features.

ground *n* the solid surface of the earth; soil; the background, as in design; the connection of an electrical conductor with the earth; (*pl*) a basis for belief, action, or argument; the area about and relating to a building; a tract of land; sediment. * *vti* to set on the ground; to run aground or cause to run aground; to base, found, or establish; to instruct in the first principles of; to prevent (aircraft) from flying.

grounding *n* basic general knowledge of a subject.

groundsheet *n* a waterproof sheet placed on the ground in a tent.

groundwork *n* foundation, basis.

group *n* a number of persons or things considered as a collective unit; a small musical band of players or singers; a number of companies under single ownership; two or more figures forming one artistic design. * *vti* to form into a group or groups.

grouse[1] *n* (*pl* **grouse**) a game bird; its flesh as food.

grouse[2] *vi* (*inf*) to complain.—**grouser** *n*.

grove *n* a small wood, generally without undergrowth.

grovel *vi* (*pt* **grovelled**) to lie and crawl in a prostrate position as a sign of respect, fear or humility. —**groveller** *n*.

grow *vb* (*pt* **grew**, *pp* **grown**) *vi* to come into being; to be produced naturally; to develop, as a living thing; to increase in size, quantity, etc. * *vt* to cause or let grow; to raise, to cultivate. —**growable** *adj*.—**grower** *n*.

growl *vi* to make a rumbling, menacing sound such as an angry dog makes. * *vt* to express in a growling manner. * *n* a growling noise; a grumble.—**growler** *n*.

growth *n* the act or process of growing; progressive increase, development; something that grows or has grown; an abnormal formation of tissue, as a tumour.

grub *vb* (*pt* **grubbed**) *vi* to dig in the ground; to work hard. * *vt* to clear (ground) of roots; to uproot. * *n* the worm-like larva of a beetle; (*sl*) food.

grubby *adj* (**grubbier, grubbiest**) dirty, soiled.—**grubbiness** *n*.

grudge *n* a deep feeling of resentment or ill will. * *vt* to be reluctant to give or admit something.—**grudging** *adj*. —**grudgingly** *adv*.

gruelling, grueling (*US*) *adj* severely testing, exhausting.

gruesome *adj* causing horror or loathing.

gruff *adj* rough or surly; hoarse.—**gruffly** *adv*.—**gruffness** *n*.

grumble *vti* to mutter in discontent; to make a rumbling sound.—*also n*. —**grumbler** *n*.

grumpy *adj* (**grumpier, grumpiest**) bad-tempered, peevish.—**grumpily** *adv*.—**grumpiness** *n*.

grunt *vi* to make a gruff guttural sound like a pig; to say or speak in such a manner.—*also n*.

guarantee *n* a pledge or security for another's debt or obligation; a pledge to replace something substandard, etc; an assurance that something will be done as specified; something offered as a pledge or security; a guarantor. * *vt* to give a guarantee for; to promise.

guarantor *n* a person who gives a guaranty or guarantee.

guard *vt* to watch over and protect; to defend; to keep from escape or trouble; to restrain. * *vi* to keep watch (against); to act as a guard. * *n* defence; protection; a posture of readiness for defence; a device to protect against injury or loss; a person or group that guards; (*boxing, fencing, cricket*) a defensive attitude; an official in charge of a train.

guarded *adj* discreet; cautious.—**guardedly** *adv*.

guardian *n* a custodian; a person legally in charge of a minor or someone incapable of taking care of their own affairs.—**guardianship** *n*.

guerrilla, guerilla *n* a member of a small force of irregular soldiers, making surprise raids.—*also adj*.

guess *vt* to form an opinion of or state with little or no factual knowledge; to judge correctly by doing this; to think or suppose. * *n* an estimate based on guessing.—**guesser** *n*.

guest *n* a person entertained at the home, club,

etc of another; any paying customer of a hotel, restaurant, etc; a performer appearing by special invitation.

guesthouse *n* a private home or boarding-house offering accommodation.

guestroom *n* a room kept for guests.

guffaw *n* a crude noisy laugh.—*also vi.*

guidance *n* leadership; advice or counsel.

guide *vt* to point out the way for; to lead; to direct the course of; to control. * *n* a person who leads or directs others; a person who shows and explains points of interest; something that provides a person with guiding information; a device controlling the motion of something; a book of basic instruction; (*with cap*) a member of the girls' organization equivalent to the Scouts.

guidebook *n* a book containing directions and information for tourists.

guided missile *n* a military missile whose course is controlled by radar or internal instruments, etc.

guide dog *n* a dog trained to guide people who are blind.

guild *n* a club, society; an association of people with common interests formed for mutual aid and protection, as craftsmen in the Middle Ages.

guile *n* craftiness, deceit.—**guileful** *adj.*—**guileless** *adj.*

guillotine *n* an instrument for beheading by a heavy blade descending between grooved posts; a device or machine for cutting paper; a rule for limiting time for discussion in a legislature.—*also vt.*

guilt *n* the fact of having done a wrong or committed an offence; a feeling of self-reproach from believing one has done a wrong.

guiltless *adj* innocent.

guilty *adj* (**guiltier, guiltiest**) having guilt; feeling or showing guilt.—**guiltily** *adv.*—**guiltiness** *n.*

guinea *n* a former English gold coin equal to 21 shillings (£1.05).

guinea pig *n* a rodent-like animal commonly kept as a pet, and often used in scientific experiments; a person or thing subject to an experiment.

guise *n* an external appearance, aspect; an assumed appearance, pretence.

guitar *n* a stringed musical instrument with a long, fretted neck, and a flat body, which is plucked with a plectrum or the fingers.—**guitarist** *n.*

gulf *n* a large area of ocean reaching into land; a wide, deep chasm; a vast separation.

gull *n* any of numerous long-winged web-footed sea birds.

gullet *n* the oesophagus; the throat.

gullible *adj* easily deceived.—**gullibility** *n.*—**gullibly** *adv.*

gully *n* a narrow trench cut by running water after rain; (*cricket*) a fielding position between the slips and point. * *vt* to make gullies in.

gulp *vt* to swallow hastily or greedily; to choke back as if swallowing. * *n* a gulping or swallowing; a mouthful.

gum[1] *n* the firm tissue that surrounds the teeth.

gum[2] *n* a sticky substance found in certain trees and plants; an adhesive; chewing gum. * *vb* (*pt* **gummed**) *vt* to coat or unite with gum. * *vi* to become sticky or clogged.

gumboot *n* a rubber, waterproof boot, a wellington.

gumption *n* (*inf*) shrewd practical common sense; initiative.

gun *n* a weapon with a metal tube from which a projectile is discharged by an explosive; the shooting of a gun as a signal or salute; anything like a gun. * *vb* (*pt* **gunned**) *vi* to shoot or hunt with a gun. * *vt* (*inf*) to shoot (a person); (*sl*) to advance the throttle of an engine.

gunboat *n* a small armed ship.

gunman *n* an armed gangster; a hired killer.

gunner *n* a soldier, etc who helps fire artillery; a naval warrant officer in charge of a ship's guns.

gunpowder *n* an explosive powder used in guns, for blasting, etc.

gurgle *vi* (*liquid*) to make a low bubbling sound; to utter with this sound.—*also n.*

gush *vi* to issue plentifully; to have a sudden flow; to talk or write effusively. * *vt* to cause to gush. * *n* a sudden outpouring.—**gushy** *adj.*

gusset *n* a small triangular piece of cloth inserted in a garment to strengthen or enlarge a part.

gust *n* a sudden brief rush of wind; a sudden outburst. * *vi* to blow in gusts. —**gusty** *adj.*—**gustily** *adv.*

gusto *n* great enjoyment, zest.

gut *n* (*often pl*) the bowels or the stomach; the intestine; tough cord made from animal intestines; (*pl*) (*sl*) daring; courage. * *vt* (*pt* **gutted**) to remove the intestines from; to destroy the interior of.

gutter *n* a channel for carrying off water, esp at

a roadside or under the eaves of a roof; a channel or groove to direct something (as of a bowling alley); the lowest condition of human life. * *adj* marked by extreme vulgarity or indecency. * *vt* to provide with a gutter. * *vi* to flow in rivulets; (*candle*) to melt unevenly; (*candle flame*) to flutter.—**guttering** *n.*

guttersnipe *n* a dirty child who plays in the streets, esp slum areas.

guttural *adj* formed or pronounced in the throat; harsh-sounding.—**gutturally** *adv.*

guy[1] *n* a rope, chain, etc, for fixing or steadying anything. * *vt* to fix or steady with a guy.

guy[2] *n* an effigy of Guy Fawkes made from old clothes stuffed with newspapers, etc burnt on the anniversary of the Gunpowder Plot (5 November); (*inf*) a man or boy; (*pl*) (*inf*) men or women; a shabby person. * *vt* to tease.

guzzle *vti* to gulp down food or drink greedily.—**guzzler** *n.*

gym *n* (*inf*) a gymnasium.

gymnasium *n* a room or building equipped for physical training and sports.

gymnast *n* a person skilled in gymnastics.

gymnastics *n* (*used as sing*) training in exercises devised to strengthen the body; (*pl*) gymnastic exercises; (*pl*) feats of dexterity or agility.

gynaecology, gynecology (*US*) *n* the branch of medicine that deals with the diseases and disorders of the female reproductive system.—**gynaecological** *adj.*—**gynaecologist** *n.*

gypsy *n* (*with cap*) a member of a travelling people, orig from India, now spread throughout Europe and North America; a person who looks or lives like a Gypsy.—*also* **gipsy**.

gyrate *vi* to revolve; to whirl or spiral. —**gyration** *n.*—**gyratory** *adj.*

H

haberdasher *n* a dealer in sewing accessories; in US, a dealer in men's clothing.—**haberdashery** *n.*

habit *n* a distinctive costume, as of a nun, etc; a thing done often and hence easily; a usual way of doing things; an addiction, esp to narcotics. * *vt* to clothe.

habitual *adj* having the nature of a habit; regular.—**habitually** *adv.*

hack[1] *vt* to cut or chop (at) violently; to clear (vegetation) by chopping; (*comput*) to gain illegal access to confidential data. * *n* a gash or notch; a harsh, dry cough.

hack[2] *n* a riding horse for hire; an old worn-out horse; a mediocre or unexceptional writer; a coach for hire; (*inf*) a taxicab. * *vti* to ride a horse cross-country. * *adj* banal, hackneyed.

hackneyed *adj* made trite or banal through overuse.

had *see* **have**.

haddock *n* (*pl* **haddock**) an important Atlantic food fish related to the cod.

haemorrhage, hemorrhage (*US*) *n* the escape of blood from a blood vessel; heavy bleeding. * *vi* to bleed heavily.

haemorrhoids, hemorrhoids (*US*) *npl* swollen or bleeding veins around the anus.—*also* **piles**.

haggard *n adj* having an exhausted, untidy look.

haggle *vi* to bargain; barter.—**haggler** *n.*

hail[1] *vt* to greet; to summon by shouting or signalling, as a taxi; to welcome with approval, to acclaim. * *vi* to originate from. * *interj* an exclamation of tribute, greeting, etc. * *n* a shout to gain attention; a distance within which one can be heard calling.—**hailer** *n.*

hail[2] *n* frozen raindrops; something, as abuse, bullets, etc, sent forcefully in rapid succession. * *vti* to pour down like hail.

hailstone *n* a pellet of hail.

hair *n* a threadlike growth from the skin of mammals; a mass of hairs, esp on the human head; a threadlike growth on a plant.

haircut *n* a shortening and styling of hair by cutting it; the style of cutting.

hair-do *n* a particular style of hair after cutting, etc.

hairdresser *n* a person who cuts, styles, colours, etc hair.

hairpiece *n* a wig or toupee; an additional piece of hair attached to a person's real hair.

hairpin *n* U-shaped pin used to hold hair in place.

hairpin bend *n* a sharply curving bend in a road, etc.

hair-raising *adj* terrifying, shocking.

hairstyle *n* the way in which hair is arranged.—**hairstylist** *n.*

hairy *adj* (**hairier, hairiest**) covered with hair; (*inf*) difficult, dangerous.—**hairiness** *n.*

hake *n* (*pl* **hake**) a marine food fish related to the cod.

half *n* (*pl* **halves**) either of two equal parts of

something; (*inf*) a half-price ticket for a bus, etc; (*inf*) half a pint. * *adj* being a half; incomplete; partial. * *adv* to the extent of a half; (*inf*) partly.

halfback *n* (*football, hockey*) a player occupying a position between the forwards and the fullbacks; a player in this position in other sports.

half-caste *n* a person whose parents are of different races.

half-hearted *adj* with little interest, enthusiasm, etc.

half-hour *n* 30 minutes; the point 30 minutes after the beginning of an hour.

half-time *n* (*sport*) an interval between two halves of a game.

halfway *adj* midway between two points, etc.

halibut *n* a large marine flatfish used as food.

hall *n* a public building with offices, etc; a large room for exhibits, gatherings, etc; the main house on a landed estate; a college building, esp a dining room; a vestibule at the entrance of a building; a hallway.

hallmark *n* a mark used on gold, silver or platinum articles to signify a standard of purity, weight, date of manufacture; a mark or symbol of high quality; a characteristic feature. * *vt* to stamp with a hallmark.

hallo *see* **hello**.

hallucination *n* the apparent perception of sights, sounds, etc that are not actually present; something perceived in this manner.—**hallucinatory** *adj*.

halo *n* (*pl* **haloes, halos**) a circle of light, as around the sun; a symbolic ring of light around the head of a saint in pictures; the aura of glory surrounding an idealized person or thing.

halt[1] *n* a temporary interruption or cessation of progress; a minor station on a railway line. * *vti* to stop or come to a stop.

halt[2] *vi* to falter; to hesitate.—**halting** *adj*.

halve *vt* to divide equally into two; to reduce by half; (*golf*) to play one hole in the same number of strokes as one's opponent.

halves *see* **half**.

ham *n* the upper part of a pig's hind leg, salted, smoked, etc; the meat from this area; (*inf*) the back of the upper thigh; (*inf*) an actor who overacts; (*inf*) a licensed amateur radio operator. * *vt* (*pt* **hammed**) to speak or move in an exaggerated manner, to overact.

hamburger *n* ground beef; a cooked patty of such meat, often in a bread roll with pickle, etc.

hamlet *n* a very small village.

hammer *n* a tool for pounding, driving nails, etc, having a heavy head and a handle; a thing like this in shape or use, as the part of the gun that strikes the firing pin; a bone of the middle ear; a heavy metal ball attached to a wire thrown in athletic contests. * *vti* to strike repeatedly, as with a hammer; to drive, force, or shape, as with hammer blows; (*inf*) to defeat utterly.

hammock *n* a length of strong cloth or netting suspended by the ends and used as a bed.

hamper[1] *vt* to hinder; to interfere with; to encumber.

hamper[2] *n* a large, usu covered, basket for storing or transporting food and crockery, etc.

hand *n* the part of the arm below the wrist, used for grasping; a side or direction; possession or care; control; an active part; a promise to marry; skill; one having a special skill; handwriting; applause; help; a hired worker; a source; one of a ship's crew; anything like a hand, as a pointer on a clock; the breadth of a hand, four inches when measuring the height of a horse; the cards held by a player at one time; a round of card play; (*inf*) applause. * *adj* of, for, or controlled by the hand. * *vt* to give as with the hand; to help or conduct with the hand. * *vi* (*with* **on**) to pass to the next.

handbag *n* a woman's small bag for carrying personal items.

handbook *n* a book containing useful instructions.

handcuff *n* (*usu pl*) either of a pair of connected steel rings for shackling the wrists of a prisoner. * *vt* to manacle.

handful *n* as much as will fill the hand; a few; (*inf*) a person who is difficult to handle or control.

handicap *n* a mental or physical impairment; a contest in which difficulties are imposed on, or advantages given to, contestants to equalize their chances; such a difficulty or advantage; any hindrance. * *vt* (*pt* **handicapped**) to give a handicap to; to hinder.—**handicapper** *n*.

handicraft *n* a skill involving the hands, such as basketwork, pottery, etc; an item of pottery, etc made by hand.

handkerchief *n* a small cloth for blowing the nose, etc.

handle *vt* to touch, hold, or move with the hand; to manage or operate with the hands; to manage, deal with; to buy and sell (goods).

* *vi* to react in a specified way. * *n* a part of anything designed to be held or grasped by the hand.—**handleable** *adj*.—**handling** *n*.

handlebar *n* (*often pl*) the curved metal bar with a grip at each end used to steer a bicycle, etc; a bushy moustache with curved ends.

handmade *adj* made by hand, carefully crafted.

handsome *adj* good-looking; dignified; generous; ample.—**handsomely** *adv*.—**handsomeness** *n*.

handy *adj* (**handier, handiest**) convenient, near; easy to use; skilled with the hands.—**handily** *adv*.—**handiness** *n*.

handyman *n* a person who does odd jobs.

hang *vb* (*pt* **hung**) *vt* to support from above, esp by a rope, chain, etc, to suspend; (*door, etc*) to attach by hinges to allow to swing freely; to decorate with pictures, or other suspended objects; (*wallpaper*) to stick to a wall; to exhibit (works of art); to prevent (a jury) from coming to a decision; (*pt* **hanged**) to put to execute or kill by suspending by the neck. * *vi* to be suspended, so as to dangle loosely; to fall or droop; (*clothing, etc*) to fall or flow in a certain direction; to lean, incline, or protrude; to depend; to remain in the air; to be in suspense; (*pt* **hanged**) to die by hanging; (*with* **about, around**) to loiter; (*with* **back**) to hesitate, be reluctant; (*with* **out**) to meet regularly at a particular place. * *n* the way in which anything hangs; (*sl*) a damn.

hangar *n* a shelter for aircraft.

hanger *n* a device on which something is hung.

hanger-on *n* a sycophantic follower.

hang-glider *n* an unpowered aircraft consisting of a metal frame over which a lightweight material is stretched, with a harness for the pilot suspended below.—**hang gliding** *n*.

hangover *n* the unpleasant after-effects of excessive consumption of alcohol; something surviving from an earlier time.

hang-up *n* an emotional preoccupation with something.

hank *n* a coiled or looped bundle of wool, rope, etc.

hanker *vi* (*with* **after, for**) to desire longingly.—**hankering** *n*.

hanky, hankie *n* (*inf*) a handkerchief.

haphazard *adj* not planned; random. * *adv* by chance.—**haphazardly** *adv*.

happen *vi* to take place; to be, occur, or come by chance.

happening *n* an occurrence; an improvization.

happy *adj* (**happier, happiest**) fortunate; having, expressing, or enjoying pleasure or contentment; pleased; appropriate, felicitous.—**happily** *adv*.—**happiness** *n*.

happy-go-lucky *adj* irresponsible; carefree.

harass *vt* to annoy, to irritate; to trouble (an enemy) by constant raids and attacks.—**harassment** *n*.

harbour, harbor (*US*) *n* a protected inlet for anchoring ships; any place of refuge. * *vt* to shelter or house; (*grudge, etc*) to keep in the mind secretly. * *vi* to take shelter.

hard *adj* firm, solid, not easily cut or punctured; difficult to comprehend; difficult to accomplish; difficult to bear, painful; severe, unfeeling, ungenerous; indisputable, intractable; (*drugs*) addictive and damaging to health; (*weather*) severe; (*currency*) stable in value; (*news*) definite, not speculative; (*drink*) very alcoholic; (*water*) having a high mineral content that prevents lathering with soap; (*colour, sound*) harsh. * *adv* with great effort or intensity; earnestly, with concentration; so as to cause hardness; with difficulty; with bitterness or grief; close, near by.—**hardness** *n*.

hardback *n* a book bound with a stiff cover.—*also adj*.

hardboard *n* a stiff board made of compressed wood chips.

hard-boiled *adj* (*eggs*) boiled until solid; (*inf*) unfeeling.

hard cash *n* payment in coins and notes as opposed to cheque, etc.

harden *vti* to make or become hard.—**hardener** *n*.

hardly *adv* scarcely; barely; with difficulty; not to be expected.

hard sell *n* an aggressive selling technique.

hardship *n* something that causes suffering or privation.

hard up *adj* (*inf*) short of money.

hardware *n* articles made of metal as tools, nails, etc; (*comput*) the mechanical and electronic components that make up a computer system.

hardy *adj* (**hardier, hardiest**) bold, resolute; robust; vigorous; able to withstand exposure to physical or emotional hardship.—**hardily** *adv*.—**hardiness** *n*.

hare *n* any of various timid, swift, long-eared mammals, resembling but larger than the rabbit.

harebrained *adj* flighty; foolish.

harelip *n* a congenital deformity of the upper lip in the form of a vertical fissure.

harem, hareem *n* the usu secluded part of a

Muslim household where the women live; the women in a harem.

harm *n* hurt; damage; injury. * *vt.* to inflict hurt, damage, or injury upon.

harmful *adj* hurtful.—**harmfully** *adv.*

harmless *adj* not likely to cause harm.—**harmlessly** *adv.*—**harmlessness** *n.*

harmonic *adj* (*mus*) of or in harmony. * *n* an overtone; (*pl*) the science of musical sounds.

harmonica *n* a small wind instrument that produces tones when air is blown or sucked across a series of metal reeds; a mouth-organ.

harmonious *adj* fitting together in an orderly and pleasing manner; agreeing in ideas, interests, etc; melodious. —**harmoniously** *adv.*

harmonium *n* a keyboard musical instrument whose tones are produced by thin metal reeds operated by foot bellows.

harmonize *vi* to be in harmony; to sing in harmony. * *vt* to make harmonious.—**harmonization** *n.*

harmony *n* a pleasing agreement of parts in colour, size, etc; agreement in action, ideas, etc; the pleasing combination of musical tones in a chord.

harness *n* the leather straps and metal pieces by which a horse is fastened to a vehicle, plough, etc; any similar fastening or attachment, eg for a parachute, hang-glider. * *vt* to put a harness on; to control so as to use the power of.

harp *n* a stringed musical instrument played by plucking. * *vi* (*with* **on** *or* **upon**) to talk persistently (on some subject).—**harpist** *n.*

harpoon *n* a barbed spear with an attached line, for spearing whales, etc.—*also vt.*

harpsichord *n* a musical instrument resembling a grand piano whose strings are plucked by a mechanism rather than struck.

harrow *n* a heavy frame with spikes, spring teeth, or disks for breaking up and levelling ploughed ground. * *vt* to draw a harrow over (land); to cause mental distress to.—**harrowing** *adj.*

harsh *adj* unpleasantly rough; jarring on the senses or feelings; rigorous; cruel.—**harshly** *adv.*—**harshness** *n.*

harvest *n* (the season of) gathering in the ripened crops; the yield of a particular crop; the reward or product of any exertion or action. * *vti* to gather in (a crop). * *vt* to win by achievement. —**harvester** *n.*

has *see* **have**.

hash[1] *n* a chopped mixture of reheated cooked meat and vegetables. * *vt* to chop up (meat or vegetables) for hash; to mix or mess up.

hash[2] *n* (*inf*) hashish.

hashish *n* resin derived from the leaves and shoots of the hemp plant, smoked or chewed as an intoxicant.

haste *n* quickness of motion.

hasten *vt* to accelerate; to cause to hurry. * *vi* to move or act with speed.

hasty *adj* (**hastier, hastiest**) done in a hurry; rash, precipitate.—**hastily** *adv.* —**hastiness** *n.*

hat *n* a covering for the head.

hatch[1] *n* a small door or opening (as on an aircraft or spaceship); an opening in the deck of a ship or in the floor or roof of a building; a lid for such an opening; a hatchway.

hatch[2] *vt* to produce (young) from the egg, esp by incubating; to devise (eg a plot). * *vi* to emerge from the egg; to incubate.

hatch[3] *vt* (*drawing, engraving*) to shade using closely spaced parallel lines or incisions.

hatchback *n* a sloping rear end on a car with a door; a car of this design.

hatchet *n* a small axe with a short handle.

hate *vt* to feel intense dislike for. * *vi* to feel hatred; to wish to avoid. * *n* a strong feeling of dislike or contempt; the person or thing hated.

hateful *adj* deserving or arousing hate.—**hatefully** *adv.*

hatred *n* intense dislike or enmity.

hat trick *n* (*cricket*) the taking of three wickets with three successive bowls; the scoring of three successive goals, points, etc in any game.

haughty *adj* (**haughtier, haughtiest**) having or expressing arrogance.—**haughtily** *adv.*—**haughtiness** *n.*

haul *vti* to move by pulling; to transport by truck, etc. * *n* the act of hauling; the amount gained, caught, etc at one time; the distance over which something is transported.

haulage *n* the transport of commodities; the charge for this.

haulier *n* a person or business that transports goods by road.

haunch *n* the part of the body around the hips; the leg and loin of a deer, sheep, etc.

haunt *vt* to visit often or continually; to recur repeatedly to. * *vi* to linger; to appear habitually as a ghost. * *n* a place often visited.

have *vt* (*pres t* **has**, *pr p* **having**, *pt* **had**) to have in one's possession; to possess as an attribute; to hold in the mind; to experience; to give birth to; to allow, or tolerate; to arrange or hold; to engage in; to cause, compel, or require to be; to to be obliged; (*sl*) to have sexual intercourse with; to be pregnant with; (*inf*) to hold at a disadvantage; (*inf*) to deceive; to accept or receive; to consume food, drink, etc; to show some quality; to perplex.

haven *n* a place where ships can safely anchor; a refuge.

haversack *n* a canvas bag similar to a knapsack but worn over one shoulder.

havoc *n* widespread destruction or disorder.

hawk[1] *n* any of numerous birds of prey; a person who advocates aggressive or intimidatory action.—**hawkish** *adj*.

hawk[2] *vti* to clear the throat (of) audibly.

hawk[3] *vt* to offer goods for sale, as in the street.

hawker *n* a person who goes about offering goods for sale.

hay *n* grass cut and dried for fodder.

hay fever *n* an allergic reaction to pollen causing irritation of the nose and eyes.

haystack, hayrick *n* a pile of stacked hay ready for storing.

haywire *adj* (*inf*) out of order; disorganized.

hazard *n* risk; danger; an obstacle on a golf course. * *vt* to risk.

hazardous *adj* dangerous; risky.

haze *n* a thin vapour of fog, smoke, etc in the air; slight vagueness of mind. * *vti* to make or become hazy.

hazy *adj* (**hazier, haziest**) misty; vague .—**hazily** *adv*.—**haziness** *n*.

he *pron* the male person or animal named before; a person (male or female). * *n* a male person or animal.

head *n* the part of an animal or human body containing the brain, eyes, ears, nose and mouth; the top part of anything; the foremost part; the chief person; (*pl*) a unit of counting; the striking part of a tool; mind; understanding; the topic of a chapter, etc; crisis, conclusion; pressure of water, steam, etc; the source of a river, etc; froth, as on beer. * *adj* at the head, top or front; coming from in front; chief, leading. * *vt* to command; to lead; to cause to go in a specified direction; to set out; to travel (in a particular direction); to strike (a football) with the head.—**headless** *adj*.

headache *n* a continuous pain in the head; (*inf*) a cause of worry or trouble.

heading *n* something forming the head, top, or front; the title, topic, etc of a chapter, etc; the direction in which a vehicle is moving.

headland *n* a promontory.

headlight, headlamp *n* a light at the front of a vehicle.

headline *n* printed lines at the top of a newspaper article giving the topic; a brief news summary. * *vt* to give featured billing or publicity to.

headlong *adj* with the head first; with uncontrolled speed or force; rashly.—*also adv*.

headmaster, headmistress *n* the principal of a school.

head-on *adj* with the head or front foremost; without compromise.—*also adv*.

headquarters *n* the centre of operations of one in command, as in an army; the main office in any organization.

headrest *n* a support for the head.

headroom *n* space overhead, as in a doorway or tunnel.

headstrong *adj* determined to do as one pleases.

head waiter *n* the head of the dining-room staff in a restaurant.

headway *n* forward motion; progress.

headwind *n* a wind blowing against the direction of a ship or aircraft.

heady *adj* (**headier, headiest**) (*alcoholic drinks*) intoxicating; invigorating, exciting; impetuous.—**headily** *adv*.—**headiness** *n*.

heal *vti* to make or become healthy; to cure; (*wound, etc*) to repair by natural processes.—**healer** *n*.

health *n* physical and mental well-being; freedom from disease, etc; the condition of body or mind; a wish for health and happiness, as in a toast.

healthy *adj* (**healthier, healthiest**) having or producing good health; beneficial; sound.—**healthily** *adv*.—**healthiness** *n*.

heap *n* a mass or pile of jumbled things; (*pl*) (*inf*) a large amount. * *vt* to throw in a heap; to pile high; to fill (a plate, etc) full or to overflowing.

hear *vb* (*pt* **heard**) *vt* to perceive by the ear; to listen to; to conduct a hearing of (a law case, etc); to be informed of; to learn. * *vi* to be able to hear sounds; (*with* **of** *or* **about**) to be told.—**hearer** *n*.

hearing *n* the sense by which sound is perceived by the ear; an opportunity to be heard; the distance over which something can be heard, earshot.

hearing aid *n* a small electronic amplifier worn behind the ear to improve hearing.

hearsay *n* rumour, gossip.

hearse *n* a vehicle for transporting a coffin to a funeral.

heart *n* the hollow, muscular organ that circulates the blood; the central, vital, or main part; the human heart as the centre of emotions, esp sympathy, courage, etc; a conventional design representing a heart; one of a suit of playing cards marked with such a symbol in red.

heartache *n* sorrow or grief.

heart attack *n* a sudden instance of abnormal heart functioning, esp coronary thrombosis.

heartbeat *n* the rhythmic contraction and dilation of the heart.

heartbreak *n* overwhelming sorrow or grief.—**heartbreaking** *adj*.—**heartbroken** *adj*.

heartburn *n* a burning sensation in the lower chest.

heartfelt *adj* sincere.

hearth *n* the floor of a fireplace and surrounding area; this as symbolic of house and home.

heartily *adv* vigorously, enthusiastically; sincerely.

heartless *adj* unfeeling.—**heartlessly** *adv*.—**heartlessness** *n*.

hearty *adj* (**heartier, heartiest**) warm and friendly; unrestrained, as laughter; strong and healthy; nourishing and plentiful.—**heartiness** *n*.

heat *n* energy produced by molecular agitation; the quality of being hot; the perception of hotness; hot weather or climate; strong feeling, esp anger, etc; a single bout, round, or trial in sports; the period of sexual excitement and readiness for mating in female animals; (*sl*) coercion. * *vti* to make or become warm or hot; to make or become excited.

heated *adj* made hot; excited, impassioned.—**heatedly** *adv*.

heater *n* a device that provides heat; (*sl*) a gun.

heath *n* an area of uncultivated land with scrubby vegetation; any of various shrubby plants that thrive on sandy soil, eg heather.

heathen *n* (*pl* **heathens, heathen**) anyone not acknowledging the God of Christian, Jew, or Muslim belief; a person regarded as irreligious, uncivilized, etc.

heather *n* a common evergreen shrub of northern and alpine regions with small stalkless leaves and tiny usu purplish pink flowers.

heating *n* a system of providing heat, as central heating; the warmth provided.

heat wave *n* a prolonged period of hot weather.

heave *vb vt* to lift or move, esp with great effort; to utter (a sigh, etc) with effort; (*inf*) to throw. * *vi* to rise and fall rhythmically; to vomit; to pant; to gasp; to haul; (*pt* **hove**) (*with* **to**) (*ship*) to come to a stop. * *n* the act or effort of heaving.

heaven *n* (*usu pl*) the visible sky; (*sometimes cap*) the dwelling place of God and his angels where the blessed go after death; any place or state of great happiness; (*pl*) *interj* an exclamation of surprise.

heavenly *adj* of or relating to heaven or heavens; divine; (*inf*) excellent, delightful.—**heavenliness** *n*.

heavy *adj* (**heavier, heaviest**) hard to lift or carry; of more than the usual, expected, or defined weight; to an unusual extent; hard to do; stodgy, hard to digest; cloudy; (*industry*) using massive machinery to produce basic materials, as chemicals and steel; (*ground*) difficult to make fast progress on; clumsy; dull, serious. * *n* (*theatre*) a villain; (*sl*) a person hired to threaten violence, a thug.—**heavily** *adv*.—**heaviness** *n*.

heavyweight *n* a professional boxer weighing more than 175 pounds (79 kg) or wrestler weighing over 209 pounds (95 kg); (*inf*) a very influential or important individual.

Hebrew *n* a member of an ancient Semitic people; an Israelite; a Jew; the ancient Semitic language of the Hebrews; its modern form.—*also adj*.

heckle *vti* to harass (a speaker) with questions or taunts.—**heckler** *n*.

hectic *adj* involving intense excitement or activity.—**hectically** *adv*.

he'd = he had, he would.

hedge *n* a fence consisting of a dense line of bushes or small trees; a barrier or means of protection against something, esp financial loss; an evasive or noncommittal answer or statement. * *vt* to surround or enclose with a hedge; to place secondary bets as a precaution. * *vi* to avoid giving a direct answer in an argument or debate.

hedgehog *n* a small insectivorous mammal with sharp spines on the back.

heed *vt* to pay close attention (to). * *n* careful attention.—**heedful** *adj*.

heedless *adj* inattentive; thoughtless. —**heedlessly** *adv*.

heel[1] *n* the back part of the foot, under the ankle; the part covering or supporting the heel in stockings, socks, etc or shoes; a solid attachment forming the back of the sole of a shoe; (*inf*) a despicable person. * *vt* to furnish with a heel; to follow closely; (*inf*) to provide with money, etc. * *vi* to follow along at the heels of someone.

heel² *vti* to tilt or become tilted to one side, as a ship.

hefty *adj* (**heftier, heftiest**) (*inf*) heavy; large and strong; big.—**heftily** *adv*.—**heftiness** *n*.

heifer *n* a young cow that has not calved.

height *n* the topmost point; the highest limit; the distance from the bottom to the top; altitude; a relatively great distance above a given level; an eminence; a hill.

heighten *vti* to make or come higher or more intense.

heir *n* a person who inherits or is entitled to inherit another's property, title, etc.

heiress *n* a woman or girl who is an heir, esp to great wealth.

heirloom *n* any possession handed down from generation to generation.

held *see* **hold¹**.

helicopter *n* a kind of aircraft lifted and moved, or kept hovering, by large rotary blades mounted horizontally.

hell *n* (*Christianity*) the place of punishment of the wicked after death; the home of devils and demons; any place or state of supreme misery or discomfort; (*inf*) a cause of this. * *interj* (*inf*) an exclamation of anger, surprise, etc.

he'll = he will.

hellish *adj* of, pertaining to or resembling hell; very wicked; (*inf*) very unpleasant.

hello *interj* an expression of greeting. * *n* the act of saying "hello."—*also* **hallo, hullo**.

helm *n* the tiller or wheel used to steer a ship; a position of control or direction, authority.

helmet *n* protective headgear worn by soldiers, policemen, divers, etc.

helmsman *n* a person who steers.—**helmswoman** *nf*.

help *vt* to make things better or easier for; to aid; to assist; to remedy; to keep from; to serve or wait on. * *vi* to give aid; to be useful. * *n* the action of helping; aid; assistance; a remedy; a person that helps, esp a hired person. —**helper** *n*.

helpful *adj* giving help; useful.—**helpfully** *adv*.—**helpfulness** *n*.

helping *n* a single portion of food.

helpless *adj* unable to manage alone, dependent on others; weak and defenceless.—**helplessly** *adv*.—**helplessness** *n*.

hem *n* the edge of a garment, etc turned back and stitched or fixed. * *vt* (*pt* **hemmed**) to finish (a garment) with a hem; (*with* **in**) to enclose, confine.—**hemmer** *n*.

hemisphere *n* half of a sphere or globe; any of the halves (northern, southern, eastern, or western) of the earth.—**hemispherical** *adj*.

hemp *n* a widely cultivated Asian herb of the mulberry family; its fibre, used to mmke rope, sailcloth, etc; a narcotic drug obtained from different varieties of this plant (—*also* **cannabis, marijuana**).

hen *n* the female of many birds, esp the chicken.

hence *adv* from here; from this time; from this reason.

henceforth, henceforward *adv* from now on.

henchman *n* a trusted helper or follower.

henpeck *vt* to nag and domineer over (one's husband).—**henpecked** *adj*.

her *pron* the objective case of **she**. * *adj* of or belonging to her.

herald *n* a person who conveys news or messages; a forerunner, harbinger; (*Middle Ages*) an official at a tournament. * *vt* to usher in; to proclaim.

heraldry *n* the study of genealogies and coats of arms; ceremony; pomp. —**heraldic** *adj*.

herb *n* any seed plant whose stem withers away annually; any plant used as a medicine, seasoning, etc.—**herby** *adj*.

herd *n* a large number of animals, esp cattle, living and feeding together. * *vi* to assemble or move animals together. * *vt* to gather together and move as if a herd; to tend, as a herdsman.—**herder** *n*.

here *adv* at or in this place; to or into this place; now; on earth.

hereafter *adv* after this, in some future time or state. * *n* (*with* **the**) the future, life after death.

hereby *adv* by this means.

hereditary *adj* descending by inheritance; transmitted to offspring.

heredity *n* the transmission of genetic material that determines physical and mental characteristics from one generation to another.

heresy *n* a religious belief regarded as contrary to the orthodox doctrine of a church; any belief or opinion contrary to established or accepted theory.

heretic *n* a dissenter from an established belief or doctrine.—**heretical** *adj*.

heritage *n* something inherited at birth; anything deriving from the past or tradition; historical sites, traditions, practices, etc regarded as the valuable inheritance of contemporary society.

hermetic *adj* perfectly closed and airtight.—**hermetically** *adv*.

hermit *n* a person who lives in complete solitude, esp for religious reasons; a recluse.

hernia *n* the protrusion of an organ, esp part of the intestine, through an opening in the wall of the cavity in which it sits; a rupture.—**hernial** *adj*.

hero *n* (*pl* **heroes**) a person of exceptional bravery; a person admired for superior qualities and achievements; the central male character in a novel, play, etc.

heroic *adj* of or like a hero; of or about heroes and their deeds; daring, risky.—**heroically** *adv*.

heroin *n* a powerfully addictive drug derived from morphine.

heroine *n* a woman with the attributes of a hero; the leading female character in a novel, film or play.

heroism *n* the qualities or conduct of a hero.

heron *n* a slim long-necked wading bird.

herring *n* (*pl* **herrings, herring**) a small food fish.

hers *pron* something or someone belonging to her.

herself *pron* the reflexive form of **she** or **her**.

he's = he is; he has.

hesitant *adj* hesitating.—**hesitantly** *adv*.—**hesitancy** *n*.

hesitate *vi* to be slow in acting due to uncertainty or indecision; to be reluctant (to); to falter or stammer when speaking.—**hesitating** *adj*.—**hesitation** *n*.

het-up *adj* (*inf*) agitated, annoyed.

hew *vb* (*pp* **hewed** *or* **hewn**) *vt* to strike or cut with blows using an axe, etc; to shape with such blows. * *vi* to conform (to a rule, principle, etc).—**hewer** *n*.

hexagon *n* a polygon having six sides and six angles.—**hexagonal** *adj*.—**hexagonally** *adv*.

heyday *n* a period of greatest success, happiness, etc.

hi *interj* an exclamation of greeting.

hibernate *vi* to spend the winter in a dormant condition like deep sleep; to be inactive.—**hibernation** *n*.

hiccup *n* a sudden involuntary spasm of the diaphragm followed by inhalation and closure of the glottis producing a characteristic sound; (*inf*) a minor setback. * *vt* (*pt* **hiccuped** *or* **hiccupped**) to have hiccups.

hide[1] *vb* (*pt* **hid**, *pp* **hidden, hid**) *vt* to conceal, put out of sight; to keep secret; to screen or obscure from view. * *vi* to conceal oneself. * *n* a camouflaged place of concealment used by hunters, bird-watchers, etc.

hide[2] *n* the raw or dressed skin of an animal; (*inf*) the human skin.

hideous *adj* visually repulsive; horrifying.—**hideously** *adv*.

hiding *n* (*inf*) a thrashing.

hierarchy *n* a group of persons or things arranged in order of rank, grade, etc.—**hierarchical** *adj*.

high *adj* lofty, tall; extending upward a (specified) distance; situated at or done from a height; above others in rank, position, etc; greater in size, amount, cost, etc than usual; raised or acute in pitch; (*meat*) slightly bad; (*inf*) intoxicated; (*inf*) under the influence of drugs. * *adv* in or to a high degree, rank, etc. * *n* a high level, place, etc; an area of high barometric pressure; (*inf*) a euphoric condition induced by alcohol or drugs.

highbrow *n* (*inf*) an intellectual.—*also adj*.

high-flyer, high-flier *n* an ambitious person; a person of great ability in any profession.

high-handed *adj* overbearing.

highjack *see* **hijack**.

highlight *n* the lightest area of a painting, etc; the most interesting or important feature; (*pl*) lightening of areas of the hair using a bleach. * *vt* to bring to special attention; to give highlights to.

highly *adv* highly, very much; favourably; at a high level, wage, rank, etc.

highness *n* the state or quality of being high; (*with cap*) a title used in speaking to or of royalty.

high-rise *adj* (*building*) having multiple storeys.—*also n*.

high school *n* a secondary school.

highway *n* a public road; a main thoroughfare.

hijack *vt* to steal (goods in transit) by force; to force (an aircraft) to make an unscheduled flight. * *n* a hijacking.—*also* **highjack**.—**hijacker, highjacker** *n*.

hike *vi* to take a long walk. * *vt* (*inf*) to pull up. * *n* a long walk; a tramp.—**hiker** *n*.

hilarious *adj* highly amusing.—**hilariously** *adv*.—**hilarity** *n*.

hill *n* a natural rise of land lower than a mountain; a heap or mound; an slope in a road, etc.—**hilly** *adj*.

hilt *n* the handle of a sword, dagger, tool, etc.

him *pron* the objective case of **he**.

himself *pron* the reflexive or emphatic form of **he, him**.

hind[1] *adj* (**hinder, hindmost** *or* **hindermost**) situated at the back; rear.

hind[2] *n* (*pl* **hinds, hind**) a female deer.

hinder *vt* to keep back, or prevent the progress

of. * *vi* to be an obstacle.—**hinderer** *n*.—**hinderingly** *adv*.

hindrance *n* the act of hindering; an obstacle, impediment.

hinge *n* a joint or flexible part on which a door, lid, etc turns; a natural joint, as of a clam; a small piece of gummed paper for sticking stamps in an album. * *vti* to attach or hang by a hinge; to depend.

hint *n* an indirect or subtle suggestion; a slight mention; a little piece of practical or helpful advice. * *vt* to suggest or indicate indirectly. * *vi* to give a hint.

hip[1] *n* either side of the body below the waist and above the thigh.

hip[2] *n* the fruit of the wild rose.

hip[3] *interj* used as part of a cheer (**hip, hip, hurrah**).

hip[4] *adj* (*sl*) stylish, up-to-date.

hippopotamus *n* (*pl* **hippopotamuses**) a large African water-loving mammal with thick dark skin, short legs, and a very large head and muzzle.

hire *vt* to pay for the services of (a person) or the use of (a thing). * *n* the payment for the temporary use of anything.—**hirer** *n*.

hire-purchase *n* a system by which a person takes possession of an article after paying a deposit and then becomes the owner only after payment of a series of instalments is completed.

his *poss pron* of or belonging to **him**.—*also adj*.

hiss *vi* to make a sound resembling a prolonged *s*; to show disapproval by hissing. * *vt* to say or indicate by hissing. * *n* the act or sound of hissing.

historian *n* a person who writes or studies history.

historic *adj* (potentially) important or famous in history.

historical *adj* belonging to or involving history or historical methods; concerning actual events as opposed to myth or legend; based on history.—**historically** *adv*.

history *n* a record or account of past events; the study, analysis of past events; past events in total; the past events or experiences of a specific person or thing; an unusual or significant past.

hit *vti* (*pt* **hit**) to come against (something) with force; to give a blow (to), to strike; to strike with a missile; to affect strongly; to arrive at; (*with* **on**) to discover by accident or unexpectedly. * *n* a blow that strikes its mark; a collision; a successful and popular song, book, etc; (*inf*) an underworld killing; (*sl*) a dose of a drug.

hit-and-run *n* a motor vehicle accident in which the driver leaves the scene without stopping or informing the authorities.

hitch *vt* to move, pull, etc with jerks; to fasten with a hook, knot, etc; to obtain a ride by hitchhiking. * *vi* to hitchhike. * *n* a tug; a hindrance, obstruction; a kind of knot used for temporary fastening; (*inf*) a ride obtained from hitchhiking.

hitchhike *vt* to travel by asking for free lifts from motorists along the way.—**hitchhiker** *n*.

hive *n* a shelter for a colony of bees; a beehive; the bees of a hive; a crowd of busy people; a place of great activity. * *vt* to gather (bees) into a hive. * *vi* to enter a hive; (*with* **off**) to separate from a group.

HMS *abbr* = Her (or His) Majesty's Ship.

hoard *n* an accumulation of food, money, etc stored away for future use. * *vti* to accumulate and store away.—**hoarder** *n*.

hoarding *n* a temporary screen of boards erected around a construction site; a large board used for advertising.

hoarse *adj* (*voice*) rough, as from a cold; (*person*) having a hoarse voice.—**hoarsely** *adv*.—**hoarseness** *n*.

hoax *n* a deception; a practical joke. * *vt* to deceive by a hoax.—**hoaxer** *n*.

hob *n* a ledge near a fireplace for keeping kettles, etc hot; a flat surface on a cooker incorporating hot plates or burners.

hobble *vi* to walk unsteadily, to limp. * *vt* to fasten the legs of (horses, etc) loosely together to prevent straying. * *n* a limp; a rope etc used to hobble a horse.

hobby *n* a spare-time activity carried out for personal amusement.

hock[1] *vt* (*sl*) to give something in security for a loan.

hock[2] *n* the joint bending backward on the hind leg of a horse, etc.

hock[3] *n* a variety of German white wine.

hockey *n* an outdoor game played by two teams of 11 players with a ball and clubs curved at one end; ice hockey.

hoe *n* a long-handled tool for weeding, loosening the earth, etc. * *vti* (*pr p* **hoeing**, *pt* **hoed**) to dig, weed, till, etc with a hoe.

hog *n* a castrated male pig raised for its meat; (*inf*) a selfish, greedy, or filthy person. * *vt* (*pt* **hogged**) to take more than one's due; to hoard greedily.

hoist *vt* to raise aloft, esp with a pulley, crane, etc. * *n* a hoisting; an apparatus for lifting.

hold[1] *vb* (*pt* **held**) *vt* to take and keep in one's possession; to grasp; to maintain in a certain position or condition; to retain; to contain; to own, to occupy; to support, sustain; to remain firm; to carry on, as a meeting; to regard; to believe, to consider; to bear or carry oneself; (*with* **back**) to withhold; to restrain; (*with* **down**) to restrain; (*inf*) to manage to retain one's job, etc; (*with* **forth**) to offer (eg an inducement); (*with* **off**) to keep apart; (*with* **up**) to delay; to hinder; to commit an armed robbery. * *vi* to go on being firm, loyal, etc; to remain unbroken or unyielding; to be true or valid; to continue; (*with* **back**) to refrain; (*with* **forth**) to speak at length; (*with* **off**) to wait, to refrain; (*with* **on**) to maintain a grip on; to persist; (*inf*) to keep a telephone line open. * *n* the act or manner of holding; grip; a dominating force on a person.—**holder** *n*.

hold[2] *n* the storage space in a ship or aircraft used for cargo.

holdall *n* a portable container for miscellaneous articles.

holding *n* (*often pl*) property, esp land, stocks and bonds.

hold-up *n* a delay; an armed robbery.

hole *n* a hollow place; a cavity; a pit; an animal's burrow; an aperture; a perforation; a small, squalid, dingy place; (*inf*) a difficult situation; (*golf*) a small cavity into which the ball is hit; the tee, the fairway, etc leading to this. * *vti* to make a hole in (something); to drive into a hole; (*with* **up**) to hibernate; (*inf*) to hide oneself.

holey *adj* full of holes.

holiday *n* a period away from work, school, etc for travel, rest or recreation; a day of freedom from work, etc, esp one set aside by law. * *vi* to spend a holiday..

holiday-maker *n* a person on holiday.

holiness *n* sanctity; (*with cap*) the title of the Pope.

hollow *adj* having a cavity within or below; recessed, concave; empty or worthless. * *n* a hole, cavity; a depression, a valley.* *vti* to make or become hollow.—**hollowly** *adv*.

holly *n* an evergreen shrub with prickly leaves and red berries.

holster *n* a leather case attached to a belt for a pistol.

holy *adj* (**holier, holiest**) dedicated to religious use; without sin; deserving reverence.

Holy Ghost *n* the Holy Spirit.

Holy Spirit *n* the Third Person of the Trinity.

homage *n* a public demonstration of respect or honour towards someone or something.

home *n* the place where one lives; the city, etc where one was born or reared; a place thought of as home; a household and its affairs; an institution for the aged, orphans, etc. * *adj* of one's home or country; domestic. * *adv* at, to, or in the direction of home; to the point aimed at. * *vi* (*birds*) to return home; to be guided onto a target; to head for a destination; to send or go home.

homeland *n* the country where a person was born.

homely *adj* (**homelier, homeliest**) simple, everyday; crude; not good-looking.—**homeliness** *n*.

home-made *adj* made, or as if made, at home.

homeopath *n* a medical practitioner of homeopathy.—*also* **homoeopath, homeopathist, homoeopathist**.

homeopathy *n* the system of treating disease by small quantities of drugs that cause symptoms similar to those of the disease.—*also* **homoeopathy**. —**homeopathic, homoeopathic** *adj*. —**homeopathically, homoeopathically** *adv*.

homesick *adj* longing for home.—**homesickness** *n*.

homeward *adj* going towards home. * *adv* homewards.

homework *n* work, esp piecework, done at home; schoolwork to be done outside the classroom; preliminary study for a project.

homicide *n* the killing of a person by another; a person who kills another. —**homicidal** *adj*.

homoeopath, homoeopathy *see* **homeopath, homeopathy**.

homogeneous *adj* composed of parts that are of identical or a similar kind or nature; of uniform structure.—**homogeneity** *n*.

homosexual *adj* sexually attracted towards a person of the same sex. * *n* a homosexual person.—**homosexuality** *n*.

honest *adj* truthful; trustworthy; sincere or genuine; gained by fair means; frank, open.

honestly *adv* in an honest manner; really.

honesty *n* the quality of being honest; a plant that forms transparent seed pods.

honey *n* (*pl* **honeys**) a sweet sticky yellowish substance that bees make as food from the nectar of flowers; sweetness; its colour; (*inf*) darling. * *adj* of, resembling honey; much loved.

honeycomb *n* the structure of six-sided wax

cells made by bees to hold their honey, eggs, etc; anything arranged like this. * *vt* to fill with holes like a honeycomb.

honeymoon *n* the vacation spent together by a newly married couple.—*also vi*.—**honeymooner** *n*.

honk *n* (a sound like) the call of the wild goose; the sound made by an old-fashioned motor horn.—*also vti*.

honorary *adj* given as an honour; (*office*) voluntary, unpaid.

honour, honor (*US*) *n* high regard or respect; glory; fame; good reputation; integrity; chastity; high rank; distinction; (*with cap*) the title of certain officials, as judges; cards of the highest value in certain card games. * *vt* to respect greatly; to do or give something in honour of; to accept and pay (a cheque when due, etc).

honourable, honorable (*US*) *adj* worthy of being honoured; honest; upright; bringing honour; (*with cap*) a title of respect for certain officials, as Members of Parliament, when addressing each other.—**honourably** *adv*.

hood[1] *n* a loose covering to protect the head and back of the neck; any hood-like thing as the (folding) top of a car, etc; a car bonnet.

hood[2] *n* (*inf*) a hoodlum.

hoodwink *vt* to mislead by trickery.

hoof *n* (*pl* **hoofs, hooves**) the horny covering on the ends of the feet of certain animals, as horses, cows, etc.

hook *n* a piece of bent or curved metal to catch or hold anything; a fishhook; something shaped like a hook; a strike, blow, etc, in which a curving motion is involved. * *vt* to seize, fasten, hold, as with a hook; (*rugby*) to pass the ball backwards from a scrum.

hooligan *n* a lawless young person.—**hooliganism** *n*.

hoop *n* a circular band of metal or wood; an iron band for holding together the staves of barrels; anything like this, as a child's toy or ring in a hoop skirt. * *vt* to bind (as if) with hoops.

hoot *n* the sound that an owl makes; a similar sound, as made by a train whistle; a shout of scorn; (*inf*) laughter; (*inf*) an amusing person or thing. * *vi* to utter a hoot; to blow a whistle, etc. * *vt* to express (scorn) of (someone) by hooting.

hooter *n* something that hoots, such as a car horn; (*sl*) a nose.

hooves *see* **hoof**.

hop[1] *vi* (*pt* **hopped**) to jump up on one leg; to leap with all feet at once, as a frog, etc; (*inf*) to make a quick trip. * *n* a hopping movement; (*inf*) an informal dance; a trip, esp in an aircraft.

hop[2] *n* a climbing plant with small cone-shaped flowers; (*pl*) the dried ripe cones, used for flavouring beer.

hope *n* a feeling that what is wanted will happen; the object of this; a person or thing on which one may base some hope. * *vt* to want and expect. * *vi* to have hope (for).

hopeful *adj* filled with hope; inspiring hope or promise of success. * *n* a person who hopes to or looks likely to be a success.

hopefully *adv* in a hopeful manner; it is hoped.

hopeless *adj* without hope; offering no grounds for hope or promise of success; impossible to solve; (*inf*) incompetent.—**hopelessly** *adv*.—**hopelessness** *n*.

horde *n* a crowd or throng; a swarm.

horizon *n* the apparent line along which the earth and sky meet; the limit of a person's knowledge, interest, etc.

horizontal *adj* level; parallel to the plane of the horizon.—**horizontally** *adv*.

hormone *n* a product of living cells formed in one part of the organism and carried to another part, where it takes effect; a synthetic compound having the same purpose.—**hormonal** *adj*.

horn *n* a bony outgrowth on the head of certain animals; the hard substance of which this is made; any projection like a horn; a wind instrument, esp the French horn or trumpet; a device to sound a warning.

horned *adj* having horns.

hornet *n* a large wasp with a severe sting.

horny *adj* (**hornier, horniest**) like horn; hard; callous; (*sl*) sexually aroused.

horoscope *n* a chart of the signs and positions of planets, etc, by which astrologers profess to predict future events, esp in the life of an individual.

horrible *adj* arousing horror; (*inf*) very bad, unpleasant, etc.—**horribly** *adv*.

horrid *adj* terrible; horrible.—**horridly** *adv*.

horrify *vt* to fill with horror.

horror *n* the strong feeling caused by something frightful or shocking; strong dislike; a person, thing inspiring horror.

hors-d'oeuvre *n* an appetizer served at the beginning of a meal.

horse *n* four-legged, solid-hoofed herbivorous mammal with a flowing mane and a tail, domesticated for carrying loads or riders, etc;

cavalry; a vaulting horse; a frame with legs to support something.

horse chestnut *n* a large tree with large palmate leaves and erect clusters of flowers.

horseman *n* a person skilled in the riding or care of horses.—**horsemanship** *n*.

horsepower *n* a unit for measuring the power of engines, etc, equal to 746 watts or 33,000 foot-pounds per minute.

horseradish *n* a tall herb of the mustard family; a sauce or relish made with its pungent root.

horseshoe *n* a flat U-shaped, protective metal plate nailed to a horse's hoof; anything shaped like this.

horticulture *n* the art or science of growing flowers, fruits, and vegetables.—**horticultural** *adj*.—**horticulturist** *n*.

hose[1] *n* a flexible tube used to convey fluids. * *vt* to spray with a hose.

hose[2] *n* (*pl* **hose**) stockings, socks, tights collectively.

hosiery *n* stockings; socks.

hospitable *adj* offering a generous welcome to guests or strangers; sociable.—**hospitably** *adv*.

hospital *n* an institution where the sick or injured are given medical treatment.

hospitality *n* the act, practice, or quality of being hospitable.

host[1] *n* a person who receives or entertains a stranger or guest at his house; an animal or plant on or in which another lives; a compere on a television or radio programme. * *vti* to act as a host (to a party, television programme, etc).

host[2] *n* a very large number of people or things.

host[3] *n* the wafer of bread used in the Eucharist or Holy Communion.

hostage *n* a person given or kept as security until certain conditions are met.

hostel *n* a lodging place for the homeless, travellers, or other groups.

hostess *n* a woman acting as a host; a woman who entertains guests at a nightclub, etc.

hostile *adj* of or being an enemy; unfriendly.—**hostilely** *adv*.

hostility *n* enmity, antagonism; (*pl*) deliberate acts of warfare.

hot *adj* (**hotter, hottest**) of high temperature; very warm; giving or feeling heat; causing a burning sensation on the tongue; full of intense feeling; following closely; electrically charged; (*inf*) recent, new; (*inf*) radioactive; (*inf*) stolen. * *adv* in a hot manner.—**hotly** *adv*.—**hotness** *n*.

hot dog *n* a sausage, esp a frankfurter, served in a long soft roll.

hotel *n* a commercial establishment providing lodging and meals for travellers, etc.

hotelier *n* the owner or manager of a hotel.

hothead *n* an impetuous person.—**hot-headed** *adj*.

hothouse *n* a heated greenhouse for raising plants; an environment that encourages rapid growth.

hotplate *n* a heated surface for cooking or keeping food warm; a small portable heating device.

hound *n* a dog used in hunting; a contemptible person. * *vt* to hunt or chase as with hounds; to urge on by harassment.—**hounder** *n*.

hour *n* a period of 60 minutes, a 24th part of a day; the time for a specific activity; the time; a special point in time; the distance covered in an hour; (*pl*) the customary period for work, etc.

hourly *adj* occurring every hour; done during an hour; frequent. * *adv* at every hour; frequently.

house *n* a building to live in, esp by one person or family; a household; a family or dynasty including relatives, ancestors and descendants; the audience in a theatre; a business firm; a legislative assembly. * *vt* to provide accommodation or storage for; to cover, encase.

house arrest *n* detention in one's own house, as opposed to prison.

houseboat *n* a boat furnished and used as a home.

housebreaker *n* a burglar; a person employed to demolish buildings.—**housebreaking** *n*.

household *n* all those people living together in the same house. * *adj* pertaining to running a house and family; domestic; familiar.

housekeeper *n* a person who runs a home, esp one hired to do so.

housekeeping *n* the daily running of a household; (*inf*) money used for domestic expenses; routine maintenance of equipment, records, etc in an organization.

house warming *n* a party given to celebrate moving into a new house.

housewife *n* the woman who keeps house.—**housewifery** *n*.

housework *n* the cooking, cleaning, etc involved in running a home.

housing *n* houses collectively; the provision of accommodation; a casing enclosing a piece of machinery, etc; a slot or groove in a piece of wood, etc to receive an insertion.

housing estate *n* accommodation, shops, leisure facilities, etc planned as a single unit.

hovel *n* a small miserable dwelling.

hover *vi* (*bird, etc*) to hang in the air stationary; to hang about, to linger.

hovercraft *n* a land or water vehicle that travels supported on a cushion of air.

how *adv* in what way or manner; by what means; to what extent; in what condition.

howl *vi* to utter the long, wailing cry of wolves, dogs, etc; to utter a similar cry of anger, pain, etc; to shout or laugh in pain, amusement, etc. * *vt* to utter with a howl; to drive by howling. * *n* the wailing cry of a wolf, dog, etc; any similar sound.

howler *n* (*inf*) a stupid mistake.

HP *abbr* = hire purchase; horsepower; high pressure; Houses of Parliament.

HQ *abbr* = headquarters.

hub *n* the centre part of a wheel; a centre of activity.

hubbub *n* a confused noise of many voices; an uproar.

huddle *vti* to crowd together in a confined space; to curl (oneself) up. * *n* a confused crowd or heap.

hue *n* colour; a particular shade or tint of a colour.

huff *n* a state of smouldering resentment. * *vi* to blow; to puff.—**huffy** *adj*.—**huffily** *adv*.

hug *vb* (*pt* **hugged**) *vt* to hold or squeeze tightly with the arms; to cling to; to keep close to. * *vi* to embrace one another. * *n* a strong embrace.—**huggable** *adj*.

huge *adj* very large, enormous.—**hugely** *adv*.—**hugeness** *n*.

hulk *n* the body of a ship, esp if old and dismantled; a large, clumsy person or thing.

hulking *adj* unwieldy, bulky.

hull *n* the outer covering of a fruit or seed; the framework of a ship. * *vt* to remove the hulls of; to pierce the hull of (a ship, etc).

hullo *see* **hello**.

hum *vb* (*pt* **hummed**) *vi* to make a low continuous vibrating sound; to hesitate in speaking and utter an inarticulate sound; (*inf*) to be lively, busy; (*sl*) to stink. * *vt* to sing with closed lips. * *n* a humming sound; a murmur; (*sl*) a stink.

human *adj* of or relating to human beings; having the qualities of humans as opposed to animals; kind, considerate. * *n* a human being.

humane *adj* kind, compassionate, merciful.—**humanely** *adv*.

humanity *n* the human race; the state or quality of being human or humane; philanthropy; kindness; (*pl*) the study of literature and the arts, as opposed to the sciences.

humble *adj* having a low estimation of one's abilities; modest, unpretentious; servile. * *vt* to lower in condition or rank; to humiliate.—**humbly** *adv*.—**humbleness** *n*.

humbug *n* fraud, sham, hoax; an insincere person; a peppermint-flavoured sweet. * *vt* (*pt* **humbugged**) to cheat or impose upon; to hoax.

humdrum *adj* dull, ordinary, boring.

humid *adj* (*air*) moist, damp.

humidity *n* (a measure of the amount of) dampness in the air.

humiliate *vt* to cause to feel humble; to lower the pride or dignity of.—**humiliation** *n*.

humility *n* the state of being humble.

humorist *n* a person who writes or speaks in a humorous manner.

humorous *adj* funny, amusing; causing laughter.—**humorously** *adv*.—**humorousness** *n*.

humour, humor (*US*) *n* the ability to appreciate or express what is funny, amusing, etc; the expression of this; temperament, disposition; state of mind; (*formerly*) any of the four fluids of the body (blood, phlegm, yellow and black bile) that were thought to determine temperament. * *vt* to indulge; to gratify by conforming to the wishes of.—**humourless** *adj*.

hump *n* a rounded protuberance; a fleshy lump on the back of an animal (as a camel or whale); a deformity causing curvature of the spine. * *vt* to hunch; to arch.

humpback *n* a hunchback.—**humpbacked** *adj*.

hunch *n* a hump; (*inf*) an intuitive feeling. * *vt* to arch into a hump. * *vi* to move forward jerkily.

hunchback *n* a person with curvature of the spine.

hundred *adj, n* ten times ten; the symbol for this(100, C, c); the hundredth in a series or set.

hundredweight *n* a unit of weight, equal to 112 pounds in Britain and 100 pounds in the US.

hung *see* **hang**.

hunger *n* (a feeling weak or empty from) a need for food; a strong desire. * *vi* to feel hunger; to have a strong desire (for).

hungry *adj* (**hungrier, hungriest**) desiring

food; craving for something; greedy.—**hungrily** *adv*.

hunt *vti* to seek out to kill or capture (game) for food or sport; to search (for); to chase. * *n* a chase; a search; a party organized for hunting.

hunter *n* a person who hunts; a horse used in hunting.—**huntress** *nf*.

hunting *n* the art or practice of one who hunts; a pursuit; a search.

hurdle *n* a portable frame of bars for temporary fences or for jumping over by horses or runners; an obstacle. (*pl*) a race over hurdles.—**hurdler** *n*.

hurl *vt* to throw violently; to utter vehemently.—*also n*.

hurrah *interj* an exclamation of approval or joy.

hurricane *n* a violent tropical cyclone with winds of at least 74 miles per hour.

hurried *adj* performed with great haste.—**hurriedly** *adv*.

hurry *n* rush; urgency; eagerness to do, go, etc. * *vt* to cause to move or happen more quickly. * *vi* to move or act with haste.

hurt *vb* (*pt* **hurt**) *vt* to cause physical pain to; to injure, damage; to offend. * *vi* to feel pain; to cause pain.—**hurtful** *adj*.

hurtle *vti* to move or throw with great speed and force.

husband *n* a man to whom a woman is married. * *vt* to conserve; to manage economically.

hush *vti* to make or become silent. * *n* a silence or calm.

husk *n* the dry covering of certain fruits and seeds; any dry, rough, or useless covering. * *vt* to strip the husk from.

husky[1] *adj* (**huskier, huskiest**) (*voice*) hoarse; rough-sounding; hefty, strong. —**huskily** *adv*.—**huskiness** *n*.

husky[2] *n* an Arctic sled dog.

hustle *vt* to jostle or push roughly or hurriedly; to force hurriedly; (*sl*) to obtain by rough or illegal means. * *vi* to move hurriedly. * *n* an instance of hustling.—**hustler** *n*.

hut *n* a very plain or crude little house or cabin.

hutch *n* a pen or coop for small animals; a hut.

hyacinth *n* a plant of the lily family with spikes of bell-shaped flowers; the orange gemstone jacinth; a light violet to moderate purple.

hyaena *see* **hyena**.

hybrid *n* the offspring of two plants or animals of different species; a mongrel. * *adj* crossbred.

hydrant *n* a large pipe with a valve for drawing water from a main.

hydraulic *adj* operated by water or other liquid, esp by moving through pipes under pressure; of hydraulics.—**hydraulically** *adv*.

hydraulics *npl* (*used as sing*) the science dealing with the mechanical properties of liquids and their application in engineering.

hydroelectricity *n* electricity generated by water power.—**hydroelectric** *adj*.

hydrogen *n* a flammable, colourless, odourless, tasteless, gaseous chemical element, the lightest substance known.

hyena *n* a nocturnal, carnivorous, scavenging mammal like a wolf.—*also* **hyaena**.

hygiene *n* the principles and practice of health and cleanliness.—**hygienic** *adj*.—**hygienically** *adv*.

hymn *n* a song of praise to God or other object of worship.

hyphen *n* a punctuation mark (-) used to join two syllables or words, or to divide words into parts. * *vt* to hyphenate.

hypnosis *n* (*pl* **hypnoses**) a relaxed state resembling sleep in which the mind responds to external suggestion.

hypnotism *n* the act of inducing hypnosis; the study and use of hypnosis. —**hypnotist** *n*.

hypnotize *vt* to put in a state of hypnosis; to fascinate.

hypocrisy *n* a falsely pretending to possess virtues, beliefs, etc; an example of this.—**hypocrite** *n*.—**hypocritical** *adj*.—**hypocritically** *adv*.

hypothesis *n* (*pl* **hypotheses**) something assumed for the purpose of argument; a theory to explain some fact that may or may not prove to be true; supposition; conjecture.

hypothetical *adj* based on hypothesis, conjectural.—**hypothetically** *adv*.

hysteria *n* a mental disorder marked by excitability, anxiety, imaginary organic disorders, etc; frenzied emotion or excitement.

hysteric *n* a hysterical person; (*pl*) fits of hysteria.

hysterical *adj* caused by hysteria; suffering from hysteria; (*inf*) extremely funny.—**hysterically** *adv*.

I

I *pron* the person who is speaking or writing, used in referring to himself or herself.

ice *n* water frozen solid; a sheet of this; a portion of ice cream or water ice; (*sl*) diamonds. * *vti* (*often with* **up** *or* **over**) to freeze; to cool with ice; to cover with icing.

iceberg *n* a great mass of mostly submerged ice floating in the sea.

icebox *n* a compartment in a refrigerator for making and storing ice; a refrigerator.

ice cream *adj* a sweet frozen food, made from flavoured milk or cream.

ice hockey *n* indoor or outdoor hockey played on ice by two teams of six skaters with curved sticks and a puck.

icicle *n* a hanging tapering length of ice formed when dripping water freezes.

icing *n* a semi-solid sugary mixture covering cakes, etc.

icon *n* an image; (*Eastern Church*) a sacred image, usu on a wooden panel.

icy *adj* (**icier, iciest**) full of, made of, or covered with ice; slippery or very cold; cold in manner.—**icily** *adv*.—**iciness** *n*.

I'd = I had, I should, I would.

idea *n* a mental impression of anything; a vague impression, notion; an opinion or belief; a scheme; a supposition; a person's conception of something; a significance or purpose.

ideal *adj* existing in the mind or as an idea; satisfying an ideal, perfect. * *n* the most perfect conception of anything; a person,thing regarded as perfect; a standard for attainment or imitation; an aim or principle.—**ideally** *adv*.

identical *adj* exactly the same; having the same origin.—**identically** *adv*.

identification *n* the act of identifying; the state of being identified; that which identifies.

identify *vt* to consider to be the same, equate; to establish the identity of; to associate closely; to regard (oneself) as similar to another.—**identifier** *n*.

identity *n* the state of being exactly alike; the distinguishing characteristics of a person, personality; the state of being the same as a specified person or thing.

ideology *n* the doctrines, beliefs or opinions of an individual, social class, political party, etc.—**ideological** *adj*.—**ideologist, ideologue** *n*.

idiocy *n* mental deficiency; stupidity, imbecility; something stupid, foolish.

idiom *n* an accepted phrase or expression with a different meaning from the literal; the usual way in which the words of a language are used to express thought; the dialect of a people, region, etc; the characteristic style of a school of art, literature, etc—**idiomatic** *adj*.—**idiomatically** *adv*.

idiosyncrasy *n* a type of behaviour or characteristic peculiar to a person or group; a quirk, eccentricity.—**idiosyncratic** *adj*.

idiot *n* a severely mentally retarded adult; (*inf*) a foolish or stupid person.

idiotic *adj* stupid; senseless.—**idiotically** *adv*.

idle *adj* not employed, unoccupied; not in use; averse to work; useless; worthless. * *vt* to waste or spend (time) in idleness. * *vi* to move slowly or aimlessly; (*engine*) to operate without transmitting power.—**idleness** *n*.—**idler** *n*.—**idly** *adv*.

idol *n* an image or object worshipped as a god; a person who is intensely loved, admired or honoured.

idolize *vt* to make an idol of, for worship; to love to excess.—**idolization** *n*.

i.e. *abbr* = *id est*, that is.

if *conj* on condition that; in the event that; supposing that; even though; whenever; whether.

igloo *n* an Eskimo house built of blocks of snow and ice.

ignite *vti* to set fire to; to catch fire; to burn or cause to burn.

ignition *n* an act or instance of igniting; the starting of an internal combustion engine; the mechanism that ignites an internal combustion engine.

ignorant *adj* lacking knowledge; uninformed, uneducated; resulting from or showing lack of knowledge.—**ignorance** *n*.—**ignorantly** *adv*.

ignore *vt* to disregard; to deliberately refuse to notice someone.

ill *adj* not in good health; harmful; bad; hostile; faulty; unfavourable. * *adv* badly, wrongly; hardly, with difficulty. * *n* trouble; harm; evil.

I'll = I shall, I will.

ill-advised *adj* unwise.

ill at ease *adj* uneasy, embarrassed.

illegal *adj* against the law.—**illegally** *adv*.—**illegality** *n*.

illegible *adj* impossible to read.—**illegibly** *adv*.—**illegibility** *n*.

illegitimate *adj* born of parents not married to each other; contrary to law, rules, or logic.—**illegitimately** *adv*.—**illegitimacy** *n*.

illicit *adj* improper; unlawful.—**illicitly** *adv*.

illiterate *adj* uneducated, esp not knowing how to read or write. * *n* an illiterate person.—**illiterately** *adv*.—**illiteracy** *n*.

ill-natured *adj* spiteful.
illness *n* a state of ill-health; sickness.
illogical *adj* not logical or reasonable.—**illogically** *adv*.—**illogicality** *n*.
ill-treat *vt* to treat unkindly, unfairly, etc.—**ill-treatment** *n*.
illuminate *vt* to give light to; to light up; to make clear; to inform; to decorate as with gold or lights.—**illumination** *n*.—**illuminative** *adj*.
illusion *n* a false idea or conception; an unreal or misleading image or appearance.—**illusional, illusionary** *adj*.
illusory, illusive *adj* deceptive; based on illusion.
illustrate *vt* to explain, as by examples; to provide (books, etc) with explanatory pictures, charts, etc; to serve as an example.—**illustrative** *adj*.—**illustrator** *n*.
illustration *n* the act of illustrating; the state of being illustrated; an example that explains or corroborates; a picture or diagram in a book, etc.
illustrious *adj* distinguished, famous. —**illustriousness** *n*.
ill-will *n* antagonism, hostility.
I'm = I am.
image *n* a representation of a person or thing; the visual impression of something in a lens, mirror, etc; a copy; a likeness; a mental picture; the concept of a person, product, etc held by the public at large. * *vt* to make a representation of; to reflect; to imagine.
imagery *n* the work of the imagination; mental pictures; figures of speech; images in general or collectively.
imaginary *adj* existing only in the imagination.
imagination *n* the image-forming power of the mind, or the power of the mind that modifies the conceptions, esp the higher form of this power exercised in art and poetry; creative ability; resourcefulness in overcoming practical difficulties, etc.
imaginative *adj* having or showing imagination; produced by imagination.—**imaginatively** *adv*.
imagine *vt* to form a mental image of; to believe falsely; (*inf*) to suppose; to guess. * *vi* to employ the imagination.
imbalance *n* a lack of balance, as in proportion, emphasis, etc.
imbecile *n* an adult with a mental age of a three-to eight-year-old child; an idiotic person. * *adj* stupid or foolish.—**imbecility** *n*.
imitate *vt* to try to follow as a pattern or model; to mimic humorously, impersonate; to copy, reproduce.—**imitator** *n*.
imitation *n* an act or instance of imitating; a copy; an act of mimicking or impersonation.
immaculate *adj* spotless; flawless; pure, morally unblemished.—**immaculately** *adv*.
immaterial *adj* spiritual as opposed to physical; unimportant.
immature *adj* not mature.—**immaturity** *n*.
immediate *adj* acting or occurring without delay; next, nearest, without intervening agency; next in relationship; in close proximity, near to; directly concerning or touching a person or thing.—**immediacy** *n*.
immediately *adv* without delay; directly; near, close by. * *conj* as soon as.
immense *adj* very large in size or extent; limitless; (*inf*) excellent.—**immensely** *adv*.
immerse *vt* to plunge into a liquid; to absorb or engross; to baptize by total submergence.—**immersible** *adj*.
immersion heater *n* an electric element for heating liquids, esp water in a domestic hot-water tank.
immigrant *n* a person who immigrates; a person recently settled in a country but not born there.
immigrate *vi* to come into a new country, esp to settle permanently.—**immigration** *n*.—**immigratory** *adj*.
imminent *adj* about to happen; impending.—**imminence** *n*.—**imminently** *adv*.
immobilize *vt* to make immobile.—**immobilization** *n*.
immoral *adj* against accepted standards of proper behaviour; sexually degenerate; corrupt; wicked.—**immorally** *adv*.—**immorality** *n*.
immortal *adj* living for ever; enduring; having lasting fame. * *n* an immortal being or person; (*pl*) the gods of classical mythology.—**immortality** *n*.
immortalize *vt* to render immortal; to bestow lasting fame upon.—**immortalization** *n*.
immune *adj* not susceptible to a specified disease through inoculation or natural resistance; conferring immunity; exempt from a certain obligation, tax, duty, etc.
immunize *vt* to make immune, esp against infection.—**immunization** *n*.
impact *n* violent contact; a shocking effect; the force of a body colliding with another. * *vt* to force tightly together. * *vi* to hit with force.—**impaction** *n*.

impair *vt* to make worse, less, etc.—**impairment** *n*.

impale *vt* to fix on, or pierce through, with something pointed.—**impalement** *n*.

impartial *adj* not favouring one side more than another, unbiased.—**impartiality** *n*.—**impartially** *adv*.

impassable *adj* (*roads, etc*) incapable of being travelled through or over.—**impassability** *n*.—**impassably** *adv*.

impatient *adj* lacking patience; intolerant of delay, etc; restless.—**impatience** *n*.—**impatiently** *adv*.

impeach *vt* to question a person's honesty; to try (a public official) on a charge of wrongdoing.—**impeachment** *n*.

impeccable *adj* without defect or error; faultless.—**impeccability** *n*.—**impeccably** *adv*.

impede *vt* to obstruct or hinder the progress of.

impediment *n* something that impedes; an obstruction; a physical defect, as a stammer that prevents fluency of speech.

impend *vi* to be imminent; to threaten.—**impending** *adj*.

imperative *adj* urgent, pressing; authoritative; obligatory; designating or of the mood of a verb that expresses a command, entreaty, etc. * *n* a command; (*gram*) the imperative mood of a verb.

imperceptible *adj* not able to be detected by the mind or senses; slight, minute, gradual.—**imperceptibility** *n*.—**imperceptibly** *adv*.

imperfect *adj* having faults, flaws, mistakes, etc; defective; incomplete; (*gram*) designating a verb tense that indicates a past action or state as incomplete or continuous. * (*gram*) an imperfect tense.

imperfection *n* the state or quality of being imperfect; a defect, fault.

imperial *adj* of an empire, emperor, or empress; majestic; of great size or superior quality; of the British non-metric system of weights and measures.—**imperially** *adv*.

impersonal *adj* not referring to any particular person; cold, unfeeling; not existing as a person; (*verb*) occurring only in the third person singular, usu with "it" as subject.—**impersonality** *n*.—**impersonally** *adv*.

impersonate *vt* to assume the role of another person as entertainment or for fraud.—**impersonation** *n*.—**impersonator** *n*.

impertinent *adj* impudent; insolent; irrelevant.—**impertinence** *n*.—**impertinently** *adv*.

impervious *adj* incapable of being penetrated, as by water; not readily receptive (to) or affected (by).

impetuous *adj* acting or done suddenly with impulsive energy.—**impetuosity** *n*.—**impetuously** *adv*.

impetus *n* the force with which a body moves against resistance; driving force or motive.

impinge *vi* (*with* **on, upon**) to have an impact; to encroach.—**impingement** *n*.

implausible *adj* not plausible.—**implausibility** *n*.—**implausibly** *adv*.

implement *n* something used in a given activity. * *vt* to carry out, put into effect.—**implementation** *n*.

implicate *vt* to show to have a part, esp in a crime; to imply.

implication *n* an implicating or being implicated; that which is implied; an inference not expressed but understood; deduction.

implicit *adj* implied rather than stated explicitly; unquestioning, absolute.—**implicitly** *adv*.

implore *vt* to request earnestly; to plead, entreat.—**imploringly** *adv*.

imply *vt* to hint, suggest indirectly; to indicate or involve as a consequence.

impolite *adj* not polite, rude.—**impolitely** *adv*.—**impoliteness** *n*.

imponderable *adj* not able to be weighed or measured. * *n* something difficult to measure or assess.

import *vt* to bring (goods) in from a foreign country for sale or use; to mean; to signify. * *vi* to be of importance, to matter. * *n* something imported; meaning; importance.—**importable** *adj*.—**importer** *n*.

importance *n* the quality of being important; a high place in public estimation; high self-esteem.

important *adj* having great significance or consequence; (*person*) having power, authority, etc.—**importantly** *adv*.

impose *vt* to put (a burden, tax, punishment) on or upon; to force (oneself) on others; to lay pages of type or film and secure them. * *vi* (*with* **on** *or* **upon**) to take advantage of; to cheat or defraud.

imposing *adj* impressive because of size, appearance, dignity, etc.—**imposingly** *adv*.

impossibility *n* the character of being impossible; that which cannot be, or be supposed to be, done.

impossible *adj* not capable of existing, being done, or happening; (*inf*) unendurable, outrageous.—**impossibly** *adv*.

impostor, imposter *n* a person who acts fraudulently by impersonating another.

impotent *adj* lacking in necessary strength, powerless; (*man*) unable to engage in sexual intercourse.—**impotence** *n*.—**impotently** *adv*.

impound *vt* to take legal possession of; to shut up (an animal) in a pound.

impoverish *vt* to make poor; to deprive of strength.—**impoverishment** *n*.

impracticable *adj* not able to be carried out, not feasible.—**impracticability** *n*.—**impracticably** *adv*.

impractical *adj* not practical; not competent in practical skills.—**impracticality** *n*.—**impractically** *adv*.

imprecise *adj* not precise; ill-defined.—**imprecisely** *adv*.—**imprecision** *n*.

impregnable *adj* secure against attack, unyielding.—**impregnability** *n*.—**impregnably** *adv*.

impregnate *vt* to cause to become pregnant, to fertilize; to saturate, soak (with); to pervade.—**impregnation** *n*.

impresario *n* the manager of an opera, a concert series, etc.

impress[1] *vt* to make a strong, usu favourable, impression on; to fix deeply in the mind; to stamp with a mark; to imprint. * *n* an imprint, a mark.

impress[2] *vt* to coerce into military service.—**impressment** *n*.

impression *n* the effect produced in the mind by an experience; a mark produced by imprinting; a vague idea, notion; the act of impressing or being impressed; a notable or strong influence on the mind or senses; the number of copies of a book printed at one go; an impersonation or act of mimicry.

impressionable *n* easily impressed or influenced.—**impressionability** *n*.—**impressionably** *adv*.

impressive *adj* tending to impress the mind or emotions; arousing wonder or admiration.—**impressiveness** *n*.

imprison *vt* to put in a prison; to confine, as in a prison.—**imprisonment** *n*.

improbable *adj* unlikely to be true or to happen.—**improbability** *n*.—**improbably** *adv*.

impromptu *adj, adv* unrehearsed, unprepared. * *n* something impromptu, as a speech.

improper *adj* lacking propriety, indecent; incorrect; not suitable or appropriate.—**improperly** *adv*.

impropriety *n* the quality of being improper; indecency; an improper act, etc.

improve *vt* to make or become better.—**improvable** *adj*.—**improver** *n*.

improvement *n* the act of improving or being improved; an alteration that improves or adds to the value of something.

improvise *vti* to compose, perform, recite, etc without preparation; to make or do with whatever is at hand.—**improvisation** *n*.—**improviser** *n*.

impulse *n* a sudden push or thrust; a stimulus transmitted through a nerve or a muscle; a sudden instinctive urge to act.

impulsive *adj* tending to act on impulse; forceful, impelling; acting momentarily.—**impulsively** *adv*.—**impulsiveness** *n*.

impunity *n* exemption or freedom from punishment or harm.

impure *adj* unclean; adulterated.

impurity *n* a being impure; an impure substance or constituent.

in *prep* inside; within; at; as contained by; during; at the end of; not beyond; affected by; being a member of; wearing; using; because of; into. * *adv* to or at a certain place; so as to be contained by a certain space, condition, etc; (*games*) batting, in play. * *adj* that is in power; inner; inside; gathered, counted, etc; (*inf*) currently smart, fashionable, etc.

in. *abbr* = inch(es).

inability *n* lack of ability.

inaccessible *adj* not accessible, unapproachable.—**inaccessibility** *n*.—**inaccessibly** *adv*.

inaccurate *adj* not accurate, imprecise.—**inaccuracy** *n*.—**inaccurately** *adv*.

inactive *adj* not active.—**inactively** *adv*.—**inactivity** *n*.

inadequate *adj* not adequate; not capable.—**inadequacy** *n*.—**inadequately** *adv*.

inadmissible *adj* not admissible, esp as evidence.—**inadmissibility** *n*.

inadvertent *adj* not attentive or observant, careless; due to oversight.—**inadvertence, inadvertency** *n*.—**inadvertently** *adv*.

inadvisable *adj* not advisable; inexpedient.—**inadvisably** *adv*.

inane *adj* lacking sense, silly.—**inanely** *adv*.—**inanity** *n*.

inanimate *adj* not animate; showing no signs of life; dull.—**inanimately** *adv*.—**inanimation** *n*.

inappropriate *adj* unsuitable.—**inappropriately** *adv*.—**inappropriateness** *n*.

inarticulate *adj* not expressed in words; incapable of being expressed in words; incapable of coherent or effective expression of ideas, feelings, etc.—**inarticulately** *adv*.

inasmuch *adv* in like degree; (*with* **as**) seeing that; because.

inattentive *adj* not attending; neglectful.—**inattention** *n*.

inaudible *adj* unable to be heard.—**inaudibility** *n*.—**inaudibly** *adv*.

inaugural *n* of or pertaining to an inauguration; a speech made at an inauguration.

inaugurate *vt* to admit ceremonially into office; to open (a building, etc) formally to the public; to cause to begin, initiate.—**inauguration** *n*.

inborn *adj* present from birth; hereditary.

inbred *adj* innate; produced by inbreeding.

inbreed *vti* (*pt* **inbred**) to breed by continual mating of individuals of the same or closely related stocks.

Inc. *abbr* = Incorporated.

incapable *adj* lacking capability; not able or fit to perform an activity.—**incapability** *n*.—**incapably** *adv*.

incapacitate *vt* to weaken, to disable; to make ineligible.—**incapacitation** *n*.

incarnate *adj* endowed with a human body; personified. * *vt* to give bodily form to; to be the type or embodiment of.—**incarnation** *n*.

incendiary *adj* pertaining to arson; (*bomb*) designed to start fires; tending to stir up or inflame. * *n* a person that sets fire to a building, etc maliciously, an arsonist; an incendiary substance (as in a bomb); a person who stirs up violence, etc.

incense[1] *vt* to make extremely angry.

incense[2] *n* a substance that gives off a fragrant odour when burned; the fumes so produced; any pleasant odour.

incessant *adj* never ceasing; continual, constant.—**incessantly** *adv*.

incest *n* sexual intercourse between persons too closely related to marry legally.

inch *n* a measure of length equal to one twelfth of a foot (2.54 cm); a very small distance or amount. * *vti* to move very slowly, or by degrees.

incidence *n* the degree or range of occurrence or effect.

incidental *adj* happening in connection with something more important; happening by chance. * *npl* miscellaneous items, minor expenses.

incidentally *adv* in passing, as an aside.

incinerator *n* a furnace for burning rubbish.

incipient *adj* beginning to be or appear; initial.—**incipience** *n*.

incision *n* incising; a cut made into something, esp by a surgeon into a body.

incisive *adj* keen, penetrating; decisive; biting.—**incisively** *adv*.—**incisiveness** *n*.

incite *vt* to urge to action; to rouse.—**incitement** *n*.

inclination *n* a propensity or disposition, esp a liking; a deviation from the horizontal or vertical; a slope; inclining or being inclined; a bending movement, a bow.

incline *vi* to lean, to slope; to be disposed towards an opinion or action. * *vt* to cause to bend (the head or body) forwards; to cause to deviate, esp from the horizontal or vertical. * *n* a slope.

include *vt* to enclose, contain; to comprise as part or a larger group, amount, etc.—**inclusion** *n*.

inclusive *adj* comprehensive; including the limits specified.—**inclusively** *adv*.

incognito *adj, adv* under an assumed name or identity. * *n* (*pl* **incognitos**) a person appearing or living incognito; the name assumed by such a person.—**incognita** *nf*.

incoherent *adj* lacking organization or clarity; inarticulate in speech or thought.—**incoherence** *n*.—**incoherently** *adv*.

income *n* the money etc received for labour or services, or from property, investments, etc.

income tax *n* a tax levied on the net income of a person or business.

incoming *adj* coming; accruing. * *n* the act of coming in; that which comes in; income.

incompatible *adj* not able to exist together in harmony; antagonistic; inconsistent.—**incompatibility** *n*. —**incompatibly** *adv*.

incompetent *adj* lacking the necessary ability, skill, etc. * *n* an incompetent person.—**incompetence** *n*.—**incompetently** *adv*.

incomplete *adj* unfinished; lacking a part or parts.—**incompletely** *adv*.—**incompleteness** *n*.

incomprehensible *adj* not to be understood or grasped by the mind; inconceivable.—**incomprehension** *n*.

inconclusive *adj* leading to no definite result; ineffective; inefficient.—**inconclusively** *adv*.—**inconclusiveness** *n*.

incongruous *adj* lacking harmony or agreement of parts; unsuitable; inappropriate.—**incongruity** *n*.—**incongruously** *adv*.

inconsequential, inconsequent *adj* not following logically; irrelevant.—**inconsequen-**

tially, inconsequently *adv*.

inconsiderate *adj* uncaring about others; thoughtless.—**inconsiderately** *adv*.—**inconsiderateness, inconsideration** *n*.

inconsistent *adj* not compatible with other facts; contradictory; irregular, fickle.—**inconsistency** *n*.—**inconsistently** *adv*.

inconspicuous *adj* not conspicuous.—**inconspicuously** *adv*.—**inconspicuousness** *n*.

inconstant *adj* subject to change; unstable; variable; fickle; capricious.—**inconstancy** *n*.

incontinent *adj* unable to control the excretion of bodily wastes; lacking sexual restraint.—**incontinence** *n*.

inconvenience *n* want of convenience; unfitness; that which incommodes; disadvantage. * *vt* to put to inconvenience; to annoy.—**inconvenient** *adj*.

incorrect *adj* faulty; inaccurate; improper.—**incorrectly** *adv*.

incorruptible *adj* incapable of physical corruption, decay or dissolution; incapable of being bribed; not liable to moral perversion or contamination.—**incorruptibly** *adv*.

increase *vti* to make or become greater in size, quality, amount, etc. * *n* increasing or becoming increased; the result or amount by which something increases.—**increasingly** *adv*.

incredible *adj* unbelievable; (*inf*) wonderful.—**incredibly** *adv*.

incredulous *adj* not able or willing to accept as true; unbelieving.—**incredulity** *n*.—**incredulously** *adv*.

increment *n* (the amount of) an increase; an addition.—**incremental** *adj*.

incriminate *vt* to involve in or indicate as involved in a crime or fault.—**incrimination** *n*.—**incriminatory** *adj*.

incubator *n* an apparatus in which eggs are hatched by artificial heat; an apparatus for nurturing premature babies until they can survive unaided.

incur *vt* (*pt* **incurred**) to bring upon oneself (something undesirable).

incurable *adj* incapable of being cured; beyond the power of skill or medicine; lacking remedy; incorrigible. * *n* a person diseased beyond cure.—**incurably** *adv*.

incursion *n* an invasion or raid into another's territory, etc.

indebted *adj* in debt; owing gratitude.—**indebtedness** *n*.

indecent *adj* offending against accepted standards of decent behaviour.—**indecency** *n*.—**indecently** *adv*.

indecision *n* not able to make a decision; hesitation.

indecisive *adj* inconclusive; irresolute.—**indecisively** *adv*.—**indecisiveness** *n*.

indeed *adv* truly, certainly. * *interj* expressing irony, surprise, disbelief, etc.

indefinable *adj* that cannot be defined.—**indefinably** *adv*.

indefinite *adj* not certain, undecided; imprecise, vague; having no fixed limits.—**indefinitely** *adv*.—**indefiniteness** *n*.

indelible *adj* not able to be removed or erased; (*pen, ink, etc*) making an indelible mark.—**indelibly** *adv*.

indemnify *vt* to insure against loss, damage, etc; to repay (for damage, loss, etc).—**indemnification** *n*.

indentation *n* a being indented; a notch, cut, inlet, etc; a dent; a spacing in from the margin (—*also* **indention, indent**).

independence *n* the state of being independent.

independent *adj* freedom from the influence or control of others; self-governing; self-determined; not adhering to any political party; not connected with others; not depending on another for financial support. * *n* a person who is independent in thinking, action etc.—**independently** *adv*.

indescribable *adj* unable to be described; too beautiful, horrible, intense, etc for words.

index *n* (*pl* **indexes, indices**) an alphabetical list of names, subjects, items, etc mentioned in a printed book, usu listed alphabetically at the end of the text; a figure showing ratio or relative change, as of prices or wages; any indication or sign; a pointer or dial on an instrument; the exponent of a number. * *vt* to make an index of or for.—**indexer** *n*.

index finger *n* the forefinger.

index-linked *adj* (*salary, pension, etc*) linked directly to changes in the cost-of-living index.

Indian *n* a native of India; an American Indian, the original inhabitants of the continent of America.

indicate *vt* to point out; to show or demonstrate; to be a sign or symptom of; to state briefly, suggest.—**indication** *n*.

indicative *adj* serving as a sign (of); (*gram*) denoting the mood of the verb that affirms or denies.

indicator *n* a thing that indicates or points; a measuring device with a pointer, etc; an instrument showing the operating condition of a piece of machinery, etc; a device giving updated information, such as a departure board in a railway station or airport; a flashing light used to warn of a change in direction of a vehicle.

indict *vt* to charge with a crime; to accuse.

indictable *adj* subject to being indicted; making one liable to indictment.

indictment *n* a formal written statement framed by a prosecuting authority charging a person of a crime.

indifferent *adj* showing no concern, uninterested; unimportant; impartial; average; mediocre.—**indifference** *n.* —**indifferently** *adv.*

indigenous *adj* existing naturally in a particular country, region, or environment; native.

indigestible *adj* difficult or impossible to digest.—**indigestibility** *n.*

indigestion *n* a pain caused by difficulty in digesting food.

indignant *adj* expressing anger, esp at mean or unjust action.—**indignantly** *adv.*

indignation *n* anger at something regarded as unfair, wicked, etc.

indignity *n* humiliation; treatment making one feel degraded, undignified.

indirect *adj* not straight; roundabout; secondary; dishonest.—**indirectly** *adv.*

indiscreet *adj* not discreet; tactless.—**indiscreetly** *adv.*

indiscretion *n* an indiscreet act; rashness.

indiscriminate *adj* not making a careful choice; confused; random; making no distinctions.—**indiscriminately** *adv.*—**indiscrimination** *n.*

indispensable *adj* absolutely essential.—**indispensability** *n.*—**indispensably** *adv.*

indisposed *adj* ill or sick; reluctant; disinclined.

indisputable *adj* unquestionable; certain.—**indisputability** *n.*—**indisputably** *adv.*

indistinct *adj* not clearly marked; dim; not distinct.—**indistinctly** *adv.*—**indistinctness** *n.*

individual *adj* existing as a separate thing or being; of, by, for, or relating to a single person or thing. * *n* a single thing or being; a person.

individualist *n* a person who thinks or behaves with marked independence.—**individualism** *n.*—**individualistic** *adj.*

individuality *n* the condition of being individual; separate or distinct existence; distinctive character.

indoctrinate *vt* to systematically instruct in doctrines, ideas, beliefs, etc.—**indoctrination** *n.*

indolent *adj* idle; lazy.—**indolently** *adv.*—**indolence** *n.*

indoor *adj* done, used, or situated within a building.

indoors *adv* in or into a building.

indubitable *adj* not capable of being doubted.—**indubitably** *adv.*

induce *vt* to persuade; to bring on; to draw (a conclusion) from particular facts; to bring about (an electric or magnetic effect) in a body by placing it within a field of force.

inducement *n* something that induces; a stimulus; a motive.

induction *n* the act or an instance of inducting, eg into office; reasoning from particular premises to general conclusions; the inducing of an electric or magnetic effect by a field of force.—**inductive** *adj.*

indulge *vt* to satisfy (a desire); to gratify the wishes of; to humour. * *vi* to give way to one's desire.

indulgence *n* indulging or being indulged; a thing indulged in; a favour or privilege; (*RC Church*) a remission of punishment still due for a sin after the guilt has been forgiven.

indulgent *adj* indulging or characterized by indulgence; lenient.—**indulgently** *adv.*

industrial *adj* relating to or engaged in industry; used in industry; having many highly developed industries.—**industrially** *adv.*

industrialist *n* a person who owns or manages an industrial enterprise.

industrialize *vti* to make or become industrial.—**industrialization** *n.*

industrious *adj* hard-working.—**industriously** *adv.*—**industriousness** *n.*

industry *n* organized production or manufacture of goods; manufacturing enterprises collectively; a branch of commercial enterprise producing a particular product; any large-scale business activity; the owners and managers of industry; diligence.

inebriated *adj* drunken.—**inebriation** *n.*

inedible *adj* not fit to be eaten.

ineffective *adj* not effective.—**ineffectively** *adv.*

ineffectual *adj* not effectual; futile. —**ineffectually** *adv.*

inefficiency *n* the quality or condition of being inefficient; an instance of inefficiency or incompetence.

inefficient *adj* not efficient.—**inefficiently** *adv.*

ineligible *adj* not eligible.—**ineligibility** *n.*

inept *adj* unsuitable; unfit; foolish; awkward; clumsy.—**ineptitude** *n*.—**ineptly** *adv*.
inequality *n* lack of equality in size, status, etc; unevenness.
inert *adj* without power to move or to resist; inactive; dull; slow; with few or no active properties.—**inertly** *adv*.—**inertness** *n*.
inertia *n* (*physics*) the tendency of matter to remain at rest (or continue in a fixed direction) unless acted on by an outside force; disinclination to act.
inestimable *adj* not to be estimated; beyond measure or price; incalculable; invaluable.—**inestimably** *adv*.
inevitable *adj* sure to happen; unavoidable. * something that is inevitable.—**inevitability** *n*.—**inevitably** *adv*.
inexact *adj* not strictly true or correct.—**inexactitude** *n*.—**inexactly** *adv*.
inexhaustible *adj* not to be exhausted or spent; unfailing; unwearied.—**inexhaustibly** *adv*.
inexorable *adj* unable to be persuaded by persuasion or entreaty, relentless.—**inexorably** *adv*.
inexpensive *adj* cheap.—**inexpensively** *adv*.
inexperience *n* want of experience or of the knowledge that comes by experience.
inexperienced *adj* lacking experience; unpractised; unskilled; unversed.
inexplicable *adj* not to be explained, made plain, or intelligible; not to be interpreted or accounted for.—**inexplicably** *adv*.
inextricable *adj* that cannot be disentangled, solved, or escaped from.—**inextricably** *adv*.
infallible *adj* incapable of being wrong; dependable; reliable.—**infallibility** *n*.—**infallibly** *adv*.
infamous *adj* having a bad reputation; notorious; causing a bad reputation; scandalous.
infamy *n* ill fame; public disgrace; ignominy.
infancy *n* early childhood; the beginning or early existence of anything.
infant *n* a very young child; a baby.
infantile *adj* of infants; like an infant, babyish.
infantry *n* soldiers trained to fight on foot.
infatuate *vt* to inspire with intense, foolish, or short-lived passion.—**infatuated** *adj*.—**infatuation** *n*.
infect *vt* to contaminate with disease-causing microorganisms; to taint; to affect, esp so as to harm.—**infective** *adj*.
infection *n* an infecting or being infected; an infectious disease; a diseased condition.
infectious *adj* (*disease*) able to be transmitted; a disease caused by the spread of bacteria in the body, etc; causing or transmitted by infection; tending to spread to others.
infer *vt* (*pt* **inferred**) to conclude by reasoning from facts or premises, to deduce; to accept as a fact or consequence.—**inferable, inferible** *adj*.
inference *n* an inferring; something inferred or deduced; a reasoning from premises to a conclusion.—**inferential** *adj*.
inferior *adj* lower in position, rank, degree, or quality. * *n* an inferior person.—**inferiority** *n*.
inferiority complex *n* (*psychol*) an acute sense of inferiority expressed by a lack of confidence or in exaggerated aggression.
infernal *adj* of hell; hellish; fiendish; (*inf*) irritating, detestable.—**infernally** *adv*.
inferno *n* (*pl* **infernos**) hell; intense heat; a devastating fire.
infertile *adj* not fertile.—**infertility** *n*.
infest *vt* to overrun in large numbers, usu so as to be harmful; to be parasitic in or on.—**infestation** *n*.
infidelity *n* unfaithfulness, esp in marriage.
infighting *n* (*boxing*) exchanging punches at close quarters; intense competition within an organization.—**infighter** *n*.
infiltrate *vti* to filter or pass gradually through or into; to permeate; to penetrate (enemy lines, etc) gradually or stealthily, eg as spies.—**infiltration** *n*.—**infiltrator** *n*.
infinite *adj* endless, limitless; very great; vast.—**infinitely** *adv*.
infinitive *n* (*gram*) the form of a verb without reference to person, number or tense.
infinity *n* the condition or quality of being infinite; an unlimited number, quantity, or time period.
infirmary *n* a hospital or place for the treatment of the sick.
infirmity *n* being infirm; a physical weakness.
inflame *vti* to arouse, excite, etc or to become aroused, excited, etc; to undergo or cause to undergo inflammation.
inflammable *adj* able to catch fire, flammable; easily excited.
inflammation *n* an inflaming or being inflamed; redness, pain, heat, and swelling in the body, due to injury or disease.
inflate *vti* to fill or become filled with air or gas; to puff up with pride; to increase beyond what is normal, esp the supply of money or credit.—**inflatable** *adj*.
inflation *n* an inflating or being inflated; an increase in the currency in circulation or a

marked expansion of credit, resulting in a fall in currency value and a sharp rise in prices.
inflexible *adj* not flexible; stiff, rigid; fixed; unyielding.—**inflexibility** *n.*—**inflexibly** *adv.*
inflict *vt* to impose (pain, a penalty, etc) on a person or thing.—**infliction** *n.*
influence *n* the power to affect others; the power to produce effects by having wealth, position, ability, etc; a person with influence. * *vt* to have influence on.
influential *adj* having or exerting great influence.—**influentially** *adv.*
influenza *n* a contagious feverish virus disease marked by muscular pain and inflammation of the respiratory system.
influx *n* a sudden inflow of people or things to a place.
inform *vt* to provide knowledge of something to. * *vi* to give information to the police, etc, esp in accusing another.
informal *adj* not formal; not according to fixed rules or ceremony, etc; casual.—**informally** *adv.*
informality *n* the lack of regular, customary, or legal form; an informal act.
information *n* something told or facts learned; news; knowledge; data stored in or retrieved from a computer.
informative *adj* conveying information, instructive.
informer *n* a person who informs on another, esp to the police for a reward.
infrared *n* (*radiation*) having a wavelength longer than light but shorter than radio waves; of, pertaining to, or using such radiation.
infrequent *adj* seldom occurring; rare.—**infrequence, infrequency** *n.*
infringe *vt* to break or violate, esp an agreement or a law.—**infringement** *n.*
infuriate *vt* to enrage; to make furious.—**infuriating** *adj.*
ingenious *adj* clever, resourceful, etc; made or done in an original or clever way.—**ingeniously** *adv.*—**ingenuity** *n.*
ingot *n* a brick-shaped mass of cast metal, esp gold or silver.
ingrained *adj* (*habits, feelings, etc*) firmly established; (*dirt*) deeply embedded.—*also* **engrained**.
ingratiate *vt* to bring oneself into another's favour.
ingratitude *n* absence of gratitude; insensibility to kindness.
ingredient *n* something included in a mixture; a component.
inhabit *vt* to live in; to occupy; to reside.
inhabitant *n* a person or animal inhabiting a specified place.
inhale *vti* to breathe in.—**inhalation** *n.*
inherit *vt* to receive (property, a title, etc) under a will or by right of legal succession; to possess by genetic transmission. * *vi* to receive by inheritance; to succeed as heir.—**inheritor** *n.*
inheritance *n* the action of inheriting; something inherited.
inhibit *vt* to restrain; to prohibit.—**inhibiter** *n.*
inhibition *n* an inhibiting or being inhibited; a mental process that restrains or represses an action, emotion, or thought.
inhospitable *adj* not hospitable; affording no shelter; barren; cheerless.—**inhospitably** *adv.*—**inhospitality** *n.*
inhuman *adj* lacking in the human qualities of kindness, pity, etc; cruel, brutal, unfeeling; not human.
inimitable *adj* impossible to imitate; matchless.—**inimitably** *adv.*
iniquity *n* wickedness; great injustice.
initial *adj* of or at the beginning. * *n* the first letter of each word in a name; a large letter at the beginning of a chapter, etc. * *vt* (*pt* **initialled**) to sign with initials.—**initially** *adv.*
initiate *vt* to bring (something) into practice or use; to teach the fundamentals of a subject to; to admit as a member into a club, etc, esp with a secret ceremony. * *n* an initiated person.—**initiation** *n.*—**initiator** *n.*—**initiatory** *adj.*
initiative *n* the action of taking the first step; ability to originate new ideas or methods.
inject *vt* to force (a fluid) into a vein, tissue, etc, esp with a syringe; to introduce (a remark, quality, etc), to interject.
injection *n* an injecting; a substance that is injected.
injure *vt* to harm physically or mentally; to hurt, do wrong to.
injury *n* physical damage; harm.
injustice *n* the state or practice of being unfair; an unjust act.
ink *n* a coloured liquid used for writing, printing, etc; the dark protective secretion of an octopus, etc. * *vt* to cover, mark, or colour with ink.
inkling *n* a hint; a vague notion.
inlaid *see* **inlay**.
inland *adj* of or in the interior of a country. * *n* an inland region. * *adv* into or toward this region.
in-law *n* a relative by marriage.

inlay *vt* (*pt* **inlaid**) to decorate a surface by inserting pieces of metal, wood, etc. * *n* inlaid work; material inlaid.

inlet *n* a narrow strip of water extending into a body of land; an opening; a passage, pipe, etc for liquid to enter a machine, etc.

inmate *n* a person confined with others in a prison or institution.

inn *n* a small hotel; a restaurant or public house, esp in the countryside.

innate *adj* existing from birth; inherent; instinctive.—**innately** *adv*.

inner *adj* further within; inside, internal; private, exclusive. * *n* (*archery*) the innermost ring on a target.

innocent *adj* not guilty of a particular crime; free from sin; blameless; harmless; inoffensive; simple, credulous, naive. * *n* an innocent person, as a child.—**innocence** *n*.—**innocently** *adv*.

innocuous *adj* harmless.—**innocuously** *adv*.—**innocuousness** *n*.

innovate *vi* to introduce new methods, ideas, etc; to make changes.—**innovation** *n*.—**innovative, innovatory** *adv*.

innuendo *n* (*pl* **innuendoes, innuendos**) a hint or sly remark, usu derogatory; an insinuation.

inoculate *vt* to inject a serum or a vaccine into, esp in order to create immunity; to protect as if by inoculation.—**inoculation** *n*.

inopportune *adj* unseasonable; untimely.

inordinate *adj* excessive.—**inordinately** *adv*.

inorganic *adj* not having the structure or characteristics of living organisms; denoting a chemical compound not containing carbon.—**inorganically** *adv*.

inpatient *n* a patient being treated while remaining in hospital.

input *n* what is put in, as power into a machine, data into a computer, etc. * *vt* (*pt* **input** *or* **inputted**) to put in; to enter (data) into a computer.

inquest *n* a judicial inquiry held by a coroner, esp into a case of violent or unexplained death; (*inf*) any detailed inquiry or investigation.

inquire *vi* to request information about; (*usu with* **into**) to investigate. * *vt* to ask about.—*also* **enquire**.—**inquirer, enquirer** *n*.

inquiry *n* the act of inquiring; a search by questioning; an investigation; a question; research.—*also* **enquiry**.

inquisitive *adj* eager for knowledge; unnecessarily curious; prying.—**inquisitively** *adv*.—**inquisitiveness** *n*.

inroad *n* a raid into enemy territory; an encroachment or advance.

insane *adj* not sane, mentally ill; of or for insane people; very foolish.—**insanely** *adv*.

insanitary *adj* unclean, likely to cause infection or ill-health.

insanity *n* derangement of the mind or intellect; lunacy; madness.

insatiable *adj* not easily satisfied; greedy.—**insatiability** *n*.—**insatiably** *adv*.

inscribe *vt* to mark or engrave (words, etc) on (a surface); to add (a person's name) to a list; to dedicate (a book) to someone; to autograph; to fix in the mind.

inscription *n* an inscribing; words, etc, inscribed on a tomb, coin, etc.

inscrutable *adj* hard to understand, incomprehensible; enigmatic.—**inscrutability** *n*.—**inscrutably** *adv*.

insect *n* any of a class of small arthropods with three pairs of legs, a head, thorax, and abdomen and two or four wings.

insecticide *n* a substance for killing insects.

insecure *adj* not safe; feeling anxiety; not dependable.—**insecurely** *adv*.

insecurity *n* the condition of being insecure; lack of confidence or sureness; instability; something insecure.

insensible *adj* unconscious; unaware; indifferent; imperceptible.—**insensibility** *n*.—**insensibly** *adv*.

inseparable *adj* not able to be separated; closely attached, as romantically.

insert *vt* to put or fit (something) into something else. * *n* something inserted.—**insertion** *n*.

inshore *adj, adv* near or towards the shore.

inside *n* the inner side, surface, or part; (*pl*: *inf*) the internal organs, stomach, bowels. * *adj* internal; known only to insiders; secret. * *adv* on or in the inside; within; indoors; (*sl*) in prison. * *prep* in or within.

inside out *adj* reversed; with the inner surface facing the outside.

insider *n* a person within a place or group; a person with access to confidential information.

insidious *adj* marked by slyness or treachery; more dangerous than seems evident.—**insidiously** *adv*.—**insidiousness** *n*.

insight *n* the ability to see and understand clearly the inner nature of things, esp by intuition; an instance of such understanding.—**insightful** *adj*.

insignificant *adj* having little or no importance; trivial; worthless; small, inadequate.—**insignificance** *n.*—**insignificantly** *adv.*
insincere *adj* not sincere; hypocritical.—**insincerely** *adv.*—**insincerity** *n.*
insinuate *vt* to introduce or work in slowly, indirectly, etc; to hint.—**insinuation** *n.*
insipid *adj* lacking any distinctive flavour; uninteresting, dull.—**insipidity** *n.*—**insipidly** *adv.*—**insipidness** *n.*
insist *vi* (*often with* **on** *or* **upon**) to take and maintain a stand. * *vt* to demand strongly; to declare firmly.
insistent *adj* insisting or demanding.—**insistence** *n.*—**insistently** *adv.*
insolent *adj* disrespectful; impudent, arrogant; rude.—**insolence** *n.*—**insolently** *adv.*
insoluble *adj* incapable of being dissolved; impossible to solve or explain.—**insolubility** *n.*—**insolubly** *adv.*
insolvent *adj* unable to pay one's debts; bankrupt.—**insolvency** *n.*
insomnia *n* abnormal inability to sleep.
inspect *vt* to look at carefully; to examine or review officially.—**inspection** *n.*
inspector *n* an official who inspects in order to ensure compliance with regulations, etc; a police officer ranking below a superintendent.—**inspectorate** *n.*
inspiration *n* an inspiring; any stimulus to creative thought; an inspired idea, action, etc.—**inspirational** *adj.*
inspire *vt* to stimulate, as to some creative effort; to motivate by divine influence; to arouse (a thought or feeling) in (someone); to cause.—**inspiring** *adj.*
install, instal *vt* (*pt* **installed**) to formally place in an office, rank, etc; to establish in a place; to settle in a position or state.—**installer** *n.*
installation *n* the act of installing or being installed; machinery, equipment, etc that has been installed.
instalment, installment (*US*) *n* a sum of money to be paid at regular specified times; any of several parts, as of a magazine story or television serial.
instance *n* an example; a step in proceeding; an occasion. * *vt* to give as an example.
instant *adj* immediate; (*food*) concentrated or precooked for quick preparation. * *n* a moment; a particular moment.
instantly *adv* immediately.
instead *adv* in place of the one mentioned.
instep *n* the upper part of the arch of the foot, between the ankle and the toes.
instigate *vt* to urge on, goad; to initiate.—**instigation** *n.*—**instigator** *n.*
instil, instill (*US*) *vt* (*pt* **instilled**) to put (an idea, etc) in or into (the mind) gradually.—**instillation** *n.*—**instilment, instillment** *n.*
instinct *n* the inborn tendency to behave in a way characteristic of a species; a natural or acquired tendency; a knack.
instinctive, instinctual *adj* of, relating to, or prompted by instinct.—**instinctively, instinctually** *adv.*
institute *vt* to organize, establish; to start, initiate. * *n* an organization for the promotion of science, art, etc; a school, college, or department of a university specializing in some field.
institution *n* an established law, custom, etc; an organization having a social, educational, or religious purpose; the building housing it; (*inf*) a long-established person or thing.
instruct *vt* to provide with information; to teach; to give instructions to; to authorize.—**instructor** *n.*—**instructress** *nf.*
instruction *n* an order, direction; the act or process of teaching or training; knowledge imparted; (*comput*) a command in a program to perform a particular operation; (*pl*) orders, directions; detailed guidance.—**instructional** *adj.*
instructive *adj* issuing or containing instructions; giving information, educational.—**instructively** *adv.*
instrument *n* a thing by means of which something is done; a tool or implement; any of various devices for indicating, measuring, controlling, etc; any of various devices producing musical sound; a formal document. * *vt* to orchestrate.
instrumental *adj* serving as a means of doing something; helpful; of, performed on, or written for a musical instrument or instruments.
instrumentalist *n* a person who plays a musical instrument.
insubordinate *adj* not submitting to authority; rebellious.—**insubordination** *n.*
insufferable *adj* intolerable; unbearable.—**insufferably** *adv.*
insufficient *adj* not sufficient.—**insufficiency** *n.*—**insufficiently** *adv.*
insular *adj* of or like an island or islanders; narrow-minded; illiberal.—**insularity** *n.*
insulate *vt* to set apart; to isolate; to cover with a nonconducting material in order to prevent the escape of electricity, heat, sound, etc.—**insulation** *n.*—**insulator** *n.*

insulin *n* a hormone that controls absorption of sugar by the body, secreted by islets of tissue in the pancreas.
insult *vt* to treat with indignity or contempt; to offend. * *n* an insulting remark or act.
insuperable *adj* unable to be overcome.—**insuperability** *n.*—**insuperably** *adv.*
insurance *n* insuring or being insured; a contract purchased to guarantee compensation for a specified loss by fire, death, etc; the amount for which something is insured; the business of insuring against loss.
insure *vt* to take out or issue insurance on; to ensure. * *vi* to contract to give or take insurance.—**insurer** *n.*
insurrection *adj* a rising or revolt against established authority.—**insurrectionist** *n.*
intact *adj* unimpaired; whole.
intake *n* the place in a pipe, etc where a liquid or gas is taken in; a thing or quantity taken in, as students, etc; the process of taking in.
intangible *adj* that cannot be touched, incorporeal; representing value but without material being, as good will; indefinable. * *n* something that is intangible.—**intangibility** *n.*—**intangibly** *adv.*
integral *adj* necessary for completeness; whole or complete; made up of parts forming a whole. * *n* the result of a mathematical integration.—**integrally** *adv.*
integrate *vti* to make whole or become complete; to bring (parts) together into a whole; to remove barriers imposing segregation upon (racial groups); to abolish segregation; (*math*) to find the integral of.—**integration** *n.*
integrity *n* honesty, sincerity; completeness, wholeness; an unimpaired condition.
intellect *n* the ability to reason or understand; high intelligence; a very intelligent person.
intellectual *adj* of, involving, or appealing to the intellect; requiring intelligence. * *n* an intellectual person.
intelligence *n* the ability to learn or understand; the ability to cope with a new situation; news or information; those engaged in gathering secret, esp military, information.
intelligent *adj* having or showing intelligence; clever, wise, etc.—**intelligently** *adv.*
intelligible *adj* able to be understood; clear.—**intelligibility** *n.*—**intelligibly** *adv.*
intemperate *adj* indulging excessively in alcoholic drink; unrestrained; (*climate*) extreme.—**intemperance** *n.*—**intemperately** *adv.*
intend *vt* to mean, to signify; to propose, have in mind as an aim or purpose.
intense *adj* very strong, concentrated; passionate, emotional.—**intensely** *adv.*
intensify *vti* to make or become more intense.—**intensification** *n.*
intensity *n* the state or quality of being intense; density, as of a negative plate; the force or energy of any physical agent.
intensive *adj* of or characterized by intensity; thorough; denoting careful attention given to patients right after surgery, etc.—**intensively** *adv.*
intent *adj* firmly directed; having one's attention or purpose firmly fixed. * *n* intention; something intended; purpose or meaning.—**intently** *adv.*—**intentness** *n.*
intention *n* a determination to act in a specified way; anything intended.
intentional *adj* done purposely.—**intentionally** *adv.*
inter *vt* (*pt* **interred**) to bury.
interact *vi* to act upon each other.—**interaction** *n.*
intercede *vi* to intervene on another's behalf; to mediate.
intercept *vt* to stop or catch in its course. * *n* a point of intersection of two geometric figures; interception by an interceptor.—**interception** *n.*
interchange *vt* to give and receive one thing for another; to exchange, to put (each of two things) in the place of the other; to alternate. * *n* an interchanging; a junction on a motorway designed to prevent traffic intersecting.
interchangeable *adj* able to be interchanged.—**interchangeability** *n.*
intercom *n* (*inf*) a system of intercommunicating, as in an aircraft.
interconnect *vti* to connect by reciprocal links.—**interconnection** *n.*
intercourse *n* a connection by dealings or communication between individuals or groups; sexual intercourse, copulation.
interest *n* a feeling of curiosity about something; the power of causing this feeling; a share in, or a right to, something; anything in which one has a share; benefit; money paid for the use of money; the rate of such payment. * *vt* to excite the attention of; to cause to have a share in; to concern oneself with.
interested *adj* having or expressing an interest; affected by personal interest, not impartial.
interesting *n* engaging the attention.
interfere *vi* to clash; to come between; to

intervene; to meddle; to obstruct.

interference *n* an interfering; (*radio, TV*) the interruption of reception by atmospherics or by unwanted signals.

interim *n* an intervening period of time. * *adj* provisional, temporary. * *adv* meanwhile.

interior *adj* situated within; inner; inland; private. * *n* the interior part, as of a room, country, etc.

interjection *n* an interjecting; an interruption; an exclamation.

interlock *vti* to lock or become locked together; to join with one another.

interloper *n* a person who meddles; an intruder.

interlude *n* anything that fills time between two events, as music between acts of a play.

intermarry *vi* (*different races, religions, etc*) to become connected by marriage; to marry within one's close family.—**intermarriage** *n.*

intermediary *n* a mediator. * *adj* acting as a mediator; intermediate.

intermediate *adj* in the middle; in between.

intermission *n* an interval of time between parts of a performance.

intermittent *adj* stopping and starting again at intervals; periodic.—**intermittently** *adv.*

intern *vt* to detain and confine within an area, esp during wartime.—**internment** *n.*

internal *adj* of or on the inside; of or inside the body; intrinsic; domestic.—**internally** *adv.*

international *adj* between or among nations; concerned with the relations between nations; for the use of all nations; of or for people in various nations. * *n* a sporting competition between teams from different countries; a member of an international team of players.—**internationally** *adv.*

interplay *n* the action of two things on each other, interaction.

interpret *vt* to explain; to translate; to construe; to give one's own conception of, as in a play or musical composition. * *vi* to translate between speakers of different languages.—**interpretation** *n.*

interpreter *n* a person who translates orally for persons speaking in different languages; (*comput*) a program that translates an instruction into machine code.

interrogate *vti* to question, esp formally.—**interrogation** *n.*—**interrogator** *n.*

interrogative *adj* asking a question. * *n* a word used in asking a question.—**interrogatively** *adv.*

interrogatory *adj* questioning.

interrupt *vt* to break into (a discussion, etc) or break in upon (a speaker, worker, etc); to make a break in the continuity of. * *vi* to interrupt an action, talk, etc.—**interrupter** *n.*—**interruption** *n.*

intersect *vti* to cut or divide by passing through or crossing; (*lines, roads, etc*) to meet and cross.

intersection *n* an intersecting; the place where two lines, roads, etc meet or cross.

intersperse *vt* to scatter or insert among other things; to diversify with other things scattered here and there.

intertwine *vti* to twine or twist closely together.

interval *n* a space between things; the time between events; (*mus*) the difference of pitch between two notes.

intervene *vi* to occur or come between; to occur between two events, etc; to come in to modify, settle, or hinder some action, etc.—**intervention** *n.*

interview *n* a meeting in which a person is asked about his or her views, etc, as by a newspaper or television reporter; a published account of this; a formal meeting at which a candidate for a job is questioned and assessed by a prospective employer. * *vt* to have an interview with.—**interviewer** *n.*

intestate *adj* having made no will. * *n* a person who dies intestate.—**intestacy** *n.*

intestine *n* the lower part of the alimentary canal between the stomach and the anus.—**intestinal** *adj.*

intimacy *n* close or confidential friendship; familiarity; sexual relations.

intimate *adj* most private or personal; very close or familiar, esp sexually; deep and thorough. * *n* an intimate friend. * *vt* to indicate; to make known; to hint or imply.—**intimately** *adv.*

intimation *n* the act of intimating; a notice, announcement.

intimidate *vt* to frighten; to discourage, silence, etc esp by threats.—**intimidation** *n.*

into *prep* to the interior or inner parts of; to the middle; to a particular condition; (*inf*) deeply interested or involved in.

intolerable *adj* unbearable.—**intolerably** *adv.*

intolerance *n* lack of toleration of the opinions or practices of others; inability to bear or endure.—**intolerant** *adj.*

intonation *n* intoning; variations in pitch of the speaking voice; an accent.

intoxicate *vt* to make drunken; to elate; to poison.

intoxication *n* drunkenness; great excitement; poisoning.

intractable *adj* unmanageable, uncontrollable; (*problem, illness, etc*) difficult to solve, alleviate, or cure.—**intractability** *n*.—**intractably** *adv*.

intransigent *adj* unwilling to compromise, irreconcilable.—**intransigence** *n*.

intransitive *adj* (*gram*) denoting a verb that does not take a direct object.—**intransitively** *adv*.

intravenous *adj* into a vein.—**intravenously** *adv*.

intrepid *adj* bold; fearless; brave.—**intrepidity** *n*.—**intrepidly** *adv*.

intricate *adj* difficult to understand; complex, complicated; involved, detailed.—**intricacy** *n*.—**intricately** *adv*.

intrigue *n* a secret or underhand plotting; a secret or underhanded plot or scheme; a secret love affair. * *vi* to carry on an intrigue. * *vt* to excite the interest or curiosity of.

intrinsic *adj* belonging to the real nature of a person or thing; inherent.—**intrinsically** *adv*.

introduce *vt* to make (a person) acquainted by name (with other persons); to bring into use or establish; to present (a bill, etc) for consideration or approval (by parliament, etc); to present a radio or television programme; to bring into or insert.

introduction *n* an introducing or being introduced; the presentation of one person to another; preliminary text in a book; a preliminary passage in a musical composition.

introductory *adj* serving as an introduction; preliminary.

introspection *n* examination of one's own mind and feelings, etc.—**introspective** *adj*.

introvert *n* a person who is more interested in his or her own thoughts, feelings, etc than in external objects or events. * *adj* characterized by introversion (—*also* **introverted**).—**introversion** *n*.

intrude *vti* to force (oneself) upon others unasked.—**intruder** *n*.

intrusion *n* the act or an instance of intruding; the forcible entry of molten rock into and between existing rocks.—**intrusively** *adv*.

intuition *n* a perceiving of the truth of something immediately without reasoning or analysis; a hunch, an insight.—**intuitively** *adv*.

inundate *vt* to cover as with a flood; to deluge.—**inundation** *n*.

invade *vt* to enter (a country) with hostile intentions; to encroach upon; to penetrate; to crowd into as if invading.—**invader** *n*.

invalid[1] *adj* not valid.

invalid[2] *n* a person who is ill or disabled. * *vt* to cause to become an invalid; to disable; to cause to retire from the armed forces because of ill-health or injury.

invalidate *vt* to render not valid; to deprive of legal force.—**invalidation** *n*.

invaluable *adj* too valuable to be measured in money.—**invaluably** *adv*.

invariable *adj* never changing; constant.—**invariably** *adv*.

invasion *n* the act of invading with military forces; an encroachment, intrusion.

invective *n* the use of violent or abusive language or writing.

invent *vt* to think up; to think out or produce (a new device, process, etc); to originate; to fabricate (a lie, etc).—**inventor** *n*.

invention *n* something invented; inventiveness.

inventive *adj* pertaining to invention; skilled in inventing.—**inventiveness** *n*.

inventory *n* an itemized list of goods, property, etc, as of a business; the store of such goods for such a listing; a list of the property of an individual or an estate. * *vt* to make an inventory of; to enter in an inventory.

inverse *adj* reversed in order or position; opposite, contrary. * *n* an inverse state or thing.—**inversely** *adv*.

invert *vt* to turn upside down or inside out; to reverse in order, position or relationship.

invertebrate *adj* without a backbone. * *n* an animal without a backbone.

invest *vt* to commit (money) to property, stocks and shares, etc for profit; to devote effort, time, etc on a particular activity; to install in office with ceremony; to furnish with power, authority, etc. * *vi* to invest money.

investigate *vti* to search (into); to inquire, examine.—**investigator** *n*.

investigation *n* the act of investigating; an inquiry; a search to uncover facts, etc.

investiture *n* the act or right of giving legal possession; the ceremony of investing a person with an office, robes, title, etc.

investment *n* the act of investing money productively; the amount invested; an activity in which time, effort or money has been invested.

investor *n* a person who invests money.

inveterate *adj* firmly established, ingrained;

habitual.—**inveteracy** *n*.—**inveterately** *adv*.
invidious *adj* tending to provoke ill-will, resentment or envy; (*decisions, etc*) unfairly discriminating.—**invidiously** *adv*.—**invidiousness** *n*.
invigorate *vt* to fill with vigour and energy; to refresh.—**invigorating** *adj*.
invincible *adj* unconquerable.—**invincibility** *n*.—**invincibly** *adv*.
inviolate *adj* not violated; unbroken, unharmed.
invisible *adj* unable to be seen; hidden.—**invisibility** *n*.—**invisibly** *adv*.
invitation *n* a message used in inviting.
invite *vt* to ask to come somewhere or do something; to ask for; to give occasion for; to tempt; to entice. * *n* (*inf*) an invitation.
inviting *adj* attractive, enticing.—**invitingly** *adv*.
invoice *n* a list of goods dispatched, usu with particulars of their price and quantity. * *vt* to submit an invoice for or to.
invoke *vt* to call on (God, etc) for help, blessing, etc; to resort to (a law, etc) as pertinent; to implore.
involuntary *adj* not done by choice; not consciously controlled.—**involuntarily** *adv*.—**involuntariness** *n*.
involve *vt* to affect or include; to require; to occupy, to make busy; to complicate; to implicate.—**involvement** *n*.
invulnerable *adj* not capable of being wounded or hurt in any way.—**invulnerability** *n*.
inward *adj* situated within or directed to the inside; relating to or in the mind or spirit. * *adv* inwards.
inwardly *adv* within; in the mind or spirit; towards the inside or centre.
inwards *adv* towards the inside or interior; in the mind or spirit.
iodine *n* a nonmetallic element, found in seawater and seaweed, whose compounds are used in medicine and photography.
iota *n* the ninth letter of the Greek alphabet; a very small quantity; a jot.
IOU *n* a written note promising to pay a sum of money to the holder.
IQ *abbr* = Intelligence Quotient.
irascible *adj* easily angered; hot-tempered.—**irascibility** *n*.—**irascibly** *adv*.
irate *adj* enraged, furious.—**irately** *adv*.
iris *n* (*pl* **irises, irides**) the round, pigmented membrane surrounding the pupil of the eye; (*pl* **irises**) a perennial herbaceous plant with sword-shaped leaves and brightly coloured flowers.
Irish *adj* of Ireland or its people. * *n* the Celtic language of Ireland.
irk *vt* to annoy, irritate.
irksome *adj* tedious; tiresome.
iron *n* a metallic element, the most common of all metals; a tool, etc of this metal; a heavy implement with a heated flat underface for pressing cloth; (*pl*) shackles of iron; firm strength; power; any of certain golf clubs with angled metal heads. * *adj* of iron; like iron, strong and firm. * *vti* to press with a hot iron.
ironic, ironical *adj* of or using irony.—**ironically** *adv*.
ironmonger *n* a dealer in metal utensils, tools, etc; a hardware shop.—**ironmongery** *n*.
ironworks *n* a factory where iron is smelted, cast, or wrought.
irony *n* an expression in which the intended meaning of the words is the opposite of their usual sense; an event or result that is the opposite of what is expected.
irrational *adj* not rational, lacking the power of reason; senseless; unreasonable; absurd.—**irrationality** *n*.—**irrationally** *adv*.
irreconcilable *adj* not able to be brought into agreement; incompatible.—**irreconcilably** *adv*.
irredeemable *adj* not able to be redeemed.—**irredeemably** *adv*.
irrefutable *adj* unable to deny or disprove; indisputable.—**irrefutably** *adv*.
irregular *adj* not regular, straight or even; not conforming to the rules; imperfect; (*troops*) not part of the regular armed forces.—**irregularly** *adv*.
irregularity *n* departure from a rule, order or method; crookedness.
irrelevant *adj* not pertinent; not to the point.—**irrelevance** *n*.—**irrelevantly** *adv*.
irreparable *adj* that cannot be repaired, rectified or made good.—**irreparably** *adv*.
irreplaceable *adj* unable to be replaced.—**irreplaceability** *n*.
irrepressible *adj* unable to be controlled or restrained.—**irrepressibly** *adv*.
irreproachable *adj* blameless; faultless.—**irreproachably** *adv*.
irresistible *adj* not able to be resisted; overpowering; fascinating; very charming, alluring.—**irresistibly** *adv*.
irresolute *adj* lacking resolution, uncertain, hesitating.—**irresolutely** *adv*.—**irresoluteness** *n*.—**irresolution** *n*.
irrespective *adj* (*with* **of**) regardless.—**irrespectively** *adv*.

irresponsible *adj* not showing a proper sense of the consequences of one's actions; unable to bear responsibility.—**irresponsibility** *n.*—**irresponsibly** *adv.*

irreverent *adj* not reverent, disrespectful.—**irreverence** *n.*—**irreverently** *adv.*

irrevocable *adj* unable to be revoked, unalterable.

irrigate *vt* to supply (land) with water as by means of artificial ditches, pipes, etc; (*med*) to wash out (a cavity, wound, etc).—**irrigation** *n.*—**irrigator** *n.*

irritable *adj* easily annoyed, irritated, or provoked; (*med*) excessively sensitive to a stimulus.—**irritability** *n.*—**irritably** *adv.*

irritate *vt* to provoke to anger; to annoy; to make inflamed or sore.—**irritation** *n.*

is *see* **be**.

Islam *n* the Muslim religion, a monotheistic religion founded by Mohammed; the Muslim world.—**Islamic** *adj.*

island *n* a land mass smaller than a continent and surrounded by water; anything like this in position or isolation.

islander *n* a native or inhabitant of an island.

isle *n* an island, esp a small one.

isn't = is not.

isolate *vt* to set apart from others; to place alone; to quarantine a person or animal with a contagious disease; to separate a constituent substance from a compound.—**isolation** *n.*

isotope *n* any of two or more forms of an element having the same atomic number but different atomic weights.—**isotopic** *adj.*

issue *n* an outgoing; an outlet; a result; offspring; a point under dispute; a sending or giving out; all that is put forth at one time (an issue of bonds, a periodical, etc). * *vi* to go or flow out; to result (from) or end (in); to be published. * *vt* to let out; to discharge; to give or deal out, as supplies; to publish.

isthmus *n* (*pl* **isthmuses, isthmi**) a narrow strip of land having water at each side and connecting two larger bodies of land.

it *pron* the thing mentioned; the subject of an impersonal verb; a subject or object of indefinite sense in various constructions. * *n* the player, as in tag, who must catch another.

Italian *adj* of Italy or its people. * *n* a native of Italy; the Italian language.

italic *adj* denoting a type in which the letters slant upward to the right (*this is italic type*). * *n* (*usu pl*) italic type or handwriting.

itch *n* an irritating sensation on the surface of the skin causing a need to scratch; an insistent desire. * *vi* to have or feel an irritating sensation in the skin; to feel a restless desire.

itchy *adj* (**itchier, itchiest**) pertaining to or affected with an itch.—**itchiness** *n.*

item *n* an article; a unit; a separate thing; a bit of news or information; (*inf*) a couple having an affair.

itemize *vt* to specify the items of; to set down by items.—**itemization** *n.*

itinerant *adj* travelling from place to place. * *n* a traveller.

itinerary *n* a route; a record of a journey; a detailed plan of a journey.

it'll = it will, it shall.

its *poss pron* relating to or belonging to it.

it's = it is, it has.

itself *pron* the reflexive and emphatic form of **it**.

ITV *abbr* = Independent Television.

ivory *n* the hard, creamy-white substance forming the tusks of elephants, etc; any substance like ivory; creamy white. * *adj* of or like ivory; creamy white.

ivy *n* a climbing or creeping vine with a woody stem and evergreen leaves.

J

jab *vti* (*pt* **jabbed**) to poke or thrust roughly; to punch with short, straight blows. * *n* a sudden thrust or stab; (*inf*) an injection with a hypodermic needle.

jabber *vti* to speak or say rapidly, incoherently, or foolishly. * *n* such talk.

jack *n* any of various mechanical or hydraulic devices used to lift something heavy; a playing card with a knave's picture on it, ranking below the queen; a small flag flown on a ship's bow as a signal or to show nationality; (*bowls*) a small white ball used as a target. * *vt* to raise by means of a jack.

jacket *n* a short coat; an outer covering, as the removable paper cover of a book.

jackknife *n* a pocket-knife; a dive in which the diver touches his feet with knees straight and then straightens out. * *vi* (*articulated lorry*) to lose control so that the trailer and cab swing against each other.

jackpot *n* the accumulated stakes in certain games, as poker.

jade *n* a hard, ornamental semiprecious stone; its light green colour.

jaded *adj* tired, exhausted; satiated.

jagged *adj* having sharp projecting points; notched or ragged.—**jaggedly** *adv*.

jail *n* a prison. * *vt* to send to or confine in prison.—*also* **gaol**.

jailer *n* a person in charge of prisoners in a jail.—*also* **gaoler**.

jam[1] *n* a preserve made from fruit boiled with sugar until thickened; (*inf*) something easy or desirable.

jam[2] *vb* (*pt* **jammed**) *vt* to press or squeeze into a confined space; to crowd full with people or things; to cause (machinery) to become wedged and inoperable; to cause interference to a radio signal rendering it unintelligible. * *vi* to become stuck or blocked; (*sl*) to play in a jam session. * *n* a crowded mass or congestion in a confined space; a blockage caused by jamming; (*inf*) a difficult situation.

jamb *n* the straight vertical side post of a door, etc.

jangle *vi* to make a harsh or discordant sound, as bells. * *vt* to cause to jangle; to irritate.—*also n.*

janitor *n* a person who looks after a building, doing routine maintenance, etc.—**janitorial** *adj*.

January *n* the first month of the year, having 31 days.

Japanese *adj* of Japan, its people or language. * *n* the language of Japan.

jar[1] *vb* (*pt* **jarred**) *vi* to make a harsh, discordant noise; to have an irritating effect (on one); to vibrate from an impact; to clash. * *vt* to jolt. * *n* a grating sound; a vibration due to impact; a jolt.

jar[2] *n* a short cylindrical glass vessel with a wide mouth; (*inf*) a pint of beer.

jargon *n* the specialized or technical vocabulary of a science, profession, etc; obscure and usu pretentious language.

jasmine *n* any of a genus of climbing shrubs with fragrant white or yellow flowers.

jaundice *n* a condition characterized by yellowing of the skin, caused by excess of bile in the bloodstream; bitterness; resentment; prejudice.

jaundiced *adj* affected with jaundice; jealous, envious, disillusioned.

jaunt *n* a short journey, usu for pleasure. * *vi* to make such a journey.

jaunty *adj* (**jauntier, jauntiest**) sprightly or self-confident in manner.—**jauntily** *adv*.—**jauntiness** *n*.

javelin *n* a light spear, esp one thrown some distance in a contest.

jaw *n* one of the bones in which teeth are set; either of two movable parts that grasp or crush something, as in a vice; (*sl*) a friendly chat, gossip. * *vi* (*sl*) to talk boringly and at length.

jaywalk *vi* to walk across a street carelessly without obeying traffic rules or signals.—**jaywalker** *n*.

jazz *n* a general term for American popular music, characterized by syncopated rhythms and embracing ragtime, blues, swing, jive, and bebop; (*sl*) pretentious or nonsensical talk or actions. * *vt* (*sl*) (*with* **up**) to enliven or embellish.—**jazzy** *adj*.—**jazziness** *n*.

jealous *adj* apprehensive of or hostile towards someone thought of as a rival; envious of, resentful; anxiously vigilant or protective.—**jealously** *adv*.

jealousy *n* suspicious fear or watchfulness, esp the fear of being supplanted by a rival.

jeans *npl* trousers made from denim.

jeep *n* a small robust vehicle with heavy duty tyres and four-wheel drive for use on rough terrain, esp by the military.

jeer *vt* to laugh derisively. * *vi* to scoff (at). * *n* a jeering remark.

jelly *n* a soft, gelatinous food made from fruit syrup or meat juice; any substance like this.—**jellied** *adj*.

jellyfish *n* a sea creature with a nearly transparent body and long tentacles.

jeopardize *vt* to endanger, put at risk.

jeopardy *n* great danger or risk.

jerk[1] *n* a sudden sharp pull or twist; a sudden muscular contraction or reflex; (*inf*) a stupid person. * *vti* to move with a jerk; to pull sharply; to twitch.

jerk[2] *vt* to preserve (meat) by cutting it into long strips and drying it in the sun. * *n* jerked meat (—*also* **jerky**).

jerkin *n* a close-fitting sleeveless jacket.

jerky *adj* (**jerkier, jerkiest**) moving with jerks.—**jerkily** *adv*.—**jerkiness** *n*.

jersey *n* any plain machine-knitted fabric of natural or man-made fibres; a knitted sweater. * *adj* pertaining to the island of Jersey or its breed of cattle.

jest *n* a joke; a thing to be laughed at. * *vi* to jeer; to joke.

jet[1] *n* a hard, black, compact mineral that can be polished and is used in jewellery; a lustrous black.—**jet-black** *adj*.

jet[2] *n* a stream of liquid or gas suddenly emitted; a spout for emitting a jet; a jet-propelled aircraft. * *vti* (*pt* **jetted**) to gush out in a stream; (*inf*) to travel or convey by jet.

jet engine *n* an engine, such as a gas turbine, producing jet propulsion.

jetsam *n* cargo thrown overboard from a ship in distress to lighten it, esp such cargo when washed up on the shore.

jettison *vt* to abandon, to throw overboard.

jetty *n* a wharf; a small pier.

Jew *n* a person descended, or regarded as descended, from the ancient Hebrews; a person whose religion is Judaism.

jewel *n* a precious stone; a gem; a piece of jewellery; someone or something highly esteemed; a small gem used as a bearing in a watch.

jeweller, jeweler (*US*) *n* a person who makes, repairs or deals in jewellery, watches, etc.

jewellery, jewelry(*US*) *n* jewels such as rings, brooches, etc, worn for decoration.

Jewish *adj* of or like Jews.

jib *n* a triangular sail extending from the foremast in a ship; the projecting arm of a crane. * *vti* (*pt* **jibbed**) to pull (a sail) round to the other side; (*sail*) to swing round.

jibe *see* **gibe**.

jiffy, jiff *n* (*inf*) a very short time.

jigsaw *n* a saw with a narrow fine-toothed blade for cutting irregular shapes; a picture on wood or board cut into irregular pieces for re-assembling for amusement.

jilt *vt* to discard (a lover) unfeelingly, esp without warning.

jingle *n* a metallic tinkling sound like a bunch of keys being shaken together; a catchy verse or song with easy rhythm, simple rhymes, etc. * *vti* (to cause) to make a light tinkling sound.

jinx *n* (*inf*) someone or something thought to bring bad luck.

jitter *vi* (*inf*) to feel nervous or act nervously. * *npl* (*inf*) (*with* **the**) an uneasy nervous feeling; fidgets.

job *n* a piece of work done for pay; a task; a duty; the thing or material being worked on; work; employment; (*sl*) a criminal enterprise; (*inf*) a difficult task. * *adj* hired or done by the job. * *vti* (*pt* **jobbed**) to deal in (goods) as a jobber; to sublet (work, etc).

jobless *adj* unemployed.

jockey *n* a person whose job is riding horses in races. * *vti* to act as a jockey; to manœuvre for a more advantageous position; to swindle or cheat.

jocular *adj* joking; full of jokes.—**jocularity** *n*.—**jocularly** *adv*.

jog *vb* (*pt* **jogged**) *vt* to give a slight shake or nudge to; to rouse, as the memory. * *vi* to move up and down with an unsteady motion; to run at a relaxed trot for exercise; (*horse*) to run at a jog-trot. * *n* a slight shake or push; a nudge; a slow walk or trot.—**jogger** *n*.

join *vti* to bring and come together (with); to connect; to unite; to become a part or member of (a club, etc); to participate (in a conversation, etc); (*with* **up**) to enlist in the armed forces; to unite, connect. * *n* a joining; a place of joining.

joiner *n* a carpenter who finishes interior woodwork; (*inf*) a person who is involved in many clubs and activities, etc.

joint *n* a place where, or way in which, two things are joined; any of the parts of a jointed whole; the parts where two bones move on one another in an animal; a division of an animal carcass made by a butcher; (*sl*) a cheap bar or restaurant; (*sl*) a gambling or drinking den; (*sl*) a cannabis cigarette. * *adj* common to two or more; sharing with another. * *vt* to connect by a joint or joints; to divide (an animal carcass) into parts for cooking.

jointly *adv* in common.

joist *n* any of the parallel beams supporting the floor-boards or the laths of a ceiling.

joke *n* something said or done to cause laughter; a thing done or said merely in fun; a person or thing to be laughed at. * *vi* to make jokes.

joker *n* a person who jokes; (*sl*) a person; an extra playing card made use of in certain games.

jolly *adj* (**jollier, jolliest**) merry; full of fun; delightful; (*inf*) enjoyable. * *vti* (*inf*) to try to make (a person) feel good; to make fun of (someone).

jolt *vt* to give a sudden shake or knock to; to move along jerkily; to surprise or shock suddenly. * *n* a sudden jar or knock; an emotional shock.

jostle *vti* to shake or knock roughly; to collide or come into contact (with); to elbow for position.—*also n*.

jot *n* a very small amount. * *vt* (*pt* **jotted**) to note (down) briefly.

jotter *n* a notebook.

journal *n* a daily record of happenings, as a diary; a newspaper or periodical; (*bookkeeping*) a book of original entry for recording transactions; that part of a shaft or axle that turns in a bearing.

journalese *n* a facile style of writing found in many magazines, newspapers, etc.

journalism *n* the work of gathering news for, or producing a newspaper, magazine or news broadcast.—**journalist** *n*.—**journalistic** *adj*.

journey *n* a travelling or going from one place to another; the distance covered when travelling. * *vi* to make a journey.

jowl *n* the lower jaw; (*usu pl*) the cheek; the loose flesh around the throat; the similar flesh in an animal, as a dewlap.

joy *n* intense happiness; something that causes this.—**joyless** *adj*.—**joylessly** *adv*.—**joylessness** *n*.

joyful *adj* filled with, expressing, or causing joy.—**joyfully** *adv*.—**joyfulness** *n*.

joyous *adj* joyful.—**joyously** *adv*.—**joyousness** *n*.

joy-ride *n* (*inf*) a car ride, often in a stolen vehicle and at reckless speed, just for pleasure.—**joy-rider** *n*.—**joy-riding** *n*.

JP *abbr* = Justice of the Peace.

Jr. *abbr* = Junior.

jubilant *adj* joyful and triumphant; elated; rejoicing.—**jubilation** *n*.

jubilee *n* a 50th or 25th anniversary; a time of rejoicing.

judge *n* a public official with authority to hear and decide cases in a court of law; a person chosen to settle a dispute or decide who wins; a person qualified to decide on the relative worth of anything. * *vti* to hear and pass judgment (on) in a court of law; to determine the winner of (a contest) or settle (a dispute); to form an opinion about; to criticize or censure; to suppose, think.

judgment, judgement *n* a judging; a deciding; a legal decision; an opinion; the ability to come to a wise decision; censure.

judicial *adj* of judges, courts, or their functions; jurisdiction; judges or courts collectively.—**judicially** *adv*.

judicious *adj* possessing or characterized by sound judgment.—**judiciously** *adv*.

judo *n* a Japanese system of unarmed combat, adapted as a competitive sport from jujitsu.

jug *n* a vessel for holding and pouring liquids, with a handle and curved lip; a pitcher; (*sl*) prison. * *vt* (*pt* **jugged**) to stew meat (esp hare) in an earthenware pot; (*sl*) to put into prison.—**jugful** *n*.

juggernaut *n* a terrible, irresistible force; a large heavy truck.

juggle *vi* to toss up balls, etc and keep them in the air. * *vt* to manipulate skilfully; to manipulate so as to deceive. * *n* a juggling.—**juggler** *n*.

juice *n* the liquid part of fruit, vegetables or meat; liquid secreted by a bodily organ; (*inf*) vitality; (*inf*) electric current; (*inf*) petrol.

juicy *adj* (**juicier, juiciest**) full of juice; (*inf*) very interesting; (*inf*) highly profitable.—**juicily** *adv*.—**juiciness** *n*.

jukebox *n* a coin-operated automatic record or CD player.

July *n* the seventh month of the year, having 31 days.

jumble *vt* (*often with* **up**) to mix together in a disordered mass. * *n* items mixed together in a confused mass; articles for a jumble sale.

jumble sale *n* a sale of second-hand clothes, books, etc to raise money for charity.

jumbo *n* (*pl* **jumbos**) something very large of its kind.

jumbo jet *n* a very large jet airliner.

jump *vi* to spring or leap from the ground, a height, etc; to jerk; (*often with* **at**) to act swiftly and eagerly; to pass suddenly, as to a new topic; to rise suddenly, as prices; (*sl*) to be lively. * *vt* to leap or pass over (something); to leap upon; to cause (prices, etc) to rise; to fail to turn up (for trial when out on bail); (*inf*) to attack suddenly; (*inf*) to react to prematurely; (*sl*) to leave suddenly. * *n* a jumping; a distance jumped; a sudden transition; an obstacle; a nervous start.

jumper *n* a knitted garment for the upper body; a sleeveless dress for wearing over a blouse, etc.

jumpy *adj* (**jumpier, jumpiest**) moving in jerks, etc; easily startled, apprehensive.—**jumpily** *adv*.—**jumpiness** *n*.

junction *n* a place or point where things join; a place where roads or railway lines, etc meet, link or cross each other.

juncture *n* a junction; a point of time; a crisis.

June *n* the sixth month of the year, having 30 days.

jungle *n* an area overgrown with dense tropical trees and other vegetation, etc; any scene of wild confusion, disorder, or of ruthless competition for survival.

junior *adj* younger in age; of more recent or lower status; of juniors. * *n* a person who is younger, of lower rank, etc; a young person employed in minor capacity in an office; a member of a junior school; (*inf*) (*with cap*) the younger son, in US often used after the name if the same as the father's.

juniper *n* an evergreen shrub that yields purple berries.

junk[1] *n* a flat-bottomed sailing vessel prevalent in the China Seas.

junk[2] *n* discarded useless objects; (*inf*) rubbish, trash; (*sl*) any narcotic drug, such as heroin. * *vt* (*inf*) to scrap.

junk shop *n* a shop selling miscellaneous second-hand goods.

junta *n* a group of people, esp military, who assume responsibility for the government of a country following a coup d'état or revolution.

jurisdiction *n* the right or authority to apply the law; the exercise of such authority; the limits of territory over which such authority extends.

jurisprudence *n* the science or philosophy of law; a division of law.—**jurisprudential** *adj*.

juror *n* a member of a jury; a person who takes an oath.

jury *n* a body of usu 12 people sworn to hear evidence and to deliver a verdict on a case; a committee or panel that decides winners in a contest.

just *adj* fair, impartial; deserved, merited; proper, exact; conforming strictly with the facts. * *adv* exactly; nearly; only; barely; a very short time ago; immediately; (*inf*) really; justly, equitably; by right.—**justly** *adv*.—**justness** *n*.

justice *n* justness, fairness; the use of authority to maintain what is just; the administration of law; a judge.

jut *vti* (*pt* **jutted**) to stick out; to project. * *n* a part that juts.

juvenile *adj* young; immature; of or for young persons. * *n* a young person.

juxtapose *vt* to place side by side.—**juxtaposition** *n*.

K

kaleidoscope *n* a small tube containing bits of coloured glass reflected by mirrors to form symmetrical patterns as the tube is rotated; anything that constantly changes. —**kaleidoscopic** *adj*.

kangaroo *n* an Australian mammal with short forelegs and strong, large hind legs for jumping.

karat *see* **carat**.

keel *n* one of the main structural members of a ship extending along the bottom from stem to stern to which the frame is attached; any structure resembling this. * *vti* (to cause) to turn over.

keen[1] *adj* eager, enthusiastic; intellectually acute, shrewd; having a sharp point or fine edge; (*senses*) perceptive, penetrating; extremely cold and piercing; intense; (*prices*) very low so as to be competitive.—**keenly** *adv*.—**keenness** *n*.

keen[2] *n* a dirge or lament for the dead. * *vi* to lament the dead.

keep *vb* (*pt* **kept**) *vt* to celebrate, observe; to fulfil; to protect, guard; to take care of; to preserve; to provide for; to make regular entries in; to maintain in a specified state; to hold for the future; to hold and not let go. * *vi* to stay in a specified condition; to continue, go on; to refrain or restrain oneself; to stay fresh, not spoil. * *n* food and shelter; care and custody; the inner stronghold of a castle.

keeper *n* one who guards, watches, or takes care of persons or things.

keeping *n* care, charge; observance; agreement, conformity.

keepsake *n* something kept in memory of the giver.

keg *n* a small barrel.

kennel *n* a small shelter for a dog, a doghouse; (*often pl*) a place where dogs are bred or kept. * *vt* (*pt* **kennelled**) to keep in a kennel.

kept *see* **keep**.

kerb *n* a line of raised stone forming the edge of a pavement.—**kerbstone** *n*.

kernel *n* the inner edible part of a fruit or nut; the essential part of anything.

kerosene, kerosine *n* a fuel oil distilled from petroleum, paraffin.

ketchup *n* any of various thick sauces, esp one made from puréed tomato, for meat, fish, etc.—*also* **catchup, catsup**

kettle *n* a container with a handle and spout for boiling water.

kettledrum *n* a musical instrument consisting of a hollow metal body with a parchment head, the tension of which controls the pitch and is adjusted by screws.

key[1] *n* a device for locking and unlocking something; a thing that explains or solves, as the legend of a map, a code, etc; a controlling position, person, or thing; one of a set of parts or levers pressed in a keyboard or typewriter, etc; (*mus*) a system of related tones based on a keynote and forming a given scale; style or mood of expression; a roughened surface for improved adhesion of plaster, etc; an electric circuit breaker. * *vt* to furnish with a key; to bring into harmony. * *adj* controlling; important.

key² *n* a low island or reef.

keyboard *n* a set of keys in a piano, organ, computer, etc.

keyhole *n* an opening (in a lock) into which a key is inserted.

keynote *n* the basic note of a musical scale; the basic idea or ruling principle. * *vt* to give the keynote of; to give the keynote speech at.

khaki *adj* dull yellowish-brown. * *n* (*pl* **khakis**) strong, twilled cloth of this colour; *(often pl)* a khaki uniform or trousers.

kick *vt* to strike with the foot; to drive, force, etc as by kicking; to score (a goal, etc) by kicking. * *vi* to strike out with the foot; to recoil, as a gun; (*inf*) to complain; (*with* **off**) (*football*) to give the ball the first kick to start play; (*inf*) to start. * *n* an act or method of kicking; a sudden recoil; (*inf*) a thrill; (*inf*) an intoxicating effect.—**kicker** *n*.

kickoff *n* (*football*) a kick putting the ball into play; the beginning or start of proceedings, eg a discussion.

kid *n* a young goat; soft leather made from its skin; (*inf*) a child. * *vti* (*pt* **kidded**) (*inf*) to tease or fool playfully; (*goat*) to bring forth young.

kidnap *vt* (*pt* **kidnapped**) to seize and hold to ransom, as of a person.—**kidnapper** *n*.

kidney *n* (*pl* **kidneys**) either of a pair of glandular organs excreting waste products from the blood as urine; an animal's kidney used as food.

kill *vt* to cause the death of; to destroy; to neutralize (a colour); to spend (time) on trivial matters; to turn off (an engine, etc); (*inf*) to cause severe discomfort or pain to. * *n* the act of killing; an animal or animals killed.—**killer** *n*.

killing *adj* (*inf*) tiring; very amusing; causing death, deadly. * *n* the act of killing, murder; (*inf*) a sudden (financial) success.

kiln *n* a furnace or large oven for baking or drying (lime, bricks, pottery, etc).

kilo *n* kilogram; kilometre.

kilogram, kilogramme *n* a unit of weight and mass, equal to 1000 grams or 2.2046 pounds.

kilometre, kilometer (*US*) *n* a unit of length equal to 1000 metres or 0.62 mile.—**kilometric** *adj*.

kilowatt *n* a unit of electrical power, equal to 1000 watts.

kilt *n* a knee-length skirt made from tartan material pleated at the sides, worn as part of the Scottish Highland dress for men and women.

kimono *n* a loose Japanese robe.

kin *n* relatives; family.

kind¹ *n* sort; variety; class; a natural group or division; essential character.

kind² *adj* sympathetic; friendly; gentle; benevolent.—**kind-hearted** *adj*.—**kindness** *n*.

kindergarten *n* a class or school for very young children.

kindle *vt* to set on fire; to excite (feelings, interest, etc). * *vi* to catch fire; to become aroused or excited.

kindly *adj* (**kindlier, kindliest**) kind; gracious; agreeable; pleasant. * *adv* in a kindly manner; favourably.—**kindliness** *n*.

kindred *n* a person's family or relatives; family relationship; resemblance. * *adj* related; like, similar.

kinetic *adj* of or produced by movement.

king *n* the man who rules a country and its people; a man with the title of ruler, but with limited power to rule; man supreme in a certain sphere; something best in its class; the chief piece in chess; a playing card with a picture of a king on it, ranking above a queen; (*draughts*) a piece that has been crowned.

kingdom *n* a country headed by a king or queen; a realm, domain; any of the three divisions of the natural world: animal: vegetable, mineral.

kingfisher *n* a short-tailed diving bird that feeds chiefly on fish.

king-size, king-sized *adj* larger than standard size.

kink *n* a tight twist or curl in a piece of string, rope, hair, etc; a painful cramp in the neck, back, etc; an eccentricity of personality. * *vti* to form or cause to form a kink or kinks.

kinky *adj* (**kinkier, kinkiest**) full of kinks; (*inf*) eccentric; (*inf*) sexually bizarre.—**kinkily** *adv*.—**kinkiness** *n*.

kiosk *n* a small open structure used for selling newspapers, confectionery, etc; a public telephone booth.

kipper *n* a kippered herring, etc. * *vt* to cure (fish) by salting and drying or smoking.

kiss *vti* to touch with the lips as an expression of love, affection or in greeting; to touch the lips with those of another person as a sign of love or desire; to touch lightly. * *n* an act of kissing; a light, gentle touch.

kit *n* clothing and personal equipment, etc;

tools and equipment for a specific purpose; a set of parts with instructions ready to be assembled. * *vt* (*pt* **kitted**) (*usu with* **out** *or* **up**) to provide with kit.

kitbag *n* a strong cylindrical bag carried over one shoulder used for holding kit, esp by military personnel.

kitchen *n* a place where food is prepared and cooked.

kite *n* a bird of prey with long narrow wings and a forked tail; a light frame covered with a thin covering for flying in the wind.

kith *n* friends and relations, now only in **kith and kin.**

kitten *n* a young cat; the young of other small mammals. * *vti* to give birth to kittens.

kitty *n* the stakes in a game of poker or other gambling game; a shared fund of money.

kleptomania *n* an uncontrollable impulse to steal.—**kleptomaniac** *n*.

knack *n* an ability to do something easily; a trick; a habit.

knapsack *n* a bag for carrying equipment or supplies on the back.

knave *n* (*formerly*) a tricky or dishonest man; the jack in a pack of playing cards.—**knavery** *n*.—**knavish** *adj*.

knead *vt* to squeeze and press together (dough, clay, etc) into a uniform lump with the hands; to make (bread, etc) by kneading; to squeeze and press with the hands.

knee *n* the joint between the thigh and the lower part of the human leg; anything shaped like a bent knee. * *vt* (*pt* **kneed**) to hit or touch with the knee.

kneecap *n* the small bone covering and protecting the front part of the knee-joint. * *vt* (*pt* **kneecapped**) to maim by shooting into the kneecap.—**kneecapping** *n*.

kneel *vi* (*pt* **knelt**) to go down on one's knee or knees; to remain in this position.

knell *n* the sound of a bell rung slowly and solemnly at a death or funeral; a warning of death, failure, etc. * *vi* (*bell*) to ring a knell; to summon, announce, etc (as if) by a knell.

knelt *see* **kneel.**

knew *see* **know.**

knickers *npl* an undergarment covering the lower body and having separate leg holes, worn by women and girls.

knife *n* (*pl* **knives**) a flat piece of steel, etc, with a sharp edge set in a handle, used to cut or as a weapon; a sharp blade forming part of a tool or machine. * *vt* to cut or stab with a knife.

knight *n* (*Middle Ages*) a medieval mounted soldier; a man who for some achievement is given honorary rank entitling him to use "Sir" before his given name; a chessman shaped like a horse's head. * *vt* to make (a man) a knight.—**knighthood** *n*.—**knightly** *adv*.

knit *vb* (*pt* **knitted** *or* **knit**) *vt* to form (fabric or a garment) by interlooping yarn using knitting needles or a machine; to cause (eg broken bones) to grow together; to link or join together closely; to draw (the brows) together. * *vi* to make knitted fabric from yarn by means of needles; to grow together; to become joined or united. * *n* a knitted garment or fabric.—**knitter** *n*.

knitting *n* work being knitted.

knitting needle *n* a long thin eyeless needle, usu made of plastic or steel, used in knitting.

knitwear *n* knitted clothing.

knob *n* a rounded lump or protuberance; a handle, usu round, of a door, drawer, etc.

knock *vi* to strike with a sharp blow; to rap on a door; to bump, collide; (*engine*) to make a thumping noise; (*with* **off**) (*inf*) to finish work. * *vt* to strike; (*inf*) to criticize; (*with* **about, around**) to wander around aimlessly; to treat roughly; (*with* **back**) (*inf*) to drink, swallow quickly; to reject, refuse; (*with* **down**) to indicate a sale at an auction; (*with* **down** *or* **off**) to hit so as to cause to fall; (*with* **off**) (*inf*) to complete hastily; (*inf*) to reduce in price; (*sl*) to steal; (*with* **out**) to make unconscious or exhausted; to eliminate in a knockout competition; (*inf*) to amaze. * *n* a knocking, a hit, a rap.

knockdown *adj* cheap; (*furniture*) easy to dismantle.

knocker *n* a device hinged against a door for use in knocking.

knock-kneed *adj* having inward-curving legs.

knockout *n* a punch or blow that produces unconsciousness; a contest in which competitors are eliminated at each round; (*inf*) an attractive or extremely impressive person or thing.

knot *n* a lump in a thread, etc formed by a tightened loop or tangling; a fastening made by tying lengths of rope, etc; an ornamental bow; a small group, cluster; a hard mass of wood where a branch grows out from a tree, which shows as a roundish, cross-grained piece in a board; a unit of speed of one nautical mile per hour; something that ties closely, esp the bond of marriage. * *vti* (*pt* **knotted**) to make or form a knot (in); to entangle or become entangled.

knotty *adj* (**knottier, knottiest**) full of knots; hard to solve; puzzling.

know *vt* (*pt* **knew**, *pp* **known**) to be well-informed about; to be aware of; to be acquainted with; to recognize or distinguish.

know-how *n* practical skill, experience.

knowing *adj* having knowledge; shrewd; clever; implying a secret understanding.—**knowingly** *adv*.

knowledge *n* what one knows; the body of facts, etc accumulated over time; fact of knowing; range of information or understanding; the act of knowing.

knowledgeable, knowledgable *adj* having knowledge or intelligence; well-informed.

known *see* **know**.

knuckle *n* a joint of the finger, esp at the roots of the fingers; the knee of an animal used as food. * *vi* (*with* **down**) (*inf*) to start to work hard; (*with* **under**) to yield, to give in.

KO *abbr* = knockout.

Koran *n* the sacred book of the Muslims.

kW *abbr* = kilowatt(s).

L

l *abbr* = litre(s).

lab *n* (*inf*) laboratory.

label *n* a slip of paper, cloth, metal, etc attached to anything to provide information about its nature, contents, ownership, etc; a term of generalized classification. * *vt* (*pt* **labelled**) to attach a label to; to designate or classify (as).

laboratory *n* a room or building where scientific work and research is carried out.

laborious *adj* requiring much work; hard-working; laboured.—**laboriously** *adv*.—**laboriousness** *n*.

labour, labor (*US*) *n* work, physical or mental exertion; a specific task; all wage-earning workers; workers collectively; the process of childbirth. * *vi* to work; to work hard; to move with difficulty; to suffer (delusions, etc); to be in childbirth. * *vt* to develop in unnecessary detail.

labour camp *n* a penal colony where forced labour takes place.

labourer, laborer (*US*) *n* a person who labours, esp a person whose work requires strength rather than skill.

labyrinth *n* a structure containing winding passages through which it is hard to find one's way; a maze.—**labyrinthine** *adj*.

lace *n* a cord, etc used to draw together and fasten parts of a shoe, a corset, etc; a delicate ornamental fabric of openwork design using fine cotton, silk, etc. * *vt* to fasten with a lace or laces; to intertwine, weave; to fortify (a drink, etc) with a dash of spirits.

lack *n* the fact or state of not having any or not having enough; the thing that is needed. * *vti* to be deficient in or entirely without.

lackadaisical *adj* showing lack of energy or interest; listless.—**lackadaisically** *adv*.

laconic *adj* using few words; concise.—**laconically** *adv*.

lacquer *n* a glossy varnish. * *vt* to coat with lacquer, to make glossy.

lad *n* a boy; a young man; a fellow, chap.

ladder *n* a portable metal or wooden framework with rungs between two vertical supports for climbing up and down; something that resembles a ladder in form or use.

laden *adj* loaded with cargo; burdened.

ladle *n* a long-handled, cup-like spoon for scooping liquids; a device like a ladle in shape or use.

lady *n* a polite term for any woman; (*with cap*) a title of honour given to various ranks of women in the British peerage.

ladybird *n* a small, usu brightly-coloured beetle.

ladylike *adj* like or suitable for a lady; refined, polite.

lag[1] *vi* (*pt* **lagged**) to fall behind, hang back; to fail to keep pace in movement or development; to weaken in strength or intensity. * *n* a falling behind; a delay.

lag[2] *vt* (*pt* **lagged**) to insulate (pipes, etc) with lagging.

lag[3] *n* (*sl*) a convict; a term of imprisonment.

lager *n* a light beer that has been aged for a certain period.

lagging *n* insulating material used to lag pipes, boilers, etc.

lagoon *n* a shallow lake or pond, esp one connected with a larger body of water; the water enclosed by a circular coral reef.

laid *see* **lay[2]**.

laid back *adj* relaxed, easy-going.

lain *see* **lie[2]**.

lair *n* the dwelling or resting place of a wild animal; (*inf*) a secluded place, a retreat.

laity *n* laymen, as opposed to clergymen.

lake[1] *n* a large inland body of water.

lake[2] *n* a purplish-red pigment, originally made from lac.

lamb *n* a young sheep; its flesh as food; (*inf*) an innocent or gentle person. * *vi* to give birth to a lamb; to tend (ewes) at lambing time.
lame *adj* disabled or crippled, esp in the feet or legs; stiff and painful; weak, ineffectual. * *vt* to make lame.—**lamely** *adv*.—**lameness** *n*.
lament *vti* to feel or express deep sorrow (for); to mourn. * *n* a lamenting; an elegy, dirge, etc mourning some loss or death.
lamentable *adj* distressing, deplorable.—**lamentably** *adv*.
laminated *adj* built in thin sheets or layers.
lamp *n* any device producing light, either by electricity, gas, or by burning oil, etc; a holder or base for such a device; any device for producing therapeutic rays.
lampoon *n* a piece of satirical writing attacking someone. * *vt* to ridicule maliciously in a lampoon.—**lampooner** *n*.—**lampoonery** *n*.—**lampoonist** *n*.
lamppost *n* a post supporting a street lamp.
lance *n* a long wooden spear with a sharp iron or steel head. * *vt* to pierce (as if) with a lance; to open a boil, etc with a lancet.
land *n* the solid part of the earth's surface; ground, soil; a country and its people; property in land. * *vt* to set (an aircraft) down on land or water; to put on shore from a ship; to bring to a particular place; to catch (a fish); to get or secure (a job, prize, etc); to deliver (a blow). * *vi* to go ashore from a ship; to come to port; to arrive at a specified place; to come to rest.
landing *n* the act of coming to shore or to the ground; the place where persons or goods are loaded or unloaded from a ship; a platform at the end of a flight of stairs.
landing stage *n* a platform for landing goods or people from a ship.
landing strip *n* an airstrip.
landlady *n* a woman who owns and rents property; a woman who owns and runs a boarding house, pub, etc.
landlocked *adj* surrounded by land.
landlord *n* a man who owns and rents property; a man who owns and runs a boarding house, pub, etc.
landlubber *n* a person who has had little experience of the sea.
landmark *n* any prominent feature of the landscape distinguishing a locality; an important event or turning point.
landowner *n* a person who owns land.
landscape *n* an expanse of natural scenery seen in one view; a picture of natural, inland scenery. * *vt* to make (a plot of ground) more attractive, as by adding lawns, bushes, trees, etc.
landslide *n* the sliding of a mass of soil or rocks down a slope; an overwhelming victory, esp in an election.
lane *n* a narrow road, path, etc; a path or strip specifically designated for ships, aircraft, cars, etc; one of the narrow strips dividing a running track, swimming pool, etc for athletes and swimmers; one of the narrow passages along which balls are bowled in a bowling alley.
language *n* human speech or the written symbols for speech; any means of communicating; a special set of symbols used for programming a computer; the speech of a particular nation, etc; the particular style of verbal expression characteristic of a person, group, profession, etc.
languid *adj* lacking energy or vitality; apathetic, not interested; drooping, sluggish.—**languidly** *adv*.—**languidness** *n*.
languish *vi* to lose strength and vitality; to pine; to suffer neglect or hardship; to assume a pleading or melancholic expression.
lank *adj* tall and thin; long and limp.—**lankly** *adv*.—**lankness** *n*.
lanky *adj* (**lankier, lankiest**) lean, tall, and ungainly.—**lankily** *adv*.—**lankiness** *n*.
lantern *n* a portable transparent case for holding a light; a structure with windows on top of a door or roof to provide light and ventilation; the light-chamber of a lighthouse.
lap[1] *vti* (*pt* **lapped**) to take in (liquid) with the tongue; (*waves*) to flow gently with a splashing sound.
lap[2] *n* the flat area from waist to knees formed by a person sitting; the part of the clothing covering this.
lap[3] *n* an overlapping; a part that overlaps; one complete circuit of a race track. * *vb* (*pt* **lapped**) *vt* to fold (over or on); to wrap. * *vi* to overlap; to extend over something in space or time.
lapel *n* a part of a suit, coat, jacket, etc folded back and continuous with the collar.—**lapelled** *adj*.
lapse *n* a small error; a decline or drop to a lower condition, degree, or state; a moral decline; a period of time elapsed; the termination of a legal right or privilege through disuse. * *vi* to depart from the usual or accepted standard, esp in morals; to pass out of

existence or use; to become void or discontinued; (*time*) to slip away.

larceny *n* theft.—**larcenous** *adj*.

lard *n* melted and clarified pig fat. * *vt* to insert strips of bacon or pork fat (in meat) before cooking; to embellish.

larder *n* a room or cupboard where food is stored.

large *adj* great in size, amount, or number; bulky; big; spacious; bigger than others of its kind; operating on a big scale.—**largeness** *n*.

largely *adv* much, in great amounts; mainly, for the most part.

lark[1] *n* any of a family of songbirds.

lark[2] *n* a playful or amusing adventure; a harmless prank. * *vi* (*usu with* **about**) to have fun, frolic.

larva *n* (*pl* **larvae**) the immature form of many animals after emerging from an egg before transformation into the adult state, eg a caterpillar.—**larval** *adj*.

laryngitis *n* inflammation of the larynx.

larynx *n* (*pl* **larynges, larynxes**) the structure at the upper end of the windpipe, containing the vocal cords.

lascivious *adj* lecherous, lustful; arousing sexual desire.—**lasciviously** *adv*.—**lasciviousness** *n*.

laser *n* a device that produces an intense beam of coherent light or other electromagnetic radiation.

lash *vt* to strike forcefully (as if) with a lash; to fasten or secure with a cord, etc; to attack with criticism or ridicule. * *vi* to move quickly and violently; (*rain, waves, etc*) to beat violently against; (*with* **out**) to attack physically or verbally. * *n* the flexible part of a whip; an eyelash; a stroke (as if) with a whip.

lass, lassie *n* a young woman or girl.

lasso *n* (*pl* **lassoes, lassos**) a long rope or leather thong with a running noose for catching horses, cattle, etc. * *vt* (*pr p* **lassoing,** *pt* **lassoed**) to catch (as if) with a lasso.

last[1] *n* a shoemaker's model of the foot on which boots and shoes are made or repaired. * *vt* to shape with a last.

last[2] *vi* to remain in existence, use, etc; to endure. * *vt* to continue during; to be enough for.

last[3] *adj* being or coming after all the others in time or place; only remaining; the most recent; least likely; conclusive. * *adv* after all the others; most recently; finally. * *n* the one coming last.

lasting *adj* enduring.—**lastingly** *adv*.

lastly *adv* at the end, in the last place, finally.

last-minute *adj* at the last possible time when something can be done.

latch *n* a fastening for a door, gate, or window, esp a bar, etc that fits into a notch. * *vti* to fasten with a latch.

latchkey *n* the key of an outer door.

late *adj, adv* after the usual or expected time; at an advanced stage or age; near the end; far on in the day or evening; just prior to the present; deceased; not long past; until lately; out of office.—**lateness** *n*.

lately *adv* recently, in recent times.

latent *adj* existing but not yet visible or developed.—**latency** *n*.

lateral *adj* of, at, from, towards the side.—**laterally** *adv*.

lath *n* a thin narrow strip of wood used in constructing a framework for plaster, etc.

lathe *n* a machine that rotates wood, metal, etc for shaping.

lather *n* a foam made by soap or detergent mixed with water; frothy sweat; a state of excitement or agitation. * *vti* to cover with or form lather.

Latin *adj* of ancient Rome, its people, their language, etc; denoting or of the languages derived from Latin (Italian, Spanish, etc), the peoples who speak them, their countries, etc. * *n* a native or inhabitant of ancient Rome; the language of ancient Rome; a person, as a Spaniard or Italian, whose language is derived from Latin.

latitude *n* the distance from north or south of the equator, measured in degrees; a region with reference to this distance; extent; scope; freedom from restrictions on actions or opinions.—**latitudinal** *adj*.—**latitudinally** *adv*.

latrine *n* a lavatory, as in a military camp.

latter *adj* later; more recent; nearer the end; being the last mentioned of two.

latterly *adv* recently.

lattice *n* a network of crossed laths or bars.

laudable *adj* praiseworthy.

laugh *vi* to emit explosive inarticulate vocal sounds expressive of amusement, joy or derision. * *vt* to utter or express with laughter. * *n* the act or sound of laughing; (*inf*) an amusing person or thing.—**laughingly** *adv*.

laughable *adj* causing laughter; ridiculous.—**laughably** *adv*.

laughing stock *n* an object of ridicule.

laughter *n* the act or sound of laughing.

launch[1] *vt* to throw, hurl or propel forward; to cause (a vessel) to slide into the water; (*rocket,* *missile*) to set off; to put into action; to put a new product onto the market. * *vi* to involve oneself enthusiastically. * *n* the act or occasion of launching.

launch[2] *n* an open, or partly enclosed, motor boat.

launching pad, launch pad *n* a platform from which a spacecraft is launched.

launder *vti* to wash and iron clothes. * *vt* to legitimize (money) obtained from criminal activity by passing it through foreign banks, or investing in legitimate businesses, etc.

launderette, laundrette *n* an establishment equipped with coin-operated washing machines and driers for public use.

laundry *n* a place where clothes are washed and ironed; clothes sent to be washed and ironed.

laureate *adj* crowned with laurel leaves as a mark of honour. * *n* a poet laureate.

laurel *n* an evergreen shrub with large, glossy leaves; the leaves used by the ancient Greeks as a symbol of achievement.

lava *n* molten rock flowing from a volcano; the solid substance formed as this cools.

lavatory *n* a sanitary device for the disposal of faeces and urine; a room equipped with this, a toilet.

lavender *n* the fragrant flowers of a perennial shrub dried and used in sachets; a pale purple.

lavish *vt* to give or spend freely. * *adj* abundant, profuse; generous; extravagant.—**lavishly** *adv*.—**lavishness** *n*.

law *n* all the rules of conduct in an organized community as upheld by authority; any one of such rules; obedience to such rules; the study of such rules, jurisprudence; the seeking of justice in courts under such rules; the profession of lawyers, judges, etc; (*inf*) the police; a sequence of events occurring with unvarying uniformity under the same conditions; any rule expected to be observed.

law-abiding *adj* obeying the law.

lawbreaker *n* a person who violates the law.

lawful *adj* in conformity with the law; recognized by law.—**lawfully** *adv*.

lawless *adj* not regulated by law; not in conformity with law, illegal.—**lawlessly** *adv*.—**lawlessness** *n*.

lawn[1] *n* a fine sheer cloth of linen or cotton.

lawn[2] *n* land covered with closely cut grass, esp around a house.

lawn mower *n* a hand-propelled or power-driven machine to cut lawn grass.

lawn tennis *n* tennis played on a grass court.

lawsuit *n* a suit between private parties in a law court.

lawyer *n* a person whose profession is advising others in matters of law or representing them in a court of law.

lax *adj* slack, loose; not tight; not strict or exact.—**laxly** *adv*.—**laxness** *n*.

laxative *n* a substance that promotes emptying of the bowels.—*also adj*.

laxity *n* the state or quality of being lax, laxness.

lay[1] *see* **lie**[2].

lay[2] *vt* (*pt* **laid**) to put down; to allay or suppress; to place in a resting position; to place or set; to place in a correct position; to produce (an egg); (*sl*) to have sexual intercourse with; to devise; to present or assert; to stake a bet; (*with* **off**) to suspend from work temporarily or permanently; (*with* **on**) to supply; (*with* **out**) to plan in detail; to arrange for display; to prepare (a corpse) for viewing; (*inf*) to spend money, esp lavishly. * *vi* (*inf*) to leave (a person or thing) alone. * *n* a way or position in which something is situated; (*sl*) an act of sexual intercourse; a sexual partner.

lay[3] *n* a simple narrative poem, esp as intended to be sung; a ballad.

lay[4] *adj* of or pertaining to those who are not members of the clergy; not belonging to a profession.

layabout *n* a loafer, lazy person.

lay-by *n* a place where motorists can stop at the side of a road without obstructing other traffic.

layer *n* a single thickness, fold, etc. * *vi* to separate into layers; to form by superimposing layers.

layman *n* a person who is not a member of the clergy; a non-specialist, someone who does not possess professional knowledge.

layout *n* the manner in which anything is laid out, esp arrangement of text and pictures on the pages of a newspaper or magazine, etc; the thing laid out.

laze *vti* to idle or loaf.

lazy *adj* (**lazier, laziest**) disinclined to work or exertion; encouraging or causing indolence; sluggishly moving.—**lazily** *adv*.—**laziness** *n*.

lb *abbr* = pound.

lead[1] *vb* (*pt* **led**) *vt* to show the way, esp by going first; to direct or guide on a course; to direct by influence; to be head of (an expedition, orchestra, etc); to be ahead of in a contest; to live, spend (one's life). * *vi* to show the way, as by going first; (*with* **to**) to tend in a certain direction; to be or go first. * *n* the role of a leader; first place; the amount or distance ahead; anything that leads, as a clue; the leading role in a play, etc; the right of playing first in cards or the card played.

lead[2] *n* a heavy, soft, bluish-grey, metallic element; a weight for sounding depths at sea, etc; bullets; a stick of graphite, used in pencils; (*print*) a thin strip of metal used to space lines of type. * *adj* of or containing lead. * *vt* (*pt* **leaded**) to cover, weight, or space out with lead.

leaden *adj* made of lead; very heavy; dull grey; gloomy.

leader *n* the person who goes first; the principal first violin-player in an orchestra; the director of an orchestra; the inspiration or head of a movement, such as a political party; a person whose example is followed; a leading article in a newspaper.

leadership *n* the act of leading; the ability to be a leader; the leaders of an organization or movement collectively.

leading[1] *adj* capable of guiding or influencing; principal; in first position.

leading[2] *n* a covering of lead; (*print*) the body of a type, larger than the size, giving space.

leaf *n* (*pl* **leaves**) any of the flat, thin (usu green) parts growing from the stem of a plant; a sheet of paper; a very thin sheet of metal; a hinged or removable part of a table top. * *vi* to bear leaves; (*with* **through**) to turn the pages of.

leaflet *n* a small or young leaf; a sheet of printed information (often folded), esp advertising matter distributed free. * *vi* to distribute leaflets (to).

league[1] *n* an association of nations, groups, etc for promoting common interests; an association of sports clubs that organizes matches between members; any class or category. * *vti* to form into a league.

league[2] *n* (*formerly*) a varying measure of distance, averaging about three miles (5km).

leak *n* a crack or hole through which liquid or gas may accidentally pass; the liquid or gas passing through such an opening; confidential information made public deliberately or accidentally. * *vi* to (let) escape though an opening; to disclose information surreptitiously.

lean[1] *adj* thin, with little flesh or fat; spare; meagre. * *n* meat with little or no fat.—**leanness** *n*.

lean[2] *vb* (*pt* **leaned** *or* **leant**) *vi* to bend or slant from an upright position; to rest supported (on or against); to rely or depend for help (on). * *vt* to cause to lean.

leaning *n* inclination, tendency.

leap *vb* (*pt* **leaped** *or* **leapt**) *vi* to jump; (*with* **at**) to accept something offered eagerly. * *vt* to pass over by a jump; to cause to leap. * *n* an act of leaping; bound; space passed by leaping; an abrupt transition.

leapfrog *n* a game in which one player vaults over another's bent back. * *vi* (*pt* **leapfrogged**) to vault in this manner; to advance in alternate jumps.

leap year *n* a year with an extra day (29 February) occurring every fourth year.

learn *vti* (*pt* **learnt** *or* **learned**) to gain knowledge of or skill in; to memorize; to become aware of, realize.—**learner** *n*.

learned *adj* having learning; erudite; acquired by study, experience, etc.—**learnedly** *adv*.

learning *n* a gaining of knowledge; the acquiring of knowledge or skill through study.

lease *n* a contract by which an owner lets land, property, etc to another person for a specified period. * *vt* to grant by or hold under lease.

leash *n* a cord, strap, etc by which a dog or animal is held in check. * *vt* to hold or restrain on a leash.

least *adj* smallest in size, degree, etc; slightest. * *adv* to the smallest degree. * *n* the smallest in amount.

leather *n* material made from the skin of an animal prepared by removing the hair and tanning; something made of leather. * *vt* to cover with leather; to thrash.

leave[1] *n* permission to do something; official authorization to be absent; the period covered by this.

leave[2] *vb* (*pt* **left**) *vt* to depart from; to cause or allow to remain in a specified state; to cause to remain behind; to refrain from consuming or dealing with; to have remaining at death, to bequeath; to have as a remainder; to allow to stay or or continue doing without interference; to entrust or commit to another; to abandon. * *vi* to depart.

lecherous *adj* characterized by or encouraging lechery.

lectern *n* a reading stand in a church; any similar reading support.

lecture *n* an informative talk to a class, etc; a lengthy reprimand. * *vti* to give a lecture (to); to reprimand.—**lecturer** *n*.

led *see* **lead**[1].

ledge *n* a narrow horizontal surface resembling a shelf projecting from a wall, rock face, etc; an underwater ridge of rocks; a rock layer containing ore.

ledger *n* a book in which a record of debits, credits, etc is kept.

lee *n* a shelter; the side or part away from the wind.

leech *n* a blood-sucking worm; a person who clings to or exploits another.

leek *n* a vegetable that resembles a greatly elongated green onion.

leer *n* a sly, oblique or lascivious look.—*also vi.*

leeway *n* the distance a ship or aircraft has strayed sideways of its course; freedom of action as regards expenditure of time, money, etc.

left[1] *see* **leave**[2].

left[2] *adj* of or on the side that is towards the west when one faces north; worn on the left hand, foot, etc. * *n* the left side; (*often cap*) of or relating to the left in politics; the left hand; (*boxing*) a blow with the left hand.

left-hand *adj* of or towards the left side of a person or thing; for use by the left hand.

left-handed *adj* using the left hand in preference to the right; done or made for use with the left hand; ambiguous, backhanded. * *adv* with the left hand.

left luggage office *n* a temporary repository for luggage at a railway station, etc.—*also* **checkroom**.

leftovers *npl* unused portions of something, esp uneaten food.

left-wing *adj* of or relating to the liberal faction of a political party, organization, etc.—**left-winger** *n.*

leg *n* one of the limbs on which humans and animals support themselves and walk; the part of a garment covering the leg; anything shaped or used like a leg; a branch or limb of a forked object; a section, as of a trip; any of a series of games or matches in a competition.

legacy *n* money, property, etc left to someone in a will; something passed on by an ancestor or remaining from the past.

legal *adj* of or based on law; permitted by law; of or for lawyers.—**legally** *adv.*

legalize *vt* to make lawful.—**legalization** *n.*

legation *n* a diplomatic minister and staff; the headquarters of a diplomatic minister.

legend *n* a story handed down from the past; a notable person or the stories of his or her exploits; an inscription on a coin, etc; a caption; an explanation of the symbols used on a map.

legendary *adj* of, based on, or presented in legends; famous, notorious.

leggings *npl* protective outer coverings for the lower legs; a leg-hugging fashion garment for women.

legible *adj* able to be read.—**legibly** *adv.*—**legibility** *n.*

legion *n* an infantry unit of the ancient Roman army; a large body of soldiers; a large number, a multitude.

legislate *vi* to make or pass laws. * *vt* to bring about by legislation.

legislation *n* the act or process of law-making; the laws themselves.

legislative *adj* of legislation or a legislature; having the power to make laws.

legislator *n* a member of a legislative body.

legislature *n* the body of people who have the power of making laws.

legitimate *adj* lawful; reasonable, justifiable; conforming to accepted rules, standards, etc; (*child*) born of parents married to each other.—**legitimacy** *n.*—**legitimately** *adv.*

leisure *n* ease, relaxation, esp freedom from employment or duties. * *adj* free and unoccupied.—**leisured** *adj.*

leisurely *adj* relaxed, without hurry.—**leisureliness** *n.*

lemon *n* (a tree bearing) a small yellow oval fruit with an acid pulp; pale yellow; (*sl*) a person or thing considered disappointing or useless.—**lemony** *adj.*

lemonade *n* a lemon-flavoured drink.

lend *vb* (*pt* **lent**) *vt* to give the use of something temporarily in expectation of its return; to provide (money) at interest; to give, impart. * *vi* to make loans.—**lender** *n.*

length *n* the extent of something from end to end, usu the longest dimension; a specified distance or period of time; something of a certain length taken from a larger piece; a long expanse; (*often pl*) the degree of effort put into some action.

lengthen *vti* to make or become longer.

lengthways, lengthwise *adv* in the direction of the length.

lengthy *adj* (**lengthier, lengthiest**) long, esp too long.—**lengthily** *adv.*—**lengthiness** *n.*

lenient *adj* not harsh or severe; merciful.—**leniency** *n.*—**leniently** *adv.*

lens *n* a curved piece of transparent glass, plastic, etc used in optical instruments to form an image; any device used to focus electromagnetic rays, sound waves, etc; a similar transparent part of the eye that focuses light rays on the retina.

Lent *n* the forty weekdays from Ash Wednesday to Easter, observed by Christians as a period of fasting and penitence.—**Lenten** *adj*.

lentil *n* any of several leguminous plants with edible seeds; their seed used for food.

Leo *n* (*astrol*) the 5th sign of the zodiac, in astrology operative 22 July-21 August; (*astron*) the Lion, a constellation in the northern hemisphere.

leopard *n* a large tawny feline with black spots found in Africa and Asia.—*also* **panther**.

leotard *n* a skintight one-piece garment worn by dancers and others engaged in strenuous exercise.

leper *n* a person with leprosy.

leprosy *n* a chronic infectious bacterial disease of the skin, often resulting in disfigurement.—**leprous** *adj*.

lesbian *n* a female homosexual. * *adj* of or characteristic of lesbians.—**lesbianism** *n*.

less *adj* not so much, not so great, etc; fewer; smaller. * *adv* to a smaller extent. * *n* a smaller amount. * *prep* minus.

lessen *vti* to make or become less.

lesson *n* something to be learned or studied; something that has been learned or studied; a unit of learning or teaching; (*pl*) a course of instruction; a selection from the Bible, read as a part of a church service.

lest *conj* in order, or for fear, that not; that.

let[1] *n* a stoppage; (*tennis*) a minor obstruction of the ball that requires a point to be replayed.

let[2] *vb* (*pr p* **letting,** *pt* **let**) *vt* to allow, permit; to rent; to assign (a contract); to cause to run out, as blood; as an auxiliary in giving suggestions or commands (*let us go*); (*with* **down**) to lower; to deflate; to disappoint; to untie; to lengthen; (*with* **off**) to allow to leave (a ship, etc); to fire (a gun) or explode (a bomb); to release; to deal leniently with; (*with* **out**) to release; to reveal; to rent out; to make a garment larger; (*with* **up**) to relax; to cease. * *vi* to be rented; (*with* **on**) (*inf*) to pretend; (*inf*) to indicate one's awareness (of a secret, etc). * *n* the letting of property or accommodation.

let-down *n* a disappointment.

lethal *adj* deadly.—**lethality** *n*.—**lethally** *adv*.

lethargy *n* an abnormal drowsiness; sluggishness; apathy.—**lethargic** *adj*.—**lethargically** *adv*.

letter *n* a symbol representing a phonetic value in a written language; a character of the alphabet; a written or printed message; (*pl*) literature; learning; knowledge; literal meaning. * *vt* to mark with letters.

letter bomb *n* an explosive device concealed in an envelope and sent through the post.

letter box *n* a slit in the doorway of a house or building through which letters are delivered; a postbox.

lettering *n* the act or process of inscribing with letters; letters collectively; a title; an inscription.

lettuce *n* a plant with succulent leaves used in salads.

leukaemia, leukemia (*US*) *n* a chronic disease characterized by an abnormal increase in the number of white blood cells in body tissues and the blood.

level *n* a horizontal line or plane; a position in a scale of values; a flat area or surface; an instrument for determining the horizontal. * *adj* horizontal; having a flat surface; at the same height, rank, position, etc; steady. * *vti* (*pt* **levelled**) to make or become level; to demolish; to raise and aim (a gun, criticism, etc).—**levelly** *adv*.—**leveller** *n*.

level crossing *n* a place where a road and railway or two railway lines cross at the same level.

level-headed *adj* having an even temper and sound judgment.

lever *n* a bar used for prising or moving something; a means to an end; a device consisting of a bar turning about a fixed point; any device used in the same way, eg to operate machinery. * *vt* to raise or move (as with) a lever.

leverage *n* the action of a lever; the mechanical advantage gained by the use of a lever; power, influence.

levity *n* excessive frivolity; lack of necessary seriousness.

levy *vt* to collect by force or authority, as a tax, fine, etc; an amount levied; to enrol or conscript troops; to prepare for or wage war. * *n* a levying; the amount levied.

lewd *adj* indecent; lustful; obscene.—**lewdly** *adv*.—**lewdness** *n*.

liability *n* a being liable; something for which one is liable; (*inf*) a handicap, disadvantage; (*pl*) debts, obligations, disadvantages.

liable *adj* legally bound or responsible; subject to; likely (to).

liaison *n* intercommunication as between units

of a military force; an illicit love affair; a thickening for sauces, soups, etc, as egg yolks or cream.

liar *n* a person who tells lies.

libel *n* any written or printed matter tending to injure a person's reputation unjustly; (*inf*) any defamatory or damaging assertion about a person. * *vt* (*pt* **libelled**) to utter or publish a libel against.—**libellous** *adj*.

liberal *adj* ample, abundant; not literal or strict; tolerant; (*education*) contributing to a general broadening of the mind, non-specialist; favouring reform or progress. * *n* a person who favours reform or progress.—**liberally** *adv*.

liberate *vt* to set free from foreign occupation, slavery, etc.—**liberation** *n*.—**liberator** *n*.

liberty *n* freedom from slavery, captivity, etc; the right to do as one pleases, freedom; a particular right, freedom, etc granted by authority; an impertinent attitude; authorized leave granted to a sailor.

Libra *n* (*astrol*) the 7th sign of the zodiac, operative 24 September-23 October; a constellation represented as a pair of scales.

librarian *n* a person in charge of a library or trained in librarianship.

library *n* a collection of books, tapes, records, photographs, etc for reference or borrowing; a room, building or institution containing such a collection; (*comput*) a set of, usu general purpose, programs or subroutines for use in programming.

libretto *n* (*pl* **librettos, libretti**) the text to which an opera, oratorio, etc is set.—**librettist** *n*.

lice *see* **louse**.

licence, license (*US*) *n* a formal or legal permission to do something specified; a document granting such permission; freedom to deviate from rule, practice, etc; excessive freedom, an abuse of liberty.

license *vt* to grant a licence to or for; to permit.

licentious *adj* morally unrestrained; lascivious.—**licentiousness** *n*.

lichen *n* any of various small plants consisting of an alga and a fungus living in symbiotic association, growing on stones, trees, etc.

lick *vt* to draw the tongue over, esp to taste or clean; (*flames, etc*) to flicker around or touch lightly; (*inf*) to thrash; (*inf*) to defeat. * *n* a licking with the tongue; (*inf*) a sharp blow; (*inf*) a short, rapid burst of activity.

lid *n* a removable cover as for a box, etc; an eyelid.—**lidded** *adj*.

lido *n* an open air swimming pool and recreational complex for public use.

lie[1] *n* an untrue statement made with intent to deceive; something that deceives or misleads. * *vi* (*pr p* **lying,** *pt* **lied**) to speak untruthfully with an intention to deceive; to create a false impression.

lie[2] *vi* (*pr p* **lying,** *pt* **lay,** *pp* **lain**) to be or put oneself in a reclining or horizontal position; to rest on a support in a horizontal position; to be in a specified condition; to be situated; to exist. * *n* the way in which something is situated.

lieutenant *n* a commissioned army officer ranking below a captain; a naval officer next below a lieutenant commander; a deputy, a chief assistant to a superior.—**lieutenancy** *n*.

life *n* (*pl* **lives**) that property of plants and animals (ending at death) that enables them to use food, grow, reproduce, etc; the state of having this property; living things collectively; the time a person or thing exists; one's manner of living; one's animate existence; vigour, liveliness; (*inf*) a life sentence; a biography. * *adj* of animate being; lifelong; using a living model; of or relating to or provided by life insurance.

lifebelt *n* an inflatable ring to support a person in the water; a safety belt.

lifeboat *n* a small rescue boat carried by a ship; a specially designed and equipped rescue vessel that helps those in distress along the coastline.

lifeguard *n* an expert swimmer employed to prevent drownings.

life jacket *n* a sleeveless jacket or vest of buoyant material to keep a person afloat.

lifeless *adj* dead; unconscious; dull.—**lifelessly** *adv*.—**lifelessness** *n*.

lifelike *adj* resembling a real life person or thing.

lifeline *n* a rope for raising or lowering a diver; a rope for rescuing a person, eg as attached to a lifebelt; a vitally important channel of communication or transport.

lifelong *adj* lasting one's whole life.

life preserver *n* a club used as a weapon of self-defence; a lifebelt or life jacket.

lifetime *n* the length of time that a person lives or something lasts.

lift *vt* to bring to a higher position, raise; to raise in rank, condition, etc; (*sl*) to steal; to revoke. * *vi* to exert oneself in raising something; to rise; to go up; (*fog, etc*) to disperse; (*with* **off**) (*rocket, etc*) to take off. * *n* act or fact of lifting; distance through which a thing is lifted; elevation of mood, etc; elevated position or carriage; a ride in the direction in which one is going; help of any kind; a cage or platform for moving something from one level to another (—*also* **elevator**); upward air pressure maintaining an aircraft in flight.

liftoff *n* the vertical thrust of a spacecraft, etc at launching; the time of this.

ligament *n* a band of tissue connecting bones; a unifying bond.

light[1] *n* the agent of illumination that stimulates the sense of sight; electromagnetic radiation such as ultraviolet, infrared or X-rays; brightness, illumination; a source of light, as the sun, a lamp, etc; daylight; a thing used to ignite something; a window; knowledge, enlightenment; aspect or appearance. * *adj* having light; bright; pale in colour. * *adv* palely. * *vt* (*pt* **lit** *or* **lighted**) to ignite; to cause to give off light; to furnish with light; to brighten, animate.

light[2] *adj* having little weight; not heavy; less than usual in weight, amount, force, etc; of little importance; easy to bear; easy to digest; happy; dizzy, giddy; not serious; moderate; moving with ease; producing small products. * *adv* lightly. * *vi* (*pt* **lighted** *or* **lit**) to come to rest after travelling through the air; to dismount, to alight; to come or happen on or upon; to strike suddenly, as a blow.—**lightly** *adv*.—**lightness** *n*.

lighten[1] *vti* to make or become light or lighter; to shine, flash.

lighten[2] *vti* to make or become lighter in weight; to make or become more cheerful; to mitigate.

lighter[1] *n* a small device that produces a naked flame to light cigarettes.

lighter[2] *n* a large barge used in loading or unloading larger ships.

light-headed *adj* dizzy; delirious.

light-hearted *adj* carefree.

lighthouse *n* a tower with a bright light to guide ships.

lighting *n* the process of giving light; equipment for illuminating a stage, television set, etc; the distribution of light on an object, as in a work of art.

lightning *n* a discharge or flash of electricity in the sky. * *adv* fast, sudden.

lightning conductor, lightning rod *n* a metal rod placed high on a building and grounded to divert lightning from the structure.

lightweight *adj* of less than average weight; trivial, unimportant. * *n* a person or thing of less than average weight; a professional boxer weighing 130-135 pounds (59-61 kg); a person of little importance or influence.

light year *n* the distance light travels in one year.

like[1] *adj* having the same characteristics; similar; equal. * *adv* (*inf*) likely. * *prep* similar to; characteristic of; in the mood for; indicative of; as for example. * *conj* (*inf*) as; as if. * *n* an equal; counterpart.

like[2] *vt* to be pleased with; to wish. * *vi* to be so inclined.

likelihood *n* probability.

likely *adj* (**likelier, likeliest**) reasonably to be expected; suitable; showing promise of success.* *adv* probably.—**likeliness** *n*.

like-minded *adj* sharing the same tastes, ideas, etc.

liken *vt* to compare.

likewise *adv* the same; also.

liking *n* fondness; affection; preference.

lilac *n* a shrub with large clusters of tiny, fragrant flowers; a pale purple. * *adj* lilac coloured.

lily *n* a bulbous plant having typically trumpet-shaped flowers; its flower.

lily of the valley *n* a small plant of the lily family with white bell-shaped flowers.

limb *n* a projecting appendage of an animal body, as an arm, leg, or wing; a large branch of a tree; a participating member, agent; an arm of a cross.

limber[1] *adj* flexible, able to bend the body easily. * *vti* to make or become limber.

limber[2] *n* the detachable wheeled section of a gun carriage.

limbo[1] *n* (*pl* **limbos**) (*Christianity*) the abode after death assigned to unbaptized souls; a place for lost, unwanted, or neglected persons or things; an intermediate stage or condition between extremes.

limbo[2] *n* (*pl* **limbos**) a West Indian dance that involves bending over backwards and passing under a horizontal bar that is progressively lowered.

lime[1] *n* a white calcium compound used for making cement and in agriculture. * *vt* to treat or cover with lime.

lime[2] *n* a small yellowish-green fruit with a juicy, sour pulp; the tree that bears it; its colour.

lime[3] *n* the linden tree.

limelight *n* intense publicity; a type of lamp, formerly used in stage lighting, in which lime was heated to produce a brilliant flame.

limerick *n* a type of humorous verse consisting of five lines.

limestone *n* a type of rock composed mainly of calcium carbonate.

limit *n* a boundary; (*pl*) bounds; the greatest amount allowed; (*inf*) as much as one can tolerate. * *vt* to set a limit to; to restrict.

limitation *n* the act of limiting or being limited; a hindrance to ability or achievement.

limited *adj* confined within bounds; lacking imagination or originality.

limousine *n* a large luxury car.

limp[1] *vi* to walk with or as with a lame leg. * *n* a lameness in walking.

limp[2] *adj* not firm; lethargic; wilted; flexible.—**limply** *adv*.—**limpness** *n*.

limpet *n* a mollusc with a low conical shell that clings to rocks.

line[1] *vt* to put, or serve as, a lining in.

line[2] *n* a length of cord, rope, or wire; a cord for measuring, making level; a system of conducting fluid, electricity, etc; a thin threadlike mark; anything resembling such a mark, as a wrinkle; edge, limit, boundary; border, outline, contour; a row of persons or things, as printed letters across a page; a succession of persons, lineage; a connected series of things; the course a moving thing takes; a course of conduct, actions, etc; a whole system of transportation; a person's trade or occupation; a field of experience or interest; (*inf*) glib, persuasive talk; a verse; the forward combat position in warfare; fortifications, trenches or other defences used in war; a stock of goods; a piece of information; a short letter, note; (*pl*) all the speeches of a character in a play. * *vt* to mark with lines; to form a line along; to cover with lines; to arrange in a line. * *vi* to align.

linear *adj* of, made of, or using a line or lines; narrow and long; in relation to length only.—**linearity** *n*.

linen *n* thread or cloth made of flax; household articles (sheets, cloths, etc) made of linen or cotton cloth.

liner *n* a large passenger ship or aircraft travelling a regular route.

linesman *n* an official in certain games who assists the referee in deciding when the ball is out of play, etc.

line-up *n* an arrangement of persons or things in a line, eg for inspection.

linger *vi* to stay a long time; to delay departure; to dawdle or loiter; to dwell on in the mind; to remain alive though on the point of death.

lingo *n* (*pl* **lingoes**) (*inf*) a dialect, jargon, etc.

linguist *n* a person who is skilled in speaking foreign languages.

linguistic *adj* of or pertaining to language or linguistics.—**linguistically** *adv*.

linguistics *n* (*used as sing*) the science of language.

lining *n* a material used to cover the inner surface of a garment, etc; any material covering an inner surface.

link *n* a single loop or ring of a chain; something resembling a loop or ring or connecting piece; a person or thing acting as a connection, as in a communication system, machine or organization. * *vti* to connect or become connected.

links *npl* (*also used as sing*) flat sandy soil; a golf course, esp by the sea.

link-up *n* a linking together.

linoleum *n* a floor covering of coarse fabric backing with a smooth, hard decorative coating.

lint *n* scraped and softened linen used to dress wounds; fluff.

lintel *n* the horizontal crosspiece spanning a doorway or window.

lion *n* a large, flesh-eating feline mammal with a shaggy mane in the adult male; a person of great courage or strength.—**lioness** *nf*.

lip *n* either of the two fleshy flaps that surround the mouth; anything like a lip, as the rim of a jug; (*sl*) insolent talk. * *vt* (*pt* **lipped**) to touch with the lips; to kiss; to utter.

lip service *n* support expressed but not acted upon.

lipstick *n* a small stick of cosmetic for colouring the lips; the cosmetic itself.

liqueur *n* a sweet and variously flavoured alcoholic drink.

liquid *n* a substance that, unlike a gas, does not expand indefinitely and, unlike a solid, flows readily. * *adj* in liquid form; clear; limpid; flowing smoothly and musically, as verse; (*assets*) readily convertible into cash.—**liquidity** *n*.

liquidate *vt* to settle the accounts of; to close a (bankrupt) business and distribute its assets among its creditors; to convert into cash; to eliminate, kill.—**liquidation** *n*.—**liquidator** *n*.

liquidize *vt* to make liquid.

liquor *n* an alcoholic drink; any liquid, esp that in which food has been cooked.

liquorice, licorice (*US*) *n* a black extract made

from the root of a European plant, used in medicine and confectionery; a liquorice-flavoured sweet.

lisp *vi* to substitute the sounds *th* (as in *thin*) for *s* or *th* (as in *then*) for *z*; a speech defect or habit involving such pronunciation; to utter imperfectly. * *vt* to speak or utter with a lisp.—*also n.*

list[1] *n* a series of names, numbers, words, etc written or printed in order. * *vt* to make a list of; to enter in a directory, etc.

list[2] *vti* to tilt to one side, as a ship. * *n* such a tilting.

listen *vi* to try to hear; to pay attention, take heed; (*with* **in**) to overhear a conversation, eg on the telephone; to tune into a radio broadcast; to eavesdrop.

listener *n* a person who listens; a person listening to a radio broadcast.

listless *adj* lacking energy or enthusiasm because of illness, dejection, etc; languid.—**listlessly** *adv*.—**listlessness** *n*.

lit *see* **light**[1], **light**[2].

litany *n* a type of prayer in which petitions to God are recited by a priest and elicit set responses by the congregation; any tedious or automatic recital.

literacy *n* the ability to read and write.

literal *adj* in accordance with the exact meaning of a word or text; in a basic or strict sense; prosaic, unimaginative; real.—**literally** *adv*.

literary *adj* of or dealing with literature; knowing much about literature.

literate *adj* able to read and write; educated.—*also n.*

literature *n* the writings of a period or of a country, esp those valued for their excellence; of style or form; all the books and articles on a subject; (*inf*) any printed matter.

lithe *adj* supple, flexible.

litigate *vti* to bring or contest in a lawsuit.—**litigation** *n*.

litre, liter (*US*) *n* a measure of liquid capacity in the metric system, equivalent to 1.76 pints.

litter *n* rubbish scattered about; young animals produced at one time; straw, hay, etc used as bedding for animals; a stretcher for carrying a sick or wounded person. * *vt* to make untidy; to scatter about carelessly.

little *adj* not great or big, small in size, amount, degree, etc; short in duration; small in importance or power; narrow-minded. * *n* small in amount, degree, etc. * *adv* less, least, slightly; not much; not in the least.

liturgy *n* the prescribed form of service of a church.—**liturgical** *adj*.—**liturgically** *adv*.

live[1] *vi* to have life; to remain alive; to endure; to pass life in a specified manner; to enjoy a full life; to reside. * *vt* to carry out in one's life; to spend; pass.

live[2] *adj* having life; of the living state or living beings; of present interest; still burning; unexploded; carrying electric current; broadcast during the actual performance.

livelihood *n* employment; a means of living.

lively *adj* (**livelier, liveliest**) full of life; spirited; exciting; vivid; keen. * *adv* in a lively manner.—**liveliness** *n*.

liver *n* the largest glandular organ in vertebrate animals, which secretes bile, etc and is important in metabolism; the liver of an animal used as food; a reddish-brown colour.

livery *n* an identifying uniform, as that worn by a servant.

lives *see* **life**.

livestock *n* (farm) animals raised for use or sale.

livid *adj* (*skin*) discoloured, as from bruising; greyish in colour; (*inf*) extremely angry.

living *adj* having life; still in use; true to life, vivid; of life, for living in. * *n* a being alive; livelihood; manner of existence.

living room *n* a room in a house used for general entertainment and relaxation.

living wage *n* a wage sufficient to maintain a reasonable standard of comfort.

lizard *n* a reptile with a slender body, four legs, and a tapering tail.

llama *n* a South American animal, related to the camel, used for carrying loads and as a source of wool.

load *n* an amount carried at one time; something borne with difficulty; a burden; (*often pl*) (*inf*) a great amount. * *vt* to put into or upon; to burden; to oppress; to supply in large quantities; to alter, as by adding a weight to dice or an adulterant to alcoholic drink; to put a charge of ammunition into (a firearm); to put film into (a camera); (*comput*) to install a program in memory. * *vi* to take on a load.

loaded *adj* (*sl*) having plenty of money; drunk; under the influence of drugs.

loaf[1] *n* (*pl* **loaves**) a mass of bread of regular shape and standard weight; food shaped like this; (*sl*) the head.

loaf[2] *vi* to pass time in idleness.—**loafer** *n*.

loam *n* rich and fertile soil.—**loamy** *adj*.

loan *n* the act of lending; something lent, esp money. * *vti* to lend.

loath *adj* unwilling.—*also* **loth**.

loathe *vt* to dislike intensely; to detest.—**loathing** *n*.

lobby *n* an entrance hall of a public building; a person or group that tries to influence legislators. * *vti* to try to influence (legislators) to support a particular cause or take certain action.

lobe *n* a rounded projection, as the lower end of the ear; any of the divisions of the lungs or brain.

lobster *n* any of a family of edible sea crustaceans with four pairs of legs and a pair of large pincers.

local *adj* of or belonging to a particular place; serving the needs of a specific district; of or for a particular part of the body. * *n* an inhabitant of a specific place; (*inf*) a pub serving a particular district.—**locally** *adv*.

locality *n* a neighbourhood or a district; a particular scene, position, or place; the fact or condition of having a location in space and time.

locate *vt* to determine or indicate the position of something; to set in or assign to a particular position.

location *n* a specific position or place; a locating or being located; a place outside a studio where a film is (partly) shot; (*comput*) an area in memory where a single item of data is stored.

loch *n* (*Scot*) a lake.

lock[1] *n* a fastening device on doors, etc, operated by a key or combination; part of a canal, dock, etc in which the level of the water can be changed by the operation of gates; the part of a gun by which the charge is fired; a controlling hold, as used in wrestling. * *vt* to fasten with a lock; to shut; to fit, link; to jam together so as to make immovable. * *vi* to become locked; to interlock.

lock[2] *n* a curl of hair; a tuft of wool, etc.

locker *n* a small cupboard, chest, etc that can be locked, esp one for storing possessions in a public place.

locket *n* a small ornamental case, usu holding a lock of hair, photograph or other memento, hung from the neck.

lockjaw *n* tetanus.

locomotive *n* an electric, steam, or diesel engine on wheels, designed to move a railway train. * *adj* of locomotion.

locust *n* a type of large grasshopper often travelling in swarms and destroying crops; a type of hard-wooded leguminous tree.

lodge *n* a small house at the entrance to a park or stately home; a country house for seasonal leisure activities; a resort hotel or motel; the local chapter or hall of a fraternal society; a beaver's lair. * *vt* to house temporarily; to shoot, thrust, etc firmly (in); to bring before legal authorities; to confer upon. * *vi* to live in a place for a time; to live as a paying guest; to come to rest and stick firmly (in).

lodger *n* a person who lives in a rented room in another's home.

lodging *n* a temporary residence; (*pl*) accommodation rented in another's house.

loft *n* a space under a roof; a storage area under the roof of a barn or stable; a gallery in a church or hall. * *vt* to send into a high curve.

lofty *adj* (**loftier, loftiest**) (*objects*) of a great height, elevated; (*person*) noble, haughty, superior in manner.—**loftily** *adv*.—**loftiness** *n*.

log *n* a section of a felled tree; a device for ascertaining the speed of a ship; a record of speed, progress, etc, esp one kept on a ship's voyage or aircraft's flight. * *vb* (*pt* **logged**) *vt* to record in a log; to sail or fly (a specified distance). * *vi* (*with* **on, off**) (*comput*) to establish or disestablish communication with a mainframe computer from a remote terminal in a multi-user system.—**logger** *n*.

logbook *n* an official record of a ship's or aircraft's voyage or flight; an official document containing details of a vehicle's registration.

logic *n* correct reasoning, or the science of this; way of reasoning; what is expected by the working of cause and effect.—**logician** *n*.

logical *adj* conforming to the rules of logic; capable of reasoning according to logic.—**logically** *adv*.—**logicality** *n*.

logistics *n* (*used as sing*) the science of the organization, transport and supply of military forces; the planning and organization of any complex activity.—**logistic** *adj*.

loin *n* (*usu pl*) the lower part of the back between the hipbones and the ribs; the front part of the hindquarters of an animal used for food.

loiter *vi* to linger or stand about aimlessly.—**loiterer** *n*.

loll *vi* to lean or recline in a lazy manner, to lounge; (*tongue*) to hang loosely.

lollipop *n* a flat boiled sweet at the end of a stick.

lone *adj* by oneself; isolated; without companions, solitary.

lonely *adj* (**lonelier, loneliest**) isolated; unhappy at being alone; (*places*) remote, rarely visited.

loner *n* a person who avoids the company of others.

long[1] *adj* measuring much in space or time; having a greater than usual length, quantity, etc; tedious, slow; far-reaching; well-supplied. * *adv* for a long time; from start to finish; at a remote time.

long[2] *vi* to desire earnestly, esp for something not likely to be attained.

long-distance *adj* travelling or communicating over long distances.

longhand *n* ordinary handwriting, as opposed to shorthand.

longing *n* an intense desire.

longitude *n* distance east or west of the prime meridian, expressed in degrees or time.

long jump *n* an athletic event consisting of a horizontal running jump.

long-playing *adj* of or relating to an LP record.

long-range *adj* reaching over a long distance or period of time.

long-sighted *adj* only seeing distant objects clearly.

long-standing *adj* having continued for a long time.

long-suffering *adj* enduring pain, provocation, etc patiently.

long-term *adj* of or extending over a long time.

long wave *n* a radio wave of a frequency less than 300 kHz.

long-winded *adj* speaking or writing at great length; tiresome.

loo *n* (*inf*) a lavatory.

look *vi* to try to see; to see; to search; to appear, seem; to be facing in a specified direction; (*with* **in**) to pay a brief visit; (*with* **up**) to improve in prospects. * *vt* to direct one's eyes on; to have an appearance befitting. * *n* the act of looking; a gaze, glance; appearance; aspect; (*with* **after**) to take care of; (*with* **over**) to examine; (*with* **up**) to research (for information, etc) in book; to visit.

look-alike *n* a person that looks like another.

lookout *n* a place for keeping watch; a person assigned to watch.

loom[1] *n* a machine or frame for weaving yarn or thread. * *vt* to weave on a loom.

loom[2] *vi* to come into view indistinctly and often threateningly; to come ominously close, as an impending event.

loop *n* a figure made by a curved line crossing itself; a similar rounded shape in cord, rope, etc crossed on itself; anything forming this figure; (*comput*) a set of instructions in a program that are executed repeatedly; an intrauterine contraceptive device; a segment of film or magnetic tape. * *vt* to make a loop of; to fasten with a loop. * *vi* to form a loop or loops.

loophole *n* a means of evading an obligation, etc; a slit in a wall for looking or shooting through.

loose *adj* free from confinement or restraint; not firmly fastened; not tight or compact; not precise; inexact; (*inf*) relaxed. * *vt* to release; to unfasten; to untie; to detach; (*bullet*) to discharge. * *vi* to become loose.—**loosely** *adv*.—**looseness** *n*.

loosen *vti* to make or become loose or looser.

loot *n* goods taken during warfare, civil unrest, etc; (*sl*) money. * *vti* to plunder, pillage.—**looter** *n*.

lop *vt* (*pt* **lopped**) to sever the branches or twigs from a tree; to cut off or out as superfluous.

lopsided *adj* having one side larger in weight, height, or size than the other; badly balanced.

lord *n* a ruler, master or monarch; a male member of the nobility; (*with cap and* **the**) God; a form of address used to certain peers, bishops and judges.

lordly *adj* (**lordlier, lordliest**) noble; haughty; arrogant.

lordship *n* the rank or authority of a lord; rule, dominion; (*with* **his** *or* **your**) a title used in speaking of or to a lord.

lore *n* knowledge; learning, esp of a traditional nature; a particular body of tradition.

lorry *n* a large motor vehicle for transporting heavy loads, a truck.

lose *vb* (*pt* **lost**) *vt* to have taken from one by death, accident, removal, etc; to be unable to find; to fail to keep, as one's temper; to fail to see, hear, or understand; to fail to have, get, etc; to fail to win; to cause the loss of; to wander from (one's way, etc); to squander. * *vi* to suffer (a) loss.—**loser** *n*.

loss *n* a losing or being lost; the damage, trouble caused by losing; the person, thing, or amount lost.

lost *adj* no longer possessed; missing; not won; destroyed or ruined; having wandered astray; wasted.

lot *n* an object, such as a straw, slip of paper, etc drawn from others at random to reach a decision by chance; the decision thus arrived at; one's share by lot; fortune; a plot of ground; a group of persons or things; an item or set of items put up for auction; (*often pl*) (*inf*) a great amount; much; (*inf*) sort.

loth *see* **loath**.

lotion *n* a liquid for cosmetic or external medical use.

lottery *n* a system of raising money by selling numbered tickets that offer the chance of winning a prize; an enterprise, etc which may or may not succeed.

loud *adj* characterized by or producing great noise; emphatic; (*inf*) obtrusive or flashy.—**loudly** *adv*.—**loudness** *n*.

loudspeaker *n* a device for converting electrical energy into sound.

lounge *vi* to move, sit, lie, etc in a relaxed way; to spend time idly. * *n* a room with comfortable furniture for sitting, as a waiting room at an airport, etc; a comfortable sitting room in a hotel or private house.

louse *n* (*pl* **lice**) any of various small wingless insects that are parasitic on humans and animals; any similar but unrelated insects that are parasitic on plants; (*inf*) (*pl* **louses**) a mean, contemptible person.

lousy *adj* (**lousier, lousiest**) infested with lice; (*sl*) disgusting, of poor quality, or inferior; (*sl*) well supplied (with).

lout *n* a clumsy, rude person.—**loutish** *adj*.

lovable, loveable *adj* easy to love or feel affection for.

love *n* a strong liking for someone or something; a passionate affection for another person; the object of such affection; (*tennis*) a score of zero. * *vti* to feel love (for).

love affair *n* a romantic or sexual relationship between two people.

lovely *adj* (**lovelier, loveliest**) beautiful; (*inf*) highly enjoyable.—**loveliness** *n*.

lover *n* a person in love with another person; a person, esp a man, having an extramarital sexual relationship; (*pl*) a couple in love with each other; someone who loves a specific person or thing.

loving *adj* affectionate.—**lovingly** *adv*.

low[1] *n* the sound a cow makes, a moo. * *vi* to make this sound.

low[2] *adj* not high or tall; below the normal level; less in size, degree, amount, etc, than usual; deep in pitch; depressed in spirits; humble, of low rank; vulgar, coarse; not loud. * *adv* in or to a low degree, level, etc. * *n* a low level, degree, etc; a region of low barometric pressure.

loyal *adj* firm in allegiance to a person, cause, country, party, etc, faithful; demonstrating unswerving allegiance.—**loyally** *adv*.—**loyalty** *n*.

lozenge *n* a four-sided diamond-shaped figure; a cough drop, sweet, etc, originally diamond-shaped.

LP *n* a long-playing record, usu 12 inches (30.5 cm) in diameter and played at a speed of 33.33 revolutions per minute.

Ltd *abbr* = limited liability (used by private companies only).

lubricant *n* a substance that lubricates.

lubricate *vt* to coat or treat (machinery, etc) with oil or grease to lessen friction; to make smooth, slippery, or greasy. * *vi* to act as a lubricant.—**lubrication** *n*.—**lubricator** *n*.

lucid *adj* easily understood; sane.—**lucidly** *adv*.—**lucidity** *n*.

luck *n* chance; good fortune.

lucky *adj* (**luckier, luckiest**) having or bringing good luck.—**luckily** *adv*.

lucrative *adj* producing wealth or profit; profitable.—**lucrativeness** *n*.

ludicrous *adj* absurd, laughable.—**ludicrously** *adv*.

lug[1] *vt* (*pt* **lugged**) to pull or drag along with effort.

lug[2] *n* an ear-like projection by which a thing is held or supported.

luggage *n* the suitcases and other baggage containing the possessions of a traveller.

lukewarm *adj* barely warm, tepid; lacking enthusiasm.

lull *vt* to soothe, to calm; to calm the suspicions of, esp by deception. * *n* a short period of calm.

lullaby *n* a song to lull children to sleep.

lumbago *n* rheumatic pain in the lower back.

lumber[1] *n* timber, logs, beams, boards, etc, roughly cut and prepared for use; articles of unused household furniture that are stored away; any useless articles. * *vi* to cut down timber and saw it into lumber. * *vt* to clutter with lumber; to heap in disorder.

lumber[2] *vi* to move heavily or clumsily.

lumberjack *n* a person employed to fell trees and transport and prepare timber.

luminous *adj* emitting light; glowing in the dark; clear, easily understood.

lump *n* a small, compact mass of something, usu without definite shape; an abnormal swelling; a dull or stupid person. * *adj* in a lump or lumps. * *vt* to treat or deal with in a mass. * *vi* to become lumpy.

lumpy *adj* (**lumpier, lumpiest**) filled or covered with lumps.—**lumpily** *adv*.—**lumpiness** *n*.

lunacy *n* insanity; utter folly.

lunar *adj* of or like the moon.
lunatic *adj* insane; utterly foolish. * *n* an insane person.
lunch *n* a light meal, esp between breakfast and dinner. * *vi* to eat lunch.
luncheon *n* lunch, esp a formal lunch.
luncheon voucher *n* a voucher, issued to an employee in addition to pay, that can be exchanged for food in certain restaurants.
lung *n* either of the two sponge-like breathing organs in the chest of vertebrates.
lunge *n* a sudden forceful thrust, as with a sword; a sudden plunge forward. * *vti* to move, or cause to move, with a lunge.
lurch *vi* to lean or pitch suddenly to the side.—*also n.*
lure *n* something that attracts, tempts or entices; a brightly coloured fishing bait; a device used to recall a trained hawk; a decoy for wild animals. * *vt* to entice, attract, or tempt.
lurid *adj* vivid, glaring; shocking; sensational.—**luridly** *adv.*—**luridness** *n.*
lurk *vi* to lie hidden in wait; to loiter furtively.
luscious *adj* delicious; richly sweet; delighting any of the senses.—**lusciously** *adv.*—**lusciousness** *n.*
lush[1] *adj* tender and juicy; of or showing abundant growth.—**lushly** *adv.*—**lushness** *n.*
lush[2] *n* (*sl*) an alcoholic.
lust *n* strong sexual desire (for); an intense longing for something. * *vi* to feel lust.—**lustful** *adj.*—**lustfully** *adv.*
lustre, luster (*US*) *n* gloss; sheen; brightness; radiance; brilliant beauty or fame; glory.—**lustrous** *adj.*
lusty *adj* (**lustier, lustiest**) strong; vigorous; healthy.—**lustily** *adv.*—**lustiness** *n.*
lute *n* an old-fashioned stringed instrument.
luxuriant *adj* profuse, abundant; ornate; fertile.—**luxuriance** *n.*
luxurious *adj* constituting luxury; indulging in luxury; rich, comfortable.—**luxuriously** *adv.*—**luxuriousness** *n.*
luxury *n* indulgence and pleasure in sumptuous and expensive food, accommodation, clothes, etc; (*often pl*) something that is costly and enjoyable but not indispensable. * *adj* relating to or supplying luxury.
lying *see* **lie**[1], **lie**[2].
lynch *vt* to murder (an accused person) by mob action, without lawful trial, as by hanging.
lynx *n* (*pl* **lynxes, lynx**) a wild feline of Europe and North America with spotted fur.
lyre *n* an ancient musical instrument of the harp family.
lyric *adj* denoting or of poetry expressing the writer's emotion; of, or having a high voice with a light, flexible quality. * *n* a lyric poem; (*pl*) the words of a popular song.
lyrical *adj* lyric; (*inf*) expressing rapture or enthusiasm.

M

m *abbr* = metre(s); mile(s); million(s).
MA *abbr* = Master of Arts; Massachusetts.
mac, mack *n* (*inf*) mackintosh.
macaroni *n* pasta in the form of tubes.
mace[1] *n* a staff used as a symbol of authority by certain institutions.
mace[2] *n* an aromatic spice made from the external covering of the nutmeg.
machine *n* a structure of fixed and moving parts, for doing useful work; an organization functioning like a machine; the controlling group in a political party; a device, as the lever, etc that transmits, or changes the application of energy. * *vt* to shape or finish by machine-operated tools. * *adj* of machines; done by machinery.
machine gun *n* an automatic gun, firing a rapid stream of bullets.—*also vt.*
machinery *n* machines collectively; the parts of a machine; the framework for keeping something going.
machinist *n* one who makes, repairs, or operates machinery.
mackerel *n* (*pl* **mackerel, mackerels**) a common oily food fish.
mackintosh, macintosh *n* a waterproof raincoat.
mad *adj* (**madder, maddest**) insane; frantic; foolish and rash; infatuated; (*inf*) angry.
madam *n* a polite term of address to a woman; a woman in charge of a brothel; (*inf*) a precocious little girl.
madden *vti* to make or become insane, angry, or wildly excited.—**maddening** *adj.*—**maddeningly** *adv.*
made *see* **make**
made-to-measure *adj* (*garment*) made according to the customers individual measurements or requirements.
madly *adv* in an insane manner; at great speed, force; (*inf*) excessively.
madman *n* an insane person.—**madwoman** *nf.*
madness *n* insanity; foolishness; excitability.

magazine *n* a military store; a space where explosives are stored, as in a fort; a supply chamber, as in a camera, a rifle, etc; a periodical publication containing articles, fiction, photographs, etc.
magenta *n* a purplish-red dye; purplish red.—*also adj*.
maggot *n* a wormlike larva, as of the housefly.—**maggoty** *adj*.
magic *n* the use of charms, spells, etc to supposedly influence events by supernatural means; any mysterious power; the art of producing illusions by sleight of hand, etc. * *adj* of or relating to magic; possessing supposedly supernatural powers; (*inf*) wonderful. * *vt* (*pt* **magicked**) to influence, produce or take (away) by or as if by magic.—**magical** *adj*.—**magically** *adv*.
magician *n* one skilled in magic; a conjurer.
magistrate *n* a public officer empowered to administer the law.
magnanimous *adj* noble and generous in conduct or spirit, not petty.—**magnanimously** *adv*.
magnate *n* a very wealthy or influential person.
magnet *n* any piece of iron or steel that has the property of attracting iron; anything that attracts.
magnetic *adj* of magnetism or a magnet; producing or acting by magnetism; having the ability to attract or charm people.—**magnetically** *adv*.
magnetism *n* the property, quality, or condition of being magnetic; the force to which this is due; personal charm.
magnification *n* magnifying or being magnified; the degree of enlargement of something by a lens, microscope, etc.
magnificent *adj* splendid, stately or sumptuous in appearance; superb, of very high quality.—**magnificence** *n*.—**magnificently** *adv*.
magnify *vt* to exaggerate; to increase the apparent size of (an object) as (with) a lens.—**magnifier** *n*.
magnitude *n* greatness of size, extent, etc; importance; (*astron*) the apparent brightness of a star.
magnolia *n* a spring-flowering shrub or tree with evergreen or deciduous leaves and showy flowers.
magpie *n* a black and white bird of the crow family; a person who chatters; an acquisitive person.
mahogany *n* the hard, reddish-brown wood of a tropical tree; a reddish-brown colour.
maid *n* a maiden; a woman servant.
maiden *n* a girl or young unmarried woman. * *adj* unmarried or virgin; untried; first; (*cricket*) (*over*) without runs.—**maidenhood** *n*.—**maidenliness** *n*.—**maidenly** *adv*.
maiden name *n* the surname of a woman before marriage.
mail[1] *n* a body armour made of small metal rings or links.
mail[2] *n* letters, packages, etc transported and delivered by the post office; a postal system. * *vt* to send by mail.
mail order *n* an order for goods to be sent by post.
maim *vt* to cripple; to mutilate.
main *adj* chief in size, importance, etc; principal. * *n* (*often pl but used a sing*) a principal pipe in a distribution system for water, gas, etc; the essential point.
mainland *n* the principal land mass of a continent, as distinguished from nearby islands.
maintain *vt* to preserve; to support, to sustain; to keep in good condition; to affirm.—**maintainable** *adj*.
maintenance *n* upkeep; (*financial*) support, esp of a spouse after a divorce.
maisonette *n* a small house; self-contained living quarters, usu on two floors with its own entrance, as part of a larger house.
maize *n* corn; a light yellow colour.
majestic *adj* dignified; imposing.—**majestically** *adv*.
majesty *n* grandeur; (*with cap*) a title used in speaking to or of a sovereign.
major *adj* greater in size, importance, amount, etc; (*surgery*) very serious, life-threatening; (*mus*) higher than the corresponding minor by half a tone. * *vi* to specialize (in a field of study). * *n* in US, an officer ranking just above a captain, in UK, a lieutenant-colonel; (*mus*) a major key, chord or scale.
majority *n* the greater number or part of; the excess of the larger number of votes cast for a candidate in an election; full legal age; the military rank of a major.
make *vb* (*pt* **made**) *vt* to cause to exist, occur, or appear; to build, create, produce, manufacture, etc; to prepare for use; to amount to; to have the qualities of; to acquire, earn; to understand; to do, execute; to cause or force; to arrive at, reach; (*with* **believe**) to imagine, pretend; (*with* **good**) to make up for, pay compensation; (*with* **out**) to write out; to complete (a form, etc) in writing; to attempt

to understand; to discern, identify; (*with* **up**) to invent, fabricate, esp to deceive; to prepare; to make complete; to put together; to settle differences between. * *vi* (*with* **do**) to manage with what is available; (*with* **for**) to go in the direction of; to bring about; (*with* **good**) to become successful or wealthy; (*with* **off**) to leave in haste; (*with* **out**) to pretend; to fare, manage; (*with* **up**) to become reconciled; to compensate for; to put on make-up for the stage. * *n* style, brand, or origin; manner of production.—**maker** *n*.

make-believe *adj* imagined, pretended.—*also n*.

makeshift *adj* being a temporary substitute.—*also n*.

make-up *n* the cosmetics, etc used by an actor; cosmetics generally; the way something is put together, composition; nature, disposition.

making *n* the act or process of making, creation; (*pl*) earnings; (*pl*) potential; (*pl*) (*sl*) the materials for rolling a cigarette.

maladjusted *adj* poorly adjusted, esp to the social environment.—**maladjustment** *n*.

malaise *n* a feeling of discomfort or of uneasiness.

malaria *n* an infectious disease caused by mosquito bites, and characterized by recurring attacks of fevers and chills.—**malarial** *adj*.

male *adj* denoting or of the sex that fertilizes the ovum; of, like, or suitable for men and boys; masculine. * *n* a male person, animal or plant.

malevolent *adj* ill-disposed towards others; spiteful, malicious.—**malevolence** *n*.—**malevolently** *adv*.

malfunction *n* faulty functioning. * *vi* to function wrongly.

malice *n* active ill will, intention to inflict injury upon another.—**malicious** *adj*.—**maliciously** *adv*.—**maliciousness** *n*.

malign *adj* harmful; evil. * *vt* to slander; to defame.—**malignity** *n*.—**malignly** *adv*.

malignant *adj* having a wish to harm others; injurious; (*disease*) rapidly spreading, resistant to treatment, esp of a tumour.—**malignancy** *n*.—**malignantly** *adv*.

malinger *vi* to feign illness in order to evade work, duty.—**malingerer** *n*.

malleable *adj* pliable; capable of being shaped.—**malleability** *n*.

mallet *n* a small, usu wooden-headed, short-handled hammer; a long-handled version for striking the ball in the games of polo and croquet.

malnutrition *n* lack of nutrition.

malpractice *n* professional misconduct, esp by a medical practitioner.

malt *n* a cereal grain, such as barley, which is soaked and dried and used in brewing; (*inf*) malt liquor, malt whisky.—**malty** *adj*.

mammal *n* any member of a class of warm-blooded vertebrates that suckle their young with milk.—**mammalian** *adj*.

mammoth *n* an extinct elephant with long, curved tusks. * *adj* enormous.

man *n* (*pl* **men**) a human being, esp an adult male; the human race; an adult male with manly qualities, eg courage, virility; a male servant; an individual person; a person with specific qualities for a task, etc; an ordinary soldier, as opposed to an officer; a member of a team, etc; a piece in games such as chess, draughts, etc; a husband. * *vt* (*pt* **manned**) to provide with men for work, defence, etc.

manage *vt* to control the movement or behaviour of; to have charge of; to direct; to succeed in accomplishing. * *vi* to carry on business; to contrive to get along.—**manageable** *adj*.

management *n* those carrying out the administration of a business; the managers collectively; the technique of managing or controlling.

manager *n* a person who manages a company, organization, etc; an agent who looks after the business affairs of an actor, writer, etc; a person who organizes the training of a sports team; a person who manages efficiently.—**managerial** *adj*.—**managerially** *adv*.

manageress *n* a woman who manages a business, shop, etc.

managing *adj* administering; controlling; having authority.

mandarin *n* (*formerly*) a high-ranking bureaucrat of the Chinese empire; any high-ranking official, esp one given to pedantic sometimes obscure public pronouncements; (*with cap*) the Beijing dialect that is the official pronunciation of the Chinese language; the fruit of a small spiny Chinese tree that has been developed in cultivation (—*also* **tangerine**).

mandate *n* an order or command; the authority to act on the behalf of another, esp the will of constituents expressed to their representatives in legislatures. * *vt* to entrust by mandate.

mandatory *adj* compulsory.

mandolin, mandoline *n* a stringed instrument similar to a lute, with four or five pairs of strings.
mane *n* long hair that grows on the back of the neck of the horse, lion, etc.
manful *adj* showing courage and resolution.—**manfully** *adv*.
mangle[1] *vt* to crush, mutilate; to spoil, ruin.
mangle[2] *n* a machine for drying and pressing sheets, etc between rollers. * *vt* to smooth through a mangle.
mango *n* (*pl* **mangoes**) a yellow-red fleshy tropical fruit with a firm central stone.
mangy *adj* (**mangier, mangiest**) having mange; scruffy, shabby.—**manginess** *n*.
manhandle *vt* to handle roughly; to move by human force.
manhole *n* a hole through which one can enter a sewer, drain, etc.
manhood *n* the state or time of being a man; virility; courage, etc.
manhunt *n* a hunt for a fugitive.—**manhunter** *n*.
mania *n* a mental disorder displaying sometimes violent behaviour and great excitement; great excitement or enthusiasm; a craze.
maniac *n* a madman; a person with wild behaviour; a person with great enthusiasm for something.—**maniacal** *adj*.
manicure *n* trimming, polishing etc of fingernails.—*also vt*.—**manicurist** *n*.
manifest *adj* obvious, clearly evident. * *vt* to make clear; to display, to reveal. * *n* a list of a ship's or aircraft's cargo; a list of passengers on an aircraft.—**manifestation** *n*.—**manifestly** *adv*.
manifesto *n* (*pl* **manifestoes, manifestos**) a public printed declaration of intent and policy issued by a government or political party.
manipulate *vt* to work or handle skilfully; to manage shrewdly or artfully, often in an unfair way.—**manipulation** *n*.—**manipulative** *adj*.—**manipulator** *n*.
mankind *n* the human race.
manly *adj* (**manlier, manliest**) appropriate in character to a man; strong; virile.—**manliness** *n*.
man-made *adj* manufactured or created by man; artificial, synthetic.
manner *n* a method of way of doing something; behaviour; type or kind; habit; (*pl*) polite social behaviour.—**mannerly** *adj*.
mannerism *n* an idiosyncracy.
manoeuvre, maneuver (*US*) *n* a planned and controlled movement of troops, warships, etc; a skilful or shrewd move; a stratagem. * *vti* to perform or cause to perform manoeuvres; to manage or plan skilfully; to move, get, make, etc by some scheme.—**manoeuvrable** *adj*.,
manor *n* a landed estate; the main house on such an estate; (*sl*) a police district.—**manorial** *adj*.
manpower *n* power furnish ed by human strength; the collective availability for work of people in a given area.
mansion *n* a large, imposing house.
manslaughter *n* the killing of a human being by another, esp when unlawful but without malice.
mantel *n* the facing above a fireplace; the shelf above a fireplace.—*also* **mantelpiece, mantelshelf**.
manual *adj* of the hands; operated, done, or used by the hand; involving physical skill or hard work rather than the mind. * *n* a handy book for use as a guide, reference, etc; a book of instructions.—**manually** *adv*.
manufacture *vt* to make, esp on a large scale, using machinery; to invent, fabricate. * *n* the production of goods by manufacturing.—**manufacturer** *n*.
manure *n* animal dung used to fertilize soil. * *vt* to spread manure on.
manuscript *n* a book or document that is handwritten or typewritten as opposed to printed; an author's original handwritten or typewritten copy as submitted to a publisher before typesetting and printing.
many *adj* numerous. * *n* a large number of persons or things.
map *n* a representation of all or part of the earth's surface, showing either natural features as continents and seas, etc or man-made features as roads, railroads etc. * *vt* (*pt* **mapped**) to make a map of.
maple *n* a tree with two-winged fruits, grown for shade, wood, or sap; its hard light-coloured wood; the flavour of the syrup or sugar made from the sap of the sugar maple.
mar *vt* (*pt* **marred**) to blemish, to spoil, to impair.
marathon *n* a foot race of 26 miles, 385 yards (42.195 km); any endurance contest.
maraud *vi* to roam in search of plunder.—**marauder** *n*.—**marauding** *adj*.
marble *n* a hard limestone rock that takes a high polish; a block or work of art made of marble; a little ball of stone, glass, etc; (*pl*) a children's game played with such balls; (*pl*)

(*sl*) wits. * *adj* of or like marble.

March *n* the third month of the year having 31 days.

march *vi* to walk with regular steps, as in military formation; to advance steadily. * *vt* to make a person or group march. * *n* a steady advance; a regular, steady step; the distance covered in marching; a piece of music for marching.

mare *n* a mature female horse, mule, donkey.

margarine *n* a butter substitute made from vegetable and animal fats, etc.

margin *n* a border, edge; the blank border of a printed or written page; an amount beyond what is needed; provision for increase, error, etc; (*commerce*) the difference between cost and selling price.

marginal *adj* written in the margin; situated at the margin or border; close to the lower limit of acceptability; very slight, insignificant; (*British politics*) denoting a constituency where the sitting MP has only a small majority. * *n* a marginal constituency.—**marginally** *adv*.

marigold *n* a plant with a yellow or orange flower.

marijuana, marihuana *n* a narcotic obtained by smoking the dried flowers and leaves of the hemp plant.—*also* **cannabis, pot**.

marina *n* a small harbour with docks, services, etc for pleasure craft.

marine *adj* of, in, near, or relating to the sea; maritime; nautical; naval. * *n* a soldier trained for service on land or sea; naval or merchant ships.

marital *adj* of marriage, matrimonial.

maritime *adj* on, near, or living near the sea; of navigation, shipping, etc.

mark[1] *n* a spot, scratch, etc on a surface; a distinguishing sign or characteristic; a cross made instead of a signature; a printed or written symbol, as a punctuation mark; a brand or label on an article showing the maker, etc; an indication of some quality, character, etc; a grade for academic work; a standard of quality; impression, influence, etc; a target; (*sl*) a potential victim for a swindle. * *vt* to make a mark or marks on; to identify as by a mark; to show plainly; to heed; to grade, rate; (*Brit football*) to stay close to an opponent so as to hinder his play.

mark[2] *n* the basic monetary unit of Germany.

marked *adj* having a mark or marks; noticeable; obvious.—**markedly** *adv*.

marker *n* one that marks; something used for marking.

market *n* a meeting of people for buying and selling merchandise; a space or building in which a market is held; the chance to sell or buy; demand for (goods, etc); a region where goods can be sold; a section of the community offering demand for goods. * *vti* to offer for sale; to sell, buy domestic provisions.—**marketability** *n*.—**marketable** *adj*.

marketing *n* act of buying or selling; all the processes involved in moving goods from the producer to the consumer.

marksman *n* one who is skilled at shooting.—**marksmanship** *n*.

marmalade *n* a jam-like preserve made from oranges, sugar and water.

maroon[1] *n* a dark brownish red (—*also adj*); a type of distress rocket.

maroon[2] *vt* to abandon alone, esp on a desolate island; to leave helpless and alone.

marquee *n* a large tent used for entertainment; a canopy over an entrance, as to a theatre.

marquess *n* (*UK*) a title of nobility ranking between a duke and an earl.

marquis *n* (*Europe*) a nobleman equivalent in rank to a British marquess.

marriage *n* the legal contract by which a woman and man become wife and husband; a wedding, either religious or civil; a close union.—**marriageable** *adj*.

marrow *n* the fatty tissue in the cavities of bones; the best part or essence of anything; a widely grown green fruit eaten as a vegetable.

marry *vt* to join as wife and husband; to take in marriage; to unite. * *vi* to get married.

marsh *n* an area of boggy, poorly drained land.—**marshiness** *n*.—**marshy** *adj*.

marshal *n* in some armies, a general officer of the highest rank; an official in charge of ceremonies, parades, etc. * *vt* (*pt* **marshalled**) (*ideas, troops*) to arrange in order; to guide.

martial *adj* warlike; military.—**martially** *adv*.

martial law *n* rule by military authorities over civilians, as during a war or political emergency.

martyr *n* a person tortured for a belief or cause; a person who suffers from an illness. * *vt* to kill as a martyr; to make a martyr of.—**martyrdom** *n*.

marvel *n* anything wonderful; a miracle. * *vti* (*pt* **marvelled**) to become filled with wonder, surprise, etc.—**marvellous** *adj*.

Marxism *n* the theory and practice developed

by Karl Marx and Friedrich Engels advocating public ownership of the means of production and the dictatorship of the proletariat until the establishment of a classless society.—**Marxist** *adj*, *n*.

marzipan *n* a paste made from ground almonds, sugar and egg white, used to coat cakes or make confectionery.

mascara *n* a cosmetic for darkening the eyelashes.

mascot *n* a person, animal or thing thought to bring good luck.

masculine *adj* having characteristics of or appropriate to the male sex; (*gram*) of the male gender.—**masculinity** *n*.

mask *n* a covering to conceal or protect the face; a moulded likeness of the face; anything that conceals or disguises; a respirator placed over the nose and mouth to aid or prevent inhalation of a gas; (*surgery*) a protective gauze placed over the nose and mouth to prevent the spread of germs; (*photog*) a screen used to cover part of a sensitive surface to prevent exposure by light. * *vt* to cover or conceal as with a mask; to disguise one's intentions or character.—**masked** *adj*.

mason *n* a person skilled in working or building with stone; (*with cap*) a Freemason.

masonry *n* stonework.

masquerade *n* a ball or party at which fancy dress and masks are worn; a pretence, false show. * *vi* to take part in a masquerade; to pretend to be what one is not.—**masquerader** *n*.

mass *n* a quantity of matter of indefinite shape and size; a large quantity or number; bulk; size; the main part; (*physics*) the property of a body expressed as a measure of the amount of material contained in it; (*pl*) the common people, esp the lower social classes; (*with cap*) The celebration of the Eucharist. * *adj* of or for the masses or for a large number. * *vti* to gather or form into a mass.

massacre *n* the cruel and indiscriminate killing of many people or animals. * *vt* to kill in large numbers.

massage *n* a kneading and rubbing of the muscles to stimulate the circulation of the blood. * *vt* to give a massage to.

masseur *n* a man who gives a massage professionally.—**masseuse** *nf*.

massive *adj* big, solid, or heavy; large and imposing; relatively large in comparison to normal; extensive.—**massively** *adv*.—**massiveness** *n*.

mass media *npl* newspapers, radio, television, and other means of communication with large numbers of people.

mast *n* a tall vertical pole used to support the sails on a ship; a vertical pole from which a flag is flown; a tall structure supporting a television or radio aerial.

master *n* a man who rules others or has control over something, esp the head of a household; an employer; an owner of an animal or slave; the captain of a merchant ship; a male teacher in a private school; an expert craftsman; a writer or painter regarded as great; an original from which a copy can be made, esp a phonograph record or magnetic tape; (*with cap*) a title for a boy; one holding an advanced academic degree. * *adj* being a master; chief; main; controlling. * *vt* to be for become master of; (*in art, etc*) to become expert.

masterly *adj* expert; skilful.—**masterliness** *n*.

mastermind *n* a very clever person, esp one who plans or directs a project. * *vt* to be the mastermind of.

masterpiece *n* a work done with extraordinary skill; the greatest work of a person or group.

mastery *n* control as by a master; victory; expertise.

masturbate *vi* to manually stimulate one's sexual organs to achieve orgasm without sexual intercourse.—**masturbation** *n*.

mat[1] *n* a piece of material of woven fibres, etc, used for protection, as under a vase, etc, or on the floor; a thick pad used in wrestling, gymnastics, etc; anything interwoven or tangled into a thick mass. * *vti* (*pt* **matted**) to cover as with a mat; to interweave or tangle into a thick mass.

mat[2] *see* **matt**.

match[1] *n* a thin strip of wood or cardboard tipped with a chemical that ignites under friction.

match[2] *n* any person or thing equal or similar to another; two persons or things that go well together; a contest or game; a mating or marriage. * *vt* to join in marriage; to put in opposition (with, against); to be equal or similar to; (*one thing*) to suit to another. * *vi* to be equal, similar, suitable, etc.

matchbox *n* a small box for holding matches.

matchless *adj* unequalled.—**matchlessly** *adv*.

mate[1] *n* an associate or colleague; (*inf*) a friend; one of a matched pair; a marriage partner; the male or female of paired animals; an officer of a merchant ship, ranking below the master.

* *vti* to join as a pair; to couple in marriage or sexual union.

mate² *vt* to checkmate.

material *adj* of, derived from, or composed of matter, physical; of the body or bodily needs, comfort, etc, not spiritual; important, essential, etc. * *n* what a thing is, or may be made of; elements or parts; cloth, fabric; (*pl*) tools, etc needed to make or do something; a person regarded as fit for a particular task, position, etc.

materialize *vt* to give material form to. * *vi* to become fact; to make an unexpected appearance.—**materialization** *n*.

maternal *adj* of, like, or from a mother; related through the mother's side of the family.—**maternally** *adv*.

maternity *n* motherhood; motherliness. * *adj* relating to pregnancy.

math *n* (*inf*) mathematics.

mathematical, mathematic *adj* of, like or concerned with mathematics; exact and precise.—**mathematically** *adv*.

mathematics *n* (*used as sing*) the science dealing with quantities, forms, space, etc and their relationships by the use of numbers and symbols; (*sing or pl*) the mathematical operations or processes used in a particular problem, discipline, etc. —**mathematician** *n*.

maths *n* (*used as sing or pl*) (*inf*) mathematics.

matinée *n* an afternoon performance of a play, etc.

matriarch *n* a woman who heads or rules her family or tribe.—**matriarchal** *adj*.

matriculate *vti* to enrol, esp as a student.—**matriculation** *n*.

matrimony *n* the act or rite of marriage; the married state.—**matrimonial** *adj*.—**matrimonially** *adv*.

matron *n* a wife or widow, esp one of mature appearance and manner; a woman in charge of domestic and nursing arrangements in a school, hospital or other institution.—**matronly** *adv*.

matt *adj* without lustre, dull.—*also* **mat**.

matter *n* what a thing is made of; material; whatever occupies space and is perceptible to the senses; any specified substance; content of thought or expression; a quantity; a thing or affair; significance; trouble, difficulty; pus. * *vi* to be of importance.

matter-of-fact *adj* relating to facts, not opinions, imagination, etc.

matting *n* a coarse material, such as woven straw or hemp, used for making mats.

mattress *n* a casing of strong cloth filled with cotton, foam rubber, coiled springs, etc, used on a bed.

mature *adj* mentally and physically well-developed, grown-up; (*fruit, cheese, etc*) ripe; (*bill*) due; (*plan*) completely worked out. * *vti* to make or become mature; to become due.—**maturely** *adv*.—**matureness** *n*.

maturity *n* the state of being mature; full development; the date a loan becomes due.

maudlin *adj* foolishly sentimental; tearfully drunk.

maul *vt* to bruise or lacerate; to paw.

mausoleum *n* a large tomb.

mauve *n* any of several shades of pale purple. * *adj* of this colour.

mawkish *adj* maudlin; insipid.—**mawkishly** *adv*.—**mawkishness** *n*.

max. *abbr* = maximum.

maxim *n* a concise rule of conduct; a precept.

maximum *n* (*pl* **maxima, maximums**) the greatest quantity, number, etc. * *adj* highest; greatest possible reached.

May *n* the fifth month of the year having 31 days.

may *vb aux* (*past* **might**) *expressing* possibility; permission; wish or hope.

maybe *adv* perhaps.

Mayday *n* the international radio-telephone signal indicating a ship or aircraft in distress.

May Day *n* the first day of May, celebrated as a traditional spring festival; observed in many countries as a labour holiday.

mayhem *n* violent destruction, confusion.

mayonnaise *n* a salad dressing made from egg yolks whisked with oil and lemon juice or vinegar.

mayor *n* the chief administrative officer of a municipality.

mayoress *n* the wife of a mayor; a female mayor.

maze *n* a confusing, intricate network of pathways; a confused state.

me *pers pron* the objective case of I.

meadow *n* a piece of land where grass is grown for hay; low, level, moist grassland.

meagre, meager (*US*) *adj* thin, emaciated; lacking in quality or quantity.—**meagrely** *adv*.—**meagreness** *n*.

meal¹ *n* any of the times for eating, as lunch, dinner, etc; the food served at such a time.

meal² *n* any coarsely ground edible grain; any substance similarly ground.—**mealiness** *n*.—**mealy** *adj*.

mealy-mouthed *adj* not outspoken and blunt; euphemistic; devious in speech.

mean[1] *adj* selfish, ungenerous; despicable; shabby; bad-tempered; (*sl*) difficult; (*sl*) expert.—**meanly** *adv*.—**meanness** *n*.

mean[2] *adj* halfway between extremes; average. * *n* what is between extremes.

mean[3] *vb* (*pt* **meant**) *vt* to have in mind; to intend; to intend to express; to signify. * *vi* to have a (specified) degree of importance, effect, etc.

meander *n* a winding path esp a labyrinth; a winding of a stream or river. * *vi* (*river*) to wind; to wander aimlessly.—**meandering** *adj*.

meaning *n* sense; significance; import. * *adj* significant.—**meaningful** *adj*.—**meaningless** *adj*.

meant *see* **mean**[3].

meantime, meanwhile *adv* in or during the intervening time; at the same time. * *n* the intervening time.

measles *n* (*used as sing*) an acute, contagious viral disease, characterized by small red spots on the skin.

measly *adj* (**measlier, measliest**) (*inf*) slight, worthless; having measles.

measure *n* the extent, dimension, capacity, etc of anything; a determining of this, measurement; a unit of measurement; any standard of valuation; an instrument for measuring; a definite quantity measured out; a course of action; a statute, law; a rhythmical unit. * *vt* to find out the extent, dimensions etc of, esp by a standard; to mark off by measuring; to be a measure of. * *vi* to be of specified measurements.—**measurable** *adj*.—**measurably** *adv*.

measured *adj* set or marked off by a standard; rhythmical, regular; carefully planned or considered.

measurement *n* a measuring or being measured; an extent or quantity determined by measuring; a system of measuring or of measures.

meat *n* animal flesh; food as opposed to drink; the essence of something.

meaty *adj* (**meatier, meatiest**) full of meat; full of substance.

mechanic *n* a person skilled in maintaining or operating machines, cars, etc.

mechanical *adj* of or using machinery or tools; produced or operated by machinery; done as if by a machine, lacking thought or emotion; of the science of mechanics.—**mechanically** *adv*.

mechanics *n* (*used as sing*) the science of motion and the action of forces on bodies; knowledge of machinery; (*pl*) the technical aspects of something.

mechanism *n* the working parts of a machine; any system of interrelated parts; any physical or mental process by which a result is produced.

mechanize *vt* to make mechanical; to equip with machinery or motor vehicles.—**mechanization** *n*.—**mechanized** *adj*.

medal *n* a small, flat piece of inscribed metal, commemorating some event or person or awarded for some distinction.

medallion *n* a large medal; a design, portrait, etc shaped like a medal; a medal worn on a chain around the neck.

medallist, medalist (*US*) *n* one awarded a medal.

meddle *vi* to interfere in another's affairs.—**meddler** *n*.—**meddlesome** *adj*.

media *see* **medium**.

mediaeval *see* **medieval**.

mediate *vt* to intervene (in a dispute); to bring about agreement. * *vi* to be in an intermediate position; to be an intermediary.—**mediation** *n*.—**mediator** *n*.

medical *adj* relating to the practice or study of medicine. * *n* (*inf*) a medical examination.—**medically** *adv*.

medicine *n* any substance used to treat or prevent disease; the science of preventing, treating or curing disease.—**medicinal** *adj*.—**medicinally** *adv*.

medieval *adj* of or like the Middle Ages.—also **mediaeval**.

mediocre *adj* average; ordinary; inferior.—**mediocrity** *n*.

meditate *vi* to think deeply; to reflect.—**meditative** *adj*.

meditation *n* the act of meditating; contemplation of spiritual or religious matters.

Mediterranean *n* the Mediterranean Sea. * *adj* of, or relating to (the area around) the Mediterranean Sea; denoting a subdivision of the Caucasian race characterized by a slender build and dark complexion; (*climate*) marked by hot, dry summers and warm, wet winters.

medium *n* (*pl* **media, mediums**) the middle state or condition; a substance for transmitting an effect; any intervening means, instrument, or agency; (*pl* **media**) a means of communicating information (eg newspapers, television, radio); (*pl* **mediums**) a person claiming to act as an intermediary between the living and the dead. * *adj* midway; average.

medley *n* (*pl* **medleys**) a miscellany; a musical piece made up of various tunes or passages.

meek *adj* patient, long-suffering; submissive.—**meekly** *adv*.—**meekness** *n*.

meet *vb* (*pt* **met**) *vt* to encounter, to come together; to make the acquaintance of; to contend with, deal with; to experience; to be perceived by (the eye, etc); (*demand, etc*) to satisfy; (*bill, etc*) to pay. * *vi* to come into contact with; to be introduced. * *n* a meeting to hunt or for an athletics competition.

meeting *n* a coming together; a gathering.

megaphone *n* a device to amplify and direct the voice.

melancholy *n* gloominess or depression; sadness. * *adj* sad; depressed.—**melancholia** *n*.—**melancholic** *adj*.

mellow *adj* (*fruit*) sweet and ripe; (*wine*) matured; (*colour, light, sound*) soft, not harsh; kind-hearted and understanding. * *vti* to soften through age; to mature.—**mellowness** *n*.

melodrama *n* a play, film, etc filled with overdramatic emotion and action; drama of this genre; sensational events or emotions.—**melodramatic** *adj*.—**melodramatically** *adv*.

melody *n* a tune; a pleasing series of sounds.—**melodic** *adj*.—**melodious** *adj*.

melon *n* the large juicy many-seeded fruit of trailing plants, as the watermelon, cantaloupe.

melt *vti* (*pp* **melted** *or* **molten**) to make or become liquid; to dissolve; to fade or disappear; to soften or be softened emotionally.—**melting** *adj*.—**meltingly** *adv*.

meltdown *n* the melting of the fuel core of a nuclear reactor; the drastic collapse of almost anything.

melting point *n* the temperature at which a solid melts.

member *n* a person belonging to a society or club; a part of a body, such as a limb; a representative in a legislative body; a distinct part of a complex whole.

membership *n* the state of being a member; the number of members of a body; the members collectively.

membrane *n* a thin pliable sheet or film; the fibrous tissue that covers or lines animal organs.—**membranous, membranaceous** *adj*.

memento *n* (*pl* **mementos, mementoes**) a reminder, esp a souvenir.

memo *n* (*pl* **memos**) a memorandum.

memoir *n* an historical account based on personal experience; (*pl*) an autobiographical record.

memorable *adj* worth remembering; easy to remember.—**memorably** *adv*.

memorandum *n* (*pl* **memorandums**) an informal written communication as within an office; (*pl* **memoranda**) a note to help the memory.

memorial *adj* serving to preserve the memory of the dead. * *n* a remembrance; a monument.

memorize *vt* to learn by heart, to commit to memory.—**memorization** *n*.

memory *n* the process of retaining and reproducing past thoughts and sensations; the sum of things remembered; an individual recollection; commemoration; remembrance; the part of a computer that stores information (—*also* **store**).

men *see* **man**.

menace *n* a threat; (*inf*) a nuisance. * *vt* to threaten.—**menacing** *adj*.—**menacingly** *adv*.

menagerie *n* a place where wild animals are kept for exhibition; a collection of wild animals.

mend *vt* to repair; (*manners, etc*) to reform, improve. * *vi* to become better. * *n* the act of mending; a repaired area in a garment, etc.

menial *adj* consisting of work of little skill; servile. * *n* a domestic servant; a servile person.

meningitis *n* inflammation of the membranes enveloping the brain or spinal cord.

menopause *n* the time of life during which a woman's menstrual cycle ceases permanently.—**menopausal** *adj*.

menstruation *n* the monthly discharge of blood from the uterus.—**menstrual** *adj*.—**menstruate** *vi*.

mental *adj* of, or relating to the mind; occurring or performed in the mind; having a psychiatric disorder; (*inf*) crazy, stupid.—**mentally** *adv*.

mentality *n* intellectual power; disposition, character.

mention *n* a brief reference to something in speech or writing; an official recognition or citation. * *vt* to refer to briefly; to remark; to honour officially.—**mentionable** *adj*.

menu *n* the list of dishes served in a restaurant; a list of options on a computer display.

mercantile *adj* of merchants or trade.

mercenary *adj* working or done for money only. * *n* a soldier hired to fight for a foreign army.

merchandise *n* commercial goods. * *vti* to sell, trade.
merchant *n* a trader; a retailer; (*sl*) a person fond of a particular activity.
merchant navy *n* commercial shipping.
merciful *adj* compassionate, humane.—**mercifulness** *n*.
merciless *adj* cruel, pitiless; without mercy.—**mercilessly** *adv*.—**mercilessness** *n*.
mercury *n* a heavy silvery liquid metallic element used in thermometers etc.
mercy *n* clemency; compassion; kindness; pity.
mere *adj* nothing more than; simple, unmixed.
merely *adv* simply; solely.
merge *vti* to blend or cause to fuse together gradually; to (cause to) combine, unite.
merger *n* a combining together, esp of two or more commercial organizations.
meridian *n* the imaginary circle on the surface of the earth passing through the north and south poles.
meringue *n* a mixture of egg whites beaten with sugar and baked; a small cake or shell made from this, usu filled with cream.
merit *n* excellence; worth; (*pl*) (*of a case*) rights and wrongs; a deserving act. * *vt* to be worthy of, to deserve.—**meritorious** *adj*.
mermaid *n* (*legend*) a woman with a fish's tale.
merry *adj* (**merrier, merriest**) cheerful; causing laughter; lively; (*inf*) slightly drunk.—**merrily** *adv*.—**merriment** *n*.
merry-go-round *n* a revolving platform of hobbyhorses, etc, a carousel, a roundabout.
mesh *n* an opening between cords of a net, wires of a screen, etc; a net; a network; a snare; (*geared wheels, etc*) engagement. * *vt* to entangle, ensnare. * *vi* to become entangled or interlocked.
mesmerize *vt* to hypnotize; to fascinate.
mess *n* a state of disorder or untidiness, esp if dirty; a muddle; an unsightly or disagreeable mixture; a portion of soft and pulpy or semi-liquid food; a building where service personnel dine; a communal meal. * *vti* to make a mess (of), bungle; to eat in company; to potter (about).
message *n* any spoken, written, or other form of communication; the chief idea that the writer, artist, etc seeks to communicate in a work.
messenger *n* a person who carries a message.
messy *adj* (**messier, messiest**) dirty; confused; untidy.—**messily** *adv*.—**messiness** *n*.
met *see* **meet**.
metabolism *n* the total processes in living organisms by which tissue is formed, energy produced and waste products eliminated.—**metabolic** *adj*.
metal *n* any of a class of chemical elements which are often lustrous, ductile solids, and are good conductors of heat, electricity, etc, such as gold, iron, copper, etc; any alloy of such elements as brass, bronze, etc; anything consisting of metal.—**metalled** *adj*.
metallic *adj* of, relating to, or made of metal; similar to metal.
metallurgy *n* the science of separating metals from their ores and preparing them for use by smelting, refining, etc.—**metallurgical** *adj*.—**metallurgist** *n*.
metamorphosis *n* (*pl* **metamorphoses**) a complete change of form, structure, substance, character, appearance, etc; transformation; the marked change in some animals at a stage in their growth, eg chrysalis to butterfly.—**metamorphic** *adj*.—**metamorphose** *vi*.
metaphor *n* a figure of speech in which a word or phrase is used for another of which it is an image.—**metaphorical** *adj*.—**metaphorically** *adv*.
metaphysics *n* (*used as sing*) the branch of philosophy that seeks to explain the nature of being and reality; speculative philosophy in general.—**metaphysical** *adj*.
mete *vt* to allot; to portion (out).
meteor *n* a small particle of matter which travels at great speed through space and becomes luminous through friction as it enters the earth's atmosphere; a shooting star.
meter *n* a device for measuring and recording a quantity of gas, water, time, etc supplied; a parking meter. * *vt* to measure using a meter.
method *n* the mode or procedure of accomplishing something; orderliness of thought; an orderly arrangement or system.
methodical *adj* orderly, systematic.—**methodically** *adv*.
methylated spirit *n* a form of alcohol, adulterated to render it undrinkable, used as a solvent.
meticulous *adj* very precise about small details.—**meticulously** *adv*.—**meticulousness** *n*.
metre[1], **meter** (*US*) *n* rhythmic pattern in verse, the measured arrangement of syllables according to stress; rhythmic pattern in music.
metre[2], **meter** (*US*) *n* the basic unit of length in the metric system, consisting of 100 centimetres and equal to 39.37 inches.
metric *adj* based on the metre as a standard of

measurement; of, relating to, or using the metric system.

metrical *adj* of, relating to, or composed in rhythmic metre.

metrication *n* conversion of an existent system of units into the metric system.

metric system *n* a decimal system of weights and measures based on the metre, litre and kilogram.

metronome *n* an instrument that beats musical tempo.

metropolis *n* the main city, often a capital of a country, state, etc; any large and important city.—**metropolitan** *adj*.

mettle *n* courage, spirit.

mew *vi* (*cat*) to emit a high-pitched cry.

mezzanine *n* an intermediate storey between others; a theatre balcony.

mice *see* **mouse**.

microbe *n* a microscopic organism, esp a disease-causing bacterium.

microfilm *n* film on which documents, etc, are recorded in reduced scale. * *vt* to record on microfilm.

microphone *n* an instrument for transforming sound waves into electric signals, esp for transmission, or recording.—*also* **mike**.

microscope *n* an optical instrument for making magnified images of minute objects by means of a lens or lenses.

microscopic *adj* of, with, like, a microscope; visible only through a microscope; very small.—**microscopically** *adv*.

mid *adj* middle. * *prep* amid.

midday *n* the middle of the day, noon.

middle *adj* halfway between two given points, times, etc; intermediate; central. * *n* the point halfway between two extremes; something intermediate; the waist.

middle age *n* the time between youth and old age.—**middle-aged** *adj*.

Middle Ages *npl* the period of European history between about Ad 500 and 1500.

middle class *n* the class between the lower and upper classes, mostly composed of professional and business people.—**middle-class** *adj*.

middleman *n* a dealer between producer and consumer; an intermediary.

middling *adj* of medium quality, size, etc; second-rate. * *adv* moderately.

midge *n* a small gnat-like insect with a painful bite.

midget *n* a very small person, a dwarf; something small of its kind.—*also adj*.

midnight *n* twelve o'clock at night.

midriff *n* the middle part of the torso between the abdomen and the chest.

midst *n* middle. * *prep* amidst, among.

midway *adv* halfway.

midwife *n* a person trained to assist women before, during, and after childbirth.—**midwifery** *n*.

might[1] *see* **may**.

might[2] *n* power, bodily strength.

mightn't = might not.

mighty *adj* (**mightier, mightiest**) powerful, strong; massive; (*inf*) very.—**mightily** *adv*.—**mightiness** *n*.

migraine *n* an intense, periodic headache, usu limited to one side of the head.

migrant *n* a person or animal that moves from one region or country to another; an itinerant agricultural labourer. * *adj* migrating.

migrate *vi* to settle in another country or region; (*birds, animals*) to move to another region with the change in season.—**migration** *n*.—**migratory** *adj*.

mike *see* **microphone**.

mild *adj* (*temper*) gentle; (*weather*) temperate; bland; feeble.—**mildly** *adv*.—**mildness** *n*.

mildew *n* a fungus that attacks some plants or appears on damp cloth, etc as a whitish coating. * *vti* to affect or be affected with mildew.—**mildewy** *adj*.

mile *n* a unit of linear measure equal to 5,280 feet (1.61 km); the nautical mile is 6,075 feet (1.85 km).

mileage *n* total miles travelled; an allowance per mile for travelling expenses; the average number of miles that can be travelled, as per litre of fuel.

milestone *n* a stone marking the number of miles to a place; an important event in life, history, etc.

milieu *n* (*pl* **milieus, milieux**) environment, esp social setting.

militant *adj* ready to fight, esp for some cause; combative.—*also n*.—**militancy** *n*.—**militantly** *adv*.

military *adj* relating to soldiers or to war; warlike. * *n* the armed forces.

militia *n* an army composed of civilians called out in time of emergency.

milk *n* a white nutritious liquid secreted by female mammals for feeding their young. * *vt* to draw milk from; to extract money, etc, from; to exploit.—**milkiness** *n*.—**milky** *adj*.

milkman *n* a person who delivers milk to homes.

mill *n* an apparatus for grinding by crushing between rough surfaces; a building where grain is ground into flour; a factory. * *vt* to produce or grind in a mill; (*coins*) to put a raised edge on. * *vi* to move around confusedly.—**miller** *n*.
millennium *n* (*pl* **millennia, millenniums**) a period of a thousand years.—**millennial** *adj*.
millet *n* a cereal grass used for grain and fodder.
milli- *prefix* a thousandth part.
millimetre, millimeter (*US*) *n* a thousandth (0.001) of a metre.
milliner *n* a designer or seller of women's hats.—**millinery** *n*.
million *n* a thousand thousands, the number one followed by six zeros: 1,000,000; (*inf*) a very large number.—**millionth** *adj*.
millionaire *n* a person who owns at least a million of money; one who is extremely rich.
millstone *n* a stone used for grinding corn; a heavy burden.
mime *n* a theatrical technique using action without words; a mimic. * *vi* act or express using gestures alone; (*singers, musicians*) to perform as if singing or playing live to what is actually a prerecorded piece of music.
mimic *n* a person who imitates, esp an actor skilled in mimicry. * *adj* related to mimicry; make-believe; sham. * (*pt* **mimicked**) to imitate or ridicule.
mimicry *n* practice, art, or way of mimicking.
min. *abbr* = minimum; minute(s).
minaret *n* a high, slender tower on a mosque from which the call to prayer is made.
mince *vt* to chop or cut up into small pieces; to diminish or moderate one's words. * *vi* to speak or walk with affected daintiness.—**mincing** *adj*.—**mincingly** *adv*.
mincemeat *n* a mixture of chopped apples, raisins, etc used as a pie filling.
mind *n* the faculty responsible for intellect, thought, feelings, speech; memory; intellect; reason; opinion; sanity. * *vt* to object to, take offence to; to pay attention to; to obey; to take care of; to be careful about; to care about. * *vi* to pay attention; to be obedient; to be careful; to object.
mindful *adj* heedful, not forgetful.—**mindfully** *adv*.
mindless *adj* unthinking, stupid; requiring little intellectual effort.—**mindlessly** *adv*.
mine[1] *poss pron* belonging to me.
mine[2] *n* an excavation from which minerals are dug; an explosive device concealed in the water or ground to destroy enemy ships, personnel, or vehicles that pass over or near them; a rich supply or source. * *vt* to excavate; to lay explosive mines in an area. * *vi* to dig or work a mine.
mine detector *n* a device for indicating the whereabouts of explosive mines.
minefield *n* an area sown with explosive mines; a situation containing hidden problems.
miner *n* a person who works in a mine.
mineral *n* an inorganic substance, found naturally in the earth; any substance neither vegetable nor animal. * *adj* relating to or containing minerals.
mineralogy *n* the science of minerals.—**mineralogical** *adj*.—**mineralogically** *adv*.—**mineralogist** *n*.
mineral water *n* water containing mineral salts or gases, often with medicinal properties.
minesweeper *n* a ship for clearing away explosive mines.—**minesweeping** *n*.
mingle *vti* to mix; to combine.
miniature *adj* minute, on a small scale. * *n* a painting or reproduction on a very small scale.
minibus *n* a small bus for carrying up to twelve passengers.
minimal *adj* very minute; least possible.—**minimally** *adv*.
minimize *vt* to reduce to or estimate at a minimum.—**minimization** *n*.
minimum *n* (*pl* **minima, minimums**) the least possible amount; the lowest degree or point reached.
mining *n* the act, process, or industry of excavating from the earth; (*mil*) the laying of explosive mines.
minister *n* a clergyman serving a church; an official heading a government department; a diplomat. * *vi* to serve as a minister in a church; to give help (to).—**ministerial** *adj*.—**ministerially** *adv*.
ministry *n* the act of ministering; the clergy; the profession of a clergyman; a government department headed by a minister; the building housing a government department.
mink *n* any of several carnivorous weasel-like mammals valued for its durable soft fur.
minnow *n* a small, slender freshwater fish.
minor *adj* lesser in size, importance, degree, extent, etc; (*mus*) lower than the corresponding major by a semitone. * *n* a person under full legal age.
minority *n* the smaller part or number; a politi-

cal or racial group smaller than the majority group; the state of being under age.

minstrel *n* a travelling entertainer and musician, esp in the Middle Ages.

mint[1] *n* the place where money is coined; a large amount of money; a source of supply. * *adj* unused, in perfect condition. * *vt* (*coins*) to imprint; to invent.

mint[2] *n* an aromatic plant whose leaves are used for flavouring.

minuet *n* (the music for) a slow, graceful dance in triple time.

minus *prep* less; (*inf*) without. * *adj* involving subtraction; negative; less than. * *n* a sign (-), indicating subtraction or negative quantity.

minute[1] *n* the sixtieth part of an hour or a degree; a moment; (*pl*) an official record of a meeting. * *vt* to record or summarize the proceedings (of).

minute[2] *adj* tiny; detailed; exact.—**minutely** *adv*.—**minuteness** *n*.

miracle *n* an extraordinary event attributed to the supernatural; an unusual or astounding event; a remarkable example of something.—**miraculous** *adj*.—**miraculously** *adv*.

mirage *n* an optical illusion in which a distant object or expanse of water seems to be nearby, caused by light reflection from hot air; anything illusory or fanciful.

mirror *n* a smooth surface that reflects images; a faithful depiction. * *vt* (*pt* **mirrored**) to reflect or depict faithfully.

mirth *n* merriment, esp with laughter.—**mirthful** *adj*.—**mirthless** *adj*.

mis- *prefix* wrong(ly); bad(ly); no, not.

misadventure *n* an unlucky accident; bad luck.

misanthrope, misanthropist *n* a person who hates or distrusts mankind.—**misanthropic** *adj*.—**misanthropically** *adv*.—**misanthropy** *n*.

misapprehension *n* misunderstanding.

misappropriate *vt* to appropriate wrongly or dishonestly; to embezzle.—**misappropriation** *n*.

misbehave *vi* to behave badly.—**misbehaviour** *n*.

miscalculate *vti* to calculate wrongly.—**miscalculation** *n*.

miscarriage *n* the spontaneous expulsion of a foetus prematurely; mismanagement or failure.

miscellaneous *adj* consisting of various kinds; mixed.—**miscellaneously** *adv*.

miscellany *n* a mixed collection; a book comprising miscellaneous writings, etc.

mischief *n* wayward behaviour; damage.

mischievous *adj* harmful, prankish.—**mischievously** *adv*.—**mischievousness** *n*.

misconception *n* a mistaken idea.

misconduct *n* dishonest management; improper behaviour.—*also vt*.

misconstrue *vt* to misinterpret.—**misconstruction** *n*.

misdemeanour, misdemeanor (*US*) *n* (*law*) a minor offence, a misdeed.

miser *n* a greedy, stingy person who hoards money for its own sake.—**miserliness** *n*.—**miserly** *adj*.

miserable *adj* wretched; unhappy; causing misery; bad, inadequate; pitiable.—**miserableness** *n*.—**miserably** *adv*.

misery *n* extreme pain, unhappiness, or poverty; a cause of suffering.

misfire *vi* (*engine, etc*) to fail to ignite, start; to fail to succeed.—*also n*.

misfit *n* something that fits badly; a maladjusted person.—*also vti*.

misfortune *n* ill luck; trouble; a mishap.

misgiving *n* a feeling of misapprehension, mistrust.

misguided *adj* foolish; mistaken.

mishap *n* an unfortunate accident.

misinform *vt* to supply with wrong information.—**misinformation** *n*.

misjudge *vt* to judge wrongly, to form a wrong opinion.—**misjudgment, misjudgement** *n*.

mislay *vt* (*pt* **mislaid**) to lose something temporarily; to put down or install improperly.

mislead *vt* (*pt* **misled**) to deceive; to give wrong information to; to lead into wrongdoing.

misleading *adj* deceptive; confusing.

misnomer *n* an incorrect or unsuitable name or description.

misplace *vt* to put in a wrong place; (*trust, etc*) to place unwisely.—**misplacement** *n*.

misprint *vt* to print incorrectly. * *n* an error in printing.

misrepresent *vt* to represent falsely; to give an untrue idea of.—**misrepresentation** *n*.—**misrepre-sentative** *adj*.

miss[1] *n* (*pl* **misses**) a girl; (*with cap*) a title used before the surname of an unmarried woman or girl.

miss[2] *vt* to fail to reach, hit, find, meet, hear; to omit; to fail to take advantage of; to regret or discover the absence or loss of. * *vi* to fail to hit; to fail to be successful; to misfire, as an engine. * *n* a failure to hit, reach, obtain, etc.

missal *n* a book containing the prayers for Mass.

misshapen *adj* badly shaped; deformed.
missile *n* an object, as a rock, spear, rocket, etc, to be thrown, fired, or launched.
missing *adj* absent; lost.
mission *n* a group of people sent by a church, government, etc to carry out a special duty or task; the sending of an aircraft or spacecraft on a special assignment; a vocation.
missionary *n* a person who tries to convert unbelievers to his/her religious faith.—*also adj.*
misspent *adj* wasted, frittered away.
mist *n* a large mass of water vapour, less dense than a fog; something that dims or obscures. * *vti* to cover or be covered, as with mist.—**mistily** *adv*.—**mistiness** *n*.—**misty** *adj*.
mistake *vb* (*pt* **mistook**, *pp* **mistaken**) * *vt* to misunderstand; to misinterpret. * *vi* to make a mistake. * *n* a wrong idea, answer, etc; an error of judgment; a blunder; a misunderstanding.—**mistakable, mistakeable** *adj*.
mistaken *adj* erroneous, ill-judged.—**mistakenly** *adv*.
mister *n* (*inf*) sir; (*with cap*) the title used before a man's surname.
mistletoe *n* an evergreen parasitic plant with white berries used as a Christmas decoration.
mistreat *vt* to treat wrongly or badly.—**mistreatment** *n*.
mistress *n* a woman who is head of a household; a woman with whom a man is having a prolonged affair; a female schoolteacher; (*with cap*) the title used before a married woman's surname.
mistrust *n* lack of trust. * *vti* to doubt; to suspect.—**mistrustful** *adj*. —**mistrustfully** *adv*
misunderstand *vt* (*pt* **misunderstood**) to fail to understand correctly.—**misunderstood** *adj*.
misunderstanding *n* a mistake as to sense; a quarrel or disagreement.
misuse *vt* to use for the wrong purpose or in the wrong way; to ill-treat, abuse. * *n* improper or incorrect use.
mitigate *vti* to become or make less severe.—**mitigable** *adj*.—**mitigating** *adj*.—**mitigation** *n*.
mitre, miter (*US*) *n* the headdress of a bishop; a diagonal joint between two pieces of wood to form a corner. * *vt* to join with a mitre corner.
mitt *n* a glove covering the hand but only the base of the fingers; (*sl*) a hand; a boxing glove; a baseball glove.
mitten *n* a glove with a thumb but no separate fingers.
mix *vt* to blend together in a single mass; to make by blending ingredients, as a cake; to combine; (*with* **up**) to make into a mixture; to make disordered; to confuse or mistake. * *vi* to be mixed or blended; to get along together. * *n* a mixture.
mixed *adj* blended; made up of different parts, classes, races, etc; confused.
mixed-up *adj* (*inf*) perplexed, mentally confused.
mixer *n* a device that blends or mixes; a person considered in terms of their ability (good or bad) to get on with others; a soft drink added to an alcoholic beverage.
mixture *n* the process of mixing; a blend made by mixing.
mix-up *n* a mistake; confusion, muddle; (*inf*) a fight.
moan *n* a low mournful sound as of sorrow or pain. * *vti* to utter a moan; to complain.—**moaner** *n*.
moat *n* a deep ditch surrounding a fortification or castle, usu filled with water.
mob *n* a disorderly or riotous crowd; a contemptuous term for the masses; (*sl*) a gang of criminals. * *vt* (*pt* **mobbed**) to attack in a disorderly group; to surround.
mobile *adj* movable, not fixed; easily changing; characterized by ease in change of social status; capable of moving freely and quickly; (*inf*) having transport. * *n* a suspended structure of wood, metal, etc with parts that move in air currents.—**mobility** *n*.
moccasin *n* a flat shoe based on Amerindian footwear; any soft, flexible shoe resembling this.
mock *vt* to imitate or ridicule; to behave with scorn; to defy; (*with* **up**) to make a model of. * *n* ridicule; an object of scorn. * *adj* false, sham, counterfeit.—**mocking** *n*, *adj*.—**mockingly** *adv*.
mockery *n* derision, ridicule, or contempt; imitation, esp derisive; someone or something that is mocked; an inadequate person, thing, or action.
mock-up *n* a full-scale working model of a machine, etc.
MOD *abbr* = Ministry of Defence.
mod cons *npl* (*inf*) modern conveniences.
mode *n* a way of acting, doing or existing; a style or fashion; form; (*mus*) any of the scales used in composition; (*statistics*) the predominant item in a series of items; (*gram*) mood.—

modal *adj*.—**modality** *n*.
model *n* a pattern; an ideal; a standard worth imitating; a representation on a smaller scale, usu three-dimensional; a person who sits for an artist or photographer; a person who displays clothes by wearing them. * *adj* serving as a model; representative of others of the same style. * *vb* (*pt* **modelled**) *vt* (*with* **after, on**) to create by following a model; to display clothes by wearing. * *vi* to serve as a model for an artist, etc.—**modeller** *n*.—**modelling** *n*.
moderate *vti* to make or become moderate; to preside over. * *adj* having reasonable limits; avoiding extremes; mild, calm; of medium quality, amount, etc. * *n* a person who holds moderate views.—**moderately** *adv*.—**moderation** *n*.
modern *adj* of the present or recent times, contemporary; up-to-date.—**modernity** *n*.
modernize *vti* to make or become modern.—**modernization** *n*.
modest *adj* moderate; having a humble opinion of oneself; unpretentious.—**modestly** *adv*.—**modesty** *n*.
modicum *n* a small quantity.
modify *vt* to lessen the severity of; to change or alter slightly; (*gram*) to limit in meaning, to qualify.—**modifiable** *adj*.—**modification** *n*.—**modifier** *n*.
module *n* a unit of measurement; a self-contained unit, esp in a spacecraft.—**modular** *adj*.
mohair *n* the long, fine hair of the Angora goat; the silk cloth made from it.
moist *adj* damp; slightly wet.—**moistly** *adv*.—**moistness** *n*.
moisten *vti* to make or become moist.
moisture *n* liquid in a diffused, absorbed, or condensed state.
moisturize *vt* (*skin, air, etc*) to add moisture to.—**moisturizer** *n*.
molar *n* a back tooth, used for grinding food.
molasses *n* (*used as sing*) the thick brown sugar that is produced during the refining of sugar; treacle.
mole[1] *n* a spot on the skin, usu dark-coloured and raised.
mole[2] *n* a small burrowing insectivore with soft dark fur; a spy within an organization.
mole[3] *n* a large breakwater.
mole[4] *n* the basic SI unit of substance.
molecule *n* the simplest unit of a substance, retaining the chemical properties of that substance; a small particle.—**molecular** *adj*.
molest *vt* to annoy; to attack or assault, esp sexually.—**molestation** *n*.—**molester** *n*.
mollusc, mollusk (*US*) *n* an invertebrate animal usu enclosed in a shell, as oysters, etc.
molten *adj* melted by heat.
moment *n* an indefinitely brief period of time; a definite point in time; a brief time of importance.
momentary *adj* lasting only for a moment.
momentous *adj* very important.—**momentously** *adv*.
momentum *n* (*pl* **momenta, momentums**) the impetus of a moving object, equal to the product of its mass and its velocity.
monarch *n* a sovereign who rules by hereditary right.—**monarchic** *adj*.—**monarchical** *adj*.
monarchy *n* a government headed by a monarch; a kingdom.
monastery *n* the residence of a group of monks, or nuns.
monastic *adj* of monks or monasteries. * *n* a monk; a recluse.—**monastically** *adv*.—**monasticism** *n*.
Monday *n* the second day of the week.
monetary *adj* of the coinage or currency of a country; of or relating to money.
money *n* (*pl* **moneys, monies**) coins or paper notes authorized by a government as a medium of exchange; property; wealth.
mongrel *n* an animal or plant of mixed or unknown breed, esp a dog.—*also adj*.
monitor *n* a student chosen to help the teacher; any device for regulating the performance of a machine, aircraft, etc; a screen for viewing the image being produced by a television camera; a display screen connected to a computer. * *vti* (*TV or radio transmissions, etc*) to observe or listen to for political or technical reasons; to watch or check on; to regulate or control, a machine, etc.—**monitory** *adj*.
monk *n* a male member of a religious order living in a monastery.
monkey *n* (*pl* **monkeys**) any of the primates except man and the lemurs, esp the smaller, long-tailed primates; a mischievous child; (*sl*) £500 or $500. * *vi* (*inf*) to play, trifle, or meddle.
monkey nut *n* a peanut.
monkey wrench *n* a large wrench with an adjustable jaw.
mono- *prefix* alone, sole, single.
monochrome *n* a painting, drawing, or print in a single colour.
monocle *n* a single eyeglass held in place by the face muscles.

monogram *n* the embroidered or printed initials of one's name on clothing, stationery, etc.—**monogrammed** *adj*.

monologue, monolog *n* a long speech; a soliloquy, a skit, etc for one actor only.

monopolize *vt* to get, have, or exploit a monopoly of; to get full control of.—**monopolization** *n*.

monopoly *n* exclusive control in dealing in a particular commodity or supplying a service; exclusive use or possession; that which is exclusively controlled; such control granted by a government.—**monopolist** *n*.—**monopolistic** *adj*.

monosyllable *n* a word of one syllable.—**monosyllabic** *adj*.

monotone *n* an utterance or musical tone without a change in pitch; a tiresome sameness of style, colour, etc.—**monotonous** *adj*.—**monotonously** *adv*.—**monotony** *n*.

monsoon *n* a seasonal wind of southern Asia; the rainy season.

monster *n* any greatly malformed plant or animal; an imaginary beast; a very wicked person; a very large animal or thing. * *adj* very large, huge.—**monstrosity** *n*.

monstrous *adj* abnormally developed; enormous; horrible.—**monstrously** *adv*.

montage *n* a rapid sequence of film shots, often superimposed; the art or technique of assembling various elements, esp pictures or photographs; such an assemblage.

month *n* any of the twelve divisions of the year; a calendar month.

monthly *adj* continuing for a month; done, happening, payable, etc, every month. * *n* a monthly periodical. * *adv* once a month; every month.

monument *n* an obelisk, statue or building that commemorates a person or an event; an exceptional example.

monumental *adj* of, like, or serving as a monument; colossal; lasting.—**monumentally** *adv*.

mood *n* a temporary state of mind or temper; a gloomy feeling; a predominant feeling or spirit; (*gram*) that form of a verb indicating mode of action; (*mus*) mode.

moody *adj* (**moodier, moodiest**) gloomy; temperamental.—**moodily** *adv*.—**moodiness** *n*.

moon *n* the natural satellite that revolves around the earth and shines by reflected sunlight; any natural satellite of another planet; something shaped like the moon. * *vi* to behave in an idle or abstracted way.

moonbeam *n* a ray of moonlight.

moonlight *n* the light of the moon. * *vi* (*inf*) to have a secondary (usu night-time) job.

moonlit *adj* lit by the moon.

moor[1] *n* a tract of open wasteland, usu covered with heather and often marshy.

moor[2] *vti* (*a ship*) to secure or be secured by cable or anchor.

mooring *n* the act of mooring; the place where a ship is moored; (*pl*) the lines, cables, etc by which a ship is moored.

moose *n* (*pl* **moose**) the largest member of the deer family, native to North America.

moot *adj* debatable; hypothetical. * *vt* to propose for discussion.

mop *n* a rag, sponge, etc fixed to a handle for washing floors or dishes; a thick or tangled head of hair. * *vt* (*pt* **mopped**) to wash with a mop.

mope *vi* to be gloomy and apathetic.—**mopey** *adj*.

moped *n* a light, motor-assisted bicycle.

moral *adj* of or relating to character and human behaviour, particularly as regards right and wrong; virtuous, esp in sexual conduct; capable of distinguishing right from wrong; probable, although not certain; psychological, emotional. * *n* a moral lesson taught by a fable, event, etc; (*pl*) principles; ethics. —**moralist** *n*.—**moralistic** *adj*.—**morally** *adv*.

morale *n* moral or mental condition with respect to courage, discipline, confidence, etc.

morality *n* virtue; moral principles; a particular system of moral principles.

morass *n* a bog, marsh.

morbid *adj* diseased, resulting as from a diseased state of mind; gruesome.—**morbidly** *adv*.—**morbidness** *n*.

more *adj* (*superl* **most**) greater; further; additional(—*also compar of* **many, much**). * *adv* to a greater extent or degree; again; further.

moreover *adv* in addition to what has been said before; besides.

morgue *n* a place where the bodies of unknown dead or those dead of unknown causes are temporarily kept prior to burial; a collection of reference materials, eg newspaper clippings.

morning *n* the part of the day from midnight or dawn until noon; the early part of anything.

moron *n* an adult mentally equal to a 8 to 12-year-old child; (*inf*) a very stupid person.—**moronic** *adj*.

morose *adj* sullen, surly; gloomy.—**morosely** *adv*.—**moroseness** *n*.

morphine *n* an alkaloid derived from opium,

used as an anaesthetic and sedative.

Morse code *n* a code in which letters are represented by dots and dashes or long and short sounds, and are transmitted by visual or audible signals.

morsel *n* a small quantity of food; a small piece of anything.

mortal *adj* subject to death; causing death, fatal; hostile; very intense. * *n* a human being.—**mortally** *adv*.

mortality *n* state of being mortal; death on a large scale, as from war; number or frequency of deaths in a given period relative to population.

mortar *n* a mixture of cement or lime with sand and water used in building; an artillery piece that fires shells at low velocities and high trajectories; a bowl in which substances are pounded with a pestle.

mortgage *n* a transfer of rights to a piece of property usu as security for the payment of a loan or debt that becomes void when the debt is paid.—*also vt*.

mortify *vti* to subdue by repression or penance; to humiliate or shame; to become gangrenous.—**mortification** *n*.

mortuary *n* a place of temporary storage for dead bodies.

mosaic *n* a surface decoration made by inlaying small pieces (of glass, stone, etc) to form figures or patterns; a design made in mosaic.—*also adj*.

Moslem *see* **Muslim**.

mosque *n* a place of worship for Muslims.

mosquito *n* (*pl* **mosquitoes**) a small two-winged bloodsucking insect.

moss *n* a very small green plant that grows in clusters on rocks, moist ground, etc.—**mossy** *adj*.

most *adj* (*compar* **more**) greatest in number; greatest in amount or degree; in the greatest number of instances(—*also superl of* **many**, **much**). * *adv* in or to the greatest degree or extent. * *n* the greatest amount or degree; (*with pl*) the greatest number (of).

mostly *adv* for the most part; mainly, usually.

MOT *abbr* = Ministry of Transport.

motel *n* an hotel for motorists with adjacent parking.

moth *n* a four-winged chiefly night-flying insect related to the butterfly.

mothball *n* a small ball of camphor or naphthalene used to protect stored clothes from moths.

moth-eaten *adj* eaten into by moths; dilapidated; outmoded.

mother *n* a female who has given birth to offspring; an origin or source. * *adj* of or like a mother; native. * *vt* to be the mother of or a mother to.—**motherhood** *n*.

mother-in-law *n* the mother of one's spouse.

motherly *adj* of, proper to a mother; like a mother.—**motherliness** *n*.

mother-of-pearl *n* the iridescent lining of the shell of the pearl oyster.

motif *see* **motive**.

motion *n* activity, movement; a formal suggestion made in a meeting, law court, or legislative assembly; evacuation of the bowels. * *vti* to signal or direct by a gesture.

motionless *adj* not moving, still.

motion picture *n* a film, movie.

motive *n* something (as a need or desire) that causes a person to act; a recurrent theme in a musical composition (—*also* **motif**). * *adj* moving to action; of or relating to motion.

motley *adj* multicoloured; composed of diverse elements.

motor *n* anything that produces motion; a machine for converting electrical energy into mechanical energy; a motor car. * *adj* producing motion; of or powered by a motor; of, by or for motor vehicles; of or involving muscular movements. * *vi* to travel by car.

motorbike *n* a motorcycle.

motorboat *n* a boat propelled by an engine or motor.

motorcycle *n* a two-wheeled motor vehicle.—**motorcyclist** *n*.

motorist *n* a person who drives a car.

motor scooter *n* a small-wheeled motorcycle with an enclosed engine.

motorway *n* a road with controlled access for fast-moving traffic.—*also* **freeway** *n*.

mottled *adj* marked with blotches of various colours.

motto *n* (*pl* **mottoes, mottos**) a short saying adopted as a maxim or ideal.

mould[1], **mold** (*US*) *n* a fungus producing a furry growth on the surface of organic matter. * *vi* to become mouldy.—**mouldiness** *n*.—**mouldy** *adj*.

mould[2], **mold** (*US*) *n* a hollow form in which something is cast; a pattern; something made in a mould; distinctive character. * *vt* to make in or on a mould; to form, shape, guide.

moult, molt (*US*) *vi* to shed hair, skin, horns, etc prior to replacement of new growth.—*also n*.

mound *n* an artificial bank of earth or stones;

a heap or bank of earth. * *vt* to form into a mound.

mount[1] *n* a high hill.

mount[2] *vi* to increase. * *vt* to climb, ascend; to get up on (a horse, platform, etc); to provide with horses; (*a jewel*) to fix on a support; (*a picture*) to frame. * *n* a horse for riding; (*for a picture*) a backing.

mountain *n* a land mass higher than a hill; a vast number or quantity. * *adj* of or in mountains.

mountaineer *n* one who climbs mountains.

mountaineering *n* the technique of climbing mountains.

mountainous *adj* having many mountains; very high; huge.

mourn *vti* (*someone dead*) to grieve for; (*something regrettable*) to feel or express sorrow for.—**mourner** *n*.

mournful *adj* expressing grief or sorrow; causing sorrow.—**mournfully** *adv*.

mourning *adj* grieving. * *n* the expression of grief; dark clothes worn by mourners.

mouse *n* (*pl* **mice**) a small rodent with a pointed snout, long body and slender tail; a timid person; a hand-held device used to position the cursor and control software on a computer screen.

moustache, mustache (*US*) *n* the hair on the upper lip.

mousy, mousey *adj* (**mousier, mousiest**) mouse-like; grey-brown in colour; quiet, stealthy; timid, retiring.

mouth *n* (*pl* **mouths**) the opening in the head through which food is eaten, sound uttered or words spoken; the lips; opening, entrance, as of a bottle, etc. * *vt* to say, esp insincerely; to form words with the mouth without uttering sound. * *vi* to utter pompously; to grimace.

mouthful *n* as much (food) as fills the mouth; a word or phrase that is difficult to say correctly; (*sl*) a pertinent remark.

mouth organ *n* a harmonica.

mouthwatering *adj* appetizing; tasty.

movable, moveable *adj* that may be moved. * *npl* personal property.

move *vt* to shift or change place; to set in motion; to rouse the emotions; to put (a motion) formally. * *vi* to go from one place to another; to walk, to carry oneself; to change place; to evacuate the bowels; to propose a motion as in a meeting; to change residence; (*chess, draughts, etc*) to change the position of a piece on the board. * *n* the act of moving; a movement, esp in board games; one's turn to move; a premeditated action.—**mover** *n*.

movement *n* act of moving; the moving part of a machine, esp a clock; the policy and activities of a group; a trend, eg in prices; a division of a musical work; tempo.

movie *n* a cinema film, motion picture; (*pl*) the showing of a motion picture; the motion-picture medium or industry.

moving *adj* arousing the emotions; changing position; causing motion.—**movingly** *adv*.

mow *vti* (*pt* **mowed** *or* **mown**) (*grass, etc*) to cut from with a sickle or lawn mower; (*with* **down**) to cause to fall like cut grass.—**mower** *n*.

MP *abbr* = Member of Parliament.

mpg *abbr* = miles per gallon.

mph *abbr* = miles per hour.

Mr *n* (*pl* **Messrs**) used as a title before a man's name or an office he holds.

Mrs *n* used as a title before a married woman's name.

Ms *n* the title used before a woman's name instead of Miss or Mrs.

much *adj* (*compar* **more**, *superl* **most**) plenty. * *adv* considerably; to a great extent.

muck *n* moist manure; black earth with decaying matter; mud, dirt, filth. * *vt* to spread manure; to make dirty; (*with* **out**) to clear of muck. * *vi* to move or load muck; (*with* **about, around**) to engage in useless activity.—**muckiness** *n*.—**mucky** *adj*.

mucus *n* the slimy secretion that keeps mucous membranes moist.

mud *n* soft, wet earth.

muddle *vt* to confuse; to mix up. * *n* confusion, mess.

muddy *adj* (**muddier, muddiest**) like or covered with mud; not bright or clear; confused. * *vti* to make or become dirty or unclear.—**muddily** *adv*.—**muddiness** *n*.

mudguard *n* a screen on a wheel to catch mud splashes.

muff[1] *n* a warm soft fur cover for warming the hands.

muff[2] *n* a bungling performance; failure to hold a ball when trying to catch it. * *vti* to bungle.

muffin *n* baked yeast roll.

muffle *vt* to wrap up for warmth or to hide; (*sound*) to deaden by wrapping up.

muffler *n* a long scarf; any means of deadening sound; the silencer of a motor vehicle.

mug *n* a cylindrical drinking cup, usu of metal or earthenware; its contents; (*sl*) the face; (*sl*) a fool. * *vb* (*pt* **mugged**) *vt* to assault, usu with intent to rob.

muggy *adj* (**muggier, muggiest**) (*weather*) warm, damp and close.

mule[1] *n* the offspring of a male donkey and a female horse; a machine for spinning cotton; an obstinate person.—**mulish** *adj*.—**mulishly** *adv*.—**mulishness** *n*.

mule[2] *n* a slipper without a heel.

mull[1] *vti* (*inf*) to ponder (over).

mull[2] *vt* (*wine, etc*) to heat, sweeten and spice.—**mulled** *adj*.

mult-, multi- *prefix* much, many.

multiple *adj* of many parts; manifold; various; complex. * *n* (*math*) a number exactly divisible by another.

multiple sclerosis *n* a disease of the nervous system with loss of muscular coordination, etc.

multiplication *n* the act of multiplying; the process of repeatedly adding a quantity to itself a certain number of times, or any other process which has the same result.

multiply *vti* to increase in number, degree, etc; to find the product (of) by multiplication.

multitude *n* a large number (of people).—**multitudinous** *adj*.

mum[1], **mummy** *n* (*inf*) mother.

mum[2] *adj* silent, not speaking.

mumble *vti* to speak indistinctly, mutter. * *n* a mumbled utterance.—**mumbler** *n*.—**mumbling** *adj*.

mummy[1] *see* **mum**[1].

mummy[2] *n* a carefully preserved dead body, esp an embalmed corpse of ancient Egypt.—**mummification** *n*.—**mummify** *vt*.

mumps *npl* (*used as sing or pl*) an acute contagious virus disease characterized by swelling of the salivary glands.

munch *vti* to chew steadily.

mundane *adj* routine, everyday; banal; worldly.—**mundanely** *adv*.

municipal *adj* of or concerning a city, town, etc or its local government.—**municipally** *adv*.

municipality *n* a city or town having corporate status and powers of self-government; the governing body of a municipality.

munitions *npl* war supplies, esp weapons and ammunition.

mural *adj* relating to a wall. * *n* a picture or design painted directly onto a wall.

murder *n* the intentional and unlawful killing of one person by another; (*inf*) something unusually difficult or dangerous to do or deal with.—*also vt*.—**murderer** *n*.—**murderous** *adj*.—**murderously** *adv*.

murky *adj* (**murkier, murkiest**) dark, gloomy; darkly vague or obscure.—**murkily** *adv*.—**murkiness** *n*.

murmur *n* a continuous low, indistinct sound; a mumbled complaint; (*med*) an abnormal sound made by the heart. * *vti* to make a murmur; to say in a murmur.—**murmurous** *adj*.

muscle *n* fibrous tissue that contracts and relaxes, producing bodily movement; strength; brawn; power. * *vi* (*inf*) to force one's way (in).—**muscular** *adj*.—**muscularity** *n*.—**muscularly** *adv*.

muse *vti* to ponder, meditate.—**musing** *adj*.

museum *n* a building for exhibiting objects of artistic, historic or scientific interest.

mushroom *n* a fleshy fungus with a capped stalk, some varieties of which are edible. * *vi* to gather mushrooms; to spread rapidly, to increase.

music *n* the art of combining tones into a composition having structure and continuity; vocal or instrumental sounds having rhythm, melody or harmony; an agreeable sound.

musical *adj* of or relating to music or musicians; having the pleasant tonal qualities of music; having an interest in or talent for music. * *n* a play or film incorporating dialogue, singing and dancing.—**musically** *adv*.

musician *n* one skilled in music, esp a performer.

Muslim *n* an adherent of Islam.—*also adj*.

muslin *n* a fine cotton cloth.

mussel *n* an edible marine bivalve shellfish.

must *aux vb expressing*: necessity; probability; certainty. **n* (*inf*) something that must be done, had, etc.

mustard *n* the powdered seeds of the mustard plant used as a condiment; a brownish-yellow colour; (*sl*) zest.

muster *vt* to assemble or call together, as troops for inspection or duty; to gather. * *vi* to be assembled, as troops. * *n* gathering; review; assembly.

musty *adj* (**mustier, mustiest**) mouldy, damp; stale.

mute *adj* silent; dumb; (*colour*) subdued. * *n* a person who is unable to speak; a device that softens the sound of a musical instrument. * *vt* to lessen the sound of a musical instrument.—**mutely** *adv*.—**muteness** *n*.

mutilate *vt* to maim; to damage by removing an essential part of.—**mutilation** *n*.—**mutilator** *n*.

mutiny *vi* to revolt against authority in military

service.—*also n*.—**mutineer** *n*.—**mutinous** *adj*.—**mutinously** *adv*.

mutter *vti* to utter in a low tone or indistinctly; to grumble.—**muttering** *n*.

mutton *n* the edible flesh of sheep.

mutual *adj* given and received in equal amount; having the same feelings one for the other; shared in common.—**mutuality** *n*.—**mutually** *adv*.

muzzle *n* the projecting nose or mouth of an animal; a strap fitted over the jaws to prevent biting; the open end of a gun barrel. * *vt* to put a muzzle on; to silence or gag.

my *poss adj* of or belonging to me.

myself *pron* emphatic and reflexive form of I; in my normal state.

mystery *n* something unexplained and secret; a story about a secret crime, etc; secrecy.—**mysterious** *adj*.—**mysteriously** *adv*.

mystic *adj* having a meaning beyond normal human understanding; magical. * *n* one who seeks direct knowledge of God or spiritual truths by self-surrender.—**mysticism** *n*.

mystify *vt* to bewilder, confuse.—**mystification** *n*.

myth *n* a fable; a fictitious event; a traditional story of gods and heroes, taken to be true.—**mythical** *adj*.—**mythically** *adv*.

mythology *n* myths collectively; the study of myths.—**mythological** *adj*.—**mythologist** *n*.

N

nab *vt* (*pt* **nabbed**) (*sl*) to catch, arrest.

nag[1] *vti* (*pt* **nagged**) to scold constantly; to harass; to be felt persistently. * *n* a person who nags.

nag[2] (*inf*) a horse.

nail *n* a horny plate covering the end of a human finger or toe; a thin pointed metal spike for driving into wood as a fastening or hanging device. * *vt* to fasten with nails; to fix, secure; (*inf*) to catch or hit; (*inf*) to arrest.

naive, **naïve** *adj* inexperienced; unsophisticated; (*argument*) simple.—**naively, naïvely** *adv*.—**naivety, naiveté, naïveté** *n*.

naked *adj* bare, without clothes; without a covering; without addition or ornament; (*eye*) without optical aid.—**nakedness** *n*.

name *n* a word or term by which a person or thing is called; a title; reputation; authority. * *vt* to give a name to; to call by name; to designate; to appoint to an office; (*a date, price, etc*) to specify.

name-dropping *n* the practice of mentioning the names of famous or important people as if they were friends, in order to impress others.—**name-dropper** *n*.

nameless *adj* without a name; obscure; anonymous; unnamed; indefinable; too distressing or horrifying to be described.

namely *adv* that is to say.

namesake *n* a person or thing with the same name as another.

nanny, nannie *n* a child's nurse; (*inf*) a grandmother.

nap[1] *n* a short sleep, doze. * *vi* (*pt* **napped**) to take a nap.

nap[2] *n* a hairy surface on cloth or leather; such a surface.

napalm *n* a substance added to petrol to form a jelly-like compound used in firebombs and flame-throwers. * *vt* to attack or burn with napalm.

nape *n* the back of the neck.

napkin *n* a square of cloth or paper for wiping fingers or mouth or protecting clothes at table, a serviette; a nappy.

nappy *n* a piece of absorbent material wrapped around a baby to absorb or retain its excreta.—*also* **diaper**, **napkin**.

narcotic *adj* inducing sleep. * *n* a drug, often addictive, used to relieve pain and induce sleep.

narrate *vt* (*a story*) to tell, relate; to give an account of; (*film, TV*) to provide a spoken commentary for.—**narration** *n*.—**narrator** *n*.

narrative *n* a spoken or written account of a sequence of events, experiences, etc; the art or process of narration.—*also adj*.

narrow *adj* small in width; limited; with little margin; (*views*) prejudiced or bigoted. * *n* (*usu pl*) the narrow part of a pass, street, or channel. * *vti* to make or grow narrow; to decrease; to contract.—**narrowly** *adv*.—**narrowness** *n*.

narrow-minded *adj* prejudiced, bigoted; illiberal.—**narrow-mindedness** *n*.

nasal *adj* of the nose; sounded through the nose. * *n* a sound made through the nose.—**nasally** *adv*.

nasty *adj* (*pl* **nastier, nastiest**) unpleasant; offensive; ill-natured; disagreeable; (*problem*) hard to deal with; (*illness*) serious or dangerous.—**nastily** *adv*.—**nastiness** *n*.

nation *n* people of common territory, descent, culture, language, or history; people united under a single government.

national *adj* of a nation; common to a whole nation, general. * *n* a citizen or subject of a specific country.—**nationally** *adv*.

nationalism *n* patriotic sentiments, principles, etc; a policy of national independence or self-government; fanatical patriotism, chauvinism.—**nationalist** *n*.—**nationalistic** *adj*.

nationality *n* the status of belonging to a nation by birth or naturalization; a nation or national group.

nationalize *vt* to make national; to convert into public or government property.—**nationalization** *n*.

native *adj* inborn; natural to a person; innate; (*language, etc*) of one's place of birth; relating to the indigenous inhabitants of a country or area; occurring naturally. * *n* a person born in the place indicated; a local inhabitant; an indigenous plant or animal; an indigenous inhabitant, esp a non-White under colonial rule.

natter *vi* (*inf*) to chat, talk aimlessly.—*also n*.

natural *adj* of or produced by nature; not artificial; innate, not acquired; true to nature; lifelike; normal; at ease; (*mus*) not flat or sharp. * *n* (*inf*) a person or thing considered to have a natural aptitude (for) or to be an obvious choice (for); (*inf*) a certainty; (*mus*) a natural note or a sign indicating one.—**naturalness** *n*.

natural history *n* the study of nature, esp the animal, mineral and vegetable world.

naturalism *n* (*arts*) the theory or practice of describing nature, character, etc, in realistic detail.—**naturalistic** *adj*.

naturalist *n* a person who studies natural history; a person who advocates or practises naturalism.

naturalize *vt* to confer citizenship upon (a person of foreign birth); (*plants*) to become established in a different climate. * *vi* to become established as if native.—**naturalization** *n*.

naturally *adv* in a natural manner, by nature; of course.

natural selection *see* **selection**.

nature *n* the phenomena of physical life not dominated by man; the entire material world as a whole, or forces observable in it; the essential character of anything; the innate character of a person, temperament; kind, class; vital force or functions; natural scenery.

naught *see* **nought**.

naughty *adj* (**naughtier, naughtiest**) mischievous or disobedient; titillating.—**naughtily** *adv*.—**naughtiness** *n*.

nausea *n* a desire to vomit; disgust.

nauseate *vti* to arouse feelings of disgust; to feel nausea or revulsion.—**nauseating** *adj*.

nautical *adj* of ships, sailors, or navigation.

nautical mile *see* **mile**.

naval *adj* of the navy; of ships.

nave *n* the central space of a church, distinct from the chancel and aisles.

navel *n* the small scar in the abdomen caused by severance of the umbilical cord; a central point.

navigable *adj* (rivers, seas) that can be sailed upon or steered through.—**navigability** *n*.

navigate *vti* to steer or direct a ship, aircraft, etc; to travel through or over (*water, air, etc*) in a ship or aircraft; to find a way through, over, etc, and to keep to a course.—**navigator** *n*.

navigation *n* the act, art or science of navigating; the method of calculating the position of a ship, aircraft, etc.

navvy *n* a labourer, esp one who works on roads or railways.

navy *n* (*often* with cap) the warships of a nation; a nation's entire sea force, including ships, men, stores, etc; navy blue.

navy blue *n* an almost black blue.

near *adj* close, not distant in space or time; closely related, intimate; approximate, (*escape, etc*) narrow. * *adv* to or at a little distance; close by; almost. * *prep* close to. * *vti* to approach; to draw close to.—**nearness** *n*.

nearby *adj* neighbouring; close by in position.

nearly *adv* almost, closely.

near-sighted *adj* short-sighted, myopic.—**near-sightedness** *n*.

neat *adj* clean and tidy; skilful; efficiently done; well made; (*alcoholic drink*) undiluted; (*sl*) nice, pleasing, etc.—**neatly** *adv*.—**neatness** *n*.

nebulous *adj* indistinct; formless.

necessarily *adv* as a natural consequence.

necessary *adj* indispensable; required; inevitable. * *n* something necessary; (*pl*) essential needs.

necessitate *vt* to make necessary; to compel.

necessity *n* a prerequisite; something that cannot be done without; compulsion; need.

neck *n* the part of the body that connects the head and shoulders; that part of a garment nearest the neck; a neck-like part, esp a narrow strip of land; the narrowest part of a bottle; a strait. * *vti* (*sl*) to kiss and caress.

necklace *n* a string or band, often of precious stones, beads, or pearls, worn around the neck.

née, nee *adj* (*literally*) born: indicating the maiden name of a married woman.

need *n* necessity; a lack of something; a requirement; poverty. * *vt* to have a need for; to require; to be obliged.

needle *n* a small pointed piece of steel for sewing; a larger pointed rod for knitting or crocheting; a stylus; the pointer of a compass, gauge, etc; the thin, short leaf of the pine, spruce, etc; the sharp, slender metal tube at the end of a hypodermic syringe. * *vt* to goad, prod, or tease.

needless *adj* not needed, unnecessary; uncalled for, pointless.—**needlessly** *adv*.—**needlessness** *n*.

needy *adj* (**needier, neediest**) in need, very poor.

negation *n* a negative statement, denial; the opposite or absence of something; a contradiction.

negative *adj* expressing or meaning denial or refusal; lacking positive attributes; (*math*) denoting a quantity less than zero, or one to be subtracted; (*photog*) reversing the light and shade of the original subject, or having the colours replaced by complementary ones; (*elect*) of the charge carried by electrons; producing such a charge. * *n* a negative word, reply, etc; refusal; something that is the opposite or negation of something else; (*in debate, etc*) the side that votes or argues for the opposition; (*photog*) a negative image on transparent film or a plate. * *vt* to refuse assent, contradict; to veto.—**negatively** *adv*.

neglect *vt* to pay little or no attention to; to disregard; to leave uncared for; to fail to do something. * *n* disregard; lack of attention or care.

negligée, negligee *n* a woman's loosely fitting dressing gown.

negligence *n* lack of attention or care; an act of carelessness; a carelessly easy manner.—**negligent** *adj*.—**negligently** *adv*.

negligible *adj* that need not be regarded; unimportant; trifling.

negotiable *adj* able to be legally negotiated; (*bills, drafts, etc*) transferable.—**negotiability** *n*.

negotiate *vti* to discuss, bargain in order to reach an agreement or settlement; to settle by agreement; (*fin*) to obtain or give money value for (a bill); (*obstacle, etc*) to overcome.—**negotiation** *n* —**negotiator** *n*.

Negro *n* (*pl* **Negroes**) a member of the dark-skinned, indigenous peoples of Africa; a member of the Negroid group; a person with some Negro ancestors.—*also adj*.—**Negress** *nf*.

neighbour, neighbor (*US*) *n* a person who lives near another; a person or thing situated next to another; a fellow human being.

neighbourhood, neighborhood (*US*) *n* a particular community, area, or district; the people in an area.

neighbouring, neighboring (*US*) *adj* adjoining, nearby.

neighbourly, neighborly (*US*) *adj* characteristic of a neighbour, friendly.—*also adv*.—**neighbourliness** *n*.

neither *adj, pron* not one or the other (of two); not either. * *conj* not either; also not.

neon *n* an inert gaseous element that gives off a bright orange glow, used in lighting and advertisements.

nephew *n* the son of a brother or sister.

nerve *n* any of the fibres or bundles of fibres that transmit impulses of sensation or of movement between the brain and spinal cord and all parts of the body; courage, coolness in danger; (*inf*) audacity, boldness; (*pl*) nervousness, anxiety. * *vt* to give strength, courage, or vigour to.

nerve-racking, nerve-wracking *adj* straining the nerves, stressful.

nervous *adj* excitable, highly strung; anxious, apprehensive; affecting or acting on the nerves or nervous system.

nervous breakdown *n* a (usu temporary) period of mental illness resulting from severe emotional strain or anxiety.

nest *n* a structure or place where birds, fish, mice, etc, lay eggs or give birth to young; a place where young are nurtured; a swarm or brood; a lair; a cosy place; a set of boxes, tables, etc of different sizes, designed to fit together. * *vi* to make or occupy a nest.

nestle *vti* to rest snugly; to lie snugly, as in a nest; to lie sheltered or half-hidden.

net[1] *n* an openwork material of string, rope, or twine knotted into meshes; a piece of this used to catch fish, to divide a tennis court, etc; a snare. * *vti* (*pt* **netted**) to snare or enclose as with a net; to hit (a ball) into a net or goal.

net[2], **nett** *adj* clear of deductions, allowances or charges. * *n* a net amount, price, weight, profit, etc. * *vt* to clear as a profit.

netball *n* a game for two teams of seven players, in which points are scored by putting a ball through an elevated horizontal ring.

netting *n* netted fabric.

nettle *n* a wild plant with stinging hairs. * *vt* to irritate, annoy.

network *n* an arrangement of intersecting lines; a group of people who co-operate with each other; a chain of interconnected operations, computers, etc; (*radio*, *TV*) a group of broadcasting stations connected to transmit the same programme simultaneously. * *vt* to broadcast on a network; (*comput*) to interconnect systems so that information, software, and peripheral devices, such as printers, can be shared.

neurosis *n* (*pl* **neuroses**) a mental disorder with symptoms such as anxiety and phobia.

neurotic *adj* suffering from neurosis; highly strung; of or acting upon the nerves. * *n* someone with neurosis.

neuter *adj* (*gram*) of gender, neither masculine nor feminine; (*biol*) having no sex organs; having undeveloped sex organs in the adult. * *n* a neuter person, word, plant, or animal. * *vt* to castrate or spay.

neutral *adj* nonaligned; not taking sides with either party in a dispute or war; having no distinctive characteristics; (*colour*) dull; (*chem*) neither acid nor alkaline; (*physics*) having zero charge. * *n* a neutral state, person, or colour; a position of a gear mechanism in which power is not transmitted.—**neutrality** *n*.

never *adv* at no time, not ever; not at all; in no case; (*inf*) surely not.

nevertheless *adv* all the same, notwithstanding; in spite of, however.

new *adj* recently made, discovered, or invented; seen, known, or used for the first time; different, changed; recently grown, fresh; unused; unaccustomed; unfamiliar; recently begun. * *adv* again; newly; recently.

newborn *adj* newly born; reborn.

newcomer *n* a recent arrival.

newly *adv* recently, lately.

new moon *n* the moon when first visible as a crescent.

news *npl* current events; recent happenings; the mass media's coverage of such events; a programme of news on television or radio; information not known before.

newsagent, **newsdealer** *n* a retailer of newspapers, magazines, etc.

newsflash *n* an important news item broadcast separately and often interrupting other programmes.

newspaper *n* a printed periodical containing news published daily or weekly.

New Year's (Day) *n* the first day of a new year; 1 January, a legal holiday in many countries.

next *adj* nearest; immediately preceding or following; adjacent. * *adv* in the nearest time, place, rank, etc; on the first subsequent occasion.

next of kin *n* the nearest relative of a person.

NHS *abbr* = National Health Service.

nib *n* a pen point.

nibble *vti* to take small bites at (food, etc); to bite (at) lightly and intermittently.—**nibbler** *n*.

nice *adj* pleasant, attractive, kind, good, etc; particular, fastidious; delicately sensitive.—**nicely** *adv*.—**niceness** *n*.

niche *n* a shallow recess in a wall for a statue, etc; a place, use, or work for which a person or thing is best suited.

nick *n* a small cut, chip, etc, made on a surface; (*slang*) a police station, prison. * *vt* to make a nick in; to wound superficially; (*sl*) to steal; (*sl*) to arrest.

nickel *n* a silvery-white metallic element used in alloys and plating; a US or Canadian coin worth five cents.

nickname *n* a substitute name, often descriptive, given in fun; a familiar form of a proper name. * *vt* to give as a nickname.

nicotine *n* a poisonous alkaloid present in tobacco.

niece *n* the daughter of a brother or sister.

niggling *adj* finicky, fussy; petty; gnawing, irritating.

night *n* the period of darkness from sunset to sunrise; nightfall; a specified or appointed evening.

nightcap *n* a cap worn in bed; (*inf*) an alcoholic drink taken just before going to bed.

nightclub *n* a place of entertainment for drinking, dancing, etc, at night.

nightdress *n* a loose garment worn in bed by women and girls.

nightfall *n* the close of the day.

nightie, nighty *n* (*inf*) a nightdress, nightgown.

nightingale *n* a songbird celebrated for its musical song at night.

nightlife *n* social entertainment at night, esp in towns.

nightly *adj*, *adv* done or happening by night or every night.

nightmare *n* a frightening dream; any horrible experience.—**nightmarish** *adj*.
night school *n* an educational institution where classes are held in the evening.
night-time *n* night.
night watchman *n* the person who guards a building at night.
nil *n* nothing.
nimble *adj* agile; quick.—**nimbly** *adv*.
nine *adj, n* one more than eight. * *n* the symbol for this (9, IX, ix); the ninth in a series or set; something having nine units as members.
nineteen *adj, n* one more than eighteen. * *n* the symbol for this (19, XIX, xix).—**nineteenth** *adj*.
ninety *adj, n* nine times ten. * *n* the symbol for this (90, XC, xc); (*in pl*) **nineties**; the numbers from 90 to 99; the same numbers in a life or century.—**ninetieth** *adj*.
ninth *adj, n* next after eighth; one of nine equal parts of a thing.
nip[1] *vt* (*pt* **nipped**) to pinch, pinch off; to squeeze between two surfaces; (*dog*) to give a small bite; to prevent the growth of; (*plants*) to have a harmful effect on because of cold. * *n* a pinch; a sharp squeeze; a bite; severe frost or biting coldness.
nip[2] *n* a small drink of spirits. * *vti* to drink in nips.
nipple *n* the small protuberance on a breast or udder through which the milk passes, a teat; a teat-like rubber part on the cap of a baby's bottle; a projection resembling a nipple.
nippy *adj* (**nippier, nippiest**) (*inf*) quick, nimble; (*weather*) frosty; (*motor car*) small but powerful.
nitrogen *n* a gaseous element forming nearly 78 per cent of air.
No, no[1] *abbr* = number.
no[2] *adv* (*used to express denial or disagreement*) not so, not at all, by no amount. * *adj* not any; not a; not one, none; not at all; by no means. * *n* (*pl* **noes, nos**) a denial; a refusal; a negative vote or voter.
nobility *n* nobleness of character, mind, birth, or rank; the class of people of noble birth.
noble *adj* famous or renowned; excellent in quality or character; of high rank or birth. * *n* a person of high rank in society.—**nobleman** *n*.—**nobly** *adv*.
nobody *n* a person of no importance. * *pron* no person.
nod *vti* (*pt* **nodded**) to incline the head quickly, esp in agreement or greeting; to let the head drop, be drowsy; to indicate by a nod; (*with* **off**) (*inf*) to fall asleep. * *n* a quick bob of the head; a sign of assent or command.
noise *n* a sound, esp a loud, disturbing or unpleasant one; a din; unwanted fluctuations in a transmitted signal; (*pl*) conventional sounds, words, etc made in reaction, such as sympathy. * *vt* to make public.
noisy *adj* (**noisier, noisiest**) making much noise; turbulent, clamorous.—**noisily** *adv*.—**noisiness** *n*.
nomad *n* one of a people or tribe who move in search of pasture; a wanderer.—**nomadic** *adj*.
no-man's-land *n* an unclaimed piece of land; a strip of land, esp between armies, borders; an ambiguous area, subject, etc.
nominal *adj* of or like a name; existing in name only; having minimal real worth, token.—**nominally** *adv*.
nominate *vt* to appoint to an office or position; (*candidate*) to propose for election.—**nominator** *n*.
nomination *n* the act or right of nominating; the state of being nominated.
nominee *n* a person who is nominated.
non- *prefix* not, reversing the meaning of a word.
nonchalant *adj* calm; cool, unconcerned, indifferent.—**nonchalance** *n*.—**nonchalantly** *adv*.
noncommittal *adj* not revealing one's opinion.—**noncommittally** *adv*.
nondescript *adj* hard to classify, indeterminate; lacking individual characteristics. * *n* a nondescript person or thing.
none *pron* no one; not anyone; (*pl verb*) not any; no one. * *adv* not at all.
nonentity *n* a person or thing of no significance.
nonflammable *adj* not easily set on fire.
nonplus *vt* (*pt* **nonplussed**) to cause to be so perplexed that one cannot, go, speak, act further.
nonsense *n* words, actions, etc, that are absurd and have no meaning.—*also adj*.—**nonsensical** *adj*.
nonstop *adj* (*train, plane, etc*) not making any intermediate stops; not ceasing. * *adv* without stopping or pausing.
noodle[1] *n* (*often pl*) pasta formed into a strip.
noodle[2] *n* (*inf*) a foolish person; (*sl*) the head.
nook *n* a secluded corner, a retreat; a recess.
noon *n* midday; twelve o'clock in the day.
nor *conj* and not; not either.
norm *n* a standard or model, esp the standard

of achievement of a large group.—**normative** *adj*.

normal *adj* regular; usual; stable mentally. * *n* anything normal; the usual state, amount, etc.—**normalcy** *n*.—**normality** *n*.—**normally** *adv*.

north *n* one of the four points of the compass, opposite the sun at noon, to the right of a person facing the sunset; the direction in which a compass needle points; (*often with cap*) the northern part of one's country or the earth. * *adj* in, of, or towards the north; from the north. * *adv* in or towards the north.

northeast *adj, n* (of) the direction midway between north and east.

northern *adj* of or in the north.

northward *adj* towards or in the north.—*also adv*.—**northwards** *adv*.

northwest *adj, n* (of) the direction midway between north and west.

Norwegian *adj, n* (of or relating to) the language, people, etc, of Norway.

nose *n* the part of the face above the mouth, used for breathing and smelling, having two nostrils; the sense of smell; anything like a nose in shape or position. * *vt* to discover as by smell; to nuzzle; to push (away, etc) with the front forward. * *vi* to sniff for; to inch forwards; to pry.

nose dive *n* a swift downward plunge of an aircraft, nose first; any sudden sharp drop, as in prices.—*also vi*.

nosey *see* **nosy**.

nostalgia *n* yearning for past times or places.

nostalgic *adj* feeling or expressing nostalgia; longing for one's youth.—**nostalgically** *adv*.

nostril *n* one of the two external openings of the nose for breathing and smelling.

nosy *adj* (**nosier, nosiest**) (*inf*) inquisitive, snooping.—**nosily** *adv*.—**nosiness** *n*.—*also* **nosey**.

not *adv expressing* denial, refusal, or negation.

notable *adj* worthy of being noted or remembered; remarkable, eminent. * *n* an eminent or famous person.—**notably** *adv*.

notch *n* a V-shaped cut in an edge or surface; (*inf*) a step, degree; a narrow pass with steep sides. * *vt* to cut notches in.

note *n* a brief summary or record, written down for future reference; a memorandum; a short letter; notice, attention; an explanation or comment on the text of a book; a musical sound of a particular pitch; a sign representing such a sound; a piano or organ key; the vocal sound of a bird. * *vt* to notice, observe; to write down; to annotate.

notebook *n* a book with blank pages for writing in.

noted *adj* celebrated, well-known.

notepaper *n* paper for writing letters.

nothing *n* no thing; not anything; nothingness; a zero; a trifle; a person or thing of no importance or value. * *adv* in no way, not at all.

notice *n* an announcement; a warning; a placard giving information; a short article about a book, play, etc; attention, heed; a formal warning of intention to end an agreement at a certain time. * *vt* to observe; to remark upon. * *vi* to be aware of.

noticeable *adj* easily noticed or seen.—**noticeably** *adv*.

notice board *n* a board on which notices, bulletins, etc, are pinned for public information.

notify *vt* to inform; to report, give notice of.

notion *n* a general idea; an opinion; a whim;.

notorious *adj* widely known, esp unfavourably.—**notoriously** *adv*.

notwithstanding *prep* in spite of. * *adv* nevertheless. * *conj* although.

nougat *n* a chewy sweet consisting of sugar paste with nuts.

nought *n* nothing; a zero.—*also* **naught**.

noun *n* (*gram*) a word that names a person, a living being, an object, action etc; a substantive.

nourish *vt* to feed; to encourage the growth of; to raise, bring up.

nourishing *adj* containing nourishment; health-giving; beneficial.

nourishment *n* food; the act of nourishing.

novel *n* a relatively long prose narrative that is usually fictitious and in the form of a story. * *adj* new and unusual.

novelist *n* a writer of novels.

novelty *n* a novel thing or occurrence; a new or unusual thing; (*pl*) cheap, small objects for sale.

November *n* the eleventh month, having 30 days.

novice *n* a person on probation in a religious order before taking final vows; a beginner.

now *adv* at the present time; by this time; at once; nowadays. * *conj* since; seeing that. * *n* the present time. * *adj* of the present time.

nowadays *adv* in these days; at the present time.

nowhere *adv* not in, at, or to anywhere.

nozzle *n* the spout at the end of a hose, pipe, etc.

nuance *n* a subtle difference in meaning, colour, etc.

nuclear *adj* of or relating to a nucleus; using nuclear energy; having nuclear weapons.

nuclear energy *n* energy released as a result of nuclear fission or fusion.

nuclear fission *n* the splitting of a nucleus of an atom either spontaneously or by bombarding it with particles.

nuclear fusion *n* the combining of two nuclei into a heavier nucleus, releasing energy in the process.

nuclear power *n* electrical or motive power produced by a nuclear reactor.

nuclear reactor *n* a device in which nuclear fission is maintained and harnessed to produce energy.

nucleus *n* (*pl* **nuclei**, **nucleuses**) the central part of core around which something may develop, or be grouped or concentrated; the centrally positively charged portion of an atom; the part of an animal or plant cell containing genetic material.

nude *adj* naked; bare; undressed. * *n* a naked human figure, esp in a work of art; the state of being nude.—**nudity** *n*.

nudge *vt* to touch gently with the elbow to attract attention or urge into action; to push slightly.—*also n*.

nuisance *n* a person or thing that annoys or causes trouble.

null *adj* without legal force; invalid.

nullify *vt* to make null, to cancel out.—**nullification** *n*.

numb *adj* deadened; having no feeling (due to cold, shock, etc). * *vt* to make numb.—**numbness** *n*.

number *n* a symbol or word indicating how many; a numeral identifying a person or thing by its position in a series; a single issue of a magazine; a song or piece of music, esp as an item in a performance; (*inf*) an object singled out; a total of persons or things; (*gram*) the form of a word indicating singular or plural; a telephone number; (*pl*) arithmetic; (*pl*) numerical superiority. * *vti* to count; to give a number to; to include or be included as one of a group; to limit the number of; to total.

numberplate *n* a plate on the front or rear of a motor vehicle that displays its registration number.

numeral *n* a symbol or group of symbols used to express a number (eg two = 2 or II, etc).

numerical, numeric *adj* of or relating to numbers; expressed in numbers.

numerous *adj* many, consisting of many items.

nun *n* a woman belonging to a religious order.

nurse *n* a person trained to care for the sick, injured or aged; a person who looks after another person's child or children. * *vt* to tend, to care for; (*baby*) to feed at the breast; (*hatred*) to foster; to tend with an eye to the future.

nursery *n* a room set aside for children; a place where children may be left in temporary care; a place where young trees and plants are raised for transplanting.

nursery rhyme *n* a short traditional poem or song for children.

nursery school *n* a school for young children, usu under five.

nursery slope *n* a gently inclined slope for novice skiers.

nursing *n* the profession of a nurse.

nursing home *n* an establishment providing care for convalescent, chronically ill, or disabled people.

nut *n* a kernel (sometimes edible) enclosed in a hard shell; a usu metallic threaded block screwed on the end of a bolt; (*sl*) a mad person; (*sl*) a devotee, fan.

nutcracker *n* (usu *pl*) a tool for cracking nuts; a bird with speckled plumage.

nutmeg *n* the aromatic kernel produced by a tree, grated and used as a spice.

nutrition *n* the act or process by which plants and animals take in and assimilate food in their systems; the study of the human diet.—**nutritional** *adj*.

nutritious *adj* efficient as food; health-giving, nourishing.

nylon *n* any of numerous strong, tough, elastic, synthetic materials used esp in plastics and textiles; (*pl*) stockings made of nylon.

O

oaf *n* (*pl* **oafs**) a loutish or stupid person.—**oafish** *adj*.—**oafishness** *n*.

oak *n* a tree with a hard durable wood, having acorns as fruits.

OAP *abbr* = old age pensioner.

oar *n* a pole with a flat blade for rowing a boat; an oarsman.

oasis *n* (*pl* **oases**) a fertile place in a desert; a refuge.

oath *n* a solemn declaration to a god or a higher authority that one will speak the truth or keep a promise; a swear word; a blasphemous expression.

oatmeal *n* ground oats; a porridge of this; a pale greyish-brown colour.
oats *npl* a cereal grass widely cultivated for its edible grain; the seeds.
obedience *n* the condition of being obedient; observance of orders, instructions, etc; respect for authority.
obedient *adj* obeying; compliant; submissive to authority, dutiful.—**obediently** *adv*.
obelisk *n* a four-sided tapering pillar usu with a pyramidal top.
obey *vti* to carry out (orders, instructions); to comply (with); to submit (to).
obituary *n* an announcement of a person's death, often with a short biography.
object *n* something that can be recognized by the senses; a person or thing towards which action, feeling, etc, is directed; a purpose or aim; (*gram*) a noun or part of a sentence governed by a transitive verb or a preposition. * *vti* to state or raise an objection; to oppose; to disapprove.—**objector** *n*.
objection *n* the act of objecting; a ground for, or expression of, disapproval.
objectionable *adj* causing an objection; disagreeable.—**objectionably** *adv*.
objective *adj* relating to an object; not influenced by opinions or feelings; impartial; having an independent existence of its own, real; (*gram*) of, or appropriate to an object governed by a verb or a preposition. * *n* the thing or placed aimed at; (*gram*) the objective case.—**objectively** *adv*.—**objectivity** *n*.
obligation *n* the act of obligating; a moral or legal requirement; a debt; a favour; a commitment to pay a certain amount of money; the amount owed.
obligatory *adj* binding, not optional; compulsory.
oblige *vt* to compel by moral, legal, or physical force; (*person*) to make grateful for some favour; to do a favour for.
obliging *adj* ready to do favours, agreeable.—**obligingly** *adv*.
oblique *adj* slanting, at an angle; diverging from the straight; indirect, allusive. * *n* an oblique line.—**obliquely** *adv*.
obliterate *vt* to wipe out, to erase, to destroy.—**obliteration** *n*.
oblivion *n* a state of forgetting or being forgotten; a state of mental withdrawal.
oblivious *adj* forgetful, unheeding; unaware (of).
oblong *adj* rectangular. * *n* any oblong figure.
obnoxious *adj* objectionable; highly offensive.—**obnoxiously** *adv*.—**obnoxiousness** *n*.
oboe *n* an orchestral woodwind instrument having a mouthpiece with a double reed.—**oboist** *n*.
obscene *adj* indecent, lewd; offensive to a moral or social standard.—**obscenely** *adv*.
obscenity *n* the state or quality of being obscene; an obscene act, word, etc.
obscure *adj* not clear; dim; indistinct; remote, secret; not easily understood; inconspicuous; unimportant, humble. * *vt* to make unclear, to confuse; to hide.—**obscurely** *adv*.
obscurity *n* the state or quality of being obscure; an obscure thing or person.
obsequious *adj* subservient; fawning.—**obsequiously** *adv*.
observance *n* the observing of a rule, duty, law, etc; a ceremony or religious rite.
observant *adj* watchful; attentive, mindful.—**observantly** *adv*.
observation *n* the act or faculty of observing; a comment or remark; careful noting of the symptoms of a patient, movements of a suspect, etc prior to diagnosis, analysis or interpretation.
observatory *n* a building for astronomical observation; an institution whose primary purpose is making such observations.
observe *vt* to notice; to perceive; (*a law, etc*) to keep to or adhere to; to arrive at as a conclusion; to examine scientifically. * *vi* to take notice; to make a comment (on).—**observable** *adj*.
observer *n* a person who observes; a delegate who attends a formal meeting but may not take part; an expert analyst and commentator in a particular field.
obsess *vt* to possess or haunt the mind of; to preoccupy.—**obsessive** *adj, n*.—**obsessively** *adv*.
obsession *n* a fixed idea, often associated with mental illness; a persistent idea or preoccupation; the condition of obsessing or being obsessed.
obsolescent *adj* becoming obsolete, going out of date.—**obsolescence** *n*.
obsolete *adj* disused, out of date.
obstacle *n* anything that hinders something; an obstruction.
obstacle race *n* a race in which the competitors negotiate various obstacles.
obstetrics *n* (*used as sing*) the branch of medicine concerned with the care and treatment of women during pregnancy and childbirth.—**obstetric** *adj*.—**obstetrician** *n*.

obstinate *adj* stubborn, self-willed; intractable; persistent.—**obstinacy** *n*.—**obstinately** *adv*.

obstreperous *adj* unruly, turbulent, noisy.

obstruct *vt* to block with an obstacle; to impede; to prevent, hinder; to keep (light, etc) from.

obstruction *n* that which obstructs; the act or an example of obstructing; a hindrance, obstacle.

obstructive *adj* tending to obstruct; preventing, hindering.—**obstructively** *adv*.

obtain *vt* to get, to acquire, to gain. * *vi* to be prevalent, hold good.—**obtainable** *adj*.

obtrusive *adj* apt to obtrude, pushy; protruding, sticking out.—**obtrusively** *adv*.—**obtrusiveness** *n*.

obtuse *adj* mentally slow; not pointed; dull, stupid; (*geom*) greater than a right angle.—**obtusely** *adv*.—**obtuseness** *n*.

obviate *vt* to make unnecessary; (*danger, difficulty*) to prevent, clear away.

obvious *adj* easily seen or understood; evident.—**obviously** *adv*.—**obviousness** *n*.

occasion *n* a special occurrence or event; a time when something happens; an opportunity; reason or grounds; a subsidiary cause. * *vt* to cause; to bring about.

occasional *adj* infrequent, not continuous; intermittent; produced for an occasion; (*a cause*) incidental.

occupation *n* the act of occupying; the state of being occupied; employment or profession; a pursuit.—**occupational** *adj*.

occupy *vt* to live in; (*room, office*) to take up or fill; (*a position*) to hold; to engross (one's mind); (*city, etc*) to take possession of.—**occupier** *n*.

occur *vi* (*pt* **occurred**) to happen; to exist; to come into the mind of.

occurrence *n* a happening, an incident, an event; the act or fact of occurring.

ocean *n* a large stretch of sea, esp one of the earth's five oceans; a huge quantity or expanse.

ochre, ocher (*US*) *n* a yellow to orange-coloured clay used as a pigment.

o'clock *adv* indicating the hour; indicating a relative direction or position, twelve o'clock being directly ahead or above.

octave *n* (*mus*) the eighth full tone above or below a given tone, the interval of eight degrees between a tone and either of its octaves, or the series of tones within this interval.

October *n* the tenth month of the year, having 31 days.

octopus *n* (*pl* **octopuses**) a mollusc having a soft body and eight tentacles covered with suckers.

odd *adj* eccentric; peculiar; occasional; not divisible by two; with the other of the pair missing; extra or left over. * *npl* probability; balance of advantage in favour of one against another; excess of one number over another, esp in betting; likelihood; disagreement; strife; miscellaneous articles, scraps.—**oddly** *adv*.—**oddness** *n*.

oddity *n* the state of being odd; an odd thing or person; peculiarity.

oddment *n* an odd piece left over, esp of fabric.

ode *n* a lyric poem marked by lofty feeling and dignified style.

odious *adj* causing hatred or offence; disgusting.—**odiously** *adv*.—**odiousness** *n*.

odour, odor (*US*) *n* smell; scent; aroma; a characteristic or predominant quality.

odourless, odorless (*US*) *adj* without odour.

of *prep* from; belonging or relating to; concerning; among; by; during; owing to.

off *adv* away, from; detached, gone; unavailable; disconnected; out of condition; entirely. * *prep* away from; not on. * *adj* distant; no longer operating; cancelled; (*food or drink*) having gone bad; on the right-hand side; (*runners, etc*) having started a race.

offal *n* the entrails of an animal eaten as food.

off-colour *adj* unwell; risqué.

offence, offense (*US*) *n* an illegal action, crime; a sin; an affront, insult; a cause of displeasure or anger.

offend *vt* to affront, displease; to insult. * *vi* to break a law.—**offender** *n*.

offensive *adj* causing offence; repulsive, disagreeable; insulting; aggressive. * *n* an attack; a forceful campaign for a cause, etc.—**offensively** *adv*.—**offensiveness** *n*.

offer *vt* to present for acceptance or rejection; to show willingness (to do something); to present for consideration; to bid; (*a prayer*) to say. * *vi* to present itself; to declare oneself willing. * *n* something offered; a bid or proposal.

offering *n* a gift, present; a sacrifice.

offhand *adv* impromptu; without thinking. * *adj* inconsiderate; curt, brusque; unceremonious.

office *n* a room or building where business is carried out; the people there; (*with cap*) the location, staff, of authority of a Government department, etc; a task or function; a position of authority; a duty; a religious ceremony, rite.

officer *n* an official; a person holding a position of authority in a government, business, club, military services, etc; a policeman.

official *adj* of an office or its tenure; properly authorized; formal. * *n* a person who holds a public office.—**officially** *adv*.

officious *adj* interfering, meddlesome; offering unwanted advice.—**officiously** *adv*.—**officiousness** *n*.

offing *n* the near or foreseeable future.

off-licence *n* a licence to sell alcohol for consumption off the premises; a place so licensed.

off-peak *adj* denoting use of a service, etc, in a period of lesser demand.

offset *vt* (*pr p* **offsetting**, *pt* **offset**) to compensate for, counterbalance. * *n* compensation; a method of printing in which an image is transferred from a plate to a rubber surface and then to paper; a sloping ledge on the face of a wall.

offshore *adv* at sea some distance from the shore.

offside *adj*, *adv* illegally in advance of the ball.

offspring *n* a child, progeny; a result.

offstage *adj*, *adv* out of sight of the audience; behind the scenes.

often *adv* many times, frequently.

ogle *vti* to gape at; to make eyes at; to look at lustfully.

oil *n* a greasy, combustible liquid substance obtained from animal, vegetable, or mineral matter; petroleum; an oil painting; (*pl*) paint mixed by grinding a pigment in oil. * *vt* to smear with oil, lubricate.

oilcan *n* a container with a long spout for releasing oil for lubricating in individual drops.

oilfield *n* an area on land or under the sea that produces petroleum.

oil painting *n* a painting in oils; the art of painting in oils; (*inf*) a good-looking person.

oilskin *n* fabric made waterproof by treatment with oil; a waterproof garment of oilskin or a plastic-coated fabric.

oil slick *n* a mass of oil floating on the surface of water.

oil well *n* a well from which petroleum is extracted.

oily *adj* (**oilier**, **oiliest**) like or covered with oil; greasy; too suave or smooth, unctuous.—**oiliness** *n*.

ointment *n* a fatty substance used on the skin for healing or cosmetic purposes; a salve.

OK, **okay** *adj*, *adv* (*inf*) all right; correct(ly). * *n* (*pl* **OK's, okays**) approval.

old *adj* aged; elderly, not young; having lived or existed for a long time; long used, not new; former; of the past, not modern; experienced; worn out; of long standing.

old-fashioned *adj* out of date; in a fashion of an older time.

olive *n* an evergreen tree cultivated for its edible hard-stoned fruit and oil; its fruit; a yellow-green colour. * *adj* of a yellow-green colour.

olive oil *n* an edible yellow oil obtained from the fruit of the olive by pressing.

Olympic Games, Olympics *n* (*used as sing or pl*) an ancient athletic contest revived in 1896 as an international meeting held every four years in a different country.

omelette, **omelet** (*US*) *n* eggs beaten and cooked flat in a pan.

omen *n* a sign or warning of impending happiness or disaster.

ominous *adj* relating to an omen; foreboding evil; threatening.—**ominously** *adv*.

omission *n* something that has been left out or neglected; the act of omitting.

omit *vt* (*pt* **omitted**) to leave out; to neglect to do, leave undone.

omni- *prefix* all; universally.

on *prep* in contact with the upper surface of; supported by, attached to, or covering; directed toward; at the time of; concerning, about; using as a basis, condition or principle; immediately after; (*sl*) using; addicted to. * *adv* (so as to be) covering or in contact with something; forward; (*device*) switched on; continuously in progress; due to take place; (*actor*) on stage; on duty. * *adj* (*cricket*) designating the part of the field on the batsman's side in front of the wicket. * *n* (*cricket*) the on side.

once *adv* on one occasion only; formerly; at some time. * *conj* as soon as. * *n* one time.

oncoming *adj* approaching.

one *adj* single; undivided, united; the same; a certain unspecified (time, etc). * *n* the first and lowest cardinal number; an individual thing or person; (*inf*) a drink; (*inf*) a joke. * *pron* an indefinite person, used to apply to many people; someone.

oneself *pron reflex form of* one.

one-way *adj* (*traffic*) restricted to one direction; requiring no reciprocal action or obligation.

ongoing *adj* progressing, continuing.
onion *n* an edible bulb with a pungent taste and odour.
onlooker *n* a spectator.
only *adj* alone of its kind; single, sole. * *adv* solely, merely; just; not more than. * *conj* except that, but.
onset *n* a beginning; an assault, attack.
onslaught *n* a fierce attack.
onto *prep* to a position on.
onus *n* responsibility, duty; burden.
onward *adj* advancing, forward. * *adv* onwards.
onwards *adv* to the front, ahead, forward.
onyx *n* a limestone similar to marble with layers of colour.
ooze *vti* to flow or leak out slowly; to seep; to exude. * *n* soft mud or slime.
opal *n* a white or bluish stone with a play of iridescent colours.
opaque *adj* not letting light through; neither transparent nor translucent.—**opaquely** *adv*.—**opaqueness** *n*.
open *adj* not closed; accessible; uncovered, unprotected; not fenced; free from trees; spread out, unfolded; public; lacking reserve; (*a person*) forthcoming; generous; readily understood; liable (to); unrestricted; (*syllable*) ending with a vowel; (*consonant*) made without stopping the stream of breath. * *vti* to make or become accessible; to unfasten; to begin; to expand, unfold; to come into view. * *n* a wide space; (*sport*) a competition that any player can enter.—**openness** *n*.
opening *n* a gap, aperture; a beginning; a chance; a job opportunity. * *adj* initial.
openly *adv* frankly; publicly.
open-minded *adj* unprejudiced.—**open-mindedness** *n*.
opera *n* a dramatic work represented through music and song; plural form of **opus**.
operate *vi* to work, to function; to produce a desired effect; to carry out a surgical operation. * *vt* (*a machine*) to work or control; to carry on, run.
operatic *adj* of or relating to opera; exaggerated, overacting.
operation *n* a method of operating; a procedure; a military action; a surgical procedure.
operational *adj* of or relating to an operation; functioning; ready for use; involved in military activity.—**operationally** *adv*.
operative *adj* functioning; in force, effective; of, by surgery. * *n* a mechanic; a secret agent; a private detective.
operator *n* a person who operates or works a machine, esp a telephone switchboard; a person who owns or runs a business; a person who manipulates.
operetta *n* a short or light opera.
opinion *n* a belief that is not based on proof; judgment; estimation, evaluation; a formal expert judgment; professional advice.
opinionated *adj* unduly confident in one's opinions, dogmatic.
opium *n* a narcotic drug produced from an annual Eurasian poppy.
opponent *n* a person who opposes another; an adversary, antagonist. * *adj* opposing.
opportune *adj* well-timed; convenient.—**opportunely** *adv*.
opportunist *n* a person who forms or adapts his or her views or principles to benefit from opportunities; to seize opportunities as they may arise.—**opportunism** *n*.
opportunity *n* chance; a favourable combination of circumstances.
oppose *vt* to put in front of or in the way of; to place in opposition; to resist; to fight against; to balance against.—**opposer** *n*.
opposite *adj* placed on opposed sides of; face to face; diametrically different; contrary. * *n* a person or thing that is opposite; an antithesis. * *prep*, *adv* across from.
opposition *n* the act of opposing or the condition of being opposed; resistance; antithesis; hostility; a political party opposing the government; (*astron*) the diametrically opposite position of two heavenly bodies, when 180 degrees apart.
oppress *vt* to treat unjustly; to subjugate; to weigh down in the mind.—**oppressor** *n*.
oppression *n* the act of oppressing; the state of being oppressed; persecution; physical or mental distress.
oppressive *adj* tyrannical; burdensome; (*weather*) sultry, close.—**oppressively** *adv*.—**oppressiveness** *n*.
opt *vi* to choose or to exercise an option.
optical *adj* of or relating to the eye or light; optic; aiding or correcting vision; visual.—**optically** *adv*.
optician *n* a person who makes or sells optical aids.
optimism *n* a tendency to take the most cheerful view of things; hopefulness; the belief that good must ultimately prevail.—**optimist** *n*.—**optimistic** *adj*.—**optimistically** *adv*.
optimum *n* the best, most favourable condition.—*also adj*.

option *n* the act of choosing; the power to choose; a choice; the right to buy, sell or lease at a fixed price within a specified time.

optional *adj* left to choice; not compulsory.—**optionally** *adv*.

opulent *adj* wealthy; luxuriant.—**opulence** *n*.

opus (*pl* **opuses, opera**) an artistic or literary work; a musical composition.

or *conj denoting* an alternative; the last in a series of choices.

oracle *n* a place in ancient Greece where a deity was consulted; the response given (often ambiguous); a wise adviser; sage advice.—**oracular** *adj*.

oral *adj* of the mouth; (*drugs*) taken by mouth; spoken, not written. * *n* a spoken examination.—**orally** *adv*.

orange *n* a round, reddish-yellow, juicy, edible citrus fruit; the tree bearing it; its colour. * *adj* orange-coloured.

oration *n* a formal or public speech.

orator *n* an eloquent public speaker.

oratorio *n* (*pl* **oratorios**) a sacred story set to music for voices and instruments.

orb *n* a sphere or globe; an ornamental sphere surmounted by a cross, esp as carried by a sovereign at a coronation.

orbit *n* (*astron*) a curved path along which a planet or satellite moves; a field of action or influence; the eye socket; (*physics*) the path of an electron around the nucleus of an atom. * *vti* to put (a satellite, etc) into orbit; to circle round.—**orbital** *adj*.

orchard *n* an area of land planted with fruit trees.

orchestra *n* a group of musicians playing together under a conductor; their instruments; the space (or pit) in a theatre where they sit; the stalls of a theatre.—**orchestral** *adj*.

orchid *n* a plant with unusually shaped flowers in brilliant colours comprising three petals of uneven size.

ordain *vti* to confer holy orders upon; to appoint; to decree; to order, to command.

ordeal *n* a severe trial or test; an exacting experience.

order *n* arrangement; method; relative position; sequence; an undisturbed condition; tidiness; rules of procedure; an efficient state; a class, group, or sort; a religious fraternity; a style of architecture; an honour or decoration; an instruction or command; a rule or regulation; a state or condition, esp with regard to functioning; a request to supply something; the goods supplied; (*zool*) divisions between class and family or genus. * *vti* to put or keep (things) in order; to arrange; to command; to request (something) to be supplied.

orderly *adj* in good order; well-behaved; methodical. * *n* a hospital attendant; a soldier attending an officer.—**orderliness** *n*.

ordinal *adj* showing position in a series. * *n* an ordinal number.

ordinary *adj* normal, usual; common; plain, unexceptional.—**ordinarily** *adv*.

ordination *n* the act of ordaining or being ordained; admission to the ministry.

ore *n* a substance from which minerals can be extracted.

organ *n* a usu large and complex musical wind instrument with pipes, stops, and a keyboard; a part of an animal or plant that performs a vital or natural function; the means by which anything is done; a medium of information or opinion, a periodical.

organic *adj* of or relating to bodily organs; (disease) affecting a bodily organ; of, or derived from, living organisms; systematically arranged; structural; (*chem*) of the class of compounds that are formed from carbon; (vegetables, etc) grown without the use of artificial fertilizers or pesticides.—**organically** *adv*.

organism *n* an animal or plant, any living thing; an organized body.

organist *n* a person who plays an organ.

organization *n* the act or process of organizing; the state of being organized; arrangement, structure; an organized body or association.

organize *vt* to arrange in an orderly way; to establish; to institute; to persuade to join a cause, group, etc; to arrange for.—**organizer** *n*.

orgasm *n* the climax of sexual excitement.—**orgasmic** *adj*.

orgy *n* a wild party or gathering of people, with excessive drinking and indiscriminate sexual activity; over-indulgence in any activity.

Orient *n* the East, or Asia, esp the Far East.

orient, orientate *vti* to adjust (oneself) to a particular situation; to arrange in a direction, esp in relation to the points of the compass; to face or turn in a particular direction.

oriental *adj* of the Orient, its people or languages.

orifice *n* an opening or mouth of a cavity.

origin *n* the source or beginning of anything; ancestry or parentage.

original *adj* relating to the origin or beginning; earliest, primitive; novel; unusual; inventive, creative. * *n* an original work, as of art or literature; something from which copies are made; a creative person; an eccentric.—**originality** *n*.—**originally** *adv*.

originate *vti* to initiate or begin; to bring or come into being.—**origination** *n*.—**originator** *n*.

ornament *n* anything that enhances the appearance of a person or thing; a small decorative object. * *vt* to adorn, to decorate with ornaments.

ornamental *adj* serving as an ornament; decorative, not useful.—**ornamentally** *adv*.

ornate *adj* richly adorned; (*style*) highly elaborate.—**ornately** *adv*.—**ornateness** *n*.

ornithology *n* the study of birds.—**ornithological** *adj*.—**ornithologist** *n*.

orphan *n* a child whose parents are dead. * *vt* to cause to become an orphan.—*also adj*.

orphanage *n* a residential institution for the care of orphans.

orthodox *adj* conforming with established behaviour or opinions; not heretical; generally accepted, conventional; (*with cap*) of or relating to a conservative political or religious group.

orthopaedics, **orthopedics** (*US*) *n* the study and surgical treatment of bone and joint disorders.—**orthopaedic** *adj*.—**orthopaedist** *n*.

oscillate *vi* to swing back and forth as a pendulum; to waver, vacillate between extremes of opinion, etc.—**oscillation** *n*.

ostensible *adj* apparent; seeming; pretended.—**ostensibly** *adv*.

ostentation *n* a showy, pretentious display.—**ostentatious** *adj*.—**ostentatiously** *adv*.

osteopathy *n* the treatment of disease by manipulation of the bones and muscles, often as an adjunct to medical and surgical measures.—**osteopath** *n*.

ostracize *vt* to exclude, banish from a group, society, etc.—**ostracism** *n*.

ostrich *n* a large, flightless, swift-running African bird.

other *adj* second; remaining; different; additional. * *pron* the other one; some other one.

otherwise *adv* if not, or else; differently.

otter *n* a fish-eating mammal with smooth fur and a flat tail.

ought *aux vb* expressing obligation or duty; to be bound, to be obliged (to).

ounce *n* a unit of weight, equal to one sixteenth of a pound or 28.34 grams; one sixteenth of a pint, one fluid ounce.

our *poss adj*, *pron* relating or belonging to us.

ours *pron* belonging to us.

ourselves *pron* emphatic and reflexive form of we.

oust *vt* to eject, expel, esp by underhand means; to remove forcibly.

out *adv* not in; outside; in the open air; to the full extent; beyond bounds; no longer holding office; ruled out, no longer considered; loudly and clearly; no longer included (in a game, fashion, etc); in error; on strike; at an end; extinguished; into the open; published; revealed; (*radio conversation*) transmission ends. * *prep* out of; out through; outside. * *adj* external; outward. * *n* an exit; means of escape.

outboard *adj* (*engine*) outside a ship, etc. * *n* an engine attached to the outside of a boat.

outbreak *n* a sudden eruption (of disease, strife, etc).

outburst *n* a bursting out; a spurt; an explosion of anger, etc.

outcast *n* a person who is rejected by society.

outclass *vt* to surpass or excel greatly.

outcome *n* the result, consequence.

outcry *n* protest; uproar.

outdo *vt* (*pt* **outdid**, *pp* **outdone**) to surpass, to do more than, to excel.

outdoor *adj* existing, taking place, or used in the open air.

outdoors *adv* in or into the open air; out of doors. * *n* the open air, outside world.

outer *adj* further out or away.

outer space *n* any region of space beyond the earth's atmosphere.

outfit *n* the equipment used in an activity; clothes worn together, an ensemble; a group of people associated in an activity. * *vt* (*pt* **outfitted**) to provide with an outfit or equipment.

outfitter *n* a supplier of equipment or clothes.

outgoing *adj* departing; retiring; sociable, forthcoming. * *n* an outlay; (*pl*) expenditure.

outing *n* a pleasure trip; an excursion.

outlandish *adj* unconventional; strange; fantastic.

outlaw *vt* to declare illegal. * *n* an outlawed person; a habitual or notorious criminal.

outlay *n* a spending (of money); expenditure.

outlet *n* an opening or release; a means of expression; a market for goods or services.

outline *n* a profile; a general indication; a rough sketch or draft.—*also vt*.

outlive *vt* to live longer than, outlast; to live

through; to survive.
outlook *n* mental attitude; view; prospect.
outlying *adj* detached; remote, distant.
outmoded *adj* old-fashioned.
outpatient *n* a person treated at, but not resident in, a hospital.
outpost *n* (*mil*) a post or detachment at a distance from a main force.
output *n* the quantity (of goods, etc) produced, esp over a given period; information delivered by a computer, esp to a printer; (*elect*) the useful voltage, current, or power delivered.—*also vt*.
outrage *n* an extremely vicious or violent act; a grave insult or offence; great anger, etc, aroused by this.—*also vt*.—**outrageous** *adj*.
outright *adj* complete, downright, direct. * *adv* at once; without restrictions.
outset *n* the start, beginning.
outside *n* the outer part or surface, the exterior. * *adj* outer; outdoor; (*chance*, *etc*) slight. * *adv* on or to the outside. * *prep* on or to the exterior of; beyond.
outsider *n* a person or thing not included in a set, group, etc, a non-member; a contestant not thought to have a chance in a race.
outsize *adj* of a larger than usual size.
outskirts *npl* districts remote from the centre, as of a city.
outspoken *adj* candid in speech, frank, blunt.
outstanding *adj* excellent; distinguished, prominent; unpaid; unresolved, still to be done.
outward *adj* directed towards the outside; external; clearly apparent. * *adv* outwards.
outwardly *adv* externally.
outweigh *vt* to count for more than, to exceed in value, weight, or importance.
outwit *vt* (*pt* **outwitted**) to get the better of, defeat, by wit or cunning.
oval *adj* egg-shaped; elliptical. * *n* anything oval.
ovary *n* one of the two female reproductive organs producing eggs.—**ovarian** *adj*.
ovation *n* enthusiastic applause or public welcome.
oven *n* an enclosed, heated compartment for baking or drying.
over *prep* higher than; on top of; across; to the other side of; above; more than; concerning. * *adv* above; across; in every part; completed; from beginning to end; up and down; in addition; too. * *adj* upper; excessive; surplus; finished; remaining. * *n* (*cricket*) the number of balls bowled before changing ends.
over- *prefix* in excess, too much; above.
overact *vti* to act in an exaggerated manner, to overdo a part.
overall *adj* including everything. * *adv* as a whole; generally. * *n* a loose protective garment; (*pl*) a one-piece protective garment covering body and legs.
overawe *vt* to restrain by awe, to daunt.
overbalance *vti* to fall over; to upset; to outweigh. * *n* a surplus.
overbearing *adj* domineering; overriding.
overboard *adv* over the side of a ship, etc; (*inf*) to extremes of enthusiasm.
overcast *adj* clouded over.
overcharge *vt* (*battery*) to overload; to fill to excess; to demand too high a price (from). * *n* an excessive or exorbitant charge or load.
overcoat *n* a warm, heavy topcoat.
overcome *vti* (*pt* **overcame,** *pp* **overcome**) to get the better of, to prevail; to render helpless or powerless, as by tears, laughter, emotion, etc; to be victorious; to surmount obstacles, etc.
overdo *vt* (*pt* **overdid,** *pp* **overdone**) to do to excess; to overact; to cook (food) too much.—**overdone** *adj*.
overdose *n* an excessive dose —*also vti*.
overdraft *n* an overdrawing, an amount overdrawn, at a bank.
overdraw *vti* (*pt* **overdrew,** *pp* **overdrawn**) to draw in excess of a credit balance; to exaggerate in describing; to make an overdraft.
overestimate *vt* to set too high an estimate on or for.—*also n*.
overflow *vti* (*pp* **overflown**) to flow over, to flood; to exceed the bounds (of); to abound (with emotion, etc). * *n* that which overflows; surplus, excess; an outlet for surplus water, etc.
overgrown *adj* grown beyond the normal size; rank; ungainly.
overhaul *vt* to examine for, or make, repairs; to overtake.—*also n*.
overhead *adj*, *adv* above the head; in the sky. * *n* (often *pl*) the general, continuing costs of a business, as of rent, light, etc.
overhear *vt* (*pt* **overheard**) to hear without the knowledge of the speaker.
overjoyed *adj* highly delighted.
overland *adj*, *adv* by, on, or across land.
overlap *vt* (*pt* **overlapped**) to extend over (a thing or each other) so as to coincide in part.—*also n*.
overload *vt* to put too great a burden on; (*elect*) to charge with too much current.

overlook *vt* to fail to notice; to look at from above; to excuse.
overnight *adv* for the night; in the course of the night; suddenly. * *adj* done in the night; lasting the night; sudden.
overpass *n* a road crossing another road, path, etc, at a higher level; the upper level of such a crossing.
overpower *vt* to overcome by superior force, to subdue; to overwhelm.
overpowering *adj* overwhelming; compelling; unbearable.
overrate *vt* to value or assess too highly.
override *vt* (*pt* **overrode**, *pp* **overridden**) to ride over; to nullify; to prevail.
overrule *vt* to set aside by higher authority; to prevail over.
overseas *adj*, *adv* across or beyond the sea; abroad.
overshadow *vt* to throw a shadow over; to appear more prominent or important than.
overshoot *vt* (*pt* **overshot**) to shoot or send beyond (a target, etc); (*aircraft*) to fly or taxi beyond the end of a runway when landing or taking off.—*also n.*
oversight *n* a careless mistake or omission; supervision.
oversleep *vi* (*pt* **overslept**) to sleep beyond the intended time.
overspill *vi* (*pt* **overspilt** *or* **overspilled**) to spill over, overflow. * *n* that which overspills; excess.—*also adj*.
overt *adj* openly done, unconcealed; (*law*) done with evident intent, deliberate.—**overtly** *adv*.
overtake *vt* (*pt* **overtook**, *pp* **overtaken**) to catch up with and pass; to come upon suddenly.
overthrow *vt* (*pt* **overthrew**, *pp* **overthrown**) to throw over, overturn; (*government*, *etc*) to bring down by force.—*also n*.
overtime *adv* beyond regular working hours. * *n* extra time worked; payment for this.
overtone *n* an additional subtle meaning; an implicit quality; (*mus*) a harmonic; the colour of light reflected (as by a paint).
overture *n* an initiating of negotiations; a formal offer, proposal; (*mus*) an instrumental introduction to an opera, etc.
overturn *vti* to upset, turn over; to overthrow.
overweight *adj* weighing more than the proper amount. * *n* excess weight.
overwhelm *vt* to overcome totally; to submerge; to crush; to overpower with emotion.
overwhelming *adj* irresistible; uncontrollable; vast; vastly superior; extreme.
overwork *vti* to work or use too hard or too long.
overwrought *adj* over-excited; too elaborate.
owe *vti* to be in debt; to be obliged to pay; to feel the need to give, do, etc, as because of gratitude.
owing *adj* due, to be paid; owed; (*with* **to**) because of, on account of.
owl *n* a nocturnal bird of prey with a large head and eyes; a person of nocturnal habits, solemn appearance, etc.—**owlish** *adj*.
own[1] *vti* to possess; to acknowledge, admit; to confess to.
own[2] *adj* belonging to oneself or itself, often used reflexively (*my own*, *their own*).
owner *n* one who owns, a possessor, a proprietor.—**ownership** *n*.
ox *n* (*pl* **oxen**) a cud-chewing mammal of the cattle family; a castrated bull.
oxide *n* a compound of oxygen with another element.
oxtail *n* the tail of an ox, esp skinned and used for stews, soups, etc.
oxygen *n* a colourless, odourless, tasteless, highly reactive gaseous element forming part of air, water, etc, and essential to life and combustion.
oxygen mask *n* an apparatus worn over the nose and mouth through which oxygen passes from a storage tank.
oxygen tent *n* a canopy over a hospital bed, etc, within which a supply of oxygen is maintained.
oyster *n* an edible marine bivalve shellfish.
oz *abbr* = ounce(s).
ozone *n* a condensed form of oxygen; (*inf*) bracing seaside air.
ozone layer *n* a layer of ozone in the upper atmosphere that absorbs ultraviolet rays from the sun.

P

p *abbr* = page; penny, pence.
p.a. *abbr* = per annum.
pace *n* a single step; the measure of a single stride; speed of movement. * *vti* to measure by paces; to walk up and down; to determine the pace in a race; to walk with regular steps.—**pacer** *n*.
pacemaker *n* a person who sets the pace in a race; an electronic device inserted in the

heart, used to regulate heartbeat.

pacify *vt* to soothe; to calm; to restore peace to.—**pacification** *n*.

pack *n* a load or bundle (esp one carried on the back); a set of playing cards; a group or mass; a number of wild animals living together; an organized troop (as of Cub Scouts); a compact mass (as of snow); a small package used as a container for goods for sale. * *vt* to put together in a bundle or pack; (*suitcase*) to fill; to crowd; to press tightly so as to prevent leakage; to carry in a pack; to send (off); (*sl: gun, etc*) to carry; (*sl: punch*) to deliver with force. * *vi* (*snow, ice*) to form into a hard mass; to assemble one's belongings in suitcases or boxes. * *adj* used for carrying packs, loads, etc.—**packer** *n*.

package *n* a parcel, a wrapped bundle; several items, arrangements, etc offered as a unit. * *vt* to make a parcel of; to group together several items, etc.

packet *n* a small box or package; (*sl*) a considerable sum; a vessel carrying mail, etc, between one port and another.

pack ice *n* sea ice formed into a mass by the crushing together of floes, etc.

packing *n* material for protecting packed goods or for making airtight or watertight; the act of filling a suitcase, box, etc.

pact *n* an agreement or treaty.

pad[1] *n* the dull sound of a footstep. * *vi* (*pt* **padded**) to walk, esp with a soft step.

pad[2] *n* a piece of a soft material or stuffing; several sheets of paper glued together at one edge; the cushioned thickening of an animal's sole; a piece of folded absorbent material used as a surgical dressing; a flat concrete surface; (*sl*) one's own home or room. * *vt* (*pt* **padded**) to stuff with soft material; to fill with irrelevant information.

padding *n* stuffing; anything unimportant or false added to achieve length or amount.

paddle[1] *vi* to wade about or play in shallow water.

paddle[2] *n* a short oar with a wide blade at one or both ends; a implement shaped like this, used to hit, beat or stir. * *vti* (*canoe, etc*) to propel by a paddle; to beat as with a paddle; to spank.

paddock *n* an enclosed field in which horses are exercised.

paddy *n* threshed unmilled rice; a rice field.

padlock *n* a detachable lock used to fasten doors etc. * *vt* to secure with a padlock.

padre *n* (*sl*) a priest or chaplain.

paediatrics, pediatrics (*US*) *n* the branch of medicine dealing with children and their diseases.—**paediatric** *adj*.—**paediatrician** *n*.

pagan *n* a heathen; a person who has no religion.—*also adj*.—**paganism** *n*.

page[1] *n* a boy attendant at a formal function (as a wedding); a uniformed boy employed to run errands. * *vt* to summon by messenger, loudspeaker, etc.

page[2] *n* a sheet of paper in a book, newspaper etc. * *vt* (*a book*) to number the pages of.—*also* **paginate**.

pageant *n* a spectacular procession or parade; representation in costume of historical events; a mere show.—*also adj*.—**pageantry** *n*.

pageboy *n* a page; a medium-length hairstyle with ends of hair turned under.

paid *see* **pay**.

pail *n* a bucket.

pain *n* physical or mental suffering; hurting; (*pl*) trouble, exertion. * *vt* to cause distress to.

pained *adj* hurt, offended.

painful *adj* giving pain, distressing.—**painfully** *adv*.—**painfulness** *n*.

painkiller *n* (*inf*) a medicine that relieves pain.

painless *adj* without pain.—**painlessly** *adv*.

painstaking *adj* very careful, laborious.—**painstakingly** *adv*.

paint *vt* (*a picture*) to make using oil pigments, etc; to depict with paints; to cover or decorate with paint; to describe. * *vi* to make a picture. * *n* a colouring pigment; a dried coat of paint.

painter[1] *n* a person who paints, esp an artist.

painter[2] *n* a bow rope for tying up a boat.

painting *n* the act or art of applying paint; a painted picture.

pair *n* a set of two things that are equal, suited, or used together; any two persons or animals regarded as a unit. * *vti* to form a pair (of); to mate.

pal *n* a close friend.—**pally** *adj*.

palace *n* the official residence of a sovereign, president or bishop; a large stately house or public building.

palatable *adj* (*taste*) pleasant; (*fig*) pleasant or acceptable.—**palatably** *adv*.

palate *n* the roof of the mouth; taste; mental relish.

pale[1] *n* a fence stake; a boundary; (*her*) a vertical stripe in the middle of a shield.

pale[2] *adj* (*complexion*) with less colour than usual; (*colour, light*) faint, wan, dim. * *vti* to make or become pale.—**paleness** *n*.

palette *n* a small, wooden board on which coloured paints are mixed.

pall[1] *n* a heavy cloth over a coffin; (*of smoke*) a mantle.
pall[2] *vi* to become boring; to become satiated.
pallet[1] *n* a portable platform for lifting and stacking goods.
pallet[2] *n* a straw bed.
pallid *adj* wan, pale.—**pallidness** *n*.
palm[1] *n* the underside of the hand between fingers and wrist. * *vt* to conceal in or touch with the palm; (*with* **off**) to pass off by fraud, foist.
palm[2] *n* a tropical branchless tree with fan-shaped leaves; a symbol of victory.
Palm Sunday *n* the Sunday before Easter.
palpable *adj* tangible; easily perceived, obvious.—**palpably** *adj*.
paltry *adj* almost worthless; trifling.—**paltrily** *adv*.—**paltriness** *n*.
pamper *vt* to overindulge; to coddle, spoil.
pamphlet *n* a thin, unbound booklet; a brochure.
pan[1] *n* a wide metal container, a saucepan; (*of scales*) a tray; the bowl of a lavatory. * *vi* (*pt* **panned**) (*with* **out**) (*inf*) to turn out, esp to turn out well; to succeed.
pan[2] *vt* (*pt* **panned**) to wash gold-bearing gravel in a pan; (*inf*) to disparage, find fault with.
pan[3] *vti* (*pt* **panned**) (*film camera*) to move horizontally to follow an object or provide a panoramic view.—*also n*.
panacea *n* a cure-all, universal remedy.
pancake *n* a round, thin cake made from batter and cooked on a griddle; a thing shaped thus. * *vi* (*aircraft*) to descend vertically in a level position.
panda *n* a large black and white bear-like herbivore.
pandemonium *n* uproar; chaos.
pander *n* a pimp. * *vi* (*somebody's desires or weaknesses*) to gratify.
pane *n* a sheet of glass in a frame of a window, door, etc.—**paned** *adj*.
panel *n* a usu rectangular section or division forming part of a wall, door, etc; a board for instruments or controls; a lengthwise strip in a skirt, etc; a group of selected persons for judging, discussing, etc. * *vt* (*pt* **panelled**) to decorate with panels.
panelling, paneling (*US*) *n* panels collectively; sheets of wood, plastic, etc, used for panels.
pang *n* a sudden sharp pain or feeling.
panic *n* a sudden overpowering fright or terror.—*also adj*. * *vti* (*pt* **panicked**) to affect or be affected with panic.—**panicky** *adj*.
pannier *n* a large basket for carrying loads on the back of an animal or the shoulders of a person; a bag or case slung over the rear wheel of a bicycle or motorcycle.
panorama *n* a complete view in all directions; a comprehensive presentation of a subject; a constantly changing scene.—**panoramic** *adj*.
pansy *n* a garden flower of the violet family, with velvety petals; (*sl*) an effeminate boy or man.
pant *vi* to breathe noisily, gasp; to yearn (for or after something). * *vt* to speak while gasping.
panther *n* a leopard, esp black; a cougar or jaguar.
panties *npl* (*inf*) short underpants.
pantomime *n* a Christmas theatrical entertainment with music and jokes; a drama without words, using only actions and gestures; mime. * *vti* to mime.
pantry *n* a small room or cupboard for storing cooking ingredients and utensils, etc.
pants *npl* trousers; underpants.
panty hose *n* tights.
papacy *n* the office or authority of the pope; papal system of government.
papal *adj* of the pope or the papacy.
paper *n* the thin, flexible material made from pulped rags, wood, etc which is used to write on, wrap in, or cover walls; a single sheet of this; an official document; a newspaper; an essay or lecture; a set of examination questions; (*pl*) personal documents. * *adj* like or made of paper. * *vt* to cover with wallpaper.—**papery** *adj*.
paperback *n* a book bound in a flexible paper cover.
paperweight *n* a small heavy object for keeping papers in place.
paperwork *n* clerical work of any kind.
papier-mâché *n* a substance made of paper pulp mixed with size, glue, etc, and moulded into various objects when moist.
paprika *n* a mild red condiment ground from the fruit of certain peppers.
par *n* the standard or normal level; the established value of a currency in foreign-exchange rates; the face value of stocks, shares, etc; (*golf*) the score for a hole by a perfect player; equality.
parable *n* a short story using everyday events to illustrate a religious or moral point.
parachute *n* a fabric umbrella-like canopy used to retard speed of fall from an aircraft. * *vti* to drop, descend by parachute.—**parachutist** *n*.
parade *n* a ceremonial procession; an assem-

bly of troops for review; ostentatious display; public walk, promenade. * *vti* to march or walk through, as for display; to show off; to assemble in military order.

paradise *n* heaven; (*Bible*) the Garden of Eden; any place of perfection.

paradox *n* a self-contradictory statement that may be true; an opinion that conflicts with common beliefs; something with seeming contradictory qualities or phases.—**paradoxical** *adj*.—**paradoxically** *adv*.

paraffin *n* a distilled oil used as fuel.

paragraph *n* a subdivision in a piece of writing used to separate ideas, marked by the beginning of a new line; a brief mention in a newspaper. * *vt* to divide into paragraphs.

parallel *adj* equidistant at every point and extended in the same direction; side by side; never intersecting; similar, corresponding. * *n* a parallel line, surface, etc; a likeness, counterpart; comparison; a line of latitude. * *vt* (*pt* **paralleled**) to make or be parallel; to compare.

paralyse, paralyze (*US*) *vt* to affect with paralysis; to bring to a stop.—**paralytic** *adj*, *n*.

paralysis *n* (*pl* **paralyses**) a partial or complete loss of voluntary muscle function or sensation in any part of the body; a condition of helpless inactivity.

paramount *adj* of great importance.

paranoia *n* a mental illness characterized by delusions of grandeur and persecution; (*inf*) unfounded fear, suspicion.—**paranoid** *adj*, *n*.—**paranoiac** *adj*, *n*.

paraphernalia *npl* personal belongings; accessories; (*law*) what a wife possesses in her own right.

paraphrase *n* expression of a passage in other words in order to clarify meaning. * *vt* to restate.

parasite *n* an organism that lives on and feeds off another without rendering any service in return; a person who sponges off another.—**parasitic** *adj*.—**parasitically** *adv*.

paratroops *npl* troops dropped by parachute into the enemy area.—**paratrooper** *n*.

parcel *n* a tract or plot of land; a wrapped bundle; a package; a collection or group of persons, animals, or things. * *vt* (*pt* **parcelled**) to wrap up into a parcel; (*with* **out**) to apportion.

parch *vti* to make or become hot and dry, thirsty; to scorch, roast.—**parched** *adj*.

parchment *n* the skin of a sheep, etc prepared as a writing material; paper like parchment.

pardon *vt* to forgive; to excuse; to release from penalty. * *n* forgiveness; remission of penalty.—**pardonable** *adj*.

parent *n* a father or a mother; an organism producing another; a source.—**parental** *adj*.—**parenthood** *n*.

parenthesis *n* (*pl* **parentheses**) an explanatory comment in a sentence contained within brackets and set in a sentence, independently of grammatical sequence; the brackets themselves ().—**parenthetical** *adj*.

parish *n* an ecclesiastical area in the charge of one clergyman; the congregation of a church.

parishioner *n* an inhabitant of a parish.

parity *n* equality; equality of value at a given ratio between different kinds of money, etc; being at par.

park *n* land kept as a game preserve or recreation area; a piece of ground in an urban area kept for ornament or recreation; an enclosed stadium, esp for ball games; a large enclosed piece of ground attached to a country house. * *vti* (*vehicle*) to leave in a certain place temporarily; (*vehicle*) to manoeuvre into a parking space.

parking lot *n* a car park.

parking meter *n* a coin-operated machine that registers the purchase of parking time for a motor vehicle.

parliament *n* a legislative assembly made up of representatives of a nation or part of a nation.—**parliamentarian** *n*.

parliamentary *adj* of, used in, or enacted by a parliament; conforming to the rules of a parliament; having a parliament.

parlour, parlor (*US*) *n* a room in a house used primarily for conversation or receiving guests; a room or a shop used for business.

parochial *adj* of or relating to a parish; narrow; provincial in outlook.—**parochialism** *n*.

parody *n* a satirical or humorous imitation of a literary or musical work or style. * *vt* to make a parody of.—**parodist** *n*.

parole *n* word of honour; the release of a prisoner before his sentence has expired, on condition of future good behaviour. * *vt* to release on parole.

parquet *n* an inlaid hard wood flooring; the stalls of a theatre.

parrot *n* a tropical or subtropical bird with brilliant plumage and the ability to mimic human speech; one who repeats another's words without understanding. * *vt* to repeat mechanically.

parry *vt* to ward off, turn aside. * *n* a defensive movement in fencing.

parsley *n* a bright green herb used to flavour or garnish some foods.

parsnip *n* a long tapered root used as a vegetable.

parson *n* a priest of a parish, vicar; (*inf*) any clergyman.

part *n* a section; a portion (of a whole); an essential, separable component of a piece of equipment or a machine; the role of an actor in a play; a written copy of his/her words; (*mus*) one of the melodies of a harmony; the music for it; duty, share; one of the sides in a conflict; a parting of the hair; (*pl*) qualities, talent. * *vt* to separate; to comb the hair so as to leave a parting. * *vi* to become separated; to go different ways.

partial *adj* incomplete; biased, prejudiced; (*with* **to**) having a liking or preference for.—**partiality** *n*.—**partially** *adv*.

participate *vi* to join in or take part with others (in some activity).—**participant** *n*.

participation *n* the act of participating; the state of being related to a larger whole.

participle *n* (*gram*) a verb form used as an adjective.—**participial** *adj*.

particle *n* a tiny portion of matter; a speck; a very small part; (*gram*) a word that cannot be used alone, a prefix, a suffix.

particular *adj* referring or belonging to a specific person or thing; distinct; exceptional; careful; fastidious. * *n* a detail, single item; (*pl*) detailed information.

particularly *adv* very; especially; in detail.

parting *n* a departure; a breaking or separating; a dividing line in combing hair. * *adj* departing, esp dying; separating; dividing.

partisan *n* a strong supporter of a person, party, or cause.—*also adj*.—**partisanship** *n*.

partition *n* division into parts; that which divides into separate parts; a dividing wall between rooms. * *vt* to divide.

partly *adv* in part; to some extent.

partner *n* one of two or more persons jointly owning a business who share the risks and profits; one of a pair who dance or play a game together; either member of a married or non-married couple. * *vt* to be a partner (in or of).

partridge *n* a stout-bodied game bird of the grouse family.

part-time *adj* working fewer than the full number of hours.—**part time** *adv*.—**part-timer** *n*.

party *n* a group of people united for political or other purpose; a social gathering; a person involved in a contract or lawsuit; a small company, detachment; a person consenting, accessory; (*inf*) an individual. * *vi* to attend social parties. * *vt* to give a party for. * *adj* of or for a party.

pass *vb* (*pt* **passed**) *vi* to go past; to go beyond or exceed; to move from one place or state to another; (*time*) to elapse; to go; to die; to happen; (*with* **for**) to be considered as; (*in exam*) to be successful; (*cards*) to decline to make a bid; (*law*) to be approved by a legislative assembly. * *vt* to go past, through, over, etc; (*time*) to spend; to omit; (*law*) to enact; (*judgment*) to pronounce; to excrete; (*in test, etc*) to gain the required marks; to approve. * *n* a narrow passage or road; a permit; (*in a test, etc*) success; transfer of (a ball) to another player; a gesture of the hand; (*inf*) an uninvited sexual approach.

passable *adj* fairly good, tolerable; (*a river, etc*) that can be crossed.—**passably** *adv*.

passage *n* act or right of passing; transit; transition; a corridor; a channel; a route or crossing; a lapse of time; a piece of text or music.

passenger *n* a traveller in a public or private conveyance; one who does not pull his/her weight.

passer-by *n* (*pl* **passers-by**) one who happens to pass or go by.

passing *adj* transient; casual. * *n* departure, death.

passion *n* compelling emotion, such as love, hate, envy; ardent love, esp sexual desire; (*with cap*) the suffering of Christ on the cross; the object of any strong desire.

passionate *adj* moved by, showing, strong emotion or desire; intense; sensual.—**passionately** *adv*.

passive *adj* acted upon, not acting; submissive; (*gram*) denoting the voice of a verb whose subject receives the action.—**passively** *adv*.—**passiveness** *n*.—**passivity** *n*.

passport *n* an official document giving the owner the right to travel abroad; something that secures admission or acceptance.

password *n* a secret term by which a person is recognized and allowed to pass; any means of admission; a sequence of characters required to access a computer system.

past *adj* completed; ended; in time already elapsed. * *adv* by. * *prep* beyond (in time, place, or amount). * *n* time that has gone by; the history of a person, group, etc; a personal background that is hidden or questionable.

pasta *n* the flour paste from which spaghetti, noodles, etc is made; any dish of cooked pasta.

paste *n* a soft plastic mixture; flour and water forming dough or adhesive; a fine glass used for artificial gems. * *vt* to attach with paste; (*sl*) to beat, thrash.

pastel *n* a substance made of chalk, used for drawing; a drawing made with such; a soft, pale colour. * *adj* delicately coloured.

pasteurize *vt* (*milk, etc*) to sterilize by heat or radiation to destroy harmful organisms.—**pasteurization** *n*.

pastille *n* an aromatic or medicated lozenge.

pastime *n* a hobby; recreation, diversion.

pastoral *adj* of shepherds or rural life; pertaining to spiritual care, esp of a congregation.—**pastorally** *adv*.

pastry *n* dough made of flour, water, and fat used for making pies, tarts, etc; (*pl*) baked goods.

pasture *n* land covered with grass for grazing livestock; the grass growing on it. * *vt* (*cattle, etc*) to put out to graze in a pasture.—**pasturage** *n*.

pasty[1] *n* meat, etc enclosed in pastry and baked; a turnover.

pasty[2] *adj* (**pastier, pastiest**) like paste; pallid and unhealthy in appearance.

pat[1] *vti* (*pt* **patted**) to strike gently with the palm of the hand or a flat object; to shape or apply by patting. * *n* a light tap, usu with the palm of the hand; a light sound; a small lump of shaped butter.

pat[2] *adj* apt; exact; glib.—*also adv*.

patch *n* a piece of cloth used for mending; a scrap of material; a shield for an injured eye; a black spot of silk, etc worn on the face; an irregular spot on a surface; a plot of ground; a bandage; an area or spot. * *vt* to repair with a patch; to piece together; to mend in a makeshift way.

patchwork *n* needlework made of pieces sewn together; something made of various bits.

patchy *adj* (**patchier, patchiest**) irregular; uneven; covered with patches.—**patchily** *adv*.—**patchiness** *n*.

pâté *n* a spread made of liver, herbs, etc.

patent *adj* plain; apparent; open to public inspection; protected by a patent. * *n* a government document, granting the exclusive right to produce and sell an invention, etc for a certain time; the right so granted; the thing protected by such a right. * *vt* to secure a patent for.

patent leather *n* leather with a hard, glossy finish.

paternal *adj* fatherly in disposition; related through the father.—**paternally** *adv*.

paternity *n* fatherhood; origin or descent from a father.

path *n* a way worn by footsteps; a track for people on foot; a direction; a course of conduct.

pathetic *adj* inspiring pity; (*sl*) uninteresting, inadequate.—**pathetically** *adv*.

pathologist *n* a medical specialist who diagnoses by interpreting the changes in tissue and body fluid caused by a disease.

pathology *n* the branch of medicine that deals with the nature of disease, esp its functional and structural effects; any abnormal variation from a sound condition.—**pathological** *adj*.—**pathologically** *adv*.

pathway *n* a path; (*chem*) a sequence of enzyme-catalyzed reactions.

patience *n* the capacity to endure or wait calmly; a card game for one.

patient *adj* even-tempered; able to wait or endure calmly; persevering. * *n* a person receiving medical, dental, etc treatment.—**patiently** *adv*.

patio *n* (*pl* **patios**) an inner courtyard open to the sky; a paved area adjoining a house, for outdoor lounging, dining, etc.

patriot *n* one who strongly supports and serves his or her country.—**patriotic** *adj*.—**patriotically** *adv*.—**patriotism** *n*.

patrol *vti* (*pt* **patrolled**) to walk around a building or area in order to watch, guard, inspect. * *n* the act of going the rounds; a unit of persons or vehicles employed for reconnaissance, security, or combat; a subdivision of a Scout or Guide group.

patron *n* a regular client or customer; a person who sponsors and supports the arts, charities, etc; a protector.

patronage *n* the support given or custom brought by a patron; clientele; business; trade; the power to grant political favours; such favours.

patronize *vt* to treat with condescension; to sponsor or support; to be a regular customer of.—**patronizing** *adj*.—**patronizingly** *adv*.

patter[1] *vi* to make quick tapping sounds, as if by striking something; to run with light steps. * *n* the sound of tapping or quick steps.

patter[2] *vi* to talk rapidly and glibly. * *vt* to repeat speech, to gabble. * *n* glib speech; chatter; lingo.

pattern *n* a decorative arrangement; a model to be copied; instructions to be followed to make something; a regular way of acting or doing; a predictable route, movement, etc. * *vt* to make or do in imitation of a pattern.—**patterned** *adj*.

paunch *n* the belly, esp a potbelly.

pauper *n* a very poor person; (*formerly*) a person dependent on charity.—**pauperism** *n*.

pause *n* a temporary stop, esp in speech, action or music. * *vi* to cease in action temporarily, wait; to hesitate.

pave *vt* (*a road, etc*) to cover with concrete to provide a hard level surface.—**paving** *n*.

pavement *n* flat slabs, tiles, etc, forming a surface; a paved path adjacent to a road for pedestrians.

pavilion *n* a building at a sports ground used by players; a temporary building for exhibitions; a domed tent.

paw *n* a foot of a mammal with claws; (*sl*) a hand. * *vti* to touch, dig, hit, etc with paws; to maul; to handle clumsily or roughly.

pawn[1] *n* the piece of lowest value in chess; a person used to advance another's purpose.

pawn[2] *vt* to deposit an article as security for a loan; to wager or risk. * *n* a thing pawned; the state of being given as a pawn.

pawnbroker *n* a person licensed to lend money at interest on personal property left with him as security.

pay *vti* (*pt* **paid**) to give (money) to in payment for a debt, goods or services; to give in compensation; to yield a profit; to bear a cost; to suffer a penalty; (*homage, attention*) to give. * *n* payment for services or goods; salary, wages.—**paying** *adj*.—**payer** *n*.

payable *adj* that must be paid, due; to be paid on a specified date.

payee *n* one to whom money is paid.

payment *n* the act of paying; amount paid; reward.

payroll *n* a list of employees and their wages; the actual money for paying wages.

pc *abbr* = per cent; postcard.

pea *n* the edible, round, green seed of a climbing leguminous annual plant.

peace *n* tranquillity, stillness; freedom from contention, violence or war; a treaty that ends a war.

peaceable *adj* inclined to peace.—**peaceably** *adv*.

peaceful *adj* having peace; tranquil; quiet.—**peacefully** *adv*.—**peacefulness** *n*.

peach *n* a round, sweet, juicy, downy-skinned stone-fruit; the tree bearing it; a yellowish pink colour; (*sl*) a well-liked person or thing.

peacock *n* a male bird with a large brilliantly coloured fan-like tail (*nf* **peahen**); a man who is a show-off.

peak *n* the summit of a mountain; the highest point; the pointed end of anything; maximum value; the eyeshade of a cap, visor. * *vti* (*politician, actor, etc*) to reach or cause to reach the height of power, popularity; (*prices*) to reach and stay at the highest level.

peal *n* a reverberating sound as of thunder, laughter, bells, etc; a set of bells, the changes rung on them. * *vti* to sound in peals, ring out.

peanut *n* a leguminous plant with underground pods containing edible seeds; the pod or any of its seeds; (*pl*: *sl*) a trifling sum.

peanut butter *n* a food paste made by grinding roasted peanuts.

pear *n* a common juicy fruit of tapering oval shape; the tree bearing it.

pearl *n* the lustrous white round gem produced by oysters; mother-of-pearl; anything resembling a pearl intrinsically or physically; one that is choice and precious; a bluish medium grey.—**pearly** *adj*.

peasant *n* an agricultural labourer.

peat *n* decayed vegetable matter from bogs, which is dried and cut into blocks for fuel or used as a fertilizer.—**peaty** *adj*.

pebble *n* a small rounded stone; an irregular, grainy surface.—**pebbled** *adj*.—**pebbly** *adj*.

peck *vt* to strike with the beak or a pointed object; to pick at one's food; (*inf*) to kiss lightly; to nag.—*also n*.

peckish *adj* (*sl*) hungry.

peculiar *adj* belonging exclusively (to); special; distinct; characteristic; strange.—**peculiarly** *adv*.

peculiarity *n* an idiosyncrasy; a characteristic; an oddity.

pecuniary *adj* of or consisting of money.

pedal *n* a lever operated by the foot. * *vt* (*pt* **pedalled**) to operate, propel by pressing pedals with the foot.

pedant *n* a person who attaches too much importance to insignificant details.—**pedantic** *adj*.—**pedantically** *adv*.

peddle *vt* to go from place to place selling small goods; (*drugs*) to sell.

pedestal *n* the base that supports a column, statue, etc.

pedestrian *adj* on foot; dull, commonplace. * *n* a person who walks.

pedigree *n* a line of descent of an animal; a recorded purity of breed of an individual; a genealogy; lineage; derivation.—*also adj.*

pedlar *n* a peddler.

peek *vi* to look quickly or furtively.—*also n.*

peel *vt* to remove skin or rind from; to bare. * *vi* to flake off, as skin or paint. * *n* rind, esp that of fruit and vegetables.—**peeling** *n.*

peep[1] *vi* to make shrill noises as a young bird. * *n* a peeping sound.

peep[2] *vi* to look hastily or furtively; to look through a slit or narrow opening; to be just showing. * *n* a furtive or hurried glance, a glimpse; (*of day*) the first appearance.

peer[1] *vi* to look closely; to look with difficulty; to peep out.

peer[2] *n* an equal in rank, ability, etc; a nobleman.—**peeress** *nf.*

peerage *n* the rank or title of a peer; peers collectively; a book with a list of peers.

peeved *adj* annoyed, resentful.

peevish *adj* fretful, irritable.—**peevishly** *adv.*—**peevishness** *n.*

peg *n* a tapered piece (of wood) for securing or hanging things on, for marking position, or for adjusting the strings of an instrument; a predetermined level at which (a price) is fixed; (*a fact or opinion*) used as a support, pretext, or reason; (*mus*) one of the movable parts for tuning the string of an instrument. * *vti* (*pt* **pegged**) to fasten or mark with a peg; (*a price*) to keep steady; to work steadily, persevere.

pejorative *adj* disparaging, derogatory.—**pejoratively** *adv.*

Pekingese, Pekinese *n* a breed of small dog with long, silky hair, short legs, and a pug nose.

pelican *n* a large fish-eating waterbird with an expandable pouched bill.

pellet *n* a small ball, a pill; a piece of shot.

pelmet *n* a canopy for a window frame to hide rods, etc; a valance.

pelt[1] *vt* to throw missiles, or words, at. * *vi* (*rain*) to fall heavily; to hurry, rush. * *n* a rush.

pelt[2] *n* a usu undressed skin of an animal with its hair, wool, or fur.

pelvis *n* the bony cavity that joins the lower limbs to the body; the bones forming this.—**pelvic** *adj.*

pen[1] *n* an implement used with ink for writing or drawing. * *vt* (*pt* **penned**) to write, compose.

pen[2] *n* a small enclosure for cattle, poultry, etc; a small place of confinement. * *vt* (*pt* **penned**) to enclose in a pen, shut up.

penal *adj* relating to, liable to, or prescribing punishment; punitive.—**penally** *adv.*

penalize *vt* to impose a penalty; to put under a disadvantage.—**penalization** *n.*

penalty *n* a punishment attached to an offence; suffering or loss as a result of one's own mistake; a disadvantage imposed for breaking a rule as in football; a fine.

penance *n* voluntary suffering to atone for a sin; a sacramental rite consisting of confession, absolution, and penance.

pence *see* **penny**.

pencil *n* a pointed rod-shaped instrument with a core of graphite or crayon for writing, drawing, etc; a set of convergent light rays or straight lines; a fine paintbrush. * *vt* (*pt* **pencilled**) to write, draw, or colour with a pencil; (*with* **in**) to commit tentatively.

pendant, pendent *n* a hanging ornament; a complement or match. * *adj* (*usu* **pendent**) hanging; projecting; undecided.

pending *adj* undecided; unfinished; imminent. * *prep* during; until, awaiting.

pendulum *n* a weight suspended from a fixed point so as to swing freely; such a device used to regulate the movement of a clock; something that swings to and fro.

penetrate *vti* to thrust, force a way into or through something; to pierce; to permeate; to understand.—**penetrable** *adj.*—**penetrability** *n.*

penetrating *adj* acute, discerning; (*voice*) easily heard through other sounds.

penetration *n* the capability, act, or action of penetrating; acute insight.

pen friend *n* a friend made and kept through exchanging letters.

penguin *n* a flightless, marine bird with black and white plumage, usu found in the Antarctic.

penicillin *n* an antibiotic produced synthetically from moulds.

peninsula *n* a piece of land almost surrounded by sea.—**peninsular** *adj.*

penis *n* the male copulative organ in mammals and humans.

penitent *adj* feeling regret for sin, repentant, contrite. * *n* a person who atones for sin.—**penitence** *n.*—**penitently** *adv.*

penitentiary *n* a state or federal prison in the US.

penknife *n* a small knife, usually with one folding blade, that fits into the pocket.

pennant *n* a long tapering flag used for identifying vessels and for signalling; such a flag symbolizing a championship.

penniless *adj* having no money; poor.

penny *n* (*pl* **pence** *denoting sum*, **pennies** *denoting separate coins*) a bronze coin of the UK worth one hundredth of a pound; (*formerly*) a bronze coin worth one twelfth of a shilling, or one two hundred and fortieth of a pound; a US or Canadian cent.

pension *n* a periodic payment to a person beyond retirement age, or widowed, or disabled; a periodic payment in consideration of past services. * *vt* to grant a pension to; (*with* **off**) to dismiss or retire from service with a pension.—**pensionable** *adj*.

pensioner *n* a person who receives a pension; a senior citizen.

pensive *adj* thoughtful, musing; wistful, melancholic.—**pensively** *adv*.—**pensiveness** *n*.

pentagon *n* (*geom*) a polygon with five sides; (*with cap*) the US military leadership.—**pentagonal** *adj*.

Pentecost *n* a Christian festival on the seventh Sunday after Easter; Whit Sunday.

penthouse *n* an apartment on the flat roof or in the top floor of a building.

pent-up *adj* (*emotion*) repressed, confined.

penultimate *adj* last but one.

people *n* the body of enfranchised citizens of a state; a person's family, relatives; the persons of a certain place, group, or class; persons considered indefinitely; human beings; (*pl*) all the persons of a racial or ethnic group, typically having a common language, institutions, homes, and folkways. * *vt* to populate with people.

pep *n* (*inf*) energy, vigour.

pepper *n* a sharp, hot condiment made from the fruit of various plants; the fruit of the pepper plant, which can be red, yellow, or green, sweet or hot, and is eaten as a vegetable. * *vt* to sprinkle or flavour with pepper; to hit with small shot; to pelt; to beat.

peppermint *n* a pungent and aromatic mint; its oil used for flavouring; a sweet flavoured with peppermint.

pep talk *n* (*inf*) a vigorous talk made with the intention of arousing enthusiasm, increasing confidence, etc.

per *prep* for or in each; through, by, by means of; (*inf*) according to.

per annum *adv* yearly; each year.

perceive *vt* to become aware of, apprehend, through the senses; to recognize.

per cent *adv* in, for each hundred; (*inf*) percentage.

percentage *n* rate per hundred parts; a proportion; (*inf*) profit, gain.

perceptible *adj* able to be perceived; discernible.—**perceptibility** *n*.—**perceptibly** *adv*.

perception *n* the act or faculty of perceiving; discernment; insight; a way of perceiving, view.

perceptive *adj* able to perceive; observant.—**perceptively** *adv*.—**perceptiveness** *n*.

perch[1] *n* (*pl* **perch**) a spiny-finned chiefly freshwater edible fish.

perch[2] *n* a pole on which birds roost or alight; an elevated seat or position. * *vti* to alight, rest, on a perch; to balance (oneself) on; to set in a high position.

percolator *n* a coffee pot in which boiling water is forced through coffee grounds.

percussion *n* impact, collision; shock, sound, caused by this; (*med*) tapping the body to discover the condition of an organ by the sounds; musical instruments played by striking with sticks or hammers, eg cymbals, drums, etc.—**percussionist** *n*.—**percussive** *adj*.

peremptory *adj* urgent; absolute; dogmatic; dictatorial.—**peremptorily** *adv*.—**peremptoriness** *n*.

perennial *adj* perpetual; lasting throughout the year. * *n* (*bot*) a plant lasting more than two years.—**perennially** *adv*.

perfect *adj* faultless; exact; excellent; complete. * *n* (*gram*) a verb form expressing completed action or designating a present state that is the result of an action in the past. * *vt* to improve; to finish; to make fully accomplished in anything.—**perfectly** *adv*.

perfection *n* the act of perfecting; the quality or condition of being perfect; great excellence; faultlessness; the highest degree; a perfect person or thing.

perfectionist *n* one who demands the highest standard; one who holds that moral perfection may be attained in this world.—**perfectionism** *n*.

perforate *vt* to pierce; to make a hole or row of holes, by boring through.

perforation *n* the act of perforating; the condition of being perforated; a hole; a row of holes to facilitate tearing.

perform *vti* to carry out, do; to put into effect; to act; to execute; to act before an audience; to play a musical instrument.—**performing** *adj*.

performance *n* the act of performing; a dramatic production; an act or action.

performer *n* a person who performs, esp one who entertains an audience.

perfume *n* a pleasing odour; fragrance; a mixture containing fragrant essential oils and a fixative. * *vt* to scent; to put perfume on.

perfunctory *adj* superficial, hasty; done merely as a matter of form, half-hearted; done carelessly; indifferent.—**perfunctorily** *adv*.

perhaps *adv* possibly, maybe.

peril *n* danger, jeopardy; risk, hazard.

perilous *adj* dangerous.— **perilously** *adv*.

perimeter *n* a boundary around an area; (*math*) the curve or line bounding a closed figure, its length.

period *n* a portion of time; menstruation; an interval of time as in an academic day, playing time in a game, etc; an age or era in history, epoch; a stage in life; (*gram*) a full stop (.); (*astron*) a planet's time of revolution. * *interj* an exclamation used for emphasis.

periodic *adj* relating to a period; recurring at regular intervals, cyclic; intermittent.—**periodically** *adv*.

periodical *adj* periodic. * *n* a magazine, etc issued at regular intervals.

peripheral *adj* incidental, superficial; relating to a periphery.

periphery *n* the outer surface or boundary of an area; the outside surface of anything.

periscope *n* a device with mirrors that enables the viewer to see objects above or around an obstacle or above water, as from a submarine.

perish *vi* to be destroyed or ruined; to die, esp violently.

perishable *adj* (*food*) liable to spoil or decay. * *n* something perishable, esp food.—**perishability** *n*.

perjure *vt* to commit perjury, swear falsely.

perjury *n* (*law*) the crime of giving false witness under oath, swearing to what is untrue.

perk *n* (*inf*) a privilege, gain or profit incidental to regular wages; a tip, gratuity.

perk up *vti* to recover self-confidence; to become lively or cheerful; to prick up, as of a dog's ears; to smarten, trim.—**perky** *adj*.

perm *vt* (*inf*) (*hair*) to give a permanent wave. —*also n*.

permanence *n* the condition or quality of being permanent.

permanent *adj* lasting, or intended to last, indefinitely. * *n* a straightening or curling of hair by use of chemicals or heat lasting through many washings.—**permanently** *adv*.

permeate *vti* to fill every part of, saturate; to pervade, be diffused (through); to pass through by osmosis.—**permeable** *adj*.—**permeability** *n*.

permissible *adj* allowable.

permission *n* authorization; consent.

permissive *adj* allowing permission; lenient; sexually indulgent.—**permissively** *adv*.—**permissiveness** *n*.

permit *vti* (*pt* **permitted**) to allow to be done; to authorize; to give opportunity. * *n* a licence.

permutation *n* any radical alteration; a change in the order of a series; any of the total number of groupings within a group; an ordered arrangement of a set of objects.

pernicious *adj* destructive; very harmful.—**perniciously** *adv*.—**perniciousness** *n*.

perpendicular *adj* upright, vertical; (*geom*) at right angles (to).—*also n*.

perpetrate *vt* (*something evil, criminal, etc*) to do; (*a blunder, etc*) to commit.—**perpetration** *n*.—**perpetrator** *n*.

perpetual *adj* continuous; everlasting; (*plant*) blooming continuously throughout the season.—**perpetually** *adv*.

perpetuity *n* endless duration, eternity; perpetual continuance; an annuity payable forever.

perplex *vt* to puzzle, bewilder, confuse; to complicate.—**perplexity** *n*.

persecute *vt* to harass, oppress, esp for reasons of race, religion, etc; to worry persistently.—**persecution** *n*.—**persecutor** *n*.

persevere *vi* to persist, maintain effort in face of difficulties.—**perseverance**, **perseveringly** *adv*.

persist *vi* to continue in spite of obstacles or opposition; to persevere; to last.—**persistence** *n*.—**persistency** *n*.

persistent *adj* persevering; stubborn.—**persistently** *adv*.

person *n* a human being, individual; the body (including clothing) of a human being; (*in a play*) a character; one who is recognized by law as the subject of rights and duties; (*gram*) one of the three classes of personal pronouns and verb forms, referring to the person(s) speaking, spoken to, or spoken of.

personable *adj* pleasing in personality and appearance.

personal *adj* concerning a person's private affairs, or his/her character, habits, body, etc; done in person; (*law*) of property that is movable; (*gram*) denoting person.

personality *n* one's individual characteristics; excellence or distinction of social and personal traits; a person with such qualities; a celebrity.

personally *adv* in person; in one's own opinion; as though directed to oneself.

personify *vt* to think of, represent, as a person; to typify.—**personification** *n*.

personnel *n* the employees of an organization or company; the department that hires them.

perspective *n* objectivity; the art of drawing so as to give an impression of relative distance or solidity; a picture so drawn; relation, proportion, between parts of a subject; vista, prospect.—*also adj*.

perspire *vi* to sweat.—**perspiration** *n*.

persuade *vt* to convince; to induce by argument, reasoning, advice, etc.

persuasion *n* the act of persuading; a conviction or opinion; a system of religious beliefs; a group adhering to such a system.

persuasive *adj* able to persuade; influencing the mind or emotions.—**persuasively** *adv*.—**persuasiveness** *n*.

pert *adj* impudent, cheeky; sprightly.—**pertly** *adv*.

pertinent *adj* relevant; to the point.—**pertinence** *n*.—**pertinently** *adv*.

perturb *vt* to trouble; to agitate.

perusal *n* a careful reading.

pervade *vt* to permeate or spread through; to be rife among.—**pervasive** *adj*.

perverse *adj* deviating from right or truth; persisting in error; wayward; contrary.—**perversely** *adv*.—**perverseness** *n*.—**perversity** *n*.

perversion *n* an abnormal way of obtaining sexual gratification, eg sadism; a perverted form or usage of something.

pervert *vt* to corrupt; to misuse; to distort. * *n* a person who is sexually perverted.

pessimism *n* a tendency to see in the world what is bad rather than good; a negative outlook that always expects the worst.—**pessimist** *n*.—**pessimistic** *adj*.

pest *n* anything destructive, esp a plant or animal detrimental to man as rats, flies, weeds, etc; a person who pesters or annoys.

pester *vt* to annoy or irritate persistently.

pesticide *n* any chemical for killing pests.

pestle *n* a usu club-shaped tool for pounding or grinding substances in a mortar. * *vt* to beat, pound, or pulverize with a pestle.

pet *n* a domesticated animal kept as a companion; a person treated as a favourite. * *adj* kept as a pet; spoiled, indulged; favourite; particular. * *vti* (*pt* **petted**) to stroke or pat gently; to caress; (*inf*) to kiss, embrace, etc in making love.

petal *n* any of the leaf-like parts of a flower's corolla.—**petalled, petaled** *adj*.

peter out *vi* to come to an end; to dwindle to nothing.

petite *adj* (*woman*) small and trim in figure.

petition *n* a formal application or entreaty to an authority; a written demand for action by a government, etc, signed by a number of people. * *vti* to present a petition to; to ask humbly.—**petitionary** *adj*.—**petitioner** *n*.—**petitioning** *n*.

petrol *n* a liquid fuel or solvent distilled from petroleum.

petroleum *n* a crude oil occurring naturally in certain rock strata and distilled to yield petrol, paraffin, etc.

petticoat *n* an underskirt; a slip; (*inf*) woman.

petty *adj* (**pettier, pettiest**) trivial; small-minded; minor.—**pettily** *adv*.—**pettiness** *n*.

petty officer *n* a non-commissioned officer in the navy.

petulant *adj* showing impatience or irritation; bad-humoured.—**petulance** *n*.—**petulantly** *adv*.

pew *n* a wooden, bench-like seat in a church, often enclosed; (*sl*) a chair.

pewter *n* an alloy of tin and lead with a silvery-grey colour; dishes, etc, made of pewter.

phantom *n* a spectre or apparition. * *adj* illusionary.

pharmacist *n* one licensed to practise pharmacy.

pharmacy *n* the preparation and dispensing of drugs and medicines; a pharmacist's shop, a drug store.

phase *n* an amount of the moon's or a planet's surface illuminated at a given time; a characteristic period in a regularly recurring sequence of events or stage in a development. * *vt* to do by stages or gradually; (*with* **out**) (*making, using, etc*) to stop gradually.

PhD *abbr* = Doctor of Philosophy.

pheasant *n* a richly coloured game bird.

phenomenon *n* (*pl* **phenomena, phenomenons**) anything perceived by the senses as a fact; a fact or event that can be scientifically described; a remarkable thing or person.

phial *n* a small glass bottle; a vial.

philanthropy *n* love of mankind, esp as demonstrated by benevolent or charitable actions.—**philanthropic** *adj*.—**philanthropi-**

cally *adv*.—**philanthropist** *n*.
philately *n* the study and collecting of postage and imprinted stamps; stamp collecting.—**philatelic** *adj*.—**philatelist** *n*.
philosopher *n* a person who studies philosophy; a person who acts calmly and rationally.
philosophical *adj* of, relating to, or according to philosophy; serene; temperate; resigned.—**philosophically** *adv*.
philosophy *n* the study of the principles underlying conduct, thought, and the nature of the universe; general principles of a field of knowledge; a particular system of ethics; composure; calmness.
phlegm *n* a thick mucus discharged from the throat, as during a cold; sluggishness; apathy.
phlegmatic *adj* unemotional, composed; sluggish.
phobia *n* an irrational, excessive, and persistent fear of some thing or situation.—**phobic** *adj*.
phone *n*, *vti* (*inf*) (to) telephone.
phonetics *npl* (*used as sing*) the science concerned with pronunciation and the representation of speech sounds.
phonograph *n* a gramophone or record player.
phony, phoney *adj* (**phonier, phoniest**) (*inf*) not genuine. * *n* a fake; an insincere person.
phosphate *n* a compound of phosphorus.
phosphorus *n* a metalloid element; a phosphorescent substance or body, esp one that glows in the dark.
photo *see* **photograph**.
photo- *prefix* = light; a photographic process.
photocopy *n* a photographic reproduction of written or printed work. * *vt* to copy in this way.—**photocopier** *n*.
photogenic *adj* likely to look attractive in photographs; (*biol*) generating light.—**photogenically** *adv*.
photograph *n* an image produced by photography.—*also* **photo**.
photography *n* the art or process of recording images permanently and visibly by the chemical action of light on sensitive material, producing prints, slides or film.—**photographer** *n*.—**photographic** *adj*.—**photographically** *adv*.
phrase *n* a group of words that does not contain a finite verb but which expresses a single idea by itself; a pointed saying; a high-flown expression; (*mus*) a short, distinct musical passage. * *vt* to express orally, put in words; (*mus*) to divide into melodic phrases.
phrase book *n* a book containing idiomatic expressions of a foreign language and their translations.
physical *adj* relating to the world of matter and energy, the human body, or natural science. * *n* a general medical examination.—**physically** *adv*.
physician *n* a doctor of medicine.
physicist *n* a specialist in physics.
physics *n* the branch of science concerned with matter and energy and their interactions in the fields of mechanics, acoustics, optics, heat, electricity, magnetism, radiation, atomic structure and nuclear phenomena; the physical processes and phenomena of a particular system.
physiology *n* the science of the functioning and processes of living organisms.—**physiological** *adj*.—**physiologically** *adv*.—**physiologist** *n*.
physiotherapy *n* the treatment of disorders and disease by physical and mechanical means (as massage, exercise, water, heat, etc).—**physiotherapist** *n*.
physique *n* bodily structure and appearance; build.
pianist *n* a person who plays the piano.
piano *n* (*pl* **pianos**) a large stringed keyboard instrument in which each key operates a felt-covered hammer that strikes a corresponding steel wire or wires.
piccolo *n* (*pl* **piccolos**) a small shrill flute.
pick *n* a heavy tool with a shaft and pointed crossbar for breaking ground; a tool for picking, such as a toothpick or icepick; a plectrum; right of selection; choice; best (of). * *vti* to break up or remove with a pick; to pluck at; to nibble (at), eat fussily; to contrive; to choose; (*fruit, etc*) to gather; to steal from a pocket; (*lock*) to force open; (*with* **up**) to lift; to acquire; to call for; to recover; (*inf*) to make the acquaintance of casually; to learn gradually; to resume; to give a lift to; to increase speed.
pickaxe, pickax (*US*) *n* a pick.
picket *n* a pointed stake; a patrol or group of men selected for a special duty; a person posted by strikes outside a place of work to persuade others not to enter. * *vt* (*pt* **picketed**) to tether to a picket; to post as a military picket; to place pickets, or serve as a picket (at a factory, etc).
pickle *n* vegetables preserved in vinegar; (*inf*) a plight, mess. * *vt* to preserve in vinegar.
pickpocket *n* a person who steals from pockets.

pick-up *n* the act of picking up; a person or thing picked up; (*elect*) a device for picking up current; the power to accelerate rapidly; the balanced arm of a record player; a light truck with an enclosed cab and open body.

picnic *n* a usu informal meal taken on an excursion and eaten outdoors; an outdoor snack; the food so eaten; an easy or agreeable task. * *vi* (*pt* **picnicked**) to have a picnic.—**picnicker** *n*.

pictorial *adj* relating to pictures, painting,or drawing; containing pictures; expressed in pictures; graphic.—**pictorially** *adv*.

picture *n* drawing, painting, photography, or other visual representation; a scene; an impression or mental image; a vivid description; a cinema film. * *vt* to portray, describe in a picture; to visualize.

picturesque *adj* striking, vivid, usually pleasing; making an effective picture.—**picturesquely** *adv*.

pidgin *n* a jargon for trade purposes, using words and grammar from two or more different languages.

pie *n* a baked dish of fruit, meat, etc, with an under or upper crust of pastry, or both.

piebald *adj* covered with patches of two colours. * *n* a piebald horse, etc.

piece *n* a distinct part of anything; a single object; a literary, dramatic, artistic, or musical composition; (*sl*) a firearm; a man in chess or draughts; an opinion, view; a short distance. * *vt* to fit together, join.

piecemeal *adv* gradually; bit by bit.

piecework *n* work paid for according to the quantity produced.

pier *n* a structure supporting the spans of a bridge; a structure built out over water and supported by pillars, used as a landing place, promenade, etc; a heavy column used to support weight.

pierce *vt* to cut or make a hole through; to force a way into; (*fig*) to touch or move. * *vi* to penetrate.

piercing *adj* penetrating; keen; (*cold, pain*) acute.—**piercingly** *adv*.

piety *n* religious devoutness; the characteristic of being pious.

pig *n* a domesticated animal with a broad snout and fat body raised for food; a swine; a greedy or filthy person; an oblong casting of metal poured from the smelting furnace; (*sl*) a policeman. * *vi* (*pt* **pigged**) (*sow*) to give birth; (*inf*) to live in squalor.—**piggish** *adj*.

pigeon *n* a bird with a small head and a heavy body; (*inf*) an object of special concern.

pigeonhole *n* a small compartment for filing papers, etc; a category usu failing to reflect actual complexities. * *vt* to file, classify; to put aside for consideration, shelve.

pigeon-toed *adj* having the toes turned in.

piggy bank *n* a container for coins shaped like a pig.

pigheaded *adj* stupidly stubborn.

piglet *n* a young pig.

pigment *n* paint; a naturally occurring substance used for colouring.—**pigmentation** *n*.

pigmy *see* **pygmy**.

pigsty *n* a pen for pigs; a dirty hovel.

pigtail *n* a tight braid of hair.

pike *n* a sharp point or spike; the top of a spear; a long-snouted fish, important as a food and game fish.

pilchard *n* a fish of the herring family.

pile[1] *n* a heap or mound of objects; a large amount; a lofty building; a pyre; (*sl*) a fortune. * *vt* (*with* **up**, **on**) to heap or stack; to load; to accumulate. * *vi* to become heaped up; (*with* **up**, **out**, **on**) to move confusedly in a mass.

pile[2] *n* a vertical beam driven into (the ground) as a foundation for a building, etc. * *vt* to support with piles; to drive piles into.

pile[3] *n* the nap of a fabric or carpet; soft, fine fur or wool.

pile[4] *n* a haemorrhoid.

pile-up *n* an accumulation of tasks, etc; (*inf*) a collision of several vehicles.

pilgrim *n* a person who makes a pilgrimage.

pilgrimage *n* a journey to a holy place as an act of devotion; any long journey; a life's journey.

pill *n* medicine in round balls or tablet form; (*with cap*) an oral contraceptive.

pillage *n* looting, plunder. * *vti* to plunder, esp during war.—**pillager** *n*.

pillar *n* a slender, vertical structure used as a support or ornament; a column; a strong supporter of a cause.

pillar box *n* a red box for receiving letters for mailing, often columnar.

pillion *n* a seat behind the driver for a passenger on a motorcycle, etc.

pillory *n* (*formerly*) stocks in which criminals were put as punishment. * *vt* to expose to public scorn and ridicule.

pillow *n* a cushion that supports the head during sleep; something that supports to equalize or distribute pressure. * *vti* to rest on, serve as, a pillow.

pillowcase, pillowslip *n* a removable cover for a pillow.
pilot *n* a person who operates an aircraft; one who directs ships in and out of harbour; a guide; a television show produced as a sample of a proposed series. * *vt* to direct the course of, act as pilot; to lead or guide.
pilot light *n* a burning gas flame used to light a larger jet; an electric indicator light.
pimp *n* a prostitute's agent.—*also vt.*
pimple *n* a small, raised, inflamed swelling of the skin.—**pimpled, pimply** *adj*.
pin *n* a piece of metal or wood used to fasten things together; a small piece of pointed wire with a head; an ornament or badge with a pin or clasp for fastening to clothing; (*bowling*) one of the clubs at which the ball is rolled. * *vt* (*pt* **pinned**) to fasten with a pin; to hold, fix; (*with* **down**) to get (someone) to commit himself or herself as to plans, etc; (*a fact, etc*) to establish.
pinafore *n* a sleeveless garment worn over a dress, blouse, etc.
pincers *npl* a tool with two handles and jaws used for gripping and drawing out nails, etc; a grasping claw, as of a crab.
pinch *vti* to squeeze or compress painfully; to press between the fingers; to nip; (*sl*) to steal; (*sl*) to arrest. * *n* a squeeze or nip; what can be taken up between the finger and thumb, a small amount; a time of stress; an emergency.
pine[1] *n* an evergreen coniferous tree with long needles and well-formed cones; a tree of the pine family; its wood.
pine[2] *vi* to languish, waste away through longing or mental stress; (*with* **for**) to yearn.
pineapple *n* a tropical plant; its juicy, fleshy, yellow fruit.
ping *n* a high-pitched ringing sound. * *vti* to strike with a ping, emit a ping.
ping-pong *n* a name for table tennis; (*with caps*) a trade name for table tennis equipment.
pink[1] *n* a garden plant, including carnation, with a fragrant flower; a pale red colour; a huntsman's red coat; the highest type. * *adj* pink-coloured; (*inf*) radical in political views.
pink[2] *vt* to stab, pierce; (*cloth, etc*) to cut a zigzag edge on; to perforate with pinking shears.
pink[3] *vi* (*engine*) to make a metallic noise like knocking.
pinnacle *n* a slender tower crowning a roof, etc; a rocky peak of a mountain; the highest point, climax.
pinpoint *vt* to locate or identify very exactly.
pinstripe *n* a very narrow stripe in suit fabrics, etc.
pint *n* a liquid measure equal to half a quart or one eighth of a gallon; (*inf*) a drink of beer.
pin-up *n* (*sl*) a photograph of a naked or partially naked person; a person who has been so photographed; a photograph of a famous person.
pioneer *n* a person who initiates or explores new areas of enterprise, research, etc.—*also vti.*
pious *adj* devout; religious; sanctimonious.—**piously** *adv*.
pip *n* the seed in a fleshy fruit, eg apple, orange.
pipe *n* a tube of wood, metal etc for making musical sounds; (*pl*) the bagpipes; a stem with a bowl for smoking tobacco; a long tube or hollow body for conveying water, gas, etc. * *vt* to play on a pipe; (*gas, water, etc*) to convey by pipe; to lead, summon with the sound of a pipe(s); to trim with piping.
pipeline *n* a pipe (often underground) used to convey oil, gas, etc; a direct channel for information; the processes through which supplies pass from source to user.
piper *n* a person who plays a pipe, esp bagpipes.
piping *n* a length of pipe, pipes collectively; a tube-like fold of material used to trim seams; a strip of icing, cream, for decorating cakes, etc; the art of playing a pipe or bagpipes; a high-pitched sound. * *adj* making a high-pitched sound.
piping hot *adj* very hot.
pique *n* resentment, ill-feeling. * *vt* to cause resentment in; to offend.
piracy *n* robbery at sea; the hijacking of a ship or aircraft; infringement of copyright; unauthorized use of patented work.
pirate *n* a person who commits robbery at sea; a hijacker; one who infringes copyright. * *vti* to take by piracy; to publish or reproduce in violation of a copyright.
pirouette *n* a spin on the toes in ballet.—*also vi.*
Pisces *n* the Fishes, in astrology the twelfth sign of the zodiac, operative from 19 February - 20 March.
pistol *n* a small, short-barrelled handgun.
piston *n* a disc that slides to and fro in a close-fitting cylinder, as in engines, pumps.
pit *n* a deep hole in the earth; a (coal) mine; a scooped-out place for burning something; a sunken or depressed area below the adjacent

floor area; a space at the front of the stage for the orchestra; the area in a securities or commodities exchange in which members do the trading; the scar left by smallpox, etc; the stone of a fruit; a place where racing cars refuel. * *vti* (*pt* **pitted**) to set in competition; to mark or become marked with pits; to make a pit stop.

pitch[1] *vti* (*tent, etc*) to erect by driving pegs, stakes, etc, into the ground; to set the level of; (*mus*) to set in key; to express in a style; to throw, hurl; to fall heavily, plunge, esp forward. * *n* a throw; height, intensity; a musical tone; a place where a street trader or performer works; distance between threads (of a screw); amount of slope; a sound wave frequency; a sports field; (*cricket*) the area between the wickets; sales talk.

pitch[2] *n* the black, sticky substance from distillation of tar, etc; any of various bituminous substances. * *vt* to smear with pitch.

pitch-black *adj* black, or extremely dark.

pitch-dark *adj* completely dark.

pitcher *n* a large water jug; (*baseball*) the player who pitches the ball.

pitchfork *n* a long-handled fork for tossing hay, etc. * *vt* to lift with this; to thrust suddenly or willy-nilly into.

piteous *adj* arousing pity; heart-rending.—**piteously** *adv*.

pitfall *n* concealed danger; unexpected difficulty.

pith *n* the soft tissue inside the rind of citrus fruits; the gist, essence; importance.

pithy *adj* (**pithier, pithiest**) like or full of pith; concise and full of meaning.—**pithily** *adv*.—**pithiness** *n*.

pitiable *adj* deserving pity, lamentable, wretched.—**pitiably** *adv*.

pitiful *adj* causing pity, touching; contemptible, paltry.—**pitifully** *adv*.

pitiless *adj* without pity, ruthless.—**pitilessly** *adv*.—**pitilessness** *n*.

pittance *n* a very small quantity or allowance of money.

pity *n* sympathy with the distress of others; a cause of grief; a regrettable fact. * *vt* to feel pity for.

pivot *n* a pin on which a part turns, fulcrum; a key person upon whom progress depends; a cardinal point or factor. * *vt* (*pt* **pivoted**) to turn or hinge (on) a pivot; to attach by a pivot. * *vi* to run on, or as if on, a pivot.—**pivotal** *adj*.

pixy, pixie *n* a fairy or elf.

placard *n* a poster or notice for public display.

placate *vt* to appease; to pacify.—**placatory** *adj*.

place *n* a locality, spot; a town or village; a building, residence; a short street, a square; space, room; a particular point, part, position, etc; the part of space occupied by a person or thing; a position or job; a seat; rank, precedence; a finishing position in a race. * *vt* to put; to put in a particular place; to find a place or seat for; to identify; to estimate; to rank; (*order*) to request material from a supplier. * *vi* to finish second or among the first three in a race.

place mat *n* a small mat serving as an individual table cover for a person at a meal.

placid *adj* calm, tranquil.—**placidity**, **placidness** *n*.—**placidly** *adv*.

plagiarize *vt* to appropriate writings from another author.—**plagiarism** *n*.—**plagiarist** *n*.

plague *n* a highly contagious and deadly disease; (*inf*) a person who is a nuisance. * *vt* to afflict with a plague; (*inf*) to annoy, harass.

plaice *n* (*pl* **plaice**) any of various flatfishes, esp a flounder.

plaid *n* a long wide piece of woollen cloth used as a cloak in Highland dress; cloth with a tartan or chequered pattern.

plain *adj* level, flat; understandable; straightforward; manifest, obvious; blunt; unadorned; not elaborate; not coloured or patterned; not beautiful; ugly; pure; unmixed. * *n* a large tract of level country.

plain clothes *n* ordinary clothes, not uniform, as worn by a policeman on duty.—*also adj*.

plainly *adv* clearly, intelligibly.

plaintiff *n* (*law*) a person who brings a civil action against another.

plait *n* intertwined strands of hair, straw, etc; a pigtail.—*also vti*.

plan *n* a scheme or idea; a drawing to scale of a building; a diagram, map; any outline or sketch. * *vti* (*pt* **planned**) to make a plan of; to design; to arrange beforehand, intend; to make plans.

plane[1] *n* a tall tree with large broad leaves.

plane[2] *n* a tool with a steel blade for smoothing level wooden surfaces. * *vt* to smooth with a plane.

plane[3] *n* any level or flat surface; a level of attainment; one of the main supporting surfaces of an aeroplane; an aeroplane. * *adj* flat or level. * *vi* to fly while keeping the wings motionless; to skim across the surface of water; to travel by aeroplane.

planet *n* a celestial body that orbits the sun or other star.

plank *n* a long, broad, thick board; one of the policies forming the platform of a political party. * *vt* to cover with planks.

plankton *n* the microscopic organisms that float on seas, lakes, etc.

plant *n* a living organism with cellulose cell walls, which synthesizes its food from carbon dioxide, water and light; a soft-stemmed organism of this kind, as distinguished from a tree or shrub; the machinery, buildings, etc of a factory, etc; (*sl*) an act of planting; (*sl*) something or someone planted. * *vt* (*seeds, cuttings*) to put into the ground to grow; to place firmly in position; to found or establish; (*sl*) to conceal something in another's possession in order to implicate.

plantation *n* a large cultivated planting of trees; an estate where tea, rubber, cotton, etc, is grown, cultivated by local labour.

plaque *n* an ornamental tablet or disc attached to or inserted in a surface; a film of mucus on the teeth that harbours bacteria.

plasma *n* the colourless liquid part of blood, milk, or lymph; a collection of charged particles resembling gas but conducting electricity and affected by a magnetic field.

plaster *n* an adhesive dressing for cuts; a mixture of sand, lime and water that sets hard and is used for covering walls and ceilings. * *vt* to cover as with plaster; to apply like a plaster; to make lie smooth and flat; to load to excess.—**plasterer** *n*.

plastered *adj* (*sl*) intoxicated.

plaster of Paris *n* gypsum and water made into a quick-setting paste.

plastic *adj* able to be moulded; pliant; made of plastic; (*art*) relating to modelling or moulding. * *n* any of various nonmetallic compounds, synthetically produced, that can be moulded, cast, squeezed, drawn, or laminated into objects, films, or filaments.

plastic surgery *n* surgery to repair deformed or destroyed parts of the body.

plate *n* a flat sheet of metal on which an engraving is cut; an illustration printed from it; a full-page illustration separate from text; a sheet of metal photographically prepared with text, etc, for printing from; a sheet of glass with sensitized film used as a photographic negative; a trophy as prize at a race; a coating of metal on another metal; utensils plated in silver or gold; plated ware; a flat shallow dish from which food is eaten; a helping of food; the part of a denture that fits the palate; (*inf*) a denture. * *vt* (*a metal*) to coat with a thin film of another metal; to cover with metal plates.

plateau *n* (*pl* **plateaux, plateaus**) a flat, elevated area of land; a stable period; a graphic representation showing this.

plate glass *n* rolled, ground, and polished sheet glass.

platform *n* a raised floor for speakers, musicians, etc; a stage; a place or opportunity for public discussion; the raised area next to a railway track where passengers board trains; a statement of political aims.

platinum *n* a valuable, silvery-white metal used for jewellery, etc.

platitude *n* a dull truism; a commonplace remark.

platoon *n* a military unit consisting of two or more sections.

platter *n* an oval flat serving dish.

plausible *adj* apparently truthful or reasonable.—**plausibility** *n*.—**plausibly** *adv*.

play *vi* to amuse oneself (with toys, games, etc); to act carelessly or trifle (with somebody's feelings); to gamble; to act on the stage or perform a musical instrument; (*light*) to flicker, shimmer; (*water*) to discharge or direct on. * *vt* to participate in a sport; to be somebody's opponent in a game; to perform a dramatic production; (*instrument*) to produce music on; (*hose*) to direct; (*fish*) to give line to; to bet on. * *n* fun, amusement; the playing of, or manner of playing, a game; the duration of a game; a literary work for performance by actors; gambling; scope, freedom to move.—**playful** *adj*.—**playfully** *adv*.—**playfulness** *n*.

player *n* a person who plays a specified game or instrument; an actor.

playground *n* an area outdoors for children's recreation.

playgroup *n* an organized, regular meeting for the shared supervision of children at play.

playing card *n* one of a set of 52 cards used for playing games, each card having an identical pattern on one side and its own symbol on the reverse.

playing field *n* a place for playing sport.

playpen *n* a portable usu collapsible enclosure in which a young child may be left to play safely.

plaything *n* a toy; a thing or person treated as a toy.

playwright *n* a writer of plays.

plea *n* (*law*) an answer to a charge, made by the accused person; a request; an entreaty.
plead *vti* (*pt* **pleaded, plead** *or* **pled**) to beg, implore; to give as an excuse; to answer (guilty or not guilty) to a charge; to argue (a law case).
pleasant *adj* agreeable; pleasing.—**pleasantly** *adv*.—**pleasantness** *n*.
pleasantry *n* a polite or amusing remark.
please *vti* to satisfy; to give pleasure to; to be willing; to have the wish. * *adv* as a word to express politeness or emphasis in a request; an expression of polite affirmation.—**pleasing** *adj*.—**pleasingly** *adv*.
pleasure *n* enjoyment, recreation; gratification of the senses; preference.—**pleasurable** *adj*.—**pleasurably** *adv*.
pleat *n* a double fold of cloth, etc pressed or stitched in place.—*also vt*.
plebiscite *n* a direct vote of the electorate on a political issue such as annexation, independent nationhood, etc.
plectrum *n* a thin piece of metal, etc for plucking the strings of a guitar, etc.
pledge *n* a solemn promise; security for payment of a debt; a token or sign; a toast. * *vt* to give as security; to pawn; to bind by solemn promise; to drink a toast to.
plentiful *adj* abundant, copious.
plenty *n* an abundance; more than enough; a great number. * *adv* (*sl*) quite.
pleurisy *n* inflammation of the membranes enclosing the lung.
pliable *adj* easily bent or moulded; easily influenced.—**pliability** *n*.
pliers *npl* a tool with hinged arms and jaws for cutting, shaping wire.
plight[1] *n* a dangerous situation; a predicament.
plight[2] *vt* to pledge, vow solemnly.—*also n*.
plod *vi* (*pt* **plodded**) to walk heavily and slowly, to trudge; to work or study slowly and laboriously.—**plodder** *n*.
plough, plow (*US*) *n* a farm implement for turning up soil; any implement like this, as a snowplough. * *vt* to cut and turn up with a plough; to make a furrow (in), to wrinkle; to force a way through; to work at laboriously; (*with* **into**) to run into; (*with* **back**) to reinvest; (*sl*) to fail an examination.—**ploughman** *n*.
plover *n* a wading bird with a short tail and a bill like a pigeon's.
ploy *n* a tactic or manoeuvre to outwit an opponent; an occupation or job; an escapade.
pluck *vt* to pull off or at; to snatch; to strip off feathers; (*fruit, flowers, etc*) to pick; (*person*) to remove from one situation in life and transfer to another. * *vi* to make a sharp pull or twitch. * *n* a pull or tug; heart, courage; dogged resolution.
plucky *adj* (**pluckier, pluckiest**) brave, spirited.—**pluckily** *adv*.—**pluckiness** *n*.
plug *n* a stopper used for filling a hole; a device for connecting an appliance to an electricity supply; a cake of tobacco; a kind of fishing lure; (*inf*) a free advertisement usu incorporated in other matter. * *vti* (*pt* **plugged**) to stop up with a plug; (*sl*) to shoot or punch; (*inf*) to seek to advertise by frequent repetition; (*inf*) to work doggedly.
plum *n* an oval smooth-skinned sweet stone-fruit; a tree bearing it; a reddish-purple colour; a choice thing.
plumb *n* a lead weight attached to a line, for determining depth or verticality; any of various weights. * *adj* perfectly vertical. * *adv* vertically; in a direct manner; (*inf*) entirely. * *vt* to test by a plumb; to examine minutely and critically; to weight with lead; to seal with lead; to supply with or install as plumbing. * *vi* to work as a plumber.
plumber *n* a person who installs and repairs water or gas pipes.
plumbing *n* the system of pipes used in water or gas supply, or drainage; the plumber's craft.
plume *n* a large or ornamental bird's feather; a feathery ornament or thing; something resembling a feather in structure or density. * *vt* (*feathers*) to preen; to adorn with feathers; to indulge (oneself) with an obvious display of self-satisfaction.
plummet *n* a plumb. * *vi* (*pt* **plummeted**) to fall in a perpendicular manner; to drop sharply and abruptly.
plump[1] *adj* rounded, chubby. * *vti* to make or become plump; to swell.—**plumpness** *n*.
plump[2] *vti* to fall, drop or sink, or come into contact suddenly and heavily; (*someone, something*) to favour or give support. * *n* a sudden drop or plunge or the sound of this. * *adv* straight down, straight ahead; abruptly; bluntly.
plunder *vt* to steal goods by force, to loot. * *n* plundering; booty.—**plunderer** *n*.
plunge *vti* to immerse, dive suddenly; to penetrate quickly; to hurl oneself or rush; (*horse*) to start violently forward.
plural *adj* more than one; consisting of o r containing more than one kind or class. * *n*

(*gram*) the form referring to more than one person or thing.

plus *prep* added to; in addition to. * *adj* indicating addition; positive. * *n* the sign (+) indicating a value greater than zero; an advantage or benefit; an extra.

plush *n* a velvet-like fabric with a nap. * *adj* made of plush; (*inf*) luxurious.

ply[1] *vti* to work at diligently and energetically; to wield; to subject to persistently; (*goods*) to sell; to go to and fro, run regularly; to keep busy.

ply[2] *n* a layer or thickness, as of cloth, plywood, etc; any of the twisted strands in a yarn, etc. * *vt* to twist together.

plywood *n* a construction material consisting of several thin layers of wood glued together.

PM *abbr* = prime minister.

p.m. *abbr* = post meridiem.

pneumatic *adj* concerning wind, air, or gases; operated by or filled with compressed air.

pneumonia *n* acute inflammation of the lungs.

PO *abbr* = post office; petty officer.

poach[1] *vt* to cook (an egg without its shell, fish, etc) in or over boiling water.

poach[2] *vti* to catch game or fish illegally; to trespass for this purpose; to encroach on, usurp another's rights, etc; to steal another's idea, employee, etc.—**poacher** *n*.—**poaching** *n*.

pocket *n* a small bag or pouch, esp in a garment, for carrying small articles; an isolated or enclosed area; a deposit (as of gold, water, or gas). * *adj* small enough to put in a pocket. * *vt* to put in one's pocket, to steal; (*ball*) to put in a pocket; to envelop; to enclose; (*money*) to take dishonestly; to suppress.—**pocketful** *adj*.

pocketbook *n* a wallet; a woman's purse; monetary resources; a small esp paperback book.

pocketknife *n* a penknife.

pocket money *n* money for occasional expenses; a child's allowance.

pod *n* a dry fruit or seed vessel, as of peas, beans, etc; a protective container or housing; a detachable compartment on a spacecraft. * *vi* (*pt* **podded**) to remove the pod from.

podgy *adj* (**podgier, podgiest**) short and fat, squat.

poem *n* an arrangement of words, esp in metre, often rhymed, in a style more imaginative than ordinary speech; a poetic thing.

poet *n* the writer of a poem; a person with imaginative power and a sense of beauty.

poetic, poetical *adj* of poets or poetry; written in verse; imaginative, romantic, like poetry.—**poetically** *adv*.

poet laureate *n* (*pl* **poets laureate**) the official poet of a nation, appointed to write poems celebrating national events, etc.

poetry *n* the art of writing poems; poems collectively; poetic quality or spirit.

poignant *adj* piercing; incisive; deeply moving.—**poignantly** *adv*.

point *n* a dot or tiny mark used in writing or printing (eg a decimal point, a full stop); a location; a place in a cycle, course, or scale; a unit in scoring or judging; the sharp end of a knife or pin; a moment of time; one of thirty-two divisions of the compass; a fundamental reason or aim; the tip; a physical characteristic; a railway switch; a unit of size in printing equal to one seventy-second of an inch; a unit used in quoting the prices of stocks, bonds and commodities; a headland or cape. * *vti* to give point to; to sharpen; to aim (at); to extend the finger (at or to); to indicate something; to call attention (to).

point-blank *adj* aimed straight at a mark; direct, blunt.—*also adv*.

pointed *adj* having a point; pertinent; aimed at a particular person or group; conspicuous.—**pointedly** *adv*.

pointer *n* a rod or needle for pointing; an indicator; a breed of hunting dogs.

pointless *adj* without a point; irrelevant, aimless.—**pointlessly** *adv*.

poise *vt* to balance; to hold supported without motion; (*the head*) to hold in a particular way; to put into readiness. * *vi* to become drawn up into readiness; to hover. * *n* a balanced state; self-possessed assurance of manner; gracious tact; bearing, carriage.—**poised** *adj*.

poison *n* a substance that through its chemical action usu destroys or injures an organism; any corrupt influence; an object of aversion or abhorrence. * *vt* to administer poison in order to kill or injure; to put poison into; to influence wrongfully.—**poisoner** *n*.—**poisonous** *adj*.—**poisonously** *adv*.

poke *vt* to thrust (at), jab or prod; (*hole, etc*) to make by poking; (*sl*) to hit. * *vi* to jab (at); to pry or search (about or around). * *n* a jab; a prod or nudge; a thrust.

poker[1] *n* a metal rod for poking or stirring fire.

poker[2] *n* a card game in which a player bets that the value of his hand is higher than that of the hands held by others.

poker face *n* an expressionless face, concealing a person's thoughts or feelings.—**poker-faced** *adj*.

poky *adj* (**pokier, pokiest**) small and uncomfortable.

polar *adj* of or near the North or South Pole; of a pole; having positive and negative electricity; directly opposite.

polar bear *n* a large creamy-white bear that inhabits arctic regions.

polarize *vt* (*light waves*) to cause to vibrate in a definite pattern; to give physical polarity to; to break up into opposing factions; to concentrate.—**polarization** *n*.

pole[1] *n* a long slender piece of wood, metal, etc; a flagstaff. * *vt* to propel, support with a pole.

pole[2] *n* either end of an axis, esp of the earth; either of two opposed forces, parts, etc, as the ends of a magnet, terminals of a battery, etc; either of two opposed principles.

polemic *n* a controversy or argument over doctrine; (*pl*) art of controversy.—**polemical** *adj*.

pole vault *n* a field event in which competitors jump over a high bar using a long flexible pole.

police *n* the governmental department for keeping order, detecting crime, law enforcement, etc; the members of such a department; any similar organization. * *vt* to control, protect, etc with police or a similar force.

policeman *n* a member of a police force.—**policewoman** *nf*.

policy[1] *n* a written insurance contract.

policy[2] *n* political wisdom, statecraft; a course of action selected from among alternatives; a high-level overall plan embracing the general principles and aims of an organization, esp a government.

polish *vti* to make or become smooth and shiny by rubbing (with a cloth and polish); (*fig*) to give elegance or culture to; (*with* **off**) (*inf: meal, job, etc*) to finish completely. * *n* smoothness; elegance of manner; a finish or gloss; a substance, such as wax, used to polish.—**polisher** *n*.

polished *adj* accomplished; smoothly or professionally done or performed; (*of rice*) having had the husk removed.

polite *adj* courteous; well-bred; refined.—**politely** *adv*.—**politeness** *n*.

political *adj* relating to politics or government; characteristic of political parties or politicians.—**politically** *adv*.

politician *n* a person engaged in politics, often used with implications of seeking personal or partisan gain, scheming, etc.

politics *npl* the science and art of government; political activities, beliefs or affairs; factional scheming for power.

polka *n* a lively dance; the music for this.

polka dot *n* any of a pattern of small round dots on cloth.

poll *n* a counting, listing, etc of persons, esp of voters; the number of votes recorded; an opinion survey; (*pl*) a place where votes are cast. * *vti* to receive the votes (of); to cast a vote; to canvass or question in a poll.

pollen *n* the yellow dust, containing male spores, that is formed in the anthers of flowers.

pollination *n* the transfer of pollen from the anthers of a flower to the stigma, esp by insects.— **pollinate** *vti*.

pollute *vt* to contaminate with harmful substances; to make corrupt; to profane.—**polluter** *n*.

pollution *n* the act of polluting; the state of being polluted; contamination by chemicals, noise, etc.

polo *n* a game played on horseback by two teams, using a wooden ball and long-handled mallets.

polo neck *n* a high collar turned over at the top; a sweater with such a collar.

polyester *n* any of a number of synthetic polymeric resins used for adhesives, plastics, and textiles.

polygamy *n* the practice of being married to more than one person at a time.—**polygamist** *n*.—**polygamous** *adj*.

polytechnic *n* a college that provides instruction in many applied sciences and technical subjects.

polythene, polyethylene *n* a light, plastic, multipurpose material.

pomegranate *n* an edible fruit with many seeds; the widely cultivated tropical tree bearing it.

pommel *n* the rounded, upward-projecting front part of a saddle; a knob on the hilt of a sword. * *vt* to pummel.

pomp *n* stately ceremony; ostentation.

pompous *adj* stately; self-important.—**pompously** *adv*.—**pomposity** *n*.—**pompousness** *n*.

pond *n* a body of standing water smaller than a lake.

ponder *vti* to think deeply; to consider carefully.

ponderous *adj* heavy; awkward; dull; lifeless.—**ponderously** *adv*.

pontiff *n* the Pope; a bishop.
pontificate *vi* to speak sententiously, pompously or dogmatically; to officiate at a pontifical mass.
pontoon[1] *n* a boat or cylindrical float forming a support for a bridge.
pontoon[2] *n* a gambling game with cards in which players try to obtain points better than the banker's but not more than 21.—*also* **blackjack**.
pony *n* a small horse, a bronco, mustang, etc of the western US.
pony tail *n* a style of arranging hair to resemble a pony's tail.
poodle *n* a breed of dog with a solid-coloured curly coat of many colours and sizes.
pool[1] *n* a small pond; a puddle; a small collection of liquid; a tank for swimming.
pool[2] *n* a game of billiards played on a table with six pockets; a combination of resources, funds, supplies, people, etc for some common purpose; the parties forming such a combination. * *vti* to contribute to a common fund, to share.
poor *adj* having little money, needy; deserving pity, unfortunate; deficient; disappointing; inferior. * *n* those who have little.—**poorness** *n*.
poorly *adv* insufficiently, badly. * *adj* not in good health.
pop[1] *n* a short, explosive sound, a shot; any carbonated, nonalcoholic beverage. * *vti* (*pt* **popped**) to make or cause a pop; to shoot; to go or come quickly (in, out, up); (*corn, maize*) to roast until it pops; to put suddenly; (*eyes*) to bulge.
pop[2] *adj* in a popular modern style. * *n* pop music; pop art; pop culture.
pop[3] *n* (*inf*) father; (*inf*) a name used to address an old man.
popcorn *n* a kind of corn or maize, which when heated pops or puffs up.
pope *n* bishop of Rome, head of the RC Church.
poplar *n* a slender, quick-growing tree of the willow family.
poplin *n* a sturdy corded fabric.
poppy *n* an annual or perennial plant with showy flowers; a strong reddish colour.
populace *n* the common people; the masses; all the people in a country, region, etc.
popular *adj* of the people; well liked; pleasing to many people; easy to understand.—**popularly** *adv*.
popularity *n* the condition or quality of being popular.
popularize *vt* to make popular; to make generally accepted or understood.—**popularization** *n*.
population *n* all the inhabitants or the number of people in an area.
populous *adj* densely inhabited.
porcelain *n* a hard, white, translucent variety of ceramic ware.—*also adj*.
porch *n* a covered entrance to a building; an open or enclosed gallery or room on the outside of a building.
porcupine *n* a large rodent covered with protective quills.
pore[1] *n* a tiny opening, as in the skin, plant leaves, stem, etc, for absorbing and discharging fluids.
pore[2] *vti* to look with steady attention; to study closely.
pork *n* the flesh of a pig used as food.
pornography *n* writings, pictures, films, etc, intended primarily to arouse sexual desire.—**pornographic** *adj*.—**pornographer** *n*.
porous *adj* having pores; able to absorb air and fluids, etc.—**porousness** *n*.
porpoise *n* any of several small whales, esp a black blunt-nosed whale of the north Atlantic and Pacific; any of several bottle-nosed dolphins.
porridge *n* a thick food, usu made by boiling oats or oatmeal in water or milk.
port[1] *n* a harbour; a town with a harbour where ships load and unload cargo; airport; a place where goods may be cleared through customs.
port[2] *n* a porthole; an opening, as in a valve face, for the passage of steam, etc; a hole in an armoured vehicle for firing a weapon; a circuit in a computer for inputting or outputting data.
port[3] *n* the left of an aircraft or ship looking forward.—*also adj*.
port[4] *n* a strong, sweet, fortified dark red wine.
portable *adj* capable of being carried or moved about easily.—**portability** *n*.
portal *n* an impressive gate or doorway.
portcullis *n* a grating that can be lowered to bar entrance to a castle.
portent *n* an omen, warning.
porter[1] *n* a doorman or gatekeeper.
porter[2] *n* a person who carries luggage, etc, for hire at a station, airport, etc; a railway attendant for passengers; a dark brown beer.
porthole *n* an opening (as a window) with a cover or closure esp in the side of a ship or aircraft; a port through which to shoot; an

opening for intake or exhaust of a fluid.

portico *n* (*pl* **porticoes, porticos**) a covered walkway with columns supporting the roof.

portion *n* a part, a share, esp an allotted part; a helping of food; destiny. * *vt* to share out.

portly *adj* (**portlier, portliest**) dignified; stout.

portrait *n* a painting, photograph, etc, of a person, esp of the face; (*of person*) a likeness; a vivid description.

portray *vt* to make a portrait of; to depict in words; to play the part of in a play, film, etc.— **portrayal** *n*.

pose *n* a position or attitude, esp one held for an artist or photographer; an attitude deliberately adopted for effect. * *vti* to propound, assert; to assume an attitude for effect; to sit for a painting, photograph; to set oneself up (as).

posh *adj* (*inf*) elegant; fashionable.

position *n* place, situation; a position occupied; posture; a job; state of affairs; point of view. * *vt* to place or locate.

positive *adj* affirmative; definite; sure; marked by presence, not absence, of qualities; expressed clearly, or in a confident manner; constructive; empirical; (*elect*) charged with positive electricity; (*math*) greater than zero, plus; (*gram*) of adjective or adverb, denoting the simple form; (*photog*) having light, shade, colour as in the original. * *n* a positive quality or quantity; a photographic print made from a negative.

posse *n* a body of people summoned by a sheriff to assist in keeping the peace, etc.

possess *vt* to own, have, keep; to dominate or control the mind of.

possession *n* ownership; something possessed; (*pl*) property.

possessive *adj* of or indicating possession; (*gram*) denoting a case, form or construction expressing possession; having an excessive desire to possess or dominate.—**possessively** *adv*.

possibility *n* the state of being possible; a possible occurrence, a contingency.

possible *adj* that may be or may happen; feasible, practicable; (*inf*) tolerable.—**possibly** *adv*.

post[1] *n* a piece of wood, metal, etc, set upright to support a building, sign, etc; the starting point of a race. * *vt* (*poster, etc*) to put up; to announce by posting notices; (*name*) to put on a posted or published list.

post[2] *n* a fixed position, esp where a sentry or group of soldiers is stationed; a position or job; a trading post; a settlement. * *vt* to station in a given place.

post[3] *n* the official conveyance of letters and parcels, mail; letters, parcels, etc, so conveyed; collection or delivery of post, mail. * *vt* to send a letter or parcel; to keep informed.—**postal** *adj*.

postage *n* the charge for sending a letter, etc, as represented by stamps.

postcard *n* a card, usu decorative, for sending messages by post.

postdate *vt* to write a future date on a letter or cheque.

poster *n* a usu decorative or ornamental printed sheet for advertising.

poste restante *n* the department of a post office that will hold mail until it is called for.

posterity *n* future generations; all of a person's descendants.

postgraduate *n* a person pursuing study after obtaining a university degree.—*also adj*.

posthumous *adj* (*child*) born after its father's death; (*award, etc*) given after one's death.—**posthumously** *adv*.

postman *n* a person who collects or delivers mail.

postmark *n* the post office mark cancelling the stamp on a letter by showing the date, place of posting.

postmaster *n* the manager of a post office.

postmortem *n* an examination of a corpse to determine the cause of death; an autopsy.—*also adj*.

post office *n* the building where postage stamps are sold and other postal business conducted; (*with caps*) a government department handling the transmission of mail.

postpone *vt* to put off, delay to a future date.—**postponement** *n*.

postscript *n* (*abbr* **PS**) a note added to a letter after completion.

postulate *vt* to assume to be true; to demand or claim. * *n* a position taken as self-evident; (*math*) an unproved assumption taken as basic; an axiom.—**postulation** *n*.

posture *n* a pose; a body position; an attitude of mind; an official stand or position. * *vti* to pose in a particular way; to assume a pose.

posy *n* a small bunch of flowers.

pot[1] *n* a deep, round cooking vessel; an earthenware or plastic container for plants; a framework for catching fish or lobster; (*inf*) a large amount (as of money); (*inf*) all the money bet at a single time. * *vb* (*pt* **potted**) *vt* to put or preserve in a pot. * *vi* to take a pot shot, shoot.

pot[2] *n* (*sl*) cannabis.
potash *n* potassium carbonate.
potato *n* (*pl* **potatoes**) a starchy, oval tuber eaten as a vegetable.
potency *n* the quality or condition of being potent; power; strength.
potent *adj* powerful; influential; intoxicating; (*a male*) able to have sexual intercourse.—**potently** *adv*.
potential *adj* possible, but not yet actual. * *n* the unrealized ability to do something.—**potentiality** *n*.—**potentially** *adv*.
pothole *n* a hole worn in a road by traffic; (*geol*) a deep hole or cave in rock caused by the action of water.
potholing *n* an activity involving the exploration of deep underground caves.—**potholer** *n*.
potion *n* a mixture of liquids, such as poison.
pot shot *n* a random or easy shot.
potter[1] *vi* to busy oneself idly; to spend time. —*also* **putter**.
potter[2] *n* a person who makes earthenware vessels.
pottery *n* earthenware vessels; a workshop where such articles are made.
potty[1] *adj* (**pottier, pottiest**) (*inf*) slightly crazy; trivial, petty.
potty[2] *n* (*inf*) a chamber pot.
pouch *n* a small bag or sack; a bag for mail; a sacklike structure, as that on the abdomen of a kangaroo, etc, for carrying young.
poultice *n* a hot moist dressing applied to a sore part of the body.
poultry *n* domesticated birds kept for meat or eggs.
pounce *vi* to swoop or spring suddenly (upon) in order to seize; to make a sudden assault or approach.—*also n*.
pound[1] *n* a unit of weight equal to 16 ounces (*abbr* **lb**); a unit of money in the UK and other countries, symbol £.
pound[2] *vt* to beat into a powder or a pulp; to hit hard. * *vi* to deliver heavy blows repeatedly (at or on); to move with heavy steps; to throb; (*with* **away**) to work hard and continuously.
pound[3] *n* a municipal enclosure for stray animals; a depot for holding impounded personal property, eg cars, until claimed; a place or condition of confinement.
pour *vti* to cause to flow in a stream; to flow continuously; to rain heavily; to serve tea or coffee.—**pourer** *n*.
pout *vti* to push out (the lips); to look sulky. * *n* a thrusting out of the lips; (*pl*) a fit of pique.
poverty *n* the condition of being poor; scarcity.
powder *n* any substance in tiny, loose particles; a specific kind of powder, esp for medicinal or cosmetic use; fine dry light snow. * *vti* to sprinkle or cover with powder; to reduce to powder.
powdery *adj* like powder; easily crumbled.
power *n* ability to do something; political, social or financial control or force; a person or state with influence over others; legal force or authority; physical force; a source of energy; (*math*) the result of continued multiplication of a quantity by itself a specified number of times. * *adj* operated by electricity, a fuel engine, etc; served by an auxiliary system that reduces effort; carrying electricity. * *vt* to supply with a source of power.—**powered** *adj*.
powerful *adj* mighty; strong; influential.—**powerfully** *adv*.
powerless *adj* without power; helpless; feeble.—**powerlessly** *adv*.—**powerlessness** *n*.
power station, power plant *n* a building where electric power is generated.
powwow *n* an American Indian ceremony (as for victory in war); (*inf*) any conference or get-together. * *vi* to confer, chat.
pox *n* a virus disease marked by pustules; (*arch*) smallpox; syphilis; a plague; a curse.
practicable *adj* able to be practised; possible, feasible.—**practicability** *n*.
practical *adj* concerned with action, not theory; workable; suitable; trained by practice; virtual, in effect.
practical joke *n* a prank intended to embarrass or to cause discomfort.
practically *adv* in a practical manner; virtually.
practice *n* action; habit, custom; repetition and exercise to gain skill; the exercise of a profession.
practise, practice (*US*) *vti* to repeat an exercise to acquire skill; to put into practice; to do habitually or frequently; (*profession*) to work at.
practitioner *n* a person who practises a profession.
pragmatic *adj* practical; testing the validity of all concepts by their practical results.—**pragmatically** *adv*.
prairie *n* a large area of level or rolling land predominantly in grass; a dry treeless plateau.
praise *vt* to express approval of, to commend; to glorify, to worship. * *vi* to express praise.

* *n* commendation; glorification.—**praiseworthy** *adj*.

pram *n* a four-wheeled carriage for a baby.

prance *vi* (*horse*) to spring on the hind legs, bound; (*person*) to walk or ride in a showy manner; to swagger.—*also n*.

prank *n* a mischievous trick or joke; a ludicrous act.

prattle *vti* to talk in a childish manner; to babble. * *n* empty chatter.

prawn *n* an edible marine shrimp-like crustacean.

pray *vti* to offer prayers to God; to implore.

prayer *n* supplication, entreaty, praise or thanks to God; the form of this; the act of praying; (*pl*) devotional services; something prayed for.

preach *vi* to advocate in an earnest or moralizing way. * *vt* to deliver a sermon; (*patience, etc*) to advocate.—**preacher** *n*.

preamble *n* an introductory part to a document, speech, or story, stating its purpose.

precarious *adj* dependent on chance; insecure; dangerous.—**precariously** *adv*.—**precariousness** *n*.

precaution *n* a preventive measure; care taken beforehand; careful foresight.—**precautionary** *adj*.

precede *vti* to be, come or go before in time, place, order, rank, or importance.

precedence *n* priority; the right of higher rank.

precedent *n* a previous and parallel case serving as an example; (*law*) a decision, etc, serving as a rule.

preceding *adj* coming or going before; former.

precept *n* a rule of moral conduct; a maxim; an order issued by a legally constituted authority to a subordinate.

precinct *n* (usu *pl*) an enclosure between buildings, walls, etc; a limited area; an urban area where traffic is prohibited; (*pl*) environs; in US, a police district or a subdivision of a voting ward.

precious *adj* of great cost or value; beloved; very fastidious; affected; thoroughgoing. * *adv* (*sl*) very.—**preciousness** *n*.

precipice *n* a cliff or overhanging rock face.

precipitate *vti* to throw from a height; to cause to happen suddenly or too soon; (*chem*) to separate out; to rain; to fall as rain, snow, dew, etc.—**precipitately** *adv*.

precipitation *n* the act of precipitating; undue haste; rain, snow, etc; the amount of this.

precipitous *adj* of or like a precipice; sheer, steep.—**precipitously** *adv*.

precis, précis *n* (*pl* **precis, précis**) a summary or abstract.—*also vt*.

precise *adj* clearly defined, exact; accurate; punctilious; particular.—**precisely** *adv*.

preclude *vt* to rule out in advance; to make impossible.—**preclusion** *n*.—**preclusive** *adj*.

precocious *adj* prematurely ripe or developed.—**precociously** *adv*.

preconceive *vt* to form an idea or opinion of before actual experience.

precondition *n* a requirement that must be met beforehand, a prerequisite. * *vt* (*organism, patient*) to prepare to behave or react in a certain way under certain conditions.

precursor *n* a predecessor; a substance from which another substance is formed.—**precursory** *adj*.

predator *n* a person who preys, plunders or devours; a carnivorous animal.

predatory *adj* living on prey, of or relating to a predator; characterized by hunting or plundering.

predecessor *n* a former holder of a position or office; an ancestor.

predestine *vt* to foreordain; to destine beforehand.

predicament *n* a difficult or embarrassing situation.

predicate *vt* to state as a quality or attribute; to base (on facts, conditions etc). * *n* (*gram*) that which is stated about the subject.

predict *vt* to foretell; to state (what one believes will happen).—**predictable** *adj*.—**predictably** *adv*.

prediction *n* the act of predicting; that which is predicted; a forecast or prophecy.

predominant *adj* ruling over, controlling; influencing.—**predominance** *n*.

predominantly *adv* mainly.

predominate *vt* to rule over; to have influence or control over; to prevail; to be greater in number, intensity, etc.

pre-eminent *adj* distinguished above others; outstanding.—**pre-eminence** *n*.—**pre-eminently** *adv*.

pre-empt *vt* to take action to check other action beforehand; to gain the right to buy (public land) by settling on it; to seize before anyone else can; (*scheduled TV, radio programme*) to replace; (*in bridge*) to bid highly to exclude bids from opponents.—**pre-emption** *n*.—**pre-emptive** *adj*.

preen *vti* (*birds*) to clean and trim the feathers; to congratulate (oneself) for achievement; to groom (oneself); to gloat.

prefab *n* (*inf*) a prefabricated building.
preface *n* an introduction or preliminary explanation; a foreword or introduction to a book; a preamble. * *vt* to serve as a preface; to introduce.
prefect *n* a person placed in authority over others; a student monitor in a school; in some countries, an administrative official.
prefer *vt* (*pt* **preferred**) to like better; to promote, advance; to put before (a court) for consideration.
preferable *adj* deserving preference; superior; more desirable.—**preferably** *adv*.
preference *n* the act of preferring, choosing, or favouring one above another; that which is chosen or preferred; prior right; advantage given to one person, country, etc, over others.
preferential *adj* giving or receiving preference.—**preferentially** *adv*.
prefix *vt* to put at the beginning of or before; to put as an introduction. * *n* a syllable or group of syllables placed at the beginning of a word, affecting its meaning.
pregnant *adj* having a foetus in the womb; significant, meaningful; imaginative; filled (with) or rich (in).—**pregnancy** *n*.
prehistoric *adj* of the period before written records began.—**prehistory** *n*.
prejudge *vt* to pass judgment on before a trial; to form a premature opinion.—**prejudgment, prejudgement** *n*.
prejudice *n* a judgment or opinion made without adequate knowledge; bias; intolerance or hatred of other races, etc; (*law*) injury or disadvantage due to another's action. * *vt* to affect or injure through prejudice.—**prejudiced** *adj*.
preliminary *adj* preparatory; introductory. * *n* an event preceding another; a preliminary step or measure; (*in school*) a preparatory examination.
prelude *n* an introductory act or event; an event preceding another of greater importance; (*mus*) a movement which acts as an introduction.—*also vt*.
premarital *adj* (*sex*) taking place before marriage.
premature *adj* occurring before the expected or normal time; too early, hasty.—**prematurely** *adv*.—**prematureness**, **prematurity** *n*.
premier *adj* principal; first. * *n* the head of a government, a prime minister.—**premiership** *n*.
premiere *n* the first public performance of a play, film, etc. * *vt* to give a premiere of. * *vi* to have a first performance; to appear for the first time as a star performer.
premise *n* a proposition on which reasoning is based; something assumed or taken for granted; (*pl*) a piece of land and its buildings. * *vt* to state as an introduction; to postulate; to base on certain assumptions.
premium *n* a reward, esp an inducement to buy; a periodical payment for insurance; excess over an original price; something given free or at a reduced price with a purchase; a high value or value in excess of expectation. * *adj* (*goods*) high quality.
premonition *n* a foreboding; a feeling of something about to happen.
preoccupied *adj* absent-minded, lost in thought; (*with* **with**) having one's attention completely taken up by.
prep *abbr* = preparatory school.
preparation *n* the act of preparing; a preparatory measure; something prepared, as a medicine, cosmetic, etc.
preparatory *adj* serving to prepare; introductory. * *adv* by way of preparation; in a preparatory manner.
preparatory school *n* a private school that prepares students for an advanced school or college.
prepare *vt* to make ready in advance; to fit out, equip; to cook; to instruct, teach; to put together. * *vi* to make oneself ready.
prepared *adj* subjected to a special process or treatment.
preponderate *vi* to be greater in number, amount, influence, etc; to predominate, prevail; to weigh more.—**preponderance** *n*.—**preponderant** *adj*.
preposition *n* a word used before a noun or pronoun to show its relation to another part of the sentence.—**prepositional** *adj*.
preposterous *adj* ridiculous; laughable; absurd.—**preposterously** *adv*.—**preposterousness** *n*.
prerequisite *n* a condition, etc, that must be fulfilled prior to something else. * *adj* required beforehand.
prerogative *n* a privilege or right accorded through office or hereditary rank.
presbytery *n* a ruling body in presbyterian churches consisting of the ministers and representative elders from congregations within a district; the house of a Roman Catholic priest.
prescribe *vt* to designate; to ordain; (*rules*) to

lay down; (*medicine, treatment*) to order, advise.

prescription *n* act of prescribing; (*med*) a written instruction to a pharmacist for the preparation of a drug; (*law*) establishment of a right or title through long use.

presence *n* being present; immediate surroundings; personal appearance and bearing; impressive bearing, personality, etc; something (as a spirit) felt or believed to be present.

presence of mind *n* readiness of resource in an emergency, etc; the ability to say the right thing.

present[1] *adj* being at the specified place; existing or happening now; (*gram*) denoting action or state now or action that is always true. * *n* the time being; now; the present tense.

present[2] *n* a gift.

present[3] *vt* to introduce someone, esp socially; (*a play, etc*) to bring before the public, exhibit; to make a gift or award; to show; to perform; (*law*) to lay a charge before a court; (*weapon*) to point in a particular direction. * *vi* to present a weapon; to become manifest; to come forward as a patient.

presentable *adj* of decent appearance; fit to go into company.

presentation *n* act of presenting; a display or exhibition; style of presenting; something offered or given; a description or persuasive account; (*med*) the position of a fetus in the uterus.

presently *adv* in a short while, soon.

preservation *n* the act of preserving or securing; a state of being preserved or repaired.

preservative *adj* preserving. * *n* something that preserves or has the power of preserving, esp an additive.

preserve *vt* to keep safe from danger; to protect; (*food*) to can, pickle, or prepare for future use; to keep or reserve for personal or special use. * *vi* to make preserves; to raise and protect game for sport. * *n* (*usu pl*) fruit preserved by cooking in sugar; an area restricted for the protection of natural resources, esp one used for regulated hunting, etc; something regarded as reserved for certain persons.

preside *vi* to take the chair or hold the position of authority; to take control or exercise authority.

president *n* the head of state of a republic; the highest officer of a company, club, etc.—**presidency** *n*.—**presidential** *adj*.

press *vt* to act on with steady force or weight; to push against, squeeze, compress, etc; (*clothes, etc*) to iron; to embrace closely; to force, compel; to entreat; to emphasize; to trouble; to urge on; (*record*) to make from a matrix. * *vi* to weigh down; to crowd closely; to go forward with determination. * *n* pressure, urgency, etc; a crowd; a machine for crushing, stamping, etc; a machine for printing; a printing or publishing establishment; the gathering and distribution of news and those who perform these functions; newspapers collectively; any of various pressure devices; an upright closet for storing clothes.

press conference *n* a group interview given to members of the press by a politician, celebrity, etc.

pressing *adj* urgent; calling for immediate attention; importunate. * *n* a number of records made at one time from a master.

pressure *n* the act of pressing; a compelling force; a moral force; compression; urgency; constraint; (*physics*) force per unit of area. * *vt* to pressurize.

pressure group *n* a group of people organized to alert public opinion, legislators, etc, to a particular area of interest.

pressurize *vt* to keep nearly normal atmospheric pressure inside an aeroplane, etc, as at high altitudes; to exert pressure on; to attempt to compel, press.

prestige *n* standing in the eyes of people; commanding position in people's minds.

prestigious *adj* imparting prestige or distinction.

presumably *adv* as may be presumed.

presume *vt* to take for granted, suppose. * *vi* to assume to be true; to act without permission; to take liberties; (*with* **on**, **upon**) to take advantage of.

presumption *n* a supposition; a thing presumed; a strong probability; effrontery.

presumptuous *adj* tending to presume; bold; forward.—**presumptuously** *adv*.—**presumptuousness** *n*.

presuppose *vt* to assume beforehand; to involve as a necessary prior condition.—**presupposition** *n*.

pretence, pretense (*US*) *n* the act of pretending; a hypocritical show; a fraud, a sham.

pretend *vti* to claim, represent, or assert falsely; to feign, make believe; to lay claim (to).

pretentious *adj* claiming great importance; ostentatious.—**pretentiously** *adv*.—**pretentiousness** *n*.

pretext *n* a pretended reason to conceal a true one; an excuse.

pretty *adj* (**prettier, prettiest**) attractive in a dainty, graceful way. * *adv* (*inf*) fairly, moderately.—**prettily** *adv*.—**prettiness** *n*.

prevail *vi* to overcome; to predominate; to be customary or in force.

prevailing *adj* generally accepted, widespread; predominant.

prevalent *adj* current; predominant; widely practised or experienced.—**prevalence** *n*.

prevent *vt* to keep from happening; to hinder.—**preventable, preventible** *adj*.—**prevention** *n*.

preventive, preventative *adj* serving to prevent, precautionary. * *n* something used to prevent disease.

preview *n* an advance, restricted showing, as of a film; a showing of scenes from a film to advertise it. * *vt* to view or show in advance of public presentation; to give a preliminary survey.

previous *adj* coming before in time or order; prior, former.—**previously** *adv*.

prey *n* an animal killed for food by another; a victim. * *vi* (*with* **on**, **upon**) to seize and devour prey; (*person*) to victimize; to weigh heavily on the mind.

price *n* the amount, usu in money, paid for anything; the cost of obtaining some benefit; value, worth. * *vt* to set the price of something; to estimate a price; to deprive by raising prices excessively.

priceless *adj* very expensive; invaluable; (*inf*) very amusing, odd, or absurd.

prick *n* a sharp point; a puncture or piercing made by a sharp point; the wound or sensation inflicted; a qualm (of conscience); (*inf*) penis; (*offensive*) a spiteful person usu with authority. * *vti* to affect with anguish, grief, or remorse; to pierce slightly; to cause a sharp pain to; to goad, spur; (*the ears*) to erect; (*with* **out**) to transfer seedlings.

prickle *n* a thorn, spine or bristle; a pricking sensation. * *vti* to feel or cause to feel a pricking sensation.

prickly *adj* having prickles; tingling; irritable.—**prickliness** *n*.

prickly heat *n* a skin eruption caused by inflammation of the sweat glands.

pride *n* feeling of self-worth or esteem; excessive self-esteem; conceit; a sense of one's own importance; a feeling of elation due to success; the cause of this; splendour; a herd (of lions). * *vti* to be proud of; to take credit for.

priest *n* in various churches, a person authorized to perform sacred rites; an Anglican, Eastern Orthodox, or Roman Catholic clergyman ranking below a bishop.—**priestliness** *n*.—**priestly** *adj*.

priestess *n* a priest who is a woman; a woman regarded as a leader (as of a movement).

priesthood *n* the office of priest; priests collectively.

prig *n* a smug, self-righteous person.—**priggish** *adj*.

prim *adj* (**primmer, primmest**) proper, formal and precise in manner; demure.—**primly** *adv*.—**primness** *n*.

primarily *adv* mainly.

primary *adj* first; earliest; original; first in order of time; chief; elementary. * *n* a person or thing that is highest in rank, importance, etc; in US, a preliminary election at which candidates are chosen for the final election.

primary school *n* a school for children up to the age of 11 or 12.

primate *n* an archbishop or the highest ranking bishop in a province, etc; any of the highest order of mammals, including man.

prime[1] *adj* first in rank, importance, or quality; chief; (*math*) of a number, divisible only by itself and 1. * *n* the best time; the height of perfection; full maturity; full health and strength.

prime[2] *vt* to prepare or make something ready; to pour liquid into (a pump) or powder into (a firearm); to paint on a primer.

prime minister *n* the head of the government in a parliamentary democracy.

primer[1] *n* a simple book for teaching; a small introductory book on a subject.

primer[2] *n* a detonating device; a first coat of paint or oil.

primeval *adj* of the first age of the world; primitive.

primitive *adj* of the beginning or the earliest times; crude; simple; basic. * *n* a primitive person or thing.—**primitively** *adv*.

primrose *n* a perennial plant with pale yellow flowers.

prince *n* the son of a sovereign; a ruler ranking below a king; the head of a principality; any pre-eminent person.

princess *n* a daughter of a sovereign; the wife of a prince; one outstanding in a specified respect.

principal *adj* first in rank or importance; chief. * *n* a principal person; a person who organizes; the head of a college or school; the leading player in a ballet, opera, etc; (*law*) the person who commits a crime; a person for whom another acts as agent; a capital sum lent or invested; a main beam or rafter.

principality *n* the position of responsibility of a principal; the rank and territory of a prince.

principally *adv* mainly.

principle *n* a basic truth; a law or doctrine used as a basis for others; a moral code of conduct; a chemical constituent with a characteristic quality; a scientific law explaining a natural action; the method of a thing's working.

print *vti* to stamp (a mark, letter, etc) on a surface; to produce (on paper, etc) the impressions of inked type, etc; to produce (a book, etc); to write in letters resembling printed ones; to make (a photographic print). * *n* a mark made on a surface by pressure; the impression of letters, designs, etc, made from inked type, a plate, or block; an impression made by a photomechanical process; a photographic copy, esp from a negative.

printer *n* a person engaged in printing; a machine for printing from; a device that produces printout.

printing *n* the activity, skill, or business of producing printed matter; a style of writing using capital letters; the total number of books, etc, printed at one time.

printout *n* a printed record produced automatically (as by a computer).

prior *adj* previous; taking precedence (as in importance). * *n* the superior ranking below an abbot in a monastery; the head of a house or group of houses in a religious community.—**prioress** *nf*.

priority *n* precedence in rank, time, or place; preference; something requiring specified attention.

priory *n* a religious house under a prior or prioress.

prise *vt* to force (open, up) with a lever, etc.

prism *n* (*geom*) a solid whose ends are similar, equal, and parallel plane figures and whose sides are parallelograms; a transparent body of this form usu with triangular ends used for dispersing or reflecting light.—**prismatic** *adj*.

prison *n* a building used to house convicted criminals for punishment and suspects remanded in custody while awaiting trial; a jail.

prisoner *n* a person held in prison or under arrest; a captive; a person confined by a restraint.

pristine *adj* pure; in an original, unspoiled condition.

privacy *n* being private; seclusion; secrecy; one's private life.

private *adj* of or concerning a particular person or group; not open to or controlled by the public; for an individual person; not holding public office; secret. * *n* (*pl*) the genitals; an enlisted man of the lowest military rank in the army.—**privately** *adv*.

privet *n* a white-flowered evergreen shrub used for hedges.

privilege *n* a right or special benefit enjoyed by a person or a small group; a prerogative. * *vt* to bestow a privilege on.

privileged *adj* having or enjoying privileges; not subject to disclosure in a court of law.

privy *adj* private; having access to confidential information. * *n* a lavatory, esp one outside; (*law*) a person with an interest in an action.

prize *n* an award won in competition or a lottery; a reward given for merit; a thing worth striving for. * *adj* given as, rewarded by, a prize. * *vt* to value highly.

prizefight *n* a professional boxing match.—**prizefighter** *n*.

pro[1] *adv, prep* in favour of. * *n* (*pl* **pros**) an argument for a proposal or motion.

pro[2] *adj,n* professional.

probability *n* that which is probable; likelihood; (*math*) the ratio of the chances in favour of an event to the total number.

probable *adj* likely; to be expected.

probation *n* testing of character or skill; release from prison under supervision by a probation officer; the state or period of being on probation.—**probationary** *adj*.

probe *n* a flexible surgical instrument for exploring a wound; a device, as an unmanned spacecraft, used to obtain information about an environment; an investigation. * *vt* to explore with a probe; to examine closely; to investigate.

probity *n* honesty, integrity, uprightness.

problem *n* a question for solution; a person, thing or matter difficult to cope with; a puzzle; (*math*) a proposition stating something to be done; an intricate unsettled question.

problematic, problematical *adj* presenting a problem; questionable; uncertain.

procedure *n* an established mode of conducting business, esp in law or in a meeting; a practice; a prescribed or traditional course; a step taken as part of an established order of steps.—**procedural** *adj*.

proceed *vi* to go on, esp after stopping; to come from; to continue; to carry on; to issue; to take action; to go to law.

proceeding *n* an advance or going forward; (*pl*) steps, action, in a lawsuit; (*pl*) published records of a society, etc.

proceeds *npl* the total amount of money brought in; the net amount received.

process *n* a course or state of going on; a series of events or actions; a method of operation; forward movement; (*law*) a court summons; the whole course of proceedings in a legal action. * *vt* to handle something following set procedures; (*food, etc*) to prepare by a special process; (*law*) to take action; (*film*) to develop.

procession *n* a group of people in marching in order, as in a parade.

proclaim *vt* to announce publicly and officially; to tell openly; to praise.

proclamation *n* the act of proclaiming; an official notice to the public.

procrastinate *vti* to defer action, to delay.—**procrastination** *n*.

procreate *vt* to bring into being, to engender offspring.—**procreation** *n*.

procure *vt* to obtain by effort; to get and make available for promiscuous sexual intercourse; to bring about. * *vi* to procure women.—**procurement** *n*.

prod *vt* (*pt* **prodded**) to poke or jab, as with a pointed stick; to rouse into activity. * *n* the action of prodding; a sharp object; a stimulus.

prodigal *adj* wasteful; extravagant; openhanded. * *n* a wastrel; a person who squanders money.

prodigious *adj* enormous, vast; amazing.—**prodigiously** *adv*.

prodigy *n* an extraordinary person, thing or act; a gifted child.

produce *vt* to bring about; to bring forward, show; to yield; to cause; to manufacture, make; to give birth to; (*play, film*) to put before the public. * *vi* to yield something. * *n* that which is produced, esp agricultural products.

producer *n* someone who produces, esp a farmer or manufacturer; a person who finances or supervises the putting on of a play or making of a film; an apparatus or plant for making gas.

product *n* a thing produced by nature, industry or art; a result; an outgrowth; (*math*) the number obtained by multiplying two or more numbers together.

production *n* the act of producing; a thing produced; a work presented on the stage or screen or over the air.

productive *adj* producing or capable of producing; fertile.—**productively** *adv*.—**productiveness** *n*.

productivity *n* the state of being productive; the ratio of the output of a manufacturing business to the input of materials, labour, etc.

profane *adj* secular, not sacred; showing no respect for sacred things; irreverent; blasphemous; not possessing esoteric or expert knowledge. * *vt* to desecrate; to debase by a wrong, unworthy or vulgar use.—**profanely** *adv*.

profess *vt* to affirm publicly, declare; to claim to be expert in; to declare in words or appearance only.

profession *n* an act of professing; avowal, esp of religious belief; an occupation requiring specialized knowledge and often long and intensive academic preparation; the people engaged in this; affirmation; entry into a religious order.

professional *adj* of or following a profession; conforming to the technical or ethical standards of a profession; earning a livelihood in an activity or field often engaged in by amateurs; having a specified occupation as a permanent career; engaged in by persons receiving financial return; pursuing a line of conduct as though it were a profession.—*also n*.—**professionally** *adv*.

professor *n* a faculty member of the highest academic rank at a university; a teacher at a university, college, etc.—**professorial** *adj*.—**professorship** *n*.

proficient *adj* skilled, competent.—**proficiency** *n*.—**proficiently** *adv*.

profile *n* a side view of the head as in a portrait, drawing, etc; a biographical sketch; a graph representing a person's abilities. * *vt* to represent in profile; to produce (as by writing, drawing, etc) a profile of.

profit *n* gain; the excess of returns over expenditure; the compensation to entrepreneurs resulting from the assumption of risk; (*pl*) the excess returns from a business; advantage, benefit. * *vti* to be of advantage (to), benefit; to gain.

profitable *adj* yielding profit, lucrative; beneficial; useful.—**profitability** *n*.—**profitably** *adv*.

profiteer *vi* to make exorbitant profits, esp in wartime.—*also n*.—**profiteering** *n*.

profound *adj* at great depth; intellectually deep; abstruse, mysterious.—**profoundly** *adv*.

profuse *adj* abundant; generous; extravagant.—**profusely** *adv*.—**profuseness** *n*.
profusion *n* an abundance.
progeny *n* offspring; descendants; outcome.
program *n* a sequence of instructions fed into a computer. * *vti* (*pt* **programmed** *or* **programed**) to feed a program into a computer; to write a program.
programme, program (*US*) *n* a printed list containing details of a ceremony, of the actors in a play, etc; a scheduled radio or television broadcast; a curriculum or syllabus for a course of study; a plan or schedule. * *vt* (*pt* **programmed**) to prepare a plan or schedule.
progress *n* a movement forwards or onwards, advance; satisfactory growth or development; a tour from place to place in stages. * *vi* to move forward, advance; to improve. * *vt* (*project*) to take to completion.
progression *n* progress; advancement by degrees; (*math*) a series of numbers, each differing from the succeeding according to a fixed law; (*mus*) a regular succession of chords.
progressive *adj* advancing, improving; proceeding by degrees; continuously increasing; aiming at reforms. * *n* a person who believes in moderate political change, esp social improvement by government action.—**progressively** *adv*.—**progressiveness** *n*.
prohibit *vt* to forbid by law; to prevent.—**prohibitory** *adj*.
prohibition *n* the act of forbidding; an order that forbids; a legal ban on the manufacture and sale of alcoholic drinks.—**prohibitionist** *n*.
prohibitive *adj* forbidding; so high as to prevent purchase, use, etc, of something.—**prohibitively** *adv*.
project *n* a plan, scheme; an undertaking; a task carried out by students, etc, involving research. * *vt* to throw forward; (*light, shadow, etc*) to produce an outline of on a distance surface; to make objective or externalize; (*one's voice*) to make heard at a distance; (*feeling, etc*) to attribute to another; to imagine; to estimate, plan, or figure for the future. * *vi* to jut out; to come across vividly; to make oneself heard clearly.
projectile *n* a missile; something propelled by force. * *adj* throwing forward; capable of being thrown forward.
projection *n* the act of projecting or the condition of being projected; a thing projecting; the representation on a plane surface of part of the earth's surface; a projected image; an estimate of future possibilities based on a current trend; a mental image externalized; an unconscious attribution to another of one's own feelings and motives.
projector *n* an instrument that projects images from transparencies or film; an instrument that projects rays of light; a person who promotes enterprises.
proletariat *n* the lowest social or economic class of a community; wage earners; the industrial working class.—**proletarian** *adj*.
proliferate *vi* to grow or reproduce rapidly.—**proliferation** *n*.
prolific *adj* producing abundantly; fruitful.
prologue, prolog (*US*) *n* the introductory lines of a play, speech, or poem; an introductory event.
prolong *vt* to extend or lengthen in space or time; to spin out.
prom *n* a promenade; a dance.
promenade *n* an esplanade; a ball or dance.; a leisurely walk. * *vti* to take a promenade (along, through).
prominence *n* the state of being prominent; a projection; relative importance; celebrity, fame.
prominent *adj* jutting, projecting; standing out, conspicuous; widely and favourably known; distinguished.—**prominently** *adv*.
promiscuous *adj* indiscriminate, esp in sexual liaisons.—**promiscuity** *n*.—**promiscuously** *adv*.—**promiscuousness** *n*.
promise *n* a pledge; an undertaking to do or not to do something; an indication, as of a successful future. * *vti* to pledge; to undertake; to give reason to expect.
promising *adj* likely to turn out well; hopeful.
promontory *n* a peak of high land that juts out into a body of water.
promote *vt* to encourage; to advocate; to raise to a higher rank; (*employee, student*) to advance from one grade to the next higher grade; (*product*) to encourage sales by advertising, publicity, or discounting.
promoter *n* a person who promotes, esp one who organizes and finances a sporting event or pop concert; a substance that increases the activity of a catalyst.
promotion *n* an elevation in position or rank; the furtherance of the sale of merchandise through advertising, publicity, or discounting.—**promotional** *adj*.
prompt *adj* without delay; quick to respond; immediate; of or relating to prompting ac-

tors. * *vt* to urge; to inspire; (*actor*) to remind of forgotten words, etc (as in a play). * *n* something that reminds; a time limit for payment of an account; the contract by which this time is fixed.—**promptly** *adv*.

prompter *n* one that prompts, esp a person who sits offstage and reminds actors of forgotten lines.

promptness *n* alacrity in action or decision; quickness; punctuality.

prone *adj* face downwards; lying flat, prostrate; inclined or disposed (to).—**proneness** *n*.

prong *n* a spike of a fork or other forked object.—**pronged** *adj*.

pronoun *n* a word used to represent a noun (eg *I, he, she, it*).

pronounce *vt* to utter, articulate; to speak officially, pass (judgment); to declare formally.—**pronounceable** *adj*.

pronounced *adj* marked, noticeable.

pronouncement *n* a formal announcement, declaration; a confident assertion.

pronunciation *n* articulation; the way a word is pronounced.

proof *n* evidence that establishes the truth; the fact, act, or process of validating; test; demonstration; a sample from type, etc, for correction; a trial print from a photographic negative; the relative strength of an alcoholic liquor. * *adj* resistant; impervious, impenetrable. * *vt* to make proof against (water).

prop[1] *vt* (*pt* **propped**) to support by placing something under or against. * *n* a rigid support; a thing or person giving support.

prop[2] *see* **property**.

prop[3] *abbr* = propeller.

propaganda *n* the organized spread of ideas, doctrines, etc, to promote a cause; the ideas, etc, so spread.—**propagandist** *n, adj*.

propel *vt* (*pt* **propelled**) to drive or move forward.—**propellant, propellent** *n*.

propeller *n* a mechanism to impart drive; a device having two or more blades in a revolving hub for propelling a ship or aircraft.

propensity *n* a natural inclination; disposition, tendency.

proper *adj* own, individual, peculiar; appropriate, fit; correct, conventional; decent, respectable; in the most restricted sense; (*sl*) thorough.

properly *adv* in the right way; justifiably; (*sl*) thoroughly.

property *n* a quality or attribute; a distinctive feature or characteristic; one's possessions; real estate, land; a movable article used in a stage setting (—*also* **prop**).

prophecy *n* a message of divine will and purpose; prediction.

prophesy *vti* to predict with assurance or on the basis of mystic knowledge; to foretell.

prophet *n* a religious leader regarded as, or claiming to be, divinely inspired; one who predicts the future.—**prophetess** *nf*.

prophetic, prophetical *adj* of a prophet or prophecy; prophesying events.—**prophetically** *adv*.

proportion *n* the relationship between things in size, quantity, or degree; ratio; symmetry, balance; comparative part or share; (*math*) the equality of two ratios; a share or quota; (*pl*) dimensions. * *vt* to put in proper relation with something else; to make proportionate (to).

proportional *adj* of proportion; aiming at due proportion; proportionate.—**proportionality** *n*.—**proportionally** *adv*.

proportionate *adj* in due pro portion, corresponding in amount. * *vt* to make proportionate.—**proportionately** *adv*.

proposal *n* a scheme, plan, or suggestion; an offer of marriage.

propose *vt* to present for consideration; to suggest; to intend; to announce the drinking of a toast to; (*person*) to nominate; to move as a resolution. * *vi* to make an offer (of marriage).—**proposer** *n*.

proposition *n* a proposal for consideration; a plan; a request for sexual intercourse; (*inf*) a proposed deal, as in business; (*inf*) an undertaking to be dealt with; (*math*) a problem to be solved.

proprietor *n* an owner.—**proprietress** *nf*.—**proprietorial** *adj*.

propulsion *n* the act of propelling; something that propels.

prosaic *adj* commonplace, matter-of-fact, dull.—**prosaically** *adv*.

prose *n* ordinary language without metre. * *adj* in prose; humdrum, dull.

prosecute *vt* to bring legal action against; to pursue. * *vi* to institute and carry on a legal suit or prosecution.

prosecution *n* the act of prosecuting, esp by law; the prosecuting party in a legal case.

prosecutor *n* a person who prosecutes, esp in a criminal court.

prospect *n* a wide view, a vista; (*pl*) measure of future success; future outlook; expectation; a likely customer, candidate, etc. * *vti* to explore or search (for).—**prospector** *n*.

prospective *adj* likely; anticipated, expected.

prospectus *n* a printed statement of the features of a new work, enterprise, etc; something (as a condition or statement) that forecasts the course or nature of a situation.

prosper *vi* to thrive; to flourish; to succeed.

prosperity *n* success; wealth.—**prosperous** *adj*.—**prosperously** *adv*.

prostitute *n* a person who has sexual intercourse for money; (*fig*) one who deliberately debases his or her talents (as for money). * *vt* to offer indiscriminately for sexual intercourse, esp for money; to devote to corrupt or unworthy purposes.

prostrate *adj* lying face downwards; helpless; overcome; lying prone or supine. * *vt* to throw oneself down; to lie flat; to humble oneself.—**prostration** *n*.

protagonist *n* the main character in a drama, novel, etc; a supporter of a cause.

protect *vt* to defend from danger or harm; to guard; to maintain the status and integrity of, esp through financial guarantees; to foster or shield from infringement or restriction; to restrict competition through tariffs and trade controls.—**protector** *n*.

protection *n* the act of protecting; the condition of being protected; something that protects; shelter; defence; patronage; the taxing of competing imports to foster home industry; the advocacy or theory of this (—*also* **protectionism**); immunity from prosecution or attack obtained by the payment of money.

protective *adj* serving to protect, defend, shelter.—**protectively** *adv*.

protégé *n* a person guided and helped in his career by another person.—**protégée** *nf*.

protein *n* a complex organic compound containing nitrogen that is an essential constituent of food.

protest *vi* to object to; to remonstrate. * *vt* to assert or affirm; to execute or have executed a formal protest against; to make a statement or gesture in objection to. * *n* public dissent; an objection; a complaint; a formal statement of objection.—**protestation** *n*.—**protester** *n*.

Protestant *n* a member or adherent of one of the Christian churches deriving from the Reformation; a Christian not of the Orthodox or Roman Catholic Church, who adheres to the principles of the Reformation.—**Protestantism** *n*.

protocol *n* a note, minute or draft of an agreement or transaction; the ceremonial etiquette accepted as correct in official dealings, as between heads of state or diplomatic officials; the formatting of data in an electronic communications system; the plan of a scientific experiment or treatment.

proton *n* an elementary particle in the nucleus of all atoms, carrying a unit positive charge of electricity.

prototype *n* an original model or type from which copies are made.

protracted *adj* extended, prolonged; long-drawn-out.—**protractedly** *adv*.

protrude *vti* to thrust outwards or forwards; to obtrude; to jut out, project.—**protrusive** *adj*.

protuberance *n* a swelling, prominence.—**protuberant** *adj*.

proud *adj* having too high an opinion of oneself; arrogant, haughty; having proper self-respect; satisfied with one's achievements.—**proudly** *adv*.

prove *vti* (*pt* **proved** *or* **proven**) to try out, test, by experiment; to establish or demonstrate as true using accepted procedures; to show (oneself) to be worthy or capable; to turn out (to be), esp after trial or test; to rise.

proverb *n* a short traditional saying expressing a truth or moral instruction; an adage.

proverbial *adj* of or like, a proverb; generally known.—**proverbially** *adv*.

provide *vti* to arrange for; to supply; to prepare; to afford (an opportunity); to make provision for (financially).—**provider** *n*.

provided, providing *conj* on condition (that).

providence *n* foresight, prudence; God's care and protection.

province *n* an administrative district or division of a country; the jurisdiction of an archbishop; (*pl*) the parts of a country removed from the main cities; a department of knowledge or activity.

provincial *adj* of a province or provinces; having the way, speech, etc of a certain province; country-like; rustic; unsophisticated. * *n* an inhabitant of the provinces or country areas; a person lacking sophistication.—**provincially** *adv*.

provision *n* a requirement; something provided for the future; a stipulation, condition; (*pl*) supplies of food, stores. * *vt* to supply with stores.

provisional *adj* temporary; conditional.—**provisionally** *adv*.

proviso *n* (*pl* **provisos, provisoes**) a condition,

stipulation; a limiting clause in an agreement, etc.

provocation *n* the act of provoking or inciting; a cause of anger, resentment, etc.

provocative *adj* intentionally provoking, esp to anger or sexual desire; (*remark*) stimulating argument or discussion.—**provocatively** *adv*.

provoke *vt* to anger, infuriate; to incite, to arouse; to give rise to; to irritate, exasperate.

prow *n* the forward part of a ship, bow.

prowess *n* bravery, gallantry; skill.

prowl *vi* to move stealthily, esp in search of prey.—*also n*.

prowler *n* one that moves stealthily, esp an opportunist thief.

proximity *n* nearness in place, time, series, etc.

proxy *n* the authority to vote or act for another; a person so authorized.—*also adj*.

prudence *n* the quality of being prudent; caution; discretion; common sense.

prudent *adj* cautious; sensible; managing carefully; circumspect.—**prudently** *adv*.

prune[1] *n* a dried plum.

prune[2] *vti* (*plant*) to remove dead or living parts from; to cut away what is unwanted or superfluous.

pry *vi* to snoop into other people's affairs; to inquire impertinently.

PS *abbr* = postscript.

psalm *n* a sacred song or hymn, esp one from the Book of Psalms in the Bible.

pseudo *adj* false, pretended.

pseudonym *n* a false named adopted as by an author.—**pseudonymous** *adj*.

psyche *n* the spirit, soul; the mind, esp as a functional entity governing the total organism and its interactions with the environment.

psychiatry *n* the branch of medicine dealing with disorders of the mind, including psychoses and neuroses.—**psychiatric** *adj*.—**psychiatrist** *n*.

psychic, psychical *adj* of the soul or spirit; of the mind; having sensitivity to, or contact with, forces that cannot be explained by natural laws. * *n* a person apparently sensitive to nonphysical forces; a medium; psychic phenomena.

psychoanalysis *n* a method of treating neuroses, phobias, and some other mental disorders by analysing emotional conflicts, repressions, etc.—**psychoanalyse** *vt*.—**psychoanalyst** *n*.

psychology *n* the science that studies the human mind and behaviour; mental state.—**psychological** *adj*.—**psychologically** *adv*.—**psychologist** *n*.

psychopath *n* a person suffering from a mental disorder that results in antisocial behaviour and lack of guilt.—**psychopathic** *adj*.

PTO *abbr* = please turn over.

pub *n* a public house, an inn.

puberty *n* the stage at which the reproductive organs become functional.

public *adj* of, for, or by the people generally; performed in front of people; for the use of all people; open or known to all; acting officially for the people. * *n* the people in general; a particular section of the people, such as an audience, body of readers, etc; open observation.—**publicly** *adv*.

publication *n* public notification; the printing and distribution of books, magazines, etc; something published as a periodical, book, etc.

public house *n* a tavern or bar licensed to sell alcoholic drinks; an inn.

publicity *n* any information or action that brings a person or cause to public notice; work concerned with such promotional matter; notice by the public.

public relations *n* relations with the general public of a company, institution, etc, as through publicity.

public school *n* a school maintained by public money and supervised by local authorities; in England, a private secondary school, usu boarding.

publish *vt* to make generally known; to announce formally; (*book*) to issue for sale to the public. * *vi* to put out an edition; to have one's work accepted for publication.

publisher *n* a person or company that prints and issues books, magazines, etc.

publishing *n* the business of the production and distribution of books, magazines, recordings, etc.

puce *n*, *adj* (a) purplish brown.

puck *n* a hard rubber disc used in ice hockey.

pucker *vti* to draw together in creases, to wrinkle. * *n* a wrinkle or fold.

pudding *n* a dessert; a steamed or baked dessert; a suet pie.

puddle *n* a small pool of water, esp stagnant, spilled, or muddy water.

puerile *adj* juvenile; childish.

puff *n* a sudden short blast or gust; an exhalation of air or smoke; a light pastry; a pad for applying powder; a flattering notice, advertisement. * *vti* to emit a puff; to breathe hard, pant; to put out of breath; to praise with exaggeration; to swell; to blow, smoke, etc, with puffs.

puffin *n* a sea bird that has a short neck and a brightly coloured laterally compressed bill.

puffy *adj* (**puffier, puffiest**) inflated, swollen; panting.—**puffily** *adv*.

pugnacious *adj* fond of fighting, belligerent.—**pugnaciousness** *n*.—**pugnacity** *n*.

pull *vt* to tug at; to pluck; to move or draw towards oneself; to drag; to rip; to tear; (*muscle*) to strain; (*inf*) to carry out, perform; (*inf*) to restrain; (*inf*: *gun, etc*) to draw out; (*inf*) to attract. * *vi* to carry out the action of pulling something; to be capable of being pulled; to move (away, ahead, etc). * *n* the act of pulling or being pulled; a tug; a device for pulling; (*inf*) influence; (*inf*) drawing power.

pulley *n* (*pl* **pulleys**) a wheel with a grooved rim for a cord, etc, used to raise weights by downward pull or change of direction of the pull; a group of these used to increase applied force; a wheel driven by a belt.

pullover *n* a buttonless garment with or without sleeves pulled on over the head.

pulp *n* a soft, moist, sticky mass; the soft, juicy part of a fruit or soft pith of a plant stem; ground-up, moistened fibres of wood, rags, etc, used to make paper; a book or magazine printed on cheap paper and often dealing with sensational material. * *vti* to make or become pulp or pulpy; to produce or reproduce (written matter) in pulp form.—**pulpiness** *n*.—**pulpy** *adj*.

pulpit *n* a raised enclosed platform, esp in a church, from which a clergyman preaches; preachers as a group.

pulsate *vi* to beat or throb rhythmically; to vibrate, quiver.—**pulsation** *n*.

pulse[1] *n* a rhythmic beat or throb, as of the heart; a place where this is felt; an underlying opinion or sentiment or an indication of it; a short radio signal. * *vti* to throb, pulsate.

pulse[2] *n* the edible seeds of several leguminous plants, such as beans, peas and lentils; the plants producing them.

pulverize *vti* to reduce to a fine powder; to demolish, smash; to crumble.—**pulverization** *n*.

puma *n* a large tawny American animal of the cat family, a cougar or mountain lion.

pummel *vt* (*pt* **pummelled**) to strike repeatedly with the fists, to thump.

pump[1] *n* a device that forces a liquid or gas into, or draws it out of, something. * *vti* to move (fluids) with a pump; to remove water, etc, from; to drive air into with a pump; to draw out, move up and down, pour forth, etc, as a pump does; (*inf*) to obtain information through questioning.

pump[2] *n* a light low shoe or slipper; a rubber-soled shoe.

pumpkin *n* a large, round, orange fruit of the gourd family widely cultivated as food.

pun *n* a play on words of the same sound but different meanings, usu humorous.—*also vi*.

punch[1] *vt* to strike with the fist; to prod or poke; to stamp, perforate with a tool; (*cattle*) to herd. * *n* a blow with the fist; (*inf*) vigour; a machine or tool for punching.

punch[2] *n* a hot, sweet drink made with fruit juices, often mixed with wine or spirits.

punctual *adj* being on time; prompt.—**punctuality** *n*.—**punctually** *adv*.

punctuate *vt* to use certain standardized marks in (written matter) to clarify meaning; to interrupt; to emphasize. * *vi* to use punctuation marks.

punctuation *n* the act of punctuating; the state of being punctuated; a system of punctuation.

puncture *n* a small hole made by a sharp object; the deflation of a tyre caused by a puncture. * *vt* to make useless or ineffective as if by a puncture; to deflate. * *vi* to become punctured.

pundit *n* a learned person; an expert; a critic, esp a columnist.

pungent *adj* having an acrid smell or a sharp taste; caustic; bitter.—**pungency** *n*.—**pungently** *adv*.

punish *vt* to subject a person to a penalty for a crime or misdemeanour; to chastise; to handle roughly.

punishable *adj* liable to legal punishment.

punishment *n* a penalty for a crime or misdemeanour; rough treatment; the act of punishing or being punished.

punt[1] *n* a long flat-bottomed square-ended river boat usu propelled with a pole. * *vti* to propel or convey in a punt.

punt[2] *vt* to kick a dropped ball before it reaches the ground. * *n* such a kick.

puny *adj* (**punier, puniest**) of inferior size, strength, or importance; feeble.

pup *n* a young dog, a puppy; a young fox, seal, rat, etc. * *vi* (*pt* **pupped**) to give birth to pups.

pupil[1] *n* a child or young person taught under the supervision of a teacher or tutor; a person who has been taught or influenced by a famous or distinguished person.

pupil[2] *n* the round, dark opening in the centre of the iris of the eye through which light passes.

puppet *n* a doll moved by strings attached to its limbs or by a hand inserted in its body; a person controlled by another.—*also adj.*—**puppeteer** *n.*—**puppetry** *n.*

puppy *n* a young domestic dog less than a year old.

purchase *vt* to buy; to obtain by effort or suffering. * *n* the act of purchasing; an object bought; leverage for raising or moving loads; means of achieving advantage.—**purchaser** *n.*

pure *adj* clean; not contaminated; not mixed; chaste, innocent; free from taint or defilement; mere; that and that only; abstract and theoretical; (*mus*) not discordant, perfectly in tune.—**pureness** *n.*

purge *vt* to cleanse, purify; (*nation, party, etc*) to rid of troublesome people; to clear (oneself) of a charge; to clear out the bowels of. * *n* the act or process of purging; a purgative; the removal of persons believed to be disloyal from an organization, esp a political party.

purify *vti* to make or become pure; to cleanse; to make ceremonially clean; to free from harmful matter.—**purification** *n.*—**purifier** *n.*

purist *n* someone who is a stickler for correctness in language, style, etc.

puritan *adj* a person who is extremely strict in religion or morals; (*with cap*) an extreme Protestant of Elizabethan or Stuart times.—*also adj.*—**puritanic, puritanical** *adj.*

purity *n* the state of being pure.

purl *vt* to knit a stitch by drawing its base loop from front to back of the fabric.—*also n.*

purple *n* a dark, bluish red; crimson cloth or clothing, esp as a former emblem of royalty. * *adj* purple-coloured; royal; (*writing style*) over-elaborate.

purport *vt* to claim to be true; to imply; to be intended to seem. * *n* significance; apparent meaning.

purpose *n* objective; intention; aim; function; resolution, determination. * *vti* to intend, design.

purposeful *adj* determined, resolute; intentional.—**purposefully** *adv.*—**purposefulness** *n.*

purr *vi* (*cat*) to make a low, murmuring sound of pleasure.—**purring** *n.*

purse *n* a small pouch or bag for money; finances, money; a sum of money for a present or a prize; a handbag. * *vt* to pucker, wrinkle up.

purser *n* an officer on a passenger ship in charge of accounts, tickets, etc; an airline official responsible for the comfort and welfare of passengers.

pursue *vt* to follow; to chase; to strive for; to seek to attain; to engage in; to proceed with. * *vi* to follow in order to capture.—**pursuer** *n.*

pursuit *n* the act of pursuing; an occupation; a pastime.

pus *n* a yellowish fluid produced by infected sores.

push *vti* to exert pressure so as to move; to press against or forward; to impel forward, shove; to urge the use, sale, etc, of; (*inf*) to approach an age; (*inf*) to sell drugs illegally; to make an effort. * *n* a thrust, shove; an effort; an advance against opposition; (*inf*) energy and drive.

pushchair *n* a wheeled metal and canvas chair for a small child.

pushover *n* (*inf*) something easily done, as a victory over an opposing team; (*inf*) a person easily taken advantage of.

pushy *adj* (**pushier, pushiest**) (*inf*) assertive; forceful; aggressively ambitious.—**pushily** *adv.*—**pushiness** *n.*

puss, pussy *n* an informal name for a cat.

put *vti* (*pr p* **putting,** *pt* **put**) to place, set; to cast, throw; to apply, direct; to bring into a specified state; to add (to); to subject to; to submit; to estimate; to stake; to express; to translate; to propose; (*a weight*) to hurl. * *adj* fixed.

putrid *adj* rotten or decayed and foul-smelling.

putt *vti* (*golf*) to hit (a ball) with a putter. * *n* in golf, a stroke to make the ball roll into the hole.

putter *n* (*golf*) a straight-faced club used in putting.

putty *n* a soft, plastic mixture of powdered chalk and linseed oil used to fill small cracks, fix glass in window frames, etc.

puzzle *vt* to bewilder; to perplex. * *vi* to be perplexed; to exercise one's mind, as over a problem. * *n* bewilderment; a difficult problem; a toy or problem for testing skill or ingenuity; a conundrum.

puzzling *adj* perplexing, bewildering, inexplicable.

pygmy *n* an undersized person.—*also* **pigmy**.
pyjamas, pajamas (*US*) *npl* a loosely fitting sleeping suit of jacket and trousers.
pylon *n* a tower-like structure supporting electric power lines.
pyramid *n* (*geom*) a solid figure having a polygon as base, and whose sides are triangles sharing a common vertex; a huge structure of this shape, as a royal tomb of ancient Egypt; an immaterial structure built on a broad supporting base and narrowing gradually to an apex.
python *n* a large, nonpoisonous snake that kills by constriction.

Q

quack[1] *n* the cry of a duck. * *vi* to make a sound like a duck.
quack[2] *n* an untrained person who practises medicine fraudulently; one who pretends to have knowledge he does not have.—*also adj*.
quad *n* quadrangle; quadruplet.
quadrangle *n* (*geom*) a plane figure with four sides and four angles, a rectangle; a court enclosed by buildings.—**quadrangular** *adj*.
quadruped *n* a four-footed animal.—**quadrupedal** *adj*.
quadruple *adj* four times as much or as many; made up of or consisting or four; having four divisions or parts. * *vti* to make or become four times as many.
quadruplet *n* one of four children born at birth.
quagmire *n* soft, wet ground; a difficult situation.
quail[1] *vi* to cower, to shrink back with fear.
quail[2] *n* a small American game bird.
quaint *adj* attractive or pleasant in an odd or old-fashioned style.—**quaintly** *adv*.—**quaintness** *n*.
quake *vi* to tremble or shiver, esp with fear or cold; to quiver. * *n* a shaking or tremor; (*inf*) an earthquake.
Quaker *n* a popular name for a member of the Society of Friends, a religious sect advocating peace and simplicity.—**Quakerism** *n*.
qualification *n* qualifying; a thing that qualifies; a quality or acquirement that makes a person fit for a post, etc; modification; limitation; (*pl*) academic achievements.
qualify *vti* to restrict; to describe; to moderate; to modify, limit; to make or become capable or suitable; to fulfil conditions; to pass a final examination; (*gram*) to limit the meaning of.
qualitative *adj* of or depending on quality; determining the nature, not the quality, of components.—**qualitatively** *adv*.
quality *n* a characteristic or attribute; degree of excellence; high standard. * *adj* of high quality.
qualm *n* a doubt; a misgiving; a scruple; a sudden feeling of faintness or nausea.
quandary *n* a predicament; a dilemma.
quantitative, quantitive *adj* capable of being measured; relating to size or amount.—**quantitatively, quantitively** *adv*.
quantity *n* an amount that can be measured, counted or weighed; a large amount; the property by which a thing can be measured; a number or symbol expressing this property.
quarantine *n* a period of isolation imposed to prevent the spread of disease; the time or place of this. * *vt* to put or keep in quarantine.
quarrel *n* an argument; an angry dispute; a cause of dispute. * *vi* (*pt* **quarrelled**) to argue violently; to fall out (with); to find fault (with).
quarrelsome *adj* contentious; apt to quarrel.
quarry[1] *n* an excavation for the extraction of stone, slate, etc; a place from which stone is excavated; a source of information, etc. * *vti* to excavate (from) a quarry; to research.
quarry[2] *n* a hunted animal, prey.
quart *n* a liquid measure equal to a quarter of a gallon or two pints; a dry measure equal to two pints.
quarter *n* a fourth of something; one fourth of a year; one fourth of an hour; (in US) 25 cents, or a coin of this value; any leg of a four-legged animal with the adjoining parts; a particular district or section; (*pl*) lodgings; a particular source; an unspecified person or group; a compass point other than the cardinal points; mercy; (*her*) any of four quadrants of a shield. * *vti* to share or divide into four; to provide with lodgings; to lodge; to range over (an area) in search (of). * *adj* constituting a quarter.
quarterfinal *n* one of four matches held before the semifinals in a tournament.—*also adj*.
quarterly *adj* occurring, issued, or spaced at three-month intervals; (*her*) divided into quarters. * *adv* once every three months; (*her*) in quarters. * *n* a publication issued four times a year.
quartermaster *n* (*mil*) an officer in charge of stores; (*naut*) a petty officer in charge of steering, etc.

quartet, **quartette** *n* a set or group of four; a piece of music composed for four instruments or voices; a group of four instrumentalists or voices.

quartz *n* a crystalline mineral, a form of silica, usu colourless and transparent.

quash *vt* (*rebellion etc*) to put down; to suppress; to make void.

quasi *adv* seemingly; as if. * *prefix* almost, apparently.

quaver *vi* to tremble, vibrate; to speak or sing with a quivering voice. * *n* a trembling sound or note; (*mus*) a note having half the duration of a crotchet, an eighth note.—**quavery** *adj*.

quay *n* a loading wharf or landing place for vessels.

queasy *adj* (**queasier, queasiest**) nauseous; easily upset; over-scrupulous.—**queasily** *adv*.—**queasiness** *n*.

queen *n* a female sovereign and head of state; the wife or widow of a king; a woman considered pre-eminent; the egg-laying female of bees, wasps, etc; a playing card with a picture of a queen; (*chess*) the most powerful piece; (*sl*) a male homosexual, esp one who ostentatiously takes a feminine role. * *vi* (*with* **it**) to act like a queen, esp to put on airs. * *vt* (a pawn) to promote to a queen in chess.—**queenly** *adj*.

queen mother *n* a queen dowager who is the mother of a ruling sovereign.

queer *adj* strange, odd, curious; (*inf*) eccentric; (*sl*) homosexual. * *n* a (male) homosexual. * *vt* (*sl*) to spoil the success of.—**queerness** *n*.

quell *vt* to suppress; to allay.

quench *vt* (*thirst*) to satisfy or slake; (*fire*) to put out, extinguish; (*steel*) to cool; to suppress.—**quenchable** *adj*.

query *n* a question; a question mark; doubt. * *vti* to question; to doubt the accuracy of.

quest *n* a search, seeking, esp involving a journey. * *vti* to search (about) for, seek.—**quester** *n*.—**questingly** *adv*.

question *n* an interrogative sentence; an inquiry; a problem; a doubtful or controversial point; a subject of debate before an assembly; a part of a test or examination. * *vti* to ask questions (of); to interrogate intensively; to dispute; to subject to analysis.—**questioner** *n*.

questionable *adj* doubtful; not clearly true or honest.—**questionably** *adv*.

question mark *n* a punctuation mark (?) used at the end of a sentence to indicate a question, or to express doubt about something; something unknown.

questionnaire *n* a series of questions designed to collect statistical information; a survey made by the use of questionnaire.

queue *n* a line of people, vehicles, etc awaiting a turn. * *vi* (*pr p* **queuing,** *pt* **queued**) to wait in turn.

quibble *n* a minor objection or criticism. * *vi* to argue about trifling matters.

quick *adj* rapid, speedy; nimble; prompt; responsive; alert; eager to learn. * *adv* in a quick manner. * *n* the sensitive flesh below a fingernail or toenail; the inmost sensibilities.—**quickly** *adv*.—**quickness** *n*.

quicken *vti* to speed up or accelerate; to make alive; to come to life; to invigorate.

quicksand *n* loose wet sand easily yielding to pressure in which persons, animals, etc may be swallowed up.

quickstep *n* a ballroom dance in quick time; its music.

quick-witted *adj* mentally alert; quick in repartee.—**quick-wittedness** *n*.

quid *n* (*sl*) a pound (sterling).

quiet *adj* silent, not noisy; still, not moving; gentle, not boisterous; unobtrusive, not showy; placid, calm; monotonous, uneventful; undisturbed. * *n* stillness, peace, repose; an undisturbed state. * *vti* to quieten.—**quietly** *adv*.—**quietness** *n*.

quieten *vti* to make or become quiet; to calm, soothe.

quill *n* the hollow stem of a feather; anything made of this, as a pen; a stiff, hollow spine of a hedgehog or porcupine.

quilt *n* a thick, warm bedcover; a bedspread; a coverlet of two cloths sewn together with padding between. * *vti* to stitch together like a quilt; to make a quilt.—**quilter** *n*.—**quilting** *n*.

quin *n* a quintuplet.

quinine *n* a bitter crystalline alkaloid used in medicine; one of its salts used esp as an antimalarial and a bitter tonic.

quintet, **quintette** *n* a set or group of five; a piece of music composed for five instruments or voices; a group of five instrumentalists or voices.

quintuple *adj* fivefold; having five divisions or parts; five times as much or as many. * *vti* to multiply by five. * *n* a number five times greater than another.

quintuplet *n* one of five offspring produced at one birth.

quip *n* a witty remark; a gibe. * *vt* (*pt* **quipped**) to make a clever or sarcastic remark.
quirk *n* an unexpected turn or twist; a peculiarity of character or mannerism.—**quirky** *adj*.—**quirkiness** *n*.
quit *vti* (*pt* **quitted** *or* **quit**) to leave; to stop or cease; to resign; to free from obligation; to admit defeat. * *adj* free from; released from.
quite *adv* completely; somewhat, fairly; really.
quits *adj* even; on equal terms by payment or revenge.
quiver[1] *vi* to shake; to tremble, shiver. * *n* a shiver, vibration.—**quivery** *adj*.
quiver[2] *n* a case for holding arrows.
quiz *n* (*pl* **quizzes**) a form of entertainment where players are asked questions of general knowledge; a short written or oral test. * *vt* (*pt* **quizzed**) to interrogate; to make fun of.
quizzical *adj* humorous and questioning.—**quizzically** *adv*.
quoit *n* a ring of metal, plastic, etc thrown in quoits; (*pl*) a game in which rings are thrown at or over a peg.
quorum *n* the minimum number that must be present at a meeting or assembly to make its proceedings valid.
quota *n* a proportional share; a prescribed amount; a part to be contributed.
quotation *n* the act of quoting; the words quoted; an estimated price.
quotation mark *n* a punctuation mark used to indicate the beginning (' *or* ") and the end (' *or* ") of a quoted passage.
quote *vt* to cite; to refer to; to repeat the words of a novel, play, poem, speech, etc exactly; to adduce by way of authority; to set off by quotation marks; to state the price of (something). * *n* (*inf*) something quoted; a quotation mark.—**quotable** *adj*.

R

rabbi *n* (*pl* **rabbis**) the religious and spiritual leader of a Jewish congregation.
rabbit *n* a small burrowing mammal of the hare family with long ears, a short tail, and long hind legs; their flesh as food; their fur.
rabble *n* a disorderly crowd, a mob; the common herd.
rabid *adj* infected with rabies; raging; fanatical.
rabies *n* an acute, infectious, viral disease transmitted by the bite of an infected animal.
raccoon *n* a small nocturnal carnivore of North America that lives in trees; its yellowish grey fur.
race[1] *n* any of the divisions of humankind distinguished esp by colour of skin; any geographical, national, or tribal ethnic grouping; a subspecies of plants or animals; distinctive flavour or taste.
race[2] *n* a contest of speed; a rapid current of water. * *vi* to run at top speed or out of control; to compete in a race; (*engine*) to run without a working load. * *vt* to cause to race; to contest against.
racecourse, racetrack (*US*) *n* a track over which races are run, esp an oval track for racing horses.
racehorse *n* a horse bred and trained for racing.
racial *adj* of or relating to any of the divisions of humankind distinguished by colour, etc.
racialism, racism *n* a belief in the superiority of some races over others; prejudice against or hatred of other races; discriminating behaviour towards people of another race.—**racist** *n*.
rack *n* a frame for holding or displaying articles; an instrument for torture by stretching; the triangular frame for setting up balls in snooker; a toothed bar to engage with the teeth of a wheel; extreme pain or anxiety. * *vt* (*person*) to stretch on a rack; to arrange in or on a rack; to torture, torment; to move parts of machinery with a toothed rack.
racket[1] *n* a bat strung with nylon, for playing tennis, etc. (*pl*) a game for two or four players played in a four-walled court (—*also* **racquet**).
racket[2] *n* noisy confusion; din; an obtaining of money illegally; any fraudulent business.
racy *adj* lively, spirited; risqué.—**racily** *adv*.
radar *n* a system or device for detecting objects such as aircraft by using the reflection of radio waves.
radiance *n* the condition of being radiant; brilliant light; dazzling beauty.
radiant *adj* shining; beaming with happiness; sending out rays; transmitted by radiation.—**radiantly** *adv*.
radiate *vt* (*light, heat, etc*) to emit in rays; (*happiness, love, etc*) to give forth. * *vi* to spread out as if from a centre; to shine; to emit rays.
radiation *n* radiant particles emitted as energy; rays emitted in nuclear decay; (*med*) treatment using a radioactive substance.

radiator *n* an apparatus for heating a room; a cooling device for a vehicle engine.

radical *adj* of or relating to the root or origin; fundamental; favouring basic change. * *n* a person who advocates fundamental political or social change.—**radicalism** *n.*

radio *n* the transmission of sounds or signals by electromagnetic waves through space, without wires, to a receiving set; such a set; broadcasting by radio as an industry, etc. * *adj* of, using, used in, or sent by radio. * *vti* to transmit, or communicate with, by radio.

radio- *prefix* radial; radio; using radiant energy.

radioactive *adj* giving off radiant energy in the form of particles or rays caused by the disintegration of atomic nuclei.—**radioactivity** *n.*

radiography *n* the production of X-rays for use in medicine, industry, etc.—**radiographer** *n.*

radiology *n* a branch of medicine concerned with the use of radiant energy (as X-rays and radium) in the diagnosis and treatment of disease.—**radiologist** *n.*

radish *n* a pungent root eaten raw as a salad vegetable.

radium *n* a highly radioactive metallic element.

radius *n* (*pl* **radii** *or* **radiuses**) (*geom*) a straight line joining the centre of a circle or sphere to its circumference; a thing like this, a spoke; a sphere of activity; (*anat*) the thicker of the two bones of the forearm.

raffia *n* a kind of palm; fibre from its leaves used in basket-making, etc.

raffle *n* a lottery with prizes. * *vt* to offer as a prize in a raffle.

raft *n* a platform of logs, planks, etc strapped together to float on water.

rafter *n* one of the inclined, parallel beams that support a roof.

rag *n* a torn or waste scrap of cloth; a shred; (*inf*) a sensationalist newspaper; (*pl*) tattered or shabby clothing.

ragbag *n* a bag for scraps; a miscellaneous collection, jumble.

rage *n* violent anger; passion; frenzy; fashion, craze. * *vi* to behave with violent anger; to storm; to spread rapidly; to be prevalent.

ragged *adj* jagged; uneven; irregular; worn into rags; tattered.—**raggedly** *adv.*—**raggedness** *n.*

raid *n* a sudden attack to assault or seize. * *vt* to make a raid on; to steal from.—**raider** *n.*

rail[1] *n* a horizontal bar from one post to another, as in a fence, etc; one of a pair of parallel steel lines forming a track; a railway, railroad.

rail[2] *vi* to speak angrily.

railing *n* a fence of rails and posts; rails collectively.

railroad *n* a railway. * *vt* to force unduly; (*bill, etc*) to push forward fast; to imprison hastily, esp unjustly.

railway, railroad (*US*) *n* a track of parallel steel rails along which carriages are drawn by locomotive engines; a complete system of such tracks.

rain *n* water that falls from the clouds in the form of drops; a shower; a large quantity of anything falling like rain; (*pl*) the rainy season in the tropics. * *vti* (*of rain*) to fall; to fall like rain; (*rain, etc*) to pour down.

rainbow *n* the arc containing the colours of the spectrum formed in the sky by the sun's rays in falling rain or mist. * *adj* many-coloured.

raincoat *n* a waterproof coat.

rainfall *n* a fall of rain; the amount of rain that falls on a given area in a specified time.

rainproof *adj* rain-resisting.

rainy *adj* (**rainier, rainiest**) full of rain; wet.

raise *vt* to elevate; to lift up; to set or place upright; to stir up, rouse; to increase in size, amount, degree, intensity, etc; to breed, bring up; (*question, etc*) to put forward; to collect or levy; (*siege*) to abandon. * *n* a rise in wages.

raisin *n* a sweet, dried grape.

raja, rajah *n* an Indian or Malay prince or ruler; an Indian title.

rake[1] *n* a tool with a row of teeth and a handle for gathering, scraping or smoothing. * *vt* to scrape, gather as with a rake; to sweep with gaze or gunshot; (*with* **in**: *money, etc*) to gather a great amount rapidly; (*with* **up**: *past misdemeanours, etc*) to bring to light.

rake[2] *n* the incline or slope of a mast, stern, etc.

rake[3] *n* a dissolute man.

rakish *adj* jaunty, dashing; dissolute. —**rakishly** *adv.*—**rakishness** *n.*

rally *vti* to bring or come together; to recover strength, revive; to take part in a rally. * *n* a large assembly of people; a recovery; (*tennis*) a lengthy exchange of shots; a competitive test of driving and navigational skills.

ram *n* a male sheep; a battering device; a piston; (*with cap*) Aries, the first sign of the zodiac. * *vt* (*pt* **rammed**) to force or drive; to crash; to cram; to thrust violently.

ramble *vi* to wander or stroll about for pleasure; (*plant*) to straggle; to write or talk aimlessly. * *n* a leisurely walk in the countryside.
rambler *n* a person who rambles; a climbing rose.
rambling *adj* spread out, straggling; circuitous; disconnected; disjointed. * *n* the act of walking for pleasure.
ramification *n* a branching out; an offshoot; a consequence.
ramp *n* a sloping walk or runway joining different levels; a wheeled staircase for boarding a plane; a sloping runway for launching boats, as from trailers.
rampage *n* angry or violent behaviour. * *vi* to rush about in an angry or violent manner.
rampant *adj* dominant; luxuriant, unrestrained; violent; rife, prevalent; (*her*) (of a lion) standing on its hind legs.
rampart *n* an embankment surrounding a fortification; a protective wall.
ramshackle *adj* dilapidated.
ran *see* **run**.
ranch *n* a large farm for raising cattle, horses, or sheep; a style of house with all the rooms on one floor. * *vi* to own, manage, or work on a ranch.—**rancher** *n*.
rancid *adj* having an unpleasant smell and taste, as stale fats or oil.—**rancidity, rancidness** *n* .
rancour, rancor (*US*) *n* bitter hate or spite.—**rancorous** *adj*.—**rancorously** *adv*.
random *adj* haphazard; left to chance.
randy *adj* (**randier, randiest**) (*sl*) lustful, sexually aroused.
rang *see* **ring**[2].
range *n* a row; a series of mountains, etc; scope, compass; the distance a vehicle, etc can travel without refuelling; the distance a bullet, etc can travel, or from gun to target; fluctuation; a large open area for grazing livestock; a place for testing rockets in flight; a place for shooting or golf practice; a cooking stove. * *vt* to place in order or a row; to establish the range of; (*livestock*) to graze on a range. * *vi* to be situated in a line; to rank or classify; (*gun*) to point or aim; to vary (inside limits).
ranger *n* a forest or park warden.
rank[1] *n* a line of objects; a line of soldiers standing abreast; high standing or position; status; (*pl*) ordinary members of the armed forces. * *vti* to arrange in a line; to have a specific position in an organization or on a scale; (*with* **with**) to be counted among.
rank[2] *adj* growing uncontrollably; utter, flagrant; offensive in odour or flavour.
rank and file *n* ordinary soldiers; ordinary members, as distinguished from their leaders.
rankle *vi* to fester; to cause continuous resentment or irritation.
ransack *vt* to plunder; to search thoroughly.
ransom *n* the release of a captured person or thing; the price paid for this. * *vt* to secure release of by payment.
rant *vi* to speak loudly or violently; to preach noisily. * *n* loud, pompous talk.
rap *n* a sharp blow; a knock; (*inf*) talk, conversation; (*sl*) arrest for a crime; (*sl*) a song that is rapped. * *vti* (*pt* **rapped**) to strike lightly or sharply; to knock; (*sl*) to criticize sharply; (*with* **out**) to utter abruptly; (*sl*) to speak a song accompanied by an insistent electronic rhythm.
rape[1] *n* the act of forcing a woman to have sexual intercourse against her will; a plundering. * *vti* to commit rape (upon).—**rapist** *n*.
rape[2] *n* a bright yellow plant of the mustard family grown for its leaves and oily seeds.
rapid *adj* at great speed; fast; sudden; steep. * *npl* a part of a river where the current flows swiftly.—**rapidity** *n*.—**rapidly** *adv*.
rapport *n* a sympathetic relationship; accord.
rapture *n* the state of being carried away with love, joy, etc; intense delight, ecstasy.—**rapturous** *adj*.—**rapturously** *adv*.
rare[1] *adj* unusual; seldom seen; exceptionally good; (*gas*) of low density, thin. *adv*.—**rareness** *n*.
rare[2] *adj* not completely cooked, partly raw; underdone.
rarefy *vti* to make or become less dense; to thin out; to expand without the addition of matter; to make more spiritual or refined.—**rarefied** *adj*.
rarely *adv* almost never; exceptionally, unusually.
rarity *n* rareness; a rare person or thing.
rascal *n* a rogue; a villain; a mischievous person.
rase *see* **raze**.
rash[1] *adj* reckless; impetuous.—**rashly** *adv*.—**rashness** *n*.
rash[2] *n* a skin eruption of spots, etc.
rasher *n* a thin slice of bacon or ham.
rasp *n* a coarse file; a grating sound. * *vt* to scrape with a rasp. * *vi* to produce a grating sound.—**rasping** *n*.

raspberry *n* a shrub with white flowers and red berry-like fruits; the fruit produced; (*inf*) a sound of dislike or derision.

rat *n* a long-tailed rodent similar to a mouse but larger; (*sl*) a sneaky, contemptible person. * *vi* (*pt* **ratted**) to hunt or catch rats; to betray or inform on someone.

ratchet *n* a device with a toothed wheel that moves in one direction only.

rate *n* the amount, degree, etc of something in relation to units of something else; price, esp per unit; degree. * *vt* to fix the value of; to rank; to regard or consider; (*sl*) to think highly of. * *vi* to have value or status.

rather *adv* more willingly; preferably; somewhat; more accurately; on the contrary; (*inf*) yes, certainly.

ratify *vt* to approve formally; to confirm.

rating *n* an assessment; an evaluation, an appraisal, as of credit worthiness; classification by grade, as of military personnel; (*radio, TV*) the relative popularity of a programme according to sample polls.

ratio *n* the number of times one thing contains another; the quantitative relationship between two classes of objects; proportion.

ration *n* (*food, petrol*) a fixed amount or portion; (*pl*) food supply. * *vt* to supply with rations; (*food, petrol*) to restrict the supply of.

rational *adj* of or based on reason; reasonable; sane.—**rationally** *adv*.

rationale *n* the reason for a course of action; an explanation of principles.

rationalize *vti* to make rational; to justify one's reasons for an action; to cut down on personnel or equipment; to substitute a natural for a supernatural explanation.—**rationalization** *n*.

rat race *n* continual hectic competitive activity.

rattle *vi* to clatter. * *vt* to make a series of sharp, quick noises; to clatter; to recite rapidly; to chatter; (*inf*) to disconcert, fluster. * *n* a rattling sound; a baby's toy that makes a rattling sound; a voluble talker; the rings on the tail of a rattlesnake.

rattlesnake *n* a venomous American snake with a rattle in its tail.

raucous *adj* hoarse and harsh-sounding; loud and rowdy.

ravage *vt* to ruin, destroy; to plunder, lay waste. * *n* destruction; ruin; (*pl*) the effects of this.

rave *vi* to speak wildly or as if delirious; (*inf*) to enthuse. * *n* enthusiastic praise.—**raving** *adj*.

raven *n* a large crow-like bird with glossy black feathers. * *adj* of the colour or sheen of a raven.

ravenous *adj* very hungry; greedy.—**ravenously** *adv*.

ravine *n* a deep, narrow gorge, a large gully.

ravioli *n* small cases of pasta filled with highly seasoned chopped meat or vegetables.

ravish *vt* to violate; to rape; to captivate.

ravishing *adj* charming, captivating.

raw *adj* uncooked; unrefined; in a natural state, crude; untrained, inexperienced; sore, skinned; damp, chilly; (*inf*) harsh or unfair.—**rawness** *n*.

raw material *n* something out of which a finished article is made; something with a potential for development, improvement, etc.

ray[1] *n* a beam of light that comes from a bright source; any of several lines radiating from a centre; a beam of radiant energy, radioactive particles, etc; a tiny amount.

ray[2] *n* any of various fishes with a flattened body and the eyes on the upper surface.

rayon *n* a textile fibre made from a cellulose solution; a fabric of such fibres.

raze *vt* to demolish; to erase; to level to the ground.—*also* **rase**.

razor *n* a sharp-edged instrument for shaving.

Rd *abbr* = road.

re *prep* concerning, with reference to.

reach *vti* to arrive at; to extend as far as; to make contact with; to pass, hand over; to attain, realize; to stretch out the hand; to extend in influence, space, etc; to carry, as sight, sound, etc; to try to get. * *n* the act or power of reaching; extent; mental range; scope; a continuous extent, esp of water.

react *vi* to act in response to a person or stimulus; to have a mutual or reverse effect; to revolt; (*chem*) to undergo a chemical reaction.

reaction *n* an action in response to a stimulus; a revulsion of feeling; exhaustion after excitement, etc; opposition to new ideas; (*chem*) an action set up by one substance in another.

reactionary *adj, n* (a person) opposed to political or social change.

reactor *n* a person or substance that undergoes a reaction; (*chem*) a vessel in which a reaction occurs; a nuclear reactor.

read *vti* (*pt* **read**) to understand something written; to speak aloud (from a book); to study by reading; to interpret, divine; to register, as a gauge; to foretell; (of a computer) to obtain (information) from; (*sl*) to hear and understand (a radio communication, etc); (*with* **about**, **of**) to learn by reading; to be phrased in certain words. * *adj* well-informed.

reader *n* a person who reads; one who reads aloud to others; a proofreader; a person who evaluates manuscripts; a textbook, esp on reading; a unit that scans material for computation or storage; a senior lecturer.

readership *n* all the readers of a certain publication, author, etc.

readily *adv* in a ready manner; willingly, easily.

reading *n* the act of one who reads; any material to be read; the amount measured by a barometer, meter, etc; a particular interpretation of a play, etc.

ready *adj* (**readier, readiest**) prepared; fit for use; willing; inclined, apt; prompt, quick; handy. * *n* the state of being ready, esp the position of a firearm aimed for firing; (*sl*) money. * *vt* to make ready.—**readiness** *n*.

ready-made *adj* made in standard sizes, not to measure.

real *adj* existing, actual, not imaginary; true, genuine, not artificial; (*law*) immovable, consisting of land or houses. * *adv* (*sl*) very; really.

real estate *n* property; land.

realism *n* practical outlook; (*art, literature*) the ability to represent things as they really are; (*philos*) the doctrine that the physical world has an objective existence.—**realist** *n*.

realistic *adj* matter-of-fact, not visionary; lifelike; of or relating to realism.—**realistically** *adv*.

reality *n* the fact or condition of being real; an actual fact or thing; truth.

realize *vt* to become fully aware of; (*ambition, etc*) to make happen; to cause to appear real; to convert into money, be sold for.—**realization** *n*.

really *adv* in fact, in reality; positively, very. * *interj* indeed.

realm *n* a kingdom, country; domain, region; sphere.

ream *n* a quantity of paper varying from 480 to 516 sheets; (*pl*: *inf*) a great amount.

reap *vti* to harvest; to gain (a benefit).

rear[1] *n* the back part or position, esp of an army; (*sl*) the rump. * *adj* of, at, or in the rear.

rear[2] *vt* to raise; (*children*) to bring up; to educate, nourish, etc. * *vi* (*horse*) to stand on the hind legs.

reason *n* motive or justification (of an action or belief); the mental power to draw conclusions and determine truth; a cause; moderation; sanity; intelligence. * *vti* to think logically (about); to analyse; to argue or infer.

reasonable *adj* able to reason or listen to reason; rational; sensible; not expensive; moderate, fair.—**reasonableness** *n*.—**reasonably** *adv*.

reassure *vt* to hearten; to give confidence to; to free from anxiety.—**reassurance** *n*.

rebate *n* a refund of part of an amount paid; discount.

rebel *n* a person who refuses to conform with convention. * *vi* (*pt* **rebelled**) to rise up against authority; to dissent.—**rebellion** *n*.—**rebellious** *adj*.

rebound *vi* to spring back after impact; to bounce back; to recover. * *n* a recoil; an emotional reaction.

rebuff *vt* to snub, repulse; to refuse unexpectedly.—*also n*.

rebuke *vt* to reprimand, chide. * *n* censure, a reprimand.

rebut *vt* (*pt* **rebutted**) to disprove or refute by argument, etc.—**rebuttal** *n*.

recall *vt* to call back; to bring back to mind, remember; to revoke. * *n* remembrance; a summons to return; the removal from office by popular vote.

recant *vti* to repudiate or retract a former opinion, declaration, or belief.—**recantation** *n*.

recap *vti* (*pt* **recapped**) to recapitulate. * *n* (*inf*) recapitulation.

recapitulate *vt* to state again, to summarize.—**recapitulation** *n*.

recapture *vt* to capture again; (*a lost feeling, etc*) to discover anew, regain. * *n* the act of recapturing; a thing or feeling recaptured.

recce *n* (*sl*) reconnaissance. * *vti* (*pt* **recced** *or* **recceed**) (*sl*) to reconnoitre.

recede *vi* to move back; to withdraw, retreat; to slope backwards; to grow less; to decline in value.

receding *adj* sloping backwards; disappearing from view; (*hair*) ceasing to grow at the temples.

receipt *n* the act of receiving; a written proof of this; (*pl*) amount received from business. * *vt* to acknowledge and mark as paid; to write a receipt for.

receive *vt* to acquire, to be given; to experience, to be subjected to; to admit, to allow; to greet on arrival; to accept as true; (*stolen* *goods*) to take in; to transfer electrical signals. * *vi* to be a recipient; to convert radio waves into perceptible signals.

receiver *n* a person who receives; equipment that receives electronic signals, esp on a telephone; (*law*) a person appointed to manage or hold in trust property in bankruptcy or pending a lawsuit.

recent *adj* happening lately, fresh; not long established, modern.—**recently** *adv*.

receptacle *n* a container.

reception *n* the act of receiving or being received; a welcome; a social gathering; a response, reaction; the quality of the sound or image produced by a radio or TV set.

receptionist *n* a person employed to receive visitors to an office, hotel, hospital, etc.

receptive *adj* able or quick to take in ideas or impressions.

recess *n* a temporary halting of work, a vacation; a hidden or inner place; an alcove or niche. * *vti* to place in a recess; to form a recess in; to take a recess.

recipe *n* a list of ingredients and directions for preparing food; a method for achieving an end.

recipient *n* a person who receives.

reciprocal *adj* done by each to the other; mutual; complementary; interchangeable; (*gram*) expressing a mutual relationship. * *n* (*math*) an expression so related to another that their product is 1.—**reciprocally** *adv*.—**reciprocity** *n*.

reciprocate *vti* to give in return; to repay; (*mech*) to move alternately backwards and forwards.—**reciprocating** *adj*.—**reciprocation** *n*.

recital *n* the act of reciting; a detailed account, narrative; a statement of facts; (*mus*) a performance given by an individual musician.

recite *vti* to repeat aloud from memory; to recount, enumerate; to repeat (a lesson).

reckless *adj* rash, careless, incautious.—**recklessly** *adv*.—**recklessness** *n*.

reckon *vti* to count; to regard or consider; to think; to calculate; (*with* **with**) to take into account.

reckoning *n* a calculation; the settlement of an account.

reclaim *vt* to recover, win back from a wild state or vice; (*wasteland*) to convert into land fit for cultivation; (*plastics, etc*) to obtain from waste materials.—**reclaimable** *adj*.—**reclamation** *n*.

recline *vti* to cause or permit to lean or bend backwards; to lie down on the back or side.—**reclinable** *adj*.

recluse *n* a person who lives in solitude; a hermit.

recognition *n* the act of recognizing; identification; acknowledgment, admission.

recognize *vt* to know again, identify; to greet; to acknowledge formally; to accept, admit.—**recognizable** *adj*.

recoil *vti* to spring back, kick, as a gun; to shrink or flinch. * *n* the act of recoiling, a rebound.

recollect *vti* to recall; to remind (oneself) of something temporarily forgotten; to call something to mind.

recollection *n* the act of recalling to mind; a memory, impression; something remembered; tranquillity of mind; religious contemplation.

recommend *vt* to counsel or advise; to commend or praise; to introduce favourably.—**recommendable** *adj*.—**recommendation** *n*.

recompense *n* to reward or pay an equivalent; to compensate. * *n* reward; repayment; compensation.

reconcile *vt* to re-establish friendly relations; to bring to agreement; to make compatible; to resolve; to settle; to make resigned (to); (*financial account*) to check with another account for accuracy.—**reconcilable** *adj*.—**reconciliation** *n*.

recondition *vt* to repair and restore to good working order.

reconnaissance *n* a survey of an area, esp for obtaining military information about an enemy.

reconnoitre, reconnoiter (*US*) *vti* to make a reconnaisance (of).

reconsider *vt* to consider afresh, review; to modify.—**reconsideration** *n*.

reconstruct *vt* to build again; to build up, as from remains, an image of the original; to supply missing parts by conjecture.—**reconstruction** *n*.

record *vti* to preserve evidence of; to write down; to chart; to register, enrol; to register permanently by mechanical means; (*sound or visual images*) to register on a disc, tape, etc for later reproduction; to celebrate. * *n* a written account; a register; a report of proceedings; the known facts about anything or anyone; an outstanding performance or achievement that surpasses others previously recorded; a grooved vinyl disc for playing on a record player; (*comput*) data in machine-readable form.

recorder *n* an official who keeps records; a machine or device that records; a tape recorder; a wind instrument of the flute family.

recording *n* what is recorded, as on a disc or tape; the record.

record player *n* an instrument for playing records through a loudspeaker.

recount *vt* to narrate the details of, to tell.

re-count *vt* to count again. * *n* a second counting of votes.

recoup *vti* to make good (financial losses); to regain; to make up for something lost.

recourse *n* a resort for help or protection when in danger; that to which one turns when seeking help.

recover *vti* to regain after losing; to reclaim; to regain health or after losing emotional control.—**recoverable** *adj*.

re-cover *vt* to put a new cover on.

recovery *n* the act or process of recovering; the condition of having recovered; reclamation; restoration; a retrieval of a capsule, etc after a space flight.

re-create *vt* to create over again, esp mentally.

recreation *n* relaxation of the body or mind; a sport, pastime or amusement.—**recreational** *adj*.

recruit *n* a soldier newly enlisted; a member newly joined; a beginner. * *vti* to enlist; to increase or maintain the numbers of; to restore, refresh.—**recruitment** *n*.

rectangle *n* a four-sided geometric figure with all its angles right angles.—**rectangular** *adj*.

rectify *vt* to put right, correct; to amend; (*chem*) to refine by repeated distillation; (*elect*) to convert to direct current.—**rectifiable** *adj*.

rector *n* in some churches, a clergyman in charge of a parish; the head of certain schools, colleges, etc.

rectory *n* the house of a minister or priest.

recuperate *vti* to get well again; to recover (losses, etc).—**recuperation** *n*.

recur *vi* (*pt* **recurred**) to be repeated in thought, talk, etc; to occur again or at intervals.—**recurrence** *n*.—**recurrent** *adj*.

red *adj* (**redder, reddest**) of the colour of blood; politically left-wing. * *n* the colour of blood; any red pigment; a communist.

red carpet *n* a strip of red carpet for dignitaries to walk on; a grand or impressive welcome or entertainment.

Red Cross *n* a red cross on a white ground, the symbol of the International Red Cross, a society for the relief of suffering in time of war and disaster.

red currant *n* a cultivated red clustered fruit.

redden *vti* to make or become red; to blush.

reddish *adj* tinged with red.—**reddishness** *n*.

redeem *vt* to recover by payment; to regain; to deliver from sin; to pay off; to restore to favour; to make amends for.—**redeemable** *adj*.—**redeemer** *n*.

redeploy *vt* (*troops, workers*) to assign to new positions or activities.—**redeployment** *n*.

red-handed *adj* caught in the act of committing a crime.

redhead *n* a person having red hair.—**redheaded** *adj*.

red herring *n* a herring cured to a dark brown colour; something that diverts attention from the real issue.

red-hot *adj* glowing with heat; extremely hot; very excited, angry, etc; very new.

redirect *vt* to change the direction or course of; to readdress.—**redirection** *n*.

red light *n* a warning signal, a cautionary sign; a deterrent.—*also adj*.

redolent *adj* having a strong scent, fragrant; reminiscent (of).—**redolence** *n*.

redouble *vti* to double again; to make or become twice as much.

redress *vt* to put right, adjust; to compensate, make up for. * *n* remedy; compensation.

red tape *n* rigid adherence to bureaucratic routine and regulations, causing delay.

reduce *vt* to diminish or make smaller in size, amount, extent, or number; to lower in price; to simplify; to make thin; to subdue; to bring or convert (to another state or form).—**reducible** *adj*.—**reduction** *n*.

redundant *adj* surplus to requirements; (*person*) deprived of one's job as being no longer necessary; (*words*) unnecessary to the meaning, excessive.—**redundancy** *n*.

reed *n* a tall grass found in marshes; a thin piece of cane in the mouthpiece of a musical instrument; a person or thing too weak to rely on; one easily swayed or overcome.

reef *n* a ridge of rocks, sand, or coral in water; a hazardous obstruction; a vein of ore.

reek *n* a strong smell. * *vi* to give off smoke, fumes or a strong or offensive smell.

reel[1] *n* a winding device; a spool or bobbin; thread wound on this; a length of film, about 300m (1,000ft). * *vt* to wind on to a reel; (*with* **in**) to draw in (fish, etc) by means of a reel; (*with* **off**) to tell, write, etc, with fluency; (*with* **out**) to unwind from a reel.

reel[2] *vi* to stagger or sway about; to be dizzy or in a whirl. * *n* a staggering motion.
reel[3] *n* a lively Scottish or Irish dance; the music for it. * *vi* to dance a reel.
ref. *abbr* = with reference to.
refectory *n* the dining hall of a monastery, college, etc.
refer *vti* (*pt* **referred**) to attribute, assign (to); (*with* **to**) to direct, have recourse (to); to relate to; to mention or allude to; to direct attention (to).—**referable** *adj*.
referee *n* an arbitrator; an umpire; a judge.
reference *n* the act of referring; a mention or allusion; a testimonial; a person who gives a testimonial; a direction to a passage in a book; a passage referred to.
reference book *n* a book for reference rather than general reading, eg a yearbook, directory.
referendum *n* (*pl* **referenda**, **referendums**) the submission of an issue directly to the vote of the electorate, a plebiscite.
refill *vt* to fill again. * *n* a replacement pack for an empty permanent container; a providing again.
refine *vti* to purify; to make free from impurities or coarseness; to make or become cultured.
refined *adj* polished, cultured; affected.
refinement *n* fineness of manners or taste; an improvement; a fine distinction.
refinery *n* a plant where raw materials, eg sugar, oil, are refined.
reflect *vt* (*light*, *heat*, *etc*) to throw back; to bend aside or back; to show an image of, as a mirror; to express. * *vi* to reproduce to the eye or mind; to mirror; to meditate; (*with* **upon**) to ponder; (*with* **on**) to discredit, disparage.
reflection, reflexion *n* a reflecting back, turning aside; the action of changing direction when a ray strikes and is thrown back; reflected heat, light or colour; a reflected image; meditation, thought; reconsideration; reproach.
reflector *n* a disc, instrument, strip or other surface that reflects light or heat.
reflex *n* an involuntary response to a stimulus. * *adj* (*angle*) of more than 180 degrees; (*camera*) with a full-size viewfinder using the main lens.
reflexive *adj* (*pron*, *verb*) referring back to the subject.—**reflexively** *adv*.
reform *vti* to improve; to make or become better by the removal of faults; to amend; to abolish abuse. * *n* improvement or transformation, esp of an institution; removal of social ills.—**reformed** *adj*.
reformer *n* a person who advocates or works for reform; an apparatus for changing molecular structure.
refrain[1] *vi* to abstain (from).
refrain[2] *n* recurring words in a song or poem; a chorus.
refresh *vt* to revive; to give new energy to; to make cool; to take a drink.
refresher *n* something that refreshes, esp a drink; a reminder; a training course to renew one's skill or knowledge.
refreshment *n* the act of refreshing; a restorative; (*pl*) food and drink; a light meal.
refrigerator *n* something that refrigerates; a chamber for keeping food, etc, cool; an apparatus for cooling.
refuel *vti* (*pt* **refuelled**) to supply with or take on fresh fuel.
refuge *n* a protection or shelter from danger; a retreat, sanctuary.
refugee *n* a person who flees to another country to escape political or religious persecution.
refund *vti* to repay; to reimburse. * *n* a refunding or the amount refunded.
refusal *n* the act or process of refusing; the choice of refusing or accepting.
refurbish *vt* to renovate or re-equip.—**refurbishment** *n*.
refuse[1] *n* rubbish, garbage, waste.
refuse[2] *vt* to decline, reject; to withhold, deny. * *vi* (*horse*) to decline to jump.
refute *vt* to rebut; to disprove.—**refutable** *adj*.—**refutably** *adv*.—**refutation** *n*.
regain *vt* to get back, recover; to reach again.
regal *adj* royal; relating to a king or queen.
regalia *npl* royal badges or prerogatives; the badges of an order, office, or membership; finery.
regard *vt* to gaze at, observe; to hold in respect; to consider; to heed, take into account. * *n* a look; attention; reference; respect, esteem; (*pl*) good wishes, greetings.
regarding *prep* with reference to, about.
regardless *adj* having no regard to. * *adv* (*inf*) in spite of everything; without heeding the cost, consequences, etc.
regatta *n* a meeting for yacht or boat races.
regency *n* the status or authority of a regent; rule by a regent; (*with cap*) in British history, the period 1810-20.
regent *n* a person who rules or administers a

country during the sovereign's minority, absence, or incapacity; a member of a governing board (as of a university).

regime *n* a political or ruling system.

regiment *n* a military unit, smaller than a division, consisting usu of a number of battalions. * *vt* to organize in a strict manner; to subject to order or conformity.—**regimental** *adj.*

regimentation *n* the act of regimenting; excessive orderliness.

region *n* a large, indefinite part of the earth's surface; one of the zones into which the atmosphere is divided; an administrative area of a country; a part of the body.—**regional** *adj.*

register *n* an official list; a written record, as for attendance; the book containing such a record or list; a tone of voice; a variety of language appropriate to a subject or occasion; (*comput*) a device in which data can be stored and operated on; (*print*) exact alignment; a device for indicating speed, etc; a plate regulating draught. * *vti* to record; to enter in or sign a register; to correspond exactly; to entrust a letter to the post with special precautions for safety; to express emotion facially; to make or convey an impression.

registered *adj* recorded officially; qualified formally or officially.

registrar *n* a person who keeps records, esp one in an educational institution in charge of student records; a hospital doctor below a specialist in rank.

registration *n* the act of registering; the condition of having registered.

registry *n* registration; a place where records are kept; an official record book.

registry office *n* an office where civil marriages are held, and births and deaths recorded.

regret *vt* (*pt* **regretted**) to feel sorrow, grief, or loss; to remember with longing; (*with* **that**) to repent of. * *n* disappointment; sorrow; grief; (*pl*) polite refusal.—**regretful** *adj.*—**regretfully** *adv.*

regrettable *adj* to be regretted; deserving blame.—**regrettably** *adv.*

regular *adj* normal; habitual, not casual; at fixed intervals; according to rule, custom, or practice; uniform, consistent; symmetrical; fully qualified; belonging to a standing army; (*inf*) thorough, complete; (*inf*) pleasant, friendly. * *n* a professional soldier; (*inf*) a person who attends regularly.—**regularity** *n.*—**regularly** *adv.*

regulate *vt* to control according to a rule; to cause to conform to a standard or needs; to adjust so as to put in good order.—**regulatory** *adj.*

regulation *n* the act of regulating; a being regulated; a prescribed rule, decree. * *adj* normal, standard.

rehabilitate *vt* (*prisoner etc*) to help adapt to society after a stay in an institution; to put back in good condition; to restore to rights or privileges; (*sick person etc*) to help to adjust to normal conditions after illness.—**rehabilitation** *n.*

rehash *n* old materials put in a new form. * *vt* to dish up again.

rehearse *vti* to practise repeatedly before public performance; to recount, narrate in detail.—**rehearsal** *n.*

reign *n* the rule of a sovereign; the period of this; influence; domination. * *vi* to rule; to prevail.

reimburse *vt* to repay; to refund (for expense or loss).—**reimbursable** *adj.*—**reimbursement** *n.*

rein *n* the strap of a bridle for guiding or restraining a horse; (*pl*) a means of control or restraint. * *vt* to control with the rein; to restrain.

reincarnation *n* the incarnation of the soul after death in another body.—**reincarnate** *adj, vt.*

reindeer *n* a large deer with branched antlers found in northern regions.

reinforce *vt* (*army etc*) to strengthen with fresh troops; (*a material*) to add to the strength of.—**reinforcement** *n.*

reinstate *vt* to restore to a former position, rank, or condition.—**reinstatement** *n.*

reiterate *vt* to repeat; to say or do again or many times.—**reiteration** *n.*

reject *vt* to throw away, to discard; to refuse to accept, to decline; to rebuff. * *n* a thing or person rejected.—**rejection** *n.*

rejoice *vi* to feel joyful or happy.

rejuvenate *vt* to give youthful vigour to.—**rejuvenation** *n.*

relapse *vi* to fall back into a worse state after improvement; to return to a former vice. * *n* the recurrence of illness after apparent recovery.

relate *vt* to narrate, recount; to show a connection. * *vi* to have a formal relationship (with).

related *adj* connected, allied; akin.

relation *n* the way in which one thing stands in respect to another, footing; reference, regard; connection by blood or marriage; a relative; a narration, a narrative; (*pl*) the connections between or among persons, nations, etc; (*pl*) one's family and in-laws.

relationship *n* the tie or degree of kinship or intimacy; affinity; (*inf*) an affair.

relative *adj* having or expressing a relation; corresponding; pertinent; comparative, conditional; respective; meaningful only in relationship; (*gram*) referring to a previous noun, clause, etc. * *n* a person related by blood or marriage.—**relatively** *adv*.

relax *vti* to slacken; to make or become less severe or strict; to make (the muscles) less rigid; to take a rest.

relaxation *n* the act of relaxing; the condition of being relaxed; recreation.

relay *n* a team of fresh horses, men, etc to relieve others; a race between teams, each member of which goes a part of the distance; (*elect*) a device for enabling a weak current to control others; a relayed broadcast. * *vt* (*pt* **relayed**) (*news, etc*) to spread in stages; to broadcast signals.

release *vt* to set free; to let go; to relinquish; (*film, etc*) to issue for public exhibition; (*information*) to make available; (*law*) to make over to another. * *n* a releasing, as from prison, work, etc; a device to hold or release a mechanism; a news item, etc, released to the public; (*law*) a written surrender of a claim.

relegate *vt* to move to an inferior position; to demote; to banish.—**relegation** *n*.

relent *vi* to soften in attitude; to become less harsh or severe.

relentless *adj* pitiless; unremitting.

relevant *adj* applying to the matter in hand, pertinent; to the point.—**relevance** *n*.—**relevancy** *n*.

reliable *adj* dependable, trustworthy.—**reliability** *n*.—**reliably** *adv*.

relic *n* an object, fragment, or custom that has survived from the past; part of a saint's body or belongings; (*pl*) remains of the dead.

relief *n* the sensation following the easing or lifting of discomfort or stress; release from a duty by another person; a person who takes the place of another on duty; that which relieves; aid; assistance to the needy or victims of a disaster; the projection of a carved design from its ground; distinctness, vividness. * *adj* providing relief in disasters etc.

relieve *vt* to bring relief or assistance to; to release from obligation or duty; to ease; (*with* **oneself**) to empty the bladder or bowels. * *vi* to give relief; to break the monotony of; to bring into relief, to stand out.

religion *n* a belief in God or gods; a system of worship and faith; a formalized expression of belief.

relinquish *vt* to give up; to renounce or surrender.—**relinquishment** *n*.

relish *n* an appetizing flavour; a distinctive taste; enjoyment of food or an experience; a spicy accompaniment to food; gusto, zest. * *vt* to like the flavour of; to enjoy, appreciate.

reluctant *adj* unwilling, loath; offering resistance.—**reluctance** *n*.—**reluctantly** *adv*.

rely *vi* to depend on; to trust.

remain *vi* to stay behind or in the same place; to continue to be; to survive, to last; to be left over. * *npl* anything left after use; a corpse.

remainder *n* what is left, the rest; (*math*) the result of subtraction, the quantity left over after division; (*books*) unsold stock; (*law*) the residual interest in an estate.

remand *vt* to send back into custody for further evidence.—*also n*.

remark *vti* to notice; to observe; to pass a comment (upon). * *n* a brief comment.

remarkable *adj* unusual; extraordinary; worthy of comment.—**remarkably** *adv*.

remedial *adj* providing a remedy; correcting; relating to the teaching of people with learning difficulties.

remedy *n* a medicine or any means to cure a disease; anything that puts something else to rights. * *vt* to cure; to put right.

remember *vti* to recall; to bear in mind; to mention (a person) to another as sending regards; to exercise or have the power of memory.

remembrance *n* a reminiscence; a greeting or gift recalling or expressing friendship or affection; the extent of memory; an honouring of the dead or a past event.

remind *vt* to cause to remember.

reminder *n* a thing that reminds, esp a letter from a creditor.

reminisce *vi* to think, talk, or write about past events.

reminiscence *n* the recalling of a past experience; (*pl*) memoirs.

reminiscent *adj* reminding, suggestive (of); recalling the past.

remission *n* the act of remitting; the reduction

in length of a prison term; the lessening of the symptoms of a disease; pardon, forgiveness.

remit *vti* (*pt* **remitted**) to forgive; to refrain from inflicting (a punishment) or exacting (a debt); to abate, moderate; to send payment (by post); (*law*) to refer to a lower court for reconsideration. * *n* the act of referring; an area of authority.

remittance *n* the sending of money or a payment (by post); the payment or money sent.

remnant *n* a small remaining fragment or number; an oddment or scrap; a trace; an unsold or unused end of piece goods.

remorse *n* regret and guilt for a misdemeanour; compassion.—**remorseful** *adj*.—**remorsefully** *adv*.

remorseless *adj* ruthless, cruel; relentless.—**remorselessly** *adv*.—**remorselessness** *n*.

remote *adj* far apart or distant in time or place; out of the way; not closely related; secluded; aloof; vague, faint.—**remotely** *adv*.

remote control *n* the control of a device or activity from a distance, usu by means of an electric circuit or the making or breaking of radio waves.

removal *n* the act of removing; a change of home or office; dismissal.

remove *vti* to take away and put elsewhere; to dismiss, as from office; to get rid of; to kill; to go away. * *n* a stage in gradation; a degree in relationship.—**removable** *adj*.

remunerate *vt* to pay for a service; to reward.—**remuneration** *n*.

rend *vti* (*pt* **rent**) to tear, to wrench (apart); to be torn apart.

render *vt* (*payments, accounts, etc*) to submit, as for approval;to give back; to pay back; to perform; to represent as by drawing; to translate, interpret; to cause to be; (*fat*) to melt down.

rendering *n* interpretation, translation.

rendezvous *n* (*pl* **rendezvous**) an arranged meeting; a place to meet; a popular haunt; the process of bringing two spacecraft together. * *vi* to meet by appointment.

renegade *n* a deserter; a person who is faithless to a principle, party, religion, or cause.

renew *vti* to restore to freshness or vigour; to begin again; to make or get anew; to replace; to grant or obtain an extension of.—**renewable** *adj*.—**renewal** *n*.

renounce *vt* to abandon formally; to give up; to disown.

renovate *vt* to renew; to restore to good condition; to do up, repair.—**renovation** *n*.—**renovator** *n*.

renown *n* fame, celebrity.

renowned *adj* famous, illustrious.

rent[1] *see* **rend**.

rent[2] *n* regular payment to another for the use of a house, machinery, etc. * *vti* to occupy as a tenant; to hire; to let for rent.

rental *n* an amount paid or received as rent; a house, car, etc, for rent; an act of renting; a business that rents something.

renunciation *n* the act of renouncing; formal abandonment; repudiation.

rep *abbr* = representative; repertory.

repair *vt* to mend; to restore to good working order; to make amends for. * *n* the act of repairing; a place repaired; condition as to soundness.

repartee *n* a witty reply; skill in making such replies.

repay *vt* (*pt* **repaid**) to pay back; to refund.—**repayable** *adj*.—**repayment** *n*.

repeal *vt* to annul, to rescind; to revoke.—*also n*.

repeat *vti* to say, write, or do again; to reiterate; to recite after another or from memory; to reproduce; to recur. * *n* a repetition, encore; anything said or done again, as a re-broadcast of a TV programme; (*mus*) a passage to be repeated; the sign for this.—**repeatable** *adj*.

repeatedly *adv* many times, over and over again.

repel *vt* (*pt* **repelled**) to drive back; to beat off, repulse; to reject; to hold off; to cause distaste; (*water, dirt*) to be resistant to.

repellent *adj* distasteful, unattractive; capable of repelling. * *n* a substance that repels, esp a spray for protection against insects.

repent *vi* to wish one had not done something; to feel remorse or regret (for); to regret and change from evil ways.—**repentance** *n*.—**repentant** *adj*.

repercussion *n* a rebound; a reverberation; a far-reaching, often indirect reaction to an event.

repertoire *n* the stock of plays, songs, etc, that a company, singer, etc, can perform.

repertory *n* a repertoire; the system of alternating several plays through a season with a permanent acting group.

repetition *n* the act of repeating; something repeated, a copy.—**repetitive** *adj*.

replace *vt* to put back; to take the place of, to substitute for; to supersede.—**replaceable** *adj*.—**replacement** *n*.

replenish *vt* to stock again, refill.—**replenishment** *n*.

replete *adj* filled, well provided; stuffed, gorged.

replica *n* an exact copy; a reproduction.

reply *vti* to answer, respond; to give as an answer. * *n* an answer.

report *vti* to give an account of; to tell as news; to take down and describe for publication; to make a formal statement of; to complain about or against; to inform against; to present oneself (for duty). * *n* an account of facts; the formal statement of the findings of an investigation; a newspaper, radio or TV account of an event; a rumour; a sharp, loud noise, as of a gun.

reporter *n* a person who gathers and reports news for a newspaper, radio or TV; a person authorized to make statements concerning law decisions or legislative proceedings.

reprehensible *adj* blameworthy, culpable.

represent *vt* to portray; to describe; to typify; to stand for, symbolize; to point out; to perform on the stage; to act as an agent for; to deputize for; to serve as a specimen, example, etc, of.—**representable** *adj*.

representation *n* the act of representing or being represented, as in a parliamentary assembly; a portrait, reproduction; (*pl*) a presentation of claims, protests, views, etc.

representative *adj* typical; portraying; consisting of or based on representation of the electorate by delegates. * *n* an example or type; a person who acts for another; a delegate, agent, salesman, etc.

repress *vt* to suppress, restrain; (*emotions*) to keep under control; to exclude involuntarily from the conscious mind.—**repression** *n*.—**repressive** *adj*.

reprieve *vt* to postpone or commute the punishment of; to give respite to.—*also n*.

reprimand *n* a formal rebuke. * *vt* to reprove formally.

reprisal *n* an act of retaliation for an injury done.

reproach *vt* to accuse of a fault; to blame. * *n* a rebuke; a source of shame or disgrace.—**reproachful** *adj*.

reproduce *vti* to make a copy, duplicate, or likeness of; to produce offspring; to multiply.

reproduction *n* the act of reproducing; the process by which plants and animals breed; a copy or likeness; a representation.—**reproductive** *adj*.

reprove *vt* to rebuke, censure.—**reprovingly** *adv*.

reptile *n* any of a class of cold-blooded, air-breathing vertebrates with horny scales or plates; a grovelling or despised person.—**reptilian** *adj*.

republic *n* a government in which the people elect the head of state and in which the people and their elected representatives have supreme power; a country governed in this way.

republican *adj* of, characteristic of, or supporting a republic. * *n* an advocate of republican government; (*with cap*) a member of the US Republican party.—**republicanism** *n*.

repudiate *vt* to reject, disown; to refuse to acknowledge or pay; to deny.—**repudiation** *n*.

repugnant *adj* distasteful, offensive; contradictory; incompatible.—**repugnance** *n*.

repulse *vt* to drive back; to repel; to reject. * *n* a rebuff, rejection; a defeat, check.

repulsion *n* a feeling of disgust; aversion; (*physics*) the tendency of bodies to repel each other.

repulsive *adj* disgusting; detestable; exercising repulsion.—**repulsively** *adv*.

reputable *adj* of good repute, respectable.—**reputably** *adv*.

reputation *n* the estimation in which a person or thing is held; good name, honour.

repute *vt* to consider to be, to deem. * *n* reputation.

reputed *adj* generally reported; supposed.

reputedly *adv* in common estimation; by repute.

request *n* an asking for something; a petition; a demand; the thing asked for. * *vt* to ask for earnestly.

requiem *n* a mass for the dead; music for this.

require *vt* to demand; to need, call for; to order, command.

requirement *n* a need or want; an essential condition.

requisite *adj* needed; essential, indispensable. * *n* something required or indispensable.

requisition *n* a formal request, demand, or order, as for military supplies; the taking over of private property, etc for military use. * *vt* to order; to take by requisition.

rescind *vt* to annul, cancel.

rescue *vt* to save (a person, thing) from captivity, danger, or harm; to free forcibly from legal custody.—*also n*.—**rescuer** *n*.

research *n* a diligent search; a systematic and careful investigation of a particular subject; a scientific study. * *vi* to carry out an investigation; to study.—**researcher** *n*.

resemble *vt* to be like, to have a similarity to.—**resemblance** *n*.
resent *vt* to be indignant about; to begrudge; to take badly.—**resentful** *adj*.—**resentfully** *adv*.—**resentment** *n*.
reservation *n* the act of reserving; (*of tickets, accommodation, etc*) a holding until called for; a limitation or proviso; (*pl*) doubt, scepticism; land set aside for a special purpose.
reserve *vt* to hold back for future use; to retain; to have set aside; (*tickets, hotel room, etc*) to book. * *n* something put aside for future use; land set aside for wild animals; (*sport*) a substitute; (*mil*) a force supplementary to a regular army; a restriction or qualification; reticence of feelings; caution.—**reservable** *adj*.
reserved *adj* set apart, booked; uncommunicative, lacking cordiality.—**reservedly** *adv*.
reservoir *n* a tank or artificial lake for storing water; an extra supply or store.
reside *vi* to live in a place permanently; to be vested or present in.
residence *n* the act of living in a place; the period of residing; the house where one lives permanently; the status of a legal resident; a building used as a home.
residential *adj* of or relating to residence; used for private homes.
residue *n* a remainder; a part left over; what is left of an estate after payment of debts and legacies.
resign *vti* to give up (employment, etc); to relinquish; to yield to; to reconcile (oneself).
resignation *n* the resigning of office, etc; the written proof of this; patient endurance.
resigned *adj* submissive, acquiescent; accepting the inevitable.
resilient *adj* elastic, springing back; buoyant; (*person*) capable of carrying on after suffering hardship.—**resilience** *n*.—**resiliently** *adv*.
resin *n* a sticky substance exuded in the sap of trees and plants and used in medicines, varnishes, etc; a similar synthetic substance used in plastics.—**resinous** *adj*.
resist *vti* to fight against; to be proof against; to oppose or withstand.
resistance *n* the act of resisting; the power to resist, as to ward off disease; opposition, esp to an occupying force; hindrance; (*elect*) nonconductivity, opposition to a steady current.
resolute *adj* determined; firm of purpose, steadfast.—**resolutely** *adv*.—**resoluteness** *n*.
resolution *n* the act of resolving or the state of being resolved; determination; a fixed intention; the formal decision or opinion of a meeting; analysis, disintegration; (*med*) the dispersion of a tumour, etc; the picture definition in a TV.
resolve *vt* to break into component parts, dissolve; to convert or be converted (into); to analyse; to determine, make up one's mind; to solve, settle; to vote by resolution; to dispel (doubt); to explain; to conclude; (*med: tumour*) to disperse. * *n* a fixed intention; resolution; courage.
resonant *adj* ringing; resounding, echoing.
resort *n* a popular holiday location; a source of help, support, etc; recourse. * *vi* to have recourse to; to turn (to) for help, etc.
resound *vti* to echo; to reverberate; to go on sounding; to be much talked of; to spread (fame).
resounding *adj* echoing; notable; thorough.
resource *n* source of help; an expedient; the ability to cope with a situation; a means of diversion; (*pl*) wealth; assets; raw materials.
resourceful *adj* able to cope in difficult situations; ingenious.—**resourcefulness** *n*.
respect *n* esteem; consideration; regard; (*pl*) good wishes; reference; relation. * *vt* to feel or show esteem or regard to; to treat considerately.
respectable *adj* worthy of esteem; well-behaved; proper, correct, well-conducted; of moderate quality or size.—**respectability** *n*.—**respectably** *adv*.
respective *adj* proper to each, several.
respectively *adv* in the indicated order.
respiration *n* the act or process of breathing.
respite *n* a temporary delay; a period of rest or relief; a reprieve.
resplendent *adj* dazzling, shining brilliantly; magnificent.
respond *vti* to answer; to reply; to show a favourable reaction; to be answerable; (*with* **to**) to react.
response *n* an answer; a reaction to stimulation.
responsibility *n* being responsible; a moral obligation or duty; a charge or trust; a thing one is responsible for.
responsible *adj* having control (over); (*with* **for**) accountable (for); capable of rational conduct; trustworthy; involving responsibility.—**responsibly** *adv*.
responsive *adj* responding; sensitive to influence or stimulus; sympathetic.
rest[1] *n* stillness, sleep; inactivity; the state of not moving; relaxation; tranquillity; a sup-

port or prop; a pause in music, etc; a place of quiet. * *vti* to take a rest; to give rest to; to be still; to lie down; to relax; to be fixed (on); to lean, support or be supported; to put one's trust (in).

rest^2 *n* the remainder; the others. * *vi* to remain.

restaurant *n* a place where meals can be bought and eaten.

restful *adj* peaceful.—**restfully** *adv*.—**restfulness** *n*.

rest home *n* an old people's home; a convalescent home.

restitution *n* the restoring of something to its owner; a reimbursement, as for loss.

restive *adj* impatient; fidgety.

restless *adj* unsettled; agitated.—**restlessly** *adv*.—**restlessness** *n*.

restoration *n* the act of restoring; reconstruction; renovation; (*with cap*) the re-establishment of the monarchy in Britain in 1660 under Charles II.

restore *vt* to give or put back; to re-establish; to repair; to renovate; to bring back to the original condition.—**restorer** *n*.

restrain *vt* to hold back; to restrict; (*person*) to deprive of freedom.

restrained *adj* moderate; self-controlled; without exuberance.

restraint *n* the ability to hold back; something that restrains; control of emotions, impulses, etc.

restrict *vt* to keep within limits, circumscribe.

restricted *adj* affected by restriction; limited; not generally available.

restriction *n* restraint; limitation; a limiting regulation.—**restrictive** *adj*.

rest room *n* a room equipped with toilets, washbowls, etc for the use of the public.

result *vi* to have as a consequence; to terminate in. * *n* a consequence; an outcome; a value obtained by mathematical calculation; (*sport*) the final score; (*pl*) a desired effect.

resume *vti* to begin again; to continue after a stop or pause; to proceed after interruption.—**resumption** *n*.

resurgence *n* a revival; a renewal of activity.—**resurgent** *adj*.

resurrection *n* a revival; a rising from the dead; (*with cap*) the rising of Christ from the dead.

resuscitate *vti* to revive when apparently dead or unconscious.—**resuscitation** *n*.

retail *n* selling directly to the consumer in small quantities. * *adv* at a retail price. * *vti* to sell or be sold by retail.—*also adj*.—**retailer** *n*.—**retailing** *n*.

retain *vt* to keep possession of; to keep in the mind, to remember; to keep in place, support; to hire the services of.

retainer *n* that which returns; (*formerly*) a servant to a family, a dependant; a fee to retain the services of.

retaliate *vti* to revenge oneself, usu by returning like for like; to strike back; to cast back (an accusation).—**retaliation** *n*.—**retaliatory** *adj*.

retarded *adj* slow in physical or mental development.

retch *vi* to heave as if to vomit.

rethink *vt* (*pt* **rethought**) to consider or think about again, esp with a change in mind.

reticent *adj* reserved in speech; uncommunicative.—**reticence** *n*.

retina *n* (*pl* **retinas, retinae**) the innermost part of the eye, on which the image is formed.

retinue *n* a body of attendants.

retire *vi* to give up one's work when pensionable age is reached; to withdraw; to retreat; to go to bed. * *vt* (*troops*) to withdraw from use; to compel to retire from a position, work, etc.—**retirement** *n*.

retiring *adj* unobtrusive; shy.

retort *vi* to reply sharply or wittily. * *n* a sharp or witty reply; a vessel with a funnel bent downwards used in distilling; a receptacle used in making gas and steel.

retract *vti* to draw in or back; to withdraw (a statement, opinion, etc); to recant.—**retractable** *adj*.—**retraction** *n*.

retreat *vi* to withdraw, retire; to recede. * *n* a withdrawal, esp of troops; a sign for retiring; a quiet or secluded place, refuge; seclusion for religious devotion.

retrial *n* a second trial.

retribution *n* deserved reward; something given or exacted in compensation, esp punishment.

retrieve *vt* to recover; to revive; (*a loss*) to make good; (*comput*) to obtain information from data stored in a computer. * *vi* (*dogs*) to retrieve game.—**retrievable** *adj*.—**retrieval** *n*.

retriever *n* any of several breeds of dogs capable of being trained for retrieving.

retrospect *n* a looking back; a mental review of the past.—**retrospection** *n*.

return *vi* to come or go back; to reply; to recur. * *vt* to give or send back; to repay; to yield; to answer; to elect. * *n* something returned; a recurrence; recompense; (*pl*) yield, revenue;

a form for computing (income) tax.
reunion *n* a meeting following separation; a social gathering of former colleagues.
reunite *vt* to unite again; to reconcile. * *vi* to become reunited.
rev *vt* (*pt* **revved**) (*inf*) (*with* **up**) to increase the speed of an engine. * *n* revolution per minute.
revamp *vt* to renovate, to rework, remodel; to transform. * *n* the process of revamping; something revamped.
reveal *vt* (*something hidden or secret*) to make known; to expose; to make visible.
reveille *n* a morning bugle call to wake soldiers.
revel *vi* (*pt* **revelled**) (*with* **in**) to take pleasure or delight in; to make merry. * *n* (*pl*) merrymaking; entertainment.—**reveller** *n.*—**revelry** *n.*
revelation *n* the act of revealing; the disclosure of something secret; a communication from God to man; an illuminating experience.
revenge *vt* to inflict punishment in return for; to satisfy oneself by retaliation; to avenge. * *n* the act of revenging; retaliation; a vindictive feeling.—**revenger** *n.*
revengeful *adj* keen for revenge; vindictive.
revenue *n* the total income produced by taxation; gross income from a business or investment.
reverberate *vi* to rebound, recoil; to be reflected in; to resound, to echo.—**reverberation** *n.*
reverence *n* profound respect; devotion; a gesture of respect (such as a bow). * *vt* to hold in respect.
reverent *adj* feeling or expressing reverence.—**reverently** *adv.*
reverie *n* a daydream; (*mus*) a dreamy piece.—*also* **revery**.
reversal *n* the act or process of reversing.
reverse *vti* to turn in the opposite direction; to turn outside in, upside down, etc; to move backwards; (*law*) to revoke or annul. * *n* the contrary or opposite of something; the back, esp of a coin; a setback; a mechanism for reversing. * *adj* opposite, contrary; causing movement in the opposite direction.
reversion *n* return to a former condition or type; right to future possession.—**reversionary** *adj.*
revert *vi* to go back (to a former state); to take up again (a former subject); (*biol*) to return to a former or primitive type; (*law*) to go back to a former owner or his heirs.—**revertible** *adj.*
review *n* an evaluation; a survey; a reconsideration; a critical assessment; a periodical containing critical essays; an official inspection of ships or troops. * *vt* to re-examine; to inspect formally; to write an assessment of.
reviewer *n* a person who writes a review, esp for a newspaper, a critic.
revise *vt* to correct and amend; to prepare a new, improved version of; to study again (for an examination).—**revision** *n.*
revival *n* the act of reviving; recovery from a neglected or depressed state; renewed performance (of a play); renewed interest in; religious awakening.
revive *vti* to return to life; to make active again; to take up again.—**reviver** *n.*
revoke *vt* to cancel; to rescind. * *vi* (*cards*) to fail to follow suit.—**revocable** *adj.*—**revocation** *n.*
revolt *vt* to rebel; to overturn; to shock. * *vi* to feel great disgust. * *n* rebellion; uprising; loathing.
revolting *adj* extremely offensive.—**revoltingly** *adv.*
revolution *n* the act of revolting; a motion round a centre or axis; a single completion of an orbit or rotation; a great change; an overthrow of a government, social system, etc.
revolutionary *adj* of, advocating revolution; radically new. * *n* a person who takes part in or favours revolution.
revolutionize *vt* to cause a complete change in.
revolve *vt* to travel or cause to travel in a circle or orbit; to rotate.
revolver *n* a handgun with a magazine that revolves to reload.
revue *n* a musical show with skits, dances, etc, often satirizing recent events.
revulsion *n* disgust; aversion; a sudden change or reversal of feeling.
reward *n* something that is given in return for something done; money offered, as for the capture of a criminal. * *vt* to give a reward.
rewarding *adj* (*experience, activity, etc*) pleasing, profitable.
rewrite *vt* to write again; to revise. * *n* something rewritten; revision.
rhapsody *n* an enthusiastic speech or writing; (*mus*) an irregular instrumental composition of an epic, heroic or national character.
rhetoric *n* the art of effective speaking and writing; skill in using speech; insincere language.
rhetorical *adj* of or relating to rhetoric; high-flown, bombastic. —**rhetorically** *adv.*
rheumatic *adj* of, relating to or suffering from

rheumatism. * *n* a person who has rheumatism.

rheumatism *n* a disorder causing pain in muscles and joints.

rhinoceros *n* (*pl* **rhinoceroses**, **rhinoceros**) a large, thick-skinned mammal with one or two horns on the nose.—*also* **rhino**.

rhododendron *n* an evergreen shrub with large flowers.

rhubarb *n* a plant with large leaves and edible (when cooked) pink stalks; (*inf*) a noisy quarrel.

rhyme *n* the repetition of sounds usu at the ends of lines in verse; such poetry or verse; a word corresponding with another in end sound. * *vti* to form a rhyme (with); to put into rhyme.

rhythm *n* a regular recurrence of beat, accent or silence in the flow of sound, esp of words and music; a measured flow.—**rhythmic**, **rhythmical** *adj*.—**rhythmically** *adv*.

rib *n* one of the curved bones of the chest attached to the spine; any rib-like structure; a leaf vein; a vein of an insect's wing; a ridge or raised strip, as of knitting; a ridge of a mountain. * *vt* (*pt* **ribbed**) to provide with ribs; to form vertical ridges in knitting; (*inf*) to tease or ridicule.

ribald *adj* irreverent; humorously vulgar.

ribbon *n* silk, satin, velvet, etc, woven into a narrow band; a piece of this; a strip of cloth, etc, inked for use, as in a typewriter; (*pl*) torn shreds.

rice *n* an annual cereal grass cultivated in warm climates; its starchy food grain.

rich *adj* having much money, wealthy; abounding in natural resources, fertile; costly, fine; (*food*) sweet or oily, highly flavoured; deep in colour; (*inf*) full of humour. * *n* wealthy people collectively; (*pl* **riches**) wealth, abundance.—**richly** *adv*.—**richness** *n*.

rickets *n* a children's disease marked by softening of the bones, caused by vitamin D deficiency.

rickety *adj* shaky, unsteady.

rickshaw *n* a light, two-wheeled man-drawn vehicle, orig used in Japan.

ricochet *vi* (*pt* **ricocheted** *or* **ricochetted**) (*bullet*) to rebound or skip along ground or water. * *n* a rebound or glancing off; (*bullet*) a hit made after ricocheting.

rid *vt* (*pt* **rid** *or* **ridded**) to free from; to dispose (of).

riddance *n* clearance; disposal.

ridden[1] *see* **ride**.

ridden[2] *adj* oppressed by; full of.

riddle[1] *n* a puzzling question; an enigma; a mysterious person or thing.

riddle[2] *n* a coarse sieve. * *vt* to sieve or sift; to perforate with holes; to spread through, permeate.

ride *vb* (*pt* **rode**, *pp* **ridden**) *vti* to be carried along or travel in a vehicle or on an animal, bicycle, etc; to be supported or move on the water; to lie at anchor; to travel over a surface; to move on the body; (*inf*) to continue undisturbed. * *vt* (*horse*, *bicycle etc*); to sit on and control; to oppress, dominate; (*inf*) to torment. * *n* a trip or journey in a vehicle or on horseback, on a bicycle, etc; a thing to ride at a fairground.

rider *n* a person who rides; an addition to a document, amending a clause; an additional statement; something used to move along another piece.

ridge *n* a narrow crest or top; the ploughed earth thrown up between the furrows; a line where two slopes meet; (*of land etc*) a raised strip or elevation; a range of hills. * *vti* to form into ridges, wrinkle.—**ridged** *adj*.

ridicule *n* mockery, derision. * *vt* to make fun of, to mock.

ridiculous *adj* deserving ridicule; preposterous, silly.—**ridiculously** *adv*.—**ridiculousness** *n*.

rife *adj* widespread; prevalent.

riffraff *n* disreputable persons; refuse, rubbish.

rifle[1] *n* a shoulder gun with a spirally grooved bore.

rifle[2] *vti* to steal; to look through (a person's papers or belongings).

rift *n* a split; a cleft; a fissure. * *vti* to split.

rig *vt* (*pt* **rigged**) (*naut*) to equip with sails and tackle; to set up in working order; to manipulate fraudulently. * *n* the way sails, etc, are rigged; equipment or gear for a special purpose; a type of truck.

rigging *n* the ropes for supporting masts and sails; (*in theatre*) a network of ropes and pulleys to support and maintain scenery.

right *adj* correct, true; just or good; appropriate; fit, recovered; opposite to left; conservative; designating the side meant to be seen. * *adv* straight; directly; completely, exactly; correctly, properly; to or on the right side. * *n* that which is just or correct; truth; fairness; justice; privilege; just or legal claim; (*pl*) the correct condition. * *vti* to set or become upright; to correct; to redress.—**rightness** *n*.

right angle *n* an angle of 90 degrees.
righteous *adj* moral, virtuous.—**righteously** *adv*.—**righteousness** *n*.
rightful *adj* legitimate; having a just claim.—**rightfully** *adv*.—**rightfulness** *n*.
right-hand *adj* of or towards the right side of a person or thing; for use by the right hand.
right-handed *adj* using the right hand; done or made for use with the right hand. * *adv* with the right hand.
right-hand man *n* an important and supportive assistant.
rightly *adv* in truth; in the right; with good reason; properly.
right-of-way *n* a public path over private ground; the right to use this; precedence over other traffic.
right-wing *adj* of or relating to the conservative faction of a political party, organization, etc.—**right-winger** *n*.
rigid *adj* stiff, inflexible; severe, strict.—**rigidity** *n*.—**rigidly** *adv*.—**rigidness** *n*.
rigmarole *n* nonsense; a foolishly involved procedure.
rigour, rigor (*US*) *n* harsh inflexibility; severity; strictness.—**rigorous** *adj*.
rim *n* a border or raised edge, esp of something circular; the outer part of a wheel. * *vt* (*pt* **rimmed**) to supply or surround with a rim; to form a rim.
rimless *adj* lacking a rim; (*glasses*) without a frame.
rind *n* crust; peel; bark.
ring[1] *n* a circular band, esp of metal, worn on the finger, in the ear, etc; a hollow circle; a round enclosure; an arena for boxing, etc; a group of people engaged in secret or criminal activity to control a market, etc. * *vt* (*pt* **ringed**) to encircle, surround; to fit with a ring.
ring[2] *vti* (*pt* **rang** *or* **rung**) to emit a bell-like sound; to resound; to peal; to sound a bell; to telephone; (*with* **up**) to total and record esp by means of a cash register; to achieve. * *n* a ringing sound; a resonant note; a set of church bells.
ringlet *n* a curling lock of hair.
rink *n* an expanse of ice for skating; a smooth floor for roller skating; an alley for bowling.
rinse *vt* to wash lightly; to flush under clean water to remove soap. * *n* the act of rinsing; a preparation for tinting the hair.
riot *n* violent public disorder; uproar; unrestrained profusion; (*inf*) something very funny. * *vi* to participate in a riot.—**rioter** *n*.—**rioting** *n*.
riotous *adj* tumultuous, disorderly; luxurious, wanton.—**riotously** *adv*.—**riotousness** *n*.
rip *vti* (*pt* **ripped**) to cut or tear apart roughly; to split; (*with* **off**, **out**) to remove in a violent or rough manner; (*inf*) to rush, speed; (*with* **into**) to attack, esp verbally. * *n* a tear; a split.
rip cord *n* a cord for releasing a parachute.
ripe *adj* ready to be eaten or harvested; fully developed; mature.—**ripely** *adv*.—**ripeness** *n*.
ripen *vt* to grow or make ripe.
ripple *n* a little wave on the surface of water; the sound of this. * *vti* to have or form little waves on the surface (of).
rise *vi* (*pt* **rose**, *pp* **risen**) to get up; to stand up; to ascend; to increase in value or size; to swell; to revolt; to be provoked; to originate; to tower; to slope up; (*voice*) to reach a higher pitch; to ascend from the grave; (*fish*) to come to the surface. * *n* an ascent; origin; an increase in price, salary, etc; an upward slope.
risk *n* chance of loss or injury; hazard; danger, peril. * *vt* to expose to possible danger or loss; to take the chance of.
risky *adj* (**riskier, riskiest**) dangerous.
risqué *adj* verging on indecency; slightly offensive.
rissole *n* a fried cake of minced meat, egg, and breadcrumbs.
rite *n* a ceremonial practice or procedure, esp religious.
ritual *adj* relating to rites or ceremonies. * *n* a fixed (religious) ceremony.—**ritually** *adv*.
rival *n* one of two or more people, organizations or teams competing with each other for the same goal. * *adj* competing; having comparable merit or claim. * *vt* (*pt* **rivalled**) to strive to equal or excel; to be comparable to; to compete.
rivalry *n* emulation; competition.
river *n* a large natural stream of fresh water flowing into an ocean, lake, etc; a copious flow.
riverbed *n* the channel formed by a river.
riverside *n* the bank of a river.
rivet *n* a short, metal bolt for holding metal plates together. * *vt* (*pt* **riveted**) to join with rivets; to fix one's eyes upon immovably; to engross one's attention.—**riveter** *n*.
Riviera *n* the coast of the northern Mediterranean from southeast France to northwest Italy.
road *n* a surfaced track for travelling on; a highway; a street; a way or route; an anchorage for ships.
road block *n* a barrier erected across a road to halt traffic.

road hog *n* a car driver who obstructs other vehicles by encroaching on the others' traffic lane.

roadside *n* the border of a road.—*also adj.*

roadway *n* the strip of land over which a road passes; the main part of a road, used by vehicles.

roadworthy *adj* (*vehicle*) fit for the road.—**roadworthiness** *n.*

roam *vti* to wander about, to travel.

roar *vti* to make a loud, full, growling sound, as a lion, wind, fire, the sea; to utter loudly, as in a rage; to bellow; to guffaw.—*also n.*

roaring *adj* boisterous, noisy; brisk.

roast *vti* (*meat, etc*) to cook with little or no moisture, as in an oven; (*coffee, etc*) to process by exposure to heat; to expose to great heat; (*inf*) to criticize severely; to undergo roasting. * *n* roasted meat; a cut of meat for roasting; a picnic at which food is roasted.

rob *vb* (*pt* **robbed**) *vt* to seize forcibly; to steal from; to plunder. * *vi* to commit robbery.—**robber** *n.*

robbery *n* theft from a person by intimidation or by violence.

robe *n* a long flowing outer garment; the official dress of a judge, academic, etc; a bathrobe or dressing gown; a covering or wrap; (*pl*) ceremonial vestments. * *vti* to put on or dress in robes.

robin *n* a songbird with a dull red breast.

robot *n* a mechanical device that acts in a seemingly human way; a mechanism guided by automatic controls.

robust *adj* strong, sturdy; vigorous.—**robustly** *adv.*—**robustness** *n.*

rock[1] *n* a large stone or boulder; a person or thing providing foundation or support; (*geol*) a natural mineral deposit including sand, clay, etc; a hard sweet; (*inf*) a diamond, ice.

rock[2] *vti* to move to and fro, or from side to side; to sway strongly; to shake. * *n* a rocking motion; rock and roll.

rock and roll *n* popular music that incorporates country and blues elements and is usu played with a heavily accented beat.

rock bottom *n* the lowest or most fundamental part or level. * *adj* very lowest.

rocker *n* a rocking chair; a curved support on which a cradle, etc rocks.

rockery, rock garden *n* a garden among rocks for alpine plants.

rocket *n* any device driven forward by gases escaping through a rear vent. * *vi* to move in or like a rocket; to soar.

rocking chair *n* a chair mounted on rockers.

rocking horse *n* a toy horse fixed on rockers or springs.

rocky *adj* (**rockier, rockiest**) having many rocks; like rock; rugged, hard; shaky, unstable.

rod *n* a stick; a thin bar of metal or wood; a staff of office; a wand; a fishing rod; (*sl*) a pistol.

rode *see* **ride**.

rodent *n* any of several relatively small gnawing animals with two strong front teeth.

rodeo *n* (*pl* **rodeos**) the rounding up of cattle; a display of cowboy skill.

roe[1] *n* the eggs or sperm of fish.

roe[2] *n* a small reddish brown deer (—*also* **roe deer**); the female red deer.

rogue *n* a scoundrel; a rascal; a mischievous person; a wild animal that lives apart from the herd.—**roguish** *adj.*—**roguishly** *adv.*

role *n* a part in a film or play taken by an actor; a function.

roll *n* a scroll; anything wound into cylindrical form; a list or register; a turned-over edge; a rolling movement; a small cake of bread; a trill of some birds; an undulation; the sound of thunder; the beating of drumsticks. * *vi* to move by turning over or from side to side; to move like a wheel; to curl; to move in like waves; to flow. * *vt* to cause to roll; to turn on its axis; to move on wheels; to press with a roller; (*dice*) to throw; to beat rapidly, as a drum.

roll call *n* the reading aloud of a list of names to check attendance.

rolled gold *n* a thin coating of gold attached to another metal by passing through heavy rollers.

roller *n* a revolving cylinder used for spreading paint, flattening surfaces; a large wave; (*sl*) a Rolls Royce car.

roller skate *n* a four-wheeled skate strapped on to shoes.—**roller skating** *n.*

rolling pin *n* a wooden, plastic or stone cylinder for rolling out pastry.

rolling stock *n* all the vehicles of a railway.

Roman *adj* of or relating to the city of Rome or its ancient empire, or the Latin alphabet; Roman Catholic. * *n* an inhabitant or citizen of Rome; a Roman Catholic.

Roman Catholic *adj* belonging to the Christian church that is headed by the Pope.—*also n.*

romance *n* a prose narrative; a medieval tale of chivalry; a series of unusual adventures; a novel dealing with this; an atmosphere of awe or wonder; a love story; a love affair; a picturesque falsehood. * *vi* to write romantic fiction; to exaggerate.

Roman numerals *npl* the letters I, V, X, L, C, D and M used to represent numbers in the manner of the ancient Romans.

romantic *adj* of or given to romance; strange and picturesque; imaginative; (*art, etc*) preferring passion and imagination to proportion and finish.—**romantically** *adv*.

romp *vi* to play boisterously. * *n* a noisy game; a frolic; an easy win.

rompers *npl* a child's one-piece garment; a jumpsuit.

roof *n* (*pl* **roofs**) the upper covering of a building; the top of a vehicle; an upper limit. * *vt* to provide with a roof, to cover.

roofing *n* materials for a roof.

rook[1] *n* a crow-like bird.

rook[2] *n* (*chess*) a piece with the power to move horizontally or vertically, a castle.

room *n* space; unoccupied space; adequate space; a division of a house, a chamber; scope or opportunity; those in a room; (*pl*) lodgings. * *vi* to lodge.

roommate *n* a person with whom one shares a room or rooms.

roomy *adj* (**roomier, roomiest**) having ample space; wide.—**roominess** *n*.

roost *n* a bird's perch or sleeping-place; a place for resting. * *vi* to rest or sleep on a roost; to settle down, as for the night.

rooster *n* an adult male domestic fowl, a cockerel.

root[1] *n* the part of a plant, usu underground, that anchors the plant, draws water from the soil, etc; the embedded part of a tooth, a hair, etc; a supporting or essential part; an origin or source; (*math*) the factor of a quantity which multiplied by itself gives the quantity; (*mus*) the fundamental note of a chord; (*pl*) plants with edible roots. * *vti* to take root; to become established; (*with* **out**) to tear up, to eradicate.

root[2] *vti* to dig up with the snout; to search about, rummage; (*with* **for**) (*inf*) to encourage a team by cheering.

rope *n* a thick cord or thin cable made of twisted fibres or wires; a string or row of things braided or threaded together; a thickening in a liquid. * *vt* to tie, bind, divide or enclose with a rope; to lasso; (*liquid*) to become ropy.—**ropy** *adj*.

rosary *n* a string of beads for keeping count of prayers; a series of prayers.

rose[1] *see* **rise**.

rose[2] *n* a prickly-stemmed plant with fragrant flowers of many delicate colours; its flower; a rosette; a perforated nozzle; a pinkish red or purplish red.

rosé *n* a pink wine made from skinless red grapes or by mixing white and red wine.

rosemary *n* a fragrant shrubby mint used in cookery and perfumery.

rosette *n* a rose-shaped bunch of ribbon; a carving, etc, in the shape of a rose.

roster *n* a list or roll, as of military personnel; a list of duties.

rostrum *n* (*pl* **rostrums**, **rostra**) a platform or stage for public speaking.

rosy *adj* (**rosier, rosiest**) of the colour of roses; having pink, healthy cheeks; optimistic, hopeful.—**rosily** *adv*.—**rosiness** *n*.

rot *vti* (*pt* **rotted**) to decompose; to decay; to become degenerate. * *n* decay; corruption; several different diseases affecting timber or sheep; (*inf*) nonsense.

rota *n* a turn in succession; a list or roster of duties.

rotary *adj* revolving; turning like a wheel.

rotate *vti* to turn around an axis like a wheel; to follow a sequence.

rotation *n* the action of rotating; a regular succession, as of crops to avoid exhausting the soil.

rotor *n* a rotating part of a machine or engine.

rotten *adj* decayed, decomposed; corrupt; (*inf*) bad, nasty.—**rottenness** *n*.

rotund *adj* rounded; spherical; plump.

rouble *n* a coin and monetary unit of Russia.

rouge *n* a red cosmetic for colouring the cheeks; a red powder for polishing jewellery, etc. * *vti* to colour (the face) with rouge.

rough *adj* uneven; not smooth; ill-mannered; violent; rude, unpolished; shaggy; coarse in texture; unrefined; violent, boisterous; stormy; wild; harsh, discordant; crude, unfinished; approximate; (*inf*) difficult. * *n* rough ground; (*golf*) any part of a course with grass, etc, left uncut; a first sketch. * *vt* to make rough; to sketch roughly. * *adv* in a rough manner.—**roughly** *adv*.—**roughness** *n*.

roulette *n* a gambling game played with a revolving disc and a ball; a toothed wheel for making perforations.

round *adj* circular, spherical, or cylindrical in form; curved; plump; (*math*) expressed to the nearest ten, hundred, etc, not fractional; considerable; candid; (*style*) flowing, balanced;

(*vowel*) pronounced with rounded lips. * *adv* circularly; on all sides; from one side to another; in a ring; by indirect way; through a recurring period of time; in circumference; in a roundabout way; about; near; here and there; with a rotating movement; in the opposite direction; around. * *prep* encircling; on every side of; in the vicinity of; in a circuit through; around. * *n* anything round; a circuit; (*of shots*) a volley; a unit of ammunition; a series or sequence; a turn; (*golf*) a circuit of a course; a stage of a contest; (*mus*) a kind of canon. * *vt* to make or become round or plump; (*math*) to express as a round number; to complete; to go or pass around. * *vi* to make a circuit; to turn; to reverse direction.—**roundly** *adv*.—**roundness** *n*.

roundabout *adj* indirect, circuitous. * *n* a circuitous route; a merry-go-round; a crossroad where traffic circulates around a traffic island.

rounded *adj* curved or round; flowing, not angular.

round trip *n* a journey to a place and back again.

roundup *n* a driving together of livestock; (*inf*) the detention of several prisoners; a summary, as of news.

rouse *vti* to provoke; to stir up; to awaken; to wake up; to become active.

rousing *adj* stirring; vigorous.

rout[1] *n* a noisy crowd, a rabble; a disorderly retreat. * *vt* to defeat and put to flight.

rout[2] *vti* to grub up, as a pig; to search haphazardly; to make a furrow in (as wood or metal); to cause to emerge, esp from bed; to come up with; to uncover.

route *n* a course to be taken; the roads travelled on a journey. * *vt* to plan the route of; to send (by a specified route).

routine *n* a procedure that is regular and unvarying; a sequence of set movements, as in a dance, skating, etc.—*also adj*.

row[1] *n* a line of persons or things; a line of seats (in a theatre, etc).

row[2] *vti* to propel with oars; to transport by rowing. * *n* an act or instance of rowing.—**rower** *n*.

row[3] *n* a noisy quarrel or dispute; a scolding; noise, disturbance. * *vi* to quarrel; to scold.

rowdy *adj* (**rowdier, rowdiest**) rough and noisy, disorderly. * *n* a rowdy person, a hooligan.—**rowdiness, rowdyism** *n*.

royal *adj* relating to or fit for a king or queen; regal; under the patronage of a king or queen; founded by a king or queen; of a kingdom, its government, etc. * *n* a type of topsail; a stag with a head of twelve points; (*inf*) a member of a royal family.—**royally** *adv*.

royalist *n* a person who advocates monarchy.

royalty *n* the rank or power of a king or queen; a royal person or persons; a share of the proceeds from a patent, book, song, etc, paid to the owner, author, etc.

rpm *abbr* = revolutions per minute.

RSVP *abbr* = réspondez s'il vous plaît.

rub *vti* (*pt* **rubbed**) to move (a hand, cloth, etc) over the surface of with pressure; to wipe, scour; to clean or polish; (*with* **away**, **off**, **out**) to remove or erase by friction; to chafe, grate; to fret; to take a rubbing of; (*with* **along**) to manage somehow; (*with* **down**) to rub vigorously with a towel; to smooth down. * *n* the act or process of rubbing; a drawback, difficulty.

rubber[1] *n* an elastic substance made synthetically or from the sap of various tropical plants; an eraser.

rubber[2] *n* a group of three games at whist, bridge, etc; the deciding game.

rubber-stamp *vt* (*inf*) to give automatic approval without investigation.

rubbish *n* refuse; garbage, trash; nonsense. * *vt* (*inf*) to criticize.—**rubbishy** *adj*.

rubble *n* rough broken stone or rock; builders' rubbish.

ruby *n* a deep red, transparent, valuable precious stone. * *adj* of the colour of a ruby.

rucksack *n* a bag worn on the back by hikers.

rudder *n* a flat vertical piece of wood or metal hinged to the stern of a ship or boat or the rear of an aircraft to steer by; a guiding principle.

ruddy *adj* (**ruddier, ruddiest**) reddish pink; (*complexion*) of a healthy, red colour.

rude *adj* uncivil, ill-mannered; uncultured, coarse; harsh, brutal; crude, roughly made; in a natural state, primitive; vigorous, hearty.—**rudely** *adv*.—**rudeness** *n*.

rudiment *n* a first stage; a first slight beginning of something; an imperfectly developed organ; (*pl*) elements, first principles.

rudimentary *adj* elementary; imperfectly developed or represented only by a vestige.

rueful *adj* regretful; dejected; showing good-humoured self-pity.—**ruefully** *adv*.

ruff *n* a pleated collar or frill worn round the neck; a fringe of feathers or fur round the neck of a bird or animal.

ruffian *n* a brutal lawless person; a villain.

ruffle *vti* to disturb the smoothness of, to

disarrange; to irritate; to agitate; to upset; to swagger about; to be quarrelsome; to flutter. * *n* pleated material used as a trim; a frill; a bird's ruff; a dispute, a quarrel.

rug *n* a thick heavy fabric used as a floor covering; a thick woollen wrap or coverlet.

Rugby *n* a football game for two teams of 15 players played with an oval ball.

rugged *adj* rocky; rough, uneven; strong; stern; robust.—**ruggedly** *adv*.—**ruggedness** *n*.

ruin *n* destruction; downfall, wrecked state; the cause of this; a loss of fortune; (*pl*) the remains of something destroyed, decayed, etc. * *vti* to destroy; to spoil; to bankrupt; to come to ruin.

ruinous *adj* in ruins; causing ruin, disastrous.

rule *n* a straight-edged instrument for drawing lines and measuring; government; the exercise of authority; a regulation, an order; a principle, a standard; habitual practice; the code of a religious order; a straight line. * *vti* to govern, to exercise authority over; to manage; to draw (lines) with a ruler; (*with* **out**) to exclude, to eliminate; to make impossible.

ruler *n* a person who governs; a strip of wood, metal, etc, with a straight edge, used in drawing lines, measuring, etc.

ruling *adj* governing; reigning; dominant. * *n* an authoritative pronouncement.

rum *n* a spirit made from sugar cane.

rumble *vti* to make a low heavy rolling noise; to move with such a sound; (*sl*) to see through, find out. * *n* the dull deep vibrating noise of thunder, etc.

rummage *n* odds and ends; a search by ransacking. * *vti* to search thoroughly; to ransack; to fish (out).

rummage sale *n* a jumble sale.

rumour, rumor (*US*) *n* hearsay, gossip; common talk not based on definite knowledge; an unconfirmed report, story. * *vt* to report by way of rumour.

rump *n* the hindquarters of an animal's body; the buttocks; the back end.

rumpus *n* a commotion; a din.

run *vb* (*pt* **ran**) *vi* to go by moving the legs faster than in walking; to hurry; to flee; to flow; to operate; to be valid; to compete in a race, election, etc; (*colours*), to merge. * *vt* (*a car, etc*) to drive; (*a business, etc*) to manage; (*a story*) to publish in a newspaper; (*temperature*) to suffer from a fever; (*with* **out**) to exhaust a supply; (*inf*) to desert; (*with* **over**) (*vehicle*) to knock down a person or animal; to overflow; to exceed a limit; to rehearse quickly; (*with* **up**) to incur or amass. * *n* an act of running; a trip; a flow; a series; prevalence; a trend; an enclosure for chickens, etc; free and unrestricted access to all parts; (*in tights, etc*) a ladder.

runaway *n* a person or animal that has run away.

rundown *n* a summary.

run-down *adj* dilapidated.

rung[1] *see* **ring**[2].

rung[2] *n* the step of a ladder; the crossbar of a chair.

runner *n* an athlete; a person who runs; a smuggler; a groove or strip on which something glides.

runner bean *n* a climbing plant that produces long green edible pods.

runner-up *n* (*pl* **runners-up**) the competitor who finishes second in a race, contest, etc.

running *n* the act of moving swiftly; that which runs or flows; a racing, managing, etc. * *adj* moving swiftly; kept for a race; being in motion; continuous; discharing pus. * *adv* in succession.

runny *adj* (**runnier, runniest**) tending to flow.

run-of-the-mill *adj* average, mediocre.

runt *n* an unusually small animal, esp the smallest of a litter of pigs; a person of small stature.

runway *n* a landing strip for aircraft.

rupture *n* a breach; a severance, quarrel; the act of bursting or breaking; hernia. * *vti* to cause or suffer a rupture.

rural *adj* relating to the country or agriculture.—**rurally** *adv*.

ruse *n* a trick, deception.

rush[1] *vti* to move, push, drive, etc, swiftly or impetuously; to make a sudden attack (on); to do with unusual haste; to hurry. * *adj* marked by or needing extra speed or urgency. * *n* a sudden surge; a sudden demand; a press, as of business, requiring unusual haste; an unedited film print.

rush[2] *n* a marsh plant; its slender pithy stem; a worthless thing.

rush hour *n* the time at the beginning and end of the working day when traffic is at its heaviest.

rusk *n* a sweet or plain bread sliced and rebaked until dry and crisp.

rust *n* a reddish oxide coating formed on iron or steel when exposed to moisture; a reddish brown colour; a red mould on plants; the fungus causing this. * *vti* to form rust (on); to deteriorate, as through disuse.

rustle *n* a crisp, rubbing sound as of dry leaves, paper, etc. * *vti* to make or move with a rustle; to hustle; to steal (cattle); (*with* **up**) (*inf*) to collect or get together.

rusty *adj* (**rustier, rustiest**) coated with rust; rust-coloured, faded; out of practice; antiquated.—**rustiness** *n*.

rut[1] *n* a track worn by wheels; an undeviating mechanical routine. * *vt* (*pt* **rutted**) to mark with ruts.

rut[2] *n* the seasonal period of sexual excitement in certain male animals, eg deer. * *vi* (*pt* **rutted**) *(deer, etc)* to be in rut.

ruthless *adj* cruel; merciless.—**ruthlessly** *adv*.—**ruthlessness** *n*.

rye *n* a hardy annual grass; its grain, used for making flour and whiskey; a whiskey made from rye.

S

sabbath *n* a day of rest and worship observed on a Saturday by Jews, Sunday by Christians and Friday by Muslims.

sabbatical *n* a year's leave from a teaching post, often paid, for research or travel.

sabotage *n* deliberate damage of machinery, or disruption of public services, by enemy agents, disgruntled employees, etc, to prevent their effective operation. * *vt* to practise sabotage on; to spoil, disrupt.

saccharin *n* a non-fattening sugar substitute.

saccharine *adj* containing sugar; excessively sweet.

sack[1] *n* a large bag made of coarse cloth used as a container; the contents of this; a loose-fitting dress or coat; (*sl: with* **the**) dismissal. * *vt* to put into sacks; (*sl*) to dismiss.

sack[2] *n* the plunder or destruction of a place. * *vt* to plunder or loot.

sacking *n* the coarse cloth used for sacks; the storming and plundering of a place.

sacrament *n* a religious ceremony forming outward and visible sign of inward and spiritual grace, esp baptism and the Eucharist; the consecrated elements in the Eucharist, esp the bread; a sacred symbol or pledge.—**sacramental** *adj*.

sacred *adj* regarded as holy; consecrated to a god or God; connected with religion; worthy of or regarded with reverence, sacrosanct.

sacrifice *n* the act of offering ceremonially to a deity; the slaughter of an animal (or person) to please a deity; the surrender of something valuable for the sake of something more important; loss without return; something sacrificed, an offering. * *vt* to slaughter or give up as a sacrifice; to give up for a higher good; to sell at a loss.—**sacrificial** *adj*.

sacrilege *n* violation of anything holy or sacred.

sacrosanct *adj* inviolable; very holy.

sad *adj* (**sadder, saddest**) expressing grief or unhappiness; sorrowful; deplorable.—**sadly** *adv*.—**sadness** *n*.

sadden *vti* to make or become sad.

saddle *n* a seat, usu of leather, for a rider on a horse, bicycle, etc; a ridge connecting two mountain peaks; a joint of mutton or venison consisting of the two loins. * *vt* to put a saddle on; to burden, encumber.

saddlebag *n* a bag hung from the saddle of a horse or bicycle.

sadism *n* sexual pleasure obtained from inflicting cruelty upon another; extreme cruelty.—**sadist** *n*.—**sadistic** *adj*.

safari *n* (*pl* **safaris**) a journey or hunting expedition.

safe *adj* unhurt; out of danger; reliable; secure; involving no risk; trustworthy; giving protection; prudent; sure; incapable of doing harm. * *n* a locking metal box or compartment for valuables.—**safely** *adv*.

safeguard *n* anything that protects against injury or danger; a proviso against foreseen risks. * *vt* to protect.

safekeeping *n* the act or process of keeping safely; protection.

safety *n* freedom from danger; the state of being safe.

safety belt *n* a belt worn by a person working at a great height to prevent falling; a seatbelt in a car.

safety pin *n* a pin with a guard to cover the point.

saffron *n* a crocus whose bright yellow stigmas are used as a food colouring and flavouring; an orange-yellow colour.

sag *vi* (*pt* **sagged**) to droop downwards in the middle; to sink or hang down unevenly under pressure.

sage[1] *adj* wise through reflection and experience. * *n* a person of profound wisdom.—**sagely** *adv*.

sage[2] *n* a herb with leaves used for flavouring food; sagebrush.

Sagittarius *n* the Archer, ninth sign of the zodiac; in astrology, operative 22 November - 20 December.

sago *n* a type of Asian palm; its starchy pith used in puddings.
said *see* **say**.
sail *n* a piece of canvas used to catch the wind to propel or steer a vessel; sails collectively; anything like a sail; an arm of a windmill; a voyage in a sailing vessel. * *vt* to navigate a vessel; to manage (a vessel). * *vi* to be moved by sails; to travel by water; to glide or pass smoothly; to walk in a stately manner.
sailing *n* the act of sailing; the motion or direction of a ship, etc on water; a departure from a port.
sailing boat, sailboat (*US*) *n* a boat that is propelled by a sail or sails.
sailor *n* a person who sails; one of a ship's crew.
saint *n* a person who is very patient, charitable, etc; a person who is canonized by the Roman Catholic church.—**sainthood** *n*.
sake *n* behalf; purpose; benefit; interest.
salad *n* a dish, usu cold, of vegetables, fruits, meat, eggs, etc; lettuce, etc, used for this.
salad dressing *n* a cooked or uncooked sauce of oil, vinegar, spices, etc, to put on a salad.
salary *n* fixed, regular payment for non-manual work, usu paid monthly.
sale *n* the act of selling; the exchange of goods or services for money; the market or opportunity of selling; an auction; the disposal of goods at reduced prices; the period of this.
saleroom, salesroom *n* a place where goods are displayed for sale; an auction room.
salesman *n* a person who sells either in a given territory or in a shop.—**saleswoman** *nf*.
salient *adj* projecting outwards; conspicuous; noteworthy; leaping, gushing.
saliva *n* the liquid secreted by glands in the mouth that aids digestion.—**salivary** *adj*.
sallow *adj* (*complexion*) an unhealthy yellow colour, a pale brown colour.—**sallowness** *n*.
salmon *n* (*pl* **salmon**) a large silvery edible fish that lives in salt water and spawns in fresh water; salmon pink.
saloon *n* a large reception room; a large cabin for the social use of a ship's passengers; a four-seater car with a boot; a place where alcoholic drinks are sold and consumed.
salt *n* a white crystalline substance (sodium chloride) used as a seasoning or preservative; piquancy, wit; (*chem*) a compound of an acid and a base; (*pl*) mineral salt as an aperient. * *adj* containing or tasting of salt; preserved with salt; pungent. * *vt* to flavour, pickle or sprinkle with salt; to give flavour or piquancy to (as a story); (*with* **away**) to hoard; to keep for the future.—**salty** *adj*.
salt cellar *n* a vessel for salt at the table; a saltshaker.
salutary *adj* beneficial, wholesome.—**salutarily** *adv*.—**salutariness** *n*.
salute *n* a gesture of respect or greeting; (*mil*) a motion of the right hand to the head, or of a rifle; a discharge of guns, etc, as a military mark of honour. * *vti* to make a salute (to); to greet; to kiss; to praise or honour.
salvage *n* the rescuing of a ship or property from loss at sea, by fire, etc; the reward paid for this; the thing salvaged; waste material intended for further use. * *vt* to save from loss or danger.
salvation *n* the act of saving or the state of being saved; in Christianity, the deliverance from evil; a means of preservation.
salvo *n* (**salvoes, salvos**) a firing of several guns or missiles simultaneously; a sudden burst; a spirited verbal attack.
same *adj* identical; exactly similar; unchanged; uniform, monotonous; previously mentioned. * *pron* the same person or thing. * *adv* in like manner.
sample *n* a specimen; a small part representative of the whole; an instance. * *vt* (*food, drink*)to taste a small quantity of; to test by taking a sample.
sanatorium, sanitarium (*US*) *n* (*pl* **sanatoriums, sanitariums**) an establishment for the treatment of convalescents or the chronically ill.—*also*
sanctimonious *adj* pretending to be holy; hypocritically pious or righteous.—**sanctimoniously** *adv*.
sanction *n* express permission, authorization; a binding influence; a penalty by which a law is enforced, esp a prohibition on trade with a country that has violated international law. * *vt* to permit; to give authority.
sanctity *n* the condition of being holy or sacred.
sanctuary *n* a sacred place; the part of a church around the altar; a place where one is free from arrest or violence, an asylum; a refuge; an animal reserve.
sand *n* very fine rock particles; (*pl*) a desert; a sandy beach. * *vt* to smooth or polish with sand or sandpaper; to sprinkle with sand.
sandal *n* a shoe consisting of a sole strapped to the foot; a low slipper or shoe.
sandpaper *n* a paper coated on one side with sand or another abrasive, used to smooth or

polish. * *vt* to rub with sandpaper.

sandstone *n* a sedimentary rock of compacted sand.

sandwich *n* two slices of bread with meat, cheese, or other filling between; anything in a sandwich-like arrangement. * *vt* to place between two things or two layers; to make such.a place for.

sandy *adj* (**sandier, sandiest**) of, like, or sprinkled with sand; yellowish grey.—**sandiness** *n.*

sane *adj* mentally sound, not mad; reasonable, sensible.—**sanely** *adv.*—**saneness** *n.*

sang *see* **sing**.

sanguine *adj* confident, hopeful; blood-red; (*complexion*) ruddy.

sanitary *adj* relating to the promotion and protection of health; relating to the supply of water, drainage, and sewage disposal; hygienic.

sanitary towel *n* an absorbent pad worn externally during menstruation.

sanitation *n* the science and practice of achieving hygienic conditions; drainage and disposal of sewage.

sanity *n* the condition of being sane; mental health.

sank *see* **sink**.

Santa Claus *n* a legendary fat, white-bearded old man who brings presents to children at Christmas.—*also* **Father Christmas**.

sap *n* the vital juice of plants; energy and health; (*inf*) a fool. * *vt* (*pt* **sapped**) to drain of sap; to exhaust the energy of; to weaken or undermine.

sapling *n* a young tree; a youth.

sapphire *n* a transparent blue precious stone; a deep pure blue.—*also adj.*

sarcasm *n* a scornful or ironic remark; the use of this.—**sarcastic** *adj.*—**sarcastically** *adv.*

sardine *n* a small, edible seafish.

sash[1] *n* a band of satin or ribbon worn around the waist or over the shoulder, often as a badge of honour.

sash[2] *n* a frame for holding the glass of a window, esp one that slides vertically.

sat *see* **sit**.

Satan *n* the devil, the adversary of God.—**satanic** *adj.*

satchel *n* a bag with shoulder straps for carrying school books, etc.

satellite *n* a planet orbiting another; a man-made object orbiting the earth, moon, etc, to gather scientific information or for communication; a nation economically dependent on a more powerful one.

satin *n* a fabric of woven silk with a smooth, shiny surface on one side. * *adj* of or resembling satin.

satire *n* a literary work in which folly or evil in people's behaviour are held up to ridicule; trenchant wit, sarcasm.—**satirical** *adj.*—**satirically** *adv.*

satisfaction *n* the act of satisfying or the condition of being satisfied; that which satisfies; comfort; atonement, reparation.

satisfactory *adj* giving satisfaction; adequate; acceptable; convincing.—**satisfactorily** *adv.*—**satisfactoriness** *n.*

satisfy *vi* to be enough for; to fulfil the needs or desires of. * *vt* to give enough to; (*hunger, desire etc.*) to appease; to please; to gratify; to comply with; (*creditor*) to discharge, to pay in full; to convince; to make reparation to; (*guilt, etc*) to atone for.

saturate *vt* to soak thoroughly; to fill completely.

Saturday *n* the seventh and last day of the week.

sauce *n* a liquid or dressing served with food to enhance its flavour; stewed or preserved fruit eaten with other food or as a dessert; (*inf*) impudence. * *vt* to season with sauce; to make piquant; (*sl*) to cheek.

saucepan *n* a deep cooking pan with a handle and lid.

saucer *n* a round shallow dish placed under a cup; a shallow depression; a thing shaped like a saucer.

saucy *adj* (**saucier, sauciest**) rude, impertinent; sprightly.—**saucily** *adv.*—**sauciness** *n.*

saunter *vi* to walk in a leisurely or idle way. * *n* a stroll.

sausage *n* minced seasoned meat, esp pork, packed into animal gut or other casing.

savage *adj* fierce; wild; untamed; uncivilized; ferocious; primitive. * *n* a member of a primitive society; a brutal, fierce person or animal.—**savagely** *adv.*—**savageness** *n.*

savagery *n* the state of being a savage; an act of violence or cruelty; an uncivilized state.

save *vt* to rescue from harm or danger; to keep, to accumulate; to set aside for future use; to avoid the necessity of; (*energy etc*) to prevent waste of; (*theol*) to deliver from sin. * *vi* to avoid waste, expense, etc; to economize; to store up money or goods; (*sports*) to keep an opponent from scoring or winning. * *n* (*sports*) the act of preventing one's opponent from scoring. * *conj*, prep except, but.

saving *adj* thrifty, economical; (*clause*) containing a reservation; redeeming. * *n* what is saved; (*pl*) money saved for future use. * *prep* except; with apology to.

savings bank *n* a bank receiving small deposits and holding them in interest-bearing accounts.

saviour, savior (*US*) *n* a person who saves another from harm or danger; (*with cap*) Jesus Christ.

savour, savor (*US*) *n* the flavour or smell of something; a distinctive quality. * *vti* to season; to enjoy; to have a specified taste or smell; to smack (of); to appreciate critically.

savoury, savory (*US*) *adj* having a good taste or smell; spicy, not sweet; reputable. * *n* a savoury dish at the beginning or end of dinner; (*pl*) snacks served with drinks.—**savouriness** *n*.

saw[1] *see* **see**[1]

saw[2] *n* a tool with a toothed edge for cutting wood, etc. * *vti* (*pt* **sawed,** *pp* **sawn**) to cut or shape with a saw; to use a saw; to make a to-and-fro motion.

sawdust *n* fine particles of wood caused by sawing.

sawmill *n* a mill where timber is cut into logs or planks.

sawn *see* **saw**[2].

saxophone *n* a brass wind instrument with a single reed and about twenty finger-keys.

say *vb* (*pt* **said**) *vt* to speak, to utter; to state in words; to affirm, declare; to recite; to estimate; to assume. * *vi* to tell; to express in words. * *n* the right or opportunity to speak; a share in a decision.

saying *n* a common remark; a proverb or adage.

scab *n* a dry crust on a wound or sore; a plant disease characterized by crustaceous spots; a worker who refuses to join a strike or who replaces a striking worker.—**scabby** *adj*.

scaffold *n* a raised platform for the execution of a criminal; capital punishment; scaffolding.

scaffolding *n* a temporary framework of wood and metal for use by workmen constructing a building, etc; materials for a scaffold.

scald *vt* to burn with hot liquid or steam; to heat almost to boiling point; to immerse in boiling water (to sterilize). * *n* an injury caused by hot liquid or steam.

scale[1] *n* (*pl*) a machine or instrument for weighing; one of the pans or the tray of a set of scales; (*pl with cap*) Libra, the seventh sign of the zodiac. * *vti* to weigh in a set of scales; to have a specified weight on a set of scales.

scale[2] *n* one of the thin plates covering a fish or reptile; a flake (of dry skin); an incrustation on teeth, etc. * *vti* to remove the scales from; to flake off.

scale[3] *n* a graduated measure; an instrument so marked; (*math*) the basis for a numerical system, 10 being that in general use; (*mus*) a series of tones from the keynote to its octave, in order of pitch; the proportion that a map, etc, bears to what it represents; a series of degrees classified by size, amount, etc; relative scope or size. * *vt* (*wall*) to go up or over; (*model*) to make or draw to scale; to increase or decrease in size.

scallop *n* an edible shellfish with two fluted, fan-shaped shells; one of a series of curves in an edging. * *vt* to cut into scallops.—**scalloped** *adj*.

scalp *n* the skin covering the skull, usu covered with hair. * *vti* to cut the scalp from; to criticize sharply; (*inf*) (*tickets, etc*) to buy and resell at higher prices.

scalpel *n* a short, thin, very sharp knife used esp for surgery.

scamper *vi* to run away quickly or playfully. * *n* a brisk or playful run or movement.

scan *vb* (*pt* **scanned**) *vt* (*page etc*) to look through quickly; to scrutinize; (*med*) to examine with a radiological device; (*TV*) to pass an electronic beam over; (*radar*) to detect with an electronic beam; (*poem*) to conform to a rhythmical pattern; to check for recorded data by means of a mechanical or electronic device; (*human body*) to make a scan of in a scanner. * *vi* to analyse the pattern of verse. * *n* the act of scanning or an instance of being scanned.

scandal *n* a disgraceful event or action; talk arising from immoral behaviour; a feeling of moral outrage; the thing or person causing this; disgrace; malicious gossip.

scandalize *vt* to shock the moral feelings of; to defame.

scandalous *adj* causing scandal; shameful; spreading slander.

Scandinavia *n* the region comprising Norway, Sweden, and Denmark, and sometimes Iceland.—**Scandinavian** *adj*.

scant *adj* limited; meagre; insufficient; scanty; grudging.

scanty *adj* (**scantier, scantiest**) barely adequate; insufficient; small.—**scantily** *adv*.—**scantiness** *n*.

scapegoat *n* a person who bears the blame for

others; one who is the object of irrational hostility.

scar[1] *n* a mark left after the healing of a wound or sore; a blemish resulting from damage or wear. * *vti* (*pt* **scarred**) to mark with or form a scar.

scar[2] *n* a protruding or isolated rock; a precipitous crag; a rocky part of a hillside.

scarce *adj* not in abundance; hard to find; rare.—**scarceness** *n*.

scarcely *adv* hardly, only just; probably not or certainly not.

scarcity *n* the state of being scarce; a dearth, deficiency.

scare *vti* to startle; to frighten or become frightened; to drive away by frightening. * *n* a sudden fear; a period of general fear; a false alarm.

scarecrow *n* a wooden figure dressed in clothes for scaring birds from crops; a thin or tattered person; something frightening but harmless.

scaremonger *n* a person who causes fear or panic by spreading rumours; an alarmist.

scarf *n* (*pl* **scarves**) a rectangular or square piece of cloth worn around the neck, shoulders or head for warmth or decoration.

scarlet *n* a bright red with a tinge of orange; scarlet cloth or clothes. * *adj* scarlet coloured; immoral or sinful.

scarlet fever *n* an acute contagious disease marked by a sore throat, fever, and a scarlet rash.

scathing *adj* bitterly critical; cutting, withering.—**scathingly** *adv*.

scatter *vti* to throw loosely about; to sprinkle; to dissipate; to put or take to flight; to disperse; to occur at random. * *n* a scattering or sprinkling.

scatterbrain *n* a frivolous, heedless person.—**scatterbrained** *adj*.

scattered *adj* dispersed widely, spaced out; straggling.

scavenge *vi* to gather things discarded by others; (*animal*) to eat decaying matter.—**scavenger** *n*.

scene *n* the place in which anything occurs; the place in which the action of a play or a story occurs; a section of a play, a division of an act; the stage of a theatre; a painted screen, etc, used on this; an unseemly display of strong emotion; a landscape; surroundings; a place of action; (*inf*) an area of interest or activity (eg *the music scene*).

scenery *n* painted screens, etc, used to represent places, as in a play, film, etc; an aspect of a landscape, esp of beautiful or impressive countryside.

scenic *adj* relating to natural scenery; picturesque; of or used on the stage.—**scenically** *adv*.

scent *n* a perfume; an odour left by an animal, by which it can be tracked; the sense of smell; a line of pursuit or discovery. * *vt* to recognize by the sense of smell; to track by smell; to impart an odour to, to perfume; to get wind of, to detect.

scented *adj* perfumed.

sceptic, skeptic (*US*) *n* a person who questions opinions generally accepted; a person who doubts religious doctrines, an agnostic; an adherent of scepticism.

sceptical, skeptical (*US*) *adj* doubting; questioning.—**sceptically** *adv*.

scepticism, skepticism (*US*) *n* an attitude of questioning criticism, doubt; (*philos*) the doctrine that absolute knowledge is unattainable.

sceptre, scepter (*US*) *n* the staff of office held by a monarch on a ceremonial occasion; sovereignty.

schedule *n* a timetable; a list, inventory or tabulated statement; a timed plan for a project. * *vt* to make a schedule; to plan.

scheme *n* a plan; a project; a systematic arrangement; a diagram; an underhand plot. * *vti* to devise or plot.—**schemer** *n*.

scheming *adj* cunning; intriguing.

schism *n* a division or separation into two parties, esp of a church; the sin of this; discord, disharmony.

schizophrenia *n* a mental disorder characterized by withdrawal from reality and deterioration of the personality; the presence of mutually contradictory qualities or parts.—**schizophrenic** *adj*, *n*.

scholar *n* a pupil, a student; a learned person; the holder of a scholarship.

scholarly *adj* learned, erudite, academic.

scholarship *n* an annual grant to a scholar or student, usu won by competitive examination; learning, academic achievement.

school[1] *n* a shoal of porpoises, whales, or other aquatic animals of one kind swimming together.

school[2] *n* an educational establishment; its teachers and students; a regular session of teaching; formal education, schooling; a particular division of a university; a place or means of discipline; a group of thinkers, artists, writers, holding similar principles.

* *vt* to train; to teach; to control or discipline.

schoolboy *n* a boy who attends school.

schoolgirl *n* a girl who attends school.

schooling *n* instruction in school.

schoolmaster *n* a man who teaches in school.

schoolmistress *n* a woman who teaches in school.

schoolteacher *n* a person who teaches in school.

schooner *n* a sailing ship with two or more masts rigged with fore-and-aft sails; a large drinking glass for sherry or beer.

sciatica *n* pain along the sciatic nerve, esp in the back of the thigh; (*loosely*) pain in the lower back or adjacent parts.

science *n* knowledge gained by systematic experimentation and analysis, and the formulation of general principles; a branch of this; skill or technique.

science fiction *n* highly imaginative fiction typically involving actual or projected scientific phenomena.

scientific *adj* of or concerned with science; based on or using the principles and methods of science; systematic and exact; having or showing expert skill.—**scientifically** *adv*.

scientist *n* a specialist in a branch of science, as in chemistry, etc.

scintillating *adj* sparkling; amusing.

scissor *vt* to cut with scissors, to clip. * *npl* a tool for cutting paper, hair, etc, consisting of two fastened pivoted blades whose edges slide past each other; a gymnastic feat in which the leg movements resemble the opening and closing of scissors.

scoff[1] *vti* to jeer (at) or mock. * *n* an expression or object of derision; mocking words, a taunt.

scoff[2] *vt* (*sl*) to eat quickly and greedily.

scold *vi* to reprove angrily; to tell off.

scone *n* a small, round cake made from flour and fat which is baked and spread with butter, etc.

scoop *n* a small shovel-like utensil as for taking up flour, ice cream, etc; the bucket of a dredge, etc; the act of scooping or the amount scooped up at one time; (*inf*) a piece of exclusive news; (*inf*) the advantage gained in being the first to publish or broadcast this. * *vt* to shovel, lift or hollow out with a scoop; (*inf*) to obtain as a scoop; (*inf: rival newspaper etc*) to forestall with a news item.

scooter *n* a child's two-wheeled vehicle with a footboard and steering handle; a motor scooter.

scope *n* the opportunity to use one's abilities; extent; range;.an instrument for viewing.

scorch *vti* to burn or be burned on the surface; to wither from over-exposure to heat; to singe; (*inf*) to drive or cycle furiously.

scorcher *n* (*inf*) a very hot day.

scorching *adj* (*inf: weather*) very hot; scathing.

score *n* the total number of points made in a game or examination; a notch or scratch; a line indicating deletion or position; a group of twenty; a written copy of a musical composition showing the different parts; the music composed for a film; a grievance for settling; a reason or motive; (*inf*) the real facts; a bill or reckoning; (*pl*) an indefinite, large number. * *vt* to mark with cuts; (*mus*) to arrange in a score, to orchestrate; to gain or record points, as in a game; to evaluate in testing. * *vi* to make points, as in a game; to keep the score of a game; to gain an advantage, a success, etc; (*sl*) to be successful in seduction.—**scorer** *n*.

scorn *n* extreme contempt or disdain; the object of this. * *vt* to treat with contempt, to despise; to reject or refuse as unworthy.—**scornful** *adj*.—**scornfully** *adv*.

Scorpio *n* the eighth sign of the zodiac in astrology, operative from 23 October - 21 November.

scorpion *n* a small, tropical, insect-like animal with pincers and a jointed tail with a poisonous sting.

Scot *n* a native or inhabitant of Scotland; a member of a Celtic people from Ireland that settled in northern Britain in the 5th and 6th centuries.

Scotch *n* whisky made in Scotland.

scotch *vt* (*a rumour*) to stamp out.

Scots *adj* of or pertaining to Scotland, its law, money, and people, and the Scots language. * *n* the dialect of English developed in Lowland Scotland.

Scottish *adj* of or relating to Scotland and its people.

scoundrel *n* a rascal; a dishonest person.

scour[1] *vt* to clean by rubbing with an abrasive cloth; to flush out with a current of water; to purge. * *n* the act or process of scouring; a place scoured by running water; scouring action; damage done by scouring.

scour[2] *vt* to hasten over or along, to range over, esp in search or pursuit.

scourge *n* a whip; a means of inflicting punishment; a person who harasses and causes widespread and great affliction; a pest. * *vt* to flog; to punish harshly.

scout *n* a person, plane, etc, sent to observe the enemy's strength, etc; a person employed to find new talent or survey a competitor, etc; (*with cap*) a member of the Scouting Association, an organization for young people. * *vti* to reconnoitre; to go in search of (something).

scowl *n* a contraction of the brows in an angry or threatening manner; a sullen expression. * *vi* to make a scowl; to look sullen.

scraggy *adj* (**scraggier, scraggiest**) thin and bony, gaunt.

scram *vi* (*pt* **scrammed**) (*sl*) to get out, to go away at once.

scramble *vi* to move or climb hastily on all fours; to scuffle or struggle for something; to move with urgency or panic. * *vt* to mix haphazardly; to stir (slightly beaten eggs) while cooking; (*transmitted signals*) to make unintelligible in transit. * *n* a hard climb or advance; a disorderly struggle; a rapid emergency take-off of fighter planes; a motorcycle rally over rough ground.—**scrambler** *n*.

scrap[1] *n* a small piece; a fragment of discarded material; (*pl*) bits of food. * *adj* in the form of pieces, leftovers, etc; used and discarded. * *vt* (*pt* **scrapped**) to discard; to make into scraps.

scrap[2] *n* (*inf*) a fight or quarrel.—*also vi*.

scrapbook *n* a book for pasting clippings, etc, in.

scrape *vt* to rub with a sharp or abrasive object so as to clean, smooth or remove; to eke out or to be economical; to amass in small portions; to draw along with a grating or vibration; to get narrowly past, to graze; to draw back the foot in making a bow. * *n* the act of scraping; a grating sound; an abrasion, scratch; an awkward predicament.

scraper *n* an instrument for scraping; a grating or edge for scraping mud from boots.

scrapheap *n* a pile of discarded material or things.

scrappy *adj* (**scrappier, scrappiest**) disjointed; fragmentary; full of gaps.—**scrappiness** *n*.

scratch *vt* to mark with a sharp point; to scrape with the nails or claws; to rub to relieve an itch; to chafe; to write awkwardly; (*writing etc*) to strike out; to withdraw from a race, etc. * *vi* to use nails or claws to tear or dig. * *n* the act of scratching; a mark or sound made by this; a slight injury; a starting line for a race; a scribble. * *adj* taken at random, haphazard, impromptu; without a handicap.

scrawl *n* careless or illegible handwriting; a scribble. * *vti* to draw or write carelessly.

scrawny *adj* (**scrawnier, scrawniest**) skinny; bony.

scream *vti* to utter a piercing cry, as of pain, fear, etc; to shout; to shriek. * *n* a sharp, piercing cry; (*inf*) a very funny person or thing.

scree *n* loose shifting stones; a slope covered with these.

screech *n* a harsh, high-pitched cry. * *vti* to utter a screech, to shriek.

screen *n* a movable partition or framework to conceal, divide, or protect; a shelter or shield from heat, danger or view; an electronic display (as in a television set, computer terminal, etc); a surface on which films, slides, etc are projected; the motion picture industry; a coarse wire mesh over a window or door to keep out insects; a sieve. * *vt* to conceal or shelter; to grade by passing through a screen; to separate according to skill, etc; (*a film*) to show on a screen.

screening *n* a showing of a film; a metal or plastic mesh, as for window screens; the refuse matter after sieving.

screw *n* a metal cylinder or cone with a spiral thread around it for fastening things by being turned; any spiral thing like this; a twist or turn of a screw; a twist of paper; pressure; a propeller with revolving blades on a shaft. * *vt* to fasten, tighten etc with a screw; to oppress; to extort, to cheat out of something due; (*sl, vulg*) to have sexual intercourse with; (*with* **up**) to gather (courage, etc). * *vi* to go together or come apart by being turned like a screw; to twist or turn with a writhing movement; (*sl, vulg*) to have sexual intercourse; (*with* **up**) to bungle.

screwdriver *n* a tool like a blunt chisel for turning screws; a drink of vodka and orange juice.

screwy *adj* (*sl*) (**screwier, screwiest**) eccentric, odd.

scribble *vti* to draw or write hastily or carelessly, to scrawl; to be a writer. * *n* hasty writing, a scrawl.—**scribbler** *n*.

script *n* handwriting; a style of writing; the text of a stage play, screenplay or broadcast; a plan of action; (*print*) type that resembles handwriting. * *vt* to write a script (for).

scriptural *adj* of or based on the Bible or Scripture.

scripture *n* any sacred writing; (*with cap, often pl*) the Jewish Bible or Old Testament; the Christian Bible or Old and New Testaments. * *adj* contained in or quoted from the Bible.

scriptwriter *n* a writer of screenplays for films, TV, etc; a screenwriter —**scriptwriting** *n.*

scroll *n* a roll of parchment or paper with writing on it; an ornament like this; (*her*) a ribbon with a motto; a list. * *vti* (*comput*) to move text across a screen; to decorate with scrolls.

scrounge *vti* (*inf*) to seek or obtain (something) for nothing.—**scrounger** *n.*

scrub[1] *n* an arid area of stunted trees and shrubs; such vegetation; anything small or mean. * *adj* small, stunted, inferior, etc.

scrub[2] *vti* (*pt* **scrubbed**) to clean vigorously, to scour; to rub hard; (*inf*) to remove, to cancel. * *n* the act of scrubbing.

scruff *n* the back of the neck, the nape.

scruffy *adj* (**scruffier, scruffiest**) shabby; unkempt.—**scruffily** *adv.*—**scruffiness** *n.*

scrum *n* a scrummage.

scrummage *n* (*Rugby football*) a play consisting of a tussle between rival forwards in a compact mass for possession of the ball. * *vi* to form a scrum(mage).

scruple *n* (*usu pl*) a moral principle or belief causing one to doubt or hesitate about a course of action. * *vti* to hesitate owing to scruples.

scrupulous *adj* careful; conscientious; thorough.—**scrupulously** *adv.*—**scrupulousness** *n.*

scrutinize *vti* to look closely at, to examine narrowly; to make a scrutiny.

scrutiny *n* a careful examination; a critical gaze; an official inspection of votes cast in an election.

scuff *vti* to drag the feet, to shuffle; to wear or mark the surface of by doing this.

scuffle *n* a confused fight; the sound of shuffling. * *vi* to fight confusedly; to move by shuffling.

scullery *n* a room for storage or kitchen work, such as washing dishes, etc.

sculptor *n* a person skilled in sculpture.

sculpture *n* the art of carving wood or forming clay, stone, etc, into figures, statues, etc; a three-dimensional work of art; a sculptor's work. * *vt* to carve, adorn or portray with sculptures; to shape, mould or form like sculpture.—**sculptural** *adj.*

scum *n* a thin layer of impurities on top of a liquid; refuse; despicable people.

scurrilous *adj* abusive; grossly offensive.

scurry *vi* (*pt* **scurried**) to hurry with quick, short steps, to scamper. * *n* a bustle; a flurry (as of snow).

scurvy *n* a disease caused by a deficiency of vitamin C. * *adj* base; contemptible.

scuttle[1] *vi* to run quickly; to hurry away. * *n* a short swift run; a hurried pace.

scuttle[2] *n* a bucket with a lip for storing coal.

scuttle[3] *n* (*naut*) a hatchway, a hole with a cover in a ship's deck or side. * *vt* to sink a ship by making holes in it.

scythe *n* a two-handed implement with a large curved blade for cutting grass, etc. * *vti* to cut with a scythe; to mow down.

sea *n* the ocean; a section of this; a vast expanse of water; a heavy wave, the swell of the ocean; something like the sea in size; the seafaring life. * *adj* marine, of the sea.

seaboard *n, adj* (land) bordering on the sea.

sea breeze *n* a wind that blows from the sea to the land.

seafood *n* edible fish or shellfish from the sea.

sea front *n* the waterfront of a seaside place.

seagoing *adj* (*ship*) made for use on the open sea.

seagull *n* a gull.

seal[1] *n* an engraved stamp for impressing wax, lead, etc; wax, lead, etc, so impressed; that which authenticates or pledges; a device for closing or securing tightly. * *vt* to fix a seal to; to close tightly or securely; to shut up; to mark as settled, to confirm.

seal[2] *n* an aquatic mammal with four webbed flippers; the fur of some seals; a dark brown. * *vi* to hunt seals.

sealant *n* a thing that seals, as wax, etc; a substance for stopping a leak, making watertight, etc.

sealer *n* a person or ship whose business is hunting seals.

sea level *n* the level of the surface of the sea in relation to the land.

sea lion *n* a large seal of the Pacific Ocean that has a roar and, in the male, a mane.

seam *n* the line where two pieces of cloth are stitched together; (*geol*) a stratum of coal, oil, etc, between thicker ones; a line or wrinkle. * *vt* to join with a seam; to furrow.

seaman *n* a sailor; a naval rank.

seamy *adj* (**seamier, seamiest**) unpleasant or sordid.

seance, séance *n* a meeting of spiritualists to try to communicate with the dead.

seaplane *n* an aeroplane with floats that allow it to take off from and land on water.

seaport *n* a port, harbour or town accessible to oceangoing ships.

search *vi* to look around to find something; to explore. * *vt* to examine or inspect closely; to probe into. * *n* the act of searching; an investigation; a quest.—**searcher** *n*.
searching *adj* keen, piercing; examining thoroughly.—**searchingly** *adv*.
searchlight *n* a powerful ray of light projected by an apparatus on a swivel; the apparatus.
search warrant *n* a legal document that authorizes a police search.
seashore *n* land beside the sea or between high and low water marks; the beach.
seasick *adj* affected with nausea brought on by the motion of a ship.
seaside *n* seashore.
season *n* one of the four equal parts into which the year is divided: spring, summer, autumn, or winter; a period of time; a time when something is plentiful or in use; a suitable time; (*inf*) a season ticket. * *vt* (*food*) to flavour by adding salt, spices, etc; to make mature or experienced; (*wood*) to dry until ready for use. * *vi* to become experienced.
seasonal *adj* of or relating to a particular season.
seasoning *n* salt, spices, etc, used to enhance the flavour of food; the process of making something fit for use.
season ticket *n* a ticket or set of tickets valid for a number of concerts, games, journeys, etc, during a specified period.
seat *n* a piece of furniture for sitting on, such as a chair, bench, etc; the part of a chair on which one sits; the buttocks, the part of the trousers covering them; a way of sitting (on a horse, etc); the chief location, or centre; a part at or forming a base; the right to sit as a member; a parliamentary constituency; a large country house. * *vt* to place on a seat; to provide with seats; to settle.
seatbelt *n* an anchored strap worn in a car or aeroplane to secure a person to a seat.
seaweed *n* a mass of plants growing in or under water; a sea plant, esp a marine alga.
seaworthy *adj* fit to go to sea; able to withstand sea water, watertight.
sec. *abbr* = second.
secluded *adj* private; sheltered; kept from contact with other people.
seclusion *n* the state of being secluded; privacy, solitude.
second *adj* next after first; alternate; another of the same kind; next below the first in rank, value, etc. * *n* a person or thing coming second; another; an article of merchandise not of first quality; an aid or assistant, as to a boxer, duellist; the gear after low gear; one sixtieth of a minute of time or of an angular degree; (*pl*) (*inf*) another helping of food. * *adv* in the second place, group, etc. * *vt* to act as a second (to); (*a motion, resolution, etc*) to support; (*mil*) to place on temporary service elsewhere.
secondary *adj* subordinate; second in rank or importance; in the second stage; derived, not primary; relating to secondary school. * *n* that which is secondary; a delegate, a deputy.—**secondarily** *adv*.
secondary school *n* a school between elementary or primary school and college or university.
second class *n* the class next to the first in a classification. * *adj* (second-class) relating to a second class; inferior, mediocre; (*seating, accommodation*) next in price and quality to first class; (*mail*) less expensive and handled more slowly (than first class).
second-hand *adj* bought after use by another; derived, not original.—*also adv.*
secondly *adv* in the second place.
second-rate *adj* of inferior quality.
second thought *n* a change in thought or decision after consideration.
secrecy *n* the state of being secret; the ability to keep secret.
secret *adj* not made public; concealed from others; hidden; private; remote. * *n* something hidden; a mystery; a hidden cause.—**secretly** *adv*.
secretariat *n* an administrative office or staff, as in a government.
secretary *n* a person employed to deal with correspondence, filing, telephone calls of another or of an association; the head of a state department.—**secretarial** *adj*.
secretive *adj* given to secrecy; uncommunicative, reticent.—**secretively** *adv*.—**secretiveness** *n*.
sect *n* a religious denomination; a group of people united by a common interest or belief; a faction.
section *n* the act of cutting; a severed or separable part; a division; a distinct portion; a slice; a representation of anything cut through to show its interior; (*geom*) the cutting of a solid by a plane; a plane figure formed by this. * *vti* to cut or separate into sections; to represent in sections; to become separated or cut into parts.
sector *n* (*geom*) a space enclosed by two radii

of a circle and the arc they cut off; a distinctive part (as of an economy); a subdivision; (*mil*) an area of activity .

secular *adj* having no connection with religion or the church; worldly.

secularize *vt* to change from religious to civil use or control.—**secularization** *n*.

secure *adj* free from danger, safe; stable; firmly held or fixed; confident, assured (of); reliable. * *vt* to make safe; to fasten firmly; to protect; to confine; to fortify; to guarantee; to gain possession of.—**securely** *adv*.

security *n* the state of being secure; a financial guarantee, surety; a pledge for repayment, etc; a protection or safeguard; a certificate of shares or bonds.

sedate[1] *adj* calm; composed; serious and unemotional.—**sedately** *adv*.—**sedateness** *n*.

sedate[2] *vti* to calm or become calm by the administration of a sedative.

sedation *n* the act of calming or the condition of being calmed, esp by sedatives; the administration of sedatives to calm a patient.

sedative *n* a drug with a soothing, calming effect. * *adj* having a soothing, calming effect.

sediment *n* matter that settles at the bottom of a liquid; (*geol*) matter deposited by water or wind.—**sedimentary** *adj*.

seduce *vt* to lead astray; to corrupt; to entice into unlawful sexual intercourse.—**seducer** *n*.

seduction *n* the act of seducing; temptations; attraction.

seductive *adj* tending to seduce; enticing, alluring.—**seductively** *adv*.

see[1] *vt* (*pt* **saw,** *pp* **seen**) to perceive with the eyes; to observe; to grasp with intelligence; to ascertain; to take care (that); to accompany; to visit to meet; to consult;(*guests*) to receive. * *vi* to have the faculty of sight; to make inquiry; to consider, to reflect; to understand.

see[2] *n* the diocese of a bishop.

seed *n* the small, hard part (ovule) of a plant from which a new plant grows; such seeds collectively; the source of anything; sperm or semen; descendants; (*tennis*) a seeded tournament player. * *vti* to sow (seed); to produce or shed seed; to remove seeds from; (*tennis*) to arrange (a tournament) so that the best players cannot meet until later rounds.

seedling *n* a young plant raised from seed, not from a cutting; a young tree before it is a sapling.

seedy *adj* (**seedier, seediest**) full of seeds; out of sorts, indisposed; shabby; rundown.—**seedily** *adv*.—**seediness** *n*.

seeing *n* vision, sight. * *adj* having sight; observant. * *conj* in view of the fact that; since.

seek *vti* (*pt* **sought**) to search for; to try to find, obtain, or achieve; to resort to; (*with* **to**) to try to, to endeavour; (*with* **out**) to try to secure the society of.—**seeker** *n*.

seem *vi* to appear (to be); to give the impression of; to appear to oneself.

seen *see* **see**[1].

seep *vi* to ooze gently, to leak through.

seer *n* a person who sees visions, a prophet.

seesaw *n* a plank balanced across a central support so that it is tilted up and down by a person sitting on each end; an up-and-down movement like this; vacillation. * *vi* to move up and down; to fluctuate. * *adj, adv* alternately rising and falling.

seethe *vi* to be very angry inwardly; to swarm (with people).

segment *n* a section; a portion; one of the two parts of a circle or sphere when a line is drawn through it. * *vti* to cut or separate into segments.

segregate *vti* to set apart from others, to isolate; to separate racial or minority groups.

seize *vt* to grasp; to capture; to take hold of suddenly or forcibly; to attack or afflict suddenly. * *vi* (*machinery*) to become jammed.—**seizable** *adj*.

seizure *n* the act of seizing; what is seized; a sudden attack of illness, an apoplectic stroke.

seldom *adv* not often, rarely.

select *vti* to choose or pick out. * *adj* excellent; choice; limited (eg in membership); exclusive.

selection *n* the act of selecting; what is or are selected; the process by which certain animals or plants survive while others are eliminated.—*also* **natural selection**.

selective *adj* having the power of selection; highly specific in activity or effect.

self *n* (*pl* **selves**) the identity, character, etc, of any person or thing; one's own person as distinct from all others; one's own interests or advantage. * *adj* (*colour*) matching, uniform.

self- *prefix* of itself or oneself; by, for, in relation to, itself or oneself; automatic.

self-assured *adj* confident.—**self-assurance** *n*.

self-catering *adj* catering for oneself.

self-centred, self-centered (*US*) *adj* preoccupied with one's own affairs.—**self-centredness** *n.*

self-coloured, self-colored (*US*) *adj* of a single colour.

self-confident *adj* sure of one's own powers.—**self-confidence** *n.*

self-conscious *adj* embarrassed or awkward in the presence of others, ill at ease.—**self-consciousness** *n.*

self-contained *adj* complete in itself; showing self-control; uncommunicative.

self-control *n* control of one's emotions, desires, etc, by the will.—**self-controlled** *adj.*

self-defence, self-defense (*US*) *n* the act of defending oneself; (*law*) a plea for the justification for the use of force.

self-employed *adj* earning one's living in one's own business or profession, not employed by another; working freelance.

self-evident *adj* evident without proof or explanation.—**self-evidence** *n.*

self-indulgence *n* undue gratification of one's desires, appetites, or whims.—**self-indulgent** *adj.*

self-interest *n* regard to one's own advantage.

selfish *adj* chiefly concerned with oneself; lacking consideration for others.—**selfishly** *adv.*—**selfishness** *n.*

selfless *adj* with no thought of self, unselfish.—**selflessness** *n.*

self-portrait *n* an artist or author's painting or account of himself or herself.

self-possessed *adj* cool and collected.

self-reliant *adj* relying on one's own powers; confident.—**self-reliance** *n.*

self-respect *n* proper respect for oneself, one's standing and dignity.—**self-respecting** *adj.*

self-righteous *adj* thinking oneself better than others; priggish.—**self-righteousness** *n.*

self-sacrifice *n* the sacrifice of one's own interests, welfare, etc, to secure that of others.

self-satisfied *adj* smugly conceited.

self-service *adj* serving oneself in a cafe, shop, filling station, etc.

self-sufficient *adj* independent; supporting oneself (eg in growing food) without the help of others.—**self-sufficiency** *n.*

sell *vb* (*pt* **sold**) *vt* to exchange (goods, services, etc) for money or other equivalent; to offer for sale; to promote; to deal in. * *vi* (*with* **off**) to clear out (stock) at bargain prices; (*with* **out**) to sell off, to betray for money or reward; (*inf*) to disappoint, to trick; to make sales; to attrect buyers. * *n* an act or instance of selling; (*inf*) a disappointment, a trick, a fraud.—**seller** *n.*

sellout *n* a show, game, etc, for which all the tickets are sold; (*inf*) a betrayal.

semaphore *n* a system of visual signalling using the operator's arms, flags, etc; a signalling device consisting of a post with movable arms.

semen *n* the fluid that carries sperm in men and male animals.

semi- *prefix* half; not fully; twice in a (specified period).

semibreve *n* (*mus*) a note equal to two minims.

semicircle *n* half of a circle.—**semicircular** *adj.*

semicolon *n* the punctuation mark (;) of intermediate value between a comma and a full stop.

semiconscious *adj* not fully conscious.—**semiconsciousness** *n.*

semi-detached *adj* (*house*) with another joined to it on one side.—*also n.*

semifinal *adj, n* (the match or round) before the final in a knockout tournament.—**semifinalist** *n.*

seminar *n* a group of students engaged in study or research under supervision; any group meeting to pool and disuss ideas.

semiquaver *n* (*mus*) half a quaver.

semiskilled *adj* partly skilled or trained.

semitone *n* (*mus*) an interval equal to half a tone.

semolina *n* coarse particles of grain left after the sifting of wheat.

senate *n* a legislative or governing body; (*with cap*) the upper branch of a two-body legislature in France, the US, etc; the governing body of some universities.

senator *n* a member of a senate.—**senatorial** *adj.*

send *vti* (*pt* **sent**) to cause or enable to go; to have conveyed, to dispatch (a message or messenger); to cause to move, to propel; to grant; to cause to be; (*sl*) to move (a person) to ecstasy; (*with* **down**) to expel from university; (*with* **for**) to order to be brought, to summon; (*with* **up**) (*inf*) to send to prison; to imitate or make fun of.—**sender** *n.*

send-off *n* a friendly demonstration at a departure; a start given to someone or something.

senile *adj* of or relating to old age; weakened, esp mentally, by old age.—**senility** *n.*

senior *adj* higher in rank; of or for seniors; longer in service; older (when used to distinguish between father and son with the same first name). * *n* one's elder or superior in standing; a person of advanced age; a student in the last year of college or high school.

seniority *n* the condition of being senior; status, priority, etc, in a given job.

sensation *n* awareness due to stimulation of the senses; an effect on the senses; a thrill; a state of excited interest; the cause of this.

sensational *adj* of or relating to sensation; exciting violent emotions; melodramatic.—**sensationally** *adv*.

sensationalism *n* the use of sensational writing, language, etc; the doctrine that all knowledge is obtained from sense impressions.—**sensationalist** *n*.

sense *n* one of the five human and animal faculties by which objects are perceived: sight, hearing, smell, taste, and touch; awareness; moral discernment; soundness of judgment; meaning, intelligibility; (*pl*) conscious awareness. * *vt* to perceive; to become aware of; to understand; to detect.

senseless *adj* stupid, foolish; meaningless, purposeless; unconscious.—**senselessly** *adv*.—**senselessness** *n*.

sensibility *n* the capacity to feel; over-sensitiveness; susceptibility; (*pl*) sensitive awareness or feelings.

sensible *adj* having good sense or judgment; reasonable; practical; perceptible by the senses, appreciable; conscious (of); sensitive.—**sensibleness** *n*.—**sensibly** *adv*.

sensitive *adj* having the power of sensation; feeling readily and acutely, keenly perceptive; (*skin*) delicate, easily irritated; (*wound etc*) still in a painful condition; easily hurt or shocked, tender, touchy; highly responsive to slight changes; sensory; (*photog*) reacting to light.—**sensitively** *adj*.—**sensitiveness** *n*.

sensitivity *n* (*pl* **sensitivities**) the condition of being sensitive; awareness of changes or differences; responsiveness to stimuli or feelings, esp to excess.

sensual *adj* bodily, relating to the senses rather than the mind; arousing sexual desire.—**sensuality** *n*.—**sensually** *adv*.

sensuous *adj* giving pleasure to the mind or body through the senses.—**sensuously** *adv*.—**sensuousness** *n*.

sent *see* **send.**

sentence *n* a court judgment; the punishment imposed; (*gram*) a series of words conveying a complete thought. * *vt* (*a convicted person*) to pronounce punishment upon; to condemn (to).

sentiment *n* a feeling, awareness, or emotion; the thought behind something; an attitude of mind; a tendency to be swayed by feeling rather than reason; an exaggerated emotion.

sentimental *adj* of or arising from feelings; foolishly emotional; nostalgic.

sentry *n* a soldier on guard to give warning of danger and to prevent unauthorized access.

separate *vt* to divide or part; to sever; to set or keep apart; to sort into different sizes. * *vi* to go different ways; to cease to live together as man and wife. * *adj* divided; distinct, individual; not shared. * *n* (*pl*) articles of clothing designed to be interchangeable with others to form various outfits.—**separately** *adv*.

separation *n* the act of separating or the state of being separate; a formal arrangement of husband and wife to live apart.

September *n* the ninth month of the year, having 30 days.

septic *adj* infected by micro-organisms; causing or caused by putrefaction.

sequel *n* something that follows, the succeeding part; a consequence; the continuation of a story begun in an earlier literary work, film, etc.

sequence *n* order of succession; a series of succeeding things; a single, uninterrupted episode, as in a film.

sequin *n* a shiny round piece of metal or foil sewn on clothes for decoration.

serenade *n* music sung or played at night beneath a person's window, esp by a lover. * *vt* to entertain with a serenade.

serene *adj* calm; untroubled; tranquil; clear and unclouded; (*with cap*) honoured (used as part of certain royal titles).—**serenely** *adv*.—**serenity** *n*.

sergeant *n* a noncommissioned officer ranking above a corporal in the army, air force, and marine corps; a police officer.

serial *adj* of or forming a series; published, shown or broadcast by instalments at regular intervals. * *n* a story presented in regular instalments with a connected plot.

series *n sing, pl* a succession of items or events; a succession of things connected by some likeness; a sequence, a set; a radio or television serial whose episodes have self-contained plots; a set of books issued by one publisher; (*math*) a progression of numbers or quantities according to a certain law.

serious *adj* grave, solemn, not frivolous; meaning what one says, sincere, earnest; requiring close attention or thought; important; critical.—**seriously** *adv*.—**seriousness** *n*.

sermon *n* a speech on religion or morals, esp by a clergyman; a long, serious talk of reproof, esp a tedious one.

serrated *adj* having an edge notched like the teeth of a saw.

serum *n* (*pl* **serums**, **sera**) the watery part of bodily fluid, esp liquid that separates out from the blood when it coagulates; such fluid taken from the blood of an animal immune to a disease, used as an antitoxin.

servant *n* a personal or domestic attendant; one in the service of another.

serve *vt* to work for; to do military or naval service (for); to be useful to; to meet the needs (of), to suffice; (*a customer*) to wait upon; (*food, etc*) to hand round; (*a sentence*) to undergo; to be a soldier, sailor, etc; (*of a male animal*) to copulate with; (*law*) to deliver (a summons, etc); (*naut*) to bind (a rope) with thin cord to prevent fraying; (*tennis*) to put (the ball) into play. * *vi* to be employed as a servant; to be enough. * *n* the act of serving in tennis, etc.

service *n* the act of serving; the state of being a servant; domestic employment; a department of state employ; the people engaged in it; military employment or duty; work done for others; use, assistance; attendance in a hotel, etc; a facility providing a regular supply of trains, etc; a set of dishes; any religious ceremony; an overhaul of a vehicle; (*tennis*) the act or manner of seving; (*pl*) friendly help or professional aid; a system of providing a utility, as water, gas, etc. * *vt* to provide with assistance; to overhaul.

serviceable *adj* useful; durable.—**serviceably** *adv*.—**serviceableness** *n*.

serviceman *n* a member of the armed services; a person whose work is repairing something.—**servicewoman** *nf*.

serviette *n* a small napkin.

servile *adj* of or like a slave; subservient; submissive; menial.

session *n* the meeting of a court, legislature, etc; a series of such meetings; a period of these; a period of study, classes, etc; a university year; a period of time passed in an activity.

set *vb* (*pr p* **setting**, *pt* **set**) vt to put in a specified place, condition, etc; (*trap for animals*) to fix; (*clock etc*) to adjust; (*table*) to arrange for a meal; (*hair*) to fix in a desired style; (*bone*)to put into normal position, etc; to make settled, rigid, or fixed; (*gems*) to mount; to direct; to furnish (an example) for others; to fit (words to music or music to words); (*type*) to arrange for printing. * *vi* to become firm, hard or fixed; to begin to move (out, forth, off, etc); (*sun*) to sink below the horizon; (*with* **in**) to stitch (a sleeve) within a garment; to become established; (*with* **off**) to show up by contrast; to set in motion; to cause to explode; (*with* **on**) to urge (as a dog) to attack or pursue; to go on, advance; (*with* **up**) to erect; to establish, to found; (*with* **upon**) to attack, usu with violence. * *adj* fixed, established; intentional; rigid, firm; obstinate; ready. * *n* a number of persons or things classed or belonging together; a group, a clique; the way in which a thing is set; direction; the scenery for a play, film, etc; assembled equipment for radio or television reception, etc; (*math*) the totality of points, numbers, or objects that satisfy a given condition; (*tennis*) a series of games forming a unit of a match; a rooted cutting of a plant ready for transplanting; a badger's burrow (—*also* **sett**).

setback *n* misfortune; a reversal.

settee *n* a sofa for two people.

setting *n* a background, scene, surroundings, environment; a mounting, as for a gem; the music for a song, etc.

settle *vti* to put in order; to pay (an account); to clarify; to decide, to come to an agreement; to make or become quiet or calm; to make or become firm; to establish or become established in a place, business, home, etc; to colonize (a country); to take up residence; to come to rest; (*dregs*) to fall to the bottom; to stabilize; to make or become comfortable (for resting); (*bird*) to alight; to bestow legally for life.

settlement *n* the act of settling; a sum settled, esp on a woman at her marriage; an arrangement; a small village; a newly established colony; subsidence (of buildings).

settler *n* a person who settles; an early colonist.

set-up *n* the plan, makeup, etc, of equipment used in an organization; the details of a situation, plan, etc; (*inf*) a contest, etc, arranged to result in an easy win.

seven *adj, n* one more than six. * *n* the symbol for this (7, VII, vii); the seventh in a series or set; something having seven units as members.

seventeen *adj, n* one more than sixteen. * *n* the symbol for this (17, XVII, xvii).—**seventeenth** *adj*.

seventh *adj, n* next after sixth; one of seven

equal parts of a thing. * *n* (*mus*) an interval of seven diatonic degrees; the leading note.

seventy *adj, n* seven times ten. * *n* the symbol for this (70, LXX, lxx); (in *pl*) **seventies** (70s) the numbers for 70 to 79; the same numbers in a life or century.—**seventieth** *adj*.

sever *vti* to separate, to divide into parts; to break off.—**severance** *n*.

several *adj* more than two but not very many; various; separate, distinct; respective. * *pron* (*with pl vb*) a few. * *n* (*with pl vb*) a small number (of).

severe *adj* harsh, not lenient; very strict; stern; censorious; exacting, difficult; violent, not slight; (*illness*) critical; (*art*) plain, not florid.—**severely** *adv*.—**severity** *n*.

sew *vti* (*pt* **sewed,** *pp* **sewn** *or* **sewed**) to join or stitch together with needle and thread; to make, mend, etc, by sewing; (*with* **up**) to get full control of; (*inf*) to make sure of success in.—**sewing** *n*.

sewage *n* waste matter carried away in a sewer.

sewer[1] *n* one who sews.

sewer[2] *n* an underground pipe or drain for carrying off liquid waste matter, etc; a main drain.

sewing machine *n* a machine for sewing or stitching usu driven by an electric motor.

sex *n* the characteristics that distinguish male and female organisms on the basis of their reproductive function; either of the two categories (male and female) so distinguished; males or females collectively; the state of being mal e or female; the attraction between the sexes; (*inf*) sexual intercourse.

sexual *adj* of sex or the sexes; having sex.—**sexually** *adj*.

sexy *adj* (**sexier, sexiest**) (*inf*) exciting, or intending to excite, sexual desire.

shabby *adj* (**shabbier, shabbiest**) (*clothes*) threadbare, worn, or dirty; run-down, dilapidated; (*act, trick*) mean, shameful.—**shabbily** *adv*.—**shabbiness** *n*.

shack *n* a small, crudely built house or cabin; a shanty.

shackle *n* a metal fastening, usu in pairs, for the wrists or ankles of a prisoner; a staple; anything that restrains freedom; (*pl*) fetters. * *vt* to fasten or join by a shackle; to hamper, to impede.

shade *n* relative darkness; dimness; the darker parts of anything; shadow; a shield or screen protecting from bright light; a ghost; a place sheltered from the sun; degree of darkness of a colour, esp when made by the addition of black; a minute difference; a blind; (*pl*) the darkness of approaching night; (*pl: sl*) sunglasses. * *vti* to screen from light; to overshadow; to make dark; to pass by degrees into another colour; to change slightly or by degrees.

shadow *n* a patch of shade; darkness, obscurity; the dark parts of a painting, etc; shelter, protection; the dark shape of an object produced on a surface by intercepted light; an inseparable companion; a person (as a detective, etc) who shadows; an unsubstantial thing, a phantom; a mere remnant, a slight trace; gloom, affliction. * *vt* to cast a shadow over; to cloud; to follow and watch, esp in secret. * *adj* having an indistinct pattern or darker section; (*opposition party*) matching a function or position of the party in power.

shadowy *adj* full of shadows; dim, indistinct; unsubstantial.

shady *adj* (**shadier, shadiest**) giving or full of shade; sheltered from the sun; (*inf*) of doubtful honesty, disreputable.

shaft *n* a straight rod, a pole; a stem, a shank; the main part of a column; an arrow or spear, or its stem; anything hurled like a missile; a ray of light, a stroke of lightning; a revolving rod for transmitting power, an axle; one of the poles between which a horse is harnessed; a hole giving access to a mine; a vertical opening through a building, as for a lift; a critical remark or attack; (*sl*) harsh or unfair treatment.

shaggy *adj* (**shaggier, shaggiest**) (*hair, fur, etc*) long and unkempt; rough; untidy.—**shagginess** *n*.

shake *vti* (*pt* **shook,** *pp* **shaken**) to move to and fro with quick short motions, to agitate; to tremble or vibrate; to jar or jolt; to brandish; to make or become unsteady; to weaken; to unsettle; to unnerve or become unnerved; to clasp (another's hand) as in greeting; (*with* **down**) to cause to subside by shaking; to obtain makeshift accommodation; (*sl*) to extort money from; (*with* **off**) to get rid of; (*with* **out**) to empty by shaking; to spread (a sail); (*with* **up**) to shake together, to mix; to upset. * *n* the act of shaking or being shaken; a jolt; a shock; a milkshake; (*inf*) a deal; (*pl inf*) a convulsive trembling.

shake-up *n* an extensive reorganization.

shaky *adj* (**shakier, shakiest**) unsteady; infirm; unreliable.—**shakily** *adv*.—**shakiness** *n*.

shale *n* a kind of clay rock like slate but softer.

shall *vb aux* (*pt* **should**) used formally to express the future in the 1st person and determination, obligation or necessity in the 2nd and 3rd person. The more common form is **will**.
shallow *adj* having little depth; superficial, trivial. * *n* a shallow area in otherwise deep water.—**shallowness** *n*.
sham *n* a pretence; a person or thing that is a fraud. * *adj* counterfeit; fake.
shambles *npl* a scene of great disorder.
shame *n* a painful emotion arising from guilt or impropriety; modesty; disgrace, dishonour; the cause of this; (*sl*) a piece of unfairness. * *vti* to cause to feel shame; to bring disgrace on; to force by shame (into); to humiliate by showing superior qualities.
shamefaced *adj* bashful or modest; sheepish; showing shame; ashamed.
shameful *adj* disgraceful; outrageous.
shameless *adj* immodest; impudent, brazen.
shampoo *n* a liquid cleansing agent for washing the hair; the process of washing the hair or a carpet, etc. * *vt* to wash with shampoo.
shamrock *n* a three-leaved cloverlike plant, the national emblem of Ireland.
shandy *n* beer diluted with a non-alcoholic drink (as lemonade).
shanty[1] *n* a crude hut built from corrugated iron or cardboard.
shanty[2] *n* a rhythmic working song sung by sailors.
shape *n* the external appearance, outline or contour of a thing; a figure; a definite form; an orderly arrangement; a mould or pattern; (*inf*) condition. * *vt* to give shape to; to form; to model, to mould; to determine; (*with* **up**) to develop to a definite or satisfactory form.
shapeless *adj* lacking definite form; baggy.—**shapelessness** *n*.
shapely *adj* (**shapelier, shapeliest**) well-proportioned.—**shapeliness** *n*.
share *n* an allotted portion, a part; one of the parts into which a company's capital stock is divided, entitling the holder to a share of profits. * *vti* to distribute, to apportion (out); to have or experience in common with others; to divide into portions; to contribute or receive a share of; to use jointly.
shareholder *n* a holder of shares in a property, esp a company.
shark *n* a large voracious marine fish; an extortioner, a swindler; (*sl*) an expert in a given activity.
sharp *adj* having a keen edge or fine point; pointed, not rounded; clear-cut; distinct; intense, piercing; cutting, severe; keen, biting; clever, artful; alert, mentally acute; (*mus*) raised a semitone in pitch; out of tune by being too high; (*sl*) smartly dressed. * *adv* punctually; quickly; (*mus*) above the right pitch. * *n* (*mus*) a note that is a semitone higher than the note denoted by the same letter; the symbol for this ( ).—**sharply** *adv*.—**sharpness** *n*.
sharpen *vti* to make or become sharp or sharper.
sharpener *n* something that sharpens.
shatter *vti* to reduce to fragments suddenly; to smash; to damage or be damaged severely.
shave *vti* to remove facial or body hair with a razor; to cut away thin slices, to pare; to miss narrowly, to graze. * *n* the act or process of shaving; a narrow escape or miss; a paring.
shaven *adj* shaved.
shaver *n* one who shaves; an instrument for shaving, esp an electrical one.
shaving *n* the act of using a razor or scraping; a thin slice of wood, metal, etc, shaved off.
shawl *n* a large square or oblong cloth worn as a covering for the head or shoulders or as a wrapping for a baby.
she *pron* (*obj* **her**, *poss* **her**, **hers**) the female person or thing named before or in question. * *n* a female person or animal.
sheaf *n* (*pl* **sheaves**) a bundle of reaped corn bound together; a collection of papers, etc, tied in a bundle.
shear *vti* (*pp* **sheared** *or* **shorn**) to clip or cut (through); to remove (a sheep's fleece) by clipping; to divest; (*metal*) to break off because of a heavy force or twist. * *n* a stress acting sideways on a rivet and causing a break, etc; a machine for cutting metal; (*pl*) large scissors; (*pl*) a tool for cutting hedges, etc.
sheath *n* a close-fitting cover, esp for a blade; a condom; a closefitting dress usu worn without a belt.
shed[1] *n* a hut for storing garden tools; a large roofed shelter often with one or more sides open; a warehouse.
shed[2] *vt* (*pr p* **shedding**, *pt* **shed**) (*tears*) to let fall; (*skin, etc*) to lose or cast off; to allow or cause to flow; to diffuse, radiate. * *n* a parting in the hair.
sheep *n* (*pl* **sheep**) a cud-chewing four-footed animal with a fleece and edible flesh called mutton; a bashful, submissive person.
sheepdog *n* a dog trained to tend, drive, or guard sheep.

sheepish *adj* bashful, embarrassed.—**sheepishly** *adv*.—**sheepishness** *n*.

sheepskin *n* the skin of a sheep, esp with the fleece; a rug, parchment, or leather made from it; a garment made of or lined with sheepskin.

sheer[1] *adj* pure, unmixed; downright, utter; perpendicular, extremely steep; (*fabric*) delicately fine, transparent. * *adv* outright; perpendicularly, steeply.

sheer[2] *vti* to deviate or cause to deviate from a course; to swerve. * *n* the act of sheering; the upward curve of a deck towards bow or stern; a change in a ship's course.

sheet *n* a broad thin piece of any material, as glass, plywood, metal, etc; a large rectangular piece of cloth used as inner bed clothes; a single piece of paper; (*inf*) a newspaper; a broad, flat expanse; a suspended or moving expanse (as of fire or rain).

sheet lightning *n* lightning that has the appearance of a broad sheet due to reflection and diffusion by the clouds and sky.

sheikh *n* an Arab chief.

shelf *n* (*pl* **shelves**) a board fixed horizontally on a wall or in a cupboard for holding articles; a ledge on a cliff face; a reef, a shoal.

shell *n* a hard outside covering of a nut, egg, shellfish, etc; an explosive projectile; an external framework; a light racing boat; outward show; a cartridge. * *vt* to remove the shell from; to bombard (with shells); (*with* **out**) (*inf*) to pay out (money).

shellfish *n* an aquatic animal with a shell, esp an edible one.

shelter *n* a structure that protects, esp against weather; a place giving protection, a refuge; protection. * *vti* to give shelter to, to shield, to cover; to take shelter.

shelve *vti* to place on a shelf; to defer consideration, to put aside; to slope gently, to incline.

shelving *n* material for making shelves; shelves collectively.

shepherd *n* a person who looks after sheep; a pastor. * *vt* to look after, as a shepherd; to manouevre or marshal in a particular direction.—**shepherdess** *nf*.

shepherd's pie *n* a dish of minced meat covered with a mashed potato crust.

sheriff *n* in US, the chief law enforcement officer of a county; in Scotland, a judge in an intermediate law court; in England and Wales, the chief officer of the Crown, a ceremonial post.

sherry *n* a fortified wine originally made in Spain.

Shetland pony *n* a breed of small sturdy pony with a shaggy mane.

shield *n* a broad piece of armour carried for defence, usu on the left arm; a protective covering or guard; a thing or person that protects; a trophy in the shape of a shield. * *vti* to defend; to protect; to screen.

shift *vti* (**shiftier, shiftiest**) to change position (of); to contrive, to manage; to remove, to transfer; to replace by another or others; (*gears*) to change the arrangement of. * *n* a change in position; an expedient; a group of people working in relay with others; the time worked by them; a change or transfer; a straight dress.

shifty *adj* artful, tricky; evasive.—**shiftiness** *n*.

shilling *n* a former unit of currency of the UK and other countries, worth one twentieth of a pound.

shillyshally *vi* to vacillate, to hesitate. * *n* the inability to make up one's mind.

shimmer *vi* to glisten softly, to glimmer.—*also n*.

shin *n* the front part of the leg from the knee to the ankle; the shank. * *vi* (*with* **up**) to climb (a pole, etc) by gripping with legs and hands.

shine *vti* (*pt* **shone**) to emit light; to be bright, to glow; to be brilliant or conspicuous; to direct the light of; to cause to gleam by polishing. * *n* a lustre, a gloss; (*sl*) a liking.

shingle[1] *n* a thin wedge-shaped roof tile; a small signboard.

shingle[2] *n* waterworn pebbles as on a beach; an area covered with these.—**shingly** *adj*.

shingles *npl* a virus disease marked by a painful rash of red spots.

shiny *adj* (**shinier, shiniest**) glossy, polished; worn smooth.

ship *n* a large vessel navigating deep water; its officers and crew; a spacecraft. * *vti* (*pt* **shipped**) to transport by any carrier; to take in (water) over the side; to lay (oars) inside a boat; to go on board; to go or travel by ship.

shipbuilder *n* a person or company that designs or constructs ships.—**shipbuilding** *n*.

shipment *n* goods shipped; a consignment.

shipping *n* the business of transporting goods; ships collectively.

shipshape *adj* in good order, tidy.

shipwreck *n* the loss of a vessel at sea; the remains of a wrecked ship; ruin, destruction. * *vti* to destroy by or suffer shipwreck; to ruin.

shipyard *n* a yard or shed where ships are built or repaired.

shire *n* in the UK, a county; a strong draft horse.

shirk *vti* to neglect or avoid work; to refuse to face (duty, danger, etc).—**shirker** *n*.

shirt *n* a sleeved garment of cotton, etc, for the upper body, typically having a fitted collar and cuffs and front buttons; (*inf*) one's money or resources.

shiver[1] *n* a small fragment, a splinter.

shiver[2] *vi* to shake or tremble, as with cold or fear, to shudder.—*also n*.—**shivery** *adj*.

shoal[1] *n* a large number of fish swimming together; a large crowd. * *vi* to form shoals.

shoal[2] *n* a submerged sandbank, esp one that shows at low tide; a shallow place; a hidden danger. * *vti* to come to a less deep part; to become shallower.

shock[1] *n* a shaggy mass of hair.

shock[2] *n* a violent jolt or impact; a sudden disturbance to the emotions; the event or experience causing this; the nerve sensation caused by an electrical charge through the body; a disorder of the blood circulation, produced by displacement of body fluids (due to injury); (*sl*) a paralytic stroke. * *vt* to outrage, horrify. * *vi* to experience extreme horror, outrage, etc.

shock absorber *n* a device, as on the springs of a car, that absorbs the force of bumps and jars.

shocking *adj* revolting; scandalous, improper; very bad.—**shockingly** *adv*.

shod *see* **shoe**.

shoddy *adj* (**shodier, shodiest**) made of inferior material; cheap and nasty, trashy.—**shoddily** *adv*.—**shoddiness** *n*.

shoe *n* an outer covering for the foot not enclosing the ankle; a thing like a shoe, a partial casing; a horseshoe; a drag for a wheel; a device to guide movement, provide contact, or protect against wear or slipping; a dealing box that holds several decks of cards. * *vt* (*pr p* **shoeing**, *pt* **shod**) to provide with shoes; to cover for strength or protection.

shoehorn *n* a curved piece of plastic, metal, or horn used for easing the heel into a shoe.

shoelace *n* a cord that passes through eyelets in a shoe and is tied to keep the shoe on the foot.

shoetree *n* a block of wood, plastic or metal for preserving the shape of a shoe.

shone *see* **shine**.

shook *see* **shake**.

shoot *vb* (*pt* **shot**) *vt* to discharge or fire (a gun etc); to hit or kill with a bullet, etc; (*rapids*) to be carried swiftly over; to propel quickly; to thrust out; (*bolt*) to slide home; to variegate (with another colour, etc); (*a film scene*) to photograph; (*sport*) to kick or drive (a ball, etc) at goal; (*with* **down**) to disprove (an argument); (*with* **up**) to grow rapidly, to rise abruptly. * *vi* to move swiftly, to dart; to emit; to put forth buds, to sprout; to attack or kill indiscriminately; (*sl*) to inject a narcotic into a vein. * *n* a contest, a shooting trip, etc; a new growth or sprout.

shooting *n* the act of firing a gun or letting off an arrow.

shooting star *n* a meteor.

shop *n* a building were retail goods are sold or services provided; a factory; a workshop; the details and technicalities of one's own work, and talk about these. * *vti* (*pt* **shopped**) to visit shops to examine or buy; (*sl*) to inform on (a person) to the police; (*with* **around**) to hunt for the best buy.

shop floor *n* the part of a factory where goods are manufactured; the work force employed there, usu unionized.

shopkeeper *n* a person who owns or runs a shop.—**shopkeeping** *n*.

shoplifting *n* stealing from a shop during shopping hours.—**shoplifter** *n*.

shopper *n* a person who shops; a bag for carrying shopping.

shopping *n* the act of shopping; the goods bought.—*also adj*.

shopping centre *n* a complex of shops, restaurants, and service establishments with a common parking area.

shopsoiled *adj* faded, etc, from being on display in a shop.

shop steward *n* a union member elected to negotiate with management on behalf of his colleagues.

shore[1] *n* land beside the sea or a large body of water; beach.

shore[2] *n* a prop or beam used for support. * *vt* to prop (up), to support with a shore.

shorn *see* **shear**.

short *adj* not measuring much; not long or tall; not great in range or scope; brief; concise; not retentive; curt; abrupt; less than the correct amount; below standard; deficient, lacking; (*pastry*) crisp or flaky; (*vowel*) not prolonged, unstressed; (*drink*) undiluted, neat. * *n* something short; (*pl*) trousers not covering the knee; (*pl*) an undergarment like these; a short circuit. * *adv* abruptly; concisely; without reaching the end. * *vti* to give less than what is needed; to short-change; to short-circuit.—**shortness** *n*.

shortage *n* a deficiency.

shortbread *n* a rich, crumbly cake or biscuit made with much shortening.

short-circuit *n* the deviation of an electric current by a path of small resistance; an interrupted electric current. * *vti* to establish a short-circuit in; to cut off electric current; to provide with a short cut.

shortcoming *n* a defect or inadequacy.

short cut *n* a shorter route; any way of saving time, effort, etc.

shorten *vt* to make or become short or shorter; to reduce the amount of (sail) spread; to make (pastry, etc) crisp and flaky by adding fat.

shorthand *n* a method of rapid writing using signs or contractions.—*also adj*.

short-lived *adj* not lasting or living for long.

shortly *adv* soon, in a short time; briefly; rudely.

short-sighted *adj* not able to see well at a distance; lacking foresight.—**short-sightedness** *n*.

shortwave *n* a radio wave 60 metres or less in length.

shot[1] *see* **shoot**.

shot[2] *n* the act of shooting; range, scope; an attempt; a solid projectile for a gun; projectiles collectively; small lead pellets for a shotgun; a marksman; a photograph or a continuous film sequence; a hypodermic injection, as of vaccine; a drink of alcohol.

shotgun *n* a smooth-bore gun for firing small shot at close range.

should *vb aux* used to express obligation, duty, expectation or probability, or a future condition.—*also pt of* **shall**.

shoulder *n* the joint connecting the arm with the trunk; a part like a shoulder; (*pl*) the upper part of the back; (*pl*) the capacity to bear a task or blame; a projecting part; the strip of land bordering a road. * *vti* to place on the shoulder to carry; to assume responsibility; to push with the shoulder, to jostle.

shoulder blade *n* the large flat triangular bone on either side of the back part of the human shoulder.

shout *n* a loud call; a yell. * *vti* to call loudly, to yell.

shove *vti* to drive forward; to push; to jostle. * *n* a forceful push.

shovel *n* an broad tool like a scoop with a long handle for moving loose material. * *vt* (*pt* **shovelled**) to move or lift with a shovel.

show *vti* (*pt* **showed**, *pp* **shown**) to present to view, to exhibit; to demonstrate, to make clear; to prove; to manifest, to disclose; to direct, to guide; to appear, to be visible; to finish third in a horse race; (*inf*) to arrive; (*with* **off**) to display to advantage; to try to attract admiration; to behave pretentiously; (*with* **up**) to put in an appearance, to arrive; to expose to ridicule. * *n* a display, an exhibition; an entertainment; a theatrical performance; a radio or television programme; third place at the finish (as a horse race).

show business *n* the entertainment industry.—*also* **show biz**.

showdown *n* (*inf*) a final conflict; a disclosure of cards at poker.

shower *n* a brief period of rain, hail, or snow; a similar fall, as of tears, meteors, arrows, etc; a great number; a method of cleansing in which the body is sprayed with water from above; a wash in this; a party for the presentation of gifts, esp to a bride. * *vt* to pour copiously; to sprinkle; to bestow (with gifts). * *vi* to cleanse in a shower.

showjumping *n* the competitive riding of horses to demonstrate their skill in jumping.

showroom *n* a room where goods for sale are displayed.

shrank *see* **shrink**.

shrapnel *n* an artillery shell filled with small pieces of metal that scatter on impact.

shred *n* a strip cut or torn off; a fragment, a scrap. * *vt* (*pt* **shredded**) to cut or tear into small pieces.

shrewd *adj* astute, having common sense; keen, penetrating.—**shrewdly** *adv*.—**shrewdness** *n*.

shriek *n* a loud, shrill cry, a scream. * *vti* to screech, to scream.

shrill *adj* high-pitched and piercing in sound; strident.

shrimp *n* a small edible shellfish with a long tail.

shrine *n* a container for sacred relics; a saint's tomb; a place of worship; a hallowed place.

shrink *vti* (*pt* **shrank**, *pp* **shrunk**) to become smaller, to contract as from cold, wetting, etc; to recoil (from), to flinch; to cause (cloth, etc) to contract by soaking. * *n* (*sl*) a psychiatrist.

shrinkage *n* contraction; diminution.

shrivel *vti* (*pt* **shrivelled**) to dry up or wither and become wrinkled; to curl up with heat, etc.

shroud *n* a burial cloth; anything that envelops or conceals; (*naut*) a supporting rope for a mast. * *vt* to wrap in a shroud; to envelop or conceal.

Shrove Tuesday *n* the last day before Lent.

shrub *n* a woody plant smaller than a tree with several stems rising from the same root; a bush.—**shrubby** *adj*.

shrubbery *n* an area of land planted with shrubs.

shrug *vti* (*pt* **shrugged**) to draw up and contract (the shoulders) as a sign of doubt, indifference, etc; (*with* **off**) to brush aside; to shake off; (*a garment*) to remove by wriggling out. * *n* the act of shrugging.

shrunk *see* **shrink**.

shrunken *adj* shrivelled, pinched; reduced.

shudder *vi* to tremble violently, to shiver; to feel strong repugnance. * *n* a convulsive shiver of the body; a vibration.

shuffle *vt* to scrape (the feet) along the ground; to walk with dragging steps; (*playing cards*) to change the order of, to mix; to intermingle, to mix up; (*with* **off**) to get rid of.—*also n.*

shun *vt* (*pt* **shunned**) to avoid scrupulously; to keep away from.

shunt *vti* to move to a different place; to put aside, to shelve; (*trains*) to switch from one track to another; (*sl*) to collide.—*also n.*

shut *vti* (*pr p* **shutting,** *pt* **shut**) to close; to lock, to fasten; to close up parts of, to fold together; to bar; (*with* **down**) to (cause to) stop working or operating; (*with* **in**) to confine; to enclose; to block the view from; (*with* **off**) to check the flow of; to debar; (*with* **out**) to exclude; (*with* **up**) to confine; (*inf*) to stop talking; (*inf*) to silence.

shutdown *n* a stoppage of work or activity, as in a factory.

shutter *n* a movable cover for a window; a flap device for regulating the exposure of light to a camera lens.

shuttle *n* a device in a loom for holding the weft thread and carrying it between the warp threads; a bus, aircraft, etc, making back-and-forth trips over a short route. * *vti* to move back and forth rapidly.

shuttlecock *n* a cork stuck with feathers, or a plastic imitation, hit with a racket in badminton.

shy *adj* (**shyer, shyest** *or* **shier, shiest**) very self-conscious, timid; bashful; wary, suspicious (of); (*sl*) lacking. * *vi* to move suddenly, as when startled; to be or become cautious, etc. * *n* a sudden movement.—**shyly** *adv*.—**shyness** *n*.

Siamese cat *n* a breed of domestic shorthaired cat with a fawn or grey coat, darker ears, paws, tail and face, and blue eyes.

sick *adj* unhealthy, ill; having nausea, vomiting; thoroughly tired (of); disgusted by or suffering from an excess; (*inf*) of humour, sadistic, gruesome.—**sickness** *n*.

sick bay *n* an area in a ship used as a hospital or dispen- sary; a room used for the treatment of the sick.

sicken *vti* to make or become sick or nauseated; to show signs of illness; to nauseate.

sickening *adj* disgusting.

sickle *n* a tool with a crescent-shaped blade for cutting tall grasses; anything shaped like this.

sick leave *n* absence from work due to illness.

sickly *adj* (**sicklier, sickliest**) inclined to be ill; unhealthy; causing nausea; mawkish; pale, feeble.—**sickliness** *n*.

side *n* a line or surface bounding anything; the left or right part of the body; the top or underneath surface; the slope of a hill; an aspect, a direction; a party or faction; a cause; a team; a line of descent; (*sl*) conceit. * *adj* towards or at the side, lateral; incidental. * *vi* to associate with a particular faction.

sideboard *n* a long table or cabinet for holding cutlery, crockery, etc; (*pl*) two strips of hair growing down a man's cheeks (—*also* **sideburns**).

side effect *n* a secondary and usu adverse effect, as of a drug or medical treatment.

sidelight *n* light coming from the side; a light on the side of a car, etc; incidental information.

sideline *n* a line marking the side limit of a playing area; a minor branch of business; a subsidiary interest.

sidelong *adj* oblique, not direct. * *adv* obliquely.

side-saddle *n* a saddle that enables a rider to sit with both feet on the same side of a horse. * *adv* as if sitting on a side-saddle.

sideshow *n* a minor attraction at a fair, etc; a subsidiary event.

sidetrack *vt* to prevent action by diversionary tactics; to shunt aside, to shelve. * *n* a railway siding.

sidewalk *n* a path, usu paved, at the side of a street, pavement.

sideways *adj*, *adv* towards or from one side; facing to the side.

siding *n* a short line beside a main railway track for use in shunting; a covering as of boards for the outside of a frame building.

sidle *vi* to move sideways, esp to edge along.

siege *n* the surrounding of a fortified place to cut off supplies and compel its surrender; the act of besieging; a continued attempt to gain something.

sieve *n* a utensil with a meshed wire bottom for sifting and straining; a person who cannot keep secrets. * *vt* to put through a sieve, to sift.

sift *vti* to separate coarser parts from finer with a sieve; to sort out; to examine critically; to pass as through a sieve.

sigh *vti* to draw deep audible breath as a sign of weariness, relief, etc; to make a sound like this; to pine or lament (for); to utter with a sigh.—*also n.*

sight *n* the act or faculty of seeing; what is seen or is worth seeing, a spectacle; a view or glimpse; range of vision; a device on a gun etc to guide the eye in aiming it; aim taken with this; (*inf*) anything that looks unpleasant, odd, etc. * *vti* to catch sight of; to aim through a sight.

sightless *adj* without sight, blind.—**sightlessly** *adv.*

sightseeing *n* the viewing or visitng of places of interest.—**sightseer** *n.*

sign *n* a mark or symbol; a gesture; an indication, token, trace, or symptom (of); an omen; (*math*) a conventional mark used to indicate an operation to be performed; a board or placard with publicly displayed information. * *vi* to append one's signature; to ratify thus. * *vt* to engage by written contract; to write one's name on; to make or indicate by a sign; to signal; to communicate by sign language; (*with* **away**) to relinquish by signing a deed, etc; (*with* **on**) to accept employment; to register; (*with* **off**) to complete a broadcast.

signal *n* a sign, device or gesture to intimate a warning or to give information, esp at a distance; a message so conveyed; a semaphore system used by railways; in radio, etc, the electrical impulses transmitted or received; a sign or event that initiates action. * *vti* (*pt* **signalled**) to make a signal or signals (to); to communicate by signals. * *adj* striking, notable.

signature *n* a person's name written by himself or herself; the act of signing one's own name; a characteristic mark; (*mus*) the flats and sharps after the clef showing the key; (*print*) a mark on the first pages of each sheet of a book as a guide to the binder; such a sheet when folded.

signature tune *n* a tune associated with a performer or a TV, radio programme, etc.

signet ring *n* a ring with a seal set in it.

significant *adj* full of meaning, esp a special or hidden one; momentous, important; highly expressive; indicative (of).—**significance** *n.*—**significantly** *adv.*

silence *n* absence of sound; the time this lasts; refusal to speak or make a sound; secrecy. * *vt* to cause to be silent. * *interj* be silent!

silencer *n* a device for reducing the noise of a vehicle exhaust or gun.

silent *adj* not speaking; taciturn; noiseless; still.—**silently** *adv.*

silhouette *n* the outline of a shape against light or a lighter background; a solid outline drawing, usu in solid black on white, esp of a profile. * *vt* to show up in outline; to depict in silhouette.

silk *n* a fibre produced by silkworms; lustrous textile cloth, thread or a garment made of silk; (*pl*) silk garments; (*pl*) the colours of a racing stable, worn by a jockey, etc. * *adj* of, relating to or made of silk.

silky *adj* (**silkier, silkiest**) soft and smooth like silk; glossy; suave.—**silkiness** *n.*

silly *adj* (**sillier, silliest**) foolish, stupid; frivolous; lacking in sense or judgment; being stunned or dazed. * *n* a silly person.

silt *n* a fine-grained sandy sediment carried or deposited by water. * *vti* to fill or choke up with silt.

silver *n* a ductile, malleable, greyish-white metallic element used in jewellery, cutlery, tableware, coins, etc; a lustrous, greyish white. * *adj* made of or plated with silver; silvery; (*hair*) grey; marking the 25th in a series * *vt* to coat with silver or a substance resembling silver; to make or become silvery or grey.

silver paper *n* a metallic paper coated or laminated to resemble silver, tinfoil.

silver plate *n* a plating of silver; domestic utensils made of silver or of silver-plated metal.

silversmith *n* a worker in silver.

similar *adj* having a resemblance to, like; nearly corresponding; (*geom*) corresponding exactly in shape if not size.—**similarity** *n.*—**similarly** *adv.*

simile *n* a figure of speech likening one thing to another by the use of like, as, etc.

simmer *vti* to boil gently; to be or keep on the point of boiling; to be in a state of suppressed rage or laughter; (*with* **down**) to abate. * *n* the state of simmering.

simple *adj* single, uncompounded; plain, not elaborate; clear, not complicated; easy to do, understand, or solve; artless, not sophisticated; weak in intellect; unsuspecting, credulous; sheer, mere.—**simpleness** *n.*

simplicity *n* the quality or state of being simple; absence of complications; easiness; lack of ornament, plainness, restraint; artlessness; directness; guilelessness, openness, naivety.

simplify *vt* to make simple or easy to understand.

simply *adv* in a simple way; plainly; merely; absolutely.

simulate *vt* to pretend to have or feel, to feign; (*conditions*) to reproduce in order to conduct an experiment; to imitate.—**simulation** *n.*

simulator *n* a device that simulates specific conditions in order to test actions or reactions.

simultaneous *adj* done or occurring at the same time.—**simultaneously** *adv.*

sin *n* an offence against a religious or moral principle; transgression of the law of God; a wicked act, an offence; a misdeed, a fault. * *vi* (*pt* **sinned**) to commit a sin; to offend (against).

since *adv* from then until now; subsequently; ago. * *prep* during, or continously from (then) until now; after. * *conj* from the time that; because, seeing that.

sincere *adj* genuine, real, not pretended; honest, straightforward.—**sincerely** *adv.*

sincerity *n* the quality or state of being sincere; genuineness, honesty, seriousness.

sinew *n* a cord of fibrous tissue, a tendon; (usu *pl*) the chief supporting force, a mainstay; (*pl*) muscles, brawn.

sinful *adj* guilty of sin, wicked.

sing *vti* (*pt* **sang**, *pp* **sung**) to utter (words) with musical modulations; (*a song*) to perform; to hum, to ring; to write poetry (about), to praise.—**singer** *n.*—**singing** *n.*

singe *vt* (*pr p* **singeing,** *pt* **singed**) to burn slightly; to scorch, esp to remove feathers, etc.—*also n.*

singing *n* the art or an act of singing.

single *adj* one only, not double; individual; composed of one part; alone, sole; separate; unmarried; for one; with one contestant on each side; simple; whole, unbroken; (*tennis*) played between two only; (*ticket*) for the outward journey only. * *n* a single ticket; a game between two players; a hit scoring one; a record with one tune on each side. * *vt* (*with* **out**) to pick out, to select.

single file *n* a single column of persons or things, one behind the other.

single-handed *adj*, *adv* without assistance, unaided.

single-minded *adj* having only one aim in mind.

singlet *n* an undervest.

singly *adv* alone; one by one.

singular *adj* remarkable; exceptional; unusual; eccentric, odd; (*gram*) referring to only one person or thing. * *n* (*gram*) the singular number or form of a word.

sinister *adj* inauspicious; ominous; ill-omened; evil-looking; malignant; wicked; left; (*her*) on the left side of the shield.

sink *vti* (*pt* **sank**, *pp* **sunk** *or* **sunken**) to go under the surface or to the bottom (of a liquid); to submerge in water; to go down slowly; (*wind*) to subside; to pass to a lower state; to droop, to decline; to grow weaker; to become hollow; to lower, to degrade; to cause to sink; to make by digging out; to invest; (*with* **in**) to penetrate; to thrust into; (*inf*) to be understood in full. * *n* a basin with an outflow pipe, usu in a kitchen; a cesspool; an area of sunken land.—**sinking** *n.*

sinner *n* a person who sins.

sinuous *adj* curving; winding; tortuous.—**sinuously** *adv.*

sinus *n* (*pl* **sinuses**) an air cavity in the skull that opens in the nasal cavities.

sip *vti* (*pt* **sipped**) to drink in small mouthfuls. * *n* the act of sipping; the quantity sipped.

siphon *n* a bent tube for drawing off liquids from a higher to a lower level by atmospheric pressure; a bottle with an internal tube and tap at the top for aerated water. * *vti* to draw off, or be drawn off, with a siphon.—*also* **syphon**.

sir *n* a title of respect used to address a man in speech or correspondence; (*with cap*) a title preceding the first name of a knight or baronet. * *vt* to address as "sir".

siren *n* a device producing a loud wailing sound as a warning signal; a fabled sea nymph who lured sailors to destruction with a sweet song; a seductive or alluring woman.

sirloin *n* the upper part of a loin of beef.

sirocco *n* a hot, oppressive wind that blows across southern Europe from North Africa.

sister *n* a female sibling, a daughter of the same parents; a female member or associate of the sa me race, creed, trade union, etc; a member of a religious sisterhood; one of the same kind, model, etc; a senior nurse. * *adj* (*ship, etc*) belonging to the same type.

sister-in-law *n* the sister of a husband or wife; the wife of a brother.
sisterly *adj* like a sister, kind, affectionate.
sit *vti* (*pr p* **sitting,** *pt* **sat**) to rest oneself on the buttocks, as on a chair; (*bird*) to perch; (*hen*) to cover eggs for hatching; (*legislator, etc*) to occupy a seat; (*court*) to be in session; to pose, as for a portrait; to ride (a horse); to press or weigh (upon); to be located; to rest or lie; to take an examination; to take care of a child, pet, etc, while the parents or owners are away; to cause to sit; to provide seats or seating room for; (*with* **down**) to take a seat; (*with* **for**) to represent in parliament; (*with* **in**) to attend a discussion or a musical session; to participate in a sit-in; (*with* **on**) to hold a meeting to discuss; to delay action on something; (*inf*) to suppress; to rebuke; (*with* **out**) to sit through the whole; to abstain from dancing; (*with* **up**) to straighten the back while sitting; not to go to bed; (*inf*) to be astonished.
site *n* a space occupied or to be occupied by a building; a situation; the place or scene of something. * *vt* to locate, to place.
sit-in *n* a strike in which the strikers refuse to leave the premises; civil disobedience in which demonstrators occupy a public place and refuse to leave voluntarily.
sitting *n* the state of being seated; a period of being seated, as for a meal, a portrait; a session, as of a court; a clutch of eggs. * *adj* that is sitting; being in a judicial or legislative seat; used in or for sitting; performed while sitting.
sitting room *n* a room other than a bedroom or kitchen; a parlour.
situated *adj* having a site, located; placed; provided with money, etc.
situation *n* a place, a position; a state of affairs, circumstances; a job or post.
sit-up *n* an exercise of sitting up from a prone position without using hands or legs.
six *adj, n* one more than five. * *n* the symbol for this (6, VI, vi); the sixth in a series or set; something having six units as members.
sixteen *adj, n* one more than fifteen. * *n* the symbol for this (16, XVI, xvi).—**sixteenth** *adj, n.*
sixth *n* one of six equal parts of a thing; (*mus*) an interval of six diatonic degrees; the sixth tone of a diatonic scale.—*also adv.* * *adj* next after fifth.—**sixthly** *adv.*
sixty *n* six times ten. * *n* the symbol for this (60, LX, lx); (in *pl*) sixties (60s), the numbers for 60 to 69; the same numbers in a life or century.—**sixtieth** *adj, adv.*
sizable, sizeable *adj* of some size; large.—**sizably, sizeably** *adv.*—**sizableness, sizeableness** *n.*
size[1] *n* magnitude; the dimensions or proportions of something; a graduated measurement, as of clothing or shoes. * *vt* to sort according to size; to measure; (*with* **up**) (*inf*) to make an estimate or judgment of; to meet requirements.
size[2] *n* a thin pasty substance used to glaze paper, stiffen cloth, etc. * *vt* to treat with size.
sizzle *vti* to make a hissing spluttering noise, as of frying; to be extremely hot; to be very angry; to scorch, sear or fry with a sizzling sound. * *n* a hissing sound.
skate[1] *n* a steel blade attached to a boot for gliding on ice; a boot with such a runner; a roller skate. * *vi* to move on skates.—**skater** *n.*
skate[2] *n* an edible fish of the ray family with a broad, flat body and short, spineless tail.
skateboard *n* a short, oblong board with two wheels at each end for standing on and riding.—*also vi.*
skeleton *n* the bony framework of the body of a human, an animal or plant; the bones separated from flesh and preserved in their natural position; a supporting structure, a framework; an outline, an abstract; a very thin person; something shameful kept secret. * *adj* (*staff, crew, etc*) reduced to the lowest possible level.—**skeletal** *adj.*
sketch *n* a rough drawing, quickly made; a preliminary draft; a short literary piece or essay; a short humorous item for a revue, etc; a brief outline. * *vti* to make a sketch (of); to plan roughly.
sketchy *adj* (**sketchier, sketchiest**) incomplete; vague; inadequate.—**sketchily** *adv.*—**sketchiness** *n.*
skewer *n* a long wooden or metal pin on which pieces of meat and vegetables are cooked. * *vt* to pierce and fasten on a skewer; to transfix.
ski *n* (*pl* **skis**) a long narrow runner of wood, metal or plastic that is fastened to a boot for moving across snow; a water-ski. * *vi* (*pr p* **skiing,** *pt* **skied**) to travel on skis.—**skier** *n.*
skid *vti* (*pt* **skidded**) to slide without rotating; to slip sideways; (*vehicle*) to slide sideways out of control; to cause (a vehicle) to skid. * *n* the act of skidding; a drag to reduce speed; a ship's fender; a movable support for a heavy

object; a runner on an aircraft's landing gear.
skilful, skillful (*US*) *adj* having skill; proficient, adroit.—**skilfully** *adv*.—**skilfulness** *n*.
skill *n* proficiency; expertness, dexterity; a developed aptitude or ability; a type of work or craft requiring specialist training.
skilled *adj* fully trained, expert.
skim *vti* (*pt* **skimmed**) to remove (cream, scum) from the surface of; to glide lightly over, to brush the surface of; to read superficially.
skimp *vti* to give scant measure (of), to stint; to be sparing or frugal (with).
skimpy *adj* (**skimpier, skimpiest**) small in size; inadequate, scant, meagre.—**skimpily** *adv*.—**skimpiness** *n*.
skin *n* the tissue forming the outer covering of the body; a hide; the rind of a fruit; an outer layer or casing; a film on the surface of a liquid; a vessel for water, etc, made of hide. * *vti* (*pt* **skinned**) to remove the skin from, to peel; to injure by scraping (the knee, etc); to cover or become covered with skin; (*inf*) to swindle.
skin-deep *adj* superficial.
skin diving *n* the sport of swimming underwater with scuba equipment.—**skin-diver** *n*.
skinny *adj* (**skinnier, skinniest**) very thin; emaciated.—**skinniness** *n*.
skip[1] *vti* (*pt* **skipped**) to leap or hop lightly over; to keep jumping over a rope as it is swung under one; to make omissions, to pass over, esp in reading; (*inf*) to leave (town) hurriedly, to make off; (*inf*) to miss deliberately. * *n* a skipping movement; a light jump.
skip[2] *n* a large metal container for holding building debris; a cage or bucket for hoisting workers or materials in a mine, quarry, etc.
skipper *n* the captain of a boat, aircraft, or team. * *vt* to act as skipper; to captain.
skipping rope *n* a light rope, usu with a handle at each end, that is swung over the head and under the feet while jumping.
skirmish *n* a minor fight in a war; a conflict or clash. * *vi* to take part in a skirmish.
skirt *n* a woman's garment that hangs from the waist; the lower part of a dress or coat; an outer edge, a border; (*sl*) a woman. * *vti* to border; to move along the edge (of); to evade.
skirting board *n* a narrow panel of wood at the foot of an interior wall.
skit *n* a short humorous sketch, as in the theatre.
ski tow *n* a motor-driven device that pulls skiers uphill.
skittles *n* a game in which a wooden or plastic bottle-shaped pin is knocked down by a ball.
skulk *vi* to move in a stealthy manner; to lurk.
skull *n* the bony casing enclosing the brain; the cranium.
skunk *n* a small black-and-white mammal that emits a foul-smelling liquid when frightened; its fur; (*sl*) an obnoxious or mean person.
sky *n* the apparent vault over the earth; heaven; the upper atmosphere; weather, climate.
skylight *n* a window in the roof or ceiling.
skyscraper *n* a very tall building.
skyward *adj, adv* towards the sky.—**skywards** *adv*.
slab *n* a flat, broad, thick piece (as of stone, wood, or bread, etc); something resembling this. * *vt* to cut or form into slabs; to cover or support with slabs; to put on thickly.
slack *adj* loose, relaxed, not tight; (*business*) slow, not brisk; sluggish; inattentive, careless. * *n* the part (of a rope, etc) that hangs loose; a dull period; a lull; (*pl*) trousers for casual wear. * *vti* to neglect (one's work, etc), to be lazy; (*with* **off**) to slacken (a rope, etc).—**slackness** *n*.
slacken *vti* to make or become less active, brisk, etc; to loosen or relax, as a rope; to diminish, to abate.—**slackening** *n, adj*.
slag *n* the waste product from the smelting of metals; volcanic lava.
slam *vti* (*pt* **slammed**) to shut with a loud noise, to bang; to throw (down) violently; (*inf*) to criticize severely. * *n* a sound or the act of slamming, a bang; (*inf*) severe criticism; (*bridge*) the taking of 12 or 13 tricks.
slander *n* a false and malicious statement about another; the uttering of this. * *vt* to utter a slander about, to defame.—**slanderous** *adj*.
slang *n* words or expressions used in familiar speech but not regarded as standard English; jargon of a particular social class, age group, etc. * *adj* relating to slang.
slant *vti* to incline, to slope; to tell in such way as to have a bias. * *n* a slope; an oblique position; a bias, a point of view. * *adj* sloping.—**slantly** *adv*.
slanted *adj* prejudiced, biased; sloping.
slap *n* a smack with the open hand; an insult; a rebuff. * *vt* (*pt* **slapped**) to strike with something flat; to put, hit, etc, with force. * *adv* directly, full.
slapdash *adj* impetuous; hurried; careless; haphazard. * *adv* carelessly.
slapstick *n* boisterous humour of a knockabout kind.

slash *vti* to cut gashes in, to slit; to strike fiercely (at) with a sword, etc; to reduce (prices) sharply. * *n* a cutting blow; a long slit, a gash.

slate[1] *vt* to criticize or punish severely.

slate[2] *n* a fine-grained rock easily split into thin layers; a flat plate of this or other material used in roofing; a tablet (as of slate) for writing on; a list of proposed candidates. * *adj* the colour of slate, a deep bluish-grey colour; made of slate. * *vt* to cover with slates; to suggest as a political candidate.

slaughter *n* the butchering of animals; a wholesale killing, a massacre.—*also vt*.—**slaughterer** *n*.

slaughterhouse *n* a place where animals are slaughtered, an abattoir.

slave *n* a person without freedom or personal rights, who is legally owned by another; a person under domination, esp of a habit or vice; a person who works like a slave, a drudge. * *vti* to toil hard, as a slave.

slavery *n* the condition of being a slave; bondage; drudgery; slave-owning as an institution.

sled, sledge *n* a framework on runners for travelling over snow or ice; a toboggan. * *vti* to go or convey by sledge.

sledgehammer *n* a large, heavy hammer for two hands.

sleek *adj* smooth, glossy; having a prosperous or well-groomed appearance; plausible.

sleep *n* a natural, regularly recurring rest for the body, with little or no consciousness; a period spent sleeping; a state of numbness followed by tingling. * *vti* (*pt* **slept**) to rest in a state of sleep; to be inactive; to provide beds for; (*with* **in**) to sleep on the premises; to sleep too long in the morning; (*with* **on**) to have a night's rest before making a decision; (*with* **off**) to get rid of by sleeping; (*with* **over**) to pass the night in someone else's house; (*with* **with**) to have sexual relations with.

sleeper *n* a person or thing that sleeps; a horizontal beam that carries and spreads a weight; a sleeping car; something that suddenly attains prominence or value.

sleeping bag *n* a padded bag for sleeping in, esp outdoors.

sleeping car *n* a railway carriage with berths.

sleeping pill *n* a pill that induces sleep.

sleepwalker *n* a person who walks while asleep, a somnambulist.—**sleepwalking** *n*.

sleepy *adj* (**sleepier, sleepiest**) drowsy; tired; lazy, not alert.—**sleepily** *adv*.—**sleepiness** *n*.

sleet *n* snow or hail mixed with rain. * *vi* to rain in the form of sleet.

sleeve *n* the part of a garment enclosing the arm; (*mech*) a tube that fits over a part; an open-ended cover, esp a paperboard envelope for a record.

sleeveless *adj* (*garment*) without sleeves.

sleigh *n* a light vehicle on runners for travelling over snow; a sledge.

sleight of hand *n* manual dexterity, such as in conjuring or juggling; a deception.

slender *adj* thin; slim; slight; scanty.—**slenderly** *adv*.—**slenderness** *n*.

slept *see* **sleep**.

slice *n* a thin flat piece cut from something (as bread, etc); a wedge-shaped piece (of cake, pie, etc); a portion, a share; a broad knife for serving fish, cheese, etc; (*golf*) a stroke that makes the ball curl to the right. * *vti* to divide into parts; to cut into slices; to strike (a ball) so that it curves.—**slicer** *n* —**slicing** *adj*, *n*.

slick *adj* clever, deft; smart but unsound; insincere; wily; (*inf*) smooth but superficial, tricky, etc. * *n* a patch or area of oil floating on water. * *vt* to make glossy; (*with* **up**) (*inf*) to make smart, neat, etc.

slide *vti* (*pt* **slid**) to move along in constant contact with a smooth surface, as on ice, to glide; to coast over snow and ice; to pass gradually (into); to move (an object) unobtrusively. * *n* the act of sliding, a glide; a strip of smooth ice for sliding on; a chute; the glass plate of a microscope; a photographic transparency; a landslide.

slide rule *n* a ruler with a graduated sliding part for making calculations.

sliding scale *n* a schedule for automatically varying one thing (eg wages) according to the fluctuations of another thing (eg cost of living); a flexible scale.

slight *adj* small, inconsiderable; trifling; slim; frail, flimsy. * *vt* to disregard as insignificant; to treat with disrespect, to snub. * *n* intentional indifference or neglect, discourtesy.

slightly *adv* to a small degree; slenderly.

slim *adj* slender, not stout; small in amount, degree, etc; slight. * *vti* (slimming, slimmed) to make or become slim; to reduce one's weight by diet, etc.—**slimness** *n*.

slime *n* a sticky slippery, half-liquid substance; a glutinous mud; mucus secreted by various animals (eg slugs).

sling *n* a loop of leather with a string attached

for hurling stones; a rope for lifting or hoisting weights; a bandage suspended from the neck for supporting an injured arm. * *vt* (*pt* **slung**) to throw, lift, or suspend (as) with a sling; to hurl.

slingshot *n* a catapult.

slip[1] *vti* (*pt* **slipped**) to slide, to glide; to lose one's foothold and slide; to go or put quietly or quickly; to let go, to release; to escape from; (*with* **up**) to make a slight mistake. * *n* the act of slipping; a mistake, a lapse; a woman's undergarment; a pillowcase; a slipway.

slip[2] *n* a small piece of paper; a young, slim person; a long seat or narrow pew; a shoot for grafting, a cutting; a descendant, an offspring.

slipped disc *n* a ruptured cartilaginous disc between vertebrae.

slipper *n* a light, soft, shoe worn in the house.

slippery *adj* so smooth as to cause slipping; difficult to hold or catch; evasive, unreliable, shifty.

slip road *n* a road that gives access to a main road or motorway.

slipshod *adj* having the shoes down at heel; slovenly, careless.

slip-up *n* (*inf*) an error, a lapse.

slipway *n* an inclined surface for launching or repairing ships; a sloped landing stage.

slit *vt* (*pr p* **slitting,** *pt* **slit**) to cut open or tear lengthways; to slash or tear into strips. * *n* a long cut, a slash; a narrow opening.

slither *vi* to slide, as on a loose or wet surface; to slip or slide like a snake.

slog *vti* (*pt* **slogged**) to hit hard and wildly; to work laboriously; to trudge doggedly. * *n* a hard, boring spell of work; a strenuous walk or hike; a hard, random hit.

slogan *n* a catchy phrase used in advertising or as a motto by a political party, etc.

slop *n* a puddle of spilled liquid; unappetizing semi-liquid food; (*pl*) liquid kitchen refuse. * *vti* (*pt* **slopped**) to spill or be spilled.

slope *n* rising or falling ground; an inclined line or surface; the amount or degree of this. * *vti* to incline, to slant; (*inf*) to make off, to go.

sloppy *adj* (**sloppier, sloppiest**) slushy; (*inf*) maudlin, sentimental; (*inf*) careless, untidy.—**sloppily** *adv*.—**sloppiness** *n*.

slot *n* a long narrow opening in a mechanism for inserting a coin, a slit. * *vt* (*pt* **slotted**) to fit into a slot; to provide with a slot; (*inf*) to place in a series.

slot machine *n* a machine operated by the insertion of a coin, used for gambling or dispensing drinks, etc.

slouch *vti* to sit, stand or move in a drooping, slovenly way. * *n* a drooping slovenly posture or gait; the downward droop of a hat brim; (*inf*) a poor performer, a lazy or incompetent person.

slovenly *adj* untidy, dirty; careless.—**slovenliness** *n*.

slow *adj* moving at low speed, not fast; gradual; not quick in understanding; reluctant, backward; dull, sluggish; not progressive; (*clock*) behind in time; tedious, boring; (*surface*) causing slowness. * *vti* (*also with* **up, down**) to reduce the speed (of).—**slowly** *adv*.—**slowness** *n*.

slow-motion *adj* moving slowly; denoting a filmed or taped scene with the original action slowed down.

sludge *n* soft mud or snow; sediment; sewage.

slug[1] *n* a mollusc resembling a snail but with no outer shell.

slug[2] *n* a small bullet; a disc for inserting into a slot machine; a line of type; (*inf*) a hard blow; a drink of spirits. * *vt* (*pt* **slugged**) (*inf*) to hit hard with a fist or a bat.

sluice *n* a gate regulating a flow of water; the water passing through this; an artificial water channel. * *vti* to draw off through a sluice; to wash with a stream of water; to stream out as from a sluice.

slum *n* a squalid, rundown house; (usu *pl*) an overcrowded area characterized by poverty, etc. * *vi* (*pt* **slummed**) to make do with less comfort.

slumber *vi* to sleep. * *n* a light sleep.

slump *n* a sudden fall in value or slackening in demand; (*sport*) a period of poor play. * *vi* to fall or decline suddenly; to sink down heavily; to collapse; to slouch.

slung *see* **sling**.

slur *vti* (*pt* **slurred**) to pronounce or speak indistinctly; (*letters, words*) to run together; (*mus*) to produce by gliding without a break; to make disparaging remarks. * *n* the act of slurring; a stigma, an imputation of disgrace; (*mus*) a curved line over notes to be slurred.

slush *n* liquid mud; melting snow; (*inf*) sentimental language.—**slushy** *adj*.

slut *n* a slovenly or immoral woman.—**sluttish** *adj*.

sly *adj* (**slyer, slyest** *or* **slier, sliest**) secretively cunning, wily; underhand; knowing.—**slyly** *adv*.—**slyness** *n*.

smack[1] *n* a taste; a distinctive smell or flavour;

small quantity, a trace. * *vi* to have a smell or taste (of); to have a slight trace of something.

smack[2] *vt* to strike or slap with the open hand; to kiss noisily; to make a sharp noise with the lips.—*also n.*

small *adj* little in size, number, importance, etc; modest, humble; operating on a minor scale; young; petty. * *adv* in small pieces. * *n* the narrow, curving part of the back.

smallpox *n* an acute contagious viral disease, now rare, causing the eruption of pustules which leave the skin scarred and pitted.

small talk *n* light, social conversation.

smart *n* a sudden, stinging pain. * *vi* to have or cause a sharp, stinging pain (as by a slap); to feel distress. * *adj* stinging; astute; clever, witty; fashionable; neatly dressed; (*equipment, etc*) capable of seemingly intelligent action through computer control; (*bombs, missiles*) guided to the target by lasers ensuring pinpoint accuracy.—**smartly** *adv*.—**smartness** *n*.

smarten *vti* to make or become smart.

smash *vti* to break into pieces with noise or violence; to hit, collide, or move with force; to destroy or be destroyed. * *n* a hard, heavy hit; a violent, noisy breaking; a violent collision; total failure, esp in business; (*inf*) a popular success.

smashing *n* (*inf*) excellent.

smattering *n* a slight superficial knowledge; a small number.

smear *vt* to cover with anything greasy or sticky; to make a smudge; to slander. * *n* a smudge; a slanderous attack; a deposit of blood, secretion, etc on a glass slide for examination under a microscope.

smell *n* the sense by which odours are perceived with the nose; a scent, odour, or stench; a trace. * *vti* (*pt* **smelt** *or* **smelled**) to have or perceive an odour.—**smelly** *adj*.

smile *vti* to express amusement, friendship, pleasure, etc, by a slight turning up of the corners of the mouth.—*also n.*

smirk *vi* to smile in an expression of smugness or scorn.—*also n.*

smith *n* a person who works in metal; a blacksmith.

smithy *n* a blacksmith's workshop.

smock *n* a loose shirtlike outer garment to protect the clothes.

smog *n* a mixture of fog and smoke.

smoke *n* a cloud or plume of gas and small particles emitted from a burning substance; any similar vapour; an act of smoking tobacco, etc; (*inf*) a cigar or cigarette. * *vi* to give off smoke; to (habitually) draw in and exhale the smoke of tobacco, etc. * *vt* to fumigate; to cure food by treating with smoke; to darken (eg glass) using smoke.

smoker *n* a person who habitually smokes tobacco; a train compartment where smoking is permitted.

smoky *adj* (**smokier, smokiest**) emitting smoke, esp excessively; filled with smoke; resembling smoke in appearance, flavour, smell, colour, etc.

smooth *adj* having an even or flat surface; silky; not rough or lumpy; hairless; of even consistency; calm, unruffled; gently flowing in rhythm or sound. * *vti* to make smooth; to calm; to make easier.—**smoothly** *adv*.—**smoothness** *n*.

smother *vt* to stifle, to suffocate; to put out a fire by covering it to remove the air supply; to cover over thickly; to hold back, suppress. * *vi* to undergo suffocation.—*also n.*

smoulder, smolder (*US*) *vi* to burn slowly or without flame; (*feelings*) to linger on in a suppressed state; to have concealed feelings of anger, jealousy, etc.

smudge *n* a dirty or blurred spot or area; in US, a fire made to produce dense smoke. * *vt* to make a smudge; to smear; to blur; in US, to produce smoke to protect against insects, etc. * *vi* to become smudged.

smug *adj* (**smugger, smuggest**) complacent, self-satisfied.—**smugly** *adv*.—**smugness** *n*.

smuggle *vt* to import or export (goods) secretly without paying customs duties; to convey or introduce secretly.—**smuggler** *n*.

smut *n* a speck or smudge of dirt, soot, etc; indecent talk, writing, or pictures; a fungous disease of crop plants that covers the leaves in sooty spores. * *vti* (*pt* **smutted**) to stain or become stained with smut; (*crops, etc*) to infect or become infected with smut.—**smutty** *adj*.

snack *n* a light meal between regular meals.

snag *n* a sharp point or projection; a tear, as in cloth, made by a snag, etc; an unexpected or hidden difficulty.—*also vti.*

snail *n* a mollusc having a wormlike body and a spiral protective shell; a slow-moving person or thing.

snake *n* a limbless, scaly reptile with a long, tapering body, often with salivary glands modified to produce venom; a sly, treacherous person. * *vt* to twist along like a snake. * *vi* to crawl silently and stealthily.—**snaky** *adj*.

snap *vti* (*pt* **snapped**) (*with* **at**) to bite or grasp suddenly; (*with* **at**) to speak or utter sharply; to break suddenly; to make or cause to make a sudden, cracking sound; to close, fasten, etc with this sound. * *adj* sudden. * *n* a sharp, cracking sound; a fastener that closes with a snapping sound; a crisp biscuit; a snapshot; a sudden spell of cold weather; (*inf*) vigour, energy.

snappy *adj* (**snappier, snappiest**) speaking sharply; brisk; lively; smart, fashionable.—**snappily** *adv*.

snapshot *n* a photograph taken casually with a simple camera.

snare *n* a loop of string or wire for trapping birds or animals; something that catches one unawares, a trap; a loop of gut wound with wire stretched around a snare drum that produces a rattling sound. * *vt* to trap using a snare.

snarl[1] *vi* to growl with bared teeth; to speak in a rough, angry manner. * *vt* to express in a snarling manner.—*also n*.

snarl[2] *vti* to make or become entangled or complicated. * *n* a tangle; disorder.

snatch *vt* to seize or grasp suddenly; to take as opportunity occurs. * *n* the act of snatching; a brief period; a fragment; (*inf*) a robbery.

sneak *vti* to move, act, give, put, take, etc, secretly or stealthily. * *n* a person who acts secretly or stealthily; (*inf*) a person who tells or informs on others. * *adj* without warning.—**sneaky** *adj*.

sneer *vi* to show scorn or contempt by curling up the upper lip.—*also n*.

sneeze *vi* to expel air through the nose violently and audibly.—*also n*.

snide *adj* malicious; superior in attitude; sneering.

sniff *vti* to inhale through the nose audibly; to smell by sniffing; to scoff.—*also n*.

snigger *vti* to laugh disrespectfully.—*also n*.

snip *vti* (*pt* **snipped**) to cut or clip with a single stroke of the scissors, etc. * *n* a small piece cut off; the act or sound of snipping; (*inf*) a bargain; (*inf*) a certainty, cinch.

snipe *n* (*pl* **snipe**) any of various birds with long straight flexible bills. * *vi* to shoot at individuals from a hidden position; to make sly criticisms of.—**sniper** *n*.

snippet *n* a scrap of information.

snob *n* a person who wishes to be associated with those of a higher social status, whilst acting condescendingly to those whom he or she regards as inferior.—**snobbery** *n*.—**snobbish** *adj*.

snooker *n* a game played on a billiard table with 15 red balls, 6 variously coloured balls, and a white cue ball; a position in the game where a ball lies directly between the cue ball and target ball. * *vt* to place in a snooker; (*inf*) to obstruct, thwart.

snoop *vi* (*inf*) to pry about in a sneaking way. * *n* an act of snooping; a person who pries into other people's business.—**snooper** *n*.

snooze *vi* (*inf*) to sleep lightly. * *n* (*inf*) a nap.

snore *vi* to breathe roughly and noisily while asleep.—*also n*.

snorkel *n* a breathing tube extending above the water, used in swimming just below the surface. * *vi* to swim using a snorkel.

snort *vi* to exhale noisily through the nostrils, esp as an expression of contempt or scorn. * *vt* to inhale (a drug) through the nose.

snout *n* the nose or muzzle of an animal.

snow *n* frozen water vapour in the form of white flakes; a snowfall; a mass of snow; (*sl*) cocaine or heroin. * *vi* to fall as snow.

snowball *n* snow pressed together in a ball for throwing; a drink made with advocaat and lemonade. * *vi* to throw snowballs; to increase rapidly in size.

snowdrift *n* a bank of drifted snow.

snowfall *n* a fall of snow; the amount of snow that falls in a given time or area.

snowman *n* snow piled into the shape of a human figure.

snowplough, snowplow (*US*) *n* a vehicle designed for clearing away snow.

snub[1] *vt* (*pt* **snubbed**) to insult by ignoring or making a cutting remark.—*also n*.

snub[2] *adj* short and turned up, as a nose.

snuff[1] *n* a powdered preparation of tobacco inhaled through the nostrils.

snuff[2] *n* the charred portion of a wick. * *vt* to extinguish (a candle flame).

snug *adj* (**snugger, snuggest**) cosy; warm; close-fitting.

so *adv* in this way; as shown; as stated; to such an extent; very; (*inf*) very much; therefore; more or less; also, likewise; then.

soak *vt* to submerge in a liquid; to take in, absorb; (*sl*) to extract large amounts of money from. * *vi* to become saturated; to penetrate. * *n* the act or process of soaking.

soap *n* a substance used with water to produce suds for washing; (*inf*) a soap opera. * *vt* to rub with soap.—**soapy** *adj*.

soar *vi* to rise high in the air; to glide along high

in the air; to increase; to rise in status.
sob *vi* to weep with convulsive gasps. * *vt* to speak while sobbing.
sober *adj* not drunk; serious and thoughtful; realistic, rational; subdued in colour. * *vt* to make or become sober (*often with* **up** *or* **down**).—**soberly** *adv*.
so-called *adj* commonly named or known as.
soccer *n* a football game played on a field by two teams of 11 players with a round inflated ball.
sociable *adj* friendly; companionable.—**sociability** *n*.—**sociably** *adv*.
social *adj* living or organized in a community, not solitary; relating to human beings living in society; of or intended for communal activities; sociable. * *n* an informal gathering of people, such as a party.—**socially** *adv*.
socialism *n* (a system based on) a political and economic theory advocating state ownership of the means of production and distribution.—**socialist** *n*.—**socialistic** *adj*.
social science *n* the study of human social organization and relationships using scientific methods.
social security *n* financial assistance for the unemployed, the disabled, etc to alleviate economic distress.
social work *n* any of various professional welfare services to aid the underprivileged in society.—**social worker** *n*.
society *n* the social relationships between human beings or animals organized collectively; the system of human institutional organization; a community with the same language and customs; an interest group or organization; the fashionable or privileged members of a community; companionship.
sociology *n* the study of the development and structure of society and social relationships.—**sociologist** *n*.—**sociological** *adj*.
sock[1] *n* a kind of short stocking covering the foot and lower leg.
sock[2] *vt* (*sl*) to punch hard.—*also n*.
socket *n* a hollow part into which something is inserted, such as an eye, a bone, a tooth, an electric plug, etc.
sod[1] *n* a lump of earth covered with grass; turf.
sod[2] *n* (*sl*) an obnoxious person; (*loosely*) a person, man.
soda *n* sodium bicarbonate; sodium carbonate; soda water.
soda water *n* a fizzy drink made by charging water with carbon dioxide under pressure.
sodden *adj* completely soaked through.
sodium *n* a metallic element.
sofa *n* an upholstered couch or settee with fixed back and arms.
soft *adj* malleable; easily cut, shaped, etc; not as hard as normal, desirable, etc; smooth to the touch; (*drinks*) nonalcoholic; mild, as a breeze; lenient; (*sl*) easy, comfortable; (*colour, light*) not bright; (*sound*) gentle, low; (*drugs*) non-addictive.—**softly** *adv*.—**softness** *n*.
soften *vti* to make or become soft or softer.—**softener** *n*.
software *n* the programs used in computers.
soggy *adj* (**soggier, soggiest**) soaked with water; moist and heavy.
soil[1] *n* the ground or earth in which plants grow; territory.
soil[2] *vt* to make or become dirty or stained.
solar *adj* of or from the sun; powered by light or heat from the sun; reckoned by the sun.
sold *see* **sell**.
solder *n* a metal alloy used when melted to join or patch metal parts, etc.—*also vti*.
soldier *n* a person who serves in an army, esp a non-commissioned officer. * *vi* to serve as a soldier.—**soldierly** *adj*.
sole[1] *n* the underside of the foot or shoe. * *vt* to put a new sole on (a shoe).
sole[2] *n* (*pl* **sole**) a type of flatfish used as food.
sole[3] *adj* only, being the only one; exclusive.—**solely** *adv*.
solemn *adj* serious; formal; sacred; performed with religious ceremony.—**solemnly** *adv*.—**solemness** *n*.
solicitor *n* a lawyer.
solid *adj* firm; compact; not hollow; strongly constructed; having three dimensions; neither liquid nor gaseous; unanimous. * *n* a solid substance (not liquid or gas); a three dimensional figure.—**solidly** *adv*.—**solidity** *n*.
solidarity *n* unity of interest and action.
solidify *vti* to make or become solid, compact, hard, etc.
solitaire *n* a single gemstone, esp a diamond; a card game for one (—*also* **patience**).
solitary *adj* alone; only; single; living alone; lonely.
solitude *n* the state of being alone; lack of company.
solo *n* (*pl* **solos**) a musical composition for performance by one voice or instrument; a flight by a single person in an aircraft, esp a first flight. * *vi* to perform by oneself. * *adv* alone. * *adj* unaccompanied.—**soloist** *n*.

solstice *n* either of the two times in the year at which the sun is farthest from the equator (21 June and 21 December).
soluble *adj* capable of being dissolved (usu in water); capable of being solved or answered.—**solubility** *n*.
solution *n* the act or process of answering a problem; the answer found; the dispersion of one substance in another, usu a liquid, so as to form a homogeneous mixture.
solve *vt* to work out the answer to; to clear up, resolve.
solvent *adj* capable of dissolving a substance; able to pay all debts. * *n* a liquid that dissolves substances.—**solvency** *n*.
sombre, somber (*US*) *adj* dark, gloomy or dull; dismal; sad.
some *adj* certain but not specified or known; of a certain unspecified quantity, degree, etc; a little; (*inf*) remarkable, striking, etc. * *pron* a certain unspecified quantity, number, etc.
somebody *n* an unspecified person; an important person.—*also pron*.
someday *adv* at some future day or time.
somehow *adv* in a way or by a method not known or stated.
someone *n* somebody.—*also pron*.
someplace *adv* somewhere.
somersault *n* a forward or backward roll head over heels along the ground or in mid-air.—*also vi*.
something *n, pron* a thing not definitely known, understood, etc; an important or notable thing. * *adv* to some degree. * *adj* having been formerly; being so occasionally or in only some respects.
sometime *adj* former. * *adv* at some unspecified future date.
sometimes *adv* at times, now and then.
somewhat *adv* to some extent, degree, etc; a little.
somewhere *adv* in, to or at some place not known or specified.
son *n* a male offspring or descendant.
song *n* a piece of music composed for the voice; the act or process of singing; the call of certain birds.
sonic *adj* of, producing, or involving sound waves.
son-in-law *n* a daughter's husband.
sonnet *n* a rhyming poem in a single stanza of fourteen lines.
sonny *n* a patronizing form of address to a boy.
soon *adv* in a short time; before long.
sooner or later *adv* at some future unspecified time, eventually.
soot *n* a black powder produced from flames.—**sooty** *adj*.
soothe *vt* to calm or comfort; to alleviate; to relieve (pain, etc).—**soothing** *adj*.
sophisticated *adj* refined; worldly-wise; intelligent; complex.—**sophistication** *n*.
soppy *adj* (**soppier, soppiest**) wet; (*inf*) sickly sentimental.—**soppily** *adv*.—**soppiness** *n*.
sorcerer *n* person who uses magic powers; a magician or wizard.—**sorceress** *nf*.
sordid *adj* filthy, squalid; vile; base; selfish.
sore *n* a painful or tender injury or wound; an ulcer or boil; grief; a cause of distress. * *adj* painful; tender; distressed.—**soreness** *n*.
sorely *adv* seriously, urgently.
sorrow *n* sadness; regret; an expression of grief. * *vi* to mourn, to grieve.—**sorrowful** *adj*.—**sorrowfully** *adv*.
sorry *adj* (**sorrier, sorriest**) feeling pity, sympathy, remorse or regret; pitiful; poor.
sort *n* a class, kind, or variety; quality or type. * *vt* to arrange according to kind; to classify.—**sorter** *n*.
SOS *n* an international signal code of distress; an urgent call for help or rescue.
souffle *n* a baked dish made light and puffy by adding beaten egg whites before baking.
sought *see* **seek**.
soul *n* a person's spirit; the seat of the emotions, desires; essence; character; a human being.
soul-destroying *adj* extremely boring, depressing.
soulful *adj* expressing profound sentiment.—**soulfully** *adv*.
sound[1] *adj* healthy; free from injury or damage; substantial; stable; deep (as sleep) solid; thorough.—**soundly** *adv*.—**soundness** *n*.
sound[2] *n* a narrow channel of water connecting two seas or between a mainland and an island.
sound[3] *n* vibrations transmitted through the air and detected by the ear; the sensation of hearing; any audible noise; the impression given by something. * *vi* to make a sound; to give a summons by sound. * *vt* to cause to make a sound; to voice; to make a signal or order by sound.
sound[4] *vt* to measure the depth of; to seek to discover the views and intentions of.
sound barrier *n* the increase in air resistance experienced by objects travelling close to the speed of sound.
sounding[1] *n* measurement of the depth of wa-

ter; a test, sampling, eg of public opinion.
sounding[2] *adj* resounding.
soundproof *adj* unable to be penetrated by sound. * *vt* to make soundproof by insulation, etc.
soundtrack *n* the sound accompanying a film; the area on cinema film that carries the sound recording.
soup *n* a liquid food made from boiling meat, fish, vegetables, etc, in water; (*inf*) a difficult or embarrassing situation.—**soupy** *adj*.
sour *adj* having a sharp, biting taste; spoiled by fermentation; cross; bad-tempered; distasteful or unpleasant; (*soil*) acid in reaction. * *vti* to make or become sour.—**sourly** *adv*.—**sourness** *n*.
source *n* a spring forming the head of a stream; an origin or cause; a person, book, etc, that provides information.
south *n* the direction to one's right when facing the the direction of the rising sun; the region, country, continent, etc, lying relatively in that direction. * *adj*, *adv* facing towards or situated in the south.
southeast *n* the point on a compass midway between south and east. * *adj*, *adv* at, towards, or from the southeast.—*also* **southeastern**.
southerly *adj* in, towards, or from the south. * *n* a wind from the south.
southern *adj* in, towards, or from the south; inhabiting or characteristic of the south.—**southernmost** *adj*.
southward *adj* towards the south.—**southwards** *adv*.
southwest *n* the point on a compass midway between south and west. * *adj*, *adv* at, towards, or from the southwest.—*also* **southwestern**.
souvenir *n* a keepsake, a memento.
sovereign *adj* supreme in authority or rank; (*country, state, etc*) independent. * *n* a supreme ruler; a monarch.—**sovereignty** *n*.
sow[1] *n* an adult female pig.
sow[2] *vt* (*pt* **sowed**, *pp* **sown** *or* **sowed**) to plant or scatter seed on or in the ground; to disseminate; to implant.—**sower** *n*.
soya bean, soybean (*US*) *n* a type of bean (orig from Asia) used as a source of food and oil.
spa *n* a mineral spring; a resort where there is a mineral spring.
space *n* the limitless three-dimensional expanse within which all objects exist; outer space; a specific area; an interval, empty area; room; an unoccupied area or seat. * *vt* to arrange at intervals.
spacecraft *n* a vehicle for travel in outer space.
spacious *adj* large in extent; roomy.—**spaciousness** *n*.
spade[1] *n* a tool with a broad blade and a handle used for digging.
spade[2] *n* a black symbol resembling a stylized spearhead marking one of the four suits of playing cards; a card of this suit.
span *n* a unit of length equal to a hand's breadth (about 9 inches/23 cm); the full extent between any two limits, such as the ends of a bridge or arch. * *vt* (*pt* **spanned**) to extend across.
spaniel *n* any of various breeds of dog with large drooping ears and a long silky coat.
Spanish *adj* of or pertaining to Spain. * *n* the language of Spain and Spanish Americans.
spank *vt* to slap with the flat of the hand, esp on the buttocks.—*also n*.
spanner *n* a tool with a hole or (often adjustable) jaws to grip and turn nuts or bolts, a wrench.
spare *vt* to refrain from harming or killing; to afford; to make (something) available (eg time). * *adj* kept as an extra, additional; scanty. * *n* a spare part; a spare tyre —**sparely** *adv*.—**spareness** *n*.
sparing *adj* frugal, economical.—**sparingly** *adv*.
spark *n* a fiery or glowing particle thrown off by burning material or by friction; a flash of light from an electrical discharge; a trace. * *vt* to stir up; to activate. * *vi* to give off sparks.
sparrow *n* any of various small brownish songbirds related to the finch.
sparse *adj* spread out thinly; scanty.—**sparsely** *adv*.—**sparseness, sparsity** *n*.
spasm *n* a sudden, involuntary muscular contraction; any sudden burst (of emotion or activity).
spasmodic *adj* intermittent; of or like a spasm.—**spasmodically** *adv*.
spastic *n* a person who suffers from cerebral palsy. * *adj* affected by muscle spasm.—**spasticity** *n*.
spat *see* **spit**[2].
spate *n* a large amount; a sudden outburst (as of words); a sudden flood.
spatter *vti* to scatter or spurt out in drops; to splash.—*also n*.
spatula *n* a tool with a broad, flexible blade for spreading or mixing foods, paints, etc.
spawn *n* a mass of eggs deposited by fish,

frogs, or amphibians; offspring. * *vti* to lay eggs; to produce, esp in great quantity.
spay *vt* to render (a female animal) sterile by removing the ovaries.
speak *vi* (*pt* **spoke,** *pp* **spoken**) to utter words; to talk; to to converse with; to deliver a speech; to be suggestive of something; to produce a characteristic sound.
speaker *n* a person who speaks, esp before an audience; the presiding official in a legislative assembly; a loudspeaker.
spear *n* a weapon with a long shaft and a sharp point; a blade or shoot (of grass, broccoli, etc). * *vt* to pierce with a spear.
spec *vt* to write specifications for.
special *adj* distinguished; uncommon; designed for a particular purpose; peculiar to one person or thing.—**specially** *adv*.
specialist *n* a person who concentrates on a particular area of study or activity, esp in medicine.
speciality, specialty (*US*) *n* a special skill or interest; a special product.
specialize *vi* to concentrate on a particular area of study or activity. * *vt* to adapt to a particular use or purpose.—**specialization** *n*.
species *n* (*pl* **species**) a class of plants or animals with the same main characteristics, enabling interbreeding; a distinct kind or sort.
specific *adj* explicit; definite; of a particular kind. * *n* a characteristic quality or influence; a drug effective in treating a particular disease.—**specifically** *adv*.
specification *n* a requirement; (*pl*) detailed description of dimensions, materials, etc of something.
specify *vt* to state specifically; to set down as a condition.
specimen *n* (*plant, animal, etc*) an example of a particular species; a sample; (*inf*) a person.
speck *n* a small spot; a fleck.
speckle *n* a small mark of a different colour. * *vt* to mark with speckles.
spectacle *n* an unusual or interesting scene; a large public show; an object of derision or ridicule; (*pl*) a pair of glasses.—**spectacled** *adj*.
spectacular *adj* impressive; astonishing.
spectator *n* an onlooker.
spectre, specter (*US*) *n* an apparition or ghost; a haunting mental image.
spectrum *n* (*pl* **spectra**) the range of colour which is produced when a white light is passed through a prism; any similar distribution of wave frequencies; a broad range.
speculate *vi* to theorize, to conjecture; to make investments in the hope of making a profit.—**speculation** *n*.—**speculator** *n*.
speculative *adj* of or based on speculation; engaging in speculation in finance, etc.—**speculatively** *adv*.
speech *n* the action or power of speaking; a public address or talk; language, dialect.
speechless *adj* unable to speak; silent, as from shock; impossible to express in words.—**speechlessly** *adv*.
speed *n* quickness; rapidity or rate of motion; (*photog*) the sensitivity of film to light; (*sl*) an amphetamine drug. * *vi* (*pt* **sped**) to go quickly, to hurry; (*pt* **speeded**) to drive (a vehicle) at an illegally high speed.
speedometer *n* an instrument in a motor vehicle for measuring its speed.
speedway *n* the sport of racing light motorcycles around dirt or cinder tracks; a stadium for motorcycle racing; in US, a road reserved for fast traffic.
speedy *adj* (**speedier, speediest**) quick; prompt.—**speedily** *adv*.
spell[1] *n* a sequence of words used to perform magic; fascination.
spell[2] *vb* (*pt* **spelt** *or* **spelled**) *vt* to name or write down in correct order the letters to form a word; (*letters*) to form a word when placed in the correct order; to indicate. * *vi* to spell words.
spell[3] *n* a usu indefinite period of time; a period of duty in a certain occupation or activity. * *vt* to relieve, stand in for.
spellbound *adj* entranced, enthralled.
spend *vb* (*pt* **spent**) *vt* to pay out (money); to concentrate (one's time or energy) on an activity; to pass, as time; to use up. * *vi* to pay out money.—**spender** *n*.
spendthrift *n* a person who spends money wastefully or extravagantly.
spent *adj* consumed, used up; physically drained, exhausted.
sperm *n* semen; the male reproductive cell.
spew *vti* to vomit; to flow or gush forth. * *n* something spewed.
sphere *n* a ball, globe or other perfectly round object; a field of activity or interest; a social class.—**spherical, spheric** *adj*.—**spherically** *adv*.
spice *n* an aromatic vegetable substance used for flavouring and seasoning food; these substances collectively; something that adds zest or interest. * *vt* to flavour with spice; to add zest to.

spicy *adj* (**spicier, spiciest**) flavoured with spice; pungent; (*inf*) somewhat scandalous or indecent.—**spicily** *adv*.—**spiciness** *n*.

spider *n* a small wingless creature (arachnid) with eight legs, and abdominal spinnerets for spinning silk threads to make webs.

spike *n* long heavy nail; a sharp-pointed projection, as on a shoe to prevent slipping; an ear of corn, etc; a cluster of stalkless flowers arranged on a long stem. * *vt* to pierce with a spike.—**spiky** *adj*.

spill[1] *vti* (*pt* **spilt** *or* **spilled**) to cause, esp unintentionally, to flow out of a container; to shed (blood). * *n* something spilled.—**spillage** *n*.

spill[2] *n* a splinter or thin strip of wood or twisted paper for lighting a fire, etc.

spin *vb* (*pr p* **spinning,** *pt* **spun**) *vt* to rotate rapidly; to draw out and twist fibres into thread or yarn; (*spiders, silkworm, etc*) to make a web or cocoon; to draw out (a story) to a great length; (*with* **out**) to prolong, extend; to cause to last longer, eg money. * *vi* to seem to be spinning from dizziness; (*wheels*) to turn rapidly without imparting forward motion. * *n* a swift rotation; (*inf*) a brief, fast ride in a vehicle.

spinach *n* a plant with large, green edible leaves.

spinal *adj* of or relating to the spine or spinal cord.

spinal cord *n* the cord of nerves enclosed by the spinal column.

spindly *adj* (**spindlier, spindliest**) tall and slender; frail.

spine *n* a sharp, stiff projection, as a thorn of the cactus or quill of a porcupine; a spinal column; the backbone of a book.

spineless *adj* lacking a spine; weak-willed; irresolute.—**spinelessness** *n*.

spinning wheel *n* a small household machine with a wheel-driven spindle for spinning yarn from fibre.

spinster *n* an unmarried woman.

spiral *adj* winding round in a continuous curve up or down a centre or pole. * *n* a helix; a spiral line or shape; a continuous expansion or decrease, eg in inflation. * *vi* (*pt* **spiralled**) to move up or down in a spiral curve; to increase or decrease steadily.

spire *n* the tapering point of a steeple.

spirit *n* soul; a supernatural being, as a ghost, angel, etc; (*pl*) disposition; mood; vivacity, courage, etc; real meaning; essential quality; (*usu pl*) distilled alcoholic liquor. * *vt* to carry (away, off, etc) secretly and swiftly.

spirited *adj* full of life; animated.—**spiritedly** *adv*.

spirit level *n* a glass tube filled with liquid containing an air bubble and mounted in a frame, used for testing whether a surface is level.

spiritual *adj* of the soul; religious; sacred. * *n* an emotional religious song, originating among the Black slaves in the American South.—**spirituality** *n*.—**spiritually** *adv*.

spiritualism *n* the belief that the spirits of the dead can communicate with the living, as through mediums.—**spiritualist** *n*.

spirt *see* **spurt**.

spit[1] *n* a pointed iron rod on which meat is roasted; a long narrow strip of land projecting into the water. * *vt* (*pr p* **spitting,** *pt* **spitted**) to fix as on a spit, impale.

spit[2] *vb* (*pr p* **spitting,** *pt* **spat** *or* **spit**) *vt* to eject from the mouth; to utter with scorn. * *vi* to expel saliva from the mouth; (*hot fat*) to splutter; to rain lightly. * *n* saliva.

spite *n* ill will; malice. * *vt* to annoy spitefully, to vex.—**spiteful** *adj*.

spittle *n* saliva ejected form the mouth.

splash *vt* to spatter with liquid; to move with a splash; to display prominently. * *n* something splashed; a patch of colour; a small amount, esp of a mixer added to an alcoholic drink.—**splashy** *adj*.

spleen *n* a large lymphatic organ in the upper left part of the abdomen which modifies the blood structure; spitefulness; ill humour.

splendid *adj* brilliant; magnificent; (*inf*) very good.—**splendidly** *adv*.

splendour, splendor (*US*) *n* brilliance; magnificence; grandeur.

splice *vt* to unite (two ends of a rope) by intertwining the strands; to connect (two pieces of timber) by overlapping.—*also n*.

splint *n* a rigid structure used to immobilize and support a fractured limb; a splinter of wood for lighting fires. * *vt* to put in splints.

splinter *n* a thin, sharp piece of wood, glass, or metal broken off. * *vti* to break off into splinters.—**splintery** *adj*.

split *vti* (*pr p* **splitting,** *pt* **split**) to break apart (usu into two pieces); to separate into factions; to divide into shares; to burst or tear. * *n* the act or process of splitting; a narrow gap made (as if) by splitting; a dessert consisting of sliced fruit, esp banana, with ice cream, nuts, etc; (*often pl*) the act of extending the legs in opposite directions and lowering the the body to the floor. * *adj* divided; torn; fractured.

splutter *vi* to spit out food or drops of liquid noisily; to utter words confusedly and hurriedly.—*also n.*

spoil *vb* (*pt* **spoilt** *or* **spoiled**) *vt* to damage as to make useless, etc; to impair the enjoyment, etc, of; to overindulge (a child). * *vi* to become spoiled; to decay, etc, as food. * *npl* booty, valuables seized in war; the opportunities for financial gain from holding public office.

spoil-sport *n* (*inf*) a person who spoils the fun of others.

spoke[1], **spoken** *see* **speak**.

spoke[2] *n* any of the braces extending from the hub to the rim of a wheel.

spokesman *n* a person authorized to speak on behalf of others.—**spokeswomen** *nf.*

sponge *n* a plantlike marine animal with an internal skeleton of elastic interlacing horny fibres; a piece of natural or manmade sponge for washing or cleaning. * *vt* to wipe with a sponge. **vi* (*inf*) to scrounge. —**sponginess** *n.*—**spongy** *adj.*

sponge cake *n* a sweet cake with a light porous texture.

sponsor *n* a person or organization that pays the expenses connected with an artistic production or sports event in return for advertising; in US, a business firm, etc that pays for a radio or TV programme advertising its product. * *vt* to act as sponsor for.—**sponsorship** *n.*

spontaneous *adj* arising naturally; unpremeditated.—**spontaneously** *adv.*—**spontaneity** *n.*

spook *n* (*inf*) a ghost; (*inf*) a spy. * *vt* to frighten.—**spooky** *adj.*

spool *n* a cylinder, bobbin, or reel, upon which thread, photographic film, etc, are wound. * *vt* to wind on a spool.

spoon *n* utensil with a shallow bowl and a handle, for eating, stirring, etc.—**spoonful** *n.*

sporadic *adj* occurring here and there; intermittent.—**sporadically** *adv.*

sport *n* an athletic game or pastime, often competitive and involving physical capability; good-humoured joking; (*inf*) a person regarded as fair and abiding by the rules. * *vi* to play, frolic. * *vt* (*inf*) to display, flaunt.

sporting *adj* interested in, concerned with, or suitable for sport; exhibiting sportsmanship; willing to take a risk.

sportsman *n* a person engaged in sport; a person who plays by the rules, is fair, is a good loser, etc.—**sportswoman** *nf.*—**sportsmanlike**, **sportsmanly** *adj.*—**sportsmanship** *n.*

sporty *adj* (**sportier, sportiest**) (*inf*) fond of sport; flashy, ostentatious. —**sportily** *adv.*—**sportiness** *n.*

spot *n* a small area differing in colour, etc, from the surrounding area; a stain, speck, etc; a taint on character or reputation; a small quantity or amount; a locality; (*inf*) a difficult or embarrassing situation; a place on an entertainment programme; a spotlight. * *vt* (*pt* **spotted**) to mark with spots; (*inf*) to identify or recognise; to glimpse.

spot check *n* a sudden random examination.

spotless *adj* immaculate.—**spotlessly** *adv.*

spotty *adj* (**spottier, spottiest**) marked with spots, esp on the skin; intermittent, uneven.—**spottiness** *n.*

spouse *n* (one's) husband or wife.

spout *vti* to eject in a strong jet or spurts; (*inf*) to drone on boringly. * *n* a projecting lip or tube for pouring out liquids.

sprain *n* a wrenching of a joint by sudden twisting or tearing of ligaments.—*also vt.*

sprang *see* **spring**.

sprawl *vi* to lie down with the limbs stretched out in an untidy manner; to spread out in a straggling way.—*also n.*

spray[1] *n* fine particles of a liquid; mist; an aerosol or atomizer. * *vti* to direct a spray (on); to apply as a spray.

spray[2] *n* a number of flowers on one branch; a decorative flower arrangement; an ornament resembling this.

spread *vt* (*pt* **spread**) to extend; to unfold or open; to disseminate; to distribute; to apply a coating (eg butter). * *vi* to expand in all directions. * *n* an expanse; (*inf*) a feast; food which can be spread on bread; a bed cover.

spree *n* (*inf*) excessive indulgence, eg in spending money, alcohol consumption, etc.

sprig *n* a twig with leaves on it.

sprightly *adj* (**sprightlier, sprightliest**) full of life or energy.—**sprightliness** *n.*

spring *vb* (*pt* **sprang** *or* **sprung**, *pp* **sprung**) *vi* to move suddenly, as by elastic force; to arise suddenly; to originate. * *vt* to cause to spring up, to cause to operate suddenly. * *n* a leap; the season between winter and summer; a coiled piece of wire that springs back to its original shape when stretched; the source of a stream.—**springiness** *n.*—**springy** *adj.*

springboard *n* a flexible board used by divers

and in gymnastics to provided added height or impetus.

spring-clean *vi* to clean (a house, etc) thoroughly.—*also n.*

sprinkle *vt* to scatter in droplets or particles (on something).—*also n.*

sprint *n* a short run or race at full speed. * *vi* to go at top speed.—**sprinter** *n.*

sprite *n* an elf or imp; a dainty person.

sprout *n* a new shoot on a plant; a small cabbage-like vegetable. * *vt* to put forth (shoots). * *vi* to begin to grow.

spruce[1] *adj* smart, neat, trim. * *vt* to smarten.

spruce[2] *n* an evergreen tree of the pine family with a conical head and soft light wood.

sprung *see* **spring**.

spry *adj* (**spryer, spryest** *or* **sprier, spriest**) vigorous, agile.

spun *see* **spin**.

spur *n* a small metal wheel on a rider's heel, with sharp points for urging on the horse; encouragement, stimulus; a hard sharp projection. * *vt* (*pt* **spurred**) to urge on.

spurious *adj* not legitimate or genuine; false.—**spuriously** *adv.*—**spuriousness** *n.*

spurn *vt* to reject with disdain. * *n* disdainful rejection.

spurt *vt* to gush forth in a sudden stream or jet. * *n* a sudden stream or jet; a burst of activity.—*also* **spirt**.

spy *n* a secret agent employed to collect information on rivals. * *vi* to keep under secret surveillance, act as a spy (*usu with* **on**). * *vt* to catch sight of.

sq. *abbr* = square.

squabble *vi* to quarrel noisily. * *n* a noisy, petty quarrel.—also *n.*

squad *n* a small group of soldiers which form a working unit; a section of a police force; (*sport*) a group of players from which a team is selected.

squadron *n* a unit of warships, cavalry, military aircraft, etc.

squalid *adj* filthy; neglected, sordid; degrading.—**squalidly** *adv.*—**squalor** *n.*

squander *vt* to spend extravagantly or wastefully.

square *n* a shape with four sides of equal length and four right angles; an open space in a town, surrounded by buildings; (*inf*) an old-fashioned person; an instrument for drawing right angles; the product of a number multiplied by itself. * *adj* square-shaped; (*financial account*) settled; fair, honest; equal in score; (*inf*) old-fashioned. * *vt* to make square; to multiply by itself. * *vi* to agree.—**squarely** *adv.*—**squareness** *n.*

squash[1] *vt* to squeeze, press, or crush; to suppress. * *vi* to squelch; to crowd. * *n* a crushed mass; a crowd of people pressed together; a fruit-flavoured drink; a game played in a walled court with rackets and rubber ball.—**squashy** *adj.*

squash[2] *n* (*pl* **squashes, squash**) a marrow or gourd eaten as a vegetable.

squat *vi* (*pt* **squatted**) to crouch down upon the heels; to occupy land or property, without permission or title. * *adj* short and dumpy. * *n* the act of squatting; a house that is occupied by squatters.

squatter *n* a person who squats.

squawk *n* a loud, raucous call or cry, as of a bird; (*inf*) a loud protest.—*also vi.*

squeak *vi* to make a high-pitched cry. * *n* a squeaky noise.—**squeaker** *n.*—**squeaky** *adj.*

squeal *vi* to make a shrill and prolonged cry or sound; (*sl*) to be an informer; to protest.

squeamish *adj* easily nauseated; easily shocked or disgusted.—**squeamishly** *adv.*—**squeamishness** *n.*

squeeze *vt* to press firmly, compress; to grasp tightly; to hug; to force (through, into) by pressing; to extract liquid, juice, from by pressure; to obtain (money, etc) by force, to harass. * *n* squeezing or being squeezed; a hug; a small amount squeezed from something; a crowding together; financial pressure or hardship.

squelch *vi* to walk through soft, wet ground, making a sucking noise. * *vt* to crush or squash completely. * *n* a squelching sound.

squid *n* (*pl* **squid, squids**) an edible mollusc, related to the cuttlefish, with a long body and ten arms.

squint *vi* to half close or cross the eyes; to glance sideways. * *n* crossed eyes, as caused by a visual disorder; a glance sideways; (*inf*) a look. * *adj* squinting; (*inf*) crooked.

squire *n* a country gentleman, esp the leading landowner in a district.

squirm *vi* to writhe; to wriggle; to feel embarrassed or ashamed.

squirrel *n* a bushy tailed rodent with grey or reddish fur which lives in trees and feeds on nuts.

squirt *vt* to eject liquid in a jet. * *vi* to spurt. * *n* a jet of liquid; (*inf*) an insignificant person.

St *abbr* = Saint.

St. *abbr* = Street.

stab *vt* (*pt* **stabbed**) to injure with a knife or

pointed weapon; to pain suddenly and sharply. * *vi* to thrust at (as if) with a pointed weapon. * *n* an act or instance of stabbing; a wound made by stabbing; a sudden sensation, as of emotion, pain, etc; (*inf*) an attempt.

stabilize *vti* to make or become stable or steady.

stable[1] *adj* steady or firm; firmly established; permanent; not decomposing readily.—**stability** *n*.

stable[2] *n* a building where horses or cattle are kept; a group of racehorses belonging to one owner; a group of people working for or trained by a specific establishment, as writers, performers, etc. * *vti* to put, keep, or live in a stable.

stack *n* a large neatly arranged pile (of hay, papers, records, etc); a chimney stack; (*inf*) a large amount of; a number of aircraft circling an airport waiting for permission to land. * *vt* to pile, arrange in a stack.

stadium *n* a sports ground surrounded by tiers of seats.

staff *n* (*pl* **staves**) a strong stick or pole; (*mus*) one of the five horizontal lines upon which music is written (—*also* **stave**); (*pl* **staffs**) a body of officers who help a commanding officer, or perform special duties; the workers employed in an establishment; the teachers or lecturers of an educational institution. * *vt* to provide with staff.

stag *n* a full-grown male deer. * *adj* (*party*) for men only.

stage *n* a degree or step in a process; a raised platform, esp for acting on; (*with* **the**) the theatre, the theatrical calling; any field of action or setting; a portion of a journey; a propulsion unit of a space rocket discarded when its fuel is spent. * *vt* to perform a play on the stage; to plan, organize (an event).

stage fright *n* nervousness at appearing before an audience.

stage manager *n* a person responsible for the stage arrangements prior to and during the performance of a play.

stagger *vi* to walk unsteadily, to totter. * *vt* to astound; to give a shock to; to arrange so as not to overlap; to alternate.

staggering *adj* astounding.—**staggeringly** *adv*.

stagnant *adj* (*water*) not flowing, standing still with a revolting smell; unchanging, dull.—**stagnancy** *n*.

stagnate *vi* to be, or become, stagnant.—**stagnation** *n*.

stagy, stagey *adj* (**stagier, stagiest**) theatrical, dramatic.

staid *adj* sober; sedate; old-fashioned.

stain *vt* to dye; to discolour with spots of something which cannot be removed. * *vi* to become stained; to produce stains. * *n* a discoloured mark; a moral blemish; a dye or liquid for staining materials, eg wood.

stained glass *n* coloured glass used in windows.

stainless *adj* free from stain; (materials) resistant to staining.

stair *n* a flight of stairs; a single step; (*pl*) a stairway.

staircase *n* a flight of stairs with banisters.

stairway *n* a staircase.

stake[1] *n* a sharpened metal or wooden post driven into the ground, as a marker or fence post; a post to which persons were tied for execution by burning; this form of execution. * *vt* to support with, tie or tether to a stake; to mark out (land) with stakes; (*with* **out**) to put under surveillance.

stake[2] *vt* to bet; (*inf*) to provide with money or resources. * *n* a bet; a financial interest; (*pl*) money risked on a race; (*pl*) the prize in a race

stalactite *n* an icicle-like calcium deposit hanging from the roof of a cave.

stalagmite *n* a cylindrical deposit projecting upwards from the floor of a cave, caused by the dripping of water and lime from the roof.

stale *adj* deteriorated from age; tainted; musty; stagnant; jaded.—**staleness** *n*.

stalemate *n* (*chess*) a situation in which a king can only be moved in and out of check, thus causing a draw; a deadlock.—*also vt*.

stalk[1] *n* the stem of a plant.

stalk[2] *vi* to stride in a stiff or angry way; to hunt (game, prey) stealthily.—**stalker** *n*.

stall[1] *n* a compartment for one animal in a stable; a table or stand for the display or sale of goods; a stalling of an engine; (*aircraft*) a loss of lift and downward plunge due to an excessive decrease in airspeed; (*pl*) the seats on the ground floor of a theatre. * *vti* (*car engine*) to stop or cause to stop suddenly, eg by misuse of the clutch; (*aircraft*) to lose or cause to lose lift because of an excessive reduction in airspeed.

stall[2] *vti* to play for time; to postpone or delay. * *n* (*inf*) any action used in stalling.

stalwart *adj* strong, sturdy; resolute; dependable. * *n* a loyal, hardworking supporter.

stamina *n* strength; staying power.

stammer *vti* to pause or falter in speaking; to stutter.—*also n*.—**stammerer** *n*.

stamp *vt* to put a mark on; to imprint with an official seal; to affix a postage stamp; (*with*

out) to extinguish by stamping; to suppress, eradicate, by force. * *vi* to bring the foot down heavily (on). * *n* a postage stamp; the mark cancelling a postage stamp; a block for imprinting.

stampede *n* an impulsive rush of a panic-stricken herd; a rush of a crowd.—*also vti*.

stance *n* posture; the attitude taken in a given situation.

stand *vb* (*pt* **stood**) *vi* to be in an upright position; to be on, or rise to one's feet; to make resistance; to remain unchanged; to endure, tolerate; (*with* **by**) to look on without interfering; to be available for use if required; (*with* **down**) to withdraw, resign; to leave a witness box after testifying in court; (*soldier*) to go off duty; (*with* **off**) to remain at a distance; to reach a deadlock; (*with* **up**) to rise to one's feet. * *vt* to put upright; to endure, tolerate; (*with* **by**) to remain loyal to, to defend; (*with* **off**) to (cause to) keep at a distance; to lay off (employees) temporarily; (*with* **up**) to resist; to withstand criticism, close examination, etc; (*inf*) to fail to keep an appointment with. * *n* a strong opinion; a standing position; a standstill; a place for taxis awaiting hire; (*pl*) a structure for spectators; the place taken by a witness for testifying in court; a piece of furniture for hanging things from; a stall or booth for a small retail business.

standard *n* a flag, banner, or emblem; an upright pole, pillar; an authorized weight or measure; a criterion; an established or accepted level of achievement; (*pl*) moral principles. * *adj* serving as a standard; typical.—**standardize** *vt*.

stand-by *n* a person or thing held in readiness for use in an emergency, etc.—*also adj*.

stand-in *n* a substitute; a person who takes the place of an actor during the preparation of a scene or in stunts.—*also vi*.

standing *n* status or reputation; length of service, duration. * *adj* upright; permanent; (*jump*) performed from a stationary position.

standoffish *adj* aloof, reserved.

standpoint *n* a point of view, opinion.

standstill *n* a complete halt.

stand-up *adj* (*collar*) upright; (*fight*) furious; (*comedian*) telling jokes standing alone in front of an audience.

stank *see* **stink**.

staple[1] *n* a principal commodity of trade or industry of a region, etc; a main constituent. * *adj* chief.

staple[2] *n* a U-shaped thin piece of wire for fastening. * *vt* to fasten with a staple.

star *n* any one of the celestial bodies, esp those visible by night which appear as small points of light, including planets, comets, meteors, and less commonly the sun and moon; a figure with five points; an exceptionally successful or skilful person; a famous actor, actress, musician, dancer, etc. * *vti* (*pt* **starred**) to feature or be featured as a star.

starboard *n* the right side of a ship or aircraft when facing the bow.

starch *n* a white, tasteless, food substance found in potatoes, cereal, etc; a fabric stiffener based on this. * *vt* to stiffen with starch.—**starchy** *adj*.

stare *vi* to gaze fixedly, as in horror, astonishment,etc; to glare. * *n* a fixed gaze.

stark *adj* bare; plain; blunt; utter. * *adv* completely.—**starkly** *adv*.—**starkness** *n*.

start *vi* to commence, begin; to jump involuntarily, from fright. * *vt* to begin. * *n* a beginning; a slight involuntary body movement; a career opening.

starter *n* a person who starts something, esp an official who signals the beginning of a race; a competitor in a race; the first course of a meal; a small electric motor used to start an internal combustion engine.

startle *vti* to be, or cause to be, frightened or surprised.—**startling** *adj*.

starve *vi* to die or suffer from a lack of food. * *vt* deprive (a person) of food; to deprive (of) anything necessary.—**starvation** *n*.

state *n* condition; frame of mind; position in society; ceremonious style; (*with cap*) an area or community with its own government, or forming a federation under a sovereign government. * *adj* of the state or State; public; ceremonial. * *vt* to express in words; to specify, declare officially.

stately *adj* (**statelier, stateliest**) dignified; majestic.—**stateliness** *n*.

statement *n* a formal announcement; a declaration; a document showing one's bank balance.

statesman *n* a well-known and experienced politician.—**statesmanship** *n*.

static *adj* fixed; stationary; at rest. * *n* electrical interference causing noise on radio or TV.

station *n* a railway or bus terminal or stop; headquarters (of the emergency services); military headquarters; (*inf*) a TV channel; position in society, standing. * *vt* to assign to a post, place, office.

stationary *adj* not moving.
stationer *n* a dealer in stationery, office supplies, etc.
stationery *n* writing materials, esp paper and envelopes.
station wagon *n* an estate car.
statistic *n* a fact obtained from analysing information expressed in numbers.
statistics *n* (*used as sing*) the branch of mathematics dealing with the collection, analysis and presentation of numerical data.—**statistical** *adj*.—**statistician** *n*.
statue *n* a representation of a human or animal form that is carved or moulded.
stature *n* the standing height of a person; level of attainment.
status *n* (*pl* **statuses**) social or professional position or standing; prestige; condition or standing from the point of view of the law, position of affairs.
status quo *n* the existing state of affairs.
statute *n* a law enacted by a legislature; a regulation.
statutory *adj* established, regulated, or required by statute.
staunch *adj* loyal; dependable.—**staunchly** *adv*.
stave *n* a piece of wood of a cask or barrel; (*mus*) a staff. * *vt* (*pt* **staved** *or* **stove**) (*usu with* **in**) to smash or dent inwards.
stay[1] *n* a rope supporting a mast
stay[2] *vi* to remain in a place; to wait; to reside temporarily. * *vt* to support; to endure; to stop, restrain. * *n* a suspension of legal proceedings; a short time spent as a visitor or guest.
STD *abbr* = sexually transmitted disease; subscriber trunk dialling.
steadfast *adj* firm, fixed; resolute.—**steadfastly** *adv*.
steady *adj* (**steadier, steadiest**) firm, stable; regular, constant; calm, unexcitable. * *n* (*inf*) a regular boyfriend or girlfriend. * *vti* to make or become steady.—**steadily** *adv*.—**steadiness** *n*.
steak *n* a slice of meat, esp beef or fish, for grilling or frying.
steal *vt* (*pt* **stole**, *pp* **stolen**) to take (from someone) dishonestly; to obtain secretly. * *n* (*inf*) an unbelievable bargain.
stealth *n* a manner of moving quietly and secretly.
stealthy *adj* (**stealthier, stealthiest**) acting or performed in a quiet, secret manner; unobtrusive, furtive.—**stealthily** *adv*.—**stealthiness** *n*.
steam *n* the hot mist or vapour created by boiling water. * *vi* to give off steam; to move by steam power; to cook with steam; (*with* **up**) (*glasses, windows, etc*) to become covered in condensation. * *adj* driven by steam.
steel *n* an alloy of iron and carbon; strength or courage. * *adj* of, or like, steel. * *vt* to cover with steel; to harden; to nerve (oneself).—**steely** *adj*.
steep[1] *adj* sloping sharply; (*inf*) excessive, exorbitant.—**steeply** *adv*.—**steepness** *n*.
steep[2] *vti* to soak or be soaked in a liquid; to saturate; to imbue.—*also n*.
steeple *n* a tower of a church, with or without a spire; the spire alone.
steeplechase *n* a horse race across country or on a course over jumps; a track race over hurdles and water jumps.—**steeplechaser** *n*.
steer[1] *n* a castrated male of the cattle family.
steer[2] *vti* to direct (a vehicle, ship, bicycle, etc) in the correct direction of travel.
stem[1] *n* a plant stalk; the upright slender part of anything, such as a wineglass; the root of a word. * *vi* (*pt* **stemmed**) to originate (from).
stem[2] *vt* (*pt* **stemmed**) to stop, check (the flow or tide).
stench *n* a foul odour.
stencil *n* a pierced sheet of card or metal for reproducing letters by applying paint; a design so made. * *vti* (*pt* **stencilled**) to produce (letters, etc) or designs using a stencil.
step *n* one movement of the foot ahead in walking, running, or dancing; a pace; a grade or degree; a stage towards a goal; one tread of a stair, rung of a ladder. * *vti* (*pt* **stepped**) to take a step or a number of paces.
step- *prefix* related by remarriage of a spouse or parent.
stepladder *n* a short portable ladder with flat steps fixed within a frame.
stereo *n* (*pl* **stereos**) a hi-fi or record player with two loudspeakers; stereophonic sound. * *adj* stereophonic.
stereophonic *adj* (*sound reproduction system*) using two separate channels for recording and transmission to create a spatial effect.—**stereophonically** *adv*.—**stereophony** *n*.
stereotype *n* a fixed, general image of a person or thing shared by many people.—*also vt*.
sterile *adj* unable to produce offspring, fruit, seeds, or spores; fruitless; free from germs.
sterilize *vt* to render incapable of reproduction; to free from germs.—**sterilization** *n*.
sterling *n* the British system of money. * *adj* of excellent character.

stern[1] *adj* severe; austere, harsh.—**sternly** *adv*.—**sternness** *n*.

stern[2] *n* the rear part of a boat or ship

stethoscope *n* an instrument used to detect body sounds.—**stethoscopic** *adj*.

stew *n* a meal of cooked meat with vegetables. * *vt* to cook slowly.

steward *n* a manager (of property); a race organizer; a person who serves food on an aircraft or ship and looks after passengers.

stewardess *n* a woman steward on an aircraft or ship.

stick[1] *vb* (*pt* **stuck**) *vt* to pierce or stab; to attach with glue, adhesive tape, etc. * *vi* to cling to, to adhere; to stay close to; to be held up.

stick[2] *n* a broken off shoot or branch of a tree; a walking stick; a hockey stick; a rod.

sticker *n* an adhesive label or poster.

stickler *n* a person who is scrupulous or obstinate about something.

sticky *adj* (**stickier, stickiest**) covered with adhesive or something sweet; (*weather*) warm and humid; (*inf*) difficult.—**stickiness** *n*.

stiff *adj* not flexible or supple; rigid; firm; moving with difficulty; having aching joints and muscles; formal, unfriendly; (*drink*) potent; (*breeze*) strong; (*penalty*) severe. * *n* (*sl*) a corpse. * *adv* utterly.—**stiffly** *adv*.—**stiffness** *n*.

stiffen *vti* to make or become stiff.—**stiffener** *n*.

stifle *vt* to suffocate; to smother; to suppress, hold back.

stifling *adj* excessively hot and stuffy. —**stiflingly** *adv*.

stigma *n* (*pl* **stigmas**) a social disgrace; the part of a flower that receives pollen; (*pl* **stigmata**) (*Christianity*) marks resembling the wounds of Christ thought to appear on the bodies of saintly people.

stile *n* a step, or set of steps, for climbing over a wall or fence.

still[1] *adj* motionless; calm; silent; (*drink*) not carbonated. * *n* a single photograph taken from a cinema film. **vti* to make or become still. * *adv* continuously; nevertheless. —**stillness** *n*.

still[2] *n* an apparatus for distilling liquids, esp spirits.

stillborn *adj* born dead; (*idea, project, etc*) a failure from the start, abortive.

still life *n* (*pl* **still lifes**) a painting of inanimate objects, such as flowers, fruit, etc.

stilt *n* either of a pair of poles with footrests on which one can walk, as in a circus; a supporting column.

stilted *adj* (*speech, writing*) pompous, unnaturally formal; (*conversation*) forced, intermittent.

stimulate *vt* to excite, arouse.—**stimulation** *n*.

stimulus *n* (*pl* **stimuli**) something that acts as an incentive; an agent that arouses or provokes a response in a living organism.

sting *n* a sharp pointed organ of a bee, wasp, etc, or hair on a plant, used for injecting poison; a skin wound caused by injected poison from an insect or plant; (*sl*) a swindle. * *vt* to wound with a sting; to cause to suffer mentally; to goad, incite; (*sl*) to cheat by overcharging. * *vi* to feel a sharp pain.

stingy *adj* (**stingier, stingiest**) miserly, mean.—**stingily** *adv*.—**stinginess** *n*.

stink *vi* (*pt* **stank** *or* **stunk**) to give out an offensive smell; (*sl*) to possess something in an excessive amount; (*sl*) to be extremely bad in quality. * *n* a foul smell.

stipulate *vt* to specify as a condition of an agreement.—**stipulation** *n*.

stir[1] *vb* (*pt* **stirred**) *vt* to mix, as with a spoon; to rouse; to stimulate or excite. * *vi* to be disturbed; to move oneself; to be active. * *n* a stirring movement; tumult.

stir[2] *n* (*sl*) prison.

stirring *adj* rousing, exciting.

stirrup *n* a strap and flat-bottomed ring hanging from a saddle, for a rider's foot.

stitch *n* a single in-and-out movement of a threaded needle in sewing; a single loop of a yarn in knitting or crocheting; a sudden, sharp pain, esp in the side. * *vti* to sew.

stock *n* raw material; goods on hand; shares of corporate capital, or the certificates showing such ownership; lineage, family, race; a store; the cattle, horses, etc, kept on a farm; the broth obtained by boiling meat, bones, and vegetables as a foundation for soup, etc. * *vt* to supply; to keep in store. * *adj* standard; hackneyed.

stockade *n* a defensive enclosure or barrier of stakes fixed in the ground.

stockbroker *n* a person who deals in stocks.

stocking *n* a sock; a nylon covering for a woman's leg, supported by suspenders.

stock market, stock exchange *n* the market for dealing in stocks and shares.

stockpile *n* a reserve supply of essentials.—*also vt*.

stocky *adj* (**stockier, stockiest**) short and sturdy.—**stockily** *adv*.—**stockiness** *n*.

stodgy *adj* (**stodgier, stodgiest**) (*food*) thick, heavy and indigestible; uninteresting.

stoke *vt* to stir and feed (a fire) with fuel.
stole[1], **stolen** *see* **steal**.
stole[2] *n* a long scarf or piece of fur worn on the shoulders.
stolid *adj* impassive; unemotional.—**stolidity** *n*.—**stolidly** *adv*.
stomach *n* the organ where food is digested; the belly. * *vt* to put up with.
stone *n* a small lump of rock; a precious stone or gem; the hard seed of a fruit; (*pl* **stone**) a unit of weight (14 lb./6.35 kg). * *vt* to throw stones at; to remove stones from (fruit).
stony, stoney *adj* (**stonier, stoniest**) of, like, or full of stones; unfeeling, heartless.
stood *see* **stand**.
stool *n* a seat or a support for the back when sitting, with no back or arms; matter evacuated from the bowels.
stoop *vti* to bend the body forward and downward; to degrade oneself; to deign.—*also n*.
stop *vb* (*pt* **stopped**) *vt* to halt; to prevent; to intercept; to plug or block. * *vi* to cease; to come to an end; to stay. * *n* an act or instance of stopping; an impediment; (a knob controlling) a set of organ pipes; any of the standard settings of the aperture in a camera lens (—*also* **f-stop**); a regular stopping place for a bus or train; a punctuation mark, esp full stop.
stopover *n* a short break in a journey.
stoppage *n* stopping or being stopped; an obstruction; a deduction from pay; a concerted cessation of work by employees, as during a strike.
stopper *n* a cork or bung.
storage *n* storing or being stored; an area reserved for storing; (*comput*) the storing of data in a computer memory or on disk, tape, etc.
store *n* a large supply of goods for future use; a warehouse; a shop. * *vt* to set aside; to put in a warehouse, etc; (*comput*) to put (data) into a computer memory or onto a storage device.
storey, story (*US*) *n* a horizontal division of a building; a set of rooms occupying this space.
stork *n* a long-necked and long-legged wading bird.
storm *n* a heavy fall of rain, snow, etc with strong winds; a violent commotion; a furore; (mil) an attack on a fortified place. * *vt* to rush, invade. * *vi* to be angry; to rain, snow hard.—**stormy** *adj*.
story *n* a narrative of real or imaginary events; a plot of a literary work; an anecdote; an account; (*inf*) a lie; a news article.
stout *adj* strong; short and plump; sturdy. * *n* strong dark beer.—**stoutly** *adv*.—**stoutness** *n*.
stove[1] *n* a cooker; heating apparatus.
stove[2] *see* **stave**.
stow *vt* to store, pack, in an orderly way
stowaway *n* a person who hides on a ship, car, aircraft, etc to avoid paying the fare.
straddle *vt* to have one leg or support on either side of something.
strafe *vt* to machine-gun (troops, vehicles, etc) from the air.—*also n*.
straggle *vi* to stray; to wander.—**straggler** *n*.—**straggly** *adj*.
straight *adj* (*line*) continuing in one direction, not curved or bent; direct; honest; (*sl*) heterosexual; (*alcoholic drinks*) neat, not diluted. * *adv* directly; without delay. * *n* being straight; a straight line, form, or position; a straight part of a racetrack; (*poker*) a hand containing five cards in sequence.—**straightness** *n*.
straighten *vti* to make or become straight.
straightforward *adj* honest, open; simple; easy.—**straightforwardly** *adv*.—**straightforwardness** *n*.
strain[1] *vt* to tax; to stretch; to overexert; to stress; to injure (a muscle) by overstretching; (food) to drain or sieve. * *n* overexertion; tension; an injury from straining.
strain[2] *n* a plant or animal within a species having a common characteristic; a trait; a trace.
strained *adj* (*action, behaviour*) produced by excessive effort; (*mood, atmosphere*) tense, worried.
strainer *n* a sieve or colander used for straining liquids, pasta, tea, etc.
strait *n* a channel of sea linking two larger seas; (*usu pl*) difficulty, distress.
straitjacket, straightjacket *n* a coatlike device for restraining violent people; something that restricts or limits.—*also vt*.
strait-laced, straight-laced *adj* prim, morally strict.
strand[1] *vt* to run aground; to leave helpless, without transport or money.
strand[2] *n* a single piece of thread or wire twisted together to make a rope or cable; a tress of hair.—*also vt*.
strange *adj* peculiar; odd; unknown; unfamiliar.—**strangely** *adv*.—**strangeness** *n*.
stranger *n* a person who is unknown; a new arrival to a place, town, social gathering, etc; a person who is unfamiliar with or ignorant of something.

strangle *vt* to kill by compressing the windpipe, to choke; to stifle, suppress.—**strangler** *n*.
strap *n* a narrow strip of leather or cloth for carrying or holding (a bag, etc); a fastening, as on a shoe, wristwatch. * *vti* (*pt* **strapped**) to fasten with a strap; to beat with a strap.
strapping *adj* tall, well-built.
strata *see* **stratum**.
strategic, strategical *adj* of, relating to, or important in strategy; (*weapons*) designed to strike at the enemy's homeland, not for use on the battlefield.—**strategically** *adv*.
strategy *n* the planning and conduct of war; a political, economic, or business policy.—**strategist** *n*.
stratum *n* (*pl* **strata, stratums**) a layer of sedimentary rock; a level (of society).
straw *n* the stalks of threshed grain; a tube for sucking up a drink.
strawberry *n* a soft red fruit used in desserts and jam.
stray *vi* to wander; to deviate; to digress. * *n* a domestic animal that has become lost. * *adj* random.
streak *n* a line or long mark of contrasting colour; a flash of lightning; a characteristic, a trace. * *vti* to mark with or form streaks; to run naked in public as a prank.—**streaker** *n*.
streaky *adj* (**streakier, streakiest**) marked with streaks; (*bacon*) having alternate layers of fat and lean.
stream *n* a small river, brook, etc; a flow of liquid; anything flowing and continuous. * *vi* to flow, gush.
streamer *n* a banner; a long decorative ribbon.
streamline *vt* to shape (a car, boat, etc) in a way that lessens resistance through air or water; to make more efficient, to simplify.—**streamlined** *adj*.
street *n* a public road in a town or city lined with houses; such a road with its buildings and pavements; the people living,working, etc, along a given street.
streetcar *n* a tram.
strength *n* the state or quality of being physically or mentally strong; power of exerting or withstanding pressure, stress, force; potency; effectiveness.
strengthen *vti* to make or become stronger.
strenuous *adj* vigorous; requiring exertion.—**strenuously** *adv*.—**strenuousness** *n*.
stress *n* pressure; mental or physical tension or strain; emphasis; (*physics*) a system of forces producing or sustaining strain. * *vt* to exert pressure on; to emphasize.
stretch *vt* to extend, to draw out. * *vi* to extend, spread; to extend (the limbs, body); to be capable of expanding, as in elastic material. * *n* the act of stretching or instance of being stretched; the capacity for being stretched; an expanse of time or space; (*sl*) a period of imprisonment.—**stretchy** *adj*.
stretcher *n* a portable frame for carrying the sick or injured.
strew *vt* (*pt* **strewed,** *pp* **strewn** *or* **strewed**) to scatter; to spread.
stricken *adj* suffering (from an illness); afflicted, as by something painful.
strict *adj* harsh, firm; enforcing rules rigorously; rigid.—**strictly** *adv*.—**strictness** *n*.
stride *vi* (*pt* **strode,** *pp* **stridden**) to walk with long steps. * *vt* to straddle.—*also n*.
strident *adj* loud and harsh.—**stridency** *n*.—**stridently** *adv*.
strife *n* a fight, quarrel; struggle.
strike *vb* (*pt* **struck**) *vt* to hit; to crash into; (*mil*) to attack; to ignite (a match) by friction; (*disease, etc*) to afflict suddenly; to come upon, esp unexpectedly; to delete; (*clock*) to indicate by sounding; to assume (eg an attitude); to occur to; (*medal, coin*) to produce by stamping; (*flag, tent*) to lower, take down; to come upon (oil, ore, etc) by drilling or excavation. * *vi* to cease work to enforce a demand (for higher wages or better working conditions). * *n* a stoppage of work; a military attack.
striker *n* a worker who is on strike; a mechanism that strikes, as in a clock; (*soccer*) a forward player whose primary role is to score goals.
striking *adj* impressive.—**strikingly** *adv*.
string *n* a thin length of cord or twine used for tying, fastening, etc; a stretched length of catgut, wire, or other material in a musical instrument; (*pl*) the stringed instruments in an orchestra; their players; a line or series of things. * *vt* (*pt* **strung**) to thread on a string.
stringent *adj* strict.—**stringently** *adv*.—**stringency** *n*.
strip *vb* (*pt* **stripped**) *vt* to peel off; to divest; to take away removable parts. * *vi* to undress. * *n* a long, narrow piece (of cloth, land, etc); an airstrip or runway.
stripe *n* a narrow band of a different colour form the background; a chevron worn on a military uniform to indicate rank. * *vt* to mark with a stripe.—**striped** *adj*.—**stripy** *adj*.

stripper *n* a striptease artist; a device or solvent that removes paint.

striptease *n* an erotic show where a person removes their clothes slowly and seductively to music.

strive *vi* (*pt* **strove,** *pp* **striven**) to endeavour earnestly, labour hard, to struggle, contend.

strode *see* **stride**.

stroke[1] *n* a blow or hit; (*med*) a seizure; the sound of a clock; (*sport*) an act of hitting a ball; a manner of swimming; the sweep of an oar in rowing; a movement of a pen, pencil, or paintbrush.

stroke[2] *vt* to caress; to do so as a sign of affection.

stroll *vi* to walk leisurely, to saunter.—*also n.*

strong *adj* physically or mentally powerful; potent; intense; healthy; convincing; powerfully affecting the sense of smell or taste, pungent. * *adv* effectively, vigorously.—**strongly** *adv*.

stronghold *n* a fortress; a centre of strength or support.

strove *see* **strive**.

struck *see* **strike**.

structure *n* organization; construction; arrangement of parts in an organism, or of atoms in a molecule of a substance; system, framework; order. * *vt* to organize, to arrange; to build up.—**structural** *adj*.—**structurally** *adv*.

struggle *vi* to move strenuously so as to escape; to strive; to fight; to exert strength; to make one's way (along, through, up, etc) with difficulty. * *n* a violent effort; a fight.

strum *vt* (*pt* **strummed**) to play on (a guitar, etc), by moving the thumb across the strings.

strung *see* **string**.

strut[1] *vi* (*pt* **strutted**) to walk in a proud or pompous manner.

strut[2] *n* a brace or structural support. * *vt* to brace.

stub *n* a short piece left after the larger part has been removed or used; the counterfoil of a cheque, receipt, etc. * *vt* (*pt* **stubbed**) to knock (one's toe or foot) painfully; to extinguish (a cigarette).

stubble *n* the stubs or stumps left in the ground when a crop has been harvested; any short, bristly growth, as of beard.—**stubbly** *adj*.

stubborn *adj* obstinate; persevering; determined, inflexible.—**stubbornly** *adv*.—**stubbornness** *n*.

stuck *see* **stick**.

stuck-up *adj* (*inf*) conceited; proud; snobbish.

stud[1] *n* a male animal, esp a horse, kept for breeding; a collection of horses and mares for breeding; a farm or stable for stud animals.

stud[2] *n* a large-headed nail; an ornamental fastener. * *vt* (*pt* **studded**) to cover with studs.

student *n* a person who studies or investigates a particular subject; a person who is enrolled for study at a school, college, university, etc.

studied *adj* carefully planned.

studio *n* (*pl* **studios**) the workshop of an artist, photographer, etc; (*pl*) a building where motion pictures are made; a room where TV or radio programmes are recorded.

studious *adj* given to study; careful.

study *vt* to observe an investigate (eg phenomena) closely; to learn (eg a language); to scrutinize; to follow a course (at college, etc). * *n* the process of studying; a detailed investigation and analysis of a subject; the written report of a study of something; a room for studying.

stuff *n* material; matter; textile fabrics; cloth, esp when woollen; personal possessions generally. * *vt* to cram or fill.

stuffing *n* material used to stuff or fill anything; a seasoned mixture put inside poultry, meat, vegetables etc before cooking.

stuffy *adj* (**stuffier, stuffiest**) badly ventilated; lacking in fresh air; dull, uninspired.—**stuffiness** *n*.

stumble *vi* to trip up or lose balance when walking; to falter; (*with* **across** *or* **on**) to discover by chance. * *n* a trip; a blunder.

stump *n* the part of a tree remaining in the ground after the trunk has been felled; the part of a limb, tooth, that remains after the larger part is cut off or destroyed. * *vt* (*inf*) to confuse, baffle; to campaign for an election.

stun *vt* (*pt* **stunned**) to render unconscious due to a fall or blow; to surprise completely; to shock.

stung *see* **sting**.

stunk *see* **stink**.

stunning *adj* (*inf*) strikingly attractive.

stunt[1] *vt* to prevent the growth of, to dwarf.

stunt[2] *n* a daring or spectacular feat; a project designed to attract attention. * *vi* to carry out stunts.

stupefy *vt* to dull the senses of.—**stupefaction** *n*.

stupendous *adj* wonderful, astonishing.

stupid *adj* lacking in understanding or common sense; silly; foolish; stunned.—**stupidity** *n*.—**stupidly** *adv*.

stupor *n* extreme lethargy; mental dullness.

sturdy *adj* (**sturdier, sturdiest**) firm; strong, robust.—**sturdily** *adv*.—**sturdiness** *n*.

stutter *vi* to stammer.—*also n*.

sty[1], **stye** *n* (*pl* **sties, styes**) an inflamed swelling on the eyelid.

sty[2] *n* (*pl* **sties**) a pen for pigs; any filthy place.

style *n* the manner of writing, painting, composing music peculiar to an individual or group; fashion, elegance. * *vt* to design or shape (eg hair).

stylish *adj* having style; fashionable.—**stylishly** *adv*.—**stylishness** *n*.

stylize *vt* to give a conventional style to.—**stylization** *n*.

stylus *n* (*pl* **styli, styluses**) the device attached to the cartridge on the arm of a record-player that rests in the groove of a record and transmits the vibrations that are converted to sound.

suave *adj* charming, polite.—**suavely** *adv*.—**suaveness, suavity** *n*.

sub *n* (*inf*) a submarine; a substitute; a subscription; a subeditor.

sub- *prefix* under, below; subordinate, next in rank to.

subconscious *adj* happening without one's awareness. * *n* the part of the mind that is active without one's conscious awareness.—**subconsciously** *adv*.

subdue *vt* to dominate; to render submissive; to repress (eg a desire); to soften, tone down (eg colour, etc).

subject *adj* under the power of; liable. * *n* a person under the power of another; a citizen; a topic; a theme; the scheme or idea of a work of art. * *vt* to bring under control; to make liable; to cause to undergo something.—**subjection** *n*.

subjective *adj* determined by one's own mind or consciousness; relating to reality as perceived and not independent of the mind; arising from one's own thoughts and emotions, personal.—**subjectively** *adv*.

subjunctive *adv* denoting that mood of a verb which expresses doubt, condition, wish, or hope. * *n* the subjunctive mood.

sublime *adj* noble; exalted.—**sublimely** *adv*.—**sublimity** *n*.

submarine *adj* underwater, esp under the sea. * *n* a naval vessel capable of being propelled under water, esp for firing torpedoes or missiles.

submerge, submerse *vt* to plunge or sink under water; to cover, hide.—**submergence, submersion** *n*.

submission *n* an act of submitting; something submitted, as an idea or proposal; the state of being submissive, compliant; the act of referring something for another's consideration, criticism, etc.—**submissively** *adv*.—**submissiveness** *n*.

submit *vb* (*pt* **submitted**) *vt* to surrender (oneself) to another person or force; to refer to another for consideration or judgment; to offer as an opinion. * *vi* to yield, to surrender.

subordinate *adj* secondary; lower in order, rank. * *n* a subordinate person. * *vt* to put in a lower position or rank.—**subordination** *n*.

subscribe *vt* to pay to receive regular copies (of a magazine, etc); to donate money (to a charity, campaign); to support or agree with (an opinion, faith).—**subscriber** *n*.—**subscription** *n*.

subsequent *adj* occurring or following after.—**subsequently** *adv*.

subside *vi* to sink or fall to the bottom; to settle; to diminish; to abate.—**subsidence** *n*.

subsidiary *adj* secondary; supplementary; (*company*) owned or controlled by another.—*also n*.

subsidy *n* government financial aid to a private person or company to assist an enterprise.—**subsidize** *vt*.

subsistence *n* existence; livelihood.

substance *n* matter (such as powder, liquid); the essential nature or part; significance.

substantial *adj* of considerable value or size; important; strongly built.—**substantially** *adv*.

substantiate *vt* to prove, to verify.—**substantiation** *n*.

substitute *vt* to put or act in place of another person or thing (*with* **for**); to replace (by). * *n* a person or thing that serves in place of another.—*also adj*.—**substitution** *n*.

subtitle *n* an explanatory, usu secondary, title to a book; a printed translation superimposed on a foreign language film.—*also vt*.

subtle *adj* delicate; slight; not noticeable; difficult to define, put into words; ingenious.—**subtlety** *n*.—**subtly** *adv*.

subtract *vti* to take away or deduct, as one quantity from another.—**subtraction** *n*.

suburb *n* a residential district on the outskirts of a large town or city.—**suburban** *adj*.—**suburbia** *n*.

subversive *adj* liable to subvert established authority. * *n* a person who engages in subversive activities.

subway *n* a passage under a street; an underground metropolitan electric railway.

succeed *vt* to come after, to follow; to take the

place of. * *vi* to accomplish what is attempted; to prosper.

success *n* the gaining of wealth, fame, etc; the favourable outcome (of anything attempted); a successful person or action.

successful *adj* having success.—**successfully** *adv*.

succession *n* following in sequence; a number of persons or things following in order; the act or process of succeeding to a title, throne, etc; the line of descent to succeed to something.

successive *adj* following in sequence.—**successively** *adv*.

successor *n* a person who succeeds anothe.

succinct *adj* clear, concise.—**succinctly** *adv*.—**succinctness** *n*.

succulent *adj* juicy; moist and tasty; (*plant*) having fleshy tissue. * *n* a succulent plant (eg cactus).—**succulence** *n*.

succumb *vi* to yield to superior strength or overpowering desire; to die.

such *adj* of a specified kind (eg such people, such a film); so great. * *adv* so; very.

suck *vt* to draw (a liquid, air) into the mouth; to dissolve or roll about in the mouth (as a sweet); to draw in as if by sucking (*with* **in, up** etc).—*also n*.

sucker *n* (*sl*) a person who is easily taken in or deceived; a cup-shaped piece of rubber that adheres to surfaces.

suckle *vt* to feed at the breast or udder.

sucrose *n* sugar.

suction *n* the act or process of sucking; the exertion of a force to form a vacuum.

sudden *adj* happening quickly and unexpectedly, abrupt.—**suddenly** *adv*.—**suddenness** *n*.

sue *vt* (*pr p* **suing,** *pt* **sued**) to bring a legal action against.

suede *n* leather finished with a soft nap.

suet *n* white, solid fat in animal tissue, used in cooking.

suffer *vt* to undergo; to endure; to experience. * *vi* to feel pain or distress.—**sufferer** *n*.—**suffering** *n*.

sufferable *adj* endurable.

suffice *vi* to be sufficient, adequate (for some purpose).

sufficient *adj* enough; adequate—**sufficiency** *n*.—**sufficiently** *adv*.

suffix *n* (*pl* **suffixes**) a letter, syllable, or syllables added to the end of a word to modify its meaning or to form a new derivative.

suffocate *vti* to kill or be killed by depriving of oxygen, or by inhaling a poisonous gas; to feel hot and uncomfortable due to lack of air; to prevent from developing.—**suffocation** *n*.

sugar *n* a sweet white, crystalline substance obtained from sugarcane and sugar beet * *vi* to sweeten.

sugary *adj* resembling or containing sugar; cloyingly sweet in manner, content, etc.—**sugariness** *n*.

suggest *vt* to put forward for consideration; to bring to one's mind; to evoke.—**suggestion** *n*.

suggestible *adj* easily influenced by others.—**suggestibility** *n*.

suggestive *adj* evocative; rather indecent, risqué.—**suggestively** *adv*.—**suggestiveness** *n*.

suicide *n* a person who kills himself intentionally; the act or instance of killing oneself intentionally; ruin of one's own interests.

suit *n* a set of matching garments, such as a jacket and trousers or skirt; one of the four sets of thirteen playing cards; a lawsuit. * *vt* to be appropriate; to be convenient or acceptable to.

suitable *adj* fitting; convenient (to, for).—**suitably** *adv*.—**suitability** *n*.

suitcase *n* a portable, oblong travelling case.

suite *n* a number of followers or attendants; a set, esp of rooms, furniture, pieces of music.

sulk *vi* to be sullen.

sulky *adj* (**sulkier, sulkiest**) bad-tempered, quiet and sullen, because of resentment.

sullen *adj* moody and silent; gloomy, dull.—**sullenly** *adv*.—**sullenness** *n*.

sulphur, sulfur (*US*) *n* a yellow nonmetallic element that is inflammable and has a strong odour.—**sulphuric** *adj*.

sulphuric acid *n* a powerfully corrosive acid.

sultana *n* a dried, white grape used in cooking; the wife or female relative of a sultan.

sultry *adj* (**sultrier, sultriest**) (*weather*) very hot, humid and close; (*person*) sensual; passionate.—**sultriness** *n*.

sum *n* the result of two or more things added together; the total, aggregate; a quantity of money; essence, gist. * *vt* (*pt* **summed**) to add (*usu with* **up**); to encapsulate; to summarize.

summarize *vt* to make or be a summary of.

summary *adj* concise; performed quickly, without formality. * *n* a brief account of the main points of something.—**summarily** *adv*.

summer *n* the warmest season of the year, between spring and autumn.—**summery** *adj*.

summit *n* the highest point, the peak; a meeting of world leaders.
summon *vt* to order to appear, esp in court; to convene; to gather (strength, enthusiasm, etc).
summons *n* a call to appear (in court). * *vt* to serve with a summons.
sump *n* a section of an engine for the oil to drain into.
sumptuous *adj* lavish; luxurious.—**sumptuously** *adv*.—**sumptuousness** *n*.
sun *n* the star around which the earth and other planets revolve which gives light and heat to the solar system; the sunshine. * *vt* (*pt* **sunned**) to expose oneself to the sun's rays.
sunbathe *vi* to lie in the rays of the sun or a sun lamp to get a suntan.—*also n*.
sunburn *n* inflammation of the skin from exposure to sunlight.—*also vti*.
Sunday *n* the day of the week after Saturday, regarded as a day of worship by Christians; a newspaper published on a Sunday.
sundial *n* a device that shows the time by casting a shadow on a graduated dial.
sundry *adj* miscellaneous, various. * *n* (*pl*) miscellaneous small things.
sunflower *n* a tall plant with large yellow flowers whose seeds yield oil.
sung *see* **sing**.
sunglasses *npl* tinted glasses to protect the eyes from sunlight.
sunk *see* **sink**.
sunny *adj* (**sunnier, sunniest**) (*weather*) bright with sunshine; (*person, mood*) cheerful.
sunrise *n* dawn.
sunset *n* dusk.
sunshine *n* the light and heat from the sun.
sunstroke *n* illness caused by exposure to the sun.
suntan *n* browning of the skin by the sun.
super *adj* (*inf*) fantastic, excellent; (*inf*) a superintendent, as in the police. * *n* a variety of high-octane petrol.
superannuation *n* regular contributions from employees' wages towards a pension scheme.
superb *adj* grand; excellent; of the highest quality.—**superbly** *adv*.
supercilious *adj* arrogant; haughty, disdainful. —**superciliously** *adv*. —**superciliousness** *n*.
superficial *adj* near the surface; slight, not profound; (*person*) shallow in nature.—**superficiality** *n*.—**superficially** *adv*.
superfluous *adj* exceeding what is required; unnecessary.—**superfluity** *n*.
superimpose *vt* to put or lay upon something else.
superintendent *n* a person who manages or supervises; a British police officer next above the rank of inspector.
superior *adj* higher in place, quality, rank, excellence; greater in number, power. * *n* a person of higher rank.—**superiority** *n*.
superlative *adj* of outstanding quality; (*gram*) denoting the extreme degree of comparison of adjectives and adverbs.—**superlatively** *adv*.
supermarket *n* a large self-service, shop selling food and household goods.
supernatural *adj* relating to things that cannot be explained by nature; involving ghosts, spirits, etc.—**supernaturally** *adv*.
superpower *n* a nation with great economic and military strength.
supersede *vt* to take the place of, replace.
supersonic *adj* faster than the speed of sound.—**supersonically** *adv*.
superstition *n* irrational belief based on ignorance or fear.—**superstitious** *adj*.
supervise *vti* to have charge of, direct, to superintend.—**supervision** *n*.—**supervisor** *n*.—**supervisory** *adj*.
supper *n* a meal taken in the evening, esp when dinner is eaten at midday; an evening social event; the food served at a supper; a light meal served late in the evening.
supple *adj* flexible, easily bent; lithe; (*mind*) adaptable.—**suppleness** *n*.
supplement *n* an addition or extra amount (usu of money); an additional section of a book, periodical or newspaper. * *vt* to add to.—**supplemental** *adj*.
supply *vt* to provide, meet (a deficiency, a need); to fill (a vacant place). * *n* a stock; (*pl*) provisions.—**supplier** *n*.
support *vt* to hold up, bear; to tolerate, withstand; to assist; to advocate (a cause, policy); to provide for (financially). * *n* a means of support; maintenance.
supporter *n* a person who backs a political party, sports team, etc.
suppose *vt* to assume; to presume as true without definite knowledge; to think probable; to expect. * *vi* to conjecture.
supposed *adj* believed to be on available evidence.
supposedly *adv* allegedly.
supposition *n* an assumption, hypothesis.
suppress *vt* to crush, put an end to (eg a rebellion); to restrain (a person); to subdue.—**suppression** *n*.—**suppressor** *n*.
supreme *adj* of highest power; greatest; final;

ultimate.—**supremacy** *n*.
surcharge *vt* to overcharge (a person); to charge an additional sum; to overload. * *n* an additional tax or charge; an additional or excessive load.
sure *adj* certain; without doubt; reliable, inevitable; secure; safe; dependable. * *adv* certainly.
surely *adv* certainly; securely; it is to be hoped or expected that.
surety *n* a person who undertakes responsibility for the fulfilment of another's debt; security given as a guarantee of payment of a debt.
surf *n* the waves of the sea breaking on the shore or a reef.
surface *n* the exterior face of an object; any of the faces of a solid; the uppermost level of sea or land; a flat area, such as the top of a table; superficial features. * *adj* superficial; external. * *vt* to cover with a surface, as in paving. * *vi* to rise to the surface of water.
surfboard *n* a long, narrow board used in the sport of surfing.
surfeit *n* an excessive amount.
surfing *n* the sport of riding in toward shore on the crest of a wave, esp on a surfboard.
surge *n* the rolling of the sea, as after a large wave; a sudden, strong increase, as of power.—*also vi*.
surgeon *n* a medical specialist who practices surgery.
surgery *n* the treatment of diseases or injuries by manual or instrumental operations; the consulting room of a doctor or dentist; the daily period when a doctor is available for consultation; the regular period when an MP, lawyer, etc is available for consultation.—**surgical** *adj*.—**surgically** *adv*.
surmise *n* guess, conjecture. * *vt* to infer the existence of from partial evidence.
surmount *vt* to overcome; to rise above.
surname *n* the family name. * *vt* to give a surname to.
surpass *vt* to outdo, to outshine; to excel; to exceed.
surplus *n* an amount in excess of what is required; an excess of revenues over expenditure in a financial year.
surprise *n* the act of catching unawares; an unexpected gift, event; astonishment. * *vt* to cause to feel astonished; to attack unexpectedly; to take unawares.—**surprising** *adj*.—**surprisingly** *adv*.
surreal *adj* bizarre.
surrender *vt* to relinquish or give up possession or power. * *vi* to give oneself up (to an enemy).—*also n*.
surreptitious *adj* done by stealth; clandestine, secret.—**surreptitiously** *adv*.
surround *vt* to encircle on all or nearly all sides; (*mil*) to encircle. * *n* a border around the edge of something.
surroundings *npl* the conditions, objects, etc around a person or thing; the environment.
surveillance *n* a secret watch kept over a person, esp a suspect.
survey *vt* to take a general view of; to appraise; to examine carefully; to measure and make a map of an area. * *n* a detailed study, as by gathering information and analysing it, a general view; the process of surveying an area or a house.
surveyor *n* a person who surveys land or buildings.
survival *n* surviving; a person or thing that survives; a relic.
survive *vt* to live after the death of another person; to continue, endure; to come through alive. * *vi* to remain alive (after experiencing a dangerous situation).—**survivor** *n*.
susceptible *adj* ready or liable to be affected by; impressionable.—**susceptibility** *n*.—**susceptibly** *adv*.
suspect *vt* to mistrust; to believe to be guilty; to think probable. * *n* a person under suspicion. * *adj* open to suspicion.
suspend *vt* to hang; to discontinue, or cease temporarily; to postpone; to debar temporarily from a privilege, etc.
suspender *n* a fastener for holding up stockings; (*pl*) braces.
suspense *n* mental anxiety or uncertainty; excitement.
suspension *n* suspending or being suspended; a temporary interruption or postponement; a temporary removal from office, privileges, etc; the system of springs, shock absorbers, etc that support a vehicle on its axles; (*chem*) a dispersion of fine particles in a liquid.
suspension bridge *n* a bridge carrying a roadway suspended by cables anchored to towers at either end.
suspicion *n* act of suspecting; a belief formed or held without sure proof; mistrust; a trace.—**suspicious** *adj*.—**suspiciously** *adv*.
sustain *vt* hold up, support; to maintain; to suffer (eg an injury); to nourish.
sustenance *n* nourishment.
swab *n* a wad of absorbent material, usu cotton, used to clean wounds, take specimens, etc; a mop.—*also vt*.

swagger *vi* to strut; to brag loudly. * *n* boastfulness; swinging gait.

swallow[1] *n* a small migratory bird with long wings and a forked tail.

swallow[2] *vt* to cause food and drink to move from the mouth to the stomach; to endure; to engulf; (*inf*) to accept gullibly; (*emotion, etc*) to repress.—*also n.*

swam *see* **swim**.

swamp *n* wet, spongy land; bog. * *vt* to overwhelm; to flood as with water.—**swampy** *adj.*

swan *n* a large, usu white, bird with a very long neck that lives on rivers and lakes. * *vi* (*pt* **swanned**) (*inf*) to wander aimlessly.

swap *vti* (*pt* **swapped**) (*inf*) to trade, barter. * *n* (*inf*) the act of exchanging one thing for another.—*also* **swop**.

swarm *n* a colony of migrating bees; a moving mass, crowd or throng. * *vi* to move in great numbers; to teem.

swarthy *adj* (**swarthier, swarthiest**) dark-complexioned.—**swarthiness** *n.*

swat *vt* (*pt* **swatted**) (*inf*) to hit with a sharp blow; to swipe.—*also n.*—**swatter** *n.*

sway *vi* to swing or move from one side to the other or to and fro; to lean to one side; to vacillate in judgment or opinion. * *n* influence; control.

swear *vi* (*pt* **swore,** *pp* **sworn**) to make a solemn affirmation, promise, etc, calling God as a witness; to give evidence on oath; to curse, blaspheme or use obscene language; to vow.

sweat *n* perspiration; (*inf*) hard work; (*inf*) a state of eagerness, anxiety.—*also vti.*—**sweaty** *adj.*

sweater *n* a knitted pullover.

Swede *n* a native of Sweden.

swede *n* a round root vegetable with yellow flesh.

Swedish *adj* pertaining to Sweden, its people or language. * *n* the language of Sweden.

sweep *vb* (*pt* **swept**) *vt* to clean with a broom; to remove (rubbish, dirt) with a brush. * *vi* to pass by swiftly. * *n* a movement, esp in an arc; a stroke; scope, range; a sweepstake.

sweeping *adj* wide-ranging; indiscriminate.—**sweepingly** *adv.*

sweet *adj* having a taste like sugar; pleasing to other senses; gentle; kind. * *n* a small piece of confectionery; a dessert.—**sweetly** *adv.*—**sweetness** *n.*

sweetbread *n* the pancreas or thymus of an animal used for food.

sweetcorn *n* maize, corn on the cob.

sweeten *vti* to make or become sweet or sweeter; to mollify.

sweetheart *n* a lover.

swell *vi* (*pt* **swelled,** *pp* **swollen** *or* **swelled**) to increase in size or volume; to rise into waves; to bulge out. * *n* the movement of the sea; a bulge; a gradual increase in the loudness of a musical note; (*inf*) a socially prominent person. * *adj* excellent.

swelling *n* inflammation.

swelter *vi* to suffer from heat. * *n* humid, oppressive heat.

swept *see* **sweep**.

swerve *vi* to turn aside suddenly from a line or course; to veer.—*also n.*

swift *adj* moving with great speed; rapid. * *n* a swallow-like bird.—**swiftly** *adv.*—**swiftness** *n.*

swig *vt* (*pt* **swigged**) (*inf*) to take a long drink, esp from a bottle.—*also n.*

swill *vti* to drink greedily; to guzzle; to rinse with a large amount of water. * *n* liquid refuse fed to pigs.

swim *vi* (*pt* **swam,** *pp* **swum**) to move through water by using limbs or fins; to be dizzy; to be flooded with. * *n* the act of swimming.—**swimmer** *n.*

swimming costume, swimsuit *n* a one-piece garment for swinning in.

swindle *vti* to cheat (someone) of money or property.—*also n.*—**swindler** *n.*

swine *n* (*pl* **swine**) a pig; (*inf*) an contemptible person; (*inf*) an unpleasant thing.

swing *vb* (*pt* **swung**) *vi* to sway or move to and fro, as an object hanging in air; to pivot; to shift from one mood or opinion to another; (*music*) to have a lively rhythm; (*sl*) to be hanged. * *vt* to whirl; to play swing music; to influence; to achieve, bring about. * *n* a swinging, curving or rhythmic movement; a suspended seat for swinging in; a shift from one condition to another; a type of popular jazz played by a large band and characterized by a lively, steady rhythm.

swinging *adj* (*inf*) up-to-date; lively.

swipe *n* (*inf*) a hard, sweeping blow. * *vt* (*inf*) to hit with a swipe; (*sl*) to steal.

swirl *vti* to turn with a whirling motion.—*also n.*

swish *vi* to move with a soft, whistling, hissing sound. * *n* a swishing sound. * *adj* (*inf*) smart, fashionable.

Swiss *adj* of or belonging to Switzerland. * *n* (*pl* **Swiss**) a native of Switzerland.

switch *n* a control for turning on and off an electrical device; a sudden change; a swap. * *vt* to shift, change, swap; to turn on or off (as of an electrical device).
switchback *n* a zigzag road in a mountain region; a roller coaster.
switchboard *n* an installation in a building where telephone calls are connected.
swivel *n* a coupling that permits parts to rotate. * *vi* (*pt* **swivelled**) to turn (as if) on a pin or pivot.
swoon *vt* to faint.—*also n.*
swoop *vt* to carry off abruptly. * *vi* to make a sudden attack (*usu with* **down**) as a bird in hunting.—*also n.*
swop *see* **swap**.
sword *n* a weapon with a long blade and a handle a one end.
swordfish *n* a large marine fish with a sword-like upper jaw.
swore, sworn *see* **swear**.
swot *vi* (*pt* **swotted**) (*inf*) to study hard for an examination. * *n* (*inf*) a person who studies hard.
syllable *n* word or part of a word uttered by in a single sound; one or more letters written to represent a spoken syllable.
syllabus *n* (*pl* **syllabuses**) a summary or outline of a course of study or of examination requirements; the subjects studied for a particular course.
symbol *n* a representation; an object used to represent something abstract; an arbitrary or conventional sign standing for a quality, process, relation, etc as in music, chemistry, mathematics, etc.
symbolic, symbolical *adj* of, using, or constituting a symbol.—**symbolically** *adv*.
symbolism *n* the use of symbols; a system of symbolic representation.—**symbolist** *n*.
symbolize *vt* to be a symbol; to represent by a symbol.—**symbolization** *n*.
symmetrical, symmetric *adj* having symmetry.
symmetry *n* the corresponding arrangement of one part to another in size, shape and position; balance or harmony of form resulting form this.
sympathetic *adj* having sympathy; compassionate.—**sympathetically** *adv*.
sympathize *vi* feel sympathy for; to commiserate; to be in sympathy (with).
sympathy *n* agreement of ideas and opinions; compassion; (*pl*) support for an action or cause.
symphony *n* an orchestral composition in several movements; a large orchestra for playing symphonic works.—**symphonic** *adj*.—**symphonically** *adv*.
symposium *n* (*pl* **symposiums, symposia**) a conference at which several specialists deliver short addresses on a topic; an anthology of scholarly essays.
symptom *n* a bodily sensation experienced by a patient indicative of a particular disease; an indication.
synagogue *n* the building where Jews assemble for worship and religious study.
synchronize *vti* to occur at the same time and speed; (*watches*) to adjust to show the same time.—**synchronization** *n*.
syndicate *n* an association of individuals or corporations formed for a project requiring much capital; any group, as of criminals, organized for some undertaking; an organization selling articles or features to many newspapers, etc. * *vt* to manage as or form into a syndicate; to sell (an article, etc) through a syndicate. * *vi* to form a syndicate.—**syndication** *n*.
syndrome *n* a characteristic pattern of signs and symptoms of a disease.
synonym *n* a word that has the same, or similar, meaning as another or others in the same language.
synonymous *adj* having the same meaning; equivalent.
synopsis *n* (*pl* **synopses**) a summary or brief review of a subject.
syntax *n* (*gram*) the arrangement of words in the sentences and phrases of language; the rules governing this.—**syntactic** *adj*.—**syntactically** *adv*.
synthesis *n* (*pl* **syntheses**) the process of combining separate elements of thought into a whole; the production of a compound by a chemical reaction.
synthetic *adj* produced by chemical synthesis; artificial.—**synthetically** *adv*.
syphilis *n* a contagious, infectious venereal disease.—**syphilitic** *adj*.
syphon *see* **siphon**.
syringe *n* a hollow tube with plunger at one end and a sharp needle at the other by which liquids are injected or withdrawn, esp in medicine. * *vt* to inject or cleanse with a syringe.
syrup *n* a thick sweet substance made by boiling sugar with water; the concentrated juice of a fruit or plant.—**syrupy** *adj*.

system *n* a method of working or organizing by following a set of rules; routine; organization; structure; a political regime; an arrangement of parts fitting together.

systematic *adj* constituting or based on a system; according to a system.—**systematically** *adv*.

systems analysis *n* analysis of a particular task or operation to determine how computer hardware and software may best perform it. —**systems analyst** *n*.

T

tab *n* a small tag, label or flap; (*inf*) a bill, as for expenses. * *vt* to fix a tab on.

tabby *n* a domestic cat with a striped coat, esp a female.

table *n* a piece of furniture consisting of a slab or board on legs; the people seated round a table; supply of food; a list arranged for reference or comparison. * *vt* to submit, put forward; to postpone indefinitely. * *adj* of, on or at a table.

tablecloth *n* a cloth for covering a table.

table d'hôte *n* (*pl* **tables d'hôte**) a meal at a fixed price for a set number of courses.—*also adj*.

tablespoon *n* a large serving spoon; a unit of measure in cooking.—**tablespoonful** *n*.

tablet *n* a pad of paper; a medicinal pill; a cake of solid substance, such as soap; a slab of stone.

table tennis *n* a game like tennis played on a table with small bats and balls.

taboo, tabu *n* a religious or social prohibition.—*also adj*.

tabulate *vt* to arrange (written material) in the form of a table.—**tabulation** *n*

tacit *adj* implied without being spoken; understood.—**tacitly** *adj*.

taciturn *adj* habitually silent and reserved.—**taciturnity** *n*.

tack[1] *n* a short, flat-headed nail; the course of a sailing ship; a course of action, approach; adhesiveness. * *vt* to fasten with tacks. * *vi* to change direction.

tack[2] *n* (*inf*) food.

tackle *n* a system of ropes and pulleys for lifting; equipment; rigging; (*sport*) an act of grabbing and stopping an opponent. * *vt* (*task, etc*) to attend to, undertake; (*a person*) to confront; (*sport*) to challenge with a tackle.

tacky *adj* (**tackier, tackiest**) (*paint, etc*) sticky.

tact *n* discretion in managing the feelings of others.—**tactful** *adj*.—**tactless** *adj*.

tactics *n sing* stratagem; ploy; the science or art of manoeuvring troops in the presence of the enemy.—**tactical** *adj*.—**tactician** *n*.

tadpole *n* the larva of a frog or toad, esp at the stage when the head and tail have developed.

tag[1] *n* a strip or label for identification. * *vt* to attach a tag; to mark with a tag. * *vi* (*with* **onto, after**) to trail along (behind).

tag[2] *n* a children's chasing game.

tail *n* the appendage of an animal growing from the rear; the rear part of anything; (*pl*) the side of a coin without a head on it; (*inf*) a person who keeps another under surveillance, esp a detective. * *vt* to follow closely, shadow.

tail coat *n* a man's black or grey coat cut horizontally just below the waist at the front with two long tails at the back.

tail-end *adj* tardy; being the last in line. * *n* the last.

tailor *n* a person who makes and repairs outer garments, esp. men's suits. * *vi* to work as a tailor. * *vt* to adapt to fit a particular requirement.

tailor-made *adj* specially designed for a particular purpose or person.

taint *vt* to contaminate; to infect. * *vi* to be corrupted or disgraced. * *n* a stain; corruption.

take *vb* (*pt* **took**, *pp* **taken**) *vt* to lay hold of; to grasp or seize; to gain, win; to choose, select; (*attitude, pose*) to adopt; to understand; to consume; to accept or agree to; to lead or carry with one; to use as a means of travel; (*math*) to subtract (from); to use; to steal; (*gram*) to be used with; to endure calmly. * *vi* (*plant, etc*) to start growing successfully; to become effective; to catch on; to have recourse to; to go to. * *n* (*film, TV*) the amount of film used without stopping the camera.

takeoff *n* the process of an aircraft becoming airborne.

takeover *n* the taking over of control, as in business.

taking *adj* attractive, charming; (*inf*) catching, contagious. * *n* the act of one that takes; (*pl*) earnings; profits.

talc *n* a type of smooth mineral used in ceramics and talcum powder; talcum powder.

talcum powder *n* perfumed powdered talc for the skin.

tale *n* a narrative or story; a fictitious account, a lie; idle or malicious gossip.

talent *n* any innate or special aptitude.—**talented** *adj.*

talk *vti* to speak; to converse; to discuss; to gossip; to divulge information. * *n* a discussion; a lecture; gossip; (*pl*) negotiations.

talkative *adj* given to talking a great deal.

tall *adj* above average in height; (*inf: story*) exaggerated.—**tallness** *n.*

tallboy *n* a high chest of drawers.

tally *n* reckoning, account; one score in a game. * *vi* to correspond; to keep score.

tambourine *n* a percussion hand instrument made of skin stretched over a circular frame with small jingling metal discs around the edge.

tame *adj* (*animal*) not wild, domesticated; compliant; dull, uninteresting. * *vt* (*animal*) to domesticate; to subdue; to soften.

tamper *vi* to meddle (with); to interfere (with).

tampon *n* a firm plug of cotton wool inserted in the vagina during menstruation.

tan *n* a yellowish-brown colour; suntan. * *vti* (*pt* **tanned**) to acquire a suntan through sunbathing; (*skin, hide*) to convert into leather by processing.

tandem *n* a bicycle for two riders, one behind the other.

tang *n* sharp smell or a strong taste.—**tangy** *adj.*

tangent *n* a line that touches a curve or circle at one point, without crossing it. * *adj* touching at one point.

tangerine *n* a small, sweet orange with a loose skin; the colour of this.—*also adj.*

tangible *adj* capable of being felt, seen or noticed; substantial; real.—**tangibility** *n.*

tangle *n* a mass of hair, string or wire knotted together confusedly; a complication. * *vi* to become tangled or complicated; (*with* **with**) to become involved in argument with.

tango *n* (*pl* **tangos**) a Latin American dance.—*also vi.*

tank *n* a large container for storing liquids or gases; an armoured combat vehicle, mounted with guns and having caterpillar tracks.

tankard *n* a tall, one-handled beer mug, often with a hinged lid.

tanker *n* a large ship or truck for transporting oil and other liquids.

tantalize *vt* to tease or torment by presenting something greatly desired, but keeping it inaccessible.

tantamount *adj* equivalent (to) in effect; as good as.

tantrum *n* a childish fit of bad temper.

tap[1] *n* a quick, light blow or touch; a piece of metal attached to the heel or toe of a shoe for reinforcement or to tap-dance. * *vti* (*pt* **tapped**) to strike lightly; to make a tapping sound.

tap[2] *n* a device controlling the flow of liquid through a pipe or from a container. * *vt* to pierce in order to draw fluid from; to connect a secret listening device to a telephone; (*inf*) to ask for money from; (*resources, etc*) to draw on.

tap-dance *vi* to perform a step dance in shoes with taps.—**tap-dancer** *n.*—**tap-dancing** *n.*

tape *n* a strong, narrow strip of cloth, paper, etc, used for tying, binding, etc; a tape measure; magnetic tape, as in a cassette or videotape. * *vt* to wrap with tape; to record on magnetic tape.

tape measure *n* a tape marked in inches or centimetres for measuring.

taper *n* a long thin candle. * *vti* to make or to become gradually narrower towards one end.—**tapering** *adj.*

tape recorder *n* a machine for recording and reproducing sounds or music on magnetic tape.—*also* **tape deck**.

tapestry *n* a heavy fabric woven with patterns or figures, used for wall hangings and furnishings.

tapioca *n* a starch extracted from the root of a tropical plant and used in puddings, etc.

tar *n* a thick, dark gluey substance obtained from wood, coal, peat, etc., used for surfacing roads. * *vt* to coat with tar.—**tarry** *adj.*

tarantula *n* a large, hairy spider with a poisonous bite.

tardy *adj* (**tardier, tardiest**) slow; later than expected.—**tardily** *adv.* —**tardiness** *n.*

target *n* a mark to aim at, esp in shooting; an objective or ambition.

tariff *n* a tax on imports; (*in a hotel*) a list of prices; the rate of charge for public services, such as gas or electricity.

Tarmac, Tarmacadam *n* (*trademark*) a material for surfacing roads made from crushed stones and tar; an airport runway. * *vti* (*pt* **tarmacked**) to lay down a tarmac surface.

tarnish *vi* (*metal*) to lose its lustre or discolour due to exposure to the air. * *vt* (*reputation*) to taint.—*also n.*

tarpaulin *n* canvas cloth coated with a waterproof substance.

tart[1] *adj* having a sour, sharp taste; (*speech*) sharp, severe. —**tartly** *adv.*—**tartness** *n.*

tart[2] *n* an open pastry case containing fruit, jam or custard; (*inf*) a prostitute.

tartan *n* a woollen cloth with a chequered pattern, having a distinctive design for each Scottish clan.

tartar *n* a hard, yellow, crusty deposit that forms on the teeth; a salty deposit on the sides of wine casks.

tartar sauce *n* a mayonnaise sauce with herbs, etc, eaten esp with fish.

task *n* a specific amount of work to be done; a chore.

task force *n* a small unit with a specific mission, usu military.

tassel *n* an ornamental tuft of silken threads decorating soft furnishings, clothes, etc.—**tasselled** *adj*.

taste *vt* to perceive (a flavour) by taking into the mouth; to try by eating and drinking a little; to sample; to experience. * *vi* to try by the mouth; to have a specific flavour. * *n* the sense by which flavours are perceived; a small portion; the ability to recognize what is beautiful, attractive, etc; liking; a brief experience.

tasteful *adj* showing good taste.—**tastefully** *adv*.—**tastefulness** *n*.

tasteless *adj* without taste, bland; in bad taste.—**tastelessly** *adv*.

tasty *adj* (**tastier, tastiest**) savoury; having a pleasant flavour.

tatter *n* a torn or ragged piece of cloth.—**tattered** *adj*.

tattoo[1] *n* (*pl* **tattoos**) a continuous beating of a drum; a military display of exercises and music.

tattoo[2] *vt* to make permanent patterns or pictures on the skin by pricking and marking with dyes. * *n* (*pl* **tattoos**) marks made on the skin in this way.

tatty *adj* (**tattier, tattiest**) shabby, ragged.

taught *see* **teach**.

taunt *vt* to provoke with mockery or contempt; to tease. * *n* an insult.

Taurus *n* the Bull, the second sign of the zodiac.

taut *adj* stretched tight; tense; stressed.

tavern *n* a pub, an inn.

tawdry *adj* (**tawdrier, tawdriest**) showy, cheap, and of poor quality.

tawny *adj* yellowish brown.

tax *n* a rate imposed by the government on property or persons to raise revenues; a strain. * *vt* to impose a tax (upon); to strain.

taxation *n* the act of levying taxes; the amount so raised.

taxi, taxicab *n* a car, usu fitted with a taximeter, that may be hired to transport passengers. * *vi* (*pr p* **taxiing,** *pt* **taxied**) (*aircraft*) to move along the runway before takeoff or after landing.

taxpayer *n* a person who or an organization that pays taxes.

TB *abbr* = tuberculosis.

tea *n* a shrub growing in China, India, Sri Lanka, etc; its dried, shredded leaves, which are infused in boiling water for a beverage; a light meal taken in mid-afternoon; a main meal taken in the early evening.

tea bag *n* a small porous bag containing tea leaves for infusing.

teach *vb* (*pt* **taught**) *vt* to impart knowledge to; to give lessons (to); to train; to help to learn. * *vi* to give instruction, esp as a profession.—**teachable** *adj*.

teacher *n* a person who instructs others, esp as an occupation.

teaching *n* the profession or practice of being a teacher; the act of giving instruction.

teacup *n* a small cup for drinking tea.

teak *n* a type of hard wood from an East Indian tree.

team *n* a group of people participating in a sport together; a group of people working together; two or more animals pulling a vehicle. * *vi* (*with* **up**) to join in cooperative activity.

teamwork *n* cooperation of individuals for the benefit of the team; the ability of a team to work together.

teapot *n* a vessel in which tea is made.

tear[1] *n* a drop of salty liquid appearing in the eyes when crying; anything tear-shaped.

tear[2] *vb* (*pt* **tore,** *pp* **torn**) *vt* to pull apart by force; to split. * *vi* to move with speed. * *n* a hole or split.

tearful *adj* weeping; sad.—**tearfully** *adv*.

tear gas *n* gas that irritates the eyes and nasal passages, used in riot control.

tease *vt* to separate the fibres of; to torment or irritate; to taunt playfully. * *n* a person who teases or torments; (*inf*) a flirt.—**teaser** *n*.

tea service, tea set *n* the set of cups and saucers, etc for serving tea.

teaspoon *n* a small spoon for use with tea or as a measure; the amount measured by this.—**teaspoonful** *n*.

teat *n* the nipple on a breast or udder; the mouthpiece of a baby's feeding bottle.

tea towel, tea cloth *n* a towel for drying dishes.

technical *adj* relating to, or specializing in practical, industrial, mechanical or applied sciences; (*expression, etc*) belonging to or peculiar to a particular field of activity.—**technically** *adv.*

technicality *n* a petty formality or technical point.

technician *n* a person skilled in the practice of any art, esp in practical work with scientific equipment.

technique *n* method of performing a particular task; knack.

technology *n* the application of mechanical and applied sciences to industrial use.—**technological** *adj.*—**technologist** *n.*

teddy bear *n* a stuffed toy bear.

tedious *adj* monotonous; boring.—**tedium** *n.*

tee *n* (*golf*) the place from where the first stroke is played at each hole; a small peg from which the ball is driven. * *vti* to position (the ball) on the tee.

teem[1] *vi* (*with* **with**) to be prolific or abundant in.

teem[2] *vi* to pour (with rain).

teenager *n* (*inf*) a person who is in his or her teens.

teens *npl* the years of one's life from thir*teen* to nine*teen*.—**teenage** *adj.*—**teenaged** *adj.*

tee-shirt *see* **T-shirt**.

teeter *vi* to move or stand unsteadily.

teeth *see* **tooth**.

teethe *vi* to cut one's first teeth.

teething *n* the condition in babies of the first growth of teeth.

teething troubles *npl* problems encountered in the early stages of a project, etc; pain caused by growing teeth.

teetotaller, teetotaler (*US*) *n* a person who abstains from alcoholic drinks.—**teetotal** *adj.*

telecommunication *n* communication of information over long distances by telephone and radio; (*pl*) the technology of telephone and radio communication.

telegram *n* a message sent by telegraph.

telegraph *n* a system for transmitting messages over long distances using electricity, wires and a code. * *vt* to transmit by telegraph.—**telegraphic** *adj.*—**telegraphy** *n.*

telepathy *n* the communication between people's minds of thoughts and feelings, without the need for speech or proximity.—**telepathic** *adj.*

telephone *n* an instrument for transmitting speech at a distance, esp by means of electricity. * *vt* (*someone*) to call by telephone.

telephonist *n* a person who operates a telephone switchboard.—*also* **telephone operator**.

telephoto lens *n* a camera lens that magnifies distant objects.

teleprinter *n* a telegraph apparatus with a keyboard that transmits and a printer that receives messages over a distance.

telescope *n* a tubular optical instrument for viewing objects at a distance.

televise *vt* (*a programme*) to transmit by television.

television *n* the transmission of visual images and accompanying sound through electrical and sound waves; a television receiving set; television broadcasting.

tell *vb* (*pt* **told**) *vt* to narrate; to disclose; to inform; to notify; to instruct to distinguish. * *vi* to tell tales, to inform on; to produce a marked effect.

teller *n* a bank clerk; a person appointed to count votes in an election.

telling *adj* having great impact.

telltale *n* a person who tells tales about others. * *adj* revealing what is meant to be hidden.

telly *n* (*inf*) television.

temerity *n* rashness.

temp *n* (*inf*) a temporary employee.

temp. *abbr* = temperature.

temper *n* a frame of mind; a fit of anger. * *vt* to tone down, moderate; (*steel*) to heat and cool repeatedly to bring to the correct hardness.

temperament *n* one's disposition.

temperamental *adj* easily irritated; erratic.—**temperamentally** *adv.*

temperance *n* moderation; abstinence from alcohol.

temperate *adj* mild or moderate in temperature; (*behaviour*) moderate, self-controlled.

temperature *n* degree of heat or cold; body heat above the normal.

tempest *n* a violent storm.

template *n* a pattern, gauge or mould used as a guide esp in cutting metal, stone or plastic.

temple[1] *n* a place of worship.

temple[2] *n* the region on either side of the head above the cheekbone.

tempo *n* (*pl* **tempos, tempi**) (*mus*) the speed at which music is meant to be played; rate of any activity.

temporal[1] *adj* relating to time; secular, civil.

temporal[2] *adj* of or relating to the temples of the head.

temporary *adj* lasting or used for a limited time only; not permanent.—**temporarily** *adv.*

tempt *vt* to entice to do wrong; to invite, attract, induce.—**tempter** *n.*—**temptress** *nf.*

temptation *n* the act of tempting or the state of

being tempted; something or someone that tempts.

tempting *adj* attractive, inviting.

ten *adj, n* the cardinal number next above nine. * *n* the symbol for this (10, X, x).

tenacious *adj* grasping firmly; persistent; retentive; adhesive.

tenacity *n* the state or quality of being tenacious; doggedness, obstinacy; adhesiveness, stickiness.

tenancy *n* the temporary possession by a tenant of another's property; the period of this.

tenant *n* a person who pays rent to occupy a house or flat or for the use of land or buildings; an occupant.

tend[1] *vt* to take care of; to attend (to).

tend[2] *vi* to be inclined; to move in a specific direction.

tendency *n* an inclination or leaning.

tender[1] *n* a wagon attached to locomotives to carry fuel and water; a small ship that brings stores to a larger one.

tender[2] *vt* to present for acceptance; to offer as payment. * *vi* to make an offer. * *n* an offer to provide goods or services at a fixed price.

tender[3] *adj* soft, delicate; fragile; painful, sore; sensitive; sympathetic.—**tenderly** *adv*.—**tenderness** *n*.

tenderize *vt* (*meat*) to make more tender, esp by pounding.

tendon *n* fibrous tissue attaching a muscle to a bone.

tenement *n* a building divided into flats, each occupied by a separate owner or tenant.

tenet *n* any belief or doctrine.

tennis *n* a game for two or four people, played by hitting a ball over a net with a racket.

tennis court *n* a court surfaced with clay, asphalt or grass on which tennis is played.

tenor *n* a general purpose or intent; the highest regular adult male voice, higher than a baritone and lower than an alto; a man who sings tenor.

tense[1] *n* (*gram*) the verb form that indicates the time of an action or the existence of a state.

tense[2] *adj* stretched, taut; apprehensive; nervous and highly strung. * *vti* to make or become tense.—**tensely** *adv*.—**tenseness** *n*.

tension *n* the act of stretching; the state of being stretched; (*between forces, etc*) opposition; stress; mental strain.

tent *n* a portable shelter of canvas, plastic or other waterproof fabric, which is erected on poles and fixed to the ground by ropes and pegs.

tentacle *n* a long, slender, flexible growth near the mouth of invertebrates, used for feeling, grasping or handling.

tentative *adj* provisional; not definite.—**tentatively** *adv*.—**tentativeness** *n*.

tenterhook *n* one of a series of hooks on which cloth is stretched to dry; (*pl: with* **on**) in a tense or anxious state.

tenth *adj* the last of ten; being one of ten equal parts. * *n* one of ten equal parts.

tenuous *adj* slight, flimsy, insubstantial.—**tenuousness** *n*.

tenure *n* the holding of property or a position; the period of time which a position lasts; a permanent job at a university.

tepid *adj* slightly warm, lukewarm.

term *n* a limit; any prescribed period of time; a division of an academic year; a word or expression, esp in a specialized field of knowledge; (*pl*) mutual relationship between people; (*pl*) conditions of a contract, etc. * *vt* to call, designate.

terminal *adj* being or situated at the end or extremity; (*disease*) fatal, incurable. * *n* a bus, coach or railway station at the end of the line; the point at which an electrical current enters or leaves a device; a device with a keyboard and monitor for inputting data into, or viewing it from, a computer.—**terminally** *adv*.

terminate *vti* to bring or come to an end.—**termination** *n*.

terminology *n* the terms used in any specialized subject.

terminus *n* (*pl* **termini, terminuses**) the final part; a limit; end of a transportation line.

termite *n* a wood-eating, white, ant-like insect.

terrace *n* a raised level area of earth, often part of a slope; an unroofed paved area between a house and a lawn; a row of houses; a patio or balcony; (*pl*) unroofed tiers in a football ground. * *vt* to make into a terrace.

terrain *n* the surface features of a tract of land; (*fig*) field of activity.

terrible *adj* causing great fear; dreadful; (*inf*) very unpleasant.

terribly *adv* frighteningly; (*inf*) very.

terrier *n* a type of small, active dog.

terrific *adj* of great size; (*inf*) excellent.

terrify *vt* to fill with terror, to frighten greatly.

territory *n* an area under the jurisdiction of a city or state; a wide tract of land; an area assigned to a sales person; an area of knowledge.

terror *n* great fear; an object or person inspiring fear or dread.
terrorism *n* the use of terror and violence to intimidate.— **terrorist** *n*.
terrorize *vt* to terrify; to control by terror.—**terrorization** *n*.
terse *adj* abrupt, to the point, concise.—**tersely** *adv*.
test *n* an examination; trial; a chemical reaction to test a substance or to test for an illness; a series of questions or exercises. * *vt* to examine critically.
testament *n* a will; proof; tribute; a covenant made by God with men; (*with cap*) one of the two main parts of the Bible.
test case *n* a legal action that establishes a precedent.
testicle *n* either of the two male reproductive glands that produce sperm.
testify *vti* to give evidence under oath; to serve as witness (to); (*with* **to**) to be evidence of.
testimonial *adj* relating to a testimony. * *n* a recommendation of one's character or abilities.
testimony *n* evidence; declaration of truth or fact.
testis *n* (*pl* **testes**) testicle.
test match *n* one of a series of international cricket or Rugby football matches.
test pilot *n* someone who flies new types of aircraft to test their performance and characteristics.
test tube *n* a cylinder of thin glass closed at one end, used in scientific experiments.
testy *adj* (**testier, testiest**) touchy, irritable.
tetanus *n* an intense and painful spasm of muscles, caused by the infection of a wound by bacteria; lockjaw.
tether *n* a rope or chain for tying an animal; the limit of one's endurance. * *vt* to fasten with a tether; to limit.
text *n* the main part of a printed work; the original or exact wording; a passage from the Bible forming the basis of a sermon; a subject or topic; a textbook.—**textual** *adj*.
textbook *n* a book used as a basis for instruction.
textile *n* a woven fabric or cloth. * *adj* relating to the making of fabrics.
texture *n* the characteristic appearance, arrangement or feel of a thing; the way in which threads in fabric are woven together.—**textural** *adj*.
than *conj* introducing the second element of a comparison.
thank *vt* to express gratitude to or appreciation for. * *npl* an expression of gratitude.—**thankful** *adj*.—**thankfully** *adv*.
thankless *adj* without thanks; unappreciated; fruitless, unrewarding.—**thanklessness** *n*.
Thanksgiving Day *n* a US legal holiday observed on the fourth Thursday of November.
that *demons adj, pron* (*pl* **those**) the (one) there or then, esp the latter or more distant thing. * *rel pron* who or which. * *conj* introducing noun clause or adverbial clause of purpose or consequence; because; in order that; (*preceded by* **so**, **such**) as a result.
thatch *n* roofing straw. * *vt* to cover a roof with thatch.
thaw *vi* to melt or grow liquid; to become friendly. * *vt* to cause to melt. * *n* the melting of ice or snow by warm weather.
the *demons adj* denoting a particular person or thing. * *adv* used before comparative adjectives or adverbs for emphasis.
theatre, theater (*US*) *n* a building where plays and operas are performed; the theatrical world as a whole; a setting for important events; field of operations.
theatrical *adj* relating to the theatre; melodramatic, affected.—**theatrically** *adv*.
theft *n* act or crime of stealing.
their *poss adj* of or belonging to them; his, hers, its.
theirs *poss pron* of or belonging to them; his, hers, its.
them *pron* the objective case of **they**.
theme *n* the main subject of a discussion; an idea or motif in a work; a short essay; a leading melody.—**thematic** *adj*.
themselves *pron* the reflexive form of **they** or **them**.
then *adv* at that time; afterwards; immediately; next in time. * *conj* for that reason; in that case.
theologian *n* a person who studies and interprets religious texts, etc; a teacher of theology.
theology *n* the study of God and of religious doctrine and matters of divinity.
theorem *n* a proposition that can be proved from accepted principles; law or principle.
theoretical *adj* of or based on theory, not practical application; hypothetical; conjectural.
theorize *vi* to form theories; to speculate.—**theorist** *n*.
theory *n* an explanation or system of anything; ideas and abstract principles of a science or art; speculation; a hypothesis.

therapeutic *adj* relating to the treatment of disease; beneficial.
therapy *n* the treatment of physical or mental illness.—**therapist** *n*.
there *adv* in, at or to, that place or point; in that respect; in that matter.
thereabouts *adv* at or near that place or number.
thereafter *adv* after that; according to that.
therefore *adv* for that or this reason; consequently.
therein *adv* in that place or respect.
thereon *adv* on that or it; immediately following that.
therm *n* a measurement of heat.
thermal *adj* generating heat; hot; warm; (*underwear*) of a knitted material with air spaces for insulation. * *n* a rising current of warm air.
thermometer *n* an instrument for measuring temperature.
thermonuclear *adj* of or relating to nuclear fusion or nuclear weapons that utilize fusion reactions.
Thermos *n* (*trademark*) a brand of vacuum flask.
thermostat *n* an automatic device for regulating temperatures.
thesaurus *n* (*pl* **thesauri, thesauruses**) a reference book of synonyms.
these *see* **this**.
thesis *n* (*pl* **theses**) a detailed essay written as part of a university degree; a theory expressed as a statement for discussion.
they *pers pron, pl of* **he**, **she** *or* **it**.
thick *adj* dense; fat, broad; abundant, closely set; in quick succession; crowded; (*inf*) stupid. * *adv* closely; frequently.
thicken *vti* to make or become thick.
thickset *adj* having a short, stocky body.
thick-skinned *adj* not sensitive.
thief *n* (*pl* **thieves**) a person who steals.
thigh *n* the thick part of the leg from the hip to the knee.
thimble *n* a cap or cover worn to protect the finger when sewing.
thin *adj* (**thinner, thinnest**) narrow; slim; lean; sparse, weak, watery; (*material*) fine; not dense. * *vt* to make thin; to make less crowded; to water down.—**thinly** *adv*.—**thinness** *n*.
thing *n* an inanimate object; an event; an action; (*pl*) possessions; (*inf*) an obsession.
think *vb* (*pt* **thought**) *vi* to exercise the mind in order to make a decision; to revolve ideas in the mind, to ponder; to remember; to consider. * *vt* to judge, to believe or consider; (*with* **up**) to concoct, devise.—**thinker** *n*.
third *adj* the last of three; being one of three equal parts. * *n* one of three equal parts.
thirdly *adv* in the third place; as a third point.
third party *n* (*insurance*) involving a third person.
third rate *adj* inferior.
Third World *n* the underdeveloped countries of the world (usu refers to Africa, Asia and South America).
thirst *n* a craving for drink; a longing. * *vi* to feel thirst; to have a longing.
thirsty *adj* (**thirstier, thirstiest**) having a desire to drink; dry, arid; longing or craving for.—**thirstily** *adv*.—**thirstiness** *n*.
thirteen *adj, n* three and ten.—**thirteenth** *adj, n*.
thirty *adj, n* three times ten.—**thirtieth** *adj, n*.
this *demons pron or adj* (*pl* **these**) denoting a person or thing near, just mentioned, or about to be mentioned.
thistle *n* a wild plant with prickly leaves and a purple flower.
thong *n* a piece or strap of leather to lash things together; the lash of a whip.
thorn *n* a shrub or small tree having thorns, esp hawthorn; a sharp point or prickle on the stem of a plant or the branch of a tree.
thorny *adj* (**thornier, thorniest**) prickly; (*problem*) knotty.
thorough *adj* complete, very detailed and painstaking, exhaustive.—**thoroughness** *n*.
thoroughbred *adj* bred from pure stock. * *n* a pedigree animal, esp a horse.
thoroughfare *n* a way through; a street; right of passing through.
thoroughly *adv* completely, fully; entirely, absolutely.
those *adj, pron, pl* of **that**.
though *conj* yet, even if. * *adv* however; nevertheless.
thought *pt, pp of* **think**. * *n* the act of thinking; reasoning; serious consideration; an idea; opinions collectively; design, intention.
thoughtful *adj* pensive; considerate.
thoughtless *adj* without thought; inconsiderate.
thousand *adj* ten times one hundred; (*pl*) denoting any large but unspecified number. * *n* the number 1000.—**thousandth** *adj, n*.
thrash *vt* to beat soundly; to defeat; (*with* **out**) to discuss thoroughly, until agreement is reached. * *vi* to thresh grain; to writhe.
thread *n* a fine strand or filament; a long thin piece of cotton, silk or nylon for sewing; the

spiral part of a screw; (*of reasoning*) a line. * *vt* to pass a thread through the eye of a needle; to make one's way (through).

threadbare *adj* worn, shabby.

threat *n* a declaration of an intention to inflict harm or punishment upon another.

threaten *vti* to utter threats to; to be a threat.

three *adj*, *n* the cardinal number next above two. * *n* the symbol (3, III, iii) expressing this.

three-dimensional *adj* having three dimensions.

thresh *vti* to beat out (grain) from (husks).

threshold *n* the sill at the door of a building; doorway, entrance; the starting point, beginning.

threw *see* **throw**.

thrift *n* careful management of money.—**thrifty** *adj*.

thrill *vti* to tingle with pleasure or excitement. * *n* a sensation of pleasure and excitement; a trembling or quiver.

thriller *n* a novel, film or play depicting an exciting story of mystery and suspense.

thrive *vi* (*pt* **thrived** *or* **throve**, *pp* **thrived** *or* **thriven**) to prosper, to be successful; to grow vigorously.—**thriving** *adj*.

throat *n* the front part of the neck; the passage from back of the mouth to the top part of the tubes into the lungs and stomach; an entrance.

throb *vi* (*pt* **throbbed**) to beat or pulsate rhythmically, with more than usual force; to vibrate.—*also n*.

throes *npl* violent pangs or pain.

thrombosis *n* (*pl* **thromboses**) the forming of a blood clot in the heart or in a blood vessel.

throne *n* a chair of state occupied by a monarch; sovereign power. * *vt* to place on a throne.

throttle *n* a valve controlling the flow of fuel or steam to an engine. * *vt* to choke or strangle.

through *prep* from one side or end to the other; into and then out of; covering all parts; from beginning to end of; by means of; in consequence of; up to and including. * *adv* from one end or side to the other; completely. * *adj* going without interruption; unobstructed.

throughout *prep* in every part of; from beginning to end. * *adv* everywhere; at every moment.

throw *vb* (*pt* **threw**, *pp* **thrown**) *vt* to hurl, to fling; to cast off; (*party*) to hold; (*inf*) to confuse or disconcert. * *vi* to cast or hurl through the air (with the arm and wrist); to cast dice. * *n* the act of throwing; the distance to which anything can be thrown; a cast of dice.

throwaway *adj* disposable.

throw-in *n* (*soccer*) a throw from touch to resume play.

thrush[1] *n* a bird with a brown back and spotted breast.

thrush[2] *n* a fungal disease occurring in the mouths of babies or in women's vaginas.

thrust *vti* (*pt* **thrust**) to push with force; to stab, pierce; to force into a situation. * *n* a forceful push or stab; pressure; the driving force of a propeller; forward movement; the point or basic meaning.

thud *n* a dull, heavy sound, caused by a blow or a heavy object falling. * *vi* (*pt* **thudded**) to make such a sound.

thug *n* a violent and rough person, esp a criminal.

thumb *n* the first, short, thick finger of the human hand. * *vt* (*book*) to turn (the pages) idly.

thumb index *n* a series of semicircular notches cut in the edge of a book for easier reference to particular parts.

thumbtack *n* a drawing pin.

thump *n* a heavy blow; a thud. * *vt* to strike with something heavy. * *vi* to throb or beat violently.

thunder *n* the deep rumbling or loud cracking sound after a flash of lightning; any similar sound. * *vi* to sound as thunder. * *vt* (*words*) to utter loudly.

thunderclap *n* a loud bang of thunder.

thunderous *adj* very loud; producing thunder.

thunderstorm *n* a storm with thunder and lightning.

thundery *adj* indicating thunder.

Thursday *n* the fifth day of the week.

thus *adv* in this or that way; to this degree or extent; so; therefore.

thwart *vt* to prevent, to frustrate.

thyme *n* a herb with small leaves used for flavouring savoury food.

thyroid *n* the gland in the neck affecting growth and metabolism.

tiara *n* a semicircular crown decorated with jewels.

tic *n* any involuntary, regularly repeated, spasmodic contraction of a muscle.

tick[1] *n* a small bloodsucking insect that lives on people and animals.

tick[2] *vi* to make a regular series of short sounds; to beat, as a clock; (*inf*) to work, function. * *n* the sound of a clock; a moment.

tick[3] *n* (*inf*) account, credit.
tick[4] *vt* (*often with* **off**) to check off, as items in a list. * *n* a check mark ( ) to check of f items on a list or to indicate correctness.
ticket *n* a printed card, etc, giving right of travel or entry; a label on merchandise giving size, price, etc.
tickle *vt* to touch lightly to provoke pleasure or laughter; to please or delight.
ticklish, tickly *adj* sensitive to being tickled; easily offended; difficult or delicate.
tidal *adj* relating to, or having, tides.
tiddlywinks *npl* a game whose object is to flick small plastic discs into a container by snapping them with a larger disc.
tide *n* the regular rise and fall of the seas, oceans, etc usu twice a day; a current of water; a tendency; a flood. * *vt* (*with* **over**) to help along temporarily.
tidy *adj* (**tidier, tidiest**) neat; orderly. * *vt* to make neat; to put things in order.—**tidily** *adv*.—**tidiness** *n*.
tie *vb* (*pr p* **tying,** *pt* **tied**) *vt* to bind; to fasten with a string or thread; to make a bow or knot in; to restrict. * *vi* to score the same number of points (as an opponent). * *n* a knot, bow, etc; a bond; a long narrow piece of cloth worn with a shirt; an equality in score.
tier *n* a row or rank in a series when several rows are placed one above another.
tiff *n* a petty quarrel or disagreement.
tiger *n* a large, fierce carnivorous animal of the cat family, having orange and black stripes.—**tigress** *nf*.
tight *adj* taut; fitting closely; not leaky; constricted; miserly; difficult; providing little space or time for variance; (*contest*) close; (*inf*) drunk.
tighten *vti* to make or grow tight or tighter
tightrope *n* a taut rope on which acrobats walk.
tights *npl* a one-piece garment covering the legs and lower body.
tile *n* a thin slab of baked clay used for covering roofs, floors, etc. * *vt* to cover with tiles.
till[1] *n* a drawer inside a cash register for keeping money.
till[2] *prep* until. * *conj* until.
till[3] *vt* (*land*) to cultivate for raising crops, as by ploughing.
tiller *n* the handle or lever for turning a rudder in order to steer a boat.
tilt *vi* to slope, incline, slant. * *vt* to raise one end of. * *n* a slope or angle.
timber *n* wood when used as construction material; a beam; trees collectively. * *vt* to provide with timber or beams.
time *n* the past, present and future; a particular moment; hour of the day; an opportunity; the right moment; duration; occasion; musical beat. * *vt* to regulate as to time; to measure or record the duration of.
time bomb *n* a bomb designed to explode at a predetermined time; something with a potentially delayed reaction.
timekeeper *n* a person or instrument that records or keeps time; an employee who records the hours worked by others.—**timekeeping** *n*.
time lag *n* the interval between two connected events.
timeless *adj* eternal; ageless.
timely *adj* at the right time, opportune.—**timeliness** *n*.
timer *n* a device for measuring, recording or controlling time; a device for controlling lights, heating, etc by setting an electrical clock to regulate their operations.
timetable *n* a list of times of arrivals and departures or trains, aeroplanes, etc; a schedule showing a planned order or sequence.
time zone *n* a geographical region throughout which the same standard time is used.
timing *n* the control and expression of speech or actions to create the best effect, esp in the theatre, etc.
timpani *npl* a set of kettledrums.
tin *n* a malleable metallic element; a container of tin, a can. * *adj* made of tin or tin plate. * *vt* (*pt* **tinned**)to put food into a tin.
tinfoil *n* baking foil for wrapping food; silver paper.
tinge *vt* to tint or colour. * *n* a slight tint, colour or flavour.
tingle *vi* to feel a prickling, itching or stinging sensation.—*also n*.
tinker *n* (*formerly*) a travelling mender of pots and pans. * *vi* to fiddle with; to attempt to repair.
tinkle *vi* to make a sound like a small bell ringing; to clink, to jingle; to clink repeatedly. * *n* a tinkling sound; (*inf*) a telephone call.
tin plate *n* thin sheets of iron or steel plated with tin.
tinsel *n* a shiny Christmas decoration made of long pieces of thread wound round with thin strips of metal or plastic foil; something showy but of low value.
tint *n* a shade of any colour, esp a pale one; a tinge; a hair dye. * *vt* to colour or tinge.

tiny *adj* (**tinier, tiniest**) very small.

tip[1] *n* the pointed end of anything; the end, as of a billiard cue, etc. * *vt* (*pt* **tipped**) to put a tip on.

tip[2] *vti* (*pt* **tipped**) to tilt or cause to tilt; to overturn; to empty (out, into, etc); to give a gratuity to, as a waiter, etc; (*rubbish*) to dump; to give a helpful hint or inside information to. * *n* a light tap; a gratuity; a rubbish dump; an inside piece of information; a helpful hint.

tip-off *n* a warning based on inside information.

tipple *vi* to drink alcohol regularly in small quantities. * *n* an alcoholic drink.

tipsy *adj* (**tipsier, tipsiest**) slightly drunk.

tiptoe *vi* (*pt* **tiptoed**) to walk very quietly or carefully.

tire *vt* to exhaust the strength of, to weary. * *vi* to become weary; to lose patience; to become bored.

tired *adj* weary, sleepy; hackneyed, conventional, flat; (*with* **of**) exasperated by, bored with.

tiresome *adj* tedious.

tissue *n* thin, absorbent paper used as a disposable handkerchief, etc; a very finely woven fabric; a mass of organic cells of a similar structure and function.

tit[1] *n* a songbird such as a blue tit or great tit.

tit[2] *n* (*vulg*) a woman's breast.

titanic *adj* monumental; huge.

titbit *n* a tasty morsel of food; a choice item of information.

titillate *vt* to tickle; to arouse or excite pleasurably.

title *n* the name of a book, play, piece of music, work of art, etc; the heading of a section of a book; a name denoting nobility or rank or office held, or attached to a personal name; (*law*) that which gives a legal right (to possession).

title deed *n* a deed or document proving a title or right to possession.

title role *n* the character in a play, film, etc after whom it is named.

titter *vi* to giggle, snigger. * *n* a suppressed laugh.

tittle-tattle *n* idle chat, empty gossip.

to *prep* in the direction of; towards; as far as; expressing the purpose of an action; indicating the infinitive; introducing the indirect object; in comparison with. * *adv* towards.

toad *n* an amphibious reptile, like a frog, but having a drier skin and spending less time in water.

toadstool *n* a mushroom, esp a poisonous or inedible one.

toady *n* a person who flatters insincerely. * *vi* (*with* **to**) to act in a servile manner.

toast *vt* to brown over a fire or under a grill; to warm; to drink to the health of. * *n* toasted bread; the sentiment or person to which one drinks.

toaster *n* a person who toasts; a thing that toasts, esp an electrical appliance.

toastmaster *n* the proposer of toasts at public dinners.—**toastmistress** *nf*.

tobacco *n* a plant whose dried leaves are used for smoking, chewing or snuff.

tobacconist *n* a person or shop that sells cigarettes, etc.

toboggan *n* a sledge, sled.

today *n* this day; the present age. * *adv* on this day; nowadays.

toddler *n* a young child.

toddy *n* a drink of whisky, sugar, and hot water.

toe *n* one of the five digits on the foot; the part of the shoe or sock that covers the toes.

toenail *n* the thin, hard, covering on the end of the toes.

toffee, toffy *n* a sweet of brittle but tender texture made by boiling sugar and butter together.

toga *n* a piece of cloth draped around the body, as worn by citizens in ancient Rome.

together *adv* in one place or group; in cooperation with; in unison; jointly.

toil *vi* to work strenuously; to move with great effort. * *n* hard work.

toilet *n* a lavatory; the room containing a lavatory; the act of washing and dressing oneself.

toilet paper, toilet tissue *n* an absorbent paper for cleansing after urination, etc.

toilet roll *n* a cardboard cylinder around which toilet paper is wound.

toiletry *n* a lotion, perfume, etc used in washing and dressing oneself.

toilet water *n* a diluted perfume.

token *n* a symbol, sign; an indication; a metal disc for a slot machine; a souvenir; a gift voucher. * *adj* nominal; symbolic.

told *see* **tell**.

tolerable *adj* bearable; fairly good.—**tolerably** *adv*.

tolerance *n* open-mindedness; forbearance; (*med*) ability to resist the action of a drug, etc; ability of a substance to endure heat, stress, etc without damage.

tolerant *adj* able to put up with the beliefs, actions, etc of others; broad-minded; showing tolerance to a drug, etc; capable of enduring stress, etc.

tolerate *vt* to endure, put up with, suffer.

toll[1] *n* money levied for passing over a bridge or road; the number of people killed in an accident or disaster.

toll[2] *vt* (*bell*) to ring slowly and repeatedly, as a funeral bell. * *vi* to sound, as a bell. * *n* the sound of a bell when tolling.

tomato *n* (*pl* **tomatoes**) a plant with red pulpy fruit used as a vegetable.

tomb *n* a vault in the earth for the burial of the dead.

tomboy *n* a girl who likes rough outdoor activities.

tombstone *n* a memorial stone over a grave.

tomcat *n* a male cat.

tomorrow *n* the day after today; the future.—*also adv*.

ton *n* a unit of weight equivalent to 2,000 pounds in US or 2,240 pounds in UK; (*inf*) 100 mph; (*inf: pl*) a great quantity.

tone *n* the quality of a sound; pitch or inflection of the voice; colour, shade; body condition. * *vt* to give tone to. * *vi* to harmonize (with).

tongs *npl* an instrument consisting of two arms that are hinged, used for grasping and lifting.

tongue *n* the soft, moveable organ in the mouth, used in tasting, swallowing, and speech; the ability to speak; a language; (*shoe*) a piece of leather under the laces; a jet of flame; the tongue of an animal served as food; the catch of a buckle.

tongue-tied *adj* speechless.

tongue-twister *n* a sequence of words that it is difficult to pronounce quickly and clearly.

tonic *n* a medicine that improves physical well-being; something that imparts vigour; a fizzy mineral water with a bitter taste. * *adj* relating to tones or sounds.

tonight *n* this night; the night or evening of the present day.—*also adv*.

tonnage *n* a merchant ship's capacity measured in tons; the weight of its cargo; the amount of shipping of a country or port; merchant ships collectively; a duty levied on ships based on tonnage or capacity.

tonne *n* metric ton, 1,000 kg.

tonsil *n* one of the two oval organs of soft tissue situated one on each side of the throat.

tonsillitis *n* inflammation of the tonsils.

too *adv* in addition; also, likewise; extremely; very.

took *see* **take**.

tool *n* an implement that is used by hand; a means for achieving any purpose.

toot *vi* to hoot a car horn, whistle, etc in short blasts. * *n* a hoot.—*also vt.*

tooth *n* (*pl* **teeth**) one of the white, bone-like structures arranged in rows in the mouth, used in biting and chewing; the palate; a tooth-like projection on a comb, saw, or wheel.

toothache *n* a pain in a tooth.

toothbrush *n* a small brush for cleaning teeth.

toothpaste *n* a paste for cleaning teeth, used with a toothbrush.

toothpick *n* a sliver of wood or plastic for removing food particles from between the teeth.

top[1] *n* the highest, or uppermost, part or surface of anything; the highest in rank; the crown of the head; the lid. * *adj* highest; greatest. * *vt* to cover on the top; to remove the top of or from; to rise above; to surpass.

top[2] *n* a child's toy, which is spun on its pointed base.

top hat *n* a man's tall, silk hat.

top-heavy *adj* having an upper part too heavy for the lower, causing instability.

topic *n* a subject for discussion; the theme of a speech or writing.

topical *adj* of current interest.

topless *adj* lacking a top; (*garment*) revealing the breasts; wearing such a garment.

topmost *adj* nearest the top, highest.

topple *vi* to fall over. * *vt* to cause to overbalance and fall; (*government*) to overthrow.

topsy-turvy *adj*, *adv* turned upside down; in confusion.

torch *n* a portable light powered by batteries; a device for giving off a hot flame.

torment *n* torture, anguish; a source of pain. * *vt* to afflict with extreme pain, physical or mental.—**tormentor, tormenter** *n*.

torn *see* **tear**[2].

tornado *n* (*pl* **tornadoes**) a violently whirling column of air seen as a funnel-shaped cloud that usu destroys everything in its narrow path.

torpedo *n* (*pl* **torpedoes**) a self-propelled submarine offensive weapon, carrying an explosive charge. * *vt* to attack, hit, or destroy with torpedo(es).

torpor *n* a state of lethargy.

torque *n* (*physics*) a force that causes rotation around a central point, such as an axle.

torrent *n* a rushing stream; a flood of words.—**torrential** *adj*.

torso *n* (*pl* **torsos**) the trunk of the human body.

tortoise *n* a slow-moving reptile with a dome-shaped shell into which it can withdraw.

tortoiseshell *n* a brown and yellow colour.

tortuous *adj* full of twists, involved.—**tortuously** *adv*.

torture *n* subjection to severe physical or mental pain to extort a confession, or as a punishment. —*also vt*. —**torturer** *n*.

Tory *n* a member of the Conservative Party in UK politics.—*also adj*.

toss *vt* to throw up; to pitch; to fling; (*head*) to throw back. * *vi* to be tossed about; to move restlessly.—*also n*.

toss-up *n* the throwing of a coin to decide a question.

tot[1] *n* anything little, esp a child; a small measure of spirits.

tot[2] *vt* (*pt* **totted**) (*with* **up**) to add up or total.

total *adj* whole, complete; absolute. * *n* the whole sum; the entire amount. * *vt* (*pt* **totalled**) to add up.—**totally** *adv*.

totalitarian *adj* relating to a system of government in which one political group maintains complete control, esp under a dictator. —**totalitarianism** *n*.

totter *vi* to walk unsteadily; to shake or sway as if about to fall.—**tottery** *adj*.

touch *vt* to come in contact with, esp with the hand or fingers; to reach; to affect with emotion; to tinge or tint; to border on; (*sl*) to ask for money (from). * *vi* to be in contact; to be adjacent; to allude to. * *n* the act of touching; the sense by which something is perceived through contact; a trace; understanding; a special quality or skill.

touch-and-go *adj* precarious, risky.

touchdown *n* the moment when an aircraft or spaceship lands; (*Rugby football, American football*) a placing of the ball on the ground to score.

touched *adj* emotionally affected; mentally disturbed.

touching *adj* affecting, moving.

touchline *n* (*football, etc*) the side boundary of a pitch.

touchy *adj* (**touchier, touchiest**) irritable; very risky.

tough *adj* strong; durable; hardy; rough and violent; difficult; (*inf*) unlucky.—**toughen** *vti*.—**toughness** *n*.

toupee *n* a wig or section of hair to cover a bald spot, esp worn by men.

tour *n* a turn, period, etc as of military duty; a long trip, as for sightseeing. * *vti* to go on a tour (through).

tourism *n* travelling for pleasure; the business of catering for people who do this; the encouragement of touring.

tourist *n* one who makes a tour, a sightseer, travelling for pleasure.—*also adj*.

tournament *n* a sporting event involving a number of competitors and a series of games.

tousle *vt* to make untidy, ruffle, make tangled (esp hair).

tout *vti* (*inf*) to praise highly; (*inf*) to sell betting tips on (race horses); (*inf*) to solicit business in a brazen way. * *n* (*inf*) a person who does so.

tow *vt* to pull or drag with a rope. * *n* the act of towing; a towrope.

towards, toward (*US*) *prep* in the direction of; concerning; just before; as a contribution to.

towel *n* an absorbent cloth for drying the skin after it is washed, and for other purposes.

towelling, toweling (*US*) *n* cloth for towels; a rubbing with a towel.

tower *n* a tall, narrow building, standing alone or forming part of another; a fortress. * *vi* (*with* **over**) to rise above; to loom.

tower block *n* a skyscraper.

town *n* a densely populated urban centre, smaller than a city and larger than a village; the people of a town.

townhall *n* a large building housing the offices of the town council, often with a hall for public meetings.

towpath *n* the footpath beside a river or canal.

towrope, towline *n* a strong rope or cable for towing a wheeled vehicle, ship, etc.

toxic *adj* poisonous; harmful; deadly.

toy *n* an object for children to play with; a replica; a miniature. * *vi* to trifle; to flirt.

trace *n* a mark etc left by a person, animal or thing; a barely perceptible footprint; a small quantity. * *vt* to follow by tracks; to discover the whereabouts of; (*map, etc*) to copy by following the lines on transparent paper.

track *vt* to follow the tracks of; (*satellite, etc*) to follow by radar and record position. * *n* a mark left; a footprint; parallel steel rails on which trains run; a course for running or racing; sports performed on a track, as running, hurdling; the band on which the wheels of a tractor or tank run; one piece of music on a record; a soundtrack.

tracksuit *n* a loose suit worn by athletes to keep warm.

tract[1] *n* an expanse of land or water; a part of a bodily system or organ.

tract[2] *n* a treatise.

tractor *n* a motor vehicle for pulling heavy loads and for working ploughs.

trade *n* buying and selling (of commodities); commerce; occupation; customers; business. * *vi* to buy and sell; to exchange.—**trader** *n.*

trade-in *n* a used item given in part payment when buying a replacement.

trademark *n* a name used on a product by a manufacturer to distinguish it from its competitors, esp when legally protected.—*also vt.*

tradesman *n* (*pl* **tradesmen**) a shopkeeper; a skilled worker.

trade(s) union *n* an organized association of employees of any trade or industry for the protection of their income and working conditions.

tradition *n* the handing down from generation to generation of opinions and practices; the belief or practice thus passed on; custom.—**traditional** *adj.*—**traditionally** *adv.*

traffic *n* trade; the movement or number of vehicles, pedestrians, etc, along a street, etc. * *vi* (*pt* **trafficked**) to do business (esp. in illegal drugs).

traffic circle *n* a roundabout.

traffic light *n* one of a set of coloured lights used to control traffic at street crossings, etc.

traffic warden *n* a person who is authorized to control traffic and to report parking violations, etc.

tragedy *n* a play or drama that is serious and sad, and the climax a catastrophe; an accident or situation involving death or suffering.—**tragic** *adj.*—**tragically** *adv.*

trail *vt* to drag along the ground; to have in its wake; to follow behind. * *vi* to hang or drag loosely behind; (*plant*) to climb; (*with* **off** *or* **away**) to grow weaker or dimmer. * *n* a path or track; the scent of an animal; something left in the wake.

trailer *n* a wagon, van, etc designed to be towed by a motor vehicle; a caravan; an advertisement for a film or television programme.

train *vt* to teach, to guide; to tame for use, as animals; to prepare for racing, etc; (*gun, etc*) to aim. * *vi* to do exercise or preparation. * *n* a series of railway carriages pulled by a locomotive; a sequence; the back part of a dress that trails along the floor; a retinue.

trained *adj* skilled.

trainee *n* a person who is being trained.

trainer *n* a coach or instructor in sports; a person who prepares horses for racing.

training *n* practical instruction; a course of physical exercises.

trait *n* a characteristic feature.

traitor *n* a person who commits treason or betrays his country, friends, etc.—**traitorous** *adj.*

tram *n* an electrically powered vehicle for public transport that travels along rails set into the ground.

tramlines *npl* rails for trams; the sidelines on a tennis court.

tramp *vti* to walk heavily; to tread or trample; to wander about as a tramp. * *n* a vagrant.

trample *vti* to tread under foot.

trampoline *n* a sheet of strong canvas stretched tightly on a frame, used in acrobatic tumbling.

trance *n* a state of unconsciousness, induced by hypnosis, in which some of the powers of the waking body, such as response to commands, may be retained.

tranquil *adj* quiet, calm, peaceful.—**tranquillity, tranquility** *n.*

tranquillizer *n* a drug that calms.

transact *vt* (*business*) to conduct or carry out.

transaction *n* the act of transacting; something transacted, esp a business deal; (*pl*) a record of the proceedings of a society.

transatlantic *adj* crossing the Atlantic Ocean; across, beyond the Atlantic.

transcend *vt* to rise above or beyond; to surpass.—**transcendent** *adj.*

transcript *n* a written or printed copy made by transcribing; an official copy of proceedings, etc.

transcription *n* the act of transcribing; something transcribed, esp a piece of music; a transcript; a recording made for broadcasting.

transept *n* one of the two wings of a church, at right angles to the nave.

transfer *vb* (*pt* **transferred**) *vt* to carry, convey, from one place to another; (*law*) to make over (property) to another; (*money*) to move from the control of one institution to another. * *vi* to change to another bus, etc. * *n* the act of transferring; the state of being transferred; someone or something that is transferred; a design that can be moved from one surface to another.—**transferable** *adj.*

transform *vti* to change the shape, appearance, or condition of; to convert.—**transformation** *n.*

transformer *n* a device for changing alternating current with an increase or decrease of voltage.

transfusion *n* the injection of blood into the veins of a sick or injured person.—**transfuse** *vt*.

transient *adj* temporary; of short duration, momentary.—**transience** *n*.

transistor *n* a device for amplifying sound, as in a radio or television; a small portable radio.

transit *n* a passing over or through; the carrying of people or goods.

transition *n* passage from one place or state to another; change.—**transitional** *adj*.

transitive *adj* (*gram*) denoting a verb that requires a direct object; of or relating to transition.

transitory *adj* lasting only a short time.

translate *vti* to express in another language; to explain, interpret.—**translator** *n*.

translation *n* the act of translating; something translated into another language or state; an interpretation.

transmission *n* the act of transmitting; something transmitted; a system using gears, etc, to transfer power from an engine to a moving part, esp wheels of a car; a radio or television broadcast.

transmit *vt* (*pt* **transmitted**) to send from one place or person to another; to communicate; to convey; (*radio or TV signals*) to send out.

transmitter *n* an apparatus for broadcasting television or radio programmes.

transparency *n* the state of being transparent; (*photog*) a slide.

transparent *adj* that may be easily seen through; clear, easily understood.

transplant *vt* (*plant*) to remove and plant in another place; (*med*) to remove an organ from one person and transfer it to another.—*also n*.

transport *vt* to convey from one place to another; to delight. * *n* the system of transporting goods or passengers; the carrying of troops and their equipment by sea or land; a vehicle for this purpose.—**transportable** *adj*.—**transportation** *n*.

transvestite *n* a person who gains sexual pleasure from wearing the clothes of the opposite sex.—**transvestism** *n*.

trap *n* a mechanical device or pit for snaring animals; an ambush; a trick to catch someone out; a two-wheeled horsedrawn carriage. * *vt* (*pt* **trapped**) to catch in a trap; to trick.

trapdoor *n* a hinged or sliding door in a roof, ceiling or floor.

trapeze *n* a gymnastic apparatus consisting of a horizontal bar suspended by two parallel ropes.

trapper *n* a person who traps animals, esp for their skins.

trappings *npl* trimmings; additions; ornaments.

trash *n* nonsense; refuse; rubbish.

trash can *n* a dustbin.

trauma *n* an emotional shock that may cause long-term psychological damage; an upsetting experience.—**traumatic** *adj*.

travel *vb* (*pt* **travelled**) *vi* to journey or move from one place to another. * *vt* to journey across, through. * *n* journey.

traveller, traveler (*US*) *n* a person who travels; a salesman who travels for a company.

traveller's cheque *n* a draft purchased from a bank, etc signed at the time of purchase and signed again at the time of cashing.

travesty *n* a misrepresentation; a poor imitation; a parody.

trawler *n* a boat used for trawling.

tray *n* a flat board, or sheet of metal or plastic, surrounded by a rim, used for carrying food or drink.

treacherous *adj* untrustworthy, disloyal; unstable, dangerous.

treachery *n* disloyalty, betrayal of trust.

treacle *n* a thick sticky substance obtained during the refining of sugar.—**treacly** *adj*.

tread *vti* (*pt* **trod,** *pp* **trodden**) to step or walk on, along, in, over or across; to crush or squash (with the feet); to trample (on). * *n* a step, way of walking; the part of a shoe, wheel, or tyre that touches the ground.

treason *n* the crime of betraying one's government or attempting to overthrow it; treachery.—**treasonable** *adj*.

treasure *n* wealth and riches hoarded up; a person or thing much valued. * *vt* to hoard up; to prize greatly.

treasurer *n* a person appointed to take charge of the finances of a society, government or city.

treasury *n* a place where valuable objects are deposited; the funds or revenues of a government.

treat *vt* to deal with or regard; to subject to the action of a chemical; to apply medical treatment to; to pay for another person's entertainment; to deal with in speech or writing. * *n* an entertainment paid for by another person; a pleasure seldom indulged; a unusual cause of enjoyment.

treatise *n* a formal essay in which a subject is treated systematically.

treatment *n* the application of drugs, etc, to a patient; the manner of dealing with a person or thing, esp in a novel or painting; behaviour towards someone.
treaty *n* a formal agreement between states.
treble *adj* triple, threefold; (*mus*) denoting the treble. * *n* the highest range of musical notes in singing. * *vti* to make or become three times as much.
tree *n* a tall, woody, perennial plant having a single trunk, branches and leaves.
trek *vi* (*pt* **trekked**) to travel slowly or laboriously; (*inf*) to go on foot (to). * *n* a long and difficult journey; a migration.
trellis *n* a structure of lattice work, for supporting climbing plants, etc.—**trelliswork** *n.*
tremble *vi* to shake, shiver from cold or fear; to quiver.—*also n.*
tremendous *adj* awe-inspiring; very large or great; (*inf*) wonderful; marvellous.
tremor *n* a vibration; an involuntary shaking.
trench *n* a long narrow channel in the earth, used for drainage; such an excavation made for military purposes.
trend *n* tendency; a current style or fashion.
trendy *adj* (**trendier, trendiest**) (*inf*) fashionable. * *n* (*inf*) a person who tries to be fashionable.—**trendily** *adv.*—**trendiness** *n.*
trepidation *n* a state of fear or anxiety.
trespass *vi* to intrude upon another person's property without their permission; to encroach upon, or infringe, another's rights. * *n* act of trespassing.—**trespasser** *n.*
trestle *n* a wooden framework for supporting a table top.
trial *n* a test or experiment; judicial examination; an attempt; a preliminary race, game in a competition; suffering; hardship; a person causing annoyance.
triangle *n* (*math*) a plane figure with three angles and three sides; a percussion instrument consisting of a triangular metal bar beaten with a metal stick.—**triangular** *adj.*
tribe *n* a group of people of the same race, sharing the same customs, religion, language or land.—**tribal** *adj.*—**tribesman** *n.*
tribulation *n* distress, difficulty, hardship.
tribunal *n* a court of justice; a committee that investigates and decides on a particular problem.
tribune[1] *n* in ancient Rome, a magistrate appointed to protect the rights of common people; a champion of the people.
tribune[2] *n* a raised platform or dais from which speeches are delivered.
tributary *n* a stream or river flowing into a larger one.
tribute *n* a speech, gift or action to show one's respect or thanks to someone; a payment made at certain intervals by one nation to another in return for peace.
trick *n* fraud; deception; a mischievous plan or joke; a magical illusion; a clever feat; skill, knack; the playing cards won in a round. * *adj* using fraud or clever contrivance to deceive. * *vt* to deceive, cheat.—**trickster** *n.*
trickery *n* the practice or an act of using underhand methods to achieve an aim; deception.
trickle *vti* to flow or cause to flow in drops or in a small stream.—*also n.*
tricky *adj* (**trickier, trickiest**) complicated, difficult to handle; risky; cunning, deceitful.—**trickily** *adv.*—**trickiness** *n.*
tricycle *n* a three-wheeled pedal cycle, esp for children.
trifle *vi* to treat lightly; to dally. * *n* anything of little value; a dessert of whipped cream, custard, sponge cake, sherry, etc.
trifling *adj* insignificant.
trigger *n* a catch that when pulled activates the firing mechanism of a gun. * *vt* (*with* **off**) to initiate; to set (off).
trigonometry *n* the branch of mathematics concerned with calculating the angles of triangles or the lengths of their sides.
trim *adj* (**trimmer, trimmest**) in good condition; tidy, neat; slim. * *vt* (*pt* **trimmed**) to neaten; to cut or prune; to decorate; (*aircraft*) to balance the cargo weight in. * *n* a decorative edging; a haircut that tidies.
trimming *n* decorative part of clothing; (*pl*) accompaniments.
trinity *n* a group of three; (*with cap*) in Christianity, the union of Father, Son and Holy Spirit in one God.
trinket *n* a small or worthless ornament.
trio *n* (*pl* **trios**) a set of three; (*mus*) a group of three singers or instrumentalists.
trip *vb* (*pt* **tripped**) *vi* to move or tread lightly; to stumble and fall; to make a blunder. * *vt* (*a person: often with* **up**) to cause to stumble; to activate a trip. * *n* a stumble; a journey, tour, or voyage; a slip; a mistake; a light step; a mechanical switch; (*sl*) a hallucinatory experience under the influence of a drug.
tripe *n* the stomach lining of an ox, prepared for cooking; (*inf*) rubbish, nonsense.
triple *adj* threefold; three times as many. * *vti* to treble.

triplet *n* one of three children born at one birth.
triplicate *adj* threefold.
tripod *n* a three-legged stand, as for supporting a camera.
trite *adj* dull; hackneyed.
triumph *n* a victory; success; a great achievement. * *vi* to win a victory or success; to rejoice over a victory.—**triumphal** *adj*.
triumphant *adj* feeling or showing triumph; celebratory; victorious.—**triumphantly** *adv*.
trivia *npl* unimportant details.
trivial *adj* unimportant; commonplace.
trod, trodden *see* **tread**.
trolley *n* (*pl* **trolleys**) a table on wheels for carrying or serving food; a cart for transporting luggage or shopping in a supermarket; a device that transmits electric current from an overhead wire.
trolleybus, trolley car *n* an electric bus powered from an overhead wire by means of a trolley.
trombone *n* a brass musical wind instrument whose length is varied with a U-shaped sliding section.
troop *n* a crowd of people; a group of soldiers within a cavalry regiment; (*pl*) armed forces; soldiers. * *vi* to go in a crowd.
trooper *n* a cavalryman; in US, a mounted policeman or a state policeman.
trophy *n* a cup or shield won as a prize in a competition or contest; a memento , as taken in battle or hunting.
tropic *n* one of the two parallel lines of latitude north and south of the equator; (*pl*) the regions lying between these lines.
tropical *adj* relating to the tropics; (*weather*) hot and humid.
trot *vi* (*pt* **trotted**) (*horse*) to go, lifting the feet higher than in walking and moving at a faster rate. * *n* the gait of a horse; a brisk pace.
trouble *vti* to cause trouble to; to worry; to pain; to upset; to cause inconvenience; to take pains (to). * *n* an anxiety; a medical condition causing pain; a problem; unrest or disturbance.—**troublesome** *adj*.
troubleshooter *n* a person whose work is to locate and eliminate a source of trouble or conflict.—**troubleshooting** *n*.
trough *n* a long, narrow container for water or animal feed; a channel in the ground; an elongated area of low barometric pressure.
trounce *vt* to defeat completely.
troupe *n* a travelling company, esp of actors, dancers or acrobats.—**trouper** *n*.
trousers *npl* an item of clothing covering the body from waist to ankle, with two tubes of material for the legs; pants.
trousseau *n* (*pl* **trousseaux**) the clothes and linen a bride collects for her marriage.
trout *n* (*pl* **trout**) a game fish of the salmon family living in fresh water.
trowel *n* a hand tool for gardening; a flat-bladed tool for spreading cement, etc.
truant *n* a pupil who is absent from school without permission. * *vi* to play truant.—*also adj*.—**truancy** *n*.
truce *n* an agreement between two armies or states to suspend hostilities.
truck *n* a heavy motor vehicle for transporting goods; a lorry; a vehicle open at the back for moving goods or animals. * *vt* (*goods*) to convey by truck. * *vi* to drive a truck.
trudge *vti* to travel on foot, heavily or wearily. * *n* a tiring walk.
true *adj* (**truer, truest**) conforming with fact; correct, accurate; genuine; loyal; perfectly in tune. * *adv* truthfully; rightly.
truffle *n* a round, edible underground fungus; a sweet made with chocolate, butter and sugar.
truly *adv* completely; genuinely; to a great degree.
trump *n* (*cards*) the suit that is chosen to have the highest value in one game. * *vt* to play a trump card on.
trumpet *n* a brass wind instrument consisting of a long tube with a flared end and three buttons. * *vti* to proclaim loudly.—**trumpeter** *n*.
truncate *vt* to cut the top end off; to shorten.—**truncation** *n*.
truncheon *n* a short, thick club carried by a policeman.
trundle *vt* (*an object*) to push or pull on wheels. * *vi* to move along slowly.
trunk *n* the main stem of a tree; the torso; the main body of anything; the long nose of an elephant; a strong box or chest for clothes, etc, esp on a journey; the boot of a car.
trunks *npl* a man's short, light pants for swimming.
truss *n* a supporting framework for a roof or bridge; a hernia brace. * *vt* to bind (up).
trust *n* firm belief in the truth of anything, faith in a person; confidence in; custody; a financial arrangement of investing money for another person; a business syndicate. * *adj* held in trust. * *vti* to have confidence in; to believe.—**trustful** *adj*.
trustee *n* a person who has legal control of money or property that they are keeping or

investing for another.—**trusteeship** *n.*

trustworthy *adj* reliable, dependable.

trusty *adj* (**trustier, trustiest**) trustworthy, faithful. * *n* a prisoner granted special privileges as a trustworthy person.—**trustily** *adv.*—**trustiness** *n.*

truth *n* that which is true, factual or genuine; agreement with reality.

truthful *adj* telling the truth; accurate, realistic; honest, frank.—**truthfulness** *n.*

try *vt* to test the result or effect by experiment; to determine judicially; to put strain on. * *vi* to attempt; to make an effort. * *n* an attempt, an effort; (*Rugby football*) a score made with a touchdown.

trying *adj* exasperating.

tsar *n* the title of the former ruler of Russia.—*also* **czar**.

T-shirt *n* an informal knitted cotton sweater.—*also* **tee-shirt**.

T-square *n* a T-shaped instrument for drawing and determining right angles.

tub *n* a circular container, esp for holding water.

tuba *n* a large brass instrument of bass pitch.

tubby *adj* (**tubbier, tubbiest**) plump.

tube *n* a long, thin, hollow pipe; a soft metal or plastic cylinder in which thick liquids or pastes are stored; (*inf*) in UK, the underground railway system.—**tubular** *adj.*

tuberculosis *n* an infectious disease of the lungs.—**tubercular** *adj.*

tubing *n* tubes collectively; a length of tube; the material from which tubes are made; a circular fabric.

TUC *abbr* = Trades Union Congress.

tuck *vt* to draw or gather together in a fold; (*with* **up**) to wrap snugly. * *vi* (*inf*) (*with* **into**) to eat greedily. * *n* a fold in a garment.

Tuesday *n* the third day of the week.

tuft *n* a bunch of grass, hair or feathers held together at the base; a clump.

tug *vti* (*pt* **tugged**) to pull with effort or to drag along. * *n* a strong pull; a tugboat.

tugboat *n* a small powerful boat for towing ships.

tug of war *n* a contest in which two teams tug on opposite ends of a rope to pull the opposing team over a central line; a struggle for supremacy between two opponents.

tuition *n* teaching, instruction.

tulip *n* a highly-coloured cup-shaped flower grown from bulbs.

tumble *vi* to fall over; to roll or to twist the body, as an acrobat. * *vt* to push or cause to fall. * *n* a fall; a somersault.

tumble-drier, tumble dryer *n* a machine for drying clothes with warm air.

tumbler *n* a large drinking glass without a handle or stem; an acrobat.

tummy *n* (*inf*) stomach.

tumour, tumor (*US*) *n* an abnormal growth of tissue in any part of the body.

tumult *n* a commotion; an uproar.

tumultuous *adj* disorderly; rowdy, noisy; restless.—**tumultuously** *adv.*—**tumultuousness** *n.*

tuna *n* (*pl* **tuna, tunas**) a large ocean fish of the mackerel group.

tune *n* a melody; correct musical pitch; harmony. * *vt* (*musical instrument*) to adjust the notes of; (*radio, TV etc*) to adjust the resonant frequency, etc, to a particular value.—**tuneful** *adj.*—**tunefully** *adv.*

tungsten *n* a hard malleable greyish white metallic element used in lamps, etc, and in alloys with steel.

tunic *n* a hip or knee-length loose, usu belted blouse-like garment; a close-fitting jacket worn by soldiers and policemen.

tunnel *n* an underground passage, esp one for cars or trains. * *vb* (*pt* **tunnelled**) *vt* to make a way through. * *vi* to make a tunnel.

tunny *n* (*pl* **tunnies, tunny**) tuna.

turban *n* a headdress consisting of cloth wound in folds around the head worn by men; a woman's hat of this shape.

turbine *n* a machine in which power is produced when the forced passage of steam, water, etc causes the blades to rotate.

turbot *n* a large, flat, round edible fish.

turbulent *adj* disturbed, in violent commotion.

tureen *n* a large dish for serving soup, etc.

turf *n* (*pl* **turf, turves**) the surface layer of grass and its roots; (*with* **the**) horse racing; a racetrack. * *vt* to cover with turf.

turgid *adj* swollen; pompous, bombastic.—**turgidity** *n.*—**turgidness** *n.*

turkey *n* (*pl* **turkeys, turkey**) a large bird farmed for its meat.

Turkish bath *n* a bath with steam rooms, showers, massage, etc.

turmoil *n* agitation; disturbance, confusion.

turn *vi* to revolve; to go in the opposite direction; to depend on; to appeal (to) for help; to direct (thought or attention) away from; to change in character; to be shaped on the lathe. * *vt* to change the position or direction of by revolving; to reverse; to transform;

(*age, etc*) to have just passed; to change or convert; to invert. * *n* a rotation; new direction or tendency; a place in sequence; a turning point, crisis; performer's act; an act of kindness or malice; a bend.

turning point *n* the point at which a significant change occurs.

turnip *n* a plant with a large white or yellow root, cultivated as a vegetable.

turnout *n* a gathering of people.

turnover *n* the volume of business transacted in a given period; a fruit or meat pasty; the rate of replacement of workers.

turnpike *n* a toll road, esp one that is an expressway.

turnstile *n* a mechanical gate across a footpath or entrance, which admits only one person at a time.

turntable *n* a circular, horizontal revolving platform, as in a record player.

turn-up *n* the cuff of a trouser; (*inf*) a surprise.

turpentine *n* an oily resin secreted by coniferous trees, used as a solvent and thinner for paints.—*also* **turps**.

turquoise *n* an opaque greenish-blue mineral, valued as a gem; the colour of turquoise.—*also adj.*

turret *n* a small tower on a building rising above it; a dome or revolving structure for guns, as on a warship, tank or aeroplane.—**turreted** *adj*.

turtle *n* any of an order of land , freshwater or marine reptiles having a soft body encased in a hard shell.

turtleneck *n* a high close-fitting neckline on a sweater.

tusk *n* a long, projecting tooth on either side of the mouth, as of the elephant.—**tusked** *adj*.

tussle *n* a scuffle.

tutor *n* a private teacher who instructs pupils individually; a member of staff responsible for the supervision and teaching of students in a university. * *vt* to instruct; to act as a tutor.

tutorial *n* a period of tuition by a tutor to an individual or a small group. * *adj* of or pertaining to a tutor.

tuxedo *n* a man's semi-formal suit with a tailless jacket; a dinner jacket.

TV *abbr* = television.

twang *n* a sharp, vibrant sound, as of a taut string when plucked; a nasal tone of voice. * *vt* to make a twanging sound.

tweed *n* a twilled woollen fabric used in making clothes.

tweezers *n sing* small pincers.

twelfth *adj* the last of twelve; being one of twelve equal parts.

twelve *adj* the cardinal number next after eleven. * *n* the symbol for this (12, XII, xii).

twenty *adj, n* two times ten. * *n* the symbol for this (20, XX, xx). —**twentieth** *adj*.

twice *adv* two times; two times as much; doubly.

twig[1] *n* a small branch or shoot of a tree.—**twiggy** *adj*.

twig[2] *vti* (*pt* **twigged**) (*inf*) to grasp the meaning of.

twilight *n* the dim light just after sunset and before sunrise; the final stages of something.

twill *n* a cloth woven in such a way as to produce diagonal lines across it.—**twilled** *adj*.

twin *n* either of two persons or animals born at the same birth; one thing resembling another. * *adj* double; very like another; consisting of two parts nearly alike. * *vt* (*pt* **twinned**) to pair together.

twine *n* a string of twisted fibres or hemp. * *vti* to twist together; to wind around.

twinge *n* a sudden, stabbing pain; an emotional pang.

twinkle *vi* to sparkle; to flicker.

twirl *vt* to whirl; to rotate; to wind or twist. * *vi* to turn around rapidly.

twist *vt* to unite by winding together; to coil; to confuse or distort (the meaning of); to bend. * *vi* to revolve; to write. * *n* the act or result of twisting; a twist of thread; a curve or bend; an unexpected event; a wrench.

twitch *vt* to pull with a sudden jerk. * *vi* to be suddenly jerked. * *n* a sudden muscular spasm.

two *adj, n* the cardinal number next above one. * *n* the symbol for this (2, II, ii).

two-faced *adj* deceitful, hypocritical.

two-piece *n* a garment consisting of two separate matching bits.—*also adj*.

twosome *n* a group of two; a game for two people.

tycoon *n* a powerful industrialist, etc.

type *n* a kind, class or group; sort; model; a block of metal for printing letters; style of print. * *vt* to write by means of a typewriter; to classify.

typecast *vt* (*pt* **typecast**) (*actor*) to cast in the same role repeatedly because of physical appearance, etc.

typescript *n* a typed copy of a book, document, etc.

typewriter *n* a keyboard machine for printing characters.

typhoid *n* an acute infectious disease acquired from contaminated food or water.

typhoon *n* a violent tropical cyclone originating in the western Pacific.

typhus *n* a highly contagious acute disease spread by body lice and characterized by fever, a rash and headache.—**typhous** *adj*.

typical *adj* representative of a particular type; characteristic.—**typically** *adv*.

typify *vt* to characterize.

typist *n* a person who uses a typewriter, esp as a job.

tyranny *n* the government or authority of a tyrant; harshness; oppression.

tyrant *n* a person who uses his or her power arbitrarily and oppressively.—**tyrannical** *adj*.

tyre, tire (*US*) *n* a protective, usu rubber, covering around the rim of a wheel.

U

ubiquitous *adj* existing, or seeming to exist everywhere at once.—**ubiquity** *n*.

udder *n* a milk-secreting organ containing two or more teats, as in cows.

UFO *abbr* = unidentified flying object.

ugly *adj* (**uglier, ugliest**) unsightly; unattractive; repulsive; ill tempered.—**ugliness** *n*.

UHF *abbr* = ultrahigh frequency.

UK *abbr* = United Kingdom.

ulcer *n* an open sore on the surface of the skin or a mucous membrane.—**ulcerous** *adj*

ulterior *adj* (*motives*) hidden, not evident; subsequent.

ultimate *adj* last; final; most significant; essential. * *n* the most significant thing.—**ultimately** *adv*.

ultimatum *n* (*pl* **ultimatums**) the final proposal, condition or terms in negotiations.

ultraviolet *adj* of light waves shorter than the wavelengths of visible light and longer than X-rays.

umbilical cord *n* the vascular tube connecting a foetus with the placenta through which oxygen and nutrients are passed.

umbrage *n* resentment; offence.

umbrella *n* a cloth-covered collapsible frame carried in the hand for protection from rain or sun; a general protection.

umpire *n* an official who enforces the rules in sport; an arbiter.—*also vti*.

umpteen *adj* (*inf*) an undetermined large number.—**umpteenth** *adj*.

UN *abbr* = United Nations.

un- *prefix* not; opposite of; contrary to; reversal of an action or state.

unable *adj* not able; lacking the strength, skill, power or opportunity (to do something).

unanimous *adj* showing complete agreement.—**unanimity** *n*.—**unanimously** *adv*.

unassuming *adj* unpretentious; modest.

unattached *adj* unmarried, not engaged to be married; not belonging to a particular group, organization, etc.

unattended *adj* not supervised; not accompanied.

unauthorized *adj* not endorsed by authority.

unavoidable *adj* bound to happen, inevitable; necessary, compulsory.—**unavoidably** *adv*.

unaware *adj* not conscious or aware (of); ignorant (of).

unawares *adv* by surprise; unexpectedly, without warning.

unbalanced *adj* mentally unstable; having bias or over-representing a particular view, group, interest, etc; (*bookkeeping*) not having equal debit and credit totals.

unbeliever *n* a person who does not believe, esp in a religion.

unbending *adj* severe, stern; inflexible, unchanging; rigid in behaviour or attitude.

unbridled *adj* unrestrained; (*horse*) having no bridle.

unburden *vt* to reveal or confess one's troubles, secrets, etc to another in order to relieve the mind; to take off a burden.

uncalled-for *adj* unnecessary, unwanted, unwarranted.

uncanny *adj* (**uncannier, uncanniest**) odd; unexpected; suggestive of supernatural powers; unearthly.

uncertain *adj* not knowing accurately, doubtful; (*with* **of**) not confident or sure; not fixed, variable, changeable.—**uncertainty** *n*.

uncle *n* the brother of one's father or mother; the husband of one's aunt.

uncommon *adj* rare, unusual; extraordinary.

uncompromising *adj* not prepared to compromise; inflexible, obstinate.

unconditional *adj* without restrictions or conditions, absolute.

unconscious *adj* not aware (of); lacking normal perception by the senses, insensible; unintentional. * *n* the deepest level of mind containing feelings and emotions of which one is unaware and unable to control.—

unconsciously *adv*.

uncouth *adj* lacking in manners; rough; rude.—**uncouthness** *n*.

unctuous *adj* oily; smarmy,; too suave; insincerely charming.—**unctuously** *adv*.—**unctuousness** *n*.

undaunted *adj* fearless; not discouraged.—**undauntedly** *adv*.

undecided *adj* doubtful, hesitant; (*solution, etc*) not determined.—**undecidedly** *adv*.

under *prep* lower than; beneath the surface of; below; covered by; subject to; less than, falling short of. * *adv* beneath, below, lower down. * *adj* lower in position, degree or rank; subordinate.

under- *prefix* beneath, below.

undercarriage *n* the landing gear of an aeroplane; a car's supporting framework.

underclothes *npl* underwear.—*also* **underclothing**.

undercoat *n* a coat of paint, etc, applied as a base below another; a growth of hair or fur under another; a coat worn under an overcoat.

undercover *adj* done or operating secretly.

undercurrent *n* a hidden current under water; an emotion, opinion, etc, not apparent.

undercut *vt* (*pt* **undercut**) to charge less than a competitor; to undermine.

underdog *n* the loser in an encounter, contest, etc; a person in an inferior position.

underdone *adj* not sufficiently or completely cooked.

underestimate *vti* to set too low an estimate on or for. * *n* too low an estimate.

underexpose *vt* (*photog*) to fail to expose (film) to light sufficiently long to produce a good image.—**underexposed** *adj*.—**underexposure** *n*.

underfoot *adv* underneath the foot or feet; on the ground.

undergo *vt* (*pt* **underwent,** *pp* **undergone**) to experience, suffer, endure.

undergraduate *n* a student at a college or university studying for a first degree.

underground *adj* situated under the surface of the ground; secret; of noncommercial newspapers, movies, etc that are unconventional, radical, etc. * *n* a secret group working for the overthrow of the government or the expulsion of occupying forces; an underground railway system; a subway.

undergrowth *n* shrubs, plants, etc growing beneath trees.

underhand *adv* (*sport*) with an underarm motion; underhandedly.

underhanded *adj* sly, secret, deceptive.—**underhandedly** *adv*.

underlie *vt* (*pr p* **underlying,** *pt* **underlay,** *pp* **underlain**) to be situated under; to form the basis of.

underline *vt* to put a line underneath; to emphasize.

underling *n* a person of inferior rank or status to someone else; a subordinate.

undermine *vt* to wear away, or weaken; to injure or weaken, esp by subtle or insidious means.

underneath *adv* under. * *adj* lower. * *n* the underside.—*also prep*.

underpants *npl* pants worn as an undergarment by men and boys.

underpass *n* a section of road running beneath another road, a railway, etc.

underprivileged *adj* lacking the basic rights of other members of society; poor.

underrate *vt* to undervalue, to underestimate.

underside *n* the lower surface.

underskirt *n* a woman's undergarment worn beneath the skirt, a petticoat.

understand *vb* (*pt* **understood**) *vt* to comprehend; to realize; to believe; to assume; to know thoroughly (eg a language); to accept; to be sympathetic with. * *vi* to comprehend; to believe.—**understandable** *adj*.

understanding *n* comprehension; compassion, sympathy; personal opinion, viewpoint; mutual agreement. * *adj* sympathetic.

understate *vt* to state something in restrained terms; to represent as less than is the case.—**understatement** *n*.

understudy *vti* to learn a role or part so as to be able to replace (the actor playing it); to act as an understudy (to).—*also n*

undertake *vt* (*pt* **undertook,** *pp* **undertaken**) to attempt to; to agree to; to commit oneself; to promise; to guarantee.

undertaker *n* a funeral director.

undertaking *n* enterprise; task; promise; obligation.

underwater *adj* being, carried on under the surface of the water, esp the sea; submerged; below the water line of a vessel.—*also adv*.

underwear *n* garments worn underneath one's outer clothes, next to the skin.

underworld *n* criminals as an organized group; (*myth*) Hades.

undesirable *adj* not desirable; not pleasant; objectionable.—**undesirability** *n*.—**undesirably** *adv*.

undies *npl* (*inf*) women's underwear.
undo *vt* (*pt* **undid,** *pp* **undone**) to untie or unwrap; to reverse (what has been done); to bring ruin on.
undoubted *adj* without doubt; definite, certain.—**undoubtedly** *adv*.
undress *vt* to remove the clothes from. * *vi* to take off one's clothes.
undue *adj* improper; excessive.
unduly *adv* too; excessively; improperly.
unearth *vt* to dig up from the earth; to discover; to reveal.
unearthly *adj* mysterious; eerie; supernatural; absurd, unreasonable.
uneasy *adj* uncomfortable; restless; anxious; disquieting.—**uneasily** *adv*.—**uneasiness** *n*.
uneconomic *adj* wasteful; unprofitable.
unemployed *adj* not having a job, out of work.—**unemployment** *n*.
unerring *adj* sure, unfailing.
uneven *adj* not level or smooth; variable; not divisible by two without leaving a remainder.—**unevenness** *n*.
unexpected *adj* not looked for, unforeseen.—**unexpectedly** *adv*.
unfailing *adj* not failing or giving up; persistent; constant, dependable.—**unfailingly** *adv*.
unfair *adj* unjust; unequal; against the rules.—**unfairly** *adv*.—**unfairness** *n*.
unfaithful *adj* disloyal; not abiding by a promise; adulterous.—**unfaithfully** *adv*.—**unfaithfulness** *n*.
unfasten *vt* to open or become opened; to undo or become undone; to loose.
unfeeling *adj* callous, hardhearted.—**unfeelingly** *adv*.
unfinished *adj* not finished, incomplete; in the making; crude, sketchy.
unfit *adj* unsuitable; in bad physical condition.
unflappable *adj* (*inf*) calm, not easily agitated.
unfold *vti* to open or spread out; to become revealed; to develop.
unforeseen *adj* unsuspected.
unfortunate *adj* unlucky; disastrous; regrettable. * *n* an unlucky person.
unfortunately *adv* regrettably, unluckily, unhappily.
unfounded *adj* groundless; baseless.
ungainly *adj* (**ungainlier, ungainliest**) awkward; clumsy.—**ungainliness** *n*.
ungodly *adj* (**ungodlier, ungodliest**) not religious; sinful; wicked; (*inf*) outrageous.
unguarded *adj* without protection, vulnerable; open to attack; careless; candid, frank.—**unguardedly** *adv*.
unguent *n* a lubricant or ointment.
unhappy *adj* (**unhappier, unhappiest**) not happy or fortunate; sad; wretched; not suitable.—**unhappily** *adv*.—**unhappiness** *n*.
unhealthy *adj* (**unhealthier, unhealthiest**) not healthy or fit, sick; encouraging or resulting from poor health; harmful, degrading; dangerous.—**unhealthily** *adv*.—**unhealthiness** *n*.
unicorn *n* an imaginary creature with a body like a horse and a single horn on the forehead.
uniform *adj* unchanging in form; consistent; identical. * *n* the distinctive clothes worn by members of the same organization, such as soldiers, schoolchildren.—**uniformly** *adv*.
uniformity *n* the state of being consistent or the same; dullness, monotony.
unify *vt* to make into one; to unite.—**unification** *n*.
unilateral *adj* involving one only of several parties; not reciprocal.—**unilateralism** *n*.—**unilaterally** *adv*.
uninhibited *adj* not repressed or restrained; relaxed, spontaneous.—**uninhibitedly** *adv*.
union *n* the act of uniting; a combination of several things; a confederation of individuals or groups; marriage; a trades union.
unique *adj* without equal; the only one of its kind.—**uniquely** *adv*.
unison *n* accordance of sound, concord, harmony; **in unison** simultaneously; in agreement; in harmony.
unit *n* the smallest whole number, one; a single or whole entity; (*measurement*) a standard amount; an establishment or group of people who carry out a specific function; a piece of furniture fitting together with other pieces.—**unitary** *adj*.
unite *vti* to join into one, to combine; to be unified in purpose.
United Nations *n sing or pl* an international organization of nations for world peace and security formed in 1945.
United States *n* a federation of states, esp the United States of America.
unit trust *n* a company that manages a range of investments on behalf of members of the public whose interests are looked after by an independent trust.
unity *n* oneness; harmony; concord.
universal *adj* widespread; general; relating to all the world or the universe; relating to or applicable to all mankind.—**universally** *adv*.—**universality** *n*.
universe *n* all existing things; (*astron*) the

totality of space, stars, planets and other forms of matter and energy; the world.

university *n* an institution of higher education which confers bachelors' and higher degrees; the campus or staff of a university.

unkempt *adj* uncombed; slovenly, dishevelled

unkind *adj* lacking in kindness or sympathy; harsh; cruel.—**unkindly** *adv*.—**unkindness** *n*.

unknown *adj* not known; not famous; not understood; with an unknown value. * *n* an unknown person or thing.

unleash *vt* to release from a leash; to free from restraint.

unless *conj* if not; except that.

unlikely *adj* improbable; unpromising.

unlimited *adj* without limits; boundless; not restricted.—**unlimitedly** *adv*.

unload *vti* to remove a load, discharge freight from a truck, ship, etc; to relieve of or express troubles, etc; to dispose of, dump; to empty, esp a gun.

unlock *vt* (*door, lock, etc*) to unfasten; to let loose; to reveal; to release.

unlucky *adj* (**unluckier, unluckiest**) not lucky, not fortunate; likely to bring misfortune; regrettable.—**unluckily** *adv*.

unmask *vti* to remove the mask from; to expose, show up.

unmitigated *adj* unqualified, absolute.

unnatural *adj* abnormal; contrary to nature; artificial; affected; strange; wicked.—**unnaturally** *adv*.

unpack *vti* (*suitcase, etc*) to remove the contents of; (*container, etc*) to take things out of; to unload.

unpleasant *adj* not pleasing or agreeable; nasty; objectionable.—**unpleasantly** *adv*.—**unpleasantness** *n*.

unpopular *adj* disliked; lacking general approval.—**unpopularity** *n*.

unprecedented *adj* having no precedent; unparalleled.

unpretentious *adj* modest, not boasting.

unqualified *adj* lacking recognized qualifications; not equal to; not restricted, complete.

unravel *vt* (*pt* **unravelled**) to disentangle; to solve.

unreasonable *adj* contrary to reason; lacking reason; immoderate; excessive.—**unreasonably** *adv*.

unrelenting *adj* relentless; continuous.—**unrelentingly** *adv*.

unremitting *adj* incessant.

unrest *n* uneasiness; anxiety; angry discontent verging on revolt.

unroll *vti* to open out or down from a roll; to unfold; to straighten out; to reveal or become revealed.

unruly *adj* (**unrulier, unruliest**) hard to control, restrain, or keep in order; disobedient.

unsavoury, unsavory (*US*) *adj* distasteful; disagreeable; offensive.

unscathed *adj* unharmed.

unscrew *vti* to remove a screw from; (*lid, etc*) to loosen by turning.

unscrupulous *adj* without principles.

unseemly *adj* unbecoming; inappropriate.

unsettled *adj* changeable; lacking stability; unpredictable; not concluded.

unsightly *adj* unattractive; ugly.

unskilled *adj* without special skill or training.

unspeakable *adj* bad beyond words, indescribable.

unsteady *adj* (**unsteadier, unsteadiest**) shaky, reeling; facillating.—**unsteadily** *adv*.

unthinkable *adj* inconceivable; out of the question; improbable.—**unthinkably** *adv*.

untidy *adj* (**untidier, untidiest**) not neat, disordered. * *vt* to make untidy.—**untidily** *adv*.

untie *vt* to undo a knot in, unfasten.

until *prep* up to the time of; before. * *conj* up to the time when or that; to the point, degree, etc that; before.

untimely *adj* premature; inopportune.

untold *adj* not told; too great to be counted; immeasurable.

untoward *adj* unseemly; unfavourable; adverse.

unusual *adj* uncommon; rare.

unveil *vt* to reveal; to disclose.

unwell *adj* ill, not well; (*inf*) suffering from a hangover.

unwieldy *adj* not easily moved or handled, as because of large size; awkward.—**unwieldily** *adv*.—**unwieldiness** *n*.

unwilling *adj* not willing, reluctant; said or done with reluctance.—**unwillingly** *adv*.—**unwillingness** *n*.

unwind *vt* to untangle; to undo. * *vi* to relax.

unwitting *adj* not knowing; unintentional.—**unwittingly** *adv*.

unworldly *adj* spiritual, not concerned with the material world.

unwritten *adj* not written or printed; traditional; oral.

up *adv* to, towards, in or on a higher place; to a later period; so as to be even with in time, degree, etc. * *prep* from a lower to a higher point on or along. * *adj* moving or directed upward; at an end; (*inf*) well-informed. * *vt*

(*pt* **upped**) to raise; to increase; to take up. * *n* ascent; high point.
up-and-coming *adj* promising for the future; likely to succeed.
upbringing *n* the process of educating and nurturing (a child).
update *vt* to bring up to date.
upgrade *vt* to improve, raise to a higher grade.
upheaval *n* radical or violent change.
uphill *adj* ascending, rising; difficult, arduous. * *adv* up a slope or hill; against difficulties.
uphold *vt* (*pt* **upheld**) to support, sustain; to defend.
upholstery *n* materials used to make a soft covering esp for a seat.
upkeep *n* maintenance; the cost of it.
upon *prep* on, on top of.
upper *adj* farther up; higher in position, rank, status. * *n* the part of a boot or shoe above the sole; (*sl*) a drug used as a stimulant.—*also* **upmost**.
upper case *n* capital letters.—**upper-case** *adj*.
upper class *n* people occupying the highest social rank.—*also adj*.
upright *adj* vertical, in an erect position; righteous, honest, just. * *n* a vertical post or support. * *adv* vertically.
uprising *n* a revolt; a rebellion.
uproar *n* a noisy disturbance; a commotion; an outcry.
uproot *vt* to tear out by the roots; to remove from established surroundings.
upset[1] *vt* (*pr p* **upsetting,** *pt* **upset**) to overturn; to spill; to disturb; to put out of order; to distress; to overthrow; to make physically sick.
upset[2] *n* an unexpected defeat; distress or its cause. * *adj* distressed; confused; defeated.
upshot *n* the conclusion; the result.
upside down *adj* inverted; the wrong way up; (*inf*) topsy turvy.
upstairs *adv* up the stairs; to an upper level or storey. * *n* an upper floor.
upstart *n* a person who has suddenly risen to a position of wealth and power; an arrogant person.
up-to-date *adj* modern; fashionable.
upturn *n* an upward trend; an (economic) improvement. * *vt* to turn upside down.
upward, upwards *adj* from a lower to a higher place.—*also adv*.
uranium *n* a metallic element used as a source of nuclear energy.
urban *adj* of or relating to a city.—**urbanization** *n*.
urbane *adj* sophisticated; refined.—**urbanity** *n*.
urchin *n* a raggedly dressed mischievous child; a sea urchin.
urge *vt* to drive forward; to press, plead with. * *n* an impulse, yearning.
urgency *n* the quality or condition of being urgent; compelling need; importance.
urgent *adj* impelling; persistent; calling for immediate attention.—**urgently** *adv*.
urinate *vi* to pass urine.
urn *n* a vase or large vessel; a receptacle for preserving the ashes of the dead; a large metal container for boiling water for tea or coffee.
US *abbr* = United States.
us *pron* the objective case of **we**.
USA *abbr* = United States of America.
usage *n* customary use; practice, custom; use of language.
use[1] *vt* to put to some purpose; to utilize; to exploit (a person); to partake of (drink, drugs, tobacco, etc).
use[2] *n* act of using or putting to a purpose; usage; usefulness; need (for); advantage; practice, custom.—**usable, useable** *adj*.
used *adj* not new; second-hand.
useful *adj* able to be used to good effect; (*inf*) capable, commendable.—**usefully** *adv*.
useless *adj* of no use.—**uselessly** *adv*.—**uselessness** *n*.
usher *n* one who shows people to their seats in a theatre, church, etc; a doorkeeper in a law court. * *vt* to escort to seats, etc.
USSR *abbr* = (*formerly*) Union of Soviet Socialist Republics.
usual *adj* customary; ordinary; normal.—**usually** *adv*.
usurer *n* a person who lends money at an excessively high rate of interest.
usurp *vt* to seize or appropriate unlawfully.—**usurper** *n*.
utensil *n* an implement or container, esp one for use in the kitchen.
uterus *n* (*pl* **uteri**) the womb.—**uterine** *adj*.
utilitarian *adj* designed to be of practical use.
utility *n* usefulness; a public service, such as telephone, electricity, etc; a company providing such a service.
utilize *vt* to make practical use of.—**utilization** *n*.
utmost *adj* of the greatest degree or amount; furthest. * *n* the most possible.
utter[1] *adj* absolute; complete.
utter[2] *vt* to say; to speak.—**utterance** *n*.

V

V *abbr* = volt(s).
v *abbr* = velocity; *versus* against; *vide* see; verb.
vacancy *n* emptiness; an unoccupied job or position.
vacant *adj* empty; unoccupied; (*expression*) blank.—**vacantly** *adv*.
vacate *vt* to leave empty; to give up possession of.
vacation *n* a holiday; a period of the year when universities, colleges and law courts are closed. * *vi* to go on holiday.—**vacationer** *n*
vaccinate *vt* to inoculate with vaccine as a protection against a disease.—**vaccination** *n*
vaccine *n* a preparation used for inoculation to give immunity from certain diseases.
vacuum *n* (*pl* **vacuums**) a region devoid of all matter; a region in which gas is present at low pressure; a vacuum cleaner. * *vt* to clean with a vacuum cleaner.
vacuum cleaner *n* an electrical appliance for removing dust from carpets, etc, by suction.
vacuum flask *n* a container for keeping liquids hot or cold.
vagina *n* in female mammals and humans, the canal connecting the uterus and the external sex organs.—**vaginal** *adj*.
vagrant *n* a person who has no settled home, a tramp.—**vagrancy**.
vague *adj* unclear; indistinct, imprecise; (*person*) absent-minded.—**vaguely** *adv*.—**vagueness** *n*.
vain *adj* conceited; excessively concerned with one's appearance; senseless; worthless.—**vainly** *adv*.
valentine *n* a lover or sweetheart chosen on St Valentine's Day, 14th February; a card or gift sent on that day.
valiant *adj* courageous; brave.—**valiantly** *adv*.
valid *adj* based on facts; (*objection, etc*) sound; legally acceptable; binding.—**validity** *n*.—**validly** *adv*.
valley *n* (*pl* **valleys**) low land between hills or mountains.
valuable *adj* having considerable importance or monetary worth. * *n* a personal possession of value, esp jewellery; (*pl*) valuable possessions.
valuation *n* the act of valuing; an estimated price or worth; an estimation.—**valuator** *n*.
value *n* worth, merit, importance; market value; purchasing power; relative worth; (*pl*) moral principles. * *vt* to estimate the worth of; to regard highly; to prize.—**valued** *adj*.—**valuer** *n*.
value added tax *n* a tax levied on the difference between the production cost of an item and its selling price.
valve *n* a device for controlling the flow of a gas or liquid through a pipe; (*anat*) a tube allowing blood to flow in one direction only.
van *n* a covered motor vehicle for transporting goods, etc.
vandal *n* a person who wilfully damages property.—**vandalism** *n*.—**vandalize** *vt*.
vanguard *n* the front part of an army; the leading position of any movement.
vanilla *n* extract from the orchid pod used as a flavouring.
vanish *vi* to disappear; to fade away.
vanity *n* conceit; worthlessness; something worthless.
vanity case, vanity box *n* a small case used for carrying cosmetics, etc.
vantage *n* a favourable position; a position allowing a clear view or understanding.
vapour, vapor (*US*) *n* the gaseous state of a substance normally liquid or solid; particles of water or smoke in the air.
variable *adj* liable to change; not constant. * *n* (*math*) a quantity that varies.—**variability** *n*.
variance *n* discrepancy.
variant *n* a different form.—*also adj*.
variation *n* diversity; deviation; modification.
varicose *adj* (*veins*) abnormally swollen and dilated.
variety *n* diversity; an assortment.
variety show *n* an entertainment made up of various acts, such as songs, comedy turns, etc.
various *adj* varied, different; several.—**variously** *adv*.
varnish *n* a sticky liquid which dries and forms a hard, glossy coating. * *vt* to coat with varnish.
vary *vti* to change, to diversify, modify; to become altered.
vase *n* a vessel for displaying flowers.
vast *adj* immense.—**vastly** *adv*.—*n* **vastness**.
VAT *abbr* = value added tax.
vat *n* a large barrel or tank.
Vatican *n* the residence of the pope in Rome; papal authority.
vault[1] *n* an arched ceiling or roof; a burial chamber; a strongroom for valuables; a cellar.—**vaulted** *adj*.

vault[2] *vti* to leap or jump over an obstacle.—*also n.*
VD *abbr* = venereal disease.
veal *n* the edible flesh of a calf.
veer *vi* (*wind*) to change direction; to swing around; to change from one mood or opinion to another.
vegetable *n* a herbaceous plant grown for food; (*inf*) a person who has suffered brain damage.—*also adj.*
vegetarian *n* a person who consumes a diet that excludes meat and fish. —*also adj.*—**vegetarianism** *n*.
vegetate *vi* to grow like a plant; to sprout; to lead a mentally inactive, aimless life.
vegetation *n* vegetable growth; plants in general.
vehement *adj* passionate; forceful; furious.—**vehemence** *n*.
vehicle *n* a conveyance, such as a car, bus or truck, for carrying people or goods; a medium.—**vehicular** *adj*.
veil *n* a thin fabric worn over the head or face of a woman; a nun's headdress; anything that conceals. * *vt* to put on a veil; to cover; to conceal.
vein *n* one of the vessels that convey the blood back to the heart; a seam of mineral within a rock; a branching rib in a leaf; a streak of different colour; a style or mood. * *vt* to streak.
velocity *n* speed.
velvet *n* a fabric made from silk, rayon, etc with a soft, thick pile; anything like velvet in texture.
vending machine *n* a coin-operated machine which dispenses goods.
vendor, vender *n* a person selling something.
veneer *n* an overlay of fine wood or plastic; a superficial appearance. * *vt* to cover with veneer.
venerable *adj* worthy of reverence or respect.
venereal *adj* (*disease*) resulting from sexual intercourse.
Venetian blind *n* a window blind formed of long thin horizontal slips of wood that can be pivoted.
vengeance *n* the act of taking revenge; retribution.—**vengeful** *adj*.
venison *n* the edible flesh of the deer.
venom *n* poison; spite, malice.—**venomous** *adj*.
vent *n* a small opening or slit; an outlet or flue for the escape of fumes. * *vt* to release; (*temper*) to give expression to.
ventilate *vt* to supply with fresh air; to express, to discuss.
ventilation *n* the act of ventilating; the state of being ventilated; free discussion.
ventilator *n* an appliance for ventilating a room, etc.
ventriloquism *n* the act or art of speaking so that the sounds appear to come from a source other than the actual speaker.
venture *n* a dangerous expedition; a risky undertaking. * *vti* to risk; to dare.—**venturesome** *adj*.
venue *n* the place of an action or event.
veranda, verandah *n* a roofed porch, supported by light pillars.
verb *n* (*gram*) the part of speech that expresses an action, a process, state or condition or mode of being.
verbal *adj* spoken; literal; pertaining to or characteristic of a verb.—**verbally** *adv*.
verbiage *n* use of too many words.
verbose *adj* wordy.
verdict *n* the decision of a jury at the end of a trial; decision, judgment.
verge *n* the brink; the extreme edge or margin; a grass border beside a road. * *vi* to border (on).
verger *n* a church official.
verify *vt* to confirm the truth of; to substantiate.—**verifiable** *adj*.—**verification** *n*.
vermin *n* (*used as pl*) pests, such as insects and rodents; persons dangerous to society.—**verminous** *adj*.
vermouth *n* a white wine flavoured with herbs, used in cocktails and as an aperitif.
vernacular *n* the commonly spoken language or dialect of a country or region. * *adj* native.
versatile *adj* changeable, adaptable; able to move or turn freely.—**versatility** *n*.
verse *n* a line of poetry; a stanza of a poem; a short section of a chapter in the Bible.
versed *adj* skilled or learned in a subject.
version *n* a translation from one language into another; a particular account or description.
versus *prep* against; in contrast to.
vertebra *n* (*pl* **vertebrae, vertebras**) one of the interconnecting bones of the spinal column.
vertebrate *n* an animal with a backbone.
vertical *adj* perpendicular to the horizon; upright. * *n* a vertical line or plane.
vertigo *n* a sensation of dizziness and sickness caused by a disorder of the sense of balance.—**vertiginous** *adj*.
verve *n* enthusiasm; liveliness; energy.

very *adj* complete; absolute; same. * *adv* extremely; truly; really.

vespers *npl* (*used as sing*) an Anglican service held daily in the evening.

vessel *n* a container; a ship or boat; a tube in the body along which fluids pass.

vest *n* a sleeveless undergarment; a waistcoat. * *vt* to place or settle (power, authority, etc.); to confer.

vested interest *n* a strong reason for acting in a certain way, usu for personal gain.

vestibule *n* an entrance hall or lobby.

vestige *n* a hint; a trace.

vestry *n* a room in a church where vestments, etc, are kept and parochial meetings held; a meeting for parish business.

vet *n* a veterinary surgeon. * *vt* (*pt* **vetted**) to examine, check for errors, etc.

veteran *adj* old, experienced; having served in the armed forces. * *n* a person who has served in the armed forces; a person who has given long service in a particular activity.

veterinary surgeon *n* a person trained in treating sick or injured animals.—*also* **veterinarian**.

veto *n* (*pl* **vetoes**) the right of a person or group to prohibit an action or legislation; a prohibition. * *vt* to refuse to agree to; to prohibit.

vex *vt* to annoy; to puzzle, confuse.—**vexation** *n*.

VHF *abbr* = very high frequency.

via *prep* by way of.

viable *adj* capable of growing or developing; workable; practicable.—**viability** *n*.

viaduct *n* a road or railway carried by a bridge with arches over a valley, river, etc.

vibrate *vti* to shake; to move quickly backwards and forwards; to quiver; to oscillate.—**vibration** *n*.—**vibratory** *adj*.

vicar *n* a parish priest; a clergyman in charge of a chapel.

vice[1] *n* an evil action or habit.

vice[2], **vise** (*US*) *n* a clamping device with jaws, used for holding objects firmly.

vice- *prefix* who acts in place of, or as a deputy to, another.

vice versa *adv* conversely; the other way round.

vicinity *n* a nearby area; proximity.

vicious *adj* cruel; violent; malicious; ferocious.—**viciously** *adv*.

vicissitudes *npl* ups and downs; successive changes of fortune.

victim *n* a person who has been killed or injured by an action beyond his or her control; a dupe.

victimize *vt* to make a victim.—**victimization** *n*.

victor *n* a winner; a conqueror.

Victorian *adj* of or living in the reign of Queen Victoria; old-fashioned, prudish.

victorious *adj* having won in battle or contest; emblematic of victory; triumphant.—**victoriously** *adv*.

victory *n* triumph in battle; success; achievement.

video *n* (*pl* **videos**) the transmission or recording of television programmes or films, using a television set and a video recorder and tape. * *vt* to record on video tape.

video recorder *n* the machine that plays or records on video tape.

video tape *n* a magnetic tape on which images and sounds can be recorded for reproduction on television.—**video-tape** *vt*.

vie *vi* (*pr p* **vying,** *pt* **vied**) to contend or strive for superiority.

view *n* sight; range of vision; inspection, examination; intention; scene; opinion. * *vt* to see; to consider; to examine intellectually.

viewer *n* a person who views, esp television; an optical device used in viewing.

viewfinder *n* a device in a camera showing the view to be photographed.

viewpoint *n* opinion; a place from which something can be viewed, esp a scenic panorama.

vigil *n* keeping watch at night.

vigilance *n* watchfulness; alertness.—**vigilant** *adj*.

vigour, vigor (*US*) *n* physical or mental strength; vitality.—**vigorous** *adj*.—**vigorously** *adv*.

vile *adj* wicked; evil; offensive; very bad.

villa *n* a large country or suburban house.

village *n* a collection of houses smaller than a town.

villager *n* an inhabitant of a village.

villain *n* a scoundrel; the main evil character in a play, film or novel.—**villainous** *adj*.

vindicate *vt* to justify; to absolve from blame.—**vindication** *n*.—**vindicator** *n*.

vindictive *adj* vengeful; spiteful.—**vindictiveness** *n*.

vine *n* any climbing plant, or its stem; a grapevine.

vinegar *n* a sour-tasting liquid containing acetic acid, used as a condiment and preservative.

vineyard *n* a plantation of grapevines.

vintage *n* the grape harvest of one season; wine, esp of good quality made in a particular year; wine of a particular region; the product of a particular period. * *adj* (*cars*) classic; (*wine*) of a specified year and of good quality; (*play*) characteristic of the best.

vinyl *n* a strong plastic used in floor coverings, furniture, records, etc.

viola *n* a stringed instrument of the violin family, and tuned a fifth below it.

violate *vt* to break or infringe (an agreement); to rape; to disturb (one's privacy).

violence *n* physical force intended to cause injury or destruction; natural force; passion, intensity.

violent *adj* urged or driven by force; vehement; impetuous; forcible; furious; severe.—**violently** *adv*.

violet *n* a small plant with bluish-purple flowers; a bluish-purple colour.

violin *n* a four-stringed musical instrument, played with a bow.

violinist *n* a person who plays the violin.

VIP *abbr* = Very Important Person.

viper *n* a common European venomous snake.

virgin *n* a person (esp a woman) who has never had sexual intercourse. * *adj* chaste; pure; untouched.—**virginal** *adj*.

virginity *n* the state of being a virgin; the state of being chaste, untouched, etc.

Virgo *n* the Virgin, the 6th sign of the zodiac.

virile *adj* manly; sexually potent.—**virility** *n*.

virtual *adj* in effect or essence, though not in fact or strict definition.—**virtually** *adv*.

virtue *n* moral excellence; any admirable quality; chastity; merit.

virtuoso *n* (*pl* **virtuosi**, **virtuosos**) a person highly skilled in an activity, esp in playing a musical instrument.—*also adj*.—**virtuosity** *n*.

virtuous *adj* righteous; upright; pure.—**virtuously** *adv*.

virus *n* (*pl* **viruses**) a very simple microorganism capable of replicating within living cells, producing disease; the disease caused by a virus; a harmful influence.

visa *n* an endorsement on a passport allowing the bearer to travel in the country of the government issuing it.

vis-à-vis *prep* opposite to; in face of. * *adv* facing.

viscount *n* in UK, a title of nobility next below an earl.—**viscountess** *nf*.

visibility *n* clearness of seeing or being seen.

visible *adj* that may be seen; evident.

vision *n* the power of seeing, sight; a supernatural appearance; foresight; imagination.

visionary *adj* imaginative; having foresight; existing in imagination only, not real. * *n* an imaginative person.

visit *vt* to go to see; to pay a call upon a person or place; to punish or reward with. * *vi* to see or meet someone regularly. * *n* act of going to see.

visiting card *n* a small card with the name left when paying visits.

visitor *n* a person who visits; a caller.

visor *n* a movable part of a helmet protecting the face; the peak of a cap.

vista *n* a view, as from a high place; a mental picture.

visual *adj* relating to vision or sight; visible.

visual aid *n* a film, slide or overhead projector, etc used to aid teaching.

visualize *vt* to form a mental picture of.—**visualization** *n*.

vital *adj* necessary to life; essential; lively.—**vitally** *adv*.

vitality *n* vigour; spirits; animation.

vitamin *n* organic substance, occurring naturally in foods, which is essential for good health.

vivacious *adj* lively; animated; spirited.—**vivacity** *n*.

vivid *adj* brightly coloured; graphic; lively; intense.—**vividly** *adv*.

vivisection *n* the practice of performing surgical operations on living animals for scientific research.

vocabulary *n* an alphabetical list of words with their meanings; the words of a language; an individual's use of particular words.

vocal *adj* relating to the voice; outspoken, noisy; (*phonetics*) having a vowel function.—**vocally** *adv*.

vocalist *n* a singer.

vocation *n* calling to a particular career or occupation.— **vocational** *adj*.

vociferous *adj* clamorous, noisy.—**vociferously** *adv*.

vodka *n* a spirit distilled from rye.

vogue *n* the fashion at a specified time; popularity.

voice *n* sound from the mouth; sound produced by speaking or singing; expressed opinion; the relation between a verb and its subject. * *vt* to express; to speak.

void *adj* unoccupied, empty; not legally binding. * *n* an empty space, a vacuum. * *vt* to empty; to make invalid.

volatile *adj* evaporating very quickly.

volcano *n* (*pl* **volcanoes, volcanos**) a hill or

mountain formed by ejection of lava, ashes, etc through an opening in the earth's crust.—**volcanic** *adj*.

volition *n* the exercise of the will; choice.

volley *n* (*pl* **volleys**) the multiple discharge of many missiles or small arms; a barrage; (*tennis, volleyball*) the return of the ball before it reaches the ground. * *vt* to return (a ball) before it hits the ground.

volleyball *n* a team game played by hitting a large inflated ball over a net with the hands; the ball used.

volt *n* the unit of measure of the force of an electrical current.

voltage *n* electrical force measured in volts.

volume *n* the amount of space occupied by an object; quantity, amount; intensity of sound; a book; one book of a series.

voluntary *adj* acting by choice; willing; brought about by free will; without remuneration.—**voluntarily** *adv*.

volunteer *n* a person who carries out work voluntarily; a person who freely undertakes military service.—*also vti*.

voluptuous *adj* excessively fond of pleasure; having an attractive figure.

vomit *vi* (*pt* **vomited**) to eject the contents of the stomach through the mouth, to spew. * *n* matter ejected from the stomach when vomiting.

vote *n* an indication of a choice or opinion as to a matter on which one has a right to be consulted; a ballot; decision by a majority; the right to vote; franchise. * *vi* to cast one's vote. * *vt* to elect.—**voter** *n*.

vouch *vt* to provide evidence or proof of. * *vi* to give assurance; to guarantee.

voucher *n* a written record of a transaction; a receipt; a token that can be exchanged for something else.

vow *n* a solemn or binding promise. * *vt* to promise; to resolve.

vowel *n* an open speech sound produced by continuous passage of the breath; a letter representing such a sound, as *a, e, i, o, u*.

voyage *n* a long journey, esp by ship or spacecraft. * *vi* to journey.—**voyager** *n*.

vulgar *adj* common; coarse; offensive; vernacular.—**vulgarly** *adv*.

vulnerable *adj* capable of being wounded physically or mentally; open to persuasion; easily influenced.—**vulnerability** *n*.

vulture *n* a large bird of prey having no feathers on the neck or head.

W

wad *n* a small, soft mass, as of cotton or paper; a bundle of paper money.

wade *vti* to walk through water; to pass (through) with difficulty.

wader *n* a bird that wades, eg the heron.

waffle[1] *n* a thick, crisp pancake baked in a waffle iron.

waffle[2] *vi* (*inf*) to speak or write at length without saying anything substantial.

waft *vt* to drift or float through the air. * *n* a breath, scent or sound carried through the air.

wag[1] *vti* (*pt* **wagged**) to move rapidly from side to side or up and down (as of a finger, tail).—*also n*.

wag[2] *n* a joker, a wit.

wage *vt* to carry on, esp war. * *n* (*often pl*) payment for work or services.

wager *n* a bet. * *vti* to bet.

waggle *vti* to wag.—*also n*.

wagon, waggon *n* a four-wheeled vehicle pulled by a horse or tractor, for carrying heavy goods.

wail *vi* to make a long, loud cry of sorrow or grief; to howl, to moan.—*also n*.

waist *n* the narrowest part of the human trunk, between the ribs and the hips; the narrow part of anything that is wider at the ends; the part of a garment covering the waist.

waistcoat *n* a waist-length, sleeveless garment worn immediately under a suit jacket; a vest.

waistline *n* the narrowest part of the waist; its measurement; the seam that joins the bodice and skirt of a dress, etc; the level of this.

wait *vti* to stay, or to be, in expectation or readiness; to defer or to be postponed; to remain; (*with* **at** *or* **on**) to serve food at a meal. * *n* act or period of waiting.

waiter *n* a man or woman who serves at table, as in a restaurant.—**waitress** *nf*.

waiting list *n* a list of people applying for or waiting to obtain something.

waiting room *n* a room for people to wait in at a station, hospital, etc.

waive *vt* to refrain from enforcing; to relinquish voluntarily.

wake[1] *vb* (*pt* **woke** *or* **waked,** *pp* **woken** *or* **waked**) *vi* to emerge from sleep; to become awake. * *vt* to rouse from sleep. * *n* a watch or vigil beside a corpse, on the eve of the burial.—**wakeful** *adj*.—**waken** *vti*.

wake[2] *n* the waves or foamy water left in the track of a ship; a trail.
walk *vi* to travel on foot with alternate steps. * *vt* to pass through or over; (*a dog*) to exercise; to escort on foot. * *n* the act of walking; distance walked over; gait; a ramble or stroll; a profession.—**walker** *n*.
walkie-talkie *n* a portable two-way radio transmitter and receiver.
walking stick *n* a stick used in walking, a cane.
walkover *n* an unopposed or easy victory; a horse race with only one starter.
wall *n* a vertical structure of brick, stone, etc for enclosing, dividing or protecting. * *vt* to enclose with a wall; to close up with a wall.
wallet *n* a flat pocketbook for paper money, cards etc.
wallflower *n* a fragrant plant with red or yellow flowers; a person who does not dance for lack of a partner.
wallop *vt* (*pt* **walloped**) (*inf*) to beat or defeat soundly; (*inf*) to strike hard. * *n* (*inf*) a hard blow.
wallow *vi* (*animal*) to roll about in mud; to indulge oneself in emotion.—*also n*.
wallpaper *n* decorated paper for covering the walls of a room.
walnut *n* a tree producing an edible nut with a round shell and wrinkled seed; its nut; its wood used for furniture.
walrus *n* (*pl* **walruses, walrus**) a large, thick-skinned aquatic animal, related to the seals, having long canine teeth and coarse whiskers.
waltz *n* a piece of music with three beats to the bar; a whirling or slowly circling dance. * *vti* to dance a waltz; to lead (someone) in waltz time.
wan *adj* (**wanner, wannest**) pale and sickly; feeble or weak.—**wanly** *adv*.—**wanness** *n*.
wand *n* a magician's rod.
wander *vi* to ramble with no definite destination; to go astray; to lose concentration.—*also n*.
wane *vi* to decrease, esp of the moon; to decline. * *n* decrease, decline.
want *n* lack; poverty. * *vt* to need; to require; to lack; to wish (for).
wanted *adj* sought after.
wanting *adj* lacking.
wanton *adj* malicious; wilful; sexually provocative.
war *n* military conflict between nations or parties; a conflict; a contest. * *vi* (*pt* **warred**) to make war.
ward *n* a section of a hospital; an electoral district; a division of a prison; a child placed under the supervision of a court.—**wardship** *n*.
warden *n* an official; a person in charge of a building or home; a prison governor;
warder *n* a prison officer.
wardrobe *n* a cupboard for clothes; one's clothes.
ware *n* (*pl*) merchandise, goods for sale; pottery.
warehouse *n* a building for storing goods.
warfare *n* armed hostilities; conflict.
warhead *n* the section of a missile containing the explosive.
warlike *adj* hostile.
warm *adj* moderately hot; friendly, kind; (*colours*) rich; enthusiastic. * *vt* to make warm. * *vi* to become enthusiastic (about). —**warmly** *adv*.—**warmth** *n*.
warm-hearted *adj* kind, sympathetic; affectionate.
warn *vt* to notify of danger; to caution or advise (against).—**warning** *n*.
warp *vti* to twist out of shape; to distort; to corrupt. * *n* the threads arranged lengthwise on a loom across which other threads are passed.
warrant *vt* to guarantee; to justify. * *n* a document giving authorization; a writ for arrest.
warranty *n* a pledge to replace something if it is not as represented, a guarantee.
warrior *n* a soldier, fighter.
warship *n* a ship equipped for war.
wart *n* a small, hard projection on the skin.—**warty** *adj*.
wartime *adj, n* (of) a period or time of war.
wary *adj* (**warier, wariest**) watchful; cautious.—**warily** *adv*.—**wariness** *n*.
was *see* **be**.
wash *vti* to cleanse with water and soap; to flow against or over; to sweep along by the action of water; to separate gold, etc, from earth by washing; to cover with a thin coat of metal or paint. * *n* a washing; the break of waves on the shore; the waves left behind by a boat; a liquid used for washing.
washbasin, washbowl *n* a basin or bowl, esp a bathroom fixture, for use in washing one's hands, etc.—*also* **wash-hand basin**.
washed-out *adj* faded; limp; exhausted.
washer *n* a flat ring of metal, rubber, etc, to give tightness to joints; a washing machine.
washing *n* the act of cleansing with water; a number of items washed together.

washing machine *n* a device for washing clothes.
washroom *n* cloakroom, lavatory.
wasp *n* a winged insect with a black and yellow striped body, which can sting.
wastage *n* anything lost by use or natural decay; wasteful or avoidable loss of something valuable.
waste *adj* useless; left over; uncultivated or uninhabited. * *vt* to ravage; to squander; to use foolishly; to fail to use. * *vi* to lose strength, etc as by disease. * *n* uncultivated or uninhabited land; discarded material, garbage, excrement.—**wasteful** *adj*.—**wastefully** *adv*.—**wastefulness** *n*.
watch *n* surveillance; close observation; vigil; guard; a small timepiece worn on the wrist, etc; (*naut*) a period of duty. * *vi* to look with attention; to wait for; to keep vigil. * *vt* to keep one's eyes fixed on; to guard; to tend; to observe closely; (*chance, etc*) to wait for.—**watcher** *n*.—**watchful** *adj*.—**watchfully** *adv*.—**watchfulness** *n*.
watchdog *n* a dog that guards property; a person or group that monitors safety, standards, etc.
watchmaker *n* a person who makes and repairs watches.
water *n* the substance H_2O, a clear, thin liquid, lacking taste or smell, and essential for life; any body of it, as the ocean, a lake, river, etc; bodily secretions such as tears, urine. * *vt* to moisten with water; to irrigate; to dilute with water. * *vi* (*eyes*) to smart; to salivate; to take in water.
water-closet *n* a lavatory.
watercolour, watercolor (*US*) *n* a water-soluble paint; a picture painted with watercolours.
watercress *n* a plant growing in ponds and streams, used in a salad.
waterfall *n* a fall of water over a precipice or down a hill.
watering can *n* a container with a spout for watering plants.
water line *n* a line up to which a ship's hull is submerged.
waterlogged *adj* soaked or saturated with water.
water main *n* a main pipe or conduit for carrying water.
watermark *n* a line marking the height to which water has risen; a mark impressed on paper which can only be seen when held up to the light.
watermelon *n* a large fruit with a hard green rind and edible red watery flesh.
waterproof *adj* impervious to water; watertight.—*also vt*.
watershed *n* a turning point.
water-skiing *n* the sport of planing on water by being towed by a motorboat—**water-skier** *n*.
watertight *adj* not allowing water to pass through; foolproof.
waterworks *n* (*as sing*) an establishment that supplies water to a district; (*pl: inf*) the urinary system; (*inf*) tears.
watt *n* a unit of electrical power.
wave *n* an undulation travelling on the surface of water; the form in which light and sound are thought to travel; an increase or upsurge (eg of crime); a hair curl; a movement of the hand in greeting or farewell. * *vti* to move freely backward and forward; to flutter; to undulate; to move the hand to and fro in greeting, farewell, etc.—**wavy** *adj*.
wavelength *n* the distance between the crests of successive waves of light or sound; radio frequency.
waver *vi* to hesitate; to falter.—**waverer** *n*.
wax[1] *n* beeswax; an oily substance used to make candles, polish, etc. * *vt* to rub, polish, cover or treat with wax.
wax[2] *vi* to increase in strength, size, etc.
waxwork *n* a figure or model formed of wax; (*pl*) an exhibition of such figures.
way *n* path, route; road; distance; room to advance; direction; state; means; possibility; manner of living; (*pl*) habits.
waylay *vt* (*pt* **waylaid**) to lie in wait for; to accost.
wayward *adj* wilful, stubborn; unpredictable.—**waywardness** *n*.
WC *abbr* = water-closet.
we *pron pl* of **I**; I and others.
weak *adj* lacking power or strength; feeble; ineffectual.—**weakness** *n*.
weaken *vti* to make or grow weaker.
weakling *n* a person who lacks strength of character.
wealth *n* a large amount of possessions or money; affluence; an abundance (of).—**wealthy** *adj*.
wean *vt* (*baby, animal*) to replace the mother's milk with other nourishment; to dissuade (from indulging a habit).
weapon *n* any instrument used in fighting.
wear *vb* (*pt* **wore,** *pp* **worn**) *vt* to have on the body as clothing; (*hair, etc*) to arrange in a particular way; to display; to rub away; to

impair by use; to exhaust, tire. * *vi* to be impaired by use or time; to be spent tediously. * *n* deterioration from frequent use; articles worn.—**wearer** *n*.

weary *adj* (**wearier, weariest**) tired; bored. * *vti* to make or become tired.—**weariness** *n*.—**wearisome** *adj*.

weasel *n* a small carnivorous animal with a long slender body and reddish fur.

weather *n* atmospheric conditions, such as temperature, rainfall, cloudiness, etc. * *vt* to expose to the action of the weather; to survive. * *vi* to withstand the weather.

weathercock *n* a weather vane in the form of a cock to show the wind direction.

weave *vb* (*pt* **wove,** *pp* **woven**) *vt* to interlace threads in a loom to form fabric; to construct. * *vi* to make a way through (eg a crowd), to zigzag.—**weaver** *n*.

web *n* a woven fabric; the network of fine threads spun by a spider; the membrane joining the digits of birds and animals.

webbed *adj* (*ducks, etc*) having the digits connected by a fold of skin.

wed *vti* (*pt* **wedded** *or* **wed**) to marry; to join closely.

wedding *n* marriage; the ceremony of marriage.

wedge *n* a v-shaped block of wood or metal for splitting or fastening; a wedge-shaped object. * *vti* to split or secure with a wedge; to thrust (in) tightly; to become fixed tightly.

wedlock *n* marriage.

Wednesday *n* fourth day of the week, between Tuesday and Thursday.

wee *adj* small, tiny.

weed *n* any undesired plant, esp one that crowds out desired plants; (*sl)* marijuana. * *vt* to remove weeds or anything troublesome.

weedkiller *n* a chemical or hormonal substance used to kill weeds.

week *n* the period of seven consecutive days, esp from Sunday to Sunday.

weekday *n* a day of the week other than Saturday or Sunday.

weekend *n* the period from Friday night to Sunday night—*also adv*.

weekly *adj* happening once a week or every week.

weep *vti* (*pt* **wept**) to shed tears, to cry; (*wound*) to ooze.—**weepy** *adj*.

weigh *vt* to measure the weight of; to consider carefully. * *vi* to have weight; to be burdensome.

weight *n* the amount which anything weighs; influence; any unit of heaviness. * *vt* to attach a weight to.

weightlessness *n* the state of having no or little reaction to gravity, esp in space travel.

weightlifting *n* the sport of lifting weights of a specific amount in a particular way.—**weightlifter** *n*.

weighty *adj* (**weightier, weightiest**) heavy; serious.—**weightily** *adv*.

weir *n* a low dam across a river which controls the flow of water.

weird *adj* unearthly, mysterious; eerie; bizarre.—**weirdly** *adv*.

welcome *adj* gladly received; pleasing. * *n* reception of a person or thing. * *vt* to greet kindly.

welch *see* **welsh**.

weld *vt* to unite, as metal by heating until fused or soft enough to hammer together; to join closely. * *n* a welded joint.

welfare *n* wellbeing; health; assistance or financial aid granted to the poor, the unemployed, etc.

well[1] *n* a spring; a hole bored in the ground to provide a source of water, oil, gas, etc; the open space in the middle of a staircase. * *vi* to pour forth.

well[2] *adj* (**better, best**) agreeable; comfortable; in good health. * *adv* in a proper, satisfactory, or excellent manner; thoroughly; prosperously; with good reason; to a considerable degree; fully. * *interj* an expression of surprise, etc.

well-heeled *adj* (*inf*) wealthy.

wellies *npl* (*sl*) wellingtons.

wellington (boot) *n* a rubber, waterproof boot.

well-off *adj* in comfortable circumstances; prosperous.

well-to-do *adj* prosperous.

Welsh *adj* relating to the people of Wales or their language.—*also n*.

welsh *vti* to avoid paying a gambling debt; to run off without paying.—*also* **welch**.—**welsher, welcher** *n*.

went *see* **go**.

wept *see* **weep**.

were *see* **be**.

we're = we are.

weren't = were not.

west *n* the direction of the sun at sunset; one of the four points of the compass; the region in the west of any country; (*with cap*) Europe and the Western Hemisphere. * *adj* situated in, or toward the west. * *adv* in or to the west.

westerly *adj* towards the west; blowing from

the west. * *n* a wind blowing from the west.—*also adv*.
western *adj* of or in the west. * *n* a film, novel, etc about the usu pre-20th century American West.
westward *adj* towards the west.—*also adv*.
wet *adj* (**wetter, wettest**) covered or saturated with water or other liquid; rainy; misty; not yet dry. * *n* water or other liquid; rain or rainy weather. * *vti* (*pt* **wet** *or* **wetted**) to soak; to moisten.—**wetness** *n*.
wet suit *n* a close-fitting suit worn by divers, etc, to retain body heat.
whack *vti* (*inf*) to strike sharply, esp making a sound. * *n* (*inf*) a sharp blow.
whale *n* a very large sea mammal that breathes through a blowhole, and resembles a fish in shape. * *vi* to hunt whales.
wharf *n* (*pl* **wharfs, wharves**) a platform for loading and unloading ships in harbour.
what *adj* of what sort, how much, how great. * *relative pron* that which; as much or many as. * *interj* used as an expression of surprise or astonishment.
whatever *pron* anything that; no matter what.
whatsoever *adj* whatever.
wheat *n* a cereal grain usu ground into flour for bread.
wheel *n* a solid disc or circular rim turning on an axle; a steering wheel; (*pl*) the moving forces. * *vt* to transport on wheels. * *vi* to turn round or on an axis; to move in a circular direction, as a bird.
wheelbarrow *n* a cart with one wheel in front and two handles and legs at the rear.
wheelchair *n* a chair with large wheels for invalids.
wheeze *vi* to breathe with a rasping sound; to breathe with difficulty.—*also n*.
when *adv* at what or which time * *conj* at the time at which; although; *relative pron* at which.
where *adv* at which or what place; to which place; from what source; *relative pron* in or to which.
whereabouts *adv* near or at what place; about where. * *n* approximate location.
whereas *conj* since; on the contrary.
wherever *adv* at or to whatever place.
whet *vt* (*pt* **whetted**) to sharpen by rubbing, to stimulate.
whether *conj* introducing an alternative possibility or condition.
which *adj* what one (of). * *pron* which person or thing; that. * *relative pron* person or thing referred to.
whichever *pron* whatever one that; whether one or the other; no matter which.—*also adj*.
whiff *n* a sudden puff of air, smoke or odour.
while *n* a period of time. * *conj* during the time that; whereas; although. * *vt* to pass (the time) pleasantly.
whim *n* a fancy; an irrational thought.
whimper *vi* to make a low, unhappy cry.—*also n*.
whimsical *adj* unusual, odd, fantastic.—**whimsicality** *n*.
whine *vi* (*dog*) to make a long, high-pitched cry; (*person*) to complain childishly. * *n* a plaintive cry.
whip *n* a piece of leather attached to a handle used for punishing people or driving on animals; an officer in parliament who maintains party discipline. * *vb* (*pt* **whipped**) *vt* to move, pull, throw, etc suddenly; to strike, as with a lash; (*eggs, etc*) to beat into a froth. * *vi* to move rapidly.
whip-round *n* (*inf*) an appeal among friends for contributions.
whir, whirr *n* a humming or buzzing sound. * *vti* to revolve with a buzzing noise.
whirl *n* a swift turning; confusion, commotion; (*inf*) an attempt or try. * *vti* to turn around rapidly; to spin.
whirlpool *n* a circular current or vortex of water.
whirlwind *n* a whirling column of air; rapid activity.
whisk *vt* to make a quick sweeping movement; (*eggs, cream*) to beat, whip. * *vi* to move nimbly and efficiently. * *n* a kitchen utensil for whisking; (*inf*) a small amount.
whisker *n* any of the sensory bristles on the face of a cat, etc; (*pl*) the hair growing on a man's face, esp the cheeks.—**whiskered** *adj*.
whiskey *n* whisky distilled in the US or Ireland.
whisky *n* a spirit distilled from barley or rye.
whisper *vti* to speak softly; to spread a rumour. * *n* a hushed tone; a hint, trace.
whist *n* a card game for four players in two sides, each side attempting to win the greater number of the 13 tricks.
whistle *vti* to make a shrill sound by forcing the breath through the lips; to make a similar sound with a whistle; (*wind*) to move with a shrill sound. * *n* a whistling sound; a musical instrument; a metal tube that is blown to make a shrill warning sound.
white *adj* of the colour of snow; pure; bright; (*skin*) light-coloured. * *n* the colour white;

the white part of an egg or the eye.—**whiten** *vti*.
white-collar *adj* of office and professional workers.
whitewash *n* a mixture of lime and water, used for whitening walls; concealment of the truth.—*also vt*.
Whitsun *n* the seventh Sunday after Easter; the following week.—*also* **Whit Sunday, Whitsuntide**.
whittle *vt* to pare or cut thin shavings from (wood) with a knife; (*with* **away** *or* **down**) to reduce.
whiz, whizz *vi* (*pt* **whizzed**) to make a humming sound. * *n* (*pl* **whizzes**) a humming sound; (*inf*) an expert.
WHO *abbr* = World Health Organization.
who *pron* what or which person; that.
whodunit, whodunnit *n* (*inf*) a detective novel, play, etc.
whoever *pron* anyone who; whatever person.
whole *adj* not broken, intact; containing the total amount, number, etc.; complete. * *n* the entire amount; a thing complete in itself.
wholehearted *adj* sincere, single-minded, enthusiastic.—**wholeheartedly** *adv*.
whole note *n* a semibreve.
wholesale *n* selling of goods, usu at lower prices and in quantity, to a retailer.
wholesome *adj* healthy; mentally beneficial.—**wholesomeness** *n*.
whom *pron* objective case of **who**.
whoop *n* a loud cry of excitement.
whooping cough *n* an infectious disease, esp of children, causing coughing spasms.
whore *n* a prostitute.
whose *pron* the possessive case of **who** or **which**.
why *adv* for what cause or reason? * *interj* exclamation of surprise. * *n* (*pl* **whys**) a cause.
wick *n* a cord, as in a candle or lamp, that supplies fuel to the flame.
wicked *adj* evil, immoral, sinful.—**wickedly** *adv*.—**wickedness** *n*.
wicker *n* a long, thin, flexible twig; such twigs woven together, as in making baskets.—**wickerwork** *n*.
wicket *n* a small door or gate; (*croquet*) any of the small wire arches through which the balls must be hit; (*cricket*) the stumps at which the bowler aims the ball; the area between the bowler and the batsman; a batsman's innings.
wide *adj* broad; extensive; of a definite distance from side to side; (*with* **of**) far from the aim; open fully. * *n* (*cricket*) a ball bowled beyond the reach of the batsman.—**widely** *adv*.
wide-angle *adj* (*photog*) with an angle of view of 60 degrees or more.
wide-awake *adj* fully awake; ready, alert.
widen *vti* to make or grow wide or wider.
widespread *adj* widely extended; general.
widow *n* a woman whose husband has died. * *vt* to cause to become a widow.—**widowhood** *n*.
widower *n* a man whose wife has died.
width *n* breadth.
wield *vt* (*a weapon, etc*) to brandish; to exercise power.
wife *n* (*pl* **wives**) a married woman.
wig *n* an artificial covering of real or synthetic hair for the head.
wiggle *vti* to move from side to side with jerky movements.
wild *adj* in its natural state; not tamed or cultivated; uncivilized; lacking control; disorderly; furious. —**wildly** *adv*.—**wildness** *n*.
wilderness *n* an uncultivated and desolate place.
wild-goose chase *n* a futile pursuit of something.
wildlife *n* animals in the wild.
wilful, willful (*US*) *adj* stubborn; done intentionally.—**wilfully** *adv*. —**wilfulness** *n*.
will[1] *n* power of choosing or determining; desire; determination; desire; attitude, disposition; a legal document directing the disposal of one's property after death. * *vt* to bequeath; to command.
will[2] *aux vb* used in constructions with 2nd and 3rd persons; used to show futurity, determination, obligation.
willow *n* a tree or shrub with slender, flexible branches; the wood of the willow.
willpower *n* the ability to control one's emotions and actions.
wilt *vi* to become limp, as from heat; (*plant*) to droop; to become weak or faint.
wily *adj* (**wilier, wiliest**) crafty; sly.—**wiliness** *n*.
win *vti* (*pr p* **winning,** *pt* **won**) to gain with effort; to succeed in a contest; to gain eg by luck; to achieve influence over. * *n* a success.—**winner** *n*.
wince *vi* to shrink back; to flinch (as in pain).—*also n*.
winch *n* a hoisting machine. * *vt* to hoist or lower with a winch.
wind[1] *n* a current of air; breath; scent of game; (*inf*) flatulence; tendency; (*mus*) wind instrument(s). * *vt* (*pt* **winded**) to cause to be

short of breath; to perceive by scent.

wind[2] *vb* (*pt* **wound**) *vt* to turn by cranking; to tighten the spring of a clock; to coil around something else; to encircle or cover, as with a bandage. * *vi* to turn, to twist, to meander.

windbreak *n* a shelter that breaks the force of the wind, as a line trees.

windfall *n* fruit blown off a tree; any unexpected gain, esp financial.

winding *adj* meandering.

wind instrument *n* a musical instrument played by blowing into it or by passing a current of air through it.

windmill *n* a machine operated by the force of the wind turning a set of sails.

window *n* a framework containing glass in the opening in a wall of a building, or in a vehicle, etc, for air and light.

window box *n* a narrow box on a windowsill for growing flowers, etc.

windowsill *n* a sill beneath a window.

windpipe *n* the air passage from the mouth to the lungs.

windscreen, windshield *n* a protective shield of glass in the front of a vehicle.

windscreen wiper, windshield wiper *n* a metal blade with a rubber edge that removes rain, etc, from a windscreen.

windy *adj* (**windier, windiest**) exposed to the winds; stormy; verbose.

wine *n* fermented grape juice used as an alcoholic beverage; the fermented juice of other fruits or plants.

wineglass *n* a glass, usu with a stem, for drinking wine.

wing *n* the forelimb of a bird, bat or insect, by which it flies; the main lateral surface of an aeroplane; a projecting part of a building; the side of a stage; a section of a political party. * *vti* to make one's way swiftly; to wound without killing.

wink *vi* to quickly open and close one's eye; to give a hint by winking. * *n* the act of winking; an instant.

winning *n* a victory; (*pl*) money won in gambling. * *adj* charming.

winter *n* the coldest season of the year: in the northern hemisphere from November or December to January or February. * *vi* to spend the winter.

wintry, wintery *adj* (**wintrier, wintriest**) typical of winter, cold, stormy, snowy; unfriendly, frigid.

wipe *vt* to rub a surface with a cloth in order to clean or dry it; (*with* **out**) to remove; to erase; to kill off; to destroy. * *n* a wiping.

wire *n* a flexible thread of metal; a length of this; (*US horse racing*) the finish line of a race; a telegram. * *adj* formed of wire. * *vt* to fasten, furnish, connect, etc with wire; in US, to send a telegram.

wireless *n* (*formerly*) a radio.

wiry *adj* (**wirier, wiriest**) lean, supple and sinewy.—**wiriness** *n*.

wisdom *n* the ability to use knowledge; sound judgment.

wisdom tooth *n* one of four teeth set at the end of each side of the upper and lower jaw in humans and grown last.

wise *adj* having knowledge or common sense; learned; prudent.— **wisely** *adv*.

wish *vti* to long for; to express a desire. * *n* desire; thing desired.

wishful *adj* having a wish; hopeful.

wisp *n* a thin strand; a small bunch, as of hay; anything slender.—**wispy** *adj*.

wistful *adj* pensive; sad; yearning.—**wistfully** *adv*.—**wistfulness** *n*.

wit *n* (*speech, writing*) the facility of combining ideas with humorous effect; a person with this ability; (*pl*) ability to think quickly.

witch *n* a woman who practises magic and is considered to a have dealings with the devil.

witchcraft *n* the practice of magic.

with *prep* denoting nearness or agreement; in the company of; in the same direction as; among; by means of; possessing.

withdraw *vb* (*pt* **withdrew**, *pp* **withdrawn**) *vt* to draw back or away; to remove; to retract. * *vi* to retire; to retreat.—**withdrawal** *n*.

wither *vi* to fade or become limp or dry, as of a plant. * *vt* to cause to dry up or fade.

withhold *vt* (*pt* **withheld**) to hold back; to deduct; to restrain; to refuse to grant.

within *prep* inside; not exceeding; not beyond.

without *prep* outside or out of, beyond; not having, lacking. * *adv* outside.

withstand *vt* (*pt* **withstood**) to oppose or resist, esp successfully; to endure.

witness *n* a person who gives evidence or attests a signing; testimony (of a fact). * *vt* to have first hand knowledge of; to see; to be the scene of; to serve as evidence of; to attest a signing. * *vi* to testify.

witness box, witness stand *n* an enclosure for witnesses in a court of law.

witticism *n* a witty remark.

witty *adj* (**wittier, wittiest**) full of wit.—**wittily** *adv*.—**wittiness** *n*.

wives *see* **wife**.

wizard *n* a magician; a man who practises witchcraft or magic; an expert.—**wizardry** *n.*
wk *abbr* = week.
wobble *vi* to sway unsteadily from side to side; to waver, to hesitate.—**wobbly** *adj.*
woe *n* grief, misery; (*pl*) misfortune.—**woeful** *adj.*—**woefully** *adv.*
wok *n* a large, metal, hemispherical pan used for Chinese-style cooking.
woke, woken *see* **wake**[1].
wolf *n* (*pl* **wolves**) a wild animal of the dog family that hunts in packs; a flirtatious man.
woman *n* (*pl* **women**) an adult human female; the female sex.
womanly *adj* having the qualities of a woman.
womb *n* the female organ in which offspring are developed until birth, the uterus; any womb-like cavity; a place where something is produced.
women *see* **woman**.
won *see* **win**.
wonder *n* a feeling of surprise or astonishment; something that excites such a feeling; a prodigy. * *vi* to feel wonder; to be curious; to speculate; to marvel.
wonderful *adj* marvellous.—**wonderfully** *adv.*
won't = will not.
woo *vt* to seek to attract with a view to marriage; to court; to solicit eagerly.—**wooer** *n.*
wood *n* the hard fibrous substance under the bark of trees; trees cut or sawn, timber; a thick growth of trees.
wooded *adj* covered with trees.
woodpecker *n* a bird that pecks holes in trees to extract insects.
woodwind *n* section of an orchestra in which wind instruments, originally made of wood, are played.
woodwork *n* carpentry.
woodworm *n* an insect larva that bores into wood; the damage in furniture so caused.
wool *n* the fleece of sheep and other animals; thread or yarn spun from the coats of sheep; cloth made from this yarn.
woollen, woolen (*US*) *adj* made of wool.
woolly *adj* (**woollier, woolliest**) of, like or covered with wool; indistinct, blurred; muddled. * *n* (*inf*) a woollen garment.—**woolliness** *n.*
word *n* a single unit of language in speech or writing; talk, discussion; a message; a promise; a command; information; a password; (*pl*) lyrics; (*pl*) a quarrel. * *vt* to put into words, to phrase; to flatter.
wording *n* the way in which words are used, esp in written form; a choice of words.
wordy *adj* (**wordier, wordiest**) verbose.
wore *see* **wear**.
work *n* employment, occupation; a task; the product of work; manner of working; place of work; a literary composition; (*pl*) a factory, plant. * *vi* to be employed, to have a job; to operate (a machine, etc); to produce effects. * *vt* to effect, to achieve.—**workable** *adj.*—**worker** *n.*
working *adj* spent in or used for work; functioning. * *n* operation; mode of operation; (*pl*) the manner of functioning or operating; (*pl*) the parts of a mine that are worked.
working class *n* people who work for wages, esp manual workers.
workmanship *n* technical skill; the way a thing is made, style.
work-out *n* a session of strenuous physical exercises.
workshop *n* a room or building where work is done; a seminar for specified intensive study, work, etc.
world *n* the planet earth and its inhabitants; mankind; the universe; a sphere of existence; the public.
worldly *adj* (**worldlier, worldliest**) earthly, rather than spiritual; material; experienced.
worldwide *adj* universal.
worm *n* an earthworm; an insect larva; the thread of a screw. * *vt* to work (oneself into a position) slowly or secretly; to extract information by slow and persistent means.
worn *see* **wear**.
worn-out *adj* (*machine, etc*) past its useful life; (*person*) depressed, tired.
worry *vb* to bother, pester, harass. * *vi* to be uneasy or anxious; to fret. * *n* a cause or feeling of anxiety.—**worrier** *n.*
worse *adj* (*used as compar of* **bad** *and* **ill**) less favourable; not so well as before. * *adv* with great severity. —**worsen** *vti.*
worship *n* religious adoration; a religious ritual, eg prayers; devotion. * *vb* (*pt* **worshipped**) *vt* to adore or idolize. * *vi* to participate in a religious service.—**worshipper** *n.*
worst *adj* (*used as superl of* **bad** *or* **ill**; *see also* **worse**) bad or ill in the highest degree; of the lowest quality. * *adv* to the worst degree. * *n* the least good part.
worsted *n* twisted thread or yarn made from long, combed wool.
worth *n* value; price; excellence; importance. * *adj* equal in value to; meriting.

worthless *adj* valueless; useless; of bad character.—**worthlessness** *n*.
worthwhile *adj* important or rewarding enough to justify effort.
worthy *adj* (**worthier, worthiest**) virtuous; deserving. * *n* a worthy person, a local celebrity.—**worthily** *adv*.
would *see* **will**[2].
would-be *adj* aspiring or professing to be.
wound[1] *n* any cut, bruise, hurt, or injury caused to the skin; hurt feelings. * *vt* to injure.
wound[2] *see* **wind**[2].
wove, woven *see* **weave**.
wrangle *vi* to argue; to dispute noisily. * *n* a noisy argument.
wrap *vt* (*pt* **wrapped**) to fold (paper) around (a present, purchase etc); to wind (around); to enfold. * *n* a shawl.
wrapper *n* one who or that which wraps; a book jacket; a light dressing gown.
wrath *n* intense anger; rage.—**wrathful** *adj*.
wreak *vt* inflict or exact (eg vengeance, havoc).
wreath *n* (*pl* **wreaths**) a twisted ring of leaves, flowers, etc; something like this in shape.
wreck *n* accidental destruction of a ship; a badly damaged ship; a run-down person or thing. * *vt* to destroy; to ruin.
wreckage *n* the process of wrecking; remnants from a wreck.
wren *n* small brownish songbird, with a short erect tail.
wrench *vt* to give something a violent pull or twist; to injure with a twist, to sprain; to distort. * *n* a forceful twist; a sprain; a spanner; emotional upset caused by parting.
wrestle *vti* to fight by holding and trying to throw one's opponent down; to struggle.—**wrestler** *n*.
wretch *n* a miserable or despised person.
wretched *adj* very miserable; in poor circumstances; despicable.—**wretchedly** *adv*.—**wretchedness** *n*.
wriggle *vi* to move with a twisting motion; to squirm, to writhe; to use evasive tricks.—*also n*.—**wriggler** *n*.
wring *vt* (*pt* **wrung**) to twist; to compress by twisting to squeeze water from; to pain; to obtain forcibly.
wrinkle *n* a small crease or fold on a surface. * *vti* to make or become wrinkled.
wrist *n* the joint connecting the hand with the forearm.
writ *n* (*law*) a written court order.
write *vb* (*pr p* **writing,** *pt* **wrote,** *pp* **written**) *vt* to form letters on paper with a pen or pencil; to express in writing; to compose (music, literary work,etc); to communicate by letter; (*with* **off**) to cancel a bad debt as a loss; (*inf*) to damage (a vehicle) beyond repair. * *vi* to be a writer.
write-off *n* a debt cancelled as a loss; (*inf*) a badly damaged car.
writer *n* an author; a scribe or clerk.
writhe *vi* to twist the body violently, as in pain; to squirm (under, at).
writing *n* the act of forming letters on paper, etc; a written document; authorship; (*pl*) literary works.
writing paper *n* paper treated to accept ink and used esp for letters.
written *see* **write**.
wrong *adj* not right, incorrect; mistaken, misinformed; immoral. * *n* harm; injury done to another. * *adv* incorrectly. * *vt* to do wrong to.—**wrongly** *adv*.
wrongful *adj* unwarranted, unjust.—**wrongfully** *adv*.
wrote *see* **write**.
wrought *adj* formed; made; (*metals*) shaped by hammering, etc.
wrung *see* **wring**.
wry *adj* (**wryer, wryest** *or* **wrier, wriest**) twisted, contorted; ironic.—**wryly** *adv*.—**wryness** *n*.
wt *abbr* = weight.

XYZ

Xmas *abbr* = Christmas.
X-ray, x-ray *n* radiation of very short wavelengths, capable of penetrating solid bodies, and printing on a photographic plate a shadow picture of objects not permeable by light rays. * *vt* to photograph by x-rays.
xylophone *n* a percussion instrument consisting of a series of wooden bars which are struck with small hammers.
yacht *n* a sailing or mechanically driven vessel, used for pleasure cruises or racing. * *vi* to race or cruise in a yacht.—**yachting** *n*.—**yachtsman** *n*.—**yachtswoman** *nf*.
Yank, Yankee *n* (*inf*) a citizen of the US, an American.
yank *vti* to pull suddenly, to jerk.—*also n*.
yap *vi* (*pt* **yapped**) to yelp, bark; (*sl*) to talk constantly, esp in a noisy or irritating manner.
yard[1] *n* a unit of measure of 3 feet and equivalent to 0.9144 metres.

yard[2] *n* an enclosed concrete area, esp near a building; an enclosure for a commercial activity (eg a shipyard); a garden.

yardstick *n* a standard used in judging.

yarn *n* fibres of wool, cotton etc spun into strands for weaving, knitting, etc; (*inf*) a tale or story. * *vi* to tell a yarn; to talk at length.

yawn *vi* to open the jaws involuntarily and inhale, as from drowsiness; to gape.—*also n.*

yawning *adj* gaping; wide-open; drowsy.—**yawningly** *adv*.

yd., yds *abbr* = yard(s).

year *n* a period of twelve months, or 365 or 366 days, beginning with 1 January and ending with 31 December.

yearly *adj* occurring every year; lasting a year. * *adv* once a year; from year to year.

yearn *vi* to feel desire (for); to long for.—**yearning** *n*.

yeast *n* a fungus that causes alcoholic fermentation, used in brewing and baking.

yell *vti* to shout loudly; to scream. * *n* a loud shout.

yellow *adj* of the colour of lemons, egg yolk, etc; having a yellowish skin; (*inf*) cowardly. * *n* the colour yellow. * *i* to become or turn yellow.

yelp *vti* to utter a sharp, shrill cry or bark.—*also n.*

yen[1] *n* (*pl* **yen**) the monetary unit of Japan.

yen[2] *n* (*inf*) a yearning, an ambition.

yes *adv* a word of affirmation or consent.

yesterday *n* the day before today; the recent past. * *adv* on the day before today; recently.

yet *adv* still; so far; even. * *conj* nevertheless; however; still.

yew *n* an evergreen tree or shrub with thin, sharp leaves and red berries.

Yiddish *n* a mixed German and Hebrew dialect spoken by Jews.

yield *vt* to resign; to give forth, to produce, as a crop, result, profit, etc. * *vi* to submit; to give way to physical force, to surrender. * *n* the amount yielded; the profit or return on a financial investment.

yodel *vti* (*pt* **yodelled**) to sing, alternating from the ordinary voice to falsetto.

yoga *n* a system of exercises for attaining bodily and mental control and well-being.

yoghurt, yogurt *n* a semi-liquid food made from milk curdled by bacteria.

yoke *n* a bond or tie; slavery; the wooden frame joining oxen to make them pull together; part of a garment that is fitted below the neck. * *vt* to put a yoke on; to join together.

yolk *n* the yellow part of an egg.

yonder *adv* over there.

you *pron* (*gram*) 2nd person singular or plural; the person or persons spoken to.

you'd = you would; you had.

you'll = you will; you shall.

young *adj* in the early period of life; in the first part of growth; new; inexperienced. * *n* young people; offspring.

youngster *n* a young person; a youth.

your *poss adj* of or belonging to or done by you.

you're = you are.

yours *poss pron* of or belonging to you.

yourself *pron* (*pl* **yourselves**) the emphatic and reflexive form of **you**.

youth *n* the period between childhood and adulthood; young people collectively; the early stages of something; a young man or boy.—**youthful** *adj*.—**youthfully** *adv*.

youth hostel *n* a supervised lodging for usu young travellers.

you've = you have.

zany *adj* (**zanier, zaniest**) comical; eccentric.—**zaniness** *n*.

zeal *n* fervent devotion; fanaticism.

zealous *adj* full of zeal; ardent.—**zealously** *adv*.

zebra *n* (*pl* **zebras, zebra**) a black and white striped wild animal related to the horse.

zebra crossing *n* a street crossing for pedestrians marked by black and white strips on the road.

zero *n* (*pl* **zeros**) the symbol 0; nothing; the lowest point; freezing point, 0 degrees Celsius.

zest *n* the outer part of the skin of an orange or lemon used to give flavour; enthusiasm; excitement.—**zestful** *adj*.

zigzag *n* a series of short, sharp angles in alternate directions. * *adj* having sharp turns. * *vti* (*pt* **zigzagged**) to move or form in a zigzag.

zinc *n* a bluish-white metallic element used in alloys and batteries.

zip *n* a slide fastener on clothing, bags, etc with interlocking teeth. * *vt* (*pt* **zipped**) to fasten with a zip.

zipper *n* a zip.

zither *n* a stringed instrument played by plucking.

zodiac *n* an imaginary belt in the heavens, along which the sun, moon, and planets appear to move, divided into twelve equal areas; a diagram representing this.

zombie *n* a person who is lifeless and apathetic; an automaton.

zone *n* a region, area; a subdivision; any area with a specified use or restriction.—**zonal** *adj*.

zoo *n* (*pl* **zoos**) a place where wild animals are kept for public show.

zoology *n* the study of animals with regard to their classification, structure and habits.—**zoological** *adj*.—**zoologist** *n*.

zoom *vi* to go quickly, to speed; to climb upwards sharply in an aeroplane; to rise rapidly; (*photog*) to focus in on, using a zoom lens.

zoom lens *n* (*photog*) a camera lens that makes distant objects appear closer without moving the camera.

A

aback *adv* back, backward, rearward, regressively.

abaft *prep* (*naut*) aft, astern, back of, behind.

abandon *vb* abdicate, abjure, desert, drop, evacuate, forsake, forswear, leave, quit, relinquish, yield; cede, forgo, give up, let go, renounce, resign, surrender, vacate, waive. * *n* careless freedom, dash, impetuosity, impulse, wildness.

abandoned *adj* depraved, derelict, deserted, discarded, dropped, forsaken, left, outcast, rejected, relinquished; corrupt, demoralized, depraved, dissolute, graceless, impenitent, irreclaimable, lost, obdurate, profligate, reprobate, shameless, sinful, unprincipled, vicious, wicked.

abandonment *n* desertion, dereliction, giving up, leaving, relinquishment, renunciation, surrender.

abase *vb* depress, drop, lower, reduce, sink; debase, degrade, disgrace, humble, humiliate.

abasement *n* abjection, debasement, degradation, disgrace, humbleness, humiliation, shame.

abash *vb* affront, bewilder, confound, confuse, dash, discompose, disconcert, embarrass, humiliate, humble, shame, snub.

abashment *n* confusion, embarrassment, humiliation, mortification, shame.

abate *vb* diminish, decrease, lessen, lower, moderate, reduce, relax, remove, slacken; allow, bate, deduct, mitigate, rebate, remit; allay, alleviate, appease, assuage, blunt, calm, compose, dull, mitigate, moderate, mollify, pacify, qualify, quiet, quell, soften, soothe, tranquillize.

abatement *n* alleviation, assuagement, decrement, decrease, extenuation, mitigation, moderation, remission; cessation, decline, diminution, ebb, fading, lowering, sinking, settlement; allowance, deduction, rebate, reduction.

abbey *n* convent, monastery, priory.

abbreviate *vb* abridge, compress, condense, contract, cut, curtail, epitomize, reduce, retrench, shorten.

abbreviation *n* abridgment, compression, condensation, contraction, curtailment, cutting, reduction, shortening.

abdicate *vb* abandon, cede, forgo, forsake, give up, quit, relinquish, renounce, resign, retire, surrender.

abdication *n* abandonment, abdicating, relinquishment, renunciation, resignation, surrender.

abdomen *n* belly, gut, paunch, stomach.

abduct *vb* carry off, kidnap, spirit away, take away.

abduction *n* carrying off, kidnapping, removal, seizure, withdrawal.

aberrant *adj* deviating, devious, divergent, diverging, erratic, rambling, wandering; abnormal, anomalistic, anomalous, disconnected, eccentric, erratic, exceptional, inconsequent, peculiar, irregular, preternatural, singular, strange, unnatural, unusual.

aberration *n* departure, deviation, divergence, rambling, wandering; abnormality, anomaly, eccentricity, irregularity, peculiarity, singularity, unconformity; delusion, disorder, hallucination, illusion, instability.

abet *vb* aid, assist, back, help, support, sustain, uphold; advocate, condone, countenance, encourage, favour, incite, sanction.

abettor *n* ally, assistant; adviser, advocate, promoter; accessory, accomplice, associate, confederate.

abeyance *n* anticipation, calculation, expectancy, waiting; dormancy, inactivity, intermission, quiescence, remission, reservation, suppression, suspension.

abhor *vb* abominate, detest, dislike intensely, execrate, hate, loathe, nauseate, view with horror.

abhorrence *n* abomination, antipathy, aversion, detestation, disgust, hatred, horror, loathing.

abhorrent *adj* abominating, detesting, hating, loathing; hateful, horrifying, horrible, loathsome, nauseating, odious, offensive, repellent, repugnant, repulsive, revolting, shocking.

abide *vb* lodge, rest, sojourn, stay, wait; dwell, inhabit, live, reside; bear, continue, persevere, persist, remain; endure, last, suffer, tolerate; (*with* **by**) act up to, conform to, discharge, fulfil, keep, persist in.

abiding *adj* changeless, constant, continuing, durable, enduring, immutable, lasting, permanent, stable, unchangeable.

ability *n* ableness, adroitness, aptitude, aptness, cleverness, dexterity, efficacy, efficiency, facility, might, ingenuity, knack, power, readiness, skill, strength, talent, vigour; competency, qualification; calibre, capability, capacity, expertness, faculty, gift, parts.

abject *adj* base, beggarly, contemptible, cringing, degraded, despicable, dirty, grovelling, ignoble, low, mean, menial, miserable, paltry, pitiful, poor, servile, sneaking, slavish, vile, worthless, wretched.

abjectness *n* abasement, abjection, baseness, contemptibleness, meanness, pitifulness, servility, vileness.

abjuration *n* abandonment, abnegation, discarding, disowning, rejection, relinquishment, renunciation, repudiation; disavowal, disclaimer, disclaiming, recall, recantation, repeal, retraction, reversal, revocation.

abjure *vb* abandon, discard, disclaim, disown, forgo, forswear, give up, reject, relinquish, renounce, repudiate; disavow, disclaim, recall, recant, renounce, repeal, retract, revoke, withdraw.

able *adj* accomplished, adroit, apt, clever, expert, ingenious, practical, proficient, qualified, quick, skilful, talented, versed; competent, effective, efficient, fitted, quick; capable, gifted, mighty, powerful, talented; athletic, brawny, muscular, robust, stalwart, strong, vigorous.

ablution *n* baptism, bathing, cleansing, lavation, purification, washing.

abnegation *n* abandonment, denial, renunciation, surrender.

abnormal *adj* aberrant, anomalous, divergent, eccentric, exceptional, peculiar, odd, singular, strange, uncomfortable, unnatural, unusual, weird.

abnormality *n* abnormity, anomaly, deformity, idiosyncrasy, irregularity, monstrosity, peculiarity, oddity, singularity, unconformity.

aboard *adv* inside, within, on.

abode *n* domicile, dwelling, habitation, home, house, lodging, quarters, residence, residency, seat.

abolish *vb* abrogate, annul, cancel, eliminate, invalidate, nullify, quash, repeal, rescind, revoke; annihilate, destroy, end, eradicate, extirpate, extinguish, obliterate, overthrow, suppress, terminate.

abolition *n* abrogation, annulling, annulment, cancellation, cancelling, nullification, repeal, rescinding, rescission, revocation; annihilation, destruction, eradication, extinction, extinguishment, extirpation, obliteration, overthrow, subversion, suppression.

abominable *adj* accursed, contemptible, cursed, damnable, detestable, execrable, hellish, horrid, nefarious, odious; abhorrent, detestable, disgusting, foul, hateful, loathsome, nauseous, obnoxious, shocking, revolting, repugnant, repulsive; shabby, vile, wretched.

abominate *vb* abhor, detest, execrate, hate, loathe, recoil from, revolt at, shrink from, shudder at.

abomination *n* abhorrence, antipathy, aversion, detestation, disgust, execration, hatred, loathing, nauseation; contamination, corruption, corruptness, defilement, foulness, impurity, loathsomeness, odiousness, pollution, taint, uncleanness;

annoyance, curse, evil, infliction, nuisance, plague, torment.

aboriginal *adj* autochthonal, autochthonous, first, indigenous, native, original, primary, prime, primeval, primitive, pristine.

abortion *n* miscarriage, premature labour; disappointment, failure.

abortive *adj* immature, incomplete, rudimental, rudimentary, stunted, untimely; futile, fruitless, idle, ineffectual, inoperative, nugatory, profitless, unavailing, unsuccessful, useless, vain.

abound *vb* flow, flourish, increase, swarm, swell; exuberate, luxuriate, overflow, proliferate, swarm, teem.

about *prep* around, encircling, surrounding, round; near; concerning, referring to, regarding, relating to, relative to, respecting, touching, with regard to, with respect to; all over, over, through. * *adv* around, before; approximately, near, nearly.

above *adj* above-mentioned, aforementioned, aforesaid, foregoing, preceding, previous, prior. * *adv* aloft, overhead; before, previously; of a higher rank. * *prep* higher than, on top of; exceeding, greater than, more than, over; beyond, superior to.

above-board *adj* candid, frank, honest, open, straightforward, truthful, upright. * *adv* candidly, fairly, openly, sincerely.

abrade *vb* erase, erode, rub off, scrape out, wear away.

abrasion *n* attrition, disintegration, friction, wearing down; scrape, scratch.

abreast *adv* aligned, alongside.

abridge *vb* abbreviate, condense, compress, shorten, summarize; contract, diminish, lessen, reduce.

abridgment *n* compression, condensation, contraction, curtailment, diminution, epitomizing, reduction, shortening; abstract, brief, compendium, digest, epitome, outline, précis, summary, syllabus, synopsis; deprivation, limitation, restriction.

abroad *adv* expansively, unrestrainedly, ubiquitously, widely; forth, out of doors; overseas; extensively, publicly.

abrogate *vb* abolish, annul, cancel, invalidate, nullify, overrule, quash, repeal, rescind, revoke, set aside, vacate, void.

abrogation *n* abolition, annulling, annulment, cancellation, cancelling, repeal rescinding, rescission, revocation, voidance, voiding.

abrupt *adj* broken, craggy, jagged, rough, rugged; acclivous, acclivitous, precipitous, steep; hasty, ill-timed, precipitate, sudden, unanticipated, unexpected; blunt, brusque, curt, discourteous; cramped, harsh, jerky, stiff.

abscess *n* boil, fester, pustule, sore, ulcer.

abscond *vb* bolt, decamp, elope, escape, flee, fly, retreat, run off, sneak away, steal away, withdraw.

absence *n* nonappearance, nonattendance; abstraction, distraction, inattention, musing, preoccupation, reverie; default, defect, deficiency, lack, privation.

absent *adj* abroad, away, elsewhere, gone, not present, otherwhere; abstracted, dreaming, inattentive, lost, musing, napping, preoccupied.

absolute *adj* complete, ideal, independent, perfect, supreme, unconditional, unconditioned, unlimited, unqualified, unrestricted; arbitrary, authoritative, autocratic, despotic, dictatorial, imperious, irresponsible, tyrannical, tyrannous; actual, categorical, certain, decided, determinate, genuine, positive, real, unequivocal, unquestionable, veritable.

absolutely *adv* completely, definitely, unconditionally; actually, downright, indeed, indubitably, infallibly, positively, really, truly, unquestionably.

absoluteness *n* actuality, completeness, ideality, perfection, positiveness, reality, supremeness; absolutism, arbitrariness, despotism, tyranny.

absolution *n* acquittal, clearance, deliverance, discharge, forgiveness, liberation, pardon, release, remission, shrift, shriving.

absolutism *n* absoluteness, arbitrariness, autocracy, despotism, tyranny.

absolve *vb* acquit, clear, deliver, discharge, exculpate, excuse, exonerate, forgive, free, liberate, loose, pardon, release, set free, shrive.

absorb *vb* appropriate, assimilate, drink in, imbibe, soak up; consume, destroy, devour, engorge, engulf, exhaust, swallow up, take up; arrest, engage, engross, fix, immerse, occupy, rivet.

absorbent *adj* absorbing, imbibing, penetrable, porous, receptive.

absorption *adj* appropriation, assimilation, imbibing, osmosis, soaking up; consumption, destroying, devouring, engorgement, engulfing, exhaustion, swallowing up; concentration, engagement, engrossment, immersion, occupation, preoccupation.

abstain *vb* avoid, cease, deny oneself, desist, forbear, refrain, refuse, stop, withhold.

abstemious *adj* abstinent, frugal, moderate, self-denying, sober, temperate.

abstinence *n* abstemiousness, avoidance, forbearance, moderation, self-restraint, soberness, sobriety, teetotalism, temperance.

abstinent *adj* abstaining, fasting; abstemious, restraining, self-denying, self-restraining, sober, temperate.

abstract *vb* detach, disengage, disjoin, dissociate, disunite, isolate, separate; appropriate, purloin, seize, steal, take; abbreviate, abridge, epitomize. * *adj* isolated, separate, simple, unrelated; abstracted, occult, recondite, refined, subtle, vague; nonobjective, nonrepresentational. * *n* abridgment, condensation, digest, excerpt, extract, précis, selection, summary, synopsis.

abstracted *adj* absent, absent-minded, dreaming, inattentive, lost, musing, preoccupied; abstruse, refined, subtle.

abstraction *n* absence, absent-mindedness, brown study, inattention, muse, musing, preoccupation, reverie; disconnection, disjunction, isolation, separation; abduction, appropriation, pilfering, purloining, seizure, stealing, taking.

abstruse *adj* abstract, attenuated, dark, difficult, enigmatic, hidden, indefinite, mysterious, mystic, mystical, obscure, occult, profound, recondite, remote, subtle, transcendental, vague.

absurd *adj* egregious, fantastic, foolish, incongruous, ill-advised, ill-judged, irrational, ludicrous, nonsensical, nugatory, preposterous, ridiculous, self-annulling, senseless, silly, stupid, unreasonable.

absurdity *n* drivel, extravagance, fatuity, folly, foolery, foolishness, idiocy, nonsense.

abundance *n* affluence, amplitude, ampleness, copiousness, exuberance, fertility, flow, flood, largeness, luxuriance, opulence, overflow, plenitude, profusion, richness, store, wealth.

abundant *adj* abounding, ample, bountiful, copious, exuberant, flowing, full, good, large, lavish, rich, liberal, much, overflowing, plentiful, plenteous, replete, teeming, thick.

abuse *vb* betray, cajole, deceive, desecrate, dishonour, misapply, misemploy, misuse, pervert, pollute, profane, prostitute, violate, wrong; harm, hurt, ill-use, ill-treat, injure, maltreat, mishandle; asperse, berate, blacken, calumniate, defame, disparage, lampoon, lash, malign, revile, reproach, satirize, slander, traduce, upbraid, vilify. * *n* desecration, dishonour, ill-use, misuse, perversion, pollution, profanation; ill-treatment, maltreatment, outrage; malfeasance, malversation; aspersion, defamation, disparagement, insult, invective, obloquy, opprobrium, railing, rating, reviling, ribaldry, rudeness, scurrility, upbraiding, vilification, vituperation.

abusive *adj* calumnious, carping, condemnatory, contumelious, damnatory, denunciatory, injurious, insolent, insulting, offensive, opprobrious, reproachful, reviling, ribald, rude, scurrilous, vilificatory, vituperative.

abut *vb* adjoin, border, impinge, meet, project.

abutment *n* bank, bulwark, buttress, embankment, fortification; abutting, abuttal, adjacency, contiguity, juxtaposition.

abuttal *n* adjacency, boundary, contiguity, juxtaposition, nearness, next, terminus.

abyss *n* abysm, chasm, gorge, gulf, pit.

academic *adj* collegiate, lettered, scholastic. * *n* academician, classicist, doctor, fellow, pundit, savant, scholar, student, teacher.

academy *n* college, high school, institute, school.

accede *vb* accept, acquiesce, agree, assent to, comply with, concur, consent, yield.

accelerate *vb* dispatch, expedite, forward, hasten, hurry, precipitate, press on, quicken, speed, urge on.

acceleration *n* expedition, hastening, hurrying, quickening, pickup, precipitation, speeding up, stepping up.

accent *vb* accentuate, emphasize, stress. * *n* cadence, inflection, intonation, tone; beat, emphasis, ictus.

accentuate *vb* accent, emphasize, mark, point up, punctuate, stress; highlight, overemphasize, overstress, underline, underscore.

accept *vb* acquire, derive, get, gain, obtain, receive, take; accede to, acknowledge, acquiesce in, admit, agree to, approve, assent to, avow, embrace; estimate, construe, interpret, regard, value.

acceptable *adj* agreeable, gratifying, pleasant, pleasing, pleasurable, welcome.

acceptance *n* accepting, acknowledgment, receipt, reception, taking; approbation, approval, gratification, satisfaction.

acceptation *n* construction, import, interpretation, meaning, sense, significance, signification, understanding; adoption, approval, currency, vogue.

access *vb* broach, enter, open, open up. * *n* approach, avenue, entrance, entry, passage, way; admission, admittance, audience, interview; addition, accession, aggrandizement, enlargement, gain, increase, increment; (*med*) attack, fit, onset, recurrence.

accession *n* addition, augmentation, enlargement, extension, increase; succession.

accessory *adj* abetting, additional, additive, adjunct, aiding, ancillary, assisting, contributory, helping, subsidiary, subordinate, supplemental. * *n* abettor, accomplice, assistant, associate, confederate, helper; accompaniment, attendant, concomitant, detail, subsidiary.

accident *n* calamity, casualty, condition, contingency, disaster, fortuity, incident, misadventure, miscarriage, mischance, misfortune, mishap; affection, alteration, chance, contingency, mode, modification, property, quality, state.

accidental *adj* casual, chance, contingent, fortuitous, undesigned, unintended; adventitious, dispensable, immaterial, incidental, nonessential.

acclamation *n* acclaim, applause, cheer, cry, plaudit, outcry, salutation, shouting.

acclimatization, acclimation *n* adaptation, adjustment, conditioning, familiarization, habituation, inurement, naturalization.

acclimatize, acclimate *vb* accustom, adapt, adjust, condition, familiarize, habituate, inure, naturalize, season.

acclivity *n* ascent, height, hill, rising ground, steep, upward slope.

accommodate *vb* contain, furnish, hold, oblige, serve, supply; adapt, fit, suit; adjust, compose, harmonize, reconcile, settle.

accommodation *n* advantage, convenience, privilege; adaptation, agreement, conformity, fitness, suitableness; adjustment, harmonization, harmony, pacification, reconciliation, settlement.

accompaniment *n* adjunct, appendage, attachment, attendant, concomitant.

accompany *vb* attend, chaperon, convoy, escort, follow, go with.

accomplice *n* abettor, accessory, ally, assistant, associate, confederate, partner.

accomplish *vb* achieve, bring about, carry, carry through, complete, compass, consummate, do, effect, execute, perform, perfect; conclude, end, finish, terminate.

accomplished *adj* achieved, completed, done, effected, executed, finished, fulfilled, realized; able, adroit, apt, consummate, educated, experienced, expert, finished, instructed, practised, proficient, qualified, ripe, skilful, versed; elegant, fashionable, fine, polished, polite, refined.

accomplishment *n* achievement, acquirement, attainment, qualification; completion, fulfilment.

accord *vb* admit, allow, concede, deign, give, grant, vouchsafe, yield; agree, assent, concur, correspond, harmonize, quadrate, tally. * *n* accordance, agreement, concord, concurrence, conformity, consensus, harmony, unanimity, unison.

accordant *adj* agreeable, agreeing, congruous, consonant, harmonious, suitable, symphonious.

accordingly *adv* agreeably, conformably, consistently, suitably; consequently, hence, so, thence, therefore, thus, whence, wherefore.

accost *vb* address, confront, greet, hail, salute, speak to, stop.

account *vb* assess, appraise, estimate, evaluate, judge, rate; (*with* **for**) assign, attribute, explain, expound, justify, rationalize, vindicate. * *n* inventory, record, register, score; bill, book, charge; calculation, computation, count, reckoning, score, tale, tally; chronicle, detail, description, narration, narrative, portrayal, recital, rehearsal, relation, report, statement, tidings, word; elucidation, explanation, exposition; consideration, ground, motive, reason, regard, sake; consequence, consideration, dignity, distinction, importance, note, repute, reputation, worth.

accountable *adj* amenable, answerable, duty-bound, liable, responsible.

accoutre *vb* arm, dress, equip, fit out, furnish.

accredit *vb* authorize, depute, empower, entrust.

accrue *vb* arise, come, follow, flow, inure, issue, proceed, result.

accumulate *vb* agglomerate, aggregate, amass, bring together, collect, gather, grow, hoard, increase, pile, store.

accumulation *n* agglomeration, aggregation, collection, heap, hoard, mass, pile, store.

accuracy *n* carefulness, correctness, exactness, fidelity, precision, strictness.

accurate *adj* close, correct, exact, faithful, nice, precise, regular, strict, true, truthful.

accusation *n* arraignment, charge, incrimination, impeachment, indictment.

accuse *vb* arraign, charge, censure, impeach, indict, tax.

accustom *vb* discipline, drill, familiarize, habituate, harden, inure, train, use.

ace *n* (*cards, dice*) one spot, single pip, single point; atom, bit, grain, iota, jot, particle, single, unit, whit; expert, master, virtuoso. * *adj* best, expert, fine, outstanding, superb.

acerbity *n* acidity, acridity, acridness, astringency, bitterness, roughness, sourness, tartness; acrimony, bitterness, harshness, severity, venom.

achieve *vb* accomplish, attain, complete, do, effect, execute, finish, fulfil, perform, realize; acquire, gain, get, obtain, win.

achievement *n* accomplishment, acquirement, attainment, completion, consummation, performance, realization; deed, exploit, feat, work.

acid *adj* pungent, sharp, sour, stinging, tart, vinegary.

acknowledge *vb* recognize; accept, admit, accept, allow, concede, grant; avow, confess, own, profess.

acme *n* apex, climax, height, peak, pinnacle, summit, top, vertex, zenith.

acquaint *vb* familiarize; announce, apprise, communicate, enlighten, disclose, inform, make aware, make known, notify, tell.

acquaintance *n* companionship, familiarity, fellowship, intimacy, knowledge; associate, companion, comrade, friend.

acquiesce *vb* bow, comply, consent, give way, rest, submit, yield; agree, assent, concur, consent.

acquire *vb* achieve, attain, earn, gain, get, have, obtain, procure, realize, secure, win; learn thoroughly, master.

acquirement *n* acquiring, gaining, gathering, mastery; acquisition, accomplishment, attainment.

acquit *vb* absolve, clear, discharge, exculpate, excuse, exonerate, forgive, liberate, pardon, pay, quit, release, set free, settle.

acquittal *n* absolution, acquittance, clearance, deliverance, discharge, exoneration, liberation, release.

acquittance *n* discharge; quittance, receipt.

acrid *adj* biting, bitter, caustic, pungent, sharp.

acrimonious *adj* acrid, bitter, caustic, censorious, crabbed, harsh, malignant, petulant, sarcastic, severe, testy, virulent.

acrimony *n* causticity, causticness, corrosiveness, sharpness; abusiveness, acridity, asperity, bitterness, churlishness, harshness, rancour, severity, spite, venom.

act *vb* do, execute, function, make, operate, work; enact, feign, perform, play. * *n* achievement, deed, exploit, feat, performance, proceeding, turn; bill, decree, enactment, law, ordinance, statute; actuality, existence, fact, reality.

acting *adj* interim, provisional, substitute, temporary. * *n* enacting, impersonation, performance, portrayal, theatre; counterfeiting, dissimulation, imitation, pretence.

action *n* achievement, activity, agency, deed, exertion, exploit, feat; battle, combat, conflict, contest, encounter, engagement, operation; lawsuit, prosecution.

active *adj* effective, efficient, influential, living, operative; assiduous, bustling, busy, diligent, industrious, restless; agile, alert, brisk, energetic, lively, nimble, prompt, quick, smart, spirited, sprightly, supple; animated, ebullient, fervent, vigorous.

actual *adj* certain, decided, genuine, objective, real, substantial, tangible, true, veritable; perceptible, present, sensible, tangible; absolute, categorical, positive.

actuate *vb* impel, incite, induce, instigate, move, persuade, prompt.

acumen *n* acuteness, astuteness, discernment, ingenuity, keenness, penetration, sagacity, sharpness, shrewdness.

acute *adj* pointed, sharp; astute, bright, discerning, ingenious, intelligent, keen, quick, penetrating, piercing, sagacious, sage, sharp, shrewd, smart, subtle; distressing, fierce, intense, piercing, pungent, poignant, severe, violent; high, high-toned, sharp, shrill; (*med*) sudden, temporary, violent.

adage *n* aphorism, dictum, maxim, proverb, saw, saying.

adapt *vb* accommodate, adjust, conform, coordinate, fit, qualify, proportion, suit, temper.

add *vb* adjoin, affix, annex, append, attach, join, tag; sum, sum up, total.

addict *vb* accustom, apply, dedicate, devote, habituate. * *n* devotee, enthusiast, fan; head, junkie, user.

addicted *adj* attached, devoted, given up to, inclined, prone, wedded.

addition *n* augmentation, accession, enlargement, extension, increase, supplement; adjunct, appendage, appendix, extra.

address *vb* accost, apply to, court, direct. * *n* appeal, application, entreaty, invocation, memorial, petition, request, solicitation, suit; discourse, oration, lecture, sermon, speech; ability, adroitness, art, dexterity, expertness, skill; courtesy, deportment, demeanour, tact.

adduce *vb* advance, allege, assign, offer, present; cite, mention, name.

adept *adj* accomplished, experienced, practised, proficient, skilled. * *n* expert, master, virtuoso.

adequate *adj* able, adapted, capable, competent, equal, fit, requisite, satisfactory, sufficient, suitable.

adhere *vb* cling, cleave, cohere, hold, stick; appertain, belong, pertain.

adherent *adj* adhering, clinging, sticking. * *n* acolyte, dependant, disciple, follower, partisan, supporter, vassal.

adhesion *n* adherence, attachment, clinging, coherence, sticking.

adhesive *adj* clinging, sticking; glutinous,

gummy, sticky, tenacious, viscous. * *n* binder, cement, glue, paste.

adieu *n* farewell, goodbye, parting, valediction.

adipose *adj* fat, fatty, greasy, oily, oleaginous, sebaceous.

adjacent *adj* adjoining, bordering, conterminous, contiguous, near, near to, neighbouring, touching.

adjoin *vb* abut, add, annex, append, border, combine, neighbour, unite, verge.

adjourn *vb* defer, delay, postpone, procrastinate; close, dissolve, end, interrupt, prorogue, suspend.

adjudge *vb* allot, assign, award; decide, decree, determine, settle.

adjunct *n* addition, advantage, appendage, appurtenance, attachment, attribute, auxiliary, dependency, help.

adjure *vb* beg, beseech, entreat, pray, supplicate.

adjust *vb* adapt, arrange, dispose, rectify; regulate, set right, settle, suit; compose, harmonize, pacify, reconcile, settle; accommodate, adapt, fit, suit.

administer *vb* contribute, deal out, dispense, supply; conduct, control, direct, govern, manage, oversee, superintend; conduce, contribute.

admirable *adj* astonishing, striking, surprising, wonderful; excellent, fine, rare, superb.

admiration *n* affection, approbation, approval, astonishment, delight, esteem, pleasure, regard.

admirer *n* beau, gallant, suitor, sweetheart; fan, follower, supporter.

admissible *adj* allowable, lawful, permissible, possible.

admission *n* access, admittance, entrance, introduction; acceptance, acknowledgement, allowance, assent, avowal, concession.

admit *vb* give access to, let in, receive; agree to, accept, acknowledge, concede, confess; allow, bear, permit, suffer, tolerate.

admonish *vb* censure, rebuke, reprove; advise caution, counsel, enjoin, forewarn, warn; acquaint, apprise, inform, instruct, notify, remind.

admonition *n* censure, rebuke, remonstrance; advice, caution, chiding, counsel, instruction, monition.

adolescence *n* minority, nonage, teens, youth.

adolescent *adj* juvenile, young, youthful. * *n* minor, teenager, youth.

adopt *vb* appropriate, assume; accept, approve, avow, espouse, maintain, support; affiliate, father, foster.

adore *vb* worship; esteem, honour, idolize, love, revere, venerate.

adorn *vb* beautify, decorate, embellish, enrich, garnish, gild, grace, ornament.

adroit *adj* apt, dextrous, expert, handy, ingenious, ready, skilful.

adulation *n* blandishment, cajolery, fawning, flattery, flummery, praise, sycophancy.

adult *adj* grown-up, mature, ripe, ripened. * *n* grown-up person.

adulterate *vb* alloy, contaminate, corrupt, debase, deteriorate, vitiate.

advance *adj* beforehand, forward, leading. * *vb* propel, push, send forward; aggrandize, dignify, elevate, exalt, promote; benefit, forward, further, improve, promote; adduce, allege, assign, offer, propose, propound; augment, increase; proceed, progress; grow, improve, prosper, thrive. * *n* march, progress; advancement, enhancement, growth, promotion, rise; offer, overture, proffering, proposal, proposition, tender; appreciation, rise.

advancement *n* advance, benefit, gain, growth, improvement, profit.

advantage *n* ascendancy, precedence, preeminence, superiority, upper-hand; benefit, blessing, emolument, gain, profit, return; account, behalf, interest; accommodation, convenience, prerogative, privilege.

advantageous *adj* beneficial, favourable, profitable.

advent *n* accession, approach, arrival, coming, visitation.

adventitious *adj* accidental, extraneous, extrinsic, foreign, fortuitous, nonessential.

adventure *vb* dare, hazard, imperil, peril, risk, venture. * *n* chance, contingency, experiment, fortuity, hazard, risk, venture; crisis, contingency, event, incident, occurrence, transaction.

adventurous *adj* bold, chivalrous, courageous, daring, doughty; foolhardy, headlong, precipitate, rash, reckless; dangerous, hazardous, perilous.

adversary *n* antagonist, enemy, foe, opponent.

adverse *adj* conflicting, contrary, opposing; antagonistic, harmful, hostile, hurtful, inimical, unfavourable, unpropitious; calamitous, disastrous, unfortunate, unlucky, untoward.

adversity *n* affliction, calamity, disaster, distress, misery, misfortune, sorrow, suffering, woe.

advertise *vb* advise, announce, declare, inform, placard, proclaim, publish.

advertisement *n* announcement, information, notice, proclamation.

advice *n* admonition, caution, counsel, exhortation, persuasion, suggestion, recommendation; information, intelligence, notice, notification; care, counsel, deliberation, forethought.

advisable *adj* advantageous, desirable, expedient, prudent.

advise *vb* admonish, counsel, commend, recommend, suggest, urge; acquaint, apprise, inform, notify; confer, consult, deliberate.

adviser *n* counsellor, director, guide, instructor.

advocate *vb* countenance, defend, favour, justify, maintain, support, uphold, vindicate. * *n* apologist, counsellor, defender, maintainer, patron, pleader, supporter; attorney, barrister, counsel, lawyer, solicitor.

aegis *n* defence, protection, safeguard, shelter.

aesthetic *adj* appropriate, beautiful, tasteful.

affable *adj* accessible, approachable, communicative, conversable, cordial, easy, familiar, frank, free, sociable, social; complaisant, courteous, civil, obliging, polite, urbane.

affair *n* business, circumstance, concern, matter, office, question; event, incident, occurrence, performance, proceeding, transaction; battle, combat, conflict, encounter, engagement, skirmish.

affairs *npl* administration, relations; business, estate, finances, property.

affect *vb* act upon, alter, change, influence, modify, transform; concern, interest, regard, relate; improve, melt, move, overcome, subdue, touch; aim at, aspire to, crave, yearn for; adopt, assume, feign.

affectation *n* affectedness, airs, artificiality, foppery, pretension, simulation.

affected *adj* artificial, assumed, feigned, insincere, theatrical; assuming, conceited, foppish, vain.

affection *n* bent, bias, feeling, inclination, passion, proclivity, propensity; accident, attribute, character, mark, modification, mode, note, property; attachment, endearment, fondness, goodwill, kindness, partiality, love.

affectionate *adj* attached, devoted, fond, kind, loving, sympathetic, tender.

affiliate *vb* ally, annex, associate, connect, incorporate, join, unite. * *n* ally, associate, confederate.

affinity *n* connection, propinquity, relationship; analogy, attraction, correspondence, likeness, relation, resemblance, similarity, sympathy.

affirm *vb* allege, assert, asseverate, aver, declare, state; approve, confirm, establish, ratify.

affix *vb* annex, attach, connect, fasten, join, subjoin, tack.

afflict *vb* agonize, distress, grieve, pain, persecute, plague, torment, trouble, try, wound.

affliction *n* adversity, calamity, disaster, misfortune, stroke, visitation; bitterness, depression, distress, grief, misery, plague, scourge, sorrow, trial, tribulation, wretchedness, woe.

affluent *adj* abounding, abundant, bounteous, plenteous; moneyed, opulent, rich, wealthy.

afford *vb* furnish, produce, supply, yield; bestow, communicate, confer, give, grant, impart, offer; bear, endure, support.

affray *n* brawl, conflict, disturbance, feud, fight, quarrel, scuffle, struggle.

affright *vb* affray, alarm, appal, confound, dismay, shock, startle. * *n* alarm, consternation, fear, fright, panic, terror.

affront *vb* abuse, insult, outrage; annoy, chafe, displease, fret, irritate, offend, pique, provoke, vex. * *n* abuse, contumely, insult, outrage, vexation, wrong.

afraid *adj* aghast, alarmed, anxious, apprehensive, frightened, scared, timid.

after *prep* later than, subsequent to; behind, following; about, according to; because of, in imitation of. * *adj* behind, consecutive, ensuing, following, later, succeeding, successive, subsequent; aft, back, hind, rear, rearmost, tail.* *adv* afterwards, later, next, since, subsequently, then, thereafter.

again *adv* afresh, anew, another time, once more; besides, further, in addition, moreover.

against *prep* adverse to, contrary to, in opposition to, resisting; abutting, close up to, facing, fronting, off, opposite to, over; in anticipation of, for, in expectation of; in compensation for, to counterbalance, to match.

age *vb* decline, grow old, mature. * *n* aeon, date, epoch, period, time; decline, old age, senility; antiquity, oldness.

agency *n* action, force, intervention, means, mediation, operation, procurement; charge, direction, management, superintendence, supervision.

agent *n* actor, doer, executor, operator, performer; active element, cause, force; attorney, broker, commissioner, deputy, factor, intermediary, manager, middleman.

agglomeration *n* accumulation, aggregation, conglomeration, heap, lump, pile.

agglutinate *vb* cement, fasten, glue, unite.

aggrandize *vb* advance, dignify, elevate, enrich, exalt, promote.

aggravate *vb* heighten, increase, worsen; colour, exaggerate, magnify, overstate; enrage, irritate, provoke, tease.

aggravation *n* exaggeration, heightening, irritation.

aggregate *vb* accumulate, amass, collect, heap, pile. * *adj* collected, total. * *n* amount, gross, total, whole.

aggressive *adj* assailing, assailant, assaulting, attacking, invading, offensive; pushing, self-assertive.

aggressor *n* assailant, assaulter, attacker, invader.

aggrieve *vb* afflict, grieve, pain; abuse, ill-treat, impose, injure, oppress, wrong.

aghast *adj* appalled, dismayed, frightened, horrified, horror-struck, panic-stricken, terrified; amazed, astonished, startled, thunderstruck.

agile *adj* active, alert, brisk, lively, nimble, prompt, smart, ready.

agitate *vb* disturb, jar, rock, shake, trouble; disquiet, excite, ferment, rouse, trouble; confuse, discontent, flurry, fluster, flutter; canvass, debate, discuss, dispute, investigate.

agitation *n* concussion, shake, shaking; commotion, convulsion, disturbance, ferment, jarring, storm, tumult, turmoil; discomposure, distraction, emotion, excitement, flutter, perturbation, ruffle, tremor, trepidation; controversy, debate, discussion.

agnostic *n* doubter, empiricist, sceptic.

agonize *vb* distress, excruciate, rack, torment, torture.

agony *n* anguish, distress, pangs.

agree *vb* accord, concur, harmonize, unite; accede, acquiesce, assent, comply, concur, subscribe; bargain, contract, covenant, engage, promise, undertake; compound, compromise; chime, cohere, conform, correspond, match, suit, tally.

agreeable *adj* charming, pleasant, pleasing.

agreement *n* accordance, compliance, concord, harmony, union; bargain, compact, contract, pact, treaty.

agriculture *n* cultivation, culture, farming, geoponics, husbandry, tillage.

aid *vb* assist, help, serve, support; relieve, succour; advance, facilitate, further, promote. * *n* assistance, cooperation, help, patronage; alms, subsidy, succour, relief.

ailment *n* disease, illness, sickness.
aim *vb* direct, level, point, train; design, intend, mean, purpose, seek. * *n* bearing, course, direction, tendency; design, object, view, reason.
air *vb* expose, display, ventilate. * *n* atmosphere, breeze; appearance, aspect, manner; melody, tune.
aisle *n* passage, walk.
akin *adj* allied, kin, related; analogous, cognate, congenial, connected.
alacrity *n* agility, alertness, activity, eagerness, promptitude; cheerfulness, gaiety, hilarity, liveliness, vivacity.
alarm *vb* daunt, frighten, scare, startle, terrify. * *n* alarm-bell, tocsin, warning; apprehension, fear, fright, terror.
alert *adj* awake, circumspect, vigilant, watchful, wary; active, brisk, lively, nimble, quick, prompt, ready, sprightly. * *vb* alarm, arouse, caution, forewarn, signal, warn. * *n* alarm, signal, warning.
alertness *n* circumspection, vigilance, watchfulness, wariness; activity, briskness, nimbleness, promptness, readiness, spryness.
alien *adj* foreign, not native; differing, estranged, inappropriate, remote, unallied, separated. * *n* foreigner, stranger.
alienate *vb* (*legal*) assign, demise, transfer; disaffect, estrange, wean, withdraw.
alienation *n* (*legal*) assignment, conveyance, transfer; breach, disaffection, division, estrangement, rupture; (*med*) aberration, delusion, derangement, hallucination, insanity, madness.
alike *adj* akin, analogous, duplicate, identical, resembling, similar. * *adv* equally.
aliment *n* diet, fare, meat, nutriment, provision, rations, sustenance.
alive *adj* animate, breathing, live; aware, responsive, sensitive, susceptible; brisk, cheerful, lively, sprightly.
allay *vb* appease, calm, check, compose; alleviate, assuage, lessen, moderate, solace, temper.
allege *vb* affirm, assert, declare, maintain, say; adduce, advance, assign, cite, plead, produce, quote.
allegiance *n* duty, homage, fealty, fidelity, loyalty, obligation.
allegory *n* apologue, fable, myth, parable, story, tale.
alleviate *vb* assuage, lighten, mitigate, mollify, moderate, quell, quiet, quieten, soften, soothe.
alliance *n* affinity, intermarriage, relation; coalition, combination, confederacy, league, treaty, union; affiliation, connection, relationship, similarity.
allot *vb* divide, dispense, distribute; assign, fix, prescribe, specify.
allow *vb* acknowledge, admit, concede, confess, grant, own; authorize, grant, let, permit; bear, endure, suffer, tolerate; grant, yield, relinquish, spare; approve, justify, sanction; abate, bate, deduct, remit.
allude *vb* glance, hint, mention, imply, insinuate, intimate, refer, suggest, touch.
allure *vb* attract, beguile, cajole, coax, entice, lure, persuade, seduce, tempt. * *n* appeal, attraction, lure, temptation.
allusion *n* hint, implication, intimation, insinuation, mention, reference, suggestion.
ally *vb* combine, connect, join, league, marry, unite. * *n* aider, assistant, associate, coadjutor, colleague, friend, partner.
almighty *adj* all-powerful, omnipotent.
alms *npl* benefaction, bounty, charity, dole, gift, gratuity.
alone *adj* companionless, deserted, forsaken, isolated, lonely, only, single, sole, solitary.
along *adv* lengthways, lengthwise; forward, onward; beside, together, simultaneously.
aloud *adv* audibly, loudly, sonorously, vociferously.
alter *vb* change, conform, modify, shift, turn, transform, transmit, vary.
altercation *n* bickering, contention, controversy, dispute, dissension, strife, wrangling.
alternating *adj* intermittent, interrupted.
alternative *adj* another, different, second, substitute. * *n* choice, option, preference.

although *conj* albeit, even if, for all that, notwithstanding, though.
altitude *n* elevation, height, loftiness.
altogether *adv* completely, entirely, totally, utterly.
always *adv* continually, eternally, ever, evermore, perpetually, unceasingly.
amalgamate *vb* blend, combine, commingle, compound, incorporate, mix.
amass *vb* accumulate, aggregate, collect, gather, heap, scrape together.
amateur *n* dilettante, nonprofessional.
amaze *vb* astonish, astound, bewilder, confound, confuse, dumbfound, perplex, stagger, stupefy.
amazement *n* astonishment, bewilderment, confusion, marvel, surprise, wonder.
ambassador *n* deputy, envoy, legate, minister, plenipotentiary.
ambiguous *adj* dubious, doubtful, enigmatic, equivocal, uncertain, indefinite, indistinct, obscure, vague.
ambition *n* aspiration, emulation, longing, yearning.
ambitious *adj* aspiring, avid, eager, intent.
ameliorate *vb* amend, benefit, better, elevate, improve, mend.
amenability *n* amenableness, responsiveness; accountability, liability, responsibility.
amenable *adj* acquiescent, agreeable, persuadable, responsive, susceptible; accountable, liable, responsible.
amend *vb* better, correct, improve, mend, redress, reform.
amends *npl* atonement, compensation, expiation, indemnification, recompense, reparation, restitution.
amenity *n* agreeableness, mildness, pleasantness, softness; affability, civility, courtesy, geniality, graciousness, urbanity.
amiable *adj* attractive, benign, charming, genial, good-natured, harmonious, kind, lovable, lovely, pleasant, pleasing, sweet, winning, winsome.
amicable *adj* amiable, cordial, friendly, harmonious, kind, kindly, peaceable.
amiss *adj* erroneous, inaccurate, incorrect, faulty, improper, wrong. * *adv* erroneously, inaccurately, incorrectly, wrongly.
amnesty *n* absolution, condonation, dispensation, forgiveness, oblivion.
amorous *adj* ardent, enamoured, fond, longing, loving, passionate, tender; erotic, impassioned.
amorphous *adj* formless, irregular, shapeless, unshapen; noncrystalline, structureless; chaotic, characterless, clumsy, disorganized, misshapen, unorganized, vague.
amount *n* aggregate, sum, total.
ample *adj* broad, capacious, extended, extensive, great, large, roomy, spacious; abounding, abundant, copious, generous, liberal, plentiful; diffusive, unrestricted.
amputate *vb* clip, curtail, prune, lop, remove, separate, sever.
amuse *vb* charm, cheer, divert, enliven, entertain, gladden, relax, solace; beguile, cheat, deceive, delude, mislead.
amusement *n* diversion, entertainment, frolic, fun, merriment, pleasure.
analeptic *adj* comforting, invigorating, restorative.
analogy *n* correspondence, likeness, parallelism, parity, resemblance, similarity.
analysis *n* decomposition, dissection, resolution, separation.
anarchy *n* chaos, confusion, disorder, misrule, lawlessness, riot.
anathema *n* ban, curse, denunciation, excommunication, execration, malediction, proscription.
anatomy *n* dissection; form, skeleton, structure.
ancestor *n* father, forebear, forefather, progenitor.
ancestry *n* family, house, line, lineage; descent, genealogy, parentage, pedigree, stock.
anchor *vb* fasten, fix, secure; cast anchor, take firm hold. * *n* (*naut*) ground tackle; defence, hold, security, stay.
ancient *adj* old, primitive, pristine; antiquated, antique, archaic, obsolete.
ancillary *adj* accessory, auxiliary, contributory, helpful, instrumental.
angelic *adj* adorable, celestial, cherubic,

heavenly, saintly, seraphic; entrancing, enrapturing, rapturous, ravishing.

anger *vb* chafe, displease, enrage, gall, infuriate, irritate, madden. * *n* choler, exasperation, fury, gall, indignation, ire, passion, rage, resentment, spleen, wrath.

angle *vb* fish. * *n* divergence, flare, opening; bend, corner, crotch, cusp, point; fish-hook, hook.

angry *adj* chafed, exasperated, furious, galled, incensed, irritated, nettled, piqued, provoked, resentful.

anguish *n* agony, distress, grief, pang, rack, torment, torture.

anile *adj* aged, decrepit, doting, imbecile, senile.

animadversion *n* comment, notice, observation, remark; blame, censure, condemnation, reproof, stricture.

animate *vb* inform, quicken, vitalize, vivify; fortify, invigorate, revive; activate, enliven, excite, heat, impel, kindle, rouse, stimulate, stir, waken; elate, embolden, encourage, exhilarate, gladden, hearten. * *adj* alive, breathing, live, living, organic, quick.

animosity *n* bitterness, enmity, grudge, hatred, hostility, rancour, rankling, spleen, virulence.

annals *npl* archives, chronicles, records, registers, rolls.

annex *vb* affix, append, attach, subjoin, tag, tack; connect, join, unite.

annihilate *vb* abolish, annul, destroy, dissolve, exterminate, extinguish, kill, obliterate, raze, ruin.

annotation *n* comment, explanation, illustration, note, observation, remark.

announce *vb* advertise, communicate, declare, disclose, proclaim, promulgate, publish, report, reveal, trumpet.

announcement *n* advertisement, annunciation, bulletin, declaration, manifesto, notice, notification, proclamation.

annoy *vb* badger, chafe, disquiet, disturb, fret, hector, irk, irritate, molest, pain, pester, plague, trouble, vex, worry, wound.

annul *vb* abolish, abrogate, cancel, countermand, nullify, overrule, quash, repeal, recall, reverse, revoke.

anoint *vb* consecrate, oil, sanctify, smear.

anonymous *adj* nameless, unacknowledged, unsigned.

answer *vb* fulfil, rejoin, reply, respond, satisfy. * *n* rejoinder, reply, response, retort; confutation, rebuttal, refutation.

answerable *adj* accountable, amenable, correspondent, liable, responsible, suited.

antagonism *n* contradiction, discordance, disharmony, dissonant, incompatibility, opposition.

antecedent *adj* anterior, foregoing, forerunning, precedent, preceding, previous. * *n* forerunner, precursor.

anterior *adj* antecedent, foregoing, preceding, previous, prior; fore, front.

anticipate *vb* antedate, forestall, foretaste, prevent; count upon, expect, forecast, foresee.

anticipation *n* apprehension, contemplation, expectation, hope, prospect, trust; expectancy, forecast, foresight, foretaste, preconception, presentiment.

antidote *n* corrective, counteractive, counter-poison; cure, remedy, restorative, specific.

antipathy *n* abhorrence, aversion, disgust, detestation, hate, hatred, horror, loathing, repugnance.

antique *adj* ancient, archaic, bygone, old, old-fashioned.

anxiety *n* apprehension, care, concern, disquiet, fear, foreboding, misgiving, perplexity, trouble, uneasiness, vexation, worry.

anxious *adj* apprehensive, restless, solicitous, uneasy, unquiet, worried.

apart *adv* aloof, aside, separately; asunder.

apathetic *adj* cold, dull, impassive, inert, listless, obtuse, passionless, sluggish, torpid, unfeeling.

ape *vb* counterfeit, imitate, mimic; affect. * *n* simian, troglodyte; imitator, mimic; image, imitation, likeness, type.

aperture *n* chasm, cleft, eye, gap, opening, hole, orifice, passage.

aphorism *n* adage, apothegm, byword, maxim, proverb, saw, saying.
apish *adj* imitative, mimicking; affected, foppish, trifling.
aplomb *n* composure, confidence, equanimity, self-confidence.
apocryphal *adj* doubtful, fabulous, false, legendary, spurious, uncanonical.
apologetic *adj* exculpatory, excusatory; defensive, vindictive.
apology *n* defence, justification, vindication; acknowledgement, excuse, explanation, plea, reparation.
apostate *adj* backsliding, disloyal, faithless, false, perfidious, recreant, traitorous, untrue. * *n* backslider, deserter, pervert, renegade, turncoat.
apostle *n* angel, herald, messenger, missionary, preacher; advocate, follower, supporter.
apothegm *n* aphorism, byword, dictum, maxim, proverb, saw, saying.
appal *vb* affright, alarm, daunt, dismay, frighten, horrify, scare, shock.
apparel *n* attire, array, clothes, clothing, dress, garments, habit, raiment, robes, suit, trappings, vestments.
apparent *adj* discernible, perceptible, visible; conspicuous, evident, legible, manifest, obvious, open, patent, plain, unmistakable; external, ostensible, seeming, superficial.
apparition *n* appearance, appearing, epiphany, manifestation; being, form; ghost, phantom, spectre, spirit, vision.
appeal *vb* address, entreat, implore, invoke, refer, request, solicit. * *n* application, entreaty, invocation, solicitation, suit.
appear *vb* emerge, loom; break, open; arise, occur, offer; look, seem, show.
appearance *n* advent, arrival, apparition, coming; form, shape; colour, face, fashion, feature, guise, pretence, pretext; air, aspect, complexion, demeanour, manner, mien.
appease *vb* abate, allay, assuage, calm, ease, lessen, mitigate, pacify, placate, quell, soothe, temper, tranquillize.
appellation *n* address, cognomen, denomination, epithet, style, title.
append *vb* attach, fasten, hang; add, annex, subjoin, tack, tag.
appendix *n* addition, adjunct, appurtenance, codicil; excursus, supplement.
appetite *n* craving, desire, longing, lust, passion; gusto, relish, stomach, zest; hunger.
applaud *vb* acclaim, cheer, clap, compliment, encourage, extol, magnify.
applause *n* acclamation, approval, cheers, commendation, plaudit.
applicable *adj* adapted, appropriate, apt, befitting, fitting, germane, pertinent, proper, relevant.
application *n* emollient, lotion, ointment, poultice, wash; appliance, exercise, practice, use; appeal, petition, request, solicitation, suit; assiduity, constancy, diligence, effort, industry.
apply *vb* bestow, lay upon; appropriate, convert, employ, exercise, use; addict, address, dedicate, devote, direct, engage.
appoint *vb* determine, establish, fix, prescribe; bid, command, decree, direct, order, require; allot, assign, delegate, depute, detail, destine, settle; constitute, create, name, nominate; equip, furnish, supply.
apportion *vb* allocate, allot, allow, assign, deal, dispense, divide, share.
apposite *adj* apt, fit, germane, pertinent, relevant, suitable, pertinent.
appraise *vb* appreciate, estimate, prize, rate, value.
appreciate *vb* appreciate, esteem, estimate, rate, realize, value.
apprehend *vb* arrest, catch, detain, seize, take; conceive, imagine, regard, view; appreciate, perceive, realize, see, take in; fear, forebode; conceive, fancy, hold, imagine, presume, understand.
apprehension *n* arrest, capture, seizure; intellect, intelligence, mind, reason; discernment, intellect, knowledge, perception, sense; belief, fancy, idea, notion, sentiment, view; alarm, care, dread, distrust, fear, misgiving, suspicion.
apprise *vb* acquaint, inform, notify, tell.
approach *vb* advance, approximate, come close; broach; resemble. * *n* advance,

advent; approximation, convergence, nearing, tendency; entrance, path, way.

approbation *n* approval, commendation, liking, praise; assent, concurrence, consent, endorsement, ratification, sanction.

appropriate *vb* adopt, arrogate, assume, set apart; allot, apportion, assign, devote; apply, convert, employ, use. * *adj* adapted, apt, befitting, fit, opportune, seemly, suitable.

approve *vb* appreciate, commend, like, praise, recommend, value; confirm, countenance, justify, ratify, sustain, uphold.

approximate *vb* approach, resemble. * *adj* approaching, proximate; almost exact, inexact, rough.

apt *adj* applicable, apposite, appropriate, befitting, fit, felicitous, germane; disposed, inclined, liable, prone, subject; able, adroit, clever, dextrous, expert, handy, happy, prompt, ready, skilful.

aptitude *n* applicability, appropriateness, felicity, fitness, pertinence, suitability; inclination, tendency, turn; ability, address, adroitness, quickness, readiness, tact.

arbitrary *adj* absolute, autocratic, despotic, domineering, imperious, overbearing, unlimited; capricious, discretionary, fanciful, voluntary, whimsical.

arcade *n* colonnade, loggia.

arch[1] *adj* cunning, knowing, frolicsome, merry, mirthful, playful, roguish, shrewd, sly; consummate, chief, leading, preeminent, prime, primary, principal.

arch[2] *vb* span, vault; bend, curve. * *n* archway, span, vault.

archaic *adj* ancient, antiquated, antique, bygone, obsolete, old.

archives *npl* documents, muniments, records, registers, rolls.

ardent *adj* burning, fiery, hot; eager, earnest, fervent, impassioned, keen, passionate, warm, zealous.

ardour *n* glow, heat, warmth; eagerness, enthusiasm, fervour, heat, passion, soul, spirit, warmth, zeal.

arduous *adj* high, lofty, steep, uphill; difficult, fatiguing, hard, laborious, onerous, tiresome, toilsome, wearisome.

area *n* circle, circuit, district, domain, field, range, realm, region, tract.

argue *vb* plead, reason upon; debate, dispute; denote, evince, imply, indicate, mean, prove; contest, debate, discuss, sift.

arid *adj* barren, dry, parched, sterile, unfertile; dry, dull, jejune, pointless, uninteresting.

aright *adv* correctly, justly, rightly, truly.

arise *vb* ascend, mount, soar, tower; appear, emerge, rise, spring; begin, originate; rebel, revolt, rise; accrue, come, emanate, ensue, flow, issue, originate, proceed, result.

aristocracy *n* gentry, nobility, noblesse, peerage.

arm[1] *n* bough, branch, limb, protection; cove, creek, estuary, firth, fjord, frith, inlet.

arm[2] *vb* array, equip, furnish; clothe, cover, fortify, guard, protect, strengthen.

arms *npl* accoutrements, armour, array, harness, mail, panoply, weapons; crest, escutcheon.

army *n* battalions, force, host, legions, troops; host, multitude, throng, vast assemblage.

around *prep* about, encircling, encompassing, round, surrounding. * *adv* about, approximately, generally, near, nearly, practically, round, thereabouts.

arouse *vb* animate, awaken, excite, incite, kindle, provoke, rouse, stimulate, warm, whet.

arraign *vb* accuse, censure, charge, denounce, impeach, indict, prosecute, tax.

arrange *vb* array, class, classify, dispose, distribute, group, range, rank; adjust, determine, fix upon, settle; concoct, construct, devise, plan, prepare, project.

arrant *adj* bad, consummate, downright, gross, notorious, rank, utter.

array *vb* arrange, dispose, place, range, rank; accoutre, adorn, attire, decorate, dress, enrobe, embellish, equip, garnish, habit, invest. * *n* arrangement, collection, disposition, marshalling, order; apparel, attire, clothes, dress, garments; army, battalions, soldiery, troops.

arrest *vb* check, delay, detain, hinder, hold, interrupt, obstruct, restrain, stay, stop, withhold; apprehend, capture, catch, seize, take; catch, engage, engross, fix, occupy, secure, rivet. * *n* check, checking, detention, hindrance, interruption, obstruction, restraining, stay, staying, stopping; apprehension, capture, detention, seizure.

arrive *vb* attain, come, get to, reach.

arrogance *n* assumption, assurance, disdain, effrontery, haughtiness, loftiness, lordliness, presumption, pride, scornfulness, superciliousness.

arrogate *vb* assume, claim unduly, demand, usurp.

arrow *n* bolt, dart, reed, shaft.

art *n* business, craft, employment, trade; address, adroitness, aptitude, dexterity, ingenuity, knack, readiness, sagacity, skill; artfulness, artifice, astuteness, craft, deceit, duplicity, finesse, subtlety.

artful *adj* crafty, cunning, disingenuous, insincere, sly, tricky, wily.

article *n* branch, clause, division, head, item, member, paragraph, part, point, portion; essay, paper, piece; commodity, substance, thing.

artifice *n* art, chicanery, contrivance, cunning, deception, deceit, duplicity, effort, finesse, fraud, imposture, invention, stratagem, subterfuge, trick, trickery.

artificial *adj* counterfeit, sham, spurious; assumed, affected, constrained, fictitious, forced, laboured, strained.

artless *adj* ignorant, rude, unskilful, untaught; natural, plain, simple; candid, fair, frank, guileless, honest, plain, unaffected, simple, sincere, truthful, unsuspicious.

ascend *vb* arise, aspire, climb, mount, soar, tower.

ascendancy, ascendency *n* authority, control, domination, mastery, power, predominance, sovereignty, superiority, sway.

ascertain *vb* certify, define, determine, establish, fix, settle, verify; discover, find out, get at.

ashamed *adj* abashed, confused.

ask *vb* interrogate, inquire, question; adjure, beg, conjure, crave, desire, dun, entreat, implore, invite, inquire, petition, request, solicit, supplicate, seek, sue.

aspect *n* air, bearing, countenance, expression, feature, look, mien, visage; appearance, attitude, condition, light, phase, position, posture, situation, state, view; angle, direction, outlook, prospect.

asperity *n* ruggedness, roughness, unevenness; acrimony, causticity, corrosiveness, sharpness, sourness, tartness; acerbity, bitterness, churlishness, harshness, sternness, sullenness, severity, virulence.

aspersion *n* abuse, backbiting, calumny, censure, defamation, detraction, slander, vituperation, reflection, reproach.

aspiration *n* aim, ambition, craving, hankering, hope, longing.

aspire *vb* desire, hope, long, yearn; ascend, mount, rise, soar, tower.

assail *vb* assault, attack, invade, oppugn; impugn, malign, maltreat; ply, storm.

assassinate *vb* dispatch, kill, murder, slay.

assault *vb* assail, attack, charge, invade. * *n* aggression, attack, charge, incursion, invasion, onset, onslaught; storm.

assemble *vb* call, collect, congregate, convene, convoke, gather, levy, muster; converge, forgather.

assembly *n* company, collection, concourse, congregation, gathering, meeting, rout, throng; caucus, congress, conclave, convention, convocation, diet, legislature, meeting, parliament, synod.

assent *vb* accede, acquiesce, agree, concur, subscribe, yield. * *n* accord, acquiescence, allowance, approval, approbation, consent.

assert *vb* affirm, allege, aver, asseverate, declare, express, maintain, predicate, pronounce, protest; claim, defend, emphasize, maintain, press, uphold, vindicate.

assertion *n* affirmation, allegation, asseveration, averment, declaration, position, predication, remark, statement, word; defence, emphasis, maintenance, pressing, support, vindication.

assess *vb* appraise, compute, estimate, rate, value; assign, determine, fix, impose, levy.
asseverate *vb* affirm, aver, avow, declare, maintain, protest.
assiduous *adj* active, busy, careful, constant, diligent, devoted, indefatigable, industrious, sedulous, unremitting, untiring.
assign *vb* allot, appoint, apportion, appropriate; fix, designate, determine, specify; adduce, advance, allege, give, grant, offer, present, show.
assist *vb* abet, aid, befriend, further, help, patronize, promote, second, speed, support, sustain; aid, relieve, succour; alternate with, relieve, spell.
associate *vb* affiliate, combine, conjoin, couple, join, link, relate, yoke; consort, fraternize, mingle, sort. * *n* chum, companion, comrade, familiar, follower, mate; ally, confederate, friend, partner, fellow.
association *n* combination, company, confederation, connection, partnership, society.
assort *vb* arrange, class, classify, distribute, group, rank, sort; agree, be adapted, consort, suit.
assuage *vb* allay, alleviate, appease, calm, ease, lessen, mitigate, moderate, mollify, pacify, quell, relieve, soothe, tranquillize.
assume *vb* take, undertake; affect, counterfeit, feign, pretend, sham; arrogate, usurp; beg, hypothesize, imply, postulate, posit, presuppose, suppose, simulate.
assurance *n* assuredness, certainty, conviction, persuasion, pledge, security, surety, warrant; engagement, pledge, promise; averment, assertion, protestation; audacity, confidence, courage, firmness, intrepidity; arrogance, brass, boldness, effrontery, face, front, impudence.
assure *vb* encourage, embolden, hearten; certify, insure, secure against loss, vouch for.
astonish *vb* amaze, astound, confound, daze, dumbfound, overwhelm, startle, stun, stupefy, surprise.
astute *adj* acute, cunning, deep, discerning, ingenious, intelligent, penetrating, perspicacious, quick, sagacious, sharp, shrewd.
asylum *n* refuge, retreat, sanctuary, shelter.
athletic *adj* brawny, lusty, muscular, powerful, robust, sinewy, stalwart, stout, strapping, strong, sturdy.
athletics *npl* aerobics, eurythmics, exercise, exercising, gymnastics, sports, track and field, workout.
atom *n* bit, molecule, monad, particle, scintilla.
atone *vb* answer, compensate, expiate, satisfy.
atonement *n* amends, expiation, propitiation, reparation, satisfaction.
atrocity *n* depravity, enormity, flagrancy, ferocity, savagery, villainy.
attach *vb* affix, annex, connect, fasten, join, hitch, tie; charm, captivate, enamour, endear, engage, win; (*legal*) distress, distrain, seize, take.
attack *vb* assail, assault, charge, encounter, invade, set upon, storm, tackle; censure, criticise, impugn. * *n* aggression, assault, charge, offence, onset, onslaught, raid, thrust.
attain *vb* accomplish, achieve, acquire, get, obtain, secure; arrive at, come to, reach.
attempt *vb* assail, assault, attack; aim, endeavour, seek, strive, try. * *n* effort, endeavour, enterprise, experiment, undertaking, venture; assault, attack, onset.
attend *vb* accompany, escort, follow; guard, protect, watch; minister to, serve, wait on; give heed, hear, harken, listen; be attendant, serve, tend, wait.
attention *n* care, circumspection, heed, mindfulness, observation, regard, watch, watchfulness; application, reflection, study; civility, courtesy, deference, politeness, regard, respect; addresses, courtship, devotion, suit, wooing.
attentive *adj* alive, awake, careful, civil, considerate, courteous, heedful, mindful, observant, watchful.
attenuate *vb* contract, dilute, diminish, elongate, lengthen, lessen, rarefy, reduce, slim, thin, weaken.

attest *vb* authenticate, certify, corroborate, confirm, ratify, seal, vouch; adjure, call to witness, invoke; confess, display, exhibit, manifest, prove, show, witness.

attic *n* garret, loft, upper storey.

Attic *adj* delicate, subtle, penetrating, pointed, pungent; chaste, classic, correct, elegant, polished, pure.

attire *vb* accoutre, apparel, array, clothe, dress, enrobe, equip, rig, robe. * *n* clothes, clothing, costume, dress, garb, gear, habiliment, outfit, toilet, trapping, vestment, vesture, wardrobe.

attitude *n* pose, position, posture; aspect, conjuncture, condition, phase, prediction, situation, standing, state.

attract *vb* draw, pull; allure, captivate, charm, decoy, enamour, endear, entice, engage, fascinate, invite, win.

attraction *n* affinity, drawing, pull; allurement, charm, enticement, fascination, magnetism, lure, seduction, witchery.

attribute *vb* ascribe, assign, impute, refer. * *n* characteristic, mark, note, peculiarity, predicate, property, quality.

attrition *n* abrasion, friction, rubbing.

attune *vb* accord, harmonize, modulate, tune; accommodate, adapt, adjust, attempt.

audacity *n* boldness, courage, daring, fearlessness, intrepidity; assurance, brass, effrontery, face, front, impudence, insolence, presumption, sauciness.

audience *n* assemblage, congregation; hearing, interview, reception.

augment *vb* add to, enhance, enlarge, increase, magnify, multiply, swell.

augmentation *n* accession, addition, enlargement, extension, increase.

augury *n* prediction, prognostication, prophecy, soothsaying; auspice, forerunner, harbinger, herald, omen, precursor, portent, sign.

august *adj* awe-inspiring, awful, dignified, grand, imposing, kingly, majestic, noble, princely, regal, solemn, stately, venerable.

auspicious *adj* fortunate, happy, lucky, prosperous, successful; bright, favourable, golden, opportune, promising, prosperous.

austere *adj* ascetic, difficult, formal, hard, harsh, morose, relentless, rigid, rigorous, severe, stern, stiff, strict, uncompromising, unrelenting.

authentic *adj* genuine, pure, real, true, unadulterated, uncorrupted, veritable; accurate, authoritative, reliable, true, trustworthy.

authority *n* dominion, empire, government, jurisdiction, power, sovereignty; ascendency, control, influence, rule, supremacy, sway; authorization, liberty, order, permit, precept, sanction, warranty; testimony, witness; connoisseur, expert, master.

authorize *vb* empower, enable, entitle; allow, approve, confirm, countenance, permit, ratify, sanction.

auxiliary *adj* aiding, ancillary, assisting, helpful, subsidiary. * *n* ally, assistant, confederate, help.

avail *vb* assist, benefit, help, profit, use, service.

available *adj* accessible, advantageous, applicable, beneficial, profitable, serviceable, useful.

avarice *n* acquisitiveness, covetousness, greediness, penuriousness, rapacity.

avaricious *adj* grasping, miserly, niggardly, parsimonious.

avenge *vb* punish, retaliate, revenge, vindicate.

avenue *n* access, entrance, entry, passage; alley, path, road, street, walk; channel, pass, route, way.

aver *vb* allege, assert, asseverate, avouch, declare, pronounce, protest, say.

averse *adj* adverse, backward, disinclined, indisposed, opposed, unwilling.

aversion *n* abhorrence, antipathy, disgust, dislike, hate, hatred, loathing, reluctance, repugnance.

avid *adj* eager, greedy, voracious.

avocation *n* business, calling, employment, occupation, trade, vocation; distraction, hindrance, interruption.

avoid *vb* dodge, elude, escape, eschew, shun; forebear, refrain from.

avouch *vb* allege, assert, declare, maintain, say.

avow *vb* admit, acknowledge, confess, own.

awaken *vb* arouse, excite, incite, kindle, provoke, spur, stimulate; wake, waken; begin, be excited.

award *vb* adjudge, allot, assign, bestow, decree, grant. * *n* adjudication, allotment, assignment, decision, decree, determination, gift, judgement.

aware *adj* acquainted, apprised, conscious, conversant, informed, knowing, mindful, sensible.

away *adv* absent, not present. * *adj* at a distance; elsewhere; out of the way.

awe *vb* cow, daunt, intimidate, overawe. * *n* abashment, fear, reverence; dread, fear, fearfulness, terror.

awful *adj* august, awesome, dread, grand, inspired; abashed, alarming, appalled, dire, frightful, portentous, tremendous.

awkward *adj* bungling, clumsy, inept, maladroit, unskilful; lumbering, unfit, ungainly, unmanageable; boorish; inconvenient, unsuitable.

axiom *n* adage, aphorism, apothegm, maxim, postulation, truism.

axis *n* axle, shaft, spindle.

azure *adj* blue, cerulean, sky-coloured.

B

babble *vb* blather, chatter, gibber, jabber, prate, prattle. * *n* chat, gossip, palaver, prate, tattle.

babel *n* clamour, confusion, din, discord, disorder, hubbub, jargon, pother.

baby *vb* coddle, cosset, indulge, mollycoddle, pamper, spoil. * *adj* babyish, childish, infantile, puerile; diminutive, doll-like, miniature, pocket, pocket-sized, small-scale. * *n* babe, brat, child, infant, suckling, nursling; chicken, coward, milksop, namby-pamby, sad sack, weakling; miniature; innocent.

bacchanal *n* carouse, debauchery, drunkenness, revelry, roisterousness.

back *vb* abet, aid, countenance, favour, second, support, sustain; go back, move back, retreat, withdraw. * *adj* hindmost. **adv* in return, in consideration; ago, gone, since; aside, away, behind, by; abaft, astern, backwards, hindwards, rearwards. **n* end, hind part, posterior, rear.

backbite *vb* abuse, asperse, blacken, defame, libel, malign, revile, scandalize, slander, traduce, vilify.

backbone *n* chine, spine; constancy, courage, decision, firmness, nerve, pluck, resolution, steadfastness.

backslider *n* apostate, deserter, renegade.

backward *adj* disinclined, hesitating, indisposed, loath, reluctant, unwilling, wavering; dull, slow, sluggish, stolid, stupid. **adv* aback, behind, rearward.

bad *adj* baleful, baneful, detrimental, evil, harmful, hurtful, injurious, noxious, pernicious, unwholesome, vicious; abandoned, corrupt, depraved, immoral, sinful, unfair, unprincipled, wicked; unfortunate, unhappy, unlucky, miserable; disappointing, discouraging, distressing, sad, unwelcoming; abominable, mean, shabby, scurvy, vile, wretched; defective, inferior, imperfect, incompetent, poor, unsuitable; hard, heavy, serious, severe.

badge *n* brand, emblem, mark, sign, symbol, token.

badger *vb* annoy, bait, bother, hector, harry, pester, persecute, tease, torment, trouble, vex, worry.

baffle *vb* balk, block, check, circumvent, defeat, foil, frustrate, mar, thwart, undermine, upset; bewilder, confound, disconcert, perplex.

bait *vb* harry, tease, worry. **n* allurement, decoy, enticement, lure, temptation.

balance *vb* equilibrate, pose, (*naut*) trim; compare, weigh; compensate, counteract, estimate; adjust, clear, equalize, square. **n* equilibrium, liberation; excess, remainder, residue, surplus.

bald *adj* bare, naked, uncovered, treeless; dull, inelegant, meagre, prosaic, tame, unadorned, vapid.

baleful *adj* baneful, deadly, calamitous, hurtful, injurious, mischievous, noxious, pernicious, ruinous.

balk *vb* baffle, defeat, disappoint, disconcert, foil, frustrate, thwart.

ball *n* drop, globe, orb, pellet, marble, sphere; bullet, missile, projectile, shot; assembly, dance.

balmy *adj* aromatic, fragrant, healing, odorous, perfumed.

ban *vb* anathematize, curse, execrate; interdict, outlaw. **n* edict, proclamation; anathema, curse, denunciation, execration; interdiction, outlawry, penalty, prohibition

band[1] *vb* belt, bind, cinch, encircle, gird, girdle; ally, associate, combine, connect, join, league; bar, marble, streak, stripe, striate, vein. **n* crew, gang, horde, society, troop; ensemble, group, orchestra.

band[2] *n* ligament, ligature, tie; bond, chain, cord, fetter, manacle, shackle, trammel; bandage, belt, binding, cincture, girth, tourniquet.

bandit *n* brigand, freebooter, footpad, gangster, highwayman, outlaw, robber.

baneful *adj* poisonous, venomous; deadly, destructive, hurtful, mischievous, noxious, pernicious.

bang *vb* beat, knock, maul, pommel, pound, strike, thrash, thump; slam; clatter, rattle, resound, ring. **n* clang, clangour, whang; blow, knock, lick, thump, thwack, whack.

banish *vb* exile, expatriate, ostracize; dismiss, exclude, expel.

bank[1] *vb* incline, slope, tilt; embank. **n* dike, embankment, escarpment, heap, knoll, mound; border, bound, brim, brink, margin, rim, strand; course, row, tier.

bank[2] *vb* deposit, keep, save. **n* depository, fund, reserve, savings, stockpile.

banner *n* colours, ensign, flag, standard, pennon, standard, streamer.

banter *vb* chaff, deride, jeer, joke, mock, quiz, rally, ridicule. **n* badinage, chaff, derision, jesting, joking, mockery, quizzing, raillery, ridicule.

bar *vb* exclude, hinder, obstruct, prevent, prohibit, restrain, stop. **n* grating, pole, rail, rod; barricade, hindrance, impediment, obstacle, obstruction, stop; bank, sand bar, shallow, shoal, spit; (*legal*) barristers, counsel, court, judgement, tribunal.

barbarian *adj* brutal, cruel, ferocious, fierce, fell, inhuman, ruthless, savage, truculent, unfeeling. **n* brute, ruffian, savage.

barbaric *adj* barbarous, rude, savage, uncivilized, untamed; capricious, coarse, gaudy, riotous, showy, outlandish, uncouth, untamed, wild.

bare *vb* denude, depilate, divest, strip, unsheathe; disclose, manifest, open, reveal, show. **adj* denuded, exposed, naked, nude, stripped, unclothed, uncovered, undressed, unsheltered; alone, mere, sheer, simple; bald, meagre, plain, unadorned, uncovered, unfurnished; empty, destitute, indigent, poor.

bargain *vb* agree, contract, covenant, stipulate; convey, sell, transfer. **n* agreement, compact, contract, covenant, convention, indenture, transaction, stipulation, treaty; proceeds, purchase, result.

barren *adj* childless, infecund, sterile; (*bot*) acarpous, sterile; bare, infertile, poor, sterile, unproductive; ineffectual, unfruitful, uninstructive.

barricade *vb* block up, fortify, protect, obstruct. **n* barrier, obstruction, palisade, stockade.

barrier *n* bar, barricade, hindrance, impediment, obstacle, obstruction, stop.

barter *vb* bargain, exchange, sell, trade, traffic.

base[1] *adj* cheap, inferior, worthless; counterfeit, debased, false, spurious; baseborn, humble, lowly, mean, nameless, plebeian, unknown, untitled, vulgar; abject, beggarly, contemptible, degraded, despicable, low, menial, pitiful, servile, sordid, sorry, worthless.

base[2] *vb* establish, found, ground. **n* foundation, fundament, substructure, underpinning; pedestal, plinth, stand; centre, headquarters, HQ, seat; starting point; basis, cause, grounds, reason, standpoint; bottom, foot, foundation, ground.

bashful *adj* coy, diffident, shy, timid.

basis n base, bottom, foundation, fundament, ground, groundwork.

bastard *adj* adulterated, baseborn, counterfeit, false, illegitimate, sham. **n* love child.

batch *vb* assemble, bunch, bundle, collect, gather, group. **n* amount, collection, crowd, lot, quantity.

bathe *vb* immerse, lave, wash; cover, enfold, enwrap, drench, flood, infold, suffuse. **n* bath, shower, swim.

batter[1] *vb* beat, pelt, smite; break, bruise, demolish, destroy, shatter, shiver, smash; abrade, deface, disfigure, indent, mar; incline, recede, retreat, slope. **n* batsman, striker.

batter[2] *n* dough, goo, goop, gunk, paste, pulp.

battle *vb* contend, contest, engage, fight, strive, struggle. **n* action, affair, brush, combat, conflict, contest, engagement, fight, fray.
bauble *n* gewgaw, gimcrack, knick-knack, plaything, toy, trifle, trinket.
bawdy *adj* obscene, filthy, impure, indecent, lascivious, lewd, smutty, unchaste.
bawl *vb* clamour, cry, hoot, howl, roar, shout, squall, vociferate, yell.
bay[1] *vb* bark, howl, wail, yell, yelp.
bay[2] *n* alcove, compartment, niche, nook, opening, recess.
bay[3] *n* bight, cove, gulf, inlet.
bays *npl* applause, chaplet, fame, garland, glory, honour, plaudits, praise, renown.
beach *vb* ground, maroon, strand. **n* coast, margin, rim, sands, seashore, seaside, shore, shoreline, strand, waterfront.
beacon *vb* brighten, flame, shine, signal; enlighten, illuminate, illumine, guide, light, signal. **n* lighthouse, pharos, watchtower; sign, signal.
beadle *n* apparitor, church officer, crier, servitor, summoner.
beak *n* bill, mandible, (*sl*) nose; (*naut*) bow, prow, stem.
beam *vb* beacon, gleam, glisten, glitter, shine. **n* balk, girder, joist, scantling, stud; gleam, pencil, ray, streak.
bear *vb* support, sustain, uphold; carry, convey, deport, transport, waft; abide, brook, endure, stand, suffer, tolerate, undergo; carry on, keep up, maintain; cherish, entertain, harbour; produce; cast, drop, sustain; endure, submit, suffer; act, operate, work. **n* growler, grumbler, moaner, snarler; speculator.
bearable *adj* endurable, sufferable, supportable, tolerable.
bearing *n* air, behaviour, demeanour, deportment, conduct, carriage, conduct, mien, port; connection, dependency, relation; endurance, patience, suffering; aim, course, direction; bringing forth, producing; bed, receptacle, socket.
beastly *adj* abominable, brutish, ignoble, low, sensual, vile.
beat *vb* bang, baste, belabour, buffet, cane, cudgel, drub, hammer, hit, knock, maul, pound, pummel, punch, strike, thrash, thump, thwack, whack, whip; bray, bruise, pound, pulverize; batter, pelt; conquer, defeat, overcome, rout, subdue, surpass, vanquish; pulsate, throb; dash, strike. **adj* baffled, bamboozled, confounded, mystified, nonplused, perplexed, puzzled, stumped; done, dog-tired, exhausted, tired out, worn out; beaten, defeated, licked, worsted. **n* blow, striking, stroke; beating, pulsation, throb; accent, metre, rhythm; circuit, course, round.
beatific *adj* ecstatic, enchanting, enraptured, ravishing, rapt.
beatitude *n* blessing, ecstasy, felicity, happiness.
beau *n* coxcomb, dandy, exquisite, fop, popinjay; admirer, lover, suitor, sweetheart.
beautiful *adj* charming, comely, fair, fine, exquisite, handsome, lovely, pretty.
beautify *vb* adorn, array, bedeck, deck, decorate, embellish, emblazon, garnish, gild, grace, ornament, set.
beauty *n* elegance, grace, symmetry; attractiveness, comeliness, fairness, loveliness, seemliness; belle.
become *vb* change to, get, go, wax; adorn, befit, set off, suit.
becoming *adj* appropriate, apt, congruous, decent, decorous, due, fit, proper, right, seemly, suitable; comely, graceful, neat, pretty.
bed *vb* embed, establish, imbed, implant, infix, inset, plant; harbour, house, lodge. **n* berth, bunk, cot, couch; channel, depression, hollow; base, foundation, receptacle, support, underlay; accumulation, layer, seam, stratum, vein.
bedim *vb* cloud, darken, dim, obscure.
befall *vb* betide, overtake; chance, happen,occur, supervene.
befitting *adj* appropriate, apt, becoming, decorous, fit, proper, right, suitable, seemly.
befool *vb* bamboozle, beguile, cheat, circumvent, delude, deceive, dupe, fool, hoax, hoodwink, infatuate, stupefy, trick.
befriend *vb* aid, benefit, countenance, encourage, favour, help, patronize.

beg *vb* adjure, ask, beseech, conjure, crave, entreat, implore, importune, petition, pray, request, solicit, supplicate.

beggarly *adj* destitute, needy, poor; abject, base, despicable, grovelling, low, mean, miserable, miserly, paltry, pitiful, scant, servile, shabby, sorry, stingy, vile, wretched.

begin *vb* arise, commence, enter, open; inaugurate, institute, originate, start.

beginning *n* arising, commencement, dawn, emergence, inauguration, inception, initiation, opening, outset, start, rise; origin, source.

beguile *vb* cheat, deceive, delude; amuse, cheer, divert, entertain, solace.

behaviour *n* air, bearing, carriage, comportment, conduct, demeanour, deportment, manner, manners, mien.

behest *n* bidding, charge, command, commandment, direction, hest, injunction, mandate, order, precept.

behind *prep* abaft, after, following. **adv* abaft, aft, astern, rearward. **adj* arrested, backward, checked, detained, retarded; after, behind. **n* afterpart, rear, stern, tail; back, back side, reverse; bottom, buttocks, posterior, rump.

behold *vb* consider, contemplate, eye, observe, regard, see, survey, view.

behoove *vb* become, befit, suit; be binding, be obligatory.

being *n* actuality, existence, reality, subsistence; core, essence, heart, root.

beleaguer *vb* besiege, blockade, invest; beset, block, encumber, encompass, encounter, obstruct, surround.

belief *n* assurance, confidence, conviction, persuasion, trust; acceptance, assent, credence, credit, currency; creed, doctrine, dogma, faith, opinion, tenet.

bellow *vb* bawl, clamour, cry, howl, vociferate, yell.

belt *n* band, cincture, girdle, girth, zone; region, stretch, strip.

bemoan *vb* bewail, deplore, lament, mourn.

bemused *adj* bewildered, confused, fuddled, muddled, muzzy, stupefied, tipsy.

bend *vb* bow, crook, curve, deflect, draw; direct, incline, turn; bend, dispose, influence, mould, persuade, subdue; (*naut*) fasten, make fast; crook, deflect, deviate, diverge, swerve; bow, lower, stoop; condescend, deign. **n* angle, arc, arcuation, crook, curvature, curve, elbow, flexure, turn.

beneath *prep* below, under, underneath; unbecoming, unbefitting, unworthy. **adv* below, underneath.

benediction *n* beatitude, benefit, benison, blessing, boon, grace, favour.

benefaction *n* alms, boon, charity, contribution, donation, favour, gift, grant, gratuity, offering, present.

beneficent *adj* benevolent, bounteous, bountiful, charitable, generous, kind, liberal.

beneficial *adj* advantageous, favourable, helpful, profitable, salutary, serviceable, useful, wholesome.

benefit *vb* befriend, help, serve; advantage, avail, profit. **n* favour, good turn, kindness, service; account, advantage, behalf, gain, good, interest, profit, utility.

benevolence *n* beneficence, benignity, generosity, goodwill, humanity, kindliness, kindness.

benevolent *adj* altruistic, benign, charitable, generous, humane, kind, kindhearted, liberal, obliging, philanthropic, tender, unselfish.

benign *adj* amiable, amicable, beneficent, benevolent, complaisant, friendly, gentle, good, gracious, humane, kind, kindly, obliging.

bent *adj* angled, angular, bowed, crooked, curved, deflected, embowed, flexed, hooked, twisted; disposed, inclined, prone, minded; (*with* **on**) determined, fixed on, resolved, set on. **n* bias, inclination, leaning, partiality, penchant, predilection, prepossession, proclivity, propensity

bequeath *vb* devise, give, grant, leave, will; impart, transmit.

berate *vb* chide, rate, reprimand, reprove, scold.

bereave *vb* afflict, deprive of, despoil, dispossess, divest, rob, spoil, strip.

beseech *vb* beg, conjure, entreat, implore, importune, petition, supplicate; ask, beg, crave, solicit.
beset *vb* besiege, encompass, enclose, environ, encircle, hem in, surround; decorate, embarrass, embellish, entangle, garnish, ornament, perplex, set.
beside[1] *prep* at the side of, by the side of, close to, near; aside from, not according to, out of the course of, out of the way of; not in possession of, out of.
besides[1] *prep* barring, distinct from, excluding, except, excepting, in addition to, other than, over and above, save.
beside[2], **besides**[2] *adv* additionally, also, further, furthermore, in addition, more, moreover, over and above, too, yet.
besiege *vb* beset, blockade, encircle, encompass, environ, invest, surround.
besot *vb* drench, intoxicate, soak, steep; befool, delude, infatuate, stultify, stupefy.
bespatter *vb* bedaub, befoul, besmirch, smear, spatter.
bespeak *vb* accost, address, declare, evince, forestall, imply, indicate, prearrange, predict, proclaim, solicit.
best *vb* better, exceed, excel, predominate, rival, surpass; beat, defeat, outdo, worst. **adj* chief, first, foremost, highest, leading, utmost. **adv* advantageously, excellently; extremely, greatly. **n* choice, cream, flower, pick.
bestial *adj* beast-like, beastly, brutal, degraded, depraved, irrational, low, vile; sensual.
bestow *vb* deposit, dispose, put, place, store, stow; accord, give, grant, impart.
bet *vb* gamble, hazard, lay, pledge, stake, wage, wager. **n* gamble, hazard, stake, wager.
bethink *vb* cogitate, consider, ponder, recall, recollect, reflect, remember.
betide *vb* befall, happen, occur, overtake.
betimes *adv* beforehand, early, forward, soon.
betoken *vb* argue, betray, denote, evince, imply, indicate, prove, represent, show, signify, typify.
betray *vb* be false to, break, violate; blab, discover, divulge, expose, reveal, show, tell; argue, betoken, display, evince, expose, exhibit, imply, indicate, manifest, reveal; beguile, delude, ensnare, lure, mislead; corrupt, ruin, seduce, undo.
betroth *vb* affiance, engage to marry, pledge in marriage, plight.
better *vb* advance, amend, correct, exceed, improve, promote, rectify, reform. **adj* bigger, fitter, greater, larger, less ill, preferable. **n* advantage, superiority, upper hand, victory; improvement, greater good.
between *prep* amidst, among, betwixt.
bewail *vb* bemoan, deplore, express, lament, mourn over, rue, sorrow.
beware *vb* avoid, heed, look out, mind.
bewilder *vb* confound, confuse, daze, distract, embarrass, entangle, muddle, mystify, nonplus, perplex, pose, puzzle, stagger.
bewitch *vb* captivate, charm, enchant, enrapture, entrance, fascinate, spellbind, transport.
beyond *prep* above, before, farther, over, past, remote, yonder.
bias *vb* bend, dispose, incline, influence, predispose, prejudice. **n* bent, inclination, leaning, partiality, penchant, predilection, prepossession, proclivity, propensity, slant, tendency, turn.
bicker *vb* argue, dispute, jangle, quarrel, spar, spat, squabble, wrangle.
bid *vb* charge, command, direct, enjoin, order, require, summon; ask, call, invite, pray, request, solicit; offer, propose, proffer, tender. **n* bidding, offer, proposal.
big *adj* bumper, bulking, bulky, great, huge, large, massive, monstrous; important, imposing; distended, inflated, full, swollen, tumid; fecund, fruitful, productive, teeming.
bigoted *adj* dogmatic, hidebound, intolerant, obstinate, narrow-minded, opinionated, prejudiced.
bill[1] *vb* charge, dun, invoice; programme, schedule; advertise, boost, plug, promote, publicize. **n* account, charges, reckoning, score; advertisement, banner, hoarding, placard, poster; playbill, programme, schedule; bill of exchange, cer-

tificate, money; account, reckoning, statement.

bill[2] *n* beak, mandible, (*sl*) nose; billhook, brush-cutter, hedge-bill, hedging knife; caress, fondle, kiss, toy.

billet *vb* allot, apportion, assign, distribute, quarter, station. **n* accommodation, lodgings, quarters.

billow *vb* surge, wave; heave, roll; bag, baloon, bulge, dilate, swell. **n* roller, surge, swell, wave.

bin *n* box, bunker, crib, frame, receptacle.

bind *vb* confine, enchain, fetter, restrain, restrict; bandage, tie up, wrap; fasten, lash, pinion, secure, tie, truss; engage, hold, oblige, obligate, pledge; contract, harden, shrink, stiffen.

birth *n* ancestry, blood, descent, extraction, lineage, race; being, creation, creature, offspring, production, progeny.

bit *n* crumb, fragment, morsel, mouthful, piece, scrap; atom, grain, jot, mite, particle, tittle, whit; instant, minute, moment, second.

bite *vb* champ, chew, crunch, gnaw; burn, make smart, sting; catch, clutch, grapple, grasp, grip; bamboozle, cheat, cozen, deceive, defraud, dupe, gull, mislead, outwit, overreach, trick. **n* grasp, hold; punch, relish, spice, pungency, tang, zest; lick, morsel, sip, taste; crick, nip, pain, pang, prick, sting.

bitter *adj* acrid; dire, fell, merciless, relentless, ruthless; harsh, severe, stern; afflictive, calamitous, distressing, galling, grievous, painful, poignant, sore, sorrowful.

black *adj* dark, ebony, inky, jet, sable, swarthy; dingy, dusky, lowering, murky, pitchy; calamitous, dark, depressing, disastrous, dismal, doleful, forbidding, gloomy, melancholy, mournful, sombre, sullen.

blacken *vb* darken; deface, defile, soil, stain, sully; asperse, besmirch, calumniate, defame, malign, revile, slander, traduce, vilify.

blamable *adj* blameable, blameworthy, censurable, culpable, delinquent. faulty, remiss, reprehensible.

blame *vb* accuse, censure, condemn, disapprove, reflect upon, reprehend, reproach, reprove, upbraid. **n* animadversion, censure, condemnation, disapproval, dispraise, disapprobation, reprehension, reproach, reproof; defect, demerit, fault, guilt, misdeed, shortcoming, sin, wrong.

blameless *adj* faultless, guiltless, inculpable, innocent, irreproachable, unblemished, undefiled, unimpeachable, unspotted, unsullied, spotless, stainless.

blanch *vb* bleach, fade, etiolate, whiten.

bland *adj* balmy, demulcent, gentle, mild, soothing, soft; affable, amiable, complaisant, kindly, mild, suave.

blandishment *n* cajolery, coaxing, compliment, fascination, fawning, flattery, wheedling

blank *adj* bare, empty, vacuous, void; amazed, astonished, confounded, confused, dumbfounded, nonplussed; absolute, complete, entire, mere, perfect, pure, simple, unabated, unadulterated, unmitigated, unmixed, utter, perfect.

blare *vb* blazon, blow, peal, proclaim, trumpet. **n* blast, clang, clangour, peal.

blasphemy *n* impiousness, sacrilege; cursing, profanity, swearing.

blast *vb* annihilate, blight, destroy, kill, ruin, shrivel, wither; burst, explode, kill. **n* blow, gust, squall; blare, clang, peal; burst, discharge, explosion.

blaze *vb* blazon, proclaim, publish; burn, flame, glow. **n* flame, flare, flash, glow, light.

bleach *vb* blanch, etiolate, render white, whiten.

bleak *adj* bare, exposed, unprotected, unsheltered, storm-beaten, windswept; biting, chill, cold, piercing, raw; cheerless, comfortless, desolate, dreary, uncongenial,

blemish *vb* blur, injure, mar, spot, stain, sully, taint, tarnish; asperse, calumniate, defame, malign, revile, slander, traduce, vilify. **n* blot, blur, defect, disfigurement, fault, flaw, imperfection, soil, speck, spot, stain, tarnish; disgrace, dishonour, reproach, stain, taint.

blend *vb* amalgamate, coalesce, combine, commingle, fuse, mingle, mix, unite. **n* amalgamation, combination, compound, fusion, mix, mixture, union.

bless *vb* beatify, delight, gladden; adore, celebrate, exalt, extol, glorify, magnify, praise.

blessedness *n* beatitude, bliss, blissfulness, felicity, happiness, joy.

blight *vb* blast, destroy, kill, ruin, shrivel, wither; annihilate, annul, crush, disappoint, frustrate. **n* blast, mildew, pestilence.

blind *vb* blear, darken, deprive of sight; blindfold, hoodwink. **adj* eyeless, sightless, stone-blind, unseeing; benighted, ignorant, injudicious, purblind, undiscerning, unenlightened; concealed, confused, dark, dim, hidden, intricate, involved, labyrinthine, obscure, private, remote; careless, headlong, heedless, inconsiderate, indiscriminate, thoughtless; blank, closed, shut. **n* cover, curtain, screen, shade, shutter; blinker; concealment, disguise, feint, pretence, pretext, ruse, stratagem, subterfuge.

blink *vb* nictate, nictitate, wink; flicker, flutter, gleam, glitter, intermit, twinkle; avoid, disregard, evade, gloss over, ignore, overlook, pass over. **n* glance, glimpse, sight, view, wink; gleam, glimmer, sheen, shimmer, twinkle.

bliss *n* beatification, beatitude, blessedness, blissfulness, ecstasy, felicity, happiness, heaven, joy, rapture, transport.

blithe *adj* airy, animated, blithesome, buoyant, cheerful, debonair, elated, happy, jocund, joyful, joyous, lively, mirthful, sprightly, vivacious.

bloat *vb* dilate, distend, inflate, swell.

block *vb* arrest, bar, blockade, check, choke, close, hinder, impede, jam, obstruct, stop; form, mould, shape; brace, stiffen. **n* lump, mass; blockhead, dunce, fool, simpleton; pulley, tackle; execution, scaffold; jam, obstruction, pack, stoppage.

blood *n* children, descendants, offspring, posterity, progeny; family, house, kin, kindred, line, relations; consanguinity, descent, kinship, lineage, relationship; courage, disposition, feelings, mettle, passion, spirit, temper.

bloom *vb* blossom, blow, flower; thrive, prosper. **n* blossom, blossoming, blow, efflorescence, florescence, flowering; delicacy, delicateness, flush, freshness, heyday, prime, vigour; flush, glow, rose.

blossom *vb* bloom, blow, flower. **n* bloom, blow, efflorescence, flower.

blot *vb* cancel, efface, erase, expunge, obliterate, rub out; blur, deface, disfigure, obscure, spot, stain, sully; disgrace, dishonour, tarnish. **n* blemish, blur, erasure, spot, obliteration, stain; disgrace, dishonour, stigma.

blow[1] *n* bang, beat, buffet, dab, impact, knock, pat, punch, rap, slam, stroke, thump, wallop, buffet, impact; affliction, calamity, disaster, misfortune, setback.

blow[2] *vb* breathe, gasp, pant, puff; flow, move, scud, stream, waft. **n* blast, gale, gust, squall, storm, wind.

blue *adj* azure, cerulean, cobalt, indigo, sapphire, ultramarine; ghastly, livid, pallid; dejected, depressed, dispirited, downcast, gloomy, glum, mopey, melancholic, melancholy, sad.

bluff[1] *adj* abrupt, blunt, blustering, coarse, frank, good-natured, open, outspoken; abrupt, precipitous, sheer, steep. **n* cliff, headland, height.

bluff[2] *vb* deceive, defraud, lie, mislead. **n* deceit, deception, feint, fraud, lie.

blunder *vb* err, flounder, mistake: stumble. **n* error, fault, howler, mistake, solecism.

blunt *adj* dull, edgeless, obtuse, pointless, unsharpened; insensible, stolid, thickwitted; abrupt, bluff, downright, plainspoken, outspoken, unceremonious, uncourtly. **vb* deaden, dull, numb, weaken.

blur *vb* bedim, darken, dim, obscure; blemish, blot, spot, stain, sully, tarnish. **n* blemish, blot, soil, spot, stain, tarnish; disgrace, smear.

blush *vb* colour, flush, glow, redden. **n* bloom, flush, glow, colour, reddening, suffusion.

bluster *vb* boast, brag, bully, domineer, roar, swagger, swell, vaunt. **n* boisterousness, noise, tumult, turbulence; braggadocio, bravado, boasting, gasconade, swaggering.

board *n* deal, panel, plank; diet, entertainment, fare, food, meals, provision, victuals; cabinet, conclave, committee, council; directorate; panel.

boast *vb* bluster, brag, crack, flourish, crow, vaunt. **n* blustering, boasting, bombast, brag, braggadocio, bravado, bombast, swaggering, vaunt.

bode *vb* augur, betoken, forebode, foreshadow, foretell, portend, predict, prefigure, presage, prophesy.

bodily *adj* carnal, corporeal, fleshly, physical. **adv* altogether, completely, entirely, wholly.

body *n* carcass, corpse, remains; stem, torso, trunk; aggregate, bulk, corpus, mass; being, individual, mortal creature, person; assemblage, association, band, company, corporation, corps, coterie, force, party, society, troop; consistency, substance, thickness.

boggle *vb* demur, falter, hang fire, hesitate, shrink, vacillate, waver.

boil[1] *vb* agitate, bubble, foam, froth, rage, seethe, simmer. **n* ebullience, ebullition.

boil[2] (*med*) gathering, pimple, pustule, swelling, tumour.

boisterous *adj* loud, roaring, stormy; clamouring, loud, noisy, obstreperous, tumultuous, turbulent.

bold *adj* adventurous, audacious, courageous; brave, daring, dauntless, doughty, fearless, gallant, hardy, heroic, intrepid, mettlesome, manful, manly, spirited, stouthearted, undaunted, valiant, valorous; assured, confident, self-reliant; assuming, forward, impertinent, impudent, insolent, push, rude, saucy; conspicuous, projecting, prominent, striking; abrupt, precipitous, prominent, steep.

bolster *vb* aid, assist, defend, help, maintain, prop, stay, support. **n* cushion, pillow; prop, support.

bolt *vb* abscond, flee, fly. **n* arrow, dart, missile, shaft; thunderbolt.

bombast *n* bluster, brag, braggadocio, fustian, gasconade, mouthing, pomposity, rant.

bond *vb* bind, connect, fuse, glue, join. **adj* captive, enslaved, enthralled, subjugated. **n* band, cord, fastening, ligament, ligature, link, nexus; bondage, captivity, chains, constraint, fetters, prison, shackle; attachment, attraction, connection, coupling, link, tie, union; compact, obligation, pledge, promise.

bondage *n* captivity, confinement, enslavement, enthralment, peonage, serfdom, servitude, slavery, thraldom, vassalage.

bonny *adj* beautiful, handsome, fair, fine, pretty; airy, blithe, buoyant, buxom, cheerful, jolly, joyous, merry. playful, sporty, sprightly, winsome.

bonus *n* gift, honorarium, premium, reward, subsidy.

booby *n* blockhead, dunce, fool, idiot, simpleton.

book *vb* bespeak, engage, reserve; programme, schedule; list, log, record, register. **n* booklet, brochure, compendium, handbook, manual, monograph, pamphlet, textbook, tract, treatise, volume, work.

bookish *adj* erudite, learned, literary, scholarly, studious.

boon *adj* convivial, jolly, jovial, hearty; close, intimate. **n* benefaction, favour, grant, gift, present; advantage, benefit, blessing, good, privilege.

boor *n* bumpkin, clodhopper, clown, lout, lubber, peasant, rustic, swain.

boorish *adj* awkward, bearish, clownish, course, gruff, ill-bred, loutish, lubberly, rude, rustic, uncivilized, uncouth, uneducated.

bootless *adj* abortive, fruitless, futile, profitless, vain, worthless, useless.

booty *n* loot, pillage, plunder, spoil.

border *vb* bound, edge, fringe, line, march, rim, skirt, verge; abut, adjoin, butt, conjoin, connect, neighbour. **n* brim, brink, edge, fringe, hem, margin, rim, skirt, verge; boundary, confine, frontier, limit, march, outskirts.

bore[1] *vb* annoy, fatigue, plague, tire, trouble, vex, weary, worry. **n* bother, nuisance, pest, worry.

bore[2] *vb* drill, perforate, pierce, sink, tunnel. **n* calibre, hole, shaft, tunnel.

borrow *vb* take and return, use temporarily; adopt, appropriate, imitate; dissemble, feign, simulate.

boss[1] *vb* emboss, stud; **n* knob, protuberance, stud.

boss[2] *vb* command, direct, employ, run. **n* employer, foreman, master, overseer, superintendent.

botch *vb* blunder, bungle, cobble, mar, mend, mess, patch, spoil. **n* blotch, pustule, sore; failure, miscarriage.

bother *vb* annoy, disturb, harass, molest, perplex, pester, plague, tease, trouble, vex, worry. **n* annoyance, perplexity, plague, trouble, vexation.

bottom *vb* build, establish, found. **adj* base, basic, ground, lowermost, lowest, nethermost, undermost. **n* base, basis, foot, foundation, groundwork; dale, meadow, valley; buttocks, fundament, seat; dregs, grounds, lees, sediment.

bounce *vb* bound, jump, leap, rebound, recoil, spring. **n* knock, thump; bound, jump, leap, spring, vault.

bound[1] *adj* assured, certain, decided, determined, resolute, resolved; confined, hampered, restricted, restrained; committed, contracted, engaged, pledged, promised; beholden, duty-bound, obligated, obliged.

bound[2] *vb* border, delimit, circumscribe, confine, demarcate, limit, restrict, terminate. **n* boundary, confine, edge, limit, march, margin, periphery, term, verge.

bound[3] *vb* jump, leap, spring. **n* bounce, jump, leap, spring, vault.

boundary *n* border, bourn, circuit, circumference, confine, limit, march, periphery, term, verge.

boundless *adj* endless, immeasurable, infinite, limitless, unbounded, unconfined, undefined, unlimited, vast.

bountiful *adj* beneficent, bounteous, generous, liberal, munificent, princely.

bounty *n* beneficence, benevolence, charity, donation, generosity, gift, kindness, premium, present, reward.

bourn *n* border, boundary, confine, limit; brook, burn, rill, rivulet, stream, torrent.

bow[1] *n* (*naut*) beak, prow, stem.

bow[2] *vb* arc, bend, buckle, crook, curve, droop, flex, yield; crush, depress, subdue; curtsy, genuflect, kowtow, submit. **n* arc, bend, bilge, bulge, convex, curve, flexion; bob, curtsy, genuflection, greeting, homage, obeisance; coming out, debut, introduction; curtain call, encore.

bowels *npl* entrails, guts, insides, viscera; compassion, mercy, pity, sympathy, tenderness.

box[1] *vb* fight, hit, mill, spar. **n* blow, buffet, fight, hit, spar.

box[2] *vb* barrel, crate, pack, parcel. **n* case, chest, container, crate, portmanteau, trunk.

boy *n* lad, stripling, youth.

brace *vb* make tight, tighten; buttress, fortify, reinforce, shore, strengthen, support, truss. **n* couple, pair; clamp, girder, prop, shore, stay, support, tie, truss.

brag *vb* bluster, boast, flourish, gasconade, vaunt.

branch *vb* diverge, fork, bifurcate, ramify, spread. **n* bough, offset, limb, shoot, sprig, twig; arm, fork, ramification, spur; article, department, member, part, portion, section, subdivision.

brand *vb* denounce, stigmatize, mark. **n* firebrand, torch; bolt, lightning flash; cachet, mark, stamp, tally; blot, reproach, stain, stigma.

brave *vb* dare, defy. **adj* bold, courageous, fearless, heroic, intrepid, stalwart.

bravery *n* courage, daring, fearlessness, gallantry, valour.

brawl *vb* bicker, dispute, jangle, quarrel, squabble. **n* broil, dispute, feud, fracas, fray, jangle, quarrel, row, scuffle, squabble, uproar, wrangle.

brawny *adj* athletic, lusty, muscular, powerful, robust, sinewy, stalwart, strapping, strong, sturdy.

bray *vb* clamour, hoot, roar, trumpet, vociferate. **n* blare, crash, roar, shout.

breach *n* break, chasm, crack, disruption,

fissure, flaw, fracture, opening, rent, rift, rupture; alienation, difference, disaffection, disagreement, split.

bread *n* aliment, diet, fare, food, nourishment, nutriment, provisions, regimen, victuals.

break *vb* crack, disrupt, fracture, part, rend, rive, sever; batter, burst, crush, shatter, smash, splinter; cashier, degrade, discard, discharge, dismiss; disobey, infringe, transgress, violate; intermit, interrupt, stop; disclose, open, unfold. **n* aperture, breach, chasm, fissure, gap, rent, rip, rupture; break-up, crash, debacle.

breast *vb* face, oppose, resist, stem, withstand. **n* bosom, chest, thorax; affections, conscience, heart; mammary gland, mammary organ, pap, udder.

breath *n* exhaling, inhaling, pant, sigh, respiration, whiff; animation, existence, life; pause, respite, rest; breathing space, instant, moment.

breathe *vb* live, exist; emit, exhale, give out; diffuse, express, indicate, manifest, show.

breed *vb* bear, beget, engender, hatch, produce; bring up, foster, nourish, nurture, raise, rear; discipline, educate, instruct, nurture, rear, school, teach, train; generate, originate. **n* extraction, family, lineage, pedigree, progeny, race, strain.

brevity *n* briefness, compression, conciseness, curtness, pithiness, shortness, terseness, transiency.

brew *vb* concoct, contrive, devise, excite, foment, instigate, plot. **n* beverage, concoction, drink, liquor, mixture, potation.

bribe *vb* buy, corrupt, influence, pay off, suborn. **n* allurement, corruption, enticement, graft, pay-off, subornation.

bridle *vb* check, curb, control, govern, restrain. **n* check, control, curb.

brief *vb* direct, give directions, instruct; capsulate, summarize, delineate, describe, draft, outline, sketch; (*law*) retain. **adj* concise, curt, inconsiderable, laconic, pithy, short, succinct, terse; fleeting, momentary, short, temporary, transient. **n* abstract, breviary, briefing, epitome, compendium, summary, syllabus; (*law*) precept, writ.

brigand *n* bandit, footpad, freebooter, gangster, highwayman, marauder, outlaw, robber, thug.

bright *adj* blazing, brilliant, dazzling, gleaming, glowing, light, luminous, radiant, shining, sparkling, sunny; clear, cloudless, lambent, lucid, transparent; famous, glorious, illustrious; acute, discerning, ingenious, intelligent, keen; auspicious, cheering, encouraging, exhilarating, favourable, inspiring, promising, propitious; cheerful, genial, happy, lively, merry, pleasant, smiling, vivacious.

brilliant *adj* beaming, bright, effulgent, gleaming, glistening, glittering, lustrous, radiant, resplendent, shining, sparkling splendid; admirable, celebrated, distinguished, famous, glorious, illustrious, renowned; dazzling, decided, prominent, signal, striking, unusual.

brim *n* border, brink, edge, rim, margin, skirt, verge; bank, border, coast, shore.

bring *vb* bear, convey, fetch; accompany, attend, conduct, convey, convoy, guide, lead; gain, get, obtain, procure, produce.

brisk *adj* active, alert, agile, lively, nimble, perky, quick, smart, spirited, spry.

brittle *adj* brash, breakable, crisp, crumbling, fragile, frangible, frail, shivery.

broach *vb* open, pierce, set; approach, break, hint, suggest; proclaim, publish, utter.

broad *adj* ample, expansive, extensive, large, spacious, sweeping, vast, wide; enlarged, hospitable, liberal, tolerant; diffused, open, spread; coarse, gross, indecent, indelicate, unrefined, vulgar.

broaden *vb* augment, enlarge, expand, extend, increase, spread, stretch, widen.

broken *adj* fractured, rent, ruptured, separated, severed, shattered, shivered, torn; exhausted, feeble, impaired, shaken, shattered, spent, wasted; defective, halting, hesitating, imperfect, stammering, stumbling; contrite, humble, lowly, penitent; abrupt, craggy, precipitous, rough.

broker *n* agent, factor, go-between, middleman.

brood *vb* incubate, sit. **n* issue, offspring, progeny; breed, kind, line, lineage, sort, strain.

brook *vb* abide, bear, endure, suffer, tolerate. **n* burn, beck, creek, rill, rivulet, run, streamlet.

brotherhood *n* association, clan, clique, coterie, fraternity, junta, society.

brotherly *adj* affectionate, amicable, cordial, friendly, kind.

browbeat *vb* bully, intimidate, overawe, overbear.

bruise *vb* contuse, crunch, squeeze; batter, break, maul, pound, pulverize; batter, deface, indent. **n* blemish, contusion, swelling.

brush[1] *n* brushwood, bush, scrub, scrubwood, shrubs, thicket, wilderness.

brush[2] *vb* buff, clean, polish, swab, sweep, wipe; curry, groom, rub down; caress, flick, glance, graze, scrape, skim, touch. **n* besom, broom; action, affair, collision, contest, conflict, encounter, engagement, fight, skirmish.

brutal *adj* barbaric, barbarous, brutish, cruel, ferocious, inhuman, ruthless, savage; bearish, brusque, churlish, gruff, impolite, harsh, rude, rough, truculent, uncivil.

brute *n* barbarian, beast, monster, ogre, savage; animal, beast, creature. **adj* carnal, mindless, physical; bestial, coarse, gross.

bubble *vb* boil, effervesce, foam. **n* bead, blob, fluid, globule; bagatelle, trifle; cheat, delusion, hoax.

buccaneer *n* corsair, freebooter, pirate.

buck *vb* jump, leap. **n* beau, blade, blood, dandy, fop, gallant, spark; male.

bud *vb* burgeon, germinate, push, shoot, sprout, vegetate. **n* burgeon, gem, germ, gemmule, shoot, sprout.

budget *vb* allocate, cost, estimate. **n* account, estimate, financial statement; assets, finances, funds, means, resources; bag, bundle, pack, packet, parcel, roll; assortment, batch, collection, lot, set, store.

buffet[1] *vb* beat, box, cuff, slap, smite, strike; resist, struggle against, **n* blow, box, cuff, slap, strike;

buffet[2] *n* cupboard, sideboard; refreshment counter.

buffoon *n* antic, clown, droll, fool, harlequin, jester, mountebank.

build *vb* construct, erect, establish, fabricate, fashion, model, raise, rear. **n* body, figure, form, frame, physique; construction, shape, structure.

building *n* construction, erection, fabrication; edifice, fabric, house, pile, substructure, structure,

bulk *n* dimension, magnitude, mass, size, volume; amplitude, bulkiness, massiveness; body, majority, mass.

bully *vb* browbeat, bulldoze, domineer, haze, hector, intimidate, overbear. **n* blusterer, browbeater, bulldozer, hector, swaggerer, roisterer, tyrant.

bulwark *n* barrier, fortification, parapet, rampart, wall; palladium, safeguard, security.

bump *vb* collide, knock, strike, thump. **n* blow, jar, jolt, knock, shock, thump; lump, protuberance, swelling.

bunch *vb* assemble, collect, crowd, group, herd, pack. **n* bulge, bump, bundle, hump, knob, lump, protuberance; cluster, hand, fascicle; assortment, batch, collection, group, lot, parcel, set; knot, tuft.

bundle *vb* bale, pack, package, parcel, truss, wrap. **n* bale, batch, bunch, collection, heap, pack, package, packet, parcel, pile, roll, truss.

bungler *n* botcher, duffer, fumbler, lout, lubber, mis-manager, muddler.

burden *vb* encumber, grieve, load, oppress, overlay, overload, saddle, surcharge, try. **n* capacity, cargo, freight, lading, load, tonnage, weight; affliction, charge, clog, encumbrance, impediment, grievance, sorrow, trial, trouble; drift, point, substance, tenor, surcharge.

bureau *n* chest of drawers, dresser; counting room, office.

burial *n* burying, entombment, inhumation, interment, sepulture.

burlesque *vb* ape, imitate, lampoon, mock,

ridicule, satirize. **n* caricature, extravaganza, parody, send-up, take-off, travesty.

burn[1] *n* beck, brook, gill, rill, rivulet, runnel, runlet, stream. water

burn[2] *vb* blaze, conflagrate, enflame, fire, flame, ignite, kindle, light, smoulder; cremate, incinerate; scald, scorch, singe; boil, broil, cook, roast, seethe, simmer, stew, swelter, toast; bronze, brown, sunburn, suntan, tan; bake, desiccate, dry, parch, sear, shrivel, wither; glow, incandesce, tingle, warm. **n* scald, scorch, singe; sunburn.

burning *adj* aflame, fiery, hot, scorching; ardent, earnest, fervent, fervid, impassioned, intense.

burnish *vb* brighten, buff, furbish, polish, shine. **n* glaze, gloss, patina, polish, shine.

burst *vb* break open, be rent, explode, shatter, split open. **adj* broken, kaput, punctured, ruptured, shattered, split. **n* break, breakage, breach, fracture, rupture; blast, blowout, blowup, discharge, detonation, explosion; spurt; blaze, flare, flash; cloudburst, downpour; bang, crack, crash, report, sound; fusillade, salvo, spray, volley, outburst, outbreak flare-up, blaze, eruption.

bury *vb* entomb, inearth, inhume, inter; conceal, hide, secrete, shroud.

business *n* calling, employment, occupation, profession, pursuit, vocation; commerce, dealing, trade, traffic; affair, concern, engagement, matter, transaction, undertaking; duty, function, office, task, work.

bustle *vb* fuss, hurry, scurry. **n* ado, commotion, flurry, fuss, hurry, hustle, pother, stir, tumult.

busy *vb* devote, employ, engage, occupy, spend, work. **adj* employed, engaged, occupied; active, assiduous, diligent, engrossed, industrious, sedulous, working; agile, brisk, nimble, spry, stirring; meddling, officious.

but *conj* except, excepting, further, howbeit, moreover, still, unless, yet. **adv* all the same, even, notwithstanding, still, yet.

butchery *n* massacre, murder, slaughter.

butt[1] *vb* bunt, push, shove, shunt, strike; encroach, impose, interfere, intrude, invade, obtrude. **n* buck, bunt, push, shove, shunt, thrust.

butt[2] *n* barrel, cask.

butt[3] *n* aim, goal, mark, object, point, target; dupe, gull, victim.

butt[4] *vb* abut, adjoin, conjoin, connect, neighbour. **n* end, piece, remainder, stub, stump; buttocks, posterior, rump.

buttonhole *vb* bore, catch, detain in conversation, importune.

buttress *vb* brace, prop, shore, stay, support. **n* brace, bulwark, prop, stay, support.

buxom *adj* comely, fresh, healthy, hearty, plump, rosy, ruddy, vigorous.

byword *n* adage, aphorism, apothegm, dictum, maxim, proverb, saying, saw.

C

cabal *vb* conspire, intrigue, machinate, plot. * *n* clique, combination, confederacy, coterie, faction, gang, junta, league, party, set; conspiracy, intrigue, machination, plot.

cabbalistic, cabalistic *adj* dark, fanciful, mysterious, mystic, occult, secret.

cabaret *n* tavern, inn, public house, wine shop.

cabin *n* berth, bunk, cot, cottage, crib, dwelling, hovel, hut, shack, shanty, shed.

cabinet *n* apartment, boudoir, chamber, closet; case, davenport, desk, escritoire; council, ministry.

cachinnation *n* guffaw, laugh, laughter.

cackle *vb* giggle, laugh, snicker, titter; babble, chatter, gabble, palaver, prate, prattle, titter. * *n* babble, chatter, giggle, prate, prattle, snigger, titter.

cacophonous *adj* discordant, grating, harsh, inharmonious, jarring, raucous.

cadaverous *adj* bloodless, deathlike, ghastly, pale, pallid, wan.

cage *vb* confine, immure, imprison, incarcerate. * *n* coop, pen, pound.

caitiff *adj* base, craven, pusillanimous, rascally, recreant. **n* coward, knave, miscreant, rascal, rogue, scoundrel, sneak, traitor, vagabond, villain, wretch.

cajole *vb* blandish, coax, flatter, jolly, wheedle; beguile, deceive, delude, entrap, inveigle, tempt.

calamity *n* adversity, affliction, blow, casualty, cataclysm, catastrophe, disaster, distress, downfall, evil, hardship, mischance, misery, misfortune, mishap, reverse, ruin, stroke, trial, visitation.

calculate *vb* cast, compute, count, estimate, figure, rate, reckon, weigh; tell.

calculating *adj* crafty, designing, scheming, selfish; careful, cautious, circumspect, far-sighted, politic, sagacious, wary.

calefaction *n* heating, warming; hotness, incandescence, warmth.

calendar *n* almanac, ephemeris, register; catalogue, list, schedule.

calibre *n* bore, capacity, diameter, gauge; ability, capacity, endowment, faculty, gifts, parts, scope, talent.

call *vb* christen, denominate, designate, dub, entitle, name, phrase, style, term; bid, invite, summons; assemble, convene, convoke, muster; cry, exclaim; arouse, awaken, proclaim, rouse, shout, waken; appoint, elect, ordain. **n* cry, outcry, voice; appeal, invitation, summons; claim, demand, summons; appointment, election, invitation.

calling *n* business, craft, employment, occupation, profession, pursuit, trade.

callous *adj* hard, hardened, indurated; apathetic, dull, indifferent, insensible, inured, obdurate, obtuse, sluggish, torpid, unfeeling, unsusceptible.

callow *adj* naked, unfeathered, unfledged; green, immature, inexperienced, sappy, silly, soft, unfledged, unsophisticated.

calm *vb* allay, becalm, compose, hush, lull, smooth, still, tranquillize; alleviate, appease, assuage, moderate, mollify, pacify, quiet, soften, soothe, tranquillize. **adj* halcyon, mild, peaceful, placid, quiet, reposeful, serene, smooth, still, tranquil, unruffled; collected, cool, composed, controlled, impassive, imperturbable, sedate, self-possessed, undisturbed, unperturbed, unruffled, untroubled. **n* lull; equanimity, peace, placidity, quiet, repose, serenity, stillness, tranquillity.

calorific *adj* heat, heat-producing.

calumniate *vb* abuse, asperse, backbite, blacken, blemish, defame, discredit, disparage, lampoon, libel, malign, revile, slander, traduce, vilify.

calumny *n* abuses, aspersion, backbiting, defamation, detraction, evil-speaking, insult, libel, lying, obloquy, slander, vilification, vituperation.

camarilla *n* cabal, clique, junta, ring.

camber *vb* arch, bend, curve. **n* arch, arching, convexity.

camp[1] *vb* bivouac, encamp, lodge, pitch, tent. **n* bivouac, cantonment, encampment, laager; cabal, circle, clique, coterie, faction, group, junta, party, ring, set.

camp[2] *adj* affected, artificial, effeminate, exaggerated, mannered, theatrical.

canaille *n* mob, populace, proletariat, rabble, ragbag, riffraff, scum.

canal *n* channel, duct, pipe, tube.

cancel *vb* blot, efface, erase, expunge, obliterate; abrogate, annul, countermand, nullify, quash, repeal, rescind, revoke.

candelabrum *n* candlestick, chandelier, lustre.

candid *adj* fair, impartial, just, unbiased, unprejudiced; artless, frank, free, guileless, honest, honourable, ingenuous, naive, open, plain, sincere, straightforward.

candidate *n* applicant, aspirant, claimant, competitor, probationer.

candour *n* fairness, impartiality, justice; artlessness, frankness, guilelessness, honesty, ingenuousness, openness, simplicity, sincerity, straightforwardness, truthfulness.

canker *vb* corrode, erode, rot, rust, waste; blight, consume, corrupt, embitter, envenom, infect, poison, sour. **n* gangrene, rot; bale, bane, blight, corruption, infection, irritation.

canon *n* catalogue, criterion, formula, formulary, law, regulation, rule, standard, statute.

canorous *adj* musical, tuneful.

cant[1] *vb* whine. **adj* current, partisan, popular, rote, routine, set; argotic, slangy. **n* hypocrisy; argot, jargon, lingo, slang.

cant[2] *vb* bevel, incline, list, slant, tilt, turn. **n* bevel, inclination, leaning, list, pitch, slant, tilt, turn.

cantankerous *adj* contumacious, crabbed, cross-grained, dogged, headstrong, heady, intractable, obdurate, obstinate, perverse, refractory, stiff, stubborn, wilful, unyielding.

canting *adj* affected, pious, sanctimonious, whining.

canvas *n* burlap, scrim, tarpaulin.

canvass *vb* discuss, dispute; analyze, consider, examine, investigate, review, scrutinize, sift, study; campaign, electioneer, solicit votes. **n* debate, discussion, dispute; examination, scrutiny, sifting.

canyon *n* gorge, gulch, ravine.

cap *vb* cover, surmount; complete, crown, finish; exceed, overtop, surpass, transcend; match, parallel, pattern. **n* beret, head-cover, head-dress; acme, chief, crown, head, peak, perfection, pitch, summit, top.

capability *n* ability, brains, calibre, capableness, capacity, competency, efficiency, faculty, force, power, scope, skill.

capable *adj* adapted, fitted, qualified, suited; able, accomplished, clever, competent, efficient, gifted, ingenious, intelligent, sagacious, skilful.

capacious *adj* ample, broad, comprehensive, expanded, extensive, large, roomy, spacious, wide.

capacitate *vb* enable, qualify.

capacity *n* amplitude, dimensions, magnitude, volume; aptitude, aptness, brains, calibre, discernment, faculty, forte, genius, gift, parts, power, talent, turn, wit; ability, capability, calibre, cleverness, competency, efficiency, skill; character, charge, function, office, position, post, province, service, sphere.

caparison *vb* accoutre, costume, equip, outfit, rig out. **n* accoutrements, armour, get-up, harness, housing, livery, outfit, panoply, tack, tackle, trappings, turnout.

caper *vb* bound, caracole, frisk, gambol, hop, leap, prank, romp, skip, spring. **n* bound, dance, gambol, frisk, hop, jump, leap, prance, romp, skip.

capillary *adj* delicate, fine, minute, slender.

capital *adj* cardinal, chief, essential, important, leading, main, major, pre-eminent, principal, prominent; fatal; excellent, first-class, first-rate, good, prime, splendid. *n chief city, metropolis, seat; money, estate, investments, shares, stock.

caprice *n* crotchet, fancy, fickleness, freak, humour, inconstancy, maggot, phantasy, quirk, vagary, whim, whimsy.

capricious *adj* changeable, crotchety, fanciful, fantastical, fickle, fitful, freakish, humoursome, odd, puckish, queer, uncertain, variable, wayward, whimsical.

capsize *vb* overturn, upset.

capsule *n* case, covering, envelope, sheath, shell, wrapper: pericarp, pod, seed-vessel.

captain *vb* command, direct, head, lead, manage, officer, preside. *n chief, chieftain, commander, leader, master, officer, soldier, warrior.

captious *adj* carping, caviling, censorious, critical, fault-finding, hypercritical; acrimonious, cantankerous, contentious, crabbed, cross, snappish, snarling, splenetic, testy, touchy, waspish; ensnaring, insidious.

captivate *vb* allure, attract, bewitch, catch, capture, charm, enamour, enchant, enthral, fascinate, gain, hypnotize, infatuate, win.

captivity *n* confinement, durance, duress, imprisonment; bondage, enthralment, servitude, slavery, subjection, thraldom, vassalage.

capture *vb* apprehend, arrest, catch, seize. *n apprehension, arrest, catch, catching, imprisonment, seizure; bag, prize.

carcass *n* body, cadaver, corpse, corse, remains.

cardinal *adj* capital, central, chief, essential, first, important, leading, main, preeminent, primary, principal, vital.

care *n* anxiety, concern, perplexity, trouble, solicitude, worry; attention, carefulness, caution, circumspection, heed, regard, vigilance, wariness, watchfulness; charge, custody, guardianship, keep, oversight, superintendence, ward; burden, charge, concern, responsibility.

careful *adj* anxious, solicitous, concerned, troubled, uneasy; attentive, heedful, mindful, regardful, thoughtful; cautious, canny, circumspect, discreet, leery, vigilant, watchful.

careless *adj* carefree, nonchalant, unapprehensive, undisturbed, unperplexed, unsolicitous, untroubled; disregardful, heedless, inattentive, incautious, inconsiderate, neglectful, negligent, regardless, remiss, thoughtless, unobservant, unconcerned, unconsidered, unmindful, unthinking.

carelessness *n* heedlessness, inadvertence, inattention, inconsiderateness, neglect, negligence, remissness, slackness, thoughtlessness, unconcern.

caress *vb* coddle, cuddle, cosset, embrace, fondle, hug, kiss, pet. *n cuddle, embrace, fondling, hug, kiss.

caressing *n* blandishment, dalliance, endearment, fondling.

cargo *n* freight, lading. load.

caricature *vb* burlesque, parody, send-up, take-off, travesty. *n burlesque, farce, ludicrous, parody, representation, take-off, travesty.

carious *adj* decayed, mortified, putrid, rotten, ulcerated.

cark *vb* annoy, fret, grieve, harass, perplex, worry.

carnage *n* bloodshed, butchery, havoc, massacre, murder, slaughter.

carnal *adj* animal, concupiscent, fleshly, lascivious, lecherous, lewd, libidinous, lubricous, lustful, salacious, sensual, voluptuous; bodily, earthy, mundane. natural, secular, temporal, unregenerate, unspiritual.

carol *vb* chant, hum, sing, warble. *n canticle, chorus, ditty, hymn, lay, song, warble.

carousal *n* banquet, entertainment, feast, festival, merry-making, regale; bacchanal, carouse, debauch, jamboree, jollification, orgy, revel, revelling, revelry, saturnalia, spree, wassail.

carp *vb* cavil, censure, criticize, fault.

carping *adj* captious, cavilling, censorious, hypercritical. **n* cavil, censure, fault-finding, hypercriticism.
carriage *n* conveyance, vehicle; air, bearing, behaviour, conduct, demeanour, deportment, front, mien, port.
carry *vb* bear, convey, transfer, transmit, transport; impel, push forward, urge; accomplish, compass, effect, gain, secure; bear up, support, sustain; infer, involve, imply, import, signify.
cart *n* conveyance, tumbril, van, vehicle, wagon.
carte-blanche *n* authority, power.
carve *vb* chisel, cut, divide, engrave, grave, hack, hew, indent, incise, sculpt, sculpture; fashion, form, mould, shape.
cascade *vb* cataract, descend, drop, engulf, fall, inundate, overflow, plunge, tumble. **n* cataract, fall, falls, force, linn, waterfall.
case[1] *vb* cover, encase, enclose, envelop, protect, wrap; box, pack. **n* capsule, covering, sheathe; box, cabinet, container, holder, receptacle.
case[2] *n* condition, plight, predicament, situation, state; example, instance, occurrence; circumstance, condition, contingency, event; action, argument, cause, lawsuit, process, suit, trial.
case-hardened *adj* hardened, indurated, steeled; brazen, brazen-faced, obdurate, reprobate.
cash *n* banknotes, bullion, coin, currency, money, payment, specie.
cashier *vb* break, discard, discharge, dismiss.
cast *vb* fling, hurl, pitch, send, shy, sling, throw, toss; drive, force, impel, thrust; lay aside, put off, shed; calculate, compute, reckon; communicate, diffuse, impart, shed, throw. **n* fling, throw, toss; shade, tinge, tint, touch; air, character, look, manner, mien, style, tone, turn; form, mould.
castaway *adj* abandoned, cast-off, discarded, rejected. **n* derelict, outcast, reprobate, vagabond.
caste *n* class, grade, lineage, order, race, rank, species, status.
castigate *vb* beat, chastise, flog, lambaste, lash, thrash, whip; chaste, correct, discipline, punish; criticize, flagellate, upbraid.
castle *n* citadel, fortress, stronghold.
castrate *vb* caponize, emasculate, geld; mortify, subdue, suppress, weaken.
casual *adj* accidental, contingent, fortuitous, incidental, irregular, occasional, random, uncertain, unforeseen, unintentional, unpremeditated; informal, relaxed.
casualty *n* chance, contingency, fortuity, mishap; accident, catastrophe, disaster, mischance, misfortune.
cat *n* grimalkin, kitten, puss, tabby, tomcat.
cataclysm *n* deluge, flood, inundation; disaster, upheaval.
catacomb *n* crypt, tomb, vault.
catalogue *vb* alphabetize, categorize, chronicle, class, classify, codify, file, index, list, record, tabulate. **n* enumeration, index, inventory, invoice, list, record, register, roll, schedule.
cataract *n* cascade, fall, waterfall.
catastrophe *n* conclusion, consummation, denouement, end, finale, issue, termination, upshot; adversity, blow, calamity, cataclysm, debacle, disaster, ill, misfortune, mischance, mishap, trial, trouble.
catch *vb* clutch, grasp, gripe, nab, seize, snatch; apprehend, arrest, capture; overtake; enmesh, ensnare, entangle, entrap, lime, net; bewitch, captivate, charm, enchant, fascinate, win; surprise, take unawares. **n* arrest, capture, seizure; bag, find, haul, plum, prize; drawback, fault, hitch, obstacle, rub, snag; captive, conquest.
catching *adj* communicable, contagious, infectious, pestiferous, pestilential; attractive, captivating, charming, enchanting, fascinating, taking, winning, winsome.
catechize *adj* examine, interrogate, question, quiz.
catechumen *n* convert, disciple, learner, neophyte, novice, proselyte, pupil, tyro.
categorical *adj* absolute, direct, down-

right, emphatic, explicit, express, positive, unconditional, unqualified, unreserved, utter.

category *n* class, division, head, heading, list, order, rank, sort.

catenation *n* conjunction, connection, union.

cater *vb* feed, provide, purvey.

cathartic *adj* abstergent, aperient, cleansing, evacuant, laxative, purgative. **n* aperient, laxative, physic, purgative, purge.

catholic *adj* general, universal, worldwide; charitable, liberal, tolerant, unbigoted, unexclusive, unsectarian.

cause *vb* breed, create, originate, produce; effect, effectuate, occasion, produce. **n* agent, creator, mainspring, origin, original, producer, source, spring; account, agency, consideration, ground, incentive, incitement, inducement, motive, reason; aim, end, object, purpose; action, case, suit, trial.

caustic *adj* acrid, cathartic, consuming, corroding, corrosive, eating, erosive, mordant, virulent; biting, bitter, burning, cutting, sarcastic, satirical, scalding, scathing, severe, sharp, stinging.

caution *vb* admonish, forewarn, warn. **n* care, carefulness, circumspection, discretion, forethought, heed, heedfulness, providence, prudence, wariness, vigilance, watchfulness; admonition, advice, counsel, injunction, warning.

cautious *adj* careful, chary, circumspect, discreet, heedful, prudent, wary, vigilant, wary, watchful.

cavalier *adj* arrogant, curt, disdainful, haughty, insolent, scornful, supercilious; debonair, gallant, gay. **n* chevalier, equestrian, horseman, horse-soldier, knight.

cave *n* cavern, cavity, den, grot, grotto.

cavil *vb* carp, censure, hypercriticize, object.

cavilling *adj* captious, carping, censorious, critical, hypercritical.

cavity *n* hollow, pocket, vacuole, void.

cease *vb* desist, intermit, pause, refrain, stay, stop; fail; discontinue, end, quit, terminate.

ceaseless *adj* continual, continuous, incessant, unceasing, unintermitting, uninterrupted, unremitting; endless, eternal, everlasting, perpetual.

cede *vb* abandon, abdicate, relinquish, resign, surrender, transfer, yield; convey, grant.

celebrate *vb* applaud, bless, commend, emblazon, extol, glorify, laud, magnify, praise, trumpet; commemorate, honour, keep, observe; solemnize.

celebrated *adj* distinguished, eminent, famed, famous, glorious, illustrious, notable, renowned.

celebrity *n* credit, distinction, eminence, fame, glory, honour, renown, reputation, repute; lion, notable, star.

celerity *n* fleetness, haste, quickness, rapidity, speed, swiftness, velocity.

celestial *adj* empyreal, empyrean; angelic, divine, god-like, heavenly, seraphic, supernal, supernatural.

celibate *adj* single, unmarried. **n* bachelor, single, virgin.

cellular *adj* alveolate, honeycombed.

cement *vb* attach, bind, join, combine, connect, solder, unite, weld; cohere, stick. **n* glue, paste, mortar, solder.

cemetery *n* burial-ground, burying-ground, churchyard, god's acre, graveyard, necropolis.

censor *vb* blue-pencil, bowdlerize, cut, edit, expurgate; classify, kill, quash, squash, suppress. **n* caviller, censurer, faultfinder.

censorious *adj* captious, carping, caviling, condemnatory, faultfinding, hypercritical, severe.

censure *vb* abuse, blame, chide, condemn, rebuke, reprehend, reprimand, reproach, reprobate, reprove, scold, upbraid. **n* animadversion, blame, condemnation, criticism, disapprobation, disapproval, rebuke, remonstrance, reprehension, reproach, reproof, stricture.

ceremonious *adj* civil, courtly, lofty, stately; formal, studied; exact, formal, punctilious, precise, starched, stiff.

ceremony *n* ceremonial, etiquette, form,

formality, observance, solemnity, rite; parade, pomp, show, stateliness.

certain *adj* absolute, incontestable, incontrovertible, indisputable, indubitable, positive, undeniable, undisputed, unquestionable, unquestioned; assured, confident, sure, undoubting; infallible, never-failing, unfailing; actual, existing, real; constant, determinate, fixed, settled, stated.

certainty *n* indubitability, indubitableness, inevitableness, inevitability, surety, unquestionability, unquestionableness; assurance, assuredness, certitude, confidence, conviction, surety.

certify *vb* attest, notify, testify, vouch; ascertain, determine, verify, show.

cerulean *adj* azure, blue, sky-blue.

cessation *n* ceasing, discontinuance, intermission, pause, remission, respite, rest, stop, stoppage, suspension.

cession *n* abandonment, capitulation, ceding, concession, conveyance, grant, relinquishement, renunciation, surrender, yielding.

chafe *vb* rub; anger, annoy, chagrin, enrage, exasperate, fret, gall, incense, irritate, nettle, offend, provoke, ruffle, tease, vex; fret, fume, rage.

chaff *vb* banter, deride, jeer, mock, rally, ridicule. scoff. **n* glumes, hulls, husks; refuse, rubbish, trash, waste.

chaffer *n* bargain, haggle, higgle, negotiate.

chagrin *vb* annoy, chafe, displease, irritate, mortify, provoke, vex. **n* annoyance, displeasure, disquiet, dissatisfaction, fretfulness, humiliation, ill-humour, irritation, mortification, spleen, vexation.

chain *vb* bind, confine, fetter, manacle, restrain, shackle, trammel; enslave. **n* bond, fetter, manacle, shackle, union.

chalice *n* bowl, cup, goblet.

challenge *vb* brave, call out, dare, defy, dispute; demand, require. **n* defiance, interrogation, question; exception, objection.

chamber *n* apartment, hall, room; cavity, hollow.

champion *vb* advocate, defend, uphold. **n* defender, promoter, protector, vindicator; belt-holder, hero, victor, warrior, winner.

chance *vb* befall, betide, happen, occur. **adj* accidental, adventitious, casual, fortuitous, incidental, unexpected, unforeseen. **n* accident, cast, fortuity, fortune, hap, luck; contingency, possibility; occasion, opening, opportunity; contingency, fortuity, gamble, peradventure, uncertainty; hazard, jeopardy, peril, risk.

change *vb* alter, fluctuate, modify, vary; displace, remove, replace, shift, substitute; barter, commute, exchange. **n* alteration, mutation, revolution, transition, transmutation, turning, variance, variation; innovation, novelty, variety, vicissitude.

changeable *adj* alterable, inconstant, modifiable, mutable, uncertain, unsettled, unstable, unsteadfast, unsteady, variable, variant; capricious, fickle, fitful, flighty, giddy, mercurial, vacillating, volatile, wavering.

changeless *adj* abiding, consistent, constant, fixed, immutable, permanent, regular, reliable, resolute, settled, stationary, unalterable, unchanging.

channel *vb* chamfer, cut, flute, groove. **n* canal, conduit, duct, passage; aqueduct, canal, chute, drain, flume, furrow; chamfer, groove, fluting, furrow, gutter.

chant *vb* carol, sing, warble; intone, recite; canticle, song.

chaos *n* anarchy, confusion, disorder.

chapfallen *adj* blue, crest-fallen, dejected, depressed, despondent, discouraged, disheartened, dispirited, downcast, downhearted, low-spirited, melancholy, sad.

chaplet *n* coronal, garland, wreath.

char *vb* burn, scorch.

character *n* emblem, figure, hieroglyph, ideograph, letter, mark, sign, symbol; bent, constitution, cast, disposition, nature, quality; individual, original, person, personage; reputation, repute; nature, traits; eccentric, trait.

characteristic *adj* distinctive, peculiar, singular, special, specific, typical. **n* attribute, feature, idiosyncrasy, lineament, mark, peculiarity, quality, trait.

charge *vb* burden, encumber, freight, lade, load; entrust; ascribe, impute, lay; accuse, arraign, blame, criminate, impeach, inculpate, indict, involve; bid, command, exhort, enjoin, order, require, tax; assault, attack bear down. **n* burden, cargo, freight, lading, load; care, custody, keeping, management, ward; commission, duty, employment, office, trust; responsibility, trust; command, direction, injunction, mandate, order, precept; exhortation, instruction; cost, debit, expense, expenditure, outlay; price, sum; assault, attack, encounter, onset, onslaught.

charger *n* dish, platter; mount, steed, warhorse.

charily *adv* carefully, cautiously, distrustfully, prudently, sparingly, suspiciously, warily.

charitable *adj* beneficial, beneficent, benignant, bountiful, generous, kind, liberal, open-handed; candid, considerate, lenient, mild.

charity *n* benevolence, benignity, fellow-feeling, good-nature, goodwill, kind-heartedness, kindness, tenderheartedness; beneficence, bounty, generosity, humanity, philanthropy. liberality.

charlatan *n* cheat, empiric, impostor, mountebank, pretender, quack.

charm *vb* allure, attract, becharm, bewitch, captivate, catch, delight, enamour, enchain, enchant, enrapture, enravish, fascinate, transport, win. **n* enchantment, incantation, magic, necromancy, sorcery, spell, witchery; amulet, talisman; allurement, attraction, attractiveness, fascination.

charming *adj* bewitching, captivating, delightful, enchanting, enrapturing, fascinating, lovely.

charter *vb* incorporate; hire, let. **n* franchise, immunity, liberty, prerogation, privilege, right; bond, deed, indenture, instrument, prerogative.

chary *adj* careful, cautious, circumspect, shy, wary; abstemious, careful, choice, economical, frugal, provident, saving, sparing, temperate, thrifty, unwasteful.

chase *vb* follow, hunt, pursue, track; emboss. **n* course, field-sport, hunt, hunting.

chasm *n* cavity, cleft, fissure, gap, hollow, hiatus, opening.

chaste *adj* clean, continent, innocent, modest, pure, pure-minded, undefiled, virtuous; chastened, pure, simple, unaffected, uncorrupt.

chasten *vb* correct, humble; purify, refine, render, subdue.

chastening *n* chastisement, correction, discipline, humbling.

chastise *vb* castigate, correct, flog, lash, punish, whip; chasten, correct, discipline, humble, punish, subdue.

chastity *n* abstinence, celibacy, continence, innocence, modesty, pure-mindedness, purity, virtue; cleanness, decency; chasteness, refinement, restrainedness, simplicity, sobriety, unaffectedness.

chat *vb* babble, chatter, confabulate, gossip, prate, prattle. **n* chit-chat, confabulation, conversation, gossip, prattle.

chatter *vb* babble, chat, confabulate, gossip, prate, prattle. **n* babble, chat, gabble, jabber, patter, prattle.

cheap *adj* inexpensive, low-priced; common, indifferent, inferior, mean, meretricious, paltry, poor.

cheapen *vb* belittle, depreciate.

cheat *vb* cozen, deceive, dissemble, juggle, shuffle; bamboozle, befool, beguile, cajole, circumvent, deceive, defraud, chouse, delude, dupe, ensnare, entrap, fool, gammon, gull, hoax, hoodwink, inveigle, jockey, mislead, outwit, overreach, trick. **n* artifice, beguilement, blind, catch, chouse, deceit, deception, fraud, imposition, imposture, juggle, pitfall, snare, stratagem, swindle, trap, trick, wile; counterfeit, deception, delusion, illusion, mockery, paste, sham, tinsel; beguiler, charlatan, cheater, cozener, impostor, jockey, knave, mountebank, trickster, rogue, render, sharper, seizer, shuffler, swindler, taker, tearer.

check *vb* block, bridle, control, counteract, curb, hinder, obstruct, repress, restrain; chide, rebuke, reprimand, reprove. **n* bar, barrier, block, brake, bridle, clog, control, curb, damper, hindrance, impediment, interference, obstacle, obstruction, rebuff, repression, restraint, stop, stopper.

cheep *vb* chirp, creak, peep, pipe, squeak.

cheer *vb* animate, encourage, enliven, exhilarate, gladden, incite, inspirit; comfort, console, solace; applaud, clap. **n* cheerfulness, gaiety, gladness, glee, hilarity, jollity, joy, merriment, mirth; entertainment, food, provision, repast, viands, victuals; acclamation, hurrah, huzza.

cheerful *adj* animated, airy, blithe, buoyant, cheery, gay, glad, gleeful, happy, joyful, jocund, jolly, joyous, lighthearted, lightsome, lively, merry, mirthful, sprightly, sunny; animating, cheering, cheery, encouraging, enlivening, glad, gladdening, gladsome, grateful, inspiriting, jocund, pleasant.

cheerless *adj* dark, dejected, desolate, despondent, disconsolate, discouraged, dismal, doleful, dreary, forlorn, gloomy, joyless, low-spirited, lugubrious, melancholy, mournful, rueful, sad, sombre, spiritless, woe-begone.

cherish *vb* comfort, foster, nourish, nurse, nurture, support, sustain; treasure; encourage, entertain, indulge, harbour.

chest *n* box, case, coffer; breast, thorax, trunk.

chew *vb* crunch, manducate, masticate, munch; bite, champ, gnaw; meditate, ruminate.

chicanery *n* chicane, deception, duplicity, intrigue, intriguing, sophistication, sophistry, stratagems, tergiversation, trickery, wiles, wire-pulling.

chide *vb* admonish, blame, censure, rebuke, reprimand, reprove, scold, upbraid; chafe, clamour, fret, fume, scold.

chief *adj* first, foremost, headmost, leading, master, supereminent, supreme, top; capital, cardinal, especial, essential, grand, great, main, master, paramount, prime, principal, supreme, vital. **n* chieftain, commander; head, leader.

chiffonier *n* cabinet, sideboard.

child *n* babe, baby, bairn, bantling, brat, chit, infant, nursling, suckling, wean; issue, offspring, progeny.

childbirth *n* child-bearing, delivery, labour, parturition, travail.

childish *adj* infantile, juvenile, puerile, tender, young; foolish, frivolous, silly, trifling, weak.

childlike *adj* docile, dutiful, gentle, meek, obedient, submissive; confiding, guileless, ingenuous, innocent, simple, trustful, uncrafty.

chill *vb* dampen, depress, deject, discourage, dishearten. **adj* bleak, chilly, cold, frigid, gelid. **n* chilliness, cold, coldness, frigidity; ague, rigour, shiver; damp, depression.

chime *vb* accord, harmonize. **n* accord, consonance.

chimera *n* crochet, delusion, dream, fantasy, hallucination, illusion, phantom.

chimerical *adj* delusive, fanciful, fantastic, illusory, imaginary, quixotic, shadowy, unfounded, visionary, wild.

chink[1] *vb* cleave, crack, fissure, crevasse, incise, split, slit. **n* aperture, cleft, crack, cranny, crevice, fissure, gap, opening, slit.

chink[2] *vb, n* jingle, clink, ring, ting, tink, tinkle.

chip *vb* flake, fragment, hew, pare, scrape. **n* flake, fragment, paring, scrap.

chirp *vb* cheep, chirrup, peep, twitter.

chirrup *vb* animate, cheer, encourage, inspirit.

chisel *vb* carve, cut, gouge, sculpt, sculpture.

chivalrous *adj* adventurous, bold, brave, chivalric, gallant, knightly, valiant, warlike; gallant, generous, high-minded, magnanimous.

chivalry *n* knighthood, knight-errantry; courtesy, gallantry, politeness; courage, valour.

choice *adj* excellent, exquisite, precious,

rare, select, superior, uncommon, unusual, valuable; careful, chary, frugal, sparing. *n alternative, election, option, selection; favourite, pick, preference.

choke *vb* gag, smother, stifle, strangle, suffocate, throttle; overcome, overpower, smother, suppress; bar, block, close, obstruct, stop.

choleric *adj* angry, fiery, hasty, hot, fiery, irascible, irritable, passionate, petulant, testy, touchy, waspish.

choose *vb* adopt, co-opt, cull, designate, elect, pick, predestine, prefer, select.

chop *vb* cut, hack, hew; mince; shift, veer. *n slice; brand, quality; chap, jaw.

chouse *vb* bamboozle, beguile, cheat, circumvent, cozen, deceive, defraud, delude, dupe, gull, hoodwink, overreach, swindle, trick, victimize. *n cully, dupe, gull, simpleton, tool; artifice, cheat, circumvention, deceit, deception, delusion, double-dealing, fraud, imposition, imposture, ruse, stratagem, trick, wile.

christen *vb* baptize; call, dub, denominate, designate, entitle, name, style, term, title.

chronic *adj* confirmed, continuing, deep-seated, inveterate, rooted.

chronicle *vb* narrate, record, register. *n diary, journal, register; account, annals, history, narration, recital, record.

chuckle *vb* crow, exult, giggle, laugh, snigger, titter. *n giggle, laughter, snigger, titter.

chum *n* buddy, companion, comrade, crony, friend, mate, pal.

churl *n* boor, bumpkin, clodhopper, clown, countryman, lout, peasant, ploughman, rustic; curmudgeon, hunks, miser, niggard, scrimp, skinflint.

churlish *adj* brusque, brutish, cynical, harsh, impolite, rough, rude, snappish, snarling, surly, uncivil, waspish; crabbed, ill-tempered, morose, sullen; close, close-fisted, illiberal, mean, miserly, niggardly, penurious, stingy.

churn *vb* agitate, jostle.

cicatrice *n* cicatrix, mark, scar, seam.

cicesbeo *n* beau, escort, gallant, gigolo.

cincture *n* band, belt, cestos, cestus, girdle.

cipher *n* naught, nothing, zero; character, device, monogram, symbol; nobody, nonentity.

circle *vb* compass, encircle, encompass, gird, girdle, ring; gyrate, revolve, rotate, round, turn. *n circlet, corona, gyre, hoop, ring, rondure; circumference, cordon, periphery; ball, globe, orb, sphere; compass, enclosure; class, clique, company, coterie, fraternity, set, society; bounds, circuit, compass, field, province, range, region, sphere.

circuit *n* ambit, circumambience, circumambiency, cycle, revolution, turn; bounds, district, field, province, range, region, space, sphere, tract; boundary, compass; course, detour, perambulation, round, tour.

circuitous *adj* ambiguous, devious, indirect, roundabout, tortuous, turning, winding.

circulate *vb* diffuse, disseminate, promulgate, propagate, publish, spread.

circumference *n* bound, boundary, circuit, girth, outline, perimeter, periphery.

circumlocution *n* circuitousness, obliqueness, periphrase, periphrasis, verbosity, wordiness.

circumscribe *vb* bound, define, encircle, enclose, encompass, limit, surround; confine, restrict.

circumspect *adj* attentive, careful, cautious, considerate, discreet, heedful, judicious, observant, prudent, vigilant, wary, watchful.

circumstance *n* accident, incident; condition, detail, event, fact, happening, occurrence, position, situation.

circumstantial *adj* detailed, particular; indirect, inferential, presumptive.

circumvent *vb* check, checkmate, outgeneral, thwart; bamboozle, beguile, cheat, chouse, cozen, deceive, defraud, delude, dupe, gull, hoodwink, inveigle, mislead, outwit, overreach, trick.

circumvention *n* cheat, cheating, chicanery, deceit, deception, duplicity, fraud, guile, imposition, imposture, indirection, trickery, wiles.

cistern *n* basin, pond, reservoir, tank.

citation *n* excerpt, extract, quotation; enumeration, mention, quotation, quoting.

cite *vb* adduce, enumerate, extract, mention, name, quote; call, summon.

citizen *n* burgess, burgher, denizen, dweller, freeman, inhabitant, resident, subject, townsman.

civil *adj* civic, municipal, political; domestic; accommodating, affable, civilized, complaisant, courteous, courtly, debonair, easy, gracious, obliging, polished, polite, refined, suave, urbane, well-bred, well-mannered.

civility *n* affability, amiability, complaisance, courteousness, courtesy, good-breeding, politeness, suavity, urbanity.

civilize *vb* cultivate, educate, enlighten, humanize, improve, polish, refine.

claim *vb* ask, assert, challenge, demand, exact, require. **n* call, demand, lien, requisition; pretension, privilege, right, title.

clammy *adj* adhesive, dauby, glutinous, gummy, ropy, smeary, sticky, viscid, viscous; close, damp, dank, moist, sticky, sweaty.

clamour *vb* shout, vociferate. **n* blare, din, exclamation, hullabaloo, noise, outcry, uproar, vociferation.

clan *n* family, phratry, race, sect, tribe; band, brotherhood, clique, coterie, fraternity, gang, set, society, sodality.

clandestine *adj* concealed, covert, fraudulent, furtive, hidden, private, secret, sly, stealthy, surreptitious, underhand.

clap *vb* pat, slap, strike; force, slam; applaud, cheer. **n* blow, knock, slap; bang, burst, explosion, peal, slam.

clarify *vb* cleanse, clear, depurate, purify, strain.

clash *vb* collide, crash, strike; clang, clank, clatter, crash, rattle; contend, disagree, interfere. **n* collision; clang, clangour, clank, clashing, clatter, crash, rattle; contradiction, disagreement, interference, jar, jarring, opposition.

clasp *vb* clutch, entwine, grasp, grapple, grip, seize; embrace, enfold, fold, hug. **n* buckle, catch, hasp, hook; embrace, hug.

class *vb* arrange, classify, dispose, distribute, range, rank. **n* form, grade, order, rank, status; group, seminar; breed, kind, sort; category, collection, denomination, division, group, head.

classical *adj* first-rate, master, masterly, model, standard; Greek, Latin, Roman; Attic, chaste, elegant, polished, pure, refined.

classify *vb* arrange, assort, categorize, class, dispose, distribute, group, pigeonhole, rank, systematize, tabulate.

clatter *vb* clash, rattle; babble, clack, gabble, jabber, prate, prattle. **n* clattering, clutter, rattling.

clause *n* article, condition, provision, stipulation.

claw *vb* lacerate, scratch, tear. **n* talon, ungula.

clean *vb* cleanse, clear, purge, purify, rinse, scour, scrub, wash, wipe. **adj* immaculate, spotless, unsmirched, unsoiled, unspotted, unstained, unsullied, white; clarified, pure, purified, unadulterated, unmixed; adroit, delicate, dextrous, graceful, light, neat, shapely; complete, entire, flawless, faultless, perfect, unabated, unblemished, unimpaired, whole; chaste, innocent, moral, pure, undefiled. **adv* altogether, completely, entirely, perfectly, quite, thoroughly, wholly.

cleanse *vb* clean, clear, elutriate, purge, purify, rinse, scour, scrub, wash, wipe.

clear *vb* clarify, cleanse, purify, refine; emancipate, disenthral, free, liberate, loose; absolve, acquit, discharge, exonerate, justify, vindicate; disembarrass, disengage, disentangle, extricate, loosen, rid; clean up, scour, sweep; balance; emancipate, free, liberate. **adj* bright, crystalline, light, limpid, luminous, pellucid, transparent; pure, unadulterated, unmixed; free, open, unencumbered, unobstructed; cloudless, fair, serene, sunny, unclouded, undimmed, unobscured; net; distinct, intelligible, lucid, luminous, perspicuous; apparent, conspicuous, distinct, evident, indisputable, manifest, obvious, palpable, unambiguous, undeniable, unequivocal, unmistakable, unquestionable, visible; clean, guiltless, immaculate, innocent, irreproachable, sinless, spotless, unblemished, undefiled, unspotted, unsullied; unhampered, unimpeded, unobstructed; euphonious, fluty, liquid, mellifluous, musical, silvery, sonorous.

cleave[1] *vb* crack, divide, open, part, rend, rive, sever, split, sunder.

cleave[2] *vb* adhere, cling, cohere, hold, stick.

cleft *adj* bifurcated, cloven, forked. **n* breach, break, chasm, chink, cranny, crevice, fissure, fracture, gap, interstice, opening, rent, rift.

clemency *n* mildness, softness; compassion, fellow-feeling, forgivingness, gentleness, kindness, lenience, leniency, lenity, mercifulness, mercy, mildness, tenderness.

clement *adj* compassionate, forgiving, gentle, humane, indulgent, kind, kind-hearted, lenient, merciful, mild, tender, tender-hearted.

clench *vb* close tightly, grip; fasten, fix, rivet, secure.

clergy *n* clergymen, the cloth, ministers.

clever *adj* able, apt, gifted, talented; adroit, capable, dextrous, discerning, expert, handy, ingenious, knowing, quick, ready, skilful, smart, talented.

click *vb* beat, clack, clink, tick. **n* beat, clack, clink, tick; catch, detent, pawl, ratchet.

cliff *n* crag, palisade, precipice, scar, steep.

climate *n* clime, temperature, weather; country, region.

climax *vb* consummate, crown, culminate, peak. **n* acme, consummation, crown, culmination, head, peak, summit, top, zenith.

clinch *vb* clasp, clench, clutch, grapple, grasp, grip; fasten, secure; confirm, establish, fix. **n* catch, clutch, grasp, grip; clincher, clamp, cramp, holdfast.

cling *vb* adhere, clear, stick; clasp, embrace, entwine.

clink *vb, n* chink, jingle, ring, tinkle; chime, rhyme.

clip *vb* cut, shear, snip; curtail, cut, dock, pare, prune, trim. **n* cutting, shearing; blow, knock, lick, rap, thump, thwack, thump.

clique *n* association, brotherhood, cabal, camarilla, clan, club, coterie, gang, junta, party, ring, set, sodality.

cloak *vb* conceal, cover, dissemble, hide, mask, veil. **n* mantle, surcoat; blind, cover, mask, pretext, veil.

clock *vb* mark time, measure, stopwatch; clock up, record, register. **n* chronometer, horologue, timekeeper, timepiece, timer, watch.

clog *vb* fetter, hamper, shackle, trammel; choke, obstruct; burden, cumber, embarrass, encumber, hamper, hinder, impede, load, restrain, trammel. **n* dead-weight, drag-weight, fetter, shackle, trammel; check, drawback, encumbrance, hindrance, impediment, obstacle, obstruction.

cloister *n* abbey, convent, monastery, nunnery, priory; arcade, colonnade, piazza.

close[1] *adj* closed, confined, snug, tight; hidden, private, secret; incommunicative, reserved, reticent, secretive, taciturn; concealed, retired, secluded, withdrawn; confined, motionless, stagnant; airless, oppressive, stale, stifling, stuffy, sultry; compact, compressed, dense, form, solid, thick; adjacent, adjoining, approaching, immediately, near, nearly, neighbouring; attached, dear, confidential, devoted, intimate; assiduous, earnest, fixed, intense, intent, unremitting; accurate, exact, faithful, nice, precise, strict; churlish, close-fisted, curmudgeonly, mean, illiberal, miserly, niggardly, parsimonious, penurious, stingy, ungenerous. **n* courtyard, enclosure, grounds, precinct, yard.

close[2] *vb* occlude, seal, shut; choke, clog,

estop, obstruct, stop; cease, complete, concede, end, finish, terminate; coalesce, unite; cease, conclude, finish, terminate; clinch, grapple; agree. *n* cessation, conclusion, end, finish, termination.

closet *n* cabinet, retiring-room; press, store-room.

clot *vb* coagulate, concrete. *n* coagulation, concretion, lump.

clothe *vb* array, attire, deck, dress, rig; cover,endow, envelop, enwrap, invest with, swathe.

clothes *n* apparel, array, attire, clothing, costume, dress, garb, garments, gear, habiliments, habits, raiment, rig, vestments, vesture.

cloud *vb* becloud, obnubilate, overcast, overspread; befog, darken, dim, obscure, shade, shadow. *n* cirrus, cumulus, fog, haze, mist, nebulosity, scud, stratus, vapour; army, crowd, horde, host, multitude, swarm, throng; darkness, eclipse, gloom, obscuration, obscurity.

cloudy *adj* clouded, filmy, foggy, hazy, lowering, lurid, murky, overcast; confused, dark, dim, obscure; depressing, dismal, gloomy, sullen; clouded, mottled; blurred, dimmed, lustreless, muddy.

clown *n* churl, clod-breaker, clodhopper, hind, husbandman, lubber; boor, bumpkin, churl, fellow, lout; blockhead, dolt, clodpoll, dunce, dunderhead, numbskull, simpleton, thickhead; buffoon, droll, farceur, fool, harlequin, jack-a-dandy, jack-pudding, jester, merry-andrew, mime, pantaloon, pickle-herring, punch, scaramouch, zany.

clownish *adj* awkward, boorish, clumsy, coarse, loutish, ungainly, rough, rustic; churlish, ill-bred, ill-mannered, impolite, rude, uncivil.

cloy *vb* glut, pall, sate, satiate, surfeit.

club *vb* combine, unite; beat, bludgeon, cudgel. *n* bat, bludgeon, cosh, cudgel, hickory, shillelagh, stick, truncheon; association, company, coterie, fraternity, set, society, sodality.

clump *vb* assemble, batch, bunch, cluster, group, lump; lumber, stamp, stomp, stump, trudge. *n* assemblage, bunch, cluster, collection, group, patch, tuft.

clumsy *adj* botched, cumbrous, heavy, ill-made, ill-shaped, lumbering, ponderous, unwieldy; awkward, blundering, bungling, elephantine, heavy-handed, inapt, mal adroit, unhandy, unskilled.

cluster *vb* assemble, batch, bunch, clump, collect, gather, group, lump, throng. *n* agglomeration, assemblage, batch, bunch, clump, collection, gathering, group, throng.

clutch[1] *vb* catch, clasp, clench, clinch, grab, grapple, grasp, grip, hold, seize, snatch, squeeze. *n* clasp, clench, clinch, grasp, grip, hold, seizure, squeeze.

clutch[2] *n* aerie, brood, hatching, nest.

clutches *npl* claws, paws, talons; hands, power.

clutter *vb* confuse, disarrange, disarray, disorder, jumble, litter, mess, muss; clatter. *n* bustle, clatter, clattering, racket; confusion, disarray, disorder, jumble, litter, mess, muss.

coadjutor *n* abettor, accomplice, aider, ally, assistant, associate, auxiliary, collaborator, colleague, cooperator, fellow-helper, helper, helpmate, partner.

coagulate *vb* clot, congeal, concrete, curdle, thicken.

coalesce *vb* amalgamate, blend, cohere, combine, commix, incorporate, mix, unite; concur, fraternize.

coalition *n* alliance, association, combination, compact, confederacy, confederation, conjunction, conspiracy, co-partnership, federation, league, union.

coarse *adj* crude, impure, rough, unpurified; broad, gross, indecent, indelicate, ribald, vulgar; bearish, bluff, boorish, brutish, churlish, clownish, gruff, impolite, loutish, rude, unpolished; crass, inelegant.

coast *vb* flow, glide, roll, skim, sail, slide, sweep. *n* littoral, seaboard, sea-coast, seaside, shore, strand; border.

coat *vb* cover, spread. *n* cut-away, frock, jacket; coating, cover, covering; layer.

coax *vb* allure, beguile, cajole, cog, entice, flatter, persuade, soothe, wheedle.

cobble *vb* botch, bungle; mend, patch, repair, tinker.
cobweb *adj* flimsy, gauzy, slight, thin, worthless. **n* entanglement, meshes, snare, toils.
cochleate *adj* cochlear, cochleary, cochleous, cochleated, spiral, spiry.
cockle *vb* corrugate, pucker, wrinkle.
coddle *vb* caress, cocker, fondle, humour, indulge, nurse, pamper, pet.
codger *n* churl, curmudgeon, hunks, lickpenny, miser, niggard, screw, scrimp, skinflint.
codify *vb* condense, digest, summarize, systematize, tabulate.
coerce *vb* check, curb, repress, restrain, subdue; compel, constrain, drive, force, urge.
coercion *n* check, curb, repression, restraint; compulsion, constraint, force.
coeval *adj* coetaneous, coexistent, contemporaneous, contemporary, synchronous.
coexistent *adj* coetaneous, coeval, simultaneous, synchronous.
coffer *n* box, casket, chest, trunk; money-chest, safe, strongbox; caisson.
cogent *adj* compelling, conclusive, convincing, effective, forcible, influential, irresistible, persuasive, potent, powerful, resistless, strong, trenchant, urgent.
cogitate *vb* consider, deliberate, meditate, ponder, reflect, ruminate, muse, think, weigh.
cognate *adj* affiliated, affined, akin, allied, alike, analogous, connected, kindred, related, similar.
cognizance *n* cognition, knowing, knowledge, notice, observation.
cohere *vb* agree, coincide, conform, fit, square, suit.
coherence *n* coalition, cohesion, connection, dependence, union; agreement, congruity, consistency, correspondence, harmony, intelligibility, intelligible, meaning, rationality, unity.
coherent *adj* adherent, connected, united; congruous, consistent, intelligible, logical.
cohort *n* band, battalion, line, squadron.
coil *vb* curl, twine, twirl, twist, wind. **n* convolution, curlicue, helix, knot, roll, spiral, tendril, twirl, volute, whorl; bustle, care, clamour, confusion, entanglements, perplexities, tumult, turmoil, uproar.
coin *vb* counterfeit, create, devise, fabricate, forge, form, invent, mint, originate, mould, stamp. **n* coign, corner, quoin; key, plug, prop, wedge; cash, money, specie.
coincide *vb* cohere, correspond, square, tally; acquiesce, agree, harmonize, concur.
coincidence *n* corresponding, squaring, tallying; agreeing, concurrent, concurring.
cold *adj* arctic, biting, bleak, boreal, chill, chilly, cutting, frosty, gelid, glacial, icy, nipping, polar, raw, wintry; frost-bitten, shivering; apathetic, cold-blooded, dead, freezing, frigid, indifferent, lukewarm, passionless, phlegmatic, sluggish, stoical, stony, torpid, unconcerned, unfeeling, unimpressible, unresponsive, unsusceptible, unsympathetic; dead, dull, spiritless, unaffecting, uninspiring, uninteresting. **n* chill, chilliness, coldness.
collapse *vb* break down, fail, fall. **n* depression, exhaustion, failure, faint, prostration, sinking, subsidence.
collar *vb* apprehend, arrest, capture, grab, nab, seize. **n* collarette, gorget, neckband, ruff, torque; band, belt, fillet, guard, ring, yoke.
collate *vb* adduce, collect, compare, compose.
collateral *adj* contingent, indirect, secondary, subordinate; concurrent, parallel; confirmatory, corroborative; accessory, accompanying, additional, ancillary, auxiliary, concomitant, contributory, simultaneous, supernumerary; consanguineous, related. **n* guarantee, guaranty, security, surety, warranty; accessory, extra, nonessential, unessential; consanguinean, relative.
collation *n* luncheon, repast, meal.
colleague *n* aider, ally, assistant, associate, auxiliary, coadjutor, collaborator,

companion, confederate, confrere, cooperator, helper, partner.

collect *vb* assemble, compile, gather, muster; accumulate, aggregate, amass, garner.

collected *adj* calm, composed, cool, placid, self-possessed, serene, unperturbed.

collection *n* aggregation, assemblage, cluster, crowd, drove, gathering, group, pack; accumulation, congeries, conglomeration, heap, hoard, lot, mass, pile, store; alms, contribution, offering, offertory.

colligate *vb* bind, combine, fasten, unite.

collision *n* clash, concussion, crash, encounter, impact, impingement, shock; conflict, crashing, interference, opposition.

collocate *vb* arrange, dispose, place, set.

colloquy *n* conference, conversation, dialogue, discourse, talk.

collude *vb* concert, connive, conspire.

collusion *n* connivance, conspiracy, coven, craft, deceit.

collusive *adj* conniving, conspiratorial, , dishonest, deceitful, deceptive, fraudulent.

colossal *adj* Cyclopean, enormous, gigantic, Herculean, huge, immense, monstrous, prodigious, vast.

colour *vb* discolour, dye, paint, stain, tinge, tint; disguise, varnish; disguise, distort, garble, misrepresent, pervert; blush, flush, redden, show. **n* hue, shade, tinge, tint, tone; paint, pigment, stain; redness, rosiness, ruddiness; complexion; appearance, disguise, excuse, guise, plea, pretence, pretext, semblance.

colourless *adj* achromatic, uncoloured, untinged; blanched, hueless, livid, pale, pallid; blank, characterless, dull, expressionless, inexpressive, monotonous.

colours *n* banner, ensign, flag, standard.

column *n* pillar, pilaster; file, line, row.

coma *n* drowsiness, lethargy, somnolence, stupor, torpor; bunch, clump, cluster, tuft.

comatose *adj* drowsy, lethargic, sleepy, somnolent, stupefied.

comb *vb* card, curry, dress, groom, rake, unknot, untangle; rake, ransack, rummage, scour, search. **n* card, hatchel, ripple; harrow, rake.

combat *vb* contend, contest, fight, struggle, war; battle, oppose, resist, struggle, withstand. **n* action, affair, battle, brush, conflict, contest, encounter, fight, skirmish.

combative *adj* belligerent, contentious, militant, pugnacious, quarrelsome.

combination *n* association, conjunction, connection, union; alliance, cartel, coalition, confederacy, consolidation, league, merger, syndicate; cabal, clique, conspiracy, faction, junta, ring; amalgamation, compound, mixture.

combine *vb* cooperate, merge, pool, unite; amalgamate, blend, incorporate, mix.

combustible *adj* consumable, inflammable.

come *vb* advance, approach; arise, ensue, flow, follow, issue, originate, proceed, result; befall, betide, happen, occur.

comely *adj* becoming, decent, decorous, fitting, seemly, suitable; beautiful, fair, graceful, handsome, personable, pretty, symmetrical.

comfort *vb* alleviate, animate, cheer, console, encourage, enliven, gladden, inspirit, invigorate, refresh, revive, solace, soothe, strengthen. **n* aid, assistance, countenance, help, support, succour; consolation, solace, encouragement, relief; ease, enjoyment, peace, satisfaction.

comfortable *adj* acceptable, agreeable, delightful, enjoyable, grateful, gratifying, happy, pleasant, pleasurable, welcome; commodious, convenient, easeful, snug; painless.

comfortless *adj* bleak, cheerless, desolate, drear, dreary, forlorn, miserable, wretched; broken-hearted, desolate, disconsolate, forlorn, heart-broken, inconsolable, miserable, woe-begone, wretched.

comical *adj* amusing, burlesque, comic, diverting, droll, farcical, funny, humorous, laughable, ludicrous, sportive, whimsical.

coming *adj* approaching, arising, arriving, ensuing, eventual, expected, forthcoming, future, imminent, issuing, looming, nearing, prospective, ultimate; emergent, emerging, successful; due, owed, owing. **n* advent, approach, arrival; imminence, imminency, nearness; apparition, appearance, disclosure, emergence, manifestation, materialization, occurrence, presentation, revelation, rising.

comity *n* affability, amenity, civility, courtesy, politeness, suavity, urbanity.

command *vb* bid, charge, direct, enjoin, order, require; control, dominate, govern, lead, rule, sway; claim, challenge, compel, demand, exact. **n* behest, bidding, charge, commandment, direction, hest, injunction, mandate, order, requirement, requisition; ascendency, authority, dominion, control, government, power, rule, sway, supremacy.

commander *n* captain, chief, chieftain, commandment, head, leader.

commemorate *vb* celebrate, keep, observe, solemnize.

commence *vb* begin, inaugurate, initiate, institute, open, originate, start.

commend *vb* assign, bespeak, confide, recommend, remit; commit, entrust, yield; applaud, approve, eulogize, extol, laud, praise.

commendation *n* approbation, approval, good opinion, recommendation; praise, encomium, eulogy, panegyric.

commensurate *adj* commeasurable, commensurable; co-extensive, conterminous, equal; adequate, appropriate, corresponding, due, proportionate, proportioned, sufficient.

comment *vb* animadvert, annotate, criticize, explain, interpret, note, remark. **n* annotation, elucidation, explanation, exposition, illustration, commentary, note, gloss; animadversion, observation, remark.

commentator *n* annotator, commentator, critic, expositor, expounder, interpreter.

commerce *n* business, exchange, dealing, trade, traffic; communication, communion, intercourse.

commercial *adj* mercantile, trading.

commination *n* denunciation, menace, threat, threatening.

commingle *vb* amalgamate, blend, combine, commix, intermingle, intermix, join, mingle, mix, unite.

comminute *vb* bray, bruise, grind, levigate, powder, pulverize, triturate.

commiserate *vb* compassionate, condole, pity, sympathize.

commiseration *n* compassion, pitying; condolence, pity, sympathy.

commission *vb* authorize, empower; delegate, depute. **n* doing, perpetration; care, charge, duty, employment, errand, office, task, trust; allowance, compensation, fee, rake-off.

commissioner *n* agent, delegate, deputy.

commit *vb* confide, consign, delegate, entrust, remand; consign, deposit, lay, place, put, relegate, resign; do, enact, perform, perpetrate; imprison; engage, implicate, pledge.

commix *vb* amalgamate, blend, combine, commingle, compound, intermingle, mingle, mix, unite.

commodious *adj* advantageous, ample, comfortable, convenient, fit, proper, roomy, spacious, suitable, useful.

commodity *n* goods, merchandise, produce, wares.

common *adj* collective, public; general, useful; common-place, customary, everyday, familiar, frequent, habitual, usual; banal, hackneyed, stale, threadbare, trite; indifferent, inferior, low, ordinary, plebeian, popular, undistinguished, vulgar.

commonplace *adj* common, hackneyed, ordinary, stale, threadbare, trite. **n* banality, cliché, platitude; jotting, memoir, memorandum, note, reminder.

common-sense, common-sensical *adj* practical, sagacious, sensible, sober.

commotion *n* agitation, disturbance, ferment, perturbation, welter; ado, bustle, disorder, disturbance, hurly-burly, pother, tumult, turbulence, turmoil.

communicate *vb* bestow, confer, convey, give, impart, transmit; acquaint, announce, declare, disclose, divulge, publish, reveal, unfold; commune, converse, correspond.

communication *n* conveyance, disclosure, giving, imparting, transmittal; commence, conference, conversation, converse, correspondence, intercourse; announcement, dispatch, information, message, news.

communicative *adj* affable, chatty, conversable, free, open, sociable, unreserved.

communion *n* converse, fellowship, intercourse, participation; Eucharist, holy communion, Lord's Supper, sacrament.

community *n* commonwealth, people, public, society; association, brotherhood, college, society; likeness, participancy, sameness, similarity.

compact[1] *n* agreement, arrangement, bargain, concordant, contract, covenant, convention, pact, stipulation, treaty.

compact[2] *vb* compress, condense, pack, press; bind, consolidate, unite. **adj* close, compressed, condensed, dense, firm, solid; brief, compendious, concise, laconic, pithy, pointed, sententious, short, succinct, terse.

companion *n* accomplice, ally, associate, comrade, compeer, confederate, consort, crony, friend, fellow, mate; partaker, participant, participator, partner, sharer.

companionable *adj* affable, conversable, familiar, friendly, genial, neighbourly, sociable.

companionship *n* association, fellowship, friendship, intercourse, society.

company *n* assemblage, assembly, band, bevy, body, circle, collection, communication, concourse, congregation, coterie, crew, crowd, flock, gang, gathering, group, herd, rout, set, syndicate, troop; party; companionship, fellowship, guests, society, visitor, visitors; association, copartnership, corporation, firm, house, partnership.

compare *vb* assimilate, balance, collate, parallel; liken, resemble.

comparison *n* collation, compare, estimate; simile, similitude.

compartment *n* bay, cell, division, pigeonhole, section.

compass *vb* embrace, encompass, enclose, encircle, environ, surround; beleaguer, beset, besiege, block, blockade, invest; accomplish, achieve, attain, carry, consummate, effect, obtain, perform, procure, realize; contrive, devise, intend, meditate, plot, purpose. **n* bound, boundary, extent, gamut, limit, range, reach, register, scope, stretch; circuit, round.

compassion *n* clemency, commiseration, condolence, fellow-feeling, heart, humanity, kind-heartedness, kindness, kindliness, mercy, pity, rue, ruth, sorrow, sympathy, tenderheartedness, tenderness.

compassionate *adj* benignant, clement, commiserative, gracious, kind, merciful, pitying, ruthful, sympathetic, tender.

compatible *adj* accordant, agreeable to, congruous, consistent, consonant, reconcilable, suitable.

compeer *n* associate, comrade, companion, equal, fellow, mate, peer.

compel *vb* constrain, force, coerce, drive, necessitate, oblige; bend, bow, subdue, subject.

compend *n* abbreviation, abridgement, abstract, breviary, brief, compendium, conspectus, digest, epitome, précis, summary, syllabus, synopsis.

compendious *adj* abbreviated, abridged, brief, comprehensive, concise, short, succinct, summary.

compensate *vb* counterbalance, counterpoise, countervail; guerdon, recompense, reimburse, remunerate, reward; indemnify, reimburse, repay, requite; atone.

compensation *n* pay, payment, recompense, remuneration, reward, salary; amends, atonement, indemnification, indemnity, reparation, requital, satisfaction; balance, counterpoise, equalization, offset.

compete *vb* contend, contest, cope, emulate, rival, strive, struggle, vie.

competence *n* ability, capability, capacity, fitness, qualification, suitableness; ad-

equacy, adequateness, enough, sufficiency.
competent *adj* able, capable, clever, equal, endowed, qualified; adapted, adequate, convenient, fit, sufficient, suitable.
competition *n* contest, emulation, rivalry, rivals.
competitor *n* adversary, antagonist, contestant, emulator, opponent.
compile *vb* compose, prepare, write; arrange, collect, select.
complacency *n* content, contentment, gratification, pleasure, satisfaction; affability, civility, complaisance, courtesy, politeness.
complacent *adj* contented, gratified, pleased, satisfied; affable, civil, complaisant, courteous, easy, gracious, grateful, obliging, polite, urbane.
complain *vb* bemoan, bewail, deplore, grieve, groan, grouch, grumble, lament, moan, murmur, repine, whine.
complainant *n* accuser, plaintiff.
complaining *adj* fault-finding, murmuring, querulous.
complaint *n* grievance, gripe, grumble, lament, lamentation, plaint, murmur, wail; ail, ailment, annoyance, disease, disorder, illness, indisposition, malady, sickness; accusation, charge, information.
complete *vb* accomplish, achieve, conclude, consummate, do, effect, effectuate, end, execute, finish, fulfil, perfect, perform, realize, terminate. **adj* clean, consummate, faultless, full, perfect, perform, thorough; all, entire, integral, total, unbroken, undiminished, undivided, unimpaired, whole; accomplished, achieved, completed, concluded, consummated, ended, finished.
completion *n* accomplishing, accomplishment, achieving, conclusion, consummation, effecting, effectuation, ending, execution, finishing, perfecting, performance, termination.
complex *adj* composite, compound, compounded, manifold, mingled, mixed; complicate, complicated, entangled, intricate, involved, knotty, mazy, tangled. **n* complexus, complication, involute, skein, tangle; entirety, integration, network, totality, whole; compulsion, fixation, obsession, preoccupation, prepossession; prejudice.
complexion *n* colour, hue, tint.
complexity *n* complication, entanglement, intricacy, involution.
compliance *n* concession, obedience, submission; acquiescence, agreement, assent, concurrence, consent; compliancy, yieldingness.
complicate *vb* confuse, entangle, interweave, involve.
complication *n* complexity, confusion, entanglement, intricacy; combination, complexus, mixture.
compliment *vb* commend, congratulate, eulogize, extol, flatter, laud, praise. **n* admiration, commendation, courtesy, encomium, eulogy, favour, flattery, honour, laudation, praise, tribute.
complimentary *adj* commendatory, congratulatory, encomiastic, eulogistic, flattering, laudatory, panegyrical.
comply *vb* adhere to, complete, discharge, fulfil, meet, observe, perform, satisfy; accede, accord, acquiesce, agree to, assent, consent to, yield.
component *adj* composing, constituent, constituting. **n* constituent, element, ingredient, part.
comport *vb* accord, agree, coincide, correspond, fit, harmonize, square, suit, tally.
compose *vb* build, compact, compound, constitute, form, make, synthesize; contrive, create, frame, imagine, indite, invent, write; adjust, arrange, regulate, settle; appease, assuage, calm, pacify, quell, quiet, soothe, still, tranquillize.
composed *adj* calm, collected, cool, imperturbable, placid, quiet, sedate, self-possessed, tranquil, undisturbed, unmoved, unruffled.
composite *adj* amalgamated, combined, complex, compounded, mixed; integrated, unitary. **n* admixture, amalgam, blend, combination, composition, compound, mixture, unification.

composition *n* constitution, construction, formation, framing, making; compound, mixture; arrangement, combination, conjunction, make-up, synthesize, union; invention, opus, piece, production, writing; agreement, arrangement, compromise.

compost *n* fertilizer, fertilizing, manure, mixture.

composure *n* calmness, coolness, equanimity, placidity, sedateness, quiet, self-possession, serenity, tranquillity.

compotation *n* conviviality, frolicking, jollification, revelling, revelry, rousing, wassailling; bacchanal, carousal, carouse, debauch, orgy, revel, saturnalia, wassail.

compound[1] *vb* amalgamate, blend, combine, intermingle, intermix, mingle, mix, unite; adjust, arrange, compose, compromise, settle. **adj* complex, composite. **n* combination, composition, mixture; farrago, hodgepodge, jumble, medley, mess, olio.

compound[2] *n* enclosure, garden, yard.

comprehend *vb* comprise, contain, embrace, embody, enclose, include, involve; apprehend, conceive, discern, grasp, know, imagine, master, perceive, see, understand.

comprehension *n* comprising, embracing, inclusion; compass, domain, embrace, field, limits, province, range, reach, scope, sphere, sweep; connotation, depth, force, intention; conception, grasp, intelligence, understanding; intellect, intelligence, mind, reason, understanding.

comprehensive *adj* all-embracing, ample, broad, capacious, compendious, extensive, full, inclusive, large, sweeping, wide.

compress *vb* abbreviate, condense, constrict, contract, crowd, press, shorten, squeeze, summarize.

compression *n* condensation, confining, pinching, pressing, squeezing; brevity, pithiness, succinctness, terseness.

comprise *vb* comprehend, contain, embody, embrace, enclose, include, involve.

compromise *vb* adjust, arbitrate, arrange, compose, compound, settle; imperil, jeopardize, prejudice; commit, engage, implicate, pledge; agree, compound. **n* adjustment, agreement, composition, settlement.

compulsion *n* coercion, constraint, force, forcing, pressure, urgency.

compulsory *adj* coercive, compelling, constraining; binding, enforced, imperative, necessary, obligatory, unavoidable.

compunction *n* contrition, misgiving, penitence, qualm, regret, reluctance, remorse, repentance, sorrow.

computable *adj* calculable, numerable, reckonable.

computation *n* account, calculation, estimate, reckoning, score, tally.

compute *vb* calculate, count, enumerate, estimate, figure, measure, number, rate, reckon, sum.

comrade *n* accomplice, ally, associate, chum, companion, compatriot, compeer, crony, fellow, mate, pal.

concatenate *vb* connect, join, link, unite.

concatenation *n* connection; chain, congeries, linking, series, sequence, succession.

concave *adj* depressed, excavated, hollow, hollowed, scooped.

conceal *vb* bury, cover, screen, secrete; disguise, dissemble, mask.

concede *vb* grant, surrender, yield; acknowledge, admit, allow, confess, grant.

conceit *n* belief, conception, fancy, idea, image, imagination, notion, thought; caprice, illusion, vagary, whim; estimate, estimation, impression, judgement, opinion; conceitedness, egoism, self-complacency, priggishness, priggery, self-conceit, self-esteem, self-sufficiency, vanity; crotchet, point, quip, quirk.

conceited *adj* egotistical, opinionated, opinionative, overweening, self-conceited, vain.

conceivable *adj* imaginable, picturable; cogitable, comprehensible, intelligible, rational, thinkable.

conceive *vb* create, contrive, devise, form,

plan, purpose; fancy, imagine; comprehend, fathom, think, understand; assume, imagine, suppose; bear, become pregnant.

concern *vb* affect, belong to, interest, pertain to, regard, relate to, touch; disquiet, disturb, trouble. **n* affair, business, matter, transaction; concernment, consequence, importance, interest, moment, weight; anxiety, care, carefulness, solicitude, worry; business, company, establishment, firm, house.

concert *vb* combine, concoct, contrive, design, devise, invent, plan, plot, project. **n* agreement, concord, concordance, cooperation, harmony, union, unison.

concession *n* acquiescence, assent, cessation, compliance, surrender, yielding; acknowledgement, allowance, boon, confession, grant, privilege.

conciliate *vb* appease, pacify, placate, propitiate, reconcile; engage, gain, secure, win, win over.

concise *adj* brief, compact, compendious, comprehensive, compressed, condensed, crisp, laconic, pithy, pointed, pregnant, sententious, short, succinct, summary, terse.

conclave *n* assembly, cabinet, council.

conclude *vb* close, end, finish, terminate; deduce, gather, infer, judge; decide, determine, judge; arrange, complete, settle; bar, hinder, restrain, stop; decide, determine, resolve.

conclusion *n* deduction, inference; decision, determination, judgement; close, completion, end, event, finale, issue, termination, upshot; arrangement, closing, effecting, establishing, settlement.

conclusive *adj* clinching, convincing, decisive, irrefutable, unanswerable; final, ultimate.

concoct *vb* brew, contrive, design, devise, frame, hatch, invent, mature, plan, plot, prepare, project.

concomitant *adj* accessory, accompanying, attendant, attending, coincident, concurrent, conjoined. **n* accessory, accompaniment, attendant.

concord *n* agreement, amity, friendship, harmony, peace, unanimity, union, unison, unity; accord, adaptation, concordance, consonance, harmony.

concordant *adj* accordant, agreeable, agreeing, harmonious.

concordat *n* agreement, bargain, compact, convention, covenant, stipulation, treaty.

concourse *n* confluence, conflux, congress; assemblage, assembly, collection, crowd, gathering, meeting, multitude, throng.

concrete *vb* cake, congeal, coagulate, harden, solidify, thicken. **adj* compact, consolidated, firm, solid, solidified; agglomerated, complex, conglomerated, compound, concreted; completely, entire, individualized, total. **n* compound, concretion, mixture; cement.

concubine *n* hetaera, hetaira, mistress, paramour.

concupiscence *n* lasciviousness, lechery, lewdness, lust, pruriency.

concupiscent *adj* carnal, lascivious, lecherous, lewd, libidinous, lustful, prurient, rampant, salacious, sensual.

concur *vb* accede, acquiesce, agree, approve, assent, coincide, consent, harmonize; combine, conspire, cooperate, help.

concurrent *adj* agreeing, coincident, harmonizing, meeting, uniting; associate, associated, attendant, concomitant, conjoined, united.

concussion *n* agitation, shaking; clash, crash, shock.

condemn *vb* adjudge, convict, doom, sentence; disapprove, proscribe, reprobate; blame, censure, damn, deprecate, disapprove, reprehend, reprove, upbraid.

condemnation *n* conviction, doom, judgement, penalty, sentence; banning, disapproval, proscription; guilt, sin, wrong; blame, censure, disapprobation, disapproval, reprobation, reproof.

condemnatory *adj* blaming, censuring, damnatory, deprecatory, disapproving, reproachful.

condense *vb* compress, concentrate, consolidate, densify, thicken; abbreviate, abridge, contract, curtail, diminish, epitomize, reduce, shorten, summarize; liquefy.

condescend *vb* deign, vouchsafe; descend, stoop, submit.

condescension *n* affability, civility, courtesy, deference, favour, graciousness, obeisance.

condign *adj* adequate, deserved, just, merited, suitable.

condiment *n* appetizer, relish, sauce, seasoning.

condition *vb* postulate, specify, stipulate; groom, prepare, qualify, ready, train; acclimatize, accustom, adapt, adjust, familiarize, habituate, naturalize; attune, commission, fix, overhaul, prepare, recondition, repair, service, tune. **n* case, circumstances, plight, predicament, situation, state; class, estate, grade, rank, station; arrangement, consideration, provision, proviso, stipulation; attendant, necessity, postulate, precondition, prerequisite.

condole *vb* commiserate, compassionate, console, sympathize.

condonation *n* forgiveness, overlooking, pardon.

condone *vb* excuse, forgive, pardon.

conduce *vb* contribute, lead, tend; advance, aid.

conducive *adj* conducting, contributing, instrumental, promotive, subservient, subsidiary.

conduct *vb* convoy, direct, escort, lead; administer, command, govern, lead, preside, superintend; manage, operate, regulate; direct, lead. **n* administration, direction, guidance, leadership, management; convoy, escort, guard; actions, bearing, behaviour, career, carriage, demeanour, deportment, manners.

conductor *n* guide, lead; director, leader, manager; propagator, transmitter.

conduit *n* canal, channel, duct, passage, pipe, tube.

confederacy *n* alliance, coalition, compact, confederation, covenant, federation, league, union.

confer *vb* advise, consult, converse, deliberate, discourse, parley, talk; bestow, give, grant, vouchsafe.

confess *vb* acknowledge, admit, avow, own; admit, concede, grant, recognize; attest, exhibit, manifest, prove, show; shrive.

confession *n* acknowledgement, admission, avowal.

confide *vb* commit, consign, entrust, trust.

confidence *n* belief, certitude, dependence, faith, reliance, trust; aplomb, assurance, boldness, cocksureness, courage, firmness, intrepidity, self-reliance; secrecy.

confident *adj* assured, certain, cocksure, positive, sure: bold, presumptuous. sanguine, undaunted.

confidential *adj* intimate, private, secret; faithful, trustworthy.

configuration *n* conformation, contour, figure, form, gestalt, outline, shape.

confine *vb* restrain, shut in, shut up; immure, imprison, incarcerate, impound, jail, mew; bound, circumscribe, limit, restrict. **n* border, boundary, frontier, limit.

confinement *n* restraint; captivity, duress, durance, immurement, imprisonment, incarceration; childbed, childbirth, delivery, lying-in, parturition.

confines *npl* borders, boundaries, edges, frontiers, limits, marches, precincts.

confirm *vb* assure, establish, fix, settle; strengthen; authenticate, avouch, corroborate, countersign, endorse, substantiate, verify; bind, ratify, sanction.

confirmation *n* establishment, settlement; corroboration, proof, substantiation, verification.

confiscate *vb* appropriate, forfeit, seize.

conflict *vb* clash, combat, contend, contest, disagree, fight, interfere, strive, struggle. **n* battle, collision, combat, contention, contest, encounter, fight, struggle; antagonism, clashing, disagreement, discord, disharmony, inconsistency, interference, opposition.

confluence *n* conflux, junction, meeting, union; army, assemblage, assembly, concourse, crowd, collection, horde, host, multitude, swarm.

confluent *adj* blending, concurring, flowing, joining, meeting, merging, uniting.

conform *vb* accommodate, adapt, adjust; agree, comport, correspond, harmonize, square, tally.

conformation *n* accordance, agreement, compliance, conformity; configuration, figure, form, manner, shape, structure.

confound *vb* confuse; baffle, bewilder, embarrass, flurry, mystify, nonplus, perplex, pose; amaze, astonish, astound, bewilder, dumfound, paralyse, petrify, startle, stun, stupefy, surprise; annihilate, demolish, destroy, overthrow, overwhelm, ruin; abash, confuse, discompose, disconcert, mortify, shame.

confront *vb* face; challenge, contrapose, encounter, oppose, threaten.

confuse *vb* blend, confound, intermingle, mingle, mix; derange, disarrange, disorder, jumble, mess, muddle; darken, obscure, perplex; befuddle, bewilder, embarrass, flabbergast, flurry, fluster, mystify, nonplus, pose; abash, confound, discompose, disconcert, mortify, shame.

confusion *n* anarchy, chaos, clutter, confusedness, derangement, disarrangement, disarray, disorder, jumble, muddle; agitation, commotion, ferment, stir, tumult, turmoil; astonishment, bewilderment, distraction, embarrassment, fluster, fuddle, perplexity; abashment, discomfiture, mortification, shame; annihilation, defeat, demolition, destruction, overthrow, ruin.

confute *vb* disprove, oppugn, overthrow, refute, silence.

congeal *vb* benumb, condense, curdle, freeze, stiffen, thicken.

congenial *adj* kindred, similar, sympathetic; adapted, agreeable, natural, suitable, suited; agreeable, favourable, genial.

congenital *adj* connate, connatural, inborn.

congeries *n* accumulation, agglomeration, aggregate, aggregation, collection, conglomeration, crowd, cluster, heap, mass.

congratulate *vb* compliment, felicitate, gratulate, greet, hail, salute.

congregate *vb* assemble, collect, convene, convoke, gather, muster; gather, meet, swarm, throng.

congregation *n* assemblage, assembly, collection, gathering, meeting.

congress *n* assembly, conclave, conference, convention, convocation, council, diet, meeting.

congruity *n* agreement, conformity, consistency, fitness, suitableness.

congruous *adj* accordant, agreeing, compatible, consistent, consonant, suitable; appropriate, befitting, fit, meet, proper, seemly.

conjecture *vb* assume, guess, hypothesize, imagine, suppose. surmise, suspect; dare say, fancy, presume. **n* assumption, guess, hypothesis, supposition, surmise, theory.

conjoin *vb* associate, combine, connect, join, unite.

conjugal *adj* bridal, connubial, hymeneal, matrimonial, nuptial.

conjuncture *n* combination, concurrence, connection; crisis, emergency, exigency, juncture.

conjure *vb* adjure, beg, beseech, crave, entreat, implore, invoke, pray, supplicate; bewitch, charm, enchant, fascinate; juggle.

connect *vb* associate, conjoin, combine, couple, hyphenate, interlink, join, link, unite; cohere, interlock.

connected *adj* associated, coupled, joined, united; akin, allied, related; communicating.

connection *n* alliance, association, dependence, junction, union; commerce, communication, intercourse; affinity, relationship; kindred, kinsman, relation, relative.

connive *vb* collude, conspire, plot, scheme.

connoisseur *n* critic, expert, virtuoso.

connotation *n* comprehension, depth, force, intent, intention, meaning.

connubial *adj* bridal, conjugal, hymeneal, matrimonial, nuptial.
conquer *vb* beat, checkmate, crush, defeat, discomfit, humble, master, overcome, overpower, overthrow, prevail, quell, reduce, rout, subdue, subjugate, vanquish; overcome, surmount.
conqueror *n* humbler, subduer, subjugator, vanquisher; superior, victor, winner.
conquest *n* defeat, discomfiture, mastery, overthrow, reduction, subjection, subjugation; triumph, victor; winning.
consanguinity *n* affinity, kinship, blood-relationship, kin, kindred, relationship.
conscientious *adj* careful, exact, fair, faithful, high-principled, honest, honourable, incorruptible, just, scrupulous, straightforward, uncorrupt, upright.
conscious *adj* intelligent, knowing, percipient, sentient; intellectual, rational, reasoning, reflecting, self-conscious, thinking; apprised, awake, aware, cognizant, percipient, sensible; self-admitted, self-accusing.
consecrate *vb* dedicate, devote, ordain; hallow, sanctify, venerate.
consecutive *adj* following, succeeding.
consent *vb* agree, allow, assent, concur, permit, yield; accede, acquiesce, comply. **n* approval, assent, concurrence, permission; accord, agreement, consensus, concord, cooperation, harmony, unison; acquiescence, compliance.
consequence *n* effect, end, event, issue, result; conclusion, deduction, inference; concatenation, connection, consecution; concern, distinction, importance, influence, interest, moment, standing, weight.
consequential *adj* consequent, following, resulting, sequential; arrogant, conceited, inflated, pompous, pretentious, self-important, self-sufficient, vainglorious.
conservation *n* guardianship, maintenance, preservation, protection.
conservative *adj* conservatory, moderate, moderationist; preservative; reactionary, unprogressive. **n* die-hard, reactionary, redneck, rightist, right-winger; moderate; preservative.
conserve *vb* keep, maintain, preserve, protect, save, sustain, uphold. **n* confit, confection, jam, preserve, sweetmeat.
consider *vb* attend, brood, contemplate, examine, heed, mark, mind, ponder, reflect, revolve, study, weigh; care for, consult, envisage, regard, respect; cogitate, deliberate, mediate, muse, ponder, reflect, ruminate, think; account, believe, deem, hold, judge, opine.
considerate *adj* circumspect, deliberate, discrete, judicious, provident, prudent, serious, sober, staid, thoughtful; charitable, forbearing, patient.
consideration *n* attention, cogitation, contemplation, deliberation, notice, heed, meditation, pondering, reflection, regard; consequence, importance, important, moment, significant, weight; account, cause, ground, motive, reason, sake, score.
consign *vb* deliver, hand over, remand, resign, transfer, transmit; commit, entrust; ship.
consignor *n* sender, shipper, transmitter.
consistency *n* compactness, consistence, density, thickness; agreement, compatibility, conformableness, congruity, consonance, correspondence, harmony.
consistent *adj* accordant, agreeing, comfortable, compatible, congruous, consonant, correspondent, harmonious, logical.
consolation *n* alleviation, comfort, condolence, encouragement, relief, solace.
console *vb* assuage, calm, cheer, comfort, encourage, solace, relieve, soothe.
consolidate *vb* cement, compact, compress, condense, conduce, harden, solidify, thicken; combine, conjoin, fuse, unite.
consolidation *n* solidification; combination, union.
consonance *n* accord, concord, conformity, harmony; accord, accordance, agreement, congruence, congruity, consistency, unison.

consonant *adj* accordant, according, harmonious; compatible, congruous, consistent. *n articulation, letter-sound.

consort *vb* associate, fraternize. *n associate, companion, fellow, husband, spouse, partner.

conspectus *n* abstract, brief, breviary, compend, compendium, digest, epitome, outline, precis, summary, syllabus, synopsis.

conspicuous *adj* apparent, clear, discernible, glaring, manifest, noticeable, perceptible, plain, striking, visible; celebrated, distinguished, eminent, famed, famous, illustrious, marked, noted, outstanding. pre-eminent, prominent, remarkable, signal.

conspiracy *n* cabal, collusion, confederation, intrigue, league, machination, plot, scheme.

conspire *vb* concur, conduce, cooperate; combine, compass, contrive, devise, project; confederate, contrive, hatch, plot, scheme.

constancy *n* immutability, permanence, stability, unchangeableness; regularity, unchangeableness; decision, determination, firmness, inflexibility, resolution, steadfastness, steadiness; devotion, faithfulness, fidelity, loyalty, trustiness, truth.

constant *adj* abiding, enduring, fixed, immutable, invariable, invariant, permanent, perpetual, stable, unalterable, unchanging, unvaried; certain, regular, stated, uniform; determined, firm, resolute, stanch, steadfast, steady, unanswering, undeviating, unmoved, unshaken, unwavering; assiduous, diligent, persevering, sedulous, tenacious, unremitting; continual, continuous, incessant, perpetual, sustained, unbroken, uninterrupted; devoted, faithful, loyal, true, trusty.

consternation *n* alarm, amazement, awe, bewilderment, dread, fear, fright, horror, panic, terror.

constituent *adj* component, composing, constituting, forming; appointing, electoral. *n component, element, ingredient, principal; elector, voter.

constitute *vb* compose, form, make; appoint, delegate, depute, empower; enact, establish, fix, set up.

constitution *n* establishment, formation, make-up, organization, structure; character, characteristic, disposition, form, habit, humour, peculiarity, physique, quality, spirit, temper, temperament.

constitutional *adj* congenital, connate, inborn, inbred, inherent, innate, natural, organic; lawful, legal, legitimate. *n airing, exercise, promenade, stretch, walk.

constrain *vb* coerce, compel, drive, force; chain, confine, curb, enthral, hold, restrain; draw, impel, urge.

constriction *n* compression, constraint, contraction.

construct *vb* build, fabricate, erect, raise, set up; arrange, establish, form, found, frame, institute, invent, make, organize, originate.

construction *n* building, erection, fabrication; configuration, conformation, figure, form, formation, made, shape, structure; explanation, interpretation, rendering, version.

construe *vb* analyse, explain, expound, interpret, parse, render, translate.

consult *vb* advise, ask, confer, counsel, deliberate, interrogate, question; consider, regard.

consume *vb* absorb, decay, destroy, devour, dissipate, exhaust, expend, lavish, lessen, spend, squander, vanish, waste.

consummate[1] *vb* accomplish, achieve, compass, complete, conclude, crown, effect, effectuate, end, execute, finish, perfect, perform.

consummate[2] *adj* complete, done, effected, finished, fulfilled, perfect, supreme.

consumption *n* decay, decline, decrease, destruction, diminution, expenditure, use, waste; atrophy, emaciation.

contact *vb* hit, impinge, touch; approach, be heard, communicate with, reach. *n approximation, contiguity, junction, juxtaposition, taction, tangency, touch.

contagion *n* infection; contamination, corruption, infection, taint.

contagious *adj* catching, epidemic, infectious; deadly, pestiferous, pestilential, poisonous.

contain *vb* accommodate, comprehend, comprise, embody, embrace, enclose, include; check, restrain.

contaminate *vb* corrupt, defile, deprave, infect, poison, pollute, soil, stain, sully, taint, tarnish, vitiate.

contamination *n* contaminating, defilement, defiling, polluting, pollution; abomination, defilement, impurity, foulness, infection, pollution, stain, taint, uncleanness.

contemn *vb* despise, disdain, disregard, neglect, scorn, scout, slight, spurn.

contemplate *vb* behold, gaze upon, observe, survey; consider, dwell on, meditate on, muse on, ponder, reflect upon, study, survey, think about; design, intend, mean, plan, purpose.

contemplation *n* cogitation, deliberation, meditation, pondering, reflection, speculation, study, thought; prospect, prospective, view; expectation.

contemporaneous *adj* coetaneous, coeval, coexistent, coexisting, coincident, concomitant, contemporary, simultaneous, synchronous.

contemporary *adj* coetaneous, coeval, coexistent, coexisting, coincident, concomitant, concurrent, contemporaneous, current, present, simultaneous, synchronous; advanced, modern, modernistic, progressive, up-to-date. **n* coeval, coexistent, compeer, fellow.

contempt *n* contumely, derision, despite, disdain, disregard, misprision, mockery, scorn, slight.

contemptible *adj* abject, base, despicable, haughty, insolent, insulting, low, mean, paltry, pitiful, scurvy, sorry, supercilious, vile, worthless.

contemptuous *adj* arrogant, contumelious, disdainful, haughty, insolent, insulting, scornful, sneering, supercilious.

contend *vb* battle, combat, compete, contest, fight, strive, struggle, vie; argue, debate, dispute, litigate; affirm, assert, contest, maintain.

content[1] *n* essence, gist, meaning, meat, stuff, substance; capacity, measure, space, volume.

content[2] *vb* appease, delight, gladden, gratify, humour, indulge, please, satisfy, suffice. **adj* agreeable, contented, happy, pleased, satisfied. **n* contentment, ease, peace, satisfaction.

contention *n* discord, dissension, feud, squabble, strife, quarrel, rapture, wrangle, wrangling; altercation, bickering, contest, controversy, debate, dispute, litigation, logomachy.

contentious *adj* belligerent, cross, litigious, peevish, perverse, petulant, pugnacious, quarrelsome, wrangling; captious, caviling, disputatious.

conterminous *adj* adjacent, adjoining, contiguous; co-extensive, coincident, commensurate.

contest *vb* argue, contend, controvert, debate, dispute, litigate, question; strive, struggle; compete, cope, fight, vie. **n* altercation, contention, controversy, difference, dispute, debate, quarrel; affray, battle, bout, combat, conflict, encounter, fight, match, scrimmage, struggle, tussle; competition, contention, rivalry.

contexture *n* composition, constitution, framework, structure, texture.

contiguous *adj* abutting, adjacent, adjoining, beside, bordering, conterminous, meeting, near, neighbouring, touching.

continent[1] *n* mainland, mass, tract.

continent[2] *adj* abstemious, abstinent, chaste, restrained, self-commanding, self-controlled, moderate, sober, temperate.

contingency *n* accidentalness, chance, fortuity, uncertainty; accident, casualty, event, incident, occurrence.

contingent *adj* accidental, adventitious, casual, fortuitous, incidental; conditional, dependent, uncertain. **n* proportion, quota, share.

continual *adj* constant, constant, perpetual, unceasing, uninterrupted, unremitting; endless, eternal, everlasting, interminable, perennial, permanent, perpetual, unending; constant, oft-repeated.

continuance *n* abiding, continuation, duration, endurance, lasting, persistence, stay; continuation, extension, perpetuation, prolongation, protraction; concatenation, connection, sequence, succession; constancy, endurance, perseverance, persistence.

continue *vb* endure, last, remain; abide, linger, remain, stay, tarry; endure, persevere, persist, stick; extend, prolong, perpetuate, protract.

continuous *adj* connected, continued, extended, prolonged, unbroken, unintermitted, uninterrupted.

contour *n* outline, profile.

contraband *adj* banned, forbidden, illegal, illicit, interdicted, prohibited, smuggled, unlawful.

contract *vb* abbreviate, abridge, condense, confine, curtail, diminish, epitomize, lessen, narrow, reduce, shorten; absorb, catch, incur, get, make, take; constrict, shrink, shrivel, wrinkle; agree, bargain, covenant, engage, pledge, stipulate. **n* agreement, arrangement, bargain, bond, compact, concordat, covenant, convention, engagement, pact, stipulation, treaty.

contradict *vb* assail, challenge, controvert, deny, dispute, gainsay, impugn, traverse; abrogate, annul, belie, counter, disallow, negative, contravene, counteract, oppose, thwart.

contradiction *n* controversion, denial, gainsaying; antinomy, clashing, contrariety, incongruity, opposition.

contradictory *adj* antagonistic, contrary, incompatible, inconsistent, negating, opposed, opposite, repugnant.

contrariety *n* antagonism, clashing, contradiction, contrast, opposition, repugnance.

contrary *adj* adverse, counter, discordant, opposed, opposing, opposite; antagonistic, conflicting, contradictory, repugnant, retroactive; forward, headstrong, obstinate, refractory, stubborn, unruly, wayward, perverse. **n* antithesis, converse, obverse, opposite, reverse.

contrast *vb* compare, differentiate, distinguish, oppose. **n* contrariety, difference, opposition; comparison, distinction.

contravene *vb* abrogate, annul, contradict, counteract, countervail, cross, go against, hinder, interfere, nullify, oppose, set aside, thwart.

contravention *n* abrogation, contradiction, interference, opposition, transgression, traversal, violation.

contretemps *n* accident, mischance, mishap.

contribute *vb* bestow, donate, give, grant, subscribe; afford, aid, furnish, supply; concur, conduce, conspire, cooperate, minister, serve, tend.

contribution *n* bestowal, bestowment, grant; donation, gift, offering, subscription.

contrite *adj* humble, penitent, repentant, sorrowful.

contrition *n* compunction, humiliation, penitence, regret, remorse, repentance, self-condemnation, self-reproach, sorrow.

contrivance *n* design, inventive, inventiveness; contraption, device, gadget, invention, machine; artifice, device, fabrication, machination, plan, plot, scheme, shift, stratagem.

contrive *vb* arrange, brew, concoct, design, devise, effect, form, frame, hatch, invent, plan, project; consider, plan, plot, scheme; manage, make out.

control *vb* command, direct, dominate, govern, manage, oversee, sway, regulate, rule, superintend; bridle, check, counteract, curb, check, hinder, repress, restrain. **n* ascendency, command, direction, disposition, dominion, government, guidance, mastery, oversight, regiment, regulation, rule, superintendence, supremacy, sway.

controversy *n* altercation, argument, contention, debate, discussion, disputation, dispute, logomachy, polemics, quarrel, strife; lawsuit.

contumacious *adj* disobedient, cross-grained, disrespectful, haughty, headstrong, intractable, obdurate, obstinate, pertinacious, perverse, rebellious, refractory, stiff-necked, stubborn.

contumacy *n* doggedness, haughtiness, headiness, obduracy, obstinacy, pertinacity, perverseness, stubbornness; contempt, disobedience, disrespect, insolence, insubordination, rebelliousness.

contumelious *adj* abusive, arrogant, calumnious, contemptuous, disdainful, insolent, insulting, opprobrious, overbearing, rude, scornful, supercilious.

contumely *n* abuse, affront, arrogance, contempt, contemptuousness, disdain, indignity, insolence, insult, obloquy, opprobrium, reproach, rudeness, scorn, superciliousness.

contuse *vb* bruise, crush, injure, knock, squeeze, wound.

contusion *n* bruise, crush, injury, knock, squeeze, wound.

convalescence *n* recovery, recuperation.

convene *vb* assemble, congregate, gather, meet, muster; assemble, call, collect, convoke, muster, summon.

convenience *n* fitness, propriety, suitableness; accessibility, accommodation, comfort, commodiousness, ease, handiness, satisfaction, serviceability, serviceableness.

convenient *adj* adapted, appropriate, fit, fitted, proper, suitable, suited; advantageous, beneficial, comfortable, commodious, favourable, handy, helpful, serviceable, timely, useful.

convent *n* abbey, cloister, monastery, priory.

convention *n* assembly, congress, convocation, meeting; agreement, bargain, compact, contract, pact, stipulation, treaty; custom, formality, usage.

conventional *adj* agreed on, bargained for, stipulated; accustomed, approved, common, customary, everyday, habitual, ordinary, orthodox, regular, standard, traditional, usual, wonted.

conversable *adj* affable, communicative, free, open, sociable, social, unreversed.

conversation *n* chat, colloquy, communion, confabulation, conference, converse, dialogue, discourse, intercourse, interlocution, parley, talk.

converse[1] *vb* commune; chat, confabulate, discourse, gossip, parley, talk. **n* commerce, communication, intercourse; colloquy, conversation, talk.

converse[2] *adj* adverse, contradictory, contrary, counter, opposed, opposing, opposite; *n* antithesis, contrary, opposite, reverse.

conversion *n* change, reduction, resolution, transformation, transmutation; interchange, reversal, transposition.

convert *vb* alter, change, transform, transmute; interchange, reverse, transpose; apply, appropriate, convince. **n* catechumen, disciple, neophyte, proselyte.

convey *vb* bear, bring, carry, fetch, transmit, transport, waft; abalienate, alienate, cede, consign, deliver, demise, devise, devolve, grant, sell, transfer.

conveyance *n* alienation, cession, transfer, transference, transmission; carriage, carrying, conveying, transfer, transmission.

convict *vb* condemn, confute, convince, imprison, sentence. **n* criminal, culprit, felon, malefactor, prisoner.

convivial *adj* festal, festive, gay, jolly, jovial, merry, mirthful, social.

convocation *n* assembling, convening, convoking, gathering, summoning; assembly, congress, convention, council, diet, meeting, synod.

convoke *vb* assemble, convene, muster, summon.

convoy *vb* accompany, attend, escort, guard, protect. **n* attendance, attendant, escort, guard, protection.

convulse *vb* agitate, derange, disorder, disturb, shake, shatter.

convulsion *n* cramp, fit, spasm; agitation, commotion, disturbance, shaking, tumult.

cook *vb* bake, boil, broil, fry, grill, microwave, roast, spit-roast, steam, stir-fry; falsify, garble.

cool *vb* chill, ice, refrigerate; abate, allay, calm, damp, moderate, quiet, temper. **adj* calm, collected, composed, dispassionate, placid, sedate, self-possessed, quiet, staid, unexcited, unimpassioned, undisturbed, unruffled; cold-blooded, indifferent, lukewarm, unconcerned; apathetic, chilling, freezing, frigid, repellent; bold, impertinent, impudent, self-possessed, shameless. **n* chill, chilliness, coolness; calmness, composure, coolheadedness, countenance, equanimity, poise, self-possession, self-restraint.

coop *vb* cage, confine, encage, immure, imprison. **n* barrel, box, cage, pen.

cooperate *vb* abet, aid, assist, co-act, collaborate, combine, concur, conduce, conspire, contribute, help, unite.

cooperation *n* aid, assistance, co-action, concert, concurrence, collaboration, synergy.

coordinate *vb* accord, agree, arrange, equalize, harmonize, integrate, methodize, organize, regulate, synchronize, systematize. **adj* coequal, equal, equivalent, tantamount; coincident, synchronous. **n* complement, counterpart, like, pendant; companion, fellow, match, mate.

copartnership *n* association, fraternity, partnership; company, concern, establishment, firm, house.

cope *vb* combat, compete, contend, encounter, engage, strive, struggle, vie.

copious *adj* abundant, ample, exuberant, full, overflowing, plenteous, plentiful, profuse, rich.

copiousness *n* abundance, exuberance, fullness, plenty, profusion, richness.

copse *n* coppice, grove, thicket.

copulation *n* coition, congress, coupling.

copy *vb* duplicate, reproduce, trace, transcribe; follow, imitate, pattern. **n* counterscript, duplicate, facsimile, offprint, replica, reproduction, transcript; archetype, model, original, pattern; manuscript, typescript.

cord *n* braid, gimp, line, string.

cordate *adj* cordiform, heart-shaped.

cordial *adj* affectionate, ardent, earnest, heartfelt, hearty, sincere, warm, warm-hearted; grateful, invigorating, restorative, pleasant, refreshing. **n* balm, balsam, elixir, tisane, tonic; liqueur.

core *n* centre, essence, heart, kernel.

corner *vb* confound, confuse, nonplus, perplex, pose, puzzle. **n* angle, bend, crutch, cusp, elbow, joint, knee; niche, nook, recess, retreat.

corollary *n* conclusion, consequence, deduction, induction, inference.

coronal *n* bays, chaplet, crown, garland, laurel, wreath.

corporal *adj* bodily; corporeal, material, physical.

corporeal *adj* bodily, fleshly, substantial; corporal, material, nonspiritual, physical.

corps *n* band, body, company, contingent, division, platoon, regiment, squad, squadron, troop.

corpse *n* body, carcass, corse, remains; ashes, dust.

corpulent *adj* big, burly, fat, fleshy, large, lusty, obese, plump, portly, pursy, rotund, stout.

corpuscle *n* atom, bit, grain, iota, jot, mite, molecule, monad, particle, scintilla, scrap, whit.

correct *vb* adjust, amend, cure, improve, mend, reclaim, rectify, redress, reform, regulate, remedy; chasten, discipline, punish. **adj* accurate, equitable, exact, faultless, just, precise, proper, regular, right, true, upright.

correction *n* amendment, improvement, redress; chastening, discipline, punishment.

corrective *adj* alternative, correctory, counteractive, emendatory, improving, modifying, rectifying, reformative, reformatory.

correctness *n* accuracy, exactness, faultlessness, nicety, precision, propriety, rectitude, regularity, rightness, truth.

correlate *n* complement, correlative, counterpart.

correspond *vb* accord, agree, answer, comport, conform, fit, harmonize, match, square, suit, tally; answer, belong, correlate; communicate.

correspondence *n* accord, agreement, coincidence, concurrence, conformity, congruity, fitness, harmony, match; correlation, counterposition; communication, letters, writing.

corroborate *vb* confirm, establish, ratify, substantiate, support, sustain, strengthen.

corrode *vb* canker, erode, gnaw; consume, deteriorate, rust, waste; blight, embitter, envenom, poison.

corrosive *adj* acrid, biting, consuming, cathartic, caustic, corroding, eroding, erosive, violent; consuming, corroding, gnawing, mordant, wasting, wearing; blighting, cankerous, carking, embittering, envenoming, poisoning.

corrugate *vb* cockle, crease, furrow, groove, pucker, rumple, wrinkle.

corrupt *vb* putrefy, putrid, render; contaminate, defile, infect, pollute, spoil, taint, vitiate; degrade, demoralize, deprave, pervert; adulterate, debase, falsify, sophisticate; bribe, entice. **adj* contaminated, corrupted, impure, infected, putrid, rotten, spoiled, tainted, unsound; abandoned, debauched, depraved, dissolute, profligate, reprobate, vicious, wicked; bribable, buyable.

corruption *n* putrefaction, putrescence, rottenness; adulteration, contamination, debasement, defilement, infection, perversion, pollution, vitiation; demoralization, depravation, depravity, immorality, laxity, sinfulness, wickedness; bribery, dishonesty.

corsair *n* buccaneer, picaroon, pirate, rover, sea-robber, sea-rover.

corset *n* bodice, girdle, stays.

cosmonaut *n* astronaut, spaceman.

cosmos *n* creation, macrocosm, universe, world; harmony, order, structure.

cost *vb* absorb, consume, require. **n* amount, charge, expenditure, expense, outlay, price; costliness, preciousness, richness, splendour, sumptuousness; damage, detriment, loss, pain, sacrifice, suffering.

costly *adj* dear, expensive, high-priced; gorgeous, luxurious, precious, rich, splendid, sumptuous, valuable.

costume *n* apparel, attire, dress, robes, uniform.

cosy, cozy *adj* comfortable, easy, snug; chatty, conversable, social, talkative.

coterie *n* association, brotherhood, circle, club, set, society, sodality.

cottage *n* cabin, chalet, cot, hut, lodge, shack, shanty.

couch *vb* lie, recline; crouch, squat; bend down, stoop; conceal, cover up, hide; lay, level. **n* bed, davenport, divan, lounge, seat, settee, settle, sofa.

council *n* advisers, cabinet, ministry; assembly, congress, conclave, convention, convocation, diet, husting, meeting, parliament, synod.

counsel *vb* admonish, advise, caution, recommend, warm. **n* admonition, advice, caution, instruction, opinion, recommendation, suggestion; deliberation, forethought; advocate, barrister, counsellor, lawyer.

count *vb* enumerate, number, score; calculate, cast, compute, estimate, reckon; account, consider, deem, esteem, hold, judge, regard, think; tell. **n* reckoning, tally.

countenance *vb* abet, aid, approve, assist, befriend, encourage, favour, patronize, sanction, support. **n* aspect, look, men; aid, approbation, approval, assistance, encouragement, favour, patronage, sanction, support.

counter[1] *n* abacus, calculator, computer, meter, reckoner, tabulator, totalizator; bar, buffet, shopboard, table; (*naut*) end, poop, stern, tail; chip, token.

counter[2] *vb* contradict, contravene, counteract, oppose, retaliate. **adj* adverse, against, contrary, opposed, opposite. **adv* contrariwise, contrary. **n* antithesis, contrary, converse, opposite, reverse; counterblast, counterblow, retaliation.

counteract *vb* check, contrapose, contravene, cross, counter, counterpose, defeat, foil, frustrate, hinder, oppose, resist, thwart, traverse; annul, countervail, counterbalance, destroy, neutralize, offset.

counteractive *adj* antidote, corrective, counteragent, medicine, remedy, restorative.

counterbalance *vb* balance, counterpoise; compensate, countervail.

counterfeit *vb* forge, imitate; fake, feign, pretend, sham, simulate; copy, imitate. **adj* fake, forged, fraudulent, spurious, suppositious; false, feigned, hypocritical, mock, sham, simulated, spurious; copied, imitated, resembling. **n* copy, fake, forgery, sham.

countermand *vb* abrogate, annul, cancel, recall, repeal, rescind, revoke.

counterpane *n* coverlet, duvet, quilt.

counterpart *n* copy, duplicate; complement, correlate, correlative, reverse, supplement; fellow, mate, match, tally, twin.

counterpoise *vb* balance, counteract, countervail, counterbalance, equilibrate, offset. **n* balance, counterweight.

countersign *n* password, watchword.

countervail *vb* balance, compensate, counterbalance.

country *n* land, region; countryside; fatherland, home, kingdom, state, territory; nation, people, population. **adj* rural, rustic; countrified, rough, rude, uncultivated, unpolished, unrefined.

countryman *n* compatriot, fellow-citizen; boor, clown, farmer, hind, husbandman, peasant, rustic, swain.

couple *vb* pair, unite; copulate, embrace; buckle, clasp, conjoin, connect, join, link, pair, yoke. **n* brace, pair, twain, two; bond, coupling, lea, link, tie.

courage *n* audaciousness, audacity, boldness, bravery, daring, derring-do, dauntlessness, fearlessness, firmness, fortitude, gallantry, hardihood, heroism, intrepidity, manhood, mettle, nerve, pluck, prowess, resolution, spirit, spunk, valorousness, valour.

courageous *adj* audacious, brave, bold, chivalrous, daring, dauntless, fearless, gallant, hardy, heroic, intrepid, lionhearted, mettlesome, plucky, resolute, reliant, staunch, stout, undismayed, valiant, valorous.

course *vb* chase, follow, hunt, pursue, race, run. **n* career, circuit, race, run; road, route, track, way; bearing, direction, path, tremor, track; ambit, beat, orbit, round; process, progress, sequence; order, regularity, succession, turn; behaviour, conduct, deportment; arrangement, series, system.

court *vb* coddle, fawn, flatter, ingratiate; address, woo; seek; invite, solicit. **n* area, courtyard, patio, quadrangle; addresses, civilities, homage, respects, solicitations; retinue, palace, tribunal.

courteous *adj* affable, attentive, ceremonious, civil, complaisant, courtly, debonair, elegant, gracious, obliging, polished, polite, refined, respected, urbane, well-bred, well-mannered.

courtesan *n* harlot, prostitute, strumpet, vamp, wanton, wench, whore.

courtesy *n* affability, civility, complaisance, courteousness, elegance, good-breeding, graciousness, polish, politeness, refine, urbanity.

courtly *adj* affable, ceremonious, civil, elegant, flattering, lordly, obliging, polished, polite, refined, urbane.

courtyard *n* area, court, patio, quadrangle, yard.

cove[1] *n* anchorage, bay, bight, creek, firth, fjord, inlet.

cove[2] *n* bloke, chap, character, customer, fellow, type.

covenant *vb* agree, bargain, contract, stipulate. **n* bond, deed; arrangement, bargain, compact, concordat, contract, convention, pact, stipulation, treaty.

cover *vb* overlay, overspread; cloak, conceal, curtain, disguise, hide, mask, screen, secrete, shroud, veil; defend, guard, protect, shelter, shield; case, clothe, envelop, invest, jacket, sheathe; comprehend, comprise, contain, embody, embrace, include. **n* capsule, case, covering, integument, tegument, top; cloak, disguise, screen, veil; guard, defence, protection, safeguard, shelter, shield; shrubbery, thicket, underbrush, undergrowth, underwood, woods.

covert *adj* clandestine, concealed, disguised, hidden, insidious, private, secret, sly, stealthy, underhand. **n* coppice, shade, shrubbery, thicket, underwood; asylum; defence, harbour, hiding-place, refuge, retreat, sanctuary, shelter.

covet *vb* aim after, desire, long for, yearn for; hanker after, lust after.

covetous *adj* acquisitive, avaricious, close-fisted, grasping, greedy, miserly, niggardly, parsimonious, penurious, rapacious.

cow[1] *n* bovine, heifer.

cow[2] *vb* abash, break, daunt, discourage, dishearten, frighten, intimidate, overawe, subdue.

coward *adj* cowardly, timid. **n* caitiff, craven, dastard, milksop, poltroon, recreant, skulker, sneak, wheyface.

cowardly *adj* base, chicken-hearted, coward, craven, dastardly, faint-hearted, fearful, lily-livered, mean, pusillanimous, timid, timorous, white-livered, yellow.

cower *vb* bend, cringe, crouch, fawn, shrink, squat, stoop.

coxcomb *n* beau, dandy, dude, exquisite, fop, jackanapes, popinjay, prig.

coy *adj* backward, bashful, demure, diffident, distant, modest, reserved, retiring, self-effacing, shrinking, shy, timid.

coyness *n* affectation, archness, backwardness, bashfulness, coquettishness, demureness, diffidence, evasiveness, modesty, primness, reserve, shrinking, shyness, timidity.

cozen *vb* beguile, cheat, chouse, circumvent, deceive, defraud, diddle, dupe, gull, overreach, swindle, trick, victimize.

cozy *see* **cosy**.

crabbed *adj* acrid, rough, sore, tart; acrimonious, cantankerous, captious, caustic, censorious, churlish, cross, growling, harsh, ill-tempered, morose, peevish, petulant, snappish, snarling, splenetic, surly, testy, touchy, waspish; difficult, intractable, perplexing, tough, trying, unmanageable.

crabbedness *n* acridity, acridness, roughness, sourness, tartness; acerbity, acrimonious, asperity, churlishness, harshness, ill-tempered, moodiness, moroseness, sullenness; difficulty, intractability, perplexity.

crack *vb* break; chop, cleave, split; snap; craze, madden; boast, brag, bluster, crow, gasconade, vapour, vaunt. **adj* capital, excellent, first-class, first-rate, tip-top. **n* breach, break, chink, cleft, cranny, crevice, fissure, fracture, opening, rent, rift, split; burst, clap, explosion, pop, report; snap.

cracked *adj* broken, crackled, split; crack-brained, crazed, crazy, demented, deranged, flighty, insane.

crackle *vb* crepitate, decrepitate, snap.

craft *n* ability, aptitude, cleverness, dexterity, expertness, power, readiness, skill, tact, talent; artifice, artfulness, cunning, craftiness, deceitfulness, deception, guile, shrewdness, subtlety; art, avocation, business, calling, employment, handicraft, trade, vocation; vessel.

crafty *adj* arch, artful, astute, cunning, crooked, deceitful, designing, fraudulent, guileful, insidious, intriguing, scheming, shrewd, sly, subtle, tricky, wily.

crag *n* rock; neck, throat.

craggy *adj* broken, cragged, jagged, rough, rugged, scraggy, uneven.

cram *vb* fill, glut, gorge, satiate, stuff; compress, crowd, overcrowd, press, squeeze; coach, grind.

cramp *vb* convulse; check, clog, confine, hamper, hinder, impede, obstruct, restrain, restrict. **n* convulsion, crick, spasm; check, restraint, restriction, obstruction.

crank *vb* bend, crankle, crinkle, turn, twist, wind. **n* bend, quirk, turn, twist, winding.

cranny *n* breach, break, chink, cleft, crack, crevice, fissure, gap, hole, interstice, nook, opening, rift.

crapulous *adj* crapulent, drunk, drunken, inebriated, intoxicated, tipsy.

crash *vb* break, shatter, shiver, smash, splinter. **adj* emergency, fast, intensive, rushed, speeded-up. **n* clang, clash, collision concussion, jar.

crass *adj* coarse, gross, raw, thick, unabated, unrefined.

cravat *n* neckcloth, neckerchief, necktie.

crave *vb* ask, beg, beseech, entreat, implore, petition, solicit, supplicate; desire, hanker after, long for, need, want, yearn for.

craven *n* coward, dastard, milk-sop, poltroon, recreant. **adj* cowardly, chickenhearted, lily-livered, pusillanimous, yellow.

craving *n* hankering, hungering, longing, yearning.

craw *n* crop, gullet, stomach, throat.

craze *vb* bewilder, confuse, dement, derange, madden; disorder, impair, weaken. **n* fashion, mania, mode, novelty.

crazy *adj* broken, crank, rickety, shaky, shattered, tottering; crack-brained, delirious, demented, deranged, distracted, idiotic, insane, lunatic, mad, silly.

create *vb* originate, procreate; cause, design, fashion, form, invent, occasion, produce; appoint, constitute, make.

creation *n* formation, invention, origination, production; cosmos, universe; appointment, constitution, establishment, nomination.

creator *n* author, designer, inventor, fashioner, maker, originator; god.

creature *n* animal, beast, being, body, brute, man, person; dependant, hanger-on, minion, parasite, retainer, vassal; miscreant, wretch.

credence *n* acceptance, belief, confidence, credit, faith, reliance, trust.

credentials *npl* certificate, diploma, missive, passport, recommendation, testament, testimonial, title, voucher, warrant.

credibility *n* believability, plausibility, tenability, , trustworthiness.

credit *vb* accept, believe, trust; loan, trust. **n* belief, confidence, credence, faith, reliance, trust; esteem, regard, reputableness, reputation; influence, power; honour, merit; loan, trust.

creditable *adj* estimable, honourable, meritorious, praiseworthy, reputable, respectable.

credulity *n* credulousness, gullibility, silliness, simplicity, stupidity.

credulous *adj* dupable, green, gullible, naive, over-trusting, trustful, uncritical, unsuspecting, unsuspicious.

creed *n* belief, confession, doctrine, dogma, opinion, profession, tenet.

creek *n* bay, bight, cove, fjord, inlet; rivulet, streamlet.

creep *vb* crawl; steal upon; cringe, fawn, grovel, insinuate. **n* crawl, scrabble, scramble; fawner, groveller, sycophant, toady.

crenate *adj* indented, notched, scalloped.

crepitate *vb* crack, crackle, decrepitate, snap.

crest *n* comb, plume, topknot, tuft; apex, crown, head, ridge, summit, top; arms, badge, bearings.

crestfallen *adj* chap-fallen, dejected, depressed, despondent, discouraged, disheartened, dispirited, downcast, downhearted, low-spirited, melancholy, sad.

crevice *n* chink, cleft, crack, cranny, fissure, fracture, gap, hole, interstice, opening, rent, rift.

crew *n* company, complement, hands; company, corps, gang, horde, mob, party, posse, set, squad, team, throng.

crib *vb* cage, confine, encage, enclose, imprison; pilfer, purloin. **n* manger, rack; bin, bunker; plagiarism, plunder, theft.

crick *vb* jar, rick, wrench, wrick. **n* convulsion, cramp, jarring, spasm, rick, wrench, wrick.

crime *n* felony, misdeed, misdemeanour, offence, violation; delinquency, fault, guilt, iniquity, sin, transgression, unrighteousness, wickedness, wrong.

criminal *adj* culpable, felonious, flagitious, guilty, illegal, immoral, iniquitous, nefarious, unlawful, vicious, wicked, wrong. **n* convict, culprit, delinquent, felon, malefactor, offender, sinner, transgressor.

criminate *vb* accuse, arraign, charge, convict, impeach, indict; implicate, involve.

crimp *vb* crisp, curl.

cringe *vb* bend, bow, cower, crouch, fawn, grovel, kneel, sneak, stoop, truckle.

cripple *vb* cramp, destroy, disable, enfeeble, impair, lame, maim, mutilate, paralyse, ruin, weaken.

crisis *n* acme, climax, height; conjuncture, emergency, exigency, juncture, pass, pinch, push, rub, strait, urgency.

crisp *adj* brittle, curled, friable, frizzled.

criterion *n* canon, gauge, measure, principle, proof, rule, standard, test, touchstone.

critic *n* arbiter, caviller, censor, connoisseur, judge, nit-picker, reviewer.

critical *adj* accurate, exact, nice; captious, carping, caviling, censorious, exacting; crucial, decisive, determining, important, turning: dangerous, dubious, exigent, hazardous, imminent, momentous, precarious, ticklish.

criticism *n* analysis, animadversion, appreciation, comment, critique, evaluation, judgement, review, strictures.

criticize *vb* appraise, evaluate, examine, judge.

croak *vb* complain, groan, grumble, moan, mumble, repine; die.

crone *n* hag, witch.

crony *n* ally, associate, chum, friend, mate, mucker, pal.

crook *vb* bend, bow, curve, incurvate, turn, wind. **n* bend, curvature, flexion, turn; artifice, machination, trick; criminal, thief, villain

crooked *adj* angular, bent, bowed, curved, winding, zigzag; askew, aslant, awry, deformed, disfigured, distorted, twisted, wry; crafty, deceitful, devious, dishonest, dishonourable, fraudulent, insidious, intriguing, knavish, tricky, underhanded, unfair, unscrupulous.

crop *vb* gather, mow, pick, pluck, reap; browse, nibble; clip, curtail, lop, reduce, shorten. **n* harvest, produce, yield.

cross *vb* intersect, pass over, traverse; hinder, interfere, obstruct, thwart; interbred, intermix. **adj* transverse; cantankerous, captious, crabbed, churlish, crusty, cynical, fractious, fretful, grouchy, ill-natured, ill-tempered, irascible, irritable, morose, peevish, pettish, petulant, snappish, snarling, sour, spleeny, splenetic, sulky, sullen, surly, testy, touchy, waspish. **n* crucifix, gibbet, rood; affliction, misfortune, trial, trouble, vexation; cross-breeding, hybrid, intermixture.

cross-grained *adj* cantankerous, headstrong, obdurate, peevish, perverse, refractory, stubborn, untractable, wayward.

crossing *n* intersection, overpass, traversing, under-pass.

crossways, crosswise *adv* across, over, transversely.

crotchet *n* caprice, fad, fancy, freak, quirk, vagary, whim, whimsy.

crouch *vb* cower, cringe, fawn, truckle; crouch, kneel, stoop, squat; bow, curtsy, genuflect.

croup *n* buttocks, crupper, rump.

crow *vb* bluster, boast, brag, chuckle, exult, flourish, gasconade, swagger, triumph, vapour, vaunt.

crowd *vb* compress, cram, jam, pack, press; collect, congregate, flock, herd, huddle, swarm. **n* assembly, company, concourse, flock, herd, horde, host, jam, multitude, press, throng; mob, pack, populace, rabble, rout.

crown *vb* adorn, dignify, honour; recompense, requite, reward; cap, complete, consummate, finish, perfect. **n* bays, chaplet, coronal, coronet, garland, diadem, laurel, wreath; monarchy, royalty, sovereignty; diadem; dignity, honour, recompense, reward; apex, crest, summit, top.

crowning *adj* completing, consummating, dignifying, finishing, perfecting.

crucial *adj* intersecting, transverse; critical, decisive, searching, severe, testing, trying.

crude *adj* raw, uncooked, undressed, unworked; harsh, immature, rough, unripe; crass, coarse, unrefined; awkward, immature, indigestible, rude, uncouth, unpolished, unpremeditated.

cruel *adj* barbarous, blood-thirsty, dire, fell, ferocious, inexorable, hard-hearted, inhuman, merciless, pitiless, relentless, ruthless, sanguinary, savage, truculent, uncompassionate, unfeeling, unmerciful, unrelenting; bitter, cold, hard, severe, sharp, unfeeling.

crumble *vb* bruise, crush, decay, disintegrate, perish, pound, pulverize, triturate.
crumple *vb* rumple, wrinkle.
crush *vb* bruise, compress, contuse, squash, squeeze; bray, comminute, crumble, disintegrate, mash; demolish, raze, shatter; conquer, overcome, overpower, overwhelm, quell, subdue.
crust *n* coat, coating, incrustation, outside, shell, surface.
crusty *adj* churlish, crabbed, cross, cynical, fretful, forward, morose, peevish, pettish, petulant, snappish, snarling, surly, testy, touchy, waspish; friable, hard, short.
cry *vb* call, clamour, exclaim; blubber, snivel, sob, wail, weep, whimper; bawl, bellow, hoot, roar, shout, vociferate, scream, screech, squawk, squall, squeal, yell; announce, blazon, proclaim, publish. **n* acclamation, clamour, ejaculation, exclamation, outcry; crying, lament, lamentation, plaint, weeping; bawl, bellow, howl, roar, scream, screech, shriek, yell; announcement, proclamation, publication.
crypt *n* catacomb, tomb, vault.
cuddle *vb* cosset, nestle, snuggle, squat; caress, embrace, fondle, hug, pet. **n* caress, embrace, hug.
cudgel *vb* bang, baste, batter, beat, cane, drub, thrash, thump. **n* bastinado, baton, bludgeon, club, shillelagh, stick, truncheon.
cue *vb* intimate, prompt, remind, sign, signal. **n* catchword, hint, intimation, nod, prompting, sign, signal, suggestion.
cuff *vb* beat, box, buffet, knock, pummel, punch, slap, smack, strike, thump. **n* blow, box, punch, slap, smack, strike, thump.
cul-de-sac *n* alley, dead end, impasse, pocket.
cull *vb* choose, elect, pick, select; collect, gather, glean, pluck.
culmination *n* acme, apex, climax, completion, consummation, crown, summit, top, zenith.
culpability *n* blame, blameworthiness, criminality, culpableness, guilt, remissness, sinfulness.
culpable *adj* blameable, blameworthy, censurable, faulty, guilty, reprehensible, sinful, transgressive, wrong.
culprit *n* delinquent, criminal, evil-doer, felon, malefactor, offender.
cultivate *vb* farm, fertilize, till, work; civilize, develop, discipline, elevate, improve, meliorate, refine, train; investigate, prosecute, pursue, search, study; cherish, foster, nourish, patronize, promote.
culture *n* agriculture, cultivation, farming, husbandry, tillage; cultivation, elevation, improvement, refinement.
cumber *vb* burden, clog, encumber, hamper, impede, obstruct, oppress, overload; annoy, distract, embarrass, harass, perplex, plague, torment, trouble, worry.
cumbersome *adj* burdensome, clumsy, cumbrous, embarrassing, heavy, inconvenient, oppressive, troublesome, unmanageable, unwieldy, vexatious.
cuneiform *adj* cuneate, wedge-shaped.
cunning *adj* artful, astute, crafty, crooked, deceitful, designing, diplomatic, foxy, guileful, intriguing, machiavellian, sharp, shrewd, sly, subtle, tricky, wily; curious, ingenious. **n* art, artfulness, artifice, astuteness, craft, shrewdness, subtlety; craftiness, chicane, chicanery, deceit, deception, intrigue, slyness.
cup *n* beaker, bowl, chalice, goblet, mug; cupful, draught, potion.
cupboard *n* buffet, cabinet, closet.
cupidity *n* avidity, greed, hankering, longing, lust; acquisitiveness, avarice, covetousness, greediness, stinginess.
curative *adj* healing, medicinal, remedial, restorative.
curator *n* custodian, guardian, keeper, superintendent.
curb *vb* bridle, check, control, hinder, moderate, repress, restrain. **n* bridle, check, control, hindrance, rein, restraint.
cure *vb* alleviate, correct, heal, mend, remedy, restore; kipper, pickle, preserve. **n* antidote, corrective, help, remedy, reparative, restorative, specific; alleviation, healing, restorative.
curiosity *n* interest, inquiringness, inquisi-

tiveness; celebrity, curio, marvel, novelty, oddity, phenomenon, rarity, sight, spectacle, wonder.

curious *adj* interested, inquiring, inquisitive, meddling, peering, prying, scrutinizing; extraordinary, marvellous, novel, queer, rare, singular, strange, unique, unusual; cunning, elegant, fine, finished, neat, skilful, well-wrought.

curl *vb* coil, twist, wind, writhe; bend, buckle, ripple, wave. **n* curlicue, lovelock, ringlet; flexure, sinuosity, undulation, wave, waving, winding.

curmudgeon *n* churl, lick-penny, miser, niggard, screw, scrimp, skinflint.

currency *n* publicity; acceptance, circulation, transmission; bills, coins, money, notes.

current *adj* common, general, popular, rife; circulating, passing; existing, instant, present, prevalent, widespread. **n* course, progression, river, stream, tide, undertow. **adv* commonly, generally, popularly, publicly.

curry *vb* comb, dress; beat, cudgel, drub, thrash.

curse *vb* anathematize, damn, denounce, execrate, imprecate, invoke, maledict; blast, blight, destroy, doom; afflict, annoy, harass, injure, plague, scourge, torment, vex; blaspheme, swear. **n* anathema, ban, denunciation, execration, fulmination, imprecation, malediction, malison; affliction, annoyance, plague, scourge, torment, trouble, vexation; ban, condemnation, penalty, sentence.

cursed *adj* accursed, banned, blighted, curse-laden, unholy; abominable, detestable, execrable, hateful, villainous; annoying, confounded, plaguing, scourging, tormenting, troublesome, vexatious.

cursory *adj* brief, careless, desultory, hasty, passing, rapid, slight, summary, superficial, transient, transitory.

curt *adj* brief, concise, laconic, short, terse; crusty, rude, snappish, tart.

curtail *vb* abridge, dock, lop, retrench, shorten; abbreviate, contract, decrease, diminish, lessen.

curtain *vb* cloak, cover, drape, mantle, screen, shade, shield, veil. **n* arras, drape, drop, portière, screen, shade.

curvature *n* arcuation, bend, bending, camber, crook, curve, flexure, incurvation.

curve *vb* bend, crook, inflect, turn, twist, wind. **n* arcuation, bend, bending, camber, crook, flexure, incurvation.

curvet *vb* bound, leap, vault; caper, frisk.

cushion *vb* absorb, damp, dampen, deaden, dull, muffle, mute, soften, subdue, suppress; cradle, pillow, support. **n* bolster, hassock, pad, pillow, woolsack.

cusp *n* angle, horn, point.

custodian *n* curator, guardian, keeper, sacristan, superintendent, warden.

custody *n* care, charge, guardianship, keeping, safe-keeping, protection, watch, ward; confinement, durance, duress, imprisonment, prison.

custom *n* consuetude, convention, fashion, habit, manner, mode, practice, rule, usage, use, way; form, formality, observation; patronage; duty, impost, tax, toll, tribute.

customary *adj* accustomed, common, consuetudinary, conventional, familiar, fashionable, general, habitual, gnomic, prescriptive, regular, usual, wonted.

cut *vb* chop, cleave, divide, gash, incise, lance, sever, slice, slit, wound; carve, chisel, sculpture; hurt, move, pierce, touch; ignore, slight; abbreviate, abridge, curtail, shorten. **n* gash, groove, incision, nick, slash, slice, slit; channel, passage; piece, slice; fling, sarcasm, taunt; fashion, form, mode, shape, style.

cutthroat *adj* barbarous, cruel, ferocious, murderous; competitive, exacting, exorbitant, extortionate, rivalling, ruthless, usurious, vying.**n* assassin, murderer, ruffian.

cutting *adj* keen, sharp; acid, biting, bitter, caustic, piercing, sarcastic, sardonic, satirical, severe, trenchant, wounding.

cycle *n* age, circle, era, period, revolution, round.

Cyclopean *adj* colossal, enormous, gigantic, Herculean, immense, vast.

cynical *adj* captious, carping, censorious,

churlish, crabbed, cross, crusty, fretful, ill-natured, ill-tempered, morose, peevish, pettish, petulant, sarcastic, satirical, snappish, snarling, surly, testy, touchy, waspish; contemptuous, derisive, misanthropic, pessimistic, scornful.

cynosure *n* attraction, centre.

cyst *n* pouch, sac.

D

dab *vb* box, rap, slap, strike, tap touch; coat, daub, smear. * *adj* adept, expert, proficient; pat. * *n* lump, mass, pat.

dabble *vb* dip, moisten, soak, spatter, splash, sprinkle, wet; meddle, tamper, trifle.

daft *adj* absurd, delirious, foolish, giddy, idiotic, insane, silly, simple, stupid, witless; frolicsome, merry, mirthful, playful, sportive.

dagger *n* bayonet, dirk, poniard, stiletto.

dainty *adj* delicate, delicious, luscious, nice, palatable, savoury, tender, toothsome; beautiful, charming, choice, delicate, elegant, exquisite, fine, neat; fastidious, finical, finicky, over-nice, particular, scrupulous, squeamish. * *n* delicacy, titbit, treat.

dale *n* bottom, dell, dingle, glen, vale, valley.

dalliance *n* caressing, endearments, flirtation, fondling.

dally *vb* dawdle, fritter, idle, trifle, waste time; flirt, fondle, toy.

damage *vb* harm, hurt, impair, injure, mar. * *n* detriment, harm, hurt, injury, loss, mischief.

damages *npl* compensation, fine, forfeiture, indemnity, reparation, satisfaction.

dame *n* babe, baby, broad, doll, girl; lady, madam, matron, mistress.

damn *vb* condemn, doom, kill, ruin. * *n* bean, curse, fig, hoot, rap, sou, straw, whit.

damnable *adj* abominable, accursed, atrocious, cursed, detestable, hateful, execrable, odious, outrageous.

damp *vb* dampen, moisten; allay, abate, check, discourage, moderate, repress, restrain; chill, cool, deaden, deject, depress, dispirit. * *adj* dank, humid, moist, wet. * *n* dampness, dank, fog, mist, moisture, vapour; chill, dejection, depression.

damper *n* check, hindrance, impediment, obstacle; damp, depression, discouragement, wet blanket.

dandle *vb* amuse, caress, fondle, pet, toss; dance.

danger *n* jeopardy, insecurity, hazard, peril, risk, venture.

dangerous *adj* critical, hazardous, insecure, perilous, risky, ticklish, unsafe.

dangle *vb* drape, hang, pend, sway, swing; fawn.

dank *adj* damp, humid, moist, wet.

dapper *adj* active, agile, alert, brisk, lively, nimble, quick, ready, smart, spry; neat, nice, pretty, spruce, trim.

dapple *vb* diversify, spot, variegate. * *adj* dappled, spotted, variegated.

dare *vb* challenge, defy, endanger, hazard, provoke, risk. * *n* challenge, defiance, gage.

daring *adj* adventurous, bold, brave, chivalrous, courageous, dauntless, doughty, fearless, gallant, heroic, intrepid, valiant, valorous. * *n* adventurousness, boldness, bravery, courage, dauntlessness, doughtiness, fearlessness, intrepidity, undauntedness, valour.

dark *adj* black, cloudy, darksome, dusky, ebon, inky, lightless, lurid, moonless, murky, opaque, overcast, pitchy, rayless, shady, shadowy, starless, sunless, swart, tenebrous, umbrageous, unenlightened, unilluminated; abstruse, cabbalistic, enigmatical, incomprehensible, mysterious, mystic, mystical, obscure, occult, opaque, recondite, transcendental, unillumined, unintelligible; cheerless, discouraging, dismal, disheartening, funereal, gloomy; benighted, darkened, ignorant, rude, unlettered, untaught; atrocious, damnable, infamous, flagitious, foul, horrible, infernal, nefarious, vile, wicked. * *n* darkness, dusk, murkiness, obscurity; concealment, privacy, secrecy; blindness, ignorance.

darken *vb* cloud, dim, eclipse, obscure, shade, shadow; chill, damp, depress, gloom, sadden; benight, stultify, stupefy; obscure, perplex; defile, dim, dull, stain, sully.

darkness *n* blackness, dimness, gloom, obscurity; blindness, ignorance; cheerlessness, despondency, gloom, joylessness; privacy, secrecy.

darling *adj* beloved, cherished, dear, loved, precious, treasured. * *n* dear, favourite, idol, love, sweetheart.

dart *vb* ejaculate, hurl, launch, propel, sling, throw; emit, shoot; dash, rush, scoot, spring.

dash *vb* break, destroy, disappoint, frustrate, ruin, shatter, spoil, thwart; abash, confound, disappoint, surprise; bolt, dart, fly, run, speed, rush. * *n* blow, stroke; advance, onset, rush; infusion, smack, spice, sprinkling, tincture, tinge, touch; flourish, show.

dashing *adj* headlong, impetuous, precipitate, rushing; brilliant, gay, showy, spirited.

dastardly *adj* base, cowardly, coward, cowering, craven, pusillanimous, recreant. * *n* coward, craven, milksop, poltroon, recreant.

data *npl* conditions, facts, information, premises.

date *n* age, cycle, day, generation, time; epoch, era, period; appointment, arrangement, assignation, engagement, interview, rendezvous, tryst; catch, steady, sweetheart.

daub *vb* bedaub, begrime, besmear, blur, cover, deface, defile, grime, plaster, smear, smudge, soil, sully. * *n* smear, smirch, smudge.

daunt *vb* alarm, appal, check, cow, deter, discourage, frighten, intimate, scare, subdue, tame, terrify, thwart.

dauntless *adj* bold, brave, chivalrous, courageous, daring, doughty, gallant, heroic, indomitable, intrepid, unaffrighted, unconquerable, undaunted, undismayed, valiant, valorous.

dawdle *vb* dally, delay, fiddle, idle, lag, loiter, potter, trifle.

dawn *vb* appear, begin, break, gleam, glimmer, open, rise. * *n* daybreak, dawning, cockcrow, sunrise, sun-up.

day *n* daylight, sunlight, sunshine; age, epoch, generation, lifetime, time.

daze *vb* blind, dazzle; bewilder, confound, confuse, perplex, stun, stupefy. * *n* bewilderment, confusion, discomposure, perturbation, pother; coma, stupor, swoon, trance.

dazzle *vb* blind, daze; astonish, confound, overpower, surprise. * *n* brightness, brilliance, splendour.

dead *adj* breathless, deceased, defunct, departed, gone, inanimate, lifeless; apathetic, callous, cold, dull, frigid, indifferent, inert, lukewarm, numb, obtuse, spiritless, torpid, unfeeling; flat, insipid, stagnant, tasteless, vapid; barren, inactive, sterile, unemployed, unprofitable, useless. * *adv* absolutely, completely, downright, fundamentally, quite; direct, directly, due, exactly, just, right, squarely, straight. * *n* depth, midst; hush, peace, quietude, silence, stillness.

deaden *vb* abate, damp, dampen, dull, impair, muffle, mute, restrain, retard, smother, weaken; benumb, blunt, hebetate, obtund, paralyse.

deadly *adj* deleterious, destructive, fatal, lethal, malignant, mortal, murderous, noxious, pernicious, poisonous, venomous; implacable, mortal, rancorous, sanguinary.

deal *vb* allot, apportion, assign, bestow, dispense, distribute, divide, give, reward, share; bargain, trade, traffic, treat with. * *n* amount, degree, distribution, extent, lot, portion, quantity, share; bargain, transaction.

dear *adj* costly, expensive, high-priced; beloved, cherished, darling, esteemed, precious, treasured. * *n* beloved, darling, deary, honey, love, precious, sweet, sweetie, sweetheart.

dearth *n* deficiency, insufficiency, scarcity; famine, lack, need, shortage, want.

death *n* cessation, decease, demise, departure, destruction, dissolution, dying, end, exit, mortality, passing.

deathless *adj* eternal, everlasting, immortal, imperishable, undying; boring, dull, turgid.

debacle *n* breakdown, cataclysm, collapse; rout, stampede.

debar *vb* blackball, deny, exclude, hinder, prevent, prohibit, restrain, shut out, stop, withhold.

debase *vb* adulterate, alloy, depress, deteriorate, impair, injure, lower, pervert, reduce, vitiate; abase, degrade, disgrace, dishonour, humble, humiliate, mortify, shame; befoul, contaminate, corrupt, defile, foul, pollute, soil, taint.

debate *vb* argue, canvass, contest, discuss, dispute; contend, deliberate, wrangle. * *n* controversy, discussion, disputation; altercation, contention, contest, dispute, logomachy.

debauch *vb* corrupt, deprave, pollute, vitiate; deflower, ravish, seduce, violate. * *n* carousal, orgy, revel, saturnalia.

debauchery *n* dissipation, dissoluteness, excesses, intemperance; debauch, excess, intemperance, lewdness, licentiousness, lust; bacchanal, carousal, compotation, indulgence, orgies, potation, revelry, revels, saturnalia, spree.

debilitate *vb* enervate, enfeeble, exhaust, prostrate, relax, weaken.

debility *n* enervation, exhaustion, faintness, feebleness, frailty, imbecility, infirmity, languor, prostration, weakness.

debonair *adj* affable, civil, complaisant, courteous, easy, gracious, kind, obliging, polite, refined, urbane, well-bred.

debris *n* detritus, fragments, remains, rubbish, rubble, ruins, wreck, wreckage.

debt *n* arrears, debit, due, liability, obligation; fault, misdoing, offence, shortcoming, sin, transgression, trespass.

decadence *n* caducity, decay, declension, decline, degeneracy, degeneration, deterioration, fall, retrogression.

decamp *vb* abscond, bolt, escape, flee, fly.

decapitate *vb* behead, decollate, guillotine.

decay *vb* decline, deteriorate, disintegrate, fail, perish, wane, waste, wither; decompose, putrefy, rot. * *n* caducity, decadence, declension, decline, decomposition, decrepitude, degeneracy, degeneration, deterioration, dilapidation, disintegration, fading, failing, perishing, putrefaction, ruin, wasting, withering.

deceased *adj* dead, defunct, departed, gone, late, lost.

deceit *n* artifice, cheating, chicanery, cozenage, craftiness, deceitfulness, deception, double-dealing, duplicity, finesse, fraud, guile, hypocrisy, imposition, imposture, pretence, sham, treachery, tricky, underhandedness, wile.

deceitful *adj* counterfeit, deceptive, delusive, fallacious, hollow, illusive, illusory, insidious, misleading; circumventive, cunning, designing, dissembling, dodgy, double-dealing, evasive, false, fraudulent, guileful, hypocritical, insincere, tricky, underhanded, wily.

deceive *vb* befool, beguile, betray, cheat, chouse, circumvent, cozen, defraud, delude, disappoint, double-cross, dupe, ensnare, entrap, fool, gull, hoax, hoodwink, humbug, mislead, outwit, overreach, trick.

deceiver *n* charlatan, cheat, humbug, hypocrite, knave, impostor, pretender, rogue, sharper, trickster.

decent *adj* appropriate, becoming, befitting, comely, seemly, decorous, fit, proper, seemly; chaste, delicate, modest, pure; moderate, passable, respectable, tolerable.

deception *n* artifice, cheating, chicanery, cozenage, craftiness, deceitfulness, deception, double-dealing, duplicity, finesse, fraud, guile, hoax, hypocrisy, imposition, imposture, pretence, sham, treachery, trick, underhandedness, wile; cheat, chouse, ruse, stratagem, wile.

deceptive *adj* deceitful, deceiving, delusive, disingenuous, fallacious, false, illusive, illusory, misleading.

decide *vb* close, conclude, determine, end,

settle, terminate; resolve; adjudge, adjudicate, award.

decided *adj* determined, firm, resolute, unhesitating, unwavering; absolute, categorical, positive, unequivocal; certain, clear, indisputable, undeniable, unmistakable, unquestionable.

deciduous *adj* caducous, nonperennial, temporary.

decipher *vb* explain, expound, interpret, reveal, solve, unfold, unravel; read.

decision *n* conclusion, determination, judgement, settlement; adjudication, award, decree, pronouncement, sentence; firmness, resolution.

decisive *adj* conclusive, determinative, final.

deck *vb* adorn, array, beautify, decorate, embellish, grace, ornament; apparel, attire, bedeck, clothe, dress, robe.

declaim *vb* harangue, mouth, rant, speak, spout.

declamation *n* declaiming, haranguing, mouthing, ranting, spouting.

declamatory *adj* bombastic, discursive, fustian, grandiloquent, high-flown, high-sounding, incoherent, inflated, pompous, pretentious, rhetorical, swelling, turgid.

declaration *n* affirmation, assertion, asseveration, averment, avowal, protestation, statement; announcement, proclamation, publication.

declaratory *adj* affirmative, annunciatory, assertive, declarative, definite, enunciative, enunciatory, expressive; explanatory, expository.

declare *vb* advertise, affirm, announce, assert, asseverate, aver, blazon, bruit, proclaim, promulgate, pronounce, publish, state, utter.

declension *n* decadence, decay, decline, degeneracy, deterioration, diminution; inflection, variation; declination, nonacceptance, refusal.

declination *n* bending, descent, inclination; decadence, decay, decline, degeneracy, degeneration, degradation, deterioration, diminution; aberration, departure, deviation, digression, divagation, divergence; declinature, nonacceptance, refusal.

decline *vb* incline, lean, slope; decay, droop, fail, flag, languish, pine, sink; degenerate, depreciate, deteriorate; decrease, diminish, dwindle, fade, ebb, lapse, lessen, wane; avoid, refuse, reject; inflect, vary. * *n* decadence, decay, declension, declination, degeneracy, deterioration, diminution, wane; atrophy, consumption, marasmus, phthisis; declivity, hill, incline, slope.

declivity *n* declination, descent, incline, slope.

decompose *vb* analyse, disintegrate, dissolve, distil, resolve, separate; corrupt, decay, putrefy, rot.

decomposition *n* analysis, break-up, disintegration, resolution; caries, corruption, crumbling, decay, disintegration, dissolution, putrescence, rotting.

decorate *vb* adorn, beautify, bedeck, deck, embellish, enrich, garnish, grace, ornament.

decoration *n* adorning, beautifying, bedecking, decking, enriching, garnishing, ornamentation, ornamenting; adornment, enrichment, embellishment, ornament.

decorous *adj* appropriate, becoming, befitting, comely, decent, fit, suitable, proper, sedate, seemly, staid.

decorum *n* appropriate behaviour, courtliness, decency, deportment, dignity, gravity, politeness, propriety, sedateness, seemliness.

decoy *vb* allure, deceive, ensnare, entice, entrap, inveigle, lure, seduce, tempt. * *n* allurement, lure, enticement.

decrease *vb* abate, contract, decline, diminish, dwindle, ebb, lessen, subside, wane; curtail, diminish, lessen, lower, reduce, retrench. * *n* abatement, contraction, declension, decline, decrement, diminishing, diminution, ebb, ebbing, lessening, reduction, subsidence, waning.

decree *vb* adjudge, appoint, command, decide, determine, enact, enjoin, order, ordain. * *n* act, command, edict, enactment, fiat, law, mandate, order, ordinance, precept, regulation, statute.

decrement *n* decrease, diminution, lessening, loss, waste.

decrepit *adj* feeble, effete, shattered, wasted, weak; aged, crippled, superannuated.

decry *vb* abuse, belittle, blame, condemn, denounce, depreciate, detract, discredit, disparage, run down, traduce, underrate, undervalue.

dedicate *vb* consecrate, devote, hallow, sanctify; address, inscribe.

deduce *vb* conclude, derive, draw, gather, infer.

deducible *adj* derivable, inferable.

deduct *vb* remove, subtract, withdraw; abate, detract.

deduction *n* removal, subtraction, withdrawal; abatement, allowance, defalcation, discount, rebate, reduction, reprise; conclusion, consequence, corollary, inference.

deed *n* achievement, act, action, derring-do, exploit, feat, performance; fact, truth, reality; charter, contract, document, indenture, instrument, transfer.

deem *vb* account, believe, conceive, consider, count, estimate, hold, imagine, judge, regard, suppose, think; fancy, opine.

deep *adj* abysmal, extensive, great, profound; abstruse, difficult, hard, intricate, knotty, mysterious, recondite, unfathomable; astute, cunning, designing, discerning, intelligent, insidious, penetrating, sagacious, shrewd; absorbed, engrossed; bass, grave, low; entire, great, heartfelt, thorough. * *n* main, ocean, water, sea; abyss, depth, profundity; enigma, mystery, riddle; silence, stillness.

deeply *adv* profoundly; completely, entirely, extensively, greatly, thoroughly; affectingly, distressingly, feelingly, mournfully, sadly.

deface *vb* blotch, deform, disfigure, injure, mar, mutilate, obliterate, soil, spoil, sully, tarnish.

de facto *adj* actual, real. * *adv* actually, in effect, in fact, really, truly.

defalcate *vb* abate, curtail, retrench, lop.

defalcation *n* abatement, deduction, diminution, discount, reduction; default, deficiency, deficit, shortage, shortcoming; embezzlement, fraud.

defamation *n* abuse, aspersion, back-biting, calumny, detraction, disparagement, libel, obloquy, opprobrium, scandal, slander.

defamatory *adj* abusive, calumnious, libellous, slanderous.

defame *vb* abuse, asperse, blacken, belie, besmirch, blemish, calumniate, detract, disgrace, dishonour, libel, malign, revile, slander, smirch, traduce, vilify.

default *vb* defalcate, dishonour, fail, repudiate, welsh. * *n* defalcation, failure, lapse, neglect, offence, omission, oversight, shortcoming ; defect, deficiency, deficit, delinquency, destitution, fault, lack, want.

defaulter *n* delinquent, embezzler, offender, peculator.

defeat *vb* beat, checkmate, conquer, discomfit, overcome, overpower, overthrow, repulse, rout, ruin, vanquish; baffle, balk, block, disappoint, disconcert, foil, frustrate, thwart. * *n* discomfiture, downfall, overthrow, repulse, rout, vanquishment; bafflement, checkmate, frustration.

defect *vb* abandon, desert, rebel, revolt. * *n* default, deficiency, destitution, lack, shortcoming, spot, taint, want; blemish, blotch, error, flaw, imperfection, mistake; failing, fault, foible.

defection *n* abandonment, desertion, rebellion, revolt; apostasy, backsliding, dereliction.

defective *adj* deficient, inadequate, incomplete, insufficient, scant, short; faulty, imperfect, marred.

defence *n* defending, guarding, holding, maintaining, maintenance, protection; buckler, bulwark, fortification, guard, protection, rampart, resistance, shield; apology, excuse, justification, plea, vindication.

defenceless *adj* exposed, helpless, unarmed, unprotected, unguarded, unshielded, weak.

defend *vb* cover, fortify, guard, preserve,

protect, safeguard, screen, secure, shelter, shield; assert, espouse, justify, maintain, plead, uphold, vindicate.

defender *n* asserter, maintainer, pleader, upholder; champion, protector, vindicator.

defer[1] *vb* adjourn, delay, pigeonhole, procrastinate, postpone, prorogue, protract, shelve, table.

defer[2] *vb* abide by, acknowledge, bow to, give way, submit, yield; admire, esteem, honour, regard, respect.

deference *n* esteem, homage, honour, obeisance, regard, respect, reverence, veneration; complaisance, consideration; obedience, submission.

deferential *adj* respectful, reverential.

defiance *n* challenge, daring; contempt, despite, disobedience, disregard, opposition, spite.

defiant *adj* contumacious, recalcitrant, resistant; bold, courageous, resistant.

deficiency *n* dearth, default, deficit, insufficiency, lack, meagreness, scantiness, scarcity, shortage, shortness, want; defect, error, failing, falling, fault, foible, frailty, imperfection, infirmity, weakness.

deficient *adj* defective, faulty, imperfect, inadequate, incomplete, insufficient, lacking, scant, scanty, scarce, short, unsatisfactory, wanting.

deficit *n* deficiency, lack, scarcity, shortage, shortness.

defile[1] *vb* dirty, foul, soil, stain, tarnish; contaminate, debase, poison, pollute, sully, taint, vitiate; corrupt, debauch, deflower, ravish, seduce, violate.

defile[2] *vb* file, march, parade, promenade. * *n* col, gorge, pass, passage, ravine, strait.

define *vb* bound, circumscribe, designate, delimit, demarcate, determine, explain, limit, specify.

definite *adj* defined, determinate, determined, fixed, restricted; assured, certain, clear, exact, explicit, positive, precise, specific, unequivocal.

definitive *adj* categorical, determinate, explicit, express, positive, unconditional; conclusive, decisive, final.

deflect *vb* bend, deviate, diverge, swerve, turn, twist, waver, wind.

deflower *vb* corrupt, debauch, defile, seduce.

deform *vb* deface, disfigure, distort, injure, mar, misshape, ruin, spoil.

deformity *n* abnormality, crookedness, defect, disfigurement, distortion, inelegance, irregularity, malformation, misproportion, misshapenness, monstrosity, ugliness.

defraud *vb* beguile, cheat, chouse, circumvent, cozen, deceive, delude, diddle, dupe, embezzle, gull, overreach, outwit, pilfer, rob, swindle, trick.

defray *vb* bear, discharge, liquidate, meet, pay, settle.

deft *adj* adroit, apt, clever, dab, dextrous, expert, handy, ready, skilful.

defunct *adj* dead, deceased, departed, extinct, gone; abrogated, annulled, cancelled, inoperative.

defy *vb* challenge, dare; brave, contemn, despise, disregard, face, flout, provoke, scorn, slight, spurn.

degeneracy *n* abasement, caducity, corruption, debasement, decadence, decay, declension, decline, decrease, degenerateness, degeneration, degradation, depravation, deterioration; inferiority, meanness, poorness.

degenerate *vb* decay, decline, decrease, deteriorate, retrograde, sink. * *adj* base, corrupt, decayed, degenerated, deteriorated, fallen, inferior, low, mean, perverted.

degeneration *n* debasement, decline, degeneracy, deterioration.

degradation *n* deposition, disgrace, dishonour, humiliation, ignominy; abasement, caducity, corruption, debasement, decadence, decline, degeneracy, degeneration, deterioration, perversion, vitiation.

degrade *vb* abase, alloy, break, cashier, corrupt, debase, demote, discredit, disgrace, dishonour, disparage, downgrade, humiliate, humble, lower, pervert, vitiate; deteriorate, impair, lower, sink.

degree *n* stage, step; class, grade, order,

quality, rank, standing, station; extent, measure; division, interval, space.

deify *vb* apotheosize, idolize, glorify, revere; elevate, ennoble, exalt.

deign *vb* accord, condescend, grant, vouchsafe.

deject *vb* depress, discourage, dishearten, dispirit, sadden.

dejected *adj* blue, chapfallen, crestfallen, depressed, despondent, disheartened, dispirited, doleful, downcast, downhearted, gloomy, low-spirited, miserable, sad, wretched.

delay *vb* defer, postpone, procrastinate; arrest, detain, check, hinder, impede, retard, stay, stop; prolong, protract; dawdle, linger, loiter, tarry. * *n* deferment, postponement, procrastination; check, detention, hindrance, impediment, retardation, stoppage; prolonging, protraction; dallying, dawdling, lingering, tarrying, stay, stop.

delectable *adj* agreeable, charming, delightful, enjoyable, gratifying, pleasant, pleasing.

delectation *n* delight, ecstasy, gladness, joy, rapture, ravishment, transport.

delegate *vb* appoint, authorize, mission, depute, deputize, transfer; commit, entrust. * *n* ambassador, commissioner, delegate, deputy, envoy, representative.

delete *vb* cancel, efface, erase, expunge, obliterate, remove.

deleterious *adj* deadly, destructive, lethal, noxious, poisonous; harmful, hurtful, injurious, pernicious, unwholesome.

deliberate *vb* cogitate, consider, consult, meditate, muse, ponder, reflect, ruminate, think, weigh. * *adj* careful, cautious, circumspect, considerate, heedful, purposeful, methodical, thoughtful, wary; well-advised, well-considered; aforethought, intentional, premeditated, purposed, studied.

deliberation *n* caution, circumspection, cogitation, consideration, coolness, meditation, prudence, reflection, thought, thoughtfulness, wariness; purpose.

delicacy *n* agreeableness, daintiness, deliciousness, pleasantness, relish, savouriness; bonne bouche, dainty, tidbit; elegance, fitness, lightness, niceness, nicety, smoothness, softness, tenderness; fragility, frailty, slenderness, slightness, tenderness, weakness; carefulness, discrimination, fastidiousness, finesse, nicety, scrupulousness, sensitivity, subtlety, tact; purity, refinement, sensibility.

delicate *adj* agreeable, delicious, pleasant, pleasing, palatable, savoury; elegant, exquisite, fine, nice; careful, dainty, discriminating, fastidious, scrupulous; fragile, frail, slender, slight, tender, delicate; pure, refined.

delicious *adj* dainty, delicate, luscious, nice, palatable, savory; agreeable, charming, choice, delightful, exquisite, grateful, pleasant.

delight *vb* charm, enchant, enrapture, gratify, please, ravish, rejoice, satisfy, transport. * *n* charm, delectation, ecstasy, enjoyment, gladness, gratification, happiness, joy, pleasure, rapture, ravishment, satisfaction, transport.

delightful *adj* agreeable, captivating, charming, delectable, enchanting, enjoyable, enrapturing, rapturous, ravishing, transporting.

delineate *vb* design, draw, figure, paint, sketch, trace; depict, describe, picture, portray.

delineation *n* design, draught, drawing, figure, outline, sketch; account, description, picture, portrayal.

delinquency *n* crime, fault, misdeed, misdemeanour, offence, wrong-doing.

delinquent *adj* negligent, offending. * *n* criminal, culprit, defaulter, malefactor, miscreant, misdoer, offender, transgressor, wrong-doer.

delirious *adj* crazy, demented, deranged, frantic, frenzied, light-headed, mad, insane, raving, wandering.

delirium *n* aberration, derangement, frenzy, hallucination, incoherence, insanity, lunacy, madness, raving, wandering.

deliver *vb* emancipate, free, liberate, release; extricate, redeem, rescue, save; commit, give, impart, transfer; cede, grant, relinquish, resign, yield; declare, emit, promulgate, pronounce, speak, utter; deal, discharge.

deliverance *n* emancipation, escape, liberation, redemption, release.

delivery *n* conveyance, surrender; commitment, giving, rendering, transference, transferral, transmission; elocution, enunciation, pronunciation, speech, utterance; childbirth, confinement, labour, parturition, travail.

dell *n* dale, dingle, glen, valley, ravine.

delude *vb* beguile, cheat, chouse, circumvent, cozen, deceive, dupe, gull, misguide, mislead, overreach, trick.

deluge *vb* drown, inundate, overflow, overwhelm, submerge. * *n* cataclysm, downpour, flood, inundation, overflow, rush.

delusion *n* artifice, cheat, clap-trap, deceit, dodge, fetch, fraud, imposition, imposture, ruse, snare, trick, wile; deception, error, fallacy, fancy, hallucination, illusion, mistake, mockery, phantasm.

delusive *adj* deceitful, deceiving, deceptive, fallacious, illusional, illusionary, illusive.

demand *vb* challenge, exact, require; claim, necessitate, require; ask, inquire. * *n* claim, draft, exaction, requirement, requisition; call, want; inquiry, interrogation, question.

demarcation *n* bound, boundary, confine, distinction, division, enclosure, limit, separation.

demeanour *n* air, bearing, behaviour, carriage, deportment, manner, mien.

demented *adj* crack-brained, crazed, crazy, daft, deranged, dotty, foolish, idiotic, infatuated, insane, lunatic.

dementia *n* idiocy, insanity, lunacy.

demerit *n* delinquency, fault, ill-desert.

demise *vb* alienate, consign, convey, devolve, grant, transfer; bequeath, devise, leave, will. * *n* alienation, conveyance, transfer, transference, transmission; death, decease.

demolish *vb* annihilate, destroy, dismantle, level, over-throw, overturn, pulverize, raze, ruin.

demon *n* devil, fiend, kelpie, goblin, troll.

demoniac, demoniacal *adj* demonic, demonical, devilish, diabolic, diabolical, fiendish, hellish, infernal, Mephistophelean, Mephistophelian, satanic; delirious, distracted, frantic, frenzied, feverish, hysterical, mad, overwrought, rabid.

demonstrate *vb* establish, exhibit, illustrate, indicate, manifest, prove, show.

demonstration *n* display, exhibition, manifestation, show.

demonstrative *adj* affectionate, communicative, effusive, emotional, expansive, expressive, extroverted, open, outgoing, passionate, sentimental, suggestive, talkative, unreserved; absolute, apodictic, certain, conclusive, probative; exemplificative, illustrative.

demoralize *vb* corrupt, debase, debauch, deprave, vitiate; depress, discourage, dishearten, weaken.

demulcent *adj* emollient, lenitive, mild, mollifying, sedative, soothing.

demur *vb* halt, hesitate, pause, stop, waver; doubt, object, scruple. * *n* demurral, hesitance, hesitancy, hesitation, objection, pause, qualm, scruple.

demure *adj* prudish; coy, decorous, grave, modest, priggish, prudish, sedate, sober, staid.

den *n* cavern, cave; haunt, lair, resort, retreat.

denial *n* contradiction, controverting, negation; abjuration, disavowal, disclaimer, disowning; disallowance, refusal, rejection.

denizen *n* citizen, dweller, inhabitant, resident.

denominate *vb* call, christen, designate, dub, entitle, name, phrase, style, term.

denomination *n* appellation, designation, name, style, term, title; class, kind, sort; body, persuasion, school, sect.

denote *vb* betoken, connote, designate, imply, indicate, mark, mean, note, show, signify, typify.

dénouement *n* catastrophe, unravelling; consummation, issue, finale, upshot, conclusion, termination.

denounce *vb* menace, threaten; arraign, attack, brand, censure, condemn, proscribe, stigmatize, upbraid; accuse, inform, denunciate.

dense *adj* close, compact, compressed, condensed, thick; dull, slow, stupid.

dent *vb* depress, dint, indent, pit. * *n* depression, dint, indentation, nick, notch.

dentate *adj* notched, serrate, toothed.

denude *vb* bare, divest, strip.

denunciation *n* menace, threat; arraignment, censure, fulmination, invective; exposure.

deny *vb* contradict, gainsay, oppose, refute, traverse; abjure, abnegate, disavow, disclaim, disown, renounce; disallow, refuse, reject, withhold.

depart *vb* absent, disappear, vanish; abandon, decamp, go, leave, migrate, quit, remove, withdraw; decease, die; deviate, diverge, vary.

department *n* district, division, part, portion, province; bureau, function, office, province, sphere, station; branch, division, subdivision.

departure *n* exit, leaving, parting, removal, recession, removal, retirement, withdrawal; abandonment, forsaking; death, decease, demise, deviation, exit.

depend *vb* hang, hinge, turn.

dependant *n* client, hanger-on, henchman, minion, retainer, subordinate, vassal; attendant, circumstance, concomitant, consequence, corollary.

dependence *n* concatenation, connection, interdependence; confidence, reliance, trust; buttress, prop, staff, stay, support, supporter; contingency, need, subjection, subordination.

dependency *n* adjunct, appurtenance; colony, province.

dependent *adj* hanging, pendant; conditioned, contingent, relying, subject, subordinate.

depict *vb* delineate, limn, outline, paint, pencil, portray, sketch; describe, render, represent.

deplete *vb* drain, empty, evacuate, exhaust, reduce.

deplorable *adj* calamitous, distressful, distressing, grievous, lamentable, melancholy, miserable, mournful, pitiable, regrettable, sad, wretched.

deplore *vb* bemoan, bewail, grieve for, lament, mourn, regret.

deploy *vb* display, expand, extend, open, unfold.

deportment *n* air, bearing, behaviour, breeding, carriage, comportment, conduct, demeanour, manner, mien, port.

depose *vb* break, cashier, degrade, dethrone, dismiss, displace, oust, reduce; avouch, declare, depone, testify.

deposit *vb* drop, dump, precipitate; lay, put; bank, hoard, lodge, put, save, store; commit, entrust. * *n* diluvium, dregs, lees, precipitate, precipitation, sediment, settlement, settlings, silt; money, pawn, pledge, security, stake.

depositary *n* fiduciary, guardian, trustee.

deposition *n* affidavit, evidence, testimony; deposit, precipitation, settlement; dethroning, displacement, removal.

depository *n* deposit, depot, storehouse, warehouse.

depot *n* depository, magazine, storehouse, warehouse.

depravation *n* abasement, corruption, deterioration, impairing, injury, vitiation; debasement, degeneracy, degeneration, depravity, impairment.

depraved *adj* abandoned, corrupt, corrupted, debased, debauched, degenerate, dissolute, evil, graceless, hardened, immoral, lascivious, lewd, licentious, lost, perverted, profligate, reprobate, shameless, sinful, vicious, wicked.

depravity *n* corruption, degeneracy, depravedness; baseness, contamination, corruption, corruptness, criminality, demoralization, immorality, iniquity, license, perversion, vice, viciousness, wickedness.

depreciate *vb* underestimate, undervalue, underrate; belittle, censure, decry, degrade, disparage, malign, traduce.

depreciation *n* belittling, censure, derogation, detraction, disparagement, maligning, traducing.

depredation *n* despoiling, devastation,

pilfering, pillage, plunder, rapine, robbery, spoliation, theft.

depress *vb* bow, detrude, drop, lower, reduce, sink; abase, abash, degrade, debase, disgrace, humble, humiliate; chill, damp, dampen, deject, discourage, dishearten, dispirit, sadden; deaden, lower.

depression *n* cavity, concavity, dent, dimple, dint, excavation, hollow, hollowness, indentation, pit; blues, cheerlessness, dejection, dejectedness, despondency, disconsolateness, disheartenment, dispiritedness, dole, dolefulness, downheartedness, dumps, gloom, gloominess, hypochondria, melancholy, sadness, vapours; inactivity, lowness, stagnation; abasement, debasement, degradation, humiliation.

deprivation *n* bereavement, dispossession, loss, privation, spoliation, stripping.

deprive *vb* bereave, denude, despoil, dispossess, divest, rob, strip.

depth *n* abyss, deepness, drop, profundity; extent, measure; middle, midst, stillness; astuteness, discernment, penetration, perspicacity, profoundness, profundity, sagacity, shrewdness.

deputation *n* commission, delegation; commissioners, deputies, delegates, delegation, embassies, envoys, legation.

depute *vb* accredit, appoint, authorize, charge, commission, delegate, empower, entrust.

deputy *adj* acting, assistant, vice, subordinate. * *n* agent, commissioner, delegate, envoy, factor, legate, lieutenant, proxy, representative, substitute, viceregent.

derange *vb* confound, confuse, disarrange, disconcert, disorder, displace, madden, perturb, unsettle; discompose, disconcert, disturb, perturb, ruffle, upset; craze, madden, unbalance, unhinge.

derangement *n* confusion, disarrangement, disorder, irregularity; discomposure, disturbance, perturbation; aberration, alienation, delirium, dementia, hallucination, insanity, lunacy, madness, mania.

derelict *adj* abandoned, forsaken, left, relinquished; delinquent, faithless, guilty, neglectful, negligent, unfaithful. * *n* castaway, castoff, outcast, tramp, vagrant, wreck, wretch.

dereliction *n* abandonment, desertion, relinquishement, renunciation; delinquency, failure, faithlessness, fault, neglect, negligence.

deride *vb* chaff, flout, gibe, insult, jeer, lampoon, mock, ridicule, satirize, scoff, scorn, sneer, taunt.

derision *n* contempt, disrespect, insult, laughter, mockery, ridicule, scorn.

derisive *adj* contemptuous, contumelious, mocking, ridiculing, scoffing, scornful.

derivation *n* descent, extraction, genealogy; etymology; deducing, deriving, drawing, getting, obtaining; beginning, foundation, origination, source.

derive *vb* draw, get, obtain, receive; deduce, follow, infer, trace.

derogate *vb* compromise, depreciate, detract, diminish, disparage, lessen.

derogatory *adj* belittling, depreciative, deprecatory, detracting, dishonouring, disparaging, injurious.

descant *vb* amplify, animadvert, dilate, discourse, discuss, enlarge, expatiate. * *n* melody, soprano, treble; animadversion, commentary, remarks; discourse, discussion.

descend *vb* drop, fall, pitch, plunge, sink, swoop; alight, dismount; go, pass, proceed, devolve; derive, issue, originate.

descendants *npl* offspring, issue, posterity, progeny.

descent *n* downrush, drop, fall; descending; decline, declivity, dip, pitch, slope; ancestry, derivation, extraction, genealogy, lineage, parentage, pedigree; assault, attack, foray, incursion, invasion, raid.

describe *vb* define, delineate, draw, illustrate, limn, sketch, specify, trace; detail; depict, explain, narrate, portray, recount, relate, represent; characterize.

description *n* delineation, tracing; account, depiction, explanation, narration, narrative, portrayal, recital, relation, report, representation; class, kind, sort, species.

descry *vb* behold, discover, discern, distinguish, espy, observe, perceive, see; detect, recognize.

desecrate *vb* abuse, pervert, defile, pollute, profane, violate.

desert[1] *n* due, excellence, merit, worth; punishment, reward.

desert[2] *vb* abandon, abscond, forsake, leave, quit, relinquish, renounce, resign, quit, vacate.

desert[3] *adj* barren, desolate, forsaken, lonely, solitary, uncultivated, uninhabited, unproductive, untilled, waste, wild.

deserted *adj* abandoned, forsaken, relinquished.

deserter *n* abandoner, forsaker, quitter, runaway; apostate, backslider, fugitive, recreant, renegade, revolter, traitor, turncoat.

desertion *n* abandonment, dereliction, recreancy, relinquishment.

deserve *vb* earn, gain, merit, procure, win.

desiderate *vb* desire, lack, miss, need, want.

design *vb* brew, concoct, contrive, devise, intend, invent, mean, plan, project, scheme; intend, mean, purpose; delineate, describe, draw, outline, sketch, trace. * *n* aim, device, drift, intent, intention, mark, meaning, object, plan, proposal, project, purport, purpose, scheme, scope; delineation, draught, drawing, outline, plan, sketch; adaptation, artifice, contrivance, invention, inventiveness.

designate *vb* denote, distinguish, indicate, particularize, select, show, specify, stipulate; characterize, define, describe; call, christen, denominate, dub, entitle, name, style; allot, appoint, christen.

designation *n* indication, particularization, selection, specification; class, description, kind; appellation, denomination, name, style, title.

designing *adj* artful, astute, crafty, crooked, cunning, deceitful, insidious, intriguing, Machiavellian, scheming, sly, subtle, treacherous, trickish, tricky, unscrupulous, wily.

desirable *adj* agreeable, beneficial, covetable, eligible, enviable, good, pleasing, preferable.

desire *vb* covet, crave, desiderate, fancy, hanker after, long for, lust after, want, wish, yearn for; ask, entreat, request, solicit. * *n* eroticism, lasciviousness, libidinousness, libido, lust, lustfulness, passion; eagerness, fancy, hope, inclination, mind, partiality, penchant, pleasure, volition, want, wish.

desirous *adj* avid, eager, desiring, longing, solicitous, wishful.

desist *vb* cease, discontinue, forbear, pause, stay, stop.

desolate *vb* depopulate, despoil, destroy, devastate, pillage, plunder, ravage, ruin, sack. * *adj* bare, barren, bleak, desert, forsaken, lonely, solitary, unfrequented, uninhabited, waste, wild; companionable, lonely, lonesome, solitary; desolated, destroyed, devastated, ravaged, ruined; cheerless, comfortless, companionless, disconsolate, dreary, forlorn, forsaken, miserable, wretched.

desolation *n* destruction, devastation, havoc, ravage, ruin; barrenness, bleakness, desolateness, dreariness, loneliness, solitariness, solitude, wildness; gloom, gloominess, misery, sadness, unhappiness, wretchedness.

despair *vb* despond, give up, lose hope. * *n* dejection, desperation, despondency, disheartenment, hopelessness.

despatch *see* **dispatch**.

desperado *n* daredevil, gangster, marauder, ruffian, thug, tough.

desperate *adj* despairing, despondent, desponding, hopeless; forlorn, irretrievable; extreme; audacious, daring, foolhardy, frantic, furious, headstrong, precipitate, rash, reckless, violent, wild, wretched; extreme, great, monstrous, prodigious, supreme.

desperation *n* despair, hopelessness; fury, rage.

despicable *adj* abject, base, contemptible, degrading, low, mean, paltry, pitiful, shameful, sordid, vile, worthless.

despise *vb* contemn, disdain, disregard, neglect, scorn, slight, spurn, undervalue.

despite *n* malevolence, malice, malignity, spite; contempt, contumacy, defiance. * *prep* notwithstanding.

despoil *vb* bereave, denude, deprive, dispossess, divest, strip; devastate, fleece, pillage, plunder, ravage, rifle, rob.

despond *vb* despair, give up, lose hope, mourn, sorrow.

despondency *n* blues, dejection, depression, discouragement, gloom, hopelessness, melancholy, sadness.

despondent *adj* dejected, depressed, discouraged, disheartened, dispirited, low-spirited, melancholy.

despot *n* autocrat, dictator; oppressor, tyrant.

despotic *adj* absolute, arrogant, autocratic, dictatorial, imperious; arbitrary, oppressive, tyrannical, tyrannous.

despotism *n* absolutism, autocracy, dictatorship; oppression, tyranny.

destination *n* appointment, decree, destiny, doom, fate, foreordainment, foreordination, fortune, lot, ordination, star; aim, design, drift, end, intention, object, purpose, scope; bourne, goal, harbour, haven, journey's end, resting-place, terminus.

destine *vb* allot, appoint, assign, consecrate, devote, ordain; design, intend, predetermine; decree, doom, foreordain, predestine.

destitute *adj* distressed, indigent, moneyless, necessitous, needy, penniless, penurious, pinched, poor, reduced, wanting.

destitution *n* indigence, need, penury, poverty, privation, want.

destroy *vb* demolish, overthrow, overturn, subvert, raze, ruin; annihilate, dissolve, efface, quench; desolate, devastate, devour, ravage, waste; eradicate, extinguish, extirpate, kill, uproot, slay.

destruction *n* demolition, havoc, overthrow, ruin, subversion; desolation, devastation, holocaust, ravage; annihilation, eradication, extinction, extirpation; death, massacre, murder, slaughter.

destructive *adj* baleful, baneful, deadly, deleterious, detrimental, fatal, hurtful, injurious, lethal, mischievous, noxious, pernicious, ruinous; annihilatory, eradicative, exterminative, extirpative.

desultory *adj* capricious, cursory, discursive, erratic, fitful, inconstant, inexact, irregular, loose, rambling, roving, slight, spasmodic, unconnected, unmethodical, unsettled, unsystematic, vague, wandering.

detach *vb* disengage, disconnect, disjoin, dissever, disunite, divide, part, separate, sever, unfix; appoint, detail, send.

detail *vb* delineate, depict, describe, enumerate, narrate, particularize, portray, recount, rehearse, relate, specify; appoint, detach, send. * *n* account, narration, narrative, recital, relation; appointment, detachment; item, part.

details *npl* facts, minutiae, particulars, parts.

detain *vb* arrest, check, delay, hinder, hold, keep, restrain, retain, stay, stop; confine.

detect *vb* ascertain, catch, descry, disclose, discover, expose, reveal, unmask.

detention *n* confinement, delay, hindrance, restraint, withholding.

deter *vb* debar, discourage, frighten, hinder, prevent, restrain, stop, withhold.

deteriorate *vb* corrupt, debase, degrade, deprave, disgrace, impair, spoil, vitiate; decline, degenerate, depreciate, worsen.

deterioration *n* corruption, debasement, degradation, depravation, vitiation, perversion; caducity, decadence, decay, decline, degeneracy, degeneration, impairment.

determinate *adj* absolute, certain, definite, determined, established, explicit, express, fixed, limited, positive, settled; conclusive, decided, decisive, definitive.

determination *n* ascertainment, decision, deciding, determining, fixing, settlement, settling; conclusion, judgment, purpose, resolution, resolve, result; direction, leaning, tendency; firmness, constancy, effort, endeavour, exertion, grit, persistence, stamina, resoluteness; definition, limitation, qualification.

determine *vb* adjust, conclude, decide,

end, establish, fix, resolve, settle; ascertain, certify, check, verify; impel, incline, induce, influence, lead, turn; decide, resolve; condition, define, limit; compel, necessitate.

detest *vb* abhor, abominate, despise, execrate, hate, loathe, nauseate, recoil from.

detestable *adj* abhorred, abominable, accursed, cursed, damnable, execrable, hateful, odious; disgusting, loathsome, nauseating, offensive, repulsive, sickening, vile.

dethrone *vb* depose, uncrown.

detract *vb* abuse, asperse, belittle, calumniate, debase, decry, defame, depreciate, derogate, disparage, slander, traduce, vilify; deprecate, deteriorate, diminish, lessen.

detraction *n* abuse, aspersion, calumny, censure, defamation, depreciation, derogation, disparagement, slander.

detriment *n* cost, damage, disadvantage, evil, harm, hurt, injury, loss, mischief, prejudice.

detrimental *adj* baleful, deleterious, destructive, harmful, hurtful, injurious, mischievous, pernicious, prejudicial.

devastate *vb* desolate, despoil, destroy, lay waste, harry, pillage, plunder, ravage, sack, spoil, strip, waste.

devastation *n* despoiling, destroying, harrying, pillaging, plundering, ravaging, sacking, spoiling, stripping, wasting; desolation, destruction, havoc, pillage, rapine, ravage, ruin, waste.

develop *vb* disentangle, disclose, evolve, exhibit, explicate, uncover, unfold, unravel; cultivate, grow, mature, open, progress.

development *n* disclosure, disentanglement, exhibition, unfolding, unravelling; growth, increase, maturation, maturing; evolution, growth, progression; elaboration, expansion, explication.

deviate *vb* alter, deflect, digress, diverge, sheer off, slew, tack, turn aside, wheel, wheel about; err, go astray, stray, swerve, wander; differ, vary.

deviation *n* aberration, departure, depression, divarication, divergence, turning; alteration, change, difference, variance, variation.

device *n* contraption, contrivance, gadget, invention; design, expedient, plan, project, resort, resource, scheme, shift; artifice, evasion, fraud, manoeuvre, ruse, stratagem, trick, wile; blazon, emblazonment, emblem, sign, symbol, type.

devil *n* archfiend, demon, fiend, goblin; Apollyon, Belial, Deuce, Evil One, Lucifer, Old Harry, Old Nick, Old Serpent, Prince of Darkness, Satan.

devilish *adj* demon, demonic, demonical, demoniac, demoniacal, diabolic, diabolical, fiendish, hellish, infernal, Mephistophelean, Mephistophelian, satanic; atrocious, barbarous, cruel, malevolent, malicious, malign, malignant, wicked.

devilry *n* devilment, diablerie, mischief; devilishness, fiendishness, wickedness.

devious *adj* deviating, erratic, roundabout, wandering; circuitous, confusing, crooked, labyrinthine, mazy, obscure; crooked, disingenuous, misleading, treacherous.

devise *vb* brew, compass, concert, concoct, contrive, dream up, excogitate, imagine, invent, plan, project, scheme; bequeath, demise, leave, will.

devoid *adj* bare, destitute, empty, vacant, void.

devolve *vb* alienate, consign, convey, deliver over, demise, fall, hand over, make over, pass, transfer.

devote *vb* appropriate, consecrate, dedicate, destine; set apart; addict, apply, give up, resign; consign, doom, give over.

devoted *adj* affectionate, attached, loving; ardent, assiduous, earnest, zealous.

devotee *n* bigot, enthusiast, fan, fanatic, zealot.

devotion *n* consecration, dedication, duty; devotedness, devoutness, fidelity, godliness, holiness, piety, religion, religiousness, saintliness, sanctity; adoration, prayer, worship; affection, attachment, love; ardour, devotedness, eagerness, earnestness, fervour, passion, spirit, zeal.

devotional *adj* devout, godly, pious, religious, saintly.

devour *vb* engorge, gorge, gulp down, raven, swallow eagerly, wolf; annihilate, consume, destroy, expend, spend, swallow up, waste.

devout *adj* devotional, godly, holy, pious, religious, saint-like, saintly; earnest, grave, serious, sincere, solemn.

dexterity *n* ability, address, adroitness, aptitude, aptness, art, cleverness, expertness, facility, knack, quickness, readiness, skilfulness, skill, tact.

dexterous, dextrous *adj* able, adept, adroit, apt, deft, clever, expert, facile, handy, nimble-fingered, quick, ready, skilful.

diabolic, diabolical *adj* atrocious, barbarous, cruel, devilish, fiendish, hellish, impious, infernal, malevolent, malign, malignant, satanic, wicked.

diagram *n* chart, delineation, figure, graph, map, outline, plan, sketch.

dialect *n* idiom, localism, provincialism; jargon, lingo, patois, patter; language, parlance, phraseology, speech, tongue.

dialectal *adj* idiomatic, local, provincial.

dialectic, dialectical *adj* analytical, critical, logical, rational, rationalistic.

dialogue *n* colloquy, communication, conference, conversation, converse, intercourse, interlocution; playbook, script, speech, text, words.

diaphanous *adj* clear, filmy, gossamer, pellucid, sheer, translucent, transparent.

diarrhoea *n* (*med*) flux, looseness, purging, relaxation.

diary *n* chronicle, daybook, journal, register.

diatribe *n* disputation, disquisition, dissertation; abuse, harangue, invective, philippic, reviling, tirade.

dictate *vb* bid, direct, command, decree, enjoin, ordain, order, prescribe, require. * *n* bidding, command, decree, injunction, order; maxim, precept, rule.

dictation *n* direction, order, prescription.

dictator *n* autocrat, despot, tyrant.

dictatorial *adj* absolute, unlimited, unrestricted; authoritative, despotic, dictatory, domineering, imperious, overbearing, peremptory, tyrannical.

dictatorship *n* absolutism, authoritarianism, autocracy, despotism, iron rule, totalitarianism, tyranny.

diction *n* expression, language, phraseology, style, vocabulary, wording.

dictionary *n* glossary, lexicon, thesaurus, vocabulary, wordbook; cyclopedia, encyclopedia.

dictum *n* affirmation, assertion, saying; (*law*) award, arbitrament, decision, opinion.

didactic, didactical *adj* educational, instructive, pedagogic, preceptive.

die *vb* decease, demise, depart, expire, pass on; decay, decline, fade, fade out, perish, wither; cease, disappear, vanish; faint, fall, sink.

diet[1] *vb* eat, feed, nourish; abstain, fast, regulate, slim. * *n* aliment, fare, food, nourishment, nutriment, provision, rations, regimen, subsistence, viands, victuals.

diet[2] *n* assembly, congress, convention, convocation, council, parliament.

differ *vb* deviate, diverge, vary; disagree, dissent; bicker, contend, dispute, quarrel, wrangle.

difference *n* contrariety, contrast, departure, deviation, disagreement, disparity, dissimilarity, dissimilitude, divergence, diversity, heterogeneity, inconformity, nuance, opposition, unlikeness, variation; alienation, altercation, bickering, breach, contention, contest, controversy, debate, disaccord, disagreement, disharmony, dispute, dissension, embroilment, falling out, irreconcilability, jarring, misunderstanding, quarrel, rupture, schism, strife, variance, wrangle; discrimination, distinction.

different *adj* distinct, nonidentical, separate, unlike; contradistinct, contrary, contrasted, deviating, disagreeing, discrepant, dissimilar, divergent, diverse, incompatible, incongruous, unlike, variant, various; divers, heterogeneous, manifold, many, sundry.

difficult *adj* arduous, exacting, hard, Herculean, stiff, tough, uphill; abstruse, complex, intricate, knotty, obscure, perplexing; austere, rigid, unaccommodating, uncompliant, unyielding; dainty, fastidious, squeamish.

difficulty *n* arduousness, laboriousness; bar, barrier, crux, deadlock, dilemma, embarrassment, emergency, exigency, fix, hindrance, impediment, knot, obstacle, obstruction, perplexity, pickle, pinch, predicament, stand, standstill, thwart, trial, trouble; cavil, objection; complication, controversy, difference, embarrassment, embroilment, imbroglio, misunderstanding.

diffidence *n* distrust, doubt, hesitance, hesitancy, hesitation, reluctance; bashfulness, modesty, sheepishness, shyness, timidity.

diffident *adj* distrustful, doubtful, hesitant, hesitating, reluctant; bashful, modest, over-modest, sheepish, shy, timid.

diffuse[1] *vb* circulate, disperse, disseminate, distribute, intermingle, propagate, scatter, spread, strew.

diffuse[2] *adj* broadcast, dispersed, scattered, sparse, sporadic, widespread; broad, extensive, liberal, profuse, wide; copious, loose, prolix, rambling, verbose, wordy.

diffusion *n* circulation, dispersion, dissemination, distribution, extension, propagation, spread, strewing.

diffusive *adj* expansive, permeating, wide-reaching; spreading, dispersive, disseminative, distributive, distributory.

dig *vb* channel, delve, excavate, grub, hollow out, quarry, scoop, tunnel. * *n* poke, punch, thrust.

digest[1] *vb* arrange, classify, codify, dispose, methodize, systemize, tabulate; concoct; assimilate, consider, contemplate, meditate, ponder, reflect upon, study; master; macerate, soak, steep.

digest[2] *n* code, system; abridgement, abstract, brief, breviary, compend, compendium, conspectus, epitome, summary, synopsis.

dignified *adj* august, courtly, decorous, grave, imposing, majestic, noble, stately.

dignify *vb* advance, aggrandize, elevate, ennoble, exalt, promote; adorn, grace, honour.

dignity *n* elevation, eminence, exaltation, excellence, glory, greatness, honour, place, rank, respectability, standing, station; decorum, grandeur, majesty, nobleness, stateliness; preferment; dignitary, magistrate; elevation, height.

digress *vb* depart, deviate, diverge, expatiate, wander.

digression *n* departure, deviation, divergence; episode, excursus.

dilapidate *vb* demolish, destroy, disintegrate, ruin, waste.

dilapidated *adj* decayed, ruined, run down, wasted.

dilapidation *n* decay, demolition, destruction, disintegration, disrepair, dissolution, downfall, ruin, waste.

dilate *vb* distend, enlarge, expand, extend, inflate, swell, tend, widen; amplify, descant, dwell, enlarge, expatiate.

dilation *n* amplification, bloating, distension, enlargement, expanding, expansion, spreading, swelling.

dilatory *adj* backward, behind-hand, delaying, laggard, lagging, lingering, loitering, off-putting, procrastinating, slack, slow, sluggish, tardy.

dilemma *n* difficulty, fix, plight, predicament, problem, quandary, strait.

diligence *n* activity, application, assiduity, assiduousness, attention, care, constancy, earnestness, heedfulness, industry, laboriousness, perseverance, sedulousness.

diligent *adj* active, assiduous, attentive, busy, careful, constant, earnest, hard-working, indefatigable, industrious, laborious, notable, painstaking, persevering, persistent, sedulous, tireless.

dilly-dally *vb* dally, dawdle. delay, lag, linger, loiter, saunter, trifle.

dilute *vb* attenuate, reduce, thin, weaken. * *adj* attenuated, diluted, thin, weak, wishy-washy.

dim *vb* blur, cloud, darken, dull, obscure, sully, tarnish. * *adj* cloudy, dark, dusky, faint, ill-defined, indefinite, indistinct, mysterious, obscure, shadowy; dull, obtuse; clouded, confused, darkened, faint, obscured; blurred, dulled, sullied, tarnished.

dimension *n* extension, extent, measure.

dimensions *npl* amplitude, bigness, bulk, capacity, greatness, largeness, magnitude, mass, massiveness, size, volume; measurements.

diminish *vb* abate, belittle, contract, decrease, lessen, reduce; curtail, cut, dwindle, melt, narrow, shrink, shrivel, subside, taper off, weaken.

diminution *n* abatement, abridgement, attenuation, contraction, curtailment, decrescendo, cut, decay, decrease, deduction, lessening, reduction, retrenchment, weakening.

diminutive *adj* contracted, dwarfish, little, minute, puny, pygmy, small, tiny.

din *vb* beat, boom, clamour, drum, hammer, pound, repeat, ring, thunder. * *n* bruit, clamour, clash, clatter, crash, crashing, hubbub, hullabaloo, hurly-burly, noise, outcry, racket, row, shout, uproar.

dingle *n* dale, dell, glen, vale, valley.

dingy *adj* brown, dun, dusky; bedimmed, colourless, dimmed, dulled, faded, obscure, smirched, soiled, sullied.

dint *n* blow, stroke; dent, indentation, nick, notch; force, power.

diocese *n* bishopric, charge, episcopate, jurisdiction, see.

dip *vb* douse, duck, immerse, plunge, souse; bail, ladle; dive, pitch; bend, incline, slope. * *n* decline, declivity, descent, drop, fall; concavity, depression, hole, hollow, pit, sink; bathe, dipping, ducking, sousing, swim.

diplomat *n* diplomatist, envoy, legate, minister, negotiator.

dire *adj* alarming, awful, calamitous, cruel, destructive, disastrous, dismal, dreadful, fearful, gloomy, horrible, horrid, implacable, inexorable, portentous, shocking, terrible, terrific, tremendous, woeful.

direct *vb* aim. cast, level, point, turn; advise, conduct, control, dispose, guide, govern, manage, regulate, rule; command, bid, enjoin, instruct, order; lead, show; address, superscribe. * *adj* immediate, straight, undeviating; absolute, categorical, express, plain, unambiguous; downright, earnest, frank, ingenuous, open, outspoken, sincere, straightforward, unequivocal.

direction *n* aim; tendency; bearing, course; administration, conduct, control, government, management, oversight, superintendence; guidance, lead; command, order, prescription; address, superscription.

directly *adv* absolutely, expressly, openly, unambiguously; forthwith, immediately, instantly, quickly, presently, promptly, soon, speedily.

director *n* boss, manager, superintendent; adviser, counsellor, guide, instructor, mentor, monitor.

direful *adj* awful, calamitous, dire, dreadful, fearful, gloomy, horrible, shocking, terrible, terrific, tremendous.

dirge *n* coronach, elegy, lament, monody, requiem, threnody.

dirty *vb* befoul, defile, draggle, foul, pollute, soil, sully. * *adj* begrimed. defiled, filthy, foul, mucky, nasty, soiled, unclean; clouded, cloudy, dark, dull, muddy, sullied; base, beggarly, contemptible, despicable, grovelling, low, mean, paltry, pitiful, scurvy, shabby, sneaking, squalid; disagreeable, rainy, sloppy, uncomfortable.

disability *n* disablement, disqualification, impotence, impotency, inability, incapacity, incompetence, incompetency, unfitness, weakness.

disable *vb* cripple, enfeeble, hamstring, impair, paralyse, unman, weaken; disenable, disqualify, incapacitate, unfit.

disabuse *vb* correct, undeceive.

disadvantage *n* disadvantageousness, inconvenience, unfavourableness; damage, detriment, disservice, drawback, harm, hindrance, hurt, injury, loss, prejudice.

disadvantageous *adj* inconvenient, inexpedient, unfavourable; deleterious, detrimental, harmful, hurtful, injurious, prejudicial.

disaffect *vb* alienate, disdain, dislike, disorder, estrange.
disaffected *adj* alienated, disloyal, dissatisfied, estranged.
disaffection *n* alienation, breach, disagreement, dislike, disloyalty, dissatisfaction, estrangement, repugnance, ill will, unfriendliness.
disagree *vb* deviate, differ, diverge, vary; dissent; argue, bicker, clash, debate, dispute, quarrel, wrangle.
disagreeable *adj* contrary, displeasing, distasteful, nasty, offensive, unpleasant, unpleasing, unsuitable.
disagreement *n* deviation, difference, discrepancy, dissimilarity, dissimilitude, divergence, diversity, incongruity, unlikeness; disaccord, dissent; argument, bickering, clashing, conflict, contention, dispute, dissension, disunion, disunity, jarring, misunderstanding, quarrel, strife, variance, wrangle.
disallow *vb* forbid, prohibit; disapprove, reject; deny, disavow, disclaim, dismiss, disown, repudiate.
disappear *vb* depart, fade, vanish; cease, dissolve.
disappoint *vb* baffle, balk, deceive, defeat, delude, disconcert, foil, frustrate, mortify, tantalize, thwart, vex.
disappointment *n* baffling, balk, failure, foiling, frustration, miscarriage, mortification, unfulfilment.
disapprobation *n* blame, censure, condemnation, disapproval, dislike, displeasure, reproof.
disapprove *vb* blame, censure, condemn, deprecate, dislike; disallow, reject.
disarrange *vb* agitate, confuse, derange, disallow, dishevel, dislike, dislocate, disorder, disorganize, disturb, jumble, reject, rumple, tumble, unsettle.
disarray *n* confusion, disorder; dishabille.
disaster *n* accident, adversity, blow, calamity, casualty, catastrophe, misadventure, mischance, misfortune, mishap, reverse, ruin, stroke.
disastrous *adj* adverse, calamitous, catastrophic, destructive, hapless, ill-fated, ill-starred, ruinous, unfortunate, unlucky, unpropitious, unprosperous, untoward.
disavow *vb* deny, disallow, disclaim, disown.
disband *vb* break up, disperse, scatter, separate.
disbelief *n* agnosticism, doubt, nonconviction, rejection, unbelief.
disburden *vb* alleviate, diminish, disburden, discharge, disencumber, ease, free, relieve, rid.
disbursement *n* expenditure, spending.
discard *vb* abandon, cast off, lay aside, reject; banish, break, cashier, discharge, dismiss, remove, repudiate.
discern *vb* differentiate, discriminate, distinguish, judge; behold, descry, discover, espy, notice, observe, perceive, recognize, see.
discernible *adj* detectable, discoverable, perceptible.
discerning *adj* acute, astute, clear-sighted, discriminating, discriminative, eagle-eyed, ingenious, intelligent, judicious, knowing, perspicacious, piercing, sagacious, sharp, shrewd.
discernment *n* acumen, acuteness, astuteness, brightness, cleverness, discrimination, ingenuity, insight, intelligence, judgement, penetration, perspicacity, sagacity, sharpness, shrewdness; beholding, descrying, discerning, discovery, espial, notice, perception.
discharge *vb* disburden, unburden, unload; eject, emit, excrete, expel, void; cash, liquidate, pay; absolve, acquit, clear, exonerate, free, release, relieve; cashier, discard, dismiss, sack; destroy, remove; execute, perform, fulfil, observe; annul, cancel, invalidate, nullify, rescind. * *n* disburdening, unloading; acquittal, dismissal, displacement, ejection, emission, evacuation, excretion, expulsion, vent, voiding; blast, burst, detonation, explosion, firing; execution, fulfilment, observance; annulment, clearance, liquidation, payment, satisfaction, settlement; exemption, liberation, release; flow, flux, execration.
disciple *n* catechumen, learner, pupil,

scholar, student; adherent, follower, partisan, supporter.

discipline *vb* breed, drill, educate, exercise, form, instruct, teach, train; control, govern, regulate, school; chasten, chastise, punish. * *n* culture, drill, drilling, education, exercise, instruction, training; control, government, regulation, subjection; chastisement, correction, punishment.

disclaim *vb* abandon, disallow, disown, disavow; reject, renounce, repudiate.

disclose *vb* discover, exhibit, expose, manifest, uncover; bare, betray, blab, communicate, divulge, impart, publish, reveal, show, tell, unfold, unveil, utter.

disclosure *n* betrayal, discovery, exposé, exposure, revelation, uncovering. discolour vb stain, tarnish, tinge.

discomfit *vb* beat, checkmate, conquer, defeat, overcome, overpower, overthrow, rout, subdue, vanquish, worst; abash, baffle, balk, confound, disconcert, foil, frustrate, perplex, upset.

discomfiture *n* confusion, defeat, frustration, overthrow, rout, vexation.

discomfort *n* annoyance, disquiet, distress, inquietude, malaise, trouble, uneasiness, unpleasantness, vexation.

discommode *vb* annoy, disquiet, disturb, harass, incommode, inconvenience, molest, trouble.

discompose *vb* confuse, derange, disarrange, disorder, disturb, embroil, jumble, unsettle; agitate, annoy, chafe, displease, disquiet, fret, harass, irritate, nettle, plague, provoke, ruffle, trouble, upset, vex, worry; abash, bewilder, disconcert, embarrass, fluster, perplex.

disconcert *vb* baffle, balk, contravene, defeat, disarrange, frustrate, interrupt, thwart, undo, upset; abash, agitate, bewilder, confuse, demoralize, discompose, disturb, embarrass, faze, perplex, perturb, unbalance, worry.

disconnect *vb* detach, disengage, disjoin, dissociate, disunite, separate, sever, uncouple, unlink.

disconsolate *adj* broken-hearted, cheerless, comfortless, dejected, desolate, forlorn, gloomy, heartbroken, inconsolable, melancholy, miserable, sad, sorrowful, unhappy, woeful, wretched.

discontent *n* discontentment, displeasure, dissatisfaction, inquietude, restlessness, uneasiness.

discontinuance *n* cessation, discontinuation, disjunction, disruption, intermission, interruption, separation, stop, stoppage, stopping, suspension.

discontinue *vb* cease, intermit, interrupt, quit, stop.

discord *n* contention, difference, disagreement, dissension, opposition, quarrelling, rupture, strife, variance, wrangling; cacophony, discordance, dissonance, harshness, jangle, jarring.

discordance *n* conflict, disagreement, incongruity, inconsistency, opposition, repugnance; discord, dissonance.

discordant *adj* contradictory, contrary, disagreeing, incongruous, inconsistent, opposite, repugnant; cacophonous, dissonant, harsh, inharmonious, jangling, jarring.

discount *vb* allow for, deduct, lower, rebate, reduce, subtract; disregard, ignore, overlook. * *n* abatement, drawback; allowance, deduction, rebate, reduction.

discourage *vb* abase, awe, damp, daunt, deject, depress, deject, dismay, dishearten, dispirit, frighten, intimidate; deter, dissuade, hinder; disfavour, discountenance.

discouragement *n* disheartening; dissuasion; damper, deterrent, embarrassment, hindrance, impediment, obstacle, wet blanket.

discourse *vb* expiate, hold forth, lucubrate, sermonize, speak; advise, confer, converse, parley, talk; emit, utter. * *n* address, disquisition, dissertation, homily, lecture, preachment, sermon, speech, treatise; colloquy, conversation, converse, talk.

discourteous *adj* abrupt, brusque, curt, disrespectful, ill-bred, ill-mannered, impolite, inurbane, rude, uncivil, uncourtly, ungentlemanly, unmannerly.

discourtesy *n* abruptness, brusqueness, ill-breeding, impoliteness, incivility, rudeness.

discover *vb* communicate, disclose, exhibit, impart, manifest, show, reveal, tell; ascertain, behold, discern, espy, see; descry, detect, determine, discern; contrive, invent, originate.

discredit *vb* disbelieve, doubt, question; depreciate, disgrace, dishonour, disparage, reproach. * *n* disbelief, distrust; disgrace, dishonour, disrepute, ignominy, notoriety, obloquy, odium, opprobrium, reproach, scandal.

discreditable *adj* derogatory, disgraceful, disreputable, dishonourable, ignominious, infamous, inglorious, scandalous, unworthy.

discreet *adj* careful, cautious, circumspect, considerate, discerning, heedful, judicious, prudent, sagacious, wary, wise.

discrepancy *n* contrariety, difference, disagreement, discordance, dissonance, divergence, incongruity, inconsistency, variance, variation.

discrete *adj* discontinuous, disjunct, distinct, separate; disjunctive.

discretion *n* care, carefulness, caution, circumspection, considerateness, consideration, heedfulness, judgement, judiciousness, prudence, wariness; discrimination, maturity, responsibility; choice, option, pleasure, will.

discrimination *n* difference, distinction; acumen, acuteness, discernment, insight, judgement, penetration, sagacity.

discriminatory *adj* characteristic, characterizing, discriminating, discriminative, distinctive, distinguishing.

discursive *adj* argumentative, reasoning; casual, cursory, desultory, digressive, erratic, excursive, loose, rambling, roving, wandering, wave.

discus *n* disk, quoit.

discuss *vb* agitate, argue, canvass, consider, debate, deliberate, examine, sift, ventilate.

disdain *vb* contemn, deride, despise, disregard, reject, scorn, slight, scout, spurn. * *n* arrogance, contempt, contumely, haughtiness, hauteur, scorn, sneer, superciliousness.

disdainful *adj* cavalier, contemptuous, contumelious, haughty, scornful, supercilious.

disease *n* affection, affliction, ail, ailment, complaint, disorder, distemper, illness, indisposition, infirmity, malady, sickness.

disembarrass *vb* clear, disburden, disencumber, disengage, disentangle, extricate, ease, free, release, rid.

disembodied *adj* bodiless, disincarnate, immaterial, incorporeal, spiritual, unbodied.

disembowel *vb* degut, embowel, eviscerate.

disengage *vb* clear, deliver, discharge, disembarrass, disembroil, disencumber, disentangle, extricate, liberate, release; detach, disjoin, dissociate, disunite, divide, separate; wean, withdraw.

disentangle *vb* loosen, separate, unfold, unravel, untwist; clear, detach, disconnect, disembroil, disengage, extricate, liberate, loose, unloose.

disfavour *n* disapproval, disesteem, dislike, disrespect; discredit, disregard, disrepute, unacceptableness; disservice, unkindness. **vb* disapprove, dislike, object, oppose.

disfigure *vb* blemish, deface, deform, injure, mar, spoil.

disfigurement *n* blemishing, defacement, deforming, disfiguration, injury, marring, spoiling; blemish, defect, deformity, scar, spot, stain.

disgorge *vb* belch, cast up, spew, throw up, vomit; discharge, eject; give up, relinquish, surrender, yield.

disgrace *vb* degrade, humble, humiliate; abase, debase, defame, discredit, disfavour, dishonour, disparage, reproach, stain, sully, taint, tarnish. * *n* abomination, disrepute, humiliation, ignominy, infamy, mortification, shame, scandal.

disgraceful *adj* discreditable, dishonourable, disreputable, ignominious, infamous, opprobrious, scandalous, shameful.

disguise *vb* cloak, conceal, cover, dissemble, hide, mask, muffle, screen, secrete, shroud, veil. * *n* concealment, cover, mask, veil; blind, cloak, masquerade, pretence, pretext, veneer.

disguised *adj* cloaked, masked, veiled.

disgust *vb* nauseate, sicken; abominate, detest, displease, offend, repel, repulse, revolt. * *n* disrelish, distaste, loathing, nausea; abhorrence, abomination, antipathy, aversion, detestation, dislike, repugnance, revulsion.

dish *vb* deal out, give, ladle, serve; blight, dash, frustrate, mar, ruin, spoil. * *n* bowl, plate, saucer, vessel.

dishearten *vb* cast down, damp, dampen, daunt, deject, depress, deter, discourage, dispirit.

dished *adj* baffled, balked, disappointed, disconcerted, foiled, frustrated, upset.

dishevelled *adj* disarranged, disordered, messed, tousled, tumbled, unkempt, untidy, untrimmed.

dishonest *adj* cheating, corrupt, crafty, crooked, deceitful, deceiving, deceptive, designing, faithless, false, falsehearted, fraudulent, guileful, knavish, perfidious, slippery, treacherous, unfair, unscrupulous.

dishonesty *n* deceitfulness, faithlessness, falsehood, fraud, fraudulence, fraudulency, improbity, knavery, perfidious, treachery, trickery.

dishonour *vb* abase, defame, degrade, discredit, disfavour, dishonour, disgrace, disparage, reproach, shame, taint. * *n* abasement, basement, contempt, degradation, discredit, disesteem, disfavour, disgrace, dishonour, disparagement, disrepute, ignominy, infamy, obloquy, odium, opprobrium, reproach, scandal, shame.

dishonourable *adj* discreditable, disgraceful, disreputable, ignominious, infamous, scandalous, shameful; base, false, falsehearted, shameless.

disinclination *n* alienation, antipathy, aversion, dislike, indisposition, reluctance, repugnance, unwillingness.

disinfect *vb* cleanse, deodorize, fumigate, purify, sterilize.

disingenuous *adj* artful, deceitful, dishonest, hollow, insidious, insincere, uncandid, unfair, wily.

disintegrate *vb* crumble, decompose, dissolve, disunite, pulverize, separate.

disinter *vb* dig up, disentomb, disinhume, exhume, unbury.

disinterested *adj* candid, fair, high-minded, impartial, indifferent, unbiased, unselfish, unprejudiced; generous, liberal, magnanimous.

disjoin *vb* detach, disconnect, dissever, dissociate, disunite, divide, part, separate, sever, sunder.

disjointed *adj* desultory, disconnected, incoherent, loose.

disjunction *n* disassociation, disconnection, disunion, isolation, parting, separation, severance.

dislike *vb* abominate, detest, disapprove, disrelish, hate, loathe. * *n* antagonism, antipathy, aversion, disapproval, disfavour, disgust, disinclination, displeasure, disrelish, distaste, loathing, repugnance.

dislocate *vb* disarrange, displace, disturb; disarticulate, disjoint, luxate, slip.

dislodge *vb* dismount, dispel, displace, eject, expel, oust, remove.

disloyal *adj* disaffected, faithless, false, perfidious, traitorous, treacherous, treasonable, undutiful, unfaithful, unpatriotic, untrue.

disloyalty *n* faithlessness, perfidy, treachery, treason, undutifulness, unfaithfulness.

dismal *adj* cheerless, dark, dreary, dull, gloomy, lonesome; blue, calamitous, doleful, dolorous, funereal, lugubrious, melancholy, mournful, sad, sombre, sorrowful.

dismantle *vb* divest, strip, unrig.

dismay *vb* affright, alarm, appal, daunt, discourage, dishearten, frighten, horrify, intimidate, paralyse, scare, terrify. * *n* affright, alarm, consternation, fear, fright, horror, terror.

dismember *vb* disjoint, dislimb, dislocate, mutilate; divide, separate, rend, sever.

dismiss *vb* banish, cashier, discard, discharge, disperse, reject, release, remove.

dismount *vb* alight, descend, dismantle, unhorse; dislodge, displace.

disobedient *adj* froward, noncompliant, noncomplying, obstinate, rebellious, refractory, uncomplying, undutiful, unruly, unsubmissive.

disobey *vb* infringe, transgress, violate.

disobliging *adj* ill-natured, unaccommodating, unamiable, unfriendly, unkind.

disorder *vb* confound, confuse, derange, disarrange, discompose, disorganize, disturb, unsettle, upset. * *n* confusion, derangement, disarrangement, disarray, disorganization, irregularity, jumble, litter, mess, topsy-turvy; brawl, commotion, disturbance, fight, quarrel, riot, tumult; riotousness, tumultuousness, turbulence; ail, ailment, complaint, distemper, illness, indisposition, malady, sickness.

disorderly *adj* chaotic, confused, intemperate, irregular, unmethodical, unsystematic, untidy; lawless, rebellious, riotous, tumultuous, turbulent, ungovernable, unmanageable, unruly.

disorganization *n* chaos, confusion, demoralization, derangement, disorder.

disorganize *vb* confuse, demoralize, derange, disarrange, discompose, disorder, disturb, unsettle, upset.

disown *vb* disavow, disclaim, reject, renounce, repudiate; abnegate, deny, disallow.

disparage *vb* belittle, decry, depreciate, derogate from, detract from, doubt, question, run down, underestimate, underpraise, underrate, undervalue; asperse, defame, inveigh against, reflect on, reproach, slur, speak ill of, traduce, vilify.

disparagement *n* belittlement, depreciation, derogation, detraction, underrating, undervaluing; derogation, detraction, diminution, harm, impairment, injury, lessening, prejudice, worsening; aspersion, calumny, defamation, reflection, reproach, traduction, vilification; blackening, disgrace, dispraise, indignity, reproach.

disparity *n* difference, disproportion, inequality; dissimilarity, dissimilitude, unlikeness.

dispassionate *adj* calm, collected, composed, cool, imperturbable, inexcitable, moderate, quiet, serene, sober, staid, temperate, undisturbed, unexcitable, unexcited, unimpassioned, unruffled; candid, disinterested, fair, impartial, neutral, unbiased.

dispatch, despatch *vb* assassinate, kill, murder, slaughter, slay; accelerate, conclude, dismiss, expedite, finish, forward, hasten, hurry, quicken, speed. * *n* dispatching, sending; diligence, expedition, haste, rapidity, speed; completion, conduct, doing, transaction; communication, document, instruction, letter, message, missive, report.

dispel *vb* banish, disperse, dissipate, scatter.

dispensation *n* allotment, apportioning, apportionment, dispensing, distributing, distribution; administration, stewardship; economy, plan, scheme, system; exemption, immunity, indulgence, licence, privilege.

dispense *vb* allot, apportion, assign, distribute; administer, apply, execute; absolve, excuse, exempt, exonerate, release, relieve.

disperse *vb* dispel, dissipate, dissolve, scatter, separate; diffuse, disseminate, spread; disappear, vanish.

dispirit *vb* damp, dampen, depress, deject, discourage, dishearten.

dispirited *adj* chapfallen, dejected, depressed, discouraged, disheartened, down-cast, down-hearted.

displace *vb* dislocate, mislay, misplace, move; dislodge, remove; cashier, depose, discard, discharge, dismiss, oust, replace, unseat.

display *vb* expand, extend, open, spread, unfold; exhibit, show; flaunt, parade. * *n* exhibition, manifestation, show; flourish, ostentation, pageant, parade, pomp.

displease *vb* disgruntle, disgust, disoblige, dissatisfy, offend; affront, aggravate, anger, annoy, chafe, chagrin, fret, irritate, nettle, pique, provoke, vex.

displeasure *n* disaffection, disapprobation, disapproval, dislike, dissatisfaction, distaste; anger, annoyance, indignation, irritation, pique, resentment, vexation, wrath; injury, offence.

disport *vb* caper, frisk, frolic, gambol, play, sport, wanton; amuse, beguile, cheer, divert, entertain, relax, solace.

disposal *n* arrangement, disposition; conduct, control, direction, disposure, government, management, ordering, regulation; bestowment, dispensation, distribution.

dispose *vb* arrange, distribute, marshal, group, place, range, rank, set; adjust, determine, regulate, settle; bias, incline, induce, lead, move, predispose; control, decide, regulate, rule, settle; arrange, bargain, compound; alienate, convey, demise, sell, transfer.

disposed *adj* apt, inclined, prone, ready, tending.

disposition *n* arrangement, arranging, classification, disposing, grouping, location, placing; adjustment, control, direction, disposure, disposal, management, ordering, regulation; aptitude, bent, bias, inclination, nature, predisposition, proclivity, proneness, propensity, tendency; character, constitution, humour, native, nature, temper, temperament, turn; inclination, willingness; bestowal, bestowment, dispensation, distribution.

dispossess *vb* deprive, divest, expropriate, strip; dislodge, eject, oust; disseise, disseize, evict, oust.

dispraise *n* blame, censure; discredit, disgrace, dishonour, disparagement, opprobrium, reproach, shame.

disproof *n* confutation, rebuttal, refutation.

disproportion *n* disparity, inadequacy, inequality, insufficiency, unsuitableness; incommensurateness.

disprove *vb* confute, rebel, rebut.

disputable *adj* controvertible, debatable, doubtful, questionable.

disputation *n* argumentation, controversy, debate, dispute.

disputatious *adj* argumentative, bickering, captious, caviling, contentious, dissentious, litigious, polemical, pugnacious, quarrelsome.

dispute *vb* altercate, argue, debate, litigate, question; bicker, brawl, jangle, quarrel, spar, spat, squabble, tiff, wrangle; agitate, argue, debate, ventilate; challenge, contradict, controvert, deny, impugn; contest, struggle for. * *n* controversy, debate, discussion, disputation; altercation, argument, bickering, brawl, disagreement, dissension, spat, squabble, tiff, wrangle.

disqualification *n* disability, incapitation.

disqualify *vb* disable, incapacitate, unfit; disenable, preclude, prohibit.

disquiet *vb* agitate, annoy, bother, discompose, disturb, excite, fret, harass, incommode, molest, plague, pester, trouble, vex, worry. * *n* anxiety, discomposure, disquietude, disturbance, restlessness, solicitude, trouble, uneasiness, unrest, vexation, worry.

disquisition *n* dissertation, discourse, essay, paper, thesis, treatise.

disregard *vb* contemn, despise, disdain, disobey, disparage, ignore, neglect, overlook, slight. * *n* contempt, ignoring, inattention, neglect, pretermit, oversight, slight; disesteem, disfavour, indifference.

disrelish *vb* dislike, loathe. * *n* dislike, distaste; flatness, insipidity, insipidness, nauseousness; antipathy, aversion, repugnance.

disreputable *adj* derogatory, discreditable, dishonourable, disgraceful, infamous, opprobrious, scandalous, shameful; base, contemptible, low, mean, vicious, vile, vulgar.

disrepute *n* abasement, degradation, derogation, discredit, disgrace, dishonour, ill-repute, odium.

disrespect *n* disesteem, disregard, irreverence, neglect, slight.

disrespectful *adj* discourteous, impertinent, impolite, rude, uncivil, uncourteous.

dissatisfaction *n* discontent, disquiet, inquietude, uneasiness; disapprobation, disapproval, dislike, displeasure.

dissect *vb* analyze, examine, explore, investigate, scrutinize, sift; cut apart.
dissemble *vb* cloak, conceal, cover, disguise, hide; counterfeit, dissimulate, feign, pretend.
dissembler *n* dissimulator, feigner, hypocrite, pretender, sham.
disseminate *vb* circulate, diffuse, disperse, proclaim, promulgate, propagate, publish, scatter, spread.
dissension *n* contention, difference, disagreement, discord, quarrel, strife, variance.
dissent *vb* decline, differ, disagree, refuse. * *n* difference, disagreement, nonconformity, opposition, recusancy, refusal.
dissentient *adj* disagreeing, dissenting, dissident, factious.
dissertation *n* discourse, disquisition, essay, thesis, treatise.
disservice *n* disadvantage, disfavour, harm, hurt, ill-turn, injury, mischief.
dissidence *n* disagreement, dissent, nonconformity, sectarianism.
dissimilar *adj* different, divergent, diverse, heterogeneous, unlike, various.
dissimilarity *n* dissimilitude, disparity, divergent, diversity, unlikeness, variation.
dissimulation *n* concealment, deceit, dissembling, double-dealing, duplicity, feigning, hypocrisy, pretence.
dissipate *vb* dispel, disperse, scatter; consume, expend, lavish, spend, squander, waste; disappear, vanish.
dissipation *n* dispersion, dissemination, scattering, vanishing; squandering, waste; crapulence, debauchery, dissoluteness, drunkenness, excess, profligacy.
dissociate *vb* disjoin, dissever, disunite, divide, separate, sever, sunder.
dissolute *adj* abandoned, corrupt, debauched, depraved, disorderly, dissipated, graceless, lax, lewd, licentious, loose, profligate, rakish, reprobate, shameless, vicious, wanton, wild.
dissolution *n* liquefaction, melting, solution; decomposition, putrefaction; death, disease; destruction, overthrow, ruin; termination.
dissolve *vb* liquefy, melt; disorganize, disunite, divide, loose, separate, sever; destroy, ruin; disappear, fade, scatter, vanish; crumble, decompose, disintegrate, perish.
dissonance *n* cacophony, discord, discordance, harshness, jarring; disagreement, discrepancy, incongruity, inconsistency.
dissonant *adj* discordant, grating, harsh, jangling, jarring, unharmonious; contradictory, disagreeing, discrepant, incongruous, inconsistent.
distance *vb* excel, outdo, outstrip, surpass. * *n* farness, remoteness; aloofness, coldness, frigidity, reserve, stiffness, offishness; absence, separation, space.
distant *adj* far, far-away, remote; aloof, ceremonious, cold, cool, frigid, haughty, reserved, stiff, uncordial; faint, indirect, obscure, slight.
distaste *n* disgust, disrelish; antipathy, aversion, disinclination, dislike, displeasure, dissatisfaction, repugnance.
distasteful *adj* disgusting, loathsome, nauseating, nauseous, unpalatable, unsavoury; disagreeable, displeasing, offensive, repugnant, repulsive, unpleasant.
distemper *n* ail, ailment, complaint, disease, disorder, illness, indisposition, malady, sickness.
distempered *adj* diseased, disordered; immoderate, inordinate, intemperate, unregulated.
distend *vb* bloat, dilate, enlarge, expand, increase, inflate, puff, stretch, swell, widen.
distil *vb* dribble, drip, drop; extract, separate.
distinct *adj* definite, different, discrete, disjunct, individual, separate, unconnected; clear, defined, manifest, obvious, plain, unconfused, unmistakable, well-defined.
distinction *n* discernment, discrimination, distinguishing; difference; account, celebrity, credit, eminence, fame, name, note, rank, renown, reputation, repute, respectability, superiority.
distinctive *adj* characteristic, differentiating, discriminating, distinguishing.

distinctness *n* difference, separateness; clearness, explicitness, lucidity, lucidness, perspicuity, precision.

distinguish *vb* characterize, mark; differentiate, discern, discriminate, perceive, recognize, see, single out, tell; demarcate, divide, separate; celebrate, honour, signalize.

distinguished *adj* celebrated, eminent, famous, illustrious, noted; conspicuous, extraordinary, laureate, marked, shining, superior, transcendent.

distort *vb* contort, deform, gnarl, screw, twist, warp, wrest; falsify, misrepresent, pervert.

distortion *n* contortion, deformation, deformity, twist, wryness; falsification, misrepresentation, perversion, wresting.

distract *vb* divert, draw away; bewilder, confound, confuse, derange, discompose, disconcert, disturb, embarrass, harass, madden, mystify, perplex, puzzle.

distracted *adj* crazed, crazy, deranged, frantic, furious, insane, mad, raving, wild.

distraction *n* abstraction, bewilderment, confusion, mystification, embarrassment, perplexity; agitation, commotion, discord, disorder, disturbance, division, perturbation, tumult, turmoil; aberration, alienation, delirium, derangement, frenzy, hallucination, incoherence, insanity, lunacy, madness, mania, raving, wandering.

distress *vb* afflict, annoy, grieve, harry, pain, perplex, rack, trouble; distrain, seize, take. * *n* affliction, calamity, disaster, misery, misfortune, adversity, hardship, perplexity, trial, tribulation; agony, anguish, dolour, grief, sorrow, suffering; gnawing, gripe, griping, pain, torment, torture; destitution, indigence, poverty, privation, straits, want.

distribute *vb* allocate, allot, apportion, assign, deal, dispense, divide, dole out, give, mete, partition, prorate, share; administer, arrange, assort, class, classify, dispose.

distribution *n* allocation, allotment, apportionment, assignment, assortment, dispensation, dispensing; arrangement, disposal, disposition, classification, division, dole, grouping, partition, sharing.

district *n* circuit, department, neighbourhood, province, quarter, region, section, territory, tract, ward.

distrust *vb* disbelieve, discredit, doubt, misbelieve, mistrust, question, suspect. * *n* doubt, misgiving, mistrust, question, suspicion.

distrustful *adj* doubting, dubious, suspicious.

disturb *vb* agitate, shake, stir; confuse, derange, disarrange, disorder, unsettle, upset; annoy, discompose, disconcert, disquiet, distract, fuss, incommode, molest, perturb, plague, trouble, ruffle, vex, worry; impede, interrupt, hinder.

disturbance *n* agitation, commotion, confusion, convulsion, derangement, disorder, perturbation, unsettlement; annoyance, discomposure, distraction, excitement, fuss; hindrance, interruption, molestation; brawl, commotion, disorder, excitement, fracas, hubbub, riot, rising, tumult, turmoil, uproar.

disunion *n* disconnection, disjunction, division, separation, severance; breach, feud, rupture, schism.

disunite *vb* detach, disconnect, disjoin, dissever, dissociate, divide, part, rend, separate, segregate, sever, sunder; alienate, estrange.

disuse *n* desuetude, discontinuance, disusage, neglect, nonobservance.

ditch *vb* canalize, dig, excavate, furrow, gouge, trench; abandon, discard, dump, jettison, scrap. * *n* channel, drain, fosse, moat, trench.

divagation *n* deviation, digression, rambling, roaming, straying, wandering.

divan *n* bed, chesterfield, couch, settee, sofa.

divaricate *vb* diverge, fork, part.

dive *vb* explore, fathom, penetrate, plunge, sound. * *n* drop, fall, header, plunge; bar, den, dump, joint, saloon.

diverge *vb* divide, radiate, separate; divaricate, separate; deviate, differ, disagree, vary.

divers *adj* different, manifold, many, numerous, several, sundry, various.

diverse *adj* different, differing, disagreeing, dissimilar, divergent, heterogeneous, multifarious, multiform, separate, unlike, variant, various, varying.

diversion *n* deflection, diverting; amusement, delight, distraction, enjoyment, entertainment, game, gratification, pastime, play, pleasure, recreation, sport; detour, digression.

diversity *n* difference, dissimilarity, dissimilitude, divergence, unlikeness, variation; heterogeneity, manifoldness, multifariousness, multiformity, variety.

divert *vb* deflect, distract, disturb; amuse, beguile, delight, entertain, exhilarate, give pleasure, gratify, recreate, refresh, solace.

divest *vb* denude, disrobe, strip, unclothe, undress; deprive, dispossess, strip.

divide *vb* bisect, cleave, cut, dismember, dissever, disunite, open, part, rend, segregate, separate, sever, shear, split, sunder; allocate, allot, apportion, assign, dispense, distribute, dole, mete, portion, share; compartmentalize, demarcate, partition; alienate, disunite, estrange.

divination *n* augury, divining, foretelling, incantation, magic, sooth-saying, sorcery; prediction, presage, prophecy.

divine *vb* foretell, predict, presage, prognosticate, vaticinate, prophesy; believe, conjecture, fancy, guess, suppose, surmise, suspect, think. * *adj* deiform, godlike, superhuman, supernatural; angelic, celestial, heavenly, holy, sacred, seraphic, spiritual; exalted, exalting, rapturous, supreme, transcendent. * *n* churchman, clergyman, ecclesiastic, minister, parson, pastor, priest.

division *n* compartmentalization, disconnection, disjunction, dismemberment, segmentation, separation, severance; category, class, compartment, head, parcel, portion, section, segment; demarcation, partition; alienation, allotment, apportionment, distribution; breach, difference, disagreement, discord, disunion, estrangement, feud, rupture, variance.

divorce *vb* disconnect, dissolve, disunite, part, put away, separate, sever, split up, sunder, unmarry. * *n* disjunction, dissolution, disunion, division, divorcement, parting, separation, severance.

divulge *vb* communicate, declare, disclose, discover, exhibit, expose, impart, proclaim, promulgate, publish, reveal, tell, uncover.

dizzy *adj* giddy, vertiginous; careless, heedless, thoughtless.

do *vb* accomplish, achieve, act, commit, effect, execute, perform; complete, conclude, end, finish, settle, terminate; conduct, transact; observe, perform, practice; translate, render; cook, prepare; cheat, chouse, cozen, hoax, swindle; serve, suffice. * *n* act, action, adventure, deed, doing, exploit, feat, thing; banquet, event, feast, function, party.

docile *adj* amenable, obedient, pliant, teachable, tractable, yielding.

dock[1] *vb* clip, curtail, cut, deduct, truncate; lessen, shorten.

dock[2] *vb* anchor, moor; join, meet. * *n* anchorage, basin, berth, dockage, dockyard, dry dock, harbour, haven, marina, pier, shipyard, wharf.

doctor *vb* adulterate, alter, cook, falsify, manipulate, tamper with; attend, minister to, cure, heal, remedy, treat; fix, mend, overhaul, repair, service. * *n* general practitioner, GP, healer, leech, medic, physician; adept, savant.

doctrinaire *adj* impractical, theoretical. * *n* ideologist, theorist, thinker.

doctrine *n* article, belief, creed, dogma, opinion, precept, principle, teaching, tenet.

dodge *vb* equivocate, evade, prevaricate, quibble, shuffle. * *n* artifice, cavil, evasion, quibble, subterfuge, trick.

dogged *adj* cantankerous, headstrong, inflexible, intractable, mulish, obstinate, pertinacious, perverse, resolute, stubborn, tenacious, unyielding, wilful; churlish, morose, sour, sullen, surly.

dogma *n* article, belief, creed, doctrine, opinion, precept, principle, tenet.

dogmatic *adj* authoritative, categorical,

formal, settled; arrogant, confident, dictatorial, imperious, magisterial, opinionated, oracular, overbearing, peremptory, positive; doctrinal.

dole *vb* allocate, allot, apportion, assign, deal, distribute, divide, share. * *n* allocation, allotment, apportionment, distribution; part, portion, share; alms, donation, gift, gratuity, pittance; affliction, distress, grief, sorrow, woe.

doleful *adj* lugubrious, melancholy, piteous, rueful, sad, sombre, sorrowful, woebegone, woeful; cheerless, dark, dismal, dolorous, dreary, gloomy.

dolorous *adj* cheerless, dark, dismal, gloomy; doleful, lugubrious, mournful, piteous, rueful, sad, sorrowful, woeful.

dolt *n* blockhead, booby, dullard, dunce, fool, ignoramus, simpleton.

domain *n* authority, dominion, jurisdiction, province, sway; empire, realm, territory; lands, estate; branch, department, region.

domestic *n* charwoman, help, home help, maid, servant. * *adj* domiciliary, family, home, household, private; domesticated; internal, intestine.

domesticate *vb* tame; adopt, assimilate, familiarize, naturalize.

domicile *vb* domiciliate, dwell, inhabit, live, remain, reside. * *n* abode, dwelling, habitation, harbour, home, house, residence.

dominant *adj* ascendant, ascending, chief, controlling, governing, influential, outstanding, paramount, predominant, preeminent, preponderant, presiding, prevailing, ruling.

dominate *vb* control, rule, sway; command, overlook, overtop, surmount.

domineer *vb* rule, tyrannize; bluster, bully, hector, menace, swagger, swell, threaten.

dominion *n* ascendancy, authority, command, control, domain, domination, government, jurisdiction, mastery, rule, sovereign, sovereignty, supremacy, sway; country, kingdom, realm, region, territory.

donation *n* alms, benefaction, boon, contribution, dole, donative, gift, grant, gratuity, largesse, offering, present, subscription.

done *adj* accomplished, achieved, effected, executed, performed; completed, concluded, ended, finished, terminated; carried on, transacted; rendered, translated; cooked, prepared; cheated, cozened, hoaxed, swindled; (*with* **for**) damned, dished, *hors de combat*, ruined, shelved, spoiled, wound up.

donkey *n* ass, mule; dunce, fool, simpleton.

donor *n* benefactor, bestower, giver; donator.

double *vb* fold, plait; duplicate, geminate, increase, multiply, repeat; return. * *adj* binary, coupled, geminate, paired; dual, twice, twofold; deceitful, dishonest, double-dealing, false, hollow, insincere, knavish, perfidious, treacherous, two-faced. * *adv* doubly, twice, twofold. * *n* doubling, fold, plait; artifice, manoeuvre, ruse, shift, stratagem, trick, wile; copy, counterpart, twin.

doublet *n* jacket, jerkin.

doubt *vb* demur, fluctuate, hesitate, vacillate, waver; distrust, mistrust, query, question, suspect. * *n* dubiety, dubiousness, dubitation, hesitance, hesitancy, hesitation, incertitude, indecision, irresolution, question, suspense, uncertainty, vacillation; distrust, misgiving, mistrust, scepticism, suspicion.

doubtful *adj* dubious, hesitating, sceptical, undecided, undetermined, wavering; ambiguous, dubious, enigmatical, equivocal, hazardous, obscure, problematical, unsure; indeterminate, questionable, undecided, unquestioned.

doubtless *adv* certainly, unquestionably; clearly, indisputably, precisely.

doughty *adj* adventurous, bold, brave, chivalrous, courageous, daring, dauntless, fearless, gallant, heroic, intrepid, redoubtable, valiant, valorous.

douse *see* **dowse**.

dowdy *adj* awkward, dingy, ill-dressed, shabby, slatternly, slovenly; old-fashioned, unfashionable.

dowel *n* peg, pin, pinion, tenon.

dower *n* endowment, gift; dowry; portion, share.

downcast *adj* chapfallen, crestfallen, dejected, depressed, despondent, discouraged, disheartened, dispirited, downhearted, low-spirited, sad, unhappy.

downfall *n* descent, destruction, fall, ruin.

downhearted *adj* chapfallen, crestfallen, dejected, depressed, despondent, discouraged, disheartened, dispirited, downcast, low-spirited, sad, unhappy.

downright *adj* absolute, categorical, clear, explicit, plain, positive, sheer, simple, undisguised, unequivocal, utter; aboveboard, artless, blunt, direct, frank, honest, ingenuous, open, sincere, straightforward, unceremonious.

downy *adj* lanate, lanated, lanose.

dowse, douse *vb* dip, immerse, plunge, souse, submerge.

doxy *n* mistress, paramour; courtesan, drab, harlot, prostitute, strumpet, streetwalker, whore.

doze *vb* drowse, nap, sleep, slumber. * *n* drowse, forty-winks, nap.

dozy *adj* drowsy, heavy, sleepy, sluggish.

draft *vb* detach, select; commandeer, conscript, impress; delineate, draw, outline, sketch. * *n* conscription, drawing, selection; delineation, outline, sketch; bill, cheque, order.

drag *vb* draw, haul, pull, tow, tug; trail; linger, loiter. * *n* favour, influence, pull; brake, check, curb, lag, resistance, retardation, scotch, skid, slackening, slack-off, slowing.

draggle *vb* befoul, bemire, besmirch, dangle, drabble, trail.

dragoon *vb* compel, drive, force, harass, harry, persecute. * *n* cavalier, equestrian, horse-soldier.

drain *vb* milk, sluice, tap; empty, evacuate, exhaust; dry. * *n* channel, culvert, ditch, sewer, sluice, trench, watercourse; exhaustion, withdrawal.

draught *n* current, drawing, pulling, traction; cup, dose, drench, drink, potion; delineation, design, draft, outline, sketch.

draw *vb* drag, haul, tow, tug, pull; attract; drain, suck, syphon; extract, extort; breathe in, inhale, inspire; allure, engage, entice, induce, influence, lead, move, persuade; extend, protract, stretch; delineate, depict, sketch; deduce, derive, infer; compose, draft, formulate, frame, prepare; blister, vesicate, write.

drawback *n* defect, deficiency, detriment, disadvantage, fault, flaw, imperfection, injury; abatement, allowance, deduction, discount, rebate, reduction.

drawing *n* attracting, draining, inhaling, pulling, traction; delineation, draught, outline, picture, plan, sketch.

dread *vb* apprehend, fear. * *adj* dreadful, frightful, horrible, terrible; awful, venerable. * *n* affright, alarm, apprehension, fear, terror; awe, veneration.

dreadful *adj* alarming, appalling, awesome, dire, direful, fearful, formidable, frightful, horrible, horrid, terrible, terrific, tremendous; awful, venerable.

dream *vb* fancy, imagine, think. * *n* conceit, day-dream, delusion, fancy, fantasy, hallucination, illusion, imagination, reverie, vagary, vision.

dreamer *n* enthusiast, visionary.

dreamy *adj* absent, abstracted, fanciful, ideal, misty, shadowy, speculative, unreal, visionary.

dreary *adj* cheerless, chilling, comfortless, dark, depressing, dismal, drear, gloomy, lonely, lonesome, sad, solitary, sorrowful; boring, dull, monotonous, tedious, tiresome, uninteresting, wearisome.

dregs *npl* feculence, grounds, lees, offscourings, residuum, scourings, sediment, waste; draff, dross, refuse, scum, trash.

drench *vb* dowse, drown, imbrue, saturate, soak, souse, steep, wet; physic, purge.

dress *vb* align, straighten; adjust, arrange, dispose; fit, prepare; accoutre, apparel, array, attire, clothe, robe, rig; adorn, bedeck, deck, decorate, drape, embellish, trim. * *n* apparel, attire, clothes, clothing, costume, garb, guise, garments, habiliment, habit, raiment, suit, toilet, vesture; bedizenment, bravery; frock, gown, rob.

dressing *n* compost, fertilizer, manure; forcemeat, stuffing.
dressy *adj* flashy, gaudy, showy.
driblet *n* bit, drop, fragment, morsel, piece, scrap.
drift *vb* accumulate, drive, float, wander. * *n* bearing, course, direction; aim, design, intent, intention, mark, object, proposal, purpose, scope, tendency; detritus, deposit, diluvium; gallery, passage, tunnel; current, rush, sweep; heap, pile.
drill[1] *vb* bore, perforate, pierce; discipline, exercise, instruct, teach, train. * *n* borer; discipline, exercise, training.
drill[2] *n* channel, furrow, trench.
drink *vb* imbibe, sip, swill; carouse, indulge, revel, tipple, tope; swallow, quaff; absorb. * *n* beverage, draught, liquid, potation, potion; dram, nip, sip, snifter, refreshment.
drip *vb* dribble, drop, leak, trickle; distil, filter, percolate; ooze, reek, seep, weep. * *n* dribble, drippings, drop, leak, leakage, leaking, trickle, tricklet; bore, nuisance, wet blanket.
drive *vb* hurl, impel, propel, send, shoot, thrust; actuate, incite, press, urge; coerce, compel, constrain, force, harass, oblige, overburden, press, rush; go, guide, ride, travel; aim, intend. * *n* effort, energy, pressure; airing, ride; road.
drivel *vb* babble, blether, dote, drool, slaver, slobber. * *n* balderdash, drivelling, fatuity, nonsense, prating, rubbish, slaver, stuff, twaddle.
drizzle *vb* mizzle, rain, shower, sprinkle. * *n* haar, mist, mizzle, rain, sprinkling.
droll *adj* comic, comical, farcical, funny, jocular, ludicrous, laughable, ridiculous; amusing, diverting, facetious, odd, quaint, queer, waggish. * *n* buffoon, clown, comedian, fool, harlequin, jester, punch, Punchinello, scaramouch, wag, zany.
drollery *n* archness, buffoonery, fun, humour, jocularity, pleasantry, waggishness, whimsicality.
drone *vb* dawdle, drawl, idle, loaf, lounge; hum. * *n* idler, loafer, lounger, sluggard.
drool *vb* drivel, slaver.
droop *vb* fade, wilt, wither; decline, fail, faint, flag, languish, sink, weaken; bend, hang.
drop *vb* distil, drip, shed; decline, depress, descend, dump, lower, sink; abandon, desert, forsake, forswear, leave, omit, relinquish, quit; cease, discontinue, intermit, remit; fall, precipitate. * *n* bead, droplet, globule; earring, pendant.
dross *n* cinder, lees, recrement, scoria, scum, slag; refuse, waste.
drought *n* aridity, drouth, dryness, thirstiness.
drove *n* flock, herd; collection, company, crowd.
drown *vb* deluge, engulf, flood, immerse, inundate, overflow, sink, submerge, swamp; overcome, overpower, overwhelm.
drowse *vb* doze, nap, sleep, slumber, snooze. * *n* doze, forty winks, nap, siesta, sleep, snooze.
drowsy *adj* dozy, sleepy; comatose, lethargic, stupid; lulling, soporific.
drub *vb* bang, beat, cane, cudgel, flog, hit, knock, pommel, pound, strike, thrash, thump, whack.
drubbing *n* beating, caning, cudgelling, flagellation, flogging, pommelling, pounding, thrashing, thumping, whacking.
drudge *vb* grub, grind, plod, slave, toil, work. * *n* grind, hack, hard worker, menial, plodder, scullion, servant, slave, toiler, worker.
drug *vb* dose, medicate; disgust, surfeit. * *n* medicine, physic, remedy; poison.
drunk *adj* boozed, drunken, inebriated, intoxicated, maudlin, soaked, tipsy; ablaze, aflame, delirious, fervent, suffused. * *n* alcoholic, boozer, dipsomaniac, drunkard, inebriate, lush, soak; bacchanal, bender, binge.
drunkard *n* alcoholic, boozer, carouser, dipsomaniac, drinker, drunk, inebriate, reveller, sot, tippler, toper.
dry *vb* dehydrate, desiccate, drain, exsiccate, parch. * *adj* desiccated, dried, juiceless, sapless, unmoistened; arid, droughty, parched; drouthy, thirsty; bar-

ren, dull, insipid, jejune, plain, pointless, tame, tedious, tiresome, unembellished, uninteresting, vapid; cutting, keen, sarcastic, severe, sharp, sly.

dub *vb* call, christen, denominate, designate, entitle, name, style, term.

dubious *adj* doubtful, fluctuating, hesitant, irresolute, skeptical, uncertain, undecided, unsettled, wavering; ambiguous, doubtful, equivocal, improbable, questionable, uncertain.

duck *vb* dip, dive, immerse, plunge, submerge, souse; bend, bow, dodge, stoop.

duct *n* canal, channel, conduit, pipe, tube; blood-vessel.

ductile *adj* compliant, docile, facile, tractable, yielding; flexible, malleable, pliant; extensible, tensile.

dudgeon *n* anger, indignation, ill will, ire, malice, resentment, umbrage, wrath.

due *adj* owed, owing; appropriate, becoming, befitting, bounden, fit, proper, suitable, right. * *adv* dead, direct, directly, exactly, just, right, squarely, straight. * *n* claim, debt, desert, right.

dulcet *adj* delicious, honeyed, luscious, sweet; harmonious, melodious; agreeable, charming, delightful, pleasant, pleasing.

dull *vb* blunt; benumb, besot, deaden, hebetate, obtund, paralyse, stupefy; dampen, deject, depress, discourage, dishearten, dispirit; allay, alleviate, assuage, mitigate, moderate, quiet, soften; deaden, dim, sully, tarnish. * *adj* blockish, brutish, doltish, obtuse, stolid, stupid, unintelligent; apathetic, callous, dead, insensible, passionless, phlegmatic, unfeeling, unimpassioned, unresponsive; heavy, inactive, inanimate, inert, languish, lifeless, slow, sluggish, torpid; blunt, dulled, hebetate, obtuse; cheerless, dismal, dreary, gloomy, sad, sombre; dim, lack-lustre, lustreless, matt, obscure, opaque, tarnished; dry, flat, insipid, irksome, jejune, prosy, tedious, tiresome, uninteresting, wearisome.

duly *adv* befittingly, decorously, fitly, properly, rightly; regularly.

dumb *adj* inarticulate, mute, silent, soundless, speechless, voiceless.

dumbfound, dumfound *vb* amaze, astonish, astound, bewilder, confound, confuse, nonplus, pose.

dumps *npl* blues, dejection, depression, despondency, gloom, gloominess, melancholy, sadness.

dun[1] *adj* greyish-brown, brown, drab.

dun[2] *vb* beset, importune, press, urge.

dunce *n* ass, block, blockhead, clodpole, dolt, donkey, dullard, dunderhead, fool, goose, halfwit, ignoramus, jackass, lackwit, loon, nincompoop, numskull, oaf, simpleton, thickhead, witling.

dupe *vb* beguile, cheat, chouse, circumvent, cozen, deceive, delude, gull, hoodwink, outwit, overreach, swindle, trick. * *n* gull, simpleton.

duplicate *vb* copy, double, repeat, replicate, reproduce. * *adj* doubled, twofold. * *n* copy, counterpart, facsimile, replica, transcript.

duplicity *n* artifice, chicanery, circumvention, deceit, deception, dishonesty, dissimulation, double-dealing, falseness, fraud, guile, hypocrisy, perfidy.

durable *adj* abiding, constant, continuing, enduring, firm, lasting, permanent, persistent, stable.

duration *n* continuance, continuation, permanency, perpetuation, prolongation; period, time.

duress *n* captivity, confinement, constraint, durance, hardship, imprisonment, restraint; compulsion.

dusky *adj* cloudy, darkish, dim, murky, obscure, overcast, shady, shadowy; dark, swarthy, tawny.

dutiful *adj* duteous, obedient, submissive; deferential, respectful, reverential.

duty *n* allegiance, devoirs, obligation, responsibility, reverence; business, engagement, function, office, service; custom, excise, impost, tariff, tax, toll.

dwarf *vb* lower, stunt. * *n* bantam, homunculus, manikin, midget, pygmy.

dwarfish *adj* diminutive, dwarfed, little, low, pygmy, small, stunted, tiny, undersized.

dwell *vb* abide, inhabit, live, lodge, remain, reside, rest, sojourn, stay, stop, tarry, tenant.

dwelling *n* abode, cot, domicile, dugout, establishment, habitation, home, house, hutch, lodging, mansion, quarters, residence.

dwindle *vb* decrease, diminish, lessen, shrink; decay, decline, deteriorate, pine, sink, waste away.

dye *vb* colour, stain, tinge. * *n* cast, colour, hue, shade, stain, tinge, tint.

dying *adj* expiring; mortal, perishable. * *n* death, decease, demise, departure, dissolution, exit.

dynasty *n* dominion, empire, government, rule, sovereignty.

dyspepsia *n* indigestion.

E

eager *adj* agog, avid, anxious, desirous, fain, greedy, impatient, keen, longing, yearning; animated, ardent, earnest, enthusiastic, fervent, fervid, forward, glowing, hot, impetuous, sanguine, vehement, zealous.

eagerness *n* ardour, avidity, earnestness, enthusiasm, fervour, greediness, heartiness, hunger, impatience, impetuosity, intentness, keenness, longing, thirst, vehemence, yearning, zeal.

eagle-eyed *adj* discerning, hawk-eyed, sharp-sighted.

ear[1] *n* attention, hearing, heed, regard.

ear[2] *n* head, spike.

early *adj* opportune, seasonable, timely; forward, premature; dawning, matutinal. * *adv* anon, beforehand, betimes, ere, seasonably, shortly, soon.

earn *vb* acquire, gain, get, obtain, procure, realize, reap, win; deserve, merit.

earnest *adj* animated, ardent, eager, cordial, fervent, fervid, glowing, hearty, impassioned, importune, warm, zealous; fixed, intent, steady; sincere, true, truthful; important, momentous, serious, weighty. * *n* reality, seriousness, truth; foretaste, pledge, promise; handsel, payment.

earnings *npl* allowance, emoluments, gains, income, pay, proceeds, profits, remuneration, reward, salary, stipend.

earth *n* globe, orb, planet, world; clay, clod, dirt, glebe, ground, humus, land, loam, sod, soil, turf; mankind, world.

earthborn *adj* abject, base, earthly, grovelling, low, mean, unspiritual.

earthly *adj* terrestrial; base, carnal, earthborn, low, gross, grovelling, sensual, sordid, unspiritual, worldly; bodily, material, mundane, natural, secular, temporal.

earthy *adj* clayey, earth-like, terrene; earthly, terrestrial; coarse, gross, material, unrefined.

ease *vb* disburden, disencumber, pacify, quiet, relieve, still; abate, allay, alleviate, appease, assuage, diminish, mitigate, soothe; loosen, release; facilitate, favour. * *n* leisure, quiescence, repose, rest; calmness, content, contentment, enjoyment, happiness, peace, quiet, quietness, quietude, relief, repose, satisfaction, serenity, tranquillity; easiness, facility, readiness; flexibility, freedom, liberty, lightness, naturalness, unconcern, unconstraint; comfort, elbowroom.

easy *adj* light; careless, comfortable, contented, effortless, painless, quiet, satisfied, tranquil, untroubled; accommodating, complaisant, compliant, complying, facile, indolent, manageable, pliant, submissive, tractable, yielding; graceful, informal, natural, unconstrained; flowing, ready, smooth, unaffected; gentle, lenient, mild, moderate; affluent, loose, unconcerned, unembarrassed.

eat *vb* chew, consume, devour, engorge, ingest, ravage, swallow; corrode, demolish, erode; breakfast, dine, feed, lunch, sup.

eatable *adj* edible, esculent, harmless, wholesome.

ebb *vb* abate, recede, retire, subside; decay, decline, decrease, degenerate, deteriorate, sink, wane. * *n* refluence, reflux, regress, regression, retrocedence, retrocession, retrogression, return; caducity, decay, decline, degeneration, deterioration, wane, waning; abatement, decrease, decrement, diminution.

ebullience *n* ebullition, effervescence; burst, bursting, overenthusiasm, overflow, rush, vigour.

ebullition *n* boiling, bubbling; effervescence, fermentation; burst, fit, outbreak, outburst, paroxysm.
eccentric *adj* decentred, parabolic; aberrant, abnormal, anomalous, cranky, erratic, fantastic, irregular, odd, outlandish, peculiar, singular, strange, uncommon, unnatural, wayward, whimsical. * *n* crank, curiosity, original.
eccentricity *n* ellipticity, flattening, flatness, oblateness; aberration, irregularity, oddity, oddness, peculiarity, singularity, strangeness, waywardness.
ecclesiastic[1], **ecclesiastical** *adj* churchish, churchly, clerical, ministerial, nonsecular, pastoral, priestly, religious, sacerdotal.
ecclesiastic[2] *n* chaplain, churchman, clergyman, cleric, clerk, divine, minister, parson, pastor, priest, reverend, shepherd.
echo *vb* reply, resound, reverberate, ring; re-echo, repeat. * *n* answer, repetition, reverberation; imitation.
éclat *n* acclamation, applause, brilliancy, effect, glory, lustre, pomp, renown, show, splendour.
eclipse *vb* cloud, darken, dim, obscure, overshadow, veil; annihilate, annul, blot out, extinguish. * *n* clouding, concealment, darkening, dimming, disappearance, hiding, obscuration, occultation, shrouding, vanishing, veiling; annihilation, blotting out, destruction, extinction, extinguishment, obliteration.
eclogue *n* bucolic, idyl, pastoral.
economize *vb* husband, manage, save; retrench.
economy *n* frugality, husbandry, parsimony, providence, retrenchment, saving, skimping, stinginess, thrift, thriftiness; administration, arrangement, management, method, order, plan, regulation, system; dispensation.
ecstasy *n* frenzy, madness, paroxysm, trance; delight, gladness, joy, rhapsody, rapture, ravishment, transport.
eddy *vb* gurgle, surge, spin, swirl, whirl. * *n* countercurrent; swirl, vortex, whirlpool.
edge *vb* sharpen; border, fringe, rim. * *n* border, brim, brink, bound, crest, fringe, hem, lip, margin, rim, verge; animation, intensity, interest, keenness, sharpness, zest; acrimony, bitterness, gall, sharpness, sting.
edging *n* border, frill, fringe, trimming.
edible *adj* eatable, esculent, harmless, wholesome.
edict *n* act, command, constitution, decision, decree, law, mandate, manifesto, notice, order, ordinance, proclamation, regulation, rescript, statute.
edifice *n* building, fabric, habitation, house, structure.
edify *vb* educate, elevate, enlightenment, improve, inform, instruct, nurture, teach, upbuild.
edition *n* impression, issue, number.
educate *vb* breed, cultivate, develop, discipline, drill, edify, exercise, indoctrinate, inform, instruct, mature, nurture, rear, school, teach, train.
educated *adj* cultured, lettered, literate.
education *n* breeding, cultivation, culture, development, discipline, drilling, indoctrination, instruction, nurture, pedagogics, schooling, teaching, training, tuition.
educe *vb* bring out, draw out, elicit, evolve, extract.
eerie *adj* awesome, fearful, frightening, strange, uncanny, weird.
efface *vb* blot, blot out, cancel, delete, destroy, erase, expunge, obliterate, remove, sponge.
effect *vb* cause, create, effectuate, produce; accomplish, achieve, carry, compass, complete, conclude, consummate, contrive, do, execute, force, negotiate, perform, realize, work. * *n* consequence, event, fruit, issue, outcome, result; efficiency, fact, force, power, reality; validity, weight; drift, import, intent, meaning, purport, significance, tenor.
effective *adj* able, active, adequate, competent, convincing, effectual, sufficient; cogent, efficacious, energetic, forcible, potent, powerful.
effects *npl* chattels, furniture, goods, movables, property.

effectual *adj* operative, successful; active, effective, efficacious, efficient.
effectuate *vb* accomplish, achieve, complete, do, effect, execute, fulfil, perform, secure.
effeminate *adj* delicate, feminine, soft, tender, timorous, unmanly, womanish, womanlike, womanly; camp.
effervesce *vb* bubble, ferment, foam, froth.
effete *adj* addle, barren, fruitless, sterile, unfruitful, unproductive, unprolific; decayed, exhausted, spent, wasted.
efficacious *adj* active, adequate, competent, effective, effectual, efficient, energetic, operative, powerful.
efficacy *n* ability, competency, effectiveness, efficiency, energy, force, potency, power, strength, vigour, virtue.
efficient *adj* active, capable, competent, effective, effectual, efficacious, operative, potent; able, energetic, ready, skilful.
effigy *n* figure, image, likeness, portrait, representation, statue.
effloresce *vb* bloom, flower.
efflorescence *n* blooming, blossoming, flowering.
effluence *n* discharge, efflux, effluvium, emanation, emission, flow, outflow, outpouring.
effort *n* application, attempt, endeavour, essay, exertion, pains, spurt, strain, strife, stretch, struggle, trial, trouble.
effrontery *n* assurance, audacity, boldness, brass, disrespect, hardihood, impudence, incivility, insolence, presumption, rudeness, sauciness, shamelessness.
effulgent *adj* burning, beaming, blazing, bright, brilliant, dazzling, flaming, glowing, lustrous, radiant, refulgent, resplendent, shining, splendid.
effusion *n* discharge, efflux, emission, gush, outpouring; shedding, spilling, waste; address, speech, talk, utterance.
egg *vb* (*with* **on**) encourage, incite, instigate, push, stimulate, urge; harass, harry, provoke.
ego *n* id, self, me, subject, superego.
egotism *n* self-admiration, self-assertion, self-commendation, self-conceit, self-esteem, self-importance, self-praise; egoism, selfishness.
egotistic, egotistical *adj* bumptious, conceited, egoistical, opinionated, self-asserting, self-admiring, self-centred, self-conceited, self-important, self-loving, vain.
egregious *adj* conspicuous, enormous, extraordinary, flagrant, great, gross, huge, monstrous, outrageous, prodigious, remarkable, tremendous.
egress *n* departure, emergence, exit, outlet, way out.
eject *vb* belch, discharge, disgorge, emit, evacuate, puke, spew, spit, spout, spurt, void, vomit; bounce, cashier, discharge, dismiss, disposes, eliminate, evict, expel, fire, oust; banish, reject, throw out.
elaborate *vb* develop, improve, mature, produce, refine, ripen. * *adj* complicated, decorated, detailed, dressy, laboured, laborious, ornate, perfected, studied.
elapse *vb* go, lapse, pass.
elastic *adj* rebounding, recoiling, resilient, springy; buoyant, recuperative.
elated *adj* animated, cheered, elate, elevated, excited, exhilarated, exultant, flushed, puffed up, roused.
elbow *vb* crowd, force, hustle, jostle, nudge, push, shoulder. * *n* angle, bend, corner, flexure, joining, turn.
elder *adj* older, senior; ranking; ancient, earlier, older. * *n* ancestor, senior; presbyter, prior, senator.
elect *vb* appoint, choose, cull, designate, pick, prefer, select. * *adj* choice, chosen, picked, selected; appointed, elected; predestinated, redeemed.
election *n* appointment, choice, preference, selection; alternative, freedom, freewill, liberty; predestination.
elector *n* chooser, constituent, selector, voter.
electrify *vb* charge, galvanize; astonish, enchant, excite, rouse, startle, stir, thrill.
elegance, elegancy *n* beauty, grace, propriety, symmetry; courtliness, daintiness, gentility, nicety, polish, politeness, refinement, taste.
elegant *adj* beautiful, chaste, classical,

dainty, graceful, fine, handsome, neat, symmetrical, tasteful, trim, well-made, well-proportioned; accomplished, courtly, cultivated, fashionable, genteel, polished, polite, refined.

elegiac *adj* dirgeful, mournful, plaintive, sorrowful.

elegy *n* dirge, epicedium, lament, ode, threnody.

element *n* basis, component, constituent, factor, germ, ingredient, part, principle, rudiment, unit; environment, milieu, sphere.

elementary *adj* primordial, simple, uncombined, uncomplicated, uncompounded; basic, component, fundamental, initial, primary, rudimental, rudimentary.

elevate *vb* erect, hoist, lift, raise; advance, aggrandize, exalt, promote; dignify, ennoble, exalt, greaten, improve, refine; animate, cheer, elate, excite, exhilarate, rouse.

elfin *adj* elflike, elvish, mischievous, weird.

elicit *vb* draw out, educe, evoke, extort, fetch, obtain, pump, wrest, wring; deduce, educe.

eligible *adj* desirable, preferable; qualified, suitable, worthy.

eliminate *vb* disengage, eradicate, exclude, expel, remove, separate; ignore, omit, reject.

ellipsis *n* gap, hiatus, lacuna, omission.

elliptical *adj* oval; defective, incomplete.

elocution *n* declamation, delivery, oratory, rhetoric, speech, utterance.

elongate *vb* draw, draw out, extend, lengthen, protract, stretch.

elope *vb* abscond, bolt, decamp, disappear, leave.

eloquence *n* fluency, oratory, rhetoric.

else *adv* besides, differently, otherwise.

elucidate *vb* clarify, demonstrate, explain, expound, illuminate, illustrate, interpret, unfold.

elucidation *n* annotation, clarification, comment, commentary, elucidating, explaining, explanation, exposition, gloss, scholium.

elude *vb* avoid, escape, evade, shun, slip; baffle, balk, disappoint, disconcert, escape, foil, frustrate, thwart.

elusive *adj* deceptive, deceitful, delusive, evasive, fallacious, fraudulent, illusory; equivocatory, equivocating, shuffling.

Elysian *adj* blissful, celestial, delightful, enchanting, heavenly, ravishing, seraphic.

emaciation *n* attenuation, lankness, leanness, meagreness, tabes, tabescence, thinness.

emanate *vb* arise, come, emerge, flow, issue, originate, proceed, spring.

emancipate *vb* deliver, discharge, disenthral, enfranchise, free, liberate, manumit, release, unchain, unfetter, unshackle.

emancipation *n* deliverance, enfranchisement, deliverance, freedom, liberation, manumission, release.

emasculate *vb* castrate, geld; debilitate, effeminize, enervate, unman, weaken.

embalm *vb* cherish, consecrate, conserve, enshrine, preserve, store, treasure; perfume, scent.

embargo *vb* ban, bar, blockade, debar, exclude, prohibit, proscribe, restrict, stop, withhold. * *n* ban, bar, blockade, exclusion, hindrance, impediment, prohibition, prohibitory, proscription, restraint, restriction, stoppage.

embark *vb* engage, enlist.

embarrass *vb* beset, entangle, perplex; annoy, clog, bother, distress, hamper, harass, involve, plague, trouble, vex; abash, confound, confuse, discomfit, disconcert, dumbfound, mortify, nonplus, pose, shame.

embellish *vb* adorn, beautify, bedeck, deck, decorate, emblazon, enhance, enrich, garnish, grace, ornament.

embellishment *n* adornment, decoration, enrichment, ornament, ornamentation.

embezzle *vb* appropriate, defalcate, filch, misappropriate, peculate, pilfer, purloin, steal.

embitter *vb* aggravate, envenom, exacerbate; anger, enrage, exasperate, madden.

emblem *n* badge, cognizance, device,

mark, representation, sign, symbol, token, type.

embody *vb* combine, compact, concentrate, incorporate; comprehend, comprise, contain, embrace, include; codify, methodize, systematize.

embolden *vb* animate, cheer, elate, encourage, gladden, hearten, inspirit, nerve, reassure.

embosom *vb* bury, cherish, clasp, conceal, enfold, envelop, enwrap, foster, hide, nurse, surround.

embrace *vb* clasp; accept, seize, welcome; comprehend, comprise, contain, cover, embody, encircle, enclose, encompass, enfold, hold, include. * *n* clasp, fold, hug.

embroil *vb* commingle, encumber, ensnarl, entangle, implicate, involve; confuse, discompose, disorder, distract, disturb, perplex, trouble.

embryo *n* beginning, germ, nucleus, root, rudiment.

embryonic *adj* incipient, rudimentary, undeveloped.

emendation *n* amendment, correction, improvement, rectification.

emerge *vb* rise; emanate, escape, issue; appear, arise, outcrop.

emergency *n* crisis, difficulty, dilemma, exigency, extremity, necessity, pass, pinch, push, strait, urgency; conjuncture, crisis, juncture, pass.

emigration *n* departure, exodus, migration, removal.

eminence *n* elevation, hill, projection, prominence, protuberance; celebrity, conspicuousness, distinction, exaltation, fame, loftiness, note, preferment, reputation, repute, renown.

eminent *adj* elevated, high, lofty; celebrated, conspicuous, distinguished, exalted, famous, illustrious, notable, prominent, remarkable, renowned.

emissary *n* messenger, scout, secret agent, spy.

emit *vb* breathe out, dart, discharge, eject, emanate, exhale, gust, hurl, jet, outpour, shed, shoot, spurt, squirt.

emollient *adj* relaxing, softening. soothing. * *n* softener.

emolument *n* compensation, gain, hire, income, lucre, pay, pecuniary, profits, salary, stipend, wages; advantage, benefit, profit, perquisites.

emotion *n* agitation, excitement, feeling, passion, perturbation, sentiment, sympathy, trepidation.

emphasis *n* accent, stress; force, importance, impressiveness, moment, significance, weight.

emphatic *adj* decided, distinct, earnest, energetic, expressive, forcible, impressive, intensive, positive, significant, strong, unequivocal.

empire *n* domain, dominion, sovereignty, supremacy; authority, command, control, government, rule, sway.

empirical, empiric *adj* experimental, experiential; hypothetical, provisional, tentative; charlatanic, quackish.

employ *vb* busy, devote, engage, engross, enlist, exercise, occupy, retain; apply, commission, use. * *n* employment, service.

employee *n* agent, clerk, employee, hand, servant, workman.

employment *n* avocation, business, calling, craft, employ, engagement, occupation, profession, pursuit, trade, vocation, work.

emporium *n* market, mart, shop, store.

empower *vb* authorize, commission, permit, qualify, sanction, warrant; enable.

empty *vb* deplete, drain, evacuate, exhaust; discharge, disembogue; flow, embogue. * *adj* blank, hollow, unoccupied, vacant, vacuous, void; deplete, destitute, devoid, hungry; unfilled, unfurnished, unsupplied; unsatisfactory, unsatisfying, unsubstantial, useless, vain; clear, deserted, desolate, exhausted, free, unburdened, unloaded, waste; foolish, frivolous, inane, senseless, silly, stupid, trivial, weak.

empyrean, empyreal *adj* aerial, airy, ethereal, heavenly, refined, sublimated, sublimed.

emulation *n* competition, rivalry, strife, vying; contention, envy, jealousy.

enable *vb* authorize, capacitate, commission, empower, fit, permit, prepare, qualify, sanction, warrant.

enact *vb* authorize, command, decree, establish, legislate, ordain, order, sanction; act, perform, personate, play, represent.

enactment *n* act, decree, law, edict, ordinance.

enamour *vb* bewitch, captivate, charm, enchant, endear, fascinate.

enchain *vb* bind, confine, enslave, fetter, hold, manacle, restrain, shackle.

enchant *vb* beguile, bewitch, charm, delude, fascinate; captivate, catch, enamour, win; beatify, delight, enrapture, rapture, ravish, transport.

enchanting *adj* bewitching, blissful, captivating, charming, delightful, enrapturing, fascinating, rapturous, ravishing.

enchantment *n* charm, conjuration, incantation, magic, necromancy, sorcery, spell, witchery; bliss, delight, fascination, rapture, ravishment, transport.

encase *vb* encircle, enclose, incase, infix, set; chase, emboss, engrave, inlay, ornament.

encage *vb* confine, coop up, impound, imprison, shut up.

encircle *vb* belt, circumscribe, encompass, enclose, engird, enring, environ, gird, ring, span, surround, twine; clasp, embrace, enfold, fold.

enclose, inclose *vb* circumscribe, corral, coop, embosom, encircle, encompass, environ, fence in, hedge, include, pen, shut in, surround; box, cover, encase, envelop, wrap.

encomium *n* applause, commendation, eulogy, laudation, panegyric, praise.

encompass *vb* belt, compass, encircle, enclose, engird, environ, gird, surround; beset, besiege, hem in, include, invest, surround.

encounter *vb* confront, face, meet; attack, combat, contend, engage, strive, struggle. * *n* assault, attack, clash, collision, meeting, onset; action, affair, battle, brush, combat, conflict, contest, dispute, engagement, skirmish.

encourage *vb* animate, assure, cheer, comfort, console, embolden, enhearten, fortify, hearten, incite, inspirit, instigate, reassure, stimulate, strengthen; abet, aid, advance, approve, countenance, favour, foster, further, help, patronize, promote, support.

encroach *vb* infringe, invade, intrude, tench, trespass, usurp.

encumber *vb* burden, clog, hamper, hinder, impede, load, obstruct, overload, oppress, retard; complicate, embarrass, entangle, involve, perplex.

encumbrance *n* burden, clog, deadweight, drag, embarrassment, hampering, hindrance, impediment, incubus, load; claim, debt, liability, lien.

end *vb* abolish, close, conclude, discontinue, dissolve, drop, finish, stop, terminate; annihilate, destroy, kill; cease, terminate. * *n* extremity, tip; cessation, close, denouement, ending, expiration, finale, finis, finish, last, period, stoppage, wind-up; completion, conclusion, consummation; annihilation, catastrophe, destruction, dissolution; bound, limit, termination, terminus; consequence, event, issue, result, settlement, sequel, upshot; fragment, remnant, scrap, stub, tag, tail; aim, design, goal, intent, intention, object, objective, purpose.

endanger *vb* compromise, hazard, imperil, jeopardize, peril, risk.

endear *vb* attach, bind, captivate, charm, win.

endearment *n* attachment, fondness, love, tenderness; caress, blandishment, fondling.

endeavour *vb* aim, attempt, essay, labour, seek, strive, struggle, study, try. * *n* aim, attempt, conatus, effort, essay, exertion, trial, struggle, trial.

endless *adj* boundless, illimitable, immeasurable, indeterminable, infinite, interminable, limitless, unlimited; dateless, eternal, everlasting, never-ending, perpetual, unending; deathless, ever-enduring, ever-living, immortal, imperishable, undying.

endorse, indorse *vb* approve, back, confirm, guarantee, ratify, sanction, superscribe, support, visé, vouch for, warrant; superscribe.

endow *vb* bequeath, clothe, confer, dower, endue, enrich, gift, indue, invest, supply.

endowment *n* bequest, boon, bounty, gift, grant, largesse, present; foundation, fund, property, revenue; ability, aptitude, capability, capacity, faculty, genius, gift, parts, power, qualification, quality, talent.

endurance *n* abiding, bearing, sufferance, suffering, tolerance, toleration; backbone, bottom, forbearance, fortitude, guts, patience, resignation.

endure *vb* bear, support, sustain; experience, suffer, undergo, weather; abide, brook, permit, pocket, swallow, tolerate, stomach, submit, withstand; continue, last, persist, remain, wear.

enemy *n* adversary, foe; antagonist, foeman, opponent, rival.

energetic *adj* active, effective, efficacious, emphatic, enterprising, forceful, forcible, hearty, mettlesome, potent, powerful, strenuous, strong, vigorous.

energy *n* activity, dash, drive, efficacy, efficiency, force, go, impetus, intensity, mettle, might, potency, power, strength, verve, vim; animation, life, manliness, spirit, spiritedness, stamina, vigour, zeal.

enervate *vb* break, debilitate, devitalize, emasculate, enfeeble, exhaust, paralyse, relax, soften, unhinge, unnerve, weaken.

enfeeble *vb* debilitate, devitalize, enervate, exhaust, relax, unhinge, unnerve, weaken.

enfold, infold *vb* enclose, envelop, fold, enwrap, wrap; clasp, embrace.

enforce *vb* compel, constrain, exact, force, oblige, require, urge.

enfranchise *vb* emancipate, free, liberate, manumit, release.

engage *vb* bind, commit, obligate, pledge, promise; affiance, betroth, plight; book, brief, employ, enlist, hire, retain; arrest, allure, attach, draw, entertain, fix, gain, win; busy, commission, contract, engross, occupy; attack, encounter; combat, contend, contest, fight, interlock, struggle; embark, enlist; agree, promise, stipulate, undertake, warrant.

engagement *n* appointment, assurance, contract, obligation, pledge, promise, stipulation; affiancing, betrothment, betrothal, plighting; avocation, business, calling, employment, enterprise, occupation; action, battle, combat, encounter, fight.

engender *vb* bear, beget, breed, create, generate, procreate, propagate; cause, excite, incite, occasion, produce.

engine *n* invention, machine; agency, agent, device, implement, instrument, means, method, tool, weapon.

engorge *vb* bolt, devour, eat, gobble, gorge, gulp, swallow; glut, obstruct, stuff.

engrave *vb* carve, chisel, cut, etch, grave, hatch, incise, sculpt; grave, impress, imprint, infix.

engross *vb* absorb, engage, occupy, take up; buy up, forestall, monopolize.

engrossment *n* absorption, forestalling, monopoly.

engulf, ingulf *vb* absorb, overwhelm, plunge, swallow up.

enhance *vb* advance, aggravate, augment, elevate, heighten, increase, intensify, raise, swell.

enhearten *vb* animate, assure, cheer, comfort, console, embolden, encourage, hearten, incite, inspirit, reassure, stimulate.

enigma *n* conundrum, mystery, problem, puzzle, riddle.

enigmatic, enigmatical *adj* ambiguous, dark, doubtful, equivocal, hidden, incomprehensible, mysterious, mystic, obscure, occult, perplexing, puzzling, recondite, uncertain, unintelligible.

enjoin *vb* admonish, advise, urge; bid, command, direct, order, prescribe, require; prohibit, restrain.

enjoy *vb* like, possess, relish.

enjoyment *n* delight, delectation, gratification, happiness, indulgence, pleasure, satisfaction; possession.

enkindle *vb* inflame, ignite, kindle; excite, incite, instigate, provoke, rouse, stimulate.

enlarge *vb* amplify, augment, broaden, develop, dilate, distend, expand, extend, grow, increase, magnify, widen; aggrandize, engreaten, ennoble, expand, exaggerate, greaten; swell.

enlighten *vb* illume, illuminate, illumine; counsel, educate, civilize, inform, instruct, teach.

enlist *vb* enrol, levy, recruit, register; enrol, list; embark, engage.

enliven *vb* animate, invigorate, quicken, reanimate, rouse, wake; exhilarate, cheer, brighten, delight, elate, gladden, inspire, inspirit, rouse.

enmity *n* animosity, aversion, bitterness, hate, hatred, hostility, ill-will, malevolence, malignity, rancour.

ennoble *vb* aggrandize, dignify, elevate, engreaten, enlarge, exalt, glorify, greaten, raise.

ennui *n* boredom, irksomeness, languor, lassitude, listlessness, tedium, tiresomeness, weariness.

enormity *n* atrociousness, atrocity, depravity, flagitiousness, heinousness, nefariousness, outrageousness, villainy, wickedness.

enormous *adj* abnormal. exceptional, inordinate, irregular; colossal, Cyclopean, elephantine, Herculean, huge, immense, monstrous, vast, gigantic, prodigious, titanic, tremendous.

enough *adj* abundant, adequate, ample, plenty, sufficient. * *adv* satisfactorily, sufficiently. * *n* abundance, plenty, sufficiency.

enquire *see* **inquire**.

enrage *vb* anger, chafe, exasperate, incense, inflame, infuriate, irritate, madden, provoke.

enrapture *vb* beatify, bewitch, delight, enchant, enravish, entrance, surpassingly, transport.

enrich *vb* endow; adorn, deck, decorate, embellish, grace, ornament.

enrobe *vb* clothe, dress, apparel, array, attire, invest, robe.

enrol *vb* catalogue, engage, engross, enlist, list, register; chronicle, record.

ensconce *vb* conceal, cover, harbour, hide, protect, screen, secure, settle, shelter, shield, snugly.

enshrine *vb* embalm, enclose, entomb; cherish, treasure.

ensign *n* banner, colours, eagle, flag, gonfalcon, pennon, standard, streamer; sign, signal, symbol; badge, hatchment.

enslave *vb* captivate, dominate, master, overmaster, overpower, subjugate.

ensnare *vb* catch, entrap; allure, inveigle, seduce; bewilder, confound, embarrass, encumber, entangle, perplex.

ensue *vb* follow, succeed; arise, come, flow, issue, proceed, result, spring.

entangle *vb* catch, ensnare, entrap; confuse, enmesh, intertwine, intertwist, interweave, knot, mat, ravel, tangle; bewilder, embarrass, encumber, ensnare, involve, nonplus, perplex, puzzle.

enterprise *n* adventure, attempt, cause, effort, endeavour, essay, project, undertaking, scheme, venture; activity, adventurousness, daring, dash, energy, initiative, readiness, push.

enterprising *adj* adventurous, audacious, bold, daring, dashing, venturesome, venturous; active, adventurous, alert, efficient, energetic, prompt, resourceful, smart, spirited, stirring, strenuous, zealous.

entertain *vb* fete, receive, regale, treat; cherish, foster, harbour, hold, lodge, shelter; admit, consider; amuse, cheer, divert, please, recreate.

entertainment *n* hospitality; banquet, collation, feast, festival, reception, treat; amusement, diversion, pastime, recreation, sport.

enthusiasm *n* ecstasy, exaltation, fanaticism; ardour, earnestness, devotion, eagerness, fervour, passion, warmth, zeal.

enthusiast *n* bigot, devotee, fan, fanatic, freak, zealot; castle-builder, dreamer, visionary.

entice *vb* allure, attract, bait, cajole, coax, decoy, inveigle, lure, persuade, prevail on, seduce, tempt, wheedle, wile.

enticement *n* allurement, attraction, bait,

blandishment, inducement, inveiglement, lure, persuasion, seduction.

entire *adj* complete, integrated, perfect, unbroken, undiminished, undivided, unimpaired, whole; complete, full, plenary, thorough; mere, pure, sheer, unalloyed, unmingled, unmitigated, unmixed.

entitle *vb* call, characterize, christen, denominate, designate, dub, name, style; empower, enable, fit for, qualify for.

entomb *vb* bury, inhume, inter.

entrails *npl* bowels, guts, intestines, inwards, offal, viscera.

entrance[1] *n* access, approach, avenue, incoming, ingress; adit, avenue, aperture, door, doorway, entry, gate, hallway, inlet, lobby, mouth, passage, portal, stile, vestibule; beginning, commencement, debut, initiation, introduction; admission, entrée.

entrance[2] *vb* bewitch, captivate, charm, delight, enchant, enrapture, fascinate, ravish, transport.

entrap *vb* catch, ensnare; allure, entice, inveigle, seduce; embarrass, entangle, involve, nonplus, perplex, pose, stagger.

entreat *vb* adjure, beg, beseech, crave, enjoin, implore, importune, petition, pray, solicit, supplicate.

entreaty *n* adjuration, appeal, importunity, petition, prayer, request, solicitation, suit, supplication.

entrée *n* access, admission, admittance.

entrench, intrench *vb* furrow; circumvallate, fortify; encroach, infringe, invade, trench, trespass.

entrenchment, intrenchment *n* entrenching; earthwork, fortification; defence, protection, shelter; encroachment, inroad, invasion.

entrust *vb* commit, confide, consign.

entwine *vb* entwist, interlace, intertwine, interweave, inweave, twine, twist, weave; embrace, encircle, encumber, interlace, surround.

enumerate *vb* calculate, cite, compute, count, detail, mention, number, numerate, reckon, recount, specify, tell.

enunciate *vb* articulate, declare, proclaim, promulgate, pronounce, propound, publish, say, speak, utter.

envelop *vb* encase, enfold, enwrap, fold, pack, wrap; cover, encircle, encompass, enshroud, hide, involve, surround.

envelope *n* capsule, case, covering, integument, shroud, skin, wrapper, veil, vesture, wrap.

envenom *vb* poison, taint; embitter, malign; aggravate, enrage, exasperate, incense, inflame, irritate, madden, provoke.

environ *n* begird, belt, embrace, encircle, encompass, enclose, engrid, envelop, gird, hedge, hem, surround; beset, besiege, encompass, invest.

environs *npl* neighbourhood, vicinage, vicinity.

envoy *n* ambassador, legate, minister, plenipotentiary; courier, messenger.

envy *vb* hate; begrudge, grudge; covet, emulate, desire. * *n* enviousness, hate, hatred, ill-will, jealousy, malice, spite; grudge, grudging.

enwrap *vb* absorb, cover, encase, engross, envelop, infold, involve, wrap, wrap up.

ephemeral *adj* brief, diurnal, evanescent, fleeting, flitting, fugacious, fugitive, momentary, occasional, short-lived, transient, transitory.

epic *adj* Homeric, heroic, narrative.

epicure *n* gastronome, glutton, gourmand, gourmet; epicurean, sensualist, Sybarite, voluptuary.

epidemic *adj* general, pandemic, prevailing, prevalent. * *n* outbreak, pandemia, pestilence, plague, spread, wave.

epidermis *n* cuticle, scarf-skin.

epigrammatic *adj* antithetic, concise, laconic, piquant, poignant, pointed, pungent, sharp, terse.

episcopal *adj* Episcopalian, pontifical, prelatic.

epistle *n* communication, letter, missive, note.

epithet *n* appellation, description, designation, name, predicate, title.

epitome *n* abbreviation, abridgement, abstract, breviary, brief, comment, compendium, condensation, conspectus, digest, summary, syllabus, synopsis.

epitomize *vb* abbreviate, abridge, abstract, condense, contract, curtail, cut, reduce, shorten, summarize.

epoch *n* age, date, era, period, time.

equable *adj* calm, equal, even, even-tempered, regular, steady, uniform, serene, tranquil, unruffled.

equal *vb* equalize, even, match. * *adj* alike, coordinate, equivalent, like, tantamount; even, level, equable, regular, uniform; equitable, even-handed, fair, impartial, just, unbiased; co-extensive, commensurate, corresponding, parallel, proportionate; adequate, competent, fit, sufficient. * *n* compeer, fellow, match, peer; rival.

equanimity *n* calmness, composure, coolness, peace, regularity, self-possession, serenity, steadiness.

equestrian *adj* equine, horse-like, horsy. * *n* horseman, rider; cavalier, cavalryman, chevalier, horse soldier, knight.

equilibrist *n* acrobat, balancer, funambulist, rope-walker.

equip *vb* appoint, arm, furnish, provide, rig, supply; accoutre, array, dress.

equipage *n* accoutrements, apparatus, baggage, effects, equipment, furniture; carriage, turnout, vehicle; attendance, procession, retinue, suite, train.

equipment *n* accoutrement, apparatus, baggage, equipage, furniture, gear, outfit, rigging.

equipoise *n* balance, equilibrium.

equitable *adj* even-handed, candid, honest, impartial, just, unbiased, unprejudiced, upright; adequate, fair, proper, reasonable, right.

equity *n* just, right; fair play, fairness, impartiality, justice, rectitude, reasonableness, righteousness, uprightness.

equivalent *adj* commensurate, equal, equipollent, tantamount; interchangeable, synonymous. * *n* complement, coordinate, counterpart, double, equal, fellow, like, match, parallel, pendant, quid pro quo.

equivocal *adj* ambiguous; doubtful, dubious, enigmatic, indeterminate, problematical, puzzling, uncertain.

equivocate *vb* dodge, evade, fence, palter, prevaricate, shuffle, quibble.

equivocation *n* evasion, paltering, prevarication, quibbling, shuffling; double entendre, double meaning, quibble.

era *n* age, date, epoch, period, time.

eradicate *vb* extirpate, root, uproot; abolish, annihilate, destroy, obliterate.

erase *vb* blot, cancel, delete, efface, expunge, obliterate, scrape out.

erasure *n* cancellation, cancelling, effacing, expunging, obliteration.

erect *vb* build, construct, raise, rear; create, establish, form, found, institute, plant. * *adj* standing, unrecumbent, uplifted, upright; elevated, vertical, perpendicular, straight; bold, firm, undaunted, undismayed, unshaken, unterrified.

erelong *adv* early, quickly, shortly, soon, speedily.

eremite *n* anchoret, anchorite, hermit, recluse, solitary.

ergo *adv* consequently, hence, therefore.

erode *vb* canker, consume, corrode, destroy, eat away, fret, rub.

erosive *adj* acrid, cathartic, caustic, corroding, corrosive, eating, virulent.

erotic *adj* amorous, amatory, arousing, seductive, stimulating, titillating.

err *vb* deviate, ramble, rove, stray, wander; blunder, misjudge, mistake; fall, lapse, nod, offend, sin, stumble, trespass, trip.

errand *n* charge, commission, mandate, message, mission, purpose.

errant *adj* adventurous, rambling, roving, stray, wandering.

erratic *adj* nomadic, rambling, roving, wandering; moving, planetary; abnormal, capricious, deviating, eccentric, irregular, odd, queer, strange.

erratum *n* correction, corrigendum, error, misprint, mistake.

erroneous *adj* false, incorrect, inaccurate, inexact, mistaken untrue, wrong.

error *n* blunder, fallacy, inaccuracy, misapprehension, mistake, oversight; delinquency, fault, iniquity, misdeed, misdoing, misstep, obliquity, offence, shortcoming, sin, transgression, trespass, wrongdoing.

erudition *n* knowledge, learning, lore, scholarship.

eruption *n* explosion, outbreak, outburst; sally; rash.

escape *vb* avoid, elude, evade, flee from, shun; abscond, bolt, decamp, flee, fly; slip. * *n* flight; release; passage, passing; leakage.

eschew *vb* abstain, avoid, elude, flee from, shun.

escort *vb* convey, guard, protect; accompany, attend, conduct. * *n* attendant, bodyguard, cavalier, companion, convoy, gallant, guard, squire; protection, safe conduct, safeguard; attendance, company.

esculent *adj* eatable, edible, wholesome.

esoteric *adj* hidden, inmost, inner, mysterious, private, recondite, secret.

especial *adj* absolute, chief, distinct, distinguished, marked, particular, peculiar, principal, singular, special, specific, uncommon, unusual; detailed, minute, noteworthy.

espousal *n* affiancing, betrothing, espousing, plighting; adoption, defence, maintenance, support.

espouse *vb* betroth, plight, promise; marry, wed; adopt, champion, defend, embrace, maintain, support.

espy *vb* descry, detect, discern, discover, observe, perceive, spy, watch.

esquire *n* armiger, attendant, escort, gentleman, squire.

essay[1] *vb* attempt, endeavour, try. * *n* aim, attempt, effort, endeavour, exertion, struggle, trial.

essay[2] *n* article, composition, disquisition, dissertation, paper, thesis.

essence *n* nature, quintessence, substance; extract, part; odour, perfume, scent; being, entity, existence, nature.

essential *adj* fundamental, indispensable, important, inward, intrinsic, necessary, requisite, vital; diffusible, pure, rectified, volatile.

establish *vb* fix, secure, set, settle; decree, enact, ordain; build, constitute, erect, form, found, institute, organize, originate, pitch, plant, raise; ensconce, ground, install, place, plant, root, secure; approve, confirm, ratify, sanction; prove, substantiate, verify.

estate *n* condition, state; position, rank, standing; division, order; effects, fortune, possessions, property; interest.

esteem *vb* appreciate, estimate, rate, reckon, value; admire, honour, like, prize, respect, revere, reverence, value, venerate, worship; account, believe, consider, deem, fancy, hold, imagine, suppose, regard, think. * *n* account, appreciation, consideration, estimate, estimation, judgement, opinion, reckoning, valuation; credit, honour, regard, respect, reverence.

estimable *adj* appreciable, calculable, computable; admirable, credible, deserving, excellent, good, meritorious, precious, respectful, valuable, worthy.

estimate *vb* appraise, appreciate, esteem, prise, rate, value; assess, calculate, compute, count, gauge, judge, reckon. * *n* estimation, judgement, valuation; calculation, computation.

estimation *n* appreciation, estimate, valuation; esteem, estimate, judgement, opinion; honour, reckoning, regard, respect, reverence.

estop *vb* bar, impede, preclude, stop.

estrange *vb* withdraw, withhold; alienate, divert; disaffect, destroy.

estuary *n* creek, inlet, fiord, firth, frith, mouth.

etch *vb* corrode, engrave.

eternal *adj* absolute, inevitable, necessary, self-active, self-existent, self-originated; abiding, ceaseless, endless, ever-enduring, everlasting, incessant, interminable, never-ending, perennial, permanent, perpetual, sempiternal, unceasing, unending; deathless, immortal, imperishable, incorruptible, indestructible, never-dying, undying; immutable, unchangeable; constant, continual, continuous, incessant, persistent, unbroken, uninterrupted.

ethereal *adj* aerial, airy, celestial, empyreal, heavenly, unworldly; attenuated, light, subtle, tenuous, volatile; delicate, fairy, flimsy, fragile, rare, refined, subtle.

eulogize *vb* applaud, commend, extol, laud, magnify, praise.

eulogy *n* discourse, eulogium, panegyric, speech; applause, encomium, commendation, laudation, praise.

euphonious *adj* clear, euphonic, harmonious, mellifluous, mellow, melodious, musical, silvery, smooth, sweet-toned.

evacuant *adj* abstergent, cathartic, cleansing, emetic, purgative. * *n* cathartic, purgative.

evacuate *vb* empty; discharge, clean out, clear out, eject, excrete, expel, purge, void; abandon, desert, forsake, leave, quit, relinquish, withdraw.

evade *vb* elude, escape; avoid, decline, dodge, funk, shun; baffle, elude, foil; dodge, equivocate, fence, palter, prevaricate, quibble, shuffle.

evanescence *n* disappearance, evanishing, evanishment, vanishing; transience, transientness, transitoriness.

evanescent *adj* ephemeral, fleeting, flitting, fugitive, passing, short-lived, transient, transitory, vanishing.

evaporate *vb* distil, volatilize; dehydrate, dry, vaporize; disperse, dissolve, fade, vanish.

evaporation *n* distillation, volatilization; dehydration, drying, vaporization; disappearance, dispersal, dissolution.

evasion *n* artifice, avoidance, bluffing, deceit, dodge, equivocation, escape, excuse, funking, prevarication, quibble, shift, subterfuge, shuffling, sophistical, tergiversation.

evasive *adj* elusive, elusory, equivocating, prevaricating, shuffling, slippery, sophistical.

even *vb* balance, equalize, harmonize, symmetrize; align, flatten, flush, level, smooth, square. * *adj* flat, horizontal, level, plane, smooth; calm, composed, equable, equal, peaceful, placid, regular, steady, uniform, unruffled; direct, equitable, fair, impartial, just, straightforward. * *adv* exactly, just, verily; likewise. * *n* eve, evening, eventide, vesper.

evening *n* dusk, eve, even, eventide, nightfall, sunset, twilight.

event *n* circumstance, episode, fact, happening, incident, occurrence; conclusion, consequence, end, issue, outcome, result, sequel, termination; adventure, affair.

eventful *adj* critical, important, memorable, momentous, remarkable, signal, stirring.

eventual *adj* final, last, ultimate; conditional, contingent, possible. * *adv* always, aye, constantly, continually, eternally, ever evermore, forever, incessantly, perpetually, unceasingly.

everlasting *adj* ceaseless, constant, continual, endless, eternal, ever-during, incessant, interminable, never-ceasing, never-ending, perpetual, unceasing, unending, unintermitting, uninterrupted; deathless, ever-living, immortal, imperishable, never-dying, undying.

evermore *adv* always, constantly, continually, eternally, ever, forever, perpetually.

everyday *adj* accustomed, common, commonplace, customary, habitual, routine, usual, wonted.

evict *vb* dispossess, eject, thrust out.

evidence *vb* evince, make clear, manifest, prove, show, testify, vouch. * *n* affirmation, attestation, averment, confirmation, corroboration, deposition, grounds, indication, proof, testimony, token, trace, voucher, witness.

evident *adj* apparent, bald, clear, conspicuous, distinct, downright, incontestable, indisputable, manifest, obvious, open, overt, palpable, patent, plain, unmistakable.

evil *adj* bad, ill; base, corrupt, malicious, malevolent, malign, nefarious, perverse, sinful, vicious, vile, wicked, wrong; bad, deleterious, baleful, baneful, destructive, harmful, hurtful, injurious, mischievous, noxious, pernicious, profane; adverse, calamitous, diabolic, disastrous, unfortunate, unhappy, unpropitious, woeful. * *n* calamity, disaster, ill, misery, misfortune, pain, reverse, sorrow, suffering, woe; badness, baseness, corruption, depravity, malignity, sin, viciousness, wickedness; bale, bane, blast, canker, curse, harm, injury, mischief, wrong.

evince *vb* establish, evidence, manifest, prove, show; disclose, display, exhibit, indicate, reveal.

eviscerate *vb* disembowel, embowel, gut.

evoke *vb* arouse, elicit, excite, provoke, rouse.

evolve *vb* develop, educe, exhibit, expand, open, unfold, unroll.

exacerbate *vb* aggravate, embitter, enrage, exasperate, excite, inflame, infuriate, irritate, provoke, vex.

exact *vb* elicit, extort, mulch, require, squeeze; ask, claim, compel, demand, enforce, requisition, take. * *adj* rigid, rigorous, scrupulous, severe, strict; diametric, express, faultless, precise, true; accurate, close, correct, definite, faithful, literal, undeviating; accurate, critical, delicate, fine, nice, sensitive; careful, methodical, punctilious, orderly, punctual, regular.

exacting *adj* critical, difficult, exactive, rigid, extortionary.

exaction *n* contribution, extortion, oppression, rapacity, tribute.

exactness *n* accuracy, correctness, exactitude, faithfulness, faultlessness, fidelity, nicety, precision, rigour; carefulness, method, precision, regularity, rigidness, scrupulousity, scrupulousness, strictness.

exaggerate *vb* enlarge, magnify, overcharge, overcolour, overstate, romance, strain, stretch.

exalt *vb* elevate, erect, heighten, lift up, raise; aggrandize, dignify, elevate, ennoble; bless, extol, glorify, magnify, praise.

exalted *adj* elated, elevated, high, highflown, lofty, lordly, magnificent.

examination *n* inspection, observation; exploration, inquiry, inquisition, investigation, perusal, research, search, scrutiny, survey; catechism, probation, review, test, trial.

examine *vb* inspect, observe; canvass, consider, explore, inquire, investigate, scrutinize, study, test; catechize, interrogate.

example *n* archetype, copy, model, pattern, piece, prototype, representative, sample, sampler, specimen, standard; exemplification, illustration, instance, precedent, warning.

exanimate *adj* dead, defunct, inanimate, lifeless; inanimate, inert, sluggish, spiritless, torpid.

exasperate *vb* affront, anger, chafe, enrage, incense, irritate, nettle, offend, provoke, vex; aggravate, exacerbate, inflame, rouse.

exasperation *n* annoyance, exacerbation, irritation, pro- vocation; anger, fury, ire, passion, rage, wrath; aggravation, heightening, increase, worsening.

excavate *vb* burrow, cut, delve, dig, hollow, hollow out, scoop, trench.

exceed *vb* cap, overstep, surpass, transcend; excel, outdo, outstrip, outvie, pass.

excel *vb* beat, eclipse, outdo, outrival, outstrip, outvie, surpass; cap, exceed, transcend.

excellence *n* distinction, eminence, preeminence, superiority, transcendence; fineness, fitness, goodness, perfection, purity, quality, superiority; advantage; goodness, probity, uprightness, virtue, worth.

excellent *adj* admirable, choice, crack, eminent, first-rate, prime, sterling, superior, tiptop, transcendent; deserving, estimable, praiseworthy, virtuous, worthy.

except *vb* exclude, leave out, omit, reject. * *conj* unless. * *prep* bar, but, excepting, excluding, save.

exceptional *adj* aberrant, abnormal, anomalous, exceptive, irregular, peculiar, rare, special, strange, superior, uncommon, unnatural, unusual.

excerpt *vb* cite, cull, extract, quote, select, take. * *n* citation, extract, quotation, selection.

excess *adj* excessive, unnecessary, redundant, spare, superfluous, surplus. * *n* disproportion, fulsomeness, glut, oversupply, plethora, redundance, redundancy, surfeit, superabundance, superfluity; overplus, remainder, surplus; debauchery, dissipation, dissoluteness, intemperance, immoderation, overindulgence, unrestraint; extravagance, immoderation, overdoing.

excessive *adj* disproportionate, exuberant, superabundant, superfluous, undue; extravagant, enormous, inordinate, outrageous, unreasonable; extreme, immoderate, intemperate; vehement, violent.

exchange *vb* barter, change, commute, shuffle, substitute, swap, trade, truck; bandy, interchange. * *n* barter, change, commutation, dealing, shuffle, substitution, trade, traffic; interchange, reciprocity; bazaar, bourse, fair, market.

excise[1] *n* capitation, customs, dues, duty, tariff, tax, taxes, toll.

excise[2] *vb* cancel, cut, delete, edit, efface, eradicate, erase, expunge, extirpate, remove, strike out.

excision *n* destruction, eradication, extermination, extirpation.

excitable *adj* impressible, nervous, sensitive, susceptible; choleric, hasty, hotheaded, hot-tempered, irascible, irritable, passionate, quick-tempered.

excite *vb* animate, arouse, awaken, brew, evoke, impel, incite, inflame, instigate, kindle, move, prompt, provoke, rouse, spur, stimulate; create, elicit, evoke, raise; agitate, discompose, disturb, irritate.

excitement *n* excitation, exciting; incitement, motive, stimulus; activity, agitation, bustle, commotion, disturbance, ferment, flutter, perturbation, sensation, stir, tension; choler, heat, irritation, passion, violence, warmth.

exclaim *vb* call, cry, declare, ejaculate, shout, utter, vociferate.

exclude *vb* ban, bar, blackball, debar, ostracize, preclude, reject; hinder, prevent, prohibit, restrain, withhold; except, omit; eject, eliminate, expel, extrude.

exclusive *adj* debarring, excluding; illiberal, narrow, narrow-minded, selfish, uncharitable; aristocratic, choice, clannish, cliquish, fastidious, fashionable, select, snobbish; only, sole, special.

excommunicate *vb* anathematize, ban, curse, denounce, dismiss, eject, exclude, expel, exscind, proscribe, unchurch.

excoriate *vb* abrade, flay, gall, scar, scarify, score, skin, strip.

excrement *n* dejections, dung, faeces, excreta, excretion, ordure, stool.

excrescence *n* fungus, growth, knob, lump, outgrowth, protuberance, tumour, wart.

excrete *vb* discharge, eject, eliminate, separate.

excruciate *vb* agonize, rack, torment, torture.

exculpate *vb* absolve, acquit, clear, discharge, exonerate, free, justify, release, set right, vindicate.

excursion *n* drive, expedition, jaunt, journey, ramble, ride, sally, tour, trip, voyage, walk; digression, episode.

excursive *adj* devious, diffuse, digressive, discursive, erratic, rambling, roaming, roving, wandering.

excusable *adj* allowable, defensible, forgivable, justifiable, pardonable, venial, warrantable.

excursus *n* discussion, disquisition, dissertation.

excuse *vb* absolve, acquit, exculpate, exonerate, forgive, pardon, remit; extenuate, justify; exempt, free, release; overlook. * *n* absolution, apology, defence, extenuation, justification, plea; colour, disguise, evasion, guise, pretence, pretext, makeshift, semblance, subterfuge.

execrable *adj* abhorrent, abominable, accursed, cursed, damnable, detestable, hateful, odious; disgusting, loathsome, nauseating, nauseous, obnoxious, offensive, repulsive, revolting, sickening, vile.

execrate *vb* curse, damn, imprecate; abhor, abominate, detest, hate, loathe.

execute *vb* accomplish, achieve, carry out, complete. consummate, do, effect, effectuate, finish, perform, perpetrate; administer, enforce, seal, sign; behead, electrocute, guillotine, hang.

execution *n* accomplishment, achievement, completion, consummation, operation, performance; warrant, writ; beheading, electrocution, hanging.

executive *adj* administrative, commanding, controlling, directing, managing, ministerial, officiating, presiding, ruling. * *n* administrator, director, manager.

exegetic, exegetical *adj* explanatory, explicative, explicatory, expository, hermeneutic, interpretative.

exemplary *adj* assiduous, close, exact, faithful, punctual, punctilious, rigid, rigorous, scrupulous; commendable, correct, good, estimable, excellent, praiseworthy, virtuous; admonitory, condign, monitory, warning.

exemplify *vb* evidence, exhibit, illustrate, manifest, show.

exempt *vb* absolve, except, excuse, exonerate, free, release, relieve. * *adj* absolved, excepted, excused, exempted, free, immune, liberated, privileged, released.

exemption *n* absolution, dispensation, exception, immunity, privilege, release.

exercise *vb* apply, busy, employ, exert, praxis, use; effect, exert, produce, wield; break in, discipline, drill, habituate, school, train; practise, prosecute, pursue; task, test, try; afflict, agitate, annoy, burden, pain, trouble. * *n* appliance, application, custom, employment, operation, performance, play, plying, practice, usage, use, working; action, activity, effort, exertion, labour, toil, work; discipline, drill, drilling, schooling, training; lesson, praxis, study, task, test, theme.

exert *vb* employ, endeavour, exercise, labour, strain, strive, struggle, toil, use, work.

exertion *n* action, exercise, exerting, use; attempt, effort, endeavour, labour, strain, stretch, struggle, toil, trial.

exhalation *n* emission, evaporation; damp, effluvium, fog, fume, mist, reek, smoke, steam, vapour.

exhale *vb* breathe, discharge, elect, emanate, emit, evaporate, reek; blow, expire, puff.

exhaust *vb* drain, draw, empty; consume, destroy, dissipate, expend, impoverish, lavish, spend, squander, waste; cripple, debilitate, deplete, disable, enfeeble, enervate, overtire, prostrate, weaken.

exhaustion *n* debilitation, enervation, fatigue, lassitude, weariness.

exhibit *vb* demonstrate, disclose, display, evince, expose, express, indicate, manifest, offer, present, reveal, show; offer, present, propose.

exhibition *n* demonstration, display, exposition, manifestation, representation, spectacle, show; allowance, benefaction, grant, pension, scholarship.

exhilarate *vb* animate, cheer, elate, enliven, gladden, inspire, inspirit, rejoice, stimulate.

exhilaration *n* animating, cheering, elating, enlivening, gladdening, rejoicing, stimulating; animation, cheer, cheerfulness, gaiety, gladness, glee, good spirits, hilarity, joyousness.

exhort *vb* advise, caution, encourage, incite, persuade, stimulate, urge, warm; preach.

exhume *vb* disentomb, disinhume, disinter, unbury, unearth.

exigency, exigence *n* demand, necessity, need, requirement, urgency, want; conjuncture, crisis, difficulty, distress, emergency, extremity, juncture, nonplus, quandary, pass, pinch, pressure, strait.

exiguous *adj* attenuated, diminutive, fine, small, scanty, slender, tiny.

exile *vb* banish, expatriate, expel, ostracize, proscribe. * *n* banishment, expatriation, expulsion, ostracism, proscription, separation; outcast, refugee.

exist *vb* be, breathe, live; abide, continue, endure, last, remain.

existence *n* being, subsisting, subsistence; being, creature, entity, essence, thing; animation, continuation, life, living, vitality, vivacity.

exit *vb* depart, egress, go, leave. * *n* departure, withdrawal; death, decrease, demise, end; egress, outlet.

exonerate *vb* absolve, acquit, clear, exculpate, justify, vindicate; absolve, discharge, except, exempt, free, release.

exorbitant *adj* enormous, excessive, extravagant, inordinate, unreasonable.

exorcise *vb* cast out, drive away, expel; deliver, purify; address, conjure.

exordium *n* introduction, opening, preamble, preface, prelude, proem, prologue.

exotic *adj* extraneous, foreign; extravagant.

expand *vb* develop, open, spread, unfold, unfurl; diffuse, enlarge, extend, increase, stretch; dilate, distend, enlarge.

expanse *n* area, expansion, extent, field, stretch.

expansion *n* expansion, opening, spreading; diastole, dilation, distension, swelling; development, diffusion, enlargement, increase; expanse, extent, stretch.

ex parte *adj* biased, one-sided, partisan.

expatiate *vb* amplify, decant, dilate, enlarge, range, rove.

expatriate *vb* banish, exile, expel, ostracize, proscribe. * *adj* banished, exiled, refugee. * *n* displaced person, emigrant, exile.

expect *vb* anticipate, await, calculate, contemplate, forecast, foresee, hope, reckon, rely.

expectancy *n* expectance, expectation; abeyance, prospect.

expectation *n* anticipation, expectance, expectancy, hope, prospect; assurance, confidence, presumption, reliance, trust.

expedient *adj* advisable, appropriate, convenient, desirable, fit, proper, politic, suitable; advantageous, profitable, useful. * *n* contrivance, device, means, method, resort, resource, scheme, shift, stopgap, substitute.

expedite *vb* accelerate, advance, dispatch, facilitate, forward, hasten, hurry, precipitate, press, quicken, urge.

expedition *n* alacrity, alertness, celerity, dispatch, haste, promptness, quickness, speed; enterprise, undertaking; campaign, excursion, journey, march, quest, voyage.

expeditious *adj* quick, speedy, swift, rapid; active, alert, diligent, nimble, prompt, punctual, swift.

expel *vb* dislodge, egest, eject, eliminate, excrete; discharge, eject, evacuate, void; bounce, discharge, exclude, exscind, fire, oust, relegate, remove; banish, disown, excommunicate, exile, expatriate, ostracize, proscribe, unchurch.

expend *vb* disburse, spend; consume, employ, exert, use; dissipate, exhaust, scatter, waste.

expenditure *n* disbursement, outlay, outlaying, spending; charge, cost, expenditure, outlay.

expensive *adj* costly, dear, high-priced; extravagant, lavish, wasteful.

experience *vb* endure, suffer; feel, know; encounter, suffer, undergo. * *n* endurance, practice, trial; evidence, knowledge, proof, test, testimony.

experienced *adj* able, accomplished, expert, instructed, knowing, old, practised, qualified, skilful, trained, thoroughbred, versed, veteran, wise.

experiment *vb* examine, investigate, test, try. * *n* assay, examination, investigation, ordeal, practice, proof, test, testimony, touchstone, trial.

expert *adj* able, adroit, apt, clever, dextrous, proficient, prompt, quick, ready, skilful. * *n* adept, authority, connoisseur, crack, master, specialist.

expertise *n* adroitness, aptness, dexterity, facility, promptness, skilfulness, skill.

expiate *vb* atone, redeem, satisfy.

expiration n death, decease, demise, departure, exit; cessation, close, conclusion, end, termination.

expire *vb* cease, close, conclude, end, stop, terminate; emit, exhale; decease, depart, die, perish.

explain *vb* demonstrate, elucidate, expound, illustrate, interpret, resolve, solve, unfold, unravel; account for, justify, warrant.

explanation *n* clarification, description, elucidation, exegesis, explication, exposition, illustration, interpretation; account, answer, deduction, justification, key, meaning, secret, solution, warrant.

explicit *adj* absolute, categorical, clear, definite, determinate, exact, express, plain, positive, precise, unambiguous, unequivocal, unreserved.

explode *vb* burst, detonate, discharge, displode, shatter, shiver; contemn, discard, repudiate, scorn, scout.
exploit *vb* befool, milk, use, utilize. * *n* achievement, act, deed, feat.
explore *vb* examine, fathom, inquire, inspect, investigate, prospect, scrutinize, seek.
explosion *n* blast, burst, bursting, clap, crack, detonation, discharge, displosion, fulmination, pop.
exponent *n* example, illustration, index, indication, specimen, symbol, type; commentator, demonstrator, elucidator, expounder, illustrator, interpreter.
expose *vb* bare, display, uncover; descry, detect, disclose, unearth; denounce, mask; subject; endanger, jeopardize, risk, venture.
exposé *n* exhibit, exposition, manifesto; denouncement, divulgement, exposure, revelation.
exposition *n* disclosure, interpretation; commentary, critique, elucidation, exegesis, explanation, explication, interpretation; display, show.
expound *vb* develop, present, rehearse, reproduce, unfold; clear, elucidate, explain, interpret.
express *vb* air, assert, asseverate, declare, emit, enunciate, manifest, utter, vent, signify, speak, state, voice; betoken, denote, equal, exhibit, indicate, intimate, present, represent, show, symbolize. * *adj* categorical, clear, definite, determinate, explicit, outspoken, plain, positive, unambiguous; accurate, close, exact, faithful, precise, true; particular, special; fast, nonstop, quick, rapid, speedy, swift. * *n* dispatch, message.
expression *n* assertion, asseveration, communication, declaration, emission, statement, utterance, voicing; language, locution, phrase, remark, saying, term, word; air, aspect, look, mien.
expressive *adj* indicative, meaningful, significant; demonstrative, eloquent, emphatic, energetic, forcible, lively, strong, vivid; appropriate, sympathetic, well-modulated.
expulsion *n* discharge, eviction, expelling, ousting; elimination, evacuation, excretion; ejection, excision, excommunication, extrusion, ostracism, separation.
expunge *vb* annihilate, annul, cancel, delete, destroy, efface, erase, obliterate, wipe out.
expurgate *vb* clean, cleanse, purge, purify; bowdlerize, emasculate.
exquisite *adj* accurate, delicate, discriminating, exact, fastidious, nice, refined; choice, elect, excellent, precious, rare, valuable; complete, consummate, matchless, perfect; acute, keen, intense, poignant. * *n* beau, coxcomb, dandy, fop, popinjay.
extant *adj* existent, existing, present, surviving, undestroyed, visible.
extempore *adj* extemporaneous, extemporary, impromptu, improvised. * *adv* offhand, suddenly, unpremeditatedly, unpreparedly.
extend *vb* reach, stretch; continue, elongate, lengthen, prolong, protract, widen; augment, broaden, dilate, distend, enlarge, expand, increase; diffuse, spread; give, impart, offer, yield; lie, range.
extensible *adj* ductile, elastic, extendible, extensile, protractible, protractile.
extension *n* augmentation, continuation, delay, dilatation, dilation, distension, enlargement, expansion, increase, prolongation, protraction.
extensive *adj* broad, capacious, comprehensive, expanded, extended, far-reaching, large, wide, widespread.
extent *n* amplitude, expanse, expansion; amount, bulk, content, degree, magnitude, size, volume; compass, measure, length, proportions, reach, stretch; area, field, latitude, range, scope; breadth, depth, height, width.
extenuate *vb* diminish, lessen, reduce, soften, weaken; excuse, mitigate, palliate, qualify.
exterior *adj* external, outer, outlying, outside, outward, superficial, surface; extrinsic, foreign. * *n* outside, surface; appearance.
exterminate *vb* abolish, annihilate, de-

stroy, eliminate, eradicate, extirpate, uproot.

external *adj* exterior, outer, outside, outward, superficial; extrinsic, foreign; apparent, visible.

extinct *adj* extinguished, quenched; closed, dead, ended, lapsed, terminated, vanished.

extinction *n* death, extinguishment; abolishment, abolition, annihilation, destruction, excision, extermination, extirpation.

extinguish *vb* choke, douse, put out, quell, smother, stifle, suffocate, suppress; destroy, nullify, subdue; eclipse, obscure.

extirpate *vb* abolish, annihilate, deracinate, destroy, eradicate, exterminate, uproot, weed.

extol *vb* celebrate, exalt, glorify, laud, magnify, praise; applaud, commend, eulogize, panegyrize.

extort *vb* elicit, exact, extract, force, squeeze, wrench, wrest, wring.

extortion *n* blackmail, compulsion, demand, exaction, oppression, overcharge, rapacity, tribute; exorbitance.

extortionate *adj* bloodsucking, exacting, hard, harsh, oppressive, rapacious, rigorous, severe; exorbitant, unreasonable.

extra *adj* accessory, additional, auxiliary, collateral; another, farther, fresh, further, more, new, other, plus, ulterior; side, spare, supernumerary, supplemental, supplementary, surplus; extraordinary, extreme, unusual. * *adv* additionally, also, beyond, farthermore, furthermore, more, moreover, plus. * *n* accessory, appendage, collateral, nonessential, special, supernumerary, supplement; bonus, premium; balance, leftover, remainder, spare, surplus.

extract *vb* extort, pull out, remove, withdraw; derive, distil, draw, express, squeeze; cite, determine, derive, quote, select. * *n* citation, excerpt, passage, quotation, selection; decoction, distillation, essence, infusion, juice.

extraction *n* drawing out, derivation, distillation, elicitation, essence, pulling out; birth, descent, genealogy, lineage, origin, parentage.

extraneous *adj* external, extrinsic, foreign; additional, adventitious, external, superfluous, supplementary, unessential.

extraordinary *adj* abnormal, amazing, distinguished, egregious, exceptional, marvellous, monstrous, particular, peculiar, phenomenal, prodigious, rare, remarkable, signal, singular, special, strange, uncommon, unprecedented, unusual, unwonted, wonderful.

extravagance *n* excess, enormity, exorbitance, preposterousness, unreasonableness; absurdity, excess, folly, irregularity, wildness; lavishness, prodigality, profuseness, profusion, superabundance; waste.

extravagant *adj* excessive, exorbitant, inordinate, preposterous, unreasonable; absurd, foolish, irregular, wild; lavish, prodigal, profuse, spendthrift.

extreme *adj* farthest, outermost, remotest, utmost, uttermost; greatest, highest; final, last, ultimate; drastic, egregious, excessive, extravagant, immoderate, intense, outrageous, radical, unreasonable. * *n* end, extremity, limit; acme, climax, degree, height, pink; danger, distress.

extremity *n* border, edge, end, extreme, limb, termination, verge.

extricate *vb* clear, deliver, disembarrass, disengage, disentangle, liberate, release, relieve.

extrinsic *adj* external, extraneous, foreign, outside, outward, superabundance, superfluity.

exuberance *n* abundance, copiousness, flood, luxuriance, plenitude; excess, lavishness, overabundance, overflow, overgrowth, over-luxuriance, profusion, rankness, redundancy, superabundance, superfluity.

exuberant *adj* abounding, abundant, copious, fertile, flowing, luxuriant, prolific, rich; excessive, lavish, overabundant, overflowing, over-luxuriant, profuse, rank, redundant, superabounding, superabundant, wanton.

exude *vb* discharge, excrete, secrete, sweat; infiltrate, ooze, percolate.

exult *vb* gloat, glory, jubilate, rejoice, transport, triumph, taunt, vault.

exultation *n* delight, elation, joy, jubilation, transport, triumph.

eye *vb* contemplate, inspect, ogle, scrutinize, survey, view, watch. * *n* estimate, judgement, look, sight, vision, view; inspection, notice, observation, scrutiny, sight, vigilance, watch; aperture, eyelet, peephole, perforation; bud, shoot.

F

fable *n* allegory, legend, myth, parable, story, tale; fabrication, falsehood, fiction, figment, forgery, untruth.

fabric *n* building, edifice, pile, structure; conformation, make, texture, workmanship; cloth, material, stuff, textile, tissue, web.

fabricate *vb* build, construct, erect, frame; compose, devise, fashion, make, manufacture; coin, fake, feign, forge, invent.

fabrication *n* building, construction, erection; manufacture; fable, fake, falsehood, fiction, figment, forgery, invention, lie.

fabulous *adj* amazing, apocryphal, coined, fabricated, feigned, fictitious, forged, imaginary, invented, legendary, marvellous, mythical, romancing, unbelievable, unreal.

façade *n* elevation, face, front.

face *vb* confront; beard, buck, brave, dare, defy, front, oppose; dress, level, polish, smooth; cover, incrust, veneer. * *n* cover, facet, surface; breast, escarpment, front; countenance, features, grimace, physiognomy, visage; appearance, expression, look, semblance; assurance, audacity, boldness, brass, confidence, effrontery, impudence.

facet *n* cut, face, lozenge, surface.

facetious *adj* amusing, comical, droll, funny, humorous, jocose, jocular, pleasant, waggish, witty; entertaining, gay, lively, merry, sportive, sprightly.

facile *adj* easy; affable, approachable, complaisant, conversable, courteous, mild; compliant, ductile, flexible, fluent, manageable, pliable, pliant, tractable, yielding; dextrous, ready, skilful.

facilitate *vb* expedite, help.

facility *n* ease, easiness; ability, dexterity, expertness, knack, quickness, readiness; ductility, flexibility, pliancy; advantage, appliance, convenience, means, resource; affability, civility, complaisance, politeness.

facsimile *n* copy, duplicate, fax, reproduction.

fact *n* act, circumstance, deed, event, incident, occurrence, performance; actuality, certainty, existence, reality, truth.

faction *n* cabal, clique, combination, division, junta, party, side; disagreement, discord, disorder, dissension, recalcitrance, recalcitrancy, refractoriness, sedition, seditiousness, tumult, turbulence, turbulency.

factious *adj* litigious, malcontent, rebellious, recalcitrant, refractory, seditious. turbulent.

factitious *adj* artful, artificial, conventional, false, unnatural, unreal.

factor *n* agent, bailiff, broker, consignee, go-between, steward, component, element, ingredient; influence, reason.

factory *n* manufactory, mill, work, workshop.

faculty *n* ability, capability, capacity, endowment, power, property, quality; ableness, address, adroitness, aptitude, aptness, clearness, competency, dexterity, efficiency, expertness, facility, forte, ingenuity, knack, qualification, quickness, readiness, skill, skilfulness, talent, turn; body, department, profession; authority, prerogative, license, privilege, right.

fade *vb* disappear, die, evanesce, fall, faint, perish, vanish; decay, decline, droop, fall, languish, wither; bleach, blanch, pale; disperse, dissolve.

faeces *npl* dregs, lees, sediment, settlings; dung, excrement, ordure, settlings.

fag *vb* droop, flag, sink; drudge, toil; fatigue, jade, tire, weary. * *n* drudgery, fatigue, work; drudge, grub, hack; cigarette, smoke.

fail *vb* break, collapse, decay, decline, fade, sicken, sink, wane; cease, disappear; fall, miscarry, miss; neglect, omit; bankrupt, break.

failing *adj* deficient, lacking, needing, wanting; declining, deteriorating, fading, flagging, languishing, sinking, waning, wilting; unsuccessful. * *prep* lacking, needing, wanting. * *n* decay, decline; failure, miscarriage; defect, deficiency, fault, foible, frailty, imperfection, infirmity, shortcoming, vice, weakness; error, lapse, slip; bankruptcy, insolvency.

failure *n* defectiveness, deficiency, delinquency, shortcoming; fail, miscarriage, negligence, neglect, nonobservance, nonperformance, omission, slip; abortion, botch, breakdown, collapse, fiasco, fizzle; bankruptcy, crash, downfall, insolvency, ruin; decay, declension, decline, loss.

fain *adj* anxious, glad, inclined, pleased, rejoiced, well-pleased. * *adv* cheerfully, eagerly, gladly, joyfully, willingly.

faint *vb* swoon; decline, fade, fail, languish, weaken. * *adj* swooning; drooping, exhausted, feeble, languid, listless, sickly, weak; gentle, inconsiderable, little, slight, small, soft, thin; dim, dull, indistinct, perceptible, scarce, slight; cowardly, dastardly, faint-hearted, fearful, timid, timorous; dejected, depressed, discouraged, disheartened, dispirited. * *n* blackout, swoon.

faint-hearted *adj* cowardly, dastardly, faint, fearful, timid, timorous.

fair[1] *adj* spotless, unblemished, unspotted, unstained, untarnished; blond, light, white; beautiful, comely, handsome, shapely; clear, cloudless, pleasant, unclouded; favourable, prosperous; hopeful, promising, propitious; clear, distinct, open, plain, unencumbered, unobstructed; candid, frank, honest, honourable, impartial, ingenuous, just, unbiased, upright; equitable, proper; average, decent, indifferent, mediocre, moderate, ordinary, passable, reasonable, respectful, tolerable.

fair[2] *n* bazaar, carnival, exposition, festival, fete, funfair, gala, kermess.

fairy *n* brownie, elf, demon, fay, sprite.

faith *n* assurance, belief, confidence, credence, credit, dependence, reliance, trust; creed, doctrine, dogma, persuasion, religion, tenet; constancy, faithfulness, fidelity, loyalty, truth, truthfulness.

faithful *adj* constant, devoted, loyal, staunch, steadfast, true; honest, upright, reliable, trustworthy, trusty; reliable, truthful; accurate, close, conscientiousness, exact, nice, strict.

faithless *adj* unbelieving; dishonest, disloyal, false, fickle, fluctuating, inconstant, mercurial, mutable, perfidious, shifting, treacherous, truthless, unsteady, untruthful, vacillating, variable, wavering.

fall *vb* collapse, depend, descend, drop, sink, topple, tumble; abate, decline, decrease, depreciate, ebb, subside; err, lapse, sin, stumble, transgress, trespass, trip; die, perish; befall, chance, come, happen, occur, pass; become, get; come, pass. * *n* collapse, comedown, descent, downcome, dropping, falling, flop, plop, tumble; cascade, cataract, waterfall; death, destruction, downfall, overthrow, ruin, surrender; comeuppance, degradation; apostasy, declension, failure, lapse, slip; decline, decrease, depreciation, diminution, ebb, sinking, subsidence; cadence, close; declivity, inclination, slope.

fallacious *adj* absurd, deceptive, deceiving, delusive, disappointing, erroneous, false, illusive, illusory, misleading; paralogistic, sophistical, worthless.

fallacy *n* aberration, deceit, deception, delusion, error, falsehood, illusion, misapprehension, misconception, mistake, untruth; non sequitur, paralogism, sophism, sophistry.

fallibility *n* frailty, imperfection, uncertainty.

fallible *adj* erring, frail, ignorant, imperfect, uncertain, weak.

fallow *adj* left, neglected, uncultivated, unsowed, untilled; dormant, inactive, inert.

false *adj* lying, mendacious, truthless, untrue, unveracious; dishonest, dishonourable, disingenuous, disloyal, double-faced, double-tongued, faithless, false-hearted, perfidious, treacherous, unfaithful; fictitious, forged, made-up, unreliable, untrustworthy; artificial, bastard, bogus, counterfeit, factitious, feigned, forged, hollow, hypocritical, make-believe, pretended, pseudo, sham, spurious, suppositious; erroneous, improper, incorrect, unfounded, wrong; deceitful, deceiving, deceptive, disappointing, fallacious, misleading.

false-hearted *adj* dishonourable, disloyal, double, double-tongued, faithless, false, perfidious, treacherous.

falsehood *n* falsity; fabrication, fib, fiction, lie, untruth; cheat, counterfeit, imposture, mendacity, treachery.

falsify *vb* alter, adulterate, belie, cook, counterfeit, doctor, fake, falsely, garble, misrepresent, misstate, represent; disprove; violate.

falsity *n* falsehood, untruth, untruthfulness.

falter *vb* halt, hesitate, lisp, quaver, stammer, stutter; fail, stagger, stumble, totter, tremble, waver; dodder.

fame *n* bruit, hearsay, report, rumour; celebrity, credit, eminence, glory, greatness, honour, illustriousness, kudos, lustre, notoriety, renown, reputation, repute.

familiar *adj* acquainted, aware, conversant, well-versed; amicable, close, cordial, domestic, fraternal, friendly, homely, intimate, near; affable, accessible, companionable, conversable, courteous, civil, friendly, kindly, sociable, social; easy, free and easy, unceremonious, unconstrained; common, frequent, well-known. * *n* acquaintance, associate, companion, friend, intimate.

familiarity *n* acquaintance, knowledge, understanding; fellowship, friendship, intimacy; closeness, friendliness, sociability; freedom, informality, liberty; disrespect, overfreedom, presumption; intercourse.

familiarize *vb* accustom, habituate, inure, train, use.

family *n* brood, household, people; ancestors, blood, breed, clan, dynasty, kindred, house, lineage, race, stock, strain, tribe; class, genus, group, kind, subdivision.

famine *n* dearth, destitution, hunger, scarcity, starvation.

famish *vb* distress, exhaust, pinch, starve.

famous *adj* celebrated, conspicuous, distinguished, eminent, excellent, fabled, famed, far-famed, great, glorious, heroic, honoured, illustrious, immortal, notable, noted, notorious, remarkable, renowned, signal.

fan[1] *vb* agitate, beat, move, winnow; blow, cool, refresh, ventilate; excite, fire, increase; rouse, stimulate. * *n* blower, cooler, punkah, ventilator.

fan[2] *n* admirer, buff, devotee, enthusiast, fancier, follower, pursuer, supporter.

fanatic *n* bigot, devotee, enthusiast, visionary, zealot.

fanatical *adj* bigoted, enthusiastic, frenzied, mad, rabid, visionary, wild, zealous.

fanciful *adj* capricious, crotchety, imaginary,
visionary, whimsical; chimerical, fantastical, ideal, imaginary, wild.

fancy *vb* apprehend, believe, conjecture, imagine, suppose, think; conceive, imagine. * *adj* elegant, fine, nice, ornamented; extravagant, fanciful, whimsical. * *n* imagination; apprehension, conceit, conception, impression, idea, image, notion, thought; approval, fondness, inclination, judgement, liking, penchant, taste; caprice, crotchet, fantasy, freak, humour, maggot, quirk, vagary, whim, whimsy; apparition, chimera, daydream, delusion, hallucination, megrim, phantasm, reverie, vision.

fanfaron *n* blatherskite, blusterer, braggadocio, bully, hector, swaggerer, vapourer.

fang *n* claw, nail, talon, tooth; tusk.

fantastic *adj* chimerical, fanciful, imaginary, romantic, unreal, visionary; bizarre, capricious, grotesque, odd, quaint, queer, strange, whimsical, wild.

far *adj* distant, long, protracted, remote; farther, remoter; alienated, estranged, hostile. * *adv* considerably, extremely, greatly, very much; afar, distantly, far away, remotely.

farce *n* burlesque, caricature, parody, travesty; forcemeat, stuffing.

farcical *adj* absurd, comic, droll, funny, laughable, ludicrous, ridiculous.

fardel *n* bundle, burden, load, pack; annoyance, burden, ill, trouble.

fare *vb* go, journey, pass, travel; happen, prosper, prove; feed, live, manage, subsist. * *n* charge, price, ticket money; passenger, traveller; board, commons, food, table, victuals, provisions; condition, experience, fortune, luck, outcome.

farewell *n* adieu, leave-taking, valediction; departure, leave, parting, valedictory.

far-fetched *adj* abstruse, catachrestic, forced, recondite, strained.

farrago *n* gallimaufry, hodgepodge, hotchpotch, jumble, medley, miscellany, mixture, potpourri, salmagundi.

farther *adj* additional; further, remoter, ulterior. * *adv* beyond, further; besides, furthermore, moreover.

farthingale *n* crinoline, hoop, hoop skirt.

fascinate *vb* affect, bewitch, overpower, spellbind, stupefy, transfix; absorb, captivate, catch, charm, delight, enamour, enchant, enrapture, entrance.

fascination *n* absorption, charm, enchantment, magic, sorcery, spell, witchcraft, witchery.

fash *vb* harass, perplex, plague, torment, trouble, vex, worry. * *n* anxiety, care, trouble, vexation.

fashion *vb* contrive, create, design, forge, form, make, mould, pattern, shape; accommodate, adapt, adjust, fit, suit. * *n* appearance, cast, configuration, conformation, cut, figure, form, make, model, mould, pattern, shape, stamp; manner, method, sort, wake; conventionalism, conventionality, custom, fad, mode, style, usage, vogue; breeding, gentility; quality.

fashionable *adj* modish, stylish; current, modern, prevailing, up-to-date; customary, usual; genteel, well-bred.

fast[1] *adj* close, fastened, firm, fixed, immovable, tenacious, tight; constant, faithful, permanent, resolute, staunch, steadfast, unswerving, unwavering; fortified, impregnable, strong; deep, profound, sound; fleet, quick, rapid, swift; dissipated, dissolute, extravagant, giddy, reckless, thoughtless, thriftless, wild. * *adv* firmly, immovably, tightly; quickly, rapidly, swiftly; extravagantly, prodigally, reckless, wildly.

fast[2] *vb* abstain, go hungry, starve. * *n* abstention, abstinence, diet, fasting, starvation.

fasten *vb* attach, bind, bolt, catch, chain, cleat, fix, gird, lace, lock, pin, secure, strap, tether, tie; belay, bend; connect, hold, join, unite.

fastidious *adj* critical, dainty, delicate, difficult, exquisite, finical, hypercritical, meticulous, overdelicate, overnice, particular, precise, precious, punctilious, queasy, squeamish.

fat *adj* adipose, fatty, greasy, oily, oleaginous, unctuous; corpulent, fleshy, gross, obese, paunchy, portly, plump, pudgy, pursy; coarse, dull, heavy, sluggish, stupid; lucrative, profitable, rich; fertile, fruitful, productive, rich. * *n* adipose tissue, ester, grease, oil; best part, cream, flower; corpulence, fatness, fleshiness, obesity, plumpness, stoutness.

fatal *adj* deadly, lethal, mortal; baleful, baneful, calamitous, catastrophic, destructive, mischievous, pernicious, ruinous; destined, doomed, foreordained, inevitable, predestined.

fatality *n* destiny, fate; mortality; calamity, disaster.

fate *n* destination, destiny, fate; cup, die, doom, experience, lot, fortune, portion, weird; death, destruction, ruin.

fated *adj* appointed, destined, doomed, foredoomed, predetermined, predestinated, predestined, preordained.

fatherly *adj* benign, kind, paternal, protecting, tender.
fathom *vb* comprehend, divine, penetrate, reach, understand; estimate, gauge, measure, plumb, probe, sound.
fathomless *adj* abysmal, bottomless, deep, immeasurable, profound; impenetrable, incomprehensible, obscure.
fatigue *vb* exhaust, fag, jade, tire, weaken, weary. * *n* exhaustion, lassitude, tiredness, weariness; hardship, labour, toil.
fatuity *n* foolishness, idiocy, imbecility, stupidity; absurdity, folly, inanity, infatuation, madness.
fatuous *adj* dense, drivelling, dull, foolish, idiotic, stupid, witless; infatuated, mad, senseless, silly, weak.
fault *n* blemish, defect, flaw, foible, frailty, imperfection, infirmity, negligence, obliquity, offence, shortcoming, spot, weakness; delinquency, error, indiscretion, lapse, misdeed, misdemeanour, offence, peccadillo, slip, transgression, trespass, vice, wrong; blame, culpability.
faultless *adj* blameless, guiltless, immaculate, innocent, sinless, spotless, stainless; accurate, correct, perfect, unblemished.
faulty *adj* bad, defective, imperfect, incorrect; blameable, blameworthy, censurable, culpable, reprehensible.
faux pas *n* blunder, indiscretion, mistake.
favour *vb* befriend, countenance, encourage, patronize; approve; ease, facilitate; aid, assist, help, oblige, support; extenuate, humour, indulge, palliate, spare. * *n* approval, benignity, countenance, esteem, friendless, goodwill, grace, kindness; benefaction, benefit, boon, dispensation, kindness; championship, patronage, popularity, support; gift, present, token; badge, decoration, knot, rosette; leave, pardon, permission; advantage, cover, indulgence, protection; bias, partiality, prejudice.
favourable *adj* auspicious, friendly, kind, propitious, well-disposed, willing; conductive, contributing, propitious; adapted, advantage, beneficial, benign, convenient, fair, fit, good, helpful, suitable.
favourite *adj* beloved, darling, dear; choice, fancied, esteemed, pet, preferred.
fawn *vb* bootlick, bow, creep, cringe, crouch, dangle, kneel, stoop, toady, truckle.
fealty *n* allegiance, homage, loyalty, obeisance, submission; devotion, faithfulness, fidelity, honour, loyalty.
fear *vb* apprehend, dread; revere, reverence, venerate. * *n* affright, alarm, apprehension, consternation, dismay, dread, fright, horror, panic, phobia, scare, terror; disquietude, flutter, perturbation, palpitation, quaking, quivering, trembling, tremor, trepidation; anxiety, apprehension, concern, misdoubt, misgiving, qualm, solicitude; awe, dread, reverence, veneration.
fearful *adj* afraid, apprehensive, haunted; chicken-hearted, chicken-livered, cowardly, faint-hearted, lily-livered, nervous, pusillanimous, timid, timorous; dire, direful, dreadful, frightful, ghastly, horrible, shocking, terrible.
fearless *adj* bold, brave, courageous, daring, dauntless, doughty, gallant, heroic, intrepid, unterrified, valiant, valorous.
feasible *adj* achievable, attainable, possible, practicable, suitable.
feast *vb* delight, gladden, gratify, rejoice. * *n* banquet, carousal, entertainment, regale, repast, revels, symposium, treat; celebration, festival, fete, holiday; delight, enjoyment, pleasure.
feat *n* accomplishment, achievement, act, deed, exploit, performance, stunt, trick.
feather *n* plume; kind, nature, species.
featly *adv* adroitly, dextrously, nimbly, skilfully.
feature *vb* envisage, envision, picture, visualize; imagine; specialize; appear in, headline, star. * *n* appearance, aspect, component; conformation, fashion, make; characteristic, item, mark, particularity, peculiarity, property, point, trait; leader, lead item, special; favour, expression, lineament; article, film, motion picture, movie, story; highlight, high spot.
fecund *adj* fruitful, impregnated, productive, prolific, rich.

fecundity *n* fertility, fruitfulness, productiveness.

federation *n* alliance, allying, confederation, federating, federation, leaguing, union, uniting; affiliation, coalition, combination, compact, confederacy, entente, federacy, league, copartnership.

fee *vb* pay, recompense, reward. * *n* account, bill, charge, compensation, honorarium, remuneration, reward, tip; benefice, fief, feud.

feeble *adj* anaemic, debilitated, declining, drooping, enervated, exhausted, frail, infirm, languid, languishing, sickly; dim, faint, imperfect, indistinct.

feed *vb* contribute, provide, supply; cherish, eat, nourish, subsist, sustain. * *n* fodder, food, foodstuff, forage, provender.

feel *vb* apprehend, intuit, perceive, sense; examine, handle, probe, touch; enjoy, experience, suffer; prove, sound, test, try; appear, look, seem; believe, conceive, deem, fancy, infer, opine, suppose, think. * *n* atmosphere, feeling, quality; finish, surface, texture.

feeling *n* consciousness, impression, notion, perception, sensation; atmosphere, sense, sentience, touch; affecting, emotion, heartstrings, impression, passion, soul, sympathy; sensibility, sentiment, susceptibility, tenderness; attitude, impression, opinion.

feign *vb* devise, fabricate, forge, imagine, invent; affect, assume, counterfeit, imitate, pretend, sham, simulate.

feint *n* artifice, blind, expedient, make-believe, pretence, stratagem, trick.

felicitate *vb* complicate, congratulate; beatify, bless, delight.

felicitous *adj* appropriate, apt, fit, happy, ingenious, inspired, opportune, pertinent, seasonable, skilful, well-timed; auspicious, fortunate, prosperous, propitious, successful.

felicity *n* blessedness, bliss, blissfulness, gladness, happiness, joy; appropriateness, aptitude, aptness, felicitousness, fitness, grace, propriety, readiness, suitableness; fortune, luck, success.

fell[1] *vb* beat, knock down, level, prostrate; cut, demolish, hew.

fell[2] *adj* barbarous, bloodthirsty, bloody, cruel, ferocious, fierce, implacable, inhuman, malicious, malign, malignant, pitiless, relentless, ruthless, sanguinary, savage, unrelenting, vandalistic; deadly, destructive.

fellow *adj* affiliated, associated, joint, like, mutual, similar, twin. * *n* associate, companion, comrade; compeer, equal, peer; counterpart, mate, match, partner; member; boy, character, individual, man, person.

fellowship *n* brotherhood, companionship, comradeship, familiarity, intimacy; participation; partnership; communion, converse, intercourse; affability, kindliness, sociability, sociableness.

felon *n* convict, criminal, culprit, delinquent, malefactor, outlaw; inflammation, whitlow.

felonious *adj* atrocious, cruel, felon, heinous, infamous, malicious, malign, malignant, nefarious, perfidious, vicious, villainous.

female *adj* delicate, gentle, ladylike, soft; fertile, pistil-bearing, pistillate.

feminine *adj* affectionate, delicate, gentle, graceful, modest, soft, tender; female, ladylike, maidenly, womanish, womanly; effeminateness, effeminacy, softness, unmanliness, weakness, womanliness.

fen *n* bog, marsh, moor, morass, quagmire, slough, swamp.

fence *vb* defend, enclose, fortify, guard, protect, surround; circumscribe, evade, equivocate, hedge, prevaricate; guard, parry. * *n* barrier, hedge, hoarding, palings, palisade, stockade, wall; defence, protection, guard, security, shield; fencing, swordplay, swordsmanship; receiver.

fenny *adj* boggy, fennish, swampy, marshy.

feral, ferine *adj* ferocious, fierce, rapacious, ravenous, savage, untamed, wild.

ferment *vb* agitate, excite, heat; boil, brew, bubble, concoct, heat, seethe. * *n* barm, leaven, yeast; agitation, commotion, fever, glow, heat, tumult.

ferocious *adj* feral, fierce, rapacious, ravenous, savage, untamed, wild; barbarous, bloody, bloodthirsty, brutal, cruel, fell, inhuman, merciless, murderous, pitiless, remorseless, ruthless, sanguinary, truculent, vandalistic, violent.

ferocity *n* ferociousness, ferocity, fierceness, rapacity, savageness, wildness; barbarity, cruelty, inhumanity.

fertile *adj* bearing, breeding, fecund, prolific; exuberant, fruitful, luxuriant, plenteous, productive, rich, teeming; female, fruit-bearing, pistillate.

fertility *n* fertileness, fertility; abundance, exuberant, fruitfulness, luxuriance, plenteousness, productiveness, richness.

fervent *adj* burning, hot, glowing, melting, seething; animated, ardent, earnest, enthusiastic, fervid, fierce, fiery, glowing, impassioned, intense, passionate, vehement, warm, zealous.

fervour *n* heat, warmth; animation, ardour, eagerness, earnestness, excitement, fervency, intensity, vehemence, zeal.

fester *vb* corrupt, rankle, suppurate, ulcerate; putrefy, rot. * *n* abscess, canker, gathering, pustule, sore, suppination; festering, rankling.

festival *n* anniversary, carnival, feast, fete, gala, holiday, jubilee; banquet, carousal, celebration, entertainment, treat.

festive *adj* carnival, convivial, festal, festival, gay, jolly, jovial, joyful, merry, mirthful, uproarious.

festivity *n* conviviality, festival, gaiety, jollity, joviality, joyfulness, joyousness, merrymaking, mirth.

festoon *vb* adorn, decorate, embellish, garland, hoop, ornament. * *n* decoration, embellishment, garland, hoop, ornament, ornamentation.

fetch *vb* bring, elicit, get; accomplish, achieve, effect, perform; attain, reach. * *n* artifice, dodge, ruse, stratagem, trick.

fetid *adj* foul, malodorous, mephitic, noisome, offensive, rancid, rank, rank-smelling, stinking, strong-smelling.

fetish *n* charm, medicine, talisman.

fetter *vb* clog, hamper, shackle, trammel; bind, chain, confine, encumber, hamper, restrain, tie, trammel. * *n* bond, chain, clog, hamper, shackle.

feud *vb* argue, bicker, clash, contend, dispute, quarrel. * *n* affray, argument, bickering, broil, clashing, contention, contest, discord, dissension, enmity, fray, grudge, hostility, jarring, quarrel, rupture, strife, vendetta.

fever *n* agitation, excitement, ferment, fire, flush, heat, passion.

fey *adj* clairvoyant, ethereal, strange, unusual, whimsical; death-smitten, doomed.

fiasco *n* failure, fizzle.

fiat *n* command, decree, order, ordinance.

fibre *n* filament, pile, staple, strand, texture, thread; stamina, strength, toughness.

fickle *adj* capricious, changeable, faithless, fitful, inconstant, irresolute, mercurial, mutable, shifting, unsettled, unstable, unsteady, vacillating, variable, veering, violate, volatile, wavering.

fiction *n* fancy, fantasy, imagination, invention; novel, romance; fable, fabrication, falsehood, figment, forgery, invention, lie.

fictitious *adj* assumed, fabulous, fanciful, feigned, imaginary, invented, mythical, unreal; artificial, counterfeit, dummy, false, spurious, suppositious.

fiddle *vb* dawdle, fidget, interfere, tinker, trifle; cheat, swindle, tamper. * *n* fraud, swindle; fiddler, violin, violinist.

fiddle-de-dee *interj* fudge, moonshine, nonsense, stuff.

fiddle-faddle *n* frivolity, gabble, gibberish, nonsense, prate, stuff, trifling, trivia, twaddle.

fidelity *n* constancy, devotedness, devotion, dutifulness, faithfulness, fealty, loyalty, true-heartedness, truth; accuracy, closeness, exactness, faithfulness, precision.

fidget *vb* chafe, fret, hitch, twitch, worry. * *n* fidgetiness, impatience, restlessness, uneasiness.

fiduciary *adj* confident, fiducial, firm, steadfast, trustful, undoubting, unwavering; reliable, trustworthy. * *n* depositary, trustee.

field *n* clearing, glebe, meadow; expanse, extent, opportunity, range, room, scope, surface; department, domain, province, realm, region.

fiendish *adj* atrocious, cruel, demoniac, devilish, diabolical, hellish, implacable, infernal, malevolent, malicious, malign, malignant.

fierce *adj* barbarous, brutal, cruel, fell, ferocious, furious, infuriate, ravenous, savage; fiery, impetuous, murderous, passionate, tearing, tigerish, truculent, turbulent, uncurbed, untamed, vehement, violent.

fiery *adj* fervent, fervid, flaming, heated, hot, glowing, lurid; ardent, fierce, impassioned, impetuous, inflamed, passionate, vehement.

fight *vb* battle, combat, war; contend, contest, dispute, feud, oppose, strive, struggle, wrestle; encounter, engage; handle, manage, manoeuvre. * *n* affair, affray, action, battle, brush, combat, conflict, confrontation, contest, duel, encounter, engagement, melée, quarrel, struggle, war; brawl, broil, riot, row, skirmish; fighting, pluck, pugnacity, resistance, spirit, temper.

figment *n* fable, fabrication, falsehood, fiction, invention.

figurative *adj* emblematical, representative, symbolic, representative, typical; metaphorical, tropical; florid, flowery, ornate, poetical.

figure *vb* adorn, diversify, ornament, variegate; delineate, depict, represent, signify, symbolize, typify; conceive, image, imagine, picture; calculate, cipher, compute; act, appear, perform. * *n* configuration, conformation, form, outline, shape; effigy, image, likeness, representative; design, diagram, drawing, pattern; image, metaphor, trope; emblem, symbol, type; character, digit, number, numeral.

filament *n* cirrus, fibre, fibril, gossamer, hair, strand, tendril, thread.

filch *vb* crib, nick, pilfer, purloin, rob, snitch, seal, thieve.

file[1] *vb* order, pigeonhole, record, tidy. * *n* data, dossier, folder, portfolio; column, line, list, range, rank, row, series, tier.

file[2] *vb* burnish, furbish, polish, rasp, refine, smooth.

filibuster *vb* delay, frustrate, obstruct, play for time, stall, temporize. * *n* frustrater, obstructionist, thwarter; adventurer, buccaneer, corsair, freebooter, pirate.

fill *vb* occupy, pervade; dilate, distend, expand, stretch, trim; furnish, replenish, stock, store, supply; cloy, congest, content, cram, glut, gorge, line, pack, pall, sate, satiate, satisfy, saturate, stuff, suffuse, swell; engage, fulfil, hold, occupy, officiate, perform.

film *vb* becloud, cloud, coat, cover, darken, fog, mist, obfuscate, obscure, veil; photograph, shoot, take. * *n* cloud, coating, gauze, membrane, nebula, pellicle, scum, skin, veil; thread.

filter *vb* filtrate, strain; exude, ooze, percolate, transude. * *n* diffuser, colander, riddle, sieve, sifter, strainer.

filth *n* dirt, nastiness, ordure; corruption, defilement, foulness, grossness, impurity, obscenity, pollution, squalor, uncleanness, vileness.

filthy *adj* defiled, dirty, foul, licentious, nasty, obscene, pornographic, squalid, unclean; corrupt, gross, impure, unclean; miry, mucky, muddy.

final *adj* eventual, extreme, last, latest, terminal, ultimate; conclusive, decisive, definitive, irrevocable.

finale *n* conclusion, end, termination.

finances *npl* funds, resources, revenues, treasury; income, property.

find *vb* discover, fall upon; gain, get, obtain, procure; ascertain, notice, observe, perceive, remark; catch, detect; contribute, furnish, provide, supply. * *n* acquisition, catch, discovery, finding, plum, prize, strike.

fine[1] *vb* filter, purify, refine. * *adj* comminuted, little, minute, small; capillary, delicate, small; choice, light; exact, keen, sharp; attenuated, subtle, tenuous, thin; exquisite, fastidious, nice, refined, sensitive, subtle; dandy, excellent, superb, superior; beautiful, elegant, handsome, magnificent, splendid; clean, pure, unadulterated.

fine[2] *vb* amerce, mulct, penalize, punish. * *n* amercement, forfeit, forfeiture, mulct, penalty, punishment.

finery *n* decorations, frippery, gewgaws, ornaments, splendour, showiness, trappings, trimmings, trinkets.

finesse *vb* manipulate, manoeuvre. * *n* artifice, contrivance, cunning, craft, manipulation, manoeuvre, manoeuvring, ruses, stratagems, strategy, wiles.

finger *vb* handle, manipulate, play, purloin.

finical *adj* critical, dainty, dapper, fastidious, foppish, jaunty, overnice, overparticular, scrupulous, spruce, squeamish, trim.

finish *vb* accomplish, achieve, complete, consummate, execute, fulfil, perform; elaborate, perfect, polish; close, conclude, end, terminate. * *n* elaboration, elegance, perfection, polish; close, end, death, termination, wind-up.

finite *adj* bounded, circumscribed, conditioned, contracted, definable, limited, restricted, terminable.

fire *vb* ignite, kindle, light; animate, enliven, excite, inflame, inspirit, invigorate, rouse, stir up; discharge, eject, expel, hurl. * *n* combustion; blaze, conflagration; discharge, firing; animation, ardour, enthusiasm, fervour, fervency, fever, force, heat, impetuosity, inflammation, intensity, passion, spirit, vigour, violence; light, lustre, radiance, splendour; imagination, imaginativeness, inspiration, vivacity; affliction, persecution, torture, trouble.

firm[1] *adj* established, coherent, confirmed, consistent, fast, fixed, immovable, inflexible, rooted, secure, settled, stable; compact, compressed, dense, hard, solid; constant, determined, resolute, staunch, steadfast, steady, unshaken; loyal, robust, sinewy, stanch, stout, sturdy, strong.

firm[2] *n* association, business, company, concern, corporation, house, partnership.

firmament *n* heavens, sky, vault, welkin.

firmness *n* compactness, fixedness, hardness, solidity; stability, strength; constancy, soundness, steadfastness, steadiness.

first *adj* capital, chief, foremost, highest, leading, prime, principal; earliest, eldest, original; maiden; elementary, primary, rudimentary; aboriginal, primal, primeval, primitive, pristine. * *adv* chiefly, firstly, initially, mainly, primarily, principally; before, foremost, headmost; before, rather, rather than, sooner, sooner than. * *n* alpha, initial, prime.

first-rate *adj* excellent, prime, superior.

fissure *n* breach, break, chasm, chink, cleft, crack, cranny, crevice, fracture, gap, hole, interstice, opening, rent, rift.

fit[1] *vb* adapt, adjust, suit; become, conform; accommodate, equip, prepare, provide, qualify. * *adj* capacitated, competent, fitted; adequate, appropriate, apt, becoming, befitting, consonant, convenient, fitting, good, meet, pertinent, proper, seemly, suitable.

fit[2] *n* convulsion, fit, paroxysm, qualm, seizure, spasm, spell; fancy, humour, whim; mood, pet, tantrum; interval, period, spell, turn.

fitful *adj* capricious, changeable, convulsive, fanciful, fantastic, fickle, humoursome, impulsive, intermittent, irregular, odd, spasmodic, unstable, variable, whimsical; checkered, eventful.

fitness *n* adaptation, appropriateness, aptitude, aptness, pertinence, propriety, suitableness; preparation, qualification.

fix *vb* establish, fasten, place, plant, set; adjust, correct, mend, repair; attach, bind, clinch, connect, fasten, lock, rivet, stay, tie; appoint, decide, define, determine, limit, seal, settle; consolidate, harden, solidify; abide, remain, rest; congeal, stiffen. * *n* difficulty, dilemma, quandary, pickle, plight, predicament.

flabbergast *vb* abash, amaze, astonish, astound, confound, confuse, disconcert, dumbfound, nonplus.

flabby *adj* feeble, flaccid, inelastic, limp, soft, week, yielding.

flaccid *adj* baggy, drooping, flabby, inelastic, lax, limber, limp, loose, pendulous, relaxed, soft, weak, yielding.

flag[1] *vb* droop, hang, loose; decline, droop, fail, faint, lag, languish, pine, sink, succumb, weaken, weary; stale, pall.

flag[2] *vb* indicate, mark, semaphore, sign, signal. * *n* banner, colours, ensign, gonfalon, pennant, pennon, standard, streamer.

flagellate *vb* beat, castigate, chastise, cudgel, drub, flog, scourge, thrash, whip.

flagitious *adj* abandoned, atrocious, corrupt, flagrant, heinous, infamous, monstrous, nefarious, profligate, scandalous, villainous, wicked.

flagrant *adj* burning, flaming, glowing, raging; crying, enormous, flagitious, glaring, monstrous, nefarious, notorious, outrageous, shameful, wanton, wicked.

flake *vb* desquamate, scale. * *n* lamina, layer, scale.

flamboyant *adj* bright, gorgeous, ornate, rococo.

flame *vb* blaze, shine; burn, flash, glow, warm. * *n* blaze, brightness, fire, flare, vapour; affection, ardour, enthusiasm, fervency, fervour, keenness, warmth.

flaming *adj* blazing; burning, bursting, exciting, glowing, intense, lambent, vehement, violent.

flap *vb* beat, flutter, shake, vibrate, wave. * *n* apron, fly, lap, lappet, tab; beating, flapping, flop, flutter, slap, shaking, swinging, waving.

flare *vb* blaze, flicker, flutter, waver; dazzle, flame, glare; splay, spread, widen. * *n* blaze, dazzle, flame, glare.

flash *vb* blaze, glance, glare, glisten, light, shimmer, scintillate, sparkle, twinkle. * *n* instant, moment, twinkling.

flashy *adj* flaunting, gaudy, gay, loud, ostentatious, pretentious, showy, tawdry, tinsel.

flat *adj* champaign, horizontal, level; even, plane, smooth, unbroken; low, prostrate, overthrow; dull, frigid, jejune, lifeless, monotonous, pointless, prosaic, spiritless, tame, unanimated, uniform, uninteresting; dead, flashy, insipid, mawkish, stale, tasteless, vapid; absolute, clear, direct, downright, peremptory, positive. * *adv* flatly, flush, horizontally, level. * *n* bar, sandbank, shallow, shoal, strand; champaign, lowland, plain; apartment, floor, lodging, storey.

flatter *vb* compliment, gratify, praise; blandish, blarney, butter up, cajole, coax, coddle, court, entice, fawn, humour, inveigle, wheedle.

flattery *n* adulation, blandishment, blarney, cajolery, fawning, obsequiousness, servility, sycophancy, toadyism.

flaunt *vb* boast, display, disport, flourish, parade, sport, vaunt; brandish.

flaunting *adj* flashy, garish, gaudy, ostentatious, showy, tawdry.

flavour *n* gust, gusto, relish, savour, seasoning, smack, taste, zest; admixture, lacing, seasoning; aroma, essence, soul, spirit.

flaw *n* break, breach, cleft, crack, fissure, fracture, gap, rent, rift; blemish, defect, fault, fleck, imperfection, speck, spot.

flay *vb* excoriate, flay; criticize.

fleck *vb* dapple, mottle, speckle, spot, streak, variegate. * *n* speckle, spot, streak.

flecked *adj* dappled, mottled, piebald, spotted, straked, striped, variegated.

flee *vb* abscond, avoid, decamp, depart, escape, fly, leave, run, skedaddle.

fleece *vb* clip, shear; cheat, despoil, pluck, plunder, rifle, rob, steal, strip.

fleer *vb* mock, jeer, gibe, scoff, sneer.

fleet[1] *n* armada, escadrille, flotilla, navy, squadron; company, group.

fleet[2] *adj* fast, nimble, quick, rapid, speedy, swift.

fleeting *adj* brief, caducous, ephemeral, evanescent, flitting, flying, fugitive, passing, short-lived, temporary, transient, transitory.

fleetness *n* celerity, nimbleness, quickness, rapidity, speed, swiftness, velocity.

flesh *n* food, meat; carnality, desires; kindred, race, stock; man, mankind, world.

fleshly *adj* animal, bodily, carnal, lascivious, lustful, lecherous, sensual.

fleshy *adj* corpulent, fat, obese, plump, stout.

flexibility *n* flexibleness, limbersome, lithesome, pliability, pliancy, suppleness; affability, complaisance, compliance, disposition, ductility, pliancy, tractableness, tractability, yielding.

flexible *adj* flexible, limber, lithe, pliable, pliant, supple, willowy; affable, complaisant, ductile, docile, gentle, tractable, tractile, yielding.

flexose, flexuous *adj* bending, crooked, serpentine, sinuate, sinuous, tortuous, waxy, winding.

flibbertigibbet *n* demon, imp, sprite.

flight[1] *n* flying, mounting, soaring, volition; shower, flight; steps, stairs.

flight[2] *n* departure, fleeing, flying, retreat, rout, stampede; exodus, hegira.

flighty *adj* capricious, deranged, fickle, frivolous, giddy, light-headed, mercurial, unbalanced, volatile, wild, whimsical.

flimsy *adj* slight, thin, unsubstantial; feeble, foolish, frivolous, light, puerile, shallow, superficial, trashy, trifling, trivial, weak; insubstantial, sleazy.

flinch *vb* blench, flee, recoil, retreat, shirk, shrink, swerve, wince, withdraw.

fling *vb* cast, chuck, dart, emit, heave, hurl, pitch, shy, throw, toss; flounce, wince. * *n* cast, throw, toss.

flippancy *n* volubility; assuredness, glibness, pertness.

flippant *adj* fluent, glib, talkative, voluble; bold, forward, frivolous, glib, impertinent, inconsiderate, irreverent, malapert, pert, saucy, trifling.

flirt *vb* chuck, fling, hurl, pitch, shy, throw, toss; flutter, twirl, whirl, whisk; coquet, dally, philander. * *n* coquette, jilt, philanderer; jerk.

flirtation *n* coquetry, dalliance, philandering.

flit *vb* flicker, flutter, hover; depart, hasten, pass.

flitting *adj* brief, ephemeral, evanescent, fleeting, fugitive, passing, short, transient, transitory.

float *vb* drift, glide, hang, ride, sail, soar, swim, waft; launch, support.

flock *vb* collect, congregate, gather, group, herd, swarm, throng. * *n* collection, group, multitude; bevy, company, convoy, drove, flight, gaggle, herd, pack, swarm, team, troupe; congregation.

flog *vb* beat, castigate, chastise, drub, flagellate, lash, scourge, thrash, whip.

flood *vb* deluge, inundate, overflow, submerge, swamp. * *n* deluge, freshet, inundation, overflow, tide; bore, downpour, eagre, flow, outburst, spate, rush; abundance, excess.

floor *vb* deck, pave; beat, confound, conquer, overthrow, prevail, prostrate, puzzle; disconcert, nonplus. * *n* storey; bottom, deck, flooring, pavement, stage.

florid *adj* bright-coloured, flushed, red-faced, rubicund; embellished, figurative, luxuriant, ornate, rhetorical, rococo.

flounce[1] *vb* fling, jerk, spring, throw, toss, wince. * *n* jerk, spring.

flounce[2] *n* frill, furbelow, ruffle.

flounder *vb* blunder, flop, flounce, plunge, struggle, toss, tumble, wallow.

flourish *vb* grow, thrive; boast, bluster, brag, gasconade, show off, vaunt, vapour; brandish, flaunt, swing, wave. * *n* dash, display, ostentation, parade, show; bombast, fustian, grandiloquence; brandishing, shake, waving; blast, fanfare, tantivy.

flout *vb* chaff, deride, fleer, gibe, insult, jeer, mock, ridicule, scoff, sneer, taunt. * *n* gibe, fling, insult, jeer, mock, mockery, mocking, scoff, scoffing, taunt.

flow *vb* pour, run, stream; deliquesce, liquefy, melt; arise, come, emanate, follow, grow, issue, proceed, result, spring; glide; float, undulate, wave, waver; abound, run. * *n* current, discharge, flood, flux, gush, rush, stream, trickle; abundance, copiousness.

flower *vb* bloom, blossom, effloresce; develop. * *n* bloom, blossom; best, cream, elite, essence, pick; freshness, prime, vigour.

flowery *adj* bloomy, florid; embellished, figurative, florid, ornate, overwrought.

flowing *adj* abundant, copious, fluent, smooth.

fluctuate *vb* oscillate, swing, undulate, vibrate, wave; change, vary; vacillate, waver.

flue *n* chimney, duct; flew, fluff, nap, floss, fur.

fluency *n* liquidness, smoothness; affluence, copiousness; ease, facility, readiness.

fluent *adj* current, flowing, gliding, liquid; smooth; affluent, copious, easy, facile, glib, ready, talkative, voluble.

fluff *vb* blunder, bungle, forget, fumble, mess up, miscue, misremember, muddle, muff. * *n* down, flew, floss, flue, fur, lint, nap; cobweb, feather, gossamer, thistledown; blunder, bungle, fumble, muff.

flume *n* channel, chute, mill race, race.

flummery *n* chaff, frivolity, froth, moonshine, nonsense, trash, trifling; adulation, blandishment, blarney, flattery; brose, porridge, sowens.

flunky, **flunkey** *n* footman, lackey, livery servant, manservant, valet; snob, toady.

flurry *vb* agitate, confuse, disconcert, disturb, excite, fluster, hurry, perturb. * *n* gust, flaw, squall; agitation, bustle, commotion, confusion, disturbance, excitement, flutter, haste, hurry, hurry-scurry, perturbation, ruffle, scurry.

flush[1] *vb* flow, rush, start; glow, mantle, redden; animate, elate, elevate, erect, excite; cleanse, drench. * *adj* bright, fresh, glowing, vigorous; abundant, affluent, exuberant, fecund, fertile, generous, lavish, liberal, prodigal, prolific, rich, wealthy, well-supplied; even, flat, level, plane. * *adv* evenly, flat, level; full, point-blank, right, square, squarely, straight. * *n* bloom, blush, glow, redness, rosiness, ruddiness; impulse, shock, thrill.

flush[2] *vb* disturb, rouse, start, uncover.

fluster *vb* excite, flush, heat; agitate, disturb, flurry, hurry, perturb, ruffle; confound, confuse, discompose, disconcert. * *n* glow, heat; agitation, flurry, flutter, hurry, hurry-scurry, perturbation, ruffle.

fluted *adj* channelled, corrugated, grooved.

flutter *vb* flap, hover; flirt, flit; beat, palpitate, quiver, tremble; fluctuate, oscillate, vacillate, waver. * *n* agitation, tremor; hurry, commotion, confusion, excitement, flurry, fluster, hurry-scurry, perturbation, quivering, tremble, tumult, twitter.

flux *n* flow, flowing; change, mutation, shifting, transition; diarrhoea, dysentery, looseness; fusing, melting, menstruum, solvent.

fly[1] *vb* aviate, hover, mount, soar; flap, float, flutter, play, sail, soar, undulate, vibrate, wave; burst, explode; abscond, decamp, depart, flee, vanish; elapse, flit, glide, pass, slip.

fly[2] *adj* alert, bright, sharp, smart, wide-awake; astute, cunning, knowing, sly; agile, fleet, nimble, quick, spry.

foal *n* colt, filly.

foam *vb* cream, froth, lather, spume; boil, churn, ferment, fume, seethe, simmer, stew. * *n* bubbles, cream, froth, scum, spray, spume, suds.

fodder *n* feed, food, forage, provender, rations.

foe *n* adversary, antagonist, enemy, foeman, opponent.

fog *vb* bedim, bemist, blear, blur, cloud, dim, enmist, mist; addle, befuddle, confuse, fuddle, muddle. * *n* blear, blur, dimness, film, fogginess, haze, haziness, mist, smog, vapour; befuddlement, confusion, fuddle, maze, muddle.

foggy *adj* blurred, cloudy, dim, dimmed, hazy, indistinct, misty, obscure; befuddled, bewildered, confused, dazed, muddled, muddy, stupid.

foible *n* defect, failing, fault, frailty, imperfection, infirmity, penchant, weakness.

foil[1] *vb* baffle, balk, check, checkmate, circumvent, defeat, disappoint, frustrate, thwart.

foil[2] *n* film, flake, lamina; background, contrast.

foist *vb* impose, insert, interpolate, introduce, palm off, thrust.

fold[1] *vb* bend, cover, double, envelop, wrap; clasp, embrace, enfold, enwrap, gather, infold, interlace; collapse, fail. * *n* double, doubling, gather, plait, plicature.

fold[2] *n* cot, enclosure, pen.

foliaceous *adj* foliate, leafy; flaky, foliated,

lamellar, lamellate, lamellated, laminated, scaly, schistose.

folk *n* kindred, nation, people.

follow *vb* ensue, succeed; chase, dog, hound, pursue, run after, trail; accompany, attend; conform, heed, obey, observe; cherish, cultivate, seek; practise, pursue; adopt, copy, imitate; arise, come, flow, issue, proceed, result, spring.

follower *n* acolyte, attendant, associate, companion, dependant, retainer, supporter; adherent, admirer, disciple, partisan, pupil; copier, imitator.

folly *n* doltishness, dullness, imbecility, levity, shallowness; absurdity, extravagance, fatuity, foolishness, imprudence, inanity, indiscretion, ineptitude, nonsense, senselessness; blunder, faux pas, indiscretion, unwisdom.

foment *vb* bathe, embrocate, stupe; abet, brew, encourage, excite, foster, instigate, promote, stimulate.

fond *adj* absurd, baseless, empty, foolish, senseless, silly, vain, weak; affectionate, amorous, doting, loving, overaffectionate, tender.

fondle *vb* blandish, caress, coddle, cosset, dandle, pet.

fondness *n* absurdity, delusion, folly, silliness, weakness; liking, partiality, predilection, preference, propensity; appetite, relish, taste.

food *n* aliment, board, bread, cheer, commons, diet, fare, meat, nourishment, nutriment, nutrition, pabulum, provisions, rations, regimen, subsistence, sustenance, viands, victuals; feed, fodder, forage, provender.

fool *vb* jest, play, toy, trifle; beguile, cheat, circumvent, cozen, deceive, delude, dupe, gull, hoodwink, overreach, trick. * *n* blockhead, dolt, driveller, idiot, imbecile, nincompoop, ninny, nitwit, simpleton; antic, buffoon, clown, droll, harlequin, jester, merry-andrew, punch, scaramouch, zany; butt, dupe.

foolery *n* absurdity, folly, foolishness, nonsense; buffoonery, mummery, tomfoolery.

foolhardy *adj* adventurous, bold, desperate, harebrained, headlong, hot-headed, incautious, precipitate, rash, reckless, venturesome, venturous.

foolish *adj* brainless, daft, fatuous, idiotic, inane, inept, insensate, irrational, senseless, shallow, silly, simple, thick-skulled, vain, weak, witless; absurd, ill-judged, imprudent, indiscreet, nonsensical, preposterous, ridiculous, unreasonable, unwise; childish, contemptible, idle, puerile, trifling, trivial, vain.

foolishness *n* doltishness, dullness, fatuity, folly, imbecility, shallowness, silliness, stupidity; absurdity, extravagance, imprudence, indiscretion, nonsense; childishness, puerility, triviality.

footing *n* foothold, purchase; basis, foundation, groundwork, installation; condition, grade, rank, standing, state, status; settlement, establishment.

footman *n* footboy, menial, lackey, runner, servant.

footpad *n* bandit, brigand, freebooter, highwayman, robber.

footpath *n* footway, path, trail.

footprint *n* footfall, footmark, footstep, trace, track.

footstep *n* footmark, footprint, trace, track; footfall, step, tread; mark, sign, token, trace, vestige.

fop *n* beau, coxcomb, dandy, dude, exquisite, macaroni, popinjay, prig, swell.

foppish *adj* coxcombical, dandified, dandyish, dressy, finical, spruce, vain.

forage *vb* feed, graze, provender, provision, victual; hunt for, range, rummage, search, seek; maraud, plunder, raid. * *n* feed, fodder, food, pasturage, provender; hunt, rummage, search.

foray *n* descent, incursion, invasion, inroad, irruption, raid.

forbear *vb* cease, desist, hold, pause, stop, stay; abstain, refrain; endure, tolerate; avoid, decline, shun; abstain, omit, withhold.

forbearance *n* abstinence, avoidance, forbearing, self-restraint, shunning, refraining; indulgence, leniency, long-suffering, mildness, moderation, patience.

forbid *vb* ban, debar, disallow, embargo, enjoin, hinder, inhibit, interdict, prohibit, proscribe, taboo, veto.

forbidding *adj* abhorrent, disagreeable, displeasing, odious, offensive, repellant, repulsive, threatening, unpleasant.

force *vb* coerce, compel, constrain, necessitate, oblige; drive, impel, overcome, press, urge; ravish, violate. * *n* emphasis, energy, head, might, pith, power, strength, stress, vigour, vim; agency, efficacy, efficiency, cogency, potency, validity, virtue; coercion, compulsion, constraint, enforcement, vehemence, violence; army, array, battalion, host, legion, phalanx, posse, soldiery, squadron, troop.

forcible *adj* all-powerful, cogent, impressive, irresistible, mighty, potent, powerful, strong, weighty; impetuous, vehement, violent, unrestrained; coerced, coercive, compulsory; convincing, energetic, effective, efficacious, telling, vigorous.

forcibly *adv* mightily, powerfully; coercively, compulsorily, perforce, violently; effectively, energetically, vigorously.

ford *n* current, flood, stream; crossing, wading place.

fore *adj* anterior, antecedent, first, foregoing, former, forward, preceding, previous, prior; advanced, foremost, head, leading.

forebode *vb* augur, betoken, foreshow, foretell, indicate, portend, predict, prefigure, presage, prognosticate, promise, signify.

foreboding *n* augury, omen, prediction, premonition, presage, presentiment, prognostication.

forecast *vb* anticipate, foresee, predict; calculate, contrive, devise, plan, project, scheme. * *n* anticipation, foresight, forethought, planning, prevision, prophecy, provident.

foreclose *vb* debar, hinder, preclude, prevent, stop.

foredoom *vb* foreordain, predestine, preordain.

forego *see* **forgo**.

foregoing *adj* antecedent, anterior, fore, former, preceding, previous, prior.

foregone *adj* bygone, former, past, previous.

foreign *adj* alien, distant, exotic, exterior, external, outward, outlandish, remote, strange, unnative; adventitious, exterior, extraneous, extrinsic, inappropriate, irrelevant, outside, unnatural, unrelated.

foreknowledge *n* foresight, prescience, prognostication.

foremost *adj* first, front, highest, leading, main, principal.

foreordain *vb* appoint, foredoom, predestinate, predetermine, preordain.

forerunner *n* avant-courier, foregoer, harbinger, herald, precursor, predecessor; omen, precursor, prelude, premonition, prognosticate, sign.

foresee *vb* anticipate, forebode, forecast, foreknow, foretell, prognosticate, prophesy.

foreshadow *vb* forebode, predict, prefigure, presage, presignify, prognosticate, prophesy.

foresight *n* foreknowledge, prescience, prevision; anticipation, care, caution, forecast, forethought, precaution, providence, prudence.

forest *n* wood, woods, woodland.

forestall *vb* hinder, frustrate, intercept, preclude, prevent, thwart; antedate, anticipate, foretaste; engross, monopolize, regrate.

foretaste *n* anticipation, forestalling, prelibation.

foretell *vb* predict, prophesy; augur, betoken, forebode, forecast, foreshadow, foreshow, portend, presage, presignify, prognosticate, prophesy.

forethought *n* anticipation, forecast, foresight, precaution, providence, prudence.

forever *adv* always, constantly, continually, endlessly, eternally, ever, evermore, everlastingly, perpetually, unceasingly.

forewarn *vb* admonish, advise, caution, dissuade.

forfeit *vb* alienate, lose. * *n* amercement, damages, fine, forfeiture, mulct, penalty.

forfend *vb* avert, forbid, hinder, prevent, protect.

forge *vb* beat, fabricate, form, frame, hammer; coin, devise, frame, invent; counterfeit, falsify, feign. * *n* furnace, ironworks, smithy.

forgery *n* counterfeit, fake, falsification, imitation.

forgetful *adj* careless, heedless, inattentive, mindless, neglectful, negligent, oblivious, unmindful.

forgive *vb* absolve, acquit, condone, excuse, exonerate, pardon, remit.

forgiveness *n* absolution, acquittal, amnesty, condoning. exoneration, pardon, remission, reprieve.

forgiving *adj* absolutory, absolvatory, acquitting, clearing, excusing, pardoning, placable, releasing.

forgo *vb* abandon, cede, relinquish, renounce, resign, surrender, yield.

fork *vb* bifurcate, branch, divaricate, divide. * *n* bifurcation, branch, branching, crotch, divarication, division.

forked *adj* bifurcated, branching, divaricated, furcate, furcated.

forlorn *adj* abandoned, deserted, forsaken, friendless, helpless, lost, solitary; abject, comfortless, dejected, desolate, destitute, disconsolate, helpless, hopeless, lamentable, pitiable, miserable, woebegone, wretched.

form *vb* fashion model, mould, shape; build, conceive, construct, create, fabricate, make, produce; contrive, devise, frame, invent; compose, constitute, develop, organize; discipline, educate, teach, train. * *n* body, build, cast, configuration, conformation, contour, cut, fashion, figure, format, mould, outline, pattern, shape; formula, formulary, method, mode, practice, ritual; class, kind, manner, model, order, sort, system, type; arrangement, order, regularity, shapeliness; ceremonial, ceremony, conventionality, etiquette, formality, observance, ordinance, punctilio, rite, ritual; bench, seat; class, rank; arrangement, combination, organization.

formal *adj* explicit, express, official, positive, strict; fixed, methodical, regular, rigid, set, stiff; affected, ceremonious, exact, precise, prim, punctilious, starchy. starched; constitutive, essential; external, outward, perfunctory; formative, innate, organic, primordial.

formality *n* ceremonial, ceremony, conventionality, etiquette, punctilio, rite, ritual.

formation *n* creation, genesis, production; composition, constitution; arrangement, combination, disposal, disposition.

formative *adj* creative, determinative, plastic, shaping; derivative, inflectional, nonradical.

former *adj* antecedent, anterior, earlier, foregoing, preceding, previous, prior; late, old-time, quondam; by, bygone, foregone, gone, past.

formidable *adj* appalling, dangerous, difficult, dreadful, fearful, frightful, horrible, menacing, redoubtable, shocking, terrible, terrific, threatening, tremendous.

forsake *vb* abandon, desert, leave, quit; drop, forgo, forswear, relinquish, renounce, surrender, yield.

forsooth *adv* certainly, indeed, really, surely, truly.

forswear *vb* abandon, desert, drop, forsake, leave, quit, reject, renounce; abjure, deny, eschew, perjure, recant, repudiate, retract.

fort *n* bulwark, castle, citadel, defence, fastness, fortification, fortress, stronghold.

forthwith *adv* directly, immediately, instantly, quickly, straightaway.

fortification *n* breastwork, bulwark, castle, citadel, defence, earthwork, fastness, fort, keep, rampart, redoubt, stronghold, tower.

fortify *vb* brace, encourage, entrench, garrison, protect, reinforce, stiffen, strengthen; confirm, corroborate.

fortitude *n* braveness, bravery, courage, determination, endurance, firmness, hardiness, patience, pluck, resolution, strength, valour.

fortuitous *adj* accidental, casual, chance, contingent, incidental.

fortunate *adj* favoured, happy, lucky, prosperous, providential, successful; advantageous, auspicious, favourable, happy, lucky, propitious, timely.

fortune *n* accident, casualty, chance, contingency, fortuity, hap, luck; estate, possessions, property, substance; affluence, felicity, opulence, prosperity, riches, wealth; destination, destiny, doom, fate, lot, star; event, issue, result; favour, success.

forward *vb* advance, aid, encourage, favour, foster, further, help, promote, support; accelerate, dispatch, expedite, hasten, hurry, quicken, speed; dispatch, post, send, ship, transmit. * *adj* ahead, advanced, onward; anterior, front, fore, head; prompt, eager, earnest, hasty, impulsive, quick, ready, willing, zealous; assuming, bold, brazen, brazen-faced, confident, flippant, impertinent, pert, presumptuous, presuming; advanced, early, premature. * *adv* ahead, onward.

foster *vb* cosset, feed, nurse, nourish, support, sustain; advance, aid, breed, cherish, cultivate, encourage, favour, foment, forward, further, harbour, patronize, promote, rear, stimulate.

foul *vb* besmirch, defile, dirty, pollute, soil, stain, sully; clog, collide, entangle, jam. * *adj* dirty, fetid, filthy, impure, nasty, polluted, putrid, soiled, stained, squalid, sullied, rank, tarnished, unclean; disgusting, hateful, loathsome, noisome, odious, offensive; dishonourable, underhand, unfair, sinister; abominable, base, dark, detestable, disgraceful, infamous, scandalous, scurvy, shameful, wile, wicked; coarse, low, obscene, vulgar; abusive, foul-mouthed, foul-spoken, insulting, scurrilous; cloudy, rainy, rough, stormy, wet; feculent, muddy, thick, turbid; entangled, tangled.

foul-mouthed *adj* abusive, blackguardy, blasphemous, filthy, foul, indecent, insolent, insulting, obscene, scurrilous.

found *vb* base, fix, ground, place, rest, set; build, construct, erect, raise; colonize, establish, institute, originate, plant; cast, mould.

foundation *n* base, basis, bed, bottom, footing, ground, groundwork, substructure, support; endowment, establishment, settlement.

founder[1] *n* author, builder, establisher, father, institutor, originator, organizer, planter.

founder[2] *n* caster, moulder.

founder[3] *vb* sink, swamp, welter; collapse, fail, miscarry; fall, stumble, trip.

fountain *n* fount, reservoir, spring, well; jet, upswelling; cause, fountainhead, origin, original, source.

foxy *adj* artful, crafty, cunning, sly, subtle, wily.

fracas *n* affray, brawl, disturbance, outbreak, quarrel, riot, row, uproar, tumult,

fractious *adj* captious, cross, fretful, irritable, peevish, pettish, perverse, petulant, querulous, snappish, splenetic, touchy, testy, waspish.

fracture *vb* break, crack, split. * *n* breaking, rupture; breach, break, cleft, crack, fissure, flaw, opening, rift, rent.

fragile *adj* breakable, brittle, delicate, frangible; feeble, frail, infirm, weak.

fragility *n* breakability, breakableness, brittleness, frangibility, frangibleness; feebleness, frailty, infirmity, weakness.

fragment *vb* atomize, break, fracture, pulverize, splinter. * *n* bit, chip, fraction, fracture, morsel, part, piece, remnant, scrap.

fragrance *n* aroma, balminess, bouquet, odour, perfume, redolence, scent, smell.

fragrant *adj* ambrosial, aromatic, balmy, odoriferous, odorous, perfumed, redolent, spicy, sweet, sweet-scented, sweet-smelling.

frail *adj* breakable, brittle, delicate, fragile, frangible, slight; feeble, infirm, weak.

frailty *n* feebleness, frailness, infirmity, weakness; blemish, defect, failing, fault, foible, imperfection, peccability, shortcoming.

frame *vb* build, compose, constitute, construct, erect, form, make, mould, plan, shape; contrive, devise, fabricate, fashion, forge, invest, plan. * *n* body, carcass, framework, framing, shell, skeleton; constitution, fabric, form, structure, scheme, system; condition, humour, mood, state, temper.

franchise *n* privilege, right; suffrage, vote; exemption, immunity.

frangible *adj* breakable, brittle, fragile.

frank *adj* artless, candid, direct, downright, frank-hearted, free, genuine, guileless, ingenuous, naive, open, outspoken, outright, plain, plain-spoken, point-blank, sincere, straightforward, truthful, unequivocal, unreserved, unrestricted.

frankness *n* candour, ingenuousness, openness, outspokenness, plain speaking, truth, straightforwardness.

frantic *adj* crazy, distracted, distraught, frenzied, furious, infuriate, mad. outrageous, phrenetic, rabid, raging, raving, transported, wild.

fraternity *n* association, brotherhood, circle, clan, club, company, fellowship, league, set, society, sodality; brotherliness.

fraternize *vb* associate, coalesce, concur, consort, cooperate, harmonize, sympathize, unite.

fraud *n* artifice, cheat, craft, deception, deceit, duplicity, guile, hoax, humbug, imposition, imposture, sham, stratagem, treachery, trick, trickery, wile.

fraudulent *adj* crafty, deceitful, deceptive, dishonest, false, knavish, treacherous, trickish, tricky, wily.

fraught *adj* abounding, big, burdened, charged, filled, freighted, laden, pregnant, stored, weighted.

fray[1] *n* affray, battle, brawl, broil, combat, fight, quarrel, riot.

fray[2] *vb* chafe, fret, rub, wear; ravel, shred.

freak *adj* bizarre, freakish, grotesque, monstrous, odd, unexpected, unforeseen. * *n* caprice, crotchet, fancy, humour, maggot, quirk, vagary, whim, whimsey; antic, caper, gambol; abnormality, abortion, monstrosity.

freakish *adj* capricious, changeable, eccentric, erratic, fanciful, humoursome, odd, queer, whimsical.

free *vb* deliver, discharge, disenthral, emancipate, enfranchise, enlarge, liberate, manumit, ransom, release, redeem, rescue, save; clear, disencumber, disengage, extricate, rid, unbind, unchain, unfetter, unlock; exempt, immunize, privilege. * *adj* bondless, independent, loose, unattached, unconfined, unentangled, unimpeded, unrestrained, untrammelled; autonomous, delivered, emancipated, freeborn, liberated, manumitted, ransomed, released, self-governing; clear, exempt, immune, privileged; allowed, permitted; devoid, empty, open, unimpeded, unobstructed, unrestricted; affable, artless, candid, frank, ingenuous, sincere, unreserved; bountiful, charitable, free-hearted, generous, hospitable, liberal, munificent, openhanded; immoderate, lavish, prodigal; eager, prompt, ready, willing; available, gratuitous, spontaneous; careless, lax, loose; bold, easy, familiar, informal, overfamiliar, unconstrained. * *adv* openly, outright, unreservedly, unrestrainedly, unstintingly; freely, gratis, gratuitously.

freebooter *n* bandit, brigand, despoiler, footpad, gangster, highwayman, marauder, pillager, plunderer, robber; buccaneer, pirate, rover.

freedom *n* emancipation, independence, liberation, liberty, release; elbowroom, margin, play, range, scope, swing; franchise, immunity, privilege; familiarity, laxity, license, looseness.

freethinker *n* agnostic, deist, doubter, infidel, sceptic, unbeliever.

freeze *vb* congeal, glaciate, harden, stiffen; benumb, chill.

freight *vb* burden, charge, lade, load. * *n* burden, cargo, lading, load.

frenzy *n* aberration, delirium, derangement, distraction, fury, insanity, lunacy, madness, mania, paroxysm, rage, raving, transport.

frequent *vb* attend, haunt, resort, visit. * *adj* iterating, oft-repeated; common, customary, everyday, familiar, habitual, persistent, usual; constant, continual, incessant.

fresh *adj* new, novel, recent; renewed, revived; blooming, flourishing, green, undecayed, unimpaired, unfaded, unobliterated, unwilted, unwithered, well-preserved; sweet; delicate, fair, fresh-coloured, ruddy, rosy; florid, hardy, healthy, vigorous, strong; active, energetic, unexhausted, unfatigued, unwearied, vigorous; keen, lively, unabated, undecayed, unimpaired, vivid; additional, further; uncured, undried, unsalted, unsmoked; bracing, health-giving, invigorating, refreshing, sweet; brink, stiff, strong; inexperienced, raw, uncultivated, unpracticed, unskilled, untrained, unused.

freshen *vb* quicken, receive, refresh, revive.

fret[1] *vb* abrade, chafe, fray, gall, rub, wear; affront, agitate, annoy, gall, harass, irritate, nettle, provoke, ruffle, tease, vex, wear, worry; ripple, roughen; corrode; fume, peeve, rage, stew. * *n* agitation, fretfulness, fretting, irritation, peevishness, vexation.

fret[2] *vb* diversify, interlace, ornament, variegate. * *n* fretwork, interlacing, ornament; ridge, wale, whelk.

fretful *adj* captious, cross, fractious, ill-humoured, ill-tempered, irritable, peevish, pettish, petulant, querulous, short-tempered, snappish, spleeny, splenetic, testy, touchy, uneasy, waspish.

friable *adj* brittle, crisp, crumbling, powdery, pulverable.

friction *n* abrasion, attrition, grating, rubbing; bickering, disagreement, dissension, wrangling.

friend *adj* benefactor, chum, companion, comrade, crony, confidant, intimate; adherent, ally, associate, confrere, partisan; advocate, defender, encourager, favourer, patron, supporter, well-wisher.

friendly *adj* affectionate, amiable, benevolent, favourable, kind, kind-hearted, kindly, well-disposed; amicable, cordial, fraternal, neighbourly; conciliatory, peaceable, unhostile.

friendship *n* affection, attachment, benevolence, fondness, goodness, love, regard; fellowship, intimacy; amicability, amicableness, amity, cordiality, familiarity, fraternization, friendliness, harmony.

fright *n* affright, alarm, consternation, dismay, funk, horror, panic, scare, terror.

frighten *vb* affright, alarm, appal, daunt, dismay, intimidate, scare, stampede, terrify.

frightful *adj* alarming, awful, dire, direful, dread, dreadful, fearful, horrible, horrid, shocking, terrible, terrific; ghastly, grim, grisly, gruesome, hideous.

frigid *adj* cold, cool, gelid; dull, lifeless, spiritless, tame, unanimated, uninterested, uninteresting; chilling, distant, forbidding, formal, freezing, prim, repellent, repelling, repulsive, rigid, stiff.

frill *n* edging, frilling, furbelow, gathering, ruche, ruching, ruffle; affectation, mannerism.

fringe *vb* border, bound, edge, hem, march, rim, skirt, verge. * *n* border, edge, edging, tassel, trimming. * *adj* edging, extra, unofficial.

frisk *vb* caper, dance, frolic, gambol, hop, jump, play, leap, romp, skip, sport, wanton.

frisky *adj* frolicsome, coltish, gay, lively, playful, sportive.

frivolity *n* flummery, folly, fribbling, frippery, frivolousness, levity, puerility, trifling, triviality.

frivolous *adj* childish, empty, flighty, flimsy, flippant, foolish, giddy, idle, light, paltry. petty, puerile, silly, trashy, trifling, trivial, unimportant, vain, worthless.

frolic *vb* caper, frisk, gambol, lark, play, romp, sport. * *n* escapade, gambol, lark, romp, skylark, spree, trick; drollery, fun, play, pleasantry, sport.

frolicsome *adj* coltish, fresh, frolic, gamesome, gay, lively, playful, sportive.

front *vb* confront, encounter, face, oppose. * *adj* anterior, forward; foremost, frontal, headmost. * *n* brow, face, forehead; assurance, boldness, brass, effrontery, impudence; breast, head, van, vanguard; anterior, face, forepart, obverse; facade, frontage.

frontier *n* border, boundary, coast, confine, limits, marches.

frosty *adj* chill, chilly, cold, icy, stinging, wintry; cold, cold-hearted, frigid, indifferent, unaffectionate, uncordial, unimpassioned, unloving; dull-hearted, lifeless, spiritless, unanimated; frosted, grey-hearted, hoary, white.

froth *vb* bubble, cream, foam, lather, spume. * *n* bubbles, foam, lather, spume; balderdash, flummery, nonsense, trash, triviality.

frothy *adj* foamy, spumy; empty, frivolous, light, trifling, trivial, unsubstantial, vain.

froward *adj* captious, contrary, contumacious, cross, defiant, disobedient, fractious, impudent, intractable, obstinate, peevish, perverse, petulant, refractory, stubborn, ungovernable, untoward, unyielding, wayward, wilful.

frown *vb* glower, lower, scowl.

frowzy, frowsy *adj* fetid, musty, noisome, rancid, rank, stale; disordered, disorderly, dowdy, slatternly, slovenly.

frugal *adj* abstemious, careful, chary, choice, economical, provident, saving, sparing, temperate, thrifty, unwasteful.

fruit *n* crop, harvest, produce, production; advantage, consequence, effect, good, outcome, product, profit, result; issue, offspring, young.

fruitful *adj* abounding, productive; fecund, fertile, prolific; abundant, exuberant, plenteous, plentiful, rich, teeming.

fruition *n* completion, fulfilment, perfection; enjoyment.

fruitless *adj* acarpous, barren, sterile, infecund, unfertile, unfruitful, unproductive, unprolific; abortive, bootless, futile, idle, ineffectual, profitless, unavailing, unprofitable, useless, vain.

frumpish, frumpy *adj* cross, cross-grained, cross-tempered, dowdy, grumpy, irritable, shabby, slatternly, snappish.

frustrate *vb* baffle, balk, check, circumvent, defeat, disappoint, disconcert, foil, thwart; cross, hinder, outwit.

frustrated *adj* balked, blighted, dashed, defeated, foiled, thwarted; ineffectual, null, useless, vain.

fuddled *adj* befuddled, boozy, corned, crapulous, drunk, groggy, high, inebriated, intoxicated, muddled, slewed, tight, tipsy.

fugacious *adj* evanescent, fleeting, fugitive, transient, transitory.

fugitive *adj* escaping, fleeing, flying; brief, ephemeral, evanescent, fleeting, flitting, fugacious, momentary, short, short-lived, temporal, temporary, transient, transitory, uncertain, unstable, volatile. * *n* émigré, escapee, evacuee, fleer, outlaw, refugee, runaway.

fulfil *vb* accomplish, complete, consummate, effect, effectuate, execute, realize; adhere, discharge, do, keep, obey, observe, perform; answer, fill, meet, satisfy.

full *adj* brimful, filled, flush, replete; abounding, replete, well-stocked; bagging, flowing, loose, voluminous; chock-full, cloyed, crammed, glutted, gorged, overflowing, packed, sated, satiated, saturated, soaked, stuffed, swollen; adequate, complete, entire, mature, perfect; abundant, ample, copious, plenteous, plentiful, sufficient; clear, deep, distinct, loud, rounded, strong; broad, large, capacious, comprehensive, extensive, plump; circumstantial, detailed, exhaustive. * *adv* completely, fully; directly, exactly, precisely.

fullness *n* abundance, affluence, copiousness, plenitude, plenty, profusion; glut, satiety, sating, repletion; completeness, completion, entireness, perfection; clearness, loudness, resonance, strength; dilation, distension, enlargement, plumpness, rotundity, roundness, swelling.

fully *adv* abundantly, amply, completely, copiously, entirely, largely, plentifully, sufficiently.

fulminate *vb* detonate, explode; curse, denounce, hurl, menace, threaten, thunder.

fulsome *adj* excessive, extravagant, fawning; disgusting, nauseous, nauseating, offensive, repulsive; coarse, gross, lustful, questionable.

fumble *vb* bungle, grope, mismanage, stumble; mumble, stammer, stutter.

fume *vb* reek, smoke, vaporize. * *n* effluvium exhalation, reek, smell, smoke, steam, vapour; agitation, fret, fry, fury, passion, pet, rage, storm.

fun *adj* amusing, diverting, droll, entertaining. * *n* amusement, diversion, drollery, frolic, gaiety, humour, jesting, jocularity, jollity, joy, merriment, mirth, play, pranks, sport, pleasantry, waggishness.

function *vb* act, discharge, go, operate, officiate, perform, run, serve, work. * *n* discharge, execution, exercise, operation, performance, purpose, use; activity, business, capacity, duty, employment, occupation, office, part, province, role; ceremony, rite; dependant, derivative.

fund *vb* afford, endow, finance, invest, provide, subsidise, support; garner, hoard, stock, store. * *n* accumulation, capital, endowment, reserve, stock; store, supply; foundation.

fundament *n* bottom, buttocks, seat.

fundamental *adj* basal, basic, bottom, cardinal, constitutional, elementary, essential, indispensable, organic, principal, primary, radical. * *n* essential, principal, rule.

funeral *n* burial, cremation, exequies, internment, obsequies.

funereal *adj* dark, dismal, gloomy, lugubrious, melancholy, mournful, sad, sepulchral, sombre, woeful.

funk *vb* blanch, shrink, quail. * *n* stench, stink; fear, fright, panic.

funny *adj* amusing, comic, comical, diverting, droll, facetious, farcical, humorous, jocose, jocular, laughable, ludicrous, sportive, witty; curious, odd, queer, strange. * *n* jest, joke; cartoon, comic.

furbish *vb* burnish, brighten, polish, renew, renovate, rub, shine.

furious *adj* angry, fierce, frantic, frenzied, fuming, infuriated, mad, raging, violent, wild; boisterous, fierce, impetuous, stormy, tempestuous, tumultuous, turbulent, vehement.

furnish *vb* appoint, endow, provide, supply; decorate, equip, fit; afford, bestow, contribute, give, offer, present, produce, yield.

furniture *n* chattels, effects, household goods, movables; apparatus, appendages, appliances, equipment, fittings, furnishings; decorations, embellishments, ornaments.

furore *n* commotion, craze, enthusiasm, excitement, fad, fury, madness, mania, rage, vogue.

furrow *vb* chamfer, channel, cleave, corrugate, cut, flute, groove, hollow; pucker, seam, wrinkle. * *n* chamfer, channel, cut, depression, fluting, groove, hollow, line, seam, track, trench, rot, wrinkle.

further *vb* advance, aid, assist, encourage, help, forward, promote, succour, strengthen. * *adj* additional. * *adv* also, besides, farther, furthermore, moreover.

furtive *adj* clandestine, hidden, secret, sly, skulking, sneaking, sneaky, stealthy, stolen, surreptitious.

fury *n* anger, frenzy, fit, furore, ire, madness, passion, rage; fierceness, impetuosity, turbulence, turbulency, vehemence; bacchant, bacchante, bedlam, hag, shrew, termagant, virago, vixen.

fuse *vb* dissolve, melt, liquefy, smelt; amalgamate, blend, coalesce, combine, commingle, intermingle, intermix, merge, unite. * *n* match.

fusion *n* liquefaction, melting; amalgamation, blending, commingling, commixture, intermingling, intermixture, union; coalition, merging.

fuss *vb* bustle, fidget; fret, fume, worry. * *n* ado, agitation, bother, bustle, commotion, disturbance, excitement, fidget, flurry, fluster, fret, hurry, pother, stir, worry.

fustian *n* bombast, claptrap, rant, rodomontade; balderdash, inanity, nonsense, stuff, trash, twaddle.

fusty *adj* ill-smelling, malodorous, mildewed, mouldy, musty, rank.

futile *adj* frivolous, trifling, trivial; bootless, fruitless, idle, ineffectual, profitless, unavailing, unprofitable, useless, vain, valueless, worthless.

futility *n* frivolousness, triviality; bootlessness, fruitlessness, uselessness, vanity, worthlessness.

future *adj* coming, eventual, forthcoming, hereafter, prospective, subsequent. * *n* hereafter, outlook, prospect.

G

gabble *vb* babble, chatter, clack, gibber, gossip, prate, prattle. * *n* babble, chatter, clack, gap, gossip, jabber, palaver, prate, prattle, twaddle.

gadabout *n* idler, loafer, rambler, rover, vagrant; gossip, talebearer, vagrant.

gaffer *n* boss, foreman, overseer, supervisor.

gag[1] *n* jape, jest, joke, stunt, wisecrack.

gag[2] *vb* muffle, muzzle, shackle, silence, stifle, throttle; regurgitate, retch, throw up, vomit; choke, gasp, pant. * *n* muzzle.

gage *n* pawn, pledge, security, surety; challenge, defiance, gauntlet, glove.

gaiety *n* animation, blithesomeness, cheerfulness, glee, hilarity, jollity, joviality, merriment, mirth, vivacity.

gain *vb* achieve, acquire, earn, get, obtain, procure, reap, secure; conciliate, enlist, persuade, prevail, win; arrive, attain, reach; clear, net, profit. * *n* accretion, addition, gainings, profits, winnings; acquisition, earnings, emolument, lucre; advantage, benefit, blessing, good, profit.

gainful *adj* advantageous, beneficial, profitable; lucrative, paying, productive, remunerative.

gainsay *vb* contradict, controvert, deny, dispute, forbid.

gait *n* carriage, pace, step, stride, walk.

galaxy *n* assemblage, assembly, cluster, collection, constellation, group.

gale *n* blast, hurricane, squall, storm, tempest, tornado, typhoon.

gall[1] *n* effrontery, impudence; bile; acerbity, bitterness, malice, maliciousness, malignity, rancour, spite.

gall[2] *vb* chafe, excoriate, fret, hurt; affront, annoy, exasperate, harass, incense, irritate, plague, provoke, sting, tease, vex.

gallant *adj* fine, magnificent, showy, splendid, well-dressed; bold, brave, chivalrous, courageous, daring, fearless, heroic, high-spirited, intrepid, valiant, valorous; chivalrous, fine, honourable, high-minded, lofty, magnanimous, noble. * *n* beau, blade, spark; lover, suitor, wooer.

gallantry *n* boldness, bravery, chivalry, courage, courageousness, fearlessness, heroism, intrepidity, prowess, valour; courtesy, courteousness, elegance, politeness.

galling *adj* chafing, irritating, vexing.

gallop *vb* fly, hurry, run, rush, scamper, speed.

gamble *vb* bet, dice, game, hazard, plunge, speculate, wager. * *n* chance, risk, speculation; bet, punt, wager.

gambol *vb* caper, cut, frisk, frolic, hop, jump, leap, romp, skip. * *n* frolic, hop, jump, skip.

game[1] *vb* gamble, sport, stake. * *n* amusement, contest, diversion, pastime, play, sport; adventure, enterprise, measure, plan, project, scheme, stratagem, undertaking; prey, quarry, victim.

game[2] *adj* brave, courageous, dauntless, fearless, gallant, heroic, intrepid, plucky, unflinching, valorous; enduring, persevering, resolute, undaunted; ready, eager, willing.

game[3] *adj* crippled, disabled, halt, injured, lame.

gameness *n* bravery, courage, grit, heart, mettle, nerve, pith, pluck, pluckiness, spirit, stamina.

gamesome *adj* frisky, frolicsome, lively, merry, playful, sportive, sprightly, vivacious.

gammon *vb* bamboozle, beguile, cheat, circumvent, deceive, delude, dupe, gull, hoax, humbug, inveigle, mislead, overreach, outwit. * *n* bosh, hoax, humbug, imposition, nonsense.

gang *n* band, cabal, clique, company, coterie, crew, horde, party, set, troop.

gaol *see* **jail**.

gap *n* breach, break, cavity, chasm, chink, cleft, crack, cranny, crevice, hiatus, hollow, interval, interstice, lacuna, opening, pass, ravine, rift, space, vacancy.

gape *vb* burst open, dehisce, open, stare, yawn.

garb *vb* attire, clothe, dress. * *n* apparel, attire, clothes, costume, dress, garments, habiliment, habit, raiment, robes, uniform, vestment.

garbage *n* filth, offal, refuse, remains, rubbish, trash, waste.

garble *vb* corrupt, distort, falsify, misquote, misrepresent, mutilate, pervert.

gargantuan *adj* big, Brobdingnagian, colossal, enormous, gigantic, huge, prodigious, tremendous.

garish *adj* bright, dazzling, flashy, flaunting, gaudy, glaring, loud, showy, staring, tawdry.

garland *vb* adorn, festoon, wreathe. * *n* chaplet, coronal, crown, festoon, wreath.

garment *n* clothes, clothing, dress, habit, vestment.

garner *vb* accumulate, collect, deposit, gather, hoard, husband, reserve, save, store, treasure.

garnish *vb* adorn, beautify, bedeck, decorate, deck, embellish, grace, ornament, prank, trim. * *n* decoration, enhancement, ornament, trimming.

garrulous *adj* babbling, loquacious, prating, prattling, talkative.

gasconade *n* bluster, boast, brag, bravado, swagger, vaunt, vapouring.

gasp *vb* blow, choke, pant, puff. * *n* blow, exclamation, gulp, puff.

gather *vb* assemble, cluster, collect, convene, group, muster, rally; accumulate, amass, garner, hoard, huddle, lump; bunch, crop, cull, glean, pick, pluck, rake, reap, shock, stack; acquire, gain, get, win; conclude, deduce, derive, infer; fold, plait, pucker, shirr, tuck; condense, grow, increase, thicken.

gathering *n* acquisition, collecting, earning, gain, heap, pile, procuring; assemblage, assembly, collection, company, concourse, congregation, meeting, muster; abscess, boil, fester, pimple, pustule, sore, suppuration, tumour, ulcer.

gauche *adj* awkward, blundering, bungling, clumsy, inept, tactless, uncouth.

gaudy *adj* bespangled, brilliant, brummagem, cheap, flashy, flaunting, garish, gimcrack, glittering, loud, ostentatious, overdecorated, sham, showy, spurious, tawdry, tinsel.

gauge *vb* calculate, check, determine, weigh; assess, estimate, guess, reckon. * *n* criterion, example, indicator, measure, meter, touchstone, yardstick; bore, depth, height, magnitude, size, thickness, width.

gaunt *adj* angular, attenuated, emaciated, haggard, lank, lean, meagre, scraggy, skinny, slender, spare, thin.

gawky *adj* awkward, boorish, clownish, clumsy, green, loutish, raw, rustic, uncouth, ungainly.

gay *adj* bright, brilliant, dashing, fine, showy; flashy, flaunting, garish, gaudy, glittering, loud, tawdry, tinsel; airy, blithe, blithesome, cheerful, festive, frivolous, frolicsome, gladsome, gleeful, hilarious, jaunty, jolly, jovial, light-hearted, lively, merry, mirthful, sportive, sprightly, vivacious.

gear *vb* adapt, equip, fit, suit, tailor. * *n* apparel, array, clothes, clothing, dress, garb; accoutrements, appliances, appointments, appurtenances, array, harness, goods, movables, subsidiaries; harness, rigging, tackle, trappings; apparatus, machinery, mechanics.

gelid *adj* chill, chilly, cold, freezing, frigid, icy.

gem *n* jewel, stone, treasure.

genealogy *n* ancestry, descent, lineage, pedigree, stock.

general *adj* broad, collective, generic, popular, universal, widespread; catholic, ecumenical; common, current, ordinary, usual; inaccurate, indefinite, inexact, vague.

generally *adv* commonly, extensively, universally, usually.

generate *vb* beget, breed, engender, procreate, propagate, reproduce, spawn; cause, form, make, produce.

generation *n* creation, engendering, formation, procreation, production; age, epoch, era, period, time; breed, children, family, kind, offspring, progeny, race, stock.

generosity *n* disinterestedness, high-mindedness, magnanimity, nobleness; bounteousness, bountifulness, bounty, charity, liberality, openhandedness.

generous *adj* high-minded, honourable, magnanimous, noble; beneficent, bountiful, charitable, free, hospitable, liberal, munificent, open-handed; abundant, ample, copious, plentiful, rich.

genial *adj* cheering, encouraging, enlivening, fostering, inspiring, mild, warm; agreeable, cheerful, cordial, friendly, hearty, jovial, kindly, merry, mirthful, pleasant.

genius *n* aptitude, aptness, bent, capacity, endowment, faculty, flair, gift, talent, turn; brains, creative power, ingenuity, inspiration, intellect, invention, parts, sagacity, wit; adeptness, master, master hand, proficiency; character, disposition, naturalness, nature; deity, demon, spirit.

genteel *adj* aristocratic, courteous, gentlemanly, lady-like, polished, polite, refined, well-bred; elegant, fashionable, graceful, stylish.

gentility *n* civility, courtesy, good breeding, politeness, refinement, urbanity.

gentle *adj* amiable, bland, clement, compassionate, humane, indulgent, kind, kindly, lenient, meek, merciful, mild, moderate, soft, tender, tender-hearted; docile, pacific, peaceable, placid, quiet, tame, temperate, tractable; bland, easy, gradual, light, slight; soft; high-born, noble, well-born; chivalrous, courteous, cultivated, knightly, polished, refined, well-bred.

gentlemanly *adj* civil, complaisant, courteous, cultivated, delicate, genteel, honourable, polite, refined, urbane, well-bred.

genuine *adj* authentic, honest, proper, pure, real, right, true, unadulterated, unalloyed, uncorrupted, veritable; frank, native, sincere, unaffected.

genus *n* class, group, kind, order, race, sort, type.

germ *n* embryo, nucleus, ovule, ovum, seed, seed-bud; bacterium, microbe, microorganism; beginning, cause, origin, rudiment, source.

germane *adj* akin, allied, cognate, related; apposite, appropriate, fitting, pertinent, relevant, suitable.

germinate *vb* bud, burgeon, develop, generate, grow, pollinate, push, shoot, sprout, vegetate.

gesture *vb* indicate, motion, signal, wave. * *n* action, attitude, gesticulation, gesturing, posture, sign, signal.

get *vb* achieve, acquire, attain, earn, gain, obtain, procure, receive, relieve, secure, win; finish, master, prepare; beget, breed, engender, generate, procreate.

gewgaw *n* bauble, gimcrack, gaud, kickshaw, knick-knack, plaything, trifle, toy, trinket.

ghastly *adj* cadaverous, corpse-like, deathlike, deathly, ghostly, lurid, pale, pallid, wan; dismal, dreadful, fearful, frightful, grim, grisly, gruesome, hideous, horrible, shocking, terrible.

ghost *n* soul, spirit; apparition, phantom, revenant, shade, spectre, spook, sprite, wraith.

giant *adj* colossal, enormous, Herculean, huge, large, monstrous, prodigious, vast. * *n* colossus, cyclops, Hercules, monster.

gibberish *n* babble, balderdash, drivel, gabble, gobbledygook, jabber, nonsense, prate, prating.

gibe, jibe *vb* deride, fleer, flout, jeer, mock, ridicule, scoff, sneer, taunt. * *n* ridicule, sneer, taunt.

giddiness *n* dizziness, head-spinning, vertigo.

giddy *adj* dizzy, head-spinning, vertiginous; careless, changeable, fickle, flighty, frivolous, hare-brained, headlong, heedless, inconstant, irresolute, light-headed, thoughtless, unsteady, vacillating, wild.

gift *n* alms, allowance, benefaction, bequest, bonus, boon, bounty, contribution, donation, dowry, endowment, favour, grant, gratuity, honorarium, largesse, legacy, offering, premium, present, prize, subscription, subsidy, tip; faculty, talent.

gifted *adj* able, capable, clever, ingenious, intelligent, inventive, sagacious, talented.

gigantic *adj* colossal, Cyclopean, enormous, giant, herculean, huge, immense, prodigious, titanic, tremendous, vast.

giggle *vb, n* cackle, grin, laugh, snigger, snicker, titter.

gild *vb* adorn, beautify, bedeck, brighten, decorate, embellish, grace, illuminate.

gimcrack *adj* flimsy, frail, puny; base, cheap, paltry, poor. * *n* bauble, knick-knack, toy, trifle.

gird *vb* belt, girdle; begird, encircle, enclose, encompass, engird, environ, surround; brace, support. * *n* band, belt, cincture, girdle, girth, sash, waistband.

gist *n* basis, core, essence, force, ground, marrow, meaning, pith, point, substance.

give *vb* accord, bequeath, bestow, confer, devise, entrust, present; afford, contribute, donate, furnish, grant, proffer, spare, supply; communicate, impart; deliver, exchange, pay, requite; allow, permit, vouchsafe; emit, pronounce, render, utter; produce, yield; cause, occasion; apply, devote, surrender; bend, sink, recede, retire, retreat, yield.

glad *adj* delighted, gratified, happy, pleased, rejoicing, well-contented; animated, blithe, cheerful, cheery, elated, gladsome, jocund, joyful, joyous, light, light-hearted, merry, playful, radiant; animating, bright, cheering, exhilarating, gladdening, gratifying, pleasing.

gladden *vb* bless, cheer, delight, elate, enliven, exhilarate, gratify, please, rejoice.

gladiator *n* prize-fighter, sword-player, swordsman.

gladness *n* animation, cheerfulness, delight, gratification, happiness, joy, joyfulness, joyousness, pleasure.

gladsome *adj* airy, blithe, blithesome, cheerful,
delighted, frolicsome, glad, gleeful, jocund, jolly, jovial, joyful, joyous, light-hearted, lively, merry, pleased, sportive, sprightly, vivacious.

glamour *n* bewitchment, charm, enchantment, fascination, spell, witchery.

glance *vb* coruscate, gleam, glisten, glister, glitter, scintillate, shine; dart, flit; gaze, glimpse, look, view. * *n* gleam, glitter; gleam, look, view.

glare *vb* dazzle, flame, flare, gleam, glisten, glitter, sparkle; frown, gaze, glower. * *n* flare, glitter.

glaring *adj* dazzling, gleaming, glistening, glittering; barefaced, conspicuous, extreme, manifest, notorious, open.

glassy *adj* brilliant, crystal, crystalline, gleaming, lucent, shining, transparent.

glaze *vb* burnish, calender, furbish, gloss, polish. * *n* coat, enamel, finish, glazing, polish, varnish.

gleam *vb* beam, coruscate, flash, glance, glimmer, glitter, shine, sparkle. * *n* beam, flash, glance, glimmer, glimmering, glow, ray; brightness, coruscation, flashing, gleaming, glitter, glittering, lustre, splendour.

glean *vb* collect, cull, gather, get, harvest, pick, select.

glee *n* exhilaration, fun, gaiety, hilarity, jocularity, jollity, joviality, joy, liveliness, merriment, mirth, sportiveness, verve.

glib *adj* slippery, smooth; artful, facile, flippant, fluent, ready, talkative, voluble.

glide *vb* float, glissade, roll on, skate, skim, slide, slip; flow, lapse, run, roll. * *n* gliding, lapse, sliding, slip.

glimmer *vb* flash, flicker, gleam, glitter, shine, twinkle. * *n* beam, gleam, glimmering, ray; glance, glimpse.

glimpse *vb* espy, look, spot, view. * *n* flash, glance, glimmering, glint, look, sight.

glitter *vb* coruscate, flare, flash, glance, glare, gleam, glisten, glister, scintillate, shine, sparkle. * *n* beam, beaming, brightness, brilliancy, coruscation, gleam, glister, lustre, radiance, scintillation, shine, sparkle, splendour.

gloaming *n* dusk, eventide, nightfall, twilight.

gloat *vb* exult, gaze, rejoice, stare, triumph.

globe *n* ball, earth, orb, sphere.

globular *adj* globate, globated, globe-shaped, globose, globous, round, spheral, spheric, spherical.

globule *n* bead, drop, particle, spherule.

gloom *n* cloud, darkness, dimness, gloominess, obscurity, shade, shadow; cheerlessness, dejection, depression, despondency, downheartedness, dullness, melancholy, sadness.

gloomy *adj* dark, dim, dusky, obscure; cheerless, dismal, lowering, lurid; crestfallen, dejected, depressed, despondent, disheartened, dispirited, downcast, downhearted, glum, melancholy, morose, sad, sullen; depressing, disheartening, dispiriting, heavy, saddening.

glorify *vb* adore, bless, celebrate, exalt, extol, honour, laud, magnify, worship; adorn, brighten, elevate, ennoble, make bright.

glorious *adj* celebrated, conspicuous, distinguished, eminent, excellent, famed, famous, illustrious, pre-eminent, renowned; brilliant, bright, grand, magnificent, radiant, resplendent, splendid; consummate, exalted, high, lofty, noble, supreme.

glory *vb* boast, exult, vaunt. * *n* celebrity, distinction, eminence, fame, honour, illustriousness, praise, renown; brightness, brilliancy, effulgence, lustre, pride, resplendence, splendour; exaltation, exceeding, gloriousness, greatness, grandeur, nobleness; bliss, happiness.

gloss[1] *vb* coat, colour, disguise, extenuate, glaze, palliate, varnish, veneer, veil. * *n* coating, lustre, polish, sheen, varnish, veneer; pretence, pretext.

gloss[2] *vb* annotate, comment, elucidate, explain, interpret. * *n* annotation, comment, commentary, elucidation, explanation, interpretation, note.

glove *n* gantlet, gauntlet, handwear, mitt, mitten; challenge.

glow *vb* incandesce, radiate, shine; blush, burn, flush, redden. * *n* blaze, brightness, brilliance, burning, incandescence, luminosity, reddening; ardour, bloom, enthusiasm, fervency, fervour, flush, impetuosity, vehemence, warmth.

glower *vb* frown, glare, lower, scowl, stare. * *n* frown, glare, scowl.

glum *adj* churlish, crabbed, crestfallen, cross-grained, crusty, depressed, frowning, gloomy, glowering, moody, morose, sour, spleenish, spleeny, sulky, sullen, surly.

glut *vb* block up, cloy, cram, gorge, satiate, stuff. * *n* excess, saturation, surfeit, surplus.

glutinous *adj* adhesive, clammy, cohesive, gluey, gummy, sticky, tenacious, viscid, viscous.

glutton *n* gobbler, gorger, gourmand, gormandizer, greedy-guts, lurcher, pig.

gnarled *adj* contorted, cross-grained, gnarly, knotted, knotty, snaggy, twisted.

go *vb* advance, move, pass, proceed, progress repair; act, operate; be about, extravagate, fare, journey, roam, rove, travel, walk, wend; depart, disappear, cease; elapse, extend, lead, reach, run; avail, concur, contribute, tend, serve; eventuate, fare, turn out; afford, bet, risk, wager. * *n* action, business, case, chance, circumstance, doings, turn; custom, fad, fashion, mode, vogue; energy, endurance, power, stamina, verve, vivacity.

goad *vb* annoy, badger, harass, irritate, sting, worry; arouse, impel, incite, instigate, prod, spur, stimulate, urge. * *n* incentive, incitement, pressure, stimulation.

goal *n* bound, home, limit, mark, mete, post; end, object; aim, design, destination.

gobble *vb* bolt, devour, gorge, gulp, swallow.

goblin *n* apparition, elf, bogey, demon, gnome, hobgoblin, phantom, spectre, sprite.

god *n* almighty, creator, deity, divinity, idol, Jehovah, omnipotence, providence.

godless *adj* atheistic, impious, irreligious, profane, ungodly, wicked.
godlike *adj* celestial, divine, heavenly, supernal.
godly *adj* devout, holy, pious, religious, righteous, saint-like, saintly.
godsend *n* fortune, gift, luck, present, windfall.
golden *adj* aureate, brilliant, bright, gilded, resplendent, shining, splendid; excellent, precious; auspicious, favourable, opportune, propitious; blessed, delightful, glorious, halcyon, happy.
good *adj* advantageous, beneficial, favourable, profitable, serviceable, useful; adequate, appropriate, becoming, convenient, fit, proper, satisfactory, suitable, well-adapted; decorous, dutiful, honest, just, pious, reliable, religious, righteous, true, upright, virtuous, well-behaved, worthy; admirable, capable, excellent, genuine, healthy, precious, sincere, sound, sterling, valid, valuable; benevolent, favourable, friendly, gracious, humane, kind, merciful, obliging, well-disposed; fair, honourable, immaculate, unblemished, unimpeachable, unimpeached, unsullied, untarnished; cheerful, companionable, lively, genial, social; able, competent, dextrous, expert, qualified, ready, skilful, thorough, well-qualified; credit-worthy; agreeable, cheering, gratifying, pleasant. * *n* advantage, benefit, boon, favour, gain, profit, utility; interest, prosperity, welfare, weal; excellence, righteousness, virtue, worth.
good breeding *n* affability, civility, courtesy, good manners, polish, politeness, urbanity.
goodbye *n* adieu, farewell, parting.
goodly *adj* beautiful, comely, good-looking, graceful; agreeable, considerate, desirable, happy, pleasant.
good-natured *adj* amiable, benevolent, friendly, kind, kind-hearted, kindly.
goodness *n* excellence, quality, value, worth; honesty, integrity, morality, principle, probity, righteousness, uprightness, virtue; benevolence, beneficence, benignity, good-will, humaneness, humanity, kindness.
goods *npl* belongings, chattels, effects, furniture, movables; commodities, merchandise, stock, wares.
goodwill *n* benevolence, kindness, good nature; ardour, earnestness, heartiness, willingness, zeal; custom, patronage.
gore *vb* horn, pierce, stab, wound.
gorge[1] *vb* bolt, devour, eat, feed, swallow; cram, fill, glut, gormandize, sate, satiate, stuff, surfeit. * *n* craw, crop, gullet, throat.
gorge[2] *n* canyon, defile, fissure, notch, ravine.
gorgeous *adj* bright, brilliant, dazzling, fine, glittering, grand, magnificent, resplendent, rich, shining, showy, splendid, superb.
Gorgon *n* bugaboo, fright, hobgoblin, hydra, ogre, spectre.
gory *adj* bloody, ensanguined, sanguinary.
gospel *n* creed, doctrine, message, news, revelation, tidings.
gossip *vb* chat, cackle, clack, gabble, prate, prattle, tattle. * *n* babbler, busybody, chatterer, gossipmonger, newsmonger, quidnunc, tale-bearer, tattler, tell-tale; cackle, chat, chit-chat, prate, prattle, tattle.
gourmet *n* connoisseur, epicure, epicurean.
govern *vb* administer, conduct, direct, manage, regulate, reign, rule, superintend, supervise; guide, pilot, steer; bridle, check, command, control, curb, restrain, rule, sway.
government *n* autonomy, command, conduct, control, direction, discipline, dominion, guidance, management, regulation, restraint, rule, rulership, sway; administration, cabinet, commonwealth, polity, sovereignty, state.
governor *n* commander, comptroller, director, head, headmaster, manager, overseer, ruler, superintendent, supervisor; chief magistrate, executive; guardian, instructor, tutor.
grab *vb* capture, clutch, seize, snatch.
grace *vb* adorn, beautify, deck, decorate, embellish; dignify, honour. * *n* benignity, condescension, favour, good-will, kind-

ness, love; devotion, efficacy, holiness, love, piety, religion, sanctity, virtue; forgiveness, mercy, pardon, reprieve; accomplishment, attractiveness, charm, elegance, polish, propriety, refinement; beauty, comeliness, ease, gracefulness, symmetry; blessing, petition, thanks.

graceful *adj* beautiful, becoming, comely, easy, elegant; flowing, natural, rounded, unlaboured; appropriate; felicitous, happy, tactful.

graceless *adj* abandoned, corrupt, depraved, dissolute, hardened, incorrigible, irreclaimable, lost, obdurate, profligate, reprobate, repugnant, shameless,

gracious *adj* beneficent, benevolent, benign, benignant, compassionate, condescending, favourable, friendly, gentle, good-natured, kind, kindly, lenient, merciful, mild, tender; affable, civil, courteous, easy, familiar, polite.

grade *vb* arrange, classify, group, order, rank, sort. * *n* brand, degree, intensity, stage, step, rank; gradient, incline, slope.

gradual *adj* approximate, continuous, gentle, progressive, regular, slow, successive.

graduate *vb* adapt, adjust, proportion, regulate. * *n* alumna, alumnus, laureate, postgraduate.

graft *vb* ingraft, inoculate, insert, transplant. * *n* bud, scion, shoot, slip, sprout; corruption, favouritism, influence, nepotism.

grain *n* kernel, ovule, seed; cereals, corn, grist; atom, bit, glimmer, jot, particle, scintilla, scrap, shadow, spark, tittle, trace, whit; disposition, fibre, humour, temper, texture; colour, dye, hue, shade, stain, texture, tincture, tinge.

granary *n* corn-house, garner, grange, store-house.

grand *adj* august, dignified, elevated, eminent, exalted, great, illustrious, lordly, majestic, princely, stately, sublime; fine, glorious, gorgeous, magnificent, pompous, lofty, noble, splendid, superb; chief, leading, main, pre-eminent, principal, superior.

grandee *n* lord, noble, nobleman.

grandeur *n* elevation, greatness, immensity, impressiveness, loftiness, vastness; augustness, dignity, eminence, glory, magnificence, majesty, nobility, pomp, splendour, state, stateliness.

grandiloquent *adj* bombastic, declamatory, high-minded, high-sounding, inflated, pompous, rhetorical, stilted, swelling, tumid, turgid.

grant *vb* accord, admit, allow, sanction; cede, concede, give, impart, indulge; bestow, confer, deign, invest, vouchsafe; convey, transfer, yield. * *n* admission, allowance, benefaction, bestowal, boon, bounty, concession, donation, endowment, gift, indulgence, largesse, present; conveyance, cession.

graphic *adj* descriptive, diagrammatic, figural, figurative, forcible, lively, pictorial, picturesque, striking, telling, vivid, well-delineated, well-drawn.

grapple *vb* catch, clutch, grasp, grip, hold, hug, seize, tackle, wrestle.

grasp *vb* catch, clasp, clinch, clutch, grapple, grip, seize; comprehend, understand. * *n* clasp, grip, hold; comprehension, power, reach, scope, understanding.

grasping *adj* acquisitive, avaricious, covetous, exacting, greedy, rapacious, sordid, tight-fisted.

grate *vb* abrade, rub, scrape, triturate; comminute, rasp; creak, fret, grind, jar, vex. * *n* bars, grating, latticework, screen; basket, fire bed.

grateful *adj* appreciative, beholden, indebted, obliged, sensible, thankful; pleasant, welcome.

gratification *n* gratifying, indulgence, indulging, pleasing, satisfaction, satisfying; delight, enjoyment, fruition, pleasure, reward.

gratify *vb* delight, gladden, please; humour, fulfil, grant, indulge, requite, satisfy.

gratifying *adj* agreeable, delightful, grateful, pleasing, welcome.

grating *adj* disagreeable, displeasing, harsh, irritating, offensive. * *n* grate, partition.

gratis *adv* freely, gratuitously.
gratitude *n* goodwill, gratitude, indebtedness, thankfulness.
gratuitous *adj* free, spontaneous, unrewarded, voluntary; assumed, baseless, groundless, unfounded, unwarranted, wanton.
gratuity *n* benefaction, bounty, charity, donation, endowment, gift, grant, largesse, present.
grave[1] *n* crypt, mausoleum, ossuary, pit, sepulchre, sepulture, tomb, vault.
grave[2] *adj* cogent, heavy, important, momentous, ponderous, pressing, serious, weighty; dignified, sage, sedate, serious, slow, solemn, staid, thoughtful; dull, grim, plain, quiet, sober, sombre, subdued; cruel, hard, harsh, severe; despicable, dire, dismal, gross, heinous, infamous, outrageous, scandalous, shameful, shocking; heavy, hollow, low, low-pitched, sepulchral.
grave[3] *vb* engrave, impress, imprint, infix; carve, chisel, cut, sculpt.
gravel *vb* bewilder, embarrass, nonplus, perplex, pose, puzzle, stagger. * *n* ballast, grit, sand, shingle.
graveyard *n* burial ground, cemetery, churchyard, god's acre, mortuary, necropolis.
gravity *n* heaviness, weight; demureness, sedateness, seriousness, sobriety, thoughtfulness; importance, moment, momentousness, weightiness.
graze *vb* brush, glance, scrape, scratch; abrade, shave, skim; browse, crop, feed, pasture. * *n* abrasion, bruise, scrape, scratch.
great *adj* ample, big, bulky, Cyclopean, enormous, gigantic, Herculean, huge, immense, large, pregnant, vast; decided, excessive, high, much, pronounced; countless, numerous; chief, considerable, grand, important, leading, main, pre-eminent, principal, superior, weighty; celebrated, distinguished, eminent, exalted, excellent, famed, famous, far-famed, illustrious, noted, prominent, renowned; august, dignified, elevated, grand, lofty, majestic, noble, sublime; chivalrous, generous, high-minded, magnanimous; fine, magnificent, rich, sumptuous.
greatness *n* bulk, dimensions, largeness, magnitude, size; distinction, elevation, eminence, fame, importance, renown; augustness, dignity, grandeur, majesty, loftiness, nobility, nobleness, sublimity; chivalry, generosity, magnanimity, spirit.
greed, greediness *n* gluttony, hunger, omnivorousness, ravenousness, voracity; avidity, covetousness, desire, eagerness, longing; avarice, cupidity, graspingness, grasping, rapacity, selfishness.
greedy *adj* devouring, edacious, gluttonous, insatiable, insatiate, rapacious, ravenous, voracious; desirous, eager; avaricious, grasping, selfish.
green *adj* aquamarine, emerald, olive, verdant, verdure, viridescent, viridian; blooming, flourishing, fresh, undecayed; fresh, new, recent; immature, unfledged, unripe; callow, crude, inexpert, ignorant, inexperienced, raw, unskilful, untrained, verdant, young; unseasoned; conservationist, ecological, environmentalist. * *n* common, grass plot, lawn, sward, turf, verdure.
greenhorn *n* beginner, novice, tyro.
greet *vb* accost, address, complement, hail, receive, salute, welcome.
greeting *n* compliment, salutation, salute, welcome.
grief *n* affliction, agony, anguish, bitterness, distress, dole, heartbreak, misery, regret, sadness, sorrow, suffering, tribulation, mourning, woe; grievance, trial; disaster, failure, mishap.
grievance *n* burden, complaint, hardship, injury, oppression, wrong; affliction, distress, grief, sorrow, trial, woe.
grieve *vb* afflict, aggrieve, agonize, discomfort, distress, hurt, oppress, pain, sadden, wound; bewail, deplore, mourn, lament, regret, sorrow, suffer.
grievous *adj* afflicting, afflictive, burdensome, deplorable, distressing, heavy, lamentable, oppressive, painful, sad, sorrowful; baleful, baneful, calamitous, destructive, detrimental, hurtful, injurious,

mischievous, noxious, troublesome; aggravated, atrocious, dreadful, flagitious, flagrant, gross, heinous, iniquitous, intense, intolerable, severe, outrageous, wicked.

grill *vb* broil, griddle, roast, toast; sweat; cross-examine, interrogate, question; torment, torture. * *n* grating, gridiron; cross-examination, cross-questioning.

grim *adj* cruel, ferocious, fierce, harsh, relentless, ruthless, savage, stern, unyielding; appalling, dire, dreadful, fearful, frightful, grisly, hideous, horrid, horrible, terrific.

grimace *vb, n* frown, scowl, smirk, sneer.

grime *n* dirt, filth, foulness, smut.

grimy *adj* begrimed, defiled, dirty, filthy, foul, soiled, sullied, unclean.

grind *vb* bruise, crunch, crush, grate, grit, pulverize, rub, triturate; sharpen, whet; afflict, harass, oppress, persecute, plague, trouble. * *n* chore, drudgery, labour, toil.

grip *vb* clasp, clutch, grasp, hold, seize. * *n* clasp, clutch, control, domination, grasp, hold.

grisly *adj* appalling, frightful, dreadful, ghastly, grim, grey, hideous, horrible, horrid, terrible, terrific.

grit *vb* clench, grate, grind. * *n* bran, gravel, pebbles, sand; courage, decision, determination, firmness, perseverance, pluck, resolution, spirit.

groan *vb* complain, lament, moan, whine; creak. * *n* cry, moan, whine; complaint; grouse, grumble.

groom *vb* clean, dress, tidy; brush, tend; coach, educate, nurture, train. * *n* equerry, hostler, manservant, ostler, servant, stable-hand, valet, waiter.

groove *n* channel, cut, furrow, rabbet, rebate, recess, rut, scoring; routine.

gross *vb* accumulate, earn, make. * *adj* big, bulky, burly, fat, great, large; dense, dull, stupid, thick; beastly, broad, carnal, coarse, crass, earthy, impure, indelicate, licentious, low, obscene, unbecoming, unrefined, unseemly, vulgar, rough, sensual; aggravated, brutal, enormous, flagrant, glaring, grievous, manifest, obvious, palpable, plain, outrageous, shameful; aggregate, entire, total, whole. * *n* aggregate, bulk, total, whole.

grossness *n* bigness, bulkiness, greatness; density, thickness; coarseness, ill-breeding, rudeness, vulgarity; bestiality, brutality, carnality, coarseness, impurity, indelicacy, licentiousness, sensuality.

grotesque *adj* bizarre, extravagant, fanciful, fantastic, incongruous, odd, strange, unnatural, whimsical, wild; absurd, antic, burlesque, ludicrous, ridiculous.

ground *vb* fell, place; base, establish, fix, found, set; instruct, train. * *n* area, clod, distance, earth, loam, mould, sod, soil, turf; country, domain, land, region, territory; acres, estate, field, property; base, basis, foundation, groundwork, support; account, consideration, excuse, gist, motive, opinion, reason.

groundless *adj* baseless, causeless, false, gratuitous, idle, unauthorized, unfounded, unjustifiable, unsolicited, unsought, unwarranted.

grounds *npl* deposit, dregs, grouts, lees, precipitate, sediment, settlings; accounts, arguments, considerations, reasons, support; campus, gardens, lawns, premises, yard.

group *vb* arrange, assemble, dispose, order. * *n* aggregation, assemblage, assembly, body, combination, class, clump, cluster, collection, order.

grove *n* copse, glade, spinney, thicket, wood, woodland.

grovel *vb* cower, crawl, creep, cringe, fawn, flatter, sneak.

grovelling *adj* creeping, crouching, squat; abject, base, beggarly, cringing, fawning, low, mean, servile, slavish, sneaking, undignified, unworthy, vile.

grow *vb* enlarge, expand, extend, increase, swell; arise, burgeon, develop, germinate, shoot, sprout, vegetate; advance, extend, improve, progress, thrive, wax; cultivate, produce, raise.

growl *vb* complain, croak, find fault, gnarl, groan, grumble, lament, murmur, snarl. * *n* croak, grown, snarl; complaint.

growth *n* augmentation, development, expansion, extension, growing, increase;

burgeoning, excrescence, formation, germination, pollution, shooting, sprouting, vegetation; cultivation, produce, product, production; advance, advancement, development, improvement, progress; adulthood, maturity.

grub *vb* clear, dig, eradicate, root. * *n* caterpillar, larvae, maggot; drudge, plodder.

grudge *vb* begrudge, envy, repine; complain, grieve, murmur. * *n* aversion, dislike, enmity, grievance, hate, hatred, ill-will, malevolence, malice, pique, rancour, resentment, spite, venom.

gruff *adj* bluff, blunt, brusque, churlish, discourteous, grumpy, harsh, impolite, rough, rude, rugged, surly, uncivil, ungracious.

grumble *vb* croak, complain, murmur, repine; gnarl, growl, snarl; roar, rumble. * *n* growl, murmur, complaint, roar, rumble.

grumpy *adj* crabbed, cross, glum, moody, morose, sour, sullen, surly.

guarantee *vb* assure, insure, pledge, secure, warrant. * *n* assurance, pledge, security, surety, warrant, warranty.

guard *vb* defend, keep, patrol, protect, safeguard, save, secure, shelter, shield, watch. * *n* aegis, bulwark, custody, defence, palladium, protection, rampart, safeguard, security, shield; keeper, guardian, patrol, sentinel, sentry, warden, watch, watchman; conduct, convoy, escort; attention, care, caution, circumspection, heed, watchfulness.

guarded *adj* careful, cautious, circumspect, reserved, reticent, wary, watchful.

guardian *n* custodian, defender, guard, keeper, preserver, protector, trustee, warden.

guerdon *n* recompense, remuneration, requital, reward.

guess *vb* conjecture, divine, mistrust, surmise, suspect; fathom, find out, penetrate, solve; believe, fancy, hazard, imagine, reckon, suppose, think. * *n* conjecture, divination, notion, supposition, surmise.

guest *n* caller, company, visitant.

guidance *n* conduct, control, direction, escort, government, lead, leadership, pilotage, steering.

guide *vb* conduct, escort, lead, pilot; control, direct, govern, manage, preside, regulate, rule, steer, superintend, supervise. * *n* cicerone, conductor, director, monitor, pilot; adviser, counsellor, instructor, mentor; clew, directory, index, key, thread; guidebook, itinerary, landmark.

guild *n* association, brotherhood, company, corporation, fellowship, fraternity, society, union.

guile *n* art, artfulness, artifice, craft, cunning, deceit, deception, duplicity, fraud, knavery, ruse, subtlety, treachery, trickery, wiles, wiliness.

guileless *adj* artless, candid, frank, honest, ingenuous, innocent, open, pure, simple-minded, sincere, straightforward, truthful, undesigning, unsophisticated.

guilt *n* blame, criminality, culpability, guiltless; ill-desert, iniquity, offensiveness, wickedness, wrong; crime, offence, sin.

guiltless *adj* blameless, immaculate, innocent, pure, sinless, spotless, unpolluted, unspotted, unsullied, untarnished.

guilty *adj* criminal, culpable, evil, sinful, wicked, wrong.

guise *n* appearance, aspect, costume, dress, fashion, figure, form, garb, manner, mode, shape; air, behaviour, demeanour, mien; cover, custom, disguise, habit, pretence, pretext, practice.

gulf *n* abyss, chasm, opening; bay, inlet; whirlpool.

gull *vb* beguile, cheat, circumvent, cozen, deceive, dupe, hoax, overreach, swindle, trick. * *n* cheat, deception, hoax, imposition, fraud, trick; cat's paw, dupe.

gullibility *n* credulity, naiveness, naivety, overtrustfulness, simplicity, unsophistication.

gullible *adj* confiding, credulous, naive, over-trustful, simple, unsophisticated, unsuspicious.

gumption *n* ability, astuteness, cleverness,

capacity, common sense, discernment, penetration, power, sagacity, shrewdness, skill; courage, guts, spirit.

gun *n* blunderbuss, cannon, carbine, firearm, musket, pistol, revolver, rifle, shotgun.

gurgle *vb* babble, bubble, murmur, purl, ripple. * *n* babbling, murmur, ripple.

gush *vb* burst, flood, flow, pour, rush, spout, stream; emotionalize, sentimentalize. * *n* flow, jet, onrush, rush, spurt, surge; effusion, effusiveness, loquacity, loquaciousness, talkativeness.

gushing *adj* flowing, issuing, rushing; demonstrative, effusive, sentimental.

gust *vb* blast, blow, puff. * *n* blast, blow, squall; burst, fit, outburst, paroxysm.

gusto *n* enjoyment, gust, liking, pleasure, relish, zest.

gusty *adj* blustering, blustery, puffy, squally, stormy, tempestuous, unsteady, windy.

gut *vb* destroy, disembowel, embowel, eviscerate, paunch. * *n* bowels, entrails, intestines, inwards, viscera.

gutter *n* channel, conduit, kennel, pipe, tube.

guttural *adj* deep, gruff, hoarse, thick, throaty.

guy *vb* caricature, mimic, ridicule. * *n* boy, man, person; dowdy, eccentric, fright, scarecrow.

guzzle *vb* carouse, drink, gorge, gormandize, quaff, swill, tipple, tope.

gyrate *vb* revolve, rotate, spin, whirl.

H

habiliment *n* apparel, attire, clothes, costume, dress, garb, garment, habit, raiment, robes, uniform, vesture, vestment.
habit *vb* accoutre, array, attire, clothe, dress, equip, robe. * *n* condition, constitution, temperament; addiction, custom, habitude, manner, practice, rule, usage, way, wont; apparel, costume, dress, garb, habiliment.
habitation *n* abode, domicile, dwelling, headquarters, home, house, lodging, quarters, residence.
habitual *adj* accustomed, common, confirmed, customary, everyday, familiar, inveterate, ordinary, regular, routine, settled, usual, wonted.
habituate *vb* accustom, familiarize, harden, inure, train, use.
habitude *n* custom, practice, usage, wont.
hack[1] *vb* chop, cut, hew, mangle, mutilate, notch; cough, rasp. * *n* cut, cleft, incision, notch; cough, rasp.
hack[2] *vb* ride. * *adj* hired, mercenary; banal, hackneyed, pedestrian, uninspired, unoriginal. * *n* horse, nag, pony; hireling, mercenary; journalist, scribbler, writer.
hackneyed *adj* banal, common, commonplace, overworked, pedestrian, stale, threadbare, trite.
hag *n* beldame, crone, fury, harridan, jezebel, she-monster, shrew, termagant, virago, vixen, witch.
haggard *adj* intractable, refractory, unruly, untamed, wild, wayward; careworn, emaciated, gaunt, ghastly, lank, lean, meagre, raw, spare, thin, wasted, worn.
haggle *vb* argue, bargain, cavil, chaffer, dispute, higgle, stickle; annoy, badger, bait, fret, harass, tease, worry.
hail[1] *vb* acclaim, greet, salute, welcome; accost, address, call, hallo, signal. * *n* greeting, salute.
hail[2] *vb* assail, bombard, rain, shower, storm, volley. * *n* bombardment, rain, shower, storm, volley.
halcyon *adj* calm, golden, happy, palmy, placid, peaceful, quiet, serene, still, tranquil, unruffled, undisturbed.
hale *adj* hardy, healthy, hearty, robust, sound, strong, vigorous, well.
halfwit *n* blockhead, dunce, moron, simpleton.
halfwitted *adj* doltish, dull, dull-witted, feeble-minded, foolish, sappy, shallow, silly, simple, soft, stolid, stupid, thick.
hall *n* chamber, corridor, entrance, entry, hallway, lobby, passage, vestibule; manor, manor-house; auditorium, lecture-room.
halloo *vb* call, cry, shout. * *n* call, cry, hallo, holla, hollo, shout.
hallow *vb* consecrate, dedicate, devote, revere, sanctify, solemnize; enshrine, honour, respect, reverence, venerate.
hallowed *adj* blessed, holy, honoured, revered, sacred.
hallucination *n* blunder, error, fallacy, mistake; aberration, delusion, illusion, phantasm, phantasy, self-deception, vision.
halo *n* aura, aureole, glory, nimbus.
halt[1] *vb* cease, desist, hold, rest, stand, stop. * *n* end, impasse, pause, standstill, stop.
halt[2] *vb* hesitate, pause, stammer, waver; falter, hobble, limp. * *adj* crippled, disabled, lame. * *n* hobble, limp.
hammer *vb* beat, forge, form, shape; excogitate, contrive, invent.
hammer and tongs *adv* earnestly, energetically, resolutely, strenuously, vigorously, zealously.
hamper *vb* bind, clog, confine, curb, embarrass, encumber, entangle, fetter,

hinder, impede, obstruct, prevent, restrain, restrict, shackle, trammel. * *n* basket, box, crate, picnic basket; embarrassment, encumbrance, fetter, handicap, impediment, obstruction, restraint, trammel.

hand *vb* deliver, give, present, transmit; conduct, guide, lead. * *n* direction, part, side; ability, dexterity, faculty, skill, talent; course, inning, management, turn; agency, intervention, participation, share; control, possession, power; artificer, artisan, craftsman, employee, labourer, operative, workman; index, indicator, pointer; chirography, handwriting.

handbook *n* guidebook, manual.

handcuff *vb* bind, fetter, manacle, shackle. * *n* fetter, manacle, shackle.

handful *n* fistful, maniple, smattering.

handicap *vb* encumber, hamper, hinder, restrict. * *n* disadvantage, encumbrance, hampering, hindrance, restriction.

handicraft *n* hand manufacture, handwork, workmanship.

handle *vb* feel, finger, manhandle, paw, touch; direct, manage, manipulate, use, wield; discourse, discuss, treat. * *n* haft, helve, hilt, stock.

handsome *adj* admirable, comely, finelooking, stately, well-formed, well-proportioned; appropriate, suitable, becoming, easy, graceful; generous, gracious, liberal, magnanimous, noble; ample, large, plentiful, sufficient.

handy *adj* adroit, clever, dextrous, expert, ready, skilful, skilled; close, convenient, near.

hang *vb* attach, swing; execute, truss; decline, drop, droop, incline; adorn, drape; dangle, depend, impend, suspend; rely; cling, loiter, rest, stick; float, hover, pay.

hangdog *adj* ashamed, base, blackguard, low, villainous, scurvy, sneaking.

hanger-on *n* dependant, minion, parasite, vassal.

hanker *vb* covet, crave, desire, hunger, long, lust, want, yearn.

hap *n* accident, chance, fate, fortune, lot.

haphazard *adj* aimless, chance, random.

hapless *adj* ill-fated, ill-starred, luckless, miserable, unfortunate, unhappy, unlucky, wretched.

happen *vb* befall, betide, chance, come, occur.

happily *adv* fortunately, luckily; agreeably, delightfully, prosperously, successfully.

happiness *n* brightness, cheerfulness, delight, gaiety, joy, light-heartedness, merriment, pleasure; beatitude, blessedness, bliss, felicity, enjoyment, welfare, wellbeing.

happy *adj* blessed, blest, blissful, cheerful, contented, joyful, joyous, lighthearted, merry; charmed, delighted, glad, gladdened, gratified, pleased; fortunate, lucky, prosperous, successful; able, adroit, apt, dextrous, expert, ready, skilful; befitting, felicitous, opportune, pertinent, seasonable, well-timed; auspicious, bright, favourable, propitious.

harangue *vb* address, declaim, spout. * *n* address, bombast, declamation, oration, rant, screed, speech, tirade.

harass *vb* exhaust, fag, fatigue, jade, tire, weary; annoy, badger, distress, gall, heckle, disturb, harry, molest, pester, plague, tantalize, tease, torment, trouble, vex, worry.

harbour *vb* protect, lodge, shelter; cherish, entertain, foster, indulge. * *n* asylum, cover, refuge, resting place, retreat, sanctuary, shelter; anchorage, destination, haven, port.

hard *adj* adamantine, compact, firm, flinty, impenetrable, marble, rigid, solid, resistant, stony, stubborn, unyielding; difficult, intricate, knotty, perplexing, puzzling; arduous, exacting, fatiguing, laborious, toilsome, wearying; austere, callous, cruel, exacting, hard-hearted, incorrigible, inflexible, insensible, insensitive, obdurate, oppressive, reprobate, rigorous, severe, unfeeling, unkind, unsusceptible, unsympathetic, unyielding, untender; calamitous, disagreeable, distressing, grievous, painful, unpleasant; acid, alcoholic, harsh, rough, sour; excessive, intemperate. * *adv* close, near; diligently, earnestly, energetically, incessantly, laboriously; distressfully, painfully, rigorously, severely; forcibly, vehemently, violently.

harden *vb* accustom, discipline, form, habituate, inure, season, train; brace, fortify, indurate, nerve, steel, stiffen, strengthen.

hardened *adj* annealed, case-hardened, tempered, indurated; abandoned, accustomed, benumbed, callous, confirmed, deadened, depraved, habituated, impenitent, incorrigible, inured, insensible, irreclaimable, lost, obdurate, reprobate, seared, seasoned, steeled, trained, unfeeling.

hard-headed *adj* astute, collected, cool, intelligent, sagacious, shrewd, well-balanced, wise.

hardhearted *adj* cruel, fell, implacable, inexorable, merciless, pitiless, relentless, ruthless, unfeeling, uncompassionate, unmerciful, unpitying, unrelenting.

hardihood *n* audacity, boldness, bravery, courage, decision, firmness, fortitude, intrepidity, manhood, mettle, pluck, resolution, stoutness; assurance, audacity, brass, effrontery, impudence.

hardly *adv* barely, scarcely; cruelly, harshly, rigorously, roughly, severely, unkindly.

hardship *n* fatigue, toil, weariness; affliction, burden, calamity, grievance, hardness, injury, misfortune, privation, suffering, trial, trouble.

hardy *adj* enduring, firm, hale, healthy, hearty, inured, lusty, rigorous, robust, rugged, sound, stout, strong, sturdy, tough; bold, brave, courageous, daring, heroic, intrepid, manly, resolute, stout-hearted, valiant.

harebrained *adj* careless, changeable, flighty, giddy, harum-scarum, headlong, heedless, rash, reckless, unsteady, volatile, wild.

hark *interj* attend, hear, hearken, listen.

harlequin *n* antic, buffoon, clown, droll, fool, jester, punch, fool.

harm *vb* damage, hurt, injure, scathe; abuse, desecrate, ill-use, ill-treat, maltreat, molest. * *n* damage, detriment, disadvantage, hurt, injury, mischief, misfortune, prejudice, wrong.

harmful *adj* baneful, detrimental, disadvantageous, hurtful, injurious, mischievous, noxious, pernicious, prejudicial.

harmless *adj* innocent, innocuous, innoxious; inoffensive, safe, unoffending.

harmonious *adj* concordant, consonant, harmonic; dulcet, euphonious, mellifluous, melodious, musical, smooth, tuneful; comfortable, congruent, consistent, correspondent, orderly, symmetrical; agreeable, amicable, brotherly, cordial, fraternal, friendly, neighbourly.

harmonize *vb* adapt, attune, reconcile, unite; accord, agree, blend, chime, comport, conform, correspond, square, sympathize, tally, tune.

harmony *n* euphony, melodiousness, melody; accord, accordance, agreement, chime, concord, concordance, consonance, order, unison; adaptation, congruence, congruity, consistency, correspondence, fairness, smoothness, suitableness; amity, friendship, peace.

harness *vb* hitch, tackle. * *n* equipment, gear, tackle, tackling; accoutrements, armour, array, mail, mounting.

harp *vb* dwell, iterate, reiterate, renew, repeat.

harping *n* dwelling, iteration, reiteration, repetition.

harrow *vb* harass, lacerate, rend, tear, torment, torture, wound.

harry *vb* devastate, pillage, plunder, raid, ravage, rob; annoy, chafe, disturb, fret, gall, harass, harrow, incommode, pester, plague, molest, tease, torment, trouble, vex, worry.

harsh *adj* acid, acrid, astringent, biting, caustic, corrosive, crabbed, rough, sharp, sour, tart; cacophonous, discordant, grating, jarring, metallic, raucous, strident, unmelodious; abusive, austere, crabbed, crabby, cruel, disagreeable, hard, ill-natured, ill-tempered, morose, rigorous, severe, stern, unfeeling; bearish, bluff, blunt, brutal, gruff, rude, uncivil, ungracious.

harshness *n* roughness; acerbity, asperity, austerity, churlishness, crabbedness, hardness, ill-nature, ill-temper, moroseness, rigour, severity, sternness, unkindness; bluffness, bluntness, churlishness, gruffness, incivility, ungraciousness, rudeness.

harum-scarum *adj* hare-brained, precipitate, rash, reckless, volatile, wild.

harvest *vb* gather, glean, reap. * *n* crops, produce, yield; consequence, effect, issue, outcome, produce, result.

haste *n* alacrity, celerity, dispatch, expedition, nimbleness, promptitude, quickness, rapidity, speed, urgency, velocity; flurry, hurry, hustle, impetuosity, precipitateness, precipitation, press, rashness, rush, vehemence.

hasten *vb* haste, hurry; accelerate, dispatch, expedite, precipitate, press, push, quicken, speed, urge.

hasty *adj* brisk, fast, fleet, quick, rapid, speedy, swift; cursory, hurried, passing, slight, superficial; ill-advised, rash, reckless; headlong, helter-skelter, pell-mell, precipitate; abrupt, choleric, excitable, fiery, fretful, hot-headed, irascible, irritable, passionate, peevish, peppery, pettish, petulant, testy, touchy, waspish.

hatch *vb* brew, concoct, contrive, excogitate, design, devise, plan, plot, project, scheme; breed, incubate.

hate *vb* abhor, abominate, detest, dislike, execrate, loathe, nauseate. * *n* abomination, animosity, antipathy, detestation, dislike, enmity, execration, hatred, hostility, loathing.

hateful *adj* malevolent, malicious, malign, malignant, rancorous, spiteful; abhorrent, abominable, accursed, damnable, detestable, execrable, horrid, odious, shocking; disgusting, foul, loathsome, nauseous, obnoxious, offensive, repellent, repugnant, repulsive, revolting, vile.

hatred *n* animosity, enmity, hate, hostility, ill-will, malevolence, malice, malignity, odium, rancour; abhorrence, abomination, antipathy, aversion, detestation, disgust, execration, horror, loathing, repugnance, revulsion.

haughtiness *n* arrogance, contempt, contemptuousness, disdain, hauteur, insolence, loftiness, pride, self-importance, snobbishness, stateliness, superciliousness.

haughty *adj* arrogant, assuming, contemptuous, disdainful, imperious, insolent, lofty, lordly, overbearing, overweening, proud, scornful, snobbish, supercilious.

haul *vb* drag, draw, lug, pull, tow, trail, tug. * *n* heaving, pull, tug; booty, harvest, takings, yield.

haunt *vb* frequent, resort; follow, importune; hover, inhabit, obsess. * *n* den, resort, retreat.

hauteur *n* arrogance, contempt, contemptuousness, disdain, haughtiness, insolence, loftiness, pride, self-importance, stateliness, superciliousness.

have *vb* cherish, exercise, experience, keep, hold, occupy, own, possess; acquire, gain, get, obtain, receive; accept, take.

haven *n* asylum, refuge, retreat, shelter; anchorage, harbour, port.

havoc *n* carnage, damage, desolation, destruction, devastation, ravage, ruin, slaughter, waste, wreck.

hawk-eyed *adj* eagle-eyed, sharp-sighted.

hazard *vb* adventure, risk, venture; endanger, imperil, jeopardize. * *n* accident, casualty, chance, contingency, event, fortuity, stake; danger, jeopardy, peril, risk, venture.

hazardous *adj* dangerous, insecure, perilous, precarious, risky, uncertain, unsafe.

haze *n* fog, har, mist, smog; cloud, dimness, fume, miasma, obscurity, pall.

hazy *adj* foggy, misty; cloudy, dim, nebulous, obscure; confused, indefinite, indistinct, uncertain, vague.

head *vb* command, control, direct, govern, guide, lead, rule; aim, point, tend; beat, excel, outdo, precede, surpass. * *adj* chief, first, grand, highest, leading, main, principal; adverse, contrary. * *n* acme, summit, top; beginning, commencement, origin, rise, source; chief, chieftain, commander, director, leader, master, principal, superintendent, superior; intellect, mind, thought, understanding; branch, category, class, department, division, section, subject, topic; brain, crown, headpiece, intellect, mind, thought, understanding; cape, headland, point, promontory.

headiness *n* hurry, precipitation, rashness; obstinacy, stubbornness.

headless *adj* acephalous, beheaded; leaderless, undirected; headstrong, heady, imprudent, obstinate, rash, senseless, stubborn.

headlong *adj* dangerous, hasty, heady, impulsive, inconsiderate, perilous, precipitate, rash, reckless, ruinous, thoughtless; perpendicular, precipitous, sheer, steep. * *adv* hastily, headfirst, helter-skelter, hurriedly, precipitately, rashly, thoughtlessly.

headstone *n* cornerstone, gravestone.

headstrong *adj* cantankerous, cross-grained, dogged, forward, headless, heady, intractable, obstinate, self-willed, stubborn, ungovernable, unruly, violent, wayward.

heady *adj* hasty, headlong, impetuous, impulsive, inconsiderate, precipitate, rash, reckless, rushing, stubborn, thoughtless; exciting, inebriating, inflaming, intoxicating, spirituous, strong.

heal *vb* amend, cure, remedy, repair, restore; compose, harmonize, reconcile, settle, soothe.

healing *adj* curative, palliative, remedial, restoring, restorative; assuaging, assuasive, comforting, composing, gentle, lenitive, mild, soothing.

health *n* healthfulness, robustness, salubrity, sanity, soundness, strength, tone, vigour.

healthy *adj* active, hale, hearty, lusty, sound, vigorous, well; bracing, healthful, health-giving, hygienic, invigorating, nourishing, salubrious, salutary, wholesome.

heap *vb* accumulate, augment, amass, collect, overfill, pile up, store. * *n* accumulation, collection, cumulus, huddle, lot, mass, mound, pile, stack.

hear *vb* eavesdrop, hearken, heed, listen, overhear; ascertain, discover, gather, learn, understand; examine, judge.

heart *n* bosom, breast; centre, core, essence, interior, kernel, marrow, meaning, pith; affection, benevolence, character, disposition, feeling, inclination, love, mind, passion, purpose, will; affections, ardour, emotion, feeling, love; boldness, courage, fortitude, resolution, spirit.

heartache *n* affliction, anguish, bitterness, distress, dole, grief, heartbreak, sorrow, woe.

heartbroken *adj* broken-hearted, cheerless, comfortless, desolate, disconsolate, forlorn, inconsolable, miserable, woebegone, wretched.

hearten *vb* animate, assure, cheer, comfort, console, embolden, encourage, enhearten, incite, inspire, inspirit, reassure, stimulate.

heartfelt *adj* cordial, deep, deep-felt, hearty, profound, sincere, warm.

hearth *n* fireplace, fireside, forge, hearthstone.

heartily *adv* abundantly, completely, cordially, earnestly, freely, largely, sincerely, vigorously.

heartless *adj* brutal, cold, cruel, hard, harsh, merciless, pitiless, unfeeling, unsympathetic; spiritless, timid, timorous, uncourageous.

heart-rending *adj* affecting, afflicting, anguishing, crushing, distressing.

hearty *adj* cordial, deep, earnest, fervent, heartfelt, profound, sincere, true, unfeigned, warm; active, animated, energetic, fit, vigorous, zealous; convivial, hale, healthy, robust, sound, strong, warm; abundant, full, heavy; nourishing, nutritious, rich.

heat *vb* excite, flush, inflame; animate, rouse, stimulate, stir. * *n* calorie, caloricity, torridity, warmth; excitement, fever, flush, impetuosity, passion, vehemence, violence; ardour, earnestness, fervency, fervour, glow, intensity, zeal; exasperation, fierceness, frenzy, rage.

heath *n* field, moor, wasteland, plain.

heathen *adj* animist, animistic; pagan, paganical, paganish, paganistic, unconverted; agnostic, atheist, atheistic, gentile, idolatrous, infidel, irreligious; barbarous, cruel, inhuman, savage. * *n* atheist, gentile, idolater, idolatress, infidel, pagan, unbeliever; barbarian, philistine, savage.

heave *vb* elevate, hoist, lift, raise; breathe, exhale; cast, fling, hurl, send, throw, toss; dilate, expand, pant, rise, swell; retch, throw up; strive, struggle.

heaven *n* empyrean, firmament, sky, welkin; bliss, ecstasy, elysium, felicity, happiness, paradise, rapture, transport.

heavenly *adj* celestial, empyreal, ethereal; angelic, beatific, beatified, cherubic, divine, elysian, glorious, god-like, sainted, saintly, seraphic; blissful, delightful, divine, ecstatic, enrapturing, enravishing, exquisite, golden, rapturous, ravishing, exquisite, transporting.

heaviness *n* gravity, heft, ponderousness, weight; grievousness, oppressiveness, severity; dullness, languor, lassitude, sluggishness, stupidity; dejection, depression, despondency, gloom, melancholy, sadness, seriousness.

heavy *adj* grave, hard, onerous, ponderous, weighty; afflictive, burdensome, crushing, cumbersome, grievous, oppressive, severe, serious; dilatory, dull, inactive, inanimate, indolent, inert, lifeless, listless, sleepy, slow, sluggish, stupid, torpid; chapfallen, crestfallen, crushed, depressed, dejected, despondent, disconsolate, downhearted, gloomy, low-spirited, melancholy, sad, sobered, sorrowful; difficult, laborious; tedious, tiresome, wearisome, weary; burdened, encumbered, loaded; clammy, clayey, cloggy, ill-raised, miry, muddy, soggy; boisterous, deep, energetic, loud, roaring, severe, stormy, strong, tempestuous, violent; cloudy, dark, dense, gloomy, lowering, overcast.

hebetate *adj* blunt; dull, obtuse, sluggish, stupid, stupefied.

hectic *adj* animated, excited, fevered, feverish, flushed, heated, hot.

hector *vb* bluster, boast, bully, menace, threaten; annoy, fret, harass, harry, irritate, provoke, tease, vex, worry. * *n* blusterer, bully, swaggerer.

hedge *vb* block, encumber, hinder, obstruct, surround; enclose, fence, fortify, guard, protect; disappear, dodge, evade, hide, skulk, temporize. * *n* barrier, hedgerow, fence, limit.

heed *vb* attend, consider, mark, mind, note, notice, observe, regard. * *n* attention, care, carefulness, caution, circumspection, consideration, heedfulness, mindfulness, notice, observation, regard, wariness, vigilance, watchfulness.

heedful *adj* attentive, careful, cautious, circumspect, mindful, observant, observing, provident, regardful, watchful, wary.

heedless *adj* careless, inattentive, neglectful, negligent, precipitate, rash, reckless, thoughtless, unmindful, unminding, unobserving, unobservant.

heft *n* handle, haft, helve; bulk, weight.

hegemony *n* ascendancy, authority, headship, leadership, predominance, preponderance, rule.

height *n* altitude, elevation, tallness; acme, apex, climax, eminence, head, meridian, pinnacle, summit, top, vertex, zenith; eminence, hill, mountain; dignity, exaltation, grandeur, loftiness, perfection.

heighten *vb* elevate, raise; ennoble, exalt, magnify, make greater; augment, enhance, improve, increase, strengthen; aggravate, intensify.

heinous *adj* aggravated, atrocious, crying, enormous, excessive, flagitious, flagrant, hateful, infamous, monstrous, nefarious, odious, villainous.

heir *n* child, inheritor, offspring, product.

helical *adj* screw-shaped, spiral, winding.

hellish *adj* abominable, accursed, atrocious, curst, damnable, damned, demoniacal, detestable, devilish, diabolical, execrable, fiendish, infernal, monstrous, nefarious, satanic.

helm *n* rudder, steering-gear, tiller, wheel; command, control, direction, rein, rule.

help *vb* relieve, save, succour; abet, aid, assist, back, cooperate, second, serve, support, sustain, wait; alleviate, ameliorate, better, cure, heal, improve, remedy, restore; control, hinder, prevent, repress, resist, withstand; avoid, forbear, control. * *n* aid, assistance, succour, support; relief, remedy; assistant, helper, servant.

helper *adj* aider, abettor, ally, assistant, auxiliary, coadjutor, colleague, helpmate, partner, supporter.

helpful *adj* advantageous, assistant, auxiliary, beneficial, contributory, convenient, favourable, kind, profitable, serviceable, useful.

helpless *adj* disabled, feeble, imbecile, impotent, infirm, powerless, prostrate, resourceless, weak; abandoned, defenceless, exposed, unprotected; desperate, irremediable, remediless.

helpmate *n* companion, consort, husband, partner, wife; aider, assistant, associate, helper.

helter-skelter *adj* disorderly, headlong, irregular, pell-mell, precipitate. * *adv* confusedly, hastily, headlong, higgledy-piggledy, pell-mell, precipitately, wildly.

hem *vb* border, edge, skirt; beset, confine, enclose, environ, surround, sew; hesitate. * *n* border, edge, trim.

henchman *n* attendant, follower, retainer, servant, supporter.

herald *vb* announce, proclaim, publish. * *n* announcer, crier, publisher; harbinger, precursor, proclaimer.

heraldry *n* blazonry, emblazonry.

herbage *n* greenery, herb, pasture, plants, vegetation.

herculean *adj* able-bodied, athletic, brawny, mighty, muscular, powerful, puissant, sinewy, stalwart, strong, sturdy, vigorous; dangerous, difficult, hard, laborious, perilous, toilsome, troublesome; colossal, Cyclopean, gigantic, great, large, strapping.

herd *vb* drive, gather, lead, tend; assemble, associate, flock. * *n* drover, herder, herdsman, shepherd; crowd, multitude, populace, rabble; assemblage, assembly, collection, drove, flock, pack.

hereditary *adj* ancestral, inheritable, inherited, patrimonial, transmitted.

heresy *n* dissent, error, heterodoxy, impiety, recusancy, unorthodoxy.

heretic *n* dissenter, dissident, nonconformist, recusant, schismatic, sectarian, sectary, separatist, unbeliever.

heretical *adj* heterodox, impious, schismatic, schismatical, sectarian, unorthodox.

heritage *n* estate, inheritance, legacy, patrimony, portion.

hermetic *adj* airtight, impervious; cabbalistic, emblematic, emblematical, magical, mysterious, mystic, mystical, occult, secret, symbolic, symbolical.

hermit *n* anchoress, anchoret, anchorite, ascetic, eremite, monk, recluse, solitaire, solitary.

heroic *adj* bold, brave, courageous, daring, dauntless, fearless, gallant, illustrious, intrepid, magnanimous, noble, valiant; desperate, extravagant, extreme, violent.

heroism *n* boldness, bravery, courage, daring, endurance, fearlessness, fortitude, gallantry, intrepidity, prowess, valour.

hesitate *vb* boggle, delay, demur, doubt, pause, scruple, shilly-shally, stickle, vacillate, waver; falter, stammer, stutter.

hesitation *n* halting, misgiving, reluctance; delay, doubt, indecision, suspense, uncertainty, vacillation; faltering, stammering, stuttering.

heterodox *adj* heretical, recusant, schismatic, unorthodox, unsound; apocryphal, uncanonical.

heterogeneous *adj* contrasted, contrary, different, dissimilar, diverse, incongruous, indiscriminate, miscellaneous, mixed, opposed, unhomogeneous, unlike.

hew *vb* chop, cut, fell, hack; fashion, form, shape, smooth.

hiatus *n* blank, break, chasm, gap, interval, lacuna, opening, rift.

hidden *adj* blind, clandestine, cloaked, close, concealed, covered, covert, enshrouded, latent, masked, occult, private, secluded, secret, suppressed, undiscovered, veiled; abstruse, cabbalistic, cryptic, dark, esoteric, hermetic, inward, mysterious, mystic, mystical, obscure, oracular, recondite.

hide *vb* bury, conceal, cover, secrete, suppress, withhold; cloak, disguise, eclipse, hoard, mask, screen, shelter, veil.

hideous *adj* abominable, appalling, awful, dreadful, frightful, ghastly, ghoulish, grim, grisly, horrible, horrid, repulsive, revolting, shocking, terrible, terrifying.

hie *vb* hasten, speed.

hieratic *adj* consecrated, devoted, priestly, sacred, sacerdotal.

hieroglyph *n* picture-writing, rebus, sign, symbol.

hieroglyphic *adj* emblematic, emblematical, figurative, obscure, symbolic, symbolical.

higgle *vb* hawk, peddle; bargain, chaffer, haggle, negotiate.

higgledy-piggledy *adj* chaotic, confused, disorderly, jumbled. * *adv* confusedly, in disorder, helter-skelter, pell-mell.

high *adj* elevated, high-reaching, lofty, soaring, tall, towering; distinguished, eminent, pre-eminent, prominent, superior; admirable, dignified, exalted, great, noble; arrogant, haughty, lordly, proud, supercilious; boisterous, strong, tumultuous, turbulent, violent; costly, dear, pricey; acute, high-pitched, high-toned, piercing, sharp, shrill; tainted, malodorous. * *adv* powerfully, profoundly; eminently, loftily; luxuriously, richly.

high-flown *adj* elevated, presumptuous, proud, lofty, swollen; extravagant, high-coloured, lofty, overdrawn, overstrained; bombastic, inflated, pompous, pretentious, strained, swollen, turgid.

high-handed *adj* arbitrary, despotic, dictatorial, domineering, oppressive, overbearing, self-willed, violent, wilful.

highly strung *adj* ardent, excitable, irascible, nervous, quick, tense; high-spirited, sensitive.

high-minded *adj* arrogant, haughty, lofty, proud; elevated, high-toned; generous honourable, magnanimous, noble, spiritual.

highwayman *n* bandit, brigand, footpad, freebooter, marauder, outlaw, robber.

hilarious *adj* boisterous, cheerful, comical, convivial, riotous, uproarious, jovial, joyful, merry, mirthful, noisy.

hilarity *n* cheerfulness, conviviality, exhilarated, gaiety, glee, jollity, joviality, joyousness, merriment, mirth.

hill *n* ascent, ben, elevation, eminence, hillock, knoll, mount, mountain, rise, tor.

hind *adj* back, hinder, hindmost, posterior, rear, rearward.

hinder *vb* bar, check, clog, delay, embarrass, encumber, impede, interrupt, obstruct, oppose, prevent, restrain, retard, stop, thwart.

hindrance *n* check, deterrent, encumbrance, hitch, impediment, interruption, obstacle, obstruction, restraint, stop, stoppage.

hinge *vb* depend, hang, rest, turn.

hint *vb* allude, glance, imply, insinuate, intimate, mention, refer, suggest. * *n* allusion, clue, implication, indication, innuendo, insinuation, intimation, mention, reminder, suggestion, taste, trace.

hire *vb* buy, rent, secure; charter, employ, engage, lease, let. * *n* allowance, bribe, compensation, pay, remuneration, rent, reward, salary, stipend, wages.

hireling *n* employee, mercenary, myrmidon.

hirsute *adj* bristled, bristly, hairy, shaggy; boorish, course, ill-bred, loutish, rough, rude, rustic,
uncouth, unmannerly.

hiss *vb* shrill, sibilate, whistle, whir, whiz; condemn, damn, ridicule. * *n* fizzle, hissing, sibilant, sibilation, sizzle.

historian *n* annalist, autobiographer, biographer, chronicler, narrator, recorder.

history *n* account, autobiography, annals, biography, chronicle, genealogy, memoirs, narration, narrative, recital, record, relation, story.

hit *vb* discomfit, hurt, knock, strike; accomplish, achieve, attain, gain, reach, secure, succeed, win; accord, fit, suit; beat, clash, collide, contact, smite. * *n* blow, collision, strike, stroke; chance, fortune, hazard, success, venture.

hitch *vb* catch, impede, stick, stop; attach,

connect, fasten, harness, join, tether, tie, unite, yoke. * *n* catch, check, hindrance, impediment, interruption, obstacle; knot, noose.

hoar *adj* ancient, grey, hoary, old, white.

hoard *vb* accumulate, amass, collect, deposit, garner, hive, husband, save, store, treasure. * *n* accumulation, collection, deposit, fund, mass, reserve, savings, stockpile, store.

hoarse *adj* discordant, grating, gruff, guttural, harsh, husky, low, raucous, rough.

hoary *adj* grey, hoar, silvery, white; ancient, old, venerable.

hoax *vb* deceive, dupe, fool, gammon, gull, hoodwink, swindle, trick. * *n* canard, cheat, deception, fraud, humbug, imposition, imposture, joke, trick, swindle.

hobble *vb* falter, halt, hop, limp; fasten, fetter, hopple, shackle, tie. * *n* halt, limp; clog, fetter, shackle; embarrassment, difficulty, perplexity, pickle, strait.

hobgoblin *n* apparition, bogey, bugbear, goblin, imp, spectre, spirit, sprite.

hobnail *n* bumpkin, churl, clodhopper, clown, lout, rustic.

hocus-pocus *n* cheater, impostor, juggler, sharper, swindler, trickster; artifice, cheat, deceit, deception, delusion, hoax, imposition, juggle, trick.

hodgepodge *n* farrago, hash, hotchpotch, jumble, medley, miscellany, mixture, ragout, stew.

hog *n* beast, glutton, pig; grunter, porker, swine.

hoggish *adj* brutish, filthy, gluttonish, piggish, swinish; grasping, greedy, mean, selfish, sordid.

hoist *vb* elevate, heave, lift, raise, rear. * *n* elevator, lift.

hold *vb* clasp, clinch, clutch, grasp, grip, seize; have, keep, occupy, possess, retain; bind, confine, control, detain, imprison, restrain, restrict; connect, fasten, fix, lock; arrest, check, stay, stop, suspend, withhold; continue, keep up, maintain, manage, prosecute, support, sustain; cherish, embrace, entertain; account, believe, consider, count, deem, entertain, esteem, judge, reckon, regard, think; accommodate, admit, carry, contain, receive, stow; assemble, conduct, convene; endure, last, persist, remain; adhere, cleave, cling, cohere, stick. * *n* anchor, bite, clasp, control, embrace, foothold, grasp, grip, possession, retention, seizure; prop, stay, support; claim, footing, vantage point; castle, fort, fortification, fortress, stronghold, tower; locker, storage, storehouse.

hole *n* aperture, opening, perforation; abyss, bore, cave, cavern, cavity, chasm, depression, excavation, eye, hollow, pit, pore, void; burrow, cover, lair, retreat; den, hovel, kennel.

holiday *n* anniversary, celebration, feast, festival, festivity, fete, gala, recess, vacation.

holiness *n* blessedness, consecration, devotion, devoutness, godliness, piety, purity, religiousness, righteousness, sacredness, saintliness, sanctity, sinlessness.

hollow *vb* dig, excavate, groove, scoop. * *adj* cavernous, concave, depressed, empty, sunken, vacant, void; deceitful, faithless, false, false-hearted, hollow-hearted, hypocritical, insincere, pharisaical, treacherous, unfeeling; deep, low, muffled, reverberating, rumbling, sepulchral. * *n* basin, bowl, depression; cave, cavern, cavity, concavity, dent, dimple, dint, depression, excavation, hole, pit; canal, channel, cup, dimple, dig, groove, pocket, sag.

holocaust *n* carnage, destruction, devastation, genocide, massacre.

holy *adj* blessed, consecrated, dedicated, devoted, hallowed, sacred, sanctified; devout, godly, pious, pure, religious, righteous, saintlike, saintly, sinless, spiritual.

homage *n* allegiance, devotion, fealty, fidelity, loyalty; court, deference, duty, honour, obeisance, respect, reverence, service; adoration, devotion, worship.

home *adj* domestic, family; close, direct, effective, penetrating, pointed. * *n* abode, dwelling, seat, quarters, residence.

homely *adj* domestic, familiar, house-like;

coarse, commonplace, homespun, inelegant, plain, simple, unattractive, uncomely, unpolished, unpretentious.

homespun *adj* coarse, homely, inelegant, plain, rude, rustic, unpolished.

homicide *n* manslaughter, murder.

homily *n* address, discourse, lecture, sermon.

homogeneous *adj* akin, alike, cognate, kindred, similar, uniform.

honest *adj* equitable, fair, faithful, honourable, open, straight, straightforward; conscientious, equitable, reliable, sound, square, true, trustworthy, trusty, uncorrupted, upright, virtuous; aboveboard, faithful, genuine, thorough, unadulterated; creditable, decent, proper, reputable, respectable, suitable; chaste, decent; candid, direct, frank, ingenuous, sincere, unreserved.

honesty *n* equity, fairness, faithfulness, fidelity, honour, integrity, justice, probity, trustiness, trustworthiness, uprightness; truth, truthfulness, veracity; genuineness, thoroughness; candour, frankness, ingenuousness, openness, sincerity, straightforwardness, unreserve.

honorary *adj* formal, nominal, titular, unofficial, unpaid.

honour *vb* dignify, exalt, glorify, grace; respect, revere, reverence, venerate; adore, hallow, worship; celebrate, commemorate, keep, observe. * *n* civility, deference, esteem, homage, respect, reverence, veneration; dignity, distinction, elevation, nobleness; consideration, credit, fame, glory, reputation; high-mindedness, honesty, integrity, magnanimity, probity, uprightness; chastity, purity, virtue; boast, credit, ornament, pride.

honourable *adj* elevated, famous, great, illustrious, noble; admirable, conscientious, fair, honest, just, magnanimous, true, trustworthy, upright, virtuous, worshipful; creditable, esteemed, estimable, equitable, proper, respected, reputable, right.

honours *npl* dignities, distinctions, privilege, titles; adornments, beauties, decorations, glories; civilities.

hood *n* capuche, coif, cover, cowl, head.

hoodwink *vb* blind, blindfold; cloak, conceal, cover, hide; cheat, circumvent, cozen, deceive, delete, dupe, fool, gull, impose, overreach, trick.

hook *vb* catch, ensnare, entrap, hasp, snare; bend, curve. * *n* catch, clasp, fastener, hasp; snare, trap; cutter, grass-hook, reaper, reaping-hook, sickle.

hooked *adj* aquiline, bent, crooked, curved, hamate, unciform.

hoop *vb* clasp, encircle, enclose, surround. * *n* band, circlet, girdle, ring; crinoline, farthingale.

hoot *vb* boo, cry, jeer, shout, yell; condemn, decry, denounce, execrate, hiss. * *n* boo, cry, jeer, shout, yell.

hop *vb* bound, caper, frisk, jump, leap, skip, spring; dance, trip; halt, hobble, limp. * *n* bound, caper, dance, jump, leap, skip, spring.

hope *vb* anticipate, await, desire, expect, long; believe, rely, trust. * *n* confidence, belief, faith, reliance, sanguineness, sanguinity, trust; anticipation, desire, expectancy, expectation.

hopeful *adj* anticipatory, confident, expectant, fond, optimistic, sanguine; cheerful, encouraging, promising.

hopeless *adj* abject, crushed, depressed, despondent, despairing, desperate, disconsolate, downcast, forlorn, pessimistic, woebegone; abandoned, helpless, incurable, irremediable, remediless; impossible, impracticable, unachievable, unattainable.

horde *n* clan, crew, gang, troop; crowd, multitude, pack, throng.

horn *vb* gore, pierce. * *n* trumpet, wind instrument; beaker, drinking cup, cornucopia; spike, spur; cusp, prong, wing.

horrid *adj* alarming, awful, bristling, dire, dreadful, fearful, frightful, harrowing, hideous, horrible, horrific, horrifying, rough, terrible, terrific; abominable, disagreeable, disgusting, odious, offensive, repulsive, revolting, shocking, unpleasant, vile.

horrify *vb* affright, alarm, frighten, shock,

terrify, terrorise.

horror *n* alarm, awe, consternation, dismay, dread, fear, fright, panic; abhorrence, abomination, antipathy, aversion, detestation, disgust, hatred, loathing, repugnance, revulsion; shuddering.

horse *n* charger, cob, colt, courser, filly, gelding, mare, nag, pad, palfrey, pony, stallion, steed; cavalry, horseman; buck, clotheshorse, frame, sawhorse, stand, support.

horseman *n* cavalier, equestrian, rider; cavalryman, chasseur, dragoon, horse-soldier.

hospitable *adj* attentive, bountiful, kind; bountiful, cordial, generous, liberal, open, receptive, sociable, unconstrained, unreserved.

host[1] *n* entertainer, innkeeper, landlord, master of ceremonies, presenter, proprietor, owner, receptionist.

host[2] *n* array, army, legion; assemblage, assembly, horde, multitude, throng.

host[3] *n* altar bread, bread, consecrated bread, loaf, wafer.

hostile *adj* inimical, unfriendly, warlike; adverse, antagonistic, contrary, opposed, opposite, repugnant.

hostilities *npl* conflict, fighting, war, warfare.

hostility *n* animosity, antagonism, enmity, hatred, ill-will, unfriendliness; contrariness, opposition, repugnance, variance.

hot *adj* burning, fiery, scalding; boiling, flaming, heated, incandescent, parching, roasting, torrid; heated, oppressive, sweltering, warm; angry, choleric, excitable, furious, hasty, impatient, impetuous, irascible, lustful, passionate, touchy, urgent, violent; animated, ardent, eager, fervent, fervid, glowing, passionate, vehement; acrid, biting, highly flavoured, highly seasoned, peppery, piquant, pungent, sharp, stinging.

hotchpotch *n* farrago, jumble, hodgepodge, medley, miscellany, stew.

hotel *n* inn, public house, tavern.

hot-headed *adj* furious, headlong, headstrong, hot-brained, impetuous, inconsiderate, passionate, precipitate, rash, reckless, vehement, violent.

hound *vb* drive, incite, spur, urge; bate, chase, goad, harass, harry, hunt, pursue.

house *vb* harbour, lodge, protect, shelter. * *n* abode, domicile, dwelling, habitation, home, mansion, residence; building, edifice; family, household; kindred, race, lineage, tribe; company, concern, firm, partnership; hotel, inn, public house, tavern.

housing *n* accommodation, dwellings, houses; casing, container, covering, protection, shelter.

hovel *n* cabin, cot, den, hole, hut, shed.

hover *vb* flutter; hang; vacillate, waver.

however *adv* but, however, nevertheless, notwithstanding, still, though, yet.

howl *vb* bawl, cry, lament, ululate, weep, yell, yowl. * *n* cry, yell, ululation.

hoyden *n* romp, tomboy.

hoydenish *adj* bad-mannered, boisterous, bold, ill-behaved, ill-taught, inelegant, romping, rough, rude, rustic, tomboyish, uncouth, ungenteel, unladylike, unruly.

hubbub *n* clamour, confusion, din, disorder, disturbance, hullabaloo, racket, riot, outcry, tumult, uproar.

huckster *n* hawker, peddler, retailer.

huddle *vb* cluster, crowd, gather; crouch, curl up, nestle, snuggle. * *n* confusion, crowd, disorder, disturbance, jumble, tumult.

hue *n* cast, colour, complexion, dye, shade, tinge, tint, tone.

huff *vb* blow, breathe, exhale, pant, puff. * *n* anger, fume, miff, passion, pet, quarrel, rage, temper, tiff.

hug *vb* clasp, cling, cuddle, embrace, grasp, grip, squeeze; cherish, nurse, retain. * *n* clasp, cuddle, embrace, grasp, squeeze.

huge *adj* bulky, colossal, Cyclopean, elephantine, enormous, gigantic, herculean, immense, stupendous, vast,

huggermugger *adj* clandestine, secret, sly; base, contemptible, mean, unfair; confused, disorderly, slovenly.

hull *vb* husk, peel, shell. * *n* covering, husk, rind, shell.

hullabaloo *n* clamour, confusion, din, disturbance, hubbub, outcry, racket, vociferation, uproar.
hum *vb* buzz, drone, murmur; croon, sing.
humane *adj* accommodating, benevolent, benign, charitable, clement, compassionate, gentle, good-hearted, kind, kind-hearted, lenient, merciful, obliging, tender, sympathetic; cultivating, elevating, humanizing, refining, rational, spiritual.
humanity *n* benevolence, benignity, charity, fellow-feeling, humaneness, kind-heartedness, kindness, philanthropy, sympathy, tenderness; humankind, mankind, mortality.
humanize *vb* civilize, cultivate, educate, enlighten, improve, polish, reclaim, refine, soften.
humble *vb* abase, abash, break, crush, debase, degrade, disgrace, humiliate, lower, mortify, reduce, sink, subdue. * *adj* meek, modest, lowly, simple, submissive, unambitious, unassuming, unobtrusive, unostentatious, unpretending; low, obscure, mean, plain, poor, small, undistinguished, unpretentious.
humbug *vb* cheat, cozen, deceive, hoax, swindle, trick. * *n* cheat, dodge, gammon, hoax, imposition, imposture, deception, fraud, trick; cant, charlatanism, charlatanry, hypocrisy, mummery, quackery; charlatan, impostor, fake, quack.
humdrum *adj* boring, dronish, dreary, dry, dull, monotonous, prosy, stupid, tedious, tiresome, wearisome.
humid *adj* damp, dank, moist, wet.
humiliate *vb* abase, abash, debase, degrade, depress, humble, mortify, shame.
humiliation *n* abasement, affront, condescension, crushing, degradation, disgrace, dishonouring, humbling, indignity, mortification, self-abasement, submissiveness, resignation.
humility *n* diffidence, humbleness, lowliness, meekness, modesty, self-abasement, submissiveness.
humorist *n* comic, comedian, droll, jester, joker, wag, wit.
humorous *adj* comic, comical, droll, facetious, funny, humorous, jocose, jocular, laughable, ludicrous, merry, playful, pleasant, sportive, whimsical, witty.
humour *vb* favour, gratify, indulge. * *n* bent, bias, disposition, predilection, prosperity, temper, vein; mood, state; caprice, crotchet, fancy, freak, vagary, whim, whimsy, wrinkle; drollery, facetiousness, fun, jocoseness, jocularity, pleasantry, wit; fluid, moisture, vapour.
hunch *vb* arch, jostle, nudge, punch, push, shove. * *n* bunch, hump, knob, protuberance; nudge, punch, push, shove; feeling, idea, intuition, premonition.
hungry *adj* covetous, craving, desirous, greedy; famished, starved, starving; barren, poor, unfertile, unproductive.
hunk *n* chunk, hunch, lump, slice.
hunt *vb* chase, drive, follow, hound, pursue, stalk, trap, trail; poach, shoot; search, seek. * *n* chase, field-sport, hunting, pursuit.
hurl *vb* cast, dart, fling, pitch, project, send, sling, throw, toss.
hurly-burly *n* bustle, commotion, confusion, disturbance, hurl, hurly, uproar, tumult, turmoil.
hurricane *n* cyclone, gale, storm, tempest, tornado, typhoon.
hurried *adj* cursory, hasty, slight, superficial.
hurry *vb* drive, precipitate; dispatch, expedite, hasten, quicken, speed; haste, scurry. * *n* agitation, bustle, confusion, flurry, flutter, perturbation, precipitation; celerity, haste, dispatch, expedition, promptitude, promptness, quickness.
hurt *vb* damage, disable, disadvantage, harm, impair, injure, mar; bruise, pain, wound; afflict, grieve, offend; ache, smart, throb. * *n* damage, detriment, disadvantage, harm, injury, mischief; ache, bruise, pain, suffering, wound.
hurtful *adj* baleful, baneful, deleterious, destructive, detrimental, disadvantageous, harmful, injurious, mischievous, noxious, pernicious, prejudicial, unwholesome.
husband *vb* economize, hoard, save, store.
husbandry *n* agriculture, cultivation, farming, geoponics, tillage; economy,

frugality, thrift.

hush *vb* quiet, repress, silence, still, suppress; appease, assuage, calm, console, quiet, still. * *n* quiet, quietness, silence, stillness.

hypocrite *n* deceiver, dissembler, impostor, pretender.

hypocritical *adj* deceiving, dissembling, false, insincere, spurious, two-faced.

hypothesis *n* assumption, proposition, supposition, theory.

hypothetical *adj* assumed, imaginary, supposed, theoretical.

hysterical *adj* frantic, frenzied, overwrought, uncontrollable; comical, uproarious.

I

ice *vb* chill, congeal, freeze. * *n* crystal; frosting, sugar.
icy *adj* glacial; chilling, cold, frosty; cold-hearted, distant, frigid, indifferent, unemotional.
idea *n* archetype, essence, exemplar, ideal, model, pattern, plan, model; fantasy, fiction, image, imagination; apprehension, conceit, conception, fancy, illusion, impression, thought; belief, judgement, notion, opinion, sentiment, supposition.
ideal *adj* intellectual, mental; chimerical, fancied, fanciful, fantastic, illusory, imaginary, unreal, visionary, shadowy; complete, consummate, excellent, perfect; impractical, unattainable, utopian. * *n* criterion, example, model, standard.
identical *adj* equivalent, same, selfsame, tantamount.
identity *n* existence, individuality, personality, sameness.
ideology *n* belief, creed, dogma, philosophy, principle.
idiocy *n* fatuity, feebleness, foolishness, imbecility, insanity.
idiosyncrasy *n* caprice, eccentricity, fad, peculiarity, singularity.
idiot *n* blockhead, booby, dunce, fool, ignoramus, imbecile, simpleton.
idiotic *adj* fatuous, foolish, imbecile, irrational, senseless, sottish, stupid.
idle *adj* inactive, unemployed, unoccupied, vacant; indolent, inert, lazy, slothful, sluggish; abortive, bootless, fruitless, futile, groundless, ineffectual, unavailing, useless, vain; foolish, frivolous, trashy, trifling, trivial, unimportant, unprofitable. * *vb* dally, dawdle, laze, loiter, potter, waste; drift, shirk, slack.
idler *n* dawdler, doodle, drone, laggard, lazybones, loafer, lounger, slacker, slowcoach, sluggard, trifler.
idol *n* deity, god, icon, image, pagan, simulacrum, symbol; delusion, falsity, pretender, sham; beloved, darling, favourite, pet.
idolater *n* heathen, pagan; admirer, adorer, worshipper.
idolize *vb* canonize, deify; adore, honour, love, reverence, venerate.
idyll *n* eclogue, pastoral.
if *conj* admitting, allowing, granting, provided, supposing, though, whether. * *n* condition, hesitation, uncertainty.
igneous *adj* combustible, combustive, conflagrative, fiery, molten.
ignite *vb* burn, inflame, kindle, light, torch.
ignoble *adj* base-born, low, low-born, mean, peasant, plebeian, rustic, vulgar; contemptible, degraded, insignificant, mean, worthless; disgraceful, dishonourable, infamous, low, unworthy.
ignominious *adj* discreditable, disgraceful, dishonourable, disreputable, infamous, opprobrious, scandalous, shameful; base, contemptible, despicable.
ignominy *n* abasement, contempt, discredit, disgrace, dishonour disrepute, infamy, obloquy, odium, opprobrium, scandal, shame.
ignoramus *n* blockhead, duffer, dunce, fool, greenhorn, novice, numskull, simpleton.
ignorance *n* benightedness, darkness, illiteracy, nescience, rusticity; blindness, unawareness.
ignorant *adj* blind, illiterate, nescient, unaware, unconversant, uneducated, unenlightened, uninformed, uninstructed, unlearned, unread, untaught, untutored, unwitting.
ignore *vb* disregard, neglect, overlook, reject, skip.
ill *adj* bad, evil, faulty, harmful, iniquitous,

naughty, unfavourable, unfortunate, unjust, wicked; ailing, diseased, disordered, indisposed, sick, unwell, wrong; crabbed, cross, hateful, malicious, malevolent, peevish, surly, unkind, ill-bred; ill-favoured, ugly, unprepossessing. * *adv* badly, poorly, unfortunately. * *n* badness, depravity, evil, mischief, misfortune, wickedness; affliction, ailment, calamity, harm, misery, pain, trouble.

ill-advised *adj* foolish, ill-judged, imprudent, injudicious, unwise.

ill-bred *adj* discourteous, ill-behaved, ill-mannered, impolite, rude, uncivil, uncourteous, uncourtly, uncouth.

illegal *adj* contraband, forbidden, illegitimate, illicit, prohibited, unauthorized, unlawful, unlicensed.

illegible *adj* indecipherable, obscure, undecipherable, unreadable.

illegitimate *adj* bastard, misbegotten, natural.

ill-fated *adj* ill-starred, luckless, unfortunate, unlucky.

ill-favoured *adj* homely, ugly, offensive, plain, unpleasant.

ill humour *n* fretfulness, ill-temper, peevishness, petulance, testiness.

illiberal *adj* close, close-fisted, covetous, mean, miserly, narrow, niggardly, parsimonious, penurious, selfish, sordid, stingy, ungenerous; bigoted, narrow-minded, uncharitable, ungentlemanly, vulgar.

illicit *adj* illegal, illegitimate, unauthorized, unlawful, unlegalized, unlicensed; criminal, guilty, forbidden, improper, wrong.

illimitable *adj* boundless, endless, immeasurable, immense, infinite, unbounded, unlimited, vast.

illiterate *adj* ignorant, uneducated, uninstructed, unlearned, unlettered, untaught, untutored.

ill-judged *adj* foolish, ill-advised, imprudent, injudicious, unwise.

ill-mannered *adj* discourteous, ill-behaved, ill-bred, impolite, rude, uncivil, uncourteous, uncourtly, uncouth, unpolished.

ill-natured *adj* disobliging, hateful, malevolent, unamiable, unfriendly, unkind; acrimonious, bitter, churlish, crabbed, cross, cross-grained, crusty, ill-tempered, morose, perverse, petulant, sour, spiteful, sulky, sullen, wayward.

illness *n* ailing, ailment, complaint, disease, disorder, distemper, indisposition, malady, sickness.

illogical *adj* absurd, fallacious, inconsistent, inconclusive, inconsequent, incorrect, invalid, unreasonable, unsound.

ill-proportioned *adj* awkward, ill-made, ill-shaped, misshapen, misproportioned, shapeless.

ill-starred *adj* ill-fated, luckless, unfortunate, unhappy, unlucky.

ill temper *n* bad temper, crabbedness, crossness, grouchiness, ill nature, moroseness, sulkiness, sullenness.

ill-tempered *adj* acrimonious, bad-tempered, crabbed, cross, grouchy, ill-natured, morose, sour, sulky, surly.

ill-timed *adj* inapposite, inopportune, irrelevant, unseasonable, untimely.

ill-treat *vb* abuse, ill-use, injure, maltreat, mishandle, misuse.

illude *vb* cheat, deceive, delude, disappoint, mock, swindle, trick.

illuminate *vb* illume, illumine, light; adorn, brighten, decorate, depict, edify, enlighten, inform, inspire, instruct, make wise.

illusion *n* chimera, deception, delusion, error, fallacy, false appearance, fantasy, hallucination, mockery, phantasm.

illusive, illusory *adj* barmecide, deceitful, deceptive, delusive, fallacious, imaginary, make-believe, mock, sham, unsatisfying, unreal, unsubstantial, visionary, tantalizing.

illustrate *vb* clarify, demonstrate, elucidate, enlighten, exemplify, explain; adorn, depict, draw.

illustration *n* demonstration, elucidation, enlightenment, exemplification, explanation, interpretation; adornment, decoration, picture.

illustrative *adj* elucidative, elucidatory, exemplifying.

illustrious *adj* bright, brilliant, glorious, radiant, splendid; celebrated, conspicuous, distinguished, eminent, famed, famous, noble, noted, remarkable, renowned, signal.

ill will *n* animosity, dislike, enmity, envy, grudge, hate, hatred, hostility, ill nature, malevolence, malice, malignity, rancour, spleen, spite, uncharitableness, unkindness, venom.

image *n* idol, statue; copy, effigy, figure, form, imago, likeness, picture, resemblance, representation, shape, similitude, simulacrum, statue, symbol; conception, counterpart, embodiment, idea, reflection.

imagery *n* dream, phantasm, phantom, vision.

imaginable *adj* assumable, cogitable, conceivable, conjecturable, plausible, possible, supposable, thinkable.

imaginary *adj* chimerical, dreamy, fancied, fanciful, fantastic, fictitious, ideal, illusive, illusory, invented, quixotic, shadowy, unreal, utopian, visionary, wild; assumed, conceivable, hypothetical, supposed.

imagination *n* chimera, conception, fancy, fantasy, invention, unreality; position; contrivance, device, plot, scheme.

imaginative *adj* creative, dreamy, fanciful, inventive, poetical, plastic, visionary.

imagine *vb* conceive, dream, fancy, imagine, picture, pretend; contrive, create, devise, frame, invent, mould, project; assume, suppose, hypothesize; apprehend, assume, believe, deem, guess, opine, suppose, think.

imbecile *adj* cretinous, drivelling, fatuous, feeble, feeble-minded, foolish, helpless, idiotic, imbecilic, inane, infirm, witless. * *n* dotard, driveller.

imbecility *n* debility, feebleness, helplessness, infirmity, weakness; foolishness, idiocy, silliness, stupidity, weak-mindedness.

imbibe *vb* absorb, assimilate, drink, suck, swallow; acquire, gain, gather, get, receive.

imbroglio *n* complexity, complication, embarrassment, entanglement, misunderstanding.

imbrue *vb* drench, embrue, gain, moisten, soak, stain, steep, wet.

imbue *vb* colour, dye, stain, tincture, tinge, tint; bathe, impregnate, infuse, inoculate, permeate, pervade, provide, saturate, steep.

imitate *vb* copy, counterfeit, duplicate, echo, emulate, follow, forge, mirror, reproduce, simulate; ape, impersonate, mimic, mock, personate; burlesque, parody, travesty.

imitation *adj* artificial, fake, man-made, mock, reproduction, synthetic. * *n* aping, copying, imitation, mimicking, parroting; copy, duplicate, likeness, resemblance; mimicry, mocking; burlesque, parody, travesty.

imitative *adj* copying, emulative, imitating, mimetic, simulative; apeish, aping, mimicking.

imitator *n* copier, copycat, copyist, echo, impersonator, mimic, mimicker, parrot.

immaculate *adj* clean, pure, spotless, stainless, unblemished, uncontaminated, undefiled, unpolluted, unspotted, unsullied, untainted, untarnished; faultless, guiltless, holy, innocent, pure, saintly, sinless, stainless.

immanent *adj* congenital, inborn, indwelling, inherent, innate, internal, intrinsic, subjective.

immaterial *adj* bodiless, ethereal, extramundane, impalpable, incorporeal, mental, metaphysical, spiritual, unbodied, unfleshly, unsubstantial; inconsequential, insignificant, nonessential, unessential, unimportant.

immature *adj* crude, green, imperfect, raw, rudimental, rudimentary, unfinished, unformed, unprepared, unripe, unripened, youthful; hasty, premature, unseasonable, untimely.

immaturity *n* crudeness, crudity, greenness, imperfection, rawness, unpreparedness, unripeness.

immeasurable *adj* bottomless, boundless,

illimitable, immense, infinite, limitless, measureless, unbounded, vast.

immediate *adj* close, contiguous, near, next, proximate; intuitive, primary, unmeditated; direct, instant, instantaneous, present, pressing, prompt.

immediately *adv* closely, proximately; directly, forthwith, instantly, presently, presto, pronto.

immemorial *adj* ancient, hoary, olden.

immense *adj* boundless, illimitable, infinite, interminable, measureless, unbounded, unlimited; colossal, elephantine, enormous, gigantic, huge, large, monstrous, mountainous, prodigious, stupendous, titanic, tremendous, vast.

immensity *n* boundlessness, endlessness, limitlessness, infiniteness, infinitude, infinity; amplitude, enormity, greatness, hugeness, magnitude, vastness.

immerse *vb* baptize, bathe, dip, douse, duck, overwhelm, plunge, sink, souse, submerge; absorb, engage, engross, involve.

immersion *n* dipping, immersing, plunging; absorption, engagement; disappearance; baptism.

imminent *adj* close, impending, near, overhanging, threatening; alarming, dangerous, perilous.

immobile *adj* fixed, immovable, inflexible, motionless, quiescent, stable, static, stationary, steadfast; dull, expressionless, impassive, rigid, stiff, stolid.

immobility *n* fixedness, fixity, immovability, immovableness, motionlessness, stability, steadfastness, unmovableness; dullness, expressionlessness, inflexibility, rigidity, stiffness, stolidity.

immoderate *adj* excessive, exorbitant, extravagant, extreme, inordinate, intemperate, unreasonable.

immodest *adj* coarse, gross, indecorous, indelicate, lewd, shameless; bold, brazen, forward, impudent, indecent; broad, filthy, impure, indecent, obscene, smutty, unchaste.

immodesty *n* coarseness, grossness, indecorum, indelicacy, shamelessness; impurity, lewdness, obscenity, smuttiness, unchastity; boldness, brass, forwardness, impatience.

immolate *vb* kill, sacrifice.

immoral *adj* antisocial, corrupt, loose, sinful, unethical, vicious, wicked, wrong; bad, depraved, dissolute, profligate, unprincipled; abandoned, indecent, licentious.

immorality *n* corruption, corruptness, criminality, demoralization, depravity, impurity, profligacy, sin, sinfulness, vice, wickedness; wrong.

immortal *adj* deathless, ever-living, imperishable, incorruptible, indestructible, indissoluble, never-dying, undying, unfading; ceaseless, continuing, eternal, endless, everlasting, never-ending, perpetual, sempiternal; abiding, enduring, lasting, permanent. * *n* god, goddess; genius, hero.

immortality *n* deathlessness, incorruptibility, incorruptibleness, indestructibility; perpetuity.

immortalize *vb* apotheosize, enshrine, glorify, perpetuate.

immovable *adj* firm, fixed, immobile, stable, stationary; impassive, steadfast, unalterable, unchangeable, unshaken, unyielding.

immunity *n* exemption, exoneration, freedom, release; charter, franchise, liberty, license, prerogative, privilege, right.

immure *vb* confine, entomb, imprison, incarcerate.

immutability *n* constancy, inflexibility, invariability, invariableness, permanence, stability, unalterableness, unchangeableness.

immutable *adj* constant, fixed, inflexible, invariable, permanent, stable, unalterable, unchangeable, undeviating.

imp *n* demon, devil, elf, flibbertigibbet, hobgoblin, scamp, sprite; graft, scion, shoot.

impact *vb* collide, crash, strike. * *n* brunt, impression, impulse, shock, stroke, touch; collision, contact, impinging, striking.

impair *vb* blemish, damage, deface, deteriorate, injure, mar, ruin, spoil, vitiate;

decrease, diminish, lessen, reduce; enervate, enfeeble, weaken.

impale *vb* hole, pierce, puncture, spear, spike, stab, transfix.

impalpable *adj* attenuated, delicate, fine, intangible; imperceptible, inapprehensible, incorporeal, indistinct, shadowy, unsubstantial.

impart *vb* bestow, confer, give, grant; communicate, disclose, discover, divulge, relate, reveal, share, tell.

impartial *adj* candid, disinterested, dispassionate, equal, equitable, evenhanded, fair, honourable, just, unbiased, unprejudiced, unwarped.

impassable *adj* blocked, closed, impenetrable, impermeable, impervious, inaccessible, pathless, unattainable, unnavigable, unreachable.

impassioned *adj* animated, ardent, burning, excited, fervent, fervid, fiery, glowing, impetuous, intense, passionate, vehement, warm, zealous.

impassive *adj* calm, passionless; apathetic, callous, indifferent, insensible, insusceptible, unfeeling, unimpressible, unsusceptible.

impassivity *n* calmness, composure, indifference, insensibility, insusceptibility, passionlessness, stolidity.

impatience *n* disquietude, restlessness, uneasiness; eagerness, haste, impetuosity, precipitation, vehemence; heat, irritableness, irritability, violence.

impatient *adj* restless, uneasy, unquiet; eager, hasty, impetuous, precipitate, vehement; abrupt, brusque, choleric, fretful, hot, intolerant, irritable, peevish, sudden, testy, violent.

impeach *vb* accuse, arraign, charge, indict; asperse, censure, denounce, disparage, discredit, impair, impute, incriminate, lessen.

impeachment *n* accusation, arraignment, indictment; aspersion, censure, disparagement, imputation, incrimination, reproach.

impeccable *adj* faultless, immaculate, incorrupt, innocent, perfect, pure, sinless, stainless, uncorrupt.

impede *vb* bar, block, check, clog, curb, delay, encumber, hinder, interrupt, obstruct, restrain, retard, stop, thwart.

impediment *n* bar, barrier, block, check, curb, difficulty, encumbrance, hindrance, obstacle, obstruction, stumbling block.

impel *vb* drive, push, send, urge; actuate, animate, compel, constrain, embolden, incite, induce, influence, instigate, move, persuade, stimulate.

impend *vb* approach, menace, near, threaten.

impending *adj* approaching, imminent, menacing, near, threatening.

impenetrable *adj* impermeable, impervious, inaccessible; cold, dull, impassive, indifferent, obtuse, senseless, stolid, unsympathetic; dense, proof.

impenitence *n* hardheartedness, impenitency, impenitentness, obduracy, stubbornness.

impenitent *adj* hardened, hard-hearted, incorrigible, irreclaimable, obdurate, recusant, relentless, seared, stubborn, uncontrite, unconverted, unrepentant.

imperative *adj* authoritative, commanding, despotic, domineering, imperious, overbearing, peremptory, urgent; binding, obligatory.

imperceptible *adj* inaudible, indiscernible, indistinguishable, invisible; fine, impalpable, inappreciable, gradual, minute.

imperfect *adj* abortive, crude, deficient, garbled, incomplete, poor; defective, faulty, impaired.

imperfection *n* defectiveness, deficiency, faultiness, incompleteness; blemish, defect, fault, flaw, lack, stain, taint; failing, foible, frailty, limitation, vice, weakness.

imperial *adj* kingly, regal, royal, sovereign; august, consummate, exalted, grand, great, kingly, magnificent, majestic, noble, regal, royal, queenly, supreme, sovereign, supreme, consummate.

imperil *vb* endanger, expose, hazard, jeopardize, risk.

imperious *adj* arrogant, authoritative, commanding, compelling, despotic, dictatorial, domineering, haughty, imperative, lordly, magisterial, overbearing, tyrannical, urgent, compelling.

imperishable *adj* eternal, everlasting, immortal, incorruptible, indestructible, never-ending, perennial, unfading.

impermeable *adj* impenetrable, impervious.

impermissible *adj* deniable, insufferable, objectionable, unallowable, unallowed, unlawful.

impersonate *vb* act, ape, enact, imitate, mimic, mock, personate; embody, incarnate, personify, typify.

impersonation *n* incarnation, manifestation, personification; enacting, imitation, impersonating, mimicking, personating, representation.

impertinence *n* irrelevance, irrelevancy, unfitness, impropriety; assurance, boldness, brass, brazenness, effrontery, face, forwardness, impudence, incivility, insolence, intrusiveness, presumption, rudeness, sauciness, pertness.

impertinent *adj* inapplicable, inapposite, irrelevant; bold, forward, impudent, insolent, intrusive, malapert, meddling, officious, pert, rude, saucy, unmannerly.

imperturbability *n* calmness, collectedness, composure, dispassion, placidity, placidness, sedateness, serenity, steadiness, tranquility.

imperturbable *adj* calm, collected, composed, cool, placid, sedate, serene, tranquil, unmoved, undisturbed, unexcitable, unmoved, unruffled.

impervious *adj* impassable, impenetrable, impermeable.

impetuosity *n* force, fury, haste, precipitancy, vehemence, violence.

impetuous *adj* ardent, boisterous, brash, breakneck, fierce, fiery, furious, hasty, headlong, hot, hot-headed, impulsive, overzealous, passionate, precipitate, vehement, violent.

impetus *n* energy, force, momentum, propulsion.

impiety *n* irreverence, profanity, ungodliness; iniquity, sacreligiousness, sin, sinfulness, ungodliness, unholiness, unrighteousness, wickedness.

impinge *vb* clash, dash, encroach, hit, infringe, strike, touch.

impious *adj* blasphemous, godless, iniquitous, irreligious, irreverent, profane, sinful, ungodly, unholy, unrighteous, wicked.

implacable *adj* deadly, inexorable, merciless, pitiless, rancorous, relentless, unappeasable, unforgiving, unpropitiating, unrelenting.

implant *vb* ingraft, infix, insert, introduce, place.

implement *vb* effect, execute, fulfil. * *n* appliance, instrument, tool, utensil.

implicate *vb* entangle, enfold; compromise, concern, entangle, include, involve.

implication *n* entanglement, involvement, involution; connotation, hint, inference, innuendo, intimation; conclusion, meaning, significance.

implicit *adj* implied, inferred, understood; absolute, constant, firm, steadfast, unhesitating, unquestioning, unreserved, unshaken.

implicitly *adv* by implication, silently, tacitly, unspokenly, virtually, wordlessly.

implore *vb* adjure, ask, beg, beseech, entreat, petition, pray, solicit, supplicate.

imply *vb* betoken, connote, denote, import, include, infer, insinuate, involve, mean, presuppose, signify.

impolicy *n* folly, imprudence, ill-judgement, indiscretion, inexpediency.

impolite *adj* bearish, boorish, discourteous, disrespectful, ill-bred, insolent, rough, rude, uncivil, uncourteous, ungentle, ungentlemanly, ungracious, unmannerly, unpolished, unrefined.

impoliteness *n* boorishness, discourteousness, discourtesy, disrespect, ill-breeding, incivility, insolence, rudeness, unmannerliness.

impolitic *adj* ill-advised, imprudent, indiscreet, inexpedient, injudicious, unwise.

import *vb* bring in, introduce, transport; betoken, denote, imply, mean, purport, signify. * *n* goods, importation, merchandise; bearing, drift, gist, intention, interpretation, matter, meaning, purpose, sense, signification, spirit, tenor; consequence, importance, significance, weight.

importance *n* concern, consequence, gravity, import, moment, momentousness, significance, weight, weightiness; consequence, pomposity, self-importance.

important *adj* considerable, grave, material, momentous, notable, pompous, ponderous, serious, significant, urgent, valuable, weighty; esteemed, influential, prominent, substantial; consequential, pompous, self-important.

importunate *adj* busy, earnest, persistent, pertinacious, pressing, teasing, troublesome, urgent.

importune *vb* ask, beset, dun, ply, press, solicit, urge.

importunity *n* appeal, beseechment, entreaty, petition, plying, prayer, pressing, suit, supplication, urging; contention, insistence; urgency.

impose *vb* lay, place, put, set; appoint, charge, dictate, enjoin, force, inflict, obtrude, prescribe, tax; (*with* **on, upon**) abuse, cheat, circumvent, deceive, delude, dupe, exploit, hoax, trick, victimize.

imposing *adj* august, commanding, dignified, exalted, grand, grandiose, impressive, lofty, magnificent, majestic, noble, stately, striking.

imposition *n* imposing, laying, placing, putting; burden, charge, constraint, injunction, levy, oppression, tax; artifice, cheating, deception, dupery, fraud, imposture, trickery.

impossibility *n* hopelessness, impracticability, inability, infeasibility, unattainability; inconceivability.

impossible *adj* hopeless, impracticable, infeasible, unachievable, unattainable; inconceivable, self-contradictory, unthinkable.

impost *n* custom, duty, excise, rate, tax, toil, tribute.

impostor *n* charlatan, cheat, counterfeiter, deceiver, double-dealer, humbug, hypocrite, knave, mountebank, pretender, quack, rogue, trickster.

imposture *n* artifice, cheat, deceit, deception, delusion, dodge, fraud, hoax, imposition, ruse, stratagem, trick, wile.

impotence *n* disability, feebleness, frailty, helplessness, inability, incapability, incapacity, incompetence, inefficaciousness, inefficacy, inefficiency, infirmity, powerlessness, weakness.

impotent *adj* disabled, enfeebled, feeble, frail, helpless, incapable, incapacitated, incompetent, inefficient, infirm, nerveless, powerless, unable, weak; barren, sterile.

impound *vb* confine, coop, engage, imprison.

impoverish *vb* beggar, pauperize; deplete, exhaust, ruin.

impracticability *n* impossibility, impracticableness, impracticality, infeasibility, unpracticability.

impracticable *adj* impossible, infeasible; intractable, obstinate, recalcitrant, stubborn, thorny, unmanageable; impassable, insurmountable.

impracticality *n* impossibility, impracticableness, impractibility, infeasibility, unpracticability; irrationality, unpracticalness, unrealism, unreality, unreasonableness.

imprecate *vb* anathematize, curse, execrate, invoke, maledict.

imprecation *n* anathema, curse, denunciation, execration, invocation, malediction.

imprecatory *adj* appealing, beseeching, entreating, imploratory, imploring, imprecatory, pleading; cursing, damnatory, execrating, maledictory.

impregnable *adj* immovable, impenetrable, indestructible, invincible, inviolable, invulnerable, irrefrangible, secure, unconquerable, unassailable, unyielding.

impregnate *vb* fecundate, fertilize, fructify; dye, fill, imbrue, imbue, infuse, permeate, pervade, saturate, soak, tincture, tinge.

impress *vb* engrave, imprint, print, stamp; affect, move, strike; fix, inculcate; draft, enlist, levy, press, requisition. * *n* impression, imprint, mark, print, seal, stamp;

cognizance, device, emblem, motto, symbol.

impressibility *n* affectibility, impressionability, pliancy, receptiveness, responsiveness, sensibility, sensitiveness, susceptibility.

impressible *adj* affectible, excitable, impressionable, pliant, receptive, responsive, sensitive, soft, susceptible, tender.

impression *n* edition, imprinting, printing, stamping; brand, dent, impress, mark, stamp; effect, influence, sensation; fancy, idea, instinct, notion, opinion, recollection.

impressive *adj* affecting, effective, emphatic, exciting, forcible, moving, overpowering, powerful, solemn, speaking, splendid, stirring, striking, telling, touching.

imprint *vb* engrave, mark, print, stamp; impress, inculcate. * *n* impression, mark, print, sign, stamp.

imprison *vb* confine, jail, immure, incarcerate, shut up.

imprisonment *n* captivity, commitment, confinement, constraint, durance, duress, incarceration, restraint.

improbability *n* doubt, uncertainty, unlikelihood.

improbable *adj* doubtful, uncertain, unlikely, unplausible.

improbity *n* dishonesty, faithlessness, fraud, fraudulence, knavery, unfairness.

impromptu *adj* extempore, improvised, offhand, spontaneous, unpremeditated, unprepared, unrehearsed. * *adv* extemporaneously, extemporarily, extempore, offhand, ad-lib.

improper *adj* immodest, inapposite, inappropriate, irregular, unadapted, unapt, unfit, unsuitable, unsuited; indecent, indecorous, indelicate, unbecoming, unseemly; erroneous, inaccurate, incorrect, wrong.

impropriety *n* inappropriateness, unfitness, unsuitability, unsuitableness; indecorousness, indecorum, unseemliness.

improve *vb* ameliorate, amend, better, correct, edify, meliorate, mend, rectify, reform; cultivate; gain, mend, progress; enhance, increase, rise.

improvement *n* ameliorating, amelioration, amendment, bettering, improving, meliorating, melioration; advancement, proficiency, progress.

improvidence *n* imprudence, thriftlessness, unthriftiness.

improvident *adj* careless, heedless, imprudent, incautious, inconsiderate, negligent, prodigal, rash, reckless, shiftless, thoughtless, thriftless, unthrifty, wasteful.

improvisation *n* ad-libbing, contrivance, extemporaneousness, extemporariness, extemporization, fabrication, invention; (*mus*) extempore, impromptu.

improvise *vb* ad-lib, contrive, extemporize, fabricate, imagine, invent.

imprudence *n* carelessness, heedlessness, improvidence, incautiousness, inconsideration, indiscretion, rashness.

imprudent *adj* careless, heedless, ill-advised, ill-judged, improvident, incautious, inconsiderate, indiscreet, rash, unadvised, unwise.

impudence *n* assurance, audacity, boldness, brashness, brass, bumptiousness, cheek, cheekiness, effrontery, face, flippancy, forwardness, front, gall, impertinence, insolence, jaw, lip, nerve, pertness, presumption, rudeness, sauciness, shamelessness.

impudent *adj* bold, bold-faced, brazen, brazen-faced, cool, flippant, forward, immodest, impertinent, insolent, insulting, pert, presumptuous, rude, saucy, shameless.

impugn *vb* assail, attack, challenge, contradict, dispute, gainsay, oppose, question, resist.

impulse *n* force, impetus, impelling, momentum, push, thrust; appetite, inclination, instinct, passion, proclivity; incentive, incitement, influence, instigation, motive, instigation.

impulsive *adj* impelling, moving, propulsive; emotional, hasty, heedless, hot, impetuous, mad-cap, passionate, quick, rash, vehement, violent.

impunity *n* exemption, immunity, liberty, licence, permission, security.

impure *adj* defiled, dirty, feculent, filthy, foul, polluted, unclean; bawdy, coarse, immodest, gross, immoral, indelicate, indecent, lewd, licentious, loose, obscene, ribald, smutty, unchaste; adulterated, corrupt, mixed.

impurity *n* defilement, feculence, filth, foulness, pollution, uncleanness; admixture, coarseness, grossness, immodesty, indecency, indelicacy, lewdness, licentiousness, looseness, obscenity, ribaldry, smut, smuttiness, unchastity, vulgarity.

imputable *adj* ascribable, attributable, chargeable, owing, referable, traceable, owing.

imputation *n* attributing, charging, imputing; accusation, blame, censure, charge, reproach.

impute *vb* ascribe, attribute, charge, consider, imply, insinuate, refer.

inability *n* impotence, incapacity, incapability, incompetence, incompetency, inefficiency; disability, disqualification.

inaccessible *adj* unapproachable, unattainable.

inaccuracy *n* erroneousness, impropriety, incorrectness, inexactness; blunder, defect, error, fault, mistake.

inaccurate *adj* defective, erroneous, faulty, incorrect, inexact, mistaken, wrong.

inaccurately *adv* carelessly, cursorily, imprecisely, incorrectly, inexactly, mistakenly, unprecisely, wrongly.

inactive *adj* inactive; dormant, inert, inoperative, peaceful, quiet, quiescent; dilatory, drowsy, dull, idle, inanimate, indolent, inert, lazy, lifeless, lumpish, passive, slothful, sleepy, stagnant, supine.

inactivity *n* dilatoriness, idleness, inaction, indolence, inertness, laziness, sloth, sluggishness, supineness, torpidity, torpor.

inadequacy *n* inadequateness, insufficiency; defectiveness, imperfection, incompetence, incompetency, incompleteness, insufficiency, unfitness, unsuitableness.

inadequate *adj* disproportionate, incapable, insufficient, unequal; defective, imperfect, inapt, incompetent, incomplete.

inadmissible *adj* improper, incompetent, unacceptable, unallowable, unqualified, unreasonable.

inadvertence, inadvertency *n* carelessness, heedlessness, inattention, inconsiderateness, negligence, thoughtlessness; blunder, error, oversight, slip.

inadvertent *adj* careless, heedless, inattentive, inconsiderate, negligent, thoughtless, unobservant.

inadvertently *adv* accidently, carelessly, heedlessly, inconsiderately, negligently, thoughtlessly, unintentionally.

inalienable *adj* undeprivable, unforfeitable, untransferable.

inane *adj* empty, fatuous, vacuous, void; foolish, frivolous, idiotic, puerile, senseless, silly, stupid, trifling, vain, worthless.

inanimate *adj* breathless, dead, extinct; dead, dull, inert, lifeless, soulless, spiritless.

inanition *n* emptiness, inanity, vacuity; exhaustion, hunger, malnutrition, starvation, want.

inanity *n* emptiness, foolishness, inanition, vacuity; folly, frivolousness, puerility, vanity, worthlessness.

inapplicable *adj* inapposite, inappropriate, inapt, irrelevant, unfit, unsuitable, unsuited.

inapposite *adj* impertinent, inapplicable, irrelevant, nonpertinent; inappropriate, unfit, unsuitable.

inappreciable *adj* impalpable, imperceptible, inconsiderable, inconspicuous, indiscernible, infinitesimal, insignificant, negligible, undiscernible, unnoticed.

inappropriate *adj* inapposite, unadapted, unbecoming, unfit, unsuitable, unsullied.

inapt *adj* inapposite, unapt, unfit, unsuitable; awkward, clumsy, dull, slow, stolid, stupid.

inaptitude *n* awkwardness, inapplicability, inappropriateness, inaptness, unfitness, unsuitableness.

inarticulate *adj* blurred, indistinct, thick; dumb, mute.

inartificial *adj* artless, direct, guileless,

ingenuous, naive, simple, simple-minded, sincere, single-minded.

inasmuch as *conj* considering that, seeing that, since.

inattention *n* absent-mindedness, carelessness, disregard, heedlessness, inadvertence, inapplication, inconsiderateness, neglect, remissness, slip, thoughtlessness, unmindfulness, unobservance

inattentive *adj* absent-minded, careless, disregarding, heedless, inadvertent, inconsiderate, neglectful, remiss, thoughtless, unmindful, unobservant.

inaudible *adj* faint, indistinct, muffled; mute, noiseless, silent, still.

inaugurate *vb* induct, install, introduce, invest; begin, commence, initiate, institute, originate.

inauguration *n* beginning, commencement, initiation, institution, investiture, installation, opening, origination.

inauspicious *adj* bad, discouraging, ill-omened, ill-starred, ominous, unfavourable, unfortunate, unlucky, unpromising, unpropitious, untoward.

inborn *adj* congenital, inbred, ingrained, inherent, innate, instinctive, native, natural.

incalculable *adj* countless, enormous, immense, incalculable, inestimable, innumerable, sumless, unknown, untold.

incandescence *n* candescence, glow, gleam, luminousness, luminosity.

incandescent *adj* aglow, candent, candescent, gleaming, glowing, luminous, luminant, radiant.

incantation *n* charm, conjuration, enchantment, magic, necromancy, sorcery, spell, witchcraft, witchery.

incapability *n* disability, inability, incapacity, incompetence.

incapable *adj* feeble, impotent, incompetent, insufficient, unable, unfit, unfitted, unqualified, weak.

incapacious *adj* cramped, deficient, incommodious, narrow, scant.

incapacitate *vb* cripple, disable; disqualify, make unfit.

incapacity *n* disability, inability, incapability, incompetence; disqualification, unfitness.

incarcerate *vb* commit, confine, immure, imprison, jail, restrain, restrict.

incarnate *vb* body, embody, incorporate, personify. * *adj* bodied, embodied, incorporated, personified.

incarnation *n* embodiment, exemplification, impersonation, manifestation, personification.

incautious *adj* impolitic, imprudent, indiscreet, uncircumspect, unwary; careless, headlong, heedless, inconsiderate, negligent, rash, reckless, thoughtless.

incendiary *adj* dissentious, factious, inflammatory, seditious. * *n* agitator, firebrand, fire-raiser.

incense[1] *vb* anger, chafe, enkindle, enrage, exasperate, excite, heat, inflame, irritate, madden, provoke.

incense[2] *n* aroma, fragrance, perfume, scent; admiration, adulation, applause, laudation.

incentive *n* cause, encouragement, goad, impulse, incitement, inducement, instigation, mainspring, motive, provocation, spur, stimulus.

inception *n* beginning, commencement, inauguration, initiation, origin, rise, start.

incertitude *n* ambiguity, doubt, doubtfulness, indecision, uncertainty.

incessant *adj* ceaseless, constant, continual, continuous, eternal, everlasting, never-ending, perpetual, unceasing, unending, uninterrupted, unremitting.

inchoate *adj* beginning, commencing, inceptive, incipient, initial.

incident *n* circumstance, episode, event, fact, happening, occurrence. * *adj* happening; belonging, pertaining, appertaining, accessory, relating, natural; falling, impinging.

incidental *adj* accidental, casual, chance, concomitant, contingent, fortuitous, subordinate; adventitious, extraneous, nonessential, occasional.

incinerate *vb* burn, char, conflagrate, cremate, incremate.

incipient *adj* beginning, commencing, inchoate, inceptive, originating, starting.

incised *adj* carved, cut, engraved, gashed, graved, graven.

incision *n* cut, gash, notch, opening, penetration.
incisive *adj* cutting; acute, biting, sarcastic, satirical, sharp; acute, clear, distinct, penetrating, sharp-cut, trenchant.
incite *vb* actuate, animate, arouse, drive, encourage, excite, foment, goad, hound, impel, instigate, prod, prompt, provoke, push, rouse, spur, stimulate, urge.
incitement *n* encouragement, goad, impulse, incentive, inducement, motive, provocative, spur, stimulus.
incivility *n* discourteousness, discourtesy, disrespect, ill-breeding, ill-manners, impoliteness, impudence, inurbanity, rudeness, uncourtliness, unmannerliness.
inclemency *n* boisterousness, cruelty, harshness, rigour, roughness, severity, storminess, tempestuousness, tyranny.
inclement *adj* boisterous, harsh, rigorous, rough, severe, stormy; cruel, unmerciful.
inclination *n* inclining, leaning, slant, slope; trending, verging; aptitude, bent, bias, disposition, penchant, predilection, predisposition, proclivity, proneness, propensity, tendency, turn, twist; desire, fondness, liking, taste, partiality, predilection, wish; bow, nod, obeisance.
incline *vb* lean, slant, slope; bend, nod, verge; tend; bias, dispose, predispose, turn; bow. * *n* ascent, descent, grade, gradient, rise, slope.
inclose *see* **enclose**.
include *vb* contain, hold; comprehend, comprise, contain, cover, embody, embrace, incorporate, involve, take in.
inclusive *adj* comprehending, embracing, encircling, enclosing, including, taking in.
incognito, incognita *adj* camouflaged, concealed, disguised, unknown. * *n* camouflage, concealment, disguise.
incoherent *adj* detached, loose, nonadhesive, noncohesive; disconnected, incongruous, inconsequential, inconsistent, uncoordinated; confused, illogical, irrational, rambling, unintelligible, wild.
income *n* earnings, emolument, gains, interest, pay, perquisite, proceeds, profits, receipts, rents, return, revenue, salary, wages.
incommensurate *adj* disproportionate, inadequate, insufficient, unequal.
incommode *vb* annoy, discommode, disquiet, disturb, embarrass, hinder, inconvenience, molest, plague, trouble, upset, vex.
incommodious *adj* awkward, cumbersome, cumbrous, inconvenient, unhandy, unmanageable, unsuitable, unwieldy; annoying, disadvantageous, harassing, irritating, vexatious.
incommunicative *adj* exclusive, unsociable, unsocial, reserved.
incomparable *adj* matchless, inimitable, peerless, surpassing, transcendent, unequalled, unparalleled, unrivalled.
incompatibility *n* contrariety, contradictoriness, discrepancy, incongruity, inconsistency, irreconcilability, unsuitability, unsuitableness
incompatible *adj* contradictory, incongruous, inconsistent, inharmonious, irreconcilable, unadapted, unsuitable.
incompetence *n* inability, incapability, incapacity, incompetency; inadequacy, insufficiency; disqualification, unfitness.
incompetent *adj* incapable, unable; inadequate, insufficient; disqualified, incapacitated, unconstitutional, unfit, unfitted.
incomplete *adj* defective, deficient, imperfect, partial; inexhaustive, unaccompanied, uncompleted, unexecuted, unfinished.
incomprehensible *adj* inconceivable, inexhaustible, unfathomable, unimaginable; inconceivable, unintelligible, unthinkable.
incomputable *adj* enormous, immense, incalculable, innumerable, prodigious.
inconceivable *adj* incomprehensible, incredible, unbelievable, unimaginable, unthinkable.
inconclusive *adj* inconsequent, inconsequential, indecisive, unconvincing. illogical, unproved, unproven.
incongruity *n* absurdity, contradiction, contradictoriness, contrariety, discord-

ance, discordancy, discrepancy, impropriety, inappropriateness, incoherence, incompatibility, inconsistency, unfitness, unsuitableness.

incongruous *adj* absurd, contradictory, contrary, disagreeing, discrepant, inappropriate, incoherent, incompatible, inconsistent, inharmonious, unfit, unsuitable.

inconsequent *adj* desultory, disconnected, fragmentary, illogical, inconclusive, inconsistent, irrelevant, loose.

inconsiderable *adj* immaterial, insignificant, petty, slight, small, trifling, trivial, unimportant.

inconsiderate *adj* intolerant, uncharitable, unthoughtful; careless, heedless, giddy, hare-brained, hasty, headlong, imprudent, inadvertent, inattentive, indifferent, indiscreet, light-headed, negligent, rash, thoughtless.

inconsistency *n* incoherence, incompatibility, incongruity, unsuitableness; contradiction, contrariety; changeableness, inconstancy, instability, vacillation, unsteadiness.

inconsistent *adj* different, discrepant, illogical, incoherent, incompatible, incongruous, inconsequent, inconsonant, irreconcilable, unsuitable; contradictory, contrary; changeable, fickle, inconstant, unstable, unsteady, vacillating, variable.

inconsolable *adj* comfortless, crushed, disconsolate, forlorn, heartbroken, hopeless, woebegone.

inconstancy *n* changeableness, mutability, variability, variation, fluctuation, faithlessness, fickleness, capriciousness, vacillation, uncertainty, unsteadiness, volatility.

inconstant *adj* capricious, changeable, faithless, fickle, fluctuating, mercurial, mutable, unsettled, unsteady, vacillating, variable, varying, volatile, wavering; mutable, uncertain, unstable.

incontestable *adj* certain, incontrovertible, indisputable, indubitable, irrefrangible, sure, undeniable, unquestionable.

incontinence *n* excess, extravagance, indulgence, intemperance, irrepressibility, lasciviousness, lewdness, licentiousness, prodigality, profligacy, riotousness, unrestraint, wantonness, wildness.

incontinent *adj* debauched, lascivious, lewd, licentious, lustful, prodigal, unchaste, uncontrolled, unrestrained.

incontrovertible *adj* certain, incontestable, indisputable, indubitable, irrefutable, sure, undeniable, unquestionable.

inconvenience *vb* discommode; annoy, disturb, molest, trouble, vex. * *n* annoyance, disadvantage, disturbance, molestation, trouble, vexation; awkwardness, cumbersomeness, incommodiousness, unwieldiness; unfitness, unseasonableness, unsuitableness.

inconvenient *adj* annoying, awkward, cumbersome, cumbrous, disadvantageous, incommodious, inopportune, troublesome, uncomfortable, unfit, unhandy, unmanageable, unseasonable, unsuitable, untimely, unwieldy, vexatious.

incorporate *vb* affiliate, amalgamate, associate, blend, combine, consolidate, include, merge, mix, unite; embody, incarnate. * *adj* incorporeal, immaterial, spiritual, supernatural; blended, consolidated, merged, united.

incorporation *n* affiliation, alignment, amalgamation, association, blend, blending, combination, consolidation, fusion, inclusion, merger, mixture, unification, union, embodiment, incarnation, personification.

incorporeal *adj* bodiless, immaterial, impalpable, incorporate, spiritual, supernatural, unsubstantial.

incorrect *adj* erroneous, false, inaccurate, inexact, untrue, wrong; faulty, improper, mistaken, ungrammatical, unbecoming, unsound.

incorrectness *n* error, inaccuracy, inexactness, mistake.

incorrigible *adj* abandoned, graceless, hardened, irreclaimable, lost, obdurate, recreant, reprobate, shameless; helpless, hopeless, irremediable, irrecoverable, irreparable, irretrievable, irreversible, remediless.

incorruptibility *n* unpurchasableness; deathlessness, immortality, imperishableness, incorruptibleness, incorruption, indestructibility.

incorruptible *adj* honest, unbribable; imperishable, indestructible, immortal, undying, deathless, everlasting.

increase *vb* accrue, advance, augment, enlarge, extend, grow, intensify, mount, wax; multiply; enhance, greaten, heighten, raise, reinforce; aggravate, prolong. * *n* accession, accretion, accumulation, addition, augmentation, crescendo, development, enlargement, expansion, extension, growth, heightening, increment, intensification, multiplication, swelling; gain, produce, product, profit; descendants, issue, offspring, progeny.

incredible *adj* absurd, inadmissible, nonsensical, unbelievable.

incredulity *n* distrust, doubt, incredulousness, scepticism, unbelief.

incredulous *adj* distrustful, doubtful, dubious, sceptical, unbelieving.

increment *n* addition, augmentation, enlargement, increase.

incriminate *vb* accuse, blame, charge, criminate, impeach.

incubate *vb* brood, develop, hatch, sit.

inculcate *vb* enforce, implant, impress, infix, infuse, ingraft, inspire, instil.

inculpable *adj* blameless, faultless, innocent, irreprehensible, irreproachable, irreprovable, sinless, unblamable, unblameable.

inculpate *vb* accuse, blame, censure, charge, incriminate, impeach, incriminate.

inculpatory *adj* criminatory, incriminating.

incumbent *adj* binding, devolved, devolving, laid, obligatory; leaning, prone, reclining, resting. * *n* holder, occupant.

incur *vb* acquire, bring, contract.

incurable *adj* cureless, hopeless, irrecoverable, remediless; helpless, incorrigible, irremediable, irreparable, irretrievable, remediless.

incurious *adj* careless, heedless, inattentive, indifferent, uninquisitive, unobservant, uninterested.

incursion *n* descent, foray, raid, inroad, irruption.

incursive *adj* aggressive, hostile, invasive, predatory, raiding.

incurvate *vb* bend, bow, crook, curve. * *adj* (*bot*) aduncous, arcuate, bowed, crooked, curved, hooked.

indebted *adj* beholden, obliged, owing.

indecency *n* impropriety, indecorum, offensiveness, outrageousness, unseemliness; coarseness, filthiness, foulness, grossness, immodesty, impurity, obscenity, vileness.

indecent *adj* bold, improper, indecorous, offensive, outrageous, unbecoming, unseemly; coarse, dirty, filthy, gross, immodest, impure, indelicate, lewd, nasty, obscene, pornographic, salacious, shameless, smutty, unchaste.

indecipherable *adj* illegible, undecipherable, undiscoverable, inexplicable, obscure, unintelligible, unreadable.

indecision *n* changeableness, fickleness, hesitation, inconstancy, irresolution, unsteadiness, vacillation.

indecisive *adj* dubious, hesitating, inconclusive, irresolute, undecided, unsettled, vacillating, wavering.

indecorous *adj* coarse, gross, ill-bred, impolite, improper, indecent, rude, unbecoming, uncivil, unseemly.

indecorum *n* grossness, ill-breeding, ill manners, impoliteness, impropriety, incivility, indecency, indecorousness.

indeed *adv* absolutely, actually, certainly, in fact, in truth, in reality, positively, really, strictly, truly, verily, veritably. * *interj* really! you don't say so! is it possible!

indefatigable *adj* assiduous, never-tiring, persevering, persistent, sedulous, tireless, unflagging, unremitting, untiring, unwearied.

indefeasible *adj* immutable, inalienable, irreversible, irrevocable, unalterable.

indefensible *adj* censurable, defenceless, faulty, unpardonable, untenable; inexcusable, insupportable, unjustifiable, unwarrantable, wrong.

indefinite *adj* confused, doubtful, equivocal, general, imprecise, indefinable, indecisive, indeterminate, indistinct, inexact, inexplicit, lax, loose, nondescript, obscure, uncertain, undefined, undetermined, unfixed, unsettled, vague.

indelible *adj* fast, fixed, ineffaceable, ingrained, permanent.

indelicacy *n* coarseness, grossness, indecorousness, indecorum, impropriety, offensiveness, unseemliness, vulgarity; immodesty, indecency, lewdness, unchastity; foulness, obscenity.

indelicate *adj* broad, coarse, gross, indecorous, intrusive, rude, unbecoming, unseemly; foul, immodest, indecent, lewd, obscene, unchaste, vulgar.

indemnification *n* compensation, reimbursement, remuneration, security.

indemnify *vb* compensate, reimburse, remunerate, requite, secure.

indent *vb* bruise, jag, notch, pink, scallop, serrate; bind, indenture.

indentation *n* bruise, dent, depression, jag, notch.

indenture *vb* bind, indent. * *n* contract, instrument; indentation.

independence *n* freedom, liberty, self-direction; distinctness, nondependence, separation; competence, ease.

independent *adj* absolute, autonomous, free, self-directing, uncoerced, unrestrained, unrestricted, voluntary; (*person*) self-reliant, unconstrained, unconventional.

indescribable *adj* ineffable, inexpressible, nameless, unutterable.

indestructible *adj* abiding, endless, enduring, everlasting, fadeless, imperishable, incorruptible, undecaying.

indeterminate *adj* indefinite, uncertain, undetermined, unfixed.

index *vb* alphabetize, catalogue, codify, earmark, file, list, mark, tabulate. * *n* catalogue, list, register, tally; indicator, lead, mark, pointer, sign, signal, token; contents, table of contents; forefinger; exponent.

indicate *vb* betoken, denote, designate, evince, exhibit, foreshadow, manifest, mark, point out, prefigure, presage, register, show, signify, specify, tell; hint, imply, intimate, sketch, suggest.

indication *n* hint, index, manifestation, mark, note, sign, suggestion, symptom, token.

indicative *adj* significant, suggestive, symptomatic; (*gram*) affirmative, declarative.

indict *vb* (*law*) accuse, charge, present.

indictment *n* (*law*) indicting, presentment; accusation, arraignment, charge, crimination, impeachment.

indifference *n* apathy, carelessness, coldness, coolness, heedlessness, inattention, insignificance, negligence, unconcern, unconcernedness, uninterestedness; disinterestedness, impartiality, neutrality.

indifferent *adj* apathetic, cold, cool, dead, distant, dull, easy-going, frigid, heedless, inattentive, incurious, insensible, insouciant, listless, lukewarm, nonchalant, perfunctory, regardless, stoical, unconcerned, uninterested, unmindful, unmoved; equal; fair, medium, middling, moderate, ordinary, passable, tolerable; mediocre, so-so; immaterial, unimportant; disinterested, impartial, neutral, unbiased.

indigence *n* destitution, distress, necessity, need, neediness, pauperism, penury, poverty, privation, want.

indigenous *adj* aboriginal, home-grown, inborn, inherent, native.

indigent *adj* destitute, distressed, insolvent, moneyless, necessitous, needy, penniless, pinched, poor, reduced.

indigested *adj* unconcocted, undigested; crude, ill-advised, ill-considered, ill-judged; confused, disorderly, ill-arranged, unmethodical.

indigestion *n* dyspepsia, dyspepsy.

indignant *adj* angry, exasperated, incensed, irate, ireful, provoked, roused, wrathful, wroth.

indignation *n* anger, choler, displeasure, exasperation, fury, ire, rage, resentment, wrath.

indignity *n* abuse, affront, contumely, dishonour, disrespect, ignominy, insult, obloquy, opprobrium, outrage, reproach, slight.

indirect *adj* circuitous, circumlocutory, collateral, devious, oblique, roundabout, sidelong, tortuous; deceitful, dishonest, dishonorable, unfair; mediate, remote, secondary, subordinate.

indiscernible *adj* imperceptible, indistinguishable, invisible, undiscernible, undiscoverable.

indiscipline *n* laxity, insubordination.

indiscreet *adj* foolish, hasty, headlong, heedless, imprudent, incautious, inconsiderate, injudicious, rash, reckless, unwise.

indiscretion *n* folly, imprudence, inconsiderateness, rashness; blunder, faux pas, lapse, mistake, misstep.

indiscriminate *adj* confused, heterogeneous, indistinct, mingled, miscellaneous, mixed, promiscuous, undiscriminating, undistinguishable, undistinguishing.

indispensable *adj* essential, expedient, necessary, needed, needful, requisite.

indisputable *adj* certain, incontestable, indubitable, infallible, sure, undeniable, undoubted,
unmistakable, unquestionable.

indisposed *adj* ailing, ill, sick, unwell; averse, backward, disinclined, loath, reluctant, unfriendly, unwilling.

indisposition *n* ailment, illness, sickness; aversion, backwardness, dislike, disinclination, reluctance, unwillingness.

indisputable *adj* certain, incontestable, indutitable, infallible, sure, undeniable, undoubted, unmistakable, unquestionable.

indissoluble *adj* abiding, enduring, firm, imperishable, incorruptible, indestructible, lasting, stable, unbreakable.

indistinct *adj* ambiguous, doubtful, uncertain; blurred, dim, dull, faint, hazy, misty, nebulous, obscure, shadowy, vague; confused, inarticulate, indefinite, indistinguishable, undefined, undistinguishable.

indistinguishable *adj* imperceptible, indiscernible, unnoticeable, unobservable; chaotic, confused, dim, indistinct, obscure, vague.

indite *vb* compose, pen, write.

individual *adj* characteristic, distinct, identical, idiosyncratic, marked, one, particular, personal, respective, separate, single, singular, special, unique; peculiar, proper; decided, definite, independent, positive, self-guided, unconventional. * *n* being, character, party, person, personage, somebody, someone; type, unit.

individuality *n* definiteness, indentity, personality; originality, self-direction, self-determination, singularity, uniqueness.

individualize *vb* individuate, particularize, singularize, specify.

indivisible *adj* incommensurable, indissoluble, inseparable, unbreakable, unpartiable.

indocile *adj* cantankerous, contumacious, dogged, froward, inapt, headstrong, intractable, mulish, obstinate, perverse, refractory, stubborn, ungovernable, unmanageable, unruly, unteachable.

indoctrinate *vb* brainwash, imbue, initiate, instruct, rehabilitate, teach.

indoctrination *n* grounding, initiation, instruction, rehabilitation.

indolence *n* idleness, inactivity, inertia, inertness, laziness, listlessness, sloth, slothfulness, sluggishness.

indolent *adj* easy, easy-going, inactive, inert, lazy, listless, lumpish, otiose, slothful, sluggish, supine.

indomitable *adj* invincible, unconquerable, unyielding.

indorse *see* **endorse**.

indubitable *adj* certain, evident, incontestable, incontrovertible, indisputable, sure, undeniable, unquestionable.

induce *vb* actuate, allure, bring, draw, drive, entice, impel, incite, influence, instigate, move, persuade, prevail, prompt, spur, urge; bring on, cause, effect, motivate, lead, occasion, produce.

inducement *n* allurement, draw, enticement, instigation, persuasion; cause, consideration, impulse, incentive, incitement, influence, motive, reason, spur, stimulus.

induct *vb* inaugurate, initiate, install, institute, introduce, invest.

induction *n* inauguration, initiation, institution, installation, introduction; conclusion, generalization, inference.

indue *vb* assume, endow, clothe, endue, invest, supply.

indulge *vb* gratify, license, revel, satisfy, wallow, yield to; coddle, cosset, favour, humour, pamper, pet, spoil; allow, cherish, foster, harbour, permit, suffer.

indulgence *n* gratification, humouring, pampering; favour, kindness, lenience, lenity, liberality, tenderness; (*theol*) absolution, remission.

indulgent *adj* clement, easy, favouring, forbearing, gentle, humouring, kind, lenient, mild, pampering, tender, tolerant.

indurate *vb* harden, inure, sear, strengthen.

induration *n* hardening, obduracy.

industrious *adj* assiduous, diligent, hardworking, laborious, notable, operose, sedulous; brisk, busy, persevering, persistent.

industry *n* activity, application, assiduousness, assiduity, diligence; perseverance, persistence, sedulousness, vigour; effort, labour, toil.

inebriated *adj* drunk, intoxicated, stupefied.

ineffable *adj* indescribable, inexpressible, unspeakable, unutterable.

ineffaceable *adj* indelible, indestructible, inerasable, inexpungeable, ingrained.

ineffectual *adj* abortive, bootless, fruitless, futile, inadequate, inefficacious, ineffective, inoperative, useless, unavailing, vain; feeble, inefficient, powerless, impotent, weak.

inefficacy *n* ineffectualness, inefficiency.

inefficient *adj* feeble, incapable, ineffectual, ineffective, inefficacious, weak.

inelastic *adj* flabby, flaccid, inductile, inflexible, irresilient.

inelegant *adj* abrupt, awkward, clumsy, coarse, constrained, cramped, crude, graceless, harsh, homely, homespun, rough, rude, stiff, tasteless, uncourtly, uncouth, ungainly, ungraceful, unpolished, unrefined.

ineligible *adj* disqualified, unqualified; inexpedient, objectionable, unadvisable, undesirable.

inept *adj* awkward, improper, inapposite, inappropriate, unapt, unfit, unsuitable; null, useless, void, worthless; foolish, nonsensical, pointless, senseless, silly, stupid.

ineptitude *n* inappositeness, inappropriateness, inaptitude, unfitness, unsuitability, unsuitable-ness; emptiness, nullity, uselessness, worthlessness; folly, foolishness, nonsense, pointlessness, senselessness, silliness, stupidity.

inequality *n* disproportion, inequitableness, injustice, unfairness; difference, disparity, dissimilarity, diversity, imparity, irregularity, roughness, unevenness; inadequacy, incompetency, insufficiency.

inequitable *adj* unfair, unjust.

inert *adj* comatose, dead, inactive, lifeless, motionless, quiescent, passive; apathetic, dronish, dull, idle, indolent, lazy, lethargic, lumpish, phlegmatic, slothful, sluggish, supine, torpid.

inertia *n* apathy, inertness, lethargy, passiveness, passivity, slothfulness, sluggishness.

inestimable *adj* incalculable, invaluable, precious, priceless, valuable.

inevitable *adj* certain, necessary, unavoidable, undoubted.

inexact *adj* imprecise, inaccurate, incorrect; careless, crude, loose.

inexcusable *adj* indefensible, irremissible, unallowable, unjustifiable, unpardonable.

inexhaustible *adj* boundless, exhaustless, indefatigable, unfailing, unlimited.

inexorable *adj* cruel, firm, hard, immovable, implacable, inflexible, merciless, pitiless, relentless, severe, steadfast, unbending, uncompassionate, unmerciful, unrelenting, unyielding.

inexpedient *adj* disadvantageous, ill-judged, impolitic, imprudent, indiscreet, injudicious, inopportune, unadvisable, unprofitable, unwise.

inexperience *n* greenness, ignorance, rawness.

inexperienced *adj* callow, green, raw, strange, unacquainted, unconversant, undisciplined, uninitiated, unpractised, unschooled, unskilled, untrained, untried, unversed, young.

inexpert *adj* awkward, bungling, clumsy, inapt, maladroit, unhandy, unskilful, unskilled.

inexpiable *adj* implacable, inexorable, irreconcilable, unappeasable; irremissible, unatonable, unpardonable.

inexplicable *adj* enigmatic, enigmatical, incomprehensible, inscrutable, mysterious, strange, unaccountable, unintelligible.

inexpressible *adj* indescribable, ineffable, unspeakable, unutterable; boundless, infinite, surpassing.

inexpressive *adj* blank, characterless, dull, unexpressive.

inextinguishable *adj* unquenchable.

in extremis *adv* moribund.

inextricable *adj* entangled, intricate, perplexed, unsolvable.

infallibility *n* certainty, infallibleness, perfection.

infallible *adj* certain, indubitable, oracular, sure, unerring, unfailing.

infamous *adj* abominable, atrocious, base, damnable, dark, detestable, discreditable, disgraceful, dishonorable, disreputable, heinous, ignominious, nefarious, odious, opprobrious, outrageous, scandalous, shameful, shameless, vile, villainous, wicked.

infamy *n* abasement, discredit, disgrace, dishonour, disrepute, ignominy, obloquy, odium, opprobrium, scandal, shame; atrocity, detestableness, disgracefulness, dishonorableness, odiousness, scandalousness, shamefulness, villainy, wickedness.

infancy *n* beginning, commencement; babyhood, childhood, minority, nonage, pupillage.

infant *n* babe, baby, bairn, bantling, brat, chit, minor, nursling, papoose, suckling, tot.

infantile *adj* childish, infantine, newborn, tender, young; babyish, childish, weak; babylike, childlike.

infatuate *vb* befool, besot, captivate, delude, prepossess, stultify.

infatuation *n* absorption, besottedness, folly, foolishness, prepossession, stupefaction.

infeasible *adj* impractical, unfeasible.

infect *vb* affect, contaminate, corrupt, defile, poison, pollute, taint, vitiate.

infection *n* affection, bane, contagion, contamination, corruption, defilement, pest, poison, pollution, taint, virus, vitiation.

infectious *adj* catching, communicable, contagious, contaminating, corrupting, defiling, demoralizing, pestiferous, pestilential, poisoning, polluting, sympathetic, vitiating.

infecund *adj* barren, infertile, sterile, unfruitful, unproductive, unprolific.

infecundity *n* unfruitfulness.

infelicitous *adj* calamitous, miserable, unfortunate, unhappy, wretched; inauspicious, unfavourable, unpropitious; ill-chosen, inappropriate, unfitting.

infer *vb* collect, conclude, deduce, derive, draw, gather, glean, guess, presume, reason.

inference *n* conclusion, consequence, corollary, deduction, generalization, guess, illation, implication, induction, presumption.

inferior *adj* lower, nether; junior, minor, secondary, subordinate; bad, base, deficient, humble, imperfect, indifferent, mean, mediocre, paltry, poor, second-rate, shabby.

inferiority *n* juniority, subjection, subordination, mediocrity; deficiency, imperfection, inadequacy, shortcoming.

infernal *adj* abominable, accursed, atrocious, damnable, dark, demoniacal, devilish, diabolical, fiendish, fiendlike, hellish, malicious, nefarious, satanic, Stygian.

infertility *n* barrenness, infecundity, sterility, unfruitfulness, unproductivity.

infest *vb* annoy, disturb, harass, haunt, molest, plague, tease, torment, trouble, vex, worry; beset, overrun, possess, swarm, throng.

infidel *n* agnostic, atheist, disbeliever, heathen, heretic, sceptic, unbeliever.

infidelity *n* adultery, disloyality, faithlessness, treachery, unfaithfulness; disbelief, scepticism, unbelief.

infiltrate *vb* absorb, pervade, soak.

infinite *adj* boundless, endless, illimitable, immeasurable, inexhaustible, interminable, limitless, measureless, perfect, unbounded, unlimited; enormous, immense, stupendous, vast; absolue, eternal, self-determined, self-existent, unconditioned.

infinitesimal *adj* infinitely small; microscopic, miniscule.

infinity *n* absoluteness, boundlessness, endlessness, eternity, immensity, infiniteness, infinitude, interminateness, self-determination, self-existence, vastness.

infirm *adj* ailing, debilitated, enfeebled, feeble, frail, weak, weakened; faltering, irresolute, vacillating, wavering; insecure, precarious, unsound, unstable.

infirmity *n* ailment, debility, feebleness, frailness, frailty, weakness; defect, failing, fault, foible, weakness.

infix *vb* fasten, fix, plant, set; implant, inculcate, infuse, ingraft, instil.

inflame *vb* animate, arouse, excite, enkindle, fire, heat, incite, inspirit, intensify, rouse, stimulate; aggravate, anger, chafe, embitter, enrage, exasperate, incense, infuriate, irritate, madden, nettle, provoke.

inflammability *n* combustibility, combustibleness, inflammableness.

inflammable *adj* combustible, ignitible; excitable.

inflammation *n* burning, conflagration; anger, animosity, excitement, heat, rage, turbulence, violence.

inflammatory *adj* fiery, inflaming; dissentious, incendiary, seditious.

inflate *vb* bloat, blow up, distend, expand, swell, sufflate; elate, puff up; enlarge, increase.

inflated *adj* bloated, distended, puffed-up, swollen; bombastic, declamatory, grandiloquent, high-flown, magniloquent, overblown, pompous, rhetorical, stilted, tumid, turgid.

inflation *n* enlargement, increase, overenlargement, overissue; bloatedness, distension, expansion, sufflation; bombast, conceit, conceitedness, self-conceit, self-complacency, self-importance, self-sufficiency, vaingloriousness, vainglory.

inflect *vb* bend, bow, curve, turn; (*gram*) conjugate, decline, vary.

inflection *n* bend, bending, crook, curvature, curvity, flexure; (*gram*) accidence, conjugation, declension, variation; (*mus*) modulation.

inflexibility *n* inflexibleness, rigidity, stiffness; doggedness, obstinacy, perinacity, stubbornness; firmness, perseverance, resolution, tenacity.

inflexible *adj* rigid, rigorous, stiff, unbending; cantankerous, cross-grained, dogged, headstrong, heady, inexorable, intractable, obdurate, obstinant, pertinacious, refractory, stubborn, unyielding, wilful; firm, immovable, persevering, resolute, steadfast, unbending.

inflict *vb* bring, impose, lay on.

infliction *n* imposition, inflicting; judgment, punishment.

inflorescence *n* blooming, blossoming, flowering.

influence *vb* affect, bias, control, direct, lead, modify, prejudice, prepossess, sway; actuate, arouse, impel, incite, induce, instigate, move, persuade, prevail upon, rouse. * *n* ascendancy, authority, control, mastery, potency, predominance, pull, rule, sway; credit, reputation, weight; inflow, inflowing, influx; magnetism, power, spell.

influential *adj* controlling, effective, effectual, potent, powerful, strong; authoritative, momentous, substantial, weighty.

influx *n* flowing in, introduction.

infold *see* **enfold**.

inform *vb* animate, inspire, quicken; acquaint, advise, apprise, enlighten, instruct, notify, teach, tell, tip, warn.

informal *adj* unceremonious, unconventional, unofficial; easy, familiar, natural, simple; irregular, nonconformist, unusual.

informality *n* unceremoniousness; unconventionality; ease, familiarity, naturalness, simplicity; noncomformity, irregularity, unusualness.

informant *n* advertiser, adviser, informer, intelligencer, newsmonger, notifier, relator; accuser, complainant, informer.

information *n* advice, data, intelligence, knowledge, notice; advertisement, enlightenment, instruction, message, tip, word, warning; accusation, complaint, denunciation.

informer *n* accuser, complainant, informant, snitch.

infraction *n* breach, breaking, disobedience, encroachment, infringement, nonobservance, transgression, violation.

infrangible *adj* inseparable, inviolable, unbreakable.

infrequency *n* rareness, rarity, uncommonness, unusualness.

infrequent *adj* rare, uncommon, unfrequent, unusual; occasional, scant, scarce, sporadic.

infringe *vb* break, contravene, disobey, intrude, invade, transgress, violate.

infringement *n* breach, breaking, disobedience, infraction, nonobservance, transgression, violation.

infuriated *adj* angry, enraged, furious, incensed, maddened, raging, wild.

infuse *vb* breathe into, implant, inculcate, ingraft, insinuate, inspire, instil, introduce; macerate, steep.

infusion *n* inculcation, instillation, introduction; infusing, macerating, steeping.

ingathering *n* harvest.

ingenious *adj* able, adroit, artful, bright, clever, fertile, gifted, inventive, ready, sagacious, shrewd, witty.

ingenuity *n* ability, acuteness, aptitude, aptness, capacity, capableness, cleverness, faculty, genius, gift, ingeniousness, inventiveness, knack, readiness, skill, turn.

ingenuous *adj* artless, candid, childlike, downright, frank, generous, guileless, honest, innocent, naive, open, openhearted, plain, simple-minded, sincere, single-minded, straightforward, transparent, truthful, unreserved.

ingenuousness *n* artlessness, candour, childlikeness, frankness, guilelessness, honesty, naivety, open-heartedness, openness, sincerity, single-mindedness, truthfulness.

inglorious *adj* humble, lowly, mean, nameless, obscure, undistinguished, unhonoured, unknown, unmarked, unnoted; discreditable, disgraceful, humiliating, ignominous, scandalous, shameful.

ingloriousness *n* humbleness, lowliness, meanness, namelessness, obscurity; abasement, discredit, disgrace, dishonour, disrepute, humiliation, infamy, ignominousness, ignominy, obloquy, odium, opprobrium, shame.

ingraft *vb* graft, implant, inculcate, infix, infuse, instil.

ingrain *vb* dye, imbue, impregnate.

ingratiate *vb* insinuate.

ingratitude *n* thanklessness, ungratefulness, unthankfulness.

ingredient *n* component, constituent, element.

ingress *n* entrance, entré, entry, introgression.

ingulf *see* **engulf**.

inhabit *vb* abide, dwell, live, occupy, people, reside, sojourn.

inhabitable *adj* habitable, livable.

inhabitant *n* citizen, denizen, dweller, inhabiter, resident.

inhalation *n* breath, inhaling, inspiration; sniff, snuff.

inhale *vb* breathe in, draw in, inbreathe, inspire.

inharmonious *adj* discordant, inharmonic, out of tune, unharmonious, unmusical.

inhere *vb* cleave to, stick, stick fast; abide, belong, exist, lie, pertain, reside.

inherent *adj* essential, immanent, inborn, inbred, indwelling, ingrained, innate, inseparable, intrinsic, native, natural, proper; adhering, sticking.

inherit *vb* get, receive.
inheritance *n* heritage, legacy, patrimony; inheriting.
inheritor *n* heir, (*law*) parcener.
inhibit *vb* bar, check, debar, hinder, obstruct, prevent, repress, restrain, stop; forbid, interdict, prohibit.
inhibition *n* check, hindrance, impediment, obstacle, obstruction, restraint; disallowance, embargo, interdict, interdiction, prevention, prohibition.
inhospitable *adj* cool, forbidding, unfriendly, unkind; bigoted, illiberal, intolerant, narrow, prejudiced, ungenerous, unreceptive; barren, wild.
inhospitality *n* inhospitableness, unkindness; illiberality, narrowness.
inhuman *adj* barbarous, brutal, cruel, fell, ferocious, merciless, pitiless, remorseless, ruthless, savage, unfeeling; nonhuman.
inhumanity *n* barbarity, brutality, cruelty, ferocity, savageness; hard-heartedness, unkindness.
inhume *vb* bury, entomb, inter.
inimical *adj* antagonistic, hostile, unfriendly; adverse, contrary, harmful, hurtful, noxious, opposed, pernicious, repugnant, unfavourable.
inimitable *adj* incomparable, matchless, peerless, unequalled, unexampled, unmatched, unparagoned, unparalleled, unrivalled, unsurpassed.
iniquitous *adj* atrocious, criminal, flagitious, heinous, inequitable, nefarious, sinful, wicked, wrong, unfair, unjust, unrighteous.
iniquity *n* injustice, sin, sinfulness, unrighteousness, wickedness, wrong; crime, misdeed, offence.
initial *adj* first; beginning, commencing, incipient, initiatory, introductory, opening, original; elementary, inchoate, rudimentary.
initiate *vb* begin, commence, enter upon, inaugurate, introduce, open; ground, indoctrinate, instruct, prime, teach.
initiation *n* beginning, commencement, inauguration, opening; admission, entrance, introduction; indoctrinate, instruction.
initiative *n* beginning; energy, enterprise.
initiatory *adj* inceptive, initiative.
inject *vb* force in, interject, insert, introduce, intromit.
injudicious *adj* foolish, hasty, ill-advised, ill-judged, imprudent, incautious, inconsiderate, indiscreet, rash, unwise.
injunction *n* admonition, bidding, command, mandate, order, precept.
injure *vb* damage, disfigure, harm, hurt, impair, mar, spoil, sully, wound; abuse, aggrieve, wrong; affront, dishonour, insult.
injurious *adj* baneful, damaging, deadly, deleterious, destructive, detrimental, disadvantageous, evil, fatal, hurtful, mischievous, noxious, pernicious, prejudicial, ruinous; inequitable, iniquitous, unjust, wrongful; contumelious, detractory, libellous, slanderous.
injury *n* evil, ill, injustice, wrong; damage, detriment, harm, hurt, impairment, loss, mischief, prejudice.
injustice *n* inequity, unfairness; grievance, iniquity, injury, wrong.
inkhorn *n* inkbottle, inkstand.
inkling *n* hint, intimation, suggestion, whisper.
inky *adj* atramentous, black, murky.
inland *adj* domestic, hinterland, home, upcountry; interior, internal.
inlet *n* arm, bay, bight, cove, creek; entrance, ingress, passage.
inmate *n* denizen, dweller, guest, intern, occupant.
inmost *adj* deepest, innermost.
inn *n* hostel, hostelry, hotel, pub, public house, tavern.
innate *adj* congenital, constitutional, inborn, inbred, indigenous, inherent, inherited, instinctive, native, natural, organic.
inner *adj* interior, internal.
innermost *adj* deepest, inmost.
innkeeper *n* host, innholder, landlady, landlord, tavernkeeper.
innocence *n* blamelessness, chastity, guilelessness, guiltlessness, purity, simplicity, sinlessness, stainlessness; harmlessness, innocuousness, innoxiousness, inoffensiveness.

innocent *adj* blameless, clean, clear, faultless, guiltless, immaculate, pure, sinless, spotless, unfallen, upright; harmless, innocuous, innoxious, inoffensive; lawful, legitimate, permitted; artless, guileless, ignorant, ingenuous, simple. * *n* babe, child, ingénue, naif, naive, unsophisticate.

innocuous *adj* harmless, innocent, inoffensive, safe.

innovate *vb* change, introduce.

innovation *n* change, introduction; departure, novelty.

innuendo *n* allusion, hint, insinuation, intimation, suggestion.

innumerable *adj* countless, numberless.

inoculate *vb* infect, vaccinate.

inoffensive *adj* harmless, innocent, innocuous, innoxious, unobjectionable, unoffending.

inoperative *adj* inactive, ineffectual, inefficacious, not in force.

inopportune *adj* ill-timed, inexpedient, infelicitous, mistimed, unfortunate, unhappy, unseasonable, untimely.

inordinate *adj* excessive, extravagant, immoderate, intemperate, irregular.

inorganic *adj* inanimate, unorganized; mineral.

inquest *n* inquiry, inquisition, investigation, quest, search.

inquietude *n* anxiety, disquiet, disquietude, disturbance, restlessness, uneasiness.

inquire, enquire *vb* ask, catechize, interpellate, interrogate, investigate, query, question, quiz.

inquiry, enquiry *n* examination, exploration, investigation, research, scrutiny, study; interrogation, query, question, quiz.

inquisition *n* examination, inquest, inquiry, investigation, search.

inquisitive *adj* curious, inquiring, scrutinizing; curious, meddlesome, peeping, peering, prying.

inroad *n* encroachment, foray, incursion, invasion, irruption, raid.

insalubrious *adj* noxious, unhealthful, unhealthy, unwholesome.

insane *adj* abnormal, crazed, crazy, delirious, demented, deranged, distracted, lunatic, mad, maniacal, unhealthy, unsound.

insanity *n* craziness, delirium, dementia, derangement, lunacy, madness, mania, mental aberration, mental alienation.

insatiable *adj* greedy, rapacious, voracious; insatiate, unappeasable.

inscribe *vb* emblaze, endorse, engrave, enroll, impress, imprint, letter, mark, write; address, dedicate.

inscrutable *adj* hidden, impenetrable, incomprehensible, inexplicable, mysterious, undiscover-able, unfathomable, unsearchable.

inscrutableness *n* impenetrability, incomprehensibility, incomprehensibleness, inexplicability, inscrutability, mysteriousness, mystery, unfathomableness, unsearchableness.

insecure *adj* risky, uncertain, unconfident, unsure; exposed, ill-protected, unprotected, unsafe; dangerous, hazardous, perilous; infirm, shaking, shaky, tottering, unstable, weak, wobbly.

insecurity *n* riskiness, uncertainty; danger, hazardousness, peril; instability, shakiness, weakness, wobbliness.

insensate *adj* dull, indifferent, insensible, torpid; brutal, foolish, senseless, unwise; inanimate, insensible, insentient, nonpercipient, unconscious, unperceiving.

insensibility *n* dullness, insentience, lethargy, torpor; apathy, indifference, insusceptibility, unfeelingness, dullness, stupidity; anaesthesia, coma, stupor, unconsciousness.

insensible *adj* imperceivable, imperceptible, undiscoverable; blunted, brutish, deaf, dull, insensate, numb, obtuse, senseless, sluggish, stolid, stupid, torpid, unconscious; apathetic, callous, phlegmatic, impassive, indifferent, insensitive, insentient, unfeeling, unimpressible, unsusceptible.

insensibly *adv* imperceptibly.

insentient *adj* inert, nonsentient, senseless; inanimate, insensible, insensate, nonpercipient, unconscious, unperceiving.

inseparable *adj* close, friendly, intimate, together; indissoluble, indivisible, inseverable.

insert *vb* infix, inject, intercalate, interpolate, introduce, inweave, parenthesize, place, put, set.

inside *adj* inner, interior, internal; confidential, exclusive, internal, private, secret. * *adv* indoors, within. * *n* inner part, interior; nature.

insidious *adj* creeping, deceptive, gradual, secretive; arch, artful, crafty, crooked, cunning, deceitful, designing, diplomatic, foxy, guileful, intriguing, Machiavellian, sly, sneaky, subtle, treacherous, trickish, tricky, wily.

insight *n* discernment, intuition, penetration, perception, perspicuity, understanding.

insignia *npl* badges, marks.

insignificance *n* emptiness, nothingenss, paltriness, triviality, unimportance.

insignificant *adj* contemptible, empty, immaterial, inconsequential, inconsiderable, inferior, meaningless, paltry, petty, small, sorry, trifling, trivial, unessential, unimportant.

insincere *adj* deceitful, dishonest, disingenuous, dissembling, dissimulating, double-faced, double-tongued, duplicitous, empty, faithless, false, hollow, hypocritical, pharisaical, truthless, uncandid, untrue.

insincerity *n* bad faith, deceitfulness, dishonesty, disingenuousness, dissimulation, duplicity, falseness, faithlessness, hypocrisy.

insinuate *vb* hint, inculcate, infuse, ingratiate, instil, intimate, introduce, suggest.

insipid *adj* dead, dull, flat, heavy, inanimate, jejune, lifeless, monotonous, pointless, prosaic, prosy, spiritless, stupid, tame, unentertaining, uninteresting; mawkish, savourless, stale, tasteless, vapid, zestless.

insipidity, insipidness *n* dullness, heaviness, lifelessness, prosiness, stupidity, tameness; flatness, mawkishness, staleness, tastlessness, unsavouriness, vapidness, zestlessness.

insist *vb* demand, maintain, urge.

insistence *n* importunity, solicitousness, urging, urgency.

insnare *see* **ensnare**.

insolence *n* impertinence, impudence, malapertness, pertness, rudeness, sauciness; contempt, contumacy, contumely, disrespect, frowardness, insubordination.

insolent *adj* abusive, contemptuous, contumelious, disrespectful, domineering, insulting, offensive, overbearing, rude, supercilious; cheeky, impertinent, impudent, malapert, pert, saucy; contumacious, disobedient, froward, insubordinate.

insoluble *adj* indissoluble, indissolvable, irreducible; inexplicable, insolvable.

insolvable *adj* inexplicable.

insolvent *adj* bankrupt, broken, failed, ruined.

insomnia *n* sleeplessness, wakefulness.

inspect *vb* examine, investigate, look into, pry into, scrutinize; oversee, superintend, supervise.

inspection *n* examination, investigation, scrutiny; oversight, superintendence, supervision.

inspector *n* censor, critic, examiner, visitor; boss, overseer, superintendent, supervisor.

inspiration *n* breathing, inhalation; afflatus, fire, inflatus; elevation, exaltation; enthusiasm.

inspire *vb* breathe, inhale; infuse, instil; animate, cheer, enliven, inspirit; elevate, exalt, stimulate; fill, imbue, impart, inform, quicken.

inspirit *vb* animate, arouse, cheer, comfort, embolden, encourage, enhearten, enliven, fire, hearten, incite, invigorate, quicken, rouse, stimulate.

instable *see* **unstable**.

instability *n* changeableness, fickleness, inconstancy, insecurity, mutability.

install, instal *vb* inaugurate, induct, introduce; establish, place, set up.

installation *n* inauguration, induction, instalment, investiture.

instalment *n* earnest, payment, portion.
instance *vb* adduce, cite, mention, specify. * *n* case, example, exemplification, illustration, occasion; impulse, incitement, instigation, motive, prompting, request, solicitation.
instant *adj* direct, immediate, instantaneous, prompt, quick; current, present; earnest, fast, imperative, importunate, pressing, urgent; ready cooked. * n flash, jiffy, moment, second, trice, twinkling; hour, time.
instantaneous *adj* abrupt, immediate, instant, quick, sudden.
instantaneously *adv* forthwith, immediately, presto, quickly, right away.
instauration *n* reconstitution, reconstruction, redintegration, re-establishment, rehabilitation, reinstatement, renewal, renovation, restoration.
instead *adv* in lieu, in place, rather.
instigate *vb* actuate, agitate, encourage, impel, incite, influence, initiate, move, persuade, prevail upon, prompt, provoke, rouse, set on, spur on, stimulate, stir up, tempt, urge.
instigation *n* encouragement, incitement, influence, instance, prompting, solicitation, urgency.
instil, instill *vb* enforce, implant, impress, inculcate, ingraft; impart, infuse, insinuate.
instillation *n* infusion, insinuation, introduction.
instinct *n* natural impulse.
instinctive *adj* automatic, inherent, innate, intuitive, involuntary, natural, spontaneous; impulsive, unreflecting.
institute[1] *n* academy, college, foundation, guild, institution, school; custom, doctrine, dogma, law, maxim, precedent, principle, rule, tenet.
institute[2] *vb* begin, commence, constitute, establish, found, initial, install, introduce, organize, originate, start.
institution *n* enactment, establishment, foundation, institute, society; investiture; custom, law, practice.
instruct *vb* discipline, educate, enlighten, exercise, guide, indoctrinate, inform, initiate, school, teach, train; apprise, bid, command, direct, enjoin, order, prescribe to.
instruction *n* breeding, discipline, education, indoctrination, information, nurture, schooling, teaching, training, tuition; advice, counsel, precept; command, direction, mandate, order.
instructor *n* educator, master, preceptor, schoolteacher, teacher, tutor.
instrument *n* appliance, apparatus, contrivance, device, implement, musical instrument, tool, utensil; agent, means, medium; charter, deed, document, indenture, writing.
instrumental *adj* ancillary, assisting, auxiliary, conducive, contributory, helpful, helping, ministerial, ministrant, serviceable, subservient, subsidiary.
instrumentality *n* agency, intermediary; intervention, means, mediation.
insubordinate *adj* disobedient, disorderly, mutinous, refractory, riotous, seditious, turbulent, ungovernable, unruly.
insubordination *n* disobedience, insurrection, mutiny, revolt, riotousness, sedition; indiscipline, laxity.
insufferable *adj* intolerable, unbearable, unendurable, insupportable; abominable, detestable, disgusting, execrable, outrageous.
insufficiency *n* dearth, defectiveness, deficiency, lack, inadequacy, inadequateness, incapability, incompetence, paucity, shortage.
insufficient *adj* deficient, inadequate, incommensurate, incompetent, scanty; incapable, incompetent, unfitted, unqualified, unsuited, unsatisfactory.
insular *adj* contracted, illiberal, limited, narrow, petty, prejudiced, restricted; isolated, remote.
insulate *vb* detach, disconnect, disengage, disunite, isolate, separate.
insulation *n* disconnection, disengagement, isolation, separation.
insult *vb* abuse, affront, injure, offend, outrage, slander, slight. * *n* abuse, affront, cheek, contumely, indignity, insolence, offence, outrage, sauce, slight.
insulting *adj* abusive, arrogant, contume-

lious, impertinent, impolite, insolent, rude, vituperative.

insuperable *adj* impassable, insurmountable.

insupportable *adj* insufferable, intolerable, unbearable, unendurable.

insuppressible *adj* irrepressible, uncontrollable.

insurance *n* assurance, security.

insure *vb* assure, guarantee, indemnify, secure, underwrite.

insurgent *adj* disobedient, insubordinate, mutinous, rebellious, revolting, revolutionary, seditious. * *n* mutineer, rebel, revolter, revolutionary.

insurmountable *adj* impassable, insuperable.

insurrection *n* insurgence, mutiny, rebellion, revolt, revolution, rising, sedition, uprising.

intact *adj* scathless, unharmed, unhurt, unimpaired, uninjured, untouched; complete, entire, integral, sound, unbroken, undiminished, whole.

intangible *adj* dim, impalpable, imperceptible, indefinite, insubstantial, intactile, shadowy, vague; aerial, phantom, spiritous.

intangibility *n* imperceptibility, insubstantiality, intangibleness, shadowiness, vagueness.

integral *adj* complete, component, entire, integrant, total, whole.

integrity *n* goodness, honesty, principle, probity, purity, rectitude, soundness, uprightness, virtue; completeness, entireness, entirety, wholeness.

integument *n* coat, covering, envelope, skin, tegument.

intellect *n* brains, cognitive faculty, intelligence, mind, rational faculty, reason, reasoning, faculty, sense, thought, understanding, wit.

intellectual *adj* cerebral, intelligent, mental, scholarly, thoughtful. * *n* academic, highbrow, pundit, savant, scholar.

intelligence *n* acumen, apprehension, brightness, discernment, imagination, insight, penetration, quickness, sagacity, shrewdness, understanding, wits; information, knowledge; advice, instruction, news, notice, notification, tidings; brains, intellect, mentality, sense, spirit.

intelligent *adj* acute, alert, apt, astute, brainy, bright, clear-headed, clear-sighted, clever, discerning, keen-eyed, keen-sighted, knowing, long-headed, quick, quick-sighted, sagacious, sensible, sharp-sighted, sharp-witted, shrewd, understanding.

intelligibility *n* clarity, comprehensibility, intelligibleness, perspicuity.

intelligible *adj* clear, comprehensible, distinct, evident, lucid, manifest, obvious, patent, perspicuous, plain, transparent, understandable.

intemperate *adj* drunken; excessive, extravagant, extreme, immoderate, inordinate, unbridled, uncontrolled, unrestrained; self-indulgent.

intend *vb* aim at, contemplate, design, determine, drive at, mean, meditate, propose, purpose, think of.

intendant *n* inspector, overseer, superintendent, supervisor.

intense *adj* ardent, earnest, fervid, passionate, vehement; close, intent, severe, strained, stretched, strict; energetic, forcible, keen, potent, powerful, sharp, strong, vigorous, violent; acute, deep, extreme, exquisite, grievous, poignant.

intensify *vb* aggravate, concentrate, deepen, enhance, heighten, quicken, strengthen, whet.

intensity *n* closeness, intenseness, severity, strictness; excess, extremity, violence; activity, energy, force, power, strength, vigour; ardour, earnestness, vehemence.

intensive *adj* emphatic, intensifying.

intent *adj* absorbed, attentive, close, eager, earnest, engrossed, occupied, preoccupied, zealous; bent, determined, decided, resolved, set. * *n* aim, design, drift, end, import, intention, mark, meaning, object, plan, purport, purpose, purview, scope, view.

intention *n* aim, design, drift, end, import, intent, mark, meaning, object, plan, purport, purpose, purview, scope, view.

intentional *adj* contemplated, deliberate, designed, intended, preconcerted, predetermined, premeditated, purposed, studied, voluntary, wilful.
inter *vb* bury, commit to the earth, entomb, inhume, inurn.
intercalate *vb* insert, interpolate.
intercede *vb* arbitrate, interpose, mediate; entreat, plead, supplicate.
intercept *vb* cut off, interrupt, obstruct, seize.
intercession *n* interposition, intervention, mediation; entreaty, pleading, prayer, supplication.
intercessor *n* interceder, mediator.
interchange *vb* alternate, change, exchange, vary. * *n* alternation.
interchangeableness *n* interchangeability.
interchangeably *adv* alternately.
intercourse *n* commerce, communication, communion, connection, converse, correspondence, dealings, fellowship, truck; acquaintance, intimacy.
interdict *vb* debar, forbid, inhibit, prohibit, prescribe, proscribe, restrain from. * *n* ban, decree, interdiction, prohibition.
interest *vb* affect, concern, touch; absorb, attract, engage, enlist, excite, grip, hold, occupy. * *n* advantage, benefit, good, profit, weal; attention, concern, regard, sympathy; part, participation, portion, share, stake; discount, premium, profit.
interested *adj* attentive, concerned, involved, occupied; biassed, patial, prejudiced; selfish, self-seeking.
interesting *adj* attractive, engaging, entertaining, pleasing.
interfere *vb* intermeddle, interpose, meddle; clash, collide, conflict.
interference *n* intermeddling, interposition; clashing, collision, interfering, opposition.
interim *n* intermediate time, interval, meantime.
interior *adj* inmost, inner, internal, inward; inland, remote; domestic, home. * *n* inner part, inland, inside.
interjacent *adj* intermediate, interposed, intervening, parenthetical.
interject *vb* comment, inject, insert, interpose.
interjection *n* exclamation.
interlace *vb* bind, complicate, entwine, intersperse, intertwine, interweave, inweave, knit, mix, plait, twine, twist, unite.
interlard *vb* difersify, interminate, intersperse, intertwine, mix, vary.
interline *vb* insert, write between.
interlineal *adj* interlinear, interlined.
interlink, interlock *vb* connect, interchain, interrelate, join.
interlocution *n* colloquy, conference, dialogue, interchange.
interlocutor *n* respondent, speaker.
interloper *n* intruder, meddler.
intermeddle *vb* interfere, interpose, meddle.
intermediary *n* go-between, mediator.
intermediate *adj* interjacent, interposed, intervening, mean, median, middle, transitional.
interment *n* burial, entombment, inhumation, sepulture.
interminable *adj* boundless, endless, illimitable, immeasurable, infinite, limitless, unbounded, unlimited; long-drawn-out, tedious, wearisome.
intermingle *vb* blend, commingle, commix, intermix, mingle, mix.
intermission *n* cessation, interruption, interval, lull, pause, remission, respite, rest, stop, stoppage, suspension.
intermit *vb* interrupt, intervene, stop, suspend; discontinue, give over, leave off; abate, subside.
intermittent *adj* broken, capricious, discontinuous, fitful, flickering, intermitting, periodic, recurrent, remittent, spasmodic.
intermix *vb* blend, commingle, commix, intermingle, mingle, mix.
internal *adj* inner, inside, interior, inward; incorporeal, mental, spiritual; deeper, emblematic, hidden, higher, metaphorical, secret, symbolical, under; genuine, inherent, intrinsic, real, true; domestic, home, inland, inside.
international *adj* cosmopolitan, universal.

internecine *adj* deadly, destructive, exterminating, exterminatory, interneciary, internecinal, internecive, mortal.
interpellate *vb* interrogate, question.
interpellation *n* interruption; intercession, interposition; interrogation, questioning.
interplay *n* interaction.
interpolate *vb* add, foist, insert, interpose; (*math*) intercalate, introduce.
interpose *vb* arbitrate, intercede, intervene, mediate; interfere, intermeddle, interrupt, meddle, tamper; insert, interject, put in, remark, sandwich, set between; intrude, thurst in.
interposition *n* intercession, interpellation, intervention, mediation.
interpret *vb* decipher, decode, define, elucidate, explain, expound, solve, unfold, unravel; construe, render, translate.
interpretation *n* meaning, sense, signification; elucidation, explanation, explication, exposition; construction, rendering, rendition, translation, version.
interpreter *n* expositor, expounder, translator.
interrogate *vb* ask, catechize, examine, inquire of, interpellate, question.
interrogation *n* catechizing, examination, examining, interpellation, interrogating, questioning; inquiry, query, question.
interrogative *adj* interrogatory, questioning.
interrupt *vb* break, check, disturb, hinder, intercept, interfere with, obstruct, pretermit, stop; break, cut, disconnect, disjoin, dissever, dissolve, disunite, divide, separate, sever, sunder; break off, cease, discontinue, intermit, leave off, suspend.
interruption *n* hindrance, impediment, obstacle, obstruction, stop, stoppage; cessation, discontinuance, intermission, pause, suspension; break, breaking, disconnecting, disconnection, disjunction, dissolution, disunion, disuniting, division, separation, severing, sundering.
intersect *vb* cross, cut, decussate, divide, interrupt.
intersection *n* crossing.
interspace *n* interlude, interstice, interval.
intersperse *vb* intermingle, scatter, sprinkle; diversify, interlard, mix.
interstice *n* interspace, interval, space; chink, crevice.
interstitial *adj* intermediate, intervening.
intertwine *vb* interlace, intertwine, interweave, inweave, twine.
interval *n* interim, interlude, interregnum, pause, period, recess, season, space, spell, term; interstice, skip.
intervene *vb* come between, interfere, mediate; befall, happen, occur.
intervening *adj* interjacent, intermediate; interstitial.
intervention *n* interference, interposition; agency, mediation.
interview *n* conference, consultation, parley; meeting.
interweave *vb* interlace, intertwine, inweave, weave; intermingle, intermix, mingle, mix.
intestinal *adj* domestic, interior, internal.
intestines *npl* bowels, entrails, guts, insides, inwards, viscera.
intimacy *n* close acquaintance, familiarity, fellowship, friendship; closeness, nearness.
intimate[1] *adj* close, near; familiar, friendly; bosom, chummy, close, dear, homelike, special; confidential, personal, private, secret; detailed, exhaustive, first-hand, immediate, penetrating, profound; cosy, warm. * *n* chum, confidant, companion, crony, friend.
intimate[2] *vb* allude to, express, hint, impart, indicate, insinuate, signify, suggest, tell.
intimately *adv* closely, confidentially, familiarly, nearly, thoroughly.
intimation *n* allusion, hint, innuendo, insinuation, suggestion.
intimidate *vb* abash, affright, alarm, appal, browbeat, bully, cow, daunt, dishearten, dismay, frighten, overawe, scare, subdue, terrify, terrorize.
intimidation *n* fear, intimidating, terror, terrorism.
intolerable *adj* insufferable, insupportable, unbearable, unendurable.
intolerance *n* bigotry, narrowness; impa-

tience, rejection.
intolerant *adj* bigoted, narrow, proscriptive; dictatorial, impatient, imperious, overbearing, supercilious.
intonation *n* cadence, modulation, tone; musical recitation.
in toto *adv* entirely, wholly.
intoxicate *vb* fuddle, inebriate, muddle.
intoxicated *adj* boozy, drunk, drunken, fuddled, inebriated, maudlin, mellow, muddled, stewed, tight, tipsy.
intoxication *n* drunkenness, ebriety, inebriation, inebriety; excitement, exhilaration, infatuation.
intractability *n* cantankerousness, contrariety, inflexibility, intractableness, obduracy, obstinacy, perverseness, perversity, pig-headedness, stubbornness, wilfulness.
intractable *adj* cantankerous, contrary, contumacious, cross-grained, dogged, froward, headstrong, indocile, inflexible, mulish, obdurate, obstinate, perverse, pig-headed, refractory, restive, stubborn, tough, uncontrollable, ungovernable, unmanageable, unruly, unyielding, wilful.
intrench *see* **entrench**.
intrenchment *see* **entrenchment**.
intrepid *adj* bold, brave, chivalrous, courageous, daring, dauntless, doughty, fearless, gallant, heroic, unappalled, unawed, undaunted, undismayed, unterrified, valiant, valorous.
intrepidity *n* boldness, bravery, courage, daring, dauntlessness, fearlessness, gallantry, heroism, intrepidness, prowess, spirit, valour.
intricacy *n* complexity, complication, difficulty, entanglement, intricateness, involution, obscurity, perplexity.
intricate *adj* complicated, difficult, entangled, involved, mazy, obscure, perplexed.
intrigue *vb* connive, conspire, machinate, plot, scheme; beguile, bewitch, captivate, charm, fascinate. * *n* artifice, cabal, conspiracy, deception, finesse, Machiavelianism, machination, manoeuvre, plot, ruse, scheme, stratagem, wile; amour, liaison, love affair.
intriguing *adj* arch, artful, crafty, crooked, cunning, deceitful, designing, diplomatic, foxy, Machiavelian, insidious, politic, sly, sneaky, subtle, tortuous, trickish, tricky, wily.
intrinsic *adj* essential, genuine, real, sterling, true; inborn, inbred, ingrained, inherent, internal, inward, native, natural.
intrinsically *adv* essentially, really, truly; inherently, naturally.
introduce *vb* bring in, conduct, import, induct, inject, insert, lead in, usher in; present; begin, broach, commence, inaugurate, initiate, institute, start.
introduction *n* exordium, preface, prelude, proem; introducing, ushering in; presentation.
introductory *adj* precursory, prefatory, preliminary, proemial.
introspection *n* introversion, self-contemplation.
intrude *vb* encroach, impose, infringe, interfere, interlope, obtrude, trespass.
intruder *n* interloper, intermeddler, meddler, stranger.
intrusion *n* encroachment, infringement, intruding, obtrusion.
intrusive *adj* obtrusive, trespassing.
intuition *n* apprehension, cognition, insight, instinct; clairvoyance, divination, presentiment.
intuitive *adj* instinctive, intuitional, natural; clear, distinct, full, immediate.
intumesce *vb* bubble up, dilate, expand, swell.
intumescence *n* inturgescence, swelling, tumefaction, turgescence.
inundate *vb* deluge, drown, flood, glut, overflow, overwhelm, submerge.
inundation *n* cataclysm, deluge, flood, glut, overflow, superfluity.
inure *vb* accustom, discipline, familiarize, habituate, harden, toughen, train, use.
inutile *adj* bootless, ineffectual, inoperative, unavailing, unprofitable, useless.
invade *vb* encroach upon, infringe, violate; attack, enter in, march into.
invalid[1] *adj* baseless, fallacious, false, inoperative, nugatory, unfounded, unsound, untrue, worthless; (*law*) null,

void.

invalid² *adj* ailing, bedridden, feeble, frail, ill, infirm, sick, sickly, valetudinary, weak, weakly. * *n* convalescent, patient, valetudinarian.

invalidate *vb* abrogate, annul, cancel, nullify, overthrow, quash, repeal, reverse, undo, unmake, vitiate.

invalidity *n* baselessness, fallaciousness, fallacy, falsity, unsoundness.

invaluable *adj* inestimable, priceless.

invariable *adj* changeless, constant, unchanging, uniform, unvarying; changeless, immutable, unalterable, unchangeable.

invariableness *n* changelessness, constancy, uniformity, unvaryingness; changelessness, immutability, unchangeableness, invariability.

invasion *n* encroachment, incursion, infringement, inroad; aggression, assault, attack, foray, raid.

invective *n* abuse, censure, contumely, denunciation, diatribe, railing, reproach, sarcasm, satire, vituperation.

inveigh *vb* blame, censure, condemn, declaim against, denounce, exclaim against, rail at, reproach, vituperate.

inveigle *vb* contrive, devise; concoct, conceive, create, design, excogitate, frame, imagine, originate; coin, fabricate, forge, spin.

invent *vb* concoct, contrive, design, devise, discover, fabricate, find out, frame, originate.

invention *n* creation, discovery, ingenuity, inventing, origination; contrivance, design, device; coinage, fabrication, fiction, forgery.

inventive *adj* creative, fertile, ingenious.

inventor *n* author, contriver, creator, originator.

inventory *n* account, catalogue, list, record, roll, register, schedule.

inverse *adj* indirect, inverted, opposite, reversed.

inversion *n* inverting, reversing, transposal, transposition.

invert *vb* capsize, overturn; reverse, transpose.

invertebrate *adj* invertebral; spineless.

invest *vb* put money into; confer, endow, endue; (*mil*) beset, besiege, enclose, surround; array, clothe, dress.

investigate *vb* canvass, consider, dissect, examine, explore, follow up, inquire into, look into, overhaul, probe, question, research, scrutinize, search into, search out, sift, study.

investigation *n* examination, exploration, inquiry, inquisition, overhauling, research, scrutiny, search, sifting, study.

investiture *n* habilitation, induction, installation, ordination.

investment *n* money invested; endowment; (*mil*) beleaguerment, siege; clothes, dress, garments, habiliments, robe, vestment.

inveteracy *n* inveterateness, obstinacy.

inveterate *adj* accustomed, besetting, chronic, confirmed, deep-seated, habitual, habituated, hardened, ingrained, long-established, obstinate.

invidious *adj* disagreeable, envious, hateful, odious, offensive, unfair.

invigorate *vb* animate, brace, energize, fortify, harden, nerve, quicken, refresh, stimulate, strengthen, vivify.

invincible *adj* impregnable, indomitable, ineradicable, insuperable, insurmountable, irrepressible, unconquerable, unsubduable, unyielding.

inviolable *adj* hallowed, holy, inviolate, sacramental, sacred, sacrosanct, stainless.

inviolate *adj* unbroken, unviolated; pure, stainless, unblemished, undefiled, unhurt, uninjured, unpolluted, unprofaned, unstained; inviolable, sacred.

invisibility *n* imperceptibility, indistinctness, invisibleness, obscurity.

invisible *adj* impalpable, imperceptible, indistinguishable, intangible, unapparent, undiscernable, unperceivable, unseen.

invitation *n* bidding, call, challenge, solicitation, summons.

invite *vb* ask, bid, call, challenge, request, solicit, summon; allure, attract, draw on, entice, lead, persuade, prevail upon.

inviting *adj* alluring, attractive, bewitching, captivating, engaging, fascinating, pleasing, winning; prepossessing, promising.

invocation *n* conjuration, orison, petition, prayer, summoning, supplication.

invoice *vb* bill, list. * *n* bill, inventory, list, schedule.

invoke *vb* adjure, appeal to, beseech, beg, call upon, conjure, entreat, implore, importune, pray, pray to, solicit, summon, supplicate.

involuntary *adj* automatic, blind, instinctive, mechanical, reflex, spontaneous, unintentional; compulsory, reluctant, unwilling.

involve *vb* comprise, contain, embrace, imply, include, lead to; complicate, compromise, embarrass, entangle, implicate, incriminate, inculpate; cover, envelop, enwrap, surround, wrap; blend, conjoin, connect, join, mingle; entwine, interlace, intertwine, interweave, inweave.

invulnerability *n* invincibility, invulnerableness.

invulnerable *adj* incontrovertible, invincible, unassailable, irrefragable.

inward[1] *adj* incoming, inner, interior, internal; essential, hidden, mental, spiritual; private, secret.

inward[2], **inwards** *adv* inwardly, towards the inside, within.

inweave *vb* entwine, interlace, intertwine, interweave, weave together.

iota *n* atom, bit, glimmer, grain, jot, mite, particle, scintilla, scrap, shadow, spark, tittle, trace, whit.

irascibility *n* hastiness, hot-headedness, impatience, irascibleness, irritability, peevishness, petulance, quickness, spleen, testiness, touchiness.

irascible *adj* choleric, cranky, hasty, hot, hot-headed, impatient, irritable, nettlesome, peevish, peppery, pettish, petulant, quick, splenetic, snappish, testy, touchy, waspish.

irate *adj* angry, incensed, ireful, irritated, piqued.

ire *n* anger, choler, exasperation, fury, indignation, passion, rage, resentment, wrath.

ireful *adj* angry, furious, incensed, irate, raging, passionate.

iridescent *adj* irisated, nacreous, opalescent, pavonine, prismatic, rainbow-like.

iris *n* rainbow; (*bot*) fleur-de-lis, flower-de-luce; diaphragm of the eye.

irksome *adj* annoying, burdensome, humdrum, monotonous, tedious, tiresome, wearisome, weary, wearying.

iron *adj* ferric, ferrous.

ironic, ironical *adj* mocking, sarcastic.

irons *npl* chains, fetters, gyves, hampers, manacles, shackles.

irony *n* mockery, raillery, ridicule, sarcasm, satire.

irradiate *vb* brighten, illume, illuminate, illumine, light up, shine upon.

irrational *adj* absurd, extravagant, foolish, injudicious, preposterous, ridiculous, silly, unwise; unreasonable, unreasoning, unthinking; brute, brutish; aberrant, alienated, brainless, crazy, demented, fantastic, idiotic, imbecilic, insane, lunatic.

irrationality *n* absurdity, folly, foolishness, unreasonableness; brutishness.

irreclaimable *adj* hopeless, incurable, irrecoverable, irreparable, irretrievable, irreversible, remediless; abandoned, graceless, hardened, impenitent, incorrigible, lost, obdurate, profligate, recreant, reprobate, shameless, unrepentant.

irreconcilable *adj* implacable, inexorable, inexpiable, unappeasable; incompatible, incongruous, inconsistent.

irrecoverable *adj* hopeless, incurable, irremediable, irreparable, irretrievable, remediless.

irrefragable *adj* impregnable, incontestable, incontrovertible, indisputable, invincible, irrefutable, irresistible, unanswerable, unassailable, undeniable.

irrefutable *adj* impregnable, incontestable, incontrovertible, indisputable, invincible, irrefragable, irresistible, unanswerable, unassailable, undeniable.

irregular *adj* aberrant, abnormal, anomalistic, anomalous, crooked, devious, eccentric, erratic, exceptional, heteromorphous, raged, tortuous, unconformable, unusual; capricious, changeable, desultory, fitful, spasmodic, uncertain, unpunctual, unsettled, variable; disordered, disorderly, improper, uncanonical, unparliamentary, unsystematic; asymmetric, uneven, unsymmetrical; disorderly, dissolute, immoral, loose, wild. * *n* casual, freelance, hireling, mercenary.

irregularity *n* aberration, abnormality, anomaly, anomalousness, singularity; capriciousness, changeableness, uncertainty, variableness; asymmetry; disorderliness, dissoluteness, immorality, laxity, looseness, wildness.

irrelevance, irrelevancy *n* impertinency, inapplicability, nonpertinency.

irrelevant *adj* extraneous, foreign, illogical, impertinent, inapplicable, inapposite, inappropriate, inconsequent, unessential, unrelated.

irreligion *n* atheism, godlessness, impiety, ungodliness.

irreligious *adj* godless, ungodly, undevout; blasphemous, disrespectful, impious, irreverent, profane, ribald, wicked.

irremediable *adj* hopeless, incurable, immedicable, irrecoverable, irreparable, remediless.

irremissible *adj* binding, inexpiable, obligatory, unatonable, unpardonable.

irreparable *adj* irrecoverable, irremediable, irretrievable, remediless.

irreprehensible *adj* blameless, faultless, inculpable, innocent, irreproachable, irreprovable, unblamable.

irrepressible *adj* insuppressible, uncontrollable, unquenchable, unsmotherable.

irreproachable *adj* blameless, faultless, inculpable, innocent, irreprehensible, irreprovable, unblamable.

irresistible *adj* irrefragable, irrepressible, overpowering, overwhelming, resistless.

irresolute *adj* changeable, faltering, fickle, hesitant, hesitating, inconstant, mutable, spineless, uncertain, undecided, undetermined, unsettled, unstable, unsteady, vacillating, wavering.

irrespective *adj* independent, regardless.

irresponsible *adj* unaccountable; untrustworthy.

irretrievable *adj* incurable, irrecoverable, irremediable, irreparable, remediless.

irreverence *n* blasphemy, impiety, profaneness, profanity; disesteem, disrespect.

irreverent *adj* blasphemous, impious, irreligious, profane; disrespectful, slighting.

irreversible *adj* irrepealable, irrevocable, unalterable, unchangeable; changeless, immutable, invariable.

irrevocable *adj* irrepealable, irreversible, unalterable, unchangeable.

irrigate *vb* moisten, wash, water, wet.

irrigation *n* watering.

irritability *n* excitability, fretfulness, irascibility, peevishness, petulance, snappishness, susceptibility, testiness.

irritable *adj* captious, choleric, excitable, fiery, fretful, hasty, hot, irascible, passionate, peppery, peevish, pettish, petulant, snappish, splenetic, susceptible, testy, touchy, waspish.

irritate *vb* anger, annoy, chafe, enrage, exacerbate, exasperate, fret, incense, jar, nag, nettle, offend, provoke, rasp, rile, ruffle, vex; gall, tease; (*med*) excite, inflame, stimulate.

irritation *n* irritating; anger, exacerbation, exasperation, excitement, indignation, ire, passion, provocation, resentment, wrath; (*med*) excitation, inflammation, stimulation; burn, itch.

irruption *n* breaking in, bursting in; foray, incursion, inroad, invasion, raid.

island *n* atoll, isle, islet, reef.

isochronal *adj* isochronous, uniform.

isolate *vb* detach, dissociate, insulate, quarantine, segregate, separate, set apart.

isolated *adj* detached, separate, single, solitary.

isolation *n* detachment, disconnection, insulation, quarantine, segregation, separation; loneliness, solitariness, solitude.

issue *vb* come out, flow out, flow forth, gush, run, rush out, spout, spring, spurt, well; arise, come, emanate, ensue, flow, follow, originate, proceed, spring; end, eventuate, result, terminate; appear, come out, deliver, depart, debouch, discharge, emerge, emit, put forth, send out; distribute, give out; publish, utter. * *n* conclusion, consequence, consummation, denouement, end, effect, event, finale, outcome, result, termination, upshot; antagonism, contest, controversy; debouchment, delivering, delivery, discharge, emergence, emigration, emission, issuance; flux, outflow, outpouring, stream; copy, edition, number; egress, exit, outlet, passage out, vent, way out; escape, sally, sortie; children, offspring, posterity, progeny.

itch *vb* tingle. * *n* itching; burning, coveting, importunate craving, teasing desire, uneasy hankering.

itching *n* itch; craving, longing, importunate craving, desire, appetite, hankering.

item *adv* also, in like manner. * *n* article, detail, entry, particular, point.

iterate *vb* reiterate, repeat.

itinerant *adj* nomadic, peripatetic, roaming, roving, travelling, unsettled, wandering.

itinerary *n* guide, guidebook; circuit, route.

J

jabber *vb* chatter, gabble, prate, prattle.
jacket *n* casing, cover, sheath; anorak, blazer coat, doublet, jerkin.
jaded *adj* dull, exhausted, fatigued, satiated, tired, weary.
jagged *adj* cleft, divided, indented, notched, serrated, ragged, uneven.
jail, gaol *n* bridewell, (*sl*) clink, dungeon, lockup, (*sl*) nick, penitentiary, prison.
jam *vb* block, crowd, crush, press. * *n* block, crowd, crush, mass, pack, press.
jangle *vb* bicker, chatter, dispute, gossip, jar, quarrel, spar, spat, squabble, tiff, wrangle. * *n* clang, clangour, clash, din, dissonance.
jar[1] *vb* clash, grate, interfere, shake; bicker, contend, jangle, quarrel, spar, spat, squabble, tiff, wrangle; agitate, jolt, jounce, shake. * *n* clash, conflict, disaccord, discord, jangle, dissonance; agitation, jolt, jostle, shake, shaking, shock, start.
jar[2] *n* can, crock, cruse, ewer, flagon.
jarring *adj* conflicting, discordant, inconsistent, inconsonant, wrangling.
jargon *n* gabble, gibberish, nonsense, rigmarole: argot, cant, lingo, slang; chaos, confusion, disarray, disorder, jumble.
jaundiced *adj* biased, envious, prejudiced.
jaunt *n* excursion, ramble, tour, trip.
jaunty *adj* airy, cheery, garish, gay, fine, fluttering, showy, sprightly, unconcerned.
jealous *adj* distrustful, envious, suspicious; anxious, apprehensive, intolerant, solicitous, zealous.
jealousy *n* envy, suspicion, watchfulness.
jeer *vb* deride, despise, flout, gibe, jape, jest, mock, scoff, sneer, spurn, rail, ridicule, taunt. * *n* abuse, derision, mockery, sneer, ridicule, taunt.
jeopardize *vb* endanger, hazard, imperil, risk, venture.
jeopardy *n* danger, hazard, peril, risk, venture.
jerk *vb, n* flip, hitch, pluck, tweak, twitch, yank.
jest *vb* banter, joke, quiz. * *n* fun, joke, pleasantry, raillery, sport.
jester *n* humorist, joker, wag; buffoon, clown, droll, fool, harlequin, punch.
jibe *see* **gibe**.
jiffy *n* instant, moment, second, twinkling, trice.
jilt *vb* break with, deceive, disappoint, discard. * *n* coquette, flirt, light-o'-love.
jingle *vb* chink, clink, jangle, rattle, tinkle. * *n* chink, clink, jangle, rattle, tinkle; chorus, ditty, melody, song.
jocose *adj* comical, droll, facetious, funny, humorous, jesting, jocular, merry, sportive, waggish, witty.
jocund *adj* airy, blithe, cheerful, debonair, frolicsome, jolly, joyful, joyous, lively, merry, playful.
jog *vb* jostle, notify, nudge, push, remind, warn; canter, run, trot. * *n* push, reminder.
join *vb* add, annex, append, attach; cement, combine, conjoin, connect, couple, dovetail, link, unite, yoke; amalgamate, assemble, associate, confederate, consolidate.
joint *vb* fit, join, unite. * *adj* combined, concerted, concurrent, conjoint. * *n* connection, junction, juncture, hinge, splice.
joke *vb* banter, jest, frolic, rally. * *n* crank, jest, quip, quirk, witticism.
jolly *adj* airy, blithe, cheerful, frolicsome, gamesome, facetious, funny, gay, jovial, joyous, merry, mirthful, jocular, jocund, playful, sportive, sprightly, waggish; bouncing, chubby, lusty, plump, portly, stout.

jolt *vb* jar, shake, shock. * *n* jar, jolting, jounce, shaking.
jostle *vb* collide, elbow, hustle, joggle, shake, shoulder, shove.
jot *n* ace, atom, bit, corpuscle, iota, grain, mite, particle, scrap, whit.
journal *n* daybook, diary, log; gazette, magazine, newspapers, periodical.
journey *vb* ramble, roam, rove, travel: fare, go, proceed. * *n* excursion, expedition, jaunt, passage, pilgrimage, tour, travel, trip, voyage.
jovial *adj* airy, convivial, festive, jolly, joyous, merry, mirthful.
joy *n* beatification, beatitude, delight, ecstasy, exultation, gladness, glee, mirth, pleasure, rapture, ravishment, transport; bliss, felicity, happiness.
joyful *adj* blithe, blithesome, buoyant, delighted, elate, elated, exultant, glad, happy, jocund, jolly, joyous, merry, rejoicing.
jubilant *adj* exultant, exulting, rejoicing, triumphant.
judge *vb* conclude, decide, decree, determine, pronounce; adjudicate, arbitrate, condemn, doom, sentence, try, umpire; account, apprehend, believe, consider, deem, esteem, guess, hold, imagine, measure, reckon, regard, suppose, think; appreciate, estimate. * *n* adjudicator, arbiter, arbitrator, bencher, justice, magistrate, moderator, referee, umpire, connoisseur, critic.
judgment, judgement *n* brains, ballast, circumspection, depth, discernment, discretion, discrimination, intelligence, judiciousness, penetration, prudence, sagacity, sense, sensibility, taste, understanding, wisdom, wit; conclusion, consideration, decision, determination, estimation, notion, opinion, thought; adjudication, arbitration, award, censure, condemnation, decree, doom, sentence.
judicious *adj* cautious, considerate, cool, critical, discriminating, discreet, enlightened, provident, politic, prudent, rational, reasonable, sagacious, sensible, sober, solid, sound, staid, wise.
jug *n* cruse, ewer, flagon, pitcher, vessel.
juicy *adj* lush, moist, sappy, succulent, watery; entertaining, exciting, interesting, lively, racy, spicy.
jumble *vb* confound, confuse, disarrange, disorder, mix, muddle. * *n* confusion, disarrangement, disorder, medley, mess, mixture, muddle.
jump *vb* bound, caper, clear, hop, leap, skip, spring, vault. * *n* bound, caper, hop, leak, skip, spring, vault; fence, hurdle, obstacle; break, gap, interruption, space; advance, boost, increase, rise; jar, jolt, shock, start, twitch.
junction *n* combination, connection, coupling, hook-up, joining, linking, seam, union; conjunction, joint, juncture.
junta *n* cabal, clique, combination, confederacy, coterie, faction, gang, league, party, set.
just *adj* equitable, lawful, legitimate, reasonable, right, rightful; candid, even-handed, fair, fair-minded, impartial; blameless, conscientious, good, honest, honourable, pure, square, straightforward, virtuous; accurate, correct, exact, normal, proper, regular, true; condign, deserved, due, merited, suitable.
justice *n* accuracy, equitableness, equity, fairness, honesty, impartiality, justness, right; judge, justiciary.
justifiable *adj* defensible, fit, proper, right, vindicable, warrantable.
justification *n* defence, exculpation, excuse, exoneration, reason, vindication, warrant.
justify *vb* approve, defend, exculpate, excuse, exonerate, maintain, vindicate, support, warrant.
justness *n* accuracy, correctness, fitness, justice, precision, propriety.
juvenile *adj* childish, immature, puerile, young, youthful. * *n* boy, child, girl, youth.
juxtaposition *n* adjacency, contiguity, contact, proximity.

K

keen[1] *adj* ardent, eager, earnest, fervid, intense, vehement, vivid; acute, sharp; cutting; acrimonious, biting, bitter, caustic, poignant, pungent, sarcastic, severe; astute, discerning, intelligent, quick, sagacious, sharp-sighted, shrewd.

keen[2] *vb* bemoan, bewail, deplore, grieve, lament, mourn, sorrow, weep. * *n* coronach, dirge, elegy, lament, lamentation, monody, plaint, requiem, threnody.

keenness *n* ardour, eagerness, fervour, vehemence, zest; acuteness, sharpness; rigour, severity, sternness; acrimony, asperity, bitterness, causticity, causticness, pungency; astuteness, sagacity, shrewdness.

keep *vb* detain, hold, retain; continue, preserve; confine, detain, reserve, restrain, withhold; attend, guard, preserve, protect; adhere to, fulfil; celebrate, commemorate, honour, observe, perform, solemnize; maintain, support, sustain; husband, save, store; abide, dwell, lodge, stay, remain; endure, last. * *n* board, maintenance, subsistence, support; donjon, dungeon, stronghold, tower.

keeper *n* caretaker, conservator, curator, custodian, defender, gaoler, governor, guardian, jailer, superintendent, warden, warder, watchman.

keeping *n* care, charge, custody, guard, possession; feed, maintenance, support; agreement, conformity, congruity, consistency, harmony.

keepsake *n* memento, souvenir, token.

ken *n* cognizance, sight, view.

key *adj* basic, crucial, essential, important, major, principal. * *n* lock-opener, opener; clue, elucidation, explanation, guide, solution, translation; (*mus*) keynote, tonic; clamp, lever, wedge.

kick *vb* boot, punt; oppose, rebel, resist, spurn. * *n* force, intensity, power, punch, vitality; excitement, pleasure, thrill.

kidnap *vb* abduct, capture, carry off, remove, steal away.

kill *vb* assassinate, butcher, dispatch, destroy, massacre, murder, slaughter, slay.

kin *adj* akin, allied, cognate, kindred, related. * *n* affinity, consanguinity, relationship; connections, family, kindred, kinsfolk, relations, relatives, siblings.

kind[1] *adj* accommodating, amiable, beneficent, benevolent, benign, bland, bounteous, brotherly, charitable, clement, compassionate, complaisant, gentle, good, good-natured, forbearing, friendly, generous, gracious, humane, indulgent, lenient, mild, obliging, sympathetic, tender, tender-hearted.

kind[2] *n* breed, class, family, genus, race, set, species, type; brand, character, colour, denomination, description, form, make, manner, nature, persuasion, sort, stamp, strain, style,

kindle *vb* fire, ignite, inflame, light; animate, awaken, bestir, exasperate, excite, foment, incite, provoke, rouse, stimulate, stir, thrill, warm.

kindliness *n* amiability, benevolence, benignity, charity, compassion, friendliness, humanity, kindness, sympathy; gentleness, mildness, softness.

kindly *adj* appropriate, congenial, kindred, natural, proper; benevolent, considerate, friendly, gracious, humane, sympathetic, well-disposed. * *adv* agreeably, graciously, humanely, politely, thoughtfully.

kindness *n* benefaction, charity, favour; amiability, beneficence, benevolence, benignity, clemency, generosity, goodness, grace, humanity, kindliness, mildness, philanthropy, sympathy, tenderness.

kindred *adj* akin, allied, congenial, connected, related, sympathetic. * *n* affinity, consanguinity, flesh, relationship; folks, kin, kinsfolk, kinsmen, relations, relatives.

king *n* majesty, monarch, sovereign.

kingdom *n* dominion, empire, monarchy, rule, sovereignty, supremacy; region, tract; division, department, domain, province, realm.

kingly *adj* imperial, kinglike, monarchical, regal, royal, sovereign; august, glorious, grand, imperial, imposing, magnificent, majestic, noble, splendid.

kink *n* cramp, crick, curl, entanglement, knot, loop, twist; crochet, whim, wrinkle.

kinsfolk *n* kin, kindred, kinsmen, relations, relatives.

kit *n* equipment, implements, outfit, set, working.

knack *n* ability, address, adroitness, aptitude, aptness, dexterity, dextrousness, expertness, facility, quickness, readiness, skill.

knave *n* caitiff, cheat, miscreant, rascal, rogue, scamp, scapegrace, scoundrel, sharper, swindler, trickster, villain.

knavery *n* criminality, dishonesty, fraud, knavishness, rascality, scoundrelism, trickery, villainy.

knavish *adj* dishonest, fraudulent, rascally, scoundrelly, unprincipled, roguish, trickish, tricky, villainous.

knell *vb* announce, peal, ring, toll. * *n* chime, peal, ring, toll.

knife *vb* cut, slash, stab. * *n* blade, jackknife, lance.

knit *vb* connect, interlace, join, unite, weave.

knob *n* boss, bunch, hunch, lump, protuberance, stud.

knock *vb* clap, cuff, hit, rap, rattle, slap, strike, thump; beat, blow, box. * *n* blow, slap, smack, thump; blame, criticism, rejection, setback.

knoll *n* hill, hillock, mound.

knot *vb* complicate, entangle, gnarl, kink, tie, weave. * *n* complication, entanglement; connection, tie; joint, node, knag; bunch, rosette, tuft; band, cluster, clique, crew, gang, group, pack, set, squad.

knotty *adj* gnarled, hard, knaggy, knurled, knotted, rough, rugged; complex, difficult, harassing, intricate, involved, perplexing, troublesome.

know *vb* apprehend, comprehend, cognize, discern, perceive, recognize, see, understand; discriminate, distinguish.

knowing *adj* accomplished, competent, experienced, intelligent, proficient, qualified, skilful, well-informed; aware, conscious, percipient, sensible, thinking; cunning, expressive, significant.

knowingly *adv* consciously, intentionally, purposely, wittingly.

knowledge *n* apprehension, command, comprehension, discernment, judgment, perception, understanding, wit; acquaintance, acquirement, attainments, enlightenment, erudition, information, learning, lore, mastery, scholarship, science; cognition, cognizance, consciousness, ken, notice, prescience, recognition.

knowledgeable *adj* aware, conscious, experienced, well-informed; educated, intelligent, learned, scholarly.

knuckle *vb* cringe, crouch, stoop, submit, yield.

L

laborious *adj* assiduous, diligent, hardworking, indefatigable, industrious, painstaking, sedulous, toiling; arduous, difficult, fatiguing, hard, Herculean, irksome, onerous, tiresome, toilsome, wearisome.

labour *vb* drudge, endeavour, exert, strive, toil, travail, work. * *n* drudgery, effort, exertion, industry, pains, toil, work; childbirth, delivery, parturition.

labyrinth *n* entanglement, intricacy, maze, perplexity, windings.

labyrinthine *adj* confused, convoluted, intricate, involved, labyrinthian, labyrinthic, perplexing, winding.

lace *vb* attach, bind, fasten, intertwine, tie, twine. * *n* filigree, lattice, mesh, net, netting, network, openwork, web.

lacerate *vb* claw, cut, lancinate, mangle, rend, rip, sever, slash, tear, wound; afflict, harrow, rend, torture, wound.

lack *vb* need, want. * *n* dearth, default, defectiveness, deficiency, deficit, destitution, insufficiency, need, scantiness, scarcity, shortcoming, shortness, want.

lackadaisical *adj* languishing, sentimental, pensive.

laconic *adj* brief, compact, concise, pithy, sententious, short, succinct, terse.

lad *n* boy, schoolboy, stripling, youngster, youth.

lading *n* burden, cargo, freight, load.

ladylike *adj* courtly, genteel, refined, well-bred.

lag *vb* dawdle, delay, idle, linger, loiter, saunter, tarry.

laggard *n* idler, lingerer, loiterer, lounger, saunterer, sluggard.

lair *n* burrow, couch, den, form, resting place.

lambent *adj* flickering, gliding, gleaming, licking, touching, twinkling.

lame *vb* cripple, disable, hobble. * *adj* crippled, defective, disabled, halt, hobbling, limping; feeble, insufficient, poor, unsatisfactory, weak.

lament *vb* complain, grieve, keen, moan, mourn, sorrow, wail, weep; bemoan, bewail, deplore, regret. * *n* complaint, lamentation, moan, moaning, plaint, wailing; coronach, dirge, elegy, keen, monody, requiem, threnody.

lamentable *adj* deplorable, doleful, grievous, lamented, melancholy, woeful; contemptible, miserable, pitiful, poor, wretched.

lamentation *n* dirge, grief, lament, moan, moaning, mourning, plaint, ululation, sorrow, wailing.

lampoon *vb* calumniate, defame, lash, libel, parody, ridicule, satirize, slander. * *n* calumny, defamation, libel, parody, pasquinade, parody, satire, slander.

land *vb* arrive, debark, disembark. * *n* earth, ground, soil; country, district, province, region, reservation, territory, tract, weald.

landlord *n* owner, proprietor; host, hotelier, innkeeper.

landscape *n* prospect, scene, view.

language *n* dialect, speech, tongue, vernacular; conversation; expression, idiom, jargon, parlance, phraseology, slang, style, terminology; utterance, voice.

languid *adj* drooping, exhausted, faint, feeble, flagging, languishing, pining, weak; dull, heartless, heavy, inactive, listless, lukewarm, slow, sluggish, spiritless, torpid.

languish *vb* decline, droop, fade, fail, faint, pine, sicken, sink, wither.

languor *n* debility, faintness, feebleness, languidness, languishment, weakness; apathy, ennui, heartlessness, heaviness, lethargy, listlessness, torpidness, torpor, weariness.

lank *adj* attenuated, emaciated, gaunt, lean, meagre, scraggy, slender, skinny, slim, starveling, thin.

lap[1] *vb* drink, lick, mouth, tongue; plash, ripple, splash, wash; quaff, sip, sup, swizzle, tipple. * *n* draught, dram, drench, drink, gulp, lick, swig, swill, quaff, sip, sup, suck; plash, splash, wash.

lap[2] *vb* cover, enfold, fold, turn, twist, swaddle, wrap; distance, pass, outdistance, overlap. * *n* fold, flap, lappet, lapel, ply, plait; ambit, beat, circle, circuit, cycle, loop, orbit, revolution, round, tour, turn, walk.

lapse *vb* glide, sink, slide, slip; err, fail, fall. * *n* course, flow, gliding; declension, decline, fall; error, fault, indiscretion, misstep, shortcoming, slip.

larceny *n* pilfering, robbery, stealing, theft, thievery.

large *adj* big, broad, bulky, colossal, elephantine, enormous, heroic, great, huge, immense, vast; broad, expanded, extensive, spacious, wide; abundant, ample, copious, full, liberal, plentiful; capacious, comprehensive.

lascivious *adj* concupiscent, immodest, incontinent, goatish, lecherous, lewd, libidinous, loose, lubricious, lustful, prurient, salacious, sensual, unchaste, voluptuous, wanton.

lash[1] *vb* belay, bind, strap, tie; fasten, join, moor, pinion, secure.

lash[2] *vb* beat, castigate, chastise, flagellate, flail, flay, flog, goad, scourge, swinge, thrash, whip; assail, censure, excoriate, lampoon, satirize, trounce. * *n* scourge, strap, thong, whip; cut, slap, smack, stroke, stripe.

lass *n* damsel, girl, lassie, maiden, miss.

lassitude *n* dullness, exhaustion, fatigue, languor, languidness, prostration, tiredness, weariness.

last[1] *vb* abide, carry on, continue, dwell, endure, extend, maintain, persist, prevail, remain, stand, stay, survive.

last[2] *adj* hindermost, hindmost, latest; conclusive, final, terminal, ultimate; eventual, endmost, extreme, farthest, ultimate; greatest, highest, maximal, maximum, most, supreme, superlative, utmost; latest, newest; aforegoing, foregoing, latter, preceding; departing, farewell, final, leaving, parting, valedictory. * *n* conclusion, consummation, culmination, end, ending, finale, finis, finish, termination.

last[3] *n* cast, form, matrix, mould, shape, template.

lasting *adj* abiding, durable, enduring, fixed, perennial, permanent, perpetual, stable.

lastly *adv* conclusively, eventually, finally, ultimately.

late *adj* behindhand, delayed, overdue, slow, tardy; deceased, former; recent. * *adv* lately, recently, sometime; tardily.

latent *adj* abeyant, concealed, hidden, invisible, occult, secret, unseen, veiled.

latitude *n* amplitude, breadth, compass, extent, range, room, scope; freedom, indulgence, liberty; laxity.

latter *adj* last, latest, modern, recent.

lattice *n* espalier, grating, latticework, trellis.

laud *vb* approve, celebrate, extol, glorify, magnify, praise.

laudable *adj* commendable, meritorious, praiseworthy.

laugh *vb* cackle, chortle, chuckle, giggle, guffaw, snicker, snigger, titter. * *n* chortle, chuckle, giggle, guffaw, laughter, titter.

laughable *adj* amusing, comical, diverting, droll, farcical, funny, ludicrous, mirthful, ridiculous.

laughter *n* cackle, chortle, chuckle, glee, giggle, guffaw, laugh, laughing.

launch *vb* cast, dart, dispatch, hurl, lance, project, throw; descant, dilate, enlarge, expiate; begin, commence, inaugurate, open, start.

lavish *vb* dissipate, expend, spend, squander, waste. * *adj* excessive, extravagant, generous, immoderate, overliberal, prodigal, profuse, thriftless, unrestrained, unstinted, unthrifty, wasteful.

law *n* act, code, canon, command, commandment, covenant, decree, edict, enactment, order, precept, principle, statute, regulation, rule; jurisprudence; litigation, process, suit.

lawful *adj* constitutional, constituted, legal, legalized, legitimate; allowable, authorized, permissible, warrantable; equitable, rightful, just, proper, valid.

lawless *adj* anarchic, anarchical, chaotic, disorderly, insubordinate, rebellious, reckless, riotous, seditious, wild.

lawyer *n* advocate, attorney, barrister, counsel, counsellor, pettifogger, solicitor.

lax *adj* loose, relaxed, slow; drooping, flabby, soft; neglectful, negligent, remiss; dissolute, immoral, licentious, seditious, wild.

lay[1] *vb* deposit, establish, leave, place, plant, posit, put, set, settle, spread; arrange, dispose, locate, organize, position; bear, produce; advance, lodge, offer, submit; allocate, allot, ascribe, assign, attribute, charge, impute; concoct, contrive, design, plan, plot, prepare; apply, burden, encumber, impose, saddle, tax; bet, gamble, hazard, risk, stake, wager; allay, alleviate, appease, assuage, calm, relieve, soothe, still, suppress; disclose, divulge, explain, reveal, show, unveil; acquire, grab, grasp, seize; assault, attack, beat up; discover, find, unearth; bless, confirm, consecrate, ordain. * *n* arrangement, array, form, formation; attitude, aspect, bearing, demeanour, direction, lie, pose, position, posture, set.

lay[2] *adj* amateur, inexpert, nonprofessional; civil, laic, laical, nonclerical, nonecclesiastical, nonreligious, secular, temporal, unclerical.

lay[3] *n* ballad, carol, ditty, lied, lyric, ode, poem, rhyme, round, song, verse.

layer *n* bed, course, lay, seam, stratum.

laziness *n* idleness, inactivity, indolence, slackness, sloth, fulness, sluggishness, tardiness.

lazy *adj* idle, inactive, indolent, inert, slack, slothful, slow, sluggish, supine, torpid.

lead *vb* conduct, deliver, direct, draw, escort, guide; front, head, precede; advance, excel, outstrip, pass; allure, entice, induce, persuade, prevail; conduce, contribute, serve, tend. * *adj* chief, first, foremost, main, primary, prime, principal. * *n* direction, guidance, leadership; advance; precedence, priority.

leader *n* conductor, director, guide; captain, chief, chieftain, commander, head; superior, dominator, victor.

leading *adj* governing, ruling; capital, chief, first, foremost, highest, principal, superior.

league *vb* ally, associate, band, combine, confederate, unite. * *n* alliance, association, coalition, combination, combine, confederacy, confederation, consortium, union.

leak *vb* drip, escape, exude, ooze, pass, percolate, spill. * *n* chink, crack, crevice, hole, fissure, oozing, opening; drip, leakage, leaking, percolation.

lean[1] *adj* bony, emaciated, gaunt, lank, meagre, poor, skinny, thin; dull, barren, jejune, meagre, tame; inadequate, pitiful, scanty, slender; bare, barren, infertile, unproductive.

lean[2] *vb* incline, slope; bear, recline, repose, rest; confide, depend, rely, trust.

leaning *n* aptitude, bent, bias, disposition, inclination, liking, predilection, proneness, propensity, tendency.

leap *vb* bound, clear, jump, spring, vault; caper, frisk, gambol, hop, skip. * *n* bound, jump, spring, vault; caper, frisk, gambol, hop, skip.

learn *vb* acquire, ascertain, attain, collect, gain, gather, hear, memorize.

learned *adj* erudite, lettered, literate, scholarly, well-read; expert, experienced, knowing, skilled, versed, well-informed.

learner *n* beginner, novice, pupil, student, tyro.

learning *n* acquirements, attainments, culture, education, information, knowledge, lore, scholarship, tuition.

least *adj* meanest, minutest, smallest, tiniest.

leave[1] *vb* abandon, decamp, go, quit, vacate, withdraw; desert, forsake, relinquish, renounce; commit, consign, refer; cease, desist from, discontinue, refrain, stop; allow, let, let alone, permit; bequeath, demise, desist, will.

leave[2] *n* allowance, liberty, permission, licence, sufferance; departure, retirement, withdrawal; adieu, farewell, goodbye.

leaven *vb* ferment, lighten, raise; colour, elevate, imbue, inspire, lift, permeate, tinge; infect, vitiate. * *n* barm, ferment, yeast; influence, inspiration.

leavings *npl* bits, dregs, fragments, leftovers, pieces, relics, remains, remnants, scraps.

lecherous *adj* carnal, concupiscent, incontinent, lascivious, lewd, libidinous, lubricious, lustful, wanton, salacious, unchaste.

lechery *n* concupiscence, lasciviousness, lewdness, lubriciousness, lubricity, lust, salaciousness, salacity.

lecture *vb* censure, chide, reprimand, reprove, scold, sermonize; address, harangue, teach. * *n* censure, lecturing, lesson, reprimand, reproof, scolding; address, discourse, prelection.

ledge *n* projection, ridge, shelf.

lees *npl* dregs, precipitate, refuse, sediment, settlings.

leg *n* limb, prop.

legacy *n* bequest, gift, heirloom; heritage, inheritance, tradition.

legal *adj* allowable, authorized, constitutional, lawful, legalized, legitimate, proper, sanctioned.

legalize *vb* authorize, legitimate, legitimatize, legitimize, permit, sanction.

legend *n* fable, fiction, myth, narrative, romance, story, tale.

legendary *adj* fabulous, fictitious, mythical, romantic.

legible *adj* clear, decipherable, fair, distinct, plain, readable; apparent, discoverable, recognizable, manifest.

legion *n* army, body, cohort, column, corps, detachment, detail, division, force, maniple, phalanx, platoon; squad; army, horde, host, multitude, number, swarm, throng. * *adj* many, multitudinous, myriad, numerous.

legislate *vb* enact, ordain.

legitimacy *n* lawfulness, legality; genuineness.

legitimate *adj* authorized, lawful, legal, sanctioned; genuine, valid; correct, justifiable, logical, reasonable, warrantable, warranted.

leisure *n* convenience, ease, freedom, liberty, opportunity, recreation, retirement, vacation.

lend *vb* advance, afford, bestow, confer, furnish, give, grant, impart, loan, supply.

lengthen *vb* elongate, extend, produce, prolong, stretch; continue, protract.

lengthy *adj* diffuse, lengthened, long, long-drawn-out, prolix, prolonged, protracted.

lenience, leniency *n* clemency, compassion, forbearance, gentleness, lenity, mercy, mildness, tenderness.

lenient *adj* assuasive, lenitive, mitigating, mitigative, softening, soothing; clement, easy, forbearing, gentle, humouring, indulgent, long-suffering, merciful, mild, tender, tolerant.

lesion *n* derangement, disorder, hurt, injury.

less *adj* baser, inferior, lower, smaller; decreased, fewer, lesser, reduced, smaller, shorter; * *adv* barely, below, least, under; decreasingly. * *prep* excepting, lacking, minus, sans, short of, without.

lessen *vb* abate, abridge, contract, curtail, decrease, diminish, narrow, reduce, shrink; degrade, lower; dwindle, weaken.

lesson *n* exercise, task; instruction, precept; censure, chiding, lecture, lecturing, rebuke, reproof, scolding.

let[1] *vb* admit, allow, authorize, permit, suffer; charter, hire, lease, rent.

let[2] *vb* hinder, impede, instruct, prevent. * *n* hindrance, impediment, interference, obstacle, obstruction, restriction.

lethal *adj* deadly, destructive, fatal, mortal, murderous.

lethargic *adj* apathetic, comatose, drowsy, dull, heavy, inactive, inert, sleepy, stupid, stupefied, torpid.

lethargy *n* apathy, coma, drowsiness, dullness, hypnotism, inactiveness, inactivity, inertia, sleepiness, sluggishness, stupefaction, stupidity, stupor, torpor.

letter *n* epistle, missive, note.

lettered *adj* bookish, educated, erudite, learned, literary, versed, well-read.

levee *n* ceremony, entertainment, reception, party, soiree; embankment.

level *vb* equalize, flatten, horizontalize, smooth; demolish, destroy, raze; aim, direct, point. * *adj* equal, even, flat, flush, horizontal, plain, plane, smooth. * *n* altitude, degree, equality, evenness, plain, plane, smoothness; deck, floor, layer, stage, storey, tier.

levity *n* buoyancy, facetiousness, fickleness, flightiness, flippancy, frivolity, giddiness, inconstancy, levity, volatility.

levy *vb* collect, exact, gather, tax; call, muster, raise, summon. * *n* duty, tax.

lewd *adj* despicable, impure, lascivious, libidinous, licentious, loose, lustful, profligate, unchaste, vile, wanton, wicked.

liability *n* accountableness, accountability, duty, obligation, responsibility, tendency; exposedness; debt, indebtedness, obligation.

liable *adj* accountable, amenable, answerable, bound, responsible; exposed, likely, obnoxious, subject.

liaison *n* amour, intimacy, intrigue; connection, relation, union.

libel *vb* calumniate, defame, lampoon, satirize, slander, vilify. * *n* calumny, defamation, lampoon, satire, slander, vilification, vituperation.

liberal *adj* beneficent, bountiful, charitable, disinterested, free, generous, munificent, open-hearted, princely, unselfish; broad-minded, catholic, chivalrous, enlarged, high-minded, honourable, magnanimous, tolerant, unbiased, unbigoted; abundant, ample, bounteous, full, large, plentiful, unstinted; humanizing, liberalizing, refined, refining.

liberality *n* beneficence, bountifulness, bounty, charity, disinterestedness, generosity, kindness, munificence; benefaction, donation, gift, gratuity, present; broad-mindedness, catholicity, candour, impartiality, large-mindedness, magnanimity, toleration.

liberate *vb* deliver, discharge, disenthral, emancipate, free, manumit, ransom, release.

libertine *adj* corrupt, depraved, dissolute, licentious, profligate, rakish. * *n* debauchee, lecher, profligate, rake, roue, voluptuary.

liberty *n* emancipation, freedom, independence, liberation, self-direction, self-government; franchise, immunity, privilege; leave, licence, permission.

libidinous *adj* carnal, concupiscent, debauched, impure, incontinent, lascivious, lecherous, lewd, loose, lubricious, lustful, salacious, sensual, unchaste, wanton, wicked.

licence *n* authorization, leave, permission, privilege, right; certificate, charter, dispensation, imprimatur, permit, warrant; anarchy, disorder, freedom, lawlessness, laxity, liberty.

license *vb* allow, authorize, grant, permit, warrant; suffer, tolerate.

licentious *adj* disorderly, riotous, uncontrolled, uncurbed, ungovernable, unrestrained, unruly, wanton; debauched, dissolute, lax, libertine, loose, profligate, rakish; immoral, impure, lascivious, lecherous, lewd, libertine, libidinous, lustful, sensual, unchaste, wicked.

lick *vb* beat, flog, spank, thrash; lap, taste. * *n* blow, slap, stroke; salt-spring.

lie[1] *vb* couch, recline, remain, repose, rest; consist, pertain.

lie[2] *vb* equivocate, falsify, fib, prevaricate, romance. * *n* equivocation, falsehood, falsification, fib, misrepresentation, prevarication, untruth; delusion, illusion.

lief *adv* freely, gladly, willingly.

life *n* activity, alertness, animation, briskness, energy, sparkle, spirit, sprightliness, verve, vigour, vivacity; behaviour, conduct, deportment; being, duration, existence, lifetime; autobiography, biography, curriculum vitae, memoirs, story.

lifeless *adj* dead, deceased, defunct, extinct, inanimate; cold, dull, flat, frigid, inert, lethargic, passive, pulseless, slow, sluggish, tame, torpid.

lift *vb* elevate, exalt, hoist, raise, uplift. * *n* aid, assistance, help; elevator.

light[1] *vb* alight, land, perch, settle. * *adj* porous, sandy, spongy, well-leavened; loose, sandy; free, portable, unburdened, unencumbered; inconsiderable, moderate, negligible, slight, small, trifling, trivial, unimportant; ethereal, feathery, flimsy, gossamer, insubstantial, weightless; easy, effortless, facile; fickle, frivolous, unsettled, unsteady, volatile; airy, buoyant, carefree, light-hearted, lightsome; unaccented, unstressed, weak.

light[2] *vb* conflagrate, fire, ignite, inflame, kindle; brighten, illume, illuminate, illumine, luminate, irradiate, lighten. * *adj* bright, clear, fair, lightsome, luminous, pale, pearly, whitish. * *n* dawn, day, daybreak, sunrise; blaze, brightness, effulgence, gleam, illumination, luminosity, phosphorescence, radiance, ray; candle, lamp, lantern, lighthouse, taper, torch; comprehension, enlightenment, information, insight, instruction, knowledge; elucidation, explanation, illustration; attitude, construction, interpretation, observation, reference, regard, respect, view.

lighten[1] *vb* allay, alleviate, ease, mitigate, palliate; disburden, disencumber, relieve, unburden, unload.

lighten[2] *vb* brighten, gleam, shine; light, illume, illuminate, illumine, irradiate; enlighten, inform; emit, flash.

light-headed *adj* dizzy, giddy, vertiginous; confused, delirious, wandering; addle-pated, frivolous, giddy, heedless, indiscreet, light, rattle-brained, thoughtless, volatile.

light-hearted *adj* blithe, blithesome, carefree, cheerful, frolicsome, gay, glad, gladsome, gleeful, happy, jocund, jovial, joyful, lightsome, merry.

lightness *n* flightiness, frivolity, giddiness, levity, volatility; agility, buoyancy, facility.

like[1] *vb* approve, please; cherish, enjoy, love, relish; esteem, fancy, regard; choose, desire, elect, list, prefer, select, wish. * *n* liking, partiality, preference.

like[2] *adj* alike, allied, analogous, cognate, corresponding, parallel, resembling, similar; equal, same; likely, probable. * *adv* likely, probably. * *n* counterpart, equal, match, peer, twin.

likelihood *n* probability, verisimilitude.

likely *adj* credible, liable, possible, probable; agreeable, appropriate, convenient, likable, pleasing, suitable, well-adapted, well-suited. * *adv* doubtlessly, presumably, probably.

likeness *n* appearance, form, parallel, resemblance, semblance, similarity, similitude; copy, counterpart, effigy, facsimile, image, picture, portrait, representation.

liking *n* desire, fondness, partiality, wish; appearance, bent, bias, disposition, inclination, leaning, penchant, predisposition, proneness, propensity, tendency, turn.

limb *n* arm, extremity, leg, member; bough, branch, offshoot.

limit *vb* bound, circumscribe, define; check, condition, hinder, restrain, restrict. * *n* bound, boundary, bourn, confine, frontier, march, precinct, term, termination, terminus; check, hindrance, obstruction, restraint, restriction.

limitation *n* check, constraint, restraint, restriction.

limitless *adj* boundless, endless, eternal, illimitable, immeasurable, infinite, never-ending, unbounded, undefined, unending, unlimited.

limp[1] *vb* halt, hitch, hobble, totter. * *n* hitch, hobble, shamble, shuffle, totter.

limp[2] *adj* drooping, droopy, floppy, sagging, weak; flabby, flaccid, flexible, limber, pliable, relaxed, slack, soft.

limpid *adj* bright, clear, crystal, crystalline, lucid, pellucid, pure, translucent, transparent.

line *vb* align, line up, range, rank, regiment; border, bound, edge, fringe, hem, interline, march, rim, verge; seam, stripe, streak, striate, trace; carve, chisel, crease, cut, crosshatch; define, delineate, describe. * n mark, streak, stripe; cable, cord, rope, string, thread; rank, row; ancestry, family, lineage, race, succession;

course, method; business, calling, employment, job, occupation, post, pursuit.

lineage *n* ancestry, birth, breed, descendants, descent, extraction, family, forebears, forefathers, genealogy, house, line, offspring, progeny, race.

lineament *n* feature, line, outline, trait.

linen *n* cloth, fabric, flax, lingerie.

linger *vb* dally, dawdle, delay, idle, lag, loiter, remain, saunter, stay, tarry, wait.

link *vb* bind, conjoin, connect, fasten, join, tie, unite. * *n* bond, connection, connective, copula, coupler, joint, juncture; division, member, part, piece.

liquefy *vb* dissolve, fuse, melt, thaw.

liquid *adj* fluid; clear, dulcet, flowing, mellifluous, mellifluent, melting, soft. * *n* fluid, liquor.

list[1] *vb* alphabetize, catalogue, chronicle, codify, docket, enumerate, file, index, inventory, record, register, tabulate, tally; enlist, enroll; choose, desire, elect, like, please, prefer, wish. * *n* catalogue, enumeration, index, inventory, invoice, register, roll, schedule, scroll, series, table, tally; border, bound, limit; border, edge, selvedge, strip, stripe; fillet, listel.

list[2] *vb* cant, heel, incline, keel, lean, pitch, tilt, tip. * *n* cant, inclination, incline, leaning, pitch, slope, tilt, tip.

listen *vb* attend, eavesdrop, hark, hear, hearken, heed, obey, observe.

listless *adj* apathetic, careless, heedless, impassive, inattentive, indifferent, indolent, languid, torpid, vacant, supine, thoughtless, vacant.

listlessness *n* apathy, carelessness, heedlessness, impassivity, inattention, indifference, indolence, languidness, languor, supineness, thoughtlessness, torpor, torpidity, vacancy.

literally *adv* actually, really; exactly, precisely, rigorously, strictly.

literary *adj* bookish, book-learned, erudite, instructed, learned, lettered, literate, scholarly, well-read.

literature *n* erudition, learning, letters, lore, writings.

lithe *adj* flexible, flexile, limber, pliable, pliant, supple.

litigation *n* contending, contest, disputing, lawsuit.

litigious *adj* contentious, disputatious, quarrelsome; controvertible, disputable.

litter *vb* derange, disarrange, disorder, scatter, strew; bear. * *n* bedding, couch, palanquin, sedan, stretcher; confusion, disarray, disorder, mess, untidiness; fragments, rubbish, shreds, trash.

little *adj* diminutive, infinitesimal, minute, small, tiny, wee; brief, short, small; feeble, inconsiderable, insignificant, moderate, petty, scanty, slender, slight, trivial, unimportant, weak; contemptible, illiberal, mean, narrow, niggardly, paltry, selfish, stingy. * *n* handful, jot, modicum, pinch, pittance, trifle, whit.

live[1] *vb* be, exist; continue, endure, last, remain, survive; abide, dwell, reside; fare, feed, nourish, subsist, support; continue, lead, pass.

live[2] *adj* alive, animate, living, quick; burning, hot, ignited; bright, brilliant, glowing, lively, vivid; active, animated, earnest, glowing, wide-awake.

livelihood *n* living, maintenance, subsistence, support, sustenance.

liveliness *n* activity, animation, briskness, gaiety, spirit, sprightliness, vivacity.

lively *adj* active, agile, alert, brisk, energetic, nimble, quick, smart, stirring, supple, vigorous, vivacious; airy, animated, blithe, blithesome, buoyant, frolicsome, gleeful, jocund, jolly, merry, spirited, sportive, sprightly, spry; bright, brilliant, clear, fresh, glowing, strong, vivid; dynamic, forcible, glowing, impassioned, intense, keen, nervous, piquant, racy, sparkling, strenuous, vigorous.

living *adj* alive, breathing, existing, live, organic, quick; active, lively, quickening. * *n* livelihood, maintenance, subsistence, support; estate, keeping; benefice.

load *vb* freight, lade; burden, cumber, encumber, oppress, weigh. * *n* burden, freightage, pack, weight; cargo, freight, lading; clog, deadweight, encumbrance, incubus, oppression, pressure.

loafer *n* (*sl*) bum, idler, lounger, vagabond, vagrant.

loath *adj* averse, backward, disinclined, indisposed, reluctant, unwilling.

loathe *vb* abhor, abominate, detest, dislike, hate, recoil.

loathing *n* abhorrence, abomination, antipathy, aversion, detestation, disgust, hatred, horror, repugnance, revulsion.

loathsome *adj* disgusting, nauseating, nauseous, offensive, palling, repulsive, revolting, sickening; abominable, abhorrent, detestable, execrable, hateful, odious, shocking.

local *adj* limited, neighbouring, provincial, regional, restricted, sectional, territorial, topical.

locality *n* location, neighbourhood, place, position, site, situation, spot.

locate *vb* determine, establish, fix, place, set, settle.

lock[1] *vb* bolt, fasten, padlock, seal; confine; clog, impede, restrain, stop; clasp, embrace, encircle, enclose, grapple, hug, join, press. * *n* bolt, fastening, padlock; embrace, grapple, hug.

lock[2] *n* curl, ringlet, tress, tuft.

lodge *vb* deposit, fix, settle; fix, place, plant; accommodate, cover, entertain, harbour, quarter, shelter; abide, dwell, inhabit, live, reside, rest; remain, rest, sojourn, stay, stop. * *n* cabin, cot, cottage, hovel, hut, shed; cave, den, haunt, lair; assemblage, assembly, association club, group, society.

lodging *n* abode, apartment, dwelling, habitation, quarters, residence; cover, harbour, protection, refuge, shelter.

loftiness *n* altitude, elevation, height; arrogance, haughtiness, pride, vanity; dignity, grandeur, sublimity.

lofty *adj* elevated, high, tall, towering; arrogant, haughty, proud; eminent, exalted, sublime; dignified, imposing, majestic, stately.

logical *adj* close, coherent, consistent, dialectical, sound, valid; discriminating, rational, reasoned.

loiter *vb* dally, dawdle, delay, dilly-dally, idle, lag, linger, saunter, stroll, tarry.

loneliness *n* isolation, retirement, seclusion, solitariness, solitude; desolation, dreariness, forlornness.

lonely *adj* apart, dreary, isolated, lonesome, remote, retired, secluded, separate, sequestrated, solitary; alone, lone, companionless, friendless, unaccompanied; deserted, desolate, forlorn, forsaken, withdrawn.

lonesome *adj* cheerless, deserted, desolate, dreary, gloomy, lone, lonely.

long[1] *vb* anticipate, await, expect; aspire, covet, crave, desire, hanker, lust, pine, wish, yearn.

long[2] *adj* drawn-out, extended, extensive, far-reaching, lengthy, prolonged, protracted, stretched; diffuse, long-winded, prolix, tedious, wearisome; backward, behindhand, dilatory, lingering, slack, slow, tardy.

longing *n* aspiration, coveting, craving, desire, hankering, hunger, pining, yearning.

long-suffering *adj* enduring, forbearing, patient. * *n* clemency, endurance, forbearing.

look *vb* behold, examine, notice, see, search; consider, inspect, investigate, observe, study, contemplate, gaze, regard, scan, survey, view; anticipate, await, expect; heed, mind, watch; face, front; appear, seem. * *n* examination, gaze, glance, peep, peer, search; appearance, aspect, complexion; air, aspect, manner, mien.

loophole *n* aperture, crenellation, loop, opening; excuse, plea, pretence, pretext, subterfuge.

loose *vb* free, liberate, release, unbind, undo, unfasten, unlash, unlock, untie; ease, loosen, relax, slacken; detach, disconnect, disengage. * *adj* unbound, unconfined, unfastened, unsewn, untied; disengaged, free, unattached; relaxed; diffuse, diffusive, prolix, rambling, unconnected; ill-defined, indefinite, indeterminate, indistinct, vague; careless, heedless, negligent, lax, slack; debauched, dissolute, immoral, licentious, unchaste, wanton.

loosen *vb* liberate, relax, release, separate, slacken, unbind, unloose, untie.

looseness *n* easiness, slackness; laxity, levity; lewdness, unchastity, wantonness, wickedness; diarrhoea, flux.

loot *vb* pillage, plunder, ransack, rifle, rob, sack. * *n* booty, plunder, spoil.

lop *vb* cut, truncate; crop, curtail, dock, prune; detach, dissever, sever.

loquacious *adj* garrulous, talkative, voluble, wordy; noisy, speaking, talking; babbling, blabbing, tattling, tell-tale.

loquacity *n* babbling, chattering, gabbling, garrulity, loquaciousness, talkativeness, volubility.

lord *n* earl, noble, nobleman, peer, viscount; governor, king, liege, master, monarch, prince, ruler, seigneur, seignior, sovereign, superior; husband, spouse.

lordly *adj* aristocratic, dignified, exalted, grand, lofty, majestic, noble; arrogant, despotic, domineering, haughty, imperious, insolent, masterful, overbearing, proud, tyrannical; large, liberal.

lordship *n* authority, command, control, direction, domination, dominion, empire, government, rule, sovereignty, sway; manor, domain, seigneury, seigniory.

lore *n* erudition, knowledge, learning, letters, scholarship; admonition, advice, counsel, doctrine, instruction, lesson, teaching, wisdom.

lose *vb* deprive, dispossess, forfeit, miss; dislodge, displace, mislay, misspend, squander, waste; decline, fall, succumb, yield.

loss *n* deprivation, failure, forfeiture, privation; casualty, damage, defeat, destruction, detriment, disadvantage, injury, overthrow, ruin; squandering, waste.

lost *adj* astray, missing; forfeited, missed, unredeemed; dissipated, misspent, squandered, wasted; bewildered, confused, distracted, perplexed, puzzled; absent, absent-minded, abstracted, dreamy, napping, preoccupied; abandoned, corrupt, debauched, depraved, dissolute, graceless, hardened, incorrigible, irreclaimable, licentious, profligate, reprobate, shameless, unchaste, wanton; destroyed, ruined.

lot *n* allotment, apportionment, destiny, doom, fate; accident, chance, fate, fortune, hap, haphazard, hazard; division, parcel, part, portion.

loth *adj* averse, disinclined, disliking, reluctant, unwilling

loud *adj* high-sounding, noisy, resounding, sonorous; deafening, stentorian, strong, stunning; boisterous, clamorous, noisy, obstreperous, tumultuous, turbulent, uproarious, vociferous; emphatic, impressive, positive, vehement; flashy, gaudy, glaring, loud, ostentatious, showy, vulgar.

lounge *vb* loll, recline, sprawl; dawdle, idle, loaf, loiter.

love *vb* adore, like, worship. * *n* accord, affection, amity, courtship, delight, fondness, friendship, kindness, regard, tenderness, warmth; adoration, amour, ardour, attachment, passion; devotion, inclination, liking; benevolence, charity, goodwill.

lovely *adj* beautiful, charming, delectable, delightful, enchanting, exquisite, graceful, pleasing, sweet, winning; admirable, adorable, amiable.

loving *adj* affectionate, dear, fond, kind, tender.

low[1] *vb* bellow, moo.

low[2] *adj* basal, depressed, profound; gentle, grave, soft, subdued; cheap, humble, mean, plebeian, vulgar; abject, base, base-minded, degraded, dirty, grovelling, ignoble, low-minded, menial, scurvy, servile, shabby, slavish, vile; derogatory, disgraceful, dishonourable, disreputable, unbecoming, undignified, ungentlemanly, unhandsome, unmanly; exhausted, feeble, reduced, weak; frugal, plain, poor, simple, spare; lowly, reverent, submissive; dejected, depressed, dispirited.

lower[1] *vb* depress, drop, sink, subside; debase, degrade, disgrace, humble, humiliate, reduce; abate, decrease, diminish, lessen. * *adj* baser, inferior, less, lesser, shorter, smaller; subjacent, under.

lower[2] *vb* blacken, darken, frown, glower, threaten.

lowering *adj* dark, clouded, cloudy, lurid,

murky, overcast, threatening.

lowliness *n* humbleness, humility, meekness, self-abasement, submissiveness.

lowly *adj* gentle, humble, meek, mild, modest, plain, poor, simple, unassuming, unpretending, unpretentious; low-born, mean, servile.

loyal *adj* constant, devoted, faithful, patriotic, true.

loyalty *n* allegiance, constancy, devotion, faithfulness, fealty, fidelity, patriotism.

lubricious *adj* slippery, smooth; uncertain, unstable, wavering; impure, incontinent, lascivious, lecherous, lewd, libidinous, licentious, lustful, salacious, unchaste, wanton.

lucid *adj* beaming, bright, brilliant, luminous, radiant, resplendent, shining, clear, crystalline, diaphanous, limpid, lucent, pellucid, pure, transparent; clear, distinct, evident, intelligible, obvious, perspicuous, plain; reasonable, sane, sober, sound.

luck *n* accident, casualty, chance, fate, fortune, hap, haphazard, hazard, serendipity, success.

luckless *adj* ill-fated, ill-starred, unfortunate, unhappy, unlucky, unpropitious, unprosperous, unsuccessful.

lucky *adj* blessed, favoured, fortunate, happy, successful; auspicious, favourable, propitious, prosperous.

lucrative *adj* advantageous, gainful, paying, profitable, remunerative.

ludicrous *adj* absurd, burlesque, comic, comical, droll, farcical, funny, laughable, odd, ridiculous, sportive.

lugubrious *adj* complaining, doleful, gloomy, melancholy, mournful, sad, serious, sombre, sorrowful.

lukewarm *adj* blood-warm, tepid, thermal; apathetic, cold, dull, indifferent, listless, unconcerned, torpid.

lull *vb* calm, compose, hush, quiet, still, tranquillize; abate, cease, decrease, diminish, subside. * *n* calm, calmness, cessation.

lumber[1] *vb* rumble, shamble, trudge.

lumber[2] *n* refuse, rubbish, trash, trumpery; wood.

luminous *adj* effulgent, incandescent, radiant, refulgent, resplendent, shining; bright, brilliant, clear; clear, lucid, lucent, perspicuous, plain.

lunacy *n* aberration, craziness, dementia, derangement, insanity, madness, mania.

lunatic *adj* crazy, demented, deranged, insane, mad, psychopathic. * *n* madman, maniac, psychopath.

lurch *vb* appropriate, filch, pilfer, purloin, steal; deceive, defeat, disappoint, evade; ambush, lurk, skulk; contrive, dodge, shift, trick; pitch, sway.

lure *vb* allure, attract, decoy, entice, inveigle, seduce, tempt. * *n* allurement, attraction, bait, decoy, enticement, temptation.

lurid *adj* dismal, ghastly, gloomy, lowering, murky, pale, wan; glaring, sensational, startling, unrestrained.

lurk *vb* hide, prowl, skulk, slink, sneak, snoop.

luscious *adj* delicious, delightful, grateful, palatable, pleasing, savoury, sweet.

lush *adj* fresh, juicy, luxuriant, moist, sappy, succulent, watery.

lust *vb* covet, crave, desire, hanker, need, want, yearn. * *n* cupidity, desire, longing; carnality, concupiscence, lasciviousness, lechery, lewdness, lubricity, salaciousness, salacity, wantonness.

lustful *adj* carnal, concupiscent, hankering, lascivious, lecherous, licentious, libidinous, lubricious, salacious.

lustily *adv* strongly, vigorously.

lustiness *n* hardihood, power, robustness, stoutness, strength, sturdiness, vigour.

lustre *n* brightness, brilliance, brilliancy, splendour.

lusty *adj* healthful, lively, robust, stout, strong, sturdy, vigorous; bulky, burly, corpulent, fat, large, stout.

luxuriance *n* exuberance, profusion, superabundance.

luxuriant *adj* exuberant, plenteous, plentiful, profuse, superabundant.

luxuriate *vb* abound, delight, enjoy, flourish, indulge, revel.

luxurious *adj* epicurean, opulent, pampered, self-indulgent, sensual, sybaritic, voluptuous.

luxury *n* epicureanism, epicurism, luxuriousness, opulence, sensuality, voluptuousness; delight, enjoyment, gratification, indulgence, pleasure; dainty, delicacy, treat.

lying *adj* equivocating, false, mendacious, untruthful, untrue.

lyric *adj* dulcet, euphonious, lyrical, mellifluous, mellifluent, melodic, melodious, musical, poetic, silvery, tuneful.

lyrical *adj* ecstatic, enthusiastic, expressive, impassion; dulcet, lyric, mellifluous, mellifluent, melodic, melodious, musical, poetic.

M

macabre *adj* cadaverous, deathlike, deathly, dreadful, eerie, frightening, frightful, ghoulish, grim, grisly, gruesome, hideous, horrid, morbid, unearthly, weird.
mace *n* baton, staff, truncheon.
macerate *vb* harass, mortify, torture; digest, soak, soften, steep.
Machiavellian *adj* arch, artful, astute, crafty, crooked, cunning, deceitful, designing, diplomatic, insidious, intriguing, shrewd, sly, subtle, tricky, wily.
machination *n* artifice, cabal, conspiracy, contrivance, design, intrigue, plot, scheme, stratagem, trick.
machine *n* instrument, puppet, tool; machinery, organization, system; engine.
mad *adj* crazed, crazy, delirious, demented, deranged, distracted, insane, irrational, lunatic, maniac, maniacal; enraged, furious, rabid, raging, violent; angry, enraged, exasperated, furious, incensed, provoked, wrathful; distracted, infatuated, wild; frantic, frenzied, raving.
madden *vb* annoy, craze, enrage, exasperate, inflame, infuriate, irritate, provoke.
madness *n* aberration, craziness, dementia, derangement, insanity, lunacy, mania; delirium, frenzy, fury, rage.
magazine *n* depository, depot, entrepot, receptacle, repository, storehouse, warehouse; pamphlet, paper, periodical.
magic *adj* bewitching, charming, enchanting, fascinating, magical, miraculous, spellbinding. * *n* conjuring, enchantment, necromancy, sorcery, thaumaturgy, voodoo, witchcraft; char, fascination, witchery.
magician *n* conjurer, enchanter, juggler, magus, necromancer, shaman, sorcerer, wizard.
magisterial *adj* august, dignified, majestic, pompous; authoritative, despotic, domineering, imperious, dictatorial.
magnanimity *n* chivalry, disinterestedness, forbearance, high-mindedness, generosity, nobility.
magnificence *n* brilliance, éclat, grandeur, luxuriousness, luxury, majesty, pomp, splendour.
magnificent *adj* elegant, grand, majestic, noble, splendid, superb; brilliant, gorgeous, imposing, lavish, luxurious, pompous, showy, stately.
magnify *vb* amplify, augment, enlarge; bless, celebrate, elevate, exalt, extol, glorify, laud, praise; exaggerate.
magnitude *n* bulk, dimension, extent, mass, size, volume; consequence, greatness, importance; grandeur, loftiness, sublimity.
maid *n* damsel, girl, lass, lassie, maiden, virgin; maidservant, servant.
maiden *adj* chaste, pure, undefiled, virgin; fresh, new, unused. * *n* girl, maid, virgin.
maidenly *adj* demure, gentle, modest, maidenlike, reserved.
maim *vb* cripple, disable, disfigure, mangle, mar, mutilate. * *n* crippling, disfigurement, mutilation; harm, hurt, injury, mischief.
main[1] *adj* capital, cardinal, chief, leading, principal; essential, important, indispensable, necessary, requisite, vital; enormous, huge, mighty, vast; pure, sheer; absolute, direct, entire, mere. * *n* channel, pipe; force, might, power, strength, violence.
main[2] *n* high seas, ocean; continent, mainland.
maintain *vb* keep, preserve, support, sustain, uphold; hold, possess; defend, vindicate, justify; carry on, continue, keep

up; feed, provide, supply; allege, assert, declare; affirm, aver, contend, hold, say.

maintenance *n* defence, justification, preservation, support, sustenance, vindication; bread, food, livelihood, provisions, subsistence, sustenance, victuals.

majestic *adj* august, dignified, imperial, imposing, lofty, noble, pompous, princely, stately, regal, royal; grand, magnificent, splendid, sublime.

majesty *n* augustness, dignity, elevation, grandeur, loftiness, stateliness.

majority *n* bulk, greater, mass, more, most, plurality, preponderance, superiority; adulthood, manhood.

make *vb* create; fashion, figure, form, frame, mould, shape; cause, construct, effect, establish, fabricate, produce; do, execute, perform, practice; acquire, gain, get, raise, secure; cause, compel, constrain, force, occasion; compose, constitute; go, journey, move, proceed, tend, travel; conduce, contribute, effect, favour, operate; estimate, judge, reckon, suppose, think. * *n* brand, build, constitution, construction, form, shape, structure.

maker *n* creator, god; builder, constructor, fabricator, framer, manufacturer; author, composer, poet, writer.

maladministration *n* malversation, misgovernment, misrule.

maladroit *adj* awkward, bungling, clumsy, inept, inexpert, unhandy, unskilful, unskilled.

malady *n* affliction, ailment, complaint, disease, disorder, illness, indisposition, sickness.

malcontent *adj* discontented, dissatisfied, insurgent, rebellious, resentful, uneasy, unsatisfied. * *n* agitator, complainer, fault-finder, grumbler, spoilsport.

malediction *n* anathema, ban, curse, cursing, denunciation, execration, imprecation, malison.

malefactor *n* convict, criminal, culprit, delinquent, evildoer, felon, offender, outlaw.

malevolence *n* hate, hatred, ill-will, malice, malignity, rancour, spite, spitefulness, vindictiveness.

malevolent *adj* evil-minded, hateful, hostile, ill-natured, malicious, malignant, mischievous, rancorous, spiteful, venomous. vindictive.

malice *n* animosity, bitterness, enmity, grudge, hate, ill-will, malevolence, maliciousness, malignity, pique, rancour, spite, spitefulness, venom, vindictiveness.

malicious *adj* bitter, envious, evil-minded, ill-disposed, ill-natured, invidious, malevolent, malignant, mischievous, rancorous, resentful, spiteful, vicious.

malign *vb* abuse, asperse, blacken, calumniate, defame, disparage, revile, scandalize, slander, traduce, vilify. * *adj* malevolent, malicious, malignant, ill-disposed; baneful, injurious, pernicious, unfavourable, unpropitious.

malignant *adj* bitter, envious, hostile, inimical, malevolent, malicious, malign, spiteful, rancorous, resentful, virulent; heinous, pernicious; ill-boding, unfavourable, unpropitious; dangerous, fatal.

malignity *n* animosity, hatred, ill-will, malice, malevolence, maliciousness, rancour, spite; deadliness, destructiveness, fatality, harmfulness, malignancy, perniciousness, virulence; enormity, evilness, heinousness.

malpractice *n* dereliction, malversation, misbehaviour, misconduct, misdeed, misdoing, sin, transgression.

maltreat *vb* abuse, harm, hurt, ill-treat, ill-use, injure.

mammoth *adj* colossal, enormous, gigantic, huge, immense, vast.

man *vb* crew, garrison, furnish; fortify, reinforce, strengthen. * *n* adult, being, body, human, individual, one, person, personage, somebody, soul; humanity, humankind, mankind; attendant, butler, dependant, liege, servant, subject, valet, vassal; employee, workman.

manacle *vb* bind, chain, fetter, handcuff, restrain, shackle, tie. * *n* bond, chain, handcuff, gyve, hand-fetter, shackle.

manage *vb* administer, conduct, direct, guide, handle, operate, order, regulate, superintend, supervise, transact, treat; control, govern, rule; handle, manipulate, train, wield; contrive, economize, husband, save.

manageable *adj* controllable, docile, easy, governable, tamable, tractable.

management *n* administration, care, charge, conduct, control, direction, disposal, economy, government, guidance, superintendence, supervision, surveillance, treatment.

manager *n* comptroller, conductor, director, executive, governor, impresario, overseer, superintendent, supervisor.

mandate *n* charge, command, commission, edict, injunction, order, precept, requirement.

manful *adj* bold, brave, courageous, daring, heroic, honourable, intrepid, noble, stout, strong, undaunted, vigorous.

mangily *adv* basely, foully, meanly, scabbily, scurvily, vilely.

mangle[1] *vb* hack, lacerate, mutilate, rend, tear; cripple, crush, destroy, maim, mar, spoil.

mangle[2] *vb* calender, polish, press, smooth.

manhood *n* virility; bravery, courage, firmness, fortitude, hardihood, manfulness, manliness, resolution; human nature, humanity; adulthood, maturity.

mania *n* aberration, craziness, delirium, dementia, derangement, frenzy, insanity, lunacy, madness; craze, desire, enthusiasm, fad, fanaticism.

manifest *vb* declare, demonstrate, disclose, discover, display, evidence, evince, exhibit, express, reveal, show. * *adj* apparent, clear, conspicuous, distinct, evident, glaring, indubitable, obvious, open, palpable, patent, plain, unmistakable, visible.

manifestation *n* disclosure, display, exhibition, exposure, expression, revelation.

manifold *adj* complex, diverse, many, multifarious, multiplied, multitudinous, numerous, several, sundry, varied, various.

manipulate *vb* handle, operate, work.

manliness *n* boldness, bravery, courage, dignity, fearlessness, firmness, heroism, intrepidity, nobleness, resolution, valour.

manly *adj* bold, brave, courageous, daring, dignified, firm, heroic, intrepid, manful, noble, stout, strong, undaunted, vigorous; male, masculine, virile.

manner *n* fashion, form, method, mode, style, way; custom, habit, practice; degree, extent, measure; kind, kinds, sort, sorts; air, appearance, aspect, behaviour, carriage, demeanour, deportment, look, mien; mannerism, peculiarity; behaviour, conduct, habits, morals; civility, deportment.

mannerly *adj* ceremonious, civil, complaisant, courteous, polite, refined, respectful, urbane, well-behaved, well-bred.

manners *npl* conduct, habits, morals; air, bearing, behaviour, breeding, carriage, comportment, deportment, etiquette.

manoeuvre *vb* contrive, finesse, intrigue, manage, plan, plot, scheme. * *n* evolution, exercise, movement, operation; artifice, finesse, intrigue, plan, plot, ruse, scheme, stratagem, trick.

mansion *n* abode, dwelling, dwelling house, habitation, hall, residence, seat.

mantle *vb* cloak, cover, discover, obscure; expand, spread; bubble, cream, effervesce, foam, froth, sparkle. * *n* chasuble, cloak, toga; cover, covering, hood.

manufacture *vb* build, compose, construct, create, fabricate, forge, form, make, mould, produce, shape. * *n* constructing, fabrication, making, production.

manumission *n* deliverance, emancipation, enfranchisement, freedom, liberation, release.

manumit *vb* deliver, emancipate, enfranchise, free, liberate, release.

manure *vb* enrich, fertilize. * *n* compost, dressing, fertilizer, guano, muck.

many *adj* abundant, diverse, frequent, innumerable, manifold, multifarious, multifold, multiplied, multitudinous, numerous, sundry, varied, various. * *n* crowd, multitude, people.

map *vb* chart, draw up, plan, plot, set out,

sketch. * *n* chart, diagram, outline, plot, sketch.

mar *vb* blot, damage, harm, hurt, impair, injure, ruin, spoil, stain; deface, deform, disfigure, maim, mutilate.

marauder *n* bandit, brigand, desperado, filibuster, freebooter, outlaw, pillager, plunderer, ravager, robber, rover.

march *vb* go, pace, parade, step, tramp, walk. * *n* hike, tramp, walk; parade, procession; gait, step, stride; advance, evolution, progress.

marches *npl* borders, boundaries, confines, frontiers, limits, precincts.

margin *n* border, brim, brink, confine, edge, limit, rim, skirt, verge; latitude, room, space, surplus.

marine *adj* oceanic, pelagic, saltwater, sea; maritime, naval, nautical. * *n* navy, shipping; sea-dog, sea soldier, soldier; sea piece, seascape.

mariner *n* navigator, sailor, salt, seafarer, seaman, tar.

marital *adj* connubial, conjugal, matrimonial.

maritime *adj* marine, naval, nautical, oceanic, sea, seafaring, seagoing; coastal, seaside.

mark *vb* distinguish, earmark, label; betoken, brand, characterize, denote, designate, engrave, impress, imprint, indicate, print, stamp; evince, heed, note, notice, observe, regard, remark, show, spot. * *n* brand, character, characteristic, impression, impress, line, note, print, sign, stamp, symbol, token, race; evidence, indication, proof, symptom, trace, track, vestige; badge; footprint; bull's-eye, butt, object, target; consequence, distinction, eminence, fame, importance, notability, position, preeminence, reputation, significance.

marked *adj* conspicuous, distinguished, eminent, notable, noted, outstanding, prominent, remarkable.

marriage *n* espousals, nuptials, spousals, wedding; matrimony, wedlock; union; alliance, association, confederation.

marrow *n* medulla, pith; cream, essence, quintessence, substance.

marsh *n* bog, fen, mire, morass, quagmire, slough, swamp.

marshal *vb* arrange, array, dispose, gather, muster, range, order, rank; guide, herald, lead. * *n* conductor, director, master of ceremonies, regulator; harbinger, herald, pursuivant.

marshy *adj* boggy, miry, mossy, swampy, wet.

martial *adj* brave, heroic, military, soldier-like, warlike.

marvel *vb* gape, gaze, goggle, wonder. * *n* miracle, prodigy, wonder; admiration, amazement, astonishment, surprise.

marvellous *adj* amazing, astonishing, extraordinary, miraculous, prodigious, strange, stupendous, wonderful, wondrous; improbable, incredible, surprising, unbelievable.

masculine *adj* bold, hardy, manful, manlike, manly, mannish, virile; potent, powerful, robust, strong, vigorous; bold, coarse, forward.

mask *vb* cloak, conceal, cover, disguise, hide, screen, shroud, veil. * *n* blind, cloak, disguise, screen, veil; evasion, pretence, plea, pretext, ruse, shift, subterfuge, trick; masquerade; bustle, mummery.

masquerade *vb* cover, disguise, hide, mask, revel, veil. * *n* mask, mummery, revel, revelry.

Mass *n* communion, Eucharist.

mass *vb* accumulate, amass, assemble, collect, gather, rally, throng. * *adj* extensive, general, large-scale, widespread. * *n* cake, clot, lump; assemblage, collection, combination, congeries, heap; bulk, dimension, magnitude, size; accumulation, aggregate, body, sum, total, totality, whole.

massacre *vb* annihilate, butcher, exterminate, kill, murder, slaughter, slay. * *n* annihilation, butchery, carnage, extermination, killing, murder, pogrom, slaughter.

massive *adj* big, bulky, colossal, enormous, heavy, huge, immense, ponderous, solid, substantial, vast, weighty.

master *vb* conquer, defeat, direct, govern,

overcome, overpower, rule, subdue, subjugate, vanquish; acquire, learn. * *adj* cardinal, chief, especial, grand, great, main, leading, prime, principal; adept, expert, proficient. * *n* director, governor, lord, manager, overseer, superintendent, ruler; captain, commander; instructor, pedagogue, preceptor, schoolteacher, teacher, tutor; holder, owner, possessor, proprietor; chief, head, leader, principal.

masterly *adj* adroit, clever, dextrous, excellent, expert, finished, skilful, skilled; arbitrary, despotic, despotical, domineering, imperious.

mastery *n* command, dominion, mastership, power, rule, supremacy, sway; ascendancy, conquest, leadership, preeminence, superiority, upper-hand, victory; acquisition, acquirement, attainment; ability, cleverness, dexterity, proficiency, skill.

masticate *vb* chew, eat, munch.

match *vb* equal, rival; adapt, fit, harmonize, proportion, suit; marry, mate; combine, couple, join, sort; oppose, pit; correspond, suit, tally. * *n* companion, equal, mate, tally; competition, contest, game, trial; marriage, union.

matchless *adj* consummate, excellent, exquisite, incomparable, inimitable, peerless, perfect, surpassing, unequalled, unmatched, unparalleled, unrivalled.

mate *vb* marry, match, wed; compete, equal, vie; appal, confound, crush, enervate, subdue, stupefy. * *n* associate, companion, compeer, consort, crony, friend, fellow, intimate; companion, equal, match; assistant, subordinate; husband, spouse, wife.

material *adj* bodily, corporeal, nonspiritual, physical, temporal; essential, important, momentous, relevant, vital, weighty. * *n* body, element, stuff, substance.

maternal *adj* motherlike, motherly.

matrimonial *adj* conjugal, connubial, espousal, hymeneal, marital, nuptial, spousal.

matrimony *n* marriage, wedlock.

matter *vb* import, signify, weigh. * *n* body, content, sense, substance; difficulty, distress, trouble; material, stuff; question, subject, subject matter, topic; affair, business, concern, event; consequence, import, importance, moment, significance; discharge, purulence, pus.

mature *vb* develop, perfect, ripen. * *adj* complete, fit, full-grown, perfect, ripe; completed, prepared, ready, well-considered, well-digested.

maturity *n* completeness, completion, matureness, perfection, ripeness.

mawkish *adj* disgusting, flat, insipid, nauseous, sickly, stale, tasteless, vapid; emotional, feeble, maudlin, sentimental.

maxim *n* adage, aphorism, apothegm, axiom, byword, dictum, proverb, saw, saying, truism.

maze *vb* amaze, bewilder, confound, confuse, perplex. * *n* intricacy, labyrinth, meander; bewilderment, embarrassment, intricacy, perplexity, puzzle, uncertainty.

mazy *adj* confused, confusing, intricate, labyrinthian, labyrinthic, labyrinthine, perplexing, winding.

meagre *adj* emaciated, gaunt, lank, lean, poor, skinny, starved, spare, thin; barren, poor, sterile, unproductive; bald, barren, dry, dull, mean, poor, prosy, feeble, insignificant, jejune, scanty, small, tame, uninteresting, vapid.

mean[1] *vb* contemplate, design, intend, purpose; connote, denote, express, imply, import, indicate, purport, signify, symbolize.

mean[2] *adj* average, medium, middle; intermediate, intervening. * *n* measure, mediocrity, medium, moderation; average; agency, instrument, instrumentality, means, measure, method, mode, way.

mean[3] *adj* coarse, common, humble, ignoble, low, ordinary, plebeian, vulgar; abject, base, base-minded, beggarly, contemptible, degraded, dirty, dishonourable, disingenuous, grovelling, low-minded, pitiful, rascally, scurvy, servile, shabby, sneaking, sorry, spiritless, unfair, vile; illiberal, mercenary, miserly, narrow, narrow-minded, niggardly, parsimonious, penurious, selfish, sordid, stingy, ungenerous, unhandsome; contemptible, despicable, diminutive, insignificant, paltry, petty, poor, small, wretched.

meaning *n* acceptation, drift, import, intention, purport, purpose, sense, signification.

means *npl* instrument, method, mode, way; appliance, expedient, measure, resource, shift, step; estate, income, property, resources, revenue, substance, wealth, wherewithal.

measure *vb* mete; adjust, gauge, proportion; appraise, appreciate, estimate, gauge, value. * *n* gauge, meter, rule, standard; degree, extent, length, limit; allotment, share, proportion; means, step; foot, metre, rhythm, tune, verse.

measureless *adj* boundless, endless, immeasurable, immense, limitless, unbounded, unlimited, vast.

meat *n* aliment, cheer, diet, fare, feed, flesh, food, nourishment, nutriment, provision, rations, regimen, subsistence, sustenance, viands, victuals.

mechanic *n* artificer, artisan, craftsman, hand, handicraftsman, machinist, operative, workman.

meddle *vb* interfere, intermeddle, interpose, intrude.

meddlesome *adj* interfering, intermeddling, intrusive, officious, prying.

mediate *vb* arbitrate, intercede, interpose, intervene, settle. * *adj* interposed, intervening, middle.

mediation *n* arbitration, intercession, interposition, intervention.

mediator *n* advocate, arbitrator, interceder, intercessor, propitiator, umpire.

medicine *n* drug, medicament, medication, physic; therapy.

mediocre *adj* average, commonplace, indifferent, mean, medium, middling, ordinary.

meditate *vb* concoct, contrive, design, devise, intend, plan, purpose, scheme; chew, contemplate, ruminate, study; cogitate, muse, ponder, think.

meditation *n* cogitation, contemplation, musing, pondering, reflection, ruminating, study, thought.

meditative *adj* contemplative, pensive, reflective, studious, thoughtful.

medium *adj* average, mean, mediocre, middle. * *n* agency, channel, intermediary, instrument, instrumentality, means, organ; conditions, environment, influences; average, means.

medley *n* confusion, farrago, hodgepodge, hotchpotch, jumble, mass, melange, miscellany, mishmash, mixture.

meed *n* award, guerdon, premium, prize, recompense, remuneration, reward.

meek *adj* gentle, humble, lowly, mild, modest, pacific, soft, submissive, unassuming, yielding.

meekness *n* gentleness, humbleness, humility, lowliness, mildness, modesty, submission, submissiveness.

meet *vb* cross, intersect, transact; confront, encounter, engage; answer, comply, fulfil, gratify, satisfy; converge, join, unite; assemble, collect, convene, congregate, forgather, muster, rally. * *adj* adapted, appropriate, befitting, convenient, fit, fitting, proper, qualified, suitable, suited.

meeting *n* encounter, interview; assemblage, assembly, audience, company, concourse, conference, congregation, convention, gathering; assignation, encounter, introduction, rendezvous; confluence, conflux, intersection, joining, junction, union; collision.

melancholy *adj* blue, dejected, depressed, despondent, desponding, disconsolate, dismal, dispirited, doleful, down, downcast, downhearted, gloomy, glum, hypochondriac, low-spirited, lugubrious, moody, mopish, sad, sombre, sorrowful, unhappy; afflictive, calamitous, unfortunate, unlucky; dark, gloomy, grave, quiet. * *n* blues, dejection, depression, despondency, dismals, dumps, gloom, gloominess, hypochondria, sadness, vapours.

melee *n* affray, brawl, broil, contest, fight, fray, scuffle.

mellifluous, mellifluent *adj* dulcet, euphonic, euphonical, euphonious, mellow,

silver-toned, silvery, smooth, soft, sweet.
mellow *vb* mature, ripen; improve, smooth, soften, tone; pulverize; perfect. * *adj* mature, ripe; dulcet, mellifluous, mellifluent, rich, silver-toned, silvery, smooth, soft; delicate; genial, good-humoured, jolly, jovial, matured, softened; mellowy, loamy, unctuous; perfected, well-prepared; disguised, fuddled, intoxicated, tipsy.
melodious *adj* arioso, concordant, dulcet, euphonious, harmonious, mellifluous, mellifluent, musical, silvery, sweet, tuneful.
melody *n* air, descant, music, plainsong, song, theme, tune.
melt *vb* dissolve, fuse, liquefy, thaw; mollify, relax, soften, subdue; dissipate, waste; blend, pass, shade.
member *n* arm, leg, limb, organ; component, constituent, element, part, portion; branch, clause, division, head.
memento *n* memorial, remembrance, reminder, souvenir.
memoir *n* account, autobiography, biography, journal, narrative, record, register.
memorable *adj* celebrated, distinguished, extraordinary, famous, great, illustrious, important, notable, noteworthy, remarkable, signal, significant.
memorandum *n* minute, note, record.
memorial *adj* commemorative, monumental. * *n* cairn, commemoration, memento, monument, plaque, record, souvenir; memorandum, remembrance.
memory *n* recollection, remembrance, reminiscence; celebrity, fame, renown, reputation; commemoration, memorial.
menace *vb* alarm, frighten, intimidate, threaten. * *n* danger, hazard, peril, threat, warning; nuisance, pest, troublemaker.
menage *n* household, housekeeping, management.
mend *vb* darn, patch, rectify, refit, repair, restore, retouch; ameliorate, amend, better, correct, emend, improve, meliorate, reconcile, rectify, reform; advance, help; augment, increase.
mendacious *adj* deceitful, deceptive, fallacious, false, lying, untrue, untruthful.
mendacity *n* deceit, deceitfulness, deception, duplicity, falsehood, lie, untruth.
mendicant *n* beggar, pauper, tramp.
menial *adj* base, low, mean, servile, vile. * *n* attendant, bondsman, domestic, flunkey, footman, lackey, serf, servant, slave, underling, valet, waiter.
mensuration *n* measurement, measuring; survey, surveying.
mental *adj* ideal, immaterial, intellectual, psychiatric, subjective.
mention *vb* acquaint, allude, cite, communicate, declare, disclose, divulge, impart, inform, name, report, reveal, state, tell. * *n* allusion, citation, designation, notice, noting, reference.
mentor *n* adviser, counsellor, guide, instructor, monitor.
mephitic *adj* baleful, baneful, fetid, foul, mephitical, noisome, noxious, poisonous, pestilential.
mercantile *adj* commercial, marketable, trading.
mercenary *adj* hired, paid, purchased, venal; avaricious, covetous, grasping, mean, niggardly, parsimonious, penurious, sordid, stingy. * *n* hireling, soldier.
merchandise *n* commodities, goods, wares.
merchant *n* dealer, retailer, shopkeeper, trader, tradesman.
merciful *adj* clement, compassionate, forgiving, gracious, lenient, pitiful; benignant, forbearing, gentle, humane, kind, mild, tender, tender-hearted.
merciless *adj* barbarous, callous, cruel, fell, hard-hearted, inexorable, pitiless, relentless, remorseless, ruthless, savage, severe, uncompassionate, unfeeling, unmerciful, unrelenting, unrepenting, unsparing.
mercurial *adj* active, lively, nimble, prompt, quick, sprightly; cheerful, lighthearted; changeable, fickle, flighty, inconstant, mobile, volatile.
mercy *n* benevolence, clemency, compassion, gentleness, kindness, lenience, leniency, lenity, mildness, pity, tenderness; blessing, favour, grace; discretion, dis-

posal; forgiveness, pardon.

mere *adj* bald, bare, naked, plain, sole, simple; absolute, entire, pure, sheer, unmixed. * *n* lake, pond, pool.

meretricious *adj* deceitful, brummagem, false, gaudy, make-believe, sham, showy, spurious, tawdry.

merge *vb* bury, dip, immerse, involve, lose, plunge, sink, submerge.

meridian *n* acme, apex, climax, culmination, summit, zenith; midday, noon, noontide.

merit *vb* deserve, earn, incur; acquire, gain, profit, value. * *n* claim, right; credit, desert, excellence, goodness, worth, worthiness.

meritorious *adj* commendable, deserving, excellent, good, worthy.

merriment *n* amusement, frolic, gaiety, hilarity, jocularity, jollity, joviality, laughter, liveliness, mirth, sport, sportiveness.

merry *adj* agreeable, brisk, delightful, exhilarating, lively, pleasant, stirring; airy, blithe, blithesome, buxom, cheerful, comical, droll, facetious, frolicsome, gladsome, gleeful, hilarious, jocund, jolly, jovial, joyous, light-hearted, lively, mirthful, sportive, sprightly, vivacious.

mess *n* company, set; farrago, hodgepodge, hotchpotch, jumble, medley, mass, melange, miscellany, mishmash, mixture; confusion, muddle, perplexity, pickle, plight, predicament.

message *n* communication, dispatch, intimation, letter, missive, notice, telegram, wire, word.

messenger *n* carrier, courier, emissary, envoy, express, mercury, nuncio; forerunner, harbinger, herald, precursor.

metamorphic *adj* changeable, mutable, variable.

metamorphose *vb* change, mutate, transfigure, transform, transmute.

metamorphosis *n* change, mutation, transfiguration, transformation, transmutation.

metaphorical *adj* allegorical, figurative, symbolic, symbolical.

metaphysical *adj* abstract, allegorical, figurative, general, intellectual, parabolic, subjective, unreal.

mete *vb* dispense, distribute, divide, measure, ration, share. * *n* bound, boundary, butt, limit, measure, term, terminus.

meteor *n* aerolite, falling star, shooting star.

method *n* course, manner, means, mode, procedure, process, rule, way; arrangement, classification, disposition, order, plan, regularity, scheme, system.

methodical *adj* exact, orderly, regular, systematic, systematical.

metropolis *n* capital, city, conurbation.

mettle *n* constitution, element, material, stuff; character, disposition, spirit, temper; ardour, courage, fire, hardihood, life, nerve, pluck, sprightliness, vigour.

mettlesome *adj* ardent, brisk, courageous, fiery, frisky, high-spirited, lively, spirited, sprightly.

mew *vb* confine, coop, encase, enclose, imprison; cast, change, mould, shed.

microscopic *adj* infinitesimal, minute, tiny.

middle *adj* central, halfway, mean, medial, mid; intermediate, intervening. * *n* centre, halfway, mean, midst.

middleman *n* agent, broker, factor, go-between, intermediary.

mien *n* air, appearance, aspect, bearing, behaviour, carriage, countenance, demeanour, deportment, look, manner.

might *n* ability, capacity, efficacy, efficiency, force, main, power, prowess, puissance, strength.

mighty *adj* able, bold, courageous, potent, powerful, puissant, robust, strong, sturdy, valiant, valorous, vigorous; bulky, enormous, huge, immense, monstrous, stupendous, vast.

migratory *adj* nomadic, roving, shifting, strolling, unsettled, wandering, vagrant.

mild *adj* amiable, clement, compassionate, gentle, good-natured, indulgent, kind, lenient, meek, merciful, pacific, tender; bland, pleasant, soft, suave; calm, kind, placid, temperate, tranquil; assuasive, compliant, demulcent, emollient, lenitive, mollifying, soothing.

mildness *n* amiability, clemency, gentleness, indulgence, kindness, meekness, moderation, softness, tenderness, warmth.

mildew *n* blight, blast, mould, must, mustiness, smut, rust.

milieu *n* background, environment, sphere, surroundings.

militant *adj* belligerent, combative, contending, fighting.

military *adj* martial, soldier, soldierly, warlike. * *n* army, militia, soldiers.

mill *vb* comminute, crush, grate, grind, levigate, powder, pulverize. * *n* factory, manufactory; grinder; crowd, throng.

mimic *vb* ape, counterfeit, imitate, impersonate, mime, mock, parody. * *adj* imitative, mock, simulated. * *n* imitator, impersonator; mime, mocker, parodist, parrot.

mince[1] *vb* chop, cut, hash, shatter. * *n* forcemeat, hash, mash, mincemeat.

mince[2] *vb* attenuate, diminish, extenuate, mitigate, palliate, soften; pose, sashay, simper, smirk.

mind[1] *vb* attend, heed, mark, note, notice, regard, tend, watch; obey, observe, submit; design, incline, intend, mean; recall, recollect, remember, remind; beware, look out, watch out. * *n* soul, spirit; brains, common sense, intellect, reason, sense, understanding; belief, consideration, contemplation, judgement, opinion, reflection, sentiment, thought; memory, recollection, remembrance; bent, desire, disposition, inclination, intention, leaning, purpose, tendency, will.

mind[2] *vb* balk, begrudge, grudge, object, resent.

mindful *adj* attentive, careful, heedful, observant, regardful, thoughtful.

mindless *adj* dull, heavy, insensible, senseless, sluggish, stupid, unthinking; careless, forgetful, heedless, neglectful, negligent, regardless.

mine *vb* dig, excavate, quarry, unearth; sap, undermine, weaken; destroy, ruin. * *n* colliery, deposit, lode, pit, shaft.

mingle *vb* blend, combine, commingle, compound, intermingle, intermix, join, mix, unite.

miniature *adj* bantam, diminutive, little, small, tiny.

minion *n* creature, dependant, favourite, hanger-on, parasite, sycophant; darling, favourite, flatterer, pet.

minister *vb* administer, afford, furnish, give, supply; aid, assist, contribute, help, succour. * *n* agent, assistant, servant, subordinate, underling; administrator, executive; ambassador, delegate, envoy, plenipotentiary; chaplain, churchman, clergyman, cleric, curate, divine, ecclesiastic, parson, pastor, preacher, priest, rector, vicar.

ministry *n* agency, aid, help, instrumentality, interposition, intervention, ministration, service, support; administration, cabinet, council, government.

minor *adj* less, smaller; inferior, junior, secondary, subordinate, younger; inconsiderable, petty, unimportant, small.

minstrel *n* bard, musician, singer, troubadour.

mint *vb* coin, stamp; fabricate, fashion, forge, invent, make, produce. * *adj* fresh, new, perfect, undamaged. * *n* die, punch, seal, stamp; fortune, (*inf*) heap, million, pile, wad.

minute[1] *adj* diminutive, fine, little, microscopic, miniature, slender, slight, small, tiny; circumstantial, critical, detailed, exact, fussy, meticulous, nice, particular, precise.

minute[2] *n* account, entry, item, memorandum, note, proceedings, record; instant, moment, second, trice, twinkling.

miracle *n* marvel, prodigy, wonder.

miraculous *adj* supernatural, thaumaturgic, thaumaturgical; amazing, extraordinary, incredible, marvellous, unaccountable, unbelievable, wondrous.

mirror *vb* copy, echo, emulate, reflect, show. * *n* looking-glass, reflector, speculum; archetype, exemplar, example, model, paragon, pattern, prototype.

mirth *n* cheerfulness, festivity, frolic, fun, gaiety, gladness, glee, hilarity, festivity, jollity, joviality, joyousness, laughter, merriment, merry-making, rejoicing, sport.

mirthful *adj* cheery, cheery, festive, frolicsome, hilarious, jocund, jolly, merry, jovial, joyous, lively, playful, sportive, vivacious; comic, droll, humorous, facetious, funny, jocose, jocular, ludicrous, merry, waggish, witty.

misadventure *n* accident, calamity, catastrophe, cross, disaster, failure, ill-luck, infelicity, mischance, misfortune, mishap, reverse.

misanthrope *n* cynic, egoist, egotist, man-hater, misanthropist.

misapply *vb* abuse, misuse, pervert.

misapprehend *vb* misconceive, mistake, misunderstand.

misbehaviour *n* ill-behaviour, ill-conduct, incivility, miscarriage, misconduct, misdemeanour, naughtiness, rudeness.

miscarriage *n* calamity, defeat, disaster, failure, mischance, mishap; misbehaviour, misconduct, ill-behaviour.

miscellaneous *adj* confused, diverse, diversified, heterogeneous, indiscriminate, jumbled, many, mingled, mixed, promiscuous, stromatic, stromatous, various.

miscellany *n* collection, diversity, farrago, gallimaufry, hodgepodge, hotchpotch, jumble, medley, mishmash, melange, miscellaneous, mixture, variety.

mischance *n* accident, calamity, disaster, ill-fortune, ill-luck, infelicity, misadventure, misfortune, mishap.

mischief *n* damage, detriment, disadvantage, evil, harm, hurt, ill, injury, prejudice; ill-consequence, misfortune, trouble; devilry, wrong-doing.

mischievous *adj* destructive, detrimental, harmful, hurtful, injurious, noxious, pernicious; malicious, sinful, vicious, wicked; annoying, impish, naughty, troublesome, vexatious.

misconceive *vb* misapprehend, misjudge, mistake, misunderstand.

misconduct *vb* botch, bungle, misdirect, mismanage. * *n* bad conduct, ill-conduct, misbehaviour, misdemeanour, rudeness, transgression; ill-management, mismanagement.

misconstrue *vb* misread, mistranslate; misapprehend, misinterpret, mistake, misunderstand.

miscreant *adj* corrupt, criminal, evil, rascally, unprincipled, vicious, villainous, wicked. * *n* caitiff, knave, ragamuffin, rascal, rogue, ruffian, scamp, scoundrel, vagabond, villain.

misdemeanour *n* fault, ill-behaviour, misbehaviour, misconduct, misdeed, offence, transgression, trespass.

miser *n* churl, curmudgeon, lickpenny, money-grabber, niggard, penny-pincher, pinch-fist, screw, scrimp, skinflint.

miserable *adj* afflicted, broken-hearted, comfortless, disconsolate, distressed, forlorn, heartbroken, unhappy, wretched; calamitous, hapless, ill-starred, pitiable, unfortunate, unlucky; poor, valueless, worthless; abject, contemptible, despicable, low, mean, worthless.

miserly *adj* avaricious, beggarly, close, close-fisted, covetous, grasping, mean, niggardly, parsimonious, penurious, sordid, stingy, tight-fisted.

misery *n* affliction, agony, anguish, calamity, desolation, distress, grief, heartache, heavy-heartedness, misfortune, sorrow, suffering, torment, torture, tribulation, unhappiness, woe, wretchedness.

misfortune *n* adversity, affliction, bad luck, blow, calamity, casualty, catastrophe, disaster, distress, hardship, harm, ill, infliction, misadventure, mischance, mishap, reverse, scourge, stroke, trial, trouble, visitation.

misgiving *n* apprehension, distrust, doubt, hesitation, suspicion, uncertainty.

mishap *n* accident, calamity, disaster, ill luck, misadventure, mischance, misfortune.

misinterpret *vb* distort, falsify, misapprehend, misconceive, misconstrue, misjudge.

mislead *vb* beguile, deceive, delude, misdirect, misguide.

mismanage *vb* botch, fumble, misconduct, mishandle, misrule.

misprize *vb* slight, underestimate, underrate, undervalue.

misrepresent *vb* belie, caricature, distort,

falsify, misinterpret, misstate, pervert.
misrule *n* anarchy, confusion, disorder, malad-ministration, misgovernment, mismanagement.
miss[1] *vb* blunder, err, fail, fall short, forgo, lack, lose, miscarry, mistake, omit, overlook, trip; avoid, escape, evade, skip, slip; feel the loss of, need, want, wish. * *n* blunder, error, failure, fault, mistake, omission, oversight, slip, trip; loss, want.
miss[2] *n* damsel, girl, lass, maid, maiden.
misshapen *adj* deformed, ill-formed, ill-shaped, ill-proportioned, misformed, ugly, ungainly.
missile *n* projectile, weapon.
mission *n* commission, legation; business, charge, duty, errand, office, trust; delegation, deputation, embassy.
missive *n* communication, epistle, letter, message, note.
mist *vb* cloud, drizzle, mizzle, smog. * *n* cloud, fog, haze; bewilderment, obscurity, perplexity.
mistake *vb* misapprehend, miscalculate, misconceive, misjudge, misunderstand; confound, take; blunder, err. * *n* misapprehension, miscalculation, misconception, mistaking, misunderstanding; blunder, error, fault, inaccuracy, oversight, slip, trip.
mistaken *adj* erroneous, inaccurate, incorrect, misinformed, wrong.
mistrust *vb* distrust, doubt, suspect; apprehend, fear, surmise, suspect. * *n* doubt, distrust, misgiving, suspicion.
misty *adj* cloudy, clouded, dark, dim, foggy, obscure, overcast.
misunderstand *vb* misapprehend, misconceive, misconstrue, mistake.
misunderstanding *n* error, misapprehension, misconception, mistake; difference, difficulty, disagreement, discord, dissension, quarrel.
misuse *vb* desecrate, misapply, misemploy, pervert, profane; abuse, ill-treat, maltreat, ill-use; fritter, squander, waste. * *n* abuse, perversion, profanation, prostitution; ill-treatment, ill-use, ill-usage, misusage; misapplication, solecism.
mitigate *vb* abate, alleviate, assuage, diminish, extenuate, lessen, moderate, palliate, relieve; allay, appease, calm, mollify, pacify, quell, quiet, reduce, soften, soothe; moderate, temper.
mitigation *n* abatement, allaying, alleviation, assuagement, diminution, moderation, palliation, relief.
mix *vb* alloy, amalgamate, blend, commingle, combine, compound, incorporate, interfuse, interlard, mingle, unite; associate, join. * *n* alloy, amalgam, blend, combination, compound, mixture.
mixture *n* admixture, association, intermixture, union; compound, farrago, hash, hodgepodge, hotchpotch, jumble, medley, melange, mishmash; diversity, miscellany, variety.
moan *vb* bemoan, bewail, deplore, grieve, groan, lament, mourn, sigh, weep. * *n* groan, lament, lamentation, sigh, wail.
mob *vb* crowd, jostle, surround, swarm, pack, throng. * *n* assemblage, crowd, rabble, multitude, throng, tumult; dregs, canaille, populace, rabble, riffraff, scum.
mobile *adj* changeable, fickle, expressive, inconstant, sensitive, variable, volatile.
mock *vb* ape, counterfeit, imitate, mimic, take off; deride, flout, gibe, insult, jeer, ridicule, taunt; balk, cheat, deceive, defeat, disappoint, dupe, elude, illude, mislead. * *adj* assumed, clap-trap, counterfeit, fake, false, feigned, make-believe, pretended, spurious. * *n* fake, imitation, phoney, sham; gibe, insult, jeer, scoff, taunt.
mockery *n* contumely, counterfeit, deception, derision, imitation, jeering, mimicry, ridicule, scoffing, scorn, sham, travesty.
mode *n* fashion, manner, method, style, way; accident, affection, degree, graduation, modification, quality, variety.
model *vb* design, fashion, form, mould, plan, shape. * *adj* admirable, archetypal, estimable, exemplary, ideal, meritorious, paradigmatic, perfect, praiseworthy, worthy. * *n* archetype, design, mould, original, pattern, protoplast, prototype, type; dummy, example, form; copy, fac-

simile, image, imitation, representation.
moderate *vb* abate, allay, appease, assuage, blunt, dull, lessen, soothe, mitigate, mollify, pacify, quell, quiet, reduce, repress, soften, still, subdue; diminish, qualify, slacken, temper; control, govern, regulate. * *adj* abstinent, frugal, sparing, temperate; limited, mediocre; abstemious, sober; calm, cool, judicious, reasonable, steady; gentle, mild, temperate, tolerable.
moderation *n* abstemiousness, forbearance, frugality, restraint, sobriety, temperance; calmness, composure, coolness, deliberateness, equanimity, mildness, sedateness.
modern *adj* fresh, late, latest, new, novel, present, recent, up-to-date.
modest *adj* bashful, coy, diffident, humble, meek, reserved, retiring, shy, unassuming, unobtrusive, unostentatious, unpretending, unpretentious; chaste, proper, pure, virtuous; becoming, decent, moderate.
modesty *n* bashfulness, coyness, diffidence, humility, meekness, propriety, prudishness, reserve, shyness, unobtrusiveness; chastity, purity, virtue; decency, moderation.
modification *n* alteration, change, qualification, reformation, variation; form, manner, mode, state.
modify *vb* alter, change, qualify, reform, shape, vary; lower, moderate, qualify, soften.
modish *adj* fashionable, stylish; ceremonious, conventional, courtly, genteel.
modulate *vb* attune, harmonize, tune; inflict, vary; adapt, adjust, proportion.
moiety *n* half; part, portion, share.
moil *vb* drudge, labour, toil; bespatter, daub, defile, soil, splash, spot, stain; fatigue, weary, tire.
moist *adj* damp, dank, humid, marshy, muggy, swampy, wet.
moisture *n* dampness, dankness, humidity, wetness.
mole *n* breakwater, dike, dyke, jetty, mound, pier, quay.
molecule *n* atom, monad, particle.
molest *vb* annoy, badger, bore, bother, chafe, discommode, disquiet, disturb, harass, harry, fret, gull, hector, incommode, inconvenience, irritate, oppress, pester, plague, tease, torment, trouble, vex, worry.
mollify *vb* soften; appease, calm, compose, pacify, quiet, soothe, tranquillize; abate, allay, assuage, blunt, dull, ease, lessen, mitigate, moderate, relieve, temper; qualify, tone down.
moment *n* flash, instant, jiffy, second, trice, twinkling, wink; avail, consequence, consideration, force, gravity, importance, significance, signification, value, weight; drive, force, impetus, momentum.
momentous *adj* grave, important, serious, significant, vital, weighty.
momentum *n* impetus, moment.
monarch *n* autocrat, despot; chief, dictator, emperor, king, potentate, prince, queen, ruler, sovereign.
monastery *n* abbey, cloister, convent, lamasery, nunnery, priory.
monastic *adj* coenobitic, coenobitical, conventual, monkish, secluded.
money *n* banknotes, cash, coin, currency, riches, specie, wealth.
moneyed, monied *adj* affluent, opulent, rich, well-off, well-to-do.
monitor *vb* check, observe, oversee, supervise, watch. * *n* admonisher, admonitor, adviser, counsellor, instructor, mentor, overseer.
monomania *n* delusion, hallucination, illusion, insanity, self-deception.
monopolize *vb* control, dominate, engross, forestall.
monotonous *adj* boring, dull, tedious, tiresome, undiversified, uniform, unvaried, unvarying, wearisome.
monotony *n* boredom, dullness, sameness, tedium, tiresomeness, uniformity, wearisomeness.
monster *adj* enormous, gigantic, huge, immense, mammoth, monstrous. * *n* enormity, marvel, prodigy, wonder; brute, demon, fiend, miscreant, ruffian, villain, wretch.

monstrous *adj* abnormal, preternatural, prodigious, unnatural; colossal, enormous, extraordinary, huge, immense, stupendous, vast; marvellous, strange, wonderful; bad, base, dreadful, flagrant, frightful, hateful, hideous, horrible, shocking, terrible.

monument *n* memorial, record, remembrance, testimonial; cairn, cenotaph, gravestone, mausoleum, memorial, pillar, tomb, tombstone.

mood *n* disposition, humour, temper, vein.

moody *adj* capricious, humoursome, variable; angry, crabbed, crusty, fretful, ill-tempered, irascible, irritable, passionate, pettish, peevish, petulant, snappish, snarling, sour, testy; cross-grained, dogged, frowning, glowering, glum, intractable, morose, perverse, spleeny, stubborn, sulky, sullen, wayward; abstracted, gloomy, melancholy, pensive, sad, saturnine.

moonshine *n* balderdash, fiction, flummery, fudge, fustian, nonsense, pretence, stuff, trash, twaddle, vanity.

moor[1] *vb* anchor, berth, fasten, fix, secure, tie.

moor[2] *n* bog, common, heath, moorland, morass, moss, wasteland.

moot *vb* agitate, argue, debate, discuss, dispute. * *adj* arguable, debatable, doubtful, unsettled.

mopish *adj* dejected, depressed, desponding, downcast, down-hearted, gloomy, glum, sad.

moral *adj* ethical, good, honest, honourable, just, upright, virtuous; abstract, ideal, intellectual, mental. * *n* intent, meaning, significance.

morals *npl* ethics, morality; behaviour, conduct, habits, manners.

morass *n* bog, fen, marsh, quagmire, slough, swamp.

morbid *adj* ailing, corrupted, diseased, sick, sickly, tainted, unhealthy, unsound, vitiated; depressed, downcast, gloomy, pessimistic, sensitive.

mordacious *adj* acrid, biting, cutting, mordant, pungent, sharp, stinging; caustic, poignant, satirical, sarcastic, scathing, severe.

mordant *adj* biting, caustic, keen, mordacious, nipping, sarcastic.

moreover *adv, conj* also, besides, further, furthermore, likewise, too.

morning *n* aurora, daybreak, dawn, morn, morningtide, sunrise.

morose *adj* austere, churlish, crabbed, crusty, dejected, desponding, downcast, downhearted, gloomy, glum, melancholy, moody, sad, severe, sour, sullen, surly.

morsel *n* bite, mouthful, titbit; bit, fragment, part, piece, scrap.

mortal *adj* deadly, destructive, fatal, final, human, lethal, perishable, vital. * *n* being, earthling, human, man, person, woman.

mortality *n* corruption, death, destruction, fatality.

mortification *n* chagrin, disappointment, discontent, dissatisfaction, displeasure, humiliation, trouble, shame, vexation; humility, penance, self-abasement, self-denial; gangrene, necrosis.

mortify *vb* annoy, chagrin, depress, disappoint, displease, disquiet, dissatisfy, harass, humble, plague, vex, worry; abase, abash, confound, humiliate, restrain, shame, subdue; corrupt, fester, gangrene, putrefy.

mortuary *n* burial place, cemetery, churchyard, graveyard, necropolis; charnel house, morgue.

mostly *adv* chiefly, customarily, especially, generally, mainly, particularly, principally.

mote *n* atom, corpuscle, flaw, mite, particle, speck, spot.

motherly *adj* affectionate, kind, maternal, paternal, tender.

motion *vb* beckon, direct, gesture, signal. * *n* action, change, drift, flux, movement, passage, stir, transit; air, gait, port; gesture, impulse, prompting, suggestion; proposal, proposition.

motionless *adj* fixed, immobile, quiescent, stable, stagnant, standing, stationary, still, torpid, unmoved.

motive *adj* activating, driving, moving,

operative. * *n* cause, consideration, ground, impulse, incentive, incitement, inducement, influence, occasion, prompting, purpose, reason, spur, stimulus.

motley *adj* coloured, dappled, mottled, speckled, spotted, variegated; composite, diversified, heterogeneous, mingled, mixed.

mottled *adj* dappled, motley, piebald, speckled, spotted, variegated.

mould[1] *vb* carve, cast, fashion, form, make, model, shape. * *n* cast, character, fashion, form, matrix, pattern, shape; material, matter, substance.

mould[2] *n* blight, mildew, mouldiness, must, mustiness, rot; fungus, lichen, mushroom, puffball, rust, smut, toadstool; earth, loam, soil.

moulder *vb* crumble, decay, perish, waste.

mouldy *adj* decaying, fusty, mildewed, musty.

mound *n* bank, barrow, hill, hillock, knoll, tumulus; bulwark, defence, rampart.

mount[1] *n* hill, mountain, peak.

mount[2] *vb* arise, ascend, climb, rise, soar, tower; escalate, scale; embellish, ornament; bestride, get upon. * *n* charger, horse, ride, steed.

mountain *n* alp, height, hill, mount, peak; abundance, heap, mound, stack.

mountebank *n* charlatan, cheat, impostor, pretender, quack.

mourn *vb* bemoan, bewail, deplore, grieve, lament, sorrow, wail.

mournful *adj* afflicting, afflictive, calamitous, deplorable, distressed, grievous, lamentable, sad, woeful; doleful, heavy, heavy-hearted, lugubrious, melancholy, sorrowful, tearful.

mouth *vb* clamour, declaim, rant, roar, vociferate. * *n* chaps, jaws; aperture, opening, orifice; entrance, inlet; oracle, mouthpiece, speaker, spokesman.

movables *npl* chattels, effects, furniture, goods, property, wares.

move *vb* dislodge, drive, impel, propel, push, shift, start, stir; actuate, incite, instigate, rouse; determine, incline, induce, influence, persuade, prompt; affect, impress, touch, trouble; agitate, awaken, excite, incense, irritate; propose, recommend, suggest; go, march, proceed, walk; act, live; flit, remove. * *n* action, motion, movement.

movement *n* change, move, motion, passage; emotion; crusade, drive.

moving *adj* impelling, influencing, instigating, persuading, persuasive; affecting, impressive, pathetic, touching.

mucous *adj* glutinous, gummy, mucilaginous, ropy, slimy, viscid.

mud *n* dirt, mire, muck, slime.

muddle *vb* confuse, disarrange, disorder; fuddle, inebriate, stupefy; muff, mull, spoil. * *n* confusion, disorder, mess, plight, predicament.

muddy *vb* dirty, foul, smear, soil; confuse, obscure. * *adj* dirty, foul, impure, slimy, soiled, turbid; bothered, confused, dull, heavy, stupid; incoherent, obscure, vague.

muffle *vb* cover, envelop, shroud, wrap; conceal, disguise, involve; deaden, soften, stifle, suppress.

mulish *adj* cross-grained, headstrong, intractable, obstinate, stubborn.

multifarious *adj* different, divers, diverse, diversified, manifold, multiform, multitudinous, various.

multiloquence *n* garrulity, loquacity, loquaciousness, talkativeness.

multiply *vb* augment, extend, increase, spread.

multitude *n* numerousness; host, legion; army, assemblage, assembly, collection, concourse, congregation, crowd, horde, mob, swarm, throng; commonality, herd, mass, mob, pack, populace, rabble.

mundane *adj* earthly, secular, sublunary, temporal, terrene, terrestrial, worldly.

munificence *n* benefice, bounteousness, bountifulness, bounty, generosity, liberality.

munificent *adj* beneficent, bounteous, bountiful, free, generous, liberal, princely.

murder *vb* assassinate, butcher, destroy, dispatch, kill, massacre, slaughter, slay; abuse, mar, spoil. * *n* assassination, butchery, destruction, homicide, killing, manslaughter, massacre.

murderer *n* assassin, butcher, cut-throat, killer, manslaughterer, slaughterer, slayer.

murderous *adj* barbarous, bloodthirsty, bloody, cruel, fell, sanguinary, savage.

murky *adj* cheerless, cloudy, dark, dim, dusky, gloomy, hazy, lowering, lurid, obscure, overcast.

murmur *vb* croak, grumble, mumble, mutter; hum, whisper. * *n* complaint, grumble, mutter, plaint, whimper; hum, undertone, whisper.

muscular *adj* sinewy; athletic, brawny, powerful, lusty, stalwart, stout, strong, sturdy, vigorous.

muse *vb* brood, cogitate, consider, contemplate, deliberate, dream, meditate, ponder, reflect, ruminate, speculate, think. * *n* abstraction, musing, reverie.

music *n* harmony, melody, symphony.

musical *adj* dulcet, harmonious, melodious, sweet, sweet-sounding, symphonious, tuneful.

musing *adj* absent-minded, meditative, preoccupied. * *n* absent-mindedness, abstraction, contemplation, daydreaming, meditation, muse, reflection, reverie, rumination.

muster *vb* assemble, collect, congregate, convene, convoke, gather, marshal, meet, rally, summon. * *n* assemblage, assembly, collection, congregation, convention, convocation, gathering, meeting, rally.

musty *adj* fetid, foul, fusty, mouldy, rank, sour, spoiled; hackneyed, old, stale, threadbare, trite; ill-favoured, insipid, vapid; dull, heavy, rusty, spiritless.

mutable *adj* alterable, changeable; changeful, fickle, inconstant, irresolute, mutational, unsettled, unstable, unsteady, vacillating, variable, wavering.

mutation *n* alteration, change, variation.

mute *vb* dampen, lower, moderate, muffle, soften. * *adj* dumb, voiceless; silent, speechless, still, taciturn.

mutilate *vb* cripple, damage, disable, disfigure, hamstring, injure, maim, mangle, mar.

mutinous *adj* contumacious, insubordinate, rebellious, refractory, riotous, tumultuous, turbulent, unruly; insurgent, seditious.

mutiny *vb* rebel, revolt, rise, resist. * *n* insubordination, insurrection, rebellion, revolt, revolution, riot, rising, sedition, uprising.

mutter *vb* grumble, muffle, mumble, murmur.

mutual *adj* alternate, common, correlative, interchangeable, interchanged, reciprocal, requited.

myopic *adj* near-sighted, purblind, short-sighted.

myriad *adj* innumerable, manifold, multitudinous, uncounted. * *n* host, million(s), multitude, score(s), sea, swarm, thousand(s).

mysterious *adj* abstruse, cabbalistic, concealed, cryptic, dark, dim, enigmatic, enigmatical, hidden, incomprehensible, inexplicable, inscrutable, mystic, mystical, obscure, occult, puzzling, recondite, secret, sphinx-like, unaccountable, unfathomable, unintelligible, unknown.

mystery *n* enigma, puzzle, riddle, secret; art, business, calling, trade.

mystical *adj* abstruse, cabbalistic, dark, enigmatical, esoteric, hidden, inscrutable, mysterious, obscure, occult, recondite, transcendental; allegorical, emblematic, emblematical, symbolic, symbolical.

mystify *vb* befog, bewilder, confound, confuse, dumbfound, embarrass, obfuscate, perplex, pose, puzzle.

myth *n* fable, legend, tradition; allegory, fiction, invention, parable, story; falsehood, fancy, figment, lie, untruth.

mythical *adj* allegorical, fabled, fabulous, fanciful, fictitious, imaginary, legendary, mythological.

N

nab *vb* catch, clutch, grasp, seize.

nag[1] *vb* carp, fuss, hector, henpeck, pester, torment, worry. * *n* nagger, scold, shrew, tartar.

nag[2] *n* bronco, crock, hack, horse, pony, scrag.

naive *adj* artless, candid, ingenuous, natural, plain, simple, unaffected, unsophisticated.

naked *adj* bare, nude, uncovered; denuded, unclad, unclothed, undressed; defenceless, exposed, open, unarmed, unguarded, unprotected; evident, manifest, plain, stark, unconcealed, undisguised; mere, sheer, simple; bare, destitute, rough, rude, unfurnished, unprovided; uncoloured, unexaggerated, unvarnished.

name *vb* call, christen, denounce, dub, entitle, phrase, style, term; mention; denominate, designate, indicate, nominate, specify. * *n* appellation, cognomen, denomination, designation, epithet, nickname, surname, sobriquet, title; character, credit, reputation, repute; celebrity, distinction, eminence, fame, honour, note, praise, renown.

narcotic *adj* stupefacient, stupefactive, stupefying. * *n* anaesthetic, anodyne, dope, opiate, sedative, stupefacient, tranquillizer.

narrate *vb* chronicle, describe, detail, enumerate, recite, recount, rehearse, relate, tell.

narration *n* account, description, chronicle, history, narrative, recital, rehearsal, relation, story, tale.

narrow *vb* confine, contract, cramp, limit, restrict, straiten. * *adj* circumscribed, confined, contracted, cramped, incapacious, limited, pinched, scanty, straitened; bigoted, hidebound, illiberal, ungenerous; close, near.

nastiness *n* defilement, dirtiness, filth, filthiness, foulness, impurity, pollution, squalor, uncleanness; indecency, grossness, obscenity, pornography, ribaldry, smut, smuttiness.

nasty *adj* defiled, dirty, filthy, foul, impure, loathsome, polluted, squalid, unclean; gross, indecent, indelicate, lewd, loose, obscene, smutty, vile; disagreeable, disgusting, nauseous, odious, offensive, repulsive, sickening; aggravating, annoying, pesky, pestering, troublesome.

nation *n* commonwealth, realm, state; community, people, population, race, stock, tribe.

native *adj* aboriginal, autochthonal, autochthonous, domestic, home, indigenous, vernacular; genuine, intrinsic, natural, original, real; congenital, inborn, inbred, inherent, innate, natal. * *n* aborigine, autochthon, inhabitant, national, resident.

natty *adj* dandyish, fine, foppish, jaunty, neat, nice, spruce, tidy.

natural *adj* indigenous, innate, native, original; characteristic, essential; legitimate, normal, regular; artless, authentic, genuine, ingenious, unreal, simple, spontaneous, unaffected; bastard, illegitimate.

nature *n* universe, world; character, constitution, essence; kind, quality, species, sort; disposition, grain, humour, mood, temper; being, intellect, intelligence, mind.

naughty *adj* bad, corrupt, mischievous, perverse, worthless.

nausea *n* queasiness, seasickness; loathing, qualm; aversion, disgust, repugnance.

nauseous *adj* abhorrent, disgusting, distasteful, loathsome, offensive, repulsive,

revolting, sickening.
naval *adj* marine, maritime, nautical.
navigate *vb* cruise, direct, guide, pilot, plan, sail, steer.
navy *n* fleet, shipping, vessels.
near *vb* approach, draw close. * *adj* adjacent, approximate, close, contiguous, neighbouring, nigh; approaching, forthcoming, imminent, impending; dear, familiar, friendly, intimate; direct, immediate, short, straight; accurate, literal; narrow, parsimonious.
nearly *adv* almost, approximately, well-nigh; closely, intimately, pressingly; meanly, parsimoniously, penuriously, stingily.
neat *adj* clean, cleanly, orderly, tidy, trim, unsoiled; nice, smart, spruce; chaste, pure, simple; excellent, pure, unadulterated; adroit, clever, exact, finished; dainty, nice.
nebulous *adj* cloudy, hazy, misty.
necessary *adj* inevitable, unavoidable; essential, expedient, indispensable, needful, requisite; compelling, compulsory, involuntary. * *n* essential, necessity, requirement, requisite.
necessitate *vb* compel, constrain, demand, force, impel, oblige.
necessitous *adj* destitute, distressed, indigent, moneyless, needy, penniless, pinched, poor, poverty-stricken; narrow, pinching.
necessity *n* inevitability, inevitableness, unavoidability, unavoidableness; compulsion, destiny, fatality, fate; emergency, urgency; exigency, indigence, indispensability, indispensableness, need, needfulness, poverty, want; essentiality, essentialness, requirement, requisite.
necromancy *n* conjuration, divination, enchantment, magic, sorcery, witchcraft, wizardry.
necropolis *n* burial ground, cemetery, churchyard, crematorium, graveyard, mortuary.
need *vb* demand, lack, require, want. * *n* emergency, exigency, extremity, necessity, strait, urgency, want; destitution, distress, indigence, neediness, penury, poverty, privation.
needful *adj* distressful, necessitous, necessary; essential, indispensable, requisite.
needless *adj* superfluous, unnecessary, useless.
needy *adj* destitute, indigent, necessitous, poor.
nefarious *adj* abominable, atrocious, detestable, dreadful, execrable, flagitious, heinous, horrible, infamous, iniquitous, scandalous, vile, wicked.
negation *n* denial, disavowal, disclaimer, rejection, renunciation.
neglect *vb* condemn, despise, disregard, forget, ignore, omit, overlook, slight. * *n* carelessness, default, failure, heedlessness, inattention, omission, remissness; disregard, disrespect, slight; indifference, negligence.
negligence *n* carelessness, disregard, heedlessness, inadvertency, inattention, indifference, neglect, remissness, slackness, thoughtlessness; defect, fault, inadvertence, omission, shortcoming.
negligent *adj* careless, heedless, inattentive, indifferent, neglectful, regardless, thoughtless.
negotiate *vb* arrange, bargain, deal, debate, sell, settle, transact, treat.
neighbourhood *n* district, environs, locality, vicinage, vicinity; adjacency, nearness, propinquity, proximity.
neighbourly *adj* attentive, civil, friendly, kind, obliging, social.
neophyte *n* beginner, catechumen, convert, novice, pupil, tyro.
nerve *vb* brace, energize, fortify, invigorate, strengthen. * *n* force, might, power, strength, vigour; coolness, courage, endurance, firmness, fortitude, hardihood, manhood, pluck, resolution, self-command, steadiness.
nervous *adj* forcible, powerful, robust, strong, vigorous; irritable, fearful, shaky, timid, timorous, weak, weakly.
nestle *vb* cuddle, harbour, lodge, nuzzle, snug, snuggle.
nettle *vb* chafe, exasperate, fret, harass, incense, irritate, provoke, ruffle, sting,

tease, vex.

neutral *adj* impartial, indifferent; colourless, mediocre.

neutralize *vb* cancel, counterbalance, counterpoise, invalidate, offset.

nevertheless *adv* however, nonetheless, notwithstanding, yet.

new *adj* fresh, latest, modern, novel, recent, unused; additional, another, further; reinvigorated, renovated, repaired.

news *n* advice, information, intelligence, report, tidings, word.

nice *adj* accurate, correct, critical, definite, delicate, exact, exquisite, precise, rigorous, strict; dainty, difficult, exacting, fastidious, finical, punctilious, squeamish; discerning, discriminating, particular, precise, scrupulous; neat, tidy, trim; fine, minute, refined, subtle; delicate, delicious, luscious, palatable, savoury, soft, tender; agreeable, delightful, good, pleasant.

nicety *n* accuracy, exactness, niceness, precision, truth, daintiness, fastidiousness, squeamishness; discrimination, subtlety.

niggard *n* churl, curmudgeon, miser, screw, scrimp, skinflint.

niggardly *adj* avaricious, close, close-fisted, illiberal, mean, mercenary, miserly, parsimonious, penurious, skinflint, sordid, stingy.

nigh *adj* adjacent, adjoining, contiguous, near; present, proximate. * *adv* almost, near, nearly.

nimble *adj* active, agile, alert, brisk, lively, prompt, quick, speedy, sprightly, spry, swift, tripping.

nobility *n* aristocracy, dignity, elevation, eminence, grandeur, greatness, loftiness, magnanimity, nobleness, peerage, superiority, worthiness.

noble *adj* dignified, elevated, eminent, exalted, generous, great, honourable, illustrious, magnanimous, superior, worthy; choice, excellent; aristocratic, gentle, high-born, patrician; grand, lofty, lordly, magnificent, splendid, stately. * *n* aristocrat, grandee, lord, nobleman, peer.

noctambulist *n* sleepwalker, somnambulist.

noise *vb* bruit, gossip, repeat, report, rumour. * *n* ado, blare, clamour, clatter, cry, din, fuss, hubbub, hullabaloo, outcry, pandemonium, racket, row, sound, tumult, uproar, vociferation.

noiseless *adj* inaudible, quiet, silent, soundless.

noisome *adj* bad, baneful, deleterious, disgusting, fetid, foul, hurtful, injurious, mischievous, nocuous, noxious, offensive, pernicious, pestiferous, pestilential, poisonous, unhealthy, unwholesome.

noisy *adj* blatant, blustering, boisterous, brawling, clamorous, loud, uproarious, riotous, tumultuous, vociferous.

nomadic *adj* migratory, pastoral, vagrant, wandering.

nominal *adj* formal, inconsiderable, minimal, ostensible, pretended, professed, so-called, titular.

nominate *vb* appoint, choose, designate, name, present, propose.

nonchalant *adj* apathetic, careless, cool, indifferent, unconcerned.

nondescript *adj* amorphous, characterless, commonplace, dull, indescribable, odd, ordinary, unclassifiable, uninteresting, unremarkable.

nonentity *n* cipher, futility, inexistence, inexistency, insignificance, nobody, nonexistence, nothingness.

nonplus *vb* astonish, bewilder, confound, confuse, discomfit, disconcert, embarrass, floor, gravel, perplex, pose, puzzle.

nonsensical *adj* absurd, foolish, irrational, senseless, silly, stupid.

norm *n* model, pattern, rule, standard.

normal *adj* analogical, legitimate, natural, ordinary, regular, usual; erect, perpendicular, vertical.

notable *adj* distinguished, extraordinary, memorable, noted, remarkable, signal; conspicuous, evident, noticeable, observable, plain, prominent, striking; notorious, rare, well-known. * *n* celebrity, dignitary, notability, worthy.

note *vb* heed, mark, notice, observe, regard, remark; record, register; denote, designate. * *n* memorandum, minute, record; annotation, comment, remark, scholium; indication, mark, sign, symbol, token; account, bill, catalogue, reckoning; billet, epistle, letter; consideration, heed, notice, observation; celebrity, consequence, credit, distinction, eminence, fame, notability, notedness, renown, reputation, respectability; banknote, bill, promissory note; song, strain, tune, voice.

noted *adj* celebrated, conspicuous, distinguished, eminent, famed, famous, illustrious, notable, notorious, remarkable, renowned, well-known.

nothing *n* inexistence, nonentity, nonexistence, nothingness, nullity; bagatelle, trifle.

notice *vb* mark, note, observe, perceive, regard, see; comment on, mention, remark; attend to, heed. * *n* cognizance, heed, note, observation, regard; advice, announcement, information, intelligence, mention, news, notification; communication, intimation, premonition, warning; attention, civility, consideration, respect; comments, remarks.

notify *vb* advertise, announce, declare, publish, promulgate; acquaint, apprise, inform.

notion *n* concept, conception, idea; apprehension, belief, conceit, conviction, expectation, estimation, impression, judgement, opinion, sentiment, view.

notoriety *n* celebrity, fame, figure, name, note, publicity, reputation, repute, vogue.

notorious *adj* apparent, egregious, evident, notable, obvious, open, overt, manifest, patent, well-known; celebrated, conspicuous, distinguished, famed, famous, flagrant, infamous, noted, remarkable, renowned.

notwithstanding *conj* despite, however, nevertheless, yet. * *prep* despite.

nourish *vb* feed, nurse, nurture; maintain, supply, support; breed, educate, instruct, train; cherish, encourage, foment, foster, promote, succour.

nourishment *n* aliment, diet, food, nutriment, nutrition, sustenance.

novel *adj* fresh, modern, new, rare, recent, strange, uncommon, unusual. * *n* fiction, romance, story, tale.

novice *n* convert, proselyte; initiate, neophyte, novitiate, probationer; apprentice, beginner, learner, tyro.

noxious *adj* baneful, deadly, deleterious, destructive, detrimental, hurtful, injurious, insalubrious, mischievous, noisome, pernicious, pestilent, poisonous, unfavourable, unwholesome.

nude *adj* bare, denuded, exposed, naked, uncovered, unclothed, undressed.

nugatory *adj* frivolous, insignificant, trifling, trivial, vain, worthless; bootless, ineffectual, inefficacious, inoperative, null, unavailing, useless.

nuisance *n* annoyance, bore, bother, infliction, offence, pest, plague, trouble.

null *adj* ineffectual, invalid, nugatory, useless, void; characterless, colourless.

nullify *vb* abolish, abrogate, annul, cancel, invalidate, negate, quash, repeal, revoke.

numb *vb* benumb, deaden, stupefy. * *adj* benumbed, deadened, dulled, insensible, paralysed.

number *vb* calculate, compute, count, enumerate, numerate, reckon, tell; account, reckon. * *n* digit, figure, numeral; horde, multitude, numerousness, throng; aggregate, collection, sum, total.

numerous *adj* abundant, many, numberless.

nuncio *n* ambassador, legate, messenger.

nunnery *n* abbey, cloister, convent, monastery.

nuptial *adj* bridal, conjugal, connubial, hymeneal, matrimonial.

nuptials *npl* espousal, marriage, wedding.

nurse *vb* nourish, nurture; rear, suckle; cherish, encourage, feed, foment, foster, pamper, promote, succour; economize, manage; caress, dandle, fondle. * *n* auxiliary, orderly, sister; amah, *au pair*, babysitter, nanny, nursemaid, nurserymaid,

nurture *vb* feed, nourish, nurse, tend; breed, discipline, educate, instruct, rear, school, train. * *n* diet, food, nourishment; breeding, discipline, education, instruction, schooling, training, tuition; attention, nourishing, nursing.

nutriment *n* aliment, food, nourishment, nutrition, pabulum, subsistence, sustenance.

nutrition *n* diet, food, nourishment, nutriment.

nutritious *adj* invigorating, nourishing, strengthening, supporting, sustaining.

nymph *n* damsel, dryad, lass, girl, maid, maiden, naiad.

O

oaf *n* blockhead, dolt, dunce, fool, idiot, simpleton.

oath *n* blasphemy, curse, expletive, imprecation, malediction; affirmation, pledge, promise, vow.

obduracy *n* contumacy, doggedness, obstinacy, stubbornness, tenacity; depravity, impenitence.

obdurate *adj* hard, harsh, rough, rugged; callous, cantankerous, dogged, firm, hardened, inflexible, insensible, obstinate, pigheaded, unfeeling, stubborn, unbending, unyielding; depraved, graceless, lost, reprobate, shameless, impenitent, incorrigible, irreclaimable.

obedience *n* acquiescence, agreement, compliance, duty, respect, reverence, submission, submissiveness, subservience.

obedient *adj* acquiescent, compliant, deferential, duteous, dutiful, observant, regardful, respectful, submissive, subservient, yielding.

obeisance *n* bow, courtesy, curtsy, homage, reverence, salutation.

obelisk *n* column, pillar.

obese *adj* corpulent, fat, fleshy, gross, plump, podgy, portly, stout.

obesity *n* corpulence, corpulency, embonpoint, fatness, fleshiness, obeseness, plumpness.

obey *vb* comply, conform, heed, keep, mind, observe, submit, yield.

obfuscate *vb* cloud, darken, obscure; bewilder, confuse, muddle.

object[1] *vb* cavil, contravene, demur, deprecate, disapprove of, except to, impeach, oppose, protest, refuse.

object[2] *n* particular, phenomenon, precept, reality, thing; aim, butt, destination, end, mark, recipient, target; design, drift, goal, intention, motive, purpose, use, view.

objection *n* censure, difficulty, doubt, exception, protest, remonstrance, scruple.

objurgate *vb* chide, reprehend, reprove.

oblation *n* gift, offering, sacrifice.

obligation *n* accountability, accountableness, responsibility; agreement, bond, contract, covenant, engagement, stipulation; debt, indebtedness, liability.

obligatory *adj* binding, coercive, compulsory, enforced, necessary, unavoidable.

oblige *vb* bind, coerce, compel, constrain, force, necessitate, require; accommodate, benefit, convenience, favour, gratify, please; obligate, bind.

obliging *adj* accommodating, civil, complaisant, considerate, kind, friendly, polite.

oblique *adj* aslant, inclined, sidelong, slanting; indirect, obscure.

obliterate *vb* cancel, delete, destroy, efface, eradicate, erase, expunge.

oblivious *adj* careless, forgetful, heedless, inattentive, mindless, negligent, neglectful.

obloquy *n* aspersion, backbiting, blame, calumny, censure, contumely, defamation, detraction, disgrace, odium, reproach, reviling, slander, traducing.

obnoxious *adj* blameworthy, censurable, faulty, reprehensible; hateful, objectionable, obscene, odious, offensive, repellent, repugnant, repulsive, unpleasant, unpleasing.

obscene *adj* broad, coarse, filthy, gross, immodest, impure, indecent, indelicate, ribald, unchaste, lewd, licentious, loose, offensive, pornographic, shameless, smutty; disgusting, dirty, foul.

obscure *vb* becloud, befog, blur, cloud, darken, eclipse, dim, obfuscate, obnubilate, shade; conceal, cover, equivocate, hide. * *adj* dark, darksome, dim, dusky, gloomy, lurid, murky, rayless, shadowy, sombre, unenlightened, unilluminated; abstruse, blind, cabbalistic, difficult, doubtful, enigmatic, high, incomprehensible, indefinite, indistinct, intricate, involved, mysterious, mystic, recondite, undefined, unintelligible, vague; remote, secluded; humble, inglorious, nameless, renownless, undistinguished, unhonoured, unknown, unnoted, unnoticed.

obsequious *adj* cringing, deferential, fawning, flattering, servile, slavish, supple, subservient, sycophantic, truckling.

observant *adj* attentive, heedful, mindful, perceptive, quick, regardful, vigilant, watchful.

observation *n* attention, cognition, notice, observance; annotation, note, remark; experience, knowledge.

observe *vb* eye, mark, note, notice, remark, watch; behold, detect, discover, perceive, see; express, mention, remark, say, utter; comply, conform, follow, fulfil, obey; celebrate, keep, regard, solemnize.

obsolete *adj* ancient, antiquated, antique, archaic, disused, neglected, old, old-fashioned, obsolescent, out-of-date, past, passé, unfashionable.

obstacle *n* barrier, check, difficulty, hindrance, impediment, interference, interruption, obstruction, snag, stumbling block.

obstinacy *n* contumacy, doggedness, headiness, firmness, inflexibility, intractability, obduracy, persistence, perseverance, perversity, resoluteness, stubbornness, tenacity, wilfulness.

obstinate *adj* cross-grained, contumacious, dogged, firm, headstrong, inflexible, immovable, intractable, mulish, obdurate, opinionated, persistent, pertinacious, perverse, resolute, self-willed, stubborn, tenacious, unyielding, wilful.

obstreperous *adj* boisterous, clamorous, loud, noisy, riotous, tumultuous, turbulent, unruly, uproarious, vociferous.

obstruct *vb* bar, barricade, block, blockade, block up, choke, clog, close, glut, jam, obturate, stop; hinder, impede, oppose, prevent; arrest, check, curb, delay, embrace, interrupt, retard, slow.

obstruction *n* bar, barrier, block, blocking, check, difficulty, hindrance, impediment, obstacle, stoppage; check, clog, embarrassment, interruption, obturation.

obtain *vb* achieve, acquire, attain, bring, contrive, earn, elicit, gain, get, induce, procure, secure; hold, prevail, stand, subsist.

obtrude *vb* encroach, infringe, interfere, intrude, trespass.

obtrusive *adj* forward, interfering, intrusive, meddling, officious.

obtuse *adj* blunt; blockish, doltish, dull, dull-witted, heavy, stockish, stolid, stupid, slow, unintellectual, unintelligent.

obviate *vb* anticipate, avert, counteract, preclude, prevent, remove.

obvious *adj* exposed, liable, open, subject; apparent, clear, distinct, evident, manifest, palatable, patent, perceptible, plain, self-evident, unmistakable, visible.

occasion *vb* breed, cause, create, originate, produce; induce, influence, move, persuade. * *n* casualty, event, incident, occurrence; conjuncture, convenience, juncture, opening, opportunity; condition, necessity, need, exigency, requirement, want; cause, ground, reason; inducement, influence; circumstance, exigency.

occasional *adj* accidental, casual, incidental, infrequent, irregular, uncommon; causative, causing.

occasionally *adv* casually, sometimes.

occult *adj* abstruse, cabbalistic, hidden, latent, secret, invisible, mysterious, mystic, mystical, recondite, shrouded, undetected, undiscovered, unknown, unrevealed, veiled. * *n* magic, sorcery, witchcraft.

occupation *n* holding, occupancy, possession, tenure, use; avocation, business, calling, craft, employment, engagement, job, post, profession, trade, vocation.

occupy *vb* capture, hold, keep, possess;

cover, fill, garrison, inhabit, take up, tenant; engage, employ, use.

occur *vb* appear, arise, offer; befall, chance, eventuate, happen, result, supervene.

occurrence *n* accident, adventure, affair, casualty, event, happening, incident, proceeding, transaction.

odd *adj* additional, redundant, remaining; casual, incidental; inappropriate, queer, unsuitable; comical, droll, erratic, extravagant, extraordinary, fantastic, grotesque, irregular, peculiar, quaint, singular, strange, uncommon, uncouth, unique, unusual, whimsical.

odds *npl* difference, disparity, inequality; advantage, superiority, supremacy.

odious *adj* abominable, detestable, execrable, hateful, shocking; hated, obnoxious, unpopular; disagreeable, forbidding, loathsome, offensive.

odium *n* abhorrence, detestation, dislike, enmity, hate, hatred; odiousness, repulsiveness; obloquy, opprobrium, reproach, shame.

odorous *adj* aromatic, balmy, fragrant, perfumed, redolent, scented, sweet-scented, sweet-smelling.

odour *n* aroma, fragrance, perfume, redolence, scent, smell.

offal *n* carrion, dregs, garbage, refuse, rubbish, waste.

offence *n* aggression, attack, assault; anger, displeasure, indignation, pique, resentment, umbrage, wrath; affront, harm, injury, injustice, insult, outrage, wrong; crime, delinquency, fault, misdeed, misdemeanour, sin, transgression, trespass.

offend *vb* affront, annoy, chafe, displease, fret, gall, irritate, mortify, nettle, provoke, vex; molest, pain, shock, wound; fall, sin, stumble, transgress.

offender *n* convict, criminal, culprit, delinquent, felon, malefactor, sinner, transgressor, trespasser.

offensive *adj* aggressive, attacking, invading; disgusting, loathsome, nauseating, nauseous, repulsive, sickening; abominable, detestable, disagreeable, displeasing, execrable, hateful, obnoxious, repugnant, revolting, shocking, unpalatable, unpleasant; abusive, disagreeable, impertinent, insolent, insulting, irritating, opprobrious, rude, saucy, unpleasant. * *n* attack, onslaught.

offer *vb* present, proffer, tender; exhibit; furnish, propose, propound, show; volunteer; dare, essay, endeavour, venture. * *n* overture, proffering, proposal, proposition, tender, overture; attempt, bid, endeavour, essay.

offhand *adj* abrupt, brusque, casual, curt, extempore, impromptu, informal, unpremeditated, unstudied. * *adv* carelessly, casually, clumsily, haphazardly, informally, slapdash; ad-lib, extemporaneously, extemporarily, extempore, impromptu.

office *n* duty, function, service, work; berth, place, position, post, situation; business, capacity, charge, employment, trust; bureau, room.

officiate *vb* act, perform, preside, serve.

officious *adj* busy, dictatorial, forward, impertinent, interfering, intermeddling, meddlesome, meddling, obtrusive, pushing, pushy.

offset *vb* balance, counteract, counterbalance, counterpoise. * *n* branch, offshoot, scion, shoot, slip, sprout, twig; counterbalance, counterpoise, set-off, equivalent.

offspring *n* brood, children, descendants, issue, litter, posterity, progeny; cadet, child, scion.

often *adv* frequently, generally, oftentimes, repeatedly.

ogre *n* bugbear, demon, devil, goblin, hobgoblin, monster, spectre.

old *adj* aged, ancient, antiquated, antique, archaic, elderly, obsolete, olden, old-fashioned, superannuated; decayed, done, senile, worn-out; original, primitive, pristine; former, preceding, pre-existing.

oleaginous *adj* adipose, fat, fatty, greasy, oily, sebaceous, unctuous.

omen *n* augury, auspice, foreboding, portent, presage, prognosis, sign, warning.

ominous *adj* inauspicious, monitory, portentous, premonitory, threatening, unpropitious.

omission *n* default, failure, forgetfulness, neglect, oversight.

omit *vb* disregard, drop, eliminate, exclude, miss, neglect, overlook, skip.

omnipotent *adj* almighty, all-powerful.

omniscient *adj* all-knowing, all-seeing, all-wise.

oneness *n* individuality, singleness, unity.

onerous *adj* burdensome, difficult, hard, heavy, laborious, oppressive, responsible, weighty.

one-sided *adj* partial, prejudiced, unfair, unilateral, unjust.

only *adj* alone, single, sole, solitary. * *adv* barely, merely, simply.

onset *n* assault, attack, charge, onslaught, storm, storming.

onus *n* burden, liability, load, responsibility.

ooze *vb* distil, drip, drop, shed; drain, exude, filter, leak, percolate, stain, transude. * *n* mire, mud, slime.

opaque *adj* dark, dim, hazy, muddy; abstruse, cryptic, enigmatic, enigmatical, obscure, unclear.

open *vb* expand, spread; begin, commence, initiate; disclose, exhibit, reveal, show; unbar, unclose, uncover, unlock, unseal, untie. * *adj* expanded, extended, unclosed, spread wide; aboveboard, artless, candid, cordial, fair, frank, guileless, hearty, honest, sincere, openhearted, single-minded, undesigning, undisguised, undissembling, unreserved; bounteous, bountiful, free, generous, liberal, munificent; ajar, uncovered; exposed, undefended, unprotected; clear, unobstructed; accessible, public, unenclosed, unrestricted; mild, moderate; apparent, debatable, evident, obvious, patent, plain, undetermined.

opening *adj* commencing, first, inaugural, initiatory, introductory. * *n* aperture, breach, chasm, cleft, fissure, flaw, gap, gulf, hole, interspace, loophole, orifice, perforation, rent, rift; beginning, commencement, dawn; chance, opportunity, vacancy.

openly *adv* candidly, frankly, honestly, plainly, publicly.

openness *n* candour, frankness, honesty, ingenuousness, plainness, unreservedness.

operate *vb* act, function, work; cause, effect, occasion, produce; manipulate, use, run.

operation *n* manipulation, performance, procedure, proceeding, process; action, affair, manoeuvre, motion, movement.

operative *adj* active, effective, effectual, efficient, serviceable, vigorous; important, indicative, influential, significant. * *n* artisan, employee, labourer, mechanic, worker, workman.

opiate *adj* narcotic, sedative, soporiferous, soporific. * *n* anodyne, drug, narcotic, sedative, tranquillizer.

opine *vb* apprehend, believe, conceive, fancy, judge, suppose, presume, surmise, think.

opinion *n* conception, idea, impression, judgment, notion, sentiment, view; belief, persuasion, tenet; esteem, estimation, judgment.

opinionated *adj* biased, bigoted, cocksure, conceited, dictatorial, dogmatic, opinionative, prejudiced, stubborn.

opponent *adj* adverse, antagonistic, contrary, opposing, opposite, repugnant. * *n* adversary, antagonist, competitor, contestant, counteragent, enemy, foe, opposite, opposer, party, rival.

opportune *adj* appropriate, auspicious, convenient, favourable, felicitous, fit, fitting, fortunate, lucky, propitious, seasonable, suitable, timely, well-timed.

opportunity *n* chance, convenience, moment, occasion.

oppose *vb* combat, contravene, counteract, dispute, obstruct, oppugn, resist, thwart, withstand; check, prevent; confront, counterpoise.

opposite *adj* facing, fronting; conflicting, contradictory, contrary, different, diverse, incompatible, inconsistent, irreconcilable; adverse, antagonistic, hostile, inimical, opposed, opposing, repugnant. * *n* contradiction, contrary, converse, reverse.

opposition *n* antagonism, antinomy, contrariety, inconsistency, repugnance; counteraction, counter-influence, hostility, resistance; hindrance, obstacle, obstruction, oppression, prevention.

oppress *vb* burden, crush, depress, harass, load, maltreat, overburden, overpower, overwhelm, persecute, subdue, suppress, tyrannize, wrong.

oppression *n* abuse, calamity, cruelty, hardship, injury, injustice, misery, persecution, severity, suffering, tyranny; depression, dullness, heaviness, lassitude.

oppressive *adj* close, muggy, stifling, suffocating, sultry.

opprobrious *adj* abusive, condemnatory, contemptuous, damnatory, insolent, insulting, offensive, reproachable, scandalous, scurrilous, vituperative; despised, dishonourable, disreputable, hateful, infamous, shameful.

opprobrium *n* contumely, scurrility; calumny, disgrace, ignominy, infamy, obloquy, odium, reproach.

oppugn *vb* assail, argue, attack, combat, contravene, oppose, resist, thwart, withstand.

option *n* choice, discretion, election, preference, selection.

optional *adj* discretionary, elective, nonobligatory, voluntary.

opulence *n* affluence, fortune, independence, luxury, riches, wealth.

opulent *adj* affluent, flush, luxurious, moneyed, plentiful, rich, sumptuous, wealthy.

oracular *adj* ominous, portentous, prophetic; authoritative, dogmatic, magisterial, positive; aged, grave, wise; ambiguous, blind, dark, equivocal, obscure.

oral *adj* nuncupative, spoken, verbal, vocal.

oration *n* address, declamation, discourse, harangue, speech.

orb *n* ball, globe, sphere; circle, circuit, orbit, ring; disk, wheel.

orbit *vb* circle, encircle, revolve around. * *n* course, path, revolution, track.

ordain *vb* appoint, call, consecrate, elect, experiment, constitute, establish, institute, regulate; decree, enjoin, enact, order, prescribe.

order *vb* adjust, arrange, methodize, regulate, systematize; carry on, conduct, manage; bid, command, direct, instruct, require. * *n* arrangement, disposition, method, regularity, symmetry, system; law, regulation, rule; discipline, peace, quiet; command, commission, direction, injunction, instruction, mandate, prescription; class, degree, grade, kind, rank; family, tribe; brotherhood, community, fraternity, society; sequence, succession.

orderly *adj* methodical, regular, systematic; peaceable, quiet, well-behaved; neat, shipshape, tidy.

ordinance *n* appointment, command, decree, edict, enactment, law, order, prescript, regulation, rule, statute; ceremony, observance, sacrament, rite, ritual.

ordinary *adj* accustomed, customary, established, everyday, normal, regular, settled, wonted, everyday, regular; common, frequent, habitual, usual; average, commonplace, indifferent, inferior, mean, mediocre, second-rate, undistinguished; homely, plain.

organization *n* business, construction, constitution, organism, structure, system.

organize *vb* adjust, constitute, construct, form, make, shape; arrange, coordinate, correlate, establish, systematize.

orgy *n* carousal, debauch, debauchery, revel, saturnalia.

orifice *n* aperture, hole, mouth, perforation, pore, vent.

origin *n* beginning, birth, commencement, cradle, derivation, foundation, fountain, fountainhead, original, rise, root, source, spring, starting point; cause, occasion; heritage, lineage, parentage.

original *adj* aboriginal, first, primary, primeval, primitive, primordial, pristine; fresh, inventive, novel; eccentric, odd, peculiar. * *n* cause, commencement, origin, source, spring; archetype, exemplar, model, pattern, prototype, protoplast, type.

originate *vb* arise, begin, emanate, flow,

proceed, rise, spring; create, discover, form, invent, produce.
originator *n* author, creator, former, inventor, maker, parent.
orison *n* petition, prayer, solicitation, supplication.
ornament *vb* adorn, beautify, bedeck, bedizen, decorate, deck, emblazon, garnish, grace. * *n* adornment, bedizenment, decoration, design, embellishment, garnish, ornamentation.
ornate *adj* beautiful, bedecked, decorated, elaborate, elegant, embellished, florid, flowery, ornamental, ornamented.
orthodox *adj* conventional, correct, sound, true.
oscillate *vb* fluctuate, sway, swing, vacillate, vary, vibrate.
ostensible *adj* apparent, assigned, avowed, declared, exhibited, manifest, presented, visible; plausible, professed, specious.
ostentation *n* dash, display, flourish, pageantry, parade, pomp, pomposity, pompousness, show, vaunting; appearance, semblance, showiness.
ostentatious *adj* boastful, dashing, flaunting, pompous, pretentious, showy, vain, vainglorious; gaudy.
ostracize *vb* banish, boycott, exclude, excommunicate, exile, expatriate, expel, evict.
oust *vb* dislodge, dispossess, eject, evict, expel.
outbreak *n* ebullition, eruption, explosion, outburst; affray, broil, conflict, commotion, fray, riot, row; flare-up, manifestation.
outcast *n* exile, expatriate; castaway, pariah, reprobate, vagabond.
outcome *n* conclusion, consequence, event, issue, result, upshot.
outcry *n* cry, scream, screech, yell; bruit, clamour, noise, tumult, vociferation.
outdo *vb* beat, exceed, excel, outgo, outstrip, outvie, surpass.
outlandish *adj* alien, exotic, foreign, strange; barbarous, bizarre, uncouth.
outlaw *vb* ban, banish, condemn, exclude, forbid, make illegal, prohibit. * *n* bandit, brigand, crook, freebooter, highwayman, lawbreaker, marauder, robber, thief.
outlay *n* disbursement, expenditure, outgoings.
outline *vb* delineate, draft, draw, plan, silhouette, sketch. * *n* contour, profile; delineation, draft, drawing, plan, rough draft, silhouette, sketch.
outlive *vb* last, live longer, survive.
outlook *n* future, prospect, sight, view; lookout, watch-tower.
outrage *vb* abuse, injure, insult, maltreat, offend, shock, injure. * *n* abuse, affront, indignity, insult, offence.
outrageous *adj* abusive, frantic, furious, frenzied, mad, raging, turbulent, violent, wild; atrocious, enormous, flagrant, heinous, monstrous, nefarious, villainous; enormous, excessive, extravagant, unwarrantable.
outré *adj* excessive, exorbitant, extravagant, immoderate, inordinate, overstrained, unconventional.
outrun *vb* beat, exceed, outdistance, outgo, outstrip, outspeed, surpass.
outset *n* beginning, commencement, entrance, opening, start, starting point.
outshine *vb* eclipse, outstrip, overshadow, surpass.
outspoken *adj* abrupt, blunt, candid, frank, plain, plainspoken, unceremonious, unreserved.
outstanding *adj* due, owing, uncollected, ungathered, unpaid, unsettled; conspicuous, eminent, prominent, striking.
outward *adj* exterior, external, outer, outside.
outwit *vb* cheat, circumvent, deceive, defraud, diddle, dupe, gull, outmanoeuvre, overreach, swindle, victimize.
overawe *vb* affright, awe, browbeat, cow, daunt, frighten, intimidate, scare, terrify.
overbalance *vb* capsize, overset, overturn, tumble, upset; outweigh, preponderate.
overbearing *adj* oppressive, overpowering; arrogant, dictatorial, dogmatic, domineering, haughty, imperious, overweening, proud, supercilious.
overcast *vb* cloud, darken, overcloud, overshadow, shade, shadow. **adj* cloudy, darkened, hazy, murky, obscure.

overcharge *vb* burden, oppress, overburden, overload, surcharge; crowd, overfill; exaggerate, overstate, overstrain.

overcome *vb* beat, choke, conquer, crush, defeat, discomfit, overbear, overmaster, overpower, overthrow, overturn, overwhelm, prevail, rout, subdue, subjugate, surmount, vanquish.

overflow *vb* brim over, fall over, pour over, pour out, shower, spill; deluge, inundate, submerge. * *n* deluge, inundation, profusion, superabundance.

overhaul *vb* overtake; check, examine, inspect, repair, survey. * *n* check, examination, inspection.

overlay *vb* cover, spread over; overlie, overpress, smother; crush, overpower, overwhelm; cloud, hide, obscure, overcast. * *n* appliqué, covering, decoration, veneer.

overlook *vb* inspect, oversee, superintend, supervise; disregard, miss, neglect, slight; condone, excuse, forgive, pardon, pass over.

overpower *vb* beat, conquer, crush, defeat, discomfit, overbear, overcome, overmaster, overturn, overwhelm, subdue, subjugate, vanquish.

overreach *vb* exceed, outstrip, overshoot, pass, surpass; cheat, circumvent, deceive, defraud.

override *vb* outride, outweigh, pass, quash, supersede, surpass.

overrule *vb* control, govern, sway; annul, cancel, nullify, recall, reject, repeal, repudiate, rescind, revoke, reject, set aside, supersede, suppress.

oversight *n* care, charge, control, direction, inspection, management, superintendence, supervision, surveillance; blunder, error, fault, inadvertence, inattention, lapse, miss, mistake, neglect, omission, slip, trip.

overt *adj* apparent, glaring, open, manifest, notorious, patent, public, unconcealed.

overthrow *vb* overturn, upset, subvert; demolish, destroy, level; beat, conquer, crush, defeat, discomfit, foil, master, overcome, overpower, overwhelm, rout, subjugate, vanquish, worst. * *n* downfall, fall, prostration, subversion; destruction, demolition, ruin; defeat, discomfiture, dispersion, rout.

overturn *vb* invert, overthrow, reverse, subvert, upset.

overture *n* invitation, offer, proposal, proposition.

overweening *adj* arrogant, conceited, consequential, egotistical, haughty, opinionated, proud, supercilious, vain, vainglorious.

overwhelm *vb* drown, engulf, inundate, overflow, submerge, swallow up, swamp; conquer, crush, defeat, overbear, overcome, overpower, subdue, vanquish.

overwrought *adj* overdone, overelaborate; agitated, excited, overexcited, overworked, stirred.

own[1] *vb* have, hold, possess; avow, confess; acknowledge, admit, allow, concede.

own[2] *adj* particular, personal, private.

owner *n* freeholder, holder, landlord, possessor, proprietor.

P

pace *vb* go, hasten, hurry, move, step, walk. * *n* amble, gait, step, walk.
pacific *adj* appeasing, conciliatory, ironic, mollifying, placating, peacemaking, propitiatory; calm, gentle, peaceable, peaceful, quiet, smooth, tranquil, unruffled.
pacify *vb* appease, conciliate, harmonize, tranquillize; allay, appease, assuage, calm, compose, hush, lay, lull, moderate, mollify, placate, propitiate, quell, quiet, smooth, soften, soothe, still.
pack *vb* compact, compress, crowd, fill; bundle, burden, load, stow. * *n* bale, budget, bundle, package, packet, parcel; burden, load; assemblage, assembly, assortment, collection, set; band, bevy, clan, company, crew, gang, knot, lot, party, squad.
pact *n* agreement, alliance, bargain, bond, compact, concordat, contract, convention, covenant, league, stipulation.
pagan *adj* heathen, heathenish, idolatrous, irreligious, paganist, paganistic. * *n* gentile, heathen, idolater.
pageantry *n* display, flourish, magnificence, parade, pomp, show, splendour, state.
pain *vb* agonize, bite, distress, hurt, rack, sting, torment, torture; afflict, aggrieve, annoy, bore, chafe, displease, disquiet, fret, grieve, harass, incommode, plague, tease, trouble, vex, worry; rankle, smart, shoot, sting, twinge. * *n* ache, agony, anguish, discomfort, distress, gripe, hurt, pang, smart, soreness, sting, suffering, throe, torment, torture, twinge; affliction, anguish, anxiety, bitterness, care, chagrin, disquiet, dolour, grief, heartache, misery, punishment, solicitude, sorrow, trouble, uneasiness, unhappiness, vexation, woe, wretchedness.
painful *adj* agonizing, distressful, excruciating, racking, sharp, tormenting, torturing; afflicting, afflictive, annoying, baleful, disagreeable, displeasing, disquieting, distressing, dolorous, grievous, provoking, troublesome, unpleasant, vexatious; arduous, careful, difficult, hard, severe, sore, toilsome.
pains *npl* care, effort, labour, task, toilsomeness, trouble; childbirth, labour, travail.
painstaking *adj* assiduous, careful, conscientious, diligent, hardworking, industrious, laborious, persevering, plodding, sedulous, strenuous.
paint *vb* delineate, depict, describe, draw, figure, pencil, portray, represent, sketch; adorn, beautify, deck, embellish, ornament. * *n* colouring, dye, pigment, stain; cosmetics, greasepaint, make-up.
pair *vb* couple, marry, mate, match. * *n* brace, couple, double, duo, match, twosome.
pal *n* buddy, chum, companion, comrade, crony, friend, mate, mucker.
palatable *adj* acceptable, agreeable, appetizing, delicate, delicious, enjoyable, flavourful, flavoursome, gustative, gustatory, luscious, nice, pleasant, pleasing, savoury, relishable, tasteful, tasty, toothsome.
palaver *vb* chat, chatter, converse, patter, prattle, say, speak, talk; confer, parley; blandish, cajole, flatter, wheedle. * *n* chat, chatter, conversation, discussion, language, prattle, speech, talk; confab, confabulation, conference, conclave, parley, powwow; balderdash, cajolery, flummery, gibberish.
pale *vb* blanch, lose colour, whiten. * *adj* ashen, ashy, blanched, bloodless, pallid, sickly, wan, white; blank, dim, obscure, spectral. * *n* picket, stake; circuit, enclo-

sure; district, region, territory; boundary, confine, fence, limit.

pall[1] *n* cloak, cover, curtain, mantle, pallium, shield, shroud, veil.

pall[2] *vb* cloy, glut, gorge, satiate, surfeit; deject, depress, discourage, dishearten, dispirit; cloak, cover, drape, invest, overspread, shroud.

palliate *vb* cloak, conceal, cover, excuse, extenuate, hide, gloss, lessen; abate, allay, alleviate, assuage, blunt, diminish, dull, ease, mitigate, moderate, mollify, quell, quiet, relieve, soften, soothe, still.

pallid *adj* ashen, ashy, cadaverous, colourless, pale, sallow, wan, whitish.

palm[1] *vb* foist, impose, obtrude, pass off; handle, touch.

palm[2] *n* bays, crown, laurels, prize, trophy, victory.

palmy *adj* flourishing, fortunate, glorious, golden, halcyon, happy, joyous, prosperous, thriving, victorious.

palpable *adj* corporeal, material, tactile, tangible; evident, glaring, gross, intelligible, manifest, obvious, patent, plain, unmistakable.

palpitate *vb* flutter, pulsate, throb; quiver, shiver, tremble.

palter *vb* dodge, equivocate, evade, haggle, prevaricate, quibble, shift, shuffle, trifle.

paltry *adj* diminutive, feeble, inconsiderable, insignificant, little, miserable, petty, slender, slight, small, sorry, trifling, trivial, unimportant, wretched.

pamper *vb* baby, coddle, fondle, gratify, humour, spoil.

panacea *n* catholicon, cure-all, medicine, remedy.

panegyric *adj* commendatory, encomiastic, encomiastical, eulogistic, eulogistical, laudatory, panegyrical. * *n* eulogy, laudation, praise, paean, tribute.

pang *n* agony, anguish, distress, gripe, pain, throe, twinge.

panic *vb* affright, alarm, scare, startle, terrify; become terrified, overreact. * *n* alarm, consternation, fear, fright, jitters, terror.

pant *vb* blow, gasp, puff; heave, palpitate, pulsate, throb; languish; desire, hunger, long, sigh, thirst, yearn. * *n* blow, gasp, puff.

parable *n* allegory, fable, story.

paraclete *n* advocate, comforter, consoler, intercessor, mediator.

parade *vb* display, flaunt, show, vaunt. * *n* ceremony, display, flaunting, ostentation, pomp, show; array, pageant, review, spectacle; mall, promenade.

paradox *n* absurdity, contradiction, mystery.

paragon *n* flower, ideal, masterpiece, model, nonpareil, pattern, standard.

paragraph *n* clause, item, notice, passage, section, sentence, subdivision.

parallel *vb* be alike, compare, conform, correlate, match. * *adj* abreast, concurrent; allied, analogous, correspondent, equal, like, resembling, similar. * *n* conformity, likeness, resemblance, similarity; analogue, correlative, counterpart.

paramount *adj* chief, dominant, eminent, pre-eminent, principal, superior, supreme.

paraphernalia *n* accoutrements, appendages, appurtenances, baggage, belongings, effects, equipage, equipment, ornaments, trappings.

parasite *n* bloodsucker, fawner, flatterer, flunky, hanger-on, leech, spaniel, sycophant, toady, wheedler.

parcel *vb* allot, apportion, dispense, distribute, divide. * *n* budget, bundle, package; batch, collection, group, lot, set; division, part, patch, pierce, plot, portion, tract.

parched *adj* arid, dry, scorched, shrivelled, thirsty.

pardon *vb* condone, forgive, overlook, remit; absolve, acquit, clear, discharge, excuse, release. * *n* absolution, amnesty, condonation, discharge, excuse, forgiveness, grace, mercy, overlook, release.

parentage *n* ancestry, birth, descent, extraction, family, lineage, origin, parenthood, pedigree, stock.

pariah *n* outcast, wretch.

parish *n* community, congregation, parishioners; district, subdivision.

parity *n* analogy, correspondence, equality, equivalence, likeness, sameness, similarity.

parody *vb* burlesque, caricature, imitate, lampoon, mock, ridicule, satirize, travesty. * *n* burlesque, caricature, imitation, ridicule, satire, travesty.

paroxysm *n* attack, convulsion, exacerbation, fit, outburst, seizure, spasm, throe.

parsimonious *adj* avaricious, close, close-fisted, covetous, frugal, grasping, grudging, illiberal, mean, mercenary, miserly, near, niggardly, penurious, shabby, sordid, sparing, stingy, tightfisted.

parson *n* churchman, clergyman, divine, ecclesiastic, incumbent, minister, pastor, priest, rector.

part *vb* break, dismember, dissever, divide, sever, subdivide, sunder; detach, disconnect, disjoin, dissociate, disunite, separate; allot, apportion, distribute, divide, mete, share; secrete. * *n* crumb, division, fraction, fragment, moiety, parcel, piece, portion, remnant, scrap, section, segment, subdivision; component, constituent, element, ingredient, member, organ; lot, share; concern, interest, participation; allotment, apportionment, dividend; business, charge, duty, function, office, work; faction, party, side; character, cue, lines, role; clause, paragraph, passage.

partake *vb* engage, participate, share; consume, eat, take;evince, evoke, show, suggest.

partial *adj* component, fractional, imperfect, incomplete, limited; biased, influential, interested, one-sided, prejudiced, prepossessed, unfair, unjust, warped; fond, indulgent.

participate *vb* engage in, partake, perform, share.

particle *n* atom, bit, corpuscle, crumb, drop, glimmer, grain, granule, iota, jot, mite, molecule, morsel, mote, scrap, shred, snip, spark, speck, whit.

particular *adj* especial, special, specific; distinct, individual, respective, separate, single; characteristic, distinctive, peculiar; individual, intimate, own, personal, private; notable, noteworthy; circumstantial, definite, detailed, exact, minute, narrow, precise; careful, close, conscientious, critical, fastidious, nice, scrupulous, strict; marked, odd, singular, strange, uncommon. * *n* case, circumstance, count, detail, feature, instance, item, particularity, point, regard, respect.

parting *adj* breaking, dividing, separating; final, last, valedictory; declining, departing. * *n* breaking, disruption, rupture, severing; detachment, division, separation; death, departure, farewell, leave-taking.

partisan *adj* biased, factional, interested, partial, prejudiced. * *n* adherent, backer, champion, disciple, follower, supporter, votary; baton, halberd, pike, quarterstaff, truncheon, staff.

partition *vb* apportion, distribute, divide, portion, separate, share. * *n* division, separation; barrier, division, screen, wall; allotment, apportionment, distribution.

partner *n* associate, colleague, copartner, partaker, participant, participator; accomplice, ally, coadjutor, confederate; companion, consort, spouse.

partnership *n* association, company, copartnership, firm, house, society; connection, interest, participation, union.

parts *npl* abilities, accomplishments, endowments, faculties, genius, gifts, intellect, intelligence, mind, qualities, powers, talents; districts, regions.

party *n* alliance, association, cabal, circle, clique, combination, confederacy, coterie, faction, group, junta, league, ring, set; body, company, detachment, squad, troop; assembly, gathering; partaker, participant, participator, sharer; defendant, litigant, plaintiff; individual, one, person, somebody; cause, division, interest, side.

pass[1] *vb* devolve, fall, go, move, proceed; change, elapse, flit, glide, lapse, slip; cease, die, fade, expire, vanish; happen, occur; convey, deliver, send, transmit, transfer; disregard, ignore, neglect; exceed, excel, surpass; approve, ratify, sanction; answer, do, succeed, suffice, suit; express, pronounce, utter; beguile, wile.

pass[2] *n* avenue, ford, road, route, way; defile, gorge, passage, ravine; authorization, licence, passport, permission, ticket; condition, conjecture, plight, situation, state; lunge, push, thrust, tilt; transfer, trick.

passable *adj* admissible, allowable, mediocre, middling, moderate, ordinary, so-so, tolerable; acceptable, current, receivable; navigable, traversable.

passage *n* going, passing, progress, transit; evacuation, journey, migration, transit, voyage; avenue, channel, course, pass, path, road, route, thoroughfare, vennel, way; access, currency, entry, reception; act, deed, event, feat, incidence, occurrence, passion; corridor, gallery, gate, hall; clause, paragraph, sentence, text; course, death, decease, departure, expiration, lapse; affair, brush, change, collision, combat, conflict, contest, encounter, exchange, joust, skirmish, tilt.

passenger *n* fare, itinerant, tourist, traveller, voyager, wayfarer.

passionate *adj* animated, ardent, burning, earnest, enthusiastic, excited, fervent, fiery, furious, glowing, hot-blooded, impassioned, impetuous, impulsive, intense, vehement, warm, zealous; hot-headed, irascible, quick-tempered, tempestuous, violent.

passive *adj* inactive, inert, quiescent, receptive; apathetic, enduring, long-suffering, nonresistant, patient, stoical, submissive, suffering, unresisting.

past *adj* accomplished, elapsed, ended, gone, spent; ancient, bygone, former, obsolete, outworn. * *adv* above, extra, beyond, over. * *prep* above, after, beyond, exceeding. * *n* antiquity, heretofore, history, olden times, yesterday.

pastime *n* amusement, diversion, entertainment, hobby, play, recreation, sport.

pastor *n* clergyman, churchman, divine, ecclesiastic, minister, parson, priest, vicar.

pat[1] *vb* dab, hit, rap, tap; caress, chuck, fondle, pet. * *n* dab, hit, pad, rap, tap; caress.

pat[2] *adj* appropriate, apt, fit, pertinent, suitable. * *adv* aptly, conveniently, fitly, opportunely, seasonably.

patch *vb* mend, repair. * *n* repair; parcel, plot, tract.

patent *adj* expanded, open, spreading; apparent, clear, conspicuous, evident, glaring, indisputable, manifest, notorious, obvious, public, open, palpable, plain, unconcealed, unmistakable. * *n* copyright, privilege, right.

paternity *n* derivation, descent, fatherhood, origin.

path *n* access, avenue, course, footway, passage, pathway, road, route, track, trail, way.

pathetic *adj* affecting, melting, moving, pitiable, plaintive, sad, tender, touching.

patience *n* endurance, fortitude, long-sufferance, resignation, submission, sufferance; calmness, composure, quietness; forbearance, indulgence, leniency; assiduity, constancy, diligence, indefatigability, indefatigableness, perseverance, persistence.

patient *adj* meek, passive, resigned, submissive, uncomplaining, unrepining; calm, composed, contented, quiet; indulgent, lenient, long-suffering; assiduous, constant, diligent, indefatigable, persevering, persistent. * *n* case, invalid, subject, sufferer.

patrician *adj* aristocratic, blue-blooded, highborn, noble, senatorial, well-born. * *n* aristocrat, blue blood, nobleman.

patron *n* advocate, defender, favourer, guardian, helper, protector, supporter.

patronize *vb* aid, assist, befriend, countenance, defend, favour, maintain, support; condescend, disparage, scorn.

pattern *vb* copy, follow, imitate. * *n* archetype, exemplar, last, model, original, paradigm, plan, prototype; example, guide, sample, specimen; mirror, paragon; design, figure, shape, style, type.

paucity *n* deficiency, exiguity, insufficiency, lack, poverty, rarity, shortage.

paunch *n* abdomen, belly, gut, stomach.

pauperism *n* beggary, destitution, indigence, mendicancy, mendicity, need, poverty, penury, want.

pause *vb* breathe, cease, delay, desist, rest, stay, stop, wait; delay, forbear, intermit, stay, stop, tarry, wait; deliberate, demur, hesitate, waver. * *n* break, caesura, cessation, halt, intermission, interruption, interval, remission, rest, stop, stoppage, stopping, suspension; hesitation, suspense, uncertainty; paragraph.

pawn[1] *n* cat's-paw, dupe, plaything, puppet, stooge, tool, toy.

pawn[2] *vb* bet, gage, hazard, lay, pledge, risk, stake, wager. * *n* assurance, bond, guarantee, pledge, security.

pay *vb* defray, discharge, discount, foot, honour, liquidate, meet, quit, settle; compensate, recompense, reimburse, requite, reward; punish, revenge; give, offer, render. * *n* allowance, commission, compensation, emolument, hire, recompense, reimbursement, remuneration, requital, reward, salary, wages.

peace *n* calm, calmness, quiet, quietness, repose, stillness; accord, amity, friendliness, harmony; composure, equanimity, imperturbability, placidity, quietude, tranquillity; agreement, armistice.

peaceable *adj* pacific, peaceful; amiable, amicable, friendly, gentle, inoffensive, mild; placid, quiet, serene, still, tranquil, undisturbed, unmoved.

peaceful *adj* quiet, undisturbed; amicable, concordant, friendly, gentle, harmonious, mild, pacific, peaceable; calm, composed, placid, serene, still.

peak *vb* climax, culminate, top; dwindle, thin. * *n* acme, apex, crest, crown, pinnacle, summit, top, zenith.

peaked *adj* piked, pointed, thin.

peasant *n* boor, countryman, clown, hind, labourer, rustic, swain.

peculate *vb* appropriate, defraud, embezzle, misappropriate, pilfer, purloin, rob, steal.

peculiar *adj* appropriate, idiosyncratic, individual, proper; characteristic, eccentric, exceptional, extraordinary, odd, queer, rare, singular, strange, striking, uncommon, unusual; individual, especial, particular, select, special, specific.

peculiarity *n* appropriateness, distinctiveness, individuality, speciality; characteristic, idiosyncrasy, oddity, peculiarity, singularity.

pedantic *adj* conceited, fussy, officious, ostentatious, over-learned, particular, pedagogical, pompous, pragmatical, precise, pretentious, priggish, stilted.

pedlar *n* chapman, costermonger, hawker, packman, vendor.

pedigree *adj* purebred, thoroughbred. * *n* ancestry, breed, descent, extraction, family, genealogy, house, line, lineage, race, stock, strain.

peer[1] *vb* gaze, look, peek, peep, pry, squinny, squint; appear, emerge.

peer[2] *n* associate, co-equal, companion, compeer, equal, equivalent, fellow, like, mate, match; aristocrat, baron, count, duke, earl, grandee, lord, marquis, noble, nobleman, viscount.

peerless *adj* excellent, incomparable, matchless, outstanding, superlative, unequalled, unique, unmatched, unsurpassed.

peevish *adj* acrimonious, captious, churlish, complaining, crabbed, cross, crusty, discontented, fretful, ill-natured, ill-tempered, irascible, irritable, pettish, petulant, querulous, snappish, snarling, splenetic, spleeny, testy, waspish; forward, headstrong, obstinate, self-willed, stubborn; childish, silly, thoughtless, trifling.

pellucid *adj* bright, clear, crystalline, diaphanous, limpid, lucid, transparent.

pelt[1] *vb* assail, batter, beat, belabour, bombard, pepper, stone, strike; cast, hurl, throw; hurry, rush, speed, tear.

pelt[2] *n* coat, hide, skin.

pen[1] *vb* compose, draft, indite, inscribe, write.

pen[2] *vb* confine, coop, encage, enclose, impound, imprison, incarcerate. * *n* cage, coop, corral, crib, hutch, enclosure, paddock, pound, stall, sty.

penalty *n* chastisement, fine, forfeiture, mulct, punishment, retribution.

penance *n* humiliation, maceration, mortification, penalty, punishment.

penchant *n* bent, bias, disposition, fondness, inclination, leaning, liking, predilection, predisposition, proclivity, proneness, propensity, taste, tendency, turn.

penetrate *vb* bore, burrow, cut, enter, invade, penetrate, percolate, perforate, pervade, pierce, soak, stab; affect, sensitize, touch; comprehend, discern, perceive, understand.

penetrating *adj* penetrative, permeating, piercing, sharp, subtle; acute, clear-sighted, discerning, intelligent, keen, quick, sagacious, sharp-witted, shrewd.

penetration *n* acuteness, discernment, insight, sagacity.

penitence *n* compunction, contrition, qualms, regret, remorse, repentance, sorrow.

penitent *adj* compunctious, conscience-stricken, contrite, regretful, remorseful, repentant, sorrowing, sorrowful. * *n* penance-doer, penitentiary, repentant.

penniless *adj* destitute, distressed, impecunious, indigent, moneyless, pinched, poor, necessitous, needy, pensive, poverty-stricken, reduced.

pensive *adj* contemplative, dreamy, meditative, reflective, sober, thoughtful; grave, melancholic, melancholy, mournful, sad, serious, solemn.

penurious *adj* inadequate, ill-provided, insufficient, meagre, niggardly, poor, scanty, stinted; avaricious, close, close-fisted, covetous, illiberal, grasping, grudging, mean, mercenary, miserly, near, niggardly, parsimonious, sordid, stingy, tightfisted.

penury *n* beggary, destitution, indigence, need, poverty, privation, want.

people *vb* colonize, inhabit, populate. * *n* clan, country, family, nation, race, state, tribe; folk, humankind, persons, population, public; commons, community, democracy, populace, proletariat; mob, multitude, rabble.

perceive *vb* behold, descry, detect, discern, discover, discriminate, distinguish, note, notice, observe, recognize, remark, see, spot; appreciate, comprehend, know, understand.

perceptible *adj* apparent, appreciable, cognizable, discernible, noticeable, perceivable, understandable, visible.

perception *n* apprehension, cognition, discernment, perceiving, recognition, seeing; comprehension, conception, consciousness, perceptiveness, perceptivity, understanding, feeling.

perchance *adv* haply, maybe, mayhap, peradventure, perhaps, possibly, probably.

percolate *vb* drain, drip, exude, filter, filtrate, ooze, penetrate, stain, transude.

percussion *n* collision, clash, concussion, crash, encounter, shock.

perdition *n* damnation, demolition, destruction, downfall, hell, overthrow, ruin, wreck.

peremptory *adj* absolute, authoritative, categorical, commanding, decisive, express, imperative, imperious, positive; determined, resolute, resolved; arbitrary, dogmatic, incontrovertible.

perennial *adj* ceaseless, constant, continual, deathless, enduring, immortal, imperishable, lasting, never-failing, permanent, perpetual, unceasing, undying, unfailing, uninterrupted.

perfect *vb* accomplish, complete, consummate, elaborate, finish. * *adj* completed, finished; complete, entire, full, unqualified, utter, whole; capital, consummate, excellent, exquisite, faultless, ideal; accomplished, disciplined, expert, skilled; blameless, faultless, holy, immaculate, pure, spotless, unblemished.

perfection *n* completeness, completion, consummation, correctness, excellence, faultlessness, finish, maturity, perfection, perfectness, wholeness; beauty, quality.

perfidious *adj* deceitful, dishonest, disloyal, double-faced, faithless, false, false-hearted, traitorous, treacherous, unfaithful, untrustworthy, venal.

perfidy *n* defection, disloyalty, faithlessness, infidelity, perfidiousness, traitorousness, treachery, treason.

perforate *vb* bore, drill, penetrate, pierce, pink, prick, punch, riddle, trepan.

perform *vb* accomplish, achieve, compass, consummate, do, effect, transact; complete, discharge, execute, fulfil, meet, observe, satisfy; act, play, represent.

performance *n* accomplishment, achievement, completion, consummation, discharge, doing, execution, fulfilment; act, action, deed, exploit, feat, work; composition, production; acting, entertainment, exhibition, play, representation, hold; execution, playing.

perfume *n* aroma, balminess, bouquet, fragrance, incense, odour, redolence, scent, smell, sweetness.

perfunctory *adj* careless, formal, heedless, indifferent, mechanical, negligent, reckless, slight, slovenly, thoughtless, unmindful.

perhaps *adv* haply, peradventure, perchance, possibly.

peril *vb* endanger, imperil, jeopardize, risk. * *n* danger, hazard, insecurity, jeopardy, pitfall, risk, snare, uncertainty.

perilous *adj* dangerous, hazardous, risky, unsafe.

period *n* aeon, age, cycle, date, eon, epoch, season, span, spell, stage, term, time; continuance, duration; bound, conclusion, determination, end, limit, term, termination; clause, phrase, proposition, sentence.

periodical *adj* cyclical, incidental, intermittent, recurrent, recurring, regular, seasonal, systematic. * *n* magazine, paper, review, serial, weekly.

periphery *n* boundary, circumference, outside, perimeter, superficies, surface.

perish *vb* decay, moulder, shrivel, waste, wither; decease, die, expire, vanish.

perishable *adj* decaying, decomposable, destructible; dying, frail, mortal, temporary.

perjured *adj* false, forsworn, perfidious, traitorous, treacherous, untrue.

permanent *adj* abiding, constant, continuing, durable, enduring, fixed, immutable, invariable, lasting, perpetual, persistent, stable, standing, steadfast, unchangeable, unchanging, unfading, unmovable.

permissible *adj* admissible, allowable, free, lawful, legal, legitimate, proper, sufferable, unprohibited.

permission *n* allowance, authorization, consent, dispensation, leave, liberty, licence, permit, sufferance, toleration, warrant.

permit *vb* agree, allow, endure, let, suffer, tolerate; admit, authorize, consent, empower, license, warrant. * *n* leave, liberty, licence, passport, permission, sanction, warrant.

pernicious *adj* baleful, baneful, damaging, deadly, deleterious, destructive, detrimental, disadvantageous, fatal, harmful, hurtful, injurious, malign, mischievous, noisome, noxious, prejudicial, ruinous; evil-hearted, malevolent, malicious, malignant, mischief-making, wicked.

perpetrate *vb* commit, do, execute, perform.

perpetual *adj* ceaseless, continual, constant, endless, enduring, eternal, ever-enduring, everlasting, incessant, interminable, never-ceasing, never-ending, perennial, permanent, sempiternal, unceasing, unending, unfailing, uninterrupted.

perplex *vb* complicate, encumber, entangle, involve, snarl, tangle; beset, bewilder, confound, confuse, corner, distract, embarrass, fog, mystify, nonplus, pother, puzzle, set; annoy, bother, disturb, harass, molest, pester, plague, tease, trouble, vex, worry.

persecute *vb* afflict, distress, harass, molest, oppress, worry; annoy, beset, importune, pester, solicit, tease.

perseverance *n* constancy, continuance, doggedness, indefatigableness, persistence, persistency, pertinacity, resolution, steadfastness, steadiness, tenacity.

persevere *vb* continue, determine, endure, maintain, persist, remain, resolve, stick.

persist *vb* continue, endure, last, remain; insist, persevere.

persistent *adj* constant, continuing, enduring, fixed, immovable, persevering, persisting, steady, tenacious; contumacious, dogged, indefatigable, obdurate, obstinate, pertinacious, perverse, pigheaded, stubborn.

personable *adj* comely, good-looking, graceful, seemly, well-turned-out.

personal *adj* individual, peculiar, private, special; bodily, corporal, corporeal, exterior, material, physical.

personate *vb* act, impersonate, personify, play, represent; disguise, mast; counterfeit, feign, simulate.

perspective *n* panorama, prospect, view, vista; proportion, relation.

perspicacious *adj* keen-sighted, quick-sighted, sharp-sighted; acute, clever, discerning, keen, penetrating, sagacious, sharp-witted, shrewd.

perspicacity *n* acumen, acuteness, astuteness, discernment, insight, penetration, perspicaciousness, sagacity, sharpness, shrewdness.

perspicuity *n* clearness, distinctness, explicitness, intelligibility, lucidity, lucidness, perspicuousness, plainness, transparency.

perspicuous *adj* clear, distinct, explicit, intelligible, lucid, obvious, plain, transparent, unequivocal.

perspire *vb* exhale, glow, sweat, swelter.

persuade *vb* allure, actuate, entice, impel, incite, induce, influence, lead, move, prevail upon, urge; advise, counsel; convince, satisfy; inculcate, teach.

persuasion *n* exhortation, incitement, inducement, influence; belief, conviction, opinion; creed, doctrine, dogma, tenet; kind, sort, variety.

persuasive *adj* cogent, convincing, inducing, inducible, logical, persuading, plausible, sound, valid, weighty.

pert *adj* brisk, dapper, lively, nimble, smart, sprightly, perky; bold, flippant, forward, free, impertinent, impudent, malapert, presuming, smart, saucy.

pertain *vb* appertain, befit, behove, belong, concern, refer, regard, relate.

pertinacious *adj* constant, determined, firm, obdurate, persevering, resolute, staunch, steadfast, steady; dogged, headstrong, inflexible, mulish, intractable, obstinate, perverse, stubborn, unyielding, wayward, wilful.

pertinent *adj* adapted, applicable, apposite, appropriate, apropos, apt, fit, germane, pat, proper, relevant, suitable; appurtenant, belonging, concerning, pertaining, regarding.

perturb *vb* agitate, disquiet, distress, disturb, excite, trouble, unsettle, upset, vex, worry; confuse.

pervade *vb* affect, animate, diffuse, extend, fill, imbue, impregnate, infiltrate, penetrate, permeate.

perverse *adj* bad, disturbed, oblique, perverted; contrary, dogged, headstrong, mulish, obstinate, pertinacious, perversive, stubborn, ungovernable, intractable, unyielding, wayward, wilful; cantankerous, churlish, crabbed, cross, cross-grained, crusty, cussed, morose, peevish, petulant, snappish, snarling, spiteful, spleeny, surly, testy, touchy, wicked, wrong-headed; inconvenient, troublesome, untoward, vexatious.

perversion *n* abasement, corruption, debasement, impairment, injury, prostitution, vitiation.

perverted *adj* corrupt, debased, distorted, evil, impaired, misguiding, vitiated, wicked.

pessimistic *adj* cynical, dark, dejected, depressed, despondent, downhearted, gloomy, glum, melancholy, melancholic, morose, sad.

pest *n* disease, epidemic, infection, pestilence, plague; annoyance, bane, curse, infliction, nuisance, scourge, trouble.

pestilent *adj* contagious, infectious, malignant, pestilential; deadly, evil, injurious, malign, mischievous, noxious, poisonous; annoying, corrupt, pernicious, troublesome, vexatious.

petition *vb* ask, beg, crave, entreat, pray, solicit, sue, supplicate. * *n* address, appeal, application, entreaty, prayer, request, solicitation, supplication, suit.

petrify *vb* calcify, fossilize, lapidify; benumb, deaden; amaze, appal, astonish, astound, confound, dumbfound, paralyse, stun, stupefy.

petty *adj* diminutive, frivolous, inconsiderable, inferior, insignificant, little, mean, slight, small, trifling, trivial, unimportant.

petulant *adj* acrimonious, captious, cavilling, censorious, choleric, crabbed, cross, crusty, forward, fretful, hasty, ill-humoured, ill-tempered, irascible, irritable, peevish, perverse, pettish, querulous, snappish, snarling, testy, touchy, waspish.

phantom *n* apparition, ghost, illusion, phantasm, spectre, vision, wraith.

pharisaism *n* cant, formalism, hypocrisy, phariseeism, piety, sanctimoniousness, self-righteousness.

phenomenal *adj* marvellous, miraculous, prodigious, wondrous.

philanthropy *n* alms-giving, altruism, benevolence, charity, grace, humanitarianism, humanity, kindness.

philosophical, philosophic *adj* rational, reasonable, sound, wise; calm, collected, composed, cool, imperturbable, sedate, serene, stoical, tranquil, unruffled.

phlegmatic *adj* apathetic, calm, cold, cold-blooded, dull, frigid, heavy, impassive, indifferent, inert, sluggish, stoical, tame, unfeeling.

phobia *n* aversion, detestation, dislike, distaste, dread, fear, hatred.

phrase *vb* call, christen, denominate, designate, describe, dub, entitle, name, style. * *n* diction, expression, phraseology, style.

phraseology *n* diction, expression, language, phrasing, style.

physical *adj* material, natural; bodily, corporeal, external, substantial, tangible, sensible.

physiognomy *n* configuration, countenance, face, look, visage.

picaroon *n* adventurer, cheat, rogue; buccaneer, corsair, freebooter, marauder, pirate, plunderer, sea-rover.

pick *vb* peck, pierce, strike; cut, detach, gather, pluck; choose, cull, select; acquire, collect, get; pilfer, steal. * *n* pickaxe, pike, spike, toothpick.

picture *vb* delineate, draw, imagine, paint, represent. * *n* drawing, engraving, painting, print; copy, counterpart, delineation, embodiment, illustration, image, likeness, portraiture, portrayal, semblance, representation, resemblance, similitude; description.

picturesque *adj* beautiful, charming, colourful, graphic, scenic, striking, vivid.

piece *vb* mend, patch, repair; augment, complete, enlarge, increase; cement, join, unite. * *n* amount, bit, chunk, cut, fragment, hunk, part, quantity, scrap, shred, slice; portion; article, item, object; composition, lucubration, work, writing.

pied *adj* irregular, motley, mottled, particoloured, piebald, spotted, variegated.

pierce *vb* gore, impale, pink, prick, stab, transfix; bore, drill, excite, penetrate, perforate, puncture; affect, move, rouse, strike, thrill, touch.

piety *n* devotion, devoutness, holiness, godliness, grace, religion, sanctity.

pile[1] *vb* accumulate, amass; collect, gather, heap, load. * *n* accumulation, collection, heap, mass, stack; fortune, wad; building, edifice, erection, fabric, pyramid, skyscraper, structure, tower; reactor, nuclear reactor.

pile[2] *n* beam, column, pier, pillar, pole, post.

pile[3] *n* down, feel, finish, fur, fluff, fuzz, grain, nap, pappus, shag, surface, texture.

pilfer *vb* filch, purloin, rob, steal, thieve.

pilgrim *n* journeyer, sojourner, traveller, wanderer, wayfarer; crusader, devotee, palmer.

pilgrimage *n* crusade, excursion, expedition, journey, tour, trip.

pillage *vb* despoil, loot, plunder, rifle, sack, spoil, strip. * *n* depredation, destruction, devastation, plundering, rapine, spoliation; despoliation, plunder, rifling, sack, spoils.

pillar *n* column, pier, pilaster, post, shaft, stanchion; maintainer, prop, support, supporter, upholder.

pilot *vb* conduct, control, direct, guide, navigate, steer. * *adj* experimental, model, trial. * *n* helmsman, navigator, steersman; airman, aviator, conductor, director, flier, guide.

pinch *vb* compress, contract, cramp, gripe,

nip, squeeze; afflict, distress, famish, oppress, straiten, stint; frost, nip; apprehend, arrest; economize, spare, stint. * *n* gripe, nip; pang, throe; crisis, difficulty, emergency, exigency, oppression, pressure, push, strait, stress.

pine *vb* decay, decline, droop, fade, flag, languish, waste, wilt, wither; desire, long, yearn.

pinion *vb* bind, chain, fasten, fetter, maim, restrain, shackle. * *n* pennon, wing; feather, quill, pen, plume, wing; fetter.

pinnacle *n* minaret, turret; acme, apex, height, peak, summit, top, zenith.

pious *adj* filial; devout, godly, holy, religious, reverential, righteous, saintly.

piquant *adj* biting, highly flavoured, piercing, prickling, pungent, sharp, stinging; interesting, lively, racy, sparkling, stimulating; cutting, keen, pointed, severe, strong, tart.

pique *vb* goad, incite, instigate, spur, stimulate, urge; affront, chafe, displease, fret, incense, irritate, nettle, offend, provoke, sting, vex, wound. * *n* annoyance, displeasure, irritation, offence, resentment, vexation.

pirate *vb* copy, crib, plagiarize, reproduce, steal. * *n* buccaneer, corsair, freebooter, marauder, picaroon, privateer, seadog, sea-robber, sea-rover, sea wolf.

pit *vb* match, oppose; dent, gouge, hole, mark, nick, notch, scar. * *n* cavity, hole, hollow; crater, dent, depression, dint, excavation, well; abyss, chasm, gulf; pitfall, snare, trap: auditorium, orchestra.

pitch *vb* fall, lurch, plunge, reel; light, settle, rest; cast, dart, fling, heave, hurl, lance, launch, send, toss, throw; erect, establish, fix, locate, place, plant, set, settle, station. * *n* degree, extent, height, intensity, measure, modulation, rage, rate; declivity, descent, inclination, slope; cast, jerk, plunge, throw, toss; place, position, spot; field, ground; line, patter.

piteous *adj* affecting, distressing, doleful, grievous, mournful, pathetic, rueful, sorrowful, woeful; deplorable, lamentable, miserable, pitiable, wretched; compassionate, tender.

pith *n* chief, core, essence, heart, gist, kernel, marrow, part, quintessence, soul, substance; importance, moment, weight; cogency, force, energy, strength, vigour.

pithy *adj* cogent, energetic, forcible, powerful; compact, concise, brief, laconic, meaty, pointed, short, sententious, substantial, terse; corky, porous.

pitiable *adj* deplorable, lamentable, miserable, pathetic, piteous, pitiable, woeful, wretched; abject, base, contemptible, despicable, disreputable, insignificant, low, paltry, mean, rascally, sorry, vile, worthless.

pitiably *adv* deplorably, distressingly, grievously, lamentably, miserably, pathetically, piteously, woefully, wretchedly.

pitiful *adj* compassionate, kind, lenient, merciful, mild, sympathetic, tender, tenderhearted; deplorable, lamentable, miserable, pathetic, piteous, pitiable, wretched; abject, base, contemptible, despicable, disreputable, insignificant, mean, paltry, rascally, sorry, vile, worthless.

pitiless *adj* cruel, hardhearted, implacable, inexorable, merciless, unmerciful, relentless, remorseless, unfeeling, unpitying, unrelenting, unsympathetic.

pittance *n* allowance, allotment, alms, charity, dole, gift; driblet, drop, insufficiency, mite, modicum, trifle.

pity *vb* commiserate, condole, sympathize. * *n* clemency, commiseration, compassion, condolence, fellow-feeling, grace, humanity, leniency, mercy, quarter, sympathy, tenderheartedness.

pivot *vb* depend, hinge, turn. * *n* axis, axle, centre, focus, hinge, joint.

place *vb* arrange, bestow, commit, deposit, dispose, fix, install, lay, locate, lodge, orient, orientate, pitch, plant, pose, put, seat, set, settle, situate, stand, station, rest; allocate, arrange, class, classify, identify, order, organize, recognize; appoint, assign, commission, establish, induct, nominate. * *n* area, courtyard, square; bounds, district, division, locale, locality, location, part, position, premises, quarter, region, scene, site, situation, spot, station, tract, whereabouts; calling, charge, employment, function, occupation, office, pitch, post; calling, condition, grade, precedence, rank, sphere, stakes, standing; abode, building, dwelling, habitation, mansion, residence, seat; city, town, village; fort, fortress, stronghold; paragraph, part, passage, portion; ground, occasion, opportunity, reason, room; lieu, stead.

placid *adj* calm, collected, composed, cool, equable, gentle, peaceful, quiet, serene, tranquil, undisturbed, unexcitable, unmoved, unruffled; halcyon, mild, serene.

plague *vb* afflict, annoy, badger, bore, bother, pester, chafe, disquiet, distress, disturb, embarrass, harass, fret, gall, harry, hector, incommode, irritate, molest, perplex, tantalize, tease, torment, trouble, vex, worry. * *n* disease, pestilence, pest; affliction, annoyance, curse, molestation, nuisance, thorn, torment, trouble, vexation, worry.

plain *adj* dull, even, flat, level, plane, smooth, uniform; clear, open, unencumbered, uninterrupted; apparent, certain, conspicuous, evident, distinct, glaring, manifest, notable, notorious, obvious, overt, palpable, patent, prominent, pronounced, staring, transparent, unmistakable, visible; explicit, intelligible, perspicuous, unambiguous, unequivocal; homely, ugly; aboveboard, blunt, crude, candid, direct, downright, frank, honest, ingenuous, open, openhearted, sincere, single-minded, straightforward, undesigning, unreserved, unsophisticated: artless, common, natural, simple, unaffected, unlearned; absolute, mere, unmistakable; clear, direct, easy; audible, articulate, definite; frugal, homely; unadorned, unfigured, unornamented, unvariegated. * *n* expanse, flats, grassland, pampas, plateau, prairie, steppe, stretch.

plaint *n* complaint, cry, lament, lamentation, moan, wail.

plaintiff *n* accuser, prosecutor.

plaintive *adj* dirge-like, doleful, grievous, melancholy, mournful, piteous, rueful, sad, sorrowful, woeful.

plan *vb* arrange, calculate, concert, delineate, devise, diagram, figure, premeditate, project, represent, study; concoct, conspire, contrive, design, digest, hatch, invent, manoeuvre, machinate, plot, prepare, scheme. * *n* chart, delineation, diagram, draught, drawing, layout, map, plot, sketch; arrangement, conception, contrivance, design, device, idea, method, programme, project, proposal, proposition, scheme, system; cabal, conspiracy, intrigue, machination; custom, process, way.

plane *vb* even, flatten, level, smooth; float, fly, glide, skate, skim, soar. * *adj* even, flat, horizontal, level, smooth. * *n* degree, evenness, level, levelness, smoothness; aeroplane, aircraft; groover, jointer, rabbet, rebate, scraper.

plant *vb* bed, sow; breed, engender; direct, point, set; colonize, furnish, inhabit, settle; establish, introduce; deposit, establish, fix, found, hide. * *n* herb, organism, vegetable; establishment, equipment, factory, works.

plaster *vb* bedaub, coat, cover, smear, spread. * *n* cement, gypsum, mortar, stucco.

plastic *adj* ductile, flexible, formative, mouldable, pliable, pliant, soft.

platitude *n* dullness, flatness, insipidity, mawkishness; banality, commonplace, truism; balderdash, chatter, flummery, fudge, jargon, moonshine, nonsense, palaver, stuff, trash, twaddle, verbiage.

plaudit *n* acclaim, acclamation, applause, approbation, clapping, commendation, encomium, praise.

plausible *adj* believable, credible, probable, reasonable; bland, fair-spoken, glib, smooth, suave.

play *vb* caper, disport, frisk, frolic, gambol, revel, romp, skip, sport; dally, flirt, idle, toy, trifle, wanton; flutter, hover, wave; act, impersonate, perform, personate, represent; bet, gamble, stake, wager. * *n* amusement, exercise, frolic, gambols, game, jest, pastime, prank, romp, sport; gambling, gaming; act, comedy, drama, farce, performance, tragedy; action, motion, movement; elbowroom, freedom, latitude, movement, opportunity, range, scope, sweep, swing, use.

playful *adj* frisky, frolicsome, gamesome, jolly, kittenish, merry, mirthful, rollicking, sportive; amusing, arch, humorous, lively, mischievous, roguish, skittish, sprightly, vivacious.

plead *vb* answer, appeal, argue, reason; argue, defend, discuss, reason, rejoin; beg, beseech, entreat, implore, petition, sue, supplicate.

pleasant *adj* acceptable, agreeable, delectable, delightful, enjoyable, grateful, gratifying, nice, pleasing, pleasurable, prepossessing, seemly, welcome; cheerful, enlivening, good-humoured, gracious, likable, lively, merry, sportive, sprightly, vivacious; amusing, facetious, humorous, jocose, jocular, sportive, witty.

please *vb* charm, delight, elate, gladden, gratify, pleasure, rejoice; content, oblige, satisfy; choose, like, prefer.

pleasure *n* cheer, comfort, delight, delectation, elation, enjoyment, exhilaration, joy, gladness, gratifying, gusto, relish, satisfaction, solace; amusement, diversion, entertainment, indulgence, refreshment, treat; gratification, luxury, sensuality, voluptuousness; choice, desire, preference, purpose, will, wish; favour, kindness.

plebeian *adj* base, common, ignoble, low, lowborn, mean, obscure, popular, vulgar. * *n* commoner, peasant, proletarian.

pledge *vb* hypothecate, mortgage, pawn, plight; affiance, bind, contract, engage, plight, promise. * *n* collateral, deposit, gage, pawn; earnest, guarantee, security; hostage, security.

plenipotentiary *n* ambassador, envoy, legate, minister.

plenitude *n* abundance, completeness, fullness, plenteousness, plentifulness, plenty, plethora, profusion, repletion.

plentiful *adj* abundant, ample, copious, full, enough, exuberant, fruitful, luxuriant, plenteous, productive, sufficient.

plenty *n* abundance, adequacy, affluence, amplitude, copiousness, enough, exuberance, fertility, fruitfulness, fullness, overflow, plenteousness, plentifulness, plethora, profusion, sufficiency, supply.

pleonastic *adj* circumlocutory, diffuse, redundant, superfluous, tautological, verbose, wordy.

plethora *n* fullness, plenitude, repletion; excess, redundance, redundancy, superabundance, superfluity, surfeit.

pliable *adj* flexible, limber, lithe, lithesome, pliable, pliant, supple; adaptable, compliant, docile, ductile, facile, manageable, obsequious, tractable, yielding.

plight[1] *n* case, category, complication, condition, dilemma, imbroglio, mess, muddle, pass, predicament, scrape, situation, state, strait.

plight[2] *vb* avow, contract, covenant, engage, honour, pledge, promise, propose, swear, vow. * *n* avowal, contract, covenant, oath, pledge, promise, troth, vow, word; affiancing, betrothal, engagement.

plod *vb* drudge, lumber, moil, persevere, persist, toil, trudge.

plot[1] *vb* connive, conspire, intrigue, machinate, scheme; brew, concoct, contrive, devise, frame, hatch, compass, plan, project; chart, map. * *n* blueprint, chart, diagram, draft, outline, plan, scenario, skeleton; cabal, combination, complicity, connivance, conspiracy, intrigue, plan, project, scheme, stratagem; script, story, subject, theme, thread, topic.

plot[2] *n* field, lot, parcel, patch, piece, plat, section, tract.

pluck[1] *vb* cull, gather, pick; jerk, pull, snatch, tear, tug, twitch.

pluck[2] *n* backbone, bravery, courage, daring, determination, energy, force, grit, hardihood, heroism, indomitability, indomitableness, manhood, mettle, nerve, resolution, spirit, valour.

plump[1] *adj* bonny, bouncing, buxom, chubby, corpulent, fat, fleshy, full-figured, obese, portly, rotund, round, sleek, stout, well-rounded; distended, full, swollen, tumid.

plump[2] *vb* dive, drop, plank, plop, plunge, plunk, put; choose, favour, support * *adj* blunt, complete, direct, downright, full, unqualified, unreserved.

plunder *vb* desolate, despoil, devastate, fleece, forage, harry, loot, maraud, pillage, raid, ransack, ravage, rifle, rob, sack, spoil, spoliate, plunge. * *n* freebooting, devastation, harrying, marauding, rapine, robbery, sack; booty, pillage, prey, spoil.

ply[1] *vb* apply, employ, exert, manipulate, wield; exercise, practise; assail, belabour, beset, press; importune, solicit, urge; offer, present.

ply[2] *n* fold, layer, plait, twist; bent, bias, direction, turn.

pocket *vb* appropriate, steal; bear, endure, suffer, tolerate. * *n* cavity, cul-de-sac, hollow, pouch, receptacle.

poignant *adj* bitter, intense, penetrating, pierce, severe, sharp; acrid, biting, mordacious, piquant, prickling, pungent, sharp, stinging; caustic, irritating, keen, mordant, pointed, satirical, severe.

point *vb* acuminate, sharpen; aim, direct, level; designate indicate, show; punctuate. * *n* apex, needle, nib, pin, prong, spike, stylus, tip; cape, headland, projection, promontory; eve, instant, moment, period, verge; place, site, spot, stage, station; condition, degree, grade, state; aim, design, end, intent, limit, object, purpose; nicety, pique, punctilio, trifle; position, proposition, question, text, theme, thesis; aspect, matter, respect; characteristic, peculiarity, trait; character, mark, stop; dot, jot, speck; epigram, quip, quirk, sally, witticism; poignancy, sting.

point-blank *adj* categorical, direct, downright, explicit, express, plain, straight. * *adv* categorically, directly, flush, full, plainly, right, straight.

pointless *adj* blunt, obtuse; aimless, dull, flat, fruitless, futile, meaningless, vague, vapid, stupid.

poise *vb* balance, float, hang, hover, support, suspend. * *n* aplomb, balance, composure, dignity, equanimity, equilibrium, equipoise, serenity.

poison *vb* adulterate, contaminate, corrupt, defile, embitter, envenom, impair, infect, intoxicate, pollute, taint, vitiate. * *adj* deadly, lethal, poisonous, toxic. * *n* bane, canker, contagion, pest, taint, toxin, venom, virulence, virus.

poisonous *adj* baneful, corruptive, deadly, fatal, noxious, pestiferous, pestilential, toxic, venomous.

poke *vb* jab, jog, punch, push, shove, thrust; interfere, meddle, pry, snoop. * *n* jab, jog, punch, push, shove, thrust; bag, pocket, pouch, sack.

pole[1] *n* caber, mast, post, rod, spar, staff, stick; bar, beam, pile, shaft; oar, paddle, scull.

pole[2] *n* axis, axle, hub, pivot, spindle.

poles *npl* antipodes, antipoles, counterpoles, opposites.

policy *n* administration, government, management, rule; plan, plank, platform, role; art, address, cunning, discretion, prudence, shrewdness, skill, stratagem, strategy, tactics; acumen, astuteness, wisdom, wit.

polish *vb* brighten, buff, burnish, furbish, glaze, gloss, scour, shine, smooth; civilize, refine. * *n* brightness, brilliance, brilliancy, lustre, splendour; accomplishment, elegance, finish, grace, refinement.

polished *adj* bright, burnished, glossed, glossy, lustrous, shining, smooth; accomplished, cultivated, elegant, finished, graceful, polite, refined.

polite *adj* attentive, accomplished, affable, chivalrous, civil, complaisant, courtly, courteous, cultivated, elegant, gallant, genteel, gentle, gentlemanly, gracious, mannerly, obliging, polished, refined, suave, urbane, well, well-bred, well-mannered.

politic *adj* civic, civil, political; astute, discreet, judicious, long-headed, noncommittal, provident, prudent, prudential, sagacious, wary, wise; artful, crafty, cunning, diplomatic, expedient, foxy, ingenious, intriguing, Machiavellian, shrewd, skilful, sly, subtle, strategic, timeserving, unscrupulous, wily; well-adapted, well-devised.

political *adj* civic, civil, national, politic, public.

pollute *vb* defile, foul, soil, taint; contaminate, corrupt, debase, demoralize, deprave, impair, infect, pervert, poison, stain, tarnish, vitiate; desecrate, profane; abuse, debauch, defile, deflower, dishonour, ravish, violate.

pollution *n* abomination, contamination, corruption, defilement, foulness, impurity, pollutedness, taint, uncleanness, vitiation.

poltroon *n* coward, crave, dastard, milksop, recreant, skulk, sneak.

pomp *n* display, flourish, grandeur, magnificence, ostentation, pageant, pageantry, parade, pompousness, pride, show, splendour, state, style.

pompous *adj* august, boastful, bombastic, dignified, gorgeous, grand, inflated, lofty, magisterial, ostentatious, pretentious, showy, splendid, stately, sumptuous, superb, vainglorious.

ponder *vb* cogitate, consider, contemplate, deliberate, examine, meditate, muse, reflect, study, weigh.

ponderous *adj* bulky, heavy, massive, weighty; dull, laboured, slow-moving; important, momentous; forcible, mighty.

poniard *n* dagger, dirk, stiletto.

poor *adj* indigent, necessitous, needy, pinched, straitened; destitute, distressed, embarrassed, impecunious, impoverished, insolvent, moneyless, penniless, poverty-stricken, reduced, seedy, unprosperous; emaciated, gaunt, spare, lank, lean, shrunk, skinny, spare, thin; barren, fruitless, sterile, unfertile, unfruitful, unproductive, unprolific; flimsy, inadequate, insignificant, insufficient, paltry, slender, slight, small, trifling, trivial, unimportant, valueless, worthless; decrepit, delicate, feeble, frail, infirm, unsound, weak; inferior, shabby, valueless, worthless; bad, beggarly, contemptible, despicable, humble, inferior, low, mean, pitiful, sorry; bald, cold, dry, dull, feeble, frigid, jejune, languid, meagre, prosaic, prosing, spiritless, tame, vapid, weak; ill-fated, ill-starred, inauspicious, indifferent, luckless, miserable, pitiable, unfavourable, unfortunate, unhappy, unlucky, wretched; deficient, imperfect, inadequate, insufficient, mediocre, scant, scanty; faulty, unsatisfactory; feeble.

populace *n* citizens, crowd, inhabitants, masses, people, public, throng.

popular *adj* lay, plebeian, public; comprehensible, easy, familiar, plain; acceptable, accepted, accredited, admired, approved, favoured, liked, pleasing, praised, received; common, current, prevailing, prevalent; cheap, inexpensive.

pore[1] *n* hole, opening, orifice, spiracle.

pore[2] *vb* brood, consider, dwell, examine, gaze, read, study.

porous *adj* honeycombed, light, loose, open, penetrable, perforated, permeable, pervious, sandy.

porridge *n* broth, gruel, mush, pap, pottage, soup.

port[1] *n* anchorage, harbour, haven, shelter; door, entrance, gate, passageway; embrasure, porthole.

port[2] *n* air, appearance, bearing, behaviour, carriage, demeanour, deportment, mien, presence.

portable *adj* convenient, handy, light, manageable, movable, portative, transmissible.

portend *vb* augur, betoken, bode, forebode, foreshadow, foretoken, indicate, presage, procrastinate, signify, threaten.

portent *n* augury, omen, presage, prognosis, sign, warning; marvel, phenomenon, wonder.

portion *vb* allot, distribute, divide, parcel; endow, supply. * *n* bit, fragment, morsel, part, piece, scrap, section; allotment, contingent, dividend, division, lot, measure, quantity, quota, ration, share; inheritance.

portly *adj* dignified, grand, imposing, magisterial, majestic, stately; bulky, burly, corpulent, fleshy, large, plump, round, stout.

portray *vb* act, draw, depict, delineate, describe, paint, picture, represent, pose, position, sketch.

pose *vb* arrange, place, set; bewilder, confound, dumbfound, embarrass, mystify, nonplus, perplex, place, puzzle, set, stagger; affect, attitudinize. * *n* attitude, posture; affectation, air, facade, mannerism, pretence, role.
position *vb* arrange, array, fix, locate, place, put, set, site, stand. * *n* locality, place, post, site, situation, spot, station; relation; attitude, bearing, posture; affirmation, assertion, doctrine, predication, principle, proposition, thesis; caste, dignity, honour, rank, standing, status; circumstance, condition, phase, place, state; berth, billet, incumbency, place, post, situation.
positive *adj* categorical, clear, defined, definite, direct, determinate, explicit, express, expressed, precise, unequivocal, unmistakable, unqualified; absolute, actual, real, substantial, true, veritable; assured, certain, confident, convinced, sure; decisive, incontrovertible, indisputable, indubitable, inescapable; imperative, unconditional, undeniable; decided, dogmatic, emphatic, obstinate, overbearing, overconfident, peremptory, stubborn, tenacious.
possess *vb* control, have, hold, keep, obsess, obtain, occupy, own, seize.
possession *n* monopoly, ownership, proprietorship; control, occupation, occupancy, retention, tenancy, tenure; bedevilment, lunacy, madness, obsession; (*pl*) assets, effects, estate, property, wealth.
possessor *n* owner, proprietor.
possible *adj* conceivable, contingent, imaginable, potential; accessible, feasible, likely, practical, practicable, workable.
possibly *adv* haply, maybe, mayhap, peradventure, perchance, perhaps.
post[1] *vb* advertise, announce, inform, placard, publish; brand, defame, disgrace, vilify; enter, slate, record, register. * *n* column, picket, pier, pillar, stake, support.
post[2] *vb* establish, fix, place, put, set, station. * *n* billet, employment, office, place, position, quarter, seat, situation, station.
post[3] *vb* drop, dispatch, mail. * *n* carrier, courier, express, mercury, messenger, postman; dispatch, haste, hurry, speed.
posterior *adj* after, ensuing, following, later, latter, postprandial, subsequent. * *n* back, buttocks, hind, hinder, rump.
posterity *n* descendants, offspring, progeny, seed; breed, brood, children, family, heirs, issue.
postpone *vb* adjourn, defer, delay, procrastinate, prorogue, retard.
postscript *n* addition, afterthought, appendix, supplement.
postulate *vb* assume, presuppose; beseech, entreat, solicit, supplicate. * *n* assumption, axiom, conjecture, hypothesis, proposition, speculation, supposition, theory.
posture *vb* attitudinize, pose. * *n* attitude, pose, position; condition, disposition, mood, phase, state.
pot *n* kettle, pan, saucepan, skillet; can, cup, mug, tankard; crock, jar, jug.
potency *n* efficacy, energy, force, intensity, might, power, strength, vigour; authority, control, influence, sway.
potent *adj* efficacious, forceful, forcible, intense, powerful, strong, virile; able, authoritative, capable, efficient, mighty, puissant, strong; cogent, influential.
potentate *n* emperor, king, monarch, prince, sovereign, ruler.
potential *adj* able, capable, inherent, latent, possible. * *n* ability, capability, dynamic, possibility, potentiality, power.
pother *vb* beset, bewilder, confound, confuse, embarrass, harass, perplex, pose, puzzle, tease. * *n* bustle, commotion, confusion, disturbance, flutter, fuss, huddle, hurly-burly, rumpus, tumult, turbulence, turmoil.
pound[1] *vb* beat, strike, thump; bray, bruise, comminute, crush, levigate, pulverize, triturate; confound, coop, enclose, impound.
pound[2] *n* enclosure, fold, pen.
pour *vb* cascade, emerge, flood, flow, gush, issue, rain, shower, stream.
pouting *adj* bad-tempered, cross, ill-humoured, moody, morose, sulky, sullen.

poverty *n* destitution, difficulties, distress, impecuniosity, impecuniousness, indigence, necessity, need, neediness, penury, privation, straits, want; beggary, mendicancy, pauperism, pennilessness; dearth, jejuneness, lack, scantiness, sparingness, meagreness; exiguity, paucity, poorness, smallness; humbleness, inferiority, lowliness; barrenness, sterility, unfruitfulness, unproductiveness.

power *n* ability, ableness, capability, cogency, competency, efficacy, faculty, might, potency, validity, talent; energy, force, strength, virtue; capacity, susceptibility; endowment, faculty, gift, talent; ascendancy, authoritativeness, authority, carte blanche, command, control, domination, dominion, government, influence, omnipotence, predominance, prerogative, pressure, proxy, puissance, rule, sovereignty, sway, warrant; governor, monarch, potentate, ruler, sovereign; army, host, troop.

powerful *adj* mighty, potent, puissant; able-bodied, herculean, muscular, nervous, robust, sinewy, strong, sturdy, vigorous, vivid; able, commanding, dominating, forceful, forcible, overpowering; cogent, effective, effectual, efficacious, efficient, energetic, influential, operative, valid.

practicable *adj* achievable, attainable, bearable, feasible, performable, possible, workable; operative, passable, penetrable.

practical *adj* hardheaded, matter-of-fact, pragmatic, pragmatical; able, experienced, practised, proficient, qualified, trained, skilled, thoroughbred, versed; effective, useful, virtual, workable.

practice *n* custom, habit, manner, method, repetition; procedure, usage, use; application, drill, exercise, pursuit; action, acts, behaviour, conduct, dealing, proceeding.

practise *vb* apply, do, exercise, follow, observe, perform, perpetrate, pursue.

practised *adj* able, accomplished, experienced, instructed, practical, proficient, qualified, skilled, thoroughbred, trained, versed.

pragmatic *adj* impertinent, intermeddling, interfering, intrusive, meddlesome, meddling, obtrusive, officious, over-busy; earthy, hard-headed, matter-of-fact, practical, pragmatical, realistic, sensible, stolid.

praise *vb* approbate, acclaim, applaud, approve, commend; celebrate, compliment, eulogize, extol, flatter, laud; adore, bless, exalt, glorify, magnify, worship. * *n* acclaim, approbation, approval, commendation; encomium, eulogy, glorification, laud, laudation, panegyric; exaltation, extolling, glorification, homage, tribute, worship; celebrity, distinction, fame, glory, honour, renown; desert, merit, praiseworthiness.

praiseworthy *adj* commendable, creditable, good, laudable, meritorious.

prank *n* antic, caper, escapade, frolic, gambol, trick.

prate *vb* babble, chatter, gabble, jabber, palaver, prattle, tattle. * *n* chatter, gabble, nonsense, palaver, prattle, twaddle.

pray *vb* ask, beg, beseech, conjure, entreat, implore, importune, invoke, petition, request, solicit, supplicate.

prayer *n* beseeching, entreaty, imploration, petition, request, solicitation, suit, supplication; adoration, devotion(s), litany, invocation, orison, praise, suffrage.

preach *vb* declare, deliver, proclaim, pronounce, publish; inculcate, press, teach, urge; exhort, lecture, moralize, sermonize.

preamble *n* foreword, introduction, preface, prelude, prologue.

precarious *adj* critical, doubtful, dubious, equivocal, hazardous, insecure, perilous, unassured, riskful, risky, uncertain, unsettled, unstable, unsteady.

precaution *n* care, caution, circumspection, foresight, forethought, providence, prudence, safeguard, wariness; anticipation, premonition, provision.

precautionary *adj* preservative, preventative, provident.

precede *vb* antedate, forerun, head, herald, introduce, lead, utter.

precedence *n* advantage, antecedence, lead, pre-eminence, preference, priority, superiority, supremacy.

precedent *n* antecedent, authority, custom, example, instance, model, pattern, procedure, standard, usage.

precept *n* behest, bidding, canon, charge, command, commandment, decree, dictate, edict, injunction, instruction, law, mandate, ordinance, ordination, order, regulation; direction, doctrine, maxim, principle, teaching, rubric, rule.

preceptor *n* instructor, lecturer, master, pedagogue, professor, schoolteacher, teacher, tutor.

precinct *n* border, bound, boundary, confine, environs, frontier, enclosure, limit, list, march, neighbourhood, purlieus, term, terminus; area, district.

precious *adj* costly, inestimable, invaluable, priceless, prized, valuable; adored, beloved, cherished, darling, dear, idolized, treasured; fastidious, overnice, over-refined, precise.

precipice *n* bluff, cliff, crag, steep.

precipitate *vb* advance, accelerate, dispatch, expedite, forward, further, hasten, hurry, plunge, press, quicken, speed. * *adj* hasty, hurried, headlong, impetuous, indiscreet, overhasty, rash, reckless; abrupt, sudden, violent.

precipitous *adj* abrupt, cliffy, craggy, perpendicular, uphill, sheer, steep.

precise *adj* accurate, correct, definite, distinct, exact, explicit, express, nice, pointed, severe, strict, unequivocal, well-defined; careful, scrupulous; ceremonious, finical, formal, prim, punctilious, rigid, starched, stiff.

precision *n* accuracy, correctness, definiteness, distinctness, exactitude, exactness, nicety, preciseness.

preclude *vb* bar, check, debar, hinder, inhibit, obviate, prevent, prohibit, restrain, stop.

precocious *adj* advanced, forward, overforward, premature.

preconcert *vb* concoct, prearrange, predetermine, premeditate, prepare.

precursor *n* antecedent, cause, forerunner, predecessor; harbinger, herald, messenger, pioneer; omen, presage, sign.

precursory *adj* antecedent, anterior, forerunning, precedent, preceding, previous, prior; initiatory, introductory, precursive, prefatory, preliminary, prelusive, prelusory, premonitory, preparatory, prognosticative.

predatory *adj* greedy, pillaging, plundering, predacious, rapacious, ravaging, ravenous, voracious.

predestination *n* doom, fate, foredoom, foreordainment, foreordination, necessity, predetermination, preordination.

predicament *n* attitude, case, condition, plight, position, posture, situation, state; corner, dilemma, emergency, exigency, fix, hole, impasse, mess, pass, pinch, push, quandary, scrape.

predict *vb* augur, betoken, bode, divine, forebode, forecast, foredoom, foresee, forespeak, foretell, foretoken, forewarn, portend, prognosticate, prophesy, read, signify, soothsay.

predilection *n* bent, bias, desire, fondness, inclination, leaning, liking, love, partiality, predisposition, preference, prejudice, prepossession.

predisposition *n* aptitude, bent, bias, disposition, inclination, leaning, proclivity, proneness, propensity, willingness.

predominant *adj* ascendant, controlling, dominant, overruling, prevailing, prevalent, reigning, ruling, sovereign, supreme.

predominate *vb* dominate, preponderate, prevail, rule.

pre-eminent *adj* chief, conspicuous, consummate, controlling, distinguished, excellent, excelling, paramount, peerless, predominant, renowned, superior, supreme, surpassing, transcendent, unequalled.

preface *vb* begin, introduce, induct, launch, open, precede. * *n* exordium, foreword, induction, introduction, preamble, preliminary, prelude, prelusion, premise, proem, prologue, prolusion.

prefatory *adj* antecedent, initiative, introductory, precursive, precursory, preliminary, prelusive, prelusory, preparatory, proemial.

prefer *vb* address, offer, present, proffer, tender; advance, elevate, promote, raise; adopt, choose, elect, fancy, pick, select, wish.

preference *n* advancement, choice, election, estimation, precedence, priority, selection.

preferment *n* advancement, benefice, dignity, elevation, exaltation, promotion.

pregnant *adj* big, enceinte, parturient; fraught, full, important, replete, significant, weighty; fecund, fertile, fruitful, generative, potential, procreant, procreative, productive, prolific.

prejudice *vb* bias, incline, influence, turn, warp; damage, diminish, hurt, impair, injure. * *n* bias, intolerance, partiality, preconception, predilection, prejudgement, prepossession, unfairness; damage, detriment, disadvantage, harm, hurt, impairment, injury, loss, mischief.

prejudiced *adj* biased, bigoted, influenced, one-sided, partial, partisan, unfair.

preliminary *adj* antecedent, initiatory, introductory, precedent, precursive, precursory, prefatory, prelusive, prelusory, preparatory, previous, prior, proemial. * *n* beginning, initiation, introduction, opening, preamble, preface, prelude, start.

prelude *n* introduction, opening, overture, prelusion, preparation, voluntary; exordium, preamble, preface, preliminary, proem.

premature *adj* hasty, ill-considered, precipitate, unmatured, unprepared, unripe, unseasonable, untimely.

premeditation *n* deliberation, design, forethought, intention, prearrangement, predetermination, purpose.

premise *vb* introduce, preamble, preface, prefix. * *n* affirmation, antecedent, argument, assertion, assumption, basis, foundation, ground, hypothesis, position, premiss, presupposition, proposition, support, thesis, theorem.

premium *n* bonus, bounty, encouragement, fee, gift, guerdon, meed, payment, prize, recompense, remuneration, reward; appreciation, enhancement.

premonition *n* caution, foreboding, foreshadowing, forewarning, indication, omen, portent, presage, presentiment, sign, warning.

preoccupied *adj* absent, absentminded, abstracted, dreaming, engrossed, inadvertent, inattentive, lost, musing, unobservant.

prepare *vb* adapt, adjust, fit, qualify; arrange, concoct, fabricate, make, order, plan, procure, provide.

preponderant *adj* outweighing, overbalancing, preponderating.

prepossessing *adj* alluring, amiable, attractive, bewitching, captivating, charming, engaging, fascinating, inviting, taking, winning.

preposterous *adj* absurd, excessive, exorbitant, extravagant, foolish, improper, irrational, monstrous, nonsensical, perverted, ridiculous, unfit, unreasonable, wrong.

prerogative *n* advantage, birthright, claim, franchise, immunity, liberty, privilege, right.

presage *vb* divine, forebode; augur, betoken, bode, foreshadow, foretell, foretoken, indicate, portend, predict, prognosticate, prophesy, signify, soothsay. * *n* augury, auspice, boding, foreboding, foreshowing, indication, omen, portent, prognostication, sign, token; foreknowledge, precognition, prediction, premonition, presentiment, prophecy.

prescribe *vb* advocate, appoint, command, decree, dictate, direct, enjoin, establish, institute, ordain, order.

presence *n* attendance, company, inhabitance, inhabitancy, nearness, neighbourhood, occupancy, propinquity, proximity, residence, ubiquity, vicinity; air, appearance, carriage, demeanour, mien, personality.

present[1] *adj* near; actual, current, existing, happening, immediate, instant, living; available, quick, ready; attentive, favourable. * *n* now, time being, today.

present² *n* benefaction, boon, donation, favour, gift, grant, gratuity, largesse, offering.

present³ *vb* introduce, nominate; exhibit, offer; bestow, confer, give, grant; deliver, hand; advance, express, prefer, proffer, tender.

presentiment *n* anticipation, apprehension, foreboding, forecast, foretaste, forethought, prescience.

presently *adv* anon, directly, forthwith, immediately, shortly, soon.

preservation *n* cherishing, conservation, curing, maintenance, protection, support; safety, salvation, security; integrity, keeping, soundness.

preserve *vb* defend, guard, keep, protect, rescue, save, secure, shield; maintain, uphold, sustain, support; conserve, economize, husband, retain. * *n* comfit, compote, confection, confiture, conserve, jam, jelly, marmalade, sweetmeat; enclosure, warren.

preside *vb* control, direct, govern, manage, officiate.

press *vb* compress, crowd, crush, squeeze; flatten, iron, smooth; clasp, embrace, hug; force, compel, constrain; emphasize, enforce, enjoin, inculcate, stress, urge; hasten, hurry, push, rush; crowd, throng; entreat, importune, solicit. * *n* crowd, crush, multitude, throng; hurry, pressure, urgency; case, closet, cupboard, repository.

pressing *adj* constraining, critical, distressing, imperative, importunate, persistent, serious, urgent, vital.

pressure *n* compressing, crushing, squeezing; influence, force; compulsion, exigency, hurry, persuasion, press, stress, urgency; affliction, calamity, difficulty, distress, embarrassment, grievance, oppression, straits; impression, stamp.

prestidigitation *n* conjuring, juggling, legerdemain, sleight-of-hand.

prestige *n* credit, distinction, importance, influence, reputation, weight.

presume *vb* anticipate, apprehend, assume, believe, conjecture, deduce, expect, infer, surmise, suppose, think; consider, presuppose; dare, undertake, venture.

presumption *n* anticipation, assumption, belief, concession, conclusion, condition, conjecture, deduction, guess, hypothesis, inference, opinion, supposition, understanding; arrogance, assurance, audacity, boldness, brass, effrontery, forwardness, haughtiness, presumptuousness; probability.

presumptuous *adj* arrogant, assuming, audacious, bold, brash, forward, irreverent, insolent, intrusive, presuming; foolhardy, overconfident, rash.

pretence *n* affectation, cloak, colour, disguise, mask, semblance, show, simulation, veil, window-dressing; excuse, evasion, fabrication, feigning, makeshift, pretext, sham, subterfuge; claim, pretension.

pretend *vb* affect, counterfeit, deem, dissemble, fake, falsify, feign, sham, simulate; act, imagine, lie, profess; aspire, claim.

pretension *n* assertion, assumption, claim, demand, pretence; affectation, airs, conceit, ostentation, pertness, pretentiousness, priggishness, vanity.

pretentious *adj* affected, assuming, conceited, conspicuous, ostentatious, presuming, priggish, showy, tawdry, unnatural, vain.

preternatural *adj* abnormal, anomalous, extraordinary, inexplicable, irregular, miraculous, mysterious, odd, peculiar, strange, unnatural.

pretext *n* affectation, appearance, blind, cloak, colour, guise, mask, pretence, semblance, show, simulation, veil; excuse, justification, plea, vindication.

pretty *adj* attractive, beautiful, bonny, comely, elegant, fair, handsome, neat, pleasing, trim; affected, foppish. * *adv* fairly, moderately, quite, rather, somewhat.

prevail *vb* overcome, succeed, triumph, win; obtain, predominate, preponderate, reign, rule.

prevailing *adj* controlling, dominant, effectual, efficacious, general, influential, operative, overruling, persuading, predominant, preponderant, prevalent, ruling, successful.

prevalent *adj* ascendant, compelling, efficacious, governing, predominant, prevailing, successful, superior; extensive, general, rife, widespread.

prevaricate *vb* cavil, deviate, dodge, equivocate, evade, palter, pettifog, quibble, shift, shuffle, tergiversate.

prevent *vb* bar, check, debar, deter, forestall, help, hinder, impede, inhibit, intercept, interrupt, obstruct, obviate, preclude, prohibit, restrain, save, stop, thwart.

prevention *n* anticipation, determent, deterrence, deterrent, frustration, hindrance, interception, interruption, obstruction, preclusion, prohibition, restriction, stoppage.

previous *adj* antecedent, anterior, earlier, foregoing, foregone, former, precedent, preceding, prior.

prey *vb* devour, eat, feed on, live off; exploit, intimidate, terrorize; burden, distress, haunt, oppress, trouble, worry. * *n* booty, loot, pillage, plunder, prize, rapine, spoil; food, game, kill, quarry, victim; depredation, ravage.

price *vb* assess, estimate, evaluate, rate, value. * *n* amount, cost, expense, outlay, value; appraisal, charge, estimation, excellence, figure, rate, quotation, valuation, value, worth; compensation, guerdon, recompense, return, reward.

priceless *adj* dear, expensive, precious, inestimable, invaluable, valuable; amusing, comic, droll, funny, humorous, killing, rich.

prick *vb* perforate, pierce, puncture, stick; drive, goad, impel, incite, spur, urge; cut, hurt, mark, pain, sting, wound; hasten, post, ride. * *n* mark, perforation, point, puncture; prickle, sting, wound.

pride *vb* boast, brag, crow, preen, revel in. * *n* conceit, egotism, self-complacency, self-esteem, self-exaltation, self-importance, self-sufficiency, vanity; arrogance, assumption, disdain, haughtiness, hauteur, insolence, loftiness, lordliness, pomposity, presumption, superciliousness, vainglory; decorum, dignity, elevation, self-respect; decoration, glory, ornament, show, splendour.

priest *n* churchman, clergyman, divine, ecclesiastic, minister, pastor, presbyter.

prim *adj* demure, formal, nice, precise, prudish, starch, starched, stiff, strait-laced.

primary *adj* aboriginal, earliest, first, initial, original, prime, primitive, primeval, primordial, pristine; chief, main, principal; basic, elementary, fundamental, preparatory: radical.

prime[1] *adj* aboriginal, basic, first, initial, original, primal, primary, primeval, primitive, primordial, pristine; chief, foremost, highest, leading, main, paramount, principal; blooming, early; capital, cardinal, dominant, predominant; excellent, first-class, first-rate, optimal, optimum, quintessential, superlative; beginning, opening. * *n* beginning, dawn, morning, opening; spring, springtime, youth; bloom, cream, flower, height, heyday, optimum, perfection, quintessence, zenith.

prime[2] *vb* charge, load, prepare, undercoat; coach, groom, train, tutor.

primeval *adj* original, primitive, primordial, pristine.

primitive *adj* aboriginal, first, fundamental, original, primal, primary, prime, primitive, primordial, pristine; ancient, antiquated, crude, old-fashioned, quaint, simple, uncivilized, unsophisticated.

prince *n* monarch, potentate, ruler, sovereign; dauphin, heir apparent, infant; chief, leader, potentate.

princely *adj* imperial, regal, royal; august, generous, grand, liberal, magnanimous, magnificent, majestic, munificent, noble, pompous, splendid, superb, titled; dignified, elevated, high-minded, lofty, noble, stately.

principal *adj* capital, cardinal, chief, essential, first, foremost, highest, leading, main, pre-eminent, prime. * *n* chief, head, leader; head teacher, master.

principally *adv* chiefly, essentially, especially, mainly, particularly.

principle *n* cause, fountain, fountainhead, groundwork, mainspring, nature, origin, source, spring; basis, constituent, element, essence, substratum; assumption, axiom, law, maxim, postulation; doctrine, dogma, impulse, maxim, opinion, precept, rule, tenet, theory; conviction, ground, motive, reason; equity, goodness, honesty, honour, incorruptibility, integrity, justice, probity, rectitude, righteousness, trustiness, truth, uprightness, virtue, worth; faculty, power.

prink *vb* adorn, deck, decorate; preen, primp, spruce.

print *vb* engrave, impress, imprint, mark, stamp; issue, publish. * *n* book, periodical, publication; copy, engraving, photograph, picture; characters, font, fount, lettering, type, typeface.

prior *adj* antecedent, anterior, earlier, foregoing, precedent, preceding, precursory, previous, superior.

priority *n* antecedence, anteriority, precedence, pre-eminence, pre-existence, superiority.

priory *n* abbey, cloister, convent, monastery, nunnery.

prison *n* confinement, dungeon, gaol, jail, keep, lockup, penitentiary, reformatory; can, clink, cooler, jug.

pristine *adj* ancient, earliest, first, former, old, original, primary, primeval, primitive, primordial.

privacy *n* concealment, secrecy; retirement, retreat, seclusion, solitude.

private *adj* retired, secluded, sequestrated, solitary; individual, own, particular, peculiar, personal, special, unofficial; confidential, privy; clandestine, concealed, hidden, secret. * *n* GI, soldier, tommy.

privation *n* bereavement, deprivation, dispossession, loss; destitution, distress, indigence, necessity, need, want; absence, negation; degradation.

privilege *n* advantage, charter, claim, exemption, favour, franchise, immunity, leave, liberty, licence, permission, prerogative, right.

privy *adj* individual, particular, peculiar, personal, private, special; clandestine, secret; retired, sequestrated.

prize[1] *vb* appreciate, cherish, esteem, treasure, value.

prize[2] *adj* best, champion, first-rate, outstanding, winning. * *n* guerdon, honours, meed, premium, reward; cup, decoration, medal, laurels, palm, trophy; booty, capture, lot, plunder, spoil; advantage, gain, privilege.

probability *n* chance, prospect, likelihood, presumption; appearance, credibility, credibleness, likeliness, verisimilitude.

probable *adj* apparent, credible, likely, presumable, reasonable.

probably *adv* apparently, likely, maybe, perchance, perhaps, presumably, possibly, seemingly.

probation *n* essay, examination, ordeal, proof, test, trial; novitiate.

probe *vb* examine, explore, fathom, investigate, measure, prove, scrutinize, search, sift, sound, test, verify. * *n* examination, exploration, inquiry, investigation, scrutiny, study.

probity *n* candour, conscientiousness, equity, fairness, faith, goodness, honesty, honour, incorruptibility, integrity, justice, loyalty, morality, principle, rectitude, righteousness, sincerity, soundness, trustworthiness, truth, truthfulness, uprightness, veracity, virtue, worth.

problem *adj* difficult, intractable, uncontrollable, unruly. * *n* dilemma, dispute, doubt, enigma, exercise, proposition, puzzle, riddle, theorem.

problematic *adj* debatable, disputable, doubtful, dubious, enigmatic, problematical, puzzling, questionable, suspicious, uncertain, unsettled.

procedure *n* conduct, course, custom, management, method, operation, policy, practice, process; act, action, deed, measure, performance, proceeding, step, transaction.

proceed *vb* advance, continue, go, pass, progress; accrue, arise, come, emanate, ensue, flow, follow, issue, originate, result, spring.

proceeds *npl* balance, earnings, effects,

gain, income, net, produce, products, profits, receipts, returns, yield.

process *vb* advance, deal with, fulfil, handle, progress; alter, convert, refine, transform. * *n* advance, course, progress, train; action, conduct, management, measure, mode, operation, performance, practice, procedure, proceeding, step, transaction, way; action, case, suit, trial; outgrowth, projection, protuberance.

procession *n* cavalcade, cortege, file, march, parade, retinue, train.

proclaim *vb* advertise, announce, blazon, broach, broadcast, circulate, cry, declare, herald, promulgate, publish, trumpet; ban, outlaw, proscribe.

proclamation *n* advertisement, announcement, blazon, declaration, promulgation, publication; ban, decree, edict, manifesto, ordinance.

proclivity *n* bearing, bent, bias, determination, direction, disposition, drift, inclination, leaning, predisposition, proneness, propensity, tendency, turn; aptitude, facility, readiness.

procrastinate *vb* adjourn, defer, delay, postpone, prolong, protract, retard; neglect, omit; lag, loiter.

procrastination *n* delay, dilatoriness, postponement, protraction, slowness, tardiness.

procreate *vb* beget, breed, engender, generate, produce, propagate.

procurable *adj* acquirable, compassable, obtainable.

procurator *n* agent, attorney, deputy, proctor, proxy, representative, solicitor.

procure *vb* acquire, gain, get, obtain; cause, compass, contrive, effect.

procurer *n* bawd, pander, pimp.

prodigal *adj* abundant, dissipated, excessive, extravagant, generous, improvident, lavish, profuse, reckless, squandering, thriftless, unthrifty, wasteful. * *n* spendthrift, squanderer, waster, wastrel.

prodigality *n* excess, extravagance, lavishness, profusion, squandering, unthriftiness, waste, wastefulness.

prodigious *adj* amazing, astonishing, astounding, extraordinary, marvellous, miraculous, portentous, remarkable, startling, strange, surprising, uncommon, wonderful, wondrous; enormous, huge, immense, monstrous, vast.

prodigy *n* marvel, miracle, phenomenon, portent, sign, wonder; curiosity, monster, monstrosity.

produce *vb* exhibit, show; bear, beget, breed, conceive, engender, furnish, generate, hatch, procreate, yield; accomplish, achieve, cause, create, effect, make, occasion, originate; accrue, afford, give, impart, make, render; extend, lengthen, prolong, protract; fabricate, fashion, manufacture. * *n* crop, fruit, greengrocery, harvest, product, vegetables, yield.

producer *n* creator, inventor, maker, originator; agriculturalist, farmer, greengrocer, husbandman, raiser.

product *n* crops, fruits, harvest, outcome, proceeds, produce, production, returns, yield; consequence, effect, fruit, issue, performance, production, result, work.

production *n* fruit, produce, product; construction, creation, erection, fabrication, making, performance; completion, fruition; birth, breeding, development, growth, propagation; opus, publication, work; continuation, extension, lengthening, prolongation.

productive *adj* copious, fertile, fruitful, luxuriant, plenteous, prolific, teeming; causative, constructive, creative, efficient, life-giving, producing.

proem *n* exordium, foreword, introduction, preface, prelims, prelude, prolegomena.

profane *vb* defile, desecrate, pollute, violate; abuse, debase. * *adj* blasphemous, godless, heathen, idolatrous, impious, impure, pagan, secular, temporal, unconsecrated, unhallowed, unholy, unsanctified, worldly, unspiritual; impure, polluted, unholy.

profanity *n* blasphemy, impiety, irreverence, profaneness, sacrilege.

profess *vb* acknowledge, affirm, allege, aver, avouch, avow, confess, declare, own, proclaim, state; affect, feign, pretend.

profession *n* acknowledgement, assertion, avowal, claim, declaration; avocation, evasion, pretence, pretension, protestation, representation; business, calling, employment, engagement, occupation, office, trade, vocation.

proffer *vb* offer, propose, propound, suggest, tender, volunteer. * *n* offer, proposal, suggestion, tender.

proficiency *n* advancement, forwardness, improvement; accomplishment, aptitude, competency, dexterity, mastery, skill.

proficient *adj* able, accomplished, adept, competent, conversant, dextrous, expert, finished, masterly, practised, skilled, skilful, thoroughbred, trained, qualified, well-versed. * *n* adept, expert, master, master-hand.

profit *vb* advance, benefit, gain, improve. * *n* aid, clearance, earnings, emolument, fruit, gain, lucre, produce, return; advancement, advantage, benefit, interest, perquisite, service, use, utility, weal.

profitable *adj* advantageous, beneficial, desirable, gainful, productive, useful; lucrative, remunerative.

profitless *adj* bootless, fruitless, unprofitable, useless, valueless, worthless.

profligate *adj* abandoned, corrupt, corrupted, degenerate, depraved, dissipated, dissolute, graceless, immoral, shameless, vicious, vitiated, wicked. * *n* debauchee, libertine, rake, reprobate, roué.

profound *adj* abysmal, deep, fathomless; heavy, undisturbed; erudite, learned, penetrating, sagacious, skilled; deeply felt, far-reaching, heartfelt, intense, lively, strong, touching, vivid; low, submissive; abstruse, mysterious, obscure, occult, subtle, recondite; complete, thorough.

profundity *n* deepness, depth, profoundness.

profuse *adj* abundant, bountiful, copious, excessive, extravagant, exuberant, generous, improvident, lavish, overabundant, plentiful, prodigal, wasteful.

profusion *n* abundance, bounty, copiousness, excess, exuberance, extravagance, lavishness, prodigality, profuseness, superabundance, waste.

progenitor *n* ancestor, forebear, forefather.

progeny *n* breed, children, descendants, family, issue, lineage, offshoot, offspring, posterity, race, scion, stock, young.

prognostic *adj* foreshadowing, foreshowing, foretokening. * *n* augury, foreboding, indication, omen, presage, prognostication, sign, symptom, token; foretelling, prediction, prophecy.

prognosticate *vb* foretell, predict, prophesy; augur, betoken, forebode, foreshadow, foreshow, foretoken, indicate, portend, presage.

prognostication *n* foreknowledge, foreshowing, foretelling, prediction, presage; augury, foreboding, foretoken, indication, portent, prophecy.

progress *vb* advance, continue, proceed; better, gain, improve, increase. * *n* advance, advancement, progression; course, headway, ongoing, passage; betterment, development, growth, improvement, increase, reform; circuit, procession.

prohibit *vb* debar, hamper, hinder, preclude, prevent; ban, disallow, forbid, inhibit, interdict.

prohibition *n* ban, bar, disallowance, embargo, forbiddance, inhibition, interdict, interdiction, obstruction, prevention, proscription, taboo, veto.

prohibitive *adj* forbidding, prohibiting, refraining, restrictive.

project *vb* cast, eject, fling, hurl, propel, shoot, throw; brew, concoct, contrive, design, devise, intend, plan, plot, purpose, scheme; delineate, draw, exhibit; bulge, extend, jut, protrude. * *n* contrivance, design, device, intention, plan, proposal, purpose, scheme.

projectile *n* bullet, missile, shell.

projection *n* delivery, ejection, emission, propulsion, throwing; contriving, designing, planning, scheming; bulge, extension, outshoot, process, prominence, protuberance, salience, saliency, salient, spur; delineation, map, plan.

proletarian *adj* mean, plebeian, vile, vulgar. * *n* commoner, plebeian.

proletariat *n* commonality, hoi polloi, masses, mob, plebs, working class.

prolific *adj* abundant, fertile, fruitful, generative, productive, teeming.

prolix *adj* boring, circumlocutory, discursive, diffuse, lengthy, long, long-winded, loose, prolonged, protracted, prosaic, rambling, tedious, tiresome, verbose, wordy.

prologue *n* foreword, introduction, preamble, preface, preliminary, prelude, proem.

prolong *vb* continue, extend, lengthen, protract, sustain; defer, postpone.

promenade *vb* saunter, walk. * *n* dance, stroll, walk; boulevard, esplanade, parade, walkway.

prominent *adj* convex, embossed, jutting, projecting, protuberant, raised, relieved; celebrated, conspicuous, distinguished, eminent, famous, foremost, influential, leading, main, noticeable, outstanding; conspicuous, distinctive, important, manifest, marked, principal, salient.

promiscuous *adj* confused, heterogeneous, indiscriminate, intermingled, mingled, miscellaneous, mixed; abandoned, dissipated, dissolute, immoral, licentious, loose, unchaste, wanton.

promise *vb* covenant, engage, pledge, subscribe, swear, underwrite, vow; assure, attest, guarantee, warrant; agree, bargain, engage, stipulate, undertake. * *n* agreement, assurance, contract, engagement, oath, parole, pledge, profession, undertaking, vow, word.

promising *adj* auspicious, encouraging, hopeful, likely, propitious.

promote *vb* advance, aid, assist, cultivate, encourage, further, help, promote; dignify, elevate, exalt, graduate, honour, pass, prefer, raise.

promotion *n* advancement, encouragement, furtherance; elevation, exaltation, preferment.

prompt *vb* actuate, dispose, impel, incite, incline, induce, instigate, stimulate, urge; remind; dictate, hint, influence, suggest. * *adj* active, alert, apt, quick, ready; forward, hasty; disposed, inclined, prone; early, exact, immediate, instant, precise, punctual, seasonable, timely. * *adv* apace, directly, forthwith, immediately, promptly. * *n* cue, hint, prompter, reminder, stimulus.

promptly *adv* apace, directly, expeditiously, forthwith, immediately, instantly, pronto, punctually, quickly, speedily, straightway, straightaway, summarily, swiftly.

promptness *n* activity, alertness, alacrity, promptitude, readiness, quickness.

promulgate *vb* advertise, announce, broadcast, bruit, circulate, declare, notify, proclaim, publish, spread, trumpet.

prone *adj* flat, horizontal, prostrate, recumbent; declivitous, inclined, inclining, sloping; apt, bent, disposed, inclined, predisposed, tending; eager, prompt, ready.

pronounce *vb* articulate, enunciate, frame, say, speak, utter; affirm, announce, assert, declare, deliver, state.

proof *adj* firm, fixed, impenetrable, stable, steadfast. * *n* essay, examination, ordeal, test, trial; attestation, certification, conclusion, conclusiveness, confirmation, corroboration, demonstration, evidence, ratification, substantiation, testimony, verification.

prop *vb* bolster, brace, buttress, maintain, shore, stay, support, sustain, truss, uphold. * *n* support, stay; buttress, fulcrum, pin, shore, strut.

propaganda *n* inculcation, indoctrination, promotion.

propagate *vb* continue, increase, multiply; circulate, diffuse, disseminate, extend, promote, promulgate, publish, spread, transmit; beget, breed, engender, generate, originate, procreate.

propel *vb* drive, force, impel, push, urge; cast, fling, hurl, project, throw.

propensity *n* aptitude, bent, bias, disposition, inclination, ply, proclivity, proneness, tendency.

proper *adj* individual, inherent, natural, original, particular, peculiar, special, specific; adapted, appropriate, becoming, befitting, convenient, decent, decorous, demure, fit, fitting, legitimate, meet, pertinent, respectable, right, seemly, suitable; accurate, correct, exact, fair, fastidious, formal, just, precise; actual, real.

property *n* attribute, characteristic, disposition, mark, peculiarity, quality, trait, virtue; appurtenance, assets, belongings, chattels, circumstances, effects, estate, goods, possessions, resources, wealth; ownership, possession, proprietorship, tenure; claim, copyright, interest, participation, right, title.

prophecy *n* augury, divination, forecast, foretelling, portent, prediction, premonition, presage, prognostication; exhortation, instruction, preaching.

prophesy *vb* augur, divine, foretell, predict, prognosticate.

propinquity *n* adjacency, contiguity, nearness, neighbourhood, proximity, vicinity; affinity, connection, consanguinity, kindred, relationship.

propitiate *vb* appease, atone, conciliate, intercede, mediate, pacify, reconcile, satisfy.

propitious *adj* benevolent, benign, friendly, gracious, kind, merciful; auspicious, encouraging, favourable, fortunate, happy, lucky, opportune, promising, prosperous, thriving, timely, well-disposed.

proportion *vb* adjust, graduate, regulate; form, shape. * *n* arrangement, relation; adjustment, commensuration, dimension, distribution, symmetry; extent, lot, part, portion, quota, ratio, share.

proposal *n* design, motion, offer, overture, proffer, proposition, recommendation, scheme, statement, suggestion, tender.

propose *vb* move, offer, pose, present, propound, proffer, put, recommend, state, submit, suggest, tender; design, intend, mean, purpose.

proposition *vb* accost, proffer, solicit. * *n* offer, overture, project, proposal, suggestion, tender, undertaking; affirmation, assertion, axiom, declaration, dictum, doctrine, position, postulation, predication, statement, theorem, thesis.

proprietor *n* lord, master, owner, possessor, proprietary.

propriety *n* accuracy, adaptation, appropriation, aptness, becomingness, consonance, correctness, fitness, justness, reasonableness, rightness, seemliness, suitableness; conventionality, decency, decorum, demureness, fastidiousness, formality, modesty, properness, respectability.

prorogation *n* adjournment, continuance, postponement.

prosaic *adj* commonplace, dull, flat, humdrum, matter-of-fact, pedestrian, plain, prolix, prosing, sober, stupid, tame, tedious, tiresome, unentertaining, unimaginative, uninspired, uninteresting, unromantic, vapid.

proscribe *vb* banish, doom, exile, expel, ostracize, outlaw; exclude, forbid, interdict, prohibit; censure, condemn, curse, denounce, reject.

prosecute *vb* conduct, continue, exercise, follow, persist, pursue; arraign, indict, sue, summon.

prospect *vb* explore, search, seek, survey. * *n* display, field, landscape, outlook, perspective, scene, show, sight, spectacle, survey, view, vision, vista; picture, scenery; anticipation, calculation, contemplation, expectance, expectancy, expectation, foreseeing, foresight, hope, presumption, promise, trust; likelihood, probability.

prospectus *n* announcement, conspectus, description, design, outline, plan, programme, sketch, syllabus.

prosper *vb* aid, favour, forward, help; advance, flourish, grow rich, thrive, succeed; batten, increase.

prosperity *n* affluence, blessings, happiness, felicity, good luck, success, thrift, weal, welfare, well-being; boom, heyday.

prosperous *adj* blooming, flourishing, fortunate, golden, halcyon, rich, successful, thriving; auspicious, booming, bright, favourable, good, golden, lucky, promising, propitious, providential, rosy.

prostrate *vb* demolish, destroy, fell, level, overthrow, overturn, ruin; depress, exhaust, overcome, reduce. * *adj* fallen, prostrated, prone, recumbent, supine; helpless, powerless.

prostration *n* demolition, destruction, overthrow; dejection, depression, exhaustion.

prosy *adj* prosaic, unpoetic, unpoetical; dull, flat, jejune, stupid, tedious, tiresome, unentertaining, unimaginative, uninteresting.

protect *vb* cover, defend, guard, shield; fortify, harbour, house, preserve, save, screen, secure, shelter; champion, countenance, foster, patronize.

protector *n* champion, custodian, defender, guardian, patron, warden.

protest *vb* affirm, assert, asseverate, attest, aver, avow, declare, profess, testify; demur, expostulate, object, remonstrate, repudiate. * *n* complaint, declaration, disapproval, objection, protestation.

prototype *n* archetype, copy, exemplar, example, ideal, model, original, paradigm, precedent, protoplast, type.

protract *vb* continue, extend, lengthen, prolong; defer, delay, postpone.

protrude *vb* beetle, bulge, extend, jut, project.

protuberance *n* bulge, bump, elevation, excrescence, hump, lump, process, projection, prominence, roundness, swelling, tumour.

proud *adj* assuming, conceited, contended, egotistical, overweening, self-conscious, self-satisfied, vain; arrogant, boastful, haughty, high-spirited, highly strung, imperious, lofty, lordly, presumptuous, supercilious, uppish, vainglorious.

prove *vb* ascertain, conform, demonstrate, establish, evidence, evince, justify, manifest, show, substantiate, sustain, verify; assay, check, examine, experiment, test, try.

proverb *n* adage, aphorism, apothegm, byword, dictum, maxim, precept, saw, saying.

proverbial *adj* acknowledged, current, notorious, unquestioned.

provide *vb* arrange, collect, plan, prepare, procure; gather, keep, store; afford, contribute, feed, furnish, produce, stock, supply, yield; cater, purvey; agree, bargain, condition, contract, covenant, engage, stipulate.

provided, providing *conj* granted, if, supposing.

provident *adj* careful, cautious, considerate, discreet, farseeing, forecasting, forehanded, foreseeing, prudent; economical, frugal, thrifty.

province *n* district, domain, region, section, territory, tract; colony, dependency; business, calling, capacity, charge, department, duty, employment, function, office, part, post, sphere; department, division, jurisdiction.

provincial *adj* annexed, appendant, outlying; bucolic, countrified, rude, rural, rustic, unpolished, unrefined; insular, local, narrow. * *n* peasant, rustic, yokel.

provision *n* anticipation, providing; arrangement, care, preparation, readiness; equipment, fund, grist, hoard, reserve, resources, stock, store, supplies, supply; clause, condition, prerequisite, proviso, reservation, stipulation.

provisions *npl* eatables, fare, food, provender, supplies, viands, victuals.

proviso *n* clause, condition, provision, stipulation.

provocation *n* incentive, incitement, provocativeness, stimulant, stimulus; affront, indignity, insult, offence; angering, vexation.

provoke *vb* animate, arouse, awaken, excite, impel, incite, induce, inflame, instigate, kindle, move, rouse, stimulate; affront, aggravate, anger, annoy, chafe, enrage, exacerbate, exasperate, incense, infuriate, irritate, nettle, offend, pique, vex; cause, elicit, evoke, instigate, occasion, produce, promote.

provoking *adj* aggravating, annoying, exasperating, irritating, offensive, tormenting, vexatious, vexing.

prowess *n* bravery, courage, daring, fearlessness, gallantry, heroism, intrepidity, valour; aptitude, dexterity, expertness, facility.

proximity *n* adjacency, contiguity, nearness, neighbourhood, propinquity, vicinage, vicinity.

proxy *n* agent, attorney, commissioner, delegate, deputy, lieutenant, representative, substitute.

prudence *n* carefulness, caution, circumspection, common sense, considerateness, discretion, forecast, foresight, judgment, judiciousness, policy, providence, sense, tact, wariness, wisdom.

prudent *adj* cautious, careful, circumspect, considerate, discreet, foreseeing, heedful, judicious, politic, provident, prudential, wary, wise.

prudish *adj* coy, demure, modest, precise, prim, reserved, strait-laced.

prune *vb* abbreviate, clip, cut, dock, lop, thin, trim; dress, preen.

prurient *adj* covetous, craving, desiring, hankering, itching, lascivious, libidinous, longing, lustful.

pry *vb* examine, ferret, inspect, investigate, peep, peer, question, scrutinize, search; force, lever, prise.

public *adj* civil, common, countrywide, general, national, political, state; known, notorious, open, popular, published, well-known. * *n* citizens, community, country, everyone, general public, masses, nation, people, population; audience, buyers, following, supporters.

publication *n* advertisement, announcement, disclosure, divulgement, divulgence, proclamation, promulgation, report; edition, issue, issuance, printing.

publicity *n* daylight, currency, limelight, notoriety, spotlight; outlet, vent.

publish *vb* advertise, air, bruit, announce, blaze, blazon, broach, communicate, declare, diffuse, disclose, disseminate, impart, placard, post, proclaim, promulgate, reveal, tell, utter, vent, ventilate.

pucker *vb* cockle, contract, corrugate, crease, crinkle, furrow, gather, pinch, purse, shirr, wrinkle. * *n* crease, crinkle, fold, furrow, wrinkle.

puerile *adj* boyish, childish, infantile, juvenile, youthful; foolish, frivolous, idle, nonsensical, petty, senseless, silly, simple, trifling, trivial, weak.

puffy *adj* distended, swelled, swollen, tumid, turgid; bombastic, extravagant, inflated, pompous.

pugnacious *adj* belligerent, bellicose, contentious, fighting, irascible, irritable, petulant, quarrelsome.

puissant *adj* forcible, mighty, potent, powerful, strong.

pull *vb* drag, draw, haul, row, tow, tug; cull, extract, gather, pick, pluck; detach, rend, tear, wrest. * *n* pluck, shake, tug, twitch, wrench; contest, struggle; attraction, gravity, magnetism; graft, influence, power.

pulsate *vb* beat, palpitate, pant, throb, thump, vibrate.

pulverize *vb* bruise, comminute, grind, levigate, triturate.

pun *vb* assonate, alliterate, play on words. * *n* assonance, alliteration, clinch, conceit, double-meaning, paranomasia, play on words, quip, rhyme, witticism, wordplay.

punctilious *adj* careful, ceremonious, conscientious, exact, formal, nice, particular, precise, punctual, scrupulous, strict.

punctual *adj* exact, nice, precise, punctilious; early, prompt, ready, regular, seasonable, timely.

puncture *vb* bore, penetrate, perforate, pierce, prick. * *n* bite, hole, sting, wound.

pungent *adj* acid, acrid, biting, burning, caustic, hot, mordant, penetrating, peppery, piercing, piquant, prickling, racy, salty, seasoned, sharp, smart, sour, spicy, stimulating, stinging; acute, acrimonious, cutting, distressing, irritating, keen, painful, peevish, poignant, pointed, satirical, severe, tart, trenchant, waspish.

punish *vb* beat, castigate, chasten, chastise, correct, discipline, flog, lash, scourge, torture, whip.

punishment *n* castigation, chastening, chastisement, correction, discipline, infliction, retribution, scourging, trial; judgment, nemesis, penalty.

puny *adj* feeble, inferior, weak; dwarf, dwarfish, insignificant, diminutive, little, petty, pygmy, small, stunted, tiny, underdeveloped, undersized.

pupil *n* beginner, catechumen, disciple,

learner, neophyte, novice, scholar, student, tyro.

pupillage *n* minority, nonage, tutelage, wardship.

puppet *n* doll, image, manikin, marionette; cat's-paw, pawn, tool.

purchase *vb* buy, gain, get, obtain, pay for, procure; achieve, attain, earn, win. * *n* acquisition, buy, gain, possession, property; advantage, foothold, grasp, hold, influence, support.

pure *adj* clean, clear, fair, immaculate, spotless, stainless, unadulterated, unalloyed, unblemished, uncorrupted, undefiled, unpolluted, unspotted, unstained, unsullied, untainted, untarnished; chaste, continent, guileless, guiltless, holy, honest, incorrupt, innocent, modest, sincere, true, uncorrupt, upright, virgin, virtuous; genuine, perfect, real, simple, true, unadorned; absolute, essential, mere, sheer, thorough; classic, classical.

purge *vb* cleanse, clear, purify; clarify, defecate, evacuate; deterge, scour; absolve, pardon, shrive. * *n* elimination, eradication, expulsion, removal, suppression; cathartic, emetic, enema, laxative, physic.

purify *vb* clean, cleanse, clear, depurate, expurgate, purge, refine, wash; clarify, fine.

puritanical *adj* ascetic, narrow-minded, overscrupulous, prim, prudish, rigid, severe, strait-laced, strict.

purity *n* clearness, fineness; cleanness, correctness, faultlessness, immaculacy, immaculateness; guilelessness, guiltlessness, holiness, honesty, innocence, integrity, piety, simplicity, truth, uprightness, virtue; excellence, genuineness; homogeneity, simpleness; chasteness, chastity, continence, modesty, pudency, virginity.

purlieus *npl* borders, bounds, confines, environs, limits, neighbourhood, outskirts, precincts, suburbs, vicinage, vicinity.

purloin *vb* abstract, crib, filch, pilfer, rob, steal, thieve.

purport *vb* allege, assert, claim, maintain, pretend, profess; denote, express, imply, indicate, mean, signify, suggest. * *n* bearing, current, design, drift, gist, import, intent, meaning, scope, sense, significance, signification, spirit, tendency, tenor.

purpose *vb* contemplate, design, intend, mean, meditate; determine, resolve. * *n* aim, design, drift, end, intent, intention, object, resolution, resolve, view; plan, project; meaning, purport, sense; consequence, effect.

pursue *vb* chase, dog, follow, hound, hunt, shadow, track; conduct, continue, cultivate, maintain, practise, prosecute; seek, strive; accompany, attend.

pursuit *n* chase, hunt, race; conduct, cultivation, practice, prosecution, pursuance; avocation, calling, business, employment, fad, hobby, occupation, vocation.

pursy *adj* corpulent, fat, fleshy, plump, podgy, pudgy, short, thick; short-breathed, short-winded; opulent, rich.

purview *n* body, compass, extent, limit, reach, scope, sphere, view.

push *vb* elbow, crowd, hustle, impel, jostle, shoulder, shove, thrust; advance, drive, hurry, propel, urge; importune, persuade, tease. * *n* pressure, thrust; determination, perseverance; emergency, exigency, extremity, pinch, strait, test, trial; assault, attack, charge, endeavour, onset.

pusillanimous *adj* chicken, chicken-hearted, cowardly, dastardly, faint-hearted, feeble, lily-livered, mean-spirited, spiritless, timid, recreant, timorous, weak.

pustule *n* abscess, blain, blister, blotch, boil, fester, gathering, pimple, sore, ulcer.

put *vb* bring, collocate, deposit, impose, lay, locate, place, set; enjoin, impose, inflict, levy; offer, present, propose, state; compel, constrain, force, oblige; entice, incite, induce, urge; express, utter.

putative *adj* deemed, reckoned, reported, reputed, supposed.

putrefy *vb* corrupt, decay, decompose,

fester, rot, stink.

putrid *adj* corrupt, decayed, decomposed, fetid, rank, rotten, stinking.

puzzle *vb* bewilder, confound, confuse, embarrass, gravel, mystify, nonplus, perplex, pose, stagger; complicate, entangle.* *n* conundrum, enigma, labyrinth, maze, paradox, poser, problem, riddle; bewilderment, complication, confusion, difficulty, dilemma, embarrassment, mystification, perplexity, point, quandary, question.

pygmy *adj* diminutive, dwarf, dwarfish, Lilliputian, little, midget, stunted, tiny. * *n* dwarf, Lilliputian, midget.

Q

quack[1] *vb, n* cackle, cry, squeak.
quack[2] *adj* fake, false, sham. * *n* charlatan, empiric, humbug, impostor, mountebank, pretender.
quadruple *adj* fourfold, quadruplicate.
quagmire *n* bog, fen, marsh, morass, slough, swamp; difficulty, impasse, muddle, predicament.
quail *vb* blench, cower, droop, faint, flinch, shrink, tremble.
quaint *adj* antiquated, antique, archaic, curious, droll, extraordinary, fanciful, odd, old-fashioned, queer, singular, uncommon, unique, unusual; affected, fantastic, far-fetched, whimsical; artful, ingenious.
quake *vb* quiver, shake, shiver, shudder; move, vibrate. * *n* earthquake, shake, shudder.
qualification *n* ability, accomplishment, capability, competency, eligibility, fitness, suitability; condition, exception, limitation, modification, proviso, restriction, stipulation; abatement, allowance, diminution, mitigation.
qualified *adj* accomplished, certificated, certified, competent, fitted, equipped, licensed, trained; adapted, circumscribed, conditional, limited, modified, restricted.
qualify *vb* adapt, capacitate, empower, entitle, equip, fit; limit, modify, narrow, restrain, restrict; abate, assuage, ease, mitigate, moderate, reduce, soften; diminish, modulate, temper, regulate, vary.
quality *n* affection, attribute, characteristic, colour, distinction, feature, flavour, mark, nature, peculiarity, property, singularity, timbre, tinge, trait; character, condition, disposition, humour, mood, temper; brand, calibre, capacity, class, description, excellence, grade, kind, rank, sort, stamp, standing, station, status, virtue; aristocracy, gentility, gentry, noblesse, nobility.
qualm *n* agony, pang, throe; nausea, queasiness, sickness; compunction, remorse, uneasiness, twinge.
quandary *n* bewilderment, difficulty, dilemma, doubt, embarrassment, perplexity, pickle, plight, predicament, problem, puzzle, strait, uncertainty.
quantity *n* content, extent, greatness, measure, number, portion, share, size; aggregate, batch, amount, bulk, lot, mass, quantum, store, sum, volume; duration, length.
quarrel *vb* altercate, bicker, brawl, carp, cavil, clash, contend, differ, dispute, fight, jangle, jar, scold, scuffle, spar, spat, squabble, strive, wrangle. * *n* altercation, affray, bickering, brawl, breach, breeze, broil, clash, contention, contest, controversy, difference, disagreement, discord, dispute, dissension, disturbance, feud, fight, fray, imbroglio, jar, miff, misunderstanding, quarrelling, row, rupture, spat, squabble, strife, tiff, tumult, variance, wrangle.
quarrelsome *adj* argumentative, choleric, combative, contentious, cross, discordant, disputatious, dissentious, fiery, irascible, irritable, petulant, pugnacious, ugly, wranglesome.
quarter *vb* billet, lodge, post, station; allot, furnish, share. * *n* abode, billet, dwelling, habitation, lodgings, posts, quarters, stations; direction, district, locality, location, lodge, position, region, territory; clemency, mercy, mildness.
quash *vb* abate, abolish, annul, cancel, invalidate, nullify, overthrow; crush, extinguish, repress, stop, subdue, suppress.
queasy *adj* nauseated, pukish, seasick, sick, squeamish.

queer *vb* botch, harm, impair, mar, spoil. * *adj* curious, droll, extraordinary, fantastic, odd, peculiar, quaint, singular, strange, uncommon, unusual, whimsical; gay, homosexual.

quell *vb* conquer, crush, overcome, overpower, subdue; bridle, check, curb, extinguish, lay, quench, rein in, repress, restrain, stifle; allay, calm, compose, hush, lull, pacify, quiet, quieten, still, tranquillize; alleviate, appease, blunt, deaden, dull, mitigate, mollify, soften, soothe.

quench *vb* extinguish, put out; check, destroy, repress, satiate, stifle, still, suppress; allay, cool, dampen, extinguish, slake.

querulous *adj* bewailing, complaining, cross, discontented, dissatisfied, fretful, fretting, irritable, mourning, murmuring, peevish, petulant, plaintive, touchy, whining.

query *vb* ask, enquire, inquire, question; dispute, doubt. * *n* enquiry, inquiry, interrogatory, issue, problem, question.

quest *n* expedition, journey, search, voyage; pursuit, suit; examination, enquiry, inquiry; demand, desire, invitation, prayer, request, solicitation.

question *vb* ask, catechize, enquire, examine, inquire, interrogate, quiz, sound out; doubt, query; challenge, dispute. * *n* examination, enquiry, inquiry, interpellation, interrogation; enquiry, inquiry, interrogatory, query; debate, discussion, disquisition, examination, investigation, issue, trial; controversy, dispute, doubt; motion, mystery, point, poser, problem, proposition, puzzle, topic.

questionable *adj* ambiguous, controversial, controvertible, debatable, doubtful, disputable, equivocal, problematic, problematical, suspicious, uncertain, undecided.

quibble *vb* cavil, equivocate, evade, prevaricate, shuffle. * *n* equivocation, evasion, pretence, prevarication, quirk, shift, shuffle, sophism, subtlety, subterfuge.

quick *adj* active, agile, alert, animated, brisk, lively, nimble, prompt, ready, smart, sprightly; expeditious, fast, fleet, flying, hurried, rapid, speedy, swift; adroit, apt, clever, dextrous, expert, skilful; choleric, hasty, impetuous, irascible, irritable, passionate, peppery, petulant, precipitate, sharp, unceremonious, testy, touchy, waspish; alive, animate, live, living.

quicken *vb* animate, energize, resuscitate, revivify, vivify; cheer, enliven, invigorate, reinvigorate, revive, whet; accelerate, dispatch, expedite, hasten, hurry, speed; actuate, excite, incite, kindle, refresh, sharpen, stimulate; accelerate, live, take effect.

quickly *adv* apace, fast, immediately, nimbly, quick, rapidly, readily, soon, speedily, swiftly.

quickness *n* celerity, dispatch, expedition, haste, rapidity, speed, swiftness, velocity; agility, alertness, activity, briskness, liveliness, nimbleness, promptness, readiness, smartness; adroitness, aptitude, aptness, dexterity, facility, knack; acumen, acuteness, keenness, penetration, perspicacity, sagacity, sharpness, shrewdness.

quiescent *adj* at rest, hushed, motionless, quiet, resting, still; calm, mute, placid, quiet, serene, still, tranquil, unagitated, undisturbed, unruffled.

quiet *adj* hushed, motionless, quiescent, still, unmoved; calm, contented, gentle, mild, meek, modest, peaceable, peaceful, placid, silent, smooth, tranquil, undemonstrative, unobtrusive, unruffled; patient; retired, secluded. * *n* calmness, peace, repose, rest, silence, stillness.

quieten *vb* arrest, discontinue, intermit, interrupt, still, stop, suspend; allay, appease, calm, compose, lull, pacify, sober, soothe, tranquillize; hush, silence; alleviate, assuage, blunt, dull, mitigate, moderate, mollify, soften.

quip *n* crank, flout, gibe, jeer, mock, quirk, repartee, retort, sarcasm, sally, scoff, sneer, taunt, witticism.

quit *vb* absolve, acquit, deliver, free, release; clear, deliver, discharge from, free, liberate, relieve; acquit, behave, conduct;

carry through, perform; discharge, pay, repay, requite; relinquish, renounce, resign, stop, surrender; depart from, leave, withdraw from; abandon, desert, forsake, forswear. * *adj* absolved, acquitted, clear, discharged, free, released.

quite *adv* completely, entirely, exactly, perfectly, positively, precisely, totally, wholly.

quiver *vb* flicker, flutter, oscillate, palpitate, quake, play, shake, shiver, shudder, tremble, twitch, vibrate. * *n* shake, shiver, shudder, trembling.

quixotic *adj* absurd, chimerical, fanciful, fantastic, fantastical, freakish, imaginary, mad, romantic, utopian, visionary, wild.

quiz *vb* examine, question, test; peer at; banter, hoax, puzzle, ridicule. * *n* enigma, hoax, jest, joke, puzzle; jester, joker, hoax.

quota *n* allocation, allotment, apportionment, contingent, portion, proportion, quantity, share.

quotation *n* citation, clipping, cutting, extract, excerpt, reference, selection; estimate, rate, tender.

quote *vb* adduce, cite, excerpt, extract, illustrate, instance, name, repeat, take; estimate, tender.

R

rabble *n* commonality, horde, mob, populace, riffraff, rout, scum, trash.

rabid *adj* frantic, furious, mad, raging, wild; bigoted, fanatical, intolerant, irrational, narrow-minded, rampant.

race[1] *n* ancestry, breed, family, generation, house, kindred, line, lineage, pedigree, stock, strain; clan, folk, nation, people, tribe; breed, children, descendants, issue, offspring, progeny, stock.

race[2] *vb* career, compete, contest, course, hasten, hurry, run, speed. * *n* career, chase, competition, contest, course, dash, heat, match, pursuit, run, sprint; flavour, quality, smack, strength, taste.

rack *vb* agonize, distress, excruciate, rend, torment, torture, wring; exhaust, force, harass, oppress, strain, stretch, wrest. * *n* agony, anguish, pang, torment, torture; crib, manger; neck, crag; dampness, mist, moisture, vapour.

racket *n* clamour, clatter, din, dissipation, disturbance, fracas, frolic, hubbub, noise, outcry, tumult, uproar; game, graft, scheme, understanding.

racy *adj* flavoursome, palatable, piquant, pungent, rich, spicy, strong; forcible, lively, pungent, smart, spirited, stimulating, vigorous, vivacious.

radiance *n* brightness, brilliance, brilliancy, effluence, efflux, emission, glare, glitter, light, lustre, refulgence, resplendence, shine, splendour.

radiant *adj* beaming, brilliant, effulgent, glittering, glorious, luminous, lustrous, resplendent, shining, sparkling, splendid; ecstatic, happy, pleased.

radiate *vb* beam, gleam, glitter, shine; emanate, emit; diffuse, spread.

radical *adj* constitutional, deep-seated, essential, fundamental, ingrained, inherent, innate, native, natural, organic, original, uncompromising; original, primitive, simple, uncompounded, underived; complete, entire, extreme, fanatic, insurgent, perfect, rebellious, thorough, total. * *n* etymon, radix, root; fanatic, revolutionary.

rage *vb* bluster, boil, chafe, foam, fret, fume, ravage, rave. * *n* excitement, frenzy, fury, madness, passion, rampage, raving, vehemence, wrath; craze, fashion, mania, mode, style, vogue.

ragged *adj* rent, tattered, torn; contemptible, mean, poor, shabby; jagged, rough, rugged, shaggy, uneven; discordant, dissonant, inharmonious, unmusical.

raid *vb* assault, forage, invade, pillage, plunder. * *n* attack, foray, invasion, inroad, plunder.

rail *vb* abuse, censure, inveigh, scoff, scold, sneer, upbraid.

raillery *n* banter, chaff, irony, joke, pleasantry, ridicule, satire.

raiment *n* array, apparel, attire, clothes, clothing, costume, dress, garb, garments, habiliment, habit, vestments, vesture.

rain *vb* drizzle, drop, fall, pour, shower, sprinkle, teem; bestow, lavish. * *n* cloudburst, downpour, drizzle, mist, shower, sprinkling.

raise *vb* boost, construct, erect, heave, hoist, lift, uplift, upraise, rear; advance, elevate, ennoble, exalt, promote; aggravate, amplify, augment, enhance, heighten, increase, invigorate; arouse, awake, cause, effect, excite, originate, produce, rouse, stir up, occasion, start; assemble, collect, get, levy, obtain; breed, cultivate, grow, propagate, rear; ferment, leaven, work.

rake[1] *vb* collect, comb, gather, scratch; ransack, scour.

rake[2] *n* debauchee, libertine, profligate,

roué.

rakish *adj* debauched, dissipated, dissolute, lewd, licentious; cavalier, jaunty.

ramble *vb* digress, maunder, range, roam, rove, saunter, straggle, stray, stroll, wander. * *n* excursion, rambling, roving, tour, trip, stroll, wandering.

rambling *adj* discursive, irregular; straggling, strolling, wandering.

ramification *n* arborescence, branching, divarication, forking, radiation; branch, division, offshoot, subdivision; consequence, upshot.

ramify *vb* branch, divaricate, extend, separate.

rampant *adj* excessive, exuberant, luxuriant, rank, wanton; boisterous, dominant, headstrong, impetuous, predominant, raging, uncontrollable, unbridled, ungovernable, vehement, violent.

rampart *n* bulwark, circumvallation, defence, fence, fortification, guard, security, wall.

rancid *adj* bad, fetid, foul, fusty, musty, offensive, rank, sour, stinking, tainted.

rancorous *adj* bitter, implacable, malevolent, malicious, malign, malignant, resentful, spiteful, vindictive, virulent.

rancour *n* animosity, antipathy, bitterness, enmity, gall, grudge, hate, hatred, ill-will, malevolence, malice, malignity, spite, venom, vindictiveness.

random *adj* accidental, casual, chance, fortuitous, haphazard, irregular, stray, wandering.

range *vb* course, cruise, extend, ramble, roam, rove, straggle, stray, stroll, wander; bend, lie, run; arrange, class, dispose, rank. * *n* file, line, row, rank, tier; class, kind, order, sort; excursion, expedition, ramble, roving, wandering; amplitude, bound, command, compass, distance, extent, latitude, reach, scope, sweep, view; register.

rank[1] *vb* arrange, class, classify, range. * *n* file, line, order, range, row, tier; class, division, group, order, series; birth, blood, caste, degree, estate, grade, position, quality, sphere, stakes, standing; dignity, distinction, eminence, nobility.

rank[2] *adj* dense, exuberant, luxuriant, overabundant, overgrown, vigorous, wild; excessive, extreme, extravagant, flagrant, gross, rampant, sheer, unmitigated, utter, violent; fetid, foul, fusty, musty, offensive, rancid; fertile, productive, rich; coarse, disgusting.

ransack *vb* pillage, plunder, ravage, rifle, sack, strip; explore, overhaul, rummage, search thoroughly.

ransom *vb* deliver, emancipate, free, liberate, redeem, rescue, unfetter. * *n* money, payment pay-off, price; deliverance, liberation, redemption, release.

rant *vb* declaim, mouth, spout, vociferate. * *n* bombast, cant, exaggeration, fustian.

rapacious *adj* predacious, preying, raptorial; avaricious, grasping, greedy, ravenous, voracious.

rapid *adj* fast, fleet, quick, swift; brisk, expeditious, hasty, hurried, quick, speedy.

rapine *n* depredation, pillage, plunder, robbery, spoliation.

rapt *adj* absorbed, charmed, delighted, ecstatic, engrossed, enraptured, entranced, fascinated, inspired, spellbound.

rapture *vb* enrapture, ravish, transport. * *n* delight, exultation, enthusiasm, rhapsody; beatification, beatitude, bliss, ecstasy, felicity, happiness, joy, spell, transport.

rare[1] *adj* sparse, subtle, thin; extraordinary, infrequent, scarce, singular, strange, uncommon, unique, unusual; choice, excellent, exquisite, fine, incomparable, inimitable.

rare[2] *adj* bloody, underdone.

rarity *n* attenuation, ethereality, etherealness, rarefaction, rareness, tenuity, tenuousness, thinness; infrequency, scarcity, singularity, sparseness, uncommonness, unwontedness.

rascal *n* blackguard, caitiff, knave, miscreant, rogue, reprobate, scallywag, scapegrace, scamp, scoundrel, vagabond, villain.

rash[1] *adj* adventurous, audacious, careless, foolhardy, hasty, headlong, headstrong, heedless, incautious, inconsiderate, indiscreet, injudicious, impetuous, impulsive, incautious, precipitate, quick, rapid, reckless, temerarious, thoughtless, unguarded, unwary, venturesome.

rash² *n* breaking-out, efflorescence, eruption; epidemic, flood, outbreak, plague, spate.

rashness *n* carelessness, foolhardiness, hastiness, heedlessness, inconsideration, indiscretion, precipitation, recklessness, temerity, venturesomeness.

rate¹ *vb* appraise, compute, estimate, value. * *n* cost, price; class, degree, estimate, rank, value, valuation, worth; proportion, ration; assessment, charge, impost, tax.

rate² *vb* abuse, berate, censure, chide, criticize, find fault, reprimand, reprove, scold.

ratify *vb* confirm, corroborate, endorse, establish, seal, settle, substantiate; approve, bind, consent, sanction.

ration *vb* apportion, deal, distribute, dole, restrict. * *n* allowance, portion, quota, share.

rational *adj* intellectual, reasoning; equitable, fair, fit, just, moderate, natural, normal, proper, reasonable, right; discreet, enlightened, intelligent, judicious, sagacious, sensible, sound, wise.

raucous *adj* harsh, hoarse, husky, rough.

ravage *vb* consume, desolate, despoil, destroy, devastate, harry, overrun, pillage, plunder, ransack, ruin, sack, spoil, strip, waste. * *n* desolation, despoilment, destruction, devastation, havoc, pillage, plunder, rapine, ruin, spoil, waste.

ravenous *adj* devouring, ferocious, gluttonous, greedy, insatiable, omnivorous, ravening, rapacious, voracious.

ravine *n* canyon, cleft, defile, gap, gorge, gulch, gully, pass.

raving *adj* delirious, deranged, distracted, frantic, frenzied, furious, infuriated, mad, phrenetic, raging. * *n* delirium, frenzy, fury, madness, rage.

ravish *vb* abuse, debauch, defile, deflower, force, outrage, violate; captivate, charm, delight, enchant, enrapture, entrance, overjoy, transport; abduct, kidnap, seize, snatch, strip.

raw *adj* fresh, inexperienced, unpractised, unprepared, unseasoned, untried, unskilled; crude, green, immature, unfinished, unripe; bare, chafed, excoriated, galled, sensitive, sore; bleak, chilly, cold, cutting, damp, piercing, windswept; uncooked.

ray *n* beam, emanation, gleam, moonbeam, radiance, shaft, streak, sunbeam.

raze *vb* demolish, destroy, dismantle, extirpate, fell, level, overthrow, ruin, subvert; efface, erase, obliterate.

reach *vb* extend, stretch; grasp, hit, strike, touch; arrive at, attain, gain, get, obtain, win. * *n* capability, capacity, grasp.

readily *adv* easily, promptly, quickly; cheerfully, willingly.

readiness *n* alacrity, alertness, expedition, quickness, promptitude, promptness; aptitude, aptness, dexterity, easiness, expertness, facility, quickness, skill; preparation, preparedness, ripeness; cheerfulness, disposition, eagerness, ease, willingness.

ready *vb* arrange, equip, organize, prepare. * *adj* alert, expeditious, prompt, quick, punctual, speedy; adroit, apt, clever, dextrous, expert, facile, handy, keen, nimble, prepared, prompt, ripe, quick, sharp, skilful, smart; cheerful, disposed, eager, free, inclined, willing; accommodating, available, convenient, near, handy; easy, facile, fluent, offhand, opportune, short, spontaneous.

real *adj* absolute, actual, certain, literal, positive, practical, substantial, substantive, veritable; authentic, genuine, true; essential, internal, intrinsic.

realize *vb* accomplish, achieve, discharge, effect, effectuate, perfect, perform; apprehend, comprehend, experience, recognize, understand; externalize, substantiate; acquire, earn, gain, get, net, obtain, produce, sell.

reality *n* actuality, certainty, fact, truth, verity.

really *adv* absolutely, actually, certainly, indeed, positively, truly, verily, veritably.

reap *vb* acquire, crop, gain, gather, get,

harvest, obtain, receive.

rear[1] *adj* aft, back, following, hind, last. * *n* background, reverse, setting; heel, posterior, rear end, rump, stern, tail; path, trail, train, wake.

rear[2] *vb* construct, elevate, erect, hoist, lift, raise; cherish, educate, foster, instruct, nourish, nurse, nurture, train; breed, grow; rouse, stir up.

reason *vb* argue, conclude, debate, deduce, draw from, infer, intellectualize, syllogize, think, trace. * *n* faculty, intellect, intelligence, judgement, mind, principle, sanity, sense, thinking, understanding; account, argument, basis, cause, consideration, excuse, explanation, gist, ground, motive, occasion, pretence, proof; aim, design, end, object, purpose; argument, reasoning; common sense, reasonableness, wisdom; equity, fairness, justice, right; exposition, rationale, theory.

reasonable *adj* equitable, fair, fit, honest, just, proper, rational, right, suitable; enlightened, intelligent, judicious, sagacious, sensible, wise; considerable, fair, moderate, tolerable; credible, intellectual, plausible, well-founded; sane, sober, sound; cheap, inexpensive, low-priced.

rebate *vb* abate, bate, blunt, deduct, diminish, lessen, reduce; cut, pare, rabbet. * *n* decrease, decrement, diminution, lessening; allowance, deduction, discount, reduction.

rebel *vb* mutiny, resist, revolt, strike. * *adj* insubordinate, insurgent, mutinous, rebellious. * *n* insurgent, mutineer, traitor.

rebellion *n* anarchy, insubordination, insurrection, mutiny, resistance, revolt, revolution, uprising.

rebellious *adj* contumacious, defiant, disloyal, disobedient, insubordinate, intractable, obstinate, mutinous, rebel, refractory, seditious.

rebuff *vb* check, chide, oppose, refuse, reject, repel, reprimand, resist, snub. * *n* check, defeat, discouragement, opposition, rejection, resistance, snub.

rebuke *vb* blame, censure, chide, lecture, upbraid, reprehend, reprimand, reprove, scold, silence. * *n* blame, censure, chiding, expostulation, remonstrance, reprimand, reprehension, reproach, reproof, reproval; affliction, chastisement, punishment.

recall *vb* abjure, abnegate, annul, cancel, countermand, deny, nullify, overrule, recant, repeal, repudiate, rescind, retract, revoke, swallow, withdraw; commemorate, recollect, remember, retrace, review, revive. * *n* abjuration, abnegation, annulment, cancellation, nullification, recantation, repeal, repudiation, rescindment, retraction, revocation, withdrawal; memory, recollection, remembrance, reminiscence.

recant *vb* abjure, annul, disavow, disown, recall, renounce, repudiate, retract, revoke, unsay.

recapitulate *vb* epitomize, recite, rehearse, reiterate, repeat, restate, review, summarize.

recede *vb* desist, ebb, retire, regress, retreat, retrograde, return, withdraw.

receive *vb* accept, acquire, derive, gain, get, obtain, take; admit, shelter, take in; entertain, greet, welcome; allow, permit, tolerate; adopt, approve, believe, credit, embrace, follow, learn, understand; accommodate, carry, contain, hold, include, retain; bear, encounter, endure, experience, meet, suffer, sustain.

recent *adj* fresh, new, novel; latter, modern, young; deceased, foregoing, late, preceding, retiring.

reception *n* acceptance, receipt, receiving; entertainment, greeting, welcome; levee, soiree, party; admission, credence; belief, credence, recognition.

recess *n* alcove, corner, depth, hollow, niche, nook, privacy, retreat, seclusion; break, holiday, intermission, interval, respite, vacation; recession, retirement, retreat, withdrawal.

reciprocal *adj* alternate, commutable, complementary, correlative, correspondent, mutual.

recital *n* rehearsal, repetition, recitation; account, description, detail, explanation, narration, relation, statement, telling.

recite *vb* declaim, deliver, rehearse, repeat; describe, mention, narrate, recount, relate, tell; count, detail, enumerate, number, recapitulate.

reckless *adj* breakneck, careless, desperate, devil-may-care, flighty, foolhardy, giddy, harebrained, headlong, heedless, inattentive, improvident, imprudent, inconsiderate, indifferent, indiscreet, mindless, negligent, rash, regardless, remiss, thoughtless, temerarious, uncircumspect, unconcerned, unsteady, volatile, wild.

reckon *vb* calculate, cast, compute, consider, count, enumerate, guess, number; account, class, esteem, estimate, regard, repute, value.

reckoning *n* calculation, computation, consideration, counting; account, bill, charge, estimate, register, score; arrangement, settlement.

reclaim *vb* amend, correct, reform; recover, redeem, regenerate, regain, reinstate, restore; civilize, tame.

recline *vb* couch, lean, lie, lounge, repose, rest.

recluse *adj* anchoritic, anchoritical, cloistered, eremitic, eremitical, hermitic, hermitical, reclusive, solitary. * *n* anchorite, ascetic, eremite, hermit, monk, solitary.

reclusive *adj* recluse, retired, secluded, sequestered, sequestrated, solitary.

recognition *n* identification, memory, recollection, remembrance; acknowledgement, appreciation, avowal, comprehension, confession, notice; allowance, concession.

recognize *vb* apprehend, identify, perceive, remember; acknowledge, admit, avow, confess, own; allow, concede, grant; greet, salute.

recoil *vb* react, rebound, reverberate; retire, retreat, withdraw; blench, fail, falter, quail, shrink. * *n* backstroke, boomerang, elasticity, kick, reaction, rebound, repercussion, resilience, revulsion, ricochet, shrinking.

recollect *vb* recall, remember, reminisce.

recollection *n* memory, remembrance, reminiscence.

recommend *vb* approve, commend, endorse, praise, sanction; commit; advise, counsel, prescribe, suggest.

recommendation *n* advocacy, approbation, approval, commendation, counsel, credential, praise, testimonial.

recompense *vb* compensate, remunerate, repay, requite, reward, satisfy; indemnify, redress, reimburse. * *n* amends, compensation, indemnification, indemnity, remuneration, repayment, reward, satisfaction; requital, retribution.

reconcilable *adj* appeasable, forgiving, placable; companionable, congruous, consistent.

reconcile *vb* appease, conciliate, pacify, placate, propitiate, reunite; content, harmonize, regulate; adjust, compose, heal, settle.

recondite *adj* concealed, dark, hidden, mystic, mystical, obscure, occult, secret, transcendental.

record *vb* chronicle, enter, note, register. * *n* account, annals, archive, chronicle, diary, docket, enrolment, entry, file, list, minute, memoir, memorandum, memorial, note, proceedings, register, registry, report, roll, score; mark, memorial, relic, trace, track, trail, vestige; memory, remembrance; achievement, career, history.

recount *vb* describe, detail, enumerate, mention, narrate, particularize, portray, recite, relate, rehearse, report, tell.

recover *vb* recapture, reclaim, regain; rally, recruit, repair, retrieve; cure, heal, restore, revive; redeem, rescue, salvage, save; convalesce, recuperate.

recreant *adj* base, cowardly, craven, dastardly, faint-hearted, mean-spirited, pusillanimous, yielding; apostate, backsliding, faithless, false, perfidious, treacherous, unfaithful, untrue. * *n* coward, dastard; apostate, backslider, renegade.

recreation *n* amusement, cheer, diversion, entertainment, fun, game, leisure, pastime, play, relaxation, sport.

recreational *adj* amusing, diverting, entertaining, refreshing, relaxing, relieving.

recruit *vb* repair, replenish; recover, refresh, regain, reinvigorate, renew, renovate, restore, retrieve, revive, strengthen, supply. * *n* auxiliary, beginner, helper, learner, novice, tyro.

rectify *vb* adjust, amend, better, correct, emend, improve, mend, redress, reform, regulate, straighten.

rectitude *n* conscientiousness, equity, goodness, honesty, integrity, justice, principle, probity, right, righteousness, straightforwardness, uprightness, virtue.

recumbent *adj* leaning, lying, prone, prostrate, reclining; idle, inactive, listless, reposing.

recur *vb* reappear, resort, return, revert.

recusancy *n* dissent, heresy, heterodoxy, nonconformity.

redeem *vb* reform, regain, repurchase, retrieve; free, liberate, ransom, rescue, save; deliver, reclaim, recover, reinstate; atone, compensate for, recompense; discharge, fulfil, keep, perform, satisfy.

redemption *n* buying, compensation, recovery, repurchase, retrieval; deliverance, liberation, ransom, release, rescue, salvation; discharge, fulfilment, performance.

redolent *adj* aromatic, balmy, fragrant, odoriferous, odorous, scented, sweet, sweet-smelling.

redoubtable *adj* awful, doughty, dreadful, formidable, terrible, valiant.

redound *vb* accrue, conduce, contribute, result, tend.

redress *vb* amend, correct, order, rectify, remedy, repair; compensate, ease, relieve. * *n* abatement, amends, atonement, compensation, correction, cure, indemnification, rectification, repair, righting, remedy, relief, reparation, satisfaction.

reduce *vb* bring; form, make, model, mould, remodel, render, resolve, shape; abate, abbreviate, abridge, attenuate, contract, curtail, decimate, decrease, diminish, lessen, minimize, shorten, thin; abase, debase, degrade, depress, dwarf, impair, lower, weaken; capture, conquer, master, overpower, overthrow, subject, subdue, subjugate, vanquish; impoverish, ruin; resolve, solve.

redundant *adj* copious, excessive, exuberant, fulsome, inordinate, lavish, needless, overflowing, overmuch, plentiful, prodigal, superabundant, replete, superfluous, unnecessary, useless; diffuse, periphrastic, pleonastic, tautological, verbose, wordy.

reel[1] *n* capstan, winch, windlass; bobbin, spool.

reel[2] *vb* falter, flounder, heave, lurch, pitch, plunge, rear, rock, roll, stagger, sway, toss, totter, tumble, wallow, welter, vacillate; spin, swing, turn, twirl, wheel, whirl. * *n* gyre, pirouette, spin, turn, twirl, wheel, whirl.

re-establish *vb* re-found, rehabilitate, reinstall, reinstate, renew, renovate, replace, restore.

refer *vb* commit, consign, direct, leave, relegate, send, submit; ascribe, assign, attribute, impute; appertain, belong, concern, pertain, point, relate, respect, touch; appeal, apply, consult; advert, allude, cite, quote.

referee *vb* arbitrate, judge, umpire. * *n* arbiter, arbitrator, judge, umpire.

reference *n* concern, connection, regard, respect; allusion, ascription, citation, hint, intimation, mark, reference, relegation.

refine *vb* clarify, cleanse, defecate, fine, purify; cultivate, humanize, improve, polish, rarefy, spiritualize.

refined *adj* courtly, cultured, genteel, polished, polite; discerning, discriminating, fastidious, sensitive; filtered, processed, purified.

refinement *n* clarification, filtration, purification, sublimation; betterment, improvement; delicacy, cultivation, culture, elegance, elevation, finish, gentility, good breeding, polish, politeness, purity, spirituality, style.

reflect *vb* copy, imitate, mirror, reproduce; cogitate, consider, contemplate, deliberate, meditate, muse, ponder, ruminate, study, think.

reflection *n* echo, shadow; cogitation, consideration, contemplation, deliberation, idea, meditation, musing, opinion, remark, rumination, thinking, thought; aspersion, blame, censure, criticism, disparagement, reproach, slur.

reflective *adj* reflecting, reflexive; cogitating, deliberating, musing, pondering, reasoning, thoughtful.

reform *vb* amend, ameliorate, better, correct, improve, mend, meliorate, rectify, reclaim, redeem, regenerate, repair, restore; reconstruct, remodel, reshape. * *n* amendment, correction, progress, reconstruction, rectification, reformation.

reformation *n* amendment, emendation, improvement, reform; adoption, conversion, redemption; refashioning, regeneration, reproduction, reconstruction.

refractory *adj* cantankerous, contumacious, cross-grained, disobedient, dogged, headstrong, heady, incoercible, intractable, mulish, obstinate, perverse, recalcitrant, self-willed, stiff, stubborn, sullen, ungovernable, unmanageable, unruly, unyielding.

refrain[1] *vb* abstain, cease, desist, forbear, stop, withhold.

refrain[2] *n* chorus, song, undersong.

refresh *vb* air, brace, cheer, cool, enliven, exhilarate, freshen, invigorate, reanimate, recreate, recruit, reinvigorate, revive, regale, slake.

refreshing *adj* comfortable, cooling, grateful, invigorating, pleasant, reanimating, restful, reviving.

refuge *n* asylum, covert, harbour, haven, protection, retreat, safety, sanction, security, shelter.

refulgent *adj* bright, brilliant, effulgent, lustrous, radiant, resplendent, shining.

refund *vb* reimburse, repay, restore, return. * *n* reimbursement, repayment.

refuse[1] *n* chaff, discard, draff, dross, dregs, garbage, junk, leavings, lees, litter, lumber, offal, recrement, remains, rubbish, scoria, scum, sediment, slag, sweepings, trash, waste.

refuse[2] *vb* decline, deny, withhold; disallow, disavow, exclude, rebuff, reject, renege, renounce, repel, repudiate, repulse, revoke, veto.

refute *vb* confute, defeat, disprove, overcome, overthrow, rebut, repel, silence.

regain *vb* recapture, recover, re-obtain, repossess, retrieve.

regal *adj* imposing, imperial, kingly, noble, royal, sovereign.

regale *vb* delight, entertain, gratify, refresh; banquet, feast.

regard *vb* behold, gaze, look, notice, mark, observe, remark, see, view, watch; attend to, consider, heed, mind, respect; esteem, honour, revere, reverence, value; account, believe, estimate, deem, hold, imagine, reckon, suppose, think, treat, use. * *n* aspect, gaze, look, view; attention, attentiveness, care, concern, consideration, heed, notice, observance; account, reference, relation, respect; admiration, affection, attachment, deference, esteem, estimation, favour, honour, interest, liking, love, respect, reverence, sympathy, value; account, eminence, note, reputation, repute; condition, matter, point.

regardful *adj* attentive, careful, considerate, deferential, heedful, mindful, observing, thoughtful, watchful.

regarding *prep* concerning, respecting, touching.

regardless *adj* careless, disregarding, heedless, inattentive, indifferent, mindless, neglectful, negligent, unconcerned, unmindful, unobservant. * *adv* however, irrespectively, nevertheless, nonetheless, notwithstanding.

regenerate *vb* reproduce; renovate, revive; change, convert, renew, sanctify. * *adj* born-again, converted, reformed, regenerated.

regime *n* administration, government, rule.

region *n* climate, clime, country, district, division, latitude, locale, locality, province, quarter, scene, territory, tract; area, neighbourhood, part, place, portion, spot, space, sphere, terrain, vicinity.

register *vb* delineate, portray, record, show. * *n* annals, archive, catalogue, chronicle, list, record, roll, schedule; clerk, registrar, registry; compass, range.

regret *vb* bewail, deplore, grieve, lament,

repine, sorrow; bemoan, repent, mourn, rue. * *n* concern, disappointment, grief, lamentation, rue, sorrow, trouble; compunction, contrition, penitence, remorse, repentance, repining, self-condemnation, self-reproach.

regular *adj* conventional, natural, normal, ordinary, typical; correct, customary, cyclic, established, fixed, habitual, periodic, periodical, recurring, reasonable, rhythmic, seasonal, stated, usual; steady, constant, uniform, even; just, methodical, orderly, punctual, systematic, unvarying; complete, genuine, indubitable, out-and-out, perfect, thorough; balanced, consistent, symmetrical.

regulate *vb* adjust, arrange, dispose, methodize, order, organize, settle, standardize, time, systematize; conduct, control, direct, govern, guide, manage, rule.

regulation *adj* customary, mandatory, official, required, standard. * *n* adjustment, arrangement, control, disposal, disposition, law, management, order, ordering, precept, rule, settlement.

rehabilitate *vb* reinstate, re-establish, restore; reconstruct, reconstitute, reintegrate, reinvigorate, renew, renovate.

rehearsal *n* drill, practice, recital, recitation, repetition; account, history, mention, narration, narrative, recounting, relation, statement, story, telling.

rehearse *vb* recite, repeat; delineate, depict, describe, detail, enumerate, narrate, portray, recapitulate, recount, relate, tell.

reign *vb* administer, command, govern, influence, predominate, prevail, rule. * *n* control, dominion, empire, influence, power, royalty, sovereignty, power, rule, sway.

reimburse *vb* refund, repay, restore; compensate, indemnify, requite, satisfy.

rein *vb* bridle, check, control, curb, guide, harness, hold, restrain, restrict. * *n* bridle, check, curb, harness, restraint, restriction.

reinforce *vb* augment, fortify, strengthen.

reinstate *vb* re-establish, rehabilitate, reinstall, replace, restore.

reject *vb* cashier, discard, dismiss, eject, exclude, pluck; decline, deny, disallow, despise, disapprove, disbelieve, rebuff, refuse, renounce, repel, repudiate, scout, slight, spurn, veto. * *n* cast-off, discard, failure, refusal, repudiation.

rejoice *vb* cheer, delight, enliven, enrapture, exhilarate, gladden, gratify, please, transport; crow, exult, delight, gloat, glory, jubilate, triumph, vaunt.

rejoin *vb* answer, rebut, respond, retort.

relate *vb* describe, detail, mention, narrate, recite, recount, rehearse, report, tell; apply, connect, correlate.

relation *n* account, chronicle, description, detail, explanation, history, mention, narration, narrative, recital, rehearsal, report, statement, story, tale; affinity, application, bearing, connection, correlation, dependency, pertinence, relationship; concern, reference, regard, respect; alliance, nearness, propinquity, rapport; blood, consanguinity, cousinship, kin, kindred, kinship, relationship; kinsman, kinswoman, relative.

relax *vb* loose, loosen, slacken, unbrace, unstrain; debilitate, enervate, enfeeble, prostrate, unbrace, unstring, weaken; abate, diminish, lessen, mitigate, reduce, remit; amuse, divert, ease, entertain, recreate, unbend.

release *vb* deliver, discharge, disengage, exempt, extricate, free, liberate, loose, unloose; acquit, discharge, quit, relinquish, remit. * *n* deliverance, discharge, freedom, liberation; absolution, dispensation, excuse, exemption, exoneration; acquaintance, clearance.

relentless *adj* cruel, hard, impenitent, implacable, inexorable, merciless, obdurate, pitiless, rancorous, remorseless, ruthless, unappeasable, uncompassionate, unfeeling, unforgiving, unmerciful, unpitying, unrelenting, unyielding, vindictive.

relevant *adj* applicable, appropriate, apposite, apt, apropos, fit, germane, pertinent, proper, relative, suitable.

reliable *adj* authentic, certain, constant, dependable, sure, trustworthy, trusty, unfailing.

reliance *n* assurance, confidence, credence, dependence, hope, trust.

relic *n* keepsake, memento, memorial, remembrance, souvenir, token, trophy; trace, vestige.

relics *npl* fragments, leavings, remainder, remains, remnants, ruins, scraps; body, cadaver, corpse, remains.

relict *n* dowager, widow.

relief *n* aid, alleviation, amelioration, assistance, assuagement, comfort, deliverance, ease, easement, help, mitigation, reinforcement, respite, rest, succour, softening, support; indemnification, redress, remedy; embossment, projection, prominence, protrusion; clearness, distinction, perspective, vividness.

relieve *vb* aid, comfort, help, spell, succour, support, sustain; abate, allay, alleviate, assuage, cure, diminish, ease, lessen, lighten, mitigate, remedy, remove, soothe; indemnify, redress, right, repair; disengage, free, release, remedy, rescue.

religious *adj* devotional, devout, god-fearing, godly, holy, pious, prayerful, spiritual; conscientious, exact, rigid, scrupulous, strict; canonical, divine, theological.

relinquish *vb* abandon, desert, forsake, forswear, leave, quit, renounce, resign, vacate; abdicate, cede, forbear, forgo, give up, surrender, yield.

relish *vb* appreciate, enjoy, like, prefer; season, flavour, taste. * *n* appetite, appreciation, enjoyment, fondness, gratification, gusto, inclination, liking, partiality, predilection, taste, zest; cast, flavour, manner, quality, savour, seasoning, sort, tang, tinge, touch; appetizer, condiment.

reluctance *n* aversion, backwardness, disinclination, dislike, loathing, repugnance, unwillingness.

reluctant *adj* averse, backward, disinclined, hesitant, indisposed, loath, unwilling.

rely *vb* confide, count, depend, hope, lean, reckon, repose, trust.

remain *vb* abide, continue, endure, last; exceed, persist, survive; abide, continue, dwell, halt, inhabit, rest, sojourn, stay, stop, tarry, wait.

remainder *n* balance, excess, leavings, remains, remnant, residue, rest, surplus.

remark *vb* heed, notice, observe, regard; comment, express, mention, observe, say, state, utter. * *n* consideration, heed, notice, observation, regard; annotation, comment, gloss, note, stricture; assertion, averment, comment, declaration, saying, statement, utterance.

remarkable *adj* conspicuous, distinguished, eminent, extraordinary, famous, notable, noteworthy, noticeable, pre-eminent, rare, singular, strange, striking, uncommon, unusual, wonderful.

remedy *vb* cure, heal, help, palliate, relieve; amend, correct, rectify, redress, repair, restore, retrieve. * *n* antidote, antitoxin, corrective, counteractive, cure, help, medicine, nostrum, panacea, restorative, specific; redress, reparation, restitution, restoration; aid, assistance, relief.

remembrance *n* recollection, reminiscence, retrospection; keepsake, memento, memorial, memory, reminder, souvenir, token; consideration, regard, thought.

reminiscence *n* memory, recollection, remembrance, retrospective.

remiss *adj* backward, behindhand, dilatory, indolent, languid, lax, lazy, slack, slow, tardy; careless, dilatory, heedless, idle, inattentive, neglectful, negligent, shiftless, slothful, thoughtless.

remission *n* abatement, decrease, diminution, lessening, mitigation, moderation, reduction, relaxation; cancellation, discharge, release, relinquishment; intermission, interruption, pause, rest, stop, stoppage, suspense, suspension; absolution, acquittal, excuse, exoneration, forgiveness, indulgence, pardon.

remit *vb* replace, restore, return; abate, bate, diminish, relax; release; absolve, condone, excuse, forgive, overlook, pardon; relinquish, resign, surrender; consign, forward, refer, send, transmit. * *n* authorization, brief, instructions, orders.

remnant *n* remainder, remains, residue, rest, trace; fragment, piece, scrap.

remorse *n* compunction, contrition, penitence, qualm, regret, repentance, reproach, self-reproach, sorrow.

remorseless *adj* cruel, barbarous, hard, harsh, implacable, inexorable, merciless, pitiless, relentless, ruthless, savage, uncompassionate, unmerciful, unrelenting.

remote *adj* distant, far, out-of-the-way; alien, far-fetched, foreign, inappropriate, unconnected, unrelated; abstracted, separated; inconsiderable, slight; isolated, removed, secluded, sequestrated.

removal *n* abstraction, departure, dislodgement, displacement, relegation, remove, shift, transference; elimination, extraction, withdrawal; abatement, destruction; discharge, dismissal, ejection, expulsion.

remove *vb* carry, dislodge, displace, shift, transfer, transport; abstract, extract, withdraw; abate, banish, destroy, suppress; cashier, depose, discharge, dismiss, eject, expel, oust, retire; depart, move.

remunerate *vb* compensate, indemnify, pay, recompense, reimburse, repay, requite, reward, satisfy.

remuneration *n* compensation, earnings, indemnity, pay, payment, recompense, reimbursement, reparation, repayment, reward, salary, wages.

remunerative *adj* gainful, lucrative, paying, profitable; compensatory, recompensing, remuneratory, reparative, requiting, rewarding.

rend *vb* break, burst, cleave, crack, destroy, dismember, dissever, disrupt, divide, fracture, lacerate, rive, rupture, sever, shiver, snap, split, sunder, tear.

render *vb* restore, return, surrender; assign, deliver, give, present; afford, contribute, furnish, supply, yield; construe, interpret, translate.

rendition *n* restitution, return, surrender; delineation, exhibition, interpretation, rendering, representation, reproduction; translation, version.

renegade *adj* apostate, backsliding, disloyal, false, outlawed, rebellious, recreant, unfaithful. * *n* apostate, backslider, recreant, turncoat; deserter, outlaw, rebel, revolter, traitor; vagabond, wretch.

renew *vb* rebuild, recreate, re-establish, refit, refresh, rejuvenate, renovate, repair, replenish, restore, resuscitate, revive; continue, recommence, repeat; iterate, reiterate; regenerate, transform.

renounce *vb* abjure, abnegate, decline, deny, disclaim, disown, forswear, neglect, recant, repudiate, reject, slight; abandon, abdicate, drop, forgo, forsake, desert, leave, quit, relinquish, resign.

renovate *vb* reconstitute, re-establish, refresh, refurbish, renew, restore, revamp; reanimate, recreate, regenerate, reproduce, resuscitate, revive, revivify.

renown *n* celebrity, distinction, eminence, fame, figure, glory, honour, greatness, name, note, notability, notoriety, reputation, repute.

renowned *adj* celebrated, distinguished, eminent, famed, famous, honoured, illustrious, remarkable, wonderful.

rent[1] *n* breach, break, crack, cleft, crevice, fissure, flaw, fracture, gap, laceration, opening, rift, rupture, separation, split, tear; schism.

rent[2] *vb* hire, lease, let. * *n* income, rental, revenue.

repair[1] *vb* mend, patch, piece, refit, retouch, tinker, vamp; correct, recruit, restore, retrieve. * *n* mending, refitting, renewal, reparation, restoration.

repair[2] *vb* betake oneself, go, move, resort, turn.

repairable *adj* curable, recoverable, reparable, restorable, retrievable.

reparable *adj* curable, recoverable, repairable, restorable, retrievable.

reparation *n* renewal, repair, restoration; amends, atonement, compensation, correction, indemnification, recompense, redress, requital, restitution, satisfaction.

repay *vb* refund, reimburse, restore, return; compensate, recompense, remunerate, reward, satisfy; avenge, retaliate, revenge.

repeal *vb* abolish, annul, cancel, recall, rescind, reverse, revoke. * *n* abolition, abrogation, annulment, cancellation, rescission, reversal, revocation.

repeat *vb* double, duplicate, iterate; cite, narrate, quote, recapitulate, recite, rehearse; echo, renew, reproduce. * *n* duplicate, duplication, echo, iteration, recapitulation, reiteration, repetition.

repel *vb* beat, disperse, repulse, scatter; check, confront, oppose, parry, rebuff, resist, withstand; decline, refuse, reject; disgust, revolt, sicken.

repellent *adj* abhorrent, disgusting, forbidding, repelling, repugnant, repulsive, revolting, uninviting.

repent *vb* atone, regret, relent, rue, sorrow.

repentance *n* compunction, contriteness, contrition, penitence, regret, remorse, self-accusation, self-condemnation, self-reproach.

repentant *adj* contrite, penitent, regretful, remorseful, rueful, sorrowful, sorry.

repercussion *n* rebound, recoil, reverberation; backlash, consequence, result.

repetition *n* harping, iteration, recapitulation, reiteration; diffuseness, redundancy, tautology, verbosity; narration, recital, rehearsal, relation, retailing; recurrence, renewal.

repine *vb* croak, complain, fret, grumble, long, mope, murmur.

replace *vb* re-establish, reinstate, reset; refund, repay, restore; succeed, supersede, supplant.

replenish *vb* fill, refill, renew, re-supply; enrich, furnish, provide, store, supply.

replete *adj* abounding, charged, exuberant, fraught, full, glutted, gorged, satiated, well-stocked.

repletion *n* abundance, exuberance, fullness, glut, profusion, satiation, satiety, surfeit.

replica *n* autograph, copy, duplicate, facsimile, reproduction.

reply *vb* answer, echo, rejoin, respond. * *n* acknowledgement, answer, rejoinder, repartee, replication, response, retort.

report *vb* announce, annunciate, communicate, declare; advertise, broadcast, bruit, describe, detail, herald, mention, narrate, noise, promulgate, publish, recite, relate, rumour, state, tell; minute, record. * *n* account, announcement, communication, declaration, statement; advice, description, detail, narration, narrative, news, recital, story, tale, talk, tidings; gossip, hearsay, rumour; clap, detonation, discharge, explosion, noise, repercussion, sound; fame, reputation, repute; account, bulletin, minute, note, record, statement.

repose[1] *vb* compose, recline, rest, settle; couch, lie, recline, sleep, slumber; confide, lean. * *n* quiet, recumbence, recumbency, rest, sleep, slumber; breathing time, inactivity, leisure, respite, relaxation; calm, ease, peace, peacefulness, quietness, quietude, stillness, tranquillity.

repose[2] *vb* place, put, stake; deposit, lodge, reposit, store.

repository *n* conservatory, depository, depot, magazine, museum, receptacle, repertory,
storehouse, storeroom, thesaurus, treasury, vault.

reprehend *vb* accuse, blame, censure, chide, rebuke, reprimand, reproach, reprove, upbraid.

reprehensible *adj* blameable, blameworthy, censurable, condemnable, culpable, reprovable.

reprehension *n* admonition, blame, censure, condemnation, rebuke, reprimand, reproof.

represent *vb* exhibit, express, show; delineate, depict, describe, draw, portray, sketch; act, impersonate, mimic, personate, personify; exemplify, illustrate, image, reproduce, symbolize, typify.

representation *n* delineation, exhibition, show; impersonation, personation, simulation; account, description, narration, narrative, relation, statement; image, likeness, model, portraiture, resemblance, semblance; sight, spectacle; expostulation, remonstrance.

representative *adj* figurative, illustrative,

symbolic, typical; delegated, deputed, representing. * *n* agent, commissioner, delegate, deputy, emissary, envoy, legate, lieutenant, messenger, proxy, substitute.

repress *vb* choke, crush, dull, overcome, overpower, silence, smother, subdue, suppress, quell; bridle, chasten, chastise, check, control, curb, restrain; appease, calm, quiet.

reprimand *vb* admonish, blame, censure, chide, rebuke, reprehend, reproach, reprove, upbraid. * *n* admonition, blame, censure, rebuke, reprehension, reproach, reprobation, reproof, reproval.

reprint *vb* republish. * *n* reimpression, republication; copy.

reproach *vb* blame, censure, rebuke, reprehend, reprimand, reprove, upbraid; abuse, accuse, asperse, condemn, defame, discredit, disparage, revile, traduce, vilify. * *n* abuse, blame, censure, condemnation, contempt, contumely, disapprobation, disapproval, expostulation, insolence, invective, railing, rebuke, remonstrance, reprobation, reproof, reviling, scorn, scurrility, upbraiding, vilification; abasement, discredit, disgrace, dishonour, disrepute, indignity, ignominy, infamy, insult, obloquy, odium, offence, opprobrium, scandal, shame, slur, stigma.

reproachful *adj* abusive, censorious, condemnatory, contemptuous, contumelious, damnatory, insolent, insulting, offensive, opprobrious, railing, reproving, sacrifice, scolding, scornful, scurrilous, upbraiding, vituperative; base, discreditable, disgraceful, dishonourable, disreputable, infamous, scandalous, shameful, vile.

reprobate *vb* censure, condemn, disapprove, discard, reject, reprehend; disallow; abandon, disown. * *adj* abandoned, base, castaway, corrupt, depraved, graceless, hardened, irredeemable, lost, profligate, shameless, vile, vitiated, wicked. * *n* caitiff, castaway, miscreant, outcast, rascal, scamp, scoundrel, sinner, villain.

reproduce *vb* copy, duplicate, emulate, imitate, print, repeat, represent; breed, generate, procreate, propagate.

reproof *n* admonition, animadversion, blame, castigation, censure, chiding, condemnation, correction, criticism, lecture, monition, objurgation, rating, rebuke, reprehension, reprimand, reproach, reproval, upbraiding.

reprove *vb* admonish, blame, castigate, censure, chide, condemn, correct, criticize, inculpate, lecture, objurgate, rate, rebuke, reprimand, reproach, scold, upbraid.

reptilian *adj* abject, crawling, creeping, grovelling, low, mean, treacherous, vile, vulgar.

repudiate *vb* abjure, deny, disavow, discard, disclaim, disown, nullify, reject, renounce.

repugnance *n* contrariety, contrariness, incompatibility, inconsistency, irreconcilability, irreconcilableness, unsuitability, unsuitableness; contest, opposition, resistance, struggle; antipathy, aversion, detestation, dislike, hatred, hostility, reluctance, repulsion, unwillingness.

repugnant *adj* incompatible, inconsistent, irreconcilable; adverse, antagonistic, contrary, hostile, inimical, opposed, opposing, unfavourable; detestable, distasteful, offensive, repellent, repulsive.

repulse *vb* check, defeat, refuse, reject, repel. * *n* repelling, repulsion; denial, refusal; disappointment, failure.

repulsion *n* abhorrence, antagonism, anticipation, aversion, discard, disgust, dislike, hatred, hostility, loathing, rebuff, rejection, repugnance, repulse, spurning.

repulsive *adj* abhorrent, cold, disagreeable, disgusting, forbidding, frigid, harsh, hateful, loathsome, nauseating, nauseous, odious, offensive, repellent, repugnant, reserved, revolting, sickening, ugly, unpleasant.

reputable *adj* creditable, estimable, excellent, good, honourable, respectable, worthy.

reputation *n* account, character, fame, mark, name, repute; celebrity, credit, distinction, eclat, esteem, estimation, glory, honour, prestige, regard, renown, report, respect; notoriety.

repute *vb* account, consider, deem, esteem, estimate, hold, judge, reckon, regard, think.

request *vb* ask, beg, beseech, call, claim, demand, desire, entreat, pray, solicit, supplicate. * *n* asking, entreaty, importunity, invitation, petition, prayer, requisition, solicitation, suit, supplication.

require *vb* beg, beseech, bid, claim, crave, demand, dun, importune, invite, pray, requisition, request, sue, summon; need, want; direct, enjoin, exact, order, prescribe.

requirement *n* claim, demand, exigency, market, need, needfulness, requisite, requisition, request, urgency, want; behest, bidding, charge, command, decree, exaction, injunction, mandate, order, precept.

requisite *adj* essential, imperative, indispensable, necessary, needful, needed, required. * *n* essential, necessity, need, requirement.

requite *vb* compensate, pay, remunerate, reciprocate, recompense, repay, reward, satisfy; avenge, punish, retaliate, satisfy.

rescind *vb* abolish, abrogate, annul, cancel, countermand, quash, recall, repeal, reverse, revoke, vacate, void.

rescue *vb* deliver, extricate, free, liberate, preserve, ransom, recapture, recover, redeem, release, retake, save. * *n* deliverance, extrication, liberation, redemption, release, salvation.

research *vb* analyse, examine, explore, inquire, investigate, probe, study. * *n* analysis, examination, exploration, inquiry, investigation, scrutiny, study.

resemblance *n* affinity, agreement, analogy, likeness, semblance, similarity, similitude; counterpart, facsimile, image, representation.

resemble *vb* compare, liken; copy, counterfeit, imitate.

resentful *adj* angry, bitter, choleric, huffy, hurt, irascible, irritable, malignant, revengeful, sore, touchy.

resentment *n* acrimony, anger, annoyance, bitterness, choler, displeasure, dudgeon, fury, gall, grudge, heartburning, huff, indignation, ire, irritation, pique, rage, soreness, spleen, sulks, umbrage, vexation, wrath.

reservation *n* reserve, suppression; appropriation, booking, exception, restriction, saving; proviso, salvo; custody, park, reserve, sanctuary.

reserve *vb* hold, husband, keep, retain, store. * *adj* alternate, auxiliary, spare, substitute. * *n* reservation; aloofness, backwardness, closeness, coldness, concealment, constraint, suppression, reservedness, retention, restraint, reticence, uncommunicativeness, unresponsiveness; coyness, demureness, modesty, shyness, taciturnity; park, reservation, sanctuary.

reserved *adj* coy, demure, modest, shy, taciturn; aloof, backward, cautious, cold, distant, incommunicative, restrained, reticent, self-controlled, unsociable, unsocial; bespoken, booked, excepted, held, kept, retained, set apart, taken, withheld.

reside *vb* abide, domicile, domiciliate, dwell, inhabit, live, lodge, remain, room, sojourn, stay.

residence *n* inhabitance, inhabitancy, sojourn, stay, stop, tarrying; abode, domicile, dwelling, habitation, home, house, lodging, mansion.

residue *n* leavings, remainder, remains, remnant, residuum, rest; excess, overplus, surplus.

resign *vb* abandon, abdicate, abjure, cede, commit, disclaim, forego, forsake, leave, quit, relinquish, renounce, surrender, yield.

resignation *n* abandonment, abdication, relinquishment, renunciation, retirement, surrender; acquiescence, compliance, endurance, forbearance, fortitude, longsufferance, patience, submission, sufferance.

resist *vb* assail, attack, baffle, block, check, confront, counteract, disappoint, frustrate, hinder, impede, impugn, neutralize, obstruct, oppose, rebel, rebuff, stand against, stem, stop, strive, thwart, withstand.

resolute *adj* bold, constant, decided, determined, earnest, firm, fixed, game, hardy, inflexible, persevering, pertinacious, relentless, resolved, staunch, steadfast, steady, stout, stouthearted, sturdy, tenacious, unalterable, unbending, undaunted, unflinching, unshaken, unwavering, unyielding.

resolution *n* boldness, disentanglement, explication, unravelling; backbone, constancy, courage, decision, determination, earnestness, energy, firmness, fortitude, grit, hardihood, inflexibility, intention, manliness, pluck, perseverance, purpose, relentlessness, resolve, resoluteness, stamina, steadfastness, steadiness, tenacity.

resolve *vb* analyse, disperse, scatter, separate, reduce; change, dissolve, liquefy, melt, reduce, transform; decipher, disentangle, elucidate, explain, interpret, unfold, solve, unravel; conclude, decide, determine, fix, intend, purpose, will. * *n* conclusion, decision, determination, intention, will; declaration, resolution.

resonant *adj* booming, clangorous, resounding, reverberating, ringing, roaring, sonorous, thundering, vibrant.

resort *vb* frequent, haunt; assemble, congregate, convene, go, repair. * *n* application, expedient, recourse; haunt, refuge, rendezvous, retreat, spa; assembling, confluence, concourse, meeting; recourse, reference.

resound *vb* echo, re-echo, reverberate, ring; celebrate, extol, praise, sound.

resource *n* dependence, resort; appliance, contrivance, device, expedient, instrumentality, means, resort.

resources *npl* capital, funds, income, money, property, reserve, supplies, wealth.

respect *vb* admire, esteem, honour, prize, regard, revere, reverence, spare, value, venerate; consider, heed, notice, observe. * *n* attention, civility, courtesy, consideration, deference, estimation, homage, honour, notice, politeness, recognition, regard, reverence, veneration; consideration, favour, goodwill, kind; aspect, bearing, connection, feature, matter, particular, point, reference, regard, relation.

respects *npl* compliments, greetings, regards.

respectable *adj* considerable, estimable, honourable, presentable, proper, upright, worthy; adequate, moderate; tolerable.

respectful *adj* ceremonious, civil, complaisant, courteous, decorous, deferential, dutiful, formal, polite.

respire *vb* breathe, exhale, live.

respite *vb* delay, relieve, reprieve. * *n* break, cessation, delay, intermission, interval, pause, recess, rest, stay, stop; forbearance, postponement, reprieve.

resplendent *adj* beaming, bright, brilliant, effulgent, lucid, glittering, glorious, gorgeous, luminous, lustrous, radiant, shining, splendid.

respond *vb* answer, reply, rejoin; accord, correspond, suit.

response *n* answer, replication, rejoinder, reply, retort.

responsible *adj* accountable, amenable, answerable, liable, trustworthy.

rest[1] *vb* cease, desist, halt, hold, pause, repose, stop; breathe, relax, unbend; repose, sleep, slumber; lean, lie, lounge, perch, recline, ride; acquiesce, confide, trust; confide, rely, trust; calm, comfort, ease. * *n* fixity, immobility, inactivity, motionlessness, quiescence, quiet, repose; hush, peace, peacefulness, quietness, relief, security, stillness, tranquillity; cessation, intermission, interval, lull, pause, relaxation, respite, stop, stay; siesta, sleep, slumber; death; brace, stay, support; axis, fulcrum, pivot.

rest[2] *vb* be left, remain. * *n* balance, remainder, remnant, residuum; overplus, surplus.

restaurant *n* bistro, café, cafeteria, chophouse, eatery, eating house, pizzeria, trattoria.

restitution *n* restoration, return; amends, compensation, indemnification, recompense, rehabilitation, remuneration, reparation, repayment, requital, satisfaction.

restive *adj* mulish, obstinate, stopping,

stubborn, unwilling; impatient, recalcitrant, restless, uneasy, unquiet.

restless *adj* disquieted, disturbed, restive, sleepless, uneasy, unquiet, unresting; changeable, inconstant, irresolute, unsteady, vacillating; active, astatic, roving, transient, unsettled, unstable, wandering; agitated, fidgety, fretful, turbulent.

restoration *n* recall, recovery, re-establishment, reinstatement, reparation, replacement, restitution, return; reconsideration, redemption, reintegration, renewal, renovation, repair, resuscitation, revival; convalescence, cure, recruitment, recuperation.

restorative *adj* curative, invigorating, recuperative, remedial, restoring, stimulating. * *n* corrective, curative, cure, healing, medicine, remedy, reparative, stimulant.

restore *vb* refund, repay, return; caulk, cobble, emend, heal, mend, patch, reintegrate, re-establish, rehabilitate, reinstate, renew, repair, replace, retrieve; cure, heal, recover, revive; resuscitate.

restrain *vb* bridle, check, coerce, confine, constrain, curb, debar, govern, hamper, hinder, hold, keep, muzzle, picket, prevent, repress, restrict, rule, subdue, tie, withhold; abridge, circumscribe, narrow.

restraint *n* bridle, check, coercion, control, compulsion, constraint, curb, discipline, repression, suppression; arrest, deterrence, hindrance, inhibition, limitation, prevention, prohibition, restriction, stay, stop; confinement, detention, imprisonment, shackles; constraint, stiffness, reserve, unnaturalness.

restrict *vb* bound, circumscribe, confine, limit, qualify, restrain, straiten.

restriction *n* confinement, limitation; constraint, restraint; reservation, reserve.

result *vb* accrue, arise, come, ensue, flow, follow, issue, originate, proceed, spring, rise; end, eventuate, terminate. * *n* conclusion, consequence, deduction, inference, outcome; corollary, effect, end, event, eventuality, fruit, harvest, issue, product, sequel, termination; decision, determination, finding, resolution, resolve, solution, verdict.

resume *vb* continue, recommence, renew, restart, summarize.

résumé *n* abstract, curriculum vitae, epitome, recapitulation, summary, synopsis.

resuscitate *vb* quicken, reanimate, renew, resurrect, restore, revive, revivify.

retain *vb* detain, hold, husband, keep, preserve, recall, recollect, remember, reserve, save, withhold; engage, maintain.

retainer *n* adherent, attendant, dependant, follower, hanger-on, servant.

retaliate *vb* avenge, match, repay, requite, retort, return, turn.

retaliation *n* boomerang, counterstroke, punishment, repayment, requital, retribution, revenge.

retard *vb* check, clog, hinder, impede, obstruct, slacken; adjourn, defer, delay, postpone, procrastinate.

reticent *adj* close, reserved, secretive, silent, taciturn, uncommunicative.

retinue *n* bodyguard, cortege, entourage, escort, followers, household, ménage, suite, tail, train.

retire *vb* discharge, shelve, superannuate, withdraw; depart, leave, resign, retreat.

retired *adj* abstracted, removed, withdrawn; apart, private, secret, sequestrated, solitary.

retirement *n* isolation, loneliness, privacy, retreat, seclusion, solitude, withdrawal.

retiring *adj* coy, demure, diffident, modest, reserved, retreating, shy, withdrawing.

retort *vb* answer, rejoin, reply, respond. * *n* answer, rejoinder, repartee, reply, response; crucible, jar, vessel, vial.

retract *vb* reverse, withdraw; abjure, cancel, disavow, recall, recant, revoke, unsay.

retreat *vb* recoil, retire, withdraw; recede. * *n* departure, recession, recoil, retirement, withdrawal; privacy, seclusion, solitude; asylum, cove, den, habitat, haunt, niche, recess, refuge, resort, shelter.

retrench *vb* clip, curtail, cut, delete, dock,

lop, mutilate, pare, prune; abridge, decrease, diminish, lessen; confine, limit; economize, encroach.

retribution *n* compensation, desert, judgement, nemesis, penalty, recompense, repayment, requital, retaliation, return, revenge, reward, vengeance.

retrieve *vb* recall, recover, recoup, recruit, re-establish, regain, repair, restore.

retrograde *vb* decline, degenerate, recede, retire, retrocede. * *adj* backward, inverse, retrogressive, unprogressive.

retrospect *n* recollection, re-examination, reminiscence, re-survey, review, survey.

return *vb* reappear, recoil, recur, revert; answer, reply, respond; recriminate, retort; convey, give, communicate, reciprocate, recompense, refund, remit, repay, report, requite, send, tell, transmit; elect. * *n* payment, reimbursement, remittance, repayment; recompense, recovery, recurrence, renewal, repayment, requital, restitution, restoration, reward; advantage, benefit, interest, profit, rent, yield.

reunion *n* assemblage, assembly, gathering, meeting, re-assembly; rapprochement, reconciliation.

reveal *vb* announce, communicate, confess, declare, disclose, discover, display, divulge, expose, impart, open, publish, tell, uncover, unmask, unseal, unveil.

revel *vb* carouse, disport, riot, roister, tipple; delight, indulge, luxuriate, wanton. * *n* carousal, feast, festival, saturnalia, spree.

revelry *n* bacchanal, carousal, carouse, debauch, festivity, jollification, jollity, orgy, revel, riot, rout, saturnalia, wassail.

revenge *vb* avenge, repay, requite, retaliate, vindicate. * *n* malevolence, rancour, reprisal, requital, retaliation, retribution, vengeance, vindictiveness.

revengeful *adj* implacable, malevolent, malicious, malignant, resentful, rancorous, spiteful, vengeful, vindictive.

revenue *n* fruits, income, produce, proceeds, receipts, return, reward, wealth.

reverberate *vb* echo, re-echo, resound, return.

revere *vb* adore, esteem, hallow, honour, reverence, venerate, worship.

reverence *vb* adore, esteem, hallow, honour, revere, venerate, worship. * *n* adoration, awe, deference, homage, honour, respect, veneration, worship.

reverential *adj* deferential, humble, respectful, reverent, submissive.

reverse *vb* invert, transpose; overset, overthrow, overturn, quash, subvert, undo, unmake; annul, countermand, repeal, rescind, retract, revoke; back, back up, retreat. * *adj* back, converse, contrary, opposite, verso. * *n* back, calamity, check, comedown, contrary, counterpart, defeat, opposite, tail; change, vicissitude; adversity, affliction, hardship, misadventure, mischance, misfortune, mishap, trial.

revert *vb* repel, reverse; backslide, lapse, recur, relapse, return.

review *vb* inspect, overlook, reconsider, re-examine, retrace, revise, survey; analyse, criticize, discuss, edit, judge, scrutinize, study. * *n* reconsideration, re-examination, re-survey, retrospect, survey; analysis, digest, synopsis; commentary, critique, criticism, notice, review, scrutiny, study.

revile *vb* abuse, asperse, backbite, calumniate, defame, execrate, malign, reproach, slander, traduce, upbraid, vilify.

revise *vb* reconsider, re-examine, review; alter, amend, correct, edit, overhaul, polish.

revive *vb* reanimate, reinspire, reinspirit, reinvigorate, resuscitate, revitalize, revivify; animate, cheer, comfort, invigorate, quicken, reawaken, recover, refresh, renew, renovate, rouse, strengthen; reawake, recall.

revocation *n* abjuration, recall, recantation, repeal, retraction, reversal.

revoke *vb* abolish, abrogate, annul, cancel, countermand, invalidate, quash, recall, recant, repeal, repudiate, rescind, retract.

revolt *vb* desert, mutiny, rebel, rise; disgust, nauseate, repel, sicken. * *n* defection, desertion, faithlessness, inconstancy; disobedience, insurrection, mutiny, outbreak, rebellion, sedition, strike, uprising.

revolting *adj* abhorrent, abominable, disgusting, hateful, monstrous, nauseating, nauseous, objectionable, obnoxious, offensive, repulsive, shocking, sickening; insurgent, mutinous, rebellious.

revolution *n* coup, disobedience, insurrection, mutiny, outbreak, rebellion, sedition, strike, uprising; change, innovation, reformation, transformation, upheaval; circle, circuit, cycle, lap, orbit, rotation, spin, turn..

revolve *vb* circle, circulate, rotate, swing, turn, wheel; devolve, return; consider, mediate, ponder, ruminate, study.

revulsion *n* abstraction, shrinking, withdrawal; change, reaction, reversal, transition; abhorrence, disgust, loathing, repugnance.

reward *vb* compensate, gratify, indemnify, pay, punish, recompense, remember, remunerate, requite. * *n* compensation, gratification, guerdon, indemnification, pay, recompense, remuneration, requital; bounty, bonus, fee, gratuity, honorarium, meed, perquisite, premium, remembrance, tip; punishment, retribution.

rhythm *n* cadence, lilt, pulsation, swing; measure, metre, number.

ribald *adj* base, blue, coarse, filthy, gross, indecent, lewd, loose, low, mean, obscene, vile.

rich *adj* affluent, flush, moneyed, opulent, prosperous, wealthy; costly, estimable, gorgeous, luxurious, precious, splendid, sumptuous, superb, valuable; delicious, luscious, savoury; abundant, ample, copious, enough, full, plentiful, plenteous, sufficient; fertile, fruitful, luxuriant, productive, prolific; bright, dark, deep, exuberant, vivid; harmonious, mellow, melodious, soft, sweet; comical, funny, humorous, laughable.

riches *npl* abundance, affluence, fortune, money, opulence, plenty, richness, wealth, wealthiness.

rickety *adj* broken, imperfect, shaky, shattered, tottering, tumbledown, unsteady, weak.

rid *vb* deliver, free, release; clear, disburden, disencumber, scour, sweep; disinherit, dispatch, dissolve, divorce, finish, sever.

riddance *n* deliverance, disencumberment, extrication, escape, freedom, release, relief.

riddle[1] *vb* explain, solve, unriddle. * *n* conundrum, enigma, mystery, puzzle, rebus.

riddle[2] *vb* sieve, sift, perforate, permeate, spread. * *n* colander, sieve, strainer.

ridge *n* chine, hogback, ledge, saddle, spine, rib, watershed, weal, wrinkle.

ridicule *vb* banter, burlesque, chaff, deride, disparage, jeer, mock, lampoon, rally, satirize, scout, taunt. * *n* badinage, banter, burlesque, chaff, derision, game, gibe, irony, jeer, mockery, persiflage, quip, raillery, sarcasm, satire, sneer, squib, wit.

ridiculous *adj* absurd, amusing, comical, droll, eccentric, fantastic, farcical, funny, laughable, ludicrous, nonsensical, odd, outlandish, preposterous, queer, risible, waggish.

rife *adj* abundant, common, current, general, numerous, plentiful, prevailing, prevalent, replete.

riffraff *n* horde, mob, populace, rabble, scum, trash.

rifle *vb* despoil, fleece, pillage, plunder, ransack, rob, strip.

rift *vb* cleave, rive, split. * *n* breach, break, chink, cleft, crack, cranny, crevice, fissure, fracture, gap, opening, reft, rent.

rig *vb* accoutre, clothe, dress. * *n* costume, dress, garb; equipment, team.

right *vb* adjust, correct, regulate, settle, straighten, vindicate. * *adj* direct, rectilinear, straight; erect, perpendicular, plumb, upright; equitable, even-handed, fair, just, justifiable, honest, lawful, legal, legitimate, rightful, square, unswerving; appropriate, becoming, correct, conventional, fit, fitting, meet, orderly, proper, reasonable, seemly, suitable, well-done; actual, genuine, real, true, unquestionable; dexter, dextral, right-handed. * *adv* equitably, fairly, justly, lawfully, rightfully, rightly; correctly, fitly, properly, suitably, truly; actually, exactly, just, really, truly, well. * *n* authority, claim, liberty, permission, power, privilege, title; equity, good, honour, justice, lawfulness, legality, propriety, reason, righteousness, truth.

righteous *adj* devout, godly, good, holy, honest, incorrupt, just, pious, religious, saintly, uncorrupt, upright, virtuous; equitable, fair, right, rightful.

righteousness *n* equity, faithfulness, godliness, goodness, holiness, honesty, integrity, justice, piety, purity, right, rightfulness, sanctity, uprightness, virtue.

rightful *adj* lawful, legitimate, true; appropriate, correct, deserved, due, equitable, fair, fitting, honest, just, legal, merited, proper, reasonable, suitable.

rigid *adj* firm, hard, inflexible, permanent, stiff, stiffened, unbending, unpliant, unyielding; bristling, erect, precipitous, steep; austere, conventional, correct, exact, formal, harsh, meticulous, precise, rigorous, severe, sharp, stern, strict, unmitigated; cruel.

rigmarole *n* balderdash, flummery, gibberish, gobbledegook, jargon, nonsense, palaver, trash, twaddle, verbiage.

rigour *n* hardness, inflexibility, rigidity, rigidness, stiffness; asperity, austerity, harshness, severity, sternness; evenness, strictness; inclemency.

rile *vb* anger, annoy, irritate, upset, vex.

rim *n* brim, brink, border, confine, curb, edge, flange, girdle, margin, ring, skirt.

ring[1] *vb* circle, encircle, enclose, girdle, surround. * *n* circle, circlet, girdle, hoop, round, whorl; cabal, clique, combination, confederacy, coterie, gang, junta, league, set.

ring[2] *vb* chime, clang, jingle, knell, peal, resound, reverberate, sound, tingle, toll; call, phone, telephone. * *n* chime, knell, peal, tinkle, toll; call, phone call, telephone call.

riot *vb* carouse, luxuriate, revel. * *n* affray, altercation, brawl, broil, commotion, disturbance, fray, outbreak, pandemonium, quarrel, squabble, tumult, uproar; dissipation, excess, luxury, merrymaking, revelry.

riotous *adj* boisterous, luxurious, merry, revelling, unrestrained, wanton; disorderly, insubordinate, lawless, mutinous, rebellious, refractory, seditious, tumultuous, turbulent, ungovernable, unruly, violent.

ripe *adj* advanced, grown, mature, mellow, seasoned, soft; fit, prepared, ready; accomplished, complete, consummate, finished, perfect, perfected.

ripen *vb* burgeon, develop, mature, prepare.

rise *vb* arise, ascend, clamber, climb, levitate, mount; excel, succeed; enlarge, heighten, increase, swell, thrive; revive; grow, kindle, wax; begin, flow, head, originate, proceed, spring, start; mutiny, rebel, revolt; happen, occur. * *n* ascension, ascent, rising; elevation, grade, hill, slope; beginning, emergence, flow, origin, source, spring; advance, augmentation, expansion, increase.

risible *adj* amusing, comical, droll, farcical, funny, laughable, ludicrous, ridiculous.

risk *vb* bet, endanger, hazard, jeopardize, peril, speculate, stake, venture, wager. * *n* chance, danger, hazard, jeopardy, peril, venture.

rite *n* ceremonial, ceremony, form, formulary, ministration, observance, ordinance, ritual, rubric, sacrament, solemnity.

ritual *adj* ceremonial, conventional, formal, habitual, routine, stereotyped. * *n* ceremonial, ceremony, liturgy, observance, rite, sacrament, service; convention, form, formality, habit, practice, protocol.

rival *vb* emulate, match, oppose. * *adj* competing, contending, emulating, emulous, opposing. * *n* antagonist, competitor, emulator, opponent.

rive *vb* cleave, rend, split.

river *n* affluent, current, reach, stream, tributary.

road *n* course, highway, lane, passage, path, pathway, roadway, route, street, thoroughfare, track, trail, turnpike, way.

roam *vb* jaunt, prowl, ramble, range, rove, straggle, stray, stroll, wander.

roar *vb* bawl, bellow, cry, howl, vociferate, yell; boom, peal, rattle, resound, thunder. * *n* bellow, roaring; rage, resonance, storm, thunder; cry, outcry, shout; laugh, laughter, shout.

rob *vb* despoil, fleece, pilfer, pillage, plunder, rook, strip; appropriate, deprive, embezzle, plagiarize.

robber *n* bandit, brigand, desperado, depredator, despoiler, footpad, freebooter, highwayman, marauder, pillager, pirate, plunderer, rifler, thief.

robbery *n* depredation, despoliation, embezzlement, freebooting, larceny, peculation, piracy, plagiarism, plundering, spoliation, theft.

robe *vb* array, clothe, dress, invest. * *n* attire, costume, dress, garment, gown, habit, vestment; bathrobe, dressing gown, housecoat.

robust *adj* able-bodied, athletic, brawny, energetic, firm, forceful, hale, hardy, hearty, iron, lusty, muscular, powerful, seasoned, self-assertive, sinewy, sound, stalwart, stout, strong, sturdy, vigorous.

rock[1] *n* boulder, cliff, crag, reef, stone; asylum, defence, foundation, protection, refuge, strength, support; gneiss, granite, marble, slate, etc.

rock[2] *vb* calm, cradle, lull, quiet, soothe, still, tranquillize; reel, shake, sway, teeter, totter, wobble.

rogue *n* beggar, vagabond, vagrant; caitiff, cheat, knave, rascal, scamp, scapegrace, scoundrel, sharper, swindler, trickster, villain.

roguish *adj* dishonest, fraudulent, knavish, rascally, scoundrelly, trickish, tricky; arch, sportive, mischievous, puckish, waggish, wanton.

role *n* character, function, impersonation, part, task.

roll *vb* gyrate, revolve, rotate, turn, wheel; curl, muffle, swathe, wind; bind, involve, enfold, envelop; flatten, level, smooth, spread; bowl, drive; trundle, wheel; gybe, lean, lurch, stagger, sway, yaw; billow, swell, undulate; wallow, welter; flow, glide, run. * *n* document, scroll, volume; annals, chronicle, history, record, rota; catalogue, inventory, list, register, schedule; booming, resonance, reverberation, thunder; cylinder, roller.

rollicking *adj* frisky, frolicking, frolicsome, jolly, jovial, lively, swaggering.

romance *vb* exaggerate, fantasize. * *n* fantasy, fiction, legend, novel, story, tale; exaggeration, falsehood, lie; ballad, idyll, song.

romantic *adj* extravagant, fanciful, fantastic, ideal, imaginative, sentimental, wild; chimerical, fabulous, fantastic, fictitious, imaginary, improbable, legendary, picturesque, quixotic, sentimental. * *n* dreamer, idealist, sentimentalist, visionary.

romp *vb* caper, gambol, frisk, sport. * *n* caper, frolic, gambol.

room *n* accommodation, capacity, compass, elbowroom, expanse, extent, field, latitude, leeway, play, scope, space, swing; place, stead; apartment, chamber, lodging; chance, occasion, opportunity.

roomy *adj* ample, broad, capacious, comfortable, commodious, expansive, extensive, large, spacious, wide.

root[1] *vb* anchor, embed, fasten, implant, place, settle; confirm, establish. * *n* base, bottom, foundation; cause, occasion, motive, origin, reason, source; etymon, radical, radix, stem.

root[2] *vb* destroy, eradicate, extirpate, exterminate, remove, unearth, uproot; burrow, dig, forage, grub, rummage; applaud, cheer, encourage.

rooted *adj* chronic, confirmed, deep, established, fixed, radical.

roseate *adj* blooming, blushing, rose-coloured, rosy, rubicund; hopeful.

rostrum *n* platform, stage, stand, tribune.

rosy *adj* auspicious, blooming, blushing, favourable, flushed, hopeful, roseate, ruddy, sanguine.

rot *vb* corrupt, decay, decompose, degenerate, putrefy, spoil, taint. * *n* corruption, decay, decomposition, putrefaction.

rotary *adj* circular, rotating, revolving, rotatory, turning, whirling.

rotten *adj* carious, corrupt, decomposed, fetid, putrefied, putrescent, putrid, rank, stinking; defective, unsound; corrupt, deceitful, immoral, treacherous, unsound, untrustworthy.

rotund *adj* buxom, chubby, full, globular, obese, plump, round, stout; fluent, grandiloquent.

roué *n* debauchee, libertine, profligate, rake.

rough *vb* coarsen, roughen; manhandle, mishandle, molest. * *adj* bumpy, craggy, irregular, jagged, rugged, scabrous, scraggy, scratchy, stubby, uneven; approximate, cross-grained, crude, formless, incomplete, knotty, rough-hewn, shapeless, sketchy, uncut, unfashioned, unfinished, unhewn, unpolished, unwrought, vague; bristly, bushy, coarse, disordered, hairy, hirsute, ragged, shaggy, unkempt; austere, bearish, bluff, blunt, brusque, burly, churlish, discourteous, gruff, harsh, impolite, indelicate, rude, surly, uncivil, uncourteous, ungracious, unpolished, unrefined; harsh, severe, sharp, violent; astringent, crabbed, hard, sour, tart; discordant, grating, inharmonious, jarring, raucous, scabrous, unmusical; boisterous, foul, inclement, severe, stormy, tempestuous, tumultuous, turbulent, untamed, violent, wild; acrimonious, brutal, cruel, disorderly, riotous, rowdy, severe, uncivil, unfeeling, ungentle. * *n* bully, rowdy, roughneck, ruffian; draft, outline, sketch, suggestion; unevenness.

round *vb* curve; circuit, encircle, encompass, surround. * *adj* bulbous, circular, cylindrical, globular, orbed, orbicular, rotund, spherical; complete, considerable, entire, full, great, large, unbroken, whole; chubby, corpulent, plump, stout, swelling; continuous, flowing, harmonious, smooth; brisk, quick; blunt, candid, fair, frank, honest, open, plain, upright. * *adv* around, circularly, circuitously. * *prep* about, around. * *n* bout, cycle, game, lap, revolution, rotation, succession, turn; canon, catch, dance; ball, circle, circumference, cylinder, globe, sphere; circuit, compass, perambulation, routine, tour, watch.

roundabout *adj* circuitous, circumlocutory, indirect, tortuous; ample, broad, extensive; encircling, encompassing.

rouse *vb* arouse, awaken, raise, shake, wake, waken; animate, bestir, brace, enkindle, excite, inspire, kindle, rally, stimulate, stir, whet; startle, surprise.

rout *vb* beat, conquer, defeat, discomfit, overcome, overpower, overthrow, vanquish; chase away, dispel, disperse, scatter. * *n* defeat, discomfiture, flight, ruin; concourse, multitude, rabble; brawl, disturbance, noise, roar, uproar.

route *vb* direct, forward, send, steer. * *n* course, circuit, direction, itinerary, journey, march, road, passage, path, way.

routine *adj* conventional, familiar, habitual, ordinary, standard, typical, usual; boring, dull, humdrum, predictable, tiresome. * *n* beat, custom, groove, method, order, path, practice, procedure, round, rut.

rove *vb* prowl, ramble, range, roam, stray, struggle, stroll, wander.

row[1] *n* file, line, queue, range, rank, series, string, tier; alley, street, terrace.

row[2] *vb* argue, dispute, fight, quarrel, squabble. * *n* affray, altercation, brawl, broil, commotion, dispute, disturbance, noise, outbreak, quarrel, riot, squabble, tumult, uproar.

royal *adj* august, courtly, dignified, generous, grand, imperial, kingly, kinglike, magnanimous, magnificent, majestic, monarchical, noble, princely, regal, sovereign, splendid, superb.

rub *vb* abrade, chafe, grate, graze, scrape; burnish, clean, massage, polish, scour, wipe; apply, put, smear, spread. * *n* caress, massage, polish, scouring, shine, wipe; catch, difficulty, drawback, impediment, obstacle, problem.

rubbish *n* debris, detritus, fragments, refuse, ruins, waste; dregs, dross, garbage, litter, lumber, scoria, scum, sweepings, trash, trumpery.

rubicund *adj* blushing, erubescent, florid, flushed, red, reddish, ruddy.

rude *adj* coarse, crude, ill-formed, rough, rugged, shapeless, uneven, unfashioned, unformed, unwrought; artless, barbarous, boorish, clownish, ignorant, illiterate, loutish, raw, savage, uncivilized, uncouth, uncultivated, undisciplined, unpolished, ungraceful, unskilful, unskilled, untaught, untrained, untutored, vulgar; awkward, barbarous, bluff, blunt, boorish, brusque, brutal, churlish, gruff, ill-bred, impertinent, impolite, impudent, insolent, insulting, ribald, saucy, uncivil, uncourteous, unrefined; boisterous, fierce, harsh, severe, tumultuous, turbulent, violent; artless, inelegant, rustic, unpolished; hearty, robust.

rudimentary *adj* elementary, embryonic, fundamental, initial, primary, rudimental, undeveloped.

rue *vb* deplore, grieve, lament, regret, repent.

rueful *adj* dismal, doleful, lamentable, lugubrious, melancholic, melancholy, mournful, penitent, regretful, sad, sorrowful, woeful.

ruffian *n* bully, caitiff, cutthroat, hoodlum, miscreant, monster, murderer, rascal, robber, roisterer, rowdy, scoundrel, villain, wretch.

ruffle *vb* damage, derange, disarrange, dishevel, disorder, ripple, roughen, rumple; agitate, confuse, discompose, disquiet, disturb, excite, harass, irritate, molest, plague, perturb, torment, trouble, vex, worry; cockle, flounce, pucker, wrinkle. * *n* edging, frill, ruff; agitation, bustle, commotion, confusion, contention, disturbance, excitement, fight, fluster, flutter, flurry, perturbation, tumult.

rugged *adj* austere, bristly, coarse, crabbed, cragged, craggy, hard, hardy, irregular, ragged, robust, rough, rude, scraggy, severe, seamed, shaggy, uneven, unkempt, wrinkled; boisterous, inclement, stormy, tempestuous, tumultuous, turbulent, violent; grating, harsh, inharmonious, unmusical, scabrous.

ruin *vb* crush, damn, defeat, demolish, desolate, destroy, devastate, overthrow, overturn, overwhelm, seduce, shatter, smash, subvert, wreck; beggar, impoverish. * *n* damnation, decay, defeat, demolition, desolation, destruction, devastation, discomfiture, downfall, fall, loss, perdition, prostration, rack, ruination, shipwreck, subversion, undoing, wrack, wreck; bane, mischief, pest.

ruination *n* demolition, destruction, overthrow, ruin, subversion.

ruinous *adj* decayed, demolished, dilapidated; baneful, calamitous, damnatory, destructive, disastrous, mischievous, noisome, noxious, pernicious, subversive, wasteful.

rule *vb* bridle, command, conduct, control, direct, domineer, govern, judge, lead, manage, reign, restrain; advise, guide, persuade; adjudicate, decide, determine, establish, settle; obtain, prevail, predominate. * *n* authority, command, control, direction, domination, dominion, empire, government, jurisdiction, lordship, mastery, mastership, regency, reign, sway; behaviour, conduct; habit, method, order, regularity,

routine, system; aphorism, canon, convention, criterion, formula, guide, law, maxim, model, precedent, precept, standard, system, test, touchstone; decision, order, prescription, regulation, ruling.

ruler *n* chief, governor, king, lord, master, monarch, potentate, regent, sovereign; director, head, manager, president; controller, guide, rule; straight-edge.

ruminate *vb* brood, chew, cogitate, consider, contemplate, meditate, muse, ponder, reflect, think.

rumour *vb* bruit, circulate, report, tell. * *n* bruit, gossip, hearsay, report, talk; news, report, story, tidings; celebrity, fame, reputation, repute.

rumple *vb* crease, crush, corrugate, crumple, disarrange, dishevel, pucker, ruffle, wrinkle. * *n* crease, corrugation, crumple, fold, pucker, wrinkle.

run *vb* bolt, career, course, gallop, haste, hasten, hie, hurry, lope, post, race, scamper, scour, scud, scuttle, speed, trip; flow, glide, go, move, proceed, stream; fuse, liquefy, melt; advance, pass, proceed, vanish; extend, lie, spread, stretch; circulate, pass, press; average, incline, tend; flee; pierce, stab; drive, force, propel, push, thrust, turn; cast, form, mould, shape; follow, perform, pursue, take; discharge, emit; direct, maintain, manage. * *n* race, running; course, current, flow, motion, passage, progress, way, wont; continuance, currency, popularity; excursion, gallop, journey, trip, trot; demand, pressure; brook, burn, flow, rill, rivulet, runlet, runnel, streamlet.

rupture *vb* break, burst, fracture, sever, split. * *n* breach, break, burst, disruption, fracture, split; contention, faction, feud, hostility, quarrel, schism.

rural *adj* agrarian, bucolic, country, pastoral, rustic, sylvan.

ruse *n* artifice, deception, deceit, fraud, hoax, imposture, manoeuvre, sham, stratagem, trick, wile.

rush *vb* attack, career, charge, dash, drive, gush, hurtle, precipitate, surge, sweep, tear. * *n* dash, onrush, onset, plunge, precipitance, precipitancy, rout, stampede, tear.

rust *vb* corrode, decay, degenerate. * *n* blight, corrosion, crust, mildew, must, mould, mustiness.

rustic *adj* country, rural; awkward, boorish, clownish, countrified, loutish, outlandish, rough, rude, uncouth, unpolished, untaught; coarse, countrified, homely, plain, simple, unadorned; artless, honest, unsophisticated. * *n* boor, bumpkin, clown, countryman, peasant, swain, yokel.

ruthless *adj* barbarous, cruel, fell, ferocious, hardhearted, inexorable, inhuman, merciless, pitiless, relentless, remorseless, savage, truculent, uncompassionate, unmerciful, unpitying, unrelenting, unsparing.

S

sable *adj* black, dark, dusky, ebony, sombre.

sabulous *adj* gritty, sabulose, sandy.

sack[1] *n* bag, pouch.

sack[2] *vb* despoil, devastate, pillage, plunder, ravage, spoil. * *n* desolation, despoliation, destruction, devastation, havoc, ravage, sacking, spoliation, waste; booty, plunder, spoil.

sacred *adj* consecrated, dedicated, devoted, divine, hallowed, holy; inviolable, inviolate; sainted, venerable.

sacrifice *vb* forgo, immolate, surrender. * *n* immolation, oblation, offering; destruction, devotion, loss, surrender.

sacrilege *n* desecration, profanation, violation.

sacrilegious *adj* desecrating, impious, irreverent, profane.

sad *adj* grave, pensive, sedate, serious, sober, sombre, staid.

saddle *vb* burden, charge, clog, encumber, load.

sadly *adv* grievously, miserable, mournfully,
sorrowfully; afflictively, badly, calamitously; darkly; gravely, seriously, soberly.

sadness *n* dejection, depression, despondency, melancholy, mournful, sorrow, sorrowfulness; dolefulness, gloominess, grief, mournfulness, sorrow; gravity, sedateness, seriousness.

safe *adj* undamaged, unharmed, unhurt, unscathed; guarded, protected, secure, snug, unexposed; certain, dependable, reliable, sure, trustworthy; good, harmless, sound, whole. * *n* chest, coffer, strongbox.

safeguard *vb* guard, protect. * *n* defence, protection, security; convoy, escort, guard, safe-conduct; pass, passport.

sagacious *adj* acute, apt, astute, clear-sighted, discerning, intelligent, judicious, keen, penetrating, perspicacious, rational, sage, sharp-witted, wise, shrewd.

sagacity *n* acuteness, astuteness, discernment, ingenuity, insight, penetration, perspicacity, quickness, readiness, sense, sharpness, shrewdness, wisdom.

sage *adj* acute, discerning, intelligent, prudent, sagacious, sapient, sensible, shrewd, wise; judicious, well-judged; grave, serious, solemn. * *n* philosopher, pundit, savant.

sailor *n* mariner, navigator, salt, seafarer, seaman, tar.

saintly *adj* devout, godly, holy, pious, religious.

sake *n* end, cause, purpose, reason; account,
consideration, interest, regard, respect, score.

saleable *adj* marketable, merchantable, vendible.

salacious *adj* carnal, concupiscent, incontinent, lascivious, lecherous, lewd, libidinous, loose, lustful, prurient, unchaste, wanton.

salary *n* allowance, hire, pay, stipend, wages.

salient *adj* bounding, jumping, leaping; beating, springing, throbbing; jutting, projecting, prominent; conspicuous, remarkable, striking.

saline *adj* briny, salty.

sally *vb* issue, rush. * *n* digression, excursion, sortie, run, trip; escapade, frolic; crank, fancy, jest, joke, quip, quirk, sprightly, witticism.

salt *adj* saline, salted, salty; bitter, pungent, sharp. * *n* flavour, savour, seasoning, smack, relish, taste; humour, piquancy, poignancy, sarcasm, smartness, wit, zest; mariner, sailor, seaman, tar.

salubrious *adj* beneficial, benign, healthful, healthy, salutary, sanitary, wholesome.

salutary *adj* healthy, healthful, helpful, safe, salubrious, wholesome; advantageous, beneficial, good, profitable, serviceable, useful.

salute *vb* accost, address, congratulate, greet, hail, welcome. * *n* address, greeting, salutation.

salvation *n* deliverance, escape, preservation, redemption, rescue, saving.

same *adj* ditto, identical, selfsame; corresponding, like, similar.

sample *vb* savour, sip, smack, sup, taste; test, try; demonstrate, exemplify, illustrate, instance. * *adj* exemplary, illustrative, representative. * *n* demonstration, exemplification, illustration, instance, piece, specimen; example, model, pattern.

sanctify *vb* consecrate, hallow, purify; justify, ratify, sanction.

sanctimonious *adj* affected, devout, holy, hypocritical, pharisaical, pious, self-righteous.

sanction *vb* authorize, countenance, encourage, support; confirm, ratify. * *n* approval, authority, authorization, confirmation, countenance, endorsement, ratification, support, warranty; ban, boycott, embargo, penalty.

sanctity *n* devotion, godliness, goodness, grace, holiness, piety, purity, religiousness, saintliness.

sanctuary *n* altar, church, shrine, temple; asylum, protection, refuge, retreat, shelter.

sane *adj* healthy, lucid, rational, reasonable, sober, sound.

sang-froid *n* calmness, composure, coolness, imperturbability, indifference, nonchalance, phlegm, unconcern.

sanguinary *adj* bloody, gory, murderous; barbarous, bloodthirsty, cruel, fell, pitiless, savage, ruthless.

sanguine *adj* crimson, florid, red; animated, ardent, cheerful, lively, warm; buoyant, confident, enthusiastic, hopeful, optimistic; full-blooded.

sanitary *adj* clean, curative, healing, healthy, hygienic, remedial, therapeutic, wholesome.

sanity *n* normality, rationality, reason, saneness, soundness.

sapient *adj* acute, discerning, intelligent, knowing, sagacious, sage, sensible, shrewd, wise.

sarcastic *adj* acrimonious, biting, cutting, mordacious, mordant, sardonic, satirical, sharp, severe, sneering, taunting.

sardonic *adj* bitter, derisive, ironical, malevolent, malicious, malignant, sarcastic.

satanic *adj* devilish, diabolical, evil, false, fiendish, hellish, infernal, malicious.

satellite *adj* dependent, subordinate, tributary, vassal. * *n* attendant, dependant, follower, hanger-on, retainer, vassal.

satiate *vb* fill, sate, satisfy, suffice; cloy, glut, gorge, overfeed, overfill, pall, surfeit.

satire *n* burlesque, diatribe, invective, fling, irony, lampoon, pasquinade, philippic, ridicule, sarcasm, skit, squib.

satirical *adj* abusive, biting, bitter, censorious, cutting, invective, ironical, keen, mordacious, poignant, reproachful, sarcastic, severe, sharp, taunting.

satirize *vb* abuse, censure, lampoon, ridicule.

satisfaction *n* comfort, complacency, contentment, ease, enjoyment, gratification, pleasure, satiety; amends, appeasement, atonement, compensation, indemnification, recompense, redress, remuneration, reparation, requital, reward.

satisfactory *adj* adequate, conclusive, convincing, decisive, sufficient; gratifying, pleasing.

satisfy *vb* appease, content, fill, gratify, please, sate, satiate, suffice; indemnify, compensate, liquidate, pay, recompense, remunerate, requite; discharge, settle; assure, convince, persuade; answer, fulfil, meet.

saturate *vb* drench, fill, fit, imbue, soak, steep, wet.

saturnine *adj* dark, dull, gloomy, grave, heavy, leaden, morose, phlegmatic, sad, sedate, sombre; melancholic, mournful, serious, unhappy; mischievous, naughty, troublesome, vexatious, wicked.

sauce *n* cheekiness, impudence, insolence; appetizer, compound, condiment, relish, seasoning.

saucy *adj* bold, cavalier, disrespectful, flippant, forward, immodest, impertinent, impudent, insolent, pert, rude.

saunter *vb* amble, dawdle, delay, dilly-dally, lag, linger, loiter, lounge, stroll, tarry. * *n* amble, stroll, walk.

savage *vb* attack, lacerate, mangle, maul. * *adj* rough, uncultivated, wild; rude, uncivilized, unpolished, untaught; bloodthirsty, feral, ferine, ferocious, fierce, rapacious, untamed, vicious; beastly, bestial, brutal, brutish, inhuman; atrocious, barbarous, barbaric, bloody, brutal, cruel, fell, fiendish, hardhearted, heathenish, merciless, murderous, pitiless, relentless, ruthless, sanguinary, truculent; native, rough, rugged. * *n* barbarian, brute, heathen, vandal.

save *vb* keep, liberate, preserve, rescue; salvage, recover, redeem; economize, gather, hoard, husband, reserve, store; hinder, obviate, prevent, spare. * *prep* but, deducting, except.

saviour *n* defender, deliverer, guardian, protector, preserver, rescuer, saver.

savour *vb* affect, appreciate, enjoy, like, partake, relish; flavour, season. * *n* flavour, gusto, relish, smack, taste; fragrance, odour, smell, scent.

savoury *adj* agreeable, delicious, flavourful, luscious, nice, palatable, piquant, relishing.

saw *n* adage, aphorism, apothegm, axiom, byword, dictum, maxim, precept, proverb, sententious saying.

say *vb* declare, express, pronounce, speak, tell, utter; affirm, allege, argue; recite, rehearse, repeat; assume, presume, suppose. * *n* affirmation, declaration, speech, statement; decision, voice, vote.

saying *n* declaration, expression, observation, remark, speech, statement; adage, aphorism, byword, dictum, maxim, proverb, saw.

scale[1] *n* basin, dish, pan; balance.

scale[2] *n* flake, lamina, lamella, layer, plate.

scale[3] *vb* ascend, climb, escalate, mount. * *n* graduation.

scamp *n* cheat, knave, rascal, rogue, scapegrace, scoundrel, swindler, trickster, villain.

scamper *vb* haste, hasten, hie, run, scud, speed, trip.

scan *vb* examine, investigate, scrutinize, search, sift.

scandal *vb* asperse, defame, libel, traduce. * *n* aspersion, calumny, defamation, obloquy, reproach; discredit, disgrace, dishonour, disrepute, ignominy, infamy, odium, opprobrium, offence, shame.

scandalize *vb* offend; asperse, backbite, calumniate, decry, defame, disgust, lampoon, libel, reproach, revile, satirize, slander, traduce, vilify.

scandalous *adj* defamatory, libellous, opprobrious, slanderous; atrocious, disgraceful, disreputable, infamous, inglorious, ignominious, odious, shameful.

scanty *adj* insufficient, meagre, narrow, scant, small; hardly, scarce, short, slender; niggardly, parsimonious, penurious, scrimpy, skimpy, sparing.

scar[1] *vb* hurt, mark, wound. * *n* cicatrice, cicatrix, seam; blemish, defect, disfigurement, flaw, injury, mark.

scar[2] *n* bluff, cliff, crag, precipice.

scarce *adj* deficient, wanting; infrequent, rare,
uncommon. * *adv* barely, hardly, scantily.

scarcely *adv* barely, hardly, scantily.

scarcity *n* dearth, deficiency, insufficiency, lack, want; infrequency, rareness, rarity, uncommonness.

scare *vb* affright, alarm, appal, daunt, fright, frighten, intimidate, shock, startle, terrify. * *n* alarm, fright, panic, shock, terror.

scathe *vb* blast, damage, destroy, injure, harm, haste. * *n* damage, harm, injury, mischief, waste.

scatter *vb* broadcast, sprinkle, strew; diffuse, disperse, disseminate, dissipate, distribute, separate, spread; disappoint, dispel, frustrate, overthrow.

scene *n* display, exhibition, pageant, representation, show, sight, spectacle, view; place, situation, spot; arena, stage.

scent *vb* breathe in, inhale, nose, smell, sniff; detect, smell out, sniff out; aromatize, perfume. * *n* aroma, balminess, fragrance, odour, perfume, smell, redolence.

sceptic *n* doubter, freethinker, questioner, unbeliever.

sceptical *adj* doubtful, doubting, dubious, hesitating, incredulous, questioning, unbelieving.

scepticism *n* doubt, dubiety, freethinking, incredulity, unbelief.

schedule *vb* line up, list, plan, programme, tabulate. * *n* document, scroll; catalogue, inventory, list, plan, record, register, roll, table, timetable.

scheme *vb* contrive, design, frame, imagine, plan, plot, project. * *n* plan, system, theory; cabal, conspiracy, contrivance, design, device, intrigue, machination, plan, plot, project, stratagem; arrangement, draught, diagram, outline.

schism *n* division, separation, split; discord, disunion, division, faction, separation.

scholar *n* disciple, learner, pupil, student; don, fellow, intellectual, pedant, savant.

scholarship *n* accomplishments, acquirements, attainments, erudition, knowledge, learning; bursary, exhibition, foundation, grant, maintenance.

scholastic *adj* academic, bookish, lettered, literary; formal, pedantic.

school *vb* drill, educate, exercise, indoctrinate, instruct, teach, train; admonish, control, chide, discipline, govern, reprove, tutor. * *adj* academic, collegiate, institutional, scholastic, schoolish. * *n* academy, college, gymnasium, institute, institution, kindergarten, lyceum, manège, polytechnic, seminary, university; adherents, camarilla, circle, clique, coterie, disciples, followers; body, order, organization, party, sect.

schooling *n* discipline, education, instruction, nurture, teaching, training, tuition.

scintillate *vb* coruscate, flash, gleam, glisten, glitter, sparkle, twinkle.

scoff *vb* deride, flout, jeer, mock, ridicule, taunt; gibe, sneer. * *n* flout, gibe, jeer, sneer, mockery, taunt; derision, ridicule.

scold *vb* berate, blame, censure, chide, rate,
reprimand, reprove; brawl, rail, rate, reprimand, upbraid, vituperate. * *n* shrew, termagant, virago, vixen.

scope *n* aim, design, drift, end, intent, intention, mark, object, purpose, tendency, view; amplitude, field, latitude, liberty, margin, opportunity, purview, range, room, space, sphere, vent; extent, length, span, stretch, sweep.

scorch *vb* blister, burn, char, parch, roast, sear, shrivel, singe.

score *vb* cut, furrow, mark, notch, scratch; charge, note, record; impute, note; enter, register. * *n* incision, mark, notch; account, bill, charge, debt, reckoning; consideration, ground, motive, reason.

scorn *vb* condemn, despise, disregard, disdain, scout, slight, spurn. * *n* contempt, derision, disdain, mockery, slight, sneer; scoff.

scornful *adj* contemptuous, defiant, disdainful, contemptuous, regardless.

scot-free *adj* untaxed; clear, unhurt, uninjured, safe.

scoundrel *n* cheat, knave, miscreant, rascal, reprobate, rogue, scamp, swindler, trickster, villain.

scour[1] *vb* brighten, buff, burnish, clean, cleanse, polish, purge, scrape, scrub, rub, wash, whiten; rake; efface, obliterate, overrun.

scour[2] *vb* career, course, range, scamper, scud, scuttle; comb, hunt, rake, ransack, rifle, rummage, search.

scourge *vb* lash, whip; afflict, chasten, chastise, correct, punish; harass, torment. * *n* cord, cowhide, lash, strap, thong, whip; affliction, bane, curse, infliction, nuisance, pest, plague, punishment.

scout *vb* contemn, deride, disdain, despise, ridicule, scoff, scorn, sneer, spurn; investigate, probe, search. * *n* escort, lookout, precursor, vanguard.

scowl *vb* frown, glower, lower. * *n* frown,

glower, lower.

scraggy *adj* broken, craggy, rough, rugged, scabrous, scragged, uneven; attenuated, bony, emaciated, gaunt, lank, lean, meagre, scrawny, skinny, thin.

scrap[1] *vb* discard, junk, trash. * *n* bit, fragment, modicum, particle, piece, snippet; bite, crumb, morsel, mouthful; debris, junk, litter, rubbish, rubble, trash, waste.

scrap[2] *vb* altercate, bicker, dispute, clash, fight, hassle, quarrel, row, spat, squabble, tiff, tussle, wrangle. * *n* affray, altercation, bickering, clash, dispute, fight, fray, hassle, melee, quarrel, row, run-in, set-to, spat, squabble, tiff, tussle, wrangle.

scrape *vb* bark, grind, rasp, scuff; accumulate, acquire, collect, gather, save; erase, remove. * *n* difficulty, distress, embarrassment, perplexity, predicament.

scream *vb* screech, shriek, squall, ululate. * *n* cry, outcry, screech, shriek, shrill, ululation.

screen *vb* cloak, conceal, cover, defend, fence, hide, mask, protect, shelter, shroud. * *n* blind, curtain, lattice, partition; defence, guard, protection, shield; cloak, cover, veil, disguise; riddle, sieve.

screw *vb* force, press, pressurize, squeeze, tighten, twist, wrench; oppress, rack; distort. * *n* extortioner, extortionist, miser, scrimp, skinflint; prison guard; sexual intercourse.

scrimmage *n* brawl, melee, riot, scuffle, skirmish.

scrimp *vb* contract, curtail, limit, pinch, reduce, scant, shorten, straiten.

scrimpy *adj* contracted, deficient, narrow, scanty.

scroll *n* inventory, list, parchment, roll, schedule.

scrub[1] *adj* contemptible, inferior, mean, niggardly, scrubby, shabby, small, stunted. * *n* brushwood, underbrush, underwood.

scrub[2] *vb* clean, cleanse, rub, scour, scrape, wash.

scruple *vb* boggle, demur, falter, hesitate, object, pause, stickle, waver. * *n* delicacy, hesitancy, hesitation, nicety, perplexity, qualm.

scrupulous *adj* conscientious, fastidious, nice, precise, punctilious, rigorous, strict; careful, cautious, circumspect, exact, vigilant.

scrutinize *vb* canvass, dissect, examine, explore, investigate, overhaul, probe, search, sift, study.

scrutiny *n* examination, exploration, inquisition, inspection, investigation, search, searching, sifting.

scud *vb* flee, fly, haste, hasten, hie, post, run, scamper, speed, trip.

scuffle *vb* contend, fight, strive, struggle. * *n* altercation, brawl, broil, contest, encounter, fight, fray, quarrel, squabble, struggle, wrangle.

sculpt vb carve, chisel, cut, sculpture; engrave, grave.

scurrilous *adj* abusive, blackguardly, contumelious, foul, foul-mouthed, indecent, infamous, insolent, insulting, offensive, opprobrious, reproachful, ribald, vituperative; coarse, gross, low, mean, obscene, vile, vulgar.

scurry *vb* bustle, dash, hasten, hurry, scamper, scud, scutter. * *n* burst, bustle, dash, flurry, haste, hurry, scamper, scud, spurt.

scurvy *adj* scabbed, scabby, scurfy; abject, bad, base, contemptible, despicable, low, mean, pitiful, sorry, vile, vulgar, worthless; malicious, mischievous, offensive.

scuttle[1] *vb* hurry, hustle, run, rush, scamper, scramble, scud, scurry. * *n* dash, drive, flurry, haste, hurry, hustle, race, rush, scamper, scramble, scud, scurry.

scuttle[2] *vb* capsize, founder, go down, sink, overturn, upset. * *n* hatch, hatchway.

seal *vb* close, fasten, secure; attest, authenticate, confirm, establish, ratify, sanction; confine, enclose, imprison. * *n* fastening, stamp, wafer, wax; assurance, attestation, authentication, confirmation, pledge, ratification.

seamy *adj* disreputable, nasty, seedy, sordid, unpleasant.

sear *vb* blight, brand, cauterize, dry, scorch, wither. * *adj* dried up, dry, sere, withered.

search *vb* examine, explore, ferret, inspect,investigate, overhaul, probe, ransack, scrutinize, sift; delve, hunt, forage, inquire, look, rummage. * *n* examination, exploration, hunt, inquiry, inspection, investigation, pursuit, quest, research, seeking, scrutiny.

searching *adj* close, keen, penetrating, trying; examining, exploring, inquiring, investigating, probing, seeking.

seared *adj* callous, graceless, hardened, impenitent, incorrigible, obdurate, shameless, unrepentant.

season *vb* acclimatize, accustom, form, habituate, harden, inure, mature, qualify, temper, train; flavour, spice. * *n* interval, period, spell, term, time, while.

seasonable *adj* appropriate, convenient, fit, opportune, suitable, timely.

seasoning *n* condiment, flavouring, relish, salt, sauce.

seat *vb* establish, fix, locate, place, set, station. * *n* place, site, situation, station; abode, capital, dwelling, house, mansion, residence; bottom, fundament; bench, chair, pew, settle, stall, stool.

secede *vb* apostatize, resign, retire, withdraw.

secluded *adj* close, covert, embowered, isolated, private, removed, retired, screened, sequestrated, withdrawn.

seclusion *n* obscurity, privacy, retirement, secrecy, separation, solitude, withdrawal.

second[1] *n* instant, jiffy, minute, moment, trice.

second[2] *vb* abet, advance, aid, assist, back, encourage, forward, further, help, promote, support, sustain; approve, favour. * *adj* inferior, second-rate, secondary; following, next, subsequent; additional, extra, other; double, duplicate. * *n* another, other; assistant, backer, supporter.

secondary *adj* collateral, inferior, minor, subsidiary, subordinate. * *n* delegate, deputy, proxy.

secrecy *n* clandestineness, concealment, furtiveness, stealth, surreptitiousness.

secret *adj* close, concealed, covered, covert, cryptic, hid, hidden, mysterious, privy, shrouded, veiled, unknown, unrevealed, unseen; cabbalistic, clandestine, furtive, privy, sly, stealthy, surreptitious, underhand; confidential, private, retired, secluded, unseen; abstruse, latent, mysterious, obscure, occult, recondite, unknown. * *n* confidence, enigma, key, mystery.

secretary *n* clerk, scribe, writer; escritoire, writing-desk.

secrete[1] *vb* bury, cache, conceal, disguise, hide, shroud, stash; screen, separate.

secrete[2] *vb* discharge, emit, excrete, exude, release, secern.

secretive *adj* cautious, close, reserved, reticent, taciturn, uncommunicative, wary.

sect *n* denomination, faction, schism, school.

section *n* cutting, division, fraction, part, piece, portion, segment, slice.

secular *adj* civil, laic, laical, lay, profane, temporal, worldly.

secure *vb* guard, protect, safeguard; assure, ensure, guarantee, insure; fasten; acquire, gain, get, obtain, procure. * *adj* assured, certain, confident, sure; insured, protected, safe; fast, firm, fixed, immovable, stable; careless, easy, undisturbed, unsuspecting; heedless, inattentive, incautious, negligent, overconfident.

security *n* bulwark, defence, guard, palladium, protection, safeguard, safety, shelter; bond, collateral, deposit, guarantee, pawn, pledge, stake, surety, warranty; carelessness, heedlessness, overconfidence, negligence; assurance, assuredness, certainty, confidence, ease.

sedate *adj* calm, collected, composed, contemplative, cool, demure, grave, placid, philosophical, quiet, serene, serious, sober, still, thoughtful, tranquil, undisturbed, unemotional, unruffled.

sedative *adj* allaying, anodyne, assuasive, balmy, calming, composing, demulcent, lenient, lenitive, soothing, tranquillizing. * *n* anaesthetic, anodyne, hypnotic, narcotic, opiate.

sedentary *adj* inactive, motionless, sluggish, torpid.

sediment *n* dregs, grounds, lees, precipitate, residue, residuum, settlings.
sedition *n* insurgence, insurrection, mutiny, rebellion, revolt, riot, rising, treason, tumult, uprising, uproar.
seditious *adj* factious, incendiary, insurgent, mutinous, rebellious, refractory, riotous, tumultuous, turbulent.
seduce *vb* allure, attract, betray, corrupt, debauch, deceive, decoy, deprave, ensnare, entice, inveigle, lead, mislead.
seductive *adj* alluring, attractive, enticing, tempting.
sedulous *adj* active, assiduous, busy, diligent, industrious, laborious, notable, painstaking, persevering, unremitting, untiring.
see *vb* behold, contemplate, descry, glimpse, sight, spot, survey; comprehend, conceive, distinguish, espy, know, notice, observe, perceive, recognize, remark, understand; beware, consider, envisage, regard, visualize; experience, feel, suffer; examine, inspire, notice, observe; discern, look; call on, visit.
seed *n* semen, sperm; embryo, grain, kernel, matured ovule; germ, original; children, descendants, offspring, progeny; birth, generation, race.
seedy *adj* faded, old, shabby, worn; destitute, distressed, indigent, needy, penniless, pinched, poor.
seek *vb* hunt, look, search; court, follow, prosecute, pursue, solicit; attempt, endeavour, strive, try.
seem *vb* appear, assume, look, pretend.
seeming *adj* apparent, appearing, ostensible, specious. * *n* appearance, colour, guise, look, semblance.
seemly *adj* appropriate, becoming, befitting, congruous, convenient, decent, decorous, expedient, fit, fitting, meet, proper, right, suitable; beautiful, comely, fair, good-looking, graceful, handsome, pretty, well-favoured.
seer *n* augur, diviner, foreteller, predictor, prophet, soothsayer.
segment *n* bit, division, part, piece, portion, section, sector.
segregate *vb* detach, disconnect, disperse, insulate, part, separate.
segregation *n* apartheid, discrimination, insulation, separation.
seize *vb* capture, catch, clutch, grab, grapple, grasp, grip, snatch; confiscate, impress, impound; apprehend, comprehend; arrest, take.
seldom *adv* infrequently, occasionally, rarely.
select *vb* choose, cull, pick, prefer. * *adj* choice, chosen, excellent, exquisite, good, picked, rare, selected.
selection *n* choice, election, pick, preference.
self-conscious *adj* awkward, diffident, embarrassed, insecure, nervous.
self-control *n* restraint, willpower.
self-important *adj* assuming, consequential, proud, haughty, lordly, overbearing, overweening.
selfish *adj* egoistic, egotistical, greedy, illiberal, mean, narrow, self-seeking, ungenerous.
self-possessed *adj* calm, collected, composed, cool, placid, sedate, undisturbed, unexcited, unruffled.
self-willed *adj* contumacious, dogged, headstrong, obstinate, pig-headed, stubborn, uncompliant, wilful.
sell *vb* barter, exchange, hawk, market, peddle, trade, vend.
semblance *n* likeness, resemblance, similarity; air, appearance, aspect, bearing, exterior, figure, form, mien, seeming, show; image, representation, similitude.
seminal *adj* important, original; germinal, radical, rudimental, rudimentary, unformed.
seminary *n* academy, college, gymnasium, high school, institute, school, university.
send *vb* cast, drive, emit, fling, hurl, impel, lance, launch, project, propel, throw, toss; delegate, depute, dispatch; forward, transmit; bestow, confer, give, grant.
senile *adj* aged, doddering, superannuated; doting, imbecile.
senior *adj* elder, older; higher.
seniority *n* eldership, precedence, priority, superiority.
sensation *n* feeling, sense, perception;

excitement, impression, thrill.
sensational *adj* exciting, melodramatic, startling, thrilling.
sense *vb* appraise, appreciate, estimate, notice, observe, perceive, suspect, understand. * *n* brains, intellect, intelligence, mind, reason, understanding; appreciation, apprehension, discernment, feeling, perception, recognition, tact; connotation, idea, implication, judgment, notion, opinion, sentiment, view; import, interpretation, meaning, purport, significance; sagacity, soundness, substance, wisdom.
senseless *adj* apathetic, inert, insensate, unfeeling; absurd, foolish, ill-judged, nonsensical, silly, unmeaning, unreasonable, unwise; doltish, foolish, simple, stupid, witless, weak-minded.
sensible *adj* apprehensible, perceptible; aware, cognizant, conscious, convinced, persuaded, satisfied; discreet, intelligent, judicious, rational, reasonable, sagacious, sage, sober, sound, wise; observant, understanding; impressionable, sensitive.
sensitive *adj* perceptive, sentient; affected, impressible, impressionable, responsive, susceptible; delicate, tender, touchy.
sensual *adj* animal, bodily, carnal, voluptuous; gross, lascivious, lewd, licentious, unchaste.
sentence *vb* condemn, doom, judge. * *n* decision, determination, judgment, opinion, verdict; doctrine, dogma, opinion, tenet; condemnation, conviction, doom; period, proposition.
sententious *adj* compendious, compact, concise, didactic, laconic, pithy, pointed, succinct, terse.
sentiment *n* judgment, notion, opinion; maxim, saying; emotion, tenderness; disposition, feeling, thought.
sentimental *adj* impressible, impressionable, over-emotional, romantic, tender.
sentinel *n* guard, guardsman, patrol, picket, sentry, watchman.
separate *vb* detach, disconnect, disjoin, disunite, dissever, divide, divorce, part, sever, sunder; eliminate, remove, withdraw; cleave, open. * *adj* detached, disconnected, disjoined, disjointed, dissociated, disunited, divided, parted, severed; discrete, distinct, divorced, unconnected; alone, segregated, withdrawn.
separation *n* disjunction, disjuncture, dissociation; disconnection, disseverance, disseveration, disunion, division, divorce; analysis, decomposition.
sepulchral *adj* deep, dismal, funereal, gloomy, grave, hollow, lugubrious, melancholy, mournful, sad, sombre, woeful.
sepulchre *n* burial place, charnel house, grave, ossuary, sepulture, tomb.
sequel *n* close, conclusion, denouement, end, termination; consequence, event, issue, result, upshot.
sequence *n* following, graduation, progression, succession; arrangement, series, train.
sequestrated *adj* hidden, private, retired, secluded, unfrequented, withdrawn; seized.
seraphic *adj* angelic, celestial, heavenly, sublime; holy, pure, refined.
serene *adj* calm, collected, placid, peaceful, quiet, tranquil, sedate, undisturbed, unperturbed, unruffled; bright, calm, clear, fair, unclouded.
serenity *n* calm, calmness, collectedness, composure, coolness, imperturbability, peace, peacefulness, quiescence, sedateness, tranquillity; brightness, calmness, clearness, fairness, peace, quietness, stillness.
serf *n* bondman, servant, slave, thrall, villein.
serfdom *n* bondage, enslavement, enthralment, servitude, slavery, subjection, thraldom.
series *n* chain, concatenation, course, line, order, progression, sequence, succession, train.
serious *adj* earnest, grave, demure, pious, resolute, sedate, sober, solemn, staid, thoughtful; dangerous, great, important, momentous, weighty.
sermon *n* discourse, exhortation, homily, lecture.
serpentine *adj* anfractuous, convoluted, crooked, meandering, sinuous, spiral,

tortuous, twisted, undulating, winding.

servant *n* attendant, dependant, factotum, helper, henchman, retainer, servitor, subaltern, subordinate, underling; domestic, drudge, flunky, lackey, menial, scullion, slave.

serve *vb* aid, assist, attend, help, minister, oblige, succour; advance, benefit, forward, promote; content, satisfy, supply; handle, officiate, manage, manipulate, work.

service *vb* check, maintain, overhaul, repair. * *n* labour, ministration, work; attendance, business, duty, employ, employment, office; advantage, benefit, good, gain, profit; avail, purpose, use, utility; ceremony, function, observance, rite, worship.

serviceable *adj* advantageous, available, beneficial, convenient, functional, handy, helpful, operative, profitable, useful.

servile *adj* dependent, menial; abject, base, beggarly, cringing, fawning, grovelling, low, mean, obsequious, slavish, sneaking, sycophantic, truckling.

servility *n* bondage, dependence, slavery; abjection, abjectness, baseness, fawning, meanness, obsequiousness, slavishness, sycophancy.

servitor *n* attendant, dependant, footman, lackey, retainer, servant, squire, valet, waiter.

servitude *n* bondage, enslavement, enthralment, serfdom, service, slavery, thraldom.

set[1] *vb* lay, locate, mount, place, put, stand, station; appoint, determine, establish, fix, settle; risk, stake, wager; adapt, adjust, regulate; adorn, stud, variegate; arrange, dispose, pose, post; appoint, assign, predetermine, prescribe; estimate, prize, rate, value; embarrass, perplex, pose; contrive, produce; decline, sink; congeal, concern, consolidate, harden, solidify; flow, incline, run, tend; (*with* **about**) begin, commence; (*with* **apart**) appropriate, consecrate, dedicate, devote, reserve, set aside; (*with* **aside**) abrogate, annul, omit, reject; reserve, set apart; (*with* **before**) display, exhibit; (*with* **down**) chronicle, jot down, record, register, state, write down; (*with* **forth**) display, exhibit, explain, expound, manifest, promulgate, publish, put forward, represent, show; (*with* **forward**) advance, further, promote; (*with* **free**) acquit, clear, emancipate, liberate, release; (*with* **off**) adorn, decorate, embellish; define, portion off; (*with* **on**) actuate, encourage, impel, influence, incite, instigate, prompt, spur, urge; attack, assault, set upon; (*with* **out**) display, issue, publish, proclaim, prove, recommend, show; (*with* **right**) correct, put in order; (*with* **to rights**) adjust, regulate; (*with* **up**) elevate, erect, exalt, raise; establish, found, institute; (*with* **upon**) assail, assault, attack, fly at, rush upon. * *adj* appointed, established, formal, ordained, prescribed, regular, settled; determined, fixed, firm, obstinate, positive, stiff, unyielding; immovable, predetermined; located, placed, put. * *n* attitude, position, posture; scene, scenery, setting.

set[2] *n* assortment, collection, suit; class, circle, clique, cluster, company, coterie, division, gang, group, knot, party, school, sect.

setback *n* blow, hitch, hold-up, rebuff; defeat, disappointment, reverse.

set-off *n* adornment, decoration, embellishment, ornament; counterbalance, counterclaim, equivalent.

settle *vb* adjust, arrange, compose, regulate; account, balance, close up, conclude, discharge, liquidate, pay, pay up, reckon, satisfy, square; allay, calm, compose, pacify, quiet, repose, rest, still, tranquillize; confirm, decide, determine, make clear; establish, fix, set; fall, gravitate, sink, subside; abide, colonize, domicile, dwell, establish, inhabit, people, place, plant, reside; (*with* **on**) determine on, fix on, fix upon; establish. * *n* bench, seat, stool.

settled *adj* established, fixed, stable; decided, deep-rooted, steady, unchanging; adjusted, arranged; methodical, orderly, quiet; common, customary, everyday, ordinary, usual, wonted.

set-to *n* combat, conflict, contest, fight.

sever *vb* divide, part, rend, separate, sunder; detach, disconnect, disjoin, disunite.

several *adj* individual, single, particular; distinct, exclusive, independent, separate; different, divers, diverse, manifold, many, sundry, various.

severance *n* partition, separation.

severe *adj* austere, bitter, dour, hard, harsh, inexorable, morose, painful, relentless, rigid, rigorous, rough, sharp, stern, stiff, strait-laced, unmitigated, unrelenting, unsparing; accurate, exact, methodical, strict; chaste, plain, restrained, simple, unadorned; biting, caustic, cruel, cutting, harsh, keen, sarcastic, satirical, trenchant; acute, afflictive, distressing, excruciating, extreme, intense, stringent, violent; critical, exact.

severity *n* austerity, gravity, harshness, rigour, seriousness, sternness, strictness; accuracy, exactness, niceness; chasteness, plainness, simplicity; acrimony, causticity, keenness, sharpness; afflictiveness, extremity, keenness, stringency, violence; cruelty.

sew *vb* baste, bind, hem, stitch, tack.

sex *n* gender, femininity, masculinity, sexuality; coitus, copulation, fornication, love-making.

shabby *adj* faded, mean, poor, ragged, seedy, threadbare, worn, worn-out; beggarly, mean, paltry, penurious, stingy, ungentlemanly, unhandsome.

shackle *vb* chain, fetter, gyve, hamper, manacle; bind, clog, confine, cumber, embarrass, encumber, impede, obstruct, restrict, trammel. * *n* chain, fetter, gyve, hamper, manacle.

shade *vb* cloud, darken, dim, eclipse, obfuscate, obscure; cover, ensconce, hide, protect, screen, shelter. * *n* darkness, dusk, duskiness, gloom, obscurity, shadow; cover, protection, shelter; awning, blind, curtain, screen, shutter, veil; degree, difference, kind, variety; cast, colour, complexion, dye, hue, tinge, tint, tone; apparition, ghost, manes, phantom, shadow, spectre, spirit.

shadow *vb* becloud, cloud, darken, obscure, shade; adumbrate, foreshadow, symbolize, typify; conceal, cover, hide, protect, screen, shroud. * *n* penumbra, shade, umbra, umbrage; darkness, gloom, obscurity; cover, protection, security, shelter; adumbration, foreshadowing, image, prefiguration, representation; apparition, ghost, phantom, shade, spirit; image, portrait, reflection, silhouette.

shadowy *adj* shady, umbrageous; dark, dim, gloomy, murky, obscure; ghostly, imaginary, impalpable, insubstantial, intangible, spectral, unreal, unsubstantial, visionary.

shady *adj* shadowy, umbrageous; crooked.

shaft *n* arrow, missile, weapon; handle, helve; pole, tongue; axis, spindle; pinnacle, spire; stalk, stem, trunk.

shaggy *adj* rough, rugged.

shake *vb* quake, quaver, quiver, shiver, shudder, totter, tremble; agitate, convulse, jar, jolt, stagger; daunt, frighten, intimidate; endanger, move, weaken; oscillate, vibrate, wave; move, put away, remove, throw off. * *n* agitation, concussion, flutter, jar, jolt, quaking, shaking, shivering, shock, trembling, tremor.

shaky *adj* jiggly, quaky, shaking, tottering, trembling.

shallow *adj* flimsy, foolish, frivolous, puerile, trashy, trifling, trivial; empty, ignorant, silly, slight, simple, superficial, unintelligent.

sham *vb* ape, feign, imitate, pretend; cheat, deceive, delude, dupe, impose, trick. * *adj* assumed, counterfeit, false, feigned, mock, make-believe, pretended, spurious. * *n* delusion, feint, fraud, humbug, imposition, imposture, pretence, trick.

shamble *vb* hobble, shuffle.

shambles *npl* abattoir, slaughterhouse; confusion, disorder, mess.

shame *vb* debase, degrade, discredit, disgrace, dishonour, stain, sully, taint, tarnish; abash, confound, confuse, discompose, disconcert, humble, humiliate; deride, flout, jeer, mock, ridicule, sneer. * *n* contempt, degradation, derision, discredit, disgrace, dishonour, disrepute, ignominy, infamy, obloquy, odium, opprobrium; abashment, chagrin, confusion, embarrassment, humiliation, mortification; reproach, scandal; decency, decorousness, decorum, modesty, propriety, seemliness.

shamefaced *adj* bashful, diffident, overmodest.

shameful *adj* atrocious, base, disgraceful, dishonourable, disreputable, heinous, ignominous, infamous, nefarious, opprobrious, outrageous, scandalous, vile, villainous, wicked; degrading, indecent, unbecoming.

shameless *adj* assuming, audacious, boldfaced, brazen, brazen-faced, cool, immodest, impudent, indecent, indelicate, insolent, unabashed, unblushing; abandoned, corrupt, depraved, dissolute, graceless, hardened, incorrigible, irreclaimable, lost, obdurate, profligate, reprobate, sinful, unprincipled, vicious.

shape *vb* create, form, make, produce; fashion, model, mould; adjust, direct, frame, regulate; conceive, conjure up, figure, image, imagine. * *n* appearance, aspect, fashion, figure, form, guise, make; build, cast, cut, model, mould, pattern; apparition, image.

shapeless *adj* amorphous, formless; grotesque, irregular, rude, uncouth, unsymmetrical.

shapely *adj* comely, symmetrical, trim, well-formed.

share *vb* apportion, distribute, divide, parcel out, portion, split; partake, participate; experience, receive. * *n* part, portion, quantum; allotment, allowance, contingent, deal, dividend, division, interest, lot, proportion, quantity, quota.

sharer *n* communicant, partaker, participator.

sharp *adj* acute, cutting, keen, keen-edged, knife-edged, razor-edged, trenchant; acuminate, needle-shaped, peaked, pointed, ridged; apt, astute, canny, clear-sighted, clever, cunning, discerning, discriminating, ingenious, inventive, keen-witted, penetrating, perspicacious, quick, ready, sagacious, sharp-witted, shrewd, smart, subtle, witty; acid, acrid, biting, bitter, burning, high-flavoured, high-seasoned, hot, mordacious, piquant, poignant, pungent, sour, stinging; acrimonious, biting, caustic, cutting, harsh, mordant, sarcastic, severe, tart, trenchant; cruel, hard, rigid; afflicting, distressing, excruciating, intense, painful, piercing, shooting, sore, violent; nipping, pinching; ardent, eager, fervid, fierce, fiery, impetuous, strong; high, screeching, shrill; attentive, vigilant; severe; close, exacting, shrewd, cold, crisp, freezing, icy wintry. * *adv* abruptly, sharply, suddenly; exactly, precisely, punctually.

sharp-cut *adj* clear, distinct, well-defined.

sharpen *vb* edge, intensify, point.

sharper *n* cheat, deceiver, defrauder, knave, rogue, shark, swindler, trickster.

sharply *adv* rigorously, roughly, severely; acutely, keenly; vehemently, violently; accurately, exactly, minutely, trenchantly, wittily; abruptly, steeply.

sharpness *n* acuteness, keenness, trenchancy; acuity, spinosity; acumen, cleverness, discernment, ingenuity, quickness, sagacity, shrewdness, smartness, wit; acidity, acridity, piquancy, pungency, sting, tartness; causticness, incisiveness, pungency, sarcasm, satire, severity; afflictiveness, intensity, painfulness, poignancy; ardour, fierceness, violence; discordance, dissonance, highness, screechiness, squeakiness, shrillness.

sharp-sighted *adj* clear-sighted, keen, keen-eyed, keen-sighted.

sharp-witted *adj* acute, clear-sighted, cunning, discerning, ingenious, intelligent, keen, keen-sighted, long-headed, quick, sagacious, sharp, shrewd.

shatter *vb* break, burst, crack, rend, shiver, smash, splinter, split; break up, derange, disorder, overthrow.

shave *vb* crop, cut off, mow, pare; slice; graze, skim, touch.

shaver *n* boy, child, youngster; bargainer, extortioner, sharper.

shear *vb* clip, cut, fleece, strip; divest; break off.

sheath *n* case, casing, covering, envelope,

scabbard, sheathing.
sheathe *vb* case, cover, encase, enclose.
shed[1] *n* cabin, cot, hovel, hut, outhouse, shack, shelter.
shed[2] *vb* effuse, let fall, pour out, spill; diffuse, emit, give out, scatter, spread; cast, let fall, put off, slough, throw off.
sheen *n* brightness, gloss, glossiness, shine, spendour.
sheep *n* ewe, lamb, ram.
sheepish *adj* bashful, diffident, overmodest, shamefaced, timid, timorous.
sheer[1] *adj* perpendicular, precipitous, steep, vertical; clear, downright, mere, pure, simple, unadulterated, unmingled, unmixed, unqualified, utter; clear; fine, transparent. * *adv* outright; perpendicularly, steeply.
sheer[2] *vb* decline, deviate, move aside, swerve. * *n* bow, curve.
shelf *n* bracket, console, ledge, mantelpiece.
shell *vb* exfoliate, fall off, peel off; bombard. * *n* carapace, case, covering, shard; bomb, grenade, sharpnel; framework.
shelter *vb* cover, defend, ensconce, harbour, hide, house, protect, screen, shield, shroud. * *n* asylum, cover, covert, harbour, haven, hideaway, refuge, retreat, sanctuary; defence, protection, safety, screen, security, shield; guardian, protector.
shelve *vb* dismiss, put aside; incline, slope.
shepherd *vb* escort, guide, marshal, usher; direct, drive, drove, herd, lead; guard, tend, watch over. * *n* drover, grazier, herder, herdsman; chaplain, churchman, clergyman, cleric, divine, ecclesiastic, minister, padre, parson, pastor; chaperon, duenna, escort, guide, squire, usher.
shield *vb* cover, defend, guard, protect, shelter; repel, ward off; avert, forbid, forfend. * *n* aegis, buckler, escutcheon, scutcheon, targe; bulwark, cover, defence, guard, palladium, protection, rampart, safeguard, security, shelter.
shift *vb* alter, change, fluctuate, move, vary; chop, dodge, swerve, veer; contrive, devise, manage, plan, scheme, shuffle. * *n* change, substitution, turn; contrivance, expedient, means, resort, resource; artifice, craft, device, dodge, evasion, fraud, mask, ruse, stratagem, subterfuge, trick, wile; chemise, smock.
shiftless *adj* improvident, imprudent, negligent, slack, thriftless, unresourceful.
shifty *adj* tricky, undependable, wily.
shillyshally *vb* hesitate, waver. * *n* hesitation, irresolute, wavering.
shimmer *vb* flash, glimmer, glisten, shine. * *n* blink, glimmer, glitter, twinkle.
shin *vb* climb, swarm. * *n* shinbone, tibia.
shindy *n* disturbance, riot, roughhouse, row, spree, uproar.
shine *vb* beam, blaze, coruscate, flare, give light, glare, gleam, glimmer, glisten, glitter, glow, lighten, radiate, sparkle; excel. * *n* brightness, brilliancy, glaze, gloss, polish, sheen.
shining *adj* beaming, bright, brilliant, effulgent, gleaming, glowing, glistening, glittering, luminous, lustrous, radiant, resplendent, splendid; conspicuous, distinguished, illustrious.
shiny *adj* bright, clear, luminous, sunshiny, unclouded; brilliant, burnished, glassy, glossy, polished.
ship *n* boat, craft, steamer, vessel.
shipshape *adj* neat, orderly, tidy, trim, well-arranged.
shipwreck *vb* cast away, maroon, strand, wreck. * *n* demolition, destruction, miscarriage, overthrow, perdition, ruin, subversion, wreck.
shirk *vb* avoid, dodge, evade, malinger, quit, slack; cheat, shark, trick.
shiver[1] *vb* break, shatter, splinter. * *n* bit, fragment, piece, slice, sliver, splinter.
shiver[2] *vb* quake, quiver, shake, shudder, tremble. * *n* shaking, shivering, shuddering, tremor.
shivery[1] *adj* brittle, crumbly, frangible, friable, shatterable, splintery.
shivery[2] *adj* quaking, quavering, quivering, shaky, trembly, tremulous; chilly, shivering.
shoal[1] *vb* crowd, throng. * *n* crowd, horde, multitude, swarm, throng.
shoal[2] *n* sandbank, shallows; danger.
shock *vb* appall, horrify; disgust, disquiet,

disturb, nauseate, offend, outrage, revolt, scandalize, sicken; astound, stagger, stun; collide with, jar, jolt, shake, strike against; encounter, meet. * *n* agitation, blow, offence, stroke, trauma; assault, brunt, conflict; clash, collision, concussion, impact, percussion.

shocking *adj* abominable, detestable, disgraceful, disgusting, execrable, foul, hateful, loathsome, obnoxious, odious, offensive, repugnant, repulsive, revolting; appalling, awful, dire, dreadful, fearful, frightful, ghastly, hideous, horrible, horrid, horrific, monstrous, terrible.

shoot *vb* catapult, expel, hurl, let fly, propel; discharge, fire, let off; dart, fly, pass, pelt; extend, jut, project, protrude, protuberate, push, put forth, send forth, stretch; bud, germinate, sprout; (*with* **up**) grow increase, spring up, run up, start up. * *n* branch, offshoot, scion, sprout, twig.

shop *n* emporium, market, mart, store; workshop.

shore[1] *n* beach, brim, coast, seabord, seaside, strand, waterside.

shore[2] *vb* brace, buttress, prop, stay, support. * *n* beam, brace, buttress, prop, stay, support.

shorn *adj* cut-off; deprived.

short *adj* brief, curtailed; direct, near, straight; compendious, concise, condensed, laconic, pithy, terse, sententious, succinct, summary; abrupt, curt, petulant, pointed, sharp, snappish, uncivil; defective, deficient, inadequate, insufficient, niggardly, scanty, scrimpy; contracted, desitute, lacking, limited, minus, wanting; dwarfish, squat, undersized; brittle, crisp, crumbling, friable. * *adv* abruptly, at once, forthwith, suddenly.

shortcoming *n* defect, deficiency, delinquency, error, failing, failure, fault, imperfection, inadequacy, remissness, slip, weakness.

shorten *vb* abbreviate, abridge, curtail, cut short; abridge, contract, diminish, lessen, retrench, reduce; cut off, dock, lop, trim; confine, hinder, restrain, restrict.

shortening *n* abbreviation, abridgment, contraction, curtailment, diminution, retrenchment, reduction.

shorthand *n* brachygraphy, stenography, tachygraphy.

short-lived *adj* emphemeral, transient, transitory.

shortly *adv* quickly, soon; briefly, concisely, succinctly, tersely.

short-sighted *adj* myopic, nearsighted, purblind; imprudent, indiscreet.

shot[1] *n* discharge; ball, bullet, missile, projectile; marksman, shooter.

shot[2] *adj* chatoyant, iridescent, irisated, moiré, watered; intermingled, interspersed, interwoven.

shoulder *vb* bear, bolster, carry, hump, maintain, pack, support, sustain, tote; crowd, elbow, jostle, press forward, push, thrust. * *n* projection, protuberance.

shoulder blade *n* blade bone, omoplate, scapula, shoulder bone.

shout *vb* bawl, cheer, clamour, exclaim, halloo, roar, vociferate, whoop, yell. * *n* cheer, clamour, exclamation, halloo, hoot, huzza, outcry, roar, vociferation, whoop, yell.

shove *vb* jostle, press against, propel, push, push aside; (*with* **off**) push away, thrust away.

show *vb* blazon, display, exhibit, flaunt, parade, present; indicate, mark, point out; disclose, discover, divulge, explain, make clear, make known, proclaim, publish, reveal, unfold; demonstrate, evidence, manifest, prove, verify; conduct, guide, usher; direct, inform, instruct, teach; expound, elucidate, interpret; (*with* **off**) display, exhibit, make a show, set off; (*with* **up**) expose. * *n* array, exhibition, representation, sight, spectacle; blazonry, bravery, ceremony, dash, demonstration, display, flourish, ostentation, pageant, pageantry, parade, pomp, splendour, splurge; likeness, resemblance, semblance; affectation, appearance, colour, illusion, mask, plausibility, pose, pretence, pretext, simulation, speciousness; entertainment, production.

showy *adj* bedizened, dressy, fine, flashy, flaunting, garish, gaudy, glaring, gor-

geous, loud, ornate, smart, swanky, splendid; grand, magnificent, ostentatious, pompous, pretentious, stately, sumptuous.
shred *vb* tear. * *n* bit, fragment, piece, rag, scrap, strip, tatter.
shrew *n* brawler, fury, scold, spitfire, termagant, virago, vixen.
shrewd *adj* arch, artful, astute, crafty, cunning, Machiavellian, sly, subtle, wily; acute, astute, canny, discerning, discriminating, ingenious, keen, knowing, penetrating, sagacious, sharp, sharp-sighted.
shrewdness *n* address, archness, art, artfulness, astuteness, craft, cunning, policy, skill, slyness, subtlety; acumen, acuteness, discernment, ingenuity, keenness, penetration, perspicacity, sagacity, sharpness, wit.
shrewish *adj* brawling, clamorous, froward, peevish, petulant, scolding, vixenish.
shriek *vb* scream, screech, squeal, yell, yelp. * *n* cry, scream, screech, yell.
shrill *adj* acute, high, high-toned, high-pitched, piercing, piping, sharp.
shrine *n* reliquary, sacred tomb; altar, hallowed place, sacred place.
shrink *vb* contract, decrease, dwindle, shrivel, wither; balk, blench, draw back, flinch, give way, quail, recoil, retire, swerve, wince, withdraw.
shrivel *vb* dry, dry up, parch; contract, decrease, dwindle, shrink, wither, wrinkle.
shroud *vb* bury, cloak, conceal, cover, hide, mask, muffle, protect, screen, shelter, veil. * *n* covering, garment; grave clothes, winding sheet.
shrub *n* bush, dwarf tree, low tree.
shrubby *adj* bushy.
shudder *vb* quake, quiver, shake, shiver, tremble. * *n* shaking, shuddering, trembling, tremor.
shuffle *vb* confuse, disorder, intermix, jumble, mix, shift; cavil, dodge, equivocate, evade, prevaricate, quibble, vacillate; struggle. * *n* artifice, cavil, evasion, fraud, pretence, pretext, prevarication, quibble, ruse, shuffling, sophism, subterfuge, trick.
shun *vb* avoid, elude, eschew, escape, evade, get clear of.
shut *vb* close, close up, stop; confine, coop up,
enclose, imprison, lock up, shut up; (*with* **in**) confine, enclose; (*with* **off**) bar, exclude, intercept; (*with* **up**) close up, shut; confine, enclose, fasten in, imprison, lock in, lock up.
shy *vb* cast, chuck, fling, hurl, jerk, pitch, sling, throw, toss; boggle, sheer, start aside. * *adj* bashful, coy, diffident, reserved, retiring, sheepish, shrinking, timid; cautious, chary, distrustful, heedful, wary. * *n* start; fling, throw.
sibilant *adj* buzzing, hissing, sibilous.
sick *adj* ailing, ill, indisposed, laid-up, unwell, weak; nauseated, queasy; disgusted, revolted, tired, weary; diseased, distempered, disordered, feeble, morbid, unhealthy, unsound, weak; languishing, longing, pining.
sicken *vb* ail, disease, fall sick, make sick; nauseate; disgust, weary; decay, droop, languish, pine.
sickening *adj* nauseating, nauseous, palling, sickish; disgusting, distasteful, loathsome, offensive, repulsive, revolting.
sickly *adj* ailing, diseased, faint, feeble, infirm, languid, languishing, morbid, unhealthy, valetudinary, weak, weakly.
sickness *n* ail, ailment, complaint, disease, disorder, distemper, illness, indisposition, invalidism, malady, morbidity; nausea, qualmishness, queasiness.
side *vb* border, bound, edge, flank, frontier, march, rim, skirt, verge; avert, turn aside; (*with* **with**) befriend, favour, flock to, join with, second, support. * *adj* flanking, later, skirting; indirect, oblique; extra, odd, off, spare. * *n* border, edge, flank, margin, verge; cause, faction, interest, party, sect.
sideboard *n* buffet, dresser.
side by side abreast, alongside, by the side.
sidelong *adj* lateral, oblique. * *adv* laterally, obliquely; on the side.
sidewalk *n* footpath, footway, pavement.

sideways, sidewise *adv* laterally. * *adv* athwart, crossways, crosswise, laterally, obliquely, sidelong, sidewards.
siesta *n* doze, nap.
sift *vb* part, separate; bolt, screen, winnow; analyse, canvass, discuss, examine, fathom, follow up, inquire into, investigate, probe, scrutinze, sound, try.
sigh *vb* complain, grieve, lament, mourn. * *n* long breath, sough, suspiration.
sight *vb* get sight of, perceive, see. * *n* cognizance, ken, perception, view; beholding, eyesight, seeing, vision; exhibition, prospect, representation, scene, show, spectacle, wonder; consideration, estimation, knowledge; examination, inspection.
sightless *adj* blind, eyeless, unseeing.
sightly *adj* beautiful, comely, handsome.
sign *vb* indicate, signal, signify; countersign, endorse, subscribe. * *n* emblem, index, indication, manifestation, mark, note, proof, signal, signification, symbol, symptom, token; beacon; augury, auspice, foreboding, miracle, omen, portent, presage, prodigy, prognostic, wonder; type; countersign, password.
signal *vb* flag, glance, hail, nod, nudge, salute, sign, signalize, sound, speak, touch, wave, wink. * *adj* conspicuous, eminent, extraordinary, memorable, notable, noteworthy, remarkable. * *n* cue, indication, mark, sign, token.
signalize *vb* celebrate, distinguish, make memorable.
signature *n* mark, sign, stamp; autograph, hand.
significance *n* implication, import, meaning, purport, sense; consequence, importance, moment, portent, weight; emphasis, energy, expressiveness, force, impressiveness.
significant *adj* betokening, expressive, indicative, significative, signifying; important, material, momentous, portentous, weighty; forcible, emphatic, expressive, telling.
signification *n* expression; acceptation, import, meaning, purport, sense.
signify *vb* betoken, communication, express, indicate, intimate; denote, imply, import, mean, purport, suggest; announce, declare, give notice of, impart, make known, manifest, proclaim, utter; augur, foreshadow, indicate, portend, represent; matter, weigh.
silence *vb* hush, muzzle, still; allay, calm, quiet. * *interj* be silent, be still, hush, soft, tush, tut, whist. * *n* calm, hush, lull, noiselessness, peace, quiet, quietude, soundlessness, stillness; dumbness, mumness, muteness, reticence, speechlessness, taciturnity.
silent *adj* calm, hushed, noiseless, quiet, soundless, still; dumb, inarticulate, mum, mute, nonvocal, speechless, tacit; reticent, taciturn, uncommunicative.
silken *adj* flossy, silky, soft.
silkiness *n* smoothness, softness.
silly *adj* brainless, childish, foolish, inept, senseless, shallow, simple, stupid, weak-minded, witless; absurd, extravagant, frivolous, imprudent, indiscreet, nonsensical, preposterous, trifling, unwise. * *n* ass, duffer, goose, idiot, simpleton.
silt *n* alluvium, deposit, deposition, residue, settlement, settlings, sediment.
silver *adj* argent, silvery; bright, silvery, white; clear, mellifluous, soft.
similar *adj* analogous, duplicate, like, resembling, twin; homogeneous, uniform.
similarity *n* agreement, analogy, correspondence, likeness, parallelism, parity, resemblance, sameness, semblance, similitude.
simile *n* comparison, metaphor, similitude.
similitude *n* image, likeness, resemblance; comparison, metaphor, simile.
simmer *vb* boil, bubble, seethe, stew.
simper *vb* smile, smirk.
simple *adj* bare, elementary, homogeneous, incomplex, mere, single, unalloyed, unblended, uncombined, uncompounded, unmingled, unmixed; chaste, plain, homespun, inornate, natural, neat, unadorned, unaffected, unembellished, unpretentious, unstudied, unvarnished; artless, downright, frank, guileless, inartificial, ingenuous, naive, open, simple-hearted,

simple-minded, sincere, single-minded, straightforward, true, unconstrained, undesigning, unsophisticated; credulous, fatuous, foolish, shallow, silly, unwise, weak; clear, intelligible, understandable, uninvolved, unmistakable.

simple-hearted *adj* artless, frank, ingenuous, open, simple, single-hearted.

simpleton *n* fool, greenhorn, nincompoop, ninny.

simplicity *n* chasteness, homeliness, naturalness, neatness, plainness; artlessness, frankness, naivety, openness, simplesse, sincerity; clearness; gullibility, folly, silliness, weakness.

simply *adv* artlessly, plainly, sincerely, unaffectedly; barely, merely, of itself, solely; absolutely, alone.

simulate *vb* act, affect, ape, assume, counterfeit, dissemble, feign, mimic, pretend, sham.

simulation *n* counterfeiting, feigning, personation, pretence.

simultaneous *adj* coeval, coincident, concomitant, concurrent, contemporaneous, synchronous.

sin *vb* do wrong, err, transgress, trespass. * *n* delinquency, depravity, guilt, iniquity, misdeed, offence, transgression, unrighteousness, wickedness, wrong.

since *conj* as, because, considering, seeing that. * *adv* ago, before this; from that time. * *prep* after, from the time of, subsequently to.

sincere *adj* pure, unmixed; genuine, honest, inartificial, real, true, unaffected, unfeigned, unvarnished; artless, candid, direct, frank, guileless, hearty, honest, ingenuous, open, plain, single, straightforward, truthful, undissembling, upright, whole-hearted.

sincerity *n* artlessness, candour, earnestness, frankness, genuineness, guilelessness, honesty, ingenuousness, probity, truth, truthfulness, unaffectedness, veracity.

sinew *n* ligament, tendon; brawn, muscle, nerve, strength.

sinewy *adj* able-bodied, brawny, firm, Herculean, muscular, nervous, powerful, robust, stalwart, strapping, strong, sturdy, vigorous, wiry.

sinful *adj* bad, criminal, depraved, immoral, iniquitous, mischievous, peccant, transgressive, unholy, unrighteous, wicked, wrong.

sinfulness *n* corruption, criminality, depravity, iniquity, irreligion, ungodliness, unholiness, unrighteousness, wickedness.

sing *vb* cantillate, carol, chant, hum, hymn, intone, lilt, troll, warble, yodel.

singe *vb* burn, scorch, sear.

singer *n* cantor, caroler, chanter, gleeman, prima donna, minstrel, psalmodist, songster, vocalist.

single *vb* (*with* **out**) choose, pick, select, single. * *adj* alone, isolated, one only, sole, solitary; individual, particular, separate; celibate, unmarried, unwedded; pure, simple, uncompounded, unmixed; honest, ingenuous, sincere, unbiased, uncorrupt, upright.

single-handed *adj* alone, by one's self, unaided, unassisted.

single-minded *adj* artless, candid, guileless, ingenuous, sincere.

singleness *n* individuality, unity; purity, simplicity; ingenuousness, integrity, sincerity, uprightness.

singular *adj* eminent, exceptional, extraordinary, rare, remarkable, strange, uncommon, unusual, unwonted; particular, unexampled, unparalleled, unprecedented; unaccountable; bizarre, curious, eccentric, fantastic, odd, peculiar, queer; individual, single; not complex, single, uncompounded, unique.

singularity *n* aberration, abnormality, irregularity, oddness, rareness, rarity, strangeness, uncommonness; characteristic, idiosyncrasy, individuality, particularity, peculiarity; eccentricity, oddity.

sinister *adj* baleful, injurious, untoward; boding ill, inauspicious, ominous, unlucky; left, on the left hand.

sink *vb* droop, drop, fall, founder, go down, submerge, subside; enter, penetrate; collapse, fail; decay, decline, decrease, dwindle, give way, languish, lose strength; engulf, immerse, merge, submerge, submerse; dig, excavate, scoop out; abase, bring down, crush, debase, degrade, depress, diminish, lessen, lower, overbear; destroy, overthrow, overwhelm, reduce, ruin, swamp, waste. * *n* basin, cloaca, drain.

sinless *adj* faultless, guiltless, immaculate, impeccable, innocent, spotless, unblemished, undefiled, unspotted, unsullied, untarnished.

sinner *n* criminal, delinquent, evildoer, offender, reprobate, wrongdoer.

sinuosity *n* crook, curvature, flexure, sinus, tortuosity, winding.

sinuous *adj* bending, crooked, curved, curvilinear, flexuous, serpentine, sinuate, sinuated, tortuous, undulating, wavy, winding.

sip *vb* drink, suck up, sup; absorb, drink in. * *n* small draught, taste.

sire *vb* father, reproduce; author, breed, conceive, create, generate, originate, produce, propagate. * *n* father, male parent, progenitor; man, male person; sir, sirrah; author, begetter, creator, father, generator, originator.

siren *adj* alluring, bewitching, fascinating, seducing, tempting. * *n* mermaid; charmer, Circe, seducer, seductress, tempter, temptress.

sit *vb* be, remain, repose, rest, stay; bear on, lie, rest; abide, dwell, settle; perch; brood, incubate; become, be suited, fit.

site *vb* locate, place, position, situate, station. * *n* ground, locality, location, place, position, seat, situation, spot, station, whereabouts.

sitting *n* meeting, session.

situation *n* ground, locality, location, place, position, seat, site, spot, whereabouts; case, category, circumstances, condition, juncture, plight, predicament, state; employment, office, place, post, station.

size *n* amplitude, bigness, bulk, dimensions, expanse, greatness, largeness, magnitude, mass, volume.

skeleton *n* framework; draft, outline, sketch.

sketch *vb* design, draft, draw out; delineate, depict, paint, portray, represent. * *n* delineation, design, draft, drawing, outline, plan, skeleton.

sketchy *adj* crude, incomplete, unfinished.

skilful *adj* able, accomplished, adept, adroit, apt, clever, competent, conversant, cunning, deft, dexterous, dextrous, expert, handy, ingenious, masterly, practised, proficient, qualified, quick, ready, skilled, trained, versed, well-versed.

skill *n* ability, address, adroitness, aptitude, aptness, art, cleverness, deftness, dexterity, expertise, expertness, facility, ingenuity, knack, quickness, readiness, skilfulness; discernment, discrimination, knowledge, understanding, wit.

skim *vb* brush, glance, graze, kiss, scrape, scratch, sweep, touch lightly; coast, flow, fly, glide, sail, scud, whisk; dip into, glance at, scan, skip, thumb over, touch upon.

skin *vb* pare, peel; decorticate, excoriate, flay. * *n* cuticle, cutis, derm, epidermis, hide, integument, pellicle, pelt; hull, husk, peel, rind.

skinflint *n* churl, curmudgeon, lickpenny, miser, niggard, scrimp.

skinny *adj* emaciated, lank, lean, poor, shrivelled, shrunk, thin.

skip *vb* bound, caper, frisk, gambol, hop, jump, leap, spring; disregard, intermit, miss, neglect, omit, pass over, skim. * *n* bound, caper, frisk, gambol, hop, jump, leap, spring.

skirmish *vb* battle, brush, collide, combat, contest, fight, scuffle, tussle. * *n* affair, affray, battle, brush, collision, combat, conflict, contest, encounter, fight, scuffle, tussle.

skirt *vb* border, bound, edge, fringe, hem, march, rim; circumnavigate, circumvent, flank, go along. * *n* border, boundary, edge, margin, rim, verge; flap, kilt, overskirt, petticoat.

skittish *adj* changeable, fickle, inconstant; hasty, volatile, wanton; shy, timid, timorous.

skulk *vb* hide, lurk, slink, sneak.

skulker *n* lurker, sneak; shirk, slacker,

malingerer.
skull *n* brain pan, cranium.
sky *n* empyrean, firmament, heaven, heavens, welkin.
sky-blue *adj* azure, cerulean, sapphire, sky-coloured.
skylarking *n* carousing, frolicking, sporting.
slab *adj* slimy, thick, viscous. * *n* beam, board, layer, panel, plank, slat, table, tablet; mire, mud, puddle, slime.
slabber *vb* drivel, slaver, slobber; drop, let fall, shed, spill.
slack *vb* ease off, let up; abate, ease up, relax, slacken; malinger, shirk; choke, damp, extinguish, smother, stifle. * *adj* backward, careless, inattentive, lax, negligent, remiss; abated, dilatory, diminished, lingering, slow, tardy; loose, relaxed; dull, idle, inactive, quiet, sluggish. * *n* excess, leeway, looseness, play; coal dust, culm, residue.
slacken *vb* abate, diminish, lessen, lower, mitigate, moderate, neglect, remit, relieve, retard, slack; loosen, relax; flag, slow down; bridle, check, control, curb, repress, restrain.
slackness *n* looseness; inattention, negligence, remissness; slowness, tardiness.
slander *vb* asperse, backbite, belie, brand, calumniate, decry, defame, libel, malign, reproach, scandalize, traduce, vilify; detract from, disparage. * *n* aspersion, backbiting, calumny, defamation, detraction, libel, obloquy, scandal, vilification.
slanderous *adj* calumnious, defamatory, false, libellous, malicious, maligning.
slang *n* argo, cant, jargon, lingo.
slant *vb* incline, lean, lie obliquely, list, slope. * *n* inclination, slope, steep, tilt.
slap *vb* dab, clap, pat, smack, spank, strike. * *adv* instantly, quickly, plumply. * *n* blow, clap.
slapdash *adv* haphazardly, hurriedly, precipitately.
slash *vb* cut, gash, slit. * *n* cut, gash, slit.
slashed *adj* cut, slit; (*bot*) jagged, laciniate, multifid.
slattern *adj* slatternly, slovenly, sluttish. * *n* drab, slut, sloven, trollop.
slatternly *adj* dirty, slattern, slovenly, sluttish, unclean, untidy. * *adv* carelessly, negligently, sluttishly.
slaughter *vb* butcher, kill, massacre, murder, slay. * *n* bloodshed, butchery, carnage, havoc, killing, massacre, murder, slaying.
slaughterer *n* assassin, butcher, cutthroat, destroyer, killer, murderer, slayer.
slave *vb* drudge, moil, toil. * *n* bondmaid, bondservant, bondslave, bondman, captive, dependant, henchman, helot, peon, serf, thrall, vassal, villein; drudge, menial.
slavery *n* bondage, bond-service, captivity, enslavement, enthralment, serfdom, servitude, thraldom, vassalage, villeinage; drudgery, mean labour.
slavish *adj* abject, beggarly, base, cringing, fawning, grovelling, low, mean, obsequious, servile, sycophantic; drudging, laborious, menial, servile.
slay *vb* assassinate, butcher, dispatch, kill, massacre, murder, slaughter; destroy, ruin.
slayer *n* assassin, destroyer, killer, murderer, slaughterer.
sledge *n* drag, sled; cutter, pung, sleigh.
sleek *adj* glossy, satin, silken, silky, smooth.
sleekly *adv* evenly, glossily, nicely, smoothly.
sleep *vb* catnap, doze, drowse, nap, slumber. * *n* dormancy, hypnosis, lethargy, repose, rest, slumber.
sleeping *adj* dormant, inactive, quiescent.
sleepwalker *n* night-walker, noctambulist, somnambulist.
sleepwalking *n* somnambulism.
sleepy *adj* comatose, dozy, drowsy, heavy, lethargic, nodding, somnolent; narcotic, opiate, slumberous, somniferous, somnific, soporiferous, soporific; dull, heavy, inactive, lazy, slow, sluggish, torpid.
sleight *n* adroitness, dexterity, manoeuvring.
sleight of hand *n* conjuring, hocus-pocus, jugglery, legerdemain, prestdigitation.
slender *adj* lank, lithe, narrow, skinny,

slim, spindly, thin; feeble, fine, flimsy, fragile, slight, tenuous, weak; inconsiderable, moderate, small, trivial; exiguous, inadequate, insufficient, lean, meagre, pitiful, scanty; abstemious, light, simple, spare, sparing.

slice *vb* cut, divide, part, section; cut off, sever. * *n* chop, collop, piece.

slick *adj* glassy, glossy, polished, sleek, smooth; alert, clever, cunning, shrewd, slippery, unctuous. *vb* burnish, gloss, lacquer, polish, shine, sleek, varnish; grease, lubricate, oil.

slide *vb* glide, move smoothly, slip. * *n* glide, glissade, skid, slip.

sliding *adj* gliding, slippery, uncertain. * *n* backsliding, falling, fault, lapse, transgression.

slight *vb* cold-shoulder, disdain, disregard, neglect, snub; overlook; scamp, skimp, slur. * *adj* inconsiderable, insignificant, little, paltry, petty, small, trifling, trivial, unimportant, unsubstantial; delicate, feeble, frail, gentle, weak; careless, cursory, desultory, hasty, hurried, negligent, scanty, superficial; flimsy, perishable; slender, slim. * *n* discourtesy, disregard, disrespect, inattention, indignity, neglect.

slightingly *adv* contemptuously, disrespectfully, scornfully, slightly.

slightly *adv* inconsiderably, little, somewhat; feebly, slenderly, weakly; cursorily, hastily, negligently, superficially.

slim *vb* bant, diet, lose weight, reduce, slenderize. * *adj* gaunt, lank, lithe, narrow, skinny, slender, spare; inconsiderable, paltry, poor, slight, trifling, trivial, unsubstantial, weak; insufficient, meagre.

slime *n* mire, mud, ooze, sludge.

slimy *adj* miry, muddy, oozy; clammy, gelatinous, glutinous, gummy, lubricious, mucilaginous, mucous, ropy, slabby, viscid, viscous.

sling *vb* cast, fling, hurl, throw; hang up, suspend.

slink *vb* skulk, slip away, sneak, steal away.

slip *vb* glide, slide; err, mistake, trip; lose, omit; disengage, throw off; escape, let go, loose, loosen, release, . * *n* glide, slide, slipping; blunder, lapse, misstep, mistake, oversight, peccadillo, trip; backsliding, error, fault, impropriety, indiscretion, transgression; desertion, escape; cord, leash, strap, string; case, covering, wrapper.

slippery *adj* glib, slithery, smooth; changeable, insecure, mutable, perilous, shaky, uncertain, unsafe, unstable, unsteady; cunning, dishonest, elusive, faithless, false, knavish, perfidious, shifty, treacherous.

slipshod *adj* careless, shuffling, slovenly, untidy.

slit *vb* cut; divide, rend, slash, split, sunder. * *n* cut, gash.

slobber *vb* drivel, drool, slabber, slaver; daub, obscure, smear, stain.

slobbery *adj* dank, floody, moist, muddy, sloppy, wet.

slope *vb* incline, slant, tilt. * *n* acclivity, cant, declivity, glacis, grade, gradient, incline, inclination, obliquity, pitch, ramp.

sloping *adj* aslant, bevelled, declivitous, inclining, oblique, shelving, slanting.

sloppy *adj* muddy, plashy, slabby, slobbery, splashy, wet.

sloth *n* dilatoriness, slowness, tardiness; idleness, inaction, inactivity, indolence, inertness, laziness, lumpishness, slothfulness, sluggishness, supineness, torpor.

slothful *adj* dronish, idle, inactive, indolent, inert, lazy, lumpish, slack, sluggish, supine, torpid.

slouch *vb* droop, loll, slump; shamble, shuffle. * *n* malingerer, shirker, slacker; shamble, shuffle, stoop.

slouching *adj* awkward, clownish, loutish, lubberly, uncouth, ungainly.

slough[1] *n* bog, fen, marsh, morass, quagmire; dejection, depression, despondence, despondency.

slough[2] *vb* cast, desquamate, excuviate, moult, shed, throw off; cast off, discard, divest, jettison, reject. * *n* cast, desquamation.

sloven *n* slattern, slob, slouch, slut.

slovenly *adj* unclean, untidy; blowsy, disorderly, dowdy, frowsy, loose, slatternly, tacky, unkempt, untidy; careless, heedless, lazy, negligent, perfunctory.

slow *vb* abate, brake, check, decelerate, diminish, lessen, mitigate, moderate, modulate, reduce, weaken; delay,detain, retard; ease, ease up, relax, slack, slacken, slack off. * *adj* deliberate, gradual; dead, dull, heavy, inactive, inert, sluggish, stupid; behindhand, late, tardy, unready; delaying, dilatory, lingering, slack.

sludge *n* mire, mud; slosh, slush.

sluggard *n* dawdler, drone, idler, laggard, lounger, slug.

sluggish *adj* dronish, drowsy, idle, inactive, indolent, inert, languid, lazy, listless, lumpish, phlegmatic, slothful, torpid; slow; dull, stupid, supine, tame.

sluice *vb* drain, drench, flood, flush, irrigate. * *n* floodgate, opening, vent.

slumber *vb* catnap, doze, nap, repose, rest, sleep. * *n* catnap, doze, nap, repose, rest, siesta, sleep.

slumberous *adj* drowsy, sleepy, somniferous, somnific, soporific.

slump *vb* droop, drop, fall, flop, founder, sag, sink, sink down; decline, depreciate, deteriorate, ebb, fail, fall away, lose ground, recede, slide, slip, subside, wane. * *n* droop, drop, fall, flop, lowering, sag, sinkage; decline, depreciation, deterioration, downturn, downtrend, subsidence, ebb, falling off, wane; crash, recession, smash.

slur *vb* asperse, calumniate, disparage, depreciate, reproach, traduce; conceal, disregard, gloss over, obscure, pass over, slight. * *n* mark, stain; brand, disgrace, reproach, stain, stigma; innuendo.

slush *n* slosh, sludge.

slushy *vb* plashy, sloppy, sloshy, sludgy.

slut *n* drab, slattern, sloven, trollop.

sluttish *adj* careless, dirty, disorderly, unclean, untidy.

sly *adj* artful, crafty, cunning, insidious, subtle, wily; astute, cautious, shrewd; arch, knowing, clandestine, secret, stealthy, underhand.

smack[1] *vb* smell, taste. * *n* flavour, savour, tang, taste, tincture; dash, infusion, little, space, soupçon, sprinkling, tinge, touch; smattering.

smack[2] *vb* slap, strike; crack, slash, snap; buss, kiss. * *n* crack, slap, slash, snap; buss, kiss.

small *adj* diminutive, Lilliputian, little, miniature, petite, pygmy, tiny, wee; infinitesimal, microscopic, minute; inappreciable, inconsiderable, insignificant, petty, trifling, trivial, unimportant; moderate, paltry, scanty, slender; faint, feeble, puny, slight, weak; illiberal, mean, narrow, narrow-minded, paltry, selfish, sorded, ungenerous, unworthy.

small talk *n* chat, conversation, gossip.

smart[1] *vb* hurt, pain, sting; suffer. * *adj* keen, painful, poignant, pricking, pungent, severe, sharp, stinging.

smart[2] *adj* active, agile, brisk, fresh, lively, nimble, quick, spirited, sprightly, spry; effective, efficient, energetic, forcible, vigorous; adroit, alert, clever, dexterous, dextrous, expert, intelligent, stirring; acute, apt, pertinent, ready, witty; chic, dapper, fine, natty, showy, spruce, trim.

smartness *n* acuteness, keenness, poignancy, pungency, severity, sharpness; efficiency, energy, force, vigour; activity, agility, briskness, liveliness, nimbleness, sprightliness, spryness, vivacity; alertness, cleverness, dexterity, expertise, expertness, intelligence, quickness; acuteness, aptness, pertinency, wit, wittiness; chic, nattiness, spruceness, trimness.

smash *vb* break, crush, dash, mash, shatter. * *n* crash, debacle, destruction, ruin; bankruptcy, failure.

smattering *n* dabbling, smatter, sprinkling.

smear *vb* bedaub, begrime, besmear, daub, plaster, smudge; contaminate, pollute, smirch, smut, soil, stain, sully, tarnish. * *n* blot, blotch, daub, patch, smirch, smudge, spot, stain; calumny, defamation, libel, slander.

smell *vb* scent, sniff, stench, stink. * *n* aroma, bouquet, fragrance, fume, odour, perfume, redolence, scent, stench, stink; sniff, snuff.

smelt *vb* fuse, melt.

smile *vb* grin, laugh, simper, smirk. * *n* grin, simper, smirk.

smite *vb* beat, box, collide, cuff, knock, strike, wallop, whack; destroy, kill, slay; afflict, chasten, punish; blast, destroy.

smitten *adj* attracted, captivated, charmed, enamoured, fascinated, taken; destroyed, killed, slain; smit, struck; afflicted, chastened, punished.

smock *n* chemise, shift, slip; blouse, gaberdine.

smoke *vb* emit, exhale, reek, steam; fumigate, smudge; discover, find out, smell out. * *n* effluvium, exhalation, fume, mist, reek, smother, steam, vapour; fumigation, smudge.

smoky *adj* fuliginous, fumid, fumy, smudgy; begrimed, blackened, dark, reeky, sooty, tanned.

smooth *vb* flatten, level, plane; ease, lubricate; extenuate, palliate, soften; allay, alleviate, assuage, calm, mitigate, mollify. * *adj* even, flat, level, plane, polished, unruffled, unwrinkled; glabrous, glossy, satiny, silky, sleek, soft, velvet; euphonious, flowing, liquid, mellifluent; fluent, glib, voluble; bland, flattering, ingratiating, insinuating, mild, oily, smooth-tongued, soothing, suave, unctuous.

smoothly *adv* evenly; easily, readily, unobstructedly; blandly, flatteringly, gently, mildly, pleasantly, softly, soothingly.

smooth-tongued *adj* adulatory, cozening, flattering, plausible, smooth, smooth-spoken.

smother *vb* choke, stifle, suffocate; conceal, deaden, extinguish, hide, keep down, repress, suppress; smoke, smoulder.

smudge *vb* besmear, blacken, blur, smear, smut, smutch, soil, spot, stain. * *n* blur, blot, smear, smut, spot, stain.

smug *adj* complacent, self-satisfied; neat, nice, spruce, trim.

smuggler *n* contrabandist, runner.

smut *vb* blacken, smouch, smudge, soil, stain, sully, taint, tarnish. * *n* dirt, smudge, smutch, soot; nastiness, obscenity, ribaldry, smuttiness; pornography.

smutty *adj* coarse, gross, immodest, impure, indecent, indelicate, loose, nasty; dirty, foul, nasty, soiled, stained.

snack *n* bite, light meal, nibble.

snag *vb* catch, enmesh, entangle, hook, snare, sniggle, tangle. * *n* knarl, knob, knot, projection, protuberance, snub; catch, difficulty, drawback, hitch, rub, shortcoming, weakness; obstacle.

snaky *adj* serpentine, snaking, winding; artful, cunning, deceitful, insinuating, sly, subtle.

snap *vb* break, fracture; bite, catch at, seize, snatch at, snip; crack; crackle, crepitate, decrepitate, pop. * *adj* casual, cursory, hasty, offhand, sudden, superficial. * *n* bite, catch, nip, seizure; catch, clasp, fastening, lock; crack, fillip, flick, flip, smack; briskness, energy, verve, vim.

snappish *adj* acrimonious, captious, churlish, crabbed, cross, crusty, froward, irascible, ill-tempered, peevish, perverse, pettish, petulant, snarling, splenetic, surly, tart, testy, touchy, waspish.

snare *vb* catch, ensnare, entangle, entrap. * *n* catch, gin, net, noose, springe, toil, trap, wile.

snarl[1] *vb* girn, gnarl, growl, grumble, murmur. * *n* growl, grumble.

snarl[2] *vb* complicate, disorder, entangle, knot; confuse, embarrass, ensnare. * *n* complication, disorder, entanglement, tangle; difficulty, embarrassment, intricacy.

snatch *vb* catch, clutch, grasp, grip, pluck, pull, seize, snip, twich, wrest, wring, * *n* bit, fragment, part, portion; catch, effort.

sneak *vb* lurk, skulk, slink, steal; crouch, truckle. * *adj* clandestine, concealed, covert, hidden, secret, sly, underhand. * *n* informer, telltale; lurker, shirk.

sneaky *adj* furtive, skulking, slinking; abject, crouching, grovelling, mean; clandestine, concealed, covert, hidden, secret, sly, underhand.

sneer *vb* flout, gibe, jeer, mock, rail, scoff;

(*with* **at**) deride, despise, disdain, laugh at, mock, rail at, scoff, spurn. * *n* flouting, gibe, jeer, scoff.
snicker *vb* giggle, laugh, snigger, titter.
sniff *vb* breathe, inhale, snuff; scent, smell.
snip *vb* clip, cut, nip; snap, snatch. * *n* bit, fragment, particle, piece, shred; share, snack.
snivel *vb* blubber, cry, fret, sniffle, snuffle, weep, whimper, whine.
snivelly *adj* snotty; pitiful, whining.
snob *n* climber, toady.
snooze *vb* catnap, doze, drowse, nap, sleep, slumber. * *n* catnap, nap, sleep, slumber.
snout *n* muzzle, nose; nozzle.
snowy *adj* immaculate, pure, spotless, unblemished, unstained, unsullied, white.
snub[1] *vb* abash, cold-shoulder, cut, discomfit, humble, humiliate, mortify, slight, take down. * *n* check, rebuke, slight.
snub[2] *vb* check, clip, cut short, dock, nip, prune, stunt. * *adj* pug, retroussé, snubbed, squashed, squat, stubby, turned-up.
snuff[1] *vb* breathe, inhale, sniff; scent, smell; snort.
snuff[2] *vb* (*with* **out**) annihilate, destroy, efface, extinguish, obliterate.
snuffle *vb* sniffle; snort, snuff.
snug *adj* close, concealed; comfortable, compact, convenient, neat, trim.
snuggle *vb* cuddle, nestle, nuzzle.
so *adv* thus, with equal reason; in such a manner; in this way, likewise; as it is, as it was, such; for this reason, therefore; be it so, thus be it. * *conj* in case that, on condition that, provided that.
soak *vb* drench, moisten, permeate, saturate, wet; absorb, imbibe; imbue, macerate, steep.
soar *vb* ascend, fly aloft, glide, mount, rise, tower.
sob *vb* cry, sigh convulsively, weep.
sober *vb* (*with* **up**) calm down, collect oneself, compose oneself, control oneself, cool off, master, moderate, simmer down. * *adj* abstemious, abstinent, temperate, unintoxicated; rational, reasonable, sane, sound; calm, collected, composed, cool, dispassionate, moderate, rational, reasonabler, regular, restrained, steady, temperate, unimpassioned, unruffled, well-regulated; demure, grave, quiet, sedate, serious, solemn, sombre, staid; dark, drab, dull-looking, quiet, sad, subdued.
sobriety *n* abstemiousness, abstinence, soberness, temperance; calmness, coolness, gravity, sedateness, sober-mindedness, staidness, thoughtfulness; gravity, seriousness, solemnity.
sobriquet *n* appellation, nickname, nom de plume, pseudonym.
sociability *n* companionableness, comradeship, good fellowship, sociality.
sociable *adj* accessible, affable, communicative, companionable, conversable, friendly, genial, neighbourly, social.
social *adj* civic, civil; accessible, affable, communicative, companionable, familiar, friendly, hospitable, neighbourly, sociable; convivial, festive, gregarious. * *n* conversazione, gathering, get-together, party, reception, soiree.
society *n* association, companionship, company, converse, fellowship; the community, populace, the public, the world; élite, *monde*; body, brotherhood, copartnership, corporation, club, fraternity, partnersnip, sodality, union.
sodden *adj* drenched, saturated, soaked, steeped, wet; boiled, decocted, seethed, stewed.
sofa *n* couch, davenport, divan, ottoman, settee.
soft *adj* impressible, malleable, plastic, pliable, yielding; downy, fleecy, velvety, mushy, pulpy, squashy; compliant, facile, irresolute, submissive, undecided, weak; bland, mild, gentle, kind, lenient, soft-hearted, tender; delicate; easy, even, quiet, smooth-going, steady; effeminate, luxurious, unmanly; dulcet, fluty, mellifluous, melodious, smooth. * *interj* hold, stop.
soften *vb* intenerate, mellow, melt, tenderize; abate, allay, alleviate, appease, assuage, attemper, balm, blunt, calm, dull,

ease, lessen, make easy, mitigate, moderate, mollify, milden, qualify, quell, quiet, relent, relieve, soothe, still, temper; extenuate, modify, palliate, qualify; enervate, weaken.

soil[1] *n* earth, ground loam, mould; country, land.

soil[2] *vb* bedaub, begrime, bemire, besmear, bespatter, contaminate, daub, defile, dirty, foul, pollute, smirch, stain, sully, taint, tarnish. * *n* blemish, defilement, dirt, filth, foulness; blot, spot, stain, taint, tarnish.

sojourn *vb* abide, dwell, live, lodge, remain, reside, rest, stay, stop, tarry, visit. * *n* residence, stay.

solace *vb* cheer, comfort, console, soothe; allay, assuage, mitigate, relieve, soften. * *n* alleviation, cheer, comfort, consolation, relief.

soldier *n* fighting man, man-at-arms, warrior; GI, private.

soldierly *adj* martial, military, warlike; brave, courageous, gallant, heroic, honourable, intrepid, valiant.

sole *adj* alone, individual, one, only, single, solitary, unique.

solecism *n* barbarism, blunder, error, faux pas, impropriety, incongruity, mistake, slip.

solemn *adj* ceremonial, formal, ritual; devotional, devout, religious, reverential, sacred; earnest, grave, serious, sober; august, awe-inspiring, awful, grand, imposing, impressive, majestic, stately, venerable.

solemnity *n* celebration, ceremony, observance, office, rite; awfulness, sacredness, sanctity; gravity, impressiveness, seriousness.

solemnize *vb* celebrate, commemorate, honour, keep, observe.

solicit *vb* appeal to, ask, beg, beseech, conjure, crave, entreat, implore, importune, petition, pray, press, request, supplicate, urge; arouse, awaken, entice, excite, invite, summon; canvass, seek.

solicitation *n* address, appeal, asking, entreaty, imploration, importunity, insistence, petition, request, suit, supplication, urgency; bidding, call, invitation, summons.

solicitor *n* attorney, law agent, lawyer; asker, canvasser, drummer, petitioner, solicitant.

solicitous *adj* anxious, apprehensive, careful, concerned, disturbed, eager, troubled, uneasy.

solicitude *n* anxiety, care, carefulness, concern, perplexity, trouble.

solid *adj* congealed, firm, hard, impenetrable, rock-like; compact, dense, impermeable, massed; cubic; sound, stable, stout, strong, substantial; just, real, true, valid, weighty; dependable, faithful, reliable, safe, staunch, steadfast, trustworthy, well established.

solidarity *n* communion of interests, community, consolidation, fellowship, joint interest, mutual responsibility.

solidify *vb* compact, congeal, consolidate, harden, petrify.

solidity *n* compactness, consistency, density, firmness, hardness, solidness; fullness; massiveness, stability, strength; dependability, gravity, justice, reliability, soundness, steadiness, validity, weight; cubic content, volume.

soliloquy *n* monologue.

solitariness *n* isolation, privacy, reclusion, retirement, seclusion; loneliness, solitude.

solitary *adj* alone, companionless, lone, lonely, only, separate, unaccompanied; individual, single, sole; desert, deserted, desolate, isolated, lonely, remote, retired, secluded, unfrequented.

solitude *n* isolation, loneliness, privacy, recluseness, retiredness, retirement, seclusion, solitariness; desert, waste, wilderness.

solution *n* answer, clue, disentanglement, elucidation, explication, explanation, key, resolution, unravelling, unriddling; disintegration, dissolution, liquefaction, melting, resolution, separation; breach, disconnection, discontinuance, disjunction, disruption.

solve *vb* clear, clear up, disentangle, elucidate, explain, expound, interpret, make

plain, resolve, unfold.
solvent *n* diluent, dissolvent, menstruum.
somatic *adj* bodily, corporeal.
sombre *adj* cloudy, dark, dismal, dull, dusky, gloomy, murky, overcast, rayless, shady, sombrous, sunless; doleful, funereal, grave, lugubrious, melancholy, mournful, sad, sober.
some *adj* a, an, any, one; about, near; certain, little, moderate, part, several.
somebody *n* one, someone, something; celebrity, VIP.
somehow *adv* in some way.
something *n* part, portion, thing; somebody; affair, event, matter.
sometime *adj* former, late. * *adv* formerly, once; now and then, at one time or other, sometimes.
sometimes *adv* at intervals, at times, now and then, occasionally; at a past period, formerly, once.
somewhat *adv* in some degree, more or less, rather, something. * *n* something, a little, more or less, part.
somewhere *adv* here and there, in one place or another, in some place.
somnambulism *n* sleepwalking, somnambulation.
somnambulist *n* night-walker, noctambulist, sleepwalker, somnambulator, somnambule.
somniferous *adj* narcotic, opiate, slumberous, somnific, soporific, soporiferous.
somnolence *n* doziness, drowsiness, sleepiness, somnolency.
somnolent *adj* dozy, drowsy, sleepy.
son *n* cadet, heir, junior, scion.
song *n* aria, ballad, canticle, carol, ditty, glee, lay, lullaby, snatch; descant, melody; anthem, hymn, poem, psalm, strain; poesy, poetry, verse.
sonorous *adj* full-toned, resonant, resounding, ringing, sounding; high-sounding, loud.
soon *adv* anon, before long, by and by, in a short time, presently, shortly; betimes, early, forthwith, promptly, quick; gladly, lief, readily, willingly.
soot *n* carbon, crock, dust.
soothe *vb* cajole, flatter, humour; appease, assuage, balm, calm, compose, lull, mollify, pacify, quiet, soften, still, tranquillize; allay, alleviate, blunt, check, deaden, dull, ease, lessen, mitigate, moderate, palliate, qualify, relieve, repress, soften, subdue, temper.
soothsayer *n* augur, diviner, foreteller, necromancer, predictor, prophet, seer, sorcerer, vaticinator.
sooty *adj* black, dark, dusky, fuliginous, murky, sable.
sophism *n* casuistry, fallacy, paralogism, paralogy, quibble, specious argument.
sophist *n* quibbler.
sophistical *adj* casuistical, fallacious, illogical, quibbling, subtle, unsound.
soporific *adj* dormitive, hypnotic, narcotic, opiate, sleepy, slumberous, somnific, somniferous, soporiferous, soporous.
soppy *adj* drenched, saturated, soaked, sopped; emotional, mawkish, sentimental.
soprano *n* (*mus*) descant, discant, treble.
sorcerer *n* charmer, conjurer, diviner, enchanter, juggler, magician, necromancers, seer, shaman, soothsayer, thaumaturgist, wizard.
sorcery *n* black art, charm, divination, enchantment, necromancy, occultism, shamanism, spell, thaumaturgy, voodoo, witchcraft.
sordid *adj* base, degraded, low, mean, vile; avaricious, close-fisted, covetous, illiberal, miserly, niggardly, penurious, stingy, ungenerous.
sore *adj* irritated, painful, raw, tender, ulcerated; aggrieved, galled, grieved, hurt, irritable, vexed; afflictive, distressing, severe, sharp, violent. * *n* abscess, boil, fester, gathering, imposthume, pustule, ulcer; affliction, grief, pain, sorrow, trouble.
sorely *adv* greatly, grievously, severely, violently.
sorrily *adv* despicably, meanly, pitiably, poorly, wretchedly.
sorrow *vb* bemoan, bewail, grieve, lament, mourn, weep. * *n* affliction, dolour, grief,

heartache, mourning, sadness, trouble, woe.

sorrowful *adj* afflicted, dejected, depressed, grieved, grieving, heartsore, sad; baleful, distressing, grievous, lamentable, melancholy, mournful, painful; disconsolate, dismal, doleful, dolorous, drear, dreary, lugubrious, melancholy, piteous, rueful, woebegone, woeful.

sorry *adj* afflicted, dejected, grieved, pained, poor, sorrowful; distressing, pitiful; chagrined, mortified, pained, regretful, remorseful, sad, vexed; abject, base, beggarly, contemptible, despicable, low, mean, paltry, insignificant, miserable, shabby, worthless, wretched.

sort *vb* arrange, assort, class, classify, distribute, order; conjoin, join, put together; choose, elect, pick out, select; associate, consort, fraternize; accord, agree with, fit, suit. * *n* character, class, denomination, description, kind, nature, order, race, rank, species, type; manner, way.

sortie *n* attack, foray, raid, sally.

so-so *adj* indifferent, mediocre, middling, ordinary, passable, tolerable.

sot *n* blockhead, dolt, dullard, dunce, fool, simpleton; drunkard, tippler, toper.

sottish *adj* doltish, dull, foolish, senseless, simple, stupid; befuddled, besotted, drunken, insensate, senseless, tipsy.

sotto voce *adv* in a low voice, in an undertone, softly.

sough *n* murmur, sigh; breath, breeze, waft.

soul *n* mind, psyche, spirit; being, person; embodiment, essence, personification, spirit, vital principle; ardour, energy, fervour, inspiration, vitality.

soulless *adj* dead, expressionless, lifeless, unfeeling.

sound[1] *adj* entire, intact, unbroken, unhurt, unimpaired, uninjured, unmutilated, whole; hale, hardy, healthy, hearty, vigorous; good, perfect, undecayed; sane, well-balanced; correct, orthodox, right, solid, valid, well-founded; legal; deep, fast, profound, unbroken, undisturbed; forcible, lusty, severe, stout.

sound[2] *n* channel, narrows, strait.

sound[3] *vb* resound; appear, seem; play on; express, pronounce, utter; announce, celebrate, proclaim, publish, spread. * *n* noise, note, tone, voice, whisper.

sound[4] *vb* fathom, gauge, measure, test; examine, probe, search, test, try.

sounding *adj* audible, resonant, resounding, ringing, sonorous; imposing, significant.

soundless *adj* dumb, noiseless, silent; abysmal, bottomless, deep, profound, unfathomable, unsounded.

soundly *adv* satisfactorily, thoroughly, well; healthily, heartily; forcibly, lustily, severely, smartly, stoutly; correctly, rightly, truly; firmly, strongly; deeply, fast, profoundly.

soundness *n* entireness, entirety, integrity, wholeness; healithness, vigour, saneness, sanity; correctness, orthodoxy, rectitude, reliability, truth, validity; firmness, solidity, strength, validity.

soup *n* broth, consommé, purée.

sour *vb* acidulate; embitter, envenom. * *adj* acetose, acetous, acid, astringent, pricked, sharp, tart, vinegary; acrimonious, crabbed, cross, crusty, fretful, glum, ill-humoured, ill-natured, ill-tempered, peevish, pettish, petulant, snarling, surly; bitter, disagreeable, unpleasant; austere, dismal, gloomy, morose, sad, sullen; bad, coagulated, curdled, musty, rancid, turned.

source *n* beginning, fountain, fountainhead, head, origin, rise, root, spring, well; cause, original.

sourness *n* acidity, sharpness, tartness; acrimony, asperity, churlishness, crabbedness, crossness, discontent, harshness, moroseness, peevishness.

souse *vb* pickle; dip, douse, immerse, plunge, submerge.

souvenir *n* keepsake, memento, remembrance, reminder.

sovereign *adj* imperial, monarchical, princely, regal, royal, supreme; chief, commanding, excellent, highest, paramount, predominant, principal, supreme, utmost; efficacious, effectual. * *n* autocrat, monarch, suzerain; emperor, empress, king, lord, potentate, prince, princess, queen, ruler.

sovereignty *n* authority, dominion, empire, power, rule, supremacy, sway.

sow *vb* scatter, spread, strew; disperse, disseminate, propagate, spread abroad; plant; besprinkle, scatter.

space *n* expanse, expansion, extension, extent, proportions, spread; accommodation, capacity, room, place; distance, interspace, interval.

spacious *adj* extended, extensive, vast, wide; ample, broad, capacious, commodious, large, roomy, wide.

span *vb* compass, cross, encompass, measure, overlay. * *n* brief period, spell; pair, team, yoke.

spank *vb* slap, strike.

spar[1] *n* beam, boom, pole, sprit, yard.

spar[2] *vb* box, fight; argue, bicker, contend, dispute, quarrel, spat, squabble, wrangle.

spare *vb* lay aside, lay by, reserve, save, set apart, set aside; dispense with, do without, part with; forbear, omit, refrain, withhold; exempt, forgive, keep from; afford, allow, give, grant; save; economize, pinch. * *adj* frugal, scanty, sparing, stinted; chary, parsimonious; emaciated, gaunt, lank, lean, meagre, poor, thin, scraggy, skinny, raw-boned; additional, extra, supernumerary.

sparing *adj* little, scanty, scarce; abstemious, meagre, spare; chary, economical, frugal, parsimonious, saving; compassionate, forgiving, lenient, merciful.

spark *vb* scintillate, sparkle; begin, fire, incite, instigate, kindle, light, set off, start, touch off, trigger. * *n* scintilla, scintillation, sparkle; beginning, element, germ, seed.

sparkle *vb* coruscate, flash, gleam, glisten, glister, glitter, radiate, scintillate, shine, twinkle; bubble, effervesce, foam, froth. * *n* glint, scintillation, spark; luminosity, lustre.

sparkling *adj* brilliant, flashing, glistening, glittering, glittery, twinkling; bubbling, effervescing, eloquent, foaming, frothing, mantling; brilliant, glowing, lively, nervous, piquant, racy, spirited, sprightly, witty.

sparse *adj* dispersed, infrequent, scanty, scattered, sporadic, thin.

spartan *adj* bold, brave, chivalric, courageous, daring, dauntless, doughty, fearless, hardy, heroic, intrepid, lion-hearted, undaunted, valiant, valorous; austere, exacting, hard, severe, tough, unsparing; enduring, long-suffering, self-controlled, stoic.

spasm *n* contraction, cramp, crick, twitch; fit, paroxysm, seizure, throe.

spasmodic *adj* erratic, fitful, intermittent, irregular, sporadic; convulsive, paroxysmal, spasmodical, violent.

spat *vb* argue, bicker, dispute, jangle, quarrel, spar, squabble, wrangle.

spatter *vb* bespatter, besprinkle, plash, splash, sprinkle; spit, sputter.

spawn *vb* bring forth, generate, produce. * *n* eggs, roe; fruit, offspring, product.

speak *vb* articulate, deliver, enunciate, express, pronounce, utter; announce, confer, declare, disclose, mention, say, tell; celebrate, make known, proclaim, speak abroad; accost, address, greet, hail; exhibit; argue, converse, dispute, talk; declaim, discourse, hold forth, harangue, orate, plead, spout, treat.

speaker *n* discourse, elocutionist, orator, prolocutor, spokesman; chairman, presiding officer.

speaking *adj* rhetorical, talking; eloquent, expressive; lifelike. * *n* discourse, talk, utterance;

declamation, elocution, oratory.

spear *n* dart, gaff, harpoon, javelin, lance, pike; shoot, spire.

special *adj* specific, specifical; especial, individual, particular, peculiar, unique; exceptional, extraordinary, marked, particular, uncommon; appropriate, express.

speciality, specialty *n* particularity; feature, forte, pet subject.

species *n* assemblage, class, collection, group; description, kind, sort, variety; (*law*) fashion, figure, form, shape.

specific *adj* characteristic, especial, particular, peculiar; definite, limited, precise, specified.

specification *n* characterization, designation; details, particularization.

specify *vb* define, designate, detail, indicate, individualize, name, show, particularize.

specimen *n* copy, example, model, pattern, sample.

specious *adj* manifest, obvious, open, showy; flimsy, illusory, ostensible, plausible, sophistical.

speck *n* blemish, blot, flaw, speckle, spot, stain; atom, bit, corpuscle, mite, mote, particle, scintilla.

spectacle *n* display, exhibition, pageant, parade, representation, review, scene, show, sight; curiosity, marvel, phenomenon, wonder.

spectacles *npl* glasses, goggles, shades.

spectator *n* beholder, bystander, observer, onlooker, witness.

spectral *adj* eerie, ghostlike, ghostly, phantomlike, shadowy, spooky, weird, wraithlike.

spectre, specter *n* apparition, banshee, ghost, goblin, hobgoblin, phantom, shade, shadow, spirit, sprite, wraith.

spectrum *n* appearance, image, representation.

speculate *vb* cogitate, conjecture, contemplate, imagine, meditate, muse, ponder, reflect, ruminate, theorize, think; bet, gamble, hazard, risk, trade, venture.

speculation *n* contemplation, intellectualization; conjecture, hypothesis, scheme, supposition, reasoning, reflection, theory, view.

speculative *adj* contemplative, philosophical, speculatory, unpractical; ideal, imaginary, theoretical; hazardous, risky, unsecured.

speculator *n* speculatist, theorist, theorizer; adventurer, dealer, gambler, trader.

speech *n* articulation, language, words; dialect, idiom, locution, tongue; conversation, oral communication, parlance, talk, verbal intercourse; mention, observation, remark, saying; address, declaration, discourse, harangue, oration, palaver.

speechless *adj* dumb, gagged, inarticulate, mute, silent; dazed, dumbfounded, flabbergasted, shocked.

speed *vb* hasten, hurry, rush, scurry; flourish, prosper, succeed, thrive; accelerate, expedite, hasten, hurry, quicken, press forward, urge on; carry through, dispatch, execute; advance, aid, assist, help; favour. * *n* acceleration, celerity, dispatch, expedition, fleetness, haste, hurry, quickness, rapidity, swiftness, velocity; good fortune, good luck, prosperity, success; impetuosity.

speedy *adj* fast, fleet, flying, hasty, hurried, hurrying, nimble, quick, rapid, swift; expeditious, prompt, quick; approaching, early, near.

spell[1] *n* charm, exorcism, hoodoo, incantation, jinx, witchery; allure, bewitchment, captivation, enchantment, entrancement, fascination.

spell[2] *vb* decipher, interpret, read, unfold, unravel, unriddle.

spell[3] *n* fit, interval, period, round, season, stint, term, turn.

spellbound *adj* bewitched, charmed, enchanted, entranced, enthralled, fascinated.

spend *vb* disburse, dispose of, expend, lay out, part with; consume, dissipate, exhaust, lavish, squander, use up, wear, waste; apply, bestow, devote, employ, pass.

spendthrift *n* prodigal, spender, squanderer, waster.

spent *adj* exhausted, fatigued, played out, used up, wearied, worn out.

spew *vb* cast up, puke, throw up, vomit; cast forth, eject.

spheral *adj* complete, perfect, symmetrical.

sphere *n* ball, globe, orb, spheroid; ambit, beat, bound, circle, circuit, compass, department, function, office, orbit, province, range, walk; order, rank, standing; country, domain, quarter, realm, region.

spherical *adj* bulbous, globated, globous, globular, orbicular, rotund, round, spheroid; planetary.

spice *n* flavour, flavouring, relish, savour,

taste; admixture, dash, grain, infusion, particle, smack, soupçon, sprinkling, tincture.

spicily *adv* pungently, wittily.

spicy *adj* aromatic, balmy, fragrant; keen, piquant, pointed, pungent, sharp; indelicate, off-colour, racy, risqué, sensational, suggestive.

spill *vb* effuse, pour out, shed. * *n* accident, fall, tumble.

spin *vb* twist; draw out, extend; lengthen, prolong, protract, spend; pirouette, turn, twirl, whirl. * *n* drive, joyride, ride; autorotation, gyration, loop, revolution, rotation, turning, wheeling; pirouette, reel, turn, wheel, whirl.

spindle *n* axis, shaft.

spine *n* barb, prickle, thorn; backbone; ridge.

spinose *adj* briery, spinous, spiny, thorny.

spiny *adj* briery, prickly, spinose, spinous, thorny; difficult, perplexed, troublesome.

spiracle *n* aperture, blowhole, orifice, pore, vent.

spiral *adj* cochlear, cochleated, curled, helical, screw-shaped, spiry, winding. * *n* helix, winding, worm.

spire *n* curl, spiral, twist, wreath; steeple; blade, shoot, spear, stalk; apex, summit.

spirit *vb* animate, encourage, excite, inspirit; carry off, kidnap. * *n* immaterial substance, life, vital essence; person, soul; angel, apparition, demon, elf, fairy, genius, ghost, phantom, shade, spectre, sprite; disposition, frame of mind, humour, mood, temper; spirits; ardour, cheerfulness, courage, earnestness, energy, enterprise, enthusiasm, fire, force, mettle, resolution, vigour, vim, vivacity, zeal; animation, cheerfulness, enterprise, esprit, glow, liveliness, piquancy, spice, spunk, vivacity, warmth; drift, gist, intent, meaning, purport, sense, significance, tenor; character, characteristic, complexion, essence, nature, quality, quintessence; alcohol, liquor; (*with* **the**) Comforter, Holy Ghost, Paraclete.

spirited *adj* active, alert, animated, ardent, bold, brisk, courageous, earnest, frisky, high-mettled, high-spirited, high-strung, lively, mettlesome, sprightly, vivacious.

spiritless *adj* breathless, dead, extinct, lifeless; dejected, depressed, discouraged, dispirited, low-spirited; apathetic, cold, dull, feeble, languid, phlegmatic, sluggish, soulless, torpid, unenterprising; dull, frigid, heavy, insipid, prosaic, prosy, stupid, tame, uninteresting.

spiritual *adj* ethereal, ghostly, immaterial incorporeal, psychical, supersensible; ideal, moral, unwordly; divine, holy, pure, sacred; ecclesiastical.

spiritualize *vb* elevate, etherealize, purify, refine.

spirituous *adj* alcoholic, ardent, spiritous.

spit[1] *vb* impale, thrust through, transfix.

spit[2] *vb* eject, throw out; drivel, drool, expectorate, salivate, slobber, spawl, splutter. * *n* saliva, spawl, spittle, sputum.

spite *vb* injure, mortify, thwart; annoy, offend, vex. * *n* grudge, hate, hatred, ill-nature, ill-will, malevolence, malice, maliciousness, malignity, pique, rancour, spleen, venom, vindictiveness.

spiteful *adj* evil-minded, hateful, ill-disposed, ill-natured, malevolent, malicious, malign, malignant, rancorous.

spittoon *n* cuspidor.

splash *vb* dabble, dash, plash, spatter, splurge, swash, swish. * *n* blot, daub, spot.

splay *adj* broad, spreading out, turned out, wide.

spleen *n* anger, animosity, chagrin, gall, grudge, hatred, ill-humour, irascibility, malevolence, malice, malignity, peevishness, pique, rancour, spite.

spleeny *adj* angry, fretful, ill-tempered, irritable, peevish, spleenish, splenetic.

splendid *adj* beaming, bright, brilliant, effulgent, glowing, lustrous, radiant, refulgent, resplendent, shining; dazzling, gorgeous, imposing, kingly, magnificent, pompous, showy, sumptuous, superb; celebrated, conspicuous, distinguished, eminent, excellent, famous, glorious, illustrious, noble, pre-eminent, remarkable, signal; grand, heroic, lofty, noble, sublime.

splendour *n* brightness, brilliance, brilliancy, lustre, radiance, refulgence; display, éclat, gorgeousness, grandeur, magnificence, parade, pomp, show, showiness, stateliness; celebrity, eminence, fame, glory, grandeur, renown; grandeur, loftiness, nobleness, sublimity.

splenetic *adj* choleric, cross, fretful, irascible, irritable, peevish, pettish, petulant, snappish, testy, touchy, waspish; churlish, crabbed, morose, sour, sulky, sullen; gloomy, jaundiced.

splice *vb* braid, connect, join, knit, mortise.

splinter *vb* rend, shiver, sliver, split. * *n* fragment, piece.

split *vb* cleave, rive; break, burst, rend, splinter; divide, part, separate, sunder. * *n* crack, fissure, rent; breach, division, separation.

splotch *n* blot, daub, smear, spot, stain.

splutter *vb* sputter, stammer, stutter.

spoil *vb* despoil, fleece, loot, pilfer, plunder, ravage, rob, steal, strip, waste; corrupt, damage, destroy, disfigure, harm, impair, injure, mar, ruin, vitiate; decay, decompose. * *n* booty, loot, pillage, plunder, prey; rapine, robbery, spoliation, waste.

spoiler *n* pillager, plunderer, robber; corrupter, destroyer.

spokesman *n* mouthpiece, prolocutor, speaker.

spoliate *vb* despoil, destroy, loot, pillage, plunder, rob, spoil.

spoliation *n* depradation, deprivation, despoliation, destruction, robbery; destruction, devastation, pillage, plundering, rapine, ravagement.

sponge *vb* cleanse, wipe; efface, expunge, obliterate, rub out, wipe out.

sponger *n* hanger-on, parasite.

spongy *adj* absorbent, porous, spongeous; rainy, showery, wet; drenched, marshy, saturated, soaked, wet.

sponsor *vb* back, capitalize, endorse, finance, guarantee, patronize, promote, support, stake, subsidize, take up, underwrite. * *n* angel, backer, guarantor, patron, promoter, supporter, surety, underwriter; godfather, godmother, godparent.

spontaneity *n* improvisation, impulsiveness, spontaneousness.

spontaneous *adj* free, gratuitous, impulsive, improvised, instinctive, self-acting, self-moving, unbidden, uncompelled, unconstrained, voluntary, willing.

sporadic *adj* dispersed, infrequent, isolated, rare, scattered, separate, spasmodic.

sport *vb* caper, disport, frolic, gambol, have fun, make merry, play, romp, skip; trifle; display, exhibit. * *n* amusement, diversion, entertainment, frolic, fun, gambol, game, jollity, joviality, merriment, merry-making, mirth, pastime, pleasantry, prank, recreation; jest, joke; derision, jeer, mockery, ridicule; monstrosity.

sportive *adj* frisky, frolicsome, gamesome, hilarious, lively, merry, playful, prankish, rollicking, sprightly, tricksy; comic, facetious, funny, humorous, jocose, jocular, lively, ludicrous, mirthful, vivacious, waggish.

spot *vb* besprinkle, dapple, dot, speck, stud, variegate; blemish, disgrace, soil, splotch, stain, sully, tarnish; detect, discern, espy, make out, observe, see, sight. * *n* blot, dapple, fleck, freckle, maculation, mark, mottle, patch, pip, speck, speckle; blemish, blotch, flaw, pock, splotch, stain, taint; locality, place, site.

spotless *adj* perfect, undefaced, unspotted; blameless, immaculate, innocent, irreproachable, pure, stainless, unblemished, unstained, untainted, untarnished.

spotted *adj* bespeckled, bespotted, dotted, flecked, freckled, maculated, ocellated, speckled, spotty.

spousal *adj* bridal, conjugal, connubial, hymeneal, marital, matrimonial, nuptial, wedded.

spouse *n* companion, consort, husband, mate, partner, wife.

spout *vb* gush, jet, pour out, spirit, spurt, squirt; declaim, mouth, speak, utter. * *n* conduit, tube; beak, nose, nozzle, waterspout.

sprain *vb* overstrain, rick, strain, twist,

wrench, wrick.

spray[1] *vb* atomize, besprinkle, douche, gush, jet, shower, splash, splatter, spout, sprinkle, squirt. * *n* aerosol, atomizer, douche, foam, froth, shower, sprinkler, spume.

spray[2] *n* bough, branch, shoot, sprig, twig.

spread *vb* dilate, expand, extend, mantle, stretch; diffuse, disperse, distribute, radiate, scatter, sprinkle, strew; broadcast, circulate, disseminate, divulge, make known, make public, promulgate, propagate, publish; open, unfold, unfurl; cover, extend over, overspread. * *n* compass, extent, range, reach, scope, stretch; expansion, extension; circulation, dissemination, propagation; cloth, cover; banquet, feast, meal.

spree *n* bacchanal, carousal, debauch, frolic, jollification, orgy, revel, revelry, saturnalia.

sprig *n* shoot, spray, twig; lad, youth.

sprightliness *n* animation, activity, briskness, cheerfulness, frolicsomeness, gaiety, life, liveliness, nimbleness, vigour, vivacity.

sprightly *adj* airy, animated, blithe, blithesome, brisk, buoyant, cheerful, debonair, frolicsome, joyous, lively, mercurial, vigorous, vivacious.

spring *vb* bound, hop, jump, leap, prance, vault; arise, emerge, grow, issue, proceed, put forth, shoot forth, stem; derive, descend, emanate, flow, originate, rise, start; fly back, rebound, recoil; bend, warp; grow, thrive, wax. * *adj* hopping, jumping, resilient, springy. * *n* bound, hop, jump, leap, vault; elasticity, flexibility, resilience, resiliency, springiness; fount, fountain, fountainhead, geyser, springhead, well; cause, origin, original, principle, source; seed time, springtime.

springe *n* gin, net, noose, snare, trap.

springiness *n* elasticity, resilience, spring; sponginess, wetness.

springy *adj* bouncing, bounding, elastic, rebounding, recoiling, resilient.

sprinkle *vb* scatter, strew; bedew, besprinkle, dust, powder, sand, spatter; wash, cleanse, purify, shower.

sprinkling *n* affusion, baptism, bedewing, spattering, splattering, spraying, wetting; dash, scattering, seasoning, smack, soupçon, suggestion, tinge, touch, trace, vestige.

sprite *n* apparition, elf, fairy, ghost, goblin, hobgoblin, phantom, pixie, shade, spectre, spirit.

sprout *vb* burgeon, burst forth, germinate, grow, pullulate, push, put forth, ramify, shoot, shoot forth. * *n* shoot, sprig.

spruce *vb* preen, prink; adorn, deck, dress, smarten, trim. * *adj* dandyish, dapper, fine, foppish, jaunty, natty, neat, nice, smart, tidy, trig, trim.

spry *adj* active, agile, alert, brisk, lively, nimble, prompt, quick, ready, smart, sprightly, stirring, supple.

spume *n* foam, froth, scum, spray.

spumy *adj* foamy, frothy, spumous.

spur *vb* gallop, hasten, press on, prick; animate, arouse, drive, goad, impel, incite, induce, instigate, rouse, stimulate, urge forward. * *n* goad, point, prick, rowel; fillip, impulse, incentive, incitement, inducement, instigation, motive, provocation, stimulus, whip; gnarl, knob, knot, point, projection, snag.

spurious *adj* bogus, counterfeit, deceitful, false, feigned, fictitious, make-believe, meretricious, mock, pretended, sham, supposititious, unauthentic.

spurn *vb* drive away, kick; contemn, despise, disregard, flout, scorn, slight; disdain, reject, repudiate.

spurt *vb* gush, jet, spirt, spout, spring out, stream out, well. * *n* gush, jet, spout, squirt; burst, dash, rush.

sputter *vb* spawl, spit, splutter, stammer.

spy *vb* behold, discern, espy, see; detect, discover, search out; explore, inspect, scrutinize, search; shadow, trail, watch. * *n* agent, detective, double agent, mole, scout, undercover agent.

squabble *vb* brawl, fight, quarrel, scuffle, struggle, wrangle; altercate, bicker, contend, dispute, jangle. * *n* brawl, dispute, fight, quarrel, rumpus, scrimmage.

squad *n* band, bevy, crew, gang, knot, lot, relay, set.

squalid *adj* dirty, filthy, foul, mucky, slovenly, unclean, unkempt.
squalidness *n* filthiness, foulness, squalidity, squalor.
squall *vb* bawl, cry, cry out, scream, yell. * *n* bawl, cry, outcry, scream, yell; blast, flurry, gale, gust, hurricane, storm, tempest.
squally *adj* blustering, blustery, gusty, stormy, tempestuous, windy.
squander *vb* dissipate, expend, lavish, lose, misuse, scatter, spend, throw away, waste.
squanderer *n* lavisher, prodigal, spendthrift, waster.
square *vb* make square, quadrate; accommodate, adapt, fit, mould, regulate, shape, suit; adjust, balance, close, make even, settle; accord, chime in, cohere, comport, fall in, fit, harmonize, quadrate, suit. * *adj* four-square, quadrilateral, quadrate; equal, equitable, exact, fair, honest, just, upright; adjusted, balanced, even, settled; true, suitable. * *n* four-sided figure, quadrate, rectangle, tetragon; open area, parade, piazza, plaza.
squash *vb* crush, mash.
squashy *adj* pulpy, soft.
squat *vb* cower, crouch; occupy, plant, settle. * *adj* cowering, crouching; dumpy, pudgy, short, stocky, stubby, thickset.
squeal *vb* creak, cry, howl, scream, screech, shriek, squawk, yell; betray, inform on. * *n* creak, cry, howl, scream, screech, shriek, squawk, yell.
squeamish *adj* nauseated, qualmish, queasy, sickish; dainty, delicate, fastidious, finical, hypercritical, nice, overnice, particular, priggish.
squeeze *vb* clutch, compress, constrict, grip, nip, pinch, press; drive, force; crush, harass, oppress; crowd, force through; press; (*with* **out**) extract. * *n* congestion, crowd, crush, throng; compression.
squelch *vb* crush, quash, quell, silence, squash, suppress.
squib *n* firework, fuse; lampoon, pasquinade, satire.
squint *vb* look askance, look obliquely, peer. * *adj* askew, aslant, crooked, oblique, skew, skewed, twisted.
squire *vb* accompany, attend, escort, wait on.
squirm *vb* twist, wriggle, writhe.
squirt *vb* eject, jet, splash, spurt.
stab *vb* broach, gore, jab, pierce, pink, spear, stick, transfix, transpierce; wound. * *n* cut, jab, prick, thrust; blow, dagger-stroke, injury, wound.
stability *n* durability, firmness, fixedness, immovability, permanence, stableness, steadiness; constancy, firmness, reliability.
stable *adj* established, fixed, immovable, immutable, invariable, permanent, unalterable, unchangeable; constant, firm, staunch, steadfast, steady, unwavering; abiding, durable, enduring, fast, lasting, permanent, perpetual, secure, sure.
staff *n* baton, cane, pole, rod, stick, wand; bat, bludgeon, club, cudgel, mace; prop, stay, support; employees, personnel, team, workers, work force.
stage *vb* dramatize, perform, present, produce, put on. * *n* dais, platform, rostrum, scaffold, staging, stand; arena, field; boards, playhouse, theatre; degree, point, step; diligence, omnibus, stagecoach.
stagey *adj* bombastic, declamatory, dramatic, melodramatic, ranting, theatrical.
stagger *vb* reel, sway, totter; alternate, fluctuate, overlap, vacillate, vary; falter, hesitate, waver; amaze, astonish, astound, confound, dumbfound, nonplus, pose, shock, surprise.
stagnant *adj* close, motionless, quiet, standing; dormant, dull, heavy, inactive, inert, sluggish, torpid.
stagnate *vb* decay, deteriorate, languish, rot, stand still, vegetate.
staid *adj* calm, composed, demure, grave, sedate, serious, settled, sober, solemn, steady, unadventurous.
stain *vb* blemish, blot, blotch, discolour, maculate, smirch, soil, splotch, spot, sully, tarnish; colour, dye, tinge; contaminate, corrupt, debase, defile, deprave, disgrace, dishonour, pollute, taint. * n blemish, blot, defect, discoloration, flaw, imperfection, spot, tarnish; contamina-

tion, disgrace, dishonour, infamy, pollution, reproach, shame, taint, tarnish.

stainless *adj* spotless, unspotted, untarnished; blameless, faultless, innocent, guiltless, pure, spotless, uncorrupted, unsullied.

stairs *npl* flight of steps, staircase, stairway.

stake[1] *vb* brace, mark, prop, secure, support. * *n* pale, palisade, peg, picket, post, stick.

stake[2] *vb* finance, pledge, wager; hazard, imperil, jeopardize, peril, risk, venture. * *n* bet, pledge, wager; adventure, hazard, risk, venture.

stale *adj* flat, fusty, insipid, mawkish, mouldy, musty, sour, tasteless, vapid; decayed, effete, faded, old, time-worn, worn-out; common, commonplace, hackneyed, stereotyped, threadbare, trite.

stalk[1] *n* culm, pedicel, peduncle, petiole, shaft, spire, stem, stock.

stalk[2] *vb* march, pace, stride, strut, swagger; follow, hunt, shadow, track, walk stealthily.

stall[1] *n* stable; cell, compartment, recess; booth, kiosk, shop, stand.

stall[2] *vb* block, delay, equivocate, filibuster, hinder, postpone, procrastinate, temporize; arrest, check, conk out, die, fail, halt, stick, stop.

stalwart *adj* able-bodied, athletic, brawny, lusty, muscular, powerful, robust, sinewy, stout, strapping, strong, sturdy, vigorous; bold, brave, daring, gallant, indomitable, intrepid, redoubtable, resolute, valiant, valorous. * *n* backer, member, partisan, supporter.

stamina *n* energy, force, lustiness, power, stoutness, strength, sturdiness, vigour.

stammer *vb* falter, hesitate, stutter. * *n* faltering, hesitation, stutter.

stamp *vb* brand, impress, imprint, mark, print. * *n* brand, impress, impression, print; cast, character, complexion, cut, description, fashion, form, kind, make, mould, sort, type.

stampede *vb* charge, flee, panic. * *n* charge, flight, rout, running away, rush.

stanch *see* **staunch**[1].

stanchion *n* prop, shore, stay, support.

stand *vb* be erect, remain upright; abide, be fixed, continue, endure, hold good, remain; halt, pause, stop; be firm, be resolute, stand ground, stay; be valid, have force; depend, have support, rest; bear, brook, endure, suffer, sustain, weather; abide, admit, await, submit, tolerate, yield; fix, place, put, set upright; (*with* **against**) oppose, resist, withstand; (*with* **by**) be near, be present; aid, assist, defend, help, side with, support; defend, make good, justify, maintain, support, vindicate; (*naut*) attend, be ready; (*with* **fast**) be fixed, be immovable; (*with* **for**) mean, represent, signify; aid, defend, help, maintain, side with, support; (*with* **off**) keep aloof, keep off; not to comply; (*with* **out**) be prominent, jut, project, protrude; not comply, not yield, persist; (*with* **up for**) defend, justify, support, sustain, uphold; (*with* **with**) agree. * *n* place, position, post, standing place, station; halt, stay, stop; dais, platform, rostrum; booth, stall; opposition, resistance.

standard[1] *n* banner, colours, ensign, flag, gonfalon, pennon, streamer.

standard[2] *adj* average, conventional, customary, normal, ordinary, regular, usual; accepted, approved, authoritative, orthodox, received; formulary, prescriptive, regulation. * *n* canon, criterion, model, norm, rule, test, type; gauge, measure, model, scale; support, upright.

standing *adj* established, fixed, immovable, settled; durable, lasting, permanent; motionless, stagnant. * *n* position, stand, station; continuance, duration, existence; footing, ground, hold; condition, estimation, rank, reputation, status.

standpoint *n* point of view, viewpoint.

standstill *n* cessation, interruption, stand, stop; deadlock.

stanza *n* measure, staff, stave, strophe, verse.

staple *adj* basic, chief, essential, fundamental, main, primary, principal. * *n* fibre, filament, pile, thread; body, bulk, mass, substance.

star *vb* act, appear, feature, headline, lead,

perform, play; emphasize, highlight, stress, underline. * *adj* leading, main, paramount, principal; celebrated, illustrious, well-known. * *n* heavenly body, luminary; asterisk, pentacle, pentagram; destiny, doom, fate, fortune, lot; diva, headliner, hero, heroine, lead, leading lady, leading man, prima ballerina, prima donna, principal, protagonist.

starchy *adj* ceremonious, exact, formal, precise, prim, punctilious, rigid, starched, stiff.

stare *vb* gape, gaze, look intently, watch.

stark *adj* rigid, stiff; absolute, bare, downright, entire, gross, mere, pure, sheer, simple. * *adv* absolutely, completely, entirely, fully, wholly.

starry *adj* astral, sidereal, star-spangled, stellar; bright, brilliant, lustrous, shining, sparkling, twinkling.

start *vb* begin, commence, inaugurate, initiate, institute; discover, invent; flinch, jump, shrink, startle, wince; alarm, disturb, fright, rouse, scare; depart, set off, take off; arise, call forth, evoke, raise; dislocate, move suddenly, spring. * *n* beginning, commencement, inauguration, outset; fit, jump, spasm, twitch; impulse, sally.

startle *vb* flinch, shrink, start, wince; affright, alarm, fright, frighten, scare, shock; amaze, astonish, astound.

startling *adj* abrupt, alarming, astonishing, shocking, sudden, surprising, unexpected, unforeseen, unheard of.

starvation *n* famine, famishment.

starve *vb* famish, perish; be in need, lack, want; kill, subdue.

starveling *adj* attenuated, emaciated, gaunt, hungry, lank, lean, meagre, scraggy, skinny, thin. * *n* beggar, mendicant, pauper.

state *vb* affirm, assert, aver, declare, explain, expound, express, narrate, propound, recite, say, set forth, specify, voice. * *adj* civic, national, public. * *n* case, circumstances, condition, pass, phase, plight, position, posture, predicament, situation, status; condition, guise, mode, quality, rank; dignity, glory, grandeur, magnificence, pageantry, parade, pomp, spendour; body politic, civil community, commonwealth, nation, realm.

statecraft *n* diplomacy, political subtlety, state management, statesmanship.

stated *adj* established, fixed, regular, settled; detailed, set forth, specified.

stately *adj* august, dignified, elevated, grand, imperial, imposing, lofty, magnificent, majestic, noble, princely, royal; ceremonious, formal, magisterial, pompous, solemn.

statement *n* account, allegation, announcement, communiqué, declaration, description, exposition, mention, narration, narrative, recital, relation, report, specification; assertion, predication, proposition, pronouncement, thesis.

statesman *n* politician.

station *vb* establish, fix, locate, place, post, set. * *n* location, place, position, lost, seat, situation; business, employment, function, occupation, office; character, condition, degree, dignity, footing, rank, standing, state, status; depot, stop, terminal.

stationary *adj* fixed, motionless, permanent, quiescent, stable, standing, still.

statuary *n* carving, sculpture, statues.

statue *n* figurine, image, statuette.

stature *n* height, physique, size, tallness; altitude, consequence, elevation, eminence, prominence.

status *n* caste, condition, footing, position, rank, standing, station.

statute *n* act, decree, edict, enactment, law, ordinance, regulation.

staunch[1], **stanch** *vb* arrest, block, check, dam, plug, stem, stop.

staunch[2] *adj* firm, sound, stout, strong; constant, faithful, firm, hearty, loyal, resolute, stable, steadfast, steady, strong, trustworthy, trusty, unwavering, zealous.

stave *vb* break, burst; (*with* **off**) adjourn, defer, delay, postpone, procrastinate, put off, waive.

stay *vb* abide, dwell, lodge, rest, sojourn, tarry; continue, halt, remain, stand still, stop; attend, delay, linger, wait; arrest, check, curb, hold, keep in, prevent, rein in, restrain, withhold; delay, detain, hinder, obstruct; hold up, prop, shore up, support, sustain, uphold. * *n* delay, repose, rest, sojourn; halt, stand, stop; bar, check, curb, hindrance, impediment, interruption, obstacle, obstruction, restraint, stumbling block; buttress, dependence, prop, staff, support, supporter.

stead *n* place, room.

steadfast *adj* established, fast, firm, fixed, stable; constant, faithful, implicit, persevering, pertinacious, resolute, resolved, staunch, steady, unhesitating, unreserved, unshaken, unwavering, wholehearted.

steadiness *n* constancy, firmness, perseverance, persistence, resolution, steadfastness; fixedness, stability.

steady *vb* balance, counterbalance, secure, stabilize, support. * *adj* firm, fixed, stable; constant, equable, regular, undeviating, uniform, unremitting; persevering, resolute, staunch, steadfast, unchangeable, unwavering.

steal *vb* burglarize, burgle, crib, embezzle, filch, peculate, pilfer, plagiarize, poach, purloin, shoplift, thieve; creep, sneak, pass stealthily.

stealing *n* burglary, larceny, peculation, shoplifting, robbery, theft, thievery.

stealth *n* secrecy, slyness, stealthiness.

stealthy *adj* clandestine, furtive, private, secret, skulking, sly, sneaking, surreptitious, underhand.

steam *vb* emit vapour, fume; evaporate, vaporize; coddle, cook, poach; navigate, sail; be hot, sweat. * *n* vapour; effluvium, exhalation, fume, mist, reek, smoke.

steamboat *n* steamer, steamship.

steamy *adj* misty, moist, vaporous; erotic, voluptuous.

steed *n* charger, horse, mount.

steel *vb* case-harden, edge; brace, fortify, harden, make firm, nerve, strengthen.

steep[1] *adj* abrupt, declivitous, precipitous, sheer, sloping, sudden. * *n* declivity, precipice.

steep[2] *vb* digest, drench, imbrue, imbue, macerate, saturate, soak.

steeple *n* belfry, spire, tower, turret.

steer *vb* direct, conduct, govern, guide, pilot, point.

steersman *n* conductor, guide, helmsman, pilot.

stellar *adj* astral, starry, star-spangled, stellary.

stem[1] *vb* (*with* **from**) bud, descend, generate, originate, spring, sprout. * *n* axis, stipe, trunk; pedicel, peduncle, petiole, stalk; branch, descendant, offspring, progeny, scion, shoot; ancestry, descent, family, generation, line, lineage, pedigree, race, stock; (*naut*) beak, bow, cutwater, forepart, prow; helm, lookout; etymon, radical, radix, origin, root.

stem[2] *vb* breast, oppose, resist, withstand; check, dam, oppose, staunch, stay, stop.

stench *n* bad smell, fetor, offensive odour, stink.

stenography *n* brachygraphy, shorthand, tachygraphy.

stentorian *adj* loud-voiced, powerful, sonorous, thundering, trumpet-like.

step *vb* pace, stride, tramp, tread, walk. * *n* footstep, pace, stride; stair, tread; degree, gradation, grade, interval; advance, advancement, progression; act, action, deed, procedure, proceeding; footprint, trace, track, vestige; footfall, gait, pace, walk; expedient, means, measure, method; round, rundle, rung.

steppe *n* pampa, prairie, savannah.

sterile *adj* barren, infecund, unfruitful, unproductive, unprolific; bare, dry, empty, poor; (*bot*) acarpous, male, staminate.

sterility *n* barrenness, fruitlessness, infecundity, unfruitfulness, unproductiveness.

sterling *adj* genuine, positive, pure, real, sound, standard, substantial, true.

stern[1] *adj* austere, dour, forbidding, grim, severe; bitter, cruel, hard, harsh, inflexible, relentless, rigid, rigorous, severe, strict, unrelenting; immovable, incorruptible, steadfast, uncompromising.

stern[2] *n* behind, breach, hind part, posterior, rear, tail; (*naut*) counter, poop, rudderpost, tailpost; butt, buttocks, fundament, rump.

sternness *n* austerity, rigidity, severity; asperity, cruelty, harshness, inflexibility, relentlessness, rigour.

sternum *n* (*anat*) breastbone, sternon.

stertorous *adj* hoarsely breathing, snoring.

stew *vb* boil, seethe, simmer, stive. * *n* ragout; confusion, difficculty, mess, scrape.

steward *n* chamberlain, majordomo, seneschal; manciple, purveyor.

stick[1] *vb* gore, penetrate, pierce, puncture, spear, stab, transfix; infix, insert, thrust; attach, cement, glue, paste; fix in, set; adhere, cleave, cling, hold; abide, persist, remain, stay, stop; doubt, hesitate, scruple, stickle, waver; (*with* **by**) adhere to, be faithful, support. * *n* prick, stab, thrust.

stick[2] *n* birch, rod, switch; bat, bludgeon, club, cudgel, shillelah; cane, staff, walking stick; cue, pole, spar, stake.

stickiness *n* adhesiveness, glutinousness, tenacity, viscosity, viscousness.

stickle *vb* altercate, contend, contest, struggle; doubt, hesitate, scruple, stick, waver.

sticky *adj* adhesive, clinging, gluey, glutinous, gummy, mucilaginous, tenacious, viscid, viscous.

stiff *adj* inflexible, rigid, stark, unbending, unyielding; firm, tenacious, thick; obstinate, pertinacious, strong, stubborn; absolute, austere, dogmatic, inexorable, peremptory, positive, rigorous, severe, straitlaced, strict, stringent, uncompromising; ceremonious, chilling, constrained, formal, frigid, prim, punctilious, stately, starchy, stilted; abrupt, cramped, crude, graceless, harsh, inelegant.

stiff-necked *adj* contumacious, cross-grained, dogged, headstrong, intractable, mulish, obdurate, obstinate, stubborn, unruly.

stiffness *n* hardness, inflexibility, rigidity, rigidness, rigour, starkness; compactness, consistence, denseness, density, thickness; contumaciousness, inflexibility, obstinacy, pertinacity, stubbornness; austerity, harshness, rigorousness, severity, sternness, strictness; constraint, formality, frigidity, precision, primness, tenseness.

stifle *vb* choke, smother, suffocate; check, deaden, destroy, extinguish, quench, repress, stop, suppress; conceal, gag, hush, muffle, muzzle, silence, smother, still.

stigma *n* blot, blur, brand, disgrace, dishonour, reproach, shame, spot, stain, taint, tarnish.

stigmatize *vb* brand, defame, discredit, disgrace, dishonour, post, reproach, slur, villify.

stiletto *n* dagger, dirk, poniard, stylet; bodkin, piercer.

still[1] *vb* hush, muffle, silence, stifle; allay, appease, calm, compose, lull, pacify, quiet, smooth, tranquillize; calm, check, immobilize, restrain, stop, subdue, suppress. * *adj* hushed, mum, mute, noiseless, silent; calm, placid, quiet, serene, stilly, tranquil, unruffled; inert, motionless, quiescent, stagnant, stationary. * *n* hush, lull, peace, quiet, quietness, quietude, silence, stillness, tranquillity; picture, photograph, shot.

still[2] *n* distillery, still-house; distillatory, retort, stillatory.

still[3] *adv, conj* till now, to this time, yet; however, nevertheless, notwithstanding; always, continually, ever, habitually, uniformly; after that, again, in continuance.

stilted *adj* bombastic, fustian, grandiloquent, grandiose, high-flown, high-sounding, inflated, magniloquent, pompous, pretentious, stilty, swelling, tumid, turgid.

stimulant *adj* exciting, stimulating, stimulative. * *n* bracer, cordial, pick-me-up, tonic; fillip, incentive, provocative, spur, stimulus.

stimulate *vb* animate, arouse, awaken, brace, encourage, energize, excite, fire, foment, goad, impel, incite, inflame, inspirit, instigate, kindle, prick, prompt, provoke, rally, rouse, set on, spur, stir up, urge, whet, work up.

stimulus *n* encouragement, fillip, goad, incentive, incitement, motivation, motive, provocation, spur, stimulant.

sting *vb* hurt, nettle, prick, wound; afflict,

cut, pain.

stinging *adj* acute, painful, piercing; biting, nipping, pungent, tingling.

stingy *adj* avaricious, close, close-fisted, covetous, grudging, mean, miserly, narrow-hearted, niggardly, parsimonious, penurious.

stink *vb* emit a stench, reek, smell bad. * *n* bad smell, fetor, offensive odour, stench.

stint *vb* bound, confine, limit, restrain; begrudge, pinch, scrimp, skimp, straiten; cease, desist, stop. * *n* bound, limit, restraint; lot, period, project, quota, share, shift, stretch, task, time, turn.

stipend *n* allowance, compensation, emolument, fee, hire, honorarium, pay, remuneration, salary, wages.

stipulate *vb* agree, bargain, condition, contract, covenant, engage, provide, settle terms.

stipulation *n* agreement, bargain, concordat, condition, contract, convention, covenant, engagement, indenture, obligation, pact.

stir *vb* budge, change place, go, move; agitate, bestir, disturb, prod; argue, discuss, moot, raise, start; animate, arouse, awaken, excite, goad, incite, instigate, prompt, provoke, quicken, rouse, spur, stimulate; appear, happen, turn up; get up, rise; (*with* **up**) animate, awaken, incite, instigate, move, provoke, quicken, rouse, stimulate. * *n* activity, ado, agitation, bustle, confusion, excitement, fidget, flurry, fuss, hurry, movement; commotion, disorder, disturbance, tumult, uproar.

stirring *adj* active, brisk, diligent, industrious, lively, smart; animating, arousing, awakening, exciting, quickening, stimulating.

stitch *vb* backstitch, baste, bind, embroider, fell, hem, seam, sew, tack, whip.

stive *vb* stow, stuff; boil, seethe, stew; make close, hot or sultry.

stock *vb* fill, furnish, store, supply; accumulate, garner, hoard, lay in, reposit, reserve, save, treasure up. * *adj* permanent, standard, standing. * *n* assets, capital, commodities, fund, principal, shares; accumulation, hoard, inventory, merchandise, provision, range, reserve, store, supply; ancestry, breed, descent, family, house, line, lineage, parentage, pedigree, race; cravat, neckcloth; butt, haft, hand; block, log, pillar, post, stake; stalk, stem, trunk.

stockholder *n* shareholder.

stocking *n* hose, sock.

stock market *n* stock exchange; cattle market.

stocks *npl* funds, public funds, public securities; shares.

stockstill *adj* dead-still, immobile, motionless, stationary, still, unmoving.

stocky *adj* chubby, chunky, dumpy, plump, short, stout, stubby, thickset.

stoic, stoical *adj* apathetic, cold-blooded, impassive, imperturbable, passionless, patient, philosophic, philosophical, phlegmatic, unimpassioned.

stoicism *n* apathy, coldness, coolness, impassivity, indifference, insensibility, nonchalance, phlegm.

stolen *adj* filched, pilfered, purloined; clandestine, furtive, secret, sly, stealthy, surreptitious.

stolid *adj* blockish, doltish, dull, foolish, heavy, obtuse, slow, stockish, stupid.

stolidity *n* doltishness, dullness, foolishness, obtuseness, stolidness, stupidity.

stomach *vb* abide, bear, brook, endure, put up with, stand, submit to, suffer, swallow, tolerate. * *n* abdomen, belly, gut, paunch, pot, tummy; appetite, desire, inclination, keenness, liking, relish, taste.

stone *vb* cover, face, slate, tile; lapidate, pelt. * *n* boulder, cobble, gravel, pebble, rock; gem, jewel, precious stone; cenotaph, gravestone, monument, tombstone; nut, pit; adamant, agate, flint, gneiss, granite, marble, slate, etc.

stony *adj* gritty, hard, lapidose, lithic, petrous, rocky; adamantine, flinty, hard, inflexible, obdurate; cruel, hard-hearted, inexorable, pitiless, stony-hearted, unfeeling, unrelenting.

stoop *vb* bend forward, bend down, bow, lean, sag, slouch, slump; abase, cower,

cringe, give in, submit, succumb, surrender; condescend, deign, descend, vouchsafe; fall, sink. * *n* bend, inclination, sag, slouch, slump; descent, swoop.
stop *vb* block, blockade, close, close up, obstruct, occlude; arrest, check, halt, hold, pause, stall, stay; bar, delay, embargo, hinder, impede, intercept, interrupt, obstruct, preclude, prevent, repress, restrain, staunch, suppress, thwart; break off, cease, desist, discontinue, forbear, give over, leave off, refrain from; intermit, quiet, quieten, terminate; lodge, tarry. * *n* halt, intermission, pause, respite, rest, stoppage, suspension, truce; block, cessation, check, hindrance, interruption, obstruction, repression; bar, impediment, obstacle; full stop, point.
stopcock *n* cock, faucet, tap.
stoppage *n* arrest, block, check, closure, hindrance, interruption, obstruction, prevention.
stopper *n* cork, plug, stopple.
store *vb* accumulate, amass, cache, deposit, garner, hoard, husband, lay by, lay in, lay up, put by, reserve, save, store up, stow away, treasure up; furnish, provide, replenish, stock, supply. * *n* accumulation, cache, deposit, fund, hoard, provision, reserve, stock, supply, treasure, treasury; abundance, plenty; storehouse; emporium, market, shop.
storehouse *n* depository, depot, godown, magazine, repository, store, warehouse.
storm *vb* assail, assault, attack; blow violently; fume, rage, rampage, rant, rave, tear. * *n* blizzard, gale, hurricane, squall, tempest, tornado, typhoon, whirlwind; agitation, clamour, commotion, disturbance, insurrection, outbreak, sedition, tumult, turmoil; adversity, affliction, calamity, distress; assault, attack, brunt, onset, onslaught; violence.
storminess *n* inclemency, roughness, tempestuousness.
stormy *adj* blustering, boisterous, gusty, squally, tempestuous, windy; passionate, riotous, rough, turbulent, violent, wild; agitated, furious.
story *n* annals, chronicle, history, record; account, narration, narrative, recital, record, rehearsal, relation, report, statement, tale; fable, fiction, novel, romance; anecdote, incident, legend, tale; canard, fabrication, falsehood, fib, figure, invention, lie, untruth.
storyteller *n* bard, chronicler, narrator, raconteur.
stout *adj* able-bodied, athletic, brawny, lusty, robust, sinewy, stalwart, strong, sturdy, vigorous; courageous, hardy, indomitable, stouthearted; contumacious, obstinate, proud, resolute, stubborn; compact, firm, solid, staunch; bouncing, bulky, burly, chubby, corpulent, fat, heavy, jolly, large, obese, plump, portly, stocky, strapping, thickset.
stouthearted *adj* fearless, heroic, redoubtable; bold, brave, courageous, dauntless, doughty, firm, gallant, hardy, indomitable, intrepid, resolute, valiant, valorous.
stow *vb* load, pack, put away, store, stuff.
straddle *vb* bestride.
straggle *vb* rove, wander; deviate, digress, ramble, range, roam, stray, stroll.
straggling *adj* rambling, roving, straying, strolling, wandering; scattered.
straight *adj* direct, near, rectilinear, right, short, undeviating, unswerving; erect, perpendicular, plumb, right, upright, vertical; equitable, fair, honest, honourable, just, square, straightforward. * *adv* at once, directly, forthwith, immediately, straightaway, straightway, without delay.
straightaway, straightway *adv* at once, directly, forthwith, immediately, speedily, straight, suddenly, without delay.
straighten *vb* arrange, make straight, neaten, order, tidy.
straight-laced *see* **strait-laced**.
strain[1] *vb* draw tightly, make tense, stretch, tighten; injure, sprain, wrench; exert, overexert, overtax, rack; embrace, fold, hug, press, squeeze; compel, constrain, force; dilute, distill, drain, filter, filtrate, ooze, percolate, purify, separate; fatigue, overtask, overwork, task, tax, tire. * *n* stress, tenseness, tension, tensity; effort, exertion, force, overexertion; burden, task, tax; sprain, wrech; lay, melody,

movement, snatch, song, stave, tune.

strain² *n* manner, style, tone, vein; disposition, tendency, trait, turn; descent, extraction, family, lineage, pedigree, race, stock.

strait *adj* close, confined, constrained, constricted, contracted, narrow; rigid, rigorous, severe, strict; difficult, distressful, grievous, straitened. * *n* channel, narrows, pass, sound.

straits *npl* crisis, difficulty, dilemma, distress, embarrassment, emergency, exigency, extremity, hardship, pass, perplexity, pinch, plight, predicament.

straiten *vb* confine, constrain, constrict, contract, limit; narrow; intensify, stretch; distress, embarrass, perplex, pinch, press.

straitened *adj* distressed, embarrassed limited, perplexed, pinched.

strait-laced, straight-laced *adj* austere, formal, prim, rigid, rigorous, stern, stiff, strict, uncompromising.

straitness *n* narrowness, rigour, severity, strictness; difficulty, distress, trouble; insufficiency, narrowness, scarcity, want.

strand¹ *vb* abandon, beach, be wrecked, cast away, go aground, ground, maroon, run aground, wreck. * *n* beach, coast, shore.

strand² *n* braid, cord, fibre, filament, line, rope, string, tress.

stranded *adj* aground, ashore, cast away, lost, shipwrecked, wrecked.

strange *adj* alien, exotic, far-fetched, foreign, outlandish, remote; new, novel; curious, exceptional, extraordinary, irregular, odd, particular, peculiar, rare, singular, surprising, uncommon, unusual; abnormal, anomalous, extraordinary, inconceivable, incredible, inexplicable, marvellous, mysterious, preternatural, unaccountable, unbelievable, unheard of, unique, unnatural, wonderful; bizarre, droll, grotesque, quaint, queer; inexperienced, unacquainted, unfamiliar, unknown; bashful, distant, distrustful, reserved, shy, uncommunicative.

strangeness *n* foreignness; bashfulness, coldness, distance, reserve, shyness, uncommunicativeness; eccentricity, grotesqueness, oddness, singularity, uncommonness, uncouthness.

stranger *n* alien, foreigner, newcomer, immigrant, outsider; guest, visitor.

strangle *vb* choke, contract, smother, squeeze, stifle, suffocate, throttle, tighten; keep back, quiet, repress, still, suppress.

strap *vb* beat, thrash, whip; bind, fasten, sharpen, strop. * *n* thong; band, ligature, strip, tie; razor-strap, strop.

strapping *adj* big, burly, large, lusty, stalwart, stout, strong, tall.

stratagem *n* artifice, cunning, device, dodge, finesse, intrigue, machination, manoeuvre, plan, plot, ruse, scheme, trick, wile.

strategic, strategical *adj* calculated, deliberate, diplomatic, manoeuvering, planned, politic, tactical; critical, decisive, key, vital.

strategy *n* generalship, manoeuvering, plan, policy, stratagem, strategetics, tactics.

stratum *n* band, bed, layer.

straw *n* culm, stalk, stem; button, farthing, fig, penny, pin, rush, snap.

stray *vb* deviate, digress, err, meander, ramble, range, roam, rove, straggle, stroll, swerve, transgress, wander. * *adj* abandoned, lost, strayed, wandering; accidental, erratic, random, scattered.

streak *vb* band, bar, striate, stripe, vein; dart, dash, flash, hurtle, run, speed, sprint, stream, tear. * *n* band, bar, belt, layer, line, strip, stripe, thread, trace, vein; cast, grain, tone, touch, vein; beam, bolt, dart, dash, flare, flash, ray, stream.

streaky *adj* streaked, striped, veined.

stream *vb* course, flow, glide, pour, run, spout; emit, pour out, shed; emanate, go forth, issue, radiate; extend, float, stretch out, wave. * *n* brook, burn, race, rill, rivulet, run, runlet, runnel, trickle; course, current, flow, flux, race, rush, tide, torrent, wake, wash; beam, gleam, patch, radiation, ray, streak.

streamer *n* banner, colours, ensign, flag, pennon, standard.

street *n* avenue, highway, road, way.

strength *n* force, might, main, nerve, potency, power, vigour; hardness, solidity, toughness; impregnability, proof; brawn, grit, healthy, lustiness, muscle, robustness, sinew, stamina, thews, vigorousness; animation, courage, determination, firmness, fortitude, resolution, spirit; cogency, efficacy, soundness, validity; emphasis, energy; security, stay, support; brightness, brilliance, clearness, intensity, vitality, vividness; body, excellence, virtue; impetuosity, vehemence, violence; boldness.

strengthen *vb* buttress, recruit, reinforce; fortify; brace, energize, harden, nerve, steel, stimulate; freshen, invigorate, vitalize; animate, encourage; clench, clinch, confirm, corroborate, establish, fix, justify, sustain, support.

strenuous *adj* active, ardent, eager, earnest, energetic, resolute, vigorous, zealous; bold, determined, doughty, intrepid, resolute, spirited, strong, valiant.

stress *vb* accent, accentuate, emphasize, highlight, point up, underline, underscore; bear, bear upon, press, pressurize; pull, rack, strain, stretch, tense, tug. * *n* accent, accentuation, emphasis; effort, force, pull, strain, tension, tug; boisterousness, severity, violence; pressure, urgency.

stretch *vb* brace, screw, strain, tense, tighten; elongate, extend, lengthen, protract, pull; display, distend, expand, spread, unfold, widen; sprain, strain; distort, exaggerate, misrepresent. * *n* compass, extension, extent, range, reach, scope; effort, exertion, strain, struggle; course, direction.

strict *adj* close, strained, tense, tight; accurate, careful, close, exact, literal, particular, precise, scrupulous; austere, inflexible, harsh, orthodox, puritanical, rigid, rigorous, severe, stern, strait-laced, stringent, uncompromising, unyielding.

stricture *n* animadversion, censure, denunciation, criticism, compression, constriction, contraction.

strife *n* battle, combat, conflict, contention, contest, discord, quarrel, struggle, warfare.

strike *vb* bang, beat, belabour, box, buffet, cudgel, cuff, hit, knock, lash, pound, punch, rap, slap, slug, smite, thump, whip; impress, imprint, stamp; afflict, chastise, deal, give, inflict, punish; affect, astonish, electrify, stun; clash, collide, dash, touch; surrender, yield; mutiny, rebel, rise.

stringent *adj* binding, contracting, rigid, rigorous, severe, strict.

strip[1] *n* piece, ribbon, shred, slip.

strip[2] *vb* denude, hull, skin, uncover; bereave, deprive, deforest, desolate, despoil, devastate, disarm, dismantle, disrobe, divest, expose, fleece, loot, shave; plunder, pillage, ransack, rob, sack, spoil; disrobe, uncover, undress.

strive *vb* aim, attempt, endeavour, exert, labour, strain, struggle, toil; contend, contest, fight, tussle, wrestle; compete, cope.

stroke[1] *n* blow, glance, hit, impact, knock, lash, pat, percussion, rap, shot, switch, thump; attack, paralysis, stroke; affliction, damage, hardship, hurt, injury, misfortune, reverse, visitation; dash, feat, masterstroke, touch.

stroke[2] *vb* caress, feel, palpate, pet, knead, massage, nuzzle, rub, touch.

stroll *vb* loiter, lounge, ramble, range, rove, saunter, straggle, stray, wander. * *n* excursion, promenade, ramble, rambling, roving, tour, trip, walk, wandering.

strong *adj* energetic, forcible, powerful, robust, sturdy; able, enduring; cogent, firm, valid.

structure *vb* arrange, constitute, construct, make, organize. * *n* arrangement, conformation, configuration, constitution, construction, form, formation, make, organization; anatomy, composition, texture; building, edifice, fabric, framework, pile.

struggle *vb* aim, endeavour, exert, labour, strive, toil, try; battle, contend, contest, fight, wrestle; agonize, flounder, writhe. * n effort, endeavour, exertion, labour, pains; battle, conflict, contention, contest, fight, strife; agony, contortions, distress.

stubborn *adj* contumacious, dogged, headstrong, heady, inflexible, intractable, mulish, obdurate, obstinate, perverse, positive, refractory, ungovernable, unmanageable, unruly, unyielding, willful; constant, enduring, firm, hardy, persevering, persistent, steady, stoical, uncomplaining, unremitting; firm, hard, inflexible, stiff, strong, tough, unpliant, studied.

studious *adj* contemplative, meditative, reflective, thoughtful; assiduous, attentive, desirous, diligent, eager, lettered, scholarly, zealous.

study *vb* cogitate, lucubrate, meditate, muse, ponder, reflect, think; analyze, contemplate, examine, investigate, ponder, probe, scrutinize, search, sift, weigh. * *n* exercise, inquiry, investigation, reading, research, stumble; cogitation, consideration, contemplation, examination, meditation, reflection, thought; stun; model, object, representation, sketch; den, library, office, studio.

stunning *adj* deafening, stentorian; dumbfounding, stupefying.

stunted *adj* checked, diminutive, dwarfed, dwarfish, lilliputian, little, nipped, small, undersized.

stupendous *adj* amazing, astonishing, astounding, marvellous, overwhelming, surprising, wonderful; enormous, huge, immense, monstrous, prodigious, towering, tremendous, vast.

stupid *adj* brainless, crass, doltish, dull, foolish, idiotic, inane, inept, obtuse, pointless, prosaic, senseless, simple, slow, sluggish, stolid, tedious, tiresome, witless.

stupor *n* coma, confusion, daze, lethargy, narcosis, numbness, stupefaction, torpor.

sturdy *adj* bold, determined, dogged, firm, hardy, obstinate, persevering, pertinacious, resolute, stiff, stubborn, sturdy; athletic, brawny, forcible, lusty, muscular, powerful, robust, stalwart, stout, strong, thickset, vigorous, well-set.

style *vb* address, call, characterize, denominate, designate, dub, entitle, name, term. * *n* dedication, expression, phraseology, turn; cast, character, fashion, form, genre, make, manner, method, mode, model, shape, vogue, way; appellation, denomination, designation, name, title; chic, elegance, smartness; pen, pin, point, stylus.

stylish *adj* chic, courtly, elegant, fashionable, genteel, modish, polished, smart.

suave *adj* affable, agreeable, amiable, bland, courteous, debonair, delightful, glib, gracious, mild, pleasant, smooth, sweet, oily, unctuous, urbane.

subdue *vb* beat, bend, break, bow, conquer, control, crush, defeat, discomfit, foil, master, overbear, overcome, overpower, overwhelm, quell, rout, subject, subjugate, surmount, vanquish, worst; allay, choke, curb, mellow, moderate, mollify, reduce, repress, restrain, soften, suppress, temper.

subject *vb* control, master, overcome, reduce, subdue, subjugate, tame; enslave, enthral; abandon, refer, submit, surrender. * *adj* beneath, subjacent, underneath; dependent, enslaved, inferior, servile, subjected, subordinate, subservient; conditional, obedient, submissive; disposed, exposed to, liable, obnoxious, prone. * *n* dependent, henchman, liegeman, slave, subordinate; matter, point, subject matter, theme, thesis, topic; nominative, premise; case, object, patient, recipient; ego, mind, self, thinking.

subjoin *vb* add, affix, annex, append, join, suffix.

subjugate *vb* conquer, enslave, enthral, master, overcome, overpower, overthrow, subdue, subject, vanquish.

sublimate *vb* alter, change, repress.

sublime *adj aloft, elevated, high,* sacred; eminent, exalted, grand, great, lofty, mighty; august, glorious, magnificent, majestic, noble, stately, solemn, sublunary; elated, elevated, eloquent, exhilarated, raised.

submission *n* capitulation, cession, relinquishment, surrender, yielding; acquiescence, compliance, obedience, resignation; deference, homage, humility, lowliness, obeisance, passiveness, prostration, self-abasement, submissiveness.

submissive *adj* amenable, compliant, docile, pliant, tame, tractable, yielding; acquiescent, long-suffering, obedient, passive, patient, resigned, unassertive, uncomplaining, unrepining; deferential, humble, lowly, meek, obsequious, prostrate, self-abasing.

submit *vb* cede, defer, endure, resign, subject, surrender, yield; commit, propose, refer; offer;

acquiesce, bend, capitulate, comply, stoop, succumb.

subordinate *adj* ancillary, dependent, inferior, junior, minor, secondary, subject, subservient, subsidiary. * *n* assistant, dependant, inferior, subject, underling.

subscribe *vb* accede, approve, agree, assent, consent, yield; contribute, donate, give, offer, promise.

subscription *n* aid, assistance, contribution, donation, gift, offering.

subsequent *adj* after, attendant, ensuing, later, latter, following, posterior, sequent, succeeding.

subservient *adj* inferior, obsequious, servile, subject, subordinate; accessory, aiding, auxiliary, conducive, contributory, helpful, instrumental, serviceable, useful.

subside *vb* settle, sink; abate, decline, decrease, diminish, drop, ebb, fall, intermit, lapse, lessen, lower, lull, wane.

subsidence *n* settling, sinking; abatement, decline, decrease, descent, ebb, diminution, lessening.

subsidiary *adj* adjutant, aiding, assistant, auxiliary, cooperative, corroborative, helping, subordinate, subservient.

subsidize *vb* aid, finance, fund, sponsor, support, underwrite.

subsidy *n* aid, bounty, grant, subvention, support, underwriting.

subsist *vb* be, breathe, consist, exist, inhere, live, prevail; abide, continue, endure, persist, remain; feed, maintain, ration, support.

subsistence *n* aliment, food, livelihood, living, maintenance, meat, nourishment, nutriment, provision, rations, support, sustenance, victuals.

substance *n* actuality, element, groundwork, hypostasis, reality, substratum; burden, content, core, drift, essence, gist, heart, import, meaning, pith, sense, significance, solidity, soul, sum, weight; estate, income, means, property, resources, wealth.

substantial *adj* actual, considerable, essential, existent, hypostatic, pithy, potential, real, subsistent, virtual; concrete, durable, positive, solid, tangible, true; corporeal, bodily, material; bulky, firm, goodly, heavy, large, massive, notable, significant, sizable, solid, sound, stable, stout, strong, well-made; cogent, just, efficient, influential, valid, weighty.

substantially *adv* adequately, essentially, firmly, materially, positively, really, truly.

substantiate *vb* actualize, confirm, corroborate, establish, prove, ratify, verify.

subterfuge *n* artifice, evasion, excuse, expedient, mask, pretence, pretext, quirk, shift, shuffle, sophistry, trick.

subtle *adj* arch, artful, astute, crafty, crooked, cunning, designing, diplomatic, intriguing, insinuating, sly, tricky, wily; clever, ingenious; acute, deep, discerning, discriminating, keen, profound, sagacious, shrewd; airy, delicate, ethereal, light, nice, rare, refined, slender, subtle, thin, volatile.

subtlety *n* artfulness, artifice, astuteness, craft, craftiness, cunning, guile, subtleness; acumen, acuteness, cleverness, discernment, intelligence, keenness, sagacity, sharpness, shrewdness; attenuation, delicacy, fitness, nicety, rareness, refinement.

subtract *vb* deduct, detract, diminish, remove, take, withdraw.

suburbs *npl* environs, confines, neighbourhood, outskirts, precincts, purlieus, vicinage.

subversive *adj* destructive, overthrowing, pervasive, ruining, upsetting. * *n* collaborator, dissident, insurrectionist, saboteur, terrorist, traitor.

subvert *vb* invert, overset, overthrow, overturn, reverse, upset; demolish, destroy, extinguish, raze, ruin; confound, corrupt, injure, pervert.
succeed *vb* ensue, follow, inherit, replace; flourish, gain, hit, prevail, prosper, thrive, win.
success *n* attainment, issue, result; fortune, happiness, hit, luck, prosperity, triumph.
successful *adj* auspicious, booming, felicitous, fortunate, happy, lucky, prosperous, victorious, winning.
succession *n* chain, concatenation, cycle, consecution, following, procession, progression, rotation, round, sequence, series, suite; descent, entail, inheritance, lineage, race, reversion.
succinct *adj* brief, compact, compendious, concise, condensed, curt, laconic, pithy, short, summary, terse.
succour *vb* aid, assist, help, relieve; cherish, comfort, encourage, foster, nurse. * *n* aid, assistance, help, relief, support.
succulent *adj* juicy, luscious, lush, nutritive, sappy.
succumb *vb* capitulate, die, submit, surrender, yield.
sudden *adj* abrupt, hasty, hurried, immediate, instantaneous, rash, unanticipated, unexpected, unforeseen, unusual; brief, momentary, quick, rapid.
sue *vb* charge, court, indict, prosecute, solicit, summon, woo; appeal, beg, demand, entreat, implore, petition, plead, pray, supplicate.
suffer *vb* feel, undergo; bear, endure, sustain, tolerate; admit, allow, indulge, let, permit.
sufferable *adj* allowable, bearable, endurable, permissible, tolerable.
sufferance *n* endurance, inconvenience, misery, pain, suffering; long-suffering, moderation, patience, submission; allowance, permission, toleration.
suffice *vb* avail, content, satisfy, serve.
sufficient *adj* adequate, ample, commensurate, competent, enough, full, plenteous, satisfactory; able, equal, fit, qualified, responsible.
suffocate *vb* asphyxiate, choke, smother, stifle, strangle.
suffrage *n* ballot, franchise, voice, vote; approval, attestation, consent, testimonial, witness.
suggest *vb* advise, allude, hint, indicate, insinuate, intimate, move, present, prompt, propose, propound, recommend.
suggestion *n* allusion, hint, indication, insinuation, intimation, presentation, prompting, proposal, recommendation, reminder.
suit *vb* accommodate, adapt, adjust, fashion, fit, level, match; accord, become, befit, gratify, harmonize, please, satisfy, tally. * *n* appeal, entreaty, invocation, petition, prayer, request, solicitation, supplication; courtship, wooing; action, case, cause, process, prosecution, trial; clothing, costume, habit.
suitable *adj* adapted, accordant, agreeable, answerable, apposite, applicable, appropriate, apt, becoming, befitting, conformable, congruous, convenient, consonant, correspondent, decent, due, eligible, expedient, fit, fitting, just, meet, pertinent, proper, relevant, seemly, worthy.
suite *n* attendants, bodyguard, convoy, cortege, court, escort, followers, staff, retainers, retinue, train; collection, series, set, suit; apartment, rooms.
sulky *adj* aloof, churlish, cross, cross-grained, dogged, grouchy, ill-humoured, ill-tempered, moody, morose, perverse, sour, spleenish, spleeny, splenetic, sullen, surly, vexatious, wayward.
sullen *adj* cross, crusty, glum, grumpy, ill-tempered, moody, morose, sore, sour, sulky; cheerless, cloudy, dark, depressing, dismal, foreboding, funereal, gloomy, lowering, melancholy, mournful, sombre; dull, heavy, slow, sluggish; intractable, obstinate, perverse, refractory, stubborn, vexatious; baleful, evil, inauspicious, malign, malignant, sinister, unlucky, unpropitious.
sully *vb* blemish, blot, contaminate, deface, defame, dirty, disgrace, dishonour, foul, smirch, soil, slur, spot, stain, tarnish.
sultry *adj* close, damp, hot, humid, muggy,

oppressive, stifling, stuffy, sweltering.

sum *vb* add, calculate, compute, reckon; collect, comprehend, condense, epitomize, summarize. * *n* aggregate, amount, total, totality, whole; compendium, substance, summary; acme, completion, height, summit.

summary *adj* brief, compendious, concise, curt, laconic, pithy, short, succinct, terse; brief, quick, rapid. * *n* abridgement, abstract, brief, compendium, digest, epitome, precis, résumé, syllabus, synopsis.

summit *n* acme, apex, cap, climax, crest, crown, pinnacle, top, vertex, zenith.

summon *vb* arouse, bid, call, cite, invite, invoke, rouse; convene, convoke; charge, indict, prosecute, subpoena, sue.

sumptuous *adj* costly, dear, expensive, gorgeous, grand, lavish, luxurious, magnificent, munificent, pompous, prodigal, rich, showy, splendid, stately, superb.

sunburnt *adj* bronzed, brown, ruddy, tanned.

sunder *vb* break, disconnect, disjoin, dissociate, dissever, disunited, divide, part, separate, sever.

sundry *adj* different, divers, several, some, various.

sunny *adj* bright, brilliant, clear, fine, luminous, radiant, shining, unclouded, warm; cheerful, genial, happy, joyful, mild, optimistic, pleasant, smiling.

superannuated *adj* aged, anile, antiquated, decrepit, disqualified, doting, effete, imbecile, passé, retired, rusty, time-worn, unfit.

superb *adj* august, beautiful, elegant, exquisite, grand, gorgeous, imposing, magnificent, majestic, noble, pompous, rich, showy, splendid, stately, sumptuous.

supercilious *adj* arrogant, condescending, contemptuous, dictatorial, domineering, haughty, high, imperious, insolent, intolerant, lofty, lordly, magisterial, overbearing, overweening, proud, scornful, vainglorious.

superficial *adj* external, flimsy, shallow, untrustworthy.

superfluity *n* excess, exuberance, redundancy, superabundance, surfeit.

superfluous *adj* excessive, redundant, unnecessary.

superintend *vb* administer, conduct, control, direct, inspect, manage, overlook, oversee, supervise.

superintendence *n* care, charge, control, direction, guidance, government, inspection, management, oversight, supervision, surveillance.

superior *adj* better, greater, high, higher, finer, paramount, supreme, ultra, upper; chief, foremost, principal; distinguished, matchless, noble, pre-eminent, preferable, sovereign, surpassing, unrivalled, unsurpassed; predominant, prevalent. * *n* boss, chief, director, head, higher-up, leader, manager, principal, senior, supervisor.

superiority *n* advantage, ascendency, lead, odds, predominance, pre-eminence, prevalence, transcendence; excellence, nobility, worthiness.

superlative *adj* consummate, greatest, incomparable, peerless, pre-eminent, supreme, surpassing, transcendent.

supernatural *adj* abnormal, marvellous, metaphysical, miraculous, otherworldly, preternatural, unearthly.

supernumerary *adj* excessive, odd, redundant, superfluous.

supersede *vb* annul, neutralize, obviate, overrule, suspend; displace, remove, replace, succeed, supplant.

supervise *vb* administer, conduct, control, direct, inspect, manage, overlook, oversee, superintend.

supine *adj* apathetic, careless, drowsy, dull, idle, indifferent, indolent, inert, languid, lethargic, listless, lumpish, lazy, negligent, otiose, prostrate, recumbent, sleepy, slothful, sluggish, spineless, torpid.

supplant *vb* overpower, overthrow, undermine; displace, remove, replace, supersede.

supple *adj* elastic, flexible, limber, lithe, pliable, pliant; compliant, humble, submissive, yielding; adulatory, cringing, fawning, flattering, grovelling, obsequious, oily, parasitical, servile, slavish, sycophantic.

supplement *vb* add, augment, extend, reinforce, supply. * *n* addendum, addition, appendix, codicil, complement, continuation, postscript.

suppliant *adj* begging, beseeching, entreating, imploring, precative, precatory, praying, suing, supplicating. * *n* applicant, petitioner, solicitor, suitor, supplicant.

supplicate *vb* beg, beseech, crave, entreat, implore, importune, petition, pray, solicit.

supplication *n* invocation, orison, petition, prayer; entreaty, petition, prayer, request, solicitation.

supply *vb* endue, equip, furnish, minister, outfit, provide, replenish, stock, store; afford, accommodate, contribute, furnish, give, grant, yield. * *n* hoard, provision, reserve, stock, store.

support *vb* brace, cradle, pillow, prop, sustain, uphold; bear, endure, undergo, suffer, tolerate; cherish, keep, maintain, nourish, nurture; act, assume, carry, perform, play, represent; accredit, confirm, corroborate, substantiate, verify; abet, advocate, aid, approve, assist, back, befriend, champion, countenance, encourage, favour, float, hold, patronize, relieve, reinforce, succour, vindicate. * *n* bolster, brace, buttress, foothold, guy, hold, prop, purchase, shore, stay, substructure, supporter, underpinning; groundwork, mainstay, staff; base, basis, bed, foundation; keeping, living, livelihood, maintenance, subsistence, sustenance; confirmation, evidence; aid, assistance, backing, behalf, championship, comfort, countenance, encouragement, favour, help, patronage, succour.

suppose *vb* apprehend, believe, conceive, conclude, consider, conjecture, deem, imagine, judge, presume, presuppose, think; assume, hypothesize; imply, posit, predicate, think; fancy, opine, speculate, surmise, suspect, theorize, wean.

supposition *n* conjecture, guess, guesswork, presumption, surmise; assumption, hypothesis, postulation, theory, thesis; doubt, uncertainty.

suppress *vb* choke, crush, destroy, overwhelm, overpower, overthrow, quash, quell, quench, smother, stifle, subdue, withhold; arrest, inhibit, obstruct, repress, restrain, stop; conceal, extinguish, keep, retain, secret, silence, stifle, strangle.

supremacy *n* ascendancy, domination, headship, lordship, mastery, predominance, pre-eminence, primacy, sovereignty.

supreme *adj* chief, dominant, first, greatest, highest, leading, paramount, predominant, pre-eminent, principal, sovereign.

sure *adj* assured, certain, confident, positive; accurate, dependable, effective, honest, infallible, precise, reliable, trustworthy, undeniable, undoubted, unmistakable, well-proven; guaranteed, inevitable, irrevocable; fast, firm, safe, secure, stable, steady.

surely *adv* assuredly, certainly, infallibly, sure, undoubtedly; firmly, safely, securely, steadily.

surety *n* bail, bond, certainty, guarantee, pledge, safety, security.

surfeit *vb* cram, gorge, overfeed, sate, satiate; cloy, nauseate, pall. * *n* excess, fullness, glut, oppression, plethora, satiation, satiety, superabundance, superfluity.

surge *vb* billow, rise, rush, sweep, swell, swirl, tower. * *n* billow, breaker, roller, wave, white horse.

surly *adj* churlish, crabbed, cross, crusty, discourteous, fretful, gruff, grumpy, harsh, ill-natured, ill-tempered, morose, peevish, perverse, pettish, petulant, rough, rude, snappish, snarling, sour, sullen, testy, touchy, uncivil, ungracious, waspish; dark, tempestuous.

surmise *vb* believe, conclude, conjecture, consider, divine, fancy, guess, imagine, presume, suppose, think, suspect. * *n* conclusion, conjecture, doubt, guess, notion, possibility, supposition, suspicion, thought.

surmount *vb* clear, climb, crown, overtop, scale, top, vault; conquer, master, overcome, overpower, subdue, vanquish; exceed, overpass, pass, surpass, transcend.

surpass *vb* beat, cap, eclipse, exceed, excel, outdo, outmatch, outnumber, outrun, outstrip, override, overshadow, overtop, outshine, surmount, transcend.

surplus *adj* additional, leftover, remaining, spare, superfluous, supernumerary, supplementary. * *n* balance, excess, overplus, remainder, residue, superabundance, surfeit.

surprise *vb* amaze, astonish, astound, bewilder, confuse, disconcert, dumbfound, startle, stun. * *n* amazement, astonishment, blow, shock, wonder.

surprising *adj* amazing, astonishing, astounding, extraordinary, marvellous, unexpected, remarkable, startling, strange, unexpected, wonderful.

surrender *vb* cede, sacrifice, yield; abdicate, abandon, forgo, relinquish, renounce, resign, waive; capitulate, comply, succumb. * *n* abandonment, capitulation, cession, delivery, relinquishment, renunciation, resignation, yielding.

surreptitious *adj* clandestine, fraudulent, furtive, secret, sly, stealthy, unauthorized, underhand.

surround *vb* beset, circumscribe, compass, embrace, encircle, encompass, environ, girdle, hem, invest, loop.

surveillance *n* care, charge, control, direction, inspection, management, oversight, superintendence, supervision, surveyorship, vigilance, watch.

survey *vb* contemplate, observe, overlook, reconnoitre, review, scan, scout, view; examine, inspect, scrutinize; oversee, supervise; estimate, measure, plan, plot, prospect. * *n* prospect, retrospect, sight, view; examination, inspection, reconnaissance, review; estimating, measuring, planning, plotting, prospecting, work-study.

survive *vb* endure, last, outlast, outlive.

susceptible *adj* capable, excitable, impressible, impressionable, inclined, predisposed, receptive, sensitive.

suspect *vb* believe, conclude, conjecture, fancy, guess, imagine, judge, suppose, surmise, think; distrust, doubt, mistrust. * *adj* doubtful, dubious, suspicious.

suspend *vb* append, hang, sling, swing; adjourn, arrest, defer, delay, discontinue, hinder, intermit, interrupt, postpone, stay, withhold; debar, dismiss, rusticate.

suspicion *n* assumption, conjecture, dash, guess, hint, inkling, suggestion, supposition, surmise, trace; apprehension, distrust, doubt, fear, jealousy, misgiving, mistrust.

suspicious *adj* distrustful, jealous, mistrustful, suspect, suspecting; doubtful, questionable.

sustain *vb* bear, bolster, fortify, prop, strengthen, support, uphold; maintain, nourish, perpetuate, preserve; aid, assist, comfort, relieve; brave, endure, suffer, undergo; approve, confirm, ratify, sanction, validate; confirm, establish, justify, prove.

sustenance *n* maintenance, subsistence, support; aliment, bread, food, nourishment, nutriment, nutrition, provisions, supplies, victuals.

swagger *vb* bluster, boast, brag, bully, flourish, hector, ruffle, strut, swell, vapour. * *n* airs, arrogance, bluster, boastfulness, braggadocio, ruffling, strut.

swain *n* clown, countryman, hind, peasant, rustic; adorer, gallant, inamorata, lover, suitor, wooer.

swallow *vb* bolt, devour, drink, eat, englut, engorge, gobble, gorge, gulp, imbibe, ingurgitate, swamp; absorb, appropriate, arrogate, devour, engulf, submerge; consume, employ, occupy; brook, digest, endure, pocket, stomach; recant, renounce, retract. * *n* gullet, oesophagus, throat; inclination, liking, palate, relish, taste; deglutition, draught, gulp, ingurgitation, mouthful, taste.

swamp *vb* engulf, overwhelm, sink; capsize, embarrass, overset, ruin, upset, wreck. * *n* bog, fen, marsh, morass, quagmire, slough.

sward *n* grass, lawn, sod, turf.

swarm *vb* abound, crowd, teem, throng.

* *n* cloud, concourse, crowd, drove, flock, hive, horde, host, mass, multitude, press, shoal, throng.

swarthy *adj* black, brown, dark, dark-skinned, dusky, tawny.

sway *vb* balance, brandish, move, poise, rock, roll, swing, wave, wield; bend, bias, influence, persuade, turn, urge; control, dominate, direct, govern, guide, manage, rule; hoist, raise; incline, lean, lurch, yaw. * *n* ascendency, authority, command, control, domination, dominion, empire, government, mastership, mastery, omnipotence, predominance, power, rule, sovereignty; bias, direction, influence, weight; preponderance, preponderation; oscillation, sweep, swing, wag, wave.

swear *vb* affirm, attest, avow, declare, depose, promise, say, state, testify, vow; blaspheme, curse.

sweep *vb* clean, brush; graze, touch; rake, scour, traverse. * *n* amplitude, compass, drive, movement, range, reach, scope; destruction, devastation, havoc, ravage; curvature, curve.

sweeping *adj* broad, comprehensive, exaggerated, extensive, extravagant, general, unqualified, wholesale.

sweet *adj* candied, cloying, honeyed, luscious, nectareous, nectarous, sugary, saccharine; balmy, fragrant, odorous, redolent, spicy; harmonious, dulcet, mellifluous, mellow, melodious, musical, pleasant, soft, tuneful, silver-toned, silvery; beautiful, fair, lovely; agreeable, charming, delightful, grateful, gratifying; affectionate, amiable, attractive, engaging, gentle, mild, lovable, winning; benignant, serene; clean, fresh, pure, sound. * *n* fragrance, perfume, redolence; blessing, delight, enjoyment, gratification, joy, pleasure; candy, treat.

swell *vb* belly, bloat, bulge, dilate, distend, expand, inflate, intumesce, puff, swell, tumefy; augment, enlarge, increase; heave, rise, surge; strut, swagger. * *n* swelling; augmentation, excrescence, protuberance; ascent, elevation, hill, rise; force, intensity, power; billows, surge, undulation, waves; beau, blade, buck, coxcomb, dandy, exquisite, fop, popinjay.

swerve *vb* deflect, depart, deviate, stray, turn, wander; bend, incline, yield; climb, swarm, wind.

swift *adj* expeditious, fast, fleet, flying, quick, rapid, speedy; alert, eager, forward, prompt, ready, zealous; instant, sudden.

swiftness *n* celerity, expedition, fleetness, quickness, rapidity, speed, velocity.

swindle *vb* cheat, con, cozen, deceive, defraud, diddle, dupe, embezzle, forge, gull, hoax, overreach, steal, trick, victimize. * *n* cheat, con, deceit, deception, fraud, hoax, imposition, knavery, roguery, trickery.

swindler *n* blackleg, cheat, defaulter, embezzler, faker, fraud, impostor, jockey, knave, peculator, rogue, sharper, trickster.

swing *vb* oscillate, sway, vibrate, wave; dangle, depend, hang; brandish, flourish, whirl; administer, manage. * *n* fluctuation, oscillation, sway, undulation, vibration; elbow-room, freedom, margin, play, range, scope, sweep; bias, tendency.

swoop *vb* descend, pounce, rush, seize, stoop, sweep. * *n* clutch, pounce, seizure; stoop, descent.

sword *n* brand, broadsword, claymore, cutlass, epee, falchion, foil, hanger, rapier, sabre,
scimitar.

sybarite *n* epicure, voluptuary.

sycophancy *n* adulation, cringing, fawning, flattery, grovelling, obsequiousness, servility.

sycophant *n* cringer, fawner, flunky, hanger-on, lickspittle, parasite, spaniel, toady, wheedler.

syllabus *n* abridgement, abstract, breviary, brief, compendium, digest, epitome, outline, summary, synopsis.

symbol *n* badge, emblem, exponent, figure, mark, picture, representation, representative, sign, token, type.

symbolic, symbolical *adj* emblematic, figurative, hieroglyphic, representative, significant, typical.

symmetry *n* balance, congruity, evenness, harmony, order, parallelism, proportion, regularity, shapeliness.

sympathetic *adj* affectionate, commiserating, compassionate, condoling, kind, pitiful, tender.

sympathy *n* accord, affinity, agreement, communion, concert, concord, congeniality, correlation, correspondence, harmony, reciprocity, union; commiseration, compassion, condolence, fellow-feeling, kindliness, pity, tenderness, thoughtfulness.

symptom *n* diagnostic, indication, mark, note, prognostic, sign, token.

symptomatic *adj* characteristic, indicative, symbolic, suggestive.

synonymous *adj* equipollent, equivalent, identical, interchangeable, similar, tantamount.

synopsis *n* abridgement, abstract, compendium, digest, epitome, outline, precis, résumé, summary, syllabus.

system *n* method, order, plan.

systematic *adj* methodic, methodical, orderly, regular.

T

tabernacle *n* pavilion, tent; cathedral, chapel, church, minster, synagogue, temple.
table *vb* enter, move, propose, submit, suggest. * *n* plate, slab, tablet; board, counter, desk, stand; catalogue, chart, compendium, index, list, schedule, syllabus, synopsis, tabulation; diet, fare, food, victuals.
tableau *n* picture, scene, representation.
taboo *vb* forbid, interdict, prohibit, proscribe. * *adj* banned, forbidden, inviolable, outlawed, prohibited, proscribed. * *n* ban, interdict, prohibition, proscription.
tacit *adj* implicit, implied, inferred, silent, understood, unexpressed, unspoken.
taciturn *adj* close, dumb, laconic, mum, reserved, reticent, silent, tight-lipped, uncommunicative.
tack *vb* add, affix, append, attach, fasten, tag; gybe, yaw, zigzag. * *n* nail, pin, staple; bearing, course, direction, heading, path, plan, procedure.
tackle *vb* attach, grapple, seize; attempt, try, undertake. * *n* apparatus, cordage, equipment, furniture, gear, harness, implements, rigging, tackling, tools, weapons.
tact *n* address, adroitness, cleverness, dexterity, diplomacy, discernment, finesse, insight, knack, perception, skill, understanding.
tail *vb* dog, follow, shadow, stalk, track. * *adj* abridged, curtailed, limited, reduced. * *n* appendage, conclusion, end, extremity, stub; flap, skirt; queue, retinue, train.
taint *vb* imbue, impregnate; contaminate, corrupt, defile, inflect, mildew, pollute, poison, spoil, touch; blot, stain, sully, tarnish. * *n* stain, tincture, tinge, touch; contamination, corruption, defilement, depravation, infection, pollution; blemish, defect, fault, flaw, spot.
take *vb* accept, obtain, procure, receive; clasp, clutch, grasp, grip, gripe, seize, snatch; filch, misappropriate, pilfer, purloin, steal; abstract, apprehend, appropriate, arrest, bag, capture, ensnare, entrap; attack, befall, smite; capture, carry off, conquer, gain, win; allure, attract, bewitch, captivate, charm, delight, enchant, engage, fascinate, interest, please; consider, hold, interrupt, suppose, regard, understand; choose, elect, espouse, select; employ, expend, use; claim, demand, necessitate, require; bear, endure, experience, feel, perceive, tolerate; deduce, derive, detect, discover, draw; carry, conduct, convey, lead, transfer; clear, surmount; drink, eat, imbibe, inhale, swallow. * *n* proceeds, profits, return, revenue, takings, yield.
tale *n* account, fable, legend, narration, novel, parable, recital, rehearsal, relation, romance, story, yarn; catalogue, count, enumeration, numbering, reckoning, tally.
talent *n* ableness, ability, aptitude, capacity, cleverness, endowment, faculty, forte, genius, gift, knack, parts, power, turn.
talk *vb* chatter, communicate, confer, confess, converse, declaim, discuss, gossip, pontificate, speak. * *n* chatter, communication, conversation, diction, gossip, jargon, language, rumour, speech, utterance.
talkative *adj* chatty, communicative, garrulous, loquacious, voluble.
tally *vb* accord, agree, conform, coincide, correspond, harmonize, match, square, suit. * *n* match, mate; check, counterpart, muster, roll call; account, reckoning.

tame *vb* domesticate, reclaim, train; conquer, master, overcome, repress, subdue, subjugate. * *adj* docile, domestic, domesticated, gentle, mild, reclaimed; broken, crushed, meek, subdued, unresisting, submissive; barren, commonplace, dull, feeble, flat, insipid, jejune, languid, lean, poor, prosaic, prosy, spiritless, tedious, uninteresting, vapid.

tamper *vb* alter, conquer, dabble, damage, interfere, meddle; intrigue, seduce, suborn.

tang *n* aftertaste, flavour, relish, savour, smack, taste; keenness, nip, sting.

tangible *adj* corporeal, material, palpable, tactile, touchable; actual, certain, embodied, evident, obvious, open, perceptible, plain, positive, real, sensible, solid, stable, substantial.

tangle *vb* complicate, entangle, intertwine, interweave, mat, perplex, snarl; catch, ensnare, entrap, involve, catch; embarrass, embroil, perplex. * *n* complication, disorder, intricacy, jumble, perplexity, snarl; dilemma, embarrassment, quandary, perplexity.

tantalize *vb* balk, disappoint, frustrate, irritate, provoke, tease, torment, vex.

tantamount *adj* equal, equivalent, synonymous.

tantrum *n* fit, ill-humour, outburst, paroxysm, temper, whim.

tap[1] *vb* knock, pat, rap, strike, tip, touch. * *n* pat, tip, rap, touch.

tap[2] *vb* broach, draw off, extract, pierce; draw on, exploit, mine, use, utilize; bug, eavesdrop, listen in. * *n* faucet, plug, spigot, spout, stopcock, valve; bug, listening device, transmitter.

tardiness *n* delay, dilatoriness, lateness, procrastination, slackness, slowness.

tardy *adj* slow, sluggish, snail-like; backward, behindhand, dilatory, late, loitering, overdue, slack.

tarn *n* bog, fen, marsh, morass, swamp.

tarnish *vb* blemish, deface, defame, dim, discolour, dull, slur, smear, soil, stain, sully. * *n* blemish, blot, soiling, spot, stain.

tarry *vb* delay, dally, linger, loiter, remain, stay, stop, wait; defer; abide, lodge, rest, sojourn.

tart *adj* acid, acidulous, acrid, astringent, piquant, pungent, sharp, sour; acrimonious, caustic, crabbed, curt, harsh, ill-humoured, ill-tempered, keen, petulant, sarcastic, severe, snappish, testy.

task *vb* burden, overwork, strain, tax. * *n* drudgery, labour, toil, work; business, charge, chore, duty, employment, enterprise, job, mission, stint, undertaking; assignment, exercise, lesson.

taste *vb* experience, feel, perceive, undergo; relish, savour, sip. * *n* flavour, gusto, relish, savour, smack, piquancy; admixture, bit, dash, fragment, hint, infusion, morsel, mouthful, sample, shade, sprinkling, suggestion, tincture; appetite, desire, fondness, liking, partiality, predilection; acumen, cultivation, culture, delicacy, discernment, discrimination, elegance, fine-feeling, grace, judgement, polish, refinement; manner, style.

tasteful *adj* appetizing, delicious, flavoursome, palatable, savoury, tasty, toothsome; aesthetic, artistic, attractive, elegant.

tasteless *adj* flat, insipid, savourless, stale, watery; dull, mawkish, uninteresting, vapid.

tattle *vb* babble, chat, chatter, jabber, prate, prattle; blab, gossip, inform. * *n* gabble, gossip, prate, prattle, tittle-tattle, twaddle.

taunt *vb* censure, chaff, deride, flout, jeer, mock, scoff, sneer, revile, reproach, ridicule, twit, upbraid. * *n* censure, derision, gibe, insult, jeer, quip, quirk, reproach, ridicule, scoff.

taut *adj* strained, stretched, tense, tight.

tautology *n* iteration, pleonasm, redundancy, reiteration, repetition, verbosity, wordiness.

tavern *n* bar, chophouse, hostelry, inn, pub, public house.

tawdry *adj* flashy, gaudy, garish, glittering, loud, meretricious, ostentatious, showy.

tax *vb* burden, demand, exact, load, overtax, require, strain, task; accuse, charge.

* *n* assessment, custom, duty, excise, impost, levy, rate, taxation, toll, tribute; burden, charge, demand, requisition, strain; accusation, censure.

teach *vb* catechize, coach, discipline, drill, edify, educate, enlighten, inform, indoctrinate, initiate, instruct, ground, prime, school, train, tutor; communicate, disseminate, explain, expound, impart, implant, inculcate, infuse, instil, interpret, preach, propagate; admonish, advise, counsel, direct, guide, signify, show.

teacher *n* coach, educator, inculcator, informant, instructor, master, pedagogue, preceptor, schoolteacher, trainer, tutor; adviser, counsellor, guide, mentor; pastor, preacher.

tear *vb* burst, slit, rive, rend, rip; claw, lacerate, mangle, shatter, rend, wound; sever, sunder; fume, rage, rant, rave. * *n* fissure, laceration, rent, rip, wrench.

tease *vb* annoy, badger, beg, bother, chafe, chagrin, disturb, harass, harry, hector, importune, irritate, molest, pester, plague, provoke, tantalize, torment, trouble, vex, worry.

tedious *adj* dull, fatiguing, irksome, monotonous, tiresome, trying, uninteresting, wearisome; dilatory, slow, sluggish, tardy.

teem *vb* abound, bear, produce, swarm; discharge, empty, overflow.

teeming *adj* abounding, fraught, full, overflowing, pregnant, prolific, replete, swarming.

tell *vb* compute, count, enumerate, number, reckon; describe, narrate, recount, rehearse, relate, report; acknowledge, announce, betray, confess, declare, disclose, divulge, inform, own, reveal; acquaint, communicate, instruct, teach; discern, discover, distinguish; express, mention, publish, speak, state, utter.

temper *vb* modify, qualify; appease, assuage, calm, mitigate, mollify, moderate, pacify, restrain, soften, soothe; accommodate, adapt, adjust, fit, suit. * *n* character, constitution, nature, organization, quality, structure, temperament, type; disposition, frame, grain, humour, mood, spirits, tone, vein; calmness, composure, equanimity, moderation, tranquillity; anger, ill-temper, irritation, spleen, passion.

temperament *n* character, constitution, disposition, habit, idiosyncrasy, nature, organization, temper.

temperate *adj* abstemious, ascetic, austere, chaste, continent, frugal, moderate, self-controlled, self-denying, sparing; calm, cool, dispassionate, mild, sober, sedate.

tempest *n* cyclone, gale, hurricane, squall, storm, tornado; commotion, disturbance, excitement, perturbation, tumult, turmoil.

temporal *adj* civil, lay, mundane, political, profane, secular, terrestrial, worldly; brief, ephemeral, evanescent, fleeting, momentary, short-lived, temporal, transient, transitory.

temporary *adj* brief, ephemeral, evanescent, fleeting, impermanent, momentary, short-lived, transient, transitory.

tempt *vb* prove, test, try; allure, decoy, entice, induce, inveigle, persuade, seduce; dispose, incite, incline, instigate, lead, prompt, provoke.

tempting *adj* alluring, attractive, enticing, inviting, seductive.

tenable *adj* defensible, maintainable, rational, reasonable, sound.

tenacious *adj* retentive, unforgetful; adhesive, clinging, cohesive, firm, glutinous, gummy, resisting, retentive, sticky, strong, tough, unyielding, viscous; dogged, fast, obstinate, opinionated, opinionative, pertinacious, persistent, resolute, stubborn, unwavering.

tenacity *n* retentiveness, tenaciousness; adhesiveness, cohesiveness, glutinosity, glutinousness, gumminess, toughness, stickiness, strength, viscidity; doggedness, firmness, obstinacy, perseverance, persistency, pertinacity, resolution, stubbornness.

tend¹ *vb* accompany, attend, graze, guard, keep, protect, shepherd, watch.

tend² *vb* aim, exert, gravitate, head, incline, influence, lead, lean, point, trend, verge;

conduce, contribute.

tendency *n* aim, aptitude, bearing, bent, bias, course, determination, disposition, direction, drift, gravitation, inclination, leaning, liability, predisposition, proclivity, proneness, propensity, scope, set, susceptibility, turn, twist, warp.

tender[1] *vb* bid, offer, present, proffer, propose, suggest, volunteer. * *n* bid, offer, proffer, proposal; currency, money.

tender[2] *adj* callow, delicate, effeminate, feeble, feminine, fragile, immature, infantile, soft, weak, young; affectionate, compassionate, gentle, humane, kind, lenient, loving, merciful, mild, pitiful, sensitive, sympathetic, tender-hearted; affecting, disagreeable, painful, pathetic, touching, unpleasant.

tenebrous *adj* cloudy, dark, darksome, dusky, gloomy, murky, obscure, shadowy, shady, sombre, tenebrious.

tenement *n* abode, apartment, domicile, dwelling, flat, house.

tenet *n* belief, creed, position, dogma, doctrine, notion, opinion, position, principle, view.

tenor *n* cast, character, cut, fashion, form, manner, mood, nature, stamp, tendency, trend, tone; drift, gist, import, intent, meaning, purport, sense, significance, spirit.

tense *vb* flex, strain, tauten, tighten. * *adj* rigid, stiff, strained, stretched, taut, tight; excited, highly strung, intent, nervous, rapt.

tentative *adj* essaying, experimental, provisional, testing, toying.

tenure *n* holding, occupancy, occupation, possession, tenancy, tenement, use.

term *vb* call, christen, denominate, designate, dub, entitle, name, phrase, style. * *n* bound, boundary, bourn, confine, limit, mete, terminus; duration, period, season, semester, span, spell, termination, time; denomination, expression, locution, name, phrase, word.

termagant *n* beldam, hag, scold, shrew, spitfire, virago, vixen.

terminal *adj* bounding, limiting; final, terminating, ultimate. * *n* end, extremity, termination; bound, limit; airport, depot, station, terminus.

terminate *vb* bound, limit; end, finish, close, complete, conclude; eventuate, issue, prove.

termination *n* ending, suffix; bound, extend, limit; end, completion, conclusion, consequence, effect, issue, outcome, result.

terms *npl* conditions, provisions, stipulations.

terrestrial *adj* earthly, mundane, subastral, subcelestial, sublunar, sublunary, tellurian, worldly. * *n* earthling, human.

terrible *adj* appalling, dire, dreadful, fearful, formidable, frightful, gruesome, hideous, horrible, horrid, shocking, terrific, tremendous; alarming, awe-inspiring, awful, dread; great, excessive, extreme, severe.

terrific *adj* marvellous, sensational, superb; immense, intense; alarming, dreadful, formidable, frightful, terrible, tremendous.

terrify *vb* affright, alarm, appal, daunt, dismay, fright, frighten, horrify, scare, shock, startle, terrorize.

territory *n* country, district, domain, dominion, division, land, place, province, quarter, region, section, tract.

terror *n* affright, alarm, anxiety, awe, consternation, dismay, dread, fear, fright, horror, intimidation, panic, terrorism.

terse *adj* brief, compact, concise, laconic, neat, pithy, polished, sententious, short, smooth, succinct.

test *vb* assay; examine, prove, try. * *n* attempt, essay, examination, experiment, ordeal, proof, trial; criterion, standard, touchstone; example, exhibition; discrimination, distinction, judgment.

testify *vb* affirm, assert, asseverate, attest, avow, certify, corroborate, declare, depose, evidence, state, swear.

testimonial *n* certificate, credential, recommendation, voucher; monument, record.

testimony *n* affirmation, attestation, confession, confirmation, corroboration, declaration, deposition, profession; evidence, proof, witness.

testy *adj* captious, choleric, cross, fretful, hasty, irascible, irritable, quick, peevish, peppery, pettish, petulant, snappish, splenetic, touchy, waspish.

tetchy *adj* crabbed, cross, fretful, irritable, peevish, sullen, touchy.

tether *vb* chain, fasten, picket, stake, tie. * *n* chain, fastening, rope.

text *n* copy, subject, theme, thesis, topic, treatise.

texture *n* fabric, web, weft; character, coarseness, composition, constitution, fibre, fineness, grain, make-up, nap, organization, structure, tissue.

thankful *adj* appreciative, beholden, grateful, indebted, obliged.

thankfulness *n* appreciation, gratefulness, gratitude.

thankless *adj* profitless, ungracious, ungrateful, unthankful.

thaw *vb* dissolve, liquefy, melt, soften, unbend.

theatre *n* opera house, playhouse; arena, scene, seat, stage.

theatrical *adj* dramatic, dramaturgic, dramaturgical, histrionic, scenic, spectacular; affected, ceremonious, meretricious, ostentatious, pompous, showy, stagy, stilted, unnatural.

theft *n* depredation, embezzlement, fraud, larceny, peculation, pilfering, purloining, robbery, spoliation, stealing, swindling, thieving.

theme *n* composition, essay, motif, subject, text, thesis, topic, treatise.

theoretical *adj* abstract, conjectural, doctrinaire, ideal, hypothetical, pure, speculative, unapplied.

theory *n* assumption, conjecture, hypothesis, idea, plan, postulation, principle, scheme, speculation, surmise, system; doctrine, philosophy, science; explanation, exposition, philosophy, rationale.

therefore *adv* accordingly, afterward, consequently, hence, so, subsequently, then, thence, whence.

thesaurus *n* dictionary, encyclopedia, repository, storehouse, treasure.

thick *adj* bulky, chunky, dumpy, plump, solid, squab, squat, stubby, thickset; clotted, coagulated, crass, dense, dull, gross, heavy, viscous; blurred, cloudy, dirty, foggy, hazy, indistinguishable, misty, obscure, vaporous; muddy, roiled, turbid; abundant, frequent, multitudinous, numerous; close, compact, crowded, set, thickset; confused, guttural, hoarse, inarticulate, indistinct; dim, dull, weak; familiar, friendly, intimate, neighbourly, well-acquainted. * *adv* fast, frequently, quick; closely, densely, thickly. * *n* centre, middle, midst.

thicket *n* clump, coppice, copse, covert, forest, grove, jungle, shrubbery, underbrush, undergrowth, wood, woodland.

thief *n* depredator, filcher, pilferer, lifter, marauder, purloiner, robber, shark, stealer; burglar, corsair, defaulter, defrauder, embezzler, footpad, highwayman, housebreaker, kidnapper, pickpocket, pirate, poacher, privateer, sharper, swindler, peculator.

thieve *vb* cheat, embezzle, peculate, pilfer, plunder, purloin, rob, steal, swindle.

thin *vb* attenuate, dilute, diminish, prune, reduce, refine, weaken. * *adj* attenuated, bony, emaciated, fine, fleshless, flimsy, gaunt, haggard, lank, lanky, lean, meagre, peaked, pinched, poor, scanty, scraggy, scrawny, slender, slight, slim, small, sparse, spindly.

thing *n* being, body, contrivance, creature, entity, object, something, substance; act, action, affair, arrangement, circumstance, concern, deed, event, matter, occurrence, transaction.

think *vb* cogitate, contemplate, dream, meditate, muse, ponder, reflect, ruminate, speculate; consider, deliberate, reason, undertake; apprehend, believe, conceive, conclude, deem, determine, fancy, hold, imagine, judge, opine, presume, reckon, suppose, surmise; design, intend, mean, purpose; account, count, deem, esteem, hold, regard; compass, design, plan, plot. * *n* assessment, contemplation, deliberation, meditation, opinion, reasoning, reflection.

thirst *n* appetite, craving, desire, hunger, longing, yearning; aridity, drought, dryness.

thirsty *adj* arid, dry, parched; eager, greedy, hungry, longing, yearning.

thorn *n* prickle, spine; annoyance, bane, care, evil, infliction, nettle, nuisance, plague, torment, trouble, scourge.

thorny *adj* briary, briery, prickly, spinose, spinous, spiny; acuminate, barbed, pointed, prickling, sharp, spiky; annoying, difficult, harassing, perplexing, rugged, troublesome, trying, vexatious.

thorough, thoroughgoing *adj* absolute, arrant, complete, downright, entire, exhaustive, finished, perfect, radical, sweeping, total unmitigated, utter; accurate, correct, reliable, trustworthy.

though *conj* admitting, allowing, although, granted, granting, if, notwithstanding, still. * *adv* however, nevertheless, still, yet.

thought *n* absorption, cogitation, engrossment, meditation, musing, reflection, reverie, rumination; contemplation, intellect, ratiocination, thinking, thoughtfulness; application, conception, consideration, deliberation, idea, pondering, speculation, study; consciousness, imagination, intellect, perception, understanding; conceit, fancy, notion; conclusion, judgment, motion, opinion, sentiment, supposition, view; anxiety, attention, care, concern, provision, regard, solicitude, thoughtfulness; design, expectation, intention, purpose.

thoughtful *adj* absorbed, contemplative, deliberative, dreamy, engrossed, introspective, pensive, philosophic, reflecting, reflective, sedate, speculative; attentive, careful, cautious, circumspect, considerate, discreet, heedful, friendly, kindhearted, kindly, mindful, neighbourly, provident, prudent, regardful, watchful, wary; quiet, serious, sober, studious.

thoughtless *adj* careless, casual, flighty, heedless, improvident, inattentive, inconsiderate, neglectful, negligent, precipitate, rash, reckless, regardless, remiss, trifling, unmindful, unthinking; blank, blockish, dull, insensate, stupid, vacant, vacuous.

thraldom *n* bondage, enslavement, enthralment, serfdom, servitude, slavery, subjection, thrall, vassalage.

thrash *vb* beat, bruise, conquer, defeat, drub, flog, lash, maul, pommel, punish, thwack, trounce, wallop, whip.

thread *vb* course, direction, drift, tenor; reeve, trace. * *n* cord, fibre, filament, hair, line, twist; pile, staple.

threadbare *adj* napless, old, seedy, worn; common, commonplace, hackneyed, stale, trite, worn-out.

threat *n* commination, defiance, denunciation, fulmination, intimidation, menace, thunder, thunderbolt.

threaten *vb* denounce, endanger, fulminate, intimidate, menace, thunder; augur, forebode, foreshadow, indicate, portend, presage, prognosticate, warn.

threshold *n* doorsill, sill; door, entrance, gate; beginning, commencement, opening, outset, start.

thrift *n* economy, frugality, parsimony, saving, thriftiness; gain, luck, profit, prosperity, success.

thriftless *adj* extravagant, improvident, lavish, profuse, prodigal, shiftless, unthrifty, wasteful.

thrifty *adj* careful, economical, frugal, provident, saving, sparing; flourishing, prosperous, thriving, vigorous.

thrill *vb* affect, agitate, electrify, inspire, move, penetrate, pierce, rouse, stir, touch. * *n* excitement, sensation, shock, tingling, tremor.

thrilling *adj* affecting, exciting, gripping, moving, sensational, touching.

thrive *vb* advance, batten, bloom, boom, flourish, prosper, succeed.

throng *vb* congregate, crowd, fill, flock, pack, press, swarm. * *n* assemblage, concourse, congregation, crowd, horde, host, mob, multitude, swarm.

throttle *vb* choke, silence, strangle, suffocate.

throw *vb* cast, chuck, dart, fling, hurl, lance, launch, overturn, pitch, pitchfork, send, sling, toss, whirl. * *n* cast, fling, hurl, launch, pitch, sling, toss, whirl; chance, gamble, try, venture.

thrust *vb* clap, dig, drive, force, impel, jam, plunge, poke, propel, push, ram, run, shove, stick. * *n* dig, jab, lunge, pass, plunge, poke, propulsion, push, shove, stab, tilt.

thump *vb* bang, batter, beat, belabour, knock, punch, strike, thrash, thwack, whack. * *n* blow, knock, punch, strike, stroke.

thwart *vb* baffle, balk, contravene, counteract, cross, defeat, disconcert, frustrate, hinder, impede, oppose, obstruct, oppugn; cross, intersect, traverse.

tickle *vb* amuse, delight, divert, enliven, gladden, gratify, please, rejoice, titillate.

ticklish *adj* dangerous, precarious, risky, tottering, uncertain, unstable, unsteady; critical, delicate, difficult, nice.

tide *n* course, current, ebb, flow, stream.

tidings *npl* advice, greetings, information, intelligence, news, report, word.

tidy *vb* clean, neaten, order, straighten. * *adj* clean, neat, orderly, shipshape, spruce, trig, trim.

tie *vb* bind, confine, fasten, knot, lock, manacle, secure, shackle, fetter, yoke; complicate, entangle, interlace, knit; connect, hold, join, link, unite; constrain, oblige, restrain, restrict. * *n* band, fastening, knot, ligament, ligature; allegiance, bond, obligation; bow, cravat, necktie.

tier *n* line, rank, row, series.

tiff *n* fit, fume, passion, pet, miff, rage.

tight *adj* close, compact, fast, firm; taut, tense, stretched; impassable, narrow, strait.

till *vb* cultivate, plough, harrow.

tillage *n* agriculture, cultivation, culture, farming, geoponics, husbandry.

tilt *vb* cant, incline, slant, slope, tip; forge, hammer; point, thrust; joust, rush. * *n* awning, canopy, tent; lunge, pass, thrust; cant, inclination, slant, slope, tip.

time *vb* clock, control, count, measure, regulate, schedule. * *n* duration, interim, interval, season, span, spell, tenure, term, while; aeon, age, date, epoch, eon, era; term; cycle, dynasty, reign; confinement, delivery, parturition; measure, rhythm.

timely *adj* acceptable, appropriate, apropos, early, opportune, prompt, punctual, seasonable, well-timed.

timid *adj* afraid, cowardly, faint-hearted, fearful, irresolute, meticulous, nervous, pusillanimous, skittish, timorous, unadventurous; bashful, coy, diffident, modest, shame-faced, shrinking.

tincture *vb* colour, dye, shade, stain, tinge, tint; flavour, season; imbue, impregnate, impress, infuse. * *n* grain, hue, shade, stain, tinge, tint, tone; flavour, smack, spice, taste; admixture, dash, infusion, seasoning, sprinkling, touch.

tinge *vb* colour, dye, stain, tincture, tint; imbue, impregnate, impress, infuse. * *n* cast, colour, dye, hue, shade, stain, tincture, tint; flavour, smack, spice, quality, taste.

tint *n* cast, colour, complexion, dye, hue, shade, tinge, tone.

tiny *adj* diminutive, dwarfish, Lilliputian, little, microscopic, miniature, minute, puny, pygmy, small, wee.

tip[1] *n* apex, cap, end, extremity, peak, pinnacle, point, top, vertex.

tip[2] *vb* incline, overturn, tilt; dispose of, dump. * *n* donation, fee, gift, gratuity, perquisite, reward; inclination, slant; hint, pointer, suggestion; strike, tap.

tirade *n* abuse, denunciation, diatribe, harangue, outburst.

tire *vb* exhaust, fag, fatigue, harass, jade, weary; bore, bother, irk.

tiresome *adj* annoying, arduous, boring, dull, exhausting, fatiguing, fagging, humdrum, irksome, laborious, monotonous, tedious, wearisome, vexatious.

tissue *n* cloth, fabric; membrane, network, structure, texture, web; accumulation, chain, collection, combination, conglomeration, mass, series, set.

titanic *adj* colossal, Cyclopean, enormous, gigantic, herculean, huge, immense, mighty, monstrous, prodigious, stupendous, vast.

title *vb* call, designate, name, style, term. * *n* caption, legend, head, heading; appellation, application, cognomen, completion, denomination, designation, epithet, name; claim, due, ownership, part, possession, prerogative, privilege, right.

tittle *n* atom, bit, grain, iota, jot, mite, particle, scrap, speck, whit.

tittle-tattle *vb, n* babble, cackle, chatter, discourse, gabble, gossip, prattle.

toast *vb* brown, dry, heat; honour, pledge, propose, salute. * *n* compliment, drink, pledge, salutation, salute; favourite, pet.

toil *vb* drudge, labour, strive, work. * *n* drudgery, effort, exertion, exhaustion, grinding, labour, pains, travail, work; gin, net, noose, snare, spring, trap.

toilsome *adj* arduous, difficult, fatiguing, hard, laborious, onerous, painful, severe, tedious, wearisome.

token *adj* nominal, superficial, symbolic. * *n* badge, evidence, index, indication, manifestation, mark, note, sign, symbol, trace, trait; keepsake, memento, memorial, reminder, souvenir.

tolerable *adj* bearable, endurable, sufferable, supportable; fair, indifferent, middling, ordinary, passable, so-so.

tolerance *n* endurance, receptivity, sufferance, toleration.

tolerate *vb* admit, allow, indulge, let, permit, receive; abide, brook, endure, suffer.

toll[1] *n* assessment, charge, customs, demand, dues, duty, fee, impost, levy, rate, tax, tribute; cost, damage, loss.

toll[2] *vb* chime, knell, peal, ring, sound. * *n* chime, knell, peal, ring, ringing, tolling.

tomb *n* catacomb, charnel house, crypt, grave, mausoleum, sepulchre, vault.

tone *vb* blend, harmonize, match, suit. * *n* note, sound; accent, cadence, emphasis, inflection, intonation, modulation; key, mood, strain, temper; elasticity, energy, force, health, strength, tension, vigour; cast, colour, manner, hue, shade, style, tint; drift, tenor.

tongue *n* accent, dialect, language, utterance, vernacular; discourse, parlance, speech, talk; nation, race.

too *adv* additionally, also, further, likewise, moreover, overmuch.

toothsome *adj* agreeable, dainty, delicious, luscious, nice, palatable, savoury.

top *vb* cap, head, tip; ride, surmount; outgo, surpass. * *adj* apical, best, chief, culminating, finest, first, foremost, highest, leading, prime, principal, topmost, uppermost. * *n* acme, apex, crest, crown, head, meridian, pinnacle, summit, surface, vertex, zenith.

topic *n* business, question, subject, text, theme, thesis; division, head, subdivision; commonplace, dictum, maxim, precept, proposition, principle, rule; arrangement, scheme.

topple *vb* fall, overturn, tumble, upset.

torment *vb* annoy, agonize, distress, excruciate, pain, rack, torture; badger, fret, harass, harry, irritate, nettle, plague, provoke, tantalize, tease, trouble, vex, worry. * *n* agony, anguish, pang, rack, torture.

tornado *n* blizzard, cyclone, gale, hurricane, storm, tempest, typhoon, whirlwind.

torpid *adj* benumbed, lethargic, motionless, numb; apathetic, dormant, dull, inactive, indolent, inert, listless, sleepy, slothful, sluggish, stupid.

torpor *n* coma, insensibility, lethargy, numbness, torpidity; inaction, inactivity, inertness, sluggishness, stupidity.

torrid *adj* arid, burnt, dried, parched; burning, fiery, hot, parching, scorching, sultry, tropical, violent.

tortuous *adj* crooked, curved, curvilineal, curvilinear, serpentine, sinuate, sinuated, sinuous, twisted, winding; ambiguous, circuitous, crooked, deceitful, indirect, perverse, roundabout.

torture *vb* agonize, distress, excruciate, pain, rack, torment.* *n* agony, anguish, distress, pain, pang, rack, torment.

toss *vb* cast, fling, hurl, pitch, throw; agitate, rock, shake; disquiet, harass, try; roll, writhe. * *n* cast, fling, pitch, throw.

total *vb* add, amount to, reach, reckon. * *adj* complete, entire, full, whole; integral, undivided. * *n* aggregate, all, gross, lump, mass, sum, totality, whole.

totter *vb* falter, reel, stagger, vacillate; lean, oscillate, reel, rock, shake, sway,

tremble, waver; fail, fall, flag.
touch *vb* feel, graze, handle, hit, pat, strike, tap; concern, interest, regard; affect, impress, move, stir; grasp, reach, stretch; melt, mollify, soften; afflict, distress, hurt, injure, molest, sting, wound. * *n* hint, smack, suggestion, suspicion, taste, trace; blow, contract, hit, pat, tap.
touchiness *n* fretfulness, irritability, irascibility, peevishness, pettishness, petulance, snappishness, spleen, testiness.
touching *adj* affecting, heart-rending, impressive, melting, moving, pathetic, pitiable, tender; abutting, adjacent, bordering, tangent.
touchy *adj* choleric, cross, fretful, hot-tempered, irascible, irritable, peevish, petulant, quick-tempered, snappish, splenetic, tetchy, testy, waspish.
tough *adj* adhesive, cohesive, flexible, tenacious; coriaceous, leathery; clammy, ropy, sticky, viscous; inflexible, intractable, rigid, stiff; callous, hard, obdurate, stubborn; difficult, formidable, hard, troublesome. * *n* brute, bully, hooligan, ruffian, thug.
tour *vb* journey, perambulate, travel, visit. * *n* circuit, course, excursion, expedition, journey, perambulation, pilgrimage, round.
tow *vb* drag, draw, haul, pull, tug. * *n* drag, lift, pull.
tower *vb* mount, rise, soar, transcend. * *n* belfry, bell tower, column, minaret, spire, steeple, turret; castle, citadel, fortress, stronghold; pillar, refuge, rock, support.
towering *adj* elevated, lofty; excessive, extreme, prodigious, violent.
toy *vb* dally, play, sport, trifle, wanton. * *n* bauble, doll, gewgaw, gimmick, knick-knack, plaything, puppet, trinket; bagatelle, bubble, trifle; play, sport.
trace *vb* follow, track, train; copy, deduce, delineate, derive, describe, draw, sketch. * *n* evidence, footmark, footprint, footstep, impression, mark, remains, sign, token, track, trail, vestige, wake; memorial, record; bit, dash, flavour, hint, suspicion, streak, tinge.
track *vb* chase, draw, follow, pursue, scent, track, trail. * *n* footmark, footprint, footstep, spoor, trace, vestige; course, pathway, rails, road, runway, trace, trail, wake, way.
trackless *adj* pathless, solitary, unfrequented, unused.
tract[1] *n* area, district, quarter, region, territory; parcel, patch, part, piece, plot, portion.
tract[2] *n* disquisition, dissertation, essay, homily, pamphlet, sermon, thesis, tractate, treatise.
tractable *adj* amenable, docile, governable, manageable, submissive, willing, yielding; adaptable, ductile, malleable, plastic, tractile.
trade *vb* bargain, barter, chaffer, deal, exchange, interchange, sell, traffic. * *n* bargaining, barter, business, commerce, dealing, traffic; avocation, calling, craft, employment, occupation, office, profession, pursuit, vocation.
traditional *adj* accustomed, apocryphal, customary, established, historic, legendary, old, oral, transmitted, uncertain, unverified, unwritten.
traduce *vb* abuse, asperse, blemish, brand, calumniate, decry, defame, depreciate, disparage, revile, malign, slander, vilify.
traducer *n* calumniator, defamer, detractor, slanderer, vilifier.
traffic *vb* bargain, barter, chaffer, deal, exchange, trade. * *n* barter, business, chaffer, commerce, exchange, intercourse, trade, transportation, truck.
tragedy *n* drama, play; adversity, calamity, catastrophe, disaster, misfortune.
tragic *adj* dramatic; calamitous, catastrophic, disastrous, dreadful, fatal, grievous, heart-breaking, mournful, sad, shocking, sorrowful.
trail *vb* follow, hunt, trace, track; drag, draw, float, flow, haul, pull. * *n* footmark, footprint, footstep, mark, trace, track.
train *vb* drag, draw, haul, trail, tug; allure, entice; discipline, drill, educate, exercise, instruct, school, teach; accustom, break in, familiarize, habituate, inure, prepare, rehearse, use. * *n* trail, wake; entourage, cortege, followers, retinue, staff, suite;

chain, consecution, sequel, series, set, succession; course, method, order, process; allure, artifice, device, enticement, lure, persuasion, stratagem, trap.

trait *n* line, mark, stroke, touch; characteristic, feature, lineage,particularity, peculiarity, quality.

traitor *n* apostate, betrayer, deceiver, Judas, miscreant, quisling, renegade, turncoat; conspirator, deserter, insurgent, mutineer, rebel, revolutionary.

traitorous *adj* faithless, false, perfidious, recreant, treacherous; insidious, treasonable.

trammel *vb* clog, confine, cramp, cumber, hamper, hinder, fetter, restrain, restrict, shackle, tie. * *n* bond, chain, fetter, hindrance, impediment, net, restraint, shackle.

tramp *vb* hike, march, plod, trudge, walk. * *n* excursion, journey, march, walk; landloper, loafer, stroller, tramper, vagabond, vagrant.

trample *vb* crush, tread; scorn, spurn.

trance *n* dream, ecstasy, hypnosis, rapture; catalepsy, coma.

tranquil *adj* calm, hushed, peaceful, placid, quiet, serene, still, undisturbed, unmoved, unperturbed, unruffled, untroubled.

tranquillity *n* calmness, peace, peacefulness, placidity, placidness, quiet, quietness, serenity, stillness, tranquilness.

tranquillize *vb* allay, appease, assuage, calm, compose, hush, lay, lull, moderate, pacify, quell, quiet, silence, soothe, still.

transact *vb* conduct, dispatch, enact, execute, do, manage, negotiate, perform, treat.

transaction *n* act, action, conduct, doing, management, negotiation, performance; affair, business, deal, dealing, incident, event, job, matter, occurrence, procedure, proceeding.

transcend *vb* exceed, overlap, overstep, pass, transgress; excel, outstrip, outrival, outvie, overtop, surmount, surpass.

transcendent *adj* consummate, inimitable, peerless, pre-eminent, supereminent, surpassing, unequalled, unparalleled, unrivalled, unsurpassed; metempiric, metempirical, noumenal, super-sensible.

transcript *n* duplicate, engrossment, rescript.

transfer *vb* convey, dispatch, move, remove, send, translate, transmit, transplant, transport; abalienate, alienate, assign, cede, confer, convey, consign, deed, devise, displace, forward, grant, pass, relegate. * *n* abalienation, alienation, assignment, bequest, carriage, cession, change, conveyance, copy, demise, devisal, gift, grant, move, relegation, removal, shift, shipment, transference, transferring, transit, transmission, transportation.

transfigure *vb* change, convert, dignify, idealize, metamorphose, transform.

transform *vb* alter, change, metamorphose, transfigure; convert, resolve, translate, transmogrify, transmute.

transgress *vb* exceed, transcend, overpass, overstep; break, contravene, disobey, infringe, violate; err, intrude, offend, sin, slip, trespass.

transgression *n* breach, disobedience, encroachment, infraction, infringement, transgression, violation; crime, delinquency, error, fault, iniquity, misdeed, misdemeanour, misdoing,
offence, sin, slip, trespass, wrongdoing.

transient *adj* diurnal, ephemeral, evanescent, fleeting, fugitive, impertinent, meteoric, mortal, passing, perishable, short-lived, temporary, transitory, volatile; hasty, imperfect, momentary, short.

transitory *adj* brief, ephemeral, evanescent, fleeting, flitting, fugacious, momentary, passing, short, temporary, transient.

translate *vb* remove, transfer, transport; construe, decipher, decode, interpret, render, turn.

translucent *adj* diaphanous, hyaline, pellucid, semi-opaque, semi-transparent.

transmit *vb* forward, remit, send; communicate, conduct, radiate; bear, carry, convey.

transparent *adj* bright, clear, diaphanous, limpid, lucid; crystalline, hyaline, pellucid, serene, translucent, transpicuous, unclouded; open, porous, transpicuous; evident, obvious, manifest, patent.

transpire *vb* befall, chance, happen, occur; evaporate, exhale.

transport *vb* bear, carry, cart, conduct, convey, fetch, remove, ship, take, transfer, truck; banish, expel; beatify, delight, enrapture, enravish, entrance, ravish. * *n* carriage, conveyance, movement, transportation, transporting; beatification, beatitude, bliss, ecstasy, felicity, happiness, rapture, ravishment; frenzy, passion, vehemence, warmth.

transude *vb* exude, filter, ooze, percolate, strain.

trap *vb* catch, ensnare, entrap, noose, snare, springe; ambush, deceive, dupe, trick; enmesh, tangle, trepan. * *n* gin, snare, springe, toil; ambush, artifice, pitfall, stratagem, trepan.

trappings *npl* adornments, decorations, dress, embellishments, frippery, gear, livery, ornaments, paraphernalia, rigging; accoutrements, caparisons, equipment, gear.

trash *n* dregs, dross, garbage, refuse, rubbish, trumpery, waste; balderdash, nonsense, twaddle.

travel *vb* journey, peregrinate, ramble, roam, rove, tour, voyage, walk, wander; go, move, pass. * *n* excursion, expedition, journey, peregrination, ramble, tour, trip, voyage, walk.

traveller *n* excursionist, explorer, globetrotter, itinerant, passenger, pilgrim, rover, sightseer, tourist, trekker, tripper, voyager, wanderer, wayfarer.

traverse *vb* contravene, counteract, defeat, frustrate, obstruct, oppose, thwart; ford, pass, play, range.

travesty *vb* imitate, parody, take off. * *n* burlesque, caricature, imitation, parody, take-off.

treacherous *adj* deceitful, disloyal, faithless, false, false-hearted, insidious, perfidious, recreant, sly, traitorous, treasonable, unfaithful, unreliable, unsafe, untrustworthy.

treachery *n* betrayal, deceitfulness, disloyalty, double-dealing, faithlessness, foul play, infidelity, insidiousness, perfidiousness, treason, perfidy.

treason *n* betrayal, disloyalty, lèse-majesté, lese-majesty, perfidy, sedition, traitorousness, treachery.

treasonable *adj* disloyal, traitorous, treacherous.

treasure *vb* accumulate, collect, garner, hoard, husband, save, store; cherish, idolize, prize, value, worship. * *n* cash, funds, jewels, money, riches, savings, valuables, wealth; abundance, reserve, stock, store.

treasurer *n* banker, bursar, purser, receiver, trustee.

treat *vb* entertain, feast, gratify, refresh; attend, doctor, dose, handle, manage, serve; bargain, covenant, negotiate, parley. * *n* banquet, entertainment, feast; delight, enjoyment, entertainment, gratification, luxury, pleasure, refreshment.

treatise *n* commentary, discourse, dissertation, disquisition, monograph, tractate.

treatment *n* usage, use; dealing, handling, management, manipulation; doctoring, therapy.

treaty *n* agreement, alliance, bargain, compact, concordat, convention, covenant, entente, league, pact.

tremble *vb* quake, quaver, quiver, shake, shiver, shudder, vibrate, wobble. * *n* quake, quiver, shake, shiver, shudder, tremor, vibration, wobble.

tremendous *adj* colossal, enormous, huge, immense; excellent, marvellous, wonderful; alarming, appalling, awful, dreadful, fearful, frightful, horrid, horrible, terrible.

tremor *n* agitation, quaking, quivering, shaking, trembling, trepidation, tremulousness, vibration.

tremulous *adj* afraid, fearful, quavering, quivering, shaking, shaky, shivering, timid, trembling, vibrating.

trench *vb* carve, cut; ditch, channel, entrench, furrow. * *n* channel, ditch, drain, furrow, gutter, moat, pit, sewer, trough;

dugout, entrenchment, fortification.

trenchant *adj* cutting, keen, sharp; acute, biting, caustic, crisp, incisive, pointed, piquant, pungent, sarcastic, sententious, severe, unsparing, vigorous.

trend *vb* drift, gravitate, incline, lean, run, stretch, sweep, tend, turn. * *n* bent, course, direction, drift, inclination, set, leaning, tendency, trending.

trepidation *n* agitation, quaking, quivering, shaking, trembling, tremor; dismay, excitement, fear, perturbation, tremulousness.

trespass *vb* encroach, infringe, intrude, trench; offend, sin, transgress. * *n* encroachment, infringement, injury, intrusion, invasion; crime, delinquency, error, fault, sin, misdeed, misdemeanour, offence, transgression; trespasser.

trial *adj* experimental, exploratory, testing. * *n* examination, experiment, test; experience, knowledge; aim, attempt, effort, endeavour, essay, exertion, struggle; assay, criterion, ordeal, prohibition, proof, test, touchstone; affliction, burden, chagrin, dolour, distress, grief, hardship, heartache, inclination, misery, mortification, pain, sorrow, suffering, tribulation, trouble, unhappiness, vexation, woe, wretchedness; action, case, cause, hearing, suit.

tribe *n* clan, family, lineage, race, sept, stock; class, distinction, division, order.

tribulation *n* adversity, affliction, distress, grief, misery, pain, sorrow, suffering, trial, trouble, unhappiness, woe, wretchedness.

tribunal *n* bench, judgement seat; assizes, bar, court, judicature, session.

tribute *n* subsidy, tax; custom, duty, excise, impost, tax, toll; contribution, grant, offering.

trice *n* flash, instant, jiffy, moment, second, twinkling.

trick *vb* cheat, circumvent, cozen, deceive, defraud, delude, diddle, dupe, fob, gull, hoax, overreach. * *n* artifice, blind, deceit, deception, dodge, fake, feint, fraud, game, hoax, imposture, manoeuvre, shift, ruse, swindle, stratagem, wile; antic, caper, craft, deftness, gambol, sleight; habit, mannerism, peculiarity, practice.

trickle *vb* distil, dribble, drip, drop, ooze, percolate, seep. * *n* dribble, drip, percolation, seepage.

tricky *adj* artful, cunning, deceitful, deceptive, subtle, trickish.

trifle *vb* dally, dawdle, fool, fribble, palter, play, potter, toy. * *n* bagatelle, bauble, bean, fig, nothing, triviality; iota, jot, modicum, particle, trace.

trifling *adj* empty, frippery, frivolous, inconsiderable, insignificant, nugatory, petty, piddling, shallow, slight, small, trivial, unimportant, worthless.

trill *vb* shake, quaver, warble. * *n* quaver, shake, tremolo, warbling.

trim *vb* adjust, arrange, prepare; balance, equalize, fill; adorn, array, bedeck, decorate, dress, embellish, garnish, ornament; clip, curtail, cut, lop, mow, poll, prune, shave, shear; berate, chastise, chide, rebuke, reprimand, reprove, trounce; fluctuate, hedge, shift, shuffle, vacillate. * *adj* compact, neat, nice, shapely, snug, tidy, well-adjusted, well-ordered; chic, elegant, finical, smart, spruce. * *n* dress, embellishment, gear, ornaments, trappings, trimmings; case, condition, order, plight, state.

trinket *n* bagatelle, bauble, bijoux, gewgaw, gimcrack, knick-knack, toy, trifle.

trinkets *npl* bijouterie, jewellery, jewels, ornaments.

trip *vb* caper, dance, frisk, hop, skip; misstep, stumble; bungle, blunder, err, fail, mistake; overthrow, supplant, upset; catch, convict, detect. * *n* hop, skip; lurch, misstep, stumble; blunder, bungle, error, failure, fault, lapse, miss, mistake, oversight, slip; circuit, excursion, expedition, jaunt, journey, ramble, route, stroll, tour.

trite *adj* banal, beaten, common, commonplace, hackneyed, old, ordinary, stale, stereotyped, threadbare, usual, worn.

triturate *vb* beat, bray, bruise, grind, pound, rub, thrash; comminute, levigate, pulverize.

triumph *vb* exult, rejoice; prevail, succeed, win; flourish, prosper, thrive; boast, brag, crow, gloat, swagger, vaunt. * *n* celebration, exultation, joy, jubilation, jubilee, ovation; accomplishment, achievement, conquest, success, victory.

triumphant *adj* boastful, conquering, elated, exultant, exulting, jubilant, rejoicing, successful, victorious.

trivial *adj* frivolous, gimcrack, immaterial, inconsiderable, insignificant, light, little, nugatory, paltry, petty, small, slight, slim, trifling, trumpery, unimportant.

trollop *n* prostitute, slattern, slut, whore.

troop *vb* crowd, flock, muster, throng. * *n* company, crowd, flock, herd, multitude, number, throng; band, body, party, squad, troupe.

trophy *n* laurels, medal, palm, prize.

troth *n* candour, sincerity, truth, veracity, verity; allegiance, belief, faith, fidelity, word; betrothal.

trouble *vb* agitate, confuse, derange, disarrange, disorder, disturb; afflict, ail, annoy, badger, concern, disquiet, distress, fret, grieve, harass, molest, perplex, perturb, pester, plague, torment, vex, worry. * *n* adversity, affliction, calamity, distress, dolour, grief, hardship, misfortune, misery, pain, sorrow, suffering, tribulation, woe; ado, annoyance, anxiety, bother, care, discomfort, embarrassment, fuss, inconvenience, irritation, pains, perplexity, plague, torment, vexation, worry; commotion, disturbance, row; bewilderment, disquietude, embarrassment, perplexity, uneasiness.

troublesome *adj* annoying, distressing, disturbing, galling, grievous, harassing, painful, perplexing, vexatious, worrisome; burdensome, irksome, tiresome, wearisome; importunate, intrusive, teasing; arduous, difficult, hard, inconvenient, trying, unwieldy.

troublous *adj* agitated, disquieted, disturbed, perturbed, tumultuous, turbulent.

trough *n* hutch, manger; channel, depression, hollow, furrow.

truant *vb* be absent, desert, dodge, malinger, shirk, skive. * *n* absentee, deserter, idler, laggard, loiterer, lounger, malingerer, quitter, runaway, shirker, vagabond.

truce *n* armistice, breathing space, cessation, delay, intermission, lull, pause, recess, reprieve, respite, rest.

truck *vb* barter, deal, exchange, trade, traffic. * *n* lorry, van, wagon.

truckle *vb* roll, trundle; cringe, crouch, fawn, knuckle, stoop, submit, yield.

truculent *adj* barbarous, bloodthirsty, ferocious, fierce, savage; cruel, malevolent, relentless; destructive, deadly, fatal, ruthless.

true *adj* actual, unaffected, authentic, genuine, legitimate, pure, real, rightful, sincere, sound, truthful, veritable; substantial, veracious; constant, faithful, loyal, staunch, steady; equitable, honest, honourable, just, upright, trusty, trustworthy, virtuous; accurate, correct, even, exact, right, straight, undeviating. * *adv* good, well.

truism *n* axiom, commonplace, platitude.

trumpery *adj* pinchbeck, rubbishy, trashy, trifling, worthless. * *n* deceit, deception, falsehood, humbug, imposture; frippery, rubbish, stuff, trash, trifles.

truncheon *n* club, cudgel, nightstick, partisan, staff; baton, wand.

trunk *n* body, bole, butt, shaft, stalk, stem, stock, torso; box, chest, coffer.

trundle *vb* bowl, revolve, roll, spin, truckle, wheel.

truss *vb* bind, bundle, close, cram, hang, pack. * *n* bundle, package, packet; apparatus, bandage, support.

trust *vb* confide, depend, expect, hope, rely; believe, credit; commit, entrust. * *n* belief, confidence, credence, faith; credit, tick; charge, deposit; commission, duty, errand; assurance, conviction, expectation, hope, reliance, secutrity.

trustful *adj* confiding, trusting, unquestioning, unsuspecting; faithful, trustworthy, trusty.

trustworthy *adj* confidential, constant, credible, dependable, faithful, firm, honest, incorrupt, upright, reliable, responsible, straightforward, staunch, true, trusty, uncorrupt, upright.

truth *n* fact, reality, veracity; actuality, authenticity, realism; canon, law, oracle, principle; right, truthfulness, veracity; candour, fidelity, frankness, honesty, honour, ingenuousness, integrity, probity, sincerity, virtue; constancy, devotion, faith, fealty, loyalty, steadfastness; accuracy, correctness, exactitude, exactness, nicety, precision, regularity, trueness.

truthful *adj* correct, reliable, true, trustworthy, veracious; artless, candid, frank, guileless, honest, ingenuous, open, sincere, straightforward, trusty.

truthless *adj* canting, disingenuous, dishonest, false, faithless, hollow, hypocritical, insincere, pharisaical, treacherous, unfair, untrustworthy.

try *vb* examine, prove, test; attempt, essay; adjudicate, adjudge, examine, hear; purify, refine; sample, sift, smell, taste; aim, attempt, endeavour, seek, strain, strive. * *n* attempt, effort, endeavour, experiment, trial.

trying *adj* difficult, fatiguing, hard, irksome, tiresome, wearisome; afflicting, afflictive, calamitous, deplorable, dire, distressing, grievous, hard, painful, sad, severe.

tryst *n* appointment, assignation, rendezvous.

tube *n* bore, bronchus, cylinder, duct, hollow, hose, pipe, pipette, worm.

tuft *n* brush, bunch, crest, feather, knot, plume, topknot, tussock; clump, cluster, group.

tug *vb* drag, draw, haul, pull, tow, wrench; labour, strive, struggle. * *n* drag, haul, pull, tow, wrench.

tuition *n* education, instruction, schooling, teaching, training.

tumble *vb* heave, pitch, roll, toss, wallow; fall, sprawl, stumble, topple, trip; derange, disarrange, dishevel, disorder, disturb, rumple, tousle. * *n* collapse, drop, fall, plunge, spill, stumble, trip.

tumbler *n* acrobat, juggler; glass.

tumid *adj* bloated, distended, enlarged, puffed-up, swelled, swollen, turgid; bombastic, declamatory, fustian, grandiloquent, grandiose, high-flown, inflated, pompous, puffy, rhetorical, stilted, swelling.

tumour *n* boil, carbuncle, swelling, tumefaction.

tumult *n* ado, affray, agitation, altercation, bluster, brawl, disturbance, ferment, flurry, feud, fracas, fray, fuss, hubbub, huddle, hurly-burly, melee, noise, perturbation, pother, quarrel, racket, riot, row, squabble, stir, turbulence, turmoil, uproar.

tumultuous *adj* blustery, breezy, bustling, confused, disorderly, disturbed, riotous, turbulent, unruly.

tune *vb* accord, attune, harmonize, modulate; adapt, adjust, attune. * *n* air, aria, melody, strain, tone; agreement, concord, harmony; accord, order.

tuneful *adj* dulcet, harmonious, melodious, musical.

turbid *adj* foul, impure, muddy, thick, unsettled.

turbulence *n* agitation, commotion, confusion, disorder, disturbance, excitement, tumult, tumultuousness, turmoil, unruliness, uproar; insubordination, insurrection, mutiny, rebellion, riot, sedition.

turbulent *adj* agitated, disturbed, restless, tumultuous, wild; blatant, blustering, boisterous, brawling, disorderly, obstreperous, tumultuous, uproarious, vociferous; factious, insubordinate, insurgent, mutinous, raging, rebellious, refractory, revolutionary, riotous, seditious, stormy, violent.

turf *n* grass, greensward, sod, sward; horse racing, racecourse, race-ground.

turgid *adj* bloated, distended, protuberant, puffed-up, swelled, swollen, tumid; bombastic, declamatory, diffuse, digressive, fustian, high-flown, inflated, grandiloquent, grandiose, ostentatious, pompous, puffy, rhetorical, stilted.

turmoil *n* activity, agitation, bustle, commotion, confusion, disorder, disturbance, ferment, flurry, huddle, hubbub, hurly-burly, noise, trouble, tumult, turbulence, uproar.

turn *vb* revolve, rotate; bend, cast, defect, inflict, round, spin, sway, swivel, twirl, twist, wheel; crank, grind, wind; deflect, divert, transfer, warp; form, mould, shape; adapt, fit, manoeuvre, suit; alter, change, conform, metamorphose, transform, transmute, vary; convert, persuade, prejudice; construe, render, translate; depend, hang, hinge, pivot; eventuate, issue, result, terminate; acidify, curdle, ferment. * *n* cycle, gyration, revolution, rotation, round; bending, deflection, deviation, diversion, doubling, flection, flexion, flexure, reel, retroversion, slew, spin, sweep, swing, swirl, swivel, turning, twist, twirl, whirl, winding; alteration, change, variation, vicissitude; bend, circuit, drive, ramble, run, round, stroll; bout, hand, innings, opportunity, shift, spell; act, action, deed, office; convenience, occasion, purpose; cast, fashion, form, guise, manner, mould, phase, shape; aptitude, bent, bias, disposition, faculty, genius, gift, inclination, leaning, proclivity, proneness, propensity, talent, tendency.

turncoat *n* apostate, backslider, deserter, recreant, renegade, traitor, wretch.

turpitude *n* baseness, degradation, depravity, vileness, wickedness.

turret *n* cupola, minaret, pinnacle.

tussle *vb* conflict, contend, contest, scuffle, struggle, wrestle. * *n* conflict, contest, fight, scuffle, struggle.

tutelage *n* care, charge, dependence, guardianship, protection, teaching, tutorage, tutorship, wardship.

tutor *vb* coach, educate, instruct, teach; discipline, train. * *n* coach, governess, governor, instructor, master, preceptor, schoolteacher, teacher.

twaddle *vb* chatter, gabble, maunder, prate, prattle. * *n* balderdash, chatter, flummery, gabble, gibberish, gobbledegook, gossip, jargon, moonshine, nonsense, platitude, prate, prattle, rigmarole, stuff, tattle.

tweak *vb, n* jerk, pinch, pull, twinge, twitch.

twig[1] *n* bough, branch, offshoot, shoot, slip, spray, sprig, stick, switch.

twig[2] *vb* catch on, comprehend, discover, grasp, realize, recognize, see, understand.

twin *vb* couple, link, match, pair. * *adj* double, doubled, duplicate, geminate, identical, matched, matching, second, twain. * *n* corollary, double, duplicate, fellow, likeness, match.

twine *vb* embrace, encircle, entwine, interlace, surround, wreathe; bend, meander, wind; coil, twist. * *n* convolution, coil, twist; embrace, twining, winding; cord, string.

twinge *vb* pinch, tweak, twitch. * *n* pinch, tweak, twitch; gripe, pang, spasm.

twinkle *vb* blink, twink, wink; flash, glimmer, scintillate, sparkle. * *n* blink, flash, gleam, glimmer, scintillation, sparkle; flash, instant, jiffy, moment, second, tick, trice, twinkling.

twinkling *n* flashing, sparkling, twinkle; flash, instant, jiffy, moment, second, tick, trice.

twirl *vb* revolve, rotate, spin, turn, twist, twirl. * *n* convolution, revolution, turn, twist, whirling.

twist *vb* purl, rotate, spin, twine; complicate, contort, convolute, distort, pervert, screw, wring; coil, writhe; encircle, wind, wreathe. * *n* coil, curl, spin, twine; braid, roll; change, complication, development, variation; bend, convolution, turn; defect, distortion, flaw, imperfection; jerk, pull, sprain, wrench; aberration, characteristic, eccentricity, oddity, peculiarity, quirk.

twit[1] *vb* banter, blame, censure, reproach, taunt, tease, upbraid.

twit[2] *n* blockhead, fool, idiot, nincompoop, nitwit.

twitch *vb* jerk, pluck, pull, snatch. * *n* jerk, pull; contraction, pull, quiver, spasm, twitching.

type *n* emblem, mark, stamp; adumbration, image, representation, representative, shadow, sign, symbol, token; archetype, exemplar, model, original, pattern, prototype, protoplast, standard; character, form, kind, nature, sort; figure, letter, text, typography.

typical *adj* emblematic, exemplary, figurative, ideal, indicative, model, representative, symbolic, true.

typify *vb* betoken, denote, embody, exemplify, figure, image, indicate, represent, signify.

tyrannical *adj* absolute, arbitrary, autocratic, cruel, despotic, dictatorial, domineering, high, imperious, irresponsible, severe, tyrannical, unjust; galling, grinding, inhuman, oppressive, overbearing, severe.

tyranny *n* absolutism, autocracy, despotism, dictatorship, harshness, oppression.

tyrant *n* autocrat, despot, dictator, oppressor.

tyro *n* beginner, learner, neophyte, novice; dabbler, smatterer.

U

ubiquitous *adj* omnipresent, present, universal.
udder *n* nipple, pap, teat.
ugly *adj* crooked, homely, ill-favoured, plain, ordinary, unlovely, unprepossessing, unshapely, unsightly; forbidding, frightful, gruesome, hideous, horrible, horrid, loathsome, monstrous, shocking, terrible, repellent, repulsive; bad-tempered, cantankerous, churlish, cross, quarrelsome, spiteful, surly, spiteful, vicious.
ulcer *n* boil, fester, gathering, pustule, sore.
ulterior *adj* beyond, distant, farther; hidden, personal, secret, selfish, undisclosed.
ultimate *adj* conclusive, decisive, eventual, extreme, farthest, final, last. * *n* acme, consummation, culmination, height, peak, pink, quintessence, summit.
ultra *adj* advanced, beyond, extreme, radical.
umbrage *n* shadow, shade; anger, displeasure, dissatisfaction, dudgeon, injury, offence, pique, resentment.
umpire *vb* adjudicate, arbitrate, judge, referee. * *n* adjudicator, arbiter, arbitrator, judge, referee.
unabashed *adj* bold, brazen, confident, unblushing, undaunted, undismayed.
unable *adj* impotent, incapable, incompetent, powerless, weak.
unacceptable *adj* disagreeable, distasteful, offensive, unpleasant, unsatisfactory, unwelcome.
unaccommodating *adj* disobliging, noncompliant, uncivil, ungracious.
unaccomplished *adj* incomplete, unachieved, undone, unperformed, unexecuted, unfinished; ill-educated, uncultivated, unpolished.
unaccountable *adj* inexplicable, incomprehensible, inscrutable, mysterious, unintelligible; irresponsible, unanswerable.
unaccustomed *adj* uninitiated, unskilled, unused; foreign, new, strange, unfamiliar, unusual.
unaffected *adj* artless, honest, naive, natural, plain, simple, sincere, real, unfeigned; chaste, pure, unadorned; insensible, unchanged, unimpressed, unmoved, unstirred, untouched.
unanimity *n* accord, agreement, concert, concord, harmony, union, unity.
unanimous *adj* agreeing, concordant, harmonious, like-minded, solid, united.
unassuming *adj* humble, modest, reserved, unobtrusive, unpretending, unpretentious.
unattainable *adj* inaccessible, unobtainable.
unavailing *adj* abortive, fruitless, futile, ineffectual, ineffective, inept, nugatory, unsuccessful, useless, vain.
unbalanced *adj* unsound, unsteady; unadjusted, unsettled.
unbearable *adj* insufferable, insupportable, unendurable.
unbecoming *adj* inappropriate, indecent, indecorous, improper, unbefitting, unbeseeming, unseemly, unsuitable.
unbelief *n* disbelief, dissent, distrust, incredulity, incredulousness, miscreance, miscreancy, nonconformity; doubt, freethinking, infidelity, scepticism.
unbeliever *n* agnostic, deist, disbeliever, doubter, heathen, infidel, sceptic.
unbending *adj* inflexible, rigid, stiff, unpliant, unyielding; firm, obstinate, resolute, stubborn.
unbiased *adj* disinterested, impartial, indifferent, neutral, uninfluenced, unpreju-

diced, unwarped.

unbind *vb* loose, undo, unfasten, unloose, untie; free, unchain, unfetter.

unblemished *adj* faultless, guiltless, immaculate, impeccable, innocent, intact, perfect, pure, sinless, spotless, stainless, undefiled, unspotted, unsullied, untarnished.

unblushing *adj* boldfaced, impudent, shameless.

unbounded *adj* absolute, boundless, endless, immeasurable, immense, infinite, interminable, measureless, unlimited, vast; immoderate, uncontrolled, unrestrained, unrestricted.

unbridled *adj* dissolute, intractable, lax, licensed, licentious, loose, uncontrolled, ungovernable, unrestrained, violent, wanton.

unbroken *adj* complete, entire, even, full, intact, unimpaired; constant, continuous, fast, profound, sound, successive, undisturbed; inviolate, unbetrayed, unviolated.

unbuckle *vb* loose, unfasten, unloose.

uncanny *adj* inopportune, unsafe; eerie, eery, ghostly, unearthly, unnatural, weird.

unceremonious *adj* abrupt, bluff, blunt, brusque, course, curt, gruff, plain, rough, rude, ungracious; casual, familiar, informal, offhand, unconstrained.

uncertain *adj* ambiguous, doubtful, dubious, equivocal, indefinite, indeterminate, indistinct, questionable, unsettled; insecure, precarious, problematical; capricious, changeable, desultory, fitful, fluctuating, irregular, mutable, shaky, slippery, unreliable, variable.

unchaste *adj* dissolute, incontinent, indecent, immoral, lascivious, lecherous, libidinous, lewd, loose, obscene, wanton.

unchecked *adj* uncurbed, unhampered, unhindered, unobstructed, unrestrained, untrammelled.

uncivil *adj* bearish, blunt, boorish, brusque, discourteous, disobliging, disrespectful, gruff, ill-bred, ill-mannered, impolite, irreverent, rough, rude, uncomplaisant, uncourteous, uncouth, ungentle, ungracious, unmannered, unseemly.

unclean *adj* abominable, beastly, dirty, filthy, foul, grimy, grubby, miry, muddy, nasty, offensive, purulent, repulsive, soiled, sullied; improper, indecent, indecorous, obscene, polluted, risqué, sinful, smutty, unholy, uncleanly.

uncomfortable *adj* disagreeable, displeasing, disquieted, distressing, disturbed, uneasy, unpleasant, restless; cheerless, close, oppressive; dismal, miserable, unhappy.

uncommon *adj* choice, exceptional, extraordinary, infrequent, noteworthy, odd, original, queer, rare, remarkable, scarce, singular, strange, unexampled, unfamiliar, unusual, unwonted.

uncommunicative *adj* close, inconversable, reserved, reticent, taciturn, unsociable, unsocial.

uncomplaining *adj* long-suffering, meek, patient, resigned, tolerant.

uncompromising *adj* inflexible, narrow, obstinate, orthodox, rigid, stiff, strict, unyielding.

unconcerned *adj* apathetic, careless, indifferent.

unconditional *adj* absolute, categorical, complete, entire, free, full, positive, unlimited, unqualified, unreserved, unrestricted.

uncongenial *adj* antagonistic, discordant, displeasing, ill-assorted, incompatible, inharmonious, mismatched, unsuited, unsympathetic.

uncouth *adj* awkward, boorish, clownish, clumsy, gawky, inelegant, loutish, lubberly, rough, rude, rustic, uncourtly, ungainly, unpolished, unrefined, unseemly; odd, outlandish, strange, unfamiliar, unusual.

uncover *vb* denude, divest, lay bare, strip; disclose, discover, expose, reveal, unmask, unveil; bare, doff; open, unclose, unseal.

unctuous *adj* adipose, greasy, oily, fat, fatty, oleaginous, pinguid, sebaceous; bland, lubricious, smooth, slippery; bland, fawning, glib, obsequious, plausible, servile, suave, sycophantic; fervid, gushing.

uncultivated *adj* fallow, uncultured, unreclaimed, untilled; homely, ignorant, illiterate, rude, uncivilized, uncultured, uneducated, unfit, unlettered, unpolished, unread, unready, unrefined, untaught; rough, savage, sylvan, uncouth, wild.

undaunted *adj* bold, brave, courageous, dauntless, fearless, intrepid, plucky, resolute, undismayed.

undefiled *adj* clean, immaculate, pure, spotless, stainless, unblemished, unspotted, unsullied, untarnished; honest, innocent, inviolate, pure, uncorrupted, unpolluted, unstained.

undemonstrative *adj* calm, composed, demure, impassive, modest, placid, quiet, reserved, sedate, sober, staid, tranquil.

undeniable *adj* certain, conclusive, evident, incontestable, incontrovertible, indisputable, indubitable, obvious, unquestionable.

under *prep* below, beneath, inferior to, lower than, subordinate to, underneath. * *adv* below, beneath, down, lower.

underestimate *vb* belittle, underrate, undervalue.

undergo *vb* bear, endure, experience, suffer, sustain.

underhand *adj* clandestine, deceitful, disingenuous, fraudulent, hidden, secret, sly, stealthy, underhanded, unfair. * *adv* clandestinely, privately, secretly, slyly, stealthily, surreptitiously; fraudulently, unfairly.

underling *n* agent, inferior, servant, subordinate.

undermine *vb* excavate, mine, sap; demoralize, foil, frustrate, thwart, weaken.

understand *vb* apprehend, catch, comprehend, conceive, discern, grasp, know, penetrate, perceive, see, seize, twig; assume, interpret, take; imply, mean.

understanding *adj* compassionate, considerate, forgiving, kind, kindly, patient, sympathetic, tolerant. * *n* brains, comprehension, discernment, faculty, intellect, intelligence, judgement, knowledge, mind, reason, sense.

undertake *vb* assume, attempt, begin, embark on, engage in, enter upon, take in hand; agree, bargain, contract, covenant, engage, guarantee, promise, stipulate.

undertaking *n* adventure, affair, attempt, business, effort, endeavour, engagement, enterprise, essay, move, project, task, venture.

undesigned *adj* spontaneous, unintended, unintentional, unplanned, unpremeditated.

undigested *adj* crude, ill-advised, ill-considered, ill-judged; confused, disorderly, ill-arranged, unmethodical.

undivided *adj* complete, entire, whole; one, united.

undo *vb* annul, cancel, frustrate, invalidate, neutralize, nullify, offset, reverse; disengage, loose, unfasten, unmake, unravel, untie; crush, destroy, overturn, ruin.

undoubted *adj* incontrovertible, indisputable, indubitable, undisputed, unquestionable, unquestioned.

undress *vb* denude, dismantle, disrobe, unclothe, unrobe, peel, strip. * *n* disarray, nakedness, nudity; mufti, negligee.

undue *adj* illegal, illegitimate, improper, unlawful, excessive, disproportionate, disproportioned, immoderate, unsuitable; unfit.

undulation *n* billowing, fluctuation, pulsation, ripple, wave.

undying *adj* deathless, endless, immortal, imperishable.

unearthly *adj* preternatural, supernatural, uncanny, weird.

uneasy *adj* disquieted, disturbed, fidgety, impatient, perturbed, restless, restive, unquiet, worried; awkward, stiff, ungainly, ungraceful; constraining, cramping, disagreeable, uncomfortable.

unending *adj* endless, eternal, everlasting, interminable, never-ending, perpetual, unceasing.

unequal *adj* disproportionate, disproportioned, ill-matched, inferior, irregular, insufficient, not alike, uneven.

unequalled *adj* exceeding, incomparable, inimitable, matchless, new, nonpareil, novel, paramount, peerless, pre-eminent, superlative, surpassing, transcendent, unheard of, unique, unparalleled, unrivalled.

unequivocal *adj* absolute, certain, clear, evident, incontestable, indubitable, positive; explicit, unambiguous, unmistakable.

uneven *adj* hilly, jagged, lumpy, ragged, rough, rugged, stony; motley, unequal, variable, variegated.

uneventful *adj* commonplace, dull, eventless, humdrum, quiet, monotonous, smooth, uninteresting.

unexceptionable *adj* excellent, faultless, good, irreproachable.

unexpected *adj* abrupt, sudden, unforeseen.

unfair *adj* dishonest, dishonourable, faithless, false, hypocritical, inequitable, insincere, oblique, one-sided, partial, unequal, unjust, wrongful.

unfaithful *adj* adulterous, derelict, deceitful, dishonest, disloyal, false, faithless, fickle, perfidious, treacherous, unreliable; negligent; changeable, inconstant, untrue.

unfamiliar *adj* bizarre, foreign, new, novel, outlandish, queer, singular, strange, uncommon, unusual.

unfashionable *adj* antiquated, destitute, disused, obsolete, old-fashioned, unconventional.

unfavourable *adj* adverse, contrary, disadvantageous, discouraging, ill, inauspicious, inimical, inopportune, indisposed, malign, sinister, unfriendly, unlucky, unpropitious, untimely; foul, inclement.

unfeeling *adj* apathetic, callous, heartless, insensible, numb, obdurate, torpid, unconscious, unimpressionable; adamantine, cold-blooded, cruel, hard, merciless, pitiless, stony, unkind, unsympathetic.

unfit *vb* disable, disqualify, incapacitate. * *adj* improper, inappropriate, incompetent, inconsistent, unsuitable; ill-equipped, inadequate, incapable, unqualified, useless; debilitated, feeble, flabby, unhealthy, unsound.

unflagging *adj* constant, indefatigable, never-ending, persevering, steady, unfaltering, unremitting, untiring, unwearied.

unflinching *adj* firm, resolute, steady, unshrinking.

unfold *vb* display, expand, open, separate, unfurl, unroll; declare, disclose, reveal, tell; decipher, develop, disentangle, evolve, explain, illustrate, interpret, resolve, unravel.

unfortunate *adj* hapless, ill-fated, ill-starred, infelicitous, luckless, unhappy, unlucky, unprosperous, unsuccessful, wretched; calamitous, deplorable, disastrous; inappropriate, inexpedient.

unfrequented *adj* abandoned, deserted, forsaken, lone, solitary, uninhabited, unoccupied.

unfruitful *adj* barren, fruitless, sterile; infecund, unprolific; unprofitable, unproductive.

ungainly *adj* awkward, boorish, clownish, clumsy, gawky, inelegant, loutish, lubberly, lumbering, slouching, stiff, uncourtly, uncouth, ungraceful.

ungentlemanly *adj* ill-bred, impolite, rude, uncivil, ungentle, ungracious, unmannerly.

unhappy *adj* afflicted, disastrous, dismal, distressed, drear, evil, inauspicious, miserable, painful, unfortunate, wretched.

unhealthy *adj* ailing, diseased, feeble, indisposed, infirm, poorly, sickly, toxic, unsanitary, unsound, toxic, venomous.

uniform *adj* alike, constant, even, equable, equal, smooth, steady, regular, unbroken, unchanged, undeviating, unvaried, unvarying. * *n* costume, dress, livery, outfit, regalia, suit.

uniformity *n* constancy, continuity, permanence, regularity, sameness, stability; accordance, agreement, conformity, consistency, unanimity.

unimportant *adj* immaterial, inappreciable, inconsequent, inconsequential, inconsiderable, indifferent, insignificant, mediocre, minor, paltry, petty, small, slight, trifling, trivial.

unintentional *adj* accidental, casual, fortuitous, inadvertent, involuntary, spontaneous, undesigned, unmeant, unplanned, unpremeditated, unthinking.

uninterrupted *adj* continuous, endless, incessant, perpetual, unceasing.

union *n* coalescence, coalition, combination, conjunction, coupling, fusion, incorporation, joining, junction, unification, uniting; agreement, concert, concord, concurrence, harmony, unanimity, unity; alliance, association, club, confederacy, federation, guild, league.

unique *adj* choice, exceptional, matchless, only, peculiar, rare, single, sole, singular, uncommon, unexampled, unmatched.

unison *n* accord, accordance, agreement, concord, harmony.

unite *vb* amalgamate, attach, blend, centralize, coalesce, confederate, consolidate, embody, fuse, incorporate, merge, weld; associate, conjoin, connect, couple, link, marry; combine, join; harmonize, reconcile; agree, concert, concur, cooperate, fraternize.

universal *adj* all-reaching, catholic, cosmic, encyclopedic, general, ubiquitous, unlimited; all, complete, entire, total, whole.

unjust *adj* inequitable, injurious, partial, unequal, unfair, unwarranted, wrong, wrongful; flagitious, heinous, influenced, iniquitous, nefarious, unrighteous, wicked; biased, prejudiced, uncandid.

unjustifiable *adj* indefensible, unjust, unreasonable, unwarrantable; inexcusable, unpardonable.

unknown *adj* unappreciated, unascertained; undiscovered, unexplored, uninvestigated; concealed, dark, enigmatic, hidden, mysterious, mystic; anonymous, incognito, inglorious, nameless, obscure, renownless, undistinguished, unheralded, unnoted.

unladylike *adj* ill-bred, impolite, rude, uncivil, ungentle, ungracious, unmannerly.

unlamented *adj* unmourned, unregretted.

unlimited *adj* boundless, infinite, interminable, limitless, measureless, unbounded; absolute, full, unconfined, unconstrained, unrestricted; indefinite, undefined.

unlucky *adj* baleful, disastrous, ill-fated, ill-starred, luckless, unfortunate, unprosperous, unsuccessful; ill-omened, inauspicious; miserable, unhappy.

unmanageable *adj* awkward, cumbersome, inconvenient, unwieldy; intractable, unruly, unworkable, vicious; difficult, impractical.

unmatched *adj* matchless, unequalled, unparalleled, unrivalled.

unmitigated *adj* absolute, complete, consummate, perfect, sheer, stark, thorough, unqualified, utter.

unnatural *adj* aberrant, abnormal, anomalous, foreign, irregular, prodigious, uncommon; brutal, cold, heartless, inhuman, unfeeling, unusual; affected, artificial, constrained, forced, insincere, self-conscious, stilted, strained; factitious.

unpleasant *adj* disagreeable, displeasing, distasteful, obnoxious, offensive, repulsive, unlovely, ungrateful, unacceptable, unpalatable, unwelcome.

unpremeditated *adj* extempore, impromptu, offhand, spontaneous, undesigned, unintentional, unstudied.

unprincipled *adj* bad, crooked, dishonest, fraudulent, immoral, iniquitous, knavish, lawless, profligate, rascally, roguish, thievish, trickish, tricky, unscrupulous, vicious, villainous, wicked.

unqualified *adj* disqualified, incompetent, ineligible, unadapted, unfit; absolute, certain, consummate, decided, direct, downright, full, outright, unconditional, unmeasured, unrestricted, unmitigated; exaggerated, sweeping.

unreal *adj* chimerical, dreamlike, fanciful, flimsy, ghostly, illusory, insubstantial, nebulous, shadowy, spectral, visionary, unsubstantial.

unreasonable *adj* absurd, excessive, exorbitant, foolish, ill-judged, illogical, immoderate, impractical, injudicious, irrational, nonsensical, preposterous, senseless, silly, stupid, unfair, unreasoning, unwarrantable, unwise.

unreliable *adj* fallible, fickle, irresponsible, treacherous, uncertain, undependable, unstable, unsure, untrustworthy.

unremitting *adj* assiduous, constant, continual, diligent, incessant, indefatigable, persevering, sedulous, unabating, unceasing.

unrepentant *adj* abandoned, callous, graceless, hardened, impenitent, incorrigible, irreclaimable, lost, obdurate, profligate, recreant, seared, shameless.

unrequited *adj* unanswered, unreturned, unrewarded.

unreserved *adj* absolute, entire, full, unlimited; above-board, artless, candid, communicative, fair, frank, guileless, honest, ingenuous, open, sincere, single-minded, undesigning, undissembling; demonstrative, emotional, open-hearted.

unresisting *adj* compliant, long-suffering, non-resistant, obedient, passive, patient, submissive, yielding.

unresponsive *adj* irresponsive, unsympathetic.

unrestrained *adj* unbridled, unchecked, uncurbed, unfettered, unhindered, unobstructed, unreserved; broad, dissolute, incontinent, inordinate, lax, lewd, licentious, loose, wanton; lawless, wild.

unrestricted *adj* free, unbridled, unconditional, unconfined, uncurbed, unfettered, unlimited, unqualified, unrestrained; clear, open, public, unobstructed.

unrevealed *adj* hidden, occult, secret, undiscovered, unknown.

unrewarded *adj* unpaid, unrecompensed.

unriddle *vb* explain, expound, solve, unfold, unravel.

unrighteous *adj* evil, sinful, ungodly, unholy, vicious, wicked, wrong; heinous, inequitable, iniquitous, nefarious, unfair, unjust.

unripe *adj* crude, green, hard, immature, premature, sour; incomplete, unfinished.

unrivalled *adj* incomparable, inimitable, matchless, peerless, unequalled, unexampled, unique, unparalleled.

unrobe *vb* disrobe, undress.

unroll *vb* develop, discover, evolve, open, unfold; display, lay open.

unromantic *adj* literal, matter-of-fact, prosaic.

unroot *vb* eradicate, extirpate, root out, uproot.

unruffled *adj* calm, peaceful, placid, quiet, serene, smooth, still, tranquil; collected, composed, cool, imperturbable, peaceful, philosophical, placid, tranquil, undisturbed, unexcited, unmoved.

unruly *adj* disobedient, disorderly, fractious, headstrong, insubordinate, intractable, mutinous, obstreperous, rebellious, refractory, riotous, seditious, turbulent, ungovernable, unmanageable, wanton, wild; lawless, obstinate, rebellious, stubborn, vicious.

unsafe *adj* dangerous, hazardous, insecure, perilous, precarious, risky, treacherous, uncertain, unprotected.

unsaid *adj* tacit, unmentioned, unspoken, unuttered.

unsanctified *adj* profane, unhallowed, unholy.

unsatisfactory *adj* insufficient; disappointing; faulty, feeble, imperfect, poor, weak.

unsatisfied *adj* insatiate, unsated, unsatiated, unstaunched; discontented, displeased, dissatisfied, malcontent; undischarged, unpaid, unperformed, unrendered.

unsavoury *adj* flat, insipid, mawkish, savourless, tasteless, unflavoured, unpalatable, vapid; disagreeable, disgusting, distasteful, nasty, nauseating, nauseous, offensive, rank, revolting, sickening, uninviting, unpleasing.

unsay *vb* recall, recant, retract, take back.

unscathed *adj* unharmed, uninjured.

unschooled *adj* ignorant, uneducated, uninstructed; undisciplined, untrained.

unscrupulous *adj* dishonest, reckless, ruthless, unconscientious, unprincipled, unrestrained.

unsealed *adj* open, unclosed.

unsearchable *adj* hidden, incomprehensible, inscrutable, mysterious.

unseasonable *adj* ill-timed, inappropriate, infelicitous, inopportune, untimely; late, too late; inexpedient, undesireable, unfit, ungrateful, unsuitable, unwelcome;

premature, too early.
unseasonably *adv* malapropos, unsuitably, untimely.
unseasoned *adj* inexperienced, unaccustomed, unqualified, untrained; immoderate, inordinate, irregular; green; fresh, unsalted.
unseeing *adj* blind, sightless.
unseemly *adj* improper, indecent, inappropriate, indecorous, unbecoming, uncomely, unfit, unmeet, unsuitable.
unseen *adj* undiscerned, undiscovered, unobserved, unperceived; imperceptible, indiscoverable, invisible, latent.
unselfish *adj* altruistic, devoted, disinterested, generous, high-minded, impersonal, liberal, magnanimous, self-denying, self-forgetful, selfless, self-sacrificing.
unserviceable *adj* ill-conditioned, unsound, useless; profitless, unprofitable.
unsettle *vb* confuse, derange, disarrange, disconcert, disorder, disturb, trouble, unbalance, unfix, unhinge, upset.
unsettled *adj* changeable, fickle, inconstant, restless, transient, unstable, unsteady, vacillating, wavering; inequable, unequal; feculent, muddy, roiled, roily, turbid; adrift, afloat, homeless, unestablished, uninhabited; open, tentative, unadjusted, undecided, undetermined; due, outstanding, owing, unpaid; perturbed, troubled, unnerved.
unshackle *vb* emancipate, liberate, loose, release, set free, unbind, unchain, unfetter.
unshaken *adj* constant, firm, resolute, steadfast, steady, unmoved.
unshapen *adj* deformed, grotesque, ill-formed, ill-made, ill-shaped, misshapen, shapeless, ugly, uncouth.
unsheltered *adj* exposed, unprotected.
unshrinking *adj* firm, determined, persisting, resolute, unblenching, unflinching.
unshroud *vb* discover, expose, reveal, uncover.
unsightly *adj* deformed, disagreeable, hideous, repellent, repulsive, ugly.
unskilful, unskillful *adj* awkward, bungling, clumsy, inapt, inexpert, maladroit, rough, rude, unhandy, unskilled, unversed.
unskilled *adj* inexperienced, raw, undisciplined, undrilled, uneducated, unexercised, unpractised, unprepared, unschooled; unskilful.
unslaked *adj* unquenched, unslacked.
unsleeping *adj* unslumbering, vigilant, wakeful, watchful.
unsmirched *adj* undefiled, unpolluted, unspotted.
unsociable *adj* distant, reserved, retiring, segregative, shy, solitary, standoffish, taciturn, uncommunicative, uncompanionable, ungenial, unsocial; inhospitable, misanthropic, morose.
unsoiled *adj* clean, spotless, unspotted, unstained, unsullied, untarnished.
unsophisticated *adj* genuine, pure, unadulterated; good, guileless, innocent, undepraved, unpolluted, invitiated; artless, honest, ingenuous, naive, natural, simple, sincere, straightforward, unaffected, undesigning, unstudied.
unsound *adj* decayed, defective, impaired, imperfect, rotten, thin, wasted, weak; broken, disturbed, light, restless; diseased, feeble, infirm, morbid, poorly, sickly, unhealthy, weak; deceitful, erroneous, fallacious, false, faulty, hollow, illogical, incorrect, invalid, ill-advised, irrational, questionable, sophistical, unreasonable, unsubstantial, untenable, wrong; dishonest, false, insincere, unfaithful, untrustworthy, untrue; insubstantial, unreal; heretical, heterodox, unorthodox.
unsparing *adj* bountiful, generous, lavish, liberal, profuse, ungrudging; harsh, inexorable, relentless, rigorous, ruthless, severe, uncompromising, unforgiving.
unspeakable *adj* indescribable, ineffable, inexpressible, unutterable.
unspiritual *adj* bodily, carnal, fleshly, sensual.
unspotted *adj* clean, spotless, unsoiled, unstained, unsullied, untarnished; faultless, immaculate, innocent, pure, stainless, unblemished, uncorrupted, undefiled, untainted.

unstable *adj* infirm, insecure, precarious, top-heavy, tottering, unbalanced, unballasted, unreliable, unsafe, unsettled, unsteady; changeable, erratic, fickle, inconstant, irresolute, mercurial, mutable, vacillating, variable, wavering, weak, volatile.—*also* **instable**.

unstained *adj* colourless, uncoloured, undyed, untinged; clean, spotless, unspotted.

unsteady *adj* fluctuating, oscillating, unsettled; insecure, precarious, unstable; changeable, desultory, ever-changing, fickle, inconstant, irresolute, mutable, unreliable, variable, wavering; drunken, jumpy, tottering, vacillating, wobbly, tipsy.

unstinted *adj* abundant, ample, bountiful, full, large, lavish, plentiful, prodigal, profuse.

unstrung *adj* overcome, shaken, unnerved, weak.

unstudied *adj* extempore, extemporaneous, impromptu, offhand, spontaneous, unpremeditated; inexpert, unskilled, unversed.

unsubdued *adj* unbowed, unbroken, unconquered, untamed.

unsubmissive *adj* disobedient, contumacious, indocile, insubordinate, obstinate, perverse, refractory, uncomplying, ungovernable, unmanageable, unruly, unyielding.

unsubstantial *adj* airy, flimsy, gaseous, gossamery, light, slight, tenuous, thin, vaporous; apparitional, bodiless, chimerical, cloudbuilt, dreamlike, empty, fantastical, ideal, illusory, imaginary, imponderable, moonshiny, spectral, unreal, vague, visionary; erroneous, fallacious, flimsy, groundless, illogical, unfounded, ungrounded, unsolid, unsound, untenable, weak.

unsuccessful *adj* abortive, bootless, fruitless, futile, ineffectual, profitless, unavailing, vain; ill-fated, ill-starred, luckless, unfortunate, unhappy, unlucky, unprosperous.

unsuitable *adj* ill-adapted, inappropriate, malapropos, unfit, unsatisfactory, unsuited; improper, inapplicable, inapt, incongruous, inexpedient, infelicitous, unbecoming, unbeseeming, unfitting.

unsuited *adj* unadapted, unfitted, unqualified.

unsullied *adj* chaste, clean, spotless, unsoiled, unspotted, unstained, untarnished; immaculate, pure, stainless, unblemished, uncorrupted, undefiled, untainted, untouched, virginal.

unsupplied *adj* destitute, unfurnished, unprovided.

unsupported *adj* unaided, unassisted; unbacked, unseconded, unsustained, unupheld.

unsurpassed *adj* matchless, peerless, unequalled, unexampled, unexcelled, unmatched, unparagoned, unparalleled, unrivalled.

unsusceptible *adj* apathetic, cold, impassive, insusceptible, phlegmatic, stoical, unimpressible, unimpressionable.

unsuspecting *adj* confiding, credulous, trusting, unsuspicious.

unsuspicious *adj* confiding, credulous, gullible, simple, trustful, unsuspecting.

unsustainable *adj* insupportable, intolerable; controvertible, erroneous, unmaintainable, untenable.

unswerving *adj* direct, straight, undeviating; constant, determined, firm, resolute, staunch, steadfast, steady, stable, unwavering.

unsymmetrical *adj* amorphous, asymmetric, disproportionate, formless, irregular, unbalanced.

unsystematic, unsystematical *adj* casual, disorderly, haphazard, irregular, planless, unmethodical.

untainted *adj* chaste, clean, faultless, fresh, healthy, pure, sweet, wholesome; spotless, unsoiled, unstained, unsullied, untarnished; immaculate, stainless, unblemished, uncorrupted, undefiled, unspotted.

untamable *adj* unconquerable.

untamed *adj* fierce, unbroken, wild.

untangle *vb* disentangle, explain, explicate.

untarnished *adj* chaste, clean, spotless,

unsoiled, unspotted, unstained, unsullied; immaculate, pure, spotless, stainless, unblemished, uncorrupted, undefiled, unspotted, unsullied, untainted, virginal, virtuous.

untaught *adj* illiterate, unenlightened, uninformed, unlettered; ignorant, inexperienced, undisciplined, undrilled, uneducated, uninitiated, uninstructed, untutored.

untenable *adj* indefensible, unmaintainable, unsound; fallacious, hollow, illogical, indefensible, insupportable, unjustifiable, weak.

untenanted *adj* deserted, empty, tenantless, uninhabited, unoccupied.

unterrified *adj* fearless, unappalled, unawed, undismayed, undaunted, unscared.

unthankful *adj* thankless, ungrateful.

unthinking *adj* careless, heedless, inconsiderate, thoughtless, unreasoning, unreflecting; automatic, mechanical.

unthoughtful *adj* careless, heedless, inconsiderable, thoughtless.

unthrifty *adj* extravagant, improvident, lavish, prodigal, profuse, thriftless, wasteful.

untidy *adj* careless, disorderly, dowdy, frumpy, mussy, slatternly, slovenly, unkempt, unneat.

untie *vb* free, loose, loosen, unbind, unfasten, unknot, unloose; clear, resolve, solve, unfold.

until *adv, conj* till, to the time when; to the place, point, state or degree that; * *prep* till, to.

untimely *adj* ill-timed, immature, inconvenient, inopportune, mistimed, premature, unseasonable, unsuitable; ill-considered, inauspicious, uncalled for, unfortunate. * *adv* unseasonably, unsuitably.

untinged *adj* achromatic, colourless, hueless, uncoloured, undyed, unstained.

untiring *adj* persevering, incessant, indefatigable, patient, tireless, unceasing, unfatiguable, unflagging, unremitting, unwearied, unwearying.

untold *adj* countless, incalculable, innumerable, uncounted, unnumbered; unrelated, unrevealed.

untouched *adj* intact, scatheless, unharmed, unhurt, uninjured, unscathed; insensible, unaffected, unmoved, unstirred.

untoward *adj* adverse, froward, intractable, perverse, refractory, stubborn, unfortunate; annoying, ill-timed, inconvenient, unmanageable, vexatious; awkward, uncouth, ungainly, ungraceful.

untrained *adj* green, ignorant, inexperienced, raw, unbroken, undisciplined, undrilled, uneducated, uninstructed, unpractised, unskilled, untaught, untutored.

untrammelled *adj* free, unhampered.

untried *adj* fresh, inexperienced, maiden, new, unassayed, unattempted, unattested, virgin; undecided.

untrodden *adj* pathless, trackless, unbeaten.

untroubled *adj* calm, careless, composed, peaceful, serene, smooth, tranquil, undisturbed, unvexed.

untrue *adj* contrary, false, inaccurate, wrong; disloyal, faithless, perfidious, recreant, treacherous, unfaithful.

untrustworthy *adj* deceitful, dishonest, inaccurate, rotten, slippery, treacherous, undependable, unreliable; disloyal, false; deceptive, fallible, illusive, questionable.

untruth *n* error, faithlessness, falsehood, falsity, incorrectness, inveracity, treachery; deceit, deception, fabrication, fib, fiction, forgery, imposture, invention, lie, misrepresentation, misstatement, story.

untutored *adj* ignorant, inexperienced, undisciplined, undrilled, uneducated, uninitiated, uninstructed, untaught; artless, natural, simple, unsophisticated.

untwist *vb* disentangle, disentwine, ravel, unravel, unwreathe.

unused *adj* idle, unemployed, untried; new, unaccustomed, unfamiliar.

unusual *adj* abnormal, curious, exceptional, extraordinary, odd, peculiar, queer, rare, recherché, remarkable, singular, strange, unaccustomed, uncommon, unwonted.

unutterable *adj* incommunicable, indescribable, ineffable, inexpressible, unspeakable.

unvarnished *adj* unpolished; candid, plain, simple, true, unadorned, unembellished.

unvarying *adj* constant, invariable, unchanging.

unveil *vb* disclose, expose, reveal, show, uncover, unmask.

unveracious *adj* false, lying, mendacious, untruthful.

unversed *adj* inexperienced, raw, undisciplined, undrilled, uneducated, unexercised, unpractised, unprepared, unschooled; unskilful.

unviolated *adj* inviolate, unbetrayed, unbroken.

unwarlike *adj* pacific, peaceful.

unwarped *adj* impartial, unbiased, undistorted, unprejudiced.

unwarrantable *adj* improper, indefensible, unjustifiable.

unwary *adj* careless, hasty, heedless, imprudent, incautious, indiscreet, precipitate, rash, reckless, remiss, uncircumspect, unguarded.

unwavering *adj* constant, determined, firm, fixed, resolute, settled, staunch, steadfast, steady, unhesitating.

unwearied *adj* unfatigued; constant, continual, incessant, indefatigable, persevering, persistent, unceasing, unremitting, untiring.

unwelcome *adj* disagreeable, unacceptable, ungrateful, unpleasant, unpleasing.

unwell *adj* ailing, delicate, diseased, ill, indisposed, sick.

unwept *adj* unlamented, unmourned, unregretted.

unwholesome *adj* baneful, deleterious, injurious, insalubrious, noisome, noxious, poisonous, unhealthful, unhealthy; injudicious, pernicious, unsound; corrupt, tainted.

unwieldy *adj* bulky, clumsy, cumbersome, cumbrous, elephantine, heavy, hulking, large, massy, ponderous, unmanageable, weighty.

unwilling *adj* averse, backward, disinclined, indisposed, laggard, loath, opposed, recalcitrant, reluctant; forced, grudging.

unwind *vb* unravel, unreel, untwine, wind off; disentangle.

unwise *adj* brainless, foolish, ill-advised, ill-judged, impolitic, imprudent, indiscreet, injudicious, inexpedient, senseless, silly, stupid, unwary, weak.

unwitnessed *adj* unknown, unseen, unspied.

unwittingly *adv* ignorantly, inadvertently, unconsciously, undesignedly, unintentionally, unknowingly.

unwonted *adj* infrequent, rare, uncommon, unusual; unaccustomed, unused.

unworthy *adj* undeserving; bad, base, blameworthy, worthless; shameful, unbecoming, vile; contemptible, derogatory, despicable, discreditable, mean, paltry, reprehensible, shabby.

unwrap *vb* open, unfold.

unwrinkled *adj* smooth, unforrowed.

unwritten *adj* oral, traditional, unrecorded; conventional, customary.

unwrought *adj* crude, rough, rude, unfashioned, unformed.

unyielding *adj* constant, determined, indomitable, inflexible, pertinacious, resolute, staunch, steadfast, steady, tenacious, uncompromising, unwavering; headstrong, intractable, obstinate, perverse, self-willed, stiff, stubborn, wayward, wilful; adamantine, firm, grim, hard, immovable, implastic, inexorable, relentless, rigid, unbending.

unyoke *vb* disconnect, disjoin, part, separate.

unyoked *adj* disconnected, separated; licentious, loose, unrestrained.

upbraid *vb* accuse, blame, chide, condemn, criticize, denounce, fault, reproach, reprove, revile, scold, taunt, twit.

upheaval *n* elevation, upthrow; cataclysm, convulsion, disorder, eruption, explosion, outburst, overthrow.

uphill *adj* ascending, upward; arduous, difficult, hard, laborious, strenuous, toilsome, wearisome.

uphold *vb* elevate, raise; bear up, hold up, support, sustain; advocate, aid, champion, countenance, defend, justify, maintain, vindicate.

upland *n* down, fell, ridge, plateau.

uplift *vb* raise, upraise; animate, elevate, inspire, lift, refine. * *n* ascent, climb, elevation, lift, rise, upthrust; exaltation, inspiration, uplifting; improvement, refinement.

upon *prep* on, on top of, over; about, concerning, on the subject of, relating to; immediately after, with.

upper hand *n* advantage, ascendancy, control, dominion, mastership, mastery, pre-eminence, rule, superiority, supremacy, whip hand.

uppermost *adj* foremost, highest, loftiest, supreme, topmost, upmost.

uppish *adj* arrogant, assuming, haughty, perky, proud, smart.

upright *adj* erect, perpendicular, vertical; conscientious, equitable, fair, faithful, good, honest, honourable, incorruptible, just, pure, righteous, straightforward, true, trustworthy, upstanding, virtuous.

uprightness *n* erectness, perpendicularity, verticality; equity, fairness, goodness, honesty, honour, incorruptibility, integrity, justice, probity, rectitude, righteousness, straightforwardness, trustiness, trustworthiness, virtue, worth.

uproar *n* clamour, commotion, confusion, din, disturbance, fracas, hubbub, hurly-burly, noise, pandemonium, racket, riot, tumult, turmoil, vociferation.

uproarious *adj* boisterous, clamorous, loud, noisy, obstreperous, riotous, tumultuous.

uproot *vb* eradicate, extirpate, root out.

upset *vb* capsize, invert, overthrow, overtumble, overturn, spill, tip over, topple, turn turtle; agitate, confound, confuse, discompose, disconcert, distress, disturb, embarrass, excite, fluster, muddle, overwhelm, perturb, shock, startle, trouble, unnerve, unsettle; checkmate, defeat, overthrow, revolutionize, subvert; foil, frustrate, nonplus, thwart. * *adj* disproved, exposed, overthrown; bothered, confused, disconcerted, flustered, mixed-up, perturbed; shocked, startled, unsettled; beaten, defeated, overcome, overpowered, overthrown; discomfited, distressed, discomposed, overexcited, overwrought, shaken, troubled, unnerved. * *n* confutation, refutation; foiling, frustration, overthrow, revolution, revulsion, ruin, subversdion, thwarting.

upshot *n* conclusion, consummation, effect, end, event, issue, outcome, result, termination.

upside down *adj* bottom side up, bottom up, confused, head over heels, inverted, topsy-turvy.

upstart *n* adventurer, arriviste, parvenu, snob, social cimber, yuppie.

upturned *adj* raised, uplifted; retroussé.

upward *adj* ascending, climbing, mounting, rising, uphill. * *adv* above, aloft, overhead, up; heavenwards, skywards.

urbane *adj* civil, complaisant, courteous, courtly, elegant, mannerly, polished, polite, refined, smooth, suave, well-mannered.

urbanity *n* amenity, civility, complaisance, courtesy, politeness, smoothness, suavity.

urchin *n* brat, child, kid, ragamuffin, rascal, scrap, squirt, tad.

urge *vb* crowd, drive, force on, impel, press, press on, push, push on; beg, beseech, conjure, entreat, exhort, implore, importune, ply, solicit, tease; animate, egg on, encourage, goad, hurry, incite, instigate, quicken, spur, stimulate. * *n* compulsion, desire, drive, impulse, longing, pressure, wish, yearning.

urgency *n* drive, emergency, exigency, haste, necessity, press, pressure, push, stress; clamorousness, entreaty, insistence, importunity, instance, solicitation; goad, incitement, spur, stimulus.

urgent *adj* cogent, critical, crucial, crying, exigent, immediate, imperative, important, importunate, insistent, instant, pertinacious, pressing, serious.

urinal *n* chamber, chamber pot, lavatory, pot, potty, jordan, toilet.

urinate *vb* make water, pee, pee-pee, piddle, piss, stale, wee.

usage *n* treatment; consuetude, custom,

fashion, habit, method, mode, practice, prescription, tradition, use.
use *vb* administer, apply, avail oneself of, drive, employ, handle, improve, make use of, manipulate, occupy, operate, ply, put into action, take advantage of, turn to account, wield, work; exercise, exert, exploit, practice, profit by, utilize; absorb, consume, exhaust, expend, swallow up, waste, wear out; accustom, familiarize, habituate, harden, inure, train; act toward, behave toward, deal with, manage, treat; be accustomed, be wont. * *n* appliance, application, consumption, conversion, disposal, exercise, employ, employment, practice, utilization; adaptability, advantage, avail, benefit, convenience, profit, service, usefulness, utility, wear; exigency, necessity, indispensability, need, occasion, requisiteness; custom, habit, handling, method, treatment, usage, way.
useful *adj* active, advantageous, available, availing, beneficial, commodious, conducive, contributory, convenient, effective, good, helpful, instrumental, operative, practical, profitable, remunerative, salutary, suitable, serviceable, utilitarian; available, helpful, serviceable, valuable.
usefulness *n* advantage, profit, serviceableness, utility, value.
useless *adj* abortive, bootless, fruitless, futile, helpless, idle, incapable, incompetent, ineffective, ineffectual, inutile, nugatory, null, profitless, unavailing, unprofitable, unproductive, unserviceable, valueless, worthless; good for nothing, waste.
usher *vb* announce, forerun, herald, induct, introduce, precede; conduct, direct, escort, shepherd, show. * *n* attendant, conductor, escort, shepherd, squire.
usual *adj* accustomed, common, customary, everyday, familiar, frequent, general, habitual, normal, ordinary, prevailing, prevalent, regular, wonted.
usurp *vb* appropriate, arrogate, assume, seize.
usurpation *n* assumption, dispossession, infringement, seizure.
usury *n* interest; exploitation, extortion, profiteering.
utensil *n* device, implement, instrument, tool.
utility *n* advantageousness, avail, benefit, profit, service, use, usefulness; happiness, welfare.
utilize *vb* employ, exploit, make use of, put to use, turn to account, use.
utmost *adj* extreme, farthest, highest, last, main, most distant, remotest; greatest, uttermost. * *n* best, extreme, maximum, most.
Utopian *adj* air-built, air-drawn, chimerical, fanciful, ideal, imaginary, visionary, unreal.
utricle *n* bladder, cyst, sac, vesicle.
utter[1] *adj* complete, entire, perfect, total; absolute, blank, diametric, downright, final, peremptory, sheer, stark, thorough, thoroughgoing, unconditional, unqualified, total.
utter[2] *vb* articulate, breathe, deliver, disclose, divulge, emit, enunciate, express, give forth, pronounce, reveal, speak, talk, tell, voice; announce, circulate, declare, issue, publish.
utterance *n* articulation, delivery, disclosure, emission, expression, pronouncement, pronunciation, publication, speech.
utterly *adv* absolutely, altogether, completely, downright, entirely, quite, totally, unconditionally, wholly.
uttermost *adj* extreme, farthest; greatest, utmost.

V

vacant *adj* blank, empty, unfilled, void; disengaged, free, unemployed, unoccupied, unencumbered; thoughtless, unmeaning, unthinking, unreflective; uninhabited, untenanted.

vacate *vb* abandon, evacuate, relinquish, surrender; abolish, abrogate, annul, cancel, disannul, invalidate, nullify, overrule, quash, rescind.

vacillate *vb* dither, fluctuate, hesitate, oscillate, rock, sway, waver.

vacillation *n* faltering, fluctuation, hesitation, inconstancy, indecision, irresolution, reeling, rocking, staggering, swaying, unsteadiness, wavering.

vacuity *n* emptiness, inanition, vacancy; emptiness, vacancy, vacuum, void; expressionlessness, inanity, nihility.

vacuous *adj* empty, empty-headed, unfilled, vacant, void; inane, unintelligent.

vacuum *n* emptiness, vacuity, void.

vagabond *adj* footloose, idle, meandering, rambling, roving, roaming, strolling, vagrant, wandering. * *n* beggar, castaway, landloper, loafer, lounger, nomad, outcast, tramp, vagrant, wanderer.

vagary *n* caprice, crotchet, fancy, freak, humour, whim.

vagrant *adj* erratic, itinerant, roaming, roving, nomadic, strolling, unsettled, wandering. * *n* beggar, castaway, landloper, loafer, lounger, nomad, outcast, tramp, vagabond, wanderer.

vague *adj* ambiguous, confused, dim, doubtful, indefinite, ill-defined, indistinct, lax, loose, obscure, uncertain, undetermined, unfixed, unsettled.

vain *adj* baseless, delusive, dreamy, empty, false, imaginary, shadowy, suppositional, unsubstantial, unreal, void; abortive, bootless, fruitless, futile, ineffectual, nugatory, profitless, unavailing, unprofitable; trivial, unessential, unimportant, unsatisfactory, unsatisfying, useless, vapid, worthless; arrogant, conceited, egotistical, flushed, high, inflated, opinionated, ostentatious, overweening, proud, self-confident, self-opinionated, vainglorious; gaudy, glittering, gorgeous, showy.

valediction *n* adieu, farewell, goodbye, leave-taking.

valet *n* attendant, flunky, groom, lackey, servant.

valetudinarian *adj* delicate, feeble, frail, infirm, sickly.

valiant *adj* bold, brave, chivalrous, courageous, daring, dauntless, doughty, fearless, gallant, heroic, intrepid, lion-hearted, redoubtable, Spartan, valorous, undaunted.

valid *adj* binding, cogent, conclusive, efficacious, efficient, good, grave, important, just, logical, powerful, solid, sound, strong, substantial, sufficient, weighty.

valley *n* basin, bottom, canyon, dale, dell, dingle, glen, hollow, ravine, strath, vale.

valorous *adj* bold, brave, courageous, dauntless, doughty, intrepid, stout.

valour *n* boldness, bravery, courage, daring, gallantry, heroism, prowess, spirit.

valuable *adj* advantageous, precious, profitable, useful; costly, expensive, rich; admirable, estimable, worthy. * *n* heirloom, treasure.

value *vb* account, appraise, assess, estimate, price, rate, reckon; appreciate, esteem, prize, regard, treasure. * *n* avail, importance, usefulness, utility, worth; cost, equivalent, price, rate; estimation, excellence, importance, merit, valuation.

valueless *adj* miserable, useless, worthless.

vandal *n* barbarian, destroyer, savage.

vandalism *n* barbarism, barbarity, savagery.
vanish *vb* disappear, dissolve, fade, melt.
vanity *n* emptiness, falsity, foolishness, futility, hollowness, insanity, triviality, unreality, worthlessness; arrogance, conceit, egotism, ostentation, self-conceit.
vanquish *vb* conquer, defeat, outwit, overcome, overpower, overthrow, subdue, subjugate; crush, discomfit, foil, master, quell, rout, worst.
vapid *adj* dead, flat, insipid, lifeless, savourless, spiritless, stale, tasteless; dull, feeble, jejune, languid, meagre, prosaic, prosy, tame.
vapour *n* cloud, exhalation, fog, fume, mist, rack, reek, smoke, steam; daydream, dream, fantasy, phantom, vagary, vision, whim, whimsy.
variable *adj* changeable, mutable, shifting; aberrant, alterable, capricious, fickle, fitful, floating, fluctuating, inconstant, mobile, mutable, protean, restless, shifting, unsteady, vacillating, wavering.
variance *n* disagreement, difference, discord, dissension, incompatibility, jarring, strife.
variation *n* alteration, change, modification; departure, deviation, difference, discrepancy, innovation; contrariety, discordance.
variegated *adj* chequered, dappled, diversified, flecked, kaleidoscopic, mottled, multicoloured, pied, spotted, striped.
variety *n* difference, dissimilarity, diversity, diversification, medley, miscellany, mixture, multiplicity, variation; kind, sort.
various *adj* different, diverse, manifold, many, numerous, several, sundry.
varnish *vb* enamel, glaze, japan, lacquer; adorn, decorate, embellish, garnish, gild, polish; disguise, excuse, extenuate, gloss over, palliate. * *n* enamel, lacquer, stain; cover, extenuation, gloss.
vary *vb* alter, metamorphose, transform; alternate, exchange, rotate; diversify, modify, variegate; depart, deviate, swerve.
vassal *n* bondman, liegeman, retainer, serf, slave, subject, thrall.
vassalage *n* bondage, dependence, serfdom, servitude, slavery, subjection.
vast *adj* boundless, infinite, measureless, spacious, wide; colossal, enormous, gigantic, huge, immense, mighty, monstrous, prodigious, tremendous; extraordinary, remarkable.
vaticination *n* augury, divination, prediction, prognostication, prophecy.
vault[1] *vb* arch, bend, curve, span. * *n* cupola, curve, dome; catacomb, cell, cellar, crypt, dungeon, tomb; depository, strongroom.
vault[2] *vb* bound, jump, leap, spring; tumble, turn. * *n* bound, leap, jump, spring.
vaunt *vb* advertise, boast, brag, display, exult, flaunt, flourish, parade.
veer *vb* change, shift, turn.
vegetate *vb* blossom, develop, flourish, flower, germinate, grow, shoot, sprout, swell; bask, hibernate, idle, stagnate.
vehemence *n* impetuosity, violence; ardour, eagerness, earnestness, enthusiasm, fervency, fervour, heat, keenness, passion, warmth, zeal; force, intensity.
vehement *adj* furious, high, hot, impetuous, passionate, rampant, violent; ardent, burning, eager, earnest, enthusiastic, fervid, fiery, keen, passionate, sanguine, zealous; forcible, mighty, powerful, strong.
veil *vb* cloak, conceal, cover, curtain, envelop, hide, invest, mask, screen, shroud. * *n* cover, curtain, film, shade, screen; blind, cloak, disguise, mask, muffler, visor.
vein *n* course, current, lode, seam, streak, stripe, thread, wave; bent, character, faculty, humour, mood, talent, turn.
velocity *n* acceleration, celerity, expedition, fleetness, haste, quickness, rapidity, speed, swiftness.
velvety *adj* delicate, downy, smooth, soft.
venal *adj* corrupt, mean, purchasable, sordid.
vend *vb* dispose, flog, hawk, retail, sell.
venerable *adj* grave, respected, revered, sage, wise; awful, dread, dreadful; aged, old, patriarchal.

venerate *vb* adore, esteem, honour, respect, revere.
veneration *n* adoration, devotion, esteem, respect, reverence, worship.
vengeance *n* retaliation, retribution, revenge.
venial *adj* allowed, excusable, pardonable, permitted, trivial.
venom *n* poison, virus; acerbity, acrimony, bitterness, gall, hate, ill-will, malevolence, malice, maliciousness, malignity, rancour, spite, virulence.
venomous *adj* deadly, poisonous, septic, toxic, virulent; caustic, malicious, malignant, mischievous, noxious, spiteful.
vent *vb* emit, express, release, utter. * *n* air hole, hole, mouth, opening, orifice; air pipe, air tube, aperture, blowhole, bunghole, hydrant, plug, spiracle, spout, tap, orifice; effusion, emission, escape, outlet, passage; discharge, expression, utterance.
ventilate *vb* aerate, air, freshen, oxygenate, purify; fan, winnow; canvass, comment, discuss, examine, publish, review, scrutinize.
venture *vb* adventure, dare, hazard, imperil, jeopardize, presume, risk, speculate, test, try, undertake. * *n* adventure, chance, hazard, jeopardy, peril, risk, speculation, stake.
venturesome *adj* adventurous, bold, courageous, daring, doughty, enterprising, fearless, foolhardy, intrepid, presumptuous, rash, venturous.
veracious *adj* reliable, straightforward, true, trustworthy, truthful; credible, genuine, honest, unfeigned.
veracity *n* accuracy, candour, correctness, credibility, exactness, fidelity, frankness, honesty, ingenuousness, probity, sincerity, trueness, truth, truthfulness.
verbal *adj* nuncupative, oral, spoken, unwritten.
verbose *adj* diffusive, long-winded, loquacious, talkative, wordy.
verdant *adj* fresh, green, verdure, verdurous; green, inexperienced, raw, unsophisticated.
verdict *n* answer, decision, finding, judgement, opinion, sentence.
verge *vb* bear, incline, lean, slope, tend; approach, border, skirt. * *n* mace, rod, staff; border, boundary, brink, confine, edge, extreme, limit, margin; edge, eve, point.
verification *n* authentication, attestation, confirmation, corroboration.
verify *vb* attest, authenticate, confirm, corroborate, prove, substantiate.
verily *adv* absolutely, actually, confidently, indeed, positively, really, truly.
verity *n* certainty, reality, truth, truthfulness.
vermicular *adj* convoluted, flexuose, flexuous, meandering, serpentine, sinuous, tortuous, twisting, undulating, waving, winding, wormish, wormlike.
vernacular *adj* common, indigenous, local, mother, native, vulgar. * *n* cant, dialect, jargon, patois, speech.
versatile *adj* capricious, changeable, erratic, mobile, variable; fickle, inconstant, mercurial, unsteady; adaptable, protean, plastic, varied.
versed *adj* able, accomplished, acquainted, clever, conversant, practised, proficient, qualified, skilful, skilled, trained.
version *n* interpretation, reading, rendering, translation.
vertex *n* apex, crown, height, summit, top, zenith.
vertical *adj* erect, perpendicular, plumb, steep, upright.
vertiginous *adj* rotatory, rotary, whirling; dizzy, giddy.
vertigo *n* dizziness, giddiness.
verve *n* animation, ardour, energy, enthusiasm, force, rapture, spirit.
very *adv* absolutely, enormously, excessively, hugely, remarkably, surpassingly. * *adj* actual, exact, identical, precise, same; bare, mere, plain, pure, simple.
vesicle *n* bladder, blister, cell, cyst, follicle.
vest *vb* clothe, cover, dress, envelop; endow, furnish, invest. * *n* dress, garment, robe, vestment, vesture, waistcoat.
vestibule *n* anteroom, entrance hall, lobby,

porch.

vestige *n* evidence, footprint, footstep, mark, record, relic, sign, token.

veteran *adj* adept, aged, experienced, disciplined, seasoned, old. * *n* campaigner, old soldier; master, past master, old-timer, old-stager.

veto *vb* ban, embargo, forbid, interdict, negate, prohibit. * *n* ban, embargo, interdict, prohibition, refusal.

vex *vb* annoy, badger, bother, chafe, cross, distress, gall, harass, harry, hector, molest, perplex, pester, plague, tease, torment, trouble, roil, spite, worry; affront, displease, fret, irk, irritate, nettle, offend, provoke; agitate, disquiet, disturb.

vexation *n* affliction, agitation, chagrin, discomfort, displeasure, disquiet, distress, grief, irritation, pique, sorrow, trouble; annoyance, curse, nuisance, plague, torment; damage, troubling, vexing.

vexed *adj* afflicted, agitated, annoyed, bothered, disquieted, harassed, irritated, perplexed, plagued, provoked, troubled, worried.

vibrate *vb* oscillate, sway, swing, undulate, wave; impinge, quiver, sound, thrill; fluctuate, hesitate, vacillate, waver.

vibration *n* nutation, oscillation, vibration.

vicarious *adj* commissioned, delegated, indirect, second-hand, substituted.

vice *n* blemish, defect, failing, fault, imperfection, infirmity; badness, corruption, depravation, depravity, error, evil, immorality, iniquity, laxity, obliquity, sin, viciousness, vileness, wickedness.

vicinity *n* nearness, proximity; locality, neighbourhood, vicinage.

vicious *adj* abandoned, atrocious, bad, corrupt, degenerate, demoralized, depraved, devilish, diabolical, evil, flagrant, hellish, immoral, iniquitous, mischievous, profligate, shameless, sinful, unprincipled, wicked; malicious, spiteful, venomous; foul, impure; debased, faulty; contrary, refractory.

viciousness *n* badness, corruption, depravity, immorality, profligacy.

vicissitude *n* alteration, interchange; change, fluctuation, mutation, revolution, variation.

victim *n* martyr, sacrifice, sufferer; prey; cat's-paw, cull, cully, dupe, gull, gudgeon, puppet.

victimize *vb* bamboozle, befool, beguile, cheat, circumvent, cozen, deceive, defraud, diddle, dupe, fool, gull, hoax, hoodwink, overreach, swindle, trick.

victor *n* champion, conqueror, vanquisher, winner.

victorious *adj* conquering, successful, triumphant, winning.

victory *n* achievement, conquest, mastery, triumph.

victuals *npl* comestibles, eatables, fare, food, meat, provisions, repast, sustenance, viands.

vie *vb* compete, contend, emulate, rival, strive.

view *vb* behold, contemplate, eye, inspect, scan, survey; consider, inspect, regard, study. * *n* inspection, observation, regard, sight; outlook, panorama, perspective, prospect, range, scene, survey, vista; aim, intent, intention, design, drift, object, purpose, scope; belief, conception, impression, idea, judgement, notion, opinion, sentiment, theory; appearance, aspect, show.

vigilance *n* alertness, attentiveness, carefulness, caution, circumspection, observance, watchfulness.

vigilant *adj* alert, attentive, careless, cautious, circumspect, unsleeping, wakeful, watchful.

vigorous *adj* lusty, powerful, strong; active, alert, cordial, energetic, forcible, strenuous, vehement, vivid, virile; brisk, hale, hardy, robust, sound, sturdy, healthy; fresh, flourishing; bold, emphatic, impassioned, lively, nervous, piquant, pointed, severe, sparkling, spirited, trenchant.

vigour *n* activity, efficacy, energy, force, might, potency, power, spirit, strength; bloom, elasticity, haleness, health, heartiness, pep, punch, robustness, soundness, thriftiness, tone, vim, vitality; enthusiasm, freshness, fire, intensity, liveliness, piquancy, strenuousness, vehemence, verve, raciness.

vile *adj* abject, base, beastly, beggarly, brutish, contemptible, despicable, disgusting, grovelling, ignoble, low, odious, paltry, pitiful, repulsive, scurvy, shabby, slavish, sorry, ugly; bad, evil, foul, gross, impure, iniquitous, lewd, obscene, sinful, vicious, wicked; cheap, mean, miserable, valueless, worthless.

vilify *vb* abuse, asperse, backbite, berate, blacken, blemish, brand, calumniate, decry, defame, disparage, lampoon, libel, malign, revile, scandalize, slander, slur, traduce, vituperate.

villain *n* blackguard, knave, miscreant, rascal, reprobate, rogue, ruffian, scamp, scapegrace, scoundrel.

villainous *adj* base, mean, vile; corrupt, depraved, knavish, unprincipled, wicked; atrocious, heinous, outrageous, sinful; mischievous, sorry.

vindicate *vb* defend, justify, uphold; advocate, avenge, assert, maintain, right, support.

vindication *n* apology, excuse, defence, justification.

vindictive *adj* avenging, grudgeful, implacable, malevolent, malicious, malignant, retaliative, revengeful, spiteful, unforgiving, unrelenting, vengeful.

violate *vb* hurt, injure; break, disobey, infringe, invade; desecrate, pollute, profane; abuse, debauch, defile, deflower, outrage, ravish, transgress.

violent *adj* boisterous, demented, forceful, forcible, frenzied, furious, high, hot, impetuous, insane, intense, stormy, tumultuous, turbulent, vehement, wild; fierce, fiery, fuming, heady, heavy, infuriate, passionate, obstreperous, strong, raging, rampant, rank, rapid, raving, refractory, roaring, rough, tearing, towering, ungovernable; accidental, unnatural; desperate, extreme, outrageous, unjust; acute, exquisite, poignant, sharp.

virago *n* amazon, brawler, fury, shrew, tartar, vixen.

virgin *adj* chaste, maidenly, modest, pure, undefiled, stainless, unpolluted, vestal, virginal; fresh, maiden, untouched, unused. * *n* celibate, damsel, girl, lass, maid, maiden.

virile *adj* forceful, manly, masculine, robust, vigorous.

virtual *adj* constructive, equivalent, essential, implicit, implied, indirect, practical, substantial.

virtue *n* chastity, goodness, grace, morality, purity; efficacy, excellence, honesty, integrity, justice, probity, quality, rectitude, worth.

virtuous *adj* blameless, equitable, exemplary, excellent, good, honest, moral, noble, righteous, upright, worthy; chaste, continent, immaculate, innocent, modest, pure, undefiled; efficacious, powerful.

virulent *adj* deadly, malignant, poisonous, toxic, venomous; acrid, acrimonious, bitter, caustic.

visage *n* aspect, countenance, face, guise, physiognomy, semblance.

viscera *n* bowels, entrails, guts, intestines.

viscous *adj* adhesive, clammy, glutinous, ropy, slimy, sticky, tenacious.

visible *adj* observable, perceivable, perceptible, seeable, visual; apparent, clear, conspicuous, discoverable, distinct, evident, manifest, noticeable, obvious, open, palpable, patent, plain, revealed, unhidden, unmistakable.

vision *n* eyesight, seeing, sight; eyeshot, ken; apparition, chimera, dream, ghost, hallucination, illusion, phantom, spectre.

visionary *adj* imaginative, impractical, quixotic, romantic; chimerical, dreamy, fancied, fanciful, fantastic, ideal, illusory, imaginary, romantic, shadowy, unsubstantial, utopian, wild. * *n* dreamer, enthusiast, fanatic, idealist, optimist, theorist, zealot.

vital *adj* basic, cardinal, essential, indispensable, necessary, needful; animate, alive, existing, life-giving, living; paramount.

vitality *n* animation, life, strength, vigour, virility.

vitiate *vb* adulterate, contaminate, corrupt, debase, defile, degrade, deprave, deteriorate, impair, infect, injure, invalidate, poison, pollute, spoil.

vitiation *n* adulteration, corruption, degeneracy, degeneration, degradation, depravation, deterioration, impairment, injury, invalidation, perversion, pollution, prostitution.

vituperate *vb* abuse, berate, blame, censure, denounce, overwhelm, rate, revile, scold, upbraid, vilify.

vituperation *n* abuse, blame, censure, invective, reproach, railing, reviling, scolding, upbraiding.

vivacious *adj* active, animated, breezy, brisk, buxom, cheerful, frolicsome, gay, jocund, light-hearted, lively, merry, mirthful, spirited, sportive, sprightly.

vivacity *n* animation, cheer, cheerfulness, gaiety, liveliness, sprightliness.

vivid *adj* active, animated, bright, brilliant, clear, intense, fresh, lively, living, lucid, quick, sprightly, strong; expressive, graphic, striking, telling.

vivify *vb* animate, arouse, awake, quicken, vitalize.

vixen *n* brawler, scold, shrew, spitfire, tartar, virago.

vocabulary *n* dictionary, glossary, lexicon, wordbook; language, terms, words.

vocation *n* call, citation, injunction, summons; business, calling, employment, occupation, profession, pursuit, trade.

vociferate *vb* bawl, bellow, clamour, cry, exclaim, rant, shout, yell.

vociferous *adj* blatant, clamorous, loud, noisy, obstreperous, ranting, stunning, uproarious.

vogue *adj* fashionable, modish, stylish, trendy. * *n* custom, fashion, favour, mode, practice, repute, style, usage, way.

voice *vb* declare, express, say, utter. * *n* speech, tongue, utterance; noise, notes, sound; opinion, option, preference, suffrage, vote; accent, articulation, enunciation, inflection, intonation, modulation, pronunciation, tone; expression, language, words.

void *vb* clear, eject, emit, empty, evacuate. * *adj* blank, empty, hollow, vacant; clear, destitute, devoid, free, lacking, wanting, without; inept, ineffectual, invalid, nugatory, null; imaginary, unreal, vain. * *n* abyss, blank, chasm, emptiness, hole, vacuum.

volatile *adj* gaseous, incoercible; airy, buoyant, frivolous, gay, jolly, lively, sprightly, vivacious; capricious, changeable, fickle, flighty, flyaway, giddy, harebrained, inconstant, light-headed, mercurial, reckless, unsteady, whimsical, wild.

volition *n* choice, determination, discretion, option, preference, will.

volley *n* fusillade, round, salvo; blast, burst, discharge, emission, explosion, outbreak, report, shower, storm.

voluble *adj* fluent, garrulous, glib, loquacious, talkative.

volume *n* book, tome; amplitude, body, bulk, compass, dimension, size, substance, vastness; fullness, power, quantity.

voluminous *adj* ample, big, bulky, full, great, large; copious, diffuse, discursive, flowing.

voluntary *adj* free, spontaneous, unasked, unbidden, unforced; deliberate, designed, intended, purposed; discretionary, optional, willing.

volunteer *vb* offer, present, proffer, propose, tender.

voluptuary *n* epicure, hedonist, sensualist.

voluptuous *adj* carnal, effeminate, epicurean, fleshy, licentious, luxurious, sensual, sybaritic.

vomit *vb* discharge, eject, emit, puke, regurgitate, spew, throw up.

voracious *adj* devouring, edacious, greedy, hungry, rapacious, ravenous.

vortex *n* eddy, maelstrom, whirl, whirlpool.

votary *adj* devoted, promised. * *n* adherent, devotee, enthusiast, follower, supporter, votarist, zealot.

vote *vb* ballot, elect, opt, return; judge, pronounce, propose, suggest. * *n* ballot, franchise, poll, referendum, suffrage, voice.

vouch *vb* affirm, asseverate, attest, aver, declare, guarantee, support, uphold, verify, warrant.

vouchsafe *vb* accord, cede, deign, grant, stoop, yield.
vow *vb* consecrate, dedicate, devote; asseverate. * *n* oath, pledge, promise.
voyage *vb* cruise, journey, navigate, ply, sail. * *n* crossing, cruise, excursion, journey, passage, sail, trip.
vulgar *adj* base-born, common, ignoble, lowly, plebeian; boorish, cheap, coarse, discourteous, flashy, homespun, garish, gaudy, ill-bred, inelegant, loud, rustic, showy, tawdry, uncultivated, unrefined; general, ordinary, popular, public; base, broad, loose, low, gross, mean, ribald, vile; inelegant, unauthorized.
vulgarity *n* baseness, coarseness, grossness, meanness, rudeness.
vulnerable *adj* accessible, assailable, defenceless, exposed, weak.

W

waddle *vb* toddle, toggle, waggle, wiggle, wobble.
waft *vb* bear, carry, convey, float, transmit, transport. * *n* breath, breeze, draught, puff.
wag[1] *vb* shake, sway, waggle; oscillate, vibrate, waver; advance, move, progress, stir. * *n* flutter, nod, oscillation, vibration.
wag[2] *n* humorist, jester, joker, wit.
wage *vb* bet, hazard, lay, stake, wager; conduct, undertake.
wager *vb* back, bet, gamble, lay, pledge, risk, stake. * *n* bet, gamble, pledge, risk, stake.
wages *npl* allowance, compensation, earnings, emolument, hire, pay, payment, remuneration, salary, stipend.
waggish *adj* frolicsome, gamesome, mischievous, roguish, tricksy; comical, droll, facetious, funny, humorous, jocular, jocose, merry, sportive.
wagon *n* cart, lorry, truck, van, waggon, wain.
wail *vb* bemoan, deplore, lament, mourn; cry, howl, weep. * *n* complaint, cry, lamentation, moan, wailing.
waist *n* bodice, corsage, waistline.
wait *vb* delay, linger, pause, remain, rest, stay, tarry; attend, minister, serve; abide, await, expect, look for. * *n* delay, halt, holdup, pause, respite, rest, stay, stop.
waiter, waitress *n* attendant, lackey, servant, servitor, steward, valet.
waive *vb* defer, forgo, surrender, relinquish, remit, renounce; desert, reject.
wake[1] *vb* arise, awake, awaken; activate, animate, arouse, awaken, excite, kindle, provoke, stimulate. * *n* vigil, watch, watching.
wake[2] *n* course, path, rear, track, trail, wash.
wakeful *adj* awake, sleepless, restless; alert, observant, vigilant, wary, watchful.
wale *n* ridge, streak, stripe, welt, whelk.
walk *vb* advance, depart, go, march, move, pace, saunter, step, stride, stroll, tramp. * *n* amble, carriage, gait, step; beat, career, course, department, field, province; conduct, procedure; alley, avenue, cloister, esplanade, footpath, path, pathway, pavement, promenade, range, sidewalk, way; constitutional, excursion, hike, ramble, saunter, stroll, tramp, turn.
wall *n* escarp, parapet, plane, upright.
wallet *n* bag, knapsack, pocketbook, purse, sack.
wan *adj* ashen, bloodless, cadaverous, colourless, haggard, pale, pallid.
wand *n* baton, mace, truncheon, sceptre.
wander *vb* forage, prowl, ramble, range, roam, rove, stroll; deviate, digress, straggle, stray; moon, rave. * *n* amble, cruise, excursion, ramble, stroll.
wane *vb* abate, decrease, ebb, subside; decline, fail, sink. * *n* decrease, diminution, lessening; decay, declension, decline, failure.
want *vb* crave, desire, need, require, wish; fail, lack, neglect, omit. * *n* absence, defect, default, deficiency, lack; defectiveness, failure, inadequacy, insufficiency, meagreness, paucity, poverty, scantiness, scarcity, shortness; requirement; craving, desire, longing, wish; destitution, distress, indigence, necessity, need, penury, poverty, privation, straits.
wanton *vb* caper, disport, frisk, frolic, play, revel, romp, sport; dally, flirt, toy, trifle. * *adj* free, loose, unchecked, unrestrained, wandering; abounding, exuberant, luxuriant, overgrown, rampant; airy, capricious, coltish, frisky, playful, skit-

tish, sportive; dissolute, irregular, licentious, loose; carnal, immoral, incontinent, lascivious, lecherous, lewd, libidinous, light, lustful, prurient, salacious, unchaste; careless, gratuitous, groundless, heedless, inconsiderate, needless, perverse, reckless, wayward, wilful. * *n* baggage, flirt, harlot, light-o'-love, prostitute, rake, roué, slut, whore.

war *vb* battle, campaign, combat, contend, crusade, engage, fight, strive. * *n* contention, enmity, hostility, strife, warfare.

warble *vb* sing, trill, yodel. * *n* carol, chant, hymn, hum.

ward *vb* guard, watch; defend, fend, parry, protect, repel. * *n* care, charge, guard, guardianship, watch; defender, guardian, keeper, protector, warden; custody; defence, garrison, protection; minor, pupil; district, division, precinct, quarter; apartment, cubicle.

warehouse *n* depot, magazine, repository, store, storehouse.

wares *npl* commodities, goods, merchandise, movables.

warfare *n* battle, conflict, contest, discord, engagement, fray, hostilities, strife, struggle, war.

warily *adv* carefully, cautiously, charily, circumspectly, heedfully, watchfully, vigilantly.

wariness *n* care, caution, circumspection, foresight, thought, vigilance.

warlike *adj* bellicose, belligerent, combative,
hostile, inimical, martial, military, soldierly, watchful.

warm *vb* heat, roast, toast; animate, chafe, excite, rouse. * *adj* lukewarm, tepid; genial, mild, pleasant, sunny; close, muggy, oppressive; affectionate, ardent, cordial, eager, earnest, enthusiastic, fervent, fervid, glowing, hearty, hot, zealous; excited, fiery, flushed, furious, hasty, keen, lively, passionate, quick, vehement, violent.

warmth *n* glow, tepidity; ardour, fervency, fervour, zeal; animation, cordiality, eagerness, earnestness, enthusiasm, excitement, fervency, fever, fire, flush, heat, intensity, passion, spirit, vehemence.

warn *vb* caution, forewarn; admonish, advise; apprise, inform, notify; bid, call, summon.

warning *adj* admonitory, cautionary, cautioning, monitory. * *n* admonition, advice, caveat, caution, monition; information, notice; augury, indication, intimation, omen, portent, presage, prognostic, sign, symptom; call, summons; example, lesson, sample.

warp *vb* bend, bias, contort, deviate, distort, pervert, swerve, turn, twist. * *n* bent, bias, cast, crook, distortion, inclination, leaning, quirk, sheer, skew, slant, slew, swerve, twist, turn.

warrant *vb* answer for, certify, guarantee, secure; affirm, assure, attest, avouch, declare, justify, state; authorize, justify, license, maintain, sanction, support, sustain, uphold. * *n* guarantee, pledge, security, surety, warranty; authentication, authority, commission, verification; order, pass, permit, summons, subpoena, voucher, writ.

warrantable *adj* admissible, allowable, defensible, justifiable, lawful, permissible, proper, right, vindicable.

warrior *n* champion, captain, fighter, hero, soldier.

wary *adj* careful, cautious, chary, circumspect, discreet, guarded, heedful, prudent, scrupulous, vigilant, watchful.

wash *vb* purify, purge; moisten, wet; bathe, clean, flush, irrigate, lap, lave, rinse, sluice; colour, stain, tint. * *n* ablution, bathing, cleansing, lavation, washing; bog, fen, marsh, swamp, quagmire; bath, embrocation, lotion; laundry, washing.

washy *adj* damp, diluted, moist, oozy, sloppy, thin, watery, weak; feeble, jejune, pointless, poor, spiritless, trashy, trumpery, unmeaning, vapid, worthless.

waspish *adj* choleric, fretful, irascible, irritable, peevish, petulant, snappish, testy, touchy; slender, slim, small-waisted.

waste *vb* consume, corrode, decrease, diminish, emaciate, wear; absorb, deplete, devour, dissipate, drain, empty, exhaust, expend, lavish, lose, misspend, misuse, scatter, spend, squander; demolish, desolate, destroy, devastate, devour, dilapidate, harry, pillage, plunder, ravage, ruin, scour, strip; damage, impair, injure; decay, dwindle, perish, wither. * *adj* bare, desolated, destroyed, devastated, empty, ravaged, ruined, spoiled, stripped, void; dismal, dreary, forlorn; abandoned, bare, barren, uncultivated, unimproved, uninhabited, untilled, wild; useless, valueless, worthless; exuberant, superfluous. * *n* consumption, decrement, diminution, dissipation, exhaustion, expenditure, loss, wasting; destruction, dispersion, extravagance, loss, squandering, wanton; decay, desolation, destruction, devastation, havoc, pillage, ravage, ruin; chaff, debris, detritus, dross, excrement, husks, junk, matter, offal, refuse, rubbish, trash, wastrel, worthlessness; barrenness, desert, expanse, solitude, wild, wilderness.

wasteful *adj* destructive, ruinous; extravagant, improvident, lavish, prodigal, profuse, squandering, thriftless, unthrifty.

watch *vb* attend, guard, keep, oversee, protect, superintend, tend; eye, mark, observe. * *n* espial, guard, outlook, wakefulness, watchfulness, watching, vigil, ward; alertness, attention, inspection, observation, surveillance; guard, picket, sentinel, sentry, watchman; pocket watch, ticker, timepiece, wristwatch.

watchful *adj* alert, attentive, awake, careful, circumspect, guarded, heedful, observant, vigilant, wakeful, wary.

watchword *n* catchword, cry, motto, password, shibboleth, word.

waterfall *n* cascade, cataract, fall, linn.

watery *adj* diluted, thin, waterish, weak; insipid, spiritless, tasteful, vapid; moist, wet.

wave *vb* float, flutter, heave, shake, sway, undulate, wallow; brandish, flaunt, flourish, swing; beckon, signal. * *n* billow, bore, breaker, flood, flush, ripple, roll, surge, swell, tide, undulation; flourish, gesture, sway; convolution, curl, roll, unevenness.

waver *vb* flicker, float, undulate, wave; reel, totter; falter, fluctuate, flutter, hesitate, oscillate, quiver, vacillate.

wax *vb* become, grow, increase, mount, rise.

way *n* advance, journey, march, progression, transit, trend; access, alley, artery, avenue, beat, channel, course, highroad, highway, passage, path, road, route, street, track, trail; fashion, manner, means, method, mode, system; distance, interval, space, stretch; behaviour, custom, form, guise, habit, habitude, practice, process, style, usage; device, plan, scheme.

wayfarer *n* itinerant, nomad, passenger, pilgrim, rambler, traveller, walker, wanderer.

wayward *adj* capricious, captious, contrary, forward, headstrong, intractable, obstinate, perverse, refractory, stubborn, unruly, wilful.

weak *adj* debilitated, delicate, enfeebled, enervated, exhausted, faint, feeble, fragile, frail, infirm, invalid, languid, languishing, shaky, sickly, spent, strengthless, tender, unhealthy, unsound, wasted, weakly; accessible, defenceless, unprotected, vulnerable; light, soft, unstressed; boneless, cowardly, infirm; compliant, irresolute, pliable, pliant, undecided, undetermined, unsettled, unstable, unsteady, vacillating, wavering, yielding; childish, foolish, imbecile, senseless, shallow, silly, simple, stupid, weak-minded, witless; erring, foolish, indiscreet, injudicious, unwise; gentle, indistinct, low, small; adulterated, attenuated, diluted, insipid, tasteless, thin, watery; flimsy, frivolous, poor, sleazy, slight, trifling; futile, illogical, inconclusive, ineffective, ineffectual, inefficient, lame, unconvincing, unsatisfactory, unsupported, unsustained, vague, vain; unsafe, unsound, unsubstantial, untrustworthy; helpless, impotent, powerless; breakable, brittle, delicate, frangible; inconsiderable, puny, slender, slight, small.

weaken *vb* cramp, cripple, debilitate, devitalize, enervate, enfeeble, invalidate, relax, sap, shake, stagger, undermine, unman, unnerve, unstring; adulterate, attenuate, debase, depress, dilute, exhaust, impair, impoverish, lessen, lower, reduce.

weakness *n* debility, feebleness, fragility, frailty, infirmity, languor, softness; defect, failing, fault, flaw; fondness, inclination, liking.

weal *n* advantage, good, happiness, interest, profit, utility, prosperity, welfare; ridge, streak, stripe.

wealth *n* assets, capital, cash, fortune, funds, goods, money, possessions, property, riches, treasure; abundance, affluence, opulence, plenty, profusion.

wean *vb* alienate, detach, disengage, withdraw.

wear *vb* bear, carry, don; endure, last; consume, impair, rub, use, waste. * *n* corrosion, deterioration, disintegration, erosion, wear and tear; consumption, use; apparel, array, attire, clothes, clothing, dress, garb, gear.

wearied *adj* apathetic, bored, exhausted, fagged, fatigued, jaded, tired, weary, worn.

weariness *n* apathy, boredom, ennui, exhaustion, fatigue, languor, lassitude, monotony, prostration, sameness, tedium.

wearisome *adj* annoying, boring, dull, exhausting, fatiguing, humdrum, irksome, monotonous, prolix, prosaic, slow, tedious, tiresome, troublesome, trying, uninteresting, vexatious.

weary *vb* debilitate, exhaust, fag, fatigue, harass, jade, tire. * *adj* apathetic, bored, drowsy, exhausted, jaded, spent, tired, worn; irksome, tiresome, wearisome.

weave *vb* braid, entwine, interlace, lace, mat, plait, pleat, twine; compose, construct, fabricate, make.

wed *vb* contract, couple, espouse, marry, unite.

wedding *n* bridal, espousal, marriage, nuptials.

wedlock *n* marriage, matrimony.

ween *vb* fancy, imagine, suppose, think.

weep *vb* bemoan, bewail, complain, cry, lament, sob.

weigh *vb* balance, counterbalance, lift, raise; consider, deliberate, esteem, examine, study.

weight *vb* ballast, burden, fill, freight, load; weigh. * *n* gravity, heaviness, heft, tonnage; burden, load, pressure; consequence, efficacy, emphasis, importance, impressiveness, influence, moment, pith, power, significance, value.

weighty *adj* heavy, massive, onerous, ponderous, unwieldy; considerable, efficacious, forcible, grave, important, influential, serious, significant.

weird *adj* eerie, ghostly, strange, supernatural, uncanny, unearthly, witching.

welcome *vb* embrace, greet, hail, receive. * *adj* acceptable, agreeable, grateful, gratifying, pleasant, pleasing, satisfying. * *n* greeting, reception, salutation.

welfare *n* advantage, affluence, benefit, happiness, profit, prosperity, success, thrift, weal, wellbeing.

well[1] *vb* flow, gush, issue, jet, pour, spring. * *n* fount, fountain, reservoir, spring, wellhead, wellspring; origin, source; hole, pit, shaft.

well[2] *adj* hale, healthy, hearty, sound; fortunate, good, happy, profitable, satisfactory, useful. * *adv* accurately, adequately, correctly, efficiently, properly, suitably; abundantly, considerably, fully, thoroughly; agreeably, commendably, favourably, worthily.

wellbeing *n* comfort, good, happiness, health, prosperity, welfare.

welter *vb* flounder, roll, toss, wallow. * *n* confusion, jumble, mess.

wet *vb* dabble, damp, dampen, dip, drench, moisten, saturate, soak, sprinkle, water. * *adj* clammy, damp, dank, dewy, dripping, humid, moist; rainy, showery, sprinkly. * *n* dampness, humidity, moisture, wetness.

whack *vb, n* bang, beat, rap, strike, thrash, thump, thwack.

wharf *n* dock, pier, quay.

wheedle *vb* cajole, coax, flatter, inveigle, lure.

wheel *vb* gyrate, revolve, roll, rotate, spin,

swing, turn, twist, whirl, wind. * *n* circle, revolution, roll, rotation, spin, turn, twirl.

whet *vb* grind, sharpen; arouse, awaken, excite, provoke, rouse, stimulate; animate, inspire, kindle, quicken, warm.

whiff *vb, n* blast, gust, puff.

whim *n* caprice, crotchet, fancy, freak, frolic, humour, notion, quirk, sport, vagary, whimsy, wish.

whimsical *adj* capricious, crotchety, eccentric, erratic, fanciful, frolicsome, odd, peculiar, quaint, singular.

whine *vb* cry, grumble, mewl, moan, snivel, wail, whimper. * *n* complaint, cry, grumble, moan, sob, wail, whimper.

whip *vb* beat, lash, strike; flagellate, flog, goad, horsewhip, scourge, slash; hurt, sting; jerk, snap, snatch, whisk. * *n* bullwhip, cane, crop, horsewhip, knout, lash, scourge, switch, thong.

whipping *n* beating, castigation, dusting, flagellation, flogging, thrashing.

whirl *vb* gyrate, pirouette, roll, revolve, rotate, turn, twirl, twist, wheel. * *n* eddy, flurry, flutter, gyration, rotation, spin, swirl, twirl, vortex.

whit *n* atom, bit, grain, iota, jot, mite, particle, scrap, speck, tittle.

white *adj* argent, canescent, chalky, frosty, hoary, ivory, milky, silver, snowy; grey, pale, pallid, wan; candid, clean, chaste, immaculate, innocent, pure, spotless, unblemished.

whole *adj* all, complete, entire, intact, integral, total, undivided; faultless, firm, good, perfect, strong, unbroken, undivided, uninjured; healthy, sound, well. * *adv* entire, in one. * *n* aggregate, all, amount, ensemble, entirety, gross, sum, total, totality.

wholesome *adj* healthy, healthful, invigorating, nourishing, nutritious, salubrious, salutary; beneficial, good, helpful, improving, salutary; fresh, sound, sweet.

wholly *adv* altogether, completely, entirely, fully, totally, utterly.

whoop *vb* halloo, hoot, roar, shout, yell. * *n* bellow, hoot, roar, shout, yell.

whore *n* bawd, courtesan, drab, harlot, prostitute, streetwalker, strumpet.

wicked *adj* abandoned, abominable, depraved, devilish, godless, graceless, immoral, impious, infamous, irreligious, irreverent, profane, sinful, ungodly, unholy, unprincipled, unrighteous, vicious, vile, worthless; atrocious, bad, black, criminal, dark, evil, heinous, ill, iniquitous, monstrous, nefarious, unjust, villainous.

wide *adj* ample, broad, capacious, comprehensive, distended, expanded, large, spacious, vast; distant, remote; prevalent, rife, widespread. * *adv* completely, farthest, fully.

wield *vb* brandish, flourish, handle, manipulate, ply, work; control, manage, sway, use.

wild *adj* feral, undomesticated, untamed; desert, desolate, native, rough, rude, uncultivated; barbarous, ferocious, fierce, savage, uncivilized; dense, luxuriant, rank; disorderly, distracted, frantic, frenzied, furious, impetuous, irregular, mad, outrageous, raving, turbulent, ungoverned, uncontrolled, violent; dissipated, fast, flighty, foolish, giddy, harebrained, heedless, ill-advised, inconsiderate, reckless, thoughtless, unwise; boisterous, rough, stormy; crazy, extravagant, fanciful, grotesque, imaginary, strange. * *n* desert, waste, wilderness.

wilderness *n* desert, waste, wild.

wilful *adj* cantankerous, contumacious, dogged, headstrong, heady, inflexible, intractable, mulish, obdurate, obstinate, perverse, pig-headed, refractory, self-willed, stubborn, unruly, unyielding; arbitrary, capricious; deliberate, intended, intentional, planned, premeditated.

will *vb* bid, command, decree, direct, enjoin, ordain; choose, desire, elect, wish; bequeath, convey, demise, devise, leave. * *n* decision, determination, resoluteness, resolution, self-reliance; desire, disposition, inclination, intent, pleasure, purpose, volition, wish; behest, command, decree, demand, direction, order, request, requirement.

willing *adj* adaptable, amenable, compliant, desirous, disposed, inclined, minded; deliberate, free, intentional, spontaneous, unasked, unbidden, voluntary; cordial, eager, forward, prompt, ready.

willingly *adv* cheerfully, gladly, readily, spontaneously, voluntarily.

wily *adj* arch, artful, crafty, crooked, cunning, deceitful, designing, diplomatic, foxy, insidious, intriguing, politic, sly, subtle, treacherous, tricky.

win *vb* accomplish, achieve, acquire, catch, earn, effect, gain, gather, get, make, obtain, procure, reach, realize, reclaim, recover; gain, succeed, surpass, triumph; arrive; allure, attract, convince, influence, persuade. * *n* conquest, success, triumph, victory.

wind[1] *n* air, blast, breeze, draught, gust, hurricane, whiff, zephyr; breath, breathing, expiration, inspiration, respiration; flatulence, gas, windiness.

wind[2] *vb* coil, crank, encircle, involve, reel, roll, turn, twine, twist; bend, curve, meander, zigzag. * *n* bend, curve, meander, twist, zigzag.

winding *adj* circuitous, devious, flexuose, flexuous, meandering, serpentine, tortuous, turning, twisting. * *n* bend, curve, meander, turn, twist.

windy *adj* breezy, blowy, blustering, boisterous, draughty, gusty, squally, stormy, tempestuous; airy, empty, hollow, inflated. **winning** *adj* alluring, attractive, bewitching, brilliant, captivating, charming, dazzling, delightful, enchanting, engaging, fascinating, lovely, persuasive, pleasing, prepossessing; conquering, triumphant, victorious.

winnow *vb* cull, glean, divide, fan, part, select, separate, sift.

winsome *adj* blithe, blithesome, bonny, buoyant, charming, cheerful, debonair, jocund, light-hearted, lively, lovable, merry, pleasant, sportive, winning.

wintry *adj* arctic, boreal, brumal, cold, frosty, icy, snowy.

wipe *vb* clean, dry, mop, rub. * *n* mop, rub, blow, hit, strike; gibe, jeer, sarcasm, sneer, taunt.

wisdom *n* depth, discernment, farsightedness, foresight, insight, judgement, judiciousness, prescience, profundity, prudence, sagacity, sapience, sense, solidity, understanding, wiseness; attainment, edification, enlightenment, erudition, information, knowledge, learning, lore, scholarship; reason.

wise *adj* deep, discerning, enlightened, intelligent, judicious, penetrating, philosophical, profound, rational, seasonable, sensible, sage, sapient, solid, sound; erudite, informed, knowing, learned, scholarly; crafty, cunning, designing, foxy, politic, sly, subtle, wary, wily.

wish *vb* covet, desire, hanker, list, long; bid, command, desire, direct, intend, mean, order, want. * *n* behest, desire, intention, mind, pleasure, want, will; craving, desire, hankering, inclination, liking, longing, want, yearning.

wistful *adj* contemplative, engrossed, meditative, musing, pensive, reflective, thoughtful; desirous, eager, earnest, longing.

wit *n* genius, intellect, intelligence, reason, sense, understanding; brightness, banter, cleverness, drollery, facetiousness, fun, humour, jocularity, piquancy, point, raillery, satire, sparkle, whim; conceit, epigram, jest, joke, pleasantry, quip, quirk, repartee, sally, witticism; humorist, joker, wag.

witch *n* charmer, enchantress, fascinator, sorceress; crone, hag, sibyl.

witchcraft *n* conjuration, enchantment, magic, necromancy, sorcery, spell.

withdraw *vb* abstract, deduct, remove, retire, separate, sequester, sequestrate, subduct, subtract; disengage, wean; abjure, recall, recant, relinquish, resign, retract, revoke; abdicate, decamp, depart, dissociate, retire, shrink, vacate.

wither *vb* contract, droop, dry, sear, shrivel, wilt, wizen; decay, decline, languish, pine, waste.

withhold *vb* check, detain, hinder, repress, restrain, retain, suppress.

withstand *vb* confront, defy, face, oppose, resist.

witless *adj* daft, dull, foolish, halfwitted,

obtuse, senseless, shallow, silly, stupid, unintelligent.

witness *vb* corroborate, mark, note, notice, observe, see. * *n* attestation, conformation, corroboration, evidence, proof, testimony; beholder, bystander, corroborator, deponent, eyewitness, onlooker, spectator, testifier.

witty *adj* bright, clever, droll, facetious, funny, humorous, jocose, jocular, pleasant, waggish; alert, penetrating, quick, sparkling, sprightly.

wizard *n* charmer, diviner, conjurer, enchanter, magician, necromancer, seer, soothsayer, sorcerer.

woe *n* affliction, agony, anguish, bitterness, depression, distress, dole, grief, heartache, melancholy, misery, sorrow, torture, tribulation, trouble, unhappiness, wretchedness.

woeful *adj* afflicted, agonized, anguished, burdened, disconsolate, distressed, melancholy, miserable, mournful, piteous, sad, sorrowful, troubled, unhappy, wretched; afflicting, afflictive, calamitous, deplorable, depressing, disastrous, distressing, dreadful, tragic, tragical, grievous, lamentable, pitiable, saddening.

wonder *vb* admire, gape, marvel; conjecture, ponder, query, question, speculate. * *n* amazement, astonishment, awe, bewilderment, curiosity, marvel, miracle, prodigy, surprise, stupefaction, wonderment.

wonderful *adj* amazing, astonishing, astounding, awe-inspiring, awesome, awful, extraordinary, marvellous, miraculous, portentous, prodigious, startling, stupendous, surprising.

wont *adj* accustomed, customary, familiar, habitual, ordinary, usual. * *n* custom, habit, practice, rule, usage.

wonted *adj* accustomed, common, conventional, customary, everyday, familiar, frequent, habitual, ordinary, regular, usual.

wood *n* coppice, copse, covert, forest, greenwood, grove, spinney, thicket, woodland.

word *vb* express, phrase, put, say, state, term, utter. * *n* expression, name, phrase, term, utterance; account, advice, information, intelligence, message, news, report, tidings; affirmation, assertion, averment, avowal, declaration, statement; conversation, speech; agreement, assurance, engagement, parole, pledge, plight, promise; behest, bidding, command, direction, order, precept; countersign, password, signal, watchword.

wordy *adj* circumlocutory, diffuse, garrulous, inflated, lengthened, long-winded, loquacious, periphrastic, rambling, talkative, tedious, verbose, windy.

work *vb* act, operate; drudge, fag, grind, grub, labour, slave, sweat, toil; move, perform, succeed; aim, attempt, strive, try; effervesce, ferment, leaven, rise; accomplish, beget, cause, effect, engender, manage, originate, produce; exert, strain; embroider, stitch. * *n* exertion, drudgery, grind, labour, pain, toil; business, employment, function, occupation, task; action, accomplishment, achievement, composition, deed, feat, fruit, handiwork, opus, performance, product, production; fabric, manufacture; ferment, leaven; management, treatment.

workman *n* journeyman, employee, labourer, operative, worker, wright; artisan, craftsman, mechanic.

world *n* cosmos, creation, earth, globe, nature, planet, sphere, universe.

worldly *adj* common, earthly, human, mundane, sublunary, terrestrial; carnal, fleshly, profane, secular, temporal; ambitious, grovelling, irreligious, selfish, proud, sordid, unsanctified, unspiritual; sophisticated, worldly-wise.

worry *vb* annoy, badger, bait, beset, bore, bother, chafe, disquiet, disturb, fret, gall, harass, harry, hector, infest, irritate, molest, persecute, pester, plague, tease, torment, trouble, vex. * *n* annoyance, anxiety, apprehensiveness, care, concern, disquiet, fear, misgiving, perplexity, solicitude, trouble, uneasiness, vexation.

worship *vb* adore, esteem, honour, revere,

venerate; deify, idolize; aspire, pray. * *n* adoration, devotion, esteem, homage, idolatry, idolizing, respect, reverence; aspiration, exultation, invocation, laud, praise, prayer, supplication.

worst *vb* beat, choke, conquer, crush, defeat, discomfit, foil, master, overpower, overthrow, quell, rout, subdue, subjugate, vanquish.

worth *n* account, character, credit, desert, excellence, importance, integrity, merit, nobleness, worthiness, virtue; cost, estimation, price, value.

worthless *adj* futile, meritless, miserable, nugatory, paltry, poor, trifling, unproductive, unsalable, unserviceable, useless, valueless, wretched; abject, base, corrupt, degraded, ignoble, low, mean, vile.

worthy *adj* deserving, fit, suitable; estimable, excellent, exemplary, good, honest, honourable, reputable, righteous, upright, virtuous. * *n* celebrity, dignitary, luminary, notability, personage, somebody, VIP.

wound *vb* damage, harm, hurt, injure; cut, gall, harrow, irritate, lacerate, pain, prick, stab; annoy, mortify, offend. * *n* blow, hurt, injury; damage, detriment; anguish, grief, pain, pang, torture.

wraith *n* apparition, ghost, phantom, spectre, vision.

wrangle *vb* argue, bicker, brawl, cavil, dispute, jangle, jar, quarrel, squabble, spar, spat. * *n* altercation, argument, bickering, brawl, contest, controversy, jar, quarrel, squabble.

wrap *vb* cloak, cover, encase, envelop, muffle, swathe, wind. * *n* blanket, cape, cloak, cover, overcoat, shawl.

wrath *n* anger, choler, exasperation, fury, heat, resentment, indignation, ire, irritation, offence, passion, rage.

wrathful *adj* angry, enraged, exasperated, furious, hot, indignant, infuriated, irate, mad, passionate, provoked, rageful.

wreak *vb* execute, exercise, indulge, inflict, work.

wreath *n* chaplet, curl, festoon, garland, ring, twine.

wreathe *vb* encircle, festoon, garland, intertwine, surround, twine, twist.

wreck *vb* founder, shipwreck, strand; blast, blight, break, devastate, ruin, spoil. * *n* crash, desolation, destruction, perdition, prostration, ruin, shipwreck, smash, undoing.

wrench *vb* distort, pervert, twist, wrest, wring; sprain, strain; extort, extract. * *n* twist, wring; sprain, strain; monkey wrench, spanner.

wrest *vb* force, pull, strain, twist, wrench, wring.

wrestle *vb* contend, contest, grapple, strive, struggle.

wretch *n* outcast, pariah, pilgarlic, troglodyte, vagabond, victim, sufferer; beggar, criminal, hound, knave, miscreant, rascal, ruffian, rogue, scoundrel, villain.

wretched *adj* afflicted, comfortless, distressed, forlorn, sad, unfortunate, unhappy, woebegone; afflicting, calamitous, deplorable, depressing, pitiable, sad, saddening, shocking, sorrowful; bad, beggarly, contemptible, mean, paltry, pitiful, poor, shabby, sorry, vile, worthless.

wring *vb* contort, twist, wrench; extort, force, wrest; anguish, distress, harass, pain, rack, torture.

wrinkle[1] *vb* cockle, corrugate, crease, gather, pucker, rumple. * *n* cockle, corrugation, crease, crimp, crinkle, crumple, fold, furrow, gather, plait, ridge, rumple.

wrinkle[2] *n* caprice, fancy, notion, quirk, whim; device, tip, trick.

writ *n* decree, order, subpoena, summons.

write *vb* compose, copy, indite, inscribe, pen, scrawl, scribble, transcribe.

writer *n* amanuensis, author, clerk, penman, scribe, secretary.

writhe *vb* contort, distort, squirm, twist, wriggle.

written *adj* composed, indited, inscribed, penned, transcribed.

wrong *vb* abuse, encroach, injure, maltreat, oppress. * *adj* inequitable, unfair, unjust, wrongful; bad, criminal, evil, guilty, immoral, improper, iniquitous, reprehensible, sinful, vicious, wicked; amiss, improper, inappropriate, unfit, unsuitable; erroneous, false, faulty, inaccurate, incorrect, mistaken, untrue. * *adv* amiss, erroneously, falsely, faultily, improperly, inaccurately, incorrectly, wrongly. * *n* foul, grievance, inequity, injury, injustice, trespass, unfairness; blame, crime, dishonesty, evil, guilt, immorality, iniquity, misdeed, misdoing, sin, transgression, unrighteousness, vice, wickedness, wrongdoing; error, falsity.

wroth *adj* angry, enraged, exasperated, furious, incensed, indignant, irate, passionate, provoked, resentful.

wrought *adj* done, effected, performed, worked.

wry *adj* askew, awry, contorted, crooked, distorted, twisted.

XYZ

xanthous *adj* blonde, fair, light-complexioned, xanthic, yellow.
xiphoid *adj* ensiform, gladiate, sword-like, sword-shaped.
Xmas *n* Christmas, Christmastide, Noel, Yule, Yuletide.
X-ray *n* roentgen ray, röntgen ray.
xylograph *n* cut, woodcut, wood engraving.
xylographer *n* wood engraver.
xylophagous *adj* wood-eating, wood-nourished.

yap *vb* bark, cry, yelp. * *n* bark, cry, yelp.
yard *n* close, compound, court, courtyard, enclosure, garden.
yarn *n* anecdote, boasting, fabrication, narrative, story, tale, untruth.
yawn *vb* dehisce, gape, open wide. * *n* gap, gape, gulf.
yearn *vb* crave, desire, hanker after, long for.
yell *vb* bawl, bellow, cry out, howl, roar, scream, screech, shriek, squeal.* *n* cry, howl, roar, scream, screech, shriek.
yellow *adj* aureate, gilded, gilt, gold, golden, lemon, primrose, saffron, xanthic, xanthous.
yelp *vb* bark, howl, yap; complain, bitch, grouse. * *n* bark, sharp cry, howl.
yet *adv* at last, besides, further, however, over and above, so far, still, thus far, ultimately.* *conj* moreover, nevertheless, notwithstanding, now.
yield *vb* afford, bear, bestow, communicate, confer, fetch, furnish, impart, produce, render, supply; accede, accord, acknowledge, acquiesce, allow, assent, comply, concede, give, grant, permit; abandon, abdicate, cede, forgo, give up, let go, quit, relax, relinquish, resign, submit, succumb, surrender, waive. * *n* earnings, income, output, produce, profit, return, revenue.
yielding *adj* accommodating, acquiescent, affable, compliant, complaisant, easy, manageable, obedient, passive, submissive, unresisting; bending, flexible, flexile, plastic, pliant, soft, supple, tractable; fertile, productive.
yoke *vb* associate, bracket, connect, couple, harness, interlink, join, link, unite. * *n* bond, chain, ligature, link, tie, union; bondage, dependence, enslavement, service, servitude, subjection, vassalage; couple, pair.
yokel *n* boor, bumpkin, countryman, peasant, rustic.
yore *adj* ancient, antique, old, olden. * *n* long ago, long since, olden times.
young *adj* green, ignorant, inexperienced, juvenile, new, recent, youthful. * *n* young people, youth; babies, issue, brood, offspring, progeny, spawn.
youngster *n* adolescent, boy, girl, lad, lass, stripling, youth.
youth *n* adolescence, childhood, immaturity, juvenile, juvenility, minority, nonage, pupillage, wardship; boy, girl, lad, lass, schoolboy, schoolgirl, slip, sprig, stripling, youngster.
youthful *adj* boyish, childish, girlish, immature, juvenile, puerile, young.

zany *adj* comic, comical, crazy, droll, eccentric, funny, imaginative, scatterbrained; clownish, foolish, ludicrous, silly. * *n* buffoon, clown, droll, fool, harlequin, jester, punch.
zeal *n* alacrity, ardour, cordiality, devotedness, devotion, earnestness, eagerness, energy, enthusiasm, fervour, glow, heartiness, intensity, jealousness, passion, soul, spirit, warmth.

zealot *n* bigot, devotee, fanatic, freak, partisan.

zealous *adj* ardent, burning, devoted, eager, earnest, enthusiastic, fervent, fiery, forward, glowing, jealous, keen, passionate, prompt, ready, swift, warm.

zenith *n* acme, apex, climax, culmination, heyday, pinnacle, prime, summit, top, utmost, height.

zero *n* cipher, naught, nadir, nil, nothing, nought.

zest *n* appetite, enjoyment, exhilaration, gusto, liking, piquancy, relish, thrill; edge, flavour, salt, savour, tang, taste; appetizer, sauce.

zone *n* band, belt, cincture, girdle, girth; circuit, clime, region.

zymotic *adj* bacterial, fermentative, germinating.

Appendices

Commonly Misspelt Words

All of us have problem words that cause spelling difficulties but there are some words that are generally misspelt. These include:

A

abbreviation
abscess
absence
abysmal
accelerator
accessible
accessories
accommodate
accompaniment
accumulate
accurate
accustomed
achieve
aching
acknowledge
acknowledgement/
acknowledgment
acquaint
acquaintance
acquiesce
acquiescence
acquire
acquit
acquittal
acreage
across
actual
additional
address
adequate
adieu
adjacent
admissible
admittance
adolescence
adolescent
advantageous
advertisement
advice
advise
aerate
aerial
aesthetic
affect
affiliation
afforestation
aggravate
aggravation
aggregate
aggression
aggressive
aghast
agnosticism
agoraphobia
agreeable
agreed
aisle
alcohol
alfresco
alibis
align
alignment
allege
allergic
alleys
alligator
allocate
allotment
allotted
almond
alms
alphabetically
already
although
aluminium
ambiguous
amethyst
ammunition
anachronism
anaesthetic
analyse
analysis
anarchist
ancestor
ancestry
anemone
angrily
anguish
annihilate
annihilation
anniversary
announcement
annulled
annulment
anonymous
anorak
answered
Antarctic
antibiotic
antithesis
anxiety
apartheid
apologize
appalling
apparently
appearance
appendicitis
appreciate
approval
aquarium
aquiline
arbiter
arbitrary
arbitration
archaeology
architectural
Arctic
arguably
arrangement
arrival
artichoke
ascend
ascent
asphalt
asphyxiate
asphyxiation
assassin
assassinate
assessment
assistance
associate
asthma
asthmatic
astrakhan
atheist
atrocious
attach
attendant
attitude
aubergine
auburn

auctioneer
audible
aural
automatic
autumn
awful
awkward

B

bachelor
bagatelle
baggage
bailiff
ballast
ballerina
banana
banister
bankruptcy
banquet
barbecue
barometer
barrister
basically
basis
bassoon
battalion
bazaar
beautiful
befriend
beguile
behaviour
beleaguer
belief
believe
belligerent
benefited
bequeath
berserk
besiege
bettered
bevelled
bewitch
bias
bicycle
biennial
bigamous
bigoted
bilingual
biscuit
bivouacked
blancmange
blasphemous
blasphemy
bleary
blitz
bodily
bonfire
bootee
borough
bouquet
bourgeois
boutique
bracketed
braille
brassiere
breadth
breathalyser
brief
broccoli
brochure
bronchitis
bruise
brusque
buccaneer
Buddhist
budding
budgerigar
budgeted
buffeted
bulletin
bumptious
bungalow
buoyancy
buoyant
bureau
bureaucracy
business
buttoned

C

cabbage
cafeteria
caffeine
camouflage
campaign
campaigned
cancelled
cancerous
candour
cannabis
cannibal
canvassing
capability
capillary
capitalist
caravan
carbohydrate
carburettor
career
caress
caries
carriage
cartoonist
cashier
cassette
castanets
casualty
catalogue
catarrh
catechism
catering
cauliflower
cautious
ceiling
cellophane
cemetery
centenary
centilitre
centimetre
certainty
champagne
championed
chancellor
changeable
channelled
characteristic
chasm
chauffeur
cheetah
cherish
chief
chilblain
chintz
chiropody
chisel
choreographer
choreography
chronically
chrysanthemum
cigarette
cinnamon
circuitous
cistern
civilian
claustrophobia
clientele
clique
coalesce
cocoa
coconut
coffee
cognac
coincidence

laryngitis
larynx
lassitude
latitude
laundered
launderette
layette
league
leanness
ledger
legendary
legible
legitimate
length
lengthened
leukaemia
levelled
liaise
liaison
lieu
lieutenant
lilac
limousine
lineage
linen
lingerie
linguist
liqueur
literature
litre
livelihood
loneliness
loosened
loquacious
lorgnette
lucrative
lucre
luggage
lugubrious
luminous
luscious
lustre
luxurious
lyric

M

macabre
maelstrom
magician
magnanimous
mahogany
maintenance
malaise
malaria
malignant
manageable
management
mannequin
manoeuvre
mantelpiece
manually
margarine
marijuana
marquee
martyr
marvellous
marzipan
masochist
massacre
matinee
mayonnaise
meagre
measurement
medallion
medieval
mediocre
melancholy
meningitis
meringue
messenger
meteorological
metropolitan
microphone
midday
migraine
mileage
milieu
millionaire
mimicked
mimicry
miniature
miraculous
mirrored
miscellaneous
mischief
mischievous
misogynist
misshapen
misspell
misspent
modelled
modelling
morgue
mortgage
mosquito
mountaineer
moustache
multitudinous
muscle
museum
mysterious
mythical

N

naive
narrative
naughty
nausea
nautical
necessary
necessity
negligence
negligible
negotiate
neighbourhood
neither
neurotic
neutral
niche
niece
ninetieth
ninth
nocturnal
nonentity
notably
noticeably
notoriety
nuance
numbered
numerate
numerous
nutrient
nutritious

O

obedient
obese
obituary
oblige
oblique
oblivious
obnoxious
obscene
obscenity
obsessive
obstetrician
occasion
occupancy
occupier
occupying
occurred
occurrence

octogenarian
odorous
odour
offence
offered
official
officious
ominous
omission
omitted
oneself
opaque
ophthalmic
opinion
opponent
opportunity
opposite
orchestra
ordinary
original
orthodox
orthopaedic
oscillate
ostracize
outlying
outrageous
overdraft
overrate
overreach
overwrought
oxygen

P

pacifist
pageant
pamphlet
panacea
panegyric
panicked
papered
parachute
paraffin
paragraph
paralyse
paralysis
paraphernalia
parcelled
parliament
paroxysm
parquet
partially
participant
particle
partner
passenger
passers-by
pastime
patterned
pavilion
peaceable
peculiar
pejorative
pencilled
penicillin
peppered
perceive
perennial
perilous
permissible
permitted
pernicious
perpetrate
persistence
personnel
persuasion
perusal
pessimism
pessimistically
pesticide
phantom
pharmacy
pharyngitis
pharynx
phenomenon
phial
phlegm
physician
physiotherapist
picketed
picnic
picnicked
picturesque
pioneered
pious
piteous
pitiful
plaintiff
plausible
pleurisy
pneumonia
poignant
politician
pollution
polythene
porridge
portrait
portray
positive
possession
possibility
posthumous
potatoes
precede
precedent
precinct
precipice
precocious
preference
preferred
prejudice
preliminary
prepossessing
prerequisite
prerogative
prescription
presence
preservative
prestige
prestigious
pretentious
prevalent
priest
primitive
procedure
proceed
procession
professional
profiteering
prohibit
promiscuous
pronunciation
propeller
proposal
proprietor
prosecute
protagonist
protein
provocation
prowess
psalm
psyche
psychiatric
psychic
publicly
pursuit
putative
pyjamas

Q

quarrelsome
questionnaire
queue
quintet

R

rabies
radioed
radios
railing
rancour
ransack
rapturous
reassurance
rebelled
rebellious
recalcitrant
receipt
receive
recommend
reconnaissance
reconnoitre
recruitment
recurrence
redundant
referee
reference
referred
regatta
regrettable
regretted
rehabilitation
reign
relevant
relief
relieve
reminisce
reminiscence
remuneration
rendezvous
repertoire
repetitive
reprieve
reprisal
requisite
rescind
resemblance
reservoir
resistance
resourceful
responsibility
restaurant
restaurateur
resurrection
resuscitate
retrieve
reunion
reveille
revelry
revenue
reversible
rhapsody
rheumatism
rhododendron
rhomboid
rhubarb
rhyme
rhythm
ricochet
righteous
rigorous
rigour
risotto
riveted
rogue
roughage
roulette
royalty
rucksack
ruinous
rummage
rumour

S

sabotage
sacrilege
saddened
salmon
salvage
sanctuary
sandwich
sanitary
sapphire
satellite
scaffolding
scandalous
scenic
sceptre
schedule
scheme
schizophrenic
schooner
sciatica
science
scissors
scruple
scrupulous
scurrilous
scythe
secretarial
secretary
sedative
sedentary
sensitive
separate
sergeant
serrated
serviceable
serviette
settee
shampooed
shattered
sheikh
sheriff
shield
shovelled
shuddered
siege
significant
silhouette
simply
simultaneous
sincerely
sixtieth
skeleton
skilful
slanderous
slaughter
sleigh
sleight of hand
sluice
smattering
smithereens
snivelled
soccer
solemn
solicitor
soliloquy
soloist
sombre
somersault
sophisticated
sovereign
spaghetti
spectre
spherical
sphinx
sponsor
spontaneity
spontaneous
squabble
squandered
squawk
staccato
staggered
stammered
statistics

statutory
stealth
stereophonic
stirrup
storage
strait-laced
straitjacket
strategic
strength
strenuous
stupor
suave
subpoena
subtle
succeed
successful
successor
succinct
succulent
succumb
suddenness
suede
sufficient
suffocate
suicide
sullenness
summoned
supercilious
superfluous
supersede
supervise
supervisor
supplementary
surgeon
surveillance
surveyor
susceptible
suspicious
sweetener
sycamore
symmetry
sympathize
symphony
synagogue
syndicate
synonym
syringe

T

tableau
taciturn
taffeta
tangerine
tangible
tattoo
technique
teenager
televise
temperature
tenuous
terrifically
terrifying
territory
terrorist
therapeutic
therefore
thief
thinness
thirtieth
thorough
thoroughfare
threshold
thrombosis
throughout
thwart
thyme
tightened
titivate
tobacconist
toboggan
toffee
tomatoes
tomorrow
tonsillitis
topsy turvy
tornadoes
torpedoes
torpor
tortoiseshell
tortuous
totalled
tourniquet
towelling
trafficked
tragedy
traitorous
tranquillity
tranquillizer
transcend
transferable
transferred
transparent
travelled
traveller
tremor
troublesome
trousseau
truism
trustee
tsetse
tuberculosis
tumour
tunnelled
tureen
turquoise
twelfth
typhoon
tyranny

U

unanimous
unconscious
undoubted
unduly
unequalled
unique
unnecessary
unremitting
unrequited
unrivalled
upheaval
uproarious

V

vaccinate
vacuum
vague
vanilla
variegate
vehement
vendetta
veneer
ventilator
verandah
vermilion
veterinary
vetoes
vice versa
vicissitude
vicissitudes
vigorous
vigour
viscount
visibility
vivacious
vociferous
voluminous
volunteered
vulnerable

W

walkie-talkie
walloped
warrior
wastage
watered
weakened
wearisome
Wednesday
weight
weird
whereabouts
wherewithal
widened
width
wield
wintry
witticism
wizened
woebegone
wooden
woollen
worsened
worship
worshipped
wrapper
wrath
wreak
writhe

X

xylophone

Y

yield
yoghurt

Z

zealous
zigzagged

Weights and Measures

MEASUREMENT OF MASS OR WEIGHT

Imperial		*Metric*
16 drams	= 1 ounce (oz)	= 28.3495 g
16 oz	= 1 pound (lb)	= 0.45359 kg
100 lb	= 1 short hundredweight	= 45.3592 kg
112 lb	= 1 long hundredweight	= 50.8024 kg
2000 lb	= 1 short ton	= 0.9072 tonnes
2240 lb	= 1 long ton	= 1.01605 tonnes

Metric		*Imperial*
	1 milligram (mg)	= 0.015 grain (gr)
10 mg	= 1 centigram (cg)	= 0.1543 gr
10 cg	= 1 decigram (dg)	= 1.5433 gr
10 dg	= 1 gram (g)	= 0.0353 oz
10 g	= 1 decagram (dag)	= 0.353 oz
10 dag	= 1 hectogram (hg)	= 3.527 oz
10 hg	= 1 kilogram (kg)	= 2.205 lb
1000kg	= 1 tonne (metric ton)	= 1.1023 short tons
		= 0.9842 long ton
		= 2204.62 lb

LINEAR MEASURE

Imperial		*Metric*	
	1 inch (in)	= 25.4 mm	
12 in	= 1 foot (ft)	= 0.3048 m	
3 ft	= 1 yard (yd)	= 0.9144 m	
2 yds	= 6 ft	= 1 fathom (fm)	= 1.8288 m
5.5 yds	= 16.5 ft	= 1 rod	= 5.0292 m
4 rod	= 22 yds	= 66 ft	= 1 chain (20.12 m)
10 chain	= 220 yds	= 660 ft	= 1 furlong (fur) (0.2012 km)
8 fur	= 1760 yds	= 5280 ft	= 1 mile (mi) (1.609 km)
3 mi	= 1 league	= 4.828 km	

Metric		*Imperial*
	1 millimeter (mm)	= 0 03937 in
10 mm	= 1 centimeter (cm)	= 0.3937 in
10 cm	= 1 decimeter (dm)	= 3.937 in
10 dm	= 1 meter (m)	= 39.37 in
10 m	= 1 decameter (dam)	= 10.936 yds
10 dam	= 1 hectometer (hm)	= 109.36 yds
10 hm	= 1 kilometer (km)	= 0.6214 mi

SQUARE MEASURE

Imperial		*Metric*
	1 sq inch (sq in)	= 6.4516 cm^2
144 sq in	= 1 sq foot (sq ft)	= 0.0929 m^2
9 sq ft	= 1 sq yard (sq yd)	= 0.8361 m^2
30$^1/_4$ sq yds	= 1 sq perch	= 25.2929 m^2
40 sq perch	= 1 rood	= 0.1012 ha
4 roods/4840 sq yds	= 1 acre	= 0.4047 ha
640 acres	= 1 sq mile (sq mi)	= 2.5900 km^2

Metric		*Imperial*
	1 sq millimeter (mm^2)	= 0.00155 sq in
100 mm^2	= 1 sq centimeter (cm^2)	= 0.1550 sq in
100 cm^2	= 1 sq decimeter (dm^2)	= 15.5000 sq in
100 dm^2	= 1 sq meter (m^2)	= 10.7639 sq ft
		= 1.196 sq yds
100 m^2	= 1 sq decameter (dam^2)	= 1076.391 sq ft
100 dam^2	= 1 sq hectometer (hm^2)	= 0.00386 sq mi
100 hm^2	= 1 sq kilometer (km^2)	= 0.3861 sq mi
100 m^2	= 1 are	= 119.6 sq yds
1000 m^2	= 10 ares	= 1 dekare (1195.99 sq yds)
10 000 m^2	= 100 ares	= 1 hectare (ha) (2.471 acres)

LIQUID MEASURE

Imperial		*Metric*
5 fl oz	= 1 gill	= 0.148 l
4 gills	= 1 pint (pt)	= 0.568 l
2 pt	= 1 quart (qt)	= 1.136 l
4 qt=1 gallon (gal)	= 4.546 l	

US and British equivalents

US	*British*
1 fluid ounce	1.0408 fl oz
1 pint	0.8327 pt
1 gallon	0.8327 gal

Metric		*Imperial*
10 milliliters (ml)	=1 centiliter (cl)	= 0.02113 pt
10 cl	=1 deciliter (dl)	= 0.2113 pt
10 dl	=1 liter (1)	= 2.113 pt
		= 0.2642 gal
10 l	=1 decaliter (dal)	= 2.642 gal
10 dal	=1 hectoliter (hl)	= 26.42 gal
10 hl	=1 kiloliter (kl)	= 264.17 gal

CUBIC MEASURE

Imperial		*Metric*
	1 cubic inch (cu in)	= 16.39 cm^3
1728 cu in	= 1 cubic foot (cu ft)	= 0.02832 m^3
27 cu ft	= 1 cubic yard (cu yd)	= 0.7646 m^3

Metric	*Imperial*	
1000 cubic millimeters (mm^3)	= 1 cubic centimeter (cm^3)	= 0.0610 cu in
1000 cubic centimeters (cm^3)	= 1 cubic decimeter (dm^3)	= 61.024 cu in
1000 cubic decimeters (dm^3)	= 1 cubic meter (m^3)	= 35.3147 cu ft

TEMPERATURE

Equations for conversion:

°Fahrenheit	= ($^9/_5$ x x°C) + 32
°Centigrade	= $^5/_9$ x (x°F −32)
°Kelvin	= x°C + 273.15

Normal temperature of human body	36.9°C	= 98.4°F
Freezing point	0°C	= 32°F
Boiling point	100°C	= 212°F